Heinrich August Jäschke

A Tibetan-English dictionary

With special reference to the prevailing dialects

Heinrich August Jäschke

A Tibetan-English dictionary
With special reference to the prevailing dialects

ISBN/EAN: 9783742845504

Manufactured in Europe, USA, Canada, Australia, Japa

Cover: Foto ©Andreas Hilbeck / pixelio.de

Manufactured and distributed by brebook publishing software
(www.brebook.com)

Heinrich August Jäschke

A Tibetan-English dictionary

A TIBETAN-ENGLISH

DICTIONARY

WITH SPECIAL REFERENCE TO THE PREVAILING DIALECTS.

TO WHICH IS ADDED

AN ENGLISH-TIBETAN VOCABULARY.

BY

H. A. JÄSCHKE,

LATE MORAVIAN MISSIONARY AT KYÈLANG, BRITISH LAHOUL.

PREPARED AND PUBLISHED AT THE CHARGE OF THE SECRETARY OF STATE FOR INDIA IN COUNCIL.

LONDON 1881.

PREFACE.

This work represents a new and thoroughly revised edition of a Tibetan-German Dictionary, which appeared in a lithographed form between the years 1871 and 1876.

During a residence, which commenced in 1857 and extended over a number of years, on the borders of Tibet and among Tibetan tribes, I and my colleagues gathered the materials for this Dictionary.

We had to take primarily into account the needs of missionaries entering upon new regions, and then of those who might hereafter follow into the same field of enterprize. The chief motive of all our exertions lay always in the desire to facilitate and to hasten the spread of the Christian religion and of Christian civilization, among the millions of Buddhists, who inhabit Central Asia, and who speak and read in Tibetan idioms.

A yet more definite object influenced my own personal linguistic researches, in as much as I had undertaken to make preparations for the translation of the Holy Scriptures into the Tibetan speech. I approached and carried forward this task by way of a careful examination of the full sense and exact range of words in their ordinary and common usage. For it seemed to me that, if Buddhist readers were to be brought into contact with Biblical and Christian ideas, the introduction to so foreign and strange a train of thought, and one making the largest demands upon the character and the imagination, had best be made through the medium of a phraseology and diction as simple, as clear, and as popular as possible. My instrument must be, as in the case of every successful translator of the Bible, so to say, not a technical, but the vulgar tongue.

Thus, in contrast to the business of the European philologist, engaged in the same domain, who quite rightly occupies himself with the analysis and commentary of a literary language, the vocabulary and terminology of which he finds mainly deposited in the speculative writings of the Buddhist philosophers, it became my duty to embrace every opportunity, with which my presence on the spot favoured me, to trace the living powers of words and of expressions through their consecutive historical applications, till I reached their last signification in their modern equivalents, as these are embodied in the provincial dialects of the native tribes of our own time.

These circumstances, it is hoped, will excuse and explain the system of my work.

As an inventory of the whole treasure of the language, as a finished key to its literature, this Dictionary, when judged by the high standard of modern lexicography, may seem inadequate; I have, for instance, been unable to consult, much as I could have wished to have done so, all the original and translated treatises in Tibetan which, down to the present, have appeared in Europe, and the reader of a Tibetan work may thus, here and there, look in vain for the assistance he expects. On the other hand, a consistent attempt is here made for the first time, 1. to give a rational account of the development of the values and meanings of words in this language; 2. to distinguish precisely the various transitions in periods of literature and varieties of dialect; 3. to make sure of each step by the help of accurate and copious illustrations and examples. I have done my utmost to arrive at certainty where, heretofore, much was mere guess-work, and I cherish the hope that, from this point of view, my contribution will be welcomed by the comparative philologist, and will be serviceable to the general cause of learning, as well as a useful volume within that narrower circle, whose requirements I was specially bound not to overlook, of persons whose main purpose is to be taught how to write and speak the modern Tibetan tongue.

There are two chief periods of literary activity to be noticed in studying the origin and growth of Tibetan literature and the landmarks in the history of the language. The first is the Period of Translations which, however, might also be entitled the Classical Period, for the sanctity of the religious message conferred a corresponding reputation and tradition of excellence upon the form, in which it was conveyed. This period begins in the first half of the seventh century, when Thonmi Sambhota, the minister of king Srongtsangampo, was sent to India to learn Sanskrit. His invention of the Tibetan alphabet gave a twofold impulse: for several centuries the wisdom of India and the ingenuity of Tibet laboured in unison and with the greatest industry and enthusiasm at the work of translation. The tribute due to real genius must be awarded to these early pioneers of Tibetan grammar. They had to grapple with the infinite wealth and refinement of Sanskrit, they had to save the independence of their own tongue, while they strove to subject it to the rule of scientific principles, and it is most remarkable, how they managed to produce translations at once literal and faithful to the spirit of the original. The first masters had made for their later disciples a comparatively easy road, for the style and contexts of the writings, with which the translators had to deal, present very uniform features. When once typical patterns had been furnished, it was possible for the literary manufacture to be extended by a sort of mechanical process.

A considerable time elapsed before natives of Tibet began to indulge in compositions of their own. When they did so, the subject matter, chosen by them to operate upon, was either of an historical or a legendary kind. In this Second Period the language shows much resemblance to the modern tongue, approaching most closely the present idiom of Central Tibet. We find a greater freedom in construction, a tendency to use abbreviated forms (thus the mere verbal root is often inflected in the place of a complete infinitive), and a certain number of new grammatical combinations.

The present language of the people has as many dialects, as the country has provinces. Indeed, as in most geographically similar districts, well nigh every separate mountain valley has its own singularities as to modes of utterance and favourite collocations of words. Especially is it interesting to note, in respect to pronunciation, how the old consonants, which would seem to have been generally sounded and spoken twelve centuries ago, when the Tibetan written character came into existence, and which, at any rate, are marked by the primitive system of writing, remain still extant; every one of them can still be disinterred, somewhere or other, from some local peculiarity of language, and thus even the very diversity of modern practice can be made to bear testimony to the standards imposed by what was termed above the Classical Period. (Compare my Essay on the Phonetic System of the Tibetan language in the Monthly Reports of the Royal Academy of Science at Berlin 1867, p. 148 etc.)

I have already adverted to the circumstances which, especially in the case of the student, who has for immediate object to learn how to read and write the Tibetan language, render existing dictionaries almost if not quite useless. They give but scanty information concerning modes of construction, variations and limits of actual application, shades of meaning etc. In my own case, I was forced from the beginning to compile my own German-Tibetan dictionary, and found myself for all practical purposes thrown back upon my own resources. But the cause of truth appears to require a further word or two in regard to the Lexicon by Professor I. J. Schmidt of St. Petersburg, the relation of that work to its predecessors having been left by its author in some obscurity.

The first Tibetan dictionary, intended for European students, was published at Serampore, as long ago as 1826. It contains the collections, amassed in view of a dictionary and grammar, by a Roman Catholic missionary, who was stationed in eastern Tibet or close to the frontier in Bhotan. There was nothing to assist him, except the scanty contributions, given by Georgi, in his Alphabetum Tibetanum. He had to cope with an entirely unworked language. He evidently took the one way possible of making acquaintance with it, sufficient to enable him to understand, to speak, to read and write. Each word or sentence was jotted down, as soon as it was heard, or was committed to writing, at the request of the learner, by some native expert. After a while, the attempt could be made to master a book. In the instance of our missionary, Padma Sambhava's book of legends appears to have been selected, a work which represents rather a low level of literature, yet just on that account, perhaps, as a specimen of popular and current literature, not unsuitable to start from. Then, step by step, as best he could, our missionary had to possess himself of some abstract views, which would serve as a preliminary basis for a grammar. And had it been granted to this first occupant of the field to reduce his materials to an ordered system and to prepare them himself for publication, it is possible, that in Europe the knowledge of the Tibetan language might have reached, some fifty years earlier, the stage at which it has now arrived. The very name of that Roman Catholic missionary, however, has been lost. The papers which he left behind him, unsorted and unsifted, came into the hands of Major Latter, an English officer, and were passed on by him to Mr. Schröter, a missionary in Bengal. English was substituted for the Italian of the manuscript, and the East India Company made a grant which defrayed the cost of the Tibetan types and the further expenses of printing. But there was no Tibetan scholar to correct the proofs. The author himself would doubtless, on reconsideration, have detected and dismissed much erroneous or unnecessary matter. As it was, many additional mistakes crept in during the passage through the press. Thus the work, though it has a richer vocabulary than can be found in the later dictionaries, cannot on any questionable point be accepted as an authority, and has only value for those who are already competent, for themselves, to weigh and decide upon the statements and interpretations it advances. I have not been able to extract from it much that was serviceable to me. Nevertheless, any one who knows by experience what time and toil such a work must have cost, though its design remained unfulfilled and its object unaccomplished, will not easily be able to repress his indignation at the tone, in which this book in the preface to his Grammar (p. VI) is recklessly and absolutely condemned by Professor Schmidt.

High praise, however, is awarded by the Professor to a second work, the Tibetan-English Dictionary by Csoma de Körös, which appeared in 1834. This work deserves all eulogy; but the Professor's manner, which imitates that of a master commending a pupil, is, though on other grounds, as unwarranted and as offensive in this as in the former case. The work of Csoma de Körös is that of an original investigator and the fruit of almost unparalleled determination and patience. The compiler, in order to dedicate himself to the study of Tibetan literature, lived like a monk for years among the inmates of a Tibetan monastery. It is to be regretted that, with the knowledge he certainly must have possessed of the later language and literature, he should have restricted the scope of his labours to the earlier periods of literature, and when in his Grammar conversational phrases are quoted as examples, they are almost without exception in the dialect of the Kangyur, and of little practical value.

This Tibetan-English dictionary by Csoma has been adapted for a German public by Professor I. J. Schmidt of St. Petersburg. The translation from English into German is good; in the general alphabetical arrangement improvements have been introduced, and such as are in conformity with the spirit of the language; moreover, three Mongolian dictionaries have been consulted, and from these a certain number of words have been supplemented. But it cannot be said that even on the work of revision Professor Schmidt has bestowed much pains. For example, Csoma's rough grouping of words under the principal headings is left unaltered, though here especially a reduction to alphabetical order was obviously required. Mistakes and superfluities, very pardonable in the case of a first issue of an original publication, are repeated in this translation, and these cannot be so readily overlooked and condoned, when they are made at second hand, and are sanctioned and subscribed to by one, who has assumed so severe a critical and editorial attitude.

The national dictionaries of Tibet itself, so far as I have met with such, are either little handbooks, meant only to furnish a correct orthography, or they are glossaries of antiquated forms. The absence of an alphabetical order in them makes the business of reference very troublesome. It is by great good luck that one sometimes finds an otherwise unknown word after a prolonged search.

My own dictionary, in the main, pursues the object and accepts the plan of the work, which was published by Mr. Schröter. As I said at the beginning, I have not restricted myself to the Classical Period, but I have endeavoured to deal with the Tibetan language as a whole, though I do not pretend to have performed this task exhaustively. My dictionary derives its matter and its principles, so far as possible, equally from the literature and from the speech of the people. Each word has been made the object of observation in its relation to the context as it occurs in books, and in its value and place among others when it is used in common conversation, and then the attempt has been made to define its range and to fix its meaning.

All the words, cited by Csoma and Schmidt, even such as I myself had never seen or heard, I have embodied in this work, stating, in each case, the source from whence I drew them.

The signification in Sanskrit has been added, whenever this seemed likely to be useful or interesting to the student of Tibetan literature. Of proper names only the most important are given.

The great number of diacritical marks will perhaps prove irksome to the English reader; yet, they were not to be dispensed with, if the pronunciation of Tibetan letters and words was to be represented with any degree of exactness, and the method of Prof. Lepsius seemed the most eligible among all the systems available for my purpose. The student, however, need not be disheartened, as he is not obliged to make himself acquainted with all the minutiae of the system, but need only direct his attention to the peculiarities of that dialect, within the limits of which his inquiries, for the time, are confined. And by-the-by it may be observed, that the multitude of little marks, of manifold description, cannot be startling to the Indian reader, who was ever necessitated to make himself familiar with systems quite as complicated, as e.g. the Urdu alphabet.

One word more of apology. Of publications in general it has been said, that "when human care has done its best, there will be found a certain percentage of error". And the probability is but too great, that this dictionary will exhibit a number of deficiencies and faults, in the English text as well as in the Tibetan transcript. Still, I venture to hope that an indulgent Public will be ready to make every reasonable allowance, in consideration of the peculiar difficulties, which attach to the execution of a work like the present, and which, moreover, were not a little increased, in this instance, by the fact that the compositors of the press were altogether unacquainted with English.

I should be guilty of great ingratitude, if I were not to mention my obligations to two friends, without whose kind and efficient aid it would have been impossible for me, in my present infirm state, to complete this work, which was commenced in the days of health and vigour, viz. to the Rev. T. Reichelt, formerly a Missionary of the Moravian Church in South Africa, and to Mr. F. W. Petersen, a relative of mine.

Further, I desire to record my obligations for various acts of kindness, encouragement, assistance and advice, during the prosecution of my researches and the completion of my work, to A. C. Burnell Esq. M. R. A. S., in India; Dr. E. Schlagintweit in Bavaria, Dr. Thomson and Dr. Aitchison of Kew, Dr. Kurz of Calcutta, and R. Laing Esq. M.A., Fellow of Corpus Christi College, Oxford.

Not the least debt of gratitude is that which I owe to Dr. R. Rost in London, Secretary of the Royal Asiatic Society, to whose exertions, indeed, the execution of this work is, properly speaking, entirely due, inas much as he kindly interested the Indian Government on behalf of my undertaking.

Herrnhut, January 1881.

H. A. J.

INTRODUCTION.

I. THE TIBETAN ALPHABET.

CONSONANTS.

The names of all the Consonants sound in a, pronounced like the a in the English word 'far'.

ཀ *ka* pronounced like the French c — car
ཁ *k̔a* like the English c or k — cart
ག *ga* harder than the English (hard) g
ང *ṅa* ng — pang
ཅ *ča* the soft English g — ginger
ཆ *č̔a* ch — chart
ཇ *ja* j — jar
ཉ *nya* the French gn — campagne
ཏ *ta* the French t — tard
ཐ *t̔a* the English t — tart
ད *da* dart
ན *na* nard
པ *pa* the French p — pas
ཕ *p̔a* the English p — part
བ *ba* bard
མ *ma* mart
ཙ *tsa* (ts) parts
ཚ *t̔sa* (aspirated)
ཛ *dza* (ds) — guards
ཝ *wa* waft
ཞ *ža* (zh) like the English s in leisure
ཟ *za* like the English z — zeal
འ *.a* (basis for vowels)
ཡ *) *ya* yard
ར **) *ra* rasp
ལ *la* last
ཤ *ša* (sh) — sharp
ས *sa* salve
ཧ *ha* half
ཨ *'a* (basis for vowels)

*) ཡ *ya*, when combined, as second consonant, with k- and p-sounds, or with m, is written under the first letter, assuming the shape of ྱ, thus ཀྱ *kya*, པྱ *pya*, མྱ *mya* etc.

**) ར *ra*, when combined as second letter, with k-, t- and p-sounds is written under the first, in the shape of ྲ, thus: ཀྲ, *kra*, ཏྲ *tra*, བྲ *bra* etc. — When combined with another consonant as *first* letter, it is written over the second, thus: རྐ *rka*, རྔ *rṅa*, རྡ *rda* etc., but it is seldom heard in speaking.

The so-called Sanskrit Cerebrals are represented in Tibetan letters by ཊ, ཋ, ཌ, ཎ, ཥ,

and when in this dictionary they are transcribed, they are marked by a dot underneath: *ṭ, ṭ́, ḍ, ṇ, ṣ*.

The figure ˂ (*wa-zur* or small *wa*) attached to the foot of a letter, is often used to distinguish homonyms in writing, e.g. ཚ *tsa* hot and ཚྭ *tsa* (*tswa*) salt.

The dot, which stands at the end of every syllable and of every word, is called Tseg (*tseg*) and is indispensable for a correct writing or reading.

When ག stands as a prefix, it is, when transcribed, represented by *γ*, e.g. གཅིག་ *γčig*, གཏམ་ *γtam* etc.

VOWELS.

The alphabetical order of the vowels is: a, i, u, e, o; they have in Tibetan the same sound as they have in German, Italian, and most other European languages: *a* sounds like the English a in 'far', *i* like ee in 'peer' or i in 'pin', *u* like u in 'rule' or in 'pull', *e* like a in 'fate' or e in 'met', *o* like o in 'note' or in 'not'.

As the vowel a is inherent in every consonant, so that even a single letter may form a word, e.g. བ་ *ba* (cow), ས་ *sa* (earth), there is no special character or letter required for this vowel. The other four vowels are represented by little hooks, ི standing for *i*, ུ for *u*, ེ for *e*, ོ for *o*. The marks for *i*, *e*, *o* are placed over the letter, that for *u* under it. Examples: པདྨ་ *pad-ma*, རི་ *ri*, མེ་ *me*, བུ་མོ་ *bu-mo*.

The letter ཨ is used as a basis for initial vowels, thus: ཨ་མ་ *'a-ma;* the letter འ serves as a basis for initial and final vowels: འོ་མ་ *˂o-ma*, དགའ་ *dga*.

The vowel-sounds of འ, when transcribed, are indicated by the mark ˂: འ *˂a*, འི *˂i*, འུ *˂u*, འེ *˂e*, འོ་ *˂o*, whilst the ཨ-vowels are denoted by the mark ' placed over the respective letters: ཨ *'a*, ཨི *'i*, ཨུ *'u*, ཨེ *'e*, ཨོ *'o*. — The real nature of the letters འ and ཨ is treated of in the latter part of the Introduction.

Whenever འ is a prefixed letter, the mark ˳, in transcribing, is put under the consonant following the འ e.g. འདུ *˳du*, འགྲོ་བ་ *˳gro-ba*.

Note. For a ready 'finding of words' in the Dictionary, it should be borne in mind, that the articles are arranged in the alphabetical order of the *initial* consonants *and* their *prefixed* and *superscribed* letters. Thus: ཀ—དཀ—བཀ—རྐ—སྐ—བསྐ—; ཁ—མཁ—འཁ— etc. etc.

II. PRONUNCIATION.

With regard to the language, with which I am dealing, it must, on the one hand, be admitted, that distinctions between sounds and, especially, variations in the mode of expressing their values as embodied in a written character, are far more numerous in Tibetan than either in Sanskrit or Hindi, in which two languages there is really little or no opening for mistake or ambiguity in this respect. But on the other hand, Tibetan is scarcely more irregular than French pronunciation, and a few definite rules enjoy universally recognized acceptation.

There is, however, one special difficulty in the case of Tibetan which, at the present stage of that language, renders it practically impossible to set up an equable and authoritative standard of pronunciation, and this is the existence of a great number of independent and well-defined *dialects*. An attempt to deal partially with this difficulty, — to append, let me suppose, to every word from three to five different pronunciations would involve a waste of time and an extension of space quite disproportionate to the value of the result. And yet, if one has to strike a preference in favour of one particular dialect, it is very hard to determine, which is to be selected. At first sight, it might seem the most natural course to fix upon the speech of the best educated classes in the capital city Lhasa. But when this method was followed, or when at least an endeavour was made to act upon it, by Georgi and then by Schröter, only scant approval was bestowed upon it by European critics, and there were and are several reasonable arguments to be urged against its adoption. Of all the dialects this presents to the European ear and tongue the greatest difficulties, and accommodates itself least readily to the written character. Moreover, in my own case, I have to add that I do not consider myself sufficiently master of it to care to risk its application to each individual word. Besides, modern political circumstances make this dialect, for the present, the least available for general use.

Csoma chose a much more manageable and a much more widely circulating mode of pronunciation, though one which presents problems of its own, when it has to be fitted to the written character: the West-Tibetan dialect. Here again, in representing each separate word, one has, in reality, to make choice between two, three or four pronunciations, of which one agrees best with the written character, another conforms closest to the rules of spelling, a third recommends itself as that most frequent in conversational language. In my own smaller Tibetan dictionary I went no farther than to distinguish between two principal groups, which I termed West-Tibetan and Central-Tibetan; but in a more scientific work like the present I may permit myself to call more minute attention to the niceties and refinements of the language before us. I have, accordingly, published a number of specimens from my note-book, in which I kept a collection of typical words, of which I availed myself as often as I had the opportunity of meeting the representatives of remote districts, and of enquiring concerning their manner of speech at home. Whenever in this collection a word had not been entered on sound native authority, or had not been sufficiently discussed, I preferred to mark it with a note of interrogation, and not to allow any conclusion from analogy, or any theory of pronunciation to interfere with the design of my handy-book and its simple and unprejudiced statement of fact. I may therefore, I hope, claim for this list a high degree of trustworthiness, even among collections of the kind, into which words can sometimes have slipped, as they had been heard once, and perhaps were not heard again.

In order to denote the pronunciation, I follow the scheme of Professor Lepsius. Some objections have been urged against this scheme; yet, amongst all systems of the kind, so far as I have become acquainted with them, I have no hesitation in affirming that of Professor Lepsius to be the best, and it is certainly also that most appropriate for my purpose. A thorough study of the 'Standard Alphabet by R. Lepsius, 2nd edition, London, Williams and Norgate. Berlin, Hertz, 1863' may be recommended to all persons, who interest themselves in phonetic investigations. As I can scarcely take it for granted, that the work mentioned will be already in the hands of every one, who may consult my dictionary, I shall endeavour, as briefly as possible, to indicate its essential plan and principles. Its rules may be stated as follows:

In order to mark sound, Lepsius uses the letters of the ordinary Latin alphabet. Where these are insufficient, he calls in the aid of a few Greek letters. Letters are used with the powers they most generally possess in European languages. (Thus z has its usual force, and does not stand for the peculiar sound ts, which belongs to it in the German language alone.) Sounds which lack exact representation are indicated by *diacritical marks*, placed above or below the letters which most nearly correspond. Every simple sound is represented by one and only one simple mark. Explosive and fricative consonants (these terms will be explained below) are denoted by different letters.

The following marks or signs are for *vowels:* the well known sign(˘) for a short, and (¯) for a long vowel; the mark of a modified vowel (¨), German ä, ö, ü, is placed by Lepsius, for practical reasons, below, not above the vowel (a̤, o̤. ṳ); a dot under the vowel denotes a close vowel-sound (ẹ = a in fate, ọ in note); a horizontal line under the vowel denotes a more open vowel-sound (e̱ in 'there', o̱ in 'or, cord', which, indeed, supersedes the a̤ mentioned above); the mark (˜) above the vowel indicates a nasal quality, the breath passing, while uttering the sound, to a considerable extent through the nose (the French '*an, in, on, un*' = *ã, ẹ̃, õ̱, ṳ̃*).

In marking *consonants*, there is first the distinction to be noted, that they are partly *explosives*, formed by a rapid process of closing and re-opening the passage of the air at a certain point, partly *fricatives* and *liquids*, formed by a partial process of compressing or narrowing the air-passage; and secondly, they are distinguished in regard to the exact spot, where the process of articulation takes place. The lowest articulation takes place in the *faucal region*, close to the larynx (here, for example, h is formed); next comes the guttural region, at the throat, near the soft palate and uvula (here k is formed); it is marked, when necessary, with a dot above the consonant; then the *palatal region*, the hard palate, (here the German ch is formed in 'ich'); the mark is a stroke like the acute accent in Greek over the consonant; then the *dental region*, at the teeth and gums (d, t, s, sh), and finally the *labial region*, at the lips (b, p, m). There exists a further class of consonants in the Indian languages, and also in modern Tibetan, which are styled *cerebrals;* they are most of them modified dentals, formed by bending or curling the tongue upwards, and bringing the tip of it into contact with the hard palate in the centre or toward the hinder part of its roof; mark, a dot under the consonant.

Many of these letters, in order to become audible, require in pronouncing them a certain *vocalic effort*; others, to say the least, allow or suggest such an effort; the mark of these vocalized consonants is a small *ring* under the letter. When this vocalic effort is made by the medium of the nasal channel alone, the oral passage being simultaneously closed at some one of the points indicated above, we get the nasal consonants as a result. When the stoppage is made at the guttural point, ng is obtained (to be marked *ṅ*); at the dental point, n; at the labial point, m. In order to conform with the two final rules, cited above from Lepsius, the Greek letter χ is used to represent the German ch, when it is guttural and hard, as in the word 'doch'; use is made of the Greek γ, when it is soft or accompanied by a vocalic tone (the Dutch g); χ́ gives the force of a palatal ch (German 'ich' = *iχ́*, 'milch' = milχ́); ϑ is used to represent the strong English th (as in 'through'); δ renders the softer or vocalized tone (as in 'that'); a hard, sharp and hissing s or ss (as in 'yes', 'press') is marked as s; the soft vocalic s (as in 'his', 'rise') is represented by z; the hard rushing sound sh, German sch, is rendered by š; the sound of the French j by ž. If one attempts to give at the palatal point, where the English y (in 'year'), or the German j (in 'Jahr') is formed, the sound sh, German sch, one obtains the palatal ś̌, or the softened and vocalized ź̌. In the Dictionary ȝ and ẑ have been substituted for these marks.

Further, in many languages, what are properly combinations of two consonants come to be regarded as simple forms, this happening, either because they are gradual growths upon an original simpler form, or because they have a natural affinity to each other. Thus properly dental sibilants should be distinguished thus: *tš*, *dž*; but for the sake of simplicity Lepsius, in his second edition, marks them *č* and *ǰ*, or, with their palatal force, *ć* and *j́* (instead of *č́* and *ǰ́*).

A further example of the combination of consonants is presented in what is known as *aspiration*, when the letter *h* is brought into more or less intimate connexion with another consonant. This introduces us to a very important distinction, belonging to the Tibetan language, which it is necessary to explain at some length, in accordance with which explosive consonants, as they have the force of tenues, mediae, or aspiratae, are treated. The tenues are produced by a sudden opening of the air-passage at one of the points above mentioned: throat, teeth, lips, such opening being unaccompanied by any sensible operation of the breath whatsoever. Thus, when quite exactly sounded, k, t, p, are produced. The mediae, g, d, b, are produced by the same process, carried out in a milder and less abrupt way, (the peculiar English pronunciation will come under consideration later). The aspiratae require a decided pressure by the breath (they will be found marked by the spiritus asper above the letter: *k̔, t̔, p̔*). In northern Germany, in England, and in Scandinavia, modern educated speech recognizes only mediae and aspiratae, for we give an aspirated sound to every k, t and p. The French and the Magyars distinguish consciously the pure tenues from the mediae; on the other hand they ignore the aspiratae. Tibetan pronunciation makes room and requires a mark for all three gradations. Nay more, it augments the class of explosive consonants or mutae by the addition of the dental sibilants in all three ranks or grades of aspiration: ཅ, ཆ, ཇ and ཙ, ཚ, ཛ, or according to the Standard Alphabet: *ć, č, j́* and *ts, t̔s, dz*. At a later stage of the language some further modifications were introduced, which we shall subsequently allude to.

Let us now, passing from these general observations, draw attention to a few details of the Phonetic Table, which has been drawn up in deference to a wish that reached me from several quarters.

The first column of the Table, now under review, gives the ancient literal pronunciation, as it was in vogue in the seventh century of our era, and was settled at the time of the invention of the alphabet. Such a pronunciation relies, after all, for its justification on the hypothesis, that the inventors of the alphabet had for their first object to reproduce, as exactly as possible, an artistic reflection of the natural value of sounds as spoken by their contemporaries: that, therefore, a later pronunciation is most in conformity with the original genius of the language, if it gives with the greatest distinctness a special power to each written character. A reference to the Table will amply illustrate the fact, that a pronunciation, adopted on these principles, has actually maintained itself in one or the other provincial dialect, and it is very interesting to notice, that the purest and most striking forms of this survival have their homes in those districts, which are most remote from and least subject to the disintegrating and dissolving influences of the actual centre of Tibetan civilisation, the capital Lhasa. Thus the prefixes and the superscribed consonants, for the most part, are still sounded at each extremity of the whole territory, within which the language is spoken, both on the Western and the Eastern frontier, alike in Khams, which borders on China, and in Balti, which merges into Kashmere. Moreover, in both localities the same minor irregularities occur, transgressions against an exact rendering of the pronunciation according to the letters, the same frequent transformations of the tenues into the aspiratae, g and d (compare lower down) becoming *γ* or *χ*, b becoming w. Now, about twenty degrees of longitude separate Balti from Khams, and the former, embracing Islam, long since cut itself adrift from spiritual and religious cohesion with Tibet, and there, too, the dialect in other respects has greatly deteriorated, has admitted many foreign elements and has fallen altogether from the position of a literary language. The resemblances and correspondences noted can, therefore, scarcely be accounted for in any other way, than by assuming that an old and strong instinct of speech lived on in oral tradition for more than ten centuries on the outskirts of the Tibetan domain, which in the intermediate provinces has gradually surrendered and submitted to the spirit of change.

Columns 2—6 contain, on most pages, the provincial dialects in their geographical sequence from West to East. The dialects of Ladak, Lahoul and Spiti correspond to what in my smaller Tibetan dictionary I called the dialect of Western Tibet. The last named, Spiti, represents in some respects the transition to the dialects of Eastern Tibet, under which heading Tsang and Ü are to be classed. At the date of the publication of my former dictionary I was unacquainted with the dialect of Khams. Where a space is left vacant in the columns, the provincial pronunciation agrees with the model provided under column 1. Towards the end of the Table, where the anomalies become much more frequent, I have for the sake of clearness repeated the word.

The sign ◂ (which does not occur in this Table) was pronounced = ཝ, or བ in the substantive terminations *ba* and *bo* (v. Dict. p. 362), viz. = the English w, so that རྭ sounded exactly like the French word *roi.*

The *Accent* has seldom been marked, because, as in our Teutonic dialects, it generally rests on the root of the word. In the case of compounds, it more frequently falls on the last than on the first of the component parts. But accentuation, altogether, is not of great significance in this language.

With regard to *Quantity,* vowels are pronounced shorter, even in open syllables, than is the case for instance in England and Germany. This applies particularly to the Central Provinces. Absolutely long vowels occur only as a peculiarity of dialect. They indicate that a consonant has been dropped, in most provinces, s, in Ü, gs, in Tsang, l. A long vowel may also indicate the blending of vowels. But when in Ü and Tsang the d, (as in *čė'-pa*) and when in Lahoul the g (as in *ťo', p̀u'-ròn*) is partially dropped, the vowel likewise maintains a short abrupt pronunciation. Moreover, the region, to which I have just referred, is that in which the spoken language has been greatly affected by a foreign linguistic principle. A system of Tones has been introduced under manifestly Chinese auspices. I am told by European students of reputation, who have made the Tonic languages of Eastern Asia their special department, that only the first principles of what are known as the *high and low Tones*, have made their way into Tibetan. Here, as in the languages of Farther India, generally, which possess an alphabetic system of writing, the Tone is determined by the initial consonant of the word. This I have generally indicated in column 7, which column applies only to the Spiti, Ťsang and Ü dialects. The system of Tones, as in Siam and elsewhere, has become of paramount importance in determining distinctions between words. An inhabitant of Lhasa, for example, finds the distinction between ཤ and ཞ, or between ས and ཟ, not in the consonant, but in the Tone, pronouncing ཤ and ས with a high note (as my Tibetan authorities were wont to describe it 'with a woman's voice', shrill and rapidly), ཞ and ཟ, on the contrary with a low note, and, as it appeared to me, more breathed and floating. This latter distinction is still more apparent with regard to those low-toned aspirates, that in the course of time were introduced in Central Tibet instead of the mediae, in contraposition to which now the original aspirates are used as high-toned; so more particularly in the dialect of Spiti. The low-toned aspirate I have indicated by h, the high-toned by the mark of the spiritus asper ʽ.

Those letters of the alphabet, which as simple initial consonants have a deep tone, become with a superscribed letter or with a prefix high-toned, so also ལ, when subscribed. The tenues remain, it would appear, unaffected by the Tone. With reference to the modifying effect of a final *n*, *d*, and *ṅ*, in different provinces, the Table may be consulted. The characterisation of the rushing sounds as 'palatals' is no doubt correct and agrees with the generally prevailing pronunciation; but the learner need not consider it as being of much importance.

The two letters, འ and ཨ, introduce us to a very interesting linguistic phenomenon. We meet here with the idea of the *vowel absolute*, the pure vocalic note, freed altogether from any presence of a consonant. This vowel-tone is rendered by the letter of the alphabet འ, in contradistinction to ཨ, which represents the Semitic א, the spiritus lenis of the Greeks, the audible re-opening of the air passage of the larynx. The difference may be observed, for example, in the manner of uttering the words, 'the lily, an endogen' and in the pronunciation of 'Lilian' (a name), in Tibetan ལི་ལི་ཨན་ and ལི་ལི་འན་. Thus, whenever in the middle of a word one vowel succeeds another (hence also in all diphthongs), འ is used. Again, in Tibetan, as in every form of human speech, it cannot but be the commonest of occurrences for a vowel to follow a consonant, and the strict rule might seem to require the vocalic tone to be always indicated, which, according to Csoma, was originally done. However, as the Tibetan language, adopting the principle from Sanskrit, deems the sound of *a* to be naturally inherent in every consonant, while the other four vowels, as mere subspecies of the vowel absolute, are indicated by little hooks above or below the letter, and as the end of a syllable is always marked by a dot (called *tseg*), the function of འ in this capacity was soon seen to be quite superfluous. Its use is necessary only to obviate ambiguities, when for instance one of the five letters, used as prefixes, precedes a consonant with *a*; e.g. the word མད་, would be read *'mad';* whereas མདའ་, written thus, implies that the vowel does not precede but follow the consonant d, and consequently the m is prefix, and the word to be read *'mda'*. If the vowel is not *a*, the sign of such vowel suffices, e.g. མདོ་ *mdo;* མདའོ་ *mdao*, standing now for མདའོའ་. Some practical difficulty attends the pronunciation of the pure vowel as an initial letter. In order that the effect of the consonant ཨ may not be produced, it is necessary, after opening the larynx, to allow the tone gently to set in and then to let it gradually gain fulness and force. I shall indicate this process by the mark ˱. The sound would be still more accurately represented than it is in the Table, thus: *˱aár-po, ˱uúg-pa* etc. Improper are the expedients of some of the dialects, the sound being hardened to *γ* in Khams, to ཨ in Western Tibet; also Csoma's device of indicating it by an h is inadequate. This is a case in which the true pronunciation has been preserved in the Central Provinces, perhaps, because it almost necessarily implies the effort connected with the low Tone, above referred to, so that, when the invading system of Tones had here established its authority, it acted as a conservative element.

Finally, this vocalic tone can be used in connexion with certain consonants. It is unnecessary to indicate it in Tibetan, when it accompanies liquidae (*m, n, ṅ, r, l*) and sibilants; but with the mutae it must be marked, where the effect is that, with which we are familiar in the case of the English mediae, b, d, g, j, for instance in 'be, do, go, jew'. In Tibetan the vocalic effect accompanies aspirates too, and is marked by འ, placed as a prefix, which I transcribe thus ₒ, e.g. འདུ་ *ₒdu* = the English do. The pause on the tone is of course in the case of mutae a very short one. Here again, though only in the case of the mediae, we find this peculiarity preserved in its purity in Central Tibet. It is not difficult to understand, how, if one is careless about closing the nasal passage, a nasal articulation of this prefix can easily grow common. This has happened throughout Khams, and in the rest of Tibet at least in compound words; at Lhasa it is considered inelegant, as is also the sounding of any prefix. On the other hand, the dialect of Central Tibet neglects the distinction between མ and འ and pronounces the former only as a vocalic initial. In words from the Sanscrit the འ is used in some respect as a 'mora', to denote a long syllable, e. g. ཤྲཱི for श्री; hence the opinion of Lamas of Lhasa, that it expresses prosodical length, when used as above in མདའ.

མྱ་ *mya*, is not found in use in any of the dialects. The sole confirmation of its literal pronunciation depends upon the word *myań-ba* which, perhaps a thousand years ago, found its way into the Bu-nan language (Tibar-skad, Cunningh.) and which the people of Lahoul, when speaking Tibetan, pronounce *nyań-wa*. The process of transition to the cerebral ṭ-sounds in the words *krad-pa* etc. is in many places not yet completed, so that the sound of r is still more or less clearly distinguishable. The *Prefixes* have always constituted the most perplexing phenomena in the Tibetan language. At the time of the invention of the alphabet they must have represented a sort of anticipatory sound in close connexion with the initial consonant of the word. Certain seeming impossibilities of pronunciation, when one has, for instance, to deal with a prefix together with a threefold initial consonant (བསྒྲ་, བསྐྲ་) become less formidable, and not more embarrassing than those which meet us, for example, in the Polish language, when we ascertain that in Balti and Khams the three explosive prefixes are pronounced as fricatives, in which case *v* must be written for *w*. Thus གཅིག་ *γči-wa*, བཀྲ་ *wkra*, བསྒྲགས་ *wsgrugs* call for no greater exertions, than do the Polish *chciwy*, *wkrótce*, *wskroś*. Our strongest ground for assuming this fricative pronunciation to be that of antiquity is, I think, that, had it been explosive, words like གསུ་, གསོན་ would have coincided with གྲུ་, སྒྲོན་. Yet it must be acknowledged that a pronunciation *bču*, *bka* etc. exists, side by side with *wču*, *wka* etc. — མ, as a liquid, offers no difficulty. — འ, as a prefix, is no consonant.

A doubt must still cling to ད, and I do not venture to determine its ancient pronunciation. It is by a strange anomaly that, in most dialects, when prefixed to བ, both it and the initial consonant die away into a spiritus lenis; and almost still more singular it is, that where it still asserts an independent force, in Khams and in Balti, it is sounded like ག with the power of *γ*. The investigations of Lepsius go indeed to prove, that ད and ག are complements to each other; but how came, at the beginning, two letters to be chosen as signs for one and the same sound? Most probably the original sound was ð, which then very soon passed into *γ*. The variations between r and s in Ladak afford no sure hold for drawing inferences.

The purpose, for which the Phonetic Table was drawn up, will have been attained, if I succeed in convincing my readers, 1. that for scientific objects the pronunciation, as it is given in Column 1, is the most suitable, and that with a good conscience it can be recommended in the place of that introduced by Csoma; 2. that its system is regular enough to render it unnecessary to give the pronunciation of every individual word throughout the work; 3. that I present in this Table, in regard to the various dialects, as much in the way of results as, down to the present, it has been possible for European students to acquire and to put into shape for the service of a European public.

III. PHONETIC TABLE FOR COMPARING THE DIFFERENT DIALECTS.

The columns 2—6 are arranged according to the geographical site of the provinces from West to East.

I. Words containing only simple consonants and vowels.

1	2	3	4	5	6	7
	West. Tibet		Central Prov.			
	Ladak	Lahoul	Spiti	Tsang, Ü	Khams	
ka-ra						
kug = cook		*ku'*				
kun				*kṳn*	*kṳn*	
ḱaṅ-pa						in C. high-toned
gaṅ			*ghaṅ*	*ghaṅ*		
ṅal				*ṅā* Ts.		in C. deep-toned
ṅan-pa				*ṅem-pa* Ü.		
c̀i					*c̀e*	
čad-pa				*čẹ̤'-pa*		
čan-pa				*čem-pa*		high-toned
čen-po				*čem-po*		
ja			*jha*	*jha*		deep-toned
nyin					*nyen*	
tib-ril				*tib-rī* Ts.	*teb-rel*	
t́aṅ					*t́eṅ*	
t́ab = *t́ăp*						high-toned
t́og		*tŏ'*				
t́od-pa				*t́o̤'-pa*		
da			*dha*	*dha*		
dud-pa			*dhud-pa*	*dhṳ'-pa*		deep-toned
nad = *năt*				*nẹ'*		
ṕan-pa				*ṕem-pa*		high-toned
ṕug-ron		*ṕu'-ron*		*ṕug-ro̤n*		
ba			*bha*	*bha*	*wa*	
bal			*bhal*	*bhā* Ts. *bhal* Ü.	*wal*	
bu			*bhu*	*bhu*	*wo̤*	
bu-mo			*bhu-mo*	*bhu-mo*	*wo̤-mo*	deep-toned
bod			*bhod*	*bho̤'*	*wod*	
mig		*mi'*				
me						
t́sil				*t́sī*	*t́sel*	high-toned
dza-ti						
wa-tse						
z̀a			*s̀a*	*s̀a*	*ža*	
z̀ag		*z̀a'*	*s̀ag*	*s̀ag*	*žag*	
za			*sa*	*sa*		
zan			*san*	*sen*		
‹ar-po	*'ar-po*	*'ar-po*			*γar-po*	
‹ug-pa	*'ug-pa*	*'ug-pa*			*γug-pa*	
‹o-ma	*'a-ma*	*'o-ma*			*γo-ma*	in C. deep-toned
‹od	*'od*	*'od*		*o͡‹ọ'*	*γod*	
‹ol-mo	*'ol-mo*	*'ol-mo*		*o͡‹ó-mo* Ts.	*γol-mo*	
yaṅ					*yeṅ*	
yan-pa				*yā-ga*		
yal-ga				*yem-pa*		
yin					*yen*	
yul				*yū*, *yṳ̄* Ts.		

1	2	3	4	5	6	7
	West. Tibet		Central Prov.			
	Ladak	Lahoul	Spiti	Tsang, Ü	Khams	
yod				*yọ'*		
ral				*rā̤*		deep-toned
rol-mo				*rō-mo* Ts		
lo-ma						
ša						
šel						high-toned
sa						
'a-ma						

II. Words terminating in བ་ or བོ་.

1	2 Ladak	3 Lahoul	4 Spiti	5 Tsang, Ü	6 Khams	7
za-ba		*za-wa*	*sa-wa*	*sa-wa*		deep-toned
ži-ba		*ži-wa*	*ši-wa*	*ši-wa*	*ži-wa*	
ši-ba		*ši-wa*	*ši-wa*	*ši-wa*	*ši-wa*	high-toned
žu-ba		*žu-wa*	*šu-wa*	*šu-wa*	*žu-wa*	
jo-bo		*jo-wo*	*jho-wo*	*jho-wo*		deep-toned
dar-ba		*dar-wa*	*dhar-wa*	*dhar-wa*		
sol-ba		*sol-wa*		*sō-wa* Ts.		high-toned

III. Words terminating in ས.

1	2 Ladak	3 Lahoul	4 Spiti	Kun.	5 Tsang, Ü	6 Khams	7
k̔as	*k̔as, k̔ẹ̄*	*k̔ai, k̔ẹ̄*	*k̔ẹ̄*	*k̔ā*	*k̔ẹ̄*	*k̔ē*	high-toned
ris	*ris, rī*	*rī*	*rī*	*rī*	*rī*	*rī*	
gus	*gus, gṻ*	*gui, gṻ*	*ghụi*	*gū*	*ghṻ*	*gṻ*	
dus	*dus, dṻ*	*dui, dṻ*	*dhụi*	*dū*	*dhṻ*	*dṻ*	deep-toned
des	*des, dē*	*dē*	*dhē*	*dē*	*dhē*	*dī*	
k̔os	*k̔os, k̔ọ̄*	*k̔oi, k̔ọ̄̈*	*k̔ọ̄*	*k̔ọ*	*k̔ọ̄̈*	*kō̤*	high-toned
gos	*gos, gọ̄*	*goi, gọ̄*	*ghọ̄*	*gō*	*ghọ̄̈*	*gọ̄̈*	deep-toned
'os	*'os, 'ọ̄*	*'oi, 'ọ̄̈*	*'ọ̄̈*	*ō*	*'ọ̄̈*	*γọ̄̈*	
č̔os	*č̔os, č̔ọ̄*	*č̔oi, č̔ọ̄̈*	*č̔ọ̄*	*č̔ō*	*č̔ọ̄̈*	*č̔ọ̄̈*	high-toned
nags	*nag(s)*	*nag*		?	*nag, nā*	*nāg*	deep-toned
rigs	*rig(s)*	*rig*		?	*rig, rī*	and	
t̔ugs	*t̔ug(s)*	*t̔ug*		?	*t̔ug, t̔ụ̄*	so forth	high-toned
legs	*leg(s)*	*leg*		?	*leg, lē*		deep-toned
p̔ogs	*p̔og(s)*	*p̔og*		?	*p̔og, p̔ō*		
t̔abs	*t̔ab(s)*	*t̔ab*	*t̔au*		*t̔ab*	*t̔ab*	
č̔ibs	*č̔ib(s)*	*č̔ib*	*č̔iu͡*		*č̔ib*	*č̔ib*	high-toned
šubs	*šub(s)*	*šub*	*šū*		*šub*	*šub*	
p̔ebs	*p̔eb(s)*	*p̔eb*	*p̔ĕü͡*		*p̔eb*	*p̔eb*	
'obs	*'ob(s)*	*'ob*	*'ŏü͡*		*'o͡ŏb*	*γob*	deep-toned
t̔ams-čád	*t̔am(s)-čád*	*t̔am-čád*	*t̔am-čád*		*t̔am-čẹ̄'*	*t̔am-čad*	high-toned
goms-pa	*gom(s)-pa*	*gom-pa*	*ghom-pa*		*ghom-pa*	*gom-pa*	deep-toned

IV. Words with diphthongs.

1	2 Ladak	3 Lahoul	4 Spiti	5 Tsang, Ü	6 Khams	7
k̔ai	*k̔ẹ̄*	*k̔ai, k̔ẹ̄*		*k̔ẹ̄*	*k̔ē*	high-toned
čü, čī	*čī*	*čī*		*čī*	*čī*	
bui	*bui, bṻ*	*bui, bṻ*	*bhui*	*bhṻ*	*bṻ*	deep-toned
dĕī͡	*dei*		*dhĕī͡*	*dhĕī͡*	*dī*	
soí					*sọ̄*	high-toned
gă͡ü			*ghăü*	*ghau*	*ga-γọ*	
lĕü͡					and so forth	
mĭü͡						deep-toned
ră͡ŏ					(*ra-γo*)	
reo						

1	2	3	4	5	6	7
	West. Tibet		Central Prov.			
	Ladak	Lahoul	Spiti	Tsang, Ü	Khams	
rio						
roo, rō						deep-toned
ruo						

V. Words with subscribed letters.

kyaṅ					kyeṅ	
kyir-kyir					kyer-kyér	
kyu					kyo̤	
k̔yi					k̔ye	
k̔yu					k̔yo̤	high-toned
k̔yed				k̔yĕ'		
k̔yod				k̔yö̤'		
gyi			ghyi	ghyi		deep-toned
gyon-pa	Pur. Bal.; Ld.		ghyon-pa	ghyo̤m-pa		
p̔yag	p̔yag čag	čag	čag	čag	čag	
p̔yi	p̔i	p̔i	či	či	či	
p̔yug-po	p̔yug-po čug-po	čug-po	čug-po	čug-po	čug-po	high-toned
p̔ye	p̔e	p̔e	če	če	če?	
p̔yogs	čog(s)	čog	čog	čog Ts. čō Ü.	čog	
bya-mo	bya-mo ǰa-mo	ǰa-mo	?	ǰha-mo	?	
byi-ba, byi-wa	bi-wa	bi-wa	?	ǰhi-wa	?	deep-toned
bye-ma	?	be-ma	?	ǰhe-ma	?	
byos	?	ǰos, ǰoi, ǰö̤	?	ǰhö̤	?	
mya-ṅán	?	nya-ṅán	nya-ṅán	nya-ṅe̤n	?	high-toned
krad-pa	?	ṭad-pa	ṭad-pa	ṭē̤'-pa Ts. vlg. ke̤'-pa Ü.	?	
k̔rag	k̔rag	ṭ̔ag	ṭ̔äg	ṭ̔äg	ṭ̔äg	
k̔rims		ṭ̔im(s)	ṭ̔im	ṭ̔im	ṭ̔em	high-toned
k̔rus	?	ṭ̔us; ṭ̔ṳ̈	ṭ̔ui	ṭ̔ṳ̈	ṭ̔ṳ̈	
k̔roṅ-po	?	ṭ̔oṅ-pa	ṭ̔oṅ-pa	ṭ̔o̤m-pa	ṭ̔oṅ-pa	
gri	gri	dri, ḍi	ḍhi	ḍhi	ḍi	deep-toned
droṅ-mo		ḍoṅ-mo	ḍhoṅ-mo	ḍhoṅ-mo	ḍoṅ-mo	
p̔ru-gu	p̔ru-gu	ṭ̔u-gu	ṭ̔u-ghu	ṭ̔u-ghu	ṭ̔o̤-go̤	high-toned
bra-bo, bra-wo		bra-wo, ḍa-wo	ḍha-wo	ḍha-wo	ḍa-wo	deep-toned
braṅ-sa	(B. blaṅ-sa)	ḍaṅ-sa	ḍhaṅ-sa	ḍhaṅ-sa	ḍaṅ-sa	
sraṅ-ma	stran-ma?	ṡran-ma	ṡran-ma	ṡrém-ma vulg. sem-ma	stran-ma	high-toned
sriṅ-mo	strin-mo B.	ṡriṅ-mo	ṡriṅ-mo	ṡriṅ-mo vulg. siṅ-mo	striṅ-mo	
hrul-po	ṡrul-po	ṡrul-po	ṡrul-po	šrul-po	šrul-po	deep-toned
klog-pa	?	log-pa	log-pa	log-pa	?	
glog	γlog B.	log	log	log	γlog	high-toned
bla-ma	?	la-ma	la-ma	la-ma	wla-ma	
zla-ba, zla-wa	lza B.	(l)da-wa	da-wa	da-wa	lda-wa	?
rlaṅs-pa		(r)laṅ(s)-pa	lã-pa	laṅ-pa	rleṅ-pa	high-toned
sla-mo	?	la-mo	la-mo̤	la-mo	sla-mo	

VI. Words with superscribed letters.

rkaṅ-pa	?	(r)kuṅ-pa	kaṅ-pa	kaṅ-pa	rkeṅ-pa	these and all
rgad-po	?	(r)gad-po	gad-po	ge̤'-po	rgad-po	the rest are
rṅa	?	(r)ṅa	ṅa	ṅa	rṅa	high-toned
rǰes	?	žes, žē	ǰē?	ǰē	rǰī	

1	2	3	4	5	6	7
	West. Tibet		Central Prov.			
	Ladak	Lahoul	Spiti	Tsang, Ü	Khams	
rnyiṅ-pa	*(r)nyiṅ-pa*	*nyiṅ-pa*	*nyiṅ-pa*	*nyiṅ-pa*	*rnyiṅ-pa*	
rta	*rta, sta, ta*	*ta*	*ta*	*ta*	*rta*	
rdo	*(r)do*	*do*	*do*	*do*	*rdo*	
rṅon-po	*(r)ṅon-po*	*ṅon-po*	*ṅon-po*	*ṅo̤m-po*	*rṅon-po*	
rba	*wa*	*ba*	*ba*	*ba*	*rwa?*	
rmig-pa	*mig-pa*	*mig-pa*	*mig-ba*	*mig-pa*	*rmig-pa*	
rtsa	*sa*	*sa*	?	*tsa*	?	Pur. Bal.
rtswa	*sa*	*sa*	?	*tsa*	?	*rtsoṅ, stsoṅ*
rdza-ma	*za-ma*	*za-ma*	?	*dza-ma*	?	
lṅa	*ṅa, šṅa*	*ṅa*	*ṅa*	*ṅa*	*lṅa*	
lċaṅ-ma	*lċaṅ-ma*	*ċaṅ-ma*	*ċaṅ-ma*	*ċaṅ-ma*	*lċeṅ-ma*	*lċaṅ-ma*
ljaṅ-k'u	*(l)jaṅ-k'u*	*jaṅ-k'u*	*jaṅ-k'u*	*jaṅ-k'u*	*ljeṅ-k'u*	
ltad-mo	*(l)tad-mo*	*tad-mo*	*tad-mo*	*tė'-mo*	*ltad-mo*	*ltad-mo*
ldag-pa	*(l)dag-pa*	*dag-pa*	*ḍag-pa*	*dag-pa*	*ldag-pa*	
lham	*lam*	*lam*	*lam*	*hlam* or *χlam*	*lham*	*lham*
skom	*skom*	*kom*	*kom*	*kom*	*skom*	*skom*
skra	*šra*	*šra, ṭa*	*ṭa*	*ṭa*	*štra*	
sgo	*γo*	*go*	*go*	*go*	*sgo*	*sgo*
sgra	*ḍa, ra*	*ḍa, ra*	*ḍa*	*ḍa*	*zdra*	
sṅon-po	*ṅon-po*	*ṅon-po*	*ṅon-po*	*ṅo̤m-po*	*sṅon-po*	
snyiṅ	*nyiṅ*	*nyiṅ*	*nyin*	*nyiṅ*	*snyeṅ*	
stag	*stag*	*tag*	*tag*	*tag*	*stag*	
sdoṅ-po	*(s)doṅ-po*	*doṅ-po*	*doṅ-po*	*doṅ-po*	*sdoṅ-po*	
sna	*na*	*na*	*na*	*na*	*sna*	
spu	*(s)pu*	*pu*	*pu*	*pu*	*spo̤*	
spyod-pa	*(s)ċod-pa*	*ċod-pa*	*ċod-pa*	*ċö'-pa*	*šwod-pa*	
sprĕü	also *šrĕü*	*ṭĕü*	*ṭĕü*	*ṭĕü*	*štre-yü*	
sbal-ba	*(s)bal-wa*	*bal-wa*	*bal-wa*	*bā-wa* Ts. *bal-wa* Ü.	*zwal-wa*	
sbyar-ba	*žar-wa*	*žar-wa*	*žar-wa*	*jar-wa*	*zwar-wa*	
sbraṅ-bu	also *ḍaṅ-bu*	*ḍaṅ-bu*	*ḍaṅ-bu*	*ḍaṅ-bu*	*ḍeṅ-wo̤*	
sman	*(s)man*	*man*	*man*	*me̤n*	*sman*	
smyon-pa	*nyon-pa*	*nyon-pa*	*nyon-pa*	*nyo̤m-pa*	*snyon-pa*	
smra-ba	*mra-wa*	*mra-wa*	?	*m(r)a-wa*	*šna-wa*	
stsal-ba	*(s)tsal-wa*	*tsal-wa*	*tsal-wa*	*tsā-wa* Ts. *tsal-wa* Ü.	*stsal-wa*	

VII. Words with prefixed letters.

γċes-pa	*ċes-pa*	*ċē-pa*	*ċē-pa*	*ċē-pa*	*γċī-pa*	
γtam	*tam*	*tam*	*tam*	*tam*	*γtām*	
γduṅ-ba	*ḍuṅ-wa*	*duṅ-wa*	*duṅ-wa*	*duṅ-wa*	*γduṅ-wa*	
γnaṅ-ba	*naṅ-wa*	*naṅ-wa*	*naṅ-wa*	*naṅ-wa*	*γneṅ-wa*	
γnam	*nam*	*nam*	*nam*	*nam*	*γnam*	Bal. *γnam*
γtsaṅ-po	*tsaṅ-po*	*tsaṅ-po*	*tsaṅ-po*	*tsaṅ-po*	*γtseṅ-po*	
γžu	*žu*	*žu*	*šu*	*šu*	*γžo̤*	
γzig	*zig*	*zi'*	*sig*	*sig*	*γzig*	
γyog-po	*yog-po*	*yo'-po*	*yog-po*	*yög-po*	*(γ)yog-po*	
γšer-pa	*šer-pa*	*šer-pa*	*šer-pa*	*šer-pa*	*γšer-pa*	or *gšer-pa*
γser	*ser*	*ser*	*ser*	*ser*	*γser*	Bal. *γser*
dkar-po	*kar-po*	*kar-po*	*kar-po*	*kar-po*	*γkar-po*	
dkyil	*kyil*	*kyil*	*kyil*	*kyil*	*γkyil*	
dgu	*gu*	*gu*	*gu*	*gu*	*γgo̤*	
dgra	*ḍa*	*ḍa*	*ḍa*	*ḍa*	*(γ)ḍa*	Bal. *χṅul*
dṅul	*ṅul* (vulgo	*mul*) *ṅul*	*ṅul*	*ṅü* Ts. *ṅul* Ü.	*γṅul*	or *χmul*
dpe-ċa	*pe-ċa*	*pe-ċa*	*pe-ċa*	*pe-ċa*	*γpe-ċa*	*γpe-ċa*

1	2	3	4	5	6	7
	West. Tibet		Central Prov.			
	Ladak	Lahoul	Spiti	Tsaug, Ü	Khams	
ma-dpe	*mas-pe*	*mar-pe*	*ma-pe*	*ma-pe*	*maγ-pe?*	
dpyid	*(s)pid*	*pid*	*ćid*	*ći'*	*χśid*	
dbaṅ	*uaṅ*	*uaṅ*	*uaṅ*	*uaṅ* (vlg. *aṅ*)	*γweṅ*	
dbu	*'u**	*'u*	*'u*	*'u*	*wọ*	* = ཨུ་ etc.
dbugs	*'ug(s)*	*'u'*	*'ug*	*'ug* Ts. *'ü* Ü.	*wug*	
dbul-po	*'ul-po*	*'ul-po*	*'ul-po*	*'ü-po* Ts. *'ul-po, ụl-po* Ü.	*γwọl-po*	
dben-pa	*'en-pa*	*'en-pa*	*'en-pa*	*'em-pa*	*γwen-pa*	
dbyar	*yar*	*yar*	*yar*	*yar*	*wyer*	
dmar-po	*mar-po*	*mar-po*	*mar-po*	*mar-po*	*(γ)mar-po*	
dmyal-ba	*nyal-wa*	*nyal-wa*	*nyal-wa*	*nyä-wa* Ts. *nyal-wa* Ü.	*mnyal-wa*	
bka, vka	*ka*	*ka*	*ka*	*kā*	*vka*	
bkra-śis	*ṭa-śi(s)*	*ṭa-śī*	*ṭa-śī*	*ṭa-śī*	*bṭa-śī*	
bgo-ba	*go-wa*	*go-wa*	*go-wa*	*go-wa*	*vgo-wa*	
brgyad	*gyad*	*gyad*	*gyad*	*gyẹ'*	*vrgyad*	Bal. *vrgyad*
bću	*ću*	*ću*	*ću*	*ću*	*vću, bću*	
bćug-sum	*ćug-súm*	*ćug-um*	*ću-súm?*	*ću-súm* *ću-sum*	*vćug-súm*	
bćub-ži	*ćub-ži*	*ćub-ží*	*ću-ži*	*ću-ží*	*vćub-ži?*	
brǰed-pa	*žed-pa*	*žed-pa*	*ǰed-pa*	*ǰĕ'-pa*	*vrǰed-pa*	
btum-pa	*tum-pa*	*tum-pa*	*tum-pa*	*tūm-pa*	*btọm-pa*	
bdun	*dun*	*dun*	*dun*	*dụn*	*vdun*	Bal. *vdun*
brtse-ba	*se-wa.*	*se-wa*	*tse-wa*	*tse-wa*	*vrtse-wa*	
brdzun	*zun*	*zun*	*dzun*	*dzun*	*vrdzun*	Pur. *rdzun*
bži	*ži*	*ži*	*śi*	*śi*	*vže*	
bžib-ću	*žib-ću*	*žib-ću*	*śi-ću?*	*śí-ću*	*vžeb-ću?*	
bzaṅ-po	*zaṅ-po*	*zaṅ-po*	*saṅ-po*	*saṅ-po*	*vzeṅ-po*	
bśal-ba	*śal-wa*	*śal-wa*	*śal-wa*	*śä-wa*	*vśel-wa*	
bsu-ba	*su-wa*	*su-wa*	*su-wa*	*su-wa*	*vsọ-wa*	
bsreg-pa	*śreg-pa*	*śreg-pa*	*śreg-pa*	*śreg-pa* *(seg-pa)*	*vstrag-pa*	
bslab-pa	*lab-pa*	*lab-pa*	*lab-pa*	*lab-pa*	*vslab-pa*	
mṅar	*ḱar*	*ḱar*	*ḱar*	*ḱar*	*mḱar*	
mgo	*go*	*go*	*˳go*	*˳go*	*mgo*	
mgron	*ḍon*	*ḍon*	*ḍon*	*˳ḍọn*	*mḍon*	
mṅar-(b)wa	*ṅar-wa*	*ṅar-wa*	*ṅar-wa*	*ṅar-wa*	*mṅar-wa*	
mčin-pa	*čin-pa*	*čin-pa*	*čin-pa*	*čim-ga*	*mčen-pa*	
mǰiṅ-pa	*ǰiṅ-pa*	*ǰiṅ-pa*	*˳ǰiṅ-pa*	*˳ǰiṅ-pa*	*mǰiṅ-pa*	
mṫiṅ	*ṫiṅ*	*ṫiṅ*	*ṫiṅ*	*ṫiṅ*	*(m)ṫeṅ*	
mda	*da*	*da*	*˳da*	*˳da*	*mḍa*	
mṫso	*ṫso*	*ṫso*	*ṫso*	*ṫso*	*mṫso*	
mdzo	*dzo*	*dzo*	*˳dzo*	*˳dzo*	*mdzo*	
˳ḱol-ba	*ḱol-wa*	*ḱol-wa*	*ḱol-wa*	*ḱö-wa* Ts.	*ṅḱol-wa*	
˳gul-ba	*gul-wa*	*gul-wa*	*˳gul-wa*	*˳gü-wa* Ts *˳gul-wa* Ü.	*ṅgul-wa*	
˳čam-pa	*čam-pa*	*čam-pa*	*čam-pa*	*čam-pa*	*nčam-pa*	
˳ǰam-po	*ǰam-po*	*ǰam-po*	*˳ǰam-po*	*˳ǰam-po*	*nǰam-po*	
˳ṫag-pa	*ṫag-pa*	*ṫag-pa*	*ṫag-pa*	*ṫag-pa*	*nṫag-pa*	
γge-˳dún	*gen-dun*	*gen-dun*	*ge(n)-dún*	*ge(n)-dụn* Ts. *ge-˳dụn* Ü.	*γgen-dún?*	
˳dod-pa	*dod-pa*	*dod-pa*	*˳dod-pa*	*˳dọ̈'-pa*	*ndod-pa*	—
˳ṗur-ba	*ṗur-wa*	*ṗur-wa*	*ṗur-wa*	*ṗur-wa*	*mṗur-wa*	
˳ṗyi-ba	*ṗi-wa*	*ṗi-wa*	*ṗi-wa*	*či-wa*	*nči-wa*	
˳prod-pa	*ṭ́od-pa*	*ṭ́od-pa*	*ṭ́od-pa*	*ṭ́ọ̈'-pa*	*nṭ́od-pa*	

1	2	3	4	5	6	7
	West. Tibet		Central Prov.			
	Ladak	Lahoul	Spiti	Tsang, Ü	Khams	
˳bab-pa	*bab-pa*	*bab-pa*	*˳bab-pa*	*˳bab-pa*	*mbab-pa*	
vka-˳bùm	*kam-bum*	*kam-bum*	*kam-bùm*	*ka(m)-bùm*	*vkam-bùm*	
˳tsir-wa	*tsir-wa*	*tsir-wa*	*tsir-wa*	*tsir-wa*	*ntsir-wa*	
˳dzin-pa	*dzin-pa*	*dzin-pa*	*dzin-pa*	*dzim-pa*	*ndzen-pa*	

ABBREVIATIONS.

abbr. = abbreviated, abbreviation
acc. according to
accus. accusative case
act. active, -ly
adj. adjective
adv. adverb, -ially
A. R. Asiatic Researches
Ar. Arabic
B. books, book-language
Bal. Balti, the most westerly of the districts, in which the Tibetan language is spoken.
Bhar. Bharata, a dialogue, ed. by Dr. A. Schiefner.
Bhot. Bhotan, province.
Burn. I. Burnouf, Introduction au Buddhism Indien.
» II. Burnouf, Lotus de la bonne loi.
C. Central Tibet, esp. the provinces Ü and Tsang.
c. cum, with
c.c. construitur cum, construed with.
c.c.a. construed with the accusative, etc.
ccapir construitur cum accusativo personae, instrumentativo rei
ccirdp construitur cum instrumentativo rei, dativo personae etc.
cf. confer, compare
Chr. P. Christian writings by Protestant missionaries.
Chr. R. Christian writings by Roman Catholic missionaries.
cog. cognate, related in origin
col. colloquial, -ly
collect. collective, -ly
com. commonly
comp. compound -s
conj. conjunction
contr. contracted
corr. correct, -ly
correl. correlative, -ly
Cs. Csoma de Körös, Tibetan-English Dictionary.
Cunn. Cunningham, General, Ladak and the surrounding country.
dat. dative case
deriv. derivative
Desg. Desgodins, La Mission du Tibet de 1855—1870.
Do. or Dom. Do-mang, a collection of incantations.
dub. dubious
Dzl. Dzanglun, an ancient collection of Legends of Buddha.
e.g. = exempli gratia, for instance
eleg. elegant, -ly
elsewh. elsewhere
emphat. emphatical, -ly
erron. erroneous, -ly
esp. especially
euphemist. euphemistical, -ly
expl. explain, explanation
extr. extremo, towards the end of a longer article.
fem. feminine gender
fig. figurative, -ly
frq. frequent, -ly
fut. future tense
gen. general, -ly
gen. genitive case
Glr. Gyalrabs, a history of the kings of Tibet.
Gram. native grammarians or grammatical works
Gyatch. Gyatcherrolpa, Biography of Buddha.
Hd. Hindi language.
Hook. Dr. Hooker, Himalayan Journals.
ibid. ibidem, in the same place.
id. idem, the same
i. e. id est, that is
imp. imperative mood
impers. impersonal, -ly
incorr. incorrect, -ly
inf. infinitive mood
init. initio, at the beginning of a longer article.
inst. instead
instr. instrumentative case
interj. interjection
interr. interrogative, -ly
intrs. intransitive
i.o. instead of
irr. irregular, -ly
Kh. Khams, eastern part of Tibet.
Köpp. Köppen, Die Religion des Buddha.
Kun. Kunawur, province under English protection.
Lat. Latin
Ld. Ladak, province.
Ld.-Glr. Ladak-Gyalrabs, a history of Tibet, ed. by Dr. E. Schlagintweit.
Lew. Lewin, Manual of Tibetan.
Lex., Lexx. Lexicons, native dictionaries.
Lh. Lahoul, province.
Lis. Lishigurkhang, glossary.
lit. literally, also literature
Ma. Ma-ong-lung-bstan, a kind of Tibetan Apocalypse.

masc.	=	masculine gender
Med.		medical works
med.		medio, about the middle of a longer article
metaph.		metaphorical, -ly
meton.		metonymical, -ly
Mil.		Milaraspa's hundred thousand Songs.
Mil. nt.		Milaraspai nam-tar, Milaraspa's autobiography.
Mng.		Man-ngag-rgyud, a medical work.
n.		name
neut.		neuter gender
nif.		ni fallor, if I am not mistaken
n.p.		noun proper
N.T.		New Testament
num.		numeral
obs.		obsolete
opp.		as opposed to
p.		page
partic.		participle
pass.		passive, -ly
perh.		perhaps
Pers.		Persian
pers.		person, personal
pf.		perfect tense
pl.		plural number
pleon.		pleonastic, -ally
p. n.		proper name
po.		poetically
pop.		popular language
postp.		postposition
prep.		preposition
prob.		probably
pron.		pronoun
prop.		properly
prov.		provincialism, provincial, -ly
Pth.		Padma thangyig, a collection of legends of Padma Sambhava.
Pur.		Purig, province.
q. v.		quod vide, which see
rel.		relative
resp.		respectful, -ly
Sambh. or Sb.		Shambhala, a fabulous country in the north and a book: Guide to Sb.
sbst.		substantive
Sch.		Prof. Is. J. Schmidt, Tibetisch-Deutsches Wörterbuch.
„		„ „ Tibetische Grammatik.
Schf.		Dr. A. Schiefner.
Schl.	=	Dr. E. Schlagintweit, Buddhism in Tibet.
Schr.		Schröter, editor of the first Tibetan Dictionary.
S.g.		Shad-gyud, a medical work.
Sik.		Sikkim, province
sim.		similar in meaning, similarly
sing.		singular number
s.l.c.		si lectio certa, if the reading is to be depended upon
S.O.		Ser-od, a religious work.
Sp.		Spiti, province.
Ssk.		Sanskrit
Stg.		Stan-gyur, a collection of commentaries.
symb. num.		symbolical numeral
syn. or synon.		synonymous
Tar.		Taranatha, history of the propagation of Buddhism in India.
termin.		terminative case
Thgr.		Thos-grol, Direction for the departed soul to find the way to eternal happiness.
Thgy.		Thargyan, scientific treatises.
Trig.		Triglot, a collection of Buddhist terms in Sanskrit, Tibetan and Mongolian.
trop.		tropically, figuratively
trs.		transitive
Ts.		Tsang, province of Central Tibet.
Ü		Ü, „ „ „ „
Urd.		Urdu, a dialect of Hindustani.
v.		vide, see
vb.		verb
vb. a.		verb active
vb. n.		verb neuter
vulg.		vulgar, low expression
vulgo		in common life
W.		Western Tibet.
Was.		Prof. W. Wasiljew, Der Buddhismus.
Wdk.		Waidurya Karpo, a mathematical work.
Wdn.		Waidurya Nonpo, a medical work.
w.e.		without explanation
Will.		Williams, Sanskrit-English Dictionary.
Wls.		Wilson, Sanskrit Dictionary.
Wts.		Wai-tsang-thu-shi, a description of Tibet, originally Chinese, ed. by Klaproth.
Z.		Zangskar, a Kashmere-Tibetan province.
Zam.		Zamatog, a treatise on Tibetan grammar and orthography.

EMENDATION.

Page 122, 1st. column, 4th. line from the top, after dignity, are to be inserted the following words: 2. *Cs.* exaggeration. *sgro-$_o$dogs-pa* 1. *Sch.* to bestow the peacock's feather.

Other misprints in the English text will be easily recognized as such, and hardly require a specification.

TIBETAN-ENGLISH DICTIONARY.

ཀ

ཀ་ *ka* 1. the letter **k**, tenuis, = French *c* in *car*. — 2. as numerical figure, used in marking the volumes of a work: **one**. — *ka-ḱo* **alphabetical register** *Sch.* — *ká-pa* the first volume of a work. — *ka-dpé* **a-b-c-book.** — *ka-ṗréṅ*, *ka smad sum-ču*, *kā-li* the Tibetan **alphabet**.

ཀ་ *ka* 1. an additional syllable, so-called article, affixed to some substantives, numerals and pronouns, v. the grammars. — 2. **pillar**, v. *ka-ba*.

ཀྭ་ *ka (kva)* **oh!**

ཀ་ཀ་ *ka-ká* **excrement,** (nursery word), **ka-ka taṅ-če* W.* = French: *faire caca.*

ཀཱ་ཀ་ *kā-ka Ssk.* **crow.**

ཀཾ་ཀ་ *kaṅ-ka, Ssk.* **कङ्क**, **heron.**

ཀ་ཀ་ཎི་ *ka-ka-ni* a small coin of ancient India *Cs.*

ཀ་ཀ་རང་ *ka-ka-ráṅ* **cucumber** *Kun.*

ཀ་ཀོ་ལ་ *ka-ko-la, Ssk.* **कक्कोल**, a plant bearing a berry the inner part of which is a waxlike and aromatic substance. — *ka-ko* prob. means the same.

ཀ་ཁ་ *ka-ḱá* the **a-b-c, alphabet**; *ka-ḱai ḱo* **alphabetical register,** *ka-ḱai dpe* **a-b-c-book**; *ka-ḱa-pa* **abecedarian.**

ཀ་ཁོལ་མ་ *ka-ḱól-ma* v. *ḱol-ma.*

ཀ་ཅ་ *ká-ča* also *ká-ča*, **goods, things**; *ká-čai ṙjés-su ̥bráṅs-pai rgyálpo* n. of a demon.

ཀ་ཏ་ཡ་ *ká-ta-ya*, also *ka-tya.* n. of a locality *Mil.*

ཀ་ཏུ་ *ka-tu* v. *ke-tu.*

ཀ་ཏོ་ར་ *ka-tó-ra*, more correctly *ka-ṭo-ra*, *Hd.*, **metal cup, dish, basin.**

ཀ་ཕ་ར་ *ka-ṗa-ra Kun.* a sort of **peach.**

ཀ་དག་ *ka-dág*, also *ka-nas dag*, pure from the beginning *Lex.*

ཀ་དར་ *ka-dár* (from خبردار *Urd.?*) only in the phrase: **ka-dar čo-če** **to be cautious, take care, take heed,** *-la*, of.

ཀ་པཱ་ལ་ *ka-pā-la Ssk.* **skull.**

ཀ་པི་ཏ་ *ka-pi-ta* **gum, resin** *Sch.*

ཀཾ་པོ་རྩེ་ *kam-po-rtse*, absurd spelling instead of *kam-bo-ja Wdk.*

ཀ་བ་ *ká-ba* **ka-wa** 1. **pillar, post**; *k. ̥dzug-pa* to erect a pillar. — 2. a large vein or artery in the abdomen. — **Comp.** *ka-skéd* shaft of a column. — *ká čan* having columns. — *ka-γčig-sgo-γčig* a small house, poor cottage; also a mode of capital punishment is said to be called so, when the culprit is fastened to a pillar in a dungeon until he dies of hunger. — *ka-γčig-pa* having one pillar, *ka-máṅ-ma* having many pillars. — *ka-čén* the principal p. (cf. στῦλος Gal. 2. 9) *Tar.* 182. 10. — *ka-rtén* base of a p. *Lex.* — *ka-stégs*, *ka-γdán* pedestal, base of a p. — *ka-spúṅs* many pillars. — *ka-méd* without a pillar; helpless, destitute. — *ka-rtsé*, *ka-γdáṅ-rtse* **capital of a pillar.** — *ka wá-*

čan, súl-čan a channeled pillar. — *ka-gžú* capital of a pillar. — *ka-gžu-gdúṅ* beam of the capital (pillars are mostly made of wood).

ཀ་བེད་ *ka-béd* prob. a sort of **gourd** *Wdṅ.*

ཀ་མ་རུ་ *ka-ma-ru* 1. **alabaster** *Sch.* — 2. n. of a country.

ཀ་མ་ལ་ཤི་ལ་ *ka-ma-la-śi-la* n of a famous ancient pandita or Brahmanical scholar.

ཀ་མུལ་རྡོ་རྒྱུད་ *ka-mul-rdo-rgyúd* is said to denote a sort of **alabaster** or of **steatite** in *C.*

ཀ་ཙ་ལིན་དི་ *ka-tsa-lindi* n. of a fabulous, very smooth, stuff or cloth, *Gyatch.*

ཀ་རྩམ་ *ka-rtsam, Ld. *ka-sam**, prob. a sort of **oats**; differing from *yug-po*, accounted superior to buckwheat, but inferior to wheat.

ཀ་ཚིགས་ཆེན་པོ་ *ka-tsigs-čén-po* title of a book cited in *Glr.*

ཀྭ་ཡེ་ *ka-yé (kwa-ye)* **oh! holla! hear!** so e. g. at the beginning of a royal proclamation *Pth.*

ཀ་ར་ *ká-ra C. & B.* **sugar**; *šel-ka-ra* crystallized s., sugar-candy, *rgyál-mo-ka-ra* id. *Sch.*; *byé-ma-ka-ra* ground sugar. — *ka-ra-ǰa* tea with sugar; *Sch.* 'a sweet soup'? — *ka-ra tog-tóg* sugar in lumps. — *kara-šiṅ* sugar-cane. (*W. ka-ru*).

ཀ་ར་བཱི་ར་ *ka-ra-bī-ra*, also *ka-ra-wi-ra (Ssk.)* **oleander flower**, *Nerium odorum.*

ཀ་རཉྫ་ *ka-rañ-dza Ssk.* a medicinal fruit, *Galedupa arborea.*

ཀ་རནྡ་ ཎྜ *ka-ran-dha Pth.* more correctly *ka-raṇ-ḍa, Ssk.*, a species of **duck**.

ཀ་རུ་ *ká-ru* **wedge.**

ཀ་ལཱ་པ་ *ka-lā-pa* a fabulous place or country in the north of Asia; also n. of a grammar *Cs.*

ཀ་ལ་པིང་ཀ་ *ka-la-piṅ-ka Cs.*: 'Ssk., n. of a bird', *Will.*: '*kalāpin* peacock; the Indian cuckoo'.

ཀ་ལ་ཤ་ *ka-la-śa Ssk.* **pitcher, jar.**

ཀ་ལག་ *ká-lag W.* **mud,** mixture of earth and water used instead of clay (*C. & B.: ǰim-pa*); the word is also used for other similar compounds.

ཀ་ལནྟ་ཀ་ *ka-lan-taka Ssk.* n. of a bird.

ཀ་ལི་ *ka-li* 1. **skull** *Lex.* — 2. = *ka-lé W.*

ཀཱ་ལི་ *kā-li* the **Tib. alphabet,** v. *ka.*

ཀ་ལིང་ག་ *ka-liṅ-ga Ssk.* n. of different tracts in the eastern part of India; *Sch.*: 'Korea', without giving further explanation; perh. Mongol writers call it so?

ཀ་ལིབ་ *ka-lib, Ar.* قالب **bullet-mould** *W.*

ཀ་ལེ་ *ka-lé*, also *ka-léb*, **saddle-cloth.**

ཀཱ་ཤ་ *kā-śa Ssk.* a sort of grass, Saccharum spontaneum; Tibetans often seem to mistake it for *ku-śa* q. v.

ཀཱ་ཤི་ཀ་ *ka-śi-ka Ssk.*, adj. of Kāsi (Banāras): inhabitant of Banāras; *ka-śi-kai ras*, a sort of fine **cottoncloth.**

ཀ་ས་ *ká-sa*, also **ká-so, kas** (perh. a mutilated form of *bka-stsal*) resp. **yes, Sir! very well, Sir! at your service!** (*W.* also: **ká-sa-ǰu** v. *žu*) *W.* frq., also *C.* ni f., never in *B.*

ཀག་གིས་ *kág-gis* **suddenly** *Sch.*

ཀག་མ་ *kág-ma* **mischief, harm, injury** *Cs.*

ཀང་ཀ་ *kaṅ-ka Ssk.* **heron.**

ཀང་དང་ཀིང་ *kaṅ-daṅ-kiṅ* n. of a terrifying deity *Glr.*, prob. = *kiṅ-káṅ*, which is said to signify Rāhula (v. *sgra-gčan & drag-gšed.* in *drag-pa*).

ཀཎྚ་ཀཱ་རི་ *kaṇḍa-kā-ri Ssk.* ('thorny') Wilson: *Solanum Jaquini;* in *Lh.* a sort of wild Rubus.

ཀད་ *kad, Ld.* sometimes instead of the affix *ka*, e. g. *gnyis-kád, tsaṅ-kád;* perh. also in *mnyam-kád, Thgy.?*

ཀན་ *kan Med.* = *bad-kan.*

ཀན་མ་ *kán-ma* **middle finger.**

ཀབ་ཟ་ *káb-za* (قبضه *Ar.*) *W.* **hilt, handle** of a sword.

ཀབ་ཤ་ *káb-ša* (كفش *Pers.*) **shoe**; in *W.* esp. the leather shoes of Hindu fashion, which are also bought by wealthier Tibetans.

ཀམ་བོ་ཛ་ *kam-bo-dza Ssk.* n. of a country in the northwest of India, *Wdn.: kam-po-rtse.*

ཀཽ་ *kau* **watermelon** *Sch.*

ཀར་ *kar*, also *kar-kar*, **great pain, suffering** *Lex.*

ཀརྐ་ཏ་ *karka-ta Ssk.* the constellation of **Cancer.**

ཀར་སྐྱིན་ *kár-skyin* **loan**, when respectfully requested, cf. *skyin.*

ཀར་ཆག་ *kar-čág* **register, list.**

ཀརྨ་ *kárma Ssk.* ('deed, action'); *kar-ma-pa* (in Nepal *karmika*) name of a philosophical school of Buddhism.

ཀར་ཡོལ་ *kar-yól* **porcelain, china-ware, -cup** etc.

ཀར་ལང་བ་ *kár-laṅ-ba*, also *kér-laṅ-ba*, **to stand up, to rise.**

ཀར་ཤ་པ་ཎི་ or ཎ་ *kar-ša-pa-ni* or *na, Ssk.* **कार्षापण**, a coin in ancient India, or rather a weight of gold and silver, of different value (not = 'cowries', as *Sch.* seems to think).

ཀལ་ཡ་ *kál-ya*, also *kal-yór*, *W.* col. instead of *kar-yól*, the former seems to be a corruption of قلعی.

ཀི་ *ki* numerical figure: 31, *ki-pa* the 31st (volume).

ཀི་ཀང་ *ki-káṅ* **wild leek** *Sch.*

ཀི་གུ་ *ki-gu* n. of the vowel-sign for *i*, ི.

ཀི་མ་ *ki-ma Dzl.* [illegible] acc. to *Schf.* a corruption of the Chinese *khin*, a lyre with 7 strings. (Pilgrim. of Fa-Hian Calc. 1848 p. 265).

ཀི་ཙི་ *ki-tsi* **tickling** *W.*, **ki-tsi kúg-če** **to tickle.**

ཀིང་ཀང་ *kiṅ-káṅ* v. *kaṅ-daṅ-kiṅ.*

ཀིམ་པ་ *kim-pa* n. of a fruit, *Lex.*

ཀུ་ *ku* numerical figure: 61; *kú-pa* the 61st (volume).

ཀུ་ *ku*, *kú-sgra B.*, **kú-čo* W.* **clamour.**

ཀུ་ན་ལ་ *ku-na-la*, *ku-nā-la Ssk.*, n. of a bird in the Himalaya.

ཀུ་བ་ *kú-ba Wdn.* **gourd.**

ཀུ་བེ་ར་ *ku-be-ra Ssk.* the god of riches, also *Nag-ku-bera*, *Rnam-tos-kyi-bú*, *Rnam-tos-sras*, *Lag-na-rdó-rje* etc.

ཀུ་མུ་ད་ *ku-mu-da Ssk.* the flower of the red and white **lotus**, *Nymphaea rubra* and *esculenta.*

ཀུ་ཡ་ *kú-ya* **sediment of urine** *Med.*

ཀུ་རུ་ཀུལ་ལེ་ *ku-ru-kul-le* n. of a female deity *Mil.*

ཀུ་རུག་ *ku-rúg Ld.* **colt of an ass.**

ཀུ་རེ་ *ku-ré*, also *ku-res* **jest, joke**, *ku-re byed-pa* **to jest**, cf. *kyal-ka.*

ཀུ་ལིག་ *ku-lig* **key**, also **lock;** more accurately: **pé-ku-lig** key, *čúg-ku-lig* lock, padlock; **ku-lig-búr-* (or *bor-*) *tse** in *Ld.* a contrivance used instead of a doorlatch. *W.*

ཀུ་ཤ་ *ku-ša* a sort of grass, Poa cynosuroides, often used in sacred ceremonies.

ཀུ་ཤུ་ *ku-šu* **apple** *Dzl.*; *W.* (Cf. *sli*).

ཀུ་སུ་མ་ *ku-su-ma Ssk.* **flower.**

ཀུ་ཧུ་ *ku-hu* **ring-dove** *Cs.* (*Ssk.*: the cry of the cuckoo).

ཀུག་ *kug*, also *kug-kúg*, **crooked; a hook;** *gri-kug* a curved knife, short sabre; *lčags-kug* an iron hook; *nya-kug* a fishing-hook; **kug-kug ǰhé-pa* C.* **taṅ-če* W.* **to bend, curve; clinch** (a nail); **go kug taṅ-če* W.* **to nod**, **lag kug taṅ-če* W.* **to beckon.** (Cf. *kum-pa.*)

ཀུག་རྩེ་ *kug-rtse*, **kug-se** **cuckoo** *W.*

ཀུན་ *kun (C.: *kyn*)* **all, every, each; whole;** *spui kúñ-bu kún-nas* from every pore *Dzl.; dé-dag kun* all these; *γžan kun* all the others; also pleon. *kun tams-čád* all of them, they altogether; *kún-gyis mtóñ-ba, tós-pa* seen, heard by every body, generally known; *kún-tu* 1. into all, in all etc. 2. adv. everywhere, in every direction; *kun-tu-bzáñ-po* Allgood, n. of the first of the celestial Bodhisattwas, *Samanta-bhadra,* sometimes confounded with Adibuddha, *tóg-mai Sañs-rgyas;* in later works even a *Kun-tu-bzáñ-mo Yum* is mentioned *Thgr.; kún-tu rgyú-ba* to go everywhere, wander about; *Kun-tu-rgyu* परिव्राजक n. of a class of Brahmans, itinerant monks, *Dzl.; kún-nas* **from everywhere, round about, wholly, thoroughly** e. g. overpowered by passions, cleansed from sin *Dzl.; kún-nas* ̥*dod-pa* to wish from the bottom of the heart *Thgy.*

Comp. *kun-dkris* **general corruptness, misery, sin** *Lex.* — *Kun-kyáb* comprising, pervading all things. — *Kun-mkyén-(pa)* **omniscient.** — *Kun-dgá-bo, Ssk. ānandā,* n. of the favourite disciple of Buddha; *Kun-dga* is to this time frequently used as a name of (female) persons. — *Kun-dga-rá-ba,* also *kun-dga Thgy.,* or *kun-ra, Ssk.* आराम or संघाराम 'garden of all joys' 1. the **grove** in which a monastery is situated. 2. the **monastery.** 3. in Tibet, which is destitute of groves, more particularly the **auditory** or **library** of a monastery — *Kun-brtágs,* in the Mahayána: a personal, erroneous supposition *Was.* — *Kun-̥dús* **all-gathering, all-uniting.** — *Kun-dbáñ* **almighty.** — *Kun-rdzób* **altogether vain, delusive;** *kun-rdzób-kyi bdén-pa* subjective truth *Was.* — *Kun-γži* lit.: the primary cause of all things, viz.: 1. the **soul** or **spirit,** *kun-γžii sems* (opp. to ̥*byúñ-ba bžii lus* the body consisting of the 4 elements), *kun-γžii séms-la po mo ma mčis-te* as no difference of sex exists in souls (we, though being women, would beg etc.) *Mil.* 2. With more precise distinction: *kun-γži* **soul** as the seat of the passions, opp. to *sems-nyid,* the very soul, the spirit as the seat of reason *Mil.* 3. To the followers of the Adibuddha doctrine *kun-γži* is = **God, Adibuddha,** *kun-γžii Sañs-rgyas.* — *Kun-γzigs* **all-seeing.** — *Kun-slóñ Lex.* v. *sloñ-ba.*

ཀུན་ད་ *kun-da Ssk.* **jessamine.**

ཀུན་དུ་རུ་ *kun-du-ru Ssk.* **incense,** Boswellia.

ཀུམ་པ་ *kúm-pa,* also *kum-kúm, kúm-po,* **crooked, shriveled, dried up;** **kum tán-če* W.* **to bend** together, **to double.** (Cf. *skúm-pa).*

ཀུམ་བྷ་ *kum-bha Ssk.* earthen **jar.**

ཀུམ་བྷི་ར་ *kum-bhi-ra Ssk.* **crocodile.**

ཀེ་ *ke* numeral: 91, *ke-pa* the 91st (volume).

ཀེ་ཀེ་རུ་ *ke-ke-ru,* also *kerketana & ketaka Ssk.* 'n. of a precious white stone' *Cs.;* our Ssk. dictionaries give but the last of these names, and as its only signification the name of the tree Pandanus odoratissima.

ཀེ་ཏ་ར་ *ke-ta-ra Sambh.,* n. of a mountain, prob. Kedāra, part of the Himalaya. *Will.*

ཀེ་ཏུ་ *ke-tu Ssk.* **a fiery meteor, shooting star; the descending node.**

ཀེ་རྩེ་ *ke-rtsé* v. *keu-rtsé.*

ཀེ་རེ་ *ke-ré* v. *kye-ré.*

ཀེ་ལ་ཤ, ཀཻ་ལ་ཤ་ *ke-la-ša, kai-la-ša Cs.,* कैलास *Will.,* n. of a lofty region of the Himalaya, mythological rather than geographical, seems to be the same as Ti-se q. v., though modern geographers apply the name to different ranges.

ཀེ་ལན་ *ke-lan;* the fraternity or association, which Huc mentions under this name (Voy. II ch. 6), seemed to be totally unknown to our Tashilhunpo Lama, although the expectation of a final war between Buddhist believers and infidels, in which the latter will be destroyed, is widely spread through Tibet.

ཀེ་ཤུ་ཀ *ke-šu-ka Wdñ.* n. of a plant, perhaps *kèčuka*, Arum Colocasia, with edible root; or = *keṅ-su-ka?*

ཀེག་མ་ *kég-ma* = ཀག་མ་ *kág-ma Cs.*

ཀེང་རུས་ *keṅ-rús* **skeleton.**

ཀེང་ཤུ་ཀ *keṅ-šu-ka Lex., Sambh., Wdñ.,* n. of a tree.

ཀེའུ་རྩེ་ *keu-rtse*, also *ke-rtse*, **jacket** *Mil.*

ཀེའུ་རི་ *keu-ri* n. of a female terrifying deity *Thgr.*

ཀེའུ་ལེ་ *keu-le Dzl.* ⁓, 1: *keu-lei rgya*, acc. to the Mongol version: **customary seal.** — dubious.

ཀེར་གྱིས་ *kér-gyis* **suddenly** *Sch.*

ཀེར་བ་ *kér-ba* **to raise, lift up,** e. g. the finger towards heaven *Glr.; ker láṅ-ba* **to rise, stand up.**

ཀོ་ *ko* 1. num.: 121; *kó-pa* the 121st (volume). — 2. affix, = *ka col. Ld.* — 3. **all, whole** *Schr.*, cf. *kob.*

ཀོ་ཀོ་ *ko-kó* 1. also *ko-sko*, **throat, chin** *Sch., ko-sko ̥degs Lex.?* 2. = *ka-ka W.*

ཀོ་ཀོ་ཐང་མ་ *ko-ko-ťáṅ-ma* n. of a country in or near Ceylon *Pth.*

ཀོ་ཉོན་ཙེ་ *ko-nyon-tsé*, also *ko-nyol-tsé, ko-lon-tsé* the kernel of the pine-apple *Cs.;* more particularly the edible seed of the Neosa-pine in the valley of the Sutledj; also *skan-nyan-tsé Kun.*

ཀོ་ཋ་ *ko-ťa, Ssk.* कोठ, a kind of **leprosy** *Wdñ.*

ཀོ་པང་ཙེ་ *ko-paṅ-tsé* a sort of **tea** *Schr.*

ཀོ་ཕོངས་ *ko-póṅs* **guitar** *Ld.;* it is tuned in 3 fourths.

ཀོ་བ་ *kó-ba* 1. **hide, skin.** — 2. **leather,** **kó-wa nyé-ǩan** **tanner** *C.; gláṅ-ko* **neat's leather.** — *ko-krád* **leather-shoe.** — *kó-mǩan* 1. **tanner.** 2. (acc. to some also:) conductor of a leather-boat, **boatman.** — *ko-btúm* 'leather-wrapping' is said to be a criminal punishment in *C.*, in different degrees of severity, e. g. **lúg-pa ko-túm**, when the culprit's hands are cut off, the stumps sewed up in leather, and the wretch thrown as a beggar upon public charity etc. — *ko-ťág* **strap, thong.** — *ko-̥ťágs Cs.:* a small instrument of leather to weave lace with. — *ko-gdán* a piece of leather put under the saddle *Sch.* — *ko-lpágs* **hide, leather.** — *ko-̥bügs Sch.:* three-edged needle for leather. — *ko-ťság* **leather-sieve.** — *ko-rúl* a rotten hide.

ཀོ་བོ་ *kó-bo* n. of a country *Wdk.*

ཀོ་མ་ *kó-ma* n. of a bird *Wdñ.*

ཀོ་ཝག་ *ko-wág* is meant to express the voice of a raven.

ཀོ་ར་ *ko-ra, Hindi* **कोरा,** more tibetanized *ko-rás*, unbleached coarse cotton cloth.

ཀོ་རེ་ *ko-ré*, in compounds *kor W.*, **cup** for drinking; *šiṅ-kor* wooden cup, a utensil every Tibetan carries with him in his bosom; *šél-kor* (European) **tumbler.** (Cf. *ṗór-pa*).

ཀོ་ལོང་ *ko-lóṅ*, a dubious word. *Sch.* has *ko-loṅ-ba* to hate, envy, but in a passage in *Mil.*, where the connection admits of no doubt, *ko-loṅ mdzad-pa* must be taken for: to disdain.

ཀོ་ཤམ་བི་ *ko-šam-bi Dzl., Glr., Ssk.:* **कौशाम्बी** n. of an ancient city on the Ganges, in the Doab.

ཀོ་ས་ལ *ko-sa-la Sambh., Ssk.:* **कोसला,** = *Ayodhya*, Oude.

ཀོག་པ་ *kóg-pa* I. subst., also *skóg-pa, skógs-pa* **shell, peel, rind;** *šún-kog* id.; *ṗyi-kog* exterior shell, **bark;** *kóg-pa šu-ba* **to peel, pare.** — II. vb. n. **to splinter off, to chink;** *kog laṅ-ba* 1. id. 2. **to** rise suddenly and run away.

ཀོང་ *koṅ*, also *koṅ-kóṅ*, 1. **concave, excavated.** — 2. **crooked,** **pi-ši ťsig-pa koṅ-kóṅ čo** the cat makes a crooked back *W.* — *kóṅ-po* 1. **cup, bowl.** 2. **crucible.** 3. **breach, gap** *Sch.* 4. n. of a province S. E. of Lhasa. — *kóṅ-bu* small cup, bowl. — *mčód-kóṅ* offering-bowl; *snág-koṅ* **inkstand** for black **ink**, *mtsál-koṅ* for red ink, vermilion; **lúg-koṅ** **casting-mould** *C.*

ཀོད་ *kod* ('a gathering'?) 1. *lag-kód Ld.* an armful of corn, a **sheaf.** 2. affix = *kad, ka, ko: *nyis-kód, ṅa-kód** all the two, all the five *Ld.*

ཀོབ་ *kob* all, *Ld.* col.

ཀོར་ *kor*, root denoting anything round or concave, hence: *kor-kór* 1. adj. **round,** circular *C.* (= **kyir-kyir* W.*); roundish, globular *C.*; concave, deep, as a soup-plate (opp. to flat) *W.* 2. sbst. a thick **loaf** of bread, (opp. to a flat, thin cake) *C.*; **a pan,** saucepan *W.*; a hollow in the ground, a pit not very deep *W.*; *stód-kor* a little circle above a letter, *Ssk.* anuswara; *kl̄ád-kor* id., a dot, zero, naught; *ydúb-kor* bracelet *Cs.*; *pád-kor* a certain way of folding the fingers, so as to represent the form of a lotus-flower; *˷ód-kor* a radiant circle *Cs.* Cf. *skór-ba, ˳kór-ba, ko-ré.*

ཀོར་དོ་བ་ *kor-do-ba* **boot** *Ld.?*

ཀོལ་ཏོ་ *kol-to* **dumb, mute** *Sp.?*

ཀོས་ཀོ་ *kós-ko* = *ko-ko; kos-snyúṅ* with a pointed chin *Sch.*

ཀྱ་སིར་རླུང་ *kya-sir-rlúṅ* v. *kyiṅ.*

ཀྱག་ *kyag,* also *kyag-kyág,* **thick,** run into clots *Cs.*

ཀྱག་ཀྱོག་ *kyag-kyóg* **curved, crooked;** **go kyag-kyóg čo-če* W.* to shake one's head, viz. slowly, in meditating; **ri-mo kyag-(ga-) kyog-(gé)** **a flourish** (in writing) *W.* Cf. *kyog-kyóg.*

ཀྱང་ *kyaṅ* I. adj., also *kyaṅ-kyáṅ, kyaṅ-po,* **straight, slender,** as a stick; **kyaṅ-kyaṅ riṅ-mo** **tall, slender,** as a man, a tree etc. *W.* — II. adv. = *yaṅ,* **too, also,** always used enclitically, after the letters g, d, b, s.

ཀྱང་ཀྱོང་ *kyaṅ-kyóṅ,* also **kyaṅ-ṅa-kyoṅ-ṅé**, **indolent, lazy, idle** *W.*; **kyaṅ-kyoṅ čo-če** to lounge, to be idle *W.*

ཀྱར་ཀྱར་ *kyar-kyár,* also *kyar-po* **flat,** not globular *Cs.*

ཀྱར་ཀྱོར་ *kyar-kyór,* also **kyar-ra-kyor-ré**, **still feeble,** as convalescents after a disease.

ཀྱལ་ཀ་ *kyal-ka* 1. **joke, jest,** in words (*Lis. ku-rei tsig*). — 2. **jocular trick,** *ku-re daṅ kyál-kai pyir* by way of jest, for fun. — 3. any **worthless, foolish, indecent talk** *Stg.*

ཀྱལ་ཀྱལ་ *kyal-kyál Lex.* w. e.; *Sch.: kyal-kyal-ba* to go round (?).

ཀྱལ་ཀྱོལ་ *kyal-kyól* = *kyar-kyór, dúd-˳gro kyal-kyól ˳ga* some poor ill-conditioned beast, speaking of cattle, *Mil. nt.*

ཀྱི་ *kyi,* affix I. to sbst.-roots, ending in d, b, s: sign of the genitive case. — II. to verbal roots, after the same final letters, and then without an essential difference from *kyis,* to which we add in this place also examples of the other terminations *gi(s), gyi(s), yi(s), i* (the *s* by itself is not used after verbal roots): a. in the sense of a gerund, meaning **by** (doing something), **because,** *dgós-kyis ˳óṅ-ṅo* we come because it is necessary . . . , or more freq. **though,** *dgai* though she is glad . . . *Dzl.,* in which case it may often be rendered in English by **but:** she is glad, but . . . ; *zas bzáṅ-po mi ˳dód-kyis ťa-mál-pa zos* he did not care for dainties, but ate vulgar food *Dzl.*; or it has to be omitted: *bdén-pa yin-gyis rdzún-pa ma yin* it is true, no fiction *Dzl.* — b. as an adjective, forming, like *kyin* (q. v.), with *˳dug* or *yod* a periphrastical present tense e. g. *˳groi ˳dug* he is walking, *˷oṅ-gi yod* he is coming. — c. at the end of a sentence in the sense of a finite verb and more particularly in the 1. pers. fut.: *˳gyod mi rmoi* I shall not make you suffer for it *Dzl., ṅas grogs byá-yis* I shall help *Glr., bžag-gi,* and: *bžág-gis* I shall put *Glr.* This use of *kyi(s)* is said to be quite common at the present time in *C.*, whereas in *W.* not only the whole gerundial use, but even the distinction of *kyi, gyi, gi* in the genitive case of a sbst. has disappeared from colloquial language, instead of which the last consonant is repeated and the vowel i added: *ṡiṅ-ṅi* of the wood, **yid-di** of the mind, **bál-li** of the wool.

Note 1. *kyi(s)* when combined with adjective roots, includes the verb to be, e. g. *máṅ-gi* = *máṅ-po yin-gyi*. — 2. In colloquial language and later literature the genitive of the verbal root often takes the place of the genit. infinitivi, which seldom occurs in the old classical style, e. g. *nam ˳tsoi bár-du* lifelong. — 3. *ji nús kyi(s), ji t̔úb-kyi(s)* or vulg. **t̔úb-bi**, as much as (I, you etc.) can (could etc.) — 4. *kyi(s)*, when denoting an antithesis, is often followed by a pleonastical *˛óṅ-kyaṅ*.

ཀྱི་ལྕེ་ *kyi-lċe* a medic. plant, Gentiana decumbens *L.*, *k. dkár-po* a variety of it with white flowers.

ཀྱི་ལྡིར་ *kyi-ldir* **iron hoop** *Ld.?*

ཀྱི་བུན་ *kyi-bún* **a feeling cold, a chill** *Sch.*

ཀྱི་ཧུད་ *kyi-húd* the sound of weeping, lamentation.

ཀྱིག་རྩེ་ *kyig-rtse* **unburnt brick** *Sch.*

ཀྱིང་སིར་རླུང་ *kyiṅ-sir-rlúṅ* *Mil.* also *kya-s. l., C.*, an onomatopoetic word: **a blowing wind.**

ཀྱིན་ *kyin*, used alternatively with *gyin* and *gin*, after a vowel: *yin*, denotes a partic. present, e. g. *smón-lam ˛débs-kyin soṅ* proceed on your way praying! With *yod* or *˛dug* it forms a periphrastical present tense: *smón-lam ˳débs-kyin yod* he is praying (just now); in *Ld.* even as a real subst.: **ṡúg-ra ˳tón-gyin (žig) daṅ** 'with a whistling sound proceeding from it', **dó-yin-daṅ** 'together with walking' = in walking.

ཀྱིར་ཀྱིར་ *kyir-kyir* *W.* (= *kor-kór C.*) **round, circular**; a round thing, **disk**, e. g. the little silver saucer which the women of *Lh.* wear as an ornament on the crown of their head; *kyir-mo* id., esp. **a rupee** *Ld.*; **da kyir-kyir** the disk of the moon.

ཀྱིས་ *kyis*, after d, b, s. 1. sign of the instrumentative case, and therefore generally indicating the personal subject of the action. — 2. combined with verbal roots = *kyi*.

ཀྱེ་ *kye* **oh! holla!** in calling to somebody; in solemnly addressing a person or an auditory; also merely the sign of the vocative case *B.* (in *W.* **wa!**) *kye-kyé* id. emphatically.

ཀྱཻ་ abbrev. for *kye-kyé* v. *kye*.

ཀྱེ་ག་ *kyé-ga* n. of a bird. *Med.*

ཀྱེ་ཕང་(པ་) *kye-p̔áṅ-(pa)* n. of an idol in Lh., consisting like most of the popular idols in those countries of a wooden stick or log decked with rags, but much dreaded and revered; said to be identical with *Pe-dkar* in *C.* Its worship probably dates from a time before Buddhism was introduced.

ཀྱེ་མ་ *kyé-ma* **oh! alas!** mostly expressive of sorrow, often combined with *kyi-hud*; also sign of the vocative case. Seldom it expresses joy. — *kye-mao* id.

ཀྱེ་རེ་ *kye-ré* **upright, erect;** **kye-re laṅ-wa**, resp. **žeṅ-wa C.*, *kyer-kyér-la dad-ċe*, resp. *žaṅ-ċe** *W.* to stand; **˛go kyer ǰhé-pa** to raise one's head, to look up *C.* Cf. *kyer-ba*.

ཀྱེ་ཧུད་ *kye-húd*, = *kyi-hud*.

ཀྱེ་ཧོ་ *kye-hó* **hollo! heigh! well!** also like the **behold** of the Holy Scriptures.

ཀྱེད་ཀྱེད་ *kyed-kyéd*, also *braṅ-kyéd*, with the upper part of the body stretched forward *Ld.*

ཀྱེར་ *kyer*, v. *kye-re*.

ཀྱོ་བ་ *kyó-ba* **hook** *Sch.*

ཀྱོག་ *kyog*, also *kyog-kyóg*, *kyóg-po*, **crooked, bent, winding.** *rtse kyog* with its point bent, crooked at the top. *Med.*

ཀྱོང་ *kyoṅ*, also *kyoṅ-kyóṅ*, *kyoṅ-po* 1. **hard,** as e. g. stale bread, *ču kyóṅ-po* hard water; **obstinate, unmanageable**; *kyoṅ-˳búr* a sort of relievo-work in metal. — 2. **oblong** *Cs.* — *Sch.*: *kyóṅ-k̔a* **quarrel,** *kyoṅ-rgyó* cause of a quarrel (?). Cf. *gyoṅ*, *k̔a-gyoṅ*.

ཀྱོང་ *kyoṅ*, also *kyóṅ-bu*, **small shovel, scraper** *Sch.*

ཀྱོམ་ *kyom*, also *kyóm-kyom*, 1. **flexible,** but without elasticity, **flabby, loose, lax.** — 2. also *Kyom-Kyóm*, **of irregular shape,** not rectilinear.

ཀྱོར་ *kyor*, also *kyor-kyór* **weak, feeble, unfortified** *Cs.*

ཀྱོལ་ *kyol*, also *kyol-kyól* = *kyor Cs.*

ཀྲག་ *krag* v. *bkrag.*

ཀྲང་ངེ་ *kraṅ-ṅé* **standing,** *kraṅ sdod-pa* to **stand** *Zam. Cf. kroṅ.*

ཀྲད་པ་ *krád-pa* **leather half-boot** or **shoe,** as it is worn by the lower class of people, often with a woolen leg; *krad-rgyún Cs.* a long narrow piece of leather to fasten the sole to the upper-leather; **tad-kyi* W. *ṭạ-kyi* C.* (or *gyi*, from *gyi-na?*) a worn-out leather sole.

ཀྲབ་ཀྲབ་ *krab-kráb* v. *ₒKrab-pa.*

ཀྲམ་ *kram W.* **cabbage,** *kram-mṅár* sweet or fresh cabbage; *kram-skyúr* sour or macerated cabbage *Cs.* (?)

ཀྲི་ཀྲི་ *kṛi-kṛi* n. of a fabulous king of India *Glr.*, not mentioned in the Ssk. dictionaries.

ཀྲིཥྞ་སཱ་ར་ *krišṇa-sā-ra Ssk.* **the spotted antelope** *Pth.*

ཀྲུ་ཀྲུ་ *kru-krú W.* **windpipe,** **ṭu-ṭú dam-te ši-ċe** to be strangled.

ཀྲེ་ནག་ *kre-nág* **smut** of a kettle *Sch.* (= *sre-nag?*)

ཀྲོང་ཀྲོང་ *kroṅ-króṅ* **standing upright,** e. g. books (opp. to **gyél-Kan** laid down, lying *W.*); when used of persons it means also: standing on one's knees, kneeling in an upright position.

ཀྲོན་ཀྲོན་ *kron-krón* **hanging,** **ton-ton-la dug-ċe** to hang, to be suspended in the air W.

ཀླ་ཀློ་ *kla-klo* 1. *Ssk.* म्लेच्छ **barbarian.** — 2. in later times: **Moslem, Mahometan; Mahometanism.** *Was.*

ཀླག་ཅོར་ *klag-ċor* **clamour, noise** *Cs.*

ཀླད་ *klad*, acc. to *Liš.* = *goṅ* what is above; hence *klád-pa*, also *glad*, 1. **head.** 2. **brain,** and *klad-ma* **beginning, top** *Sch.*; *gur-klád* chimney of a felt-tent. — *klad-kor* v. *kor.* — *klad-rgyá* the skin covering the brain, **pia mater**; *klad-rgyas*, = *lhá-ba*, 'the bloody marrow in the bones' *Sch.*, or simply **'brain'** *Schf.* — *klad-sgo* the **fontanel** in the infant cranium *Sch.* — *klad-čúṅ* the **cerebellum** *Sch.* — *klad-ẏžúṅ* **spinal marrow.** — *klad-ẏzér* **headache** *Med.* — *klad-šúbs* = *klad-rgyá Sch.*

ཀླན་ཀ་ *klan-ka* 1. **censure, blame** *Cs.*, *klan byéd-pa*, *ₒdebs-pa* to blame, cf. *skur-klán.* — 2. *klan tsol-ba* to seek **brawls** *Pth.*

ཀླན་པ་ *klán-pa* v. *klon-pa.*

ཀླུ་ *klu*, *Ssk.* नाग, originally: hooded snake, cobra di capello; in this specific sense, however, it is never used in Tibetan, whereas every child knows and believes in the mythological signification: **serpent-demon,** a demigod with a human head and the body of a serpent, living in fountains, rivers etc., commanding over great treasures, causing rain and certain maladies, and becoming dangerous when in anger; *ẏdúg-pa* is therefore a usual epitheton of such demons. *klui skad* means the Prakrit language, *klui yi-ge* the Nagari character of *Ssk.* letters, viz. that which is called *varttula*, in contrast to the holy *landza*, *lhai yi-ge.* — *klui ẏnod-pa* or *skyon* diseases of unknown origin. — *klu-mo* a female serpent-demon. —

klu-sgrúb, prop. n., Nagarjuna, a famous Buddhist divine. — *klu-mdúd* Codonopsis ovata. — *klu-nad* = *klui-ẏnod-pa.* — *klu-ṗrúg* a young Lu. — *klu-smán* 'n. of a medicine' *Cs.*, but *sman* and *klu-smán* are also synonyms for *klu*, *Glr.*, *Mil.* etc.

ཀླུང་ *kluṅ* **river,** more com. *ču-klúṅ*, *B.*

ཀླུངས་ *kluṅs* 1. **cultivated land, field,** *klúṅs-su skye* it grows on cultivated ground *Wdṅ.* — 2. **a complex of fields,** *dkar-*

mdaṅs-kyi kluṅ ťsáṅ-ma all the fields belonging to Kardang (n. of a village).

ཀླུབ་པ་ *klúb-pa*, *pf. klubs*, **to cover**, e. g. the body with ornaments *Pth.*

ཀློག་ *klog* v. *klog-pa.*

ཀློག་པ་ *klóg-pa* I. *sbst.* **earwax** *Sch.* — II. *vb.*, *pf. (b)klags*, *ft. (b)klag*, *imp. klog, lhogs*, **to read**, *B.*, *C.*, *yid-kyis klóg-pa* to read without uttering a sound; *klog-pa* or *klog sbst.* reading, *klog bzáṅ-po šés-pa Mil.* to be a good reader; *klóg-gi slób-dpon* a reading-teacher. — *klóg-gra* a reading-school. — *klóg-ťabs, klóg-ťsul* art, way of reading.

ཀློང་ *kloṅ* acc. to *Lex.* = *Ssk. urmi*, **wave**; in the living language it is used for **middle**; in ancient literature for **expanse**, esp. *nám-mk'ai* of the heavens, *rgyá-mťsoi* of the sea; *raṅ-byúṅ kloṅ yaṅs brjod-méd* the unspeakably vast uncreated space; hence: the space of heaven, the heavens, *klóṅ-du ldíṅ-ba* to soar, to hover in the sky. This vagueness of meaning makes the word suited to the idle fancies of mysticism, as in: *klóṅ-du ͼgyúr-ba*, which seems to denote a soaring into mystic perfection. — *dba-klóṅ Sch.:* wave; Tibetans of to-day, and *Schr.:* the midst of the waves. — *kloṅ-brdól Glr.* was explained by Lamas: emerging from amidst the waves. (The significations 'depth, abyss, plenty, body' added by *Sch.* seem to be erroneous). *Cf. dkyel.*

ཀློན་པ་ *klón-pa*, also *klán-pa*, **to mend, patch** v. also *lhán-pa.*

ཀྵ་ཡ་ *kša-ya Ssk.* prop. **phthisis pulmonalis;** but acc. to Tib. pathology *kša-ya nág-po* denotes a bilious disease, prob. **icterus niger, black jaundice.**

དཀགས་པོ་ *dkágs-po W.* for *dka-bo.*

དཀན་ *dkan*, also *rkan (Ld. *skan*)* 1. **the palate,** *yá-dkan*, the upper, *má-dkan* the lower part of the palate; **kán-ḍa ͼdéb-pa** **to smack** *C.; dkan-ɉnyér* the wrinkles of the roof of the mouth *Cs.* — 2. *dkan yzár-po Lex.* w. e, *Sch.* steep declivity, precipice.

དཀའ་བ་ *dka-ba* 1. adj., also *-bo*, seld. *-mo*, **difficult**, *slób-pa dká-ba* learning is difficult *Dzl.*, gen. with supine: *slób-tu* or *slób-par dka* it is difficult to learn, or with the root: *go-dká* difficult to understand; *dkár-ba byuṅ* it has become difficult, it is difficult (to me, to him etc.) — 2. sbst. *dká-ba* **pains, exertion, hardship, suffering,** *dká-ba méd-par* without difficulty, easily, *dka-ba spyod-pa* to undergo hardships = to use exercises of penance (**तपस, कष्ट**).

dka-ͼgrél Cs. 'a difficult commentary', acc. to Tib. dictionaries = **पञ्जिका** perpetual commentary, lit.: explanation of difficulties. — *dka-ťúb, dka-spyód, dka-spyád* 1. **penance.** 2. **penitent;** *dka-ťúb-pa, dka-spyód-pa, dká-ťub-čan*, penitent, *ͼťsó-ba dka-ťúb-ba rtén-pa* to live as a penitent. — *dka-sdúg* **trouble,** *dka-sdúg máṅ-po byéd-pa* to take great pains *C.* — *dka-ťségs* = *dká-ba.* — *dka-lás* 1. **a troublesome work.** 2. **trouble, distress.**

དཀར་བ་ *dkár-ba* I. adj., also *-po*, seld. *-mo* 1. **white, whitish, gray.** — 2. **morally good,** standing on the side of virtue — 3. candid, sincere? *las dkár-po* good action; *k'a-zás dkár-po* v. *dkar-zás; dkár-la dmar-mdáṅs-čan* white and red of complexion *Pth.*

II. sbst. **whiteness.** — *dkár-mo* sbst. 1. the goddess Durga. — 2. **white rice** *Cs.*

Comp. *dkar-skya* **light-gray.** — *dkar-k'úṅ* 1. **window-hole** in a wall *W.* — 2. opening for the smoke in the roof *C.* — *dkar-goṅ C.* a piece of quartz, (acc. to popular belief porcelain is made of quartz,) hence *Cs.:* 'porcelain-clay.' — *dkar-rgyá* **rose-coloured.** — *dkar-čág* **register.** — *dkar-tog* = *dkar-zas.* — *dkar-mé* a light (?), *dkar-mé sbor-ba Sch.* 'to light a candle.' — *dkar-dmar* **light-red** *Sch.* — *dkar-rtsi* **white-wash,** consisting of lime or some other earthy colour *C.*, *W.* — *dkar-zás, k'a-zás dkar-po, dkar-tóg* **clean food, lenten**

diet, viz. esp. milk, curd, cheese or butter, as *dkar-ɣsúm Schf. Tar.* (Germ. translat. p. 335); also honey, fruit. — *dkar-yól,* resp. *C.* **žal-kar, W. sol-kar** **porcelain, china-ware,** cups or plates of porcelain, *dkar-yol sgrig-pa* to place the china-service on the table, for: to lay the cloth. — *dkar-ɣyá W.* **tin, pewter,** **kar-yá dań žár-če** **to solder.** — *dkar-sér* **yellowish white.** — *dkar-ɣsál* 1. **shining white,** *sku-mdog dkar-ɣsál gáńs-ri ˳dra* of a bright white colour like a glacier *Glr.* 2. **window** *Sch.* (?)

དཀུ་ *dku* 1. the **side** of a person's body *Cs.*, *dkur* or *dkú-la rtén-pa* to carry a thing at one's side *Zam.; dku brtólba* to open the side (in child-birth, v. *mńal).* — 2. v. *dkú-ba. Comp. dku-lči* a heavy feeling in the side, as a symptom of pregnancy. — *dku-mda* (**kúm-da**) *W.* (= *mčan-mda?)* **pocket** in the clothes. — *dku-nád* apparently a disease of the kidneys. — *dku-zlúm, Lex.* **कक्षि** cavity of the abdomen, womb.

དཀུ་ལྟོ་ *dkú-lto* **craft, cunning, trick, stratagem,** esp. if under specious pretence one person induces another to do a thing that proves hurtful to him.

དཀུ་བ་ *dkú-ba* **'sweet scent'** *Cs.; Zam.:* = **पूति stench.**

དཀོན་མཆོག་ *dkon-mčog (W.: *kon-čóg, kon-čóg, C.: kon-čó')* 1. **the most precious thing.** Buddhism has always sought the highest good not in anything material, but in the moral sphere, looking with indifference, and indeed with contempt, on everything merely relating to matter. It is not, however, moral perfection or the happiness attained thereby, which is understood by the 'most precious thing', but the mediator or mediators who procure that happiness for mankind, viz. Buddha, (the originator of the doctrine), the doctrinal scriptures and the corporate body of priests, **त्रिरत्न**, *dkon-mčóg ɣsum.* Now, although this triad cannot by any means be placed on a level with the Christian doctrine of a triune God, yet it will be easily understood, how the innate desire of man to adore and worship something supernatural, together with the hierarchical tendency of the teaching class, have afterwards contributed to convert the acknowledgment of human activity for the benefit of others (for such it was undoubtedly on the part of the founder himself and his earlier followers) into a devout, and by degrees idolatrous adoration of these three agents, especially as Buddha's religious doctrine did not at all satisfy the deeper wants of the human mind, and as its author himself did not know anything of a God standing apart and above this world. For whatever in Buddhism is found of beings to whom divine attributes are assigned, has either been transferred from the Indian and other mythologies, and had accordingly been current among the people before the introduction of Buddhism, or is a product of philosophical speculation, that has remained more or less foreign to the people at large. — 2. As then the original and etymological signification of the word is no longer current, and as to every Tibetan *'dkon-mčog'* suggests the idea of some supernatural power, the existence of which he feels in his heart, and the nature and properties of which he attributes more or less to the three agents mentioned above, we are fully entitled to assign to the word *dkon-mčog* also the signification of **God,** though the sublime conception which the Bible connects with this word, viz. that of a personal, absolute, omnipotent being, will only with the spread of the Christian religion be gradually introduced and established.

Note 1. *rań-grub-dkon-mčog* with *Schr.* is evidently the appellation of the Christian God adopted by the Rom. Cath. missionaries of those times. — 2. In the older writings *dkon-mčog* occurs (as far as I know) never without *ɣsum,* and combinations such as *dkon-mčog-la mčod-pa byed-pa* or *ysol-ba ˌdebs-pa,* as well as *bla-ma dkon-mčog,* are to be found only in writings of a comparatively recent date. — 3. Instead of the phrase of asseveration: *dkon-mčog šes,* God knows! the mere words *dkon-mčog ysum* are frequently used in the same sense.

དཀོན་པ་ *dkón-pa C., B., -mo W.* **rare, scarce,** and therefore **dear, precious, valuable** (in an objective sense, cf. *ycés-pa) ˌjig-rtén-na dkón-no* is exceedingly rare in the world *Dzl., ˌjig-rtén-na dkón-par bzáṅ-ṅo* it is of a beauty rarely to be met with in the world *Dzl.; k̔yod ˳dra mtóṅ-na dkón-rgyu med* to see a person like you, is nothing particular *Mil.; k̔e bdé-mo-la lhá čos dkon* with a prattler religion is scarce, there is generally not much religion about him *Mil.* — *dkon-nór* riches, valuables *Mil.*

དཀོར་ *dkór* 1. **wealth, riches.** — 2. *mtil-dkor, yaṅ-dkor, sa-dkor* are expressions current in *C.* which I could not get sufficiently explained. — *dkor-nór* = *nor.* — *dkor-pa Cs., dkor-mi Sch.* **treasurer.** — *dkor-mdzód* frq., **treasury.** — *dkor-rdzogs* (pronounce **kor-zog(s)**) n. of a monastery in southern Ladak, situated 16 000 feet high.

དཀྱར་ *dkyar Z., Ld.,* a sort of **snow-shoes.** *(Sch.:* 'stocking-boots'?)

དཀྱིལ་ *dkyil* **the middle,** *dkyil-du, -na* in the middle, c. genit. in the midst of, amidst; *dkyil-nas* from the middle, from amidst; relative to time: **yar-ri kyil-la* W.,* in the middle of summer. *dkyil-ma* the middle one, e. g. room, = dwelling-room *Ld.*

Comp. *dkyil-dkrúṅ* v. *skyil-dkrúṅ.* — *dkyil-ˌk̔or* 1. **circle, circumference,** frq. 2. **figure,** e. g. *dkyil-ˌk̔or gru-bži-pa* **quadrangle, square;** a certain mystical figure; **diagram, model.** 3. **a circle of objects,** *ˌk̔or-gyi dkyil-ˌk̔or* the circle of the attendants. 4. **the area of a circle, disk,** e. g. of the sun; *žál-gyi dkyil-k̔or bstan* = he showed his full countenance *Pth.* 5. **sphere,** *rlúṅ-gi dkyil-ˌk̔or* the atmosphere, *mé̆i-dkyil-˳k̔or* the sphere of fire, and similarly of the other elements, *lhai dkyil-˳k̔or* may perh. likewise be translated by: the sphere of the power of a certain god. In mysticism and magic, however, several other more or less arbitrary significations are assigned to the word, e. g. it is said to be used for *lús-kyi dkyil-ˌk̔or* the whole extent or bulk of the body, = the body, *dkyil-ˌk̔or-gyi ynás-su ˳čáṅ-ba* to wear on one's body (e. g. an amulet); or instead of *čós-kyi dky.: dkyil k̔or mtóṅ-ba* to behold the whole extent of religious doctrine (?).

Note. In Lex. *dkyil* is said to be = मध्य; perh. merely because *dkyil-ˌk̔or* is used for मण्डल? But *mán-dal-gyi dkyil-k̔or* is the Buddhistic map of the world, representing mount Sumeru with the surrounding continents etc.

དཀྱུ་བ་ *dkyú-ba* 1 **to run a race** *Cs.* — 2. **to wring out, to filter** *Sch.* — 3. **to caper about** *Ld.* — *dkyú-byai rta* race-horse *Cs., dkyu-sa* race-course *Cs.*

དཀྱུག་པ་ *dkyúg-pa* **to lose colour** by washing *Ld.,* perh. more correctly *skyúg-pa.*

དཀྱུས་ *dkyus* 1. **length,** *dkyús-su* in length, *dkyus-riṅ* **long** *C., spyan-dkyús* length from one corner of the eye to the other (e. g. in an image) *C. (Sch.:* bold, insolent?) — 2. **untruth, falsehood, lie.** Tar. 108. 7. *dkyus-nyid* seems to be used so, whilst 188, 5 is totally obscure.

དཀྱུས་མ་ *dkyús-ma* **common, every-day,** e. g. *na-bza* every-day clothes, *dbu-ža* work-day hat; hence *mi dkyús-ma* common people (without office or authority) *C.*

དཀྱེལ་ *dkyel* seems to be acc. to *Cs.* a synonym of *kloṅ.* I only met with the word *dkyél-po če* in a medical work; *Sch.* explains it by **universe,** and a native Lex. by *k̔aṅ yáṅs-pa* the wide house, which possibly may signify the same.

དཀྲི་བ་ *dkri-ba pf. dkris, vb. a.* (cf. *˳k̔ri-ba)* **to wind, to wind up,** *grú-gu* a clew or ball of thread, *lús-la gos* (or *gós-*

kyis) dkr., **to wrap** a garment round the body; *rtsá-bar ₒḱór-lo dkris-pai ɣčeu Med.* was explained to me: a magic spell in circular writing, wrapped round the lower end of a clyster-pipe, *fig.: sér-snas kún-nas dkris* quite **ensnared** in avarice; *kun-dkris* 'all-ensnaring' = sin. — *dkri-ma (Glr.* 47. where the text has *drima)* means very likely **necker-chief,** which col. is called **kog-ṫi* or *ḱa-ṫi C. 'og-śri, ḱa-śri, kya-śri* W.* — In the sense of *ₒkrid-pa* to conduct *(Sch.)* it never came to my notice.

དཀྲིགས་པ་ *dkrigs-pa* 1. **darkened, obscured, dim,** = *krigs-pa.* — also *dkrigs-ṗrág,* term for a very large number, *Cs.:* a 100 000 billion, acc. to *Zam.* = *ɣtáms-pa,* which *Cs.* renders, a 1000 billion. The one may be, after all, as correct as the other, for all these large numbers are, of course, not meant to be used in serious calculations, but are mere imitations of fantastic Indian extravagancies.

དཀྲུག་པ་ *dkrúg-pa pf. dkrugs (W. *śrug-če*)* **to stir, stir up, agitate** (as the storm does the sea); **to trouble, disturb, confound** (as enemies of religion confound the doctrine, or as passions disturb the mind); *dkrugs-śiṅ* 1. **stirring-stick, twirling-stick.** 2. **disturber, enemy** e.g. of the doctrine *Glr.* — *dkrugs Schr.:* turning-lathe (?) — *dkrugs-ma Schr.:* quarrel. — *Dzl.* ༢༧༧. *dkrugs byéd-pa* dubious; a safer reading is *dkú-lto byéd-pa.*

དཀྲུང་ *dkruṅ* v. *skyil.*

དཀྲུམ་པ་ *dkrúm-pa Cs. & Sch.:* **broken.**

དཀྲོག་པ་ *dkróg-pa (= skróg-pa)* 1. **to stir, churn** frq. 2. **to rouse, scare up,** *Glr.* — 3. **to wag** e. g. the tail *W.*

དཀྲོལ་བ་ *dkról-ba* v. *ₒkról-ba.*

བཀག་པ་ *bkag-pa* v. *ₒgégs-pa; bkág-ča byéd-pa* **to forbid** *Sch.*

བཀང་བ་ *bkáṅ-ba* v. *géṅs-pa* to fill.

བཀད་ *bkad? Lex.* quote *ṫágs-kyi bkad,* which was explained to me by: the crossing of threads in weaving; similar: *mgó-spui bkad, mgo-bkád* the crossing or entangling of the hair on the head. — *bkád-pa* seems = *ₒḱad-pa.*

བཀད་ས་ *bkád-sa* 1. **a bake-house, kitchen, cook's shop** *Lex.* — 2. **open hall** or **shed,** erected on festive occasions *Tib.-Ssk. Glossary; Tar.* 18, 12.

བཀན་པ་ *bkán-pa* **to put, to press,** *rkáṅ-pa rtsig-pa-la* one's foot against a wall; **to apply,** *ɣšó-mo* the plane, *lág-pa* the hand *Zam.,* to put the hand on or to something (or: stretch it out? *Sch.)*

བཀབ་པ་ *bkáb-pa* v. *ₒgébs-pa.*

བཀའ་ *bka (resp.* for *ɣtam, ṫsig, skad)* **word, speech** of a respected person (wherefore **order, commandment** may often be substituted for it), *rgyál-poi bka* the word of the king, *bká-la ɣtsógs-pa* to belong to the word, i. e. to be under the commandment or dominion (of somebody) *Glr.; rgyál-bai bka* the word of Buddha (this is named as one of the five 'means of grace', so to speak, Glr. fol. 70; the four others are: *mdo-rgyúd* the sacred writings *(sutra* and *tantra), bstan-bčós* doctrinal and scientific writings *(śāstra), luṅ* oral benedictions and instructions of Lamas, *man-ṅág* admonitions given by them). After quotations *bka* or *bkao (= skad & skad-do)* means: thus says (the holy book or teacher). *bka* as first part of a compound is frequently used to give the word adjoined the character of respectfulness, and is therefore not to be translated separately.

Phrases and compounds: *bka bkód-pa* **to publish, proclaim; publication, proclamation** *C.* — *bka-bkyón* (col. **kab-kyon*)* 'verbal blows' **reprimand, rebuke** (given by a superior), *bka-bkyón byéd-pa, mdzád-pa B. C., *tón-če, ṗiṅ-če* W., bka bkyón-pa,* all of them construed with dat., **to rebuke** somebody. — *bka-bḱrims* **law, commandment,** *rgyál-poi bka-ḱrims ɣnyán-pas* by the cruel order of the king *Dzl.* — *bka bgró-ba* **to consult, to deliberate,** *naṅ-blón bču* *daṅ bka-žib-tu bgrós-pa-la* deliberating carefully with the ten ministers of the interior *Pth.* (*Schr.* gives also, *bka-grós ₒdri-ba* to ask, — *bgéd-pa* to give advice), — *bka-ₒgyur* (**ká-gyur,** com. **kan-gyur, kan-dyúr,** in Mongolia **kan-jur**) the word of Buddha, as translated from the original Sanskrit, the holy scriptures of the Buddhists (100 volumes). — *bka ₒgrol-ba* **to dismiss** *Pth.*, *bka-bkrol* **leave of absence,** *ysol-ba* to ask for, *ynaṅ-ba* to grant leave *Schr.* — *bka-rgya, bka-šog,* resp. for *rgya-ma* and *šog-bu,* letter or paper from a superior etc., **diploma, missive, communication** etc. *bka-rgyúd* 1. = *bkai rgyud* 'thread of the word', the oral tradition of the word of Buddha, which is supposed to have been delivered through a continual series of teachers and disciples besides the written scriptures; *bka-rgyud bla-ma* a Lama deriving his religious knowledge in this manner from Buddha himself *Mil.* 2. perh. also = *bka daṅ rgyud* 'word and tantra', oral and written instruction; *bka-rgyúd-pa* n. of a Lama-sect *Schl.* 73.; *bka-bsgos* **commandment, precept.** — *bka-sgyúr* order, *bka-sgyúr ynaṅ-ba* to issue an order *C.* — *bka sgyúr-ba* 1. to translate the words (of Buddha etc.) 2. to issue an order (viz. in the name of a superior). — *bka sgrog-pa* 1. to publish an order. 2. to proclaim, read, preach the word. — *bka yčog-pa* to act against an order, *yab-kyi bka bčag-tu med* the order of the father must be obeyed *Glr.* — *bka-čéms* resp. for *ka-čéms* **testament.** — *bka-mčid* resp. for *mčid,* words or speech of a superior or any person to be honoured. — *bka nyan-pa ccg.* 1. *vb.* **to obey.** 2. *adj.* **obedient,** *bka mi nyan-pa* 1. to disobey. 2. disobedient. *bka ynyan* 'the cruel commander', acc. to a Lex. = *btsan-pai sa-bdag* 'the mighty lord of the ground', is said to be the first of gods, either Siva or a pre-buddhistic deity. — **ka taṅ-ce** *W.* **to permit.** — *bka btags-pa* (*Lex.*: = *krims bsgrags-pa*) **a proclaimed order,** cf. *bkar.* — *bka-rtags Cs.*: **mark, seal, precept, maxim** (?) — *bka-stod Sch.*: **'a subaltern, agent'** (?) — *bka-taṅ* **order, edict.** — *bka-drin* resp. for *drin,* **favour, grace, kindness, benefit,** *bka-drinmdzád-pa* to bestow a favour, *mi-la* upon somebody; *blá-mai bka-drin-gyis* through the kindness of his (your) reverence *Mil.*; *bka-drin-čé* the usual phrase of acknowledgment, as our: you are very kind! many thanks! *B.* and *col.* — *bka-druṅ* **secretary** (of a high person) *C.* — *bka-ydáms,* = *žal-ydáms* **advice, counsel, instruction;** *bka-ydáms-pa* 1. **adviser** *Sch.* 2. n. of a sect of red Lamas, founded by Brom-ston *Schl.* 73. — *bka-ₒdógs-pa* **to proclaim; proclamation.** — *bka-bsdú-ba* collection of the doctrine *Tar.* — **ka-nán** **instruction** *C.* — *bka ynáṅ-ba* 1. *vb.* **to order, command; grant, permit;** 2. *sbst.* **order; permission;** *ṅed bód-kyi rgyál-poi btsún-mo-la bka ynáṅ-bar žu* I beg you will give her as a consort to my (the Tibetan) king *Glr.* — *bka-pébs Sch.* **a supreme order.** — *bka-príṅ* **message.** — *bka ₒbáb-pa* the going forth of an order, *bka-ₒbáb* order, edict *Schr.* — *bka-ₒbúm,* vulg. **kam-búm**, the hundred thousand precepts (title of a book). — *bka stsol-ba, pf. stsal* (*stsál-to, stsál-pa*), resp. for *smrá-ba* **to speak, to say** (acc. to circumstances: to command, ask, beg, relate, answer etc.), esp. in ancient literature, in which it is almost invariably used of Buddha and of kings. — *bka-blo-bdé Lex.*: = सुवचस् speaking well, eloquently; *Sch.*: *bka-blo-bdé-ba* to acknowledge to be wrong (?); *bka-blón,* (*bkai blón-po Glr.* f. 94) **prime minister;** any **high official.** — *bka-šóg* any writing of a superior, **decree, diploma, passport, official paper, letter.** — *bka yšágs* 1. **a high official, counsellor.** *C.* 2. **court of justice, judgment-hall.**

བཀར་ *bkar term.* of *bka* in or to the word etc; *bkar ₒdógs-pa Cs.* **to legalize,** *Dzl.* cap. 4: **to proclaim, publish.** *bkár-btags-pa* **published; publication.**

བཀར་བ་ bkár-ba v. dgár-ba.

བཀལ་བ་ bkál-ba v. ˳k'ál-ba and ˏgél-ba.

བཀས་ bkas instr. of bka; bkás-pa v. ˏgés-pa.

བཀུ་བ་ bk'ú-ba Lex.: **to extract,** to make an extract of a drug by drawing out the juice (k'ú-ba ˳byin-pa); bkús-te ˏbór-ba id.; smán-bku medicinal extract.

བཀུག་ bkug v. kug; bkúg-pa v. ˏgúgs-pa.

བཀུམ་ bkum v. kum; bkúm-pa v. ˏgúms-pa.

བཀུར་བ་ bkúr-ba I. 1. vb. **to honour, esteem** (synon. mčód-pa), máṅ-pos bkúr-bai rgyál-po, **महासम्मत**, the king honoured by many, frq.; kún-gyis bkúr-žiṅ mčód-pai ˏos worthy of general honour and respect Mil.; mis bkúr-bar mi ˏgyur is not esteemed by men Dzl. — 2. sbst. **honour;** more frq., bkúr-sti, **honour, respect, homage, mark of honour,** bkúr-stis mčód-pa to distinguish (a person) by marks of respect Zam.; ráṅ-la bkúr-sti ˳byuṅ dus when honour is shown to yourself Mil.; bkúr-sti byéd-pa to do honour frq.; to make a reverence, to salute. — II. pf. of ˳k'úr-ba **to carry;** in the term máṅ-pos bkúr-bai rgyál-po the legend combines this signification with the preceding one Glr.

བཀོག་པ་ bkóg-pa v. ˏgóg-pa.

བཀོང་བ་ bkóṅ-ba v. ˏgóṅ-ba.

བཀོད་པ་ bkód-pa v. ˏgód-pa.

བཀོན་པ་ bkón-pa v. ˳k'ón-pa.

བཀོབ་ལྟ་ bkób-lta (*kób-ta*) **the plan** of an undertaking W. (vulg. pronunciation for bkod-blta?)

བཀོར་འདྲེ་ bkór-˳dré Mil. seems to be a kind of goblins.

བཀོལ་བ་ bkól-ba v. k'ól-ba.

བཀྱལ་བ་ bkyál-ba Cs.: **to talk nonsense,** v. kyál-ka; bkyál-pai ṅag = kyál-ka Lex.

བཀྱིག་པ་ bkyig-pa v. ˳k'yig-pa.

བཀྱེ་བ་ bkyé-ba v. ˏgyéd-pa.

བཀྱེད་པ་ bkyéd-pa **to bend back, recline** (vb. nt.), rgyaṅs byéd-de bending or turning far aside.

བཀྱོན་པ་ bkyón-pa **to beat** (= rdúṅ-ba) Mil. nt.; bka bkyon-pa resp. to chastise with words, **to scold,** frq. (v. bka, phrases); Schr. mentions also bkyon-bkyál chiding.

བཀྲ་བ་ bkra-ba (Lex.: = **चित्र**, cf. also k'rá-bo) 1. **variegated.** — 2. **beautiful, blooming** (of complexion); **glossy, well-fed** (of animals); ša-bkrá n. of a cutaneous disease.

Comp. bkra-bzáṅ n. of a mountain in Tibet. — bkra-lam-mé v. k'ra-lam-mé. — bkra-šis Ssk. **मङ्गल** 1. **happiness, prosperity, blessing,** ˳báṅs-rnams-la bkra-šis šog happiness to my people! may they prosper! Glr.; *nád-med tsád-med ṭa-ši p'un-sum-tsóg žu* I wish you good health and immeasurable and perfect happiness! (new year's wish in W.); bkra-šis-kyi ču holy water Glr.; bkra-šis-kyi mál-k'ri nuptial bed Cs.; bkra šis-kyi tsig or smon-lam blessing, benediction; *ṭa-ši šig!* Good bye! May you be happy! *k'yód-la ṭa-ši čo!* I wish you joy! (also ironically) W.; bkra-šis-šiṅ being happy, enjoying prosperity Glr.; bkra-šis srúṅ-bai gó-ča instruments used for insuring happiness (to a new-born infant) Lt. — 2. sacrificial ceremony by which blessings are to be drawn down, bkra-šis byéd-pa or mčód-pa or *yóg-če* (W., barley being scattered — yyog-pa — on that occasion), to perform this ceremony. — bkra-šis-pa **propitious, lucky,** perh. also: **happy;** bkra-šis-pai ltas lucky signs; bkra-šis-pai rtags lucky configurations or semblances (such as e. g. devout imagination seeks to discover in the outlines of mountains etc. Glr. fol. 58.) bkra-šis-ma n. of a goddess, Sch.: goddess of glory Dzl. — bkra-mi-šis **misfortune, calamity,** bkra-mi-šis-pa unhappy; **calamity**, *bkra-mi-śis-pa t'ams-čád* all manner of calamities. (The expression *bkra-mi-śis* c dat. for: 'Woe to . . .' in our translation of the New Test. does not rest upon classic authority, but has been adopted as analogous to the above mentioned *bkra-śis śog.*) *bkra-śis-čos-rdzoṅ* (**ta-śi-čo-dzóṅ**) 'Tassisudon' in Bhot., *bkra-śis-lhun-po* (**ta-śi-hlum-po**) 'Tashilunpo' in Tsaṅ.

བཀྲག་ *bkrag* 1. **brightness, lustre** = *mdaṅs*, also *bkrag-mdáṅs*, e. g. of jewels. 2. **beautiful appearance, colour,** of the face or skin, also *śa-bkrág*; *śa bkrag-mdaṅs* pure **gloss** of the skin *Mil.*; *bkrág-čan* **bright**. *bkrag-čór* without gloss, **dim.**

བཀྲབ་པ་ *bkráb-pa* 1. **to select, choose;** *mčóg-tu bkrab* **exquisite, choice** *Lex.* — 2 = *ₒk'rúb-pa, skráb-pa W.*

བཀྲམ་པ་ *bkrám-pa* v. *ₑgrém-pa.*

བཀྲལ་བ་ *bkrál-ba* 1. *pf.* of *ₑgrél-ba Cs.*, *Tar.* 124, 14. — 2. **to appoint**, *lás-la* to a business.

བཀྲས་པ་ *bkrás-pa* 1. *Sch.*: *pf.* of a verb *bkrá-ba*, adorned, decorated (?) 2. *Cs.*: *bkras* abbreviation for *bkra-śís*, *bkras-btags* for *bkra-śis k'a-btags* = *k'a-btags.*

བཀྲི་བ་ *bkri-ba* 1. for *dkri-ba* to wrap. — 2. for *ₒkríd-pa* to conduct. — 3. to try to acquire, **to search for** *Dzl.* ༢༩ **to lay up,** = **śri-če* W.*

བཀྲིས་ *bkris* abbrev. for *bkra-śis.*

བཀྲིས་པ་ *bkris-pa* for *dkris-pa* v. *dkri-ba.*

བཀྲུ་, བཀྲུས་ *bkru, bkrus*, v. *ₒk'rúd-pa.*

བཀྲུག་པ་ 1. *Dzl.* ༡༤༥ 1. prob. an incorrect reading. 2. prov. instead of *dkrúg-pa*, v. *ja bkrúg.*

བཀྲེན་པ་ *bkrén-pa* 1. *Cs.* **poor, indigent, hungry,** *sai p'yogs bkr.* a poor, barren country *Stg.* — 2. **miserly, stingy** *C.*

བཀྲེས་པ་ *bkrés-pa vb.* **to be hungry;** *adj.* **hungry;** *sbst.* **hunger** *B., C.* where it is now used as the respectful term; *bkres-skóm* hunger and thirst; *bkres-skóm-pa-las čóg-par ₒbyin-te* leading after hunger and thirst to satiety; *bkrés-ṅáb-pa Sch.*: to have a ravenous appetite.

བཀྲོངས་ *bkroṅs* v. *ₑgróṅs-pa.*

བཀྲོལ་བ་ *bkrol-ba* v. *ₑgról-ba.*

བཀླག་པ་ *bklag-pa* v. *klóg-pa.*

རྐ་ *rka* 1. **a small furrow** conveying water from a conduit (*yúr-ba*) to trees or plants; **furrow** between the beds of a garden; hence: 2. **flower-bed.**

རྐང་ *rkaṅ* (*Ld.* **skaṅ, χaṅ**) 1. **marrow,** *rkaṅ-már* id.; *rkáṅ-bro-ma* tasting of marrow *Sch.*; *rkáṅ-gi k'óṅ-nas byáms-pa* love from the innermost heart *Thgy.* — 2. the upper part of the arm or thigh, or the large **marrow-bones** of them, *dpúṅ-rkaṅ, rlá-rkaṅ Med.* — 3. **kernel** of a nut etc. *W.* — 4. = *rkaṅ-pa* no. 5, **stalk;** also **quill** of a feather. — 5. in compounds for *rkáṅ-pa.*

རྐང་པ་ *rkaṅ-pa* (resp. *žabs*) 1. **foot.** — 2. **leg.** — 3 (cf. *lag-pa*) **hind-foot.** — 4. **lower part, lower end,** e. g. of a letter, *rkaṅ-pa-čan* 'having a foot', so the nine letters are called that extend below the line (ཀ, ཁ etc.) *Glr.* — 5. **stem, stalk,** esp. leaf-stalk, *lo-rkáṅ.* — 6. **verse,** metrical line; *ts'ig-rkáṅ*, prop.: *ts'igs-su-bčad-pai rkáṅ-pa, id.*, *ts'ig-rkáṅ mt'ar nyis-śád t'ob* at the close of a verse a double *shad* is placed; hence: **verse** of the Bible *Chr. Prot.* — 7. **base, foundation,** *rdzu-ₒp'rúl-gyi rkáṅ-pa bži Dzl.* the four 'pillars' of performing miracles (ऋद्धिपाद) *Trigl. fol.* 17.

Comp. **kaṅ-kyóg** **bandy-legged** *C.* — *rkaṅ-krí* a piece of cloth to wrap round the legs (*Lat.: tibiale*) *Sch.* — *rkaṅ-ₒk'úm Lex.* w. e., prob. having a foot contracted by disease — *rkaṅ-ₒk'ór* **bandy-legged** *Sch.* *rkaṅ-mgyógs pa* **nimble-footed,** *rkaṅ-mgyógs-kyi rdzas lham-la byúgs-te* oiling his boots with swiftfootedness, a miraculous ointment imparting this gift *Glr., Tar.* 67. — *rkaṅ-ₑgró* a vassal or subject paying his duty by serving as a messenger or porter *Cs.* — *rkan-ₒgros* or *-brós* 1. **walking on foot.** 2. **domestic cattle; breeding-cattle.** — *rkan-rgyu Cs.:* 'the hollow of the sole'. — *rkan-ycig-pa* **one-footed.** — *rkan-rjén* **bare-footed.** — *rkan-rjés* **footstep, trace.** — *rkan-ynyis-pa* **two-footed, a biped,** po. for **man, mankind.** — *rkan-stégs* **footstool; trestle.** — *rkan-tán* **on foot,** *rkan-tán-pa* **pedestrian. foot-soldier,** *rkan-tán-du grúl-ba (Sch.* also: *rkan-tán-ba)* to walk, to go on foot. — *rkan-mtil* **sole** of the foot. — *rkan-ₒtún* (erron. also *-tun) Ssk.* पादप 'drinking with the foot' po. for: **tree** *Mil.* — *rkan-dún* trumpet made of a human thigh-bone (*Hook.* I 173). — *rkan-drúg-pa, rkan-drúg-ldan-pa* **six-footed; insect,** *po.* — *rkan-ydúb* **foot-ring** (ornament). — *rkan-ₒdrén* (v. also *žabs-ₒdrén)* **disgrace,** *rkan ₒdrén-pa* c. genit. to get a person into disgrace, to deprive him of his honour and good name, to be a disgrace to another, e. g. a son to his father by criminal actions etc. *rkan-rdúm* **a maimed foot; lame** *Cs.* — *rkán-snam* **trowsers,** *snám-bui rkán-snam ycig* one pair of cloth-trowsers. *rkan pags lhun S. g.* fol. 9? — *rkan-pyin* felt for covering the legs, v. *rkan-dkri.* — *rkan-ból* upper part of the foot. — *rkan-bám* a disease in the foot, *Sch.:* gout. *rkan-ₒbrós* or *bros* v. *rkan-ₒgrós.* — *rkan-tségs* v. *tségs.* — *rkan-mdzub-ₒdzér-pa Sch.:* **corn** (on the toe). — *rkan-mdzér* **iron pricks** fastened to the feet for climbing mountains. — *rkan-bži-pa* **four-footed; quadruped.** — *rkan-lág* hands and feet, *rkan-lag bšál-ba Lt., Schr.:* 'numbness or rheumatic pain in hands and feet'; *rkan-lág sér-kar ₒon* hands and feet chap *Sch.* — *rkan-lám* **foot-path.** *rkan-šin* **treadle,** of a loom. — *rkan-šúbs* **stocking, sock.** — *rkan sór* **toe.**

རྐན་ *rkan* v. *dkan.*

རྐམ་པ་ *rkám-pa* I. *vb.* **to desire, to long,** *nór-la* for money. II. *sbst.* 1. **longing** (*cf.* *kam* extr.) — 2. v. *skam-pa.*

རྐུ་བ་ *rkú-ba, pf. (b)rkus, ft. brku, imp. rkus,* **to steal, to rob,** *brkú-bya* to be stolen, *brkú-byai rdzas* things that may be stolen.

རྐུན་མ་ *rkún-ma* 1. **thief** frq. 2. **theft.** *rk. byéd-pa (W.: *co-ce*)* to steal; **kún-ma zos son* W.* it has been carried away by a thief; **ka-kún gyáb-ce* W.* 'to steal with the mouth', to promise to pay without ever doing so, or: to deny having known a thing missing, until all inquiry has ceased and it may be safely appropriated (a common practice of servants in India); *dur-rkún* robber of graves. — *rkún-tabs-su blan-ba* to take away thievishly *Stg.* — *rkún-nor* stolen goods. — *rkún-po, fem. -mo* **thief.** — *rkún-dpon* the head of a gang of thieves or robbers *Cs.* — *rkún-zla* a thief's accomplice.

རྐུབ་ *rkub (Lex.* पायु) 1. **the anus** *B.* — 2. **vulva** *W., C.* — 3. **backside, posteriors** *C.* — *rkub-stégs* **sitting-bench** *C.* — *rkub-tsós* **buttocks** *Cs.*

རྐེ་བ་ *rké-ba (cf. skémpa)* **lean, meagre** *Cs.*

རྐེད་པ་ *rkéd-pa,* also *skéd-pa, W.: *skéd-pa** 1. **the waist,** *sén-ges mcóns-sar was mcons rkéd-pa ₒcag* if the fox takes a lion's leap, he breaks his neck *Mil.;* **skyed kug tán-ce* W.* **to bow;** **sked-zér** (?) the arms **a-kimbo** *W.;* more particularly that part where the girdle is worn, **loins;** *rked-rgyán* ornament of the girdle; *rkéd-pa-nas gri bton* he took a knife from his girdle *Pth.;* **ké-pa bhab** 'her waist fell', euphem. expression for: she has got her menses *C.* — 2. **the middle** of a building, of a mountain, **kar-skyéd* W.* the middle story of a castle; *rkéd-pa tsam brtsigs tsár nas* when the building was half finished *Glr.;* *Ti-sei rkéd-pa-na yar bslebs son* he is already half-way up the Ti-se *Mil.*

རྐོ་བ་ *rkó-ba, pf. (b)rkos, ft. brko, imp. rkos* 1. **to dig, dig-out, to hoe,** e. g. *sa* earth; *rko-byéd* digger; po. also a spade, mattock; *brkó-byai sa* soil to be turned up. — 2. **to engrave** *(cf. ₒbúr-ba); brko-spyád* **a gouge** *Sch.; brkós ma* **sculpture.**

རྐོ་མ་ *rkó-ma* n. of a bird *Wdn.*, prob. = *ko-ma.*

རྐོག་མ་ *rkóg-ma* v. *lkóg-ma.*

རྐོང་པ་ *rkóṅ-pa Cs.:* **itch,** *za-rkóṅ* id.; *Lt.: rkóṅ-po.* Others describe it as a scabby eruption of the skin, chiefly affecting animals, but occasionally also men *C.*

རྐོད་པ་ *rkód-pa,* = *rkó-ba Ts.*

རྐོན་པ་ *rkón-pa,* also *skón-pa* 1. **basket;** the word is said to be used in Kun.; perh. also the Ladakian word **kun-dúm*,* a large cylindrical or bottle-shaped basket, may be traced to the same form. I never found it in books. — 2. **net,** fowler's net *Lex.*

རྐྱག(པ) *rkyag(-pa),* also *skyag(-pa),* **dirt, excrement;** **kyág-pa tóṅ-wa* C., *kyág táṅ-če* W.* to cack, vulg. — *mig-skyág* the impurity in the eyes *Cs.; *na-skyág** ear-wax *W.*

རྐྱང་ *rkyaṅ* **the wild ass** or horse of Central Asia, Chigitai, *p̔o-rkyáṅ* male, *mo-rkyaṅ* female of it; *rkyaṅ dár-ma* a young wild ass, *rkyaṅ-rgan* an old one, *Cs.* — *rkyaṅ-ču* n. of a lake in the south of *Ld.,* in the neighbourhood of which these animals are particularly numerous.

རྐྱང་པ་ *rkyaṅ-pa* **simple, single;** *ras rkyaṅ* a single sheet of cotton cloth *Dzl., Mil.; *mi kyaṅ** a single i. e. free, unemployed man, one that carries no burden *C.; yi-ge rkyáṅ-pa* a letter that forms by itself a syllable, or one that is not *brtségs-pa* and without any other consonant or a vowel-sign superscribed; *rkyáṅ-pai graṅs* are called 1, 10, 100 and the further powers of 10; *miṅ rkyáṅ-pa* a word that has no affix-denoting case etc. attached. — **kyaṅ, kyaṅ-kyáṅ, kyáṅ-ka, k̔a-(r)kyáṅ*,* col. (in *B. ṡa-stag)* **only, nothing but,** **p̔é-ča ṅags k̔ár-kyaṅ dug** the book contains nothing but charms. — **kyaṅ-kyáṅ** also: living by one's self, childless *W.* — **kyaṅ-ltab** single folded.

རྐྱང་བ་ *rkyáṅ-ba* v. *rkyóṅ-ba.*

རྐྱང་མ་ *rkyáṅ-ma* n. of a vein, v. rtsa.

རྐྱན་ *rkyan (Ld. *skyan*)* 1. a brass-vessel like a tea-pot, with a spout, *rag-rkyan id.; *o-kyan* W.* milk-pot. — 2. **pot-belly, paunch** *Sch.*

རྐྱལ་ཀ་ *rkyál-ka,* sometimes for *kyál-ka.*

རྐྱལ་པ་ *rkyál-pa,* **कृति, leather bag** *frq.; p̔úṅ-po mi-ytsaṅ-rdzás-kyi rkyál-pa* a poetical term for the body *Mil.; rkyal-bu (*kyal-lu*)* **small bag, pouch;** *ra-rkyál* bag of goatskin; *p̔ye-rkyál (*če-kyal* C., *p̔e-ky.* W.)* bag for flour.

རྐྱལ་བ་ *rkyál-ba* **to swim,** **kyal gyáb-če* W. id.; rkyal rtséd-pa* to amuse one's self by swimming.

རྐྱེན་ *rkyen,* **प्रत्यय** *Will.: 'with Buddhists: a co-operating cause, the concurrent occasion of an event as distinguished from its proximate* (or rather primary, original) *cause', rgyu* **हेतु.** (The right meaning was given already by *Schr.,* whereas afterwards, by a mistake of *Cs.,* the totally erroneous sense of 'effect, consequence' has become current among philologists.) 1. **cause, occasion,** *rkyén-gis* c. gen. **by, on account of,** *čii rkyén-gis* whereby? *dei rkyén-gyis* thereby, therefore, *dei rgyu dei rkyén-gyis id.* As a medical term, opp. to *rgyu* (the anthropological or primary cause of a disease) it denotes the pathological or secondary cause of it. — 2. **event, occurrence, accident, case, circumstance,** in a general sense, in as far as the Buddhist conceives every thing that happens in the mutual connexion of cause and effect; *rkyen ṅán-pa* unfortunate accident; *rkyen ṅán-pas ˳das* he has perished by a fatal accident *Glr.; tse ˳dir byúṅ-bai rkyen ṅán-rnams* the adversities of the present life *Mil.; raṅ mi ˳dód-pai rkyen* an event disagreeable to one's own self; *bló-bur rkyen* a sudden accident *Mil.; rkyen dé-la brtén-nas* owing to that circumstance *Tar.* 8. 1. *méd-pai rkyén-la bltás-te* or *brtén-te C.* considering the case of not being . . . , not having . . . , thus *nad-kyi rkyen, či-bai rkyen* stands also for: a case of disease, of death; *˳gal-*

rkyén any circumstance or event adverse to the success of an action, **obstacle, hinderance**, any thing opposite or hostile to the existence of another thing, *mtun-rkyén*, **a happy, favorable circumstance, furtherance, assistance, supply**, *mtun-rkyén byéd-pa* c. genit. to assist in, to help to; *mtun-rkyén ₒdzom-po* altogether successful. — 3. **misfortune, ill luck, calamity**, *rkyen zlóg-pa* to avert a misfortune, *tégs-pa* to endure, *túb-pa* to brave it *Mil.* — *cf. rgyu.*

རྐྱོང་བ་ *rkyóṅ-ba pf. & ft. brkyaṅ*, **to stretch, extend, stretch forth** (one's hand to a person), **put out** (the tongue), **spread, distend** (the wings, a curtain), *žabs ɣnyis brkyaṅ-bskúm* one leg stretched out, the other drawn in *Pth.; *kyaṅ-šád-če* W.* to stretch one's limbs. — *brkyaṅ-šiṅ* 1. 'extending-wood', an instrument of torture in Tibet, a wooden frame on which the extended arms and legs of the delinquent are fastened down, whilst burning pitch or sealing-wax is dropped on his naked breast, which procedure is called *brkyaṅ-šiṅ sprád-pa, brkyaṅ-šiṅ-la bčúg-pa* or *brkyáṅ-ba* 2. **cross** *Chr. Prot.* This word has been adopted on account of its etymological signification, although it differs in its form and use from the σταυρός of the N. T., which is unknown in Tibet and India. Additional explanation will be at any rate required on the part of missionaries; but much more so in the case of the *Kro-če (Ital. croce)* of the Rom. Cath. missionaries of the last century. In favour of the word *ɣsal-šiṅ*, pointed stake for empaling a delinquent, speaks the circumstance, that this is also the original and classical signification of σταυρός, and that Buddhists from their own legends are well acquainted with the idea of martyrdom inflicted in this manner. Still *ɣsal-šiṅ* leads to a conception of the death of Christ historically untrue and revolting to our feelings and is therefore better not employed; moreover it is to be assumed that in the times of the Evangelists σταυρός was the term generally used for cross, whilst in the case of *ɣsal-šiṅ* no Tibetan thinks of anything else but empaling.

རྐྱོང་ཙེ་ *rkyóṅ-tse W.*, resp. **zim-kyoṅ, zim-tiṅ**, **lamp, candle**, (spelling uncertain).

ལྐུགས་པ་ *lkúgs-pa* 1. **dumb, mute**; *ka lkúgs-par byed-pa* to put to silence *Do.*; *lkúgs-pa-pa* a dumb man, *-ma* woman *Cs.* — 2. **dull, stupid** *Sch.*

ལྐོག་ *lkog* **secrecy**, *lkóg-gi čúṅ-ma Cs.*: a wife kept secretly, a private concubine, *lkóg-tu* in secrect, secretly frq.: *lkóg-tu gyúr-pa, lkyog-gyúr*, परोक्ष, secret, hidden, out of sight *Mil., Tar.*; *lkóg-tu gléṅ-ba* to converse secretly; *lk. sdód-pa* to keep in retirement. — *lkog-rṅan* a reward given secretly, a bribe. — *lkog-čós Sch.*: 'a secret doctrine'; but *lkog-čos byéd-pa* is gen. understood: to apply one's self to religious studies or exercises in secret. — *lkog ǰab byéd-pa* to hide one's self in a lurking place: *lkog ǰab byed-nas lta-ba* to watch, to witness from a lurking-place. — *lkog-zán zá-ba Sch.* to take usury-interest in secret. — *lkog-láb* backbiting, slander.

ལྐོག་མ་ *lkóg-ma* (vulg. **og-ma**) 1. **gullet, oesophagus.** — 2. **wind-pipe.** — 3. **throat.** — 4. **neck.** *lkóg-mai lha-góṅ Sch.*, (acc. to others: *lhar-gór*) the larynx, **koi lkóg-ma** or **og-ma šraṅ soṅ* W.* his throat is swollen, he has the croup. — — *lkog-dkár* a small nocturnal carnivorous quadruped with a white throat, marten? — *lkog-gágs* hoarseness of voice *Cs.* — *lkog-šál* **dew-lap** (of oxen). — *lkog-sóg* **craw, maw** (of birds) *Cs.*

ལྐོབ་ *lkob* **fat, heavy, plump** *Sch.*

ལྐོལ་མདུད་ *lkol-mdúd*, also *'ol-mdúd*, **larynx.**

སྐ་ཅིག་ *ska-čig* v. *skad čig, skad* no. 4.

སྐ་ཅོག་ *ska-čóg* n. of a grammarian *Zam.*

སྐ་བ་ *ská-ba* **thick** (of fluids, *cf. slá-ba*); *ska-slád (Ld.: *kas-lád*)* **consistence, density.** — *W.: *skán-te**.

སྐ་རགས་ *ska-rágs B. & C.*, also *ske-rágs*, *W.* **kye-rágs**, *resp.* *sku-rágs* **girdle**, *ska-rags* *ₒčiṅ-ba* to put on the girdle, *ska-rágs bšur-ba Sch.*: a girdle with a clasp (?).

སྐག་ *skag* 1. *Cs.*: = *kag*, *keg*, **mischief; unlucky.** — 2. v. *rgyu-skar*.

སྐང་བ་ *skáṅ-ba* = *skoṅ-ba*; *skaṅ-ysó* 1. **satisfaction** *Sch.* — 2. a kind of **expiatory sacrifice**, to make amends for a duty not performed.

སྐང་ཤ་ *skaṅ-ša Sch.*: **sods** cut out.

སྐད་ *skad* (*C.*: **ka̤**) 1. **voice, sound, cry** (*cf. sgra*), *gláṅ-po-čei skad lta-bui sgra* a sound like the voice of an elephant, **ka̤'-la čig-pa dho̤n mi-čig-pa** *C.* (words) equal as to sound, but of different sense (= homophone), *sdug-bsṅál-bai skad ₒbyíṅ-pa*, *snyiṅ-žei skad dón-pa* to utter lamentable cries; *skad stér-ba Sch.*, **ke̤' gyúg-pa** *C.*, **skad táṅ-če** *W.* **to sound**; **ke̤' taṅ-wa** *C.* **skad gyab-če** *W. ccdp.* **to call** to a person; *skad mtún-par* with one voice, with one accord. — 2. **speech, words, talk, news,** **ka̤' či naṅ ₒdug** what is your pleasure? what did you say, Sir? *C.*; *zér-ba de či-skad yiṅ* the (words) spoken what speech are they? = what do they mean? *Pth.*; *ₒdi-skad-(du)* in these words, thus, (before a literally quoted speech), *dé-skad-(čes)* id. (after it); it is also used in a more general sense instead of *dé-ltar*: *dé-skad ma byed* don't do that *Mil.*; *skad smrá-ba* to give account, to relate *Ld.-Glr. fol.* 12. b. *Schl.*, acc. to another reading instead of *sra smrás-te*; *skad byéd-pa id.*, *rmi-lám-du byúṅ-ba skad byás-te* reporting it as having been revealed to him by a dream *Pth.* — 3. **language,** *bód-skad* the Tibetan language, *rgya-gár-skad* the Sanskrit language, *bód-skad-du*, *col.* *-la*, into or in the Tib. language, *yúl-skad-du* into or in the provincial dialect. — 4. **a snap** with the fingers, always with *čig*: *skád-čig-(ma)*, gen. as a measure of time: **a moment**; also adv.: for a moment, *skád-čig-la* in a moment, instantly, in one moment, *skád-čig de-nyid-la* in the very same moment. (Some mathematical books compute the *skád-čig* = ¹/₄‴, others as long as ¹/₃″).

Comp. and Deriv. *skad-ₒgágs* **hoarseness of the voice,** *Cs.* — *skad-ṅán* 1. **a bad voice.** 2. **cry, screaming.** — *skád-čan* having a voice, **sounding.** — *skád-ča* 1. *C.*: discourse, conversation, **ka̤'-ča láb-pa** or **ǰhé'-pa** to converse, to have a chat. 2. *C.* talk, rumour, **mii ká'-ča re** it is (but) talk of the people. 3. *W.*: news, tidings, intelligence. — *skad-čé*, *-čén* 1. **a loud voice** *Sch.* 2. n. of an animal *Lt.* — *skad-ynyá Sch.*: **a high voice.** — *skad-snyán sgyúr-ba Mil.* to sing or whistle in a quavering, warbling manner, of birds, flute- players etc., *ₒgyúr-skad* a singing or playing of this kind. — *skad-dód* **an equivalent word,** *čúṅ-mai sk.* another word for wife *Gramm.* — *skád-pa* v. the separate article below. — *skad-ₒdzér Cs.* = *skad-ₒgágs*. — *skad-bzáṅ* 1. **a good voice.** 2. *W.*: **good news.** — *skad-lúgs* **dialect.** — *skad-lóg* **clamour, screaming.** — *skad-ysáṅs mto Sch.*: **a loud voice,** *skad-ysáṅ nyams-čúṅ ₒgyur* the voice is getting weak *Wdṅ.*

སྐད་ *skad* **ladder,** v. *skás-ka*.

སྐད་པ་ *skád-pa* I. vb. 1. **to say, tell, relate,** *žiṅ-k'áms šig yód-do skád-par tos* that a land (of bliss) exists I heard say *Mil.*; more frq. at the end of a sentence *skád-do* or *skad* for: it is said (= dicitur), *grags skad id. Mil.* — 2. **to name, call,** *skád-pa* partic. = *byá-ba* **named, called.** — 3. *Ld.*: **skád-če*, *χád-če** **to measure, take measure.**—II. sbs. **interpreter; language-master, teacher.**

སྐན་ཏེ་ *skán-te*, *W.* instead of *ská-ba* **thick, turbid.**

སྐབས་ *skabs* 1. **time, opportunity, case, circumstances;** *mtóṅ-(bai) skabs* opportunity of seeing, *skabs rnyéd-pa* to find an opportunity, *skábs-su* or *skabs-skábs-su* now and then, under certain circumstances, *skábs-su* or *skabs* with genit. at the time of, on occasion of, during, while, when; *dé-ka skáb-su* in a moment, instantly, *skabs ₒdir* now, here, in this case, in this place (of a book etc.) frq., *skabs re* once, for a time, **skabs-tóg* Ld. (col.)* now, *bár-skabs* **interval, interlapse of time** *Tar.; dús-skabs, ťsé-skabs, γnás-skabs,* **time, state, situation,** *skabs daṅ sbyár-ba, dús-skabs daṅ bstún-pa* fit for, adapted, suited to the occasion. — 2. *Cs.* **'mode, method',** or perh. rather, **way, manner;** so the word seems to be used in *Wdṅ.: ldúm-bui skabs la-pʼúg daṅ skyé-lugs ₒdrá-bar* the manner (nature) of the plant being similar to that of a radish as to growth. — 3. **section, chapter** *(cf. γtam* no. 3), so esp.in *Tar.; skabs bču* the ten sections of Buddhistical theology, also: one that has absolved them.

སྐམ་ *skam* v. *skám-pa* and *-po.*

སྐམ་པ་ *skam-pa* I. *vb.* 1. = *rkám-pa* **to long for.** — 2. = *ském-pa (bskam-pa).* — II. *sbst.* 1. = *rkám-pa* **longing,** 2. **a pair of tongs;** *skam-čúṅ* small tongs, **pincers;** also several other instruments of a similar shape. — III. *adj.*, com. *skám-po* **dry,** *skam-rlón* 1. **dry and wet.** — 2. **dryness** in a relative sense, **skam-ši* Ld.* **very lean** (like a mummy), *skám-sa* **the dry land, the shore,** *skam* id., *skám-sar pʼyin-pa, skam-la sléb-pa* to get ashore, *skam-lam* **journey by land** *Wts.; *skam-saṅ* Ld.* **meat perfectly dried.**

སྐར་ *skar;* this and the compounds *skar-ka* and *skar-ťsad* v. under *ska-ba; skar-kúṅ* etc. under *skar-ma.*

སྐར་བ་ *skar-ba Cs.:* 'a penning of cattle, assortment, separation, to pen, to fold, to separate'. But as these significations seem to belong to the spelling *bkar-ba* and *dgar-ba,* it will be safer to confine the verb *skar-ba, pf. bskar, imp. skor,* to the following, 1. **to hang up,** **skar-taṅ-če, čár-la skár-če** id. *Ld.* (e. g. clothes). — 2. **to weigh,** and **skar** **weight,** **gau ṅul gui skar** a little box weighing 9 rupees (about 4 ounces); **skár-ka** or *-k̔a** **weight;** **skar-ťsád** **measure, scale.** *W., C.* — 3. **skar-tág táṅ-če** **to inquire rigorously; to restrict, to bind down, to flog;** **skar-lčág** a rigorous inquiring, a flogging *W.*, also *C.*

སྐར་མ་ *skár-ma Ssk.* तारा 1. **star,** fixed star, *nyi zla γza skar* sun, moon, planets and stars; sometimes it is used generally: **skar-čén** a very large, uncommonly bright star, esp. Venus when appearing as evening- or morning-star; *nyin-moi skár-ma* a star seen in the day-time (a thing of very rare occurrence). — 2. **constellation, asterism;** *btsas-skár* constellation of nativity *Med; γyaṅ-skár* propitious constellation (such are the nakšatras no. [illegible] to [illegible], v. *rgyu-skár*).

Comp, *skár-k̔uṅ* (the same word as *dkar-k̔uṅ,* but of a different etymology) **window.** — *skar-k̔óṅs Cs.:* 'the angular distance between two stars or planets' (?) — *skar-líṅ* a weight ('5 points' on the steelyard for gold) = 1 žo or $^1/_{20}$ ounce; as money = $^1/_3$ rupee. — *skar-čú* 'star-water'; bathing under the constellation *skár-ma rib-či* (prob. *rewati,* the 28th *nakšatra,* is meant) in October is considered beneficial for every kind of complaint, because *Saṅs-rgyás smán-pai rgyál-po* (quasi 'Buddha Aesculapius', to whom the origin of the medical science is ascribed by Tibetan Buddhists), bathed in that season, and therefore Tibetans, though not particularly fond of washing and bathing in general, are said to follow this example pretty frequetnly. — *skar-mdá (Cs.:* 'ignis fatuus'?) **a shooting star,** *ltuṅ* or *sa-la dril* is coming down, *ₒpʼaṅs Mil. id.* — *skar-dpyád, -rtsís* **astrology.** — *skar-pʼrán* **a small star.** — *skar-ťsógs* the starry host. — *skar-ₒdzín* 'star-catching', making one's self sure of a propitious constellation, e. g. for an intended journey, by a sham departure, conveying luggage or goods to the next village etc., but then interrupting and postponing it to a more convenient time.

སྐལ་བ་ *skál-ba* Ssk. भाग, *resp.* *sku-skál* 1. **portion, share**; *bgo-skál* allotted portion; *zas-skál* portion of food, **ration**; *rañ-skál* personal share; *nor-skál* or *ẏal-nór Glr.* hereditary portion, **inheritance**; *skál-ba ma čád-par* without being shortened of his portion *Mil.*; *ma mtóñ-ba skál-ba ma mčis-pa ₒdra* it does not seem to fall to my lot to see my mother. — *skal-čád* dried up, withered *Sch.* (?) — 2. in a special sense: the portion of good or bad fortune that falls to a man's lot, as a consequence of his former actions, **lot, fate, destiny**, a. relatively: *skál-ba bzáñ-po, ñán-pa* good, bad fortune; *tse ₒdii grogs-skál* the matrimonial share of the present life, the connubial fate for which a person is predestinated *Glr.* (The Buddhist priests pretend to be able to calculate the *skál-ba* of any one after his death) b. in a positive and good sense, denoting either prosperity and blessing as a consequence of good actions, or those actions themselves as being pious and meritorious, so that *skal-ldán* means **happy, blessed** as well as **pious, devout**, and *skal-méd* **unhappy, irreligious, impious.** *skal-ldán* are all those who have devoted themselves to virtue and treasured up more or less good works, and who may expect to be promoted in proportion. The term **worthy**, therefore, though not quite correct as to the word itself, is still very appropriate as it regards the subject; even **venerable, holy** may be applied occasionally, cf. भगवत् and भगवान्. Also some single blessing or spiritual gift may be meant by *skál-ba* and so the Ommanipadmehūm is called the *čos-skál*, 'the religious treasure', of Tibet *Glr.*

སྐས་ཀ་ *skás-ka B., C., skás-ka, skás-pa C., skrás-ka* (pronounced **té-ka C., šrás-ka, šré-ka W.*), even *skas, skad* **ladder**, generally consisting of the notched trunk of a tree; *rkyáñ-skad C.* 'single ladder', the same, compared with two or three of them joined together, to make a sort of staircase with broader steps; **do-tá C., do-šrás, do-šré* W.* a flight of stone-steps; **gya-šrás, gya-šré W., gya-ke* C.* (*Schr.*) a regular **staircase** as in European houses; *gru-skás Glr.* prob.: flight of steps at the corner of a building; *gro-skad Glr.* fol. 7 appeared to be unknown to those that were consulted; *skas-kyi rim-pa Cs.* **steps**; **šra-ldañ, šral-dáñ* W.* **spokes** of a ladder; *skas ẓgram Cs.* the two **side-pieces** of a staircase or ladder; *skas ₒdzug-pa* to apply a ladder *Schr., Cs.*

སྐུ *sku, Ssk.* काय, sometimes मूर्त्ति 1. also *sku-lus, sku-ẏzugs, resp.* for *lus*: **body**; by being prefixed to the names of parts of the body and even of everything that has reference to the bodily existence of a person, it imparts to them the character of respectful terms: *sku-stod, -smad* the upper, lower, part of the body; *sku-ša* flesh; *sku-mtsál* (*for sku-krag*) blood *Cs.*; *sku-mdóg* colour of the skin, *sku-ná* age; *sku-tse* lifetime, life; *sku-káms* state of health; *sku-skál* portion, share, *sku-čás* goods, stores *Mil.*, *sku-bsód* virtue, happiness *Tar.*; *sku-skyés* a present (given to or received from a respected personage); *sku-ₒbág* image, statue *Glr.*; *sku-mdun-pa* (*C.: *kun-dụn-pa**) or *-druñ-pa* attendant of a man of rank; **ku-jar-wa** ('adherent', v. *ₒbyar-ba*) *id. C.*; *sku-nye Sch.* relation, kinsman; *sku-ẏšegs-pa* dying, death (of a king etc.) *Glr.*; *sku-bstod* praise *Sch.*; *sku-šogs* (acc. to *Cs.* instead of *sku ẏšogs* 'the side' = your presence) a title of honour, when we should say: your or his honour, your or his worship, in *W.* only for clerical dignitaries, in *C.* also for other persons of rank. Even buildings (monasteries etc.) are honoured by these respectful expressions: *sku-dkar ẏsol-ba* to 'administer' whitewash. — 2. in a special sense: **the person of Buddha**, whom philosophers represent in three forms of existence called *sku-ẏsum* त्रिकाय, viz.: *čós-kyi sku*, धर्मकाय, *loñs-spyód-kyi sku* संभोगकाय and *sprúl-pai sku* निर्माणकाय. These three 'persons', however, have as little as *dkon-mčog-ẏsum* any thing in common with the Christian Trinity, nor even with the Indian Trimūrtti, for the first state, the 'body of law', the absolute body, is Buddha in the Nirvāna, the so-called first world of abstract existence i. e. non-existence, which is the ultimate aim and end of every existence and the ideal aspired to by every believing Buddhist; the second state, the 'body of happiness or glory' is Buddha in the perfection of a conscious and active life of bliss in the second world (heaven or Elysium), which state however is inferior to the first; the third, the 'body of transformation and incarnation', is Buddha in the third or visible world, as man on earth. Notwithstanding the altogether abstract character of *čós-sku,* as a philosophical conception, Buddhistic fancy is pleased to represent it as a visible image of Buddha, shining in the colours of the rainbow, or at least as a brilliant apparition of light, though impalpable and unapproachable; and this is not only a notion of the vulgar, but is acknowledged also in literature. More recent speculators have even added a *ňo-bo-nyid-kyi sku* superior to the three, viz. that which is **eternal** in the essence of a Buddha, even *čós-sku,* the absolute body, being described by these philosophers as transient. The unintelligible passage in *Cs.*'s dictionary, p. 305 b. might be corrected thus: 'adding to the former three as a fourth' etc. — To this signification belong the compounds *sku-rím, resp.* for *rim-ₒgro* **reverence, respect,** particularly in the special sense of a solemn **sacrificial ceremony,** performed on public and private occassions, e. g. in cases of disease; *sku-rim byéd-pa* to perform such a ceremony. — *sku-rtén, sku-ťsáb, sku-γzúgs, sku-ₒdrá (W. *kun-ḍá*)* **image of Buddha** etc. — 3. **image, statue,** of Buddha or other holy persons, *γsér-sku* a gold image, *rdó-sku* a stone image, *ₒǰim-sku* an image of clay, *bris-sku* a painted image, *ₒbúr-sku* a basso-relievo, *rkós-sku* an engraved, *blúgs-* or *ḷdugs-sku* a molten, *ťágs-sku* a woven image *Cs.* — *sku-ₒbúm* 'mausoleum' or acc. to another etymology 'the 100 000 images', n. of the famous monastery Kumbúm east of the Kokonor (v. Travels of Huc and Gabet). — *sku γsuṅ ťugs* 1. (cf. *sku* no. 1) resp. f. *lus ṅag yid* the three spheres of a man's doings or sufferings, works, words and thoughts. — 2. the *rten γsum,* the three representations of Buddha: the image of his person, the books containing his doctrine, the pyramid *(mčod-rtén)* as the symbol of his grace. — *sku-lha-rgyál-po* five deities of degenerated Buddhism *Schl.* 157.

སྐུ་རུ་ *skú-ru* a **paddle-wheel,** without a rim; such are the water-wheels of all the mills in the Himalaya *skú-ru-ka* **the figure of a cross** + ×. The latter is common in books as an abbreviation like our 'etc.', to save the repeated writing at full length of the same sentence, as refrains etc.

སྐུགས་ *skugs* **the stake** in a game or wager received by the winner. — *skugs-stóṅ Sch. id.?*

སྐུང་བ་ *skuṅ-ba pf. bskuṅs, ft. bskuṅ* 1. **to hide in the ground.** — 2. **to bury, to inter.** — 3. **to tie** in a doubled or twisted position, e. g. a corpse before it is burnt, **to cord** on all sides. — *bskúṅs-sa* **lurking-place, hiding-place** *Mil.*

སྐུད་ *skud sbst.* v. *skúd-pa.*

སྐུད་པ་ *skúd-pa* I. *sbst.* **thread, yarn; wire;** *skúd-pa γčód-pa* to cut off the thread, also *fig. Cs.* to divorce; *ras-skúd* cotton thread, *lčags-skúd* iron wire; *ťson-skúd* coloured thread; *skud-ró* the thread-ends of a seam; *skúd-bris-mkan* an embroiderer.

II. *vb. pf. bskus, ft. bsku, imp. skus, col. kú-wa C. *skú-ce* W.* **to smear** **tá-gir-la mar skú-ce** to butter the bread *W.*, **di-la nág-po ma sku** don't make that dirty *W.*; **to besmear, to daub** *snyiṅ-po(-la) snúm-gyis* a wick with grease *Dzl.*; *sgó-la rtsi* **to paint** a door; *spós-kyis skúd-pa* **to anoint;** *skud* **ointment,** **šra-skúd** **pomatum** *W.*

སྐུད་པོ *skúd-po* 1. **brother-in-law** *Cs.* — 2. **father-in-law.**

སྐུན་བུ *skún-bu* = *kóṅ-bu Lex.*

སྐུམ་པ *skúm-pa pf. bskums, ft. bskum, imp. skum(s)* **to contract, to draw in,** e.g. the leg.

སྐུར་པ *skúr-pa,* also *skur-kláṅ, skur-žúṅ* **abuse,** occasionally **blasphemy;** *skur-°debs-pa, byed-pa, smra-ba* **to abuse,** viz.: persons to whom respect is due, esp. holy men or things, e.g. *°pʿágs-pa-la* the venerable *Dzl.; dkon-mčóg γsum mi bdén-par ltá-žiṅ skúr-pa °débspa* to blaspheme by denying the 'Three Most Precious' *Thgy. sgro-skúr* v. *sgro.*

སྐུར་བ *skúr-ba* I. *pf. skur,* at the end of a sentence *skúr-ro,* sometimes for *skúr-pa °debs-pa Mil.* —

II. *pf. ft. & imp. bskur, pf.* at the end of a sentence *bskur-to* 1. **to send, to transmit,** e.g. news, objects, also an army, but not a messenger; *mdún-du skúr-ba* to send on in advance, to have carried before, e.g. a banner; *skur γnaṅ mdzád-pa* resp.: to be pleased to send. — 2. **to give, hand over, deliver, consign, give in charge, commit,** e.g. an army to a general; *dbaṅ skúr-ba* to invest with power, **to authorize,** *ǰi dgá-bar gyid-du dbaṅ skúr čig* give me power, permission, to do what I like *Dzl.; rgyál-por dbaṅ skúrba* to authorize somebody to be a ruler, to appoint, create, designate as king. The ceremony observed in such a case is a kind of anointing or baptism, pouring holy water on the crown of the head, *spyi-bo-nas dbaṅ skúr-ba,* and as supernatural powers are supposed to be active during this process, *dbaṅ skúr-ba* means also: **to bless, consecrate, endow** with miraculous power; esp. four mystical powers of meditation are imparted in this way.

སྐུལ་བ *skúl-ba pf. bskul,* at the end of a sentence *bskúl-to, Ssk.* चुद्, **to exhort, admonish, enjoin,** *mi žig las byéd-par* a person to do a thing; **to appoint,** *mi žig lás-la,* in the same sense; **to impose,** *mi žig-la las,* work on somebody, — perh. a mere provincialism; *dei tsig-gis bskúl-nas* **induced** by his words; *rnám-šes las daṅ nyon-móṅs-kyis bskúl-nas* the (departed) soul **urged on, influenced, driven,** by its former works and sins *S. g.; lha-srín mčod skul kyaṅ* though I tried **to determine, to bring round,** the gods and the evil spirits by sacrifices *Pth.; gliṅ sogs drág-tu skúl-šiṅ* flutes and other (instruments) **calling,** resounding, fortissimo and so animating the actors; **yid skúl-če* W.* **to remind, admonish;** **šaṅ** (for *γčaṅ*) **skúl-če** **to rouse** by shaking. — *bskúl-ba* and more frq. *bskul-ma* **exhortation, admonition;** *bskúl-ma °débs-pa, C.* also *skúl-rgyag-pa, skul-čág byéd-pa Mil. nt.* **to admonish, exhort.** — **skúl-kʿan W.* **overseer.**

སྐེ *ske, vulg. skye,* seld. *skya,* **neck, throat,** *frq.;* neck of a bottle *Cs.; *skye tsir táṅ-če, *kyig-če, sdúm-če* W.* **to choke, strangle,** **skyé-la tág-pa tág-na sád-če* id.; ske γčód-pa, γtúb-pa, °brég-pa* **to behead, slaughter;** *sker °tʿám-pa* to seize by the throat, to worry *Sch.; sker dógs-pa* to tie round the neck e. g. an amulet; *ske-°kʿór* necklace *Schr.; ske-čá* ornament for the neck, **necklace** *Mil.; ske-stóṅ Med., Sch.:* cavity of the throat; *ske-rmá Sch.:* a wound of the throat, a jugular gland that has opened.

སྐེ་ཚེ *ske-tsé Wdṅ., Ssk.* **राजिका** Sinapis ramosa, **black mustard; mustard seed,** a grain of m. s.

སྐེག་ཚོས *skeg-tsós* **paint, rouge** (for the face) *Sch.*

སྐེད་པ *skéd-pa* v. *rkéd-pa.*

སྐེམ་པ *ském-pa* I. *vb. pf. bskams, ft. bskam, imp. skom(s)* **to make dry, lean, meagre; to dry up; exsiccate.** — II. *adj.,* also *ském-po,* **dry, dried up; meagre.** — *skem-byéd* a demon that causes drought *Lt.* — *skem-nád Bhar.* consumption.

སྐོ་བ *skó-ba, pf. (b)skos, ft. bsko, imp. skos* 1. **to appoint, nominate, commission, charge** a person, *lás-su* with a work *Dzl.,* much more freq.: *rgyál-por,* *dpón-du* to be king, chief; *rgyál-sar skó-ba* to raise to the throne; *ma bskós-šiṅ* without mandate, unbidden *Glr.* — 2. *lás-la bskós-pa* **destined** to the works i. e. destined to a man in consequence of his works; *ṅéd-kyi las-bskós* my **destiny, fate, lot** *Mil.*

Note. The signification: to elect, to choose *(Cs., Sch.)* cannot be proved and was expressly denied by Tibetans.

སྐོ་ཙེ་ *sko-tsé* 1. a kind of wild onion *Cs.* — 2. a mixture of the leaves of several kinds of leek, pounded, formed into balls and dried; when used, a small portion is broken off, fried in butter and then added to the food. This spice forms a lucrative article of commerce and is exported from *Ld.* to Cashmere and from *Lh.* to India.

སྐོག་པ་ *skóg-pa* v. *kóg-pa.*

སྐོང་ *skoṅ* v. under *koṅ.*

སྐོང་བ་ *skóṅ-ba* *pf. bskaṅs, ft. bskaṅ, imp. skoṅ(s)* 1. **to fulfil,** e. g. a hope, a vow etc., **nyiṅ** the desire *W.*; *k'a skóṅ-ba* to fill up what is open, to make up a deficiency *Zam.*, also *dgé-bai k'a-skoṅ* to fulfil perfectly the laws of virtue, *k'a-skóṅ, k'a-bskáṅs, k'as-skoṅ* 1. **appendix, supplement,** *ɣšám-du k'a-skóṅ-du bšad* will be said, described, below in the appendix *Wdṅ.* 2. By Tibetan copyists of books a short prayer is called so, consisting of a stanza of 4 verses, which they are accustomed to write down or recite after having finished the copy of a work, in order to make amends for the mistakes they may have committed. — *t'ugs-dám bskaṅ-rdzás* a certain ceremony v. *Schl.* 260. — 2. v. *dpa.*

སྐོན་པ་ *skón-pa* I. *sbst.* v. *rkón-pa.* — II. *vb. pf. & ft. bskon* **to dress,** to clothe another person (*resp. ɣsól-ba).*

སྐོབས་ *skobs* = *skabs Schr., Sch.*

སྐོམ་ *skom* 1. **thirst,** *skóm-gyis ɣdúṅs-pa* tormented by thirst *Dzl.* — 2. *resp.* *žal-skóm,* **drink;** *zas (daṅ) skom* food and drink. — 3. *i.o. skam* the **dry land** *Glr., provinc.* — *skóm-pa* 1. **to thirst, to be thirsty.** 2. **the thirst.** 3. **thirsty,** *skóm-pa-dag ni skóm-pa daṅ brál-bar ˳gyur* the thirsty will get rid of their thirst *S. O.* — *skom-dád (dad-pa* = *˳dod-pa)* **thirst** *Med.* — *skom-t'sád* **burning thirst** *Mil.* — **skóm-ri** **thirst** *W.*

སྐོར་ *skor* (*cf. kor*) 1. **circle,** *mig-skor* eyeball *W.*; *sba-skór* hoop of bamboo *Schr.* — 2. **appurtenances,** *yi-ge ˳bri-bai skor* writing utensils, *t'áb-kyi skor* everything that belongs to the fire-place *C.* (perh. provinc.) — 3. **section, division,** e. g. of a book, similar to *leu*, chapter *Mil., Tar.* — 4. **repetition,** *skor ldáb-pa* to repeat *Schr.* — 5. **theme, subject,** *gaṅ skór-la ˳bri ˳dug* what is the subject of this writing? Answer: *rtai skór-la* a horse *C.*; *de skór-la* on that account, therefore *Ld.* — 6. *skor, skór-zas* **food presented to Lamas;** laymen are deterred from laying their hands on it by the mysteriously menacing verse: *skór-zas zá-la lčag-gi ˳grám-pa dgos* he that eats Lama's food, wants iron jaws. — 7. v. *skór-ba* no. II.

སྐོར་བ་ *skór-ba* I. *vb. pf. & ft. bskor* 1. **to surround, encircle, enclose, besiege** *cca & d.*; also of inanimate objects: *dé-la skór-bai ri* the mountains surrounding it *Glr.*; *ri nágs-kyis bskór-ba Sambh.* a mountain surrounded by a forest. — 2. **to go, move, ride round a thing;** esp. the reverential ceremony of प्रदक्षिण transferred from Brahmanism to Buddhism, which consists in going round a holy object with one's right side turned towards it — one of the most meritorious and indispensible religious duties in the eyes of a Buddhist; *č'ós-skor-la byon* they walked round in the religious direction, i. e. according to the precepts of Buddhism, *bón-skor-du soṅ* in the Bon manner, i. e. the opposite direction *Mil.*; *p'yag daṅ skór-ba byéd-pa,* as a specification of religious duties: to make salutations and circumambulations.

3. **to wander through, traverse,** *rgyál-ḱams*, the countries, *Mil.* — 4. **to return, go home** *Sch.* — 5. **to turn round, twist,** *mii ltág-pa* a man's neck, i.e. to choke, to strangle him *Glr.*

Phrases: *mgo skór-ba, mgo skor byéd-pa* (*W.* **čo-če**) **to befool, delude, deceive** a person, by intoxication or flattery *Glr.*, also by a flood of words. — **ḱa kór-wa C., kór-če* W.* to make one alter his sentiments, to divert one from a plan etc. — **lan** or **dugs skór-če** to take vengeance *W.* — **si kór-če* (v. *rtsis*) *W.* **to count, calculate.** — *tsógs-kyi ḱórlo skór-ba* to arrange the objects of the *maṇḍal* (q.v.) in a circle n.f. — *skor lóg-pa, skor lóg-la ͼgró-ba* to go round the wrong way *Mil.*; **pé-ra kor-re-lóg táṅ-če** to talk foolishly, to twaddle *W.* — **lag kór-če** the putting a seal under a document which is done by several persons one after another *W.*

Comp. *skór-ḱaṅ Glr.*, prob. = *skór-lam.* — *skor-rgyúgs* turning the enemy, getting into his rear *Mil.* — *skór-mḱan, skór-pa* **a turner** *Cs.* — *skor-spyád, skor-šiṅ* a turner's **lathe** *Cs.* — *skor-ťig* **a pair of compasses.** — *skor-dbyúg* a sling, for throwing *Sch.* — *skor-lám* 1. the pathway round-about a monastery, used for the holy processions. 2. a veranda surrounding a house. 3. col. also: round-about way.

II. 1. **the going, moving round, encircling** etc. — 2. **the way** round a thing, = *skor-lám*, in the compounds: *náṅ-skor* the inner, *bár-skor* the middle, *p̔yi-skor* the outer roundway, *p̔yi-skor čén-po* the outermost. — *sá-skor* round-about way, by-way.

སྐོལ་བ་ *skól-ba* pf. & ft. *bskol* **to boil** (vb. act., cf. *ͼḱól-ba*).

སྐོས་པ་ *skós-pa* 1. v. *skó-ba.* — 2. *Sch.*: 'to order', but this is *sgó-ba.*

སྐྱ་ *skya* 1. **oar** *C., Thgy.*; *skya-léb* id.; *skya-m̔yúg* **rudder**; *skya rgyáb-pa* **to row** *Schr.* — 2. **spatula** *Schr.* — 3. **pot-ladle,** *C.* — 4. **wall** of stone or clay, *bár-skya*, partition-wall, **bhár-kya ča'-pa** to make a partition-wall *C.*

སྐྱ་ཀ་ *skyá-ka, skyá-ga Lt.*, n. of a bird, *Cs.*: **magpie.**

སྐྱ་བ་ *skyá-ba* I. vb. 1. pf. *bskyas*, ft. *bskya* 1. *Lex.*: = *ͼp̔ó-ba* **to change place,** cf. *skyas.* — 2. **to carry, convey** to a place (a quantity of stones, wood, water etc.) *W.*, v. *skyéd-pa.* — 3. *Sch.* **to swim** (?)

II. sbst. 1. **kettle** *Sch.* — 2. prob. = *skya* 1.

སྐྱ་བོ་ *skya-bo*, *Ssk.* **पाण्डर** and **पाण्डु**, **whitish gray, yellowish-white;** **skya čág-če* to fry or toast a thing so that its whitish colour turns partially into brown *Ld.*; *mi skya* one clothed in light-gray, (not in red or yellow, as monks are), a layman; *sṅo-skya* **light-blue,** *ǰaṅ-skyá* **light-green,** and so of the other colours; therefore *ser-skya* ought to denote **light-yellow,** but it is also used as an equivalent of **कपिल**, n. of a saint, (Ser-skyai-ͼgroṅ = Kapilavastu, an ancient city in Oude, and Buddha's birth-place); originally: 'monkey-coloured', **tawny,** *lto-skyá* 'pale' i. e. poor, insipid, miserable food *Mil.nt.*

Comp. **kya-ko-ré, kya-ťe-ré** **pale, white** *C.* — *skya-skyá* id. *Sch.* — *skya-nár,* **पाटलि** n. of a flower, Bignonia graveolens; *Skya-nár-gyi-bu* n. of a city of Old-India Pāṭaliputra, now Patna. — *skya-snár* acc. to *Stg.* the colour of the skin of the Indians, **brown.** — *skya-rbáb Cs.*: a kind of dropsy, *Sch.*: a grayish oedematic swelling; *skya-rbab-skráṅs Lex.* — **skya-már** **fresh** (i. e. not melted) **butter** *W.* — **skya 'ód* W.*, *skya-réṅs* **morning-twilight, dawn.** — *skya-lám* = *skyá-bo Thgy., C.* — *skya-šéṅ* 1. n. of a tree. 2. translation of Pandu, *skya-séṅ-gi bu* a Pandava. — *skya-sér* 1. *Sch.*: **tawny,** cf. *ser-skya.* 2. 'white and yellow' viz.: men, **lay-men and priests** *Mil.nt.*

སྐྱ་རུ་ར་ *skyá-ru-ra* n. of a drug *Med.*

སྐྱག་པ་ *skyág-pa* 1. = *rkyág-pa.* — 2. pf. *bskyags*, ft. *bskyag*, imp. *skyog* to spend, lay out, expend; *skyag-sgó* **expenditure,** *skyag-ṫó* **account of expenses.** — 3. *W.:* **skyag táṅ-če** **to slaughter, to murder.**

སྐྱང་ནུལ་ *skyaṅ-núl* **pavement, clay-floor, mud-floor** *Lex., Cs.; skaṅ-núl byéd-pa* **to pave, to plaster** (*Sch.* also; to rub, polish).

སྐྱབས་ *skyabs* (*cf. skyób-pa*) *Ssk.* **शरण protection, defence, help, assistance;** *me-čú-la skyabs* is a protection against water and fire; *skyabs méd-do* I am (or: he is etc.) lost! *skyabs byéd-pa, skyábs-su ˌgyúr-ba* ccgp. **to protect, help, save** a person, frq. with *srog-gi* added; *skyábs-su ˌgró-ba* eleg. *mčiba, W.:* **skyab čól-la yóṅ-če** to seek help, *mii* or *mi-la* of some body, *skyabs-ˌgrós* 1. the seeking of help, **शरण गमन** 2. the formula *Saṅs-rgyás-kyi skyabs-su mčio, čós-kyi sky. mčio, dge-ˌdún-gyi sky. mčio,* the Buddhistic creed or confession of faith.

Comp. *skyabs-mgón* **helper, protector, deliverer;** this is applied to certain highly esteemed and respected persons, mythological as well as living, ni f.; *Chr. Pr.* use it for **Saviour, Redeemer, Christ.** — *skyabs-ˌgrós* v. above. — *skyabs-γnás* 1. **place of refuge,** shelter; also of persons, = **helper,** frq; *mi-la skyabs-γnás byéd-pa Mil.* to take refuge to a person, to seek his assistance. 2. seld. for *skyábs-su γnás-pa* **client,** *ṅá-yi skyábs-γnas ṗó-mo-rnams* all my clients, men and women *Glr.* — *skyabs-sbyin* a gesture of the right hand, like that for giving benediction *Glr.* — *skyabs-yúl* = *skyabs-γnás.* 1.

སྐྱར་གོག་ *skyár-gog* **naked** *Pur.*

སྐྱར་པོ་ *skyár-po Sch.:* **snipe, wood-cock;** *skyar-čúṅ Sch.:* **'a large snipe'** (??); *skyár-mo Sch.* **heron;** *skyar-léb Sch.* **spoonbill;** *ču-skyar Cs.* **duck,** *Sch.:* **bittern,** but the **कादम्ब** of the *Lex.*, 'a kind of goose' speaks in favour of *Cs.*

སྐྱར་བ་ *skyár-ba* v. *skyór-ba.*

སྐྱས་ *skyas* a changing of abode; *skyas ˌdébs-pa* to change one's dwelling-place (cf. *skya-ba*), *skyas čén-po ˌdébs-pa* to die

སྐྱས་མ་ *skyás-ma* 1. v. *skyes.* — 2. *Sik.:* **fern.**

སྐྱི་ *skyi Cs.:* the outward side of a skin or hide (opp. to *ša*); *skyi γyá-ba* to shiver, tremble with fear *Cs.* **Comp.:** *skyi-dkár Cs.* dressed leather; hide. — *skyi-lpágs Sch.:* chamois, wash-leather. — *skyi-búṅ Mil.?* — *skyi-bún* prob. an itching of the skin *Mil.?* — *skyi-šá* 1. outward and inward side of a hide. 2. *Sch.:* the anus.

སྐྱི་བ་ *skyi-ba* I. sbst. 1. a medicinal plant *Med.* — 2. also **kyi-u, ṗi-liṅ kyi-u,** **potato** *C.*

II. vb. pf. *bskyis,* ft. *bskyi,* imp. *skyis* **to borrow,** esp. money or goods (cf. *γyár-ba* and *skyin-pa*).

སྐྱིག་པ་ *skyig-pa* **to hickup;** *skyig-bu* **the hickup** *Med.*

སྐྱིང་སེར་ *skyiṅ-sér Mil.,* eagle, vulture.

སྐྱིད་པ་ *skyid-pa* vb., sbst., adj.: **to be happy, happiness** (*Ssk.* सौख्य), **happy;** *skyid-do* (I, thou etc.) am, art etc. happy; *bdé-žiṅ skyid-la* being happy and glad; *skyid-pai nyi-ma* sun of felicity, propitious day *Glr.; skyid-po* = *skyid-pa* adj., frq., *skyid-de-ba* id. *Tar.* 5, 19.

Comp. *skyid-glu* song of joy. — *skyid-mgo* beginning of happiness *Mil.* — *skyid-sdúg* good and ill luck, happiness and misery; *skyid sdug ji byuṅ kyaṅ* whatever may happen *Glr.; skyid sdug bsré-ba* to share pleasure and pain. — *skyid-čú* n. of the tributary of the Ya-ru-tsaṅ-po, on which Lhasa is situated.

སྐྱིན་ *skyin* **wild mountain goat,** Capra ibex.

སྐྱིན་གོར་ *skyin-gór* **lizard** *Lex.,* = *da-byid.*

སྐྱིན་ཐང་ *skyin-ṫáṅ Sch.:* **hail, sleet.**

སྐྱིན་པ་ *skyin-pa, W.* **skyin-po**, resp. *kar-skyin* **a loan,** a thing borrowed; money advanced without interest; *skyin-pa skyi-ba* to ask a loan; *ṅá-la ˌdi skyin-du ˌtsal* he asked me to lend him this *Dzl.; skyin-pa lén-pa Cs.* to take on credit; *skyin-pa spród-pa, ˌjal-ba* to pay back or return a loan *Cs.; nór-skyin* a loan of goods or money, *gós-skyin* of clothes. — *skyin-mi Schr.* debtor. — *skyin-ťsáb C.:* the pledge for a loan; acc. to others, however, it just means the object lent or its equivalent when being returned.

སྐྱིབས་ *skyibs* everything giving **shelter** from above, an overhanging rock, a roof etc.: **čar skyib** shelter from rain; **ḍag-skyib** under a *p̓a-boṅ* q. v. (*gyam* is much larger, *p̓úg-pa* deeper) *W.*; *bka-sky.* प्रघाण, a covered terrace or small portico before a house.

སྐྱིལ་བ་ *skyil-ba,* pf. & ft. *bskyil* 1. **to bend,** esp. the legs when sitting on the ground after Oriental fashion, also another's leg by a kick from behind; to bend the bow. — 2. **to pen up, shut up,** cattle, **to dam up,** a river, also: *ču rdziṅ-du skyil-ba* **to collect** water into a pond *Glr.*, or *rdziṅ-bu sky.*; to dam up a pond (but not 'to dig it' *Schr.*); **to keep back, retain, detain** a person *W.*; **k̓a kyil-če** to keep a person from doing something, to dissuade from *W.* — *skyil-krúṅ,* also *skyil-mo-krúṅ,* the posture of **sitting cross-legged,** *skyil-krúṅ byéd-pa* (resp. *mdzád-pa*), *skyil-mo-krúṅ-gis* (or *du*) *ḥdúg-pa* (resp. *bžúgs-pa*) to assume such a posture; *séms-dpai skyil-krúṅ* the usual manner of sitting, in which the feet are not seen, *rdo-rjei sky.* the posture in which the soles of the feet are seen turned upwards, *rdzógs-pai sky.* another posture requiring particular practice. (The spelling *dkyil-krúṅ,* though frequent, is expressly rejected by grammarians.) — **skyil-díṅ* W.* a small hole filled with water. — **skil-ldir* W.* **handle, ring** fixed to a thing, for carrying it, hanging it up etc.

སྐྱུ་གང་ *skyu-gáṅ Lex.* w.e., *Sch.*: a **gulp, draught.**

སྐྱུ་རུ་ *skyú-ru* a sour fruit *Med.*; *skyú-ru-ra Med.* (*Lex.*: अम्लक wood-sorrel) the same (?); in later times the word seems to have been used also for the **olive,** and *skyú-ru-šiṅ* **the olive tree,** which in *Sik.* is called *k̓a-skyúr-poi šiṅ.*

སྐྱུ་རུམ་ *skyu-rúm Cs.*: '**condiment, sauce, pickle**', acc. to others, at least in *W.*, only the resp. word for *spags:* 1. **sauce, gravy.** 2. **dish, mess.**

སྐྱུག་པ་ *skyúg-pa* pf. *skyugs.* 1. **to vomit, eject,** e.g. blood, *skyúg-tu ḥjúg-pa* to cause to vomit, *skyúg-pa drén-pa* to excite vomiting *Tar.*; *skyúgs-pa* (partic. pf.), *ṅan-skyúgs,* **the vomit** (it is the food of certain demons, and being boiled in it, is one of the punishments of hell). — 2 to lose colour, **to stain.**

Comp. *skyug-ldád* **rumination,** chewing the cud; *Sch.* also: **eructation.** — *skyúg-bro-ba* nausea, *skyúg-bro-bai nad* disease of nausea; *skyúg-bro-bas* from disgust; *skyug-bro C.* also **impure** with regard to religion, = *W. *ťsid-du*.* — *skyug-smán* **an emetic.** — *skyúg-log-pa Sch.* to feel disgust.

སྐྱུང་ཀ་ *skyúṅ-ka,* also *lčúṅ-ka,* **jack-daw** (black, with a red bill); *skyúṅ-kas zos Lex.* eaten or stolen by a jack-daw.

སྐྱུང་བ་ *skyúṅ-ba* pf. *bskyuṅs,* ft. *bskyuṅ,* imp. *skyuṅ(s) Cs.* **to leave behind, to lay aside,** e.g. a task *Lex.*, pride *S.g.*

སྐྱུད་པ་ *skyúd-pa* 1. *Cs.*: **to forget, leave off.** 2. *Sch.*: **to comminute; to swallow.** (?)

སྐྱུར་བ་ *skyúr-ba* I. adj. **sour,** sbst. **acidity;** more frq.: *skyúr-po C.*, *-mo W.* adj. **sour,** *Ssk.* अम्ल; *skyur ḥgyúr-pa* 1. to turn sour. 2. to suffer a substance to turn sour, v. *ḥgyur-pa.* — *k̓a(-ša)-skyúr-po* **olive,** *k̓a (ša)-skyur-pói šiṅ* olive tree *Sik.* — *skyúr-k̓u Cs.*, *raṅ-skyúr Cs.*, *skyúr-ru* (*Sik.*), *skúr-mo Lh.* a sour liquid, **vinegar.** (Vinegar seems to be little known as yet in Tibet, and the above mentioned expressions may have been framed by different persons on different occasions, but are not in general use. The same may be said of *Cs.*'s *skyúr-pa* and *skyur-rtsí* for **acid** in a chemical sense.)

II. vb. pf. & ft. *bskyur* 1. **to throw, to cast,** *p̓yir* out, *lhuṅ-zéd nám-mk̓a-la bskyur-nas* having flung his mendicant's-bowl up into the air *Dzl.*, *čur skyúr-ba* to throw into the water, *rgyáb-tu* behind one's self = to turn one's back upon a thing; **to throw away, throw down,** a stone, a corpse etc.; **to eject,** *lúd-pa* phlegm; **to throw off,** a rider; **to give up, abandon,** a work; **to forsake,** a friend; **to abort.** — *skyúr-ma* **abortion** *W.* (?) — *ču skyúr, γyaṅskyúr* capital punishment in *C.*, when the delinquent, with a weight fastened to his neck, is thrown from a rock into a river.

སྐྱུས་ *skyus? Sch.: skyus tóg-pa* **altogether;** *skyús-su klóg-pa Gramm.:* to pronounce **jointly,** viz. two consonants without a vowel between them.

སྐྱེ་ *ske* 1 v. *ske.* — 2. v. *skyed* and *skyé-ba.*

སྐྱེ་བ་ *skyé-ba* I. vb. (जन) pf. *skyes* 1. **to be born;** *ṅá-la* (seld. *las) bu skyés-pa yin* I have given birth to a son *Glr.; pó-skyes* a man, *mó skyes* a woman, female; *skye-rga-na-ₒči-bai sdug-bsṅál* the evil of birth, old age, sickness and death (which constitute what in the opinion of the Buddhist is the greatest evil of all, that of existence); *tóg-ma skyés-nas, má-la skyés-nas B.,* *'á-ma skyé-sa-na* *W.* from one's birth; *sKye či-* (or *ši-*) *méd pa* subject neither to birth nor to death, eternal; *skye-ₒgag-méd-Thgy., Lex.,* is said to mean the same. In the special sense of the doctrine of metempsychosis *skyé-ba* has often to be rendered by: **to be re-born,** *mi-ru* as man, *bur* as (somebody's) son. — *mi skyé-bai čós-la bzód-pa* v. *bzód-pa.* — *W.:* *skyé-če* 1. as inf. **to be born, reborn.** 2. as sbst. the being born; **birth.** 3. as adj. being with child, **pregnant; big with young,** also *sKyé-če-ma*. — 2. **to become, to begin to exist, arise,** *nad kun mi skye, skyés-paaṅ ži-bai pyir* ut ne morbus ullus nascatur, natus quoque sedetur *Med.; skye-ba daṅ ₒjig-pa* to arise and pass away; frq. of thoughts, passions etc. (the person as well as the thing in the accus.): *Kyeu Krós-pai sems skyés-te* the youth — thoughts of wrath arising (in him). — 3. **to grow** *(nasci) lúṅ-pa ₒbru skyé-ba* valleys where corn grows; *ru mgó-la skye* a horn is growing on the head. — 4. **to grow** *(crescere) čer or čen-por skyé-ba* to grow up, to grow tall; *ras kyaṅ lús-Kyi tsád-du skyés-so* the garment also grew in proportion to the growth of the body, or: with the body *Dzl.; rtúl-pod-par skyés-so* he grew up a valiant man, became a valiant man; **to bud, germinate, sprout,** *sbáns-te skye čúg-ce* to accelerate the germinating of the seed by maceration *W.;* even = *ₒpél-ba Dzl.* ??? ? — 5. sometimes = *skyá-ba* 2. unless in that case *kyé-če* should be spelled *bskyás-čes W.*

II. sbst. (जाति) 1. the being born, the **birth,** *skyé-ba mto-ba, skye-mtó or mtón* **high birth;** of high birth, **noble, man,** male; *skyé-ba dmá-ba, skye-dmá, -dmán* **low birth;** of low birth, **ignoble, woman,** *mi-lus tob kyaṅ skyé-ba dman* born a human being, it is true, but only a female *Mil.; skyes-dmán* col. *kyer mán* in *C.* the usual word for **woman** and **wife,** *ṅe Kyer mén* my wife. — In the special Buddhistic sense: **re-birth** *mir skyé-ba bžén-pa* to take or assume re-birth as a human being; also **period of re-birth** = **existence, life,** *skyé-ba ₒdi-la* in this, my present, period of life; *skyé-ba bdun* seven periods of life; also **manner of re-birth,** v. *skye-γnás*; in a concrete sense: the **re-born individual,** *yúm-gyi skyé-ba yin* she is the re-birth of the queen dowager, the re-born q. d. — 2. the **arising** etc. — 3. the **growing** etc.

Comp. *skye-dgú* v. *skyé-bo.* — *skye-ₒgró* = *ₒgroba* being (q.v.) — *skye-sgó* 1. **entrance to re-birth,** viz. to one of the six regions of birth, v. *ₒgró-ba* II., *skye-sgó γčód-pa* to lock it up. 2. **face,** *légs-pa* a handsome, *žan-pa* an ugly face; also *Ka-sgó skye-ₒbras légs-pa* is said for: having a handsome exterior *C.* — *skye-mčéd* (आयतन) the five (or six) seats, i. e. **organs, of the senses** (the sixth is मनस् the inner sense); the **senses** themselves; this conception, however, has been greatly altered and varied by the fanciful theories of medical and philosophical authors, cf. *Burn.* I, 500. *Was.* (240). — *skye-γnás* 1. **birthplace; station** or **locality** of a plant.

2. **class** or **region of birth** or re-birth, **class of beings** (v. *₍gró-ba*); *byol són-gi skye-ba* the being born as an animal. 3. **manner of birth** उपपाद्य, *skyé-ba bži*, also चतुर्योनि. the four kinds or ways of being born: *mṅál-las* (or *nas*) out of a womb (so, acc. to Stg., elephants and some men are born), *sgo-ṅá-las* out of an egg (birds, some *klu*, some men), *drod-γšér-las* out of heat and humidity (insects, some men etc.), *rdzús-te* in a supernatural way (so the *lha*, the Buddhas, when they spring from lotus-flowers; also the inhabitants of infernal regions, souls in the bardo and some men). — *skye-γzúgs* prob. = *byad-γzúgs* **stature, figure.** — *skye-rábs* **series of the births** of a man, **history** of them, and esp. so of the births of Buddha, — so in the title of a work. — *skye-šíṅ* = *skyed-šíṅ Wdn.*

སྐྱེ་བོ་ *skyé-bo* 1. **being,** (animans) *mi-la-sogs-pa sKyé-bo* man and the other living beings *Dzl.* — 2. **human being, man,** gen. as a collective noun: **mankind,** *ₒKrúl-bčas skyé-bo* infatuated men *Pth.; skyé-bo mKás-pa γžán-rnams* other sensible people *Tar.; skyé-bo máṅ-poi yid-du ₍óṅ-ba* universally beloved *Dom.; mí nag skyé-bo* **laymen** (on account of the dimness of their religious knowledge); *so-sói skyé-bo* पृथग्जन (cf. *Will.)* the lower clergy, common monks *Tar.*, but also simple laymen, if they are not quite without religious knowledge; *skye-bo-čog, (skyeo-čog Cs.* is a less accurate pronunciation), *skyé-dgú*, or (less correctly) *rgu*, **men, mankind**; *skye-dgui-bdág-mo* प्रजापती fem. pr. n., the aunt and first governess of Buddha *Glr., Gyatch.*, also a name of *dpal-lhá-mo's* q.v.

སྐྱེ་ཙེ་ *skye-ťsé* = *ske-ťsé Lex.*, **mustard.**

སྐྱེ་རགས་ *skyé-rágs W.* for *ska-rags* **girdle.**

སྐྱེག *skyeg Cs.:* = *kég, kag* **misfortune.** But *rtsis-kyi skyeg Lex.* w.e.?

སྐྱེགས་ *skyegs* 1. n. of a bird: *ču-sky. Lex.* w.c., *Sch.:* **coot, water-hen;** *ri-skyégs Lex.* w.e., *Cs.:* a large singing-bird, *Sch.;* **grouse, heath-cock.** — 2. *rgya-skyégs* **shell-lac.**

སྐྱེང་བ་ *skyeṅ-ba* and *skyeṅs-pa* **to be ashamed,** also *Ka-skyeṅ-ba*, B. and col. frq.

སྐྱེང་སེར་རླུང་ *skyeṅ-ser-rluṅ* also *skye-* or *skya-ser-luṅ Mil.*, **cold wind.**

སྐྱེད་ *skyed* and *skye*, 1. **growth, increase,** *skyed če-bar ₍gyur-ba* to grow much; *γžan-gyi zla-skyed-pas dei žag-skyed če* his daily growth was greater than the growth of others in a month etc. *Pth.* — 2. **progress, the getting on, improvement** *skyed yoṅ* progress comes, I am making progress *Mil.;* **profit, gain** *nad-la skyed med* (this) is of no **use** for that disease, of no **benefit** *S.g. fol.* 10. — 3. **interest** *C.*, *dṅul-skyed* of money, *ₒbru-skyed* of corn *C.*, *skyed-du γtoṅ-ba* to give on interest *Cs.; skyed ṗog pa Cs.:* 'to be the full term of payment', more accurately: *skyed ṗog* I (you, he etc.) am struck or hit by the term of payment; *skyed-čan* yielding interest, profit *Cs.*

སྐྱེད་སྒོ་ *skyed-sgo Mil.nt.* prob. = *rgyal-sgo* principal door.

སྐྱེད་པ་ *skyed-pa* I. vb pf. *bskyed*, act. to *skye-ba*, in *W.* pronounced alike: **skye-če** 1. **to generate, procreate;** seldom in a physical sense: *bskyed-pai yab* ὁ γεννήσας πατήρ *Pth.*, (opp. to *bltams-pai yum Pth.*, for which however *skyed-ma Cs.* does not seem to be an appropriate substitute). — 2. **to produce, form, cause** (opp. to *med-par byed-pa* to destroy, annihilate) e. g. diseases, fear, roots of virtue, merit, *bsod-nams-kyi ťsogs, sa-bon* (fig.) *Dzl.*, *ₒbras-bu* retribution; **to reproduce,** *zad-pa* what has been consumed *Med.;* to create certain thoughts or affections either in one's self or in others: *spró-ba bskyed-pas dei ṗa-má yan spró-ba čúṅ-zad skyés-nas* by his own rejoicing also to his parents a little joy arising *Dzl.* 22. 5; *ťams-čad-kyis brtson-₍grús bskyed-do* they all created zeal, took great pains *Dzl.; čes bsam-pa bskyéd-nas* thus they thought. — 3. **to cause to germinate** or **grow,** *yúr-bai čú-yis žiṅ skyed*

ˌ*dra* just as the water of the ditch makes the fields green *Med.; sá-bon Dzl.* (v. before, but it may as well be referred to this signification); *ɣsos skyéd-pa* **to bring up, to nurse up** *Dzl.; skyed sriṅ-ba* id. *Glr.* — 4. = *skyá-ba,* **to bring on, carry, convey** to a place *Pth.*

Comp. *skyed-mos-ťsál* **grove, park.** — *skyed-rdzógs,* instead of *skyed-rím* and *rdzogs-rím,* **उत्सक्रम** and **सम्पन्नक्रम**, two kinds or degrees of meditation. — *skyed-ṡiṅ Cs.:* a planted tree (?) prob. a fruit-tree, *Dzl.*

II sbst. 1. **the generating, producing** etc. — 2. = *skyed,* e. g. *skyéd-pa lén-pa* **to gain flesh, to thrive** *C.* — 3. = *rkéd-pa.*

སྐྱེན་པ་ *skyén-pa* adj. 1. **quick, swift** *Lex., ḱró-* or *sdáṅ-skyen-pa* quick to wrath *Stg.; byéd-skyen-pa* rash, hasty, precipitate *Glr.* — 2. **nimble, dexterous** *C. W.;* ˌ*ṗóṅ-skyen-pa* dexterous in shooting, **a skilful** archer *Dzl.* (Besides: vb. to make haste, to strive; sbst. zeal, ardour; adj. strong *Cs., Sch.* ??)

སྐྱེམ་པ་ *skyém-pa* resp. **to be thirsty.**

སྐྱེམས་ *skyems* resp. 1. **thirst.** — 2. **drink, beverage,** esp. **beer,** also *žal-skyéms* or *-skyoms, skyems* ˌ*drén-pa* to offer or set before an honoured person something to drink, *bžés-pa* to accept of it, to take it; *skyems-la ɣsol-rés byéd-pa* to drink beer in company *Glr.; ɣṡegs-skyéms* a carousal on the departure of an honoured person; *ɣser-skyéms* beer together with grains of corn, as an offering to the gods for the good success of an enterprise, a journey etc., in religious dancing-festivals, *ɣser-skyéms-pa* sbst. the priest or dancer who offers it. — *skyems-čáṅ* **beer.** — *skyems-čú* **drinkable water.** — **skyéms-ḍaṅ* W.* (?) **brandy.** — *skyéms-ťsúgs Sch.:* **cup, dish.** — *skyéms-siṅ* **small-beer.**

སྐྱེར་པ་ *skyér-pa Lex.:* **हरित** curcuma, **turmeric;** in *W.* **barberry.**

སྐྱེར་དམན་ vulgo for *ske-dmán* **woman** *C.* (v. *skye-ba* II).

སྐྱེལ་བ་ *skyél-ba,* pf. & ft. *bskyel,* imp. *skyol* 1. **to conduct, accompany,** resp. *ɣdan-skyél-ba; skyól-la ṡog* conduct him hither! *Pth.; *skyel-la-la** (for **skyél-wa-la**) *soṅ* he has gone to accompany (him) *W.* — *bsu-bskyál* going to meet, and accompanying on departing *Dzl., ɣṡegs-skyél byéd-pa* resp. to accompany an honoured person on departing, to see him off *Mil.* — 2. **to convey, bring, take** e. g. a child to a place, food to somebody, *Dzl., C. W.* id.; **to carry off, to take away** *C.: *ṡiṅ ma kyal čig** do not bring any more wood! more accurately **kyal ṡog** bring! **kyal soṅ** take away! — 3. **to send** *B. & C.* e.g. clothes to somebody *Dzl.* — 4. **to risk, to stake,** *raṅ-srog Mil.* — 5. *C.:* **to use, to employ** **bá-laṅ lẹ ǰhé-pa-la** an ox for work; **to spend,** **lẹ ǰhé-pa-la mi-ťse** one's whole life in working, **lé-lọ náṅ-na** in idleness. — 6. **ḱa kyél-wa* C.* to kiss; *ɣnód-pa skyél-ba, B. *kyal-wa* C. W.* col., **to do harm, to hurt, inflict an injury, to play** one **a trick;** *mna skyel-ba B., C. W.,* **to swear,** take an oath; **lo kyél-če* W.* **to rely, depend upon, confide in.** — *skyel-ťuṅ byéd-pa = ɣṡegs-skyél byéd-pa,* (prop.: to accompany one to a short distance). — *skyel-bdár Lex.,* also col., present of the departing person to those that accompany him. — *skyel-ma* **an escort, convoy;** *skyél-mar yod* he is a guide (to me) *Mil.; skyél-ma žu* we ask for a safe-conduct *Glr.; dmag daṅ bčás-pai skyél-ma* a military escort *Glr.*

སྐྱེས་ *skyes,* also *skyás-ma, skyós-ma, ḱyós-ma,* resp. *ɣnaṅ-skyés,* **a present,** *skyes skúr-ba* to give or send a present; ˌ*byon-skyés, ṗebs-skyes* a present given to or received from somebody on his arrival. — *sḱyas-čáṅ* a present of beer, *skyes-ḱúr* of cakes, *skyes-nór* of merchandise or money; *skyes-lán* a present made in return *Cs.*

སྐྱེས་སྡོང་ *skyes-sdóṅ Sik.* **banana, plantain.**

སྐྱེས་ནག་ *skyes-nág,* also *skye-nág C.* **widower.**

སྐྱེས་པ་ *skyés-pa* 1. pt. pf. of *skyé-ba.* — 2. sbst. **man, male person,** *skyés-pa* *daṅ bud-méd*, men and women *B. & C.*; emphatically: *rgyál-po ɣčig-po skyés-pa yin* the king alone is a man *Dzl.*; **husband** *Glr.*; = *skyés-bu* **a holy man?**

སྐྱེས་བུ་ *skyés-bu*, *Ssk.* **पुरुष** **man, people**; *skyés-bu gaṅ* **whosoever; man** opp. to the rest of nature *Med.*; **one** (French: *on*), *skyés-bu lág-pa brkyáṅ-ba tsám-gyis* as quick as one stretches out his hand *Dzl.* — Though this word may also be applied to culprits and criminals (*Pth.*), it is chiefly used of **holy men**: *skyés-bu dám-pa* the saint; *dad-ldán sky.* the believing, the faithful *Glr.*; *skyés-bu čén-po*, **महापुरुष** the great saint, in Buddhistic writings nearly identical with Buddha; *skyés-bu mčog* id. (For the 32 chief characteristics and the 80 subordinate marks distinguishing such a person refer to *Köppen.* I. 433. *Burn.* II. 553 ff. *Gyatch.* c. VII.)

སྐྱེས་མ་ *skyés-ma* 1. fem. of *skyés-pa*, she that has been born *Mil.* — 2. **fern**, = *skyás-ma Sik.*

སྐྱོ་ངོགས་ *skyo-ṅógs* *Cs.*: **quarrel**, *Lex.* = *˳krug-lóṅ*.

སྐྱོ་བ་ *skyóba* 1. vb. **to be weary**, c.c.r: *bdag kyim-gyis skyó-ste* I being weary of living in the world *Dzl.*; in a more general sense: **to be ill-humoured, grieved, vexed, to feel an aversion** *Tar.* 12. 13; *skyo mi šés-par* or *skyo mi šés-pa tsám-du* without being tired, **indefatigably**; *nam skyo-na* when he was tired of it *Dzl.* — 2. sbst. **weariness** *˳tsol-˳tsól-nas skyó-ba yaṅ skyé-bar dug* we are quite tired of that constant seeking *Mil.*; *yid yóṅs-su mi skyó-ba* **indefatigableness, perseverance** *Thgy.* — *skyó-mo* adj., **sems skyó-mo rag** I feel **discontented, disheartened** *Ld.*

Comp. *skyo-grógs* **comforter, companion** *Glr., Mil.* — *skyo-glú Cs.*: **a mournful song.** — *skyo-ṅál, skyo-dúb* **weariness**, *skyo-ṅal-méd-pai dád-pa* unwearied faith *Mil.* — *skyo-šás* **disgust, aversion.** — *skyo-sáṅs* **recreation**, *skyo-sáns-la ˳gró-ba*, resp. *˳byon-pa* to take a walk or a ride, to promenade. — *skyo-bsún-pa* to be grieved *Sch.*

སྐྱོ་མ་ *skyó-ma* 1. **pap** of parched meal and beer; any **pap, paste** or **dough**; *skyó-ma ˳byúg-pa* to spread paste (upon a wound, as a salve) *Med.*; *ša-skyó Med.* ? (it may denote a paste of meat as well as one of mushrooms). — 2. **blame, slander**, *skyó-ma máṅ-la* when he slanders a great deal *Mil.*

སྐྱོགས་ *skyogs* 1. **scoop, ladle.** — **me-kyóg** **coal-shovel** *C.*; **žu-kyóg** **melting-spoon, crucible** *C. W.* — 3. **drinking-cup, bowl, goblet.** — *ɣser-skyógs, dṅul-skyógs* gold, silver goblet. *žal-skyógs C. B.*, **don-skyógs** *W.* resp.: drinking-cup. *krag-skyógs* bowl for drinking blood, a skull used for that purpose *Pth.*; **kyog-žáb sal** may I ask your honour for the foot of your cup (viz the remnant of your drink)? *W.* — 3. *srab-skyógs Cs.*: **the rein of a bridle.** —

སྐྱོགས་ལྟོ་འབུ་ *skyógs-lto-˳bu* **snail** *W.* **'ol-skyógs** id.

སྐྱོགས་པ་ *skyógs-pa* **to turn**, *mgrin-pa* the neck, = to look round, back, *Mil.*, also = to turn away, aside *C.*

སྐྱོང་བ་ *skyoṅ-ba*, pf. *bskyaṅs*, ft. *bskyaṅ*, imp. *(b)skyoṅ(s)* Ssk. **पा, रक्ष** **to guard; to keep, to tend**, cattle; **to defend**, the religion; **to save, preserve**, the life, the body; **support, to take care of**, poor people, e.g. *drin bzáṅ-pos* by benefits, favours. *tábs-kyis* by various means; **to attend to; to be given to**, *tugs-dám* meditation, *lag-léṅ* exercise; *rgyal-srid skyóṅ-ba* to rule, govern a kingdom, *čos bžin-du* in conformity with the law of religion, justly. — *čos-skyóṅ* **'protector, defender of religion'**, **धर्मपाल**, is used for a certain individual deity, or = *˳ʒig-rten-skyóṅ*, or for a class of magicians in the monasteries of *C.*, v. *Schl.* 157. *Kö.* II. 259. — *˳ʒig-rteṅ-skyóṅ*, **लोकपाल** **'guardian of the world'**; there are four of them, identical with *rgyal-čen bži* the four great spirit-kings, q.v. — *skyoṅ-dál* **assistance** *C.*, **kyoṅ-dhál ʒhe'-pa** to help. — *skyoṅ-ma* = *brtán-ma* the goddess of the earth.

སྐྱོད་པ་ *skyód-pa* pf. & ft. *bskyod*, *Ssk.* **चल.** 1. **to move, to agitate**, *rlúṅ-gis yál-ga* skyod-na when the wind agitates the branches *Dzl.*; **to shake**; hence *Mi-skyód-pa*, Akshobhya, n. of the second Dhyani-Buddha. — 2. *W.*: resp. **to go, to walk**, (= *yšégs-pa*, *byón-pa B. C.*) *nán-du skyod* step in, if you please! — 3. *W.*: **to go down, to set**, of the sun, moon etc., **to expire, to pass, to elapse**, of time.

སྐྱོན *skyon* दोष 1. **fault, defect** (opp. to *yón-tan*), *skyon gaṅ yaṅ med* I have not to complain of anything, I do not want anything *Dzl.*; **damage, harm, disadvantage, misfortune**, *ḱrul-pa-la skyon či yod* what harm is there in erring? *Thgy.*; C.: *mi kyon, kyon me'*, no harm, no matter (*W.* more freq.: *mi sto*); *yžán-gyi skyon tós-na dgá-ba* rejoicing in the calamities of others, malicious *Glr.*; *skyón-du mťóṅ-bá* to consider it a loss *Glr.* — 2. **bodily defect, fault**, as lameness; **derangement, disorder** in the mixture of the humours *Med.* — 3. **spiritual defect, sin, vicious quality**, *rdzún-du smrá-bai skyon* the sin of lying *Dzl.*; *skyón-gyis ma gos* not defiled by sin; *lar skyon če* but that is very bad (of you) *Glr.*; *skyon byéd-pa Cs.* to commit a fault, *sél-ba Lex.* to remove, amend, correct a fault, *spáṅ-ba* to leave off, to quit it; *mi-la skyon bébs-pa, dógs-pa* (col. *tág-pa, tág-če*) to charge one with a crime, to calumniate *Glr.*; *yžán-gyi skyon gléṅ-ba, rjód-pa*, to name the faults of others, to speak ill of them, to slander *B., C., Schr.* also: to blame, criticise. — *skyón-čan* 1. **faulty, defective, incorrect**, e.g. *dag-yig* the spelling of a word. 2. **sinful**, subject to vice. — 4. symb. num: 18.

སྐྱོན་པ *skyón-pa* pf. (*b*)*skyon* **to put astride** upon a thing, (causative form to *žón-pa*), *mi žig rtá-la* (or *rtá-ru*) to cause a man to mount, to go on horseback: to fix something on a stick; *mi žig ysál-šiṅ-la* **to empale** a man.

སྐྱོབ་པ *skyób-pa*, pf. (*b*)*skyabs*, ft. *bskyab*, imp. *skyób(s) Ssk.* त्रा **to protect, defend, preserve, save** frq., *jigs-pa-las* from fear, *jig-pa-las* from destruction; *bskyáb-pa* the protecting power, the preserving cause *Mil.* (ui f.).

སྐྱོབས *skyobs* **help, assistance**, seldom for *skyabs*; *skyóbs-ma Thgy.* id.; *šrog-kyób* col. preservation of life, escape; also: he that saves another's life, helper.

སྐྱོམ་པ *skyóm-pa*, pf. *bskyoms*, ft. *bskyom*, imp. *skyom(s) Cs.*: **to shake, agitate, stir up.** *Lexx.* give: *ču skyóm-pa* and *snód skyom-pa*, to stir the water, to shake a vessel.

སྐྱོར *skyor* = *ḱyor*, the hollow of the hand filled with a fluid, e.g. *ču-skyór* a handful of water.

སྐྱོར་བ *skyór-ba* I. vb. pf. & ft. *bskyar* 1. **to hold up, to prop**, — 2. **to paste.** — 2. **to repeat**, *bskyár-te btaṅ* it was repeatedly sent *Dzl.*; to repeat word for word what the teacher says, in order to learn it by heart *Mil.*; to say over again; to **recite by heart** (opp. to *sgróg-pa* to read); *glu de rjes skyór-nas ma bláṅs-na* if one does not sing the hymn afterwards repeatedly *Mil.*; *kyor jaṅ jhé'-pa* *C.* to practise repeatedly.

II. sbst. **enclosure, fence.**

སྐྱོལ་བ *skyól-ba* sometimes for *skyél-ba*.

སྐྱོས་མ *skyós-ma* v. *skyes*.

སྐྲ *skra*, resp. *dbu-skrá* (*C.*: *ṭa*, *W.*: *šra*) **the hair** of the head, *šra-ló* *Ld.* id., used caressingly in speaking to children and women; *skra daṅ ḱá-spu* the hair of the head and of the beard; *skra bsgril ba Cs.*: plaited or curled hair; *skra nyag yčig* a single hair. — *skrá-čan* having long hair. — *skra-do-kér* the hair plaited together on the crown of the head, as Buddha and Hindu-women wear it. — *skra-mdúd* the bow of ribands at the end of the long plaits of the women in *Ld.* etc. — *skra-tsáb Cs.*: **false hair, a peruke.** — *skra-šeṅ Sch.* thin hair.

སྐྲག་པ *skrág-pa*, with instr., **to be terrified, frightened by, afraid of** something *jigs-skrag-pa, dṅáṅs-skr.* id. *B., C.*

སྐྲང་བ་ *skráṅ-ba* pf. *skraṅs*, **to swell**, **skraṅs-soṅ** it is swollen, a tumour, a bile, a weal has formed itself *W.*; *skráṅs-po Sch.* a swelling, tumour; *skraṅs-₀búr Sch.* an abscess not yet open.

སྐྲན་ *skran* 1. *Ssk.* गुल्म *Cs.*: a fleshy etc. excrescence in the abdomen, a concretion under the skin, in the bowels, womb etc., *Sch.* also: a swelling of the glands. Wise (Commentary on Hindoo Medicine) says, that very different diseases are comprised unter the term *gúlma*, tumours of the pylorus, partial enlargements of the liver, diseases of the large intestines, fixed and moveable swellings; — perhaps also herniae, which I did not find mentioned elsewhere. — In *S.g.* I found *skran-nád* described as a consequence of great fatigue and want of breath, and *skran-γzér* as pain in consequence of suppressed winds. — 2. *rdo-skrán*, *bad-skrán*, two sorts of **steatite** *C.*

སྐྲབ་པ་ *skráb-pa Cs.*: 'to beat the ground with one's feet,' **to stamp, tread,** cf. *₀k'ráb-pa*; *Lex.*: *bró-skrab-pa*, to dance.

སྐྲས་ཀ་ *skrás-ka* v. *skás-ka*.

སྐྲི་བ་ *skri-ba* 1. *Cs.* **to conduct** (?) 2. *W.* **ṡri-ċe** f. *dkri-ba*.

སྐྲུ་བ་ *skrú-ba* pf. *bskrus* ft. *bskru*, *Sch.*: to wait; the latter would suit well in a passage of *Mil.*, perh. also in *zás-la skru* of the *Lexx.*; but *ṡiṅ-skrus-pa Lexx.* remains unexplained.

སྐྲུན་པ་ *skrún-pa* pf. & ft. *bskrun* **to produce,** fruits *Mil.*, a root of virtue (v. *rtsá-ba*) *Stg.*

སྐྲུམ་ *skrum* **meat,** resp. viz. when spoken of as the food of respected persons.

སྐྲོག་པ་ *skróg-pa* = *dkróg-pa*, perh. also f. *skrág-pa*. *Lexx.* *ḍá-ru skróg-po* **to beat** the drum: *W.* **koṗóṅ ṡróg-ċe** **to play** on the guitar.

སྐྲོད་པ་ *skród-pa* pf. & ft. *bskrad* **to expel, drive out, eject,** out of the country *Dzl.*, *Mil.*; to deprive of cast; **ṡrád-de taṅ ċe** to expel a thief publicly out of the village *W.*

བཀ..., བསྐ...; words beginning with these letters will in most cases be found arranged under rk.. and sk..

བསྐང་རྫས་ *bskaṅ-rdzás* a sacrificial ceremony v. *Schl.* 360.

བསྐ་བ་ *bská-ba*, *Ssk.* कषाय, **astringent,** as to taste, *Cs.* erron.: bitter.

བསྐལ་པ་ *bskál-pa*, *Ssk.* कल्प, **a kalpa,** a fabulous period of time; the fantastical reveries of the Buddhists concerning this subject v. *Kö.* I. 266, also *Will.* under *kalpa*. *bskál-pa čén-po* the great kalpa; *bár-(gyi) bskal-pa* the intervening or middle 'kalpa'; *bsk. bzáṅ-po* the happy, blessed period, viz. in which Buddhas appear; *bskál-pa ṅán-pa* the] bad 'kalpa'; *bskal-mé* conflagration of the universe.

བསྐུ་བ་ *bskú-ba* v. *skúd-pa* II vb.

ཁ

ཁ *k'a* 1. the letter **k'**, aspirated, like c in '*call*'. — 2. numerical figure: **two**, *k'a-pa* the second volume.

ཁ་ *k'a* I. additional syllable, = *ka*, but less frequent. —

II. in compounds instead of *k'á-ba* **bitter** and *k'á-ba* **snow**; for the latter signification it is in *W.* the only form existing.

III. i. o. *k'ag* **part,** *k'a γnyis-su* into two parts (e. g. to cleave) *Stg.*; **k'a-ghàṅ** one part; in a special sense: the sixth part of a rupee *C.*; *ḱa-ċig* part, **some, several**, frq.

IV. (also *Ssk.* ཁ) resp. *žal*, cf. *ḱá-po* 1. **mouth**, *ḱa ḱa* bitter mouth, bitter taste *Med.*; *ḱa dúl-po* (soft mouth), manageable, tractable, *ḱa gyóṅ-po* hard-mouthed, refractory; *ḱa sgyúr-ba* (= *ḱa-lo sgy.*) to govern, to rein the mouth (of a horse), to lead, guide, influence other persons *Glr*, to turn off (a river) *Tar.*; *ḱa ᶜṫén-pa* (to pull the mouth) to stop a beast of draught *Tar.*; *ḱa ₒbyed-pa, W,* **ṕé-ċe** to open one's mouth, *γdáṅs-pa* to open it wide, *ₒdzúm-pa, W.,* **ċug-ċe** to shut it; *ḱa brdáb-pa* (or *kráb-pa?*) **to smack;** **ḱa dab** (or **ṭab**) **zér-wa** to produce a smacking, snapping sound, col.; *ḱa rég-pa* c. dat. to put one's mouth to a thing, in order to eat or drink it; *ḱa ḍúg-pa* c. dat. **to interfere, to meddle with;** *ḱa ṫál-ba* 1. col. = *ḱa ḍug-pa*, 2. *Cs.:* **to promise;** *ḱa γtúgs-pa, ḱa ₒo γtúgs-pa, ḱá-la ₒo byéd-pa, ḱa sbyór-ba B., C.,* **ḱa lán-ċe* W.,* **ḱa kyél-wa* C.* **to kiss;** **ḱa kyé-ċe* W.,* **to inveigh,** to give ill language; *ḱa bsré-ba* to have intercourse, social connexion with one another, viz. in eating, drinking and smoking together, which is a matter of no little social consequence; *ḱa ₒdzin byéd-pa* c.genit. to receive friendly, to be kind to, assist *Mil.*; *ḱa γtád-pa Glr.* 16. 3. was explained: to bring together personally, to confront, = *ḱa sprád-pa*; *ḱa ₒbúb-tu nyal-ba* to lie in that position; *ḱa bsláṅ-ba* the contrary of the preceding; *ḱa ₒóg-tu bltás-te ṡi-ba* to be killed by a precipitous fall. Especially: the speaking mouth, *ḱá-nas,* col. also **ḱá-na**, **orally,** by word of mouth, e. g. to state, report, **ḱá-ne zér-na** in the colloquial language *C.*; **ḱa dé-mo ṅyiṅ sóg-po* W.* hypocritical; *ḱá-la slá-te dón-la bka* easily spoken after, but difficult to be understood (e. g. a doctrine); **ḱa ṡór soṅ** 'my (his etc.) mouth has run away', **nor soṅ** 'has erred', the former denoting inconsiderate talk, the latter a lapsus linguae; *ḱas lén-pa, bláṅ-ba* 1. 'to anticipate with the mouth', **to promise** frq., with direct speech or term. inf., sometimes also with the term. of a sbst. e. g. *brán-du ḱas blaṅs* he promised or engaged himself as a servant, — also: **to presume, to arrogate** *Mil.* 2. 'to accept, adopt with the mouth', **to acknowledge, admit** *Tar.*; *ḱas ₒċé-ba B., ḱa ṫál-ba Cs.,* to promise; *ḱa sṅá-ba, sṅás-pa* to blurt out, speak out inconsiderately; *ḱa ₒċám-pa, mṫún-pa, col.* **ṫúg-pa** to agree upon; *ḱa sdóm-pa, mnán-pa* to silence, *W.*; **ḱa kág-ċe, kyíl-ċe** id.; *ḱa skyór-ba, slú-ba* to speak cunningly, to try to persuade etc.; *ḱa róg-pa,* more freq. **ḱa róg-(te) dúg-pa, dád-pa,* **to be silent;** *ḱa ᶜṕáṅ-ba Tar.,* prob. = *ḱa ₒḱyam dbyúg-pa C.* to divulge ill rumours; *ḱa lóg-pa* to reply, contradict; *ḱa gáṅ dgar smrá-ba* (**gaṅ tad, gaṅ dran zér-ċe* W.*) to talk at random; *ḱa- (la) nyán-pa* **to obey.** *ḱa nyán-po* **obedient** (resp. *bka* i.o. *ḱa*); *γsál-ḱa* clear, intelligible language; *ḱa ṅán-du smrá-ba, W.:* **ḱa sóg-po zér-ċe** to use ill language; also without **ṅán-pa** or **sóg-po, ḱa zér-ċe** or **ḱa ṫóṅ-wa** means the same. — 2. **mouth, opening, orifice,** of a vessel, cavern, pit etc., *ḱa γċód-pa, ᶜgébs-pa* to cover, shut an opening; *ḱa ₒbyéd-pa* to open, is also used of a book, a letter etc. (for holy books *žal* is employed i.o. *ḱa*); *ḱa ₒbye-ba* to open or unclose itself, to begin to appear, *ḱa ₒbú-ba* id., of flowers; *ḱa búb-tu* the opening turned downward, *ḱa bslán-du* turned upward; *ḱa-ṫúg skóṅ-ba* to fill to the brim; *ḱa skóṅ-ba* to fill up a void, to make up a deficiency, *γžan-nas* or *las* from elsewhere; *ḱa naṅ* the inward brim, *ḱa ṗyi* the outer edge *Glr.* — 3. **the front side, face,** *ḱa lhor stón-pa* or *ltá-ba* to be directed southwards *Glr.* — 4. **surface,** *ḱa ₒbri-ba,* to be diminished, of a fluid the surface of which is sinking; *ḱá ᶜṗri-ba* to diminish, to make less, by taking away from the surface; **the outside,** *ḱa dkar γtiṅ nag* outside white, inside black, fig. *Mil.*; in a special sense: **colour,** v. *ḱá-dóg*; therefore *ḱá-ru, ḱá-na, ḱá-la, ḱar* 1. **on, upon, above,** *ṡiṅ-ḱar* upon the tree (e. g. he sits), up the tree (he climbs) *Dzl.*; *ču Kar* on the water; *pyogs bži Ká-ru* all round *Glr.* 2. **on, at,** *ču Kar* on the river side, *mtso Kar pebs* he came to the lake *Pth.* 3. **above, besides,** = *stéṅ-du Mil.* 4. **towards, in the face of,** *mtson Kar sra* proof against thrust or blow *Mil.* 5. **at the time of, when,** *sléb-pai Kar, sleb Kar, ₒbyon Kar* when (he) arrived; *ré-bai Kar* in the hope of; — *Ká-nas* down from, away from, *rta Ká-nas ₒbébs-pa* to alight from the horse *Glr.*; **Ká-na, Ká-ne, Ká-la** col. for *sgó-nas*, **tábs-si Ká-na** by way of the opportunity, on occasion, **yun riṅ-gi Ká-ne** by little and little, gradually. — 5. **sharpness, edge,** of a knife etc., **Ka túg-po soṅ** the edge has become blunt, **log soṅ** has become bad; **Ka mi ₒdug** the edge is wanting; *meī, čui, rluṅ-gi Ka nón-pa* to suppress the sharpness of the fire, water, wind, to stop the flames, floods etc. (viz. by means of incantations) *Glr.*; **Ka tón-če, píṅ-če* W.* to grind, to sharpen; *Ka lén-pa* to become sharp *Sch.*

V. **yesterday,** also: **the day before yesterday,** *Kai nyin* id., cf. *Ka-rtsaṅ.*

Compounds. *Ka-dkri (C. *-ṭi*, W. *-šri*)* **neck-cloth,** sometimes worn as a protection against cold. — *Ká-skóṅ, Kas-skóṅ* **appendix,** of a book. — *Ka-skyur-po* **olive, olive-tree** *Sik.* — *Ka-Ka-sán* or *siṅ* about two months ago *C.* — *Ka-Kébs* **cover, lid** *Sch.* — *Ka-Kór, Ka-Kyér* **border** *Sch.* — *Ka-Kral Cs.*: respect, regard, with respect to. — *Ka-ₒKór* the circumference of the mouth *Cs.* — *Ka-gáṅ* (cf. *Ka* III) **quadrate, square,** *Ka-gáṅ-ba* square *adj.*, *Ka-gáṅ-ma* id., e.g. pieces of cloth so shaped. — *Ka-gáb Sch.* **cover, lid.** — *Ka-góṅ* **snow-ball.** — *Ka-grú* corner of the mouth. — *Ka-mgál* v. *Ka-só.* — *Ka-rgán Mil.* privilege of old age n. f. — *Ka-rgód Sch.*: ill language; a slanderer. *Ka-rgyúg Glr.* acc. to the context: idle talk, unfounded assertion. — *Ka-rgyúd* or *-gyún*, resp. *žal-rgyun*, oral tradition, esp. certain mystical doctrines not allowed to be written down. — *Ka-bsgós* advice, = *Ká-ta;* commandment, cf. *bka-bsgós.* — *Ka-mńár* bitter and sweet. — *Ka-čig* (v. *Ka* III) **some,** — *Ka-γčáṅ* clever talking, cf. *Ka sbyáṅ-po* **eloquent.** *(Cs.*: fair words?) — *Ka-γčód* **cover, lid; cork.** — *Ka-bčól Sch.* idle talk, prattle. — *Ka-čág Mil.*, was explained: **abuse,** ill language. — *Ka-čád*, resp. *žal-čád* **agreement, convention, covenant,** **K. zúm-če* W.* to conclude a convention. — *Ka-čár Mil.* snow and rain; *Ka-ma-čár* both falling promiscuously, sleet. — *Ka-čiṅs* the appeasing of wild beasts etc. by witchcraft *Mil.* — *Ka-čú* 1. spittle *Cs.* 2. snow-water. — *Ka-če* 1. a large mouth. 2. a person that has to command over much (cf. *Ka-drág, Ka-žán).* 3. n. of a mask in the religious plays. 4. n. of a country, Cashmere, v. below. — *Ka-čéms* **last will,** *Ka-čéms ₒjóg-pa* to make a testament. — *Ka-čos* **hypocrisy.** — *Ka-mču* 1. **lip.** 2. *Sch.*: word, voice (?) 3. **quarrel, dispute.** — *Ka-rjé* 1. great lord, mighty personage *Cs.* (?) 2. good luck, good fortune *Cs.*; but in *C.* it is only used for **fortune = goods, wealth.** — *Ka-nyúṅ Sch* sparing of words, **laconic.** — *Ká-ta*, also *Ká-lta* **good advice, lesson,** *byéd-pa* or *ₒjóg-pa* to give, *C. W.* — *Ka-tód-la* (or *-na) Ld.* = *Ka-tóg la,* **on, upon.** — *Ka-tón Cs.*: 'a reading or saying with a loud voice' *(Lex.* पठन), better: **the saying by heart,** *klóg-gam Ka-tón-du dón-nas* reading or saying by heart, *Ka-tón-du šés-pa* to know by heart *Dzl.*; gen. in reference to religious texts. — *Ka-γtám Cs.* **tradition.** — *Ka-stóṅ* not yet having eaten anything. — *Ka-túg C.* to the brim. — *Ka-tóg-la* or *-na,* = *Ká-la,* **above, upon,** on the top or surface of, *Ka-tóg-tu* id.; *Ka-tóg-nas* down from. — *Ka-tór Sch.* pustules in the mouth. — *Ka-dig, Ka-ldig-mKan W.* **stammerer.** — *Ka-dóg,* also *Ka* (v. *Ka* IV. 4.) **colour** *skra mtón-mtiṅ-gi Ka-dóg-tu gyúr-to* the hair became blue *Dzl.*; *Ka sgyur-ba* to change colour, *Ka ₒgyur* the colour changes, cf. also *mdog.* — *Ka-drág* 1. **mighty.** 2 **haughty.** — *Ka-draṅ W.* **over-against, just before, opposite, straight on.** — *Ka-šdáms,* = *Ká-ta, γdáms-Ka,* **advice** *W.* — *Ka-ₒdár*

Cs.: 'one who speaks too fast', *Sch.:* 'too loud'. — *ḱa-˳dig* **cork, bung, stopple.** — *ḱa-nan* **yesterday morning** *C.* — *ḱá-nar-čan* **oblong.** — *ḱa-nin* **last year.** — *ḱá-po* sometimes f. *ḱa* 1. **mouth,** e.g. **ḱá-po dúl-mo** *W.*, **ḱá dúl-po C.*, tractable. 2. **speech** *Mil.* 3. **bitter** *C.* — *ḱá-lpágs* **lip,** *góṅ-ma* upper, *˶óg-ma* lower lip; *W.:* **ḱál-pag (s) pág-če, dáb-če** to smack. — *ḱá-spu* hair of the beard, *skra dan ḱá-spu* hair of the head and beard, frq. — *ḱá-p̓ó* **boasting,** *ḱa-p̓o-čé* id. — *ḱa-pór* = *p̓ór-pa,* **a cup.** — *ḱa-p̓yis* **napkin.** — *ḱá-ba* v. below. — *ḱa-bád* the humidity of the air or the moisture of the earth caused by snow. — *ḱa-búb* mouth or face being turned downwards. — *ḱa-brág* v. below. — *ḱa-rbád Cs.:* 'a boast, proud speech'; others: idle talk. — *ḱa-sbyáṅ* **eloquence** *Mil.*, *ḱa-sbyáṅ-po* eloquent, cf. *ḱa-yčáṅ?* — *ḱa-ma-čár* **sleet,** rain and snow. — *ḱa-múr* bit (bridle) *Sch* — *ḱa-rtsáṅ, ḱa-sáṅ* 1. *B. C.* **yesterday forenoon,** *ḱa-rtsáṅ-gi byis-pa* the boy that was here yesterday forenoon *Mil.* 2. *W.* (**kar-sáṅ**) **the day before yesterday;** some days ago; **kar-sáṅ za-nyi-ma** last sunday: **ḱar-sáṅ (s)tón-ka** last autumn. — *ḱa-ťsa* 1. **bitter and acrid** *Med.* 2. **'hot in the mouth'** *a.* a very acrid sort of radish, e.g. horse-radish. *b.* aphthae, thrush, a disease of the mouth, incident to horses, cows, sheep. *c. ḱa-ťsá riṅ-ṅe-ba Mil. nt.* daily warm food. — *ḱa-ťsúb* **snow-storm.** — *ḱa-ťsó* **boasting,** *ḱa-ťsó šin-tu čé-ba* a great swaggerer *Glr.* — *ḱa-ťsón* v. below. — *ḱa-mťsúl* **muzzle, mouth** (of a dog etc.); the lower part of the human face col. — *ḱa-˳ťsóg* abuse? **ḱa-ťsóg čém-po** *C.* **a** great abuser, reviler. — *ḱa-žán* the contrary of *ḱa-ḍrág,* low, unimportant, having no authority, *ḱa-žán-pai sdug-bsṅál* the misfortune of being of low birth *Mil.* — *ḱa-žé* 1. 'mouth and mind', *ḱa-žé mi mťsúṅs-pa* **hypocrisy, hypocrite** *C.* 2. 'mouth-mind', meaning the same as the phrase just mentioned: **hypocrisy** *Mil.*, *ḱa-že-méd-pa* unfeigned, sincere *Mil.* — *ḱa-žéṅ* **breadth, expanse,** e.g. of the heavens *Mil.* — *ḱa-zás* **food, victuals** *B. C.* — *ḱá-ya* lit.: 'being one's partner or match as to speaking', also *ḱai ya,* — gen.: **partner; match;** **ḱá-ya ǰhé'-pa** *C.* to assist, **ḱọ ḱẹ ya** (or **ḱa-ya) ṅe mi ťub** I am not his match, not able to compete with him; with regard to things: I am not equal to the task. — *ḱa-ras* **neck-cloth,** cf. *ḱa-dkri.* — *ḱá-ru-ťsa* **alum** *Méd.* — *ḱa-rúd* **snow-slip, avalanche,** — *ḱa-ró* taste in the mouth. — *ḱa rog* v. *ḱa* IV. 1. extr. — *ḱa-lán* 'mouth-requital' 1. **thanks-giving** *Mil.* 2. **reply,** esp. angry reply. — 3. **requital** for food received *C.* — *ḱa-leb* **cover, lid.** — *ḱá-lo* 1. 'mouth leaves', *sṅoi ḱá-lo Mil.* the young, tender leaves of several wild herbs, used as vegetables. 2. v. below. — *ḱa-šá* 1. v. *ḱa-skyúr-po.* — *ḱá-sá šá-ba S.g.*, 'snow-deer', **elk** *Sch.;* shoe-leather from the skin of this animal is mentioned in *Mil.*, and is known in Tibet. In *Sik.* however **the deer** of the neighbouring Tarai is called *ḱa-ša,* in other parts of the country **the spotted deer,** — *ḱa-šágs* **jest, joke,** **ḱa-šág ťáb-če, táṅ-če** *W.* to jest. — *ḱa-šúgs-čan, -šéd-čan W.* **eloquent.** — *ḱa-šés Cs.* **some.** — *ḱa-šób* col. **lies, falsehoods; obscene talk; idle talk.** *ḱa-bšád* **talk, gossip** *Mil.* — *ḱa-sáṅ* v. *ḱa-rtsáṅ.* — *ḱa-síṅ* several weeks ago *Cs.* — *ḱa-só* mouth and teeth; similar: *ḱa-mgál* mouth and jawbone, **ḱá-so** or **ḱa-gál čag yin** I shall break your chops *W.* — *ḱá-sró? Ld.* **ḱa-šró lám-če** to fry (meat) in butter. — *ḱa-slób,* = *ḱa-tón,* learnt by heart, (used by children) *W.* — *ḱa-lhág* remnant of a meal *Mil.*

ཁྭ་ *ḱa (ḱwa?)* v. *ḱwa-ta.*

ཁ་ག་པོ་ *ḱá-ga-po Sch.:* difficult (?).

ཁ་ཅུལ་ *ḱa-čúl W.* col. for *ḱa-če-yul,* **Cashmere.**

ཁ་ཆེ་ *ḱa-čé* **Cashmere;** amongst other things it produces much saffron, hence *ḱa-če-skyes* **saffron;** in Cashmere Buddhism was once flourishing (v. the legend relative to its being introduced there: Introduction du Buddhisme dans le Kashmir par L. Feer Paris 1866), but afterwards it came under Mahometan rulers, and *Ka-čé* denotes therefore now in *C.* a mussulman (cf. Huc & Gabet's journey); *Ka-čéi dpé-ča* the koran *Schr.*; *Ka-čéi ₒgrón-kaṅ* an inn kept by a mussulman *Mil.*

ཁྭ་ཏ་ *Ká-ta (Kva-ta?) Ssk.* 1. **crow.** — 2. **raven,** = *bya-róg, po-róg.* — 3. *Ka-ta krá-bo* **magpie.**

ཁ་ཏོ་ཤིང་ *Ká-to-šiṅ* is said to be = *ɣsál-šiṅ*, a pointed stake used for the execution of criminals.

ཁ་ཊྭཱཾ་ག་ *Ka-ṭváṅ-ga, Ka-ṭv.*, gen. pronounced *Ka-tóm-ga Ssk., Will.*: 'a club or staff with a skull at the top', the weapon of Siva, also carried by ascetics; Tibetans refer it also to the trident.

ཁ་བཏགས་ *Ka-btágs* **handkerchief or scarf of salutation**, a piece of veil-like and generally worthless silk-fabric, about as large as a small pocket-handkerchief, which in Tibet is given or sent, with or without other presents, to the person one intends to visit; cf. Huc's journey.

ཁ་འདད་ *Ka-ₒdá*, v. *Kan-da.*

ཁ་བ་ *Ká-ba* I. col. *C.* **Ká-po**, *W.* **Kán-te**, *Bal.* **χo** **bitter.** — II. *W.* **Ka** **snow,** *Ká-ba duṅ ltar ɣsal* bright as snow and shells *Pth.*; *Ká-ba ₒbab*, col. **Ka yoṅ** it snows; **Ka páṅ-če** *W.* to remove the snow (with a shovel); *Ká-ba-čan* snowy, and as a subst.: the snow-country, Tibet; *Ká-ba-čan-pai séms-čan-rnams* the Tibetan beings *Glr.* — III. correspondently to the Arabian word قهوة the missionaries in *Lh.* have given to *Ka-ba* the signification of **coffee,** which is otherwise unknown in Tibet.

ཁ་བད་ *Ka-bád* 1. the architectural ornament of a Tibetan house formed by the projecting ends of the beams which support the roof (not 'parapet' *Cs.*) — 2. v. *ka.*

ཁ་བྲག་ *Ka-brág* **fork** (not generally used in eating); any forked object.

ཁ་སྨོ་ *Ká-mo Cs.* **enchantment, irresistible influence.**

ཁ་ཚར་ *Ka-tsár* **fringes, threads,** such as the loose threads at the end of a web.

ཁ་ཚོན་ *Ka-tsón Sch.* decision; but in the only passage where I met with this word, viz. *Dzl.* ༢༥༧ 13, this meaning is not applicable, but something like surface or width.

ཁ་ཞུར་ *Ka-žúr Sch.* **water-hen.**

ཁ་ཟུར་ *Ka-zúr (Ssk.* खर्जूर, *Hindi* खजूर) col. *Ka-zúr-pa-ni* **date,** *Ka-zur šiṅ* date-tree.

ཁ་གཟེ་ *Ka-ɣzé* 1. *W.*: **rake** (gardening). — 2. *Sp.*: a carrier's **load,** **Ka-zé-pa** a cooly.

ཁ་ཡོག་ *Ka-yóg* **a false charge,** *C.*: **ma nyé-pe Ka-yóg ǰhuṅ** he was innocently accused.

ཁ་ར་ *Ká-ra* 1. *W.* f *ká-ra* **sugar.** — 2. *Sch.*: **trough, manger.**

ཁ་རི་ *Ka-ri*, or *Ka-rú*, v. *Kál-ri.*

ཁ་རོག་ *Ka-rog*, v. *Ka rog-pa*, *Ka* IV. 1. towards the end.

ཁ་ལེ་ *Ká-le* v. *Kyá-le.*

ཁ་ལོ་ *Ká-lo* 1. v. *Ka* Comp. — 2. *Schr.* **prow** of a ship, others: **helm;** the word is very often used in the phrase: *Ka-lo sgyur-ba*, esp. *gru-ɣziṅs-kyi*, to turn a ship, to steer, to lead, govern, rule, *Ka-lo sgyur-mkas-pa* skilful in driving, *Ka-lo-pa* a charioteer. — 3. *Cs.*: the glans penis.

ཁ་ཤྱ་ *Ka-šya* n. of a mountainous country in the N.E. of India *Tar.* 21. 10.

ཁ་སུར་ *Ka-súr* v. *Ka-zur.*

ཁག་ *Kag* 1. **a task; charge, business, duty; responsibility; importance;** *Kag ₒKúr-ba* to be charged with, *kág ₒgél-ba* to lay upon; **kag tég-pa** or **kyág-pa** *C.* to warrant, become responsible; *dér ₒtsó-ba yóṅ-ba kag teg* I warrant you will get something to eat there *Mil.*; **Kag -tég, Kag-Kyág** *C.* a bail; *Kág-čan* important. — 2. *W.*: **part,** *bču-Kág* the tenth part, tithe, **Kag-nyi čo-té čád-če** to cut in two; **division, section** (of a book); **place,** **Kág nyi-la pog soṅ** I have hurt myself in two places; **Kag čig-la rúb-če** to press towards one point; in a more general sense: **Kag čig-la 'i* *sás-ka čos** finish this work at once! — *yul-Kág* **province, district**; *rgyal-Kág* **kingdom.** — 3. *W.*: **Kug** or **Kág-ga tág-če** **to hang** (by the neck).

ཁག་པོ་ *Kág po C.* 1. **difficult** *(W.* **Kág(s)-po**); **hard** (to bear), **Kág-po ǰhuṅ** it proved hard, **Kág-po ǰhě-pa** to suffer want. — 2. **bad, spoiled, rotten,** **mar Kág-po soṅ** the butter has become rancid.

ཁག་ལ་ (?) *Kág-la, Md.*: **Kág-la mar** **fresh** butter, just made.

ཁང་ *Kaṅ C.*: vulg. f. *Koṅ*, sometimes also in books.

ཁང་པ་ *Káṅ-pa* **house,** *káṅ-pa-la W.* home, at home; in compounds also for a part of the house: **room, story, floor** etc., *steṅ-, bár-, ˎóg-Kaṅ* upper story, middle story, ground-floor *Glr.*; *bár-ma, dkyil-ma* or *ȷzúṅ-Kaṅ* means also the usual dwelling-room, opp. to *pugs* and *sgo* (v. *sgo*): *bzó-Káṅ* **workshop;** *báṅ-Kaṅ* **store-house, store-room;** *sgó-Kaṅ* **entrance, vestibule;** *skór-Kaṅ* (*Glr.* 68, 9) seems to be a passage running round a building; **šóg-Kaṅ** *W.* the scooping-form or **mould** used in the manufacture of paper; **tsás-Kaṅ** **bed** (garden).

Kaṅ-glá **house-rent.** — *Kaṅ-čúṅ* house or room reserved for decrepit parents; *Kaṅ-čúṅ-pa* inhabitant of such; *yaṅ-Kaṅ-čúṅ-pa* such a person of the second degree, (if, during his life, his son enters into the same right). — *kaṅ-stóṅ* **an empty house,** which is thought a fit place for sorcery and necromancy. — *Káṅ-bu* 1. little house, **cottage.** 2. **room,** *mya-ṅán-gyi K.* room of mourning *Dzl.* — *Kaṅ-mig* **room.** — *Kaṅ-rtsá* **foundation of a house** *Sch.* — *Kaṅ-žábs* **flooring** of a room. — *Kaṅ-bzáṅs* **residence,** chiefly of gods. — *kaṅ-rúl Sch.* **a house in ruins.**

ཁང་བུ་ *Káṅ-bu Pth.* n. of a (fabulous) country.

ཁད་ *Kad* 1. **litter, barrow.** — 2. **like, as,** = *ltar Glr.* — 3. = *Kod, Kad-snyáms* v. *ˏKod-snyóms.*

ཁད་པ་ *Kad-pa*, 1. the same as *ˏKód-pa* **to stick fast, to be seized, stopped, impeded,** v. *ˏKad-pa;* hence also *ma-Kád* = *ma-ťág* **as soon as:** *dbugs čad ma-Kád-du* as soon as the breathing ceases *Thgr.*; **de ma-Kád** instantly, directly, *bu skyes-ma-Kád čig Glr.* a child born **just now.** — 2. **to approach, draw near,** with *la, núb-la Kád-pai tse* when the evening drew near *Pth.*; frq. with the perfect-root of a verb: *dbugs čád-la Kád-pai dus* when the ceasing of the breath approaches *Thgr.*; *zin-la Kad yód-pa-la* as we were just about to seize him; *Kád-du* postpos. c.a.: *rtiṅ-pa Kád-du* **as far as** the heel *Mil.*; *Kád-kyis* adv. **by degrees** *Mil.*; *Kád-la, Kád-du* id. *Tar.*

ཁན་པ་ *Kán-pa*, also *Kén-pa* 1. sbst. *Schr.*: wormwood, probably a mistake for *Kám-pa.* — 2. vb. **to add** (arithm.) *Wdk.*

ཁན་ད་ *Kán-da*, more correctly *Káṇ-ḍa*, also spelled *Ká-ˏdá, Ssk*, treacle or molasses partially dried, **candy;** *dé-la Kán-da bčos-pa* the candy made of it *Med.*; *skyér-Kan-da* candied *skyer-pa.*

ཁན་མན་ *Kan-máṅ* (corrupted from *Ka-dmaṅ?*) **modest** *Lh.*

ཁབ་ *Kab* 1. **court, residence** of a prince, *rgyál-poi Káb-kyi mi-rnams* courtiers. — 2. **wife, spouse,** *Kab čén-ma* the first wife (in rank); *dé-la Kab ˎós-pa ma rnyéd-nas* as there was not found a wife worthy of him *Glr.*; *ˏdi ȷnyis ṅai Káb-tu byúṅ-ba rmis-so* I dreamt that these two would become my wives *Glr.*; *Káb-tu bžés-pa* to take for a wife, to marry. *(Schr.* has even a verb: *čúṅ-mar Káb-pa.)* — 3. **needle,** *Kab-rtse* point of a needle, *kab-rál(?) Sch.* needle-case, *Kab-mig* eye of a needle, *Káb-mig-tu skúd-pa ˏǰúg-pa* or *rgyúd-pa* to thread a needle; *pra-Káb* a small needle, *sbom-Káb, mo-Káb Dzl., ťa Káb W., blo-Káb W., Kab-rúl W.* a large, thick needle, packing-needle; *Kab-spú* **bristle** *Sik.*; *Kab-lén (rdo)* **loadstone, magnet.**

ཁབ་ཏ་ཀ་ *Kab-tá-ka* col. **knapsack, pouch.**

ཁབ་ལེ་ *Káb-le* (or *las?*) *W.* **difficult.**

ཁབས་ *Kabs* n. of a disease *Med.*

ཁམ་ *ḱam* 1. **a bit,** a small piece of anything, *ḱam-čuṅ* a small bit, *ḱam-gáṅ*, *ḱam γčig* a mouthful, *ḱam-ts̓ád-du γčód-pa* to cut 'in the size of bits' *Dzl.* (infernal punishment); *ḱam-zán* a mouthful of food *Mil.; zas ḱam γčig* id. — 3. *W., C.* **appetite,** **zá-če-la ḱam yoṅ** *W.* I get an appetite for eating; **ḱam dig soṅ** *W.* I have no appetite; *ḱam-lóg* want of appetite, **nausea,** aversion (*Cs.* also: hatred); **ḱam-lóg-pa** inclined to nausea, easily sickened *C.; *ḱam-lóg-ḱaṅ** *W.* id.; **ḱam-ḱám čo dug, nyíṅ ḱam-ḱám čo dug** (with *la*) *W.* he has a desire, a longing for, perh. only provincial pronunciation for *rkám-pa.*

ཁམ་ཁུམ་ *ḱam-ḱúm* high and low *Schr.* (?)

ཁམ་དར་ *ḱam-dár* **walnut** *Sch.*

ཁམ་པ་ *ḱám-pa* 1. **fox-coloured, sorrel, brownish.** — 2. **porcelain-clay, china-clay.** — 3. **Tanacetum tomentosum,** a very aromatic plant, frequent on high mountains.

ཁམ་ཕོར་ *ḱam-p̓ór* a cup made of dough, used as a lamp in sacrificing.

ཁམ་བིར་ *ḱam-bir* (perh the *Ar.-Hd.* خمير leaven) thick bread-cakes leavened with butter-milk *Ld.*

ཁམ་བུ་ *ḱám-bu* 1. **apricot** *B., C., ḱám-bui ts̓i-gu* the stone of an apricot; *ḱam-bu-mar* the oil pressed out of apricot-stones, smelling and tasting of bitter almonds *Med.; mṅa-ris ḱám-bu* dried apricots, v. *p̓á-tiṅ.* — 2. **peach** *Sik.* — 3. v. *ḱam.*

ཁམ་གཡག *ḱam-γyág Sch.* cherries, morels; these not being known in Tibet, the word must be either of Khotan or Chinese origin, or else the signification of 'stones of apricots' is to be adopted, as given in *Wts.*

ཁམས་ *ḱams* (*Ssk.* धातु) 1. physical constitution of the body, **state of health,** *ḱams bdé ba* healthy constitution, good health; *rje-btsún-gyi ḱams bde lágs-sam?* is your Reverence well? asks a layman, and the Lama answers: *ṅa šín-tu bde; ḱyed ḱams bde-am?* I am quite well: are you well? *Mil.; W.* more frq.: **ḱam-záṅ-po**, *C.* also *ḱam saṅ* good health; *ḱams-rmyá Med.*, acc. to *Cs.* **nausea,** feeling sick; *ḱams-sós Sch.:* rest, comfort, health, prob. more accurately: recreation, recovery, restoration (of health), so*: ḱams sós-par gyur Mil.;* sometimes it seems to be a synonym of *lus,* body, *ḱams dúb-pa bsóṅ-ba* to recreate the exhausted body *Mil.nt.* fig.: *γnod-sems-méd-pai ḱams šas če* the peaceable disposition predominates *Stg.* — 2. (synon. of *yul*) **empire, realm, territory, domain;** *yul-ḱáms* empire, in a geographical and political sense, e.g. Nepaul *Glr.; rgyal-ḱáms* 1. for *rgyál-poi ḱams* kingdom, *ḱa-ba-čan-gyi rgyal-ḱáms* the kingdom of Tibet. 2. for *rgyál-bai ḱams* the empire of Buddha, the world; *rgyal-ḱáms ̥grím-pa* to roam over the kingdoms, the countries *Mil.;* **region, dominion,** *bar-snáṅ-gyi ḱams* the aërial regions, where the *lha* live *Pth.*; in physiology: *mḱris-pai ḱams* the dominion of bile *Med.; ḱams γsum* the three worlds acc. to Buddhistic speculation, viz. the earth with the six heavens of the gods, as the 'region of desire', *̥dód-pai ḱams;* above this is the 'region of form', *γzúgs-kyi ḱams,* and ultimately follows the 'region of formlessness', *γzugs-med-pai ḱams.* — 3. **element** (syn. *̥byúṅ-ba*), *ḱams drug* the six elements of some philosophical systems, consisting, besides the four elements familiar to us, also of *nám-mḱa* and *rnam-šés,* the ether and the substance of the mind. In chronology, in naming the single years of the cycle, five elements are assumed, which (according to Chinese theory) are wood, fire, earth, iron, water. — 4. p.n. **Khams,** Great Tibet, the parts between Ü and China; *smad-mdo-ḱams-sgóṅ γsum* the low-land, the three provinces Do, Kham, and Gong, cf. *mṅa-ris; ḱáms-pa* a man from Khams.

ཁར་རྩང་ *ḱar-rstáṅ* v. *ḱa-rtsáṅ.*

ཁར་གོང་ *ḱar-góṅ* **steatite, soapstone,** *Sch.*, prob. = *dkar-goṅ.*

ཁར་རྐྱང་ *k̔ar-rkyáṅ* v. *k̔a-rkyáṅ*.

ཁར་རྩང་ *k̔ar-rtsáṅ* v. *k̔a-rtsáṅ*.

ཁརྶ་པ་ཎི་ or ཁ་སརྤ་ཎ་ *k̔arsa-pa-ni* or *k̔a-sar-pa-na* n. of a deity *Glr.*; *Tar.* p. 110 gives a (rather absurd) legend concerning the origin of the name.

ཁལ་ *k̔al* 1. (cf. *sgal)* **burden, load,** *k̔al ˳k̔yér-ba* to carry a burden; *k̔ál-gyi stéṅ-du* on the top of the luggage *Glr.*; *k̔al ˳gél-ba* to load a burden, to put a load upon, *k̔al ˳bógs-pa* to take off the burden, to unload; **load, freight;** as a fixed quantity, *lúg-k̔al* a sheep-load, *bóṅ-k̔al* load of an ass; *˳brui k̔al* a load of corn. — 2. **bushel,** a dry measure = 20 bre; therefore = a score or 20 things of the same kind; in *W.* **k̔al-ĉig** frq. for *nyi-šu*, also with respect to persons; *gžór-k̔al* a 'measuring-score', 20 *bre*, actually measured, as is usual with corn; *˳dégs-k̔al* a 'weighing-score', the weight of 20 points on the steel-yard *(rgya-ma)*, in weighing wood, hay, butter etc.

ཁལ་ཁ་ *k̔ál-k̔a* n. of a Mongol tribe, Khal-ka.

ཁལ་ཁོལ་ *k̔al-k̔ól* **stunned, insensible** *Thgy.*

ཁལ་ཅག་ *k̔al-ĉág* the best sort of wool for manufacturing shawls, coming from Jang-thang.

ཁལ་པ་ *k̔ál-pa* 1. **wether,** castrated ram. — 2. **sow-thistle,** Sonchus.

ཁལ་མ་ *k̔ál-ma* **beast of burden, sumpter-mule** *B., C.* *k̔ál-ma-rnams bzán-la skyél-ba* to drive beasts of burden to the pasture, to turn them on grass-land *Glr.*; *Schr.*; **mi k̔al nyís-kyi la* C.* payment for carriers and beasts of burden; though in *W.* it might be understood as: payment for twice twenty men.

ཁལ་རི་, ཁལ་རུ་ *k̔al-rí, k̔al-rú*, also *k̔a-rí, k̔a-rú* twenty bushels.

ཁས་ *k̔as* instr. of *k̔a*; *k̔as-lén-pa* etc. v. *k̔a*, 4; *kas-skóṅ* = *k̔á-skóṅ*, q.v.; *kas-stóṅ* with an empty stomach; *k̔as-dmán, kas-žán,* **weak, poor.**

ཁི་ *k̔i* numerical figure: 32.

ཁིའུ་ *k̔iu C.*: **k̔yiu** **a cutting-out knife.**

ཁུ *k̔u* 1. numerical figure: 62. — 2. for *k̔ú-lu* (?) *Lál.*

ཁུ་གུ་ *k̔ú-gu Cs.* '1. uncle. 2. an address'(?)

ཁུ་ཏུ་ *k̔ú-tu* **a hut, cottage,** constructed of branches *Lh.*

ཁུ་ནུ་ *k̔ú-nu* p. n. **Kunawar,** also Bissáhar, country on the upper Sutledj, bordering on Tibet, and inhabited in the northern part by Tibetans. Here are situated Kanám, a monastery with a considerable collection of Tibetan books, and Poo, a missionary station of the Church of the United Brethren, founded 1865.

ཁུ་བ་ *k̔ú-ba* 1. **fluid, liquid,** also (but less frq.) *k̔u-ĉú*; *lhuṅ-bzéd bkrús-pai k̔ú-ba*, the fluid in which a beggar's bowl has been washed *Tar.*; *k̔rús-k̔u* dish-wash, swill *Tar.*; *˳brás-k̔u Cs.*: rice-soup, *Schr.*: rice-water; *šiṅ-k̔u, rtsá-k̔u* the sap of trees, of plants *Cs.*; *šá-k̔u* broth, gravy; *már-k̔u* melted butter. — 2. **semen virile,** *k̔u-ba byin-pa* emittere semen; *k̔u-k̔rág* the mixture of the semen with the uterine blood, by which process, acc. to Indian physiology, the fetus is formed, *Med., Ssk.* **संक्लेद.**

ཁུ་བོ་ *k̔ú-bo* **uncle,** on the father's side *B.* and *C.*; *p̔a-k̔ú* father and uncle; *k̔u-dbón* and *k̔u-tsán* uncle and nephew. But owing to polyandry, the degrees of kindred lose their precision, in as far as all the brothers that have become the husbands of one wife may be called 'father' by the children.

ཁུ་བྱུག་ *k̔u-byúg B.*, also *k̔u-gyúg* and *yug.* **cuckoo,** called *byá-yi rgyál-po* and described as a sweetly singing bird, whence prob. *Cs.* has conjectured nightingale, which however is scarcely known in Tibet. — *k̔u-byug-rtsá* n. of a medicinal herb.

ཁུ་མག་ *k̔u-mág Lh.* purse, money-bag, col. for *k̔ug-ma.*

ཁུ་ཚུར་ *k̔u-tsúr Cs.* the clinched hand, **fist,** *k̔u-tsúr snún-pa (Sch.* also *rgyáb-pa)* to strike with the fist. This signification, however, seemed not to be known to the Lamas consulted, who interpreted the word: a religious gesture, the fore-finger being raised, and the others drawn back. Some native dictionaries have मुष्टि fist, others खटक half-closed fist.

ཁུ་ཡུ་ *Ḱu-yú*, in *C.* also *'a-yú*, **hornless,** having no horns, used of cattle *Sch.*

ཁུ་ལུ་ *Ḱú-lu* 1. the short woolly hair of the yak. — 2. *Lh.*: venereal disease, **syphilis.**

ཁུ་ལེ་ *Ḱú-le Sch.*: **steel-yard** and its weight; but *Dzl.* ११, 17 the word refers to an ordinary pair of scales and denotes that **scale** of the two which contains the weights.

ཁུག་, ཁུགས་ *Ḱug*, *Ḱugs* **corner,** concave angle, **nook;** of rivers, lakes etc.: **creek, bay, gulf, cove,** also *ču-ḱúg*; *Ḱúg-tu* within a recess, on the farther side of a cavity.

ཁུག་ཏ་ *Ḱúg-ta* (or *rta*), *a-li-ḱúg-ta*, a kind of **swallow** *Cs.*; the lights (lungs) of this bird are used as a remedy against pulmonary diseases, *Med.*

ཁུག་རྣ་ *Ḱug-rná* and *Ḱug-sná* **fog, mist, haze,** during a calm, esp. in spring-time.

ཁུག་པ་ *Ḱúg-pa* I sbst. 1. *Cs.*: "part of a long period of time" (?) — 2. a certain part of the body *Med.* — II. vb. 1. also *Ḱúgs-pa*, **to call** = *gúg-pa Mil.* (cf. also *γyań*). — 2. **to find; get, earn;** *nor Ḱúgs-pa-ań srid* there is a possibility that we may yet replenish our cash *Mil. nt.*; *γnyid Ḱúgs-pa* to get sleep; *srań γsum Ḱugs*, it drew i.e. weighed three ounces.

ཁུག་མ་ *Ḱúg-ma* **pouch,** little bag, *me-lčags-ḱug-ma* tinder-pouch *Mil.*; *dńúl-ḱug* money-bag, purse; *rdzóń-ḱug* *Pur.* knap-sack; *rtsám-ḱug*, resp. *žib-ḱug*, little bag for flour; *nú-ḱug* sucking-bag, for babies.

ཁུང་ *Ḱuń* **hole, pit, hollow, cavity,** originally used only of dark holes and cavities; *sna-ḱúń* nostril, *rna-ḱúń* the ear-hole, *mčan-ḱúń* arm-hole, arm-pit; *brag-ḱúń* cleft in a rock, cavern; *byi-ḱúń* mouse-hole; *čab-ḱúń* a sink; *bso-ḱúń* peep-hole; *mda-ḱúń* loop-hole; in *C.* *'i-ḱúń, mig-ḱúń, te-ḱúń* are used of any hole in walls, clothes etc., caused by decay or daily wear. *γtor-ḱúń* a sink, gutter; *ḱúń-dregs* soot of an oven or chimney *Sch.*; *ḱúń-pa*, *ḱúń-po Cs.* a large hole, *ḱún-bu* a small hole, e.g. *spui ḱún-bu* pore, passage of perspiration *Dzl.*

ཁུངས་ *Ḱuńs* 1. the original meaning perh. is **mine, pit** *Cs.* — 2. **origin, source** (fig.), *γyoi ḱuńs snubs*, he stopped the source of the deceit *Ld.-Glr. Schl.* 13, b. *Ḱúńs-čan*, and prob. of similar meaning *Ḱuńs-btsún*, of noble descent, or when applied to statements etc.: well founded; *Cs.* also fine, excellent; *Ḱuńs-méd*, *Ḱuńs ńán-pa* having no 'origin', mean, pitiful, ill founded; in the last sense it seems to be used of historical accounts, *Tar.* 43, 5, and more esp. of religious records *Pth.*, *Glr.*; *γtam-ḱúńs Tar.* 66, 18, prob.: historical source, record, document; in *Pth.* facetiously: *γtam-ḱúńs čań yin* the source of that speech is beer.

ཁུད་ *Ḱud* **coat-lap,** or any cloth serving in an emergency as a vessel; *ḱu' ze'* hold forth the lap of your coat, words frequently used to beggars, to whom the alms, chiefly consisting in flour, are poured into that receptacle, *C.*

ཁུད་པ་ *Ḱúd-pa* **pocket, pouch** *Sch.*

ཁུད་མ་ *Ḱúd-ma* **side, edge** *Cs.*; *Ḱúd-du* aside, apart, secretly; *ḱúd-du* ₒ*jog-pa* to put, to lay aside.

ཁུན་ཏི་ *Ḱún-ti*, or *ḱyen-ti*, is stated to be used in *Pur.* for **he, she.**

ཁུན་པ་ *Ḱún-pa* **to grunt** (*Sch.*: to groan).

ཁུན་བུ་ *Ḱún-bu Glr.* 97, 12?

ཁུམ(ས)་ *Ḱum(s)* v. ₒ*gum-pa*; *Ḱúms-pa*, **crooked.**

ཁུམས་ *Ḱums Sch.*: so it is said; *Mil.*: *ló-tstsa-bai snyán-pa rgyáń-nas ḱums* might be rendered: the interpreter's renown was proclaimed from afar; the word, however, is of rare occurrence.

ཁུར་ *Ḱur* 1. **burden, load,** for men, more fully: *mi-ḱur*; *Ḱúr-skyed-pas* ₒ*tsó-ba žig* one that lives by carrying loads *Tar.* — 2. rarely **porter**, carrier of a load; *Kúr-po* **load, burden**; *Kúr-bu*, col. **Kúr-ru** prop. a small load; a load in general; *Kúr-pá* carrier, cooly; *Kur-rtsá, Kur-lám* cooly-station, a day's journey, gen. 10 to 12 English miles; *Kur-rtsá-pa* a station-cooly.

ཁུར་བ་, འཁུར་བ་ *Kúr-ba, °Kúr-ba* 1. sbst. *Cs.:* **bread, food**, *Sch.* also forage, fodder. It is, however, not the common word for bread, but only for certain sorts, such as *bra-Kúr*, bread of buckwheat, *rtsabs-Kúr* q v., and more particularly it is applied to cakes and pastry-work baked in fat or oil. — 2. vb. v. *°Kúr-ba.*

ཁུར་མ་, ཁུར་མང(ས)་ *Kúr-ma, Kur-máṅ(s)* **dandelion** *C.*, used as a pot-herb and medicinal plant; as the former it is also called *Kur-tsód.*

ཁུར་ཚོས་ *Kur-tsós C.* and *B.* **cheek**, the ruddy part of the face below the eyes (cf. *°grám-pa); *Kur-tsóg W.*

ཁུལ་ *Kul* 1. *Sch.:* "the soft **down** of furs", abbreviation of *Kú-lu; Kul-mal* small basket for wool *Ts.* — 2. **ravine** *Kun.* — 3. **district, province, domain**; *lhá-sa Kul* all that belongs to Lhasa *Georgi Alph.*, **dei Kul-la °dug** is subject to him *C.*

ཁུལ་མ་ *Kúl-ma* the bottom, or the side of a thing *Cs.*

ཁེ་ *Ke* numeral, ninety-two, 92.

ཁེ་, ཁྱེ་ *Ke, Kye (Sch.: Ke-ma)* 1. **profit, gain**; *Ke-spógs B.* and *C.*, **Ke-béd* W.* id.; *Ke-tsóṅ byéd-pa* **to trade**, to traffic *Pth.; šés-Kyi Ke* gain, advantage obtained by knowledge and attainments; *Ke-pa* **tradesman**, dealer; *tsóṅ-°dus Ké-pa* trader in a market *Mil.; Ke-nyén Sch.;* profit and loss, risk; *Ke-sgrúb-pa Cs.*, **Kye-béd tób-če* W.*, to make profit, to gain, *Ke brgyáb-pa*, to make a good bargain *Sch.; *Ke-ru °do-wa* C.* to abate, to go down in price; **Ké-čuṅ, Ke-me'**, profitable, unprofitable; **Kyé-mo* W.* **cheap.** — 2. **tetter, herpes, ringworm** (eruption of the skin) *Sch.*

ཁེགས་ *Kegs* v. *Kegs.*

ཁེངས་པ་ *Kéṅs-pa* 1. partic. of *°Kéṅs-pa*, filled, replete with. — 2. adj. puffed up, **proud, haughty**, arrogant; sbst. pride etc.; *Keṅs-séms, Keṅs-drégs* pride. *Keṅs-po Med.* with reference to food: producing flatulence.

ཁེན་པ་ *Kén-pa* 1. *Schr.* worm-wood, prob. erron. for *Kám-pa.* — 2. *Sch.:* to lean, to repose on, erron. for *bKán-pa.*

ཁེབས་ *Kebs*, col., *W.: *Kyebs*, Cs.: Kébs-ma* **covering**, coverlet: **Keb sáṅ-pa**, to take the covering off *C.; čár-Kebs* a covering against rain, rain-cloak; *stéṅ-Kebs, lčóg-Kebs*, table-cloth *Cs.; tód-Kebs Lt.* **cap, hood**; *gdúṅ-Kebs*, a certain beam or board above the capital of a pillar; *gdóṅ-Kebs*, **veil**, cloth to cover the head; **dún-Kyebs* W.* **apron**; **paṅ-Kéb* C.* **napkin, apron.**

ཁེམ་ *Kem* v. *Kyem.*

ཁེར་རྒྱག་པ་ *Kér-rgyag-pa*, **to defraud; to usurp** *Sch.*

ཁེལ་བ་ *Kél-ba* prob. for *°Kél-ba*, **to load** upon; *blo Kél-ba* is said to be used in *C.* for *blo skyél-ba W.*, v. *skyél-ba* no. 6.

ཁེས་ཉིན་ *Kes-nyén* the day before yesterday *Sch.*

ཁེས་པ་ *Kés-pa C.* **to hit**, *°tsáms-la* (or *mtsáms-la?*) to hit the right thing, the exact point or line; *gnád-la* to strike the vital parts, to hit mortally, fatally.

ཁོ་ *Ko* 1. numeral, 122. — 2. *Bal.* (**χ'o**) for *Ka-ba*, bitter.

ཁོ་ *Ko* pers. pron. of the third person, **he, she, it**, but almost exclusively in col. language. In ancient writings it occurs but rarely, being either omitted or supplied by *de*, but in later works that come nearer to the present language, it is to be found the more frequently. *Koi* his, her; **Kó-pa, Kó-wa** plur. **they**, *W.* and *C.*, v. *Georgi Alph.*, in an edict; **Kó-čag, Kó-tso** id. *C.; *Kó-wa nyi* W.*, both of them: *Ko-ráṅ* 1. he himself. 2. he, = **Ko** col.; with partic.: *Ko dá-či sṅon la soṅ-ba de, Mil.*, he that just went on in advance, proceded in front.

Note. The word prob. has been originally a sbst., denoting essence, substance (like *ṅó-bo*); *má-ko, γżi-Ko, rgyú-Ko* are said to be used in *C.* for: the essential, the most important part of a thing, the main point, and the noun substantive may possibly have changed into a substantive pronoun, in a similar manner, as *ṅa*, I, is connected with *ṅó-bo;* cf. also *Kó-na, Kó-bo.*

ཁོ་ཏི *Ko-ti C.* (Chinese?) **tea-kettle.**

ཁོ་ཐག་གཅོད་པ *Ko-ťág γčód-pa* c. termin. **to despair of** *Mil.*; **to resign, to acquiesce in, to reconcile one's self to;** also *sems Ko-ťág γčód pa Pth.*

ཁོ་ན *Kó-na* adj. and adv. 1. **just, exactly, the very,** *rgyál-pos ͺdod-pa Kó-na yin* that is just what has been wished for by the king *Dsl.* ༢༠. 17. *sṅá-ma Kó-na bžin-du* just as before; *ͺdi Kó-na yin-par ṅes* he is evidently the very same (man) *Mil.*; *srin-bu Kó-na ͺdrá-ba* just like a worm *Thgy.*; *ťsul de Kó-nas* by the very same process *Tar.* 13, 12; *de Kó-na nyid-du gyur čig* just so may it happen! (at the conclusion of a prayer) *Glr.*; but *de-Ko-na-nyid,* as a philosophical term, is also the translation of the *Ssk. táttva,* essentiality, truth, implying to the Buddhist nothing but **vacuity,** the Nirvâna *Trig.* 20. — 2. **only, solely, exclusively,** *skád-čig Kó-na,* only for a moment *Dzl.* ༢༥༢, 12. *ͺdod Kó-nas brél na,* if taken up merely with lust: *séms-čan Kó-na bdé-bar ͺdód-tsa-na* as he intended only the welfare of beings *Thgy.*; *Tar.*

ཁོ་བོ *Kó-bo* mas., *Kó-mo* fem. pers. pron. 1st. person, I, pl. *Kó-bo-čag* we, indiscriminately as to the rank of persons, *B.* and *C.*; mi *Kó-boi rnam-šés* the soul of me the man, i.e. my human soul *Mil.*; also pleon. *Kó-bo ṅa.*

ཁོ་བོམ *Ko-bóm,* the Tibetan name for **Khatmandu,** the capital of Nepaul *Glr.*, *Mil.*; sometimes also called *klui ṗo-bráṅ,* prob. on account of the mineral treasures supposed to abound in that country.

ཁོ་མ *Kó-ma,* perh. misprinted for *Kom* **knapsack, wallet** *Mil.*, or else a secondary form of that word.

ཁོ་གཡུ *Ko-γyú,* occurs only in **Ko-yú skór-če* (perh. col. for *ͺKor-γyúl*) *W.* **to thrash,** which is done by driving a number of oxen fastened together round a pole that stands in the middle of the thrashing-floor.

ཁོ་ར *Kó-ra, Cs.* also *Kór-sa,* **circumference;** circumjacent space; also **fence,** surrounding **wall;** *Kó-ra Kor-yúg-tu, (Kor-) Kor-yúg-tu,* in a circle, in circumference, frq. in measuring; also round about, all round, e.g. to flow, to encompass; *Kor-yúg kún-tu* in the whole circuit, round about.

ཁོ་ལག *Ko-lág* 1. *Cs.*: **bigness,** robustness (Lex. पीरवाह), *Ko-lág-yáṅs-pa* big, prominent limbs; *Sch.*: *Ko-lág čé-ba* a large space. — 2. *Lh.*; **dumpling,** made of *rtsám-pa* and beer; *Ld.*: **pap** of *rtsám-pa* and tea, called *spags* in *C.*

ཁོག *Kog* 1. frq. for *Koṅ(-pa),* **the interior, inside;** v. also *Kóg-pa* and *Kóg-ma.* — 2. for *Kogs, ͺkogs* q.v. — 3. for *ͺgégs-pa.*

ཁོག་པ *Kóg-pa,* sometimes *Kóg-ma, Kog,* the trunk of the body, *ša-Kóg* the body of an animal cut up for food; **ša-Kóg ḍál-če, šig-ce** to cut up a carcass; **Kóg-tu, Kog náṅ-du** within the body.

ཁོག་མ *Kóg-ma C.* **pot,** earthen vessel = *ṗru; Kog-čén* large pot.

ཁོགས *Kogs* **cough** *Med.*, *Kógs-pa* to cough.

ཁོང *Koṅ,* rarely *Kóṅ-pa,* pers. pron. 3d. person, **he, she;** like *Ko* it is of far less frequency in the earlier literature than in the later; at present it is in *W.* used as the respectful word for he, but in *C.*, acc. to Lewin, as plur., = they; *Kóṅ-gi* his, her; pl. *Kóṅ-rnams, Kóṅ-čag, Kóṅ-ťso, Kóṅ-čag-rnams; Koṅ-rán* and *Koṅ-nyid* he himself; *rgyál-po Koṅ-ráṅ yin dgóṅs-nas* the king supposing that he himself was meant *Glr.*

ཁོང་པ *Kóṅ-pa* 1. prov. for *Kóṅ-pa.* — 2. **the inside,** inward parts, prov. *Kóg-pa* (*Cs.* also: the veins); *Kóṅ-du, Kóṅ-na, Kóṅ-nas* adv. and postp. **in, within, from**

within, out of; *k'óṅ-du* (also *k'oṅs-su*) *čúd-pa* or *tsúd-pa*, with or without *sems* (resp. *tugs*) being prefixed 1. **impressed on**, fixed in the mind, thoroughly understood, known. 2. very restless, **uneasy, sorry, anxious** in one's mind; — *k'óṅ-du sdú-ba* to impress on the memory, to learn (by heart) *Glr.*; *k'óṅ-nas snyiṅ p'yúṅ-ba ltar* as if their heart was torn out, *Pth.*; *snyiṅ k'oṅ rús-pai dkyil-nas ysól-ba btab* he prayed from his inmost heart *Thgy.*; *k'óṅ-nas šés-pa, smrá-ba* to know by heart, to say, recite by heart *Cs.* **k'óg-la yid-du med** *W.* I have no recollection of it; *k'óṅ-pai dród-la p'an* it helps against internal heat *Med.*; *k'óṅ-par sóṅ-bai dug bžin-no* it is like a poison that has entered into the internal parts (or the veins) *Thgy.*; **k'óg-paṅk'an-pa**, a bad character *W.*, **k'óg-pa čén-mo** *W.* generosity, magnanimity (?) —

Comp. *k'oṅ-krág*, the blood contained in the veins *Cs.* — *k'óṅ-k'ro (-ba)* **wrath, anger**; *k'óṅ-k'ro spóṅ-ba Mil.* to put away, subdue anger, **zá-ba** *C.* to 'conceive' anger, take a dislike; *k'óṅ-mi-k'ro-ba* quiet, calm, mild *Pth.* — **k'og-t'úg** col. uneasiness, **sorrow, anxiety**; **k'og-t'úg jhé-pa** *C.*, **čó-če** *W.* to be uneasy, anxious. — *k'oṅ-gáṅ* full, filled up in the inside, **solid**, *k'oṅ-stóṅ* **hollow, tubular**. — **k'og-tén, k'og-ḍén**, *W.* grudge, ill-will, **hatred**. — *k'oṅ-tsil* **suet**. — **k'oṅ-lóg** *W.* **cholera**. — **k'og-šiṅ** *W.* 1. **the core** of a tree, heart-wood. 2. **tenon**. — **k'og-šúgs** **a groan, sigh** *W.*, **k'og-šúgs táṅ-če** to sigh, to groan. — **k'og-šúbs-la sil-če** *W.* to read low, softly, whisperingly; **k'og-sil táṅ-če** *W.* to read noiselessly, so as not to be heard. — *k'oṅ-(γ)seṅ* inner caverns, not opening to the daylight; (those of the Rirab are the habitations of the Lhama-yin or Asura).

ཁོངས་ *K'oṅs* 1. sbst. (*k'óṅs-ma Cs.?*) **the middle, the midst**; *gaṅs-k'óṅs-na* in the midst of alpine snows *Mil.*; respecting time: *žág bdún-gyi k'óṅs-su* **within, during**, seven days *Pth.*, *Tar.*; respecting money: *de nyid-kyi k'óṅs-na γnás-so*, (this) is contained, included in that (sum) *Tar.* ༢༢, 15; *k'óṅs-su γtógs-pa Lex.*, *Cs.*: annexed to, united, incorporated with. — 2. adj. **crooked**; *W.*: **k'oṅs ča dug** it is **bent, curved**, e.g. paper by heat, the limbs by the gout; **k'óṅs-kan** *W.*, **k'oṅ-ril** *C.* **crippled**.

ཁོད་ *K'od* I. v. *ˎk'ód-pa* and *ˎgód-pa*. — II. inst. of *ˎk'od*.

ཁོན་པ་ *K'on-pa* **anger, grudge, resentment**; *k'on ˎdzin-pa*, *k'ón-du ˎdzin-pa* to hate, **k'ón-la k'úr-če** *W.* id.; **k'on-gúg-ste dád-če** *W.* ("to sit waiting with hatred") id.; **k'on-bér** *W.*, the sting, the burning of anger or hatred in the soul.

ཁོབ་ *K'ob* 1. fat, heavy, clumsy *Sch.* — 2. sometimes for *ˎk'ob*. — 3. v. *ˎpebs-pa*.

ཁོམ་ *K'om* **wallet, leather trunk** *C.*, *Cs.*: felt or skin bag; *γzims-k'óm Cs.* id. (prob. resp.); *k'om-ˎbóg Cs.* a cloak-bag; more accurately: the cloth in which the trunk is wrapped and carried by the porter.

ཁོམ་པ་ *K'óm-pa Schr.*; to be able, esp. **to be enabled** to do a thing by the absence of external impediments; *k'óm-pa min Cs.*, **k'óm-če mi rag** *W.* I have no time, I cannot do it now; *sdod mi k'om* I cannot sit and wait now *Pth.*; *mid mi k'óm-par* without your having time to swallow it down *Dzl.* ༢༥༠, 17. *mi-k'óm-pa brgyad*, the eight obstacles to happiness, caused by the re-birth in places or situations unfavourable to conversion *Trig.* no. 66. Acc. to *Schr.* the word is also used in that special sense: to be able to carry on a law-suit, to which there are likewise eight obstacles.

ཁོར་མོ་ཡུག་ *K'or-mo-yúg Sch.*, *k'or-yúg*, *k'ór-sa* v. *k'ó-ra*; *k'or-yúg-tu* **continually, incessantly** *Mil.*

ཁོལ་ *K'ol Cs.* = *k'ól-bu*; *k'ól-du p'yúṅ-ba*, **abridgment**, epitome *Cs.*

ཁོལ་པ་ *K'ól-pa* 1. *Cs.* **boiled**. — 2. *Sch.* **boiling, bubbling**, *zaṅs k'ól-pa* a bubbling kettle *Dzl.*

ཁོལ་པོ་ *K'ól-po*, also *k'ol-brán*, **servant**, man-servant, *k'ól-por r)és-su bzúṅ-ba* to take, to hire for a servant *Pth.*; frq. fig. *séms-kyi Kól-por ɣda* (the body) is a servant of the mind *Mil.*; *ɉig-rtén srid-pai Kól-po* a servant of the world i.e. of mammon *Mil.*

ཁོལ་བུ་ *Kól-bu* **a small piece,** *Kól-bu nyúṅ-ₒbru tsam žig kyaṅ ma lus Pth.* not so much as a grain of mustard seed is left.

ཁོལ་མ་ *Kól-ma* 1. *Cs.* 'anything boiled'; perh. more accurately: anything boiling, *ču Kól-ma* **boiling** water; *dúg-mtso Kól-ma* a boiling lake of poison. — 2. *Sch.*: an outlet for the smoke in a roof.

ཁོལ་མོ་ *Kól-mo* 1. **maid-servant** *B.* — 2. a coarse sort of **blanket** usually given to slaves *Schr.* — 3. mowed corn, **a swath** *C.*

ཁོས་ *Kos* v. *gés-pa.*

ཁོས་པ་ *Kós-pa* **wished for,** wanted *Sch.*

ཁྱ་ལེ་ *Kyá-le Cs.*, **Ká-le* W.*, as much as fills the hollow of the hand, **a handful,** e.g. of water.

ཁྱག་པ་ *Kyág-pa* to lift, v. *ₒkyog-pa.*

ཁྱག(ས)་པ་ *Kyág(s)-pa* 1. **frozen; ice.** — 2. **the frost, cold,** *Kyág-ťog-Kar* on the ice *Glr.*; *Kyág-pa ₒKyág-pai bód-yul* 'Tibet frozen up with frost' *Pth.*; **Kyág-la ɉar* (v. *byór-ba*) **soṅ* W.* it has stuck fast by freezing. — **Kyag-žu-ko-kó* Ts.* mud caused by a thaw, **snow-water.** — **Kyág-sran-čan* W.* hardened against the cold. — *Kyag-rúm, Kyag-róm* ice, pieces of ice, floating blocks of ice (also *čab-róm*); cf. *ₒKyag-pa.*

ཁྱད་ *Kyad* 1. **difference, distinction** *B.*, *C.*, *W.* **gaṅ táṅ-na Kyad med* W.* it is no matter which you give me; *ṅá-daṅ-ɉrad-pa dáṅ Kyad-méd-do* it is quite the same as if they came to myself; *séms-la Kyad byuṅ* a difference of opinion arose. — *Kyad-ċos* mark of distinction. — 2. **something excellent, superior,** *bzoi Kyad, bzo-Kyád* an excellent work of art *Glr.*; *bsgrúb-pai Kyad yoṅ* prob.: it shall be instantly performed in the very best manner *Pth.* — *Kyad-nór* the principal or chief wealth *Cs.* — *Kyad-dón* the principal sense *Sch.* — 3. syllable employed to form abstract nouns. A transition to such formations appears in the following sentence: *dkar-nag-čós-kyi če-Kyád blta Mil.* we wish to examine the difference of greatness or worth of the white and the black religion; so also whenever a certain measure is given, and in general, when such abstract nouns are used in a relative sense, as: *mťo-Kyád* **height,** *zab-Kyád* **depth,** *ɉnyug-Kyád* **wealth.** — 4. **part, division,** the same as *Kyád-par* 2; **sa-Kyád* W.* **place,** corresponding exactly to **sa-ča* C.*

Derivatives. **kye'-ťsar-čen** = *ṅó-mťsar-čan* wonderful *C.* — *Kyád-du* adv. especially, particularly, *Kyád-du ₒṗágs-pa* particularly (uncommonly) lofty, sublime *Glr.* *Kyád-par* adv. = *Kyád-du Glr.* 50, 7, and more frq. sbst.: 1. **difference, dissimilarity** *B.* and *C.*, *ṅa daṅ Kyod ɣnyis Kyád-par-če* I and you — that is a great difference *Glr.*; *de daṅ kyád-par-ma-mčis-pai rten* an image not differing from this *Glr.*; *míṅ-gi Kyád-par yin* it is (only) a difference of name *Glr.* — 2. **sort, kind,** *ₒbrás-bui Kyád-par kun* all sorts of fruit; *ri-dvágs-kyi Kyád-par žig* a particular kind of game; perh. also: **division, part,** *yúl-gyi Kyád-par* **province** *Tar.* ༢༠. 14. — 3. = *Kyad* 2. something of superior qualities, an excellent man *Tar.* ༢༠, 7. *Kyád-par-čan* **superior, excellent, capital,** *blá-ma Kyád-par-čan čig Mil.* an excellent spiritual teacher; *Kyád-par-du* adv. **particularly,** chiefly, especially. Rather obscure as to its literal sense, but of frq. use is the phrase *Kyád-du ɣsód-pa, ɣsád-pa,* c. accus. but also dat., **to despise,** e.g. *dmá-la* an inferior, *rgyu-ₒbrás* the doctrine of retribution, *ṅyon-móṅs-pa* trouble etc.

ཁྱབ་ *Kyab* v. *Kyáb-pa.*

ཁྱབ་པ་ *Kyáb-pa* **to fill, penetrate; to embrace, comprise,** c. accus., also dat., *mi-ɣtsáṅ-bas Kyáb-pai sa-ɉnyógs* a place full of dirt *Thgy.*; *ₒbrúm-pa máṅ-pos* full of, quite covered with pustules, pocks *Med.*; *mKris-*

pas filled, impregnated with bile *Med.*; *lus sems dga-bdés ḱyáb-par gyúr-nas* body and soul (filled with) full of joy *Glr.*; *bar ḱyáb-pa* to fill up an intermediate space; **to make** (a country etc.) **full** of light, religion, happiness, frq.; *ťams-čád-la drín-gyis* to embrace all creatures with benevolence; *kún-la ḱyab-pa* in grammar: capable of being joined to any word, comprising all of them, *Glr.*; *ḱyab-čé-ba* comprehensive; used also in the way of censure: everywhere and nowhere, to be met with everywhere *Mil.*; *ḱyab-ydál* or *rdól* comprehensive, extensive. — *ḱyab* seems also to be a sbst. in *ḱyab-čé-ba*, and still more so in *rgya bod yoṅs ḱyáb-tu grágs-pa-la* according to what is spoken in the whole compass of India and Tibet *Tar.* 87.

ཁྱབ་འཇུག་ *ḱyab-ǰúg* **Vishnu**, a Brahmanical divinity, appearing, like Brahma and Shiva, also in Buddhist legends, yet principally known in his quality as *yza-sgra-yčan-ʼdzin* (Râhula), conqueror of the demon that threatens to devour sun and moon; hence *ḱyab-ǰug-yzér Med.*, **ḱyab-ǰúg-gi nad* W.*, **ra-hu-lẹ nẹ* C.*, **epilepsy.**

ཁྱམས་ *ḱyams Cs., Sch.* **yard, court-yard,** *Cs.* also gallery. It is, like *ťsoms*, a space that is to be found in many Tibetan houses, and may be compared to the compluvium of the Romans, being open in the middle, and on the sides generally enclosed by verandas. *Ḱyams* may therefore be called court-yard, when it is on the same level with the ground, (so also perh. *Tar.* 89, 4, reading *ḱyams-su* for *ʼḱyams-su*); but in the upper stories such a construction is unknown in European architecture. *Ḱyams-stód* the upper court-yard, *ḱyams-smád* the lower one; *ḱyams-ťóṅs Cs.*: 'impluvium'.

ཁྱམས་ *ḱyams Cs.*: p. n. = *ḱams*, v. *ḱams* 3.

ཁྱམས་པ་, ཁྱར་པ་, ཁྱལ་པ་ *ḱyáms-pa, ḱyár-pa, ḱyál-pa* v. *ʼḱyáms-pa*, etc.

ཁྱི་ *ḱyi* **dog,** *ḱyi rmug B.* and *C.*; the dog bites, *W.*: barks; **so tab* W.*; bites; **ťam* W.* lays hold of; *ḱyi bós-nas ma brduṅ* proverb: if you call the dog, then you must not beat him *Glr.* — *ḱyi rkaṅ-ynyis Sch.* 'a bastard dog, a cur' (?) — *ḱyi-skád* the barking. — *ḱyi-ḱáṅ* **dog-kennel,** — *ḱyi-gu* **a puppy.** — *ḱyi-rgán* an old dog. — *ḱyi-rṅó* the itch of dogs. — *ḱyi-dám* 'dog's seal', a mark burnt in; **stigma** *C., W.* — *ḱyi-dúg* poison of hydrophobia *Sch.* — *ḱyi-mdúd-pa* the pairing of dogs *Sch.* — *ḱyi-pul* **dog-kennel, dog-house.** — **ḱyi-pal-ǰór* W.* Blitum virgatum. — *ḱyi-spyáṅ W.* **jackal.** — *ḱyi-po* a male dog. — *ḱyi-brú Sch.* a vicious, biting dog. — *ḱyi-sbráṅ* dog's fly. — *ḱyi-mo* a female dog, **bitch.** — *ḱyi-smyón* canine madnes, **hydrophobia** *C., W.*; also mad dog = *ḱyi smyón-pa.* — *ḱyi-rdzi* dog-keeper. — *ḱyi-yžóṅ* trough for dogs and other animals, **manger.** — *ḱyi-šig* **flea.**

ཁྱི་གུ་ *ḱyi-gu* 1. v. *ḱyi.* — 2. *W.* **bud** (of leaves and branches, not of blossoms), **eye** (of a plant).

ཁྱི་ར་ *ḱyi-ra* **chase, hunting,** esp. of single huntsmen, not of a party; stable-stand, cf. *liṅs*; **kyi-ra-la čá-če* W.* to go a hunting, **ḱyi-ra čo-če, gyáb-če, gyúg-če** id.; **ḱyi-ra-la čá-ḱan** hunter, sportsman; *ḱyi-ra-ba B.* and *C.*, **ḱyi-ra-pa* W.* huntsman.

ཁྱི་རོང་ *ḱyi-róṅ* p.n., v. *skyid-gróṅ.*

ཁྱི་ལ་བ་རི་ *ḱyi-la-wa-ri* a sort of treacle made of *seṅ-ldeṅ Wdṅ.*

ཁྱིག་ *ḱyig* v. *ʼḱyig-pa.*

ཁྱིད་ *ḱyid* breadth of the hand with the thumb extended, a span.

ཁྱིམ་ *ḱyim* (*Ssk.* गृह) 1. **house,** not as a building, but as a dwelling-place of man, **a home.** Even when in *Sik.* they speak of **šiṅ-ḱyim, nyúg-ḱyim** a house of wood, of bamboo, the idea of habitation, dwelling-place predominates in these expressions. *ḱyim-na* at home, *ḱyim-du* home (to go home); *ḱyim daṅ ḱyim-na* house for house, each in his house *Tar.* 151. 22; *ḱyim spó-ba* to remove to another place; *ḱyim skyóṅ-ba* to have a household, to gain a livelihood; *Kyim-gyi so-tsis* household, housekeeping, farming; *Kyim-gyi rig-pa* knowledge, experience in housekeeping and farming; *Kyim-med-pa* homeless, without a home; therefore esp. as opp. to the life of a homeless and unmarried priest: *Kyim-gyi byá-ba* or *las*, 1. domestic business, 2. lay-life, worldly life; cf. also many of the compounds. *Kyim-la ˏòn-ba, ɣtóṅ-ba* to get married, to be given in marriage, respecting the female part *Glr., Mil.* — 2. **the signs** of the Zodiac, which is called *Kyím-gyi ˏKór-lo*, viz. *lug* ram, *ɣlaṅ* bull, *ˏKrig-pa* (pairing) twins, *kárkata (Ssk.)* crab, *séṅ-ge* lion, *bú-mo* virgin, *sraṅ* balance, *sdig(-pa)* scorpion, *ɣžu* (bow) archer, *ču-srin* (sea-monster) capricorn, *búm-pa* water-bearer, *nya* fishes. To these 12 signs however the corresponding Tibetan figures are not ༡ to ༡༢, but o to ༡༡, as seems to be the usage in astronomical science. There is moreover a division into 27 'lunar mansions' much in use; v. *rgyu-skár*. — 3. **double-hour**, the time of two hours; or the twelfth part of the time of the apparent daily rotation of the heavens and consequently also of the zodiac, or, as we should say, the time of the passing of a sign of the zodiac through the meridian. — 4. *Cs.:* **halo**, or circle round the sun or moon. — 5. Symbolic numeral: 12.

Comp. and deriv. *Kyim-táb(s)* **husband**, frq.; also wife; *Kyim-táb-la ɣtóṅ-ba* to give in marriage, to give away a woman for a wife; *Kyim-tá b-mo* **wife**, housewife, *Cs.* — *Kyim-bdág* master of the house, **husband**; owner of a house, **citizen**; *Kyim-bdág-ma* fem. — *Kyim-pa* 1. **layman**, 2. *Cs.:* surrounded by a halo (*Kyim* 4); *Kyim-pai ṗyógs-su sbyin-pa* given away to laymen *Dzl.*; *Kyim-par ˏdug* or *ɣnas* he lives as a layman; *ṗyis Kyim-pai tsúl-čan-gyi rnál-ˏbyor-pa* a devout man, who lives outwardly like a layman *Mil.* — *Kyim-pa-pa* **a houseowner, peasant, farmer, husband**; *Kyim-pa-ma* **housewife.** — *Kyim bya* **domestic fowl, cock, hen, poultry** *W., C.* — *Kyim-mi* family of a house, household *Cs.* — *Kyim-tsáṅ* id. — *Kyim-tsér Glr.* 51, 10, usually *Kyim-mtsés, Kyim-mtsés-pa*, fem. *Kyim-mtsés-ma* **neighbour.** — *Kyim-žág, Kyim-zlá, Kyim-ló* 'a zodiacal day, month, year' (?) *Cs.* — *Kyím-sa* earth, **dust**, dirt (in a house), **sweepings** *W.*, **Kyim-sa dú-če, spúṅ-če* to sweep (a floor), to sweep together.

ཁྱིམ་ཉ་ *Kyim-nya Sch.:* **whale** (if at all correct, it must be taken as mythological signification, no Tibetan having ever known of the existence of real whales).

ཁྱུ་ *Kyu, Kyú-bo Cs., Kyú-mo Pth.* **flock, herd,** *lúg-Kyu* a flock of sheep, *mdzó-mo-Kyu* a herd of bastard cows, *ɣnág-Kyu* of horned cattle; *Kyu skóṅ-ba* to keep, tend a flock or herd; **company, band, gang, troop,** *mi-Kyu Cs.* a company of men, *bú-mo-Kyu* a bevy of girls, *dmag-Kyú* a troop of soldiers; *Kyú-nas ˏbúd-pa* to exclude from the company *Pth., C.*; *Kyu-sná ˏdrén-pa* to go before, to take the lead of a troop, a flock *Mil.*; *Kyu-mčóg* **bell-wether;** also the most distinguished amongst a number of men, the first, **chief, head** *Pth., Kyu-mčóg-ma* fem.; *Kyu tságs-pa* vb.n., *Sch.* to collect, to gather in flocks.

ཁྲུ་ *Kyu Sch.* 'ell', prob. incor. for *Kru.*

ཁྱུ་བྱུག་ *Kyu-byúg* acc. to *Lex.* = *ku-hú.*

ཁྱུག་ *Kyug* v. *ˏKyúg-pa.*

ཁྱུང་ *Kyuṅ (Sch.* also *Kyúṅ-mo)* the Garuda bird, a mythical bird, chief of the feathered race. *Kyúṅ-šog-čan* = *ṗyag-rdór.*

ཁྱུང་དཔྱད་ *Kyuṅ-dpyad* a small round **basket** of reed *Cs.*; *Kyuṅ-ril* is said to be in *C.* a large cylindrical basket, the same as *kun-dúm Ld.*, v. *rkón-pa.*

ཁྱུང་སྡེར་ *Kyuṅ-sdér* ('Garuda claw') *Med., Cs.:* n. of a medicinal root, pseudo-zedoary; *Kyuṅ-rgód Med.* id (?).

ཁྱུད་ *Kyud* v. *ˏKyúd-pa.*

ཁྱུད་མོ་ *Kyúd-mo* **rim** of a vessel *Sch.*

ཁྱུར་མིད་པ་ *ḱyur-mid-pa* **to swallow** *Med.*; *ḱyur-mid-du sóṅ-ste* suffering himself to be swallowed (from the story of an Indian idol) *Pth.*

ཁྱུས་ *ḱyus* wall-side *Ts.* (?)

ཁྱེ་ *ḱye* 1. for *ḱyeu Mil.* — 2. for *ḱe* q.v.; *ḱyé-mo* v. *ḱe.*

ཁྱེ་མ་ *ḱyé-ma* n. of a disease *Med.*

ཁྱེའུ་ *ḱyeu* (diminutive of *ḱyó-bo?*) 1. **male child, infant boy.** 2. **youth, adolescent** *B.*

ཁྱེད་ *ḱyed* pers. pron. 2nd. person, **thou,** and particularly in the plur. **you,** in *B.* eleg., in addressing superiors, but also used by superiors in speaking to inferiors, and even contemptuously: *ḱyed ltá-bui md-rabs* such vulgar, mean people, as ye are *Dzl.* — *ḱyéd-kyi* thy, your. — *ḱyed-ráṅ* (*kyed-nyíd* seems to be little used) thou thyself, you yourself; plur. particularly expressed: *ḱyéd-ċag, ḱyéd-rnams, ḱyed-ťso; dge-ťsúl ḱyéd ɣnyis* you two Getsuls *Glr.*; *ḱyed ɣsúm-po* you three (a mother speaking to her sons) *Glr.*; *ḱyéd-ċág* you, when speaking to one person *Glr.*, = *nyid-ċag.*

ཁྱེད་ *ḱyed* 1. = *ḱyid W.* 2. v. *˳ḱyéd-pa.*

ཁྱེན་ཏི་ *ḱyén-ti Pur.* **he, she,** v. *ḱún-ti.*

ཁྱེབས་ *ḱyebs* v. *ḱebs.*

ཁྱེམ་ *ḱyem* (*Sch.* also *ḱem*) **a shovel,** *W.*: **kyem daṅ ṗáṅ-ċe** to shovel away, to remove with a shovel; *ḱyém-gyi ˳dáb-ma* the blade of a shovel, *yú-ba* the handle of it *Cs.* — *gru-ḱyém, ču-kyém W.* **oar,** *lċags-ḱyém* **spade;** *me-ḱyém* fire-shovel; *wa-ḱyém* a scoop, hollow gutter-shaped shovel *Cs.*; *ḱyém-bu* spoon *Cs.*

ཁྱེར་ *ḱyer* v. *˳ḱyé-ba*; *ḱyér-so* v. *˳ḱyer-so.*

ཁྱོ་ *ḱyo B.* frq., also *ḱyó-po Pth.* 1. **man** (seldom). 2. **husband,** *ḱyo byéd-pa* ('to act a husband' cf. *byed-pa* I. 1) to take a wife; *ḱyod ṅai ḱyo mi byéd-na* if you do not marry me *Dzl.* — *ḱyo-méd* **single, unmarried.** — *kyó-mo* wife *Cs.* — *ḱyo-šúg* husband and wife, married couple; *ḱyo-šúg ɣnyís grógs-nas soṅ* these two married people went together; *ḱyo-šúg mdzá-ba-rnams* a loving couple; *ḱyim-bdag ḱyo-šúg ɣnyis* the citizen with his wife; *ɣsér-lha ḱyo-šúg ɣnyis* about the same as: Mr. and Mrs. Serlha; *ḱyo-šúg-tu sdú-ba* to join a couple in marriage *Dzl.*

ཁྱོ་ག་ *ḱyó-ga* 1. **man** emphatically, as: *skyés-bu ṅa hór-pa yaṅ ḱyó-ga yin* we Turks are men, too; **hero,** *ḱyó-ga-pa* id. — 3. **heroic deed, exploit.**

ཁྱོག་པོ་ *ḱyóg-po* **crooked, curved, bent;** *Cs.* also cunning.

ཁྱོག་ཐོང་ *ḱyog-ťóṅ* (v. *ḱyó-ga* and *ťoṅ*) *W.* **young man, youth.**

ཁྱོགས་ *ḱyogs* **litter, bier** *Pth.*, **palanquin** *Cs.* also scaffold (?) *Cs.*

ཁྱོང་ *ḱyoṅ* v. *ḱyóṅ-ba.*

ཁྱོད་ *ḱyod* pers. pron. 2nd. person sing. and plur., **thou, you;** *ḱyod-kyi* thy, thine, your; if plurality is to be especially expressed, it is done by adding *ċag*: *ḱyód-ċag Mil.*; occasionally also *ḱyód-rnams*, cf. *ḱyed*; *ḱyod-ráṅ* 1. thou thyself, you yourself. 2. thou, you (*W. *ḱyo-ráṅ**).

ཁྱོན་ *ḱyon* **size, extension, width, circumference, area, height** e.g. of Dzambuling *Dzl.*, of the Sumeru *Glr.*, of the lunar mansions or the zodiac *Glr.*; *ḱyon-yáṅs-pa* a wide extent, *ḱyoṅ-yáṅs sa-ɣži* all the wide world (earth); *ḱyon-sdóm Cs.* 1. narrow-extent. 2. sum, contents. — *ḱyón-nas* **thoroughly,** *ḱyón-nas mi sdíg-ċan* thoroughly a sinner; *ḱyón-nas med* not at all *C.*

ཁྱོམ་ཁྱོམ་ *ḱyom-ḱyóm* 1. **oblique, awry,** irregularly shaped.—2. v. *˳ḱyóm-pa.*

ཁྱོར་ *ḱyor* (*Cs. ḱyór-pa*) as much as fills the hollow of the hand, **a handful,** cf. *skyor*; *ḱyor gaṅ, ḱyor re* one handful, *ḱyor do* two handfuls.

ཁྱོལ་བ་ *ḱyól-ba* v. *˳ḱyól-ba*; *ḱyós-ma C.* = *skyós-ma, skyás-ma.*

ཁྲ་ *ḱra* 1. a small bird of prey, **sparrow-hawk, falcon,** used for hunting, also *bya-ḱrá*; *ḱra-žúr Sch.*: a species of eagles; *ḱrá-pa* falconer. — 2. v. the following article.

ཁྲ་བོ་ *K̔rá-bo* perh. also *k̔rá-mo* **piebald,** two-coloured, (not many-coloured, which is *bkrá-ba); rgya-stág-k̔rá-bo* the streaked Indian tiger *Mil.; *ṭa-ṭá* C.* id.; **ṭa-wo-pi-wo, ṭa-si-pi-si* W.* id. (spelling uncertain); *nag-k̔rá* black-spotted, so that black is the predominating colour of the whole; *dmar-k̔rá* red-spotted, red being the predominating colour. — The significations of the various compounds of *k̔ra* have all a reference to the peculiar effect produced on the eye by the blending of two or more colours together, especially when seen from a distance; so: *k̔ra-čam-mé Glr.* is said of a rainbow-tinted meteor, *k̔ra-lam-mé Mil.*, (or *lham-mé,)* of a similar phenomenon, *k̔ra-čem-čém Pth.* of a flight of birds; **ṭa-čám-se, ṭa-čem-mé, ṭa-čém-se* C., *čam-ṭá-ṭiṅ-ṅé* Ld., *ṭa-šig-ge' ṭa-ₒčig-ge, ṭa-róg-ge* C.*, — all these seem to be of nearly the same import. — These compounds have also assumed the character of an adverb, signifying, **together, altogether,** *k̔ra-me-ré Mil.* id.

ཁྲ་མ་ *K̔rá-ma* 1. *Cs.* **register, index.** — 2. *C.* **judicial decree.** — 3. a species of grain, acc. to *Wdṅ.* = *mgyogs-nás* a kind of barley growing and ripening within 60 days; v. *nas.*

ཁྲག་ *K̔rag* (in *Bal.* still pronounced **k̔rag** elsewhere **ṭag*), Cs.:* resp. *sku-mtsal*, **blood;** **ṅal-ṭág, žaṅ-ṭág* W.* vulg. blood discharged by menstruation, from which, acc. to some authorities, **paṅ-ṭág** blood of the childbed is to be distinguished; *γzuṅ-k̔rág* healthy, nourishing blood *Cs.; nad-k̔rág* bad blood *Cs.: k̔rag ₒdón-pa, W. *tón-če**, to bleed a person; *γtár-ba* id.; *k̔rag γčód-pa* to stop, to stanch the blood; *k̔rag čád-pa* vb. n. to cease to bleed, cessation of bleeding; **nyiṅ-ṭág ₒk̔ól-la rag* W.* I feel my blood boiling, e.g. from ascending a steep hill; *k̔rag ₑdzág-pa* menstruation (the plain undisguised expression): *k̔rag čág-pa* clotted blood, gore *Cs.; k̔rag-šas-čé-ba* plethoric *Med.*

Comp. *k̔rag-ₒk̔rúgs Sch.:* agitation, flutter, orgasm of the blood. — *k̔rág-čan* bloody, e.g. *ral-gri.* — *k̔rag-γčód* n. of a medicinal herb *Med., k̔rag-čags-rtá* a 'blood-bred' horse, i.e. a real horse, opp. to a metaphysical one *Mil.* — *k̔rag-ₑt̔úṅ* a class of terrifying deities *Thgr.* — **ṭág-tuṅ-bu* W.* **leech.** — *k̔rag-γzér W.* rheumatic pain (?) — *k̔rag-ró* clotted blood (?) *Med.* — *k̔rag-liṅ* a clot of blood. — *k̔rag-šór* hemorrhage, bloody flux (?) *Med.*

ཁྲག་ཁྲིག་ *K̔rag-k̔rig* one hundred thousand million, an indefinitely large number *Cs.;* acc. to *Lex.* = प्रयुत one million, cf. *dkrigs-pa.*

ཁྲག་ཁྲུག་ *K̔rag-k̔rúg Cs.* **complicate, confused;** *Zam.:* like a troop of fighting men, or like the loose leaves of a book, when out of order.

ཁྲག་ཁྲོག་ *K̔rag-k̔róg Lt.?*

ཁྲང་ *K̔raṅ* v. *mk̔raṅ.*

ཁྲད་པ་ *K̔rád-pa Cs.* stretched out; *k̔rád-por sdód-pa* to sit (with the legs) stretched out (?). *k̔rád-por skyé-ba Wdṅ.* a botanical term applied to the leaves of plants.

ཁྲབ་ *K̔rab* shield, buckler; coat of mail, scales *Sch.;* acc. to oral communication the word in the first instance denotes **scale** (scale of a fish), and secondly **coat of mail**; consequently *k̔ráb-čan* 1. scaled, scaly. 2. mailed, armed with a coat of mail; *k̔ráb-mk̔an* armourer *Glr.*

ཁྲབ་ཁྲབ་ *K̔rab-k̔ráb* 1. a weeper, one that sheds tears on every occasion *Sch.* — 2. *Mil.* 92, 4?

ཁྲམ་ཁ་ *K̔rám-k̔a* **a cut, a notch** (in wood), lines cut into wood so as to cross one another, as an ornament; *k̔rám-šiṅ* a club-like implement, carved in the manner just mentioned, representing the attribute of a god. *nyag-k̔rám* a notch.

ཁྲམ་པ་ *K̔rám-pa* I. *C.:* **a liar,** *slu-bar byéd-pai k̔rám-pa Pth.; k̔rám-ma* fem. *Cs.; k̔a-k̔rám* a lie *Mil.; k̔rám-sems-čan* **lying, mendacious** *Mil.* — II *W.:* 1. **lively, brisk, quick,** like boys, kids etc. (the contrary of *γlén-pa* slow, indolent, apathetic); **ṭám-pa čo* W.* a wish of good speed, addressed to one going on a journey, such as: good success! may all go well! — 2. **modest,** attentive to the wishes of others.

ཁྲལ་ *k̔ral (Lex.* दण्ड punishment) 1. **punishment, chastisement** for sins, **visitation;** in this sense the word is said to be used still, but much more frq. it signifies 2. **tax, tribute, duty,** service to be performed to a higher master; *k̔ral sdú-ba* to collect taxes, *ȝjál-ba, skór-ba* to pay taxes, *bkál-ba* to impose taxes; *dṅúl-kral* money-tax, tax to be paid in money, *ₒbrú-k̔ral* corn-tax, tribute paid in corn, *til-már-k̔ral* tax, tribute to be paid in sesame-oil.

ཁྲི་ *k̔ri (Cs. k̔ri-ma), k̔ri-k̔rág, k̔ri-ťsó* **ten thousand,** a myriad, *k̔ri p̔yed daṅ ȝnyis* 15 000; *nyi-k̔ri* 20 000; *bži-k̔ri* 40 000; *brgyad-k̔ri bži-stóṅ* 84 000, a number frq. occurring in legends.

ཁྲི་ *k̔ri,* also *k̔riu,* seldom *k̔rí-bo,* resp. *bžúgs-k̔ri,* **seat, chair; throne; couch; frame,** sawing-jack, trestle etc.; **gya-ṭ́i** an Indian (Anglo-Indian, European) chair; *čós-k̔ri* a professorial chair, pulpit *Pth.*, reading-desk, table for books, school-table; **nyé-ṭ́i** (v. *snyé-ba*) a contrivance to rest the head on when sleeping on the ground *W. nyál-k̔ri,* resp. *ȝzím-k̔ri,* bed-stead; *sén-ge-k̔ri* throne; *k̔ri-la bskó-ba* to raise on the throne; *k̔ri-la ₒk̔ód-pa* to preside, to hold the chair. — As the Tibetans generally sit on the bare ground, or on mats, or carpets, chairs are rather articles of luxury.

Comp. and deriv. *k̔ri-ȝdúgs* po. **the sun.** — *k̔ri-pa Cs.* **a chairman;** one sitting on a throne. — *k̔ri-ȝp̔áṅ* 1. *Cs.:* the height of a chair, a high chair. — 2. *mčod-rtén-gyi k̔ri-ȝp̔áṅ* the same as *baṅ-rim.* — *k̔ri-mún* or *món Pth., Tar.,* **prison, dungeon.** — **ṭ́i-šiṅ, ṭ́iu-šiṅ**, the common, plain word for chair.

ཁྲི་ལེ་བ་ *k̔ri-le-ba* **fear** *C.* (?)

ཁྲིག་ཁྲིག་ *k̔rig-k̔rig* 1. *so k̔rig-k̔rig byéd-pa* to gnash, grind the teeth *Mil.*; *ȝzúgs-po* to shiver, shake with cold, terror, rage *Mil.* — 2. col. for *tig-tig.*

ཁྲིགས་ *k̔rigs* **plentiful, abundant** *Sch.*; *za-ₒóg k̔rigs-se* silk-fabrics, silks, in abundance *Mil.*; *k̔rigs-se gaṅ* quite full *Sch.*; *k̔rigs-se byéd-pa* to treat, to entertain plentifully *Sch.*

ཁྲིད་, འཁྲིད་ *k̔rid, ₒk̔rid,* **instruction, teaching;** *k̔rid ₒdébs-pa* to give instruction, to instruct, *k̔rid-pas-čog* I am willing to give you instruction, you may have lessons with me *Mil.*; *k̔rid bšád-pa* to give instruction, to make admonitory speeches, to give parenetical lectures; *k̔rid záb-po* thorough instruction; *slu-k̔rid* instruction to an evil purpose, seduction, v. *slú-ba*; *sna-k̔rid Lex.* guide, leader. — *k̔rid-mk̔an* col. teacher. — *k̔rid-p̔rúg* scholar, pupil. — *k̔rid-pa* v. *ₒk̔rid-pa.*

ཁྲིམས་ *k̔rims* 1. **right,** not in the abstract sense in which the word is generally understood with us, but in more or less concrete applications, such as administration of justice, law, judgment, sometimes also implying **custom, usage, duty.** Accordingly *rgyál-po,* or *btsún-po k̔rims-méd* means an unjust king, an unprincipled priest or ecclesiastic; *k̔rims bžin-du, k̔rims daṅ mt̔un-par* conscientiously, justly; in conformity with custom, duty, law; *čos-k̔rims* religious right, coming nearest to our abstract right; when, for instance, in *Glr.* king Sroṅ-btsan-sgam-po says: *rgyál-k̔rims čós-k̔rims-su bsgyur* I have changed the right of a king into that of religion, he means to say: I have subjected my own absolute will to the higher principle of universal right. A somewhat different sense conveys *Glr.* 97, 4: *čós-k̔rims ȝjig-pai gros byas* they conspired to extirpate the religious principle of administration. — 2. **law,** *dgé-ba bču daṅ ldán-pai k̔rims* a general law, founded upon the ten virtues *Glr.*; *des čós-k̔rims daṅ rgyál-k̔rims ȝnyis ȝtán-la p̔ab,* he regulated the spiritual and secular law *Glr.* 97, 1.; *bka-k̔rims* resp. law, as a collection of precepts, **decree, commandment;** *k̔rims čá-ba* to enact a law, to publish a decree, frq.; *k̔rims sgróg-pa* to proclaim an edict; *mtó-ba k'rims-kyis ɣnon* he limited the power of the nobility by laws *Glr.*, *k'rims-yig* code of law *C.*; *k'rims* also a single **precept, rule, commandment** *Dzl.*; *Burn.* I, 630. — 3. **administration of justice,** *čós-kyi k'rims* the ecclesiastical, *dpón-gyi k'rims* the secular civil, exercised by the *k'rims-dpon; lugs ɣnyis-kyi k'rims* a twofold jurisdiction, a combination of the ecclesiastical and secular administration of justice (as it existed among the Jews); *k'rims srúṅ-ba* to observe, to act according to right, custom, duty; also to exercise jurisdiction, to govern, to reign; to bridle, to keep in check *Glr.* 95. 9.; *k'rims byéd-pa* id. ni f. — *tsúl-k'rims* a spiritual precept or duty; also a frequent man's name. — 4. **action, lawsuit,** *W.* also **ṭim-šágs** or only **šags; gaṅ žig ṭim-si ṗi-la* W.* for the sake of some law-suit, **ṭim táṅ-če** to sit in judgment, to try, to hear causes; **ṭim čǒ-pa* C.* = **ṭim táṅ-če* W.*, means also to pass sentence, to punish, **ṭim ḍág-po tóṅ-wa** to inflict a heavy punishment; *mi-la k'rims-bčad ṗog* he incurs, suffers punishment *Pth.*; **ṭim žú-če* W.* to go to law, to commence an action; **ṭim žú-k'an* W.* plaintiff; **ṭim táṅ-k'an* W.* magistrate, judge; *k'rims-dpon B., C., W.*, superior judge, chief-justice; **ṭim-kyi ḍág-po* C. id.*; *k'rims-ɣyóg* apparitor, beadle *Cs.*; *k'rims-pa* lawyer, advocate *Cs.* (seems to be little used); *k'rims-k'an* court, court of justice, tribunal; *k'rims-ra* id.; place of execution. — 5. **use, custom, usage** — that power to which people in general show the readiest obedience, and which in every sphere of life forms the greatest obstacle to reforms and improvements.

ཁྲིལ་ *k'ril* v. *ʼk'ril.*

ཁྲིས་ *k'ris? k'ris-ǰágs* **peace,** v. *ǰags.*

ཁྲུ་ *k'ru* (*k'rú-ma Cs.*) **cubit,** a measure of eighteen inches, from the elbow to the extremity of the middle finger. The average height of a man is assumed to be four cubits, that of a short man three. — *k'ru ʼǰál-ba* to measure with a cubit measure *Cs.*

ཁྲུ་བ་ *k'rú-ba* sometimes for *ʼk'ru-ba.*

ཁྲུ་གཟར་ *k'ru-ɣzár* a kind of **stew-pan** *Sch.*

ཁྲུ་སློག་ *k'ru-slóg* a pit filled with corn (?) *Sch.*; in *Mil. k'ru-slóg-pa* stands for digging, breaking up the soil, gardening.

ཁྲུང་ཁྲུང་ *k'ruṅ-k'ruṅ* (*Ssk.* क्रौञ्च) **crane,** Grus cinerea.

ཁྲུན་ *k'run* **height, length, extension** *Lex.*, *Cs.*

ཁྲུལ་ *k'rul* 1. *k'rul ɣtoṅ-ba* to let fall, to **drop** (several things at intervals), *mči-ma* tears *Mil.* — 2. **da-ṭúl* W.* **intercalary month.**

ཁྲུལ་པོ་ *k'rúl-po C.* 1. **cheerful, merry.** — 2. **fornicator.**

ཁྲུལ་མ་ *k'rúl-ma* 1. *W. *k'ú-wa ṭúl-ma** crooked handle, **crank** (spelling uncertain). — 2. *C.* **a whore.**

ཁྲུམ་ཁྲུམ་ *k'rum-k'rúm*, *Sch.*: *k'rum-k'rúm byéd-pa*, *Lt.*: *k'rum-k'rúm brdúṅ-ba* **to pound** in a mortar.

ཁྲུམས་སྟོད་ *k'rums-stód*, and *-smád*, two Nakshatras, v. *rgyu-skár* ༢༥.

ཁྲུས་ *k'rus* 1. pf. of *ʼk'ru-ba.* — 2. sbst. **bath, washing, ablution**; *k'rús-k'u*, water for bathing, washing or rinsing; dish-water; *k'rus byéd-pa* to bathe, to use baths *Dzl.*; *k'rús-la ʼgró-ba* to go to bathe *Dzl.*; *k'rus ɣsól-ba* resp. to take a bath *Glr.*, also to administer a bath to another (cf. *ɣsól-ba*) *Glr.*, *Pth.*; esp. as a religious ceremony, consisting in the sprinkling with water, and performed, when a new-born infant receives a name, when a person enters into a religious order, or in diseases and on various other occasions (cf. *Schl. Buddh.* p. 239, where the word is spelled *bkrus*). Therefore 3. **baptism,** and *k'rus ɣsol-ba* **to baptize** *Chr. R.* and *P.* — *k'rús-kyi rdziṅ*, pond, pool for bathing; *k'rus-k'áṅ* bathing-room or house; *k'rus-sdér* basin, washing-bowl *Sch.*; *k'rus-búm* sacred watering-pot; *k'rus-ɣžóṅ* bathing-tub *Sch.*; *k'rus-ɣdér* bathing-water *Sch.*, but in *Lt.* this word relates to a certain medical procedure or method of curing.

ཁྲེ་ *k̔re (Ssk.* प्रियङ्गु) **millet,** *k̔re-čáṅ* Murwa-beer *Sik.*, v. *Hook. Himal. Journ.*

ཁྲེ་ཚེ་ *k̔re-tsé* Chinese **vermicelli** *C. (*ṭ̔e-tse*)*.

ཁྲེགས་པ་ *k̔régs-pa* v. *mk̔régs-pa.*

ཁྲེལ་ *k̔rel,* resp. *t̔ugs-k̔rél* 1. **shame, shamefacedness, bashfulness, modesty;** **ṭ̔el káb-če* W.* v. *gébs-pa.* — 2. **piety,** esp. *W.* — 3. *C.* **disgust, aversion.**

Comp. and deriv. — *k̔rel-gád* a scornful laughter. — *k̔rél-čan Cs.* bashful, timid; *W.* **pious, faithful, conscientious.** — *k̔rel-ltás, k̔rel-ltos,* dread of wicked actions; *k̔rel-γdoṅ* (lit. a face capable of shame) id. — **ṭ̔él-dad-čan, ṭ̔él-₀dod-čan* W.* fond of making others ashamed. — *k̔rel-ldán* = *k̔rél-čan.* — *k̔rél-ba* vb. to make or to be ashamed, **ṭ̔el soṅ** he was ashamed, **ṭ̔él-če mi yoṅ* W.* he is not put to shame; *C.* also: to get into a passion; sbst. shame, *k̔rél-ba daṅ ṅó-ts̔a-ba med* he has no shame nor dread *Dzl.*, **ṭ̔él-wa yod* W.* it is a shame. — *k̔rel-méd (-pa), W. *k̔rel-méd- (k̔an)* shameless, insolent. — **ṭ̔él-₀o** object of disgust, *C.* — *k̔rél-yod* **chastity, modesty, decency,** *k̔rél-yod-pa* chaste etc., *k̔rél-yod-par byéd-pa* to behave chastely etc. — *k̔rel-šór* = *k̔rel-méd.*

ཁྲེས་པོ་ *k̔rés-po Thgy.* **load, burden,** = *k̔ur.*

ཁྲོ་ *k̔ro* 1. a kind of **bronze,** of about the same quality and worth as *₀k̔ár-ba,* but inferior to *li,* q.v.; *k̔ró-ču* liquid, melted bronze; *k̔ró-čus sdóm-pa* to fill up joints, grooves etc. with melted bronze, to solder *Glr.* — 2. **kettle** *Schr.*

ཁྲོ་པ་ *k̔ró-pa W.* for *k̔rod.*

ཁྲོ་བ་ *k̔ro-ba* 1. **anger, wrath,** (cf. *₀k̔ró-ba* vb.) frq; *k̔óṅ-k̔ró-ba* inward anger *Thgy.* — 2. **angry, wrathful** *Cs.; k̔ró-bar byéd-pa, ₀gyúr-ba* to be, to grow angry *Cs.; k̔ró-bo,* fem. *k̔ró-mo* angry, fierce, ferocious, e.g. *γčan-γzán* a ferocious beast; esp. applied to the 54 (or 60) deities of anger and terror (भैरव), e.g. *k̔ró-ba-čén-po* = *γšin-rje* the ruler of hades; **ṭ̔o-túm-po** furious with rage, raging with anger *C.*: *k̔ro-γnyér* distortion of the face by anger; *k̔ró-ba-ma, k̔ró-ba-čan* she whose face is wrinkled with anger, n. of a goddess *Glr.* 17, 12. — **ṭ̔o-ṭ̔á* W.* **dissatisfaction, grumbling.** — *k̔ro-món Sch.* prison (perh. *k̔ri-món).* — *k̔ro-žál* an angry, frowning countenance *Glr.*

ཁྲོག་ *k̔rog?* — *k̔rog brgyáb-pa* to drink hastily, to gulp down *Glr.; k̔rog-k̔rog* plump! the sound caused by something falling heavily on the ground *W.* — *k̔rog-smán* the raw, unprepared substance of a medicine *Sch.*

ཁྲོག་པོ་ *k̔róg-po* botanical term, used of leaves standing round the stem scattered or alternately.

ཁྲོང་ངེ་ *k̔roṅ-ṅé* **upright, straight, erect,** (cf. *kroṅ,) Glr., Mil.*

ཁྲོང་པོ་ *k̔róṅ-po, *ṭ̔óṅ-po* Ts.* **close-fisted, stingy.**

ཁྲོད་(པ་) *k̔ród (-pa), W. *ṭ̔ó (-pa)** **crowd, assemblage, mass, multitude;** *mi-k̔ród* a troop, crowd of men, *ri-k̔ród* an assemblage (mass) of mountains; *rtsva-k̔ród* a heap, stack, rick of hay; *nags-k̔ród* a dense forest, *mun-k̔ród* thick darkness; *dur-k̔ród* cemetery where the corpses are cut into pieces for the birds of prey; *dei k̔ród-du lha-γčig ₀jóg-pas* placing the princess among their (the girls') company *Glr.*; in *W.* **ṭ̔ó-pai náṅ-na** and **náṅ-du** c. genit. is the usual expression for **among.**

ཁྲོན་ *k̔ron* **claw, fang;** *k̔rón-kyis rkó-bai sde* the class of the gallinaceous birds *S.g.*

ཁྲོན་པ་ *k̔rón-pa* 1. **well, spring.** — 2. *Lh.:* a wooden **water kennel;** *k̔rón-bu* a little well; also n. of a medicinal herb, a purgative against bilious complaints *Med. k̔ron-rágs* enclosure of a well *Sch.*

ཁྲོམ་ *k̔rom* 1. **market-place, market-street, bazar;** *k̔rom skór-ba* to wander, to ride round the market *Glr.*, to ramble through; *γsaṅ-sṅágs króm-du klog* secret spells (magic formulas) are read in the market (a crime and sacrilege in the eyes of a Buddhist). — 2. **crowd of people,** multitude of persons; *krom-čén* a great crowd; *tsógs-pai krŏm-rnams* the assembled crowd *Pth.*; *p'o-krŏm* a multitude of men; *rgyal-krŏm* prob. an assembly, a gathering of kings *Mil.*; *krom dmar-nág ˬkyil-ba* a motley crowd, throng of people *Pth.*

Comp. — *krŏm-čén (po) Thgr.* chief market-place, principal street *Cs.* — *krŏm-dpon* overseer, police-officer who is charged with the supervision of the market. — *krŏm-skor-ma* harlot, strumpet *Cs.*

ཁྲོམ་པོ་ *krŏm-po Glr.*, n. of a province (?), *krŏm-po-pa* an inhabitant of it.

ཁྲོམ་མེ་ *krom-mé* sparkling, glittering, *zil-pa krom-mé* a sparkling dew-drop *Pth.*

ཁྲོམས་ *kroms* v. *ˬgrém-pa.*

ཁྲོལ་ *krol* 1. v. *ˬkról-ba* and *ˬgról-ba.* — 2. **a sound;** *król-gyis soṅ Glr.* (the ring) slid sounding (across the azure-floor); *krol-dóṅ* is said to denote a large hand-bell, and *krol-lóg* the same as *krog-króg W.* — Cf. *ˬkról-ba.* — 3. kettle (?) v. *lčags.*

ཁྲོལ་ཁྲོལ་ *krol-król* adj 1. **bright, shining,** = *król-po.* — 2. *krol-król byéd-pa Glr.*, **mig ṭol-lé ṭol-lé tá-wa** *C.* to stare, *la,* at.

ཁྲོལ་ཆ་ *król-ča* the act of forgiving, pardon *Sch.*

ཁྲོལ་པོ་ *król-po.* 1. **sparkling, glistening, dazzling,** e. g. water when the sun shines upon it; **'od ṭól-po** *W.* brightness, splendour. — 2. **distinct, intelligible,** **(s)pé-ra ṭól-po zer mi še(s)** *W.* he cannot speak distinctly.

ཁྲོལ་མོ་ *król-mo W.* **brittle, fragile,** opp. to *mnyén-po.*

ཁྲོལ་ཚགས་ *krol-tságs Lex., Cs.* **a sieve.**

ཁྲོས་པ་ *krós-pa* v. *ˬkró-ba.*

མཁན་ *mkan,* an affix to substantives and verbal roots, denoting 1. one who knows a thing thoroughly, making a trade or profession of it, *sá-mkan* one who knows the country, the road, a guide, a pilot (*Dzl.* ༢༡༥, 7); *lám-mkan* id. *Mil.*; *šiṅ-mkan,* worker in wood, carpenter, joiner etc. — 2. affixed to a verbal root, it is often (at least in later literature) equivalent to the periphrastic participle, signifying: he who in any special case performs an action; so *ˬdógs-mkan Glr.*, one who is binding, fastening; also with an objective case: *ṅai bú-mo ˬdód-mkan Glr.* such as are courting my daughter; *bsád-mkan* the man having killed, the murderer. — 3. In colloquial language, esp. in *W.*, it has on account of its more significant form entirely displaced the proper participle termination in *pa:* **dúṅ-ma kyer-kan-ni mi** *W.* the men carrying the beam; contrary to its original signification, it is even used in a passive sense: **sád-kan-ni lug** *W.* the slaughtered sheep.

མཁན་པོ་ *mkán-po (Ssk.* उपाध्याय, पण्डित) a clerical teacher, **professor,** doctor of divinity, principal of a great monastery, **abbot,** who, as such, is endowed with the *mkan-rgyúd,* or spiritual gifts, handed down from Buddha himself by transmission, viz. *dbaṅ, luṅ, krid;* next to him comes the *slób-dpon,* or professor in ordinary. *mkán-po tón-mi sámbho-ṭa* Dr. Thon-mi Sambhoṭa; *mkán-mo* **mistress, instructress** *Cs.*: *mkán-bu* **pupil, scholar** *Tar.*; *mkan-čén* a great Doctor, a head-master; *mkan-slób* for *mkán-po daṅ slób-dpon,* e.g. *blá-ma mkan-slób-kyi bka* the words of the Lamas, abbots and masters; also for *mkán-po daṅ slób-ma Glr.* 100, 4. — *mkan-rábs* the series or succession of the abbots in the great monasteries *Cs.* — *mkan-rim* the respective prospects of being elected abbot, as depending on the different ranks of the expectant individuals.

མཁའ་ *mka (Ssk.* ख) 1. **heaven, heavens,** gen. *nam-mka; mká-la* in the heavens, *mká-la p'úr-ba, rgyú-ba, ldiṅ-ba* to fly, wander, soar, in the air. — 2. **ether,** as the fifth element. — 3. symb. num.: **cipher, naught.**

Comp. — *mka-klóṅ, mka-kyáb, mka-dbyíṅs* the whole compass or extent of the heavens *Cs.* — *mk'a-ₒgró-ma*, in *Mil.* gen. *mk'a-ṗro-ma*, *Ssk.* डाकिनी, fabulous beings of more modern legends, 'wise' women of supernatural powers, sometimes represented like angels, at other times like fairies or witches. — *mk'a-mnyám Lex.* like the heavens, infinite. — *mk'a-ldiṅ* the sky-soarer, the bird Garuda, v. *k'yuṅ.* — *mk'a-spyód* wanderings through heaven *Tar.* 112, 4, also: enjoyment of heaven, enjoying or inhabiting heaven; *mk'a-spyód-du γšégs-pa* to go to heaven, to die *Mil.*

མཁར་ *mk'ar* 1. resp. *sku-mk'ár. Glr.*, **castle,** nobleman's seat or mansion, manor-house, frq.; **citadel, fort** *Pth.*; **house** in general *Mil.* — 2. termin. case of *mk'a.*

Comp. — *mk'ar-dpón* governor of a castle, commander of a fortress. — *mk'ar-lás C.* and *B.*, the work of constructing a castle, of raising an edifice; **k'ar-lén* *W.* id. — *mk'ar-srúṅ* the guard or garrison of a castle, fortress *Cs.* —

མཁར་བ་ *mk'ár-ba* 1. (also *ₒk'ár-ba*) *B.* and *C.*, **staff, stick;** *mk'ar-γsil* staff of the mendicant friars, the upper part of which is hung with jingling rings; *ṗyag-mk'ár* resp. for *mk'ár-ba.* — 2. **bronze, bell-metal,** v. *ₒk'ár-ba.*

མཁལ་མ་ *mk'ál-ma* **kidney, reins,** *mk'ál mdog* 'kidney-colour, dark red' *Cs.*

མཁས་པ་ *mk'ás-pa Ssk.* पटु, (originally like σοφός) **skilled; skilful,** in mechanical work, and so it is frq. used in col. language; further in a more general sense: *smán-pa mk'ás-pa* a skilful, clever physician; **experienced, learned, prudent, shrewd, wise;** c. accus. or dat., in a thing; *so-ts'ís-la* in farming, *č'os* in religion; *slób-ma skyóṅ-ba-la mk'ás-pa* an able tutor, pedagogue *Mil.*; *mk'as-btsun-bzáṅ* prop. denotes the qualities of a right priest: learned, conscientious, good, but sometimes it indicates only the position in society, the clerical rank, so esp. *mk'as-btsún* learned clerics, reverends *Glr.*, *mk'ás-po* or *-pa* a learned man, **a scholar,** *sṅón-gyi mk'ás-po-rnams* learned men of former times; *mk'as-grúb* id., *rgya-gár-gyi mk'as-grúb-rnams* Indian scholars; it is also used like our 'most wise', 'very learned', and similar expressions in a pompous address *Glr.*; *mk'as-mčóg* profound scholar *Zam.* I never found the word applied to inanimate things in the sense of 'wisely contrived', and the correctness of *Cs.*: *t'abs mk'ás-pos* 'by wise means' may be questioned.

མཁུན་པ་ *mk'ún-pa Sch.* v. *k'ún-pa.*

མཁུར་ཚོས་ *mk'ur-ts'ós* v. *k'ur-ts'ós.*

མཁོ་བ་ *mk'ó-ba* **desirable,** to be wished for, *mk'ó-bai yo-byád*, in *C.* also **k'o-ǰhe*,* desirable things, requisits, wants, desiderata; **hindu-tẹ́n-gyi mí-la k'ó-wẹ ts'oṅ-zóg** articles of commerce, goods, commodities, such as they are called for in Hindostan; *nyé-bar mk'ó-ba* indispensable, most necessary. Cf. *ₒk'o.*

མཁོས་པབ་ *mk'os-páb Lex.* v. *ₒk'os.*

མཁྱུད་པ་ *mk'yúd-pa Cs.*: to keep, to hold, to embrace, = *ₒk'yúd-pa*; *dpe-mk'yúd Lex.* w.e.; *Cs.*: unwillingness to lend books, *dpe-mk'yúd-čan* unwilling to lend books, *dpe-mk'yúd byed-pa* to be unwilling to lend books; *mk'yud-spyád* a sort of bag or vessel for carrying something (?); sorcery, witchcraft *Sch.*

མཁྱེན་པ་ *mk'yen-pa*, resp. for *šés-pa, rig-pa, gó-ba*, **to know,** *yab-yúm-gyis mk'yén-par mdzód-čig* my esteemed parents may know *Dzl.*; to know, one man from another, *rgyál-po mk'yén-tam* does the king, does your majesty know the . . .? (the king himself will answer: *ṅas šés-so*) *Dzl.* It is frq. used of the supernatural perception of Buddha and the saints, *bsám-ṗa dág-par mk'yén-pas* as he (the Bodhisattwa) perceived the sentiments (of his scholar) to be sincere *Dzl.*; *mk'yén-par gyúr-to* perceived, found out, discovered; **to understand,** *mk'yen sóṅ-ṅam* did you understand it? *mk'yen-rgyá-čan* possessed of much understanding, very learned *Mil.*; *mk'yén-ldan-yáṅs-pa* profoundly learned; *mk'yen-brtsé Glr.* prob.: omniscient-merciful; *t'ams-čad-mk'yén* all-knowing, a later epithet of Buddha; *ye-mk'yén, mṅon-mk'yén* = *ye-šés, mṅon-šés.* — *tugs-mkyén* is known to me only as a sbst. abstr.: the knowing, **knowledge, prophetic sight,** *rje-btsún-gyis tugs-mk'yén-gyis γzigs-pa lágs-sam* has your reverence seen by your prophetic sight? *Mil.*; acc. to *Cs.*, however, *sku-mk'yén, γsuṅ-mk'yén* and *tugs-mk'yén* are identical in meaning with *mk'yen-mk'yén*, a form of entreaty which, as a Lama told me, properly has the sense: you know yourself best what is good for me! In accordance to this explanation we find in *Mil.* after an entreaty: *blá-ma k'yed mk'yen-mk'yen.* It is gen. added without any connecting word, like our **pray,** or **please,** but sometimes it is construed with the inf.: *mdzád-pa(r) mk'yen-mk'yén,* please to do.

མཁྲང་(བ་) *mk'raṅ (-ba)*, also *k'raṅ* **hard, solid, compact;** *srá-mk'ráṅ-čan ˳gyur-méd Thgy.* **firm, hearty, sound,** of a strong and robust constitution. — *mk'ráṅ-pa* denotes the fourth stage of the development of the foetus *Thgy.*

མཁྲིག་མ་ *mk'rig-ma* **the wrist** of the hand.

མཁྲིགས་པ་ **ṭigs-pa** col. *W.* (also *Bunan*) for:

མཁྲིས་པ་ *mk'ris-pa B.* and *C.* (*Ssk.* पित्त) **bile, gall.** — 1. the vesicle of the gall, the gall-bladder, as part of the intestines. — 2. generally: the substance of the bile, the bilious fluid, which acc. to Indo-Tibetan philosophy is connected with the element of fire, and which, conformably to its functions, is divided into five species, of which physiology gives the oddest details. — *mk'ris-nád* bilious disease; *mk'ris-tsád* prob. bilious fever; *gráṅ-mk'ris* a feverish shivering, a chill.

མཁྲིས་མ་ *mk'ris-ma Lex.* w.e., perh. = *˳k'ris.*

མཁྲེགས་པ་ *mk'régs-pa, W. *ṭág-mo** (*Ssk.* सार) **hard, firm,** e.g. snow; **yo-ṭág-čan* W.* **obstinate, stiffnecked, stubborn.**

འཁང་བ་ *˳k'áṅ-ba* (not: to put a fault or crime on another *Cs.*, but:) **to hurt or offend, to annoy, to vex,** *tsúr-la ˳k'aṅ* we cause vexation to ourselves (by minding too much the affairs of others); *˳k'aṅ* **animosity.** *˳k'aṅ maṅ* there occur many collisions, quarrels *Mil.*, *dpon-slób re ˳k'aṅ ˳byuṅ* there arise mutual differences, animosities, between masters and scholars *Mil.*

འཁད་པ་ *˳k'ád-pa* esp. *W.* 1. **to sit, to sit firm,** *rtai k'á-ru* on the back of a horse. — 2. to remain sitting, **to stick fast,** to be stopped, kept back, e.g of a bird, *rnyius*, in a snare; *rkáṅ-pa ˳k'ád-de ˳gyél-ba* to get entangled with the foot so as to fall; *sgo ˳k'ad ˳dug* the door sticks. Cf. also *k'ad-pa* and *bk'ad-pa.*

འཁམ་པ་ *˳k'ám-pa* 1. **to faint away, to swoon.** — 2. *Sch.* also: to take into one's mouth.

འཁར་བ་ *˳k'ár-ba* I. sbst. 1. **staff** v. *mk'ár-ba.* — 2. **bronze, bell-metal,** *˳k'ár-(bai) čù* molten, liquid bronze, *˳k'ár-bai mé-loṅ* a metallic mirror; *˳k'ar-ṙṅá* **gong,** used in India and China instead of bells; *Cs.:* a drum of bronze; yet it is rather a large bronze disk, producing, when struck, a very loud sound like that of a bell. — *˳k'ar-γžóṅ* a dish or basin of metal; *˳k'ar-záṅs* a metallic kettle. — II. vb., in *C.* the same as *˳k'ád-pa.* — 2. in *W.* intrs. to *dgar-ba.*

འཁར་འཁུ་བ་ *˳k'ár-˳k'u-ba* to resist *Sch.*

འཁལ་བ་ *˳k'ál-ba*, pf. and fut. (imp. *k'ol?*), *W. *kál-če** 1. *B., C., W.:* **to spin,** *bal,* wool, *skúd-pa* a thread, *srád-bu* yarn. — 2. *W.* **to send, to forward,** things.

འཁུ་བ་ *˳k'ú-ba* **to offend, insult,** *Bhar.* (*Lex.* = द्रोह injury); *˳k'u-˳k'rig,* acc. to the context, denotes certain passions that disturb the tranquillity of the mind, such as malignity and covetousness; *˳k'áṅ-ba* is synon. — *Cs.*'s 'to emulate, contemn, hate, long for', and *Sch.*'s 'pride' I am not able to verify.

འཁུན་པ་ *˳k'ún-pa* **to groan,** to fetch a deep sigh, not so much as a sign of pain or sorrow, but rather as a mere physical deep and hollow sound *Med.*; *˳k'ún-sgras k'áṅ-pa k'eṅs* he filled the house with groanings *Pth.; sdáṅ-bai dgrá-la γyag ltar ₒḱun* he groans (grunts, bellows) like a yak against a fierce enemy *Mil.*

འཁུམ་པ་ *ₒḱúm-pa* pf. *ḱums* (cf. *skúm-pa*) **to shrink**, to be contracted, e.g. of the limbs, by gout; **yúr-ra raṅ-žin ₒḱúm-če yin* W.* the ditch will get narrower of itself; *ḱúms-pa* shrunk, shrivelled, contracted; fig. reduced, restricted, deprived of power.

འཁུམས་པ་ *ₒḱúms-pa Lex.* and *Cs.* to comprehend, understand; *Sch.* also: to practise, to impress on the mind.

འཁུར་བ་ *ₒḱúr-ba* I. sbst. = *ḱúr-ba*, **pastry**. II. vb., pf. and fut. *ḱur*, rarely *bkur* (v. *bkúr-ba*) 1. **to carry, convey,** *ḱur(-ru) ₒḱúr-ba* to carry a load; *mi ťég-par ₒḱúr-ba Med.* to carry too heavy loads, prop to carry what one cannot carry; **ḱur šog* C., *ḱur kyoṅ* W.* bring! fetch! **ḱur soṅ* C., *ḱur ḱyer* W.* take away! carry off! *ₒḱúr-du ťógs-te* taking up in order to carry, taking on one's back *Dzl.; *lág-par ḱúr-če* W.* to hold in one's hand. — 2. **to carry away or off,** *ro ₒḱúr-ba Pth.*, to carry away a corpse; **to take along with,** in *W.* even: **to pocket,** **sém-la ḱúr-če* W.* to take to heart; **'á-ne ₒḱúr-če** to take a wife, to marry. — *ₒḱúr-ťag* carrying-girth, rope or strap *Thgy.* Cf. *ḱur, ḱúr-ba* etc.

འཁུར་ཚོས་ *ₒḱur-tsós* v. *ḱur-tsós.*

འཁུལ་བ་ *ₒḱúl-ba* **to subdue, to subject** *Cs.; Sch.* also: to be uneasy about. *Lex.: γyóg-tu ₒḱúl-ba;* v. also *ḱul* 3. *Zam.; ḱral ₒḱúl-ba* perh. to force a tax, a rate, on a person.

འཁེགས་པ་ *ₒḱegs-pa* pf. *ḱegs* **to hinder, stop, shut off, debar,** *lam* the way *Mil.; ǰi-ltar bkag ruṅ ma ḱégs-pas Mil.*, although they prohibited, tried to proh. him), he was not prohibited; *rgyál-bai ṗyág-gis kyaṅ mi ḱégs-pa Mil.* not being hindered even by Buddha's power.

འཁེངས་པ་ *ₒḱéṅs-pa*, pf. *ḱeṅs*, **to be full,** *čus keṅs yod-pa Glr.; blo-grós ma ḱéṅs-te* his mind not being satiated *Tar.* 135, 13.

འཁེབ་པ་ *ₒḱéb-pa* pf. *ḱebs*, **to cover, to spread over,** *yoṅs-su ḱébs-té* being covered all over *Stg.; ḱa ťams-čad ḱebs-te* over the whole face *Stg.;* **to overshadow** *Dzl.* ཟཱ, 17.

འཁེལ་བ་ *ₒḱél-ba* pf. *ḱél* 1. **to put on, to load, to pack on,** = *ₒgél-ba; bču-ťóg ḱél-na* when the ten stories or lofts shall have been put on *Mil.nt.* 2. **to spin,** = *ₒḱál-ba C., Glr.*

འཁོ་བ་ *ₒḱó-ba* (vb. to *mḱó-ba*), **to wish, to want,** to think useful, serviceable, necessary, to have occasion for *Mil.; ₒḱó-ste ₒoṅ* he will be able to make use of it *Mil.; *ₒḱda mi ₒḱo** or **ₒḱó-če med* W.* I do not want it, I do not like it; *ₒḱo-bjéd* fit for use, **useful.**

འཁོགས་པ་ *ₒḱógs-pa* weak from old age, **decrepit, decayed;** *rgan* or *rgas-ₒḱógs* id.; *sṅo-ḱóg, skya-ḱóg* (sic) *Thgy.* with a complexion blue or pale from old age.

འཁོང་བ་ *ₒḱóṅ-ba* (cf. *sgóṅ-ba*) to contract one's limbs, to sit in a cowering position, **to squat; to hide one's self;** *dpa ₒḱóṅ-ba* to become discouraged, disheartened *Thgy.*

འཁོད་, ཁོད་ *ₒḱod, ḱod* 1. **surface, superficies;** *sai ₒḱod snyóms-pa* to remove inequalities of the surface, to level, to plane, *ₒḱód-snyoms-pa* levelled, made even, plain; also fig.: *bár-gyi ḱod snyoms* gaps were filled up, i.e. distinctions of rank, wealth etc. were done away with, not in consequence of a revolution, but as an act of kindness, forced upon the people by a despotic government. — 2. **a mill-stone,** **yá-ḱo'** the upper stone, **má-ḱo'** the nether stone *C.*

འཁོད་པ་ *ₒḱód-pa* **to sit down, to sit;** *bar-snáṅ-la*, suspended in the air, floating, soaring, frq. of gods and saints in legends; *rgyal-srid-la* to have been raised to the throne *Tar.;* **to live, to dwell** *Dzl.;* gen. used like a passive to *ₒgód-pa* **to be put, placed, established** (in virtue, in a doctrine, = to be converted to); *glegs-bám-du* to be put down in writing, to be recorded *Tar.* Cf. *ₒḱád-pa.*

འཁོན་པ་ ₒḱón-pa (*Lexx.* have a pf. *bkon*) 1. c.c. *dan*, **to bear a grudge** or ill-will against a person, **to be dissatisfied** with a thing; *ₒḱón-nas* when they (the states) were at war with one another (opp. to *mṫún-nas* in peaceful relations) *Glr.*; *ₒḱón-med-par* honestly, without insidious intentions, e.g. in negotiations *Glr.*: *čos dan ₒḱón-pa* to wish to keep aloof from religion, or to have done with religion; in a special sense: to be tired of the clerical profession *Glr.*; *ₒḱón-žugs-pa*, *ₒḱón-.du ₒdzin-pa* = *ₒḱón-pa*; *ₒḱon res byéd-pa Sch.* to quarrel, prob. more accurately, to have a spite against each other. — *ₒḱón-po* **dissension, discord** *Sch.* Cf. *ḱón-pa.* — 2. *C.* = *ₒḱar-ba* II.

འཁོབ་ *ₒḱób Sch.* **barbarous, rough, rude,** gen. combined with *mṫa*, *mṫa-ₒḱób*, with or without *yul*, **barbarous border-country.** So the Tibetans always designate their own country, in comparison with India, the holy land of Buddhism, as being *mṫa-ₒḱób ḱá-ba-čan.* The rarely occurring *yan-ḱób* seems to indicate a still more distant and barbarous country.

འཁོབས་པ་ *ₒḱóbs-pa* to be startled, agitated, alarmed, in one Lex. however, it is explained by *ḱyáb-pa.*

འཁོར་ *ₒḱor* 1. **circle, circumference**; the persons or objects encircling, surrounding (a certain point or place); *lté-ba dan dei ₒḱór-rnams* the navel and the circumjacent parts *Med.*; **de-ḱór-la* W.* thereabout; *nye-ₒḱór* v. *nye;* more esp. **retinue, attendants,** *ₒḱor dan bčas-pa* (सपरिवार) with attendants, suite: *ₒḱor rnám-pa bži Tar.* frq., the attendants of Buddha's hearers, divided into four classes (viz. in the earliest times: *dge-slón, dge-slón-ma, dge-snyén,* and *dge-snyén-ma;* at a later period: *nyan-ṫós, ran-sans-rgyás, byan-čub-séms-dpa,* and *so-sói skyé-bo-rnams* q.v.) *ₒḱor dgra-bčóm-pas bskór-te* surrounded by the retinue of the Arhants (v. *dgra-bčóm-pa*); *ₒḱór-du bsdús-so* he gathered them round himself as his retinue *Dzl.*; also fig.: the train of thoughts, reminiscences etc., which the soul, when passing into a new body, cannot take along with it *Thgy.*; it is also used for a single servant or attendant (*Cs.* has *ₒḱór-po* or *ₒḱór-pa* male attendant, and *ₒḱór-ma* female attendant), *ₒḱor ycig Mil.*; *ₒḱor ynyis* two attendants *Glr.*, hence *ₒḱor-rnams* sometimes for domestics, household servants; but if *ₒḱor* with a numeral is preceded by *ytsó-bo*, or a similar noun, this preceding word is acc. to the Tibetan mode of speaking included in the number given, so that *ytsó-bo ₒḱor lna* should be translated: the master and four attendants (not five). — 2. instead of *ₒḱór-ba*, or *ḱór-lo*, esp. in compound words; *lo-ₒḱór* = *lo-skór* a cycle, comprising a space of twelve years.

Comp. *ₒḱór-mḱan* **attendants** *Glr.* — *ₒḱór-ₒbáns* **subjects** *Cs.* — *ₒḱor-yyóg* = *ₒḱór* **retinue, servants** etc. — **dhun-ḱór* C.* **waiting man,** valet de chamber, = *sku-mdún-pa* which is the respectful word for it. — *nan-ₒḱór* household servants, domestics. — **ḱor-gyág* W.* **latch.** — *ₒḱor-ₒdás* v. sub *ₒḱór-ba* II.

འཁོར་བ་ *ₒḱór-ba* I. vb. (cf. *skór-ba*), **to turn round, to turn about, to go round** in a circle; *ₒḱór-gin yod* he is walking (running, flying etc.) round the . . . *Glr.*; esp. of the successive transmigrations of metempsychosis, v. II; *mgo ₒḱor* my head turns, I am getting dizzy, confused; also **I am duped,** cheated, imposed on, *ḱyéd-kyi ḱa-sbyán-gyis ned mgo mi ₒḱor* we are not to be taken in by the volubility of your tongue *Mil.*; **to pass away, to grow full, to be completed,** *lo-dús ₒḱór-ba-na* when one year was past *Glr.*; *srás-kyis lo ₒḱór-te* when the prince had completed one year, was one year old; **da bú-lon ḱor* W.* now the debt is entirely paid off, cleared: **ḱor mi ṫub** it cannot be paid off: **mi ḱor**, the sum is not full, not sufficient to cover the debt; **to walk about, roam, ramble** *W.*; **to return** from a journey, to come home: **rán-la ḱór-ba** to come or fall back (on the head of the author, originator); to come together, **to contract, to gather,** e.g.

clouds, frq. water, *ḱoi ḱá-ču ḱor* W. it makes his mouth water; *dgrá-bo ˳ḱor Mil.* enemies are collecting (we create ourselves enemies); also impersonally: *ḱor soṅ* it has become cloudy; *ynam ḱor* the sky is getting overcast, clouded; therefore even **to arise, to be produced, formed,** *zil-pa ˳ḱor* dew is produced, *yyá*, rust, even: *lus-la sras ˳ḱor* a child has been formed, produced, in the womb *Pth.* —

II. sbst. 1. the turning round or about etc.; more particularly 2. **the orb** or **round** of transmigration within the six classes of physical beings. Though the Buddhist has not a more ardent wish, than to be finally released from the repeated wanderings of the soul, yet he believes so firmly in these migrations, that he will rather follow the doctrines of his philosophers, and doubt the reality of the perception of his senses, than think it possible, that the whole theory of the *˳ḱór-ba* with all its consequences should be nothing but a product of human imagination. — *˳ḱór-bar ˳ḱór-ba* to turn round, to wander about in the orb of transmigration; *˳ḱór-bai btsón-ra, ˳dam, mtso* the dungeon, the swamp, the sea of the *˳ḱór-ba; ˳ḱór-ba-las ˳dás-pa* to escape from the *˳kór-ba,* = to enter into the Nirwana *˳ḱór-˳das* 1. abbreviation of the foregoing. 2. for *˳ḱór-ba daṅ ˳das-pa* the stay in the *˳ḱór-ba* and the escape from it; *˳ḱor ˳das ynyis-su ṅas ma mtoṅ* I have not seen that there is a difference between these two *Mil.*

འཁོར་ཡུག *˳ḱor-yúg* **a wall, rampart** *Cs.*, v. *ḱó-ra.*

འཁོར་གཡར *ḱór-yyá C.* **latch.**

འཁོར་ལོ *˳ḱór-lo* (*Ssk.* चक्र, मण्डल) **1. circle,** *tsógs-kyi ˳ḱór-lo* offerings arranged in a circle, v. *tsogs: ˳ḱór-lo ˳bri-ba* to describe a circle *Tar.* More frq.: 2. a circular body, **a disk, roll, wheel,** any modification of the cylinder, *bču-ysum-˳ḱór-lo* the column on the *mčod-rtén* consisting apparently of thirteen circular disks; *˳ḱór-lo brtsib-brgyád* the wheel with eight spokes, a frq. attribute of deities; *rdza-mḱán-gyi ˳ḱór-lo* potter's wheel; *čós-kyi ˳ḱór-lo* praying-cylinder, cf. below; also a complication of wheels, wheel-work, engine, *˳prúl-(gyi) ˳ḱór(-lo)* 'magic wheel', a phantastic attribute of gods, but also any real machine of a more ingenious construction, e.g. sugar-press *Stg.*, electrical machine etc.; *čú-tsod-˳ḱór-lo* a clock; *śiṅ-rta-˳ḱór-lo* waggon, carriage, also cart-wheel. — Figuratively: *bdé-ba daṅ sdug-bsṅál-gyi ˳ḱór-lo,* vicissitude of fortune; *dús-kyi ˳ḱór-lo* (कालचक्र) acc. to *Cs.*'s Chronological Table (*Cs.'s Gram.* p. 181) a later philosophical system, contained esp. in the *rtsa-rgyúd, Mūlatantra,* in which the Adibuddha doctrine, prophecies, chronology etc. are propounded. It was introduced into Tibet about 1000 p. Chr.; cf. also *Schl.* 45. — *˳ḱór-lo sgyúr-ba,* or *skór-ba,* with *čós-kyi,* to turn the wheel of doctrine, = to preach, to teach religion, (vulgo understood only of the turning of the praying-cylinder); **čö̗-kyi ḱór-lo̗ léṅ-mor bé'-pa* C.* to devote one's self to the preaching of religion. On the other hand: *˳ḱór-los sgyúr-bai rgyál-po* (चक्रवर्तिन्) *Will.*: 'a ruler, the wheels of whose chariot roll everywhere without obstruction, emperor, sovereign of the world, the ruler of a *ča-kra,* or country extending from sea to sea'. In this Indian explanation two different etymologies are given, the former of which is undoubtedly the original one. Buddhism and the Tibetan language have added a third signification, 'praying-wheel'; modern scholars a fourth, that of the 'orb' or round of transmigration or metempsychosis: hence the confusion attaching to the import of this word.

འཁོར་ལོག **ḱor-lóg** is said to be used in col. language instead of *ḱa-ló* 3. *W.*

འཁོར་ས *˳ḱór-sa* = *skór-lam* v. *skór-ba* I. extr.; *˳ḱór-sa bár-pa, čén-po Glr.*

འཁོར་གསུམ *˳ḱor-ysum,* lit. three circles, *Ssk. trimaṇḍala*; *Sch.*: 'everything that belongs to archery'; more correctly: arrow, knife, and spear.

འཁོལ་བ་ *ₒKól-ba* I. pf. *Kol*, cf. *skól-ba*, **to boil, to be boiling**, *ču Kol* the water is boiling; *ₒKol ₒǰúg-pa* to make boil, to set to the fire for boiling, = *skól-ba*; **to ferment** (dough), **to effervesce, to sparkle** (beer) *W.* — II. pf. *bkol*, imp. *Kol* 1. to oblige a person to be a servant or bondman, **to use as a servant**; in full: *bran-du*, also *γyóg-tu*, *ₒKól-ba*; therefore *bran-Kól*, *Kól-po* **servant, man-servant**: *bkol-spyód-kyi sdug-bsṅál* the calamity of servitude, current expression for designating the lot of animals; *γžán-dag-gis dbáṅ-med-par bkól-ba* to be enslaved by others, to be compelled to do slave-work *Thgy.*; *dgé-bai lás-la bkól-ba* to make a person minister to works of virtue. — 2. **to save, to spare**, to enjoy with moderation *Cs.*, *zúr-du . . . bkól-ba Lex.*; *Sch.*: saved, laid up, put by. — 3. *Sch.*: **to become insensible, to be asleep, to get benumbed**, in reference to the limbs; seems to be used in *Med.*

འཁོས་ *ₒKos* 1. *C.* also *ₒKós-ka* (cognate to *ₒKó-ba*), **worth, value, importance** *Cs.*; *ₒKós-čan* important, mighty, of great influence, *ₒKos-méd* the opposite of it. — 2. *ₒKós-su-ṗab-pa* **clyster** *Sch.*; one Lex. has *mKos-ṗáb*, w.e.

འཁྱག(ས)་པ་ *ₒKyág(s)-pa* 1. **to freeze** (of water, earth, provisions); **to coagulate, congeal** (melted fat etc.). — 2. **to feel cold**, *ₒKyágs-na gós gyon* if you feel cold, put on clothes *Glr.*, **kyag ǰhuṅ* C.*, **Kyágs-sa rag* W.* I feel cold; *ₒKyágs-gri* a feeling cold, a shivering (cf. *ltógs-gri*) *Mil.*; **Kyágs-ša* W.* id., the cold fit of the ague. — *ₒKyags-rúm*, *ₒKyags-róm* **ice** *Glr.*; *ₒKyags-lhám* snow-shoe *Sch.*

འཁྱམ་པ་ *ₒkyám-pa* **to run about, to wander**, e.g. *čá-med yúl-du* in an unknown country *Glr.*; *ₒKór-bar* in the orb or round of transmigration, v. *ₒKór-ba*; *ₒKyám-ste nor mi bdóg-pa žig* one who lives as a vagabond *Dzl.*; *dé-dag-ni rnám-par ₒKyám-pao* they are mistaken, on the wrong track *Wdṅ.*; *ₒKyám-du ₒǰúg-pa* to cause to ramble or rove about, to scatter; *ₒKyáms-pa* strayed, lost, wandering, vagrant; erroneous, erring *Tar.* 153, 15. — *ₒkyám-Kyi* **a vagrant dog**. — *ₒKyáms-po* 1. **a vagabond**. — 2. **n. of a** disease *Med.* — 3. erroneous *Tar.* — *ču ₒKyám-pa* inundation, flood *Ma.*

འཁྱར་བ་ *ₒKyár-ba* **to err, to go astray, to deviate from**, **yan Kyár-la ma ča* Ld.* do not step out of your rank! do not absent yourself! *ₒKyar dogs yod* one should be afraid of going astray *Thgy.*; *dpe ₒKyár-po* a defective simile; *tsig ₒkyár-po* an inadequate designation. — In *Tar.* 48, 4 *dpe ₒKyár-po* is translated 'epitome' by *Schf.*, but the whole passage is somewhat obscure.

འཁྱལ་བ་ *ₒKyál-ba* = *kyal-ka* q.v.

འཁྱི་བ་ *ₒKyi-ba Sch.*, prob. an incorrect reading for *ₒKyil-ba*.

འཁྱིག་པ་ *ₒKyig-pa*, pf. *bkyigs*, fut. *bkyig*, **to bind** (a prisoner, a bundle of straw etc.); **kye** (v. *ske*) **Kyig-pa* C.* to strangle, suffocate.

འཁྱིགས་པ་ *°Kyigs-pa* **to comprise, encompass** *Pth.*, v. *ṗáṅ-pa*.

འཁྱིད་པ་ *ₒKyid-pa*, *Sch.*: *mig ₒKyid-pa* **to turn** or **roll** one's eyes.

འཁྱིམས་པ་ *ₒKyims-pa* 1. **to be encircled** with a halo, as the sun and moon sometimes are *Cs.*; *ₒog-ₒKyims Lex.* = परिधि halo; also *ₒǰa-ód ₒKyims* a rainbow-coloured halo appears *Pth.* — 2.: **na-bún** or **múg-pa Kyims*, *dúd-pa Kyims**, fog, smoke, **comes floating on.**

འཁྱིར་བ་ *°Kyir-ba* **to turn round** in a circular course *Cs.*, *Lex.*: *γdugs ₒKyir-ba* to turn a parasol round (?).

འཁྱིལ་བ་ *ₒKyil-ba* vb. n. 1. **to wind, to twist**; *duṅ γyás-su ₒKyil-ba* a triton or trumpet-shell, wound to the right, and then considered particularly valuable, these shells generally being wound to the left; of the hair: *gyén-la ₒKyil-ba* wound or twisted (on the crown of the head) *Glr.*: *ro-smád °brúl-du ₒKyil-ba* the lower part of the body being wound into a serpent (the usual manner of representing the '*klu*'); *ₒód-du ₒKyil-žiṅ*, the body enveloping itself in light *Mil.*; to roll: *nya γser-mig ₒKyil-*

ba yod the fish rolls its golden eye *Mil.*; to whirl, to eddy, to move round rapidly, of the water, so prob. *Dzl.* ༢༣, 13; ༧༤༢, 2; *Ḱrom dmar-nág ˳Ḱyil-ba* the motley crowd in a whirling motion *Pth.*; to hang or flow down in folds, of a tent or a curtain *Glr.* 33, 12. — 2. **to flow** (whirling) **together**, used of rivulets and brooks overflowing so as to form small lakes *Mil.*; of persons: to meet, to flock or crowd together, *mi máṅ-po dé-ru ˳Ḱyil-bar gyúr-te Pth.*; **Ḱyil-ču,** and **ču-Ḱyil** col. puddle.

འཁྱུ་བ་ *˳Ḱyú-ba*, pf. *˳Ḱyus* **to run** *Lex.*

འཁྱུག་པ་ *˳Ḱyúg-pa*, pf. *Ḱyug* 1. *Cs.:* **to run;** *˳Ḱyug-po* a runner; *˳Ḱyúg-yig* running hand, current hand-writing, as is used in the writing of letters etc.; *˳Ḱyúg-po ˳Ḱyú-ba Lex.* is explained by *Sch.:* to run away hastily. The signification of running, however, seems to be obsolete, whilst the usual meaning is: 2. **to dart** or **sweep rapidly along**, frq. used of a flash of lightning, also of the rapid motion of a fish in the water *Mil.;* of spectral apparitions *Mil.;* of acute rheumatic pains; of the light: to flash, to shoot rays of light, *Ḱra-Ḱyug-Ḱyúg-pa* to gleam, to sparkle with light, to shine in various colours *Pth.; ser-˳Ḱyúg-ge-ba* glittering in yellow lustre *Mil.;* to glitter, to shine, of the rainbow; to shine through, of the veins through the cuticle etc. — **Ḱyúg-šar-čán** *W.* hasty, hurrying, careless.

འཁྱུད་པ་ *˳Ḱyúd-pa* 1. **to embrace** frq., *mgúl-nas ˳Ḱyúd-pa* to clasp round the neck, **to hug;** to encompass by spanning *Pth.* and elsewhere, cf. *˳Ḱyígs-pa.* — 2. **to glide** in or into (as serpents), *mṅál-du ˳Ḱyúg-pa* of the soul in the new conception, like the synonym *˳Ḱril-ba*, for *˳ǰúg-pa.* — 3. **to be able,** **nád-pa mál-sa-na láṅ-ṅa** (instead of *laṅ-bar) *mi Ḱyud** the sick man is not able to rise from his bed. — *blos mi ˳Ḱyúd-pa byéd-pa Thgy.* (not clear).

འཁྱུར་བ་ *˳Ḱyúr-ba Cs.:* to be separated, divorced; *Lex.: bsḱúr-bas ˳kyúr-ba,* therefore prob. the vb. n. to *skyúr-ba,* to be deserted, cast off.

འཁྱེང་བ་ *˳Ḱyéṅ-ba* seems to be = *˳géṅs-pa C.* col.

འཁྱེད་པ་ *Ḱyéd-pa* (1. cf. *˳gyed-pa*) *Cs.* **to be distributed**, e.g. food, *Dzl.* — 2. *C.* and *W.* **to be sufficient, to suffice, to be enough, to hold out,** **mi Ḱyed** there is not enough. — 3. *C.* to gain (a law-suit), **to be acquitted.** — 4. *ṗyir Ḱyéd-pa* **to bow** without uncovering one's head, as a less humble way of saluting *Mil.nt.*

འཁྱེར་བ་ *˳Ḱyér-ba* pf. *˳Ḱyer* (Northern *Ld.* **Ḱyers**), at the end of a sentence *Ḱyér-ro. Tar.* and others, (*Cs. Ḱyer-to?*), nearly the same as *˳Ḱur-ba;* (the **नय** of the Lexx.: to lead, to guide, does not fully agree with the sense in which it is generally used) — 1. **to carry away, to take away***; čus* to be carried or swept away by water; fig.: *lé-los* to be overcome, carried away by idleness *Mil.; ldé-mig Ḱyer* take the key with you! — 2. **to carry, to bring,** in a more general sense, *C.* and *B.: Ḱyer šog* bring! *Ḱyer soṅ* carry off! take away! (in a like manner as *˳Ḱúr-ba*)*; des ču bláṅ-nas Ḱyer ˳óṅ-bai lám-Ḱa-na* he having fetched water, being on his way to bring it *Pth.; Ḱyer-la šog* bring me (word), let me know (the result of your investigation) *Mil.* — *˳Ḱyér-so* 1. **appearance,** esp. a neat, handsome appearance of persons or things. 2. **advantage, superiority, pleasantness,** *Mil., C.*

འཁྱེལ་བ་ *˳Ḱyel-ba Ld.* **to hit, to strike.**

འཁྱོག་པ་ *˳Ḱyóg-pa*, pf. *Ḱyag*, imp. *Ḱyog*, **to lift, lift up,** = *˳ṫógs-pa, ṫégs-pa Glr.;* **to carry, bring,** **sól-ǰa Ḱyog** bring in the tea *C.*, cf. sub *Ḱag.*

(འ)ཁྱོག་པོ་ *˳Ḱyóg-po* or *Ḱyóg-po* **crooked, bent;** *Ḱyóg-poi ri-mo* a crooked figure, a curve, flourish, crescent etc.; *nyas ṗar ˳Ḱyog ṫsur ˳Ḱyog byás-šiṅ* the fish winding its body, writhing *Pth.; ˳Ḱyog-čan, ˳Ḱyog-˳Ḱyóg* tortuous; *˳Ḱyog-bšád* a crooked, out of the way construction or explanation. — *˳Ḱyog stón-pa* to fly into a passion (?) *Sch.*

(འ)ཁྱོགས་ ₒk̓yogs or k̓yogs **palanquin, sedan-chair, litter** *Pth.*; *ₒk̓yogs-dpyáṅ* id.; a lath or pole for carrying burdens *Sch.*

འཁྱོང་བ་ *ₒk̓yóṅ-ba* pf. and imp. *k̓yoṅ* **to bring** *W.*

འཁྱོམ་པ་ *ₒk̓yóm-pa* pf. *ₒk̓yoms* 1. **to rock, to wave,** of a ship *Schr.*, of the water *Sch.* (not quite clear); **k̓yom-k̓yom ḍo-ba** *C.* **to reel, stagger,** **čáṅ-ghi k̓yom-pa dug** he is staggering under the influence of beer; to be dizzy *Med.*; *mtso-ₒk̓yóm* dizziness, vertigo, ni. f.; *lug-glád mgo-ₒk̓ór ₒk̓yóm-pa yso* the brain of a sheep cures the swimming of the head (vertigo) *Med.*

འཁྱོར་བ་ *ₒk̓yór-ba* 1. **to miss, fail,** not to hit *Cs.* — 2. **to reel, stagger,** from intoxication. — 3. **to warp,** of wood.

འཁྱོལ་བ་ *ₒk̓yól-ba*, pf. *ₒk̓yol*, cf. *skyél-ba*, **to be carried, to be brought** (somewhere) *Pth.*; with *ynód-pa* to be done, inflicted *Mil.*; **to arrive at, come to, reach,** *sku-tsé mťá-ru* the end of life.

འཁྱོས་པ་, (འཕྱོས་པ་) *ₒk̓yós-pa* (*ₒp̓yós-pa*) *Sch.*, *ₒk̓yós-ma Mil.*, **a present, gift,** = *k̓yós ma, skyás-ma.*

འཁྲ་བ་ *ₒk̓rá-ba* I. vb., pf. prob. *ₒk̓ras* **to lean to, to incline towards** *Cs.*; *ₒk̓rá-sa* a support to lean against, a prop, back (of a chair) *Lex.* — II. adj. **hard,** = *ₒk̓ráṅ-ba, mk̓ráṅ-ba Sch.*

འཁྲབ་པ་ *ₒk̓ráb-pa*, pf. *bkrab* (?), cf. also *skráb-pa*, 1. **to strike, to beat,** in repeated strokes, as in swimming and rowing; **to thrust, stamp, thump,** tread heavily, *bro ₒk̓rab-pa* to dance in that manner *Mil.*, *Pth.* — 2. **to winnow, to fan** *Stg.*, col. **ṭáb-pa**. — 3. **mig ṭab ṭab** (or **ṭab-ṭab**) **ǰhé-pa** *C.*, **čó-če** *W.*, **to blink, twinkle, wink** with the eyes. — 4. **k̓a-šág ṭab-če** *W.* **to jest, to joke,** to crack jokes. — 5. *Sch.*: **to leap, jump,** *Schr.* for joy. — 6. **to scoop out, to bail out** *Sch.* — 7. **to fight, to combat** *C.*, *W.*

འཁྲལ་འཁྲུལ་ *ₒk̓ral-ₒk̓rúl* **confusion, disorder.**

འཁྲི་བ་ *ₒk̓ri-ba*, pf. *ₒk̓ris*, cf. *dkri-ba*, cognate to *ₒk̓ril-ba*, 1. **to wind, roll; twist** one's self, **to coil** (of snakes) *Dzl.*; *k̓yim-ťáb-kyi ₒk̓ri-ba* conjugal embrace *Pth.*; **óg-ma ṭi-se** (for *ₒk̓ri-ste*) **rag** *W.* I have a sore throat, prop. I feel my throat tied up, I am choking; fig.: *kún-la ₒk̓ris-pa*, either as an adj. 'ensnaring', or as a sbst. 'ensnarer' = sin, cf. *kun-dkris* in *dkri-ba*; *ₒk̓ri-šiṅ* = *ₒk̓ril-šiṅ.* — 2. mostly as a sbst.: **the being attached to,** given to, c.c. genit. (synonym of *čágs-pa*): *raṅ-dón-gyi*, to one's own advantage, *bu-smád-kyi* to wife and children *Mil.*; **fondness, attachment;** *žen-ₒk̓ris* id. — 3. *k̓ral ₒk̓ri-ba* **to impose** a tax *C.*, *Lex.*

འཁྲིག་པ་ *ₒk̓rig-pa* I. sbst. 1. (*Ssk.* **मिथुन**) **coitus** (of the two sexes), **copulation, pairing,** the usual, not exactly obscene, yet not euphemistic term for it; *ₒk̓rig-pa spyód-pa*, also *ₒk̓rig-čágs spyód-pa B.* and *C.*, **ṭig-pa čó-če** *W.*, to lie with etc.; *ₒk̓rig-pai čós-la rtén-pa* to indulge in lust, to be given to voluptuousness; *ₒk̓rig-skád Sch.*, *ₒk̓rig-tsig Lexx.*, obscene words, unchaste language; *ₒk̓rig-pa ₒbyin-pa* to talk smut. — 2. a sign of the zodiac, **the twins.** — 3. symb. num.: 2.

II. vb. 1. **to cohere, to stick together** *Cs.* — 2. **to be clouded** (of the sky), *ynam ₒk̓rig* the sky is getting overcast; also **ṭigs soṅ** *W.* without a sbst., it has become cloudy, dull; *ₒód-zér daṅ ₒja-ₒód ₒk̓rig-pa* wrapt in rays of light and the splendours of the rainbow *Pth.*: *ťaṅ ťams-čád mes ₒk̓rig-pa* the whole plain was enveloped in a flame of fire *Mil.* Cf. *dkrigs-pa.*

འཁྲིད་ *ₒk̓rid* v. *k̓rid.*

འཁྲིད་པ་ *ₒk̓rid-pa*, pf. *k̓rid*, fut. *bkrit*, **to lead, to conduct** men or beasts to a place; **to command, to head** (an army); **to bring** along with, *ₒk̓rid-de ma ₒóṅs-so* he has not brought (his wife) with him *Dzl.*; therefore *ₒk̓rid* equivalent to 'with': *bú-ťsa ₒk̓rid byuṅ-nas* coming out with their children

Glr. — *blo ˳ḱrid-pa* perh. a mistake for *brid-pa.*

འཁྲིམས་ *˳ḱrims, bréd(-nas)-˳ḱrims Lexx.* w.e.

འཁྲིལ་བ་ *˳ḱril-ba* 1. **to wind** or **coil round** (of serpents), **to embrace** closely, **to clasp round**, e.g. in the act of coition; *ma byams bú-la ˳ḱril* a loving mother clasping her child *Pth.*; *˳ḱril-mḱan* a plant furnished with tendrils or claspers *W.*; *˳ḱril-šiṅ Wdṅ.* a climbing plant, creeper. — 2. **to glide, slip into,** of the soul when entering another body, = *˳ḱyúd-pa.* — 3. *ḱa ˳ḱril-ba W.* to speak imperfectly (like children), **to stammer,** — 4. **to heap up,** = *˳dril-ba, sgril-ba.*

འཁྲིས་ *˳ḱris* 1. syn. with *˳gram*, **bank, shore, coast,** *rmá-čui ˳ḱris-na yód-pai mḱar,* a castle on the banks of the Hoangho *Glr.*; **ḱyo'-ráṅ-gi t́i-na yo'** *C.* it lies just before you, under your nose; *blá-mai sku-ḱris-su = blá-mai p̔yógs-la Mil.nt.* — 2. v. *˳ḱri-ba.*

འཁྲུ་བ་ *˳ḱrú-ba* 1. *Cs.* **to wash, to bathe,** = *˳ḱrud-pa,* cf. *ḱrus.* — 2. **diarrhoea, looseness**; dysentery (?); *˳ḱru-nád, ˳ḱru-sbyóṅs* (**अतिसार**) id.

འཁྲུག་པ་ *˳ḱrúg-pa* 1. vb., pf. *˳ḱrugs,* cf. *dkrug-pa, bkrug-pa,* to be in disorder, agitation, commotion, **to be disturbed**; *˳ḱrúg-par ˳gyúr-ba* to get disordered; of the blood: *rtsa ḱams-čád ˳ḱrúg-tu bčug,* it made all his blood boil *Glr.*; of the sea trq.; esp. of the mind, disturbed by wrath, fear, anxiety, or some other passion, cf. *ḱog-˳ḱrúgs*; **to quarrel, fight, contend,** *de ynyis ˳ḱrúgs-nas,* the two quarrelling; *bod če naṅ ˳ḱrúg-go,* the nobles of Tibet are contending among one another, have internal feuds; *mči-ma ˳ḱrúg-pa* tears appearing, coming forth, (lit. tears being stirred up, excited *Thgy., Mil., Tar.* — 2. sbst. **disorder, tumult, war,** also **single combat, duel,** *˳ḱrúg-pa šor* disorder arises; *˳ḱrug-dús byas* he appointed the time of the duel *Glr.*; *˳ḱrúg-dpon = dmág-dpon*; *˳ḱrúg-pa byed-pa* to take up arms, to begin war; respecting subjects: to rebel; *˳ḱrúg-pa byéd-pai dús-su* in times of war *Glr.*; *dmag-˳ḱrúg, ˳t́ab-˳ḱrúg* war. — *mi-˳ḱrúgs-pa* n. of a Buddha (not = *mi-skyód-pa*). — *˳ḱrug-lóṅ* is the explanation given by *Lexx.* for *skyo-ṅógs,* hence prob.: contest, strife. — **t́úgs-mḱan** *W.* having small cracks, flaws, of potter's ware.

འཁྲུང་བ་ *˳ḱrúṅ-ba* or *˳ḱrúṅs-pa* 1. resp. for *skyé-ba* **to be born,** *bčom-ldan-˳dás ˳ḱrúṅs-pa daṅ dus-mnyám-du* at the same time when Buddha was born *Glr.*; *ynyis-la sras ma ˳ḱrúṅs-par* as by neither of the two (queens) a son was born *Glr.*; *˳ḱruṅs-dkáḥ skyés-bu* (holy) men, such as are but rarely born (lit. with difficulty) *Mil.*; **to arise, to originate,** *˳ḱruṅs-rábs* legend of the origin . . .; *ḱyed-ráṅ-gi t́úgs-la ˳ḱrúṅs-pai t́sig* words as they may just arise in your honour's mind *Mil.*; *snyiṅ-rje t́úgs-la ˳ḱrúṅs-pas* compassion arose in the soul of his reverence *Mil.*; *tiṅ-ṅe-˳dzin ˳ḱrúṅs-pas* meditation arising. — 2. **to come up, shoot, sprout, grow,** of seeds and plants frq.

འཁྲུད་པ་ *˳ḱrúd-pa,* pf. *bḱrus,* fut. *bkru* **to wash, to bathe,** *gos* clothes, *ḱa-lág* face and hands *Dzl.*; **to wash off,** *dri-ma* dirt; fig. *sa nán-gyis ˳ḱrud Ma.* is stated to mean: the country is fleeced, thoroughly drained of its resources.

འཁྲུམས་ *˳ḱrums* **carcass, carrion,** game torn by beasts of prey, *Sch.*, (the word seems to be very little known).

འཁྲུལ་བ་ *˳ḱrúl-ba* (*Lex.: Ssk.* **भ्रम** to turn out of the way, to wander, to stray, hence perh. originally:) 1. **to be dislocated, sprained, distorted,** **t́sig t́ul** *W.* the limb is dislocated; usually: 2. **to be out, to be mistaken,** almost always used in the pf. tense, *˳ḱrúl-pa* mistaken, deceived, *ṅa mig ˳ḱrúl-pa yin-nam* does my eye deceive me? *Mil.*; *rná-ba ˳ḱrul dogs túr-re gyis* take care not to hear wrong *Mil.*; *ynyis yčig-tu ˳ḱrúl-bar byéd-pa* to make by mistake two to be one, to confound one thing with another *Tar.*; *˳di dge-slóṅ-mar ˳dód-pa ˳ḱrúl-pa yin-la* she being frustrated in her wish to become a nun *Tar.* 85, 1; *˳gró-ba ˳ḱrúl-pa* the deceived creature *Glr.*;

frq. with *snaṅ: raṅ-snáṅ ₒk̔rúl-par ₒdug* I have been mistaken, it was a deception of the senses *Mil.*; *snaṅ-ₒk̔rúl*, and *ₒk̔rul-snáṅ* **illusion, delusion**; *ₒk̔rul-snáṅ-čan* **delusive** *Glr.*; to err, as a syn. of *nór-ba: k̔yód-čag ₒk̔rúl-pai ʒig-rten-pa* ye deluded children of the world! *Mil.*; *žes ₒdón-pa-rnams ₒk̔rul* they who pronounce (read) in this manner, are mistaken; *ₐa ₒdogs ₒk̔rul* the adding of *ₐa* is a mistake; *nor-ₒk̔rúl* mistake, *nor-ₒk̔rúl sél-ba Schr.*, **tón-ce, sál-po gyáb-će**, *W.* to remove mistakes, to correct. — 3. **to be insane, deranged,** syn. of *smyós-pa Dzl.* and others. — *ₒk̔rúl-pa* 1. adj. **mistaken, deceived.** — 2. sbst. **mistake; frenzy, madness;** *ₒk̔rul-ɣži* **mistake, error;** *ₒk̔rúl-so (errandi locus)* occasion for committing mistakes, a wrong way, **peril; mistake, error,** cf. *gól-sa*; *ₒk̔rul-ₒk̔ór* artifice *Sch.*, (*Cs.:* machine, contrivance; but this is spelled more correctly *ₒp̔rul-ₒk̔ór*).

འཁྲེན་པ་ *ₒk̔rén-pa* 1. **to wish, to long for,** *zas-skóm Med.*, *k̔yim-la Lex.* — 2. *W.* **to look upon with envy, jealousy.**

འཁྲོ་བ་ *ₒk̔ró-ba*, pf. *k̔ros*, **to be angry,** *la* at.

འཁྲོག་པ་ *ₒk̔róg-pa* **to roar, rush, buzz, hum,** *rná-ba k̔úr-la ₒk̔rog Med.*, a tingling noise is caused in the ear; *rgyu-lóṅ ₒk̔róg-čiṅ* a rumbling in the bowels *Med.*; *sbo-ₒk̔róg* in the belly; *ₒk̔rog-k̔róg* roaring, rushing, buzzing.

འཁྲོལ་བ་ *ₒk̔ról-ba* pf. and fut. *dk̔rol*, imp. *k̔rol* 1. **to cause to sound, to make a noise, to play,** *ról-mo* on an instrument, **to ring** (a bell), **to beat** (a gong, cymbal): *ma dk̔ról-bar* without being played on. — 2. **to sound, resound,** **ḍód-pa ṭ ól-la rag* W.* my bowels croak; *ₒk̔ról-po* a player, performer, bell-ringer etc., cf. *k̔ról-po*: **ṭrol-lo-lo-tse* W.* a tinkling of bells.

ག

ག *ga* 1. the letter **g,** originally, and in the border countries still at the present time, as initial letter = the English hard g, as final letter = ck; in *C.* as initial deep-toned and aspirated (gh), as final letter more or less indistinct; as a prefix (in *Khams* and *Balti*) fricative = γ or χ: v. Preface. — 2. as numerical figure: 3, cf. *ka* 2.

ག་ *ga* affix (article) to some substantives, like *k̔a*.

ག་ *ga* (*C.* **gha**) 1. = *ₐga* (*C.* **gā**). — 2. = *gaṅ*.

ག་ཁྲལ་ *ga-k̔rál C.* (pron. **gha-ṭal**) **tax, duty** (on cattle and butter).

ག་ག་ *ga-gá W.* a title of honour: **the old gentleman, the old squire** e.g. **ga-gá ta-ra-čáṅ** the old Squire Tara Chand, opp. to *no-nó* the young Squire; instead of it in *C.:* **a-ǰho-lág**.

ག་ག་ཚིལ་ *ga-ga tsil,* **tickling** *Cs.*; *ga-ga-tsil byéd-pa* **to tickle.**

ག་གེ་མོ་ *ga-gé-mo* **such a one, such a thing** *Cs.*; **such and such;** v. *če-ge-mo.*

ག་གོན་ *ga-gón* **a melon** *Cs.* (some Lexx. have: cucumber, others: barley).

ག་ཅེན་, ག་ཆེན་ *ga-čén, ga-čén* **some** (people), **a good many; a good deal** *W., C.*

ག་ཆད་ *ga-čád* **without cause, involuntarily,** e.g. to weep *Med.*

ག་ཏ་ *gá-ta Ssk.*, *ga-tai sde-tsan* a particular kind of Indian hand-writing, besides Nagari and Lantsa *Glr.*

ག་ད་ *gá-da* (गदा), **club, mace.**

ག་དུར་ *ga-dúr* medicinal herb of an astringent taste.

ག་དོར་ *ga-dór Lex.* w.e.: *ša-bai ga-dor*: *Sch.* explains: the growth of a new branch on a stag's horn.

ག་འདྲས་ *ga-ₒdrás C.* (pronounced **ghandẹ**) **how?**

ག་ན་ *gá-na* = *gaṅ-na*, **where**, used interr. and correl., frq.; *gá-na-ba* and *gáṅ-na-ba* the same as a sbst., **the whereabouts** of a person, his place of residence; *rgyál-po gá-na-bar*, (or *gá-na-ba der*, *gá-na ₒdúg-par*, *gá-na bžúgs-par*) *soṅ* he went where the king was *Dzl.*, frq. — **ga-na-méd** *W.* **absolutely, at all events,** **ga-na-méd kal gos** it must be sent by all means; **ga-na-méd lóg-te taṅ yin** I shall give it back at all events (*B. čís-kyaṅ*).

ག་པུར་ *ga-pur* **camphor** *Med.*

ག་བྲ་ *ga-bra* n. of a medicine *Med.*

ག་ཙམ་ *ga-tsám* **how, how much, how many how long,** interr. and correl.; **as much as,** e.g. as much as you like (you may take) col.

ག་བཙོན་ *ga-btsón* an eruption of the skin *W.*

ག་ཚོད་ *ga-tsód C.* **how much,** **rin gha-tsọ̈** what is the price?

ག་ཞ་, ག་གཞར་, ག་ཤ་ *gá-ža*, *gá-ɣža*, *gá-ša* **a jest, joke, laughter,** *gá-ža daṅ rtséd-mo rtse Pth.* they jest and play; also adj.: inclined to jesting, **di-riṅ gá-ša mi dug** he is not in a good humour, in good spirits, to-day *W.*

ག་ཟུག་ *gá-zug W.* **how,** interr. and correl.

ག་གཟི་ *ga-ɣzi W.* **squinting.**

ག་རི་, དགའ་རིས་ *ga-ri*, *dga-ris* = *gá ža W.*; **ga-ri mi raṅ** I am in low spirits, **dejected.**

ག་རུ་ *gá-ru* = *gan-du* 1. **whither,** which way, to which place, whereto. — 2. **where,** interr. and correl.

ག་རུ་ཌ་ *ga-ru-ḍa* the Garuda-bird. v. *kyuṅ.*

ག་རེ་ *ga-ré* 1. **where is?** *B.* and col. — 2. *Ld.* a species of Lathyrus.

ག་ལ་ *gá-la* for *gáṅ-la*, *či-la C.*; **ghá-la tén-ne ne' ǰhun** owing to what, or from what cause did the disease arise? **ghá-la p̔en** to what does this serve, of what use is this? *Sch.*; **whither,** to what place? **ghá-la ₒdó-ghi yim-pa** *Ü*, where are you going to? — *gá-la-ba* = *gá-na-ba.*

ག་ལེ་ *gá-le C.* **slowly, softly, gently,** gen. in a good sense, opp. to every thing turbulent; therefore in exchanging compliments on meeting or parting: **ₒo-ná ghá-le ku žu naṅ** (perh. to be spelled *sku bžugs snaṅ*) says the person that has paid a visit, **ₒo-ná ghá-le p̔eb** he that received the visit, when taking leave of each other, both phrases implying about the same as our **farewell! good-bye!** Cf. *snaṅ-ba.*

ག་ལོག་ *ga-lóg W.* **squinting.**

ག་ཤ་ *gá-ša* 1. v. *ga-ža.* — 2. **girth** or **rope** slung across breast and shoulder in order to draw or carry anything; also **dog-harness;** also the **bandoleer** or **shoulder-belt,** worn as a badge of dignity by constables and the like officers; sobriquet for the rope of meditation, v. *sgom-t̔ág.*

ག་ཤས་ *ga-šás*, *C.* **gha-šẹ**, **some, part;** **bhú-mo yaṅ gha-šẹ čọ ǰhe'-pa yin** even girls, in part, take to religion (become nuns).

ག་ཤེད་ *ga-šéd* v. *šed.*

ག་ཤེལ་ *ga-šél* **glass-beads, glass-pearls** *Sch.*

ག་སིར་ *ga-sír*, instead of تعزیر **punishment** *Ld.*

གག་ *gag* 1. **silver** in bars, ingots, small pieces etc., **uncoined** *W.* — 2. **wad, wadding** (for loading muskets) *W.* — 3. *Cs:* = *bya-gág*, *gag-t̔sé* a water-fowl.

གག་པ་ *gág-pa Med.*, a swelling in the throat *Cs.*; *gag-lhóg* id. (?)

གང་ *gaṅ* I. interr. pron. 1. **who? which?** *B.*, *C.*, *W.*; when used adjectively, it generally follows its sbst. (so at least in good language), and if preceding it, it stands in the genit. case: *p̔yogs gaṅ* which region or part of the world? *gáṅ-gi dus* which time? in the latter case it may also mean **whose**: *gáṅ-gi lam* whose way? *p̀yi naṅ γnyis č̓os lugs gaṅ bzaṅ* which of the two doctrines, the Brahmanic or the Buddhist, is the right one? *p̀yogs gáṅ-nas oṅ, ṅo mi šés-pas* not knowing from what part of the country she comes *Glr.*; *ma ni gaṅ yin bu ni gaṅ yin bye-brág p̀yes* decide which is the mother and which the child *Dzl.*; *gaṅ žé-na* lit. 'if one asks which?' corresponds sometimes to the English 'namely, to wit, viz.'; *gáṅ-na* where? *gaṅ-la* whither? *gáṅ-nas, gáṅ-las* whence? *gáṅ-du* where? whither? *gáṅ-na-ba* = *ga-na-ba* v. above; *gáṅ-pa, yul gáṅ-pa*, col. _*gaṅ-yúl-pa*_, from what country? — 2. *C.* for *či* **what?** _*ghaṅ zér-ra(m)*_ what shall I say? _*kyọ́-kyi miṅ-la ghaṅ zér-ghyi yọ́-dhaṅ*_ what is your name? _*gháṅ-la yoṅ*_ what are you coming for? what do you want? — 2. rel., or rather correl. pron., **who, which, he who, she who, whoever, whichever, whatever,** ὅςτις: *gaṅ p̀yir ṫóṅ-ba de ni* she who follows *Dzl.*; *gaṅ gos ˳dód-pa-la gos byuṅ* whoever wanted clothes, to him they were given *Dzl.*; *rig-pa gaṅ rnó-ba čig-la stér-ro* I give it to him who is the sharpest as to sagacity *Glr.*; *ḱyód-kyi dpá-ba gaṅ yin-pa-la ḱó-bo mgu* the bravery which you have shown pleases me *Tar.* 21, 13; *rgyál-bu gáṅ-du ṫse ˳p̀ós-pai γnás-su sóṅ-ṅo* they went to the place where the prince had changed life *Dzl.*; *gáṅ-gi lam sṅón-du grub-pa des . . .* he whose way (of sanctification) will be completed first, shall . . . *Stg.* Often *ṫams-čád* or a plural-sign accompanies the partic.: *gaṅ mi šés-pa-dag* they who do not understand *Dzl.* Rarely in *B.*, but frq. in the col. language of *W.*, the *pa* after the verb is supplied by a gerundial particle, such as *na, nas*: _*gaṅ táṅ-na ḱyad med*_ which you intend to give is all the same. Sometimes, however, particularly in more modern literature, no *pa* is added to the verb at all, esp. when *gaṅ* is joined with *yin, yod,* or *dug*, so that such sentences in their form are very similar to the relative sentences of occidental languages: but that this omission of *pa*, although sanctioned by long continued use, is after all an incorrect breviloquence, and that *pa* must always be understood, appears from the frq. occurrence of the plural sign immediately after *yod* etc.: *de γnyis-kyi srid gaṅ yód-rnams* the claims to government which both of these maintained *Glr.*; *gáṅ-ṫse — dé-ṫse* **when — then**; *gaṅ žig* **whoever, if any body** etc. frq.; vulgo in *W.* often pleon. = any or some, _*gaṅ žig ṫims-si p̀i-la*_ on account of some law-suit, instead of *ṫims žig-gi p̀yir*; *gaṅ la-lá žig* is of a similar meaning, but less frq. The import of the word is still more generalized by *yaṅ* being added to *gaṅ* or to the verb: *dṅós-po gaṅ mṫoṅ yaṅ Mil.* whatever he sets his eyes upon; *gaṅ ltár-na yaṅ, gaṅ yin kyaṅ* whatsoever it may be, however that may be, be that as it may, at all events, esp. *C.*; *gaṅ-yaṅ-rúṅ-ba, gaṅ-rúṅ, gaṅ-či-yaṅ-rúṅ* whosoever he may be, whatsoever it may be, *quicunque*; *γnas gaṅ-yaṅ-rúṅ-ba-na* wherever; *gáṅ-nas gáṅ-du skyes kyaṅ* out of which class of beings and into whichsoever I shall be re-born *Dzl.* — 3. indefinite pron., used absolutely, **each, every, any, all,** when followed by a negation = **not any, none, no:** *žo dar ču sogs gaṅ yaṅ ḱa*, curdled milk, buttermilk, water, every thing tastes bitter *Med.*; *saṅs-rgyás gáṅ-gis kyaṅ ma bčágs-pa* not yet trodden by any Buddha *Glr.*; *p̀an gaṅ ṫogs gyis* be as useful as ever possible *Mil.*; *gáṅ-dag* all *Glr.* and elsewhere; *dé-dag mi ˳byuṅ gaṅ yaṅ med* these are to be found everywhere; *gáṅ-la gaṅ-˳dul* converting each in the manner best suited to him; *gáṅ-gis kyaṅ* = *čis-kyaṅ* by all means; *gáṅ-gis kyaṅ dgós-pa méd-pa* altogether useless *Mil.*; *gaṅ daṅ gaṅ Cs., Sch.* (more frq. *gaṅ daṅ či*) every thing whatsoever *Glr.*

གང་ག་ཆུང་ *gaṅ-ga-čuṅ* an officinal plant *Med.*

གང་གཱ *gaṅ-gā Ssk.* the river **Ganges.**

གང་བ་ *gáṅ-ba*, sometimes *gáṅ-po*, also *gaṅ* 1. **full**, *rin-po-čʿés baṅ-mdzód gáṅ-ba žig* a treasury full of jewels *Dzl.*; *ṫál-čʿu ḱól-mas gáṅ-ba-ste* being filled with boiling lye *Thgy.*; *γser-ṗyé bre gáṅ-po*, *γser γžóṅ-pa gaṅ* a measure filled with gold-dust, a basin full of gold; *ₒdòs-kyi náṅ-na sbrul ẏdúg-pas gáṅ-ṅo* lit.: in the ditch it was full of poisonous snakes *Dzl.*; *brgyud gáṅ-bar gyúr-to* the progeny increased *Glr.*; *mčʿód-rten ḱru gáṅ-pa Glr.* a pyramid, a full cubit in height. — 2. *W.* also **heaped** (measure), opp. to **gaṅ-čád** (lit. *bčad*) **smoothed** (measure).

གང་བུ་ *gáṅ-bu* **pod, shell, husk** (*Sch.* also also flower-bud?) *ₒod-zér-gyi gáṅ-bur ₒdríl-nas* enveloping himself in a veil of rays, wrapping himself in a garment of light (another reading: *góṅ-por* in a lump, in one mass) *Glr.*; *gaṅ-ló* an empty pod, freed from the kernels *W.*

གང་ཟག་ *gaṅ-zág* 1. **man**, as an intellectual being, **a person**; *gaṅ-zág γžán-gyis brda sprád-pas* another person describing it to you (opp. to what we know by our own perception and observation) *Mil.*; hence philosophical term for the **I** or **self**, पुद्गल *Was.*; *bstan-bčʿós-la mḱás-pai gaṅ-žág-rnams* learned or lettered men, men of science *Glr.*; esp. man in relation to religion: *čʿos ṗyi-bšól byéd-pai gaṅ-zág Mil.*, men who postpone religion, not troubling themselves about it: *ₒpʿágs-pai gaṅ-žág-rnams-kyi rgyál-po* the king of reverend persons, i.e. Buddha; *lóg-lta-čaṅ-gyi gaṅ-zág* heretical people; *gaṅ-zág ṗál-pa, ṫa-mál-pá* common people *Mil.* and others; also explicitly: people favourably disposed towards religion, religious people *Gyatch.* c. 26 & 27. (at present the word is generally understood in the latter sense); *dus ṗyis-kyi gaṅ-zág Glr.*, *ma-ₒóṅs-pai gaṅ-zág skál-ba daṅ ldán-pa Mil.* a pious posterity. The word, however, so little implies the clerical state, that it is used directly for 2. **layman**, one that has not taken orders *Dzl.* ༢༥༠, 5 and elsewhere. — 3. (resp. *žal-zág*) **tobacco-pipe**, not the hukka, but a small sort, similar to ours, gen. made of metal; *gaṅ-mgó* **bowl** of a tobacco-pipe; *gaṅ-mǰúg* mouth-piece or **tip** of it *C.*

གངས་ *gaṅs* 1. **glacier-ice, glacier**; *gáṅs-čan* adj. abounding in snow, in glaciers, also as a sbst. a glacier; *gáṅs-čan-las ₒbyúṅ-bai čʿu* the water issuing from a glacier *Med.*, and even as a p.n.: Tibet; *gáṅs-čan-gyi skad* the Tibetan language; *gáṅs-bšóg-pa* to cleave the snow, i.e. to have it trodden down by yaks sent in advance, in order thus to form a path for the travellers (v. Huc Voyage II. 421). — *gaṅs-rgyúd* a chain of snow-mountains. — *gaṅs-čen-mzod-lṅá* 'the five receptacles of the vast glacier-ice', or *gaṅs-čen-rǰé-lṅá* 'the five kings of the same', pronounced **ghaṅ-čen-ₒdzo'-ṅá**, or **ǰe-ṅá**, n. of a high mountain in Sikkim, commonly spelled Kinjinjunga; *gaṅs-čen-mtsʿó-rgyál* name of a deity (?) *Glr.* — *gaṅs-ṫigs Med.* perh. stalactite. — *gaṅs-ri* a snow- or ice-mountain, as p.n. = Ti-se. — Seldom 2. col. **ice** in general; **gaṅs-soṅ** it has frozen *W.* — 3. **snow** in general, **ghaṅ ₒbab** it snows *Ts.*; **ghaṅ-ma-čár** sleet. — 4. **the sclerotic** of the eye *Sch.*

གད་པ་ *gád-pa* 1. **a bluff**; precipitous river-banks, such as frequently inclose the mountain rivers of Tibet. — 2. In *W.* the word seems to refer more to the species of rock, which is favourable to the formation of such banks: **conglomerate**; *gad-pʿúg* a cavern in such a bank; *gad-rgyál* the gigantic walls of conglomerate rock, through which mountain rivers have cut their way.

གད་མོ་ *gád-mo* **laughing, laughter**, *ǰig-rtén-pai gád-mo* a laughter, a laughing-stock, to wordly-minded people; *ṅai gád-moi γnas* this is to me an object of laughing, it is ridiculous to me *Mil.*; *gád-mos ₒdébs-pa* to laugh at a person *Tar.* 25, 15.

གན་ *gan B.* and *W.*, *gám C.*, **nearness**, proximity, used only in such connections as *gan-du* **to, towards, up to**, *ṅai gán-du šog* come to me; *rgyál-poi gán-du* he went to the king; *ḱáṅ-pai gán-du soṅ* he went towards the house; *rgyál-poi gán-nas p̓yin* he came from the king; in col. language also c. accus.: **dóg-po gáń-du** *W.* close by the brook, and c. termin. case, **čur gán-te** *W.* hard by the water: *rir-gán-pa* one living close to a mountain or hill.

གན་ཀྱལ་ *gan-kyál,* and *rkyal,* **supine,** lying on the back, with the face upward, *gan-kyál (du) nyál-ba* to lie in that position; *ḥgyel-ba* to fall backward; *sgyél-ba* to make one fall on his back; **ghan-kyál lóg-pa** to perform a somerset, to tumble over head and heels *C.*

གན་རྒྱ་ *gan-rgyá C.,* **gam-rgya** *W.,* a **written contract, an agreement.**

གན་དར་ *gan-dár Sch.:* a silk handkerchief offered as a present in exchanging compliments on meeting, = *k̓a-btags.*

གན་མཛོད་ *gan-mdzód* **store-room, storehouse** *Sch.*

གནྡྷོ་ལ་ *gándho-la* n. of a famous temple in *rdo-rje-gdán* (Vajrâsana near Gaya in Bengal) *Tar.* 16, 4 and elsewhere frq.; yet the words in *Glr.* 8, 10: *p̓yi gándho-la náṅ-du lhá-k̓aṅ byás-pas* 'making outwardly a gandhola, inside an idolshrine', seem not to admit of a noun proper; a Lama explained it by *gtsug-lag-k̓aṅ;* more correctly perh. = *dri-gtsaṅ-k̓aṅ,* i.e. = **गन्धकूट.** Cf. also ghâṇḍhola.

གཉྫི་ར་ *gáñji-ra Glr.* 65, 8 obviously a *Ssk.* word, though not in our dictionaries; Lamas described it as an architectural ornament, consisting in small turrets or spires along the edge of a flat roof.

གབ་སྒྲ་ *gáb-sgra W.* **a belch** (vulgar).

གབ་པ་ *gáb-pa* **to hide,** to conceal one's self *Dzl.* and elsewhere frq.; *gáb-yig,* writing in secret characters, cryptography *W., C.; gáb-sa* a place of concealment, hiding-place.

གབ་སྤངས་ *gab-spáṅs Glr.,* panels or little boards beneath the cornice of a roof, often filled out with paintings.

གབ་ཙེ་, གབ་ཚེ་ *gáb-tse, gáb-tše* a tableau containing numerous mythological and astrological figures, and used for fortune-telling.

གབ་ཚད་, གབ་པའི་ཚ་བ་ *gab-tšád, gáb-pai tšá-ba* a disease *Med.;* acc. to *Schr.* a hectic, consumptive fever.

གམ་ *gam* v. *gan.*

གམ་བུ་ར་ *gám-bu-ra W.* **citron, lemon.**

གའུ་ *gau* 1. **a chest, box** *Pth.;* a little box or case; when containing amulets, it is worn suspended by a string round the neck (v. *Schl.* 174). — 2. a squeaking sound *W.,* **gau zér-če** **to squeak.**

གར་ *gar* I. (*Cs. gár-ma*) **a dance,** *gar byed-pa, W. *gár se-če*,* to dance; *glu gar rtséd-mo byéd-pa Glr.* to sing, to dance and play; *gár-mk̓an* 1. one dancing, a dancer, a performer, e.g. even Buddha or any saint, when displaying miracles. — 2. n. of a god *Tar.* 11, 17, acc. to *Schr., Siva; gar-stábs* a dancing gesture or motion. — II. = *gá-ru, gáṅ-du,* **whither, whereto, where;** *gar yaṅ* anywhere, *gár yaṅ skyé-ba* growing everywhere *Wdṅ.; gar yaṅ mi ḥgró-ba* to go nowhere, to remain where one is *Mil.; Pth.* — **gar-méd** *W.* at all events, by all means, = **ga-na-med** — *gar-báb* at random, hit or miss, at hap-hazard *Sch.*

གར་ནག་ *gar-nág* n. of a medicine *Lt.*

གར་བ་ *gár-ba* **strong.** *gar-čaṅ strong beer.*

གར་བུ་ *gár-bu* **solid,** not hollow *Sch.*

གར་མོ་ *gár-mo* **thick,** e.g. soup, = *ská-ba; gar-slá Sch.:* thick and thin; thickness.

གར་ཞ་ *gár-ža,* native name of the district called by the Hindoos Lâhul or Lâhŏl (acc to Cunningham 'Lahul' is a corruption of *lho-yul,* southern country, which latter appellation, however, is not in use in that district itself). Here, in the village of Kyelang, a missionary station was established in 1857, by the Church of the United Brethren (Moravians), together with a school and a lithographic press, for diffusing Christian knowledge by means of books and tracts.

གར་ལོག་ *gar-lóg*, *Tar.* 91, 7. 10. Transl. p. 317: 'acc. to *Was.* a rapacious mountain tribe, north-east of Tibet; in the Tibetan-Sanskrit dictionary mentioned as "Turushka". They are doubtless the same robbers, that are called 'Kolo' by Huc (II. p. 187), who were known to our Lama from Tashilhunpo as *mgo-lóg*, or *lčań-mo-mgo-lóg*, they having received this name ('queer-heads') in consequence of having their hair closely cropped. Possibly *gar-lóg* is the older and more correct form; cf. *dar-rgyas-gliń*.

གར་ཤ་ *gar-šá* the muscles of the thumb (?) *Med.*

གལ་ *gál* 1. **importance**, *gál-du ˳dzín-pa* to consider of importance, to esteem highly *Mil.*; *gál-čan Cs.*, more frq. *gal-čé-ba* important, *de mi šín-tu gál-čé-bar yód-do Glr.*, *bsláb-bya gal-čé-ba Glr.* important precepts; *gal-čúń* unimportant, insignificant; undervalued, slighted *Mil.*; *gál-po* prob. = *gal*, *Schr.*; *gal-po-čé-yi bzá-dpon* the important, indispensable master of the house *Mil.* — 2. **constraint, compulsion**, **ńa-la ghal ǰhuń* C.* I have been compelled. — 3. **trap, snare** *C*, *W.*, also *Mil.*; **gal-ltém* W.* id.; *gal ˳dzúg-pa* to set a trap or snare.

གལ་འགག་ *gál-˳gág Med.* ?

གལ་ཏ་ *gál-ta W.* **crow-bar, handspike.**

གལ་ཏེ་ *gál-te* I. sbst., *gál-te mčán-ḱuń bčug Pth.* ? — II. conj. **if, in case**, serves to introduce a conditional sentence, ending with *na* (which is the essential word, whereas *gal-te* may be left out as well): *gál-te .. ˳óń-na* if .. comes (ἐάν ... ἔλθῃ); also followed by *yań* (*kyań*), although black snow fell *Dzl.* (*nas* instead of *na*, frq. to be met with, is either merely a slip of the pen, or an impropriety of speech). — *gál-te-na* as one word, and with the signification of **perhaps**, or the Greek ἄν (not 'if', *Cs.*) I found only in a few passages of the Kye-lang manuscript of *Dzl.*, where the edition of *Sch.* has *gál-te*, which makes no sense. *gal-srid W.* = *gal-te*. In Lewin's Manual it often occurs in the sense of **but, however.**

གལ་སྨྲོད་ *gál-smdo* n. of a disease *Med.*

གལ་བ་ *gál-ba* **to force, to press** something on a person (cf. *gal* 2), *mi-la btson gal* in-door confinement is forced on men *Mil.*

གལ་རོ་ *gal-ró W.* **refuse, rubbish.**

གས་ *gas* v. *˳gás-pa*.

གི་ *gi* 1. num. for 33. — 2. affix instead of *kyi*, after *g* and *ń*; for the signification v. *kyi*.

གི་གུ་ *gi-gu* the vowel sign ི, **i**.

གི་གུ་ཞལ་, གི་གུ་ཤ་ *gi-gu-šél*, *gi-gu-šá Sch.*; 'having a white speck in the eye, wall-eyed (of horses)'.

གི་ཝང་ *gi-wáń*, *Glr.*, *gi-bám Lt.*, also *giu*, or *giu-wáń*, *Cs.*: 'n. of a concretion in the entrails of some animals, used for medicine'. But *Glr.* 35, 9 an elephant has it on its neck, and acc. to oral assertions it is to be found also in the human head; a man, for instance, is said to have *gi-wáń* in his brains, if in his sleep he is heard to utter long-drawn humming sounds.

གི་ལིང་ *gi-liń* a strong-bodied, durable horse *Sch.*

གི་ལིན་ *gi-lín Wts.* a fabulous animal.

གིང་ *giń Pth.* prob. a little drum, or the beating of it, as an accompaniment to dancing.

གིན་ *gin* affix, v. *kyin*.

གིར་མོ་ *gír-mo Ld.* the Indian **rupee**, = 5 *jau*.

གིས་ *gis* instead of *kyis* after *g* and *ń*, v. *kyis*.

གུ་ *gu* 1. num. for 63. — 2. sign of diminutives, e.g. *ḱyi-gu* puppy, little dog. — 3. **extension, extent, room, space** *gnás-sa gu-dóg*, *lhń-pa gu-dóg*, *lam gu-dóg* a narrow place, valley, road; *gu-yáṅs* (*-pa*) spacious, roomy, wide, *gu yáṅs-pa ˛dug* there is much room here.

གུ་གུ་ཤ་ *gú-gu-ša Ts.* **plate, flat dish.**

གུ་གུལ་ *gú-gul* (गुग्गुल) Amyris Agallocha, a costly incense, one kind is white, another black.

གུ་གེ་ *gú-ge* n. of a province in the south-western part of Tibet.

གུ་ཏི་ *gú-ti W.* **deaf** (?).

གུ་རུ་ *gú-ru Ssk.*, spiritual teacher, father-confessor.

གུ་རུག་ *gu-rug Ld.* **colt** or **foal** of an ass.

གུ་ལང་ *gu-láṅ* n. of a deity, resorted to by mothers for being blessed with children; acc. to *Sch.: Siva.*

གུ་ལེ་ *gú-le W.* for *gá-le* q.v.; *gú-le-la* id., **slowly, softly, gently,** without noise, **go gú-le-la čug** shut the door gently! *gu-yár Sch.* apparently the same.

གུ་སུ་ *gú-su Wdk.* **garment, dress** (?).

གུག་གེ་བ་ *gúg-ge-ba* **bent,** bent downwards (?), of leaves *Wdṅ.; gúg-pa* id.

གུག་པ་ *gúg-pa W.* to rub or scratch gently, **to tickle.**

གུང་ *guṅ* I. *Sch.:* 'the broad-headed tiger of Central Asia, Charachula' (*Mongol.*); it is said to differ from *stag*, and is not found in Tibet. — II. also *dguṅ* (*Cs. gúṅ-ma*) 1. **the middle,** *gúṅ-la* in the middle, e.g. the king in the middle (between his two wives); *stód-kyi gúṅ* (*-nas*) *ťon* taken out of the middle of the upper part *Mil.; gúṅ-du byéd-pa Thgy.* prob. to divide through the middle, to dissect (anatomically); *gúṅ sgrig-pa Sch.* 'to unite'; with respect to time: *dbyár-gyi gúṅ-la W.* in the middle of summer; *nyin-gúṅ*, and *mtsán-gúṅ* mid-day, mid-night *Cs.*; *guṅ-gnyis*, the two middle times, mid-day and mid-night; *nám-gyi guṅ-ťún-la* at the hour of midnight. — 2. **mid-day,** *guṅ ˛báb-pa* to take a noon-rest on a journey; *guṅ-tsigs* dinner *Schr.*; *guṅ sáṅs-la ˛gró-ba* (*W. *ča-če**) to take a walk about the middle of the day, at noon; perh. also generally: to take a walk; *guṅ-lón Sch.:* 'at noon', more prob.: afternoon. — 3. **mid-night,** *gúṅ-la* at midnight *Glr.*; *dguṅ-γčig* one night (?) *Sch.* — 4. (Chinese?) title of a magistrate in Lhasa, something like Privy Counsellor; v. *dguṅ*.

གུང་སྟག་ *guṅ-stág* prob. = *stag Ld.-Glr. Schl.* fol. 13, 6.

གུང་ཐང་ *guṅ-ťáṅ* n. of a monastery in *Máṅ-yul Mil.*

གུང་མོ་ *gúṅ-mo* **the middle finger;** **guṅ-dzúg* C.* id.

གུང་དམར་ལ་ཕུག་ *guṅ-dmár-la-p̔ug C.* **carrot.**

གུང་ལ་ཕུག་ *guṅ-la-p̔ug C.* **radish.**

གུད་ *gud* 1. **slope, declivity** *Cs.* — 2. **separation, solitude, seclusion** *Sch.*; *gúd-du ˛bór-ba* to place obliquely *Cs.*; *gúd-du γtégs-pa Dzl.* ༢༢༡, 18 to separate, to disperse (?) *Sch.* — 3. *C.:* **loss, damage** = *gun, god.* — 4. *Ld.:* **heavy** or **thick of hearing,** **gud-nág** quite deaf, deaf as a post. — 5. *gúd-du ǰúg pa* v. *˛gúd-pa*.

གུད་པ་ *gúd-pa* v. *˛gúd-pa*.

གུན་ *gun* (*Cs. gún-pa*) **loss, damage,** **ṅá-la gun p̔og* W.* I have suffered a loss (prop. damage has come over me).

གུན་པོ་ *gún-po Lh.* **expensive, dear.**

གུན་དུམ་ *guṅ-dúm* a bottle-shaped or cylindrical **basket** to put fruit in, *Ld.* (perh. akin to *rkón-pa*).

གུམ་པ་ *gúm-pa* v. *˛gúm-pa*.

གུར་ *gur*, resp. *bžugs-gúr*, *γzim-gúr Cs.*, also *dbu-gúr C.*, **tent,** *gos-gúr Cs.* a tent of silk, *p̔yiṅ-gúr* of felt, *sbra* and *re-gúr* of coarse yak's hair felt, *ras-gúr* of cotton cloth; *rgyal-gúr Cs.* 'a king's pavilion', *dmag-gúr* a military tent. — *gur-mčóg* a magnificent tent, or *gur-rgyál*, is used by Chr. Prot. for the tabernacle. — *gur-ťág* the tent-ropes, **gur-bér* W.*, or *gur-šiṅ Cs.* the tent-poles. — *gur-ťóg Cs.:* 'the upper covering or outer fly of a tent'. — *gur-γžól Cs.:* 'the walls of a tent'. — *gur-klád* passage for the smoke out of a tent, *gur-*

ₒgram lattice in the side of it, and *gur-lċám* stakes supporting the roof *Sch.*, — peculiar expressions relating to the felt-tents of the Mongol nomads.

གུར་ཀུམ་, གུར་གུམ་ *gur-kúm, gur-gúm* 1. **saffron,** Crocus *Glr., Lt.* — 2. **marigold,** Calendula, and similar yellow flowers *C.*

གུར་གུར་ *gur-gúr Ld.* a small **churn** used for preparing tea.

གུར་ལྤགས་ *gur-lpágs* a perforated skin, a hide full of holes *Sch.*

གུལ་གུལ་ *gul-gúl Bal.* **slowly,** for *gú-le.*

གུལ་ནག་ *gul-nág Lt.* n. of a medicine.

གུས་པ་ *gús-pa* sbst. **respect, reverence, devotion;** also adj **respectful, devout;** *dge-ₒdún-la gús-pas ṗyag ₒtsál-lo* the priesthood I respect with devotion; *ma-gús-pa* unbelieving, undevout *Thgy.*; **gus-žáb ċó-ċe* W.* to show a respectful willingness to serve; **humble,** *gús-par ₒgyúr-ba Cs.:* 'to humble one's self'; in modern letters = *ṗran,* your most humble servant.

གུས་པོ་ *gús-po C., W.,* **expensive, costly, dear.**

གེ་ *ge* num. for 93.

གེ་ཤ་ *ge-šá* a kerchief for the head hanging down behind.

གེ་སར་ *ge-sár* 1. *Cs.* n. of a flower, *Lt.* and elsewhere, prob. = केसर; it is said to grow in Nepal, and to be called also *pád-ma ge-sár.* — 2. *Sch.:* **pistil,** but, like *ze-ₒbrú,* it signifies undoubtedly the organs of fructification in general, as the natural science of Tibet is certainly not acquainted with the sexual difference in the parts of flowers; *ge-sár-ċan* the lotos flower *Sch.* — 3. n. of a fabulous king in the north of Tibet, with the epithet *dmág-gi rgyál-po Glr.* and elsewh.; *ge-sár-gyi sgruṅ* the fabulous history of the same.

གེགས་ *gegs* **hindrance, impediment, obstacle,** *gégs-med-par* without hindrance, unimpeded, *the-tsóm daṅ gegs sél-ba* to remove doubts and hindrances *Mil.*; *gegs-byéd bgegs* a malignant spirit, causing impediments or mischief *Zam.*; *ċos-mdzád yóṅs-la gegs byéd-pa* to throw obstacles in the way of all pious people *Pth.*; *saṅs-rgyás mi tób-pai gegs bži* four obstacles to attaining the Buddhaship *Thgy.*; also without a negation: *tób-pai grogs ₒgró-am gégs-su ₒgro* will you help me or hinder me in obtaining ...? *Mil.*; *ₒgrúb-pai gegs* impediment to perfection.

གེལ་པ་ *gél-pa* **branch** of a tree, *šiṅ-gel-pa.*

གོ་ *go* 1. numerical sign for 123. — 2. num. inst. of *dgú-bċú,* in the abbreviated numbers *go-ɣċig* etc., 91—99. — 3. for *gó-ċa.* — 4. for *gó-bo.*

གོ་ *gó* 1. **place, room, space** (prob. = *gu*); in this sense it is used in *go-mtsams-méd-par* without intermediate spaces, continuous; *ₒbru sna tsogs go-mtsams-med-par skyes* grain of every kind grew densely, luxuriantly; *go-mtsams-méd-par gáṅ-ba* closely filled *Tar.* 13; prob. also in *go-ċod:* 'the space is cut off, or filled i. e. the matter is done with, settled, satisfaction has been made; col. also: I have got enough, I am full, (the thing lost or missed) has been found, restored; **gho ċo' soṅ** or **ǰhuṅ* C., *go ċód-kan yod* W.* he has managed the business well, he has executed his commission satisfactorily; *des rgyál-bai gó mi ċod* by this the victory has not yet been fully decided *Mil.*; *tos bsam sgom ǰsúm-gyi go ċod* (by only once looking at the Ommanipadmehūm) every other hearing, thinking, or looking at is done away with, any thing further is rendered unnecessary *Glr.*; *kyéd-la go mi ċód-pai ċos* a doctrine not satisfactory to you *Mil.*; *bu tsab ṅa spyugs ċi ṗyir go mi ċod* why should it not be sufficient that I be condemned to exile instead of my son? *Pth.* — 2. **the proper place** of a person or thing among other persons or things, **position, rank,** condition of life, so in many of the following compounds, the word being seldom used alone: *ṗai gór* in the place, office, dignity of his father *Dzl.*; *gó-nas* according to, in proportion to *Glr.*; *go rgás-na* when rank and dignity are grown old and gone, when the position in life has been lost *Glr.*; hence *go-rgás* may be applied to an old maid (*Schr.*); *ráṅ-gi go ₒdug* that is my place, my business, like *ča;* also **place, space, spot** in a still more general sense: *'á-mai gó-na* at the place of my mother, with my mother *Glr.*; *raṅ-ₒtág-gi gó-na* near the mill *Glr.*; *go ldóg-pa* (*zlog-pa, lóg-pa*) to change place, esp. to turn to the contrary *S.g.*; *nád-go* the seat of a disease *Sch.*; *go-byéd* is mentioned as a quality of the air *S.g.*; *sprin-gyi go-bar ṗyé-nas ₒoṅs*, we came parting the space between the clouds *Mil.*; *sprín dkar ldiṅ-gi go-čóg Mil.?* — 3. **armour**, gen. *gó-čá.* —

Comp. *go-skábs* lit. a chance of taking place, of existing, *bdé-bai go-skábs gá-la yod Pth.*, where is there a possibility of being happy? — *go-skál C.* the share or portion due to a person in accordance to his rank. — *go-ḱáṅ* **arsenal** *Schr.* — *go-ḱráb* coat of mail with helmet, **armour.** — *go-grál* **rank, dignity** *Cs.* — *go-grás* id. *Cs.* — *go-rgás* v. *go* 2. — *gó-ča* 1. **armour**; often fig.: *bzód-pai gó-ča bgó-ba*, or *gón-pa*, to put on the armour of patience; *mi-ǰigs-go-ča* the harness of intrepidity. 2. **gear, implements, tools** in general, *bkra-šis srúṅ-bai gó-ča* (charmed) instruments used for securing future happiness (in behalf of a new-born infant) *Med.* — *go-mnyám C.* of equal rank. — *go-ťém* degree of dignity or rank *Cs.* — *go-ₒdún* = *sna-ₒdún*, of different sorts, **various** *Lex.* — *go-ldóg* (cf. *go-ldóg-pa*) **the contrary, reverse, opposite; wrong, perverse,** *dé-las go-ldóg* the contrary of it *Med.*: **go ǰug go-lóg-la** *W.* head fore-most; **go-lóg čó-če** *W.* to go to work in the wrong way, **go-lóg ḍi-če** to write wrong. — *go-ṗáṅ(s)* 1. **degree, rank, dignity,** *blón-poi go-ṗáṅ-la bkód-par ₒgyúr-ba Pth.* to be installed into the dignity of a minister: *go-ṗáṅ spár-ba Lex.* to raise the dignity. 2. **model, pattern,** standard of perfection (?) *Cs.* — *go-mťsáms* v. *go* no. 1. — *go-mťsón* harness and weapons. — *go-rím* 1. **order** of rank *Glr.* — 2. **succession**, successive order, turn.

གོ་ཁ་ *gó-ḱa* the place (near the hearth) for firewood *Mil.*

གོ་བ་ *gó-ba* I. vb. 1. **to understand, comprehend,** *W.* **há-go-če**; *go-dká-ba* difficult, hard to be understood, *go-slá-ba* easy to be understood, intelligible; **gho-dé-wa yoṅ** *C.* now it becomes intelligible, thus it will be understood; *go-byed-brdá Lex.* an explaining, illustrating symbol; *gó-žiṅ rtóg-pa* to take in and comprehend; *brdá-ru go* this I understand to be a symbol *Pth.*; *gó-bai yul, gó-byai yul* a subject intelligible to all *Schr.* — 2. **to mean, to imagine,** *par* that. *Glr.*; *go-nór-ba* to misunderstand, to mistake, to be mistaken. —

II. sbst. **perception, comprehension,** *gó-ba bláṅ-ba Mil.* to come to a right comprehension, a clear perception (of some philosophical or religious truth): *gó-bai ṅjál-ba Lex.*: '*ṅjál-ba* in the sense of perceiving'.

གོ་བོ་ *gó-bo* a large **eagle** or **vulture**, *C., W.* and *B.*; *go-sér* the common black-bearded vulture of the Himalaya, with a yellow neck; *go-brúṅ* excrements of it *Med.*

གོ་བྱི་ལ་ *go-byi-la Med.* n. of a poisonous medicinal fruit *Cs.*; *go-bye Med.* id.?

གོ་ཡུ་ *go-yú Med.*, n. of a flower *Cs.*

གོ་ར་ *go-rá Cs.*; 'prison, jail'; prop. a court surrounded by a wall.

གོ་རེ་ལོང་ *gó-re-lóṅ* a waiting-servant, **page** *Cs.*

གོ་ལ་ *gó-la Ssk.* **ball, bullet.**

གོ་ལོག་ *go-lóg* v. *go-ldóg* sub *go* Comp.

གོ་ཤེན་ *go-šén* v. *go-čén.*

གོ་ས་ *go-sá* **rank, dignity,** **go-sá čén-po, ťón-po** *W.* high in rank.

གོ་ཏ་མ་, གཽ་ཏ་མ་, གོའུ་ཏ་མ་ *Gó-ta-ma, Gau-ta-ma, Gou-ta-ma,* **the Gotamide**, the descendant of Gotama, which, among others, was the name of the founder of the Nyaya philosophy in India (Banerjea Dialogues on Hindoo Philosophy p. 56f.); but in the Buddhist legends it is mentioned as the name of one of the ancestors of the Sakya-race, on which account Buddha is often called Gautama. The different forms of this name are used promiscuously by Tibetan writers.

གོག་ *gog W.* for *góṅ-po* **a lump.**

གོག་ཐལ་ *gog-ťál* **ashes,** **gog-ťál yúm-ċe, yóg-ċe, tiṅ-ċe** *W.* to spread ashes (viz. on the snow, in order to increase the effects of the sun, and to accelerate the thawing of the snow).

གོག་པ་ *góg-pa* 1. **to crawl** (of little children). — 2. **to crumble off, to scale off** (of the plaster of a wall, of scurf etc.).

གོག་པོ་ *góg-po* **dilapidated, ruinous,** *ḱáṅ(-pa) góg(-po)* a house in ruins; *mḱar-góg* a dilapidated castle; of clothes: out of repair, ragged; *žiṅ-góg* a field lying waste; *dpe-góg* an antiquated, worthless book; *gog-góg Cs.:* 'the sound of a somewhat broken vessel'.

གོང་ *goṅ* 1. **price, value,** also *goṅ-ťáṅ Glr.,* frq.; *goṅ dpyád-pa* (often also *bċád-pa,* inconsistent with etymology) to apprize, to fix a price; *goṅ brgyáb-pa C.* (*goṅ* ˳*grig-pa Schr., Sch.*) id. — 2. **the above,** in space as well as in time, (in *Khams* e. g. it is used as a sbst., signifying: elevated, alpine pasture-grounds); **the above said, the former,** referring to a preceding part or passage of a book, *goṅ daṅ mťun, goṅ daṅ* ˳*drá-bar, goṅ-bžin, goṅ-mťsúṅs* as above (mentioned); *ṗrin goṅ* ˳*og* ˳*dzól-ba* to confuse a message, to make a medley of it *Glr.*; *góṅ-du, góṅ-na, góṅ-nas, góṅ-la* 1. adv. over it, on it, thereon, above, from above. 2. postp. c. genit. or accus.: on, above, over, before, *sgo góṅ-du* over the door; *yáb-kyi góṅ-du* ˳*das,* he died before his father *Glr.*; *déi góṅ-du* before this time *Glr.*; *ma ťsogs góṅ-du* before they are assembled; *góṅ-gi* the former, the above mentioned; *góṅ-gi dé-rnams* those preceding; *góṅ-du bšád-pa ltar* as has been said, explained above; *góṅ-du smós-pa* the above mentioned; *góṅ-gi . . . žes smós-pa* the above statement that . . .; *sṅa goṅ bód-kyi rgyál-po* the former (ancient) Tibetan kings; *goṅ* and ˳*og* like our subdivisions of *a* and *b*, the first and second part, division or section of a book, *ba-góṅ* and *ba-*˳*óg* Volume XV Section 1 and 2; the face and the back of a leaf: *bži-góṅ* folio 4, a. — *goṅ-sku-*˳*žógs,* a title, like our: his highness, excellence, eminence *Sch.* v. *sku.*

གོང་པོ་, གོང་བུ་ *góṅ-po, góṅ-bu, W.* **gog**, **lump, mass, heap, clot,** *šá-goṅ-po* a lump of flesh *Dzl.*; *ḱrag-góṅ* a clot of blood *Glr.*; **bol-góṅ** *C.,* **sa-góg** *W.,* clod, glebe; **ḱa-góg** *W.* snow-ball.

གོང་བ་ *góṅ-ba, W.* **góṅ-ṅa**, *gós-kyi góṅ-ba,* **collar,** *goṅ-ba-nas* ˳*dzín-pa* to seize by the collar

གོང་མ་ *góṅ-ma* a higher one, **a superior; the former,** the first named, *góṅ-ma bžin-du* like the former; *rgyál-ba góṅ-ma* the most high, the divine Buddha *Mil.*; *góṅ-ma ċe, góṅ-ma ċén-po* the most high, applied to worldly sovereigns, as: *rgya-nág góṅ-ma* the emperor of China *C.*; *góṅ-ma-rnams Mil.* the gods (the 'superi' of the ancients), among whom according to the doctrines of Buddhism the Lamas are included.

གོང་མོ་ *góṅ-mo* **ptarmigan, white grouse,** *ľhá-bya góṅ-mo B.* and *C.,* **ri-bya góṅ-mo** *W., goṅ-sróg* id. (?); *goṅ-yag Sch.:* wood-grouse, cock of the wood, Tetrao urogallus.

གོང་ཞུ་ *goṅ-žú C.* **paper lantern.**

གོད་ *god, W.* **yód-ḱa** *Dzl. gód-pa, Cs. gód-ma* 1. **loss, damage,** *god* ˳*gyúr-ba Thgy.,* **gho'-la* ˳*dó-wa** *C.,* **god-la ċá-ċe** *W.,* to suffer loss, e.g. *nór-la* or *nor,* a loss of money and property; *gód-pa* vb. id., **nor gód-da** *W.* have you had a loss? 2. *C.* **punishment.**

གོན་ *gon* the common **gourd, pumpkin** *W.*

གོན་པ་ *gón-pa* I. vb. **to put on** (clothes, shoes), *mgó-la ža gón-pa* to put on a cap.

— II. sbst. **coat, clothing** *Sch.*; **gón-če* *Lh.*, *Ld.*, **gón-ma* *Bal.* id.

གོབ་ནོན་ *gob-nón* (spelling uncertain), **gob-nón čó-če, táñ-če, gyáb-če* *W.* **to tease, vex, irritate.**

གོམ་པ་ *góm-pa* 1. **a pace, step,** *góm-pa ₒbór-ba* to make a step, to pace; *góm-pa bdun ₒbór-ba Glr.* 5, 2 and elsewh.: to make seven steps, as a ceremony, which may also be counted equivalent to a religious pilgrimage, the actual performance of which is not possible: *góm-pa ₒdór-ba* prob. = *ₒbór-ba*; *góm-pa ₒdébs-pa* and *skyél-ba Lt.* ? ? — *góm-pai stabs* the (peculiar) manner of stepping *Zam.*; **ṗrú-gu-la gom-táñ láb-če* *W.* to teach a little child to walk; **gom čág-če* to stride solemnly along; **gom-ɉór* col. a veranda (?). — 2. **the 'pas'** in dancing.

གོམས་པ་ *góms-pa* **accustomed, wonted, wont** c. dat.; *klóg-pa-la góms-šiñ* practising (the art of) reading *Dzl.*; *góms-par byéd-pa*, and *ₒgyúr-ba* c. dat. and accus., to accustom one's self to a thing, to practise; *mi góm-pa* unaccustomed; **mi dañ góm-te* *W.* accustomed to man, tame, domesticated: **ghom-kyé* *C.* a habit, custom.

གོར་མ་ *gór-mu Cs.*: a general name for stone; *Sch.*: stones, rubble, bowlder-stones.

གོར་མ་ཆག་ *gor-ma-čág*, eleg. *gor-ma-bkúm*, **certain, sure, indubitable,** *de ₒbyúñ-ba gor-ma-čág-go* his coming is quite sure *Wdñ.*; *dé yin gor-ma-čág-go* that it is this, is quite certain *Stg.* frq; *gor-ma-čág-par* adv. certainly.

གོར་མོ་ *gór-mo* 1. **round, circular** *Sch.*; *gor-gór Med.* id. — 2. *W.* **a rupee.**

གོར་ཤི་ཤ་ *gór-ši-ša* v. *tsán-da-na*.

གོལ་བ་ *gól-ba* v. *ₒgól-ba*.

གོས་ *gos* 1. resp. *ná-bza*, **garment, dress.** — 2. in some compounds **silk.** — *rgyán-gós* fine clothes *Glr.*; *rgyún-gos C.*, *W.*, an every day coat; *čos-gos* clerical garb or garments *Schl.* 170, *Burn.* I. 306, *Köpp.* I. 339, II. 266; *mtáñ-gos* a sort of petticoat worn by the monks, having many plaits and folds, like the kilt of the Highlanders, but longer and of one colour; *ṗó-gos* man's dress; *blá-gos* an upper garment, a kind of toga; *mó-gos* a woman's gown; *γzáb-gos* holiday clothes, opp. to *rgyun-gos C.*, *W.* — *gos gón-pa*, *gyón-pa* to put on, *ₒbúd-pa* to take off, *bṙje-ba* to change clothes; *brtségs-pa Sch.*: to put one garment over the other; *gos btég-pa* to tuck up, by drawing the front skirts under the girdle; *gos ldáb-pa* to lay or fold a coat together; *gos spú-ma* a coat of napped cloth.

Comp. *gos-skúd* **silk-thread.** — *gos-sgáb* **skirt** or **flap** of a coat. — *gos-sgám* box, chest, or press for clothes, **wardrobe.** — *gos-čén*, col. *go-šén*, silk fabrics, **silks.** — *gos-rnyiñ* an old coat or dress. — *gos-túñ* **trowsers** *Glr.*, *C.* — *gos-mtá* = *gos-sgab*. — *gos-nág* a black garment, a female dress. — *gos-bzáñ* a beautiful dress, fine clothes (as an object of show), festival raiment. *gos-lág* (in *W.* also pronounced **goi-lág, go-lág** in *C.* **gho-lág**) **dress, clothes,** body-linen; **gos-lág ṭú-če* *W.* to wash linen.

གོས་པ་ *gós-pa* pf. of *bgó-ba*.

གྱ་ *gya* num. instead of *brgyád-ču*, in the abbreviated numbers *gya-γčig* etc. 81—89.

གྱ་ *gya*, a root, the meaning of which is not quite settled yet; it occurs in the following combinations: *gya-gyú* (*Cs.*: crookedness?) **intrigues,** secret machinations *C.*, *W.*; *γnód-séms dañ bslú-bai gya-gyú sogs* malice, deceitful tricks and the like; *gya-gyu-čan* crafty, deceitful, fraudulent, e.g. *sems*; *gya-gyú byéd-pa* to intrigue, to plot. — *gya-ma-gyú* 1. of rivers etc.: **quiet, calm,** gently flowing along *Mil.* 2. of a man: **cautious, close, reserved,** so that one does not know what to think of him, ni f. — *gya-nyés Mil.* was explained: **marvelous, inexplicable,** of men, occurrences etc. — *gya-nóm-pa Cs.*: 'contentment, joy'; yet the context in several passages of *Mil.* suggests the signification: abundance, sufficiency. — *gya-rtsóm*, *gya-tsóm* haste, hurry, rashness *Cs.*

གྱ་བ་ *gyá-ba* **deformed, disfigured, having** lost his or her former beauty *Cs.*

གྱག་པ་ *gyág-pa* diminished *Cs.*; v. *°gyág-pa.*

གྱང་, གྱེང་ *gyaṅ, gyéṅ* **pisé**, earth or clay stamped into moulds, and frequently used as building-material in *Sp.*, *Ld.*, and other parts of Tibet; *gyaṅ-sgróm* pisé-mould; *gyaṅ-skór* pisé-wall round an estate or village *Glr.*; *gyaṅ-ra* cattle-yard constructed of pisé; *gyaṅ-tse* terrace wall of pisé *Ld.*; *gyaṅ-rím* one layer of pisé, i.e. as much as is stamped in at a time, about one ell in height; this frequently serves for a measure of the depth of the snow *Mil.*; *gyaṅ-ris* fresco or wall-painting.

གྱད་ *gyad*, also *gyád-pa*, *Ssk.* मल्ल 1. **a champion**, a man of great physical strength, **an athlete**, frq.; *da-dúṅ gyád-gyi tsal °gran* let us try once more our strength in fighting *Mil.*; *gyád-rdo* giant-stone, i.e. a stone which only a giant is able to lift *Mil.* — 2. n. of a people *Tar.* 11, 10.

གྱན་རྒྱུ་ *gyan-rgyu Med.*, *gyan-rgyui bu-ga*, *gyan-rgyui mtu?*

གྱམ་ *gyam* **a shelter, a grotto** large and wide, but not deep (cf. *skyibs*), *brág-gyam* a shelter under a rock; *gád-gyam* a grotto beneath a conglomerate rock; *ṗoṅ-gyám* (for *ṗa-boṅ-gyam*) a shelter under a beetling rock: *gyám-bu* a little cover or shelter *Cs.*

གྱར་གྱོད་ *gyar-gyód* prob. = *gyod-ḱa*, *god-pa* loss, damage.

གྱི་ *gyi* for *gyi*, after *n*, *m*, *r*, *l*; v. *kyi.*

གྱི་ན་(བ་) *gyi-na* (*-ba*) 1. **bad, coarse, mean, poor, miserable,** of food, clothes etc.; *gyi-na °ṫsó-ba* a miserable, starving life *Pth.* — 2. **unsteady, fickle** *Schr.*

གྱི་ལིང་ *gyi-liṅ Glr.* n. of an excellent breed of horses.

གྱིག་ *gyig* **caoutchouc, India rubber,** *gyig-šiṅ*, *gyig-sdóṅ* caoutchouc-tree *Sik.*

གྱིང་ *gyiṅ* n. of a deity *Pth.*, perh. = *kiṅ-káṅ.*

གྱིང་མོ་ *gyiṅ-mo W.* gently **sloping,** gradually descending or subsiding.

གྱིན་ *gyin* v. *kyin.*

གྱིམ་བག་ *gyim-bág* **amalgam**; *gyim-bág-gis °byúg-pa* to gild in the fire *Schr.*

གྱིས་ *gyis* 1. inst. of *kyis*, after liquid letters. — 2. v. *bgyid-pa.*

གྱུ་ *gyu Cs.* = *gya-gyú*; cf. also *sgyu.* — *gyú-ba* v. *°gyú-ba.*

གྱུང་རོ་ *gyúṅ-ro* v. *gyóṅ-ro*; *gyur* v. *°gyúr-ba.*

གྱེ་གུ་ *gyé-gu* **crookedness, curve; hunch, hump,** crookback, crooked; *gyé-gu-čan* of a camel, *gyé-gur °dúg-pa* being crooked, of trees, opp. to *draṅ-po*, *Stg.*

གྱེ་གོང་ *gye-góṅ* n. of a Bonpo idol (?) *Mil.*

གྱེང་ *gyéṅ* v. *gyaṅ.*

གྱེད་པ་ *gyéd-pa* v. *°gyéd-pa.*

གྱེན་ *gyen* (opp. to *ťur*) **up, upward, up-hill,** mostly followed by *du* or *la*, *gyén-du °dzég-pa* to mount up, to ascend; *gyén-du rdzé-ba* to turn up, to cock (a hat or cap); above, on the surface, *gyén-du lús-pa* to keep above (water) *Glr.* **gyen-la ḍáṅ-po** *W.* **perpendicular, vertical;** *gyen-čád* (opp. to *man-čád*) the upper part of a country, *pú-rig gyen-čád* Upper Purig, *Ld.-Glr. Schl.* 26, b. also sbst.: *gyen γzár-po* a steep ascent *C.*

གྱེར་ *gyer* v. *dgyér-ba.*

གྱེས་ *gyes* v. *°gyé-ba.*

གྱོ་མོ་ *gyó-mo* 1. **gravel, grit** *Dzl.*, *Stg.* — 2. **potsherd** *Cs.*; *gyo-dúm* id. — 3. **tile, brick** *Sch.*; *gyo-mgó* id.; clay-vessel. In an allegorical comparison of the body with a house, the hair of the head is said to be like a *ṗó-gyo mo-gyói rdza Med.?* *gyo-rtsi Wdṅ.?*

གྱོག་པ་ *gyóg-pa* **curved, crooked** *Cs.*; *gyóg-po* **left-handed, awkward** *Sch.*

གྱོགས་ *gyogs C.* pronounced **ghyog, ghyo**, for *sgyogs* **cannon,** large gun.

གྱོང་ *gyóṅ* **want, need, indigence,** *lťo-gós-kyi gyóṅ ťég-pa* to be able to endure want of food and clothes *Mil.*; *°ḱur-ba* to be reduced to want. — gyóṅ-po (cf. kyoṅ-po) **hard, harsh, rough, rude, impolite,** (*srab-*) *ḱa-gyóṅ-po* hard-mouthed; *gyoṅ-ró* a dried up body, a mummy *Sch.*; metaph. *dgra-gyóṅ* a hard, cruel, dangerous enemy; *ḱa-gyoṅ-čé* very rude, impudent *Mil.*

གྱོད་ *gyod* v. *ₒgyód-pa.*

གྱོད་ཁ་ *gyód-ḱa* **loss; quarrel, law-suit** *Sch.*

གྱོན་པ་ *gyón-pa* **to put on, to wear** = *gón-pa*; *lús-la gyón-pai gos* the garment that one wears *Dzl.*; *gyóṅ-rgyu* materials for clothing *Mil.*

གྱོས་པོ་ *gyós-po* **father-in-law,** *gyós-mo* mother-in-law, *gyos-sgyúg* parents-in-law *Dzl.*, *Stg.* (In *Ld.* this word is rather avoided, sounding, as it is pronounced there, much like the obscene *rgyó-ba.*)

གྲྭ་ *grva* 1. **angle, corner** *Dzl.* ༡༢༥, 13; **lap, lappet, extremity,** *gós-kyi grva* coat-tail *Tar.* 98, 10 (seldom used). — 2. **school,** *klóg-grva* a reading-school *Cs.*; *sgóm-grva Glr.* and elsewhere: a meditating-school; *sṅágs-grva* a school for mystical theology *Cs.*; *ₒdúl-grva Glr.* a training-school, seminary; *smán-grvá* a medical school; *rtsís-grva* a school where mathematics are taught; *yig-grva* a writing-school *Cs.* — 3. **a cell** *Cs.* (?) — 4. sometimes for *grvá-pa.*

Comp. *grvá-ḱaṅ* **school-house, school-room;** **láb-ḍa-ḱaṅ** *W.* id. — *grvá-pa* **scholar, disciple,** generally; **monk,** the lowest ecclesiastical grade; *grvá-pa byéd-pa* to become or to be a monk. — *grvá-dpon* **school-master** *Cs.* — *grva-ṗrúg* **school-boy.** — *grvá-tsáṅ* the apartments in great monasteries, where the monks belonging to the same theological confession live together. — *grva-tsógs* convention of monks. — **ḍa-šág** **cell** *C., W.* — *grva-sa* **monastery,** *grva-sa čén-po* a great monastery; a school attached to such a one; *mtsan-nyid-kyi grvá-sa žig* a school of the Tsannyidpa sect; *dei stón-pa-rnams* the teachers of such a school *Mil.*

གྲ་ཏི་ *grá-ti* **plate, dish** *Ld.*

གྲ་བ་ *grá-ba* 1. sbst., also *gra-ṗád* **'a muzzle'** *Sch.*; a net before the window, to prevent passers-by from looking into the room *Schr.* — 2. vb. **to carve in wood.**

གྲ་མ་ *grá-ma* 1. **a beard** of corn, **awn,** *ₒbru grá-ma-ċan* bearded, awned plants, such as corn etc. (opp. to *ₒbru gáṅ-bu-ċan* leguminous plants) *S.g.*; **the bones** of fish v. *nya.* — *Zam.*: a tree or shrub, prob. the Tibetan **furze,** Caragana versicolor. — 3. a disease of the genitals, perh. venereal boils (condyloma) *Med.*

གྲག་པ་ *grág-pa* I. sbst. 1. **noise, rumour, talk,** *Cs.* — 2. the principal or most distinguished amongst several persons *Mil.* — II. vb. = *ₒgrág-pa, miṅ yaṅ mi grág-par* so that not even the name is mentioned any more *Pth.*

གྲགས་པ་ *grágs-pa* I. vb. 1. **to bind** *Thgy., C., W.*, e.g. *grés-po* a load, a burden, also *grás-pa Thgy.*; perh. also *ₒgrágs-pa, ₒgrógs-pa* q.v. — 2. pf. of *ₒgrág-pa.* — II. sbst. 1. **fame, reputation,** character by report, *grágs-pa ṅán-pa* ill name, bad repute *Pth.*; **rumour, report,** *deĩ grágs-pa čén-po byuṅ* the report of it spread, was circulated; in most cases it signifies **good name, renown,** *snyán-pa daṅ grágs-pas saĩ steṅ ṫams-ċád ḱyáb-pa Glr.* the whole earth was filled with (his) fame and renown; *snyan-grágs* id. (*Cs.*: good tidings); *grágs-pa-ċan, snyán-grags-ċan* illustrious, renowned; *rgyáṅ-nas grágs-pa če-ba* of great renown, of celebrity at a distance, (of less significance when more closely examined); **fame, glory,** *rnyéd-pa daṅ grágs-pa-la čágs-pas Dzl.*, greedy of gain and fame; *grágs-pa-čén-po* is also the name of a goddess = *dpal-lhá-mo.* — *grags* = *grágs-pa*: *grágs-ₒdod-ċan* desirous of glory *Mil.*; *grágs-ċan W.* (pronounced **rág-ċán**) **famous, renowned; beautiful, splendid, glorious; proud, haughty** (in this case perh. for *drégs-pa-ċan*). — *grágs-ₒdzin-ma, Ssk.* यशोधरा, यशोवति, the second wife of Buddha, acc. to others the second name of his first wife. — 2. **cry, outcry, clamour** (perh. better written *grág-pa*), *dga-grágs ˌúr-ba* to raise shouts of joy.

གྲང་བ་ *gráṅ-ba*, *W.* **ḍáṅ-mo**, I. adj. **cold, cool,** *gráṅ-bai ɣnas* a cool place; **ḍáṅ-mo rag* W.*, **ḍháṅ-ghi ˳dúg* C.* I am cold.

II. sbst. **coldness, cold,** *gráṅ-ba ni dró-bar gyur* the cold changed into warmth *Dzl.*: **mén-ťog ḍáṅ-mo ṗog* W.* the cold has struck, killed, the flowers. — *graṅ-nád* the cold fit of the ague, **ḍhaṅ-ṭi** (lit. *mkʼris*) *C.* id. — **ḍaṅ-ṅád* W.* synon. with *grúm-bu*, **gout, rheumatism, arthritic pain;** *graṅ-dro* **cold and warmth,** *graṅ-dro-méd-pai ras-kyáṅ ˳di* this thin cloth which constitutes my clothing, in warm and in cold weather *Mil.*, v. *méd-pa;* also warmth in a relative sense, **temperature.** — *graṅ-śúm Lt.*, *graṅ-śúm byéd-pa* to shiver with cold *Schr.*

III. vb., also *graṅs-pa* 1. **to get** or **grow cold,** *gráṅs-su bčúg-pa Lex.* to let grow cold; *graṅs ˳gró-bar ˳dug* it will grow cold *Mil.; graṅ mi bya* one must not suffer (the child) to catch cold *Lt.* — 2. **to count, judge, consider,** v. *bgráṅ-ba;* also *Zam.: čes gráṅ-naaṅ* though such may be supposed; *Cs.* and *Schr.* have also *graṅ* **perhaps,** *yin graṅ* perhaps it may be so.

གྲངས་ *graṅs*, col. also **ḍaṅ-ka**, *Ssk.* संख्या **number,** frq., *lan graṅs-dú-mar* a number of times *Mil.; graṅs-méd-pa*, eleg. *graṅs-ma-mčís-pa* innumerable; *gráṅs-čan* numerous (?) *Cs.; gráṅs-čan-pa* the atheistic Sankhya sect of the Brahmans (Bun. p. 66); **ḍá-ḍáṅ žág-ḍaṅ gyáb-če* W.* to date (lit. to write down the number of month and day); *graṅs ˳débs-pa* or *rtsí-ba* to count *Cs.* — *graṅs-brdá* (*Cs.* Gram. § 235) symbolical numerals, certain nouns, which in some books are used instead of the usual numerals, e.g. *mig*, eye, for 'two'.

གྲངས་པ་ *gráṅs-pa* to grow cold, v. *gráṅ-ba* III.

གྲབ་རྒྱག *gráb-rgyág* pride, boasting *Sch.*

གྲབས་ *grabs* 1. **preparation, arrangements, measures; a contrivance,** *grabs byéd-pa* to make preparations for, to be on the point of, frq., *˳gró-bai grabs byéd-pa*, to make preparations for departing, *ɣsód-grábs ɣód-pai tsé-na* just as preparations were made for slaughtering them *Mil.; *ko kyug ḍhab ǰhe'* C.* he is getting sick, is going to vomit; *ḱáb-grabs, ˳dziṅ-grabs* the making one's self ready for combat. — 2. col. also for *gros*, **deliberation,** **ṇe čir dhab ǰhe' dug* C.* they are deliberating about me; **naṅ-náṅ-ṅi ḍabs ťún-ṇe* W.* on mutual agreement.

གྲམ་པ་ *grám-pa* 1. **swamp, marsh, fen** *Lex.* — 2. *˳grém-pa Mṅg.*

གྲལ་ *gral*, *Ssk.* पङ्क्ति 1. **row, series, class,** esp. a row of persons, *gral(-du) sgrig-pa* to order, to dispose in rows, in rank and file; *grál-gyi ťóg-ma, ltag, goṅ*, more frq. *gral-mgó* the upper end of a row, the uppermost place, the seat at the head of the table; *ťá-ma, ˌog* or *gral-mǰúg(-ɣžug)* the lower end; *gral mgó-ma* the first, the head person *Mil.; ɣyas-grál* the right-hand end, *ɣyon-grál* the left-hand end; *gral-rím C.* **claim, title,** *rgan-ɣžon-gral-rím* the right of seniority; *grál-pa* a beer-house customer; *gral-ɣtám* tap-house talk *Mil.; dbaṅ-grál* the row of supplicants for a benediction; *mčed-grógs daṅ dbaṅ-grál mťun dús-su Mil.* if you sit with your fellow-believers in one row, on one mat; **če-ḍál-la čud soṅ* W.* he has entered into the row, the class, of adults. — 2. **bench.** — 3. **proportionality** (?), **žeṅ-ríṅ ḍal-méd daṅ* W.* with his disproportioned length and breadth, his unwieldiness. — 4. **mi žig-la ḍal žig ḍíg-če* W.* (lit. *sgrig-pa*) *W.* to play **a trick** to a person.

གྲལ་མ་ *grál-ma* a small beam, **rafter,** *Cs.*; *grál-bu, gral-ṗyám S.g.* roof-laths, sticks which are laid close together and covered with earth.

གྲས་ *gras* **class, order, series; rank, dignity; tribe** *Cs.*

གྲས་པ་ *grás-pa* 1. for *drás-pa.* — 2. **to bind,** v. *grágs-pa.*

གྲི་ *gri* (so pronounced in *Pur.*) 1. **knife,** *gris ɣčód-pa*, **ḍi daṅ čád-če* W.*, to cut with a knife, but also *grir rṅám-pa, ɣsód-pa, ˳gúm-pa Ma:* to kill with a knife;

gri-só, gri-dhó, gri-ḱá the edge of a knife; *gri-lám* lit. 'the path of the knife', the cut, incision; *gri-gúg Pth.* a short, crooked sabre or sword, **falchion, cimeter;** *gri-šá* flesh of a man that has been killed with a sword, (used in sorcery). — 2. *Lt.: dar-mai gri?*

གྲི་མག་ *gri-mág* v. *grib-ma.*

གྲིན་པ་ *grin-pa Mil.*, prob. = *sgrin-po* **skilful, clever.**

གྲིབ་ *grib* 1. **shade,** *grib-kyi ṗu Glr.* the shady part of a valley on the north side of a mountain range, cf. *sribs*; *grib-ṗyogs* the side not exposed to the sun, north side, col., *grib-lhágs* the coolness of the shade, the cool shade *Sch.*; *grib-ma* **ḍi-mág* W.* **shadow** (cast by an object); *dei grib-ma gáṅ-la ṗóg-pa* on whom his shadow falls; *grib-ṫsód* a dial *Cs.* — 2. **spot, filth, defilement, contamination,** mostly in a religious sense: *grib yoṅ* pollution arises; *ro-grib* defilement by a corpse; *grib-sél* name of a Buddha; *grib-(kyis) nón-gyi γdon* a demon that defiles and poisons the food, a harpy; **ḱó-la ḍib ṗog soṅ* W. C.* he is crack-brained, not in his right mind; **ḍib-čan** stubborn, refractory, whether from stupidity, or from ill-will.

གྲིམ་པ་ *grim-pa* **to hasten, to hurry** *Sch.*

གྲིམ་ཙེ་ *grim-tse Sik.* a pair of **scissors.**

གྲིམས་ *grims Med.?* (*Lex.* **चतुरस्र** quadrangular, regular, harmonious) Schr.: intelligent, clever.

གྲིལ་ *gril* (cf. *ₒgril-ba*) **a roll,** *šog-gril* rolled paper, a paper-roll; *gos-gril* a garment folded up *Cs.*; *gril-ḱa byéd-pa* to make up a parcel *Sch.*

གྲུ་ *gru* 1. **boat, ferry, ship, vessel,** also a hide blown up with air, used for crossing rivers = **ko-ḍhú* C.*; *gru-šán* id.; *gru-šán-pa* ferry-man; *grú-la žón-pa* to go on a ferry. **Comp,** *grú-ḱa, gru-šán-ḱa, grú-btaṅ-sa C.* starting- or landing-place of a ferry. — *gru-glá, gru-btsás* fare, passage-money, a boat-man's fee. — *grú-pa* ferry-man. — *gru-dpón* ship-master, master of a vessel. — *grú-bo,* gen. *gru-γzins,* ship. — *gru-ₒdzin* (**पोतल**) ancient name of Tatta, at the mouth of the Indus, ancestral seat of the Shakya race, whence the name is transferred to the residence of the Dalai Lama in Lhasa, v. Köpp. II, 342. — 2. (*Cs. grú-ma*) **angle, corner,** convex or concave, also **edge, border, brim;** *gru-γsum, gru-bži* etc. triangle, quadrangle; *gru-γsúm-pa* triangular; *dkyil-ₒḱor gru-bži-pa žig ₒbri-ba* to draw a quadrangular figure, a square; *ₒdom-gáṅ gru-bži,* a surface six feet square; *dbyibs gru-bžir yod S.g.*; **ḍu-nar-čan* W.* rhomboidal; *gru-yon,Cs.gru-gyél,* oblique angled; *gru-dráṅ* right-angled *Cs.*; *gru-ḱún* v. *mṫo-gon.* — *yúl-gru* **place, village, town, country.** — 3. **lustre,** of precious stones, *gru-dmár* a reddish lustre *Mil.nt.*

གྲུ་གུ་ *grú-gu* 1. **clew, hank.** — 2. n. of a country.

གྲུ་ཆར་ *gru-čár* 'a fine, fertile rain' *Sch.*

གྲུ་མོ་, གྲེ་མོ་ *grú-mo, gré-mo* **elbow,** *grú-mor ḱa-ṫrám-ka bzúṅ-ba* holding a trident in his arm *Pth.*; *dé-la grú-moi ṗul-rdég čig byás-nas* pushing him with his elbow *Mil.; gru-súg byéd-pa* id.; *grú-moi ḱug,* the hollow of the elbow-joint *Glr.*

གྲུ་ཤ་ *gru-šá,* or *gru-šá,* n. of a country *Pth.*

གྲུག་པ་ *grúg-pa* to break into small pieces, **to crumble, to bruise** *Dzl.*; *grúg-pai ₒbras* bruised rice *Schr.*; *rús-pa čag-grúgs* fracture of a bone *Med.*; *grúgs-bu* something broken.

གྲུང་བ་, གྲུང་པོ་ *grúṅ-ba, grúṅ-po,* fem. *grúṅ-mo* 1. **wise, prudent** *Mil.*; also: *grúṅs-pa lags* very learned Sir! *Thgr.* — 2. **meek, mild, gentle** *Cs.*

གྲུབ་ *grub Ld.* **all,** **ḍub ši soṅ** all are dead; **ḍub zas soṅ** it has all been eaten up, (v. the next word).

གྲུབ་པ་ *grúb-pa,* pf. of *ₒgrúb-pa* 1. **made ready, complete; perfect;** (*ma grúb-pa* also: not existing); *grúb-pai raṅ-byón spyan-ras-γzigs Glr.* the perfect, by himself originated, Awalokiteswara = *lhúṅ-gyis grúb-pa; don ṫams-čád grub-pa, don-grub,* **सर्वार्थसिद्ध, सिद्धार्थ** 'the fulfilment of every wish' n. of Buddha, also of a spell or magic formula. — *grúb-pa lus Med.* either: the frame, the structure of the body, or more prob. an abbreviation of *p̀úṅ-po lṅá-las grúb-pai lus Med.*, v. *p̀úṅ-po.* — 2. **the state of perfection,** *grub-pa t̀ob-pa* to attain to this state, *grub-t̀ób* सिद्ध one that has attained to it, **a saint;** *grub-brnyés, grub-mč̀óg* id.; *grub mt̀á* (*C.*col. **d̀hum-t̀á**) *Ssk.* सिद्धान्त **opinion, theory** *Zam.; p̀yi-náṅ-gi grub-mt̀a ma ˳č̀áms-par Glr.* there being no conformity of opinion between Brahmanists and Buddhists; also n. of a philosophical work, *Was.* 262. — *ma-grúb-pa, grub-pa-méd-pa?*

གྲུམ་པ་ *grúm-pa* 1. *S.g.* n. of a burrowing animal, *Sch.:* **badger.** — 2. pf. of *˳grúm-pa* **lamed, crippled,** *grúm-po* a maimed person, a cripple; *grúm-bu, grum-nád* **gout, rheumatism,** = *t̀sig-nád; drag-grúm* gout, podagra; **s̀a-d̀úm* W.*, a feeling of lameness in the limbs.

གྲུམ་ཙེ་ *grúm-tse* a thick woolen **blanket** *Mil.nt.*

གྲུལ་བུམ་ *grul-búm* a class of demons, *grul-búm-mo* female demons; there are also horned demons of this kind.

གྲུས་པོ་ *grús-po C.* a yak two or three years old.

གྲེ་ *gre* a Naksatra, v. *rgyu-skár.*

གྲེ་ཀ་ *gré-ga C.* **a sheet of paper** (*W.*s̀og-gáṅ**)

གྲེ་བ་ *gré-ba* the fore-part of the neck, the **throat,** both the wind-pipe and the gullet; **d̀é-wa dé-mo**, or **nyán-pa dug* W.* he has a good voice, sings well; *gre (-ba) gágs(-pa) Med.* hoarseness; **d̀é-wa t̀áṅ-c̀e* Ld.* to join in singing or shouting; *gré-ba dár-ba* a snoring or rattling in the throat; **d̀e-bsál t̀áṅ-c̀e* W.* to hawk, to hem, to clear the throat.

གྲེ་བོ་ *gré-bo* a species of demons; *gré-mo* 1. female demons of this kind. — 2. v. *grú-mo.*

གྲེ་མག་ *d̀é-mág*, vulg. for *grá-ma* **awn.**

གྲེ་མོག་འབུ་ *gré-mog-˳bu W.* **ant, emmet.**

གྲེའུ་ *greu* **pea, pease,** *món-sran-greu* acc. to *Wdṅ.* = माष.

གྲེས་མ་ *grés-ma* **the flashing, lightening, shining** *Schr.*

གྲོ་ *gro* 1. **wheat,** *gro-yós* parched grains of wheat, parched corn; *gro-sóg* stalk of wheat, wheat-straw. — 2. **breakfast,** taken late in the forenoon or about noon, *gro ˳dégs-pa Glr.*, also **d̀ho ˳bóg-pa* C.* to take breakfast, = *t̀sál-ma zá-ba.* — **d̀o z̀ig* W.* a morning's march, short day's march, reaching quarters already at 10 or 11 o'cl. a.m.

གྲོ་ག་ *gró-ga, W.* also **d̀ó-wa**, the thin **bark of the birch-tree,** frq. used to write on (esp letters), or for ornamenting bows etc. *Mil.*

གྲོ་བོ་, གྲོ་མོ་ *gró-bo, gró-mo* **reddish gray.**

གྲོ་མ་ *gró-ma* 1. = *gro* 2. — 2. n. of a medicinal herb *Wdṅ.* — 3. **d̀hó-ma, gya-d̀hó* C.* **potato.**

གྲོག་པོ་ *gróg-po* (*Lex.* दरभ्र) 1. a deep **dell, ravine,** lateral valley *C.; gróg-č̀u* brook, rivulet; *grog-ȷzár* a torrent pouring down in a ravine. — 2. *W.* = *gróg-č̀a.*

གྲོག་མ་, གྲོག་མོ་ *gróg-ma, gróg-mo* **ant, emmet;** *grog-tsáṅ, grog-mk̀ár* ant-hill; *grog-spúr* acc. to some = *gróg-ma,* acc. to others some other insect.

གྲོག་ཞིང་ *grog-z̀iṅ* n. of a medicine *Wdṅ.*

གྲོགས་ *grogs*, col. **rog** 1. **friend;** the more definite form is *grógs-po*, fem. *grógs-mo; k̀a-grógs* a seeming friend, a false friend; *ytiṅ-grogs* a true friend; *sdig-pai grógs-po-la rten-na* if he attaches himself to bad friends *Dzl:; snyiṅ-gi grógs-po* intimate friend, bosom-friend *Pth.; grógs-po(r) byéd-pa* to make friendship, to enter into connexion with, to make a league, *ma-mt̀oṅ-ma-p̀rád-pai grógs-po byas,* they joined in friendship without knowing each other *Glr.* — *kye grógs-po* ho, friend! *Pth.* — 2. **associate, companion, comrade,** *grógs-po-dag* company, society *Dzl.* also used as address: comrades! friends! or more respectfully: honoured friends! honoured gentlemen! *Stg.*; **fellow**, *grógs - kyeu* play-fellow, play-mate *Dzl.*; *dpúṅ-grógs* fellow-combatant, brother in arms; *ˌdúg - grogs*, resp. *bžúgs-grogs* inmate, fellow-lodger *Mil.*, **ḍáṅ-rog** *W.*, (v. *braṅ-sa*) id.; also neighbour *W.*, *C.*; *dgá-grogs, ytán-grogs, grogs*, companion in life, **spouse, husband, wife,** *grogs mi rnyed* she cannot get a husband *Mil.*; *ṫse ˌdüi grogs-skál* a man's destination as to marriage, the matrimonial lot assigned by fate *Glr.*; *ˌdód-grogs, mdzá-grogs, bzáṅ-grogs C.* one beloved, **lover, sweet-heart,** *mál-grogs* resp. *yzím-grogs* bed-fellow (not only 'concubine' *Cs.*); *dmág-grogs* ally, confederate (in war), hence also: — 3. **assistant, fellow-labourer,** *lás-grogs* journeyman, under-workman; *grogs byéd-pa* to help; *rgán-mo mčód-rten skúd-pai grogs byas* they helped the old woman in anointing the pyramid *Dzl.*; *rtsig-grogs byéd-pa* to help in building a house; at present in *C.* a word of courteousness in making requests: **ṫẹn rog naṅ* (*ynaṅ*) be so kind as to show me; **naṅ rog dzẹ'** would you kindly give me; **dha ṅa ṫoṅ rog dzọ'** now please let me go! cf. *rogs*.

གྲོང་ *groṅ* an inhabited place, a human habitation, **house, village, town,** *brgyá-groṅ, stòṅ-groṅ* a place of a hundred, of a thousand houses or house-holds (*mi-kyim*). —

Comp. *groṅ-kyér* 1. a large town, **city,** *B.* and *C.*, *groṅ-kyer (gyi) mčog* chief city, capital *Tar.* 2. fig. **place, scene, sphere,** (e.g. this world is a scene of illusions *Mil.*) — *groṅ-graṅs* the number of houses in a village or town. — *groṅ-mčóg Mil.*, *groṅ-mčóg ˌdrim-pa, ˌgró-ba, rgyúg-pa* one that wanders about among the peasantry as a fortune-teller; clerical charlatan, hedge-priest. — *groṅ-ytám* prob. = *groṅ-tsig* — *groṅ-rdál* (*Lex.* ग्रामपद 'an extension of houses') a large town, also a suburb. — *groṅ-pa* 1. *W.* **a villager, peasant.** 2. *C.* = *groṅ*. — *gróṅ-po* = *groṅ Mil.* — *gróṅ-dpon* **village-chief,** *Sch.* — *gróṅ-mi* **peasant.** — *groṅ-tsig Lex.* **provincialism.** — *gróṅ-ṫso* **village, borough.** — *groṅ-bžis* **farm** *Sch.* — *gróṅ-yul* **village** *Mil.*

གྲོང་བ་ *groṅ-ba C.* col. for *graṅ-ba* **cold,** in *Glr.* occasionally.

གྲོད་པ་ *gród-pa* 1. **belly,** *grod-tsil* **suet.** — 2. col. **stomach**; of ruminating animals the first stomach or paunch. — 3. a dried paunch, or bullock's stomach, for keeping oil etc. *Glr.*

གྲོན་ཅན་ *grón-čan* disadvantageous, injurious, *gron-čé* very noxious, *gron-méd* harmless, innoxious *Lex.*

གྲོལ་བ་ *gról-ba* pf. of *ˌgról-ba*, as sbst. = मुक्ति the having been delivered, **deliverance** (from the pain of existence).

གྲོས་ *gros* 1. **advice, counsel,** *gros ˌdebs-pa B.* to give advice; *gros byéd-pa B.*, **ḍós gyáb-če** *W.*, to consider, to deliberate; to resolve, decide; *gros ˌdri-ba* to ask (a person's) advice, to consult (with one); *grós-ˌdri-sa* the place where advice may be asked, **an oracle** *Glr.*; *grós-pa* adviser, counsellor, senator; *grós-mi* id., head-man of a village; *gros mṫún-par* by unanimous decree, unanimously *Dzl.* — 2. **speech, talk,** = *ytam Mil. nt.* — 3. **council** (?). — 4. *Cs.*: **care, heed, caution,** *grós-čan* careful, cautious, *grós-med* careless, heedless.

གླ་ *gla* **pay, wages, fee,** *gla zá-ba* to live on wages, to work for daily wages *Dzl.*; *gla-ltó* food and wages; *glá-pa, glá-bo* (col.), *gla-mi* a day-labourer, hired workman, *glá-mo* (*Cs. glá-pa-mo*) fem.

གླ་བ་ *glá-ba* 1. **the musk-deer,** Moschus moschiferus, *glá-mo* the female of it, *gla-prúg* the young of it; *glá-bai lté-ba* musk-bag (lit. navel); *glá-rtsi* (*W.* **lar-si**), *Ssk.* कस्तूरी **musk,** *glá-rtsi-me-tog* Pedicularis megalantha, **gla-dá-ra** *W.* Delphinium moschatum, two alpine plants smelling strongly of musk; *gla-sgáṅ* n. of a medicinal root *Cs.*; *gla-glád* v. *glaṅ-glad*. — 2. n. of a pretty large tree, similar to, or the same as *stár-bu Glr.*

གླག་, བྱ་གླག *glag, bya-glág* **eagle, vulture;** *glag krá-mo Sch.*, **lag-kyi** *W.* (an eagle which is said to bark like a dog), *rgyab-glág* perh. different species of eagles.

གླག་པ་ *glág-pa* often used erroneously instead of *rlag-pa*.

གླགས་ *glags* **opportunity, occasion, possibility,** *glags ˳ts'ól-bá* to seek an occasion, to look for an opportunity; *da glags rnyéd-par dug* now the favourable point of time seems to have come *Glr.;* esp. opportunity of doing harm to another, of getting a hold on him; *glags rnyéd-par mi gyur,* he will not be able to get at you, to do you harm; *ysó-glags med* there is no possibility of helping him, he is incurable *Med.; bzód-glags med* intolerable, insupportable, frq.

གླང་ *glaṅ* (*Bal.* **χlaṅ**) 1. **ox, bullock.** — 2. **elephant.** — 3 **Taurus,** the Bull, in the zodiac.

Comp. *glaṅ-glád* 'bullock- or elephant-brains'; soap being made of such, acc. to popular belief: *C.* **soap** (*Schr. gla-glad*). — *gláṅ-to* the Indian **bison,** Bos taurus indicus, *Lh.* — *glaṅ-t'úg, glaṅ ˳óg-čan* **a bull.** — *glaṅ-dár-ma* n. of a king of Tibet, living about 1000 after Christ, notorious for his hostility against the hierarchy of the Lamas. — *glaṅ-dór* **a team** of bullocks. — *glaṅ-sná* **the trunk** or proboscis of an elephant; a plant so called on account of the long spiral spur of its corolla, Pedicularis Hookeriana. — *glaṅ-po* = *glaṅ.* — *glaṅ-po-čé, glaṅ-čén,* **elephant,** *gláṅ-mo* **a** female elephant, *glaṅ-p'rúg* the young of an elephant. — *glaṅ-bu* a young bullock, *glaṅ-rú* a bullock's horn; also a large fork used by the Tibetan soldiers to rest the musket on, when firing (Hook. II., 235). — *p'a-gláṅ* = *glaṅ-t'úg.*

གླང་, གླང་ཐབས་ *glaṅ, glaṅ-t'ábs Med., yzer-gláṅ W.,* **colic, gripes, spasms** in the stomach, and similar affections; *glaṅ-šú Med.?*

གླང་མ་ *gláṅ-ma* a large kind of alpine **willow.**

གླད་ *glad* 1. **the head,** *glád-la* round the head, e.g. to brandish a sword, *Glr.;* as postposition used in a general sense: **close over,** *čui glád-la* close over the water. — 2. **brain** *Med.,* cf. *klád-pa.*

གླད་པ་ *glád-pa* **to thin** *Sch.* Cf. *lhad, slád-pa.*

གླན་པ་ *glán-pa* 1. = *glón-pa,* **to patch, botch, mend;** *glan brgyáb-pa Sch., glán-par byéd-pa Lt.* id.; *lhán-pa glán-pa* to sew on a patch *Lex.* — 2. **to return,** *lan* an answer, to reply, rejoin *Lex.* — 3. *C.* col. for *glén-pa*; so also occasionally in books.

གླལ་བ་ *glál-ba* **to yawn.**

གླིང་ *gliṅ,* द्वीप, prop. **island,** but usually: **continent,** part of the globe, viz. one of the four imaginary parts of the earth, as taught by the geographers of Tibet, or rather of ancient India: *lus-p'ágs* the part east of the Sumeru, of a semicircular shape; *˳dzam-bu-gliṅ* in the south, triangular; *ba-glaṅ-spyód* in the west, circular; *sgra-mi-snyán* in the north, square. The general character of the first of these parts is described as being *ži-ba* tranquil; that of the second as being *rgyás-pa* rich; that of the third as being *dbaṅ-ldán* strong, and that of the fourth as being *drág-po* wild. In a more general sense: **region, country,** so Nepal is frq. denominated *rin-po-čei gliṅ* the country of jewels and treasures, Urgyan *mk'a-groi gliṅ* the country of the Dakini, as is also Lahoul, in local chronicles; *byai gliṅ* region or country of birds *Glr.;* the word is also not unfrequently a component part of the names of towns and villages. — *gliṅ-p'rán* prop. a little island, generally one of the small continents, of which there are eight, acc. to the above mentioned geographical system; also island in general. — *gliṅ-ka* a small uncultivated river-island, or low-land *C.*

གླིང་བུ་ *gliṅ-bu* (*Ssk.* वंश) **fife, flageolet,** made of one piece of wood and much like those used in Europe as play-things for children; it is the common musical instrument of herdsmen, and often consists of two pipes; *p'red-gliṅ* **flute, piccolo-flute,** mostly of metal; *dge-gliṅ* a larger musical instrument like a **hautboy**, used in sacred ceremonies; *rkaṅ-gliṅ* lit. a fife made of the human femural bone, but sometimes also of metal.

གླུ་ *glu* (*Ssk.* गीति) **song**, **tune**, mostly, though not always, of a profane nature, opp. to religious hymns; *glu-dbyáṅs*, *glu-sgrá*, id.; the word is also used of the singing of birds; *glu-čúṅ* a little song, ditty, hummed by a person *Glr.*; *glu-rés* alternate song; *glu-gar-rtséd-po* rejoicings of every kind *Glr.*; *glu lén-pa B.*, **lu gyáb-pa* C.*, **táṅ-cè* W.*, to sing.

གླུད་, བླུད་, གླུད་ཚབ་ *glud*, *blud*, *glud-tsab* **a ransom**, a thing given as a ransom, *sróg-gi glud* a ransom for one's life *Lex.*; *ḱoi glúd-du lug brgya ysód-pa*, to slaughter a hundred sheep as a ransom *Mil.*; **lǘ-la taṅ* C.* he is made an expiator, a scape-goat; **mi-lü* C.* in a special sense: a man's image which in his stead is cast away in the *ytór-ma*: therefore **ḱo mi-lü' yin* C.* he is a curse, an anathema, one deserving to be cursed (ni.f.).

གླུམ་ *glum* **boiled barley, wheat, or rice,** used instead of malt in brewing beer (not for food).

གླེ་ *gle* 1. *Glr.* 60. a small uncultivated island, = *gliṅ-ka* (*Ld.* **zal**). — 2. n. of the capital of Ladak, usually *sle*.

གླེ་འདམས་ *gle-ₒdams* n. of a distemper *Cs.*; involuntary discharge from the bowels, or of urine *Sch.*

གླེགས་ *glegs* (*Cs. glégs-ma*) **table, board, plate**; *záṅs-kyi glégs-bu* copper-plate *Tár.* 26, 10; *glegs-bám* (पुस्तक) **book,** also *dpé-ča glegs-bám Glr.*; *glegs-bám máṅ-po bžéṅs-so* he made a present of, dedicated, many books (for the use of a temple); *glegs-šiṅ* the wooden boards which in a Tibetan book supply the binding; *glegs-tág* a thong etc. fastened round a book; *glegs-čáb* a buckle, clasp, or ring attached to this thong. — *sgó-glegs* the pannel of a door; **nám-lag** writing-tablet, a small board, blackened, greased, and strewed over with scraped chalk, on which the school-children write with wood-pencils.

གླེང་བ་ *gléṅ-ba*, pf. *gleṅs* **to say, talk, converse,** *ytam* (*-du*) *gléṅ-ba* id., resp. *ysuṅ gléṅ-ba*; *'lám-la ma tar' žes gléṅs-nas* as word was sent: 'the road is not passable!' *Glr.*; *ytam gléṅ-ba ni bdág-gis byas* I have made this speech *S.O.*; *ycig gléṅ ynyis gleṅ rim-pas mčéd-de btsún-moi búr-du gléṅ-žiṅ* the rumour spreading from one to the other, until it came before the queen *Pth.*; *čós-kyi sgrog-gléṅ byéd-pa*, (resp. *mdzád-pa*), **to preach** *Glr.*; *gros-gléṅ* **council, consultation,** perh. also disputation.

Comp. and deriv. *gléṅ-brjód*, *gléṅ-mo* sbst. **conversation, discourse, lecture,** *gléṅ-brjód ma maṅ dar-ycig yson* listen a little to a short discourse *Mil.*; *čós-ytam gléṅ-mo byed* let us converse on religious subjects *Mil.*; *gléṅ-mo* the act of speaking, opp. to *yi-ge*, the act of writing, the written letter etc. *Lex.* — *gleṅ-yži* 1. **the subject** of a discourse *Cs.* 2. table of contents, **index** *S.O.* and elsewh. 3. **place, scene,** of a conversation or discourse *Stg.* frq. — *gléṅ-ba-po*, *gléṅ-mo-mḱan* a story-teller *Cs.*; *glen-ₒbúm* 'a hundred thousand stories', title of a book, *Sch.*

གླེན་པ་ *glén-pa* 1. *B.* and *C.* **stupid, foolish,** *glen lkugs bkol-spyód-kyi sdug-bsṅál* the misery of stupidity, of dumbness and of servitude (the state of animals) *Thgr.*; *byol-sóṅ-las kyaṅ glén-po* more stupid than a brute *Mil.*; **fool,** *kyód-rnams re glen* fools that you are all of you *Dzl.*; often in the sense of 'fool' in the Bible, = the wicked, the ungodly: *glén-pa yti-mug-čan* infatuated fools *Dzl.* ༢༠, 9 = profaners of holy things; **len-nág* W.* id.; **len-nág-gi pé-ra** foolish talk. — 2. *W.*: **idle, lazy, dull, imbecile,** e.g. a sickly child, an animal affected with a disease (opp. to **ṭám-pa, šáṅ-po** being in good health, active, lively).

གླེབ་པ་ *gléb-pa*, pf. *glebs*, **to make flat, plain** *Cs.*, *léb-mor gleb Lex.*

གླེམ་པ་ *glém-pa* **to press, squeeze; to crush, squash** *Stg.*, *C.*

གློ་ *glo* (*Ld.* ཧློ་ **hlo**), resp. *yžogs*, 1. **the side**, esp. of the body, *glos ṗáb-pa* to lie down on one's side (lit. by means of the side); *gló-ča* (*Ld.* *'ldó-ča**) ornaments, suspended on the side of the body, strings of pearls, shells etc., worn by women in the girdle; also in a general sense: *sráṅ-gi glo γyas γyón-na* on both sides of the street *Stg.*; perh. also side of a house, wall, in the expression: **kún-mę lo tol** the thieves broke through the wall *W.*; *glo-skár* window *Pth.* — 2. **saddle-girth** *W.* — 3. **cough**, **lo gyág-pa** *C.* to cough; (*Sch.* has: to err, to act foolishly, to lose, to neglect); **lo láṅ-wa** *C.* to cough; *gló-k'a sra* a bad cough *Sch.*; **lo-k'óg** *C.*, *W.*, cough; *glo-rgyál Lt.* a chronic cough; *glo-bstúd Lt.* a permanent short cough. — 4. Not quite clear is the etymology in *glo rdég-pa Sch.:* to be frightened, timid, and *glo rdég* (*-tu*) suddenly, = *gló-bur* q.v.

གློ་བ་ *gló-ba* **the lungs**, *gló-ba ma lṅa* prob. the five posterior lobes of the lungs, *gló-ba bu lṅa* the five anterior ones *Med.*; *gló-k'a* of a colour like the blood of the lungs, **pale-red** *Sch.*; *glo-dóṅ* **windpipe** *Cs.* — *glo-rdól* a disease of the lungs; *glo-rkó* perh. the same. — *glo-sbúbs* (*Sch. spub*) wind-pipe. — **gló-ro** *W.* prob. pulmonary consumption. — *glo lú-ba Lt.* 'convulsion of the lungs' *Cs.*, or simply: cough, v. *lú-ba.*

གློ་བུར་ *gló-bur* 1. **suddenly, instantaneously,** also *gló-bur-du*, *gló-bur-bar*; *glo-bur-du mi máṅ-po ˳či-bai sdug-bsṅál* the calamity of many men dying suddenly; *glo-bur-nád* diseases that arise on a sudden (opp. to *lhan-skyés* inherited diseases) *Med.* — *gló-bur-ba* adj., *gló-bur-bai don* the signification of suddenness *Lex.* — 2. *Cs.:* 'recently, *gló-bur-du ˳óṅs-pa* a new comer'.

གློ་འབུར་ *glo-˳bur* **a rise,** an elevation above a surface *Sch.*

གློག་ *glog* (*Bal.* and *Kh.* **χlog**), col. also *glóg ka*, **lightning**, flash of lightning; *glog ˳bar* it lightens; *glog k'yug* id.; *glog k'yúg-pai yun tsám-las ma lón-par* with the rapidity of lightning *Mil.*; *glog rgyú-ba* the flashing of light, *Dzl.*; *glog-sprín* thunder-cloud, also as a symbol of the transitoriness of things.

གློག་པ་ *glóg-pa* a disease, = *lhóg-pa.*

གློད་པ་ *glod-pa* 1. **to loosen, relax, slacken** vb.a. *Cs.* — 2. **to comfort, console; to cheer up** *Sch.*; *glód-la rgyún-du bžugs* your honour may be easy about staying here always *Mil.*, cf. *lhód-pa.* — 3. *Ü:* **to give,** *ma bzuṅ ma glód*(*-par*) without any regard to taking or giving *Glr.*

གློན་པ་, གླན་པ་ *glón-pa, glán-pa* 1. **to return an answer, to reply.** — 2. **to patch, to mend,** cf. *klón-pa* etc.

གྷནྡྷོ་ལ་ *ghán-dho-la* n. of a mountain in *Lh.*, perh. incor. instead of *gan-dho-la* q.v.; it may also be derived from घण्टा bell, and thus the word would signify the same as *dríl-bu-ri*, which is the name of another holy mountain, at the foot of which the nobleman's seat **Gondla** is situated.

དགག་པ་ *dgág-pa* v. *˳gégs-pa.*

དགང་བ་ *dgáṅ-ba* v. *˳géṅs-pa.*

དགང་གཟར་ *dgaṅ-γzár* v. *γzar.*

དགད་མོ་ *dgád-mo* v. *gád-mo.*

དགབ་པ་ *dgáb-pa* v. *˳gébs-pa.*

དགའ་བ་ *dgá-ba* (*Ld.* col. **γá-če**) I. vb. **to rejoice,** to be rejoiced or glad, *la* at, in, or of; *dé-la dgá-ste*, rejoiced at it, glad of it, — *mi dgá-ste* grieved, vexed, indignant at it; *k'rims γód-pa-la dgá-nas* if you wish to have the law introduced *Glr.*; *γsód-pa-la dgá-žiṅ* sanguinary, delighting in blood-shed *Dzl.*; *bu-mo de-nyid-la dgá-bas*, as I wish to have none other but this girl *Dzl.*; *bód-la dgá-ba γčig kyaṅ ma byuṅ* nobody took an interest in Tibet *Glr.*; *k'yed čii p̔yir mi dga* why are you so dejected, low-spirited? *dga bžin-du* with pleasure (e.g. I shall accept it); rarely with the gerund: *bram-ze da-ruṅ ˳dug-ste rab-tu dga-nas* much rejoicing, very glad, when (that) the Brahmin was still there *Dzl.*; with the termin. of the inf.: to do a thing readily, willingly, *nyán-par dgá-ba* **to like** to hear, to listen eagerly; **to be willing,** *su žig ˳dúg-par dgá-na* if anybody will stay here voluntarily *Dzl.;* **to have a mind, to intend, to wish,** *k'yod rab-tu byúṅ-bar dgá-am* do you intend to take orders? *Dzl.; bdág-gis ras ˳di . . . sbyin-par dgao* I should like to present this cloth to . . . *Dzl.: méd-par byá-bar dgá-na* as I wish to annihilate . . . *Dzl.; gar dgá-bar* (or *gar dgá-ba der*) *soṅ* go wherever you like *Dzl.;* seldom with the accus.: *˳dzóm-pa de dga-ste* as you now enjoy an abundance *Mil.;* with the instr. case: *des dgá-bar šóg-čig*, may you be cheered, comforted by it *Dzl.*; frq. absolutely: *dgá-bar byéd-pa* to make glad, to rejoice, *C.* also: to caress, to fondle.

II. sbst. **joy,** *dgá-bai γtam byéd-pa* to express one's joy *Dzl.*; *dgá-bai sems* id.; *dé-la rab-tu dgá-bai sems skyés-so* he found great delight in it *Dzl.*; compounds v. below.

III. adj. 1. **glad, pleased, enjoying,** *ṅa dgá-ba ma yin-pas* as I was not pleased with it *Dzl.; de-la mi dgá-ba, W.* **mi gá-k'an**, not favourably disposed towards, unfriendly, inimical to; *dgá-bar byéd-pa* to make glad, to delight, *bu čuṅ dgá-ba byéd-pai yo-byád* things which delight little children, play-things *Glr.* — Less frq. 2. **charming, sweet, pleasing, agreeable, beautiful,** *lhág-par dgá-ru ˳gro* she is getting more and more beautiful; *C.* in a general sense: **good,** cf. below: *dga-bdé.* — 3. as a proper name = नन्द *Tar.*

Comp. and deriv. *dga-grágs ˳úr-ba* to give cheers, to raise shouts of joy *Mil.* — *dga-grógs* a participator of joy, gen. with reference to husband or wife (col. **ga-róg**). — *dga-mgú* great joy, *dga-mgú-ba, dga-mgu-ráṅ-ba* to have great pleasure, to be very glad, to be delighted, frq., *dgá-žiṅ mgú-la yi-ráṅs-pár ˳gyúr-ba* id. *Glr.* frq.; yet *dga-mgúr spyód-pa* to indulge in sensual pleasure *Pth., Stg., bú-mo daṅ* with a girl. — *dga-stón* **feast,** public festivity; *dga-stón-gyi γdán-sa* the place of a feast *Glr.*; *bsú-ba dgá-ba* festivities of welcome *Glr.*; *dga-stón byéd-pa* to celebrate a festival; *˳gyéd-pa* to spread a feast, to distribute festival dishes; **fig.** *rná-bai dga-stón* a feast or treat to the ears *Glr.* — *dga-bdé* 1. **joy,** *lus sems dga-bdés k'yáb-par ˳gyur Glr.* 2. (*Ts.* col. **gan-dé**) **good,** = *yág-po*, (of servants, dogs etc.) *C.*; **mi-la ga-dé ǰhé'-pa** to treat a person kindly, with affection *C.* — *dga-˳dún* wedding, nuptial festivities *Sch.* (seems to be a word not generally known). — *dga-˳dól* n. of the plain of Lhasa, or at least of the northern part of it. — *dga-ldán* joyful 1. n. of a residence of gods, or of one of the heavens, *Ssk.* तुषित v. *Köpp.* I. 265. 2. n. of one of the great monasteries near Lhasa, founded by Tsongkhapa, about the year 1407, v. *Köpp.* II, 345. 3. *γžúṅ-sa dga-ldan* n. of the royal castle of residence at Lhasa; *dga-ldán-pa* n. of a sect = *dge-lúgs-pa.* — *dgá-bo* = *dga-bdé* 2. **good** *C.* — *dga-sdug-drag-žan* good and bad, strong and weak, of articles of merchandise and the like *C.* — *dga-spró* **joy,** *dga-spró dpag-tu-méd-pa t'ób-pa yin* he entered into a state of indescribable joy *Mil.* — *dgá-ma* n. of the goddess of joy *Cs.* — *dga-ma-˳dár C., W.* (col. **gá-man-dár**) the trembling with joy, the state of being enraptured, in ecstasy. — *dgá-mo* 1. **delightful, pleasing, charming,** of news, of a speech *W.*, of a landscape *Mil.* 2. **delighted, joyous, cheerful** *W.*, **sem gá-mó rag** I am cheerful; **gá-mo-čan** *W.* id.; **gá-mo ǰhé'-pa** *C.* to caress, to fondle. 3. **pure, holy** *Sch., Dzl.*, prob. also *Mil.*; *čós-pa dgá-mo* a godly priest. — *dga-ts'ór* **joy,** **k'o ga-ts'ór mán-po ǰhe'** *C.* he is very joyful; *dga-ts'ór čé-ba* **gratifying,** delightful *Mil.* — *dga-ráṅs* being glad, **rejoicing,** **dhé-la ga-ráṅ ḍhág-te** *C.* being greatly delighted with it, — *dga-ris* v. *ga-ri*, = *gá-ža.*

དགར་ *dgar* = *dgá-bar*, *raṅ-dgár* **at pleasure,** ad libitum, frq.: *či dgar Pth.* seems to mean: **why.**

དགར་བ་ *dgár-ba* I. **to separate, confine, fold up** (men, cattle, goods), *dgar-byai p'yugs* cattle to be penned in a fold *Cs.*; *γnás-nas dgár-ba* to banish, to exile; *dgár-bai dón-du* in a special sense, in particular *Sch.* — **gár - te bór-če** *W.* to set apart, exclude, shut out; to lock up, shut up, to lay up or by, to preserve; **gár-gya čó-če** *W.* to store up; **tób-či gár-če** to button up. — 2. **to hang up, to fasten, to attach,** **dhar-čóg tág-pa-la** *C.* a flag to a rope. Cf. *skár-ba.*

དགལ་བ་ *dgál-ba* v. *ₒgél-ba.*

དགས་པ་ *dgás-pa* v. *ₒgás-pa.*

དགུ་ *dgu* 1. **nine,** *dgú-bču* (*túm-pa*) ninety; *dgú-bču rtsa γčig,* or *go-čig*, *W.* **gu-bču-go-čig** ninety one etc.; *dgú-pa* 1. the ninth. 2. having, comprising, measuring, nine, e.g. *kru-dgú-pa* measuring nine cubits (in length, height etc.); *dgú-po* the nine, those nine; *lan-dgú* nine times; *dgu-nín* three years ago col. — 2. **many,** *dgú-čig* id. *Mil.*; *tabs dgus bsags,* gathered by many efforts, with great difficulty; used as sign of the plural: *skyé-dgu* men, *skye-dgui bdág-po* (*Ssk.* प्रजापति) the lord of creatures, the lord of men; *skye-dgui-bdág-mo* n. of the aunt and wet-nurse of Buddha; *yód-dgu Lex.* those that are, the existing beings; *nor yód-dgu-čog Mil.* the goods that one has, property; *bzán-dgu Lex.* the good and the brave (among men); *lus ₒdod dgur sgyúr-ba* to be changed, transformed, ad libitum *Mil.*; *nan-dgu túb-pa Lt.* to overcome every evil; *mi šes dgu šés-po Thgy.* he that knows every thing; **mi ǰhe' gu ǰhe' mi yon gu yon** *C.* if you do many things which ought not to be done, many things will take place which ought not to take place; *ši-ba yid-kyi dgú-la mi byéd-de Thgy.* not counting death among things to be thought of. — 3. inst. of *dgun, dgu-zlá* winter-month *Mil.* frq — *zer-dgu, smra-dgu??*

དགུ་ཁྲི་ *dgu-kri* **litter, bier** *C.*

དགུ་གཏོར་ *dgu-γtór,* for *tses nyer-dgúi γtor-ma,* a sacrifice on the 29th day of the month *W.*

དགུ་ཐུབ་ *dgu-túb* 'all-conquering', n. of a plant.

དགུ་ཕྲུགས་ *dgu-prúgs Mil., Thg.,* a particular kind of meditation.

དགུ་བ་ *dgú-ba* 1. vb. **to bend,** to make crooked; **go gú-če** *Ld.* to bend, bow, stop; to submit. — 2. sbst. the act of bending, bowing, **inflection.** — 3. adj. **bent, stooping;** *dgú-po, dgú-mo Cs.* id.

དགུ་རྩེགས་ *dgu-rtségs* n. of a yellow flower *Cs.*

དགུ་ཚིགས་, དགུ་ཚིགས་སྐྱ་མོ་ *dgu-tsigs, dgu-tsigs skya-mo* **the galaxy, the milky way** *Mil.*

དགུ་མཚན་ *dgu-mtsán* **prize** (of combat) *C.*

དགུག་པ་ *dgúg-pa* v. *ₒgúg-pa.*

དགུང་ *dgun,* another form for *gun* (the former of the two appears to be prevalent) 1. **the middle.** — 2. **noon, mid-day.** — 3. **mid-night.** — 4. **heaven.** *dgún-la reg* it reached up to heaven *Mil.*; *dgun snón-po* the blue heaven, *yá-gi dgun-snón* the blue heaven above *Mil.*; *dgún-du* (or *-la*) *γšégs-pa* (lit. to repair, to withdraw, to heaven) to die *Mil.* and elsewh. — 5. before dates, esp. before the word *lo,* it serves as a respectful word, and is e.g. frq. used in stating the age of a Buddha or a king; yet it occurs also in compounds, where no such bearing is discernible: *dgun-žág, dgun-zla Cs.*; *dgun-do-núb Mil.* this evening, to-night; *dgun-snyin* a year, a year of one's life; *dgun-kág* division of time (?); *dgun-bdún* a week. (*Cs.* has also *dgun-tig,* and *dgun-tig-gi dkyil-ₒkor,* which terms were prob. framed by him, and meant to denote the meridian line and meridian circle.)

དགུང་མོ་ *dgún-mo* **evening** *Sch.*, perh. a corruption of *dgón-mo.*

དགུན་, དགུན་ཀ་ *dgún, dgún-ka, W.* **gún-ka** **winter;** *dgún* is also used adverbially: in winter(-time), during winter; *dgún-dus* winter-time; *dgun-tóg, dgun-tog-tág, W.* **gun-tag-tóg*,* all the winter through; **gun tse re** *W.* every winter; *dgun grán-bai dús-na* during the cold of winter *Dzl.*; *dgun-nyi-ldog* the winter solstice; dgun-nyi-ldog-gi ťig, or kor-ťig the tropic of Capricorn Cs. (cf. the remark at the end of dgun); dgun-stód, dgun-smád the first and the last half of winter, (v. dus).

དགུམ་པ་ dgúm-pa v. ₒgúm-pa.

དགུར་, རྒུར་, སྒུར་ dgur, rgur, sgur, three different spellings of the same root, all of them pronounced *gur*, **crooked,** dbyibs-dgur of crooked stature S.g.; rgur žig stoop down! bend your back! Dzl.; sgúr-te writhing (with pain) Dzl.; sgúr-po crooked, hump-backed, by birth Lt.; with age Thgy.; C. col. *gur-gúr* id.; mgo dgúr-ba to duck, to bend vb.n.; to submit, to humble one's self (cf. dgú-ba). Cs.: dgúr-po, dgúr-mo a crooked man, a crooked woman; ťsigs-dgúr a crooked back, crook-backed; lag-dgúr having crooked hands etc.; dgur-ₒgro of a stooping gait.

དགུས་ dgus 1. instr. of dgu. — 2. C., W., **this day five days** (the present day included).

དགེ་བ་ dgé-ba (Ssk. शुभ, कुशल, श्रेयस; also स्वस्ति, कल्याण, seldom शुद्ध) 1. **happiness, welfare; happy, propitious,** dgé-žiṅ šís-pa Wdṅ. More frq.: 2. **virtue** (opp. to mi-dgé-ba, and sdig-pa), also adj. **virtuous,** sems dgé-ba a virtuous mind Glr., las dgé-ba, mi-dgé-ba good and bad actions Stg.; dgé-bai rtsá-ba roots of virtue, meritorious actions, from which afterwards the fruits of reward come forth; dgé-rtsa skyéd-pa frq., spyód-pa Thgy., byéd-pa Mil. to produce such a root, to achieve a meritorious action; dgé-ba séms-par ₒgyúr-ba to become inclined to virtue, i.e. converted Dzl.; dge-ťsógs (v. ťsogs) a virtuous work, a good deed; dgé-ba bču the ten virtues, viz. 1. srog mi ɣčód-pa, not to kill anything living (by which Buddhism has replaced our scriptural interdiction of murder); 2. ma byin-par mi lén-pa not to take what has not been given (those who closely stick to the word go even so far, that they will not touch or accept an alms, unless it be put into their hands); 3. lóg-par mi ɣyém-pa not to fornicate; 4. rdzun mi smrá-ba not to tell a lie; 5. ťsig-rtsúb mi smrá-ba not to abuse or revile; 6. ṅag-kyál (or ₒkyal) mi smrá-ba not to talk foolishness (cf. kyál-ka); 7. ṗrá-ma mi byéd-pa not to calumniate; 8. brnáb-sems mi byéd pa not to be avaricious or covetous; 9. ɣnód-sems mi byéd-pa not to think upon doing harm or mischief; 10. lóg-lta mi byéd-pa not to entertain heretic notions, or positively, yáṅ-dag-par ltá-ba Stg. to be orthodox. — 3. **fasting, abstinence,** in the phrase: dgé-ba srúṅ-ba to fast, to abstain from food, frq. — 4. **alms, charity; banquet, treat,** as a religious work, ši-dge ɣsón-dge largesses, treats, taking place at funerals, or given in one's life time Mil. (W. *yá-tra*, and *ku-rím*).

Comp. and deriv. dge-bskos **censor,** and at the same time **provost** and **beadle** in a monastery, who has to watch over strict order, and to punish the transgressors Köpp. II. 259, 276; in Ld. he is also called čos-krims-pa (vulg. *čosrimpa*). — dge-rgán **surety, moral bail,** a monk that is made answerable for the moral conduct of an other, who is placed under his care and called dge-ɣžón; also in a gen. sense: **teacher, schoolmaster.** — dge-bsnyén, fem. dge-bsnyén-ma (Ssk. उपासक and उपसिका) 1. the pious of the laymen who retaining their secular occupations have renounced the five cardinal sins (murder, theft, fornication, lying, and drunkenness) and provide for the maintenance of the priests (so in Dzl. and gen. in the earlier writings). 2. in in later times as much as **a novice, probationer, catechumen,** i.e. either a kind of clerical apprentice (the Shabi of the Mongols, śrāmanera Ssk., v. Köpp. II., 252), or one of a next higher degree, a candidate (v. Schl. 162). — dge-ltás S.g. **a propitious omen,** a favourable prognostic. — dge-ₒdún (col. *gen-dún*), prop. dge-slóṅ-gi ₒdun (Burn. II., 435) Ssk. संघ, the whole body of the clergy, **priesthood;** dge-ₒdun-dkon-mčóg the priesthood as one of the three great jewels, or as part of the godhead (in which latter sense the word now is usually understood) cf. *dkon-mčóg*; *dge-ₒdun-dpal-čén Mahāsāṅghika*, n. of a Hinayāna school *Tar.*, *Was.*; *dge-ₒdun-grúb-pa* n. p., the first Dalai Lama about the year 1400; *dge-ₒdun-rgyá-mtso* n. of the second Dalai Lama, v. *Köpp.* II., 131. — *dge-ldán* **virtuous**; *dge-ldan-pa* n. of the most numerous sect of Lamas, founded by Tsonk'apa; it is also called *dge-lúgs-pa*, or *dga-ldán-pa* from Galdan, a monastery near Lhasa which, as well as Sera and Ḍa-puṅ, belongs to his sect. The Lamas of this community wear for the most part yellow garments; they are said to approach nearer to perfection in mysticism (the highest aim of Buddhist priests) than any other sect, since they apply themselves more systematically to the preparatory studies of morality etc. — *dge-sdig* for *dge-ba daṅ sdig-pa*. — *dge-sbyóṅ Ssk.* श्रमण a Buddhist ascetic, or mendicant friar, *Burn.* I. 275. *Köpp.* I., 330. — *dge-sbyór* seems to have corresponded in its original acceptation to our conception of piety, sanctification and practical religion, but in later times the sense of expertness in the art of meditation was attached also to this word, as: *dge-sbyór p̓el* (this man's) expertness increases, is making progress *Mil.* — *dgé-rtsa* instead of *dgé-bai rtsá-ba* v. above. — *dge-rtsis* the amount of virtue, the sum of merit, *dge-rtsis rgyás-pa* a considerable amount of merit. — *dge-tsúl* 1. a young monk; in the older writings it may be understood as novice; 2. in later literature it denotes the degree next to the *dge-bsnyén*, being that of a subordinate or under-priest, *Köpp.* II. 252, 335. *Schl.* 162.; *dge-tsul-ma* a young nun, a novice. — *dge-mtsán* a lucky omen *Glr.* — *dge-γžón* v. *dge-rgán*. — *dge-γyóg* (seems to be pronounced **ger-yóg** in col. language) **constable, beadle,** a servant of the *tsógs-čén zal-ṅó*, or chief-justice of Sera and other monasteries. — *dgé-las* a good deed or action, but by later writers also applied to magic ceremonies and the like. — *dge-lúgs-pa* v. *dge-ldán-pa*. — *dge-légs* good fortune, prosperity *Glr.* — *dge-slóṅ* Gelong, 1. originally 'beggar of virtue', mendicant friar, भिक्षु one that has entirely renounced the world and become a Buddhist priest, 2. in later writings the highest clerical degree, a priest that has received the highest ordination, v. *Köpp.* I., 335. The Gelong is bound to observe all the 233 commandments of the *so-sór tar-pai mdo.* — *dge-slób-ma* a young nun *Cs.* — *dge-bšés* 1. v. *bšes-γnyén*. 2. n. of priests or monks. — *dge-sloṅ-šiṅ* is said to be a provincial name of the cedar, Cedrus Deodara.

དགེང་ལ་ *dgéṅ-la*, also *dgáṅ-la*, **on, upon, in, at** *Ts.*

དགེར་བ་ *dgér-ba* = *γyo-ba*, **to prepare,** (food), *ₒkúr-ba dgér-ba* to bake pastry; **tụ̈-ma gér-wa* C.* = *ₒtúd-pa*.

དགེས་པ་ *dgés-pa* = *dgyés-pa* frq.

དགོ་ *dgo*, in *Lexx.* explained by *dúm-bur*, to divide (?).

དགོ་བ་ *dgo-ba*, a species of **antelope**, living on high mountains, Procapra picticaudata *Hodgson*, v. *Hook.* II. 157 and 139; *dgó-ba-mo* the female of this antelope *Cs.*

དགོག་ *dgog Lexx.* w.c.; *dgog-tiṅ* **pestle** *C.*

དགོང(ས)་ *dgoṅ(s)*, also *dgóṅ(s)-mo*, *Sch.* *dgóṅ(s)-ka* 1. **evening,** *dgoṅs-γčig* one evening, once on an evening *Glr.*; *naṅ re dgoṅs re* every morning and evening; **goṅs-zdn* W.*, **góṅs-zẹ* C.*, resp. *dgoṅs-γsól* evening-meal, supper; *dgoṅs-ₒjám* resp. evening-soup; *dgóṅs-su Dzl.*, *dgóṅs-mo* and *dgoṅs Glr.* in the evening; *dgoṅs daṅ to-ráṅs* in the evening and in the morning *Med.* frq.; *dgoṅs ₒbáb-pa* to hold an evening's rest, to take up night-quarters. — 2. **supper** *C.* — 3. **a day's journey,** *dgoṅs-žág* col. id.; *rta-dgóṅs* a day's journey for one travelling on horseback, *lug-dgóṅs* a day's journey for a drove of sheep.

དགོངས་པ་ *dgóṅs-pa*, resp. for *sém-pa*, *snyám-pa* etc., and *sems*, *blo* etc. I. vb.

1. **to think, to meditate,** *dgoṅs-pa-la jug-pa* to enter into meditation *Glr.*; *ₒdi snyám-du dgóṅs-par gyur-to* he thought so in his mind *Dzl.*; *rgyál-po k̔oṅ-ráṅ yin dgóṅs-nas* the king thinking that he himself was meant, referring the allusion to himself *Glr.*; **to regard as,** *bu daṅ ₒdrá-bar dgóṅs-pa* to treat one like a son *Dzl.*; **to remember, to think of, to devise,** *mṅa-ris-kyi gdúl-bya-la* remembering those of Nari that were to be converted, thinking of the conversion of Nari *Glr.*; also with *p̔yir Pth.*; *ṅá-la t̔ugs-brtsé-bar dgoṅs-šig* remember me graciously, frq.; so in a similar manner: to hear graciously, to take a kind interest, share, or concern in, to interest one's self for, to try to promote; so our Lama explained the passage *Glr.* 101, 9: *saṅs-rgyás-kyi bstáṅ-pa-la dgóṅs-nas = bstán-pa ₒp̔él-bai p̔yir bsám-blo btáṅ-nas*; **to intend, to purpose,** with the termin. of the inf., frq., *t̔ugs-kyis ma dgoṅs-so* he did not intend, he had no mind *Pth.* — 2. **to die,** *més-kyi dgóṅs-dus-kyi mč̔ód-pa btsug Glr.* is stated to mean: he instituted sacrifices for the remembrance of his grandfather's death; and so similarly in other passages.

II. sbst., also *t̔ugs-dgóṅs,* 1. the act of **thinking, meditating, pondering,** *t̔ugs-dgóṅs gtóṅ-ba Mil.* to meditate; **thought,** *rgyál-poi t̔úgs-kyi dgóṅs-pa-la 'gáṅ-du p̔yin' snyám-pa* lit. in the king's 'mind-thoughts' was thought: where shall I go? *Glr.*; **meaning, sense,** esp. the sense of sacred words or writings, therefore *dgóṅs-pa ₒgrél-ba* to explain that sense, *dgoṅs-ₒgrél, dgoṅs-bgról* commentary; **a will, a wish,** *rgyál-poi* (or *-pos*) *dgoṅs-pa bžin-du bsgrub nús-so* I am able to fulfil your majesty's wish *Dzl.*; *skyóṅ-bai dgons-pa-čan Glr.* 104, poetically, one having the desire of protecting, one wishing to protect. — 2. **soul,** *dgóṅs-pa mya-ṅán-las ₒdás-so* his soul quitted (the abode of) misery. — 3. **permission** *C., W.,* **góṅ-pa žú-wa** to beg leave, to ask permission, **góṅ-pa táṅ-wa**, resp. **náṅ-wa** to give permission, in *Sik.* also: to grant admission; but gen. it is used for **leave of absence**, and **k̔ó-la góṅ-ḱog ǰhuṅ soṅ* C.* signifies: he has been dismissed, turned out.

དགོད་པ་ *dgód-pa* 1. **to laugh,** *Glr.*; gen. in such expressions as the following **gọ'-ḍhó* (lit. *bro*) *yim-pa* C.* to make one's self ridiculous, **a laughing-stock,** also *Glr.*; **hab-gód čó-če* W.* to set up a loud laugh, to burst out into laughter; *dgod-bág* a jest, joke *Sch.*; cf. *bgád-pa.* — 2. v. *ₒgód-pa.*

དགོན་པ་ *dgón-pa* 1. **a solitary place; desert, wilderness,** *dgón-pai gnas* a desolate place or region *Stg.*; *dgon-dúṅ* a sandy desert, sands *Sch.* (*Zam.* अकुन and *dgón-pa:* अरण्य forest). — 2. **hermitage.** — 3. **monastery,** frq.; *dgón-pa-pa* 1. a man dwelling in a desert, a hermit. 2. a man dwelling in a monastery, a monk; *dgon-pa-ma* fem.

དགོས་པ་ *dgós-pa* I. vb. implying necessity, as well as want: **to be necessary, to be obliged or compelled; to want,** to stand in need of; also where we use 'ought'; it is gen. used with the verbal root or with the termin. of the inf. present, *byed dgos*, but sometimes also of the inf. future or perfect, e.g. *rin-po-č̔es brtsigs dgós-na rin-po-č̔e méd-pas sá-las bya dgos* though it ought to have been built of precious stones, yet for want of such, it will have to be constructed of earth *Dzl.* — *la* gen. denotes the person standing in need of a thing, e.g. *ṅá-la dgos* I want, I stand in need of, but it also refers to the object for which a thing is wanted: *rgya-gár-du ₒgró-ba-la gser dgos-pa yin* for a journey to India gold is wanted (required); in such a case the termin. may also be used: *či žig-tu dgos,* for what purpose is it wanted? *zas za ma dgos* I did not want to eat *Mil.*; *dgós-pai dús-su blaṅs* they took them when they wanted them *Glr.*; *bžéṅs ma dgos* he was not obliged to erect . . . *Glr.* — In commanding, the word is used to paraphrase the imperative of a verb: *ₒóṅ-bar dgos* come! in entreating, the respectful term is chosen: *ₒbyon dgos Mil.*, or in *W.*: **skyod dgos žu** 'you must come, pray!' =

please, do come! *ₒkrid dgós-pai γsól-ba*, or *žú-ba*, a request to be taken along with (by another person) *Mil. C.*: **to wish,** *k̔yo̤' še-pa ₒdi ṅa go̤-pa yin* I wish you to know this *Lew.*

II. sbst. **necessity, want, use, purpose** (*W. dgós-če*, pronounced **gó-še(s)**), *máṅ-po ₒt̔sol dgós-pa byuṅ* we have been under the necessity of looking for you a long time *Mil.*; *ṅá-la γyui dgós-pa med* I have no use for that turkois, I do not want it *Mil.*; **t̔iṅ-la gó-še p̔i-la* W.* for future use; *dgós-pai čún-bas* as it is rather useless; *dgós-pa čii p̔yir* for what purpose? frq.

III. adj. (*C.* also **go̤-gyu**, and **go̤**, *W. *gó-še**, as in II.), **necessary, due, needful, useful,** *med kyaṅ dgos-pai k̔ral-bsdud* a tax necessarily to be paid, unrelentingly exacted *Mil.*; *ráṅ-la dgós-pai skál-ba* the portion due to you *Mil.*; *dgós-pai bslάb-bya* useful doctrines *Glr.*; *dgós-pa yin* or *yod B.* and *C.*, **gó-šes yod* W.* it is requisite; *dgas(-pa) med B.*, **go̤-gyu me̤n* C.*, **gó-še man** or **med* W.*, it is unnecessary, unfit, not wanted; *mi-dgós-pa* **useless, noxious,** *mi-dgós-pai p̔ra-mén* pernicious witchcraft *Pth.*; *dgos-byéd* **useful,** *don dgos-byéd či ₒdug* what there is in it of useful contents *Mil.*; *dgos-ₒdód* **wishes and wants,** *dgos-dód ₒbyúṅ-bai dpal* a treasure out of which all wishes and wants come, i. e. are satisfied *Glr.*; *dgos-ₒdód nags-t̔sál* a forest for wishes, i.e. a forest which grants every wish; *dgos-ₒdód* necessary expenses *Cs.*

དགྱེ་བ་ *dgyé-ba* **to bend, to be curving** or **crooked**; *dbyibs dgyé-ba* stooping, cringing, ducking *S.g.*

དགྱེར་བ་ *dgyér-ba*, *glu dgyér-ba* for *glu lén-pa* **to sing, chant,** expression of the Bonpas; the word is also pronounced **ghyér-wa**.

དགྱེལ་བ་ *dgyél-ba Sch.* = *sgyél-ba.*

དགྱེས་པ་ *dgyés-pa*, resp. for *dgá-ba*, **to rejoice, to be glad;** often with *t̔ugs*: *rgyál-poi* (or *-po*) *t̔ugs dgyes* the king rejoiced; with *la* (to rejoice) at or in, (to be glad) of; **to please, to be pleased, to choose,** *jó-bo ₒbyón-pa-la t̔ugs-dgyés-par ₒdug* it seems the lord is pleased to walk *Glr.*; *mi dgyés-te* sorrowful, sad, discouraged, dejected; angry, indignant; cf. *dgá-ba.*

དགྱེས་སུ་འཇུག་པ་ *dgyés-su ₒjúg-pa* **to bend,** to double down *Sch.*, v. *dgyé-ba.*

དགྲ་ *dgra*, also *dgrá-bo*, *Ssk.* शत्रु 1. **enemy, foe,** *sdáṅ-bai dgra* the hating enemy, (opp. to *byáms-pai γnyén*), frq. used of imaginary hostile powers, that are to be attacked and withstood only by witchcraft; *dgra γnyen med* there is no difference between friend and enemy = no such thing exists (viz in the golden age); *dgrar ₒgyúr-ba* to become an enemy (to one) *Tar.*; *dgra byéd-pa*, *dgrá-ru ldáṅ-ba*, *láṅ-ba* to act in a hostile manner, *la*, against; *dgra slóṅ-ba*, causative form, to make a person one's enemy *S.g.*; *dgrar sém-pa*, *ₒdzín-pa* to look upon one as an enemy, to take him for an enemy; *dgrar šés-pa* id.; *dgrá-bčóm-pa* Arhant, Arhat, the most perfect Buddhist saint (*Ssk.* अर्हन्त् venerable; the Buddhists, however, explain it as a compound of *ari* enemy and *han* to extirpate, he who has extirpated the enemies i.e. the passions *Burn.* I. 295, II. 287. *Köpp.* I. 400). Also *dgra bgegs ₒdúl-ba Glr.* is interpreted as referring to the subduing of spiritual enemies. — *sṅá-dgrá* a former foe, *dá-dgra* a present foe, *p̔yi-dgra* a future foe *Cs.*; *p̔yi-dgra* prob. also a foreign enemy. — *ₒči-dgra* a **mortal,** deadly enemy *Cs.* — *dgrá-ča* weapon, arms *Wdṅ.*, *dgrá-sta* battle-axe; *dgrá-lha* v. *lha.* — 2. In *W.* also **punishment,** **k̔ó-la ḍa p̔og soṅ** he was punished; also for any self-incurred misfortune: **kyód-la ḍa p̔og yin** you will draw upon yourself trouble, fatal consequences.

དགྲམ་པ་ *dgrám-pa* v. *ₒgrém-pa.*

དགྲོང་བ་ *dgróṅ-ba* v. *ₒgróṅ-ba.*

དགྲོལ་བ་ *dgról-ba* v. *ₒgról-ba.*

བགག་པ་ *bgág-pa Cs.* another form for *ₒgégs-pa.*

བགད་པ་ *bgád-pa* to laugh *Dzl.*, cf. *dgód-pa.*

བགམ་པ་ *bgám-pa* v. *ˏgám-pa.*

བགེགས་ *bgegs* 1. = *gegs*, **hindrance, obstruction**, seldom. — 2. an evil spirit, **demon, devil,** like *γdoṅ*; *bgégs-kyi rgyál-po bi-ná-ya-ka Mil.* frq. (*Ssk.* **विनायक** a remover, of obstacles; the god Ganesha etc.).

བགོ་བ་ *bgó-ba* 1. vb. 1. **to put on clothes** etc., pf., imp. *bgos*; *lham rtág-tu bgos* always wear shoes *S.g.*; esp. to put on armour. — 2. v. under *bgód-pa.*

II. sbst. **clothes, clothing,** *bgó-ba daṅ bzá-ba* food and clothes *Dzl.*

བགོད་པ་ *bgód-pa* (*bgog-pa Sch.* is perh. a provincialism) pf., imp. *bgos*, fut. *bgo*; *W.* inf. **gó-ċe**; imp. **gos ťóṅ** **to divide,** *nor* an inheritance; **to divide** in ciphering, *graṅs* a number; **to distribute,** *ṣas-ṡás-su* into shares, *mi-rnams-la* to or amongst people *Dzl.*

Comp. *bgod-byéd* **divisor** *Wdk.*, and accordingly also *bgo-byá* **dividend.** — *bgo-skál* 1. **share, lot,** *B.* and *col.* 2. **the doctrine of strict retribution** *Thgr.* frq. — **gó-k'an** *W.* **sharer, partaker, heir, joint-heir,** — *bgo-bṡá* = *bgo-skál*, *bgo-bṡá byéd-pa* to distribute, allot, apportion, *nor* the property *Thgy.*, *la* among *Stg.*

བགོམ་པ་ *bgóm-pa*, pf. *bgams Sch.*, **to walk, to step, to stride,** *góm-pa bgóm-pa Lex.* to make steps; *ˏtém pa-la bgóm-pa* to step over the threshold; *bgom ˏgró-ba* to pace, to walk slowly; *bgoms ťúb-pa* to begin to walk (?) *Sch.*

བགོར་ *bgor*, supine of *bgó-ba.*

བགོར་བ་ *bgór-ba*, *Cs.* = *ˏgór-ba.*

བགྱང་བ་ *bgyáṅ-ba*, acc. to *Zam.* = *brgyáṅ-ba*, v. *rgyóṅ-ba.*

བགྱི་བ་ *bgyi-ba*, eleg. for *byá-ba*, 1. fut. of *bgyid-pa.* — 2. sbst. **action, deed.**

བགྱིད་པ་ *bgyid-pa*, pf. *bgyis*, fut. *bgyi*, imp. *gyis*, eleg. for *byéd-pa* 1. **to make, to manufacture**; *gyis zér-bai γzugs* the images regarding to which there had been said: 'make them!' i.e. the bespoken, ordered images *Glr.*; **to do, to act, to perform,** *las bgyid-pa* to do a work, *bká bżin-du bgyio* according to the word will be acted *Dzl.*; *nye-γnás bgyid-pa* to act the disciple = to be a disciple *Dzl.*; *mi-la γnód-pa bgyis* I have hurt the man, I have done him harm *Dzl.*; *bu yód-par gyis ṡig* make, bring it about, that a child be (born)! *Dzl.*; *rgyál-bu ma ṡór-ba gyis ṡig* see that yo do not let the prince escape *Pth.* (*ba* for *bar* in the more careless popular style). — 2. **to say,** *żes bgyis* so he said *Dzl.*; *żes bgyi-ba* the so called *Dzl.*

བགྲང་བ་ *bgráṅ-ba*, pf. *bgraṅs*, **to number, count, calculate** *bsód-nams-kyi ṫsad* the amount of merits *Glr.*; *bgráṅ-bya* what may be numbered, numerable; *bgráṅ-bar mi byá-ba*, *bgráṅ-du méd-pa*, *bgraṅ-yás* innumerable; *bgraṅ-p'réṅ* rosary, beads *Glr.*, also the garland of human skulls, often seen as an attribute of terrible deities.

བགྲད་པ་ *bgrád-pa* 1. **to open wide,** *mig bgrád-pa* to stare, goggle, *k'a bgrád-pa* to gape *Glr.*, *Cs.*; *rkáṅ-pa* to part the legs wide, to straddle, cf. *bsgrád-pa.* — 2. **to scratch** *Sch.* (spelled more corr. *ˏbrád-pa*).

བགྲུང་བ་ *bgrúṅ-ba*, pf. *bgruṅs* to cause to deposit, **to strain, to depurate** *Cs.*, e.g. *rnyóg-ma* impure water *Lex.*.

བགྲུད་པ་ *bgrúd-pa*, pf. *bgrus*, fut. *bgru*, to clear from the husks, **to husk, to shell,** *bgrús-pai ˏbras Lex.* husked rice.

བགྲེ་བ་ *bgré-ba*, pf. *bgrés*, resp. **to grow old,** often with an additional *sku-nas* in years (v. *na*) *Dzl.*; *bgres-rgyúd* weakness of old age, infirmity *Pth.*: *bgrés-po*, in *W.* pronounced **ré(s)-po**, an old man, a man gray with age, hoary; **ré(s)-mo** fem.

བགྲེང་བ་ *bgréṅ-ba*, occasionally for 1. *sgréṅ-ba.* 2. *bgráṅ-ba.*

བགྲེན་པ་ *bgrén-pa*, *Sch.* = *bkrén-pa.*

བགྲོ་བ་ *bgró-ba*, pf. *bgros* (resp. *bka-bgrós mdzád-pa Pth.*) **to argue, discuss, deliberate, consider**; the subject discussed is gen. a direct quotation: *ċii p'yir ˏdi-ltar gyur ċel bgrós-nas* to converse on the cause of the present state of things *Dzl.*; *żes p'an-*

ťsùn-du bgrós-nas thus declaring their opinions to one another *Tar.*; **to ask advice,** *ċi-ltar bya žes bgrós-nas* asking what they should do *Dzl.*; **to resolve, decide,** *bgrú-bar* to do *Dzl.*; *bgro-gléṅ byéd-pa* to dispute, to debate *Lex.*

བགྲོང་བ་ *bgróṅ-ba Tar.* = *bgráṅ-ba* **to count.**

བགྲོད་ *bgrod* 1. **the walk, gait,** mode of walking. — 2. symbol. num.: 2.

བགྲོད་པ་ *bgród-pa* **to walk,** *bgród-la ṗan* this assists in learning to walk *Lt.*; **to go, wander,** *lam bgród-pa* to travel over *Glr.*; **to get through,** *ǩyód-kyis bgród-pai skabs med ruṅ* although until now you have not been able to get to this place *Mil.*; *ču bgród-par dká-ba* a river difficult to cross; *nyi-ma-lho-bgród* the sun's going to the south, in the winter half-year, the sun's south **declination,** *byaṅ-bgrod*, north declination, *bgród-dus ɣnyis S.g.* both declinations; *bud-méd-la bgród-pa* to lie with a woman *Schr.*, *Cs.*

བགྲོས་པ་ *bgrós-pa* v. *bgró-ba.*

མགར་ *mgar* n. of a noted crafty vizier of the king Srontsangampo *Glr.*

མགར་བ་ *mgár-ba* (col. **gár-ra**) **smith,** *mgár-bai bzo* smith's work; **gár-zo čó-če* W.* to forge; *mgár-ǩaṅ*, *mgár-sa* smithy; *ɣser-mgár* gold-smith *Cs.*

མགལ་ *mgal* **jaw, jaw-bone,** *ya-mgál* the upper, *ma-mgál* the lower jaw-bone; *mgal-čág* a broken jaw-bone, *mgal-búd* a dislocated jaw-bone *Cs.*

མགལ་པ་ *mgál-pa*, also *˳gál-pa* **a billet of wood;** *mgal-dúm* 1. a large piece of wood split or cut, 2. a piece of wood half-burnt *W.*, *C.*; **gal-dó, gal ťsig* W.*, **gal-ró* C.* id.; **gal-mé** a burning piece of wood, **a fire-brand; torch,** consisting of long chips or thin billets of wood; *mgal-méi ˳ǩór-lo* a circle of light produced by whirling round a fire-brand.

མགུ་བ་ *mgú-ba* **to rejoice, to be glad, joyful, content;** *mgú-nas* delighted *Mil.*, *Tar.*; *mgú-bai lan ma byuṅ* he did not receive a gratifying, satisfactory answer *Tar.* 17, 27; *ťams-čád byin yaṅ mgú-dus med* he is never content though every thing be given him *Mil.*; *mgú-bar byéd-pa*, *W.*: **gu čúg-če**, to exhilarate, to gladden, to make content; *dga-mgú-ba*, *dga-mgu-ráṅ-ba* are intensive verbs; *mgur* = *mgú-bar.*

མགུར་ *mgur* (*Ssk.* कण्ठ) resp. 1. **throat, neck,** *gyu mgur-du ṗul-nas* presenting (the great teacher) with a turkois for his neck *Ma.* — 2. **voice,** *mgur snyán-pa* a sweet, harmonious, voice *Cs.* — 3. (col. **gúr-ma**) **song, air, melody,** hence a religious song is always designated by the respectful word *mgur* (not by *glu*), although the term in itself has no immediate reference to it. *mgur (-du) ɣsúṅ-ba*, *bžés-pa* resp. for *glu lén-pa* to sing a song; *Sch.*: *mgur ťen-pa* id. — *mgur-˳búm* a hundred thousand Songs, title of the Legends of Milaraspa, which are richly interwoven with songs. — *Sch.*: *mgur bsál-ba* to clear the throat, to hawk, to hem; *čú-boi mgur* 'by-water', a tributary, a subsidiary stream (?).

མགུར་ལྷ་ *mgúr-lha* the god of hunting with the Shamans *Sch.*

མགུལ་(པ་) *mgúl (-pa) Ssk.* कन्धर 1. **neck, throat,** *mgul-du ˳dógs-pa* to tie, fasten to one's neck e.g. magic objects; *ráṅ-gi mgúl-pa ɣčód-pa* to cut one's own throat *Dzl.*; *mgúl-pa sub* his throat is stopped, choked *Mṅg.*; *mgúl(-pa)-nas ˳dzín-pa*, *˳ǰú-ba*, to seize by the throat, sometimes also used for *mgúl-pa-nas ˳ǩyúd-pa* to fall on a person's neck, to embrace. — *mgúl-nad* disease of the throat, **sore throat.** — *mgul-čiṅs dkár-po* a white **neck-cloth** *Pth.* — *mgul-dár* or *dpa-dár* a silk cloth tied round the neck as a badge of honour. — 2. **the shoulder** of a mountain *Mil.*, *ɣyón-mgul-na* on the left slope.

མགེའུ་ *mgeu* = མགོའུ་ *mgou Cs.* v. *mgo.*

མགོ་ *mgo* (*Ssk.* शिर) resp. *dbu* 1. **head,** **gó-la zug rag** I have a headache, a pain in my head *W.*; **mgo ˳ǩor** my head turns, I feel dizzy, I am getting confused, perplexed; *mgo skór-ba* to cheat, swindle, deceive; *mi-mgo ma skor* do not cheat people! *Mil.; mgo dgú-ba, dgúr-ba* v. *dgú-ba, mgo ₒfóm-pa* v. *ₒfóm-pa; mgor ȷóg-pa* to carry on the head *Sch.*; **go yúg-če* W.* to shake one's head, **kug tán-ce* W.* to nod with the head, either as a sign of affirmation, or of beckoning to a person; **kyog-kyóg čó-če** to wave the head from one side to the other, expressive of reflection. — 2. **summit, height, top,** *ri-mgo ká-bas γyogs Mil.* the hill-tops were covered with snow. — 3. **first place, principal part,** *mgo byéd-pa* to lead, to command, to be at the head *Glr.*; to educate cf. *dbu mdzád-pa*; to inspect, look after, superintend, control, *bú-mo žig-gis mgo byéd-pai mi mán-po* a number of (labouring) people looked after by a girl (the farmer's daughter) *Mil.; *ḍos gó čó-če* W.* to preside in a consultation. — 4. **beginning,** *W.*, **go-ma**; *gros-mgo* the beginning of a consultation; *mgo ₒdzúg-pa* to begin; *bod sdúg-pai mgo ₒdzugs* that was the beginning of the misfortunes of Tibet *Ma*; *brtán-gyi skyid-mgo dé-nas ṫsugs* with this my constant good-fortune commenced *Mil.; ló-mgo-la* at the beginning of the year *Mil.*; *mgó-nas* from the beginning *Dzl.* — 5. *Gram.*: a superscribed *r, l, s* e. g. *rá-mgoi ka,* ཪྐ, *k* with *r* superscribed; *dé-rnams bas ṗul sá-mgoi kao* these are the words beginning with *bsk.*

Comp. and deriv. *mgo-klád* **brain** *Cs.* — *mgo-dkyil* col. crown of the head, **vertex.** — **go-kár**, or **gar* Ld.* a tight under-garment, drawn over the head when put on, (*Ssk.* परिधान, *Hd.* अंगिरखा) something like a shirt, but not in general use. — *mgo-skór* **imposture, deceit,** *bdud-kyi mgo-skór de ṅa mi ₒdod* I detest these diabolical tricks *Mil.* — *mgo-skyá* a gray head, *mgo-skyá-čan* a gray-headed person *Cs.* — **go-kyóṅ* C., W.,* **protector, patron,** = *mgo-ₒdren.* — *mgo-kra* scald, scald-head *Sch.* — *mgo-mkrégs-čan* **obstinate, pertinacious, stubborn,** esp. in buying and bartering, selfish, bargaining, haggling: **go ṭag čó-če* W.* to have these qualities. — *mgo-rgyán* head-ornament. — *mgo-čan* **having a** head, **mí-go-čan** having a man's head, such as English rupees and other coins (bearing the image of a head) *W.* — **go-čiṅ* C., W.* = *go-ₒdrén.* — **go-(l)cág** a blow or knock on the head *Ld.* — *mgo-lčógs* little **shoots, sprouts, branches** *Sch.* — *mgo-ča* = *mgo-rgyán.* — *mgo-mjug* beginning and end (head and tail), *šiṅ ₒdii mgo mjug gaṅ yin-pa bye-brág ṗyes šig* find out which is the upper and which the lower end of this piece of wood *Dzl.* — *mgo-ȷóṅ Cs.*: 'an oblong head.' — *mgo-rjén* bare headed. — *mgo-nyóg Cs.*: 'a compressed, contracted head'. **go-nyī-pa* C.* two-headed, double-tongued: a double-dealer, backbiter. — *mgo-snyóms* indifferent, unconcerned. — **gor-tiṅ ṫsáṅ-ma** from head to heel, the whole from top to toe, = **go-lus-ča-ṫsaṅ**. — *mgo-ₒdón* = *mgo-ₒdrén,* with *byed-pa* = *mgo ₒdon-pa* to bring or draw forth, to raise, to lift up a person's head, gen. with *raṅ*, one's own head, used in the sense of: **to be self-dependent,** one's own master, to come off well, **to be uppermost** *Mil.*; *mgo ₒton-pa* id. — *mgo-ₒdrén* **protector, patron,** used frq. in letters as a complimentary title. — *mgo-nág* po. for **man** *Glr.* — *mgo-nád* **headache.** — **gó-bu* W.* **first-born.** — *mgó-ma* 1. adj. **first,** *gral-mgo-ma* first in order, the first in a row or line of persons *Mil.* 2. sbst. **the beginning** *W.*, **go-ma ṫsug-če** to begin. 3. adv. **in the beginning, at first** *W.* — *mgo-ṫsém* 'stitched at the head' denoting a book which is so stitched, that the lines run parallel to the back, whilst one stitched in our way is called *rta-mgó-ma.* — *mgo-γžim*, col. **gog-žim** **crown** of the head. — *mgou, mgeu* a small head *Cs.* — *mgo-yór* = *ṫsá-bai nad Ts.* — *mgo-γyógs* **a covering for the head** (hat, cap etc.). — *mgo-ril* 1. **a round head.** 2. **cattle without horns** *W.* — *mgo-rég* for *mgo brégs-pa* one that has his head shaved, **a monk;** *mgo-rég btsún-ma Lt.* monks and nuns, or: nuns that have their heads shaved. — **go-lus-ča-ṫsáṅ** a **complete suit of clothes,** **gor-tiṅ-ṫsáṅ-ma** id.; **go lus sum kón-če* W.* to furnish a person with new clothes; **go lus spó-če* W.* to give one's own clothes to a person (e.g. when a king honours any body by arraying him in splendid garments). — *mgo-léb* a flat head *Cs.* — *go-šóg*, resp. *u-šog* **cover,** of a copy-book etc. *Cs.* — *mgo-srin* n. of a disease *Lt.*

མགོན་པོ་ *mgón-po*, *Ssk.* नाथ **protector, patron; principal, master, lord; tutelar god;** *˳gro-mgón* protector of beings; *skyabs-mgón* v. *skyabs; čii pyir ṅai mgon mi byed* why do you not assist me? *Dzl.; lhai, bdúd-kyi, gšin-rjei mgón-po* the principal of the gods, of the devils, the lord of death *Cs.; mgón-po mčód-pa, stód-pa, rbád-pa* to honour, to praise, the tutelar god, to stir up or urge him to aid one's cause. The special tutelar god of Tibet, called *mgón-po* by preference, is Awalokiteśwara, Spyan-ras-gzigs; *˳jig-rten-mgón-po*, or *mi-mjed-žiṅ-gi mgón-po* lord of the world, *˳jig-rten gsúm-gyi mgón-po* (Hindi: *triloknāth*), lord or ruler of the three worlds, an epithet 1. of Buddha, 2. of Awalokiteśwara, 3. of the Dharma-Rājā of Bhotān.

Comp. *mgon máṅs* many patrons or defenders of religion; many small pyramidical sacred buildings *Cs.* — *mgon-méd* unprotected, *mgon-med-zas-sbyin*, अनाथपिण्डद, n. of a certain house-owner in Buddha's time, often mentioned in legends.

མགྱོགས་པ་ *mgyógs-pa*, *C.* **gyóg-po** **quick, speedy, swift;** *mgyógs-par* (seldom *mgyógs-la Mil.*) adv. **quickly, speedily, soon;** **gyog-riṅ** *W.* speedy, hasty, rash, **gyog-lám** *W., C.*, a straight, short way, a short cut; *rkaṅ-mgyógs* v. *rkaṅ.* — *su-mgyógs*, pronounced **sun-gyóg(s)** *W.*, (lit. 'who is quick?') a race, a racing or running-match.

མགྲིན་པ་ *mgrin-pa*, (*Ssk.* ग्रीवा) 1. **neck,** *mgrin riṅ-ba*, a long neck, *mgrin túṅ-ba* a short neck *Lt.*; *mgrin-sṅón* blue-necked, an epithet of gods. — 2. **throat,** as passage or organ of the voice, *mgrin gčig-tu* (to call as) with one voice, frq.; *mgrin-bzáṅ* a loud voice *Cs.*

མགྲོན་ *mgron* **feast, treat, banquet, entertainment,** *mgron gtóṅ-ba*, resp. *sku-mgrón ˳búl-ba* to entertain; **dón-taṅ-k̇an** *W.* host, entertainer; *mgrón-la ˳bod-pa*, resp. *mgrón-du spyan-˳drén-pa*, to invite to an entertainment; *mgrón-du gnyér-ba* to treat, to regale *Dzl.*; *mgrón-du ˳gró-ba* to go to an entertainment, a party *Dzl.* (cf. *˳grón-du ˳gró-ba* to go abroad); *zas-mgrón* an entertainment consisting in eating; *ja-mgrón* a tea-party; *čaṅ-mgrón* a treatment with beer or wine *Cs.*

འགག་ *˳gag* 1. **obstruction, stoppage,** esp. in comp.: *yi-ga-˳gág* want of appetite; *gčin-˳gág*, also *-dgag*, strangury. — 2. a place or spot that has to be passed by all that proceed to a certain point, **zám-pe gág-tu gúg-na kụ́m-ma ˳dzin túb** *C.* the thief may be stopped, if you are on the watch in the thoroughfare of the bridge; *ri-bo dpal-˳bár-gyi ˳gag* the place on the Palbár mountain, where there is the only passage *Mil.; sgo-˳gág* the door of the house, because through it all that enter or leave have to pass; *k̇a-˳gág* the mouth, through which every thing must pass that is eaten; fig.: *tar-lám-gyi gnad-˳gág*, the main point for obtaining salvation; *˳gag gčig-tu dril-ba* to unite, to be concentrated in one point *Mil.*

འགག་པ་ *˳gág-pa* 1. vb, (cf. *˳gegs-pa*) **to stop, to cease,** to be at a stand-still; mostly in the perfect form *˳gags; dáṅ-k̇a ˳gags* the appetite is gone *Mil.;* it is also used of the passions having been suppressed, having ceased *Mil.* — 2. sbst. **door-keeper,** v. *sgo-˳gág* sub *˳gag.*

འགང་ *˳gaṅ* v. *rgaṅ.*

འགངས་པ་ *˳gáṅspa* **difficult, troublesome** *Sch.*

འགང་(པོ་) *˳gáṅ(-po)* the **burden** of an office, business, commission, *˳gaṅ ˳k̇úr-ba* to bear such a burden, *bskúr-ba* to impose it on a person.

འགབ་ *˳gáb* = *mtá-ma, mjúg-ma,* **the end,** of a bench, a garment etc. *Mil.nt.*; as postpos. c.genit. **after, behind** *C.*

འགབ་པ་ *˳gáb-pa* 1. *Sch.:* **to take care, to be cautious; orderly, decent.** — 2.

W. **to suffice,** **mi gáb-ɖe med** the workmen will not suffice.

འགམ་པ་ *˳gám-pa*, pf. *gams Sch.*, *bgams Cs.*, fut. *bgam*, imp. *goms* 1. **to put**, or rather **throw, into the mouth**, e.g. grains of wheat, a mouthful of meal, as Tibetans use to do; *ɣye ṫúr-mgo re tsam ˳gams* I took a small spoonful of meal *Mil.* — 2. **to try,** *bgám-mo* I will try him, I shall put him to the proof *Dzl.*; *ṫsód ˳gám-pa* id. *Lex.* — 3. *W.* **to threaten, to menace.**

འགའ་ *˳ga* (*˳ga-bo Cs.?*) **some, a few, several,** *k̓yi-ra-ba ˳ga* some huntsmen *Mil.*; *ɣžón-pa ˳ga žig* some young men *Mil.*; *k̓o-ráṅ ˳ga* some of them *Mil.*; *˳ga-ré* = *˳ga žig Pth.*; *gál-te náṅ-gyis ˳ga žig bžág-na* if I appoint some by a peremptory decree *Dzl.*; *skabs ˳gar* in some cases; *lan ˳ga* (*žig*) sometimes, now and then (opp. to frequently, as well as to once, one time); *res ˳ga* 1. sometimes. 2. col. for some, several; *bar ˳ga* sometimes; *lan ˳ga* — *lan ˳ga*, *res ˳ga* — *res ˳ga*, *bar ˳ga* — *bar-˳ga* at one time — at another time, some — others; *˳ga tsam* a few, few *Thgy.*: *˳ga śás* some, part (of them) *Mil.*; *˳ga yaṅ* followed by a negation: no, no one, not any, none.

འགའ་ *˳ga Glr.*, also *˳ga-ti* n. of a place in the east of Tibet.

འགར་ *˳gar*, termin. of *˳ga*.

འགར་བ་ *˳gár-ba* 1. sbst. (*W.* also **gár-ru**, *Ts.* **˳gar, ˳gir**) masc. *˳gár-po*, fem. *˳gár-mo*, a mixed breed of cattle, of a *mdzo* (q.v.) and a common cow, or a bull and a *mdzó-mo*. — 2. vb. v. sub *dgár-ba*.

འགལ་དུམ་ *˳gál-dúm* v. *mgal*.

འགལ་བ་ *˳gál-ba*, c. *las* or *daṅ*, **to be in opposition** or **contradiction to**, as: *rtág-pa daṅ dṅós-po ɣnyis ˳gál-ba yin* the ideas of 'perpetuity' and of 'thing' are contradictory; commonly of persons: **to counteract**, to act in opposition to, **to transgress, violate, infringe, break,** a promise, law, duty; *yid daṅ mi ˳gál-bar Dzl.*, resp. *ṫugs daṅ mi ˳gal-bar*, (he gives them) to their wish, to their heart's content; *bka bžin-du mi ˳gal-bar bgyio* I shall act faithfully according to the order *Dzl.*; **gal mi dug** *W.* he has not committed anything, he is innocent; *lha* or *klu daṅ ˳gal-ba* not to honour a Lha or Lu according to duty.

Comp. *˳gal-rkyén* **mishap, untoward accident, impediment** (opp. to *mṫun-rkyen*); *˳gal-rkyen sél-ba*, or *méd-par byéd-pa*, or *zlóg-pa* to avert, to remove such accidents or impediments. — *˳gal-˳k̓rúl* **transgression,** *˳gal-˳k̓rúl spaṅs-te*, conscientiously; **gal-ṫúl só-wa** to make amends, to atone for a transgression. — *˳gal-mṫún-śes-pa Chr. Prot.*, the knowledge of what is conformable or contrary to the divine law, meant to express our **'conscience'**; the term was formed after the Tibetan phrase: *dge mi-dgé śés-pa*, or *rig-pa*, knowledge of what is virtue and what is vice; cf. however *śés-bžin*, *ɣnóṅ-ba*, and *byas-čós*. — *˳gál-ba-po Cs.*, *˳gál-po Sch.*, a transgressor. — *˳gal-ṫsábs Cs.* a great fault, a crime: *˳gal-ṫsábs-čan* faulty, criminal, a criminal (?).

འགས་པ་ *˳gás-pa*, pf. *gas* (cf *˳ges-pa*) **to be cleft** or **split,** of rocks etc.; **to chap,** of the skin, the lips; to break open, **to burst,** of a bag etc., *k̓a lṅá-ru* into five rents, in five places; **to crack, to break** or **burst asunder,** of a vessel, the heart, a fruit, *bdún-du* into seven pieces; *śiṅ-gi rigs-la byás-na ni ˳gas* if it be made of wood, it will split, crack *Glr.*

འགིའུ་ *˳giu* v. *gi-wáṅ*.

འགུ་མདའ་ *˳gu-mdá* **gun-stock,** (spelling not certain) v. *sgum-mdá*.

འགུ་བ་ *˳gú-ba*, incorr. for *mgú-ba*.

འགུག(ས)་ *˳gug(s)* **a mesh** *W.*

འགུག(ས)་པ་ *˳gúg(s)-pa*, pf. *bgug*, fut. *dgug*, imp. *k̓ug* 1. (cf. *kug*) **to bend,** to make crooked, *ɣnya ˳gugs-pa C.* to bend, bow, stoop; *mgo ˳gugs-˳gúgs-par sóṅ-ṅo* he went off bowed down, crestfallen. — 2. **to gather,** to cause a gathering, *rnág-tu* of matter, pus, to suppurate. — 3. **to call, to summon, to send for,** e.g. the gardener *Dzl.*, one's daughters *Dzl.;* **to conjure up,** ghosts, *des bdag ˳gúg-par ˳gyúr-ro* by this (charm) I may be conjured up; *blo náṅ-du k̔úg-la* calling the spirit back into its inner domain, abstracting the mind from the external world. — 4. **to draw back, to cause to return, to convey back** *Mil., C.*

འགུད་པ་ *˳gúd-pa,* pf. *gud, = rgud-pa? gúd-du bcúg-pa* **to ruin,** to reduce to an extremity *Schr.*; *rtsa byiṅ-gúd dal Med.* a pulse slow and sinking.

འགུམ་པ་ *˳gúm-pa* 1. pf. *gum, ˳gums* eleg. **to die.** — 2. pf. *bkum, fut. dkum,* imp. *k̔um(s),* **to kill,** to put to death *Dzl.* frq.; **to slaughter** (butcher), *ɣsár-du bkúm-pai ša,* meat of an animal just killed, fresh meat *Dzl.* — 3. **to bend, curve,** make crooked, to contract, v. *kum* and *skúm-pa.*

འགུལ་ *˳gul* **neck,** v. *mgul.*

འགུལ་བ་ *˳gúl-ba* (cf. *sgul-ba*) to change place or posture, **to move, shake, to be agitated,** **ri-gu ḍód-pa-la gul dug** the kid moves in the womb (of the goat); *˳gul-dká* (the limb) moves with difficulty *Med.* frq.; *˳gul yaṅ ma nús-so* (they) would not even stir (from terror) *Dzl.*; **to waver, tremble, shiver,** *˳dár-žiṅ ˳gúl-ba; sa-˳gúl* (pronounced **saṅ-gúl**) earthquake *W.*

འགེག(ས)་པ་ *˳gégs-pa* pf. *bkag,* fut. *dgag,* imp. *k̔og* **to hinder, prohibit, stop,** *bdág-gis bkág-na yaṅ ma t̔úb-kyis* though I was preventing it, I could not (carry my point) *Dzl.*; *ma bkág-ste náṅ-du btaṅ* he admitted him without impediment *Dzl.*; **kág-če med zér-k̔an-gyi ka-šóg** a warrant, a permit to traffic without hinderance, a pass-bill, and the like *W.*; **to shut, to lock** (up), **to close,** *sgo* the door *Glr., lam* the road frq., to close one's nose with the hand *Pth.*; **to retain, keep back** excretions *Med., bšaṅ-dgág* obstruction (cf. *˳gag*); **zá-če kág-te ši* W.* his food sticking fast he died; **to lock up, shut up** (things for keeping), **to pen up** (sheep, cattle), **kág-te bór-če* W.* id ; *dgag-dbyé* the ending of the seclusion, viz. of the monks who have to stay in their houses during the rainy season *Schf., Tar.* 10, 10, cf. *Kōpp.* I, 369; **to forbid,** *dgag-sgrúb Sch.*: 'to forbid and to allow'(?); *gág-pai sgra, ˳gag-ts̔ig* a prohibitive particle *Gram.*; *bkág-ča byéd-pa* to forbid, prohibit *Sch.*; **k̔a kág-če* W.* to silence, to hush; *dgág-pa* a negative, a negation; *bkág-ča* the negative side *Was.* (282).

འགེངས་པ་ *˳géṅs-pa,* pf. *bkaṅ,* fut. *dgaṅ,* imp. *k̔oṅ* 1. **to fill,** *t̔ib-ril čus* or (seld.) *čú-las,* or *t̔ib-ril-du čus,* or *ču,* (to fill) a tea-pot with water; **to soil, smear, stain,** the bed with blood *Glr.*; *dgáṅ-dka* difficult to be filled, not to be satisfied, insatiable *Stg.* — 2. **to fulfil** (more frq. *skóṅ-ba*) *t̔ugs-dám Lex.* — 3. *ɣžu ˳géṅs-pa, mda ˳géṅs-pa* to prepare bow and arrows for shooting, frq.; **tú-pag káṅ-če* W.* to load a gun.

འགེད་པ་ *˳géd-pa, Cs.* = *˳gyéd-pa.*

འགེབས་པ་ *˳gébs-pa,* pf. *bkab,* fut. *dgab,* imp. *k̔ob* (*W.* **bkob**), **to cover,** e.g. one's breast with the hand; to cover up, *k̔a* an opening, aperture; **to spread** over or on, **to set up, to put on,** a cover, lid, cork, plug etc.; **to protect,** *btsún-mo mi-ma-yin-gyis ˳gébs-su ˳júg-pa* to have the queen protected by ghosts; **to disguise,** metaph: **bkáb-ste** in disguised language, euphemistically *W.*, **káb-če p̔i-la** in order to express it euphemistically.

འགེམ་པ་ *˳gém-pa,* acc. to *Cs.* another form for *˳gúm-pa,* **to kill, to destroy;** *Schr.*: *klád-pa ˳géms-pa* to surprise; to overthrow an argument by reason; cf. *mgo-˳géms Lex.* w.e.; as a partic.: stupid *Schr.*; the few passages, where I met with the word, leave its meaning doubtful.

འགེལ་བ་ *˳gél-ba,* pf. *bkal,* fut. *dgal,* imp. *k̔ol,* 1. **to load, to lay on** a burden, *brui k̔al čig bkál-te* loaded with a load of grain *Dzl.*; fig. to put a yoke upon a person's neck, *byur* to bring down misery on a person; *W.* to bring accusations against a person, **mi 'ós-pe lás-ka žig mi žig-la kal táṅ-na* Ld.* if one is accused of an unlawful action; *k̔ral ˳gél-ba* to impose tribute *Lex.*; **to commission, to charge with, to make, appoint, constitute,** **mi žig gád-po-la kál če** *Ld.* to appoint some one to be an elder or senior, cf *˳čól-ba.* — 2. **to put, to place** on or over, *ydúṅ-ma bkál-ba* a beam placed over it *S.g.*; **to set** or **put on,** e.g. a pot on a trevet; **to hang up,** *gos-˳gel-ydáṅ* a stand to hang clothes on; fig. *˳či-bar nús-pai tog ˳gel dgos* one must set on it the roof of being able to die, i.e. one must crown the whole edifice by being free from fear of death *Mil.*

འགེས་པ་ *˳gés-pa*, pf. *bkas*, fut. *dgas*, imp. *ḱos*, trs. to *˳gás-pa*, **to split, cleave, divide,** *bkas-šiṅ Lex.* cleft or chopped wood; *dúm-bur* (to divide) into pieces *Lex.*, **to cut up** or **open,** e.g. a fish, gourd, pumpkin, *Dzl.*

འགོ་ *˳go,* = *mgo* in some figurative applications of the word: *dmág-˳go* **commander** of an army *Cs.*; *mḱár-˳go, rdzóṅ-˳go* commander of a fort *Cs.*; *˳go-snám* a sort of fine cloth made of shawl-wool, or also: Europe-cloth, i.e. broad cloth = *sag-lád*; *˳gó-pa* **officer, captain, head-man** of a village or district, esp. in *W.*; in a general sense: **kon-čóg ǰig-ten-gyi gó-pa yin** God is the ruler of the world; **koṅ-čóg-gi saṅ gó-pa med** God is the only and highest ruler; **go-pṓn* C.* **rector, director, head-master, principal** e.g. of a school; *˳gó-ma Zam.* **beginning, origin, source;** *˳gó-mi Lex.* = *˳gó-pa*; **go-yód** = *˳gó-pa Ld.*; *˳gor* in the beginning, at first, originally *Sch.*, *sér-bai ˳gor* when it began to hail *Mil.nt.*

འགོ་བ་ *˳gó-ba*, pf *gos* (or *˳gos*), cf. *bsgo-ba*, 1. **to stain,** to lose colour; **to dirty, sully** one's self, *dé-la* with it, *naṅ-skyúgs lús-la* to soil one's self with vomit. — 2. **to infect,** with a disease, *˳gó-bai nad, ˳go-nád, ˳gó-bai rims,* a contagious or epidemic disease, **a plague,** frq.

འགོག་པ་ *˳góg-pa*, pf. *bkog*, fut. *dgog?* imp. *ḱog* 1. **to take away** forcibly, **to snatch, tear away, pull out,** *rtsá-ba* a root *Lex.*, so a tooth *Schr.*; **to tear up,** e.g. a floor *W.*; **to peel** *Sch.*; **kóg-te ḱyér-če* W.* **to rob, plunder** frq.; **kóg-te ḱyers* Ld.* it has been robbed. — 2. **to take off,** a cover, a lid, a pot from the fire *W.*

འགོགས་ཀ་ *˳gógs-pa* another form for *˳gégs-pa*, **to prevent, to avert** unfortunate events, fatal consequences; **to suppress,** the symptoms of a disease by medicine; **to drive back** or **away, to expel** e.g. spirits, ghosts; **to repel** people that are trying to land.

འགོང་བ་ *˳góṅ-ba* 1 *Cs.*: to bewitch, enchant (?), *góṅ-ba-po, ˳góṅ-po* **an enchanter, sorcerer,** *góṅ-ba-mo* enchantress, sorceress *Cs.*; more frq. *˳góṅ-po* **an evil spirit, demon,** also fig. demon of concupiscence, of fear, of terror *Mil.*; *˳góṅ-mo* fem. — 2. pf. *bkoṅ*, perh. more corr. *sgóṅ-ba, spá-sgoṅ-ba Lex.* **to despond.**

འགོད་པ་ *˳gód-pa*, pf. *bgod*, fut. *dgod*, imp. *ḱod* (cf. *ḱód-pa*), the Latin *condere*, 1. **to design, to project, to plan** *Schr.* — 2. **to found, to etablish, to lay out** (a town), **to build** (a house); hence *bkód-pai rig-byéd* books on architecture *Glr.*; **to manufacture, to form, to frame.** — 3. **to put, to fix, to transfer,** into a certain state or condition, *bdé(-ba)-la Dzl.*, *bder Lex.*, into a happy state, *dge-ba-la Dzl.* into virtue, *čós-la Pth* into the true doctrine, *rnám-par ˳gról-ba-la Dzl.* into salvation, *mya-ṅán-las ˳dás-pa-la* into delivery from existence *Dzl.*; *žag-gráṅs* **to fix** a certain time or term *Schr.*; *tsad* (to determine) the measure or size of a thing *Schr.* — 4. **to set, put,** or **place in order,** *gral-ṕyám bgód-pa ˳dra* as the rafters of a roof are placed side by side *S.g.*; *mtar dgód-pa* **to add** or **affix** e.g. ciphers to a certain number *Wdk.*; *bkód-par mdzés-pá* beautiful as to arrangement, nicely ordered, *(b)rgyan dgód-pa Lex.* to arrange ornaments (tastefully), **to decorate, adorn, to construct** or **adjust** grammatical forms, sentences *Zam.* — 5. to put down in writing, **to record,** *miṅ ká-ba-la* to write names on a column *Pth.*: **to compose, draw up, write,** a narrative etc., frq.: **to mention, to insert,** in a writing: **ka kó-pa* C.* **to publish,** to make known. — 6. **to rule, to govern** *Schr.*; *byol-sóṅ bkód-pai rgyál-*

po yin he is king over all subjugated animals *Mil.*

The partic. pf. *bkód-pa* is also sbst.: 1. **plan, ground-plan, draught** of a building *Schr.* — 2. **delineation, sketch,** *žiṅ-bkód* **map.** — 3. **form, shape, figure** *Schr.* — 4. **sample, copy,** even of one's own body, e.g. when a person multiplies himself by magic virtue, = *sprúl-ba.* — 5. **building, edifice, structure,** *bkód-pa mdzes* the structure (is) beautiful *Glr.* — 6. **frame, body,** *bkód-pa lus* id. *Mil.; ṅai bkód-pa nám-mkʼai raṅ-žin* my body of an ethereal nature *Pth.*

Note. The Lexx. have for *bkód-pa* always न्यास putting down, depositing; but often it has the signification of व्यूह orderly arrangement; as vb. it comes nearest to उपरच्. As the meaning of the word is almost quite the same as that of κτίζειν and *condere*, it recommends itself as the most suitable term for **'to create',** to call into existence, *ʼgód-pa-po* for **creator,** and *bkód-pa* for **creature,** notions which are otherwise foreign to Buddhism.

འགོམས་པ་ *ʼgóm-pa, Cs.* = *góms-pa, Sch.* also = *ʼgém-pa, ʼgúm-pa.*

འགོར་ *ʼgor* 1. v. the following article. — 2. termin. of *ʼgo*, in the beginning, at first *Sch.* — 3. supine of *ʼgó-ba.*

འགོར་བ་ *ʼgór-ba* **to tarry, linger, loiter,** *W.* frq. **máṅ-po gor soṅ** you stayed away very long; **lám-la gor** he lingers on the way; **máṅ-po ma gór-te** without long delay, = *riṅ-por ma lón-par*, and *riṅ-por mi tʼogs-par B.*; *de ʼgor-ɣži yin* that impedes, delays; *zlá-ba ɣnyis ʼkor* (the work) lasted two months *Glr.*

འགོལ་བ་ *ʼgól-ba*, pf. *gol* 1. **to part, to separate** vb.n.; *ʼgól-bai ɣnas* a hermitage *Pth.*, *ʼgól-po* hermit, recluse. — 2. **to deviate, err,** go wrong or astray; *ʼgól-sa* 1. the place where two roads separate. 2. **error, mistake.**

འགོས་ *ʼgos* n. of a monastery *Tar.*

འགོས་པ་ *ʼgós-pa* v. *ʼgó-ba.*

འཁྱག་པ་ *ʼkyág-pa* cf. *skyág-pa*, **to be sold, spent, expended** *Cs.*

འགྱང་བ་ *ʼkyáṅ-ba*, pf. *ʼgyaṅs*, **to be delayed, deferred, postponed,** *pʼyir ʼgyaṅ-na* if one defers it; **nyin ʼgyaṅ žag ʼgyaṅ ǰhé-pa* C.* to delay again and again; *lo maṅ-po mi ʼgyaṅ-bar* before many years shall have passed; *dus ʼgyaṅs Lex.* w.e.

འགྱིང་བ་ *ʼgyiṅ-ba* 1. to look about haughtily, **to look down upon, to slight,** *mi-la* a person; also of things: **to despise, contemn, neglect** them *B.* and col.: **ʼgyiṅ-bhág ǰhé-pa* C.*, **gyiṅ čó-če* W.* id.; **gyiṅ-čan** supercilious, contemptuous. — 2. = *sgyiṅ-ba Glr.*; *Mil.* — *šél-kyi ʼgyiṅ-ʼkʼar* a sceptre of crystal, an attribute of gods, in pictures represented as a plain, unadorned staff.

འགྱུ་བ་ *ʼgyú-ba*, pf. *ʼgyus*, **to move quickly** to and fro, e.g. as lightning, the quivering air in a mirage, the motion and versatility of the mind etc.

འགྱུར་བ་ *ʼgyúr-ba* I. vb., pf. *gyur(-to, -pa)* imp. *gyur (-čig)*, cf. *sgyúr-ba*, 1. **to change,** to be altered *B.* and col.; *mi-rnams-kyi spyód-pa ʼgyur* the behaviour of men changes *Ma.*; *ʼgyúr-bai čos* a changeable (and therefore perishable) thing *Cs.*; and *ʼgyúr-du yód-pa* changeable, variable, *ʼgyúr-du méd-pa, ʼgyur-med* unchangeable, invariable; sometimes **to decrease, abate, vanish, die away,** *mtʼu-stóbs, nád-med-pa, ɣzi-rǰid yóṅs-su ʼgyur-ba* the total decay of strength, health, and esteem (in old age) *Thgy.*; *bdág-gi sems ma gyur, ma nyáms-so* my mind has not been altered, nor my resolution weakened *Dzl.*; also with *las: dád-pa ʼdi-las ma gyur čig* do not **depart** from that belief *Mil.* (I have therefore availed myself of this word, combined with the active (transitive) form *sems sgyúr-ba* 'to change the mind' for expressing the μετανοεῖν and μετάνοια of the N. T., though the Buddhist is wont to regard the *mi-gyúr-ba* as the thing most to be praised and desired.) With the termin. it signifies **to be changed, transformed into,** *B.* and col.; hence — 2. **to become, to grow,** *dge-slóṅ-du ʼgyúr-ba, rgyál-por ʼgyúr-ba* to become a monk, a king *Dzl.*; *skra mton-mtiṅ-gi k'a-dóg-tu gyúr-to* his hair turned azure (sky-blue) *Dzl.*; *sbrúm-par ₒgyúr-ba* to get with child; *bdún-du ₒgyur-ba* to reach the number of seven *Dzl.* (In all these cases the more recent writings and the col. language in *C.* usually have *ₒdó-wa*, *in W.* *čá-če*.) *ₒgyúr-ba* is also frq. used in conjunction with verbs: *yód-par ₒgyúr-ba* 'to become being', i.e. to begin to exist, 'to become having,' i.e. to gain possession; *sróg-la miltá-bar ₒgyúr-pai dṅós-po ₒdi-dag* these acts of having become indifferent to life, i.e. acts of contempt of death *Dzl.*; *ná-bar gyúr-na ₒdi mtóṅ-ba tsám-gyis nad sós-par ₒgyúr-ro* when taken ill, they get well again, as soon as they obtain a sight of this *Glr.*; *čaṅ mi smrá-bar gyúr-to* he became speechless *Dzl.*; *ₒgyúr-ba* denoting both the pass. voice, and the fut. tense, the context must decide in every instance, how it is to be understood: *su žig rgyal-srid byéd-par ₒgyur* who shall have the government, who shall rule? *Tar.* 21.; *de rgyál-por ₒgyúr-bar šés-so* they knew that this man is made king (for: would be made king); *K'ó-mos k'yód-kyi bu bsád-par gyúr-na* if your son has been killed by me *Dzl.*; *k'yod mi-ša zá-bar gyúr-čig* may you be obliged to eat human flesh! *Dzl.*; *čii p'yir k'yod ₒdi-ltar gyur* by what means have you come into this state? *Dzl.*; *ya-mtsán-du* (or *-par*) *ₒgyúr-ba* to be surprised, astonished; with *ɣnás-su:* **to come to a place, to arrive** at *Mil.*; *ₒdód-pai dṅos-grúb-tu ₒgyúr-ba* to be endowed with the perfect gift of wishing, viz. of having every wish fulfilled; **to happen, to take place, to occur**, *ya-mtsán-du ₒgyúr-ba či yod* lit. what is there that has wonderfully happened, what wonderful things have happened? *ɣyós-par ₒgyúr-ba* to become moving, to begin to move. — 3. **to be translated**, *bod-du* into Tibetan *Tar.*; *bka-ₒgyúr* the translated word, v. *bka*; cf. *sgyúr-ba*. — 4. joined to numbers it signifies **time** or **times**, *ɣžán-pas brgya-ₒgyúr stoṅ-ₒgyúr-du ₒp'ags-pa* a hundred times, nay a thousand, times more sublime than others *Dzl.*; *k'yód-pas brgya-ₒgyúr-bas lhág-par bzáṅ-ba yod* there are (girls) a hundred times prettier than you *Dzl.*; *ɣsum-ₒgyúr ltá-bur* three times as much *Dzl.*; *de ɣñyis-ₒgyúr tsam žig* one twice as large as that *Mil.*

II. sbst. **change, alteration, vicissitude,** *dus bžii ₒgyúr-bas* through the change of seasons *Thgy.* — *ₒgyur-skád*, or also *ₒgyur-k'úgs* singing or humming a tune in a trilling manner *Mil.*; *ₒgyur-lčam nya Mil.* perh. a fish swiftly moving to and fro; *ₒgyur-rtén bžág-pa* to pay money in hand, as an earnest that the bargain is not to be retracted. — Instead of the imp. *gyur*, *šóg* is frq. used.

འགྱེ་བ་ *ₒgyé-ba*, pf. (and imp.?) *gyes*, **to be divided**, e.g. a river that is divided into several branches; *rnám-pa ɣñyis-su* (a ray of light divided) into two parts *Dzl.*; **to separate, to part**, *bem rig ₒgyes dus* when body and soul part from each other *Mil.*; **to disperse**, of a crowd, with or without *so-sór Dzl.* and elsewh.; of a single person: **to part, withdraw, go away**, *mi-tsóg daṅ ghyē-nẹ* *C.* withdrawing from the crowd; **to issue, proceed, spread**, *dé-dag-las gyés-so* they have proceeded from those (their ancestors); of a disease: *gyén-du gyes* (opp. to *t'úr-du zug*) *Med.?*

འགྱེད་པ་ *ₒgyéd-pa* (*W.* *kyé-če*) pf. *bgyes*, fut. *bkye*, 1. **to divide** (trs.), **to scatter, disperse, diffuse**, e.g. rays of light; it is also used when the neutral form *ₒgyé-ba* would seem to be more correct; **to let proceed**, *sprúl-pa*, an emanation; hence **to send**, a messenger *Lex.* and *Schr.*; **to dismiss**, *tsogs*, an assembly *Sch.* — 2. *ₒt'áb-mo ₒgyéd-pa*, *ɣyul ₒgyéd-pa*, also *ₒgyéd-pa* alone, to fight a battle, **to fight, to combat**, *ₒgyéd-pai tse* in the dispute; similarly *ₒdzíṅ-ga bkyé-ba* **to quarrel** *Med.*; hence prob. *W.*: *k'a kyé-če* to abuse, to menace. — 3. *stón-mo ₒgyéd-pa* frq. **to give** an entertainment, banquet, prop. to dispense a feast; *nor ₒgyéd-pa* **to distribute** a property *Lex.*

འགྱེར་བ་ *ₒgyér-ba* **to drop** or let fall, to throw down *Schr.*; **to quit, abandon**, throw away *Sch.*

འགྱེལ་བ་ ˏgyél-ba, pf. gyel (-to), imp. gyel, **to fall, to tumble,** *gyel ma gyel* W. don't tumble, take care not to fall; *gyél-kan* W. lying, (not standing), e. g. a bottle.

འགྱེས་པ་ ˏgyés-pa, another form for ˏgyé-ba, ṕyi-gros-su ˏgyés-par ˏgyur back foremost they retreat Glr.

འགྱོད་པ་ ˏgyód-pa (Ssk. कौकृत्यं) vb. (W. *gyód-če*) **to repent, to grieve for,** and sbst. **repentance,** sorrow for, not only for bad, but also for good actions, when the latter are attended with disadvantage or loss; ṕyis ˏgyón-par ˏgyur you will have to repent it hereafter Dzl.; with la, to repent of a thing; ˏgyód-pa skye repentance arises, I feel repentance, I repent frq.; sems ˏgyód-par ˏgyur id.; *da gyód-pa yoṅ dug* W. id.; ˏgyód-pa med I do not regret it; ˏgyód-pa-čan repenting Pth.; ˏgyód-pai sems méd-par ḱyód-la sbyin-no I give it you readily and with all my heart Pth.; ˏgyód-med without repentance, without grudging, also: in good earnest; ˏgyod-ťsáṅs byéd-pa, ˏťól-žiṅ ˏgyód-pa, ˏgyód-čiṅ bśág-pa Dzl. to acknowledge repentingly, to confess with compunction; ˏgyod-ťsáṅs byéd-par γnáṅ-ba to accept a repentant confession = to forgive, to pardon Dzl. (p. ༤༧, ༥༧, ༦༠, ༢༢༧); ˏgyód-rmo-ba, c. la, to make repent, to make one suffer, feel, or pay (for a thing) Dzl.; γnoṅ-ˏgyód repentance proceeding from consciousness of guilt Pth.

འགྲག(ས)་པ་ ˏgrág(s)-pa, pf. grags, **to sound,** to utter a sound, of men, animals, thunder etc. Dzl.; **to cry, to shout,** dei rná-lam-du ˏgrágs-par ˏgyúr-na if it is shouted into his ear; čes grags so it is called, so he was called, by this name he goes, under that name he is known, celebrated; bód-la yi-ge med čes grags Tibet, so it is said, was without letters, without a written language; Zam.

འགྲགས་པ་ ˏgrágs-pa **to bind,** v. grágs-pa.

འགྲང་བ་ ˏgráṅ-ba 1. Cs. **to number, to count,** v. bgráṅ-ba. — 2. **to satisfy** with food, **to satiate,** *ḍáṅ-če med* W. he is insatiable; gen. only the pf. is in use: ˏgraṅs γjes after having eaten one's fill Med.; śá-ba bsád-pas mi ˏgráṅ-te not yet having enough of deer-killing Mil.

འགྲད་པ་ ˏgrád-pa Cs. = bgrád-pa, **to spread, to extend** (vb. a).

འགྲན་པ་ ˏgrán-pa (Ssk. स्पर्ध) 1. **to vie** with, **contend** with, **to strive** (for victory), wa séṅ-ge-la a fox (contending) with the lion Dzl.; čo-ˏpʰrúl in magic tricks Dzl.; rig-pa in shrewdness, cunning Glr.; ṕyug-ḱyád rnam-ťós-kyi bu daṅ ˏgrán-te to cope even with Plutus as to riches Dzl.; bstód-par ˏgran let us vie with one another in songs of praise Glr.; ˏgrán-pas čog let us now draw a parallel between (these two) Glr.; ˏgrán-du ˏǰúg-pa to cause (two persons) to strive (for the victory) Dzl. — 2. in a general sense, **to fight,** to defend one's self, to make resistance.

Comp. ˏgran-ťsig words of contention, **a quarrelling speech** Glr. — ˏgran-sems 1. **contention, emulation.** 2. **jealousy.** 3. **quarrelsome temper, spirit of controversy;** ˏgran-sems γčóg-pa to stop, put an end to contention. — ˏgrán-zla (pronounced *ḍál-za* in the north of Ld.), **rival, competitor,** equal match; ˏgrán-zla-med-pa, ˏgran-zla daṅ brál-ba, also ˏgrán-gyi do-méd, ˏgrán-ya-med, without a rival, **matchless, unequalled,** applied also to things.

འགྲམ་ ˏgram 1. **shore, bank,** ču-ˏgrám id.; ču čén-poi ˏgrám-du soṅ **they went** to the bank of a large river Dzl. — 2. **side,** sgo-ˏgrám γyás-na on the right side of the door Glr.; sgoi ṕyi-ˏgram-na before the door, outside, out of doors Pth. — 3. **wall,** ḱáṅ-pai ˏóg-ˏgram the lower wall of a house (opp. to the roof) Mil.; ˏgram-γži C., S.g. **foundation, basis,** ˏgram-γži ˏdiṅ-ba to lay a foundation. — In a more general sense: ˏgrám-du **near, close to, just by,** rgyáṅ-nas sgra čé-la ˏgrám-du don čuṅ he has a great voice, is making much noise, at a distance, but looking nearer, you do not find much in him Mil.; śiṅ-gi ˏgrám-du close to the tree.

འགྲམ་པ་ ₒ*grám-pa* **cheek** (cf. *k'ur-tsós*), **dám-pa hom soṅ** *W.* his cheeks are fallen; *lág-pa ₒgrám-pa-la rtén-pa* to lay one's hand on the cheek (in a pensive or sorrowful mood) *Dzl.*

Comp. ₒ*gram-lčág* a slap on the face, box on the ear; **ḍam-čág gyáb-čę** *W.* to box a person's ears. — ₒ*gram-ču ldaṅ* that makes one's mouth water *Sch.* — ₒ*gram-ǰug Lt.?* — **ḍam-dzóg** *C.* a blow or cuff with the fist upon the cheek, **gyúg-pa** to deal such blows. — ₒ*gram-rús* **cheek-bone, jaw-bone.** — ₒ*grám-ša* the flesh of the cheek. — ₒ*gram-γšóg* the hinder part of the jaw-bone *Sch.* — ₒ*grám-so* **cheek-tooth,** molar-tooth, grinder.

འགྲམ་ཡིག་ ₒ*gram-yig* **edict, proclamation, publication** *Sch.*

འགྲམས་པ་ ₒ*gráms-pa* **to hurt** *Lt.*; of wounds: to get inflamed, ni f. *Mil. nt.*

འགྲམས་ཚད་ ₒ*grams-tsád*, a disease, fever in consequence of great exertions *Med.*

འགྲས་པ་ ₒ*grás-pa* **to hate,** to bear ill-will, to have a spite against, **ṅa k'ó-la že ḍę ₒdug** *C.* I hate him in my heart.

འགྲིག་འགྲིག་ ₒ*grig-ₒgrig* 1. **gelatine, jelly** of meat *C.* 2. v. the following article.

འགྲིག་པ་ ₒ*grig-pa* (cf. *sgrig-pa*) **to suit, agree, correspond, to be right, adequate, sufficient,** in *B.* seldom, col. very frq., **ḍig-pa yin** *C.* that will do, I am satisfied; **da ḍig** *W.* now that will do! just enough now! **ḍig-ḍig** *W.* to be sure! quite so! of course! *ₒ*o ḍig gog** *W.* yes, to be sure! **tsó-če mi ḍig** *W.* it is not yet time for cooking; **tó-re tsúg-na ḍig-ga** *W.* will it be early enough, if I sift it to-morrow? **de yaṅ mi ḍig-pa dug** *W.* also that is not practicable; *ṅa ǰo'-yaṅ di ma ḍig-na* if my pronunciation is not correct *C.* (Lewin).

འགྲིབ་པ་ ₒ*grib-pa*, pf. *grib*, 1. **to grow less, to decrease, to be diminished,** syn. to ₒ*bri-ba; mi ₒgrib mi lúd-pa* neither to grow less nor to flow over *Dzl.*; but gen. ₒ*pél-ba* is opposed to ₒ*grib-pa*, and both words refer not only to bulk, size, and quantity, but also to strength, well-being etc., so that ₒ*grib-pa* also means to sink, decay, be reduced; *bskál-pa mar ₒgrib*, acc. to *Schr.* = Treta yuga v. *dus* 6; *mar ₒgrib-pa* also opp. to *yar skyé-ba* to be re-born in lower regions. — 2. **to grow dim, to get dark,** cf. *sgrib-pa Cs.*

འགྲིམ་ ₒ*grim*, in *lag-ₒgrim Glr.* 45: *lag-ₒgrim-gyis brgyus-pas* passing from hand to hand, v. ₒ*grim-pa* II, 1.

འགྲིམ་པ་ ₒ*grim-pa* I. sometimes for ₒ*brim-pa Pth.* II. pf. ₒ*grims* 1. **to go, walk, march about, perambulate, to rove** or **stroll** idling about, *rgyal-k'ams* over the countries *Mil.*; *γčig-pur ri-k'ród-la Mil.*; *bár-dor* in the bardo (q.v.) *Thgr.*; *mi-sér ǰúg-pai ₒgrim-sa yin* it is a resort of robbers *Mil.*; it is also used of the course of the veins in the body *Med.* — 2. *W.* **to go off, to sell,** to meet with a ready sale. — 3. *rig-pa ₒgrim-pa* v. *rig-pa.*

འགྲིལ་བ་ ₒ*gril-ba*, pf. *gril* (cf. *sgril-ba*) 1. **to be twisted** or **wrapped round,** *Dzl.* ༢༥, 17. acc. to one manuscript, for ₒ*kri-ba Sch.*; to be collected, concentrated, to flock or crowd together, *kun ₒgril-nas* all in a heap, all together *Mil.* — 2. **to be turned, rounded, made circular** or **cylindric,** e.g. a stick *Mil.* — 3. **to fall,** e.g. leaves from a tree; in *B.* seldom, in *W.* frq. (ₒ*dril-ba* is the same word).

འགྲིས་ ₒ*gris* v. ₒ*dris.*

འགྲུ་བ་ ₒ*grú-ba*, pf. *grus*, **to bestow pains** upon a thing, *slob-pa-la* upon study *Dzl.*

འགྲུབ་པ་ ₒ*grúb-pa*, pf. *grub* 1. **to be made ready, to be finished, accomplished;** ₒ*grúb-pa mi srid* it is not possible that this be accomplished *Glr.*; *ma ₒgrúb-par* before its having been finished *Glr.*; *ma-ₒgrúb-pa-rnams ₒgrúb-par ₒgyur-ro* (frq. of charms, regarding their desired effect) prob. means: all that has not yet been effected, will be accomplished by it; *grúb-pa-rnams* is applied in a special sense to the ordained Gelongs (v. *dge-slóṅ*); *šúgs-la ₒgrub* the thing is brought about quite of itself *Mil.*; so esp. in the phrase: *lhún-gyis grúb-pa* being produced spontaneously (opp. to making, procuring) e. g. clothes, food etc. were always at his disposal, viz. in a supernatural way *Dzl.*; *dpál-las grub* it devolved on me in consequence of my perfection, my superior qualities *Mil.*; *dón-la grúb-pa med kyaṅ* though it did not actually happen so (still, being meant to frighten by appearances etc.) *Glr.*; *byéd-na don čen ˳grub* if you do so, you will have many advantages (lit. great welfare) by it *Mil.*; *gru ˳grúb-pa Tar.* 25,6; 34,20 *Schf.*: to take in a full cargo, though from the wide meaning of the word, it may also signify: to accomplish a journey happily, so esp. in the passage *Tar.* 35,3 — 2. **to be made, fabricated**, *rdó-las* out of stone. — 3. **to be fulfilled, granted,** of wishes etc., also with *bžin-du.* — 4. **to be performed according to rule,** of charms; cf. *sgrúb-pa* and *grúb-pa.* — *˳grúb-sbyór* is an expression occurring in almanacs, relative to the proving true of certain astrological prognostics of good luck, similar to, but not identic with *rten-˳brél.*

འགྲུམ་པ་ *˳grúm-pa*, pf. *grum*(?), **to pinch or nip off** (the point of a thing), **to cut off, to prune, lop, clip,** the wings, *W.*, cf. *grúm-pa.*

འགྲུལ་བ་ *˳grúl-ba* I. 1. **to walk, to pass, to travel,** *˳grúl-bar byéd-pa* to cause to go, to send off, despatch, a messenger *Dzl.*; **ṅún-la ḍul* W.* walk first! take the lead! *˳grúl-ba-po, ˳grúl-po Sch., *ḍúl-k̔an, ḍúl-mi* W.* a walker, foot-traveller, pedestrian; *˳grúl-pa Sch.* id.; *˳grúl* sbst. passage, the possibility of passing, *γnya-náṅ-gi ˳grul čád-pas* the passing from Nyanaṅ being made impracticable (viz. by snow) *Mil.* — 2. fig. **to walk, to live, act,** or **behave,** **ṭim-si** (or **tim-mi*) *naṅ-tar* W.* (to live) in conformity with one's duty, in accordance to the law. — 3. **to pass, to be good, current,** of coins.

II. i. o. *brúl-ba Mil.*

འགྲུས་པ་ *˳grús-pa* 1. pf. of *˳grú-ba.* — 2. sbst. **zeal, diligence, endeavour;** more frq. *brtson-˳grús.*

འགྲེ་བ་ *˳gré-ba* 1. **to roll** one's self, *sá-la* on the ground; *˳gre-ldóg Glr.* (or *˳gre lóg Pth.*) *byéd-pa* id., e.g. from pain, despair etc.; also of horses etc. — 2. **to repeat** *Cs.*

འགྲེང་བ་ *˳gréṅ-ba* (cf. *˳sgreṅ-ba*) **to stand** (not in use in *W.*) *dóṅ-gi k̔ar ˳gréṅ-nas* standing at the top of the pit *Dzl.*; *dṅáṅs-pa ltar ˳gréṅ-bar ˳gyur* they start up as if frightened *Dzl.*; of the *p̔o-mtsán:* to be erected *Med.*; *mi ˳greṅ γsum* three lengths of a man *Tar.* — *˳gréṅ-bu,* also *˳gréṅ-po* (*Glr.*) the sign of the vowel e.

འགྲེམ(ས)་པ་ *˳grém(s)-pa,* pf. *bkram,* fut. *dgram,* imp. *k̔roms* (*W. *ṭam-če**, imp. **ṭom**) 1. **to put** or **lay down** in order, e.g. beams, spars etc. *B.* and col; **to spread out, to display,** goods, books, on the table or ground; **to scatter,** blossoms by the wind *Stg.*; **to draw,** a curtain. — 2. **to sprinkle,** water, *B.* and col. — 3. **to distribute,** for *˳brím-pa C.*

འགྲེལ་བ་ *˳grél-ba,* pf. *bkral,* another form for *˳grol-ba,* **to explain, comment, illustrate,** *dgóṅs-pa* the import (of the words or writings of the saints); *˳grél-ba Cs., ˳grel-pa Zam., Tar.* explanation, explication, commentary; *don-˳grél,* resp. *dgoṅs-˳grél* explanation of the meaning; *tsig-˳grél* explanation of a word, of the words; *γžuṅ-grél* 1. explication of the text 2. text and commentary; *raṅ-˳grél* prob. self-explanation, an explanation contained in the book itself *Wdṅ.*; *˳grél-ba-po Cs., ˳grél-po Sch., ˳grel-byéd Cs.* an explainer, commentator. (*p̔an-tsún ˳grél-ba,* and *k̔ral ˳grél-ba Lexx.*?)

འགྲོ་སྒོ་ *˳gró-sgo C.* **expense, expenditure,** of money, **ḍo-gor táṅ-ba** to lay out (money), to spend.

འགྲོ་ལྡིང་ *˳gro-ldiṅ* Dramila, country in the south of India *Schf.*; another reading gives Draviḍa (coast of Coromandel).

འགྲོ་བ་ *˳gró-ba* I. vb., pf. and imp. *soṅ,* the imp. *˳gro(s)* seldom used, 1. **to**

walk, *k'yeu ˳gro mi nús-pa góg-pa tsam* an infant, a child, that creeps only, and is not yet able to walk *Dzl.*; *˳gró-ba daṅ nyál-ba daṅ ˳dúg-pa* the walking, lying and sitting *Dzl.*; com. in a more gen. sense: **to go, to move,** *˳gró-am mi ˳gro* will you go or not? *rgyál-poi mdún-la ˳gró-bai lág-č'a* the things going, i.e. carried, before the king *Glr.*; **to go away,** *da ṅa ˳gró-bar ẑu* now I beg to be permitted to go *Pth.*; *ɣnás-nas ˳gró-ba* to go away from a place, to leave, *k'yím-nas ˳gro mi ȷ̓ód-na* if one cannot leave his house, part from home *Pth.*; **to go out,** *k'yod nyin-par rtág-tu ˳gró-na* if during the day you always go out, are from home *Dzl.*; **to travel,** *ȷ̓'an-tsún-du ˳gró-ba Dzl.*, *ȷ̓'ar ˳gro tsur ˳gró-ba Pth.* travelling there and back; *yar ˳gro mar ˳gró-ba* to travel up and down, up hill and down hill *Glr.*; *˳gró-č'os-su* as a spiritual vademecum *Mil.*; *˳gró-tse* on the way, on the road; opp. to *˳óṅ-ba* (more fully: *ȷ̓'ar ˳gro tsur ˳oṅ-ba*, col. *yoṅ-ba*) to go and to come back; hence *˳gro-tse* may also mean: on the way thither; *˳gro-˳oṅ-méd-pa* a thing that is neither going nor coming, but always remaining in its place *Mil.*; **to go, move on,** to continue one's way, esp. in the phrase *soṅ(-soṅ)-ba-las.* Connected with adverbs and postpositions: *ȷ̓'yir ˳gró-ba* to return, go home, to come back, also: to go out, *mdún-du*, *sṅón-du*, *sṅún-la ˳gró-ba* to go before, pass before, precede (*mdún-du* referring to space only, *sṅón-du* and *sṅún-du* both to space and time); *rȷ̓és-su ˳gró-ba* to follow, come after or later, to succeed, also to give one's self over to, to addict one's self to (e.g. ill courses) *Ld.-Glr. Schl.* p. 7, b; *˳gro čug, C.* let it be, let it take its course! — *rkyál-˳gro* a swimming fish *Cs.* — *dgúr* (or *rgur*)-*˳gro* = *dud-˳gro.* — *˳grúl-˳gro* pacing, walking *Cs.* — *rgyúg-˳gro* running, galloping *Cs.* — *ṅán-˳gro* going to damnation, *ṅán-soṅ* having gone to damnation, *ṅán-soṅ ɣsum* the three damned, or not saved, classes of beings (v. sub II); *ṅán-soṅ ɣsum* is opposed to *bdé-˳gro*, and often used in a general sense = 'hell'. — *sṅón-˳gro* 1. **preceding, foregoing, previous, former.** 2. **preface, introduction,** opp. to *dṅos-ɣẑi*, the thing itself, the text etc. *Thgr.* and elsewh. — *č'os t'ams-čád-kyi sṅón-˳groi sláb-bya* Petersb. Verzeichniss no. 409) does not mean: 'advice given by the former (teachers)' *Sch.*, but: introductory and preparatory doctrines. — *mčóṅ-˳gro* (going in leaps) **a frog** *Cs.* — *nyál-˳gro* (creeping, crawling) **a worm.** — *ltó-˳gro* (crawling, sliding on the belly) **worm, snake,** frq. — *dúd-˳gro* (*Ssk.*, तिर्यंच) walking in an inclined posture, **an animal,** v. sub. II. — *bdé-˳gro* going to happiness: **the happy, the blessed,** also *bdér-˳gro Was.*, opp. to *ṅán-˳gro*, v. above; usually in a gen. sense, like our 'heaven'; *bdé-˳gro mt'o-ris-kyi lus t'ób-pa* to receive a heavenly, glorified body, v. *lus.* — *˳dúr-˳gro* **trotting** *Cs.* — *˳ȷ̓'ur-gro* **a bird** *Cs.* — *˳ȷ̓'yé-˳gro* = *ltó-˳gro.* — *láṅs-˳gro* walking erect, **man.** — 2. **to get, to get into, to enter** * či-bdag-gi dbáṅ-du sóṅ-ba* having got into the power of death *S.g.*; *grál-gyi t'a-mar soṅ* they got (in a miraculous manner) to the end *Dzl.* ༢༥, 4. b.; *de nyid mig-tu sóṅ-na* if the same (a little hair) gets into the eye *Thgy.* — 3. **to find room** in, **to be contained** in, like *sóṅ-ba*: *til-rȷ̓áṅ k'al brgyád-ču ˳gró-ba ẑig* a sesame store-room that will hold 80 bushels; *k'al ɣčig ˳gró-bai ẑiṅ* as much land as can be sown with a bushel of corn (prop. a field holding a bushel) *Pth.* — 4. **to turn to, to be transformed into,** syn. to *˳gyúr-ba* and often used instead of it, but only in more recent writings, and in the col. language of *C.* (in *W.* **čá-če** is much more in use): *dúg-tu ˳gro* it turns to poison, it is changed into poison *Mil.*; *k'yi-mo ẑig-tu soṅ* she was changed into a bitch *Mil.*; *mt'ar gyúr-nas sdug-bsṅál-du ˳gró-bas-na* because they finally change and are turned into misery *Thgy.*; *lóg-par ˳gró-ba* **to take an unfavourable turn, to have a fatal issue** (of a cure) *Lt.*; *da sgrúb-ɣnas-su soṅ yod* it has now become a place of meditation, it has been transformed into sacred ground

Mil.; *stobs č̌úṅ-du ˳gró-ba* the state of declining, the decay of strength *Med.*; *č̌ól-bar ˳gro* they get intermixed, confused *Ma.*; similarly *Tar.* 210,10; *las zin ˳gró-na* when there is no more work, when work ceases. In a somewhat different sense: *mé-tog smán-la ˳gro* the blossom is used for medicines. — 5. In *W.* *˳gró-ba* is gen. joined to a supine in *te*, and used to express uncertainty or probability: **di-riṅ der léb-te ḍo** he has probably arrived there to-day; **zér-te yod ḍo** very likely he has said so; **s̀ro z̀i-te ḍo** his anger will have abated, I think. The origin of this particular use of the word may perh. be traced to such sentences as the one following: *p̀úṅ-ste ˳gro* we are going to be ruined, we are likely to be ruined. — 6. **to be spent, expended,** v. *˳gró-sgo*; **sóṅ-to** col., account of expenses.

II. sbst. **a being, a living creature,** *˳gró-ba mi* the being 'man', *Mil.*; *˳gró-ba rin-č̌én Cs.*, *˳gro-mč̌óg*, the highest being, or creature, man; *˳gró-bai rigs drúg*, *˳gro-drúg* the six classes of beings, viz. *lha, lha-ma-yín, mi, dúd-˳gro, yi-dvags, dmyál-ba-pa.* The *lha-ma-yin* are sometimes omitted, or placed after man. — *˳gro(-bai) don byéd-pa*, or *mdzád-pa* to care for the welfare of beings, which expression is frq. applied to the benevolent activity of the Bodhisatvas etc., at present as much as: to perform divine service, to officiate, = *sku-rím byéd-pa.* — *˳gro-p̀án* = *˳gro-dón Tar.* 13,16. — *˳gró-sa* 1. **way, road** *W.*, **ḍó-sa med** one cannot go there. 2. **aim, scope,** *˳gró-sar p̀yin* he reaches his aim, attains his end *Glr.* 3. **access, approach,** *˳gró-sa mi ˳dug* one cannot gain access, admission.

འགྲོགས་པ་ *˳gróg·s-pa* 1. (cf. *grogs*) **to be associated,** *ḱyo-s̀úg ɣnyis ˳gróg·s-na* husband and wife together *Dzl.*; *de daṅ ˳gróg·s-te ˳oṅs* he came with him, had joined him *Dzl.*; *˳gróg·s-te dóṅ-ṅo* let us go together *Dzl.*; *ṅa daṅ ḱyéd-rnams ˳bral-méd rtág-tu ˳grogs* I and you, we shall always remain inseparably united *Glr.*; *˳gróg·s-dgos-rnams* those with whom we are to keep close fellowship, our nearest relations and associates *S.g.* — 2. cf. *˳grág·s-pa, sgróg-pa*) **to cry, to shout** *Dzl.*, esp. joined with *˳bod.* — 3. (cf. *grás-pa, grág·s-pa* I.) **to bind, to tie,** *t́ág-pa-la dar-lčóg*, a flag to a rope; **to hang, fix, fasten,** *nyí-mai zér-la* hanging on a sun-beam *Glr.*

འགྲོང(ས)་པོ་ *˳gróṅ(s)-po*, or *˳gróṅs-pa*, **straight,** = *bsráṅs-pa, Ts.*

འགྲོང་བ་ *˳groṅ-ba* 1. pf. *groṅs* 1. resp. **to die**; *˳gróṅs-ka* the very time of one's death *Cs.*, cf. *˳č̌í-ka*; sometimes it stands 2. for *˳drén-pa, Mil.* and *C.* — 2. pf. *bkroṅs*, fut. *dgroṅs*, resp. **to be killed, murdered, put to death,** of Lamas and kings.

འགྲོད་པ་ *˳gród-pa*, = *bgród-pa*, **to go, to travel** *Glr.*

འགྲོན་ *˳gron* **alienism,** the state of being a foreigner; *˳grón-du ˳gró-ba* to go on travels, to go abroad *Dzl.*; *˳grón-po*, fem. *˳grón-mo*, guest, foreigner, stranger, traveller frq.; *˳grón-po ˳bód-mḱan* one inviting guests, an inviter col.; *ɣz̀is-˳gron* a native guest, *byés-˳gron* a foreign guest *Cs.*; *˳gron-ḱáṅ* inn, public house *Mil.*; *˳gron-ɣnyér* 1. that servant in a household who has to announce visitors, to receive and hand over requests etc.; in *W.* an official in the monasteries attending on strangers and travellers. 2. a mediator, one supporting a petition, one taking care of sacrifices etc. — *˳gron-lám* road *Cs.*

འགྲོན་པ་ *˳grón-pa*, *Cs.* = *˳gród-pa.*

འགྲོན་བུ་ *˳grón-bu* (*W.* col. **rúm-bu**) **a small shell, cowry,** at present chiefly used as ornament, or as a medicine, after having been burnt and pulverized; *˳grón-bui t́al* the ashes of this shell *Med.*; *˳gron-t́ód* an ornament for the head, consisting of cowries *Mil.*

འགྲོར་ *˳gror*, supine of *˳gró-ba.*

འགྲོལ་བ་ *˳gról-ba* I. vb. neut., pf. *grol*, **to become free, to be liberated, released from,** *bčíṅs-pa gaṅ yín-pa dé-dag ni gról-bar gyúr-to* all that were bound were released; *lus dé las* from this body *Glr.*; *nád-las* from disease, *ṅas* by me *Mil.* In a specific Buddhistic sense: *yid*, or *sems rnám-par grol* the soul or spirit is released, made free, viz. from every impediment arising from imperfect knowledge or perception, the latter being no longer subject to dimness and uncertainty, but perfectly clear; *raṅ(-sar) gról-ba* what has become clear of itself (without any study or exertion) *Glr.*; yet *raṅ gról-ba* seems also to denote: to be set free, to get released (from the *˳ḱor-ba*) through one's self; *čos-nyid-kyi gliṅ-du ˳gról-ba* to be released and elevated into the region of the highest perception *Glr.*; *˳gról-ba*, used absolutely, always signifies, like *ťár-ba*, to be released from the evil of existence.

II. vb. act., pf. *bkrol*, fut. *dgrol*, imp. *ḱrol* (*W. bkrol*, pronounced *ṭol*) 1. **to loose, untie, unbutton, unfasten**, a knot, a bag, a garment; **to put down, take off**, arms, ornaments etc. — 2. **to release, redeem, liberate,** *bčiṅs-pa-las* from fetters *Tar.* — 3. **to remove,** do away with, put an end to, *sdug-bsṅál* misery, *ťe-ťsóm* doubts. — 4. **to remove obscurities,** to free from uncertainties, **to explain, interpret, comment,** = *˳grél-ba*, e.g. *dgóṅs-pa* the sense, import *Lex.*; *˳grol-byéd*, *˳gról(-ba)-po* commentator *Cs.*

འགྲོས་ *˳gros* the act of **going, walking,** *ṕyi ˳grós-su* v. sub *˳gyés-pa*; *skyabs-˳grós* v. *skyabs*; *spyod-˳grós* manner of walking, gait, carriage; *séṅ-gei spyod-grós Mil.* the manner of a lion; also manner or mode of living, of transacting business, *dé-ťso ṅá-yi spyod-˳grós yin* these are my occupations *Mil.*; *mig-gi spyod-˳grós* the language of the eyes, of looks; *rkaṅ-grós* 1. a going or travelling on foot, a march. 2. breeding cattle, *rkaṅ-˳grós spél-ba* to breed cattle, to be a grazier. — *ču-˳grós* a current of water; *šiṅ ču-˳grós-la kyál-če* to float timber *W.* — *˳gros-čén* amble (of a horse) *Sch.*

རྒ་བ་ *rga-ba*, pf. *rgas* 1. **to be old, aged,** *rga-šis ɣzir-ba* to suffer under (the infirmities of) old age *Zam.* (cf. *skyé-ba* init.); *rgás-pai stéṅ-du* beside my being already old *Dzl.*; *rgas-ḱógs* v. *˳ḱógs-pa*. — 2. fig. **to go down, to set,** of the sun etc.; *go-rgás* v. *go* 2.

རྒ་ཝང་ཁྲད་ཀྱི་ *rga-waṅ-ḱrád-kyi*(?) **bat, flittermouse** *Ts.*

རྒྱག་ཅིག་ *rgyag-čig* a large gray species of **lizard** *Ld.*

རྒང་ *rgaṅ*, also *˳gaṅ-ɣzér-ma* **hedgehog** *Sch.*, or perh. rather **porcupine.**

རྒད་པ་ *rgád-pa*, or *rgán-pa*, **old, aged**; more frq. *rgád-po* 1. an **old man,** a man gray with old age. 2. an **elder, senior, headman** of a village; *rgád-mo* an old woman; *rgan-bgrés* old people *Sch.*; *rgan-rgón ɣnyis Sch.*: 'both the old man and the old woman' (?); *rgan-rgón-rnams-kyi skyo-gróys* the comforter of old people (so *Mil.* calls himself). — *rgan-byis* old people and children, old and young *Mil.* — *rgan-mi-máṅ* = *rgan-ɣsum.* — *gan-ťsir-žón-ťsir W.*, *geṇ-žoṇ-ḍhal-rim C.* the privileges of seniority. — *rgan-žúgs* those that are grown old *Cs.*, 'an old monk' (?) *Sch.* — *rgan-rábs* the aged, *rgan-rábs-la rim-gro byéd-pa Stg.*, *rgan-rigs ṕu-dúd-du ḱúr-ba S.g.* to respect old age. — *rgan-ɣsúm*, *rgan-mi-máṅ* the elders of a village.

རྒལ་ *rgal W.* **a ford.**

རྒལ་ཅིག་པ་ *rgal-čig-pa* = *rgyag-čig Ld.*

རྒལ་བ་ *rgál-ba*, pf. and fut. *brgal*, imp. *rgol*, c. *las*, or accus., or *la*, **to step** over (a threshold) *Glr.*; **to pass** or **climb** over (a mountain); *la brgál-bai byáṅ-ṅos* the north-side of a pass crossed *Glr.*; **to leap** over (a wall) *Dzl.*; **to ford** (a river); **to travel** through, **to sail** over, **to pass** (a river or lake), *rgyá-mťso-la gru-ɣziṅs-kyi lám-nas brgál-te* after having crossed the sea in a ship.

རྒལ་ཚིགས་ *rgal-ťsigs Sch.* = *sgal-ťsigs.*

རྒས་ *rgas*, v. *rgá-ba.*

རྒས་ཀ་ *rgás-ka* **old age**; *rgás-ka sra* a vigorous old age.

རྒུ་ *rgu* sometimes for *dgu*; *rgu-ťub* = *dgu-ťub Med.*; *-gu-drús?*

རྒུད་པ་ *rgúd-pa* **to decline, to sink, to get weak, frail,** esp. with old age *Mil.*, *Pth.*; in *W.* used in a more general sense: **gud soṅ** 1. he has grown thin. 2. he is impoverished, much reduced, in declining circumstances; *dar-rgúd* the rise and fall in the world.

རྒུན་ *rgun* **the vine; grape;** *rgun-dkár* white grapes, *rgun-nág* black, or purple grapes *W.*; *rgun-rgód W.* **raisins;** *rgun-˳brúm* grapes; raisins; *rgun (-˳brum)-śiṅ* vine; *rgun(-˳brum)-ťsás* **vineyard;** *rgun-čáṅ Mil.* **wine,** resp. *rgun-skyéms Cs.*

རྒུར་ *rgur* v. *dgur.*

རྒོ་ *rgo*, sometimes for *sgo.*

རྒོ་བ་ *rgó-ba* = *dgó-ba.*

རྒོངས་ *rgoṅs S.g.?*

རྒོངས་མོ་ *rgóṅs-mo Mil.* for *dgóṅs-mo* (?).

རྒོད་ *rgod* 1. **laughing, laughter** *S.g.* — 2. **bird of prey.** — 3. **wild.** — 4. **prudent** (v. the following word).

རྒོད་པ་ *rgód-pa* I. vb. 1. **to laugh,** aloud *Mil.*; (*Bal.* **rgód-ča**) cf. *gád-mo, dgód-pa, bgád-pa.* — 2. **to grow weak, languid,** or **indolent,** syn. to *γyéṅ-ba*, often joined with *byiṅ*, for emphasis; *rgód-bag-čan* weak, languid, indolent *Stg.*

II. adj. 1. **wild,** *ra-rgód* wild goat, *ṗag-rgód* wild boar, *γyag-rgód* wild yak or ox; *rgod-γyag-rwá* horn of the wild yak *S.g.*; *bya-rgód* vulture, bird of prey = *bya-rgyál*; *rgód-po*, and *rgod* id.; *rgód-kyi rtse-rgyál* an eagle's feather, stuck as ornament on the hat *Pth.*; *mi-rgód* a wild or savage man; a robber, ruffian; *mi-rgód byéd-pa* to rob (usually named together with murdering and lying) *Dzl.*, but as the Tibetan always attaches to this word *mi-rgód* the notion of some gigantic hairy fiend, it cannot in every instance be applied to beings really existing. — Fig. furious, angry (seldom); *dbugs-rgód Med.?* — 2. **prudent, able** *C.*, *Zam.*

རྒོད་མ་ *rgód-ma, rta rgód-ma* (*Bal.* **gún-ma** **a mare;** *rgod-skám-ma* a barren mare *Sch.*; *rgod-brún* dung of a mare *Med.*

རྒོལ་ *rgol* 1. v. *rgál-ba.* 2. v. *rgól-ba.*

རྒོལ་བ་ *rgól-ba*, pf. and fut. *brgol*, **to dispute, combat, fight,** *mi-la* with or against a man; *ṗá-rol-poi dmág-la rgól-du ˳gró-ba* they are about to fight against the hostile army *Dzl.*; *γžán-gyis rgol ma nús-so* nobody could fight them, could make head against them *Glr.*; **to offer resistance,** to make opposition, *sus kyaṅ rgól-ba ˳dzúgs-pai mi ma byuṅ* nobody arose to offer resistance *Pth.* (evidently incorrect; it should be either; *sus kyaṅ rgól-ba ˳dzúgs-pa* [inf.] *ma byuṅ*, or: *rgól-ba ˳dzúgs-pai* [partic.] *mi su yaṅ ma byuṅ*); sometimes as much as **to accuse, to charge,** *ḱyód-kyis ṅai bu bsád-do žes brgál-te* 'you have killed my son', thus accusing me *Dzl.*; *ťsur γnyis rgol* he quarrels at a double rate *Mil.*; *mi-la rgól-ba zú-ba* to find fault with another (higher in rank), to pick a quarrel with him *Mil.*; *rgól-bai žu-dón* a speech provoking a quarrel with a superior *Mil.*; *ṗas-rgól* a quarrel or contest begun by the counter-party *Sch.*; *ṗas-rgol-mi, ṗas rgól-pa mi* adversary, opponent *Dzl.* ༧༥°, 2. — *sṅá-rgol*, and *ṗyi-rgol* (*Ssk.* पूर्ववादिन् & परवादिन्) 1. acc. to *Cs.* **plaintiff** and **defendant,** but these terms are not quite adequate, as *sṅá-rgol* prop. denotes him who begins a quarrel, **the aggressor, assailant,** both in war and in common life, e.g. in court, and *ṗyi-rgol* designates him, who is intent on defending himself against the attacks and accusations of the opponent, by surpassing him in abusive language and esp. by having recourse to witchcraft. Hence *ṗyir-rgól-bai γnód-pa* is a kind of danger against which every one tries to protect himself, and chiefly again by charms and witchcraft. — 2. *sṅa-rgol* and *ṗyi-rgol* are also said to signify those students that are contending with one another in academical disputations.

རྒྱ་ *rgya* 1. resp. *ṗyag-rgyá*, **seal, stamp, mark, sign, token;** (*ṗyag-*) *rgyás ˳débs-*

pa, *Cs.* *rgya brgyáb-pa*, to seal, to stamp; to seal up, *búm-pa-la* a bottle *Glr.*; *nám-mḱai dbyiṅs-su* (to seal up) into the heavenly regions, i.e. to cause to disappear, to hide for ever *Glr.*; to confirm or pledge solemnly by a sealed document; *rí-rgya lúṅ-rgya ˳dzúg-pa* 'to seal up hills and valleys', i.e. to protect the living beings inhabiting them from being harmed by huntsmen or fishermen, an annual performance of the Dalai Lama, consisting in a variety of spells and incantations; *rgya ẏcóg-pa* to break open a seal *Cs.* — Further expressions v. compounds. — 2. (*Cs.* *rgyá-bo?*) **extent, width, size,** *rgyar dpag-tu-méd-pa* immeasurable in extent *Glr.*; *séms-čan-gyi rgyai ťsad ni či tsam* how vast must be the extent (of love) with respect to beings! *Thgy.*; *rgyá-čan* having extent, *mḱyén-rgya-čan* of extensive learning *Mil.*; *rgya-čén(-po)* of very large size, very extensive, of a building, a pond etc.; grand, enormous, prodigious, of banquets feasts, sacrifices, assemblies; c. accus. very rich in, *Schr.*; in a general sense: great, *stón-pa rgya-čé-ba* a great master or teacher *Thgy.*; *rgya-čén spyód-pai blá-ma* may be rendered: a very virtuous Lama, po.; *rgya-čúṅ* denotes the contrary of all this; *rgya-če-čúṅ* v. *rgya-ḱyón* in Compounds; *rgya-čér* adv. = *rgyás-par* in detail, at large, at full length, e.g. to explain; *rgya-čér byéd-pa* to extend *Feer Introd.* etc. p. 72; *rgya-čer-ról-pa Lalitavistara* or *Lalitavistāra*, title of a biography of Buddha, translated and edited by *Foucaux* (a conjecture concerning the signification of the Sanskrit word v. *Fouc. Rgyatcherr.* II. p. XXII.; some statements relative to the Chinese translations of this work, v. ibid. p. XVI., and *Was.* 176; on the historical value of it v. *Was.* 3, 4); *rgya bskyéd-pa Zam.*, *Cs.* to widen, augment, enlarge, extend, *rgya bskúm-pa* to contract, to diminish the extent. Lastly, it also denotes, like *dkyíl-˳ḱor*, a plain surface, a disk: *nyi zlai rgya dkar šar Mil.* the bright disks of the sun and moon appear, cf. *rgyas* in *zla-rgyás*; v. also the compounds. — 3. (*Cs.* *rgyá-mo*, perh. also *rgyá-ma*) **net**; *byá-rgya* fowling-net, *nyá-rgya* fishing-net, *ri-dags-rgya* hunting-net, — 4. for *rgyá-ma*, v. compounds. — 5. for *rgyá-mo* **beard**, *rgyá-čan* having a beard, bearded *C.* — 6. for *rgya-gár*, *rgya-gár-pa*, and *rgya-gàr-skad*. — 7. for *rgya-nág*, *rgya-nág-pa*, and *rgya-nág-skad*. — 8. for *rgya-ru*. — 9. for *rgya-skyégs*. — 10. erron. for *brgya*.

Comp. and deriv. *rgya-dkár* 1. *nyi-zlái rgya-dkár* v. above no. 2. extr. 2. *Cs.* = *rgya-gár* India, 3. *Cs.* a dog with white spots on the nose. — *rgya-skád* 1. Sanskrit language, 2. Chinese language. — *rgya-skás* (*W.* **gya-šrę**) a (European) **staircase**, cf. *skás-ka*. — *rgya-skégs*, *rgya-skyégs*, *Ssk.* लाक्षा, Williams: 'a kind of red dye, lac, obtained from an insect as well as from the resin of a particular tree'; in medical works it is mentioned as an astringent medicine; the adjectives *dkar-rgyá* light-red, and *rgya-smúg* violaceous *C.* are derived from this word. — *rgya-ḱúr Med.?* — *rgya-ḱyi* a Chinese dog. — *rgya-ḱyón* **width, extent, area** *Pth.*, col. **gya-če-čúṅ**. — *rgya-ḱri C.* **chair.** — *rgya-gár* (the 'white extent or plain') **India**, *rgya-gár-pa* an Indian, *rgya-gar-skad* Sanskrit language. — *rgya-grám* a figure like a cross; *rdo-rje-rgya-grám* shaped like a quadrifid flower; *rluṅ rgya-grám žés-pa Glr.* seems to be = *rlúṅ-gi dkyil-˳ḱor* atmosphere (connected with some phantastic association); *lám-po rgya-grám* a cross-road *Sch.* — *rgya-čáṅ* a kind of girdle *Lex.* — *rgya-čan* v. *rgya* 2 and 5. — *rgya-ču-ḱúg-pa* n. of a river in China near the Tibetan frontier (also *rgya-ču-rabs-med*) *Glr.* — *rgya-če* etc. v. *rgya* 2. — *rgya-ṭám Bhot.* = *ṭám-ka*, the third part of a rupee. — *rgya-rtags* **mark, signature, stamp** *Sch.* — *rgya-ťél* a kind of seal or stamp *Cs.* — *rgya-mťóṅs* 1. a platform, an open pavilion on the house-top, 2. a vent-hole for smoke. — *rgya-˳dré* **a quarrel** *Mil.nt.* — *rgya-nág* (the 'black extent') **China**, *rgya-nág-pa*, and *-ma* a China-man and woman; *rgyá-rnams* the Chinese *Glr.*

— *rgya-nón W.* the great royal seal, of a square form; surpassing (*nón-pa*) all others in influence and power. — *rgya-dpé* a Sanskrit book *Tar.* 33, 2. — *rgya-p̔i-liṅ* n. of the country, *rgya-p̔i-liṅ-pa*, n. of the people, through which the Tibetans heard first (prob. at the beginning of the eighteenth century) of the civilized nations of the occident, hence n. for **British India**, for Englishman, or European resident of British India, and also (sometimes without *rgya*) for Europe and European in general. The word is of course not to be found in literature. Some derive it from 'Feringhi', which term, in the slightly altered form of *p̔a-ráṅ, p̔e-ráṅ*, is current in *C.*, along with the above mentioned *rgya-p̔i-liṅ*; it is therefore not improbable, that *p̔i-liṅ* represents only the more vulgar pronunciation of the genuine Tibetan word *p̔yi-gliṅ*, an out-country, a distant foreign country and esp. **Europe**, *Chr. Prot.* — *rgya-p̔ib(s)*, *rgya-p̔úb(s)* a Chinese roof *Glr.* — *rgyá-ba* 1. vb. to be wide, extensive, pf. *rgyas* (q.v.), 2. sbst. width, extent, 3. adj. wide; *rgyá-bar ˳gyúr-ba* to extend, to increase, to become copious *Cs.*, perh. no longer in use. — *rgyá-bo* 1. *Cs.* and *Lex.* **beard.** 2. **a Chinese** *Glr.*, but not without an allusion to the former signification. — *rgya-dbáṅ rin-po-č̔é* title of the Dalai Lama, v. *Huc* II., 275, where '*kian ngan*' stands erroneously. — *rgyá-ma* 1. **a large steel-yard** *C.*, *rgyá-ma-la ˳dégs-pa* to weigh *Glr.*, **gyá-ma-la tég-ne** *C.* being weighed out by retail, e.g. meat; **gyá-ma-la ma tég-ne** *C.* wholesale. 2. a sealed paper, document. — *rgya-mi* **a Chinese.** — *rgyá-mo* 1. **net** *Cs.* 2. **a Chinese woman** *Glr.*; *rgyá-mo-bza* id. — *rgya-rmá* **the venereal disease** *Sch.* — *rgya-smúg* **violet colour** *C.* — *rgya-ts̔á* **sal ammoniac** *Med.* — *rgya-ts̔ós Med.*, perh. = *rgya-skyégs.* — *rgyá-mts̔o* 1. **sea, ocean;** *rgyá-mts̔or ˳j̔úg-pa* to go to sea *Dzl.*, *γtóṅ-ba* to let one go to sea *Dzl.*; *p̔yii rgyá-mts̔o* the outer sea, ocean; *náṅ-gi rgyá-mts̔o* an inner sea, inland sea, lake. 2. *Bal.* (**rgyám-ts̔o**) **river.** 3. **dropsy** *Mṅg.* 4. symb. num.: *four.* — *rgya-γži W.* is stated to be a kind of *γtór-ma.* — *rgya-zór Mil.* = *zor* **reaping-hook, sickle.** — *rgya-γzéb Sch.* 'a large net', *C.* a large **rake,** used in reaping. — *rgya-yúl* 1. a large country 2. China *Glr.* — *rgyá-ra, rgyá-ru*, occasionally *rgya* alone, **the Saiga-antelope** *Sch.* — *rgya-rí* **a portion of meat,** (= *sder-gáṅ* a plateful) small or large, *Pth., W. C.*; it also denotes a measure = ½ *dum*, or ¼ *lhu.* — *rgya-róg* **beard** *C.* — *rgya-láb* **talk, gossip.** — *rgya-lám*, **high-road, high-way.** — *rgya-šóg* **Chinese paper.** — *rgya-sér* 1. **gap, cleft, fissure, chasm,** in rocks, glaciers etc., 2. a dog with yellow spots about the nose *Cs.* 3. **Russia,** *rgya-sér-pa* a Russian; cf. *rgya-gár.* — *rgya-sóg* 1. *W.* **a saw** 2. *Sch.*: 'a Chuichui, or Chuichur, an infidel, a Mahometan; also Turkestan'. — *rgya-sráṅ* the open **street** (opp. to house) *Glr.*

རྒྱག་པ་ *rgyág-pa* another form for *rgyáb-pa*, used esp. in *C.*, **to throw, cast, fling,** *mda rgyág-pa* to shoot arrows *Glr.*; *brág-la č̔u rgyág-pai ˳p̔raṅ* a path along a precipice, where the water rushes against the rock, i.e. where there is a cataract *Glr.*; *dgón-pa žig rgyág-pa* **to found** a monastery (= *˳débs-pa*) *Georgi Alph. Tib.*; **gó-la zug gyag** *C.* = *mgó-nad ˳debs.*

རྒྱགས་ *rgyags*, or *brgyags*, **provisions, victuals, food,** in full: *˳ts̔ó-bai rgyags*, *˳ts̔o-rgyágs*; *lam-rgyágs* provisions for a journey; *dgun-rgyágs* prov. for the winter; *rgyágs-p̔ye*, provisions of meal or flour; *rgyags-zóṅ* merchandize to buy or barter victuals with.

རྒྱགས་པ་ *rgyágs-pa* **fat, stout,** *Schr.* also **mighty, powerful, proud;** *rgyags-p̔rúg Pth., Schr.*: bastard-child.

རྒྱང་ *rgyaṅ* (so pronounced in *Bal.*) instead of *gyaṅ*, **wall.**

རྒྱང་བ་ *rgyáṅ-ba*, for *(b)rkyáṅ-ba*, *Pth.*: *rgyáṅ-nas bžag* they laid him down with his hands and feet stretched out.

རྒྱང་མ་ *rgyáṅ-ma* **distance** 1. absolutely: *rgyáṅ(-ma)-nas* at a distance, from afar, e.g. to see, to call to; *rgyáṅ (-ma)*

-nas grágs-pa čé-ba famous, celebrated, from afar *Mil.*; *rgyáṅ-du lús-pa* lingering far behind *Sch.*; *rgyaṅ mig mi mtóṅ-mkan W.* short-sighted; *rgyaṅ mčoṅ btáṅ-gin* moving forward by long leaps; *rgyáṅ-so* *ₒdzúgs-pa* to look over *Sch.*, (ought perhaps to be spelled *rgyaṅ-zo* one looking, spying into a distance); *rgyaṅ-šél* spy-glass, *rgyaṅ-bsríṅs-pa* lengthened to a great distance *Lex.*; *rgyaṅ-pán, rgyaṅ-pén* n. of a philosophical (atheistical *Cs.*) sect in ancient India, *Tar.* 22, 8: *ₒjig-rten-rgyaṅ-pán.* — 2. used relatively: *rgyaṅ-riṅ-po* **far**, *rgyaṅ-riṅ-por soṅ* he went far away *Mil.*; *rgyaṅ-túṅ-ba* **near**; *rgyaṅ-grágs* the reach of hearing, **ear-shot**, (gen. the distance at which the sound of a trumpet may be heard, i.e. about 500 fathoms; however, as this number is much in favour with the Tibetans, such estimates are not to be depended upon). — *mig-rgyáṅ Glr.* distance of sight, i.e. the distance at which a man may be well distinguished from a woman, or a horse from an ass; — *rgyáṅs* adv. far, *rgyaṅs bkyéd-de Mil.nt.* moving far away, e.g. in order to increase one's distance from an unpleasant neighbour at table).

རྒྱང་ཙེ *rgyáṅ-tse* n. of a village and monastery in Tibet, not far from the frontier of Bhotan, *Köpp.* II., 358.

རྒྱན *rgyan* I. 1. **ornament, decoration,** *rgyán-gyis brgyán-pa* decked with ornaments *Dzl.*; *rgyan-ₒdógs-pa* to adorn one's self *Mil.*; *ka-rgyán* an ornament at the mouth, edge, or brim of a vessel, e.g. peacock's feathers about the mouth of a *búm-pa* (sacred bottle), flowers in a glass etc.; *ka-rgyán-čan* decorated in the front-part, e.g. a coat trimmed with fur of different colours, an arrow gaily painted at its notched end; *rgyán-rnams Dzl.* ornaments, *rgyán-ča* id.; *rgyan-gós Glr.* festival garment, beautiful vesture; *dbu-rgyán* an ornament of the head, a diadem. — 2. in relation to spiritual things: *séms-kyi rgyan* something good, **a blessing,** for the heart *Mil.*; *rgyán-du ₒčar* it proves a blessing, a moral advantage or benefit *Mil.*

II. 1. **a stake or pledge** at play, = *skugs*, **gyan tsúg-če* W.* to bet, to wager, e.g. a rupee: (also *rgyal? Schr.*). — 2. **lot,** *rgyan rgyáb-pa* to cast lots, without religious ceremonies, whereas *rtags-ril* and *mo* are connected with such.

རྒྱབ *rgyab*, resp. *sku-rgyáb*, *Ssk.* पृष्ठ 1. **the back** of the body, the back part of any thing; *rgyáb-kyis pyógs-pa*, in later literature also *rgyab-pyógs-pa Thgy.* to turn one's back to a person or thing, c. *la*, also fig. *Dzl.*; *rgyáb-kyis pyógs-par byéd-pa* to put to flight; *rgyab stón-pa* to turn one's back, to turn round *Glr.*; *rgyáb-tu skyúr-ba* to throw to the back, to leave behind, to give up, to quit, frq.; *rgyáb-tu ₒbór-ba* id.; *rgyab brtén-pa* to lean one's back against or upon, to lean or rest on, to rely upon, confide in *Mil.*; *rgyab byéd-pa* to protect *Sch.*; *rgyáb-tu, rgyáb-na, rgyáb-la* **behind,** behind hand; **after, back**; *rgyab-nas* from behind; *rgyab mdún gnyis-la Glr.*, **gyab daṅ dún-la** col. behind and before; *ti-seï byaṅ-rgyáb-tu sleb tse* as we came behind to the north-side of the Tise *Mil.*; *rgyáb-kyi skyed-mos-tsal-du gšégs-so* let us go into the garden behind us *Dzl.*; *rgyab-rdzi* one standing behind working people, in order to watch and superintend them. — 2. as much as one is able to carry on his back, **a load,** *drel-rgyáb gsum* three mules' loads *Glr.*

Comp. *bal-rgyáb*, or **rgyab-bál* W.* **a fleece** of wool. — *rgyab-kál* 'a back's load', a burden carried on the back *Sch.*, *Schr.* — *rgyab-sňás* a cushion or pad for the back *C.* — *rgyab-rtén* something to lean against, a safe retreat, **prop, support** *Mil.*, *rgyáb-rtén byéd-pa* to be a support *Mil.* — *rgyab-ríṅ* **serpent, snake** *Sch.* — **gyab-lóg jhé-pa* C.* 1. **to turn one's back** 2. **to rebel, revolt**; **gyab-lóg dád-če* W.* to sit backward, with the back in advance. — *rgyab-lógs* **the back, back-part, reverse** of a thing.

རྒྱབ་པ *rgyáb-pa*, pf. and fut. *brgyab*, imp. *rgyob*, **to throw, to fling,** aiming at a certain point, hence **to hit,** also **to beat** with a stick, = *rdúṅ-ba*; **to strike,** *mó-la mčus brgyáb-nas bsad* he (the male bird) killed his mate by a stroke of his bill *Bhar.*; **tsá-ge-la gyob* W.* throw into the centre! hit the mark! *sdóṅ-po-la brgyab ṗog* (the ray of light) fell upon the stem *Glr.; dé-la ċu rgyob* sprinkle this with water! *Pth.*; *ṗyugs nágs-seb-tu rgyáb-pa* to let the cattle run into the wood; **żag-ḍáṅ gyab-ċe* W.* to put down the date, to date; **la gyab-ċe** to cross a mountain pass. — *rgyáb-pa* is particularly used in *W.* in many phrases, whilst in *C. rgyág-pa*, and in *B.* *ˌdébs-pa* are more in use, as may be seen by referring to the several substantives, e.g. **lud gyáb-ċe* W.* to throw dung upon the fields, to manure; **par gyáb-pa* C.*, and **gyáb-ċe* W.*, to print; *gyáb-pa* stands also alone, elliptically: **ka gyab duġ** here (is printed) the letter *ka.*

རྒྱམ་ཚྭ་ *rgyam-tsva Med., Cs.*: 'a kind of salt, like crystal'.

རྒྱར་ *rgyar* v. *rgya* 2.

རྒྱལ་ *rgyal* 1. **victory,** in certain phrases: **gyal ṫób-ċe* W.* to gain the victory, to conquer, overcome; to win a law-suit, opp. to **ṗam ṗóg-ċe**. — 2. *Schr.* and *Sch.*: *rgyal-rgyán* **a pledge, a stake,** *rgyal btsúg-pa* to bet, wager, gamble *Sch.*; *rgyal bżag-pa* to contend with an other person about the first place, to try to get the precedence (?) *Sch.*; perh. also ornament, v. sub *rgód-pa* 2. — 3. **fine, penalty,** for theft *C.* — 4. n. of two lunar mansions, v. sub *rgyu-skár*; *rgyál-gyi zlá-ba, skár-ma rgyál-la báb-pai nyin-par, skár-ma rgyal daṅ ˌdzom-par, dpyid-zla rá-bai skár-ma rgyál-gyi nyín-par*, are dates relating to them. — 5. for *rgyál-po* and *rgyál-ba.*

རྒྱལ་བ་ *rgyál-ba* I. vb. neut. **to be victorious,** to obtain the victory, always with the sbst. in the nom. (not instr.) case, and gen. with *las,* **over** or **against,** *nág-poi ṗyógs-las* over the powers of darkness, *ˌǰigs-pa-las* over fright, fear; also *γyúl-lás* in battle; prob. also *ṫsod ltá-ba-las* to pass an examination successfully; but also without *las, rtsód-pa* (to win) in a contest *Glr.*; very frq. *rgyál-bar ˌgyúr-ba* id.; *ṅa ṗám soṅ ḱyod gyal soṅ* I have lost, thou hast won (also in business); **to be acquitted,** to gain a law-suit; *dmag-ˌḱrúgs-kyi rgyal-ṗám-gyi γnas-ṫsúl ḱol* send (us) news concerning the progress of the war; in a similar sense: *rgyal ṗam ċi-ltar byuṅ B.*; *rgyál-bar gyúr-ċig, rgyál-ba daṅ ṫse-riṅ-bar šog ċig* victory and long life! *Dzl.*

II. sbst. 1. (*Ssk.* जय) the act of conquering, **the victory,** **ḍi gyál-wa ṫob* C.* this bears away the palm or prize, this is the most excellent of all. — 2. the conquering party or person, he that prevails, **the conqueror** (opp. to *ṗám-pa* the conquered, vanquished). Much more frq.: 3. **the most high, Buddha** (*Ssk.* जिन), *rgyál-bai sku* his person, *rgyál-bai bka,* his word; *rgyal daṅ de sras* (po. instead of *rgyál-ba daṅ dei sras*) Buddha and his children, his disciples *Pth.* 1, 1; *rgyál-ba góṅ-ma* the highest Buddha, **God,** *Mil.* — 4. *rgyál-ba rin-po-ċé* His Highness, His supreme Majesty, title of the Dalai Lama.

III. adj. 1. **conquering, superior, eminent, excellent,** *rnám-par rgyál-bai ḱaṅ-bzáṅs* the most magnificent palace (of Indra) *Glr.* — 2. *W.* (gen. pronounced **gyálla**, in *Pur.* **rgyál-wa**) **good,** instead of *bzáṅ-po*; **gyál-la dád-ċe** or **lús-ċe** to continue in good condition, entire, uninjured; *mā gyalla* excellent! capital!

Comp. and deriv., belonging partly to *rgyál-ba*, partly to *rgyál-po*: **gyal-kár** **window** *C.* — **gyál-ḱa, ḱa-gyál** **victory, gain, advantage** *W.* — *rgyal-ḱág* **country, empire.** — *rgyal-ḱáms* 1. **kingdom.** 2. **realm, dominion of Buddha, the world.** — *rgyal-ḱríd Ld.* for *rgyal-srid.* — *rgyal-ḱríms* v. *ḱrims.* — *rgyal-ˌgóṅ* n. of a demon *Mil.* — *rgyal-brgyúd*, and *rgyal-rábs* 1. succession of kings of the same line or family, **dynasty** *Glr.* 2. a single **generation** of a dynasty, *rgyal-brgyúd lṅá-bċu-na* in the fiftieth degree (in the line of descent). — *rgyál-sgo* **principal door,** entrance-door, **gate** *C.* — *rgyal-sgrúṅs*, legend of the kings, esp. that of Gesar. — *rgyal-ċén bżi* the four kings of the spirits or guardians of the universe

(*ʼjig-rten-skyóṅ* v. *skyoṅ-ba*), residing just below the summit of Meru, the protectors of the gods against the Asuras, v. *Köpp.* I, 250; II, 261. — *rgyal-stód* lunar mansion v. *rgyu-skár.* — *rgyál-po* 1. **king,** *rgyál-po čʼén-po* **great king, emperor**; *rgyál-por ʼjúg-pa, bskó-ba*, to inaugurate a king, to raise to the royal throne; *mi-la rgyál-po ʼčól-ba* id. *Pth.*; *rgyál-po byéd-pa* to act the king, to be(a) king; *ṅa rgyál-po mi ʼdod* I do not wish to be king *Dzl.*; *rgyál-po mi tʼób-na* if I do not obtain royalty *Dzl.*; *ṅas ni rgyál-po mi nús-so* I cannot be king *Dzl.* The word is also used for: government-authorities, police etc.; *rgyál-poi čʼád-pa* public punishment, *rgyál-pos gsód-pa* to be publicly executed. (As a characteristic sign of Asiatic views it seems worth mentioning, that the *rgyal-po* is usually spoken of much in the same manner, as robbers, conflagrations etc. are, i.e. as a kind of calamity against which protection is to be sought, esp. by charms and spells, cf. *ʼjigs-pa*). 2. a local god, *ʼgro-tʼáṅ rgyál-po* the Dewa of Dotaṅ *Mil.* 3. fig. something excellent, superior in its kind; not only as with us the word is applied to the lion, as the king of animals, but also to distinguished flowers: the Udumbara (Ficus glomerata), to mountains, Meru and others; and col. *gaṅs-rgyál* a large glacier, *brag-rgyál* a huge rock, *smón-lam-gyi rgyál-po* a very comprehensive prayer, the *bzaṅ-spyód Glr.* 4. symb. num.: 16. — *rgyal-pʼrán* vassal or feudatory prince. — *rgyál-bu* prince. — *rgyal-blón* king and ministers, council of state. — *rgyál-mo* 1. queen. 2. pupil of the eye, together with the iris; *rgyál-moi mdaṅs nyams* the brightness of the eyeball disappears *Med.* 3. like *rgyál-po* 3, e.g. a charm of particular power. — *rgyal-smád* lunar mansion, v. *rgyu-skár.* — *rgyal-tsʼáb* (for *rgyal-poi tsʼab*) 1. vice-roy, regent. Such a vice-roy under Chinese supremacy is now the king of Tibet, who about a century ago was still an independent ruler. 2. **successor** of a king. 3. (for *rgyál-bai tsʼab*) **Maitreya,** the future Buddha. — *rgyal-mtsʼán* sign of victory, **trophy,** a kind of decoration of cloth, of a cylindrical shape, erected upon a flag-staff, or carried on a pole. — *rgyal-rábs* 1. = *rgyal-brgyúd.* 2. **history, annals,** of the kings, title of several books. — *rgyal-rigs* 1. **the royal family, house, lineage,** 2. **warrior-caste** ཀྵ་. — *rgyál-sa* 1. **a king's** or prince's **residence,** city where a court is held, and hence often **capital, metropolis.** 2. col., esp. in *W.*: **town.** 3. **throne** fig.; *rgyál-sar gsérgs-pa* to ascend the throne, *rgyal-sa bzúṅ-ba* to occupy the throne, *rgyál-sar bskó-ba* to raise to the throne, *rgyal-sa ʼpʼrog-pa* to usurp the throne; *ʼdi-nas rgyál-sa rgyai miṅ rgyál-po-la šor* from him the dominion passed over to the Chinese Ming-dynasty *Glr.* — *rgyal-srás* 1. **prince.** 2. **son of Buddha, a saint;** *sṅón-gyi rgyal-srás* saints of the olden time, of past ages. — *rgyal-srid* 1. **government, reign,** *rgyal-srid bzúṅ-ba* to enter upon the reign, to take possession of the throne. 2. *rgyal-srid sna-bdún* the seven jewels of royal government, v. *rin-čʼén.*

རྒྱས་པ་ *rgyás-pa* (prop. pf. to *rgyá-ba*) 1. vb. **to increase** in bulk or quantity, **to augment, to spread,** *bá-yi nu ltar rgyas* (the swollen uvula) gets as big as a cow's dug (these are in Tibet particularly small) *Lt.*; *ʼja-tsʼón rgyás-pa ʼdra* like an expanded rainbow *Glr.*; *bstán-pa rgyás-šin* the doctrine gaining ground, spreading *Glr.*; **to grow, develop** itself, of blossoms frq., of the body etc. — 2. adj. **extensive, large, ample, wide; copious, plentiful, manifold, numerous; rich in, abounding in; great in, strong in** cca.; **detailed, complete, full;** esp. adv. *rgyás-par* (col. **gyás-pa, gyẹ-pa**), *rgyás-par šes ʼdód-na*, often also *rgyás-par ʼdód-na* if you wish to know it fully, to hear it in detail; **tsʼáṅ-ma gyás-pa zér-na** *W.* if all the particulars are to be told; *rgyás-par byéd-pa* 1. to make bigger, to augment, to increase, to bestow or confer plentifully, *mi-la* on a person *Glr.* 2. to describe, narrate, state at large, in detail frq.; *don rgyás-par byed-pa* to be very useful, to exert a beneficial influence, *la* on, *Glr.* — *zla-ba rgyás-pa* full moon *Pth.; nya-rgyás zla-ba* id. — *rgyás-pai ťsá-ba, rgyas-ťsád* n. of a disease *Med.* — *ži-rgyás* etc. v. *gliṅ*, and *ží-ba*.

རྒྱུ་ *rgyu Ssk.* हेतु I. 1. **matter, substance, material**, *rgyu šél-las* crystal being the material; *čáṅ-rgyu* ingredients for making beer, i.e. barley, barm etc.; *rgyu dgé-ba bságs-pas ťób-pa yin* (the human body) is a substance obtained by accumulating virtue *Thgy.*; *ṅá-la dgós-rgyu čuṅ* I have few wants *Mil.*; also for substance in an emphatical sense, = nervus rerum, money *Mil.*; *bzó-rgyu* matter or substance of which any thing is made or manufactured, material *Glr.; zá-rgyu med* we have nothing to eat *Glr.*; hence **opportunity, chance, possibility,** *dá-ltar rgyu žig snáṅ-ṅo* an opportunity offers now *Dzl.*; **arrangements, preparation,** **ₒdó-gyu ǰhé-pa* C.* to make preparations for a journey. In a special sense: material, stuff for weaving, **warp, chain.** — 2. **cause, reason, motive,** main condition, *mya-ṅán-las ₒdás-pai rgyur ₒgyur* it becomes the cause of Nirwana, i.e. it leads to Nirwana *Dzl.*; in elliptical speech: *lha daṅ mii rgyur gyúr-pai dgé-ba* the virtue that leads to (the re-birth amongst) gods or men *Dzl.* ༢V, 17 (*Sch.* incorr.); in the same manner *ṅán-soṅ rgyúr-ru ₒgro; rgyus* c. genit. by reason of, on account of, in consequence of *Tar.; čii rgyus* why *Stg.*; *rgyu méd-du, méd-par* without the impulse of a foreign cause, spontaneously; without sufficient reason, without good cause, the Latin *temere*; *rgyu daṅ rkyen Cs.* and *Sch.* 'cause and effect', more correctly (cf. *rkyen*): primary and secondary cause, which, certainly, sometimes coincides with 'origin and further development', and so, too, with 'cause and effect'; *rgyu daṅ rkyen deï p̔yir, deï rgyu deï rkyén-gyis, deï rgyu-rkyén,* therefore, on that account; in *Med.*: *nyé-bai rgyu* the three anthropological causes or conditions of diseases, the three 'humours', air, bile, and phlegm; *riṅ-bai rgyu* the ultimate cause of diseases, and of every evil, viz. ignorance (*ma-rig-pa*, v. *rig-pa*); *skyéd-byed rgyu* the creative cause *Zam.*; *ₒp̔él-bai rgyu ni lté-ba* the main condition, the efficient cause, of growth is the navel-string *Med.*; *rgyu byéd-pa* to be the principal cause of, to lie at the bottom of a matter *Mil.; rgyu skyéd-pa* to lay the foundation of *Dzl.* — 3. after verbal roots *rgyu* implies necessity, like our **I am to, I have to, I am obliged to, I ought to;** in later literature, as well as in the present col. language of *C.*, it indicates the fut. tense: *čós-skor γyás-nas byéd-rgyu-la* whereas the holy circumambulation (v. *skor-ba* I, 2) ought to be performed from the right (to the left) *Mil.; sdáṅ-dgra yál-rgyu-la* as the enemy must vanish, or: is sure to come to an end *Mil.; *sol-čóg ṭal-ḍig ǰhá-gyu yín-nam* C.* am I to lay the cloth? **dhá-ta tó-ča zá-la ₒḍó-gyu yin* C.* now I will go and dine; *ṅai drúṅ-du ₒóṅ-rgyu yín-pa* those that intended to come to me (the Latin 'venturi') *Glr.; dé-la rgyal-srid γťád-rgyu-la* when the government was to be conferred upon him, when he was to enter upon his reign *Glr.; rta žón-rgyu med* (riding-) horses were not to be had *Glr.* — When appended to adjectives, it is a mere pleonastical addition: *dkón-rgyu med* that is not a very precious thing, there is nothing particular in that *Mil.; čúṅ-rgyui lha-k̔áṅ* a very small temple *Mil.; γžán-pas légs-rgyu med* he is not more beautiful than others *Glr.*; *ya-mťsán-rgyu-med* that is not to be wondered at; **gó-gyu maṇ* C.* that is useless.

Comp. *rgyu-rkyén* (v. above sub no. 2) **connection**, meaning, signification, *rgyu-rkyen bšad-du γsol* please explain to me the connection, which is often used in a general sense = what does that mean? what is that? *Glr.*, but also in a special sense relative to law-suits: **k̔yó-kyi gyu-kyén žú-la ₒdo* C.* I am going to tell what it is with you, i.e. I shall inform against you, bring an action against you. — *rgyu-čá* col. that which belongs to a thing, **an appurtenance,** necessary implement etc. —

rgyu-ₒbrás cause and effect or consequence, gen. in a moral sense: actions and their fruits (lás-kyi rgyu-ₒbrás); also the doctrine treating on this subject, the doctrine of retribution, the principal dogma of Buddhism, prop.: las-rgyu-ₒbrás-kyi čos; las-rgyu-ₒbrás-la yid-čes-pa to believe in the doctrine of retribution Glr. — rgyu-mtsán (Ssk. **निमित्त**) 1. **cause**, rgyu-mtsán ₒdri-ba to ask after the cause Glr.; rgyu-mtsán lo-rgyús ₒdri-ba to question closely, to examine rigorously Mil.; **the connection of events, the manner in which a thing has come to pass**, ṅai náṅ-nas ǰye ḱyér-bai rgyu-mtsán šod tell me how it was that you could fetch the flour from my house, how you were able to accomplish it Mil. nt. 2. **token, sign, characteristic, proof, evidence**, ₒdúg-pai rgyu-mtsán as an evidence of being... Glr.

II. instead of rgyú-ma.

རྒྱུ་བ rgyú-ba **to go, walk, move, wander, range**, of men, animals, and fig. of lifeless things, čú-la rgyú-bai ₒdab-čágs birds frequenting the water; kún-tu rgyú-ba to wander from one place to another, hence: kun-tu-rgyú itinerant monk, n. of a sect of the Brahmans Dzl.; rluṅ rgyú-bai rtsa those veins in which air is circulating, cf. rtsa and rluṅ; also c. accus.: yul, or groṅ rgyú-ba to rove through countries, through villages; rgyu-sráṅ, btsán-gyi rgyu-sráṅ the road that is frequented by the btsan (a kind of demons). — rgyu-skár v. below.

རྒྱུ་མ rgyú-ma 1. **entrails, intestines, bowels**, esp. the small intestines, opp. to loṅ-ka the large intestines; rgyu ₒḱril-ba convolvulus intestinorum Sch.(?); rgyu ₒḱróg-pa the croaking of the bowels Sch.; rgyu-sgróg the **caul**, covering the lower intestines; rgyu-stód the upper bowels, rgyu-smád the lower bowels Cs.; rgyu-nád disease of the bowels; rgyu-ɣžér **colic**. — 2. **sausage**, *gyú-ma gyáṅ-wa* C. (v. sgyóṅ-ba), *káṅ-če* W. to stuff sausages; *gyú-ma kar-gyáṅ* meat-sausage, meat-pudding, *gyú-ma nag-gyáṅ* black-pudding C.

རྒྱུ་སྐར rgyu-skár **the lunar mansions**, Ssk. **नक्षत्र**, or those 'constellations' through which the moon 'passes' in her revolution round the heavens; acc. to Wdk. and others they are the following: ༠ ta-skar (also dbyug-gu) three stars in the Ram's head; ༡ bra-nye (conceived by the Brahmans to be the image of the yoni); ༢ smin-drug, the Pleiades; ༣ be-rdzi, snar-ma; ༤ mgo, smal-po; ༥ lag; ༦ nabs-so, rgyal-stod, nam-so; ༧ rgyal-smad; ༨ skag, wa; ༩ mču, rta-pa, rta-čen (with Regulus its brightest star); ༡༠ gre, rtau, rta-čuṅ; ༡༡ dbo, ḱra; ༡༢ me-bži, bya-ma; ༡༣ nag-pa, byau (with Spica); ༡༤ sa-ri; ༡༥ sa-ga; ༡༦ lha-mtsams, lag-sor; ༡༧ snron, ldeu (with Antares); ༡༨ snrubs, sog-pa: ༡༩ ču-stod; ༢༠ ču-smad, ǰul; ༢༡ gro-bžin and byi-bžin (considered as one constellation); ༢༢ mon-gre, mon-dre; ༢༣ mon-gru, sgrog; ༢༤ ḱrums-stod; ༢༥ ḱrums-smad; ༢༦ nam-gru, še-sa.

རྒྱུག་པ rgyúg-pa, pf. brgyugs, fut. brgyug 1. **to run**, frq.; **to make haste, to hurry, to rush**, sgor to the door (out of the room) Dzl. . . . kyi tóg-tu upon . . . Dzl.; *há-la gyug* be off! get you gone! C. 1. **to start** (of a rail-way train) W.; rta-rgyúg-pa to ride full speed, **to gallop**; also sbst. **race** Glr. — 2. **to go, to pass, to circulate, to be current; to be valid, to have force.**

རྒྱུགས rgyugs Lex.; Sch.: **limit, term, aim, end**; W.: **task, lesson.**

རྒྱུགས་པ rgyúgs-pa **pride, ambition** Sch.; **grief, sorrow** Schr.(?).

རྒྱུང་བ rgyúṅ-ba **the nerves, sinews** Sch.; cf. brgyúṅs-pa.

རྒྱུད rgyud 1. Ssk. **तन्तु, तन्त्री string, cord**, but only in certain relations: the string of a bow; rgya-rgyúd Chinese string Mil.; string, chord, of a musical instrument, rgyud-máṅs harp; chain, v. lu-gu; mostly fig.: ri-rgyúd, gaṅs-rgyúd chain of mountains, ridge of snowy hills; also thread of tradition, i.e. continuous, uninterrupted tradition, so in: ḱa-rgyúd, dgoṅs-rgyúd, čos-rgyúd, bka-rgyúd (v. bka, compounds); snyan-rgyúd = bka-rgyúd, frq. in Mil.; ɣtam-rgyúd Zam. legendary tradition. — If used for expressing a succession of generations or families, the word is gen. written *brgyud*, rarely *rgyud*, e.g. *rje-btsún slob-rgyúd dań bčas-te* his reverence (the venerable divine) with his race of scholars, in as much as the disciples of a saint are frequently called his spiritual children *Mil.* — 2. **treatise, dissertation,** *Ssk.* तन्त्र, also *rgyud-sdé*, esp. the necromantic books of the mysticism of later times *Was.* (184), in four classes, the so-called four classes of Tantras (*rgyud-sdé bži*): *byá-bai rgyud, spyód-pai rgyud, rnal-ₒbyór rgyud, rnal-ₒbyór bla-na-méd-pai rgyud;* yet *rgyud bži* is also the short title of a medical work consisting of four parts: *rtsá-bai rgyud, bšád-pai rgyud, man-ńág rgyud, ṗyi-mai rgyud.* — 3. **connection, relation, reference,** e.g. of a word.(?) — 4. **character, disposition** of mind, natural quality; **heart, soul;** *rgyud bzáń-po* a good disposition, *rgyud ńán-pa* a bad disposition; *rgyud ži-ba* a mild disposition, good nature, *rgyud ₒjám-pa* a soft temperament *Cs.*; *rgyud ma-rúńs-pa* a wicked character *Thgy.; sem-gyụ̈́ C., šē-gyụ̈́ C., Mil.*, prob. also *rig-rgyúd Mil.*, character; *rań-rgyúd ńán-pai ₒgóń-po ťul* restrain the demon of your own wicked heart *Mil.*; of thoughts, feelings, passions, also of a *tiń-ńe-ḍzin* is said: *rgyúd-la skye* they arise in the soul; *rgyud smin* the mind ripens *Mil.*; in some phrases and passages it designates a man's whole personality: *ráń-gi rgyud ťóg-tu lén-pa* to take (other people's) sufferings altogether upon one's own person (not merely to heart) *Glr.; rań-rgyúd-la brtág-pa, γžan-rgyúd-la sbyár-ba* to think a matter through in one's own mind, to draw conclusions from an attentive observation of others, *Thgy.* — Concerning *rań-rgyúd*, and *γžan-rgyúd* (स्वतन्त्र & परतन्त्र) in the more recent philosophical writings, and in medical works, v. *Was.* — *rgyud-čágs Tar.* 15, 14, acc. to *Schf.* sentence, thesis, point. — *don-rgyúd, sgrub-rgyúd Mil.?*

རྒྱུད་པ *rgyúd-pa* I. vb., pf. *brgyus* and *brgyud*, fut. *brgyu*, imp. *rgyud*, 1. **to fasten** or **file** on a string, to string, *tá-gu-la brgyús-pa* strung, filed on a string *Stg.; γsér-nyag-ťag γyu brgyús-pa* a gold chain with turquoises inserted *Mil.* — 2. **to pass** through or over, **to traverse** (later literature and col.) *mú-ge rgyúd-nas ₒoń* famine passes over, prevails in the country *Ma.*; **náń-nạ nań gyúd-de ḍul* W.* he passes from one room to the other, he visits room after room; **nyúń-ti-nẹ gyúd-nạ gár-la ťon* W.* he is passing through Kullu to Gar; *lag-ₒgrim-gyis brgyús-pas* v. *ₒgrim; yig-nór brgyúd-pa* an error in writing has crept in *Tar.*; *stón-pa γsum ras-čúń-pa brgyúd-nas zer* the three teachers, using *Ras-čuń-pa* as a go-between, said ..., = they sent word by *Ras-čuń-pa* to this effect *Mil.*

II. sbst. and adj. 1. prop. a participle used a. actively; *rgyúd-pa* (or *brgyud-pa*) one that is transmitting knowledge, **a teacher;** *rgyúd-pa bzáń-poi byin-rlabs-čan* one that enjoys the blessing of having an excellent spiritual teacher *Mil.*; *ńai rgyúd-pa rdo-rje-ₒčań-čén yin Mil.* (in this instance it would be justifiable to write *brgyúd-pa*, and, regarding this as a derivative of *brgyúd*, to translate it with 'ancestor'). — b. used passively: *rdo-rje-ₒčáń-nas nyams-rtógs rgyúd-pa de ná-ro lags* he to whom knowledge was communicated by *Dor-je-čáń* is *Nāro Mil.*; *nā-ro čen-poi rgyud-pa* **a scholar** of great *Nāro Mil.* — 2. a derivative of *rgyud* 2., a Tantrika, **a mystic.**

རྒྱུད་རིས *rgyud-ris* a term used in architecture, **wall, panel** (?).

རྒྱུད་ལོང *rgyud-lóń* **bolt, door-bar** *Sch.*

རྒྱུན *rgyun*, *Ssk.* स्रोतस् a continual flowing, **the flow, current** or **stream** (seldom river; perh. *smig-rgyui rgyun Lex.* a river seen by a mirage or fata morgana(?); *gáń-gai rgyun* the river Ganges); *ču-rgyún-gyis ₒkyér-ba* to be carried away by the current; *rgyún-du žúgs-pa* v. *ₒbrás-bu bži*; frq. fig. *ťúgs-rjei rgyun* stream of grace *Glr.*, and sim. in some compounds; often in reference to time, hence *rgyún-du* **continually, perpetually, always,** *dus-rgyún-du* id.; **dhụ̄-gyụ̈n ta-bhu jhẹ̄ šig* C.* make it as usual!

snár-gyi rgyun all the time before, opp. to da-ltar now; also for **ordinarily, predominantly**, e.g. ordinarily it is white, only by way of exception it is of another colour; k'a-rgyún = ka-rgyúd tradition; rgyún-gos an every day coat, opp. to γzáb-gos; rgyun-ₒgág, and more frq. rgyun-čád an interruption of flowing, of progress, hence rgyun-čad-méd-par, or rgyun-mi-čád-par uninterruptedly; rgyun-zás daily food; rgyun-riṅ-ba lasting, of long continuance; rgyun-lám an endless, interminable way, to be pursued again and again, e.g. ₒk'ór-bai of transmigration, byaṅ-čúb-kyi of virtue, holiness *Mil.*

རྒྱུས་ rgyus 1. v. rgyu. — 2. (*Cs.* rgyús-ma) **notice, intelligence, knowledge,** ṅá-la dé-i gyus yod I am acquainted with it, I know the thing, I am up to it, frq; *W.*: *gyus yód-k'an* one that knows about it; *gyus yód-pai lam* a well-known road; ča-méd yúl-du rgyus-méd ₒk'yam as a stranger I am rambling through a foreign country *Glr.*; lo-rgyús 1. **annals, chronicle,** 2. in a general sense **history, story, tale, narrative,** lo-rgyús bšád-pa to relate a story *Glr.*, *ṅá-la lo-gyús šád-ĉe máṅ-po yod* *W.* I have much to relate, to tell; lo-rgyús žib-tu ₒdrí-ba to ask closely, to inquire minutely into a story *Mil.*; góṅ-gi lo-rgyús bšád-do he reported what was related above *Pth.*; also used of any short notice or intelligence, without reference to things past: der ₒbyóṅ-pai lo-rgyús γsuṅs he mentioned that he was going there *Mil.*

རྒྱུས་པ་ rgyus-pa the fine threads or **fibres** of which animal muscle, plants etc. are composed; rgyús-pa-čan fibrous; rgyus-skúd **catgut.**

རྒྱོ་བ་ rgyo-ba, pf. brgyos, fut. brgyo, imp. rgyos, to unite in sexual embrace. This word is an undisguised, and therefore somewhat obscene expression, which in books and in col. language is avoided, though referring to an act not criminal in itself, as *Cs.* seems to have understood it, when he translates rgyo-ba by: to abuse, constuprate, ravish; hence it is allowable, yet vulgar, to say: *'á-pa daṅ 'á-ma gyó-wa)he'* *C.*

རྒྱོང་བ་ rgyóṅ-ba, pf. brgyaṅs, fut. brgyaṅ, seems to be a secondary form of rkyóṅ-ba, **to extend, stretch, spread** (vb. *n.*); the word is to be found in *Lexx.*, but seems to be little used; brgyáṅs-pai má-tsa *Pth.* a disease consisting in some parts of the body being morbidly distended (?).

རྒྱོབ་པ་ rgyób-pa *Cs.*, a secondary form of rgyáb-pa, prob. but a provincialism.

ལྒ་ lga, also sga, **སྒ་སྐྱེར་ ginger** (fresh or dried); lga-rloṅ fresh ginger.

ལྒང་ངེ་ lgaṅ-ṅé *Pth.*: skya-lgaṅ-ṅé, is stated to mean: **perfectly white.**

ལྒང་པ་ lgáṅ-pa, lgaṅ-p'úg **urinary bladder** *Med.*

ལྒང་བུ་ lgáṅ-bu, = gáṅ-bu, **husk, pod, shell.**

ལྒའུ་ཀ་ཤེར་ lgau-γšér *Cs.* = lga-rloṅ.

ལྒོ་ lgo *Cs.* = p'a-ba-dgo-dgó **puff-ball.**

ལྒྱམ་ཚྭ་ lgyám-tswa = rgyám-tsa *Zam.*, a kind of **rock-salt.**

སྒ་ sga 1. gen. ĺčá-sga, bča-sga, **ginger,** = lga; sga-skyá *Lt.* id. (?); sgá-pi-p'o *Lt.* prob. for sga daṅ pi-pi-liṅ daṅ p'ó-ba-ri ginger and two kinds of black pepper; sga-spyód *Sch.* = sga-skyá. — 2. **saddle,** rta-sga (*Ld.* *stásga*) horse-saddle; sga bstád-pa, resp. čibs-sga bstád-pa *Glr.*, to lay the saddle on, to saddle; sga-k'ébs saddle-cloth, *Sch.*: the leather cover or coating of a saddle; sga-gló saddle-girth *W.*, *C.*; sga-lúg *Cs.*: frame of the saddle; saddle-bow, saddle-tree; sga-šá straps for fastening the travelling-baggage to the saddle, cf. ša-stág 2.

སྒ་ཕོང་ sga-p'óṅ **bat, flitter-mouse** *Sch.*

སྒང་ sgaṅ 1. a projecting **hill or spur,** on the side of a larger mountain; sgaṅ-γšóṅ elevations and depressions on a hill-side, in *Kun.* sgaṅ-k'úl; sgáṅ-k'a-la yod (the village) is situated on a mountain-spur; *sgaṅ gyáb-na* *W.* when you have passed round the extremity of the hill. — 2. ču-

sgáṅ **a blister,** caused by vesicatories, by long marches etc., *C., W.*; cf. *bsgaṅ*.

སྒང་བ་ *sgaṅ-ba*, pf. *bsgaṅs*, fut. *bsgaṅ*, **to grow** or **become full** *Cs.; bud-méd ná-so sgaṅ* a marriageable girl.

སྒབ་པ་ *sgab-pa*, secondary form of *ˌgébs-pa*, *byá-mas bú-la sgab-pa* the covering of a young bird by its mother *Glr.*; *gos-sgáb Lex.*, skirt or lap of a coat, *sgab-ťúṅ* a short skirt.

སྒམ་ *sgam* **chest, box, trunk;** *sgam-čúṅ* a little chest or box; *sgam-bu* id.; *sgam-sgo-máṅs* a chest of drawers, cabinet *C.*; *šiṅ-sgam* a wooden chest, *lčágs-sgam* an iron chest; *kó-sgam* a leather trunk; *ró-sgam*, resp. *spúr-sgam* coffin *Cs.* — syn. *sgrom*.

སྒམ་པ་ *sgám-pa*, or *sgám-po Cs.* **deep, profound,** *Sch.* also **prudent, quiet;** *Lex. blo-sgam* w.e. Only the following phrase came under my notice: *ťugs šin-tu sgám-mo* he (the prince) is very clever (as a legendary explanation and confirmation of the name *sroṅ-btsan-sgám-po*). Prob. obsolete.

སྒར་ *sgar* **camp, encampment,** *dmag-sgár* a military camp, *sgar ˌdébs-pa* to pitch a camp; *sgar-míṅ C.* watch-word, parole, = *bso-sgrá*.

སྒལ་ *sgal* **load** of a beast of burden, *rta-sgal* a horse-load, *šiṅ-rtai sgal* a cart-load, waggon-load *Cs.*; *sgal ˌgél-ba* to put on a load, *ˌpán-ba* to throw it off, *ˌbógs-pa* to take it off, *sgal bsrdú-ba* to adjust or balance it; *sgál-rta* pack-horse, *sgál-pyugs* beast of burden.

སྒལ་པ་ *sgál-pa* 1. **the small of the back,** *sgál-ˌdabs* the lumbar region *Med.* — 2 **the croup, crupper,** back of a horse *Glr.*; **gál-pa ťon dug** *W.* the back comes out, i.e. has become sore or galled; *sgal-ts̀igs-Med.*, *sgal-rus* col. backbone, spine; *sgal-rmá* a sore on a animal's back caused by the load.

སྒུ་སྟེགས་ *sgu-stégs Lex.* w.e.; *Sch.* **elbow, angle.**

སྒུ་རྡོ་ *sgu-rdó* **a sling** *Sch.*

སྒུག་པ་ *sgúg-pa*, pf. *bsgugs*, fut. *bsgug*, imp. *sgug(s)*, **to wait,** *zlá-ba γčig sgúg-pa* to wait for a month *Glr.*; **to await, to expect,** *ˌčí-ba* death *Mil.; lám-na sgúg-pa* to wait on the road *Mil.*; *sgúg-čiṅ sdód-pa, W.:* **gúg-te dád-če** to sit waiting; **'i-ru gúg-te dód** *W.* wait here! *sgug-tu ˌǰug-pa* to keep one waiting *Glr.*; **to lie in wait** (for a person), **to waylay;** *ǰág-pas sgúg-pai sa* a place where robbers are lying in ambush *Mil.*; **ǩon gúg-te dád-če** *W.* to bear a grudge, to have a spite against a person.

སྒུང་ *sguṅ Ld.* **clap, crack, crash, report** (of a gun).

སྒུད་པོ་ *sgud-po* **father-in-law,** *sgud-mo* mother-in-law *Sch.* prov.

སྒུམ་མདའ་ *sgum-mda Schr.* butt-end of a gun, **gun-stock** *C., W.*; spelling dubious.

སྒུར་ *sgur* v. *dgur*.

སྒུལ་བ་ *sgúl-ba* vb. a. (cf. *ˌgul-ba*), pf. and fut. *bsgul*, **to move, agitate,** put in motion, *rgyud kyaṅ ma sgúl-to* he could not even move the bow-string *Dzl.;* to pull (e.g. the bell-string).

སྒེའུ་ *sgeu* 1. diminutive of *sga*, **ginger,** *sgeu-γsér Med., Ssk.* आर्द्रक (*Hind. adrak*), fresh ginger. — 2. **a small door.**

སྒེག་པ་ *sgég-pa Cs.:* **to boast, brag;** yet not so much with respect to words as to looks and demeanour, so that it may be applied to the airs of coquettish girls (*sgég-čiṅ mdzés-pa* coquettish *Mil., Stg.*) as well as to the bearing of insolent youngsters and bullies. *sgég-ma* n. of a goddess; *sgég-mo Lex.* लास्या, a dancing girl.

སྒེང་ལ་ *sgéṅ-la*, or *dgeṅ-la* (?) **on, upon** *Ts.*

སྒེར་ *sger Sch.:* 'different, dissimilar, foreign'. This word I repeatedly met with in books of physical science, without finding the signification given above applicable.

སྒོ་ *sgo* 1. **door,** the aperture itself, as well as the wood-work of the door: *sgo ˌbyéd-pa, W.* **pé-če**, to open the door; **ǰúg-pa** 1. *C.* to put in a door, to hang a door on hinges 2. *W.* to close, to shut the door;

ycòd-pa 1. to shut, 2. to lock (a door); **gyág-pa, gyáb-pa* C.*, to shut (the door); *ytán-pa Sch.:* 'to lock up', prop. to bolt, to bar, v. *sgo-ytán; bkúm-pa, bskúm-pa Cs.:* resp. to shut (a door); *sgo bdúṅ-ba* to knock, to rap at the door; **go šrúg-ga rag* W.* I hear a rattling or rapping at the door. The ground floor of a house into which the door leads, is generally occupied by the cattle, hence: *sgoi p̀yugs* the cattle near the door, opp. to: *p̀úgs kyi nor* the money in the inner chamber farthest from the door, cattle and money being thus the two poles or terminating points of household property. — *rgyál-sgo* the principal door or entrance of a house or chamber (in *Ld.* also: **gyáz-go**). — *sgrig-sgo* folding-door *Cs.* — *čáb-sgo* resp. for *sgo Cs.*, cf. *ysáṅ-sgo.* — *rtá-sgo* a door which may be passed through on horseback, viz. the door or gate of a court-yard or garden, open at the top, or a high castle-gate; in the latter case syn. to *rgyál-sgo.* — *náṅ-sgo* the innermost door, *bár-sgo* the middle door, *p̀yi-sgo* the outer door *Pth.* — *tsé-sgo* v. 2, *lás-sgo* v. 3. — *šél-sgo* glass-door; wing of a window, casement; *ysáṅ-sgo* secret door; *Cs.* resp, for *sgo* (?). — 2. **the boards** that form the pane or square of a door, hence **board, plank,** v. *sgo-rṅám*; *tsé-sgo* a Chinese punishment, consisting of a thick board with an opening for the neck of the culprit, and resting on his shoulders; *sgo ygóg-pa* to put on the board of punishment. — *bsé-sgo daṅ lčágs-sgo bdun sbrags* a door constructed of sevenfold layers of leather and iron, used as a butt for shooting at. — 3. the aperture of a door, and hence **aperture** in general: *sgo kún-nas* from all the apertures (of the body); *žál-gyi sgo* resp. mouth *Dzl.*; *mṅál-sgo* the opening of the womb (v. *mṅal*) frq.; *skyé-bai sgo* id. less frq. *Thgy.*; *dkyil-ₒk̀or sgo-bži-pa* a square figure with four openings, about thus: ⌜⌝⌞⌟; the opening of a semicircle; **entrance, passage, outlet,** connecting passage, communication; also fig.: way of mediation, of bringing an agreement about, *ṅan-sóṅ-gi sgo* the entrance, the road, to misery viz.: to hell; *dbáṅ-poi sgo* the organs of sense, also *sgo lṅa* alone; *sgo-ysúm* the three media or spheres of moral activity, *lus, ṅag, yid,* action, word and thought frq.; *bzá-ba daṅ btúṅ-bai sgo ₒp̀rog-pa* to cut off the supply (of provisions) *Pth.*; *bdag čos sgor ₒjug-pa žu* I beg to allow us to enter religion, to receive us as students or disciples *Mil.*; *ₒgró-sgo Schr.* 1. also *búd-go, kyág-go W.*, expense, expenditure 2. *ḍó-go-tar šé-pa C.* to relate accurately how a thing came to pass; *lás-sgo* 'door of intercourse, of trade', a commercial place or town, emporium *Glr.* Hence *sgó-nas* with the genit. **by means of, by,** in the way of, according to, but never as connected with a person or joined to an infinitive: *tabs dú-mai sgó-nas* in different ways, variously (often coinciding with: by various means); *lus ṅag yid-kyi sgó-nas* in or by actions, words, and thoughts (e.g. to strive for virtue, cf. above *sgo-ysúm*) *Dzl.*; *rnám-pa sna-tsógs-kyi sgó-nas* in every possible way *Dzl.*; *dpei sgó-nas* (to explain) by way of comparison *Thgy.*; *mtsan-nyid-kyi sgó-nas* (to describe a thing) according to its characteristics *Thgy.*; *rigs-kyi sgó-nas* (to divide) according to the species *Lt.*; *ₒdrá-bai sgó-nas btags-miṅ ste* it being a name given to it from its resemblance to ... *Wdṅ.*; ... *la p̀rag-dóg-gi sgó-nas* from envy of ... *Mil.*; *mi-snáṅ-bai sgó-nas* by way of invisibility, by being invisible *Wdṅ.*

Comp. and deriv. *sgo-k̀áṅ* the entrance into a house, **vestibule, porch, portal.** — *sgo-k̀úṅ* opening of the door *Mil.* — *sgo-k̀yi* a door-guarding dog, **watch-dog.** — *sgo-ₒk̀ór* **hinge** of a door or gate. — *sgo-gláṅs Zam.* = *sgo-ytán* (?). — *sgo-glégs* **the board** or **plank** of a door *Cs.* — *sgo-ₒgrám* the space near the door. — *sgo-ₒdrig* (*Ld.* **sgon-ḍig**) **door-frame,** window-frame. — *sgo-rgyáb* the space behind the door, within the door *Glr.* — **go-čág** (*lčags*) *C.* **lock** of a door. — **go(g)-tán** a bar or bolt (a small beam) to secure the door with. —

sgo-ṫém **threshold,** also **the head-piece** of a door. — *sgo-bdág* = *sgo-dpón.* — *sgo-rnám* a single **board,** e.g. of the floor. — *sgó-pa,* resp. *čábs-sgo-pa* **door-keeper, porter;** *sgo-dpón* the first, principal door-keeper. — **go-ṗiṅ* W.* **door-hinge.** — *sgo-ₒp̔ár* **board** or **plank** of a door *Cs.* — *sgo-búr Ld.* **chinks** between the separate laths of a door (for of such the doors in Tibet frequently consist, owing to the scarcity of wood). — *sgó-ma* 1. **pane** or **square** of a door, **fold** of a folding-door; 2. a masked dancer in religious dramatic entertainments, representing one of the four guardians of the world (v. *rgyal-čén*). — *sgó-mo* 1. **a large door, a gate, castle-gate, town-gate;** 2. **beginning,** *rtsis-kyi sgó-mo Pth.* = *rtsis-ₒgo Cs.* (Chronol. Table) beginning of a new epoch. — *sgo-mtsáms* the small opening left between door-post and door, when the latter does not perfectly fit. — *sgo-yig Cs.* 1. **inscription,** 2. **lampoon, libel,** 3. a magisterial **advertisement** fastened to a door. — *sgo-lá* n. of a high and difficult mountain-pass between Lhasa and Paṅ, v. Huc. I. p. 244. — *sgo-sruṅ* **door-keeper, porter** *Dzl.*

སྒོ་ *sgo,* in *skyé-sgo* v. sub *sgó-po.*

སྒོང་ *sgo-ṅá* or *sgoṅ-ṅá* and *sgoṅ,* **egg, eggs, spawn,** also egg as a measure *Lt.; sgoṅ-dkrís* the pellicle, membrane of an egg *Sch.; sgóṅ-čú* the white of an egg *Sch.; sgoṅ-šún,* or *koṅ,* the shell of an egg; *sgoṅ-sér* yolk of an egg *Sch.* — *sgo-ṅa ṗyed* a scholastic term, v. *Was.* (274).

སྒོ་ཕུར་ *sgo-púr* **foreskin, prepuce** *C.* vulg.

སྒོ་པོ་ *sgó-po,* also *sgó-bo,* (*Ld.* **gó-po**) *W.* 1. **the body,** with respect to its physical nature and appearance, **gó-po čén-mo, riṅ-mo, go-riṅ, go-záṅ** tall, **gó-po čúṅ-se** of small stature, short; **róm-po** stout, lusty; **ṫá-mo** slender, thin; **dé-mo** healthy, well; **go-yál** a man that has lost his own body by gaming and become the slave of another. — 2. = *skyé-sgo* **face, countenance,** *skye-sgo legs* a beautiful face, *žán-sgo* an ugly face *Mil.* — *sgó-lo* 1. **body,** 2. **face,** as a flattering word; also directly for a nice or pretty face, **gó-lo min dug bag ṫsogs yod** she has not a pretty face, but looks like a fright *W.*

སྒོ་བ་ *sgó-ba,* pf. *bsgo* (*bsgos* in *Lexx.,* prob. obsolete) **to say,** when used of superiors, hence mostly **to bid, to order** (cf. the article *bka* init.), frq. in early literature, in later times more and more disappearing, being unknown to the common people.

སྒོ་ཙམ་ *sgo-tsám* **a little** *Sch.*

སྒོ་ལོ་ *sgó-lo* 1. v. *sgó-po.* — 2. *Ld.* also = *sgo-ṅá.*

སྒོག་པ་ *sgóg-pa,* (*Ssk.* लशुन) **garlic, leek,** (Allium); *ri-sgóg Med.* Allium sphaeroceph. *L.,* or a species allied to it; *sgog-skyá Med.* Allium nivale Jacqm. (?); *sgog-sṅón Med.* perh. A. rubellum, a blue species, very common in the Himalaya. — *sgog-tiṅ* mortar, *sgog-γtún* pestle, for bruising leek.

སྒོག་པ་ *sgóg-pa* 1. *Cs.*: 'pf. *bsgags,* fut. *bsgag,* to make one swear, *sgóg-po* one that makes a person swear.' I only met with *mna-sgóg Lex.* w. e. — 2. *γya sgóg-pa* v. *γya.*

སྒོང་ *sgoṅ* 1. v. *sgo-ṅá.* — 2. n. of a country, prob. = *koṅ Glr.* — 3. *sgoṅ-ṫóg-pa* n. of a plant *Med.*

སྒོང་བ་ *sgóṅ-ba,* pf. *bsgoṅs,* fut. *bsgoṅ,* imp. *sgoṅ* (*s*), 1. **to make round, globular** *Cs.;* so it is prob. to be understood in: *bu-rám bsgár-žiṅ bsgráṅs-nas bsgoṅs Lex.,* he having boiled down the sugar and allowed it to grow cold, formed it into balls (in this form the sugar is usually kept in Tibet). — 2. **to hide** or **conceal** a thing *Sch.,* thus in **góṅ-te bór-če* W.;* cf. also *dpá-sgoṅ-ba.*

སྒོབ་སྒོབ་ *sgob-sgób* **unable, deficient,** wanting in strength *Sch.;* **lág-pa gob-soṅ* Kun.* the hands are unable (to move), stiff (from cold).

སྒོམ་ *sgom* **reflection, meditation, contemplation,** *sgom šór-gyi dógs-pa* the fear lest contemplation should be prejudiced or rendered impossible *Mil.*; *sgom srúṅ-ba* to sustain, to preserve meditation (undisturbed) *Mil.*; *sgom-méd* without meditation *Thgr.*

སྒོམ་པ་ *sgóm-pa* 1. vb., pf. *bsgoms*, fut. *bsgom*, imp. *sgom(s)*, resp. *ṭugs sgóm-pa* (*Ssk.* भू, *causative* भावय) 1. originally: **to fancy, imagine; meditate, contemplate, consider**, c. accus. and dat.; **to have, to entertain, to produce** in one's mind, = *skyéd-pa*, e. g. *bzód-pa*, *snyiṅ-rje*, *byáms-pa* etc.; *rgyún-du nam ₒči ča-med sgom* always consider that it is uncertain at what time you shall die *Mil.*; with the accus. and termin., or with a double accus.; **to look upon**, to represent to one's self as . . ., *ₒgró-drug-sèms-čan pʻá-mar sgom* look upon the beings of the six classes as being your parents *Mil.*, viz. with the same respect and affection, or even so, that you imagine your father's or your mother's soul inhabiting just now the animal body of one of those beings; *rmi-lam sgyú-ma sgom* look upon it as being the illusion of a dream *Mil.* — 2. In later times *sgóm-pa* became the usual term for the systematic **meditation** of the Buddhist saint, so that this word, and the expressions *tiṅ-ṅe-ₒdzin-du ₒjúg-pa*, and *bsam-ytán sgrúb-pa*, which in classical writings denote the concentration of the mind upon one point or subject, e. g. upon a certain deity, *lha*, prob. imply one and the same thing. Three degrees of this systematic meditation are to be distinguished, viz. *ltá-ba* contemplation, *sgóm-pa* meditation, properly so called, (which requires *ysal daṅ mi-rtog má-ygeṅs ysum*, i. e. that it be performed in a clear and decided manner, without suffering one's self to be disturbed or distracted by any thing), and the third degree *spyód-pa*, exercise and practice, which three distinctions will be somewhat elucidated by the following: *bzá(-bai)-ytad(-so) yód-na bltá-ba min*, *byiṅ-rgod yód-na sgóm-pa min*, *bláṅ-dor yód-na spyód-pa min*, if one lives plenteously, there is no contemplation (possible); where there is inattention and a distracted mind, meditation cannot take place; where there is desire or disgust, exercise and practice are not (to be thought of) *Mil.* 14, 11. Hence contemplation would seem to be more immediately opposed to the rule of sense, meditation to the rule of imagination, practice to the rule of passion; v. also *Was.* (137), *Köpp.* I, 585. Sometimes contemplation and meditation are also opposed to *ṭós-pa*, and *bsám-pa*, hearing and knowing, as to mere acts of memory and intellect. — *sgóm(-pa)-po Cs.*, *sgom-byéd*, *sgóm-mkʻan Mil.* one that meditates, **an ascetic**; *sgóm-ma* fem. *Mil.* — *sgom-čén* 1. **a great meditator** (so *Mil.* often calls himself). 2. a kind of **field-mouse**, Lagomys badius *Hook.* II, 156. — *sgom-ṭág* 'meditating-cord', a cord or rope slung by the laxer sects round their bodies, in order to facilitate the effort of maintaining an erect and immoveable posture during meditation, which expedient of course is scorned by the more rigid devotees.

II. sbst. 1. **meditation**. — 2. *Cs.*: 'the state of being accustomed to' (prob. erron. for *goms-pa*).

སྒོམ་འབྲོག *sgom-ₒbróg* (?) **holly**, Ilex. *Sik.*

སྒོར་ *sgor* a spindle in turning-lathes? v. the next word.

སྒོར་བ་ *sgór-ba* 1. pf. and fut. *bsgar*, **to boil down**, to condense by boiling, e. g. *bu-rám* sugar. — 2. **to turn** on a lathe, *W.* **gór-la ṭen-če**.

སྒོར་མོ་ *sgór-mo* (perh. also *skór-mo*) 1. **round**, e. g. of leaves, *Wdṅ.* and elsewh. — 2. **a circle**. — 3. **a disk**, **a globe**; hence a rupee *W.*; a semi-globular bowl or vessel *W.*, *sgor-ṭig* circular line, circumference, circle; *sgor-ṭig pʻyé-ba Cs.*, *pʻyéd-ka Schr.* semicircle.

སྒོས་ *sgos*, in compounds and as adverb: **private, separate, distinct; privately** etc., opp. to *spyi*, e. g. *spyi-ydugs* a parasol for several persons, awning, shelter, *sgos-ydugs* a parasol for one person *Glr.*; *sgós-skal* share of a single person, individual lot

Mil.; *sgós-su*, or *sgos* adv., (opp. to *spyir*) particularly, especially; *sgos-(kyi), dpon* a subaltern officer *Cs.*; *sgós-pa Sch.*: 'to choose, to find the right thing'.

སྒྱིའུ, སྒྱིག་གུ *sgyiu, sgyig-gu* **bag, purse**; *sgyig-gu čád-poi dbáṅ-du sóṅ-nas* our purse being at low ebb; *dṅul-sgyig* money-bag, purse.

སྒྱིང་བ *sgyiṅ-ba*, pf. *bsgyiṅs*, fut *bsgyiṅ*, 1. acc. to *Lex.* = *Ssk.* जम्भ syn. to *gyál-ba*, **to yawn, gape,** and perh. to stretch one's self after having slept; it is almost exclusively used in describing the attitude of a dying lion, and so also the dying attitude of Buddha. — 2. perh. also = *ₒgyiṅ-ba.*

སྒྱིད(པ) *sgyid(-pa)* 1. the hollow of the knee, bend of the knee; **knee-joint;** *sgyid-pa γčód-pa* to lame the knee-joint, to hamstring (a horse) *Glr.* — 2. **the calf** (of the leg) *Mil.*; *sgyid skyúr-ba* acute pain in the knee and leg e.g. of a woman with child *Med.; Cs.*: 'to despair'? — *sgyid-ḱúṅ* the hollow of the knee *Med.* — *sgyid-ḱyól* one lame in his legs *Cs.* — *sgyid-lug-pa Lex.* w. e., *Cs.*: slothful, idle, lazy; *sgyid-lhód Sch.* id.

སྒྱིད་བུ *sgyid-bu*, also *sgyéd-bu*, **a hearth, fire-place,** consisting of (three) stones on which the kettle is placed; *lčags-sgyid* iron trevet, tripod, cf. *sgyéd-po.*

སྒྱུ *sgyu* **artifice, imposture** *Dzl.* and elsewh., *γyo-sgyú* id.; *γyo-sgyu-med-na* if he is without guile *Dzl.; sgyu-čan* artful, crafty, cunning, *Cs.* — *sgyu-ₒṗrúl-ma,* माया, the name of Buddha's mother. — *sgyú-ma,* माया, **illusion,** false show, deception of sight, opp. to *dṅos* reality; *sgyu-ma sprul-ba* to exhibit a false show *Cs.*; *ṅas snáṅ-ba tams-čád sgyú-mar šes* I know that every thing visible, the whole external world, is only an illusion *Mil.; sgyú-mai nor* apparent riches, hence riches in general *Mil.* (cf. *sgyu-lús*); *sgyú-ma-mḱan* **a juggler** *Mil.*; *sgyú-ma-mḱan-gyi mčán-bu, sgyu-mai mčán-bu* a juggler's apprentice *Lex.* — *sgyu-rtsál* **art, skill, dexterity,** frq., the Indians, and so also the Tibetans counting 64 arts (or 60 in a round number) *Tar.* 21, 2. — *sgyu-zóg* **deception, hypocrisy** *Pth.* — *sgyu-lús* 1. the immaterial, subtile and pure body of the soul in the Bardo, hell etc., hence = *yid-kyi lus Thgr.* 2. the animal and human body in general, in as much as it is only an apparent body, a phantom, when considered from a higher philosophical point of view *Mil.*

སྒྱུག་མོ *sgyúg-mo* **mother-in-law** *Stg.*; *mna-sgyúg* both daughter-in-law and mother-in-law.

སྒྱུར་བ *sgyúr-ba*, pf. and fut. *bsgyur*, (vb. a. to *ₒgyúr-ba*) 1. **to transform,** *lus ₒdod-dgúr* to transform one's body (i. e. one's self) at pleasure, (*Dzl.* ༢༦ *lus* is to be supplied, or *gyúr-te* to be read); to transform the royal prerogative into a religious one, v. *ḱrims.* — 2. **to change** (colour, one's mind), **to alter** (something written), hence **to correct, to revise.** — 3. **to give up, leave off** (customs, scruples, doubts, timidity) *Glr.*, *ṗyi-rol-pai čós-lugs* the non-Buddhist religion. — 4. **to turn** off or aside (the course of a river); **to dissuade, divert,** *las,* from *Dzl.* — 5. **to turn,** **ǰiṅ pa gyúr-če* W.* to turn round on one's heel; **ǰiṅ-pa gyúr-te ltá-če* W.* to look back; *ḱór-lo sgyúr-ba* to turn a wheel = *skór-ba*; *skad sgyúr-ba* to vary, to modulate the voice, also to hum a tune, to sing or whistle, as birds do. — 6. **to govern,** *rtai ḱa sráb-kyis,* a horse's mouth by the bridle; also fig. **gyál-pọ ḱa lǿn-gyi gyur, ḱyọ̈ ḱa čúṅ-mẹ̈ gyur* C.* the king is governed by his minister, the husband by his wife; *ₒdod-čágs ṅán-pas ḱa-sgyur* he is governed by evil passions *Mil.; ḱá-lo sgyúr-ba* to govern, prop. and fig., v. *ḱá-lo*; *šiṅ-rta sgyúr-ba* to drive a carriage; in a similar sense *dbaṅ sgyúr-ba* c. *la,* to have command or control of, to command, dominate, frq.; prob. also to possess *Mil.* — 7. **to translate,** *sgra sgyúr-ba* id. — 8. **to multiply** *Wdk.* (cf. *ₒgyúr-ba* 4, and *lóg-pa*); *bsgyúr-bya* the multiplicand *Wdk.* — 9. *Lad., Pur.* **to kill, to slaughter.** — 10. **to publish, proclaim, announce** **ka-sál gyúr-če* W.* to publish an order; *'lon gyur'* *W.* announce me! send in my name!

སྒྱེ་སྒུར་ *sgye-sgúr* **crooked** *Sch.*, better *dgye.*

སྒྱེ་བོ་ *sgyé-bo* is said to denote in *C.* one of the lower classes of officials or noblemen.

སྒྱེ་མོ་ *sgyé-mo* 1. sbst. **a bag** (not of leather); *ras-sgyé* a bag of cotton stuff *Pth.*; *sgyeu* diminutive. — 2. adj. **quiet, gentle** (of horses) *Sp.*

སྒྱེད་པོ་ *sgyéd-po* a stone for a fire-place, **hearth-stone,** three of which are so placed together, that a fire may be kindled between them and a kettle put on; *sgyid-bu* a fire-place constructed in this manner.

སྒྱེལ་བ་ *sgyél-ba,* pf. and fut. *bsgyel,* vb. a. to *ˏgyél-ba,* **to throw down, to overthrow, overturn,** *gan-kyáb* on the back *Lex.*; **to lay or put down** (a bottle, a book); **to thwart** (the charm of an enemy); **to kill** (horses); *'mi sę', ta gyel'* manslaughter and the killing of horses, *C.*

སྒྱོགས་ *sgyogs* 1. a warlike engine to shoot darts or fling stones with, **catapult, ballista,** *sgyógs-kyi ˏṗrul-ˏkór Thgr.* id.; *sgyogs-rdo* a stone flung from such a machine *Sch.*; in later times: 2. **mortar, cannon, gun,** in Tibet even at the present day without wheels, col. *'ghyog'*. — 3. a surgeon's instrument for setting broken limbs *Cs.*

སྒྱོང་བ་ *sgyóṅ-ba,* pf. *bsgyaṅs,* fut. *bsgyaṅ,* perh. originally = *sgóṅ-ba* to hide, but actually used 1. in *C.*: *'gyú-ma gyáṅ-wa'* **to fill, to stuff** (a sausage) 2. col. in *W.*: *'gyáṅ-ċe'* **to put** into (the pocket, a box, a coffin); *'gyáṅ-du bór-ċe'* **to keep, lock,** or **shut up** (things); *'úgs gyáṅ-ċe'* to hold one's breath; *gla ṗyir sgyóṅ-ba* **to retain** the wages due to another person *Sch.* The form *rgyaṅs* often occurs in *Mil.*, in passages where 'to retain, lock up, put into' or a similar term would suit very well. Other passages cannot yet be sufficiently accounted for, and upon the whole the roots *gyaṅ* and *kyaṅ* (*rgyaṅ* etc.) require to be more closely investigated.

སྒྲ་ *sgra,* *W.* also *'ra'*, 1. **a sound, noise; voice;** *há-sgra* the sound *h Glr.*; *sgrá-bċas ˏḱru* noisy evacuations take place *Lt.*; *ˏón-pa-dag sgrá-rnams ťos* the deaf hear sounds; *sgra sgróg-pa* to produce sounds, noises *Mil.*; *sgra dag γsal γsum* (read) loud, correctly, and distinctly, those three (a precept for reading or reciting); *'ngid-ra táṅ-ċe'* *W.* to snore; *'śóg-ra'* the noise made by a flight of birds passing; *miṅ-sgra* a mere word, name, or sound *Was.*, as a philosophical term. — 2. **word, syllable,** *bdág-sgra Cs.*, *bdág-poi sgra Gram.*, the name given in grammar to the so-called article *pa,* e.g. in *rtá-pa* horseman, rider; *dgág-sgra* prohibitive or negative particle. — 3. **language,** science of languages, **philology.**

Comp. *sgra-skád* (= *sgra* 1.) **sound, voice,** *sgra-skád snyán-pa* frq. — *sgrá-ċan* **sounding, sonorous.** — *sgra-čé* **far-famed, renowned** *Mil.*, *sgra čer grags-pa Stg.* id. — *sgra-snyán* 1. **a well-sounding, agreeable voice.** 2. *C.* **a guitar.** — *sgra-brnyán* **echo** *Mil.* — *sgrá-ldar* **sounding, sonorous.** — *sgra-dbyáṅs* 1. **pleasing tone, harmony, euphony,** e.g. *glu daṅ ról-moi Tar.* 2. n. of a goddess *Cs.* — *sgra-sbyór Zam., Tar., Schf.*, a coalition or connection of letters. — *sgra-mi-snyán* (a disagreeable voice) n. of a larger and two smaller northern continents of the fabulous geography of ancient India. — *sgra-ťsád* (*sgra daṅ ťsad-ma*) *Tar., Schf.*: grammar and logic; yet *yi-gei sgra-ťsád, sgra-ťsad-yi-ge Glr.* seem to denote philology.

སྒྲ་གཅན་ *sgra-γċán, Ssk.* राहु *Ráhu,* 1. a demon or monster of Indian mythology, esp. known by his being at enmity with the Sun and Moon, on whom he is continually wreaking his vengeance, occasionally swallowing them for a time and thereby causing their eclipses. The Buddhist representation of the Ráhu-legend is given by *Schl.* p. 114 — 2. *Cs.*: **the ascending node** of the moon, determining the time of the obscurations. — *sgra-γċán-*

dzin, राहुल *Rāhula* 1. 'seized by Rāhu' (*Fouc. Gyatch.* II, LVII), obscured, eclipse of the sun or moon, 2. 'catcher of Rāhu,' acc. to the Tibetan legend an epithet given to the deity *ṗyag-rdór*, acc. to Indian mythology, to Vishnu, who in Tibetan is called *k̔yab-ʼjúg* (also *k̔yab-ʼjug-ẏsól Cs.*); sometimes, however, he is identified with Rāhu himself, for the names *ẏza-sgra-ẏčan*, *ẏza-sgra-ẏčan-dzin*, *ẏza-k̔yab-ʼjúg*, *ẏza-rā-hu-la*, and even *ẏza-du-ba-ʼjug-rin* (comet!) are used promiscuously. — 3. a son and disciple of Shakyamuni, who received this name on account of an eclipse of the moon taking place at his birth, v. *Fouc. Gyatch.* II, 389.

སྒྲང་བ་ *sgrán-ba*, *Cs.*: pf. *bsgrans*, fut. *bsgran*, imp. *sgron*, 1. **to enumerate**, to reckon up separately. — 2. **to upbraid, to reproach.**

སྒྲལ་བ་ *sgrál-ba* **to cut** into small pieces, viz. the picture of an enemy whom one wishes to destroy.

སྒྲིག་པ་ *sgrig-pa*, pf. *bsgrigs*, fut. *bsgrig*, imp. *sgrig(s)*, *W.* **rig-če**, **to lay** or **put in order, to arrange, adjust,** *pan-léb* boards or planks, *so-ṗág* bricks or tiles *Glr.*, *kar-yól* plates and dishes, = to lay the cloth; *ẏdan* stuffed seats or chairs *Dzl.*; **to put** or **fit together, to join** the separate parts of an animal body *Glr.*; to put close together, side by side, hence *W.*: **žin de nyis rig-te yod** these two fields are adjacent, **ṫa dan rig-te yin** it is situated close to the border; **to compile, to write** books *Glr.* — **rig-mo** *W.* **tight, close,** e.g a joint, commissure, seam.

སྒྲིན་པོ་ *sgrin-po*, *Zam.*: = *mk̔ás-pa*, **prudent, skilful, clever,** *blo sgrin-pa* a penetrating mind *Sch.*

སྒྲིབ་པ་ *sgrib-pa* 1. vb. pf. *bsgribs*, fut. *bsgrib*, imp. *sgrib(s)*, *W.* **rib-če**, to deprive of light, **to darken, to obscure,** *W.* **rib ma rib** get out of my light! *nyi-mai ʼod-zér bsgribs-nas* the light of the sun being obscured, by clouds *Glr*, by a curtain *Zam.* — 2. sbst. the state of being darkened, **obscuration,** gen. fig., mental darkness, **sin,** also *sgrib*; *séms-čan ṫams-čád-kyi sgrib-pa sél-ba* frq., hence *sgrib-pa-rnam-sél* n. of a Boddhisatva; *sgrib-pa lna Dzl.*, the five obscurations caused by sin, prob. = पञ्चकषाय *Burn.* II, 360. — 3. adj **darkened, obscured, dark; sinner,** *bdag-rán sgrib-pa čé-am* am I so great a sinner? *Pth.* — **ḍib-ma** *C.*, **rib-ma** *W.* **shelter, fence,** e.g. at the side of a field against the wind.

སྒྲིམ་པ་ *sgrim-pa*, pf. *bsgrims*, fut. *bsgrim*, imp. *sgrim(s)*, *Cs.*: **'to hold fast, to force** or **twist together; to endeavour'**; *Sch.* also: **'to squeeze in, cram in; to be over-hasty, confused'.** Only the following phrases came to my notice: **ḱú'-pa ḍím-pa** *C.* to twist or twine a thread; **rig-pa ḍim** *C.* take care! (collect your thoughts!); **ḍim-tog-čan** *Sp.* inquisitive, curious. Some passages in *B.*, e.g. *blo-bsgrims* (explained by *blo-ʼdás Zam.*) are as yet dubious as to their sense.

སྒྲིལ་བ་ *sgril-ba*, pf. and fut. *bsgril*, *W.* **(s)ril-če**, (cf. *ʼgril-ba* 1. and *ʼk̔ril-ba*), 1. **to wind** or **wrap round** e.g. a bit of cloth round one's finger; **to roll, wrap,** or **wind up**; *ril-bur* to roll or form into a pill *Med.*; **to make fast** or **tight,** *lhód-pa* what is loose; *ṗyogs ẏčig-tu sgril-ba* to gather into a heap, **to heap** or **pile up, to sweep together**; hence *sgril-bas* (also *dril-bas Glr.*) **to sum up all,** taking all together, in short *Lt.*; *mjúg-ma sgril-ba* **to wag** the tail, *mi-la* at a person (of dogs) *Mil.*; **to roll,** e.g. a large stone to some place. — 2. **to multiply** *Wdk.*, frq.; *bsgril-ma* a doubled and twisted thread or cord *Sch.*; *sgril-šin* a wooden roll, round which paper etc. is wound; the rolling-pin of bakers. — *sgril-šóg*, *W.* **šog-ril**, rolled paper *Cs.*

སྒྲུག་པ་ *sgrug-pa*, pf. *bsgrugs*, fut. *bsgrug*, imp. *sgrug(s)*, *W.* **rúg-če(s)**, **to collect, gather, pluck, pick up** e.g. wood, flowers, vermin etc.

སྒྲུང(ས)་ *sgrun(s)*, *Ld.* **šruns**, *C.* **ḍum**, **fable, legend, tale** (to the uncultivated mind of the Tibetan, destitute of any physical and historical knowledge of the countries and people beyond the boundaries of his native soil, the difference between truth and fable is but vague and unsettled); *sgruṅ ˳čád-pa* to relate fables, stories etc.; *sṅon-rábs sgruṅ Zam.*, *sṅón-gyi sgruṅ-rgyúd Glr.*, *sgruṅ-γtám* tales of ancient times, of the days of yore; *sgrúṅ-mk'an Cs.*, *sgrúṅ-pa Sch.* the inventor or writer of fables and tales, also a narrator of tales.

སྒྲུང་བ་ *sgrúṅ-ba*, pf. *bsgruṅs*, fut. *bsgruṅ*, **1. to mix. 2. to invent, to feign** *Cs.*

སྒྲུན་པ་ *sgrún-pa*, pf. and fut. *bsgrun* **1. to compare** c. *la* and *daṅ Dzl.* — **2. to emulate, vie, contend with** *Cs.*

སྒྲུབ་པ་ *sgrúb-pa* I. vb. pf. *bsgrubs*, fut. *bsgrub*, imp. *sgrub(s)* (cf. *˳grúb-pa Ssk.* साध) **1. to complete, finish, perform, carry out,** an order, a wish, hence usually with *bžin-du Dzl.*; **to make, achieve, manufacture, obtain, attain,** *dṅúl-rdo-la dṅul bsgrúb-tu btúb-pa ltar séms-čan-la Saṅs-rgyás bsgrúb-tu btúb-pa yin-no* in like manner as silver is obtained from silver-ore, Buddha may proceed from beings *Thgy.*; *don sgrúb-pa* to attain to one's aim, to obtain a blessing, a boon; *tse ˳dii don sgrúb-pa* to care for the wants of this life; **to procure,** *rgyágs-p̔ye* flour, as provision for a journey *Mil.*; *nor sgrúb-pa* **to gain** riches; **to furnish with, to supply,** one's self or others *Mil.* — 2. *lha-sgrúb-pa* implies, in accordance to Brahmanic-Buddhistic theology, not so much the making a deity propitious to man (*Cs.*), as rendering a god subject to human power, forcing him to perform the will of man. This coercion of a god seems to be effected in a twofold manner. The practise of the common people is to perform a vast amount of prayers and conjurations, specially intended for the god that is to be made subject. Another method is adopted by saints, who are advanced in every kind of religious knowledge. They continue their *sgóm-pa*, or profound meditation, for months and years, until the deity, finally overcome, stands before them visible and tangible, nay, until they have been personally united with and, as it were, incorporated into the invoked and subjected god. Whilst the conatus, the labouring in this arduous undertaking, is often called *sgrúb-pa*, the arriving at the proposed end is designated by *˳grúb-pa*, e.g. *rgyál-pos rta-mgrin sgrúb-pa mdzád-pas ˳grúb-nas rta-skád btón-pas* etc., the king began to coerce *Taḍin* (*Hayagrîva*), and when the latter was made obsequious, so as to appear, a neighing was heard etc. *Glr.*; *sgom-sgrúb byéd-pa* for *sgóm-pa daṅ sgrúb-pa byéd-pa Mil.* — *bsgrub-k'áṅ*, *sgrub-γnás*, *sgrub-p̔úg* the house, the place, the cavern, where a saint applies himself to *sgrúb-pa*; *sgrúb-pa-po* one effectuating the coercion described above, *Sambh.* frq. — *sgrub-rtágs* tokens, proofs of perfection, of an accomplished saint. — *sgrub-t'ábs* the method of effecting the coercion, of obliging a god to make his appearance; *sgrub-byéd* 1. he that accomplishes the coercion (cf. *Schl.* p. 247). 2. a kind of bile *Med.* — *sgrub-γšén* the Bon-doctrine *Mil.*

II. sbst. 1. one that contemplates and meditates, like *sgom-čén Mil.* 2. n. of a sect of Lamas, with whom marriage is permitted.

སྒྲེ་བ་ *sgré-ba* I. *Cs.* adj. **naked,** gen. *sgren-mo.*

II. vb. pf. *bsgres*, fut. *bsgre* (cf. *˳gre-ba*) **1. to roll** *Glr.*, *Pth.* — **2. to multiply** *Wdk.* — **3. to repeat** *Cs.* — **4. to put** or **place in order, to put together, to compare,** e.g. records *Tar.* 174, 14 *Schf.*

སྒྲེ་ཟློག་ *sgre-zlóg* a sea-washed beach *Sch.*

སྒྲེག་པ་ *sgrég-pa* 1. vb. pf. *sgregs*, **to belch.** — 2. sbst. **belch, eructation,** *sgrég-pa ˳dón-pa*, *˳byin-pa Med.* **ral-ḍág* C.* a belch of a fetid smell.

སྒྲེང་བ་ *sgréṅ-ba*, pf. *bsgreṅs*, fut. *bsgreṅ*, imp. *sgreṅ(s)*, cf. *˳gréṅ-ba*, 1. **to raise, erect,** lift up, hold up, plant up, e.g. a finger, a beam etc. — 2. **to stretch out** a limb and hold it stiff *C.*

སྒྲེན་མོ་ *sgrén-mo* **naked,** *sgrén-mor ˳byúṅ-ba* to appear in a naked state, to show one's self naked *Dzl.*; *Bhar.* 59. *Schf.* 'orbus', orphaned (cog. to *bkren?*).

སྒྲོ་ *sgro* 1. a large **feather**, esp. quill-feather, used for an ornament of arrows, as a charm etc.; *sgro-mdóṅs* peacock's feather, as a badge of dignity. 2. **to elevate, exalt, increase;** *Cs.:* **to exaggerate.** *Was.* however has p. (305): 'Vorurtheil (Anerkennung des Nichtwahren), Gegensatz: *skur-ₒdébs* Lästerung (Leugnung des Wahren)', and p. (297): '*sgro-skúr* Verneinen und Lästerung'. *Cs.* renders *sgro-skúr* by 'exaggerated praise and blame'; *sgro-skúr ₒdébs-ba* occurs also in *Mil.* The phrase *sgro-ₒdógs ɣčód-pa* might therefore be rendered: to put an end to overrating and to prejudice; this meaning, however, does not suit in every instance, and acc. to expressions heard from people in *C.*, *sgro-ₒdógs ɣčód-pa* would signify: to turn to account, to work one's way up, to contest for a prize. Finally ought to be mentioned that acc. to *Schr.* *sgro-ₒdógs spyód-pa* (sic) denotes 'logic'. A connection between these heterogeneous significations is not discernible, but a clew may perhaps be found hereafter. — 3. **sack, bag** (?), *tál-sgro Glr.* was explained by: a sack full of ashes.

སྒྲོ་ག *sgro-ga C.* the little bubbles in sparkling beverages, **čáṅ-la ḍó-ga ḍug** the beer sparkles.

སྒྲོ་གུ *sgró-gu*, v. *sgróg-gu* sub *sgrog.*

སྒྲོ་བ་ *sgró-ba* I. sbst. 1. *Wdṅ.*, acc. to *Sch.* **the bark** of a species of willow, but prob. the same as *gró-ga*. — 2. *C.* **the penis.**

II. vb., pf. *bsgros*, fut. *bsgro*, imp. *sgro-Lexx.* w.e., *Cs.:* **to debate, discuss,** so that it would be only another form of *bgro-ba*; but in *C.* **ḍo-šé' ǰhé'-pa** is said to mean: **to talk at random,** to chatter away thoughtlessly.

སྒྲོག(ས)་ *sgrog(s)* **cord, rope,** for tying, fettering; **fetters** *Mil.* and *C.*; *lčags-sgróg* iron fetters, chain; *lčags-sgróg lág-pa sbrél-nas* the hands tied or chained together; *lčags-sgróg-pa* a convict put in irons; *šiṅ-sgróg* fetters made of twisted twigs *Cs.*; *lham-sgróg* **shoe-strap,** lace, latchet. — *sgróg-gu*, *sgró-gu*, *W.* **róg-bu**, **string, strap,** for binding, fastening, strapping; *Sch.* also button; *sgrog-ril Sch.* **button,** *sgrog-ril sgróg-pa* to button up.

སྒྲོག་པ་ *sgróg-pa*, pf. *bsgrags*, fut. *bsgrag*, imp. *sgrags(s)*, **to call, call out,** call to *Dzl.* and elsewh.; **to publish, proclaim, promulgate,** *ɣtam-snyán* good news *Mil.*; *ši-bai ɣtam bsgrágs-na* if his death becomes known, *Tar.*; *čos sgróg-pa*, resp. *čós-kyi sgrog-gléṅ mdzád-pa Glr.* **to preach;** *dril-sgrog-pa* to publish by ringing a bell, to publish, proclaim; *sgróg-pa-po* a proclaimer, a preacher *Cs.* — 2. **to shout, to scream,** *ṅú-skad drág-por sgrog* (the infant) weeps and screams *Lt.* — 3. *C.* (in *W.* only resp.) **to read,** *ɣsuṅ sgróg-pa* to read words of Buddha *Ma.*; even: *séms-kyis sgróg-pa* to read silently. — 4. **to bind,** like *ₒgrógs-pa;* v. also *sgrog* extr.

སྒྲོད་པ་ *sgród-pa*, another form of *ₒgród-pa* to go; not much used.

སྒྲོན་མ་ *sgrón-ma* **a lamp, lantern, torch,** *sgron-mé* a burning lamp, (prop. a lamp-fire); often fig. — *sgroṅ-pa* vb. **to light, to kindle,** *dpé-ča-la me sgrón-nas* lighting (burning) the book *Pth.* — *sgron-bskál* the enlightened age *Cs.*, opp. to *mun-bskál* the dark age. — *sgron-drégs* **lamp-black.** — *sgron-(me-)šiṅ Sch.* the yew-leaved fir, Pinus picea, which tree, however, is scarcely known in Tibet; in *Sik.* it denotes Pinus longifolia, and prob. also in every other province, the most resinous species of coniferous trees prevailing there.

སྒྲོན་པ་ *sgrón-pa*, pf. and fut. *bsgron* 1. **to cover, to lay over, adorn, decorate** *Glr.* — 2. **to light, to kindle,** v. *sgrón-ma.*

སྒྲོབ་ *sgrob* **haughtiness, arrogance, pride,** *Lexx.*

སྒྲོམ་ *sgrom* **box, chest, trunk, coffer** = *sgam*; *sgróm-bu* a small box or chest: *smyug-sgróm Cs.* = *ɣzéb-ma* a chest or trunk made of bamboo; *ro-sgróm*, *rús-pai sgrom Zam.* **coffin.**

སྒྲོལ་བ་ *sgról-ba*, pf. and fut. *bsgral* 1. **to rescue, deliver, save,** *las* from, out of, *sgról-bai ded-dpón-du ₒgyur* he becomes a guide to salvation *Glr.* — 2. **to lead,**

transport, carry, to cross (a river) by boat or ferry, *ču-bsgrál Lex.:* तीर्ण passed over; *čú-boi p̀á-rol-tu bsgrál-bar mdzód-čig* have the goodness to take me over to the other bank *Sambh.*; *ₒkór-ba bsgrál-bai gru-γzíṅs yin Glr.* it is a boat that carries over the river of transmigration. — 3. **to remove**, do away with, drive away, *ₒdré-rnams p̀yii rgyá-mtso čén-po-la bsgrál Glr.* the demons were driven to the uttermost parts of the sea; *bdud sgról-ba* to expel the devil; *sdig-čan rgyál-po sgról-bar ₒgyur* the guilty king will be removed out of the way! *Glr.*; *dgra-bgegs bsgral-bai ša k̀rag rus-pa daṅ naṅ-rol glo snyiṅ bčás-pa mčod-par ₒbul* the flesh, blood, bones, heart, lungs and entrails of slaughtered enemies of the faith are offered by us as a sacrifice. This saying, the tendency of which is often justified by the sophism, that it is an act of mercy to kill an enemy of the faith and thus prevent him from accumulating more sin, shows that even 'mild Buddhism' is not incapable of bloody fanaticism, and instances like that of king Laṅ-dar-ma of old, and of the recent martyrdom of Roman Catholic christians at Bonga confirm this fact from experience.

སྒྲོལ་མ་ *sgról-ma*, sometimes also *sgrol-yúm Cs., W.* **ról-ma**, 1. n. of two goddesses, *Ssk.* तारा, known in the history of Tibet as the white and green Tara, incarnated in the two wives of Srongtsangámpo, *Schl.* 66 and 84; *Köpp.* II., 65. — 2. a name of females, of frequent occurrence.

སྒྲོས *sgros* 1. *Cs.* **manner, method, way,** *bšád-sgros* way of explaining, instructing, informing: *sgrogs bšád-sgros Sch.:* 'the method of instruction which is to be proclaimed' (?); *γtám-sgros Cs.:* 'way or manner of speaking' (?). — 2. *Cs.* **edge, brim, lip;** *Sch.* also mark from a wound, **scar;** *žál-gyi mču-sgrós* seems to signify only 'lip'.

བརྒད་པ་ *brgád-pa* = *bgád-pa* to smile, to smile on *Stg.*

བརྒལ་ *brgal* 1. v. *rgál-ba*, 2. v. *rgól-ba.*

བརྒོལ་བ་ *brgól-ba Sch.* 'das Gegenseitige', mutual relation, contrast, contrary?

བརྒྱ་(ཐམ་པ་) *brgya (tám-pa)* **a hundred,** one hundred; *brgya-p̀rág* the hundred, a century; *brgya-p̀rág bču* 1000; *brgyá-pa* the hundredth; *brgyá-po* consisting of one hundred (cf. under *dgu*); *brgya daṅ bču-bži* 114; *brgya-nyi-šu* 120; *bži-brgya (daṅ) go-brgyád* 498; *brgyá-rtsa* v. *rtsa*; *brgyá-la (Cs.: brgya-ma-lan-γčig,* or *brgyá-lam-na?)* once among a hundred (cases or times) i.e. very rarely, e.g. *(dus) brgyá-la brnyed kyaṅ* though it be found for once at last *Mil.* frq., cf. *Schf.* Erläut. zu *Dzangl.* p. 45; also = finally, in short, the Latin *denique, Mil.nt.*; *brgyá-čan* erron. for *rgyá-čan.* — *brgya-mčód* a hecatomb of 100 lamps, offered on certain festival occasions *Sik.* — *brgyá-ₒdaṅs* about or nearly a hundred *Sch.* — *brgyá-dpon* a captain of a hundred men, the Latin centurio. — *brgya-byin* (शतक्रतु) '(honoured by) a hundred sacrifices', epithet of Indra, cf. ἑκατόμβαιος) 1. Indra. 2. n. of a medicine *Wdṅ.*

བརྒྱ་ *brgya?* 1. in *smrá-bai brgya Sch.:* noisy conversation; *Lex.* simply आलाप speech, conversation (with the remark that the word is obs. and prov.). — 2. often erron. for *rgya.*

བརྒྱང་བ་ *brgyáṅ-ba* 1. v. *rgyoṅ-ba* 2. **to call** to a person from a distance, *C.*

བརྒྱད་ *brgyad* **eight**; *brgyád-pa* the eighth, *brgyad-po* consisting of eight, *brgyád-ču* eighty, *brgyad-ču-rtsa-γčig* (*W.* **gyad-ču-gya-čig**), *gya-γčig* 81; *brgyad-brgyá* 800; *brgyad-stóṅ* 8000; *brgyad-k̀ri* 80 000.

བརྒྱད་(བ)ཀག *brgyad-(b)kág* **a reproach, rebuke,** *brgyad-kág byéd-pa* to rebuke, to chide *Dzl.*

བརྒྱན་པ་ *brgyán-pa*, vb. **to adorn, decorate; to provide with** (c. instrum.), cf. *rgyan* sbst.; *nya mgo sa-yis brgyán-pa* the letter *nya* (ཉ) being provided with an *s* above it, = *sny..*, *Zam.*

བརྒྱལ་བ་ *brgyal-ba* 1. **to sink down** senseless, **to faint;** **brgyál-te dád-če**

W. to lie in winter-sleep; *ₒo-brgyál-te* very much exhausted, v. *ₒo.* — 2. **to howl**, of the fox. *Sch.*

བརྒྱུངས་པ་ *brgyúṅs-pa Lex.*; *Cs.*: **'the marrow in the back-bone'.**

བརྒྱུད་ *brgyud*, cf. *rgyud*, *Ssk.* परम्पर **family** (*gens*), **lineage; relations, ancestors, descendants, offspring,** *mi-brgyúd* 1. = *brgyud, dei mi-brgyúd yin-pa* being of his family *Glr.* 2. people, nation, *bód-kyi mi-brgyúd* the Tibetan nation. 3: the human race, mankind *Cs.*; *rigs-brgyúd*, resp. *ydun-brgyúd* family; issue, progeny, *rigs-brgyúd ₒpél-bar ₒgyur* there will be a numerous offspring; *bla-rgyúd* succession or descent of Lamas *Cs.* — **mig ná-ċe gyúd-la yod** *W.* diseases of the eye frequently occur in that family; **dé-ne gyud mi čad yin** *W.* then the race will not die out; **spél-gyud-la bór-ċe** *W.* to set apart cattle for breeding; *brgyúd-nas brgyúd-du* from generation to generation *Cs.*; *bu ťsa brgyúd-du bdeo* he is blessed even to his children and children's children *Dzl.*

Comp. *brgyud-brgyúgs* a continuous succession *Sch.* — *brgyúd-ċan* like his progenitors *Cs.* — *brgyúd-pa* 1. belonging to a race or family. 2. v. *rgyud* and *rgyúd-pa.* — *brgyud-méd* degenerate *Cs.*, cf. *brgyúd-ċan.* — *brgyúd-ma* 1. *Cs.* = *brgyúd-ċan.* 2. *W.* fruitful, fertile. 3. *brgyud-ma-brgyab Lex.* w.e. — *brgyud-ₒdzín* a first-born male, heir and successor.

བརྒྲད་ *brgrad* is acknowledged by *Lexx.*, but evidently an incorrect form for *bgrad.*

བསྒ··· *bsg* . . . words beginning thus will for the greater part be found under *sg* . . .

བསྒག་པ་ *bsgág-pa* v. *ₒgégs-pa* and *sgóg-pa.*

བསྒང་ *bsgaṅ* (*Lexx.* = *dṅos-yži*, मुख?) **point of time, moment, instant, conjuncture,** *lo-ysar-bsgáṅ-gi lhágs-ma* a chilling gale on newyear's day *Mil.*; esp. **the proper time** or season for doing a thing, *byá-bai bsgaṅ; ₒbri-bai, zá-bai bsgaṅ* the time for writing, eating. (A different word from *sgaṅ*).

བསྒོ་བ་ *bsgó-ba* 1. v. *sgó-ba.* — 2. pf. *bsgos*, vb. n. to *ₒgó-ba*, **to soil, stain, defile,** lit. and fig., **kyon-ghyī ma gō** *C.* he was not tainted with any spot or blemish, nothing could be laid to his charge; **to infect** with disease; rarely in a good sense: *dri sna-ťsogs-kyis legs-par bsgos-pa Stg.* well **anointed** with salves and perfumes.

བསྒྲང་བ་ *bsgráṅ-ba* 1. **to enumerate, count up** (?) *Cs.* — 2. **to cause to grow cold** *Lexx.*

བསྒྲད་པ་ *bsgrád-pa Lexx.* = *bgrád-pa.*

ང

ང་ *ṅa* 1. the letter *ṅ*, sounded as a nasal guttural, the English ng in singing, in the Tibetan language often the initial letter of a word. — 2. as numerical figure: 4. — 3. as numeral adjective = *lṅá-bċu*, in the numbers 51—59.

ང་ *ṅa*, pers. pron., first person sing. and pl. **I, we,** the usual word in familiar speech; *ṅai* my, our; mine, ours; *ṅa mi rgan* old man that I am *Mil.*; *ṅa rgyál-po sroṅ-btsan-sgám-po daṅ* with me, king Srongtsangampo *Glr.*; *blá-ma ṅa* I, the Lama *Mil.*; *de mi rgan ṅai ká-la nyon* listen to my word as that of an old man *Mil.*; *ṅai ₒdi* this my (doing) *Glr.*; *ṅai rje-btsún* my honoured masters! *Mil.*; *ṅai* yid-˳ŏṅ my dearest! *Pth.*; *ṅa-ráṅ* I myself, esp. col. very frq.; **ṅa ráṅ-ka** *Ts.*, **ṅa tsog** *Ü*, *ṅa nyid, ṅa k'ó-na, ṅa bdag* (?), *ṅa-bo* (??) *Cs.* id.; *ṅa ráṅ-gi yaṅ* moreover, what concerns my own affairs *Mil.* Distinct expressions for the pl. **we** are: *ṅá-čag B.* and *C.*; **ṅá-ža** *W.*, **ṅá-ya** *Bal.*; in *W.* **ṅá-ža** seems to be used in an exclusive sense: I and my people, i.e. excluding you or the person or persons addressed, so that when Europeans use it in *Ld.* or *Lh.*, in addressing their hearers, meaning to include themselves (all of us, we and you), they are generally misunderstood; **ṅa daṅ** 'he or those with me', is said to be used in a similar manner; **ṅa daṅ nyis** both of us; *ṅa-rnams* we *Cs.* Synonyms are: *ṅed, ṅos, bdag,* **k'o-bo**; and *ṅaṅ, ṅo, dṅo, dṅos, ṅogs* may prob. bederived from the same root.

ང་རྒྱལ་ *ṅa-rgyál* ('I the first') **pride, arrogance**, frq.; *ṅa-rgyál skyéd-pa* to be proud *Dzl.*; *γčog-pa* to break (another's pride), to humble, humiliate *Mil.*; *ṅa-rgyál-čan* proud; *W.* also naughty, of children.

ང་ངུར་ *ṅa-ṅúr* a species of **duck**, v. *ṅúr-ba*; perh. Anas casarca.

ང་བ་ *ṅá-ba*, rarely for *ṅán-pa*; *dri ṅá-ba* stench *Stg.*; cf. *nyám-ṅa-ba, yá-ṅa-ba.*

ང་ར་ *ṅá-ra* (cf. *ṅad*) **air**, *ṅa gáṅs-kyi ṅá-ras mi ǰigs* I am not afraid of the air of glaciers *Mil.*; **ṅá-ra ḍáṅ-mo rag, ǰám-po rag** *W.* I perceive the air to be cold, to be mild; esp. cold air, *ṅá-ra-čan* fresh, cold.

ང་རོ་ *ṅá-ro* **a loud voice, a cry**, *kye-húd-kyi ṅá-ro ˳bód-pa* to raise woeful cries *Pth.*; *skád-kyi ṅá-ro čĕn-pos bsgrágs-so* they proclaimed, shouting at the top of their voices *Pth.*; *séṅ-gei ṅá-ro* the loud voice, the roaring, of a lion *Mil.*; *γdúg-pai ṅá-ro* prob. voices foreboding mischief *Mil.*; **the roar, roaring, rushing**, of waves etc.; *ṅá-ro sgróg-pa* to roar, to rage; in a relative sense: *skád-kyi ṅá-ro drag-žán* a loud and a low sound, the different force or effort required in producing it *Gram.*; *ṅá-ro-čan* loud, noisy, roaring; a crier, bawler, noisy fellow.

ངག་ *ṅag*, sometimes *dṅags*, resp. *γsuṅ*, **speech, talk, word,** *ṅág-gi nyés-pa* sins committed with the tongue, in words, (*rdzun, ṗrá-ma, ts'ig-rtsúb*, prob. also *kyál-ka*); *ṅág-gi lhá-mo* the goddess of speech, of eloquence, Sarasvati; *ṅág-gi dbaṅ-ṗyúg* = *˳jam-dbyáṅs* Manjusri; *ṅag ˳jám-po* kind, polite speech or words; *ṅag-˳jám smra-mk'ás* of a soft tone in speaking and prudent in words *Glr.*; *smán-pai ṅag bžin-du byed-pa* to obey the words of the physician; *ṅag sdóm-pa, ṅag bčád-pa* silence, as a monastic duty or religious exercise, resp. *γsuṅ-bčád Mil.*; *γžan-gyi ṅag γčóg-pas* not doing according to another's word, not obeying him *Tar.*, frq.; *ṅag mnyán-pa* to be obedient *Dzl.*

Comp. *ṅag-kyál*, or *-˳k'yal* = *kyál-ka.* — *ṅag-˳grós, smrá-bai ṅag-grós* 'a manner of speaking or uttering words' *Cs.* — *ṅag-rgyún* tradition, not recorded history, *Cs.* — *ṅag-snyán, snyan-ṅág, snyan-dṅágs* 1. **poetical expression, figure, metaphor.** 2. **poem**, piece of poetry *Glr.* — *ṅag-dbáṅ* 1. **eloquent.** 2. p. n., e. g. *ṅag-dbáṅ blo-bzáṅ rgyá-mtso* Dalai Lama, born 1615. — *ṅag-sbyór* arrangement of speech *Cs.* — *ṅag-ts'ig* = *ṅag.* — *ṅag-lám žú-ba* to apply to a person by word of mouth, resp.

ངང་ *ṅaṅ* (not in the earlier literature) 1. **the nature, essentiality, idiocrasy** of a person, the peculiarity of a thing, *saṅs-rgyás-kyi ṅaṅ yin* he is (partaking) of the nature of Buddha, Buddha-like (corresponding to our 'divine', which consequently might be expressed by *dkon-mčóg-gi ṅaṅ*) *Mil.*; *stón-pai ṅaṅ-nyid* the essentiality of the vacuum itself *Glr.*; frq. used only paraphrastically or pleonastically: *tiṅ-ṅe-dzin-gyi ṅáṅ-la žúgs-pa* to enter into meditation *Mil.*; *t'ugs-mnyés bžin-pai ṅáṅ-la* in a cheerful mood *Mil.*; *čágs-med-kyi ṅáṅ-la γnás-par gyis* continue in that passionless state of mind *Thgr.*; *˳jigs-skrág-gi ṅáṅ-nas ˳či-ba* to die of fear or anxiety; *ṅáṅ-nas* in general is used nearly like *sgó-nas Mil.* frq.; **character, disposition**, *ṅáṅ-bzáṅ, ṅaṅ-ṅán Sch.*; *ṅaṅ-ts'úl*, and esp.

ṅaṅ-rgyúd id., *ṅaṅ-rgyúd bzáṅ-po Wdṅ.*, *dgé-ba Glr.*, a naturally good, virtuous character; very frq.: *ṅaṅ-rgyúd riṅ-ba* forbearing, longsuffering, not easily put into a passion *Glr.*; not easily excited to action, **phlegmatic**, cool, also **ṅaṅ riṅ-wa* C.*; even *ṅaṅ* alone may have this meaning: *ṅaṅ ma ťuṅ* don't lose your patience *Mil. nt.*; *ṅáṅ-gis adv.* not only signifies spontaneously, of one's own accord, but also **slowly, gradually, gently** *Mil.* (so already *Schr.*) — 2. **dominion, sphere, province,** parallel to *kloṅ* and *dbyiṅs Mil.; *ṅa ma-ši-kai ṅáṅ-la dug** I belong to the kingdom of Christ, said one of our Christians, in order to show the meaning of **ṅaṅ**. Hence it might be used for expressing the ἐν of the N. T. (I John 5, 6 and many other passages) denoting a pertaining to, belonging to, being connected with. *ṅáṅ-la ̥ǰóg-pa (bžág-pa) Mil.* and *C.* is an expression not explained as yet.

ངང་པ་ *ṅáṅ-pa* 1. **goose,** more accurately *ṅáṅ-pa* a gander, *ṅáṅ-ma* a goose *Cs.* The domestic goose and the breeding of it is not yet known in Tibet, at least not in *W.* — 2. **a light-bay horse,** an isabel-coloured horse *Ld.-Glr.*

ངད་ *ṅad* 1. cog. to *ṅá-ra*, **air,** **ṅád-la skám-če* W.* to dry in the air; in a general sense the air in its chemical qualities, in its influence on the senses: **scent, fragrance,** *spós-kyi ṅad ldáṅ-ba* the rising of an aromatic breeze; *ṅad yal* the fragrancy, the aroma evaporates; **vapour,** *ḱá-ṅad, čú-ṅad* snowy vapour, aqueous vapour; **aromati csubstance,** *sṅó-ṅad* aromatic vegetables, such as onions *Med.*; **cold air, the cold, coldness,** v. *ṅad-čan.* — 2. *W.* (cf. *ṅár-ba, ṅár-ma*) **severity, roughness,** **ṅe ṅad ǰigs dug** he fears I might address him harshly; *ṅád-čan* 1. fragrant, fresh, cool, *W.* cold. 2. *W.* rough, impetuous.

ངན་ *ṅan* 1. **evil, mischief, misfortune,** *ṅan čén-po byas* it has done great mischief *Glr.*; esp. harm done by sorcery and witchcraft *Mil.*; *ṅan-dgú* every possible evil *Lt.* — 2. **curse, imprecation,** *ṅan ̥débs-pa, W. *táb-če**, to curse, to execrate; *mtu ṅan ̥débs-pa* to curse by means of witchcraft. Cf. *mṅan.*

ངན་པ་ *ṅán-pa*, col. also **ṅáṇ-po**, **bad,** of food etc.; **mean, miserable** *Dzl.*; **poor, humble, low,** (prop. *rigs-ṅán*), *ṅan-lóṅ* poor and blind (people) *Glr.*; *lo ṅán-pa* a year yielding no crops, an unfruitful or bad year; of men, actions etc.: **wicked,** *ṅán-pa ḱyod gnyis* ye two villains! *Glr.*; **noisome, pernicious,** *gsol-ṅán* pernicious food, i.e. poison, resp., *Glr.; ... la ṅán-du rǰód-pa* to revile, blaspheme; *mi-la mig ṅán ltá-ba* to look with an evil or envious eye upon a person *Glr.*; *ráṅ-rnams spyod ṅan byás-nas dus ṅan zer* acting badly themselves they speak of bad times *Ma.* — *ṅan-̥gro, ṅan-soṅ* v. *̥gro-ba* I. extr. — *ṅan-ṅón Cs.* mean, pitiful, very bad. — *ṅan-ṅón tsám-gyis čog šés-pa* prob.: to be satisfied with any thing, and be it ever so poor. — *ṅan-ne-ba* bad. — **ṅan-p̔e* W.* meal of parched barley, roasted meal. — *ṅán-so* 'bad place', hell; cf. *ṅán-̥gro* under *̥gró-ba* I. extr.

ངན་བུ་ *ṅán-bu C.*, **we,** eleg., = *bdag*, when speaking humbly of one's self.

ངམ་གྲོག་ *ṅam-gróg, Cs.* 'torrent', *Sch.* 'ditch filled with water, water-ditch; the bank of a river grown high and steep by having been gradually washed out by the current'; (only this latter sense of the word was authenticated to me). In *Glr.* Tibet is poetically called '*ṅam-grog-čé*', which is a very appropriate name when rendered: having large and deep erosions.

ངམ་དུར་ཅན་ *ṅám-dur-čan* given to gluttony and drinking *Stg.*

ངམ་རུ་ *ṅam-ru* n. of a disease *Med.*

ངམ་ཤུགས་ *ṅam-šúgs* **reluctantly.**

ངར་ *ṅar* 1. **fore- or front-side, forepart,** *ṅar-gdóṅ* id.; esp. of the leg, the shin-bone, also knuckle ni f.; *lag-ṅár, rkaṅ-ṇár* fore-arm, lower part of the leg; *rǰe-ṅar* seems to be an appellation for both, (in *W. *nyar** instead of it). — 2 v. *ṅár-ba* 1. —

3. termin. of *ṅa*, 'to one's self', *ṅar-₀dzin* = *blag-₀dzin*, selfishness, self-interest. *Mil.* — 4. *ṅar ₀dón-pa* to set on or against, **to instigate,** *nyams-kyi ṅar ₀dón-pa* irritations of the mind, excitements *Mil.*; *nyam-ṅár Lex.* id. (?) — 5. v. *ṅar-ṅár-po.*

ངར་སྐད་ *ṅar-skád* **the roaring,** of lions etc., *₀dón-pa, sgróg-pa Mil.*; *W.* **táṅ-če** also to call to, to shout at.

ངར་ངར་པོ་ *ṅar-ṅár-po* **hoarse, husky, wheezing,** e.g. in old age *Thgy.*; *ṅar-ṅár ₀kún-sgra* a hoarse groaning *Pth.*; *ṅar-glúd* hoarseness and phlegm *Med.*; *gré-ba ṅar-ba* a hoarse throat *Med.*

ངར་ཅན་ *ṅár-čan* v. *ṅár-ba.*

ངར་སྣབས་ *ṅar-snábs* **mucus, snivel,** (affords food to certain demons).

ངར་པ་ *ṅár-pa* **stalk** of plants *Med.*

ངར་པོ་ *ṅár-po W.* **strong, ferocious,** of the tiger etc.

ངར་བ་ *ṅár-ba* 1. **strength, force; hardness,** of steel; cold, frost, cold wind *Mil.* (cf. *ṅá-ra, ṅad*); *ṅar γtoṅ-ba, W.* **táṅ-če, čúg-če**, *Sch.* also *ldúd-pa*, to steel, to temper. — *ṅár-čan* 1. strong, vigorous 2. tempered; *ṅár-ldan* id.; *sems ṅár-ldan* a strong mind *Mil.*; *ṅar-méd* weak, soft. — 2. (v. *ṅar* 1.) a sort of flap (of breeches).

ངར་མ་ *ṅárma* 1. **irritable, passionate, impetuous** *Sch.* — 2. **strong, powerful,** e.g. a powerful protection, *Mil.*

ངལ་བ་ *ṅál-ba* **to be fatigued, tired, wearied; fatigue, weariness,** resp. *sku ṅál-ba*, or *tugs ṅál-ba*, also *mnyél-ba*; *ṅal soṅ* I am tired; *spóbs-pa ṅal* the strength decreases *Med.*; *ṅál-čad-pa, ṅál-dub-pa* intensive forms of *ṅal*; *ṅal ǰúg-pa* vb. a. **to tire, fatigue, weary;** *ṅal γsó-ba* 'to cure weariness', **to rest,** frq.; *ṅal-stégs* a rest, a sort of crutch or fork, which coolies sometimes carry with them, to support their load, whilst taking a momentary rest in standing; also any bench or seat inviting to repose. To provide such conveniences for wayfaring men is considered a meritorious act.

ངས་ *ṅas* 1. instr. of *ṅa.* — 2. *mi-ṅas Tar.* 37, 16. is undoubtedly a typographical error, instead of *mi-ṅad. Schf.* has left it without an annotation.

ངི་ *ṅi* num. fig.: 34.

ངུ་ *ṅu* num. fig.: 64.

ངུ་བ་ *ṅu-ba*, pf. *ṅus*, resp. *šum-pa*, 1. **to weep,** 2. *W.* also **to roar,** used of swelling rivers, not of the wind; *Schr.*: 'to groan like a turtle-dove'; **ṅu ma ṅu** *W.* do not weep! *ṅús-pai mči-ma* **tears** that have been shed *Dzl.*; *ga-čád ṅús-pa* weeping without a cause, hysterical weeping *Med.*; *ṅú-ru ǰúg-pa* to cause to weep *Lt.*; **ṅú-ma-god** *W.* weeping and laughing at the same time; *šes ṅús-so* thus he said weeping *Glr.*; **ṇu ḍhó-wa** (lit. *gro-ba*) *C.* to be sorrowful, sad. — *ṅú(-ba)-po Cs.*, *ṅú-mk'an* col. one weeping, a weeper. — *ṅú-šur-čan Sch.*, *ṅú-mk'an* col. a child that is continually crying. — *ṅu-₀bód, ṅu-rdzi*, *W.* **ṅu-zi**, sbst. a crying, howling, lamenting.

ངུ་རུ་ *ṅú-ru W.* for *ṅúr-ba* 1.

ངུག་པ་ *ṅúg-pa Ts.* = *ṅúr-ba* 2, **to grunt; to snore; to pur** (of cats).

ངུད་མོ་ *ṅúd-mo* **a sob** *Cs., Schr.*

ངུར་བ་ *ṅúr-ba* 1. sbst. **duck,** esp. the red wild duck, चक्रवाक Anas casarca; *ṅúr-ka* as red as fire, fiery red; *ṅur-smrig* yellowish red, **saffron colour,** the original colour of the monks' habit, though not the common high-red of the Brug-pa monks in *Sik.* and in *W.* — 2. vb. **to grunt,** of pigs and yaks.

ངུས་ *ṅus* v. *ṅu-ba.*

ངེ་ *ṅe* num. fig.: 94.

ངེད་ *ṅed* pers. person. first person, eleg. for *ṅa*, **I, we;** *ṅéd-kyi* my, our; *ṅed γnyis(-ka)* we two; *ṅed γsum(-po)* we three; *ṅed spun γsum* we three brothers *Glr.*; *ṅéd-kyi bu-dód mdzod* have the goodness to become our foster-son *Mil.*; sometimes *ṅa* and *ṅed* are used promiscuously in the same sentence, so: *ṅas* I, and directly after: *ṅéd-kyi* our *Mil.* The plural number is specially indicated in: *ṅéd-cag*, *ṅéd-ťso*, *ṅéd-rnams*, *ṅéd-dag Mil.*; *ṅéd-ċag-rnams Cs.* — *ṅed-ráṅ* 1. I myself, we ourselves. 2. I, we *Glr.*; *ṅed-nyid*, *ṅed-ḱó-na Cs.* id. (*Ld.* **ṅad**).

ངེའུ་ཅག་ *ṅeu-ċag Dzl.* ༢༥༢, 11.15. is prob. an incor. reading in *Sch.'s* edition, instead of *˳u-bu-ċag*.

ངེས་པ་ *ṅés-pa* 1. adj. **certain, true, sure, firm,** *bdág-la ṅés-pa żig stsál-du ysol* I ask you to communicate to me something certain, i.e. authentic news; *ṅés-par byéd-pa* to fix, settle, establish, ascertain, e.g. facts of chronology, v. *Wilk.* chronological table in *Cs.'s* Grammar; to ratify *Schr.*; *˳ċi-bar ṅés-pa yin* or *ṅés-so* death is certain; *de bdén-par ṅés-sam* is it certain that this is true? *Glr.*; *mi btúb-tu ṅés-na* as it is certain that I am not able (to do it) *Dzl.*; *nam ˳ḱyer ṅés-pa med* it is not certain at what time they will be carried off *Glr.*; *bdag ḱyód-kyi bu yin ṅés-na* if I am actually, for certain, your son *Pth.*; *p̀an ṅés-pai ċos* that religion which is sure to lead to salvation *Mil.*; *ṅés-pai dón-las gol* he is missing the true sense *Pth.*; *ma-ṅés-pa* untrue *Tar.* 109, 17; *ynás-la ṅés-pa méd-pa yin* as to abode I am changeable, I have no fixed abode *Mil.*; also *ṅes-méd* alone: **homeless** *Mil.*; **undefined**, *ṅes-méd-kyi rí-la* somewhere on the mountains *Mil.*; sometimes it is but a rhetorical turn, like the English **evidently, obviously,** *bú-la bkra-mi-śis ṅés-kyis*, as our son has evidently met with an accident *Dzl.*; *bud-méd yin-du ṅés-so* they are evidently women, they do not deserve to be called men *Dzl.*; also sbst. **certainty, surety, truth**; *ťsé-la*, *ṅág-la*, *lús-la ṅés-pa med* (man's) life-time, word, body have no certainty, are transient *Glr.* Hence *ṅés-pa-ċan* **real, actual,** *ṅés-pa-ċan-du* really, truly, in fact, in reality, opp. to deceitful appearances, false opinions, wrong calculations etc. *Glr.*; *ṅes-pa-nyid-du* adv. 1. in reality *Glr.* 2. truly, in truth, verily *Glr.*; *ṅés-par* adv. 1. really, certainly, to be sure, frq.; *sdig-pa byás-na rnam-par-smín-pa ṅés-par myóṅ-ste* as retribution for a sin committed is sure to take place, will certainly follow *Dzl.*; *dé-ḍra-ba żig ṅés-par yód-na* if such a one is really present *Dzl.*; *ṅés-par ċi-ba* the certain dying, the certainty of death *Thgy.*; *bdag ṅés-par byao* I will surely do it *Dzl.* 2. **by all means,** to add force to the imperative mood *Tar.* 16, 11. — 2. often it is used subjectively, esp. in *C.*, when *séms-la* is to be supplied, so that it may be rendered by **to know:** *bdén-par ṅes*, *rdzún-par ṅes* I know (I am certain) that it is true, untrue; *ṅés-pa ċer med* I am not quite sure, I do not know for certain, I do not fully understand, I do not clearly see through it *Mil.*; *séms-ċan ˳di bdág-gi p̀a-má yin ṅés-na*, if we take it for granted, if we try to realize the fact, that this being is our father or mother *Thgy.*; to remember, to bear in mind **sém-la ṅē ťúb-bam* C.* shall you be able to remember that? *ṅés-dón*, also *ydáṅ-dag-doṅ*, is said to mean immediate knowledge of the truth, which may be obtained mystically by continued contemplation, and is opp. to *dráṅ-don*, knowledge obtainable through the medium of the sacred writings *Mil.*, also *Lexx.*; *ṅes (-par) ˳byuṅ-(ba) Mil.* frq., *Schr.*: 'deliverance from the round of transmigration', *Sch.*: 'to appear, to prove true'; another explanation still: 'knowledge of one's self' is not borne out by etymology. — *ṅes-bzúṅ* acc. to *Lexx.* a synonym of *brnán-pa*, q. v. — *ṅes-(par) légs(-pa) Thgy.*, 'that which evidently is the best', is said to denote deliverance from the round of transmigration.

ངོ་ *ṅo* num. fig.: 124.

ངོ་ *ṅo* 1. resp. *żal-ṅó* (cf. *ṅó-bo*, *ṅor*, *ṅos*) **face, countenance, air, look,** as the expression of a man's personality and mind (*ṅo mdzés-pa Cs.*, and *ṅán-pa Schr.* are dubious), *bdág-gi ṅó-la yzigs-nas* when she (my mother) shall see my face, *ṅod kár-po* a cheerful face; *ṅo nág-par ˳dug-pa* to sit with a sad and gloomy face *Glr.*; *ṅo nág-par* ˳*gyúr-ba* to grow sorrowful, to turn pale with fright, pain etc.; *ṅo bab* courage fails(me); *ṅo srúṅ-ba* frq. 'to watch the countenance', to pay much or even too much regard to other people's opinions; *ṅo* ⁽*dzín-pa Mil.* seems to signify the same, and *ṅo čógs-pa* the contrary: not to comply with a person's wishes *Mil.*; *ṅo spród-pa* to lay open the features, to show the nature of a thing, to explain; *ṅo* ˳*ṗród-pa* to understand, to learn, in later literature frq.; *ṅo šés-pa* to know *ccap: ṅa ṅo kyód-kyis ma šés-na* if thou dost not know me *Mil.*; with termin. inf.: to know (that something happens); to find out, e.g. by calculation; to perceive; *ṅo mi šés-pa* 1. not to know 2. unacquaintance, ignorance 3. unknown: *ṅó-mi-šes-pa-la ldáṅ-ba* to rise before a stranger; *ṅó-mi-šes-pai yul* an unknown country *Thgy.*; *ṅo ltá-ba Glr.* is said to signify: to submit (vb. n.); **ṅo lén-če** *W.* to beg pardon, cf. *ṅos bláṅ-ba*; *ṅo ldóg-pa* or *lóg-pa* to turn away, always fig. = to desert, ˳*ḱór-bai yul ṅo lóg-na* if you will desert, get rid of, the land of transmigration; more frq.: *ṅo-lóg byéd-pa* to revolt, rebel, *rtsóm-pa* to bring about a revolt, *ṅo-lóg-mḱan* mutineer, agitator, *ṅo-lóg-čan* seditious, faithless, *ṅo zlóg-pa ccg.* to oppose, resist, not comply with a person's wish *Dzl.* — 2. **side**, like *ṅos*, esp. *W.*: **'a ṅó-la soṅ** he has gone to that side, in that direction; **sám-pa 'a ṅo 'i ṅó-a soṅ** he is absent, inattentive. — 3. **self, the thing itself**, cf. *ṅó-bo* and *ṅos*; v. ˳*ǰál-ba*; also sbst. **the self, the I**, *ṅo-tsáb* the representative of the I; cf. also *ṅo-čén*. — 4. **likelihood, prospect of**, c. genit. inf. or root, ˳*ḱyér-bai ṅo* a probability of its being taken away; *bu čig* ˳*byuṅ ṅo če* a great chance of (getting) a son. — 5. (also *ṅos*) a. **the waxing** and **waning moon**, with regard to shape; one half of the lunar month with regard to time, *yar-ṅo* the former, *mar-ṅo* the latter half; *yár-ṅo zla ltar* like the crescent moon. b. in a special sense the **increasing moon**, or the first half of the month; thus vulgo: so also in *B.*: *zlá-ba dgu ṅo bču lón-pa-na Glr.*, *ṅo bčú-nas*, *zlá-ba ṅo bčú-na Pth.* in the first half of the tenth month (to denote the duration of pregnancy).

Comp. and deriv. *ṅo dkar* v. above 1. — *ṅo-lkog* prop. adj.: **public** and **private, open** and **secret**, but it is generally used as a synonym of *zol* or *rdzun*, **fraud, imposture, deceit, eye-service.** It may be explained by its contrary: *ṅó-med lkóg-med* acting in the same manner in public as in private life, the open and the secret conduct being alike *Mil.* (cf. *ṅos*). — *ṅó-čan* natural (?) *Cs.* — *ṅo-čén* ('the greater self'), a man of influence interceding for another person, **an intercessor**; *ṅo-čén byéd-pa* to intercede *Glr.*; *mi-la ṅo-čén* ˳*čól-ba* to use a person as negotiator, to make inquiries through him *Glr.* (*Sch.* incorr.) — *ṅo-rtóg W.* 1. (like *ṅés-pa* of *B.*) **certain**, e.g. **ṅo-tóg šé-če** to know for certain. 2. (like *dṅos*, *yaṅ-dag-pa*) **real, actual; true, genuine**, ** ˳ṫul yin-na ṅo-tóg yin** is it counterfeit or genuine? illusion or reality? **ṅo-tóg sád-ḱan** the actual murderer, he who really occasioned the death. — **ṅó-stod-ḱan** *W.* he who praises another to his face, **a flatterer.** — *ṅo-nág* v. above 1. — *ṅó-bo-nyid*, **entity**, *ṅo-bo-nyid-méd-pa* non-entity *Tar.* 90, 2.; **essence, nature, substance**, e.g. *séms-kyi Mil.*; **character** *Was.* (278. 294); **marrow, main substance, quintessence** (= *snyiṅ-po*) *Glr.* and elsewh.; *ráṅ-gi ṅó-bos* in itself, according to its intrinsic nature *Mil.*; also col. **ṅó-bo ḱo-ráṅ** *C.* the thing itself, opp. to a surrogate; *ṅó-bo γčig rtógs-pa* γ*nyis Was.*: 'one quality, two (different) ideas' (*Schl.* has *ldóg-pa* instead of *rtóg-pa*). — *ṅo-*˳*bab-pa* adj. **discouraged, timorous, bashful** *W.* — *ṅó-ma* acc. to *Cs.* = *ṅo*. — *ṅó-ma-γyog C.*: master and servant. — *ṅó-mig W.* **boldness**; **ṅó-mig-čan**, or **čén-po** bold, daring, courageous; **ṅó-mig čuṅ-se** shy, timid, faint-hearted *W.* — *ṅó-tsa* ('heat of the face') 1. the act of **blushing, shame**, *ṅó-tsai* γ*nas* shameful things *Sch.*, *Schr.*; *ṅó-tsa-čan*, *ṅó-tsa-šes-pa* shamefaced, chaste, ashamed; *ṅó-tsa-med-pa*, *mi-šes-pa* shameless, barefaced, impudent; **ṅa ṅó-tsa rag** I am ashamed, **ko ṅó-tsa dug, ṅó-tsa-čan dug** *W.* he is ashamed; *ṅó-tsa byéd-pa* to be ashamed. 2. a shameful thing, *kyod ṅó-mi-tsa-la ṅó-tsar byed* you are ashamed where there is no occasion for it *Mil.*; *ṅó-tsa-ba* to be indecent, indecorous, unbecoming, *yúl-du lóg-na ṅó-tsa-la* as it would be a shame if we returned *Glr.*; *yčér-bur* ₒ*gró-ba ṅó-tsa žiṅ* as it would be indecorous to go naked *Pth.* — *ṅo-mtsár-ba* v. *mtsár-ba.* — *ṅó-ru, ṅor* 1. into the face *Sch.*, e.g. *skúd-pa* to smear; *rtsúb-pa* to say rude things to another's face *Thgy.*; *ṅo-ráṅ-du* id. 2. in the face of, before the eyes, *yžán-gyi* of others. 3. by reason of, in consequence of, *des bskúl-bai ṅor* in consequence of a summons, of a request of him *Glr.* and elsewh. — *ṅo-šés* **an acquaintance, a friend** (the usual word in *W.*). — *ṅo-só* **joy**, *ṅo-só čé-bar* ₒ*oṅ* you will have great joy, you will be delighted, highly satisfied; *sbyín-pa ṅo-só byéd-pa* to make presents to another to his full satisfaction *Mil.*, also *Tar.* 211, 2. — *ṅo-srúṅs* regard to the opinion of others, an aiming at applause *Mil.*

ངོགས་ *ṅogs* 1. **mountain-side, slope** (cf. *ṅos*); river-side, **bank, shore**, *rgyá-mtsoi Dzl.* — 2. **ford**, *ču-ṅógs* id. *C.*

ངོམ་པ་ *ṅóm-pa*, pf. *ṅoms*, 1. **to satisfy one's desire** by drinking, *krág-gis*, also *krág-las Dzl.*; *ma ṅoms* I am still thirsty; *ṅóm-par*, also *ṅoms-tsád*, ₒ*túṅ-ba* to drink one's fill; also of sleeping, *nyid ma ṅom* I have not yet had my full share of sleep; fig.: *čós-kyi bdud-rtsis*, to fill one's self with the nectar of doctrine *Dzl.*; *bltá-bas mi ṅoms mdzés-pa* so beautiful, that one cannot gaze at it long enough, frq.; also *bltá-bas mi ṅoms bžin-du* not being able to look at it sufficiently *Pth.*; *ṅoms(-pa)-méd(-pa)* insatiable. — 2. **to show** with design (boastingly, or indecently, e.g. one's nakedness) *Glr.*, *Pth.* — 3. col. for *snóm-pa* to snuffle, to pry into, to spy.

ངོར་ *ṅor* 1. v. under *ṅo*, *Comp.* — 2. n. of a monastery of the Saskya, *Wdk.* chronological table in *Cs.'s* Gram.

ངོས་ *ṅos* 1. **side**, *mdún-ṅos* front-side, front of the body *Lt.*; of a pyramid, a mountain, *lhó-ṅos* southern side or slope of a mountain, **side, margin, edge**, of a pond etc.; *rgyáb ṅos yyás-na* on the right hand behind, *yyás ṅos mdún-na* on the right hand before *Glr.*; **surface, plain**, of the table; *sai ṅos* surface of the earth *Cs.*; hence *ṅós-su* (opp. to *lkog-tu*) *Mil.*, **ṅó-la** (opp. to *sbás-te* (**bé-te**) *W.* manifestly, notoriously, publicly, openly (cf. *ṅo*); **side, direction**, like *pyogs*, *W.* — 2. a thing itself (cf. *ṅo* 3), examples v. under ₒ*jál-ba.* — 3. pers. pron. first person **I, we**; esp. in *Ld.* in epistolary correspondence, eleg. — 4. instrum. of *ṅo*, = *ṅó-yis*; *ṅos dzin-pa Mil.* (*dṅos dzin-pa Thgy.*) vb. 1. to be selfish, self-interested, also adj. selfish, cf. *ṅos* 3. 2. more frq. to perceive, to know, to discern, also *ṅó-yis dzin-pa*; *ṅos zin-par gyis šig*, know it! be sensible of it! *Thgr.*; with the termin.: to acknowledge as, to take for, to look upon as *Tar.* 189, 1. In a special sense: diagnosis, discriminating a disease *Med.* **nóṅ-ṅo láṅ-wa** *C.* (lit. *ynoṅ ṅos blaṅ-ba*) = **ṅo lén-če** v. **ṅo** 1.

དངགས་སྙན་ *dṅags-snyán* v. *ṅag* (*Lex.* = काव्य).

དངང་བ་ *dṅáṅ-ba*, pf. *dṅaṅs* 1. **to be out of breath, to pant**, to feel oppressed e.g. when plunging into cold water *C.*, but esp. when frightened and terrified, hence 2. to **be frightened, to fear, to be afraid,** *sbrúl-gyis* of a snake; *čes dṅáṅs-nas* thus he spoke in dismay *Dzl.*; *dṅáṅ-par* ₒ*gyúr-ro* you will (or would) be terrified *Dzl.*; *dṅaṅ-skrág, skrag-dṅáṅ* great fear, fright, terror; *dṅaṅ-skrág-pa* intensive form of *dṅáṅ-ba*, frq.

དངན་འཐེན་པ་ *dṅan-*ₒ*tén-pa Lex.* not to return things taken away from another.

དངར་ *dṅar* 1. for *mṅar*, **sweet** *Mil.* and elsewh. — 2. also *zil-dṅár Lex.* w.e.;

Sch.: order, succession(?); *ṫsár-du dṅar Lex., Sch.* put in order, placed in array.

དངད་མོ་ *dṅúd-mo* = *ṅúd-mo Sch.*

དངུལ་ *dṅul* (col. often **mul**) 1. **silver.** — 2. **money.** — 3. **a rupee.** — 4. **a tola** or Indian half ounce; *dṅúl-gyi ṫóg-nas dṅul ɣsúm-ċu ṫob* he gets 30 rupees out of the ready money; *dṅúl-ḱa* a silver mine, a vein of silver; *dṅul-kúg, dṅul-sgyig* money-bag, purse; *dṅúl-ċu* quicksilver, mercury; *dṅul-dúl-ma* refined silver *Sch.*; *dṅul-rmig,* lump, bar, ingot, of silver *Sch.*; **ṅul-zán(s)** *W., C.,* silvered or plated copper.

དངོ་ *dṅo* 1. **shore, bank** *Lex.* — 2. **edge** of a knife *Cs.*; fig. *rta-lċág-gi dṅo* whip-cord, lash of a whip *C.* — 3. handle of a knife(??) *Cs.*

དངོམ་པ་ *dṅóm-pa, dṅom-brjid,* **brightness, splendour**; *dṅóm-po, dṅóm-ċan* shining, bright *Cs.*; *Lex. dṅom-ċé* very bright. Cf. *rṅám-pa.*

དངོས་ *dṅos* 1. **reality, real,** *dṅos daṅ sgyú-ma* reality and illusion; *rgyál-bu dṅos* the real prince (opp. to a spurious one); **proper, true, genuine; positive** (opp. to negative) *Gram.*; **personal,** *dṅós-la yód-pa* to be personally present; *dṅós-su,* resp. *żal-dṅós-su* **bodily** e.g. to appear bodily; *ạ-yig dṅós-su med kyaṅ,* even though the *ạ* is not actually written there, *Gram.*; *dṅós-su grúb-pa méd-pa* to have no real existence *Thgy.* — 2. *Cs.*: pers. pron. I, cf. *ṅos*; *dṅos-ḍzin-pa* to be selfish *Thgy.*; *dṅos-ḍzin* **selfishness, selfinterest,** *dṅos-ḍzin ɣdón-gyis zin-pa* to be possessed by the demon of selfishness *Thgy.*; *dṅos-ḍzin-ċan* selfish, self-interested. Thus it was explained by Lamas, though it cannot be denied that sometimes the version: belief in existence, a clinging to reality, a signification equally justifiable by etymology (v. below), would be more adequate to the context. — 3. *Tar.* 150, 14: thou, you; except in this passage I did not meet with the word in this sense, yet it may be used so, in the same manner as *nyid* q.v.

Comp. and deriv. *dṅos-grúb, Ssk. siddhi,* 1. **perfection, excellence,** any thing of superior value, e.g. honour, riches, talents, and esp. wisdom, higher knowledge, and spiritual power, as far as they are not acquired by ordinary study and exercise, but have sprung from within spontaneously, or in consequence of long continued contemplation. This *dṅos-grúb* is, as it were, the Buddhist caricature of the *χαρίσματα* of the N.T. (v. I. Cor. 12,4). — 2. name of male persons, col. **ṅo-rúb** *W.* — *dṅos-ṅán* having little flesh, **ill-fed,** emaciated *Mil.* — *dṅós-ċan* **material, real** *Cs.* — *dṅós-dad* true faith, opp. to *blún-dad* 'a fool's faith', superstition *Mil.* — *dṅos-sdig* prob.: real, or still effective sin, unatoned, unexpiated sin *Dzl.* ༢༧, 14; or less emphatically: sinful actions in general ༣༠, 15. — *dṅós-po, Ssk.* भव, वस्तु, **thing, natural body,** *ser dṅúl-la sógs-pai dṅós-po Glr.*; **matter, subject,** *dgá-bai dṅós-po* matter of rejoicing *Wdṅ.*; **goods, utensils,** *dge-slóṅ-gi* wearing-apparel of a Gelong; **occurrence, event, action,** *dṅós-po sgrúb-pa* to bring a thing about, to set it on foot or a going *Dzl.*: as a philosophical term: **substance, matter,** *Was.* (270. 294); *dṅós-por ḍzin-pa* the belief in the reality of existence *Mil.* — *dṅós-ma Cs.* **natural** (opp. to artificial), natural productions. — *dṅós-miṅ* 1. **the proper** or **real name** for a thing; so *Zam.* uses the paraphrase: *pʼo-mṫsán-gyi dṅós-miṅ,* in order to avoid the plain expression *mje,* which is considered obscene. 2. **noun substantive.** *Chr. Prot.* a newly coined grammatical term. — *dṅos-med Lex.* = *Ssk. abhava, Cs.* **immaterial,** not existing, *Was.* (281): **not real.** — *dṅos-slób* a real, **a personal pupil** *Tar.* often. — *dṅos-ɣżi* (*Lex.* = *Ssk. mūla*) the main part of a thing, **the thing itself,** e.g. the subject-matter of a treatise, the ceremony itself, opp. to *snóṅ-ạgro* introduction, *sbyór-ba* preparation, and eventually also *rjes* that which follows.

མངག་པ་ *mṅág-pa,* pf. *mṅags,* **to commission, charge, delegate, send** (a messenger, commissary etc.) *Dzl.*; also used of Buddha's sending a Bodhisatva on the earth to convert all mortals. — *mṅag-γžúg* **a servant, slave,** but esp. a messenger of the gods.

མངན་པ་ *mṅán-pa* **to curse, to execrate;** *mṅan bsgrań-ba Cs.* 'enumeration of curses'; but *mṅan mi bgrań? Lex.* w.e.

མངའ་ *mṅa*, resp. for *dbań*, **might, dominion, sway,** *mṅa mdzád-pa* to govern, to rule, *la* over; *mṅa brnyés-pa* to have obtained power *Glr.; mṅa sgyúr-ba Tar.* id.; to possess (books, knowledge etc.); to have mastered, to understand thoroughly; *mṅa γsól-ba* 1. to name, nominate, appoint, *rgyál-por* a king *Pth.; btsún-mor* to declare a woman one's wife *Glr.* 2. to praise *C.*; *bkra-šís mṅa γsól-ba C.* to congratulate. — *mṅa-tʻáń* **power, might.** — *mṅa-bdág* **ruler, master, owner,** frq. — *mṅá-ba* 1. vb. resp. for *yod-pa*, **to be** (to have), *rgyál-po-la sras γsum mṅá-ste* the king having three sons *Dzl.; btsún-poi skú-la bsnyuń mi mṅa lágs-sam* (I trust) your majesty is not unwell? *Glr.* 2. adj. (partic.) being owned by, **belonging to,** *Dzl.* ༧༢, 3; **having, owning,** = *dań ldán-pa*, frq. — *mṅa-mdzád* = *mṅa-bdág.* — *mṅa-žábs Glr., mṅa-ₒóg Glr., mṅa-ris Lex.* **subject to; a subject.**

མངའ་རིས་ *mṅa-ris* p.n., in a wider sense the whole country round the sources and the upper course of the Indus and Sutledge, together with some more western parts; the Cashmere, English, and most western Chinese provinces, where Tibetans live; in a more limited sense *mṅa-ris skor γsum* denotes Rutok, Guge, and Purang. — *mṅa-ris-kʻám-bu C.* (*pá-tiń* *W.*), **dried apricots** from Balti; *mṅa-ris čʻu, mṅa-ris γtsáń-po*, also *γyas-ru-γtsáń-po*, and *rta-mčʻóg-kʻa-bab*, the principal river of Tibet.

མངར་བ་ *mṅár-ba, W.* **ṅár-mo**, *C.* **ṅár-po**, **sweet,** frq.; **mṅar γsum** the three sweets, sugar, molasses, and honey; cf. *dkar γsum.*

མངལ་ *mṅal*, resp. *lhums* (गर्भ) **womb;** *mṅál-gyi drí-mas ma gós-par* not contaminated by the impurity of the womb (so all the Buddhas are not born like other mortals, but come forth out of the side of the breast); *mṅal dań ldán-par ₒgyúr-ba* to be with child; *mṅal mi bdé-bar ₒgyúr-ba* to be taken by the labours of childbirth; *maí mṅál-nas byúń-nas rtág-par* constantly from one's birth; *mṅál-du čʻágs-pa* 1. the originating in the womb, conception, 2. the foetus or embryo *Med.; mṅál-du tʻógs-pa* a disease; *mṅál(-du) γnás (-pa)* foetus, embryo *Thgy.; mṅál-du ₒjúg-pa* to enter the womb, relative to a Buddha: his incarnating himself, his assuming flesh; *mṅál-du ₒdzín-pa Wdń.* to conceive, to be with child. — *mṅál-kʻa* mouth of the womb, orifice of the uterus *Med.* — *mṅal-grib* contamination of the womb; *Cs.* adds: original sin, yet prob. it signifies nothing more than *mṅál-gyi drí-ma* v. above; (the said contamination is considered to extend to the least contact with a woman in childbed). — *mṅál-sgo* the canal of the uterus, vagina; also in a more special sense the extreme orifice of the vagina *Med.*; frq. without any immediate physiological reference, the same as *mṅal*, e.g, when the subject of re-birth is spoken of. — *mṅal-tʻúr* a spoon used in midwifery for extracting a dead fruit (in the artificial delivering of a live child the obstetric art in Tibet is rather helpless). — *mṅal rlúgs-pa* **abortion,** *mṅal rlúgs-par byéd-pa* to cause abortion *Cs.*

མངོན་པ་ *mṅón-pa* **conspicuous, visible,** e.g. continents, because they stand out of the water; more frq. fig.: **evident, manifest, clear,** *mṅón-par ₒgyúr-ba* to become manifest; to be verified, proved, e.g. gold by refining *Dzl.* — Tibetan writers regularly translate the *Ssk. abhi* by *mṅón-pa*, hence *čʻos mṅón-pa Dzl.*, and *mṅón-pai bka Pth.*, the *Abhidharma* (v. *Köpp.* I., 595; *Was.*), *mṅon-pai sde-snod Abhidharma-piṭaka, mṅon-pa-mdzod Abhidharma kośa* (v. *Burn.* I. and *Was.*); as a vb.: to be evident, to appear clearly, *bdén-par čʻis mṅon*, from what is it evident that it is true? *Dzl.; γnód-par bgyid-du mṅón-no* they are evidently bent on doing mischief *Dzl.; mṅón-du byéd-pa* to manifest, to make public; to show something to others; *Tar.* 24, 1 should be understood: to make clear or manifest to one's self, to perceive, know, understand; *mṅón-du ₒbyin-pa* to disclose, reveal (secrets, the future) *Glr.*; to make known (one's wishes) *Glr.*; *mṅón-du ₒgyúr-ba* to be revealed or disclosed, to make one's appearance, *raṅ-byúṅ ye-šés mṅón-du gyúr-pas* as the self-originated wisdom has revealed itself to us *Mil.* — *mṅón-par* adv. manifestly, openly, evidently; often = entirely, highly, greatly, very, *mṅón-par rdzogs Was.* (246) complete fulfilment; in the sense of 'very' it may also be taken in *mṅón-par dgao*, in the legends of Buddha, 'they rejoiced very much', though also one of the other significations of *abhinanda* might help to explain these words.

Comp. *mṅón-(par) brjód(-pa)* = *abhidāna*, a collection of synonyms, of which some are mentioned in *Burn.* I. and II. — *mṅon-rtágs* **proof, argument**; sign or token of the truth of a thing *Dzl.* ༧༢, 2. — *mṅon-(par) rtógs(-pa)* 1. a clear comprehension *Was.* (287). 2. a hymnlike description of a Lha from top to toe, v. also *Schl.* 260. — *mṅon-mtʼó* re-birth as Lha or as man *Thgy.* (*Schr.*); also n. of a region in Paradise. — *mṅón-pa-pa* an Abhidharma scholar. — *mṅon-spyód Sch.* cruelty, severity; *Schf.* more corr.: **witchcraft**, *Ssk. abhičāra*, *Pth.*, *drág-po mṅon-spyód-kyi las Tar.* frq. — *mṅon-mtsán Lex.* w.e., *Sch.*; an evident sign. — *mṅón-(par) šés(-pa)*, resp. *mkʼyén(-pa)*, *Ssk. abhijñā*, a kind of **clairvoyance**, gift of supernatural perception, of which five species are enumerated, viz. assuming any form at will, seeing and hearing to any distance, knowing a man's thoughts, knowing a man's condition and antecedents; originally used as a vb.: to be clear-seeing *Pth.* — *mṅon-súm-du* 1. **openly, publicly** *Dzl.*; more frq. 2. **bodily, personally**; like *dṅós-su*, e.g. to appear, to instruct, in person (*Tar.*); to know by one's own personal experience (*W.*).

རྔ་ *rṅa* I. **kettle-drum, drum**, *ₒkʼár-rṅa* v. *ₒkʼar*; *rdzá-rṅa Glr.*, *Cs.*: 'a drum of earthen ware'; *rgyál-rṅa* the beating of drums after a victory, *bóg-rṅa* at nuptial festivities, **lhá-ṅa* Ld.* for the king; **žén-ṅa**, and **zim-ṅa* Ld.* a morning and evening serenade with an accompaniment of drums: *kʼrims-kyi rṅá-bo če brdúṅs-te* the beat or sound of the large proclamation drum (prop. law-drum) *Glr.* —

Comp. *rṅa-sgrá* 1. sound of the drum, or kettle-drum 2. n. of a Buddha, = *dón-yod-grub-pa* or Amoghasiddha. — **ṅa-lčág* W.*, *rṅa-rdég Sch.*, *rṅa-dbyúg Cs.*, *rṅa-yáb Sch.* **drum-stick.** — *rṅá-pa* **a drummer** *Cs.*, *rṅa-dpón* a chief drummer. — *rṅa-lpágs* **drum-skin.** — *rṅa-yu* handle of a kettle-drum (the larger kettle-drums being held up during the play by means of a handle or stick). — *rṅa-šiṅ* the wooden body of a drum *Cs.* — *rṅa-šón* kettle-drum music *Sch.* — *rṅa-gsáṅs* (also *rṅa-bsaṅs*) a loud beat or roll of the kettle-drum *Sch.*

II. for *rṅa-bóṅ*, and *rṅá-ma*.

རྔ་བ་ *rṅá-ba*, pf. *brṅas*, fut. *brṅa*, imp. *rṅos*, **to mow, to cut, to reap**, *ₒbru*, or *lo-tóg zór-bas* to cut the harvest with a sickle; *brtsás-ma brṅás-pa* the reaped corn; *rṅá-mkʼan* the mower, reaper.

རྔ་བོང་ *rṅa-bóṅ W.*, **ṅa-móṅ* C.*, **camel**, *rṅa-gséb* male camel, *rṅá-mo* female camel; a camel in general; *rṅa-pʼrúg* the young of a camel; *rṅa-rgód* a wild camel; *rṅa-bál* camel's hair.

རྔ་མ་ *rṅá-ma* 1. **tail.** 2. in a special sense: **yak's tail** *Mil.* — *rṅá-ma gyúg-pa Sch.*, **ṅá-ma ṭóg-če** (lit. *skrog-pa*) *W.*, to wag the tail. — *rṅa-yáb* 1. a **yak's tail**, used for fanning and dusting. 2. *rṅa-yáb*, and *rṅa-yab-gžán*, n. of two fabulous islands in the south of Asia *Cs.*

རྔན་ཆེན་ *rṅan-čén Lex.*, *C.* and *W.*, **contempt, disdain**; **ṅan-čén jhé-pa* C.*, **čó-če* W.* to despise, contemn.

རྔན་པ་ *rṅán-pa* I. sbst. 1. **reward, fee, hire, wages**; *rṅán-pa mṅáṅ-po* the wages are high; *rṅán-pa sbyin-pa* or *gtóṅ-ba* to pay wages; to bribe, to corrupt. — 2. in *C.* at present a kind of **sacrifice.**

II. vb. **to reward, to recompense,** perh. better *brṅán-pa.*

རྔབ་པ་ *rṅáb-pa* 1. (cf. *rṅam-pa*) **to desire** earnestly, **to crave,** *bkrés-rṅab-pa* to be greedy, to have a craving appetite *Lex.* — 2. *W.* col. for *rṅá-ba* **to mow;** **ṅáb-sa** (lit. *ṅáb-rtsva*) *W.* grass or corn that is to be mown or cut.

རྔབས་རྭ་ *rṅábs-rva Med.,* a hollow horn, used for sucking *Sch.*

རྔམ་པ་ *rṅám-pa* 1. sbst. (cf. *dṅom*), also *rṅam-brǰid, rṅom-brǰid,* **splendour, magnificence, majesty,** an appearance, commanding awe or inspiring terror (but not = awe *Cs.*); *rṅám-pai ṅá-ro* a voice of that kind; *rṅám-po, rṅám-čan* adj. bright, shining, grand, majestic. — 2. vb., also *rṅáms-pa,* pf. *brṅams,* **to breathe,** *rṅám-pa bde* the breathing is regular *Mṅg.*, frq.; *rṅám-pa tuṅ* short breath *Sch.*; esp. to breathe heavily, **to pant,** *rṅám-pa rgod* wild puffing *Med.*; c. dat. **to pant for, to desire ardently,** *srog γčód-pa-la* to be blood-thirsty *Ma.*; *rṅám-pai tsúl-gyis* greedily (devouring) *Thgr.*; *rṅám-čan* adj. greedy, avaricious, covetous; **za-ṅam-pa** voracious, gluttonous, ravenous *W.*; to rush upon, fly at, throw one's self on, *γžán-la* on others *Mil.*; **to rage,** to be in a fury; **to destroy** or murder in a state of fury; *mi pal-čér grir rṅom* (like *grir γsod*) the people are in numbers murdered by the sword *Ma.*; to call out in a rage, *čes krós-rṅam-nas* thus she called furious with rage *Dzl.*; *rṅáms-pai (kro)-žal* an angry face, wrathful look *Glr.*

རྔམས་ *rṅams* **height;** in height *Glr.*, *rṅáms-su* id.

རྔས་ *rṅas,* v. *sṅas.*

རྔུ་ *rṅu* **pain,** v. *zug-rṅu.*

རྔུབ་པ་ *rṅúb-pa,* pf. (*b*)*rṅubs,* fut. *brṅub,* imp. *rṅubs,* **to draw in,** *dbugs* air, *snar* into the nose *Med.*; to breathe *Med.*; *dbugs rṅub mi ˳ton* (?) is mentioned as a sign of great sadness and affliction *Pth.*

རྔུལ་ *rṅul* **perspiration, sweat,** *rṅúl-ču* id., esp. col.; *rṅul ˳du Med.*, *˳byuṅ Dzl.*, *rṅúl-ču ˳ton, *yoṅ*,* col. perspiration is breaking forth; *rṅul ˳dón-pa* to cause to sweat or perspire *Cs.*; *rṅúl-ba,* pf. *brṅul,* to sweat, to perspire *Cs.*

རྔེའུ་ *rṅeu* 1. also *rṅeu-čúṅ, rṅa-čúṅ,* a little drum, diminutive of *rṅa.* — 2. the young of a camel, v. *rṅa-móṅ.*

རྔོ་ *rṅo,* is stated to be a kind of **leprosy,** covering the whole body, of a whitish colour, itching very much, and contagious; **ṅo pog, gyab** he is affected with leprosy; *rṅó-čan* leprous (cf. *mdze*).

རྔོ་བ་ *rṅó-ba* **to be able** *Cs.*, *rṅo-tóg-pa* id., so *Fouc. Gyatch.* ၃၃၀, 9, **ṅób-če* Ld.*; *Sch.* has: *rṅo mi tóg-pa* to look at one with uncertainty, not being able to recognize; the passage of *Mil.*: *rṅo ma togs kyaṅ* is not to be explained by either of these significations; *Lex.*: *rṅo mi togs* w.e.

རྔོ་བག་ཅན་ *rṅó-bag-čan Cs.* v. *rṅom-bag-čan.*

རྔོ་ལེན་པ་ *rṅó-len-pa* **to roast, fry,** (?) *Sch.* v. *rṅód-pa.*

རྔོག་ *rṅog* 1. also *ze-rṅóg,* **the hunch** or **hump** of an animal *Lex.*, more esp. a hump consisting of fat (like that of the camel); *tsil-rṅóg* the fat around the kidneys, suet *Mil.*; *rús-kyi rṅog Lex.* w.e. — 2. *rṅog(-ma)* **the mane** of horses etc. (not of the lion, v. *ral-pa*), *rta-rṅóg* a horse's mane, *dre-rṅóg* a mule's mane; *dreu-rṅóg* a kind of stuffed seat or mattress *Cs.*, a thick-haired carpet *Sch.*; *rṅóg-čan, rṅóg-ldan* having a mane; *rṅogs-čágs* a beast that has a mane *Cs.*

རྔོད་པ་ *rṅód-pa* I. pf. *brṅos,* fut. *brṅod Cs.* (perh. erron. for *brṅo*) imp. *rṅod, rṅos, W. *ṅo-če** 1. **to parch** (barley), *ser tsam* (to parch a thing) so that it turns yellowish *Glr.* — 2. **to roast, to fry** e.g. meat in a pan.

II. **to deceive** (acc. to *Cs.* = *rṅón-pa* to deceive wild beasts, to hunt); **to seduce,** esp. to sensual indulgence, *bud-méd Lex.*; similarly *Tar.* 39, 2.

རྔོན་པ་ *rṅón-pa* 1. vb., pf. and fut. *brṅon*, **to hunt, pursue,** wild animals *Cs.*, *Sch.*; **to fish** *C.* — 2. sbst. a hunter, huntsman *Dzl.* and *Ler.*; *rṅón-pa-mo* a hunting woman, a huntress *Cs.*

རྔོབ་པ་ *rṅób-pa Ld.* **to be able,** v. *rṅó-ba*.

རྔམ་བརྗིད་ *rṅom-brjid* (cf. *rṅám-pa* 1) **splendour, stateliness, majesty;** *rṅóm-bag-čan*, also col. **ṅóm-jig-čan**, **grand, majestic;** terrible, of a judge, of terrifying deities. (A sbst. *rṅóm-bag* = *rṅom-brjid Cs.* prob. does not exist.)

ལྔ་ *lṅa* (*Bal.* '*ya*'), **five,** *lṅá-bču(-tam-pa)* fifty; *lṅa-brgya* five hundred; *lṅa-bču-rtsa-gčig* (*W.* **ṅa-bču-ṅa-čig**) or *ṅa-gčig*, fifty one etc.; *lṅá-pa* the fifth, *lṅa-po* consisting of five, cf. *dgu*; *lṅá-ga Cs.*, *lṅá-ka Pth.* all the five, each of the five. The number five very often occurs in legends, as well as in sacred science, v. the Index to *Burn.* II., and to *Fouc. Gyatch.* II. under '*Cinq*'. *lṅa-lén*, *Ssk.* पञ्चाल, n. of a country in the north of ancient India.

སྔ་ *sṅa* (पूर्व) a root signifying **before, soon, early,** rarely referring to space, and seldom used alone as adj. or adv., e.g. *Dzl.* ༢༣༥, 8: *ḥdá-ba ni há-čaṅ yaṅ sṅa čés-so* deliverance (sc. from existence) takes place much too soon; *ṅa ni tém-pa sṅa brgal yin* I was the foremost, the first, to cross the threshold *Glr.*; *bstán-pa sṅa dar bar dar pyi dar gsum* the first, intermediate, and last propagation of the doctrine *Glr.*; gen. it is used with an adjective termination, with postpositions, or in compounds.

Deriv. *sṅá-ba* 1. adj. **ancient,** belonging or referring to former **ages,** *rgya-nág-gi rgyál-po sṅá-ba* an ancient king of China *Glr.*; of an early date, long ago, . . . *las dá-lta sṅá-ba ḥdúg-gam* is it already a long time, since . . .? *Mil.*; 2. sbst. **antiquity,** the olden time; **the morning;** = *sṅá-dro*, *Mil.*; 3. vb. pf. *sṅas*, **to be the first, to come first, to be beforehand,** (φθάνειν): *rjé-yi sku mtoṅ ṅa sṅá-bas* as I was the first to see the king's face *Glr.*; *ḥgran-tsig sṅás-pa yin* you were beforehand with me in disputing *Glr.*; **ka ṅe son** *Sp.* you promised it. — *sṅá-bar* in former times, **formerly, in the morning;** *saṅ sṅá-bar* to-morrow morning *Glr.* — *sṅá-ma* adj. 1. **earlier, former, preceding, afore-said,** frq.; *sṅá-ma sṅá-ma* always the anterior in time and place; *sṅá-ma ltar*, or *bžin-du*, as before, frq. 2. **the first,** the foremost in a series or succession *Dzl.*; *ldáṅ-bai sṅá-ma* she who takes the first turn in getting up *Mil.* — *sṅá-mo* 1. **earlier, by-gone;** *sṅá-mo-nas* **long ago** *Mil.*; 2. *W.*: **the morning,** in the morning, **mā ṅá-mo** early in the morning, **tó-re ṅá-mo** to-morrow morning; also: **early enough,** in due time (opp. to **pi-mo**). — *sṅá-ru* v. *sṅar*, as a separate article. — *sṅá-na* **before, previously,** (gen. *sṅar* is used inst. of it). — *sṅá-nas* id., prop. of former times.

Comp. *sṅá-góṅ(-nas)* adv. **before, previously, at first,** a little while ago, **just now** *Mil.*; **formerly,** = late, deceased, *sṅa-góṅ yab* your late father *Glr.*; *sṅa góṅ bód-kyi rgyál-po* the earlier Tibetan kings *Glr.* — *sṅa-dgóṅs* morning and evening *Sch.* — *sṅa-sṅá* very early *Sch.* — *sṅa-čád* **formerly, hitherto,** till now, up to this time *Dzl.*, = *sṅan-čád*, *sṅon-čád*. — *sṅa-rtiṅ-du* **earlier** or **later,** not at the same time, e.g. *brós-so* they escaped *Glr.* — *sṅa-ltás* **omen, presage, prognostic;** also the fate or destiny portended. — *sṅa-tóg* 1. **forenoon.** 2. the **first-fruits** of harvest *Cs.* — *sṅa-dús* **antiquity, time of old.** — *sṅa-dro* **the morning,** the earlier part of the forenoon, 'the time before the heat of the sun'; *sṅá-dro gčig-la* in half a forenoon *Glr.*; *sṅá-dro dgóṅs-mo* morning and evening *Sch.* v. above; *saṅ sṅá-dro* to-morrow morning *Mil.* — *sṅa-pyi(r)* **sooner** or **later,** like *sṅa-rtiṅ-du* v. above *Dzl.* frq. — *sṅá-rol* **time of old, past ages** *Cs.*; *sṅá-rol-tu* before *Tar.* (cf. *sṅón-rol*). — **ṅá-lo** *W.* **last year.** — *sṅa sugs ḥdrén-pa Cs.*: 'the accenting of the first syllable'. — *sṅa-sár* **early,** *sṅa-sar-sár* very early *Cs.* — *sṅa-sór* 1. in the first place, first of all, **at first** (cf. *rtiṅ-sor*) *Glr.* 2. **anciently,** in old times *Cs.*

སྔ་སྔོ་ *ṅa-ṅó* **vegetables, greens** *Thgy.* (v. *ṅo*).

སྔག་པ་ *ṅág-pa*, also *ṅágs-pa*, pf. *bsṅags*, fut. *bsṅag*, imp. *ṅog*, **to praise, commend, extol; to recommend;** *ₒgró-bar ṅags* it is recommended to go *Wdṅ.*; *bstod-ṅág-pa* to praise, to sing praises, frq.; *ṅág-(pa-)po* a praiser, commender, *Cs.*; *ṅag-(par) ₔos(-pa)*, *ṅág-ldan* praiseworthy; praised; also n. of the horse of Buddha *Cs.* — *ṅag-ɣsól* **praise, thanks.**

སྔགས་ *ṅags* (मन्त्र, also धारणी & तन्त्र) 1. **incantation**, magical formula, a set of words, consisting mostly of a number of unmeaning Sanskrit syllables, in the recital of which however perfect accuracy is requisite; hence detailed rules and instructions for a correct pronunciation of the Sanskrit sounds have been drawn up for Tibetan devotees. (On magical formulas v. *Burn.* II., 21, and note; on Buddhist magic in general v. *Was.* 142. 177, *Köpp.* II., 29.) — *ɣzuṅs-ṅágs*, *rig-ṅágs*, and *ɣsaṅ-ṅágs* prob. = *ṅags*. — *ṅags sgrúb-pa*, *spél-ba*, *zlá-ba*, *C.* also **gyág-pa**, to recite, to pronounce charms, incantations; *ₒčáṅ-ba*, *ₒdzin-pa*, to carry (charms) about one's self. — *ṅágs-kyi ṫég-pa* Tantrayāna, Mantrayāna, v. *ṫég-pa*. — *ṅágs-pa*, *ṅágs-mḱan*, one versed in charms and their use, i.e. in orthodox and legitimate magic, as contained in the sacred books of religion. Opposed to this are *ṅan-ṅágs*, *ṅan-ṅags-mḱan*, diabolical sorcerers and necromancers, and also common swindlers, jugglers, conjurers, fortune-tellers etc. — 2. *praise, encomium Cs.*

སྔངས་ *ṅaṅs* = *dṅaṅs*, v. *dṅáṅ-ba Glr.*, *Pth.*

སྔན་ *ṅan*, for *ṅa*, *ṅon*, e.g. *ṅan-čád*, **formerly, before, previously, beforehand,** opp. to now *Mil.*; *ṅan-čád ṫó-ₒtsams-pa bzód-par ɣsol* pardon our former scoffing *Mil.*; esp. *W.*: **ṅán-la** for *ṅón-la*, *ṅar*, before, previously; **ṅán-ma** for *ṅá-ma*, **ṅán-mẹ gyál-po** the former or last king, **ṅán-ma náṅ-tar** just as before.

སྔན་བུ་ *ṅán-bu* a medicinal herb, *Wdṅ.*

སྔར་ *ṅar*, prop. *ṅá-ru*, **before, beforehand, previously, formerly, at first;** *ṅar de byás-pai ₔóg-tu* not until that has been previously done *Dzl.*; *ṅar méd-pa*, *ṅar ma byás-pa*, *ṅar ma skyés-pa* what has not existed, or has not been done before, where we only say **new**, frq.; *ṅar loṅs* get up first! *Dzl.*; *ṅár-bas kyaṅ(lhag-pár)* still more so than formerly, frq.; *ṅár-gyi* what has been hitherto in use, frq.; *ṅár-gyi yi-ge rnyiṅ-pa-rnams* the old writings of antiquity *Glr.*; *ṅar yin-na* adv. = *ṅar Mil.*; *ṅar ltar*, *ṅar bžin* as before; *ṅár-nas* from before, from former times *Mil.*; also with reference to space: foremost, ahead, in advance, on, onward, joined to verbs of motion *Dzl.*; *ṅár-ba* the former, first-mentioned (?). In the sense of a postposition (c. accus.) *ṅar* is used but seldom, as far as I know only in *spyan-ṅár*.

སྔར་མ་ *ṅár-ma* **intelligent,** quick of apprehension *Sch.*

སྔས་ *ṅas* **a bolster, pillow, cushion;** *yo-byád ṅás-su ₒjúg-pa Glr.*, *C.* col. **yo-ǰhẹ́-la ṅẹ čúg-pa** using the luggage as a pillow; *ṅas-stán*, *ṅas-ₒból*, resp. *dbu-ṅás* pillow; *rgyab-ṅás* a cushion for the back; *ṅas-mál* a couch constructed of pillows or cushions; *ṅas-ₒǰáns* (?) pillow, cushion *Cs.*; *W.* **nyẹ** for **ṅas**.

སྔས་པ་ *ṅás-pa* v. *ṅa-ba*.

སྔུན་ *ṅun*, col. for *ṅon*; *ṅún-la* c. genit. **before, ago,** like *góṅ-du*; **dá-wa nyís-si ṅún-la** two months ago; **ṅún-la soṅ** he walked in advance, or ahead; **ṅún-ma** former, last; **ṅún-ma-žag** *W.* two days before yesterday, **yan ṅún-žag** three days before yesterday.

སྔུར་བ་ *ṅúr-ba* **to snore** *Lex.* (cf. *ṅur-ba*).

སྔེའུ་ *ṅeu Lex.*, *Cs.*: a kind of pulse or pease; *Sch.* = *món-sran*, v. *greu*.

སྔོ་ *ṅo*, a root signifying **blue** or **green**; as sbst. **plant, herb, vegetable, greens** *Mil.*; *ṅo skyé-na* when it is getting green or verdant.

Comp. *ṅo-skyá* **blue bice, pale blue,** e.g.

the skin of emaciated persons *Med.*; **ṅo gyaṅ-gyáṅ** *W.* greenish-yellow (spelling dubious). — *sṅo-sgá* officinal herb, *Wdṅ.* (green ginger?) — *sṅo-ṅád* v. *ṅad.* — *sṅo-ljáṅ* **bluish green.** — *sṅo-tóg Schr.* 'unripe, sour, of fruits'(?); more corr.: green, unripe fruits. — *sṅo-drégs* green mud or mire *Sch.* — *sṅo-nág* **deep blue.** — *sṅó-ba* 1. vb. **to get green, verdant;** 2. adj., also *sṅó-bo*, more frq. *sṅón-po, sṅón-mo* **blue, green,** also used of the livid colour of diseased or famished people *Glr.* — *sṅo-smán* a medicinal herb. — *sṅo-ṫsód* **vegetables; herbs.** — *sṅo-ló* the leaf of a plant; *Cs.:* '*sṅo-ló ₒčár-ba* to become notorious'. — *sṅo-sáṅs* **pale blue** e.g. of the sky; *sṅo-sáṅs-ma* night *Sch.*

སྔོ་བ་ *sṅó-ba, Cs.* also *sṅód-pa*, pf. *bsṅos*, fut. *bsṅo*, imp. *sṅos*, 1. **to become green** *Cs.* — 2. (*Lex.* परिणाम?) **to bless,** **ṅó-wa gyáb-če** *W.*, though in most cases as a requital for a present given; *Dzl.* ༢་༣, 16: to bless, to pronounce a benediction, hence also in litanies the words of the priest seem to be indiscriminately called *sṅó-ba*, whereas the responses of the congregation of monks are termed *mṫun-ₒgyúr*; generally: **to dedicate, devote,** e.g. one's property to the *dkon-mčóg ɣsum*, i.e. in reality to the priesthood; *dgé-ba ₒgro-drug dón-du sṅos*, to devote alms, charitable gifts, to the (temporal and eternal) welfare of beings. *Mil.*; also **to design, to intend,** *ṅá-la bsṅós-pai ɣyu* the turkois intended for me (by you) *Mil.*; *Dzl.* ༧༢, 3: *sá-la ḱáṅ-bu daṅ rin-po-čér bsṅós-nas rtse-ba*, fancying the earth to consist of cottages and jewels, and thus playing with it.

སྔོག་པ་ *sṅóg-pa Lexx.*, prob. pf. *bsṅogs*, fut. *bsṅog*, imp. *sṅogs*, **to vex, to annoy**; cf. *skyo-ṅógs, skyo-sṅógs.*

སྔོན་ *sṅon = sṅa* and *sṅan*, **formerly, before, previously;** *sṅon ṫós-na* having formerly heard *Dzl.*; *sṅon máṅ-du ḱyer yaṅ* although you have taken a good deal with you before; *sṅon ₒdás-pai* or *byúṅ-bai dús-na* in by-gone times, frq.; *sṅon bčom-ldan-ₒdás* a former Buddha *Glr.*; *sṅon mi dbúl-po de* this man formerly poor *Dzl.*; *bdág-las sṅon bdág-gi ṗa* my father before me (has . . .); *sṅón-gyi* adj. former, last; *sṅón-ma* the former (when two persons or things are spoken of), *sṅón-ma-rnams* the former (persons or things) *Glr.*; **beginning,** *lha-ḱáṅ ǰig-pai sṅón-ma lhá-sa-la byás-te* making a beginning with the destruction of the temples in Lhasa *Glr.*; *sṅón-du* adv. and postp., **before,** at the head, in advance, in the front of, *sṅón-du ₒgró-ba* to go before or in advance, to precede, also of words and letters; *sṅón-du ₒjúg-pa* to put or place before, *Gram.*; *sṅón-la = sṅón-du: sṅón-la soṅ* walk first! *Mil.*; *stón-pai sṅón-du* (he died) before the Teacher (Buddha) *Tar.*; sooner, earlier, before the time supposed, *sṅón-la ṫsár-ro* they were first in finishing (their task) *Glr.*; *ₒo-ná sṅón-la ₒdi ṗul čig* oh yes, but first give me that *Mil.*; *sṅón-nas* from a former time, from the beginning *Mil.*; *sṅón-bžin* as formerly *Mil.*

Comp. *sṅon-skyés* **the first-born,** eldest son. — *sṅon-gró* v. *ₒgró-ba* compounds. — *sṅon-čál, sṅon-čád Dzl.*, v. *sṅan-čád.* — *sṅon-ₒjúg* **a prefixed letter** *Gram.* — *sṅon-dús, sṅon-ṫsé* **antiquity;** adv. **anciently,** in times of old. — *sṅon-byúṅ Cs. = sṅon-rábs.* — *sṅón-rábs* ancient race, ancient history, **antiquity,** पुराण. — *sṅón-rol* (cf. *sṅá-rol*) **former time** or **period,** *ma ɣtád-pai sṅón-rol žig-tu* formerly, in former times, when (the chair) was not yet transferred (to . . .) *Tar.* — *dus ná-niṅ sṅón-bai sṅón-rol-na* a year ago (an expression with an unnecessary redundancy of words!) *Mil.* — *sṅon-lás* **former actions.**

སྔོན་ *sṅon = sṅo, sṅón-po*, v. *sṅo.*

སྔོན་བུ་ *sṅón-bu* n. of a medicinal plant, acc. to *Cs.* poisonous; in *Lh.* Delphinium Cashmirianum, officinal. — *sṅon-bum* n. of a botanical work: 'the hundred thousand vegetables' *Cs.*

བརྔ་བ་ *brṅá-ba*, v. *rṅá-ba.*

བརྔད་པ་ *brṅád-pa Sch.:* 'ausziehen, ausreissen'.

བརྡན་པ་ brńán-pa, = rńán-pa sbst. *Glr.*, vb. *Lex.*

བརྡབ་པ་ brńáb-pa 1. *Sch.* = *brńád-pa.* — 2. *Lex.* = *rńáb-pa, rńams-pa.*

བསྡལ་བ་ *bsńál-ba* **to be faint** or exhausted *Cs.*; v. *sdug-bsńál.*

བསྡས་པ་ *bsńás-pa* to place upon a cushion *Sch.*

བསྔོ་བ་ *bsńó-ba* 1. v. *sńó-ba.* — 2. **a blessing,** cf. *sńó-ba.* — 3. *Cs.* also: **mouldy, rotten** (prob. only livid, discoloured, v. *sńo).*

ཙ

ཙ་ *ća* 1. the letter *ć*, tenuis, palatal, like the Italian ci in *ciascuno*, or c in *cicerone.* — 2. as numerical figure: 5. — 3. = *lća* **excrement,** alvine discharges, *ća ₒdór-ba* to discharge excrements *Mil.*

ཙ་ཅིར་ *ća-ćir* lark *Ld.*

ཙ་ཅུས་ *ća-ćús* **warped, distorted, awry** *Sch.*

ཙ་ཅོ་ *ća-ćó* **clamour, cries,** *snyiṅ tsim-gyi ća-ćo* shout, exclamation of joy *Pth.*; **noise,** of many people *Thgy.*; *da ćá-ćó ma zer* now do not make such a noise! (so *Mil.* rebukes the aërial spirits); **chirping, twitter** *Glr.*; *ćá-ćo-ćan* **shouting, bawling; talkative, loquacious** *Stg.*

ཙ་དར་ *ćá-dar,* also *ťsá-dar, tsá-sar,* **a sheet, blanket, toga.**

ཙ་ར་ར་ *ća-ra-rá,* or *ći-ri-ri, W.* **ćár-pa ća-ra-rá yoṅ dug**, it rains heavily, it is pouring.

ཙ་རི་ *ća-rí W.* **bug.**

ཙ་རེ་ *ća-ré* **continually, always** = *ćar.*

ཅག་ *ćag* termination of the plur. of pers. pronouns.

ཅག་ཀྲུམ་ *ćag-krúm* **cartilage, gristle;** *sna ćag-krúm* bridge of the nose.

ཅག་དཀར་ *ćag-dkár W.* **quartz.**

ཅག་ག་ *ćág-ga, C.* **ćág-ga ǰhé'-pa**, = *nyá-ra byéd-pa,* c. *la,* **to take care of;** **ćág-ga dág-po ǰhé'-pa** to look after, to keep, preserve carefully; **ćág-ga dág-po** careful, orderly, regular, tidy, of persons.

ཅག་ཅག་, ཅག་པ་ *ćag-ćág, ćág-pa* **smacking** in eating *Cs.*

ཅག་ཅེར་རེ་ *ćag-ćer-ré* closely pressed or crowded, in standing or sitting *Ld.*

ཅག་རྡོ་ *ćag-rdó* = *ćag-dkár W.*

ཅང་ *ćaṅ*, (v. *ćiaṅ, ći-yaṅ*), **every thing, any thing whatever,** *ćaṅ-śés* knowing every thing, epithet of deities or saints; more frq. followed by a negative particle and then signifying: **nothing;** **ćaṅ mi sto** it does not matter, it is indifferent (to me), frq.; **ćaṅ med** there is nothing here, or at hand; also = **ćaṅ mi sto; ćaṅ mi śés-ǩan** ignorant, stupid; blockhead, simpleton.

ཅང་ཏེའུ་ *ćaṅ-téu Glr.*, also *ćaṅ-ćaṅ-téu* (**डमरु**) a sort of **small drum** *Pth.*

ཅན་ *ćan,* affix, adjective termination, prop. signifying: **having, being provided with,** = *daṅ ldán-pa,* corresponding to the English adj. terminations -ous, -y, -ly, -ful, e.g. *ťsér-ma-ćan* thorny; sometimes also = -like or -ish: *bón-ćan* Bon-like, heretical *Mil.*, *hín-du-ćan* Hindoo-like, Hindooish; seldom affixed to verbs: *byéd-pa-ćan* a doer, maker; in *C.* also for the possessive pron.: *ṅá-ćan, kó-ćan,* my, his (her), **nag-góṅ sá-hib-ćęn** the Sahib's inkstand. It may also be affixed to a set of words that form one expression: *ťsér-ma nón-po-ćan* having sharp thorns, *séṅ-gei mgó-ćan* having a lion's head.

ཅན་ *ċan*, po., prop. *ċán-du*, postp. c. accus., **to, with,** *Koṅ ċán-du mi ˳gro* I do not go to him *Mil., Pth.; ṅa ċán-du* with me, in my presence *Mil.* The word seems to be rather obsolete; more recent editions having *gán-du* and *drúṅ-du* instead of it.

ཅན་ཅིལ་ *ċan-ċil* (?) *W.* the green shell of a walnut.

ཅན་ཅེ་, ཅན་ཅེར་, ཅན་ནེ་ *ċan-ċé, ċan-ċér, ċan-né, Sch.;* a small bowl or dish; *Cs.:* continually.

ཅན་དྲང་ *ċan-draṅ* **green, unripe** *W.* (?).

ཅན་ས་ *ċán-sa* (?) **kitchen, fire-place** *W.*

ཅབ་ཅོབ་ *ċab-ċob Cs.* **nonsense** e.g. *smrá-ba.*

ཅམ་ *ċam* 1. *Cs.* **slow**; *Lex. ċám-gyis ˳jog,* and several other passages, the sense of which is not quite clear; cf. *čam-mé.* — 2. **glistening, glittering** (?) cf. *lčam-mé.* — 3. *W.* **whole, unimpaired,** **sa** (*lit. rtsva*) **ċam-mé yod** the whole store of hay is still left (entire).

ཅམ་པ་ཏ་ལོ་ *ċám-pa-tá-lo Ts.* **mallow.**

ཅམ་པོད་ *ċam-pód Ld.* **a bunch** of flowers, sprigs etc., a handful of ears of corn.

ཅར་ *ċar* 1. *Lex. ċar-ré, Cs. ċa-ré, Sch.* also *ċar-már,* **always, continually** *Cs.* — 2. also *čar, čár-du,* with numerals, esp. *γċig-ċar* **at the same time, simultaneously,** opp. to one after the other, successively (viz. doing or suffering a thing, sleeping, dying etc.) *Dzl.*; **at once, on a sudden,** opp. to gradually *Mil.; lṅá-čar* all the five together *Thgy., γnyis-čar, drúg-čar* etc.

ཅར་རས་ *ċar-ras* v. *˳doms-ras.*

ཅལ་ *ċal Cs.:* '**noise,** *ċal-ċal* id.; *ċal-rgyúg* rumour, (false) report'; *ċal-ċól* idle talk, nonsense, *ċal-ċól γtam* id. *Mil.*

ཅས་ *ċas Pur.,* v. *ċes* 2.

ཅས་ཅུས་ *ċas-ċús Sch.* = *ċa-ċús.*

ཅི་ *ċi* num. figure: 35.

ཅི་ *ċi* I. interr. pron. in direct questions: 1. **what?** (*C.* gen. *gaṅ* instead of *ċi*) *ċi šes* (like the *Hind.* क्या जाने) who knows? col. *W.*; also pleon. at the end of a question after the . . . *am: ṅa ṅó-šes-sam ċi?* do you know me? do you? *Dzl.; ċii* of whom? whose? followed by *pyir, don, čed, slad* (*-du*): why? wherefore? inst. of *ċii pyir* also *ċi-pyir* etc.; *de ċii pyir žé-na* 'this wherefore? (= why this?) if so it is asked'. (This phrase, besides the gerundial particles — esp. *pas* — is the only way in which in *B.* the causal conjunction 'for' (*Lat. nam, enim*) can be expressed, and in translating into Tibetan, the English conjunction must therefore often be altogether omitted.) *ċii ˳brás-bu* what sort of fruit? *ċii ri* what kind of a mountain? i.e. of what consisting? *Pth.; ċi* also, like an adj., is placed after the word to which it belongs: *rgyu ċi-las* for what reason? on what account? *Thgy.* — 2. **why? wherefore?** but only in negative questions: *bdág-la des ċi ma čog* why should not that suffice me? *Thgy.; ċi mi sgrub* why do you not procure . . .? inst. of the imp. procure! *Mil.; bsám-na ċi ma legs* if you considered . . ., why would not that be a good thing? = you had better consider, you ought to consider *Mil.*; frq.: *de ˳byúṅ-na ċi ma ruṅ* if that happened, why should it not be desirable? = would that it happened! oh, may it happen! — 3. **how?** in conjunction with other words, v. below. — 4. inst. of a note of interrogation, e.g. in: *ċi γnaṅ,* for *γnáṅ-ṅam, γšégs-par ċi γnaṅ* do you allow(me) to come? *Dzl.* ཟི, 13; ཉེ, 5.

II. correlatively: **which, what; whatsoever; every thing,** much like *gaṅ,* q.v., esp. the syntactical explanations given there. *ċi,* as a correlative, ought prop. always to be written *ji,* yet not even in decidedly correlative sentences is this strictly observed: *ċi byed(-na-˳aṅ)* whatever I may do *Glr.; ċi bgyi bka nyan(-te) ṅéd-kyis bsgrub* whatever we may be bidden to do, we shall obediently perform *Pth.; ċi myur,* also *ċi myur žig-la Pth.* as quick as possible;

also c̀i alone: by all means, at all events, *spyan c̀i draṅs* he must be conducted here at all events *Glr.*

Comp. and deriv. *c̀i-ga* **what?** col. — *c̀i-dgar, c̀i dgá-bar* whatever one may wish, **at pleasure, ad libitum.** — *c̀i snyed* v. *snyed.* — **c̀i toṅ** (lit. *ɣtoṅ*) **žig** **some, something** col. — *c̀i lta-bu* **of what sort,** manner, fashion, quality or nature? *Lat. qualis.* — *c̀i ltar* **how?** in what manner? **what?** *da c̀i ltar bya, W.* **da c̀i c̀ó-c̀e**, what is now to be done? — *c̀i ltar gyúr-pai ɣtam byás-so* he related what had happened, frq. — *c̀i-ste,* followed by *na* or (rarely) *te,* in most cases = the *Lat. sin,* **but if,** if however; even supposed that; sometimes for *gál-te,* **if,** in case. — *c̀i sto* what does it matter? *śi yaṅ c̀i sto* if he dies, what does it matter? *Thgy.* (cf. *c̀aṅ*). — *c̀i-˳dra-ba* similar to what? of what kind? also: of whatever description it may be *Glr.* — *c̀i-nas* from which or what? out of which or what? by which? etc. (*Bal.:* **c̀i-ne** how?), *c̀i-nas kyaṅ* = *c̀is kyaṅ* q.v. — *c̀i tsam* **how much?** *B., W.; c̀i tsam yod kyaṅ* though he have ever so much *Mil.*; *c̀i tsám-du* how far? to what distance? — *c̀i-tsug Cs.,* col. **c̀i-zug, gá-zug** how? in what manner? — *c̀i žig* 1. **what? what a?** 2. **some one, any one, something, anything**; *c̀i žig-tu dgos* for what (purpose) is it wanted? *Dzl.*; *c̀i žig-na* once, one time, at any time *Pth.*; *c̀i žig-nas* after that, afterwards *Pth.* — *c̀i yaṅ, c̀i-aṅ, c̀aṅ* **whatever,** any thing, all kinds of things, **ṅul yȯ-na ťsóṅ-gyu c̀i yaṅ yȯ** *C.* if there is money, you may sell any thing; followed by a negative: **nothing.** — *c̀i rigs-pa* adj., *c̀i rigs-par* adv. 1. **in some measure,** to a certain degree; in part, partly *Tar.*; 2. **of every sort** *Dzl.* and elsewh. — *c̀i-la* **why? wherefore?** *Glr., W.* col.; also for the *de c̀ii pʼyir žé-na* of *B.*; further it is used inst. of an affirmative; e.g. question: shall we get rice there? answer: **ťob yin; c̀i-la mi ťob** of course, why not? **c̀i-la žu** **why! well!**

ཅི་ལིམ་ *c̀i-lim* (*Hind.* چلم) 1. the **bowl** of a hukka (water-pipe). — 2. a **hukka.**

ཅི་ཙེ་ *c̀i-tse Kun.,* also *tsé-tse,* **millet.**

ཅིག་ *c̀ig,* enclitic, a modification of *ɣc̀ig,* after *s* usually changed into *śig,* after vowels, and the liquids *ṅ, n, m, r, l* into *žig* (exceptions, however, in provincialisms and in literature are not unfrequent) 1. after nouns, the indefinite article **a,** or **a few,** when following after a plural; sometimes also untranslatable: *bud-méd-dag c̀ig* some women; *máṅ-po žig* many (sometimes expressly opp. to *máṅ-po, the* many, *Tar.* 7, 15); *gaṅ žig* v. *gaṅ;* **a little, some,** *śiṅ žig ˳ťú-ru ˳gro dgos* I must go and pick up some fire-wood *Mil.*; after infinitives: *Krims daṅ ˳gál-ba žig byéd-pa* to commit a trespass, to make one's self guilty of a transgression *Dzl.*; *ťse ˳pʼós-pa gráṅs-med-pa žig myaṅ* he suffered innumerable deaths *Dzl.*; it is even added to numerals, and not only when 'nearly', 'about' or similar words leave a given number undefined (*mi lṅa tsam žig* some five people), but also in sentences like the following: *c̀ú-mig bži žig yod* there are four springs or fountains. In all these cases, however, it may also be omitted. The numeral for 'one' ought always to be written *ɣc̀ig* and never *c̀ig,* but prefixing the *ɣ* is so often neglected (e.g. in *ťabs c̀ig-tu, lhan c̀ig* etc.) that even grammarians let it pass. — 2. when affixed to verbs (to the root of the imp. mood, or, in negative sentences, to the root of the present tense) it is a sign of the imperative. In ancient literature it is used without reference to rank, whether it be in making prayers to Buddha, or in giving orders to a servant; at present in *C.* only in the latter way; in *W.* it is of rare occurrence.

ཅིང་, ཤིང་, ཞིང་ *c̀iṅ, śiṅ, žiṅ,* a gerundial particle, the initial letter of which is changed acc. to the rules obtaining for *c̀ig*; it corresponds to the English participle in **ing,** is used in sentences beginning with **when, after, as,** and is affixed to verbal roots and adjectives, in the latter case including the auxiliary verb to be: *ɣsón-por dúr-du bc̀úg-c̀iṅ bui śa zá-bar* *gyúr-ċig* (= *bċúg-nas*, or *bċúg-ste*) may I, after having been buried alive, be obliged to eat my own son's flesh! *Dzl.*; usually however employed in the minor clauses of accessory sentences: *brós-šiṅ gáb-pas* having hid themselves after running away *Dzl.*; frq. also where coordinate ideas are in English connected by **and** or **but:** *šá-la zá-žiṅ ḱrág-la ˳ṫúṅ-ba* eating flesh and drinking blood; *čé-žiṅ légs-pa* tall and well-shaped; *drod ɣnód-ċiṅ bsil-ba ṗan* heat is hurtful (but), cold is beneficial *Lt.* It is also used like the ablative of the gerund in Latin: *nya bšór-žiṅ ˳ṫsó-o* we live by fishing (piscando) *Dzl.*; and = *kyin* (q.v.): *ri-la draṅ-sroṅ byéd-ċiṅ ˳dúg-go* he sits on the mountain acting the part of an anchorite *Dzl.*; *smre-sṅágs ˳dón-ċiṅ ˳dug* he sits wailing *Dzl.*; *raṅ-dgár ˳gró-žiṅ ɣda* he is wandering at pleasure *Mil.*; *ċes smrá-žiṅ yód-pa-la* as they were thus speaking *Glr.*; *čos stón-ċiṅ yód-pai ṫse* as he was just giving religious instruction *Tar.* 11, 12.

ཅིའུ་རི་ *ċiu-ri* n. of a female demon *Thgr.*

ཅིར་, ཅི་རུ་ *ċir, ċi-ru*, termin. of *ċi*, 1. **whereto** etc., little used. — 2. with *yaṅ:* **everywhere**, in every direction, for any purpose, by all means, with a negative: **nowhere** (so at least it is to be explained in several passages of *Pth.* and *Thgy.*).

ཅིས་ *ċis*, instr. of *ċi*, *ċis yid-čes-par ˳gyur* **by what** am I to believe it? what shall make me believe it? **whereby** can I know it to be true? *Dzl.*; *ċis kyaṅ mi skrág-pa yin* he is not to be frightened by any thing *Dzl.*; *ċis kyaṅ*, and *ċi-nas kyaṅ* frq. used as adv.; **by all means,** at all events, at any rate, *ċis kyaṅ ˳gró-na* if you wish to go by all means, at all hazards; *da ċis kyaṅ gegs byao* now I will at any rate play him a trick *Dzl.*; *ċis kyaṅ bžes-pa žu* I beg of you most earnestly to accept it *Mil.*; *ċis kyaṅ slobs* **never mind!** teach it me at any rate! *Pth.*

ཅུ་ *ċu* 1. num. figure: 65. — 2. inst. of *bċu*, used in compound numerals for the tens, when the preceding numeral ends with a consonant: *sum-ċu, drug-ċu, bdun-ċu, brgyad-ċu.*

ཅུ་གང་ *ċu-gaṅ Med., Cs.:* 'a sort of lime used for medicine'.

ཅུ་ཏི་ *ċu-ti* (*?yċu-ti*) **pig-tail, cue,** worn by boys and men in Tibet proper, *Ld.* and *Sp.* Cf. *ċo-to.*

ཅུ་ལི་, ཅོ་ལི་ *ċu-li, ċo-li* 1. *W.* **a fresh apricot.** — 2. *C.* **dried apricots** without stones. — 3. a sort of wild-growing vegetable *Sik., C.* — *ċu-li ta-gir* the pulp of apricots boiled down to a conserve and formed into cakes *W.* — *bun-ċu-li* a kind **of peach** *Kun.*

ཅུག་ཅུག་ *ċug-ċúg* = *ċag-ċág Sch.*

ཅུང་ *ċuṅ* 1. *C.* **gourd, pumpkin.** — 2. n. of a place. — 3. for *ċuṅ žig: da ḱyod ċuṅ ˳pyis-pa yin* you are **a little** too late now *Pth.*; *ċuṅ yó-ba* a little slanting *Glr.*

ཅུང་ཞིག, ཅུང་ཟད, ཆུང་ཟད་ *ċúṅ-žig, ċúṅ-zad, čúṅ-zad*, **a little,** *B.* and *C.*, *mú-ge ċúṅ-zad ċig* a partial famine *Mil.*; *ċúṅ-zad-kyi ṗyir* for the sake of a trifle, through an insignificant circumstance *Dzl.* ༢༢༥, 15; **some,** *Lat. non-nulla*, of rare occurrence, *Was.* (242); *ċuṅ žig skyéṅ-bar gyúr-nas* rather ashamed, somewhat confounded *Glr.*; *ċúṅ-žig ṗán-nam blta* I shall see, whether it will help, or has helped, a little *Mil.*; **a little while,** a short space of time, *ċúṅ-zad ċig sdod ċig* wait a little (while) *Dzl.* When followed by a negative, it may either be translated as in: *ċúṅ-zad ma bdé-ba* **a** little unwell, uneasy etc. *Mil.*, or as in: *dbaṅ ċúṅ-zad med*, there is not even a slight possibility = there is no possibility **at** all *Pth.* and elsewh.

ཅུང་ཞོ་ *ċúṅ-žo*, also *ċúṅ-žu, ċuṅ-ži, yċoṅ-ži*, a kind of white stone.

ཅུབ་ *ċub W.*, from the *Hind.* चुप, **ċub ċád-de dug** he keeps silence, holds his peace.

ཅུར་ *ċur*, in *ċur mid-pa* **to devour** food **entire** *Sch.*

ཅུར་ནི་ *ċúr-ni* **meal, flour,** only in medical writings.

ཅེ་ *ċe* numer. figure: 95.

ཅེ་ན, ཤེ་ན, ཞེ་ན *ċé-na, śé-na, žé-na* (cf. *ċig*), inst. of *ċes smrá-na*, **'if one says so, asks so'** etc., after words literally quoted, frq. (*W.* **zér-na**).

ཅེ་སྤྱང་ *ċe-spyáṅ* **jackal.**

ཅེ་རེ, ཅེར་རེ་ *ċe-ré, ċer-ré* **envious, jealous,** *mig ċe-ré* (*ċér-gyis Thgr., ċér-te Glr.*) *ltá-ba* to look with an evil or envious eye upon; *ċe-ré lóṅ-ba* dim-sighted, purblind *Cs.*

ཅེམ་མེ་བ་ *ċém-me-ba* **bright, shining,** of polished metal *Glr.*, cf. *krá-bo*.

ཅེམ་ཙེ་ *ċém-tse* **scissors** *C.*

ཅེའུ་ *ċeu* 1. a small **sucking-pipe** for drinking the Murva-beer, in which millet grains are swimming *Sik.* (v. *Hook.* I., 175). — 2. **a clyster-pipe.**

ཅེར་ *ċer*, v. *ċe-ré*.

ཅེས་ *ċes* 1. (*Lex.* इति), also *śes* and *žes* (cf. *ċig*) **so, thus,** in ancient literature regularly placed after words or thoughts that are literally quoted, and so continuing the sentence; the quotation itself is gen. preceded by *ₒdi skád-du*, or *ₒdi snyám-du*. In later literature *ċes* and the introductory words are often omitted, in col. language always. Inst. of *ċes smrás-so, ċes ysúṅs-so*, so he said, thus he spoke, so has been said or spoken, so it is said, often only *ċés-so* is used, and in like manner *ċés-pa* for *ċes smrás-pa*, this word, this speech; *ċés-pa-la sogs-pa* these and similar words; *ċés-pa ₒdi yaṅ* also the preceding poem (is written by him); *snyun žés-pa nád-kyi miṅ yin* the word *snyun* is a term for 'disease' *Zam.*; *žés(-pa) daṅ* 'such, and', if a quotation is followed by another, where we say 'further', 'moreover'; *ċés-pa-la* after words have been quoted, which form the subject of further discussion; *ċes byá-ba*, or *ċés-pa* the so called, frq. after names; *ċés-su* rarely for *ċes*. — 2. acc. to the usual spelling and pronunciation (*ċes, ċe*) of the Lamas of *Ld.* it is the ordinary termination of the infinitive in *W.* (in *Pur.* and *Bal.* *ċas*, in *Kun.* *ċā*), though etymologically as yet not accounted for; sometimes used also as a sbst. or adj. i.e. partic.: *bsád-ċes* killing, *bsád-ċes yin* it is to be killed; *skyé-ċes* pregnant, v. *skyé-ba*.

ཅོ་ *ċo* 1. num. fig.: 125. — 2. *ċo-ₒdri-ba* *Lex., C.*, **to blame, reproach, slight; to vie with.**

ཅོ་ག, ལྕོ་ག་ *ċó-ga, lċó-ga Mil.* **lark** (not common in Tibet).

ཅོ་གེར་ *ċó-ger*(?), *ċó-ger bžugs Glr., W.* vulgo: **ċó-gun dug** he sits **motionless.**

ཅོ་ཏོ་ *ċó-to*, also *ċó-ti, Cs.*: **a tuft of hair** on the head, thus *Lex.*: *ċó-toi tor-ċóg* (= *ċú-ti?*); cf. *lċaṅ-lo*.

ཅོ་རི་ *ċó-ri* = *ċor*, *č̌áṅ ċo-ri Lex.*(?).

ཅོ་ལི་ *ċó-li* = *ċu-li*.

ཅོ་ལོ་ *ċó-lo* **the prattling** or **chattering** of little children *Mil.*; cf. *ċá-ċo*.

ཅོག་ *ċog Cs.*: a plural-sign; *Schr.* all (people). This, or a similar original meaning of the word is also to be traced in an expression usual in *Ld.*: *ċóg-mdo* a place where three roads meet, v. *mdo*; cf. also *ċag*. When affixed to a word, it must be preceded by the vowel *o*, the final consonant of the root being at the same time repeated. Affixed to verbs, it seems to convert them into participles: *ₒóṅs-so-ċog-la Dzl.* ༢༥, 6, to those arrived, to the (persons) arrived, *yin-no-ċog, yód-do-ċog* those being, existing (things or persons); *Cs.*: *yċés-so-ċog* things that are valuable, precious, to a man.

ཅོག་ཅོག་པ་ *ċóg-ċog-pa W.* **grasshopper, cricket.**

ཅོག་པ་ *ċóg-pa C.* **to have leisure** *ċóg-na yoṅ go* if you have leisure, come! **ċóg-ka** **leisure,** **dhe-riṅ ċóg-ka me** to-day I have no leisure; **ċóg-ka ǰhé** is an affirmative answer, when having been asked for some little service, something like: well, I'll do it.

ཅོག་བུ་ ċóg-bu a sort of **small tent** *Cs.*

ཅོག་ཙེ་ *ċóg-tse*, v. *lċog-tse.*

ཅོག་ལ་མ་ *ċóg-la-ma* a mineral (?) *Med.*

ཅོང་ *ċoṅ* 1. *Lex.* a musical instrument, *Schr.*: a bell. — 2. *Mil: ċoṅ-la skyur-ba* to push one down a precipice in order to kill him (the only meaning the context here will admit); cf. *tson-dóṅ.* — 3. v. *γċoṅ.*

ཅོང་ཅི་ *ċóṅ-ċi* a small **bowl** or **dish** *Sch.*; v. *ċan-ċe.*

ཅོང་ཅོང་ *ċoṅ-ċóṅ* **jagged, indented, serrated.**

ཅོང་མོ་ *ċóṅ-mo*, col. for *lċúṅ-mo.*

ཅོང་བ་ *ċóṅ-ba*, *Pth.*: *ṅu-ₒbód ċóṅ-ba* acc. to the context: to raise loud lamentations, wailings (at funerals); perh. etymologically connected with *čo-ṅés.* Cf. *γċóṅ-skad.*

ཅོང་ཞི་ *ċóṅ-ži* = *ċúṅ-žo.*

ཅོང་རོང་ *ċoṅ-róṅ*, perh. = *ċoṅ-ċóṅ*, *Mil. ċoṅ-róṅ tsér-ma.*

ཅོད་པན་ *ċod-pán*, मुकुट, ornament for the head, worn by kings, **tiara, diadem, crown**; **the crest** of gallinaceous birds.

ཅོབ་དར་ *ċób-dár Ld.-Glr.*, *Schl.* p. 29, a (?).

ཅོར་གང་, ཅོར་ཅིག་ *ċor-gáṅ*, *ċór-ċig* **a mouthful, a gulp, a little** *Sch.*; cf. *ċo-ré.*

ཅོལ་ཆུང་ *ċol-čúṅ Thgy.* childish **prattle** or **babbling.**

གཅགས་པ་ *γċágs-pa* 1. **to apprehend, to grasp** (with the understanding), **to impress**, gen. with *yid-la*, on the mind, e.g. the doctrine *Dzl.*; also *bka nan-γċágs čén-po γnáṅ-ba* to give a thoroughly solid, impressive instruction; *γċágs-po byéd-pa* = *γċágs-pa*; with additional force: **do ċág-po ǰhé-pa** *C.* to impress (to one's mind) as firm as a rock. — 2. relative to persons it is synon. to *čágs-pa* **to love.**

གཅང་པོ་ *γċáṅ-po*, *W.* **šáṅ-po** **clever; lively, sprightly;** *W.* also **attentive to, regardful of;** *γċáṅ-po drúṅ-po* clever and sagacious *Mil.*, *γċaṅ-drúṅ ldán-pa* id. *Pth.*; hence also *γċaṅ* sbst. **sagacity, cleverness;** *ka-γċáṅ* clever words, clever speech *Cs.*; cf. also *ka-sbyáṅ*; *W.*: **šaṅ ċó-ċe** **to watch** for; to keep **guard**, to watch; **šaṅ-rig ċó-ċe** to be very attentive, to listen with fixed attention, **šáṅ-rig-ċan**, *C.* **ċáṅ-rig-ċen** very attentive; *W.*: **šaṅ skúl-ċe** 1. to exhort, admonish 2. to wake, to rouse from sleep; **čós-si šaṅ-skúl táṅ-ċe** to give religious exhortations, to hold parenetic lectures.

གཅད་པ་ *γċád-pa*, v. *γċód-pa.*

གཅན་(ག)ཟན་ *γċan-(γ)zán* frq. beast of prey, *Lat. fera*, but more in a systematic sense, so that the cat, and even the dog may be included; *Glr.* po. *γċan-(γ)zán tá-ma* 'the last of the beasts of prey', the cat.

གཅམ་བུ་ *γċám-bu Cs.* **humbleness, servility, flattery**, *Sch.* also **untruth, lie**; *γċám-bui ṅag*, or *tsig* a servile speech; *γċám-bu smrá-ba* to speak submissively *Stg.* (not much used).

གཅར་བ་ *γċár-ba* 1. *Sch.*: **cut out, put out, knocked out**, e.g. *mig* an eye (cf. *bċar-ba.* — 2. *Mil.?*

གཅལ་བ་ *γċál-ba*, *γċál-du bkrám-pa* **to spread, display, lay out** e.g. precious stones, jewels, on a table, on the ground, *Glr.*, also *Lex.*

གཅི་བ་ *γċi-ba* 1. vb. v. *γċid-pa.* — 2. sbst. = *γċin*; *bšaṅ γċi* both kinds of alvine discharges. *Dzl.*

གཅིག་ *γċig*, num. **one**; *γċig kyaṅ* even but one; **one and the same**, *dus γċig-tu* at the same time (whereas *dus ċig-na* once, one day, which however is also written *dus γċig-na*); *γċig byéd-pa* to unite (vb. n.), to join (in an act), to act in concert; sole, alone; **dear**, beloved, *yab γċig* dear father! *Glr.*: *šin-tu γdúṅ-bai ma γċig* my own (only) beloved mother! somebody, some one *Dzl.*, *γċig ... γċig* the one — the other, somebody or other, very frq.; *γċig-gis γċig*, *γċig-la γċig* etc. one another, each other frq.; *mi-γċig C.* **differing, different.**

Comp. and deriv. *γčig-ka* **single, only,** opp. to several, *Mil.* — *γčig-čar, γčig-čar* v. *čar.* — *γčig-čig*, pronounced **čig-čig**, **a certain, some one,** εἷς τις, *slób-ma-las γčig-čig Dzl.; bud-méd γčig-čig Dzl.* ༣༥༤, 5 (where *Sch.* has *čig-γčig* erron.); *γčig-γčig*, pronounced **čig-čig**, 1. **one at a time; separately, alone,** esp. *W.*; 2. **of the same kind, not different** *W.* (v. *Fouc. Gram.* p. 21. 42), 3. adv. **by one's self, only, solely** *W.* — *γčig-čóg* **all-sufficient** *Glr.* — *γčig-nyid Cs.* 'unity'(?) — *γčig-tu* 1. **into one,** into one body, **together,** *γčig-tu sdú-ba* to unite e.g. six countries, *Dzl.*; to contract, to simplify *C.* 2. at once, wholly, altogether *Dzl.* ༣༣, 3; 3. firstly, in the first place, *γčig-tu-ni*; then follows *γnyis-su-ni* etc. *Dzl.* 4. only, solely *Thgy.* — *γčig-dú* unity and plurality, *γčig-du-brál* not having these two qualities *Was.* (308). *γčig-pa* 1. **the first** *Wdn.* (little used). 2. **having** etc. **one,** cf. *dgu.* 3. **of one kind,** not different or manifold, *mi-γčig-pa* different *B.* and *C.* — *γčig-pu* (also *γčig-bu?*) **alone, single,** *γčig-pus mi stoṅ fúb-pa* to be able to cope alone with a thousand men *Dzl.; γčig-pur lus-pa* to remain alone behind *Glr.*; **only, sole,** *bu γčig-pu* the only son, frq. — *γčig-po* 1. **alone,** *rgyál-po γčig-po skyés-pa yin* the king alone is a man, *Dzl.* 2. **being one,** or the one, *ma γnyis-la skyés-pai bu γčig-po* thou (being the) one son of two mothers, viz. claimed by two, *Glr.* 3. *Pur.* **the one — the other.** — *γčig-śós* **the other,** when speaking of two.

གཅིད་པ་ *γčid-pa*, also *γči-ba*, pf. *γčis*, fut. *γči*, imp. *γčis*, to make water, to piss.

གཅིན་ *γčin* **urine,** *γčin γčid-pa*, or *γči-ba*, *W. táṅ-če*, to make water; *γčin śor* urine is discharged involuntarily; *γčin-rkyág*, both discharges, vulg.; *γčin-ₒgág* the retention of urine *Med.*; *γčin-snyí* gonorrhoea, clap(?) *Med.*

གཅིའུ་ *γčiu* 1. clyster-pipe = *čeu*; *γči-ui sman* clyster *Lex.* — 2. *clyster*(?) *Cs.*

གཅིལ་བ་ *γčil-ba* **to spoil, to destroy** *Sch.*

གཅུ་བ་, ལྕུ་བ་ *γčú-ba, lčú-ba*, v. *γčúd-pa; γču* or *lču-ₒkór Cs.*, *γču-skór W.*, *γčús-bu Ts.*, **screw.** — *γčú-ti* v. *ču-ti.* — *γču-dóṅ* screw-box *Cs.*

གཅུ་གལ་ *γču-gál* **importance,** *Cs.*

གཅུགས་པ་ *γčúgs-pa*, prob. not different from *γčágs-pa.* The word occurs in: *yid(-la) γčugs(-pa)* beloved, a friend *Dzl.*; *mdza-γčúgs byéd-pa* to treat amicably *Wdn.; kon-γčúgs* having conceived a hatred *Lex.*

གཅུང་པོ་ *γčúṅ-po*, resp. **a younger brother.**

གཅུད་ *γčud? γčud-(la) ₒbór(-ba) Lex.* w.e.; *Sch.*: **to forsake, to cast out, to reject;** (cog. to *čud-zán?*)

གཅུད་, ལྕུད་པ་ *γčúd-pa, lčúd-pa*, pf. *γčus, lčus*, fut. *γču, lču*, imp. *γčus*(?) **to turn,** turn round, **twist, twine, plait, braid;** **čud log táṅ-če* W.* to untwist, untwine a rope; **čus zum táṅ-te nol dug* W.* they wrestle and scuffle (prop. they fight scuffling); **sen čus gyáb-če* W.* to press and bore with the knuckle; **čús-spu** a low expression for the hair; *lág-pa γčus Zam.?*

གཅུན་པ་ *γčún-pa*, secondary form of *ₒjún-pa, Lex.*: *rtsád-nas γčún-pa*, prob. **to subdue** completely; *γčúr-žiṅ γčún-pa* prob. to beat or press a thing until it is soft.

གཅུར་བ་ *γčúr-ba*, secondary form of *ₒjur-ba*; *γčúr-pe Ld.* a coarse sort of **vermicelli.**

གཅེ་བ་ *γčé-ba* **to esteem, to hold dear, to love** *Sch.*

གཅེན་ *γčen* (*Cs. γčén-po*) resp. *Cs.*: one's **elder brother** *Dzl.* ༡༡༦, 11; acc. to *Zam.*: first-born son.

གཅེར་བ་ *γčér-ba* v. *bčér-ba.*

གཅེར་བུ་ *γčér-bu* **naked,** col., also *Mil.; γčer-nyál* id.; *Kun.*: **čer-góf**; resp. *sku γčér-bu; γčér-bu-rnams ₒgábs-par byéd-pa yin-pa* being one that covers the naked *Stg.*; *γčér-bur ₒbyin-pa* to make naked, to strip *Pth.*; *γčér-bu byúṅ-ba, W. *čer-nyál fón-če** to show one's self naked; *γčér-*

bu-pa, γčér-nyal-mk'an Mil. (*Ssk. nirgrantha* a naked man, gymnosophist; *čós-sku γčer mtóṅ-du gról-bas* having been delivered so far as to see the *čós-sku* (v. *sku*) unveiled *Glr.*

གཅེས་པ་ *γčés-pa* (*Lh.* **šé-pa-**) **dear, beloved,** ... *ltar γčés-na yaṅ* although he is to me as dear as ... *Glr.*; *ṅéd-kyi mi γčés-pa* a man dear to us, our beloved, our darling *Mil.*; *γčés-ma* a favourite, sweetheart *Cs.*; *γčes-p'rúg* dear child *Mil.*; **excellent, precious, valuable,** *šín-tu γčes-pai lṅa* the five important letters (viz. the prefixed letters) *Glr.*; *šés-pa γčes* it is of importance to know *Med.*; often as superlative: *ˏjig rtén ˏdi-na γčés-pa raṅ-srog yin* the dearest thing in the world is one's own life *Pth.*; *γčés-par byéd-pa Stg.*, *ˏdzín-pa Glr.* c. accus, *W.*: **šé-pa čó-če** gen. with the dat., to hold dear, to love, to esteem, persons or things, but not applicable to the deeper affections of the heart. — *γčes-bsdús Lex.* w.e.; *γčes-btús Cs.* choice pieces (out of books).

གཅོག་པ་ *γčóg-pa*, pf. *bčag*, imp. *čog(s)*, *W.* **čág-če**, imp. **čog** trs. to *ˏčág-pa*, **to break,** *dúm-bur* to pieces; **to break off,** or **asunder; to smash,** a glass; **to crack,** nuts; **to burst; split, blast,** a gun, a rock; fig.: **to break, to violate,** a promise, a vow, a law etc. frq., *yáb-kyi bka bčág-tu med* the word of my father may not be violated (by me) *Glr.*

གཅོང་, གཅོང་ནད་ *γčoṅ, γčoṅ-nád*, **consumption, phthisis,** *γčoṅ-čén dmú-ču* prob. dropsy in the chest or in the pericardium *Med.*; gen. any **chronic disease** **čoṅ-la ṭsu' ma soṅ-ṅam** *C.* it has not taken a chronic turn, has it? also fig.: **sem čóṅ-po dug** *C.* the heart is sick, afflicted.

གཅོང་སྐད་ *γčóṅ-skad Lex., Sch.*: **lamentations, wailings, plaintive voices,** cf. *γčóṅ-ba.*

གཅོང་བ་ *γčóṅ-ba* 1. pf. *bšoṅs*, **to excavate, wash out, undermine** through the action of water, *túr-du γčoṅ-bar mi gyúr-ro* they are not undermined (by the water) *Stg.*; *γčoṅ-roṅ* a narrow passage, a defilé *Cs.* — 2. from *γčoṅ*, **to get faint, languid, wearied** in mind, *C.*

གཅོང་ཞི་ *γčoṅ-ži*, v. *čoṅ-ži.*

གཅོད་པ་ *γčód-pa*, pf. *bčad*, fut. *γčad*, imp. *čod*, *W.* **čád-če**, imp. **čod** 1. **to cut,** ; *čád-bya γčód-pa secanda secare Gram.*; **to cut asunder,** *k'am-ṭsad-du* into small bits; **to cut off, chop off,** the hands; **to cut down, to fell,** trees; **to cut out,** the tongue *Dzl.*; **to rend asunder, to break,** a thread, a rope, chains, fetters. — 2. **to cut off** fig.: *ču*, the water, by damming it out, frq.; **to reduce,** the wages; **to cure,** a disease; **to suppress,** a passion; **to discontinue, to give up,** *zan, zas*, eating i.e. to abstain from food, to fast; *srog*, to kill, to murder, frq.; **to stop** a thing in its origin, **to obviate, prevent, avert; to avoid; to lock,** the door, frq.; ... *kyi*, or *la, bár-du γčód-pa* to throw obstacles in a person's way, to hinder, impede, frq.; *sróg-la bár-du γčód-pa dé-dag* all these life-endangering beings *Glr.*; (for more examples refer to *bar*); **to stop,** to make a pause, in reading, *šad yoṅ-na drág-por bčád-pa* making a marked stop, when there is a *shad*, *Gram.*; *rnam(-par) γčód(-pa)*, or *bčad(-pa)*, section, paragraph; stop, pause; *yoṅs-γčód* id. *Gram.*; **to decide,** *čes bčád-do* thus he decided *Dzl.*; *k'rims*, or (*Dzl.*) *žal-čé*, to pass sentence or judgment; to judge, condemn, cf. also *ṭ'ág-γčod-pa.* — 3. **to cross** (little used), *čú-bo gru-yis* a river in a boat *Glr.* — 4. *rjes γčód-pa* **to follow** the track, used both of men and dogs; **már-dzi** (to follow) the smell of butter (viz. of roast-meat), **kyúr-dzi čö'-pa** *C.* to follow the sourish smell (viz. the smell of beer); *(γ)sár-* (also *ṭsar Pth.*) *γčod-pa* to search into, to investigate, to examine or study thoroughly *Ld.-Glr. Schl.* p. 20, b. — *čád-pas γčód-pa* and other phrases v. under the respective noun. — **čö'-taṅ** *C.* **the Tibetan rupee,** having lines (*radii*) of division marked, by which they may be cut into smaller pieces. — Note: In some phrases the spelling of *ycód-pa* and the assonant verbs *spyód-pa* and *dpyód-pa* is variable.

གཅོམ་, བཅོམ་ *ycom*, *bcom*, **pride, haughtiness, arrogance**, *bskyúṅ-ba* to put it off, give it up *Lexx.*; *bcom čuṅ-ṅus Tar.* 20, 6 despondingly, low-spirited; *gros-ycóm Lex.* obs. or prov. for *gros-bcám*, v. *₀čám-pa.*

གཅོར་བ་ *ycór-ba* **to spread, scatter, disperse** *Cs.*

བཅག་པ་ *bcág-pa* v. *ycóg-pa* and *₀čág-pa.*

བཅང་ *bcaṅ? Sch.:* '*bcaṅ-rgya-čén-po* comprising much, comprehensive, very extensive; *bcaṅ-rgyár mdzad-pa* resp. to apply one's self, to bestow pains upon'.

བཅད་ཀ་ *bcád-ka W.* a whole that has been cut into, or a piece cut off.

བཅད་པོ་ *bcád-po W.* something **old, torn, worn out.**

བཅབ་པ་ *bcáb-pa* v. *₀čab-pa.*

བཅམ་བཅོམ་ *bcam-bcóm Sch.:* trivial things, medley, hodge-podge.

བཅའ་སྒ་ *bcá-sga* v. *sga.*

བཅའ་བ་ *bcá-ba* 1. v. *čá-ba.* — 2. sbst. drinking; gen. used connected with *bza-ba; bcá-ba daṅ bzá-ba*, or *bza-bca* food and drink.

བཅའ་འཕྲང་ *bca-₀pràṅ Mil.*, declivity, precipice *Sch.*

བཅའ་མག་ *bca-mág*, the usual pronunciation of *lcags-mag.*

བཅར་བ་ *bcár-ba* 1. = *bcír-ba* **to squeeze, to press** in a press *Thgy.*; **to crowd, to throng**, **yár-la bcar** *C.*, stand (or sit) more closely together! — 2. **to pull** or **force from, to wrest** *Cs.* — 3. *Lexx.: mig bcár-ba* the same as in *ycar-mig* (?). — 4. *Sch.: logs bcár-ba* to prop sideways. — 5. *Sch.: bcar bžúgs-pa* to have a permanent residence (this would however be more correctly expressed by *car*). — 6. *bcár-bai rta-bcibs*, and *lan-bcár? Lexx.* w.e.

བཅལ་བ་ *bcál-ba* v. *₀jál-ba.*

བཅས་པ་ *bcás-pa* 1. originally pf. of *₀čá-ba*, little used. — 2. adj. **together with, connected with, having, possessing, containing** a thing, with *daṅ* or termin. (the latter in prose only when a second *daṅ*, signifying 'and', occurs in the sentence); gerundially: *bcás-te*, sometimes also *bcás-pas* or *bcás-šiṅ*; adverbially: *bcás-su* frq.; *₀kor daṅ bcás-pa* (*-te, -su*) with attendance, with a retinue or suite, frq.; *bu-mo bcu bod-blón daṅ bcás-pas skór-te* surrounded by ten virgins together with the Tibetan ambassadors *Glr.*; *btsún-mo daṅ srás-su bcás-te* with (his) wife and son *Glr.*; *gos daṅ bcás-su* (to go into the water) having one's clothes on *Dzl.*; *žal ₀dzúm-pa daṅ bcás-te* with a smiling face *Glr.*; *sér-sna daṅ bcás-pa* infected with, subject to, avarice; without *daṅ* or termin. (esp. po.); *₀krúl-bcas* infatuated, fascinated *Pth.*; *₀bru-táṅ tun bcas* together with a small parcel of Dutan tea; it is also, like *rnams*, a collective sign, used in enumerations, referring to several nouns, *Wdṅ.*, or like *la-sógs-pa* and other (things), and more (such things), and the like: *rgyags daṅ bcas bskyál-lo* provisions and other necessaries we shall supply *Mil.*

བཅིང་བ་ *bciṅ-ba*, fut. of *₀čiṅ-ba* **to bind.**

བཅིངས་པ་ *bcíṅs-pa*, pf. of *₀čiṅ-ba* **to bind.** Both verbs (*bcíṅ-ba* and *bcíṅs-pa*) are also used as substantives: **bonds, fetters**, whether of a material, spiritual, or magical nature.

བཅིབ(ས)་པ་ *bcib(s)-pa* v. *₀čib-pa; Sch.* also: **carriage, conveyance.**

བཅིར་བ་ *bcír-ba* v. *₀čir-ba.*

བཅིལ་བ་ *bcil-ba* v. *₀jil-ba.*

བཅུ་ *bcu* (*Bal.* **wcu**) **ten**, *bcu tam-pa* id.; *bcu-prag* a decade; *bcu-ycig, bcu-ynyis* (*Bal.* **wcu-ñas**) eleven, twelve etc., (v. also *bco*); *bcú-pa, bcú-po* as in *dgú-pa, dgú-po.* — *bcu-skór ₀ton, bcu-gyúr ₀ton* (the field) yields a tenfold crop. — **cú-ka, cú-kai tal** *C.*, **cu-kág** *W.*, tithe, tithes; *bcu-kág-pa* a collector of tithes, *bcu-kag ₀dón-pa* to tithe, to decimate *Cs.* — *bcu-dpón* corporal, Lat. *decurio, bcu-₀og* (**cu-*

*wáy** *Ts.*) a band of ten soldiers. — *bču-yčig-žál* the eleven-faced (Awalokiteswara) *Glr.*

བཅུ་བ་ *bčú-ba* v. *˳čú-ba.*

བཅུག་པ་ *bčúg-pa* v. *˳jug-pa.*

བཅུགས་ *bčugs*, from the phrases: *sems kʻón-med-pa dan bčúgs med-pa dan ynód-pa med-pa Stg.*, and *Pratihārya Avadāna* (v. *Feer*) p. 3: *lha-byin-gyis bčugs byás-te* = देवदत्तविगृहीतेन, it appears, that *bčugs* signifies hatred, hostility, damage, loss, which when compared with *ɣčugs* seems rather strange, yet is in accordance with कौकृत्य (for this must probably be read inst. of कौकृत).

བཅུད་ *bčud* (रस) **moisture, juice, sap**, but gen. combined with the notion of a certain inherent virtue or power; *zlá-bai bčud* a fructifying moisture, to be compared in its effects to the warmth of the sun, and prob. means night-dew (if after all it is any thing real); hence **essence, nutriment**, *rkán-gis bčud ˳gyur* nourishment comes from the marrow *Med.*; *bčúd-la son*, *Mil.* also *bčúd-lu bor*, (this food) has proved a nutritious fluid, it agrees with him; *bčúd-čan* nutritious, succulent, of grass, food etc.; *bčud-méd* not nutritious, *Med.*; invigorating **cordial, quintessence**, *bčud-lén* an elixir of life; frq. fig.: *čos tʻams-čád bsdús-pai bčud Glr.*

བཅུམ་པ་ *bčúm-pa* 1. v. *˳júm-pa.* — 2. **to use artifices, to chicane** *Sch.*

བཅུར་བ་ *bčúr-ba* **1. to be flattened down** *Sch.* — 2. *Kun.* **lún-po čúr-te yon** there is a draught (here). — 3. *C.* like *bkág-pa* **to bar, obstruct, block up**, e.g. of snow obstructing a road. Cf. *˳júr-ba.*

བཅེ་, བཅེས་ *bče, bčes* v. *˳čé-ba.*

བཅེར་བ་ *bčér-ba* 1. **to heap** or **pile up** *Cs.*; *Lex.*: *šin ɣšin-por bčér-ba* to pile up wood. — 2. = *bčír-ba* 1. **to squeeze, to press** *C.*, *W.*; **to squeeze in**, *ri-brág ɣnyís-kyi bár du* something between two rocks *Pth.*; **čer tán-če** *W.* to squeeze, press, screw in; **čer-čér tán-če** *W.* to throng, to crowd.

བཅོ་ *bčo*, for *bču* in *bčo-lná* 15, and *bčo-brgyád* 18; *lo lna ɣsum bčo-lná* 3 times 5, 15 years (*lna ɣsum* standing pleon.) *Mil.*

བཅོ་བ་ *bčó-ba*, pf. and imp. *bčos*, prop. root of the fut. tense of *˳čós-pa*, but in *W.* the usual word for *byéd-pa* **to make, perform; to prepare, manufacture, construct**; employed in all kinds of phrases; **kʻó-la zún-čan čó** *W.* (he) makes him a liar.

བཅོག་ *bčog? Glr.* 99.

བཅོམ་ *bčom* for *ɣčom*, **pride.**

བཅོམ་པ་ *bčóm-pa*, pf. of *˳jóms-pa*, **conquered, subdued; having conquered** or **subdued**, e.g. *dgrá-bčoms-pa*, v. *dgra*; **victory** *Cs.*; *˳prog-bčóm*, and **čom-ṭóg** *W.* **robbery** and **acts of violence.** — *bčom-brlág* p.n., Mathura, town of ancient India, in the neighbourhood of Agra, *Zam.*, *Tar.* — *bčom-ldán* victorious *Cs.*; *bčom-ldan-˳dás* (*Kh.* **wčom-ldan-dę́**, *Ld.* **čom-dan-dás**, *C.* **čom-dān-dę́**) भगवत् *Cs.*: victorious, *Sch.*: 'the victoriously consummated', *Burn.* le bien-heureux, the usual epithet of Buddha, *Burn.* I., 71.

བཅོལ་བ་ *bčól-ba*, v. *˳čól-ba*; *bčól-ma* a thing committed to a person's charge, **a trust.**

བཅོས་པ་ *bčós-pa*, a verb of its own, though as to form resembling a participle, 1. **to treat medically**, hence **to cure, to heal**, *mkʻas kyan bčós-su med* he cannot be cured even by the best physicians *Med.*; *bčós-(pai) tʻabs* the way of treating, the method of curing *Med.*; *sman-bčós* medical treatment *Med.* — 2. to do (a thing) for the sake of appearance, for form's sake, **to affect**, *bčós-su byéd-pa* **to perform a sham work**, e.g. blowing into a blazing fire *C.*; hence as sbst.: **a false conception**, wrong idea, *bčós pa dan ˳kʻrúl-bar gyúr-ba* to give way to odd fancies, to have crotchets in the brain, e.g. in consequence of old age *Thgy.* — 3. partic.: made or contrived by art,

artificial, feigned, fictitious, *ma-bc̀ós* artless, unaffected, genuine; it also seems to denote an absence of mental activity, or a forbearance of exercising such activity, in short that indifference to the world, which is so highly valued by the Buddhist, *Mil.* — *bc̀ós-pai ras,* or *ras bc̀ós-bu,* washed or prepared cotton-cloth *Cs.*; calico, chintz *Cs.*; in *S. O.* it seems to denote a costly, valuable fabric; *bc̀ós-ma* sbst. and adj., a production of art, any thing made or contrived by art, esp. every thing imitated, counterfeit, mock, sham, not genuine, frq.; *bc̀ós-ma ma yin-pa* natural, unfeigned, genuine, e.g. respect, reverence *Glr.* — *ťsúl-bc̀os-mḱan,* one that is shamming, a hypocrite. Cf. *˳c̆ós-pa.*

ལྕ་ *lc̀a, Ld.* for *lc̀i-ba,* **excrement, dung, manure.**

ལྕ་སྒ་ *lc̀á-sga = bc̀a-sga,* **white ginger,** v. *sgá.*

ལྕ་བ་ *lc̀á-ba* 1. *Cs.:* a sort of **carrot,** *Med.* frq., but not known to the common people, at least not in *W.* — 2. **कम्बल** acc. to *Was.* a garment made of wool or felt *Tar.*

ལྕག་ *lc̀ag* 1. **rod, switch, stick, whip;** *glaṅ-lc̀ág* ox-whip; *ṙṅa-lc̀ág* kettle-drum stick; *lc̀aṅ-lc̀óg Lex.* willow-twig, osier-switch; *rta-lc̀ág* horse-whip, whip in general, also a scourge, consisting of several straps with sharp knots; *spa-lc̀ág* a cane, bamboo *Mil.*; *ber(-ma)-lc̀ág* stick *Mil.* — 2. (*lc̀ág-ma*) **stroke, blow, cut, hit,** *lc̀ag rgyáb-pa* to give a blow or cut, *rtá-la* to the horse *Glr.*; *mgo-lc̀ág* (*Ld.* **go-lc̀ág**) a blow or stroke upon the head; *˳gram-lc̀ág* a smack on the cheek, slap on the face, box on the ear *Cs.*; *ťal-lc̀ág* id. — 3. forepart of a coat of mail *Sch.* — 4. a kind of Daphne, v. *re-lc̀ag-pa.*

Comp. *lc̀ág-rdo W.* **flint,** flint-stone. — *lc̀ag-˳brás Mil.* **whip-cord,** lash of a whip; *lc̀ag-˳bréṅ,* and *lc̀ag-dṅó* id. — *lc̀ag-ťsán = rta-lc̀ág C.* — *lc̀ag-yú* **whip-stick,** handle of a whip.

ལྕག་ལྕིག་ *lc̀ag-lc̀ig Lex.* w. e.

ལྕག་པོད་ *lc̀ag-pód* **a girdle,** made of plaited and interlaced strips and resembling a chain; one *Lex.* adds: *dáṅ-mai ˳dril-du lhás-pa* (?).

ལྕགས་ *lc̀ags* 1. **iron,** *lc̀ágs-kyi* of iron; *lc̀ágs-bton-mḱan* a miner digging for iron; *rgya-lc̀ágs* Chinese iron; *ṗo-lc̀ágs* an inferior sort of iron, *mo-lc̀ágs* a finer and better sort of it, *Cs.* steel (?) — 2. an iron instrument, tool, esp. **lock** (of doors), **fetter, shackle,** *sgo ťams-c̀ad lc̀ags btab-c̀iṅ* locking every door *Pth.*; **ḱáṅ-c̀ag lág-c̀ag** *C.* fettered on hands and feet; *ṙnam-lc̀ágs* 1. thunderbolt, 2. a flash of lightning just striking an object; *me-lc̀ágs* a steel to strike fire with, fire-steel.

Comp. and deriv. *lc̀ags-kyú B.* an iron hook, esp. fishing-hook, angle; often fig.: *ťúgs-rj̀ei,* or *c̆ós-kyi lc̀ags-kyús ˳dzin-pa* to seize with the hook of grace or of religion *Dzl., Glr.* and elsewh. — *lc̀ags-dkár* tin-plate, white iron plate. — *lc̀ags-skúd* **thin wire.** — *lc̀ags-ḱém* or *ḱyém* **a spade.** — *lc̀ags-ḱról Sch.* a big iron kettle (= *W.* **c̀ag-dol** **stew-pan,** large iron pan or pot?) — *lc̀ags-mgár* iron smith, **black-smith.** — *lc̀ags-sgór* iron pan. — *lc̀ags-sgyíd* **trevet, tripod.** — *lc̀ags-sgróg* **fetter, shackle.** — *lc̀ags-c̆ás* **implements of iron, hardware.** — *lc̀ags-tig* a kind of **gentian,** cf. *tig-ta.* — *lc̀ags-ťág* **chain** or **chains.** — *lc̀ags-ťál Cs.* an iron **dish** or **plate,** prob. from *ťá-li.* — *lc̀ags-drégs* (*W.* **c̀ag-rág**) 1. **iron dross,** scoria or slag of iron; 2. **dirt** of the intestines. — *lc̀ags-rdó* 1. perh. more correctly *lc̀ag-rdó* **flint-stone.** 2. iron-stone, **iron ore** (?). — *lc̀ags-ṗrá Ů,* a kind of musket, imported from Rum (Turkey). — **c̀ag-bér** *W.* an iron bar, **crowbar, hand-spike.** — *lc̀ágs-mag, bc̀á-mag,* the Turkish چَکمَک **flint-stone, tinder-box** *W.* — *lc̀ags-ťságs* an iron **cribble** or **sieve, colander.** — *lc̀ags-zám* iron bridge. — *lc̀ags-záṅs* iron kettle. — **c̀ag-záṅ** *C.* good iron, **steel.** — *lc̀ags-ẏyá* **rust** *Med.* — *lc̀ags-ri* a wall encircling an estate, a town etc. — *lc̀ags-sláṅ* a large iron pan for roasting or kiln-drying corn. — *lčags-šáṅ* iron hoop, hasp, cramp-iron. — *lčags-sá* iron ore *Cs.* — *lčags-bsró* **smoothing-iron** *Sch.*

ལྕང་མ་ *lčáṅ-ma* **willow,** Salix viminalis, almost the only leaved tree in Tibet, frq. planted in the vicinity of villages; *rgyál-lčaṅ* the specific name of this tree in *Kun.*; *róṅ-lčaṅ*, *sér-lčaṅ* different species of it; *lčaṅ-dkár Kun.* a white kind with birch-like bark, cf. *šo*; *lčaṅ-ló* willow-leaves, 2. (**जटा**) **matted hair,** *lčáṅ-lo-čan*, or *-pa*, one with matted hair, a penitent; also n. of a place in ancient India, of another in Lhasa, and of a third on the top of the fabulous Rirab. 3. **queue, pig-tail** *C.* — *lčaṅ-rlóm* a flat willow basket *Ts.* — *lčaṅ-šiṅ* willow-tree, willow-wood. — *lčaṅ-šól Sch.*: 'the red willow'. — **čaṅ-sil* W.* coolness, shade under a willow-tree.

ལྕང་ལྕོང་ *lčaṅ-lčóṅ Cs.* = *saṅ-šóṅ* **a craggy place, a broken country.**

ལྕམ་ *lčam*, also *p̓yam*, 1. **lath, pole, rafter, spar** of a roof. In Tibet the rafters are placed horizontally, and support a layer of earth; in Mongol tents they are slanting, supporting the felt-covering. — 2. also *brag-lčám*, n. of an officinal herb used for healing wounds *Med.* — 3. *ᵒgyur-lčám* prob. denotes a glittering fish, or a fish rapidly darting along — 4. v. *lčám-mo.*

ལྕམ་མེ་བ་ *lčám-me-ba*, perh. **variegated, shining, dazzling** *Glr.*

ལྕམ་མོ་ *lčám-mo*, resp. for *spun*, and esp. for *sriṅ-mo*, acc. to *Cs.* also for *čúṅ-ma*, **a royal consort,** a great man's **sister** or **wife;** *lha-lčám* a princess *Pth.*; *lčam-čúṅ* a young princess or lady, a young unmarried lady of noble rank; *lčam-drál*, *mčéd-lčam-dral*, *lčam-sriṅ* brother and sister.

ལྕམ་པ་ *lčám-pa* 1. n. of a flower *Wdṅ.*; 2. n. of a kind of vegetables *S.g.*

ལྕི་བ་ *lčí-ba* 1. sbst. (*Ld.* **lča**, *Lh.* **či-a*, *čé-a**), **dung,** esp. of cattle; *bai lčí-ba*, *bá-lči* cow-dung; *lči-skám* dry dung (used as fuel), *lči-rlón* fresh dung. — 2. adj. **heavy,** *W.* **čin-te**, *yaṅ-lčí* 1. light and heavy; 2. weight, **yaṅ-či ḍán-ḍa čó-ce** *W.* to balance equally, to counterpoise; with regard to food, perh. heavy, oppressing the stomach; but also in a favourable sense: **substantial, nutritious;** fig.: **weighty, important,** *k̓yéd-kyi skyes daṅ bka-stsál lčí-ba des* in consequence of your weighty presents and requests *Glr.*; **nám-čog čin-te** *W.* hard of hearing; *k̓a-na-ma-t̓ó-ba lči-ba* a heavy, deadly sin, frq.

ལྕིད་ *lčid* v. *ḷjid.*

ལྕིན་ཏེ་ *lčin-te* v. *lči-ba.*

ལྕིབས་ *lčibs* denotes a. things, which serve to protect the hands, when having to deal with hot or otherwise disagreeable objects; so gloves may be called *lčibs Sch.*, but esp. *ṫsa-lčibs* (*W.* **ṫsalčib**) **pot-cloth** (to take pots from the fire), **rę-čib** *C.*, also **lag-čib** id.; hence prob. *mig-lčibs*, resp. *spyan-lčibs* **eyelid;** *mig-gi lčibs-ṫór* sty, wisp in the eye, and perh. from some remote similarity *sgo-lčibs*, *sgoi ya-lčibs* the lintel or head-piece of a door; *nya-lčibs* fishgills, *Lex.* and *Cs.*; b. contrivances to facilitate the handling of different objects, as: **the handles** of pots and vessels, the handles, **hilts, bows, ears, loops** etc. of knives, scissors, pincers and other working-tools.

ལྕུ་བ་ *lčú-ba* v. *ṗčú-ba.*

ལྕུག་པ་ *lčúg-pa Cs.*, *mnyen-lčug Lex.*, **flexible, pliant; a supple branch;** *lčug-lčúg byéd-pa* to bend repeatedly *Cs.*; *lčúg-ma* **a root-shoot** of a willow or a poplar-tree, **a rod, switch;** **čúg-gu** *C.* the bud of a twig; *lčug-p̓rán* a thin branch or twig.

ལྕུགས་ *lčugs*, *gri-yi lčugs Lex.* w.e.

ལྕུང་ཀ་ *lčúṅ-ka* = *skyúṅ-ka*, **jack-daw.**

ལྕུང་མོ་ *lčúṅ-mo* **thimble** *Glr.*

ལྕུད་པ་ *lčud-pa* v. *ṗčud-pa.*

ལྕུམ་ *lčum Med.*, *lčum-ṫsa Cs.*: 'a plant, the stalks of which are used as a purgative'; lčum-dkár prob. another species of that plant *Med.*

ལྕེ་ *lče* 1. resp. *ljags* (जिह्व) **tongue,** *lče rkyaṅ-ba* to put forth, to show the tongue *Mil.; lče brgyá-yis yon-tan čún-zad brjód-par nus ma mčis* even with a hundred tongues we should not be able sufficiently to praise the merit... *Pth.* — 2. **blade,** *Cs. gri-lče.* — 3. (अशनि) **thunderbolt,** *lče ˳bébs-pai glog* a flash of lightning accompanying a thunderbolt. — 4. **flame,** *mé-lče.*

Comp. *lče-kyigs* **the frenum** of the tongue *Cs.* — *lče-čúṅ* **uvula,** *lče-čuṅ ˳babs* inflammation of the uvula *Med.* — *lče-ɣnyis-pa* **double-tongued, deceitful,** *lče-ɣnyis byéd-pa* to be double-tongued. — *lče-t́éb, lče-˳drá* a fleshy excrescence below the tongue *Cs.* — *lče-bdé* a nimble tongue a babbler *Mil.* — *lče-spyáṅ* = *če-spyáṅ Thgy., Stg.* *lče-˳búr* a swelling on the tongue *Cs.* — *lče-myaṅ-t́sá* **alum** *Med.* — *lče-rtsá* the root of the tongue, *lče-rtsá-čan* a letter pronounced from the root of the tongue, a guttural. — *lče-rtsé* the tip of the tongue *Cs., lče-rtsé-čan* a letter sounded with the tip of the tongue, a lingual. — *lče-t́sá-(-ba)* a sharp-tasted, pungent medicinal herb *Med.* — *lče-ɣžór* a tongue-scraper *Cs.*

ལྕེག་ *lčeg* a coat of mail for a horse *Sch.*

ལྕེབ་པ་ *lčéb-pa* to go to kill one's self, **to seek death**, esp. by a leap into the water or down a precipice, but not every kind of suicide; also used of insects that fly into a flame etc.

ལྕོ་ག་ *lčó-ga*, also *lčóg-ma* or *mo* **lark.**

ལྕོག་ *lčog* 1. *B., C.* a **turret** on a housetop, pinnacle (*W.* **speu**). — 2. v. *lčóg-tse.*

ལྕོག་པོ་ *lčóg-po* prob. **low,** *lčóg-por skye* (a certain plant) is low-growing, it does not grow high.

ལྕོག་ཙེ་, ལྕོག་རྩེ་ *lčóg-tse, lčóg-rtse*, resp. *ɣsol-lčóg*, **table**, in Tibet, esp. in *W.*, a very rare piece of furniture, and always small and low; *lčog-k̓ébs* tablecloth, *lčog-k̓ébs btiṅ-ba* to lay the cloth; *rgya-lčóg* a large table, a European table; *mdun-lčóg* 'fore-table', a sort of table before an idol, for spreading offerings on it, v. e.g. *Hook.* I, 172; but it is not the same as altar.

ལྕོགས་ *lčogs, zer-lčógs* **pronunciation** *C.*(?)

ལྕོག(ས)་པ་ *lčóg(s)-pa* I. **to be agitated, to shake, to tremble,** *mé-tog mgo-lčóg Zam.* a flower shaking, waving its head (little used).

II. 1. vb. **to be able,** *de ma lčóg-na* if (he) is not able (to do that); *ji lčóg-kyi Mil.* as much as possible, to the utmost; **ṅa-ráṅ-ghi gaṅ čóg-pa** *C.* as far as I am able. More used: 2. adj. **able,** *šéd-kyis mi lčóg-pa* unable, feeble, weak, *rig-pas mi lčóg-pa* ignorant; **ṅe t́sar čig-la čóg-pa me'** I am not able to carry the whole at once *C.*; **čóg-čan** clever, skilful, handy, **čog-méd** awkward *W.*; **k̓e čog mi dug** he does not get on with his mouth, he lisps; also **k̓a čóg-pa** irreverent, disrespectful in speaking *W.*(?)

ལྕོང་ *lčoṅ, sbol-lčóṅ* a frog in its first stage of development, **tadpole** *Pth.*

ཆ

ཆ་ *č̒a* 1. the letter *č̒*, the aspirated *č*, pronounced hard and forcibly, like **ch** in *chap* or *church.* — 2. numerical figure: 6, *č̒a-pa* the sixth volume.

ཆ་ *č̒a* I. **part, portion, share** 1. opp. to the whole, *č̒a ɣsúm-du bgos* divide it in three parts! *brgyai č̒a* $\frac{1}{100}$ *Glr.; stóṅ-gi č̒a* $\frac{1}{1000}$; *baṅ-mdzód ɣsúm-č̒a ɣčig* one third of the provisions *Dzl.*; *dbui ča tsam čig γsér-gyis ma lóṅ-bar* there being still wanting about as much gold as (the weight of) his head *Glr.*; *náṅ-par sṅá-bai ča* the following day's first part, i.e. the following morning *Mil.*; *sá-ča* a piece of land *Glr.*, *C.*, also **land**, **territory**, **country** in general, *ghai sa-ča* the country of Gha *Glr.*; *zúr-ča* frontier parts, frontier province; *ča-snyoms* at equal parts, equally, e.g. *ču sbyar* mixed with the same quantity of water *Lt.*; *ča-mnyám* id., *ča-mnyám žib bteg* accurately weighed in equal parts *Lt.*; *ča tsam*, *ča ₒdra tsam* in part, in some measure; *ča ma ₒdra* or *ma mtún-pa* partly not equal, differing a little; *ča tsam šes kyaṅ* even if one knows but a little *Mil.*; *yid smon ₒos ča tsam mi γdá-bas* it being not in the least desirable; *ča-rdzógs* being complete in every part, entire, integral *Sch.* — Esp. 2. **the half**, *nám-gyi ča stod*, the first half of the night, *nám-gyi ča smad* the second, the last half of it. Hence 3. **the one part** of a pair, similar to *ya*, *lham ča γčig* the one boot; *ča sgrig-pa* to pair, to match, to couple *Sch.*; an equal, a match, *ča-mtún-pa*, *ča-ₒdrá-ba*, *C.* also **ča-lóṅ-wa**, similar, resembling *Wdṅ.* and elsewh.; *la-lá tár-pa ča-mtún dgé-ba med* some have no virtue befitting (i.e. leading to) final salvation *Thgy.*; *ča-méd* without an equal, matchless; *čá-ma-yin-pa* unfit, improper, unbecoming *Sch.*, *ṅag γčóg-pa ni ča ma yin* not obeying will not do, is out of place *Tar.* 110, 11. — 4. **a pair**, = *zuṅ Sch.*; *Zam.*: युग. — 5. **share**, **portion**, **lot**, *mtsar-sdúg bltá-bai čá-nas mnyam* being equal as to their (respective) share of beauty *Glr.*; *dmán-ča ₒdzin-pa* to choose the humbler (inferior) share, i.e. to be humble, = *dmán-sa ₒdzin-pa Mil.*; in general: *ča ₒdzin-pa* c. genit. to adhere, to be attached to a person or thing *Pth.*; *žiṅ rmó-ba ṅai ča yin* ploughing is my business, my lot, my department *Dzl.*; *čá-la* equally, in equal parts, equally divided, *ḱá-ba nyin dgu mtsan dgu babs, čá-la nyin mtsan bčo-brgyád babs Mil.* there was a fall of snow during nine days and nine nights; it fell equally portioned out to days and nights, (together) eighteen (the peculiar mode of reckoning is here to be noticed).

II. **news**, **intelligence**, **notice**, construed like *rgyus* and *γtam*; *γtám-ča ₒdri-ba* = *γtam ₒdri-ba*; *ča yod*, *ča med* like *rgyus yod* and *rgyus med*; *nam ₒči ča méd-kyi čos* the doctrine of the uncertainty of the day of death *Mil.*; ...*par ča mčis-te* there coming news or intelligence that ...; *skád-ča* v. *skad*; physically: **voice**, **sound**, *brág-ča* echo; intellectually: **prospect**, **auspices**, *Mil.*: *sróg-ča* prospects of life (as to its length and preservation), *ḱyim-ča* prospects regarding the household, *dgra-ča* prospects, expectations as to one's enemies; **lám-ča* C.* prospects of a safe journey (cf. *ṅo* 4).

III. **thing**, **things**, relating to clothes, ornaments, materials etc., cf. *čas*; **go-lus-ča-tsáṅ* W.* a complete suit of clothes; but mostly used in compounds: *ské-ča* neck-ornaments, *glo-ča* ornaments suspended to the belt or girdle, e.g. strings of shells; *dgós-ča* necessary things *Cs.*; *mčód-ča* things necessary for sacrifices, requisites for offerings *Glr.*; *mtsón-ča* weapons; *yig-ča* prob. writings, deeds, documents *Glr.*; **rẹ-ča** cottons, cotton fabrics *C.*; *lag-ča* implements, utensils, goods, baggage etc. *Glr.* — There is still to be noticed the expression: *ča-bžág-pa*, lit. to add one's own share to a thing, 1. to adhere, stick, or cling to, to follow, obey (laws); *saṅs-rgyás-kyi bká-la ča bžag* they adhere to the words of Buddha; *rgyál-poi bká-la* to obey the king's commandment. 2. to refer to(?) *C.*

ཆ་རྐྱེན་ *ča-rkyén Lex.*, *Sch.*: 'share of destiny, of fate; consequence of one's actions' (?).

ཆ་མཁན་ *čá-mḱan* **soothsayer**, **fortune-teller** *Sch.*

ཆ་ག་ *čá-ga Mil.*, **hem**, **edge**, **border**; *čá-ga ₒdebs-pa* to hem, to turn in (the edge of cloth).

ཆ་ག་འབུ་ *čá-ga-ₒbu C., Lex.* also *čá-ga-pa*, **grasshopper.**

ཆ་ཆོ་ *čá-čo Lex., Sch.*: 'things homogeneous, matched'.

ཆ་བ་ *čá-ba*, pf. and imp. *soṅ* (the regular form *čas* being nearly obs. at present), in *W.* the usual word for *ₒgro-ba* to go, in *B.* little used and only in later writings, 1. **to go,** **šór-te čá-če** to retire, to retreat slowly; **da ča yin**, or **da čen** adieu, good bye, farewell! **da čen žu** resp., your servant! (in taking leave); **'á-ru-soṅ** go thither, or that way! **'á-ru ma ča** do not go to this place, do not step this way! **to travel,** **gyál-la** (or *dé-mo, yág-po*) *ča žig** I wish you a safe journey, a pleasant trip to you! **lóg-te čá-če** to return, to go or come back; **tíṅ-la čá-če** to follow, to come after or later; **ča čug** let (him) go! give (it) up! let (it) alone! **to be gone, consumed, spent, used, wasted,** **šiṅ mán-po ča yin** a great deal of wood will go, will be consumed. — 2. **to become, grow, get, turn,** **tsan ča dug** it grows night, it is getting dark; **gas čá če** to grow old; **nág-po soṅ** that has turned black; **šés-kan čá-če** to get information; also with *la:* **bág-ma-la čá-ba** (= *bág-mar ₒgró-ba, ₒgyúr-ba*) to become a bride *Ma.*; **mán-lami ča** this is not used for medicine. — 3. with a supine (*B.*) or a verbal root (col.): **to be about, to be on the point, to be going,** *sléb-tu čá-bai tse* when they were on the point of arriving *Mil.*; *nyí-ma ₒčár-du čá-ba daṅ* when the sun was just going to rise *Mil.*; **me ši ča dug** the fire is on the point of going out; **nad ži ča dug**, the disease is decreasing. — 4. with the gerund it expresses a continuous progress, a gradual operation, an effect by little and little, **ču pél-te ča dug** the water increases from day to day. — 5. with the inf. it is used in the sense of the future tense, or like the Greek μέλλειν: **to intend, to purpose,** **či šrid-de dir šriṅ-če ča dug** how long does he (do you etc.) intend to stay? **nam lug sád-če ča dug** when are you going to kill the sheep?

ཆ་བུ་ *čá-bu*, a kind of little ornament worn in the ears *Ld.*

ཆ་བྱད་ *ča byád* 1. **thing, implement, instrument,** e.g. a musical instrument *Dzl.*, a surgical instr. *Med.* — 2. **clothing, dress,** *mi-sdúg-pai ča-byad-čan* poorly clothed, ragged *Mil.*; **external appearance,** also of animals.

ཆ་ཚམ་ *ča-tsám* v. *ča* I, 1.

ཆ་ཚད་ *ča-tsád* = *čag-tsad.*

ཆ་ཚན་ *ča-tsán* **species, division, class** *Sch.*

ཆ་འཛིན་ *ča-ₒdzin* v. *ča* I., 5.

ཆ་རྫོགས་ *ča-rdzógs* v. *ča* I, 1.

ཆ་ར་ *čá-ra* 1. **oak,** also *mon-čá-ra* (on account of its growing only on the southern ranges of the Himalaya mountains, inhabited mostly by Non-Tibetans) in several species, with pointed, evergreen leaves, a tree much inferior in beauty to the English oak. *čá-ra preu Sch.*: 'the stunted or dwarf-oak'. — 2. also *ča-ri, ča-lí, ča-lú*, a coarse sort of **blanket** made of yak's hair.

ཆ་ལ་ *čá-la* v. *ča* I., 5.

ཆ་ལག་ *čá-lag* 1. *C.* **implements, instruments,** required for the carrying on of a business. — 2. *W.* **things, effects,** luggage. — 3. *Tar.* 43, 18: *čá-lag daṅ bčás-pa rdzógs-par šés-pa Schf.*: 'the systematic and complete understanding'.

ཆ་ལང་ *ča-láṅ* joined with *rdéb-pa Lex.* and *Mil.*, meaning not known; *Wts.* gives: petite lance des bonzes.

ཆ་ལམ་ *čá-lam* = *há-lam*, **some; for the most part, rather** *C.*

ཆ་ལི་, ཆ་ལུ་ *ča-lí, ča-lú* v. sub *čá-ra.*

ཆ་ལུགས་ *ča-lúgs* **clothing, costume, appearance.**

ཆ་ཤས་ *ča-šás* **part, portion, share,** *lús-kyi ča-šás* a part of the body, a limb etc.

ཆ་ཧར་ *ča-hár* Chakhar, a Mongol tribe *Sch.*

ཆག་ čag 1. **dry fodder** for horses and other animals, as hay, barley etc.; *čag-γžoṅ* trough, manger, crib. — 2. **the fourth finger** *Med.* — 3. resp. for **shoe** *Glr.*, also *p̓yag(-lhám)*. — 4. *čag-p̓éb-pa Glr.* = *p̓yag p̓éb-pa.* — 5. **the breadth of a fist,** *čag gaṅ* id, *Mṅg.* frq. — 6. v. *čág-pa.*

ཆག་(ད)ཀྲུམ(ས)་ *čag-(d)krúm(s)* **piece, fragment** *Lex.*, *Thgy.*; **čag-ṭúm-la soṅ** *C.* it has gone to pieces.

ཆག་སྐྱ་བ་ *čag-skya-ba Sch.*: 'having only one purpose, pursuing but one aim; unremitting, indefatigable'.

ཆག་ག་ཆོག་གེ་ *čag-ga-čog-gé* (or *p̓yag-ga-p̓yog-gé?*) various things mixed up or thrown together, medley.

ཆག་གྲུམ་ *čag-grúm Lex.* = *čag-dkrúm*(?).

ཆག་རྒྱག་པ་ *čag-rgyág-pa* **to doubt** *Sch.*

ཆག་ཆག་ *čag-čág* I. 1. with *byed-pa*, *ˏdebs-pa*, **to sprinkle, besprinkle,** *čus* with water, *k̓áṅ-pa*, *lám-rnams* the house, the streets *B.*, *C.* (*W.* **čab-čáb**). — 2. *Sch.*: *čag-čóg γdab-pa* **to starch, to stiffen.**

II. *W.* **čag-čág čó-če** **to tread, to trample,** e.g. the narrow paths or furrows between garden-beds; **to clap the hands.**

ཆག་ཆད་ *čag-čád* **rent, break, rupture** *Sch.*

ཆག་དུམ་ *čag-dúm* **fragment, piece, crumb, scrap, bit.**

ཆག་འདིང་ *čag-ˏdiṅ* **doubtful, incredible** *Sch.*

ཆག་པ་ *čág-pa* 1. a large **tuft** or **bunch** of flowers, ears of corn etc. — 2. pf. of *ˏčág-pa*, **broken**; *ma-čág(s)-pa*, and esp. adv. *ma-čág(s)-par* also *čág-med-par* uninterrupted, unintermitting; uninterruptedly; *gas-čag-méd* without a crack, flaw, or chink. — 3. *lam čág-pa* v. *ˏčag-pa.*

ཆག་པོ་ *čág-po* **broken; a broken vessel, pot** etc., **a pot-sherd;** *tsel-(po) čág(-po)* a broken dosser or pannier.

ཆག་བུ་ *čág-bu*, diminutive of *čag-pa*, **a little bunch.**

ཆག་མོ་ *čág-mo* **bunch,** *ˏbrás-bu čág-mo* a fruit growing in the form of bunches or clusters, like the grapes of the vine, the berries of the elder etc. *W.*

ཆག་ཙེ་ *čág-tse* a small **grain,** e.g. of ground grits, **čág-tse-čan** **granulous**; **bág-p̓e čág-tse-čan** ground grits, *W.*; *Hind. soojee.*

ཆག་ཚད་ *čag-tsád Sch.*: **the right measure,** *dug ster čag-tsád* if a sufficient quantity of poison has been administered to a person, *Med.*

ཆག་ཤིང་ *čag-šiṅ* a wooden **splint** for a broken limb, **čug-če** to put it on *W.*

ཆགས་པ་ *čágs-pa* I. frq. for *čág-pa* 2.

II. vb. **to be begotten, produced;** *ma-čágs-pa* not begotten or produced in the usual way of propagation, but = *rdzús-te skyés-pa*, or *lhún-gyis grúb-pa Pth.* frq.; *mṅál-du čágs-pa* to be produced in the womb, as the foetus is; hence *čags* in compounds: animal, *ˏdab-čágs*, *γšog-čágs* winged animal, bird; *srog-čágs* in general: a living being, an animal, = *séms-čan*; *ˏp̓rúl-gyi tsul-čágs Glr.* prob. as much as a wonderful child, a prodigy; *šiṅ-la čágs-pa* to grow on a tree, of fruits; and in general: **to rise, arise, spring up, originate,** of the world, of new works, buildings, empires, customs, of eruptions on the skin; **zil-pa čags soṅ** *W.* dew has fallen; **to come forth, to appear,** = *ˏbyúṅ-ba*, e.g. *ˏód-du čágs-pa* to come to light, to appear *Mil.*; **ṅul čags** *W.* sweat comes forth, breaks out, I perspire; even: *ráb-tu čágs-pa* = *ráb-tu ˏbyúṅ-ba* to become a cleric (little used); *čags-rábs* genesis, history of the beginning, esp. of the world; *čags-tsúl* 1. manner of beginning, origin, procreation *Med.* 2. *W.* form, figure, demeanour, **čags-tsúl sóg-po** coarse, rude, rough.

III. 1. vb. **to love,** (ἐρᾶν), *bú-mo-la* a girl; *skyés-pa daṅ na-čúṅ γčig čágs-pa* the mutual affection between a man and a maiden; tender attachment in general, connubial, parental and filial love, *yid-la čágs-pai bú-mo-rnams* my dearly beloved daughters *Pth.*; ardent desire or longing for something, *grágs-pa-la* for glory; **to be attached to, to cling to,** e.g. *lus daṅ sróg-la čágs-pa* to life, *yúl-la* to one's home, to one's native country; often: to suffer one's self to be enticed by a thing, **to indulge in;** *čágs-par mi bya ˌjígs-par mi byá-ste* allowing neither desire nor fear to have any influence upon himself *Samb.* — 2. sbst. **love** (ἔρως), **lust, passion** for, **affection, attachment,** *čágs-pa skyés-so* he fell in love *Dzl.*; *čágs-pa spyód-pa* = *ˌkrig-pa spyód-pa.* According to Buddhistic theory all *čágs-pa* is a great evil, as it betrays a troubled state of mind, and a reprehensible attachment to external things; yet even a saint, so far advanced in dispassion and apathy as Milaraspa, may sometimes be caught in very tender affections and sensations of *čágs-pa,* very like those of other human creatures.

Comp. *čags-sdáṅ* 1. *Schr.* **love and hatred,** 2. *Glr., Pth.* **jealousy** (love showing itself in hatred), also *čags-sdáṅ-gi ṗrag-dog.* — *čags-spyód* **coition, copulation,** cf. *čágs-pa* III., 2. — *čags-žén,* also *žen-čágs* = *čágs-pa* sbst. *Mil.*; **čags-žén čó-če* W.,* to love, c. *la*; *čags-žén méd-pa* dispassionate, indifferent to all terrestrial things. — *čags-séms* = *čags-žén.* — *čágs-sred-čan Pth.* **lustful, libidinous, wanton.**

ཆང་ *čaṅ* (मद्य) resp. *skyems, ysól-čaṅ, mčód-čaṅ C.,* a fermented liquor, **beer, wine,** (not 'brandy' *Sch.*); *bu skyés-pa-la miṅ, čaṅ dráṅs-pa-la ytam* proverb: to the new-born child a name (is due), to the beer to be drunk a talk; *nás-čaṅ* beer made of barley (the usual kind); *brás-čaṅ* of rice *Glr.*; *gró-čaṅ* of wheat *Cs.*; *bú-ram-čaṅ,* or *búr-čaṅ* of sugar *Med.*; *rgún-čaṅ* wine; *sbráṅ-čaṅ Med.* honey-wine, mulse, mead? *rús-čaṅ Med.?* — *zás-čaṅ, zán-čaṅ* eating and drinking, meat and drink. — *sloṅ-, tig-,* and *bsu-čaṅ* v. sub *bág-ma.* — Fig.: *btúṅ-ba dran-šes bdúd-rtsii čaṅ* my drink is the wine of wisdom's nectar *Mil.* —

Here the process of brewing may be mentioned. When the boiled barley (*Ld.* **sbo-bód*, Ts. *ṫab**) has grown cold, some **ṗabs** (q. v.) is added, after which it is left standing for two or three days, until fermentation commences, when it is called *glum.* Having sufficiently fermented, some water is poured to it, and the beer is considered to be ready for use. If proper care is taken (and the people of Ü and Ladak generally do so), the pale beer, thus obtained, is not amiss, and sparkles a good deal, but not being hopped it does not keep long. The people of Lahoul are accustomed to press out the *glum* with their hands, instead of filtering it, and mismanage the business also in other respects, so that their *čaṅ* is a gray muddy liquor, that has hardly any resemblance to beer. The residue of malt, called *sbáṅ-ma,* may be mixed with water or milk, pressed through a strainer, and used instead of barm in baking bread, cakes etc.

Comp. *čáṅ-ḱaṅ* **beer-house, pot-house, tavern.** — *čáṅ-čan* **drinking-cup** or **bowl** *Sch, Wts.* — *čáṅ-čem-čan* **an intoxicated person.** — *čáṅ-čem-sa Lex.* prob. = *čáṅ-sa.* — *čáṅ-ˌtuṅ-mḱan* **a beer-drinker;** **čáṅ-ˌtun-ḱan máṅ-po dzom** a great beer-drinking bout takes place *W.* — **čáṅ-dad-čan** **a drunkard, tippler** *W.* — *čáṅ-tsúgs* = *čaṅ-čan Sch.* — *čáṅ-ˌṫsoṅ-gi ḱyim* **beer-house** *Dzl.* — *čáṅ-sa* 1. **beer-house** 2. **beer-carousal,** *čáṅ-sa čén-po byéd-pa* to give or arrange a great beer-drinking bout *Mil.*

ཆང་ཅུང་ *čaṅ-čúṅ* **a little** *Sch.*

ཆད་ *čad* 1. also *čad-dón, čad-mdó, W.* **čád-ka*,* **promise, engagement, agreement** *ḱa-čád* oral, verbal engagement, *lag-čád* pledge of faith by hand; *čad-dón byéd-pa, *čád-ka čó-če, zúm-če* W.,* to give a promise, make a contract; *ytóṅ-(bai) čad(-don) byéd-pa* to agree about giving; *čad-dón ltar byéd-pa* to keep, fulfil a promise; *čad-rdó* 1. the stone which is broken in the ceremony of *rdo yčóg-pa* q. v. 2. monument, memorial of a covenant. — 2. in compounds also for *čád-pa* punishment, *lus-čád* corporeal punishment.

ཆད་པ་ *čád-pa* I. sbst., resp. *bka-čád*, **punishment**; the preceding genit., contrary to our usage, is the genit. of the punishing person, thus: *rgyál-poi čád-pa* a punishment of the magistrates, i. e. a punishment decreed or inflicted by the magistrates, frq.; seldom, if ever, genit. of the punished action, and never that of the punished person. In classical language the usual construction of the words is the following: *čád-pas gčód-pa* to punish, *mi žig-la* somebody, ...*pas* or ... *pai pyir* for having ...; in more recent literature: *čád-pa gčód-pa Thgr., Glr.*; *čád-pa tób-pa* 1. to receive the fine incurred by another 2. to suffer punishment, to pay a fine; *ṅá-la čád-pa pog* punishment is inflicted on me, I am punished.

II. 1. **to promise**, e.g. *bká-lus mi ˳gál-bar* to obey. — 2. v. sub ˳*čád-pa*.

III. adj. **begotten, born, descended** from; the Tibetans are *sbreu daṅ srin-mo-nas* (or *las*) *čád-pa* the offspring of a monkey and a Rakshasi *Glr.; šá-nas čád-pai bu* a full child *Glr.*

ཆད་པོ་ *čád-po* 1. **rent, torn, worn-out, ragged, tattered**, *sgyí-gu čád-po* a leaky purse. — 2. a limited time, **a term** *Sch.*

ཆད་ཡིག *čad-yig* **a written contract**; *čad-mál-gyi yi-ge Glr.* id.

ཆད་ལུས་པ་ *čád-lus-pa* not to obtain the things hoped for, to be disappointed *Sch.*

ཆད་སོ་ *čád-so* 1. a limited time, **a term**. — 2. **a time-purchase** *Sch.* — 3. **an agreement** *Tar.*

ཆན་ *čan*, also *čan-túg Sch.*, **boiled corn** or **barley** etc.; ˳*bras-čán* rice-pap, *nas-čán* barley-pap.

ཆན་པ་ *čán-pa* a pair of **scissors**, but the common people know only **shears**, which are for various purposes; the scissors mentioned in surgical books are prob. of a nicer construction.

ཆབ་ *čab*, resp. and eleg. for *ču* 1. **water**, *dri-čáb* scented water; *sna-čáb, pyi-čáb*, water which at the beginning and close of the meetings in the large monasteries is handed round, and of which every one present takes a few drops on his tongue, as a symbol of purification, in place of the original ablutions. — 2. for other fluids, as *spyan-čáb* **tears**, *žal-čáb* **spittle**, *gsaṅ-čáb*, or *čab-gsáṅ* **urine**, *ba-čab* cow's urine (so with the Hindoos in *Lh.*, the cow being to them a sacred animal). — 3. in some compounds: **power, dominion, authority**. — *čab-rkyán* **brass can, brass-(tea) pot** with a long spout for pouring out tea, *W.*; also n. for Tibet, perh. on account of the large consumption of tea there. — *čab-kúṅ* **privy** *Cs.* — *čab-sgó* **door**, *čab-sgo-pa* **door-keeper, porter**. — **čab-ḍá** (spelling dubious) a wooden **pail**, of a similar shape as *čab-rkyán W.* — *čab-bróm, čab-róm* **ice**. — *čab-blúg C.* a vessel for rinsing one's mouth with water. *čab-mig* eleg. for *ču-mig* **fountain, spring**. — *čab-tsód* eleg. **a watch, a clock**. — *čab-˳óg* what is subjected to a person's sway, territory, dominion etc., *čab-˳óg-tu sdú-ba* to subject; *čab-˳óg-gi rgyál-po* a vassal, feudal tenant *Trig.*; *čab-˳óg-pa*, also *čab-˳báṅs* one owing allegiance to a sovereign, a subject. — *čab-šóg Cs.* eleg. for **letter, diploma** etc. — *čab-sér* eleg. for *ču-sér* **matter, pus**.

ཆབ་མ་ *čáb-ma W., C.*, also *Mil.*, **lid, valve**; **buckle, clasp**, *čáb-tse*, or *čáb-rtse C.* id.

ཆབས་ *čabs Lex. čabs-gčig Sch.* = *tabs-gčig* **together**.

ཆམ་ *čam*, in *čám-la ˳bébs-pa Lex.* w.e.; *Sch.*: to throw down, to cause to lie down; to subdue, subject; to spend, consume, **to have done with**; by this last signification it would be a syn. to *zin-pa*, and the circumstance that *čams* is used in Balti as an auxiliary vb. of the pf. tense agrees with that supposition, e. g. **zan zós-se čams** I have done eating, = *zos zin B.*

ཆམ་པ་ *čám-pa* 1. **cold** (in the head), **catarrh**; *sne-čám* id.; *gre-čam* catarrh in the throat, bronchial catarrh; *glo-čám* catarrh in the lungs; *rims-čám* an infecting or epidemic catarrh. — 2. *Cs.* = *ₒčám-pa* **accord, accordance.**

ཆམས་མེ་ *čam-mé* **slowly, by degrees, gradually** *Schr.* (cf. *čem-mé*).

ཆར་ *čar*, termin. of *ča*, 1. **into parts**, e.g. *bgó-ba* to divide into parts. — 2. **as an equal, as a match**, … *la čar mi ṗod* he is not an equal to, cannot come up to… *Thgy.*; … *dan stón-ṗrag-čar mi nye* prob.: he does not come up to… at all (lit. not for the thousandth part) *Pth.*; so in a similar manner: *brgyai čar yan mi sleb Tar.* — 3. affixed to numerals, and sometimes, though less correctly, written *čar*, q.v. The terminations of the cases mag be affixed to it: *lna čár-gyis* every fifth day *Thgy.*

ཆར་ *čar*, also *čár-pa*, 1. **rain**, *čar čén-po* a plentiful rain, *čar drág-po*, or *drag-čár* a heavy rain; *čar čén-pas* or *čé-bas* as it rained heavily *Pth.*; *čar ₒbébs-pa* to cause to rain; *čar ₒbab* it rains, *W.* **čár-pa yon**; *čár-gyi rgyun* a sudden or violent shower of rain *Tar.* — 2. at Kyelang for **watering-pot;** this utensil having never been seen there before, the word was at first applied to it jestingly, but is now generally adopted; *ču-tsâg* 'water-sieve' would be more correct.

Comp. *čar-skyibs* **a shelter, pent-roof,** protecting from rain. — *čar-k̔ébs* dress against rain, **rain-cloak.** — *čár-čan*, *čár-ldan* rainy *Cs.* — *čár-ču* **rain-water.** — *čár-dus* **rainy season.** — *čar-ₒdód (-byeu)* n. of a bird, water-ousel. — *čar-sprin* a rain-threatening cloud. — **čar-bhi** (?) *C.* rain-cloak. — *čar-rlún* rain and wind *Cs.* — **čar-šin** = *čar-skyibs W.* — *čar-lén* the coping or water-tile of a wall *Cs.*

ཆལ་ *čal*, *sku-čál* resp. **belly, abdomen,** *Cs.*

ཆལ་ཆིལ་ *čal-čil Lex.*, wavering, fluctuating *Sch.*

ཆལ་ཆོལ་ *čal-čól Tar.* 184, 20 = *ₒčal-la-ₒčol-le.*

ཆལ་མར་བརྡལ་བ་ *čál-mar brdál-ba* to spread equally, uniformly (vb. a.)

ཆས་ *čás* (*Sch. čás-ka*) cf. *ča* III., 1. **thing, tool, requisite** etc., *sé-mo-do-la sógs-pai čás-kyis brgyán-te* adorned with ornaments of pearls and other things *Mil.*; *dga-stón-gyi čas rgya čén-po* grand festival arrangements; *čas dé-rnams bšig* overturn the whole affair! *Glr.*; *bág-mar rdzón-bai čas* things to be given to her as a dowry *Tar.* 121, 5; *lčágs-čas* iron tools or utensils; *ltó-čas* food; *dmag-čas* military stores, requisites for war *Pth.*; *ₒtsó-čas* provisions *Mil.*; *lág-čas* tool, instrument *Cs.* — 2. **dress, garment**, *ṗó-čas* man's dress; *čas-gós*, *W.* **gón-če**, coat, dress; in a more general sense: **appearance, form, shape,** *búd-med-kyi čás-su byúste* appearing in the shape of a woman *Glr.*; *hór-čas byed* he puts on a Mongol dress *Ma.*; *bú-moi čás-su žugs* he puts on a girl's dress, disguises himself as a girl *Glr.*, *Pth.*; *čas sgyúr-ba* to put on, to assume another dress.

ཆས་པ་ *čás-pa*, originally the pf. of *čá-ba*, but always used as a separate vb. 1. **to set out, set forth, depart,** *čas dgós-par* as I must depart from here *Thgy.*; *bód-du čás-so* they set out for Tibet *Glr.*; *dus-gčig-tu čás-so* they departed at the same time *Dzl.*; *čás-su ₒjúg-pa* to send away, dispatch; *mgyógs-čas gtón-ba* to rush, run towards. — 2. **to set about, to begin,** *gsód-par* to kill; *ₒgró-bar čás-pa-las* when he made arrangements to depart *Dzl.*; also in the following manner; *da ṗyir ₒdón-no žes čás-pa* 'now we will return' they said, making preparations, or: saying thus, they made preparations *Dzl.*; *tugs čás-so* he had set his mind on departing *Mil.*

ཆི་ *či* num. fig.: 36.

ཆི་ཀ་ *čí-ka* **wallet, knapsack** *W.*

ཆི་ཏྲ་ *čí-tra W.* **variegated, figured,** of fabrics.

ཆི་ལི་ལི་ *či-li-li* onomatopoetic word for snuffing up scents by the nose; **žim-žim di-ma či-li-li k̔yer** *C.* sweet odours of cakes are meeting us; *mé-tog dri-ma či-li-li* the perfumes of flowers are perceptible *Mil.*

ཅིག་ *čig* = *ɣčig* **one**, as the first part of compound numbers: *čig-bču* 10, *čig-brgya* 100, *čig-ston* 1000, *čig-kri* a myriad etc.; also: *čig-rkyáṅ Lex., Schr.*: 'separate, single, one alone'; *čig-skyés Med., čig-táṅ Med.?* — *čig-túb* n. of a plant *Med.*; *Sch.* also: *čig-túb-pa* to be able to do a thing alone; *čig-dril Sch.*: rolled, wrapped, packed up (in one parcel or bundle); *čig-láb byéd-pa* to talk to one's self, to hold a soliloquy *Schr.*

ཅིང(ས)་ *čiṅ(s)* v. *ₒčiṅ-ba.*

ཅིད་པ་ *čid-pa* v. *p̀yid-ba.*

ཅིབ་པ་ *čib-pa* equal, uniform, suitable *Sch.*

ཅིབས་(པ) *čibs (-pa)* resp. **horse**, riding-horse, saddle-horse, *čibs-la ₒčib-pa* (for *rtá-la žón-pa*) to get on horseback, to mount; to go on horseback, to ride; *čibs-las ɣžól-ba* to dismount, **čibs žól-la naṅ** C. may your honour please to dismount; *kyéd-kyi čibs-su ₒbul* I give it you for a riding-horse *Mil.*

Comp. *čibs-ka ₒkrid-pa* to lead a horse by the bridle *Schr.*; *čibs-ka túb-pa* to have the command of the bridle, fig.: to be expert in ruling *Ld.-Glr.* p. 14, a, *Schl.* where *p̀yibs* is incorr.). — *čibs-čás* a horse's furniture, **harness** *Cs.* — *čibs-tur* **the head-piece** of a bridle. — *čibs-dpón* a master groom, **equerry.** — *čibs-rá* **a stable** for horses.

ཆུ་ *ču* I. num. fig.: 66.

II. sbst. (resp. *čab*) 1. **water**; *ču daṅ sai bu* is said to be a poetical name for wood; *ₒbáb-ču* lit. descending water, viz. brook, river, also rain. — 2. **brook, river,** *ču ₒkyám-po* overflowing rivers, floods *Ma.*; *táṅ-ču* a river or rivulet of the plain; *ri-ɣzár-ču* cataract, mountain torrent *Glr.* — 3. **water in the body:** *snyiṅ-ču* dropsy in the pericardium, *págs-ču* anasarca *Med.*; *págs-ču-zugs* one suffering from anasarca; v. also *ču-sér*; esp. euphem. for **urine;** *mi-ču* urine of men, *bá-ču* of cows *Med.*; *ču ni ču ₒdra* the urine is like water *Med.* — 4. v. *ču-žéṅ.*

Comp. *ču-klúṅ* **river**, e.g. *ču-kluṅ gaṅ-gá* the river Ganges *Dzl.* — *ču-klóṅ Cs.*: 'the body of a river', yet v. *kloṅ.* — *ču-dkyil* the middle of a river. — *ču-rkyál* a leather bag for water *Cs.* — *ču-skád* the voice of the waters, the sound of rushing water. — *ču-skór, raṅ-tág-ču-skór* **water-mill** *Glr.* — *ču-skyúr* n. of a bird *Thgy.*, *Sch.*: **'bittern, snipe'**; also n. of a plant. — *ču-skyúr* 1. *Lt.*: acidulous mineral waters 2. *C.*: **vinegar.** — *ču-skyés* 'water-born', the lotus *Glr.* — *ču-skyór* a handful of water. *ču-ka* the bank or brink of a river. — *ču-kúg* **bay, gulf.** — *ču-ₒkúr* containing water, po. for **cloud;** a native proposed to use this word also for **sponge,** which is a commodity hitherto unknown in Tibet. — *ču-ₒkyil* **puddle, pool.** — *ču-gáṅ* 1. full of water. 2. = *ču-sgáṅ* (v. *sgaṅ*) which latter is prob. the more correct spelling. 3. *Dzl.* ༢༢༦, 2; ༢༦༡, 18 = सत्य virtue, honesty, v. *Schf.* on this passage. — *ču-gri* a sort of knife; *Tar.* 43, 1 *Schf.* **razor;** also the attribute of a god, a weapon with a curved blade *Stg.* — *ču-gróg Sch.*: rivulet, brook; dish-water, rinsings; 'boiled water (?). — *ču-mgó C.* **source** or **head** of a river. — *ču-gágs* stoppage or retention of urine, **ischury,** *ču-gágs ₒbigs* the ischury is removed (lit. bored through) *Med.* — *ču-ₒgrám* **bank** of a river; *ču-grám-gyi šiṅ* a tree on the edge of a river, a metaphor for frail and perishable things. — *ču-rgyún* the streaming, continual flowing, **current,** often fig. — *ču-sgóṅ* the water-egg, po. for moon *Sch.* — *ču-ṅógs* v. *ṅógs.* — **čú-tu-gir** *W.* flour-dumplings, boiled in water. — **ču-stán** *W.* **swaddling-cloth.** — **ču-tág** *W.* calamus, sweet-scented flag, or some similar plant. — *ču-túms Sch.*: 'a swelling in the flesh, or a tumour filled with water'. — *ču-mtá* the side or **bank** of a river, **ču-tá tsúg-pa** (the avalanche came down) even to the river side. — *ču-dár Wdk.* a small prayer-flag stuck up close to the river, in order to avert inundations. — *ču-dúg Sch.*: 'a poisonous plant, hemlock', but Tibetans usually understand by it the stupefying power ascribed to certain rivers. — *ču-dóṅ* a deep **well.** —

— *ču-mdá* **a jet**, a spouting forth of water *Med.* — *ču-mdó* 'mouth (of a river), spout (of a tea-pot)' *Sch.*; but v. *mču.* — *ču-mdóg* the colour of urine *Med.* — *ču-rdó C.* small rounded pebbles, as in brooks. — *ču-nág* inundation, flood (?) *Ma.* — *ču-rnág* matter, pus *Sch.* — *ču-snód* 1. **pitcher, jug.** 2. *Schr.*: **chamber-pot** (yet in *W.* at least this article of luxury is not known). — *čú-pa* **water-carrier.** — *ču-pyág-pa* is enumerated among other synonyms to *grú-pa*, signifying **a ferry-man**, water-man. — *ču-prán* a little river, **brook.** — *ču-bár* 1. ('between the waters') **isthmus**, neck of land. 2. p. n. of a place in Tibet. — *ču-bál* n. of an aquatic plant *Wdn.* — *ču-bún* white paint for the face *Sch.* — *ču-bór* 1. **bubble,** also *čuí ču-búr* 2. **blister, bladder, vesicle,** e.g. occasioned by a burn or a vesicatory *Lt.* 3. **boil, ulcer, abscess** *Thgy.*, 4. *šaí ču-búr* a word describing the foetus five days after conception *Thgy.* — *čú-bur-čan* 1. n. of a hell *Thgy.* 2. the eye *Schr.* — *čú-bo* **river**, frq., *čú-bo-ri* n. of a mountain with a monastery two days' journey from Lhasa *Glr.* — *ču-byá* **a water-bird**; *Sch.*: *ču-byá dkár-po* swan, *ču-byá mgo-dmár* stork (not known in *W.*). — *ču-byí* **water-rat** *Sch.* — *ču-lbág* v. *lbag.* — *ču-sbúr* 1. *Sch.*: 'driftwood and the like', prob. more correctly: thin pieces of wood, chips, chaff etc. floating on the water. 2. **water-beetle** *Med.* — *ču-sbrúl* **water-snake,** not a mythological conception, like *klu*, but a really existing animal, though for Tibetans a somewhat faboulous one, as they have never seen the creature itself. The eel (*Sch.*) can hardly be meant by it. — *ču-mig* 1. **spring, fountain** frq. 2. n. of a vein *Med.* — *ču-rtsá* v. *ču-ču*, as a separate article. — *ču-tságs* 1. **a strainer, sieve,** 2. **watering-pot.** — *ču-tsán* 1. hot water, 2. warm water, not too hot for drinking *Med.* 3. a hot spring *Sch.* — *ču-tsód* 1. the clepsydra or **water-clock** of ancient India. 2. **clock** in general, *ču-tsod-ₒkór-lo* a wheel-clock. 3. **the Indian hour** = ½ *kyim* or 24 minutes. 4. **the European hour**; *W.*: **ču-tsód nyis ma leb** it is not yet two o'clock. — *ču-ₒdzin* po. **cloud** *Mil.* — *ču-rdzá* earthen vessel for water, **water-jar.** — *ču-žén* (*Lex.* परिणाह) **long and broad, area, superficial extent,** *ču-žén kru-brgyád-pa* eight cubits long and broad *Dzl.*; also *ču-žen-gáb-pa*, e.g. *ču-žen-gáb-pa-la dpag-tsád brgyád-ču Glr.*; *ču-žen-srab-túg* in length, breadth and height; also separately: *čur dpag-tsád* ༢༥༠༠, *žén-du yan* ༢༥༠༠, *mta-skór-du dpag-tsád* ༡༠༠༠༠ *yód-pa* 2500 miles in length, 2500 miles in breadth, 10000 in circumference; yet except in this connexion *ču* alone is never used for length. As another signification of *ču-žen-gáb-pa Schr.* mentions moreover: proportioned, symmetrical; others have: beautiful, great, considerable, which e.g. is its proper meaning in: *ču-žen-gáb-pa nya-grodha Stg.* the stately fig-tree. — *ču-zém* **water-tub.** — *ču-zlá* 1. the image, the reflexion of the moon in the water; a sort of deception of the senses by witchcraft. 2. the water-month, the first month. — *ču-yzár* a large **ladle** *Cs.* — *ču-bzóm* **a covered bucket** for carrying water. — *ču-ₒóbs* **water-ditch** *Sch.* — *ču-yar* col. water-rat (?) — *ču-rágs* **dam, dike.** — *ču-rí* 'hill of water', **billow.** — *ču-rúd* water rushing in, **inundation, deluge.** — *ču-rlábs* **wave, billow** *Dzl.* — *ču-lág* the arm of a river *Glr.* — *ču-lúd Sch.* dung, manure (?) — *ču-ló* n. of an edible plant *S.g.* — *ču-lóg* **floods.** — *ču-lón*, **dam, dike** *Tar.* 56, 15. *Lis.* — *ču-šín* wood drifted away by the water = *ču-ₒgrám-gyi šin* v. above; or the translation of कदली plantain or banana-tree with its spongy wood, in the place of which the Tibetan thinks of the *ₒóm-bu*, a shrub of similar qualities, at any rate a symbol of perishableness, of the frailty of life. — *ču-šún Sch.* surface of the water (?) — *ču-šél* v. *šel.* — *ču-ɉšón Dzl.* ༡༣༦, 17. a ravine containing water. — *ču-sá* **river-mud,** as manure. — *ču-sér* 1. animal water, **serum,** whether normal, or of a morbid character *Med.* — 2. **matter, pus.** — *ču-srán*, = ༡/༦༠ *ču-tsod*, i.e. **a minute**; the Indian or Tibetan minute is equal to 24 of our seconds, = 6 *dbugs Wdk.*, cf. *ču-tsód.* — *ču-srín* a water- or **sea-monster,** also Capricorn in the Zodiac. — *ču-lhá* **water-god** (*Varuṇa*); also = *klui rgyál-po.*

ཆུ་ཆུ་ *ču-čú,* = *la-čú,* **rhubarb,** *ču-rtsá* its root, used as dye and as a laxative *C.*

ཆུ་ཉིང་ *ču-níṅ* **four years ago** *C., W.*

ཆུ་པ་ *čú-pa* 1. *C.* a man's dress, **coat,** — 2. **water-carrier.**

ཆུ་བ་ *čú-ba* a large **sinew,** of which there are 16 acc. to Tibetan anatomy; *čú-ba ldóg-pa* a contraction of the sinews *Cs.*, *żá-ba* lameness, paralysis of the sinews *Sch.* — *ču-rgyús* (स्नायु) sinews, ligaments and nerves (there are 900 *rgyús-pa*); with respect to these, as well as to the veins, Tibetan science seems to be rather in the dark. — *ču-rtsá* 'sinew-veins', a term coming nearest to what we call the nerves. — *ču-ba-lṅa-ldán,* and *lṅa-lén Cs.* names of countries in India.

ཆུ་མ་རྩི་ *ču-ma-rtsi* a medicinal herb *Med.*

ཆུ་མ་ལོང་ *ču-ma-lóṅ,* **ṭu-gu ču-ma-loṅ** *Ld.* **an infant, baby.**

ཆུ་སོ་ *ču-só* the external and internal **urinary organs.**

ཆུག་ *čug* v. *ȷúg-pa.*

ཆུང་བ་ *čúṅ-ba* 1. adj. col. *čúṅ-ṅu, W.* also **čúṅ-se**, **little, small,** *čuṅ-čés-pas Dzl.* when he was very little; **young,** *bu čúṅ-ba* or *-ṅu* the younger or the youngest son; *lo-čúṅ* young in years; *ma-čúṅ* the younger sister of the mother; **'á-pa čúṅ-ṅu** the younger brother of the father; the younger or the youngest of the fathers (in polyandry); *čúṅ-ṅu-nas* up from infancy; *čuṅ-grógs* an early friend, friend of one's youth; *čuṅ-zád* a little, cf. *čuṅ-zad; čuṅ-(gyi) sri* a devil devouring infants, infants-devil; **nyiṅ-kʼám-, ṅo-míg-, pʼod-**, or **nyom-čúṅ-se** *W.* shy, timid. — 2. vb. **to be little, small** etc., *snyiṅ ma čuṅ čig Glr.*, be not timorous, do not fear! *ₒdún-ma rgya ma čuṅ čig* let the consultation not be trifling, let at once something of moment be consulted; *ₒdún-ma rgya mi čúṅ-bar byed-do* let us now decide on important things *Glr.*; *čúṅs-pa* pf., *čúṅs-pa yin-nam* is it too unimportant? *Mil.* (*čuṅ-ȷúg* v. *ȷa*).

ཆུང་མ་ *čúṅ-ma, C.* also **čuṅ-grógs, čuṅ-ₒdris**, resp. *btsún-mo,* **wife, consort, partner** *B., C.*; *lén-pa* to marry; *mi žig-gi čúṅ-mar byéd-pa* to be made a man's wife, to be married.

ཆུད་ *čud* occurs only in *čúd-ɣzon-pa, -ɣson-pa, -ɣsan-pa, -za-ba,* seldom *-ₒdza-ba* (*Lex.*) **to consume, spend, waste**; *čud mi zá-ba* inexhaustible.

ཆུད་པ་ *čúd-pa* = *ₒtsúd-pa, ȷúg-pa,* **to go, get in** or **into, to enter, to put in** or **into** etc., to go into a town *Dzl.*; of food entering the body *Dzl.*; *gaṅ yaṅ rúṅ-ba mi čúd-pa med* all without distinction may enter (my religion), says Buddha, in opposition to the aristocratic exclusiveness of Brahmanism *Dzl.*; *tʼúgs-su čúd-pa,* resp., to impress on one's mind; *kʼoṅ-du* v. *kʼoṅ-pa; ₒóg-tu* to subject *Tar.*; *grábs-su* c. accus. to procure, to provide or furnish one's self with a thing *Mil.*

ཆུན་ *čun,* occurs in *žiṅ-čun* one that is watering or taking care of fields, *tsʼás-čun* gardens *ₒól-čun* meadows *Ld.*

ཆུན་པོ་ *čún-po* (दामा) 1. **bunch, bundle.** 2. **tuft, tassel, ornament,** of silk, pearls etc.

ཆུན་མ་ *čún-ma* **the second wife** in rank.

ཆུན་ཙེ་ *čún-tse Bal.* **little, small.**

ཆུབ་པ་ *čúb-pa,* a corruption of *čúd-pa, kun čúb-par byao* all this is to be well impressed on the mind; *dbaṅ-po tʼams-čád-du čúb-pa* to pass through, to penetrate, every organ *Stg.*

ཆུམ་པ་ *čúm-pa, ₒȷigs-čum-pa Mil.,* **to shrink, to crouch** with fear.

ཆུར་ *čur,* termin. of *ču*; *čur ₒči-ba* to be drowned.

ཆུར་བ་ *čúr-ba* a kind of vermicelli, prepared from butter-milk boiled *Med., Ld.* **čúrpʼe**.

ཆུས་ *čus* 1. instrum. of *ču; Sch.* also *čús-γtoṅ-ba* 'to melt'; more correctly: **to gild, to plate** (in the warm or in the cold way), to overspread with a gold or silver liquid. — **after five days** *C., W.*, or, the present day included, on the sixth day, cog. to *bču.*

ཆེ་ *če* 1. num. fig.: 96. — 2. v. *če-ba.*

ཆེ་གེ་མོ་ *čé-ge-mo* **such a one,** *lo čé-ge-mo žig-la* in such and such a year *Dzl.*; *čé-ge-mo ḱyod* you so and so *Thgr.*

ཆེ་འགྲན་ *če-ₒgrán W.* being jealous of one's own honour, ni f.

ཆེ་ཐབས་ *če-ťábs* **arrogance, haughtiness,** *sde-pai če-ťabs* the arrogance of the great *Ma.*; **če-ťábs-med-ḱan* W.* affable, condescending, kind; *če-ťábs-čan* proud, arrogant, haughty; *če-ťábs byéd-pa B.*, **čo-če* W.*, **zuṅ-wa* C.*, to be arrogant, haughty.

ཆེ་དོན་ *če-dón* **a missive** to an inferior, **an edict.**

ཆེ་བ་ *čé-ba* 1. adj. **great,** (for *čén-po*); *bu čé-ba* the eldest son, the elder; *čé-bar ₒgyúr-ba* to become great or greater, to grow, increase e.g. of passions; *čé-bar ₒgró-ba, čer ₒgró-ba* id., cf. *čer*, *čé-bar byéd-pa* to make great; frq. in conjunction with nouns: *že-sdáṅ čé-ba* great with respect to anger, i.e. very prone to anger; *rigs čé-žiṅ* being of high extraction; also in compounds, v. below. — 2. sbst. **greatness, high degree** *Mil.*; **superiority, excellence,** . . . *kyi čé-ba stón-pa* to show the superiority of a thing *Mil.*; **čé-wa šrún-wa* Ld.* to behave decently, respectably. — 3. vb., pf. *čes* **to be great,** not only in *čé-žiṅ, če-o,* but also in: *ṅa-rgyál ma čé-žig* do not be great in pride, i.e. do not allow pride to become great *Mil.*, and so in similar cases; cf. *čes.*

Comp. *čé-ka Sch.*: 'chiefly; the plurality'. — *če-kyád* **greatness, size** *Dzl.* — **če-ḍál* W.*, **če-dál-la čud soṅ** he has entered the class of adults, he has come to full age. — *čé-rgyu* = *čé-ba*, cf. *rgyu* 3. — *če-brgyúd* perh. lineage by the eldest sons *Glr.* — *če-čúṅ* **great and small; size;** *če-čúṅ ni* in size. — *če-ₒdón* the coming to full age *Mil.nt.* — **če-mi* W.* **an adult.** — **če-lóṅs* C.* grown up, **adult** (*Sch.* 'chiefly'?)

ཆེ་ཞེ་ *če-žé* one's **elder sister** *Cs.*, **the elder wife** *Sch.*

ཆེ་བཞི་ *če-bži Lis.* = *bden-dpáṅ*, **witness, eye-witness; witness, testimony,** *če-bžir dris-te* being questioned as a witness, or asked for a testimony *Stg.*

ཆེད་ *čed,* as sbst. of rare occurrence, *Schr.*: reason, signification = *don; Sch.*: *čed čén-po* a great thing, an important business or affair. Mostly *čéd-du* postp. c. genit. **on account of, because of, for;** *ltá-bai čéd-du yin* it is in order to see *Pth.*; *rín-gyi čéd-du* as an equivalent *Pth.*; *lhai čéd-du ₒdzín-pa* or *γnyér-ba,* also *rjés-su ₒdzín-pa* or *γnyér-ba* to admit to the discipleship or communion of a god *Mil.* — As an adv. *čed-du* seems to signify 1. for a certain purpose, **designedly, purposely, expressly,** e.g. with *byéd-pa* to do, to make a thing; *mṅágs-pa* to send off, dispatch. — 2. **again, once more, once again,** = *p̄yir Mil.* — *dgos-čéd* the construction of any noun with *p̄yir-du, čéd-du* etc., regarded by Tib. grammarians as a case of declension.

ཆེད་དོན་ *čed-dón* v. *če-dón.*

ཆེན་པོ་ *čén-po B.* and *C.*, **čén-mo* W.*, **great** (*čén-mo* in *B.* only as fem. *Dzl.* ༧༥, b), *čén-por ₒgyúr-ba, W.* **čen čá-če**, to become great, to increase, col. also for to grow up; *skyes-bu čén-po* a great man, a man of great worth (by his talents and actions), a saint; **mi čén-mo* W.* a man of quality, of rank, a nobleman, a rich man; *čén-ma* the first wife in rank; *čen čun γnyis* the first and second wife *Glr.*; **čén-mo* W.* also: **old,** **ṭ'ú-gu lo ču čen-mo** a child ten years old.

ཆེམ་མེ་བ་ *čém-me-ba Lex., Cs.* **stillness, silence,** *čém-mer ₒdúg-pa Schr.*, *čém-mer ₒḱód-pa C.*, to sit still without speaking.

ཆེམ(ས)་ *čem(s)* in compounds: 1. *čaṅ-čém(s)* v. *čaṅ.* — 2. *ka-čém(s)*, resp. *žal-čéms(s)*, *bka-čém(s)* **farewell exhortation; last will, testament,** *srás-la ka-*

čém(s) ˳jóg-pa to deposit a testamentary disposal or devise for a son *Glr.*

ཆེམ(ས)་ཆེམ(ས)་ *čem(s)-čém(s)* 1. **the noise** made by thunder, by the shock of an earthquake etc., *˳brúg-sgra čem-čém sgrógs-pa* the rolling, roaring, clapping of thunder; *bžad-gád ˳ur čém-pa* a roaring laughter. — 2. *k'ra čem-čém* v. *k'rá-bo.*

ཆེར་ *čer* termin. of *če*, *čer ˳gró-ba* to grow, increase; *čer skyé-ba* to become great; to grow up, *čer skyés-pa* partic. grown up, adult; *da-dúṅ čer t'oṅ* go on! go on! *Mil.*; *rgyal-srid byá-ba čer ma byuṅ Glr.* his government was not (yet) of much consequence (as he was too young); *ṅés-pa čer med* this is not quite evident to me *Mil.*; perh. *Tar.* 36, 16; 101, 22; 120, 21; 169, 14 will allow a similar interpretation of *čer.* — *čér-na S.O.* yea; still more (?).

ཆེས་ *čes* 1. instrum. of *če.* — 2. pf. of *čé-ba*, as adv. **very**, *k'a-zás ṅan čés-kyi* as the food is very bad *Dzl.*; *čes sgrin-pa* very prudent or clever *Sch.*; *čes dár-bar gyúr-to* it spread very much *Tar.*

ཆེས་པ་ *čes-pa* 1. pf. of *čé-ba* to be great, *ha-čaṅ yaṅ čes-so* he is much too great *Dzl.*; *dmag-dpuṅ čes-pa* a great army; *dbaṅ čes-pas* being very mighty *Glr.*; *čar čes-pas* as it rained heavily *Pth.*; *dga čes-nas* greatly rejoicing *Mil.* — 2. **to believe**, but only when preceded by *yid* (resp. *t'ugs*), or *bden* (col.), c. *la*, also c. accus., or *par*, that, *Dzl.* ༧༦, 18.

ཆོ་ *čo* 1. num. fig.: 126. — 2. as a word for itself seldom to be met with, e.g. *Ld.-Glr. Schl.* fol. 13, 6, *Tar.* 129, 20; signification not clearly to be made out. **čó-med-pa** *C.* = *dón-med-pa* to no purpose, vain; fickle.

ཆོ་ག་ *čó-ga* (**विधि**) the way or **method** of doing a thing, e.g. of solving an arithmetical problem *Wdk.*, of curing maladies *S.g.*, esp. used of magic performances, *čó-ga-pa Cs.*, *čó-ga-mk'an Mil.*, a performer of such ceremonies. Whether it may safely be used for religious rites or ceremonies in general, is doubtful.

ཆོ་གོ་ *čo-gó Bal.* **great.**

ཆོ་ངེ་, ཆོ་ངེས་ *čo-ṅé*, *čo-ṅés*, **lamentation, wailing**, esp. lamentations for the dead, dirge, *˳débs-pa Dzl.*, *˳bód-pa*, *˳dón-pa* in more recent literature, *byéd-pa Sch.*, to lament, wail, cry, clamour; with *la* to cry to a person; the crying of a new-born child *Thgy.*

ཆོ་འཕྲུལ་ *čo-˳p'rúl* **magical trick, jugglery**, often put to *rdzu-˳p'rúl*, also used of the apparitions and doings of goblins *Mil.* Cf. *rdzu-˳p'rúl.*

ཆོ་བ་ *čó-ba* **to set on** (a dog), *čó-čo-ba* to set on repeatedly *Cs.*

ཆོ་འབྲང(ས)་ *čo-˳bráṅ(s) Mil.*; *Cs.*: the mother's family or lineage; *čo-rigs Dzl.* frq. *Cs.*: 1. the father's lineage, descent by the father's side; 2. an honourable extraction. — *čo-ris Mil.*, frq. = *čo-rigs*, also applied to things, e.g. a cane: *čo-ris yé-nas btsún-pa* a cane of an excellent kind, not coming from any mean or noxious plant.

ཆོ་ལོ་ *čó-lo* 1. **die, dice,** game at dice. — 2. **seal**(?) — *čó-lo-mk'an* a dice-player *Cs.*, *čó-lo rtsé-ba* to play at dice *Cs.*; *čó-lo-ris Glr.* the figure of a die, a square figure, in *Glr.* 47, 9 the Mongol translation substitutes a wheel, v. *˳k'ór-lo*; a checkered colouring or pattern, e.g. of cotton cloth *C.*

ཆོག་ *čog* 1. for *čó-ga*; *bón-čog Mil.* the ceremony of the Bonpos. — 2. v. *ɣčóg-pa.* — 3. v. *čóg-pa.*

ཆོག་པ་ *čóg-pa* vb., sbst., adj. 1. **to be sufficient, sufficiency, sufficient,** cedpir: *ṅéd-la dé-kas čog* it is sufficient for us, we are satisfied *Mil.*; *dris-pas* (instr. of *pai*) *čog-go Dzl.* ༢༨༧, 10 (there has been) enough of asking, = don't ask any more! *gáṅ-du bžugs kyaṅ čóg-par ˳dug* it is sufficient (for him) wherever he may live, i.e. he is satisfied with any place of living *Mil.*; *ṅéd-la nor loṅs-spyód-kyis čóg-pa yod* we have money and goods enough *Mil.*; *˳di ɣsúm-gyis čóg-na* if these three are sufficient for you *Mil.*; *rin-po-čes čóg-par* *gyúr-nas* when they had precious stones enough *Dzl.*; *ₒdí-tsam-gyis čóg-pa ma yin-no* that is not enough, that will not do *Dzl.*; *sgál-pa mi brgya žon čóg-pa* his back (is) large enough for a hundred men to ride on it *Glr.*; adv.: *čóg-par* sufficiently, e.g. *sbyín-pa* to give *Dzl.*; **ma čóg-pa** or **-ga* W.* (col. for *čóg-par*), **dúṅ-ce ma čóg-ga sad soṅ** he not only struck but killed him; *ṗyin-pas čóg-gi* it being sufficient (for the present) that I have come *Mil.*; *ťams-càd-la čóg-par gyúr-te* as all were satisfied *Dzl.*; *čóg-par ₒdzin-pa* to deem a thing sufficient, to be contented or satisfied with it; *čog šés-pa* vb., sbst., adj. to be contented, contentment, content; *ltá-bas čog mi šés-pai rdzas* a thing at which one cannot look enough *Glr.*, *Pth.*; *yo-byád-kyi* (better *kyis*) *čog šés-pa* easily satisfied as to the necessaries of life. — 2. **to be allowed, permitted, at liberty,** construed in the same manner: *ḱrid-pas čog* you may have lessons with me, I will instruct you *Mil.*; *ₒgrán-pas čog* I am quite at liberty to compete with you, we may safely compete with each other *Glr.*; *ₒťsó-ba dráṅs-pas čog* you can have meat set before you *Mil.*; with a root: *bu byin čog* then you may render up your son; hence it is in *W.* the usual word for *rúṅ-ba*, **náṅ-du ča čóg-ce yin-na man** is it allowed to enter or not? **šrád-ma za čog** eating pease is allowed, also: pease are edible; **lé-na ḱyoṅ čog ka taṅ** he issued an edict, that it should be permitted to fetch wool, i.e. he (the Maharajah of Kashmir) permitted the export of wool; **léb-na ṗul čog* when it arrives, I shall take the liberty of sending it to you.

ཚོགས་པ་ *čógs-pa* seldom for *ₒčág-pa* **to be broken** *Mil.*

ཚོང་, མཚོང་ *čoṅ, mčoṅ* a transparent, variegated, half-precious stone brought from India to *Ld.* and considered less valuable than *γzi*; perh. cornelian or sardonyx?

ཚོད་ *čod* 1. *C.* **the cutting off; deciding;** **ṭal-čǫ' gya čém-po ǯhé'-pa** to bring about a great remission of taxes, **bhu-lǫn-čǫ'** remission of debts; **sa-čǫ' gya čem-po ǯhé'-pa** to make a great way; cf. however *ṗyod*. — 2. **partition-wall** *Sch.*, *čod rgyág-pa* prob. to construct a partition-wall. — 3. v. *γčód-pa*.

ཚོད་པ་ *čód-pa* 1. **to be cut off,** *lám-sgo γnyis ḱá-bas čód-de* both approaches being cut off or obstructed by snow *Mil.*; *bčad kyaṅ mi čód-do* impossible to be severed, *caedendo non caeduntur*, *Glr.*; *mi-čód-rdó-rǰe* a diamond that cannot be cut to pieces, an epithet of a firm unbending king *Pth.* — 2. **to be decided, settled, fixed,** *goṅ-ťáṅ dpyád-kyis* (or *pas*) *mi čod Glr.* the value (of the stone) cannot be fixed, though one should attempt to apprize it i.e. it is invaluable, priceless; *go čód-pa* v. *go*.

ཚོད་པོ་ *čód-po W.* 1. **split, cut through;** 2. **distinct,** of words or writings.

ཚོན་ *čon* 1. *W.* (cog. to *čud?*) **useless,** to no purpose, *rin čon soṅ* the payment has been useless, thrown away; gen. adv. **čón-la** gratuitously, in vain, for nothing, **čón-la ḱón-ce** to hate without cause or reason; **čón-la dád-ce** to sit idle, to spend one's time unprofitably. — 2. **tent** (?), *čon-ťág* tent-rope *Mil.*, *čon-ṗúr* tent-pin.

ཚོམ(ས)་ *čom(s)* 1. **robbery,** *čóms-kyis zas ₒťsól-ba* to live on robbery *Ma.*; *čóm-po* robber *Dzl.*, *čóm-po rkún-ma* robber and thief, gen. *čom-rkún*, *čom-rkún-gyi ₒǰigs-pa* fear of robbers and thieves; *čom-rkún-pa* id. *Stg.* — 2. imp. of *ₒǰóms-pa*.

ཚོམ་པ་ *čóm-pa* **to be finished, accomplished,** *W.*, **ťó-re čom yin** to-morrow it will be finished, **da čom soṅ** now it is done, completed; cf. *čam*.

ཚོལ་ *čol* 1. **inconstant** *Cs.*; *dpyid-čol* fickle spring-weather. — 2. *Cs.*: for *čó-lo* in compounds, *rus-čol* **a die** made of bone; *šiṅ-čól* a wooden die; *duṅ-čól* shells used inst. of dice (?).

ཚོལ་ཁ་ *čol-ḱa Sch.*: 'a hole made by a blow; a nest'.

ཚོལ་ཟངས་ *čol-záṅs* a shallow shore *Sch.*

ཆོས་ čos (धर्म) 1. **doctrine**, a particular doctrine, **tenet**, or **precept**; *ysáṅ-bai čos šig* an esoteric doctrine, a mystery *Dzl.*; *k̓yád-čos* for *k̓yad-par-čan-gyi čos* a peculiar, distinguished, sublime, and therefore difficult doctrine; *ˏjig-rtén-gyi čos brgyad* the eight doctrines or principles of the world (though frq. mentioned, I found them nowhere specified) cf. Foucaux Gyatcherr., Translation p. 264; *čos-brgyád-mk̓an*, a man of the world, worldling *Mil.* — More esp. 2. **moral doctrine**, whether any separate dogma, or the sum of various doctrines, **religion** in general, both theoretically (system of morality, ethics) and practically (faith, exercise of religion); *lha-čós* the religion of the gods or (Buddhist) deities, i. e. the Buddhist religion, as the only true one, in opposition to all other heresies and false religions (*log-čós*), as well as to irreligiousness (*čos ma yin-pa*); *k̓a-čós* profession with the lips, hypocrisy *Glr.*; *ˏk̓rig-pai čós-la brtén-pa* those practising the religion of voluptuousness (an expression designedly forcible, like St. Paul's: 'whose god is their belly'); *mi-čos* v. below; *čos ˏčád-pa*, or *bšád-pa*, *stón-pa*, *smrá-ba*, *sgróg-pa*, resp. *čós-kyi sgrog-gléṅ mdzád-pa Glr.* to expound, to teach, to preach religion; *čos smrá-bai žál-la ltá-ba* to watch the mouth of the preacher *Pth.*; **čo̱ dóg-pa* C.* to read a religious book; **čos šád-k̓an* W.* a preacher; *čos ˏčád-pai ˏdun-k̓áṅ* place where sermons are delivered, church *Dzl.*; *čos nyán-pa* to hear religious discourses *Dzl.*; *čos žú-ba* to ask for religious discourses; partic.: one eagerly desiring or asking for religious instruction, an inquirer *Pth.*, *Mil.*; *čos byéd-pa* to act or live religiously, righteously, = *čos bžín-du byéd-pa*; also merely to wish to become pious, to strive after piety; *k̓yed smyiṅ-nas čos byéd-na* if you are in good earnest about religion, if piety is the aim of your heart *Mil.*; lastly in a special sense: to become or to be a monk *Pth.*; *čós-la sems sgyúr-ba Mil.* to show an inclination for religion, to turn religious; *čós-su*, or *čós-la ˏjúg-pa* 1. vb. nt. to enter into religion, to be converted, also: to go over to a religion, to turn (Buddhist), 2. vb. act. to convert, to turn a person from a bad life to a good one, to make him a believer, to make another a convert, a proselyte; *čós-la ˏgód-pa* = *ˏjúg-pa* 1; *čos spyód-pa* to practise religion; the exercise of religion, worship *S.g.*; *bka-čós* the word of Buddha, the doctrine as taught by Buddha himself; *rtógs-pai čós Thgy.* the knowledge acquired by meditation, independently of books, scarcely different from *ṅes-dón*, or *ṅon-šés*; *bstán-pai čos Thgy.* any knowledge derived from other sources. — 3. in a special sense the **religion of Buddha**, Buddhism, *dám-pai čos*, and frq. *dám-pa čos* id. (cf. ἡ πίστις Acts 6, 7); *čos daṅ bon* Buddhism and Bon-religion *Mil.*; *čós-la lóṅ-spyod-par ˏgyúr-ba* to live in the enjoyment of true faith. — 4. **religious writings**, and **writings, books, literature** in general, in as much as the Tibetans derivate every science from religion; *bón-gyi čos t̓ams-čád* all the Bon-writings *Mil.* — 5. **custom, manner, common usage, fashion**, *mi-čos* manners of the world *Mil.*; *mi-čos-kyi dús-su* as long as he lived according to the ways of the world *Mil.*; *yúl-čos-kyis* according to the custom of the country *Dzl.*; *kyád-čos* the way of distinguishing, of pointing out the characteristics *Glr.* (cf. under 1); **nature, quality**, *Dzl.* ༢༤༣, 18 cf. *čos-nyid.* — 6. **substance, being, thing**, *čos t̓ams-čád mi-rtág-pa yin-gyi* as every thing existing is perishable *Dzl.* — Other philosophical expressions containing the word *čos* v. *Was.* (296).

Comp. **čós-skad* W.* **book-language**, as opp. to *p̓ál-skad.* — *čós-sku* v. *sku.* — *čos-skyóṅ* v. *skyoṅ-ba.* — *čos-k̓ri* **reading-desk, lecturer's chair, pulpit** *Pth.*; **reading-table, school-desk.** — *čos-k̓ríms* v. *k̓ríms.* — *čos-k̓ríms-pa* v. *dge-bskós.* — *čos-ˏk̓ór* vulgo **prayer-mill**; the column of disks on the *mčod-rtén Pth.* v. *ˏk̓ór-lo* 2, also *ˏk̓ór-lo* extr. — *čos-grá* **school.** — *čos-(kyi) rgyál (-po)* 1. honorary title of kings deserving well of religion. 2. = *γšin-r̀je Schl. Buddh.* 93, 3. also as a p. n. — *čos-rgyúd* **religious tradition,** also = **confession, creed,** *r̀je-btsún-gyi čos-rgyúd* *ₒdzin-pa-rnams* those embracing the religious tradition of his reverence, his fellow-believers *Mil.*; *čos-rgyúd γčig-pa* one confessing the same faith or religion *Thgr.* — *čós-čan* 1. **pious, devout.** 2. v. *čos* 5, *ₒǰig-pai čós-čan yin* **having the properties** of perishableness, being subject to the law of mutability *Thgy.* — *čos-r̀jé* 'lord of the faith', viz. 1. Buddha *Lex.*, 2. devout or righteous lord, title of honour given to distinguished scholars *Tar. transl.* 331, and elsewh.; perh. also = *čos-rgyál.* — *čos-nyid* 1. = *čos* 5, **quality, nature,** *rgyá-mtsoi čos-nyid-kyis* in a manner peculiar to the sea, *Dzl.* ༡༢, 9 (112, 9?). 2. philosophical term: **existence, entity,** = *de-bžin-nyid* (acc. to *Thgy.*) by which the Buddhist however means a negation of being, non-existence, non-entity. — *čos-stégs W.* = *čos-k̔ri.* — *čos-stón* religious festive entertainment given to saints *Glr.* — *čos-dráṅ-po* **righteous** with regard to the laws of religion (adopted by Prot. Miss. for the scriptural term 'righteous' or 'just'), *čos-dráṅ-ba* justice, righteousness. — *čos-ldán* = *čós-čan.* — *čos-sdé* **convent, monastery,** *Wdk., Glr.* — *čós-pa* a religious man, **a divine, a monk.** — *čos-spún* **a religious brother;** such brotherhoods e.g. are formed by two devotees, before going on a pilgrimage. After having been consecrated by a priest, who consults the lot on such an occasion, they owe hospitality and mutual assistance to each other for life. — *čos-spyód* **exercise of religion;** *čos-spyód-bču* = *dgé-ba-bču.* — *čos-sbyin* is said to be frq. used in book-titles: *bkra-šis-lhún-po-nas čos-sbyin ₒdzad-méd spel p̀yir bris* written from Tashilhunpo as a religious gift for infinite increase and blessing. — *čos-blón* **a pious functionary** or official (*bdud-blon* an impious or wicked one) *Glr.* *čós-ma* a religious woman, **a nun** *Cs.* — *čos-méd* without religion, **irreligous, wicked.** — *čos-myón* **religious frenzy,** *W.:* **čos-nyón žugs** he has become deranged, his brains are turned (in consequence of meditating). — *čos-zóg* **priestcraft** *Mil.* = *čos-lúgs* religious party, **denomination, sect.** **čós-sem-čan** *W.* inclined to religion, **pious.**

མཆད་པ་ *čád-pa Lex.*: = 'tomb, sepulchre; = *pramārita Ssk.* killed, slain; *mčád-pa-med-pa* entire, perfect; *mčád-par byá-ba* = *mahimān Ssk.* greatness; also the magical power of increasing size at will'.

མཆན་ *mčan* 1. **the side of the breast,** *mčán-gyi bu* bosom-child, darling, *mčán-gyi mčis-bráṅ* bosom-wife (cf. our 'bosom-friend'); *mčán-du ₒǰúg-pa* to put into one's bosom *Glr.*; *mčán-k̔uṅ* **arm-hole, arm-pit,** often = *mčan; mčán-k̔uṅ γyás-pai rtsib-mai bár nas* (the Buddhas are born) from between the ribs of the right side (cf. *mṅal*); **čán-da** *W.* **pocket,** in clothes, cf. *dk̔ú-mda.* — 2. v. the following article.

མཆན་བུ་ *mčán-bu* 1. **apprentice,** *bzoi* in a handicraft, trade or art, *rig-pai* in a science, disciple *Cs.*, *sgyú-ma-mk̔an-gyi* appr. of a juggler, conjurer *Zam.* — 2. *yi-geï mčán-bu* words or lines, printed or written in a smaller character than the rest, and inserted in the text (called *má-yig Cs.*) like our parenthesis, but without brackets; hence 3. **note, annotation** (*Sch.* also: testimony?).

མཆི་བ་ *mči-ba,* eleg. for 1. **to come, to go,** *slád-bžin-par mčio* I shall come later *Dzl.*; **to appear,** used of a god; *skyábs-su* (to put one's self) under the protection of another person, ccd.; *ₒbáṅs-su mčio* I will obey *Mil.* — 2. **to say,** *žes mčio* thus he said.

མཆི་མ་ *mči-ma,* resp. *spyan-čáb* **a tear,** *ₒbyin-pa*; *ₒdón-pa Glr.*, *blág-pa Dzl.*, *γtóṅ-ba Mil.* to shed (tears); *ském-pa* to dry up tears *Cs.*; *ₒp̀yí-ba* to wipe off tears *Cs.*; *mči-mas brnáṅ-ba* to be choked with tears, to sob violently *Sch.*

མཆིག་ *mčig* 1. *Cs.* a stone for grinding spice etc., **a mortar**; *mčig-gu* a small mortar *Sch.*, **a pestle** *Cs.* — 2. **the nether mill-stone,** *mčig-ma* the runner or upper mill-stone, *Sch.*; *mčig skór-ba* to grind *Sch.*

མཆིང་ *mčiṅ Cs.* = *kloṅ*; one *Lex.* = *dkyil*; v. *kloṅ*.

མཆིང་བུ་ *mčiṅ-bu Cs.* = *ˌčiṅ-bu*.

མཆིད་ *mčid, bka-mčid, ysuṅ-mčid, W. *mol-čid** resp. the talk, discourse, speech (of an honoured person) *Cs.*; *mčid-lán* answer to such speech *Mil.*

མཆིན་པ་ *mčin-pa*, resp. *sku-mčin* **the liver**; *mčin-dri, mčin-ri* **the midriff** or **diaphragm**; *mčin-ḱa* liver-coloured; *mčin-nán* 'liver-pressing', first breakfast, because according to popular belief water rises from the human liver in the morning, which is depressed and appeased by taking some food; *mčin-nán byed-pa* to breakfast.

མཆིལ་པ་ *mčil-pa* 1. **fishing-hook** *Dzl.*, *mčil-pas nya ˌčór-ba* to fish with a hook, to angle *Cs.* — 2. **a little bird**, *W. *či-pa**, *Ts. *čil-pig; či-pa skyá-wo* W.* sparrow; *mčil-ḱra* sparrow-hawk; *mčil-mgó* a fabulous stone, like a bird's head, supposed to possess a variety of marvelous qualities.

མཆིལ་མ་ *mčil-ma* 1. *W. *mčil-mág**, resp. *ɉags-mčil, ɉags-čáb* **spittle**, prob. also other similar fluids *Lt.*; *ˌdór-ba* (*W. *ṕáṅ-če*) to spit; *mčil-lúd* (*W. *mčil-ldúd**) morbid saliva, e.g. of people affected with a cough or with hectic fevers; *mčil-snábs* prob. id.; *mčil-snód*, resp. *žal-bzéd*, spitting-box; *mčil-zúm, mčil-bkáb W.* slavering-bib or cloth. — 2. = *mčil-lhám Tar.* 72, 9?

མཆིལ་ལྷམ་ *mčil-lhám* **shoe, boot**, *mčil-lhám ynyis ˌdor-ba* to lose both shoes *Wdṅ.*; *mčil-lhám-mḱan* shoemaker, cobbler, seller of boots; *mčil-lhám-gyi yú-ba* the leg of a boot *Cs.*

མཆིས་པ་ *mčis-pa* 1. also *mčis-lágs-pa*, eleg. for *yod-pa*, **to be, to be there, to exist**, *du mčis* how much is there, how many are there? *Cs.*; *sú-la dám-pai čos mčis-pa* whoever has the holy doctrine *Dzl.*; *yul dbús-nas mčis-so* (he) is (comes) from the country Ü *Dzl.* — 2. pf. of *mči-ba* 1. *lam riṅ-po-nas mčis-te* having come from afar. 2. *žes mčis-pa* so-called.

མཆིས་བྲང་ *mčis-bráṅ* 1. eleg. **dwelling, abode, domicile**; also when speaking modestly of one's own dwelling: *bdág-gi mčis-bráṅ* my humble roof *Dzl.* — 2. *Lex.* **wife, partner.**

མཆིས་མལ་ *mčis-mál* **bed, bed-stead** *Cs.*

མཆུ་ *mču* 1. **lip**, *ya-mču* upper lip, *ma-mču* lower lip; *mču btud mḱas Wil.* prob.: one must be wise in lowering the lips, i.e. one must yield, giving up pouting; *ḱa-mčú*, resp. *žal-mčú* 1. **lip** 2. word, voice (?) *Sch.* 3. quarrel, strife, *ḱa-mčú rgyal-ṕám ɉi-ltar byuṅ žé-na* if one asks, which are the details of the quarrel; **ḱam-čú ɉhé-pa* C. *gyág-pa* Cs.* to quarrel. — 2. **beak** or **bill** of birds, *mčú-la ťógs-te ˌgró-ba* to fly, carrying something in the bill *S. O.*; *mču-lto* (or *ču-mdo?*) *W.* id. — 3. n. of one of the lunar mansions, v. *rgyu-skar*.

Comp. *mču-skyé* muzzle *Sch.* — *mču-sgrós* v. *sgros*. — *mču-ťár Sch.* (prob. a mis-print for *mču-ťór*) pustules, tubercular elevations on the lips. — *mču-ríṅs* long-beaked, n. of a bird, and also of an insect (a large musquito).

མཆེ་བ་ *mčé-ba*, *Cs.* also *mče-só*, **corner-tooth, canine tooth, eye-tooth, fang, tusk** of an animal, *mčé-la ytsigs-pa*, *W. *žé-če**, to show one's teeth, to grin; *mče-ba-čan-gyi sde* the class of the tusked animals, viz. the carnivora (lion, tiger, leopard), and the tusked pachydermata (elephant, boar etc.).

མཆེད་ *mčed, sku-mčéd, mčed-lčám*, resp. for spun, **brother, sister**; *mčed ɉnyis* my two brothers *Dzl.*; *srás-mo lha-lčám mčed bži* four princesses, sisters; *dei mčed* his illustrious brother, in reference to a king, prince etc. *Glr.*; esp. of gods: *mčed bži* four divine brothers *Glr.*; *mčed-grógs, grogs-mčéd* clerical brother, *mčed-grógs máṅ-po ťsógs-par* where many clerical brothers assemble; *mčed-grógs dam-ťsig yčig-pa Thgr.* betrothed brothers, religious brothers, = *čos-spún*; also *mčed-lčám* has this signification.

མཆེད་པ་ *mčéd-pa* 1. **to spread,** to gain ground, esp. of a fire, frq.; also fig.: *bdág-gi ˳dod-čágs-kyi me mčéd-pas* as the fire of voluptuousness spread or increased within me *Dzl.;* also in the following sense: *már-me γčig-la γčig mčed ltar* as one kindles one light by another *Mil.*; *γčig gleṅ γnyis gleṅ rím-pas mčéd-de* as (the news) spread more and more by gossiping people *Pth.* — *skye-mčéd* v. *skye.* — 2. = *γyó-ba, mi-mčed-pai dád-pa* = *dád-pa brtán-po.*

མཆེར་པ་ *mčér-pa* **the milt, spleen.**

མཆོག་ *mčog* **the best,** the most excellent in its kind, *skyés-bu mčog, mii mčog, rkaṅ-γnyís-rnams-kyi mčog* Buddha; *nyes-ltúṅ-gis ma ṗóg-pa* (or *na*) *mčog yin-te ṗog-rtíṅ bšágs-pa byéd-pa rab yin Mil.* the best thing is, not to have been surprised by sin, but after having been surprised, it is the best to confess it (and thus to atone for it); *γsuṅ-mčóg* chief or fundamental doctrine, main dogma, principal commandment etc. *Glr.*; *ṅa ni ˳jig-rtén ˳di-na mčog* I am the highest in the world (says Buddha immediately after his birth) *Glr.*; *γnas-mčóg* the most glorious or splendid country *Glr.*; *ro-mčóg* excellent taste or flavour *Mil.*; *mḱas-mčóg-rnams* most learned gentlemen *Zam.;* also as a complimentary word; *mi mčog ḱyod* most honoured Sir! *Pth.*; *mčog-dmán, mčog daṅ tun-móṅ, mčog daṅ ṗál-pa,* good and bad, first-rate and common, fine and ordinary, of goods etc.; eminent and ordinary, of mental gifts, talents etc.; *mčóg-tu gyúr-pa* = *mčog,* e.g. *mi-rnams-kyi náṅ-na mčóg-tu gyúr-pa γčig* one that has risen among men, so as to become their chief *Glr.*; *yúl-rnams-kyi mčóg-tu gyúr-pa* the most splendid of countries. — Adv.: *mčóg-tu* very, most, with verbs: *bón-po-la mčóg-tu mós-pa žig* a great admirer of the Bonpos *Mil.;* gen. with adjectives: *ro mčóg-tu mṅár-ba* extremely sweet; with the comparative: much, far, by far, greatly, *dé-bas mčóg-tu čeo* . . . is far or much greater than that *Dzl.*

Comp. *mčog-sbyín ṗyag-rgyá* a gesture made in practising magic, in conjuring up or exorcising ghosts. — *mčog-zúṅ* the model pair, the two most excellent amongst Buddha's disciples, Shariibú and Maudgalgyibú, v. *Köpp.* — *mčog-ríṅ* longest *Thgy.*

མཆོང་ *mčoṅ* v. *čoṅ.*

མཆོང་བ, མཆོངས་པ་ *mčóṅ-ba, mčóṅs-pa* to leap, to jump, frq., e.g. *čur* into the water; *mi-seb-la* among the people, e.g. of a mad dog).

མཆོད་པ་ *mčód-pa* (पूज्) I. vb. 1. **to honour,** revere, respect, receive with honour, *kún-gyis bkúr žiṅ mčód-pai ˳os* worthy of being honoured and praised by all; usually ccapir. (rarely dp.) in the special sense: to honour saints or deities by offering articles of food, flowers, music, the sound, odour and flavour of which they are supposed to relish, hence to treat, entertain, regale (the gods), and in a more general sense applied also to lifeless objects, e.g. to honour a sepulchre in such a manner; *Glr. mčód-pa* may therefore in English be sometimes translated by: to offer, to sacrifice, but it should always be borne in mind, that no idea of self-denial or yielding up a precious good (as is implied by the English word), or of slaughtering, as in the Greek *θύειν*, can be connected with the Tibetan word itself, though in practice bloody sacrifices, abhorred as they are by pure Buddhism in theory, are not quite unheard of, not only animals being immolated to certain deities, but also men notoriously noxious to religion slaughtered as *dmar-mčod,* red offering, to the *dgrá-lha* q.v. — 2. *C.* resp. **to eat, drink, take, taste,** (in *W.* expressed by **dón-če**).

II. sbst. **offering, oblation, libation,** *mčód-pa ˳búl-ba, W.* **ṗúl-če** frq., also *byéd-pa*; *ról-mo mčód-par ˳búl-ba* to bring an offering of music *Mil.*: *mčód-pa sna-tsógs tógs-te* carrying along with them all sorts of offerings *Glr.*; *mčód-pai kyád-par bču* the ten kinds of offerings *Tar.*; *lha-mčód* offering or libation brought to a *lha*; *°bru-mčód* an offering consisting of grain; *dus-mčód* offerings presented at certain times *Pth.*; *rgyun-mčód* daily offering; fig. *dád-pai mčód-pa Mil.*; *ytan-rág-tu sgrúb-pai mčód-pa ṗul* as a thanksgiving bring the offering of meditation! *Mil.* —

Comp. *mčód-k̇an* **house** or **place of offerings**, of worship, *Pth.*; adopted as an appellation for the temple of the Jews, as *lhá-k̇an* could not be used *Chr. Prot.* — *mčód-k̇ri* **offering-table**, Jewish **altar**, *Chr. Prot.* — *mčod-lčóg* prob. the same, *C.* — *mčod-čá Glr.* = *mčod-rdzás.* — *mčod-brjód* words of adoration, doxology. — *mčod-rtén Ssk.* **चैत्य** (religious building) and **स्तूप** (elevated place, elevation, tumulus) 1. etymologically; receptacle of offerings; 2. usually: a sacred pyramidal building, of a form varying in different countries and centuries, esp. near temples and convents, where often great numbers of these structures are to be seen. They were originally sepulchres, containing the relics of departed saints, and therefore called *ydun-rtén*; afterwards they were erected as cenotaphs, i. e. in honour of deceased saints buried elsewhere, but in more recent times they are looked upon as holy symbols of the Buddhist doctrine, v. *Köpp.* I, 533. — *mčod-stégs* offering-table, **altar.** — *mčod-stód Sch.*: an offering with a hymn of praise. — *mčod-stón* **an entertainment**, as sort of libation, given to the priests *Dzl.*; perh. also **a sacrificial feast.** — *mčod-sdóṅ* 1. *Sch.* = *mčod-rten* (?), 2. **offering-lamp** *Sch.*, 3. **the wick** of such a lamp (in this sense it is used in a little botanical book). — *mčod-ynás* 1. prop. place where there is offered, **place of sacrifice.** 2. the object to which veneration is shown, image of a god *Glr.*, **sanctuary.** 3. the offering priest, **the sacrificator.** — *mčód-pa-po* a sacrificer *Cs.* — *mčod-°búl* the offering of a sacrifice *Cs.* — *mčod-sbyin* id. (though elsewhere *mčod-pa* sbst., as a gift to deities, is distinct from *sbyin-pa* a gift to men), also: sacrificer; *mčod-sbyin-gyi °dun-k̇áṅ* house where people assemble in order to perform sacrifices; *sróg-gi mčod-sbyin* bloody offerings or sacrifices *Tar.* — *mčod-mé* **offering-lamp,** lighted in honour of a deity, and very common in the houses of Buddhists; **čod-mé ṗúl-če** *W.* to light such a lamp, (prop. to offer it). — *mčod-rdzás, mčod-čá, mčód-pai yo-byád* instruments, utensils, requisite for festival processions in honour of a deity. — *mčod-šóms* or *-bšáms* the upper shelves in the holy repositories, containing the little statues of Buddha etc.

མཆོར་པོ་ *mčór-po*, sometimes *°ṗyór-po* 1. **pretty, handsome,** neat, elegant, *ṗo mčór-po* a handsome man, *bud-méd mčór-mo* a pretty woman, esp. a smart gaily dressed female. — 2. *W.* also **vain, conceited.**

འཆག་ཅན་ *°čág-čan* col. **trodden, stamped; solid, firm, compact,** like the Hindustani *pakka.*

འཆག་པ་ *°čag-pa* I. pf. *čag* (s) 1. **to break** vb. n., *snod čag-pa* a broken vessel *Dzl.*; fig. *ṅa-rgyál čag* my pride is broken, frq.; *der-°byón-stabs čag* the opportunity of going there has been cut off *Mil.*; **lam čág-pa* (also *šog-pa*)* *C.* a. a beaten, practicable road (a road broken through, v. *°čég-pa*) b. *W.* an impracticable, broken-up road. — 2. **to be broken off,** abated, beaten down from the price, *žu-čág-med-par* there being no room for either asking or abating *Mil. nt.* —

II. also *čágs-pa*, pf. *bčags*, fut. *bčag* (imp. *°čog!*) 1. **to tread, to walk, to move,** esp. when speaking respectfully or formally, *yab-més-kyi žabs-kyis bčágs-pai sá-ča* the place where my ancestors did walk *Glr.*; *žabs čágs-pai ṗyag ṗyir °gro* follow me on my walk *Mil. nt.* — *°čág-tu* or *°čágs-su °gró-ba* to take a walk *Dzl.*; **góm-čag-če** *W.* to step along solemnly; *čág-ṗeb-pa* v. *ṗyág-ṗeb-pa.* — 2.

like ₒgró-ba in a more general sense: *bžón-pa-la, čibs-la* to ride in a carriage, on horseback *Cs.*

འཆགས་པ་ ₒ*čágs-pa* 1 v. ₒ*čág-pa*. — 2. sometimes for ₒ*čég-pa*.

འཆག(ས)་ས་ ₒ*čág(s)-sa* a place for walking, *Lexx.*, *Cs.*

འཆང་བ་ ₒ*čáṅ-ba*, pf. *bčaṅs*, fut. *bčaṅ*, imp. *čoṅ(s)*, 1. **to hold, to keep,** to take hold of, *skrá-la* by the hair *Mil.* — ₒ*čaṅ-zúṅs* handle, crook of a stick, *Mil.* — 2. **to carry, to wear,** to carry about one, e.g. amulets etc. — 3. (*yid-la*) **to keep** in memory, in one's mind. — 4. **to have, to assume,** e.g. the body of a goddess, of a Rakshasi *Pth.*

འཆངས་པ་ ₒ*čáṅs-pa W.* a (closed) handful e.g. of dough; **čáṅs-bu** a clod (of clay), a snow-ball etc. formed in the hand.

འཆད་པ་ ₒ*čád-pa* I. pf. *čad*, vb. n. to *γčód-pa*, like *čód-pa*, **to be cut** into pieces, **to be cut off, to decay,** *dúm-bur* (to fall) to pieces *Med.*; **to cease, end, stop,** of diseases *Glr.*, of life *Lex.*; **to cease to flow** or **to blow,** of water or wind; **to die away, to become extinct,** of a family, a generation; **to be consumed,** of provisions *Pth.* of bodily strength *Thgy.*; **to be decided,** *kyód-kyis bsád-par* ₒ*čád-na* you being determined to kill me *Dzl.* —

II. pf. and fut. *bšad*, imp. *šod* 1. **to explain,** ₒ*óg-tu* ₒ*čad* it will be explained below *Lt.*; *yid-la byos šig daṅ bšád-do* give heed, and I will explain it to you *Stg.*; ₒ*čad nyán-pa* to listen to an explanation *Sch.*; ₒ*jig čos γtam* ₒ*čád-pa* to teach the transitoriness of existence *Sch.* (?) — 2. **to tell, to relate.**

འཆབ་པ་ ₒ*čáb-pa*, pf. *bčabs*, fut. *bčab*, imp. *čob* **to conceal,** to keep secret, ₒ*čáb-pa-med-pai sems* a candid mind, open-heartedness *Stg.* (cog. to ₒ*jáb-pa*).

འཆམ་པ་ ₒ*čám-pa* I. vb. (pf. *bčam Lex.*), also adj. and sbst. **to accord, to agree, agreeing, agreement,** *srid-la mi* ₒ*čám-pas* as they did not agree about the government *Glr.*; ₒ*čam byéd-pa* to make agree, to reconcile *Mil.*, **čam mi čam** col. they do not agree; *ḱa* ₒ*čám-pa* to agree upon, to concert, e.g. an escape; *ḱa* ₒ*čám-par* by concert, unanimously.

II. 1. **to dance,** ₒ*čám-par byéd-pa Sch.* 2. a dancer, *ḱro* ₒ*čám-pa* a dancer with a frightful mask; *gar-*ₒ*čám(s)* a dance; ₒ*čám-po* a dancer *Glr.*; ₒ*čam-dpón* leader of a dance; ₒ*čám-yig* book or programme of a dance.

འཆའ་ ₒ*ča Ld.*, *Sp.* **cupboard.**

འཆའ་བ་ ₒ*čá-ba* I. pf. *bčas*, rarely ₒ*čas*, fut. *bča*, imp. *čos*, **to make, prepare, construct,** but used only in reference to certain things; 1. *γnas*, vulg. *ṫsaṅ*, ₒ*čá-ba Pth.* to prepare a place, house or abode, to settle; *mal* ₒ*čá-ba* to make a bed or couch *Cs.*; *dmag-sgár* ₒ*čá-ba* to pitch a camp; *ḱríms-ra* ₒ*čá-ba* to establish a court of justice *Glr.* — 2. *rgyal-ḱríms* ₒ*čá-ba* to draw up a law, to give laws, frq. — 3. *dam* ₒ*čá-ba* to make a vow, **to promise, assert, protest,** frq.; *yi-dam* ₒ*čá-ba* id.; also to utter a prayer; *dám-bča* v. sub *dam.* — 4. *skyil-krúṅ čá-ba* = *skyil-krúṅ byéd-pa*, v. *skyil-ba.* — 5. *blo-γtád* ₒ*čá-ba*, c. c. *la*, **to place confidence in.**

II. **to bite,** *γčig-la γčig* ₒ*čá-žiṅ zá-la* to bite and devour one another *Dzl.*; *so* ₒ*čá-ba* to bite with the teeth (?) *Mṅg.*, or to gnash or grind the teeth (?); *šiṅ* ₒ*čá-ba* **to gnaw** at a piece of wood *Stg.*

འཆར་རྒྱན་ ₒ*čar-rgyán*, or ₒ*čar-čán* a present given reluctantly *Sch.* (?)

འཆར་བ་ ₒ*čár-ba*, pf. *šar*, **to rise, appear,** become visible, of the sun etc., also of the sun's appearing above a mountain, from behind a cloud etc., frq.; **to shine,** *gaṅs-ri-la nyi-ma šar-ba* the shining of the sun upon a mountain covered with snow, a snowy mountain lit up by the rays of the sun *Glr.*; *γzugs-brnyán mi* ₒ*čar-ba* the not appearing of the image which is formed by the reflection of a mirror (as something strange and surprising) *Wdṅ*; *γzugs* ₒ*čár-ba byéd-pa* to cause an image to be reflected (in the water);

dpyid-ka šar spring has appeared; frq. of thoughts: *nyáms-su*, or *yid-la ₒčár-ba* (thoughts) rising in one's mind; *yid-la šar kyaṅ Mil.* though I can figure it in my mind; *grógs-su ₒčar* (they) appear as friends *Mil.*; *rgyáṅ-du ₒčar Mil.* it turned into a blessing. — *ₒčár-sgo* **thought, idea, conception,** *ₒčár-sgo ₒbyuṅ* an idea comes, a (happy) thought, a (new) light, bursts upon me *Mil.*; *ₒčar-ga Mil.* **the rising, the rise.**

འཆལ་བ་ *ₒčál-ba*, secondary form to *ₒčól-ba* II., 1. *Cs.:* **to fluctuate** mentally; in this sense prob. *Zam. ytad-méd ₒčál-ba* to fluctuate, to waver, without aim or object. — 2. **to be confused,** in disorder, *smra-ₒčál*, also *ₒčal-ytám smra Lt.*, as a morbid symptom, prob. he raves, he talks nonsense. — 3. morally: *tsul-ḱrims ₒčál-ba S.g.* **to break** one's vow, *bsláb-pa* to act contrary to the doctrine, **to violate** it *Tar.*; in a more restricted sense: — 4. **to fornicate,** to commit adultery, *bud-méd smad-ₒčál byéd-pa* a whore, harlot *Mil.*; *ₒčál-pa, -po* lecher, fornicator *Stg.*; *ₒčál-pa-rnams-kyi ṫsig* obscene language, mentioned as sub-species of *kyál-ka*; *ₒčál-mo* whore. — **čal-la-čol-lé* W.*, *čal-čól Tar.* 184, 20 confusedly, pellmell.

འཆི་བ་ *ₒči-ba*, pf. *ši*, 1. vb. **to die,** of a flame: to go out; *raṅ ₒčio* I will seek death *Dzl.*; *ₒči-ba yin* he dies, will die *S.g.*; *ₒči* or *ši-ba-las sós-par ₒgyúr-ba Dzl.* to be saved from imminent danger of death (but not: to rise from the dead); *ₒči-bar byéd-pai ču* water causing death *Sambh.*; *ši-bar gyúr-to* they perished *Pth.* — 2. sbst., the state of dying, **death,** *ₒči-ba tsám-du ₒgyúr-ba* to die almost (of grief etc.) *Mil.*; *dus-min ₒči-ba nyúṅ-ba yin* premature death rarely occurs *Sambh.*; *ₒči-ba nam yoṅ ča med Mil.* when death will come one does not know, (*W. *ši-če** to die; death; **ši soṅ** he has died, **ši yin** he will die).

Comp. *ₒči-ḱa Cs.:* 'the very act of dying,' but I doubt whether such a sbst. exists; I only know the adv. *ₒči-kar* at his very dying, at the point of death *Mil.*, when being exstinguished *Glr.* (v. *ḱar* sub *ḱa* IV. 4, 5), and *ₒči-ka-ma* 1. adj. dying, *dúd-ₒgro ₒči-ḱa-ma* a dying animal *Glr.*; 2. sbst. the dying, *ₒči-ka-ma-ru* = *či-ḱar* (doubtful); *ₒči-kar* and *ₒči-gar* may be incorrect spellings. — *ₒči-ltas*, more rarely *ₒči (-bai) rtágs* **forebodings, foretokens of death** *Med.* — *ₒči-bdág* the lord of death, perh. = *yšin-rje*, but it seems to be more a poetical expression than a mythological personage; *ₒči-bdág bdud* id. — *ₒči-nád* a disease causing death, **a fatal disease** *Tar.* — *ₒči-ba-po Cs.*; a person dying(?) — *ₒči-(ba)-méd(-pa)* immortal; cf. *ši-ba.* — Note. *ₒči ₒṗó-ba* is prob. only a rather incorrect, yet common expression for *ṫse ₒṗó-ba* to change one's place of existence, to transmigrate.

འཆིག(ས)་པ་ *ₒčig(s)-pa* **to bind** *Sch.*, prob. an incorr. spelling for *ₒkyig-pa.*

འཆིང་བ, འཆིངས་པ་ *ₒčiṅ-ba*, *ₒčiṅs-pa* I. vb., pf. *bčiṅs*, fut. *bčiṅ*, imp. *ₒčiṅ(s)*, *W. *čiṅ-če**, **to bind** (in general); **to fetter** (a prisoner) *Dzl.*; **to bind** or **tie up, to cord,** a bundle or package; **to tie round,** to put on, a girdle *Glr.*; **to bind up, to dress,** wounds; fig. **to render harmless, to neutralize, paralyze,** esp. by witchcraft, **to exorcise,** frq.; *bčiṅs ₒgról-ba* to untie, to loosen, to take off the dressings *Lt.* —

II. sbst. any binding-material 1. **ribbon,** *mgul-čiṅs* necklace, neckcloth, neckerchief. — 2. **fetter, shackle,** also fig. for magic curse, anathema. — 3. **string, tie.** — 4. **cramp, spasm** *C.*

འཆིང་བུ་ *ₒčiṅ-bu* a spurious, glass jewel (*Schf. Tar.* 142, 9); *bsam-yas-ₒčiṅ-bu* p. n. *Ma.*

འཆིབ(ས)་པ་ *ₒčib(s)-pa*, pf. *bčibs*, fut. *bčib*, imp. *čibs* resp. **to ascend, to mount,** a horse or carriage, *rtá-la*, or more correctly *čibs-la*, **to ride,** to proceed on horseback.

འཆིམས་པ་ *ₒčims-pa* **to be full, to get full** *Sch.*

འཆིར་བ་ ₒčír-ba, evidently a present-form of the pf. čír-ba, **to press, to squeeze.**

འཆུ་བ་ ₒčú-ba I. acc. to grammatical analogy 1. vb. n. to γčúd-pa, **to be twisted, distorted,** pf. ₒčus. — 2. sbst. **curvature, crookedness, distortion.** — 3. adj., more frq. ₒčús-pa **crooked, wry,** ka-ₒčús Wdṅ. the mouth being wry, distorted *Lt.*; also obstinately perverse; fig. yig-ₒčús *Med.* frq., prob. = kam-lóg.

II. pf. bčus, fut. bču, imp. čus, *W.* *ču-če*, 1. **to lade** or **scoop** (water), ču-mig-la ču to draw water from a well *Dzl.*; ču-tóm water-conduit *Sch.* — 2. **to irrigate, to water,** žiṅ a field *Cs.* (?)

III. nán-gyis ₒčú-ba-la *Tar.* 127, 6, when he was pressed hard, was urged with importunity; (this signification, however, seems to rest only on this passage).

འཆུག་པ་ ₒčúg-pa **to be mistaken** *Pth.*, v. ₒp̌yúg-pa.

འཆུན་པ་ ₒčún-pa, evidently vb. n. to ₒǰún-pa, hence 1. **to be tamed, subdued, made to yield,** stóbs-kyis by force, lás-kyis by hard work. — 2. **to confess** *Cs.* — 3. **to wrap** or **twist** *Sch.* — 4. **to fix** *Sch.* — 5. **to fix one's self** *Sch.*; ₒčál-sar ₒčun entangled in vicious indulgences *Sch.*

འཆུམ(ས)་པ་ ₒčúm(s)-pa 1. **to wish, to long for** *Lex.* — 2. **to shrink** *Cs.*

འཆེ་བ་ ₒče-ba, pf. bčes, ₒčes (*Sch.*), fut. bče, imp. čes, 1. **to assure, to promise,** kas ₒčé-ba *Lex.*, resp. žál-gyis ₒčé-ba id. — 2. resp. for smrá-ba, like γsúṅ-ba (?)

འཆེག་པ་ ₒčég-pa, also ₒčág(s)-pa, pf. bšags, fut. bšag, imp. šog, *W.* *šág-če*, 1. **to cleave, to split,** šiṅ wood; sóg-les ₒčég-pa to saw *Sch.*; ₒčeg-byéd (a thing) that cleaves, a hatchet *Cs.* — 2. **to confess, to acknowledge;** v. also bšág-pa and šóg-pa.

འཆེད་པ་ ₒčéd-pa an incorr. form of čád-pa or mčéd-pa.

འཆེམས་པ་ ₒčéms-pa, pf. bčems, fut. bčem, **to chew** *Med.*

འཆེལ་བ་ ₒčél-ba *Cs.* 1. **to believe, give credit to;** blo-ₒčél-ba (?) cól. id. — 2. *Lexx.* = žén-pa **to wish** (?).

འཆོག་ ₒčog **wall** *Sch.*

འཆོང་བ་, འཆོངས་པ་ ₒčóṅ-ba, ₒčóṅs-pa *Sch.* = ₒčáṅ-ba.

འཆོམས་པ་ ₒčóms-pa 1. = ₒčám-pa *Glr.* and *Lexx.* — 2. vb. n. to ₒǰóms-pa 4 *W.*, *da čoms soṅ* now it is done.

འཆོར་པོ་ ₒčór-po = mčor-po.

འཆོར་བ་ ₒčór-ba I. vb. n., pf. šor, 1. **to escape, slip, steal away; to drop from,** stón-mo šór-gyis as the meal escaped him, as he was deprived of the meal *Dzl.*; rtsa-krág ₒčór-ba hemorrhage, bloody flux *Med.*; bkrag-ₒčór without splendour, lustreless; nor ₒčor the money is gone, spent, lost *Thgy.*; sdóm-pa ₒčor the duty is violated *Glr.*; mé-la, čú-la ₒčór-ba to be consumed by fire, carried off by water; *čaṅ mi tuṅ dé-ne ka mi šor* *W.* I will not drink any beer, then the mouth cannot run away, i. e. then no indiscreet words will escape my mouth; **to flow out, to run,** of a leaking vessel, **to run over,** of a full one. — 2. **to come out, to break out,** frq. of fire; ₒkrúg-pa šor a quarrel, a war broke out, also of water breaking through an embankment etc. — 3. **to go over, to pass,** from one person or thing to another, rgyál-sa Bód-nas Me-nyág-la šor the supreme power passed from Tibet to Tanggút *Glr.*; γžán-gyi dbáṅ-du šor then I shall get into the power of another *Mil.*; rkún-ma-la šor it became the prey of a thief. — 4. *W.* **to run away, flee, escape, elope,** inst. of ₒbrós-pa, *šór-te ča-dug* he retires, falls back.

II. vb. a., pf. (b)šor, fut. γšor (?) 1. **to pursue, chase, hunt** after, ri-boṅ rgyas hares by means of nets; nya ₒčór-ba to fish *Dzl.*; *Cs.* also to strain (?); ₒčor-sgég a seducer; a swaggerer *Sch.* (cf. sgég-pa). — 2. **to light, kindle, set on fire** (?)

འཆོལ་པ་ ₒčól-pa 1. **disorderly, dissolute, immoral.** — 2. disorderly action or conduct, **dissoluteness,** ₒčól-pa sna-tsógs spyád-pa committing several acts of immorality *Wdṅ.* — kro-bo-ₒól-pa n. of a demon. (Cf. ₒčól-ba II).

འཆོལ་བ་ ₒčól-ba I. pf. bčol, fut. γžol (?) 1. **to entrust** a person with a thing, to commit a thing to another's charge; **to make, appoint,** *dé-la rgyál-po ₒčól-lo* they made him king *Pth.*; *btsún-mo-la rtá-rdzi bčól-lo* they made the queen tend the horses *Glr.*; *ťab-γyóg ₒčól žig* he may be employed as a kitchenboy, scullion *Pth.*; *dbaṅ-méd-du ₒčól-ba* to make one powerless, to compel by authority *Glr.*; *bčól-bai γnyer Lex.* manager; *ₒčól-bai ṅo Lex.* intercessor; *pi-waṅ-la ram-ₒdégs bčól-nas glu blaṅs* she sang with accompaniment of the guitar (lit. committing the accompaniment to the guitar) *Glr.*; **kyab čól-la** (for *ₒčol-du*) **yoṅ-če** *W.* to place one's self under another man's protection. — 2. **to commit, commend, recommend,** *lás ₒčól-ba* to commission one with an affair or transaction; resp. *ṗrin (-las) ₒčól-ba*, though *ṗrin (-las)* seems to be sometimes a mere pleonasm: *bán-so yul dei lha-sruṅ-rnams-la ṗrin-bčól mdzád-do* (the king) recommended the sepulchre to the tutelar gods of the country *Glr.*; **čól-te bór-če** *W.* to deposit a thing for temporary keeping.

II. = *ₒčál-ba* 1. *Cs.* **to change, to turn aside** (?) — 2. **to be thrown together** confusedly, e.g. of the loose leaves of a (Tibetan) book; *ₒčól-bar byéd-pa* to put in disorder, to confuse, to confound *Ma.*; *dge-sdig ₒčól-bar ₒgro* virtue and vice are confounded *Ma.*; **'i lé-ka čól dug** *W.* this affair goes wrong, turns out badly; in a special sense: **to rave, to be delirious** *C.*; **čol-láb gyáb-pa** *C.* id.; **nyúl-čol láb-pa, gyag-pa** *C.*, to talk confusedly whilst being heavy with sleep; **čól-ka** *C.* senseless talk; **čól-kan-ni ťú-gu, čol-ťúg** *W.* being of a mixed race; illegitimate or bastard child, bastard. — 3. morally: **to break a vow;** **a-ne čol son** he has broken his vow on account of a woman, i.e. by having married.

འཆོལ་མ་ ₒčól-ma *Cs.*: 1. a thing committed to another's care. — 2. **a sly, crafty woman,** *Sch.* **a dissolute woman.**

འཆོས་པ་ ₒčós-pa I. pf. bčos or ₒčos, fut. bčo, imp. čos, supine bčós-su *Dzl.* ༢, 4, *W.* **čó-če**, pf. and imp. **cos**, **to make, make ready, prepare, to construct, build,** a bow, a road etc. *Glr.*; *ₒčós-sam* am I to build? *Glr.*; *drés-ma ťág-par ₒčós-pa* to make ropes out of *drésma* (a kind of grass) prop. to work *drésma* into ropes, *Glr.*; *γzab ₒčós-pa* to adjust one's ornaments *Sch.*; *lus ₒčós-pa* to dress, to trim one's self up *Sch.*; *γsár-du ₒčós-pa* to renew, renovate, repair *Sch.*; *ltúṅ-ba ṗyir ₒčós-pa Tar.* 95, 20 perh. to retouch, amend, correct, improve. — *tsúl-ₒčos* hypocrisy, a mere outward performance of religious rites and observances *Mil.*, *tsul-ₒčos ma byas spyód-pa* to live without hypocrisy *Mil.*; *tsúl-ₒčos-mkan* hypocrite. — *tsúl-ₒčos-pa* or *bčós-pa* acc. to *Cs.* also an established rule or canon.

II. *Sch.*: **to gnaw off** (secondary form to *ₒčá-ba*).

ཇ

ཇ་ ǰa 1. the letter ǰ, media, palatal, like the Italian *gi* in Giovanni, *g* in giro; in *C.* as initial deep-sounding and aspirated, ǰh. — 2. numerical figure: 7. — 3. **tea,** resp. *γsol-ǰa.* For the trade in Central Asia it is pressed into brick-shaped lumps, a portion of which, when to be used, is pulverized and boiled, having been well compounded with butter and salt or soda (*bul*) by means of a kind of churn of bamboo (*gur-gúr*), after which it is drunk as hot as possible. Of late years tea grown on the southern slopes of the Himalaya Mountains finds its way into

Central Asia. The tea called *ₒbru-ťáṅ* is considered the best, and of other teas *Cs.* mentions *rtsé-ǰa*, *zi-liṅ-spú-ǰa* hairy (?) tea from Siling, (a province in the neighbourhood of the Kokonor); *Schr.*: *γnám-ǰa*, *míṅ-ǰa*, *ₒbó-ǰa*, *ǰa-γzúṅs*, *zau*, *hụ-čág*, *ₒu-si; bzaṅ-ǰa*, or *ko-tse* is, acc. to *Cs.*, good ordinary tea, *čuṅ-ₒǰug*, or *čuṅ-čuṅ* are sorts of inferior quality. The shepherds in *W.* make use of a surrogate, viz. the Potentilla Inglisii (*spáṅ-ǰa*), growing on the mountains at a height of 15 000 feet; poor people in *Sik.* use the leaves of the maple (*γya-lí*).

Other **comp.** *ǰa-bkrúg* (pronounced *ǰhab-ṭúg*), prob. for *ǰa-dkrúg*, **twirling-stick** *Ts.* — *ǰa-mčód*, libation of tea. — *ǰa-ₒťág*, or *btág* **grinding-stone**, in India and Tibet used for kitchen purposes inst. of our little mortars. — *ǰa-dám Sch.* **tea-pot** (?) — *ǰa-blúg W.* a little pitcher-shaped **brass vessel.** — *ǰa-ₒbíṅ* (pronounced *ǰham-bíṅ*) *C.* **tea-kettle, tea-pot.** — *ǰá-ma* the man that prepares the tea in a monastery, **tea-cook**; *ǰai dpon* head-tea-cook. — *ǰa-ríl* 1. *W.* **grinding-stone**; 2. *Lex.* **skull.** — *ǰa-sun-čan* 'a cup of tea, or: as much as a cup of tea' *Sch.* — *ǰa-seg* tea-dust *Sch.*

ཇ་ཧོད་ *ǰa-hód Lex.* **yellowish red.**

ཇག་ *ǰag* **robbing, robbery,** *ǰag rgyág-pa* to rob, to be a robber; *rku-ǰag-gyu-zól byéd-pa Glr.*; *ǰág-pa* frq. robber (not robbery *Sch.*); *ǰag-dpón* captain of a gang of robbers *Mil.*

ཇི་ *ǰi* 1. num. fig.: 37. — 2. the correlative form of the pron. *či*, **what.** For the construction of a sentence containing *či* or *ǰi*, v. *gaṅ* II. The explanation there given shows, that in correct language *ǰi* is always followed by a participle: *ǰi yód-pa de ṗul žig* offer what you have, make a libation of what you have. Owing, however, to the slight difference in the pronunciation of *či* and *ǰi*, the former is frq. written in the place of the latter; *ǰi*, of course, is used in conjunction with the same words as *či*; a few more instances may follow here: *ǰi-skad* whatever, relative to words spoken: *ṅas ǰi-skad smras kyaṅ* whatever I may say *Glr.* — *ǰi-snyéd* 1. as much as, as great as; 2. *C.* very much, every thing possible. — *ǰi-lta-ba* 1. adj. of what kind, of what nature, ... *ǰi-lta-ba bžin-du* ... *la yaṅ de-bžín-no* as it is with ... so it is with ... *Stg.* 2. sbst. quality, nature, condition *Cs.* — *ǰi-lta-bu* such as, like as, Lat. qualis. — *ǰi-ltar* adv. as, in what manner; *'á-mas ǰi-ltar zér-pa bžin-du* according to what the mother has said *Glr.* — *ǰi-ste* = *či-ste.* — *ǰi nús-kyis* to the utmost, to the best of one's ability *Dzl.* — *ǰi ma ǰi-bžin-du* (?) according to custom or common usage *Sch.* — *ǰi-mi-snyám-pai bzód-pa* a patience prepared for every event *Sch.* (?) — *ǰi-tsam* = *ǰi-snyéd*; *lo lṅa lón-pa ǰi-tsam-pa de-bžín-no* they are (as tall) as (children) five years old *Stg.*; *ǰi tsam byas kyaṅ* whatever they had done *Tar.*; *ǰi-tsam-na* or *nas* as soon as, when. — *ǰi-bžín* as, like, how, *ǰi-bžin ₒťso mi ruṅ* (he) can in no wise, by no means, continue to live *Lt.*; *ǰi-bžin-du γsuṅs* elliptically: he said how (it was), he answered according to the state of the case (*Schf.*) *Tar.* 89, 9. — *ǰi-srid* as long as.

ཇུ་ *ǰu* num. fig.: 67.

ཇུ་ཐིག་ *ǰu-ťig* denotes a way of drawing lots by threads of different colours, whence a class of Bonpos is called *ṗya-bon ǰu-ťig-čan Glr.*

ཇུ་པོ་ *ǰú-po Liś.*, *ǰu-lúm* *W.*, a globular stone used for grinding spices, = *ǰa-ríl.*

ཇུས་ *ǰus C.* **strategy.**

ཇུས་མ་ *ǰús-ma* a sort of silk stuff *Cs.*

ཇུས་ལེགས་ *ǰus-légs* 1. *Sch.*: 'possessed of good manners, of propriety of conduct, **decent, agreeable**; *ǰus-bdé* sincere' (?) — 2. *Cs.* **clever, skilled, able, experienced.** *žiṅ-gi le* in agriculture, *mag* in military matters *C.*

ཇེ་ *ǰe* 1. num. fig.: 97. — 2. a particle, used for expressing the comparative degree of an adj. or adv., and esp. a gradual growing or increase, often with termin. or *la*: *ǰe maṅ °gro* (they) go on increasing or multiplying in number *Mil.*; *ǰe γsál-du soṅ* it has become more and more clear or evident *Thgr.*; gen. repeated: *ǰe nye ǰe nye sóṅ-ste* going nearer and nearer *Mil.*; *ǰe čuṅ ǰe čúṅ-la soṅ*, also *ǰe čúṅ ǰe nyúṅ Mil.* less and less; sometimes also for the superlative degree, *Cs.*: *ǰe dáṅ-po* the very first, also *Lex.* — 3. *ǰé-žig* a little while, = *ré-žig Lex.* — 4. *Bhar.* 14, *Schf.*: 'an adhortative particle, often connected with a vocative'; *Sch.* has: *ǰe ḱyod* 'now you, you first!' — 5. = *dbyaṅs Lex.*

ཇོ་ *ǰo* 1. num. fig.: 127. — 2. v. the following word.

ཇོ་བོ་ *ǰó-bo* (आर्य) 1. *C.* **the elder brother,** also **ǰo-ǰó** and **'á-ǰo** (the latter also in *W.*), resp. *ǰo-légs.* — 2. **lord, master,** esp. **nobleman, grandee,** *W. *ǰo*, yar-lúṅ ǰó-bo Glr.* the lord of the manor of Yarlung; **ti-nán ǰo* W.* the nobleman of Tinan; *ǰo-ǰo miṅ-po* my noble brothers (says a princess) *Glr.*; in *C.* used as honorary title for noblemen and priests, in *W.* also for noble Mussulmans; in ancient times for certain divine persons, and idols, particularly for two, famous in history: *ǰó-bo mi-skyod-rdó-rǰe*, and *tsan-dán-gyi ǰó-bo*, also *ǰó-bo śá-kya, ǰó-bo rin-po-čé* v. *Glr.*

ཇོ་མོ་ *ǰó-mo* 1. **mistress**, the female head of a household, a woman that governs as mistress of her servants *Dzl.* — 2. **lady,** esp. **a cloistress, nun** *Mil.*; in *W.* frq. — 3. **goddess** (cf. sub *ǰo-bo* 2), *ǰo-mo sgrol-ma* the goddess *Dolma Glr.* — 4. p. n. *ǰo-mo-lha-ri* one of the highest mountain summits in West-Bhotan, usually called 'Chumulhari'; *ǰo-mo-ḱa-nag* another summit in southern Tibet.

མཇལ་བ་ *mǰál-ba*, imp. *mǰol*, 1. **to meet** c. *daṅ*, = *°prad-pa*, without any respect to rank, *Mil.* often. More frq. 2. resp.: **to obtain access** to an honoured person; *žal-dṅós-su mǰál-bar yod* he (the incarnated Buddha) may personally be seen and spoken to *Glr.*; **to wait on, to pay one's respects** to a person, *yab daṅ mǰal °tsál-lo* I will pay a visit to my father *Dzl.*; *ṕyis myúr-du mǰál-du yoṅ* I shall take the liberty of soon coming back *Mil.*; *rgyál-bai sku daṅ ťa-mal mǰal* to thee, Buddha, my own humble self approaches (says a prince to his father who appears to be an incarnated Buddha) *Glr.*; *mǰál-bar žú-ba* to ask for an audience *Glr.*; *mǰál-du mi btub* (they) cannot get in, cannot obtain admittance *Pth.*; **ǰal-čág čó-če** (or **čag-ǰál* Cs.*) *W.* to salute, to exchange compliments on meeting; *mǰal-ṕrád-byéd-pa* = *°ṕrad-pa*; used also of a king and his ministers: *mǰal-ṕrád daṅ dgá-bai γtam máṅ-po mdzad* (they) exchanged many compliments and expressions of joy *Pth.*; to visit or pay one's respects to holy places, as pilgrims do, **to go on a pilgrimage,** also *žal mǰál-ba Mil.*; *γnas mǰál-ba* id., *γnas-mǰál-pa* partic., a pilgrim, palmer; *°di mǰól žig* do make your pilgrimage to this place. — 3. **to understand, comprehend,** *Zam.*: '*gó-bai mǰál-ba* ज्ञा'; *don mǰál-ba* to understand the sense *Mil.*, yet cf. *°ǰál-ba* 3. — 4. often erron. for *ǰál-ba*.

Comp. *mǰál-ḱa* **audience, access, admittance,** *mǰál-ḱa γtóṅ-ba*, or *γnáṅ-ba* to give audience, *°gégs-pa* to refuse it *Mil.* — *mǰal-dár* = *ḱa-btágs.* — *mǰál-sna-pa* **an usher,** master of ceremonies *Cs.* — *mǰal-ṕyág* **salutation.** — *mǰal-máṅs* a visit paid by many together, a grand reception *Cs.*

མཇིང་པ་ *mǰíṅ-pa* 1. = *°ǰíṅ-pa.* — 2. *rtsva-mǰiṅ* **meadow** *Bhar.* 82, *Schf.*

མཇུག་ *mǰúg* what is behind, **hind part,** e.g. of the body, resp. *sku-mǰúg*, **posteriors, back-side, tail,** often also *mǰúg-ma*; *mǰug skór-ba* col. to turn one's back (on another); *mǰúg-ma sgril-ba* to wag the tail; fig.: the further progress and final issue of an affair, **the consequences** = *rǰes*, opp. to *dṅos-γži* the thing itself, and to *sṅón-°gro* the preparations *Thgy.*; **the lower end** or extremity, e.g. of a bench, a stick, a river (= mouth), of a procession, train etc.; with regard to time: **the end,** *zlá-ba brgyád-pai mǰúg-la*, at the end of the eighth month;

in general *m)úg-la, m)úg-tu* adv. and postp., = *mťar*, at the end of, at last, behind, after, with the genit. inf., or the verbal root, gen. opp. to *mgo*. — *m)úg-sgro* (*W.* *)úg-ro*) lower or inferior part, underpart, buttocks (cf. *yžug*); *m)úg-to* id. — *m)ug-btág* (for *btég*), and *m)ug-ldéb W.* wagtail. — *mgo-m)úg* above and below *Dzl.*

མཛེ་ *m)e*, resp. *ysáṅ-m)e*, **लिङ्ग, शेफ the penis;** *Zam.* avoids the term by making use of circumlocutions, others employ it, esp. *Med.*; also in vulgar use; *m)e láṅ-ba* erection of the penis; *m)e sbúbs-su nub* the penis recedes; *m)e-mgo* glans penis. — *m)e-rlig* the penis and testicles. — *m)e-šúbs* the membraneous covering or sheath of the penis.

མཛེད་པ་ *m)éd-pa*, *Zam.* **सह** suffering, enduring, bearing patiently; *Cs.*: obnoxious; *mi-m)éd* prop.: free; gen. **the world, the universe,** acc. to Buddhistic ideas; except in the last mentioned sense the word seems to be little used.

འཛག་པ་ *ₒ)ág-pa*, pf. *)ags*, *Cs.*; *Sch.*: to establish, settle, fix, found; hence prob. *bde-ₒ)ágs* and *k̔ris-ₒ)ágs*, *ₒ)ags-k̔ris* (*Lexx.* and elsewh., but not frq.) **time of prosperity,** of peace, of rest, a time without disturbances, war, epidemies etc. (*k̔ris* by itself is not known).

འཛག་པོ་ *ₒ)ág-po* 1. *Lex.* = *klu*, or n. of a Lu, also *ₒ)óg-po*. — 2. vulgo = *yág-po*.

འཛག་མ་ *ₒ)ág-ma* 1. *Sch.*: a sort of **coarse** and **thick grass** of inferior quality; so *Pth.* of a hut: *ₒ)ág-mas p̔úb-pa* covered with such grass. — 2. *Lex.* **वीरण a fragrant grass,** Andropogon muricatus. — 3. *Glr.*: **a blade** (of grass), **stalk** (of corn), *ₒ)ág-ma re" stéṅ-na* on every blade, *kú-šai ₒ)ág-ma p̔on ċig* a bundle of blades of Kusha grass; *ₒ)ag-rgód Sch.* horse-tail, pewter-grass, Equisetum. — 4. *Sik.* **squirrel,** perh. = *bya-ma-byi Sch.* (?).

འཛགས་ *ₒ)ags*, v. sub *ₒ)ág-pa*.

འཛགས་པ་ *ₒ)ágs-pa C.* **to give,** to make a present *Georgi Alph. Tib.*

འཛང་བ་ *ₒ)áṅ-ba* **to devour, swallow,** *Sch.*

འཛན་པོ་, འཛན་མོ་ *ₒ)án-po, ₒ)án-mo* **consort, husband, wife** *Cs.*

འཛན་ས་ *ₒ)án-sa*, v. *čán-sa*.

འཛབ་པ་ *ₒ)áb-pa*, pf. prob. *bžabs*, fut. *bžab*, **to sneak, slink,** creep privily; **to lie in wait,** in ambush, *tsé-la ₒ)áb-pa* to attempt a person's life *Pth.*; *)ág-ne)áb-te sad táṅ-ċe* *W.* to assassinate; *lkog ₒ)ab byéd-pa* v. *lkog*; *ₒ)áb-bus ma byin-par léṅ-pa Thgy.* to steal clandestinely. Cog. to *ₒčáb-pa*.

འཛབ་ཙེ་ *ₒ)áb-tse* nippers, tweezers.

འཛམ་མགོན་ *ₒ)am-mgón* = *ₒ)am-dpál*.

འཛམ་པ་ *ₒ)ám-pa B.*, *)ám-po* *W.*, *ₒ)am-)ám* *C.* col. (opp. to *rtsúb-pa, rtsíṅ-ge*) **soft, smooth, tender, mild,** e.g. of cloth, hair, a meadow, a plain without stones or rocks, of fruit, the air, the character of a person, a person's way of speaking (*ṅag C.*, *pé-ra* *W.*, *pé-ra)ám-po daṅ* with mild expressions, fair words, in a friendly manner), of a law; of beverages: **weak** *W.*; of a (hay-)rake: **close** *W.*; *)ám-po ṅáb-ċe* *W.* to mow off close; *ₒ)am-ₒbúd* blowing or playing (the flute) softly, piano; *ₒ)am-rtsí Med.*, seems to be a kind of medicine; *)am-sáṅ* *W.*, *C.*, plain, without ornaments.

འཛམ་དཔལ་ *ₒ)am-dpál* (**मञ्जुश्री**) *ₒ)ám-mgón* (**॰नाथ**), *ₒ)am(-pai)-dbyáṅs* (**॰घोष**) one of the two great Bodhisattvas of the northern Buddhists, the Apollo of the Tibetans, the god of wisdom, demiurge, and more particularly the tutelar god and civilizer of Nepal (v. Köpp. II, 21), incarnated in *Thonmi Sambhota*, and afterwards in king *Kri-sroṅ-sde-btsán* and others. Cf. *spyan-ras-yzigs*.

འཛམ་མ་, རྗེ་འཛམ་ *ₒ)ám-ma, r)e-ₒ)ám*, resp. for *ťug-pa*, **soup.**

འཛམ་མོ་ *ₒ)am-mo* **post-stage** *Sch.*

འཛའ་, འཛའ་ཚོན་ *ₒ)a, ₒ)a-tson* **rainbow** frq., *ₒ)a-ₒod* light, splendour of the rainbow *Pth.*; *ǰa-tson yal-ba* the vanishing of the rainbow frq.; *ǰa-lus* v. *lus.*

འཇའ་བ་ *ǰa-ba* 1. also *ǰa-mo Sch.* **lame,** gen. *ža-ba*; *ǰa-bar byed-pa* to make lame, to lame *S.g.* — 2. **to bespeak, to concert, to confederate** *Sch.*

འཇའ་ས་ *ǰa-sa*, *ǰa-mo*, **edict, diploma,** a permit *Cs.*, who declares this word to be Chinese.

འཇར་བ་ *ǰar-ba Lex.* w.e., acc. to *Cs.* = *byar-ba* **to stick together, to cohere.**

འཇལ་བ་ *ǰal-ba*, pf. *bčal*, fut. *γžal*, imp. *ǰol*, *W.* **čal-če**, 1. **to weigh,** *ǰal-byed srań* (a pair of) scales for weighing *Lex.*, *sráń-la γžal-ba Glr.* — 2. **to measure,** *riń-tuń-tsád ǰál-ba C.* to measure the length. — 3. **to appraise, to tax;** to weigh in one's mind, **to ponder;** more fully expressed by *blos-ǰal-ba* to understand *Sch.*, although native grammarians refer this signification with less probability to *mǰal-ba*. — 4. **to pay, pay back, repay,** *bú-lon* a debt, *skyin-pa* a loan, *k̔ral* a tax; **to retaliate, return, repay,** esp. with *lan*: *p̔an-lán γnód-pas* or *légs-pai lan nyés-pas* to return evil for good. The following is a Buddhist principle of law, but prob. existing only in theory: *dkon-mčóg-gi rdzás-la k̔ri ǰal, dge-dún-gyi rdzás-la brgyád-ču ǰal, p̔ál-pai rdzás-la bdún-gyur ńo brgyad ǰal* divine or sacred objects are to be repaid or made good tenthousandfold, things or property of the clergy eightyfold, of ordinary men sevenfold, and besides the object itself, hence eightfold *C.*; in *Glr.* there is the following passage: *brkús-pa la brgyad ǰal ńos dań dgu.* — 5. often erron. for *mǰál-ba*; thus prob. also in: *ǰal búl-ba* to bring a present *Sch.* (more correctly: a present of salutation). — *ǰál-k̔a* the act, or business of measuring *C.*

འཇི་བ་ *ǰi-ba* 1. *Cs.*, also *lǰi-ba*, **a flea.** — 2. *Lex.* and *Cs.*: = *ǰim-pa.* — 3. *Cs.* = *ǰám-pa* **soft, smooth.** — 4. *Sch.*: **disgusting, nasty,** e.g. of a fishy smell.

འཇིག་རྟེན་ *ǰig-rtén* (receptacle of all that is perishable) 1. **the external world:** a. acc. to the common (popular) notion: the whole earth, the universe, *ǰig-rtén-na dkón-pa*, what is rare, the only thing of its kind in the world *Dzl.*; *ǰig-rtén-gyi lha* the god of the world, a deity of the Bonpos *Mil.*; *ǰig-rtén-las dás-pa* one that has escaped from this world, one emancipated, blessed *Cs.* — b. the external world acc. to Brahmanic and Buddhist theories, as set forth: *Köpp.* I, 231; *ǰig-rtén-gyi k̔ams* id. *Glr.*; *ǰig-rtén čágs-pa* origin, beginning, *γnás-pa* duration, *ǰig-pa* destruction, *bžág-pa* arrangement of the world, cosmography (title of a volume of *Stg.*) *ǰig-rtén γsum* the three worlds, earth, heaven, and hades; *ǰig-rtén* (*γsúm-gyi*) *mgón-po* (*Triloknāth Hind.*) lord or patron of the three worlds, which is also the title of the third of the three highest Lamas, viz. of the Dharma Raja, residing in Bhotan, v. *Cunningh. Ladak* 371; Buddha *Sakya-t̔úb-pa* seems to have the same title, *Pth.* — c. fig.: *bdé-ba-čan-gyi ǰig-rtén*, or *bdé-gro mto-ris-kyi ǰig-rtén* the world of the blessed, like our 'heaven', but of rare occurrence. — 2. **world,** in a spiritual sense, *ǰig-rtén-gyi byá-ba* worldly things or affairs; *ǰig-rtén-la dgós-pa* (or *p̔án-pai*) *bsláb-bya* useful maxims of life, moral rules *Glr.*; *ǰig-rtén-gyi čos brgyad*, v. *čos*; *ǰig-rtén byéd-pa* short expression for *ǰig-rtén-gyi las byéd-pa Mil.* — 3. symb. num.: **three.** — *ǰig-rtén-pa* 1. an inhabitant of the world, or the inhabitants of the world, the world as the totality of men, and more particularly of the worldly-minded; *ǰig-rtén-pa ni ma-dúl-ba yin-pas* as the world is unconverted, in which sense also *ǰig-rtén* (by itself) seems to be used. 2. a layman.

འཇིག་པ་ *ǰig-pa* I. vb. 1. act. pf. *bžig*, fut. *γžig*, imp. (*b*)*šig*, *W.* **šig-če, šig táń-če**, **to destroy,** buildings etc., frq.: **to cut to pieces, to divide,** e.g. a killed animal *W.*; **to ruin, to annihilate,** existing institutions or things, also other people; **to abolish, annul,** a law *W.*: **to dissolve,** an enchantment; **to lay aside** an assumed appearance or manner (= to unmask one's self) *Mil.*; **to break, violate,** one's duty, a vow, *Dzl.*;

rma-ʼjig Med. was explained: **healing wounds.** *ʼjig-par byed-pa* = *ʼjig-pa*, frq. — 2. vb. n. pf. *bźig*, and more frq. *źig*, *W.* **źig-ċe, źig ča-ċe**, **to be ruined, undone,** e.g. by mischief-making people *Dzl.;* **to fall to pieces, to decay, to rot,** of the human body etc.; **to be lost, to perish,** *ʼjig-par śin-tu sla* (earthly goods) may be easily lost again *Thgy.;* **to vanish, disappear,** *ʼjig* (or *źig*)-*par ʼgyur-ba* id.; *sem źig soṅ W.* he was quite dejected or cast down; *źig ysós byed-pa B., C.,* **źig-só* (or *-sób*) *ċó-ċe* or *táṅ-ċe* W.* to 'restore from destruction', to rebuild c. dat. frq., also c. genit. *Pth.*; prob. also c. accus. — 3. **to suck,** draw out moisture *Sch.*, v. *ʼjib-pa.*

II. sbst. **decay, destruction, ruin,** entire overthrow, *skyé-ba daṅ ʼjig-pa kún-la srid-na* as it is the lot of all men to rise and to decay *Dzl.; lús-kyi mťar ʼjig-pai ltas* symptoms of the final decay of the body *Wdṅ.;* **čáṅ-la ǩoi źig-pa yod** beer proves his ruin, beer is his destruction *W.; ʼjig-pe čö-čen* C., ʼjig-pa-čan Cs.* frail, perishable.

III. adj., but only in conjunction with a negative: *mi-ʼjig-pa* **imperishable;** *mi-ʼjig rtág-pa* as explanation of a synonym *Lex.*

འཇིགས་པ་ *ʼjigs-pa* I. vb. (भी) resp. *tsábs-pa*, to be afraid of a thing, is gen. connected with the instr. (lit. 'by'), in later literature and col. with *la*, *srin-pos ʼjigs-śiṅ* from fear of the Rakshasa *Dzl.*; *dé-la ṅa mi ʼjigs* I am not afraid of that *Mil.;* in *W.* frq. in conjunction with **rag*:* **ǩó-la ʼjig rag** I am afraid of him; also relative to the future, like *dógs-pa: yi-ge máṅs-pas ʼjigs-nas = máṅ-gi dógs-nas,* fearing lest there should be too much writing, i. e. from want of room *Pth.; ʼjigs-su-ruṅ-ba* dreadful, frightful, frq.; **ʼjig-te dár-ri spé-ra zér-ċe* W.* to speak trembling and shaking with fear; **máṅ-po jig soṅ* W.* I am very much afraid; *ʼjigs-par ʼgyur-ba* to be frightened, *ʼjigs-par byéd-pa* to put in fear, to frighten.

II. sbst. (भीत) **fear, dread,** *srin-poi ʼjigs-pas* from fear of the Rakshasa *Dzl.* ༢༥, 14 (unless *srin-pos* ought to be read, as above); *ʼjigs-pa brgyad* the eight fears of life (so among the rest: *rgyál-poi ʼjigs-pa* the standing in fear of the king, who in the East is always supposed to be an arbitrary despot); *mi-ʼjigs-pa* 1. fearlessness, intrepidity; *mi-ʼjigs-pa sbyin-pa* to impart intrepidity; *mi-ʼjigs-pai lág-pa* a fearless hand, heroic vigour. 2. pardon, quarter, safety *Cs.* — *ʼjigs* (*-pa*)*-čan Cs.* 1. fearful, timorous. 2. dreadful, frightful (I never found it used in this sense).

III. adj. 1. (fearing) **fearful, timorous,** *ʼjigs-pai ʼgró-ba-rnams* timorous beings *Pth.* — 2. (feared) **dreadful, frightful,** *ʼjigs-pai mtsón-ča* dreadful weapons; *ǩyod-pas lhag-par ʼjigs-pa yod* there is something even more formidable than you are *Dzl.*

Comp. *bár-do-la ʼjigs skyób-mai smón-lam* a prayer efficacious in the Bardo-horrors *Thgr.* — *ʼjigs-skrág* **fear;** also a terrible object, *ʼjigs-skrág-tu soṅ* he has been changed into **a fright,** a monster *Mil.*; **ʼjig-tág tǫm-pa* C.* (lit. *btón-pa*) to frighten, deter; intimidate, threaten; *ʼjigs-skrág-pa* to fear, to be afraid *Dzl.* — *ʼjigs-mǩan* col. **timid, timorous.** — *ʼjigs-čan* v. *ʼjigs-pa-čan* above. — *ʼjigs-čúm-pa* v. *čum-pa.* — *ʼjigs*(*-pa*)*-po* one afraid *Cs.* (?) — *ʼjigs-byéd* one that is terrifying *Sch.*, appellation of Yamântaka, who is invoked, e.g. in drawing lots. — *ʼjigs-brál, ʼjigs-méd* **fearless, intrepid, bold;** also noun pers. — **ʼjigs-ri* W.* **fear, terror,** **ʼjig-ri tsór-ċe** to be afraid, **jig-ri kúl-ċe** to frighten, to menace, to intimidate. — *ʼjigs-sa Mil., ʼjigs-sa čé* it is a very dangerous quarter or region, in that place there is much occasion for being afraid.

འཇིང་ *ʼjiṅ* 1. acc. to *Cs.* = *mčiṅ, kloṅ,* e.g. *rgyá-mtsoi; Sch.: mtso-ʼjiṅ* the whole circumference of a lake; prob. more corr.: **the middle,** *Lex.: lus-ʼjám ʼjág-po mtsó-ʼjiṅ ʼjug* the smooth-bodied Lu alights in the middle of the lake. — 2. *srod-ʼjiṅ Lex.;* or *srod-byiṅ* **twilight.**

འཇིང་པ་ *ʼjiṅ-pa*, also *mjiṅ-pa*, **neck,** resp. *sku-ʼjiṅ; *jiṅ-pa gyúr-ċe* W.* to turn or move round (as vb. n.), *ǰiṅ-pa gyúr-te ltá-ce* W. to look round, or back; *ǰiṅ-pa čúg-ce* W. to break one's neck; *ǰiṅ-pa zúm-ce* W. to hug, to embrace; ǰiṅ-kyóg a wry neck Cs.; ǰiṅ-kúṅ the nape of the neck Glr.; ǰiṅ-ltág the back part of the neck Cs.

འཇིབ(ས)་པ་ ǰib(s)-pa (Sch. also ˏǰigs-pa) pf. bžibs (γžibs), fut. bzib (γžib), **to suck**, e.g. of a suckling baby; mčus with the lips Lex.; ḱrag ǰibs-pa to suck blood Lex.; **to suck out, in,** or **up, to imbibe, absorb**, also **to blister**, ǰib-man W. vesicatory.

འཇིབ་རྩི་ ǰib-rtsi 1. Cs. a kind of sirup. — 2. Wdn. a medicinal herb.

འཇིམ་པ་ ǰim-pa B., C., a compound of earth and water, **mud, clay, loam** etc. (W. *ḱá-lag*); ǰim-skoṅ a small cup of clay, a crucible Cs.; ǰim-γzugs a figure formed of clay Glr.; rdó-rǰei ǰim-pa v. rdó-rǰe.

འཇིལ་བ་ ǰil-ba, pf. bčil, fut. γžil, **to expel, eject, remove, turn off,** ṗyir ǰil-ba Lex. id., e.g. noxious animals, vices etc.

འཇུ་བ་ ǰú-ba I. vb. 1. pf. ǰus, **to seize, grasp, take hold of,** c. dat., dprál-bai mdá-la ǰú-ba grasping the arrow sticking in his forehead Glr.; γčig-la γčig ǰú-ba taking firmly hold of each other (in a storm at sea) Glr.; to seize a person (in taking him prisoner) Pth.; lág-pa-nas to grasp by the hand, to shake hands (in greeting) Dzl. — 2. pf. bžus, fut. bžu, W. *žú-ce (or ǰu-ce?)* **to melt, to digest,** zas ǰú-ba to digest the food; ǰu slá-ba digestible, ǰu dká-ba difficult of digestion; *ra ǰú-ce* W. to digest intoxication, to sleep the fumes of wine away; ǰu-byéd a sort of bile, the bile as the promoter of digestion Med. Cf. žú-ba II.

II. sbst. 1. **digestion**, ǰú-ba slao the digestion is in order, is easy Med.; ǰu-stóbs čuṅ the digestive power is weak Med. — 2. **a flea** Sch. = ǰi-ba.

འཇུག་ ǰug, sometimes for mǰug.

འཇུག་ངོགས་ ǰug-ṅógs Cs. **entrance, way** of access, to a tank or river, Ghāt (Hind.).

འཇུག་པ་ ǰúg-pa, I. pf. and imp. žugs, W. *žúg-ce*, vb. n., 1. **to go or walk in, to enter,** ḱáṅ-pai, or čui náṅ-du ǰúg-pa to go into the house, or into the water; rgyá-mtsor ǰúg-pa to put to sea, to set sail Dzl.; lám-du ǰúg-pa to set out, to start, to prosecute a journey; *mál-sa-la žúg-ce* W. to go to bed. In a special sense: a. of a demon, entering into a man to take possession of him, hence *ḍé-žug-ḱan* W. possessed (by a demon); ǰúg-sgo Med. the place where the demon entered the body. b. dgé-ba-la ǰúg-pa to walk in the path of virtue; acc. to Schr. ǰúg-pa by itself, without dgé-ba-la, implies the same, and in conformity with this a Lama gave the following explanation of the expression ǰúg-pai las in Thgy.: works that are a consequence of having really entered upon the practice of virtue, positive good works, opp. to the negative good works of the ten virtues. čós-la ǰúg-pa to turn to religion, to be converted; čos or bstán-pa žig-la ǰúg-pa to adopt a certain religion, a certain doctrine. c. bud-méd-la ǰúg-pa to lie with, sleep with a woman Med.; *búr-la žúg-ce* W. euph. expression for: to commit adultery. d. *dún-du žúg-ce* W. to appear, in reference to gods. e. rǰés-su ǰúg-pa v. rǰés-su. — 2. **to set or fall to, to begin,** rig-pa sbyáṅ-bas rtsóm-pa kún-la ǰug a skilled, an experienced man is prepared for anything, knows how to set about it, how to manage it Med.; gen. with the inf.: to begin to do, to commence doing a thing, rtóg-pa-la, resp. dgóṅs-pa-la ǰúg-pa to begin to think upon Dzl., Glr.; stón-pa-la ǰúg-pa to begin to show Dzl.; γčig-la γčig rnám-par brlág-pa-la žugs-pas being in the best way of entirely exterminating one another Stg. — 3. pass. of ǰúg-pa II, 3, of letters: **to be combined, to be preceded, to be followed,** zla yig sṅón-du ba žúgs-čan (words) having zl preceded by b, i.e. beginning with bzl Zam. — 4.

to take place, to exist, *če-čuṅ-Kyád žúgs-par mṅón-pas* as evidently a difference in size is existing (?) *Dzl.* ༥༩, 3.

II. pf. *bčug* (perh. also *ǰugs Lex.*), fut. *γžug*, imp. *čug, W.* **čúg-če**, vb. a., with *náṅ-du* or termin.: 1. **to put into,** e.g. meat into a pan, a key into the key-hole, a culprit into prison; **to infuse, inject,** *γžúg-par bya* this must be infused *Med.*; also fig. **nyíṅ-rus čúg-če* W.* to inspire with courage. In a special sense: a. *dé-la blo ǰúg-pa* to set one's mind on, to apply one's self to *Glr.* b. *mi žig čós-la ǰúg-pa* to convert a man, to induce him to adopt a certain religion; *ǰúg-pa* also without an object, to missionate successfully *Feer Introd. du B. au Cachem.* 68. — 2. **to make, render, appoint, constitute,** with the accus. and termin., or col. with two accus.: *mi zig rgyal-por ǰug-pa* to make one king *Dzl.*; *mṅon-du ǰug-pa* to make public or manifest, to disclose, to show *Samb.*; **siṅ čug-če* W.* to clear, clarify; frq. with the supine or root of a verb: a. **to cause, compel, prevail on,** *zar ǰug-pa* to prevail on another to eat something *Dzl.*; *skrod-du γžug-go* I shall induce (them) to expel (you) *Dzl.*; *bžugs ǰug rgyu yin* he will induce (the god) to take his abode *Glr.*; *groṅs-su ǰug-pa* to be the cause of somebody's death *Mil.*; *yid-la ǰug-tu ǰug-pa* to cause a thing to enter a person's mind, to put in mind, to remonstrate; *pél-bar ǰug-pa* (resp. *mdzad-pa*) = *spel-ba* to increase, as vb. a.; **juṅ čug-če* W.* to cause to exist, create, procure; **Kol ǰug-če* W.* = **skol-če** to cause to boil; *dar-du čug čig* cause it to spread *Glr.* b. **to command, order, bid,** *dmag dzin-du bčug* he ordered the soldiers to take (the man) prisoner (but he escaped) *Dzl.* ༢༢༢, 3; *byed-du ǰug-pa* to bid one do a thing, frq.; *btsun-mo blon-pos gebs-su bčug* he gave orders for the queen being protected by the minister. c. **to let, suffer, permit,** *smon-lam debs-su čug* allow me to say a prayer; *rtsig-tu mi ǰug* I shall not give permission to build *Glr.* d. **to give an opportunity** *Thgy.* e. in a general sense: *dal-du ǰug-pa* to do things slowly, to be slow *Mil.* — 3. **to put** grammatically: *sṅon-du ǰug-pa* to put or place before, *sṅon-ǰug* a prefixed letter, a prefix; *rǰes-ǰug* final letter, *yaṅ-ǰug* the last but one; also to put, to use a word in a certain signification, *rgyu-mtsan-la ǰug* is used with reference to cause *Gram.* — 4. **to banish, to exile** (prob. erron. for *spyúg-pa*), *byáṅ-la* to northern regions *Glr.* — 5. *sgo ǰúg-pa* v. *sgo.* — 6. inst. of *byúg-pa.*

འཇུག་པ་ *ǰúg-pa* sbst. 1. **the going into, the entering;** in a special sense 2. the beginning, **the first stage** of a disease *Mṅg.* — 3. (**अवतार**) the incarnation of a deity.

འཇུངས་པ་ *ǰúṅs-pa* **avarice,** *Dzl., Lex.*; *ǰúṅs-pa-čan* avaricious; *ǰuṅs-ǰúr* a miser, niggard.

འཇུད་མཐུན་མ་ *ǰud-mtún-ma,* or *ǰul-tún-ma Lex.* ('accessible to all') **a prostitute;** *ǰud-mtún byéd-pa* to be a harlot.

འཇུད་པ་ *ǰúd-pa,* and more frq. *dzúd-pa,* secondary forms of *ǰúg-pa.* Cf. *čúd-pa, tsúd-pa.*

འཇུན་པ་ *ǰún-pa,* pf. *bčun,* fut. *γžun* (cf. *bžun, žun*) *W.* **čún-če*, Cs.:* **to subdue,** make tame; to make confess; *W.*; **to make soft, to soften,** e.g. iron; **to punish,** by words or blows; **to convert.**

འཇུམ་པ་ *ǰúm-pa,* pf. *bčum,* fut. *γžum,* imp. *čum,* **to shudder, to shrink.** (Acc. to grammatical analogy *ǰum-pa* ought to be vb. a., to cause to shudder, and *čúm-pa* vb. n.) *ša ǰúms-pa Lex.,* contraction of the muscles, shrinking, shuddering *Sch.*

འཇུར་ *ǰur,* supine of *ǰú-ba*; *ǰur mi dod* indigestible *Sch.* (?).

འཇུར་བ་ *ǰúr-ba* 1. (pf. *bčur,* q. v.) *Cs.:* complication; *Sch.* also: to struggle against, to resist. *Pth.:* *ǰúr-bar gyúr-ba* **to be entangled;** *ǰúr-bu Sch.,* **ǰúr-pa* C.* tangled yarn; *srád-bui ǰúr (-pa) Lexx.* w. e., *Sch.*: 'the tightness of the yarn'; *ǰur-mtúg* wrinkled, as the skin is in old age *Thgy.*; *ǰur-mig* a wire-drawing plate, *ǰur-mig-nas drén-pa* to draw through this plate *Thgy.* — 2. = *dzúr-ba*

to evade, to shun, to go out of the way, *ˏjur-méd* unavoidable *Mil.*

འཇུས་ *ˏjus*, v. *ˏju-ba* I, 1.

འཇེབས་པ་ *ˏjébs-pa, ˏjébs-po,* **well-sounding** *Stg.*; *snyan - ˏjébs* harmony, euphony.

འཇེམ(ས)་པ་ *ˏjém(s)-pa* 1. **dexterity, cleverness** *Lex.* 2. **skilled, clever;** *Sch.* **decent;** *ˏjéms-po* id.

འཇོ་སྒེག *ˏjo - sgég* a coquettish, alluring, seducing attitude or posture; *Lex.*: *ˏjud-mtún ˏjo-sgég ˏjog* the harlot assumes such an attitude.

འཇོ་བ་ *ˏjó-ba*, pf. *bžos*, ft. *bžo*, imp. *ˏjos*, **to milk,** *rá - ma ˏjó - ba* to milk a goat, *ˏo-ma ˏjo-ba* 'to milk the milk'; *kyód-kyis ˏó-ma bžos dug, ṅas ni bžós-pa med,* it is you, not I, that have 'milked out the milk' *Glr.*; *ˏjó (-ba) - po, ˏjó - mkan,* milker, milk-man, *ˏjó(-ba)-mo* milkmaid; *ˏdód - ˏjoi ba* a cow that is able to fulfil every wish.

འཇོག་པ་ *ˏjóg-pa* I. pf. *bžag*, ft. *γžag*, imp. *žog*, *C.* col. **žág - pa**, 1. **to put, to place,** e.g. the foot on the ground; also to place persons, to assign them a place *Dzl., Glr.*; fig. = *ˏgód-pa* (e.g. *dgé-ba-la, byaṅ-čúb-la, byaṅ-čúb-kyi lám-la*) v. *ˏgód-pa* 3; **to put in order, to arrange,** *ˏjig-rtén-bžag-pa* the arrangement (system) of the world; *lus dráṅ - por bžág - ste* sitting straight, bolt-upright *Dzl., Mil.*; *bžág - na mi sdod* if one places her any where, she will not remain there *Mil.*; *stéṅ - du yar bžag* (the anchors) were placed above, were weighed *Pth.*; *lás-su ˏjóg-pa* to set one a task, to employ one in a certain service *Dzl.*, *rgyal-srid-la ˏjóg - pa* to appoint one to the government i.e. to make one king; *séms* (resp. *tugs*)*-la ˏjóg-pa* to take to heart *Glr., Mil.*; *lús-la grui ˏdu-šés bžág - la* if we fancy the human body to be a ship *Thgy.*; *nám-mka ráṅ-gi ṅáṅ-du žog* transfer it to the nature of the ethereal space, i.e. figure it to yourself as ether *Mil.*; *pyir ˏjóg-pa* 1. to leave behind, at home *Dzl.*; 2. to put by, to lay aside *Dzl.*; (another reading omits *pyir*). — 2. **to lay** or **put down,** a burden etc., **žóg-la žog** put (it) down and come! *C.*; *nor (γ)sog ˏjog med* heaping up treasures and depositing them was not, i.e. was never heard of; *γsóg-ˏjog-mkan* a boarder up, a miser *Cs.*; **to leave, to leave behind,** *lag - rjés* a trace or mark of activity, monumentum *Glr.*; **to leave, quit, abandon,** *ráṅ - gi yul* one's own country *Glr.*; *póṅs-par ma bžág-par* so that it is not abandoned, given up, to poverty *Thgy.*; **yúg-le žog* C.* (= **páṅ - té bor* W.*) throw it away! **to depose,** *yi - ger bris ˏjóg - pa* to depose in writing, *literis mandare Glr.*; *sá-bon, γduṅ-brgyúd ˏjóg-pa* to leave an offspring behind, to propagate the species; **to lay up, to keep,** as holy relics; **to lay aside,** *ré - žig žóg - la* setting aside, apart, for a while *Dzl.*; *mnyám-par ˏžóg-pa* v. *mnyám - pa*; *sgról-lam ˏjog* shall we turn them out or leave them? *Mil. nt.*

II. pf. *(b)žogs*, fut. *γžog*, imp. *žog*, *W.* **žog-če,** **to cut, to hew, to square,** a pen, timber etc.; **to carve, to chip,** a thin piece of wood etc.

འཇོག་པོ་ *ˏjog-po* n. of a Lu *Mil.*, = *ˏjag-po.*

འཇོང་ *ˏjoṅ* = *lčoṅ*, **tadpole.**

འཇོང་འཇོང་ *ˏjoṅ - ˏjóṅ* col., *Sch.* *ˏjóṅ - po,* **oblong, longish, oval, elliptical, cylindric, bottle-shaped** etc.; col. also applied to stature: **tall;** *ˏjoṅ - nyáms - čan Wdṅ.* oblong shaped, in relation to leaves, cones of fir etc.; *ló-ma ˏjoṅ - stábs nyág-ga-čan* split into narrow slips, wing-cleft (leaves of caraway) *Wdṅ.*; *dbyibs - ˏjóṅ* an oval form.

འཇོང་ཙེ་ *ˏjóṅ-tse Cs.* = *lčóg-tse.*

འཇོམས་པ་ *ˏjóms - pa*, pf. *bčom*, also *žom*, fut. *γžom*, imp. *čom*, *W.* **čóm-če** 1. **to conquer, subdue, oppress, suppress,** an enemy; *ˏdód-čágs-kyis kún-nas ˏjóms-pa* to be quite overpowered by lust; *nad ˏjóms - pai sman* a medicine for a disease (to overcome it); *rúb-tu γžóm-pa ˏdi* the following overpowering (charm);

bčóm-mo an exclamation like: I am done for! *perii!* — 2. **to destroy,** towns etc. *Glr.*; *bčóm-la γžág-go* id. *Glr.* — 3. **to plunder, spoil, rob,** *˳ǰóms-pai grabs byás-pa-la* as they were about to rob him *Mil.* — 4. **to finish, accomplish** *W.*, cf. *čóm-pa.*

འཇོར་ *˳ǰor* 1. *C.*, also *γžor*, **hoe, grubbing-hoe, mattock, pick-axe** (*W.* **tóg-tse**), *˳ǰór-gyis rkó-ba* to turn up with the hoe; *˳ǰór-po* a large mattock, pick-axe, spade, *˳ǰór-bu* a small one, a hoe; *˳ǰor-yú* the handle of a hoe, *˳ǰor-lčágs* the iron of a mattock *Cs.* — 2. supine of *˳ǰó-ba.*

འཇོལ་བ་ *˳ǰól-ba* I. vb. 1. **to hang down,** of a cow's udder, of the long hair on a yak's belly, of tails etc.; *˳ǰol-˳ǰól* hanging-belly, paunch. — 2. gen. *˳byól-ba* **to turn aside, to make way.**

II. sbst., also (*Cs.*) *˳ǰol-˳ǰól* and *γžól-ba*, **train, trail; retinue** *Cs.*; *˳ǰól-gos Cs.*, *˳ǰól-ber Wdk.*, *Pth.*, a robe or garment with a train; *˳ǰól-čan* having a train; *˳ǰol-méd* without a train *Cs.*

འཇོལ་ལེ་ *˳ǰol-lé* **hanging,** cf. *p̀yaṅ-ṅé*, *gród-pa ˳ǰol-lé* hanging-belly, paunch, cf. *p̀yal Lex.*

འཇོལ་མོ་ *˳ǰól-mo*, acc. to the descriptions given by natives, a bird of the size of a blackbird, of lively motions and an agreeable whistling, in the neighbourhood of Lhasa, building in willow-trees and thorn-bushes; *Cs.* has: a turkey-hen.

རྗང་མ་ *rǰáṅ-ma*, or *rdzaṅ-ma*, **store-room** *Thgy.*

རྗིད་པ་ *rǰid-pa* **lean** *Cs.*, gen. *rid-pa.*

རྗིབ་ལས་ **žib-las**(?) *W.*, **service** done in socage, compulsory service, in the fields, on roads etc.

རྗུད་པ་ *rǰúd-pa*, *rdzúd-pa*, = *rgúd-pa Lex.*

རྗུན་ *rǰun*, *nad-rǰún Mil.* a disease.

རྗེ་(བོ་) *rǰé(-bo)*, also *rǰe-u*, **lord, master,** 1. **ruler, king,** *yúl-gyi rǰe mdzád-nas* ruling over a country, acting the part of a sovereign *Glr.*; *bod-k̀áms-kyi rǰé-bor gyur* he became sovereign of Tibet *Wdk.*; *sá-yi bdág-po mi-yi rǰe Mil.* lord of the ground, ruler of the people; *rǰé-bo daṅ bran*, *rǰe-k̀ól Stg.*, master and servant; *rǰe-blón* king and minister; *rǰe či lags* sir, what does that mean? *Glr.*; also a title before names, esp. names of kings, *ǰó-bo rǰe Dipangkāra Glr.*; *rǰe-bdúd rǰe-btsán* the gentlemen devils and the gentlemen goblins (messieurs les diables et messieurs les farfadets); *rǰe dkon-mčóg-la γsól-ba ˳débs-pa Mil.* is in fact an empty phrase in the mouth of a Buddhist philosopher, but may nevertheless be used in Christian language for addressing God as 'our Lord'. — 2. **a nobleman,** a person of rank, *rǰeu(i) rigs*, *rǰe-rigs* = *rgyal-rigs* the caste of nobility. — *rǰe-dpón* (*Lex.* आर्य) = *rǰe*, master, lord, prince *Cs.*; *rǰé-ma*, also *γčés-ma Cs.*, col. **šé-ma**, a lady of rank, *rǰe-čúṅ* a young lady, a miss; *rǰé-srás* a young gentleman; also a term of address *Cs.* — *rǰe-btsún* **reverend sir,** a title of the higher priesthood, *rǰe-btsún-ma* fem. — *rǰé-sa* (or *žé-sa*) *byéd-pa* to show deference, to pay one's respects; *žé-sai γtam*, or *žé-sai skad* courteous words, esp. ceremonial and complimentary terms, e.g. *dbu* for *mgo* etc. *W.*: **yá-ša čó-če, yá-še pé-ra**.

རྗེ་ངར་ *rǰe-ṅár* the lower part of the leg, **the shank** (*W.* **sug**); *rkaṅ-lág rǰe-ṅár* the lower part of the arms and the legs *Med.*

རྗེ་བ་ *rǰé-ba*, pf. *brǰes*, fut. *brǰe*, imp. *brǰes*, *W.* **žé-če**, **to barter,** to give or take in exchange; *˳di-dag-gis brǰeo* it may be exchanged for these *Dzl.*; **zan daṅ srog žé-če** *W.* to risk one's life for the necessary food (as thieves do); *brǰé-byai nor* articles of barter; in a more general sense: **to change, to shift,** *miṅ* the name, *gos* the clothes *Dzl.*, *γnas* the place, *tse* the life, i.e. to die *Cs.* — *brǰé(-ba)-po* a barterer *Cs.*

རྗེད་པ་ *rǰéd-pa*, pf. and fut. *brǰed* 1. **to honour, reverence** c. dat., *mčód-čiṅ brǰéd-pa* id. *Dzl.*; *brǰéd-pai ˳os* venerable *Lex.* — 2. **to forget,** frq. (cf. *lus-pa*); *brǰéd-du ˳ǰúg-pa* to make forget, to cause to forget.

Comp. *rǰéd-ṅas-čan Lexx.* (मुषितस्मृति) **forgetful, oblivious;** *Cs.* gives inst. of it: *rǰéd-ṅes-čan*, but also thus no clear etymological explanation is obtained. — *rǰéd-ču* draught of oblivion, of Lethe *Cs.* — *rǰed-bsnyén* (etymology?) *sgúg-pa* technical term for the common practice of Indian servants to hide an object belonging to their master in some obscure corner, and after waiting (*sgúg-pa*) for some months, until it may be assumed that the thing is altogether forgotten (*brǰéd-pa*), to appropriate it to themselves. — *rǰéd-to* list of notes, memorandum-book, journal, diary, cash-book etc. *Glr.*, *C.*, *W.* — *rǰed-rdó* prob. monumental or **memorial stone.** — *rǰed-byáṅ* specifications or **lists of goods**, pieces of luggage etc. which the Tibetans number and mark with the letters of the alphabet. — *rǰed-byéd* 1. a demon that takes away the power of memory, also *rǰed-byéd-kyi ydon.* 2. epilepsy (अपस्मार) *Med.* — *rǰed-zás Cs.*: 'the meat of forgetfulness'.

རྗེན་ནེ་བ་ *rǰén-ne-ba* v. the following word.

རྗེན་པ་ *rǰén-pa* 1. not covered, **bare, naked,** *B., C.* (*W.*: *čer-nyál*), *rkaṅ-rǰén (-pa)* barefooted, unshod; *žabs-rǰén-par ydá-ba* or *ységs-pa*, resp., to be barefooted, to go barefoot; *ydoṅ rǰén-du sdód-pa* to sit with unveiled face, *mgo-rǰén-pa* with uncovered head, *rgyab-rǰén* with a naked back *Cs.*; *rǰén-par ˳dóṅ-pa C.* to strip perfectly; *dmar-rǰén* stark naked *Sch.*; *rál-gri rǰén-pa* a naked sword; **žén-pa toṅ* W.* give it (me) not wrapped up! *sa-rǰen* the bare ground, not covered with a carpet *Cs.*; *rǰén-ne-ba* undisguised, obvious to the understanding, manifest *Mil.* — 2. **raw,** not roasted or cooked, *ša-rǰen* raw meat, *dmar-rǰén* red raw meat; *mar-rǰén* not melted butter; *nas-rǰén* raw barley, not prepared or roasted; also the meal of it: *W.* **nar-jén** barley-flour, cf. *Sch.*: *bra-rǰén* buckwheat-meal. — *rǰen-zás Med.* (*Cs.* also *rǰen-rigs*) victuals that may be eaten raw. — 3. not ripe, **unripe** *W.*

རྗེས་ *rǰes* 1. **trace, track, mark left,** impression made (on the ground), *pyi-rǰés Med.* prob. id.; *mi-rǰés* a man's track, *rta-rǰés* a horse's track *Glr.*; *šiṅ-rtai rǰes* the track of a waggon or cart, a rut; *rkaṅ-rǰés*, resp. *žabs-rǰés*, the trace of one's foot, footprint, *rkaṅ-rǰés byuṅ* a footprint is made; *rkaṅ-rǰés ˳ǰóg-pa* to leave a footprint behind *Mil.*; *byas-rǰés* proof of an accomplished deed, whether it be the work itself or some indubitable result of it; *lag-rǰés*, resp. *pyag-rǰés* impression or mark left of one's hand, hence fig.: action, deed, charitable institution, pious legacy, whereby a person wishes to immortalize his name. — 2. **the hind part** of a thing *Sch.*(?) — 3. in relation to time: that which follows, **the consequence, the course** or **progress** of a thing, **the last,** = *mǰug.* — 4. adv. and postp. inst. of *rǰés-su*, v. below. — *rǰes ycód-pa* 1. *Sch.* to destroy, blot out, efface a track or trace, in *Med.* to eradicate the trace of a disease, to cure it thoroughly, 2. *Sch.*: to separate, disjoin the hind part(?) 3. *W.* **žes čád-če** to follow a trace or track, to find out or to come upon the track. — *rǰes dzín-pa* to 'seize' the track, to overtake *Glr.*, also to be able to follow the track, *rá-ma kyui rǰes mi zin-pa* a goat that cannot follow the flock *Mil.* — *rǰés-la, rǰés-su, rǰes*, adv. and postp., afterwards, hereafter, for the future, later; after, behind, *deï rǰés-la, de-rǰés* after that, afterwards, later *Mil.*; *dé-dag ˳dás-pai rǰés-su* after these were gone *Glr.*; *bžag-rǰés po.* = *bžág-pai ˳óg-tu Lt.*; *ṅai rǰés-su* after my death. *rǰés-su* in conjunction with verbs corresponds to the *Ssk.* अनु and is often not to be translated, or serves only to give additional force to some other word or expression: *rǰés-su ˳gró-ba, ˳bráṅ-ba* to go after, to follow, to come after; also fig.: *spyód-pa tams-čád ya-rábs-kyi rǰés-su ˳bróṅ-ba* to imitate the nobility, the free-born, in their whole demeanour *Glr.*; *lé-lo daṅ spyód-pa ṅán-pai rǰés-su ˳gró-ba* to imitate idleness and wickedness, or idle and wicked people *Ld.-Glr.*; *slób-dpon-gyi r)és-su br)ód-de* saying after the teacher *Thgy.* — *r)és-su ₒdzin-pa* **to receive** *Pth.*: *ḱól-por r)és-su bzúṅ-nas lto-gós-kyis bskyáṅ-du γsol* pray take me (the orphan) into your service, and provide me with food and clothes; to receive as a disciple or follower = *čéd-du ₒdzin-pa* frq.; **to draw after** (after death) *Mil.*; **to assist**, *ₒdi r)és-su zuṅ žig* do take care of, or provide for this man (as a future co-disciple) *Mil.*; finally with respect to charms and spells: to commit to memory or keep in memory ni f. — *r)és-su ₒ)úg-pa* 1. vb. a. **to add, affix,** 2. vb. n. **to follow**, *bdag daṅ bdág-gi r)és-su ₒ)úg-pai slób-ma-rnams* I and the disciples that follow me *Mil.*; in a similar sense: *mí-la r)és-su slób-pa* to follow another as a disciple *Dzl.* ༢༥༠, 3 (༧༥༢, 7 seems to be a corrupt reading). Also in the following phrases *r)és-su* may be understood in the sense of: afterwards, subsequently: *r)és-su drán-pa* **to remember, recollect**, keep in mind, *r)és-su drán-par byéd-pa* to bring to one's remembrance, to remind *Pth.*; *r)és-su ₒgyód-pa* **to repent** *Cs.*; pleon. or without any obvious meaning in: *r)és-su mťún-pa Thgy.* **to agree,** to accord, *r)és-su rnyéd-pa Stg.* **to find,** *r)és-su dpág-pa* **to weigh, to ponder** *Cs.*, *r)és-su snyiṅ-brtsé-ba Thgy.* **to pity,** *r)és-su bstán-pa Tar.* **to instruct,** and thus in similar expressions, esp. in one of frq. occurrence in legends: *r)és-su yi-ráṅ-ba*, resp. *r)és-su ťugs-ráṅ-ba* (*Sch.* erron. *ťúgs-pa!*) **to rejoice, to enjoy**, for which sometimes also *r)és-su ṗyógs-pa* is used, e.g. *dbyé-ba-rnams-la r)és-su yi-ráṅ-ba* to rejoice at people disagreeing, to enjoy dissensions and jarrings *Stg.*

Comp. *r)es-skyés* (अनुज) born later; younger brother. — *r)es-grúb-kyi miṅ* **by-name, surname** *Cs.* — *r)es-ₒ)úg* 1. **following,** coming after, *ṗyi-rábs r)es-ₒ)úg ťams-čád* all the following generations *Pth.* 2. **final consonant.** — *r)es-ťóg* prob. the same as *r)és-la Wdṅ.* — *r)es-ťób Mil.* is said to denote short interruptions of meditation by taking food, but no more than is absolutely necessary for the preservation of life. — *r)es-dpág* 1. consideration, deliberation. 2. *Was.* (297) a syllogism consisting of three propositions. — *r)és-ma* = *r)es* 2 hinder part *Cs.* — *r)es-méd* without leaving any traces, **trackless**, *ₒ)ig-pa* to destroy thoroughly *Glr.*

ཇེས་པ་ *r)és-pa* v. *r)é-ba.*

ཇོད་པ་ *r)ód-pa* pf. and fut. *br)od*, **to say, pronounce, utter**, e.g. a charm or magic formula; *ṅe miṅ žód-da rag* W.* I hear my name mentioned; *saṅs-rgyás-kyi mtsán-nas* to pronounce or invoke the name of Buddha *Dzl.*; **to propound, promulgate**, *čos* a religious doctrine; **to enumerate, set forth,** *légs-pa* or *nyés-pa* the good or bad qualities, actions etc., *yón-tan* the excellence or superiority of a person *Dzl.* and elsewh.; **to treat** of a subject in writing: *lhág-pa-rnams ni ₒdir br)ód-bya* we have now to treat of the rest *Zam.*; an author even says *žes bržód-de* with regard to his own words (after a bombastic poetical exordium, like the 'dixi', of Roman orators) *Glr*; *r)ód-du méd-pa* unspeakable, inexpressible, ineffable, *r)ód-du méd-čiṅ dpág-tu méd-pa* id. *Dzl.*; *br)od(-kyis) mi láṅ-ba* (or *lóṅ-ba*) id.; also vb.: to be inexpressible or inexhaustible, frq.; *re-réi miṅ-nas r)od mi laṅ* one cannot mention or enumerate them all *Mil.*; *don mdzád-pa r)od mi láṅ-ṅo* his utility is beyond description *Dzl.*; *r)ód-kyis mi láṅ-bai ṗyir mi bkod* I do not write it down, because it is impossible to relate every thing *Pth.* (v. *br)od*).

ལྗགས་ *l)ags*, resp. for *lče*, **tongue**, *l)ágs-kyis čab ₒdór-ba* to spit, to spit out; *l)ags-čáb* spittle, saliva; *l)ags-dbúgs* breath.

ལྗང་མོ་ *l)áṅ-mo* p. n. of a district 1. in Ü, 2. in Kams.

ལྗང་ཁུ་ *l)áṅ-ku*, or *l)áṅ-gu Lt.*, *W.*, **green** (gen. expressed by *ṅón-po*, notwithstanding the ambiguity), *l)aṅ-skyá* greenish white, *l)aṅ-nág* greenish black, dark green. — *l)áṅ-pa* green corn, in the first stage of its growth (in the second stage it is called *sóg-ma*, in the third *snyé-ma*). — *lo-ljáṅ-ba* having a green blade. — *ljáṅ-bu* greenness, verdure (grass, foliage, shrubs), *Lex.*: सस्य — *ljaṅ-dmár* greenish red; *ljaṅ-sér* greenish yellow.

ལྗང་དྭང་ *ljaṅ-dwáṅ* (spelling?), **solid**, not hollow, *W.*

ལྗན་ལྗིན་ *ljan-ljin* **filth, dirt, dust, sweepings**; *lúd-pa ljan-ljin maṅ* a great deal of foul mucous expectoration *Lt.*

ལྗབ་ *ljab W.* **flat, plain, even**; **ljab-ljáb-ba bor** lay or put it down flat; **ljab ċó-te dug** sit down flat (on the ground)!

ལྗི་བ་ *ljí-ba*, 1. **a flea** (*ʼji-ba*). — 2. **heavy, weighty.**

ལྗིད་པ་ *ljíd-pa*, **heaviness, weight**, *gser daṅ ljid-pa mnyám-pa dgos* it must be weighed up with gold *Glr.*; *de daṅ ljid mnyám-pa* of equal weight, equal in weight *Med.*; *ljid-ċan*, *ljid-ldán* heavy; *ljid-čé-ba* very heavy; *ljid-méd* light, not heavy; *lus tams-ċád-kyi ljid pab* he sat down with the whole weight of his body *Cs.*; *ljid-kyis nón-pa* pressing down by his(its) weight.

ལྗེན་པ་ *ljén-pa Cs.* **to enter, to penetrate**, *bló-la* one's mind, = to be perceived, understood; *tson-ljén* a die or colour penetrating and remaining fixed in cloth etc. Cf. *žén-pa*.

ལྗོངས་ *ljoṅs* **a large valley, principal** or **main valley; region, district, province** *Dzl.*; *ljoṅs daṅ yul-ʼkór* countries and provinces; *ljoṅs čén-po* a large country; *ká-ba-ċan-gyi ljoṅs ʼdi*, *gáṅs-ċan(-gyi) ljoṅs* Tibet, frq.; *nágs-ljoṅs* woody country; *smán-ljoṅs* a country of medicinal herbs *Zam.*; *mú-geï ljoṅs* a very poor country, starving country *Mil.*; *ljóṅs-la* in the valley, in the plain; *ljóṅs-mi-rnams* country-people *Cs.* — *ljoṅs (-su) rgyú-ba* to rove about, *ljoṅs sgyúr-ba* the end of the estival fast of the monks (about the end of August), when they are permitted to rove about the whole district of their monastery.

ལྗོན་པ་ *ljón-pa* a country of gods, **paradise**; *ljon-šiṅ* a tree from paradise, or any large and beautiful tree; *ljón-pai nágs* a beautiful forest.

བརྗིད་ *brjid*, *Tar.* 11, 14, but more frq. *gzi-brjid*, **brightness, splendour, lustre**, gen. of gods and saints, v. *gzi*; also *dpal-brjid Lex.*; *brjid-pa* to shine, glisten, glitter *Cs.*, *brjid-kyis brjid* shining with brightness *Lex.*

བརྗེ་བོ་ *brjé-bo* a making up, a compensation by **barter**, *brjé-bo byéd-pa Glr.*, **brjé-bo gyáb-ċe* W.*, to give an equal measure in bartering, e.g. of salt for barley.

བརྗོད་ *brjod* (cf. *rjód-pa*) **sound; talking; speech**, *brjod bdé-ba* euphony; also well-sounding, agreeable speech; *brjod mi bdé-ba* the contrary; also: **dha jọ' mi de* C.* it is not meet now to speak about it; *brjód-pa* speech, utterance; *mṅon-brjód* synonymy, explanation of words; *Cs.* also: 'a poetical term'; *mčod-brjód* praise, eulogy, *Sch.*: invocation of a deity; *če-brjód Schr.*(?), and *čéd-du brjód-pa*, *Tar.* 140, 2 acc. to *Schf.*: preface, introduction, in *C.*: to approve, sanction, commend, *Was.* (270) in the title of a book: = उदान वर्ग w.e.

Comp. *brjód-bya* sbst., *Zam.* also *brjód-pa*, = वाच्य an attribute, predicate *Lex.* — *brjod-méd* 1. a speech not earnestly meant, empty words, mere talk. 2. *Mil.*: the unspeakable, the transcendental, identified by some with the Nirvana, by others not. — *brjod-ʼdód Tar.* 210, 7: *brjod-ʼdód-tsam* acc. to *Schf.*: 'a mere supposition'; but in a passage in *Mil.* it seems to denote the (conceited) habit of constantly proposing one's own opinion, and so it might also be understood in *Tar.*

ཉ

ཉ་ *nya*, I. the letter *ny*, double-consonant, distinctly pronounced like *n* + *y* (*Ssk.* ञ), and used only as initial letter; therefore differing in its nature and sound from the *Ssk.* ञ, though representing it in Sanskrit words.

II. symb. num. for eight.

III. **fish** (मत्स्य), *nya ₒdzín-pa*, *W.* **nya zúm-ce**, *nya ₒċór-ba* (or *bšor-ba*) *Dzl.*, *nya lén-pa* (*bláṅ-ba*) *Pth.* to catch fish; *ₒdám-nya Ld.*, an eel *Cs*; *rgyál-poï ɣsól-nya* the king's table fish *Pth.*

IV. also *nyá-ču* (cf. *čú-ba*). 1. **tendon, sinew**; *W.*: **ḱáṅ-pe nya ḍid soṅ** my foot is asleep. — 2. col. **mark**, left by a blow, **a weal**, **nya laṅs** the blow has left a weal *W.*

V. 1. the fifteenth day of a lunar month, the day of the full moon. — 2. = *tses* ni f.: *zlá-bai nya drúg-la* on the sixth day of the month *Mil.*

VI. *nya Sch.* 1. lock (?) — 2. **muscle** *Med.*, *nya-bží* the four principal muscles, viz. those of the arms and the calves of the leg, v. also the compounds.

VII. **nya ċád-ce** *W.* to arrive sooner by a short cut; cf. also **ṫad-nya**.

Comp. *nya-rkyál* **the bladder** of a fish *Cs.* — *nya-skyogs* **gills.** — *nya-ḱrá* **sea-eagle,** white-tailed eagle *Sch.* — *nya-ḱráb-ċan* **carp** *Sch.* — *nya-ḱrab-čén* **sturgeon** *Sch.* — *nya-ḱróm* **fish-market.** — *nya-gáṅ* 1. full of fish *Sch.* 2. full moon *Cs.* — *nya-grá*, *nyai grá-ma* small **fish-bones.** — *nya-ₒgyúr* = *nya-lóg* 2 *S.g.*, *C.* — *nya-rgyá* **fishing-net.** — *nya-rgyáb C.*, earth heaped up (like the back of a fish) on the top of outer walls to prevent the entering of the wet. — *nya-rgyás* (*zlá-ba*) full moon *Pth.* — *nya-sgóṅ* **fish-spawn, roe** of fish. — *nya-lčibs* **fish-gills** *Cs.*; mother of pearl *Schr.* — *nya-čú* **tendon, sinew**; perh. also a large nerve in the nape of the neck. — *nya-dól* fishing-net; **nya-dól-pa** fisherman *W.* — *nyá-dós* a load of fish *Sch.* — *nya-ldir* 'a muscle' *Sch.* — *nyá-pa* **fisherman** *Cs.* — *nya-ṗyis* (*Cs.*: fish-gills) **mother of pearl** *S.g.* and col — *nya-míd Sch.*: a sea-monster (this word seems not to be generally known). — *nyá-mo* **a** (female?) **fish** *Mil.* — **nya-tsél** bow-net, kiddle *W.* **nya-tság** *C.* id. — *nya-tsíl* the fat of a fish. — *nya-tser* **fish-bones** *Sch.* — *nya-tsóṅ-pa* **fish-monger.** — *nya-ₒdzin Cs.*, **nya-kúg** *W.*, angle, fishing-hook. — *nya-zán* a fish-eater, one feeding on fish *Cs.* — *nya-rús* fish-bone *Cs.* — *nya-lóg* 1. *Cs.*: 'a contraction or sinking of the sinews'. 2. *Sik.*: **cholera** (*Urd.* هيضه) — 3. *Med.*, also *nya-lhóg*, a name for a disease. — *nyá-ša* 1. flesh of fish 2. *W.*: meat cut into long narrow strips and dried in the sun, in *C.* **ša-bcúg**. — *nya-ɣšóg* the fin of a fish *Cs.* — *nya-ság* fish-scale. — *nya-sóg* prob. the back-bone with the bones attached to it, resembling a saw.

ཉ་ག་, ཉག་ *nyá-ga*, *nyag*, a steel-yard.

ཉ་བོ་ *nyá-bo* body, figure *Sch.*

ཉ་མ་ *nyá-ma* (*Sch.*: 'mistress of the house, housewife'?) **hearer** of a Lama, without being a regular disciple *Mil.* frq.; *nyá-ma ṗó-mo-rnams Mil.* (cog. to *nyán-pa*?)

ཉ་ར་ *nyá-ra* **care,** *ryá-ra byéd-pa Sch.*, **nyá-ra ċó-ce** *W.*, to take care of, to provide for a person, to keep a thing well; **nyar go** *C.* for *nyá-ra byed dgos*; cf. *ɣnyér-ḱa*.

ཉ་ར་ཉོ་རེ་ *nya-ra-nyo-ré* **weak, feeble, frail,** e.g. of a worm *Thgy.*

ཉག་ *nyag* 1. v. *nyá-ga*. — 2. v. *nyág-ma*. — 3. also *nyág-ga*, *nyag-ḱrám*, **notch, indenture,** *ló-ma ṗrá-la nyág-ga-ċan* having multifid leaves, like those of caraway *Wdn.*; *nyág-ga méd-pa* not cleft, not indented. — 4. of wool, *nyúg-tu ˳drén-pa* to draw out into threads, to spin *Mil.*

ཉག་ཉིག་ *nyag-nyig Cs., Sch.* also *nyag-nyóg* **filth, dirt.**

ཉག་ཉུག་ *nyag-nyúg Mil.* = *sna-ťsogs* (?), of rare occurrence.

ཉག་ཐག་ *nyag-ťág* **thread; chain,** of gold *Mil.*, of iron *Mil.*; cord for stringing turkoises *Mil.*; a cable *Schr.*

ཉག་མཐིལ་ *nyag-mťil* **scale of a steel-yard,** *nyag-rdó* weight of a steel-yard.

ཉག་ཕྲན་ *nyag-ṗrán* a small beam, **a pole** *Cs.*; **an arrow**; *nyag-ṗran-mdá* arrow *Mil.*

ཉག་མ་ *nyág-ma*, also *nyag-ré*, **single**; *nyag γčig* 1. id., *skra*, or *spu nyag(-ma) γčig* a single hair, frq.; *skrá-yi nyág-ma* id. (a man has 21 000 of them *Med.*) — 2. **a minimum** *Mil.* — 3. *Sch.* also: **bachelor,** old voluntary bachelor. — *saṅs-rgyas-nyag-γčig Thgy., Pth.*, only Buddha, or nothing less than Buddha.

ཉག་མོ་ *nyág-mo Lex.* w.e.; **woman** *Sch.*

ཉག་ཤིང་ *nyág-šiṅ* **beam of a steel-yard.**

ཉང་ཀ་, ཉང་གེ་ *nyáṅ-ka, nyáṅ-ge Sp.* **currant,** Ribes.

ཉན་ཏི་ *nyán-ti Pur.* **thy, your** (?).

ཉན་པ་ *nyán-pa* (*nyán-to, nyán-tam*), imp. *nyon* 1. (also, though seldom, *mnyán-pa*) c. dat. or accus. **to hear,** to give ear to, **to listen** (cf. *ťos-pa*); *slób-dpon-gyi ťád-du čos nyán-pa* to attend to the religious instruction of the teacher; *ṅag* or *ťsig nyán-pa Dzl.*, *ḱá-la*, or resp. *żál-la*, or *bka-nyán-pa* to obey, to yield; *ṅas ǰi-ltar zér-pai ḱá-la nyán-na Glr.*, *ṅa zer nyán-na Mil.* if you listen to my word; *Tar.* 14, 14; 17, 16 c.c. *las.* — 2. **to listen secretly,** to be an eaves-dropper, **ṗag-nyen ǰhé-pa** *C.*, **ṗag-nyán čó-če, táṅ-če** *W.*, id.; *nyán-mḱan* col. *nyán(-pa)-po*, fem. *nyan(-pa)-mo, B.*, a hearer, auditor; *nyan-ťós* id.; but esp. of the personal disciples of Buddha, the Sravakas, *Köpp.* I., 419; *Burn.* I., 296; *nyan-ťós bču-drúg* the sixteen *γnas-brtán* q.v.; *nyan-ťós-ma* a female hearer; *ḱa-la nyán-po, nyán-mkan* obedient, *ḱá-la mi nyán-po* disobedient. — 3. **to be able,** later *B.*, and col., gen. with a negative: *˳gró ma nyán-pas* not being able to walk (on account of illness) *Mil.*; also like *ma btúb-pa* not being willing; without a negative: **nyán yin** *W.* yes, I shall be able; inst. of *rúṅ-ba*: **za-nyán yód-na ḱyoṅ** *W.*, bring it me, if it is still eatable.

ཉམ་ *nyam*, also *nyam-tig, nyam-yós* **cricket, locust** *Sik.*

ཉམ(ས)་ *nyam(s)*, resp. *ťugs, ťugs-nyám(s)* 1. **soul, mind,** *nyáms-kyi grogs* companions of the soul, viz. the murmuring springs and rivulets in the solitude of alpine regions *Mil.*; *nyáms-kyi čaṅ* the soul's wine, i.e. religious knowledge *Mil.*; *nyams dgá-ba* 1. well being, comfort, cheerfulness, *nyams mi-dgá-ba* an unhappy state, discomfort, *nyams-dgá glú-ru bloṅs* sing a song of joy! *Mil.* 2. gen. adj.: agreeable, delightful, charming, *nyáms-dga-bai sa-γnás* a charming country *Glr.*. — 2. **thought,** *nyams skye* or *šar* a thought rises. — 3. **strength, magnitude, height, state, manner,** *nyams-(kyi) ťsád byéd-pa Pth.* (also with *bčád-pa* or *lén-pa C.*) to try, to put to the test, e.g. one's strength; *ťugs-dám-gyi nyams sád-pa* to try the degree of a person's devotion or spiritual progress *Mil.*; *smra-nyáms, byed-nyáms* manner, — and particularly a pleasing, agreeable manner, — of speaking or dealing.

Other phrases are: *nyáms-su lén-pa* to take to heart, to interest one's self in or for a thing *Dzl.*, to commit to memory, to learn (v. below); *nyáms-su myóṅ-ba* to suffer, undergo, experience *Dzl.*; *nyams ṅá-ba* v. the compounds; *nyams bčád-pa C.* to try, to examine; *nyams ˳brú-ba C.* to irritate, provoke, vex; *nyams myóṅ-ba* = *nyáms-su myóṅ-ba*; *nyams bżág-pa* is said to be = *drán-pa nyé-bar bżág-pa*, v. *nyé-ba*; *nyams lén-pa* 1. = *nyáms-su lén-pa*, v. above, 2. col. to measure out, to take the measure, the dimensions of, to survey, *sa* land, *nor* the property, to take an inventory, to ascertain or compute the state of one's property, 3. *C.* = the following; *nyams sád-pa* ccg. 1. to try, to test, *byéd-dam mi byed* whether he will do it or not *Mil.*, to tempt, *tugs-dám-gyi nyams sád-pa* v. above. 2. to mock, scoff, trouble maliciously, provoke, irritate *C.*

Comp. *nyams-dgú* v. *nyams-tábs.* — *nyams-rgyúd Mil.* = *nyams, nyams-rgyúd-la sbyáṅs-pa*, intellectually skilled, well versed. — *nyams-ṅá* **anxiety, fear, dread,** of a thing, with the dat. or instr. *Mil.*; *nyams-ṅá-las tár-ba* to be delivered from anxiety *S.g.*; *nyams-ṅá-ba* vb. to be alarmed, to be in great anxiety *Sch.*; adj. dreadful, horrible, *nags-tsál nyams-ṅa-ba* a horrible forest *Dzl.* — *nyams-bċúg* is said to be used resp. or euphem. for *skyon*, e.g. for damage done to an image of a god by water *C.*; *nyams-čágs* sin *Schr.*; in *Thgr.* it seems to be used in this sense. — *nyáms-čún* 1. **faint, weak, languid, exhausted,** by hunger, illness etc. *Dzl.*; **poor** in learning, destitute of knowledge, ignorant *W.*; destitute of money, destitute of virtue *C.* 2. *W.* col. for *snyems-čúṅ.* — *nyams-rtógs* resp. **knowledge, cognition, perception,** *nyams-rtógs śig yod, nyams-rtógs bzáṅ-po skye* or *ₒkruṅs*, a perception, a good thought arises (in my mind); in a general sense: *nyams-rtógs-kyi mtar pyín-pa* to obtain perfect knowledge *Mil.*, frq. — *nyams-stóbs* **strength**, *zin* is gone *Med.* — *nyams-stoṅ-ysál* v. *ysál-po.* — *nyams-brtás byed-pa* **strengthening, restorative, nourishing** *Med.*, (but *nyams-brtas* he recovered, grew well, got up again *Dzl.*) — *nyams-tág-pa* **suffering, tormented, exhausted** *Dzl.*; *nyams-tág-pai skad* or *sgra* lamentation, doleful cries. — *nyams-tábs, nyams-dgú Sch.*: 'appearance, colour, figure, state' (?). — *nyams-myóṅ Tar.* **enjoyment, delight,** *nyams-myóṅ ma skyes ruṅ*, although I had no real enjoyment of it *Mil.nt.*; *tsór-bai nyams-myóṅ* prob. perception by the senses, knowledge acquired through the medium of the senses *Mil.* — *nyams-rtsál Dzl.* ༧༥, 7 **skill.** — *nyams-mtsár-ba C.* **wonderful,** most beautiful. — *nyams-lén* a memorial verse, a rhyme or verse serving to retain things in memory *Mil.*

ཉམས་པ་ *nyáms-pa* **injured, hurt,** e.g., by a fall *Dzl.*; of lifeless things: **spoiled, damaged** *C.*; **impaired, imperfect,** *stobs-nyams, dbáṅ-po nyáms-pa, yán-lag nyams Lex.* (as explanation of *żá-bo*); *smra-nyáms* (the sick person) speaks little *Med.*; **sem-nyám sóṅ-kan* W.* discouraged, disheartened; esp. relative to a violation of duty, failing in, *tsúl-krims* (or *tsúl-las*) *nyáms-pas* because he has failed in, acted against the moral law *Dzl.*; *bzód-pa nyáms-par ₒgyúr-bas* because their patience failed *Dzl.*; also **stained** *Glr.*, e.g. *krág-gis* with blood; *nyáms-par byéd-pa Wdṅ.*; *nyáms-su ₒjúg-pa Glr.* to spoil, deteriorate, destroy; *ma nyáms-pa* entire, complete, untouched, uncorrupted.

ཉར་ *nyar* 1. v. *nya-ra.* — 2. *Cs.*, also *nyar-nyár*, **oblong.**

ཉར་གདོང་ *nyár-ydóṅ W.* inst. of *ṅar-ydóṅ*, **shin, shin-bone.**

ཉལ་ཉིལ་ *nyal-nyil*, or *nyal-nyól* **filth, dirt,** foul matter, loose and dry dirt that may be removed by sweeping *Pth.*, *Dzl.*

ཉལ་བ་ *nyál-ba*, imp. *nyol*, 1. **to lie down,** e.g. before a tigress *Dzl.*; to lie down, **to sleep,** *nyal(-du) soṅ* (he) went to bed *Glr.*; *rgya-sráṅ-la nyal ₒdúg-go* (he) slept in the street *Glr.*; *mi nyal tsám-la* when people go to bed, at curfew *Mil.*; *rta nyal byéd-pa* to make a horse lie down *Glr.*; rarely of things: *rtsva nyal* the grass is laid-down (by the wind or rain) *Dzl.*; *ra ₒog nyál-bai nya* so *Zam.* calls the letter *rnya*; fig. to rest, *bdé-bar nyál-du méd-do* (he) had no rest, viz. from envy *Dzl.* ༢༦, 12. — 2. with *daṅ* or *la*, **to lie with** (a woman) *Dzl.* and elsewh. — 3. fig. **to dwell, to live** *Mil.*

Comp. *ṅyal-kri* **couch, bed, sofa** *C.* — *nyal-gós* **counterpane, quilt, blanket** *Sch.* — *nyál-po* **coition,** *nyál-po byéd-pa* to practise cohabitation, *máṅ-du* immoderately *Med.* —

nyál-bu bastard, whoreson *Ma.* — *nyál-sa* sleeping-place.

ཉི *nyi* 1. num. fig.: 38. — 2. num. inst. of *ɣnyis* in compounds, *nyi-brgyá*, *-stóṅ*, *-k'ri* etc., *nyi-k'ri* also title of a book, the Prajnâ Paramitâ, containing 28 000 Sloka. — 3. for *nyi-ma*.

ཉི་ཁུད *nyi-k'úd* a lake in Nepal *Pth.*

ཉི་མ *nyi-ma* (*Bal.* **nyó-ma**, 1. **the sun,** *˳čar* becomes visible, rises; *šar* id., also: has risen, shines; *nub, rgas, W.* also **skyod, bud**, sets, is setting; *nyi-ma nub ťse bar* (for *ťseṅ bár-du*) until sun-set *Sch.*; *nyi-mai ɣnyen* akin to the sun, the Sâkya race *Cs.*; **da nyi-ma riṅ-mo* W.* now the sun stands already high in the heavens; **nyi-ma-gaṅ-šár** sun-flower, Helianthus. — 2. **day,** = *nyin-mo*, opp. to night, frq.; **nyi-ma-ťsé* W.* the whole day, all day long; **nyi-ma-p'éd* W.* noon, mid-day; *nyi-ma ɣčig* one day, once *Dzl.*: *nyi-ma-re-rér* daily.

Comp. *nyi-dkyil* **disk of the sun** *Sch.* — *nyi-gúṅ*, *nyi-mai guṅ* **noon, mid-day;** meridian(?) *Cs.* — *nyi-dgá* seems to be the n. of a medicinal herb *Med.* — *nyi-rgás* **sun-set.** — *nyi-ldóg* **the solstice,** *dgún-nyi-ldog* winter solstice, *dbyár-nyi-ldog* summer solstice *Wdk.* — *nyi-núb* = *nyi-rgás.* — *nyi-ťsé* 1. *Sch.*: the time or duration of one day. 2. *Lex.*: = प्रदेश direction, place, country(?); *nyi-ťsé spyód-pa Lex.*: a kind of ascetic; *nyi-ťsé-ba Sch.*: ephemeral; single, simple; *Thgy.*: n. of a class of infernal beings. — *nyi-ťsód* **sun-dial,** *nyi-ťsód-kyi k'ór-lo* the circle of a sun-dial *Cs.* — *nyi-˳dzin* **eclipse** of the sun (cf. *sgra-ɣčán*). — *nyi-zér* **sun-beam,** *nyi-zér rtá-la žón-nas* riding on a sun-beam *Mil.* and elsewh.; *nyi-zér-gyi rdul* a mote floating in a sun-beam. — *nyi-zlá* sun and moon; also the figures of sun and moon connected, crowning the top of the *mčod-rtén*; *nyi-zlá bsdad mi oṅ* sun and moon will not stand still *Mil.* — *nyi-˳óg* below the sun; the earth *Was.* (49); *nyi-˳óg-gi rgyal-k'ams Glr.* id.; it seems, however, to denote a certain country, acc. to Mahâvyutpatti the same as Aparântaka, *Williams*: the western country; cf. *Schf.* on *Tar.* ?. — *nyi-˳od* **sun-shine.** — *nyi-yól* any **screen** or **shelter** from the sun's rays: awning, curtain, parasol, pent-house *Sch.*; **nyi-rib** (prop. *sgrib*) *W.* id., umbrella. — *nyi-šár* **sun-rise** *Cs.* — *nyi-lhag Sch.* a cold day (?) — Cf. *nyin-mo.*

ཉི་ཤུ *nyi-šu* (inst. of *nyis-ču*), often in conjunction with *ťám-pa*, **twenty,** *nyi-šu-rtsa-ɣčig B., C.*, **nyi-šu-nyer-ɣčig* W.*, *nyer-ɣčig*, twentyone.

ཉིག་ཉིག *nyig-nyig W.* **loose, slack, lax,** not tight or tense.

ཉིང་ཁུ *nyiṅ-ku, Ssk.* सत्त्व *Cs.*: 'heart, spirit, essence', cf. *snyiṅ-po.*

ཉིང་ཏོ *nyiṅ-to Sch.*: **sure, trustworthy,** *Lex.*: *nyiṅ-tor* = *ṅes-par.*

ཉིང་ལག *nyiṅ-lag*, a category not familiar to us; gen. mentioned together with *yán-lag*; it might be translated by: members of a second order, parts of the *yán-lag*; the exact meaning must however remain undetermined, as the Tibetans themselves are not able to give a clear definition of it. In *C.*: inner parts of the body, opp. to outer. In books, phrases like the following are to be found: *yán-lag daṅ nyiṅ-lag ťams-čád daṅ ldán-pa*; *yán-lag daṅ nyiṅ-lag ná-ba*; *yán-lag daṅ nyiṅ-lag ɣčód-pa*; evidently the *nyiṅ-lag* are smaller, but more numerous than the *yán-lag*. In *Pth.* also *nyiṅ-sprúl* is found besides *yaṅ-sprúl*, emanation of the third order; v. *sprúl-pa.*

ཉིང་མཚམས་སྦྱོར་བ *nyiṅ-mtsáms sbyór-ba* **to be re-born** *Stg.*

ཉིད *nyid* 1. **self, same,** opp. to other persons, *ma nyid* the mother herself *Dzl.*; *mi de ni rgyál-po nyid yin-no* this man are you yourself, o king! *Dzl.*; the very, just he, just it etc., *las byéd-pai ɣnas nyid-la* just where I am working *Dzl.*; *deṅ druṅ-nyid-na* (or *du*) close by, to, or before, hard by, *Thgy.*; *dus de-nyid-du* at the very moment, frq.; *mčód-bya nyid* that which is venerable par excellence *Tar.* 15, 13; *yón-*

tan nyid Tar. 15, 14 id.; *dé-nas mi riṅ-ba-nyid-na* a very short time after *Tar.*; when added to adjectives it denotes abstract nouns, as in English the terminations: -ness, -ship, -ty, -cy, -y etc., but it is chiefly limited to the language of philosophical writings, from which a few expressions only (such as *stoṅ-pa-nyid* the emptiness, the Buddhist vacuum) have found their way into col. language. — 2. In the more recent literature it is used resp. for *k̔yod*, **thou, you**; *nyid-kyi* **thy, your** *Pth.*, *Ma.*; *nyid-ráṅ* **you** (col. **nyi-ráṅ, nyo-ráṅ**) *W., C.*, resp., like the German '*Sie*'; *nyid-čag(-raṅ)* **you**, addressed to one person or to several, *C.* (in *Glr. k̔yed-čag* seems to be used in the same way). — 3. **only**, *graṅs-kyi lṅa nyid Zam.* only the numeral *lṅa; za nyid-do* the letter *za* alone (without a prefix).

ཉིན(མོ) *nyin(-mo)* 1. **day**, =*nyi-ma* 2; *nyin-gyi riṅ-la* during the day-time *Pth.; nyin-mor ᵒgyur* it dawns *Cs.; nyin-mor byed* 'making day', an epithet of the sun *Cs.; nyin* adv. in the day-time *Glr.; nyin-čig* one day, once *Dzl.; nyin čig bžin-du* daily *Dzl.*; *nyin-par* during the day-time *Dzl.;* by day-light *Dzl.; deï nyin-par* on that day, frq. *Dzl.; p̔yir nyin, p̔yi de nyin, deï p̔yi nyin* the following day, on the f.d. *Dzl.; ts̔es bčo-lṅái nyin* the 15th., on the 15th. *Glr.;* fig.: *bstán-pa nyin-par mdzád-pai skyés-bu* a saint that restores the doctrine, a reformer of faith; hence *Schr.: dád-pai nyin-byed* evangelist, apostle. — 2. **propitious day**; **ṅa ča nyin-mo mi ᵒdug* W.* this day is not propitious for me to go.

Comp. *nyin-dkár* a white, a **lucky day** *Sch.* — *nyin-gáṅ, nyin-t̔og-t̔ág* (*W. *t̔ag-t̔og**) all the day long. — *nyin-gúṅ* **noon.** — *nyin-gla* daily pay, a day's hire *Cs.* — **nyin-ts̔e-ré* W.* all the day long, the live-long day. — *nyin-mts̔án* 1. **a day and a night**, *nyin-mts̔án bčo-brgyád Mil.* for nine days and nine nights. 2. **day and night** *Dzl.*, *nyin-mts̔an-méd-par* id., frq.; *nyin-med-ts̔án-med W.* id.; *nyin-mts̔án-du* id. *Mil.; nyin-mts̔án mnyám-pa* equinox. — *nyin-žág(-γčig)* 1. a day with the night, 24 hours, divided into 12 portions of time, called *k̔yim* (q. v.): *nam-p̔yéd* midnight, *nam-p̔yed-yól* 2 o'clock a. m., *t̔o-ráṅs* 4 o'cl. a. m. (in popular language also: **ǰá-po dáṅ-po** about 2 o'cl., **nyís-pa** 3 o'cl., **súm-pa** 4 o'cl., *nam-láṅs* 6 o'cl. a. m. (i. e. the time when the sun first illumines the mountain tops; it is from this moment, and not from midnight, that in daily life the date is counted); *nyi-šár* 8 o'cl. a. m. (when the sun rises upon the valley); *dros-ᵒǰám* (col. **nyi-ďúl**) 10 o'cl. a. m.; *nyin-gúṅ, nyi-p̔yéd* 12 o'cl., noon; *p̔yed-č̔ól* (*W. *zá-ra p̔i-mo**) 2 o'cl. p. m., *myur-smád* 4 o'cl. p. m., *nyi-rgás* 6 o'cl. p. m., *srod-ᵒk̔ór* 8 o'cl. p. m. (col. **sa-rúb, srod-rúb**), *srod-č̔ól* 10 o'cl. p. m. (col. **tiṅ-nyi**) — thus acc. to *Wdk.* By adding the names of the 12 years' cycle (*nam-p̔yéd byi-ba, p̔yed-č̔ól glaṅ* etc., v. the word *lo*), these terms have been rendered still more convenient for astrological calculations. Of course, all the terms given are strictly correct only at the time of the equinoxes, and deviate at the summer and winter solstices for more than an hour from the time indicated by our clocks. 2. *nyin-žág* as symb. num.: 15. — *nyiṅ-bžin-gyis Pth.*, *nyin-ré bžin Glr.*, daily adv., with-*gyi* adj. — *nyin-lám* a day's journey *Glr.*, *rkaṅ-t̔áṅ-gi, rtá-pai, lúg-pai nyin-lam* a pedestrian's, a horseman's, a sheep-driver's daily march. — *nyin-ráṅs Tar.* (= *t̔o-ráṅs*) day-break, morning twilight *Schf.*

ཉིབ་ཕྱོགས་ *nyib-p̔yógs, W. *nyib-č̔óg(s)** the sunny side of mountains.

ཉིལ་བ་ *nyil-ba* **to decay**, to crumble to pieces, of rocks, mountains etc.; rarely to run down, of tears, to flow down, of locks of hair.

ཉིས་ *nyis* 1. instrum. of *nyi.* — 2. in compounds for *γnis.*

ཉུ་ *nyu* num. fig.: 68.

ཉུ་ཏི *nyú-ti* **pear** *Ld.*

ཉུག་པ་ *nyúg-pa* 1. **to besmear**, *spos* to perfume; **to rub gently, to stroke, to caress** *Sch.*, in this sense perh. *Gyatch V2*, 14. — 2. **to touch**, = *rég-pa* ccd. *W.*; *C.*? — 3. **to search after** (feeling, groping) *Cs.* — 4. **to put out, stretch out**, *čú-nas mgo* one's head out of the water, to look or **peep out**, resp. *dbu nyug mdzád-pa Glr.*; *nyug-nyúg-pa Tar.* 80, 21 **to stand out, to project** (*Sch.:* to run to and fro?).

ཉུག་རྩ་མེ་ཏོག་ *nyúg-rtsa mé-tog* **Carthusian pink** *C.*

ཉུག་རུམ་, ཉུང་རུམ་ *nyug-rúm*, *nyuṅ-rúm* **a eunuch** *Dzl.*

ཉུང་བ་ *nyúṅ-ba* 1. adj. col. **nyúṅ-ṅu**, **little**; **nyuṅ-ṅu žig**, *Ld.* col. **nyúṅ-ṅa-rig**, *nyúṅ-zad čig* id. *Dzl.*; *nyuṅ-šás Wdṅ.*, **a little, a few, some**; *nyúṅ-bar byéd-pa* to make less *Cs.* — 2. vb. **to be little.**

ཉུང་མ་ *nyúṅ-ma* **turnip**, *la(-p̔ug daṅ) nyuṅ (-ma)* radishes and turnips *Glr.* — *nyúṅ-k̔u*, *nyúṅ-loi ǰa* turnip-soup, turnip-tea, an infusion of dried turnip leaves, much used, e.g. in Bhotan, and considered very nourishing(?). **nyuṅ-dö* C.*, mentioned by *Wts.* p. 137. as 'navets ronds', large sweet, red turnips (perh. turnip-rooted cabbage?). — *nyuṅ-γži* seed-turnips (*Cs.* turnip-seed). — *nyúṅ-lo* a turnip leaf.

Note. In writing and speaking this word is often confounded with *yuṅ(s)* mustard, so that e.g. *yúṅ-ma* is said for turnip inst. of *nyúṅ-ma*, *nyuṅs-dkár* for white mustard, inst. of *yuṅs-dkár*.

ཉུང་རུམ་ *nyuṅ-rúm* v. *nyug-rúm.*

ཉུལ་བ་ *nyúl-ba* **to wander** or **rove about, to pass privily** or **steal** through, e.g. towns, countries, mountains *Mil.*, burying-places, tombs (as jackals) *Mil.*; (*lta*) *nyúl-pa*, *nyúl-mi Pth.*, *sa-nyúl* a spy *Cs.* (Also *γnyúl-ba*, *myúl-ba.*)

ཉེ་ *nye* num. fig.: 98.

ཉེ་ཏི་ *nyé-ṭi* a pear *Schr.* (cf. *nyú-ti*, *nyó-ti*).

ཉེ་བ་ *nyé-ba* I. vb., **to be near, to approach**, always with the supine of a verb, *dus byéd-du nyé-bas* when he was near dying *Dzl.*; *zlá-ba ťsáṅ-du nyé-bas* (when she was) near the completion of the months, i. e. the time of giving birth to a child *Dzl.*, frq.; *slób-dpon p̔yir ̥ǒṅ-du nyé-bas* when the time of the teacher's return drew near *Dzl.*; *zin-du mi nyé-ste* being not near having done *Dzl.*; even used as follows: *γnas der sléb-tu nyé-bai ťse* when he came near the place *Mil.*

II. adj., col. **nyé-mo** **near**, both as to space and time, *lam-riṅ-gi γnyén-pas k̔yim-mťses nye* the neighbour is nearer than a kinsman living far off; *ká-ba daṅ nyé-bai sar* at a place near the pillar *Glr.*; *ťag-nyé-ba* id.: *ri ťag-nyé-ba žig* a near or neighbouring hill *Ma.*; standing near, fig. being closely connected with by consanguinity: *nyé-ba-rnams C.* relations, kindred (*Dzl.* ༢༣, 13 *γnyén-pas* prob. is preferable to *mo nyé-bas*); allied by similarity: *mťsáms-med-pa lṅa daṅ de daṅ nyé-bai sdíg-pa* the five worst sins, and those coming nearest to them; near by friendship and affection: **nyé-mo yin* W.* he is closely connected with us, he is desirous to enter into an intimate connection with us; *blo*, or *snyiṅ*, or *sems nyé-ba* (or **nyé-mo**), friendly, kind, amicable, *blo nyé-ba ltar byéd-pa* to affect a friendly manner *Glr.*; **nyé-mo ǰhé'-pa* C.* to love, e.g. parents loving their children or vice versâ; *nyé-bai sras brgyad Glr.* the eight intimate disciples (of Buddha, not historical, but mythical persons, Mandshusri etc.).

III. adv. *nyé-bar* or *nyer* 1. **near**, *daṅ* to, *dé-dag daṅ nyé-bar lhá-k̔aṅ bžens* near to them he built a temple *Tar.*; *nyé-bar ̥ǒṅ-ba*, *sléb-pa*, to come near, to approach; *nyé-bar ̥gyúr-ba* id., *stóṅs-su nyé-bar ̥gyúr-ba daṅ* when it was nearly empty *Pth.*; *dár-la nyé-bar gyúr-to* it began to spread, to extend itself *Pth.*; *nyé-bar γnás-pa* to be near, to stand near, e.g. of a star *Wdṅ.* — 2. *nyé-bar byéd-pa*, with *la*, **to adhere to, to keep** (one's promise) *Pth.* — 3. *nyé-bar bžág-pa* **to make use of, to employ**, *drán-pa nyé-bar bžág-pa* (**स्मृत्युपस्थान**, *Burn.* I.,

626. उप near, though Tibetan dictionaries write अव) to make use of one's intellectual powers. To do this rightly forms part of Buddhist wisdom (v. *Köpp.* I, 436) and instruction (*Dzl.* ༡༢༥, 7, where *Sch.*'s version is incorr.), being divided into four divisions or degrees (*Burn.*); *saṅs-rgyás-la dkón-pai ̥du-šés nyé-bar bžág-pa* to apply to Buddha the notion of rareness *Tar.* 5, 13. — 4. **intensely, urgently, speedily,** *̥jigs-pa nyé-bar ži* fear is speedily allayed *Glr.*; *nad nyé-bar ̥tso* the disease is speedily cured *Thgy.*; *nyé-bar lén-pa Mil., Thgy.* to seize eagerly, to strive for earnestly, to aspire to, esp. to the re-birth as a human being; cf. also *nyer-lén*; *nyé-bar mk'ó-ba* of urgent necessity, frq. *Tar. nyer ̥pel* it increases rapidly *Med.*

IV. sbst. v. *nyé-šiṅ.*

Comp. *nye-sk'ór Sch. nye-̥k'ór* **those about us,** the company around us, *k'yed-ráṅ-gi nye-k'ór-gyi ldóm-bu-ba* a beggar belonging to the people around you *Mil.*; esp. relations, kindred, *des nye-k'ór yaṅ šúgs-kyis yoṅ* in this way family-connections are formed of themselves *Mil.* — *nye-mk'ón = nye-riṅ Cs.* (?) — *nye-grógs* **neighbour, fellow-creature** *Cs.* — *nye-čár* **now** *Sch.* — *nyé-dag Cs., nyé-du,* and most frq. *nye-̥brél* (*ɣnyen-̥brél*) **kindred, relations** (these being considered a main obstacle to moral perfection, they are to be shunned accordingly). — *nye-ɣnás* **disciple,** *k'yéd-kyi nye-ɣnás bgyio, nye-ɣnás-su mčio* I wish to become your disciple *Dzl.* — *nye-tsán, nye-rigs* **relative, kinsman.** — *nye-riṅ* 1. **near and far,** near and distant relations. 2. **distance,** *sgor nye-riṅ či-tsam yod* how far is it from here to the gate? 3. **partial,** *rgyál-po nye-riṅ čes* the king is very partial *Glr., nye-riṅ-méd-pa* impartial *Glr.* — *nye-lám* **near; now** *Sch.*

ཉེ་ཞོ *nye-žo* **damage, mishap, accident** (syn. to *bar-čad*), *nye-žo-méd-par* without an accident, safely *Dzl.*

ཉེ་རེག་པ་ *nye-rég-pa Lexx.* **to wash.**

ཉེ་ཤིང་ *nyé-šiṅ,* or *nyé-bai šiṅ Med.,* a tree the fruits of which are used as a sweet medicine.

ཉེག་མ་, ཉེག་ཐག་ *nyég-ma, nyeg-ťág,* v. *nyág-ma.*

ཉེད་པ་ *nyéd-pa = mnyéd-pa.*

ཉེན་ *nyen* 1. = *nye, nyen-k'ór,* or *nyen-skór = nye-̥k'or* **a relative,** *Pth.*: *nyen-k'ór žig yin* he is a kinsman; also alone, like *ɣnyen.* — 2. with a vb.: **danger, risk,** *myúr-du ̥jig-nyen yod* there is a danger of its being soon destroyed *Glr.*; *dmyál-bar ̥gro-nyén ɣda* there is a danger of going to hell; *sróg-gi bar-čád-du ̥gró-bai nyen yod Mil.* of risking one's life; **dúṅ-nyen** *C.* he has the chance of receiving a good beating; occasionally also: to be near, to impend, in reference to happy events; in col. language it is simply used for danger, *nyén-čan* dangerous, e.g. *lam, las, sbrul* etc.

ཉེན་པ་ *nyén-pa,* pf. *nyén-to,* **to be pained, pinched, pressed** hard, e.g. by hunger, cold, enemies; **to toil and moil, to labour hard, to drudge;** v. *baṅ.*

ཉེར་ *nyer* 1. = *nyé-bar.* — 2. v. *nyí-šu.*

ཉེར་སྣོགས་ *nyer-snógs Thgy.,* **theme, task** *Sch.*

ཉེར་ཉེར་ *nyer-nyér, nyer-že; W.* **dregs, sediment.**

ཉེར་བ་ *nyér-ba* 1. *Sch.* **to tan, curry, dress,** make soft. — 2. *W.*, also **nyer-k'ád ťáṅ-če**, **to snarl, growl.** — 3. *W.* **to tarry, stay, linger** (*snyér-ba* for *bsnár-ba?*).

ཉེར་མ་ *nyér-ma W.* for *ɣyér-ma,* **red pepper.**

ཉེར་ལེན་ *nyer-lén,* or *nyé-bar lén-pa,* is said to be = *rgyui rgyu,* original cause.

ཉེལ་བ་ *nyél-ba* taken **ill, sick** *Sch.*

ཉེས་པ་ *nyés-pa* I. sbst. any thing **wrong** or **noxious,** or liable to become so, and the consequences of it; hence 1. **evil, calamity, damage,** *nyés-pa ťams-čád deṅ lús-la ̥duo* all sorts of plagues are collecting upon his body *Dzl.*; *lo-nyés* a bad harvest, failure of crops, *lo-nyés byúṅ-bai ťse* when the harvest had been bad; in a special sense in medicine: the three **humours** of the body, air (v. *rluṅ*), bile, and phlegm, gen. called त्रिदोष *γnod-byéd nyés-pa γsum* the three noxious matters (most diseases being ascribed to a derangement of one of them). — 2. **moral fault, offence, sin, crime,** *nyés-pai skyon*, being contaminated by a crime *Dzl.; lus daṅ ṅág-gi* (or *k'ai*) *nyés-pa* sin in word and deed *Dzl.*; *nyés-pa byéd-pa* to commit a fault, a crime; to sin, frq.; also: *mi žig-la nyés-pa byuṅ* a slip has occurred to a person *Dzl.*; *bdág-la nyés-pa či žig yód-de ma γnaṅ* what crime have I committed, that you will not give me permission? *Dzl.* — 3. **punishment** *C.* **nyē-mig** id., resp. **ka-nyē*; *nye-pa p'og-k'an** he that has got a punishment.

II. vb. **to commit an offence,** *ₒdis či nyés-te bzuṅ* what offence has he committed that he is taken prisoner? *Dzl.* (cf. above); *sṅón-čad bdág-gis nyés-pa bden* it is true that formerly I committed a fault *Dzl.; sṅár ma sbrán-pa nyés-so* the not reporting sooner was a fault *Dzl.*; *γyógs-pa nyés-so* you have committed a fault by covering . . . *Dzl.; bdag nyés-na* if harm is done to me; hence *či nyés* in a general sense: *k'yod či nyés-pa smros šig* tell me what has happened to you *Dzl.*; *btsóṅ-na či nyés* quid mali, si vendideris? *Dzl.*; *mi drán-nam či nyes* is she out of her senses, or, what is the matter with her? *Dzl.; či nyés-na* why, *či nyés-na k'áṅ-pai náṅ-na rdziṅ-bu bskyil* why is there a pond within the house? *Dzl.*; *ma nyés-pai ₒgró-ba* innocent beings *Mil.*; *ma nyés-pa p'yir byuṅ* he came out again unhurt *Dzl.*; *nyés-byas* a wicked action, a sin *Cs.; nyés-ltuṅ* sin, sinful deed, trespass, *nyés-ltuṅ-gis p'og* he has been overtaken by a sin *Mil.*

ཉོ་ *nyo* 1. num. fig.: 128. — 2. **carrot** *Cs.*

ཉོ་ཏི་ *nyo-ti* **a pear** *Ld.*

ཉོ་བ་ *nyó-ba*, pf. and imp. *nyos*, 1. **to buy,** *dṅul brgyas* for a hundred rupees; *nyó-(ba-)po* a buyer, purchaser, *nyo-(ba-)mo* fem.; *nyó-mk'an* a buyer, customer; *nyó-t'o* account, bill; *nyo-ₒtsóṅ* commerce, traffic; *nyo-ₒtsóṅ byéd-pa* to trade. — 2. **to take at rent, to take the lease** (of a field, by buying the crop).

ཉོག་པ་ *nyóg-pa* **soiled, dirtied,** made unclean, e.g. of victuals *Mil.; nyóg-ma Sch.*, *ču-nyóg Lex.* muddy, foul water; *nyog-nyóg-po* confused (story) *Tar.*

ཉོགས་བྱིང་ *nyogs-byiṅ Sch.*: **too soft;** *nyog-nyóṅ Sch.* **soft, tender, weak,** inclined to weep; **šés-nyog-čan** (for *γšés-nyog-čan*) dandling, fondling *W.*

ཉོད་པ་ *nyód-pa* **food** *Lex.*

ཉོན་མོངས་པ་ *nyon-móṅs-pa* (seldom without -*pa*), *Ssk.* क्लेश 1. **misery, trouble, pain,** frq.; also used as a verb: *nyon-móṅs-šiṅ; tsá-bas nyon-móṅs-te* molested by the heat *Dzl.*; *nyon-móṅs-par ₒgyúr-ba* to get into trouble *Dzl.*; *nyon ma móṅs-sam* had you to experience any hardship? *Dzl.* — 2. in a restricted sense: **the misery of sin,** *nyon-móṅs-pa-las p'an-pai don med* this does not avail for being delivered from such misery *Dzl.*; **sin,** *nyon-móṅs-pai nad, dri-ma Dzl.*; *sér-sna-la sógs-pai nyon-móṅs-pa* avarice and other sins *S.O.*; *nyon-móṅs-pa-méd-pa* free from sin, sinless *S.O.*; *nyon-móṅs-čan-gyis nyá-ša nyos Zam.* the offender buys the flesh of a fish.

ཉོབ་ཉོབ་ *nyob-nyób* weak, feeble-minded *Sch.*

ཉོར་ *nyor* 1. v. *nyó-ba*. 2. **a rectangle** *Cs.*

ཉོལ་ *nyol*, imp. of *nyál-ba*; *nyól-ba* prov. for *nyál-ba*.

ཉོས་ *nyos*, imp. of *nyó-ba*; *nyos-mi* a slave *Cs.*

གཉང་བ་ *γnyáṅ-ba Sch.*, prob. = *rnyáṅ-ba*.

གཉན་ *γnyan* 1. a pestilential disease, epidemic, or contagious disorder, **plague,** *mdze daṅ ₒbrum-bu γnyan Ma.*; *γnyan-nád* id.; *γnyan-dúg* a poison against, or a remedy for the plague *Med.*; *dka-γnyán* a destructive plague *Sch.* — 2. a species of wild sheep, **argali** (Ovis ammon).

གཉན་པ་ *γnyán-pa* **cruel, fierce, severe,** *lha γnyán-rnams Glr.* gods of vengeance, deities of terror; *klu-γnyán* id.; *k̔rims γnyán-pa* a cruel commandment, frq.; *dam-tsig γnyán-pa* prob. a rigid vow, a solemn oath *Mil.*; of mountains: **wild, rugged, precipitous;** *γnyán-sa* a rugged country *Mil.*; in *γnyán-pai γnad* (v. *γnad*) prob.: dangerous. — *γnyán-po* sbst. *Mil.?*

གཉའ་(བ་) *γnya(-ba)* 1. **neck, nape,** *γnyá-ba brtuṅs* the neck is contracted or shortened *Med.* — *γnyá-ko* hide, or leather of a beast's neck *Cs.* — *γnya-k̔óbs* screen of the neck (attached to a helmet) *Sch.* — *γnya-rgyáb* (?) *C.* breast-work, parapet. — *γnya-rtsé* vertebra prominens, the cervical vertebra with its projecting process *Mil.* — *γnya-ts̔igs* cervical joint. — *γnya-rèṅs* stiff neck, *γnya-rèṅs-čan* 1. having a stiff neck; 2. stiffnecked, obstinate. — *γnya-šiṅ* a yoke (for oxen) *Glr.*, *Lex.* — 2. *skad-γnyá* v. *skad.*

གཉའ་ནང་ *γnya-náṅ*, or *snya-náṅ*, a village on the frontier of Nepal

གཉའ་བོ་ *γnyá-bo* **a witness,** one that gives evidence *Cs.*, *Lex.* = *dpáṅ-po*; *γnyá-bo byéd-pa* to pledge for, to be surety for; *Dzl.* ༡༡༤: *bskyi-γnyá byas*, *Sch.*: 'he made an attested loan'.

གཉི་ག་ *γnyi-ga* for *γnyis-ka Stg.*; *γnyi-zér* for *nyi-zér Lex.*

གཉིག་ཏུ་ *γnyig-tu Lex.* = *γčig-tu.*

གཉིད་ *γnyid*, resp. *mnal*, **sleep,** *γnyid-du ˳gró-ba* to fall asleep *Glr.*, *Mil.*; *W.* **nyid ma yoṅ** sleep has not come, I am sleepless; **nyid ma k̔ug, nyid k̔ug ma nyan**, also **nyid saṅ soṅ** id.; *γnyid mi t̔ub* he cannot find sleep *Med.*; *γnyid-t̔úm-pa* one uninterrupted portion of sleep *Glr.*; *γnyid mt̔úg-pa* a sound sleep, *γnyid-sráb* a light sleep, a slumber *Med.* — *γnyid-log-pa* (prop. *γnyid-kyis lóg-pa*) *Dzl.* to fall asleep, *Dzl.* ༡༤༣, 16; ༣༡༨, 9 (thus correctly translated already by *Schr.*), prob. also to sleep; *γnyid-la ˳gro-ba*, *W.* **ča-če**, to fall asleep; *γnyid t̔úg-por soṅ* he fell into a deep sleep *Mil.*; **da-rúṅ γnyid ma lóg-mk̔an-˳dug** *W.* I am still awake; *γnyid sád-pa* to awaken, to awake vb. n.; *γnyid-yúr-ba* to be overcome by sleep *Sch.*, *Tar.* 31, 22, *Pth.*, — *γnyid-rdól C.* somnambulism; **nyid-ma-mún-la ḍúl-če** id., *Ld.*; **nyi'-čól gyáb-pa** id. *C.* — *γnyid-čan* sleepy *Cs.*; *γnyid-méd* having no sleep, sleepless; *γnyid-yér* morbid sleeplessness; *γnyid-yár Med.*, *Pth.*, id.? *γnyid-lam C.* = *rmi-lam* dream.

གཉིས་ *γnyis* 1. also *γnyis šig* (v. *čig*), **two,** *de γnyis*, *γnyis-po*, *γnyis-ka* the two, both; *γnyis(-su)-méd(-pa)*; *mi-γnyis-pa Tar.*, not being two, i.e. not differing, identical, the same, *ṅa daṅ rgyál-ba γnyis-su med* I and Buddha, we are one, i.e. I am an incarnation of Buddha *Glr.*; *Cs.* also: indubitable, thus perh. used by *Mil.*; *γnyis-su ˳byúṅ-ba* to be divided into two, to become two *Glr.* — 2. **a** (married) **couple,** *brám-ze γnyis* Brahmin man and wife. — 3. **both** (v. above), in Tibetan often added, where two nouns have the same predicate, either disjunctively, and then usually followed by *re: jó-bo daṅ byams-mgón γnyis mdzó-mo reï stéṅ-du bžugs* both the lord and the Maitreya were mounted on bastard-cows *Glr.*; *ṅa-ráṅ re γnyis* either of us *Mil.*; *p̔yi naṅ γnyis čós-lugs gaṅ bzaṅ* which is the better of the two religions, the esoteric, or the exoteric? *Glr.*; — or copulatively: *k̔yo-šúg γnyis-la rás-čug γčig-las mi bdóg-ste* as they both, husband and wife, had only one cloth together *Dzl.*; — and reciprocally: *čos daṅ bon γnyis rtsód-pa* the contest between the religion of Buddha, and the religion of the Bons *Glr.*; *k̔yod daṅ ṅa γnyis bza-mi byao* we two shall marry each other *Glr.* In most cases mentioned sub 3, *γnyis-po* (the two), *γnyis-ka*, *(γ)nyi-ga*, *W.* col. also **nyi-ko, nyi-kad, nyi-kod**, *Sp.* **nyi-mo**, may be used inst. of *γnyis*; *γnyis* may also refer to several nouns on one or on both sides: *k̔yed daṅ ṅa γnyis* both you (referring to several persons) and I; but it may also be quite omitted, as in other languages: *ga daṅ bai ˳jug-tsúl* the way of employing the (two) letters g and b *Gram.*

Comp. and deriv. *γnyis-skyes* one that is **born twice** i.e. a bird *Cs.*; also one that has entered into a religious order *Cs.* — *γnyis-čár* v. *čar.* — *γnyis-γnyis* **two a piece.** — *γnyis-ldáb* **twofold, double,** v. *ldab.* — *γnyis-₀tún* (द्विप) 'drinking twice', the elephant. — *γnyis-pa* 1. **the second.** 2. **having two,** possessed of two, e.g. *mgo-γnyis-pa* having two heads. two-headed; also double-tongued, deceitful *W.* 3. **having doubts, doubting**(?) *Wdn.* — *γnyis-po* the two, both (v. above). — *γnyis-méd* v. beginning of this article. — *γnyis-₀dzín* prob. the state of being affected or influenced by contrary things: doubt, unsteadiness, wavering *Glr.*; *γnyis-₀dzin ltá-ba* prob. to look upon two things as differing, to think them different *Mil.*

གཉུག་མ་ *γnyúg-ma Cs.* **natural,** opp. to *bčós-ma* artificial, hence (*Sch.*) = *dnos-ma*; *Lexx.* = निज innate, peculiar. It occurs in the expressions: *sems γnyúg-ma,* and *γnyúg-mai sems Mil*; *γnyúg-mai ye-šés Mil.*; *;nyúg-mai don Mil.* and *Lex.*; *ma-bčós γnyúg-mai nán-du ₀dres,* perh.: is dissolved into the uncreated primordial existence *Mil.* Our Lama explained it differently in different passages, and was not certain of the true meaning of the word.

གཉུང་དཀར་ *γnyun-dkár* **rape-seed** for pressing oil; but cf. *nyún-ma.*

གཉུལ་བ་ *γnyúl-ba* = *nyúl-ba.*

གཉེ་བ་ *γnyé-ba, Glr.* also *γnyeo, smyé-bo,* **a wooer, courter.**

གཉེ་མ་ *γnyé-ma* the twisted part of the **colon** or **great gut,** *Med.* and col. (*Sch.* erron.: rectum).

གཉེན་ *γnyen,* resp. *sku-γnyén* 1. **kinsman, relative,** *byáms-pai γnyen* loving relations, frq.; *γnyén-la byáms-pa byéd-pa* to love one's relatives; *γnyén-gyi sgyúg-mo, sgyúg-mo* as a degree of relationship *Lex.*; *γnyen byéd-pa* to become related, or allied, by marriage *Dzl.* — 2. gen. *γnyén-po* **helper, friend, assistant,** esp. spiritually: *rgyud γnyén-po bzán-bar byin-gyis rlobs* bless my soul, that it may become a good spiritual helper (to these people) *Mil.*; *γnyén-po-la ma ltós-par* without looking up to a spiritual adviser *Mil.*; frq. used of supernatural helpers: *bod ₀dúl-bai γnyén-po* the promoter of the conversion of Tibet (the special Saviour of Tibet, as it were), Awalokiteswara, frq.; applied to things: **remedy, means, expedient, antidote,** *nád-la γsó-bar byéd-pai γnyén-po* **assistants** in curing maladies (e.g. medicine, diet etc.) *Med.*; *dei γnyén-por* as a remedy for *Thgy.*, frq.; *sgrúb-pai tabs mi šés-pai γnyén-por* as a remedy for helplessness in acquiring a certain object, i.e. direction or instruction how to obtain it *Thgy.*; *γnyén-po γsán-ba* mysterious helpers, or sources of good (relative to fetish-like objects frq.) —3. *Cs.*: '*γnyén-po* **adversary, antagonist, enemy**; contrary, opposite, adverse'; *Sch.*: '*γnyén-por rtén-pa* to adhere to the counter party'; *Lexx.* have '*spán-byai γnyén-po*' a *γnyén-po* to be shunned, explaining *γnyén-po* by प्रतिपक्ष (prob. to be corrected into पक्ष) opponent, adversary. Sure proofs of this signification of *γnyén-po* I seldom met with in literature, but Lewin mentions some instances scarcely to be doubted. — 4. i.o. *mnyen* and *bsnyen.*

Comp. *dpun-γnyén* **helper, assistant,** frq. — *pá-γnyén, má-γnyen* a relation on the father's side, on the mother's side *Cs.* — *bšes-γnyén* friend, esp. spiritual friend, v. *bšes.* — *γnyen-grás* (*Sch.?*), *γnyen-₀brél,* **nyen-dún-po** *W.* relations, esp. of the same blood; *γnyen-sdé, γnyen-tsán, γnyen-srid Mil.* id., col. — *γnyen-₀dún* 1. *Sch.*: '**concord, harmony,** amongst kinsmen', in which sense it seems to be used in *Stg.*: *γnyen-₀dún zád-pa yin* this harmony ceases. 2. **relations,** *pa yan ma yin, γnyen-₀dún min* neither father nor relations *Thgy.* — *γnyen-zlá* prob.: qualified, fit for matrimonial alliance (as to birth etc.), *kyéd-rnams kyan ned rgya-nág-pai γnyen-zlá yin-pas* as ye Tibetans may enter into connubial connexion with us Chinese *Glr.*; in a concrete sense: a good match, *γnyen-zlá ma rnyéd-*

kyis Dzl. ༢ᵾ, 14; k'yod daṅ γnyen-zlá min I am not allied with you by marriage, with you I am not on terms of affinity. — γnyen-šál (?) reconciliation C. — γnyen-bšés relatives and friends, also separately: k'yód-la γnyen med bšes kyaṅ med Mil.

གཉེར་བ་ γnyér-ba c. accus. **to take pains with, to take care of, to provide for,** to try to get; **to procure, to acquire,** γnyer byéd-pa id.; as a sbst. Tar. 165, 22: the procurer, provider Schf.; gen. in conjunction with don in various ways, as: bdag don žig γnyér-te as I have to look after a business Dzl. ༢༠, 7; don γnyér-ba to earn money; dón-du γnyér-ba c. accus., rarely c. dat.: to provide for, to strive to procure, nor dón-du γnyér-ba to endeavour to make money, frq.; yo-byád dón-du γnyér-ba-rnams people who desired to have goods Tar. 169, hence don-γnyér **exertion, effort, zeal,** don-γnyér čén-po dgos great exertions are necessary Mil.; in this sense prob. also Tar. 4, 8: earnest exertion (in investigating); don-γnyér byéd-pa c. la to study, investigate (a thing) Glr.; don-γnyér-čan 1. zealous, painstaking. 2. Sch. also: liked, welcome, mgron a welcome guest. — dkon-γnyér Tar. 183, 21, Schf.: administrator of valuable property; acc. to others: the first secular functionary of a γtsúg-lag-k'aṅ, about the same as **bailiff** (steward) of a convent, = lha-γnyér Georgi Alph. Tib. (in an edict); also the manager of the daily sacrifices (dgon-γnyér?); slob-γnyér **a student,** čos-slob-γnyér a religious scholar (a student of theology) Mil., slob-γnyér gáṅ-du bgyis where did you study? Mil. — γtad-γnyér byéd-pa to trust (a person with), to intrust (a thing to) Glr.; čéd-du γnyér-ba, and rjés-su γnyér-ba v. čed. — γnyér-k'a **attention, care,** γnyér-k'a byéd-pa ccg. to pay attention to, attend to, take care of Pth.; γnyér-k'a γtád-pa to commit (a thing) to a person's charge, to put a person in trust of Glr. — γnyér-pa **farm-steward,** in convents etc. — γnyér-byáṅ prob. = γnyér-k'a. — γnyer-tsáṅ **store-room, store-house,** (if under the charge of a special γnyér-pa).

གཉེར་མ་ γnyér-ma a fold of the skin, **wrinkle** Med.; γnyer-ma réṅs-pa ˳gyur the wrinkles are made straight, are smoothed Stg.; γnyér-ma-čan wrinkled; k'ro-γnyér (भृकुटि) a frown, a severe or angry look v. k'ró-ba; γnyér-ba to wrinkle, sna-góṅ γnyér-ba to knit the brows, to frown Pth.

གཉེལ་བ་ γnyél-ba = mnyél-ba Sch.

གཉོག་པ་ γnyóg-pa **to desire,** to wish earnestly Cs. v. snyóg-pa.

གཉོད་ γnyód **strength, durability, stoutness** of cloth etc., C. and W., γnyód-čan strong; γnyod-čúṅ, γnyod-méd weak; Lex. lus γnyod-čúṅ a weakly body or constitution.

གཉོད་པ་ γnyód-pa **to draw, stretch, strain** C., W.

མཉན་ mnyan C. **boat, skiff, wherry;** mnyán-pa boat-man, ferry-man.

མཉན་པ་ mnyán-pa 1. = nyán-pa Dzl. etc. — 2. v. mnyan.

མཉན་ཡོད་ mnyan-yód, श्रावस्ती, a town in the northern part of Oudh.

མཉམ་ mnyam v. the following word.

མཉམ་པ་ mnyám-pa (सम) col. *nyám-po*, 1. **like, alike, equal, same,** mnyám-po yód they are alike, equal, not differing, col.; with daṅ, seldom with the termin., lha daṅ mnyám-pa yod they are like unto the gods Pth., Glr.; zlúm-por mnyám-pa roundish Sambh.; rigs mnyám-pa of equal birth, rank Dzl.; dus mnyám-pa contemporary, simultaneous, frq. mnyám-par gyúr-ba to become equal, to be equal Dzl. — 2. **even, level, flat,** lag-mtil ltar mnyám-pa flat like the palm of the hand Glr. and elsewh.; mnyám-pa (or -par) byéd-pa to make even or level, to even, to equalize Dzl.; to divide equally; sems mnyám-pa imperturbation, evenness of mind, not to be affected by kindness or the reverse; sems mnyám-par ˳jóg-pa to compose the mind to perfect rest, for meditation, frq.; *mnyám-pa sbyór-ba* id. (?) — *mnyám-du* adv. (col. **nyám-po**) c. *dan:* together with, in company of, *blá-ma dan nyám-du ˳grogs dús-su Mil.*; *ma dan mnyám-du ˳či-ba Thgy.*; col. **na dan nyám-po sog** or merely **nyám-po sog** come along with me! **nyam són-te** going along with; *nyi-ma sár-ba dan mnyám-du* with the rising sun *Mil.*; col. **dul dan nyám-po** in walking, *ambulando*; **ten dan nyám-po** in taking it away (it was broken); **kúr-pa nyám** (to send something) by (with) a cooly. — *mnyam-méd, mnyam-brál* unequalled, matchless; *mi mnyám-pa* 1. unequal, 2. uneven. — *pyag* (or *lag*) *ynyis mnyám-bžag-tu yód-pa* both hands laid together on the stomach, *mnyám-bžag pyág-rgya-čan* id. — *mnyam-pa-nyíd*, समता, equality, parity; impartiality, justice.

མཉེད་པ་ *mnyéd-pa*, pf. and imp. *mnyes*, fut. *mnye*, *W.* col. **mnyo-če**, 1. **to rub**, between the hands or feet, e.g. ears of corn; one's body *Tar.*; esp. hides, hence **to tan, curry, dress**; *kó-ba mnyés-pa* a tanned hide, dressed leather; **sed dan nyé-če** *W.* to rub in or into with force. — 2. *Cs.* also: **to coax.**

མཉེན་པ་ *mnyén-pa*, *W.* **nyén-mo**, **flexible, pliable, supple; soft, smooth,** of the voice frq.; of the mind *Dzl.*; *mnyén-par byéd-pa* to make soft, smooth, flexible, *˳gyúr-ba* to become soft, of the skin etc. *Med.*; *mnyen-mnyél-ba* to make soft by tanning *Sch.* — *mnyen-mnyés ysin-pa* to caress, to fondle *Sch.*

མཉེལ་བ་ *mnyél-ba* 1. also *ynyél-ba*, **to tan, to dress** (hides) *Sch.* — 2. resp. for *nál-ba* **to get tired** *Pth.*

མཉེས་པ་ *mnyés-pa*, resp. for *dgá-ba*, in more recent writings and col. for the *dgyés-pa* of ancient literature, **to be glad, to take delight in**, ccd.; **to be willing, to wish,** often with *fugs*; *mnyés-par byéd-pa* to make glad, to give pleasure; e.g. to the king by presents *Glr.*, to Buddha by worshipping him *Glr.* — *mnyes-bsín-pa Lexx.*, *Sch.:* to love much; to be rejoiced at.

མཉོ་མཉོ་ཅན་ *mnyó-mnyo-čan* *W.* fondling, petting, *prú-gu-la* a child.

རྙ་ལོ་, སྙ་ལོ་ *rnyá-lo, snyá-lo*, several wild-growing species of Polygonum *Med.*

སྙང་བ་ *rnyán-ba Cs.* = *bsál-ba*, **to rinse**; *W.* to suffer diarrhoea, *rnyan-nád* diarrhoea; *rnyán-pa* diarrhetic stool; *rnyán-ma, ynyán-ma* id., ni f.

རྙང་རྙིང་ *rnyan-rnyín*, **worn-out clothes, rags** *Cs.*

རྙན་ *rnyan* = *ynyan* wild sheep, **argali.**

རྙབ་རྙབ་པ་ *rnyab-rnyáb-pa* **to seize or snatch together** *Sch.*

རྙས་ *rnyas*, sometimes used for *brnyas.*

རྙི་, སྙི་ *rnyi, snyi*, *W.* **nyiu, nyín-nu** (cf. *rnyon*) 1. **snare,** for catching wild animals, *rnyi ˳dzúg-pa* to lay snares, also fig. — 2. **trap,** *púr-rnyi* mouse-trap (consisting of a flat stone supported by a little stick (*púr-pa*). — 3. **net** *Sch.* (?).

རྙིང་པ་ *rnyín-pa* **old, ancient,** of things, e.g. clothes, *ysar-rnyín* new and old; *snár-gyi yi-ge rnyín-pa-rnams* ancient records *Glr.*; *brda-rnyín* the ancient orthography *Zam.*; *lo-rnyin* = *na-nín* last year *Wts.*; *dran-srón rnyín-pa* the old rishi, i.e. the well-known, of long standing, opp. to a new-comer *Dzl.* — *rnyín-ba* vb., pf. *brnyíns*, to grow old, *gos brnyíns* old clothes, *lham brnyíns* old shoes *Lex.*; *rnyín-bar ˳gyúr-ba* id.; *rnyín-bar byéd-pa* to wear out or away in a short time *Dzl.*

རྙིང་མ་ *rnyín-ma*, n. of the most ancient sect of Lamas, clothed in red, v. *Köpp.*; *Schl.* 72; *rnyin-ma-pa* one belonging to this sect.

རྙིད་པ་ *rnyíd-pa*, pf. *brnyid*, (*b*)*rnyis*, fut. *ynyid*, 1. **to wither, to fade,** also fig. — 2. **to grieve,** (vb. n.) *Sch.*

རྙིལ་, སྙིལ་ *rnyil, snyil, so-rnyil*, **the gums.**

རྙིལ་བ་ *rnyil-ba* v. *snyil-ba.*

རྙེད་པ་ *rnyéd-pa* I. vb., pf. *brnyed, brnyes*, fut. *brnyed*, (लभ) **to get, obtain, acquire; to meet with, find,** *B., C.*, frq.; *gán-*

ṅas rnyed where did you get that? *Dzl.*, also: whence shall I get it? *Dzl.*; *mi rnyéd-du mi ŕúṅ-ṅo* it must be got or procured by all means *Dzl.*; *ṅas rnyed* I obtain; *rnyéd-par dká-ba* दुर्लभ difficult to be obtained, found, or met with, frq.; *sdug-bsṅál daṅ bsdós-te čos rnyéd-pa* to purchase the acquisition of religion by suffering tortures *Dzl.*; *zas daṅ skom ma rnyéd-de* having nothing to eat or to drink, frq.; *don rnyéd-pa* v. *don*; *da ni ré-ba rnyéd-do* now my hopes are realized *Dzl.*; *gri rnyéd-pas* as he found a knife *Dzl.*; *skabs rnyéd-pa* to find an opportunity *Dzl.*; *btsál-na yaṅ ma rnyéd-de* not finding it in spite of every search *Dzl.*, (*W.* **ťob-če**).

II. sbst. लाभ **profit, gain, acquisition, property, goods,** *rnyéd-pa máṅ-po rnyed-pa* (or **ťób-če**) to gain much profit; *bdag rnyéd-pa daṅ ldán-na mi dga* if I have got some earnings, he envies me for them; often in conjunction with *grágs-pa* and similar expressions: riches and honour. — *rnyed sdú-ba, rnyéd-pa ṗróg-pa Sch.*: to make booty, to plunder. — *rnyed-bkúr Lex.*, prob. riches and honour. — *rnyed-nor* v. *ťob-nór*.

རྙོག་པ་ *rnyóg-pa* (cf. *nyóg-pa*) vb., pf. *brnyogs*, fut. *brnyog*, 1. **to trouble, to stir up** *Cs.*; also adj.: **thick, turbid.** **ču nyóg-pa* W.* — 2. **to rub** one's self, *ká-ba-la* against a pillar *Dzl.* (*snyóg-pa*). — **nyóg(-pa)-čan, nyóg-po* C.*, troubled, turbid, dirty; *rnyóg-pa méd-pa* clear, limpid, *mťso Wdṅ.* — *rnyóg-ma* dirty, muddy water; mud, mire, *rnyóg-ma-čan* muddy, miry.

རྙོགས་ *rnyogs Lt.? rnyogs-ťsád* a disease *Med.*

རྙོང་ *rnyoṅ* seems to be the same as *rnyi Lexx.*; *rnyóṅ-ba*, pf. *brnyoṅs*, fut. *brnyoṅ* 1. *Cs.*: 'to ensnare, entrap'. — 2. *Sch.*: 'to stretch out'. I met with *rnyoṅ* in the following expressions, not satisfactorily to be explained either by *Cs.* or by *Sch.*: *rkáṅ-pa rnyoṅ Lex.*; *dku ma rnyoṅs Lex.*; *lus rnyóṅ-ba S.g.*; frq.; *γyal-rnyóṅs S.g.*; *mgul-rgyáb zug daṅ rnyoṅ S.g.*; *rnyoṅs-ťsád Mṅg.*

སྙ་ནང་ *snya-náṅ* v. *γnya-náṅ*.

སྙ་ལོ་ *snyá-lo* v. *rnyá-lo*.

སྙག་པ་ *snyág-pa*, col. for *snyég-pa*; also in *Mil.*

སྙགས་ *snyags Lex.* w.e.; *C.* = *dbyaṅs* music, harmony.

སྙད་ *snyad* **malicious** or **false accusation** or **imputation,** *snyad ₒdzúg-pa* (*W.* **tsug-če**) to bring in an action against, to prosecute; **nyad ḍú-če* W.*, **nyę' kó-wa* C.* id., esp. to irritate, to provoke another, by accusations; *snyad ₒdágs-pa* id. *Glr.*; *snyad ₒdág-pa, W.* **dág-če** to clear one's self of an accusation, to refute it; *snyad byéd-pa* c.dat. to use as a pretence or pretext *Glr.*; **nyę' čọ'* (or *čẹ'*) *táṅ-wa* C.*, **nyad-sé tág-če* Ld.* to weary another by too great punctiliousness, ni f.; **nor-nyád čó-če* W.* to extort money by false accusations, *la* from; *snyad méd-par* without cause, pretence, or provocation *Thgy.*; **nyád-zer-čan* W.* one that makes false accusations.

སྙད་པ་ *snyád-pa*, pf. and fut. *bsnyad*, imp. *snyod*, **to relate, to report,** e.g. *lo-rgyús* a story *Pth.*, *rmi-lam* a dream *Dzl.*; *γtam snyád-pa* 1. to speak, state, inform, give notice (*W.* **lun táṅ-če**). 2. *Cs.*: 'to rehearse' (?).

སྙན་ *snyan* 1. resp. **the ear,** *rgyál-poi snyán-du ťos* it came to the king's hearing *Glr.*; *snyán-du žus* or *brjod* they told or informed him *Pth.*; *snyán-du zuṅ* listen, pay attention, give ear to! *Pth.*; *snyán-du ṗul* they sang to him or before him (lit. they made him hear) *Mil.* (cf. sub *snyán-pa*); *snyán-(gyis) γsán-pa* to hear *Mil.*; *snyan-γsán bébs-pa* to give ear to one, to hear one *Cs.*; **nyẹ̄n-žu ₒbul-wa* C.* to address a superior, to apply to him; *snyan-kúṅ* the ear-hole; *snyan-dbáṅ* the organ of hearing *Cs.*; *snyan-šál* the lap or tip of the ear *Cs.*; *snyan-ṗrá žú-ba* to slander, *mi mi-la* to calumniate one person to another. — 2. = *γnyan* **argali.**

སྙན་པ་ *snyán-pa* (यशस्) 1. sbst. **renown, glory, fame, praise, rumour,** *kyód-kyi* snyán-pa ṗyogs bċur grags every part of the world rings with thy praise; deï snyán-pa rgyáṅ-nas ťos Mil. his praises are heard far and wide; ċes deï snyán-pa brjód-ċiṅ thus speaking praisingly of him Mil.; čés-pai snyán-pa-la rtén-nas owing to a rumour of this purport Mil.; ċes snyán-pa daṅ grágs-pa čén-po byuṅ so was said far and near Mil.; deï snyán-du to his praise Mil. (cf. snyan). — 2. adj., W. *nyán-po*, **well-sounding**, sweet to hear, of voice, words etc.; *ťsor-náṅ-la nyán-po* W. pleasant to the ear; also: dge-slóṅ dbyaṅs ráb-tu snyán-pa a monk having a well-sounding voice Dzl.; ťsig snyán-par with pleasant words Dzl.; snyán-pai ťsig-gis id.; **low**, not loud; snyan-skád also C.: elegant, well-sounding, poetical language; mi snyán-pa 1. unharmonious; 2. offensive, insulting, gaṅ žig bdág-la rtsód-ċiṅ mi-snyán-brjod he who in a dispute says to me insulting words; mi-snyán-par zér-ba dáṅ-du lén-pa to put up with, to pocket offensive remarks. 3. lamentable, skad mi snyán-pa zér-ba to utter lamentable cries, plaintive tones, also of animals, Dzl.; ɣtam-snyán(-pa) 1. good, joyful news, glad tidings, byéd-pa to bring them Dzl., Mil. 2. a pleasing talk, conversation Cs. (?) — snyan-grágs v. grágs-pa. — snyan-rgyúd oral instruction of the Lamas, = bka-rgyúd. — snyan-(d)ṅág(s) v. ṅag. — 3. vb. **to praise, extol, glorify**, stód-ċiṅ snyán-par grágs-te he extolled him in songs of praise Dzl. (?)

སྙབ་པ་ snyáb-pa **to smack** with the lips Sch.

སྙམ་པ་ snyám-pa 1. vb. **to think, suppose, fancy, imagine**, bdág-ċag riṅ-po-čé btaṅ (better: ɣtaṅ) snyám-mo we think we shall give jewels Dzl. ༢༥༧, 16.; ṅa lċeb dgos snyám-nas thinking, I must seek death (v. lċéb-pa) Pth.; yón-tan daṅ ldán-par snyám-ste fancying to be possessed of excellent qualities Dzl. — 2. sbst. **thought, sense, mind, feeling**, čos byás-na snyám-pa yóṅ-gin ɣda (cf. na III., 2) we have a mind to renounce the world Mil.; similarly: ˳jigs-so snyám-pa yod re-skán I am far from any thought of fear Mil.; most frq. snyám-du bsams he thought in his mind; snyam-byéd: ṗan snyam-byéd kyaṅ though one may imagine that it will help Med.; skyúg-pa, brduṅs, dkris snyam-byéd there arises a feeling like that of nausea, like that of being beaten, of being (tightly) wrapt up, Med.

སྙི་ snyi v. rnyi.

སྙི་བ་ snyí-ba 1. adj., also snyi-bo, snyi-mo, snyiṅ-po Cs., *nyiṅ-te* W., **soft, smooth**, to the touch; **tender, delicate**, of the skin; **easily broken** or **injured**; **loose, crazy**, not durable, not strong or stout, of cloth, ropes etc.; not hard or tough, **tender**, of meat, rendered so by beating or boiling. — 2. sbst. **softness**. — 3. n. of a plant.

སྙི་ཕུལ་ snyi-ṗúl corn of luxuriant growth Sch. (?)

སྙི་མ་ snyi-ma prov. for snyé-ma; also Glr.

སྙི་ཤང་ཀ་ཏྱ་ snyi-šaṅ-ka-tya, and snyi-šaṅ-gur-rta, names of mountains in Nepal.

སྙིགས་པ་ snyígs-pa **degenerated, grown worse** Cs. snyigs-ma (कषाय) 1. **impure sediment**, már-gyi in butter; daṅs snyigs ˳byéd-pa to separate the clear (fluid) from the sediment Med. — 2. the degenerated age (iron age), prop. snyigs-(mai) dus.

སྙིང་ snyiṅ (हृद्) **the heart** 1. physically, also snyiṅ-ka, snyiṅ-ga, resp. ťugs (-ka); also **the breast**; *nyiṅ-ka ṗár-ra rag* W. I feel my heart palpitate; snyiṅ ˳dár-žiṅ ˳gul the heart trembles (with fear) Domaṅ; bdág-gi lús-kyi snyiṅ ltar ɣċes as dear to me as my own heart Glr. — 2. intellectually: **the mind**, snyiṅ dgá-ba, snyiṅ bdé-ba gladness, cheerfulness; snyiṅ daṅ mig ˳ṗróg-pa to transport, to ravish Sch.; courage, snyiṅ ma čuṅ ċig be not afraid! sentiment, feeling, will, *nyiṅ sóg-po ċó-te ma ċag* W. I have not broken it wilfully; *ḱa daṅ nyiṅ ma ḍé-te* W. hypocritical; *nyiṅ-sém dáṅ-po* W. sincere, candid; in a more general sense: snyiṅ ɣdón-gyis bslus the heart is infatuated by a demon *Glr.*; even madness may be attributed to the heart *Do.* — *snyiṅ-nas* 1. heartily, zealously, earnestly, e.g. looking for or to a thing *Dzl.*; *snyiṅ ťág-pa-nas* with all one's heart, most earnestly, devoutly, e.g. to say one's prayers *Thgy.* 2. actually, really, *ḱoṅ snyiṅ-nas mi ₒbyiṅ-ba yin* really he does not sink! (the water actually bears him) *Mil.* 3. v. *snyiṅ-po.*

Comp. and deriv. *snyiṅ-ku* v. *nyiṅ-ḱu.* — *snyiṅ-ḱáms* **courage** *Sch.* — **nyiṅ-ṭ ág ḱol* W.* my heart's blood is boiling (with anger etc.) — *snyiṅ-dgá* v. above. — *snyiṅ-čan* **courageous, spirited** *Ld.* — **nyiṅ-ču žug* W.* **afflicted with dropsy in the pericardium,** hydrocardia. — *snyiṅ-rje*, resp. *ťúgs-rje* (करुणा) **kindness, mercy, compassion,** *mi-la snyiṅ-rje sgóm-pa* to commiserate, to pity a person *Mil.*; *snyiṅ-rjes ḱyáb-pa* id. with respect to a great number of beings, to embrace with affection *Dzl.*; *snyiṅ-rjes nón-te* overpowered by compassion; **nyiṅ-že ťsór-če* W.* to have compassion; *snyiṅ-rje-čan, snyiṅ-rje daṅ ldán-pa* compassionate, merciful *Dzl.*: *snyiṅ-rje-skad* lamentation, a cry of compassion *Dzl.*; *snyiṅ-rje-mo:* 1. *ḱyod snyiṅ-rje-mo raṅ žig ₒdug* you are much to be pitied *Mil.* 2. col.: **dearest, most beloved, amiable, charming;** also *snyiṅ-rje* for *snyiṅ-rje-mo, snyiṅ-rje mdzá-bo* my poor little friend. — *snyiṅ-nyé-ba*, col. **nyiṅ nyé-mo**, **friendly, amicable, loving, affectionate; friend; friendship,** *snyiṅ-nye bú-mo* a woman connected by friendship with, a woman, the friend of (a sick person mentioned) *Lt.* — *snyiṅ-ytam* **a confidential speaking,** for exhortation, consolation, or encouragement; *brtsé-bai snyiṅ-ytam* affectionate exhortation *Glr.*; *pʻán-pai snyiṅ-ytam* useful admonition etc. *Mil.* — *snyiṅ-stobs* **courage.** — *snyiṅ-ₒdód-pa* **to wish, to desire, to long for,** *za-snyiṅ-ₒdód-pa* to wish to eat, to be craving for food *Thgy.*; *ₒgro-snyiṅ-ₒdód-pa* to wish to go. — *snyiṅ-rdúṅ-ba* palpitation of heart *Sch.* — **nyiṅ daṅ* (etymol. dubious) *čó-če* W.* ccd. to interest one's self for, to take an interest in. — *snyiṅ-sdúg W.* **liked, beloved; darling, favourite,** e.g. a child; *nyiṅ-dúg šig dug* W.* he is a general favourite; **ṅa di nyiṅ-dúg čo dug* W.* I am very fond of this, it is my favourite (pursuit etc.); but *snyiṅ-ma-sdúg* bad people *Mil.* — *snyiṅ nád-ba* 1. = *snyiṅ-nád.* 2. **'heart-sickness', grief,** on account of injury suffered from others, curable only by indemnity paid or revenge taken. — *snyiṅ-nád* **disease of the heart.** — *snyiṅ-po* (सार, गर्भ) **the chief part, main substance, quintessence,** e.g. the cream of the milk *Med.*; the soft part of a loaf, the wick of a lamp *Dzl.*; frq. fig.: the main substance of a doctrine, a book etc., *don-snyiṅ ₒbyin-pa* to give a summary, the sum and substance (of a writing); *séms-čan tams-čád saṅs-rgyás-kyi snyiṅ-po-čan yin-na* if all beings have the pith and essence of the nature of Buddha in themselves *Thgy.* 5, 8; the Ommanipadmehūm is called the *snyiṅ-po* of religion *Glr.*; *snyiṅ-po-méd-pa* worthless, null, void, *snyiṅ-pos dbén-pa* id. *Tar.* 185, 2; *de-bžiṅ-yšégs-pai snyiṅ-po* the spirit of Tathāgata *Was.*; *snyiṅ-po-byaṅ-čúb-* (or *byaṅ-čub-snyiṅ-po*) *-la mčís-pa* to become Buddha *Thgy.*; *srog(-gi) snyiṅ(-po) ₒbúl-ba Mil.* frq. to offer one's heart's blood, to pledge one's own life. — *snyiṅ-rtsa* (col.) the great veins connected with the heart, perh. = *snyiṅ-luṅ.* — *snyiṅ-rtse* the tip or apex of the heart, mentioned by *Mil.* as a particular dainty (perh. only by way of a jest). — *snyiṅ-brtse-ba*, resp. *ťúgs-brtsé-ba*, vb., also sbst. and adj., not much differing from *snyiṅ-rje*: **love, pity** etc. frq.; *Dzl.: bú-la snyiṅ-brtse-nas; ťams-čád-la snyiṅ-brtse-ba yin-na; de-dag-la snyiṅ-brtse-bai pʻyir; snyiṅ-brtse-bai sems skyés-te* etc. — *snyiṅ-ťsim* **contentment, satisfaction,** sometimes also pleasure felt at the misfortune of others *Pth.*, *snyiṅ-ťsim ₒdébs-pa* to manifest such an enjoyment. — *snyiṅ-ťsil* the fat about the heart *Cs.* — *snyiṅ-žo-ša* v. *žó-ša.* — *snyiṅ-rús*, resp. *ťugs-rús* (acc. to *Mil.*: *snyiṅ-gi rús-pa ťón-par gyis* let energy and diligence arise in you); **firmness of mind** (heart) i.e. 1. **diligence, zeal, perseverance**

Mil. and *C.* 2. **courage** *W.* — *snyiṅ-re-rjé* (*snyiṅ-rje*, with *re* placed between, v. *re*) **o the poor man!** the poor people! either standing absolute or as predicate to a preceding noun: *ₒdi-rnams snyiṅ-re-rjé* these (people) are indeed much to be pitied *Mil.*; *kyod-raṅ . . . ₒdzin-pa snyiṅ-re-rjé* you (would) comprehend that? poor wretches that you are! *Mil.*; even as an adjective: *séms-čan snyiṅ-re-rjé* the poor creatures! frq.; *snyiṅ-re-rjé-bai sdig-čan* the lamentable sinner! — *snyiṅ-rluṅ Sch.*: 'low spirits, melancholy, mental derangement'; I met with it only in *Mil.*, as signifying **heart-grief, deep sorrow,** e.g. *snyiṅ-rlúṅ drág-po ldaṅ* great affliction is caused. — *snyiṅ-lam-na Sch.*: 'in one's mind'. — **snyiṅ-lúṅ** *W.* the heart, liver, and lights of a slaughtered animal, the **pluck.** — *snyiṅ-šúbs* **pericardium.**

སྙིང་བ *snyiṅ-ba W.* **to swell** (in water), **lum nyiṅ soṅ** the soaked barley has swollen.

སྙིད་པ *snyid-pa* prob. = *rnyid-pa Pth.*

སྙིད་མོ *snyid-mo Lex.* the sister of a woman's husband.

སྙིན་པ *snyin-pa*, *snyin-po*, *snyin-te*, v. *snyi-ba.*

སྙིམ་པ་(གང་) *snyim-pa(-gaṅ)* a measure for liquids, as well as for flour, grain and the like, as much as may be taken up by both hands placed together.

སྙིལ *snyil* = *rnyil.*

སྙིལ་བ *snyil-ba*, or *rnyil-ba*, pf. and fut. *bsnyil* (cf. *nyil-ba*) 1. **to pull** or **throw down, to break down, to destroy,** houses, rocks etc.; *p̔yé-mar snyil-ba* to reduce to powder *Lex.*, *Sch.* — 2. *p̔yir* (*bskrad*) *snyil-ba Lex.*; *Sch.*: **to expel, banish, exile.**

སྙུག་པ *snyúg-pa*, also *smyúg-pa*, pf. *bsnyugs*, fut. *bsnyug*, **to dip in, to immerge.**

སྙུག་མ *snyúg-ma*, more frq. *smyúg-ma*, **reed, rush, bulrush**; *snyúg-gu* reed-pen; *snyúg-bzo* basket-work of reeds *Pth.*; *snyúg-šiṅ* bamboo.

སྙུགས *snyugs C.* **duration, continuity, time** *Cs.*; **nyúg-čen** *C* continual; *snyugs-sriṅs Lex.* protracted, lengthened out

སྙུགས་སྦྲུལ *snyugs-sbrúl* **lizard** *Sch.*

སྙུང *snyuṅ*, resp. for *nad*, *W.* **nyuṅ-zúg**, **disease, illness, sickness,** *btsún-paį skú-la snyuṅ mi mṅá-am* is your Majesty well? *Glr.*; *snyúṅ-du mdze byuṅ Glr.* leprosy arose to him as a disease, he was attacked with the disease of leprosy; *snyuṅ mdzes btab* id. *Tar.*; *snyúṅ-γži* = *nád-γži.*

སྙུང་བ *snyúṅ-ba* I. vb., pf. *bsnyuṅs*, fut. *bsnyuṅ*, 1. **to make less, to reduce, to diminish**; *Sch.*: **to disparage.** — 2. resp. **to be ill, sick, indisposed;** *t̔ugs snyúṅ-bai mi* people that are disagreeable, annoying to others *Mil.*

II. sbst. 1. the state of being ill, **illness, indisposition.** — 2. *W.* **awl, pricker, punch;** also *snyúṅ-bu.*

སྙུན *snyun* = *snyuṅ*, *skú-la snyún-gyis bzuṅ* he was taken ill *Dzl.*; *snyun ₒdri-ba Mil.*, *rmé-ba Sch.*, *γsól-ba Dzl.*, *snyún-dri žú-ba Mil.*, to inquire after a person's health; to wait on, to pay one's respects *Dzl.* ༢༤༩, 16.

སྙུན་པ *snyún-pa*, pf. and fut. *bsnyun*, **to be ill,** to labour under a disease.

སྙེ་ཐང *snye-t̔aṅ* a village and convent near Lhasa.

སྙེ་བ *snyé-ba*, pf. *bsnyes*, fut. *bsnye*, imp. *snye* **to lean against, to rest on,** *rtsig-pa-la* against a wall; **to lie down, recline, repose on,** *mál-stan-la* on a bed, *sṅás-la* on a cushion or pillow; **gyáb-nye** col. a support or cushion for leaning against with one's back. — *snye-k̔ri* v. *k̔ri.* — *snye-stán*, *snye-ₒból* **pillow** or **cushion** to rest on.

སྙེ་མ *snyé-ma*, also *snyi-ma*, 1. **ear** of corn. 2. **corn forming ears** (v. *ldáṅ-pa*), *snyé-ma míg-čan* fruitbearing ears, **nye-lóṅ** *W.* empty ears; **nye-ma t̔on** *W.* the corn blows, is in flower; **nye čág-pa** *C.* to thrash, **nye-čág-gi dhụ'-ḍo** an animal used for treading out the grain. — *snye-dkár* diseased ears. — *snye-ṅyó* = *snyé-ma* 1.

སྙེག(ས)་པ་ *snyeg(s)-pa*, pf. *bsnyegs*, fut. *bsnyeg*, imp. *snyog(s)*, *W.* **nyág-ċe**, 1. c. accus. **to hasten** or **run** after, **to pursue**, frq.; also with *ṙjés-nas*, *ṙjés-su*, *ṙjés-bžin-du*, *ṗyi-bžin-du*; *rań-ₒgró-sa snyogs* hasten towards your aim! *Mil*; *snyég-sar snyogs Lex.* id.; *bsnyég-tu*, or *snyégs-su ₒdoń-ba* to walk hastily, to make haste or speed *Dzl.* — 2. **to overtake**, *snyégs ma nús-pas* not being able to reach *Dzl.* — 3. c. dat. **to hasten** to some place, *ltád-mo-la* to the play *Mil.*; **to rise**, *ɣnám-la* rising up to heaven, as a flame, *Glr.*, a cedar *Wdń.*, frq.; **to strive** or **struggle for**, **to aspire to**, *nór-la* riches, *sde-čén-la* increase of territory, *žiń-k'ams-bzáń-la* the region of eternal bliss. — *snyég-ma* pursuer *Dzl.*

སྙེགས་ *snyegs* **straight, stretched out** *Sch.*

སྙེང་བ་ *snyéń-ba* 1. inst. of *rmyéń-ba*, to stretch *Mil.* — 2. also *snyéńs-pa*, resp. for *ₒjigs-pa*, vb. (pf. *bsnyeńs*, fut. *bsnyeń*) and sbst., *rgyál-pos ma snyeńs śig* do not be afraid of the king! *Dzl.*

སྙེད་ *snyed* I. the **crupper** attached to a saddle *Sch.* II. = *tsam*: 1. *ₒdi-snyéd* (*-čig*), *de-snyéd(-čig)* **so much, so many,** frq.; also for: **how many!** e.g. . . . *yón-tan ₒdi-snyéd mńao* how many excellent qualities has . . .! *Dzl.*; *či-snyéd*, *ji-snyéd* how much? how many? also *snyed* alone (examples v. sub *byé-ma*). — 2. after round sums: **about, near,** *stoń snyed*, also *stoń ji-snyéd Mil.* about a thousand.

སྙེན་པ་ *snyén-pa Cs.*: 1. **to come** or **go near, to approach,** gen. *bsnyén-pa.* — 2. **to gain, to procure,** inst. of *rnyéd-pa*(?).

སྙེམ(ས)་པ་ *snyém(s)-pa* 1. vb., pf. *bsnyems*, **to be proud** or **arrogant, to boast,** *ńa-rgyál snyéms-pas* to be swollen with pride *Dzl.*; *mt'u-rtsál* (to be proud) of one's strength *Dzl.* — 2. sbst. **pride, haughtiness,** *snyém-pa-čan* prideful, proud, *snyems-čuń* 1. prideless, humble, affable, kind, col. **nyom-čuń**, and **nyam-śuń**. 2. poor, indigent *C.*

སྙེས་ *snyes* v. *snyé-ba.*

སྙོ་བ་ *snyó-ba* sometimes for *smyó-ba.*

སྙོག་པ་ *snyóg-pa*, or *bsnyóg-pa*, secondary form of *snyég-pa*, esp. when signifying **to wish earnestly, to crave** for or **lust** after, also *k'a-snyóg-pa Cs.*

སྙོད་ *s'nyod*, = *go-snyód*, **caraway.**

སྙོད་པ་ *snyód-pa* I. pf. *bsnyad*, 1. **to draw out** and **twist,** as in spinning *Stg.*, *C.* — 2. *Cs.*: **to tell, to relate,** = *snyád-pa.*

II. pf. *bsnyod*, *bsnyos*, fut. *bsnyod*, **to feed,** to give to eat and to drink, *ccapir.*

སྙོན་པ་ *snyón-pa* I. 1. pf. and fut. *bsnyon*, **to deny, to disavow dishonestly,** *Dzl.* ༢༢༩, 2; ༢༥༠, 8 **to assert falsely,** *snyon byéd-pa Glr.* — 2. **nyon ḍú-ċe** *W.* is said to signify the same as **nyad ḍu-ċe** v. *snyad.*

II. inst. of *smyón-pa.*

སྙོབ་པ་ *snyób-pa*, pf. *bsnyabs*, fut. *bsnyab* 1. **to stretch out,** e.g. the hand, *Lex.* — 2. *W.* **to reach,** by stretching one's self out, **to arrive at,** **nyob mi t'ub**.

སྙོབས་ *snyobs* = *snyoms Lex.*

སྙོམ(ས)་ *snyom(s)*, *Lex.* = **तन्द्रि** I. 1. **weariness, lassitude; laziness, idleness,** *lus snyoms-lči-ba yin* one is exhausted and dull *Med.*; *snyóms-la ńúl-ba* to be tired and exhausted. — *snyóms-las* 1. **indolence, unconcern,** esp. religious indifference, *Glr.*; *snyóms-las byéd-pa*, or *drán-pa Glr.* to be lazy, indolent, indifferent; *snyóms-las-čan* adj. lazy etc. *Glr.* — 2. *Sch.*: an idle person(?).

II. col., also *Mil.*, inst. of *snyems.*

སྙོམ(ས)་པ་ *snyóm(s)-pa* I. vb., pf. *bsnyoms*, fut. *bsnyom*, to make even 1. **to level,** *ɣnas* a place, *Dzl.*; *sá-la snyóms-pa* to level with the ground, **to demolish** *Dzl.* — 2. *ṗan-ts'un* **to equalize** different things, **to arrange uniformly,** *zas* one's meals, i.e. not cold and warm promiscuously *Thgy.*; **to level, to reduce** to an equality of condition, *ltogs-ṗyúg* rich and poor (according to the principles of the communists) *Glr.*; similarly *bú-lon Tar.* 74; *t'ams-čád-la snyóms-na bdag kyań snyóms-par mdzad* *ₒtsal* I wish to be treated fairly like any other people *Dzl.* ?; *ḱá-lo snyóms-pa* to regulate (a matter), **to manage** or **direct** (a business) **justly**, uniformly *Glr.* — *snyóm-du med*, he has not his like *Dzl.*; **tag nyóm-la* C.* always uniformly, without variation.

II. sbst., also *btaṅ-snyóms*, evenness, or **calmness of mind, equanimity**, *snyóms-par ₒjúg-pa* to assume it, = *sems mnyám-par bźág-pa*, v. *mnyám-pa*. — *snyoms-ₒjúg byéd-pa* 1. id., 2. euphem. for *ₒḱrig-pa spyód-pa*. — *mgo-snyóms* impartial *Mil.* — *snyóms-po* equal, even, uniform, e.g. in every part equally thick.

སྙོལ་བ་ *snyól-ba*, pf. and fut. *bsnyal* (cf. *nyál-ba*) 1. **to lay down; to bed** a person, to assign him his couch or bed *Pth.*; **ṭú-gu mál-du* C.* (to lay) a child on its bed, to put to bed; **nyál-te żág-pa* C.*, *bór-ċe W.*, to lay or put down, opp. to *laṅ-te* etc., to set or place upright, to set on end, e.g. a book. — 2. fig.: **me nyál-wa* C.* to put the fire to bed, i.e. to scrape it together and cover it with ashes; *spu snyól-ba* to smooth down the bristling hair, i.e, to abate one's anger; *čaṅ*, *żo*, *snyól-ba* to allow the beer to ferment, the milk to curdle, in a state of rest (undisturbed).

བརྙ་བ་ *brnyá-ba*, pf. *brnyas*, 1. **to borrow** *Dzl.* ?, 12. 14; ?, 6. 2. **to seize** by force, **to usurp** *Sch.*

བརྙང་ *brnyaṅ* *Lex.* prob. = *rnyáṅ-pa*.

བརྙད་པ་ *brnyád-pa* for *bsnyád-pa*.

བརྙན་པ་ *brnyán-pa Cs.* **to borrow**; *brnyán-po* borrowed; also fig.: borrowed, reflected, *ɣzugs-brnyán* (*Lex. snaṅ-brnyán*) a reflected image प्रतिबिम्ब frq.; also image, picture in general; even a little statue *Pth.*; *rmi-lam-gyi ɣzugs-brnyán* vision, visionary image; *sgra-brnyán*, प्रतिश्रुत reflected sound, echo; *mgo-brnyán* a mask, a fearful apparition *Thgr.*, *mgo-brnyán sér-po Schl.* 234. — *ṗyag-brnyán* servant *Cs.* — *brnyán-poi gos Cs.*: 'a garment marked with the figures (sic) of the rainbow' — *brnyán-poi brnyas Lex.* interest for a loan, rent for things borrowed *Sch.*

བརྙབས་པ་ *brnyábs-pa* **diligence, painstaking; to take pains** *Sch.*

བརྙས་པ་ *brnyás-pa* I. borrowed, v. *brnyá-ba*.

II. 1. **to despise, contemn** c. dat., frq.; *ma brnyás śig* do not despise! *Dzl.*; *brnyas smád-pa* id. *Dzl.* — **contempt**, *brnyás-pa byéd-pa*, *W.* **nya-śé tág-ċe**, ccd. to despise, to treat contemptuously, frq.; *brnyas-bčos* (*Thgy. brnyas-čos*) contempt, scorn.

བརྙོངས་ *brnyoṅs* **convenient, suitable** *Sch.*

བསྙིགས་པ་ *bsnyigs-pa* 1. **to return, restore, deliver up** *Cs.* 2. **sediment**.

བསྙུག་ *bsnyug* full *Sch.*; *skyu-gaṅ bsnyug Lex.* a full draught (?).

བསྙུལ་བ་ *bsnyúl-ba* to wash *Lex.*

བསྙེན་པ་ *bsnyén-pa* 1. **to approach, to come near**, c. dat., also *drúṅ-du*, *ḱó-boi drúṅ-du bsnyen čig* come to me *Dzl.*; *góm-pa re-ré bór-źiṅ ₒči-ba-la bsnyén-pa ltar* as with every step we come nearer to our death *Thgy.*; **to join, to stick to** a person *Dzl.* — 2. **to propitiate, soothe, satisfy**, a deity *Cs.* — 3. **to accept, receive, admit** *W.*; *bsnyén-par rdzógs-pa* to be ordained, consecrated, frq.; c. *las* by *Tar.* — *dge-bsnyén* v. *dgé-ba*. — *bsnyen-bkúr* **reverence, veneration, respect**, *byéd-pa* to pay one's duty or respect, esp. to the priesthood by various services, *ṅá-la bsnyén-pa byás-te Dzl.* and elsewh., frq., also *bsnyén-źiṅ bkúr-ba Glr.*, and **nyen kúr-ċe* W.*; *bsnyén-bkur źú-ba* to ask permission for performing such services *Mil.* — *bsnyen-bsgrúb* priestly function, religious office, esp. *sṅags* q. v. — *bsnyen-ɣnás* fasting, abstinence; *bsnyen-ɣnás srúṅ-ba*, *W.* **zúm-ċe**, to abstain from food, to fast.

བསྙེར་བ་ *bsnyér-ba* to make grimaces or gesticulations *Cs.*

བསྙེལ་བ་ *bsnyél-ba, Lexx.:* resp., **to forget;** *bsnyel-méd* not forgetting or forgetful, mindful; *bsnyel-γsó-ba* to remind, to put one in mind of a thing *Mil. nt.*

བསྙོན་ *bsnyon* v. *snyon.*

བསྙོར་བ་ *bsnyór-ba, Lex. nas bsnyór-ba,* acc. to *Sch.:* to sift barley.

ཊ

ཊ་ *ṭa*, the letter *ṭ*, cerebral *t*, *Ssk.* ट.

ཊ་ཀཱ་ *ṭá-kā, Hind.* टका in *W.* imaginary coin, money of account, = 2 paisa or 1 d. — Different from it is

ཊཾ་ཀ་, ཊང་ཀ་, ཊང་ཁ་, ཏང་ཀ་ *ṭáṅ-ka, ṭaṅ-ka, ṭaṅ-k̔a, taṅ-ka, Hind.* तङ्का 1. in *C.* $\frac{2}{5}$ rupee = 9 d., v. also *γčod-taṅ* (v. *γčod-pa* comp.). — 2. a gold and silver coin *Tar.* 112, 6. — 3. *W.* **money** in general.

ཊི་ཀེད་, ཏྲི་ཀེད་ *ṭi-ked, tri-ked* **card, ticket; postage-stamp.**

ཌ

ཌ་ *ḍa*, the letter *ḍ*, cerebral *d*, *Ssk.* ड.

ཌཱ་ཀི་ *ḍá-ki* (डाकी *Hind.:* 'husband of a *Dākini, Shaksp.*) in *Mil.* prob. = *Dākini, mk̔á-₀gro-ma.*

ཌ་མ་རུ་, ཌ་རུ་ *ḍá-ma-ru, ḍá-ru,* (डमरु) a small **tympan** or **drum,** with a handle and two balls fastened to it by a strap.

ཌཱཀ་ *ḍāk*, gen. **drag**, *Hind.:* डाक, **the post, letter-post.**

ཌཎ་ཌི. *ḍaṇ-ḍi, Hind.* डण्डी, **the beam** of a pair of scales; a kind of litter.

ཏ

ཏ་ *ta*, 1. the letter t, tenuis, French t. — 2. num. fig.: 9. — 3. inst. of *btags*, v. *ya-btags.*

ཏ་ཀ་རི་ *tá-ka-ri* (*Hind.* तराकुडी) common **scales,** *Ld.*

ཏ་ཀུ་ *tá-ku W.* stick with a hook, hooked cane, **crutch;** **ta-ku-rú-ku** *Ld.* **crooked, contracted, crippled.**

ཏ་གིར་ *tá-gir W.* **bread,** esp. the flat bread-cakes of India, commonly called '*chapátee*'; **ču-ta-gir** *Ld.* boiled flour-dumplings; **túl-ta-gir** pancakes.

ཏ་བ་ *tá-ba* (Pers. تابا) gen. **tao** *W.* a flat **iron pan** without a handle.

ཏ་བག་ *tá-bag W., tár-₀bag C.,* **a plate,** **tá-bag dal-dál** *W.,* **ter-tér** *C.,* a flat plate, **kor-kór** a deep plate, soup-plate.

ཏ་བེར་ *ta-bér* (spelling?) *W.* **fence** of boards or laths.

ཏ་ཟིག་ *ta-zig*, or *ta-zig-yúl*, **Persia.** *ta-zig (-pa)* a Persian.

ཏ་ར་ཙེ་ *ta-ra-tsé* (*Pers.* ترازو) *W.* a small pair of scales, **goldweights.**

ཏ་རེ་ *ta-ré* v. *re.*

ཏ་ལ་ *tá-la* 1. ताल **the palmyra tree,** *Borassus flabelliformis* (not the date-tree *Cs.*) *B.* — 2. In more recent times, and already in *Mil.*, *tá-la* seems to denote **the plantain** or banana tree, *Musa paradisiaca.*

ཏ་ལ་ལ་ *ta-la-la* *Lex.* **lamp, lantern.**

ཏ་ལའི་བླ་མ་ *ta-lai-blá-ma* (*ta-lai Mong.* ocean, sea), the Dalai Lama, v. *Huc.* II., 155. *Köpp.* II., 120.

ཏག་ཏག་ *tag-tág* *W.* the imitative sound of knocking. **tag-tág zer** there is a knock, **tag-tág čó-če** to knock at the door.

ཏང་ *taṅ* **through,** v. *toṅ* and *lteṅ.*

ཏང་ཀུན་ *taṅ-kun* n. of a medicinal herb *Med.*

ཏང་ག་ *taṅ-ga* v. ཏཾ་ཀ་ *ṭaṅ-ka.*

ཏཏྐཱ་ལ་ *tatkā-la* *Ssk.* **the present moment** *Wdk.*

ཏན་དུར་ *tan-dúr* *Ld.* a sort of hard **cake** or bread, resembling biscuit or rusk.

ཏབ་ཏབ་ *tab-táb* v. *tob-tób.*

ཏར་ཏར་ *tar-tár*, **tar-tár-čó-če** *Ld.* to smooth (wrinkles or folds in cloth, paper etc.)

ཏལ་པ་ *tál-pa*, or *tál-ma*, *Cs.*: 'a moment', *Sch.*: 'quick, decisive, penetrating'; *tál-par*, *Cs.* also *tál-mar*, 1. **instantly, immediately, quickly** *C.*, e.g. *soṅ* go without delay! *Lex.* — 2. *Sch.*: **completely, quite through,** *γčód-pa* to hew, to cut (quite through), *ₒbigs-pa* to bore through, to perforate; also *tal ₒbigs-pa.*

ཏལ་བ་ *tál-ba* a tool with holes in it, used by nailers *Sch.*

ཏི་ *ti* 1. num. fig.: 39. — 2. Not originally Tibetan, designating 'water'; this word has found its way into *Ld.*, where it however occurs only in **kó-ti** saliva (water of the mouth), and in **ná-ti** mucus (running from the nose). — 3. v. *spyi.*

ཏི་ཀ་ *ti-ka* (टीका) **explanation, commentary.**

ཏི་ཏུག་ *ti-túg*, (*Sch.* *γti-tug*) **bad, mean, silly** *Cs.*; **obstinate, stubborn** *Schr.*

ཏི་ནག་ *ti-nág* **heath-cock** *Sch.*

ཏི་པི་ *ti-pi*(?) *W.* **cap, hat** (from the *Hind.* टोपी?).

ཏི་ཕུ་ *ti-pu*, *Sch.*: *ti-pu mjug-riṅ* **pheasant.**

ཏི་ཙ་ *ti-tsa* *Stg.*, *tú-tsa* *Sch.*, **anvil.**

ཏི་ཚ་ *ti-tsa* 1. *tig-tsa* **zinc** *Med.*; *ti-tsa sér-po* cadmia, calamine (?) *Med.* — 2. a musical instrument, constructed of metal *Sch.*

ཏི་སེ་, ཏེ་སེ་ *ti-se*, *té-se*, the snow-peaks around the lake Manasarowar in *Ṅáris*, which are considered to be the highest and holiest of mountains.

ཏིག་ *tig* 1. also *tig-tig*, *Lex.* w.e.: *Sch.*: 'certainty, surety; certain'. In col. language **tig, ḍig, ṭig, ṭig**, is frq. used for: **to be sure! well, well! very right!** also as an adj.: *nór-dag tig-tig* the right, the lawful heir. Cf. **ₒgrig; tig ltá-če, tig tsam**, *tig-tsád* v. sub *tig.* — 2. *Sik.* the great **hornet.**

ཏིག་ཏ་ *tig-ta* (from तिक्तक the n. of several bitter herbs, e.g. of Gentiana Chirayta) several species of **gentian.**

ཏིག་མེན་ *tig-mén* *Cs.*, *tig-tsé* *Ld.*, the ribands which are wound round the felt-gaiters that cover the lower part of the legs.

ཏིག་ཚ་ *tig-tsa* = *ti-tsa.*

ཏིག་རིག་ *tig-rig* *Sp.* inst. of *ta-gir.*

ཏིང་ *tiṅ* 1. a small **cup** of brass used esp. in sacrificing. — 2. the sound of metal, **tiṅ zér-ra rag** *W.* I hear a tinkling.

ཏིང་ངེ་འཛིན་ *tiṅ-ṅe-ₒdzin* (**समाधि** *Trigl.*, *Was.* also **समापत्ति**) **contemplation**, profound meditation, perfect absorption of mind, cf. *bsam-ytán*, and *sgóm-pa*; *tiṅ-ṅe-ₒdzin byéd-pa Sch.*, gen. *tiṅ-ṅe-ₒdziṅ-du ₒjúg-pa* to be absorbed in deep meditation; *tiṅ-ṅe-ₒdzin ₒkruṅ* devout meditation takes place; also meton.: the faculty, the power of meditating e.g. *ₒpel Mil.*

ཏིང་རྫིང་ *tiṅ-rjiṅ Sik.* **shrew(-mouse).**

ཏིང་ཏིང་ *tiṅ-tiṅ* **clean, well-swept** *Ld., Ts.*

ཏིང་ཏི་ལིང་ *tiṅ-ti-liṅ* **snipe** *Ld.*

ཏང་(ཏིང་)-ཤགས་ *tiṅ (-tiṅ) - šags* little bells moved by the wind *Sch.*

ཏིབ་རིལ་ *tib-ril*, resp. *ysol-tib*, **tea-pot,** *zaṅs-tib* a copper tea-pot, *rdza-tib* an earthen tea-pot.

ཏིམ་པི་ *tím-pi Mil.* goat's leather, kid-leather, from India, dyed green or blue.

ཏིམ་བུ་ *tim-bu Ts.* **funnel.**

ཏིལ་ *til* (**तिल**) **sesame,** *til-már* sesame-oil, seed-oil.

ཏུ་ *tu* 1. num. fig.: 69. — 2. an affix, denoting the terminative case, or the direction to a place, joined to the final consonants g and b; cf. *du, ru, su.*

ཏུ་པག་ *tú-pag* (*Turk.* توپک) *W.* **gun, musket, fire-lock, fowling-piece,** **gyáb-če** to discharge, fire off; **tú-pag-man** gun-powder.

ཏུ་རུ་ཀ་ *tu-ru-ka Ma.* **the Turks, Turkomans,** **तुरुष्क**, ترک.

ཏུ་ཙ་ *tú-tsa* v. *ti-tsa.*

ཏུ་ལཱ་ *tú-lā* (*Ssk., Hind.*) **a balance, pair of scales,** *C.* **tú-la tég-pa** to weigh.

ཏུག་གིན་འདུག་ *túg-gin ₒdug* 'cannot' *Sch.* (?)

ཏུག་རིང་ *tug-riṅ*, or *tug-čúm*, prob. also *tug-čém*, *Cs.*: a wooden rattle's sound or noise; *Sch.* also: the trotting of horses heard in the distance; *tug-riṅ-čan Stg.* noisy (?).

ཏུབ་ *tub*, *tub yčig-tu rgyúd-do?*

ཏུབ་ཏུག་ *tub-túg Lex.* w. e.; *Sch.*: 'either — or, whether I be able (to do it) or not' (?).

ཏུར་བ་ *túr-ba* (?) *W.* **to darn** (stockings).

ཏུར་རེ་ *túr-re* **clear, distinct,** syn. to *wál-le*; *yid túr-re ₒdug* it is clear to my mind; *túr-re bzuṅ Mil.* prob. watch it! have a sharp eye upon it! *že-sdáṅ laṅs dogs túr-re gyis Mil.* take care lest an emotion of anger arise in your mind! *túr-gyis sad Mil.* prob.: he awakes, stirs, is evidently roused; *túr-re-ba Glr.*; adj. (or abstract noun), *rjed-yeṅ-méd-par túr-re-ba* clear, firm with regard to perceptions, opinions etc., without omission or digression.

ཏེ་ *te* 1. num. fig.: 99. — 2. an affix denoting the gerund, and used after the final letters *n, r, l, s* (v. Grammar), to be translated by the participle in ing, or sentences beginning with when, after, as etc.; also used as a finite tense (though seldom in *B.*), and in that case followed by *ₒdug* or *yod*, or also without these words: **dád-de ₒdug** I sit *W.*; *ₒgró-ba yin-te Mil.* I go.

ཏེ་པོར་ *té-por Lex.* = *légs-par*; *Sch.*: very, really, actually.

ཏེ་བོར་ *té-bor Sch.* constantly, continually.

ཏེ་སེ་ *té-se* v. *ti-se.*

ཏེག་པ་ *tég-pa*, imp. *tog*, *C.*, *W.*, = *ₒtégs-pa*, **to pack up, put up; to put in or into,** **'am-bág-la** into one's bosom; **tag-ṭul** or **ṭug** preparations for a journey, **taṅ-če** *W.* to make.

ཏེའུ་ *teu? Ld.-Glr.* (*Schl.* f. 25, b); *teu sér-po; Mil.* 59, 4 of my edition; *Lex.*: *teu šiṅ-kri*, where *Sch.* translates: a square table.

ཏེལ་པ་ *tél-pa Cs.*: an instrument for burning *Med.*; *lčágs-tel* such an instrument of iron *Cs.*; *sprá-tel Lt.?*

ཏོ་ *to* 1. num. for 129. — 2. affix added to certain verbs, when they terminate a sentence.

ཏོ་ཏོ་ལིང་ལིང་ *to-to-liṅ-liṅ W.*, an adv. denoting a swinging motion;

hence *to-to-liṅ-liṅ sed sé-ċe* to play at swinging, to swing.

ཏོ་ལ་ *tó-la* for *tú-lā C.*

ཏོག་ *tog* 1. (केतु *Cs.*: **'the top** of any thing, **a top ornament'**; esp. the button on the cap of Chinese dignitaries, as a mark of distinction; *tog-dkár*, श्वेतकेतु n. of Buddha in paradise (*dga-ldán*) before his incarnation *Ld.-Glr.* 8, a.; *mdúṅ-tog* point, thorn, nail. — 2. for *fog*, and thus prob. also used in *skabs-tog* now, at present *Ld.*

ཏོག་སྒྲ་ *tóg-sgra*, *tóg-tog-sgra Lex.*, a rolling sound *Sch*, acc. to *Wdṅ.* also a cracking sound.

ཏོག་ཏིལ་ *tog-til* **a bump, a swelling,** by a knock against the head.

ཏོག་ཙེ་ *tóg-tse W.*, *tóg-rtse Lex.*, **hoe, mattock, pickaxe** *W.* (in *C.* *ₒjor*); *tog-lċags* the iron of the hoe, *tog-yu* the handle of it; *tog-leb* a spade (?) *Cs.*

ཏོང་ཏོང་བྱེད་པ་ *toṅ-tóṅ byéd-pa Lex.*, *Sch.*: to perforate; to produce a whirling noise.

ཏོབ་ཅི་ *tob-ċi W.* **button,** *tób-ċi brgyáb-ċe* to button up; cf. *tób-ču*; (buttons are not in general use in Tibet).

ཏོབ་ཏོབ་སྨྲ་བ་ *tob-tób smrá-ba* to talk confusedly *Sch.*; *W.*: *tab-táb*, or *tab-tób ma ċo* keep your temper! do not talk with such agitation!

ཏོའུ་ལོ་ *tou-lo* **polecat** *Sch.*

ཏོལ་ *tol? Mṅg. bem-tól? Sch. tol-yċód-pa* = *tal-yċód-pa* q.v.

ཏྲམ་པ་ *trám-pa* hard (of rare occurrence); *ša-trám*, *rus-tram*, *rtsa-tram*, *tram-dkár*, *tram-nág*, are different species of gout *Med.*

ཏྲི་ཀེད་ *tri-ked* v. *ṭi-ked.*

ཏྲི་ཤུ(ལ) *tri-šu(-la)*, from त्रिशूल trident *Wdk.*

ཏྲེ་ཏྲེ་ཧོ་ *tre-tre-ho* (by the context) a dangerous disease of the stomach or a serious symptom of it *Pth.*

ཏྲེ་བ་ཅན་ *tré-ba-ċan* coloured *Sch.*

ཏྲེ་སམ་ *tré-sam* a medicine in the shape of a powder *Med.*

ཏྲོན་ *tron* **diligence, industry** *Cs.*; *tron byéd-pa* to be diligent, to exert one's self.

གཏག་གཏོང་ *ytag-ytoṅ Lex.* w.e.; *ytag-ytoṅ-ba* to disperse *Sch.*

གཏང་རག་ *ytaṅ-rág* **thanks, thanksgiving,** and prob. also thank-offering, esp. rendering thanks to a deity; *ytaṅ-rág byéd-pa*, *ₒbúl-ba Mil.*, *Lt.*, *W.* *ċó-ċe, púl-ċe* to render thanks.

གཏད་ *ytad* (v. *ytód-pa*), in the direction of, **towards,** *yyón-gral-du ytad pyin-nas* going towards the left end of the row *Glr.*; *'doṅ-tád' W.* directly opposite, just over against.

གཏད་པ་ *ytád-pa* 1. vb, v. *ytód-pa*, also *brtád-pa*. — 2. sbst. **hold, steadiness, firmness,** *ytád-pa-med* it has no hold, no firmness *Mil.*; *ytad-méd ₒċál-ba Zam.* prob. to vacillate, to waver, to be unsteady.

གཏད་སོ་ *ytád-so* a refuge, resource, esp. store of provisions; *tẹ-so žág-pa* *C.* to procure such a store.

གཏན(པ) *ytán(-pa) Cs.*: 'series, order, system; a bar for a door'; *Sch.* also 'anvil', and 'to lock up'. People from *C.* knew only one signification of *ytán-pa*, viz **mortar,** = *ytun*; **bar, door-bar** occurs in *sgo-ytán C.* and *W.* But a different word seems to be *ytan*: 1. **order, system,** in the current phrase *ytán-la ₒbébs-pa* to put in order, to arrange, to reduce to a system, *bre-sráṅ* measure and weight *Glr.*, the Tibetan alphabet *Glr.*, the civil law and the canon law *Glr.*, laws, books, = to compose, draw up, write *Glr.*; *raṅ-séms ytán-pa* in a mystic sense: to regulate, compose, and purify the mind *Glr.*; also to fashion, to train *C.*, to set right *Mil.* (Cf. *bsam-ytán.*) — 2. **duration,** perh. also entireness, completeness, hence *ytán-gyi* constant, continual, *ytan-grogs* consort, partner for life *Mil.*; *ytan-méd Sch.*: 'perishable, without duration or continuity': *ytán-du* 1. **always, continually, for ever.** *ytán-du bzúgs-pa* living there continually *Tar.* 2. **entirely, completely** (which is the usual signification of *ytan-du*) e.g. to cut off, to deliver completely; *ytán-nas* id.; *ytan-krigs* agreement, stipulation, convention, *ytan-krigs byéd-pa Mil.*

Note. Owing to its second signification *ytan* is often confounded with *brtan(-po)*, or even with *bstan(-pa)*. Not only illiterate people, but well-educated Lamas from *C.* were occasionally doubtful as to the correct spelling of this word.

གཏན་ཚིགས་ *ytan-tsigs* (*Ssk.* **हेतु**, *Stg.*, *Do*, ཇེ f. 344 *ytan-tsigs-kyi de-ko-na-nyid bstán-pa* = **हेतुतत्त्वउपदेश**) 1. **argument, syllogism** *Cs.*; evidence before a court of justice *Dzl.* ༢༢༥, 6. — 2. *Sch.*: **a standing proposition,** indisputable point *Thgy.* (where in my *Ms. brtan-tsigs* is erron. written; v. the note to the preceding word). — 3. **logic, dialectics** *Cs.*; *ytan-tsigs-méd-par smrá-ba* is in *Stg.* the term applied to a kind of *kyál-ka*, evidently: illogical, irrational talk; *ytan-tsigs-su bžéd-nas Glr.* 96. wishing to clear up, to render evident (?); *ytan-tsigs-mkan* dialectician, logician.

གཏམ་ *ytam* (**कथा**) **talk, discourse, speech,** 1. in a general sense: **tam čig-pa** *C.*, **tam čig-čig** *W.*, that is one and the same talk, that means the same; *ytam bsdúr-ba* to compare depositions, to examine, to try judicially, **tam-dúr** *W.* trial, judicial examination. — 2. **news, tidings, intelligence,** *ytám bzáṅ-po* good news; *pyis ytam mi ˳dug* after which there are no further accounts *Mil.*; **tam šád-če** to tell a tale, a story *W.*; **report, rumour, fame,** *de pul zér-bai ytam rgyál-pos tós-nas* when the king heard the report that ... had been delivered up *Pth.*; *tag-riṅ-gi ytam* fame of remote matters or events; *bdág-gis ytám-du tós-na* as I have learned, have been told *Dzl.* — 3. **section, chapter** *Tar.*, frq.

Phrases. *ytam gléṅ-ba S.O.*, *Dzl.*, *ytám-du gléṅ-ba Dzl.* to speak, to converse, to discourse; *ytam byéd-pa, smrá-ba, zér-ba* id.; *ytam byar ˳groo* I shall go and speak to him *Dzl.*; the genit. preceding *ytam* always denotes the person or thing spoken of, not the person speaking; *ji-ltar gyúr-pai ytam byas* he gave an account of the manner how it had happened *Dzl.*; *mtún-pai ytam byéd-pa* to negotiate about peace *Glr.*; *čos(-kyi) ytam byéd-pa* to begin a religious conversation *Mil.*; *na dé-ltar byéd-pai ytam mi-la ma lab* do not tell any body that I am doing this *Mil.*; in a similar manner: *mi ríṅ-bai ytam bsgrág-go* he shall declare it to be unbecoming *Thgr.*; *pa-mái ytam dris* he inquired about his parents *Dzl.*; *bú-moi ytam tos* he heard of the girl *Dzl.*

Comp. *ytam-rgyúd* **tradition, oral account;** *deï ytam-rgyúd* the legend of him. — *ytam-ṅán* **ill report,** slander. — *ytam-snyán* **joyful news, glad tidings,** *sgróg-pa* to announce *Mil.* — *ytam-bsdúr* v. above. — *ytám-dpe* a proverb, a saying *Cs.* — *ytam-rtsúb* rough speech, **abusive language.** Note. In *W.* **(s)pé-ra** is more in use than **tam**.

གཏམ(ས)་པ་ *ytám(s)-pa* 1. adj **full,** *spú-gri ytám (s)-pa* quite full of razors *Thgy.*; also *Lexx.*; more frq. it is spelled *(b)ltám(s)-pa*. — 2. vb. to appoint, to commission, of rare occurrence. — 3. sbst. *Cs.*: a term for a thousand billion, yet v. the remark to *dkrigs-pa*.

གཏའ(མ་) *ytá(-ma) Lexx.* (cf. *yté-pa*) **pawn, pledge,** *ytá-mar ˳júg-pa* to pawn, to give as a pledge, *ytá-ma blú-ba* to redeem a pledge *Cs.*; **nór-ta** *W.* jewels, precious stones, given as a pledge (*Cs.*: 'pecuniary security, bail'); *mi-yta* a hostage *Cs.*

གཏར་བ་ *ytár-ba*, with *krag*, **to bleed,** to let blood *Med.*; *ytár(-bar) byéd-pa*, *rtsá-ba-la* from a vein, or also *ytár-ga ˳débs-pa* id.

གཏི་ཁེ་ *yti-ké* a kind of louse *Sch.*

གཏི་ཐུག་ *yti-tug* insane, mad *Sch.*, = *ti-tug*.

གཏི་མུག་ *yti-mug* (**तमस**) **gloom, mental darkness, ignorance, stupidity,** *glén-pa yti-mug-čan* infatuated fools *Dzl.*; *mtsán-mo yti-mug-ynyid-du soṅ* at night I fell into a profound sleep *Mil.*; in a special sense: the lowest of the three *guṇa* or psychological qualities of animated beings, **सत्त्व, रज, तमस्**, virtue, passion, stupidity, acc. to the Brahminical theory, for which however Buddhism has substituted the three moral categories: *ₒdod-čágs, že-sdán, yti-mug*, voluptuousness, anger, inconsiderateness (*Köpp.* I, 33); *yti-mug*, as for example, is the source of falsehoods told with a pretended good intention, *Stg.*; the symbol for it is the pig *Wdṅ.* Note. The philosophical term *ma-rig-pa* is altogether different from *yti-mug*.

གཏིག(ས)་པ་ *ytig(s)-pa Lex.* **to fall in drops, to drop, to drip.**

གཏིང་ *ytiṅ*, *Ld.* *ltiṅ*, **bottom,** *rgyá-mtsoï ytiṅ-dkrugs* he turned up the bottom of the sea; *ytiṅ-du núb-pa* to sink to the bottom *Cs.*; **depth,** hence *ytiṅ záb-po Dzl.*, *ytiṅ riṅ-ba* deep, *ytiṅ nyé-ba* not deep, shallow; *rgyá-mtso-bas ytiṅ-záb-bo* it is deeper than the sea *Dzl.*; *ygáṅ-sa ytiṅ-riṅ-ba* a deep abyss *Thgr.*; *čú-bo ytiṅ-záb-po žig* a deep river *Dzl.* ༢༤༢, 1. (in the third line however *záb-bo* would be the correct reading for *zab-po*); *ytiṅ-zab-ḱyád ḱru-brgyád-pa* eight cubits deep (lit. with regard to depth holding eight cubits) *Dzl.* ༡༢༦, 5; **fig.** *ytiṅ-nas* from the bottom of the heart, *ṅá-la dád-pa ytiṅ-nas gyis* believe in me with all your heart *Mil.*; *ḱa-grógs* and *ytiṅ-grógs* v. *grogs*; *ḱa-dkar-ytiṅ-nág* white without, and black within (fig.) *Mil.*; the following passage of *Mil.*: *rgyá-mtso čé-la dpe lóṅ-la ḱa-ytiṅ-méd-pai sgom čig gyis*, is not perfectly clear, yet the real sense seems to be: resembling the ocean, be so lost in contemplation, that you do not know any longer a difference between surface and bottom; *ytiṅ-rdó* a stone or piece of lead (*žá-nyei ytiṅ-rdó Pth.*) fastened to a rope, and used as plummet, as anchor, as a clock-weight, as a means for drowning delinquents etc.; **ču nyóg-po-če-la tiṅ med** *W.* a very muddy water has no depth; *ytiṅ-čan* deep, *ytiṅ-méd* shallow *Cs.*; also fig. deep, reserved, covert, difficult to fathom, to form an opinion of, and the contrary: shallow, superficial; *ytiṅ-mi-lón C.* of unknown depth; *ytiṅ-dróṅs-pa* fathomed, penetrated, ascertained *C.*

གཏིབ(ས)་པ་ *ytib(s)-pa* 1. **to be gathering,** of clouds, *sprin-ṗuṅ ytib-pa* thick clouds gathering *Wdṅ.*; *bdug-spós sprin-bžin ytib* incense wafts along like clouds *Glr.*; *mún-pa ytib Lex.*, col. also **nam-ḱa tib-tib yod** cf. *ₒtib-pa*. — 2. sometimes for *rdib-pa*.

གཏིམ་པ་ *ytim-pa* v. *tim-pa*.

གཏུག་པ་ *ytúg-pa*, pf. *ytugs*, also *btúg-pa*, cognate to *túg-pa*, 1. **to reach, to touch,** *yi-dam-gyi túgs-kar ytúgs-nas* putting or pressing (his forehead) against the breast of the image *Glr.*; *mi žig-gi žábs-la mgó-bos ytúg-pa*, or only *žábs-ytug-pa* to touch as a supplicant a person's feet (or skirt) with the brow, to cast one's self at another's feet, frq.; *btug túg-pa daṅ* was explained: when it (the danger) draws quite near *Ma.*; **to overtake, to reach,** *ni* f., e.g. *mta* the end *Lex.*; **to meet with, to join** *Tar.* 172, 14. — 2. to bring an action against a person, **to sue** *Sch.*, thus prob. *Dzl.* ༡༡༩, 3, and *Pth.* — 3. = *zád-pa* to be exhausted, to be consumed(?) *Zam. zád-pai ytúgs-pa.*—

Note. Not only *ytúg-pa*, but also many of the following words have b as well as g for their initial letter, and moreover a corresponding form beginning with *t*, of the same or nearly the same signification.

གཏུན་ *ytun*, *Sch.* also *rtun*, col. **gog-tún** (spelling dubious) 1. **pestle;** there are small ones, like ours and large ones, in shape of poles, as thick as a man's arm, and about 6 feet long, by means of which the pounding is effected in an excavation made in a rock, called *ytun-ḱúṅ*; *ytun(-gyis) rdúṅ-ba* to pound with a pestle *Dzl.*; *ytún-po* mortar *Cs.*; *ytun-bu, ytun-šiṅ* pestle *Cs.* — 2. **mallet, knocker** *Dzl.*

གཏུབ་པ་ *ytúb-pa*, more frq. *btúb-pa*, = *túb-pa*, **to be able,** *ṗyir ₒóṅ-du btúb-pa-am* shall you really be able to come back? *Dzl.*; *mi btúb-pa* very frq. not to be able to prevail upon one's self, **to be unable**, also: **to be unwilling, to have no mind** (to do a thing).

གཏུབ(ས)་པ་ *ɣtúb(s)-pa, btúb(s)-pa, Ld.* *stúb-ċe*, = *ₒtúb-pa*, **to cut to pieces, to cut up**, meat, wood etc.; in *W.* also **to mince**; (in *C. btsáb-pa*); *ɣtubs-spyád* chopper *Sch.*

གཏུམ་པ་ *ɣtúm-pa* 1. **ferocity, rage;** also adj. **furious;** *k̄ró-žiṅ ɣtúm-la snyiṅ-rje-med* in furious wrath, merciless *Dzl.*; *ɣdúg-ċiṅ ɣtún-pai klu* a Lu in a deadly rage *Sambh.*; *ɣtúm-pai sgra sgróg-pa* to roar furiously *Pth.*; *k̄ró-ɣtum-pa* furious with rage *Glr.*; *ɣtúm-žiṅ rgód-pa* obstinate and unmanageable, of a boy; *ɣtúm-po Mil., ɣtúm-ċan, ɣtum-ldán* cruel, fierce, furious *Cs.*; *blá-ma t̄ugs-ɣtúm-po ₒoṅ* the Lama grows angry *Mil. nt.*; *ɣtúm-mo* fem. a fury of a woman *Dzl.* ༢༠༠, 10; *Sch.* also: hangman (?); *rluṅ ɣtúm-mo Cs.* a furious wind, a hurricane — 2. = *btúm-pa, ₒtúm-pa*, **to veil, to cover; to wrap up**, e.g. the head; with the instr. to wrap up or cover with a thing.

གཏུམ་པོ་ *ɣtúm-po* 1. v. *ɣtúm-pa* 1. — 2. चण्ड (hot) in the more developed mysticism the power which meditating saints by dint of long continued practice may acquire of holding back their breath for a great length of time, by which means the air is supposed to be drawn from the *ró-ma* and *rkyáṅ-ma* (two veins, v. *rtsá-ba*) into the *dbú-ma* (*sróg-rtsa, ₒdú-ti*, aorta?) thus causing a feeling of uncommon warmth, comfort, and lightness inside, and finally even emancipating the body from the laws of gravity, so as to lift it up and hold it freely suspended in the air, *Mil.* frq.; v. also *Tar.* 186, 20; *ɣtúm-poi bde-dród* the feeling of warmth just mentioned *Mil.*; *ɣtúm-po ₒbar* the warmth of meditation commences *Mil.* The three above-named veins are symbolically represented by *a-shád*, i.e. the second half of an ཨ, viz. ༑, hence *a-šad-ɣtúm-po* the three veins'-meditation-warmth, *Mil.* — 3. n. of the goddess Durga or Uma.

གཏུར་བུ་ *ɣtúr-bu Lex.* w.e.; *Cs.* **bag, sack, wallet.**

གཏུལ་བ་ *ɣtúl-ba* **to grind, to pulverize,** colours, medicinal substances etc.; cf. *ₒtág-pa*.

གཏེ་པ་ *ɣté-pa W.* (*Ld.* *sté-pa*) *ɣtẹ́-ba, ɣté-ma C., ɣtéṅ-pa Lex.*, **pawn, pledge, bail** (*Sch.* also: a present); cf. *ɣtá-ma*; *ɣteu* id.? hostage? *Tar.*

གཏེར་ *ɣter* (निधि, कोष) 1. **treasure**, frq. — 2. symb. num. for 9. — *ɣter-mdzód* **a treasury.** — *ɣtér-k̄a* **a mineral vein, mine,** *nór-gyi ɣtér-k̄a rnyéd-pa* to find a mine of precious metals.

གཏོ་ *ɣto Lt., Thgy.* a magic ceremony for the purpose of averting misfortune; *ɣto-bċós* id.

གཏོག་པ་ *ɣtóg-pa* 1. also *btóg-pa, ₒtóg-pa*, **to pluck off, gather, crop, tear out** (one's hair) *Lex.* — 2. v. *se-gol.*

གཏོགས་པ་ *ɣtógs-pa* **to belong, appertain to; belonging,** *rgyál-poï ɣdúṅ-la ɣtógs-pa yin* you belong to the royal blood or family *Dzl.*; *deï náṅ-du mi ɣtógs-sam* am I not included in them? *Dzl.*; *ₒdzam-bui-gliṅ-la ɣtógs-pa* belonging to Dzambuling *Glr.*; *di lẹ́-ka daṅ ma tog* *W.* do not meddle with that! *ma-ɣtógs-pa*, gen. adv. *ma ɣtógs-par* **except, besides.** — *ɣtogs-ₒdód Sch.*: 'to love, to like, to wish; a good-for-nothing fellow' (?).

གཏོང་བ་ *ɣtóṅ-ba*, pf. *btaṅ*, fut. *ɣtaṅ*, imp. *toṅ* (*W.* *taṅ-ċe*, imp. *toṅ*) त्यज 1. **to let** a. **to let go,** to permit to go, **to dismiss,** *ċii p̄yir bdág-ċag-rnams-kyis ɣtoṅ* why should we let you go, suffer you (our teacher) to go? **to let escape** (a prisoner) *Dzl.*; **to let loose** (a dog against a person) *Mil.*; **to let go,** to quit one's hold *ma ɣtoṅ*, col. *ma taṅ* don't let him go, stop him! **to leave, abandon, renounce,** *č̄os* one's religion; more definitely: *blos ɣtóṅ-ba*, v. *blo*; *yóṅs-su ɣtóṅ-ba* to abandon altogether *Dzl.*; to leave off, to abstain from, *ɣsód-par byá-ba ɣtóṅ-ba* to leave off killing *Dzl.* b. **to let in, to admit,** *sgó-nas* through the door *Dzl.*, *nán-du γtón-ba* to permit to enter. — 2. **to let go,** i.e. to make go, **to send,** *mi* a man, a messenger, very frq.; *ₒdzam-bui-glin kún-tu btán-nas* he made him go all over the country of Dzambuling *Dzl.*; *skyél-du γtón-ba* to dispatch for conveying (a message); *lén-du γtón-ba* to send (a person) for (a thing); *ₒtsól-ba btán-ba-las* he sent out searchers (people in search) *Dzl.* ༢༠, 18., unless this passage should be read *ₒtsól-bar.* — 3. **to let have, to give,** so in *W.* almost exclusively; *sman γtón-ba* to give medicine, *γtón-tsul* the way of giving medicine, for 'a dose' *Med.*; *γtón-pod-čan* liberal, bounteous *Mil.*; *γtón-sems-ldan* id. *S.g.*; *γtón-sems* liberality, bounty; **tón zer** he says, give me! he wants to have, he tries to get *W.*; *čós-la γtón-ba* to give a person up to religion, i.e. to destine him for the priesthood, to make him take orders. — 4. **to make, to cause,** e.g. a smoke by lighting a fire *Glr.*; with the termin. **to turn into,** *byé-tan néu-tan-du* sandy plains into meadows *Glr.*; *rims(-nad) γtón-ba* to cause, **to send down,** epidemies, plagues (of gods); **to construct, fix, place,** chains before a building *Glr.*; in *W.* *(*s*)*kad tán-če** to utter sounds, **kú-čo, bó-ra tán-če** to raise, to set up a cry; **kug** or **kum tán-če** to make crooked, to bend; in forming intensive verbs: **go čád tán-če** to decapitate; **tón ton, pins ton** take out! throw out! **tsa ton** put salt into it! **ču tán-če** to water (the garden); **lud tán-če** to manure (the fields). The participle **tans-pa** is used adverbially in *Ld.*; **i-ne táns-pa à tsúg-pa** from here to there, from this place to that place (= *bzuns-te*).

གཏོད་ *γtod? γtód-la mnán-pa*, of the sun *Pth.*, of the galaxy *Mil.*, evidently denotes the disappearing of these celestial bodies by enchantment or only as a poetical figure; perh. = *γdos*, or to be explained by *γtód-pa* II.

གཏོད་པ་ *γtód-pa* I. also *γtád-pa*, pf. *btad, γtad*, fut. *γtad*, imp. *btod* (*Mil.*; *Cs. tod?*) 1. **to deliver up,** *lág-tu* into the hand, to hand over *Glr.*, to hand to a person the subject for a theme or problem *Glr.*, to commit the management of the household to another *Dzl.*, to commit a child to a teacher *Dzl.*, *dge-ₒdún-la dban* to confer important offices on the priesthood *Glr.*, *rig-pa* to teach; *γčig snyin γčig-la γtád-pa* to communicate one's feelings to one another *Glr.* — 2. **to lean against** or **upon** c. dat., e.g. to rest one's head on one's arm; to lay or put against, to, or on, one's mouth to a person's ear *Thgr.*, the tip of the tongue against the palate *Gram.* — 3. **to direct, to turn,** *mi-la mgó-bo*, one's face towards a person *Lt.*, *mi-la mdzúb-mo*, or *sdig-mdzúb* to point at a person (with the finger) *Glr.*; *sgo nub-pyógs bál-poi yúl-du γtod Glr.*, the door points south, towards Nepal; *ₒbém-la* to take aim, to aim at *Lex.*; *rná-bai dbán-po γtód-pa* to listen to, to give a person a hearing *Mil.*; *sems*, resp. *tugs, γtód-pa Mil.* id.; *ₒod-zér-la γtád-nas γzigs-pas* turning after a ray of light, following it with the eye (= *brtén-nas*) *Glr.*; also used absolutely: *dkar-kún γtód-pa* the projecting windows *S.g.* (?) — *ka γtód-pa Glr.?*

II. inst. of *rtód-pa*, **to fasten** (cows etc.) to a stake (driven into the ground), **to tedder.**

གཏོམ་པ་ *γtóm-pa* **to talk, to speak** *Sch.*, cf. *γtam* (?).

གཏོམས་པ་ *γtóms-pa* **filled up, full,** for *bltáms-pa, γtáms-pa, Sch.*

གཏོར་བ་ *γtór-ba* (*Lexx.* चपक) cf. *ₒtór-ba*, 1. **to strew, to scatter** ccirdp., *mé-tog-gis γtór-ro Dzl.* they strewed flowers, also *γtór-to Dzl.*; *ná-la sas γtór-ba* they that threw earth upon me *Dzl.*; *sá-la γtór-ba* to scatter over the ground *Glr.* — 2. **to cast, to throw,** ccar., books into the water *Glr.*, a ring into the air *Glr.*; to throw out, e.g. spittle into a person's ear, for healing purposes (= *ₒdór-ba*); **to cause to circulate** the chyle through every part of the body *Med.*; **to waste, to dissipate** *Dzl.*, occasionally with the accus. of the vessel containing the substance thrown out: *nú-*

ma γtór-ba Glr. (a cow) emptying its udder by discharging the milk. — 3. *Sch.: 'srub γtór-ba* **to rend**, to tear to pieces'.

གཏོར་མ་ *γtór-ma* **strewing-oblation**, an offering brought to malignant demons, either as a kind of exorcism or as an appeasing gift, in order to prevent their evil influences upon man; *mčód-pa daṅ γtór-ma sbyin-pa* to offer such an oblation, *γtór-mar snó-ba* to devote something for it. The ceremonies are similar to those used in *sbyin-srég Schl. Buddh.* 249; the offerings consisting of things eatable and not eatable, of blood, and even of animal and vegetable feces, scattered into the air (the benefit being shared by the *dri-za* q.v.). There are various sorts of Torma-offerings, according to the nature of the substances offered (*ču-* or *čab-γtor*, *ṗye-γtor*; *lhag-γtor*, an oblation of the fragments of a meal *Mil.*), or according to the time at which (*dgu-γtór* v. *dgu*), and the purpose for which they are offered (*mtsun-γtor* v. *mtsun*). Other names of Torma-offerings are: *blud-rgyá*, *mar-me-rgyá*, *tiṅ-lo*(?)-*rgyá*, *ča-γsúm* etc. Tormas in general belong to the ceremonies most frequently performed; *γtor-čá* are the vessels and other implements used for that purpose; *γtor-sdéb Sch.*: 'a bowl for these offerings'(?). — *γtor-zán Lex.* बलि oblation of the remnants of the daily meal to creatures of every description.

གཏོལ་ *γtol*, only in *γtol-méd*, = *ča-méd*, **not known, dubious**, *ṗó-˳am mó-˳am γtol-méd-do* one does not know yet, whether it will be a boy or a girl *Dzl.*; *či byá-bai γtol méd* not knowing what to do *Dzl.*; *gar ťál-bai γtol med* not knowing where she had gone to; *bdág-la γtol méd* I do not know any thing about it *Dzl.* — (*Sch.* has a verb *γtól-ba* to perforate, pierce; to discover, disclose; v. *rtól-ba*).

གཏོས་ *γtos* **size, width, quantity**, *ri-boi γtos tsam* as high as a mountain *Lex.*; *rim-gro γtos-čé-ba*, like *rgya-čé-ba*, great marks of honour, extraordinary homage.

བཏག་པ་ *btág-pa* v. *˳ťág-pa*.

བཏགས་པ་ *btágs-pa* v. *˳dógs-pa*, and *ka-btágs*.

བཏང་བ་ *btáṅ-ba* v. *γtóṅ-ba*.

བཏད་པ་ *btád-pa* v. *γtód-pa*.

བཏབ་པ་ *btáb-pa* v. *˳débs-pa*.

བཏང་སྙོམས་ *btaṅ-snyóms* (cf. *snyoms*) उपेक्ष complete **indifference**, perfect **apathy** (acc. to *Schr.* prop. 'a liberality perfectly impartial'?).

བཏང་བཟུང་ *btaṅ-bzúṅ Lex.* मुचिलिन्द n. of a hill where Buddha was teaching.

བཏིག་པ་ *btíg-pa*, pf. *btigs*, *Cs.* **to drop**, to let fall in drops, *rná-bar sman*, medicine into the ear, v. *˳ťíg-pa*.

བཏིང་བ་ *btíṅ-ba* v. *˳díṅ-ba*.

བཏུ་བ་ *btú-ba* v. *˳ťú-ba*.

བཏུང་བ་ *btúṅ-ba* v. *˳ťúṅ-ba*.

བཏུག་པ་ *btúg-pa* v. *γtúg-pa*.

བཏུད་པ་ *btúd-pa* v. *˳dúd-pa*.

བཏུད་མར་ *btúd-mar Glr.* in rapid or close succession, **tụ'-tụ'-pa-la* C.* id.

བཏུབ་ *btub*, *Lex.* = *ruṅ*, **fit, convenient, practicable, becoming**, *btúb-bo* it is convenient etc.; *btúb-pa* v. *γtúb-pa*.

བཏུམ་པ་ *btúm-pa*, *γtúm-pa*, 1. **to wrap round, to envelop**; hence 2. in *W.* **to shut**, a book, valuable books being wrapped up in a cloth before being laid by; *btum-ṗóg* **bunch** or **knot**, produced by money and the like being tied up in the girdle.

བཏུལ་བ་ *btúl-ba* v. *˳dúl-ba*, *γtúl-ba*.

བཏེག་པ་ *btég-pa* v. *˳dégs-pa*.

བཏོད་པ་ *btód-pa* 1. = *rtód-pa*, **to fasten** (grazing horses or cattle) by a rope to a stake, **to tedder**; *Mil.* declares relations to be the *btod-ťág* (the tedder) in the hands of the devil. — 2. **to erect, raise up, produce, cause, occasion**; *srol-btód-*

pa (*Lex.* w.c.) may accordingly imply: to introduce a custom.

བཏོན་པ་ *btón-pa* v. *˳dón-pa.*

བཏོལ་བ་ *btól-ba Sch.* = *γtól-ba.*

རྟ་ *rta* (*rtá-po C., Mil.*), resp. *čibs*, 1. **horse,** *p̔o-rta* a gelding, *mó-rta*, or *rta-rgód-ma*, a mare; *rta ˳dúl-ba* to break in, train, a horse; *rta rgyúg-pa* to gallop; to run horses for a wager, to race *Glr.*; **sta šrul-če* Ld.* id.? — 2. the lower front part of a pair of breeches, *dór-rta, ăṅ-rta.*

Comp. *rta-rkyá(-pa)*, or *-skyá(-pa)* one skilled in horsemanship. — *rta-bskrágs* (**stab-rágs* Ld.*) a clattering train of horsemen. — *rta-gál Ts.* pouch or bag of a horseman, saddle-bag. — *rta-grás* = *rta-rá.* — *rta-bgád* a horse-laugh, *rta-bgád-kyis ˳débs-pa* to set up a horse-laugh *Sch.* — *rta-mgó* a horse's head; *rta-mgó-ma* v. *go-tsém.* — *rta-mgrín* (हयग्रीव) n. of a demon (*Schl.* 110), a terrifying deity. — *rtá-sga, W. *té-ga**, **saddle.** — *rta-sgám* a large box or chest. — *rtá-sgo* v. *sgo.* — *rta-sgyél*, gen. connected with *mi-bsád*, the slaughtering of men and killing of horses. — *rta-ṅán* Tibetan horses, small, strong, unshod, v. *Hook.* II, 131, and so already in *Marco Polo's* travels. — *rta-rṅa* **horse-tail,** **te ṅá-ma yod* W.* it is (made) of horse-hair. — *rta-lčág* horse-whip; whip in general. — *rta-čág* dry fodder or provender given to horses, corn, oats. — *rta-mčóg* the best horse, a splendid horse, state-horse; gen. a fabulous horse, a sort of Pegasus, thus e.g. *Glr.* chp. 6, where it partakes of divine properties (*rtai rgyál-po čan-šés bá-la-ha*; acc. to *Schl.* p. 253 *rlúṅ-rta* is the same). — *rta-mčóg-ka-˳bab* = *γyas-ru-γtsán-po* = *mṅá-ris-ču* n. of the principal river of Tibet. — *rta-ljáṅ* he with the green horses, the sun, po. *Glr.* — *rta-rná* horse-ear, n. of one of the seven gold-mountains, surrounding the Rirab. — *rtá-pa* horseman, rider, **tá-pa ta-žón* Ld.* a balancing-board, **see-saw;** *rtá-pai dpúṅ* horse, **cavalry** *Cs.* — *rta-lpágs* a horse's skin; n. of a medicinal herb *Med.* — *rta-bábs* 1. a large stone or raised place for alighting from a horse(?) *Cs.* 2. the superstructure of a large door or gate, the arch of a gate-way, *Lex. toa-ra-ṇa*, द्वारवा? — *rta-dbyáṅs* अश्वघोष n. of a great scholar *Thgy.* — *rta-bél* a horse's front-hair *Cs.* — *rta-sbáṅs* **horse-dung.** — *rta-rmig* a horse's hoof; n. of a plant *Med.* — *rta-rmig-ma* a lump of silver bullion like a horse's hoof *Cs.* — *rta-rdzi* one that tends horses; **a groom** *Glr.* — *rta-žún* a good horse. — *rta-zám* 1. **post-station,** *rta-zám-gyi tsúgs-pa* a post-house; *rta-zám gyi spyi-dpon* postmaster-general *Cs.* 2. in *Ld.* also for *rta-zám-pa.* — *rta-zám-pa* **postillion, courier, express, estafet.** An estafet rides day and night, mounting fresh horses at certain stations, and making the way from Lé to Lhasa (for ordinary travellers a journey of 4 months) in 18 days. — *rta(i)-˳u-lag* a compulsory service consisting in the supply of horses. — *rta-rá, rta-grás* **inclosure, stable,** for horses. — *rta-šá* 1. horse-flesh. 2. the oblique abdominal muscles of the hips. — *rta-šád* **curry-comb** *Sch.* — *rta-γsár* a horse not yet broken in or dressed *Schr.* — *rta-bséb* **stallion.** — With regard to the colour of horses (*spú-k̔a*), the following distinctions are made: *rta-dkár* a gray or white horse; *rta-rkyaṅ-nág*, or *k̔am-nág Sch.* a dark-brown horse; *rta k̔ám-pa Ld.* a yellowish-brown horse (*Sch.* a dark-brown horse); *rta-k̔am-dmár Sch.* a light-bay horse, a sorrel horse; *rta k̔rá-bo* a piebald or a dappled horse *Ld.-Glr.*, *Schl.* fol. 26, a; *rta-gró Sch.* a gray horse, *rta gro-dkár* a light-gray horse, *rta gro-sṅón Sch.* a dapple-gray horse, *rta gro-dmár* a roan horse, a roan; *rta rgya-bo Sch.* a chestnut-bay horse (a bayard, a brown horse) with white breast and muzzle; *rta ṅáṅ-pa* an isabel *Ld.-Glr.*; *rta rṅog-dkár* a bright bay horse; *rta-sṅo-k̔ra, rta-sṅo-tig-čan Sch.* a dapple-gray horse; *rta-sṅo-nag Sch.* a dark-gray horse; *rta-tig-k̔ra Sch.* a spotted horse; *rta nag* a black horse; *rta-brau* = *rgya-*

bo Sch.; rta-mog-ro Glr. a yellowish-brown horse; rta zag-pa Sch. a horse having gray and white spots; rta ₒól-ba Mil., Ld.-Glr., a black horse; rta ra-rá Sch. a yellow-dun horse; rta rág-pa Ld. a tawny horse (Sch.: 'a white and red spotted horse'); rta rag-rág an ash-gray horse; rta rag-sér, or rta ser-sér Sch. a yellowish-red horse; rta sram-srám Sch. a gray horse with a black mane and tail.

རྟག་པ་ rtág-pa (नित्य) 1. **perpetual, constant, lasting, eternal.** 2. **perpetuity, duration** to all futurity, a quality which, acc. to Buddhist views, can be ascribed only to the vacuum, to absolute emptiness, the *stoṅ-pa-nyid; mi rtág-pa* not durable, perishable; *de yaṅ mi-rtag ťsul-du yda* this, too, is subject to the law of perishableness *Mil.; mi rtág-pai čos* the principle of transitoriness; *rtág-par ₒdzin-pa* to look upon (transitory things, i.e. the world) as lasting, and hence: to be worldly-minded *Glr.*; as partic. one that is earthly-minded, a worldling; *nyál-ba-la rtág-pa* steady in lying, i.e. disposed to lie down, to be continually at rest, *Stg.; rtag-čad* lasting and transitory, frq.; *rtag-par*, or more frq. *rtag-tu*, **always**, i.e. 1. continually, 2. at each time (*Dzl.* ༢༤, 5); *rtág-tu-ba* perpetuity, eternity *Cs.* — *rtág-po, Ld.* *stágs-po*, **lasting**, durable, reliable, *rtag-brtan* id. *C.; rtag-snyóm-la C.* adv. uniformly, equally. — *rtag-rés ₒkór-ba Sch.:* a constant change(?).

རྟགས་ rtags (cf. *rtógs-pa*) 1. resp. *pyag-rtágs*, **sign, token, mark, characteristic,** *tag-ži* *W.*, *tags-pa* *Ld.*, id.; *rtags byéd-pa*, vulg. *tag rgyáb-pa* to make a mark; *ráb-tu byúṅ-bai rtags yód-pa* (partic.) one having the outward marks of an ecclesiastic *Glr.*; *bkra-šis rtags* v. *bkra-šis;* **omen, prognostic,** = *ltas*, *bú-mo skyé-bai rtags* a prognostic of a girl being born *Med.*; **proof** of a thing, c. genit., frq.; *mṅon-rtágs Dzl.* id.; **proof, argument, evidence,** *či tágs-pa-ne zum* *Ld.* upon what evidence have they seized him? *tágs-pa žig gos* you must prove it, *ťágs-pa-aṅ mi dug* there is no trace, no evidence, left. — 2. **inference, deduction** *Was.* (320). — 3. **the black, the centre** of a target, *W.* *tág-la čúg-če* to take for a mark. — 4. **sexual organ,** organ of generation, *rtágs-sam bhá-ga* as two synonyms for the same thing *Wdṅ.*, *pó-rtags, mó-rtags* frq. — 5. **gift, present,** resp. *pyag-rtágs.* — 6. any mark for denoting grammatical distinctions, such as terminations etc., ni f.; *rtags ₒjúg-pa* using such marks, making grammatical distinctions, seems to imply about the same thing as our etymology, the etymological part of grammar. — *rtags-yig* 1. **stamp, type**(?) *Cs.* 2. letter of recommendation, **credentials** *W.* — *tag-ril* *W.*, **lot,** *tag-ril táṅ-če* to cast or draw lots (a half-religious proceeding) cf. *rgyan.*

རྟབ་པ་ rtáb-pa, also *rtab-rtáb-pa*, and *stáb-pa*, **to be in a hurry, to be confused, frightened,** in a state of alarm, e.g. of fowl frightened by some cause (*Zam.* = *bréd-pa*); *rtáb-po* adj.; *stab-stáb-por sóṅ-nas* having become quite startled and confounded *Pth.*; *rtab-rtób* sbst., *rtab-rtób-tu náṅ-du pyin-te* she ran into the house in haste (full of joy) *Mil.*; *rtab-rtáb-la ra mi ₒdren* I cannot help you with such speed *Mil. nt.* It is also spelled *brtabs-pa.*

རྟས་པ་ rtás-pa v. *brtá-ba.*

རྟིག་གི་ rtig-gi Ts. for *rtéu*, **foal, colt.**

རྟིང་ rtiṅ (in more recent literature and col.) what is **behind** or **after**, with regard to space, and more particularly to time, *rtiṅ-du, rtiṅ-la, rtiṅ-na* adv. **afterwards,** *rtiṅ-du bčós-so* they were made afterwards, were added later *Glr.*; postp. c. genit., or less corr. c. accus., after; *byon rtiṅ-la* after their appearance *Pth.*, *byuṅ-rtiṅ* after he has come *Mil.; de-rtiṅ-la* after that *Glr.;* *tiṅ-ne ďáṅ-če* *W.* to follow, to come after or later; *rtiṅ-ma* adj. and sbst. the last *Tar.; ytám-gyi rtiṅ-ma yin* this is my last, my farewell-speech *Glr.*; without *ma:* *dus tiṅ žig-na* *W.* some day hereafter, some future day; *tiṅ-ma žag, tiṅ-ma nyi-

ma' W. the following day; *'tiṅ-ǰúg'* remaining part, the last remainder, **di-riṅ ǰa tiṅ-ǰúg len soṅ** W. to-day I have used the last of my tea. — *rtiṅ-pa* 1. the end, extremity, lowest part, e.g. of a stick *Glr.*; gen.: 2. the heel of the foot, *rtiṅ-lċags* a spur, *rtiṅ-lċags rgyáb-pa* to prick with the spurs, to spur; *rtiṅ-ču* the Achilles-tendon.

རྟིབ་པ་ *rtib-pa*, pf. *brtibs*, fut. *brtib*, imp. *rtib(s)* **to break** or **pull down** (cf. *rdib-pa*).

རྟིའུ་ *rtiu*, sometimes for *rteu*, **a foal.**

རྟུག་པ་ *rtúg-pa* 1. **excrement, dirt** *rtug-skám* or *-ském* dry excrements *Med.*; *rgyal-srid rtúg-pa bžin-du dór-ba* to throw off royalty like dirt *Pth.*; *rtúg-pa p̓yis-pai rdo* a stone for wiping one's self *Mil.* — 2. *C.* **wind, flatulence.** — 3. *(b)rtug* v. sub *tógs-pa*.

རྟུང་བ་ *rtúṅ-ba*, pf. *brtuṅs*, fut. *brtuṅ*, also *stúṅ-ba*, **to make shorter, to shorten, to contract,** e.g. a rope, a dress; *ẏnyá-ba brtuṅs* his neck is contracted *Mṅg.*

རྟུན་ *rtun* v. *ẏtun*; *rtun-ril* **a trituration-bowl** *Sch.*

རྟུན་པ་ *rtún-pa*, *brtún-pa*, **diligence,** *rtún-pa skyed-pa* to be diligent *Zam.* Cf. *dún-pa*.

རྟུལ་པོ་ *rtúl-po*, or *rtúl-ba*, **blunt, dull,** *mtson-rtúl* a blunt weapon *Cs.*; gen. fig.: *dbáṅ-po rtúl-po* (opp. to *rnón-po* or *rnó-ba* sharp, and *˳bríṅ-po* middling) dullness, stupidity, imbecility of mind; dull, stupid; *blo-rtúl* weak intellect. — *(b)rtul-p̓ód-pa* (**वीर**) boldness, courage; bold, brave *Dzl.*

རྟེའུ་ *rteu* **foal, colt,** *rteu ˳bráṅ-ba* to bring forth **a** colt, to foal *Cs.*

རྟེན་ *rten* (cf. the next article) that which contains, keeps, or supports a thing, 1. **a hold, support,** esp. in compounds: *ka-rtén* the plinth or base of a pillar *Cs.*; *rkaṅ-rtén* (resp. *žabs-rten*) a foot-stool *Cs.*; *žu-rtén* a present given to support a supplication, and never omitted by Orientals when making a petition; **sem-tén** W. token, keep-sake; — esp. **a visible representation, a statue** or **figure** of Buddha or of other divine beings, which the pious may **take** hold of, and to which their devotions are more immediately directed (v. the explanation in *Glr.* chp. II, init.) — 2. **receptacle,** resp. *ẏduṅ-rtén*, for the bones or relics of a saint, *mčód-rten* for oblations, v. *mčód-pa*, compounds; *rig-pai rten* receptacle of the soul, i.e. the body *Schr.*; *rig-pa rtén-med-pa*, *rten daṅ brál-ba* the houseless, bodiless soul *Thgr.*; *˳ǰig-rtén* v. *˳ǰig*; *snyiṅ ni ṫse srog séms-kyi rten* the heart is the seat of life and of the soul *Mṅg.*; **seat, abode, residence,** of a deity, **sanctuary, temple** (*Dzl.*), **shrine,** *rtén-gyi ẏtsó-bo* the deity residing in a shrine *Glr.*; **visible representation, symbol,** of divine objects or beings, esp. the *rten ẏsum: skú-rten* an image of Buddha, *ẏsúṅ-rten* symbol of the doctrine, gen. consisting in a volume of the holy writings, *túgs-rten* symbol of grace, a pyramid, *Köpp.* II, 294. Hence *rten* might very suitably be used for denoting the material element in the Christian sacraments, viz. the water, and the bread and wine. — 3. **present, gift,** prop. for *žú-rten* (v. sub no. 1), and then in a more general sense, resp. *p̓yag-rtén*, W., for *p̓yag-rtágs*; also **offering, oblation.** — 4. **sex,** specified as male, female, or hermaphrodite, independently of age *S.g.*; sometimes comprising age *S.g.*; or denoting age alone, as child, man, old man *Lt.*; **calling, situation** in life *Tar.* 163, 15 (where *gyi* ought to be changed into *ni*) 176, 15; 178, 18; some compounds follow still at the end of the next article.

རྟེན་པ་ *rtén-pa* 1. vb., pf. and fut. *brten*, imp. *rton* (*brten?*), **to keep, to hold, to adhere to, to lean on,** *˳k̓ár-ba-la* on a staff *Pth.*; *ká-ba-la* against a pillar; *lág-pa ˳grám-pa-la* to lean one's head on one's hand, in meditating *Dzl.*; fig. **to depend** or **rely on,** *brtén-pai blá-ma* the priest to whom one holds; *snúm-la rtén-pa* to keep to the fat, i.e. to eat much fat *Med.*; *˳krig-pai čós-la* **to be given, addicted,** to sensuality; **ču táṅ-wa máṅ-po-la tén-ne** *C.* if one is intent on watering; *ₒtsó-ba dka-šúb-la* v. *dká-ba* compounds; *k̔yéd-kyis γsúṅ-ba-la brtén-nas* following, obeying (your) orders *Glr.*; *ṅai nús-pa-la rtén-nas* relying on my strength, i.e. by the help of my strength (you will be able to get to that place) *Mil.*; hence (*b*)*rtén-nas* is frq. used for: in consequence of, with respect to, concerning etc.: *rkyen dé-la rtén-nas* in consequence of this event (the doctrine spread) *Tar.* 8, 1; **gha-la tén-nas** why? wherefore? *C.*; *yul k̔yád-par-čan-la rtén-nas* (to sin) with regard to a noble object *Thgy.*; **to hang on, to depend on, to arise** or **issue from**; *rtéṅ-par ₒbrél-ba* v. *rten-ₒbrél*; **to be near, to border on,** **tén-te yod* W.* (the two villages) are contiguous to each other; = *γtád-pa, stón-pa* to be directed, to be situated, to lie towards, *lhó-p̔yogs-la* to be situated towards the south *Sambh.*; *ₒod-zér-la rtén-nas γzígs-pa* to look after or pursue with one's eye a ray of light, like *γtód-pa* I. 3. Cf. *stén-pa.* — 2. sbst. **that which holds, keeps up,** *rgyál-poi rtén-pao* (these) are **the supports** of kings *Dzl.*; *brtén-pa rús-pai γnás-lugs bstán-pa* 'the doctrine of the hold-giving bones', osteology *Mṅg.* 3. adj. attached to, faithful *C.*

Comp. *rtén-grogs, tse hril-por ₒgrógs-pai rtén-grogs* perh. erron. for *γtán-grogs.* — *rtén-γnas Gram.*: the case which denotes the place of a thing or person, **the locative.** — *rten-ₒbrél*, or in full: *rtén-par ₒbrél-bar ₒgyúr-ba* or *ₒbyúṅ-ba* 'the coming to pass in continuous connection' (the explanation of *Burn.* I, 623 is grammatically not quite correct) i.e.: 1. in a general sense: **the connection between cause and effect**; in a special sense, the Buddhist doctrine of the *rten-ₒbrel bču-γnyis*, **निदान**, the twelve causes of existence *Wdk.* 551 (with illustrations); *Schl.* 23, *Burn.* I. 485, *Köpp.* I., 609. 2. **the auspices** of an undertaking, in as much as the complete knowledge of the causal connection of things implies also a certain prescience of future events; *rten-ₒbrél rtóg-pa* to investigate the auspices, *šés-pa* to know them, (a physician e.g., when treating a patient, must try to find out the auspices) *Med.*; *rten-ₒbrél bzaṅ* or *legs* good auspices, *ṅan* bad auspices, frq.; so also frq. col. — *rtén-ma* **prop, support, pillar** *S.g.*, **tén-šiṅ* W.* a pole used as a prop; *rtén-sa Mil.?*

རྟོག་གེ་བ་ *rtóg-ge-ba* (**तर्क**) the act of **arguing, reasoning; dialectics** *Cs.*; *Sch.* distrust, suspicion (?); *k̔a-bšád rtóg-geï slób-dpon* seems to describe a teacher who talks in a hypocritical manner with a mere appearance of wisdom. — *rtóg-ge-pa* an arguer, disputer, reasoner, dialectician *Cs.*

རྟོག་པ་ *rtóg-pa* I. vb., pf. *brtags* (*rtogs* q.v.), *brtag*, imp. *rtog(s)*, 1. **to consider, examine, search into, look through,** c.a. (also dat.), *brtágs-na mi šes* though one meditates (upon the soul), one cannot understand or fathom it *Mil.*; frq. with a single or double indirect question: to examine whether (or whether not); *brtag-dpyód* (or *rtóg-γžig*) *γtóṅ-ba Pth*, *Mil.* id.; *brtags-dpyód* examination, trial *Zam.*; c. termin. **to discern, to recognize** as, e.g. *mk̔rís-par brtag* it is ascertained to be bile, to be caused by bile *Med.*; *so-sór rtóg-pa Stg.* prob. to recognize as being different. — 2. **to muse, to ruminate,** to trouble one's head about a thing, which is considered a fault much to be guarded against, and the more so, as religious faith as well as meditation require the mind to be strictly directed and entirely devoted to the one subject in question; hence *ma-rtóg tiṅ-ₒdzin Mil.* contemplation without any disturbing reflections and by-thoughts; cf. no. II. — 3. v. *dog-pa.*

II. sbst. 1. **consideration, deliberation, reflection,** cf. I., 2; *rtóg-pa skyé-ba, rtóg-pa-la ₒjúg-pa* to reflect on a thing, to indulge in musings *Dzl.* — 2. **scruple, hesitation,** *rtóg-pa skyés-te* to grow doubtful, hesitating *Mil.*; *rtog(-pa)-med(-pa)* simple, unsophisticated; simplicity; singleness of heart. — *dé-la rtog-ₒjúg mi byed Glr.* he does not meddle with that.

རྟོགས་པ་ *rtógs-pa* (prop. the pf. of *rtóg-pa*, like *novi* of *nosco*) 1. vb. **to per-**

ceive, to know, to understand, *dpyád-na ma rtógs-so* they did not understand, though they inquired into it *Dzl.*; *rtógs-par °gyúr-ba* to obtain information, to convince one's self of a thing *Dzl.*; *rtógs-par byéd-pa* to teach, to demonstrate, to convince a person of *Dzl.*; *má-rtógs-pa* stupid, ignorant; ignorance *Mil.* — 2. sbst. (but in Tibetan always construed as an infinitive with the accus. inst. of the genit., and with an adv. inst. of an adj.) **knowledge, perception, cognition,** frq.; *sems rtógs-pa* the knowledge of (one's own) soul *Mil.*; *mṅón-par rtógs-pa* (**अभिसमय**) clear understanding or perception, in modern Buddhism the same as *stoṅ-pa-nyid Trig.* 21. — *rtógs-pa-čan, rtogs-ldán* rich in knowledge *Mil.* — *rtógs-(pa) brjód(-pa)*, for **अवदान** cf. *Burn.* I. 64, a moral legend. — *rtogs-spyód* theory and practise, *rtogs-spyód byéd-pa* to know and to do, *rtogs-spyód la mk̔ás-pa* theoretically and practically religious. — *rtógs-°dod-čan* desirous of knowing or learning, inquisitive *Mil.* — Sometimes for *togs-pa.*

རྟོད་པ་, གཏོད་པ་, བཏོད་པ་ *rtód-pa, ytód-pa, btód-pa* 1. sbst., also *rtod-p̔úr,* **a stake,** in the ground, for teddering a horse, for securing a boat etc.; **a peg,** in a wall, for hanging up things; *rtod-t̔ág* a tedder (v. *btod-pa*); *rtód-pa brgyáb-pa* to drive in a stake or peg 2. vb. **to tedder, fasten, secure** *Dzl.*

རྟོན་པ་, བརྟོན་པ་, བརྟན་པ་ *rtón-pa, brtón-pa, brtán-pa,* with or without *yid,* ccd., **to place confidence in a person, to rely on.**

རྟོལ་ *rtol? čos-rtól Tar.* 164, 20, *Schf.* the pith or marrow of a doctrine; *rtól-skyes-kyi šés-pa Mil.?* — *brtól-šes-pa Tar.* 197, 8, *Schf.* to know thoroughly.

རྟོལ་ *rtol Cs., rtol-góg Lex.* w.e.; *Sch.*: **a bastard,** an animal of a mixed breed, *rtól-po* a male, *rtól-mo* a female bastard *Cs.*; acc. to Desgodins the cross-breed of a yak-bull and a *°gar-mo.* Cf. *ltor.*

རྟོལ་བ་ *rtól-ba,* pf. *brtol* (*Ld.* *stól-če*) 1. **to bore, to pierce,** to bore into, cci. & t., *Stg.*; to bore through, **to perforate** cca., a board etc., *sgo-ṅa* the shell of an egg (of chickens creeping out) *Sch.*, **to open** (an abscess) by a puncture; **to make an incision;** *bi-gaṅ* *W.* to bore a hole. — 2. **to come to, to get to, to arrive at,** *ynás-su* to (at) a place *Lex.* (cog. to *tál-ba, tél-ba*); *yoṅs-°dus-brtol Lex.* w.e.; *Tar.* 30, 22, *Schf.*: **पारिजातक.** the coral-tree, Erythrina indica; also a tree of paradise. (In *Dzl.* ༡༥༢, 13 the manuscript of Kyelang has: *dé-dag-las rtól-ba* it outpassed them).

ལྟ་ *lta* 1. more correctly *blta,* v. sub *ltá-ba,* I. 1., **we will see,** *Mil.*, frq. — 2. in various phrases and expressions, in which its special signification is no longer clearly discernible: a. *lta či smos Dzl.* and elsewh., the most frq. form, *lta smos či dgos Thgy.*, *lta smos či °tsal* (eleg.) *Stg.*, *W.* more distinctly: *lta dgos či yod*, also *zer dgos či yod*, **far from, not to mention, to say nothing of, how much less, how much more;** with a preceding infinitive or noun: *°di-dag °dul-ba lta či smos* to say nothing of the conversion of these! how much easier is it to convert these! *Dzl.*; *°o-skol lta či smos* how much more we! *Thgy.*; *lta žog* is much the same: *lo zlá-ba lta žog* to say nothing of years and months; *tar žog, tá-la žog* *C.* id. — b. the word is frq. used after participles or adjectives ending with *pa,* when, judging in each case from the connection in which it happens to stand, it may be deemed equivalent to: **evidently, indeed, thus then** etc., spoken either with emphasis, or ironically, or in a sorrowful tone. As it is next to impossible to learn from the Tibetans the exact import of those little words, which slightly modify the grammatical and logical relations of a sentence, European translators have generally passed them over. Cf. *Dzl.* ༡༠༠, 18, ༡༣༦, 2 (where a shad ought to be added), ༤༢, 7 (where *ste* means though), ༢༦༩, 18; *Tar.* 7, 17, 19. In *Dzl.* ༡༠༢, 7 *lta,* in accordance with the manuscript of Kyelang, is to be omitted. — c. **like, as,** (*ltá-ba* sbst. abstr., *ltá-bu* adj., *ltá-bur* or *ltar* adv.), *dú-ba ltá-bur yol-*

pa žig one having the nature or the colour of smoke *Glr.; rta bčus rgyúg-pa ltá-bui sgra* a noise as if ten horses were galloping *Glr.;... ltá-bu mḱás-pa žig* a man as wise as ... *Dzl.; p̓a-má ltá-bur gyúr-to* he was (to him) like a father *Dzl.; bai dzí-ma ltá-bù daṅ ldán-te* having eye-lashes like those of a cow *Stg.; ráṅ-la mi-mḱó-ba bú-la byiṅ-pa ltá-bu ma yin* not as if she (the mother) would give her child only what she does not want herself *Thgy.*; *žés-pa ltá-buo* is the usual expression for quoting a passage from an author, and always follows the quotation; *ḱyod ṅá-lta-bu min* you are not my equal, and also: you are not in my situation *Mil.; ˳dí-lta-bu, dé-lta-bu*, one like him, such a one as he; *či-lta-bu* what sort of? *saṅs-rgyas šes byá-ba či-lta-bu yin* the so-called Buddha, what sort of being is he? what is meant by 'Buddha'? *Dzl. či-lta-bu-la bskal-pa žes bgyi* what sort of a thing is called 'Kalpa'? *ǰi-lta-bá* v. *ǰi*; *ǰi-lta-bu* of what kind, as a rel. pron. Sometimes *lta* alone is used for *lta-bu: ḱyód-lta* your equal *Mil.*; so prob. also in the passage *Dzl.* ༡༥༧, 8, where *yód-pa lta či mtoṅ* would be = *yód-pa ltá-bu gaṅ mtoṅ* (better than taking *lta či mtoṅ* for *lta či smos Schf.*). In *Dzl.* ༢༧༥, 13, and ༢༧༧, 3 *ltá-žig* is prob. to be altered into *ltá-žog*, v. sub a, 2, above. — d. *lta* is sometimes a mere expletive, e.g. in *dá-lta* (v. *da*), and after the conditional *na* (*Dzl.* ༡༥༦, 1; ༧༦, b; ༡༢, 16, ༢༡༤, b.).

ལྟ་བ་ *ltá-ba* I. vb., pf. *bltas*, fut. *blta*, imp. *ltos, blta*, resp. *γzigs-pa* (cf. *ltos-pa*) 1. **to look** (as an act of the will, cf. *mtóṅ-ba*), **to view**, often with *mig*, or *mig-gis* (v. below); *bltás-na mi mtoṅ* though you look (for it) you do not see it *Mil.*; **nán-tan žib-ča ltos** *Ld.* look at it accurately! **tọ šig** *C.* look (before you)! have your eyes open! **tọ šig nyọn čig** *C.* attention! mind! be careful! *ltá-bas čog mi šés* I never can look enough at it; with *nas:* to look from or through, *sgo-séṅ-nas* (to peep) through the narrow opening of a door *Tar.*; *bltá-na sdúg-pa* pleasing when looked upon, charming to look at; also n. of the city of gods on the Riráb *Stg.*, and of one of the seven golden mountains around the Rirab *Glr.; ltá-ru soṅ* go there and look (at it)! **lta-la toṅ** *W.* let me look (at it)! show it me! *p̓an-tsun-du ltá-ba* to look around *Dzl.*; **čog-čóg-la**, or **yẹ-yón-la** col. id.; *p̓yi mig*, or *p̓yir* (to look) back *Dzl.*; **p̓i mig log lta-čẹ**, or **ǰiṅ-pa gyúr-te ltá-čẹ** *W.* id.; **to inspect**, ccd., rarely c.a., frq. *Glr., Dzl.; ḱyed mi-nús-pa-la bltás-na* if one views, considers, your inability *Dzl.; ṅas ma bltas-na* if I do not inspect it *Glr.*; **ghdáṅ-la tẹ ruṅ** *C.* whatever one may fix his eyes upon = whatever it may be; **to look after** or **into, to revise, to examine, to try,** *rtsa ltá-ba* to feel a person's pulse *Med.*; *p̓án-nam blta* I will see, if I can help *Mil.*; also: I will see, whether it has done good; *su če blta* let us see who is taller *Mil.*; *e' tsud ltos šig* see, if you can put it through *Glr.; rtiṅ-sor blta* we shall see that afterwards *Mil.; yáṅ-dag-par ltá-ba* to examine or search into minutely *Mil.;* **tsod ltá-ba** in col. language is the expression most in use for **to examine,** to put to the proof, **to test, to try, to sound** etc. Lastly, as a mere act of the mind: **to meditate, reflect, muse, ponder, investigate,** *du ˳dug blta* let us see how many there are *Mil.*; *lta rtog byéd-pa*, or *γtóṅ-ba Mil.* to investigate closely. Also in a mystic sense, v. *sgóm-pa* I, 2. — 2. ccd. (or accus.) and termin., to look upon a thing as, *šés-pa-la zóg-tu* to look upon knowledge as deceitful; *dkon-mčóg γsum mi bdén-par ltá-ba* to think the three treasures to be untrue, not real, = not to believe in them. — 3. c. dat. (rarely termin.): **to have regard to, to pay attention to, to take notice of,** and with a negative: **to be indifferent to, not to care about,** *sróg-la mi ltá-ba* not to care about one's life (from heroism or desperation). — 4. **to be situated** or **directed towards,** *mdo ni núb-tu lta* the lower part of the valley is situated towards the west. — 5. *ṅas bltás-pa* in my opinion;

ṅá-la bltás-na(s), or rtén-nas, with regard to me, as for me, for my sake *Glr.*; γžán-ma-rnams-la bltás-pas as far as the others are concerned, with regard to the others *Glr.* —

II. sbst. 1. the act of **looking, beholding,** v. I, 1. 2.; *ltá-ba yáṅs-šiṅ* circumspect *Glr.* — 2. **contemplation** (mystical) v. *sgóm-pa* I, 2. — 3. (**दर्शन**) **opinion, doctrine, theory, philosophical system, school** (in Tibetan a verb, cf. *rtógs-pa* II), *rtág-par ltá-ba* the theory of perpetual duration (of earthly things); *ṅán-par ltá-ba* a false opinion, = *lta-lóg.*

Comp. *lta-nyúl-pa* **a spy, scout,** *lta-nyúl byéd-pa* to spy, to explore, v. *nyúl-ba.* — *lta-stáṅs*, resp. *γzig-stáṅs Pth.* **the look,** or manner of looking, air, mien, *ži-bai lta-stáṅs* a mild look, or countenance, *Cs.*; *k̔ró-bai lta-stáṅs* an angry or fierce look *Cs.*; esp. the magical and powerful look of a saint, *lta-stáṅs šig mdzád-pa* to cast such a magical look *Mil.*; *lta-stáṅs-la bžúgs-pa, lta-stáṅs-kyi ṅáṅ-nas čá-ba Mil.* to sit, or stride along, with such a look, i.e. with great solemnity of deportment, as of one in a trance; *lta-stáṅs-bži* the four magical looks, viz.: *ˌgúgs-pai lta-stáṅs* the attracting look, *skród-pai lta-stáṅs* the repulsive look, *lhúṅ-bai lta-staṅs* the precipitating look, *réṅs-pai lta-stáṅs* the paralyzing look *Cs.*; also *séṅ-geï, gláṅ-po-čeï lta-stáṅs-kyis γzigs-pa* to look at a person with a lion's look, with an elephant's look. — *lta-lóg,* in later lit. and col. *lóg-lta,* **false sentiment,** not only false doctrine, heresy, but any irreligious impulses of the mind, perverse and sinful thoughts, e.g. *lóg-lta skyés-te* is used for conspiring against a person's life *Glr.*, giving way to doubt or weakness of faith *Glr.*, falling in love with a woman *Pth.*; *mi-la lóg-lta byéd-pa* to slander, to abuse a person *Glr.*

ལྟག་ལྕིན་ *ltag-lčin* **puff-ball** *Sch.*

ལྟག་པ་ *ltág-pa* 1. the back part of the neck, **nape** *Med.* and elsewh., frq. — 2. **the upper part** or **place,** *grál-gyi* of the divan, the seat of honour *Dzl.* — 3. **the back,** *gri-ltag* the back of a knife. — 4. *ltag ˌog-sgyúr-ba* to turn upside down *Dzl.*; *ltág-na(s), ltag,* **above,** *sgó-ltag* above the door, *gróṅ-ltag dgón-pa Mil.* the convent above and behind the village, the front-side of the houses being gen. turned towards the valley and the river; thus 'behind' is equivalent to 'higher up'; *ltág-na-med-pa* (of rare occurrence) for *blá-na-med-pa* the highest, **अनुत्तम**; *ltag skór-ba* to strangle, to suffocate *Glr.*; *ltag γčód-pa* 1. *Cs.* to cut off a man's neck, to behead. 2. *W.* to make a person change his mind, to alter his sentiments; **ṅe k̔ó-la gyóg-pa tag čad yin** I hope I shall talk him out of it, shall dissuade him from doing it; *ltag nyal-ba* to lie backward *Sch.*

Comp. *ltág-sgo* the back-door of a house, v. above. — *ltag-γčód* or *-čód* 1. **decapitation,** 2. *Sch.*: **changeable, fickle, inconstant.** *ltag-čú Med.; Sch.*: 'sinew of the neck, the covering of the neck'. — *ltag-mdúd Sch., ltag-sdúd Lt.*, the hole in the occiput, the connexion of the brain with the spinal marrow. — *ltág-spu* neck-hair, **mane,** of the horse, of the lion *Ld.-Glr.* — *ltág-ma* what is uppermost, e.g. words written over other words.

ལྟང་ *ltaṅ* 1. **a bale** of goods, carried on one side of a beast of burden, half a load, *ltaṅ γnyis* two bales, or a whole load. — 2. also *lteṅ*, *W.*: **through, quite through,** **p̔í-sta-ne náṅ-la ltaṅ toṅ dug** one sees from the outside into the interior; **ltaṅ bug toṅ** bore through! **ltaṅ t̔óṅ-te ča dug** he is passing through, he does not make a stay here. — Cf. *toṅ.*

ལྟད་མོ་ *ltád-mo,* col. also **ltán-mo**, resp. *γzigs-mo*, the looking on, **a sight, scene, spectacle,** *ltád-mo-la ˌtsogs* they came together in order to look on *Glr.*; *ltád-mo ltá-ba* to look at a scene, to be an eye-witness; *ltád-mo ltá-bai sa* a place where there is something to be seen; a theatre. — *ltád-mo-k̔aṅ* a playhouse, exhibition, puppet-show etc. — *ltád-mo-pa Pth.*, **ltád-mo-lta-mi**, **ltád-mo-la yóṅ-k̔an**

W., a spectator, a visitor; *ltád-mo-mḱan*, *ltád-mo stón-pa* a showman, actor, mimic etc. — *gróṅ-yul-gyi ltád-mo ma dran žig Mil.* forget the scenes of village life!

ལྟབ་པ་ *ltáb-pa*, pf. *bltabs*, fut. *bltab*, imp. *ltob* (*W.* **ltabs toṅ**), **to fold** or **gather up, to lay** or **put together**, **kyaṅ-tab, nyi-tab tub-če** *W.* to fold single, to fold double; *γsúm-ltab byéd-pa* to fold or bend together threefold, e.g. a corpse previous to cremation; *ltáb-ma Cs.* **a fold, crease, plait;** *ltab-gri* a clasp knife.

ལྟམ(ས)་པ་ *ltám(s)-pa*, pf. *bltams*, fut. *bltam*, 1. **to be full**, also *γtáms-pa*. — 2. resp. **to be born**, *skyéd-pai yab daṅ bltáms-pai yum* the father by whom one is begotten, and the mother by whom one is born *Pth.*

ལྟར་ *ltar* 1. also *bltar*, supine of *ltá-ba*, **in order to see;** *bltár-ruṅ-ba* visible; *Sch.*: 'pleasing to the eye'; *gaṅ ltár-na yaṅ, či ltár-na yaṅ*, be that as it may *Glr.* — 2. postp. c. a., **like, as**, after the manner of, *rí-ltar* like a mountain; *ṕyag byéd-pa ltar byéd-pa* to make a saluting gesture *Glr.*; *ṅo-šes ruṅ mi šés-pa ltar byas* although they knew . . ., they affected not to know . . . *Mil.*; *ḥbral mi ṕód-pa ltar yód-na yaṅ* being like one that cannot part with, = being scarcely able to part with, *Glr.*; *ltar snáṅ-ba* to appear like, hence prob. *ltar-snáṅ* appearance, similarity *Sch.*, (*Lex.* w.e.); *lúṅ-bstan-pa ltar* (to do a thing) in conformity with a prediction *Tar.*; also *ltár-na*, and *ltár-du*, *mi-lo ltár-na . . . yod* computed by human or terrestrial years it amounts to . . . *Thgy.*; *bód-rnams ltár-na* according to Tibetan (sources) *Tar.*; *čí-ltar(-na)* how? in what manner or way? *čí-ltar* also serves to paraphrase the English 'so that', e.g. 'he played so that all were enraptured' is thus expressed: he played — how did he play? — all were enraptured; *ǰí-ltar(-na)* as *ǰí-lta ǰí-ltar . . . dé-lta dé-ltar Sambh.* even as . . . so; *ḥdí-ltar, dé-ltar(-na)* so, thus, in that manner; *ḥdí-ltar mi rgan ḱyod* such an old fellow as you are; frq. also in referring to the words of others, where we use 'that': *dé-ltar bdén-na* if that is true.

ལྟར་ལྟར་པོ་ *ltár-ltar-po Lex., Cs.*: of a liquid nature, as an embryo first in the womb.

ལྟས་ *ltas* **prognostic, omen,** more distinctive *sṅá-ltas;* **miraculous sign, miracle, prodigy,** more accurately: *ṅo-mtsár-bai ltas; bkra-šís-pai ltas* a propitious omen; *rmí-ltas bzáṅ-po* a good sign in a dream *Pth.*; *dgé-ltas* a favourable sign; *ṅán-ltás*, or *ltas-ṅán* a bad sign *Dzl.*; *ltás-mḱan* a soothsayer, fortune-teller; *ltas stón-pa* to soothsay *Cs.*

ལྟི་རི་ *ltí-ri* **pitcher** *Sch.*

ལྟིག་ཐུང་ *ltig-túṅ C.* a person of small stature, perh. a corruption of *lte-túṅ*.

ལྟིབ་པ་ *ltib-pa* to fall through *Sch.*

ལྟིར་བ་ *ltir-ba* v. *ldir-ba*.

ལྟུང་བ་ *ltúṅ-ba* 1. vb., pf. *lhuṅ*, **to fall, to fall off, down, into;** fig.: *mtó-ba de yaṅ mtar lhúṅ-ṅo* what is high will finally fall down *Dzl.*; more esp. to fall into sin, to commit sin, hence *nyés-ltuṅ* an actual sin, a sinful deed, *ltúṅ-byed* a transgression, crime; also *ṅán-soṅ-du* (v. *ḥgró-ba* I, 5), or *dmyál-bar* to fall into damnation. — 2. sbst. **the fall,** esp. the moral fall, *ltúṅ-bas gós-pa* polluted by sin; *ltúṅ-ba bšágs-pa* confession of sin.

ལྟེ་བ་ *lté-ba* 1. **navel-string, umbilical cord,** *γčód-pa* to cut it *Med.* — 2. **navel,** *lté-bai ḱúṅ(bu) Lt.* id.; *glá-bai lté-ba* musk-bag. — 3. the middle of a thing, **centre,** *dkyil-ḥkor-gyi* of a circle; *mu-ḱyúd γsúm-gyi lté-bar* in the middle of three (concentric) circles *Lt.*; *raṅ-ťág-gi lté-ba* the axle-tree of a water-wheel *Glr.*; *sai lté-ba* the centre of the earth, in the opinion of the natives: *Tibet*; also cognomen of several fabulous kings of Tibet *Köpp.* II., 52. — *lté-ba γžuṅ-ráṅ* Lhasa, or, in a more special sense, the palace of the Dalai Lama — *lte-túg W.* = **tig-túṅ** *C.*

ལྟེང་ *lteṅ* 1. v. *ltaṅ*. — 2. *lteṅ-rgyás* n. of a Buddha.

ལྟེང་ཀ་ *ltèṅ-ka* **pool, pond** *Dzl.*

ལྟེབ་པ་ *ltéb-pa* (cog. to *ltáb-pa*), **to double down, to turn in,** *mla*, or *snè-mo* to hem, by turning in the edge, cf. *snè-mo*.

ལྟེམ་རྒྱང་ *ltem-rgyáṅ* **humour, whim, caprice,** *ltem-rgyáṅ byéd-pa* to be whimsical or capricious *Cs.*

ལྟེམ་པ་ *ltém-pa* the state of being full, e.g. a vessel full of water; **full, overflowing,** *ltém-po* full; *ltem-ltém* so full that it runs over.

ལྟོ་ *lto*, seldom *ltó-ba* (*C.*, *Mil.*) 1. **food, victuals,** *lto(b)za-ba* 1. to eat, *lto yaṅ ma zos* he did not eat anything *Glr.*; 2. to gain or get one's living *C.*; *ltó-la byin* give him to eat! *Lt.*; *lúg-la lto ster* feed the sheep; *lto γyó-ba* to prepare food *Mil.*; **to nyo šrog tsoṅ** *C.* he risks his life in order to procure food; *gla-ltó* wages and food; *lto-gós*, *lto-rgyáb*, food and clothes *Mil.*; *lto-rgyab-skyid Lex.* prob. food, clothes, and good health (comfort); **dha tó-če za gyu yin** *C.* now I will go and eat (something). — *lto-čúṅ*, *lto-rán Sch.*: a person temperate in eating. — *ltó-ₒdun-čan* **an epicure, parasite, sponger.** — *lto-žiṅ* provision ground which a person receives for his subsistence. — *žím-lto-čan* dainty-mouthed, lickerish. — 2. **goat's beard,** Tragopogon, used as a kitchen-vegetable.

ལྟོ་བ་ *ltó-ba* **belly, stomach;** also the belly of a bottle; *ltó-ba sá-la ₒbébs-pa* to prostrate one's self.

Comp. *lto-gáṅ* a full belly, also: with a full belly or stomach. — *ltó-ₒgro*, *ltós-ₒgró* 1. moving or creeping on the belly, **a worm, a snake.** 2. symb. num.: 8. — *lto(-ba)-ₒgróg(-pa) Cs.*: 'belly-fretting, a nervous excitement of the belly'. — *lto-stóṅ* with an empty stomach, **jejune, empty.** — *lto-ldir* belly of a vessel, *ltó-ldir-čan* swelling out, bellied, like vessels. — *ltó-na-ba*, *ltó-zug* stomach-ache. — *lto-ₒp̔yé* crawling or creeping on the belly, a snake; *lto-ₒp̔ye čén-po*, महोरग, a fabulous monster of the serpent kind, similar to the klu.

ལྟོག་འདྲེ་ *ltog-ₒdré* **a demon** *Sch.*; *ₒdre-ltógs* prob. the same.

ལྟོགས་པ་ *ltógs-pa* I. vb. 1. **to be hungry,** *ltógs-so* I am hungry *Cs.*, *ltógs-su ₒbór-ba* to suffer a person to hunger, to starve *Dzl.* — 2. *Sch.*: **to regret,** *ltogs nyal ma byeb* do not always lie in grief and regret! *Sch.* (?); *ltógs-par bžúgs-pa* resp. to be full of regret.

II. sbst. **hunger.**

III. adj. **hungry,** *séms-čan ltógs-pa-rnams Dzl.*; *ltógs-par ₒgyúr-ba* to grow hungry; *ltógs-gri Mil*, col. **ltóg-ri** *W.* hunger, **ṅa(-la) ltóg-ri rag** I am hungry, **k̔yod (-la) ltóg-ri rag** you are hungry, **k̔o ltóg-pa yod** he is hungry. — *ltogs-p̔yúg* hunger (i.e. poverty) and wealth *Glr.* — *ltog-tsór* the feeling of hunger, *ltogs-tsor če* I am very hungry *Mil.*

ལྟོང་ག་ *ltóṅ-ga* **notch, incision, indentation,** *mdá-ltoṅ* the notch in an arrow; **a depression,** *ri-tóṅ* in a ridge of mountains, *la-tóṅ* the indentation of a mountain-pass.

ལྟོངས་ *ltoṅs* **summit** *Mil.*, frq.

ལྟོབ་ *ltob* v. *ltáb-pa*.

ལྟོར་ *ltor*, *sras-ltór* a bastard prince *Glr.*

ལྟོས་ *ltos* 1. v. *lta-ba*. 2. *Sch.* = *γtos*.

ལྟོས་པ་ *ltós-pa* 1. vb., = *ltá-ba*, **to look** at, on, or to, c.d., *γnyén-po-la ma ltós-par* without looking to a spiritual guide *Thgy.*; *k̔yod dé-la ltos mi dgos-pa žig yin* you need not care for that *Mil.*; *ré-žiṅ ltós-pa Glr.* to look at (a thing) hopefully; *dé-la ltós-na* if I look at, consider, this *Mil.*, if one compares this with… *Thgy.*; **(s)ṅá-ltos či-čug (?) tsáṅ-ma čó-k̔an** *W.* a person acting with great circumspection. — 2. sbst. **the looking** at or on, *ltós-pa méd-par* without looking at it (e.g. in playing at dice); **relation, respect, regard** *Cs.*

སྟ་གོན་ *sta-gón* **preparation, arrangement,** *sta-gón byéd-pa* to make preparations, to prepare, arrange, fit out; *ₒtsó-*

bai sta-gón-la bžeṅs he rose to make preparations for dinner *Mil.*

སྟ་ཟུར་ *sta-zúr* **hip, hip-bone,** e.g. as the seat of strength *Mil.*; *stá-zúr yan-čád* from the hip upward *Dzl.*

སྟ་རི་ *sta-rí W.*, originally *sta-grí Mil.* and *C.*, *sta-ré B.*, **axe, hatchet**; *dgrá-sta* battle-axe *Lex.*; *star-ltág Cs.* the back of an axe or hatchet, *star-míg* the hole for putting the handle in, *star-yú* the handle, *star-só* the edge of an axe.

སྟག་ *stag* 1. **tiger**, *rgya-stág* the Bengal tiger *Mil.*; *stag-ṗrúg* a young tiger, *stág-mo* a tigress; *stag-ťsán* a tiger's den; *stag-rís* the stripes of a tiger's skin. — 2. *Tar.* 166, 2?

སྟག་ཆས་ *stag-čás Mil.* utensils carried by men about them, such as a knife, smoking-implements, weapons etc.

སྟག་པ་ *stág-pa* **birch-tree**; *stág-ma* n. of another tree.

སྟག་གཟིག་ *stag-γzíg* a not unfrequent form (which prob. has been adapted to Tibetan etymology) for *ta-zíg*, **Persia, Persian.**

སྟག་ཤ་ *stag-ša* a medicinal herb, *Glr.*, *Med.*; *stag-ša-dé-ba Glr.*

སྟག་ཤར་ *stag-šár* **a youth, young man** *C.*, *Mil.*

སྟང་ཟིལ་ *staṅ-zíl Cs.*: n. of a black stone, acc. to *Zam.* a silver-ore.

སྟངས་ *staṅs*, *Sch.* also *stáṅ-ka*, **manner, style, posture,** *góm-pai staṅs* manner of walking, gait; *brdég-staṅs byéd-pa* to assume a fighting posture *Mil.*; *ltá-staṅs* v. *ltá-ba* comp.; *stón-pai bžúgs-staṅs* the sitting posture of Buddha; *C.*: **ko ghó-ghon-taṅ dé-mo** his style of dressing is fine, he is well dressed; **tám-zer-taṅ ké-pa** eloquent; even like a mere termination for forming verbal substantives: **zá-taṅ**, or **túṅ-taṅ lég-mo** good eating, drinking.

སྟད་པ་ *stád-pa*, pf. and fut. *bstad*, imp. *stod*, **to put on, to lay on,** *rtá-la sga* to put the saddle on a horse, to saddle; *rtá-la ˳gró-čas* to load the baggage on a horse.

སྟན་ *stan* **mat, carpet,** esp. a carpet for sitting on, also **a cushion,** resp. *bžúgs-γdan;* **saddle-cloth**; *stan ˳díṅ-ba* to spread a mat (on the ground), *˳gébs-pa* to lay (a mat) on; **ču-stán** swaddling-cloth *W.*; **bol-tén** mattress, **ṭul-tén** (lit. *ṗrul-stán*) a light travelling-mattress *C.*; sometimes substratum of any kind, also of hard materials, e.g. *γtsub-stán*, *btsab-stán.*

སྟབ་ *stab* 1. v. *rtab.* — 2. *Sch.*: *stab stáṅs-pa* to suffer, to tolerate, to yield.

སྟབས་ *stabs* (cog. to *ťabs*, also syn. of *staṅs*), **mode, manner, way, measure,** *séṅ-gei stábs-kyis* (or *su*) *˳gró-ba* to walk in the manner of a lion; *gar-stábs* v. *gar*; **opportunity,** *˳byón-stabs* an opportunity for going; **tábs-si ká-na** (also **ká-ne*, or *ká-la**) *W.* when an opportunity offers; *ríṅs-stabs-su* hastily, speedily *Mil.*; **kón-stabs** dearth, famine, want *Ld.*; **ríṅ-stabs** a describing at full length, copiousness (*stabs*, in this instance, corresponds to the English termination 'ness', changing the adj. into an abstract noun).

སྟར་ *star*, for *sta-ri* q.v.

སྟར་ཀ་ *stár-ka Sch.*, *stár-ga Lex.*, *stár-ka Glr.*, **walnut,** *star-(gai) šiṅ*, *ljón-šiṅ stár-ka* walnut-tree *Glr.*; *star-skógs* nutshell; *star-sdóṅ* trunk of a walnut-tree. *stár-ka byéd-pa Ld.-Glr. Schl.* f. 15, b (?).

སྟར་བ་ *stár-ba*, pf. and fut. *bstar*, imp. *stor*, 1. **to file** on a string, e.g. pearls; **to tie fast, to fasten to,** e.g. sheep to a rope, in a bivouac, *stár-la rgyúd-pa* id. — 2. **to clean, to polish** *Lex.* — 3. *Sch.*: **to ornament, decorate** (?).

སྟར་བུ་ *stár-bu*, or *star-žún Med.*, frq., the berries of Hippophaë rhamnoides, a shrub or tree very frequent in Tibet; acc. to a *Lex.* also a kind of Rumex in India.

སྟི་བ་ *stí-ba*, pf. *bstis*, fut. *bsti*, imp. *stis*, 1. **to rest, to repose, to refresh** one's self, *sti-(bai) γnas* resting-place. — 2. **to honour** (?); (*b*)*sti-stáṅ* **honour, respect, reverence,** *byéd-pa* ccd., to show a person honour, frq.; **kó-la ti-táṅ čaṅ med** *W.* he is not esteemed at all, he enjoys no credit whatever; *bkúr-sti* id., v. *bkúr-ba.*

ཐྱིང་བ་ *stiṅ-ba*, pf. *bstiṅs*, fut. *bstiṅ*, imp. *stiṅs*, **to rebuke, scold, abuse** *Lex.*

ཐྱིབ(ས)་པ་ *stib(s)-pa* to offer (sacrifice), rarely used.

ཐྱིམ་པ་ *stim-pa*, pf. *bstims*, fut. *bstim*, imp. *stims*, prop. vb. causative to *ₒtim-pa*, gen. = *ₒtim-pa*, **to enter, penetrate, pervade, to be absorbed in**, *tugs čos-nyid-kyi klóṅ-du stim Pth.* the soul is absorbed in the expanse of the *čos-nyid.*

སྟུ་ *stu* **cunnus**, orifice of the vagina, the vulg. and obscene expression for the pudendum muliebre.

སྟུག(ས)་པ་ *stúg(s)-pa* 1. abstract noun and adj., **thickness, density, thick;** *stugs-po* adj., = *ₒtúg-pa*, *ₒtúg-po*, **thick, dense**, e.g. a forest, *Dzl.*; **sound, heavy** (sleep, clouds etc.); *dpal-stúgs* right noble, most noble *Cs.*; *stugs-po-bkód-pa Pth.* one of the heavens of Buddha. — 2. **a wind,** flatulence *C.*

སྟུང་བ་ *stúṅ-ba*, pf. *bstuṅs*, fut. *bstuṅ*, imp. *stuṅs* = *rtúṅ-ba.*

སྟུད་པ་ *stúd-pa*, pf. and fut. *bstud*, **to repeat, to reiterate,** to give or offer repeatedly (medicine, food, beer etc.), *bstúd-na* if it is repeated *Mng.*; *sbrid-pa máṅ-po stúd-čiṅ ₒoṅ* repeated sneezing ensues *Lt.*; *bstúd-nas ná-ba* to be always ill *Sch.*; cf. *btúd-mar.*

སྟུན་པ་ *stún-pa*, pf. and fut. *bstun*, prop. causative to *ₒtún-pa*, gen. = *ₒtún-pa*, **to agree,** *dgé-ba bčú-la bstún-pai rgyal-k'rims* a law agreeing with the ten virtues *Glr.*; *ₒdod-yón lṅa daṅ stún-pai loṅs-spyód* a life of pleasure in accordance with the five enjoyments *Glr.*; *dus-skábs daṅ stún-te* agreeably to the (proper) time, in due time *Glr.*; *ṅai žiṅ rmó-ba ₒdi daṅ stún-pai mgúr-ma* a song having reference to this my labour in the fields *Mil.*; *gžuṅ daṅ stún-pa Lex., Cs.*: 'to confer, to make agree with the original text'.

སྟུབ་པ་ *stúb-pa*, or *sté-pa*, *Ld.*, for *btúb-pa*, *gté-pa.*

སྟེ་ *ste* an affix for the gerund, inst. of *te*, after *g*, *ṅ*, and vowels, v. *te.* — As *ste* contains the copula, it may be added also to other words than verbs, e.g. *kyod rigs čé-žiṅ mtó-ba-ste* as you are of high and noble extraction *Dzl.*; like *ₒdi-lta-ste* it is also used for **namely, to wit, videlicet** (viz.), that is to say, esp. before translations of foreign words and names: *ši-ra-ste mgó-bo žes-byá-ba Tar.* 11, 11; 4, 11; 189, 2 and elsewh. In the latter case it may also be rendered by **or** (Lat. *sive*). After an enumeration of several things, it serves to point back, or to comprise: *ža, za, a, ya, ša, sá-ste drug-ni* the six letters *ž*, *z* etc.; *gsum ná-ro kyi-gu gréṅ-bu-ste* three signs, o, i, and e *Glr.*, *Tar.* 188, 16; *dá-ste žag bdún-na* as to the being now, in seven days, i.e. in seven days from to-day *Dzl.*; sometimes *ste* seems to stand in the place of a preceding verb, *Feer Introd.* 73, s.l.c.; at other times it is used, where its exact meaning is not obvious.

སྟེ་པོ་ *sté-po*, or *steu*, carpenter's **axe, adz,** an axe with its blade athwart the handle (*Cs.*: 'paring axe'), used by Indian and Tibetan carpenters, *Hind. basúla*, *ste-ltág* its back, *ste-yú* its handle, *ste-k'á Cs.* its edge, though in *S.g.* 32 *ste-k'a so-gnyis-pa* it must be the name of the tool itself. — *ste bžog gtóṅ-ba* to pare, to smooth, to hew with the axe. — **p'ág-ste** *W.* a plane.

སྟེགས་ *stegs*, also *stégs-bu*, any contrivance for putting things on, **a stand, board, table, stool** etc.; *ká-stegs* the pedestal or base of a pillar *Cs.*; *rkáṅ-stegs* foot-stool, jack, horse (wooden frame with legs); **kyóṅ-stag** *W.* candlestick; **čós-stag**; **čǒ-tag** *W.*, book-stand; *ₒdug-stegs* a board, stool, bench, to sit on *Cs.*; **do-tég** *C.* a stone-seat, whether artificial or natural; *snód-stegs Cs.* 'a board to put vessels on'; *p'ór-stegs* a cupboard *Cs.*; **p'ó-stag** *W.* a bench; *žabs-stegs* resp. for *rkaṅ-stegs*; **žǔn-teg** *C.* candlestick; *gžag-stegs* a board to place things on *Cs.*; *zá-stegs* dining-table *Schr.*; *gsól-stegs* id. resp., and table in general, col. **sol-tág**; *lám-stegs* seat, resting-place by the road-side *Glr.*; **ǒṅ-teg** *C.* candlestick.

སྟེང་ *steṅ* **that which is above, the upper part, top, surface,** *sai steṅ ťams-čád* the whole face of the earth *Glr.*; *sén-moi stéṅ-gi sa* the earth here upon my finger nail *Dzl.*; *stéṅ-gi nám-mḱa* the heavens above *Dzl.*; *stéṅ-gi p̀yogs* the zenith; *steṅ-ˏóg* above and below, *steṅ-ˏóg-gi ɣdon* demons of the upper and lower regions; *stéṅ-na* adv. and postp.: above, overhead, on high, up-stairs, on the surface, answering to the question where or in what place; *stéṅ-du* adv. and postp. 1. id., answering to the question whither, to what place, but also where or in what place, e.g. to sit on a lotos, to throw down to the ground, to send a thing or a messenger to a person *Dzl.*, frq. 2. above, over, moreover, besides, in addition to, *rgás-pai stéṅ-du* in addition to my old age *Dzl.*; *byás-pai stéṅ-du* he made it and besides... *Dzl.*; *bdag čós-la mi mós-pa méd-pai stéṅ-du bón ráṅ-la mos* I am not only no despiser of religion, but a regular Bon-worshipper *Mil.*; *stéṅ-nas* down from. — *stéṅ-ka* (*W.* **táṅ-ka**), also *stéṅ-tse* a terrace. — *stéṅ-ḱaṅ* upper story of a house, garret. — **steṅ-dúṅ** (?) *W.* pestle, pounder.

སྟེན་པ་ *stén-pa*, pf. and fut *bsten*, imp. *sten*, **to keep, to hold; to adhere to, to stick to, to rely** or **depend on,** almost like *rtén-pa*, but c. accus., *blá-ma mḱás-pa stén-pa* to adhere to a learned Lama; to stick or keep to certain victuals, medicines etc., using them regularly, frq.; even *sdug-bsṅál* to have to taste misfortunes *Thgy.*; **to addict one's self** (to virtues or vices), *sér-sna* to avarice *Stg.*; *mi stén-pa* = *spáṅ-ba* to avoid, shun, abstain from *Glr.*; *Cs.* also: *ɣyog stén-pa* to keep a servant in pay.

སྟེམ་པ་ *stém-pa*, pf. and fut. *stems* (= *stén-pa*?), **to hold, to support** *Mil. nt.*; **to shut** or **fasten** a door, **to secure** it by a beam or bar. *C.*

སྟེམས་ *stems* **curse** (?) *Tar.* 181, 20. Cf. *byad.*

སྟེའུ་ *steu* v. *sté-po.*

སྟེར་བ་ *stér-ba*, pf. and fut. *bster*, ccdp. 1. **to give** *B.*, *C.*, frq.; **to bestow, present, grant, concede, allow;** with the supine or root of a verb: **to let, permit,** *náṅ-du ˏgro(r)*, *náṅ-du ˏóṅ-du* to let enter to grant admission *Dzl.* — 2. *W.* in a special sense: to give to eat or to drink, **to feed** (infants, animals). — 3. **to add** (in arithmetic) *Wdk.* — **tér-go** **aid, contribution** *C.*

སྟེས་དབང་ *stes-dbaṅ Lex.*, where *staṅs-legs* is added for explanation; in *Tar.* 134, 7 *stes-dbaṅ-gis* is translated by *Schf.*: power of fate.

སྟོ་ཐག་ *sto-ťag* **rope** *Sch.*

སྟོ་བ་ *stó-ba*, most frq. in the col. phrase *čaṅ mi sto* it does not matter, it makes no difference, it is all the same (also *čaṅ mi rtog*); *Mil.*: *ši ruṅ mi stó-ba ˏdug* it does not matter if they die; *ši yaṅ či stó-ste* what does it matter if they die?

སྟོ་ར་ (?) *stó-ra W.*, a circle of dancers.

སྟོང་ *stoṅ* 1. **thousand,** *stoṅ-p̀rág* id., *stoṅ-p̀rag-brgyá-pa* (the work) containing ten thousand (viz. Sloka) *Köpp.* II, 272; *Burn.* I, 462. — *stóṅ-dpon* a commander over a thousand; *stoṅ-ˏḱór-lo* a wheel with a thousand spokes; *lus stoṅ byed Med.* that is a remedy producing a thousand good effects. — 2. **a fine for manslaughter,** to be paid in money or goods to the relatives of the person killed; *če-čúṅ-gi stoṅ byéd-pa Glr.*, to proportion this fine to the rank of the man killed. — 3. v. *stóṅ-pa.*

སྟོང་གྲོགས་ *stoṅ-grógs* v. *stóṅs-pa.*

སྟོང་པ་ *stóṅ-pa* (शून्य) **empty, clear,** *ḱáb-kyi rtsé-mo tsam ɣzúgs-pai sa stóṅ-pa* about so much clear space, as to allow the point of a needle to be stuck in *Dzl.*; **hollow,** not charged or loaded (of a gun); not written upon, **blank; indifferent,** having no distinct or definite quality, e.g. as to taste or smell; *rlúṅ-gi raṅ-bžin ni stoṅ mód-kyi* though wind (or air) in itself is without smell *Dzl.*; **waste, deserted,** *brag-stóṅ* a rocky desert, *luṅ-stóṅ* a desolate valley *Mil.*; *žaṅ-stóṅ* *Ld.*, *dom-stóṅ* *Pur.*, bare-bottomed, having the bottom bare, vulg.; *mi tóṅ-pa* *W.*, = *mi kyaṅ*, v. *rkyaṅ-pa; ḱaṅ-stóṅ* a desolate house, as a place suitable for enchantments; fig. *sem tóṅ-pa rag* *W.* I feel lonely. — *stoṅ-pa-nyid.* शून्यता, **emptiness, vacuity, the void,** the chief product of the philosophical speculations of the Buddhists, and the aim and end of all their aspirations, v. *Köpp.* I, 214; *Burn.* I, 442; 462. (Five synonyms v. *Trig.* f. 20). *stóṅ-zád-la skyél-ba* to squander, to waste, *ťse* one's life *Mil.*; *stoṅ-saṅ-ṅé* absolute vacuity, *stóṅ-saṅ-ṅé bgás-nas* making tabula rasa, keeping, retaining nothing whatever *Thgy.* — *stoṅ-gsál* v. *gsal-po.* — Adv. *stóṅ-par* in vain(?) *Mil.*

སྟོང་ཟིལ་ *stoṅ-zil(?)* *W.* Corydalis meifolia.

སྟོངས་པ་ *stóṅs-pa* 1. pf. *bstaṅs* (*Dzl.*), fut. *bstaṅ*(?), **to accompany,** *tóṅ-te ḍó-wa* *C.* to go along with a person; *ċis kyaṅ mi stóṅs-par ḥċi* I die without any thing following me *Thgy.*; more frq. *stoṅ-grógs byéd-pa* c.gp. (also dat.?) **to help, to assist** a person *Mil.* — 2. **to make empty; to be empty, to become waste** or **desolate,** *ráṅ-gi gnas stóṅs-šiṅ S.g.*, *raṅ-šúl stóṅs-nas Mil.*, your own place becoming desolate; *stóṅs-su nyé-bar gyur* it had become nearly empty, was almost spent or exhausted *Pth.*; *mis stóṅs-pai ḱáṅ-ro* ruins forsaken by men; *saṅs-rgyás-kyis stóṅs-pa Thgy.* the period during which no Buddha appears, a *mi-ḱóm-pa* v. *ḱóm-pa*; *sa-gžir stóṅs-pa* to level with the ground, to raze, to demolish entirely.

སྟོད་ *stod*, *Ssk.* उत्तर, I. **the upper, higher, former part** of a thing, **the upper half** opp. to *smad*; 1. esp. the upper part **of the body,** resp. *sku-stód Pth.*; *stod-ḱóg* the upper part of a carcase *Sch.*, also *stód-po Mil.*; *stod-ḱyébs* a sort of frill or ruffle of the Lamas; *stod-ḥgág* doublet of the Lamas, without sleeves; *stod-ťúṅ* a short coat, jacket. — 2. the upper or higher part **of a country,** *stód-pa* an inhabitant of it, highlander. — 3. with respect to time: **the first part,** of the night *Dzl.*, of life *Glr.*, of winter and the like; *stód-la* at the upper part of, above.

II. v. *stád-pa*, and *stód-pa*.

སྟོད་པ་ *stód-pa* 1. vb., pf. and fut. *bstod* ('to raise, to exalt', opp. to *smád-pa*) **to praise, commend, laud,** *bdág-stod-pa*, *W.* *ráṅ-tod-ċe*, to praise one's self, *raṅ-tod-ċan* a self-admirer, self-flatterer; **to extol, to glorify,** men, gods etc., frq.; *stod-(ċiṅ) bsṅags-pa* id.; *stod-ťsig* an epithet of praise, a commendable quality. — 2. sbst. **praise, eulogy,** also *tód-ra* *W.*; **compliments,** complimentary phrases e.g. in letters; hymn of praise, also *stod-bsṅágs*, *stod-dbyáṅs*, *stod-glú*; *stód-pa(r) byéd-pa*, *W.* *pul-ċe*, ccd. (the former also c. accus.) to praise, to extol; *stod-ḥós* laudable, commendable, worthy of praise.

སྟོན་ *ston* 1. **autumn** (more about it v. *dus*), *ston brgya mťóṅ-bar gyúr ċig* may he live to see a hundred autumns! *Lt.* — 2. **in autumn,** during autumn *B.*, frq. — 3. = *ston-ťóg*.

Comp. *stón-ka*, *stón-ḱa*, **autumn,** *stón-ka-na*, *stón-ka-la* in autumn, during autumn. — *ston-ťóg* autumnal fruit, **harvest,** *ston-ťóg sdú-ba* (*W.* also *dóg-ċe*) to gather in the produce of the fields, to harvest. — *ston-dús* **harvest-time, autumn,** — *ston-zlá* autumnal month.

སྟོན་པ་ *stón-pa* I. vb., pf. and fut. *bstan*, at the end of a sentence *bstán-no* (so prob. also in *Dzl.* ༢༠, 10 the correct reading), *W.* *(s)tán-ċe*, 1. **to show,** *lam stón-ċig B.*, *(s)tán toṅ* *W.*, *tṇ rog jhe šig* *C.* show me the way! *stón-mḱan žig yod* somebody has shown *Glr.*; *bú-mo sgo stón-mḱan* the girl that has shown the door *Mil.*, *mťsán-mḱan-la bu stón-pa* to show the soothsayer a child *Dzl.*; *lus stón-pa*, applied to deities etc.: to show one's self, to appear *Dzl.*; *rdzu-ḥprúl stón-pa* to show, to exhibit magic tricks, v. *rdzu*; *dmág-pa yin-no žes bstán-te* 'this is the bridegroom!' with these words showing, i. e. introducing him as the bridegroom

Dzl. ཀཱཌ, 3. — 2. = *ytód-pa*, **to face, to front, to look towards,** *sgo lhó-pyogs-su ston* the door faces the south *Glr.* — 3. **to point out, to indicate, describe, explain,** *čé-ba* the greatness or superiority of a thing *Mil.*; *bú-mo skyé bar ₒgyúr-bar stón-pa yin* it indicates that a girl will be born *Wdṅ.*; *ci-ₒdra žig (yod) ston dgos* give me a description of her person *Glr.*; *bstán-par byao* now I will explain that, frq.; *ji-ltar byón-pa bstán-pai leu* the chapter describing the arrival; hence **to teach,** *čos* religion; *luṅ* v. *luṅ*. — 4. *W.* **to make** one **undergo** or **suffer, to inflict** (just as **tóṅ-če** to suffer), **mi-la nag stón-pa** to torture a person, **dug-ṅálstón-pa** to plague, torment, grieve. — 5. *W.* as a vb. nt., **to show one's self, to appear,** **'i-ru tán-te yod** this appears here, this turns up or occurs here.

II. sbst. **a teacher,** frq., *lúṅ-ston-pa* **a prophet,** v. *luṅ;* the *stón-pa* par excellence is Buddha, frq.; — *ston-min,* and *tse-min* two false doctrines *Glr.* 92, 3. (the translation given by *Sch.* is but an arbitrary one).

སྟོན་མོ་ *stón-mo* **feast, banquet** (v. also *yá-tra*), *stón-mo bzáṅ-po, čén-po*, a grand, splendid feast *Dzl.*; *šóm-pa* to prepare, arrange (a feast), *byéd-pa* to give, hold, celebrate it, also c. dat. in honour of; *stón-mo ₒdrén-pa* to serve it up *Mil.*, *ₒgyéd-pa* to distribute the dishes, *dmáṅs-kyi stón-mo ₒgyéd-pa* to distribute of the viands of the table to the common people *Mil.*, *zá-ba* to eat, or partake, of such a festive entertainment *Dzl.*; *stón-mo-ynaṅ-sbyin* a present of meat, of provisions *Glr.*; *dgá-ston* festive entertainment, frq.; *rná-bai dgá-ston* a feast or treat to one's ears *Glr.*; *čós-ston* a religious feast *Glr.* (might be used for agapē, love-feast, feast of charity); *dús-ston* a periodical festival, one connected with certain times or periods *Tar.*; *bág-ston* wedding-feast, frq.; *míṅ-ston* feast given at the solemnity, when a name is given to a child; *ráb-ston* a feast after settling some important business *Cs.*; *btsás-ston* a feast given after the birth of a child; *tsógs-ston* sacrificatory feast; *yšíd-ston* funeral feast.

སྟོབ་པ་ *stób-pa*, pf. *bstab* (*Cs. bstob*), fut. *bstob Cs.*, imp. *stob*, (causative to *tob-pa?*), to put into another's mouth, esp. food, **to feed;** also applied to a mare that shoves the grass to her foal *Dzl.*; *nán-tan-gyis stób-pa* to press a person to accept of a dish etc. *Dzl.*; in a more general sense: *láṅ-ste stan stób-par byéd-pa* rising to offer one's own seat *Stg.*; to make a donation *Dzl.*; also capir.: *yo-byád tams-čád-kyis stób-pa* to provide a person with every thing within one's power *Tar.*

སྟོབས་(པོ་) *stóbs(-po)* **strength, vigour, force,** frq.; *lús-stobs* bodily, *snyiṅ-stobs* mental strength; *ₒjú-stobs* digestive power *Med.*; *stóbs-po če* of great physical strength *Dzl.*; *stóbs-kyis* by virtue, by means of; *stobs-ₒpel-nyams-brtás byéd-pa* strengthening, nourishing, of food *Med.*; *stóbs-čan, stobs-ldán*, strong, robust; *stobs-čúṅ, stobs-méd*, powerless, weak; the five powers of a Buddha v. *Burn.* II, 430; *Köpp.* I, 436; the ten powers v. *dbaṅ bču*. — *stobs-čén* 1. n. of a Lu-king, *S.O.* — 2. **rammer, pile-driver,** (or *rdob-čén?*) *C.*

སྟོར་བ་ *stór-ba* **to be lost, to perish, to go astray,** *bu stór-ro* a child has been lost *Dzl.*; *lus daṅ srog* (to lose) one's life *Dzl.*, *sems* one's senses, *lam* one's way (also fig. to err from true religion *Pth.*); **tor ma čug** *W.* do not lose it, do not drop it, carry it carefully; *stór-sa med* it cannot be lost or antiquated *Mil.* — *stór-kuṅ* for *ytór-kuṅ* drain, gutter *Lex.*

བརྟ... *brt...* v. chiefly sub *rt.*

བརྟ་བ་ *brtá-ba*, pf. *brtas*, *Lex.*: *lus sems brtas*, explained by *rgyás-pa*, **to grow wide, to extend;** gen. **to grow stout,** esp. with *nyams Dzl.*; cf. also the expression for strengthening sub *stóbs(-po)*; also *rtas byéd-pa Med.*; fig. strong or great: *ₒgyód-pa rtas* the greatest, the sincerest repentance *Pth.*; *bág-čags rtás-pa* high passion *Thgy.*

བརྟག(ས)་པ་ *brtág(s)-pa*, v. *rtóg-pa*; as sbst., preceded by a genit., **inquiry, examination**, *Stg.*, frq.; gen. c. accus. *rmi-lam brtág(s)-pa* examination of dreams *Stg.*; *rin-po-če brtág(s)-pa-la mḱás-pa* connoisseur of precious stones *Dzl.*; *brtágs-pa brgyad Tar.* 21, 2.?

བརྟད་ *brtad* a kind of imprecation, which consists in hiding the image and name of an enemy in the ground underneath an idol, and imploring the deity to kill him; *brtad ǰúg-pa* to perform that ceremony *Mil.*

བརྟད་པ་ *brtád-pa* 1. *Lex.* = *bló-bur* **new, recent.** — 2. *Sch.* **haste, speed,** for *rtáb-pa* (?) (*Tar.* 180, 2 it should prob. be *gtád-pa.*)

བརྟན་པ་ *brtán-pa* adj. and abstract noun; *brtán-po* adj., **firm, steadfast, safe; firmness** etc.; *brtán-par ynás-pa*, **tán-po dád-če** *W.*, to last, hold out, abide, continue, frq.; *brtán-pa ťób-pa* to become firm or durable (lit. to acquire firmness or durability) *Mil.*; *brtán-par ǥyúr-ba*, **tán-po čá-če** *W.* id.; *brtán-gyi skyid* a continued or abiding happiness *Mil.*; *dbaṅ brtan* their strength is holding out *Med.*; *brtán-du ǰúg-pa Glr.*, **tán-po čó-če** *W.*, to watch, keep, preserve carefully; **tán-po kur** *W.* carry it carefully or safely! *dám-bčas-pa brtán-par šes* he knew his word to be inviolable *Dzl.*; *yi-dam-la brtán-pas* because he firmly kept his word *Dzl.*; *dus brtán-gyi bdé-ba* eternal welfare, everlasting happiness *Mil.* (perh. this ought to be *ytan*).

བརྟན་མ་ *brtán-ma*, or *bstán-ma*, and *bstán-pa-mo*, n. of the goddess of the earth, (also *skóṅ-ma*, *yá-ma*), used in practising magic.

བརྟུལ་བ་ *brtúl-ba* 1. **deportment, behaviour** *Cs.* — 2. *Sch.* also diligence, painstaking(?). — *brtul-žúgs*, व्रत 1. *Cs.* manner, way of acting. 2. *Sch.* and gen.: exercise of penance, *brtul-žugs byéd-pa* or *spyód-pa*, to perform such exercises, to do penance. 3. penitent. — *brtul-žugs-čan* penitent (adj. and sbst.) — *brtul-ṗód-pa* v. *rtul-ṗód-pa.*

བསྟང་བ་ *bstáṅ-ba* v. *stóṅs-pa.*

བསྟན་པ་ *bstán-pa* 1. v. *stón-pa.* — 2. sbst. **doctrine**, a single doctrine, or a whole system of doctrines; *saṅs-rgyás-kyi bstán-pa* the doctrine or religion of Buddha, *ťub-bstán*, for *ťúb-pai bstán-pa*, id.; *ynás-lugs bstán-pa* the doctrine of the position of... *Med.*; *bstán-pa ynyis* with Urgyan Padma etc., the same as *mdoi* and *sṅágs-kyi lam*, v. *mdo* extr. — *bstán-ǥyur* the second great literary production of Buddhism, containing comments on *Kan-ǥyur*, and scientific treatises (v. *bka-gyur* in *bka*) *Köpp.* II, 280. — *bstan-bčos* (शास्त्र) a scientific work. — *bstan-rtsis* a chronological work relative to the year of Buddha's death. — *bstan-ǥdzin* follower, adherent of a doctrine, *saṅs-rgyás-kyi bstan-ǥdzin Mil.*, Buddhist; also frq. used as a noun personal. — *bstan-(b)šig* col. a destroyer of the doctrine, in general a good-for-nothing fellow, a mischief-maker, an obnoxious person or thing. — *bstan-srúṅ* 1. **a keeper, guardian of the doctrine;** perh. also = *bstan-ǥdzin.* 2. **keeper, warden, guardian** in general, *lha-ḱáṅ-gi bstan-srúṅ*; *lhá-sai bstan-srúṅ* the tutelar goddess of Lhasa, acc. to *Glr.* = *dpal-lhá-mo.* 3. in general the contrary to *bstan-bšig.*

བསྟིར་ *bstir* supine of *sti-ba*; *bstir-méd* 'restlessness', one of the infernal regions.

བསྟུགས་པ་ *bstúgs-pa* **to make lower, to lower** *Sch.* (?).

བསྟེན་པ་ *bstén-pa* 1. vb. v. *stén-pa.* 2. sbst. **confidence,** = *brtón-pa Bhar.*

བསྟོད་པ་ *bstód-pa* v. *stód-pa.*

ཐ

ཐ་ ťa, the letter ŧ aspirated, like the English t in 'tea'.

ཐ་ ťa 1. num. fig.: ten. — 2. **every thing, all, total** *Sch.* (?).

ཐ་སྐར་ *ťa-skár* a certain star, *ťa-skár-zla-ba* a month, prob. = वैशाख (April-May); *ťa-skár-gyi bu* अश्विनी twin half-gods.

ཐ་ཁབ་ *ťa-ǩáb Lh.* a large **needle.**

ཐ་ག་པ་ *ťá-ga-pa* **a weaver** *Dzl.*

ཐ་གུ་ *ťá-gu,* vulg. *ťi-gu,* 1. a short **cord** or **rope.** — 2. **string, twine,** for making garlands *Stg.*; a bell-rope *Dzl.*

ཐ་གྲུ་ *ťa-grú,* originally *ťag-grú Pth.,* **extension, width, breadth,** *ₒdzam-bu-gliṅ-gi ťa-grú kún-la Glr.* in the whole extent of Dzambuling; *ťa-grú čé-ba Pth.* extensive.

ཐ་རྒོད་ *ťa-rgód* 1. **obtuse, rounded off** *Sch.* — 2. *Mil.?*

ཐ་ཆད་ *ťa-čád* **very bad, mean** *Cs.*

ཐ་ཆུང་ *ťa-čúṅ* **the last month** of a season (v. *dus*), e.g. *dpyid-zla ťa-čúṅ* the last month of spring, opp. to *rá-ba,* (and *ₒbriṅ-po*); **the youngest** of three or more sons, opp. to *rab* (and *ₒbriṅ-po* the middle one).

ཐ་སྙད་ *ťa-snyád* 1. **appellation,** *žes ťa-snyád-du grags* so it is called *Wdṅ.*; *Tar.* 96, 13; 178, 3; *Was.* (296): **supposition; condition,** *ťa-snyád-pai bdén-pa* conditional truth. — 3. *Schr.*: **etymology,** *Cs.* only: part of grammar; so frq. used by grammarians, e.g. *ťsig daṅ ťa-snyád slób-pa* to learn spelling and etymology. — 4. In col. language I heard it used only for talking or disputing in a conceited, foolish manner, so also in *Mil.* — *Lex.* in conformity with each of these significations = व्यवहार, from व्यवह to distinguish, to name; to dispute. — *ťa-snyad-γčig-pa* n. of a school, of a system or doctrine *Tar.*; *ťa-snyad-grúb-pa* n. of a literary work.

ཐ་དད་པ་ *ťa-dád-pa* **different, various, sundry,** gen. opp. to *γčig* or *γčig-pa; dgós-pa ťa-dád-pa* the various wants of a man *Dzl.*; *ťa-mi-dád-pa* alike, equal.

ཐ་ན་ *ťá-na* **even, so much as, up to,** *ťá-na-srog-čágs gróg-sbur yaṅ-čád* even the smallest insect *Stg.*; *ťá-na yig-ₒbru re-ré yaṅ-čád* even every single letter *Thgy.*; at the close of an enumeration: **finally also** *Ld.-Glr. Schl.* 20, 6.

ཐ་པི་ཐུ་པི་ *ťa-pi-ťú-pi* **confusion, disorder** *Sch.*

ཐ་པག་ *ťá-pag* v. *ťár-dpag.*

ཐ་བ་ *ťá-ba* (= *ťú-ba*) **bad** *Mil.*

ཐ་མ་ *ťá-ma* **the last** of several things, with respect to number, time, rank, the lowest, meanest, most inferior, often opp. to *rab* and *ₒbriṅ,* and also to *ǩyád-par-čan*; it appears somewhat singular, that *γčan-zán-gyi ťá-ma* signifies a cat, and *ₒdab-čágs-kyi ťá-ma* a hen *Glr.*; *dús-kyi ťá-ma-la* in the last times *Glr.*, prob. also alluding to the general decline taking place towards the end of the Kalpa; sometimes it is to be translated: **in the last place, finally, at last** *Glr.*, like *ťá-mar Dzl.* ༢༥, 11; last = parting (parting-cup, parting-kiss); for the last time: *γnyén-gyi ťá-mas bskor* he sees his relations for the last time around him, *zás-kyi ťá-ma za* he eats for the last time *Thgy.*; *ťá-ma-la* c. genit. at the end of, after. — *ₒprád-pai ťá-ma ni ₒbral, γsón-pai ťá-ma ni ší-ba yin* the end of every meeting is parting, the end of every living is dying.

ཐ་མ་ཁ་ *ťa-ma-ǩa Cs.*, vulg. *W.* **ťá-mag**, **tobacco,** *ₒťuṅ-ba, W.* resp. **dón-če** to smoke (tobacco).

ཐ་མལ་པ་ *ta-mál-pa* (*ta-mál* abbreviated from *tá-ma-la*) 1. **mean, vulgar, plebeian**, *ta-mál-par* *₀dúg-pa* to live like the vulgar *Dzl.* — 2. **ordinary, usual**, *ta-mál-pa ma yin* that is no usual thing *Dzl.*; *ta-mál* adv. = *pal-čér*.

ཐ་ཚིག་ *ta-tsig Sch.* 'oath'; but in two passages of *Dzl.* *či ta-tsig* can only mean: **'what signifies?'**

ཐ་ར་ཐོ་རེ་ *ta-ra-to-ré W.* **wide asunder, wide**, **ta-ra-to-ré žág-pa* C.* to scatter, to throw loosely about.

ཐ་རམ་ *ta-rám* 1. *Sch.*: 'the breadth of a plain'. — 2. a medicinal herb *Med.*, in *Lh.* Plantago major.

ཐ་རུ་ *ta-rú Tar.* 20, 17, *Schf.*: 'the utmost limits', or it may be a p. n.

ཐ་ལི་ *ta-li W.*, **te-li* C.*, *Hind.* थलिया, a **tin plate**.

ཐ་ལོང་ *ta-lóṅ W.* a sort of red cloth.

ཐ་ཤལ་ *ta-šál Sch.*: 'the end, the consequence; bad'; *Bhar.*: *skyés-bu ta-šál nyid Schf.*: homo nequam, a good-for-naught.

ཐག་ *tag* 1. sometimes for *₀tag*, *Glr.* — 2. **distance** a. relatively (prob. from *tág-pa* measuring-cord, surveyor's chain) only in: *tag-riṅ-ba* adj. and abstract noun, *tag-riṅ(-po)* adj., *W.* **tag-riṅ-(mo)** **distant, a great distance,** *sa tag-riṅ(s)* a far country *Glr.*; with *daṅ* or *las* far from; *tag-mi-riṅ-ba* not far *Pth.*; *tag-riṅ(-po)-nas* from afar, from a distance *Thgy.*; *tag-nyé-ba* **near; proximity;** *W.* adj. **tag-nyé-mo**; *tag či-tsam* how far? *Cs.*; *tag-grú* v. *ta-gru.* b. absolutely, only with respect to time, in: *ma-tág* **but just, just now,** gen. with a verbal root, *sleb ma-tág yin-pa* he that has arrived just now *Glr.*; *sṅar bšad ma-tág-pa* (the passages) that have been explained just now *Gram.*; as an adv. gen. *ma-tág-tu*, or only *ma-tág*, frq., e.g. *tos ma-tág-tu* as soon as he had heard; *de ma-tág-tu* directly, immediately, in *W.* **ma-tóg-tse**. — 3. *tag-tóg* v. *tog-tág.* — 4. *tag-γčód-pa* v. *tág-pa* I.

ཐག་ཐག་ *tag-tág*, with **jhe̊-pa* C.*, **čó-če** **to knock,** *sgo* at the door.

ཐག་པ་ *tág-pa* I. **rope, cord** (in *Lh.* hempen ropes, as a foreign manufacture, are often distinguished from other ropes, by being called रस्सी, *bal-tág* rope made of wool, *ral-tág* rope of goat's hair, *rtsid-tág* rope of the long hair of the yak, *rtsa-tág*, or *pon-tág Glr.* rope of grass; *lčágs-(kyi) tág-pa* chain, wire-rope, used as fetters or otherwise; **ras-tág* W.* **bandage;** *tag-míg* **mesh** of a net *Sch.*; *tag-zó* **rope-maker's work** *Pth.* — *tág γčód-pa* vb. a. (*tag čód-pa*, or *čád-pa* vb. n. or pass.) 1. to cut a cord, *bdag nyé-du daṅ ₀brél-tag bčád-pas bde* I am glad of having cut the cord (tie) which united me with my family *Mil.*; gen. with *re*, the cord of hope, e.g. *₀gró-bai ré-tag čad* the cord of the hope of going on a journey is cut off, i.e. the journey has been given up *Glr.*; *Schr.*: *₀ó-tag γčód-pa* to wean (a child); *bló-tag-čod* deliberation is cut off, the matter is decided or resolved upon; hence frq. without *blo*: 2. **to decide, resolve, determine,** *rgyal-po bkróṅ-bar tag-bčád* it was determined to murder the king *Glr.*; *kyod γnyis ñá-la čúṅ-ma mi len tág-čód-pa-na* if you positively refuse to give me a wife *Pth.*; **tag-čád mi kyud* W.* I have no right to decide on that point; *tag-čód-pa byéd-pa* to decide, pass sentence, give judgment *Mil.*; **to be sure, decided, certain,** . . . *gróṅs-par tag-bčád-de* (cf. above) as it is quite certain that he has died *Mil.*; . . . *yod tag-čód* there are certainly . . . *Glr.*; *čos dar ₀óṅ tag-čód* it is quite certain that religion will spread *Mil.*; *ltá-bas tag-bčád-nas* being immovable in contemplation; with termin.: to know for a certainty, to understand or see clearly, *ráṅ-sems čós-skur tag-čód-čiṅ* knowing one's own mind to be vain and frail (v. *čós-sku* sub *sku* 2) *Mil.*; *snáṅ-ba séms-su* the visible world as a thought, as imaginary, i.e. as nothing *Mil.*; *tag-čód* **certainty, surety, evidence.** *₀ón-kyaṅ tag-čód byed dgos* but one should know it for certain, one must be sure of it *Mil.*; *ltá-ba tag-čód-kyi rnál-₀byor-pa* you, the ascetic, firm in meditation! *Mil.* — **tag-čo̊'-rbe̊'-čo̊'* C.* resolute.

II. prob. = *dág-pa*, in *snyiṅ* (or *že*, or *bsám-pa*) *tág-pa-nas* with a faithful heart, with all my heart, **heartily**, *že tág-pai žú-ba Mil.* a sincere prayer or entreaty.

Note. In *tag-pa* and other words beginning with *t*, (e.g. *taṅ*, *to*), *d* sometimes takes the place of *t*, and this uncertainty in the use of the initial letter dates perh. from a time, when the aspirated pronunciation of the media first began to be adopted in *C.*, and was not yet generally introduced.

ཐགས་ *tags* **texture, web**, *tags* *tág-pa* to weave *Dzl.*, *tágs-tag-mkan* col. for *tá-ga-pa*, also *tágs-mkan Pth.* a weaver; **tser-tág** *W.* thorn-hedge, fence consisting of thorn; *tags-kri* (weaver's) loom *Ld.-Glr.; tágs-gra-bu Cs.*, **tágs-kan-bu** *W.*, **spider**; *tágs-ča* weaver's implements; *tágs-gnas, tágs-ra*, a weaver's place or shop *Cs.; tags-brán byéd-pa Mil.*, **tag rán-če** *W.*, to begin the warp.

ཐགས་ཐོགས་ *tags-tógs* **impediment** *Cs.*

ཐང་ *taṅ* 1. also *táṅ-ma Mil.*, *táṅ-bu Dzl. Ms.*, **táṅ-ka** *W.*, flat country, **a plain, steppe**; also fig. like *žiṅ*, *bde-čén-gyi taṅ* land of bliss *Mil.; táṅ-la* (from the house) into the plain or steppe, = into the open air *Dzl.*; *táṅ-la ltúṅ-ba* to fall to the ground; **ma-táṅ** *W.* the unfloored bottom of a room; *gram-táṅ* a fenny or swampy plain *Cs.; spaṅ-táṅ* a green grassy plain or steppe, meadow, prairie; *byaṅ-táṅ* the northern steppes or plains of Tibet (used as a noun proper); *bye-táṅ* a sandy desert or plain; *ol-táṅ* ground covered with (snail-) clover, **pasture ground**, grassy plain; *šág-táṅ* a gravelly plain; *táṅ-du byéd-pa Cs.* to lay waste, to make a desert of, *táṅ-du gyúr-ba* to become a desert. — 2. *Cs.* **price, value**, perh. also amount; *rin-táṅ* id. *Dzl.; rín-taṅ-čan* **dear, precious**, *Mil.; yoṅ-táṅ* 1. *W.* **income, profit**, 2. *C.* = *yón-tan* **talent**, natural gift, faculty; *lo-táṅ* yearly tribute, *gčód-pa* to fix, to order it *Tar.; za-táṅ* (a person's) capability of eating *Thgy.* — 3. *W.* for *dwaṅs* **clear, serene**, **nam taṅ** a cloudless sky, fine weather; **daṅ pi-ro táṅ-te yod** (the sky) was cloudless last night. — 4. **potion** *Med.* — 5. = *bka-táṅ*, **order, command**, (*bka*) *taṅ-yig* **decree**; *pad-ma-taṅ-yig* is the abridged title of a collection of legends about Padma Sambhava. — 6. (**resin?**) *taṅ-čú* **resin, gum**, e.g. of fruit-trees. — 7. a very short space of time (the statements as to its length vary from five seconds to one minute and a half), **a moment, a little while**, gen. *taṅ gčig*, not seldom joined with *skad čig* and *yud tsam; taṅ tsam* id. *Pth.*; *čig-taṅ*, *bži-taṅ* one moment, four moments; *Lt.*, *taṅ-ré S.g.*, one after the other *Sch.* — 8. v. *taṅ-ka.* — In a few instances the meaning of *taṅ* is not quite evident.

Comp. *taṅ-krúṅ* bastard *Sch.* — *taṅ-čú* v. *taṅ* C. — *taṅ-stóṅ* uninhabited, desolate; wilderness. — *taṅ-brú Sch.* 'cedar-nuts', perh. = *ko-nyon-tsé* q.v. — *taṅ-már* tar *Cs.* — **taṅ-ma-la-la-tsé** a small lizard *Ld.* — *taṅ-gží* market-price; **taṅ-ži čag** *C.* the market-price abates. — **taṅ-zi** *W.* fata morgana — *taṅ-rág* cedar (?) *Sch.* — *taṅ-šíṅ* fir, pine.

ཐང་ཀ, ཐང་ག *táṅ-ka, táṅ-ga*, resp. *žal-táṅ*, *W.* **sku-táṅ**, *Tar. tán-sku*, **image**, prop. of human beings, at present = picture, **painting**, in a gen. sense, also of landscapes etc.

ཐང་དཀར་ *taṅ-dkár* the white-tailed eagle *Sch.*

ཐང་ཐང་ *taṅ-táṅ* v. the following word.

ཐང་པོ་ *táṅ-po*, **tense, tight, firm** (= *táṅ-po?*); *taṅ-lhód* tight and loose; also tenseness fig. *Mil.*; *táṅ-ša gčód-pa* to strain, to stretch, *čód-pa* vb. n. or pass. *Stg.*, *Mil.*, *C.*; **zúg-po taṅ-ñam** *C.* are you well? — *rkaṅ-táṅ-du* or *la* **on foot**, v. *rkáṅ-pa* comp.; *taṅ gčod-pa* **to tire, to fatigue** *Mil.*, *taṅ čod-pa* or *čad-pa* to be tired, wearied *Pth.*; **gom-táṅ láb-če* (*ṭú-gu-la*)* *W.* to lead a child in walking, to teach a child to walk; *ša-táṅ-táṅ* to the utmost of one's power *Sch.*

ཐང་སྲོམ་ *taṅ-próm* a medicinal herb *Med.*, *Wdṅ.* = *dha-tu-ra* thorn-apple (?).

ཐང་ཤ་ táṅ-ša v. sub taṅ-po; taṅ-šiṅ v. taṅ comp.

ཐད(ཀ) tád(-ka) 1. **the direction straight forward,** steṅ daṅ ˳og daṅ tád-ka tams-čád-du upward and downward, and in every other direction Stg.; steṅ-˳og-tád-kar straight upward and downward S.g.; p'o-bráṅ-gi tád-kar p'yin they came straight towards the castle; tád-ka-na directly before Thgy.; deĩ nub-tád-kyi that which is situated to the west of it Tar.; most frq. tád-du c.genit. **towards,** in straight direction; **over against; in presence of** e.g. to assemble, to propound, to lay before one, to study under a professor Dzl.; **exactly in the place of** a thing Tar. 17,1; šai tád-nas čod Tar. 159,4 prob.: cut off only from the flesh; *tẹ'-kya, tẹ'-kaṅ-la* Ts. **straight on;** tad-draṅ-na **directly before** Wdṅ.; *tad-nyá* W. **over against, opposite, facing;** tád-so-na = tád-ka-na Mil. — 2. tád-kar **each for himself** Glr. — 3. **entire, whole, untouched, safe** (integer) C. and perh. Thgy.

ཐིད་ frq. abbreviation for ཐམས་ཅད་ tams-čád, **whole, all.**

ཐན་ tan, Hind. थान, = yug, **a piece of cloth.**

ཐན་ཀོར་ tan-kór, tan-skór Lex., surrounding country Sch.

ཐན་ཐུན་ tan-tún (Schr. tad-tún) **a little** Sch.

ཐན་པ་ tán-pa **dry weather, heat, drought** Glr.

ཐབ་ tab 1. resp. ysol-táb, **fire-place, hearth,** me-táb, id.; also for **stove,** lčags-táb iron stove; tab šor 'the hearth is running over', i.e. the food placed on it runs over in boiling, a mis-hap the more serious, as the household god is offended by the evil smell caused thereby. — 2. v. sub čaṅ.

Comp.: *táb-ka* W. fire-place, *táb-ka tsam yod* how many fire-places, i.e. households, are there? — tab-kúṅ opening or mouth of a stove, furnace, or fire-place; v. also Schl. 249. — tab-ynás fire-place, furnace, oven Cs. — *tab-tsáṅ* W. kitchen. — tab-p'yis, W. *tab-p'is* clout, dish-clout, wiper. — tab-yžob burnt smell. — *tab-lás čó-kan* W. cook. — tab-yyóg kitchen-boy, scullion Pth. — tab-šiṅ fire-wood, fuel. — tab-lhá deity of the hearth.

ཐབ་ཐོབ་ tab-tób W. = tom-tóm.

ཐབས་ tabs (cog. to stabs), **opportunity, chance, possibility,** *tóṅ-or ḍúl-táb ma juṅ* W. I had no opportunity of seeing or going; *tab šig nyi-ráṅ-nẹ mi júṅ-na* W. if you offer no chance, if on your part it is not made possible; tabs mi tub Dzl. and col. I am not able, I cannot; ydan-dráṅs-pai tabs med I then shall lose the opportunity of meeting (the princess) Glr.; ˳brós-pai tabs med there is not any chance of escape Glr.; lám-la yžól-tabs med there is no occasion for stopping or tarrying on the road Mil.; **way, manner, mode,** klog-tabs way of reading, e.g. Sanskrit; rkún-tabs-su in a thievish manner, by theft Stg.; rgyál-poi tabs ytóṅ-ba to give up the way (of life) of a king, to resign the crown Dzl., tabs ycig-tu together, in company, jointly, e.g. to sit down with one another, to go together to a place, frq.; **means, measures.** tabs byéd-pa, W. *čó-če, kyóṅ-če* to use means, to take measures; blo tabs ˳tsól-ba to contrive means Ma.; tabs stón-pa to show means or ways, to give directions, to instruct Glr.; ˳tsó-tabs **livelihood, subsistence;** tabs zad there is nothing else to be done Glr.; ži-bai tábs-kyis in a fair way, amicably, not by constraint or compulsion Glr.; tábs-kyis by various means, by artifice, cunningly, craftily: tábs(-la)-mkás-pa, tábs-šes-pa, W. also *táb-čan*, **skilful, dexterous, clever, full of devices;** da bód-du ˳gró-tabs gyis šig now take steps, make preparations, for a journey to Tibet Glr.; de ysón-poi tabs yód-dam is there a means of recalling those men to life? tabs-čág Mil., *tab-šág* or *teb-šág* vulgo, a shift, make-shift, surrogate; tabs (daṅ) šes (-rab) the mystical union of art and science, or (Sch. less correctly) of matter and spirit, cf. Was. (144).

ཐམ་ག་, ཐམ་ཀ་ tám-ga, tám-ka **a seal, sign** Cs., v. dám-ka.

ཐམ་ཐམ་ *ťam-ťám Sch.* 1. also *ťám-me-ba*, **unconnected, scattered, dispersed.** — 2. *ťam-ťám (byed) -pa = ˳ťám-pa.*

ཐམ་པ་ *ťám-pa* (sometimes *ťém-pa*) **complete, full,** almost exclusively used as a pleon. addition to the tens up to hundred.

ཐམས་ཅད་ *ťams-čád* **whole, all;** added to the singular number: *rgyal-k'áms ťams-čád* the whole empire *Glr.*; *lus ťams-čád na* the whole body aches (opp. to one part of it); *bód-kyi zaṅs ťams-čád* all the copper of Tibet *Glr.*; more frq. added to a plural (though usually in the form of the singular number): all (the persons or things), *de ťams-čád*, rarely *dé-dag ťams-čád*, all those; *ťams-čád-kyis so-só-nas* all of them one by one, each.

ཐམས་པ་ *ťáms-pa (= ˳ťám-pa?), sa,* or *bye-ťáms-su ˳jug-pa* to suffer (a person or beast) to stick fast in the mud, in the sand (?) *Glr.* 84.

ཐའུ་ *ťau Wdṅ.* **capsule** (?), *Wts.* **peach** (?).

ཐར་ *ťar* v. *ťar-ťór.*

ཐར་ཐོར་(ལ་) *ťar-ťór(-la) = ťa-ra-ťo-ré* (cf. *˳ťór-ba*); **ťar čós-se dug* Ld.* sit wide asunder, not too close together! *ťar byed-pa Mil.* **to break to pieces, to smash, to crush.**

ཐར་ནུ་ *ťár-nu* a purgative *Med.*

ཐར་དཔག་ *ťar-dpág, C. *ťar-˳bág*, W. *ťá-bug** a large **plate, dish, platter.**

ཐར་བ་ *ťár-ba* **to become free, to be saved,** **ťar gos,* or *goi* W.* he must become free, *las* from; to be not hindered or prevented, **to get through, to get on, to be able to pass,** *čú-la* through the water *Mil.*; *zas mi ťar* the food cannot pass through *Med.*; to be released, acquitted, discharged, **ṭ'ím-na* C.* by a court of justice; *ťár-du ˳júg-pa* to set at liberty, to acquit, with *ťse* (col. **ťse-ťár-la táṅ-wa**) to pardon (a malefactor), to grant him his life, frq., to let live (animals) *Mil.*; often in a religious sense (with or without *rnám-par*) **to be saved, freed, released,** viz. from the transmigration of souls; more frq. the pf. *ťár-pa* 1. to be free etc., *lam ťar* the road is free, passable. 2. sbst. **freedom, liberty, happiness, eternal bliss,** मोक्ष, *ťár-pai rgyur ˳gyur* it will be serviceable for (my) liberty; *ťár- (pai) lam* the road to happiness (a common expression); *ťar-méd-kyi dmyál-ba* hell without release. 3. adj. **free,** *ťár-par ˳gyúr-ba* to become free, *byéd-pa* to make free, to liberate, to save; *ťár-sa* place of refuge, asylum *Thgy.*

ཐལ་ *ťal*, sometimes for *ťa-li*; *ťál-gyis* v. *ťál-ba* II. 3.

ཐལ་བ་ *ťál-ba* I. sbst. 1. **dust** (cf. *rdul*), **ashes,** and similar substances; *gog-ťál* ashes; **ťug-ťál** ('soup-dust') roasted barley-flour *C.* — *ťal-kár* a kind of elephant, *Cs.*, perh. the ash-coloured. — *ťál-ču* lye. — *ťal-čén* ashes of the dead; also a sort of light gray earth, representing the former, and used for bedaubing the face in masquerades *Mil.* — *ťal-ťág Ld.* unleavened bread. — *ťal-mdóg* ash-coloured, cinereous. — *ťal-pyágs* broom *Sch.* — *ťal-byí* the gray or cat-squirrel. — *ťal-ťsá* a sort of salt *Med.* — 2. *bya-ťal* **dung of birds** *Glr.*

II. vb. (*Cs.* also *˳ťál-ba*) 1. **to pass, to pass by,** **ťal ča dug* W.* he goes past, he does not come in; **zám-pa ťal ča dug**, he goes past the bridge, does not pass over it; to **miss** the mark, of an arrow or ball; *rba ťal-ťál ˳oṅ* the waves flow past *Mil.* — 2. **to go, step, pass beyond,** *lo lṅá-bču ťál-nas* when the age of fifty has been passed *Wdṅ.*; **ču-ťsód γčig ťsá-big ťal* W.* a little past one o'clock; *sṅo-ba-las ťal-nas dmar-žiṅ* Thgy., prob. inclining from blue to red; **to be in the advance** *C.*; **to project, to be prominent,** hence *ťal-ťúṅ* different lengths, one object projecting beyond another; **to play a prominent part, to take the lead** *W.*; *ťál-čes-pa* **to exceed the due measure** *Sch.*; **k'a ťal-wa** to be forward in speaking, bold. — 3. **to go or pass through,** *brág-la yar ťal mar ťal,* and *p'ar ťal ťsur ťál-du ˳gró-ba* to soar up and down before a rock, and to pass actually through it (the saints not being subject to the physical laws of matter) *Mil.*, *Thgr.*; **to shine, to light through**; *tal-ᵒbyúṅ-du ₒgró-ba* to go straightforward, to act without ceremony or disguise *Dzl.* ༧༥༢, 3; *tál-ma Sch.*, *tál-le C.*, **through and through**; *tál-gyis* **directly, straightway, unhesitatingly** *Mil.* — 4. **to come or get to, to arrive at** (*W.* **tél-če**), *tál-nas lo ysum lon* three years have elapsed since they arrived; *pa-má gar tál-bai ytol-méd*; *bzaṅ-tál* safe arrival *Thgr.*; *yár-gyi bzáṅ-tal čén-por ₒgró-ba* to arrive at, attain to (a blessed state) in a pleasant and speedy manner *Thgr.* — 5. **to be over, past, finished, done**, *tál-lo* of a song: it is over, finished *Mil.*; *drúg-ču tál-lo* the number of sixty is full; *yál-nas tál-ba Mil.* having disappeared, vanished; *stór-te* (or *stór-nas*) *tal* he is undone, it is all over with him *Mil.* frq.; *rim-gyis je nyúṅ je nyúṅ tal* by degrees it vanishes, dies away *Mil.*; *sṅar čad-tsig tal* the former agreement is no longer valid; *tal soṅ* col. = *tsar soṅ.* — *Tar.* 46, 5. 12? 172, 5: *tál-gyur-pa Schf.* **follower, adherent,** or the name of a certain sect.

ཐལ་མོ་ *tál-mo* **the palm of the hand,** *tál-mo sbyár-ba* to hold together the palms of the hands, as a gesture of devotion; *tál-mo snún-pa Dzl.*, more frq. *tal-lčág rgyáb-pa* to give a slap on the face, a box on the ear; *tal-brdáb-pa* to clap with the hands *Sch.*

ཐི་ *ti* num. fig.: 40.

ཐི་གུ་ *ti-gu* v. *tá-gu*; *ti-gu-kró-bo* (?) *C.* = **ar-gón* W.*

ཐི་བ་ *ti-ba* 1. **wood-pigeon, stock-dove** *Sch.*; *ti-bo* **plover, peewit, lapwing** *Sch.* — 2. *C.* = *té-ba.*

ཐིག་ *tig*, prob. from *ti-gu*, 1. **carpenter's cord** or string to mark lines with, **marking-string,** *tig(-gis) ₒdebs-pa* to use such a string, to draw lines. — 2. any instrument used in drawing lines; *skor-tig* a pair of compasses, *yya-tig* slate-pencil, lead-pencil; also a line drawn with a lead-pencil; **tig-ta taṅ-če* W.* c. genit. to examine, try, test. — 3. **a line,** *tig-ₒdebs-pa, rgyag-pa, rgyab-pa,* to draw lines; *guṅ-tig* the meridian line *Cs.*; *nag-tig* or *snag-tig* a black line, *tsal-tig* a red line; *tsaṅs-tig* diameter; equator *Cs.* — 4. symb. numeral for **zero.** — 5. v. *tig.*

Comp. *tig-skúd* string to mark lines with. — **tig-nyá* W.* **over against.** — *tig-nág Stg.*, *Sch.*: that part of hell, where the damned are sawn to pieces, lines being drawn upon them. — *tig-tsám* **a little.** — *tig-tsád Cs.* **proportion, symmetry,** *Ld.-Glr.* f. 27, 6, *tig-tsad byéd-pa* to proportion; **tig-tsád zúm-če* W.*, to determine the relation or proportion of things. — *tig-śiṅ* **a ruler,** to rule lines with.

ཐིག་ལེ་ *tig-le* 1. **a spot** like that of a leopard's skin, *tig-le-čan* **spotted, speckled;** *tig-ma* W.* id., of variegated woolen fabrics; *čos tig-le nyag čig Mil.*, the centre of all religion, in which finally all the different sects must unite. — 2. **zero, naught** *Wdk.* — 3. **semen virile.** — 4. **contemplation.** The two latter significations are mystically connected with each other, as will be seen from a passage of *Mil.*, which is also a fair specimen of the physiological and mystical reveries of the more recent Buddhism: *yoṅs lús-la ytúm-mo ₒbár-bas bde; rluṅ ro rkyaṅ dhú-tir čúd-pas bde; stod byaṅ-čub-séms-kyi rgyún-ₒbab bde; smad dáṅs-mai tig-le kyáb-pas bde; bar dkar dmar tug prad brtsé-bas bde; lus zag-med-bdé-bas tsim-pas bde; de rnál-ₒbyor nyáms-kyi bde drug lags,* he (the Yogi) feels well in general, when the warmth of meditation is kindled (cf. *ytúm-mo*) in his body; he feels well, when the air enters through *ró-ma* and *kyáṅ-ma* into the *dhúti*; he feels well in the upper part of his body by the flowing down of the *bódhi*; he feels well in the lower parts by the spreading of the chyle (chylous fluid, semen); he feels well in the middle, by being affected with tender compassion, when the red (the blood in the *kyáṅ-ma*) and the white (the semen in the *ró-ma*) unite; the whole body is well, being pervaded by the grateful feeling of sinlessness; this is the sixfold mental happiness of the Yogi.

ཐིགས་པ་ *tigs-pa* **a drop,** *tigs-pa re-ré-nas* in drops, by drops *Glr.; čar-tigs* a drop of rain; *γsér-tig-po* (sic) *Mil.* seems to denote a drop or globule of molten gold, which in this form is offered for sale by gold-washers.

ཐིང་ *tiṅ* v. *ₒdiṅ-ba.*

ཐིབ་པ་ *tib-pa* v. *ₒtib-pa* and *γtib-pa; tib-tib* **very dark** *Sch.; byin-rlábs tibs-tibs Pth.* seems to imply the descending of a blessing upon a person; *tib(s)-po, mo* **dense,** *Cs.* or perh. nothing but **obscure, dark,** *nags Stg.*

ཐིམ་པ་ *tim-pa,* also *ₒtím-pa, γtim-pa* and *stim-pa,* gen. with *la* or *náṅ-du,* **to disappear** by being **imbibed, absorbed; to evaporate,** of fluids; of a snake: **to creep away,** to disappear in a hole; frq. of the vanishing of rays of lights, of gods etc.; **to be melted, dissolved** (salt or sugar in water); **to sink,** *dran-méd-du* into unconsciousness *Mil.*

ཐུ་ *tu* 1. num. fig.: 70. — 2. **tu gyáb-čé* W.* **to spit,** with *la,* to spit at or on. — 3. often erron. for *mtu.*

ཐུ་བ་ *tu-ba* 1. also *tú-pa,* **skirt, coat-flap** *Glr.* — 2. rarely *ₒtú-ba,* **bad,** c.g. wood *Mil.; *gyal-tú* W.* good and bad promiscuously; *sdug-bsṅál tú-ba* a bad accident *Thgy.;* **malicious, wicked, vicious** *Glr.* — 3. vb., v. *ₒtú-ba.*

ཐུ་བོ་ *tú-bo* ज्येष्ठ **a chief; an elder brother,** *Dzl., Tar.; tú-mo Cs.:* mistress, lady (?).

ཐུ་མི་ *tu-mi* p. n., v. *ton-mi.*

ཐུ་རེ་ *tu-ré* **uninterrupted** *Sch.*

ཐུ་ལུམ་ *tu-lúm* **a lump of metal** *B.; W.* **cannon-ball:**

ཐུག་ *tug, C.* also **túg-pa*,* c. accus. **until, to,** in reference to time and space; **žag zib-ču tug** for forty days; only col.

ཐུག་ཆོམ་ *tug-čóm Sch.:* **'dreadful noise';** *Thgr. tug-tsóm; Mil. tug-sgrá* id.

ཐུག་པ་ *túg-pa* I. sbst. **soup, broth,** *ₒbras-túg* rice-soup, *bag-túg* meal-soup, gruel, *rgya-túg* Chinese soup, a sort of vermicelli-soup *C.; tug-tál* v. *tál-ba.*

II. vb. 1. **to reach, arrive at, come to,** c. dat. or termin., *tseï mtar túg-pa* to reach the natural term of life *Dzl.;* to come or go as far as *Dzl.; rús-pa-la túg-pa* to pierce to the quick *Dzl.; ši-la tug tse Mil., ₒči-bar túg-pa-la Lt.* when one is near death; ... *la túg-gi bár-du* till, until *Dzl., Tar., Pth.; bzúṅ-la tug* he was just on the point of seizing her *Dzl.; *sád-da tug* W.* going to kill; *ši-la* (or *bsád-pa-la*) *túg-pa* often means deserving death (of culprits) *Dzl.; tse ₒpó-ba-la tug kyaṅ* though life is at stake *Dzl.;* in like manner *W.: *lus šrog daṅ túg-te ča dug** he goes at the peril of his life; *tug-yas* not to be reached, endless *Cs.* — 2. **to meet, to light upon,** c. *la* or *daṅ,* = *ₒprád-pa,* esp. col. **nyi-ráṅ-la túg-ga-la yoṅs* W.* he has come to see you; **tug yin* W.* we shall meet again, = till we meet again! à revoir! *ǰág-pa daṅ túg-pa Mil.* to fall in with robbers; *γdoṅ túg-pa* = *túg-pa; či-la tug ruṅ Mil., *ghá-la tug kyaṅ* C.* whatever may happen to me; *tug-čád* agreement to meet *Sch.* — 3. col. **to touch, to hit or strike against,** *W.: *ï-ru túg-kan** here it touches, or strikes against; here is the rub; **lag-pa mi tug yin** I shall not touch it, I shall not come near with my hand; **dé-la tug kyaṅ ma tug* W.* do not even touch it!

ཐུགས་ *tugs,* resp. for *snyiṅ, yid, sems, bsám-pa, blo* etc., and whenever mental qualities or actions are spoken of in respectful language, v. below. 1. **heart, breast,** in a physical sense, gen. *túgs-ka; túgs-kyi sprúl-pa* the incarnation of a deity, originating in a ray of light which proceeds from the breast of that deity *Glr.* — 2. **heart,** in a spiritual sense, **mind, soul, spirit, will,** v. below; **design, purpose, intention,** *sbyin-pai tug zlóg-tu γsol* we beg to desist from the intention of giving *Dzl.;* **understanding, intellect** *Glr.* (v. *sgám-pa*); *túgs-*

su čúd-pa = *Kóṅ-du čúd-pa*; *túgs-su ˳byóṅ-pa* to be kept in mind, in memory *Mil.*; also = *yíd-du ˷óṅ-ba* ni f.; cf. *˳gró-ba.* — 3. *túgs-la btúgs-so* v. *˳dógs-pa.* — 4. for *túgs-rǰe* or *bka-drin*, *tugs mdzád-pa* **to grant or show a favour** *Dzl.* — 5 in the phrase *tugs mi túb-pa*, with the genit. of the inf., it is used without ceremonial distinctions for **to venture, to risk, to dare** *Dzl.*

Comp. *túgs-ka* v. above — *tugs-mKyén* resp. for *mṅon-šés Mil.* — *tugs-˳Krúgs* resp. for *Kóṅ-˳Krúgs Ma.* — *tugs-dgóṅs* = *dgóṅs-pa* II.; *tugs-dgóṅs ɣtóṅ-ba* = *bsam-bló ɣtóṅ-ba* **to muse, meditate, reflect** *Mil.* — *túgs(-su) ˳gró-ba* resp. for *yid-du ˷óṅ-ba* **to be agreeable; agreeable, pleasant, delightful; pleasure, delight,** ... *la* in (a thing) *Mil.* — *tugs-rgyál* resp. **anger, wrath, indignation** *Mil.*, *tugs-rgyál bžeṅs* anger arises, is roused. — *tugs-ṅán* **grief, sorrow, affliction** *Dzl.* — *túgs-čes-pa* resp. for *yid-čes-pa* to believe. — *túgs-rǰe* prop. respectful word for *snyiṅ-rǰe* **pity, commiseration, compassion;** gen. **grace, mercy, generosity,** *ṅa-la túgs-rǰe(s) ɣzigs* pray, look graciously upon me! *Mil.*; even thus: *sá-bon žig túgs-rǰe ɣzigs dgos*, pray, be so kind as to send me some seeds! *W.* — *túgs-rǰes ˳dzin-pa*, *túgs-rǰe mdzád-pa* id. — *túgs-rǰe-čan* **gracious, merciful, generous.** — (*lha*) *túgs-rǰe čén-po* the All-merciful, Awalokiteswara. — *tugs-dám*, prop. resp. for *yi-dam*, 1. **oath, vow, solemn promise,** e.g. *bčá-ba* to take (an oath), to make (a vow). 2. **a prayer,** a wish in the form of a prayer, = *smón-lam.* 3. **contemplation,** the act of contemplating a deity (cf. *sgóm-pa* and *sgrúb-pa*); **meditation** in general, *Mil.* frq., *tugs-dám ˳pel* meditation increases, proceeds successfully; **devotion.** 4. **a deity, a tutelar god or saint, a patron** *Glr.* — *tugs-nyid* v. *sems-nyid*, sub *sems.* — *tugs-múg* resp. for *yi(d)-múg* despair. — *tugs bdé-ba*, *mi bdé-ba*, v. *bdé-ba.* — *tugs-ɣtsigs-pa* to be cautious *Sch.*; v. however *ɣtsigs-pa.* — *tugs-brtsé-ba* **love, affection of the heart, compassion,** resp. for *snyiṅ-brtsé-ba*, frq., *tugs-brtse-bar dgóṅs-pa*, *ɣzigs-pa*, with *la*, to look upon compassionately, to remember in mercy. — *tugs-ráb Sch.* = *šes-ráb.* — *tugs-rús Mil.* = *snyiṅ-rús.* — *túgs-(kyi) sráś Mil.*, *Tar.*, **spiritual son,** an appellation given to the most distinguished scholars of saints.

ཐུང་ང་ *tuṅ-ṅa* **three years old,** of animals *Sch.*

ཐུང་བ་ *túṅ-ba*, col. *túṅ-ṅu*, *Ld.* **túṅ-se**, **short,** relative to space, time, quantity of vowels etc.; *tuṅ-ṅu ˳gro-ba* to become shorter; but the word is not so much used as 'short' is in English; *yid túṅ-ba Dzl.*, *spro túṅ-ba Wdṅ.* **passionate, hot-tempered, hasty.**

ཐུད་ *tud* **cheese** made of buttermilk, or of *čúr-pe*, butter and milk *Ld.*, *Glr.*, *Pth.*; *˷o-túd* milk-cheese, made of curd, or of milk coagulated with runnet.

ཐུན་ *tun* I. a regular amount, a fixed quantity 1. of time, a certain length of time, as long as a man is able to work without resting, **a shift,** six, four, or three hours; *Schf.* translates *Tar.* 67, 17 even by one hour; **a night-watch,** *mel-tse tun ˳Kor* the night-watch is over *Dzl.*; *tun bžii rnal-˳byor* the meditation of a whole day *Mil.*; **tun čúd-čé** *W.* (the cock) announces the watch (by crowing); *tun bzuṅ-ba Pth.* prob. to have the watch; *nam-gyi guṅ-tun-la* at or about midnight; *sród-kyi gúṅ-tun-la Mil.* prob. id. — 2. **a dose of medicine** *Med.* frq. — *tun-log?*

II. **in sorcery:** bodies or substances which are supposed to be possessed of magic virtues, such as sand, barley, certain seeds etc., *tun-dóṅ* a hole in which such substances are concealed; *tun-rá* a horn to carry them; *tun ɣsó-ba* to revive a charm *Mil. nt.*

III. one who collects, **a gatherer** (from *˳tú-ba*), *šiṅ-túṅ* one who picks up or gathers sticks *Mil.*; *rtsa-tun* a gatherer of grass, *snye-tún* a gatherer of ears of corn *Cs.*; *tun-zór* reaping-hook, sickle *Sch.*

IV. *tun*, or more frq. *tun-móṅ(s)*, **usual,**

daily, what is done or is happening every day; **common, general,** *dṅos-grub tun-moṅs* earthly goods, as well as intellectual endowments, considered as common property, but not spiritual gifts; *tun-min, tun-moṅs ma yin-pa* **unusual, uncommon,** not for every body; **čig-la čig tun-móṅ čo** take good care to live together in harmony *W.*; *tun-móṅ-du* or *su* **in common, in company, jointly;** *tun-moṅ* by itself is also used as adv., = *tun-spyir,* **in general.**

ཐུབ་པ་ *túb-pa* (शक्) I. vb., c. accus., sometimes c. dat., 1. **to get the better of, to be able to cope with, to be a match for** (an enemy), **to be able to stand or bear** (the cold etc.), **to be able to do one harm, to get at one,** *dug-gis ma tub-čiṅ* as the poison could not do him any harm *Dzl.*; **to be able to quench, extinguish, keep off** e.g. fire, hail *Glr.*; *γžán-gyis mi túb-pa* **invincible,** not to be overcome; *ṅan dgu túb-pa* to be able to subdue every thing that is bad *Lt.*; **to have under one's command** or **control, to keep under,** e.g. one's own body; **to be able to bear,** e.g. *mis túb-par dka* (water from a glacier) is not easily borne by man, i.e. does not agree with him *Med.*; *ras rkyaṅ tub-pa* to be able to bear a simple cotton dress *Mil.*; *lo brgya túb-pa* to live to (the age of) a hundred years, frq. — 2. with a supine or verbal root, **to be able,** col. the usual word, in B. gen. *nús-pa*; cf. *γtúb-pa.*

II. sbst. 1. शाक्य **a mighty one, one having power and authority,** *šā-kya-tub-pa* Buddha; a wise man, a sage, a saint in general, मुनि. — 2. symb. num. for 7.

ཐུམ(ས)་ *tum(s),* also *túm-pa Cs., túm-po Sch.,* 1. **cover, covering, wrapper,** of a book or a parcel; *rgydb-pa Sch.* to put (a cover round a thing), to wrap up; **šig-pa* C., W., *šáṅ-pa* C.* to take off (a covering); *túm-čan* having a cover. — 2. **a parcel wrapped up** (in paper etc.); *ˏbru-taṅ-túm bčas* together with a small parcel of tea.

ཐུམ་པ་ *túm-pa* 1. v. *tum.* 2. v. *γnyid.*

ཐུམ་བུ, ཐོམ་བུ་ *túm-bu, tóm-bu* **a large spoon, a ladle;** *rag-túm* a brass ladle, *zaṅs-túm* a copper ladle.

ཐུར་ *tur* 1. *Cs.* **a declivity** (?), prob. only adverbially: **down;** *tur-lám* a downhill road; *túr-la, túr-du* down, downward, *ˏgró-bu* to go down, *núb-pa* to sink down; *mgo túr-du bstán-te* head down, head over heels *Stg.*; **tí-pi túr-la súb-če* W.* to uncock one's cap. — 2. v. *túr-mgo,* and *túr-ma.*

ཐུར་མགོ་ *túr-mgo* 1. **the tip of a spoon,** *túr-mgo tsam* as a measure *Mil.* — 2. also *tór-mgo* halter, **túr-go čúg-če* W.* to bridle, to bit (a horse); **túr-la tén-če* W.* to strive, to struggle against; to rear. — *tur-tág* the rein, *tur-mta* the end of the rein.

ཐུར་བུ, ཐུར་རུ་ *túr-bu, túr-ru* **foal, colt, filly.**

ཐུར་མ་ *túr-ma, W. *tur-maṅ*,* 1. **spoon.** — 2. Chinese **chopsticks.** — 3. **a pole** *Dzl.* ༢༠༧, 4. — 4. a whole class of surgical instruments *S.g.*

ཐུལ་ *tul* 1. **egg** (acc. to Cunningham a Cashmiri word), *túl-ta-gir* pancake. — 2. v. *ˏdúl-ba,* also substantively: *tul dc min* besides this **way of converting** (people) *Pth.*; *tul ˎóg-tu ˏjúg-pa Tar.* 25, 16 to keep a tight hand over a person, to discipline one; *žiṅ-gi tul ˏdébs-pa Ld.-Glr.* to clear land for tillage, ni f.

ཐུལ་པ་ *túl-pa, Cs.* also *túl-po,* dress made of the skins of animals, **a furred coat** or **cloak** *Mil.*; *lúg-tul* dress of sheep-skin, *rá-tul* dress of goat-skin, *túl-lu* the common sheep-skin dress; **túl-čan* W.* wide, not fitting close or tight.

ཐུལ་བ་ *túl-ba* 1. pf. to *ˏdúl-ba,* **to tame, curb, check, restrain,** *Mil.*: *ṅás ˏdré-rnams túl-nas* the goblins having been subdued by me; *las nyon-moṅs túl-ba dka* it is difficult to check a sinful deed *Mil.*; participle: tamed, civilized; converted. — 2. **to roll** or **wind up** *Lh.*

ཐུལ་ལེ་ *túl-le Ld.* **impressive,** nearly the same as *túr-re.*

ཐུས་པ་ *tús-pa* 1. **bad** = *tú-ba,* prov.; 2. v. *ˏtú-ba.*

ཐེ་ *te* 1. for *té-mo*; 2. num.: 100.

ཐེ་རྟོག་ *te-rtóg* **scruple, doubt, uncertainty, hesitation,** occasionally used for *te-tsóm.*

ཐེ་བ་ *té-ba*, *C.* also **ti-ba**, pf. *tes Sch.*, the col. syn. of *ytógs-pa*, seldom in *B.*, 1. **to belong, appertain to,** c. *la.* — 2. **to occupy one's self** with a thing, **to meddle with, to interfere,** c. *daṅ* (= *ₒdri-ba*); *té-mKan* belonging together, c. *la*, belonging to a thing; **ma-té-a* W.* for *ma-té-bar*, = *ma-ytógs-par*; *te-rég* the connexion or relation of ownership, *di-la yáb-kyi te-rég med* to this my father has no claims *Mil. nt.*

ཐེ་བོ་, ཐེ་བོང་ *té-bo*, *te-bóṅ W.* **thumb,** v. *téb-mo.*

ཐེ་མོ་ *té-mo*, col. *té-tse*, diminutive *teu*, resp. *p̓yag-té* **seal, signet, stamp,** **té-tse gyáb-če*, or *náṅ-če** to seal, to stamp; *sa-té Tar.* 79, 12(?); **té-tse lag-kór táṅ-wa** to engage, to bind one's self by a seal in some common concern.

ཐེ་ཚོམ་ *te-tsóm* **doubt, scruple, uncertainty, perplexity,** *te-tsóm skyes, byed* (*W.* **čo**), *za*, *te-tsóm-du gyur* I am doubtful; *te-tsom za-ba-rnams* scrupulous, irresolute persons *Pth.*; **te-tsom maṅ-po rag* W.* I am in great perplexity, I am quite at a loss; *te-tsom žig ₒdri-ba* to utter a doubt *Dzl.*

ཐེ་རང་ *te-raṅ* v. *teu-raṅ.*

ཐེ་རེ་ *te-ré* col. **straight, upright, firm; smooth,** without folds or wrinkles; *te-ré tiṅ C.* draw (the carpet) smooth.

ཐེ་རེལ་ *te-rél W.* **incomplete, defective, unfinished,** *te-rél-la lus soṅ* (the loaf) is not whole, there has already been cut from it.

ཐེ་ལི་ *te-li* v. *ta-li.*

ཐེག་པ་ *tég-pa* 1. sbst. **यान**, 1. **vehicle, carriage, riding-beast,** *rtai tég-pa-la žon* he mounted on horseback *Dzl.*; *tég-pa lṅa-brgya bšams* he procured five hundred conveyances (horses, elephants, carriages) *Dzl.* 2. for attaining to salvation, *tég-pa ysum* **three conveyances** are generally mentioned, but in most cases only two are specified, viz. *tég-(pa) dman(-pa)*, **हीनयान**, and *teg(-pa) čen-po*, **महायान**, gen. called 'the little and the great conveyance or vehicle', by means of which the distant shore of salvation may be reached. Yet mention is also made of a *sṅágs-kyi tég-pa*, **मन्त्रयान** *mantrayāna*, e.g. *Tar.* 180, 13. For more particulars about these vehicles, and other more or less confused and contradictory notions, the works of *Köppen* and esp. *Wasiljew* may be consulted.

II. vb. 1. **to lift, raise, hold up, support** *Mil.*, *Glr.*; hence *Kri-tégs* leg of a table *Sch.*; *teg-Kúg C.* knapsack, travelling-bag. — 2. **to raise, set up** fig. *bšad-gád* to raise a loud laugh *Mil.* — 3. most. frq. **to be able to carry,** *ji tég-pa* as much as you are able to carry *Dzl.*; *mis teg-tsád yčig* as much as one man is able to carry *Tar.*; esp. with a negative: *ma teg* he was not able to hold him up *Dzl.*; *mi-teg Kur* to carry what is too heavy to be carried (by ordinary muscular strength), to strain one's self by lifting, *Med.*; to endure, tolerate, stand, *Kóṅ-rnams-kyi ṅan ma teg-par* not being able to stand their urgent demands *Mil.*; **to bear, to undergo without detriment,** *skyid teg sdug teg* to be able to bear good fortune and ill fortune. Cf. *ₒtégs-pa*, *ₒdégs-pa.* —

ཐེང་ *teṅ* 1 *teṅ-ró Mil.*, **ša-téṅ* Ld.*, the dead body of an animal killed by beasts of prey. — 2. **téṅ-la* C.* **down, downward,** e.g. **kyúr-wa, yúg-pa, bór-wa**, to fling down.

ཐེང་པོ་ *téṅ-po Pth.*, *téṅ-bu Sch.*, **téṅ-Kan* W.*, **lame, hobbling, limping.**

ཐེངས་ *teṅs* **time, times,** *teṅs lṅa* five times *Pth.*; *dbugs-teṅs čig-la* in one breathing, at a stretch; without intermission *Pth.*

ཐེན་ *ten* 1. **a little while, a moment.** — 2. v. *ₒten-pa.*

ཐེན་པ་ *tén-pa* **tax, duty, impost** *Sch.*

ཐེབ་ *teb* 1. for *tem*, **full** *Glr.* — 2. for *tabs* *Glr.*, *C.* — 3. *téb-mo*, *teb-čén* the thumb, *teb-čúṅ* the little finger; v. *mte-boṅ.*

ཐེབས་ *tebs* **series, order, succession** *Sch.*, *tebs-re byed-pa* to do successively; *tébs-pa* v. *°tebs-pa.*

ཐེམ་པ་ *tém-pa* I. 1. **threshold**, *rgál-ba* to cross it *Glr.*; *sgo-tém* door-sill, threshold; *yá-tém* head-piece of a door-frame, lintel, *ma-tém* sill, threshold *Glr.* — 2. **staircaise, stairs, flight of steps,** *tem-skás* id.; **tem-só** *W.* **step, stair;** *tem-rím* *Cs.* 1. the several steps of a staircase. 2. **rank, dignity.** — *rdo-tém* stone staircase; *ḱor-tém* winding stairs *Cs.* — II. 1. **to be full, complete,** *zla-dus tem-pa daṅ* when the time of the months was fulfilled *Glr.* frq.; *žag ɣčig ma tém-pa-la* one day being still wanting *Glr.*; *brgya tém-pa* v. *tam-pa Glr.* — 2. *W.*: **to be sufficient, enough.** — 3. **to receive** (?) *Sch.*

III. *Sch.* = *tén-pa*, **tax, impost, tribute.**

ཐེམ་བུ་ *tém-bu*, *tem-tsaṅs* **stopping, closing, shutting up; a stoppage** *Sch.*

ཐེམས་ཡིག་ *tems-yig Sch.* **memorial.**

ཐེའུ་རང་ *teu-ráṅ Glr.*, *te-bráṅ Lt.*, *te-ráṅ Ma.*, a sort of **demons.**

ཐེར་ *ter* 1. **bald, bare,** *spyi-tér Thgy.* a bald head; a bald-headed person; *ter-tér* *C.* flat. — 2. = *te-ré* (?) *pyi ter naṅ gog* strong and hale outside, decayed within *Mil.*; *ter-zúg-pa* = *rtág-pa Thgr.*

ཐེར་འབུམ་ *ter-°búm Sch.* 1 000 000 000; *ter-°bum-čén-po* 10 000 000 000.

ཐེར་མ་ *tér-ma* a kind of thin woollen cloth, a flannel-like fabric, *le-ter* made of shawl-wool, *bal-ter* of common wool.

ཐེལ་ *tel* for *te-li*, *rag-tél C.* a plate made of latten brass.

ཐེལ་བ་ *tél-ba W.* frq. = *sléb-pa* **to arrive,** cf. *tál-ba* II., 4.

ཐེལ་སེ་ *tél-se Sch.* and *Wts.* **a seal, stamp,** = *te-tse.*

ཐེས་པ་ *tés-pa Sch.* pf. to *té-ba*; = *tes-bsún Lt.?*

ཐོ་ *to* 1. num. for 130. — 2. **register, list, catalogue, index;** *to °brí-ba* to register, to make out a list or catalogue *Schr.*; *sléb-to*, *°byúṅ-to* account of receipts, *sóṅ-to*, *búd-to*, *skyág-to* account of expenditures; *btáṅ-to* account of money or goods lent out; *nyó-to* account of goods bought, bill; *lo-to* **calendar, almanac;** *dei lág-tu ṗrin-bor-to* list of orders or directions given to him (lit. laid down in his hands); *dei rgyúd-la tób-to* a list of things which his relations shall receive.

ཐོ་གར་ *to-gár Pth.*; acc. to *Sch.* **the Turkomans;** *Tar.* 18, *Schf.*: **Tukhara,** name of a people in the northwest of India; prob. the **Togarmah** of the Bible.

ཐོ་ཅོ་ *to-čo Mil.*, **a foolish joke,** unbefitting a sensible man.

ཐོ་ཕྱི་ *to-ṗyi Schr.* **love** (?), in *Pth.* it seems to signify the **sky.**

ཐོ་བ་, མཐོ་བ་ *tó-ba*, *mtó-ba*, **a large hammer,** *tó-bas rdúṅ-ba* to hammer, to forge; *rdó-to* a stone hammer, *śiṅ-to* a wooden hammer, mallet; **to-čúṅ** 1. an ordinary hammer. — 2. **the cock of a gun.** — 3. **a soldering-stick.** *Lh.*

ཐོ་འཚམ་པ་ *to-°tsám-pa* **to scorn, scoff, jeer, sneer at, vex, insult, mock,** c. *la*, by words *Dzl.*, also by actions *Dzl.*; *snan-čud to-°tsám-pa bzód-par ɣsol* pardon our having sneered at you before! *Mil.*; also *mto-mtsám-pa*, *-btsám-pa*, *-brtsám-pa.*

ཐོ་ཡོར་ *to-yór* **stone pyramid, heap of stones** (cairn).

ཐོ་རངས་ *to-ráṅs* 1. **dawn, break of day, early morning,** *to-ráṅs(-kyi) dús-su* early in the morning; 2. **the following, the next morning,** c. genit.; both also adverbially: *de daṅ m)al-bai to-ráṅs* on the morning after having met him.

ཐོ་རེ་ *tó-re W.* **to-morrow** (*B.*, *C. saṅ*).

ཐོ་རེ་བ་ *tó-re-ba*, *tor-tsál Cs.*: **a few;** *Mil.*, *tog-re-tsal* **a little while.**

ཐོ་ལུམ་ *to-lúm* v. *tu-lúm.*

ཐོ་ལེ་ *to-lé* 1. *to-lé °débs-pa* **to spit,** c. *la*, at or on *Pth.* (cf. *tu*). — 2. **button** *C.* — 3. *to-lé dkár-po C.* **chalk.** — 4. *to-le-rgyal Mil.?*

ཐོ་ལོག་ *to-lóg* C. **mule, hinny.**

ཐོག་ *tog* I. **what is uppermost** 1. **roof,** *tog ₒbúbs-pa* to cover with a roof, to roof (a house) frq.; *tog ₒgél-ba* id.; also fig. **to complete, to crown a thing** *Mil.*; **tóg-sa nán-če* W.* **to roof, to finish a roof** by beating and stamping down the earth or sods, of which the covering consists; *tog-rdzis ytón-ba Mil.* id.; also fig. **to impress,** c. **genit.,** *Mil.* — **tog-kár* W.*, the opening for the smoke in a roof. — *tog-čan* having a roof, **tóg-yog* W.* under cover. — 2. **ceiling;** *yá-tog* ceiling, *má-tog* floor of a room. — 3. **story,** *dgu-tóg* having nine stories or floors, frq. — 4. in a general sense: *tog ₒdrén-pa Mil.* **to be at the head, to lead, direct, govern;** *tog-kar*, *W.* **ka-tóg-la*,* **on, upon,** *kyág-tog-kar* on the ice *Glr.*; *tóg-tu,* and *tog-tóg* adv. **up, up to; above;** *yán-tog-tu* in the uppermost place, quite at the top, *Glr.;* postp. c. genit. (or accus.) 1. **on, upon,** e.g. to lay on, to place upon *Pth.; sems tóg-tu ljí-bar byún-nas* lying heavy, weighing heavily, upon one's mind *Glr.; nai tóg-tu byun* my heart was smitten (by that); that has touched, has grieved my heart *Mil.*; *tog-tu kel-ba Mil.*, vb. act. to it. 2. **above** *Glr.* 3. **towards,** in the direction of, e.g. running towards, *mai tog-tu Dzl.*; *yá-tog, má-tog* ad. **above, below, or up to, up stairs,** and **down, down stairs** *Mil.* 4. **to,** e.g. to send to *Dzl.* 5. *dmag-tog* **at the head of** the army, or only **with** the army. 6. **during, as long as, throughout; whilst** (*tog* gen. without *-tu*), *dgun-tog* throughout the whole winter; **dir á-ku sem tser tog** whilst her husband is here in great anxiety *Ld.; bgros-tog* during the walk. Cf. also *na-og, pi-tog* as sbst.: **morning, evening, forenoon, afternoon** *W.* 7. **directly after,** *bžos-tog ₒó-ma* fresh milk, *S.g.* (s.l.c.). — *tog-nas* 1. **above, more than,** **lo nab-čų tog-nę ma lus* Ld.* they remained, i.e. lived not more than fifty years. 2. **on the part of,** *Thgy.*, analogous to *pyógs-nas.*

II. **thunderbolt, lightning;** *tog dan sér-ba* lightning and hail, *tog-sér-gyi ynód-pa* damage done by the elements; *tog ₒbáb-pa* lightning descending, *rgyab-pa* striking, *tog-bábs-su ₒbyón-pa* to arrive, to approach quick or suddenly like lightning *Tar.*, resp.; *tóg-gis ysód-pa S.g., tog báb-ste ₒči-ba Do.* to be killed by lightning.

III. 1. **fruit, produce,** *dkár-tog* v. *dkár-po; žiń-tog* produce of the fields *Dzl.*; *lo-tóg* a year's produce; *šiń-tóg* produce of a tree or other plant, fruit; *ysar-tóg* this year's crop *S.g.*; *tog-pŕúd* first-fruits, as an offering; *tog-šás* id. (?). — 2. *W.* **fortune, wealth, property,** **ńúl-li tog** property in money, cash in hand; (*s*)*pi-tog* common property, property belonging to a community.

IV. in *ma-tog*(*-tse*) for *ma tag*, col. and *Thgy.*, s.l.c., v. *tag.* Cf. also *tog-tág, tóg-ma, tógs-pa.*

ཐོག་ཐག་ *tog-tág*, prob. augmentative of *tog*, v. *tóg-tu* 6, also *tag-tóg*, **during, as long as, throughout; quite,** *mtsan tog-tág-tu* all night long; *nyi-ma-yčig-gi bár-du tog-tág* during a whole day; *lam tog-tág gán-no* the roads were quite full (of snow) *Dzl.*

ཐོག་མ་ *tóg-ma* **what is uppermost,** 1. **the upper end, the uppermost place,** *grál-gyi tóg-ma-la ₒdúg-go* they sat down in the first, or uppermost, place *Dzl.*; gen. 2. **origin, beginning;** *tóg-mai sańs-rgyás kun-tu-bzán-po* Adibuddha Samantabhadra, so a deity is called, by which a prayer has been appointed that is supposed to be particularly efficacious; *tóg-ma čo-rigs mtó-ba* of noble birth, as regards his origin *Dzl.*; *tóg-ma btsás-pai tsé-na, tóg-ma btsás-nas, tóg-ma skyés-nas* already at his birth, from his very birth *Dzl.*; *tog-ma méd-pa-nas, dus tog-méd-nas* time out of mind, from eternity; *tóg-ma-nas* from the very beginning; of itself; as a matter of course *Dzl.; bsúbs-pai tog-tág-la* as soon as they began to fill up *Glr.*; *tog-mta-bar-du* at first, later, in conclusion (lit. in the beginning, end, and middle) *Lt.*; most frq. *tóg-mar* 1. **at first, first,** the Lat. primum, primo, and primus. — 2. postp. c. genit. **before**, with respect to time *Mil.* — *tog-drans-pa Pth., Glr., Sch.*: 'at first, begun'; our Lama explained it by **'to lead, to guide'**, v. *tog* I, 4.

ཐོག་ཚད་ *tog-tsád W.* **story** (of a house); *tóg-so Mil. nt.* id.

ཐོགས་ *togs* v. *ₒdógs-pa*, and *ₒtógs-pa*.

ཐོགས་པ་ *tógs-pa*, c. *la*, **to strike, stumble, run against** (like *túg-pa* v. 3); **to be hindered, impeded, delayed,** frq.; *mi kyi gáṅ-laaṅ tógs-pa méd-du* without being hindered by men, dogs, or anything else *Mil.*; *togs-pa-méd-pa, togs-méd, togs-brdúgs-* (or (b) *rtug-*) *méd-pa*, असङ्ग **not hindered, unimpeded, unchecked; all-searching, all-penetrating.**

ཐོང་ *toṅ, toṅ-šól* **a plough.**

ཐོང་ཁ་ *tóṅ-ka Mil., toṅ-ga Mṅg.?*

ཐོང་པ་ *tóṅ-pa* 1. *Cs.* **a ploughman.** — 2. *Cs.*: **'a ram** that is castrated, **wether;** *ra-toṅ* a castrated he-goat'; according to my authorities, however, *tóṅ-pa*, and *ra-tóṅ* signify a ram and he-goat **one year old,** *toṅ-tsér* and *ra-tsér* being the feminine forms (?) — 3. *tóṅ-pai lo Mil.* the years between childhood and manhood, **juvenile years,** *Sch. tóṅ-po*, cf. *kyóg-toṅ*.

ཐོང་སྤུ་ *tóṅ-spu* **mane of the camel** *Sch.*

ཐོངས་པ་ *tóṅs-pa Mil.?*

ཐོད་ *tod* 1. *Cs.* **a head-ornament, crown;** gen. the usual covering for the head in the East, **turban,** *la-tód Glr.* id.; *dbu-tód* resp.; *sá-yig tód-du bčiṅs-pai ka* the letter k having for a crown the letter s: སྐ *Zam.* — 2. = *tog* I.: **go-tö** *C.* **over** or **above** the door; *ka-tód-la, ka-tóg-la, ka-tód-la,* **up, upon** *Ld.* — 3. **threshold,** *yá-tod, má-tod* = *yá-re, má-re.* — 4. v. *tód-pa.* — 5. *tod-rgál čé-ba* (*toṅ?*) *Mil.*, acc. to the context: **angry, wrathful.** — 6. *tod-tód* v. *su.*

ཐོད་པ་ *tód-pa* 1. **skull, cranium;** skull of a dead person, **death's head;** *tod-skám* a dry skull, *tod-rlón* a fresh skull *Thgr.*; *tod-krág* a skull filled with blood *Thgr.*; *tod-pór* a drinking-cup made of a skull. — 2. col. **forehead, brow;** *tod-rtsá* vena frontalis *Lt.*; *tod-čiṅs, tod-kébs, tod-brgyán,* turban.

ཐོད་ལེ་ཀོར་ *tod-le-kór Lex.* **alabaster;** *Tar.* 67, 18 *Schf.* = खटिका, chalk.

ཐོན་ *ton* v. *ₒtón-pa* and *ₒdón-pa*; *tón-pa C.* also: **good, fair, beautiful;** *smrá-bar tón-pa* eloquent.

ཐོན་མི་ *tón-mi*, or *tú-mi sam-bhó-ṭa* n. of the minister that was sent to India by king Sroṅbtsansgampo, in order to procure an alphabet for writing.

ཐོབ་ *tob* 1. v. *tób-pa.* — 2. v. *ₒdebs-pa.*

ཐོབ་ཚུ་ *tob-ču Schr., *tob-če, tob-či, teb-ču* C.,* **button** (v. *tob-či*).

ཐོབ་པ་ *tob-pa* I. vb. (synon. to *rnyed-pa*, and exclusively in use in *W.*) 1. **to find,** frq. — 2. **to get, obtain,** *ṅas tob B., ṅá-la tob* col., I find, I get; *tob-par ₒgyúr-ba* id.; **to partake of, to come to,** *dád-pa* faith (to come to the faith) *Mil.*; **to obtain, to get possession of, to subject to one's power** *Dzl.*; *da-drág tob-mtár Gram.*: after (words) that have got a *da-drág*; *saṅs-rgyás, rgyál-po, bdág-po, tób-pa* (lit. to get the Buddha etc.) **to become** a Buddha, a king, a lord; **čag-dzód tob-če* W.* to become frq. (cf. *rgyál-po*). —

II. sbst. that which has been got or obtained: **the sum, result,** of a calculation etc. *Wdṅ.*

III. **tób-če(s)* W.* adj. that which is **to be got** or **received,** e.g. **búlon tób-čes-si bún-yig** a list of demands to be called in, of money owing.

Comp. *tob-rgyál byéd-pa* **to rob, pillage, plunder** (?) *Sch.*; *tob-čá* the share which one gets *C.* — *tob-táṅ Cs.* 'income, revenue'; more accurately: that which falls to one's share, as a reward or pay, for work, services etc., e.g. bits of cloth or silk, which a tailor may keep for himself. — *tob-nór* 1. **share, quota.** 2. **quotient.** — *tob-bló C.* **desire,** *bkúr-sti tób-pa* **ambition** *Schr.* — *tob-tsir* (lit. the turn of getting, receiving) **claim, right; duty, due,** *tob-tsir ṅá-la yod* I have a claim, a right to it *W.*; **tob-tsir táṅ-ce* W.* to give each his share in his turn (prop. acc. to the due turn). — *tob-rím Glr.* id. — *tob-yig* **repertory, index.** — *tob-sról* prob. = *tob-tsir*, **right of succession** *C.* — *tob-šá C.* **contest, quarrel, strife; scramble,** e. g. for money thrown among the people.

ཐོམ་བུ་ *tóm-bu* = *túm-bu.*

ཐོམས་པ་ *tóms-pa* v. *˳tóms-pa.*

ཐོར་ཁོད་ *tor-ḱód*, or *tor-gód*, **a Mongol tribe.**

ཐོར་མགོ་ *tor-mgó* v. *tur-mgó.*

ཐོར་ཅོག, ཐོར་ཙུགས་ *tor-cóg, tor-tsúgs*, (also *do-kér*) **a plaited tuft of hair, toupet,** *Lex.*: *có-toi tor-cóg*; *tor-cóg dar sna lṅa bciṅs Pth.* he bound his tuft of hair with a silk string of five colours; prob. = *ytsug-tór* q.v ; *tór-to(r) Lex.* id.

ཐོར་པ་ *tór-pa*, also *˳tór-pa Med.*, **the small-pox** *Sch.*; in *Sik. tór-ba* signifies **pimple, pustule,** but the usual word for this is *srin-tór*, and in *W. *pul-tór** has a similar meaning, whereas *tór-bu Med.* denotes a whole class of diseases, comprising dyspepsy and cutaneous disorders. — *dmar-tór* **measles** *Sch.*

ཐོར་བ་ *tór-ba* 1. v. *˳tór-ba.* — 2. v. *tór-pa.*

ཐོར་བུ་ *tór-bu* **single, separate;** *Tar.* 120, 19: *prá-mo tór-bu-pa* separate little works, books *Schf.*

ཐོར་མོ་ *tór-mo* the growing fat of cows, goats etc. in consequence of sterility *Sch.*

ཐོལ་བ་ *tól-ba* 1. v. *˳tól-ba*, pf. to *rtól-ba*, what has come forth, what has been raised, elevated(?) *Sch.* cf. *tol-tól Mṅg.*; *tol-byúṅ* to arise, to begin, suddenly *Sch.*

ཐོས་པ་ *tos-pa* 1. vb. **to hear** *B., C.* (*W.* **tsór-ce**), *rgyál-po žig-gi ytam tós-sam*, or only *rgyál-po žig tós-sam Dzl.* have you heard of a king? *˳brós-so zér-bai ytam rgyál-poi snyán-du tós-so* it came to the king's hearing that he had escaped. *Glr.* — 2. adj. *mṅán-du tós-pa* **far-famed, renowned,** frq.; *ma tós-pa* **unheard of;** *tos-gról* the title of a book which is read to the soul of a deceased person (**tö-dhól* C.*, **to-dól* W.*), and the full title of which is: *tós-pa tsám-gyis gról-ba tób-pai cos* a doctrine by the hearing of which a man is instantly saved *Thgr.*; *tos-cúṅ Mil.* **hearing little.**

ཐྲིག་ཐྲིག་ *trig-trig* **the creaking of shoes.**

ཐྭག་ *twag Ld.* the sharp sound, **the cracking,** which is heard, when a branch of a tree is breaking off; cf. *tsa-rág* and *ldim.*

མཐང་ *mtaṅ Cs.*: **the lower part of the body,** *mtaṅ-gós* a vestment for it, **a sort of petticoat** (acc. to others: toga) worn by Lamas.

མཐའ་ *mta* (cf. *tá-ma*) 1. **end, ending,** 1. relative to space: **edge, margin, brink, brim,** of a well *Glr.*, skirt of a forest, gen. *mtá-ma*; **limit, bound, border, confines, frontiers,** *mta skór-ba* to go round the confines (of a place); *mtá-las ˳dás-pa* exceeding all bounds, very great, e.g. *sdug-bsṅál Thgr.*; used even thus: *rgyál-po bžúgs-pai mtá-la bskor* to walk round him that sits on a throne *Glr.*, po.; adverbially: *dé-mta* round this (mountain) *Mil.*; *mta dbus kún-tu* in the whole country (in the frontier districts and in the central parts); *mtai rgyal-ḱams* neighbouring or border-country; *mta* id., e.g. *mta bži* the four border-countries, i.e. all the surrounding territory, frq.; *mtai nor* the treasures of the border-country *Glr.*; *mtai dmag* border-war.; in the Tibetan part of the Himalaya mountains *mta* denotes in a special sense **Hindoostan**; — in grammar: **termination,** *na ma ra la žés-rnams mtá-can* words ending in n, m, r, l; *ga-mtá* a final g. 2. relative to time: *bskál-pai mta Dzl.* the **termination** of a Kalpa; *dus-mtái me* the conflagration at the end of the world, the ecpyrosis; in a more general sense: *mta ṅán-pas* as this will end badly; *mta ycig-tu Wdṅ.* and *Tar.* 4, 7 *Sch.*: **on the one hand, in part, in a certain degree, in some respect;** *Schf.*: 'schlechthin' (?) —

mťa-γcód-pa final or definitive sentence or judgment *Sch.*; *dei mťa γcod-pai ṗyir* in order to settle it definitely, viz. by counter-proof, *Gram.*; *yaṅ-dag-mťa* the true end, i.e. objective truth *Was.* (297); **the rest, remainder,** *re-dógs-kyi mťa spaṅ* having given up also the last remnant of fear and hope *Glr.*, cf. *mťá-dag; mťá-ru, mťar* 1. **towards the end,** towards the boundary or the neighbouring country; **at the end** etc.; *mťar ťúg-pa* to reach, to attain to the end, frq.; *tsei mťar ťúg-pai graṅs* the number of those that reach the (natural) end of life *Dzl.*; *mťar-ťug-pa-méd-pa* inexhaustible *Dzl.*; *mťár-ṗyin-pa* (rarely *mťar-°kyil-ba*) id.; also absolutely as sbst. *mťár-ṗyin-pa* **a perfect, a holy person, a saint;** *mťár-ton-pa* id. (?) *Mil.*; *mťár-byed-pa* to give a work its finish *C.*, (*Sch.*: 'to destroy, demolish'?) 2. adv. **lastly, finally, in conclusion** *Dzl.*, *Thgy.*; perh. also **to the very last, wholly, altogether.** 3. postp. with genit. **after, behind,** *rgyal-rábs sum-brgyái mťar* after 300 royal generations *Glr.*; *sá-mťar śiṅ, śiṅ* is to be written after a final s, *Gram.* — 2. **aim, purpose** *Cs.* — 3. **system,** opinion *Tar.* 107, 4 *Schf.*, perh. for *grub-mťa.*

Comp. and deriv. *mťá-klas-pa Cs.* = *mťá-med-pa*, yet v. *mťas.* — *mťa-skór* **circumference, perimeter,** v. *dpag-tsád.* — *mťa-°kób* v. *°kob.* — *mťa-grú Glr.* 42? — *mťa-rgyás* **very wide** *Schr.* — *mťa-lċags* frame, of a mirror etc. *Schr.* — *mťa-ċag Med.?* — *mťa-rtén* final consonant *Gram.*; *mťa-rten-med-pa* ending with a vowel *Gram.* — *mťa-tig* boundary line *Sch.* — *mťa-ťog-ťág* **unceasing** (?) *Sch.* — *mťá-dag* **several, sundry; all,** frq.; *maṅ-tsig mťá-dag* the plural sign *mťa-dag Gram.* — *mťa-draṅs Gram.?* — *mťá ma* **the end,** *grál-gyi mťá-mai bú-mo* the girl at the end of the row (opp. to the middle or the other end, not necessarily to the beginning, like *mǰúg-ma*); **border, hem, seam,** of dresses *Dzl.*; *deṅ mťoṅ-ba mťa-ma* to-day we see (him) for the last time *Glr.* (*ťá-ma* would be more correct, like *Dzl.* ༢༠༧, 16). — *mťa-mal-pa* sometimes for *ťa-mal-pa.* — *mťá-mi* **borderer; neighbouring people.** — *mťá med-pa, mťá-yas-pa* **infinite, endless.** — *mťa-γséb Wdṅ.?*

མཐར་ *mťar* 1. v. *mťa.* 2. for *ťar.*

མཐར་སྐྱོལ་ *mťar-skyól* the bringing to an end, **carrying through, persistence, perseverance** *Mil.*

མཐར་གྱིས་ *mťár-gyis* **by turns, successively,** *Dzl.*; **by degrees, gradually.**

མཐས་ཀླས་ *mťas-klas, Zam.* = **पर्यन्त, border, limit?** cf. *mťa* compounds.

མཐིང་ *mťiṅ* acc. to *Cs.*: 'indigo', and '*mťiṅ-śiṅ* indigo-plant'; acc. to a Lama from Lhasa however: 1. **mountain-blue** (which is found, together with malachite, in the hills near Lhasa). — 2. from the resemblance: **indigo-colour** (whereas indigo as a substance is *rams*), and esp. a light **sky-blue, azure;** cf. *mťon-mťiṅ.*

མཐིང་རིལ་ *mťiṅ-ril, Lex.* a certain bird; *Sch.*: a sort of wild duck; acc. to *Pth.* a smaller bird.

མཐིའུ་ *mťiu* v. *mťeu.*

མཐིལ་ *mťil* 1. **bottom,** of a vessel, of the sea; **floor,** of a room *Glr.*; **foundation,** of a house. — 2. the lower side of a thing; **inner or lower part of a thing,** *lág-mťil* (resp. *ṗyág-mťil*) **the palm of the hand;** *lag-mťil-na* in the closed hand; *lag-mťil gaṅ* a closed handful; *rkaṅ-mťil* (resp. *żabs-mťil*) the sole of the foot; *lham-mťil* the sole of a shoe; *mťil bżi* the palms of the hands, and the soles of the feet. — 3. **the background, the far end,** of a cave, a tunnel etc. — 4. *C.*: **the centre, the principal or chief part,** of a town; **the principal place, chief city, capital,** of a country.

མཐུ་ *mťu* 1. **power, force, strength,** of the body, of the mind, of Buddha, of a prayer, of witchcraft etc.; **ability, power or authority** to do a thing; *mťu daṅ ldán-pa* **strong, powerful, efficacious, able** etc., *mťu-méd* **powerless, feeble, unable;** **mi za ťu mé'** *C.* I must eat it; *bsgrub-mi-nus-mťu-méd-la soṅ* we must be able to fulfil it *Mil.*; *mťu-*

žig-gis by an extraordinary manifestation of power or strength *Dzl.*; *klui mtu yin* that is an effect of the Lus, is produced, comes from the Lus *Stg.*; *mtus* **by virtue of**, frq.; *mtu-stóbs* = *mtu*. — 2. **magic, witchcraft**, *mtu ytóṅ-ba Mil.*, *mtu ̥débs-pa*, **tàb-ċe* W.*, to practise witchcraft, to injure a person by magic spells, to bewitch *Mil.* and col. frq.; *mtu ser brtad ysùm-po rdzógs-par bslabs* conjuring, raising tempests, exorcising ghosts, all these things I have learned thoroughly *Mil.*; *mtu-bo-čé* **high-potent, high and mighty** *Tar.*

མཐུག་ *mtug* v. *̥tug*.

མཐུད་པ་ *mtud-pa* v. *̥tud-pa*.

མཐུན་པ་ *mtún-pa*, also *̥tún-pa*, **to agree, to harmonize; agreement, harmony; agreeing** etc., 1. in a general sense, c. c. *daṅ*, . . . *yin-par don mtún-no* they agree in the opinion of her being . . . *Glr.*; *mtún-par byéd-pa* to make agree, to bring to an agreement, to make consistent, *mtún-par ̥gyúr-ba* to be made agreeing or consistent *Glr.*; *dgóṅs-pa yčig-tu mtún-pa* unanimous; *lhai lugs daṅ mtun* god-like (in deeds) *Glr.*; *rigs mtún-pa* of equal birth; *lo mtún-pa* of the same age, contemporary; *blo mtún-te* being of the same mind, similarly disposed, *čos byá-bar* with respect to religion *Glr.*; *ka mtún-par* with one mouth, *gros mtún-par* with one accord, unanimously, as one man; *grabs mtún-pa* to live in harmony; — **to be adequate, corresponding to**, e.g. *yid* (*daṅ*) *mtún-par*, resp. *túgs daṅ mtún-par*, to one's wish, as one could desire = *yid bžin-du*; *nad daṅ mtún-par* corresponding to the disease, fit or proper for the disease. — 2. in a special sense 1. viz. *yid daṅ*, **to be wished for, desirable**, particularly in *mtun-rkyén*, v. *rkyén*; also: **to wish, to like, to delight in**, *kyed-rnams-kyis mtún-pai rdzas* things wished for by you, desirable to you *Mil.*; 2. with or without *yčig-lu yčig*: *mtún-nas* whenever they (the two nations) lived in peace with each other (opp. to *̥kón-nas*) *Glr.*; *mtún-pai ytam byéd-pa* to converse amicably *Glr.*, to enter into negotiations of peace *Glr.*; *mtún-par byéd-pa* 1. v. above, 2. **to caress, to fondle, to dandle** *Glr.*; *šin-tu mtún-par yod* they are on the best terms with each other, are making love to each other *Glr.*; *mtún-po bsdad ̥dug* col. id.; *mtún-po byéd-pa* to be kind, affable, condescending *Mil.* (opp. to being proud, cold, reserved); *rgya bod ynyis mtun ̥oṅ* there will be a good understanding between China and Tibet *Glr.*; *mi mtún-pai pyogs tams-čád-las rgyál-ba* to gain the victory over all the hostile parties; *mtún-̥gyur-gyi yi-ge C.* **letter of recommendation**; *mtún-čan W.* **gentle, peaceful.**

མཐུར་ *mtur*, also *mtúr-mgo*, v. *túr-mgo*, **halter**, *rta-mtur Lex.* id.; *mtur-tág* **rein, reins** *Sch.*; *mtur-mtá* the end of the reins, e.g. to place them into the hands of another.

མཐུས་ *mtus* v. *mtu* 1.

མཐེ་བོ་ *mté-bo*, col. *mté-bóṅ*, *mte-čéṅ*, *mtéb-mo* (v. also *te bo*), **thumb**, *rkáṅ-pai mté-bo* **the big toe**; *mteb-čúṅ* the little finger, the little toe *Glr.*

མཐེའུ་ *mteu* 1. **a little hammer**; 2. *mteu-čúṅ* **the little toe.**

མཐོ་ *mto* 1. **a span**, from the end of the thumb to the end of the middle finger when extended; *mto ̥jál-ba* or *yžál-ba*, *W.* **táb-ċe**, to span, to measure by the hand with the fingers extended: *mto gáṅ*, *mto rè tsam* a span (in length), *mto do* two spans. — 2. v. *mtó-ba*.

མཐོ་གོང་ *mto-góṅ* a little triangular receptacle into which the likeness of an enemy is placed, to whom one wishes to do harm by witchcraft *W.*

མཐོ་རྒྱབ་ *mto-rgyáb* **earnest-money** *W.*

མཐོ་བ་ *mtó-ba* 1. **to be high; highness, height; high, lofty, elevated**, *B.* (cf. *mtón-po*), frq. fig.; *rigs če-žiṅ mtó-ba-ste* being of high and noble birth *Dzl.*; *dé-las mtó-ba* more elevated than that, surpassing, surmounting that; c. accus. or instrum., **high** as to (stature, rank etc.) *mtó-na* when I am high, when I rise; *mtó-ba γnón-pa* to lower what is high, to bring down, to humble, frq.; *ṅas mto-mtó byás-pas dma-dmá byuṅ* the more I was aspiring, the more I was brought low *Pth.*; *sbyín-pa mtó-ba Stg.* was explained: gifts or alms bestowed from a sincere heart. — 2. **hammer**, v. *to-ba*; *mto-po-tog* a stone used as a hammer *Cs.*

Comp.: *mto-kyad* **height, highness** *Dzl.* — *mto-dógs Pth.* (together with *γyo-sgyú*, and *ṗrag-dóg*) perh. mistrust, suspicion; **tón-dod-čan* W.* **ambitious**, aspiring, aiming at things too high. — *mto-spyód W.* a haughty manner. — *mto-dmán* 1. *Cs.* high and low, uneven; also *Schr.* 2. **height**, *mto-dmán mnyám-pa* of equal height *Glr.* — *mto-ₒtsám(s)-pa* v. *to-ₒtsám-pa.* — *mto-rís* **heaven**, abode of the gods, **paradise**, Elysium.

མཐོང་ག་ *mtóṅ-ga Sch.*, *mtoṅs-ka Pth.*, **chest, breast**, *mtóṅ-ga-nas ₒdzin-pa* to seize by the breast *Pth.*

མཐོང་བ་ *mtóṅ-ba* **to see**, 1. vb. n. to have the power of vision, often with *mig(-gis)*; *mtóṅ-bar ₒgyúr-ba* to obtain the faculty of seeing, to recover one's sight; *mtóṅ-bar byéd-pa* to make (the blind) see *Dzl.*; *mig-gis nye mtoṅ riṅ mi mtoṅ* he sees only when the object is near, not when it is far, he is short-sighted *Med.*; *nye-mtóṅ* short-sighted *Sch.* — 2. vb. a. 1. **to perceive**, by the eye, **to see, to behold**, *bód-kyi ri mtóṅ-bai ri* an eminence from whence one can see the mountains of Tibet *Glr.*; *mi γžán-gyis mtóṅ-sar* (a place) where one can be seen by others; *de bú-mos mtóṅ-bar mdzád-do* he made it visible to the girl, he made her see it *Dzl.*; *mtóṅ-ba žig yód-na* if there is one that has seen it, if there exists a witness *Dzl.*; *de mtóṅ-ste šes* seeing this, I came to know, i.e. from this I saw, I perceived; *mtoṅ tos dran reg*, frq., the seeing, hearing, touching, thinking of (e.g. a form of prayer, or magic formula); *ma ₒón-bar*, (or *ₒón-ba*) *mtóṅ-nas* as he saw his mother coming. 2. with accus. and termin.: **to regard, consider, take for**, *Thgy.*; *rdzas dkar sér-por mtoṅ Lt.* taking white things for yellow ones. 3. **to meet, find, catch.** 4. **to know, understand, perceive** (mentally) *Mil.* 5. col. **to undergo, suffer, endure**, misfortunes, pain etc. (cf. *stonpa* 4), *mi mtoṅ mtóṅ-ba* to suffer what is not to be suffered, not bearable nif., cf. *ltá-ba.*

Comp. *mtóṅ-kuṅ Cs.* **'a window'**, prob. for *mtoṅs-kuṅ.* — *mtóṅ-sgom-čan Thgy.* was explained: one who instantly knows and understands every thing he sees (?) — *mtóṅ-ₒkor*, *mtóṅ-mta*, **the reach of sight, range of vision** *Cs.*, **tóṅ-ₒkor-la bor* W.* do not take them (the horses) farther than you can see them; **the horizon** *Cs.*; *mtoṅ-dúg* ('eye-poison') **evil-eye** *Sch.*; **envy, grudge, jealousy.** — *mtoṅ-snáṅ* v. *snaṅ-ba.* — *mtoṅ-byéd* that which sees, the eye *Cs.*; the substance which is the source of vision, a species of gall, आलोचक. *Med.* — *mtoṅ-lám* the path of obtaining the power of sight, a mystical state *Was.* (139). — *mtóṅ-lugs* the way of beholding, of viewing a thing; **notion, idea, opinion** = *snáṅ-ba*, *mtóṅ-lugs γsúm-du byuṅ* three different opinions were forming *Glr.*

མཐོངས་, རྒྱ་མཐོངས་ *mtoṅs*, *rgya-mtoṅs* 1. **an opening for the smoke** in a ceiling or roof, also *mtóṅs-kuṅ.* — 2. also *mtóṅs-ka*, **pavilion, platform, open gallery**, on a flat roof *Glr.* (*Cs.*: 'impluvium, or the opening in the middle of a square building', for which, however, the Tibetan word seems to be *kyams* or *kyams-mtóṅs*).

མཐོངས་ཀ་ *mtóṅs-ka* **silk ornaments** on the borders of a painting *Cs.*

མཐོངས་པ་ *mtóṅs-pa Cs.*: **to lose one's senses**; perh. *ₒtóms-pa.*

མཐོན་ཀ་ *mtón-ka*, or *mtón-ga Lex.*; *Cs.* 1. **azure, sky-blue** (?). — 2. n. of a flower. — 3. *Glr.* one of the five celestial gems; *mtón-ka čén-po* another of these gems. —

མཐོན་པོ་ *mtón-po* **high, elevated**, *B.* and col. (cf. *mtó-ba*), of water **deep**, of the voice **loud**, of weight and measure **full**, of rank **high**; **čós-skad tón-po* W.* high-sounding words, pompous style; *tág-len tón-po* W. highly skilled, well practised. — mton-mtíṅ 'the high blue (thing)' viz. the hair of the head of Buddha, always represented as of a light sky-blue.

མཐོལ་བ་, འཐོལ་བ་ mtól-ba, ₒtól-ba, **to confess, to avow**, nyés-pa Dzl.; mtol tsáṅs (cf. ₒgyod-tsáṅs) **confession, acknowledgment**, mtol-tsáṅs byéd-pa Dzl., mtol bšags-pa to make confession, to confess, which acc. to Buddhist doctrine involves atonement and remission of sins.

མཐོས་ mtos 1. Ld. **high, elevated**, *ṭím-si saṅ tos ma len* do not take more than is right! — 2. Mil.?

འཐག་པ་ ₒtag-pa, pf. btags, fut. btag, imp. tog, 1. **to grind**, raṅ-ṭág-gis in a mill Dzl., gro wheat, ṗyé-mar to flour; to reduce to powder, **to pulverize**, by means of two stones (cf. ɣtun); **to mash**. — 2. **to weave**, snám-bu cloth; ₒtág(-pa)-po, ₒtág-mk'an **a weaver**; dar-tag-bú-mo the daughter of a silk-weaver Glr. — ₒtag-stán loom Sch. — ₒtag-rdó **mill-stone, grinding-stone**(?) Sch.

འཐང་པོ་ ₒtáṅ-po Wdṅ. a bodily defect or deformity, prob. téṅ-po.

འཐད་ ₒtad **liking, pleasure; will; joy,** v. the following article.

འཐད་པ་ ₒtád-pa I. 1. **to be pleasant, agreeable, well-pleasing** ccdp., ɣsuṅ de kun šin-tu séms-la ₒtád-pa žig byuṅ all these sayings have pleased me very much Mil. — 2. (not governing a case) **to please, to be acceptable, to be considered as good,** to be (generally) **admitted,** mi ₒtád-par mtoṅ I see that (this reading) is not generally accepted Zam.; žes-paaṅ ₒtád-do it occurs also in this form Zam.; mi-ₒtád-de **wrong!** Was. (294); **to be fit, proper, suitable** (syn. to ₒos-pa), sems zér-ba mi ₒtád-la as it is not proper to call it soul, as it cannot fitly be called soul Mil. — 3. a familiar word, very frq. used, in W. almost the only word for dgá-ba and ₒdód-pa, *sem tád-de* cheerfully, joyfully W., ₒtád-rgyu méd-pa tsam žig-la prob.: as he became angry Mil.; *sém-mi náṅ-ne tad soṅ*, also *tiṅ (q. v.) *tág-pa-ne tad-soṅ* W. I have been heartily glad; ₒtad-ₒtád-ₒdra yaṅ Mil. though apparently rejoicing; *ṅa tad-tád* W. I am very glad of that; *sem tád čúg-če* W. to make glad, to exhilarate; *sá-heb-bi žó-la mi tád-da* W. does your honour not like curdled milk? *tád-k'an* W. willing, ready; *gá-ru tád-na soṅ* W. go wherever you like; lóg-pa-ₒtad let us turn back Glr.; ráṅ-ñi ₒtád-la voluntarily, spontaneously.

II. Sch. = ₒtán-pa, ₒtad-ldán = ₒtán-po.

འཐན་ ₒtan **bad**, ₒtan-ₒdré a demon Sch.

འཐན་པ་ ₒtán-pa (cog. to brtán-po and tán-po?) Cs. also ₒtád-pa, **firmness, constancy**, in Lex. explained by ñán-tan; mi ₒtán-po a steady, resolute man Cs.

འཐབ་པ་ ₒtáb-pa **to combat, to fight**, in a battle; **to quarrel, to dispute, to brawl**; k'a-tsúb daṅ ₒtáb-pa to struggle with a snow-storm Mil.; ₒtáb-pa méd-čiṅ ši-ba to die peaceably, without a struggle; ₒtáb-pa ₒdúm-na when quarreling (persons) are reconciled; k'a-ₒtáb Cs. a fighting with the mouth, altercation; lag-ₒtáb Cs. a fighting with one's hands, a close fighting, a scuffle (Sch. gesticulation?); ₒtab-król Lex. dispute, contest; ₒtab-ₒk'rúg prob. id.; (Lex. **आयुध** weapon?); *tab-ḍhab* C. weapons, arms; ₒtab-čás ammunition, requisites for war Schr.; ₒtab-brdúṅs, á-k'ui ₒtab-brdúṅs the quarreling and thrashing of my uncle Mil.; ₒtáb-mo quarrel, fight, row, fray, battle, B. and col. frq., ₒtáb-mo byéd-pa B., *čó-če* W., to quarrel, fight etc.; ₒtáb-mó spród-pa to fight a battle, to join battle Glr.; ₒtab-, žób a dry cough Sch. — ₒtáb-rtsód altercation, quarrel, brawl, frq. — ₒtab-ya antagonist, k'yód-kyis ṅai ₒtáb-ya byed dgos thou must contend with me Glr. — bdúd-moi ₒtáb-ya a termagant, a she-devil to struggle with Mil.; ɣnás-skabs-kyi ₒtáb-ya the antagonists of life, i. e. the family and relations a secular man has to struggle with Mil. — ₒtab-rágs intrenchment, breast-work, fortification C.

འཐབ་འབུ་ ˳ṫáb-˳bu a cricket *Sch.*

འཐམ་པ་ ˳ṫám-pa, pf. ˳ṫams, 1. **to seize,** to lay hold of, **to grasp**, to take a firm hold of, esp. with the teeth (dogs), or the jaws (serpents *W.*); to sting (of bees *W.*); **to embrace,** **rkaṅ-pa ˳ṫám-če* W.* to put one's arms around a person's feet, as a supplicant; to grasp intellectually, to comprehend (?) *Glr.* — 2. **to gnash,** *so* one's teeth; **to shut closely,** *ḱa* one's mouth, frq. — 3. **to join, unite** (vb. n.), *grógs-su, grógs-por Stg.*, in friendship, *byá-bar* in an act, an undertaking *Dzl.*

འཐལ་བ་ ˳ṫál-ba v. *tal-ba.*

འཐས་པ་ ˳ṫás-pa, *Lex.* = *mḱrégs-pa*, **hard, solid;** *bag-čágs rgyúd-la ˳ṫas* prob.: inordinate desire has taken a firm hold of your minds; *sra-˳ṫás Sch.* **strong, robust, sinewy;** *á-˳ṫas-te*, and *ê-˳ṫas-kyi bag-čags Pth.?*

འཐིག་པ་ ˳ṫig-pa 1. vb. n., pf. ˳ṫigs **to drop, to fall in drops, to drop from,** *ḱrag ma ˳ṫigs-par Lt.* without any blood dropping out. — 2. vb. a., pf. *btigs*, fut. *btig* **to cause to fall in drops, to instil** etc.

འཐིང་སླད་ ˳ṫiṅ - slad *Cs.* a term of blame or abuse; *Lexx.*

འཐིབས་ ˳ṫibs **a cover, covering;** *˳ṫibs - ˳og tsud? S.g.*

འཐིབས་པ་ ˳ṫibs-pa, pf. *ṫibs* and *γṫibs* (cf. *γṫibs - pa*), **to gather,** of clouds, storms; *ná-bun bžiṅ-du ˳ṫibs-par gyúr-to* (all the Buddhas) came drawing nearer like clouds of mist *Glr.;* **to condensate,** vb. n. *ljóṅ-šiṅ ṫams-cád dgá-bai tsál-du ˳ṫibs* all the trees afford a delightful shade *Glr.;* *byiṅ ˳ṫibs* drowsiness overcomes me; po. and fig. **to grow dark or dim,** *šés-pa* consciousness *Med.* — *˳ṫibs - po* **dark, close, dense.**

འཐིམ་པ་ ˳ṫim-pa v. *ṫim-pa.*

འཐུ་བ་ ˳ṫú-ba 1. adj. v. *ṫu-ba.* — 2. vb., also *˳ṫún-pa*, pf. *˳ṫus, btus*, fut. *btu*, imp. *ṫus, btu (Cs.)*, **to gather, collect, pick up,** *šiṅ, me-tog*, frq.; *ṫus-mi* an assemblage of men, council, *Cs.*

འཐུང་བ་ ˳ṫúṅ-ba, pf. ˳ṫuṅs (*Cs.* also *btuṅs* I have drunk out), (fut. *btuṅ Cs.*), imp. ˳ṫuṅ, (*Cs.* also *btuṅ* drink out!), *W.* **ṫúṅ-če**, **to drink,** frq.; **to suck, to smoke** (tobacco), **to eat** (soup); **to be soaked, drenched** (cloth) *Dzl.*; *ṅóms - pa ˳ṫúṅ - ba* to drink one's fill *Dzl.; žo-˳ṫuṅs, ˳o-˳ṫuṅs* suckling baby; *žo-˳ṫuṅ dus-na* during the time of giving suck *Med.*; *˳ṫúṅs-pa ṫsám-gyis* immediately after drinking *Thgy.*; *˳ṫúṅs - so* they were engaged in drinking *Glr.*; *˳ṫúṅ-du rúṅ-ba, W. *ṫuṅ-čóg**, **drinkable;** *btúṅ-ba* sbst. **drink, beverage,** *bzá-ba daṅ btúṅ-ba, bza-btúṅ* (*W. *zabtúṅ**) meat and drink, frq.; *btúṅ-ču* water for drinking *Mil.* —

འཐུག་པ་, མཐུག་པ་ ˳ṫúg-pa, *mṫúg-pa*, adj. and abstr. sbst., *˳ṫúg-po* adj , **thick,** *mta-˳ṫúg* thicker toward the margin or edge *Mṅg.*; gen. of woven stuffs, opp. to *sráb-pa*; *srab-˳ṫúg* 1. **thin and thick,** 2. **thickness** relatively; also **consistency,** of liquids, opp to *slá-ba Med.;* **dense,** *nags*, frq.; **sound, heavy,** *γnyid ˳ṫúg-po* a sound sleep; **strong,** *bag - čágs ˳ṫúg - po* a strong inclination *Mil.*

འཐུད་པ་, མཐུད་པ་ ˳ṫúd - pa, *mṫúd - pa* **to make longer** by adding a piece, to piece out, to prolong, *ṗu-dúṅ W.* a sleeve; *skyé-ba ˳ṫud mi dgos* he has no need of adding a re-birth, a new period of life *Pth.*; *˳ṫud - ma* 1. **addition, prolongation,** **sróg-gi ṫúd-ma ṫáṅ-če* W.* prolonging life (by medicine, careful nursing). — 2. **aid, assistance, subsidy,** e.g. to a needy betrothed couple; also **a gift of honour,** a present, offered to a departing benefactor or respected Lama *W.*; *dmag - ˳ṫúd* **subsidies; auxiliary troops.** — 3. **help, assistance** in general.

འཐུན་ ˳ṫun **gatherer,** *šiṅ-˳ṫún* a gatherer of wood, *rtsa-˳ṫún* of grass.

འཐུབ་པ་ ˳ṫúb-pa, pf. *˳ṫubs*, fut. *γṫub*, imp. *˳ṫub, btub, W. *ṫúb-če**, **to cut into pieces,** v. *γṫúb-pa.*

འཐུམས་པ་ ˳ṫúm - pa, pf. *˳ṫums, btums*, fut. *btum*, imp. *˳ṫum, btum, W. *ṫúm-če**, **to cover** or **lay over, to put over, to** coat, záṅs-kyis *Glr.*; **to wrap up, to envelop,** v. *γtúm-pa.*

འཐུམས་ *ₒtums* **barren, sterile; addled** (eggs); *blo-ₒtúms* **stupid** *Lexx.*

འཐུར་ *ₒtur* supine of *ₒtu-ba.*

འཐུལ་བ་ *ₒtúl-ba* **to rise, to spread,** of smoke, vapours, perfumes, *ga-pur ₒtul* it smells of camphor *Lex.*; *rdul mi ₒtúl-bar byás-pai ₒóg-tu* after having laid the dust *Dzl.*; *la-lás bdug-spós ₒtul* some persons were spreading perfumes *Pth.*

འཐེགས་པ་ *ₒtégs-pa Cs.* **to set out on a journey.** (To me only **tág-če* W.* is known.) 1. **to pack up.** 2. **to depart.** It prob. signifies the same as *tég-pa, ₒdégs-pa* **to lift, raise, take up,** cf. *γži btúg-čes*, or *ₒdegs-pa* **to shift, to change,** lodgings, to remove; *teg-ḱúg* carpet-bag, knapsack.

འཐེང་ *ₒteṅ*, perh. only another spelling for *teṅ*; *Sch.* has *ₒtéṅ-la ₒbór-ba* **to throw away as unfit,** and if that be correct, it may serve to explain both significations mentioned under *teṅ.*

འཐེང་བ་ *ₒtéṅ-ba Cs.* **to be lame, to go lame,** cf. *téṅ-po*; also adj.: *bsu-mḱan byiu ₒteṅ-ma čig kyaṅ med* not even a lame chicken came to meet me *Mil. nt.*

འཐེན་པ་ *ₒtén-pa* 1. **to draw, to pull,** *gyén-la* up, upward, *mdún-du* forth, out; *p'ar ₒten tsur ₒten* they pulled to and fro, this way and that way *Pth.*; *nur-gyis* by jerks, by little and little *Glr.*; *yól-ba ₒtén-pa* a curtain drawn before *Glr.*; **u' tén-če* W.* to draw breath, to breathe; in *W.* esp. used for **to draw out** (a cork) **to take off** (a pot-lid), **to draw** or **take away** (a pot from the fire). — 2. **to stop, to stop short, to wait,** *ₒtén-pa bzaṅ* it will be advisable to stop, to wait. — In *W.* also = *rtén-pa* to lean, recline, repose on. — **gór-la tén-če* W.* to form on a lathe, to turn. — *Sch.*: *ₒten-ₒḱyér* forgetting and remembering (?).

འཐེབ་ *ₒteb* **overplus, extra, supernumerary,** *gos-ₒtéb* a supernumerary dress *Lex.*; *mal-gos ₒteb-kyis ₒtúm-pa* to wrap up in an extra blanket *Lex.*; *žag γčig ₒteb* one day over, or too much; *ₒtéb-pa* to have too much (?) *Sch.*

འཐེབས་པ་ *ₒtébs-pa*, pf. *tebs*, (prop. the passive or neuter vb. to *ₒdébs-pa*, but often not differing from it, v. *ₒdébs-pa*) 1. **to be thrown, strewed, scattered,** *sá-bon Mil.*; **to be afflicted with, befallen by,** *nád-kyis* a disease, frq., also with *lús-la Glr.*; *lan ₒtébs-pa* to answer; *γsal ₒtébs-pa* to be explained minutely; to be understood perfectly *Thgr.* — 2. *W.* **to be hit** or **struck** (= *ḱés-pa*; **'i-ru teb soṅ** I have been hit here (stung, bitten etc.); **teb čúg-te toṅ** put it down, hitting (the right place), i.e. put it just in its proper place; **mi téb-če** not to hit the mark, to miss the aim; **ma teb** the blow did not strike home; even of a prayer is said: **teb**, it has hit, it has been heard. — 3. *Cs.* in a general sense: **to take, seize, hold fast;** *ₒtebs-lčib Cs.*: 'a tailor's instrument for holding fast cloth etc. in sewing; a thimble'; but the latter is undoubtedly to be spelled *mteb* (or *teb*)-*lčibs*; v. *lčibs.*

འཐེམས་པ་ *ₒtéms-pa Cs.*: '**to shut, comprise, cover, include**; v. *ₒtams-pa*'; the *Lexx.* have only: *naṅ-čugs-ₒtéms*, and *ₒtems-nán* w.e. In *W.* it is 1. vb.n. to *ₒtams-pa*: **lág-pa tem** my hand has been squeezed in, **tém-čei čá-lag** a thing (e.g. a machine) giving chances of being squeezed. — 2. **to suffice,** = *ₒḱyéd-pa, ldáṅ-ba.*

འཐོ་འཚམས་པ་ *ₒto-ₒtsáms-pa* v. *to* etc.

འཐོག་པ་ *ₒtóg-pa Cs.* = *γtóg-pa*, *Sch.* also = *ₒtág-pa.*

འཐོགས་པ་ *ₒtógs-pa* pf. and imp. *ₒtogs*, 1. **to take, to seize, to take up,** a knife, a sword *Dzl.*, provisions in order to distribute them *Dzl.*, esp. **to carry** *Dzl.* and elsewh.; *ról-mo ₒtógs-pa Glr., Tar.* 21, 16, prob. to carry musical instruments (or to make music?); = *tób-pa* to receive, **mii lus togs re-ré*, or *togs tsád** all that have received human bodies by the metempsychosis *C., W.* — 2. = *ₒdógs-pa* with *p'an*, frq., v. *ₒdógs-pa*; *Tar.* 159, 16 = **to name, to call.**

འཐོན་པ་ ₒ*tón-pa*, pf. and imp. *ton*, vb.n. to ₒ*dón-pa*, in *W.* very frq., in *B.* less so, = *byúṅ-ba*, 1. **to come out, to go out,** **dág-sa ḱáṅ-pa-ne ton** he is just coming out of the house; *kun ṗyir* ₒ*tón-te* all coming out *Mil.*; **to remove** (from a house or place), **to leave,** **ton-čág* W.* the last farewell; **to depart, to emigrate;** *ču ṗá-gar tón-nas* when I shall be beyond the river *Mil.*; more carelessly: **yul tón-na, lúṅ-pa tón-na* W.* when one has passed through, the village, the valley; **dúṅ-du tón-če** to step or come forth (from the crowd etc.); **to rise, arise, originate,** v. *snyiṅ-rús*. — 2. for ₓ*óṅ-ba*, **to come,** esp. *Bal.* — 3. **to come from, to proceed from, to have origin,** *bod ḱo-ráṅ-nas* ₒ*tón-pa yin* these are products of Tibet itself; hence: **to occur,** like ₓ*oṅ-ba*, *tsóṅ-pas ḱúr-nas* ₒ*ton* ₒ*dug* (these goods) occur as imported, are imported; *rig-pa-čan miṅ* ₒ*ton yín-te* known as being acute, sagacious.

འཐོབ་པ་ ₒ*tób-pa*, v. *tób-pa*.

འཐོམ(ས)་པ་, ཐོམས་པ་ ₒ*tóm(s)-pa*, *tóm(s)-pa*, **to be dim, dull, clouded,** of the senses and the understanding, **nyid tóm-če* W.* **to slumber, to doze,** **nyid yúr-če** id.; *mgo-(bo)* ₒ*tom* consciousness is clouded or darkened, by intoxication, disease *Med.*; also of religious darkness *Pth.*; **mig tom-tóm ča dug* W.* he is dazzled (by the brightness of the sun); *ldoṅs-šiṅ* ₒ*tóms-par gyur* having become blind *Dzl.*

འཐོར་ ₒ*tor* **fragment,** of a book *Tar.*, cf. *tór-bu*.

འཐོར་བ་ ₒ*tór-ba*, pf. *btor*, fut. *ytor*, imp. ₒ*tor*, 1. prop. vb.n. **to be scattered,** of leaves by the wind *Dzl.*, **to fly asunder, to be dispersed; to fall to pieces, to decay,** of the body after death *Mil.*; **to burst,** of a gun; but also vb.a.: *mé-tog* ₒ*tór-ba* to strew flowers *Glr.*, *Dzl.*; ₒ*tor-*ₒ*tuṅ* **libation** *Cs.*, *ču-*ₒ*tór* libation of water *Sch.*; cf. *ytór-ba*. — 2. *W.*: **to have notches, flaws,** of edge-tools.

འཐོལ་བ་ ₒ*tól-ba* v. *mtól-ba*.

ད

ད་ *da* 1. the letter **d**, originally, and in the frontier districts also at present, pronounced like the German d, i.e. not quite so soft as the English d; in *C.* as initial aspirated and low-toned, **dh**; as final letter half dropped, and changing a preceding a, o, u into *ą*, *ǫ*, *ų*; as prefix in *Kh.* and *Bal.* = *γ*, not differing from the prefixed **g**. — *da-drág* is a term used by grammarians, for the now obsolete *d* as second final, after n, r, l, e.g. in *kund*, changing the termination *du* into *tu*; *no, ro, lo* into *to*; *nam, ram, lam* into *tam*. — 2. num. figure for 11.

ད་ *da* 1. gen. at the head of a sentence: **now, at present, just,** esp. before the imp. mood: *da kar-dáṅ-la soṅ* just go to Kardang! **directly, immediately, forthwith, instantly;** in narration sometimes (though rarely) for **then, at that time.** — 2. in col. language after the emphatical word of the sentence: **it is true, to be sure, indeed,** **loṅ da yod ṅul med** time I have, it is true, but no money.

Comp. *da-ko Sch.* = *da*. — *dá-či* **a little while ago, lately.** *Mil.* and col. — *dá-ča* **in future, henceforward.** — *da-nyid* **the present time; but just now.** — *dá-lta(r)*

1. **now, at present,** *dá-ci-nas dá-lta p̓án-la* from lately till now *Thgy.*; *dá-ltai* (or *dá-ltar-gyi*) *bár-du* until now; *dá-ltai spyód-lam* our course of acting during this life *Glr.*; *dá-ltar-gyi byá-ba*, or *dṅós-po* a person's experience or actions during the present period of his life *Dzl.*; *da-lta-nyid-du Glr.*, *da-lta-rán Mil*, *Pth.*, instantly; *dá-lta-ba Cs.*, *dá-ltar-ba Gram.*, *dus dá-lta-ba* the present time, presence; the present tense 2. *W.* **hereafter, afterwards,** **dág-sa mi gos, dál-ta toṅ** I do not want it now; give it me afterwards. — *dá-ste* **henceforth, from this time forward** *Dzl.* — *da-dúṅ* (frq. pronounced and spelled *da-rúṅ*) v. below. — *da-dé Glr.* and *C.* **now.** — *da-náṅ* **this morning.** — *dá-ni* 1. **now,** 2. **henceforth** *Glr.* *da-p̓yi(n)-čad Dzl.*, *da-p̓yis Glr.* **henceforth.** — *dá-byuṅ* a man of yesterday, **an upstart.** — *dá-tsam* about this time. — *da-ṫsúṅ* henceforth *Pth.* — *da-yzód* **but now, but just, not until now.** — **da-ráṅs* C.* = *da-naṅ*. — *da-rúṅ*, *da-dúṅ* **still, still more,** *da-rúṅ ṫoṅ* give still more! *da-rúṅ légs-par ysúṅ-bar žu* please, explain it more in detail *Ma.*; **still longer, once more,** *da-rúṅ yaṅ* again and again, over and over again; **da-rúṅ ṫsá-big ma ṫsar* W.* it is not quite finished yet. — *da-rés* (*Sch.* also *da-ré-ba?*) 1. **now, now at least, but for this time** (opp. to *sṅán-čad*, *sṅar*, *p̓yis*) *Mil.* 2. *W.* **formerly, heretofore** (opp. to *da* **now**). — *dá-lo* **this year, in this year.**

དཁ་ *dá-ḱa* **horse-shoe,** **dhá-ḱa gyáb-pa** to shoe a horse *C.*

དཅི་ *dá-ci* (*stá-ci?*) **sickle hook,** for cutting off briers *Lh.*

དཆུ་ *dá-ču* **mercury** *Med.*

དཏྲིག་ *da-trig* a medicine *Med.*

དདྲག་ *da-drág* v. the letter d.

དཕྲུག་, དྭཕྲུག་, དཚེ་ *da-p̓rúg*, *dwa-p̓rúg*, *da-tsé*, **orphan.**

དྭབ་ *dwá-ba* a plant *Med.*, yielding an acrid drug; *da-ṫsód* id.(?); *da-rgód*, and *da-yyúṅ* are two species of this plant, the former of which is considered to be of greater virtue *Wdi.*

དབག་ *dá-bag* v. *tá-bag*, *ṫar-ˌbág.*

དབེར་ *da-bér* v. *ta-bér*, *mda-bér.*

དབྱིད་ *da-byid* **lizard,** *Med.*; *Lex.* = *skyin-gór.*

དར་ *dá-ra* col. and sometimes *B.* = *dár-ba* **buttermilk.**

དལི་ *da-li* several low-growing kinds of Rhododendron.

དག་ *dag* 1. sign of the plural, eleg. for *rnams*; often added to the pronouns *de* and *ˌdi*, and sometimes to numerals; also in the combination *dag-rnams.* In translations of Sanskrit works it denotes the dual number. — 2. *ṅá-dag*, *ḱyéd-dag*, seems in *Mil.* often to be used for *ṅá-lta-bu-dag* **my equal,** or **equals** (another reading is *ṅá-lta*, v. *lta* 2). — 3. *W.* col. = *da*, esp. in the compounds **dág-sam, dóg-sa** now; also **certainly, it is true** (v. *da* 2) *Mil.* — 4. v. *dág-pa*.

དགཁ་ *dág-ḱa* is said to be used in *Ts.* for *dé-ḱa*.

དགཅི་ *dág-ci Lh.* **mint,** aromatic plant, Mentha Roylinna.

དགགདོགགེ་ *dag-ga-dog-gé Ld.* for *dog-dóg*.

དགཔ་ *dág-pa* (prop. pf. of *ˌdág-pa*), **clean, pure; cleanness, purity;** as adj. also *dág-po*, *W.* **dóg-mo**; *dág-par ˌgyúr-ba* to become clean, *dág-par byéd-pa* to make clean, to cleanse, to purify, *dág-par ˌḱrú-ba* (*W.* **dág-mo ṭú-ce**) to wash clean; more frq. fig.: **ḱa ma dhag* C.* impure, incorrect, vulgar pronunciation, cf. *sgra* 1; *rigs ma dag* impure blood or kindred; com. **pure** with regard to religion and morals, (also = **holy, sacred,** relative to lifeless objects), *lus daṅ ṅag daṅ yid-kyi las yóṅs-su dág-pa* quite pure in word and action *Dzl.*; *lus dag sems dag dbáṅ-po dag*, also *lus-ytsaṅ* etc. id.; *dág-par ˌṫsó-ba* to lead a pure, a virtuous life; *smón-lam dág-pa* is stated to mean **a sincere prayer** *Glr.*; *rnám-(par) dag(-pa)* quite pure, most holy, frq.;

hence *rnam-(par) dag(-par) rtsi-ba*, or *mdzád-pa* is used for: to justify, in a scriptural sense, by *Chr. Prot.*; *mi or ma-dág-pa* **impure; impurity,** *bkrús-na mi-dág-pa méd-do* when they have bathed they are quite clean *Dzl.* — Adv. *dág-par*, e.g. *ₒkrú-ba* v. above; *dág-tu* **assuredly, certainly** *Lt.(?)*; *dág-gis* purely = quite, entirely *S.g.(?)*; **dág-mo* W.* id., **dág-mo šrág-če** to burn completely, **dág-mo za-če** to eat all, to consume entirely. — *yán-dag-pa Skr.* सम्यक् *Trigl.*, **actual, real,** *yán-dag-par ču yin* in reality it is water *Dzl.*; more frq. construed thus: *de yin yán-dag-na* if it is really that, *btsoṅ yán-dag-na* if you are really willing to sell it, *ₒdod yán-dag-na* if you really wish it, *kyód-la yod yán-dag-na* if you really have *Dzl.*; *yán-dag-pa daṅ bdén-pai tsul bžin-du* in truth and in reality *S.O.*; *yaṅ-dag-pa ni bden-pa-ste* since that which is real is true *S.O.*; *yaṅ-dag-pa-nyid* reality *S.O.*; *dgé-bai čós-rnams yán-dag-par bláṅ-ba* to assume, to adopt, virtuous habits earnestly *Stg.*; *yáṅ-dag-par rdzógs-pa* really accomplished *S.O.*; *yaṅ-dag-par ltá-ba* to be orthodox, v. *dgé-ba bču*; *yaṅ-dag lam* the right way, = *tár-lam Mil.*; *yaṅ-dag-dón* seems to be = *ṅes-don Mil.*, but *yáṅ-dag dón-du ynyér-ba* to aim at, to aspire to, truth *Mil.*; *yáṅ-dag-pai dón-la ₒjúg-pa* to be pious *Thgy.* —

Comp. *dag-brjód* orthoepy *Cs.* — *dag-tér-ba, dag-tér byéd-pa Sch.* to clean, to cleanse; *Tar.* 189, 22; *dag-ster(-čer)mdzád-pa.* — *dag-(pai) snaṅ(-ba) Schr.* 'good opinion'(?), prob.: **a pure, sound view** or **knowledge** *Glr.*; in *Mil.* it has a similar meaning; **dhag-náṅ jón-wa* C.* to lead a holy life. — *dag-žíṅ* holy country *Sch.* — *dag-yig* orthography; *sṅón-gyi-dag-yig* the older orthography; *brda-dág* = *dag-yig.*

དག་པ་ *dág-pa, W. *dag-če**, v. *tég-pa.*

དང་ *daṅ*, postp. c. accus, **with** (Lat. cum), *ṅa daṅ* with me (often with the addition of *bčás-pa, lhan-yčig, mnyám,* q. v.), e.g. to go, speak, play, quarrel with; *bud-méd daṅ nyál-ba* to lie with a woman; in some cases it must be omitted in English, or rendered by other words, as: *groṅ-kyér daṅ nyé-ba, riṅ-ba* near the town, far from the town; *de daṅ ₒdrá-ba* equal to that. Some particular ways of using *daṅ* are the following: 1. for **and,** *yser daṅ dṅúl daṅ lčags-la-sógs-pa* gold, and silver, and iron, and the other (metals). The shad is here always put after *daṅ*, which shows that in the mind of the Tibetan *daṅ* never ceases to be a postposition; it can therefore be used only for connecting nouns and pronouns. In enumerations it is employed in different ways, and often quite arbitrarily, e.g. after every single noun or pronoun except the last one, or also after the last; it is used or omitted just as the metre may require it; or when a sum is mentioned, in the following manner: *byúṅ-ba bži ni: sa (daṅ) ču (daṅ) me (daṅ) rluṅ daṅ bžio* the four elements: earth, and water, and fire, and air, four they are; or, esp. in col. language, thus: *sa daṅ yčig, ču daṅ ynyis* etc. — 2. **distributively:** *žag daṅ žag, lo daṅ lo,* day by day, every year; *kyim daṅ kyim-na Tar.* every one in his house. — 3. after a personal pronoun col. almost like a sign of the plural: *ṅa daṅ ynyis-ka* we two, both of us. *ṅa daṅ tsán-ma* all of us. — 4. after the inf., and in *W.* after the gerund in *gin*, *nyi-ma šár-ba daṅ* at sun-rise, as soon as the sun rises, when the sun rose; *lo brgya lón-pa daṅ* when a hundred years had (or shall have) passed away, after a hundred years; *smrás-pa daṅ kyim-du soṅ* with saying so, he went home, is gen. translated: he said so and went home, and so frq. in narration; *W.: *šúg-ḍu ton daṅ** with a whistling, **tóṅ-gin žig daṅ** at beholding. — 5. after an imperative for **and,** *sgo rduṅs šig daṅ de-dag ₒoṅ-ṅo* knock at the door, and they will come *Dzl.*; *yid-la byos šig daṅ bšád-do* give heed, and I will explain it to you *Stg.*; or it is used in the following manner: *légs-par sems šig daṅ ma nór-ram* consider it well; have you not made a mistake there? *nyon čig daṅ sṅón-dus-na* listen to me!

Now, there was in olden times etc. *Dzl.* and elsewh., frq.; *lon žig dan ná-la dbán yod* do take it! I have the power, you know, i.e. I shall answer for it *Dzl.*; in more recent times it is used (also when not followed by any other words) as an imperative particle = *čig*: '*da zo dan*' *byas-pas* saying 'eat!' *Glr.*; '*da ltos dan*' *ysuns* 'now just see', he said *Mil.*; even after *žu*, which in its application is like a verb in the imperative: '*ysún-ba žu dan*' *žes zér-bas* saying 'pray, teach (us)!' *Mil.* — 6. In *W. dan* is used improperly for the instrum.: **bér-ka dan dun** strike with the stick! and for by or through with respect to persons: **yóg-po dan šab-šób zer** he cheats me, tells me a lie, through his servant.

དང་ *dan* 1. **meadow** *Lh.* — 2. *dan*, or perh. better *tan*, (cf. *tin*), **tan tán-če*, or *tan čó-če, tan šan čó-če**, **to read in a singing or drawling manner** *Ld.* — 3. *dán-du lén-pa*, c. *la*, **to submit, yield to, comply with,** *Glr.*, *Tar.*; c. accus. **submissively to put up with** (*Sch.* and *Wts.* are hardly right).

དང་ག, དང་ཁ *dán-ga, dán-ka*, 1. **appetite,** *dan-ga ˳gag* my appetite is gone, *mi bde* is bad, *Med.* and *Mil.* (*Sch.* 'the will'?). — 2. *C.* for *dám-ka*.

དང་པོ *dán-po* 1. **the first,** with respect to number, time, rank, *dán-poi ytam de sus zer Pth.* who spoke (raised) the first rumour? who was it that first got up the rumour? *dán-poi nyin-par* on the very first day; *na-tsód dán-po-la ynás-pa* being still in the prime of life *Wdn.*; the former, he that is mentioned before another, *dán-po ynyis* the two first named *Thgy.*; **the former, the earlier,** he that precedes another in point of time, = *snú-ma*, opp. to *pyi-ma*, *˳óg-ma*, **the latter.** — 2. **the first thing, part** etc., *nyin-moi dán-po-la* at the beginning of day, at day-break *Tar.*; *dan-po-nyid-du* **in the first place, before the rest, above all, before every other thing** *Thgy.*; *dán-po-nas* from the very beginning *Thgy.*, *Tar.*; *dán-por*, and very frq. *dán-po* adv., **firstly, in the first place; at first, in the beginning.** — *las-dán-po-pa* **a beginner,** *las-dán-po-pai dús-su* as long as he is only a beginner *Thgy.*; *las-dán-po-pai byis-pa* like νήπιος (child) in the N.T., *Mil.*

དང་བ *dán-ba* 1. **to be pure,** *nám-mka dán-nas Mil.*; gen. adj. **pure, clear,** *˳bras dán-ba* picked rice *Lt.*; of inclinations, dispositions, feelings: *séms-čan kún-la rab dán-ba* full of love towards all creatures; *dge-séms dán-ba* a pure, sincere disposition to virtue *S.O.*; most frq. **devout, pious; devotion, faith;** *dán-bai sems* id. (in *W.* often confounded with *yden-ba*). — 2. *lag dán-ba* = *dár-ba*, v. *darba* II. 2.

དང་ཚེ *dán-tse W.* **a field-terrace.**

དང་ར *dán-ra* (spelling dubious) **stable,** for cattle, *C.*, *W.*

དང་ལ *dán-la* 1. *Sch.* **'a tract of land abounding in springs'.** — 2. n. of a high mountain pass, north of Lhasa, called *Tantla* by Huc II., 231.

དྭངས་པ *dwáns-pa*, *C.* also **dhán-po**, **pure, clean, clear,** = *dan-ba* I., of air, water; *ynam-dwáns* a clear sky, fine weather (*W. *tan**); *dans-smug* reddish gray *Sch.* — *dwans-ma* 1. **the chyle,** *Ssk.* रस, concerning which Brahmanical and Buddhist physiology has led to a great many phantastical ideas, *Med.* frq.; also fig., mostly in an obscure and unintelligible manner. — 2. *Sch.*: **'the spirit, the soul',** a signification not found hitherto in any book, but acc. to a Lama's statement the word denotes the soul, when purified from every sin, and to be compared to a clear and limpid fluid, in which every heterogeneous matter has been precipitated. — *dans* is also not seldom met with erron. used for *dnans* and *mdans*.

དད་པ *dád-pa* 1. secondary form of *˳dód-pa* **to wish** *Dzl.* and elsewh.; hence in compounds: *skom-dád* **thirst,** **tágs-dad-čan** fond of dress or finery (cf. *˳dogs-pa*) *W.*, and in similar expressions. — 2. **to believe** (cf. श्रद्ध) in a religious sense, more significant than *yid-čes-pas* and including a devotedness full of confidence, like πιστεύειν in the N.T.; also sbst. **faith,** more fully *dád-*

pai sems, and adj. **faithful, believing**, *yón-bdag dád-pa* the faithful giver of alms *Mil.*; more fully *dád(-pa)-čan, dad-ldán*; *ma-dád-pa*, and *dad-méd* **unbelieving**; often with *mos* or *gus*: *kun dad-dad-mos-mós-su ₒdúg-pa-la Mil.*; *dad-čiṅ-gus-par ₒgyur-ba Glr.*; *dad-par ₒgyúr-ba, dád-pa byéd-pa* **to become faithful or believing, to believe**, frq.; *dád-bžin-du* full of faith; *dad-brtsón* for *dád-pa daṅ brtson-ₒgrús Tar.* — Note. **mi žig-la dád-pa ťob* W.* col. a man becomes a believer, v. *ťób-pa*; but *Tar.* 35, 1 *ṗágs-pa Dhi-ti-ka-la dád-pa ťob* means: he was brought to believe by hearing the Reverend Dhitika.

དན་དུ་ *dán-du*, and *dan-róg*, medicinal herbs *Med.*

དན་ད་ལི་ *dán-da-li*, or *dan-dál*, *Ld.* **a sieve**, gen. consisting of perforated leather and a wooden frame; *rás-dan-dul* a sieve made of cloth (inst. of leather).

དན་མོ་ *dán-mo* (spelling?) the female of the ibex, and of the musk-deer.

དམ་ *dam* (a root signifying bound, fast, fixed, from which the following compounds, as well as *sdóm-pa*, are to be derived), sbst., also *dam-tsig* and *yi(d)-dam*, resp. *ťugs-dam*, **a solemn promise; vow, oath, confirmation by oath**, like *bden-tsig*; *dam bčá-ba* 1. **to promise**, 2. **the act of promising, the promise**; also *dám-bča Mil.* and col.; *dám-bča ₒbúl-ba* resp. to make a promise, e.g. *mi ₒbáb-pai* not to descend *Mil.*; to promise solemnly *Mil.*; hence *yi-dam*, and (more popularly) *dám-bča* **the sacrament** *Chr. Prot.*; *dam bčás-pa* a promise made; *dam srúṅ-ba, dám-la ɣnás-pa*, or *nyé-bar byéd-pa, dám-bčas-pa spyód-pa, dám-bčas-pa bžin-du byéd-pa, dám-bčas-pa daṅ mi ₒgál-ba*, to keep one's promise; *nyáms-pa* to break (a promise, a vow); *dam-nyáms-kyi lás-rnams* **violations of duty**; *dám-la ₒdógs-pa* **to exorcise** demons etc. *Glr., Pth.*, but only by gentle persuasion, which induces them to promise to do no harm anymore, not by magic power (so it was expressly stated by a Lama); *dám-la ₒǰóg-pa Tar.* 125 id. (ni f.); *dám-čan, dam-tsig-čan Mil.* bound by an oath etc.; *dám-ču* prob. water which is drunk in taking an oath *Pth.*

དམ་ཁ་ *dám-k'a Glr.*, *dám-ga Wts.*, *ťám-ga Cs.*, **a seal, stamp**, resp. *ṗyag-dám*, esp. for the seals of Lamas; *dám-k'a rgyáb-pa* **to seal, to stamp**; *k'yi-dam* v. *k'yi*; *dam-rgyá* = *dám-k'a Tar.*; **dam-čúg* W.* seal of a Lama, used as an amulet.

དམ་པ་ *dám-pa*, acc. to the explanation of a Lama: **bound by an oath** or **vow, consecrated**; but *Lex.c.* render it by **परम, अग्र** i.e. = *mčog*, thus *Dzl.* ༢༢༥, 4; ༢༡, 9, and *Cs.*: **noble, brave, excellent**, which is prob. also the sense of the word when compounded with *čos, skyés-bu*, and other words. Its usual rendering, however, is 2. **holy, sacred**, *blá-ma dám-pa, skyés-bu dám-pa*, a holy Lama, a holy man, and most frq. *dám-pai čos, dám-pa čos, dám-čos*, the holy doctrine, the holy religion of Buddha. Yet, in the interpretation of passages the original meaning (noble, excellent) ought to be resorted to much oftener. So also *ɣyóg-mo dám-pa čig Glr.* signifies an excellent, a favourite female slave, but not exactly a holy or a faithful one.

དམ་པོ་ *dám-po* 1. **strong, firm; tight, narrow**, of fetters etc.; gen. adverbially *dam-du*, e.g. to bind, to lock up, to seize firmly, securely. — 2. of laws, commandments, **severe, strict, exact.**

དམ་དུམ་ *dam-dúm* **various** *Sch.*; yet cf. *dum*.

དར་ *dar* I. 1. **silk**, *dár-gyi* **of silk, silken**; *mǰal-dár* resp. for *k'a-btágs C.*; *rgyaï naṅ dar* fine Chinese silks *Thgy.* — *dar-dkár* white silk *Glr.* — *dar-skúd* silk-thread; *gos-méd dar-skúd ₒdra* stark naked *Ma.* — *dar-gós* silk dress, *Cs.* also silk-stuff. — *dar-čún* a bunch or fringe of silk *Cs.* — *dar-čén Ld-Glr.*, acc. to *Schl.* = *k'a-btágs*, yet cf. the significations given sub I. 2. — *dar-ₒtág-mk'an* a silk-weaver; *dar-ₒtag-bu-mo Glr.* the daughter of a silk-weaver. — *dar-ṗón* = *dar-čún*. — *dár-bu* a coarse kind of silk *Cs.* — *dar-búbs* a whole piece of silk-stuff rolled together. — **dhar-ma-rę'* C.* 'neither silk nor cotton', half silk half cotton; acc. to others velvet. — *dar-dmán-pa* raw silk *Schr.* — *dar-ṫsóṅ-pa* a dealer in silks, a silk-mercer. — *dar-zàb* the finest silk, frq.; a piece of such silk. — *dar-yáb* a silk fan. — *dar-yùg* a narrow ribbon-like piece of silk-stuff *Glr*, *Mil.* — *dar-liṅ* = **dhar-ma-rȩ**. — *dar-šàm* the lower border of a silk dress *Glr.* — *dar-(gyi) srin(-bu)* silk-worm. — 2. **a cloth**, made of whatever material; **flag** *Wts.*, **sail** (v. *γyór-mo*): *ꞌpyar-dár* a hoisted flag; *mduṅ-dar* a little flag fixed to a lance; **ru-dhár* C.* military banner. — *dar-lċóg* little flags fixed on houses, piles of stones, and the like (v. *Schl. Buddh.* 198). — *dar-po-čè* 1. **a large flag** fastened to a flag-staff; 2. **flag-staff, mast.** — *dar-ṫsó* a military division, squadron *Sch.* — *dar-šiṅ*, *dar-bér*, prob. flag-staff.

II. **ice, icy plain**; *dar čágs* ice is forming; also substantively = *dar*, *mṫsó-la dar-čágs btab Mil.* — *dar-zám* ice-bridge. — **dar-ǰár** ('clinging to the ice'?) *W.* a dark-gray aquatic bird.

III. v. *dar-γčig*, *dár-ba*, *dár-ma*.

དར་རྒྱས་གླིང་ *dar-rgyas-gliṅ* v. *rdo-rǰe-gliṅ.*

དར་སྒ་ *dár-sga* **walnut.**

དར་གཅིག་ *dar-γčig* (col. also *dal-γčig*), **a little while, a moment**; *dar-γčig lón-pa-na* after a little while *Glr.*; adverbially: **for a little while, for a moment** *Mil.*: **directly, instantly, in a moment** *Mil.*; *dár-tsam Sch.* id.

དར་དིར་ *dar-dir* **humming, buzzing** *Mil.*; **wailing, lamenting** *Pth.*

དར་རྡོ་ *dar-rdó* **grinding-stone** for Indian ink *Sch.*; *bdár-rdo* would perhaps be more correct.

དར་པོ་, དར་མོ་ *dár-po*, *dár-mo*, col. for *dál-po*, *dál-mo*, v. *dál-ba*.

དར་བ་ *dár-ba* I. sbst., also *dá-ra*, *dar*, **buttermilk**, *dar-γsár* fresh buttermilk.

II. vb. 1. **to be diffused, to spread**, of influence, power, opinions, diseases, *čes dár-ba* to gain much ground, to increase exceedingly *Lt.*; *dár-du ꞌǰúg-pa* (act.) to extend, enlarge, e.g. academies *Glr.*; *dar-gúd* spreading and decaying, increase and decrease; **dhár-po* C.* **grand, magnificent**, of a feast, drinking-bout. — 2. with *lag*, **to take in hand, to put hand to a work.** c. *la Dzl.*; also *dáṅ-ba*.

དར་མ་ *dár-ma* 1 **the age of manhood, manly age, prime of life.** gen. reckoned from 30 to 50, but acc. to *S.g.* from 16—70: *dár-la báb-pa*, or *dar-báb*, a person in the prime of life, frq.; *dar-gáṅ* col. id.: *dar-yól* a person beyond that age. — 2. **a man,** and *dár-mo* **a woman in the prime of life.**

དར་མོ་ *dár-mo* v. *dár-po*, *dár-ma*.

དར་སྨན་ *dar-smán* v. *dar-ṫsúr.*

དར་ཙམ་ *dár-tsam* v. *dar-γčig.*

དར་ཚིལ་ *dar-ṫsil Sch.* 'groin' (?).

དར་(མ)ཚུར་ *dar-(m)ṫsur Wdṅ.* = *dar-sman*, **alum** *Sch.*

དར་ཡ་ཀན་ *dar-ya-kan* a medicinal herb *Med.*

དལ་ཡམས་ *dal-yáms Mil.*, *rims-dál Mil.*, **epidemic disease, plague**, or perh. n. of a particular disease.

དལ་ཅིག་ *dál-čig*, col. for *dar-γčig.*

དལ་ཐོག་འཇུག་པ་ *dal-ṫóg ꞌǰug-pa* **to attack and disperse an enemy** *Sch.*

དལ་བ་ *dál-ba*, *dál-bu*, **slowness, ease, quietness, leisure** (opp. to haste, hurry, vehemence), **dhál-wa* (or *dhál-bu*) *yö'-dham* C.*, have you time? *dál-ba ži̇g-gi skábs-su* when he happened to have nothing to do *Dzl.*; *dál-bar ꞌdùg-pa* to be disengaged, unemployed; *dál-ba brgyad* **the eight conditions of rest**, the state of being free from the eight *mi-ꞌkóm-pa*; to these belong the *ꞌbyor-pa bču*, i.e. ten goods or blessings which, in part, are but more particular definitions of the eight rests, yet include also other blessings; hence both together are called *dal-ꞌbyór bčo-brgyád* (another instance of this peculiar way of reckoning v. sub *ńyiṅ-mṫsán*). As these various conditions are partly characteristics of 'humanity', and attainable only by human beings, they might be denominated 'the (eighteen) specific blessings of humanity'. Often they are also used directly for 'condition of humanity, or of human nature', this kind of existence being, from a religious point of view, the best and most desirable. *rnyed-dkái dál-ba mi lus*, and similar expressions frq. occur (*Cs.* has calmness, tranquillity of mind, evidently mistaking it for *rnal-₀byor*). *dál-ba, dál-bu, dál-po, dál-mo, W.* also **dál-čan**, **quiet, calm,** of the mind, the water; **gentle,** of the wind; **slow, lazy;** **šé-gyü' dhál-wa*, or *šé-pa dhál-wa* C.* phlegmatic disposition. — Adv. *dál-bar* (v. above), *dál-gyis, dál-bus*, **slowly, softly, gradually,** e.g. to draw, opp. to *drág-tu*; *dál-₀groi rgyun bžin* like a stream flowing gently and softly; *mi-dál-bar Dzl.* incessantly.

དལ་མོ་ *dál-mo* **chine, loin.**

དལ་བཙོང་ *dal-btsóṅ* (spelling dubious), **dal-tsóṅ táṅ-če* W.* **to carry on compulsory trade.** This is frequently done by Eastern rulers, who in time of personal need make a sale of goods, compelling people to buy at fixed prices.

དི་ *di*, num. fig.: 41.

དི་གར་ཙི་ *di-gar-či* is said to be a provincialism, and secondary form of *γži-ka-rtsé*, n. of a town near Tashilunpo.

དི་མར་ *di-mar Sch.*: 'a certain worm or insect'.

དི་རི་རི་ *di-ri-ri* **buzz, murmur, hum, low confused noise,** as of crowds, of a number of praying people, of wailing prisoners, of birds on the wing *Glr.*

དིག་ *dig*, the Persian دیگ, **a large kettle, washing-copper, brewer's copper.**

དིག་པ་ *dig-pa* 1. *Cs.* **a stammerer,** also *ka-dig*, cf. *₀dig-pa*. — 2. *C.* **reeling, staggering, intoxicated.**

དིང་དིང་ *diṅ-diṅ, gád-mo diṅ-diṅ Tar.* 158, 4 prob. an onomatopoetic word, *Schf.* **'laughing aloud'.**

དིང་སང་ *diṅ-sáṅ = deṅ-saṅ.*

དུ་ *du* 1. num. fig.: 71. — 2. for *tu* (q.v.) after final *ṅ, d, n, m, r, l.* — 3. **how many?** *bslébs-nas zlá-ba du lon* how many months is it ago that he came? — *du-dú* **how much, how many each time?** *dú-žig* how much about? *dú-ma* many, *žag dú-ma* many days; *dú-mar p̔ye* it is divided into **several** (parts) *Wdṅ.*; *lan dú-mar* **many a time, often** *Cs.*; **dú-ma rákša* C.* col. a great many, very much (perh. 'devilishly much', from *rākšas*).

དུ་བ་ *dú-ba* (cf. *dúd-pa*) **smoke,** *₀tul*, or *gyén-du ₀p̔yur* smoke rises *Zam.*; *dú-ba-pa Sp.* very poor people that pay but a trifling tax, **proletarians** (prop. 'smoke-people' that have nothing but the smoke of their fire). — *du-ba-mjug-riṅ* **a comet.** — *du-žág C.* the smoke or vapour hanging over towns and large villages in the morning.

དུག་ *dug* **poison,** *dug blúd-pa* to administer a poisoned potion to a person, to give him poison to drink; *dug-mi-γnód-par ₀gyur* he becomes proof against poison *Dom.*; *čú-la dug ₀débs-pa* to poison the water *Pth.*; *dug γsum* in a moral sense, *₀dod-čágs, γti-mug, že-sdáṅ;* sometimes *dug lṅa*, five moral poisons, are mentioned.

Comp. *dúg-čan* poisonous. — *dug-γnyén* an antidote *Cs.* — *dug-mdá* a poisoned arrow. — *dug-sbrúl* venomous serpent. — *dug-méd* not poisonous. — *dug-šóg* poisonous paper *Mil., Pth., Glr.* — *dug-sél* that which neutralizes a poison *Cs.* — *dug-srúṅ* a preservative against poison *Cs.*

དུག་ཏི་ *dúg-ti* (or *dúg-ste?*) *Ts.*, **so, thus, in this manner,** also *núg-ti.*

དུག་པོ་ *dug-po*, esp. *Ü* (= **ču-pa* Ts.*, **gon-čę* W.* **coat, garment, dress** *Mil.*

དུགས་ *dugs*, esp. in medical writings; it seems to denote 1. **heat:** *Tar.* 31, 21 *tsád-pai dugs-kyis* by the glowing heat of the day *Schf.*; *S.g.*: *čui dri dugs rláṅs-pa če* the water (i. e. urine) has a strong smell and emits much heat(?) and vapour; *Lt.* ༡༡, 4. 5; ༡༢, 4; ༣༦, 5; ༦༣, 4; ༡༣༧, 10. *čui rigs šin-tu dúgs-pa Mṅg.* adj.? — 2. **revenge, grudge, rancour,** **dug kór-če, dugs-*

*lán ldón-ĉe** to take vengeance, to revenge one's self.

དུགས་པ་ *dúgs-pa* W. 1. **to make warm, to warm,** *mé-la* at the fire, e.g. one's hands, a plate. — 2. **to light, to kindle,** **me dúg-ĉe** to light a fire; **k'áṅ-pa mes dug soṅ** the house has begun to burn, has caught fire; **zá-ĉe dug ts'ár-k'an** burnt food, a burnt meal; **dúg-di** a burnt smell.

དུང་ *duṅ* 1. **a tortoise shell,** *duṅ-rdó* a petrified tortoise shell *Cs.* — 2. **a shell,** both small shells, worn as an ornament (*skye-duṅ-p'réṅ* necklace of shells), and more particularly **the great trumpet-shell,** which is sounded on certain occasions; it is usually of a pure white, hence *duṅ-dkár* 1. **trumpet-shell,** 2. **white rose** *C.*, *dúṅ-so* snow-white teeth *Pth.*, *dúṅ-ru* snow-white horns *Mil.*; a trumpet-shell wound to the right (*γyás-su ˳k'yil-ba*) is regarded as valuable as it is rare *Glr.* — 3. **trumpet, tuba,** *duṅ ˳búd-pa* to sound, to blow a trumpet; *k'rims-duṅ* judgment-trumpet, trumpet used in courts of justice, *ĉos-duṅ* church-trumpet, trumpet used in religious ceremonies, *dmag-duṅ* war-trumpet, *líṅs-duṅ* hunting-bugle; *rkaṅ-duṅ* a trumpet or cornet made of a hollow thigh-bone; *zaṅs-duṅ* a copper trumpet, a bass tuba eight feet long; *dbaṅ-duṅ* a similar instrument, but of less dimensions; *rwa-duṅ* a trumpet of horn, *rag-duṅ* a brass trumpet. — 4. **skull** (?) *Sch.* has: *duṅ-ĉen* 1. skull, 2. = *rkaṅ-duṅ*; in *Glr.* Brahma is called *duṅ-gi ts'or-ts'ogs-ĉan.*

དུང་ངེ་ *duṅ-ṅe* **constant, continual** *Dom.*; *duṅ-ṅe-ba Thgr.* id.

དུང་དུང་ *duṅ-dúṅ* **staggering, reeling, tottering, wavering** *Sch.*

དུང་པན་ *duṅ-pán*, *C.* **dhuṅ-pén**, **basin.**

དུང་ཕྱུར་ *duṅ-˳p'yúr Pth.*, **100 million** *Sch.*

དུངས་པ་ *dúṅs-pa*, secondary form of *γdúṅs-pa*, **love,** *dád-pa daṅ dúṅs-pa žig skyés-te Mil.*, frq.; *yid-dúṅs* = *snyiṅ-brtse-ba*, frq.; **dhúṅ-bhu* C.* love, **ṭ'ú-gu-la dhúṅ-bu ǰhé-pa** cf. *γĉés-pa.*

དུད་པ་ *dúd-pa* I. sbst. (cf. *dú-ba*, and the Pers. دود) **smoke,** *W.*: **k'áṅ-mig dúd-pa má méd-k'an duγ** there comes very little smoke into the room. — *dúd-k'a Sch.* 1. having the colour of smoke, **dark-gray.** 2. **family, household.** 3. **chimney** (?). — *dúd-k'u Sch.* 'liquid soot'; prob. soot mixed with water, smut; *Lt.* compares morbid evacuations or matter ejected from the stomach with *dud-k'u.* — *dud-bál* soot *Sch.*, prob. **flocky soot.** — *dud-búr* a cloud of smoke *Cs.* — *dud-rtsi* soot, smut *Cs.* — *dud-lám* chimney.

II. vb. 1. **to tie, to knit, to knot,** v. *mdúd-pa.* — 2. pf. of *˳dúd-pa*, **stooping, bent,** hence *dúd-˳gro* **quadruped, beast, animal,** opp. to man that walks erect *Stg.*

དུན་པ་ *dún-pa* **great diligence, assiduity,** *dún-pa drág-po*; **dún-ĉan** very diligent *W.* (cf. *˳dún-pa*, and *rtun*).

དུབ་པ་ *dub-pa*, vb. **to be** or **get tired;** adj. **tired;** sbst. **fatigue;** *mi dúb-bo* they do not get tired *Dzl.*; *ṅál-žiṅ dúb-nas Glr.*; *lus daṅ ṅag yid dub Pth.* he is tired in body, mouth, and soul, i.e. he has no strength for doing, saying, or thinking anything good. — *dúb-ĉan* **tiresome** *Cs.* — *dúb-rgyu* **anxious, sorrowful** *Sch.*

དུབས་ *dubs, Stg.* frq.: *nyé-žiṅ dubs nyé-bar* acc. to the context it might mean: **very probably;** but the word seems to be little known.

དུམ་ *dum* **a piece,** frq.; as a measure or certain quantity of meat, v. *γzugs*; *dúm-po* **a large piece** *Cs.*; *dúm-bu* **a small piece,** frq.; *dúm-bur γĉóg-pa, γĉód-pa, byéd-pa* to break, to cut to pieces. — *dam-dúm* several small pieces or things *Cs.*; perh. = *dum-dúm Ld.*, e.g. *yul dum-dúm*, or *groṅ dum dúm* several scattered farms, hamlets or villages, which have together one common name.

དུར་ *dur* **tomb, grave,** *dúr-du ˳júg-pa*, *˳dzúd-pa* (*Cs.* *˳débs-pa*) **(s)kúṅ-ĉe* W.*, **to bury;** *dur rkó-ba* to dig a grave. — *dúr-rkun* grave-robber, plunderer of tombs. — *dúr-k'uṅ* **grave, tomb.** — *dúr-k'rod* acc. to etymology denotes **a cemetery, burial-**

ground, but in Tibet it signifies a place to which corpses are brought to be cut into pieces for hungry dogs and vultures, this being considered a very honourable mode of burying (or rather disposing of) dead bodies, *Köpp.* II, 322. These places of course are haunted by demons and foul spirits; *dúr-k̔rod-pa* an ascetic living at such a place, *Burn.* I, 309. — *dúr-rgyas* the last food which a dying man eats. — *dúr-sgam, dúr-sgrom* **coffin.** — *dúr-rdo* **tomb-stone** *Cs.* — *dúr-spyaṅ* **jackal.** — *dúr-p̔uṅ* **barrow, tumulus, mound, cairn.** — *dúr-byaṅ* **epitaph** *Cs.* — *dúr-ts̔un, dúr-ts̔od,* food offered to the dead *Cs.* — *dur-mts̔éd* a place for burning dead bodies *Sch.* — *dúr-sri* a grave-devil, a sort of sepulchral vampire.

དུར་བ་ *dúr-ba* 1. sbst. **weed, weeds,** *Sch.* — 2. vb. **to run** *Mil.*, *dúr-te rgyúg-pa* to run towards a place or object, to hasten to, *zás-la dúr-ba* to hasten to dinner, *lás-la* to work *C.*; cf. *ṅám-dur-čan.*

དུར་བིན་ *dur-bin W.*, the Persian دوربين **spy-glass.**

དུར་བྱ་ *dúr-bya* **a paring-axe; a hoe** *Sch.*

དུར་བྱིད་ *dur-byid* **a purgative root,** prob. = *tár-nu S.g.*, acc. to *Wdṅ.* = *tri-byi-ta* (sic), prop. त्रिवृता, Ipomoea Turpethum.

དུལ་བ་ *dúl-ba*, prop. pf. of *˳dúl-ba*, **soft,** of the skin etc.; **tame; gentle** (temper), **easy** (disposition), **mild;** also sbst. **softness** etc.; *dul-po, W.* **dúl-mo** id., but only adj.; *ma dul-ba* **untamed, rude,** *Dzl.*; **sráb-k̔a* (or *k̔á-po*) *dúl-mo** *W.* **soft-** or **tender-mouthed; tame, manageable, tractable.** *Tar.* 11, 14 a better reading prob. would be: *dbaṅ-po ˳dul-bai brjid* a splendour that dazzles the senses.

དུལ་མ་ *dúl-ma* a kind of **water-colour** made of pulverized gold and silver, for painting and writing.

དུས་ *dus* 1. **time,** in general, *dús-kyi k̔ór-lo* v. *k̔ór-lo*; *dús-kyi* means also: **happening sometimes** *Mil.*; *dus* adv., for a while, for some time *Lt.*; *deï dús-su, dus de tsa-na, dé-dus, dus der,* at the time, at this time; *dus de-nyid-du* then immediately, directly afterwards; *dáṅ-poi dus nyid-du* in the very first time; *dús-su,* or *dus-dús-su, dus ˳ga-ré,* sometimes, now and then; *de daṅ dus mnyám-du* simultaneously with that *Glr.*; *dus γčig-tu* or *la* at one and the same time, together; *dús-čig-na* (erron. *γčig*), also *dus re* (or *nam*)*-žig-gi ts̔e, dus-re* (*-žig*), once, one day, some day; *dus lan-čig* id. *Glr.*; *dus p̔yi žig-na* some future day; *dus γžan žig-na* another time; *dus či tsam-na* at what time? when? *Glr.*; *dus*(*-na*) after a genit., inf., or verbal root = when, after, *žag γnyis soṅ dus* when two days had, or will have passed *Mil.*; *ṅa bú-moi dús-na yin-te* when I was still a girl *Glr.*; *mgú-dus med* the time of being satisfied never arrives *Mil.*; *btsá-dus-te* as the time of giving birth has come *Lt.*; frq. with *˳báb-pa: bdag ˳dúl-bai dús-la bab* the time of my conversion has come; sometimes *dús-la sleb Lt.*; col.: *dus sleb* the time is come; *˳gro-bai dus ˳débs-pa Dzl., byéd-pa* frq., to fix a time for going, also thus: *nam ˳gró-bai dus byéd-pa Dzl.*; *dus kún-tu, dus rgyún-du* always; almost pleon. in: *dus dá-nas* henceforth, from this time forward *Mil.*; *de daṅ dus ˳dzom* as to time it coincides with that *Glr.* — 2. **the right time, proper season; for** is expressed by the genit. of the inf. (cf. above: the time of my conversion); *dús-su* at the right or proper time, e.g. for paying off *Glr.*; *dus ma yin-pa* the wrong time; *dus ma yin-par, dus-min* unseasonably, not in due time; esp. too soon, prematurely, e.g. to die; *dus-ma-yin-pa spóṅ-ba* to abstain from doing unseasonable things. — 3 *dus γsum* **the three times,** viz. *dá-ltai,* or *dá-ltar-gyi, ˳dás-pai,* and *ma-˳óṅs-pai,* frq., thus in *dus γsúm-gyi saṅs-rgyás* the Buddhas of the three times; often also with special reference to metempsychosis, **the present, the former,** and **the future period of life;** with respect to the times of the day: **morning, noon, evening;** besides *nyin-dus γsum,* also *mts̔án-dus γsum* occurs. —

4. season. Here Tibetans, of course, distinguish the four seasons of the temperate zone, *dpyid* spring, *dbyar* summer, *ston* autumn, *dgun* winter; but in books, originally written in India, either three are counted, *tsá-dus* hot season, *grán-dus* cold season, *čár-dus* rainy season, or more accurately six: *dpyid* (वसन्त) spring, i.e. March and April, *sos-ka* (ग्रीष्म) hot season, May, June, *dbyar* (वर्ष) rainy season, July, August, *ston* (शरत्) damp season, September, October, *dgun-stód* (हेमन्त) first part of winter, November, December, *dgun-smád* (शिशिर) last part of winter, January, February. — 5. **conjunctures, times, circumstances,** **dus dé-mo* W.*, **dhu-dé (sa-ǰám)* C.*, *dús-kyi ᵒkrúg-pa méd-pa Ld.-Glr.*, *dus bzán-po Dom.*, peace. — 6. a particular period of time, as distinguished from others, **an age,** युग (= γοῦγα कल्प), *yar-ldán*, or *rdzogs-ldán* (कृत or सत्य) *yar-rábs*, or *γsum-ldán* (त्रेता) *rtsod-ldán*, or *γnyis-ldán* (द्वापर) *snyigs-ma* (कलि), to be compared to the four ages of Greek mythology. — 7. **year** *Lt.* — 8. symb. num.: 6. — Note. *dus byéd-pa* also signifies (cf. 1 above) **to fulfil the time,** *tsei dus byéd-pa* to die, to perish, also to commit suicide *Dzl.* frq.; *ᵒči-bai dus byed-pa* id. *Wdn.* — *dus dzin-pa* to take the day-service upon one's self (?) *Dzl.* ༢༦༢, 3.

Comp. *dus-skabs* v. *skabs.* — *dus-čén*, *-bzán*, *-stón*, **festival,** *byéd-pa* to keep one. — *dus-mčód* v. *mčod-pa.* — *dus-sbyor Cs.*: **'judicial astrology',** *dus-sbyor-pa* an astrologer. — *dus-me* **comet** *Cs.* — *dus-rtsi-ba Cs.* **'the counting of time'.** — *dus-tsig Sch.*: *'dus-tsig γsár-ba* new, fresh provisions, **'produce of the year'** (?). — *dus-tsigs*, *dus-mtsams* 1. **period, epoch;** 2. **season** *Cs.* — *dus-tsód* 1. **space** or **measure of time.** 2. often for *dus*, *deĩ dus-tsód-kyi mi-rnams* the men of that time or period, *deĩ dus-tsod-la* at that time; also for hour. — *dus-zin Sch.*: 'time of depravity'. — *dus-bzán* v. above *dus-čén.* — *dus-rlábs* **'wave of time'** i.e. **ebb** and **flood, the tides,** *Stg.* — *dus-lóg* a year yielding no crops, **a sterile, bad year** *Pth.*

དེ་ *de* 1. num. figure: 101. — 2. affix of the gerund, for *te*, after a final *d.*

དེ་ *de* demonstrative pron. (in *B.* gen. placed after the word to which it belongs, in col. language before it, even without the termination of the genitive) **that, that one,** opp. to *ᵒdi* this, this one, yet with occasional exceptions. 1. when words or passages are literally quoted, the Tibetan begins with *ᵒdi-skad* or some similar expression, and places **a** *čes* or *dé-skad* **after** it. *ᵒdi*, in such a case, corresponds about to **'the following'**, *de* to **'such'**, or **'thus'**, (cf. τοῦτο and τόδε). But elsewhere *ᵒdi* may also refer to what has been said before, e.g. in a reply: *tsig ᵒdi ni bdén-pa yin-nam* is this word (that has just been said) true? *Dzl.* In the context of a narrative, however, *de* is usually employed. — 2. It frq. stands in the place of the definite article **the:** *pa de lóg-ste són-no* the father went back *Mil.*; esp. after adjectives and participles, where it adds to perspicuity: *γžón-nu de na-ré* the younger one said *Mil.*; *snón-la són-ba de* he that has gone on before *Mil.*; *deĩ dón-du*, *deĩ pyir(-du)*, *čéd-du*, *slád-du*, **therefore, on this account, for this reason;** *deĩ ᵒóg-tu* **under that, after that, afterwards;** *deĩ dús-su*, *tse(-na)* **there, then, at that time.** — 3. **he, she, it,** for *ko*, which in classical style is not in use. — 4. for *deĩ*, in *de-pyir*, *de-dus*, (abbreviations of *deĩ pyir-du*, *deĩ dús-su*, v. above). **Plural:** *dé-dag*, *dé-rnams*, *dé-tso.*

Comp. and deriv. *dé-ka*, *dé-ka*, **the very same,** *γsa dé-ka na yin* the very same snow-leopard (you saw) was I myself *Mil.*; *dé-ka ltar* **just so** *Thgy.*; *dé-ka yod* (in answer to a question) **indeed! yes, yes! to be sure!** *Mil.*, *C.*, frq.; *dé-ka lags Mil.*, id.; *de kyed lags Pth.*, oh, this ... is you?! — *de-kó-na*, *de-nyid*, col. *de-rán*, **the very same,** cf. *kó-na*; *de-nyid*, and *de-ko-na-nyid* are also sbst.: **essence, nature** *Thgy.*: *sems-kyi de-nyid* the essence of the soul

Mil. — *de-snyéd* **so many.** — *dé-lta, dé-ltar* (*-du*, or *-na*) **so**, *p'a ni dé-lta ma yin-te* as it is not so with the father *Stg.*; *dé-lta-bu* of that kind, quality, or manner, **such**, esp. in *B.* — *de-dé* = *de*, but more emphatic, **exactly that**; *de-de-bžin-no* **yes, so it is!** **dhén-ḍa, ḍe** *C.* = *dé-lta* etc. — *dé-na* **therein, in that place, there, here.** — *dé-nas* **from, thence, from that place; afterwards, then, at that time,** very frq. — *dé-pa, dé-ma Cs.* one of that place, sect, religion etc. — *dé-bas* 1. after a comparative, **than that**; 2. also *dé-bas-na, dés-na, des*, **therefore, consequently, now then** (δή) *B.* frq. — *dé-bo* = *de Cs.* — *dé-tsam* **so much**; *dé-tsam-na, dé-tsa-na*, **then, at that time.** — *dé-tsug*, *W.* gen. **dé-zug**, **so, thus.** — *dé-bžin(-du)* **according to that, thus, so;** frq. for **it**, *dé-bžin-du ynáṅ-ño* he allowed it *Dzl.*; *dé-bžin ṅó-šes-nas* perceiving it *Glr.* — *de-bžin-nyid* (तत्त्व) **essence,** *Was.* (272), **identity** (297), like *čos-nyid* and some other similar expressions, = *stoṅ-pa-nyid*, *Trigl.* fol. 20. — *dé-zug* = *dé-tsug*. — *dé-yaṅ, dé-aṅ*, 1. **this,** or **that, too; he also.** 2. **namely, to wit, viz.,** preceding specifications and detailed statements, sometimes also after a gerund, in which case it cannot be rendered in English. — *de-rag* **directly, immediately** *Sch.* — *de-ráṅ* = *de-k'ó-na, de-ráṅ yin* that is just the thing! exactly! to be sure! col. — *de-riṅ B.* and *C.* **to-day,** *de-riṅ-gi* **of this day.** — *dé-ru, der*, 1. **into that, thereinto, into that place, thither, that way.** 2. **in that, therein, in that place, there,** frq. — *dé-la* **to this, to that; in, on,** or **at this; thereat, therewith, thereto, thereon; about that, concerning that; thereof, therefore.** — *dé-las* **from, out of, from that**; after a comparative and *yžan*, **than that.** — *de-srid* to such a length of time.

དེ་བ་ *dé-ba* a medicinal herb, *Med.*

དེང་ *deṅ*, also *diṅ*, **to-day,** *déṅ-nas* from this day forward *Mil.*; *deṅ p'yin-čád* or *čad Dzl.* id.; *déṅ-gi dus* the present time or age; *deṅ-sáṅ* to-day and to-morrow; **now-a-days**; *deṅ-sáṅ lhá-rje* the physicians of the present day *Wdṅ.*; *déṅ-dus smáṅ-pa Lt.* id.

དེང་བ་ *déṅ-ba*, pf. and imp. of *ₒdéṅ-ba*, **to go, to go away**; *déṅs-pa* seems to be the same form: *so-sói ynás-su deṅs Mil.*, *ráṅ-sar déṅs-so Pth.* they went each to his own place; *nám-mk'ar deṅ Mil.* prob. it melted away, dissolved into air; *sór-mo-rnams deṅs mdzád-pa* to turn the fingers upwards (?). *Schr. déṅs-pa* to ascend.

དེད་པ་ *déd-pa*, pf. of *ₒdéd-pa*.

དེབ་(པ་) *déb*(*-ma*) **poultice, cataplasm,** applied to sores and inflamed parts of the body *Sch.*

དེབ་ཐེར་,། གཏེར་, སྟེར་ *deb-t'ér, -ytér, -stér*, tibetanized form of the Persian دفتر **documents, records, catalogues, registers, lists, books**; *deb-t'ér-pa, deb-t'er-mk'an Cs.* keeper of the archives or records, **recorder, archivist, librarian**; *déb-k'aṅ* **chancery, government office** *Schr.*; *déb-yig* **cover, envelope, stitched book** *Sch.*

དེམ་ཙི་ *dém-tsi* (perh. *Bu-nan*), **a small, narrow bridge, foot-bridge** *Lh.*

དེའང་ *déaṅ*, v. sub *de*.

དེའུ་(རེ) *déu*(*-re*) **one day, some future time,** *Dzl.* frq.; *deu ... deu ...* now ... now, at one time ... at another time *Mil.* (*Tar.* 165, 18 is prob. an incorr. reading).

དེར་ *der*, for *dé-ru*, esp. as adv., **then, at that time;** *der zad, der bas Cs.* that is all, there is nothing more, finis.

དེས་ *des* 1. instrum. of *de*; *des čog* with that it is enough, **that will do** *Sch.* — 2. for *dé-bas*, v. *de* comp.

དེས་པ་ *dés-pa Cs.*: '**fine, brave, noble, chaste**; a title'; occurs frq. in *Dzl.* as a commendable quality of women.

དོ་ *do* 1. num. figure: 131. — 2. **two, a pair, a couple,** used only in counting, measuring etc.: *žo do re* two drams of each *Med.*; **tá-bag do** *W.* two platefuls. — 3. **this,** *Schr.*: *dó-yi dón-du*; gen. only in *do-núb* this evening, to-night *Mil.*; *bdag do-núb sáṅ-gi mi* I, a man only for to-day and to-morrow *Mil.*; *Cs.* also *do-žág, do-*

mód to-day. — 4. **an equal, a match; a companion, associate,** *W.* **yá-do** **fellow, yoke-fellow, mate, comrade, consort;** *do-zla* 1. id. *Mil.*; 2. **party in a lawsuit**(?); **dó-da ṗan-tsún ẑib čé'-pa* Cs.* seems to mean: carefully to investigate (the right of) both parties; *do-med* unequalled, matchless; **dho-med zaṅ-po*, C., W.*

དོ་ཀེ(ར)་ *do-ké(r)* = *tor-tsúgs Lex.*

དོ་གར་ཁ་ *do-gar-ḱá W.* **light-blue.**

དོ་གལ་ *do-gál* **importance, weight; important, weighty** *C., W.*; **dho-ghál mi ǰhé'-pa* C., *do-gál mi čó-če* W*, to treat lightly, to make light of, to slight; **ₒdi tsig-po dho-ghál mi ₒdug* C.*, this word is unimportant, of no consequence; *do-gál-čan* important, of consequence *Cs.*

དོ་དམ་ *do-dám* **commission, charge, superintendence;** **dho-dhám ǰhé'-pa* C., *do-dám ḱúr-če* W.*, to have the superintendence, direction, or charge of a business, to have the keeping of a thing; *do-dám-pa* 1. a commissioned, authorized person, **overseer** etc.; 2. **bishop** *Chr. Prot.*

དོ་པོ་ *dó-po* **a load,** for a beast of burden, cf. *dos*; **do-góm* W.* saddle-cloth, housing; *do-lógs* the load on one side of a sumpter-horse, half a load, *do ya-ṗčig*; *do-nón-pa* the equalizing of the load, by increasing or lessening it on one of the sides.

དོ་བ་ *dó-ba* 1. Jerusalem artichoke *Sik.* — 2. secondary form of *sdó-ba* c. accus., to be a match for, to be equal in strength etc., to cope with *Mil.*; **šrog dhaṅ dhón-da re* C.* his life is at stake (*da?*).

དོ་བོ་ *dó-bo Med.*, prob. = *dó-ba* I.

དོ་མོད་ *do-mód* **to-day,** this day, v. *do.*

དོ་ར་ *do-rá Mil.?*

དོ་རེ་ *do-ré* v. *do* 2.

དོ་ཤཱ་ལཱ་ *do-šā-lā Hind.* a thick **shawl** or **wrapper** *W.*

དོ་ཤལ་ *do-šál Cs.* n. of an ornament hanging down from the shoulders; *Schr. mu-tig-gi do-šál* pearl-necklace; *Mil.* id.

དོ་སེ་ *do-sé* (from *tse?*) **now, at present** *Bal.*

དོག་ *dog* col. an auxiliary vb., acc. to Lamas of *W.* and *C.* = *rtóg-pa*, but of different pronunciation (*W.* **dog**, *C.* **dhog**). It seems to correspond to the expressions: as far as I know, as much as you know, to your knowledge etc. So a person may be asked: **yóg-mo me bar dóg-ga(m)** has your maid-servant, for what you know, lighted a fire? whilst, if the servant herself were asked, the question could only be: **me bar-ra(m)*, or *bar tsar-ra(m)**.

དོག་ *dog* sbst., in *B.* mostly *dóg-pa*, 1. **bundle, clew, skein,** e.g. of wool, weighing about two pounds, as much as one can hold conveniently with the hand or twist round it (*lag-dóg*). — 2. **capsule,** *ár-dza-kai* of the cotton plant. — 3. **ear of corn** *Lex.*; *Col.* more in use: *dog-dóg* a larger piece, *ḱá-ra dog-dóg*, lump-sugar (opp. to ground sugar); **clod, clump, lump, loaf,** **dog-dóg čó-če* W.* to form loaves; or in general: to press, to press together, to crush, to crumple; **a piece of wood, a log** *W.* (differing from *rdog*); **dág-ga-dog-gé* Ld.* broken in pieces, e.g. *ḱa-ra.*

དོག་པ་ *dóg-pa* 1. v. *dog* sbst. — 2. adj. and sbst., **narrow, narrowness;** *dóg-po, dóg-mo* adj.; *dóg-pai ynas-las tar-ba Wdṅ.*; fig. *šin-tu dóg-par gyúr-to* they were kept within narrow bounds *Glr.*; **ṭim dhóg-po* C.* strict administration of justice.

དོག་ལེ་ *dóg-le* an iron pan with a handle *C., W.*

དོགས་པ་ *dógs-pa* 1. vb., **to fear, to be afraid of, to apprehend,** gen. with the root of the pf tense, which in earlier writings is placed in the instrum. case: *nyés-pa byúṅ-gis mi dogs Dzl.*; whereas *Glr.*: *ser byuṅ dógs-pai dús-su* (fearing) when a hail-storm is threatening: *Tar.* 188, 9: *rgyal-srid ma zin-gyi(s) dógs-te* being afraid (the prince) might not be able to govern; *ma zin dógs-pas Glr.* fearing lest he should not finish the matter; *ysó-mk'an ma byuṅ dógs-nas Glr.* fearing that no deliverer would make his appearance; hence for **that not, lest** and similar expressions, *bu mis mtóṅ-gis dógs-nas* that his son might not be seen by the people *Pth.*; *že-sdáṅ laṅs dogs túr-re gyis* be on your guard lest anger should arise, take care not to grow angry! *Mil.*; *ₒgos dógs-pai lčibs* dusters to prevent (things) from getting dirty *Lex.*; *yžán-gyis ysál-bar šés-kyis dogs(-na)* using distant allusions, so that the drift of a speech is not at once clear and intelligible *Gram.*; rarely with the supine: *dé-dag bág-tu*, or *ₒbrós-su dogs* fearing lest they should become faint-hearted or take to flight *Dzl.* — 2. sbst. **apprehension, fear, scruple,** *dógs-pa skyes-te Dzl.*; also *dogs skyés-te Glr.*; *dogs bsál-ba, dogs yčód-pa* to remove doubts or apprehensions *Tar.*; *dogs dpyod ni dogs yčód-do* examining a scruple is as much as removing it *Sch.*; *re-dógs* hope and fear (things which a saint ought to be no longer subject to) frq.

དོང· *doṅ* 1. **a deep hole, pit, ditch,** an excavation deep in proportion to its breadth, e.g. a trench in fortifications, *Glr.*; *sa-dóṅ* id.; *č'u-dóṅ* **a well, a deep cistern**; *me-dóṅ* a fiery abyss, pool of fire *Dzl.*; *Sch.* proposes to use it also for **crater.** — 2. **depth, deepness, profundity**; *dóṅ-čan Cs.*, **dóṅ-po* W.*, **deep**; *doṅ-méd* not deep, shallow *Cs.* — 3. v. *ₒdóṅ-ba.*

དོང་ག· *dóṅ-ga* n. of a tropical climbing plant, and of a sweet-tasted lenient purgative *Med.*

དོང་པ· *dóṅ-pa* **padlock,** *dóṅ-pa ₒjúg-pa* to put a padlock on.

དོང་པོ, ལྡོང་པོ· *dóṅ-po, ldóṅ-po* 1. **tube,** any hollow cylindrical vessel, = *pu-ri*; *dóṅ-bu* a small ditto; *spa-dóṅ* a tube etc. of bamboo, *šiṅ-doṅ* a tube etc. of wood; *lčags-doṅ* of iron; *mda-doṅ* **a quiver,** *dóṅ-ba Glr.* id.; *dóṅ-mo, ldóṅ-mo* **a small churn,** = *gur-gúr.* — 2. **a shuttle,** made of a piece of bamboo.

དོང་ཙེ· *dóṅ-tse, Sch.* also *dóṅ-ts'e, dóṅ-rtse,* piece of money, **coin,** *ysér-gyi* gold coin *Dzl.*; esp. a small coin, used (like penny) proverbially for a small sum, *Dzl.* ༢༠༡, 9; ༤༤, 6.

དོང་ཟིལ· *doṅ-zil*(?) *W.* Corydalis meïfolia.

དོང་ཟེ· *dóṅ-ze* **wasp** *Cs.*

དོད· *dod* **an equivalent,** **ṅul méd-na dod čig tob gos* W.* if you have no money, I must receive an equivalent; *dei dod či-ₒdra yod* what is the equivalent, what shall we get for it? *Mil.*; *bu-dód* adoptive son, *ṅéd-kyi bu-dód mdzod* pray, suffer yourself to be adopted by us *Mil.*; *skad-dód* verbal equivalent, **synonym, translation** *Lex.*; *dód-du* **as an equivalent, as payment, for, instead of, at,** e.g. at a moderate price; *k'yód-kyis ṅai stóbs-kyi dod mi p'er Glr.*, gen. **mi nyn* C.*, you cannot cope with me in strength, you are no match for me.

དོད་པ· *dód-pa* **to project, to be prominent,** gen. with *ₒbur-du*; also **elongated** (Botany) *Wdṅ.*

དོན· *don* (Ssk. अर्थ), resp. (at least in some of its applications) *žabs-don Pth.* 1. **sense, meaning, signification,** *gó-ba* to understand, *ₒgrél-ba* to explain; *don rnyéd-par dká-bai yig-ₒbrú* letters the meaning of which is not easily understood *Glr.*; *don mi ₒdug* that makes no sense; *ₒdii don či yin* what does that mean? *žal ni k'ai don yin: 'žal'* signifies the same as *k'a*; *dpe bži don daṅ lṅai mgur* a psalm, containing four parables, together with their explanation, as being the fifth (part) *Mil.*; *ráṅ-gi-séms-la don gyis* refer the signification, make the application, to your own soul *Mil.*; . . . *kyi dón-du bšad*, it is explained in the sense of . . ., as having the same meaning as . . . *Gram.*; *don mt'ún-no* they agree in this sense, on that point, they say so unanimously *Glr.*; *don dé-la soms* think over this sense, i.e. over the meaning of this significant example *Mil.*; *žu-dón* application, petition, request; contents, *Tar.* 45, 19.; also opp. to *ts'ig* (word, form); *č'os-byuṅ-na spri-ti-ma zer-ba ₒdug-ste don mtun* in the *č'os-byun*, it is true, he is called Spritima, but the contents (i.e.

the things related about him) agree, are the same *Glr.*; *ṅés-don*, and *draṅ-don* v. *ṅés-pa* extr.; **idea, notion, conception** *Was.* (283); as the heading of a chapter or paragraph, e.g. *sdig-pa dág-pai don* of the expiation of sin. Rarely in a subjective sense: *don-méd byis-pa* thoughtless children *Mil.* — 2. **the true sense, the real state of the case, the truth,** (cf. *don-dám*), esp. *dón-la*, sometimes also *dón-gyis Tar.* 102, 12, **in truth, in fact, really** *Glr.* and elsewh.; to speak the truth *Thgy.*; *dón-la bltá-na* col. id.; also for: true! surely! indeed, forsooth. — 3. **intent, purpose, design; profit, advantage,** *ₒdii don ci yin* what is your meaning and intent (of doing that)? *soṅ-sóṅ-bai don med Dzl.* going on is to no purpose; *don med bžin-du* without seeing the use of it, without understanding the purpose *Wdn.*; with the genit. of the noun: **the profit, advantage, the good,** of a person, *mii don byéd-pa* to promote a person's welfare; esp. with reference to holy men, *ₒgro(-bai) don byéd-pa* to work for the welfare of (all) beings, very frq.; of priests col.: to act officially, to sacrifice; **gain, profit,** v. *ynyér-ba*; in a concrete sense: **some particular advantage, prerogative, good** or **blessing** obtained, frq.; *p̔án-pai don* a useful thing, *bdé-bai don* a gift of fortune, *rnyéd-pa* to obtain it; *dṅos-grúb mčóg-gi don* the excellency of the highest perfection; hence *dón-du* postp. c. genit. 1. **for,** for the good or the benefit of; 2. **for the sake of, on account of**; c. genit. of inf. **in order to, that**; 3. rarely: **in the place of, instead of, against, for,** *zas nór-gyi dón-du ₒtsóṅ-ba* to sell food for money *Mil.* — 4. in a general sense: **affair, concern, business,** *raṅ-(gi) don* one's own affairs, one's own interest (cf. n. 3); *γžan-(gyi) don* the interest of others; also meton. for **disinterestedness** *Mil.* (*Ssk.* परार्थ); *don máṅ-bas* on account of much business (syn. *brel-bas*) *Dzl.*; **chief or main point** (ni f.), *γsó-ba-rig-pai dón-rnams mdor sdú-ba* to sum up the principal points of medical science; *čos don γsúm-la ₒdús-te* religion being reduced to three main points (*lus, ṅag, yid*) *Glr.*; *don sgrúb-pa*, or *ₒgrúb-pa* to settle an affair, to obtain one's end, to attain to happiness. — 5. in anatomy *don lṅa* are: **the heart, lungs, liver, spleen,** and **kidneys** *Med.*; cf. *snod.* — 6. **document,** *čád-don* a written contract, agreement; *če(d)-don* a letter (to an inferior person).

Comp. *dón-čan*, *don daṅ ldán-pa* 1. **useful, profitable, expedient,** e.g. *tsig Thgy.* 2. **enjoying an advantage.** 3. having a certain sense. — *don-mtun* **a merchant** *Cs.*; *dpal daṅ ldán-pai don-mtún-dag* most honourable merchants! — *don-dág* 1. *Sch.* business, affairs (?). 2. col. = *don* 1. *don-dám* (परमार्थ), **the true sense,** subjectively: **good earnest,** col *W. yáṅs-pa man don-dám yin* it is not (said in) jest, but in good earnest; objectively: *don-dám-par dbyer-méd* in truth, (after all, upon the whole, in the end), it is all the same *Gram.*; *don-dám rnám-par ṅés-pai čos Glr.* prob. = *don-dám-pai bdén-pa* absolute truth *Was.* (293); in later times = *stoṅ-pa-nyid Trigl.* 20; *Mil.* — **don-ḍás** *W.* (lit.-*ₒbras*) = *če-dón?*

དོན་ *don* num. for *bdún-ču*, *don-γčig* etc. 71, 72 etc. to 79.

དོན་པ་ *dón-pa* for *ₒtón-pa Glr.* in one passage, prov. in *C.*

དོབ་དོབ་ *dob-dób*, *dob-dób smrá-ba* **to talk stuff, nonsense** *Sch.*

དོམ་ *dom* **the brown bear**; *dóm-bu* 1. *Sch.* the cub of a bear, 2. *Cs.*: a species of black dogs, resembling a bear.

དོམ་དོམ་ *dom-dóm Cs.*: ornamental fringes hanging down from the neck of a horse; *Wdṅ.*: *mé-tog rtá-yi dom-dóm ₒdra.*

དོམ་ར་ *dóm-ra* **screen, shade** for the eyes and the like *Sch.*

དོར་ *dor* **a pair** of draught cattle; *glaṅ-dór* a yoke of oxen

དོར་བ་ *dór-ba* v. *ₒdór-ba.*

དོར་མ་ *dór-ma* **breeches, trowsers.** *dor-t̔úṅ* short breeches, *dor-riṅ* long drawers, trowsers *Cs.*; *snam-dor* from *snam-bu*; *dór-rta* 1. that part of the breeches which covers the privy parts, v. *rta*; *γúgs-sa-moi dór-rta des γza sruṅ*, *rmá-la p̔an Wdṅ.*, the middle part of a widow's drawers prevents epilepsy and heals wounds. — 2. *W.* = *dór-ma?*

དོལ་ *dol* 1. **net,** esp. fishing-net, **tám-pa** to spread, to fix it *C.*, *W.*; (*nya-*)*dól-pa* **a fisherman,** cf. *γdól-pa.* — 2. *W.* **stew-pan.** — 3. *dol γčód-pa* **to split, to cleave** *Sch.*

དོས་ *dos* **a load** (of a beast of burden) that has to be carried by compulsory service, without being paid for; *k'al-dós* id.; *ja-dós* a load of tea carried in this manner; *dos ₒgél-ba* to load (on), to pack, *dos ₒbógs-pa* (not *ₒp'óg-pa Cs.*) to unload; *dós-pa* a conductor of such loads *Cs.*, *dos-dpon* the leader of a caravan of such loads; *dos drág-pa* 1. *Mil.* prob.: **hard compulsory service;** 2. perh. also: **severe in exacting it,** e.g. a feudal lord.

དྲ་ཅི་, དྲང་ཅི་ *drá-či, dráṅ-či Pur.* a flat basket.

དྲ་པ་ *drá-pa* a small copper coin, used in the western part of the Himalaya, **a thick paisa,** of the value of half a penny.

དྲ་བ་ *drá-ba* I. sbst. जाल, 1. **grate, lattice; net, net-work,** *lús-la drá-bar ₒbrel* (the veins) are spread throughout the body like net-work *S.g.*; *rús-pai drá-ba* the frame-work of bones, the skeleton *Thgy.*; *ₒod-zér-gyi drá-la* a pencil or aggregate of rays of light (lit. lattice-work of rays) *Glr.*; *dra míg* id., esp. col.; *lčágs-*(*kyi*) *dra*(*-mig*) **iron railings; grate; gridiron;** *rgyá-dra* **wooden rails, fence** *C.*, *W.*; *dra-*(*ba*) *p'yed*(*-pa*) *Lex.*, *Glr.* 'half-lattice', technical term for a kind of silk ornament; *drá-ba-čan* latticed, grated; *dra-lag-drá-lag-čan* having many forked ends or branches, of the horns of a stag. — 2. a bag made of net-work *Cs.*, *dra-p'ád, dra-čúṅ* id. — 3. the web of water-fowls.

II. vb., pf. *dras*, *W.* **dé-če**, **to cut, clip, lop, dress, prune, pare** (leather, cloth, paper, wings etc. with knife or scissors); also fig.: *p'ai míṅ-nas drás-te* borrowing (a syllable) from the father's name *Glr.* (twice); cf. also *Tar.* 107, 13; **téb-dhe-pa** *C.* one that cuts the strings (of a purse) on his thumb, i.e. **a cut-purse, pick-pocket;** *gos-drás* cloth cut out for a garment *Cs.*; *dras-spyád* **scissors** *Sch.*; *dra-gri Cs.*: 'a tailor's knife used for shears'; *drai* (sic) *ro Sch.*, **de-rúg, ta-de** *W.* **clippings, cuttings, remnants.**

དྲ་མ་ *drá-ma* **experienced, practised, learned** *Sch.*; so perh. *Pth.*, where however *bra-ma* and *tra-ma* is the usual form.

དྲ་ཟུ་ *dra-zu*, or **dra-su** *W.* a small pan with a handle; **a ladle.**

དྲག་ *drag* 1. *W.* **the post; any parcels** or **goods conveyed by post,** the *Hind.* डाक. — 2. **expedient, profitable, of use,** *p' úl-ba drág-gam* will it be of any use, well-applied, if I give? *Mil.*; *ji byas kyaṅ ma drag* whatever I did, it was of no use *Pth.*; *na či-ltar byás-na drag* what course will it be expedient to take? what shall I do best? *Pth.*; **či dhag, ghaṅ dhag** *C.* what is right? what is expedient? *nád-pa drág-pas čog* it is sufficient, if the patient is getting better *Mil.*

དྲག་པ་ *drág-pa* 1. **noble, of noble birth** *C.*, **drág-po** *W.*; *mi drág-pa*, or merely *drág-pa*, **a nobleman;** *drag-rigs* **nobility, gentry;** *drág-par byéd-pa* to raise to nobility, *drág-par ₒgyúr-ba* to become a nobleman *Cs.*; *drag-šos* an inferior officer or magistrate *Cs.* — 2. gen. *drágs-po*, *W.* also *drag-čan*, (*Ssk.* तीव्र, उग्र) **strong, vehement, violent** *ču drag-pa* a rapid river, violent current; *brtson-ₒgrus drag-pa ₒbád-pa* or *ₒdúṅ-pa drag-pa* unbending, unwearied application; *skad drag-pa* a powerful voice; *k'rims drag-pa* a severe punishment; *snyiṅ-rje drag* yearning compassion; **strong, forcible,** of expressions or language; moreover an epithet of terrifying deities, particularly of Siwa (*Ssk.* रुद्र), *drag-mo* fem.; *ži rgyas dbaṅ drag* v. sub *ži-ba.* — Adv. *drag-tu* **vehemently, violently,** e.g. to pull, to lament, to implore; **hastily, speedily,** e.g. to come *Wdṅ.*; *drág-por*, e.g. *drág-por bčad-de bklág-par byao* in reading a marked stop should be made *Gram.*; *ha-čaṅ mi-drág-par* very gently, softly; *drág-gis, dád-pa* to believe firmly *Mil.* — 3. *drág-pa* possessing a quality in a high degree, *dug-drag-pa Stg.* very poisonous. — 4. symb. num. 11.

Comp. *drag-nád*, v. *dreg-nád*, **gout.** — *drág-rtsal-čan* = *drág-po*, of deities. — *drag-žán* **strong and weak,** e.g. the relative force of sound *Gram.*; also **high and low,** with respect to rank. — *drag-šúl* **frightfulness,** *drag-šul-čan* **frightful, terrible, powerful; cruel,** frq., yet chiefly with respect to the power manifested by gods and sorcerers. — *drag-γšed* lit. 'cruel hangman', a terrifying deity v. *Schl.* 111, 214.

དྲགས་ *drags* adv. **very, much, greatly,** *mañ-drags Mil.* **very much**; adj. **much, strong, intense,** *bza-btuṅ-drags* eating and drinking a great deal *S.g.*; *dran-drágs* an intense, most vivid, remembrance of a person *Mil.*, an ardent longing or desire; *dga-drágs-nas* being very happy, highly rejoiced *Pth*, *C.*; *ɔgyod-drágs-nas* feeling deep repentance *Mil.*; *bsten drágs-na* if one continues it too long *S.g.*

དྲང་ *drañ* a kind of bear *Sch.*

དྲང་པོ་ *dráñ-po* (ऋजु) **straight** 1. not deviating from the direct course, not crooked or oblique, *tig*, *lam* etc. frq.; *lus dráñ-po ɔǰóg-pa* to sit straight; **ka búb-ne ḍáñ-po čó-če* W.* to place a thing straight or upright again; **ṭéd-la ḍáñ-po* W.*, horizontal. — 2. **right,** e.g. *lam*, opp. to *lóg-pa.* — 3. **sincere, honest, upright, truthful,** *dráñ-poi rañ-bžin-čan-gyi pyir* because they have an upright character *Dzl.*; *las dráñ-po* good actions, righteous deeds, opp. to *rtsúb-po* violent, unjust *Stg.*; *krims dráñ-po* 1. **a just sentence, righteous judgment,** opp. to *log-pa.* — 2. applied to men, with regard to their acting according to justice and the law (v. *krims*); *čós-drañ-po* **honest, upright,** with respect to religion and the divine law; also *dráñ-po* alone, whenever it is not to be misunderstood, may be used for our **just.** — *drañ-por*, *tsig dráñ-por smrá-ba* **to be candid, to speak the truth,** frq. *drañ-don* v. *ñés-pa* extr.

དྲང་བ་ *dráñ-ba* 1. abstract noun to *dráñ-po.* 2. pf. to *ɔdrén-pa.*

དྲང་སྲོང་ *drañ-sróñ*, ऋषि, 1. **a holy hermit,** an order of men, introduced from Brahmanism into Buddhism. These saints are looked upon partly as human beings, partly as Dewas, and at any rate as being endowed with miraculous powers *Dzl.* frq. — 2. At present the Lama that offers *sbyin-sreg* is stated to bear that name, and whilst he is attending to the sacred rites, he is not allowed to eat anything but *dkar-zas* (v. *dkar-po*). — 3. symb. num.: 7.

དྲན་དྲི་ *drán-dri Lh.* **the beam of a pair of scales,** *Hind.* डंडी.

དྲན་པ་ *drán-pa* I. vb. स्मृ, 1. **to think of,** c. accus., with or without *yid-la*, gen. to think of past events, **to remember, recollect, call to mind,** *drin* benefits, v. *drin*; *byúñ-ba-rnams* that which has happened *Glr.*; more emphatically: *rjés-su drán-pa* frq.; but also *dkon-mčóg drán-pa* to think of, to remember, God; *sdúg-po yóñ-ba de ma drán-pa yin* do not think of, do not trouble yourself about, future evils *Mil.*; *bskyis-par mi drán-no* I do not recollect having taken anything on credit *Dzl.*; *drán-pa tsám-gyis* as soon as one thinks of it, quick as thought *Thgr.*; *so-só-nas... drán-par gyis šig* every body should think of... *Dzl.* (the simple imp. seems not to be used); (*rjés-su*) *drán-par byéd-pa* also: **to remind of, to put in mind of, to revive the memory of,** = *drán-du ɔǰúg-pa*, *dran-skúl byéd-pa Lex.* — 2. **to become conscious of, to recollect,** *rmi-lam* a dream *Pth.*; *drán-par ɔgyúr-ba* to recover one's senses, to be one's self again *Dzl.*; *čiañ mi drán-pa* insensible *Dzl.*; *mi drán-pai ɔóg-tu* after they had become insensible *Dzl.* — 3. **to think of with love or affection, to be attached to, to long for,** *ǎ-ma* for the mother col.; **dran-sém* W.* **love, affection, attachment;** *dran-mčog-rje* dearest Sir! *Mil.*

II. sbst. स्मृति, स्मर, 1. **remembrance, recollection, reminiscence; memory** frq.; *drán-pa γsál-po* a retentive memory. — 2. **consciousness,** *stor* is lost; *tugs dran-méd-du tim-pa* to lose one's senses, resp. *Mil.*; *dran-méd-du brgyál-pa* id.; *drán-pa rnyéd-*

pa to recover one's senses *Pth.*; *ysó-ba* id.; *dran-ₒdzin-méd-pa* being out of one's senses (with joy) *Glr.*; **self-possession, consideration,** *dran-méd* without consideration, inconsiderate; *séms-čan smyón-pa-dag drán-pa so-sór rnyed* insane persons regained the respective faculties of their minds *S.O.*, *drán-pa yžúṅs-pa* prob. quickness of apprehension, good capacity; *drán-pa nyáms-pa* weak-minded; *dran-yód, dran-ldán,* remembering, being in one's senses *Cs.*; *dran-šés* for *drán-pa daṅ šes-ráb Mil.*; **ḍhẹm-pa maṅ-po ḱo-la šar** *C.* he is uneasy, troubled, full of scruples and apprehensions.

དྲལ་ *dral* 1. v. *lčam-mo.* 2. v. *ₒdral-ba.* 3. for *gral.*

དྲལ་ཙེ་ *dral-tse* a kind of courier or messenger *Cs.*

དྲས་ *dras* v. *dra-ba* II.

དྲི་ *dri,* col. also *dri-ma,* **odour, smell, scent,** *dri-žim(-po), dri-bsúṅ Dzl.* an agreeable smell, sweet scent; *dri-bzáṅ(-po)* 1. id., 2. *Cs.* also **saffron**; *dri-ṅán,* prob. also *dri-lóg, W.* **dri sóg-po**, *Cs. dri-mi-žim* an unpleasant smell, a stench; *dri bró-ba* to exhale an odour *Glr.*; **ḍi núm-pa** or **nóm-pa** to inhale an odour; *W.*: **kyúr-ḍi, nyiṅ-ḍi, dúg-ḍi, mé-ḍi, rúl-ḍi, hám-ḍi rag** I perceive a sour, stale, burnt, smoky, putrid, mouldy smell; **tsig-ḍi, žob-ḍi** a smell of burnt food, burnt wool; *dri lṅa* five odours or perfumes used in offering; *dri-ḱa Sch.*: urinous smell (?); *dri-ṅád* vapour, exhalation, fragrance; *dri-čan lté-ba* bag of the musk-deer; musk *Wdṅ.*; *dri-ču* scented water, perfume *Cs.* (yet cf. *dri-ma*), *dri-čén* a medicinal herb *Lt.* — *dri-ytsaṅ-ḱáṅ,* गन्धकूट, **a sacred place, a chapel,** conjectures about the etymology of the word v. *Burn.* I, 262. — *dri-ₒdzín* po., the nose. — *dri-za,* also *dri-za-mo* fem., गन्धर्व **an eater of fragrance,** in Brahmanism **the heavenly musicians,** and so also in Buddhism painted as playing on guitars, but usually (in accordance with the etymology) thought to be **aërial spirits,** that feed on odours of every description. They are supposed not only to be fond of flowers and other fragrant objects, but also to visit dunghills, flaying-places, shambles etc., the various substances of which are accordingly dedicated to them (cf. *ytór-ma*). The insects, swarming about such places, the Tibetan believes to be incarnated *dri-za.* — *dri-zai groṅ(-ḱyer)* **mirage, fata morgana.**

དྲི་བ་ *dri-ba* **question,** *dri-ba ₒdri-ba* to ask a question, *mi-la* a person; *dri-bai lan, dris-lán,* answer; *dri-rtóg ma maṅ Mil., C.,* **ḍhi gya ma ǰhé** or **če** *Cs.*, don't ask long! do not ask many questions!

དྲི་བོ་ *dri-bo* **an enchanter, sorcerer, magician,** *dri-mo* **enchantress, witch** *Mil.*

དྲི་མ་ *dri-ma,* मल, 1. **dirt, filth, impurity; excrement, ordure;** *lag-(pai) dri(-ma)* marks left by dirty fingers on books etc.; *sná-dri* mucus, snot, snivel *S.g.*; *dri-ma yzum* the three impurities, excrement, urine, sweat; but sometimes more are enumerated; frq. fig.: *nyés-pai, nyon-móṅs-pai, ḱa-na-ma-tó-bai dri-ma*; *dri-ma kun zád-nas* after all impurities have been put off *Dzl.*; *dri-ču* 1. **urine,** *ₒdór-ba* to urinate *Glr.*; *rés-ₒga raṅ-byuṅ-gi dri-ču sten* sometimes (in my extremity) I had recourse to my own water *Mil.* — 2. v. sub *dri.* — *dri-čén* feces of the intestinal canal. — *dri-ma-čan* **dirty, sluttish,** as to dress; *dri-ma-méd-pa* clean, cleanly. — 2. for *dkri-ma,* v. *dkri-ba.*

དྲིང་ *driṅ Cs.* = '*drin* **kindness, favour**;' yet, *yžan driṅ mi ₒǰog Lex.*, *yžán-gyis driṅ-la mi ₒǰog-čiṅ raṅ-gi čos žugs-so Dom.?* One dictionary renders it by प्रत्यय, knowledge; certainty, faith, confidence

དྲིན་ *drin,* resp. *bka-drin,* rarely *sku-drin Glr.,* **kindness, favour, grace,** *blá-mai drin-gyis* by the grace of my Lama, of my spiritual father, of my patron saint *Mil.*; in addressing a person, *ḱyed* (or *ḱyod*)-*kyi bka-drin-gyis* is gen. used; *mai drin* benefits conferred by a mother *Thgy.*; *drin-čan, drin-čé* **kind, gracious, benevolent; benefactor,** *drin-čan p̔a-má* the parents, these benefactors; *drin-čan már-pa,* Marpa full of grace (Milaraspa's Lama); *tse ˳di-la drin če-šós rán-gi ma yin* the greatest benefactress for this life is one's own mother; *bód-la bka-drin čé-ba lags-so* this turned out the greatest benefit for Tibet *Glr.*; *ǎ-ma drin-čén* kindest mother! (says a king to a wonder-working female saint) *Pth.*; *drin drán-pa* as a vb., **to acknowledge a kindness, to feel obliged**; as a sbst. **thankfulness, gratitude** *Thgy.*; *kyód-kyi drin rtág-tu drán-pas* as I shall always feel greatly obliged to you *Dzl.*; *dei bka-drin drán-čiṅ* full of thankfulness towards him *Dzl.*; *drin rjéd-pa* unmindful of obligations; *drin γzó-ba, drin-du γzo-ba, drin-lán glán-pa, drin-lán bsáb-pa, W.* **ḍin-zó taṅ-če** to return benefits, to show one's self grateful; *drin γzó-žiṅ lan byao* you shall not have done it for nothing *Dzl.*; *drin-lán-du* as a **gift** made in return, a return-present.

དྲིབ་ཤིལ་ (*drib-šil*) **ḍib-šil**, a corrupt form for *dril-bu γsil, Ld.*, = *γyér-ka.*

དྲིམ་ *drim* (spelling?) **stump, trunk,** of a tree or plant, deprived of top and branches *Ld.* —

དྲིའུ་ *driu* v. *dre.*

དྲིལ་ *dril*, gen. *dríl-bu,* **bell**; *dril sróg-pa* to ring the bell; to publish by ringing a bell; *dríl-lče* the tongue of a bell, the clapper; *dril-γzúgs* the body of a bell *Cs.*, *Glr.*; *dril-sgrá* the voice or sound of a bell, peal of bells; *dril-kaṅ* bell-tower, belfry; *dril-stégs* the frame of timber, on which bells are suspended.

དྲིལ་བ་ *dril-ba* v. *˳dril-ba.*

དྲིས་པ་ *dris-pa* v. *˳drí-ba.*

དྲུ་བུ་ *drú-bu* = *grú-bu, grú-gu,* **a clue** or **ball,** of wool etc.

དྲུག་ *drug* num. **six,** *drúg-pa, drúg-po* cf. *dgu*; *yi-ge drúg-pa* or *-ma* the prayer of the six letters, the Ommanipadmehūm, *Glr.*; *drúg-ču* sixty; *drúg-ču-rtsa-γčig* (*W.* **ḍug-ču-re-čig**), or *re-γčig*, sixty one; *drug-brgyá* six hundred; *drug-stóṅ* six thousand; *drug-ču-skór* a cycle of sixty years. — *drúg-sgra* the so-called article, presenting itself in the following six forms: *pa, ba, ma, po, bo, mo.*

དྲུག་དཀར་, དྲུག་དམར་ *drug-dkár, drug-dmár,* **two sorts of turkoise** *Cs.*

དྲུང་ *druṅ* the space **near,** and esp. **before** a person or thing, *po-bráṅ-gi druṅ gáṅ-na-ba der ˳dúg-nas* alighting on the place before the palace *Dzl.* ༢༥, 3; gen. with *na, du, nas.* 1. adv. **near to, near by, to or at the side of, before, to, off from;** *drúṅ-du rtóg-pa* to examine personally, face to face, orally *Dzl.*; *drúṅ-du ˳gró-ba* to go near or up to. 2. postp. c. genit. (less corr. c. accus.), *šiṅ-gi drúṅ-na* near, or under the tree, *drúṅ-du* id.; to or towards the tree; *drúṅ-nas* away from (the tree); *rgyál-poi drúṅ-du* to the king, before, in presence of (coram) the king; *drúṅ-pa,* resp. *sku-drúṅ-pa,* one standing near, **a waiting man, a page in ordinary** *Cs.* — *drúṅ-˳kor* **train, retinue.** — *drúṅ-γnas-pa* **companion, associate.** — *drúṅ-yig(-pa)* **secretary.** — *drúṅ-˳tso-ba* **private physician,** physician in ordinary *Cs.* When preceded by *žabs* it becomes a respectful term, e.g. in the direction of a letter, where it stands for our **'to'** (lit. 'to the feet of *N. N.*').

དྲུང་པོ་ *drúṅ-po* 1. **prudent, sensible, judicious, wise** *Mil.*, in conjunction with *γčáṅ-po*; so also *Pth.* *γčaṅ-drúṅ-ldaṅ-pa.* — 2. **sincere, candid** *C.* — 3. **diligent?**

དྲུངས་ *druṅs* **root,** of rare occurrence; *druṅs (-nas) pyuṅ* exterminated, destroyed root and branch, *Lex.*

དྲུངས་པ་ *drúṅs-pa* **clarified, clear** *Cs.*; *bčes-druṅs* resp. for *čaṅ,* **beer,** *Ts.*

དྲུད་ *drud* 1. v. *˳drud-pa.* — 2. *drud-drud* **pelican** *Sch.*

དྲུབ་པ་ *drúb-pa* v. *˳drúb-pa.*

དྲུམ་པ་ *drúm-pa* **to have a strong desire, to long, languish, pine.** for, *Sch.*

དྲུས་མ་ *drús-ma* **millet** *Sch.*

དྲེ་ *dre Ts., dreu Lex., ḍiu Lh., drel Glr.,* **mule,** *dré-po, pó-dre* he-mule, *dré-mo, mó-dre* she-mule.

དྲེ་བོ *dré-bo Lt.*, *dré-mo Mṅg.*, **ḍe-móṅ* W.*, **elbow.**

དྲེག་པ *drég-pa, drégs-pa* 1. any **dirt** that is removed by scraping, whereas *dri-ma* is washed off; more particularly: -- 2. **soot,** which is also used as a medicine *Wdṅ.*; *k'uṅ-drég* id.; *sgrón-dreg* lamp-black; *sláṅ-dreg* soot on a kettle; *lčágs-dreg* v. *lčags*; *tál-dreg, rdó-dreg Med.?* — *só-dreg* **tartar** incrusting the teeth *Med.* — *dreg-bál* flakes of soot. — *dreg-nád* **gout;** *dreg-grúm* id.

དྲེགས་པ *drégs-pa* 1. **pride, haughtiness, arrogance,** *k'eṅ-ḍégs* id.; *drégs-pa nyams* pride is put down, humbled; *drégs-pa skyáṅ-ba* to lay aside, to put off pride; *nór-gyis dregs* purse-proud *Lex.* — 2. **proud, haughty, arrogant,** = *drégs-pa-čan*; *drégs-pa (-čan tams-čád* the great, the proud, the people of high rank, the great ones of this world *Pth.*; in the world of spirits, with or without *bgegs*: the powerful demons. — 3. as a vb.: *ró-tsas dregs tse* when the sexual impulse **is strong** *Med.*

དྲེད *dred* (*Zam.* तरक्षु) **hyena,** which name has prob. been transferred by the inhabitants of the mountainous districts to the *dred*, an animal better known to them) **the yellow bear;** *mi-dred* a bear that devours men *Mil.*; *p'yúgs-dred* a bear destructive to cattle; *dréd-p'o* he-bear, *dréd-mo* she-bear. — *dred-tsáṅ* a bear's den. — *dred-siu-šiṅ* hazel-nut tree *Sch.*

དྲེད་པོ *dréd-po* 1. *Sch.*: **'evasive, lazy'**, yet *č'os-méd dréd-po zol-zóg γyo-rgyú-čan?* — 2. **load, burden,** esp. a heavy load *C.*, *dréd-po dréd-pa* = *k'rés-po grág-pa*, to cord a load.

དྲེད་མ *dréd-ma, rtsa-dréd-ma Glr.* = *drés-ma*; *dám-dréd-ma Mil.?*

དྲེའུ, དྲེལ *dreu, drel*, v. *dre*; *dreu-rṅóg* 1. **the mane of a mule.** — 2. **a couch,** or **stuffed-seat** *Cs.* — 3. a kind of **long-haired cloth.**

དྲེས་མ *drés-ma* 1. *C.* a kind of grass, of which ropes and shoes (of great durability) are made; *Glr. dréd-ma*; *drés-mai ge-sár S.g.* the filaments of *drés-ma*; *dres-ₒbru Cs.*, *dres-ₒbrum S.g.* the seeds of *drés-ma*. — 2. *W.* Iris kamaonensis.

དྲོ *dro* (cf. *dró-ba*), 1. **the hot time of the day,** from about 9 o'cl. a. m. till 3 o'cl. p. m.; *dró-la báb-nas* when this time arrived *Dzl.*; *sṅá-dro* the morning, *p'yi-dro* 1. the later part of the afternoon, 2. *W.* **p'i-ro** evening, night. — 2. a meal taken about noon, **lunch;** *dro btáb-pa* to lunch; *dro-lúg* a sheep intended to be eaten for a luncheon; *dro-šá* meat intended for such a purpose.

དྲོ་བ *dró-ba* 1. **to be warm,** v. *drós-pa*; gen. adj. **warm,** *dró-bai γnas* a warm place; *dró-bar ₒgyúr-ba* to grow warm. — 2. **warmth** (*bág-dro* v. sub *ur*).

དྲོགས *drogs Sch.*: 'packed up, made up into pack or parcel'.

དྲོང(ས) *droṅ(s)* v. *ₒdren-pa*.

དྲོང་མ *dróṅ-ma* **a large basket** or **dosser,** provided with a lid, and carried on the back, *Hind.* पतारा.

དྲོད *drod* 1. **warmth, heat,** e.g. of the sun; *drod-γšér* warmth and moisture; *dród-kyi šiṅ* a tropical tree *Wdṅ.*; *me-drod* 1. **the heat of the fire** *Lt.* 2. prob. **animal heat,** perh. because it is supposed to arise from a union of the fiery element with a germ originated by conception. — 2. *k'a-dród zuṅ γčig* a small piece of food, = *k'a-zás*, and prob. incorrect for *k'a-bród* enjoyment of the mouth. — *lám-la drod tób-pa Mil.* was explained: to have a cheerful mind, free from doubts and apprehensions on the way (to heaven), *drod*, therefore, seems to stand here for *brod*. — *drod-rtags*, *Mil.*, was explained as being new knowledge, new perceptions, as a fruit of long meditation; one *Lex.* has *dród-rig-pa* = मात्रज्ञ experienced or well-versed in measure.

དྲོན་མོ *drón-mo* col. **warm,** *zan-drón* warm food.

དྲོལ *drol* v. *ₒdrol-ba*.

དྲོས *dros, Sch.* = *dro*; *dros-čén* **noon, mid-day,** *dros-čúṅ* forenoon(?).

དྲོས་པ *drós-pa*, pf. of *dró-ba*, **heated, grown warm,** esp. of the ground by the heat of the sun, of men, by warm clothing; *dros soṅ* the ground has grown warm, the snow is beginning to melt; *drós-na* when it is getting warm; *di gón - na dros lags* if you put that on, you will be warm *Mil.*; *ṫse yċig drós - pai gos* warm clothing for one period of existence *Mil.* — *ma-drós-pa* n. of the Manasarowara or lake of Mapam in Nari. The Hindoos describe it as something like a northern ocean, inhabited by Nagas (v. *klu*), and the Tibetans in good faith repeat such fables, at least in their literature, although they know better.

ད་མན་ *dha-mán Ld.-Glr. Schl.* fol. 17, b., v. *lda-mán.*

དྷུ་ཏི་ *dhú-ti*, (धूति a shaker, agitator?) a word of more recent mystical physiology, 'the middle vein', = *dbú-ma* (cf. *ytúm-po* and *ṫig-le*) *Thgr., Mil., Wdṅ.* The Lamas consulted by me asserted, not quite in accordance with books, *dhu-ti* to denote a kind of *rluṅ* in the body (which would agree with धू to blow, and with πνεῦμα), a vital power closely connected with the soul, supporting it during lifetime, and leaving it only when separated by death. This would be a new or second signification of *dhu-ti*, although I cannot vouch for the correctness of the above statement, nor am I able to decide, whether *dhu-ti* and *ȧ-ba-dhuti* are quite the same. — *ȧ-ba-dhuti-pa Tár.* 187, 8 is a proper name, *Schf.*

དྷེ་ལ་ *dhe-la, Hind.* धेला, **half a paisa,** the smallest coin, equal to the tenth part of a penny, *W.*

གདག(ས)་ *ydag(s)* 1. fut. of *˳dogs-pa.* — 2. *ydags* **the light, day** *Cs.*, opp. to *sribs.* — 3. in *Stg. ydágs-pa* occurs frq. as a translation of प्रज्ञा **wisdom.**

གདང་, རྡང་ *ydaṅ, rdaṅ* (*ldaṅ?*) 1. **clothes-stand, rack** or **rail** for hanging up clothes, *ydáṅ-la gos ˳dzár-ba, ˳gél-ba*; *ydáṅ-bu* 1. **peg** or **nail,** for the same purpose. 2. *skás-kyi ydaṅ(-bu) Lex.*, **ṡral-dáṅ** *W.*, **step of a ladder.** — 2. col. for *ydeṅ.*

གདང་བ་ *ydáṅ-ba, ydáṅs-pa,* to open wide, mouth and nostrils, **to gape** *B.* and col.; *ydáṅ-pai ḱro-žál* an angry face with the mouth wide opened *Glr.*

གདངས་ *ydaṅs* 1. **music, harmony, melody,** = *dbyaṅs, snyags,* also *ydaṅs-snyan*; *ydaṅs byéd-pa* to make music *C.* — 2. resp. for *dprál-ba* **forehead** *Cs.*

གདངས་པ་ *ydáṅs-pa* 1. v. *ydáṅ-ba.* 2. resp. one recovering from illness, **convalescent,** with *snyun, bsnyuṅ-ba Lex.*; **ra daṅ** *W.* he has recovered from his drunken fit, has become sober again.

གདན་ *ydan,* आसन, resp. *bžugs-ydan W.*, **a bolster,** or seat composed of several quilts or cushions, put one upon the other (five for common people, nine for people of quality), cf. *˳bol; ydan-ḱri* **a throne** *Glr.*; *ydan-rábs* **a succession of teachers** *Tar.* 199, 4. The word is much used in polite expressions: *ydan ˳dégs-pa* **to take leave, to withdraw, to depart**; *ydán-sa* 1. **place of residence,** *bla-mai Mil.*; *dga - ston - gyi* place of a festival *Glr.* 2. **situation, position, rank,** ni f., *Mil.*; *ydán-˳dren-pa* **to invite,** = *spyán-˳dren-pa,* **to appoint, to nominate,** *dpon-du* a chief, a leader *Glr.*; **to go to meet** *Glr.*; **dan-su-ċe** *W.* id.; **dan-kyal-ċe** *W.* **to accompany,** as a mark of attention; *dan-ṗeb-pa* **to arrive** *Sch.*

གདབ་པ་ *ydáb-pa,* fut. of *˳debs-pa.*

གདམ་ཀ་ *ydám-ka W., ydam-ṅa Lex.*, **choice, election,** **dám - ka ċó - ċe** *W.* **to choose, to elect;** *ydám-ṅa byéd-pa Lex.* id.

གདམ་པ་ *ydám-pa,* fut. of *˳dóms-pa, ydáms-pa,* pf. of *˳dóms - pa,* **to advise,** *rgyál-po-la ydám-pai mdo* adviser of kings, a mirror for sovereigns *Thgy.*; *ydáms-pa* sbst. **advice, counsel, doctrine, precept,** *ydáms-ṅág, W.* **ydáms-ka, ydáms-ḱa** (cf. *ḱá-ta, ḱá-lta*), resp. *žal-ydáms, bka - ydáms* id.; *ydáms-pa ċig žu* we ask for some advice *Glr.*; *ṗán - pa ydáms - pa* a good advice; *ydams-ṅág stón-pa Lex.*, **dám-ka*, or *ḱá-ta táṅ-ċe** *W.* to give an advice, to advise; *ydams - ṅág ˳dóms - pai ṫsig* **the imperative mood,** expressing command or exhortation *Gram.*

གདའ་བ་ *ydá-ba,* eleg. for *˳dúg-pa B.* and *Khams,* 1. **to be, to be there,** *du* *yda* how many are there here? *Zam.*; *sgyúr-gin yda Glr.*; *rtóg-tu ydao* he or it may be discerned, distinguished *Dzl.*; *p̓yin-nas yda* he had arrived *Mil.*; no other negative than *mi* can precede it: *žábs-mtíl-la ču rég-pa tsám-las mi yda* the water did not reach above the soles of the shoes *Mil.* — **2.** with *par* it expresses uncertainty, vagueness, *ɣšégs-par yda* he may possibly go, *Pth.*; *ₒdi yin-pa* (col. for *par*) *yda* he seems to be this (man) *Pth.*; cf. *ₒdug-pa.* — 3. to say, cf. *mči-ba.*

གདལ་བ་ *ydál-ba* another form for *rdal-ba.*

གདིང་བ་ *ydiṅ-ba* another form for *ₒdiṅ-ba*; also sbst.: *ydiṅ-ba daṅ bgo-ba* **carpets** and **clothes,** i.e. all sorts of textures, *Stg.*

གདུ་བ་ *ydú-ba* 1. another form for *sdú-ba* **to gather, to collect.** 2. another form for *ydúṅ-ba(?) Sch.:* **to love**; cf. *rnyed-la ydu Zam.*

གདུ་བུ་ *ydú-bu Glr.*, *ydú-gu Glr.*, *ydúb-bu* the usual form, **ring for the wrist, bracelet,** or for the ankle, an ornament of Hindoo women; *lag* (resp. *p̓yag*)*-ydub* bracelet; *rkaṅ* (resp. *žabs*)*-ydub* foot-ring; *sór* (col. *ser*)*-ydub* finger-ring *Glr.*; *ɣser-ydub* gold-ring, *dṅul-ydub* silver-ring; *ɣsér-ser-ydub* a golden finger-ring; **tág-če* W.* to put on (a ring).

གདུག་པ་ *ydúg-pa* 1. **poison** = *dug, ydúg-pa ɣsum Dzl.* = *dug ɣsum; zás-su ydúg-pa zá-ba Dom.* — 2. in general: any thing hurtful, or any injury, mischief, harm done; as adj. **noxious, mischievous, dangerous,** *ydúg-pa-čan,* of animals, demons, wicked men; *dug-sbrúl ydúg-pa-čan* dangerous venemous serpents *Glr.*; *dre-srin ydúg-pa maṅ* many mischievous demons *Glr.*; *ydúg-pai bsám-pa* propensity to destroy, destructiveness, ferocity, of beasts of prey *Glr.*; *ydúg-pai ṅá-ro* wild screams *Mil.*; *ydug-rtsúb* **ferocity, malice, spite** *Mil.*; *stár-bu ydúg-pa tsér-ma-čan* **buckthorn** with horrible spines *Wdṅ.*; also for **mischief done by evil spirits** *Mil.*

གདུགས་ *ydugs* I. resp. *dbu-ydúgs* 1. **parasol, umbrella,** *B., C.* — 2. **canopy, baldachin**; *spyi-ydugs* a covering, shelter, awning, for several persons *Glr.*; *ydugs ₒbúbs-pa* to raise a canopy, to put up a shade or screen; of peacocks: to spread the tail.

II. eleg. **mid-day, noon,** *sáṅ-gi ydúgs-la* for to-morrow noon *Dzl.*; noon-tide heat (cf. *dugs*), *ydugs-méd ydóṅ-pa ydúgs-kyis ydúṅs* an unprotected face is molested by the heat *Lex.*; *ydugs-ts̓ód* 1. **noon-tide, dinner-time, 2. dinner.**

གདུང་ *yduṅ*, resp. for *rus* (*-pa*), 1. **bone, bones, remains,** esp. as *riṅ-srél,* also *yduṅ-rús, sku-ydúṅ*; *ɣser-ydúṅ, dṅul-ydúṅ* the gold and silver palls covering the remains of the highest Lamas. — 2. **family, lineage, progeny, descendants,** *rigs ni rgyal-rigs-so,yduṅ-ni gau-ta mao* as to caste, he belongs to that of the ruler, as to family, he is a descendant of Gotama; also fig.: *saṅs-rgyás-kyi yduṅ Dzl.* the spiritual children of Buddha, the saints; *yduṅ-brgyúd yod* the house, the family, is still existing *Glr.*; *yduṅ(brgyud) ₒdzin-pai sras* a first-born male, by whom the lineage may be continued, frq.; also for any single descendant *Glr.* — *yduṅ-sgróm Sch.* **coffin,** *Schr.* **funeral urn.** — *yduṅ-rtén* funeral pyramid containing relics, cf. *mčod-rten.* — *yduṅ-rabs* **generation,** *ṅá-nas yduṅ-rábs lṅá-pa-la* in the fifth degree after me *Glr.*

གདུང་བ་ *ydúṅ-ba, ydúṅs-pa* I. vb. 1. **to desire, to long for,** *zás-la, ltó-la, Glr.* and elsewh.; **duṅ duṅ čó-če* W.* id. — 2. **to love,** *šín-tu ydúṅ-bai ma yčig* my own dearly beloved mother! cf. *brtse-ydúṅ.* — 3. **to feel pain, to be pained, tormented, afflicted,** by heat or cold, thirst, lust, distress; **nyiṅ dúṅ-te* W.* sad, sorrowful; *ydúṅ-bar byéd-pa* to make sad, to distress, *ɣžán-gyi séms-la,* the mind of others. — **4. to be dried,** *nyi-mas* by the sun, of a dead body *Dzl.*

II. sbst. 1. **desire, longing, lust,** *ydúṅ-ba ži* (sensual) desire ceases *Stg.* — 2. love, *mos-gus-ydúṅ-ba dpag-méd skye* immense veneration and love arises *Glr.* — 3. **affliction, misery, distress, torment, pang,** *ydúṅ-bai skad* a plaintive voice, doleful cry *Glr.*

III. adj. 1. **longed for, earnestly desired.** — 2. **beloved**, v. above. — 3. **grieved, tormented** frq.; *yduṅ-dbyáṅs* a song expressive of longing or of grief, an elegy *Mil.*; *yduṅ-sems* love-longing *B.*, and col.; **á-ma-la dúṅ-sem-čan ˳dug* W.* he tenderly loves his mother.

གདུང་མ་ *ydúṅ-ma* **beam, piece of timber,** *má-yduṅ* principal beam, *bú-yduṅ* cross-beam; *yduṅ-ḱébs* beams projecting over the capital of a column *Glr.* — *yduṅ-sgrig* a raft *Ld.* — *yduṅ-˳débs S.g.* pedestal, base(?) — *yduṅ-zám* a bridge of timber or of poles. — *ydúṅ-šiṅ Sik.* fir-tree (Pinus abies).

གདུད་པ་ *ydúd-pa* **love, longing** *Sch.*, cf. *ydú-ba.*

གདུབ་བུ་ *ydúb-bu* v. *ydú-bu.*

གདུབ་པ་ *ydúb-pa Stg.*: *zás-la*, adj., **frugal, temperate?**

གདུམ་(པོ་) *ydúm(-po)* **a piece** *Sch.*, = *dum.*

གདུལ་ *ydul* v. *˳dul-ba.*

གདུས་ *ydus* v. *ydú-ba.*

གདེག་ *ydeg* v. *˳dégs-pa.*

གདེང་ *ydeṅ* **confidence, assurance, cheerfulness** *Mil.* very frq.; *ydeṅ tób-pa* to become confident, to take courage, to be reassured; *˳či-tse ydeṅ čiaṅ med* when dying, he has no confident hope *Mil.*; *mi-˳jigs-pai ydeṅ* a strong confidence *Mil.*, *Thgr.*; *ydeṅ-tsád* id., *de-riṅ tsam yaṅ sdód-pai ydeṅ-tsád ma mčis-pas* not being sure whether his life will be spared for one day more; *˳či-bród ydeṅ-tsád med* without confidence, without any readiness to die *Mil.*; *blo-ydeṅ Mil.* and col. = *ydeṅ.*

གདེང་བ་ *ydeṅ-ba*, pf. *ydeṅs*, *Cs.* **to threaten, to menace**; *Sch.* **to brandish** in a menacing way, *mtson-ydeṅ* brandishing a weapon *Lex.*; I also met with: *lag ydeṅ-ba Glr.* to raise and move one's hand (in a suppliant manner), cf. *dáṅ-ba* II., and: *bya yšog ydéṅ-pa* a bird with its wings raised and spread *Ma.*

གདེངས་ཀ་ *ydéṅs-ka* **head and neck of a serpent**, *sbrúl-gyi Glr.*

གདེངས་པ་ *ydéṅs-pa* 1. v. *ydéṅ-ba*. 2. = *ydeṅ*(?) **dáṅ-pa-čan* W.*, **ló-deṅ-pa* C.*, **deserving** or **enjoying confidence; faithful, trusty,** of servants, husbands, wives etc.

གདོང་(པ་) *ydoṅ(-pa)*, resp. *žal-ydoṅ*, 1. **face, countenance**, *ydoṅ skya* a pale face *Lt.*; *ydoṅ-dmar bod-yul* the country of the red-faced (more accurately: brown-faced) Tibetans *Pth.*; *ydoṅ-nág(-po)* 1. a black face; 2. **a frowning countenance**; *ydoṅ-čúṅ* dejected, disheartened, *ḱrel-méd ydoṅ-čúṅ mi byed-par* impudent and saucy *Glr.*; **doṅ-šrán táṅ-če* W.*, **doṅ-šran-te čá-wa* Kun.*, to be forward, bold, brazen-faced; *ṗág-gi ydóṅ-pa* pig's face, pig's head *Sambh.*; *ydoṅ-bži-pa* Brahma ('the four-faced'). — 2. **surface, superficies,** *sa-yžii*; **fore-part, front-part,** *dóṅ-la* adv. **in front, in advance** e.g. to go *C.*; *ydoṅ-ytád*, *Ld.*: *doṅ-stád* **just opposite**; *ydoṅ(-la)-˳déd-pa* **to push** or **press forward, to urge on** (a donkey, a coward to the fight), **to haul** (a culprit before the judge); *snáṅ-ba ydóṅ-ded-pa* to pursue one's course regardless of others (both in a good and in a bad sense) *Mil.*; *ydoṅ-ṗyis* handkerchief *Sch.*; **doṅ-si* W.* complexion, *gyur soṅ* he has changed colour; to *ṫúg-pa* and *bsú-ba* it is joined pleon.; *ydoṅ-lhógs* is stated to imply the same as *grúm-bu Lt.*

གདོད་མ་ *ydód-ma* = *yzód-ma*, **the beginning.** *ydód-mai dus*; *ydód-mar* **in the beginning, at first** *Mil.*; *ydód-kyi(s)* **first, at first, previously, before** *Mil.*; *ydód(-ma)-nas* from the beginning; *ydód-nas dág-pa* of primitive purity *Mil.* and elsewh.; *da-ydód Lex.* prob. = *da-yzód.*

གདོན་ *ydon* (**གྲཧ**) **evil spirit, demon,** causing diseases etc., *stéṅ ˳og-gi* superior and inferior (spirits), Rahu e.g. is *stéṅ-gi ydon*, an evil spirit of the aërial or heavenly regions; *stéṅ-ydon-gyis ˳či-ba Glr.* = *yzas ṗóg-pa* to die of epilepsy (*W.?*), or of apoplexy (*Sch.*); *ydon-čén bžo-lṅá*, or *bčo-brgyád*, frq.; *ydón-gyis brláms-pa Lt.*, *brlábs-pa Sch.*, infatuated or possessed by some evil spirit; *ɣdon ˳júg-pa* the entering of a demon into a person; *ɣdón-mi-za-ba* **certainty, surety**; *de byuṅ-ba-la* or *de byuṅ-bar ɣdon mi za* there is no doubt of such a thing having happened; gen. adv.: *ɣdón-mi-za-bar* undoubtedly, indubitably, *ɣdon-mi-˳ts̒al-bar Dzl.* id.

གདོན་པ་ *ɣdon-pa Cs.* fut. of *˳don-pa.*

གདོལ་པ་ *ɣdól-pa, Lexx.* = *rigs-ṅán*, चण्डाल, **an outcast**, a man of the lowest and most despised caste, still below the *dmáṅ-rigs.* The Tibetan word for this caste was perh. originally *dól-pa* fisherman, and has afterwards been transferred to all persons that gain their livelihood by the killing of animals, and consequently are despised as professional sinners.

གདོས་ *ɣdos* 1. **fetter, chain**; *ɣdos-ťág* fetter in a fig. sense, bondage, *Thgy.* — 2. **material existence** (?), **matter** (?), *ɣdos-bčás*, *(b)rdos-bčás*, **material, corporeal**, *ɣdos-bčás-kyi lus Thgr.*, frq.; *ɣdos-bčas-su grúb-pa med* (these things) are nothing material, they have no substance *Thgr.*; *ɣdos-méd* **immaterial, unsubstantial**; *ɣdós-su čé-ba* seems to be the same as *ɣdos-bčas*, and perh. also *ɣdós-pa ˳dzin Lex.* — 3. *ɣdos brgyáb-pa C.* for *W.* **k̒a kun gyáb-če**, v. *rkún-ma.*

གདོས་པ་ *ɣdós-pa* 1. = *ɣdos* (?) — 2. *Cs.* **mast, sail-yard**; acc. to Lexx. something pertaining to a ship; *ɣdós-bu* oar *Sch.*

བདག་ *bdag* 1. **self**, *ṅa bdag* for *ṅa nyid Dzl.* ༧༣, 14; gen. in the objective case: **myself, thyself, one's self**; *bdag ston ɣžan smad* to praise one's self, to blame others; *bdag sruṅ-ba* to devote one's self to solitary contemplation; or as a genit.: *bdág-gi* one's own, my, mine; *bdág-gi séms-la smad* he reproved himself *Dzl.*; *bdág-tu ˳dzin-pa*; *bdag-˳dzin* the clinging to the I, the attachment to one's own self, **egotism**, frq.; *bdag daṅ bdág-gir ˳dzin-pa* attachment to the I and mine *S.O.*; *bdág-tu ltá-bu* prob. id., *Tar.* 35,18, *Schf.*: Atmaka-theory, *bdag-méd-pai čos Tar.* 36, 1 the Anātmaka, the contrary; *bdag-méd rnám-pa ɣnyis* are mentioned in *Thgy.*, prob. = *gáṅ-zág-gi bdag-méd*, and *čós-kyi bdag-méd Mil.* c. XII.; *bdág-gir med S.O.*; *bdag-méd* ultimately coincides with *stoṅ-pa-nyid*, *Burn.* I., 462 med. In common life, *bdag-med* is also used for **another**, **dag-méd-kyi mi** id.; **dag-méd-la ma taṅ** do not give it to another; *bdag-ɣžan* I and others, one's self and others; *bdag-nyid* 1. = *bdag* **I myself, thou thyself, he himself**, *bdag-nyid-la ɣsón-čig* listen to me! *Pth.*; *rgyál-po bdag-nyid* the king himself *Dzl.*; *k̒a-čig ni bdag-nyid ráb-tu ˳byúṅ-bar ɣsol* some ask for the permission of becoming priests themselves *Dzl.*; *bdag-nyid ˳ba-žig* only for their own persons *Thgy.* 2. sbst. **the thing itself, the substance, the essence**, *byaṅ-čub-séms-kyi bdag-nyid yin* I am the essence of bōdhi, the personified bōdhi, says *Mil.*; *ťúgs-rje̊i bdag-nyid dkon-mčog-ɣsum* o grace personified, Triratna! *Glr.*; the Ommanipadmehūm is *saṅs-rgyás ťams-čád-kyi dgóṅs-pa ťams-čád ɣčig-tu bsdús-pai bdag-nyid Glr.*, i. e. the sum and substance of all the sentences of all the Buddhas concentrated in one word; *bdag-nyid-čén-po*, *čé-bai bdag-nyid* = *rdzógs-pai saṅs-rgyás* chief Buddha, Sākyathubpa, *S.O.* — 2. sbst. pronoun, first person, **I**, eleg., expressing modesty and respect to the hearer or reader, without amounting to our 'my own humble self', v. *p̒rán-bu*; plur. *bdág-čag*, *bdág-rnams*, *bdág-čag-rnams*, also in a general sense: we mortals *Thgy.*; *bdág-čag ts̒óṅ-pa-rnams* we, these merchants here *Dzl.* — 3. **the I**, the ego = *gáṅ-zag Was.* (269). — 4. **master, lord**, for *bdág-po*, v. below. — 5. in natural philosophy **the element of solid matter**; also for **air** *Stg.* — *bdág-po* 1. **proprietor, master, lord**; *bdág-poi sgra* the syllable *pa*, as denoting the active agent, i.e. him that has to do with a thing, e.g. *rtá-pa* (not to be taken as 'definite article' *Cs.*); thus in many compound words: *k̒áṅ-bdag*, *kyim-bdag* etc.; *ťúgs-rje̊i bdág-po* lord of grace, Awalokiteswara, *Glr.* init.; supreme lord, liege-lord, *klui bdág-po* = *dbáṅ-po*, *rgyál-po*; patron. 2. **husband, lord, spouse**; hence **á-ma̤ dág-po*, or *sriṅ-mo̤ dág-po**, a vulgar and obscene word of abuse. — *bdag(-po) byéd-pa* to reign over, to possess, prop. with *la*, but also with accus. *gha-sá-ča bód-kyis bdag byas* Tibet reigned over the province of Gha; *W.* also: to treat rudely, to handle roughly; *bdág-tu byás-pai bud-méd* a married woman *Thgy.*; *bdag-po-med-pa* (col. *mk'an*) **unowned,** e.g. of a dog, *Pth.*; **forlorn, friendless,** without a patron, **a vagabond;** also for an unmarried woman; also as an abusive word.

Comp. *bdag-rkyén* (as yet not found in books) seems to denote **kindness, attention, help,** received from a superior, (yet, it would seem, not without some obligation or other existing on the part of the latter, and thus the word differs from *bka-drín*). — *bdag-nyid, bdag-méd* v. above. — *bdag-bzúṅ Glr.* prob. = *bdag-po*. — *bdag-bsrúṅ* **hermit.**

བདའ་བ་ *bdá-ba* I. adj. resp. **savoury, well-tasted,** for *žim-pa*; *C.* col. **dán-te**.

II. vb., pf. *bdas* = *ˏdéd-pa,* 1. **to drive, to drive out,** *p̓yugs* cattle; **to chase, to put to flight** *Dzl.*; *lás-kyis, lás-kyi rlúṅ-gis bdás-nas* in consequence of works, of certain actions, frq. — 2. **to carry away, along,** or **off, to hurry off,** *ču-bos bdás-pai gliṅ* land carried away by water *Cs.* — 3. **to call in, collect, recover,** *bú-lon* debts *Dzl.* — 4. **to reprove, rebuke, accuse** *Sch.*; *bda-ˏdéd byéd-pa Lex., Cs.*: 1. **to drive, to carry.** 2. **to examine, to investigate.**

བདར་ *bdar* for *bda-bar.*

བདར་བ་, རྡར་བ་ *bdár-ba, rdár-ba,* **to rub,** i.e. 1. **to file, to polish** *Glr.*, **to grind, to whet;** *bdár-rdo* whet stone, hone. 2. **to rasp,** e.g. sandal-wood *Glr.*; **to grind, to pulverize,** *p̓yé-mar bdár-ba* to grind to powder, *Lexx.*; *lčágs-bdar* **a file,** *sá-bdar* **a rasp.** — 3. *so bdár-ba C.* **to gnash** or **grind the teeth;** *p̓yag bdár-ba* to sweep *B.*; *byi* and *p̓yi bdár-ba* **to clean, to polish** *Dzl.* — *Ma.* in two passages: **to pray earnestly,** which is the meaning required by the context, confirmed also by several Lamas. — *mdúṅ-du bdár-ba Lex.*: पुरस्कृ, to place in front; to lead; to appoint; show; inspect; prefer; honour. — *skyel-bdár* fee or reward given to an escort *Sch.* — *brdár-ša Sch.*: 'séms-kyi brdár-ša the nerves, sinews' (?); *bdár-ša yčód-pa,* and *rtsa-brdár yčód-pa* to examine closely *Mil.*; *raṅ-gi séms brdar-ša čod C.* take it seriously to heart.

བདལ་བ་ *bdál-ba* v. *rdál-ba.*

བདུག་པ་ *bdúg-pa* 1. vb. pf. *bdugs,* **to fumigate, to burn incense. to swing the censer** *Dzl.* — 2. sbst. **the burning of incense; perfume, frankincense,** more frq. *bdug-spós, bdug-spós-kyis bdúg-pa, Dzl.*; *bdug-spós ˏfal* odours of incense arise *Pth.*

བདུང་བ་ *bdúṅ-ba* v. *rdúṅ-ba.*

བདུད་ *bdud, Ssk.* मार, Mong. *šimnus,* the personified evil principle, **the Evil One, the Devil,** the adversary of Buddha, and he that tempts men to sin, but not like Satan of the Bible, a fallen spirit, nor like Ahriman of the Persians, an antagonist of Buddha of equal power and influence, but merely an evil genius of the highest rank, by whose defeat Buddha will finally be the more glorified. He is also identified with the god of love (Cupid), काम; v. *Köpp.* I. 88. 111. 253. In later times he has been split into four, and subsequently into numerous devils; also female devils, *bdúd-mo,* are mentioned. — *bdúd-rtsi* (अमृत, सुधा) 1. **the drink of gods, nectar,** frq.; fig.: *čos-kyi bdúd-rtsi* the nectar of the doctrine, and similar expressions; even common beer, when drunk by a Lama, may resp. be called so. — 2. a praising epithet of medicines; *bdud-rtsi-lṅa-lúm* a bath prepared of a decoction of five holy plants, viz. *šúg-pa, bá-lu, ƒse-pád, k'ím-pa,* and *ˏóm-bu.* — 3. **myrobalan,** Terminalia citrina, *Wdṅ.* — 4. a kind of brandy (?) — 5. *bdud-rtsi-dmár-po* a demon.

བདུན་ *bdun* 1. **seven,** *bdún-pa, bdún-po,* cf. *dgu*; *bdún-ču* seventy; *bdun-ču-rtsa-yčig,* (*W.* **bdun-ču-don-ɣčig**), *don-yčig,* seventy one etc.; *bdun-brgya* seven hundred, *bdun-stóṅ* seven thousand etc. — *lús-kyi bdún-po* the seven (principal) parts of the body, viz. hands, feet, shoulders, and neck, (those of holy men are of a goodly size, long and stately) *Stg.* — *bdun-p̀rág* (ἑβδομάς) seven days, a week, *S.g.* — **dún-na-tse** *W.* a child born before the natural time, a seven months' child.

བདུར་བ་ *bdur-ba Sch.* **to belong to a class** (?).

བདེ་བ་ *bde-ba* (शुभ, सुख) vb., adj., sbst., *bdé-po* adj. *Mil., C.* (of rare occurrence), *bdé-mo* adj., col., esp. *W.*, 1. **to be happy** or **well; happy; happiness;** *mi bdé-ba* the contrary of *bdé-ba;* *ṅa bdé-ste* as I am quite happy *Dzl.;* *bdeo* he is happy, prospers, flourishes; *bdé-bar byéd-pa* to make happy; *bdé-bar p̀yin-pa* to come to a state of happiness, of rest, to a place of safety; *bdé-bar ynás-pa* to be happy, to live in prosperity; *bdé-bar ytóṅ-ba* to let alone, to let another be happy; *k̀yod bdé-bar btaṅ mi yoṅ* we shall not allow you to be quiet *Mil.;* in *C.* col.: **ẑo' dé-mo-la mi ẑag** id.; *bdé-bar gyúr-čig,* resp. *bẑúgs-šig,* **be happy! farewell!** *W.* **dé-mo ča ẑig**; *bdé-bar btsá-ba B.*, **dé-mo-la kyé-če** *W.*, to be safely delivered of a child; *bde-bar ységs-pa* he that has entered into eternal bliss, the blessed, *Sch.* (*Köpp.* I, 91?) an epithet of former Buddhas, *Ssk.* सुगत; *lus daṅ sems mi-bdé-bar ˳gyúr-ba* to be bodily and spiritually afflicted *Dzl.;* *mi-bdé-bai búg-med-na* fearless of adversity *Dzl.;* *mi-bdé-bar ˳gyúr-ba* **to ache,** of parts of the body; *mṅal mi-bdé-bar ˳gyúr-ba* to be in travail, to suffer the pangs of childbirth; *sems-bdé, blo-bdé, snyiṅ-bdé* **cheerful, merry, glad;** *šin-tu t̀ugs-ma-bdé-bar dám-bčas-te* promising with a heavy heart, very reluctantly *Glr.;* *dga-bdé* v. *dgá-ba* comp.; *dus-bdé* (*-*mo** *W.*) **peace, a state of peace,** in *C.* frq. in conjunction with *ẑod-˳ǰágs* or *sa-˳ǰám;* *ẑi(-bai)-bdé(-ba)* **the happiness of rest, a happy tranquillity** *Glr.;* **peace** *Thgy.;* esp. the happiness of Nirwana *Thgy., Mil.;* *˳ǰig-rtén-gyi bdé-ba-la čágs-te* fond of a worldly life of pleasure *Dzl.;* *bdé-ba daṅ ldán-pa* happy, *bdé-ba-čan* v. below; *;nas-skábs-kyi bde-ba* a happy situation *Glr.;* *mya-ṅán-las ˳dás-pai bdé-ba t̀ób-pa* to attain to the happiness of Nirwana *Dzl.;* *dus-brtán-gyi bdé-ba-la bkod dgos* I must help him to attain to eternal bliss *Mil.;* *p̀an-bde* v. *p̀an.* — 2. **good, favourable, suited to its purpose** ... *na bdeo* (*W.* **dé-mo-yin**) the best thing will be, if I ... *Dzl.;* **gho dé-wa yoṅ** *C.* so it becomes intelligible; **good, well-qualified, well-adapted,** *k̀a lče bdé-ba* with good organs of speech *Pth.;* *smra-bdé-ẑiṅ* knowing to speak well, well-spoken *Pth.;* *nyáms-rtogs-kyi smra lče bde* a tongue skilled in speaking wisdom *Pth.;* in *W.* it is opp. to *rtsóg-po:* **lam de-mo** the road is good, may be passed without risk. — 3. in *W.* *bde* is also the usual word for **beautiful,** more accurately: *(*l*)*tá-na de-mo;* *mā de-mo** splendid indeed! **dé-mo man-na-méd** it is only for show.

Comp. *bde-skyid* **happiness, felicity,** frq.; *bdé-˳gro* going to happiness, joining the happy (spirits in heaven), also *bdér-˳gro,* opp. to *ṅán-˳gro;* usually in a general sense, like our 'heaven'; *bdé-˳gro mt̀o-ris-kyi lus t̀ób-pa* to receive a heavenly (glorified) body. — *bde-čén* felicity, consummate bliss, frq. — *bde-mčóg,* शम्बर. सम्वर, a deity of more recent Buddhism, *Schl.* 108; *Tar.* — *bde-˳ǰágs* **prosperity, welfare.** — *bde-stóṅ* (acc. to a Lama's statement for *t̀abs bdé-ba, šes-ráb stoṅ-pa-nyíd*), an expression for contemplation, v. *Was.* (144 and 141). — *bde-spyód W.*, **de-čód** *C.* **de-čý**, col. euphemism for **privy.** — *bdé-ba-čan* सुखवति, *bdé-ba-čan-gyi ẑiṅ-k̀ams* **the land of bliss,** a sort of heaven or paradise, in the far west, the abode of Dhyani Buddha Amitabha, v. *Glr.* chapt. IV., *Köpp.* II., 27. — *bde-byéd* he who or that which makes happy *Cs.*, शंकर. — *bde-byúṅ* शम्भु, शम्भव, source of happiness, n. of *Siwa;* as symb. num.: 11. — *bde-blág* **ease, content** *Cs.*, acc. to our Lama: **quickness, speed,** *nád-pa bde-blág-tu ysós-par ˳gyúr-bai mtsan-nyid Wdṅ.* a sign that the patient will soon recover. — *bde-légs* **well-being;** ... *las bde-légs-su gyúr-čig* they shall recover from ..., they shall prosper again after ... *Dom.*

བདེན་པ་ *bdén-pa,* सत्य, I. vb. 1. **to be true,** and adj. **true,** *k̀yod zér-ba bdén-no* what you say is true, you are right *Dzl.*; *bdág-gis nyés-pa bdén-gyis* it being true that I committed a fault *Dzl.*; *dé-bžin-du bden srid* it might be true after all *Glr.*; *šin-tu yaṅ bden* to be sure, that is true! *Glr.*; *de bdén-par ṅés-sam* is it quite certain that this is true? *Glr.*; *ė bden ltós-la bdén-par ₒdúg-na* ... see whether it is true, and if it is, then ... *Pth.*; *bdén-par ₒdzin-pa* to believe to be true, to take for granted *bdén-ₒdzin žig-na* the illusion being destroyed *Thgr.*; **dén-če-če* W.* (for *yid-čes-pa*) to believe, to be persuaded of the truth, frq.; *bden bden* very true indeed! certainly; *bden-bdén-ma* prob. something in which there is much truth *Tar.* — 2. to be in the right, to be right, *kyed bod-blon-rnams bden* ye Tibetan ambassadors are in your full right *Glr.*; **ṅa ȧ-sál-la dén-pa soṅ* W.* I have evidently been right.

II. sbst. 1. **truth**, in the abstract; but usually: **something true**, true words etc., *bdén-pa smra-ba* to tell or speak the truth; as adj.: **true, veracious** *Stg.*, (*W. *dén-pa zér-k'an**); *mi-bden-rdzún* this is not truth but falsehood *Glr.*; *bden-pa mtóṅ-ba* to discern, to know, the truth, a degree of Buddhist perfection *Tar.*; *bdén-pa bži* the four truths, the four realities, viz. pain, the origin of pain, the annihilation of pain, and the way of annihilating it, v. *Köpp.* I., 220. Whether, when *bdén-pa gnyis* are mentioned, they refer to two of the just named realities, or whether they always denote absolute (objective) truth (*don-dám-pai bdén-pa*) and subjective truth (*kun-rdzób-kyi bdén-pa*) as mentioned by *Was.* (293), I am not prepared to decide, nor am I able to explain the meaning of *lám-gyi bdén-pa* and *ₒgóg-pai bdén-pa* (*Thgy.* frq.). *bden-pa-nyid* seems to be a technical term for truth, though the Buddhist understands by it nothing but *stoṅ-pa-nyid*. Nevertheless, the possibility of its being misapprehended from this reason ought to be no obstacle to the word being used in its original sense, and re-established in its proper right, the more so, as Buddhist philosophy makes but a mockery of truth, by identifying it with a negation of reality. — 2. = *bden-tsig*, v. below, *Mil.*

Comp. **dén-daṅ, dén-da* W.* **in truth, certainly.** — *bden-po* **a true, a just man** *Cs.* — *bden-brál Cs.*: 1. **'void of truth, unjust.** 2. **southwest part** or **direction'.** — *bden-tsig* 1. a true word *Mil.*, but usually 2. a solemn asseveration, often combined with a prayer, to which the power of securing infallible fulfilment is ascribed *Dzl.* and elsewh., frq. — *bden-ₒdzin* v. above.

བདེར་ *bder* = *bdé-bar*; *gaṅ-bdér* **whichever you like, at your pleasure;** *či-bdér* has a similar meaning. v. *Tar.* 69, 14, and prob. also 192, 4; *bder-bkod* v. *ₒgód-pa bdér-ₒgro* v. *bdé-ba*.

བདོ་བ་ *bdó-ba* 1. *Cs.* **'abundance, exuberance'**; more corr., acc. to *Zam.*, where it is explained by *dár-ba* and तीव्र (unbounded), **to extend** (intr.) **without bounds.** — 2. with *la*, **to hurt, to injure** a person *Dom.* and elsewh.; *dgra bdó-ba* v. *sdáṅ-ba*.

བདོག་པ་ *bdóg-pa* I. vb. 1. *W.* **to get** or **take possession of, to stow away, to house,** **ston-tóg** the harvest; **to put into,** **gám-mi náṅ-du** something into a box; **to lay up or by, to keep,** esp. **dóg-te bór-če** in store, on hand; **ug náṅ-du dóg-če** to hold one's breath — 2. *B.* **to be in possession, to be possessed of,** gen. with *la*, like *yód-pa*, *dé-la rás-yúg γčig bdog* he is in possession of only one piece of cloth *Dzl.*; *Kyód-la ₒdi-ₒdra-bai slób-ma bdóg-gam* have you such scholars? *Dzl.*; *nor mi bdóg-pa Dzl.* poor; *dgón-pa ni gáṅ-na bdog Mil.* where have you (where is) your monastery? *bdág-la p̓úg-pa bdog* I have a cavern *Mil.*; in an absolute sense: *tabs bdóg-gam mi bdog* are there any means or not? *Ma.*; *W.* **yin-dog-čan** is stated to mean **proud, arrogant;** **yóg-dog-čan** one that saves money, a scraper.

II. sbst. **wealth, riches.** *B.*; cog to *bdág-po.*

བདྲལ་བ་ *bdrál-ba*, pf. of *ₒdrál ba*, *Dzl.* frq. (s. l. c.)

མདག་པ་ *mdág-pa* a sort of large **unburnt bricks** of mud or clay *Cs.*

མདག་མ་, མེ་མདག་ *mdág-ma, me-mdág,* **glowing embers, live** or **burning coals,** *mdág-mai doṅ* a pit for keeping them, e.g. for the purpose of melting metals *Stg.*

མདང་ *mdaṅ,* also *mdaṅs,* 1. *C., B.* **yesterday evening, last night,** frq.; *mdáṅ-gi rmi-lam,* also *mdaṅ-súm-gyi rmi-lam Glr., Pth.,* last night's dream. — 2. *W.* **yesterday** (cf *ḱa-rtsáṅ*); *mdaṅ-sáṅ Lex., Cs.:* 'yesterday and to-morrow, now-a-days'; perh. erron. for *deṅ-sáṅ.*

མདང་བ་ *mdáṅ-ba Sch.: mdáṅ-bai γnas* **place of cremation,** the spot where the burning of the dead takes place.

མདངས་ *mdaṅs* I. *Ssk.* **ओजस्. तेजस्,** 1. resp. *sku mdaṅs* **brightness of face, fresh and healthy complexion,** also with *bžin-gyi Cs.; mig-gi mdaṅs* bright eyes *Lt.; γzi-mdáṅs = mdaṅs; dmár-bai mdaṅs* fresh, ruddy complexion *Glr.; dmár-bai mdáṅs-kyis* with a face beaming with joy *Dzl.* and elsewh.; the brightness is destroyed by disease, *ₒpʻrog,* frq., or is fading away, *ₒčor Lt.;* in a relative sense: **appearance, exterior, look,** *mdaṅs-ṅán* bad, ugly appearance *S.g.* — 2. *Med.:* a hypothetical fluid, the most subtile part of the semen, a substance that pervades the whole body, esp. the skin, and is the primary source of vitality; cf. *Wise,* Hindu Syst. of Med., Calcutta 1845, p. 42. 54. 201. — *mdaṅs-bsgyúr* n. of a species of bile. — 3. **brightness, lustre, splendour,** in general, *nyi-mai, ₒjai B.* and col.; fig.: *dbáṅ-poi mdáṅs-ma mig ni ṅá-la med Pth.* I am destitute of the eye, that brightest of the senses, as much as: the most excellent of possessions is denied to me.

II. resp. *dprál-ba* **forehead.**

མདའ་ *mda* 1. **arrow,** *rgyáb-pa, ₒpʻén-pa* to shoot (an arrow); *smyúg-mda* an arrow of reed, *lčágs-mda* an iron arrow; *dúg-mda* a poisoned arrow *Mil.; dprál-bai mda* an arrow lodged in the forehead *Glr.; mé-mda* 1. **a fiery dart.** 2. **gun, firelock** *C.* — 2. any straight and thin pole or piece of wood, e.g. the stem or tube of a tobacco-pipe; *šiṅ-rtai mda* pole or beam of a carriage; *lčágs-mda* an iron bar or rod, a ramrod etc.; *čú-mda* a jet or shoot of water, frq.; **(s)kár-da* W.* a shooting star. — 3. = *mdo* 1. — 4. symb. num.: 5.

Comp. *mda-ḱúṅ* **loop-hole, embrasure.** — *mdá-mḱan* 1. **an archer.** 2. **an arrow-maker** *Glr.* — *mda-rgyáṅ* the range of an arrow-shot *Glr.* — *mda-sgró* the feathers of an arrow *Cs.* — *mdá-ču* the waters discharged from the lower parts of a valley, opp. to *pʻú-ču,* those of the upper part *Glr.* — *mda-ltóṅ* the notch at that end of an arrow which is placed on the bow-string *Pth.* — *mda-dár* a little flag fastened to an arrow; esp. an arrow with silk ribbons of five different colours. By hooking such an arrow into the collar of a bride, the match-maker draws her forth from among her maiden companions *Glr.* - *mda-dóṅ* **quiver.** — *mdá-pa* **an archer;** *mda-dpón* **the commander of the archers,** a high military rank *C.* — *mda-sprád* v. *spród-pa.* — *mda-bér* perh. the more correct form of *ta-bér.* — *mdá-bo* a large arrow. — *mda-mó* **arrow-lot,** a kind of fortune-telling by means of arrows. — *mda-rtsád byéd-pa* to amuse one's self with the shooting of arrows *Cs.* — *mda-tso* a troop of archers *Cs.* — *mda-γyu* bow and arrows *Dzl.* — *mdá-bzo-pa* arrow-maker. — *mda-γáb Glr.* 1. *Lex.* = *pú-šu,* **fence;** hence **parapet, railing;** yet a Lama from Tashi-lhunpo declared it to be the projecting part of the (flat) roofs of large temples, on which the parapet is erected. — 2. **a covered gallery** on the top of a house *C.*

མདུང་ *mduṅ* 1. **lance, spear, pike,** *mduṅ-skór-ba* to brandish, to whirl a spear *Cs.; mduṅ-ḱyim Dzl.* 96, 9 a frame for leaning spears against; *mdúṅ-mḱan* a maker of spears; *mduṅ-túṅ,* or *ₒtáb-mduṅ* a short lance or pike, a javelin. — *mdúṅ-togs Mil., mdúṅ-pa* a spearsman, a lancer. — *mduṅ-dár* a lance with a little flag at the top. — *mdúṅ-rtse* top of a spear, spear-head; *mdúṅ-šiṅ* shaft of a lance. — *mdúṅ-bzo-pa* =

mdúṅ-mkʿan. — *mduṅ rtse-gsúm-pa* trident. — 2. **sting,** of insects *C., W., mduṅ brgyáb-pa* to sting. — 3. *gser-mdúṅ, dṅul-mdúṅ* prob. the **two frontal muscles** *Med.*

མདུད་ *mdud Lt.* a medicine (?).

མདུད་པ་ *mdúd-pa* **a knot,** *mdúd-pa bór-ba* frq., *dúd-pa Lt., byéd-pa Cs.,* **gyáb-če* W.,* to tie or make a knot, *sgrol-ba, ʼgrol-ba,* to untie (a knot); **ḍól-dud* W.* sliding-knot, slip-knot, **šin-dud* W.* a regular knot; *skra-mdúd* knot or bow of ribbons holding together the long plaits of the women; frq. fig. *sér-snai mdúd-pa* bonds of avarice *Mil.; *nyiṅ-dud ḍól-če* W.* (to untie) to open one's heart to a person; *mdúd-pa-čan.* 1. **full of knots, knotty.** 2. **cloddy** (?) *S.g.* — *mdúd-ʼdra* a disease of the membrum virile, prob. paraphimosis *Mṅg.*

མདུན་ *mdun* **the fore-part, the front-side of a thing; the vis-à-vis,** *mdún-gyi nám-mkʿa-la* in the heavens before him, over against him, *Glr.* and elsewh.; *mdún-gyis* adv. coram, **face to face,** *mdún-gyis ltá-ba* to behold face to face; gen. c. *la, na, du, nas:* 1. adv. **before it, at it, to it, from it;** 2. postp. **before, at, to** etc.; *mdún-la ʼóṅ-ba,* or *sleb-pa* to come up or near, *ṙáṅ-gi mdún-la sleb ma bčug* he did not allow (the pursuer) to come near; *mdún-du skúr-ba* to send in advance; *mdun-du ṗyin-pa* to come near, to approach; to hasten to *Pth.; mi màṅ-po ʦʿógs-pai mdún-du* in the presence of a great number of people *Dzl.* — *sku-mdún-pa* **a waiting-man, valet de chambre,** v. *sku.* — *mdun-lčóg* v. *lčóg-tse.* — *mdun-na-ʼdon (C. *dụn-nán-dọn*)* 1. *Lex.* पुरोहित, **court-chaplain, domestic chaplain or priest;** so prob. also *Tar.* 58, 17. — 2. at present: **a high civil officer** or **functionary,** = *bka-blón,* vizier, *Stg.* and elsewh.

མདུན་མ་ *mdún-ma,* frq. in later lit.; one Lama explained it by *mós-pa,* another by: 1. **wife,** 2. **things, concerns;** *ʼjig-rtén-gyi mdún-ma* = *ʼjig-rtén-gyi bya-ba.*

མདེའུ་ *mdeu, Sch.* also *mde-ka,* **arrow-head** *B.*; *mde-ṡúl Cs.*: 'the furrows or grooves of an arrow-head'.

མདོ་ *mdo* 1. **the lower part of a valley,** where it merges into the plain (opp. to *ṗu*), = *mda;* more frq. the place where one valley opens into another, hence in general: the point where two valleys, roads (*lám-mdo*), rivers (*čú-mdo*) meet; *lám-sraṅ-mdor* at the street-corners *Dzl.; gsúm-mdo, bži-mdo, ʦʿóg-mdo* the point where three, four, several (roads etc.) meet, esp. *bži-mdo* **a crossing, cross-road,** as a place of incantations; *mdo* prop. n. (in full: *dar-rtse-mdo*) province of the eastern part of Tibet, v. *Kams*; **ʼdó-ru** in *C.* used as postp. = near, with, by, **ṅe ʼdo-ru** with me, **yul-gyi ʼdo-ru** near the village. — 2. *Ssk.* सूत्र, **aphorism, short sentence** or **rule, axiom;** hence *mdó-ru, mdor, mdó-tsam sdu-ba* to contract, abridge, epitomize, to give only the main points, frq.; *mdor(-sdu)-na* **in short, in general, altogether, on an average,** denique, frq. — 3. **Sūtra,** in the more recent Buddhist sense, religious treatise or dissertation, a sacred writing, *mdo-sdé* a collection of Sūtras, a part of the Kangyur; *mdo-sdé-pa, mdo-sde-ʼdzin* Sautrāntika, a school of philosophers, v. *Tar.; mdo-màṅ* title of several collections of Sūtras; in quoting passages: *mdó-la, mdó-las,* in the *mdo,* according to the *mdo* (viz. is said, is written etc.) *Stg.; mdo-sṅob* giving a benediction to the host for his entertainment *Mil.,* cf. *Köpp.* I, 143. At present a distinction is to be made between *mdoi* or *dbú-mai lam,* and *sṅágs-kyi lam,* i. e. between the doctrine of the sacred writings and a faithful and systematic study of them, — and of the more modern mysticism, which is mixed up with Siwaism, and seeks to obtain spiritual gifts by means of witchcraft, thus saving trouble and time; v. *Was.* (142. 177), *Köpp.* II, 29. — 4. *Cs. mdó-čan* **prudent,** *mdo-med* **imprudent,** cf. *ʼdo.* —

མདོ་ལེ་ *mdo-lé,* the tibetanized डोली *Hind.* **sedan-chair** *Pth.*

མདོག་ *mdog*, resp. *sku-mdóg*, **colour** (cf. *ḱa-dóg*) *B.*, *C.*; *mdog-légs* of a beautiful colour; *mdog-mdzés* 1. id., 2. **a rose.** *Cs.; mdog-dkar-ḱá* perh. the more corr. spelling for **do-gar-ḱá* W.*, light-blue; *mdog-ysál* a species of gall, lit. **'purifier of the skin'**, *Med.*

མདོངས་ *mdoṅs* 1. the white spot, **blaze, star** on the forehead of a horse *Glr.* and elsewh.; 2. **the eye in a peacock's feather;** *rmá-byai mdoṅs, sgro-mdóṅs, mdóṅs-sgro* **peacock's feather;** *mdóṅs-mťa-čan* **turkey-hen** *Cs.*

མདོངས་པ་ *mdóṅs-pa = ldóṅ-ba*, **blind,** physically and morally, *B.*, *mig-mdoṅs-pa, mdóṅs-par ˳gyúr-ba,* to get blind, to be made blind *Dzl.*

མདོངས་གསོལ་བ་ *mdóṅs-ysol-ba Mil.*, *mdoṅs-sól žú-ba* or *byéd-pa Cs.*, **to congratulate, to wish joy** to another *Cs.; Zam.* explains it by *˳dún-pa* to wish, another *Lex.* by *ṅó-dga* joy; in the passage of *Mil.* it seems to signify thank-offering.

མདོམས་ *mdoms*, sometimes written for *˳doms.*

མདོས་ *mdos* a cross formed of two small sticks, the ends of which are connected by coloured strings ⊕, and used in various magic ceremonies.

འདག་པ་ *˳dág-pa* 1. *Sch.:* **'clay; cleaving, adhesive, sticky.'** In *C.* = *˳ǰim-pa* (*W.* **ká-lag**) a mixture of clay and water; *˳dag-žál S.g.* prob. id.; *˳dág-pa sbyáṅ-ba* to make such a mixture, *Cs.; ˳dag-sbyár* covering, or stopping up with clay, e.g. the chinks of a wall or door, **˳dag-ǰár ˳búl-ba** to render such service to a meditating Lama as an act of piety. In *Pth.* *˳dág-pa* is mentioned as a kind of plastic art, and evidently signifies to mould, to model, to shape. — 2. = *ldág-pa Cs.*; *˳dág-gu Lex.* = *skyó-ma,* pap, pulp, prob. = *ldé-gu.* — 3. pf. *dag,* 1. **to clear, to wash away, to wipe off,** *dri-ma,* frq.; *rtá-la sol-byúg* (to clean) a horse marked or blackened with charcoal *Glr.*; *sdig-sgrib* (to wash off) the filth of sin *Glr.* 2. **to disappear,** of sinful thoughts *Glr.*, sometimes *ynás-su* to their own place, is added pleon. *Mil.* — Participle *dág-pa* clean, v. *dág-pa.*

འདང་ *˳daṅ* v. *˳dad.*

འདང་བ་ *˳dáṅ-ba Sch.* **to come to, to arrive at**; cf. also *brgya-˳daṅs*, sub *brgya.*

འདད་, འདང་ *˳dad*, *˳daṅ*, resp. *sku-˳dad* or *daṅ Lex.* **funeral-repast.**

འདབ་ *˳dab* **a train** of persons, *˳ḱor-˳dab* **retinue** *Cs.*

འདབ་མ་ *˳dáb-ma* 1. **wing,** *sprúg-pa* to shake (the wings) *Cs.*, *yyób-pa* to clap them *Cs.* — 2. **ladle, float-board** of a water-wheel. — 3. **petal,** flower-leaf, frq.; *˳dab-brgyad* eight-petaled *Glr.;* v. *Schl. Buddh.* 248. — 4. **any leaf, a broad leaf,** also *lo-˳dab.* — 5. **fan** *Cs.* — 6. **flag** *Cs.* — *˳dab-čags* a winged animal, **bird,** frq. — *˳dab-rdáṅs-pa* **full of leaves;** with leaves fully developed *Sch.* — *˳dab-yšóg* **flag-feather, quill-feather.**

འདབས་ *˳dabs*, rarely *˳dab*, **the side, lateral surface,** of a hill, of the body etc.; **surface,** *mčin-˳dabs* of the liver *Med.*; in a more general sense: *sgál-˳dabs* **the lumbar region** *Med.*; pleon.: *nágs-˳dabs-na* = *nágs-na* in the woods *Mil.*

འདམ་ *˳dam* **mud, mire, swamp,** earth and water, = *˳dág-pa*, but as a product of nature; *˳dam-rdzáb B.*, **dam-tsóg* W.* id.; *˳dám-du, ˳dam-rdzáb-la ˳byiṅ-ba* to sink into a swamp; **dam-pág(s)* W.* muddy plash, slough. — *˳dám-bu* **reed** for thatching, writing etc.; *Cs.* also **sugar-cane;** *˳dam-bu ka-ra?* prob. a species of reed in wells or ponds *Wdṅ.*; **dam-búr* W.* sugar-cane.

འདམ་ཀ་ *˳dám-ka Zam.*, *˳dám-ga, ˳dám-ṅa, ˳dám-pa Cs.* **choice, option,** *deṅ saṅ ˳dám-ka byéd-pa* to choose whether to-day or to-morrow *Zam.*; cf. *ydám-ka.*

འདམ་པ་ *˳dám-pa* (or *˳dóm(s)-pa Glr.* prov.) pf. *˳dams*, imp. *˳dom(s)*, **to choose, to select,** a bride *Glr.*; *mi-ytsáṅ-ba ˳dám-pa* such as choose impure things, cynical, lascivious characters *Stg.*; *˳dam-riṅ* choosing, turning over in one's mind a long while; *dgrá-bo yán-pa mi ytaṅ ˳dam-riṅ ťábs-kyis ydul* prob.: not losing sight of your enemy, constantly watching, put him down, as soon as an opportunity offers, *S.g.*, and hence *že-sdáṅ ₒdam-ríṅ* a long lingering, lurking grudge *S.g.*

འདའ་བ་ *ₒdá-ba*, pf. *ₒdas* (prob. vb. n. to *bdá-ba*, *ₒdéd-pa*) **to pass over, 1. to travel over, to clear a certain space,** *taṅ de* this plain *Sambh.*; *žag dú-mai lam* (to perform) many day's journeys *Dzl.* — 2. c. *las:* **to go beyond, to surpass** *Dzl.; lhá-las dás-pai spos* incense surpassing that of the gods, i.e. that which is burnt to them *S.O.*; **to exceed,** *tsád-las* the measure *Lt.*; *gráṅs-las dás-pa Tar.* surpassing number, innumerable; *bsám-byai yúl-las* (surpassing) the understanding or imagination, inconceivable *Glr.*; **to transgress, to trespass against,** *bká-las, krims-las*, a commandment, a law = *ₒgál-ba*; **to get over a thing, to get the better of, to overcome,** = *rgyál-ba;* **to go away from,** *mya-ṅán-las* q.v.; **to let go, leave off, abandon,** *čós-las* one's religion *Thgy.*; *bló-las dás-pa?* — 3. with or without *dús-las, tse,* resp. *sku,* **to depart this life, to die;** *das-po* **the deceased, defunct, late,** *Lex.*; **de-lóg* W.* the soul of a deceased person, **ghost, apparition;** the re-appearing is possible only for about forty days after death, as long as the Bardo lasts, v. *bar-do.* — 4. **to pass by,** = to disappear, *nyi-zlá ₒdás-nas* when the sun and the moon have disappeared (for a time); very frq. relative to time: **to pass away, to elapse,** *ₒdás-pai dus* the time that has passed, is gone, past time, v. *dus* 5.; *zla dgu ₒdás-nas* after nine months *Lt.*; *ₒdas-ló* the year past, *ₒdas-zlá* the month past, *ₒdas-žág* the day past; **de-zág-la* W.* **the other day, lately;** *nyin-mtsán čós-kyis ₒdá-bar bya* day and night are spent in religious exercises; *dgé-bai byá-ba kó-nas dus ₒda Tar.* (time) spent in none but works of virtue. — *ₒdá-ga (-ma) Cs.* **hour of death,** *ₒda-ga-ye-šés* मृति ज्ञान, knowledge of the hour of death (title of a book).

འདར་བ་ *ₒdár-ba* **to tremble, shudder, shiver, quake,** *gráṅ-bas ₒdar-ba* to shiver with cold; *ₒjigs-pas* (to tremble) with fear; *ₒdár-žiṅ ₒgúl-ba* id.; *ₒdár-bar ₒgyúr-ba* to begin to tremble; *ₒdar-yám Sch.* doubting, wavering, undetermined, *ₒdar-yám byéd-pa* to doubt, to waver.

འདལ་ *ₒdal* (?) *ru-ₒdál, ru-ₒdrél* **a single horn** *Sch.* — *bad-ₒdál* prov., being left exhausted on the road, sinking under fatigue.

འདལ་འདལ་ *ₒdal-ₒdál* v. *tá-bag.*

འདལ་བ་ *ₒdál-ba* = *dál-ba*, *ču-ₒdál* **still water** *Lex.*

འདི་ *ₒdi* demonstr. pron. **this,** *ṅai bu ₒdi* this my son; *ṅai ₒdi* this of me, i.e. that which I am doing just now *Glr.*, what I am experiencing just now *Mil.*; **the present, the respective,** *ₒgrúb-pa-po ₒdi* the respective performer (of an incantation) *Dom.*; such a one, *bdag miṅ ₒdi žes-byá-ba* I, such and such a one *Thgr.*, also *ₒdi daṅ ₒdi (-lta-bu)* and similar expressions, *ṅas kyód-la ₒdi daṅ ₒdi-lta-bu žig sbyin-no* I give you such and such a thing. On the difference between *ₒdi* and *de* v. *de*; the plural forms and derivatives of both of them are in conformity; only the following may be particularly mentioned: *ₒdi-ka-ráṅ* is used also for **just here, just now** *Mil.*; *ₒdi-lta-ste* **for instance, to wit, such as, viz.**; also pleon. with *žé-na: gnyis gaṅ žé-na ₒdi-lta-ste Wdṅ.; či pyir žé-na ₒdi-lta-ste Pth.*; *ₒdi-ltar* **so, in this manner,** *čii pyir kyod ₒdi-ltar gyur* in what manner have you become so, how did you get into this condition? *Dzl.* frq.; *ₒdi-ltar-ro* it ran thus, it was to this effect, of this purport *Glr.* frq.; *ṅa ₒdi-ltar yin* such I am, I am, live, go, just as you see me here *Mil.*; in the verse: *ₒdus-byas čos-rnams ₒdi-ltar blta* 'compounded things must be regarded thus' — the word *ₒdi-ltar* is meant to be accompanied by a snap of the fingers (*se-gól*, or *skád-čig-ma*); *ₒdi-nas* **from this place, from this time present, as yet, still.** *ₒdi (daṅ) pyi (-ma)* the present and the future life, frq.; *ₒdi pyid sdéb-pa, rjé-ba* to exchange this life for the future one, i.e. *tse pyi-ma blós-btaṅ-ste ₒdii don sgrúb-pa* to be earthly minded *C.*; **di-zug, ₒi-zug* W.*, so, thus; **di-riṅ* W.* to-day; *ₒdi-ru* (come) **in here, into this place; here, at this place,** frq.; **now,** seldom.

འདིག་ ₒ*dig* **stopper, stopple,** also *ka - ₒdig;* **dig-čc* Ld.* to put in a stopper; **to stop up,** to close with a stopper; **dig-ril* C.* **musket-ball.** Cf. *dig.*

འདིང་བ་ ₒ*diṅ-ba,* pf. *btiṅ, fut. ydiṅ, imp. tiṅ(s),* **to spread on the ground,** a mat, carpet etc.; **to scatter, sprinkle, strew,** grass or hay to lie upon, ashes on the snow etc.; **btin-ba** sbst. *W.* **a small carpet,** on which the Lamas use to sit; **mal-btin* C.* **bedding, pillow,** or **blanket.** — ₒ*diṅ rgyáb-pa Sch.* **to weigh in one's mind,** to consider; to suspect, to entertain a suspicion.

འདུ(ན)་ཁང་ ₒ*dú(n)-kaṅ* **meeting-house, house of assembly;** *čos ₒčád-pai* (quasi) **church, chapel** *Dzl.*

འདུ་འཁྲུག་ ₒ*du-ₒkrúg* **tumult, riot, uproar** *Cs.*

འདུ་བ་ ₒ*dú-ba,* pf. ₒ*dus,* (vb. n. to *sdúd-pa*) 1. **to come together, to assemble,** of men and animals; ₒ*dun-káṅ-du Dzl.;* ₒ*dús-sam ma ₒdus* are they already assembled? *daṅ* with (a person) *Tar.*; in order to fight *Stg.;* of things: *nyés-pa tams-čád dei lús-la ₒduo,* v. *nyes-pa;* ₒ*du-ba* and ₒ*dus-pa* sbst. **a coming together, an assembling, a gathering,** esp. in *Med.* a (somewhat indefinite) **disease, or cause of disease;** ₒ*dus-sa* **meeting-place** *Glr.*; *las-mi maṅ-po ₒdus-sa* an establishment comprizing many workmen, **manufactory, workshop, workhouse,** **dzóm-ₒdu yóṅ-gin ₒdug* C.* they flock or crowd together; *tsoṅ-ₒdus* the assembled traders or dealers, **the market** frq.; *skyabs-kun-ₒdus* 'a collection of all the refuges' is a name given to Milaraspa. — 2. **to unite, to join one another,** *kyo-šúg-tu* as husband and wife, **to get married;** in a special sense in philosophical language: 1. **to unite** (opp. to ₒ*brál-ba*), e.g. the soul uniting with an organ of sense, like *sdéb-pa, Mil.* 2. ₒ*dus-byás* composed of two or more ingredients, ₒ*dus-ma-byas* consisting of one thing, simple, elementary; only this is eternal, every thing compounded is perishable, frq. — 3. **to be pressed** or **crowded together,** **šril dús-te dug* Ld.* they stand crowded, in serried files or ranks; intellectually: *dam-čos ₒdus-pa* a compressed system of religion. — 4. ₒ*dús-pa* **to consist of** or **in,** *ynyis-su ₒdus-so* (religion) consists of two things *Thgy.; snaṅ-srid séms-su ₒdús-te yda* the external world consists of spirit, is spirit, i.e. is nothing *Mil.* — 5. col.: **to be drawn together, to contract, to shrink,** **dus ča dug* Ld.* it shrinks, e.g. wood or paper from heat; **tsa - ₒdu* C.* prob. **cramp, spasm, convulsion;** **dús-kan* Ld.* **elastic, springy.**

འདུ་བྱེད་ ₒ*du-byéd, Ssk.* संस्कार, (the Tibetan word is nothing but a literal translation of the *Ssk. saṅskāra;* cf. also ₒ*du-šés* and *púṅ-po*) 'one of the obscurest and most difficult terms of Buddhist philosophy' *Köpp.* I, 603, where the various translations are enumerated that have been attempted, such as: idea, notion, imagination (cf. *Burn.* I, 503), action (*Was.*) etc. It should, however, at once be acknowledged, that the word cannot be translated into a European language, as the meaning given to it is not the result of honest research and observation, but a product of arbitrary and wild speculation.

འདུ་འཛི་ ₒ*du-ₒdzi* **noise, bustle, din, clamour,** ₒ*du-ₒdzi méd-pai dbén-pa ₒdi* this solitude without any noise *Mil.;* ₒ*du-ₒdzí-la ynás-pa* to live in the midst of the bustle of worldly affairs; ₒ*du-žiṅ,* ₒ*du-lóṅ Cs.* id.

འདུ་ཤེས་ ₒ*du-šes, Ssk.* संज्ञा ('con-scientia') corresponds in most cases to our **idea, notion, conception, image,** although sometimes **perception, feeling, sense, thought, consciousness** may be employed for it: *nór-la rtág - tu yód - pai ₒdu - šés skyéd - pa* to combine with earthly goods the idea of constant possession *S.O.* and thus frq.; *lús-la grui ₒdu-šés ₒjúg-pa* to unite with the human body the idea of a ship, to represent the body as a ship, *Thgy.; skyó-bai ₒdu-šes byuṅ* the perception, the feeling of discomfort arises *S.g.*; *kró-bai ₒdu-šés-spáṅ-ba* to detest the idea, the thought of anger *Dzl.; dgé-bai pyógs-la ₒdu-šés čúṅ-žad kyaṅ ma yyos* no thoughts, no inclinations, tending to virtue, arose (in him), virtuous emotions never stirred in his mind; *čágs-pai* *ₒdu-ṡés-ċan* entertaining thoughts of sensual pleasure *Glr.*; *ₒdu-ṡés slar rnyéd-pa* to recover from a state of insensibility; as vb.: *ₒdu-ṡés-pa, mya-ṅan-ₒdás ťob du-ṡés-te* imagining that I shall obtain Nirwāna *Thgy.* As one of the five *pʼúṅ-po* it is translated by **idea** (*Burn.* I, 511), by **perception** (*Köpp.* I, 603). The three terms *ₒdu-ṡes-ċan*, *ₒdu-ṡes-méd-pa*, *ₒdu-ṡes-med-min* may be rendered: having the faculty of thinking, having no faculty of thinking, neither thinking nor not thinking (*Dzl.* ༢༢༦, 7), *ₒdu-ṡes-ċan* refers to human beings, the two other terms relate to celestial beings (v. *Köpp.* I, 261, 17 and 26), that are evidently so much the more excellent and exalted, as they are far above all reasoning and thinking. According to another, and (it would seem) more natural interpretation, the first of these three terms implies **rational** beings (man), the second **irrational** beings (higher animals), and the third **quite irrational** creatures (lower animals, worms, reptiles, that are not even possessed of the sensitive powers of the higher animals), whilst the 'long-lived Lhas' of the 17th. heaven are classed together with the common Lhas (who however taken strictly, belong to the 'first world') and on account of their stupidity are believed to be incapable of ever being converted, *Thgy.*

འདུག་པ་ *ₒdúg-pa* (eleg. *γdá-ba*, resp. *bžúgs-pa*) 1. **to sit**, syn. with *sdód-pa*; with *na, la* etc.; **to sit down** with termin. or *la*; **to sit up** (in bed); *ₒdúg-par ₒgyúr* **to get seated** *Dzl.* ༤༦, 6; **to remain sitting**, to keep one's seat, *Dzl.* ༤༦, 7; **to remain, to stay**, *ₒdir ma ₒdúg-par soṅ žig Dzl.*; **to remain behind, to stay at home**, with or without *pʼyir, ḱyim-na* etc. *Dzl.* — 2. **to be, to exist, to live** *Glr.*: ... *skabs-med ₒ'dug-go!'* there is no chance of ... Yes, there is! ... *ₒdug ṡés-nas* knowing that ... is still alive *Dzl.*; *dráṅ-sroṅ byéd-ċiṅ ₒdug* he lives as a hermit *Dzl.*; **to be, to live at a certain place**, *γnás-na ₒdúg-pa* the being somewhere *Gram.*; *pʼa-má gáṅ-na ₒdug* where are my parents now? **to be at home** *Dzl.* and elsewh.; **to be extant, to be found**, *ċaṅ mi ₒdug* nothing is, or was to be found, nothing was there *Mil.*; as partic. joined with, or put inst. of the possess. pron.: *ḱo-ráṅ daṅ* (*ḱoi*) *bu brgyad ₒdúg-pa* he and his eight children being with him *Mil.* (*yód-pa* is construed in the same manner); in quotations: to be found, to be written, to be met with, ... *yod zér-ba ... na ₒdug* the account of being ... is to be found in ..., *Glr.* — 3. **to be**, as copula, in *B.* often with termin.: *ḱyim-par ₒdúg-pa* to be a layman *Stg.*; *rkáṅ-pa ḱrá-bor ₒdug* the foot was variously coloured *Dzl.*; *ₒdi-rnams mi-ma-yin-du ₒdúg-pas* as these are spirits *Mil.* Generally speaking, this termin case is not to be pressed, nor always to be explained by: **to have become**, or to be translated by: **in**, as in the following: *rgya-gár-gyi yi-ger ₒdúg-pas* to be (written) in the Indian language *Glr.* — 4. **to be**, as auxiliar vb., 1. with the termin. of the inf., often merely paraphrastically, e.g. *yód-par ₒdúg-pa* = *yód-pa Glr.*; frq., however, indicating doubtfulness and uncertainty: *ṅa ni ṡaṅ ċi-bar ₒdug* may be I shall die to-morrow *Glr.*; *ḱyed ... yin-par-ₒdug* you seem to be, you are, I dare say *Mil.*; *ₒgro dgós-par ₒdug* I suppose you must go *Glr.*; *stér-bar ₒdug* it will probably be given *Glr.*; *ma mťóṅ-na mi rtógs-par ₒdug* if we had not seen it, we should probably not have known it *Mil.*; in the same manner it is used with *yód-pa*, q. v. — 2. with a verbal root, in ancient lit. hardly ever occurring, in more recent writings used paraphrastically like *ₒdúg-pa*, with the termin. of the inf. (v. above 1), but not indicating a certain tense, e.g. *rdol ₒdug* it makes its appearance, comes to light, *Glr.*, *bṡig ₒdug* they were destroyed *Glr.*; in col. language (in *W.* at least) it is gen. a sign of the pres. tense: *zer ₒdug* I say, thou sayest etc.; only in *Bal.* it indicates the fut. tense. — 3. with the gerund in *te* or *nas* vulgo for the pres. or preterite tense, frq.; in *B.* of so rare occurrence, that it is prob. to be regarded as a vulgarism to be charged on the copyists, and to be corrected accordingly. — 4. with *gin* (*B.* and col.) and *čiṅ* (*B.*), denoting **a continued action, state,** or **condition,** as in English: I am looking. — *ₒdúg-γnas*, *ₒdúg-sa*, **place of residence, abode.**

འདུད་པ་ *ₒdúd-pa*, pf. *btud*, fut. *γdud* (*Cs.*), imp. *dud*, *ťud* (*Cs.*), **to bend** or **bow down, to incline,** *rná-ba*, to incline one's ears to hear, (also used of animals), cf. our 'to prick the ears', *Dzl.*; **to bow, to make a bow,** *la*, to a person; *žábs-la* at a person's feet, to kneel down before a person.

འདུན་ *ₒdun*, *go-ₒdún*, = *sna-ťsogs* **of several kinds, divers, sundry, various,** *Lex.*

འདུན་པ་ *ₒdún-pa* 1. vb. **to desire, to wish earnestly,** with *la*, *nyán-pa-la mi ₒdún-par* they not having any desire to hear *Pth.*; *dgé-ba-la* to strive after virtue, frq.; also *ₒdún-pa* alone (without *dgé-ba-la*) id. *Thg.*; **lo čṓ-la ₒdṳ́m-pa** *C.* religious interest, concern for religion; to be zealous, to take a warm interest *Mil.* — 2. sbst. **a desire** *Thgy.*; **a supplication** *Dzl.*, *Glr.* Cf. *dún-pa.*

འདུན་མ་ *ₒdún-ma* **1. advice, counsel,** *ṅán-pa* a bad advice *Ma.*; *ₒdébs-pa* to give advice; *byéd-pa* to take a resolution *Mil.* — 2 **consultation** (v. examples sub *čúṅ-ba*), *ₒdun-grós* id.; *da-lán-gyi ₒdun-grós ₒdi-la* at this present consultation *Glr.*; **ₒdṳ́m-ma ǰhé'-pa** *C.* to consult, to confer with (a person about a matter). — **3. council,** *ₒdún-mar bsdus* they called a council together *Mil.*; esp. in compounds: *ₒdún-ḱaṅ* = *ₒdú-ḱaṅ* q.v.; *ₒdún-sa* **meeting-place, assembly,** frq.; **union, association, society,** *dge-ₒdun* an association of clerical persons. — 4. v. *ₒdum?* *γnyen-ₒdun* harmony amongst relations, *Stg.* — **5. the state of being a bride; bride,** *C.*, and perh. *Glr.*; cf. also *dga-ₒdún* sub *dgá-ba.* — 6. = *mdún-ma?*

འདུབ་སྙོམས་ *ₒdub-snyóms* *Sch.* **a state of comfort, ease;** *ₒdub-ₒḱrúgs*, an interruption of that state, discomfort.

འདུམ་པ་ *ₒdúm-pa* 1. vb. **to reconcile one's self to, to be reconciled with,** *ťáb-pa ₒdúm-na* if contending parties are reconciled with one another; *rtág-tu mi ₒdúm-mo* they are constantly at variance *Dzl.*; **dúm-ṭa** (lit. *ḱra*) *C.* contract, agreement, = *čad-don.* — 2. sbst. **concord, unison, peace** *Cs.*

འདུར་ *ₒdur* **thick and clammy** *Sch.*

འདུར་བ་ *ₒdúr-ba* **to trot;** *ₒdur-grós* **the trot.**

འདུལ་བ་ *ₒdúl-ba* I. vb., pf. *btul*, *ťul*, fut. *γdul*, imp. *ťul*, *W.* **túl-če** 1. **to tame, to break in,** *rta*; **to subdue, conquer, vanquish,** *dgra*; sometimes even **to kill, to annihilate** *Pth.* — 2. **to till, cultivate,** waste land; **to civilize,** a nation, which with the Buddhist is the same as **to convert,** frq.; **to educate, to discipline, to punish;** *γdúl-bai rigs-pa* those fit for and predestinated to conversion *Dzl.*; *γdúl-bya* id. frq.; also used substantively: *ₒgró-ba ṅá-yi γdúl-bya yin* the beings are to be converted by me *Glr.*; *bdag ḱyéd-kyi γdúl-byar šog čig* may we become your converts!

II. sbst. **विनय 1. the taming** etc. — 2. also *ₒdúl-bai sde*, the disciplinary part of the Kangyur, *ₒdul-ba-las* from, or according to the Dulwa; *ₒdúl-bai brda* an expression (taken) from the Dulwa.

འདུས་པ་ *ₒdús-pa*, v. *ₒdú-ba.*

འདེ་གུ་ *ₒdé-gu*, v. *ldé-gu.*

འདེ་བ་ *ₒdé-ba*, v. *ldé-ba.*

འདེག(ས)་པ་ *ₒdég(s)-pa*, pf. *bteg(s)*, fut. *γdeg*, imp. *ťeg*, *W.* **tág-če**. imp. **tog**, **to lift, to raise, to elevate,** the head, the tail, also fig.; *sgrón-me Glr.*, *'*od-ṭo** *W.*, to hold up a lamp, a light; also fig.: to let one's light shine to others; *grágs-pai gó-sar ₒdégs-pa* to raise to a high rank; **to support, sustain, maintain, keep up,** *Pth.*; *rám-bu ₒdégs-pa* to join in singing, to fall in with, *Dzl.* and elsewh. (*Sch.* erron. 'to bawl, to blare'); *rá-mda ₒdégs-pa* to help; for **ži tág-če** and similar phrases cf. the secondary forms *tég-pa*, *tégs-pa*, *ₒtégs-pa;* with or without *srán-la*, *rgyá-ma-la* etc.: to put on the balance, **to weigh,** *B.*; *žib-btégs* weighed accurately

Lt.; *ₒdégs-ḱal* 'a bushel by weight' *Cs.*, or rather: twenty points on the large steelyard. — *ǰug-tág* *W.* **water-wagtail.** — *dég-ḱa* *C., W.*, **weight.** — *ₒdégs-dpon* is said to denote a military dignity, but is not generally known; as 'servant waiting at table', it ought to be spelled *stégs-dpon.* — *ₒdégs-šiṅ* *Sch.* **yoke,** fitted to a person's shoulders, for carrying water-buckets etc.

འདེང་བ་ *ₒdéṅ-ba*, pf. *deṅ*, imp. *deṅ(s)*, **to go,** esp. *ṗyir déṅ-ba* **to go back, to return,** *Dzl., Lex.* Cf. *ₒdoṅ-ba.*

འདེད་པ་ *ₒdéd-pa*, pf. and imp. *ded*, sometimes preceded by *rǰés-su*, **to go** or **walk behind,** hence 1. **to drive,** cattle, the herdsman walking behind the animals, whereas of the shepherd *ₒḱrid-pa* is used; *rlúṅ-gis gru ₒded* the wind drives the ship, frq.; also to drive through (a tube) by blowing, to blow through *Glr.*; to drive (animals, birds) from a place of rest, **to rouse, start.** — 2. **to pursue, chase, run after,** *rgód-ma ₒdéd-pa* to be in the rut (of a stallion); *ded táṅ-ce* *W.* to chase, to hunt; *déd-de bó-ce* *W.* to call after a person. — 3. vb. n. **to follow in succession, to succeed,** *rim-pa bžin* successively, of generations, *Glr.* — 4. **to call in, to recover,** money, debts; *bú-lon-ₒded drág-po* a severe dun *Mil.*; *ₒdéd-mi* a driver, e.g. the person walking behind the horse of a rider, driving it on *Lt.*; **the pursuer** of a fugitive *Glr.* — Cf. *bdá-ba.*

འདེབས་ *ₒdebs* 1. **puncheon** (tool). — 2. **time, times,** = *lan* *W.*(?).

འདེབས་པ་ *ₒdébs-pa*, pf. *btab*, fut. *γtab*, imp. *tob*, supine *ₒdébs-su*, and *γdáb-tu*, *W.* *táb-ce*, imp. *tob*; **to cast, throw, strike, hit,** variously applied, cf. *rgyáb-pa*, in *B.* gen. with instr., even if there is a dative in the same sentence, v. the examples; *cog-tse-la táb-ce* *W.* to strike upon the table; *rlúṅ-gis, γdón-gyis, nád-kyis ₒdébs-pa*, to be beaten by the wind, to be possessed by a demon, to be seized with an illness, frq.; *sṅágs-kyis ₒdébs-pa* *B.*, *mtu btáb-pa* col., **to pronounce a charm against** a person or thing, with *la*; *lan, ṅo-spród, gros ₒdébs-pa*, **to answer, to explain, to advise;** *γsól-ba ₒdébs-pa* **to make a request,** *smón-lam ₒdébs-pa* to offer up a prayer; *γsal-ₒdébs byéd-pa* **to remember well** *Mil.*; *γsal-ₒdébs-su šés-pa* prob **to have a distinct recollection of a thing** *Glr.*; *rtsis ₒdébs-pa* prob. **to cast up an account, to reckon, to compute,** *dei rtsis-γdáb bdág-la med* I do not take that into account *Mil.*; *lús-la γzér(-gyis) ₒdébs-pa* *Dzl.*, *zér tab-ce*, or *gyab-ce* *W.*, knocking nails into the body; *rgyas ₒdébs-pa* **to seal;** *lud tab-ce*, or *gyáb-ce* *W.* to spread dung (on the ground), to manure; *cus ₒdebs-pa* to sprinkle with water *Dzl.*; *tsa, ša túg-pa-la ₒdébs-pa* to put salt, meat, into the soup; *sá-bon ₒdébs-pa* to sow; *gur ₒdébs-pa, sga-ₒdébs-pa*, to pitch a tent, a camp (driving in the tent-pins); also without a sbst.: *sṅar btab-pai ču-γšoṅ-du* (pitching) in the same dell where they had encamped before *Dzl.* ཉ་ཉ, 1. (*Sch.* incorr.): hence in general: **to found, to establish,** e.g. a monastery, frq.; *dus ₒdébs-pa* to fix a time.

འདེམས་པ་ *ₒdém-pa* **to prove, to examine** *Sch.*

འདེར་ *ₒder* *Glr.* prob. for *lder.*

འདོ་ *ₒdo*, for *mdo* 3., *Cs.* *ₒdo-yód* **prudent, clever,** *ₒdo-méd* *Lex.*, *Cs.* **imprudent, silly.**

འདོ་བ་ *ₒdó-ba* 1. sbst. *Sch.*: **'a breed of fine horses';** one *Lex.* has *ₒdo-rta* w. e. — 2. vb. *Cs.*: = *zló-ba*, **to say, to repeat;** *ma-ₒdos-par* **unspeakable** (?) *Dzl.* ༢༠༥, 4 (the reading of *Sch.* dubious, v. *Schf.*'s remarks on this passage).

འདོག་པ་ *ₒdóg-pa*, prob. an incorr. reading for *dógs-pa.*

འདོགས་པ་ *ₒdógs-pa*, pf. *btags* (also *γdags!*), fut. *γdag(s)*, imp. *ṫogs*, *W.* *tag-ce*, imp. *tog* or *tag toṅ*, 1. **to bind, fasten, tie to,** (opp. to *ₒgról-ba*), *W.* *ḱyi tág-te bor*, tie up, fasten, the dog well; (v. *ₒbór-ba*): *la* to a thing, frq.; also in a more general sense: **to fix, to attach,** e.g. a balcony to a house *S.g.*: **to tie round, to buckle on,** *go-mtsón lús-la* the armour *Pth.*; **to**

put on, *rgyan* gay clothes, finery, *rgyan bzáṅ-po btágs-pa* beautifully attired *Mil.*; col. also without *rgyan*, e.g. **tág-dad-čan** *W.* fond of dress and finery. — 2. in particular phrases: *bkar-ₒdógs-pa* v. *bkar*; *mi-la skyon ₒdógs-pa* **to charge a person with a fault, to upbraid**; *sgro ₒdógs-pa* v. *sgro*; *túgs-la ₒdógs-pa* **to interest one's self in** or **for, to take care of**; *kyod túgs-la mi ₒdógs-pa ₒdi či yin mi šes* why he does not interest himself in your behalf, I know not *Mil.nt.* 37, 6.; with reference to things: **to have near at heart**; *túgs-la btágs-so* you have taken great care of me, a phrase frq. used, where we should say: I am much obliged to you! though Tibetans deny its implying acknowledgment and expression of thanks. — *dám-la ₒdógs-pa* v. *dam*; *pan ₒdógs-pa* v. *pán-pa*; *miṅ ₒdógs-pa* **to give a name**; *drá-bai sgó-nas* according to likeness or analogy *Mṅg.*; *kyeui miṅ či-skad ɣdags* how is the boy to be called? *Dzl.* *miṅ mi-ɣdúṅ-ba žes* (or *mi-ɣdúṅ-bar*) *btágs-so* they named him ... *Mil.*, *Dzl.*; *miṅ* may also be wanting. — 3. *Gram.* **to join, subjoin, affix**, *rar btags ga* a *g* joined with *r*, i.e. *rg*; *ra-la ja* a *j* joined with *r*, i.e. *rj*; *sa-la btags-pai ta-yig, st*; *ya-btags*, or shorter, *yá-ta*, the *ya* which is written underneath, the subscribed *ya*, = ꣿ; *yá-ta btágs-pa yi-ge bdun*, seven letters are joined with *yá-ta(gs)* *Glr.*; *smád-ₒdogs ɣsum* the three subscribed letters, *ya*, *ra*, and *la* *Zam.*; *ₒdogs-čan* 1. having a letter subscribed; 2. an open syllable with a vowel-sign, as *go* གོ, *de* དེ, *mdo* མདོ, etc. (not *da* ད or *mda* མདའ) *Zam.*; *a-ₒdogs* consonants with *a* (འ) subscribed, syllables with a long vowel. — 4. in philosophical writings: *btágs-pa* **conditional**, not absolute, *Was.* (228. 270), *btags-méd* **nominal** *Was.* (281).

འདོང་བ་ ₒ*dóṅ-ba*, pf. and imp. *doṅ* or ₒ*doṅ*, **to go, to proceed**, *so-sór* *Dzl.* **to separate, to disperse**; *rgyál-poi tád-du* (to go) to the king; *pyi-rol-tu ₒčág-čiṅ* to take a walk *Dzl.*; *dóṅ-ṅo* let us go *Dzl.*; *lóg-la ₒdoṅ-ṅo* let us turn back *Glr.*

འདོད་པ་ ₒ*dód-pa* I. vb. (*W.* more frq. *tád-pa*), **to have a mind, to like, to be willing**, *zas bzáṅ-po mi ₒdod Dzl.*; *mi za ₒdod tsul byed* he pretends not to like this food *Lt.*; *sbyin (-par) ₒdód-pa ₒgyur* he gets inclined to give; *mi ₒdód-par ₒgyúr-ba* to feel no longer inclined; **to wish**, *nyán (-par)* to listen; *či daṅ či ₒdód-pa* whatever you may wish *Dzl.*; *rgyál-po ₒdód-pa* to wish to be a king *Dzl.*; as adj.: **wished for, desirable**, esp. with negatives, v. below; *ₒdód-par byá-ba* adj. **agreeable, pleasing, obliging, flattering**, *Stg.*, *Cs.*; **to desire, to long for**, *kyim ₒdod* I wish I were at home *Dzl.*; *me daṅ nyi-ma* (I am longing) for fire and for sunshine *Med.*; *bú-mo ṅa mi ₒdod* I do not wish for a girl; *raṅ-ₒdód-žen-pa* **self-love** *Glr.*; (*raṅ-*) *bzáṅ-ₒdod* **self-complacency, vanity**, *Glr.*; **to ask for, to demand**, *koṅ-jo ₒdód-pa-la slebs* they came in order to ask for *Koṅjo* (in marriage) *Glr.*; **to strive for, to aspire after**, *saṅs-rgya-bar* for holiness, for being like Buddha, for Buddhaship, *Dzl.*; **to be willing, to intend**; also ironically: *ná-ₒdod-pa* one that wants to grow ill, that does not take any care of himself; **to be ready, willing**, *bsnyen-bkúr byéd-par* to take charge of the waiting on (Buddha); *ₒdód-par byéd-pa* to make willing, disposed, to persuade to it *Dzl.*; **to maintain, to assert; to suppose; to pronounce to be** (cf. *ₒtád-pa?*) *Mṅg.*, *Tar.* and elsewh. frq. — *mi ₒdód-pa* to be not willing, not liking; **to detest**, *btsógs-pas kún-gyis mi ₒdód-na* as she was detested by all on account of her sluttishness *Dzl.*; **to be angry, indignant**, *žes mi ₒdód nas* thus exclaiming indignantly *Dzl.*; *mi-ₒdód-pa*, and *ma-ₒdód-pa* adj. **not wished for, disagreeable, adverse**, *mi-ₒdód-pai las* hard drudgery; *mi-ₒdod(-lóg)-pai rluṅ* adverse wind, frq.; **tsig mi-dód-pa zer-kan** *W.* one that slanders.

II. sbst. *Ssk.* काम 1. **lust, desire** in general; *ₒdód-pa kun zád-de* after all desires have ceased *Dzl.*; *ₒdód-pa-rnams-la čágs-pa* to indulge one's desires or passions; in a special sense, **carnal desire, lust, vo-**

luptuousness, = $_o$dod-čágs, frq.; meton., coitus, $_o$dód-pa spyód-pa to practise it; $_o$dód-pai dus $_o$débs-pa to agree upon the time for cohabiting *Tar.* — 2. *Ssk.* इच्छा, **a wish**, $_o$dód-pa γsum γnáṅ-na if three wishes are granted *Dzl.*; meton. the object of desire, $_o$dód-pa ťób-pa; $_o$dód-pa daṅ $_o$brál-ba to be separated from the object of one's desire. — 3. **supposition** *Tar.* 45, 21. — 4. *W.* semen virile. — 5. **Kama, Cupid,** the god of love and of lust. — 6. symb. num.: 13.

Comp. $_o$dod-ḱáms the world of sensual pleasure, the world of Brahma; $_o$Dod-ḱams-bdág-ma, prop. n. = Skye-dgui-bdág-mo, = Dpal-lhá-mo. — $_o$dód-mḱan he that wishes, seeks, sues, a **lover, suitor,** cca., nai bú-mo $_o$dód-mḱan máṅ-po $_o$dug there are here many suitors of my daughter *Glr.* — $_o$dod-dgu all wishes, lus $_o$dod-dgúr sgyúr-ba to transform one's self at pleasure *Mil., Stg.* — $_o$dód-čan, $_o$dod-ldán, $_o$dód-pa-čan eager, desirous *Cs.* — $_o$dod-čágs (राग) **passion, carnal desire, lust,** frq., $_o$dod-čágs skyés-te, $_o$dod-čágs-kyis γdúṅs-te; as the highest of the three **guna** (cf. γti-mug) it corresponds to सत्त्व, **virtue,** and is symbolized as cock or hen, though Tibetan readers probably never understand anything else by it than sensual indulgence. — $_o$dod-ǰó v. ǰó-ba. — $_o$dod-dúṅ strong desire *Cs.* — $_o$dod-dpál prop. n. **Dodpál, a** large hardware-manufactory and mint at the foot of the Potala in Lhasa. — $_o$dod-brál, $_o$dod-méd, free from passions. — $_o$dod-(paí) yón-(tan) 'wished for goods', earthly goods and pleasures, whatever is grateful to the senses, such as $_o$dód-pa lṅa, a delight to the ears, the eyes, the palate etc. — $_o$dod-lóg **unchastity, lewdness, prostitution,** spyód-pa to have illicit, esp. incestuous intercourse, daṅ with. — $_o$dód-sred-čan **avaricious, greedy** *Pth.*, yet cf. čags-sred-čan; both words prob. signify the same. — $_o$dod-lha = $_o$dod-pa 5.

འདོན་ $_o$don *Lt.*, n. of a medicine (?) dkar, dmar, skyur-$_o$don.

འདོན་པ་ $_o$dón-pa, pf. bton, fut. (*Cs.*) γdon, imp. ťon, *W.* *ťón-če*, the vulg. word for $_o$byin-pa, vb.n. to ťón-pa, $_o$byúṅ-ba, **to cause to go out** or **to come forth,** i.e. 1. **to expel, throw out, eject,** from the house, village etc.; to take out, from a box; **to draw forth; to dig out,** metals; *záṅ-ton-sa* *W.* a copper-mine; *ťón-te bór-če* *W.* **to put, set, lay, place out; to let out,** of prison *Pth.*; **to drive** or **turn away, to dismiss,** a servant, a wife etc., frq.; *ṅa ḱoi ḱa-ne čaṅ ma ton* *W.* I could not get or force any thing out of him; mčí-ma $_o$dón-pa to shed tears *Glr.*; with skad and similar words: **to utter, to set up** (a cry), **to make one's self heard;** hence 2. **to pronounce,** yi-ge γnyis-γnyís-su $_o$dón-pa to pronounce two consonants as two distinct sounds *Gram.*; to pronounce a magic formula; klóg-pa daṅ $_o$dón-pa-la góms-šiṅ practising reading and pronouncing *Dzl.*; **to say, to repeat; to recite** (sacred texts) with a singing, drawling tone, like that of mendicant friars; hence in general, to perform one's devotions; žal-$_o$dón-du mdzád-pa, *Tar.* 95, 11, prob. resp. = ḱa-ťón byéd-pa to repeat by heart; ťúgs-la $_o$dón-pa prob. to read silently. — 3. fig. **to elevate, to raise,** ḱri ťóg-tu *Pth.*, or rgyál-sar *Glr.*, to raise to the throne; mgo v. mgo-$_o$don, sub mgo compounds; γžán-gyi srog to prolong a person's life, by affording him a (scanty) subsistence *Thgy.*; *sróg-ton-ḱan(-po)* *W.* the giver of life, ζωοποιός. — 4. *ḱa ťón-če* *W.* **to sharpen** a scythe **by means of a hammer.** — 5. **to edit, to publish,** books, *Tar.* 47, 17. — 6. čos mťá-ru $_o$dón-pa to arrive at the end and scope of religious knowledge *Mil.* — 7. *W.* resp. **to take, to taste,** to eat or to drink, don yin-na would you like a taste of that? dón-ḱaṅ dining-room; dón-gir resp. for ta-gir; dón-rag for ṅ-rag.

འདོམ་པ་ $_o$dóm-pa 1. **to come together** *Lex.*, *Lt.* — 2. for $_o$dám-pa **to choose, to make a choice** *Glr.* — 3. also $_o$dóms-pa, pf. γdams, ft. γdam, imp. $_o$doms, 1. **to advise,** cf. γdám-pa. 2. **to exhort,** bag-méd-pa-rnams-la wicked persons, brtsón-par to give diligence *Tar.* 3. **to recommend** *Glr.*, **to bid, to command,** v. γdám-pa. — 4. *Cs.*: **importance; business, occupation** (?).

འདོམ(ས)་(པ) ˳*dóm*(*s*)(-*pa Cs.*) 1. a long-measure, **a fathom,** = 6 feet, ˳*dom-gáṅ* one fathom, *S.g.*, as the usual length of a man, = *k̔ru bźi; śiṅ* ˳*dom dó* a piece of wood two fathoms long *Dzl.;* ˳*dom bčui doṅ* a well ten fathoms deep; ˳*dóm-gyis*, or ˳*dóms-su* ˳*ǰál-ba* to measure by fathoms *Cs.*; ˳*dom-gaṅ-gru-bźi* 1. adj. measuring a square fathom, also a cubic fathom; 2. sbst. **a strong jail** or **dungeon.** — 2. imp. of ˳*dam-pa* **to choose.**

འདོམས ˳*doms* the pudenda, **privities,** regio pubis, ˳*doms*(-*kyi*)-*spu* the hair of that region, ˳*doms-spu* ˳*ťóg-pa* to pluck out such hair *Cs.*; *rṅa-ma* ˳*doms óg-tu* ˳*ǰúg-pa* col. to take to one's heels; ˳*doms-stóṅ* vulg. without breeches; *sdoms-lpágs* foreskin, prepuce (?); ˳*doms-γtsáṅ*(-*ma*) *C.* a pure virgin; a nun; ˳*doms-γtsáṅ-pa* a chaste monk (if not rather *sdom* is meant); ˳*doms-rás* (also *čar-rás Cs.*) a small apron to cover the privy parts *Cs.*

འདོར་བ ˳*dór-ba*, pf. and imp. *dor* (cog. to *γtór-ba, stór-ba, byi-dór, p̔yag-dár*). 1. **to throw** or **cast away,** like *γtór-ba* and ˳*bór-ba Stg.;* esp. **to throw out, to eject,** spittle, frq.; *drí-ču* ˳*dór-ba* to make water *Glr.*; fig. *srog* ˳*dór-ba* to fling away one's life *Dzl.;* **to sweep out** or **away** *Dzl.*, *Stg.* — 2. (opp. to *lén-pa, bźéd-pa*) **to decline, refuse, reject, despise,** things offered *Dzl.;* to reject, a reading, a passage *Gram.*; **to disapprove,** of an action as immoral; *blaṅ-dór*, ˳*dor-lén*, accepting and rejecting, deciding for or against, e.g. *dge-sdig-gi Glr.* — 3. **to subtract,** *dór-bai lhág-ma Wdk.* the remainder left after subtracting; perh. also **to divide.** — 4. *srog* ˳*dór-ba* also signifies: **to endanger life,** or **to deprive of life,** used e.g. of diseases *S.g.*; *góm-pa* ˳*dór-ba* (= ˳*bór-ba*), to pace, to step, to stride, frq.; *dmód-pa* ˳*dor-ba* v. *dmód-pa.*

འདོལ་ས ˳*dól-sa Lex.*, **fertile ground** or **soil** *Sch.*

འདྲ་བ ˳*drá-ba* 1. adj., *C.:* **ḍá-te**, **similar, equal** (which two notions gen. are not strictly distinguished from each other); ˳*drá-ba* ˳*dí-dag* these equal things, for: these comparisons, *Pth.*; *kyed γnyis* ˳*drá-bar* ˳*dug*, ˳*dra-ba yin*, ˳*drao*, you two resemble each other very much; with a pleon. *mnyam*: *riṅ-ťúṅ mnyám-la* ˳*drá-ba* equally long *Dzl.*; gen. with *daṅ* or accus., seldom with termin., in various applications: *k̔yed*(*daṅ*) ˳*drá-ba ni* your equals *Dzl.; bud-méd-du* ˳*drá-bai náṅ-na* amongst womanlike, effeminate (men), *Dzl.;* ˳*dii byin ťsáṅs-pa daṅ* ˳*drao* his brightness is equal to (that of) Brahma *Dzl.*; *γźán-gyi dón-laaṅ ráṅ-gi* ˳*drar séms-pa* esteeming our neighbour's advantage as high as our own *S.g.;* *ťams-čád-la bu γčig-pa daṅ drao* he behaved to all as (to) an only son *Dzl.;* with a negative: *γźan yaṅ de daṅ* ˳*drá-ste γnáṅ-ba med* others shall allow it just as little as he himself *Dzl.; Saṅs-rgyás daṅ* ˳*drá-bar byá-bai p̔yir* in order to be equal to Buddha, to come up with Buddha *Dzl.*; *brtsigs-pa mi* ˳*dra skyés-pa* ˳*dra* not as if (it had been) built, but as if it had grown up spontaneously *Glr.*; *bdag* ˳*dra bud-méd blo-dmán kyaṅ* even a stupid woman like myself; *skra* ˳*drá-ba yód-dam* whether any thing like hair is still left? *Mil.; ťéṅ-ro* ˳*dra rnyed* he found the remnants of a carcass or something like it *Mil.*; *ro daṅ* ˳*drá-ba* as much as dead *Wdṅ.*; *mnyán-pa daṅ* ˳*drá-bai bśes-γnyén* a teacher like as a ferryman (conveying to the shores of happiness) *Thgy.*; *rtag-rtág* ˳*dra yaṅ* seemingly eternal *Mil*; *skyid-skyíd* ˳*dra yaṅ* even if it appears a blessing *Mil.; rúṅ-ba daṅ* ˳*drá-na* if it appears feasible *Dzl.;* *ster dgós-pa* ˳*dra* it seems I shall be obliged to give it *Glr.; da-lán k̔yod nús-pa če-čé* ˳*dra bźin byúṅ-ste* as your strength this time at least seems to be rather great *Mil.;* *k̔yed slu-slú* ˳*dra* you might easily be ensnared *Mil.; mi-*˳*drá-ba* **unequal, unlike, different,** *sṅon-čád daṅ mi* ˳*drá-bar* quite otherwise than formerly *Dzl.*; *čós-pa mi* ˳*drá-bar* not like, not befitting, a priest *Mil.*; **various, several,** **k̔a-zé mi-ḍá-wa** *C.* several dishes; ˳*di-*˳*dra-ba, dé-*˳*dra-ba* **such;** *dé-dras*, (**dhén-dé** *C.* vulg.) **so, thus;** *či-*˳*dra-ba, ǰi-*˳*dra-ba* **of what kind** (qualis), *či-*˳*dra čig légs-*

par ston dgos you must tell me minutely how she looks, what kind of appearance she has *Glr.*; *ṗug či ˳dra čig ˳oṅ* what will be the upshot? where is this to end? *Glr.*; *ṅa ǰi-˳dra-bar de bžin ˳gyur* he becomes just what I am *Stg.*; **ghán-de* C.* col. **how?** *˳dra-˳dra* (*W.* **ḍán-ḍa**) very frq. for *˳drá-ba*, e.g. *ža-dkár-gyi rgyu ˳drá-˳dra-la tig-rtse-zer* something similar to the substance of tin is called zinc; *˳dra mi ˳dra* like and unlike; **equality, likeness, similarity,** *˳dra mi ˳dra ltá-ba* to examine the likeness *Glr.* — 2. sbst. 1. **resemblance, likeness,** v. *˳dógs-pa* 2. — 2. **form, shape, appearance, phase.** *Thg.*

འདྲངས་ *˳draṅs* v. *˳graṅs.*

འདྲད་ *˳drad* v. *˳brad.*

འདྲན་ *˳dran* v. *˳gran.*

འདྲལ་བ་ *˳drál-ba*, pf. *dral* (cf. *rál-ba* and *hrál-ba*), **to tear to pieces, to rend asunder;** also **to pull down,** a house; **to rip up, to cut open,** an animal.

འདྲི་བ་ *˳drí-ba*, pf. and imp. *˳dris,* 1. **to ask,** . . . *la, W. nas,* a person; with accus. **to enquire after** or **about** a thing; *grós-˳dri-sa* a place for asking advice, **oracle** *Glr.*; *blá-ma ˳drí-ba* to inquire after one's Lama *Mil.*; *ṗa-mái γtam* after one's parents *Dzl.*; *˳dri-bai tsʻig* **interrogative pronoun,** e.g. *či Gram.*; v. also *dri-ba.* — 2. inst. of *˳bri-ba.*

འདྲིང་བ་ *˳driṅ-ba Glr.* fol. 57, 12? another reading: *ldiṅ-ba.*

འདྲིད་པ་ *˳drid-pa* for *˳brid-pa.*

འདྲིམ་པ་ *˳drim-pa* for *˳brim-pa.*

འདྲིལ་བ་ *˳dril-ba*, pf. *dril,* I. vb. n., cf. *˳gril-ba* and *hril-ba*, 1. **to be turned, rolled round** or **twisted into** a thing, *od-zér-gyi gáṅ-bur* to be wrapped into a covering of light *Glr.*; **to gather, to flow together,** as *ṗó-bai bád-kan,* the gastric phlegm *Med.*; fig.: *blo-séms γčig-tu ˳dril-te* whilst our minds were flowing together *Glr.*; *yúl-pa-rnams ḱá-˳dril-te ṅó-log-pa* **a conspiracy** *Schr.* — 2. **to roll down,** *ri-bo ṅos-la* the slope of a hill *Thgy.* — 3. **to fall, to fall down** *W.*

II. vb. a., cf. *sgril-ba,* **to wrap up,** *rás-kyis* in a handkerchief *Glr.*, *dar sna lṅas* in five sorts of silk *Glr.*; *zaṅs-kyis* (covered or sheathed) with copper *Mil.*; **to heap together, to pile up,** *mé-tog ṗúṅ-por dril* the blossoms are aggregated, heaped together in a panicle *Wdṅ.*; *dril-bas* **in short, to sum up all, in summa** *Glr.* — *ljags ˳dril-ba Sch.*: to play with the tongue, moving it to and fro.

འདྲིས་པ་ *˳drís-pa* **to be accustomed to, to be acquainted with,** gen. with *daṅ*, *Glr.* and col.; rarely with accus.: *γnyen ǰi tsam ˳dris bžin* the more friends you get familiar with; *mig ˳dris čés-na* if persons constantly see one another, get perfectly used to one another, *Mil.*; mostly adj. (= *góms-pa*) **accustomed, used,** *mi* or *ḱáṅ-pa daṅ,* to men, to one's house; also *drís-pa* used absol. = **tame** *W.*; *drís-pa mi* an acquaintance, a sympathizing friend, an assistant *Thgy.*; *sṅar-dris-kyi mi* an old acquaintance, an old crony *Thgr.* A derivation of *drís-pa* from *˳drid-pa, ˳brid-pa,* to deceive, to bait, to decoy, and hence to tame, was suggested by some Tibetans, but is after all scarcely to be authenticated.

འདྲུ་བ་ *˳drú-ba* v. *˳brú-ba.*

འདྲུགས་པ་ *˳drúgs-pa* **to fall into small pieces, to crumble** (away) *Sch.*

འདྲུད་པ་ *˳drúd-pa*, pf. and imp. *drud* (*˳drus?*), rarely *˳brúd-pa*, 1. **to rub,** *lus* the body; **to file, to rasp,** *šiṅ* wood, *Lex.*; **to rub off, to scour,** **bé-ma daṅ W.*; **to polish, to smooth, to plane,** *ṗag-ste* with a plane *W.*; **to grind, to powder, to pulverize** (?). — 2. **to drag, to draw** or **pull along** on the ground, by a rope, *ro sá-la* a dead body on the ground (*ma-˳drús-par* without slipping (?) *Med.*) — 3. **ḍúd-de gyur toṅ* W.* move, or push it a little aside; *ḍud čád-če W.* to cut off obliquely (?).

འདྲུབ་པ་ *˳drúb-pa*, pf. and imp. *drub* (*s*) 1. **to sew** *Sch.*, so perh. *Dzl.* ༢༢༠, 11.

— 2. **to embroider** *C.* — 3. **to heal,** *rma* wounds *S.g.* — *tsem-drúb* needle-work *Sch.*

འདྲུལ་བ་ *˳drúl-ba,* pf. *drul,* gen. *rul* (q.v), **to become putrid, to rot, to putrefy,** *drúl-bar gyúr-ba* id.; *˳drúl-bar byéd-pa* to cause to be decomposed *Med.*; *rten-˳drúl* prob.: putrefied substances, *bšan-γčis ˳byin-par-byed* are removed with the faeces *Med.*

འདྲེ་ *˳dre,* also *lhá-˳dre, W.* **lán-de**, **goblin, gnome, imp, demon, evil spirit, devil,** col. the most frq. word for such beings; quite in a general sense: *klu-γnyán-la sógs-pai lha-˳dre-rnams; byá-˳dre, ˳dre-rgód Lt.* prob. two particular species of demons; *zá-˳dre* is said to be a word for 'owl'; *˳dres ˳kyér-ba* to be carried off by goblins *Ma.*; *˳dres-γnód, ˳drei γnód-pa* mischief done by evil spirits; *˳dre ˳júg-pa* the entering of evil spirits, the state of possession; *˳dré-žugs-pa* (*W.* **-kan**) one possessed by a devil, a demoniac; *skród-pa* to cast out, *˳dúl-ba* to subdue (devils).

Comp. *˳dre-˳jigs-šiṅ* = *gu-gul-šiṅ,* 'devil's fear', a resinous wood, by the burning of which goblins are smoked out. - *˳dre-paṅ-ka* n. of the fruit of *sgóṅ-tog Wdṅ.* — **de-pu* (or *bu?*)*-tsúb* W.* **whirlwind, water-spout.** — *˳dré-po* a male devil, *˳dré-mo* a female d., *˳dré-bu* a young d., an imp *Cs.* — *˳dre-me-bud* ignis fatuus, will-o'the wisp, Jack with the lantern *Schr.* — *˳dre-dmág* a goblin host. — *˳dre-lág* the left hand, the left side of the body being supposed to belong to the evil spirits *C.* — *˳dré-šig* **'devil's louse', bed-bug** *C.* — *˳dre-srin* goblins and Rakshasas, demons in general, frq.

འདྲེ་བ་ *˳dré-ba* I. pf. and imp. *˳dres,* prop. vb. n. to *bsré-ba,* 1. **to be mixed with,** *de γnyis ˳drés-(-na) Lt.* if the two are mixed with each other; *pyogs-γčig-tu ˳dres* mixed together, miscellaneous *Lex.*; *˳dres-mtsáms* (*˳tsams Tar.*) the 'limit of mixing', *rgyá-mtso daṅ gáṅ-gā ˳drés-mtsáms* the influx of the Ganga into the sea *Tar.* 178, 9; *tsig γžaṅ ma ˳drés-par* without mingling other talk with (the conversation); *ka daṅ snyiṅ ma ˳dres* a man with whom word and sentiment differ, **a hypocrite;** *čos daṅ čos ma yin-pa ˳dres* right and wrong were mixed together; in an absol. sense: *spyód-pa ˳drés-te mú-stegs-par gyúr-to* his course of life degenerated, and he became a Brahmanist *Pth.*; *dúd-˳gro ˳drés-pa* an animal of a mixed race, **half-breed, mongrel;** *ma ˳drés-par* without any confounding or mixing together, sharply discriminating *Mil.*; *ma-˳drés-pa* prob. **pure, unadulterated.** — 2. **to interfere, to meddle with,** **de lé-ka daṅ ma de* W.* do not meddle with that; **to have intercourse with, to engage in,** *B.* and col.; *ráṅ-sems blá-ma ˳drés-pas bde* through your, the Lama's, intercourse with my soul, in your society, I am happy *Mil*; *γtam ˳dré-ba* id.

II. erron. for *˳gré-ba Pth.*

འདྲེག་པ་ *˳drég-pa* v. *˳brég-pa.*

འདྲེགས་ *˳dreγs* v. *drég-pa.*

འདྲེད་པ་ *˳dréd-pa* **to slide, glide, slip,** **déd-de gyel* W.*, **˳déd-tag(?) šór-ne ˳gyel* C.* he slipped and fell.

འདྲེན་པ་ *˳drén-pa,* pf. *draṅ(s),* fut. *draṅ,* imp. *droṅ(s),* 1. **to draw, drag, pull,** a carriage *Glr.*; a person by his arm *Dzl.*; *drág-tu* violently *Dzl.*; **to draw tight,** a rope *Dzl.*; **to draw from, to pull out,** an arrow out of a wound *Glr.*; **to press** or **squeeze out,** matter, pus, *Med.*; **to tear out,** *γsóṅ-poi rgyú-ma* the intestines of a living person; fig. *ka-čig tser-sṅón-gyi rigs-suaṅ ˳dren* some reckon it (lit. **draw** it) to the species of Meconopsis *Wdṅ.*; **to cause, to effect,** *bde-čén* felicity *Thgy.*, *skyúg-pa* vomiting *Tar.* — 2. **to conduct,** water (*W.* **rán-če**); **to lead, to guide;** with or without *sna, lam ˳drén-pa* to direct a person in his way; also sbst. **guide,** *˳dren-méd* without a guide, without a king *Dzl.*; esp. to lead to happiness, felicity, frq.; opp. to *lóg-˳dren-pa* q.v.; *yúl-du-dmag* to lead an army into a country, to wage war against it, frq. — 3. **to cite, to quote,** *luṅ* a religious authority *Cs.* — 4. **to invite,** a guest; **to call, to go to meet; to cause to appear, to conjure up,** a ghost, a deity; resp. *spyán-˳dren-pa, γdán-˳dren-*

pa; also for **to fetch, to go for,** if the object is of a sacred character, e.g. relics; *spyan ma dráṅs-par ₒgró-ba* to go uninvited *Cs.* — 5. **to place before one, to serve up,** dishes, meals; **to pour out,** beer, wine etc., ccdpar., frq.; resp. with *žál-du Pth.*; **to taste,** to eat or drink what has been offered, resp. *W.* (cf. *mčód-pa, ysól-ba*). — 6. **to count, to number,** esp. with *re*, or *re-ré-nas*, separately, one by one, *Glr*, *Mil.*; **to enumerate,** *ma draṅs* ... are here not enumerated *Wdṅ.*; c. termin. **to count for, to consider, to look upon as,** *dpé-ru* as a parable, as not existing *Mil.* — 7. *W.* in a general sense: **to convey, to remove,** **zá-če ťúr-maṅ daṅ ḍen** food is conveyed by a spoon, **K̔a k̔yem daṅ ḍen** snow is removed by a shovel. — 8. further: *rkaṅ* (resp. *žabs*) *ₒdrén-pa* **to insult, to scoff, to deride** *Thgy.*, *C.* — *me ₒdrén-pa* the blazing, flaring of a flame *Sch.* — *mgo-ₒdren* v. *mgo*, comp.

འདྲེན་མ་, འདྲེས་མ་ *ₒdrén-ma, ₒdrés-ma,* **mixture, medley,** e.g. in border-districts a mixed dialect, a mixed religion; a mixed colour, e.g. gray.

འདྲོངས་པ་ *ₒdróṅs-pa* = *ₒdrén-pa*, esp. in conjunction with *spyan*: *spyán-ₒdroṅs-sam ltos šig*; *mi ₒdroṅs-na* try whether you can invite him (whether he will come); if not, then ... *Mil.*, also *Mil. nt.*

འདྲོག་པ་ *ₒdróg-pa* 1. **to wince, shrink, quiver, start,** from fear; **to shy,** of horses; *ₒdróg-čan* **shy, skittish, easily frightened** *W.* 2. — *ₒdrog-slóṅ-ba Sch.*: **to take by surprise, to deceive by cunning, to outwit;** *blo-ₒdróg Lex.* w.e.

འདྲོབ་སྐྱོང་ *ₒdrob-skyóṅ Sch.*: 'the keeper of light'(?).

རྡང་ *rdaṅ* v. *ydaṅ.*

རྡབ་པ་ *rdáb-pa* v. *rdéb-pa.*

རྡར་བ་ *rdár-ba* v. *bdár-ba.*

རྡལ་བ་ *rdál-ba*, pf. and fut. *brdal*, imp. *rdol*, also *ydál-ba, bdál-ba*, 1. **to spread,** sand, stones, manure, esp. if done by means of a stick, rake, shovel etc.; **to extend,** a canopy *Pth.*; **to cover,** *rdzíṅ-gi žabs byé-mas*, the bottom of a pond with sand *Dzl.*; fig. *dam-čos ťaṅ-mar bdál-ba-la* now when holy religion lies before you as if it were spread out in a plain, i.e. when it is accessible to all, *Mil.*; *kyab-ydál* or *rdál* spreading far and wide, all-embracing, *sems nám-mk̔a ltá-bu, čós-kyi kloṅ, čos-dbyiṅs*, and the like; *groṅ-rdál* v. sub *groṅ.* — 2. *sos-ydál Lex.* w.e.; *Sch.*: **slowly, not in a hurry.**

རྡིག་ *rdig* = *yo-byád? náṅ-gi rdig kun Mil.* seems to mean: all the utensils and furniture of a house.

རྡིགས་པ་ *rdigs-pa* **to beat** *Sch.*, prob. = *rdég-pa.*

རྡིབ་པ་ *rdib-pa*, pf. *rdibs*, vb. n. to *rtib-pa*, **to fall to pieces, to give way, to break down,** of a roof, rock, tree, the heavens. — 2. **to get dinted,** battered, like tin-vessels by a blow or knock, *C.*, *W.*

རྡུ་བ་ *rdú-ba Cs.* **thistle,** not generally known, but perh. the same as *ma-rdu.*

རྡུག་པ་ *rdúg-pa*, pf. *brdugs*, fut. *brdug*, 1. **to conquer, to vanquish**(?), *k̔lú-rnams-kyis lha-ma-yin ťúb-čiṅ rdúg-par byás-te* the Nagas having overcome and vanquished the Asuras *Stg.*; hence prob. **to annihilate, destroy, undo,** *der ťabs brdugs-pas* as all resources were destroyed *Pth.* — 2. **to strike against, to stumble at,** *C.* (cf. *ťúg-pa* II, 3); *ťogs-rdug* (or *brtug*)-*méd-pa*, v. *ťógs-pa*, without impediment.

རྡུང་ *rduṅ*, **a small mound, hillock,** *Ld.*

རྡུང་བ་ *rdúṅ-ba*, pf. *brduṅs*, fut. *brduṅ*, imp. (*b*)*rduṅ*(*s*), also *bdúṅ-ba*, **to beat, to strike,** a person, a drum etc.; **to cudgel, to drub,** also *rdúṅ-ₒťsog-pa* (*Sch. -ₒťsob-pa?*); **to beat with a hammer, to hammer,** *lčags*; *rdúṅ-du rúṅ-ba* malleable, ductile; **to knock,** *sgo* at a door; **to break to pieces, to smash,** *rdo-yis* with a stone (the sacrificial vessels) *Glr.*; **to beat out,** *brá-bo* buckwheat, with a stick; hence to beat out with a flail, **to thrash; to pound, to bray**: *stéṅ-rduṅ* a pestle *Ld.* — *bro rdúṅ-ba* **to dance.** — *yžu rdúṅ-ba* **to bend the bow,** v. *Schf.* on *Dzl.* ༢༥༢, 11. — *rdúṅ-mk̔an* **a fighter, bully;** of horses:

a kicker; of oxen, **butting.** — *rduṅ-ytág Lex.* w.e., prob. a drubbing, a sound thrashing; *rduṅ-ytag byuṅ* I have got a drubbing.

རྡུམ་པོ་ *rdúm-po Cs.* **maimed, mutilated,** *rdúm-po byéd-pa* **to mutilate**, *lag-rdum* a maimed hand, *rkaṅ-rdúm* a maimed foot, *rwa-rdúm* a mutilated horn; having a maimed hand, foot etc. *Mil.*

རྡུལ་ *rdul* **dust,** not so much as a deposited mass, but rather as particles floating in the air, **motes, atoms**; thus esp. *rdul-ṗrán, rdul-ṗrá-mo, rdul-ṗra-ráb, nyi-zér-gyi rdul*, yet less to express minuteness than infinite number; **atom**, in a philosophical sense, *ḱu-ḱrág-gi rdul ťams-čád* all the atoms of the procreative fluid *Wdṅ.*; **monad,** *rdul-ṗra-rab-ča-med*, acc. to *Was.* (279); *rdul ₒtul, ldaṅ*, dust arises *Dzl.*; *rdul mi ťúl-bar* (or *ma ldáṅ-bar*) *byéd-pa* to lay the dust *Dzl.*; *sprúg-pa, W.* **šrúg-če**, to shake off, to beat out; *rdúl-du rlóg-pa* (in this case also *ťál-bar rlóg-pa*) to crush or pound a thing, until it is reduced to powder *Lex.*; *glaṅ-rdúl Cs.*: 'a mote in the dung of an ox' (?), *Sch.*: 'a small particle of cow-dung.' — *rdo-rǰei rdul* diamond-powder (?) *Lex.*; *sól-bai rdul* coal-dust.

Comp. *rdúl-čan* **dusty.** — *rdul-ṗyágs* **dusting-whisk, dusting-brush** *Sch.* — *rdul-ťsub* a whirling cloud of dust. — *rdul-ťsón* coloured stone-dust, employed in certain ceremonies, for making figures drawn in the sand more visible *Mil. nt.* — *rdul-γzán* a blouse (?), travelling-cloak against the dust, *Wdk. fol.* 144 a Lha wears such a garment.

རྡུལ་པོ་ *rdúl-po*, prob. erron. for *rtúl-po Dzl.* ༡༣༥, 2.

རྡེ་ *rde* in compounds for *rdeu.*

རྡེ་བ་ད་རུ་ *rde-ba-da-ru Wdṅ.*, tibetanized from देवदारु, **cedar.**

རྡེག(ས)་པ་ *rdég(s)-pa*, pf. *(b)rdegs*, fut. *brdeg*, imp. *(b)rdeg(s)*, **to beat, strike, smite,** c. accus., or (less corr.) c. dat., chiefly in *B.*, *rdég-čiṅ spyód-pa*, verberando concumbere, to compel a wife by blows to fulfil the conjugal duty *Thgy.*; *mé-loṅ-la brdég-čiṅ* beating the looking-glass in anger *Glr.*; *rdeg-ₒťsóg-gi sdug-bsṅál* the ill-fortune of getting a beating *Thgy.*; **to push, thrust, knock, kick,** *ṗul-rdég* a blow with the fist, *byéd-pa* to give one *Mil.*; *rdeg-čós Lex.* w.e., *Sch.* a dance; *rdeg-čós-pa* to dance, so perh. *Thgy.*, if *brdog-čós-pa* is not a better reading, *glo-rdég(-tu)* = *glo-búr-du*, **suddenly.**

རྡེབ་པ་ *rdéb-pa*, sometimes for *sdéb-pa.*

རྡེབ(ས)་པ་ *rdéb(s)-pa*, prob. the original form, but of rare occurrence, for *rdáb-pa*, pf. *brdabs*, fut. *brdab*, 1. **to throw down with a clap,** to clap the coat-tail on the ground *Glr.*; with a clashing sound, a potsherd *Tar.*; **to fling or knock down,** a person *Mil.*; *lus sá-la* **to prostrate one's self,** very frq.; *rtas* (to be thrown) by the horse *Sch.*; **ḱa dáb-pa** 1. *C.* **to fall upon one's face.** 2. *W.* **to smack with the tongue,** also of the snapping of a spring, of the clapping down of a lid or the cover of a book; **ká-lpags déb-pa** *W.* to smack with the lips (in eating). — 2. **to throw to and fro, to toss about,** *mgó-bo rdébs-šiṅ ₒdré-ldog-pa* to turn one's head this way and that way *Pth.* — 3. **to stumble** *Sch.*, so perh. *Lt.* fol. 196, 6; *čal rdáb-pa Lex.*, *rdáb-čal-ba Sch.* to slip and stumble. — 4. **to kill, to slaughter** *Bal.* — 5. **deb-šóg šẹ̀'-pa, táṅ-wa** *C.*, **ur deb táṅ-če** *W.*, **to talk big, to exaggerate.**

རྡེའུ་, རྡེ་, རྡེལ་པོ་ *rdeu, rde, rdél-po*, dimin. of *rdo*, 1. **a little stone, pebble,** *rdeu bskúr-ba bžin* like a little stone thrown on the ground *Glr.* — 2. **the stone,** calculus, in the bladder or the kidneys, *ṗo-rdé* calculus in males, *mo-rdé* in females; *rdeu čágs-pa* the concrescence of a calculus, *rdeu ₒdón-pa* the removing it *Cs.* — *rdel-dkár* a white pebble, *rdel-ḱrá* a coloured pebble *Cs.* — *rde-ₒgrám* ('the spreading of little-stones') the counting with pebbles *Cs.* — *rde-γžál* a pavement of pebbles. — 3. **a musket-ball** *C.*, *rdeu-pár* a bullet-mould; a bullet-founder *C.*

རྡོ་ *rdo B., C., rdó-ba* in *W.* the usual form, in more recent lit. frq., 1. **stone.** — 2. **weight,** for weighing things by a balance, col.; *rdoi* of stone, *rdoi túb-pa* a stone Buddha *Glr.*; *rdo skyéd-pa, skyá-ba*, to carry or drag stones to a place; **do-čág čóg-pa* C.* a ceremony observed in making a contract, by breaking a stone and using the fractured side as a seal, cf. *mdzúg-gu ˳túd-pa*; *rdo-bčál btín-ba Sch.*: 'stones arranged according to their species'; **do-rúb-la tán-če, do-rúb tán-te sád-če* W.* to pelt, beat, or kill with stones, **to stone**; *rdo rus ťug* to the last extremity *Sch.*; *dṅúl-rdo* a stone containing silver, silver-ore *Lex.*; *sprin-rdo* a sort of marble *Cs.*; *sbrá-rdo Sch.*, (perh. *spra-rdo?*) asbestus; *mé-rdo* fire-stone, flint; *rmaṅ-rdo* foundation-stone; *zúr-rdo* corner-stone; *ysér-rdo* a stone containing gold, gold-ore *Cs.*

Comp. *rdo-klád* a stone resembling a sheep's brain, and used as a remedy for diseases of the brain *S.g.* — *rdo dkár Cs.* a white stone; *Sch.* **alabaster.** — *rdo-skrán* a kind of steatite or soap-stone. — *rdo-ká* a vein in a stone. — *rdo-kóg* a stone pot. — *rdo-mkris* gall-stone (?) *S.g.* — *rdo-rgyúd* various kinds of soft stone, as serpentine, soap-stone, chalk. — *rdo-rgyús S.g.?* **do-čág* C.* oath taken in the above mentioned ceremony. — *rdo-čál Sik.* = *rdo-yžál.* — *rdo-čár* a shower of stones; **hail** *Schr.* — *rdo-˳čáṅ, W. *dom-čáṅ**, a stone of such a size as may be grasped by the hand. — *rdo-mnyen Cs.* = *ka-ma-ru* a soft kind of stone, alabaster. — *rdo-snyiṅ* jasper *Sch.* — *rdo-ťál Cs.* stone-ashes, **calcined stone**; *Sch.* **quicklime,** *Schf. Tar.* 103, 14: **chalk;** *rdo-ťál byúgs-pa* to rough-cast, to plaster. — *rdo-drég S.g.? Sch.* dirt on stones. —*rdo-snúm* **rock-oil, petroleum** *Schr.* — **do-pé* W.* stone-dust, small particles or grains of stone. — *rdo bún-ba* a shining black stone *Cs.* — *rdó-bos* (perh. *do-bos*) **a large hammer, mallet** *Ld.* — *do-dbyúg* **a sling-stone** *S.g.* — *rdo-˳bum* a sacred heap of stones, **a mani.** — *rdo-sbóm* large, heavy stones *Sch.* — *rdo-rtsig* stone-wall — *rdo-tsád* (= *yám-bu, rta-rmig-ma Cs.*) **a bar of silver-bullion,** of about 156¼ tolas (4 pounds) in weight, the common medium of barter in Central Asia. — *rdo-žun Lt.* = *brag-žun* **bitumen, mineral pitch** (?) — *rdo-žó* **lime,** both quick lime and slaked lime *C.* — *rdo-yžál* **a stone-pavement.** — *rdo-yžógs* a cut or wrought stone *Cs.* — *rdo-zám* a stone-bridge; a rock-bridge, natural bridge formed by overhanging rocks. — *rdo-riṅ(s)* a stone pillar, obelisk, as a land-mark, monument, or an ornament of buildings *Glr.* — *rdo-ril* a globular stone *Pth.* — *rdo-léb* a stone slab to sit upon; or to write on etc. — *rdo-sraṅ* a stone weight *Cs.* — *rdo-srin Glr.* 50, 10, evidently a corruption of *dar-srin.*

རྡོ་རྗེ་ *rdó-rje*, gen. **dór-je* W. *dór-že**, **वज्र.** (*Zam.* also **उपल**) 1. **precious, stone, jewel,** esp. **diamond,** more precisely: *rdó-rje pa-lám*; *rdo-rjei ytun* a knocker made of precious stones *Dzl.*; *rdó-rjei sku* an adamantine body *Pth.*; *rdó-rjei tse* an adamantine life *Glr.*; *zag-med-rdó-rje-lta-bui tsé-la mňa brnyéd-pas Pth.* as much as immortality; *rdó-rjei ˳jim-pa*, or *rin-po-čéi ˳jim-pa Glr.* mortar composed of pulverized precious stones and water, and considered a cement of marvelous properties. — 2. **thunderbolt,** originally the weapon of Indra, with the northern Buddhists the ritual sceptre of the priests (v. *Köpp.* II, 271; *Was.* 193), held by them during their prayers in their hands and moved about in various directions; symbol of hardness and durability, also of power; source of many phantastic ideas and practices; frq. forming part of names. — 3. euphem. for *po-rtágs C.*

Comp. *rdo-rje-gliṅ* seems to be the popular spelling of the Sanitarium in British Sikkim, which by the English generally is written Darjeeling. (Here Csoma died, and Dr. Hooker staid here for some time.) Acc. to several titles of books in the Petersb. list of manuscripts, it ought properly to be spelled *dar-rgyas-gliṅ.* — *rdo-rje-rgya-grám* v. *rgya* comp. — *rdo-rje-yčód-pa*, **वज्रच्छेदिका**, title of a religious book most extensively used among Buddhists; *Was.* (145), *Burn.* I, 465. — *rdo-rje-˳čáṅ*, **वज्रपाणि**, less frq. *˳dzin*,

॰धर, also *lág-na*, or *p̒yág-na-rdo-rje*, and abbreviated *lag-*, or *p̒yag-rdór*, **holder of the sceptre**, originally the Indra of the Brahmans; in Buddhism, in the first place, the Dhyani Bodhisatva of the Dhyani Buddha Aksobhya, and secondly a terrifying deity, the guardian of the mystical doctrine (*Was.* frq.), hence confounded with the *čos-skyoṅ-bži*, as well as with *ku-be-ra*, prince of the *ynod-sbyin*, and special deity of Milaraspa; v. *Köpp.* and *Schl.* — *rdo-rje-ydán*, वज्रासन, prop. the diamond seat or throne of Buddha at Gaya, *Köpp.* I, 93, and hence also proper name applied to that town, frq. — *rdo-rje-p̒a-lám* diamond v. above. — *rdo-rje-p̒ág-mo*, वज्रवाराहि or भद्रोहि (*Wts.* 136) 'diamond-sow', a goddess of later Buddhism, frq. worshipped (also in *Lh.*, where she has a sanctuary at Markula near Triloknath), and incarnated as abbess in a nunnery, situated on an island of the lake Pal-te, v. Georgi *Alph. Tib.*, *Wts.* 135. — *rdo-rje-p̒úr-pa Glr.* an instrument the upper part of which is a dorje and the lower a purpa. — *rdo-rje-légs-pa*, abbrev. **dor-lág**, a local deity in *Lh.*, originally an honest village black-smith. — *rdo-rje-sems-dpa*, वज्रसत्त्व. gen. = *rdo-rje-ₒčáṅ* (*Was.* 188), sometimes differing from it, v. *Schl.* p. 50; also = *mi-skyód-pa*, Aksobhya; also *mi-skyoṅ-rdó-rje Glr.* Respecting the word *rdo-rje* cf. *Burn.* I, 526.

རྡོ་ར་ *rdo-ra*, or *rto-ra* **circle of dancers** *W.*

རྡོག་ *rdog C.* **root**, **dog dhaṅ ló-ma** root and leaves; **lab-dog** radish-root; yet cf. *rdóg-po*.

རྡོག་པ་ *rdóg-pa* **step, footstep; kick**, *rdóg-pa ₒbór-ba* **to step, to pace, to walk** *Cs.*; *rdóg-sgra* the sound of steps, the clattering of hoofs; *rdog-stán* a straw-mat for cleaning one's shoes *C.*; *rdóg-pai ˽óg-tu ₒjúg-pa Dzl.* ༡༥༡, 13 (*Ms.*; *Sch.*: *rdóg-pai žábs-su?*) to prostrate, to throw under one's feet; *rdóg-pas rdúṅ-ba Sch.*, *ₒp̒úl-ba Sch.*, *snón-pa*, *mnán-pa Sch.*, *rdog-p̒úl rgyáb-pa Pth.*; **dog-tó p̒úl-wa** *C.*, **dog-čóṅ gyab-če** *W.* to strike with the foot, to apply a good kick, to stamp the ground; *rdog-bstád byéd-pa* prob. id.; prop. to load, to pack on(?).

རྡོག་པོ་ *rdóg-po* (*Cs.* also *rdóg-ma*), **a grain of corn, sand, sugar; a drop of rain** *Glr.*; *sran rdog bdun* seven peas; *ₒp̒reṅ-rdog* the bead of a rosary, which often consists of grains of seed; **a piece**, *rdog-ycig* (how many turnips do you want?) one *C.*

རྡོངས་པ་ *rdóṅs-pa* v. *sdóṅs-pa*.

རྡོམ་ཆང་ *rdom-čáṅ* v. *rdo-mčáṅ*.

རྡོར་ *rdor* 1. in compound words for *rdó-rje*. — 2. n. of a monastery in Tibet *Cs.* Chronolog. Table 1223 p. C. — 3. = *sdor Cs.*

རྡོལ་པ་ *rdól-pa* **a cobbler** *Cs.*, prob. = *ydól-pa*.

རྡོལ་བ་ *rdól-ba*, pf. and fut. *brdol*, vb. n. to *rtól-ba*, 1. **to come out, to break forth from, to gush forth, to issue from,** of a well of water (issuing from) *Pth.*; **to come up, to sprout, to shoot,** of seed; **so ma dol** *W.* the teeth are not yet cutting; *k̒óṅ-nas rdól-bai glu* a song streaming forth from within *Mil.*; *mi-nad rdól-žiṅ* diseases breaking out among men *Mil.*; **to flow** or **run off,** of the water of a lake; *kloṅ rdól-ba* to come forth, to proceed from the middle or the midst of *Glr.* (the meaning of this passage is not quite clear); *rdol-yzér* an instrument for boring metals *Sch.* — 2. of vessels: **to leak, to be not tight, to have holes,** *snod žabs-brdól* a vessel with a leaky bottom *Thgy.*; also of shoes, covers, tent-cloth etc. not being watertight; **to break, to burst,** of ulcers, wounds; *glo-rdol Med.* v. *gló-ba*; *rdol-ynyán Sch.*: 'fistula; gonorrhea'. — 3. **to rave, to delirate; to be sleep-walking, lunatic,** also *bla rdól(smrá)-ba Lex*,, where it is explained by *bab-čól*; *ynyid-rdól*, *mig-rdól C.* id.

རྡོས་པ་ *rdós-pa* 1. sbst., *Cs.* = *ydos*; *lus rdos-čé Lex.* w.e. — 2. vb. n. *Sch.*: **'to break, burst, flow out,** *dbú-ba*, or *lbú-ba* the bursting of a bubble'.

ལྡ་… *lda* … *Ld.* frq. for *kla* …, *gla* …, *zla* …

ལྡ་གུ་ *ldá-gu* **discourse, speech, conversation**; *W.*: **ldá-gu tán-ċe** **to speak**; **ldá-gu šé-ċe med** one cannot understand what is spoken or said; *ldá-gu-ċan* **talkative** *Cs.*

ལྡ་མན་ *lda-mán*, *Ld.-Glr. dha-mán*, **a couple of small kettle-drums**, one hanging in front, the other behind, the latter being beaten by a second person that follows the bearer.

ལྡ་ལྡི་ *lda-ldí* a kind of ornament of silk or cotton, **a fringe** or **tassel**, *dár-gyi*, *rin-po-ċei*, esp. worn in sacrificing, *Lex.*

ལྡག་པ་ *ldág-pa*, pf. *bldags*, fut. *bldag*, imp. *ldog*, **to lick**, *k̔rag* blood; *klad ldág-pa* the brain being licked up, a punishment of hell *Thgy.*; *ná-bza-la*, or *-nas* to lick a person's coat *Mil.*; **ldag-ldog** *W.* = *p̔e-srul*, lit. **'a lick'**, i.e. a pap prepared of *rtsám-pa* and *ċaṅ*, licked from the fingers, or eaten with a spoon.

ལྡང་ *ldaṅ* 1. v. *ldáṅ-ba*. — 2. for *ɣdaṅ* **stand, frame, trestle**. — 3. *W.* **ldaṅ-ldáṅ-la kur** carry it lengthways! opp. to *p̔red*; **ldaṅ-ldáṅ-la dád-ċe** to rock with one's chair.

ལྡང་མགོ་ *ldáṅ-mgo* **the yarn-beam** of a loom *Sch.*

ལྡང་སྒོ་སྐ་ *ldáṅ-sgo-ska*. *Ssk.* शरभ, *Fouc. Gyatch.* २६८; if the text is correct, it would seem preferable to connect *ri-dags* with *ldáṅ-sgo-ska*, and to render it: 'the animal Sarabha', a fabulous eight-footed creature of the snowy mountains.

ལྡང་བ་ *ldáṅ-ba*, pf. *ldaṅs* or *laṅs*, imp. *ldoṅ*, 1. vb. n. to *sláṅ-ba*, **to rise, to get up** (cf. the more frq. secondary form *láṅ-ba*), *ₒgyél-ba-las* from a fall *Wdṅ.*; *nyál-las* from a lying position *Lex.*; *stán-las* from a seat; *ťo-ráṅs* in the morning *Lt.*; *ṅó-mi-šes-pa-la* before, or in presence of a stranger; also used of the bristling of the hair, *Lt.*, of the rising of vapours, perfumes, dust, of a wind springing up; **to extend, to spread**, *dri ṅán-pa p̔yogs bċur ldaṅ* an offensive smell is spreading in every quarter *Tar.*; *ₒk̔rúgs-pa dbús-nas* the rebellion (spread) from the province of Ü, *Ma.*; **to break out**, *mé-ro ldaṅ* the smothered flame breaks out again; in a special sense of morbid matter that has accumulated (*ɣsóg-pa*) *Med.* frq., e.g. *k̔a-zás žú-nas ldaṅ* during digestion the symptoms break out anew; *dgrá-ru ldáṅ-ba* to show one's self an enemy, to break out into hostilities frq.; **to arise, originate, break out**, of disease, despair, *Mil.*; also for: **to have risen, to stand**, but only in certain combinations, *ldaṅ dub byéd-pa* tired from having been standing (so long) *Lt.* — 2. *W.* **to suffice, to be sufficient, enough** (cf. *loṅ-ba*) = *ₒk̔yéd-pa*, of food, clothes, money; hence *ldaṅ*: **complete, perfect, entire, whole**, **ras náṅ-ša rág-ma gos ldaṅ ċig** cotton cloth with lining (sufficient) for a whole dress; **ḍú-gu gos ldaṅ nyis** woolen yarn for two complete dresses. — *ldaṅ* prob. signifies also quite through, cf. *ltaṅ* II.; *ldaṅ-tsád* occurs in medical works, and in many cases seems to imply **quantity**; *neu-ldáṅ* *Lex.* = *na-mnyám* of the same age (*Sch.* not corr.).

ལྡད་པ་ *ldád-pa* 1. vb. pf. and fut. *bldad*, imp. *ldod*, **to chew** *Zam.*, *W.*; *skyug-ldád* *Cs.*, v. *skyug bldeg-ċiṅ ldad-pa* (?) *Sch.* to chew the cud, to ruminate; *log* *Cs.* 1. id., 2. rumination, deliberate reflection; *Pur.*: **spá ldad-ċas** to taste, to try; *Ld.*: **ḍi ldad-ċe** to smell at. — 2. *Ld.* for *gládpa*

ལྡན་པ་ *ldán-pa* I. sbst., also *mdán-pa* *Lex.*, **cheek**, *ldán(-pai) so* cheek-tooth, molar tooth; *ldan-lċág* *Cs.* a blow on the cheek, a box on the ear; **dẹn-tsóg** *C.* id.; **mi dhé-la dẹ́n-tsog gyag* (or *gyab*) *soṅ, mi dhe dẹ́n-tsog-ghī máṅ-po duṅ soṅ** his ears have been soundly boxed; metaph. *grog-ldán* the cheek or side of a ravine *Mil. nt.*

II. vb. and adj. 1. originally: **to be near to, hard by**, a thing, (juxta), hence *W.* **ldán-la, ldán-du**, adv. and postp., **near to, by**, **ṅẹ ldán-la dug** sit down by my side; **šíṅ-gi ldán-du** close by the tree; **ṅai ldán-du šog** come near to me! **gám-mi ldán-du** near the box; **ťser-máṅ-ṅi ldán-la ḍúl-ċe** to go along the side of a hedge. — 2. in *B.* and *C.* only used with reference to possession (penes), mostly as partic. or adj., and construed like *bčás-pa*, **having, being possessed of, provided with**, = *čan* (which in *W.* is almost exclusively used in this sense). The objects may be things of any description, also physical and mental properties, so that *ldán-pa* differs in this respect from *bčás-pa* (*Tar.* 136, 14. 15); *nor dan ldán-pa* rich, wealthy; *sems-čan dan ldán-pa* with child; *bu dan bu-mor-ldán-pa* having children; *rig-pa dan ldán-pa* wise; with a negative: *nor dan mi ldán-pa*; *dan ldan-par ˏgyúr-ba* **to get, to obtain**, frq.; *ldán-du lén-pa Glr.* 101, 1 is stated to mean the same. Poetically, and forming part of certain expressions and names, without *dan* and *pa*, like *čan: nor-ldán, dga-ldán, ˏbyor-ldán.* — 3. *ldán-pa* and *ldan dan ˏdús-pa* seem to imply: **mixed, compound** (opp. to *rkyán-pa*) with regard to temper and disposition of mind *S.g.* — 4. **to add up, sum up**, *Wdk.* — 5. *W.* **gún-ka tsúg-pa ldan yin** it will be **enough**, it will hold out, till winter-time, prob. only a corruption of *ldán-ba.* — 6. *Pur.* = *ˏgrig*, **regularly, properly, duly, rightly.**

ལྡན་(པ་)པོ་ *ldán(-pa)-po* one that has, that is able, a man of ability *Cs.*

ལྡན་མ་ *ldán-ma* n. of a country *Ma.*

ལྡན་ཚད་ *ldan-tsád* equivalent to *ˏdus-tsád Mńg.* 35 (?).

ལྡབ་ལྡིབ་ *ldab-ldib* (*skad*) *Lex.* **silly talk, tittle-tattle.**

ལྡབ་ལྡོབ་ *ldab-ldób Lex.* w.e., *Cs.* **indolence, dullness, drowsiness**; acc. to others, **a hasty, volatile manner.**

ལྡབ་པ་ *ldáb-pa*, pf. *bldabs*, fut. *bldab*, imp. *ldob*, 1. *Cs.* **to do again, to repeat**; *skyár-ldáb Lex., Sch.:* **repeatedly, anew, afresh, again**; *nyis-ldáb Lex., Sch.:* for the second time, doubly, twice; **čú-(l)dab de san čén-mo yod* W.* it is ten times as large as that, yet cf. *ltáb-pa*; **ldáb-ste zér-na* W.* saying it once more, again, in short. — 2. ? *Ld.: *ldab zúm-te kyer** take a firm hold of him (or it) with your hand, and carry him (or it) **away!**

ལྡམ་ལྡམ་ *ldam-ldám Cs.*, *ldam-pa*, **very idle, slothful.**

ལྡམ་ལྡུམ་ *ldam-ldúm Cs.:* **'mean, pitiful, sorry, idle'.**

ལྡམ་ལྡེམ་ *ldam-ldém Ld.* **dubious, uncertain,** used of things.

ལྡར་བ་ *ldár-ba Cs.* **to be weary, tired, faint, languid**, *ldar-ldár-du ˏgyúr-ba.*

ལྡི་རི་རི་ *ldi-ri-ri* (v. *ldír-ba*) **the rolling of thunder** *Thgr.*

ལྡིག་པ་ *ldíg-pa* **to fall** or **sink through** *Sch.*

ལྡིང་བ་ *ldín-ba* **to be swimming, floating**, cf. *rkyál-ba*, *W.: *čáń-ni ka-tóg-la pabs ldin dug**, opp. to **til-la ner* or *nub;** **to be suspended, floating, soaring** (in the air), *γnám-la, nám-mka-la*; *mká-ldin* v. *mka.*

ལྡིང་ཁ་ *ldin-ka* v. *ltín-ka.*

ལྡིང་ཁང་ *ldín-kan* **a bower** formed by the branches of a tree, **the leafy canopy** of a dense wood *Mil.*; *šin γyú-lo rgyás-pai ldin-kan* the wide shady porches of turkois-leaved trees.

ལྡིང་དཔོན་ *ldin-dpon* an officer over fifty, acc. to others, over a hundred men, = *brgyd-dpon*, a sergeant, captain, distinguished by a copper button on his cap, *Hook.* II, 160. 200.; *ldin-ˏog Sch.*, *ldin-tso*, the troop under this officer's command.

ལྡིང་སེ་ *ldín-se*, or *ldin-si Ld.*, adv. **quite, very, very much**, **na ldín-se kams zán-po yod** I am quite well; **na ldín-se ma ˏtád son** I was very much displeased, very vexed; perh. also **ldins tág-pa-nas** for *γtin*, cf. *líns-pa*, or perh. in *Ld. ldin* is the form for *γtin.*

ལྡིབ་པ་ *ldib-pa* 1. vb., pf. *bldib*, *Sch.* = *ldíg-pa.* — 2. adj. *Cs.:* **not clear, not intelligible**, **ka-dib* W.* **stammering, stuttering**; *ldib-ldib* = *ldab-ldib.*

ལྡིམ་ *ldim W.* **the crash** of a falling tree, **the report** of a gun, **ldim zér-ra rag** I hear a crack.

ལྡིར་ལྡིར་ *ldir-ldir* is said to be = **di-ri-ri* C.*

ལྡིར་བ་ *ldír-ba* 1. also *ltír-ba*, **to be distended, inflated, to belly;** *lto-ldír* a big belly; *ltó-ldir-čan* big-bellied. — 2. **to rush, to roar,** of the wind *W.;* **to roll,** of the thunder, *°brag ldir* it thunders; *ldir bžin* like thunder; *ldir-sgra* a thundering, roaring noise; *ldír-čé-ba* thundering *Thgr.*

ལྡུ་གུ་ *ldú-gu* = *γdú-ba, γdú-gu.*

ལྡུག(ས)་པ་ *ldúg(s)-pa*, pf. *ldugs* (*Lex.*), *blugs* (usual form), fut. *blug*, imp. *blug(s)*, col. *blug-pa*, **to pour,** *snód-du*; *lág-ču blugs* pour some water on my hands, give me water for washing; **to sprinkle,** to strew, sand *Glr.*; **to cast, to found,** metals. Cf. *blugs* and *lugs.*

ལྡུད་པ་ *ldúd-pa*, pf., fut. and imp. *blud*, col. *blúd-pa*, **to give to drink, to water,** cattle etc., with accus. of the drink given, *dug blúd-čiṅ mi °či* he does not die by a poisoned draught, *btúṅ-ba blud* he gives (him) to drink *Thgr.*; *túg-pa légs-par blúd-čiṅ* making (another) eat plenty of soup *Lt.*; as one also says: *túg-pa °túṅ-ba* to eat soup.

ལྡུམ་ *ldum* 1. **vegetables, greens,** in general. — 2. *W.* **lettuce, salad;** *ldum-nág*, a kind of lettuce *Cs.*; *ldúm-bu* 1. *Cs.* **plant, stalked plant.** 2. prob. for *ldóm-bu Mil.;* 3. *C.* vulgar pronunciation for *sdóṅ-po.* — — *ldúm-ra* 1. *W.* **kitchen-garden;** 2. **fruit-garden, orchard,** and 3. esp. **flower-garden** (better *sdúm-ra*); *ldúm-ra-pa* **gardener** *Pth.*

ལྡུམ་པོ་, ལྡུམ་ལྡུམ་ *ldúm-po, ldum-ldúm*, 1. for *dúm-po Glr.;* 2. *Ld.* for *zlúm-po*, **round;** *Mil.* also *ldúm-la °gríl-ba* made round, rounded off.

ལྡུར་ལྡུར་ *ldur-ldúr Lex.*; *Sch.:* **roaring, rushing.**

ལྡེ་ *lde? Lexx. miṅ(-gi)-lde* w. e.; *lde-ka Sch.:* '**belonging together, of the same species**'.

ལྡེ་གུ་, ལྡེའུ་ *lde-gu, ldeu Med.* 1. *Cs.* **mixture, syrup** (?); 2. **ointment** *Wdṅ.*

ལྡེ་བ་ *ldé-ba* (*Sch.* also *°dé-ba*), pf. *(b)ldes*, fut. *blde*, imp. *ldes*, **to warm one's self,** c. accus., *me*, at the fire; *nyi-ma*, in the sun (not *me-la*).

ལྡེ་མིག་ *lde-mig B.* and *C.* (*Ts.* col. **de-mág* Bal.* **le-mig*, otherwise not in use in *W.*) 1. **key,** *lde-čáb Glr.* prob. id. — 2. **introduction, preface** *Cs.*

ལྡེའུ་ *ldeu* 1. *Cs.* also *sdeu*, a kind of **pease,** *Hind.* मुङ्ग — 2. v. *lde-gu.*

ལྡེག་པ་ *ldég-pa* (pf. *bldeg?*) **to quake, shake, tremble,** e. g. of the palace of the gods *Dzl.*

ལྡེང་ཀ་ *ldéṅ-ka, ldiṅ-ka*, v. *ltéṅ-ka*, **a pond.**

ལྡེབ་ *ldeb* 1. *Sch.* **leaf, sheet,** of paper; 2. = *ldebs* 1.

ལྡེབ་པ་ *ldéb-pa* 1. *Cs.* = *ldég-pa*; 2. *Sch.* **to bend round** or **back, to turn round, to double down.**

ལྡེབས་ *ldebs* 1. **side,** *Lex.* = *°dabs*, e.g. of a mountain *Sch.*, the flat side of a sword or knife *Cs.*; *rús-pai °búr-poi ldebs* by the side of, near, the protuberance of a bone. — 2. **compass, enclosure, fence** *Sch.* — 3. *C.*, *W.* **a large cloth,** in which a person is carried by several others, either by means of a pole, or by taking hold of the four corners. This mode of conveyance is called **Dandi** (डण्डी *Hindi*). — 4. in the *Wdṅ.* it seems to have still another signification.

ལྡེམ་ *ldem* 1. v. *ldém-pa* I. — 2. **statue, idolatrous image, idol,** standing upright, cf. *ldém-pa* II., *C.* — 3. **suspension-bridge** (?) *Ld.-Glr. Schl.* 17, a; v. *ldém-pa* III.

ལྡེམ་པ་ *ldém-pa* I. sbst. 1. *Cs.:* '**contrariety, opposition, irony**', which seems not to be quite inconsistent with the explanation given by *Zam.*, *draṅ-min*, as being an intentional concealing of the true sentiment. — *ldém(-po)* **riddle, enigma** (cf. *tsód-bya*); *mi-ldem, byá-ldem, bém-ldem* an enigma or allegory applied to men, to birds, to inanimate beings; *ldém-poi ṅag, ldém-γtam* **parable, allegory;** *ldem-dgóṅs Lex.* = *Ssk.* अभिसंधि, prob.: a concealed deceitful intention, *Sch.:* 'a mysterious opinion'; *ldem-rjód-pa Cs.* to say a riddle or parable, **ldem ṭad-če* W.* to propose a riddle, *ldem tsód-pa Cs.*, *čód-pa Sch.*, to solve a riddle. — 2. *W.* **a trap** (*C.* **pur-nyi**), **bi-ldém**

mouse-trap, **wa-ldém** fox-trap, **tsúg-ce** to put a trap.

II. adj. 1. (*Schr. ldém-po*) **straight, upright; tall, well-made,** *Mil.*, prob. also *Wdṅ.* — 2. partic. of III., **inconstant; unstable, variable, perishable** *Cs.*

III. vb., also *ldem-ldém-pa Sch.* **to move up and down,** striking, trembling, vibrating; *γśog-sgró ldém-pa* the clapping of wings *Mil.; ldem-ldém* **flexible, supple, elastic, pliant.**

ལྡེར་ *lder, Ts.* = *ldebs* I., *skyai ldér-la* **on the side** of a wall, **on** a wall, e.g. to paint, to scrawl; *rii lder.*

ལྡེར་བ་ *ldér-ba Cs.:* '1. **toughness, clamminess,** 2. **potter's clay**'. *lder-tso Cs.* 1. **clay,** 2. **an idol made of clay** *Mṅg.* — *ldér-sku Glr.* prob. = *ldér-tso* 2.; acc. to others: a picture on a wall. — *ldér-bzo* figures modelled of clay, **plastic work,** *ldér-bzoi lha Zam.* = *ldér-tso* 2.; *lder-bzoi-ldebs Lex.* a clay-enclosure (?) — *ldér-so Glr.* 88, 1. 2., by the context also **figure, image.**

ལྡོ་ *ldo* side, *Ld.* for *glo.*

ལྡོག་པ་ *ldóg-pa*, pf. and imp. *log*, vb. n. to *zlog-pa*, 1. **to come back, to return, to go home, to depart.** — 2. **to come again,** often with *pyir*, of diseases, = to relapse; in a specific religious sense v. *ₒbrás-bu bži*, frq.; *dgrar* to come forward again as an enemy, to renew the war (ni f.) *Mil.* — 3. **to change, to undergo a change),** as to colour, smell etc. *Med.*; *ₒgyúr-ldog*, and *ldog-ₒgyúr Mṅg.* **changeableness, inconstancy, fickleness.** — 4. **to turn away** (vb. n.) *las* from; *blo ldóg-pa* id. *Thgy.*; *ṅo ldóg-pa* v. *lóg-pa.* The partic. as adj.: *dé-las ldóg-pai* (the thing) **opposed** to that, **contrary** to it, *Wdṅ*; *go-ldóg* id. *Lt.; mgo-ldóg Lex.?* — *Sch.* has also *ldog-pyé-ba* **distinguished, different,** from each other, and *ldóg-pa* **reciprocal, mutual, each separately.** Cf. *lóg-pa.*

ལྡོང་བ་ *ldóṅ-ba* 1. vb., pf. *ldoṅs, loṅ,* **to become blind, to be blind; to be infatuated.** — 2. adj., also *ldóṅs-pa, mdóṅs-pa,* **blind; infatuated.** Cf. *lóṅ-ba.*

ལྡོང་མོ་ *ldóṅ-mo*, resp. *γsol-ldóṅ,* **a small churn,** used for preparing tea, = *gur-gúr*, v. sub *ǰa.* Cf **doṅ-dús* Ld.* **a stave;** *ldoṅ-rus?*

ལྡོང་རོས་ *ldoṅ-ros Cs.:* n. of a yellow earth, **bole, ochre,** used for staining the walls of houses; *ldoṅ-ros-sa Lt.*

ལྡོན་པ་ *ldón-pa* **to give** or **pay back, to return,** = *klón-pa, glón-pa*, esp. with *lan,* **to answer** *Dzl.*

ལྡོབ་པ་ *ldób-pa* **to apprehend quickly; to be witty, to be quick in repartee** *Cs.; ldobs-skyén Lex.*, explained by *śés-sla-ba* understanding readily?

ལྡོམ་པ་ *ldóm-pa? rag-ldóm-pa* is stated to be = *rag-lús-pa Ld.*

ལྡོམ་བུ་ *ldóm-bu*, less frq. *ldúm-bu*, often preceded by *ro-snyóms* **alms,** consisting of food; *ldóm-bu byéd-pa* to ask such alms; *ldóm-sa* alms-house, house where beggars receive food; *ldóm-bu-ba* a person living on alms, a beggar, *Mil., Pth.*

སྡང་བ་ *zdáṅ-ba*, pf. *sdaṅs*, I. **to be angry, wrathful,** *mi dgá-žiṅ sdáṅ-ste* growing angry, flying into a passion *Dzl.*; gen. c. *la:* **to hate, to be inimically disposed,** frq.; *sdáṅ-bai dgra* opp. to *byáms-pai γnyen*; *sdáṅ-bar séms-pai dgrá-bo* id. *Wdṅ.*; *kyim-mtses-kyi dgrá-sdaṅ-ba*, or *dgrá-bdo-ba* the neighbour's grudge; *sdáṅ(-bai) sems, sdáṅ-blo,* most frq. *že-sdáṅ,* **hatred, enmity, hostility, ill-will;** (cf. dug) *sdáṅ-ba tams-cád ǰig-pa* to subdue all hostile powers; *sṅar sdáṅ-ba* the former, the old hatred *Mil.*; *sdaṅ-mig Lex.* an angry look, a scowl.

II. for *γdáṅ-ba.*

སྡང་བུ་ *sdáṅ-bu* v. *γdáṅ-bu.*

སྡད་པ་ *sdád-pa* v. *sdód-pa.*

སྡམ་པ་ *sdám-pa* v. *sdóm-pa.*

སྡར་མ་ *sdár-ma* **trembling, timorous, timid** *Dzl., Zam.*

སྡི་བ་ *sdí-ba*, pf. *bsdis*, v. *sdíg-pa.*

སྡིག་ *sdig* 1. **thick** (?) *γsús-pa sdig Mṅg.* — 2. **foundation** *C.*, *rgyág-pa* to lay a foundation.

སྡིག་པ་ *sdig-pa* I. also *sdig-pa rwá-ċan*, col. **rá-tse**, **scorpion**, also as sign of the zodiac; *sdig-pa dkár-po, nág-po*; *sdig-rwá*, the sting of a scorpion; *sdig-dúg* the poison of a scorpion; *sdig-tsáṅ* a scorpion's nest; *sdig-srin* **crab, crawfish**, used both as food and medicine *Med.*, but not as designation for the respective sign of the zodiac, v. sub *k̔yim*; *sdig-srin-ₒbu Lt.* id.?

II. (पाप) **sin**, moral evil as a power, *sdig-pa-la yid-čes-pa Dzl.* ༢༧༣, 11 to believe in sin as such; *ₒjóms-pa* to conquer sin, as something hostile to man *Dom.*, and so meton. = sinners, adversaries; sometimes perh. for **sinfulness**, sinful state, but gen. in a concrete sense: **offence, trespass**, in thought, word, or deed, *k̔a-na-ma-t̔ó-bai sdig-pa*, or *nyés-pa* prob. a grievous sin *Dzl.*; also with a genit., *rgyál-poi sdig-pa sbyóṅ-ba* to wash away, to expiate, the king's sin; also *ₒdág-pa, sél-ba*, *W.* **ċád-ċe**; *ₒbyáṅ-ba* id., but more in an intransitive or passive sense; so also *ₒčágs-pa* (*γšág-pa, bšags-pa*) to confess, as acc. to Buddhist views, confession is almost tantamount to expiation of sin, cf. also *ₒgyód-pa* and *bzód-pa;* there seems to be, however, no word strictly corresponding to our 'forgiving' of sin; *sdig-(pai)-las* a sinful deed; *sdig-pa-la dgá-ba* **to love sin, to be wicked**; *sdig-(pai) grogs* a companion in vice, an associate in crime *Dzl.*; *sdig-pa byéd-pa, spyód-pa*, **to commit sin, to sin**; *sdig-pa mi byéd-pai yul* a country where no sins are committed, a pious country; *sdig-byéd, sdig-spyód* **impious, wicked; a wicked person**, *sdig-pa-rnams byás-pa* id. (more accurately: πολλὰ ἡμαρτηκώς) *Stg.*; *sdig-ċan* id. (*sdig-pa-ċan* seems not to be in use); *sdig-sgrib* the filth, the contamination of sin, *sdig-sgrib t̔ams-ċád sél-ba* to cleanse from every defilement of sin *Glr.* (which the Ommanipadmehūm is sufficient to do); *sdig-po* **a sinner, a bad character**, *sdig-po če* a vile sinner *Glr., Mil.*; *rdig-to-ċan*, पापोच, = *sdig-ċan*, but only as epithet of Dud; *sdig-blón* a wicked officer *Glr.*

སྡིག(ས)་པ་ *sdig(s)-pa*, pf. *bsdigs*, fut. *bsdig*, imp. *sdigs*, and *sdi-ba*, pf. *bsdis*, ft. *bsdi*, 1. **to show, to point out**, *sdigs-mdzúb* a pointing finger, ... *la sdigs-mdzúb γtád-pa* to point at... (with scorn or derision); *sdigs-mdzúb nám-mk̔a-la γtad* pointing with the fingers toward heaven, yet not in a 'menacing' (*Cs.*) way. — 2. **to aim** *C.*, *bsdi(g)s-sa* the place that is aimed at, **aim, butt; goal** *Thgy.*; *bsdis-pai p̔yógs-su* in the direction of the aim *Thgy.* — 3. **to menace, to threaten**, *čád-pas* with punishment *Mil.* (ni f.); **dig-ċe ṗi-la** *Ld.* as an alarm-shot; *ₒdi-la bdág-gis ₒjigs-pa žig-gis ma bsdigs-na* if I do not threaten him with something frightful, if I do not strike him with fear, *Dzl.*; *sdigs-mo byéd-pa* to assume a menacing attitude *Mil.*, to threaten tauntingly *Thgy.*

སྡིངས་ *sdiṅs* **a cavity** or **depression**, *spáṅ-sdiṅs* a depression on a grassy plain, *ri-sdiṅs* on a mountain-ridge; the significations given by *Cs.*, 'middle part, heart, core', were not known to our men of Tashilunpo.

སྡིབ་པ་ *sdib-pa* 1. *Sch.* = *ldib-pa*. — 2. *Tar.* 8,18 = *rtib-pa*.

སྡུག་པ་ *sdúg-pa* I. adj. **pretty, nice**, *ltá-na* to look at *Dzl.*; **tsa-dhi-dúg-pa** *C.* **mint**, Mentha, ἡδύοσμον; gen. with reference to a person: what is **agreeable, pleasing, dear**, to a person *Ssk.*: **प्रिय**, *bdág-gi bu náṅ-gi sdúg-pa-la* the most beloved of my sons *Dzl.*; *ṅai bu sdug* my dear son *Pth.*; *sdúg-par ₒdzin-pa Dzl., sém-pa Dzl.* frq., *rtsi-ba Mil.*, to love, c. dat., gen. with regard to parental love; *sdúg-par ₒgyúr-ba* to become dear to a person, to be endeared to, *Dzl.*; *mi-sdúg-pa* **not fair, ugly, disagreeable**, of the body, of a country etc.; *mi-sdúg-pai tiṅ-ṅe-ₒdzin Tar.* 10, 11 contemplating one's self and the world as a foul, putrid carcass (v. *Tar.* Transl. 285, foot of the page); *mi-sdúg-par byéd-pa* to disfigure, pollute, profane, a temple *Dzl.*; *sdúg-gu* beautiful, pretty, handsome, *bud-méd sdúg-gu t̔ams-čad* all pretty women *Dzl.*; there is also a form for the fem. gender: *sdúg-*

gu-ma Dzl.; sdú-ge-ba Cs.: 'the state of being somewhat pleasing'(?); in a prayer occurs: *bod-báṅs sdúg-ge snyiṅ-re-rjé* the good, poor Tibetans, just as in W. **sdug-pa-ṫsé** is used; often (but not necessarily) rather pityingly: *k'o sdug-pa-ṫsé* the good man (will do his utmost); **ri-pa sdug-pa-ṫsé** the good fieldmouse (speedily made off); but also: **sab dug-pa-ṫsé ā-lu ẑig toṅ* W.* good sir, give me a few potatoes!

II. vb. **to be oppressed, afflicted, grieved,** like *γdúṅ-ba, sems lás-kyis sdúg-nas* by sorrow *Mil.; *sem máṅ-po máṅ-po dug soṅ* C.* I was very, very sorry for it; ... *pas sdúg-go* we are miserable, because ... *Dzl.*; *sdúg-par ₒgyúr-ba* to become unhappy, to get into distress *Dzl.*

III. sbst., *Ssk.* दुःख, **affliction, misery, distress,** *bod sdúg-pai mgo ₒdzugs* that is the beginning of the misfortunes of Tibet *Ma.; ṅéd-la sdúg-pai ré-mos bab* (then) came our turn of being visited by affliction *Mil.*; more frq. *sdug*, and *sdug-bsṅál* (v. below) *sdúg-tu mi yoṅ ₒdug-gam* are you not in distress? *Mil.*; *sdug k'ur byéd-pa* **to undergo hardships** (voluntarily), to bear affliction (patiently), to suffer, in an emphatical sense, *Mil.; sdug mi ṫeg* you cannot endure the hardships *Mil.; *ka-dúg máṅ-po ǰhé'-pa* C.* to work hard, to drudge; *skyid-sdúg* good and adverse fortune, good luck and ill luck, very frq.; *bde-sdúg* id.; *sdug-sógs byéd-pa* (the contrary to *ṫsogs-sógs byéd-pa*) to accumulate misery upon one's self *Mil.*; **dug máṅ-po táṅ-wa* C.* to plague or vex a good deal, to inflict injury, c. *la*; *γẑan-sdúg-gi sdig-pa* the sin of having done evil to others *Mil.*; **dug zǿ'-la táṅ-wa* C.* **to torture, to put to the rack;** *sdug ₒbáb-pa* **to be in mourning** *Cs.; sdug srúṅ-ba* **to mourn** *Cs.*; *sdúg-ċan* col. **fatiguing, worrying.** — *sdug* as adj., **unhappy, miserable,** *Pth.*, is of rare occurrence.

Comp. and deriv. *sdug-k'áṅ* **a chamber of mourning,** a darkened room *Cs.* — *sdug-gós* **a mourning dress** *Cs.* — *sdug-bsṅál* the most frq. word for **misfortune, misery, suffering;** also **pain,** *sdug-bsṅál-gyis γdúṅs-pa Dzl., sdug-bsṅál myóṅ-ba* (*W. *ṫóṅ-ċe**) to be in calamity, to suffer pain; **dug-ṅál tóṅ-wa, tér-wa* C.* (**tán-ċe* W.*), to inflict pain, to grieve, to torment; *sdug-bsṅal daṅ ldán-pa, sdug-bsṅál-ċan* **unhappy, miserable; misery, distress, affliction;** **dug-ṅál ǰhé'-pa* C.* to lament, wail, moan; *sdug-bsṅál-du ₒgyúr-ba* to become sorrowful or melancholy; **ṅá-la ná-ga-ri ma ŝés-pe dug-ṅál yod* Ld.* I regret my not knowing Sanskrit; *sdug-bsṅál-ba* (vb.) **to be unhappy,** (sbst.) **the state of unhappiness,** *Thgy.*; *sdug-bsṅál-bai skad* lamentable, doleful cries. — *sdug-mṫúg C.* accumulating calamity. — *sdug-ₒdré* a demon *Sch.* — **dúg-po* C.* **wretched** (road), **savage** (dog), **ill-bred, naughty, unamiable; evil** (sbst.), *dúg-po byéd-pa* to do evil *Mil.*; **mí-la dúg-po táṅ-wa* C.* to do evil to a person, to molest, trouble, annoy, injure, a person. — *sdug-ṗóṅs-pa Stg., C.,* **poor.** — *sdug-ẑwa* a mourning-hood *Cs.* — *sdug-srán* inured to hardships; the being hardened *Mil.*

སྡུད་ *sdud* 1. *Sch.*: the **folds** of a garment; *sdúd-k'a* string for drawing together the opening of a bag, **drawing-hem.** — 2. *Cs.* **synthesis,** *ₒbyed-sdúd* analysis and synthesis.

སྡུད་པ་ *sdúd-pa*, pf. *bsdus*, fut. and likewise for the pres. tense) *bsdu*, imp. *sdus, bsdu*, vb.a. to *ₒdú-ba*, 1. **to collect, gather, lay up, amass, assemble,** riches, flowers, broken victuals, taxes, crops, earnings, men, cattle etc., frq.; **to put together, to compile,** *míṅ-rnams ... nas bsdus* the names have been put together out of ... *Glr.*; **to brush or sweep together,** *W.*: **k'yim-sa ǟl-mo-ne* (or *daṅ*)* the dust with a broom; *dbáṅ-du* **to subject, subdue,** frq. — 2. **to unite, join, combine,** *ŝiṅ γsum mgo* three pieces of wood at their upper ends *Dzl.*; six kingdoms into one *Dzl.* (to join) actions, words, and thoughts in the path of virtue *Dzl.*; *dmág-rnams k'ór-du* (joining) the troops with his retinue *Dzl.*; *k'yo-ŝúg-tu* to unite in matrimony, to give in marriage. — 3. **to condense, to comprise,** all moral precepts in three main points, the letters of the alphabet in five classes *Gram.*; esp. with *nyúṅ-ṅur,* *zúr-tsam*, **to contract, compress, abridge**, frq., *de yaṅ bsdú-na* if one shortens it still more, if it is abridged a second time *Gram.*; **dús-kan** *W.* **brief, concise, compendious;** **dú-yig** *C.* **abbreviation, abridgment;** *bsdus-ˏgrel* an abridged commentary *Tar.* 177,7; **to close, conclude, finish, terminate,** *mjug sdúd-pa* to close a train, opp. to *sna ˏdrén-pa Mṅg.*; *slár-bsdu-ba* concluding a sentence or period with the finite verb in *o*, *Gram.* — 4. *bsdús-pa* **to consist of** or **in**, c. instrum., e.g. *yi-ge drug-gis* of six letters *Thgy.* — 5. **to boil down, to inspissate** *Lt.*, *bsdús-ku*, *ydús-ku*, a preparation thus obtained *Med.*; *bsdus-ťáṅ* prob. id. *Med.* — 6. scil. *bsód-nams: bsdú-ba rnam bži* the four ways of collecting merit *Glr.* — 7. *dbugs sdúd-pa Med.?* *bsdú-ba* sbst. **collection, gathering** *Tar.* 33, 16. — *bsdus-yžom* or *ˏjom Schr.*: a machine for executing criminals constructed in such a manner, that the head is crushed by two stones striking together; *Stg.*: n. of one of the hells

སྡུམ་པ་ *sdúm-pa* 1. vb., pf. *bsdums*, fut. *bsdum*, imp. *sdum(s)*, vb.a. to *ˏdúm-pa*, **to make agree, to bring to an agreement,** *mi-mtún-pa-rnams* things not agreeing *Sch.*, **to reconcile, to conciliate,** *mi-mdzá-ba-rnams* enemies *Thgy.*; *sdúm-par byéd-pa* id.; *sdum-byéd* (resp. *mdzad*), *sdúm(-pa)-po*, *sdúm-mkan*, **conciliator, pacifier, peace-maker;** *res ˏkrúgs-pa res bsdúm-pa màṅ-du byúṅ-ṅo* at one time they were at odds, at another they were at peace with one another *Tar.* — 2. sbst. **house, mansion** *C.*; *yzim-sdum* (resp.) **bed-room;** *sdúm-ra* garden near the house, cf. *ldúm-ra*.

སྡུར་བ་ *sdúr-ba*, pf. and fut. *bsdur*, **to compare,** *go-sdúr byéd-pa* id., v. *go* 2; *nyams sdur byéd-pa C.* to compare different texts; **tam-dúr** *W.* **judicial examination, trial.**

སྡུར་ལེན་, སྡུར་བླང་ *sdur-lén*, *sdur-blaṅ*, **amber** *Ts.*, for *sbur-lén*.

སྡེ་ *sde* (*Ssk.* in compound words सेना) **part, portion,** of a whole, e.g. of a country, also *yúl-sde*, **province, district, territory,** even **village** *C.*, *bón-sde* the places or villages of the Bonpas *Glr.*; *sde-čeṅ-la myég-pa* to aim at an extension of territory *Dom.*; part of the human race: **nation, people, tribe, clan, community,** *pá-rol-gyi sde ˏjóms-pa* to conquer hostile nations; **class,** e.g. of letters: phonetical class; *sde sder bgó-ba* to divide into classes *Cs.*; classes of books: *mdó-sde* the Sūtras, v. sub *mdo*; *rgyúd-sde* the Tantras, v. sub *rgyud; sbyór-sde bži* the four volumes treating of pharmacy *Glr.*; of monks: community of monks, body of conventuals (consisting of not less than four persons); hence **convent, monastery,** *sde btsugs* he founded convents *Glr.*; *čos-sde* id.; class of religious followers, philosophical school, *sde bži* the four (principal) schools *Tar.*; *lha srin-gyi sde brgyad, lha klú-la sógs-pai sde brgyad* the eight classes of spirits, frq.; it is also used for **a great quantity, great many, lots of;** and by improper use, or by way of abbreviation for *sdé-pa*, *sde-dpon*, commander, ruler.

Comp. and deriv. *sde-skór Glr.* **district.** — *sde-krugs* **insurrection,** general revolt of a people, *byéd-pa* to excite one *Ma.* — *sde-snód ysum*, **त्रिपिटक**, **'the three baskets',** viz. the three classes of the sacred Buddhist writings, *ˏdúl-bai* (discipline), *mdo-sdéi* (Sūtras), *sṅágs-kyi sde-snód* (Mantras, i.e. metaphysics and mysticism), hence *sde-snód-la sbyáṅ-ba* to study the sacred writings *Mil.* — *sdé-pa* 1. **the chief** or **governor** of a district *C.*, = *ˏgó-pa W.*, **majordomo** of the Dalai Lama, *Köpp.* II., 134; in a general sense: **a man of quality, a nobleman** *Ma.* 2. **a letter** of a certain phonetic class, or the phonetic class itself, *sdé-pa bži-pa* the fourth phonetic class, the labials *Gram.* So the word is also used for denoting a certain class or **school** of Buddhist philosophers, *Tar.*, frq. — *sde-dpón* = *sdé-pa* 1, signifies also a class of **demons** *Dom.* — *sde-tsán* **class,** e.g. phonetic class, = *sde*; a particular kind of writing, *ná-ga-ri sde-tsán Glr.*; — *sde-yzár Sch.* **lawlessness, anarchy,** *sde-yzár čén-po* general anarchy (?) — *sde-yaṅs* (spelling?) **court, court-yard,** = *kyams.* — *sde-rigs* **dominion, territory,**

Glr. — *sde-srid* 1. **province, kingdom** *Cs.* 2. **regent, administrator**, in more recent times title of the *sdé-pa* of the Dalai Lama, and the rulers of Bhotan. *Köpp.* II., 154.

སྡེ་བ་ *sde-ba*(?) *W.* **ì-ru dé-če med** there is here no room any more.

སྡེབ་ *sdeb* (*? ˳debs*) **time, times**, = *lan W.*, e.g. four times.

སྡེབ་པ་ *sdéb-pa*, pf. *bsdebs*, fut. *bsdeb*, imp. *sdebs*, 1. **to mingle, mix, blend** (*ǰyogs*) *γčig-tu* together, *Lex.*, cf. *sbyir-ba.* — 2. **to join, unite, combine,** *drás-su sdéb-pa Mil.*, by the context: sewed well together, — but *drás-su?* — Gen. vb.n.: **to join, to unite,** *dan* with, also *la*, *sems mig dan bsdébs-nas lta, rná-ba dan bsdébs-nas nyan Mil.* the soul sees by joining the eye, it hears by joining the ear; **to join company, to associate, to hold intercourse with,** *Mil.*; also to have sexual intercourse *Pth.*, cf. *˳dré-ba, ˳grógs-pa, dzóm-pa.* — 3. **to prepare, dress, get ready** (victuals) *Sch.*, cf. *sbyór-ba.* — 4. **to exchange, barter, truck for,** **bág-p̀e ḍás-la* W.* flour for rice; in this sense prob. also used by *Mil.*; **to change,** money, **nul deb sal** please change me a rupee (not so in *C.*). — 5. **to make poetry, to compose verses,** at the end of poems: *žés-pa . . . kyis sdéb-pao* the above verses have been composed by . . .; = *sbyór-ba.*

སྡེབ་སྦྱོར་ *sdeb-sbyór* 1. **composition,** esp. poetical, **poetry,** — 2. *yi-gei sdeb-sbyór* **orthography** *Schr.*, *Cs.*, *Sch.*

སྡེར་མ་ *sdér-ma*, resp. *γsol-sdér*, **dish, platter, plate, saucer**; *sder-gáṅ* a plateful, a dish (of meat etc.), esp. *C.*

སྡེར་(མོ) *sdér(-mo)* **claw, talon,** *sdér-kyu Sch.* id.; *sdér-mo rno* a sharp claw; *sdér-čan* furnished with claws, *sder-méd* without claws; *sder-˳dzin byéd-pa* to seize with the claws *Cs.*; *stag(-gi)-sdér* a tiger's claw *Lt.*; *sder-čágs* animals provided with claws *Mil.*

སྡོ་ཁམ་ *sdo-k'ám Sch.* **belonging together, a pair**(?).

སྡོ་བ་ *sdó-ba*, pf. (*b*)*sdos*, fut. *bsdo*, imp. *sdos* (also *dó-ba* q. v.) 1. **to risk, hazard, venture,** gen. c. *dan*, also c. dat. or accus., *bdág-gi lus* one's own body *Dom.*; *lus srog dan* frq., *lus dan sróg-la Dzl.* — 2. **to bear up against,** *sdug-bsṅal*, *nyon-móṅs-pa dan*, against heavy trials, against toil and drudgery *Dzl.*; **to bid defiance,** to an enemy *Dzl.*, also **to behave with insolence, contemptuously** *Dzl.* — 3. *lág-pas Dzl.* ༡༡༩, 6(?).

སྡོང་པོ་ *sdóṅ-po* (*C.* vulg. **dúm-po** 1. **trunk, stem, body of a tree** *Glr.* — 2. **stalk,** of a plant, *pádmai* of a lotus; *sdóṅ-po k'oṅ-stoṅ* a hollow stalk *Wdṅ.*; *sdóṅ-poi sde* the class of stalked plants *Cs.* — 3. **tree,** also *šiṅ-sdóṅ(-po)* frq.; *šiṅ-sdóṅ rkaṅ-γčig* a tree of a single stem *Glr.*; *šiṅ-sdóṅ k'oṅ-rúl* a tree rotten at the core; col. fig. barren, of females, prob. jestingly. — 4. **block, log.**

Comp. *Cs.*: *sdar-sdóṅ* trunk of a walnut-tree, *šug-sdóṅ* stem of a juniper-tree; *ts̀il-sdóṅ* **a tallow-candle;** *k'yags-sdóṅ* **an icicle.** — *mčod-sdóṅ* (*Sch.* = *mčod-rtén*), in a botanical work it was explained by 'wick', = *sdoṅ-rás*, which seems to be more to the purpose, as a blossom is compared with it. — *sdoṅ-rkáṅ* v. *sdoṅ-rás.* — *sdoṅ-dúm* **stump of a tree,** *sdóṅ-dúm ts̀ig-pa* the burnt stump of a tree *Cs.* — *sdóṅ-bu Cs.* 1. **a small trunk.** 2. **stalk.** 3. **wick.** — *sdoṅ-rás*, *sdoṅ-šiṅ*, *sdoṅ-rkáṅ C.* a wick of cotton, of wood, of pith; cotton wicks are used esp. for sacred lamps.

སྡོང་བ་, སྡོངས་པ་ *sdóṅ-ba*, *sdóṅs-pa* (*Sch.* also *rdóṅs-pa*) pf. *bsdoṅs*, fut. *bsdoṅ*, **to unite, to join** (in undertakings), **to enter into a confederacy, to associate one's self with,** c. *dan* (also accus.?); *k'yod dan ṅa sdóṅ-ste ˳gro* you and I, we will go together; *sdóṅs-zla* prob. = *zla-grógs.*

སྡོད་པ་ *sdód-pa*, pf. and fut. *bsdad*, resp. *bžés-pa*, *W.* **dád-če**, 1. **to sit,** frq., **sil-la dod** *W.* sit down in the shade! *dál-bar sdód-pa* to sit still *Lt.* — 2. **to stay, to tarry, to abide,** *t̀óg-mar der bsdad* for the present I will stay here yet a little longer *Mil.*; *nyál-nas bsdad-˳dug-pa* to lie down and to continue lying *Mil.*; **ḍǫ́-du ˳ǰúg-pa** to receive hospitably, **mi ˳ǰúg-pa** to deny reception, to send away *C.*; **to stop, to halt,** in running, walking *Dzl.*;

to wait, *re žig ma bsád-par sdód-čig* wait a little yet before beginning to kill *Dzl.*; *skád-čig kyaṅ sdód-pai loṅ méd-par* without waiting even for a moment *Glr.*; *Ld.*: **ltós-te dád-če** to wait and see whether etc.; **sám-te dád-če** to wait for, hope for, to look forward to, **gúg-te dád-če** id.; *mdó-sde ˳di ˳tsó-žiṅ sdód-na* as long as the authority of this book is acknowledged *Dom.*; **zag daṅ kyir-kyir dad dug* W.* (this thing) always remains round (crooked), it will not get straight. — 3. **to be at home,** **dẹ' yọ'** he is at home, **dẹ' me'** he is not at home *C.*; **to live, reside, settle at** *B.* and col.; *bka-sdód Lex., C.*: 1. **attendant, waiting servant,** 2. **aid-de camp.**

སྡོམ་ *sdom* 1. *Lex.* and *C.* **spider.** — 2. **summary, contents,** *spii sdom* 1. **table of contents, index** *S.g.* 2. **general introductory remarks, introduction,** also *sdom-tsig; sdóm-la* **summarily, to be brief, in short.**

སྡོམ་པ་ *sdóm-pa* I. vb., pf. *bsdams, bsdoms,* fut. *bsdam, bsdom,* imp. *sdom(s), W. *dám-če** 1. **to bind,** *lčags-sgróg-gis* **to fetter** *Cs.*; **to bind or tie fast, to pinion; to bind up, to dress,** wounds. — 2. **to fasten, to fix firmly,** e.g. by a screw-vice; *kro-čús* by melted metal, i.e. to solder; *so,* to press, grind, or strike the teeth together, **to gnash,** as in anger *Pth.*; **to fasten securely,** the door *Dzl., Pth.*; *rtsá-ka* **to close** an opened vein *Med.*; hence in general, 3. **to stanch, stop, to cause to cease,** *rtsa-krág šór-ba* the bloody flux *Med.*; **to bind, constrain, render harmless, to neutralize,** *nyés-pa* an evil *Lex., Sch.* — 4 *W. *káb-ša dam dug** the shoe **pinches.** — 5. to make morally firm, **to confirm,** *spyód-pa,* one's conduct, to conform it strictly to the moral law. — 6. with or without *bdag-nyid,* **to bind one's self, to engage** *Cs.* — 7. **to add together, to cast or sum up,** *rgyud bži bsdóms-pas leu* ༡༥༤ all the four Gyud together have 154 chapters; *yóṅs-su bsdús-pa-la* taking all together *Tar.*

II. sbst. **सम्वर obligation, engagement, duty,** *sdóm-pa lén-pa Glr., ˳dzin-pa Cs.,* to enter into an engagement, to bind one's self to perform a certain duty, *mi-la ˳bógs-pa* **to bind a person by duty,** by oath, **to swear in** *Glr.* (e.g. in convents, in the relations of priests and laymen); *srúṅ-ba* to be true to one's duty, to keep one's engagements; *˳čor* a duty is violated *Glr.*; *ṅá-la sdóm-pa med* I have renounced my vow *Glr.* — *sdóm-pa ɣsum,* acc. to *Glr.* and other more recent authors, are: *so-tár* (v. *so-só*), *byaṅ-séms,* and *ɣsaṅ-sṅágs-kyi sdom-pa.*

Comp. *sdom-ltóṅ*(?) **neck-bell,** bell attached to the neck of cattle. — *sdom-byéd* 1 **one that binds,** by duty etc. 2. **an astringent medicine** *Cs.* — *sdom-ɣzér* **rivet of a pair** of scissors or tongs *Sch.*

སྡོམ་བུ་ *sdóm-bu Sch.*: **a ball; a round tassel.**

སྡོར་, རྡོར་ *sdor, rdor* 1. (like ὄψον) that which gives relish to food, **seasoning, condiment,** esp. *túg-sdor* that which gives substance to soup, viz. **meat;** *tsa-sdór* salt and meat. — 2. **spice,** *sdór-gyi rkyál-pa* spice-bag *S.g.*; *sdor-tál* spice-powder *Sch.* —

བརྡ་ *brda* (**संकेत**) **sign,** i.e. 1. **gesture,** *čágs-pa ˳dód-pai brda máṅ-du bstán-nas* making many wanton gestures (or giving hints, intimations v. 2), *lág-brda* signs with the hand, *saṅs-rgyás la ɣsól-čig čes lág-brda byas* they beckoned to him to ask Buddha *Dzl.*; **mig-da táṅ-če* W.* to give a hint with the eye, to wink. — 2. **indication, intimation, symptom, token,** *mi-rtág ˳gyúr-bai brdao* it is an indication of their frail condition *Thgy.*; **symbol** *Pth., brdar* as a symbol, symbolically; *de gaṅ yin ˳dri-bai brda stón-pa* to ask for a thing by symbolic signs, in symbolic language *Glr.*; *brda spród-pa, ˳pród-pa, sbyór-ba, ˳grol-ba* **to explain, describe, represent,** with accus., and prob. also with genit.: *yin-lugs-kyi brda ˳gról-ba Mil.* to explain the essence or nature of things (ni f.); meton. *dei brda či lags* what may be the symbolical meaning of it *Mil.* — 3. **word,** *˳bód-pai brda* interjection *Lis.*; *˳dúl-bai brda* word out of the Dulwa *Zam.*; *dris-pai brda-rnyiṅ* an obsolete word for 'being asked', *Lex.*; *brdá-sgyur-pa Sch.* **interpreter, dragoman** *Sch.*; *brdai blá-ma* is stated to be a Lama who instructs by word of mouth *Mil.*; esp. with regard to the spelling of words: *brda yaṅ mi ˳dra sna-ts̒ogs gyur* there came also into use various spellings *Zam.*; *brda - rnyíṅ* old orthography, *brda-γsár* new orthography *Zam.*; *bód-kyi brdai bstan-bčós* title of the Zamatog; *ts̒ig-brda* = *ts̒ig*, *ts̒ig-brda-yis ˳grol-ba* to explain by words *Mil.*

Comp. *brdá-skad* **language by symbolical signs** *Mil.*; prob. also nothing but the usual language by words *Glr.* — *brda-čád* (prob. for *˳čad*, from *˳čád-pa* II.), *me-loṅ-gi brda-čád* the language or evidence of the mirror; so prob. also *Tar.* 210, 22. — *brda-spród*, *brda-sbyór* 1. **explanation**, *miṅ - dón brda-spród* explanation of the import of names, title of a small Materia Medica by a certain Wairocana. 2. **orthography** *Gram.*, *Pth.* — *brda - lon Mil.* is said to be = *ts̒ig-lan*, verbal answer. — *brda-lags* 'insignis', acc. to *Cs.* in *Journ. As. Soc. Beng.* V, 384.

བརྡུལ་བ་ *brdúl-ba* 1. *Lex.* w.e.; *Sch.* **to deceive, to cheat.** 2. *Sch.* **to swing, brandish, flourish,** *γyáb-mo* a fly-flap.

བརྡོག་འཆོས་པ་ *brdog-˳čos-pa* **to slip, to slide, to lose one's footing.**

བསྡར་བ་ *bsdár-ba*, *Sch.*: *mdún-du bsdár-ba* **to hope, to expect** or **wait for** a favour. In *Dzl.* ༡༣༨, 18 the better reading (accordant with the manuscript of Kyelang) is *sdur* (= *sdú-bar*).

བསྡོགས་པ་ *bsdógs-pa*; the *Lexx.* add: *γrabs*, *Cs.* **to compose, prepare, make ready,** *nyer bsdógs-pa* id.; *sna-ťág bsdógs-pa* to wind the rope, which is fastened in the nose of an ox or a camel, round the horns or the neck of the animal.

ན

ན *na* 1. the letter **n.** — 2. num. figure: 12.

ན་ *na* **meadow,** *C.* also *ná-ma*; *nar skye* it grows on meadows, *Wdṅ.* and elsewh. (cf. *neu*).

ན་ *na* I. sbst. 1. **year** (?) v. *ná-niṅ*. — 2. **stage of life, age,** also *na-ts̒ód*, and *ná-so*, resp. *sku-ná* (also *sku-nás?*); *na-ts̒ód rgás - pas Wdṅ.* old, of an advanced age; *ná-so γžón-te Glr.* young; *sku-nás ṕrá - mo Mil.* of a tender age; *na-ts̒ód-kyi dbyé - ba* the different ages or stages of life; (*sku-*) *nár-son-pa* (*Sch.* grown old?) *Glr.*: of full age, adult, grown up; **ná-so-ts̒ir-la** *W.* according to age; *na - čúṅ girl*, maiden, virgin, *na - čúṅ bzáṅ - mo bču* ten beautiful girls *Dzl.*; *na-mnyám*, *-˳drá*, *-zlá*, *neu-ldáṅ Lex.* of the same age, coetaneous; **ná-da-to̤m-mo** *C.* a festivity given by wealthy parents on their son's birthday to him and his playmates, also **ló-da-to̤m-mo**; *na-ṕrá young*, tender; *na-γžón* = *γžón - nu*. II. postp. c. accus., signifying the place where a thing is, 1. added to substantives, **in,** (more accurately *náṅ-na* c. genit.), sometimes also to be rendered by **on, at, with, to** etc. *mdó-na* in scripture, *lo-rgyús-na* in a book of history *Glr.*; *dé - na* there, in that place; of time: *dus-γčig-na* at the same time, *dei ts̒é-na* at that time, then etc. — 2. added to verbs, either to the inf., or more frq. (col. always) to the verbal root: **in, at, during** (the doing or happening of a thing), hence a. **when, at the time of,** *bós-na* when I called *Dzl.*, *zér-ba-na* when he said *Tar.*; *bdág-gi ṕa ts̒e ṕós-na* when my father shall have died *Dzl.*; with *nam*: *nam dús-la báb-na* (*W.* **dus léb-na**) when the time comes, frq.; *nam* *₀gró-na* when I (you etc.) go, was going, shall go. — b. **if, in case, supposing that** (*èáv*), the different degrees of possibility, however, cannot be so precisely expressed by the mood in Tibetan, as in other languages; with or without a preceding *gál-te*, *èi-ste* etc. (cf. the remarks sub *gaṅ* II.); ... *ma mťóṅ na* ... *mi rtógs-par dug* if we had not seen ..., we should not have known ... *Mil.*; but in most cases also the vb., to which it is subordinate, is put in the gerund: *₀di byás-na brám-ze ma yin-pas* as I should be no longer a Brahmin, if I were to do that *Dzl.*; further: **if even** ..., how much the more ...! in asseverations: **if** ..., then indeed may ...! then I would that ...! it is well, that ..., it will be well, if ..., *na légs-so* frq.; if *légs-so* is elliptically omitted, *na* answers to: **o that! would that!** also: **I will**; in an interrogative sentence, viz. '*légs-sam*' being omitted, to: **must I? shall I?** *Mil.*: *čos byás-na snyam* (when we are with you) we think, we will be pious! *₀jig-rtén byás-na snyam* (when we have come home) we think, let us take care of temporal things! *èi drág-na* (better *èi byás-na drag*) what shall we consider the most advantageous? — c. of a more general signification: **as, since, whilst, by** (with the partic. pres.), = *te* or *pas Dzl.* frq., *dug zós-na yaṅ* even by eating poisonous things (he was not hurt) ༢༥, 3; *na* is used thus, however, only in conjunction with *yaṅ*, and *dug zós-na yaṅ* is the more popular phrase for *dug zos kyaṅ* In careless speaking or writing *na* is also used for *èé-na Thgy.* frq. — 3. pleon. added to the termination of the instr. of substantives and verbs: *rgyu dés-na* **for that reason, therefore,** *èii rgyús-na* **for what reason, why, wherefore** *Stg.*; *dé-bas-na* **hence, thus, so then, accordingly,** very frq.; *ḱúr-bas-na* because they carried *Glr.*; also added to the termination of the termin.: *ǰi-ltar-na* frq.; *γèig-tu-na*, *γnyis-su-na*, **in the first place, firstly** etc. *Dzl.*; *skád-du-na Dzl.*; *rgya-gár skád-du-na Thgy.* — 4. incorr. for *nas*, col. frq.; its being used for the termin. is very questionable, and the rare instances of this use in books may be regarded as errors in writing (e.g. *Dzl.* ༢༥༡, 17 *náṅ-na soṅ* inst. of *naṅ-du*), whereas the contrary, *du* for *na*, occurs frq., and is to be considered as sanctioned.

III. conj. **and,** *Bul* (?) — IV. v. *ná-ḱa*, *ná-ba*.

ནཁ་ *ná-ḱa*, = *spaṅ*, **greensward, turf.**

ནཱག་ *nā-ga*, *Ssk.* for *klu.*

ནཱགརི་ *nā-ga-ri* **Sanskrit, Sanskrit-letters.**

ནགི་ *na-gi Sch.* 1. **being ill**(?). 2. **the claws of a sea-monster**(?).

ནཱགེསར་ *nā-ge-sar Lt.* = Hindi, for नागकेसर, Mesua ferrea.

ནའཛང་ *na-ǰa W.* **mock-suns** and similar phenomena, v. *na-bún*.

ནཉིང་ *ná-niṅ* (*Cs.*: 'for *na-rnyiṅ*') **the last year;** gen. adv. **last year;** *ná-niṅ-gi* adj. **of last year** or **last year's** (crop).

ནབ་ *ná-ba* 1. **to be ill, sick;** inf. also the state of being ill, **illness, sickness,** *ná-ba γsó-ba* to cure it *Lt.*, though *nad* is more in use; partic.: a sick person, **patient,** *ná-ba daṅ ₀či-ba* disease and death; *skye rga na ₀či* v. *skyé-ba* I., *rgás-pa daṅ ná-ba* old and sick people; *mi-ná-ba γnás-pa* to remain in health *S.g.*; *ná-ba-pa*, *ná-ba-ma Cs.* a sick person, an invalid (male and female); *ná-mo* a female patient *Mil.*; *ná-ba-mḱan* a sickly person, an invalid *Cs.*; *ná-ba-èan* sickly, *na-ba-méd* healthy *Cs.*; *na-ťóg* after falling ill *Sch.* — 2. of the separate parts of the body: **to ache,** *rná-ba* (not *-bai*) *ná-ba* pain in the ear, earache; *lus ťams-èád na* (my) whole body aches *Dom.*; *so ná-na* having the toothache; *nán-na na* it aches, when pressed (with the fingers) *S.g.*; *klád-pa ná-ba-la* (good) for the headache, for diseases of the brain; *na-₀ǰréṅ* complication of diseases or fits *Sch.*; *na-(ba daṅ)zúg(-rṅu)*, *na-ťsá* disease and pain.

ནབུན་ *na-bún* **fog, thick mist,** *ťibs*, *₀ḱyims* comes on; *byin-rlabs-kyi* prob. **a cloud, a flood, of blessing** *Mil.*

ན་མ་ *ná-ma* 1. v. *na* I. 2. also *ná-mo* (नमस्), **praise, glory, adoration**, *na-mo gu-ru* praise to the teacher!

ནཱ་མ་ *ná-ma Ssk.* = *žes byá-ba* **so called**, frq. in titles of books.

ན་བཟའ་ *ná-bza* (**ná-za**, vulg. **náb-za, nám-za**) resp. for *gos*, **garment, dress**, frq.; *ysól-ba* to put it on.

ན་ཨུན་ *na-ún* obs. or vulg. for *na-bún*, old edition of *Mil.*

ན་རག་ *na-rag*, *Ssk.* नरक, **hell.**

ན་རམ་ *na-rám* medicinal herb, *Med.*; in *Lh.* Polygon. viviparum.

ནཱ་རི་ཀེ་ལ་ *na-ri-ke-la Ssk.* **cocoa-nut.**

ན་རེ་ *ná-re*, by form and position an adv., like *ₒdi-skad-du*; before words or sentences that are quoted literally, mostly followed by *smrás-nas, zér-ba-la*, but not always, in which latter case it stands for **'he says, he said'** etc., the noun being always put in the nom. case, never in the instr.: *ₒṗags-pa na-re* the Reverend said; rarely in accessory sentences: *gál-te yžán-dag ná-re* (not *ná-re-na*) si forte alii dixerint *Wdṅ.*; even without *gál-te* in the same sense *Thgy.* It hardly occurs in old classical literature, nor in the col. language of *W.*, but pretty frq. in later literature. In *Kun.*, however, there exists a vb. *ná-čas* (**ná-čā**), pf. *nas* (**nā**), *imp. nos* (**nō**) which is used for *zér-ba* (not in use there), and is construed with the instr.: *ă-pa-su nā soṅ* the father has said.

ན་རོ་ *ná-ro* the sign for the vowel **o**, ◡.

ནཱ་རོ་ *ná-ro* n. of a holy Lama *Mil.*; *nā-ro-pa Tar.* 181, 10 id.? *ná-roi sems-ₒdzín-gyi lčags-ṫág* a sort of puzzle.

ན་ལནྡ་ *na-landa Pth. nā-len-dra Wdk.*, n. of a monastery in Magadha.

ན་ལི་ *ná-li* **bowl, basin**, an iron or china dish *W.*

ན་ལེ་ཤག་ *na-le-śag Lt.*, *śal S.g.*, = *śi-kru Wdṅ.* (शिग्रु?) n. of an acrid medicine.

ནག་ *nag* (blackness?) **crime, offence, transgression**, v. *nág-pa* comp.; *nag-ku-be-ra* v. *ku-be-ra.*

ནག་པ་, ནག་པོ་ *nág-pa*, gen. *nág-po*, **black**, *ber ṗyi nág-pa naṅ dkár-ba* a garment outside black, inside white *Glr.*; **nág-po ma ku** do not blacken it, do not soil it! of the countenance **dark, frowning, gloomy, mournful** *Glr.*; *mi nag (-po or-pa)* a black one, a layman, (on account of his not being clad in a red or yellow clerical garb); *nág-po* n. p. **Krishna** *Tar.*, *nág-po čén-po* = महाकाल **Siwa**; *nág-mo* 1. **a black woman**, 2. **Kali, Uma**; *nág-moi-ₒbaṅs* or *k̔ol* Kālidāsa. — 3. **woman**, in general *Sch.* — *nag-ₒgrós, nág-po ₒgro-śés* 'easy to be understood' *Sch.*; acc. to our Lama from Tashilunpo *nág-po ₒgro-bśér* implies: illustrating a sentence by comparing it with similar passages; *nág-čan* 1. **a person guilty of a crime** *Sch.*; *mi nág-čan dóṅ-nas ṫár-pa* a criminal released from prison *Mil.* 2. **a married man** *Sch.* — *nag-ṫágs* **black-cattle, horned cattle** *Sch.*; v. also *ynág-pa.* — *nág-ču* n. of a river north of Lhasa, *Huc* II, 238; *nág-ču-k̔a-pa* people living on its banks, notorious for their thievish propensities. — *nag-čén, nag-nyés C.* **a heinous crime.** — *nag-ṫúm, nag-ṫóm, Sch., nag-śiṅ-ba Thgy., nag-hur-ré Sch.*, **coal-black, jet-black.** — *nag-nóg (-čan)* **dirty, dingy; not clear**, as bad print; fig. **stained, polluted**, with sin, guilt, *sems.* — *nag-ṗyógs* v. *ṗyogs.* — *nag(-ma)-ṫsúr* **a black mineral colour**, *Sch.*: **green vitriol**(?). — *nag-tsig* **a point, dot**, *W.* — *nag-zúg* (?) **darkness**, *nag-zúg-la snóm-bžin soṅ* he groped about in the dark.

ནག་ཤ་ *nág-śa Sch.*: **linden-tree, lime-tree** (hardly to be found in Tibet; the word perhaps introduced from Mongol dictionaries).

ནགས་(མ་) *nágs (-ma Glr.) B., C., W.*, **forest**, *rtsi-śiṅ-nags-kyis mdzes* beautified by forests, richly wooded *Glr.*; *ₒṫúg-po* dense forest; *nags-k̔ród* a thicket *Glr.*; *nágs-čan* woody, covered with forests; *nags-ljóṅs* woodland country, a well-wooded province; *nags-sbál Lt.* tree-frog (?); *nags-ṫsál* = *nags*, *nyám-ṅa-ba* a dreadful forest *Dzl.*; *yid-du-ₒoṅ-ba* a lovely wood *Sambh.*; *nags-(y)séb* an intersected forest, v. *(y)seb.*

ནང་ *nań* I. the space within a thing, 1. **the interior, the inside,** *pýug-pai nań kun* the whole interior of the cavern *Mil.*; *γžóń-pai, dóń-gi nań* the interior of a basin, of a pit (e.g. being filled up) *Dzl.*; *ḱáń-pai nań pyag-dár byéd-pa* to sweep the inside of a house *Dzl.* — 2. **space, room, apartment, chamber** col. — 3. **dwelling, domicile, house,** esp. *C.* — 4. meton **inmates, family, household,** **nań ťsań** *W.* the whole family. — 5. **the interior** (spiritually), **heart, mind, soul,** *ye-šés náń-na šar* wisdom begins to shine in the mind; *žen-ₒdzin nań-nas ₒgrol* affection, interest, disappears from the heart *Glr.* — 6. sometimes adv. for *náń-na.*

II. *náń-gi*, genit., used 1. as an adj.: **inner, inward, esoteric** (opp. *to pýi*), *náń-gi ḱrims, náń-ḱrims*, a private law, an esoteric precept or doctrine not intended for the public; **ge-dún-gyī náń-ťim dhań ₒgal ťse** *C.* if priests violate their special moral duties, (very different from *náń-pai ḱrims* the Buddhist law, merely opp. to Brahmanism); *náń-gi sbyin-pa* inward offerings, i.e. spiritual sacrifices, opp. to outward and material offerings; but *Dzl.* ༢༣༤, 4 it denotes personal sacrifices, the surrendering of parts of our own self, e.g. a member of the body, opp. to outward property; the meaning also reminds of Rom. 12, 1, and I Pet. 2, 5. — *náń-gi byá-ba* internal affairs *Glr.*; v. also the compounds. — 2. for *náń-na* **among, amidst,** frq. c. accus.: *bu náń-gi ťa čuń, pýug-ron náń-gi čúń-ńu Dzl.* the smallest among etc.; for *dé-dag-gi náń-na* **of it, of them, among them** etc.: *náń-gi čúń-ńu* the least of them *Dzl.*; *náń-gi lhá-mo sńá-ma* the foremost among the goddesses; sometimes more pleon., without distinct reference to a preceding noun, *Dzl.* ༡༠༥, 18; ༡༣༤, 16 (where *Sch.* prob. translates incorr.).

III. with *la, na, du, nas;* 1. as sbst., acc. to the significations given above, e.g. *nád-pai náń-du ₒjúg-pa* to go **into** the room of a sick person *Wdń.*; *dei náń-du γdan-dráńs-te* inviting **into** their house *Mil.* — 2. as adv. *náń-na* **in it, therein, within, among it** or **them**; *náń-du* and *náń-la* **thereinto, into it**; *náń-nas* out, thereout, from among; among it or them = *náń-na.* — 3. postp: **in, into, among** etc., e.g. *rdziń-gi náń-na ḱrus byéd-pa Dzl.* to bathe in a pond, *čui náń-du žúgs-pa* to go into the water; *groń-ḱyér dei nań dań pyi-rol-na* in the town and out of it *Dzl.*; **sém-mi náń-na zér-pa** *W.* he said to himself; *snai náń-nas byuń* it came out of his nose (again) *Dzl.*; *mii náń-na(s) bzáń-po žig* one very beautiful among men *Dzl.*; *gliń dé-rnams-kyi náń-na(s) mčóg-tu gyúr-pa* the most important among or of these countries *Glr.* (here at least the sing. is as frq. als the plur.); in col. language the word is much used, though often inaccurately; so it is frq. employed, where the later literature has *ńáń-la, ńáń-nas*; **wáń-gi náń-na** by force; **só-me náń-na zer gos** *W.* that should have been mentioned, when it was fresh (in remembrance); **lo tóń-ńi náń-na ťsá-pig ma ťsar** not yet quite in a thousand years, i.e. it is not full a thousand years *W.* — There is still to be noticed: *nań = nań-mo.* — *nań-méd-la* col. frq. suddenly; in *B.* of rare occurrence; *nań-méd nor rnyéd-pa* to become rich unexpectedly *S.g.*

Comp. and deriv. *nań-kyóg Sch.*: having legs bending inward, **bandy-legged.** — *nań-skór* v. *skór-ba* extr. — *nań-ḱrims* v. above. — *nań-ḱról*, vulgo *-rol*, **bowels, entrails, intestines**; also any separate part of them; *nań-ḱról dróń-ba* spasmodic contractions of the bowels *Sch.*; *nań-ḱrol-bžág* seems in *Lexx.* to be taken synon. with *mnyam-bžag.* — *nań-góg* v. *ťer.* — **nań-gyóg** *W.* **a large bolt, door-bar.** — *náń-ča = nań-ḱrol.* — *nań-čags-su* in one's self, in one's own mind *Sch.* — *náń-rje* **minister of the interior, home-minister** *Sch.* — *náń-lta Glr* 89, 11? — *nań-ťáb byéd-pa* to be involved in intestine war *Pth.*, = *nań-ₒḱrúgs.* — *nań-dág* 1. *Sch.* 'the interior being cleansed'. 2. col. (or *nań-brtags?*) v. *snań.* — *náń-don* **the intrinsic meaning, the true sense,** *náń-don rtóg-pa* to investigate, to study, the real meaning; **náń-don tóg-ḱen,* or *ghó - ken* C.*, **nán - don - čan* (or *-yod-kan)* W.* most learned, very erudite; acc. to *Cs.* more particularly the mystical sense of religious writings, a higher degree of theology, as it were; *nán - don - gyi rab-obyáms - pa* a Doctor of Divinity *Cs.* — *nan-nán-gi, nan - nán - nas* = *nan - gi, nan-nas* among. — *nán - pa* **Buddhist**, opp. to *pyi-pa*, Non-Buddhist, Brahmanist; *nán-pai lta-ba, bstán-pa, čos, stón-pa, čá-lugs*, the theory etc. of the Buddhists. — *nán-po* an intimate, a bosom - friend *Sch.* — *nán-mi* members of a household, inmates (ni f.) *Dom.* — *nán-mig* room, apartment, *C., W.* — **nan - yáns* W.* wide, spacious, roomy. — *nan-ról* = *nan-krol* — *nán-ša* lining, **nán - ša tán - wa** to cover on the inside, to line, **nán - ša - čen* C.* lined. — *nan-sél* **dissension, discrepancy.** — *nan-ysés* **reciprocal, mutual** *Wdn.* frq.

ནང་མཆོད་ *nan-mčód* **a sort of potion** (thin pap?) consisting of the 'ten impurities', viz. five kinds of flesh (also human flesh), excrements, urine, blood, marrow, and '*byan-séms dkár-po*' (?), all mixed together, transsubstantiated by charms, and changed into *bdúd-rtsi* or **nectar**, a small quantity of which is tasted by the devotees, with the Lama at their head. This delicious drink is considered of great importance by the mystics, who seek to obtain spiritual gifts by witchcraft (cf. *mdo* extr.); hence every offering is sprinkled with this potion.

ནང་ལྟར་ (*nán-ltar*) **nán-tar* W., C., *nán-žin* C.* col. for *bžin-du, ltar*, **according to, in conformity with, like, as,** c. genit. or accus., *bka nán-tar, bkai nan-tar.*

ནང་མེ་ *nán-me*, resp. for *me* **fire** *W.* (*snán-me?*).

ནང་མོ་ *nán-mo* (*ma Pth.?*) **the morning**; in the morning; *nán-mo ycig bžin-du* every morning *Pth.*; *nan re* id.; *nan re dgons re* every morning and evening; *da-nán* this morning; *da-nán ni gán-nas byon* where do you come from to-day? *Mil.*; *da-nán-gi tsó-ba* this day's breakfast *Mil.*; *nan-núb* in the morning and in the evening; *nan - núb nyi - pyéd ysúm - la* in the morning, in the evening, and at noon. — *nan-par* 1. in the morning, *nan-par snar* early in the morning *Dzl.* 2. **the morning, esp the following morning,** *nán - par - kyi skál-ba* the allowance, the ration for the following morning *Glr.*

ནངས་ *nans W.* (?) *nan - čun yod* that is a mere **trifle**, not worth while, cf. *mnog.*

ནངས་པར་ *náns-par Cs.*, **nán - la* W.*, **the day after to-morrow,** *B. ynan.*

ནད་ *nad* **disease, distemper, malady, sickness,** cf. *ná-ba*; (the Tibetan science of medicine distinguishes 404 kinds of diseases); *mi - nad pyúgs - nad* diseases among men and animals *Glr.*; *nad ysó - ba* to cure a disease, *nad otsó-ba, nad sós - par*, or *ži-bar*, or *dan brál-bar ogyúr-ba* to be cured of a disease, to get well, to recover; *nád-kyis odébs-pa, otébs-pa*, to be attacked by a disease, to be taken ill *B.*; *C.* more frq.: **né'-kyi gyáb-pa, zir-wa*, W.: *ná-la nad yon(s)**; *nád-kyi rgyu*, and *rkyen*, v. *rkyen* 1 and 2.

Comp. *nad - rkyál Wdk.* emblem of a deity (meaning not clear). — *nád - kan* **hospital** *Cs.* — *nád - go* **seat of a disease** *Sch.* — *nád-čan* **ill, sick** (little used). — *nád-pa* 1. **a sick person,** male or female. 2. adj. **ill, sick,** *séms-čan nád-pa-dag S.O.* = *nád-po* and *nád-bu* = *nad Cs.*, **nád-bu-čan* W.*, weak in health, **sickly, poorly.** — *nad - méd* **healthy, hale, in health,** (the usual word); *nad-méd-par gyúr-čig* may you recover your health, may you remain in good health, all hail to you! *Cs.* — *nád-med-pa* **health,** *nád-med-pa tób-pa, rnyéd-pa* to get well, to recover one's health; *nád-med-pa ogyúr-ba* declining health *Thgy.* — *nad tsúl* **the character of a disease** *S.g.* — *nad-yži* **seat, primary cause** of a disease(?) *Lt.* — *nad - yyóg* one attending to sick persons, **a nurse**; *nad-yyóg byéd-pa W. *čó-če**, **to nurse.**

ནན་ *nan* **the act of pressing, urging; pressure, urgency, importunity,** *kón-rnams-kyi nan ma tégs-par* not being able to resist their importunity *Mil.*; *nán-gyis* with urgency, pressingly, e.g. *žú-ba* to request, to solicit *Glr.*; *nán-gyis zar ˏǰúg-pa* to urge, to compel (a person) to eat *Dzl.*; *nán-gyis skór-ba* to press, to crowd, round *Dzl.*; *nán-gyis ˏgúg-pa* to make a person come near by calling to him *Mil.*; *nan-čágs* 1. sbst. **certainty, surety,** **da nan-čág ťob soṅ* W.* now I have certainty, now I know for sure; *nan-čags ˳ťems? Zam.* 2. adv. **certainly, surely** *W.*, *C.*; adj. **lon nan-čág* W.* certain news. — *nán-tan* 1. sbst. **earnest desire, application, exertion** *Cs.*; *byaṅ-čúb-la nán-tan byéd-pa* to strive earnestly for perfection *Dzl.*; *nán-tan-du byéd-pa Thgy.*; in *čós-kyi nán-tan ysuṅs Pth.* '*kyi*' is perh. to be cancelled. 2. adv. *C*: **certainly, positively,** **ṅe nén-ten láb-pa, nen-čág zér-pa**, I have told him so definitively, as my unalterable decision; *W.*: **earnestly, ardently, accurately,** **nán-tan žib-ča ltos** look at it, examine it, accurately! **nán-tan čos** do it well, most carefully! **nán-tan šrág-če** to burn entirely. — *nán-tar* very, *nán-tar bzaṅ Lex.*; **very much, all the more, altogether** *Mil.*; *nan-túr*, of rare occurrence, = *nán-tan*. — *nón-pa*, *ynán-pa* are cog. to *nan*.

ནན་ཏེ་ *nán-te* 1. *Ts.* for *ná-ba* **sick, ill.** — 2. *W.* **ču nán-te kyoṅ**, for *ran-te*, *˳dren-te*, conduct the water this way!

ནན་ཞག་ *nán-žag W.* **late, recent,** what has happened a few weeks or months ago.

ནབས་ *nabs* **put on** (your clothes)! *Sch.*, v. *mnáb-pa.*

ནབས་སོ་ *nábs-so* **one of the lunar mansions,** v. *rgyu-skár* ༦.

ནམ་ *nam* I. sbst. 1. **night,** *nam láṅs-te*, or *-nas*, when night departs, **at day-break,** frq.; *nam-gáṅ Sch.*: the last day of the lunar month on which there is no moonshine at all; *nam-gúṅ* **midnight,** *nám-gyi gúṅ-ťun-la* in the hour of midnight *Dom.*; *nam-stód* the first half of the night, *nam-smád* the second half of the night; *nám-gyi ča stod, smad,* id. — *nam-ṗyéd* **midnight** *Dzl.*, *Glr.*; *nam-žóṅ* (?) *Sch.* in the morning; *nam-ríṅ Sch.* a long day (??) — *nam-láṅs* **day-break,** *nam-laṅs-kyi-bar-du Dzl.* — *nam-sród* **darkness of night,** *nam-sród byiṅ soṅ-bai ṫse* as it was almost quite dark *Mil.*, **nam-šród yol sóṅ-nas* C.*, *nam-srós-nas Sch.* id. — 2. for *nam-mk'a* q. v.

II. adv. of time, also *dus-nám-žig*, 1. **when?** frq., **how long a time?** seldom; *rgyún-du nam ˳či ča med sgom* always keep in mind that you do not know when you will die *Mil.*; *dus-nám-žig-gi tsé-nas* **since when? since what time? how long ago?** *Mil.*; relatively: *nam ˳gró-bai dus byéd-pa* to appoint the time, when one is going to start *Dzl.*; *nam žig sgyú-lus ˏǰóg-pai tse*, when he shall lay aside his phantom-body *Mil.*; **nam tsúg-pa k'o ma léb-na, de tug*. . .,* as long as he has not come, so long . . . *W.* — 2. *nám(-du) yaṅ* (col. **nám-aṅ, náms-aṅ**) with a negative, **never,** in sentences relating to the past, or the future, or containing a prohibition, cf. *mi* and *ma*, *nam-yaṅ mi zíṅ-to* it will never be finished *Dzl.* ༢༧༦, 9; *sṅon nam yaṅ ma ťos* (that) has never been heard of formerly; without a negative in *B.* rarely, col. frq.: **always;** *nam žag brtan Mil.*; **nám-žag gyún-du* C.* id.

ནམ་མཁའ་ *nám-mk'a* (cf. *mk'a* and *ynam*) the space or region above us, **heaven, sky,** where the birds are flying, and the saints are soaring, where it lightens and thunders etc.; **the ether,** as the fifth element *S. g.*; **the principle of expansion and enlargement** *Wdṅ.*; *nám-mk'a daṅ mnyám-pa* like unto the heavens, as to wide expanse, frq.; inaccurately also for an **innumerable multitude,** *nám-mk'a daṅ mnyám-pai séms-čan-rnams Mil.*; *nám-mk'ai dbyiṅs*, *nám-mk'a-ldiṅ(-mo)* v. sub *mk'a*; *nám-mk'ai mtoṅs* **celestial vault, firmament** *Glr.*, *S. O.*; *nám-mk'a-mdog* the blue colour of the sky, **azure;** it is supposed to be produced by the southern side of mount Rirab, which consists entirely of azur-stone, *Mil.*; *k'yim-gyi nám-mk'a-la* in the air above the house, like *bar-snáṅ-la*, *Tar.* ༢༦, 2; *nam-˳ṗáṅs ycód-pa*, also *nam-*

dpáṅs spyód-pa *Mil.*, to cross the height of the heavens, to fly across the sky. — *nam-gru* v. *rgyu-skar*.

ནམ་ཟླ་ (*nám-zla*) pronounced **nám-da*, and *nám-la**, *Mil.*, *Pth.*, col., **season,** *nám-zla dus bži* the four seasons; *da nam-da ston šar* now autumn has set in; **da nam-da ḍaṅ-mo soṅ**; fig. *nám-da* *ₒdas* the (favourable) season has passed *Mil.*

ནམ་སོ་ *nám-so* = *nábs-so.*

ནར་ *nar* v. *na* I. and II., 2; also *ná-k'a.*

ནར་མ་ *nár-ma* adj., and *nár-mar* adv., continuous, without interruption *Sch.*; **či-ma nár-te ton or šor** *C.* torrents of tears gushed from his eyes, cf. *k'rul*; *nár-re Mil.*, more vulg. **nár-ra-ra** in a long row or file, *ₒgrúl-ba* to walk

ནར་མོ་, ནར་ནར་པོ་ *nár-mo*, *nár-nar-po* **oblong** *Mil.*, *Med.*; *k'a-nar-čan* having the shape of a rectangle; *gru-nar-čan* **rhombic, lozenge-shaped.** Cf. (*b*)*snár-ba.*

ནལ་ *nal* n. of a precious stone *Sch.*

ནལ་(མ་) *nál*(-*ma*) *Cs.* **incest, fornication;** *nal-grib* pollution by it. *nal-p'rúg* frq., **nal - lé* Ts.*, bastard-child; *nál - bu Sch.* a libidinous woman (??).

ནལ་བྱི་ *nál-byi Pth.* n. of a poison-tree.

ནས་ *nas* I. sbst. 1. **barley,** in three varieties: *mgyógs-nas* (*Ld. yáṅ-ma*, or *drug-ču-nas*, *Wdṅ. k'rá-ma*) early barley, ripening in about 60 days; *sér-mo* late barley, the best sort; *če - nas* a middling sort. — 2. **barley-corn,** *nas-tsam* as much as a barley-corn *Glr.* — *nás-čaṅ* beer brewed of barley. *nas - rǰén* v. *rǰén-pa.* — *nas - p'yé* barley-flour. — **nas - zír** (spelling not certain) aim or sight on a gun *W.*

II. postp., sign of the ablative case (almost like *las*) 1. added to sbst.: **from,** *byáṅ-p'yogs-nas* from the north, often joined with *bzúṅ-ste* (*Ld.* **táṅs-te**), commencing **from,** extending **from,** with a following **to, as far as; till, until,** with respect so space and time; **by,** *lág-pa-nas ₒdzín-pa* or *ₒǰú-ba* to take a person by the hand, *míṅ-nas rǰód-pa*, *smó-ba* to call by name, *t'igs-pa re-ré-nas* (to count) by single drops, *so - só - nas* **one by one, each by himself; through,** *dúṅ-nas bšád-pas* speaking through a trumpet *Glr.*, *sgo-sáṅ-nas ltá-ba* looking through the chink of a door *Tar.*; *sgó-nas γtóṅ - ba* to admit through the door *Dzl.*; **bi-yaṅ-ne p'aṅ** *W.* he flung it through the hole (cf. also *rgyúd - pa* I., 2); made, manufactured, built etc. **of,** *pá-gu-nas* of bricks; (made, worked, struck etc.) **with,** **lág-pa-ne duṅ** *W.* struck with the hand; denoting **distance:** *rgyaṅ - grágs γčig - nas pó-ta-la yod C.*, Potala lies within reach of the ear; *ₒdí-nas gáṅs - ri - la* far from here on the snowy mountain *Glr.*; with respect **to time: after,** *šag bdún-nas* after seven days: *dé-nas* **after that, afterwards, then.** — 2. added to verbs, as gerundial particle, rarely to the inf., gen. (col. always) to the verbal root, prop. **after, since;** also equivalent to *te*, when added to a pres. or pf. root (instances of which are to be met with almost on every page of Tibetan books); together with *ₒdug* or *yod* added to a pres. or pf. tense, col. frq., in *B.* rarely: *ṅa lčeb dgos snyám-nas yod* I think I must seek death *Pth.*; *tsós - nas yod* it is boiled *Pth.*; *só-nam-gyi byá-ba-la žúgs - nas yód-pa-la* as they began to till the ground *Glr.* — Col. also for *na.*

ནི་ *ni* I. 1. particle, col. also **niṅ**; *Cs.* justly remarks: 'an emphatical particle', serving to give force to that word or part of a sentence, which rhetorically is most important, esp. also (though not exclusively, *Sch.*) to separate the subject of a sentence from its predicate, thus adding to perspicuity: *k'yod ₒdir ₒóṅs-pa ni ṅai mt'us ₒoṅs-so* thy coming hither has been effected by my (magic) power *Dzl.*; *bdag ni brám-ze yin* myself am a Brahmin *Dzl.*; *de ni ṅa yin* that one am I; *ₒdi ni mi p'ód-do* this I am not able to do *Dzl.*; *t'a-mál-pa ni ma yin* a vulgar person she is not *Dzl.*; *des ni* it is by this (that...); *stobs ni* as to strength (I...); *gál-te nús-na ni* if he can (— well!); *da ni, šar ni, ₒdi-las ni, šṅon-čad ni* etc.; *šiṅ-mḱan ni* now, as to the carpenter, he . . . *Dzl.; dár-ba ni* now, with respect to the propagation (of the doctrine). In a similar manner it is frq. used, where we begin a new paragraph, heading it with its principal contents. In col. language the word before *ni* is rendered still more emphatic by repeating it once more after *ni*: **zer ni zer dug** *W.* (it is true) they say so; **ḍi ni ḍi-te yod** it has been written, (to be sure); **ǰhe ni ǰhe* C., *čo ni čo dug* W.* (certainly) they are working at it, (but . . .). In metrical compositions, esp. in mnemonic verses, it is often added as a mere metrical expletive, without any meaning, esp. after *daṅ*. — 2. *Ts.*: demonstrative pron., **ri ni-lẹ ni to-wa dug** this mountain is higher than that.

II. num. figure: 42.

ནི་ལ་ *ni-la* (*Hindi* नील blue) 1. *Cs.* **indigo.** — 2. *W.* **the blue pheasant** of the South Himalaya, manāl.

ནི་ལམ་, ལི་ལམ་ *ni-lam, li-lam* (*Hindi;* Shaksp.: 'from the Portuguese *leilam*') **auction, public sale.**

ནིང་ *niṅ* 1. col. for *ni*. 2. for *rnyiṅ?* v. *na-niṅ, že-niṅ.*

ནིམ་བ་ *nim-ba*, निम्ब, n. of a plant, Melia Azedarachta.

ནིའི་ལི་ *nii-li Sch.*: **the great buzzard** or **mouse-hawk** (?).

ནུ *nu* num. fig.: 72.

ནུ་བ་ *nú-ba* pf. and imp. *nus*, **to suck** *Cs.*, *nu(-ba)-po, mo*, **a suckling** *Cs.*, *nu-ḱug* sucking-bag.

ནུ་བོ་ *nú-bo*, resp. *γčuṅ-po*, *W.* **no**, **a man's younger brother** *B.* and *C.*

ནུ་མ་ *nú-ma*, *Cs.* also *čáb-nu* (resp.?), **breast,** as two correspondent parts of the body, 1. **mammary gland, female breast, bosom** *S.g.* — 2. **nipple, teat,** also of males. — 3. **dug, nipple** of a cow's udder; *nu-ḱyim, -γdan, -ₒbur, -ₒbor, Cs.* id. — *nú-ša* **the thoracic muscle.** — *nu-rtsé, nu-sór Cs.* the tip of the breasts, nipple. — *nú-žo* mother's milk, *mai nú-žo Dzl.*; *nú-žo snún-par byéd-pa* to suckle, to give suck, *Lt.*; *nú-žo skám-na* if she has no milk *Lt.*

ནུ་མོ་ *nú-mo* 1. *W.* **nó-mo**, **the younger sister of a female,** *B.* and col. — 2. v. *nú-ba*.

ནུག་སྟེ་ *núg-ste* (pronounced **núg-te**) *Ts.*, **so, thus.**

ནུད་པ་ *núd-pa* **to suckle,** *W.*: **pi-pi nud toṅ** give to suck! (= *snún-pa*).

ནུབ་ *nub* 1. **the west,** *nub-(kyi) p̀yogs(-rol)* id.; *núb-p̀yogs-su* towards the west; *nub-byáṅ* north-west; *núb-kyi* of the west, western; v. also *bdé-ba-čan*. — 2. **evening,** *do-núb* this evening, to-night.

ནུབ་པ་ *núb-pa* 1. vb., **to fall gradually, to sink,** *mṫil-la* to the bottom; **to sink in,** *pús-mo núb-pa tsam* knee-deep *Dzl.* frq.; **to go down, to set,** of the sun, moon, frq.; fig. **to decay, decline,** of religion; *núb-par ₒgyúr-ba* id.; *núb-par byéd-pa Sch.* = vb. a. *snúb-pa*. — 2. sbst. **an inhabitant of the West.**

ནུབ་མོ་ *núb-mo* **evening; in the evening,** frq.; *nub gráṅ-gi* happening every evening *Sch.*

ནུམ་ *num*, *W.* col. for *mun*.

ནུར་ནུར་པོ་ *núr-nur-po* denotes the form of the embryo in the second week: **oval, oblong;** *mér-mer-po* id.

ནུར་བ་ *núr-ba* (cf. *brnúr-ba, snúr-ba*), 1. **to change place or posture, to move a little,** **rig-te nur** (v. *sgrig-pa*) *W.* move a little nearer together, stand or sit a little closer! *núr-gyis ₒtén-pa* to pull gradually, to give short pulls *Glr.*; *p̀a-bóṅ ₒdam rdzis-pa bžiṅ-du nur* the rock yielded, i.e. received impressions, like foot-prints on soft clay, *Mil.*; **to step aside, to draw** or **fall back; to get out of its place, to be dislocated;** **p̀i núr-la ḍúl-čé, p̀i-log-la núr-če** *W.* to move slowly back. — 2. **to crumble to pieces,** *Mil.* of mountains during an unearthly storm, according to some Lamas, cf. *snúr-ba*. — 3. *Cs.*: **to approach, to come near to** (?), yet cf. *snúr-ba*.

ནུས་པ་ *nús-pa* I. 1. vb. **to be able,** to have sufficient moral or physical power, also = *ṗód-pa*; *ǰi* (or frq. *ći*) *nús-kyis* **to one's best ability; to be able to do** or **to perform,** *dká-las gaṅ yaṅ mi nus* he cannot perform any difficult task *Thgy.*; *rgyál-po mi nus* he cannot be a king; **to venture, to dare,** *ɑgro nús-pa* one that dared to go. (In *W.* **ṫúb-pa** is used almost exclusively instead of it.) — 2. adj. **able,** *nús-pa su ćé-ba lta* let us see who is more able, more efficient, who can do more, *Mil.*; *C.* also **active, diligent, assiduous.** — 3. sbst. **power, ability, faculty, capability,** c. genit: *ṅai nús-pa-la brtén-nas* by my power, through my agency (you shall obtain it) *Mil.*; *rtsig-pai nús-pa yód-dam med* whether there will be a capability of building . . . *Glr.*; **de ćós-la nús-pa med* W.* this religion has no power; *nús-pa bśig-pa ṫams-ćád* all the destructive powers; *byéd-nus-pa, stón-nus-pa* the capability of doing, of showing *Thgy.*; *rnam-smín-nus-pa* the power of retributive justice (Nemesis, as it were) *Mil.*; **efficiency, efficacy, virtue** (of a remedy), *smán-nus ɑǰoms* they hinder the efficacy of the medicines *Med.*; *nús-pa smin* the efficacy becomes complete *Mil.*; in a more particular sense: **the effect of a medicine** in the stomach (opp. to its taste etc.); there are eight different effects: *lći, snum, bsil, rtul, yaṅ, rtsub, ṫsa, rno S.g.*; *nús-pa ɣnyis daṅ ldan* they have both qualities *S.g.*; *nus-stóbs* = *nús-pa Sch.*

II. pf. of *nú-ba.*

ནེ་ *ne* num. figure: 102.

ནེ་ཐང་, ནེའུ་ཐང་ *ne-ṫáṅ, neu-ṫáṅ,* **meadow, grass-plot, green-sward,** *B.*, *C.*, *W.*

ནེ་ནེ་མོ་ *né-ne-mo* **aunt,** the father's sister, or wife of the mother's brother.

ནེ་མ་ *né-ma* **meadow, green-sward,** *C.*, *W.*

ནེ་ཙོ་ *né-tso* **parrot.**

ནེ་རེ་, ནེར་ནེར་ *ne-ré, ner nér* (v. *ner-ba*), *W.* **sediment, settlings, dregs.**

ནེ་ལེ་ *ne-lé Sch.*: **'mouse-hawk',** a species of large hawk or vulture, differing from *gó-bo*, frequently to be met with in Kullu, but not in Ladak.

ནེ་ཝེ་ *ne-we Sch.* mason's **trowel,** *ne-we rgyag-pa* to plaster, to roughcast.

ནེ་གསིང་, ནེ་བསིང་ *ne-ɣsiṅ, ne-bsiṅ* = *neu-(ɣ)siṅ.*

ནེན་པ་ *nén-pa W.* col. for *lén-pa*, **to take, lay hold of, seize; to take out, off, away; to hold.**

ནེམ་ནེམ་ *nem-ném* denotes **a nodding, waving,** or **rocking motion,** *Mil.*; cf. *nems* and *snem.*

ནེམ་བུ་ *ném-bu* **doubt, error** *Sch.*

ནེམས་ *nems*; *Stg.* describes an elastic floor in the following manner: *rkáṅ-pa bžág-na ni nems śes byéd-de, rkáṅ-pa btégs-na ni spar žes byed*: hence *nems,* **it sinks a little, gives way.**

ནེའུ་ལྡང་ *neu-ldáṅ Lex.* = *na-mnyám* one of the same age, **coetaneous, contemporary;** *Sch.*: *neu-ldán* **friend,** and *neu-ldáṅs* **protector, defender.**

ནེའུ་ལེ་ *neu-lé, Hindi* नेवला, *Ssk.* नकुल, **ichneumon,** Herpestes Pharaonis, *Liś.*; represented in *B.* as a fabulous animal, cat-like and vomiting jewels.

ནེའུ་(ག)སིང་ *neu-(ɣ)siṅ* 1. *C.* = *ne-ṫaṅ.* — 2. **grass-plots** on high mountains, **alpine pastures** (*C. spaṅ*).

ནེར་བ་ *nér-ba* **to sink, to fall gradually,** *mṫil-la* to the bottom, = *núb-pa.*

ནེར་ནེར་ *ner-nér* = **ne-ré* W.*

ནོ་ *no* 1. *W.* for *nú-bo.* — 2. num. fig.: 132.

ནོ་ནོ་ *no-nó Ld.* title of young noblemen, *no-nó ćén-mo* the eldest of a nobleman's sons, *bár-pa* the second, *ćúṅ-se* the youngest; *Sp.* title of the highest magistrate of the country.

ནོ་མོ་ *nó-mo* (*Bal. nó-ṅo*) *W.* for *nu-mo.*

ནོག་ *nog Sch.*: **cervical vertebra; hump of a camel.**

ནོག་པ་, ནོག་པོ་ *nóg-pa, nóg-po,* prob. prov. for *nág-po*; *nog-nóg* **very dark, deep-black.**

ནོང་བ་ *nóṅ-ba*, pf. *noṅs*, **to commit a fault, to make a mistake, to commit one's self**, *ċi noṅs* what have I done amiss? *bdág ma nóṅs-par ₒdi-ltar γnód-pa bgyis* I have thus been injured without my fault *Dzl.*; *nóṅs-pa* **fault, crime**, *nóṅs(-pa) mi byéd-pa* not to commit a fault or crime *Dzl.*; *bzód-pa* to pardon, to forgive, v. *bzód-pa*; *nóṅs-pa bzód-par γsól-ba* to ask pardon for a fault committed (in *C.* even: **nóṅ-pa sol-wa**); *nóṅs-pa-ċan* **culpable, liable to punishment**; **noṅ-ċan-ni (s)pe-ra** *W.* a reprehensible speech.

ནོངས་པ་ *nóṅs-pa* resp. **no more alive, dead** *Dzl.*, *rje-btsún sku ma nóṅs-par ṗébs-pa* that your Reverence has arrived safe and sound *Mil.*

ནོད་པ་, མནོད་པ་ *nód-pa, mnód-pa*, pf. and imp. *mnos*, **to receive** instruction, directions, favours, from a superior, esp. priest, *Dzl.*, *Glr.*; but also to receive punishment.

ནོན་པ་ *nón-pa* I. also *γnón-pa*, pf. *γnan, mnan*, 1. **to press**, **máṅ-po ma non** do not press too hard! **nán-te ṗé-ċe** *W.* to open a thing by pressing; with or without *rkáṅ-pas* to tread under foot, to crush; **to pour over, to cover with**, *sas, byé-mas*, with earth, with sand; **to be drenched**, *čár-pas* by a shower of rain *Dzl.*; to lay over, to overlay with *Tar.* 9, 11, 21; more frq. fig. **to oppress, suppress, overcome, conquer, humble, keep under**, *mtó-ba ḱrims-kyis* the great people by laws *Glr.*; enemies frq.; evil spirits by magic, e.g. *sri γnán-pa* by burying heads of animals in the ground, in order that the evil spirits may remain shut up there; *bgegs nón-pa* to keep the spirits away from the fields during harvest by hatchets etc. stuck in the ground; po. *ḱá-bai γdoṅ sri mnan* I have crushed, subdued, the face of the snow (i.e. its surface) that was adverse to me *Mil.*; *sa γnón-du* the sitting posture of a saint, when his left hand rests in his lap, and his right hand hangs down, keeping down, as it were, the earth and her powers; cf. *mnyam-bžág*. — Frq. also: *mya-ṅán-gyis, snyiṅ-rjes* etc. to be overcome by misery, by compassion. — 2. **to overtake, to catch, to reach**, *bdás-pas* in the pursuit *Mil.* and *W.* — 3. *sgo-ṅa* **to brood, to hatch, eggs**, *Sch.*

II. *W.* *lo tsam-non*, for *lon*, how old is he?

ནོམ་པ་ *nóm-pa*, pf. *noms*, 1. *Cs.* **to be satisfied, contented** (*ṅom-pa?*) — 2. **to seize, to lay hold of** (*snóm-pa*); *Sch.*: *noms-nyúg byéd-pa*.

ནོར་ *nor* I. (*Ssk.* धन, also वसु) 1. **wealth, property, possessions**, *nor(-la) gód-pa Mil.* to suffer a loss of property; **nor gód-da** or **ṗóg-ga** *W.* have you suffered damage or loss? **nor nyams ċó-pa** *C.*, **lén-ċe** *W.*, to examine the inventory, the amount of property; *ṗágs-pai nor bdun Mil.* the seven (spiritual) possessions of a saint, v. *Trig.* 17; proverb: **ráṅ-nor-la man mi-nor-la dhug (sc. tar to)** *C.* look upon your own property as a medicine, upon that of others as a poison; **thing, substance**, much the same as *rdzas*, *Zam.* (nif.). — 2. more or less exclusively: **money**, *nór-la ltá-ba* to care for money, to be avaricious, easily bribed etc.; *nor skyí-ba* to borrow money, *nor bsri-ba* to save money, to scrape together; *nor sog-ₒjóg-pa* to accumulate riches. — 3. *Sch.*: **cattle**, even in such phrases as: *nor ₒḱrig-pa* the pairing of cattle. *Sch.*, *nor-dpon Desg.* chief neatherd (provincialism of *C.?*). — 4. **heritage, inheritance**, *bkó-ba* to divide (it among the heirs); *ṗá-nor* heritage from the father, *má-nor* heritage from the mother. — 5 symb. num.: 8 (cf. *nór-lha*).

Comp. *nór-skal* **inheritance, hereditary portion**; *nór-skal-rnams* **funds, capital** *Mil.* — *nor-rgyún* imperishable riches *Cs.*; *nor-rgyún-ma* a goddess, *nor-ċan* **wealthy, opulent, rich** *Cs.* — *nór-bdag* 1. **a man of wealth.** 2. **an heir.** 3. **a money-changer, usurer**, *Hind.* महाजन, *nór-bdag-mo* fem. of it; also n. of a goddess; *nór-bdag-bu* heir. — *nór-ₒdus Pur.* **the gathering of taxes.** — *nór-brnab-ċan* covetous, greedy of money. — *nor-ṗyúgs* amount, or stock of cattle, *nor-ₒbrú* store of corn. — *nór-bu* v. that article

— *nor-odzín* po. **the earth.** — *nor-rdzás* = *nor* I., 1. *B.* and col. — *nór-lha* = *ku-be-ra*, god of riches; there are eight such gods.
II. v. sub *nór-ba.*

ནོར་བ་ *nór-ba* **to err, to make a mistake, to commit a fault,** *yas oǰul nór-ro* it is wrong (to write it) with the prefix *y Gram.*; *nor soṅ* it is a mistake, I (thou, he etc.) am wrong; *k'a, lág-pa, lam nor soṅ*, it was a slip of the tongue, I got hold of the wrong thing, I lost my way; to stray, *dé-las odi-ru* from one thing to another *Thgy.*; *mi-nór-ba, ma-nór-ba, nor-ba-méd-pa* **infallible,** not liable to fail, e.g. of a charm; where one cannot miss or go wrong, *lam; mi-nór-bar*, strictly according to prescription or direction. — *nór-ba, nór-pa Cs.* 1. **a wanderer,** from the right way. 2. **an error, a mistake.** — *nor-ok'rúl* id., frq.; *nór-ra-re Sch.*: he might possibly be mistaken.

ནོར་བུ་ *nór-bu* (मणि) 1. **jewel, gem, precious stone,** *nór-bu-čan* adorned with jewels, set with precious stones; *nór-bu-pa, nór-bu-mk'an Cs.* **a jeweler,** a connoisseur of gems; *nór-bu-oṗreṅ-ba* a rosary or chaplet composed of precious stones; also as title of a book; *nór-bu rin-po-čé*, चिन्तामणि, a very costly jewel; also jewel, par excellence, a fabulous precious stone, the possession of which procures inexhaustible riches; acc. to *Wdk.* 488, it has the shape of an oval fruit of the size of a large lemon. — 2. **a noun personal,** or family name, much in use. — 3. gen. pronounced **nór-ru, nór-ro**, **good, excellent, noble,** e.g. *mi, Bal., Pur.*

ནོར་སོ་ *nór-so, nór-so-čan, Wdṅ.* 173, 11; 182, 4?

ནོལ་བ་ *nól-ba* to agree, to come to terms *Cs.*

ནོས་པ་ *nós-pa* v. *nód-pa.*

ནྱ་གྲོ་དྷ་ *nya-gro-dha Ssk.*, Ficus indica, = *byaṅ-čub-šiṅ.*

གནག་པ་ *ynág-pa*, a secondary form of *nág-pa,* of rare occurrence, 1. **black;** *ynag-sbágs* **sooty** *Sch.*; *ynag-ṗyúgs* **black cattle,** esp. the yak; *ynag rta lug ysum* cattle, horses, and sheep, these three; *ynag-kyú* a herd of cattle; *ynag-rdzi* a keeper of cattle, cow-herd; *ynag-lhás* an enclosure for cattle. — 2. fig. black-hearted, **wicked, impious.** — 3. (looking black upon) **frowning;** *Glr.* fol. 96: *sems šin-tu ynág-par byuṅ* (notwithstanding their friendly appearance) they had a spite against each other in their hearts. — 4. sbst. **misfortune, grief, affliction, pain,** *ynág-pa daṅ ldán-pa* unfortunate, unhappy *Stg.*; **nag-čan* W.* **cruel, tormenting;** **nag stán-pa* Ld.* to torture, to torment. — 5. *Sch.*: (well) **considered,** (carefully) **weighed** in the mind; v. however *brnág-pa.*

གནང་བ་ *ynáṅ-ba* I. vb., pf. *ynaṅ(s)*, imp. *ynoṅ, B., C.* (in *W. stsál-ba* is gen. used for *ynáṅ-ba*) 1. **to give,** resp., i.e. only used when a person of higher rank gives or is asked to give; cf. *obúl-ba; *dág-la dá-wa čig-gi ṗog kyáb-rog náṅ-wa žu* C.* please, have the kindness to give me my month's pay; sometimes it is preceded by a pleon. *rjés-su, Cs.*, **to bestow, to confer, upon,** frq.; **to commit to,** to place under a person's care, e.g. a pupil (resp. for *ytód-pa*) *Mil.*; **to grant, to concede,** what has been asked, *ynáṅ-du ysol* (ancient lit.), *ynáṅ-ba žu* (later lit.) I request you to grant; *skur-ynáṅ mdzád-pa mk'yen-mk'yén* I beg you for the favour of sending me ... (in modern letters); **to allow, permit, approve of, assent to,** *ységs-par ynáṅ-no* he accepted the invitation, he promised to come *Dzl.*; *bdag ráb-tu obyúṅ-ba(r) ynoṅ žig* allow me to take (holy) orders, to become a priest *Dzl.*; *bdag ni sbyin-pa žig byéd-kyis ynoṅ žig* allow of my making a donation *Dzl.*; *de bžin-du ynáṅ-ṅo* yes, I permit it *Dzl.*; *yid bžin-du ynáṅ-ṅo* we allow it; do according to your pleasure! — *či ynaṅ* v. *či* I., 4. — In a looser sense: *blón-por ynáṅ-ṅo* he appointed him his minister; *mi ynáṅ-ba* **to forbid, prohibit,** *čos byar mi ynáṅ-bai k'rims bčas* he published a prohibitory law concerning the exercise of religion *Glr.*; *(bkas) ma ynaṅ Pth.* he refused it, declined to grant it, *byon-du ma ynaṅ* he refused to come *Glr.* — 2. sometimes **to command, to order**, complete form: *bka γnáṅ-ba; γnáṅ-tsig skúl-ba* to order a person to do a thing *Pth.* — 3. in complimentary phrases used in *C.* the precise meaning of *γnáṅ-ba* is not always quite obvious: *γnaṅ-rógs mdzad-pa* (v. above) to give, to help to, to assist in(?); **góṅ-pa tsóm-pa ma naṅ**, do not be put out, do not give way to any misgivings (towards me)! sometimes *snaṅ* (q.v.) would make a better sense.

II. sbst. **concession, permission, grant,** *ᵒgró-bai γnáṅ-ba žú-ba Mil.; mí-las γnáṅ-ba tób-pa* to obtain permission from a person; *bka-γnáṅ-ba* (magisterial) permission, order (of government); *γnaṅ-sbyin* very frq., **gift, donation, present,** *stón-mo γnaṅ-sbyin* a present of provisions *Glr.*; **gift of honour, reward, favour, privilege, price of victory** held out etc.

གནང(ས)་ *γnaṅs* adv. 1. **on the third day,** e.g. he came *Glr.*; gen. of the future: **the day after to-morrow,** *saṅ γnaṅs Glr.*; **tó-re náṅ-la** *W.* to-morrow and the day after to-morrow; *saṅ ᵒgro γnaṅs ᵒgro yód-pa yin* to-morrow or the day after to-morrow I must be off *Pth.*; *γnaṅs-γžés* on the third and fourth day *Lex.* — 2. *γnaṅs-čé* **rather** (too) **large,** *γnaṅs-čún* **rather** (too) **small** *Mil.nt.*

གནད་ *γnad*, *Ssk.* मर्मन्. 1. **the main point, object** or **substance, the pith, essence,** *γnad ᵒgról-ba* to explain the main point *Mil.*; *γnad-dón* the proper meaning, the pith of the matter *Tar.*, *Schf.*; **γnád-šes-mkan** *W.* one that knows a thing thoroughly, that is up to it, knows how to do it; **nė' šė'-pa, nė'-kyi žú-wa búl-wa** *C.* to excuse one's self, to defend or justify one's self (prop. to account for the circumstances that led to an action); **pog da pog; nad-du* (or *nad-čan*) *ma teb** *W.* I have hit (him), but not mortally; so *B.*: *γnád-du snún-pa* to pierce mortally. — 2. in anatomy: by *γnad bdun*, or 'the seven important parts of the body', acc. to *S.g.* are meant: flesh, fat, bones and veins, and *ču-rgyus, don,* and *snod* (*Wise*, Hindoo Medicine p. 69, gives a somewhat different explanation). — 3. in mysticism: the seven physical conditions requisite for successful meditation, *lág-pa mnyam-bžág-tu bžág-pa* (the hands joined over the stomach in such a manner, that the fore-joints of the fingers cover each other, whilst the thumbs are stretched out without touching), *lus rdo-rje-skyil-krúṅ sdód-pa, gal-tsig mda ltar sráṅ-ba, dpúṅ-pa γyód-šog-pa ltar sráṅ-ba, mig sna-rtsér ᵒbébs-pa, mču raṅ-ᵒbab-tu bžág-pa, lčé-rtse ya-dkán-la sbyár-ba;* there are also *séms-kyi γnad Mil.* certain conditions of the mind required, such as abstaining from *rtóg-pa*, speculative thinking.

གནན་པ་ *γnán-pa* v. *nón-pa.*

གནབ་པ་ *γnáb-pa* v. *mnáb-pa.*

གནམ་ *γnam* 1. **heaven, sky,** = *nám-mka; γnám-ga* id. *Cs.*; *γnám-gyi gó-la* **the sphere** or **globe of heaven** *Cs.*(?); *γnam ᵒgyúr-ba Mil.*, mentioned in connexion with an earthquake, and prob. corr. translated by *Schr.* with thunderstorm, tempest; **nam kar-kór** *W.* now the sky is cloudless, now overcast (inst. of **dkar-ᵒkor** ?); *γnám-sgo* 1. *Sch.* **the gate of heaven**(?). 2. *C.* **trap-door.** — *γnam-lčags, γnam-lče Cs.* **thunderbolt, lightning** that has struck; *γnam-stóṅ* the thirtieth day of the lunar month, the day of new moon *Pth.*; **nam-táṅ** *W.* serene sky, fine weather. — *γnam-tel-dkár-po Glr.* 99 is said to be a deity of the Horpa or Mongols, as likewise *sa-tel-nág-po*, and *bar-tel-krá-bo.* — *γnám-mda Pth.* shooting an arrow straight up into the air. — *γnám-rdo Cs.* = *γnam-lčágs, Schr.* **hail.** — *γnam-zlúm* vault of heaven *Sch.* — *γnam-yás Glr.* 95 is said to be a n. p., the name of a building. — *γnam-rú*, resp. for *γžu*, **bow** (for shooting), *Cs.* **rainbow.** — *γnám-sa* heaven and earth, *γnám-sa brdéb-pa tsam* so that heaven and earth were mixed *Glr.* — 2. v. *nam*, **faulty, incorrect.**

གནའ་བ་ *γná-ba Glr.*, *Lt.*, *rnab Sg.*, *Ld.* **ná-po*, fem. *ná-mo**, an **antelope,** found in *Ld.*, *Sp.*, *Kun.*, *Nepal* and other countries;

its flesh is well-tasted, and its hair is supposed to cure cases of poisoning(!) *Med. Hook.*, (Him. Journ. II, 132) seems to mean this animal by his 'gnow', prob. confounding *γna* with *γnyan* (q.v.) which latter, acc. to Cunningham's Ladak p. 198, and by the statements of the natives, is the argali.

གནའ་བོ *γná-bo* **ancient** *Cs.*; *γna-sṅón* **formerly, in old times** *Cs.*; *γná-dus Lex.* **former times, time of yore**; *γná-nas ma mťoṅ* never seen or heard of before *Dzl.*; *γná-rabs Cs.* men who lived in old times, the ancients.

གནའ་མི *γná-mi Lex.* w.c.; *Sch.* **witness.**

གནས *γnas* 1. **place, spot,** *B., C,* (in *W. sa(-ḱyád), sa-čá*) *dbén-pai γnas šig* a lonely place; *mťó-bai γnas* a raised place, an elevation *Dzl.*; *γnás-na ˳dúg-pa, γnás-su sdód-pa* the being somewhere, *γnás-su ˳gró-ba* the going somewhere, *γnás-nas skrod-pa* the expelling from a place *Gram.* — 2 **place of residence, abode, dwelling-place,** (in *W.* not in use) *γnas ˳bébspa Sch.*, *˳čá-ba Ma.*, *˳débs-pa*, to establish one's self at a place, **to settle,** *γnas γtóṅ-ba, šóm-pa*, **to quarter, lodge, take in,** a person *Stg.*, *γnas méd-par ˳gyúr-ba* to become homeless; a house, family, or race no longer existing, extinct, *Dzl.*; *γnás-su sóṅ-ṅo* they returned to their place, their home *Dzl.*; *γnas daṅ skyabs méd-par ˳gyúr-ba* to be at one's wit's end, not knowing what to do *Schr.* — 3. **a holy place, place of pilgrimage; hermilage, monastery;** **nás ǰal-pa, nás-kor-pa** *W.* **a pilgrim;** **dor-ǰe-líṅ-gi ne** the hermitage, or Buddhist parsonage in Darjeeling; acc. to *Sch.* also Lama, cf. *mčód-γnas.* — 4. **a clerical dignity** or **degree,** *γnas sbyín-pa* to confer such *Sch.* — 5. (cf. the Latin *locus*) **object,** like *yul*, but not so frq., *gád-moi γnas* an object of laughter; *ṅó-ťsai γnas* words, actions, which ought to be an object of shame *Schr.*; **point, head, item** *Was.* (225); **sphere. province,** fig. *S.g.*; *ríg-pai γnas lṅa* the five classes of science. — *γnas ˳gyúr-ba Sch.*: to appear embodied (?); *γnás-su ˳gyúr-ba* and *byéd-pa S.O.* and elsewh.?

གནས་པ *γnás-pa*, (imp. prob. only in the periphrastical form *γnás-par byos*) 1. **to be, live, lodge, dwell, stay,** of persons, animals and things, *mṅál-na γnás-pai ḱyeu* the babes in their mother's womb *Dom.* — 2. **to remain, hold to or on, adhere to,** e.g. a doctrine, opinion, way of acting etc., *dgé-ba bčú-la γnás-pa* to persevere in the ten virtues; *byáms-pai séms-la γnás-pa* to remain, to continue in love; in a general sense: *čós-la γnás-pa* 'one abiding in religion', a clerical person *Dzl.* ཙཱ, 13; **to exist permanently,** opp. to the moment of first taking existence *Was.* (278). — 3. **to hesitate** (?). — *ráb-tu γnás-pa* v. *ráb-tu.*

Comp. and deriv. (also of *γnas*): *γnás-skabs* 1. **state, condition,** or perh. more accurately **period,** *mṅál-gyi γnás-skabs ltár-ltar-po Lex.* 2. **temporal life,** *γnas-skabs-kyi bdé-ba* temporal happiness (opp. *to mťár-ťug-gi snyíṅ-po*, or *don, ˳brás-bu, Schr.*, the essence or result of perfection, here, therefore, = eternal felicity); *γnás-skabs-ťse-yi bar-γčód mi ˳byúṅ-žiṅ* if my temporal life be not endangered. — *γnás-ḱaṅ* **dwelling, dwelling-house** or **room** *Dzl.*; *γnás-ḱaṅ-la sógs-pa* a furnished house or room *Dzl.* — *γnas-čén* a great resort of pilgrimage, a great sanctuary *Tar.* — *γnas brtán* (loco firmus, stabilis, lit. translation of स्थविर 1. firm, 2. old) **an elder, senior,** n. of the (16) highest disciples of Buddha; afterwards, when various schools had been formed, n. of the orthodox Buddhists, *Burn.* I, 288; *Köpp.* I, 383; *Was.* (38). (*Cs.* seems to have confounded *brtan* with *brten*, when he translates: subaltern, vicar). — *γnás-po* **host, landlord, master of a house, head of a family** *C.*, *γnás-mo* fem. *Glr.* — *γnas-mál Lex.*, शयासन, sleeping-place, night-quarters, couch *Schr.*; *Cs.* dwelling-place (?) — *γnas-med* v. *γnas* 2. — *γnas γtsáṅ-mai ris* n. p., name of an abode of the gods. — *γnas-ťsáṅ* **dwelling, quarters, lodgings,** *mí-la γnas-ťsáṅ γyár-ba* to ask for a lodging; to be lodged, to be received into another's house *Tar.*; **nę-tsaṅ ˳juṅ** *C.* you will be lodged here, you may stay here (over night), *W.* **ḍáṅ-sa.** — *ɣnas-tsúl* 1. **the state** in which one is, good or bad, **condition of life,** *séms-kyi* the state of one's soul or heart. 2. **an account,** of one's state of mind. 3. **story, tale, narration; event,** col. 4. in philosophy: **the reality of being** (opp. to non-existence) *Was.* (297). — *ɣnas-ɣži* 1. = *ɣnas* 3, *Tar.* frq. 2. **the locative,** that case which relates to being **in** or **at** a place *Gram.* — *ɣnás-lugs* 1. **position, disposition, arrangement,** *lús-kyi* arrangement of the parts of the body, the science of anatomy *Med.* 2. in mystical works: *ɣnás-lugs rtógs-pa* **the knowledge of the essence of things,** the knowledge of all things, or in a Buddhist sense, of the non-existence of all things, *Tar.* and elsewh. — *ɣnas-bšád* 1. **topography and geography** col. 2. narration of legendary tales connected with some holy place. — *ɣnás-sa* (v. *ɣnás-pa*) the permanent residence of a person, or the constant place of a thing, opp. to **bór-sa** *W.* temporary place or residence; **place, room,** in general, **nę-sa yáṅ-pa dug** *W.* there is much room here. — *ɣnas-bsrúṅ* 1. *W.* ('locum tenens') **earnest, earnest-money, pledge, security;** it might also be used for **ticket,** ticket of admission etc. 2. *Sch.:* **guardian,** or **warden** of a monastery.

གནོང་ *ɣnoṅ* 1. v. *ɣnaṅ-ba.* — 2. **consciousness of guilt,** *ɣnoṅ laṅ* (his) conscience smites (him) *Mil.*; *˳gyod-čiṅ ɣnoṅ bkúr-bai sems* repentance and a sense of guilt *Dzl.*

གནོང་བ་ *ɣnóṅ-ba* 1. **to be conscious of one's guilt, to feel remorse,** to be stung in one's conscience, *ɣnóṅ-žiṅ ˳gyód-pai sgó-nas* from a consciousness of guilt *Pth.*, *ɣnoṅ-˳gyód drág-pos* id. *Pth.*; **nóṅ-ṅo láṅ-na ṭim-čǫ de** *C.* where there is repentance, it is easy to pass judgment. — 2. **to be seized with anguish,** as the effect of poisoning. —

གནོད་པ་ *ɣnód-pa* 1. vb. (cf. *snád-pa*) **to hurt, harm, injure, damage,** *rkáṅ-pa-la ɣnód-par ˳gyúr-gyi dógs-pas* in order not to hurt one's foot *Dzl.*; *ɣnód-par ˳gyúr-bai dgra* a dangerous enemy *Dzl.*; **ṅá-la nod yin** *W.* (he or it) will hurt me. — More frq.: 2. sbst. **damage, harm, injury,** *byéd-pa, skyél-ba, Glr., Mil.*, **kyál-če** *W.* **to do harm, to inflict injury, to hurt,** with *la*; *ɣnód-pa med-par, ma ˳gyur-nas* without any harm, without injury *Sch.*; *ɣnod-byed-nyés-pa* v. *nyés-pa* I. — *klui ɣnód-pa* damage done by Nagas. — *ɣnod-sbyin,* **यक्ष**, a class of demons.

གནོན་པ་ *ɣnón-pa* v. *nón-pa.*

གནོབ་ *ɣnob* v. *mnáb-pa.*

མནག་པ་ *mnág-pa Sch.* = *ɣnág-pa* 5.

མནད་མནད་ *mnad-mnád Sch.:* **falsehood, calumny;** *W.* **nad-nád čó-kan** one doing damage maliciously.

མནན་པ་ *mnán-pa* v. *nón-pa.*

མནབ་པ་, (ག)ནབ་པ་ *mnáb-pa, (ɣ)náb-pa,* resp. for *gyón-pa,* **to put on,** *ná-bza Lex.* the garment; v. also *nabs.*

མནབ་རྩལ་ *mnab-rtsál Cs.* **mean, worthless;** *Lex.* and *Sch.:* **nourishment, food,** *mnab-rtsál-gyi bu(-tsa) Cs.:* the child of an indigent person, *Sch.:* **foster-child;** the word is not much known.

མནམ་པ་ *mnám-pa* **to smell of,** c.a., *drí-ma glá-bai ríl-ma mnam* as to its smell, it smells of the dung of a musk-deer; **to smell agreeably, to exhale fragrance,** e.g. the scent of lotus *Glr.*; more frq. **to smell badly,** to spread an offensive smell, to stink, *rṅul maṅ dri mnam* profuse and badly smelling perspiration *Lt.*; *lus btsóg-pa mnám-pa* (or *-po*) *˳di Dzl.* this foul stinking body. Note: The transitive signification (to smell = to perceive by the nose) belongs only to the form *snám-pa*, and *Dzl.* ༢༥, 14 should be translated: the medicine stank.

མནའ་ *mna* **oath,** *mna ˳bór-ba, ˳dór-ba, byéd-pa, skyél-ba B.*, **kyál-če** *W.*, **to take an oath, to swear:** *lha dpáṅ-du btsúgs-nas mna byéd-pa* to swear by the Lha *Glr.*; *˳di-skad čes mna bór-ro Dzl.*; *bar daṅ mná-*

dpaṅ byéd-pa to act as a mediator and witness of the confirmation of the peace by oath *Glr.*; **mna zá-ba** *C.* **to swear falsely, to commit perjury.**

མནའ་མ་ *mná-ma Dzl.* and elsewh., *Cs.*: a son's or grand-son's wife, **a daughter-in-law**; but the word is also used for the daughter-in-law 'in spe', i.e. for the bride of the son, who is usually selected by the parents and lives with these for one or two years before being married; so also bridegroom and son-in-law are nearly synonymous; v. *bág-ma* and *mág-pa*; cf. also the Hebrew חָתָן and כַּלָּה.

མནར་བ་ *mnár-ba* **to suffer, to be tormented,** *B.*, *C.*, *sdug-bsṅál ṗúṅ-pos* under a mountain of misery *Glr.*; *nyes-méd ɣtsó-bo rgyál-poi ˏǰigs-pas mnar* the innocent lords had to suffer in consequence of the king's fears *Pth.*; *lás-kyis mnár-ba* to suffer in consequence of former actions, to be damned; *lás-kyis mnár-bai brág-srin-mo žig* a Srinmo in the state of damnation; *raṅ-nyid mnar-sdaṅ* (?) *byed* you make yourselves suffer the torments of damnation *Mil.*

མནལ་ *mnal*, resp. for *ɣnyid*, **sleep,** *mnál-du ṗéb-pa* or *ˏgró-ba* to fall asleep, *mnál-ba* to sleep, *mnál-ɣzim-pa* id.; *mnal sád-pa* to awake *Mil.*; *mnal-láb* the talking in one's sleep; *mnál-lam* **dream** *Glr.*

མནོ་བ་ *mnó-ba* 1. **to think, fancy, imagine,** *de ṅá-la zér-ba yin mnós-nas* thinking it had been said **to him.** — 2. **to think upon, to consider,** *sṅa bsam ṗyi mno méd-par* neither considering before hand, nor thinking of the consequences; *bsam-mnó ɣtóṅ-ba* id., *Mil.* (cf. *bsam-bló*).

མནོག་པ་ *mnóg-pa* **contentment** *Cs.*; *zas-mnóg Lex.* w.e.; *Sch.*: moderate fare, frugal diet; *mnog-čúṅ* insignificant, trifling, v. *naṅs.*

མནོང་བ་ *mnóṅ-ba* v. *ɣnóṅ-ba.*

མནོད་པ་ *mnód-pa* v. *nód-pa.*

མནོལ་གྲིབ་ *mnol-grib Cs.* = *mnal-grib*; *mnol-rig* **weak intellect,** want of quick perception *Sch.*

མནོས་ *mnos* 1. v. *nód-pa.* — 2. v. *mnó-ba.*

རྣ་བ་ *rná-ba* 1. resp. *snyan*, col. **nám-čog*, or *ăm-čog**, (*Pur.*, *Bal.* **rna, sna**), **the ear,** *séms-čan ˎón-pa-dag rná-bas sgrá-rnams ťos* the deaf hear; *rná-bai mé-loṅ* the drum or tympanum of the ear *Cs.*; *rná-bai dgá-ston* a treat for the ears *Glr.*; *rná-bai dbáṅ-po ɣtod* lend me your ear, listen to me *Mil.*; *ṅed rná-ba mi sun* I am not tired of hearing *Mil.*; *rnar snyán-pa* pleasant to the ear, tickling the ear *Stg.*; *rná-ba ˏdúd-pa* v. *ˏdúd-pa*; *rná-ba byá-ba, byó-ba, blág-pa Sch.*, **to listen,** *rná-ba ná-ba* disease of the ear, **ear-ache;** *rná-ba ˎúr-ba Med.* a tingling, humming, or buzzing in the ears; *rná-ba sra* hard or dull of hearing *Sch.* — 2. v. *ɣná-ba.*

Comp. *rna-kór* ear-ring *Sch.*—**na-kyág** *W.* ear-wax, cerumen. — *rna-ḱúṅ* ear-hole, *ˏčí-bai rná-ḱuṅ-du* (or *rná-bar*, or *rnar*) *brǰód-pa* to cry into a dying man's ear. — *rna-ḱébs* that part of a helmet which protects the ear *Sch.* — *rna-gyán* ornament worn in the ears, e.g. *mé-tog-gi Stg.*; *rna-čá* id., *ɣsér-gyi Mil.* — *rná-mčog* col. 1. = *rná-ba.* 2. the pan of a fire-lock. — *rna-ltág* the back-part of the ear *Cs.* — *rná-ťeg-čan, bzód-pa sgóm-pai rná-ťeg-čan* one that is able to listen to all that (stuff) with patience *Mil.* — *rna-ɣdúb* ear-ring *Cs.* — *rna-mdá ɣzér-ba C.* the piercing of the ear with an arrow, a chinese punishment. — *rna-spág* (sic), or *-spábs* ear-wax *Sch.* — *rna-rdl* an ear torn by pendants. — *rna-lúṅ Cs.* **the ear or handle of a vessel.** — *rna-šál Med.* ear-lap, tip of the ear. — *rna(-pa)-ɣšóg Lex.* and *Lt.*, perh. = *sna-ɣšog.* — *rna-slán* (**nas-lán**) a fur-cover for the ears, worn by Tibetan ladies.

རྣག་ *rnag* **matter, pus, suppuration,** *rnag smin-pa* pus grown ripe *Cs.*; *ˏdrén-pa Sch.*: 'to draw out the pus'; (I only met with *rnag sná-ˏdren-pa S.g.*, which can hardly have this signification); *rnag-rdól-ba* discharge of matter; *rnag-rtól-ba* prob. causing such a discharge by a puncture; *rnag ˏdzág-pa* the dropping or running of pus

Cs.; *rnág-par rnág-pa* to form pus, to ulcerate *Cs.* — *skráṅs-pa rnág-tu k'ug* v. *gug-pa*. — *rnag-k'rág* matter and blood. — *rnág-čan* containing pus, purulent. — *rnag-ₒbrúm* abscess *Sch.* — *rnag-šubs* prob. the core of an ulcer.

རྣགས་ *rnags W., C.*, **ready money, cash,** *nag kyaṅ* id.; *nag-zog* money and goods; *gir-mo gyad nag* *Ld.* eight rupees in cash.

རྣང་བ་ *rnáṅ-ba* pf. *brnaṅs* **to be checked, stopped, shut off**; with or without *gré-bar*, to stick fast in one's throat; **to be choked** (complete form *brnáṅs-te ₒči-ba*); *dbúgs-kyis rnáṅ-šiṅ* (his) breath stopping short (from fright) *Pth.*; *skád-kyis rnáṅ-te* not being able to utter a word *Dzl.* ༢༡, 1; *zás-kyis rnáṅ-te* the food sticking fast in his throat, *mya-ṅán-gyis* from sorrow *Dzl.*

རྣམ་ *rnam*, in compounds for *rnám-par*, v. *rnám-par* extr.

རྣམ་པ་ *rnam-pa* 1. **piece, part**, e. g. the parts of a panel of a door, *riṅ-gi nám-pa* a longitudinal piece, *žéṅ-gi nám-pa* a cross piece *W.*; *rnám-pa ɣnyis-su gyes* (a ray of light) is divided into two parts or rays; **section, distinct part of a treatise; part, ingredient**, *lús-kyi rnám-pa p'rá-rags-rnams* the subtile and the coarse ingredients of the body *Wdṅ.*; *rnám-pa kún-tu, t'ams-čád-du* in every respect, to all intents and purposes, through and through, entirely, perfectly; this phrase is used, whenever people of rank are addressed: *rnam-kún t'úgs-rje mgo-ₒdrén bka-drin mt'suṅs-brál* most honoured patron, altogether incomparable as to grace and goodness! or, *rnam-kún t'úgs-rje daṅ bka-drin mt'suns-brál*; European gentlemen are thus addressed in letters: *rnam-kún t'úgs-rje ₒgyur-méd sá-heb* most honoured Sahib, invariably kind in every respect! — 2. things or persons taken **individually**, often pleon., *ₒod-zér rnám-pa bži* four (separate) rays of light; *ǰó-bo rnam(-pa) ɣnyis* the two lords (sc. gods) *Glr.*; *bdag ₒdir ts'ogs bú-mo rnám-pa lṅa* we five girls here assembled *Mil.*; *sá-heb nám-pa nyi* *W.* the two European gentlemen; *čo-ₒp'rúl rnám-pa bčo-brgyád* the eighteen wonderful feats; *ₒbyúṅ-ba rnám-pa lṅa Wdṅ.* the five elements; *žal-zás rnám-pa Dzl.* ༤༦, 17 the separate dishes of a meal (another reading: *žal-zás-rnams*); when used in quite a general sense, the exact meaning is to be understood only by the context: *lhá-sa rnam-pa ɣnyis ts'ár-nas* after finishing the two Lhasa affairs, viz. the erecting of two buildings previously mentioned; *rnám-pa t'ams-čád mkyén-pai ye-šés S.O.*, or *spyan Dzl.*, as much as omniscience; *ɣzugs ni k'a-dóg daṅ dbyíbs-kyi rnám-pao* '*ɣzugs*' is that in which both colour and form are included *Wdṅ.* — 3. **division, class, species**, *dpuṅ rnam bži* the four species of troops (cavalry, elephants, chariots, infantry); *rnám-pa bži* of four different kinds. — 4. **manner, way**, *rnám-pa sna-ts'ógs-kyis, rnám-pa sna-ts'ógs-kyi sgó-nas* in manifold manner, variously, frq.; *rnám-pa drúg-tu* (the earth shakes) in six ways, i.e. directions (whenever extraordinary works of charity are performed by holy men) v. *Burn.* I., 262 (not 'six times' *Sch.*); *rnám-pas = sgó-nas*, or *p'yir*, *bslú-bai rnám-pas* by arts of seduction *Dzl.*; *dé-la mi dgá-bai rnám-pas* from vexation at it *Mil.*; *bsér-mai rnám-pas* in consequence of the cold wind *Mil.* — 5. **outward appearance, exterior,** आकार, as to form, figure, shape: *lčágs-kyui rnám-pa* in the shape of a hook, hooked *Wdṅ.*; *stón-pai rnám-par sprul* he assumed the appearance of the Teacher *Tar.*; *čós-skui rnám-par ₒgyúr-ba* to appear in a misty form *Glr.*; *lus ₒdi ni roi rnám-par ₒgyur* this body turns into a corpse *Thgy.*, and so in most cases with regard to the whole appearance; of colour alone it is used only, when *dbyíbs* (the shape) has already been stated, as in a passage from *Pth.*: as to its *rnám-pa* (colour), it is spotted like a leopard; **deportment, demeanour, gesture,** *yid-du ₒóṅ-bai rnám-pas* of graceful manners *Mil.*; further: **state, manner of existence,** of certain inhabitants of hell *Thgy.*; in philosophical writings: 'Form der Erkenntniss' *Was.* (274); men-

20*

tally: **disposition, temper, state of mind** *Thgy.*; **kọ nám-pa-la* = *sám-pa-la C.* in his mind.

རྣམ་པར་ *rnám-par* 1. termin. of *rnám-pa:* **into the form** etc., v. above. — 2. as postp. **like,** = the Lat. instar, *Wdṅ.* — 3. adv. (possibly an abbreviation of *rnám-pa kún-tu*), **entirely, perfectly, thoroughly;** in negative sentences: **by no means, on no account**; often only adding force to another word, *Ssk.* वि; frq. in the shorter form *rnam.*

The following expressions most in use, containing the adv. *rnám-par* or *rnam*, are alphabetically arranged with reference to the second word: *rnám-par klúb-pa* **to adorn, embellish** *Cs.* — *rnam-gráṅs* 1. **enumeration,** *rgyál-poi* of kings *Glr.* 2. **the whole amount, sum total,** *S.g.*; **full number** or **quantity,** where nothing is wanting *Glr.*90, 3.; *mtsán-gyi rnam-gráṅs* the component parts of his name according to their etymological value *Tar.*69, 3. 3. **treatise, dissertation, a paper,** *čós-kyi* frq. 4. by grammarians the signification of *de* is thus defined: *rnam-graṅs-ẏžan-brǰód-pa* demonstrative pronoun(?). — *rnam-ₒgyúr* (cf. above *rnám-pa* 5) 1. **form, figure, shape,** *yi-gei rnam-ₒgyúr* the form of the letters (written or printed) *Glr.*, or in this passage also = the graceful form of letters, caligraphy, penmanship, v. below. 2. **behaviour, demeanour,** *lus-ṅág-gi Wdṅ.*; of a sick person *S.g.*; **gesture,** e.g. devout gestures *Mil.*; *rnam-ₒgyúr rdzés-pa Pth.* mimic gestures, mimical performance, ballet. More esp.: 3. **beautiful form, graceful carriage** of the body, **graceful attitudes** (of dancers etc.) *Pth.*; *bzoi rnam-ₒgyúr* the beauty of a work *Glr.* 4. **pride** *C., W., Mil.*; *rnám-ₒgyur-čan* **fine, smart, gayly dressed; proud, vain, foppish** col. — *rnám-par rgyál-ba* conquering completely, gaining a full victory *Pth.*; *rnam-rgyál* a surname much in use; *rnam-rgyal-púṅ-pa*, acc. to *Schl.* 247 *búm-pa*, water-bottle for sacred uses. — *rnam(-par)-bčád(-pa)* section, paragraph, *rnám-par bčad-pa daṅ-po-o* first paragraph; also mark of punctuation at the end of a paragraph, i.e. double-shad. — *rnam-bču-dbaṅ-ldan* a certain way of writing the Ommanipadmehūm, v. *Schl.* p. 121; but I should rather explain it in accordance to *rnám-pa* 2, as the 'ten powerful things', scil. letters or written characters, else the words would have been: *rnám-par dbaṅ-ldán bču.* — *rnám-par ₒǰóg-pa* v. *rnam-bžág.* — *rnám-par rtóg-pa* (cf. *rtóg-pa* I. 2, and II., 2), gen. sbst. *rnam-rtóg* (विकल्प distinction; doubt, error) 1. **discrimination, perception**; so perh. *S.g.*: *rnam-rtóg ṅan bčom* the perception of what is disagreeable is weakened; **reasoning, mental investigation,** opp. to *ye-šes*, the sublime wisdom of the saint. 2. **scruple, hesitation,** *rnam-rtóg ma mdzád-par čaṅ ₒdi ẏsol* please drink this beer without any scruple! *Pth.*; so also in col. language. 3. in philosophy: **obscuration,** viz. of the clear and direct (nihilistic) knowledge of truth by reasonings in the mind of the individual, **error,** *Was.* (305). 4. in pop. language **disgust, distaste,** *rnám-rtog skyéd-pa* to feel disgust *Glr.*, *zá-ba Pth.* prob. id. — *rnám-(par) tár(-ba).* 1. **to be entirely released** or **delivered,** and sbst. **complete deliverance,** *rnam-tár ẏsum Trigl.* fol. 12, three ascetic notions (in themselves of little consequence), *stoṅ-pa-nyíd, mtsán-pa-med-pa,* and *smón-pa-med-pa.* 2. sbst. *rnam-tár* **biography, legendary tales** about a saint; **tale, story, description,** in general. — *rnam-tós-(kyi) bu, sras, rnam-sras* = Kuvera, *Ssk.* वैश्रवण. — *rnam-(par) dág (-pa)* thoroughly cleansed, frq.; by *rnam-(par) dág(-par) rtsi-ba,* or *mdzád-pa* I have attempted to express the Scriptural doctrine of δικαιοῦν or **justification.** — *rnam-ₒdúd* n. of one of the seven golden hills round Mount Meru *Glr.* — *rnam-ₒdrén* (cf. *ₒdrén-pa* 2) the saviour, Buddha; *rnam-log-ₒdrén* the reverse. — *rnam-par-snaṅ-mdzád,* वैरोचन, n. of the first of the Dhyani Buddhas. — *rnam-(par) ₒṗrul(-ba)* **sorcery, magic tricks,** *byéd-pa Dom.* — *rnam-ṗyé, rnam-ṗyéd,* prob. = *rnam-(par) dbye(-ba)* 1. **distinction, division, section.** 2. *rnam-dbyé* **case or cases,** of which the Tibetan grammarians, from an excessive regard of the Ssk. language and in fond imitation of its peculiarities, have also adopted seven in number. — *rnam-(par) smin(-pa)* **retaliation, requital,** of good or evil deeds, committed in former lives, of good actions by prosperity (*las-ₒp̓ró*), of bad ones by misery and sufferings (*lan-čágs*), very frq.; *sdig-pai rnam-par smin-pa myóṅ-ba Dzl.* — *rnam-(par) bžág(-pa)* 1. **to distinguish, to put in order, arrange, classify** *Wdṅ.*, *Thgy.*, ... *sgó-nas* according to ... (certain points or facts). 2. to consider a person or thing as fully equal or equivalent to another, to substitute one for the other, *C.*; *rnam-bžag* sbst., *Lex.* **व्यवस्था** 1. **placing apart, separating; distinction.** 2. **arrangement, position**, = *ynás-lugs* 1. — *rnam-(par) rig(-pa)* and *šés(-pa)*, as a vb., 1. **to know fully, to understand thoroughly.** 2. *rnám-par šés-pai lús-čan-rnams Dom.* **rational**, or at least **animated,** beings, opp. to inanimate nature; as a sbst., gen. *rnam-šes*, **विज्ञान**: 1. etymologically: **perfect knowledge, consciousness,** *Köpp.* I, 604. 2. in philosophy: one of the five *p̓úṅ-po*, **perceptions, cognitions**, *Was.* (of which there are six, if the knowledge acquired by the inner sense is included) also in *Mil.* frq., e. g. *sgo lṅai rnam-šes* (cf. *sgo ysum*). 3. in pop. language: **soul**, e.g. of the departed, (later literature and col.) (The significations 2 and 3, I presume, should be distinguished, as is done here, according to the different spheres in which they are used and not be explained one out of the other, as is attempted *Burn.* I, 503. *Schr.* gives here, as in most cases, the signification used in col. language.) 4. *rnam-rig Was.* (307) **idea, notion**; *Tar.* often = **न्याय**, also **चित्त**, *rnam-rig-tu bkrál-pa* 'explained in the sense of the idealists', *Schf.*; *rnam-rig dan rtóg-gei bstan-bčos* logical and dialectical Shastras. — *rnam-bšád* **explanation** *Tar.*

རྣམས་ *rnams*, in *B.* the usual sign of the plural, in col. language little used, esp. in *W.*, meaning, acc. to its etymology, **piece by piece;** hence its use is not a strict grammatical rule, but more or less arbitrary; it is mostly omitted, when the plural is otherwise indicated, e. g. after definite and indefinite numerals; it may be used, however, not only in these instances (*ₒk̓or máṅ-po-rnams* many servants), but also after collective nouns (*dge-ₒdún-rnams*), at the end of enumerations (= *de tams-čád*), after general expressions, such as: *guṅ yód(-pa)-rnams* whatever they were, after other plural-signs (... *dag-rnams* etc.). Cf. *rnám-pa* 2.

རྣར་ *rnar*, for *rná-bar*, q. v.

རྣལ་(མ་) *rnál(-ma)* I. 1. **rest** *Cs.*, *lus rnál-du ynás-par gyúr-to* his body obtained rest *Tar.*; esp. **tranquillity of mind, composedness, absence of passion,** *sems rnál-du mi ynás-par* his soul having no rest *Tar.*; *rnál-du ₒdúg-pa*, or *ₒk̓ód-pa*, *Mil.*: *rnál-mar sdód-pa* id.; *rig-pa rnál-du ₒbébs-pa* to give one's mind up to perfect rest *Thgr.*; *rnal-ₒbyór* 1. **योग**, **meditation,** nearly the same as *tiṅ-ṅe-ₒdzín* and *bsam-ytán Mil.*, but chiefly when it is considered as the business of life; *rnal-ₒbyor-rgyúd*, **योगतन्त्र**, *Tar.* frq. 2. often for *rnal-ₒbyór-pa*. — *rnal-ₒbyór-pa* **योगिन्**, **योगाचार्य**, **devotee, saint, sage, miracle-worker** frq. — 2. *Sch.* also: **personal, visible, essential** (?) — *Tar.* 201, 6. 22: *bstán-pa rnál-ma* ? — II. often for *mnal*.

རྣུར་བ་ *rnúr-ba* v. *snúr-ba*.

རྣོ་བ་ *rnó-ba B.*, རྣོན་པོ་ *rnón-po* usual form, 1. **sharp, acute, edged, pointed;** *rno-méd C.* **dull, blunt;** *rno p̓yúṅ-ba* to sharpen, grind, whet *Sch.* (like *k̓a ₒdón-pa*); *rno lén-pa* to get sharp, to be sharpened; *rno-p̓yuṅ* name of males. — 2. this word is applied by the Tibetans to the chemical qualities of things, though not quite in the same way as we do, as they ascribe a 'sharp' taste to the flesh of beasts of prey, to the bile etc. *Med.* — 3. *rig-pa rnó-ba* **sharp, clever, shrewd,** *Glr.*, *blo rnó-ba* **talented, gifted,** *dbáṅ-po rnó-ba* **acute, sagacious.**

རྣོང་ *rnoṅ Mil.? rnóṅ-la ₒṗog.*

སྣ་ *sna* 1. (resp. *šaṅs*) **the nose,** *B.;* in col. language *sna-mťsúl,* v. below; *snai rús-pa* bridge of the nose, *snai čag-krúm* cartilage of the nose; *skad sná-nas ₒdón-pa* to utter (nasal) whining tones *Mil.; sná-nas ₒk̔ríd-pa* to lead or turn by the nose; *sna ₒṗyi-ba* to blow one's nose. — 2. **trunk, proboscis,** *ṗág-pai Glr.; gláṅ-sna* v. *glaṅ.* — 3. a mountain projecting from some other mountain in a lateral direction, **a spur** *Glr.;* it might also be used for **cape, promontory.** — 4. **end,** *t̔ig-sna* the end of a string *Glr., rál-pai sna* the end of a lock of hair *Glr.;* **hem, edge, border,** *gós-kyi sna* the border of a garment *Cs.;* esp. **the nearer end, fore-part,** *ₒod čén-po žig-gi sná-la* foremost of a bright ray of light (that was approaching) *Mil.; sna ₒdrén-pa* **to lead, to head** (a body of men) cf. *mǰug-ma; dmág-sna ₒdrén-pa* to take the command of an army *Pth.;* more indefinitely, like *ₒdrén-pa:* **to draw along, to lead, to guide,** esp. with *lam,* to direct the way or course of a person, (having the person always in the genit. case); *ₒgro drúg-gi lam-sna ₒdren* as a guide he leads all beings *Mil.; *čú-na ḍem-pa* C.* **to conduct water** (by a water-course); **to bring upon, to cause,** v. below, compounds; *rnág-sna ₒdrén-pa* to cause suppuration *Med.; lám-sna ₒdzín-pa* to have taken a certain road *Mil.* — In some cases it is difficult to account for the signification, so: *sna-čén-po Cs.* **a deputy; commissioner;** *sna-lén byéd-pa* c. genit. **to shelter, harbour, lodge, take in,** *Pth., C.; sna (b)stád-pa Lex., bdág-gi sna-stád k̔yód-la re Cs.* I place my full confidence in you; **ná-do t̔óg-ne* C.,* (**nár-do gyáb-te* W.*) **ₒgyél-ba** either: to fall by striking with the fore-part of one's foot against a stone, or by striking one's foot against a stone lying before one. — 5. **sort, kind, species,** mostly with *t̔sógs (-pa), W.* with **so-só*,* **diverse, various, all sorts of,** *spos sna-t̔sógs-kyis ₒdébs-pa Dzl.* to strew all sorts of spices over ....; *rnám-pa sna-t̔sógs* frq.; less frq. *sna-maṅ Lex., sna dpag-tu-méd-pa Glr., sna-t̔sád Glr.* **of every sort;** *rín-po-če sna-bdun* seven kinds of jewels; *dár-sna lṅa* five sorts of silk; also *sna* alone is added to substantives, inst. of *sna-t̔sógs,* or = *rnams: šiṅ-snai dúd-pa* smoke from different sorts of wood *Glr.; ₒbrú-sna smíṅ-pa* the ripening of corn *Glr.; sna-γčig* a single one *Mil.; čós-sna Tar.* 166, 4 prob. is not so much a kind, as a part of doctrine, *Schf.* — 6. *mí-sna, bló-sna* v. *mi* and *blo.*

Comp. *sná-skad, *ná-kad ton* W.,* he speaks through his nose. — *sna-k̔úṅ* nostril. — *sna-k̔rág, sna-k̔rág ₒdzág-pa* a bleeding from the nose, *sna-k̔rág γčód-pa* to stop it, *čad,* it ceases, it is stanched. — *sna-k̔ríd* guide, leader; the leader of a choir. — *sná-ga* col. = *sna* 3. — *sna-góṅ* trunk, proboscis *Sch.* — *sna-sgáṅ* bridge of the nose *Cs.* — *sna-sgrá* the noise made through the nostrils *Cs.,* snuffling. — *sna-čú* a running nose, *sna-čú ₒdzag* mucus is dropping from the nose *Lt.* — *sna-čén Thgr.* a demon (?). — *sna-mčú* an elephant's trunk *Pth.* — *sna-t̔ág* 1. a rope passed through the nose of a beast to lead it by. 2. proboscis, *sna-t̔ág* or *sna-mčú sríṅ-ba* to stretch it forward *Pth.* — *sna-drí* prob. = *snabs Med.* — *sna-γdóṅ* bridge of the nose *Sch.* — *sna-ₒdág* (spelling?) *W.* **snuff.** — *sna-ₒdrén* **leader, commander;** *sdug-bsṅál-gyi sna-ₒdrén* **one that causes misfortune, author of it.** — *sna-nád* disease of the nose. — **na-či* C., *na-ṗi* W.,* pocket-handkerchief. — *sna-bábs* the glanders *Sch.* — *sná-bo* 1. **leader, commander, chief.** 2. **a guide,** *gom γsum tsam-laaṅ sná-bo dgos* about every third step one wants a guide *Mil.* — *sna-búg S.g., sna-sbúgs Cs.,* nostril. — *sna-sbyóṅ, sna-smán* snuff *Med.* — *sná-ma Lex.* w.e., *Cs.* = *sna* 4. — *sna-rtsá* root of the nose *Cs.* — *sna-rtsé* tip of the nose. — *sna-t̔sógs* v. *sna* 5. — **nam-t̔súl* W., *nam-súl* Bal.* = *sna* 1 and 2. — *sna-ₒdzúr* an aquiline or crooked nose *Cs.* — *sna-léb* a flat nose *Cs.* — *sna-šá* the flesh of the nose; the nose *Cs.; sna-šá sbyín-pa* to suffer one's self to be led by the nose *Cs.* — *sna-ysóg* 'the hair in the nostrils'; *sna-ysógs* 'the wings of the nose (alae nasi), together with the nostrils' *Sch.*; *sna-ysór* id. *Sch.* — *sna-bsál Lt.*, prob. an injection into the nose.

སྣ་ནམ་ *sna-nám* **Samarkand** *Glr.*

སྣ་སྣེམ་ *sna-sném, sna-sném ma ˳dúg-čig* do not sit here so idly, without any particular object! *Sch.*

སྣ་སྦྲང་ *sna-sbráṅ* **arrow-head** *Sch.*

སྣ་མ་ *sná-ma* 1. *Cs.*: 'the blossom of the nutmeg-tree'(?). — 2. v. *sna*, compounds.

སྣ་རུ, རྣ་རོ *sná-ru, rná-ro,* = *ná-ro Sch.*

སྣག་ *snag* 1. = *rnag Cs.* — 2. also *snág-tsa* **ink, Indian ink**, *rgya-snág* China ink, *bod-snag* Tibetan ink, *ċe-snág* Cashmere ink; **nág(-tsa) lug soṅ* W.* the ink has run, i. e. a blot has been made. — **nag-koṅ* W.*, **nag-bhum* C.*, inkstand. — *snag-tig* an ink-spot, a dash, a stroke, made with the pen. — *snag-p̔yé* ink-powder. — *snag-ris rgyág-pa* to paint over with ink. — 3. *mig-gi snág-lpags Pth.?*

སྣག(ས)་ *snag(s)* = *ma-ynyén*, **relationship by the mother's side**; *snág-gi ynyen-mtsáms* id. *Pth.*; *snag-dbón Lex.* w.e.

སྣང་བ་ *snáṅ-ba* I. vb. 1. **to emit light, to shine, to be bright**; *snáṅ-bar byéd-pa* **to fill with light, to enlighten, to illuminate**, *˳gyúr-ba* **to be filled with light, to be enlightened**, e.g. by the light of wisdom *Dzl.*; *šin-tu mi-snáṅ-bai mún-pa* darkness entirely devoid of light *Dzl.* — 2. **to be seen** or **perceived**, to show one's self, to appear, e.g. blood appears on the floor *Dzl.*; (*p̔yi*) *snáṅ-ba tams-ċád Mil.*, *p̔yi snáṅ-ba gaṅ ˳byuṅ Mil.*, *p̔yi snáṅ-bai yul Mil.*, *snaṅ-tsád Glr.*, every thing visible, all that is an object of sense, the external world; *dá-lta rgyu žig snáṅ-ṅo* now an opportunity shows itself *Dzl.*; *lus mi snaṅ yaṅ ysuṅ snáṅ-ba ma-čád-pa byuṅ* although the body had become invisible, yet the voice continued to appear, to be heard *Tar.* 127, 11; it seems even to be capable of being extended to mental perceptions, the partic. being equivalent to imaginable; **to have a certain appearance, to look** (like), *čád-pa ltar* as if it had been suddenly cut off *Wdṅ.*; *snúm-bčus* (to look) greasy *S.g.*; *˳p̔rúl-du snáṅ-ṅo* it looks like sorcery *Glr.* (cf. *˳p̔rul*); *mi-snáṅ-ba* **invisible**, *mi-snaṅ-bar ˳gyúr-ba* to disappear frq.; *btsún-mo-rnams mi snáṅ-ba daṅ* as their wives were not to be seen, were not present *Dzl.* ༧༠, 17; *mi-snáṅ bar byéd-pa* to make invisible, to efface the traces of a thing. — 3. = *yód-pa Lex.*, sometimes in *B.*, and in the col. language of certain districts; *žes p̔rál-skad-la snaṅ* so it occurs in vulgar language *Gram.*; *zér-ba snaṅ* it is said, *dicitur*, *Tar.* 34, 4, and in a similar manner 33, 22; 34, 14; prob. also: **to be in a certain state** (of health), **in a certain condition, situation** etc., *C.*: **dhá-ta ghaṅ náṅ-ghin yö̀-dham** how are you now? **čag peb žu naṅ** is the usual salutation in *C.*, like our: good morning! or: how do you do? however, the literal sense of it seems to have been forgotten, as even educated Lamas seldom know how to write it correctly. The proper way of spelling it seems to be: *p̔yag p̔eb bžud snaṅ*, and the words hardly imply much more than those addressed to inferior people, viz. *da leb soṅ* well, so you are come! well, there you are! Cf. *gá-le*.

II. sbst. (दर्शन, आलोक etc.) 1. **brightness, light**, *snáṅ-ba yód-pai dús-su* when there is light, broad day-light *Thgy.*; fig. *čós-kyi snáṅ-ba* the light of doctrine *Dzl.* — 2. **an apparation, phantom**, *mi máṅ-pos déd-pai snáṅ-ba ˳byúṅ-ṅo* there is an appearance as of being pursued by many people, i.e. a phantom of many pursuing people *Thgr.*; *rmi-lam-gyi snáṅ-ba-rnams Mṅg.* — 3. physically: **seeing, sight**, *bdag-ráṅ-gi snáṅ-ba ma dág-pa yin* my faculty of vision, my sight, is dimmed *Tar.*; more frq. intellectually: **view, opinion**, *saṅs-rgyás-kyi snáṅ-ba-la . . . yzigs-so, mi-nág-gi snáṅ-ba-la . . . mtóṅ-ṅo* by the Buddhas he was looked upon as . . ., by laymen as . . . *Glr.*; **thought**,

idea, notion, conception, c. genit., *ₒdi tʿams-ċád ráṅ-gi séms-kyi snáṅ-ba yin* all these things are only conceptions of your mind, your fancies *Thgr.*; *skyid-sdúg-gi snaṅ-ba šar Thgr.*; *ₒkyágs-pai snáṅ-ba ₒbyuṅ Mil.*; *bkres-snáṅ ye-méd-par gyúr-to* he was even without a thought of hunger *Mil.*; absolutely: **kyód-di náṅ-wa gá-ru taṅ soṅ** *W.* where are your thoughts wandering? *čʿós-la snáṅ-ba sgyur* turn your mind to religion! *Mil.*; *snáṅ-ba ₒgyúr-ba* (τὸ μετανοεῖν) change of heart, conversion (not to be confounded with *snáṅ-bar ₒgyúr-ba* v. above). *snáṅ-ba bdé-ba* **pleased, cheerful, happy** *Pth.*; in some expressions it is equivalent to **soul.** Most of the significations mentioned sub 3 seem not to have been in use in the older language. — *ₒkʿrul-snáṅ, ₒpʿrul snáṅ* **illusion, deception of the senses, deceit, error** *Mil., Glr.*, col. — *γnyis-snáṅ* the arising of two ideas in the mind, *γnyis-snáṅ-gi rtóg-pa* **hesitation, irresolution, wavering** *Mil.* — *mtʿoṅ-snáṅ* 1. **the act of seeing, the sight,** *mtʿoṅ-snáṅ-gi sprúl-pa* phantom, apparition, **tʿoṅ-náṅ dé-mo** *W.* a sight beautiful to look at, **tʿoṅ-náṅ sóg-po** of ugly appearance. 2. *Cs.*: **manner** or **mode of viewing, point of view;** *γzigs-snáṅ* id. resp.; *Pth.*: *γzigs-snáṅ-la* according to his (supernatural) **intuition** (with reference to a holy person). — *tsor-snáṅ* **the hearing,** **tsor-náṅ-la nyán-po** *W.* delightful to hear, pleasing to the ear. — *bar-snáṅ* v. *bar*. — *raṅ-snáṅ* one's own thoughts, ideas *Mil.*; **the own mind** *Glr.*; *raṅ-snáṅ ₒkʿrúl-pa* an illusion of fancy *Thgr.*; *snaṅ-grágs* **things seen and heard** *Mil.* — *snaṅ-stoṅ Mil.* frq., prob. not 'empty show, delusive appearance' *Sch.*, but: **things (really) appearing and (yet) void,** one of those frq. instances, where two words of opposite meaning are placed together, *dbyer-méd* often being added, as a tertium quid (cf. *Köpp.* I, 598). — *snaṅ-dág* (*naṅ-rtágs, brtág?? Ld. naṅ-stag*) col. **the inward man, the heart, the soul,** **naṅ-dág-la sám-pa šar soṅ** *W.* a thought has risen in my soul; **naṅ-dág čʿad soṅ** now he has felt it in his inmost soul, this will have struck home to his heart *W.*; **ṅá-la naṅ-dhág ma ǰhuṅ** *C.* I have not heard it, perceived it, minded it; **naṅ-dhág ma ǰhe** *C.*, **ma čʿo** *W.*, I was not heedful, I made a mistake! — *snáṅ-ba-mtʿa-yás* = *ₒod-dpag-méd* Amitābha, the fourth Dhyāni Buddha. — *snáṅ-me* v. *naṅ-me*. — *snaṅ-tsʿád* v. above I., 2. — *snaṅ-tsʿúl* 1. the outward appearance, of a landscape = **scenery** *Mil.*; 2. **appearance** opp. to essence, *γnas-tsʿul Was.* (297). — *snaṅ-mdzád* v. *rnám-par*. — *snaṅ-šás* **thoughts, fancies** (?) — *snaṅ-srid* (*Ssk.* संसार) **the visible, external world** frq. — *snaṅ-γsál* **shining brightlo, brilliant;** *čʿós-kyi snaṅ-γsál sgrón-me* the bright light of doctrine *Pth.* — *snaṅ-ṅor ral ₒdrum Tar.* 16 (?).

སྣད་པ *snád-pa*, pf. *bsnad*, imp. *snod*, **to hurt, to harm, to injure,** c. accus., *lus snád-nas* being hurt in the body *Dzl.*; *ṅai rta snad ₒgro* or *ₒoṅ* my horse might be hurt *Mil.*; *snád-kyis dógs-te* afraid of hurting him *Dzl.*; of horned cattle: **to butt** *Sch.*

སྣབས *snabs*, resp. *šaṅs*, **mucus, snivel, snot,** *snabs pʿyí-ba* to blow one's nose, *snabs-pʿyis* pocket-handkerchief; *snabs-lúg* snotty nose, snotty fellow *Sch.*; *snabs-lúd*, prob. also *dar-snábs Dom.* = *snabs*; *bé-snabs* thick phlegm *Cs.*; *snám-pa* v. *snom*.

སྣམ་བུ *snám-bu* **woolen cloth;** the common sort is not dyed, very coarse, and loosely woven; *snám-bu spú-čan* hairy cloth, napped cloth; *snam-pʿrúg, dbus-snám Mil.*, fine cloth; *ₒgo-snám C.* id.; *snam-sbyár Lex.* a sort of loose mantle for priests *Cs.* — **nám-ya** *W.* **trowsers.** — *snam-yúg, yúg-snam* a whole piece or roll of woolen cloth. *snam rás* woolen cloth and cotton cloth *Mil.*

སྣམ་བྲག *snam-brág* (*Ü:* **ám-bág**) **bosom,** *snam-lógs, snam-γžógs* resp. **side.**

སྣར *snar*, termin. of *sna*; *snar-bkáb Wdk.* fol. 464 **nose-band** (?) **pocket-handkerchief** (?); *snár-kyu* **guide-rope** for camels, passing through their nose.

སྣར་ཐང *nar-tʿáṅ* n. of a monastery, *Köpp.* II. 256; n. of a philologist *Gram.*

སྣར་པོ, སྣར་མོ *snár-po, snár-mo Cs.* 1. of a **white** or **light red colour** (cf. *skya-nár*). — 2. **long, oblong,** cf. *nár-mo*.

སྣར་བ་ *snár-ba* prob. the original form of *bsnár-ba.*

སྣར་མ་ *snár-ma* n. of one of the **lunar mansions,** v. *rgyu-skar* 3.

སྣལ་བ་ *snál-ba* v. *bsnál-ba.*

སྣལ་མ་ *snál-ma* **thread, silk-thread, woolen thread** etc.; **knitting-yarn,** or yarn used for other purposes; also for **warp, abb-yarn.**

སྣུན་པ་ *snún-pa*, pf. and fut. *bsnun*, 1. **to prick** *Lt.*; **to stick** or **prick into,** e.g. a stick into the ground *Mil.*, *mtson* a weapon *Lex.* — 2. **to suckle** (cf. *nú-ba*, *núd-pa*), *nú-ma* or *nú-žo snún-pa Pth.*, *Lt.*, id. — 3. **to multiply** *Wdk.* — *ɣnad snún-pa Lex.* w.e, *Sch.*: 'to excavate the interior, to get or penetrate into the inside'(?).

སྣུབ་པ་ *snúb-pa*, pf. *bsnubs*, fut. *bsnub*, imp. *snub(s)* vb.a. to *núb-pa*, **to cause to perish;** gen. fig. **to suppress, abolish, abrogate, annul, destroy, annihilate,** a religion, a custom etc.

སྣུམ་པ་ *snúm(-pa S.g.*, *-po Cs.*), 1. **fat, grease, any greasy substance,** *snúm-gyis skúd-pa* **to grease, to smear;** in *C.* esp. **oil** (*W.* **már-nag**), *snum-zád-kyi már-me* a lamp, the oil of which is consumed; also fig., *snum* being added pleon., e.g. *Mṅg.*: *lus-zúṅs snum-zád*, and parallel to it: *lus-zúṅs zad Lt.*; *rlan-snúm* raw fat, *žun-snúm* melted fat *Cs.*; *sol-snúm* cart-grease, composed of pulverized charcoal and fat *Glr.* — 2. fig. of luxuriant grass or pasture, *ri snúm-pa* a hill clothed with luxuriant pastures *C.* (cf. *rug-gé*); *snúm-la ǰám-pa* luxurious and soft *Mil.* — *snum-kóṅ* a little bowl for oil etc. — *snum-ˌkúr* a kind of pastry baked in suet. — *snum-glégs*, *W.* **num-lág**, a wooden tablet, blackened, greased, and strewed with ashes, used for writing upon with a wood-pencil, thus serving for a slate. — *snúm-čan*, *snúm-bčas*, *snum-ldán* **fat, oily, greasy.** — *snúm-dri* a smell of fat. — *snúm-nag* **oil** *Kun.* — *snúm-rtsi* a greasy liquid, **oil** etc.; **greasy, oily** *C.* *snúm-pa* vb. = *snóm-pa* I.

སྣུར་བ་ *snúr-ba*, pf. and fut. *bsnur*, vb.a. to *núr-ba*, 1. **to put** or **move out of its place, to remove, to shift** *W.*: **to move** or **draw towards one's self** *Cs.*, so *mdún-du snúr-ba Zam.* is explained by *ˌtén-pa.* — 2. *Sch.*: **to cut into pieces, to fracture, to crush,** *žib-mor* into small pieces (to reduce), to powder; so it seems to be frq. used in *Lt.*, though one *Lex.* explains it by *ˌdás-pa* (scarcely corr.). — 3. *Cs.* **to bring near = to shorten,** *dus* a term, a space of time. Cf. *brnú(r)-ba Lexx.*

སྣེ་(སྣོ་) *sné(-mo)* 1. **extremity, end,** *snál-mai Lex.*, of a thread, *ťág-sne* the end of a rope *Sch.*; **hem, seam,** *né-mo *ltáb-če* W.* to fold down and sew the edge of a piece of cloth, **to hem;** **né-mo gyáb-če* W.* to trim with cord or lace. *sne-ˌkór* **to warp, to get twisted** *Sch.* — 2. *sne-rgód*, *sne-dmár*, *sne-ťsód*, *món-sne*, *sneu*, names of plants.

སྣེམ་པ་ *sném-pa* **to shake, to cause to move slightly,** *bsném-byai sa-ɣži* a quagmire, shaking or yielding under one's feet *Sch.*; *nem-ném bsném-pa Lex.*, pf. *bsnems.*

སྣོ་བ་ *snó-ba Cs.* = *snúr-ba*, **to reduce to small pieces, to crumble.**

སྣོད་ *snod* I. sbst. (**भाजन**) 1. **vessel,** *snod-spyád* id., *Lex.* and col. frq.; *ɣser-snód* a gold vessel; *ṗye-snód* a vessel for meal or flour; *ču-snód* water-pot, pitcher; *bu-snód* **uterus, womb,** *Lt.* and col.; *snód-kyi ka* mouth of a vessel, *snód-kyi žabs* bottom or foot of a vessel, stem of a glass. — 2. in anatomy: *snod drug* (the six vessels) are: gall-bladder, stomach, the small and the large intestine, urinary bladder and spermatic vessels (in the female: uterus); *don-snód*, the six vessels and the five *don* together, v. *don* 5. — 3. with reference to religion v. *sde*, compounds. — 4. fig. 1. in ascetic language denoting **man,** as far as he is susceptible of higher and divine things; so already in *Dzl.* a man is called *snod yóṅs-su dág-pa* a very pure and holy vessel; *snod-ldán slób-ma* a disciple eager to be instructed *Mil.*; *snód-du rúṅ-ba* one fit for, worthy of (instruction); *snód-du méd-pa* unfit, insusceptible, rude, vulgar.; *ńés-par légs-pai snod mčog*, *ńes-legs bsgrúb-pai snod* *mčog* a most perfect vessel of religion (most susceptible of etc.) *Thgy.*; *snod ma yin* insusceptible of religion *Thgy.*, *Tar.* — 2. in metaphysics: *ṗyi-snód* **the external world,** or rather **inanimate nature,** *ṗyi-snód-kyi ˏjig-rtén Glr.* and elsewh. frq., opp. to *naṅ-bčúd*, viz. the sentient beings composing it; so *Mil.*; *Sch.*: matter and spirit. — II. v. *snád-pa*.

སྣོན་ *snon* **rest, remainder**(?) *Dzl.* ༢༨༢, 4, *Sch.*

སྣོན་པ་ *snón-pa*, pf. and fut. *bsnan*, 1. **to add, superadd, increase, augment,** **la nán-če** *W.* to add to the wages, to raise the wages; **ja ťsá-big nan sal** *W.* please give me some more tea! *ẏnyis bsnán-te* two being added to them, (their number) increasing by two *Mil.*; *máṅ-du snón-pa* to augment by a great number frq. — *nón-ka*, or *nón-ḱa W.*, **increase, growth, augmentation,** and in a special sense: **agio, premium**; *snón-ma*, *bsnán-ma*, id.; **puṅ-nón** *W.*, **gyab-nón** *C.*, *dmag-ťsógs snón-ma* **reinforcements, auxiliary troops.** — 2. **to add up, sum up** *Wdk.*

སྣོབ་ཟོག་ཅན་ *snób-zog-čan* (spelling?) **curious, inquisitive,** **nob-zóg čó-če** *W.* to pry into, to ferret.

སྣོམ་པ་ *snóm-pa* I. also *snúm-pa*, pf. *bsnums*, fut. *bsnum*, imp *snum(s)*; and *snám-pa*, pf. *bsnams*, fut. *bsnam*, imp. *snom(s)*, 1. **to smell,** to perceive by the nose (cf. *mnám-pa*), *snas dri-rnams bsnáms-pa* to perceive scents by the nose *Stg.*; **da num** *W.* there, smell at that! **zi núm-te ḍúl-če** *W.* to go about smelling and prying; **ṅa čiaṅ mi num** *W.* I do not smell any thing. — 2. **to grope,** **mụn-nag-la nom-nẹ čin* = *nag-zúg-la nóm-žin soṅ** *C.*, v. *nag-zúg*.

II. pf. *bsnams*, fut. *bsnam*, *W.* **nám-če**, resp. for *lén-pa*, *ˏdzin-pa*, *ťógs-pa*, *ˏčáṅ-ba*, **to take,** relics from a sepulchre *Glr.*; **to seize, to take up,** the alms-bowl *Dzl.*; **to hold,** a stick *Mil.*; **to put on,** a sacred garment; **nam yin-na** *W.* would you please (to take), would you like (to have a cup of tea etc.)?

སྣོར་བ་ *snór-ba*, pf. and fut. *bsnor*, **to confound, mingle, mix, disturb** *Cs.*

སྣོལ་བ་ *snól-ba*, pf. and fut. *bsnol*, 1. **to unite, join, put together, fit together,** e.g. bricks or stones in building *W.*; *Cs.* **to adjust**; *Sch.*: to mend holes in stockings, **to darn; to cross** one's hands, *bráṅ-ḱar*, resp. *ťúgs-kar*, on the breast *Thgr.* and elsewh. frq.; *ˏťam snól-ba* **to put together, to embrace** *Cs.*; *ltá-snol-ba* to look at each other, *ˏó-snol-ba* to kiss each other, 'and thus frq. denoting reciprocity' *Cs.* (though not to my knowledge). — 2. **to wrestle, scuffle, fight,** of boys, dogs frq., also *Mil.*; *stag snól-ba* a fighting tiger that rushes upon the enemy *Ma.*; **to contend with, fight against, subdue,** *me*, a fire *Tar.*

སྣྲུབས་, སྣྲོན་ *snrubs*, *snron*, the names of two of the lunar mansions, v. *rgyu-skár*.

སྣྲེལ་(ག)ཞི་ *snrel-(y)ži Lexx.* = *ṗred*; *Cs.* **sloping, oblique**; *Sch.*: **confusedly, pellmell**; *Cs.* also **mediocrity.**

བརྣག་པ་ *brnág-pa* 1. **to devise, contrive, to take care, to be concerned about, to strive for** or **after,** ... *žes ẏčig-tu brnágs-pas* striving only after (that one thing) *Tar.*; as sbst. *brnág-pa čoṅs* keep (it) well in your mind, pay all attention (to it)! c. genit., cf. *brnán-pa*. — 2. *Lex.* = *bzód-pa*, **to suffer, to endure**; *brnag-dka* **intolerable, insupportable** *Lex.* — 3. *Cs.*: **to be full of corrupt matter.**

བརྣང་བ་ *brnáṅ-ba* v. *rnáṅ-ba*.

བརྣན་པ་ *brnán-pa* 1. *Cs.* **to attend, to look on attentively,** *ˏbri-klóg brnán-pa* to attend while a person is reading or writing. — 2. *Sch.*: **'to be desirous of, to long for,** *čós-la* for religious instruction, *ltó-la* for food'. With the first signification agrees a quotation in *Zam.*: *nán-tan-brnan*, with the second the word **zá-nan-čan** *W.*, = *zá-brnab-čan*.

བརྣབ་སེམས་ *brnáb-sems Cs.*: **covetousness, selfishness**; *Thgy.*: *bdág-gi-la brnáb-sems* predilection for one's own things, *ẏžán-gyi-la brnáb-sems* desire for things belonging to others; *W.*: **zá-nab-čan** **greedy, ravenous;** **nór-nab-čan** **greedy of gain** or **money, covetous.**

བརྣུ་བ་, བརྣུར་བ་ *brnú-ba, brnúr-ba Lexx.; Cs.* **to draw to, to attract,** (*Sch.* also: 'to remove a thing from its place?'), prob. another form for *snúr-ba.*

བརྣོགས་པ་ *brnógs-pa* **to hide, conceal,** *Lexx.*

བསྣང་བ་ *bsnáṅ-ba* v. *rnáṅ-ba.*

བསྣད་པ་ *bsnád-pa* v. *snád-pa.*

བསྣན་པ་ *bsnán-pa* v. *snón-pa.*

བསྣམ་པ་ *bsnám-pa* v. *snóm-pa.*

བསྣར་བ་ *bsnár-ba* 1. **to extend in length, to lengthen, to pull out,** e.g. a piece of India rubber *W.* — 2. **to draw** or **drag after, to trail,** *mjúg-ma Lex.* the train of a robe, the tail etc.; fig. **to have in its train, to be attended with,** *nyon-moṅs-bsnár* the consequences of sin *Sch.*

བསྣལ་བ་ *bsnál-ba* **to spin out, to protract** *Cs.*

བསྣུན་པ་ *bsnún-pa* v. *snun-pa.*

པ

པ *pa* 1. the letter *p*, (tenuis), the French p. — 2. num. figure: 13.

པ་ *pa*, an affix, or so-called article, the same as *ba* (q. v.) which, when attached to the roots of verbs, gives them the signification of nouns, or, in other words is the sign of the infinitive and the participle; in the language of common life, however, it is frq. used for the finite tense, and for *par*; affixed to the names of things, it denotes the person that deals with the thing (*rtá-pa* horseman, *čú-pa* water-carrier); combined with names of places, it designates the inhabitant (*bód-pa* inhabitant of Tibet); with numerals, it either forms the ordinal number (*ynyis-pa* the second), or it implies a counting, measuring, containing (*bú-mo lo-ynyis-pa* a girl counting two years, i. e. a girl of two years; *k̄ru-gáṅ-pa* measuring one cubit; *súm-ču-pa* containing thirty viz. letters, like the Tibetan alphabet); frq. it has no particular signification (*rkéd-pa* etc. etc.), or it serves to distinguish different meanings (*rkaṅ* marrow, *rkáṅ-pa* foot) or dialects (*k̄á-ba B.*, **k̄a* W.* snow); *pa daṅ* with a verb, v. *daṅ* 4; in certain expressions it stands, it would seem, incorr. inst. of *pai*: *ysó-ba rig-pa* science of medicine, *grúb-pa lus* structure of the body, *dám-pa čos* holy doctrine (of Buddha).

པ་ཏ་ *pá-ta W.* **cross,** St. Andrew's cross (thus ×).

པ་ཏིལ་ *pa-til* v. *p̄a-til.*

པ་ཏོ་ *pá-to* a medicinal herb *Wdṅ.*

པ་ཏྲ, more corr. པཱ་ཏྲ, *pā-tra* (also *pa-ṭa Pth.*) *Ssk.*, **cup, basin, bowl** (esp. for sacrifices); beggar's bowl = *lhuṅ-bzed.*

པ་ཎ་ *pa-ṇa Ssk.* = *ṭaṅ-ka Tar.* 112, 6; in Bhotan 1 rupee *Schr.*; in *W.* (also **pé-ṇa**) a copper-coin = Paisa, esp. of foreign coinage.

པ་ཎི་ *pa-ṇi Hind.* पानी, **water** *Lt.*

པ་བེན་ *pa-ben* **a strip of wood, ledge, border** (?) *W.*

པ་(ཝ་)སངས་ *pa(-wa)-sáṅs* 1. the planet **Venus.** — 2. **Friday.**

པ་ཡག་པ་ *pa-yag-pa* a medicinal herb = *smug-čuṅ Med.*

པ་ཡུ་ *pa-yu* salt *Bal.*

པ་ཡོ་ཏོ་ཡོ་ *pa-yo-tó-yo*, **srog daṅ pa-yo-tó-yo taṅ-te soṅ** *Ld.* for *srog daṅ bsdos*, v. *sdo-ba.*

པ་ར་ཁ་ *pá-ra-k'a W.* **cross** (a straight one +).

པ་རང་ *pa-ráṅ* (spelling doubtful, at any rate not *p'a-raṅ*) n. of a mountain pass, 19 000 feet high, between Ladak and Spiti.

པ་རི་ *pá-ri W., pá-ru C., B.* 1. **box,** cylindrical or oval, high or flat, of wood or metal. — 2. *pá-ru,* also *pá-tra Sch.* — 3. v. *bá-ru.*

པ་ཤི་ *pa-ši Sch.* **'a teacher'**; *Lex.*: n. of a Tibetan priest that went to China.

པ་སངས་ *pa-saṅs* v. *pa-wa-saṅs.*

པག, པག་བུ་ *pag, pág-bu Bal., pág-gu Dzl., pau W., p'ag Glr., p'au Wdṅ.*: **brick**; *pág-gu byéd-pa Dzl.*; *p'ibs-pag* roof-tile *Cs.*; *wá-pag* gutter-tile *Cs.*; *rdzá-pag, só-pag Glr.* burnt-brick *Cs.; sá-pag Glr.* unburnt-brick *Cs.*; *pag(-bu)-mk'an* mason *Cs.; pag-rtsig* brick-wall *Cs.*; **pag-ťsir W.** a row or layer of bricks; frq. used as a measure = a small span, **k'a pag-tsir nyis yod** the snow is as deep as two layers of bricks. — Not quite plain is the etymology of *ʼog-pag*, *Lex.*: *ska-rágs-kyi rgyan, Sch.*: 'a girdle ornamented with glass-beads'; and of *pag-p'ór Sch.* cup or vessel with a lid.

པགས་པ་ *págs-pa, Mil.* also *-po* (cf. *lpags*) 1. **skin, hide**; *šu-ba* to skin, acc. to *Schr.* also merely to fret the skin; *págs-pai gos* skin or fur-clothing *S.g.* — 2. **foreskin,** when the connection of words does not admit of a misconception, *Mṅg.* — 3. **skin** or **peel** of fruit, **the bark** of trees, also *pags-šún*, and *šún-pags*; **pag-ťág** *C.* bark-cord, match-cord; *págs-ču* anasarca, skin-dropsy; *págs-ču-žugs* affected with this disease.

པང་ *paṅ*, ཕང་ *p'aṅ*, resp. *sku-páṅ*, 1. the bend or hollow formed by the belly and the thighs in sitting, **lap,** *B., C., W.*; *paṅ-du soṅ* he sat down on the lap of . . . *Glr.*; *paṅ-k'ebs* apron; *paṅ-k'rag* the blood flowing off during child-birth; **paṅ-big** *W.* urinary bladder; **paṅ-ri* (for *dri?*) *suṅ** *C.* she has the bloody flux; *páṅ-yyog-ma Cs.* midwife (a kinswoman generally has to officiate as such; a hired one receives a new dress for her services). — 2. the bend or hollow formed by the arm and the chest in carrying something; **bosom,** usually *páṅ-pa; šiṅ-paṅ-pa gaṅ* an armful of wood; *páṅ-par ʼk'yér-ba* to carry (a child) on the arm *Dzl.* and elsewh.; *sdoṅ-po páṅ-pas ma ʼk'yigs-pa tsam žig* a tree not to be encompassed by a man's arms *Pth.*; **paṅ-gód, paṅ-kód** *W.* an armful.

པང་ཀ་ *páṅ-ka, páṅ-k'a* 1. *W.* an implement for stirring the fire; for scraping = *rbad.* — 2. *Ts.* = *paṅ.*

པཉྩ, པན་ཙ་ *paṅtsa, pan-tsa*, seems to be the n. of a tree *B., C.; Ssk.* only: five.

པད་པ་ *pád-pa C.* = *srín-bu pád-ma*, v. *pád-ma.*

པདྨ, པད་མ་ *padma, pad-ma Ssk.* in *C.* pronounced **pé-ma** 1. **water-lily, lotos,** Nymphaea, if not nearer defined, the blue species, whilst the less frq. form *pád-mo* (acc. to *Glr.* fol. 62) seems to denote the white kind of this flower. — 2. (not in *Ssk.*, at least acc. to *Wls.* and *Williams*, though *Köpp.* II, 61 seems to dissent): **genitals,** of either sex, *Med.* — 3. *srín-bu pád-ma* **leech.** — *pad-kór, pad-skór* 1. a particular way of folding the fingers during prayer *Cs.* and *Sch.*; a certain gesture with the hand. 2. a kind of **toupet** of the women, also *pad-ló C., W.* — *pád(-ma) dkár(-do)* 1. white lotos. 2. **title** of a celebrated **Sutra,** translated by Burnouf, *Was.* (151). — *pad-dkár žal-laṅ* an astronomical work by Púgpapa, v. *Cs.* time-table. — *pad-ma-čan* full of lotos; more particularly lotos-lake, with and without *mťso Glr.* — *pad-(ma daṅ nyi-ma daṅ) zlái ydan Glr.* and elsewh., carpet with representations of lotos, sun and moon. — *pad-ma-pa-ni* lotos-bearer, name of Awalokiteswara, *Köpp.* II, 23. — *Pad-ma-ₒbyuṅ ɣnás, Ssk.* P. Sambhava, also: *U-rgyan-pád-ma*, one of the most famous divines and holy magicians, in the 8th century, from Urgyén (*Ssk.* Udayana) i.e. Kabul, who acc. to his own declaration (v. the fantastic legend concerning him, entitled: *pad-ma tʿaṅ-yig*) was greater than Buddha himself, v. *Köpp.* II, 68. — *pad-ma-ra-ga Ssk.* ruby. — *pád-rtsa* a medicinal herb *Wdṅ* (= *pe-tsé?*).

པཎྜི་ཏ *paṇḍi-ta Ssk.*, **Pandit,** Indian scholar or linguist; *paṇ-čén* great Pandit; *paṇ-čén rin-po-čé, bog-do* (Mongolian) *rin-čen*, title of the second Buddhist pope, residing at Tashilunpo, *Köpp.* II, 121. — *pan-ža* Pandit-cap.

པན་པོན *pan-pón* (also *pan-pún?*) not considered perfect in dignity, as for instance the Lamas in *Lh.*, that are married; yet cf. *ban-bón.*

པར *par* I. **form, mould,** *blúgs-par* casting-mould; *rdéu-par* bullet-mould; *blúgs-par*, as well as *šiṅ-par*, printing form, a stereotype plate cut in wood; *par rkó-ba* to cut types; *rgyáb-pa, par-du ₒdébs-pa*, to print, to stamp; *par (-yig) ₒbri-ba* to write the exemplar or manuscript for printing. — *pár-rko-pa, pár-rko-mkʿan*, cutter of types. — *pár-kʿaṅ* printing-office. — *par-rgyáb* print, **par-rgyáb tsʿógs-se** *W.* like a print or impression. — *par-snág* printing-ink. — *pár-pa* printer *Cs.* — *pár-dpon* fore-man of a printing-office. — *pár-ma* a printed work, book; *'di pár-ma yaṅ yod'* this is also to be had printed. — *par-ɣyóg* a printer's man, assistant. — *par-šóg* printing-paper. — *par-ɣži* = *par*.

II. v. *pár-ma.* — III. termin. of *pa*, also sign of the adverb; combined with verbs, it represents the supine, or adverbial sentences, commencing with **whilst, so that;** *mi byéd-par* without doing.

པར་ཏང *par-taṅ Lex.*, **a hairy carpet** *Sch.*

པར་པ་ཏ *par-pa-ta* n. of an officinal plant *Med.*

པར་བུ *par-bu Lexx., Sch.* = *pa-tra.*

པར་ཙ་སོ་ཏི *par-tsa-só-ti W.* **a kind of cotton cloth.**

པལ་ལ་ཏུ་ལ *pal-la-tú-la Hind.* **scales of a balance** *Sik.*

པས *pas* 1. the instr. of *pa;* combined with verbs, it signifies **by, in consequence of, because;** also **as, since, when.** — 2. = *las*, as sign of the comparative; after vowels, however and the final consonants d, r, l, *bas* stands in its place; *rtá-bas kʿyi čʿúṅ-ba yin* the dog is smaller than the horse; *kʿyód-pas, stág-pas, rtá-pa-bas, šnár-bas*, or *sṅá-ma-bas če*, bigger than you, than a tiger, than a rider, than formerly; it rarely stands for the partitive: *bu lṅa-brgyá-bas ɣčig*, or for *las* with the signification: except, *Mil.*

པི *pi* num. fig.: 43.

པི་ཆག *pi-čʿág* (*Turk.* چاكو) **large butcher's knife.**

པི་པི *pi-pi* 1. *Schr., Sch.* **fife, flute.** — 2. *W.* **nipple, teat;** **pi-pi ṇud táṅ-če** to suckle. — 3. **icicle** *W.*

པི་(པི་)ལིང *pi(-pi)-liṅ, Ssk.* पिप्पली, Piper longum, a spice, similar to black pepper, yet more oblong.

པི་ཕོ *pi-pʿo* v. *pi-ši.*

པི་ཙེ *pi-tse* **skin,** or **leather bag** for water etc. *Lh.*

པི་ཚི *pi-tsʿi*, and *ma-tsʿi*, interjections of anger, *Foucaux Gyatch.* २६८, *transl.* 292.

པི་ཝང *pi-wáṅ* or *pi-báṅ, Zam.* = वीणा, **guitar,** also *da-nyén-pi-waṅ C., pi-waṅ ról-mo Glr.* = *kʿó-poṅ W.; pi-waṅ rgyud ɣsum* a three-stringed guitar *Stg.*; *rgyud-máṅ* a guitar with many strings *Cs.*; *sgróg-pa* to play (the **guitar**); *pi-waṅ-mkʿan*, or *pi-waṅ-pa* a player on the guitar.

པི་ཤི *pi-ši* (perh. from the Persian) **cat,** *W.*; *pi-pʿo* male **cat**, *pi-mo* female **cat.**

པིག་མོ *pig-mo* v. *pús-mo.*

པིར *pir* **brush, pencil;** *byúg-pir* large brush, for house-painting; *bčád-pir* small brush or pencil for artistic painting, Chinese writing; *pir-ťogs(-pa)* painter *Cs.* — *pir-doṅ* receptacle or case for brushes. — *pir-spu* pencil-hair. — **pir-nyúg** *W.* = *bčad-pir*; also for lead-pencil. — *pir-šiṅ* pencil-stick.

པིར་བ་ *pir-ba* (spelling?) **to crush, to grind** (to powder) = *mnyéd-pa Ld.*

པིལ་ཙེ་ *pil-tse Ld.* **sieve.**

པིས་མོ་ *pis-mo* v. *pús-mo.*

པིསྤལ་ *pispal*, acc. to *Cs. Ssk.*, yet not to be found in *Lexx.*, **the wild fig-tree,** *Hindi: pipal.*

པུ་ *pu* num. figure for 73.

པུ་ཏི་ *pú-ti* **milfoil,** (millefolium), yarrow; *Lh.*

པུ་ཏྲི་ *pú-tri* (*Ssk.* पुत्री, daughter), a common female name (perh. *bu-ḱrid.*)

པུ་སྟི་ *pú-sti, Glr.* = *pó-ti*, **book** (perh. formed out of *pústak*).

པུ་ན་ཁ་ *Pu-na-ḱa* town in Bhotan.

པུ་བྱི་ *pú-byi* v. *spú-byi.*

པུ་ཙེ་ *pú-tse, pú-se*, a little rat-like animal, v. *bra* and *zlum; pu-tse-šel* prob. = *pu-šel-tse.*

པུ་ཚེ་ *pu-ťsé* **husks of barley** *W.; Cs.* **bran.**

པུ་རངས་ *Pu-ráṅs Mil.*, a district in *Mṅa-ris.*

པུ་རི་ *pu-ri* **tube,** any thing tubular and hollow, box of tin or wood, pen-case etc.; also = *dóṅ-po* the Tibetan shuttle; **pu-ri méd-ḱan** *W.* full, solid, not hollow, cf. *pá-ri.*

པུ་རུ་ཥ་ *pu-ru-ša Ssk.* **man; soul;** = *skyés-bu.*

པུ་ལིང་ག་ *pu-liṅ-ga Cs.: Ssk.* **masculine gender.**

པུ་ལུ་ *pú-lu* **hut,** built of stones, like those of the alpine herdsmen *W.*, (*Ts. rdzi-skyor*); *ḱyi-pul* dog-kennel.

པུ་ཤུ་ *pú-šu* **fence,** *Lex.* = *mda-yáb* and *lán-kan.*

པུ་ཤེལ་ཙེ་ *pu-šel-tse* a medicinal herb *Med.*

པུག་ཏ་ *púg-ta* (?) **shelf, partition** in a box.

པུག་མ་ *púg-ma Pur.* **collar-bone.**

པུང་པ་ *púṅ-pa, ṕúṅ-pa C., W.* **an urn-shaped vessel** of clay or wood, for water, beer etc. (seems not to be the same with *búm-pa*).

པུན་པ་ *pún-pa W., *pún-če** = *lúd-če* to run over.

པུཎྜ་རི་ཀ་ *puṇḍarika Ssk.*, **white lotos.**

པུར་ *pur Cs.* 1. **steel-yard.** — 2. *púr-gyis* v. *ₒṕur-ba.* — 3. v. *spur.*

པུལ་ *pul* v. *pú-lu.*

པུཥྐ་ར་ *puškara Ssk.* **blue lotos.**

པུསྟ་ཀ་ *pustaka Ssk.* **book.**

པུས་མོ་ *pús-mo, W. *pis-mo, pig-mo**, **knee;** *pis-mo sa-la ₒdzug-pa* to kneel; **pig-mo tsúg-če, pi-tsúg gyáb-če** *W.* id.; **pig-mo tsúg-te dad-če** to sit in kneeling (which is considered indecorous); cf. *tsog.*

པེ་ *pe* num. figure: 103.

པེ་(ད)ཀར་ *pe-(d)kár*, also *be-kár, pe-há-ra. bi-hár Lt., Glr., Mil.*, a much worshipped deity, v. *kye-ṕáṅ*, and *Schl.* 157.

པེ་ཏེ་ཧོར་ *pe-te-hor* n. of a people *Sch.*

པེ་ནེ་ *pe-ne, pé-na* v. *pa-ṇa.*

པེ་བན་ *pe-bán* (*Pers.* پیوند), **graft, scion;** **pe-bán tsúg-če** *W.* to graft.

པེ་ཙམ་ *pe-tsám* **little, small, a little** *Sch.*

པེ་ཙེ་ *pe-tsé, pi-tsí, Chin. pai-tsái,* **Chinese white cabbage** in *C.*; of late also known in Europe.

པེ་ར་ *pé-ra* **a flat basket.**

པེ་ས་ *pé-sa, paisa, Hind.*, copper coin, not quite a half-penny.

པེན་ཙེ་ *pén-tse* a kind of wood of which vessels are made *Cs.* (= *pán-tsa?*)

པོ་ *po* 1. sign of nouns, in like manner as *-pa;* it particularly designates concrete nouns and the masculine gender, frq., in contradistinction to abstract nouns with *-pa* or *-ba*, and to feminines with *-mo*; connected with a numeral, it supplies the definite article: *lňá-po* the five (just mentioned); *ynyís-po* the two, both, = *ynyís-ka*. — 2. num. figure: 133.

པོ་ཏ་ལ་ *pó-ta-la* (*Ssk.* पोत ship, ल to receive, hence: harbour, port; *Tib. gru-dźín*) 1. ancient n. of Tatta, a town not far from the mouth of the Indus. — 2. n. of a three-peaked hill near Lhasa, with the palace of the old kings of Tibet, now the seat of the Dalai Lama. (The spelling '*Buddha-la*' arises from an erroneous etymological hypothesis, and the fact of its being found even in Huc's writings may be attributed merely to a thoughtless adherence to what had become a custom; v. *Köpp.* II, 340.)

པོ་ཏི *pó-ti* (acc. to one *Lex.* a corruption of *pu-sta-ka*, for which also the form *pu-sti* seems to speak) = *glegs-bam*, **book** (of loose leaves).

པོ་ཏུམ་ *po-túm Sik.* **large wasp.**

པོ་ཏོ་ *po-tó C.* **bullock.**

པོ་ཏོག *po-tóg* v. *mťo-po-tog.*

པོ་ལ་ *po-lá* the well-known Turkish mess of **pilaw**, *Hind.* **pulao**, rice boiled with fowl; in *Ld.* however sweet rice, prepared with butter, sugar, and 'pating'; fig. *bsám-bloi pó-la byéd-pa* to concoct and deal in plans and plots.

པོ་ལོ(ན)་ཤན་ *po-lo(n)-šán* n. of the mountains bordering on China *Ld.-Glr. Schl.* 21, a (where in the translation the word has not been recognized as being a proper name).

པོག་ཕོར་ *pog-ṕór* **censer, perfuming-pan.**

པོགས་ཏ་ *pógs-ta* v. *ṕúgs-ta.*

པོད་ *pod, pon, pón-to* v. *ṕod, ṕon, ṕón-to.*

པོབ་ *pob C.* **castrated ram.**

པོལ་ *pol Ts.* = *tsá-bai nad.*

པྲ་ *pra* small **turkoises**, 1 or 2‴ in size, strung together for finger-rings, v. *tsom.*

པྲ་(མོ་) *pra(-mo) Cs.* 1. **lot**; *pra ₒdébs-pa* to cast lot. — 2. **sign, token, prognostic**; *Sch.*: *pra ₒbebs-pa* 'ein Zeichen geben, ein Bild darstellen'.

པྲ་ཅལ་ *pra-čál, spra-čál Lex.* w.e. *Sch.* **jest, joke, fun**, nonsensical talk; *byéd-pa* to make sport, to play the buffoon; *slóň-ba* to cause merriment; *pra-čál-pa*, or *-mḱan* wag, buffoon.

པྲ་ལི་ *pra-li Sch.*: hill-mouse (marmot?), hare (?); cf. *brá-ba.*

པྲང་འགོས་ *praň-ₒgós* an alpine herb, said to be very wholesome to sheep (so for instance in Purig); acc. to recent investigations, of little value. Acc. to *Cs.* = *á-króň*, but this is denied by the people of Lahoul.

པྲི་ཡང་ཀུ་ *pri-yaň-gu Ssk.*, n. of several kinds of Indian aromatic plants *Med.*

པྲོག, ཟེ་པྲོག་ *prog, ze-próg Lex.*, **the crest of a cock** *Cs.*; *próg-žu, bróg-žu, spróg-zu* = *čod-pán.*

དཔའ་(བ་) *dpá(-ba)* (शूर, वीर), also *spá-ba* 1. **bravery, strength, courage; brave, strong, courageous**; *dpa bsgóň-ba Lex.*, *ḱóň-ba Thgy.*; *góň-ba, bkóň-ba Lex.*, to despond: to dishearten (?); *šin-tu dpá-žiň* he becoming very brave *Dzl.*; *dpá-la stobs kyaň gyad daň bnyám-ste* being brave, and in strength equal to an athlete *Dzl.* — 2. **beauty; beautiful.** — 3. *W.* **taste, agreeable taste, flavour.**

Comp. *dpá-čan* 1. brave. 2. beautiful. 3. *W.* savoury. — *dpa-méd-ḱan W.* tasteless, v. also *ldád-pa.* — *dpa-čén* very brave; a great hero. — *dpa-dár* = *mgul-dár*, a piece of silk, tied round the neck, as an honourable distinction for some brave deed. — *dpa-ldán* = *dpá-čan* 1 and 2. — *dpá-bo*, वीर, 1. strong man, hero. 2. demigod. — *dpa-bo-dkár* a medicinal herb *Med.* — *dpá-mo* 1. heroine (more frq. than the masc. *dpá-bo*). 2. = *mḱa-gro-ma*, Dākini *Mil.*, *Thgr.*, *Glr.* — *dpa-tsúl Mil.* = *dpá-ba* 1. sbst., ni f.

དཔག་ཚད་ *dpag-ťsád* **mile**, acc. to *Cs.* = 4000 fathoms, hence a geographical mile; yet there are mentioned *dpag-čén* and *dpag-čúṅ*, the latter = 500 fathoms. The word seems altogether to belong more to the phantastic mythical literature, than to common life; so at least in *W.*

དཔག་པ་ *dpág-pa* v. *dpóg-pa.*

དཔག་གཡེངས་ *dpag-γyéṅs* the bustle or tumult of a festival *Ld.*

དཔག་བསམ་ཤིང་ *dpag-bsam-šiṅ* n. of a fabulous tree, that grants every wish; acc. to *Pth.* = *tsán-dan-sbrúl-gyi snyiṅ-po.*

དཔང་(པོ་) *dpáṅ(-po)* **witness**, both the deponent, and the evidence deposed. Fully authenticated are as yet only: *lha dpáṅ-du* ˳*dzúg-pa* to call a deity for a witness in taking an oath, to appeal to *Glr.*; also: *dpaṅ byéd-pa* to bear witness, to attest, v. *mna.* More conjectural are the meanings of: *blo-séms dpáṅ-du ǰóg-pa Glr.*, or *raṅ-séms dpáṅ-du* ˳*dzúg-pa Mil.*, to be sincere, to be conscious of speaking the truth; *dpáṅ-du* ˳*gyúr-ba* to be witness of, to see, to know (cf. *spyán-du* ˳*gyúr-ba*); *bden-dpáṅ Lis.* as explanation of *čé-bži*, witness or proof for the truth of a thing; **páṅ-po lóg-pa zér-čes* W.* to give false evidence (*Schr. rdzun-dpáṅ*). — *mi-dpáṅ* (*Ld.* **mir-paṅ**) *W.*, *C.*, is used as syn. to *dpáṅ-po* (also *Schr.*), 1. witness. 2. defender, advocate; *mi-dpaṅ* (or *dpaṅ-po*) *byéd-pa* c. genit. or dat., to defend in a court of justice; (*dpáṅ-pos dpóṅ-ba Sch.* seems to be unknown and doubtful).

དཔངས་ *dpaṅs* **height**; *dpáṅs-su* in height *Samb.*; *dpaṅs-mťó Lex.* high, cf. ˳*ṗaṅs.* — *dpaṅs-ťsád* great heat *Schr.* (?).

དཔར་བ་ *dpár-ba* v. *dpór-ba.*

དཔལ་ *dpal Ssk.* श्री 1. **glory, splendour, magnificence, abundance**; *dpal reg-pa-méd-pa* unattainable glory *Glr.*; *yón-tan dú-mai dpal* splendour of numerous accomplishments; *skyéd-pai dpál-la loṅs-spyód-pa* enjoying the atmost happiness *Glr.*; frq. as an epithet, or part of the names of deities, e.g. *dpal-čén hé-ru-ka*, and esp. *dpal(-ldan)lhá-mo*, *dpal-čén-mo*, Durga Uma, Kāli, the much adored spouse of Siva; ˳*dod-dgúi dpal* the fulness of all that can be desired *Glr.*; *dpál-gyi dúm-bu*, श्रीखण्ड, 1. sandal-wood. 2. *Cs.* a kind of syrup, prepared of *bsé-šiṅ*, used as a purgative. — 2. **wealth, abundance**, *Glr.* and elsewh. — 3. **welfare, happiness, blessing**, ˳*gró-bai* of creatures *Mil.* and elsewh.; *kún-gyi dpál-du* ˳*gyúr-ba* or *šár-ba* to be (become) the salvation, the saviour of all beings *Glr.* and elsewh.; *dpal skyéd-pa*, *γžán-gyi*, *ráṅ-gi dpal* to work for the elevation of others or for one's own. — 4. nobility, *dpál-gyi γnáṅ-ba* privilege of nobility; *dpál-gyi γnaṅ-šóg* diploma of nobility, *dpál-gyi γnaṅ-šóg-pa* one having a diploma of nobility *Cs.* — *dpal-ḱyád Dzl.* = *dpal* 1. — *dpal-rtúg* majesty, full glory *Sch.* — *dpal-ldán* a man's name (very common). — *dpal-ṗó* an illustrious man, *dpál-mo* an illustrious woman *Cs.* — *dpal(-gyi)-béu* is said to denote the figure ❋ *Glr.* — *dpal-byéu* glow-worm *Sch.* — *dpal-byór* 1. glory, wealth, magnificence, as a man's possession. 2. *W.* strawberry; 3. a man's name (very common).

དཔུང་ *dpuṅ* 1. **host, great number**, ˳*baṅs ťams-čád-kyi Dzl.*; esp. of soldiers. — 2. **troops, army**, *dpuṅ bži* the four species of troops: *rtai*, *gláṅ-po-čei*, *šiṅ-rtai*, and *rkaṅ-ťáṅ-gi dpuṅ* (or *dpuṅ(-bu)-čuṅ*); *dpuṅ-(gi) ťsógs*, *dmag-dpúṅ*, army frq.; *dgra-dpúṅ* hostilearmy. — 3. (auxiliaries?), **help, assistance**, **púṅ-la ťáṅ-če* W.* to send assistance. — *dpuṅ-grógs*, *-rogs*, helper. — *dpuṅ-(gi) γnyen* friend, protector, defender, assistant, frq. — **puṅ-nón* W.* reinforcement.

དཔུང་པ་ *dpúṅ-pa* 1. **shoulder**, *dpúṅ-pa ḱar* on the shoulder *Glr.*; *dpuṅ-pa daṅ dpyi γnyis* both the shoulders and hips *S.g.*; upper arm, *dpuṅ-pa-rkáṅ* upper arm-bone; *dpuṅ* ˳*ǰúm-pa Sch.* to contract the arm (?); *dpuṅ-pa-lág* upper and lower arm *Cs.*; *dpuṅ-pa-rgyán* an ornament for the arm *Cs.* — 2. **sleeve**, *gos dpúṅ-pa-čan* a garment with sleeves *Cs.*; *dpuṅ-pa-bčád* the part of a woman's dress covering the chest *Zam.*; *Sch.: dpuṅ-bčad-rás.*

དཔེ་ *dpe*, *Ld.* **spe**, 1. **pattern, model,** *dé-la dpe Glr.*, or *de dper byás-nas Zam.*, taking this for a pattern; *rgyá-yul-nas rtsis-kyi dpe blaṅs* it was from China that mathematics were learned *Glr.*; . . . *pai dpe mi ˳dug* there are no patterns for . . . *Glr.*; *dpe či ltar* with what to be compared? according to what analogy? *Thgy.*; similitude, parable, example, *mťún-pai dpe* an example that may be followed, a good example; *bzlóg-pai dpe* an example to the contrary, a warning example *Thgy.*; **pe záṅ-po*, and *ňém-pe pe,** as well as **yár-la* and *már-la žág-pe-pe*, or *mar-pe* C.* id.; *dpe stón-pa* to teach or to prove by examples; hence the participle, used substantively, serves as an epithet of the Sautrantikas, *Was.* (112); *dpe bšád-pa*, *dpe bžág-pa* = *dpe stón-pa*; *dper rǰód-pa* to set up for a parable or comparison; *dpér-na*, in later times also *dpé-ni*, *dpe byéd-na Mil.*, **pe gyáb-na* W.*, 1. (in order) to quote an example, by way of a comparison, just as if, followed by *bžín-du* or *ltar*, very frq.; 2. like our 'for instance', e.g., before enumerations, where in the older writings gen. *˳dí-lta-ste* is used; *dper ˳ós-pa Cs.* what may be compared, *dper mi ˳ós-pa* not to be compared; occasionally also: worthy or not worthy of imitation; *ḱá-dpe*, *ytám-dpe* proverb, adage *Cs.*; *˳drá-dpe* allegory, parable *S.g.*; *má-dpe W.*, *Ld.* **má-spe**, *Lh.* **már-pe**, pattern, (writing-) copy (cf. also *má-dpe* and *bú-dpe* below). — 2. **symmetry, harmony,** beauty, (in certain phrases). — 3. **book,** *ḱrims brgyad-kyi dpe* the book of the eight commandments *Dzl.*; *ká-dpe*, *ka-ḱái dpe* abc-book, primer; *pyág-dpe* resp. for *dpe*, if used by a Lama (cf. *pyag-mḱár*); *má-dpe*, *bú-dpe* original and copy of a book *Cs.*; *yig-nág dpe* a real book, not of a fig. meaning, as the book of nature, *Mil.*; *dpe rtsóm-pa* to write, to compose, *bšú-ba* to copy a book; *˳dógs-pa*, *˳tsém-pa* to bind, to stitch a book.

Comp. *dpé-ka* little book, vulgo. — *dpe-ḱáṅ* library; bookseller's shop. — *dpe-ḱri* a table to put books on, book-stand. — *dpe-mkyúd*, *˳ḱyud Cs.* v. *mḱyud-pa*. — *dpe-mgó*, *dpe-mǰúg* beginning, end, of a book. — *dpe-sgám* chest for books, book-case. — *dpé-ča* not frq. in *B.*, but vulgo the common word for book. — **dpé-ča pé-če, túm-če* W.* to open, to close a book; v. *btúm-pa*. — *dpe-rǰód* v. *dper*. — *dpe-tó* list of books. — *dpe-byád* proportion, symmetry, beauty, *dpe-byád bzáṅ-po brgyád-ču* the eighty physical perfections of Buddha. — *dpe-byád-čan* well-proportioned. — *dpé-tsoṅ-pa* bookseller. — *dpe-šúbs* case or covering for a book. — *dpe-bšús* copy of a book. — *dper* v. 1. — *dpe-brǰód* 1. example, comparison, *dpe-brǰód byéd-pa* to compare, to cite an example *Cs.*; *dpe-brǰód rtógs-pa Gram.* id. (?). 2. paradigm, example *Gram.* —

དཔེ་སྒྲ་ *dpé-sgra* (?), **(s)pé-ra* W.*, **speech,** for *ytam*; **(s)pé-ra zér-če(s)*, *táṅ-če(s)**, to speak, to talk; **i-zug (s)pé-ra ma taṅ* do not say so! **(s)pé-ra zér-če(s) med-ḱan soṅ** he became speechless (with terror etc.).

དཔེར་ན་ *dpér-na* v. sub *dpe.*

དཔོག་པ་ *dpóg-pa*, pf. *dpags*, fut. *dpag*, 1. **to measure, to proportion, to fix,** *ytóṅ-tsul če-čúṅ-la* (to proportion) the dose to the size *Lt.*; . . . *kyi tsád-las* after the measure of . . ., *Lt.*; *nad-stóbs-la* according to the violence of the disease *Lt.*; *dpag (tu) méd (-pa)*, less frq. *dpag-brál*, *dpag-yás*, immensely large, very much; *tugs dpag-méd* infinite grace, *mdzád-pa* to show *Dzl.* — 2. **to outweigh, to counterbalance.** *loṅs-spyód tams-čád-kyis mi dpóg-pa* not to be counterbalanced by all the wealth . . . *Tar.* — 3. **to weigh, to judge, to prove,** *rǰés-su dpóg-pa* to examine *Tar.*; *rǰes-dpág Zam.* **अनुमान,** inference, conclusion.

དཔོན་པོ་ *dpón-po* **master, lord,** over men (generally); (cf. *bdág-po* owner) master, over working-men, overseer, foreman, leader, *grá-pai dpon-po*, director, =

ₒgó-dpon; **dpón-po-la ča̓g p̓ul dug žu zer, t́ug-šró ma kyod, ṅa yóṅ-loṅ med** *W.* make your master my compliment, and he should not take it amiss that I had no time to come; *ḱrims-dpon* 1. prop.: superior judge, lord chief-justice. 2. now: high officer of state, prefect, = *mi-dpón*; *mḱar-dpón* commander of a fortress; *ₒḱrúg-dpon* general *Ma.*; *ₒgó-dpon* v. *go*; *brgyá-dpon* centurion, captain; *bču-dpon* corporal; *čibs-dpon* master of the horse, equerry; *rǰé-dpon* = *rǰe*; *rtá-pa-dpon* (sic) (cf. *pa* extr.) general of cavalry *Glr.*; *stégs-dpon*(?) v. *stegs*; *stoṅ-dpon* leader of a thousand (seems to be no longer in use); *déd-dpon* sea-captain; *mdá-dpon* is said to be in *C.* the modern word for general, and *ₒdégs-dpon* the same as *stóṅ-dpon*; however v. *stegs; ldiṅ-dpon* v. *ldiṅ; spyi-dpon* governor general *Cs.*; *mi-dpon* prefect; *rtsig-dpon* master-mason; *rdzóṅ-dpon* = *mḱár-dpon*; *yúl-dpon* prefect of a district *Wts.*; *rú-dpon* something like colonel; *šiṅ-dpon* master-carpenter; *slób-dpon* teacher, frq., also title of the higher and more learned Lamas, corresponding, as it were, to *M.A.*, master of arts; *ysól-dpon* head-cook, butler. — *dpón-mo* fem., *ṅai dpón-mo yin* she is my mistress *Glr.* — *dpón-yod* standing under a master or mistress. — *dpon-méd* free *Cs.* — *dpon-yyóg* master and servants, frq. — *kóṅ-ǰo dpon-yyóg* (princess) *koṅ-ǰo* and her suite *Glr.* — *dpon-tsáṅ* physician *Schr.* and *Sch.* — *dpon-yig* secretary *Schr.* — *dpon-slób* 1. inst. of *dpón-po daṅ slób-ma Ma.* and elsewh. 2. title of the four independent rulers in Bhotan, the 'Penlow' of English news-papers, acc. to the pronunciation of **pọn-lob, pọn-lo**.

དཔོར་བ་ *dpór-ba*, pf. and fut. *dpar*, **to dictate**, *Cs.*; **por-tsóm (ǰhe')-pa** *C.* id.

དཔྱ་ *dpya* **tax, duty, tribute**, *ₒbúl-ba* to pay, *Dzl.*, *ₒbébs-pa* to impose *Tar.* 21, 11; *dpya-ḱrál* id., *rgyál-poi dpya-ḱrál Lex.*; likewise *dpya-ťáṅ Cs.*

དཔྱང་བ་ *dpyáṅ-ba*, *spyáṅ-ba*, **to suspend, to make hang down**, prop. vb. a. to *p̓yáṅ-ba*, with pf. *dpyaṅs* and *spyaṅs*, imp. *dpyaṅs*, *Sch. dpyoṅs*, but also vb. n., **to rock, to pitch** (of a ship) *Pth.*; *dpyáṅ-la ytóṅ-ba* trs. *Thgy.*; **gyóg-čaṅ**, perh. more corr. **ḱyog-čáṅ**, also **p̓eb-čáṅ** *C.* sedan-chair, palanquin; *dpyaṅ-ťág*, *ₒp̓yaṅ-ťág*, cord or rope, by which a thing is suspended, e.g. a plummet, a bucket, a miner; hence fig. *ťugs-rǰei dpyaṅ-ťág yčód-pa Thgr.*; *ču-snod daṅ dpyaṅ-ťag sbá-ba* to hide the bucket together with the rope *Schr.*; a rope-swing, *dpyaṅ-ťág rtséd-pa* to swing (one's self); *dpyaṅs, spyáṅs-pai p̓an*, hanging ornaments, *dar-dpyáṅs* silk ornaments *S.g.*

དཔྱད་ *dpyad* 1. v. *dpyód-pa.* — 2. *Stg.*: an instrument to open the mouth by force; perh. also in a more general sense: crow-bar (?); *dpyád-pa* v. *dpyód-pa.*

དཔྱས་པོ་ *dpyás-po* **offence, fault, blame** *Cs.*; *dpyás-čan* faulty, blamable; *dpyas-méd* faultless, blameless *Cs.*; *dpyas ₒdógs-pa* to blame *Tar.*; cf. *ₒpyá-ba.*

དཔྱི་ *dpyi* (*Cs.* also *spyi*) *W.* *(s)pi*, **hip** *Lt.*; *dpyi-mgó Cs.*, *dpyi-zúr*, *dpyi-rús*, hip-bone; *dpyi-mig* socket of the hip-bone, perh. also vulg. = hip.

དཔྱིད་ *dpyid* (cf. Phonetic Table), **spring**, also adv. in spring *Dzl.*; cf. also *dus* 4; *dpyid-ka*, **pid-ḱa** *W.*, id., also *Glr.*; *dpyid-zla* month of spring.

དཔྱིས་ *dpyis*, *dpyis p̓yin-pa Sch.*: to come to the last, to arrive at the end; *dei rig-pa ₒdi dpyis p̓yin-pa sus kyaṅ mi šes dgóṅs-nas Schf.*: as he reflected, that no body would thoroughly understand his arguments.

དཔྱོང་བ་ *dpyóṅ-ba*, perh. primitive form of *dpyáṅ-ba.*

དཔྱོ་བ་ *dpyó-ba* **to change** *Sch.*

དཔྱོད་པ་ *dpyód-pa*, pf. and fut. *dpyad*, **to try, to examine**, *nyés-pa daṅ ma-nyés-pa* innocence and guilt, right and wrong *Dzl.*; *dpyád-na . . . ma rtógs-so* after ever so much investigating . . . they found out nothing *Dzl.*; *bye-brág-tu dpyád-pa ste* having now been separately examined *Zam.*; *sa-dpyád*, or *ri-dpyád yzigs-pa* to examine the country, or the mountains, i.e. their general features, with regard to omens and auspices *Glr.*; *sai dpyad bzáṅ-bar šés-pa* to know that this examination will turn out favourably *Glr.*; **rin čád-če** (gen. written **bčad-če**, cf. *bčód-pa* extr.) *W.* to tax, to estimate; *goṅ-ťáṅ dpyád-kyis* (or *-pas*) *mi čod Glr.* v. *čod-pa* 2; esp. in medicine: *smán-pas* ... *dpyad byás-te* ... *žes dpyad byás-so* the physician having tried, tried thus, (pronounced the following as the result of his examination) *Dzl.* ༢༥༡, 12; *sman-dpyád byéd-pa* to treat medically, *dpyad má-la bya* then the mother (not the child) must be placed under medical treatment *Lt.*; *ₒbrás-kyis btsún-moi sman-dpyád byed-pa* to cure (the illness of) the queen with rice *Dzl.*; *sman-dpyád-la mkʻás-pa* to be skilled in medical science *Dzl.*; *ča-byád dpyád-kyi γnas* instrumental therapeutics i.e. surgery *S.g.*; *rtog-dpyód, brtag-dpyád*, examination; *rtog-dpyód ráb-tu γtóṅ-ba* to examine very closely *Pth.*; *rtog-dpyód ťoṅ* examine! *Mil.*; *bzaṅ-dpyód* examining the worth of a thing. — *dpyód-pa-pa*, and *spyód-pa-pa, Ssk.* **मीमांसक**, an Indian sect of philosophers (the former of the two spellings seems to be more correct).

དཔྲལ་བ་ *dprál-ba* (resp. *γdaṅs Cs.*), **ṭál-wa**, *Ld.* **šrál-wa**, **forehead**, *dprál-bai mda* an arrow sticking in the forehead *Glr.*; *dprál-bai mig bžin-du* 'like the eye of the countenance', to designate something highly valued (as the scriptural 'apple of the eye'); *dprál-bai pʻyógs-kyi ťad dráṅ-na* just before one in front *Wdṅ.*; fig. **ṭal-wa ṅán-pa** *W.* unlucky; a luckless person.

དཔྲུལ་དཔྲུལ་ *dprul-dprúl* (or *pʻrul-pʻrúl?*), **ṭul-ṭúl-la tóṅ wa** *C.* to hang one's self.

ལྤགས་ *lpags*, as second part of compounds inst. of *pʻágs-pa*, e.g. *wá-lpags* fox-skin, *stág-lpags* tiger-skin; *šún-lpags* skin, bark, peel, shell.

སྤ་ *spa* 1. v. *dpa.* — 2. also *sba*, **cane** (seems to be distinguished from *smyúg-ma* more in a popular and practical way, than scientifically); *spa-skór* hoop of a cask *Schr.*; *spa-kʻár Mil.*, *spa-lčág Mil.*, *spa-bér Pth.*, *spa-dbyúg Lex.*, walking-cane; *spa-glíṅ* cane-flute *Sch.*; *spa-til* lunt, match, v. *pa-til*; *spa-dóṅ* or *-ldoṅ* little cask, made of bamboo, prob. = *gur-gúr dóṅ-mo*; **pa-ₒbár** *C.*, *W.* torch; *spa-dmyúg* or *-smyug*, cane *Cs.*; *pa-šíṅ Sik.* strong bamboo sticks.

སྤ་མ་ *spá-ma* 1. **juniper**, Juniperus squamosa, and some other small species; cf. *šúg-pa.* — 2. **cypress** *Sik.*

སྤག་པ་ *spág-pa* 1. v. *spóg-pa.* — 2. **kʻál-pag pág-če** *W.* **to smack** (in eating). — 3. *C.*, *W.* **to dip**, e.g. meat into the gravy; cf. the following.

སྤགས་ *spags*, resp. *skyu-rum*, 1. *C.* = *zan* (= **kʻó-lag, pág-kʻu** *Ld.*), **pap**, esp. made of tea and 'tsampa'. — 2. *W.* = **ša-rúg** *C.*), **sauce, gravy**, for dipping in (sops); **dam-pág** *W.* mire, sludge. — 3. **food, dish, mess**; *W.*, *C.* **pag na so-só**.

སྤང་ *spaṅ*, I. also *spáṅ-po*, 1. **turf, green-sward, meadow**, *mdún-na spáṅ-po mé-tog bkra* in front a flowery meadow-ground *Mil.* — 2. **moss**, also *ču-spaṅ Cs.* — 3. **bog**, *spaṅ-skóṅ* 1. p.n. ('turf-ditch'), a large valley, with a lake in it, on the frontier of **Ladak** and Rudog. 2. *spaṅ-skóṅ pʻyag-rgyá-pa* n. of an ancient work on religion *Glr.*; *spaṅ-rgyan* a medicinal herb *Med.*; *spáṅ-čan* covered with turf; *spáṅ-ču* green mud *Sch.*; *spaṅ-ljóṅs* grassy country; *spaṅ-ťáṅ* a plain covered with verdure; *spaṅ-spós* Waldheimia tridactylites, a pretty, very aromatic composite, growing on the higher alps; *spaṅ-bóg* piece of turf, sod; *spaṅ-ma Med.*, **तुत्थ**, blue vitriol; *spaṅ-rtsi S.g.* (?); *spaṅ-žún* verdigris *Sch.*; *spaṅ-ri* a grassy hill *Mil.*; *spaṅ-γšóṅ* a mountain-meadow *Mil.*

II. **board, plank**, gen. *spaṅ-léb Glr.* and vulg.; also **a slab, slate, flag** *Lh.*; *spaṅ-sgó* board or panel of a door *Cs.*; *spaṅ-kʻrí Schr.*, **ṭi-páṅ** *Ld.*, **paṅ-dáṅ** *Ld.*, book-stand.

སྤང་བ་ *spaṅ-ba* v. *spoṅ-ba.*

སྤངས་ *spaṅs*, sometimes inst. of *dpaṅs.*

སྤད་ *spad*, only in *pʻa-spád* **father and children**; cf. the more frq. *ma-smád, Lex.*

སྤན་སྤུན་ *span-spún* **brothers, relatives** *Cs.*

སྤབས་ *spabs*, *rna-spábs C.* **ear-wax**; *Lexx.* also *rṅul-* (or *rdul-?*) *gyi spabs* w.e.

སྤར་ *spar* for *par* 1, *Sch.*

སྤར་ཁ་ *spar-ka*, *spar-ka brgyad* the **pah kwah**, or eight diagrams of Chinese science, ☰☷ etc.

སྤར་བ་ *spar-ba* I. sbst., also *spar-mo* (*Ld.* **wár-mo**, acc. to the spelling *sbar-mo*) 1. **the grasping hand, paw, claw,** *spráṅ-poi spár-mor spa-dbyúg sprad* he puts the staff into the beggar's grasp (hand) *Lexx.*; **wár-mo gyáb-če* W.*, *spár-mos ˳brád-pa* to clutch, to scratch; *spár-mos ˳débs-pa Cs.*, *spar byéd-pa Sch.*, to seize with the hand, the paw, or the claws; *ydoṅ tams-čád spar-šád rgyáb-pa Pth.* to scratch the whole face ('combing it with the claws'); **sbar-˳ju* C.* rail, for taking hold of; *spár-mo ˳byéd-pa*, *bsdám-pa* to open, to close the hand *Cs.* — 2. as a measure: as much as may be grasped with the hand, **a handful** (of wood, grass, earth etc.), **(s)pár-ra yaṅ** one handful, *(s)pár-ra gaṅ do* two handfuls etc.; *spar-tsád lṅa-brgyá* 500 handfuls *S.g.*; *sa spar-gáṅ Mil.* a handful of earth.

II. vb. v. *spór-ba*.

སྤར་མ་ *spár-ma* a low-growing shrub of very hard wood *Mil. nt.*

སྤི་ཏི་ *(s)pi-ti* **Spiti,** the valley, situated to the west of Lahul, watered by the Spiti river, belonging to the British Punjáb, and inhabited by a race of pure Tibetans.

སྤིའུ་ *spiu* col. for *spéu*.

སྤུ་ *spu*, *Ssk.* रोमन्, 1. **hair** ('*pilus*', cf. *skra*), *lús-kyi* of the body in general, *Lex.*; *mgó-spu*, *ká-* or *ydóṅ-spu*, *mčán-spu*, *˳doms-spu* (or *spu-ṅán Cs.*), *bráṅ-spu*, hair of the head, the beard, arm-pits, lower-parts, chest; *bá-spu* the little hairs of the skin, frq.; *rtá-spu* horse-hair; *spu ˳pyi* or *ytog* the hair is plucked out *Lex.*, *byi* falls off *Dzl.*, *yžob byed* is singed off *Sch.*, *ldaṅ*, *laṅ Dzl.*, *lóṅ-yyo Mil.*, the hair bristles, stands on end; *spu ziṅ byed B.*, *brtse Sch.*, **se-ziṅ* W.*, a shuddering of fear comes over (me, him etc.); *tams-čád spu-ziṅ byéd-čiṅ Pth.*; *byad spus keṅs-pa* with a face all hairy *Glr.*; *spui kúṅ-bu* passage of perspiration, pore *Dzl.*; *spu nyág-ma tsám-gyi ˳gyód-pai sems* repentance as much as one single little hair *Dzl.* — 2. **feather,** *byá-spu rluṅ-gis kyer-ba* a down (feather) blown off; **feathers, plumage.**

Comp. *spú-ka* **colour** of horses and other hairy animals. — *spú-gri* 1. **razor**; also allegorically, as a title of books. 2. knife *C.* — *spú-čan* hairy. — *spu-čim* (?) false hair *Sch.* — *spú-ja* v. *ja*. — *spú-byi nág-po*, *spu-nág* also *pú-byi*, **sable** (furred animal) *Sch.* — *spú-ma* hairy, carded (cloth). — *spu-méd* hairless. — *spu-ytsaṅ-ma* v. *spus*. — *spu-hrúg* short-haired *Sch.*

སྤུ་རངས་ *spu-ráṅs Glr.* v. *pu-ráṅs*.

སྤུག་ *spug Lexx.* n. of a precious stone *Cs.*

སྤུང་ *spuṅ* **heap,** col. also for *púṅ-po*; *spúṅ-ba* pf. and imp. *-spuṅs*, to heap, accumulate, pile up (coals etc.); *rin-čén spúṅs-pa* a heap of precious stones *Glr.*

སྤུད་པ་ *spúd-pa* **to decorate**; *rgyáṅ-gyis Lex.* (cf. *spus*).

སྤུན་ *spun* 1. children of the same parents, **brothers, sisters,** *kó-mo-čag spun ynyis* we (his) two sisters *Dzl.* ༢༤༠, 17; *ṅed spun ysum* we three brothers *Glr.*; *kyed bú-mo spun lṅa-po* you five sisters *Mil.*; pleon. *bu spun ysum Tar.*; *spun yžán-rnams* his other (six elder) brothers *Tar.*; *spun-yčes* dear brother! *Chr. P.* — *pá-spun*, brothers and sisters of the same father; *má-spun* of the same mother; *spún-zla*, *(s)pun-da*, or *-la* 1. = *spun*; 2. in *C.* it is said to be used also for attorney, advocate; *spún-ma* sister, as a more particular designation of the sex. — 2. in a wider sense: **cousins, brothers-** or **sisters-in-law**; *grógs-spun* mate, comrade; *čós-spun* a brother of a religious order; *pá-spun*, *pás-spun*, several neighbours or inhabitants of a village, that have a common Lha, and thus have become **'rus-pa čig-čig'**, members of the same family; this common tie entails on them the duty, whenever a death takes place, ofearing for the cremation of the dead body (cf. *čos-spún*) *Mil.* and elsewh.; *mdza-spún* friend *Cs.* — 3. **weft, woof** in weaving.

སྤུན་པ་ *spún-pa* 1. sbst., also *sbún-pa B., C., sbur(-ma) Dzl., Ld.*, **chaff, husks** etc. — 2. adj. a botanical term, description of the stalk of a plant *Wdṅ.*

སྤུབ་པ་ *spúb-pa*, pf. *spubs*, vb. a. to *ₒbúb-pa* **to turn upside down.**

སྤུར་ *spur, pur*, also *sku-spúr*, resp. for *ro*, **dead body, corpse,** *spur sbyáṅs-pa C.* to burn a dead body; *spur-ḱaṅ* house for keeping dead bodies, or rather, in most cases, the place of cremation; *spur-sgam* or *sgrom* coffin; *spur-ťal* ashes of a dead body; *spur-ťsa* the salt for preparing a dead body; *spur-šiṅ* wood for burning a corpse.

སྤུར་བ་ *spúr-ba*, vb. a. to *ₒpúr-ba*, **to make fly, to scare up, to let fly;** *dus spúr-ba* to pass time quickly *Cs.*; *stoṅ-spúr* exaggeration, bombast *Cs.*

སྤུས་ *spus* 1. **goods, merchandize, ware,** *spus ltá-ba* to examine goods before purchase *Cs.*; **spus gyúr-če* W.*, **pu ₒgyúr-wa* Cs.* = **dal tsoṅ táṅ-če**. — 2. **goodness, beauty,** *spús-čan, spus-γtsáṅ, spus-bzáṅ*, of fine appearance; *spus-méd* ill-looking, unsightly. — 3. *Sch.*: for *spos.*

སྤེའུ་, སྤིའུ་ *speu, spiu*, **turret,** on a castle or gate *W.*, (*C. lčog*). High towers or steeples are seldom met with in Tibetan architecture; **peu gyá-čan riṅ-mo**, *mḱar* or *ḱáṅ-pa dgu-ťóg* are the terms denoting such.

སྤེག་ཤིང་ *speg-šiṅ Cs.*: n. of part of a cart.

སྤེན་ཏོག་ *spen-tog*, **ornament, finery.**

སྤེན་པ་ *spén-pa, γza-spén-pa* 1. the planet **Saturn**; the proper meaning is said to be a broom, hence the sign for it is somewhat resembling that implement *Wdk.* — 2. **Saturday.**

སྤེན་མ་ *spén-ma, spén-šiṅ*, n. of a tree, prob. tamarisk; *spen-bád* a parapet, formed of the stems of tamarisk and raised on the roofs of monasteries.

སྤེལ་བ་ *spél-ba*, vb. a. to *ₒpél-ba*, 1. **to augment, to increase,** *nor* the wealth *Lex.*, *bkra-šis* the welfare; *rkaṅ-ₒgrós spél-ba* to breed cattle *Dzl.* and elsewh.; **spel-gyúd-la bor-če* W.* to keep cattle for breeding. — 2. **to multiply** (arithm.) *Wdk.* — 3. **to spread, to propagate** (news, secrets) *Dzl.* and elsewh.; more emphatically: *spel rgyás-par*, or *sgróg-par byéd-pa* to blaze about *Sch.* — 4. **to join, to put together,** e.g. letters (almost = to spell); **to mingle, to mix;** *spél-ma* mixture, e.g. of prose and verse *Cs.*; acc. to *Was.* however, couplets, similar both as to metre and contents; composition, combination, *γser γyu spél-mai ḱri* a chair of gold and turkoises *Pth.*; *spél-mai nor* mixed goods *Cs.*; *spél-gos* clothes of various colours *Cs.*; *spel-ťsig Sch.*: a combination of verses, poetry (?); *spél-mar byéd-pa* to mix *Lex.*

སྤེས་ *spes* **edge, brim, border,** *Sch.*

སྤོ་ *spo* **summit of a mountain,** *brag-dmar spo-mťó-nas* from the height of Bragmar *Mil.*; *rdo-rje-γdán-gyi spó-la* on the top of Gayā *Pth.*; *spó-bo* 1. (top, point =) bud *Ts.* 2. district to the east of Lhasa *Glr.*

སྤོ་ཏོ་ *spo-to* 1. **bullock** *C.* — 2. n. of a village in Panyul.

སྤོ་རེ་ *spo-re* v. *spor.*

སྤོ་བ་ *spo-ba*, pf. and imp. *spos*, vb. a. to *ₒpó-ba*, **to alter, to change;** with and without *γnas* (*W. *sa**): to change the place (of residence), to remove, to shift; also to transpose, transplant; *miṅ spó-ba* to change the name *Mil.*; *gos spó-ba* to change one's dress; *mgo-lús* v. *mgo* extr.; to remove (an officer) to another station; to dismiss (a servant), *W.*, also *B.* frq.; *γžan mḱás-pa yód-na spós-pa bzaṅ* if another skilful (physician) is to be had, it will be better to dismiss (the present one); to alter, to mend, to correct *W.*; *spó-sa* a place newly occupied by nomads *Sch.*

སྤོག་པ་ *spóg-pa*, pf. *spags*, fut. *spag*, **to remove and to bring near by turns** *Cs.*; *Lexx.* w.e. —

སྤོགས་ *spogs* **gain, profit,** *ke-spógs* id.; *spogs byed-pa* to make profit, to gain money; *ṫsoṅ-spógs byéd-pa* to gain money by traffic *Dzl.*; *ṫsoṅ-spógs-la ˳gró-ba Dzl.*; *skyed-spogs* interest (of money); *spógs-su γtóṅ-ba* to give money on interest *Cs.*; **mi-póg lém-pa* C.* to demand a tax from emigrants or travellers.

སྤོང་བ་ *spóṅ-ba, spáṅ-ba,* pf. *spaṅs,* fut. *spaṅ,* imp. *spoṅ(s),* (*Ssk.* त्यज्) **1. to give up, to declare off,** *bdag daṅ bdag-gir Sambh.* to give one's self up and all that one has; *sman-dpyád mi byéd-par spóṅ-na* if he gives (the patient) over without even attempting a cure *Dzl.* ཞོ, 1; **to renounce** (all pleasures) frq.; **kód-gu-ru spaṅ mi ṗod** he cannot give up Kotgur (his former residence) or forget it; without an object: *yóṅs-su spóṅ-ba* (partic.) they (the Bodhisattvas) who entirely renounce *Thgy.*; **to shun, avoid, abstain from** (faults, sins, certain food) frq.; **to reject** = *˳dór-ba: bde-sdúg-la spaṅ-blaṅ med* between happiness and unhappiness there was no need to choose (sc. because only bliss prevailed) *Glr.*; *spoṅ-bláṅ ˳dzín-pa ẑig-pa* the cessation of every inclination and disinclination, or also, of every interest in choosing or rejecting. — 2. **to throw off, to drop,** a letter, *ṗyi-ṫség* (to omit) the dot after a syllable *Gram.*

སྤོང་བྱེད་ *spoṅ-byéd* **Vaisali,** ancient town near Allahabad, *Tar.* 7, 5 and elsewh.; also Vriji, acc. to *Schf.*

སྤོད་ *spod* **spice** *Med.*; *spod ˳débs-pa* to season; *spód-čan* seasoned.

སྤོད་པ་ *spód-pa* 1. **hermit,** *spód-ḱaṅ* hermitage *Sch.* — 2. **vow,** *spód-pa nyáms-pa* one that has broken his vow *Sch.*

སྤོབས་པ་ *spóbs-pa* (*W.* also **spós-pa**), 1. vb. **to dare, to venture,** *˳jú-bar mi spóbs-pas* not daring to take hold of *Pth.*, also *Dzl.* ཀླ༠, 4; ༢༠༢, 16; *spóbs-par byéd-pa* 1. id. 2. to enable, empower, authorize *Cs.* — 2. sbst. **courage, confidence.**

སྤོམ་ཡོར་ *spom-yór* diffuse (in words), **prolix, long-winded,** *byéd-pa, smrá-ba, čád-pa Cs.* 'to say circumstantially'.

སྤོར་ *spor, spo-ré,* **steel-yard;** *W.* particularly a little one.

སྤོར་བ་ *spór-ba, spár-ba,* pf. and fut. *spar,* 1. **to lift up,** *rdó-rje* the praying-sceptre *Dom.*; (a hatchet) to fetch a blow; *W. *šed spár-la* (or *spár-te*) *rgyob** swing (the hatchet) well and strike! **spár-la čoṅ** run and leap! cf. also *nems;* to raise, promote, advance, *go-ṗáṅ* in rank *Lex.* — 2. v. *dpór-ba.*

སྤོལ་ *spol Ts.* for **me-mé* W.* (v. *mes-po*).

སྤོས་ *spos* 1. sbst. **incense;** *bdug-spós* id.; less frq. **perfume** in general; *byug-spós* sweet-scented water or ointment; *spos sbyór-ba, sgrúb-pa,* also *rgyáb-pa* and *rgyág-pa Cs.*, to prepare incense, perfumes, *bdúg-pa* to burn (incense); *˳byúg-pa* to cover (with perfume); *rgya-spós, brag-spós, spaṅ-spós,* different kinds of perfume; *spos-(kyi) réṅ (-bu)* pastil, long and thin straws being covered with an odoriferous substance, which generally consists of pulverized *šugpa,* and sandal-wood, combined with some *gugul,* musk and the like; they are made by the Lamas, and frequently presented to travellers as an offering of welcome. *spos-dkár* frankincense, = *gugúl dkár-po.* — *spós-mḱan* perfumer. — *spos-čág* incense in pieces or cakes. — *spos-čú,* resp. *čab,* sweet-scented water, diluted ointment, *lús-la ˳byúg-pa Pth.*; *spós-čus čag-čág ˳débs-pa Pth.* to sprinkle with such water. — *spos-snod Cs.*, *spos-ṗór* (also *pog-ṗór*), censer, perfuming-pan. — *spós-ṫsoṅ-pa* = *spós-mḱan.* — *spos-γžóṅ* basin for incense *Cs.* — *spos-šél* (col. **po-šél**) amber. — 2. vb. v. *spó-ba* and *spóbs-pa.*

སྤྱ་དངོས་ *spya-dṅós Cs.* = *yo-byád; Lexx.* *spyad-dṅós* and *dṅos-spyád,* as explanations to *ka-ča.*

སྤྱང་ཀི་ *spyáṅ-ki Mil., Sg., -gi Dzl., -ku, -gu, ku Cs., Lh. *šáṅ-ku*,* **wolf.** (Wolves, where more frequent, as e. g. in Spiti, commit ravages among the sheep; but are other wise not much dreaded by man). *spyáṅ-mo* female wolf; *spyaṅ-ṗrúg* young wolf; *spyaṅ-ṫsáṅ* wolf's den; *spyaṅ-dóṅ* wolf's trap (used in *Sp.*); *spyáṅ-ku ṅú-ba* the howling of a wolf *Cs.*; *če-spyáṅ Lex.*, *lčè-spyáṅ Stg.*, *dur-spyáṅ Cs.*, **ḱyi-čáṅ* W.*, jackal. — *spyaṅ-dug-pa Cs.*, *spyaṅ-tsér Med.*, thistle, or kind of thistle, mentioned as an emetic.

སྤྱང་བ་ *spyáṅ-ba* 1. sbst. and adj.; *spyáṅ-po* adj., **skill; skilful, clever**, *Lex.*, *Glr.* and elsewh.; prob. = *yčáṅ(-po)*, q. v.; sometimes confounded with *sbyáṅ-ba*, *sbyáṅs-pa*, practiced, expert; *rig-pa spyáṅ-bas rtsóm-pa kún-la ˳ǰug Lt.* the clever man finds his way in every thing; *spyaṅ-ylén Cs.* the clever man and the dunce; *Glr.*: *spyaṅ ylen ma nór-ba čig byed dgos*, prob. to be read *˳byed*, and to be translated: then it must evidently appear, who is clever and who is stupid. — 2. vb. = *dpyáṅ-ba*.

སྤྱད *spyad* v. *spya*.

སྤྱད་པ་ *spyád-pa* v. *spyód-pa*.

སྤྱན *spyan*, resp. for *mig*, **eye**; *spyan bgrád-pa*, *ydáṅ-ba*, to stare *Cs.*; *spyan ˳gyúr-ba* v. *spyán-pa*; *spyan ˳drén-pa*, rarely *dróns-pa*, resp. for *˳drén-pa*, to invite, v. *˳drén-pa*; *spyan ˳ṗyi-ba* to wipe the eyes; *spyan btsúm-pa* to shut the eyes *Cs.*

Comp. and deriv. *spyan-kyúg* or *ḱyug* eye-brow *Cs.* — *spyan-dkyús* v. *dkyus*. — *spyan-bskyúns mdzád-pa* to protect, to preserve the eyes *Sch.* — *spyán-sṅa* before, with, in presence of a dignitary, *spyán-sṅai grá-pa-rnams* the scholars standing in presence of his Reverence *Cs.*; mostly in the termin. case: *spyán-sṅar*, as adv. and postp., *rgyál-poi spyán-sṅar ḱrid-pa* to lead (another) before the king, frq.; rarely in reference to the first pers.: *ṅai spyán-sṅar ˳oṅ* they came to me, before my face (sc. Buddha's) *Dzl.*; less corr. *spyán-sṅar mdzés-pai skúd-ris Mil.* in front (on the fore-part of the shoes) beautifully embroidered figures. — *spyán-čan* having eyes. — *spyan-lčibs* eye-lid. — *spyan-čáb* tears, *˳byin-pa* to shed; *čór-ba* to flow from; also to shed, *rgyál-bu spyan-čáb śór-ro Pth.* the prince shed tears. — *spyan-˳drén* one who invites, one that calls to dinner. — *spyán-pa Cs.* 1. eye-witness; 2. commissary; 3. *Sch.* overseer; *spyán-du ˳gyúr-ba* = *dpyáṅ-du ˳gyúr-ba*, to see, to know; *spyán-pa byéd-pa* to watch, guard, keep, protect, inspect *Sch.*; *bá-glaṅ-gi spyán-pa* cow-herd(?) *Sch.* — *spyan-˳brás* apple of the eye. — *spyan-mig-bzáṅ* the western 'king of ghosts', v. *rgyal-čén* sub *rgyál-ba*. — *spyan-dmigs Sch.*: 'the object of vision; the inclination of the mind'. — *spyan-smán* medicine for the eyes. — *spyan-rtség* the wrinkles of the eye-lids *Cs.* — *spyan-zúr Sch.*, corner of the eye. — *spyan-yzigs*, costly offerings dedicated to the gods, *Mil.*; also applied to presents of food, offered to men, *Mil.*; *˳búl-ba* to offer such; also *˳drén-pa*. — *spyan-yás*, *Sch.*, without eyes, blind. — *spyan-rás*, *Sch.* the brightness of the eye, a glance of the eye. — *spyan-ras-yzigs W.*; **čan-re-zig* Cs.*: **čen-re-sig* or *-si**, *Ssk.* अवलोकितेश्वर, the other (cf. *˳ǰam-dpal*) of the two great half-divine Bodhisattvas of the northern Buddhists, who more particularly is revered as begetter (not creator), redeemer, and ruler of men, and in the first place of the Tibetans, incarnate as king *Sroṅ-tsan-gám-po*, *Köpp.* II, 22. — *spyán-lam-du* seems to be = *drúṅ-du*, *spyán-sṅar*, *Mil.* and elsewh.

སྤྱི *spyi*, I. adj. (synon. *ťun*, also *dbyiṅs*, opp. to *sgos*) 1. **general, relating to all, standing higher than all**: **ṭim-pon či**, chief prefect, governor general *C.*; adv. *spyi*, *spyir(-du)*, less frq. *spyí-la*, *spyi-na*, *spyir-gyis*, **generally, in general**, frq. followed by *sgos(-kyis)*, *ḱyád-par*, **in particular, singly**; also like *cum tum* in Latin; *spyi daṅ ˳dir*, generally, and here, in this work, *Wdṅ.*; *spyii sdom*, v. *sdom*; — *spyii ḱog ǰi daṅ ǰi bžin-du* (?) *Sch.*: 'according to general custom'. — 2. **all**, *C.*; *lhá-ḱaṅ spyii bstan-srúṅ Glr.* — 3. for *spyi-bo*, v. below. — *spyi-sgra Cs.*, **general meaning**, more corr. *sgra-spyi*, *Was.* (294), **general expression**. — *spyi-yčér*, *spyi-ťer Cs.*, bald-headed. — *spyi-ťór* = *gtsug-tór Lex.* *spyi-ťóg*, property of the community, common property; *W.*: **pi-ťog-ne toṅ** bestow it out of the common funds! — *spyi-gdugs*, v. *sgos*. — *spyi-pa*, **head, chief, leader, superintendent**, *Sch.*;

spyi-dpon, much the same, v. *sgos*; *spyi-bo*, 1. (rarely *spyi*), **crown of the head**, top, *spyi-bor* *ₒk̔úr-ba* to carry on the head; — *spyi-bos p̔yág-ₒtsal-ba* to bow down bending the head; *žabs spyi-bor lén-pa*, frq., to place the foot of a superior on one's own head; *dei spyi-bo-nas byúg-nas*, pouring over his head, anointing him, *Domaṅ*; more frq: *spyi-bo-nas dbaṅ skúr-ba*, v *skur-ba*; *spyi-bo-nas dbaṅ bskúr-bai rgyál-po*, the anointed king; *spyi-glugs*, the vessel used for anointing (resembling a tea-pot). — 2. the end of a piece of cloth, *dar-yúg-gi*, *Glr.* — 3. name of a king of China *Glr.*; *spyi-miṅ* common appellation: *dkor ni nór-gyi spyi-miṅ*, '*dkor*' is a general word for property, *Lex.* — II. often incorr. for *ċi*, also *dpyi*.

སྤྱི་ཏི་ *spyi-ti*, a fantastic, mystical doctrine of **Urgyen-Padma**, *t̔ég-pa č̔én-po spyi-ti*, *spyi-ti yóg-brdai dkyil-k̔or Pth.*; *yáṅ-ti*, another of his doctrines.

སྤྱི་བརྟོལ་ *spyi-brtól*, *Cs.*: **impudence, impertinence**, *Sch.*: **lewd**; *spyi-brtól-čan*, impudent; *spyi-brtól byéd-pa*, to be impudent *Cs.*

སྤྱིང་བ་ *spyiṅ-ba*, pf. *spyiṅs*, imp. *spyiṅ(s)*, the vb. a. to *ₒbyiṅ-ba*, **to sink, to lower, let down, dip under**; *č̔ur*, *Lexx.*

སྤྱིན་ *spyin* (*W.* **(s)pín**), **glue, paste**: *spyin skól-ba*, to manufacture glue; *skúd-pa* (*Sch.* also *bdár-ba?*) to spread glue on; **pin daṅ ǰár-če** *W.* to glue; *ko-spyin*, glue made of skins, *nya-spyin*, fish-glue, isinglass; *bág-spyin* paste or rather a kind of putty, compounded of flour and glue; *rá-spyin* glue made of horn; *ša-spyin*, meat-jelly; *spyin-p̔or* glue-pot.

སྤྱིམས་ *spyims* (? *ċims*), *Ld.* = *spyi*; **ċimsi miṅ** = *spyi-miṅ*.

སྤྱིར་ *spyir* v. *spyi*.

སྤྱིལ་པོ་ *spyil-po*, 1. **hut** *Mil.*, *Pth.*; *rtsai*, **thatched hut** *Lex.*; *spyil-bu*, id.; *lo-mai spyil-bu*, hut constructed of twigs, fastened together on the top, **arbour**; **a cot**, a mean house. — 2. **inmate of such a one**, *Cs.*; also *spyil-pa*, fem. *-ma*.

སྤྱུག་པ་ *spyúg-pa*, pf. *spyugs*, imp. *spyug(s)*; **to expel, to turn out, to banish**; *yúl-nas* out of the country; *yul gžán-du Glr.*; *mt̔á-la*, *mt̔ar* into the neighbouring country, over the frontier (v. *mt̔a*); when the place of banishment is named, the otherwise faulty spelling *bċúg-pa* is allowable; v. *ₒǰúg-pa*.

སྤྱོ་བ་ *spyó-ba*, pf. and imp. *spyos*, **to blame, to scold** *Dzl.*; *č̔úṅ-ma rtág-tu spyó-žiṅ*, as my wife is always scolding; *ċes spyós-so* thus they spoke in a blaming way, *Dzl.*; *Cs.* also: **to mock, to ridicule** (?). synon. *γšé-ba*.

སྤྱོང་བ་ *spyóṅ-ba* = *dpyáṅ-ba*.

སྤྱོད་པ་ *spyód-pa*, I. vb., also *spyád-pa*, pf. *spyad*, *Ssk.* अचर 1. = *byéd-pa*, **to do, to act**, v. *tsáṅs-par*, yet gen. with an object in the accus. **to accomplish, perform, commit**; *sdig-pa*, *sdig-pai las*, *dgé-ba*, *dká-ba* (v. *dká-ba*), *č̔os spyod-pa*; *mi-dge-ba dé-dag spyód-na* if one commits these sins *Thgy.*; *bdag ċi spyád-pas ₒdir skyes*, what having done, or because of which doing of mine am I re-born here? *Dzl.*; even like *byéd-pa* = to be, *mṅa-ₒóg spyód-pai ₒbáṅs Glr.*, simply = subjects; rarely c. dat.: *sdíg-pa ₒbá-žig-la spyód-pa*, *Thgy.*, *dgé-ba bċú-la*, *Dzl.*, denoting a habitual doing; cf. *zá-ba*. — 2. **to treat, to deal with**, *zas-skóm légs-par spyód-pa*, (to deal with) food and drink in the right manner *S.g.*; gen. with the dat: *žiṅ-la lhú-ru spyad*, the fields were disposed of in lots, divided *Glr.*; hence gen. **to use**, to make use of, to employ, to enjoy: *ba-glaṅ nyin-par* to use an ox during the day (for ploughing) *Dzl.*; *yun-riṅ-dus-su bdé-bar spyad kyaṅ*, even if one has long and in tranquillity used, enjoyed (this world's goods), *Thgy.*; so frq. with *loṅs*: *lóṅs-spyod-pa*; to have for a sphere of activity, v. *mk̔á-spyod*, *sá-spyod*, *sa-ₒóg-spyod*; also a euphemism for sensual indulgence: *bud-méd-la spyód-pa* to use, to cohabit with, a woman, *Dzl.*; *mi-rigs-par* or *lóg-par*, to violate (a woman) *Thgy.* & others; *dga mgúr spyód-pa*, of a like meaning; the other synonymous phrases: *ˌdod-lóg spyód-pa, mi ˌós-pai spyód-pa byéd-pa, Glr., rgyál-po, čágs-pa, ˌkrig-pa spyód-pa*, belong by their construction properly to 1; so also: *bud-méd brgya spyod nus* he can get done with a hundred wives, *Lt.*

II. sbst. 1. **action, practice, execution**, opp. to *ltá-ba*, theory, esp. in mysticism, v. *sgóm-pa*. — 2. **activity**: *spyód-pa šín-tu dóg-par gyúr-to* they were much restrained, narrowly watched *Glr.; séms-kyi spyód-pa* seems to be: faculty of mind, *Wdn.* — 3. **way of acting, conduct, course of life**, = *spyód-lam; byan-čub-séms-dpai* frq; *nán-* or *nyés-spyod* bad actions, *bzán-* or *légs-spyod* good actions *Cs.; spyód-pa žib-pa*, 'the strict', a monastic order *Pth.;* **behaviour, deportment**, frq.: *spyód-pa rtsin-ba*, rude, rough, in manners *Glr.; spyód-pas skád-čig kyan mi tsugs*, of an extremely variable conduct (lit. not for one moment the same) *Glr.*

Comp. *spyod-ˌgrós* **gait and deportment** *Mil.* — *spyod-nán* = *nán-spyod, spyod-nán byéd pa.* — *spyód-tsul, Sch.* = *spyód-pa* II. *spyód-yul*, **sphere of activity**; *kún-gyi spyód-yul ˌdi ma lags*, that is not a thing to be attempted by every body *Mil.; mtón-bai spyód-pa* range of vision *Tar.*; cf. गोचर. — *spyód-lam*, 1. **demeanour, deportment, mode of life** frq.; 2. **good behaviour**, graceful demeanour, noble deportment; otherwise *spyód-pa mdzés-pa;* hence *spyód-pa dan ldán-pa, spyod-ldán* of genteel manners *Dzl.*; *spyód-pa dan mi ldán-pa Dzl.*, **čod-nán-čan* W.*, **čö-lóg ǰhé-kẹn*, C.* **rude, unmannerly, ill-bred, disobedient.** 3. *Med.*: **diet**, and more particularly **bodily exercise**; *zas-spyód*, food and exercise. 4. **attitude**: *spyód-lam rnam-bži* the four attitudes of sitting, lying, standing and walking.

སྤྱོད་པ་པ་ *spyód-pa-pa* v. *dpyód-pa*, extr.

སྤྱོད་པད་ *spyod-pad* or *dpyod-pád* (spelling not quite certain), pronunc.: **čö-pẹ**, **lemon, citron** *C.*

སྤྱོན་པ་ *spyón-pa*, rarely for *ˌbyon-pa.*

སྤྱོམ་པ་ *spyóm-pa*, pf. *spyoms*, **to boast, to exhibit with ostentation**, e.g. virtues, (the Greek *καυχᾶσθαι*). Notwithstanding the detailed explanations of the *Lexx.*, the word is after all so little known, that I never met with it in books, nor heard it used by the people. — *spyoms*, sbst., **self-praise, boasting** *Zam.*

སྤྲ་ *spra*, monkey. *Mil.*, prob. the large dark-gray, long-tailed **monkey** of the southern Himalaya; *sprá-mo*; *spra-prúg.*

སྤྲ་(ར)ཅལ་ *spra-čál* v. *pra-čál; spra-tél* v. *tél-pa.*

སྤྲ་བ་ *sprá-ba*, I. sbst. *W.* **šrá-wa**, **spunk, German tinder**, prepared of the fibres of a thistle (Cousinia); *spra-mé*, glowing tinder, *Pth.; pyi ni sprá-ba dkár-por yyogs*, white-nappy, as a botanical term, *Wdn.*, the colour of the tinder, referred to, being a light gray; *sprá-bai tóg-gu* a medicinal herb *Wdn.*

II. vb. pf. *spras*, imp. *spros*, 1. **to adorn, to decorate**: *rgyán-gyis* frq., *mtsán-dpes Mil.* and elsewh. — 2. *yčes spras, Lex.? sprá-ba byéd-pa* **to love, to caress.** — 3. perh. identical with **šrá-če(s)**, **to empty** (a dish). — 4. *spra ˌkrid-pa* **to lead, to direct right.** — Cf. also *ytsan sprá-wa.*

སྤྲ་ཚིལ་ *spra-tsíl, Med., C.* **wax** (*W.* **mum**).

སྤྲག་པ་ *sprág-pa* v. *sbrág-pa.*

སྤྲང་བ་ *sprán-ba, Cs.*, **to beg**; (the verb I never met with, and *Zam.* explains the sbst. only by *nor-méd*); *sprán-po*, **beggar**, *Dzl., Glr.*, frq. (*Wts.* 'filou', rather bold, though not far from the truth); **ṭan-lön* C.*, id.; *spran-rgán Mil.*, an old beggar; *rdzús-mai sprán-po* a sham-beggar *Glr.*; *spran-prúg* beggar boy: *spran-bán* mendicant friar *Glr.*; *spran-zás* beggar's livelihood *Mil*; *dkar-spran* begging for lenten food, also such food obtained by begging, v. *dkar-zás*; *skyur-sprán* begging for beer *Mil.*

སྤྲད་པ་ *sprád-pa* v. *spród-pa.*

སྤྲི་སྟི་མ་རྫ་ཡ. སི་ཅེན་ *spri-sti-ma-rdza-ya, si-čén*, n. of the emperor of China, during whose reign Buddhism was introduced into that country.

Glr.; acc. to Chinese accounts: *Miṅg-ti*, 58—76 after Christ.

སྤྲི་མ་ *spri-ma, spris-ma, sris-ma, W.* **śri**, **cream,** and other fatty substances, gathering on the surfaces of fluids; *ₒó-mai spris, Lt., žo(i)-spris, Wdṅ.;* gen. *ₒo-sri*, cream (of milk); *ṭúg-spri*, the greasy surface of soup; ditto of urine *Med.*

སྤྲིང་བ་ *spriṅ-ba*, pf. *spriṅs*, **to send a message, to give information, to send word;** *ṗrin*, tidings *Dzl.*; *žes spriṅ-ṅo* so I send him word *Dzl.*

སྤྲིན་ *sprin*, **ṭin**, *Ld.* **śrin**, *Bal.* **spin**, **cloud,** also as an emblem of transitoriness frq.; **śrin ṭigs, ḱor**, *W.*, clouds are spreading; *sprin-gyi ɣsèb-nas* from between the clouds *Glr.*; *glóg-sprin* thunder-cloud *Glr.*; *čár-sprin* rain-cloud; *ₒjá-sprin* cloud tinged with rainbow colours *Pth.*; *mig-sprin* v. this; *lhó-sprin* a southern cloud, picturesque expression, the clouds in Tibet generally coming from the south *Mil.*; *sprin-skyés* lightning; *sprin-dmár* clouds reddened by the sun, morning or evening red; *sprin-ṗúṅ, sprin-ṭsógs*, an accumulation of clouds; *sprin-gyi ṗó-nya* the messenger of the clouds, Meghadūta, a poëm by Kalidāsa *Tar.*

སྤྲིབས་པ་ *spribs-pa* **to be hungry** *Sch.*

སྤྲིས་མ་ *spris-ma* v. *spri-ma.*

སྤྲུ་མ་ *sprú-ma, Cs.*, **hellebore;** *sprú-dkár, -nág Med.*

སྤྲུག་པ་ *sprúg-pa*, pf. and imp. *sprugs*, **ṭúg-pa**, *W.* **śrug-če** **to shake, to shake off, to beat out,** *rdul* dust; **to stir up,** *rdul-ṭsúb*, **to raise,** whirl up dust; *lus sprúg-sil-ba, lus sprug-sil byéd-pa Glr.*, to shake one's self (used of horses); fig. *nus mṭu rtsal sprúg-pa*, to strain every nerve, to work with might and main *Pth.*; **to shake about, to stir up** (synon. **śrul-če, rum-če* W.*); *Cs.* also: to rub, to scratch, to brush??

སྤྲུལ་བ་ *sprúl-ba* (cf. *ₒṗrúl-ba*), **to juggle, to make phantoms** (*sprúl-pa*) **appear, to change, to transform** (one's self), which according to the doctrines of Buddhism is the highest acquisition of any man, that by his own holiness has assumed divine nature, viz. as long as he is capable of acting, not having yet been absorbed into the blessed state of nothingness. This power of transformation on the part of the Buddhist is the evidence of what he understands by divine omnipotence; but as this conception is a mere product of fancy, it varies in its import. On the one hand it is opposed to reality, *dṅos*; thus e.g. beings, whom no Buddha could convert through his personal agency, *sku-dṅós-kyi sgó-nas*, are converted (acc. to *Pth.*) *sprúl-pai ṭábs-kyis*. Frequently Buddha avails himself of jugglery, *rdzu-ṗrúl ston*, converting thousands of beings in a trice, *Dzl.* & elsewh.; further: *drág-poi sprúl-pa byás-pa yin Glr.*, I caused terrifying phantoms to appear, viz. the spectral bodies of executed culprits, in order to scare the rude Tibetans into the way of virtue. From the foregoing it is evident that the term in question by no means conveys the scriptural idea of **a creative and miraculous power**; the Tibetan, however, when he becomes acquainted with christianity, is always apt to substitute his *sprúl-pa* or *rdzu-ₒṗrúl*, and *sprúl-ba* for it. On the other hand, a real and material existence is as often attributed to a *sprul-pa*, when it designates the incarnate and embodied person, the Avatāra of a deity, (Mongol. Chubilgan), who like any human being is capable of acting, and exerting an influence on the material world around him, or of suffering by it, without any docetic admixture. Occasionally it is also to be translated by **emanation:** *yáṅ-sprul*, emanation of the second degree, i.e. one emanation going forth from another; *nyíṅ-sprul* or *ɣsúm-sprul*, an em. of the third degree *Pth.*; *sprúl-pa ₒgyéd-pa*, to let emanations go forth, *Lexx.* — Further: *sprúl-pa mkyén-pa*, to be an adept in the art of *sprúl-pa*, i.e. witchcraft, *Glr.*; *ri ɣnyís sprúl-te* producing two mountains by magic, *Dzl.*; ... *mṭó-ba ... bžúgs-pa sprúl-nas*, changing himself into a high enthroned person, *Dzl.*; *dge-*

sláh žig-tu, transforming himself into a friar, *Dzl.* frq.; *dúd-ₒgro ťsim-par sprúl-ba*, to satiate animals by fictitious food *Dzl.*; *ťams-čád sprúl-par ₒdúg-pa*, these were all metamorphoses, mocking phantoms, *Glr.*; *skulús-kyi sprúl-pa brgya-rtsa-brgyád mdzád-de* or *sprúl-te*, to centuple one's self, *Glr.*; *sprul-pai rgyál-po*, the phantom-king, viz. Buddha, Avalokitesvara, or some other divine person, incarnate as a king; *gań-la-gań-ₒdúl-gyi sprúl-pa*, all-converting Avatara, frq.

སྤྲེ *spre*, gen. *spreu*, rarely *sprel* (*Ld.* **šreu; spriu**) **monkey**, of a grayish yellow brown, common in the forests of the southern Himalaya, (cf. *spra*); sometimes a distinction is made between *spre* and *spra*, in which case the former is the long-tailed monkey. — *spré-mo*, female monkey, *Cs.*; yet also *spreu žár-ma*, a blind female monkey, *Dzl*; *spre-ṕrúg*, young monkey. — *spre-rtséd*, apish tricks; foolery.

སྤྲོ་བ *spró-ba* I. vb. pf. *spros*, prop. the transitive of *ₒṕró-ba* **to make go out, to disperse, to spread**; gen. however intransitive: 1. **to go out, to proceed, to spread**, of rays of light, of the wind, *Wdń.* — 2. fig. **to enlarge upon**, by way of explaining, representing, *Zam.*, *Pth.*; *γčig-las sprós-pa*, *Was.* (115), enlarging (proceeding) from the number one in an ascending progression of numbers; *rnám-par sprós-pa*, to have come to a full development and restoration from the consequences of sins, *Stg.*

II. 1. vb. (pf. unaltered), **to feel an inclination for, to delight in**: *dgé-ba-la*, in virtue, *Dzl.*; *byá-ba gáń-la yań spró-ba čuń*, feeling little inclination for doing any thing, *Thgy.*; *bsád-par spró-ba su yań ma byuń*, none was found that had a mind to kill, *Stg.*; so also *Tar.*; **to be willing, to wish**, *Tar.*; in an absolute sense: *sems*, or resp. *ťugs*, *spró-bar ₒgyúr-ba*, **to get cheerful, merry**, *Mil.* — 2. sbst. **joy, cheerfulness**: *spró-ba skyéd-pa*, to feel joy, pleasure, *Dzl.* and elsewh.; *spró-ba skyé-bai ṕyir-du*, for an encouragement, for a comfort, *Glr.*; *spro-šiń-ba Sch.*, **great** joy (cf. *šiń*); *spro-šiń-gé-ba, Sch.*, to one's wish (?); *spro ši-ba, Sch.*, 'not to be joyful', lit. the cessation of joy; *spro ťúń-ba*, 'short cheerfulness', i.e. a passionate disposition; or as adj. **passionate, irascible**, *Wdń.*; *dga-spró*, **joy**, *dga-spró dpag-tu-méd-pa ťob*, he got into a most cheerful humour, *Mil.* — **ţo-ḱáń**, *C.*, pleasure-house, summer-house, pavilion; *spro-séms* and (*Ld.*) **spro-šés, šro-šés**, joy; *spro-séms*, *Thgy.* also youthful joy, alacrity, cheerfulness in working, readiness to act.

སྤྲོག་མ *spróg-ma*; *Sch. spós-kyi spróg-ma*, **little box for frankincense.**

སྤྲོག་ཞུ *spróg-žu* v. *ṕrog*.

སྤྲོད་པ *spród-pa*, secondary form *sprad*, the vb. a. of *ṕrod-pa* (by the illiterate it is often used for *γtod-pa*, not very current in common life) 1. **to bring together, to put together, to make to meet**: *ńai blá-ma-la spród-do*, we will bring you together with our Lama, *Mil.*; so also resp. . . . *γnyis žal spród mdzád-pa*; in another passage *de dań žal-spród-du bžúgs-šiń* prob. means sitting exactly opposite to one another, (a whimsical idea, relative to two idols many miles distant from each other; possibly it should be read *γtod-du*); *bdág-čag spród-čig*, bring about a meeting between our two parties! *Dzl.*; *γyul* or *ťáb-mo*, to commit a battle; *rál-ḱa*, *Ma.*, to put the edges of the swords together, prob. meaning the same; *mťeb spród-pa*, to put the finger to the bow-string, *Glr.*; **lág-ţo' ťéb-ţo' kál-wa**, to suspend by the thumb and big toe, a kind of torture in *C.* (The special meaning: to cohabit, *Cs.*, never came to my notice). — 2. **to deliver** (a letter, message) *Pth.*; *spár-mor*, *lág-tu*, *Lex.*, to put into one's hand; **to set, to put, to propose**, **gyugs, ldem**, a task, a riddle, *W.*; **to pay** (cf. *ₒṕrod-pa*), *ṕyir sprod-pa*, to repay. — Moreover: *ńó-sprod-pa*, **to explain**, *don dań spród-pa* seems to signify the same in *Mil.*, *Pth.*; *brdá-sprod-pa*, **to explain, to describe** v. *brda*; *brda-spród*, ibid. seems to denote **grammar**.

སྤྲོས་པ *sprós-pa*. 1. pf. v. *spró-ba* I. — 2. **business, employment, activity**; *Cs.*:

'spros-pa-čan, busy, **employed, occupied;** sprós-bčas, id.; čʹós-kyi and ˳jig-rtén-gyi sprós-pa, spiritual and secular business'; *Sch.*: 'spros kun, all affairs'; I met only with sprós-pa méd-pa or čʹód-pa, or spros-brál, denoting the state of an absolute inactivity, such as belongs to Buddha in the state of čʹos-sku, (v. *sku* 2) *Pth.*, *Mil.*

ཕ

ཕ *ṗa* 1. the letter *ṗ*, aspirate, the English p in pass. — 2. num. figure: 14.

ཕ་ *ṗa* I. vulgo ཨ་ཕ་, ཨ་པ་, *ắ-ṗa*, *ắ-pa*, (*Cs.* also ཨ་ཏ་ *ắ-ta*) 1. **father**, resp. *yab* (yet also *ṗa* is used, e.g. when Milaraspa is addressed by his female disciples, as well as in prayers to defunct saints *Mil.*) — 2. a male, not castrated, animal (vulg. likewise *ắ-ṗa*). **Comp.** *ṗa-gláṅ* bull. — *ṗa-rjes-bú*, *Sch.*, a child born after its father's death. — *ṗa-rtá*, stallion. — **ṗa-nór**, patrimony *C.*, *W.* — *ṗa-spád* (*Sch.* also *ṗad*) v. *spad*; *ṗa-spún* v. *spun*. — *ṗa-ṗág*, boar. — *ṗa-má*, parents, *ṗa-má-la gús-pa*, *Stg.*; **ṗa-ma-méd-k̔an**, *W.*, orphan; also father or mother, parent; *ṗa-má-γčig-pa*, brothers and sisters born of the same parents. — *ṗa-miṅ*, relations on the father's side; *btsún-moi ṗa-miṅ bós-so*, *Glr.*, he invited the relations of his wife's father; *ṗa* (*daṅ*) *més* (*-po*), ancestors; *ṗa-més ši-bai dón-du*, for the (defunct) ancestors, *Wdṅ.*; — *ṗa-tsáb* 1. foster-father, guardian, *Sch.* 2. father to a country(?). — *ṗa-tsán*, *Mil.* 1. cousin by the father's side (patruelis) *C.* 2. also = *ṗa-spún*(?). — *ṗa-γží* = **ṗa-nór**, *C.* — *ṗa-yáṅ*, *Sch.*, step-father; — *ṗa-yúl*, fatherland, native country, frq.; *ṗa-yúl-la čʹágs-pa* or *srég-pa*, love of country. — *ṗa-γyág*, yak-bull. — *ṗa-γyár*, step-father, foster-father, *Cs.* — *ṗa-rá*, he-goat, buck.

II. root for the terms: **beyond, onward, farther on**; *ṗá-ga*, the opposite side; *čʹu ṗá-gar ťón-nas*, to get to the opposite bank or shore, *Mil.* (not frq.). — *ṗá-gi*, 1. that which is on the other side, *Sch.* 2. *C.*, also *Pth.*, *Mil.*: **yonder;** *ṗá-gii ri de*, that mountain yonder, *Pth.* 3. col.: **he.** — *ṗá-gir*, **there, thither.** — *ṗá-ṅos* = *ṗá-rol*, *ṗá-rol-tu Lh.* — *ṗá-mťa*, the other end, the other boundary, *Cs.*; *ṗa-mťa-méd*, without boundary, endless, *Cs.* — *ṗa-ṗyogs C.* = *ṗá-ga*. — *ṗa-tsád*, *ṗa-zád*, **distance;** *ṗa-tsád čig-na*, at a small distance (from the town), *Pth.*; *dé-nas ṗa-zád čig-na*, a bit farther on, *Dzl.*; *ṗa-tsad čig-tu ˳tón-nas*, stepping a little aside, *Pth.*; *ṗa-zád ˳gró-ba*, to go on, *Dzl.* frq. — *ṗa-ri* the mountain on the other side. — *ṗá-rol*, in *B.* very frq. 1. **the other side; opposite side, counterparty.** 2. for *ṗá-rol-pa*, *-na*, *-tu* v. below; *ṗá-rol-tu*, over to the other side, *skyél-ba*, to carry, *ṗyin-pa*, to get to the other side, esp. in reference to the Mahāyāna doctrine of crossing the stream of time to the shore of rest, of Nirwāṇa; gen. as sbst. = पारमिता, means of crossing (*Was.* **perfections**, *Köpp.* **cardinal-virtues**); gen. six of them are reckoned: *sbyin-pa*, *ťsúl-k̔rims*, *bzód-pa*, *brtson-˳grús*, *bsam-γtán*, *šes-ráb*; sometimes only five, at other times even ten, by adding *ťabs*, *smón-lam*, *stobs*, *ye-šés*; *sbyin-pai*, *šes-ráb-kyi ṗá-rol-tu ṗyin-pa*, to have stepped over or crossed by means of beneficence, wisdom etc. (or more naturally: to have got to the end of beneficence etc., to have fully achieved, accomplished it; sbst. the full accomplishment of etc.). — *ṗá-rol-na*, adv., **on the other side;** postp. e. gen. **beyond, behind,** with regard to space, *Sambh.*; **extending**

beyond, both as to the future and the past, e. g. *bskál-pa gráṅs-med-pai ṕá-rol-na*, innumerable Kalpas ago, frq.; *ṕá-rol-pa*, **1. one living on the other side.** 2. also *po*, **enemy, adversary,** *ṕá-rol-pai rgyál-po, ṕá-rol-pai dmag, ṕá-rol-gyi dmag-ṫsógs*, the hostile king, hostile army; *ṕá-rol γnón-pa*, to vanquish the enemy; *ṕá-rol-gyis mi ṫsúgs-par ˳gyúr-ba*, not to be molested by the enemy. 3. also *po*, **the other; the neighbour**; *ṕá-rol-gyi lén-pa*, to take away the neighbour's property; *ṕá-rol-gyi rdzas, yo-byád, nor, Stg.*; *ṕá-rol γnón-pa, Tar.* 12,20: excelling others, *Schf.* **exceedingly.** — Cf. also *ṕar* and *ṕan* II.

ཕ་གུ་ *ṕá-gu, Sch.* **wall; edge, border**; in two passages of *Glr.* the latter meaning does not suit at all, and the former not well; rather: **tile**; v. *pag.*

ཕ་ཏིང་ *ṕá-tiṅ, W.*, **sweet dried apricots**, in *C.* **ṅa-ri-k̔ám-bu**, in Hind. خوباني, in Russia *bokhari, bokharki*, also called Persian fruit, much exported from Balti, Kabul, and other countries of western Asia.

ཕ་ཏིལ་ *ṕa-til, pa-til* (*Ar.* فتيلة) *W.*, **lunt, match**; **dug-če**, to light (a match).

ཕ་བ་དགོ་དགོ་ *ṕa-ba-dgo-dgó*, **puff-ball, bull-fist** (a kind of fungus) *Wdṅ.*

ཕ་བོང་ *ṕa-bóṅ, Glr.* and elsewh., *C.*, *ṕa-˳óṅ Pth., Bal., ṕa-lóṅ Ld.*, **a large rock** or **block**, above ground.

ཕ་ཝང་ *ṕa-wáṅ*, 1. **bat** (animal) *Lt., Thgr., C.*; **ṕo-loṅ-hel-kyi, ṕa-waṅ-àṅ-kyé, -àr-k̔yi**, *W.*, **ṕa-waṅ-ṫár**, *Sik.*, id. (= *bya-waṅ*). 2. *rdo ṕa-waṅ, Ssk.* sâlagrâma, **ammonite.**

ཕ་ར་ *ṕá-ra*, 1. **breeding-buck.** — 2. v. *ṕár-ba.*

ཕ་རང་ *ṕa-ráṅ*, 1. also *ṕe-ráṅ*, = **ṕi-liṅ**, *C.*, **Feringhi, European.** — 2. vulg. **venereal disease.**

ཕ་རི་ *ṕa-ri* 1. *Lh.*, **a coarse covering** or **carpet.** — 2. a mountain on the other side.

ཕ་ལ་ *ṕá-la Ssk.*, **fruit,** *Lt.*

ཕ་ལམ་ *ṕa-lám, rdo-rje-ṕa-lám*, **diamond,** *Lt.*

ཕ་ལི་ *ṕa-li*, **shield, buckler.**

ཕ་ཤོད་ཤེད་འདུག་ *ṕa-šod šed ˳dug*, **he changes colour, turns pale,** with consternation, *Ld.*

ཕག་ *ṕag*, I. v. *pag.* — II. in *B.* gen. *ṕág-pa*, **swine, hog, pig** (introduced into *C.* from China, and largely consumed; in *W.* somewhat known from India, **ri-ṕag* and *lúṅ-ṕag** being distinguished as the wild boar and the tame hog); *ṕág-pai sna, Glr.*; *rús-pa, Med.*; *bčud*(?) *Lt.*; *ṕág-gi γdoṅ*, a pig's face, *Sambh.*; *ṕá-ṕag*, not castrated, *ṕó-ṕag*, castrated boar; *mó-ṕag*, sow. — *ṕág-k̔yu*, herd of swine. — *ṕág-mgo*, 1. **boar's head** (a valued protective against demons, it being hid in the ground under the threshold of the door). 2. *S.g.* fol. 26, it seems to be **a mineral** used in medicine. — *ṕag-rgód*, wild boar. — *ṕag-mče*, tusks of a boar. — *ṕag-ṫúṅ, Sch.*: a large boar(?). — *ṕag-ṕrúg*, young pig. — *ṕág-ma, Sch.*, gelded hog. — *ṕág-mo*, 1. sow. 2. a goddess v. *rdo-rje.* — *ṕag-ṫsáṅ*, pig-sty. — *ṕag-ṫsil*, hog's lard; bacon. — *ṕag-ṫsógs* = *ṕag-k̔yu.* — *ṕag-rdzi*, swine-herd. — *ṕag-zé*, hog's bristle, *Wdṅ.* — *ṕag-yar-ma, Sch.*, the fattening of pigs(?) — *ṕag-ril*, pig's muck(?) *Lt.* — *ṕag-ša*, pork.

III. (*Cs. ṕág-ma*), **something hidden; concealment**: *ṕág-na mi yód-pa*, a man concealed behind, *Dzl.*, *ṕág-gam gru žig-tu*, in a corner, in obscurity, *Dzl.*; **ṫsá-big ṕág-la yod**, it is somewhat hidden, cannot be seen well (from this place), *Ld.*; **ṕág-la zá-če**, to eat (dainties) by stealth, *W.*; *nyi-ma rii ṕág-tu ˳gró, Thgy.*, the sun hides himself behind the mountain; *sgo-ṕág-nas bltás-pas*, to watch, spy, lurk behind the door, *Glr.*, v. also *˳jáb, pa*; *ṕag nyan táṅ-če W.*, **to listen.** — **ṕag-sté**, *W.* ('a hidden paring-axe' v. *sté-po*) plane; **ṕag-sté gyáb-če, ďúl-če, šrúb-če**, to plane. — *ṕag-ṫsóṅ*, smuggling, *čó-če*, to smuggle, *W.* **táṅ-k̔an**, smuggler, *W.* — *ṕág-ra*, parapet. — *ṕag-rágs*, rampart, intrenchment. — *ṕag-lám*, secret path (of smugglers). — **ṕag-súg**, bribery, *C., W.*; **ṕag-súg táṅ-če**, to bribe; *zá-če*, to accept a bribe, *W.*

ཕག་ཕག་ *pag-pág*, the name given in *Pur.* to **Codonopsis ovata**, the thick roots of which plant are cooked like turnips or ground and baked; v. *klu-mdúd.*

ཕང་ *pań* I. *ₒpań* (*páń-ma*, *páń-bu Cs*) **spindle**; *pań-ló*, 1. the **whirl** of the spindle. 2. *śiń-rtai pań-ló*, **waggon wheel**, *Dzl.*

II. v. *pań.*

ཕང་འགྲོ་ *pań-ₒgró*, *Sch.*, the belly or body of a stringed instrument.

ཕང་བ་ *páń-ba*, *páńs-pa* (*Glr.* also *póńs-pa*, prov.) **to save, to spare, to use economy:** *srog* to spare one's life; *mi-páńs-te* or *-par* e.g. *ₒbúl-ba*, to give largely, not sparingly; *páń-sems*, **thriftiness**; *páń-sems-čan*, **thrifty, frugal**; **pań-sem čo-če**, *W.*, **to be thrifty, frugal.**

ཕང་མ་ *páń-ma*, **a medicinal plant**, *Med.*

ཕང་མེད་ *pań-méd*, stated to be = *rin-méd*, *Ts.*

ཕང་ལོ་ *pań-lo* v. *pań* I.

ཕང་ལོང་ *pań-lóń*, **vertebra** (?) *S.g.*

ཕཊ་ *paṭ Ssk.*, an unmeaning sound, frequently used in magic spells, on which subject Milaraspa speaks rather obstrusely.

ཕད་ *pad*, **a large bag** or **sack**, *rás-pad*, *rál-pad*, *rtsíd-pad*, sack of cotton cloth, goat's hair, yak's hair; *pad-ḱá*, *-skéd*, *-mtíl*, **the mouth, middle,** and **bottom** of a sack; *pad-gáń*, a full sack, a sackful; *pad-stóń*, an empty sack; *pád-snam*, sack-twine, sack-cloth; *pád-tsa*, very coarse sack-cloth.

ཕན་ *pan* I. sbst., **hanging ornaments,** lappets of silk, similar to the decorations of our tent-cloths, awnings etc., *ka-*, *sgo-*, *ydun-pan*, on pillars, doors, beams; *pan-ydugs*, a parasol so decorated, *S.g.*

II. = *pa* II., gen. in the combination of *pan-čád* (*Glr.* also *pan-čód*), also *pán-la* or *pan*, **towards, until:** *dá-či-nas dá-lta pán-la dar čig soń*, from 'but just' till 'just now' a moment has passed, *Thgy.*; *ná-niń-nas da pan-čád lo yčig son*, *Thgy.*; **da pan**, **until now,** *C.*; ... *nas diń-sań pan* (*-la*) *Glr.* from... till now; *pyi-ma pan-čád-du ₒgró-ba yin*, I am proceeding towards the future, *Thgy.*; *pan-čád* also **beyond:** **de pen-čę' ma do* C.* do not go any farther than that place; combined with its contrary *tsun*: *pan-tsún(-du) gró-ba*, to walk to and fro, there and back; to walk past, frq.; *pan-tsún-du púl-ba*, to push hither and thither, *Glr.*; *pan-tsún mtún-pai ytam*, assurances of mutual friendship, *Glr.*; *pan-tsun yčig-gis yčig-la yi-ge ytóń-ba*, *pyag byéd-pa*, *ynód-pa byéd-pa*, mutual correspondence, m. greetings, m. encroachment; *pan-tsún sdúr-ba sdébs-pa*, to compare with one another, to mix one with the other, *Zam.*; *ynyis-ynyis-dag pan-tsun-gyi ₒdra-bai yi-ge*, two equal letters (ă, ā etc.) at a time *Gram.*: *ma-páń-gi ₒgram pan-tsún-du* on each of the two shores of lake *Ma-pań*, *Mil.*; *don pan-tsún bsdú-rgyu yód-pa*, **correlative terms,** having reciprocal relation, *Gram.*: *pan-tsún tor-ba*, **to scatter, to disperse;** *pan-tsún-dag*, *Cs.*, both parties.

III. v. the following articles.

ཕན་དིལ་ *pán-dil W.* **kettle, pot** (of tinned copper, the common cooking-vessel in Tibet and India, having the shape of a broad urn); in *C.* **zańs(-bu)**, *Pers.* and *Hd.* دیگچی (*dēgči*); *pan-čuń*, a small vessel of that kind.

ཕན་པ་ *pán-pa* I. vb. **to be useful:** *de ni bdag-la mi pan*, that is no more of use to me; *pán-par mi ₒgyur*, it will be of no use; *bu ₒdis ńá-la pán-par dka*, this son will hardly be useful to me, *Glr.*; *pán-par dgá-ba-rnams*, such as wish to make themselves useful, they who are ready to serve, *Thgy.*; *bgród-la pan*, useful for learning to walk, *Lt.*; *nad kún-la pán-pa yin*, that is good for all diseases, *Lt.*; *ńai nád-la pán-pa yín-pas*, because I have recovered, *Glr.*; **pan soń**, it has helped, it has got better; ... *na pan*, if..., then I shall get well, *Glr.*; *pán-pa žig srid*, recovery might be possible, *Pth.*; *mi pan*, it is useless, = **hurtful;** also: **it is not enough,** *Mil.*; *mi pán-par ₒdód-pa tams-čád*, all the malevolent, *Domań*: *ḱá-la pan*, lit. 'it is a mere enjoyment of the mouth', i. e. an outward, temporary enjoyment or advantage; hence *ṕán-pa* and *ṕan-pa yin-pa*, adj., **useful**: *ṕán-pai don*, a useful thing, valuable possession, frq.; *bdag nyon-mȯńs-pa-las ṕan-pai don med*, after all it is of no use to me in my misery, *Dzl.*; *bslab-bya ṕan-pai tsig*, a wholesome instructive word, *Glr.*; *ṕan-pai grós*, useful advice, *Dzl.*

II. sbst. **use, benefit, profit**: *bstán-pa-la ṕán-pa žig byed-pa, Stg.*; *ṕan-ynod-méd-pa*, bringing neither profit nor harm, *Mil.*; *ṕán-pa dań bdé-ba, ṕan-bdé* **happiness and blessing**, very frq.; *ṕan-ₒdógs-pa, ṕan-ₒdógs byéd-pa*, **to be of use**, and adj. **profitable**, frq.; *ṕan-tógs*, **profit**; *ṕan-tógs če, Thgy.*, **čén-mo**, *W.*, **very profitable**; ... *la ṕan gań togs gyis*, render services to ... in every way possible! *Mil.*; *ṕan-grogs* a helping (useful) friend, *Pth.*; *ṕan-ynód*, profit and loss, *ṕan-bdé* v. above; *ṕan-zás*, wholesome diet, *Med.*; *ṕan-yón*, **benefit, blessing**, as a reward for a meritorious action, frq.; *ṕan-(pai) sems*, **benevolence, readiness to help.**

ཕབ་པ་ *ṕáb-pa*, I. v. *bébs-pa*. — II. *Sch.*: **to fall down** (?).

ཕབས་ *ṕabs*, 1. **dry barm** (prepared for inst. in Balti, is said to consist of flour, mixed with some ginger and aconite). — 2. **lees, yeast** (of beer).

ཕམ་པ་ *ṕám-pa* v. *ₒṕám-pa*.

ཕའུ་ *ṕau* v. *pag.*

ཕར་ *ṕar* I. sbst. **interest** (of money), *W.*: **ńúl-la ṕar kál-če**, to impose, demand interest, **čál-če**, to pay interest; **exchange, agio.**

II. in later writings and col. for *ṕa* II.; also for *ṕan-čád, ṕa-zád*: **farther**; *ṕar ₒgró-ba*, to go on; *ṕar ₒkyám-pa*, to roam farther and farther, *Thgy.*; **ṕár-tsam**, *C.*, = *ṕar*; *ṕar ₒgro tsur ₒgró-ba-rnams*, people going, travelling, hither and thither; **away, off**: *di-nas ṕar*, away from here; *ṕar mi mčio*, I do not go away, *Dzl.* ༢༤༠, 6 (*Sch.* erron. 'to the father'); *ṕar bžud*, go away!; ... *la ṕar lta-ba*, **to look** (in a certain direction) *Mil.*, **away from one's self**, as opp. to: *rań-rig-séms-la tsur ltá-ba*, to look into one's own heart *Mil.*; *glu ṕár-čig tsúr-čig lén-pa*, **alternative song**, *Mil.*; *ṕár-slob tsúr-slob yin*, they are mutually scholars one of the other, *Tar.*; *ṕar yčig láb-na tsur ynyis rgol*, if you say one word 'towards her', she gives you smartly a double charge back, *Mil.*; *ṕar-tsúr-la, W.* also = **so-sór*, **in opposite directions**; **ṕar-tsúr-la čo-če** to separate vb. a.; **do-če**, to **separate** vb. n.

Comp. *ṕár-ka, Thgy. ṕár-ka = ṕá-rol*, **the opposite side** (of a valley &.) vulgo frq. — *ṕár-ńos*, id., *čui ṕar-tsúr-gyi-lam*. — *ṕar-ṕyin* abbreviation for *ṕá-rol-tu ṕyin-pa* v. *ṕá-rol, ṕa* II. *Mil.* — **ṕár-tsam**, *C.*, = *ṕa-zád*. — *ṕar-ₒdzúg* and *tsur-rgól* prob. = *sńá-rgol* and *ṕyi-rgol*. — *ṕar-zád* = *ṕa-zád*. — *ṕár-la*, 1. = *ṕar*, **away, onward**, *Schr.* 2. = *ṕá-rol-tu, na*, esp. with regard to time: vulgo *lo yčig ṕár-la*, after one year; *W.* esp. after the gerund in *nas*: **zan zós-ne ṕár-la**, after dinner. — *ṕár-lam*, **way** or **journey thither**, *Sp.* ni f.

ཕར་བ་ *ṕár-ba*, I. 1. **wild dog** (barks, and commits its ravages like the wolf, yet being afraid of man) in *Ld.* — 2. wolf *C.*, also *ṕar-spyáń*. II. v. *ₒṕár-ba*.

ཕར་རྫས་ *ṕar-rdzás*, *Sch.*, **an old heir-loom.**

ཕལ་ *ṕal*, I.? *Ld.* 1. **ṕal čós-se* (or *te*) *dug**, **step aside! make way!** — 2. **ṕal-ṕál čá-če**, **to feel flattered.** II. v. the following.

ཕལ་པ་ *ṕál-pa*, **usual, common**; *ṕal-pai miń*, his usual (common) name, *Thgr.*; *ṕál-pa-las ṕags-par bzáń-ba*, a more than ordinary beauty *Dzl.*; *mi* or *gań-zág ṕál-pa*, common people, *Mil.*; *tsoń-ṕál-rnams bór-ro*, they left the common tradespeople behind, *Dzl.*; *ṕál-pai rdzas* v. *ₒjál-ba*; *šiń ṕál-rnams*, common trees, *Mil.*; *snod ṕál-pa*, common vessels, *Mil.*; *ṕal*, the common people; *ṕál-gyi náń-na ynás-pa*, to live among the people *Dzl.*; *ṕál-gyis rgyáb-nas ded ṕál-gyis bskór-te*, the people running after and crowding round him, *Pth.*; **ṕál-(pai) skad**, 1. *W.* the language of common life, opp. to **čós-skad**, book-language (*C.* *t̔ál-ke'**). 2. *Sch.*: **rough-copy, waste-book**; *p̔ál-po-* (*Cs.* also *-mo*) *če*, **a host, a troop**; *mi-rgód p̔al-po-če žig*, a troop or set of monsters (v. *rgód-pa* II.); gen. like *οἱ πολλοί*, the mass of the people, majority, great part or number; *p̔al-čé-ba* id. — *p̔al-čén*, **a philosophers' school**, called Mahasanghika. — *p̔al-čér*, **manifold, for the most part, ordinarily**, also = **universally**; *p̔al-čér čo-ṅés ͺdégs-so*, they raised a general lamentation *Dzl.*

ཕལ་ཅན་ *p̔ál-čan W.*, **broad, wide**, e.g. a broad valley; *p̔al-méd*, narrow.

ཕས་ *p̔as*, instrum. of *p̔a*, I. **by the father**; v. also *p̔as-spún*, sub *spun*. II. **of the opposite side, of the counter-party**, e.g. *p̔as rgól-ba*.

ཕི་ *p̔i*, 1. num. figure 44. — 2. *W.* for *p̔yi*, *p̔i-pa* for *p̔yi-pa*.

ཕི་ཀེར་ *p̔i-ker* (Urdu فکر, *Ar.* reflexion) *W.* **čaṅ p̔i-ker med** = *čaṅ mi sto* it is no matter, it makes no difference.

ཕི་ལིང་ *p̔i-liṅ* v. under *rgya*.

ཕིག་ཕིག་ *p̔ig-p̔ig*, a kind of jelly *C.*

ཕིང་ *p̔iṅ*, *Sch.*: 1. **earthen-ware pitcher.** — 2. **cup, cupping-glass.** — 3. *W.*: **sgó-p̔iṅ**, **door-hinge.**

ཕིང་པ་ *p̔iṅ-pa* v. ཕྱིང་པ་; ཕིང་བ་, ཕིང་ཅེས་ v. འཕྱིན་པ་

ཕིར་བ་ *p̔ír-ba*, **p̔ír-če** *W.* **to fall down.**

ཕུ *p̔u* numerical figure: 74.

ཕུ་ *p̔u*, I. sbst. 1. **the upper part** of an ascending valley or ravine; *p̔u bar mdo* (or *mda*), the upper, middle, and lower part of such a valley; *p̔u-ču*, mountain-torrent, frq.; *p̔ur ma ͺgro, p̔u yá-gir ma ͺgro, Glr.*, do not go to the upper part of the valley; *p̔u-lhágs*, higher situated and colder places or districts, opp. to *rgya-šód*, lower and milder parts. The not unfrequent phrase: *p̔u-t̔ág γčód-pa* or *čód-pa* was traced by our Lama to its original meaning: the upper part of the valley is shut up (with snow etc.), which is now used in a general sense; *k̔rúl-bai p̔u-t̔ág čod, Mil.*, prob. shut out all error, prevent every mistake! *p̔u-t̔ag-čód-lugs-kyi čos šig, Mil.* seems to be an instruction for making a decision; *ṅa rgás-pa daṅ séms kyi p̔u-t̔ág čód-pas ͺgró-ba mi yóṅ-bar ͺdug*, prob.: I being old and my spiritual affairs settled (not calling for further improvement), shall probably not travel any more (to India; but you may do so) *Mil.* cf. *p̔ugs*. — *p̔ú-pa*, the inhabitant of an elevated valley. Fig.: *p̔u γyo mda dkrug*, there is agitation above and below, the higher and the lower faculties of the mind are troubled, excited, *Mil.* — 2. prop. n. **Pu**, e. g. **a village in Upper Kunawar**, missionary station of the Church of the United Brethren. — 3. vulgo **the spirit** or **gaseous element of liquors**, causing them to foam, effervesce or explode, cf. *dbugs*; perh. to be referred to no. II.

II. interjection and imitative sound: *p̔u ͺdébs-pa Glr.*, **p̔u gyáb-če** *W.*, **to make pooh, to blow, to puff, to inflate**; *p̔u skoṅ*, puff it up (the skin etc.), lit.: fill it with pooh! *p̔us*, with the breath; *p̔us ͺdébs-pa Sch.* **to blow, howl, cry** (?); *sna-rtsa-p̔u*, **n. of a disease**, *Lt.*

ཕུ་དུང་ *p̔u-dúṅ*, also *p̔u-t̔úṅ Glr.*, *p̔u-rúṅ Cs.*, **sleeve**; **p̔u-rdzús** *C.* (false sleeves), *p̔u-dúṅ-* (or *-t̔uṅ-*) *rtse* (sleeve-edges) **hand-ruffles**; mittens, cuffs (to keep the wrist warm).

ཕུ་དུད་ *p̔u-dúd*, **honour, respect, esteem**; *p̔u-dúd-du byéd-pa, Glr.*, *p̔úd-du k̔úr-ba, S.g.*, to show honour, respect.

ཕུ་བ་ *p̔ú-ba*, pf. of *ͺbúd-pa*, **to blow**, col. used for the latter.

ཕུ་བོ་, ཕོ་བོ་ *p̔ú-bo*, *p̔ó-bo*, (*Sch.* also *p̔un*), a man's **elder brother**: *p̔u-nú*, the elder and the younger, i. e. the two brothers; also the elder and the younger sons (for examples refer to *tsan-dán*); in the passage of *Dzl* ༢༠༦, 14, *nu* ought to be canceled, and *p̔u-nú-mo*, ༧༦, 6. 9. should be translated by sister-in-law. *p̔u-grás, Sch.*, the elder brothers, dub.

ཕུ་རོན་ *p'u-rón Pth.*, *p'ug-rón*, (**p'ur-gón** vulg.) **pigeon**; *p'u-rón-gyi k'yu Pth.*; *p'ug-skya Sch.* of a light blue colour, like pigeons.

ཕུ་ལ་, ཕོ་ལ་ *p'ú-la*, *p'ó-la Ld.* (from the Turkish), **pilaw**, a dish of boiled rice, with butter and dried apricots.

ཕུ་ཤུད་ *p'u-šúd* **hoopoe.**

ཕུ་སེ་ *p'ú-se*, **mouse, souslik** and similar rodent quadrupeds (cf. *bra*).

ཕུག་ *p'ug*, 1. = *p'ugs.* — 2. = *sbugs*, *p'úg-pa*: *lgáṅ-p'ug-gaṅ*, **the bladder**, in reference to its capaciousness, *S.g.*; *m̀je p'úg-tu nub*, the penis recedes into its cavity, *Wdn.*; **the eye of a needle,** *Lt.* — 3. pf. and imp. of *˳bug-pa.* — 4 = *p'ub Schr.* — 5. for *p'ug-ron*, q.v.

ཕུག་པ་ *p'úg-pa*, **cavern**; *brag-p'úg*, rock-cavern, grotto; *gad-p'úg*, cavern in a steep river-bank, or in conglomerate; *dbén-p'ug*, the solitary cavern of an anchorite, *Ma.*; *p'úg-pa-pa*, n. of an astronomer of the 15th. century, v. *pád-ma*; *p'ug-rtsis*, and likewise *p'ug-lúgs Wdṅ.*, his calculations.

ཕུག་རོན་ *p'ug-rón* v. *p'u-rón.*

ཕུག་ཤུབ་ཤེ་ལེ་ *p'ug-šub-še-le* (?) *W.*, **hoopoe;** perh. = *p'u-šúd*, which occasionally is also spelled *p'u-ẏšud*

ཕུག(ས)་ *p'ug*(s), (cognate to *p'u*; also *˳búg-pa* and *sbugs*), **end, termination;** *p'ug-mda-t'úg-pai lóṅ-ka*, the entrails, the beginning and end of which lie close together, *Mil.* (*mda*, v. under *p'u*): **innermost part, an innermost apartment,** = *sbúgs*; *p'úgs-kyi nor* v. *sgo* init.; perh. also *p'úg-gi spa-rím ltá-bu Glr.* 45, 4 may be referable to this meaning. *séms-kyi p'ugs-t'ag čod-pas bde*, happy (am I), because the final aim of my mind is decided and settled, *Mil.*, evidently = *p'u-t'ag čod-pa*, the former being perh. etymologically more correct. Similarly: *bu t'se ˳dii bló-p'ugs čós-la ẏtód-čig Mil.*, may the boy direct the aim of his mind for this life unto religion! — **Time to come, futurity,** (opp. to *˳p'ral*, the present moment); *p'úgs-su*, *p'ugs-na*, **hereafter, at last, ultimately** (*Sch.* **always?**); *p'ugs-či ˳dra čig ˳oṅ*, how will it end? what will be the final issue? *Glr.*

ཕུགས་སྟ་ *p'ugs-ta*, *p'ógs-ta*, *pogs-ta*, *W.* (*Pers.* پخته), **firm, strong, durable**; *p'ugs-ta btsems*, sew it well (so that it will hold)!

ཕུང་པ་ *p'úṅ-pa* v. *p'úṅ-pa.*

ཕུང་པོ་ *p'úṅ-po*, 1. **heap**; *p'úṅ-por spúṅ-ba*, *Lex.* also *bčér-ba*, to gather into a heap; *nás-p'uṅ*, *rtsá-p'uṅ*, *lúd-p'uṅ*, *sá-p'uṅ*, a heap of barley, hay, dung, earth; **mass,** *me-múr-gyi p'úṅ-po*, a glowing mass a mass of fire; *sprin-p'uṅ*, clouds, a gathering of clouds *Glr.*; *ẏnyér-mai p'úṅ-po* (the skin becomes) a heap of wrinkles, *Thgy.*; the body is called *mi-ẏtsáṅ-ba rnám-pa sna-t'sógs-kyi p'úṅ-po*, *dug ẏsúm-gyi p'úṅ-po*, *ǰig-pai p'úṅ-po*, *zin-pai p'úṅ-po*, *Thgy.*; **accumulation, mass,** *bsod-nams-kyi*, *čós-kyi*, e.g. *čós-kyi p'úṅ-po* ༨༤༠༠༠, the whole mass of the 84 000 religious lectures of Buddha (!) *Mil.* — 2. In metaphysics: स्कन्ध, **the so-called five aggregates** (*Cs.*) or **elements of being,** viz. *ẏzugs*, *t'sór-ba*, *˳du-šes*, *˳du-byéd*, *rnam-šés*, (v. *Köpp.* I. 602, and esp. *Burn.* I. 475 and 511), which in the physical process of conception unite, so as to form a human individual or **the body** of a man, (*p'úṅ-po lṅa-las grub-pai lus Wdṅ.*) which by some of the later and more popular writers is itself called *p'úṅ-po.* So this word, as being synonymous to *lus*, has found its way into the language of the people, and not in a low sense, in as much as one of our Christian converts used the expression: *ye-šui p'úṅ-po dur-k'úṅ-ne žens.* — 3. Symb. num. for 5.

ཕུང་བ་ *p'úṅ-ba* v. འཕུང་བ་ *˳p'úṅ-ba.*

ཕུད་ *p'ud*, sbst. I. (v. *˳p'ud-pa*, pf. *p'ud*), **a thing set apart,** used particularly of the first-fruits of the field, as a meat- or drink-offering, in various applications: *zas-č'áṅ-gi p'ud* meat- and drink-offering *Glr.*; *t'óg-p'ud*, *ló-p'ud*, an offering of the first-fruits of harvest; *srús-p'ud* id., consisting of ears of corn, wound round a pillar of the house; *báṅ-ṗud*, first-fruit offering of the barn; *rdó-ṗud*, *sá-ṗud*, an offering of stones or earth, when a house is built, these materials then being used for manufacturing images of gods, *Glr.*; **initiatory present**, e.g. the first produce of a work, that has been committed to one *Glr.* (so, according to circumstances, it may be as much as **a specimen**); in a general sense, **a thing done for the first time**; *bág-mai ṗud*, prob the first cohabitation. — II. for *ṗu-dúṅ* and *ṗu-dúd*, q.v.

ཕུད་པ་ *ṗúd-pa*, I. pf. of *°búd-pa.*

II. *Cs.* sbst. 1. **spindle covered with yarn.** — 2. **hair-knot, tuft of hair**; *ṗúd-ċan*, being provided with such a one.

ཕུན་(སུམ་)ཚོགས་(པ་) *ṗun(-sum)-ṫsógs(-pa)* 1. adj. **perfect, complete**, possessing every requisite quality, e.g. *dgón-pa*, a hermit's dwelling; **excellent, exquisite, distinguished**, e.g. *ro*, taste, *bsnyén-bkur*, distinctions, marks of honour *Mil.*, *nor daṅ loṅs-spyod Domaṅ*; adv. *dgé-ba bċu ṗun-sum-ṫsógs-par spyód-pa*, *Dzl.*, to practise the ten virtues to perfection. — 2. sbst. **perfection, excellence, superior good**, frq.; *ṗa-ról-poi ṗun-sum-ṫsógs-pa-la ċágs-pa* to covet the excellent things which another possesses, *Thgy.* — 3. *ṗun-ṫsógs*, frequent **name** for **males** and **females.**

ཕུབ་ *ṗub* 1. **shield, buckler**, *Glr.*, of a convex shape, with the rim bent round; *ko-ṗúb*, a leather buckler; *ṗub-śúbs*, the cover of a buckler, *Cs.*; *ṗúb-kyi mé-loṅ*, the centre of the shield, *Cs.* — 2. v. the following.

ཕུབ་པ་ *ṗúb-pa*, pf. of *°búb-pa.*

ཕུབ་མ་ *ṗúb-ma*, **short straw**; *ṗúb-ma żig*, a small stalk, a bit of chaff; **ṗúb-ma ṫáb-ċe* or *ṫab táṅ-ċe**, to fan, to winnow; *ṗub-ldir Cs.*, chaff; *gró-ṗub*, wheat-straw.

ཕུམ་ཕུམ་ *ṗum-ṗúm*, **posterior, anus** *Pth.*

ཕུར་ *ṗur* 1. v. *ṗu* — 2. v. *°ṗúr-ba.* — 3. v. *ṗúr-pa.*

ཕུར་པ་ *ṗúr-pa*, **peg, pin, nail**; *rtsig-pur Schr.*, **ṗur-ċa* or *śa** (?) *Ld.*, a peg on a wall, to hang up things; *lċágs-ṗur*, **iron nail**; *śiṅ-ṗur*, **wooden peg**; *ṗur-rnyi* v. *rnyi*, *ṗur-bżi brkyáṅ-ba* to fasten the hands and feet of a culprit to four pegs driven into the ground, when he is to undergo the punishment of the *rkyaṅ-śiṅ*, v. *rkyoṅ-ba.* 2. **iron instrument** in the form of a short dagger, used for expelling evil spirits, and fancied to possess great power, *Schl.* 257; *sá-ṗur °débs-pa*, to stick such a dagger into the ground, whereby the subterranean demons are kept off; fig. *mig ṗúr-ṫsugs-su ltá-ba Glr.*, to look at one with a piercing glance of the eye; **lha-la sól-wa ṗúr-ṫsug-tu °déb-pa* C.*, to implore a god very earnestly. *ṗúr-bu* 1. = *ṗúr-pa*; the usual form of incantation is: *ṗúr-bus γdáb-bo, ṫó-bas brdúṅ-ṅo, ṗyág-rgyas mnán-no!* 2. (*γza*) *ṗúr-bu*, **the planet Jupiter**; its day: **Thursday.**

ཕུར་བ་ *ṗúr-ba*, *Sch.:* **to emboss**; *ṗúr-ma* or *°búr-ma*, **relief work, embossment.** — 2. **to scratch**, v. *°ṗúr-ba*; *mgo-ṗúr*, n. of a disease *Lt.*

ཕུར་བུ་ *ṗúr-bu*, v. under *ṗúr-pa.*

ཕུར་མ་ *ṗúr-ma*, v. *ṗúr-ba.* — 2. *ṗyé-mai ṗúr-ma*, **a decoration** resembling a flag.

ཕུར་མོ་ *ṗúr-mo*, a medicament *Wdn.*; *ṗur-tál? S.g.*

ཕུལ་ *ṗul* 1. **a handful**, also *ṗul-gáṅ*, e.g. of corn, *Dzl.*, beer *Lt.* (in which case = *skyor*). — 2. **end?** only in the phrase: *ṗúl-tu ṗyin-pa*, **to reach the highest degree, to be victorious**, to have the better of an argument; *yi-gei sgrá-la ṗúl-tu ṗyin*, he has finished his studies in grammar, *Glr.*; *mḱás-pai ṗúl-tu ṗyin-par gyúr-to*, he became a great scholar, *Pth.*; also *ṗul-(tu) byúṅ(-ba)*, **accomplished, perfect, eminent** *S.g.*; p. n. = *á-ti-śa.* — 3. *ṗúl-ċan*, **thick** = **róm-po* Ld.*

ཕུལ་བ་ *ṗúl-ba* v. *°ṗúl-ba* and *°búl-ba.*

ཕེ་ *ṗe* 1. *W.* for *ṗye*; *ṗé-ku-lig*, **key.** — 2. num. figure: 104.

ཕེ་རང་, ཕ་རང་ *ṗe-ráṅ*, *ṗa-ráṅ*, **Feringhi, Europeans**, *C.*

ཕེག་རྡོབ་ *ṗeg-rdób* v. under *ṗeb-pa.*

ཕེད་, ཕེན་ ṗed, ṗen *W.* for ṗyed, ṗyen; ṗed-ṗed v. ṗyad-ṗyad.

ཕེབ་པ་ ṗéb-pa, 1. pf. ṗebs, resp. **to go** *C.*; **to come** *C.* and *W.*; also *čág* (or *ṗyág*)-*ṗeb-pa*; scarcely in ancient lit., but *Glr.*, *Pth.*, *Mil.*; **nyi-rán-la ṗéb-lon yód-na** W., if you have time to come; **ₒo-nú ghá-le ṗeb* C.*, well, good bye! **dha sá-hib ṗeb**, id. in speaking to a European; *čag ṗeb žu nan* v. *snán-ba* I. extr.; *ṗéb-par smrá-ba Schr.*, to salute; *Sch.* also: to speak politely (??); *ṗéb-par ṗág-pa*, *Sch.*, to rise gracefully, to walk decently (?); *ṗéb-sgo ltar Sch.*: 'according to the given order', but cf. *ₒgro-sgo ltar* under *sgo* 3; *ṗéb-rdog-pa* 'to tramp arrival', to go to welcome a high Lama or other honoured person on his arrival with dance and music *C.*, *Lexx.*; *Cs.* however mentions *ṗeg-rdób* as a musical instrument, 'a small brazen plate for music', and in *Stg.* the same word occurs along with *sil-bsnyán*. — 2. for *ₒbab*; so it seems to be used, *Lt.*: *ťúr-du mi ṗebs*; *ṗó-bar mi ṗebs*, it won't go down his throat.

ཕེར་བ་ ṗér-ba **to be able** *Mil. nt.*, cf. also *dod*; *Cs.*: 'to become, to be fit' etc.

ཕོ་ ṗo I. num. figure: 134.

II. **man**, opp. to woman, **male**, *ṗo lo lná-bču-pa*, men of the age of fifty (opp. to *bú-mo lo-gnyis-ma*) *Ma.*; *ṗo mčór-po*, a handsome man (opp. to *bud-méd mčór-mo*) *Pth.*; as a pleonastic apposition to the pers. pron., like *mi*, *Mil.*; common in *C.*: **ṗo-ná**, I (masc.) = *ḱó-bo*; esp. in reference to animals: **male, he** (ass), **cock** (bird), *Dzl.* and elsewh.; as apposition to the names of domestic animals when castrated: *ṗo-rtá*, **gelding**; *rá-ṗo*, **a castrated he-goat.** — *ṗo-skyés*, **man, male person**, *Pth.* — *ṗo-gós*, man's dress, man's coat; *ṗo-čás*, *Mil.* id. (?) — *ṗo-čén Wts.*, *Sch.*, gelding. — *ṗo-tó Bal.*, stallion. — *ṗo-rtágs* 1. *Physiol.* = *ṗo-mtsán*. 2. *Gram.*: sign for the masculine gender, *Cs.* — *ṗo-nád*, 1. *W.* andromany, inordinate desire after men. 2. v. *ṗó-ba*. — *ṗo-mó*, man and woman, men and women, male and female; *ṗo-mó med*, no difference of sex exists. **ṗo-tsé* Bal.*, male sex. — *ṗo-mtsan*, membrum virile, man's yard, esp. the penis; the rather vague expression *ṗo-mtsán* (or *ṗo-rtágs*) *bčád-pa* is asserted to apply not to castration (*Schr.*), but only to circumcision (which, however, is not generally known in Tibet, Mussulmans being found only in some of the larger cities of the country). — *ṗo-yan Sch.* and *ṗo-ran Cs.*, *ṗo-hran C.*, an unmarried man. — **ṗo-ri* W.*, **ṗo-ré* C.* a male kid. — *ṗo-lhá*, 1. tutelary deity of a man's right side (ni f.) *Glr.* 2. *Cs.*: **Sir**, as polite address. — (Observation: The circumstance of the consonants of the alphabet and the prefix-letters being divided by Tibetan grammarians into masculine, feminine and neuter, is of no practical moment: careful investigations on that head have been made by Schiefner and Lepsius).

III. v. *ṗó-so*.

ཕོ་གྱོག་ ṗo-gyóg *Sch.* (perh. *ṗo-gyó* v. *gyo-mo*), **hollow tile.**

ཕོ་ཉ་ ṗó-nya, less frq. *ṗó-nya-ba* (*Ssk.* दूत). 1. **messenger**, e.g. sent for a physician; *ṗó-nya ytón-ba*, *ṗó-nya-mnág-pa*, to send, dispatch a messenger; *brtsi-ba*, *Cs.* to receive one (?) — 2. **ambassador, envoy.** — 3. Passages like *yšin-rjei ṗó-nya* messenger of death, angel of death, and *bdé-ba-čan-gyi ṗó-nya*, honourable epithet of a king, that is looked upon as a demi-god (similarly to ἄγγελος τοῦ παραδείσου) sufficiently justify the application of the word to the scriptural notion of **angel**, which may be rendered still more intelligible by adding *nám-mḱai*, *Chr. P.* (P. Georgi retains the Italian *angelo*, spelling it *án-ₒbye-lo*). Buddhist mythology has no available type for it, and *lha* (*Cs.*) could only be made use of, if already whole generations of the Tibetan nation had become Christians.

ཕོ་ནོ་ ṗo-nó *Bal.* for *pu-nú*.

ཕོ་བ་ ṗó-ba (resp. *sku-ťog Cs.*) 1. **stomach** — 2. the second cavity of the stomach or **reticulum** of ruminating animals (cf. *gród-pa*). *ṗo-ba ljid-pa*, *Cs.* to overcharge the stomach, to clog; *šól-ba Cs.* to purge, to cleanse; *po-bai ka Cs.*, the upper orifice of the stomach, joining the oesophagus; *po-nan*, a weak st., *bzan*, a good, sound st. *Cs.* — *po-tér*, swag-belly *Sch.*; *po-nád*, disorder of the st. — 2. v. *po*, above.

II. pf. of *₀bó-ba* for *pos Glr.*

ཕོ་བ་རི་ *pó-ba-ri*, also *-ris* or *po-ris Lt.*, **black pepper**; the col. form: *po-ba-ríl-bu* **'stomachic pills'** prob. is merely a popular etymology (similar to the English 'sparrow grass', corrupted from asparagus).

ཕོ་བྲང་ *po-brán* resp. for *kán-pa*, **house, dwelling**; often also implying **hall, castle, palace,** *B.* and col.; *slei po-bran*, the castle (palace) of Lé.

ཕོ་ཚོས་ *po-tsós Schr.* **red paint**; *dún-la po-tsós bskús-pa*, red paint put on a shell *Pth.*; *po-tsos-tsal Pth.*

ཕོ་རིས་ *po-ris* v. *po-ba-ri.*

ཕོ་རོག་ *po-róg*, **raven**, perh. also **crow**; cf. *kwá-ta*; *po-rog-mig*, **medicinal herb,** *Wdn.*

ཕོ་ལ་, ཕུ་ལ་ *pó-la*, *pú-la W.*, v. *pó-la.*

ཕོ་ལད་ *po-lád W.* **steel,** *Pers.* پولاد, فولاد.

ཕོ་ལོ་ལིང་ *po-lo-lin W.* **peppermint.**

ཕོ་ལོང་མདུད་ *po-lon-mdúd Mil.* a kind of knot, complicated, and of magic virtue.

ཕོ་ལོང་ཧེལ་ཀྱི་ *po-lon-hél-kyi* etc. v. *pa-wán.*

ཕོ་སོ་ *pó-so, W.* **haughtiness, pride;** **po-so čo-če**, to demean one's self haughtily, *W.*; **pó-so-čan**, proud, haughty, puffed up; *ká-po Mil.* bragging about things, which in reality one is not able to do; *po-tsod*, prob. the same as *po-so, Mil.*: *po-tsód mnón-šes ma ₀čad čig*, do not boast of prophetic sight.

ཕོག་ *pog*, 1. *Wts.* **beam, rafter;** *Sch.*: 'the principal beam of the roof'. — 2. v. *₀póg-pa* and *₀bóg-pa.*

ཕོགས་ *pogs*, **wages, pay, salary;** *lo-, zla-, nyin-pogs* annual, monthly salary, daily wages; *dnúl-pogs, smár-pogs, Cs.*, payment in money; *zón-pogs Cs.* payment in goods. 2. **providing for another person in natural produce**, even without any service being done in return, e.g. the maintenance of Lamas; *pogs-dód*, maintenance by an allowance of money (in exceptional cases).

ཕོང་ *pon*, v. *₀pán-ba*; *pón-ba Glr.* for *pan-ba.*

ཕོངས་པ་ *póns-pa* (cf. *₀póns-pa*) 1. **poor, needy;** *séms-čan nyam-tág-póns-dgu*, the poor and miserable creatures, *Glr.*; *sdúg-pons-pa*, id. *Stg.*, *C.* — 2. **poverty.**

ཕོད་ *pod, skár-ma pod, Cs., Sch.*, **comet.**

ཕོད་ཁ་ *pód-ka*, **masquerade garment** with long sleeves.

ཕོད་པ་ *pód-pa*, 1. **to be able,** esp. in a moral sense, **to prevail on one's self,** *₀bral-mi pód-pa ltar yód-na yan*, although he was scarcely able to part with . . . *Glr.*; *₀di ni mi pód-do*, that I cannot do (moral impossibility) *Dzl.*; *lta mi pod*, I cannot bear to see that, *Dzl.*; to be able to resist: *zas žim gos bzan su-yis pod* who can resist good food and fine clothes? hence *pod-pa-čan, Cs.*, **bold, daring;** **pod-čún-se**, *W.* **timid, cowardly.** — 2. **to come up to, to be nearly equal in worth,** with *tsam(-la)*: *deï bsód-nams tsam-la pód* it is nearly of equal merit as . . . *Dzl.*

ཕོན་(ཕོ?) *pón(-po) Glr.* and elsewh., *póbpon Cs.*, *pón-po(n)*, *pón-to*, *pod-pód, W.*, 1. **bundle, truss,** of hay, straw, reeds; **sheaf.** *C.* — 2. **bunch, wisp, cluster, umbel,** *W.*; **tuft, tassel;** *dár-pon, skúd-pon, Cs.*

ཕོབ་ *pob* v. *₀bébs-pa.*

ཕོར་པ་ *pór-pa C., B.* (*W. *kó-re**, resp. **don-kyóg**), **bowl, dish, drinking-cup,** generally made of wood and carried in the bosom, to have it always ready for use; cups made of other materials are called *lčágs-por, dnúl-por, ysér-por*, and a glass tumbler *šél-por.* The word is also applied to vessels used for other purposes: *spyin-por*, glue-pot, *pógs-por*, perfuming-pan. — *pór-pyis*, cloth for wiping the cup; *por-kúg*, id.(?); *por-šúg(šubs?)*, the pocket or fold in the coat for receiving the cup, *C.*

ཕོལ་ *p̓ol*, *W.* 1. **blister** caused by burning, *p̓ol-mig*, **a bad sore, ulcer, abscess,** *C.*, *W.* — 2. *Thgy.*, **a kind of fungus** (mould).

ཕོས་ *p̓os*, 1. v. *ˏbó-ba.* — 2. v. *ša.*

ཕྱ་, ཕྱྭ་ *p̓ya*, **lot**, *p̓ya débs-pa* to cast lots *Cs.*; **lot, fortune** *Cs.*, *p̓ya brtág-pa* to judge of lots or fortune *Cs.*; **prognostic** *Sch.*, *p̓ya-bzáṅ*, *-ṅán* good, bad fortune or prognostics *Cs.*; *nór-p̓ya*, *k̓yim-p̓ya* prognostics relative to property, family etc., in drawing lots or playing at dice; *p̓ya (daṅ) γyaṅ* lot (good luck) and blessing, *p̓ya daṅ γyaṅ ˏgúg-pa* to call forth good luck and blessing, to secure it by enchantment *Glr.*, *rgya-nág-gi p̓ya-γyáṅ nyáms-pas* as China's fortune and welfare were prejudiced *Glr.*; *p̓yá-mk̓an* fortune-teller *Cs.*, but v. also the next article.

ཕྱ་མཁན་ *p̓yá-mk̓an*, 1. = *rdzá-mk̓an*, **potter.** — 2. v. the foregoing.

ཕྱ་ཆན་ *p̓ya-čan Lt.?*

ཕྱ་ལ་ལེ་བ་ *p̓ya-la-lé-ba, Sch.*, **coarse, rude, negligent, disorderly** (?).

ཕྱ་ར་ *p̓yá-ra*, **curtain before a door,** *Schr. Sch.*

ཕྱག་ *p̓yag*, 1. resp. for *lag*, **hand;** *bčom-ldan-ˏdás-kyis p̓yag sá-la brdebs*, Buddha struck with his hand on the earth, *Dzl.*; *p̓yag brgyáṅ-ba*, to stretch forth one's hand, *Sch.*; with *la* it denotes also the imposition of hands as a holy ceremony, *W.*: **čag gyaṅ sál-čé**. — 2. **bow, compliment, reverence:** *p̓yag dáṅ-po-la*, whilst making the first bow, *Glr.*; also **compliment** in letters: ... *la p̓yag graṅs-med bčans*, with a thousand compliments to ... (a Lama even of a higher order concluded his letter to a nobleman with 10000 compliments to him as the head of the family, and then to the rest according to rank and age in a descending line with 1000, 100 etc.); therefore *p̓yag byéd-pa* (eleg. *gyid-pa*; resp. *mdzád-pa*, when e.g. a king is addressed by a Lama, *Pth.*), in *Balti* **p̓yag byá-ča,** *W.* gen. **čag p̓ul-če* or *čo-če*, resp. *ǰal-čag čo-če**, to salute, to pay one's respects, with *la*, e.g. ministers waiting on the **king,** *Glr.*; **čág-ga yoṅ**, he comes to pay his **respects,** *W.*; *p̓yag daṅ skór-ba byéd-pa*, **to make** bows and circumitions, *S.g.*; with or without a preceding *p̓yi* (vulg. *ˏton*), **to take leave, to bid adieu,** *B.* and vulgo (cf. *p̓yi* below), **dé-ne čag p̓ul yin**, *W.*, so then I shall take my leave now. — *p̓yag ˏtsál-ba*, pf. *btsal*, imp. *tsol*, to make a very low reverence, the head almost touching the ground; more at large: *γžán-gyi žábs-la mgó-bos p̓yag ˏtsál-ba*, esp. in use before Lamas and kings; in the introductions of books, also, the authors generally address both deities and readers with the phrase: *p̓yag ˏtsál-lo.* — 3. **impurity, dirt**(?); v. some of the following compounds and also *ˏp̓yág-pa.* — 4. sometimes for *čag.*

Comp. *p̓yag-mk̓ár* resp. for *mk̓ar-ba* **staff.** — *p̓yag-ˏk̓ur W.* = *p̓yag-rtén.* — *p̓yag-goṅ* the back of the hand *Cs.* — *p̓yag-rgyá* (मुद्रा) 1. resp. for *rgya* (I.) **seal;** *p̓yag-rgyás ˏdébs-pa* to seal, to confirm by a seal, v. *rgya* I. This meaning is at present hardly any longer known, but only: 2. gesture, the manner in which the hand and fingers are held by Buddha, by stage-players, Lamas or saints etc, when performing religious ceremonies or sorceries; *p̓yag-rgyás mnán-pa* to overcome evil spirits by such gesticulations *Dom.*, *ˏgról-ba* to set them free, by dissolving the charm *Pth.* There is a great number of these gesticulations. *p̓yag-rgya-čén-po* is said to be a figurative designation of the Uma-doctrine. (The other meanings given by *Cs.* and *Sch.* are rather uncertain.) — *p̓yag-ṅár* wrist *Cs.*, yet v. *ṅar* I. — *p̓yag-ča Sch.* 'wrought by the hand; an implement', resp. for *lag-ča*, v. *ča* III. extr.; *p̓yag-čás* attributes, carried in the hand, in performing religious dances, cf. *p̓yag-mtsán.* — *p̓yag-čáb* water for washing the hands and the face. — *p̓yag-mčód Mil.* for *p̓yag daṅ mčod-pa byéd-pa.* — *p̓yag-snyigs Lex.* = *p̓yag-dár.* — *p̓yag-rtágs* 1. resp. for *lag-rtágs* sign of the hand, impression of a blackened finger in the place of a seal. 2. = *p̓yag-rtén* (?). — *p̓yag-*

rtén B. and col. **a present of welcome**, frq., **a present** in general, also **a fee** *Glr.*; *p̓yag-rtén rgya-čén* immense presents *Glr.* — *p̓yag-mtil* resp. **palm of the hand.** — *p̓yag-mtéb* resp. **thumb.** — *p̓yag-dár* **sweepings, dust, rubbish**; *p̓yag-dár byed-pa Dzl.* and elsewh., *p̓yág-pa Lex.*, *gyáb-če* *W.* to sweep, to clean; *p̓yag-dar-pa* a sweeper *Dzl.*; *p̓yag-dár-gyi p̓úṅ-po, p̓yag-dar-k̓ród* dust-heap; *p̓yag-dar-k̓ród-kyi čós-gos* or *ná-bza* vestment or cowl of a mendicant friar, which according to the rules of his order is to be patched up of rags gathered from heaps of rubbish *Burn.* I, 305. (The explanation given by *Sch.* seems to rest on mere hypothesis.) — *p̓yag-na-rdó-rje, p̓yag-rdór* v. *rdo-rje-ˏčaṅ.* — *p̓yag-dpé* resp. for *dpé-ča* v. *dpe* 3. — *p̓yag-dpúṅ* resp. for arm. — *p̓yág-p̓yi* **attendant, man-servant** = *žabs-p̓yi*; *p̓yág-p̓yi byéd-pa* to be a servant; *p̓yág-p̓yi-la* or *p̓yag-p̓yir ˏbréṅ-ba* to be a follower (of a Lama); collect. train of servants, retinue. — *p̓yag-p̓yis* resp. **towel.** — *p̓yag-bris* resp. 1. **hand-writing, manuscript.** 2. **drawing** *Glr.* 3. **letter** *W.*, *brtsé-bai p̓yag-bris* your kind letter, your friendly correspondence. — *p̓yag-ˏbúl* resp. **gift, present.** — *p̓yag-sbál Cs.* resp. = *p̓yag-goṅ*; *Sch.* *p̓yag-sbál-du bčúg-pa* to hold one's hand ready for taking or receiving, v. *sbal.* — *p̓yag-smán* 1. resp. for *sman C.* 2. = *p̓yag-rtén W.* — *p̓yag-ma* **broom, duster, mop** *C.*, *Lexx.* — *p̓yag-tsaṅ Sch.*: 'the all-filling One, the all-universalizing One' (?) — *p̓yag-mtsán* the attributes or emblems of Buddha and of different deities, carried in the hands (it is indeed nothing else than what, when carried in the hands of men, is called *lag-* or *p̓yag-čás Glr.* and elsewh.). — *p̓yag-mdzúb* resp. for **finger.** — *p̓yag-mdzód* **treasurer**, of kings or in large monasteries. — *p̓yag-rdzás* resp. for *nor-rdzás Mil.* — *p̓yag-žábs* resp. for *rkaṅ-lág Schr.* — *p̓yag-ra* (prob. for *p̓yag-gra*) **privy, water-closet.** — *p̓yag-rás* resp. for **towel** *Sch.* — *p̓yag-lán* the return of a salutation, **reciprocal greeting** *Mil.* — *p̓yag-lás W.* resp. for *las* = *p̓rin-las B.* — *p̓yag-lén* resp. for *lag-lén* **practice, exercise**, also **ceremony**(?) **religious rite**(?); . . . *la-p̓yag-lén ˏdebs-pa Pth?* . . . *la-p̓yag-lén-du ˏgro-ba Mil.*(?) — *p̓yag-šiṅ* an attribute of idols, resembling a rod (birch) or besom *Wdk.* — *p̓yág-sa* = *p̓yag-ra*; *p̓yag-sén* resp. for *sén-mo*; *p̓yag-sór* resp. for *sór-mo.* — *p̓yag-sról* **law, regulation; practice, use; tradition.**

ཕྱང་ངེ་བ་ *p̓yáṅ-ṅe-ba, Cs.*: = *jól-le-ba*, **hanging down** (belly, v. *p̓yal*); *Lexx.* give **बाम**, slender, slight-made; *Sch.*: **straight, stretched**(?); *p̓yaṅ-p̓rúl* or *-ˏp̓rul Lexx.* pendent ornaments.

ཕྱད་ཕྱད་ *p̓yad-p̓yád*, vulg. *p̓ed-p̓éd*, **awkward gambols**, clumsy attempts at dancing.

ཕྱད་པ་ *p̓yád-pa*, also *ˏp̓yád-pa*, **constant, firm, persevering**; *p̓yád-par*, **always, continually, perpetually**; *Lexx.* = *rgyún-du* (of rare occurrence); *p̓yad ma p̓yod Mil.?*

ཕྱམ་ *p̓yam* = *lčam* (*Sbh.* also *k̓yam*), *p̓yam-ṅas, -rten, -stegs*, **support** (of rafters); *Sch.*: the resting-point of a beam.

ཕྱམ་ཕྱམ་པ་ *p̓yam-p̓yám-pa, Thgr.* **glittering**; cf. *lčám-me-ba.*

ཕྱམ་མེ་བ་ *p̓yám-me-ba, Glr.* **slow, not hasty, not greedy, indifferent to.**

ཕྱར་ཁ་ *p̓yár-k̓a Sch.* **blame, affront, insult** (v. *ˏp̓yá-ba?*) *p̓yar-γyáṅ Sch.* id.; *Lexx. p̓yar-γyéṅ?*

ཕྱལ་ *p̓yal*, resp. **belly, stomach**, *Cs.*; *p̓yal-p̓yaṅ-ṅe, Lexx.* = *gród-pa ˏjól-le-ba*, **paunch, swag-belly**; *p̓yál-mo* id.?

ཕྱི་ *p̓yi* (*W.* *p̓i*) I. **behind** adv.: *p̓yi-bkan-du nyál-ba Sch.*, to lie on one's back; *p̓yi-gros-su gyé-ba, Glr.*; *či-ḍo gyáb-pa* *C.*, to retreat, to recede, with the back in advance; *p̓yi lús-pa*, to lag behind; *p̓yi-rtiṅ Sch.*, **heel**; *p̓yi-sdér, Sch.* **the spur of birds**; *p̓yi-na, Cs.*; **behind**; *p̓yi-nas, Cs.*, **from behind**; *p̓i-nur-la* or *p̓i-log-la ḍúl-če*, to walk backward, *W.*; *p̓yi-γnón yoṅ*, pursuing he comes rapidly near, *Mil.*; *p̓yi mig ltá-ba*, to look round (back), *Glr.*, *p̓yi mig ma ltá-bar*, without looking round; *p̓yi mig čig γzigs-pas*, resp. just looking round (back), *Mil.*; *p̓i (mig) lóg-te ltá-če* *W.* id. — *p̓yi-p̓yir*, behind, following, e.g. *p̓yi*

˳gró-ba, to walk behind or after another person, *Pth.* — *p̓yi ˳bráṅ Lex.* (also *mčis-bráṅ*), spouse, wife. — *p̓yi-ma*, the posterior *Schr.*(?) — *p̓yi-bžin* adv. and postp., **after**; *˳gró-ba, ˳bráṅ-ba*, frq.; *ri-dags-kyi p̓yi-bžin rgyúg-pa*, to pursue game, deer; *p̓yir-bžin*, id.; *p̓yi-la*, later lit. and *C.*, id.; ... *kyi p̓yi-bžin p̓yin-pa, ˳óṅ-ba, ˳gró-ba*, to go after; v. also *p̓yir* and *p̓yis*.

II. **after**; adv.: *sṅa-p̓yi*, sooner and later; also adj.: the former, the latter; the earlier, the later; *˳di-p̓yi* sc. *tse*, the present and the future life; frq.; *dus p̓yi žig-na*, at a later period, some time afterwards *Dzl.*; *deï p̓yi nyin* on the following day *Dzl.*; *nyi-ma deï p̓yi de nyin k̓ó-na*, id., *Tar.* — *p̓yi-dgra* v. *dgra*. — *p̓yi-čad* = *p̓yin-čad* q.v. — *p̓yi-t̓og W.*, the later part of the afternoon. — *p̓yi-dro*, *p̓yi-ro* (also *Mil.*) *W.*, gen. **p̓i-t̓og, p̓i-ro** id., also evening. — *p̓yi-nas*, **in future**, in time to come, *Mil.* — *p̓yi-p̓réd Tar.*: *nyi-ma p̓yi-p̓red-kyi bar-du Schf.*, until sunset; *Schr.*: evening. — *p̓yi-p̓yág byéd-pa*, to greet for the last time, to bid farewell, to take leave. — *p̓yi-ma* adj.: **later, subsequent**, following, *sṅá-ma ma žu p̓yi-ma zá-ba*, not having digested the first (meal), to eat (consecutive) additional quantities *Lt.*; *p̓yi-ma p̓yi-ma*, each following one, every one consecutive in a series, *S.g.* and elsewh.; *nyál-bai p̓yi-ma*, the last going to bed, *Mil.*; *p̓yi-ma-rnams*, the later ones, the moderns, frq. — *p̓yi-mo* **adj. late**, *da (nyi-ma) p̓yi-mór soṅ dúg-pas*, it having grown late (in the day) *Mil.*; **'i go p̓i-mo p̓e duġ**, this door is not opened until later (in the day), *W.* **p̓i-mo čó(s)-k̓an-ni tá-gir**, the last baked, newest bread, *W.* — *p̓yi-rabs*, the later generation, posterity. Cf. *p̓yin*, *p̓yis*.

III. **outside**, *p̓yii žiṅ*, the field outside, as a third part of the property, exclusive of cattle and money (cf. *sgo* init.); *p̓yii só-nam*, husbandry, farming *Glr.*; *p̓yii-rgya-mtso*, the outer sea, the ocean, *Glr.*; *p̓yii mi Dzl.* (Ms.), people from abroad, other, strange people, not belonging to the family, *mgrón-nam p̓yi-mi-dag ˳óṅs-na*, if (when) guests or strangers come, *Dzl.*; *p̓yi-na*, **out of doors, abroad**; *p̓yi-nas*, from without, from abroad; *p̓yi-ru*, *p̓yir*, **out** (proceeding from the interior of a place to the exterior), less frq., v. *p̓yi-rol*; *p̓yi-la*, id., *B.* and *C.* frq. - *p̓yi-k̓yóg Sch.*: with knees bent outward. — *p̓yi-gliṅ* v. *rgya-p̓i-liṅ* under *rgya* comp.; *p̓yi-dgrá* v. *dgra*. — **p̓i-(s)ta-la* and *-ru**. *W.* for *p̓yi-ról-na* etc.; **p̓i-sta-la čá-če**, euphemist. for 'going to the water-closet'. — *p̓yi-náṅ*, **the outside** and **inside**, **p̓i naṅ lóg-če**, *W.*, *bsgyúr-ba*, *Schr.* to turn inside out, e.g. a bag; *lčágs-kyi sgróm-la-sógs-pa sgrom p̓yi naṅ rim-pa bdun tsam*, an iron box (coffin) and moreover a series of 7 boxes one within the other *Tar.* 28; *p̓yi naṅ gnyis-ka smin-pa*, ripe both as to the outside and inside, *Dzl.*; *p̓yi naṅ gtsaṅ*, pure as to thought and action. With respect to religion, this expression generally denotes the difference between Non-Buddhism — or in a more limited sense Brahmanism — and Buddhism; frequently *gsaṅ* is added as a third item, being explained by: *p̓yi lus naṅ ṅag gsáṅ-ba yid*, which explanation however is insufficient, e.g. in the passage: *čos p̓yi naṅ gsaṅ Pth.*, in which moreover merely a classification within the Buddhist religion seems to be spoken of. Political distinctions are made in *Glr.*: *p̓yi naṅ bar gsúm-gyi byá-ba byéd-pai blón-po*, yet without sufficiently elucidating the subject. The terms *p̓yi lta* and *naṅ lta*, *Glr.* fol. 89, as well as *p̓yi ltár-du* and *naṅ ltár-du*, *Pth.* p. 10 I am at a loss to explain. — *p̓yi-pa* 1. *B.* and col. **a Non-Buddhist**, more particularly **a Brahmanist**, also for *p̓yi-pai čos*, the doctrine of Brahma *p̓yi-pa-la dga Glr.* 2. *Chr. Prot.*: **heathen**, one that is neither a jew nor a Christian. — *p̓yi-yul* 1. *Sch.* **foreign country.** 2. *p̓yi snáṅ-bai yul*, **the external world**, opp. to: *náṅ-gi sems*, *Mil.* — *p̓yi-rol*, 1. **the outside**, *mál-gyi p̓yi-rol*, the outside of the bed, *Glr.*; *p̓yi-rol-na*, *-tu*, *-nas*, in *B.* gen. for *p̓yi-na*, *-ru*, *-nas*: adv. outside, out of doors, out, from without; postp. on the outside before (the door), (he was turned) out of (the house), (he comes) from without (the village), frq.; **p̓i-log* W.* id.; **čág-ri p̓i-log la**, outside before the (garden) wall. 2. mystic: *ɣdon bgegs p̓yi-rol-tu ₒdzin-pa*, to believe goblins and demons to be really **existing in the outer world** *Mil.* — *p̓yi-sa*, **excrements** *S.g.*; the supposed food of certain demons *Thgy.* — *p̓yi-lha?*

IV. *p̓yi-la*, **on account of**, v. *p̓yir*.

ཕྱི་ལྕག་ *p̓yi-lčág*, *Cs.*; **a blow** with the side of the hand.

ཕྱི་ཐན་ *p̓yi-tán*, **threat, menace**, *Mil. nt.*

ཕྱི་བདར་ (or བརྡར་) བྱེད་པ་ *p̓yi-bdár* (or *brdar*) *byéd-pa*, **to clean, to cleanse** *Dzl.* and elsewh.; *byád-kyi p̓yi-bdár bšól-nas kyaṅ* though you do not wash your face *Mil.*

ཕྱི་ཕུར་ *p̓yi-p̓úr*, a kind of **ornament**, similar to *p̓an*.

ཕྱི་བ་ *p̓yi-ba S.g.*, *ₒp̓yi-ba Lt.*, 1. the large **marmot** of the highlands of Asia, Arctomys Boibak. — 2. v. *ₒbyi-ba*.

ཕྱི་མོ་ *p̓yi-mo*, I. col. **ă-p̓yi, ŭ-pi**, **grandmother**, *Cs.* II. v. *p̓yi* II.

ཕྱིང་པ་ *Pur. *p̓yiṅ-pa*; Ld., Lh. *p̓iṅ-pa**, elsewh. *čiṅ-pa*, **felt**, *ₒdéd-pa*, to make felt, to mill, to full *Sch.*; *p̓yiṅ-gúr*, felt-tent, a Tartar hut; *p̓yiṅ-stán*, felt-carpet, felt-covering; *p̓yiṅ-déb Sch.*: a wrapper or cover made of felt.

ཕྱིད་ *p̓yid* = *p̓yi*, **after, following**; *p̓yid-nyin*, the day after to-morrow, *Cs.*

ཕྱིད་པ་ *p̓yid-pa* I. (v. *p̓yi* ni f.) **to retard, prolong, maintain**, with *ts̓e*: to maintain one's life, to earn a livelihood, *W.* e.g. **gár-ra čó-te** or **čós-si náṅ-ne ts̓e p̓id-če**, to maintain one's self as a smith, or by religion, (being a Lama). — II. **to freeze**, **káṅ-pa p̓id-soṅ**, the foot is frozen, suffering from chilblains; **mig p̓id soṅ**, the eyes are inflamed, snow-blind, *W.* (*C.* **čí**). — III. v. *ₒp̓yid*; *byid*.

ཕྱིན་ *p̓yin* for *p̓yi*, in certain phrases: 1. *p̓yin-čád, -čád*, **later, afterwards**, *p̓yin-čád sdom*, bound over for the time to come, e.g. not to do a thing again; *du p̓yin-čád*, from the present moment, from henceforth, frq.; *ₒdi p̓yin*, id.; *de p̓yin-čád*, rarely *de p̓yin-nas*, *Tar.* 57, 2 since, since that time, ever since. — 2. **outside**, *p̓yin rtsig-pa méd-de* as there was no wall outside *Glr.*; *p̓yin-dgrá* a foreign enemy *Glr.*; *p̓yin-las* outward business, foreign affairs *Dzl.*

ཕྱིན་ཅི་ལོག་ *p̓yin-či-lóg*, anything **wrong, incorrect, deceptive, fallacious; perversity**; *p̓yin-či-lóg-gis bslád-de* corrupt, depraved by perversity *Dzl.*; *p̓yin-či ma lóg-pao* it is infallible (of a spell), synon. to *bdén-pa*; *ltá-ba p̓yin-či ma lóg-pa* correct view, opinion *Pth.*; *p̓yin-či-lóg-tu stón-pa* to teach a false doctrine; *blo p̓yin-či ma lóg-par*, with a never erring mind *Mil.*

ཕྱིན་པ་ *p̓yin-pa* I. *B., C.* **čin-pa**, *Sp.* **p̓in-pa**, little used in *W.*: 1. **to come, to get to, advance, arrive**; *lam p̓yed tsám-du*, having got about midway, *Dzl.*; *der p̓yin-pa daṅ*, frq.; *ču p̓rág-pa tsám-du p̓yin-to*, the water reached up to his shoulders, *Dzl.*; **p̓in-na* Sp.*, is he arrived? *sbyin-pai p̓á-rol p̓yin*, that goes farther than alms-giving, surpasses it, *Glr.*: *dpag-tsád lṅar p̓yin-pa*, to be five miles in length, *Dzl.* — 2. **to go, to proceed**, *sṅón-la p̓yin-pa*, *Pth.*; *ma p̓yin-par sleb*, without going, without moving from the place, he arrives at . . . *Mil.*; *bud-méd deï rtsar ma p̓yin*, he did not go to the woman (euphemist.) *Glr.*; *stab-stob-du naṅ-du p̓yin-te*, he went in, ran in, in a great hurry. (Probably the word is cog. to *p̓yi*, and therefore = *ₒbyúṅ-ba, ₒtón-pa.*) — II. v. *ₒbyin-pa*.

ཕྱིར་ *p̓yir*; prop. the termin. of *p̓yi*: I. 1. adv. **back, towards the back, behind**; *p̓yir ₒóṅ-ba*, to come back, to return *Dzl.* and elsewh., frq.; also used in a special sense rel. to re-birth *lan-ɣčig p̓yir ₒóṅ-ba*, *p̓yir mi ₒóṅ-ba* v. *ₒbrás-bu* (*bži*); *p̓yir ₒgró-ba*, *p̓yir ₒdóṅ-ba* etc., id.; *p̓yir ₒdúg-pa*, to remain behind, at home, *Dzl.*; *p̓yir ₒǰóg-pa*, to leave behind, at home, to lay aside, to lay up, *Dzl.*; **again** (*rursus*), *p̓yir láṅ-ba*, to get up again, after having fallen; *p̓yir ldóg-pa, lóg-pa*, to come back again, to return; *p̓yir ldóg-pai lam*, the way back, the return, *Dzl.*; *p̓yir mi ldóg-pa*, the not taking place of relapses, the prevention of them, *Lt.*; *pyir zlóg-pa*, to bring back, to draw off, to divert from; *pyir sós-par ˳gyúr-ba*, to return to life; *pyir sáṅs-nas*, having come to himself again, having recovered, *Dzl.*; *pyir má-la smrás-pa*, he replied to his mother, *Dzl.*; *pyir-lóg skyón-pa*, to make one ride backward, with the face to the horse's tail. — 2. postp. e.g. **behind, after,** *ṅai pyir e' ˳gro Pth.*, will you follow me? come with me? instead of this more carelessly: *ṅa pyir Mil.*; *pyir-bžin* = *pyi-bžin* frq. —

II. **afterwards, hereafter,** at a later time *Thgy.*; *pyir ˳óṅ-ba*, to come too late *Dzl.*

III. **out,** *pyir-la* out (motion from an interior to an exterior place), *pyir ťón-pa*, *˳gró-ba*, *˳déṅ-ba*, *γšégs-pa* to go out, *skyúr-ba*, to cast out, *pyir bstán-nas*, turned inside out (the lining of a coat) *Glr.*; *pyir ˳búd-pa Sch.*: 'to put out, to remove; to come to an end, to be completely exhausted'; *sgo pyir mi γtóṅ-ba*, not to let out at the door, to keep locked in or shut up *Pth.* In *C.* also *pyi-la* is used in this sense. — *pyir-žiṅ* acc. to *Lexx.* = भूयंस more (exceeding in number or degree).

IV. postp. c.g., also *pyir-du*, more rarely *pyir-na* (*W.* **pi-la**) **on account of,** 1. (propter) = **by** or **through,** *či pyir kyod di-ltar gyur*, whereby or through what have you got into this plight? *Dzl.*; without *kyod*: where does that come from? *Dzl.*; **i nad či pi-la yoṅs**, by what has this disease been caused? *W.*; *γnód-pai pyir-du*, because I have done you harm *Mil.* 2. **for, for the sake of** (*causa*), for the good or benefit of, from love to *Dzl.*; **for the purpose of,** *brtág-pai pyir-du*, in order to try or to prove *Glr.* Whether *pyir* with the infinitive, esp. of one-rooted verbs, is to be resolved by **because** or **in order that,** can be determined only by the context.

ཕྱིས་ *pyis* I. adv. **behind,** *pyis ni sgra ˳byuṅ*, behind, i.e. behind your back, voices are heard; gen. with respect to time: **afterwards, later,** *pyis ˳byúṅ-ba*, to arise, to follow, to come later *Wdṅ.*; also in reference to things past, of a later date than others that had happened before them *Glr.*; *pyis-nas kyaṅ*, **also in future, in after times** *Mil.*; *pyis-nyin*, on the following day (= *saṅ*) *Dzl.*: at some future time, some (future) day, *Dzl.*; *da pyis* = *da pyin-čád Glr.*; *dus pyis* = *dus pyi žig-na*, subsequently, hereafter *Pth.*; *pyis skye-ba-méd-pa*, one that in future will not be re-born *Mil.*; on the other hand: *pyis skyes bu Sch.*, a son born after the death of his father; *sú-bas kyaṅ pyis* last of all *Dzl.*; *pyis-pa* v. *˳pyi-ba* (I.); it is also construed like a sbst.: ... *ťob-pai pyis šig-na*, at a time subsequent to his having obtained, = after he had obtained *Tar.* — II. sbst. in compounds: **clout, rag, duster, cloth,** *sná-pyis*, *lág-pyis*, *pyág-pyis*; *pyis-pa*, v. *˳pyi-ba* II.

ཕྱུག་པ་ *pyúg-pa* adj. **rich,** also fig.: *yón-tan du-mai dpál-gyis pyúg-par šog*, may I grow rich in the splendour of numerous accomplishments! *pyúg-po*, adj. **rich,** sbst. **a rich man,** *pyúg-po čén-po žig* a rich nobleman *Mil.*; *pyúg-mo* a rich lady; *pyug-ḱyád* riches, wealth, opulence *Dzl.*; *pyúg-par ˳gyúr-ba* to grow rich, *byéd-pa* to make rich; *pyug-dbúl* rich and poor; *pyug dbul med* no difference between rich and poor *Dzl.*

ཕྱུགས་ *pyugs*, **cattle,** *sgoi pyugs* v. *sgo*; *pyugs ˳ťsó-ba* to tend cattle *Glr.*; *pyúgs-kyi šiṅ-rta Cs.*, a bullock cart; *pyúgs-nad* disease of cattle, murrain; *nor-pyúgs*, chattels, all kinds of property *Dzl.*

ཕྱུར་བུ་ *pyúr-bu Sch.* **hay-rick, shock of sheaves, heap of sticks** (*Schr. ˳pyúr-ba*, to heap up).

ཕྱེ་ *pye W.* **pe**, resp. *γsáṅ-pye*, *žib*, 1. **flour, meal,** esp. 2. **flour of parched barley,** = *rtsám-pa*. — 3. for *pyé-ma*, **dust, powder** etc.; *pye ˳ťág-pa*, *ťság-pa*, to grind corn to flour; to sieve; *pyer ˳ťág-pa*, to reduce to flour. — 4. v. *˳byéd-pa*. — *rgyágs-pye* flour as provision for a journey *Glr.*; **ṅán-pe* W.* = *rtsám-pa*; also parched meal. *lčágs-pye* iron filings; *rdó-pye*, stone reduced to powder, small particles of stone; *spós-pye*, *tsándan-gyi pyé-ma*, sandlewood powder, fumigating powder; *bág-p̓yé* wheat flour; *brág-p̓ye* small fragments of stone, produced by stone-cutting *Glr.*; *s̀iṅ-p̓ye* saw-dust; *γsér-p̓ye* gold-dust; *p̓ye-k̓ug* flour-bag; *p̓ye-sgye* flour sack; *Cs.*: 'a double pouch for meal'; *p̓ye-snód*, flour-tub; *p̓ye-p̓ór Cs.* a box for meal; *p̓ye-p̓ád*, flour-bag; *p̓ye-baṅ*, flour-store; *p̓yé-ma*, dust, powder; saw-dust, filings etc.; *p̓yé-mar* termin. of *p̓yé-ma*; *p̓ye-már* (*Hindi* घीसत्तू) flour roasted with melted butter, sweetened with sugar, considered a dainty.

ཕྱེ་མ་ལེབ་ *p̓ye-ma-léb Lex.*, **p̓e-ma-leb-tsé** *W.*, **butterfly.**

ཕྱེད་ *p̓yed* I. **half;** *p̓yed-daṅ-γnyis* ('which with an additional ½ would be = 2') **one and a half** etc.; *brgya-p̓rág p̓yed-daṅ-γsúm*, two hundred and fifty; **yáṅ-č̓e' C.*, **yáṅ-p̓ed, p̓éd-di(saṅ) p̓ed, p̓éd-yaṅ-p̓ed** *W.* one fourth, a quarter; *yúṅ-p̓yed* one eighth (little used); *mi-p̓yéd* half a man, also used for woman *Pth.* (n.f.); *zla-p̓yéd* v. *zlá-ba*; *zla-ba-p̓yéd-pa*, lasting half a month, e.g. a disease. — *p̓yéd-ka, -pa, -ma, Cs., p̓yéd-po Cs.* and vulg. one half; *p̓yéd-ma* also: partner to one half; *ₒdii náṅ-na ṅai p̓yéd-ma žig kyaṅ yód-de*, as I have still a partner in this business; *p̓yed-krúṅ*, half a *skyil-krúṅ* (q. v.), drawing in one leg, and stretching out the other *Glr.*; *p̓yed-gliṅ*, peninsula; *p̓yed-brgyád* = *p̓yed-daṅ-brgyad* hence sbst.: half a rupee, = 7½ points on the gold-steel-yard *C.*

II. v. *ₒbyed-pa.*

ཕྱེན་ *p̓yen* (vulg. *p̓en*), **wind, flatulence** *Med.*; *γtóṅ-ba*, to let go a wind; *p̓yen s̀or soṅ*, a wind has escaped (me etc.); *p̓yen-dbúgs Cs.*, id.; *p̓yén-dri*, a low, soft wind.

ཕྱོ་ཕྱོ་ *p̓yo-p̓yó*, **č̓o-č̓ó zér-wa**, **to set on** or **at** (to set a dog at a person) *C.*

ཕྱོགས་ *p̓yogs* 1. **side, direction;** *p̓yogs gaṅ-nas* from whence? *p̓yogs der*, **there, thither,** in that direction; *yul dei p̓yógs-su* or *-la*) *soṅ*, proceed in the direction of yonder village; *ltág-pa* (for *-pai*) *p̓yógs-su Wdṅ.* towards the nape of the neck; *p̓yogs γčig-tu* or *-la* towards one side, in one direction; also for **together,** e.g. to sweep together, to heap together; vulgo also for **at the same time, at once;** *k̓yim-pai p̓yógs-su byin-pas*, bestowing on lay-men *Dzl.*; *č̓os p̓yógs-su γtóṅ-ba* to spend for pious purposes *Mil.*; in the same manner: *dge-bai p̓yógs-su*, to devote to benevolent designs *Mil.*; **for, in behalf of, for the benefit of:** *γtán-grogs p̓yógs-su s̀i-lčébs byéd-pa*, to die, to undergo death for the sake of husband or wife *Mil.*; in letters usually: *dé-p̓yogs-su*, there with you, *ₒdi-p̓yogs-su*, here with us. — 2. **quarter** of the heavens, **the cardinal points** of the horizon; *p̓yogs bži*, the four points of the compass; *p̓yogs bžir*, round about, in all directions; c. g. **round** (a person or place); *p̓yogs bži-nas*, from all sides; frequently also *p̓yogs bču*, the ten points of the compass are spoken of, which are the following: *s̀ar, s̀ar-lhó, lho, lho-núb, nub, nub-byáṅ, byaṅ, byaṅ-s̀ár, steṅ-* and *ₒóg-p̓yogs* (Zenith and Nadir); *p̓yogs-skyóṅ, p̓yogs-skyoṅ-rgyál-po, lha čén-po p̓yogs-skyoṅ-ba bču* similar to *ₒjig-rtén-skyoṅ* (v. *skyóṅ-ba*), yet ten in number; *rgya-gár-gyi s̀ár-p̓yogs-na*, to the east of India; *rgya-gár s̀ár-p̓yogs-pa-rnams*, the eastern Indians. — 3. *sa-p̓yogs*, **country, region, neighbourhood, part,** *dben-pai sa-p̓yógs*, lonely region, solitary part; *ₒjigs pai sa-p̓yógs*, an unsafe country; *yul-p̓yógs* id., *ṅai sa-p̓yógs-na* in my country *Mil., C.* — 4. **part, party,** also *p̓yogs-ris*; *γžán-la p̓yogs ₒgyúr-ba*, to take another man's part, to side with a certain person *Thgy.*; *p̓yogs-(ris) byéd-pa* c. genit. *W.*, **č̓og-(ri) čó-če**, *p̓yogs ₒdzin-pa Tar.*, *p̓yogs tsam ríg-pa Tar.* 119, 4 id.; *p̓yogs-méd* impartial, *sine ira et studio*, gen. in a Buddhist ascetic sense: indifferent to every thing; *p̓yógs-č̓a Mil., p̓yógs-lhuṅ Lex.*, prob. also *p̓yógs-žen Tar.* 184, 22, partial, interested; *p̓yogs-č̓ai rtóg-pa*, hesitation, scruples, arising from still feeling an interest in a thing *Mil.*; in a general sense it is used in: *p̓yogs-mtsúṅs-pa* **similar** *Wdṅ.*, *Tar.*; *p̓yogs-mt̓un-du Tar.* 190, 16 ought to be rendered: **appropriate, suitable, adequate;** *ráṅ-p̓yogs* one's own party, *γžán-p̓yogs* the other or opposite party; *γnyén-p̓yogs* friends, *dgrá-p̓yogs* enemies; *dkár-p̓yogs* **the good,**

the well-disposed, esp. the good spirits, *nág-pyogs, sdig-čan-gyi pyogs* **the bad, malicious,** esp. the evil spirits, devils. — 5. in popular language the word is used also with respect to time: **ka-sań-stón-čogs* Ld.*, **last autumn.**

ཕྱོགས་པ་ *pyógs-pa* I. vb. **to turn** vb.n., *čós-la* to turn to religion *Schr.*; *pyir pyógs-pa* to turn one's self back, to turn aside (*Schr. pyir pyógs-par byéd-pa*, to divert from, to dissuade from) *Tar.* 12, 14 28, 9. *ₒči-kar pyógs-pa* turned to dying = near dying? *kór-ba-la rgyáb-kyis pyógs-pa*, to turn one's back to the orb of transmigration; *mnón-du pyógs-pa*, **1. to be visible, to be evident, to be exposed to view** (?), *lho-nos-su mnón-du pyógs-pai brág-las ₒbyúń-ba* growing on a surface rock on the southside *Sambh.*; *don de mnón-du pyógs-par byá-bai pyir*, in order to bring this meaning to the light, to express it clearly *Gram.* (?). **2. to be openly** or **evidently attached to, to adhere to** (?) *rgyúd-la* to a Tantra or treatise *Sambh.*

II. adj., sbst., **attached to, following; a partizan, an adherent.**

ཕྱོད་པ་ *pyod-pa Cs.* **progress,** *pyod čé-ba*, great progress; *Lex.: sa-pyod-če* v. *čod.*

ཕྱོར་ *pyor Mil.*, prob. for *mčor.*

ཕྲ་ *pra*, *ₒpra*, **ornament** (?), **jewel** (?) *pra rgyág-pa, rgyáb-pa, ₒgód-pa, ₒdébs-pa, Sch.* also *pras sprá-ba*, to insert an ornament of jewels, to stud with jewels; *rmog-la pad-ma-rā-gai pra btáb-pa de*, this set of rubies on the helmet, this helmet studded with rubies *Glr.*; *rin-čén sna-tsógs-kyis pra bkód-pa Mil.*; *pra-tsóm* border, trimming, *Lex.*

ཕྲ་རྒྱས་ *pra-rgyás Was.* (241) = *bág-la nyál-ba*, **vanities,** i.e. passions, errors, erroneous notions.

ཕྲ་དོག་ *pra-dóg* v. *prag-dóg.*

ཕྲ་བ་ *prá-ba* 1. v. *ₒpra-ba.* — 2. *Lt.* a disease of children. — 3. adj., gen. *prá-mo* (*Cs.* also *bo*) **thin, fine, minute,** opp. to *sbóm-po* q.v., *sbrul prá-mo žig Tar.*; in a general sense, **little, small,** *séms-čan prá-mo-rnáms*; *ná-pra-mo*, little as to age, young, *Mil.*; **trifling, little, slight,** *rnám-rtog prá-mo* slight scruples, *Mil.*; *rdzun prá-mo*, a little lie, a fib, *Thgy.*; **ṭá-mo-ne tóń-wa, láb-pa**, to see, to inspect most accurately, to learn the minutest details, *C.*; **thin, high,** rel. to voice *W.*; *pra-žib Lex.*, fine and exact; *šin-tu prá-ba*, in reference to the doctrine of Buddha, implying prob. its subtilties. Cf. *pran.*

ཕྲ་མ་ *prá-ma*, **calumny, slander,** esp. through tell-tales and intermeddling persons *B.* and col.; *prá-ma byéd-pa Dzl.*, *smrá-ba Cs.*, *júg-pa B.* and *C.*, **čó-če* W.*, resp. (when referring to a person of higher rank) *gsól-ba, žú-ba*, to calumniate, slander, vilify, blacken; *prá-ma-mkan Cs.* calumniator, slanderer.

ཕྲ་མེན་ *pra-mén*, **sorcery, witchcraft** *Schr.*; so prob. *Pth.*: *mi-dgos-pai pra-mén-gyi nan-snágs*, an evil magic spell of pernicious necromancy; *pra-men-po* and *-pa* masc., *-mo* and *-ma* fem., necromancer, wizard, witch; *pra-mén rdzá-ki* (for *dzo-gi*, योगिन्) id.

ཕྲ་མོ་ *prá-mo*, v. *prá-ba*; ཕྲ་ཤགས་ *pra-šags*, v. *ₒprá-ba.*

ཕྲག་ *prag* provinc. also *dbrag, srag*, 1. **intermediate space, interstice, interval,** hence *prág-tu* = *bár-du Thgy.*; **a hollow, ravine, defile;** *smin-prág* v. *smin-ma.* — 2. after cardinal numbers it seems to correspond about to the Greek subst. termination ας: *bču-prág* a decade, *brgya-prág* a hundred (century), *stoń-prág* a thousand (chilind). *brgya-prág gčig, brgya-prag bču*; *stoń-prág bži-bču-žig*, a number of forty thousand *Dzl.*; *bdun-prág*, ἑβδομάς, week (recognized as a measure of time, but in common life not much in use).

ཕྲག་པ་ *prág-pa*, 1. sbst., resp. *sku-prág* **shoulder,** *prág-pa-la ₒgél-ba Glr.*, *tógs-pa Sambh.* to load on one's shoulder; *grógs-poi prág-pa-la ₒdzég-pa*, to mount the shoulder of one's companion *Dzl.*; **upper arm,** *prág-pa gnyis-kyi ša Dzl.*, *prag-gáń*

Lt. id. — 2. vb., also *ₒp̀rág-pa*, **to envy, to grudge,** *Cs.*; *p̀rag-dóg, p̀ra-dóg*, the envy, *p̀rag-dog skye* envy is stirring within me, I envy, frq.; *p̀rag-dóg-čan*, envious, grudging, jealous *Pth.*

ཕྲང་ *p̀raṅ*, v. *ₒp̀raṅ*.

ཕྲད་ *p̀rad, tsig-p̀rád, p̀rád-kyi yi-ge*, **particle,** e.g. *rnám-dbye-p̀rad* the signs of the cases, *kyi, la* etc.

ཕྲད་པ་ *p̀rád-pa* v. *ₒp̀rád-pa*; *p̀rád-po* for *ḱrád-po Wdṅ.*

ཕྲན, ཕྲན་བུ་ *p̀ran, p̀rán-bu*, (*Ts.* also *p̀rán-te*) = *p̀rá-mo*, **little, small, trifling,** yet more in particular phrases, and less used in books, than in common life, esp. in *C.*: **rin ṭém-bhu ṭé-dhe** (lit.: *sprad-de*) having paid, spent a trifle; **žú-ba ṭém-bhu žig** a small request; **ṭem-bhu čig** a little bit *C.*; as sbst.: 1. **part of the body** (whether in a general or a more particular sense, I have not been able to ascertain); in medical writings the *p̀ran-bui nad* form a class of their own; *yan-lág-gi p̀ran yčód-pa Glr.*, to maim, to mutilate parts of the body (not necessarily to castrate *Sch.*). — 2. **knives** and other small instruments used in surgery *Med.* — 3. *p̀ran-ráṅ* in the polite epistolary style the person of the writer, 'my own little self', 'your humble servant'; *p̀rán-la ráṅ-gi* = to me my ..., inst. of: *ṅá-la ṅa-ráṅ-gi*. — *p̀ran-tségs*, **trifles, minor matters;** *ₒdúl-ba p̀ran-tségs-kyi ɣži* the minutiae of religious discipline, Dulva.

ཕྲན་རྩག་ *p̀ran-rtság, p̀ran-ne-rtsag-tsi* stated to be = *p̀yin-či-lóg Ld.*

ཕྲན་ཚེགས་ *p̀ran-tségs* v. *p̀rán-bu* extr.

ཕྲལ་ *p̀ral* v. *p̀rál-ba*; ཕྲི་བ་ *p̀ri-ba* v. *ₒp̀ri-ba*; ཕྲིད་ *p̀rid* v. *sbrid-pa*.

ཕྲིན་ *p̀rin, ₒp̀rin*, **news, tidings, intelligence, message,** *p̀rin bzáṅ-po*, good tidings, favourable accounts; *p̀rin-bkur-mḱan*, messenger, vulgo; *p̀rin skúr-ba, spriṅ-ba* to send word, information, *ḱyér-ba*, to bring tidings, intelligence; *spród-pa, ₒp̀ród-pa* to deliver; *smrá-ba, rʼód-pa, byéd-pa* to report, to deliver messages orally; to superiors: *ɣsól-ba, žú-ba*; to inferiors: *sgó-ba, ɣsúṅ-ba; ḱó-boi p̀rin yaṅ dé-la byós šig* deliver a message to him also from me *Dzl.*; *p̀rin-ɣtam* message, report *Cs.*; *p̀rin-pa* messenger; newsmonger *Cs.*; *p̀rin-bzáṅ* gospel *Chr. Prot.*; *p̀rin-yig* letter, epistle; *p̀rin-lán* answer to a message. — *p̀rin-lás* (*W.* **čag-lás**) 1. resp. for *las* **labour, business; deed, work,** frq.; *ráb-tu-ɣnás-pai p̀rin-las mdzad* (the Buddhas) performed the work of consecrating *Glr.*; *p̀rin-lás rnam bži* the same as *ži-rgyas-dbaṅ-drág-gi p̀rin-lás Glr.*, v. explanation under *ži-ba*; *p̀rin-lás čól-ba, p̀rin-bčól byéd-pa* ccdpar. to commit a thing to another person's care or trust, e.g. before going on a journey; in reference to gods: to recommend to their protection or blessing *Glr.* and elsewh. — 2. po. for *p̀rin-lás-pa* **commissary** *Glr.*, where Avalokitesvara is called *p̀rin-lás* of all Buddhas. — 3. **efficiency, power** *Mil.*

ཕྲུ་གུ་ *p̀rú-gu* v. *p̀rug*.

ཕྲུ་བ་ *p̀rú-ba, ₒp̀rú-bu* = *ḱóg-ma* **earthen pot, pan, stew-pan.**

ཕྲུ་མ་ *p̀rú-ma, ₒp̀rú-ma* 1. **uterus, matrix of animals,** or acc. to *Cs.* merely the integuments of the eggs; acc. to some, also **the urinary bladder.** — 2. **encampment,** = *dmag-sgár Lex.*

ཕྲུག་ *p̀rug* 1. in compounds for *p̀rúg-gu, p̀rú-gu* **child, a young one** (of animals); *p̀rúg-gu-mo* a little girl *Cs.*; *p̀rúg-gu skyéd-pa* to beget children, *ɣsó-ba* to rear, to bring up (children); *p̀rúg-gu skye* a child is born; *šor* a miscarriage, abortion, takes place; *p̀rúg-gui dus* childhood; *dá-p̀rug* orphan; *nal-p̀rug* bastard; *gláṅ-p̀rug* the young one of an elephant; *séṅ-p̀rug* a lion's cub etc.; metaph. of disciples and subalterns: *tsoṅ-p̀rúg* the merchants of a caravan in their relationship to their leader *tsoṅ-dpón*. — 2. **fine cloth** or **woollen stuffs** *Wts.*, *snam-p̀rúg* id., *dbus-p̀rug* woollen goods from Ü *Mil.*

ཕྲུགས་ *p̀rugs* one day with the night, a period of 24 hours, — but this signification does not hold good in every case.

ཕྲུད་གཞོང་ *p̔rud-γžoṅ* v. *γžoṅ-pa.*

ཕྲུམ་ *p̔rum Lt.* and *S.g.*? *prum-rùs* **cartilage, gristle.**

ཕྲུམ་ཕྲུམ་ *p̔rum-p̔rùm Sik.* = *p̔um-p̔um.*

ཕྲེའུ་ *p̔reu Cs.* = *p̔rá-mo.*

ཕྲེང་བ་ *p̔réṅ-ba* v. *˳p̔réṅ-ba.*

ཕྲེད་ *p̔red*, *˳p̔red*, **cross, transverse; across, athwart, obliquely;** *p̔réd-du*, col. **ṭ̔ed-ṭ̔ed-la**, crossways, in a cross direction; *p̔réd-lam*, a path (horizontal or inclined) leading along the side of a mountain, (cf. on the other hand *˳p̔raṅ*); *p̔red-γtán* bolt or bar of a gate; **ṭ̔ed-la ḍàṅ-po**, horizontal *W.*

ཕྲོ་བོ་ *p̔rò-bo* something like: **a child's frock** or **chemise** *Ld.* (?)

ཕྲོག་ *p̔rog* etc. v. *˳p̔rog*; ཕྲོབ་, ཕྲོལ་ *p̔rob, p̔rol* v. *˳p̔rob*, *˳p̔rol.*

ཕྲོས་ *p̔ros* v. *˳p̔rò-ba.*

འཕག་པ་ *˳p̔ág-pa*, pf. *˳p̔ags*, 1. **to rise, to be raised,** e.g. a post or stake raised by the frost; **to soar up,** to fly up to heaven, a miraculous feat often performed by the saints of legends, *Dzl.* and elsewh.; of rays of light, *Dzl.* and elsewh.; fig.: to be higher, more elevated, *deï stéṅ-du* (or *dé-las*) *dpag-ṭsád brgyad-k̔ri* (or more accurately *k̔ris*) *˳p̔ágs-so Glr., Pth.*, (this region) lies by 80000 miles higher than that *Stg.*; **to grow larger, longer,** of the apparent lengthening of the teeth when aching *W.*; of horses: **to rear, to rise up** on the hind-legs; more particularly of the deifying of saints; thus the demi-god-like king Srontsansgampo in his farewell speech says: *k̔yed kun ˳p̔ágs-pai byin-rlabs yin* I am the divine instrument of your elevation (your elevation-blessing), he who will effect your ascent to heaven or deification; part. pf. *˳p̔ágs-pa* (*Ssk.* आर्य), **sublime, exalted, raised above,** *p̔ál-las ˳p̔ágs-par bzáṅ-ba* a more than ordinary beauty *Dzl.*; *γžan-pas ˳p̔ágs-par gyúr-to* he far excelled others *Dzl.*; *k̔yád-(par) ˳p̔ags-(pa)*, **distinguished, excellent, glorious,** *yúl-las k̔yad-˳p̔ags rgya-gar-yul* India, the most glorious country; *nór-sna k̔yád-par ˳p̔ágs-pa brgyai ˳búl-ba* an offering of a hundred of the most costly kinds of jewels *Pth.*; esp. in reference to holy persons, things, places etc.; title of saints, and teachers of religion, with the fem. *˳p̔ágs-ma*; *˳p̔ágs-pa* 'par excellence' is Avalokitesvara, in *W.* esp. the one, that has his throne at Triloknath in Chamba, v. *re-˳p̔ágs*; the word is also frq. used as an epithet, placed at the head of the title-pages of religious writings; lastly it is a name of common persons. — *˳p̔ágs-pai nor bdun* the seven treasures of the saints: *sbyin-pa, ṭsúl-k̔rims, dád-pa* and the like *Mil.* — *˳p̔ágs(-pai) yul* 1. elevated country, highland. 2. the holy land of the Buddhists, the tracts of the middle Ganges; *˳p̔ags-pai skad*, the Sanskrit language *Lex.* — *˳p̔ags-rgyal Tar.* and elsewh. = उज्जयिनी *Schf.*, town and district of Ujain. — 2. the word is stated to imply also **to play, to joke, to make sport** *C.*

འཕང་ *˳p̔aṅ* 1. v. *p̔aṅ* I. — 2. also *˳p̔aṅs, dpaṅs, spaṅs,* **height,** *˳p̔áṅ-du*, *˳p̔áṅs-su* in height; *k̔ri-˳p̔aṅ* v. *k̔ri*, *go-˳p̔aṅ* v. *go*; *γnam-˳p̔aṅ*, the height of the heavens *Lex., Mil.*; *dbu-˳p̔aṅ* fig. highness, sublimity, *dkon-mčóg-gi dbu-˳p̔áṅ smád-pa* to lower, to detract from the sublimity of God (v. *dkon-mčog*), to blaspheme God *Domaṅ*; *˳p̔aṅs-mt̔ó* high *Dzl.*; *˳p̔áṅs-mt̔o-ba*, *˳p̔aṅs-mt̔on-dmán* relative height *Dzl.*

འཕང་བ་ *˳p̔áṅ-ba* fut., *˳p̔aṅs-pa* pf. of. *˳p̔én-pa.*

འཕངས་པ་ *˳p̔áṅs-pa* 1. frq. for *p̔áṅs-pa* **to spare, to save** *Dzl.*; kindly and carefully to protect from harm, e.g. a drunken Lama *Thgy.*; hence prob. the version प्रेयस; *˳p̔aṅs-méd γtóṅ-sems-ldan* liberal, bounteous, without restriction *S.g.* — 2. *Glr.* also for *˳p̔óṅs-pa* provinc.

འཕན་ *˳p̔an* I. v. *p̔an* (1). — II. *˳p̔àṅ-yul Glr.*, *˳p̔án-po Huc* II, 242; name of the nearest alpine valley north of Lhasa, the inhabitants of which are said to speak an indistinct dialect.

འཕམ་པ་ *ₒṗám-pa*, pf. *ṗam*, opp. to *rgyál-ba* **to be beaten, conquered, to come off a loser, to get the worst of,** *γyúl(-las)* in battle *Dzl.*; *lha-ma-yin-las* by the Asuras *Dom.*; in law-suits, in traffic etc.; *ₒṗám-par ₒgyúr-ba B.*, **ṗam ḍó-wa* C.* id; also with *ṗam*, as if it were a sbst.: **ṗam kúr-wa* C.* to put up with, to bear a loss, damage, defeat; *ₒṗam bláṅ-ba Glr., Pth.* prob. id.; *ₒṗám-par byéd-pa* to beat, to defeat, to conquer, *rgyá-rnams ₒṗám-par byas* he conquered the Chinese *Glr.; rás-pas bón-po čós-kyis ṗám-byas-te* Raspa overcoming the Bonpo by the doctrine of Buddha (v. *čos* 3.) *Mil.; *ṗam čúg-če* or *kál-če*, W.* id.; *ṗam ṗog soṅ* I have met with a loss, I suffered damage, opp. to *gyal ťob soṅ; ṗam-rgyál ma bsrés-na* if one is not inclined now for a serious struggle, will not stand the chance of ... *Mil.*; *yid-ₒṗám-pa Mil.*, **sems ṗám-po* C.* dejection; *yid-ₒṗám-ma* a low-spirited, dejected woman *Mil.; ṗám-pa Glr., pám-po* the vanquished etc.; **ṗam-pe ṅo-lén čó-če* W.* to give in, to ask pardon; *mi-ₒṗám* 1. **invincible.** 2. **a man's name.** 3. *mi-ₒṗam mgón-po Zam.*, also *mi-ₒṗám čós-kyi rje* is stated to be = *ₒjam-dbyáṅs.*

འཕར་ *ₒṗar Cs.* in compounds: **board,** *sgo-ₒṗar* board or leaf of a door.

འཕར་བ་ *ₒṗár-ba* I. sbst. v. *ṗár-ba.*

II. vb. (vb. n. to *spór-ba*) 1. **to rebound,** of stones, **bar-náṅ-la* W.* **to splash up,** of water, **to fly up,** of sparks; **to leap, to bound, to throb,** of the veins, *rtsa ₒṗar,* the pulse is beating; **ṗar tá-če* W.*, to feel one's pulse; **nyiṅ-ka ṗar dug** his heart is throbbing, palpitating; **ṗár-ra rag** I have heart-throbbing (v. *rag*); *ₒṗár-ₒṗro čad* v. *ₒṗró-ba* 2; *sá-la ₒṗár-ba,* **to fidget, to be restless, to jump,** from fear *Pth.*; *pár-gyis ₒṗár-ba Lex.* prob. the same as *ₒṗár-ba.* — 2. *Cs.* **to be raised, elevated, promoted, advanced.**

འཕར་མ་ *ₒṗár-ma, Sch.* **'double, manifold'**; *brgya-ₒṗar-ma, Sch.* 'more than hundred'.

འཕལ་ག་ *ₒṗál-ga Cs.*, **incision, indentation, notch.**

འཕིག་པ་ *ₒṗig-pa, ṗig-pa,* pf. *ₒṗigs Sch.* = *ₒbig(s)-pa.*

འཕིར་བ་ *ₒṗír-ba Ts.* = *ₒṗúr-ba,* **to fly.**

འཕུག་པ་ *ₒṗúg-pa Sch.* = *ₒbúg(s)-pa* (?).

འཕུང་བ་ *ₒṗúṅ-ba*, pf. *ṗuṅ*, **to sink, to begin to decay, to be in declining circumstances, to get into misery,** either by one's own fault, or that of others (opp. to *ťséṅ-ba*) *Glr.* and elsewh.; *bód-yul ₒṗúṅ-bai las* a deed to the detriment of Tibet *Glr.;* in a similar manner *bód-yul ₒṗúṅ-bai ṗuṅ-góṅ*, mischievous conjurers in order to inflict an injury on Tibet *Ld.-Glr. Schl.* 21, b; *mgár-gyis rgyá-yul ṗúṅ-bar byás-pa-rnams dráṅ-nas*, remembering the calamities brought on China by Mgar *Glr.*; *ₒṗuṅ-bar ₒgyúr-ba B.*, **ṗúṅ-du ḍó-wa* C.*, **ṗuṅ čá-če* W.*, to be ruined, to perish, *ₒṗuṅ-bar byed-pa B.*, *ₒṗúṅ-la sbyór-ba Mil.*, prob. also *γtóṅ-ba, ₒjúg-pa* to ruin, to undo *Pth.*; *raṅ-ₒṗúṅ* having been reduced by one's own fault; *ₒṗuṅ-dkrol* or *krol* **the decay of fortune, ruin, destruction** *Mil.* and elsewh.; *ₒṗuṅ-γži* cause, occasion of decay *Mil.*

འཕུད་པ་ *ₒṗúd-pa* **to lay aside, to put away, to separate,** = *ₒbúd-pa Cs.* (?), *súg-pa ₒṗúd-pa*, to clear, to part the flour from the bran, to sieve *Sch.* (?)

འཕུབ་པ་ *ₒṗúb-pa* = *ₒbúb-pa* **to cover with a roof** *Sch.* (?)

འཕུར་བ་ *ₒṗúr-ba*, pf. *ṗur*, 1. **to fly;** *púr-gyis ₒṗúr-ba Lex.*, prob. id.; cf. *ṗár-ba.* — 2. **to wrap up, envelop, muffle up;** *Dzl.* ༢༡༦, 10: *rin-po-če gós-kyi mťá-mar* the gem into the skirt of the coat, and likewise *Dzl.* ༡༠༧, 13 read: *gós-mťar ṗúr-te*, inst. of *byúṅ-ste; mgo gós-kyis Mil.* (col. not used). — 3. = *mnyéd-pa* **to rub with the hand,** e.g. linen in washing, leather in tanning *Glr.*; to scratch (softly) *C.*

འཕུལ་(ཡིག) *ₒṗul(-yig)* **prefix,** *de sogs da-yig gás-ₒṗul-čan*, these and others have *d* with the prefix *g*: *bás-ₒṗul-kao* words beginning with *k* with the prefix *b*; *bá-yis ₒṗúl-bai sla*, viz. *bsla* ...; *das-ₒṗul-méd* these receive no *d* as prefix; *sa-*

ra-ld-rnams ₒṗúl-tsul ni the manner in which prefixes are joined with words beginning with *s*, *r* or *l*; *rkyaṅ-ₒṗul* words beginning with a simple consonant (to which also *ya-*, *ra-*, and *la-tags* are reckoned), preceded by a prefix; *brtsegs-ₒṗul*, words beginning with two consonants and a prefix *e.g. bska Gram.*

འཕུལ་བ་ *ₒṗúl-ba* I. v. the preceding article. — II. vb. 1. = *ₒbúl-ba*, **to give.** — 2. **to push, to jostle;** **ṗul-túg gyáb-če**, to push with the fist, with the trunk, (of elephants) etc., *W.*; *grú-moi ₒṗul-rdeg čig byéd-pa*, to jostle with the elbow *Mil.*; vulgo **ṗul-dag* or *ṫag** *W.*, **ₒṗul-tsúg** *C.*

འཕེག་ *ₒṗeg* v. *ṗeg.*

འཕེན་པ་ *ₒṗén-pa* pf. *ₒṗaṅs*, fut. (and frq. for the pres.) *ₒṗaṅ*, imp. *ṗoṅ*, *ṗaṅs*, 1. **to throw, to cast, to fling;** *nám-mḱa-la* into the air *Dzl.*; *ḱór-bar*, to throw into the orb of transmigration *Mil.*; *dmyál-bar*, to cast into hell *Thgy.*; **ḱa pán-če**, to shovel snow (out of the road, from the roof); **ṗáṅ-te bór-ra tsig-te bor** am I to throw down the wood, or pile it up? *W.*; **pu ṗáṅ-če** to cast the hair *W.*; hence *ₒṗaṅ*, spindle, and *ₒṗén-śiṅ*, acc. to *Sch.*, a weaver's shuttle (it being flung). — 2. **to fire off, to discharge, to let fly**, *mda*, an arrow, *gžan-la*, at another *Dzl.*; *ₒṗen-duṅ* dart, javelin *Stg.*; **to shoot**, *ₒṗen-mi śés-pa*, *W.* **ṗaṅ-mi-śes-ḱan**, one that does not know how to shoot. — 3. *Sch. ₒṗen-pa btaṅ-ba* **'to intend, to have a mind, to think upon, to consider'**, (yet in the only passage, in which I met with the word, in *Thgr.*, the above meaning does not seem applicable).

འཕེལ་བ་ *ₒṗél-ba* I. vb. pf. *ṗel* (སྤེལ) vb. n. to *spél-ba*, opp. to *ₒgrib-pa*, 1. **to increase, augment, multiply, enlarge**, frq.; **sum lan nyi-la tsam ṗel** how many are two times three? *W.*; *ₒṗel-ₒgrib-kyi dbáṅ-gis* in consequence of the increase and decrease *Gram.*; *ₒṗel-ₒgrib-nád*, prob. diseases arising from an excess or deficiency of humours *Wdṅ.* — 2. **to improve, to grow better,** *bsam-gtán* or *tugs-dám ₒṗél-ba yin* meditation has improved, has proceeded **better** *Mil.* — II. sbst., *Sch.* also *ₒṗél-ka*, 1. **increase.** 2. **development** *S.g.*

འཕོ་བ་ *ₒṗó-ba* pf. and imp. *ₒpos*, prop. intrans. to *spó-ba*, = *gnas-spó-ba*; 1. **to change place, shift, migrate** frq.; *myur-du ₒpos-śig*, go speedily elsewhere! *Dzl.*; in a more general sense **to change**, *ₒṗo-méd bdé-ba* changeless happiness; in a similar sense *ₒṗo-ₒgyur-méd-pai rnal-ₒbyór Mil.*; yet frq. also vb. a.: *ḱú-ba yaṅ ₒṗo yaṅ ₒṗo byás śiṅ* pouring off the gravy again and again *Pth.*; very frq. *ṫse ₒṗó-ba*, *ₒči-ₒṗó-ba*, *śi-ₒṗó-ba*, to exchange life, **to die,** (in the earlier literature the most common expression for it); the last of the above terms prob. may be explained by *či-žiṅ ₒṗó-ba*; *či-ₒṗo-ba ₒdébs-pa*, *Thgr.* frq. seems to mean: to help the soul to a happy departure. — 2. *C.* **to fall out, to shed,** of wheat and corn in general.

འཕོག་པ་ *ₒṗóg-pa*, pf. and secondary form *ṗog*, **to hit, strike, touch, befal, meet.** *mnár-bai dris ₒṗóg-pa ṫams-čád* all whom the sweet odour met, to whom it became perceptible *Dzl.*; gen. with *la*: *ₒod-zér, grib-ma mi-la ₒṗog*, a ray of light, a shadow falls upon that man *Glr.* frq.; *ḱó-la nad, ṫsád-pa, čád-pa ₒṗog*, disease, heat, punishment etc. has befallen him; *gza-ₒṗog-mkan* **an epileptic person** *W.*, *C.*; the signification: **to hurt**, seems to be less inherent to the word than dependent on contingent circumstances.

འཕོང་ *ₒṗoṅ Cs.* **archery,** *ₒṗóṅ-sa* archery ground, *ₒṗóṅ-mkan* archer, *ₒṗoṅ-skyén* good, skilful archer *Dzl.*

འཕོང་ཚོས་ *ₒṗoṅ-tsos Cs.* **buttocks;** *ₒṗoṅs* sitting-part, posteriors *Lt.*, *Wdṅ.*; *ₒṗóṅ-la skyón-pa Sch.* 'the riding of two persons on one horse'.

འཕོངས་པ་ *ₒṗóṅs-pa* 1. vb., pf. *ₒṗoṅs* or *ṗoṅs*, **to be poor, indigent;** *ₒṗóṅs-par bžúg-pa* to let (another) pine in poverty *Thgy.*; with instrum. **to be deprived of, to lose**, *rgyál-po srás-kyis ₒṗóṅs-nas* the king having lost his son *Pth.* — 2. also *ṗóṅs-pa*, sbst. **poverty,** and adj. **poor**, v. *ṕóṅs-pa*; perh. also **dejected, disheartened.**

འཕོད་པ་ *ₒṕód-pa* = *ṕód-pa*, *Cs.*; འཕོན་པོ་ *ₒṕón-po* = *ṕón-po*; འཕོབ་པ་ *ₒṕób-pa* = *ₒbébs-pa Sch.*

འཕྱ་བ་ *ₒṕyá-ba*, pf. *ₒṕyas*, acc. to *Lex.* = *smód-pa* **to blame, censure, chide;** the context however, in which the word occurs, seems to suggest the meaning: **to scoff, to deride,** (*Sch.*) e.g. *Dzl.* ༢༢༢, 13. ༡༥༤, 7. ༢༤༠, 15; also *Pth. mis ₒṕyá-ru ₒoṅ*, people will laugh at you.

འཕྱག་པ་ *ₒṕyág-pa*, pf. *ₒṕyags* or *ṕyag?* **to sweep, to clean** *Lex.*, *Pth.*; cf. *ṕyag-dár.*

འཕྱང་བ་ *ₒṕyaṅ-ba*, pf. *ₒṕyaṅs*, vb. n. to *dpyáṅ-ba*, **to hang down,** *dar sṅon-poi ge-ša ₒṕyaṅ-ba* a handkerchief of blue silk hanging down from the head *Sambh.*; *má-mču ťúr-du ₒṕyáṅ-ba* the lower lip hanging down, as a sign of death *S.g.*; **to cling to a person,** from love etc.; *rje-btsún-gyi skú-la Mil.*, to the Reverend's person (or body?); *jú-žiṅ ₒṕyáṅ-ba* to cling to, to take a firm hold of *Thgy.* — *ₒṕyaṅ-ťág* **plumb-line, sounding-line** *C.* also *dpyáṅ-ťag.* — **čáṅ-ǩem-pa** **rope-dancer,** esp. at the festivities of new-year *C.*

འཕྱང་མོ་ཉུག་ or ཡུག་ *ₒṕyaṅ-mo-nyug* or *-yug Sch.*, **singular, strange.**

འཕྱད་ *ₒṕyad Sch.* = *ṕyad.*

འཕྱན་པ་ *ₒṕyán-pa Lexx.* = *yán-pa* **to ramble, to range, roam about, wander, stray from;** *ₒṕyán-te ₒgró-ba Dzl.* ༢༦༩, 4.

འཕྱར་ཁ་ *ₒṕyár-ǩa Sch.*, **blame, affront, disgrace.**

འཕྱར་བ་ *ₒṕyár-ba*, imp. *ₒṕyor* and *ṕyor* 1. **to raise, to lift up;** *ṕrú-gu nám-mǩa-la Glr.* to lift the infant up to heaven; **to hold aloft,** e.g. the *dor-je* in practising magic, pointing it towards heaven; so also *sdig-mdzúb* to raise the finger *Mil.*; *rál-gri*, to lift up the sword to fetch a blow; to lift up the grain in a shovel, hence: **to fan, to sift, to winnow.** — 2. **to hoist,** a flag, frq.; *ₒṕyar-dár* or *dar-ₒṕyár*, a flag; in a general sense: **to hang up,** so esp. *W. *čár-la** (*Lad. *čás-la** for *čárs-la*), **bór-če** id.; **čár-la tán-če** to hang a man; *čár-šiṅ* gallows; occasionally too: to cling or stick to an object. — 3. *Cs.* **to show, to represent, to excite, to waken;** *ₒṕyar-γyeṅ*, engaging, winning behaviour (= *ₒjog-sgégs*), *ṕyár-ba byéd-pa* to assume an alluring attitude; *ₒṕyár-ǩa-čan*, tempting, graceful, charming.

འཕྱི་བ་ *ₒṕyi-ba* I. sbst. **marmot,** *ṕyi-ba.* — II. vb. pf. *ṕyis*, *ₒṕyis* 1. **to be late, to be belated, to come too late;** *gál-te ₒṕyis-na*, if I come too late *Dzl.*; *da ǩyod čuṅ ₒṕyis-pa yin* you come just a little too late *Pth.*; *ₒṕyi-mo* v. *ṕyi* II. — 2. also *ₒṕyid-pa* **to wipe, to blot out,** *mig* to wipe the eyes *Pth.*; *mčí-ma* the tears *Glr.*; **to pull out,** *spu* the hair *W.*; **to tear out,** *rlig-pa* the testicles *Sch.*; *ₒṕyi-rás Cs.*, **wiper, wiping-clout, duster;** *lág-ₒṕyi Cs.*, **towel,** v. *ṕyis* II.

འཕྱིག་པ་ *ₒṕyig-pa*, *Sch.* **to bind,** better *ₒǩyig-pa.*

འཕྱིད་པ་ *ₒṕyid-pa* v. *ₒṕyi-ba.*

འཕྱིལ་བ་ *ₒṕyil-ba* for *ₒǩyil-ba* **to wind, to twist,** (the hair) *Wdṅ.*

འཕྱུག(ས)་པ་ *ₒṕyúg(s)-pa*, rarely *čúg-pa* **to be mistaken,** also *W.*; **to miss,** *lam*, the road *Lex.*; *ču-ťsód*, to mistake the hour *Pth.*

འཕྱུར་བ་ *ₒṕyúr-ba* 1. **to mount, to rise up,** of smoke; **to overflow; inundate,** of rivers and lakes *Lex.* — 2. *Sch.* **to heap up, to accumulate?** v. *ṕyúr-bu.*

འཕྱེ་བ་ *ₒṕyé-ba*, pf. *ₒṕyes*, **to crawl, to creep,** like snakes; esp. *lto-ₒṕye*, 'belly-creeper', **snake, serpent;** *ₒṕyé-ba čén-po*, **महोरग,** name of a demon; *ₒṕyé-bo*, fem. *mo* **cripple** *Lex.* = *rkaṅ-med.*

འཕྱེན་ *ₒṕyen Mil.* = *pyən*, **wind,** *γtóṅ-ba*, to let go a wind.

འཕྱོ་བ་ *ₒpyó-ba* pf. *ₒṕyos?* 1. **to swim,** of fishes, *Mil.* — 2. **to soar, to float,** in the air *Thgy.* — 3. **to flow, heave, swell,** of fluids *Mṅg.*; *ₒṕyo-dár-ba Sch.*, to undulate. — 4. **to range, roam about, gambol,** *rtse-žiṅ ₒpyó-ba*, of deer *Mil.*; *rí-la ₒṕyo* *dgu*, po. the wild animals of the field *Sch.* — 5. *snyiṅ ₒp'yo Sch.*, 'the heart is swelling, courage is rising'; however *šés-pa ₒp'yo Med.*, seems rather to imply: consciousness gives way, is wavering, flitting; *sems ₒp'yo Lt.?*

འཕྱོང་བ་ *ₒp'yóṅ-ba Lt.* perh. = *ₒp'yáṅ-ba*; occasionally, like *ₒp'yoṅs-pa* used incorr. for *mčóṅs-pa*.

འཕྱོངས་རྒྱས་ *ₒp'yoṅs-rgyás Sch.*, **pride, haughtiness, insolence.**

འཕྱོན་མ་ *ₒp'yón-ma*, **harlot, prostitute,** *byéd-pa*, to whore, to fornicate *Lex.*

འཕྱོར་བ་ *ₒpyór-ba*, v. *p'yár-ba*, also for *čór-ba*; *ₒp'yór-po* for *mčór-po*, hence *ₒpyór-dga Sch.* **dandy, fop.**

འཕྱོས་མ་ *ₒp'yós-ma Sch.*, purchase-price of a bride.

འཕྲ་བ་ *ₒp'rá-ba* I. vb., also *prá-ba*, pf. *ₒp'ras*, **to kick, to jerk, to strike with the foot,** *ₒp'ra-šágs* a stroke or kick with the foot, *byéd-pa* to kick about with the feet, in a paroxysm of pain or anguish, *Pth.*; **ṭ'a-šag gyáb-pa**, to give one a kick. — II. = *p'rá-ba, p'rá-mo.*

འཕྲག, འཕྲག་པ་ *ₒp'rag, ₒp'rág-pa,* **to envy, grudge,** v. *p'rag.*

འཕྲང, ཕྲང་ *ₒp'raṅ, p'raṅ, lam-ₒp'ráṅ,* **a foot-path** along a narrow ledge on the side of a precipitous wall of rock (not 'a defile or narrow pass' *Sch.*), frq.; *bar-doi ₒp'raṅ* the road of the abyss of the *bar-do*, (as with us: the valley of death) frq. *Thgr.*; *bár-doi ₒp'raṅ-sgról*, prob. a prayer for deliverance from that abyss *Thgr.*

འཕྲང་འཕྲུལ་ *ₒp'raṅ-ₒp'rul Sch.* **something hanging down.**

འཕྲད་པ་ *ₒpràd-pa* pf. and fut. *p'rad* **to meet together;** *daṅ* **to meet with, to fall in with, to find;** *de daṅ p'rád-do*, you shall see him *Dzl.*; *de ni ṅa daṅ prad mi t'ub*, him I cannot admit *Dzl.*; *bdag daṅ ₒp'rád-par šog čig*, come to see me *Dzl.*; *sṅar ṅa daṅ ₒp'rád-pai ₒóg-tu* not until they have met me (sensu obscoeno) *Dzl.*; *byis-pai ro žig daṅ p'rád-do* he found the dead body of an infant *Dzl.*; *ₒp'rad-ts'ams Sch.*, intersecting line of two plains, **corner, angle.**

འཕྲབ་པ་ *ₒp'ráb-pa* = *ₒp'rá-ba* and *ₒk'ráb-pa*; *ₒp'ráb-byéd-pa* **to flutter,** of a bird wounded by a shot.

འཕྲལ, ཕྲལ་ *ₒp'ral, p'ral,* prob. to be regarded as a sbst., like *druṅ, mdun, sṅa* etc., expressing **immediate nearness;** 1. in reference **to space,** but seldom, as for instance *ₒp'rál-du k'yi k'rid-de*, having a dog near at hand *Glr.*; gen. 2. with respect **to time:** *p'ral daṅ p'ugs*, what is going to happen immediately and at a later period, presence and futurity; *ₒp'ral-p'úgs-kyi ₒgal-rkyén t'ams-čád sél-bar byed Glr.* to avert immediate and subsequent disasters; *ₒp'ral p'ugs gáṅ-la bzaṅ* that is good both for the nearest and the more distant future; *ₒp'ral daṅ yún-du* now and for a long time to come; *ₒp'ral-sog-ₒjog-méd-par* without having gathered or laid up any thing for daily use *Mil.*; *ₒp'rál-gyi ₒdug-ts'ugs ṅán-pa* a poor temporary dwelling, or also: a common, ordinary dwelling, v. no. 3; *ₒp'ral-du ša gžan ma rnyed-de* as at the moment he was not able to procure any other meat *Dzl.*; *ₒp'rál-du sleb yoṅ Mil.* I shall come immediately; *ₒp'rál-du dgós-pai yo-byád* the things necessary for daily use *Dzl.*; *ₒp'rál-du ₒbyór-ba ma yin* that is not to be had at a moment's bidding *Dzl.*; also postp. e.g.: *deï ₒp'rál-la p'an* that will help the moment directly after it; more frq. after verbal roots = *ma-t'ág-tu*: *p'ebs-p'rál* as soon as he had arrived *Mil.*; *smras-p'rál* as soon as it has been spoken *S.g.*; *skyes-p'rál* immediately after birth *Lt.*; in compounds: *p'ral-rkyén, p'ral-dgós, p'ral-p'úgs* cf. above; *p'ral-grig* finished, ready, prepared, in proper case, (vulgo, esp. in *W.*, a word much used) **ṭ'al-ḍig čó-če** to prepare, to get ready. — 3. fig., **common, ordinary, of daily occurrence, common-place.** *p'rál-skad B., C.*, (*W. *p'il-kad**) common dialect; *žes p'ral-skad-la snaṅ* so you may hear it in the language of the common people, *Gram., Wdṅ.*

འཕྲལ་བ་ *ₒp'rál-ba*, pf. *p'ral*, fut. *dbral*, imp. *p'rol*, vb.a. to *ₒbrál-ba*, **to separate, to part,** **k'a ṭ'ál-wa**, id., *C.*; *daṅ* from;

rtags daṅ ṗral he deprived them of their insignia *Glr.*; *srog daṅ ₒṗrál-ba* to put to death, to inflict capital punishment *Glr.*; *zúg-tu ₒṗrál-ba* to cut into quarters (cattle) *Mil.*; *ltó-ba ṗrál-ba* to cut open, to rip up the belly *Tar.*; *dbrál-bar dka* difficult to part, hard to be kept asunder *Lex.*

འཕྲས་པ་ *ₒṗrás-pa* 1. pf. of *ₒṗrá-ba*; as sbst. **stroke, blow, kick** with the foot, *Cs.*; *rkaṅ-ₒṗrás*, id.; *rtas-ₒṗras rgyag-pa*, the kicking of a horse; *lag-ₒṗrás*, a blow with the hand, *Cs.*; *ₒč̔i-ₒṗrás Lexx.*, *ši-ₒṗrás* vulg. (*W.* **šin-ṭ̔ás* or *ṭ̔e**), the kicking, struggling, moving in convulsions, of a dying man or animal, **agony.** (*Sch. ₒṗras*, to lie on one's side?). — 2. instrum. of *ₒṗra*, *Sch.*: *ṗras spras-pa.*

འཕྲི་བ་ *ₒṗri-ba* pf. and imp. *ṗri(s)*, fut. *dbri*, vb.a. to *ₒbri-ba*, **to lessen, diminish; to take away from,** **k̔a ṭ̔i-če** to take off at the top, e.g. from too full a measure *W.*; more in the special sense of subtracting, with different construction: *de* (or *dé-yis* or *dé-la*) *t̔ig-ro ṗri-ba-yis* 60 diminished by this, or: this being subtracted from 60; (*t̔ig-ró* = cipher six) *Wdk.*

འཕྲིག་པ་ *ₒṗrig-pa* 1. **to struggle, flutter,** *Cs.*; **to throb, pulsate,** *Lt.* — 2. *Sch.* **to desire, covet, demand.** — 3. *Sch.* **to be suspected.** — 4. **error?** *Sch.*: *ₒṗrig-ldán*, **erroneous, mistaken, faulty, incorrect.**

འཕྲིན་ *ₒṗrin* v. *ṗrin*; *ₒṗrin-pa* **to inform** *Cs.*

འཕྲུ་བ་ *ₒṗrú-ba*, འཕྲུ་མ་ *ₒṗrú-ma* v. *ṗrú-ba* etc.

འཕྲུག་པ་ *ₒṗrúg-pa*, pf. *ṗrugs*, **to scratch one's self,** *ṗrúgs-na Lt.* if one scratches; *za-ₒṗrúg byed* he scratches himself on account of an itching *Med.*

འཕྲུགས་ *ₒṗrugs S.O.*, perh. = *ṗrug* II.

འཕྲུལ་ *ₒṗrul*, **jugglery, magical deception,** the abstract noun to *sprúl-ba*, q.v.; *ₒṗrul-č̔e-ba* great in magic power *Glr.*; *ₒṗrul-gyi rgyal-po* the magic king, enchanted king, phantom-king *Glr.*; *ₒṗrúl-ghi koṅ-jo* the enchantress *Koṅ-jo Glr.*; *ₒṗrul-gyi spyan-gyis* with a magic eye, by means of magical vision *Dzl.*; *ṗá-rol ɣnón-pai ₒṗrul daṅ ldán-pa* possessing magic power for subduing an enemy *Sambh.*; *rnám-(par) ₒṗrúl (-ba)*, *č̔o-ₒṗrúl*, *rdzu-ₒṗrúl*, frq.; *sgyu-ₒṗrúl* less frq., id.; *mig-ₒṗrul*, optical deception *Cs.* — *ₒṗrul-gyi ₒk̔or-lo*, *ₒṗrul-ₒk̔or*, **magic wheel,** in ancient literature merely a phantastic attribute of gods etc.; in modern life applicable to every more complicated machine with a rotating motion, e.g. a sugar-mill *Stg.*, an electrifying machine and the like. *ₒṗrul-dgai lha*, *dga-bži-ₒṗrul-gyi lha*, *ɣžan-dga-ₒṗrul-dbaṅ-byed-kyi lha*, the names of various regions that are residences of gods. *ₒṗrul-snáṅ* 1. **delusion, mockery.** 2. n. of a monastery in Lhasa founded by the Nepal wife of *Sroṅ-btsan-sgam-po's.*

འཕྲུལ་ཐུར་ *ₒṗrul-t̔úr S.g.* seems to be **catheter.**

འཕྲུལ་བ་ *ₒṗrúl-ba*, 1. by its form intrs. to *sprúl-ba*; acc. to *Cs.* both are identical in meaning; I met with it only as an abstract noun = *ₒṗrul* in *rnám-par ₒṗrúl-ba* (v. under *ₒṗrul*), e.g. *rnám-par ₒṗrúl-ba dú-ma*, many transformations, magic tricks, for which *rnam-ₒṗrúl* gen. is used. — 2. **to be mistaken, to err, to make blunders** *Mil.*, better *ₒk̔rúl-ba.* — 3. **to separate, part, discriminate,** the good from the bad, truth from falsehood *Ld.* (= *ṗrál-ba?* like *drúṅ-po* and *dráṅ-po*).

འཕྲེ་བ་ *ₒṗre-ba* pf. *ₒṗres Cs.*, *ₒṗre byéd-pa Sch.*, **to incline, to lean against; to put down, to lay down;** *Dzl.* ཉV, 12, where however the context is not perfectly clear.

འཕྲེང་(བ་), ཕྲེང་(བ་) *ₒṗreṅ(-ba)*, *ṗreṅ(-ba)* sbst. col. *W.* **ṭ̔áṅ-ṅa**, *Ü*: **ṗaṅ**) *Ssk.* माला, **a string, a thread** or **cord,** on which things are filed, strung, or ranged, e.g. *mé-tog-gi ₒṗréṅ-ba Glr.* a wreath, garland of flowers; *ₒṗreṅ-ba dmar-po* a wreath of red flowers *Wdṅ.*; *gaṅs-rii* a circle of snow-mountains *Schr.*; *nags-kyi*, of woods *Sambh.*; *šiṅ-rtai ₒṗreṅ-ba rim-pa-bdun* 7 circles of chariots *Pth.*; *yig-ₒṗreṅ* a line of letters; *ₒṗréṅ-ba ₒdógs-pa* to bind a wreath; *ₒṗreṅ-skúd*, *ₒṗreṅ-t̔ág* the string or cord of the wreath; *ₒṗreṅ-rdóg* bead, hence *ₒphréṅ-ba* esp.: a string of beads, **rosary**; *bgraṅ-ₒphreṅ*, rosary for counting the repetitions of prayers and magic spells, being used also in arithmetic, as an aid to memory; *mú-tig-ₒphreṅ* string of pearls, rosary composed of pearls; *nor-bu-ₒphréṅ-ba* of precious stones; also title of a book; fig. *don ma go ts̒ig-gi ₒphréṅ-ba bzuṅ*, they only keep to the string of words, without understanding their import *Mil.*

འཕྲེང་བ་ *ₒphréṅ-ba* vb.n. **to love, to be fond of, greatly attached to,** with accus. of the person, *séms-la* and similar supplementary words being generally added; *blá-ma yid-la ₒphréṅ-bai rtags, bú-mo séms-la ₒphréṅ-bas Glr.*; *yáb-kyi tʻúgs-la phréṅ-bar gyúr-te*, or *ₒphréṅ-bžin-du* as she was very dear to her father *Glr.*; *šín-tu ₒphróṅ-ba žig byuṅ* an ardent longing for home came over me *Mil.nt.*

(འ)ཕྲེང་ *ₒphreṅ*, sometimes incorr. for *phraṅ*.

འཕྲེད་ *ₒphred*, v. *phred*. — **འཕྲེས་** *ₒphres*, v. *ₒphré-ba*.

འཕྲོ་བ་ *ₒphró-ba*, pf. *ₒphros*, prop. vb.n. to *spró-ba*, 1. gen. with *las*, from, **to proceed, issue, emanate from, to spread,** in most cases rel. to rays of light; *sku ₒod-zér ₒphró-ba* a body from which rays of light proceed, a body sending forth light *Glr.*; *Cs.* also relative to odours, fame etc.; occasionally in reference to descent or parentage *Thgy.* — 2. **to proceed, to go on, continue,** and *ₒphro* **continuation,** opp. to being finished, at an end (*Sch.* incorr.: 'the end'); **láb-ṭo žeṅ-ghyi čʻé-pa* C., Schr.*: the interruption of a conversation by another person; *ₒjig-pro bčad* the process of destruction came to an end *Glr.*; *sbyin-pai ₒphro čʻád kyaṅ slóṅ-mo-pai ₒphro ma čʻad Pth.* the gifts had come to an end, but not the begging; *ₒphar-ₒphro čʻad* the pulse no longer beats *Thgr.*; *čʻos-bsgyúr-ₒphro-rnams bskyur* the continuations of translating were thrown aside *Glr.*; of the soul: *yód-ₒphro-la mi yoṅ* whilst it is still existing, it does not come forth, i.e. it vanishes imperceptibly, as soon as an attempt is made to find out its seat and to demonstrate its essence *Mil.*; *ₒphro tʻúd-pa* to annex the remainder, to append the continuation; **ṭo žág-pa* C.* to lay the continuation aside; **žól-wa** to put it off, both expressions implying an interruption of work; *ₒphro lus soṅ* or *lus soṅ* a remainder is still left of what has not been used or consumed; **ₒdi ghaṅ ʼṭó-te** after this has been filled up (by pouring in the wanting quantity) *C.*

འཕྲོག་པ་ *ₒphróg-pa*, pf. and imp. *phrogs*, fut. *dbrog* 1. **to rob, take away; to deprive of,** cgpar. *nor, gos, rgyál-poi lág-nas rgyál-sa* to deprive the king of his throne *Glr.*; hence *rgyál-sa phrógs-pai mi* usurper *Glr.*; *ts̒ád-pas mii mtu-stóbs ₒphrog* the heat deprives a man of his strength *Med.*; yet also: *sems-yid ₒphróg-pa* to take another man's heart, to run away with his affections, to captivate him *Glr.*; *ₒphrog-byéd*, and also *ₒphróg-ma = dbaṅ-phyúg* 1. **ईश्वर** i.e. Shiwa, or also Indra. 2. symb. num.: 11. — *rku-ₒphróg*, robbery *Ma.*, **čʻom-** or **čʻom-ʼṭóg**, id., *W.*; **čʻóm-ʼṭóg táṅ-kan** robber, **waṅ daṅ čʻom-ʼṭóg čʻó-te** by violence, *W.* — 2. **to make one lose a thing,** *bdág-gi glaṅ phrogs* (by his negligence) he has made me lose my ox *Dzl.*; *sdóm-pa ₒphróg-tu byuṅ* my vow is lost to me, i.e. the meditation I had vowed has been disturbed, thwarted *Glr.*, to deprive a person of his power or place, **to overthrow,** kings, dignitaries etc. *Stg.*, analogous to *ɣyo-ba, ₒgul-ba, ₒkʻrugs-pa.* — 3. **to remove, do away with, expel,** demons *Glr.*

འཕྲོང་ *ₒphroṅ Glr.*, provinc. for *ₒphraṅ* and *ₒphreṅ*, v. *ₒphreṅ-ba*.

འཕྲོད་པ་ *ₒphrod-pa* 1. vb.: pf. *phrod*, vb. n. to *spród-pa*, **to have been delivered, transmitted,** *lág-tu* into the hands of a person, hence *ₒphrod-ₒdzin*, **ṭod-zin* W.* **receipt, quittance;** *ṅo* or *ṅos-ₒphrod-pa* **to know, perceive, understand;** so prob. also *snyiṅ-la ɣsál-bar ma phrod Schr.* — 2. adj. **fit, proper, suitable, agreeing with, congenial to,** *pʻó-bar* agreeing with the stomach *Med.*; *mi-ₒphrod zas* unwholesome food *Med.*; *mi-ₒphrod-pa* also signifies adverse fortune, adversity *C.*;

k̓an-pa e' ˳p̓rod če-na if the question is, whether the house is likely to prosper.

འཕྲོབ་པ་ ˳p̓rób-pa Sch. = ˳p̓ráb-pa, འཕྲོལ་བ་ ˳p̓rol-ba Sch. = ˳p̓rál-ba.

འཕྲོས་པ་ ˳p̓rós-pa v. ˳p̓ro-ba; ˳p̓ros γtón-ba Schr., ˳p̓ros-par byed-pa Sch. **to spread, to pour forth,** e.g. light, ˳p̓ros *Tar.* 48,3, acc. to *Schf.*: a detailed work; but *Tar.* 143,13?

བ

བ *ba* 1. the letter **b,** originally, and in the frontier districts still at the present day, corresponding to the English b; the pronunciation of it, however, varies a good deal in the different dialects of the country: in *C.* this letter, as an initial, is at present deep-toned and aspirated = *bh;* in *Sp.* as a final letter, it is softened down to w; and this softening of its sound prevails throughout Tibet in the substantive terminations *ba* and *bo*, when preceded by a vowel or by *ṅ, r, l*; as a prefix it is sounded in *Bal.* and *Kh.* = *b* or *w*. Regarding the irregularities in the pronunciation of initial *db* v. the Phonetic Table. — 2. num. figure: 15.

བ་ *ba* I. (also *bá-mo Cs.* ?) **cow,** ˳*dod-˳joi ba* v. *-jo-ba*; *ba-kó* cow-leather; *ba-kyú* herd of cows; *ba-glán* v. below; *ba-γčin* urine of a cow; *ba-lči* cow's dung; *ba-ču*, resp. *-čab* = *ba-γčin* (used by hindooizing Tibetans, the cow being sacred to the Hindoos); *ba-nú* 1. a cow's dug. 2. a stone resembling it in appearance *Med.*; *ba-p̓rúg* calf; *ba-rmig* a cow's hoofs; *ba-rmig-gi ču* the water collected in the impression of a cow's foot on the ground, to denote a very small quantity of water *Dzl.; ba-o* for *bai ˳ó-ma*; *ba-rdzi* cow-herd; *ba-rá* pen or stable for cows; *ba-rú* 1. a cow's horn. 2. vulg. cup for scarifying, the hollow tip of a cow's horn being used as such; *ba-šá* cow-beef.

II. affix or so-called **article,** for *pa*, to substantives the roots of which end with a vowel or with *ṅ, r, l*, except when *pa* has its particular signification, as in *ču-pa* etc. (v. *pa*); in adjectives it is either syn. with *po* (as: *dmár-bai mdaṅs*, a ruddy complexion), or it denotes **'having'** (= . . . *po-čan*, as: *sna-dmár-ba* or *sna-dmár-po-čan* having a reddish trunk), or it is the sign of the verb formed from it (*dmár-ba*, to be red), or of the abstract substantive (*dmár-ba*, redness).

བ་དཀར་ *ba-dkár* **lime, lime-stone** *Schr.*

བ་གམ་ *ba-gám*, *S.g.* and elsewh.; *Cs.*: 'low wall, parapet'; acc. to my authorities a certain part of the timber work of a roof, something like pinnacle, battlement; so also *Tar.* 80,21: the king with his retinue beheld the pinnacles of the Naga palace rising above the surface; v. *nyúg-pa* 4.

བ་གླང་ *bá-γlaṅ* **ox, bull;** **ba-laṅ tsogs** *W.*, like an ox, stubborn, stupid; also dirty, filthy, nasty, for which our vulgar expression is swinish; *ba-glaṅ-spyod* appellation for the western part of the globe, v. *γliṅ*. — 2. for *bál-γlaṅ Dzl.*

བ་ཊི་ *bá-ṭi*, *Hind.* **बाटी, a large brass dish.**

བ་ཊི་ཀ་ *bá-ṭi-ka Stg.*, a small long-measure, ¼ of a barley-corn.

བ་སྟག་ *bá-tag W.*, also *Sambh.*, 1. **root.** — 2. **stalk of fruit.**

བ་དན་ *ba-dán* 1. **पताका,** of which the word is a corruption acc. to *Lis.*, an **ensign** with pendent silk strips *Dzl.*, *Gyatch.*, *Glr.* — 2. also *šes-rab-ral-gri*, stated to be a kind of **dagger**, set upright, a semblance of which often attends apparitions of the gods; thus the signification of 'sword', given by *Sch.*, seems to be justified, and also *Schr.* refers to it under *spa-dám*; I never met with it in *B.* in that sense.

བ་དམ་ *ba-dám*, *Pers.*, *Urd.* بادام, from the *Ssk.* **वाताम्र**, 'windmango' *Shksp.*, **almond.**

བ་སྤུ་ *bá-spu* **a little hair,** the little hairs of the body, *bá-spu lan* or *ldan*, the little hairs stand up, I shudder, *B.*, *C.*; similarly: *bá-spu gyo Glr.*, *Mil.*; *ba-spu tsam yan med* (I feel no repentance) even as great as a hair *Dzl.*; *bá-spu-čan* **hairy, covered with hair,** *ba-spu-méd* bald; *bá-spui bú-ga* or *kun (-bu)* **pores.**

བ་བུ་ *bá-bu* (*Pers.* پاپوش, *pāpōš*) **a soft shoe,** *skúd-pai* knitted shoe, *pin-pai* felt-shoe, but in general they are made of wool or goat's hair.

བ་བླ་ *ba-bla* (*Ts.* **bhá-bla**) *Med.* **arsenic.**

བ་འབོག་ *ba-ₒbog W.* **clod, lump of earth.**

བ་མེན་ *ba-mén Mil.*, *Wdn.*, *Cs.* and *Sch.*: 'a species of wild cattle with large horns'; *Sch.* also: **buffalo-calf;** though in *Sambh. gans-ri-ba-mén* are spoken of.

བ་མོ་ *bá-mo* **hoar-frost,** *B.* and col.; *ba-tsa* (Campbell in Summer's Phenix p. 142, 5: *pen-cha*), inferior, **impure soda,** incrusting the ground near salt-lakes; it is mixed with the food of cattle (from which circumstance the word may be translated 'cow-salt'), occasionally also for the want of something better put into the tea; *bá-tsai skyúr-rtsi Cs.* muriatic (hydro-chloric) acid.

བཱ་ར་ཎ་སི་ *bā-ra-ṇa-si*, v. *wā-ra-ṇa-si.*

བ་རུ་ར་ *ba-ru-ra* an astringent medicament *Med.*

བ་ལ་ཧ་ *bá-la-ha*, *čan-šés bá-la-ha*, n. of a demon, v. *rta-mčóg.*

བ་ལུ་ *ba-lu* = *da-li*, various low alpine species of **Rhododendron.**

བ་ལེ་ཀ་ *bá-le-ka* medicinal plant, belonging to the climbers *Med.*

བ་ཤ་ *bá-ša* 1. v. *ba* I. — 2. prob. = *bá-ša-ha* a bitter-tasted officinal plant, acc. to *Wdn.* an Indian tree; in *Lh.* a rather insignificant radiated flower.

བ་ཤུ་ *bá-šu*, *W.* **a virulent boil, ulcer.**

བ་ཤོ་ *bá-šo Ld.*, *ba-šo-ka C.*, **currants, small raisins.**

བ་སོ་ *bá-so* **elephant's tooth, ivory;** *bá-so-mkan* worker in ivory.

བག་ *bag* I. a primary signification of this word seems to be: **a narrow space;** thus with *Sch.* fig. *bág-dog-pa* to be straitened, in necessitous circumstances, poor; in another application more frq.: *bág-tsam* a little, *nor bág-tsam re* a little money *Mil.*; *bag-ré Thgr.*, perh. the same; *dán-ga bág-tsam bde* the appetite is growing a little better *Lt.*; *tsér-ma bág-tsam yód-pa* having a few prickles *Wdn.*; *bág-tsam-pa* **slight, insignificant, trifling,** *sdug-bsnál*, a slight misfortune *Thgy.*; *ma-bdé-ba bág-tsam-la bzód-pa mi byéd-pa Mil.* to be fretting on account of a trifling mischance; most frq., however, the word has a moral bearing: **attention, care, caution,** relative to physical and moral evils or contaminations; *bag-méd*, in a gen. sense: *rá-ro dán-po bág-med-pa* the beginning of intoxication is the disappearing of attention; in a special sense (*Ssk.* **प्रमाद**): **careless, heedless, fearless;** *mi-bdé-bai* fearless of misfortune *Dzl.*; *ₒdi-lta-bui bag méd-par ₒgyur* I shall be freed from the fear of such things *Dzl.*; **fearless,** without fear or consideration, without regard to consequences or to the judgment of others etc., *čán-la bag-méd ₒdi-tsam ₒtún-ba Pth.* without shame drinking such great quantities of beer; *mi-dgé-bai las bág-med-par byéd-pa* to sin without fear or restraint *Dzl.*; *ₒdod-čágs-la bág-med-pas* to indulge in sensuality without restraint *Dzl.*; **heedlessness** with regard to good and evil *Tar.* 4, 22; **moral carelessness, indifference, want of principle,** *bág-med-la nyál-ba C.*, stated to be = *bág-la nyal-ba.* v. *bag* II; of an opposite meaning: *bag-yód(-pa)* **reverence, fear, shame,** often parallel to *ṅó-ts̓a*, *ₒdzém-pa*; **conscientiousness,** almost **religious awe**; adj. **conscientious**; *spyód-pa bág-yod-pa* conscientious dealings (pious course of life) *Dom.*; *bág-yod-par mdzód-čig* act conscientiously, take care not to commit sin (here = do not kill) *Tar.* 32, 7; *de bág-yod-pai p̔yir* as he was conscientious (here = chaste) *Tar.* 39, 2; *bag daṅ ldán-pa* id.; *bag daṅ ldán-par mdzod Glr.*; *bág-ts̓a-ba* **to be afraid**; *bag mi ts̓a* I am not afraid *Mil.*; sbst. **fear, timidity, anxiousness** *Mil., Stg.*; *bág-ts̓a méd-pa* fearlessness *Mil.*; *bag byéd-pa* c. *la*, to fear, to dread, a person *Dzl.*, to take care of, one's clothes *Dzl.*; *bag-yaṅs-su* (or *-kyis*) *Sch.* (*'cura relaxata'*) without fear, fearlessly, coolly; *bag ₒk̔úms-pa Sch.* to be afraid; *bag ₒbébs-pa* to drop, abandon, cast away all fear, *γžan-la* the dread of a person *Mil.* frq.; *bág-pa Dzl.* ༤༥, 15 *Ms.* as a vb. to be afraid, to be fearful, *dé-dag bág-tu dógs-nas* afraid lest they should take fright (another reading: *brós-su*) *bágs-kyis* with fear, with awe *Mil.*; *bágs-kyis byéd-pa* to act carefully, with caution *Dzl.* ༢༨༧, 15; *ma bags-kyis* without fear, unrestrained *Dzl.* ༢༥༥, 1 (*Ms.*; with *Sch. ma* is wanting, and both passages are rendered incorr.); *bág-po* adj. = *bág-yod-pa Cs.*; *bag-zón* dread, fear, anxiety *Sch.* —

II. **inclination? passion?** *bág-la nyál-ba Was.* (241) **'vanities** (in Chinese: lullings into security'), the usual sinful temptations, lust, anger etc.; the etymological derivation of the term is, however, not perfectly clear; *bag-méd-la nyál-ba*, which acc. to its primary signification ought to be placed sub I, is said to imply the same. More frq. *bag-čágs* denotes **passion, inclination, propensity,** gen. in a bad sense, *las-ṅan bag-čágs, ṅán-pai bag-čágs*, also occasionally without any addition, id.; *bag-čágs yid-kyi lus* the 'intellectual' body of passions *Thgr.*, v. *lus*; less frq. in a good sense: *Tar.* 32, 7 = love, affection; *bag-čágs bzaṅ, Mil.* —

III. in compounds also for *bag-p̔yé* and *bág-ma*.

བག་པ་ *bág-pa* 1. vb. **to be afraid,** v. *bag* I. — 2. **purity?** *Cs.*

བག་པོ་ *bág-po* 1. = *bag-yód Cs.* — 2. **bridegroom.**

བག་ཕྱེ་ *bag-p̔ye* (*W.* **bág-p̔e**) **wheat-flour**; *bag-skyó* thin pap or porridge of meal; *bag-zán* thick pap, dough; *bag-drón*, warm porridge; *bag-sbyár* paste; *bags-sbyín* **lute, putty,** a compound of meal and glue; *bag-léb*, resp. *bžes-bág C.* a cake of bread (*Hind. chapāti*).

བག་མ་ *bág-ma* **bride,** *lén-pa* to choose, to take frq.; *bág-ma-la* (or *bág-mar*) *lén-pa* to choose for a bride, *γtóṅ-ba* to give for a bride (wife), *ₒgró-ba, čú-ba Ma.*, **čá-ce** *W.*, to become a bride, to get married; **bág-ma ṭi-te* (or *láṅ-te*) *bór-ce**, *W.* to leave the chosen bride with her parents, sometimes for years, which frequently is the case, as betrothals, from reasons of expediency, are often brought about by the parents at a very early age. The common custom is that the young man desirous of marrying proceeds to the parents of his chosen one with the 'wooing-beer', *slóṅ-čaṅ*, which step however may remain yet a private affair; after some time he brings *tig-čaṅ*, the 'settling-beer', and finally *bsú-čaṅ*, the 'taking-home-beer', whereupon follows the wedding, *bág-ston*, and the consummation of marriage, *bza-mi byéd-pa*. — *bag-gós* **wedding-garment**; *bag-grógs-mo* **bride's maid** *Cs.*; *bag-zoṅ Cs.* (prob. more correctly: *rdzoṅs*) **dowry.**

བག་ཙམ་ *bág-tsam* v. *bag* I.

བག་ཙེ་ *bág-tse* a little **basket for wool** or **clews of wool,** *W.*

བག་ཤིས་ *bág-šis* (also *bá*x*is*, *bó*x*is* etc.) *Ar.* بخشيش 1. **fee,** drink-money. — 2. *Sp.* **a present, alms.**

བགས་ *bags* v. *bag* I.

བང་ *baṅ* 1. **foot-race,** *baṅ ni γžán-las mgyógs-pa* to be quicker in running than another; *de daṅ baṅ mnyám-par rgyúg-pa* to run with equal swiftness as ... *Pth.*; *baṅ rgyúg-pa Cs.*, **bhaṅ táṅ-wa** *C.*; **baṅ táṅ-*

če W.*; *baṅ* ˳*grán-pa* to run a race; *baṅ-rtsál sbyóṅ-ba Mil.* to exercise one's self in racing; *baṅ daṅ* ˳*gró-las-dag-gis nyén-pa* or *baṅ-*˳*grós nyén-pa* to overexert one's self in running *Med.*; **bhaṅ-gyóg, bhaṅ-čóṅ** *C.* **running-match, race**; *baṅ-čén(-pa*, also *-po) Pth., Glr.* **swift messenger, courier**; **bhaṅ-mi** *C.*, **baṅ-mi** *W.*, id. — 2. v. *báṅ-ba.*

བང་བ་ *báṅ-ba, báṅ-k̔aṅ, báṅ-mdzod* **store-room, store-house, corn magazine,** also **treasury** *Dzl.*; *šiṅ-baṅ Kun.* a large box for grain, half underground; *báṅ-p̔ud* first-fruit offering from the barn; **bhaṅ-gha** *Ts.* **repository**; (*dbus-baṅ*, pronounced:) **ü-bhäṅ** *Ts.* **cupboard, press, case.**

བང་རིམ་ *baṅ-rim = k̔ri-*˳*p̔áṅ*, the part of the *mčód-rten* which has the form of a staircase. — 2. *Sch.* 'a separate part of a house connected by a staircase' (?).

བང་སོ་ *báṅ-so* **grave, tomb,** *ɣsón-por báṅ-sor* ˳*dzúg-pa* to bury alive *Glr.*; **sepulchre, monument,** *báṅ-so* ˳*débs-pa*, or *rtsig-pa* to build a sepulchre *Glr.; báṅ-so mčód-pa* to perform funeral sacrifices, to honour a grave *Glr.*

བངས་པ་ *báṅs-pa Sch.* 1. = *sbáṅs-pa.* — 2. = *báṅ-ba.* — 3. = *báṅ-so.*

བཏྟི་ *bát-ti* (*Hindi*) 1. a weight = 2 *ser*, about 4 pounds. — 2. **balance, pair of scales**; **bát-ti tág-če** to weigh *W.*

བད་ *bad* 1. **moisture, humidity,** **šiṅ bad k̔ór-na** *W.* when wood attracts humidity; **bád-čan** moist, humid, damp, from rain or dew *W.* — 2. **hoar-frost** = *bá-mo Sch., Wts.* — 3. in compounds for *bád-kan.* — 4. **edge, border,** *bad ni ɣser* the edge is of gold *Sch.*; *mk̔ar-bád S.g.* = *k̔a-bad? bad-*˳*búr Mil.?*

བད་ཀ་ *bád-ka C.* a plant, similar to mustard, yielding oil.

བད་ཀན་ *bád-kan* mucus **phlegm,** a. as normal substance of the body comprizing 5 kinds: *rten-byéd* mucus in the joints of the neck and shoulders, *myag-byéd* in the stomach, *myoṅ-byéd* in the tongue and palate, *tsim-byéd* in the brain, eyes etc., ˳*byor-byéd* in the rest of the joints; b. in a morbid state, as a cause of disease: *bád-kan-las gyúr-pai nad* mucous diseases; *bad-kan-lhén* mucus in the cardiac regions, prob. = gastric catarrh; *bad-kan-lčags-drégs* intestinal catarrh; *bad-kan-mgul-*˳*gágs* mucous consumption; *bád-kan grúm-bu dkár-po* etc. *Med.*; *bad-kan-rlúṅ* phlegm and air, *bad-kan-mk̔ris* phlegm and bile; *bad-kan-k̔rag* phlegm and blood *Med.*

བན་ *ban* 1. *C.* **beer-jug, pitcher.** — 2. v. the following articles.

བན་ཆུང་, བན་བུན་ *ban-čúṅ, ban-búm* **a little, a bit**; *k̔yod-ráṅ nyams-ban-búm-gyi snáṅ-ba-la* you, with your little bit of spiritual light *Mil.*; *rtsi-šiṅ sna-tsógs ban-ma-búm* forest-trees of every kind not a few (or also variously mixed?) *Mil.*; *ban-če* in moderate quantity, 'tolerably many'.

བན་དྷ་ *bán-dha Sch.* **skull, cranium**; frq. spelled *bhán-dha*, hence perh. = भाण्ड vessel, in which sense it is gen. to be understood in books; accordingly it may be a skull used as a drinking-vessel.

བན་དྷེ་, བན་དེ་ *bán-dhe, bán-de*, acc. to Hodgson's learned Nepalese authority (Illustr. 75) = वन्द्य, *reverendus, salutandus*, for which also in the Tibetan language *btsún-pa* is always used as an equivalent: **a Buddhist priest**; hence originally = Buddhist in general, the term being also applied to women *Mil.*; *ban-rgán* an old priest *Glr.*; *ban-spráṅ* and *spraṅ-bán* a mendicant friar; *ban-čúṅ* ('*pen-kiong*' *Desg.* 370) pupil, disciple in a monastery; *ban-lóg* col., a priest that has turned apostate; *ban-bón Mil.* and elsewh. 1. (acc. to our Lama:) Buddhist and Bonpo. 2. (acc. to *Sch.*): **a Bon-priest,** in which case, however, the word prob. would be *bon-bán.*

བན་ཟོན་ *ban-zón Sch.*: for *bag-zón* **dread, fear.**

བབ་ *bab* v. ˳*báb-pa.*

བབ་ཅོལ་ *bab-čól* **hastiness, rashness,** want of consideration in speaking and acting = *ɣzu-lúm*; *sdig-pa bab-čól-du byéd-pa* to sin recklessly, without heed or regard *Mil.*

བབ་མོ་, བས་མོ་ *báb-mo, bás-mo* (?) *Ld.* **soft, mild;** also **chaste, modest**(corrupted from *bág-mo*?).

བབས་ *babs* 1. **sunk, settled,** v. *˳báb-pa; nú-ma-la rañ-bábs-kyi rdzas byúg-ste* rubbing the breasts with a medicine, so that they sank down of themselves, as if they were full *Glr.*; *bábs-sa* **settlement, colony** *Sch.* — 2. **shape, form, appearance** *Sch.* — 3. *rta-babs* v. *rta*, comp.

བམ་(པ་) *bám(-pa)* 1. **rotten, decayed, putrid,** *ro bám-pa* putrid corpse *Tar.*, *bam-ró*, id.; prob. also corpse in general, esp. in connection with sorcery; *bam-čén*, id.? *Thgr.* — 2. **mould,** white film on liquids; **mouldy, fusty, musty** *W.*

བམ་པོ་ *bám-po* 1. **bundle** of wood or grass *Schr.*, *Sch.* — 2. **division, section,** of books, (of greater length than a chapter); in metrical compositions it is said to comprize a number of 300 verses; *glegs-bám* v. *glegs*; *bam-šiñ Sch.* **board,** prob. = *glegs-šiñ*.

བམ་རིལ་ *bam-ríl* 1. *Sch.* **dull, weak,** from old age or long labour, **worn out,** by much usage. — 2. *W.* **mould.**

བར་ *bar* sbst. (*Cs.* also *bár-ma*) 1. **intermediate space, interstice, interval,** *mḱar ɣnyis-kyi bar zám-gyis sbrél-ba Glr.* overbridging the space between the two castles; *sa-bár* **straits, narrow sea;** *ču-bár* **isthmus, neck of land;** **páñ-gi bar, láñ-ḱe bar, ˳če bar** **shelf** of a repository, cup-board etc. *W.*; **intermediate, middle, mean,** *stod smad bar ɣsum* upper, lower and middle country *Ma.*; *bar ˳dir* here in the middle countries *Glr.*; *bár-gyi*, id., as adj. *Tar.* and elsewh.; *bár-gyi sder-čágs*, in *Wdñ.* a lizard, as an amphibium partaking of two natures; *bár-na, bár-du, bár-la* adv. and postp. c. genit. (and accus.), *lám-gyi bár-na* in the middle of the road (there is a well); on the road, in or on the way, on the journey *Dzl.*; *brág-bar btsír-ba* to be squeezed between two rocks *Thgy.*; *ló-ma dañ yál-gai bár-du* between leaves and branches *Dzl.*; *rgya bod bár-la ˳gró-bai mi* people travelling between China and Tibet *Glr.*; *deï bár-la, de-bár* between *Glr.*; **in the mean time, at the same time,** *Glr.*; *zla-ba ɣsum-gyi bár-du* (to provide for a person) for the space of 3 months *Dzl.*; *žag bdún-gyi bár-du* for seven days (he had not eaten any thing) *Dzl.*; *túñ-čin byá-bai sá-ča bár-du byon* he went as far as the country called *tuñ-čin Glr.*; *dá-ltai bár-du Glr.*, *da-tsam-gyi bár-du Dzl.*; *da-bár*, *Mil.* **until now, hitherto;** *de(i) bár(du)* id., when referring to what is past = **until then;** *˳brás-bui bár-du tób-pa* to obtain all, even to the fruit (inclusive of the fruit) *Dzl.*; *lan ɣsum-gyi bár-du* at three (different) times *Dzl.*; frq. with verbs: *rtsé-mo-la túg-gi bár-du* till even touching the top *Dzl.* and so frq.; rel. to time gen. with a negative, being then equivalent to **as long as,** *ma tób-pai bár-du* as long as it has not been obtained = until its having been obtained *Dzl.*; *ña ma ši bár-du* till or up to my death *Mil.*; *ma bsleb bár-du* as long as we have not reached, attained *Glr.*; seldom without a negation: *mya-ñán-las ˳dás-pai bár-du Dzl.* ꓡV, 4 (s. l. c.); *bár-nas* **from between,** *rtsib-mai bár-nas* from between the ribs *Glr.* — 2. fig. *bar byéd-pa* to interpose, intercede, mediate *Glr.*, cf. *bár-mi.* — 3. Termin. of *ba*, and cf. *par* III.

Comp. and deriv. **bhár-kya** partition-wall *C.* — *bar-skábs* space of time, period *Tar.* — *bar-skór* veranda, exterior gallery of the middle story of a house. — *bar-ḱañ Sch.* a building between two other houses; *Schr.* a room between two others. — *bar-gós Schr.* waist-coat. — *bár-˳ga* some, several; several times, now ... now ... *Dzl.* — *bar-čód, -čad*, perh. also *-ɣčod*, sbst. to *bar-du ɣčod-pa*, (v. *ɣčod-pa*) **hinderance, impediment; danger; damage, failure, fatal accident;** *tsé-la bar-čád ˳oñ*, or *byuñ* (my) life is in danger; *lús-kyi, sróg-gi bar-čád-du ˳gyur* id.; also: to meet with an accident, to perish, to be lost *Dzl.* and elsewh.; **bar-čad-la ši** *W.*, he met with a violent death; *bar-čád sél-ba* to protect against fatal accidents, of magic spells frq.; *ñid-la bar-čád méd-par* without meeting with an accident *Mil.*; *bar-čád rtsóm-pa* to meditate evil, to brood mischief *Mil.*; *bar-čád ma ťsúgs-par* without having played me a roguish trick *Mil.*; also in a moral sense: temptation; sin, trespass, *bár-du γčód-pa* to commit sin, to trespass *Mil.* — **bár-ta** *W.* cloth round the loins. — *bar-stóṅ Sch.* empty space. — *bár-do* 1. also *bar-ma-do* the intermediate state between death and re-birth, of a shorter or longer duration (yet not of more than 40 days, ni f.); although on the one hand it is firmly believed, that the place of re-birth (whether a man, an animal, or a god etc. go forth from it), unalterably depends on the former course of life, yet in *Thgr.* the soul is urged and instructed to proceed at once into Nirwana to Buddha (inconsistently with the general dogma). *bár-do γčód-pa Mil.* is explained as putting off and preventing the intermediate state after death, as well as re-birth, by penitentiary exercises. 2. *W.*: **hard, difficult; difficulty,** — perh. Bunan. — *bar-snáṅ* (seldom *bar-snáṅ-ba*) **atmospherical space**; *stéṅ-gi bar-snáṅ-la* in the heavens, in the air, frq.; *bar-snáṅ-la ˳ṗar* (a fragment of a blasted rock) flies up into the air; *bar-snáṅ-du* or *-la* c. genit., the common word for **over**, *goi bar-náṅ-la*, over (his) head. — **bár-pa** *W.* the middle one, e.g. of three brothers. — *bar-bár-du Ma.* **at intervals, from time to time, now and then**; *bar-bár-la* id.; **mă bar-bár-la**, at long intervals, seldom *W.* — *bár-ma* the middle one of three things *Glr.* — *bar-mi* **mediator, intercessor, umpire.** — **bar-tsód** *W.* middling, **lúṅ-po bar-tsód** a moderate wind. — *bar-mtsáms, bar-˳tsáms* **interval** (*Sch.*: room; leisure, convenience, comfort?). — *bar-lág-pa* = *bar-mi Sch.* — **bar-lhag** gap, vacancy, deficiency *W.*, **bar-lág káṅ-če** to fill up a gap or vacancy, to supply a want, or deficiency.

བར་ལྕིག་ *bar-lig W.* a **field** or **estate** let to a person for the term of his life, for usufruct.

བལ་ *bal* **wool,** *bál-gyi* woolen, *bal daṅ ldán-pa* woolly *Wdṅ.*; *bal séd-pa* the first coarse plucking of wool, *rmél-ba* the second, of the finer wool, *śiṅ-ba* the third, of the finest *W.*; **bal táb-če** to beat wool *W.*; *lug-, ra-, rńá-bal* sheep-wool, goat's and camel's hair; *rás-bal, śiṅ-bal* cotton *Cs.*; *śiṅ-bal* prob. also the down on willow-blossoms *Sch.*; *srin-bal Wdṅ.*, *Schr.*: raw silk, yet perh. also cotton; *čú-bal* a kind of moss on stones in brooks *Cs.* — *bal-skúd* a woolen thread or yarn, worsted. *bal-skyé Sch.*: mould on fermented liquors. — *bal-gláṅ*, *Cs.* also *bál-gyi glaṅ-po-čé*, a kind of elephant, for which sometimes incorr. and ambiguously *bá-laṅ* is used, *Dzl.* and elsewh. — *bal-ťér* thin woolen cloth *Cs.*; **bal-˳dáb** *W.* tuft of wool, as is used for spinning. — *bal-ṗrúg* thick woolen cloth. — *bal-yás Sch.* wool-card (?)

བལ་པོ་ *bál-po, bal(-po)-yúl* **Nepal**, frq. designated as *rin-po-čei gliṅ*, and as the favourite country of the *Klu*, or serpent-demons; *bál-po-pa*, fem. *bál-po-ma, bál-mo Glr.*, a Nepal man or woman; *bal-nyiṅ C.*, (*-snyiṅs*) a Nepal rupee; *bal-srán Tar.*, Nepal pease.

བས་ *bas* I. v. *bás-pa*. — II. instrum. of *ba*; *bas-bldágs*, 'licked by a cow', n. of a disease combined with the sensation, as if the skin had been licked off by a cow, cow-itch, cow-pox *Cs.* (?) — III. v. *pas*, where there is to be added: **to say nothing of, much less,** e.g. *ḱron ˳dom dgu-brgyá-bas brgya yaṅ ˳bru mi ṫub*, a well a hundred fathoms deep cannot be dug, to say nothing of 900 fathoms (much less one of 900 f.) *Glr.*

བས་པ་ *bás-pa* (cf. Pers., Hind. بس) *Cs.*: pf. of *byéd-pa* inst. of, *byás-pa* in the signification of **'done (with), settled'**; *bás-par byéd-pa*, id. *Sch.*; in *Bal.* frq.: **bas, byas, bas-se*, or also *byás-te yód** it is finished, completed, ready, all right; *der bas* that is all of it, nothing more is left *Sch.*; in *bgyis-su bás-kyis* after having been made, caused, occasioned *Mil.*, it stands as a sign of the preterite, similar to *zin*; or like *zad*: *mi γčig-gi smán-du ma bás-kyis* not only for one man it serves as a medicine *Dzl.*; *bas-mta* **border-country** *Sch.*

བས་མོ་ *bás-mo* v. *báb-mo*.

བི་ *bi* 1. num. figure: 45. — 2. in *W.* gen. for *byi*. — 3. *bi* and *biu Pur.* for *bya* **bird, fowl, hen.**

བི་གང་, བི་ཡང་ *bi-yàṅ, bi-yàṅ* in compounds *big*, **hole** *W.* for *bú-ga*, cf. *ˌbig-pa*; *bi-gàṅ-čan* having holes.

བི་ཏང་ *bi-taṅ*, *Lh.* **door,** prop. Bunan.

བི་ནཱ་ཡ་ཀ་ *bi-nā-ya-ka Ssk.*, v. *bgegs.*

བི་ཤྭ་ཀརྨ་ *bi-šwa-kar-ma Ssk.*, *lhai bzó-bo* the smith of the gods, the Brahman-Buddhist Vulcan *Dzl.*, *Glr.*

བི་ཥ་ *bi-ša* (*Ssk.* word for poison) n. of certain medicinal plants, e.g. *bi-ša-dkar* Polygonatum, in *Lh.*

བིག་པན་ *big-pan Cs.* **vitriol;** *Sch.* **potash, garlic-ashes;** mentioned in *S.g.* as a caustic.

བིག་བི་ལིག་ *big-bi-lig Kun.* **quail.**

བིད་བིད་ *bid-bid*(?) *Ld.* **mouth-piece of a hautboy, hautboy reed.**

བིམ་པ་ *bim-pa* **बिम्ब, बिम्ब**, Momordica monadelpha, a cucurbitaceous plant with a red fruit *Wdṅ.*, along with *ka-bed*; the fashion of Indian poets to compare red lips with the bimpa fruit, has been adopted also by the Tibetans, *Gyatch.* p. ༥༢; transl. p. 108; so also *Pth.*: *mču-sgrós bim-pa ltá-bur mdzes* (where *Sch.* gives the signification of **peach,** on which the name possibly may have been transferred, although 'lips of the shape of a peach-tree leaf' seem to be rather a strange fancy).

བིར་བིར་ *bir-bir W.* **crumbs, bits, scraps.**

བིལ་བ་ *bil-ba Ssk.* **बिल्व**, *Hind. bilb, bél,* Aegle marmelos, tree with a nourishing and wholesome fruit; the word seems to have been transferred also to the cocoa-nut.

བུ་ *bu* I. sbst., resp. *sras*, 1. **son,** common in *B.* and *C.*; **čé-bu** *W.*, the eldest son. — 2. child, *bu btsá-ba* the bringing forth of children, children being born *Dzl.*; *bu máṅ-bar ˌgyúr-ba* to get many children; *bu mi ɣsós-pa* not being able to keep a child alive *Dom.*; esp. in reference to the mother: *ma-bu*, mother and children; also transferred on animals: *rta ma brgya bu brgya* a hundred mares with as many foals *Dzl.*; the word is moreover used in many other instances, e.g. with regard to letters which in writing are placed under other letters, in reference to principal beams and smaller cross-beams, to capital and interest; also as a friendly address of a teacher to his hearers *Mil.* — The fem. *bú-mo* v. below.

Comp. *bu-ˌkrid* (or *pu-tri*?) a fem. noun proper. — *bu-grógs Cs.* **step-brother, foster-brother.** — *bu-rgyúd* **offspring, issue, progeny, generation** *Tar.* 168. 11. — *bu-dód* foster-child, adopted son, *ṅéd-kyi bu-dód mdzod* deign to be adopted by us *Mil.* — *bu-ɣdúṅ* a small cross-beam *Mil.* — *bu-nád* child-bed, *bu-nád log* the child-bed terminates unfavourably *Pth.* — *bu-snód* **uterus, womb** *Med.* — *bú-po* male child, son *Dzl.* — *bu-p̔rug* children. — *bú-mo*, vulg. also *bó-mo* 1. **daughter,** frq. 2. **girl,** *ṅa bú-moi dús-na yin-te* when I was still a girl *Glr.* — *k̔yeu daṅ bú-mo* lads and lasses *Dzl.*; **maiden, virgin;** *bú-mo ɣtsáṅ-ma, ɣsár-ma, ɣsár-pa* a girl that is still in a virgin state. 3. young woman *Dzl.*; *W.* gen. for *bud-méd*, frq. — *bu-smád*, *Cs.* also *bu-mád* family, children, nearest relations *Mil.* and elsewh. — *bu-tsá* (*Dzl.* ed. *Sch.* also *bu-tsá*) 1. **children's children** *Thgy.*; family = *bu-smád* 2. *W.*, **son,** gen. for *bu*; **boy,** **bú-tsa daṅ bó-mo**. — *bu-tsáb Cs.* = *bu-dod.* — *bu-tsás ˌbrél-ba Glr.* (acc. to the context) to cohabit. — *bu-sríṅ* brother and sister. — *bu-slób* scholar, disciple, follower of a clerical teacher, opp. to *nyá-ma* hearer, who still continues in his secular calling. — II. num. figure: 75.

བུ་ག་ *bu-ga* 1. **छिद्र**, in compounds *bug*, **hole, opening, orifice, aperture,** *bá-spui bú-ga* pore, passage of perspiration *Dzl.*; *sna-búg* nostril; *bú-ga dgu*(*-po*) the nine orifices of the body (eyes, ears, nostrils, mouth, urethra, anus); *tsáṅs-pai bú-ga* and perh. also *yid-ˌjug bú-ga Med.*, appears to be = *mtsog-ma* **the fontanel** or vacancy in the infant cranium, with which various fables are connected; **cavity, vessel,** (anatom.), also **veins** *Med.* — 2. symbol. num.: 9.

བུ་གུ་ *bú-gu* **hole**, *sgoi* key-hole *Dzl.*

བུ་སྟོན་ *bu-stón* name of a learned Lama and author of *čos-byúṅ*, about the year 1300 *Glr.*, an adherent of the Adi-buddha doctrine, v. *Cs. Gram.*

བུ་རྡོ་ *bú-rdo Sch.*, **idle talk, tittle-tattle.**

བུ་ཡུག་ *bu-yúg* **snow-storm** *Mil.*

བུ་རམ་ *bu-ram Hindi* गुड़, *gur*, hence *W.* **gu-rám**, **raw sugar, muscovado; treacle,** *Mil.*, *Lt.*; *bu-rám sgór-ba* to boil down raw sugar *Lex.*; *bu-ram-šiṅ*, *bur-šiṅ*, vulg. **gur-šiṅ** **sugar-cane**; *bu-ram-šiṅ-pa*, इक्ष्वाकु, name of the first king of the solar dynasty in India, *Glr.*; *bu-ram-čaṅ*, *bur-čaṅ* sugar-beer *Lt.*; *bur-dkár? Lt. bur-stáṅ ṗčig* (more correctly *ltaṅ*) *Sch.*, a bale of raw sugar packed up in leather.

བུ་ལོན་ *bú-lon* (cf. *bun*) **advanced money, debt,** **ṅul gyę bú-lon mi-la táṅ-če* W.* to lend a person a hundred florins; (*bú-lon byéd-pa* to contract debts *Schr.*, *Sch.*??) *bú-lon ˳jál-ba* (*W.* **džál-če**), *spród-pa Sch.* to pay a debt, *sél-ba* to put out, to cancel a debt, *dód-pa*, *bdá-ba* to call in, to recover a debt, *čágs-pa* prob. the beginning and running up of debts *Dzl.*; *bú-lon-pa* **debtor,** *dṅul brgyai* of a hundred rupees.

བུ་ཧག་ *bu-hág* v. *sbugs-hág.*

བུག་པ་ *búg-pa* 1. sbst. **hole,** *búg-pa ˳búg-pa* to bore holes *Glr.*, cog. to *bú-ga.* — 2. *Sch.*, to get holes (?).

བུག་ཞོལ་ *bug-žól* v. *sbugs.*

བུག་སུག་ *bug-súg Ld.* **birdsfoot-trefoil,** Melilotus.

བུང་བ་ *búṅ-ba* 1. a humming and stinging insect, **bee** etc.; *buṅ-lčág* sting, and also the wound caused by it; **buṅ-ba čág taṅ soṅ* W.* the bee has stung. 2 *Cs.* a bright black stone.

བུངས་ *buṅs* **mass, heap, bulk,** *buṅs-čén* a large heap *Lt.*; *dri-čui buṅs-če* a great quantity of urine *Mṅg.*; *buṅs byéd-pa* to heap one upon another, pile up. — *buṅ* **many** (?).

བུད་ *bud*, every darkening of the air through dry matter, **a cloud of dust,** more exactly *ťal-búd*; *bud-ťsub* dust from threshing; *búd-kyis btab* wrapt in vapour *Mil.*; perh. also **snow-storm** (*Sch.*), yet not exclusively.

བུད་དྷ་ *búd-dha Ssk.*, **Buddha,** n. of the founder of the religion which is called after him, occurring but rarely in Tibetan writings, and among the people (at least in *W.*) almost unknown, v. *saṅs-rgyas*; *bud-dhai ṗreṅ-ba*, **búd-dé ṭáṅ-na** **rosary** *Ts.*

བུད་པ་ *búd-pa* 1. *Sch.* = *sbúd-pa.* — 2. pf. cf. *˳búd-pa.*

བུད་མེད་ *bud-méd B.* and *C.*, 1. **woman,** *bud-méd sdúg-gu* a fair woman *Dzl.*; *bud-méd daṅ sbágs-pa* to defile, corrupt one's self with women *Dzl.* — 2. **wife, spouse,** not frq. *Dzl.* (*W. bú-mo* and *ă-ne*).

བུད་ཤིང་ *búd-šiṅ* **fire-wood, fuel,** also dung used as such; *búd-šiṅ bšág-pa* to cleave or chop wood.

བུན་ *bun* 1. = *bú-lon Mil.*, *bun ťoṅ* **lend us!** *Mil.*; *bun btáṅ-du ma nyán-pas* not willing to lend any thing *Mil.*; *ḱyéd-rnams-la bun dgós-na* if you want an advance (of money) *Mil.* — *bún-ťo*, *bún-yig* 1. **debtor's account-book.** 2. **bond** or obligation, **bill of debt.** — *bun-bdág* 1. **creditor.** 2. **money-changer, banker.** — *bún-yig* v. *bún-ťo.* — 2. **interest,** **bhun kyé'-pa** to bear interest *C.*; *bun ˳jál-ba* to pay interest *Cs.* — 3. (house) **rent** *Sch.*(?) — 4. *bun-ré Sch.* **a small matter,** cf. *ban-bún*; *bun-bún Sch.* piece-meal, scattered, dispersed. — 5. v. *˳bún-pa.*

བུན་ལོང་ *bun-lóṅ* — *ču bun-loṅ-lóṅ byed* it is whirling up and down, an expression used of boiling water which contains impurities or extraneous matter; hence *bun-lóṅ-gi snaṅ-sás* troubled, impure, sinful thoughts.

བུབ་པ་ *bub-pa* v. *˳bub-pa.*

བུབས་ *bubs* = *yug*, also *ťan* (थान *Hind.*) 1. an entire **piece of cloth** rolled up; *gos-bubs* cotton-cloth *Cs.* — 2. in a general sense one whole, something entire *Sch.*; *bubs-ril* prob. whole, entire, *bubs-ril lus S.g.* the whole body, opp. to separate parts.

བུམ་པ་ *búm-pa*, **bottle, flask**; the water-flask of the hukka; bottle-shaped ornaments in architecture, e. g. on the cenotaphs or Chodtén; *rdzá-mai* earthen-bottle, pitcher; *šél-bum* glass-bottle; *čáṅ-bum* beer-bottle; *mčód-bum Cs.* vessel used in sacrificing; *mé-bum* cupping-glass *Lt.* (cf. *puṅ-pa*).

བུར་ *bur* 1. **bolt, bar,** vertically fastened to a door etc., *ṫóg-bur* upper, *yóg-bur* lower bolt. — 2. for *bu-rám*. — 3. for *˳bur*.

བུར་རྟིང་ *bur-rtiṅ* (or perh. *tiṅ*) *Sch.*, a kind of **bell** or **gong** in temples.

བུར་ཚེ་ *búr-tse* n. of certain plants in *Ld. & Kun.*

བུལ་ *bul W.*, **bhul, bhyl, bhy* and *bhy-tog** *C.*, *Med.*, (the spellings of Campbell, *peu* — v. *bá-mo* — and of *Schl.*, *phuli*, have prob. resulted from a mistake in hearing), **soda**, not unfrequently found in Tibet as a white powder on the ground, and used as a medicine, as a ferment, as a means for giving additional flavour to tea, and for various technical purposes.

བུལ་པོ་ *búl-po* **slow, heavy, tardy,** *˳gro búl-te* slow in walking, making but tardy progress *Dzl.*; *W.*: **ḍúl-če búl-po**.

བུལ་ཧ་རི་ *bul-ha-ri*, **bul-gar** *W.*, **Russia leather, jufts.**

བུས་པ་ *bús-pa* 1. for *byís-pa Lt.* — 2. v. *˳búd-pa*.

བེ་ *be*, 1. num. figure: 105. — 2. *W.* for *bye*. — 3. for words here not noted refer to *pe*.

བེ་ཁུར་ *be-ḱur S.g.?*

བེ་གེ་ *be-gé* v. *beg-gé*.

བེ་ཅོན་ *be-čon*, also *-tson*, *Ssk.* गदा, 1. **club,** with an ornamental knob, prob. merely an attribute of gods. — 2. n. of a goddess *Thgr.*

བེ་ཏ་ *be-ta* a geographical prop. name, prob. = Himalaya, *Pth.*

བེ་ཏོ་, བེ་དོ་ *bé-to, bé-do*, vulg. **calf.**

བེ་དྷ་ *bé-dha* v. *˳bé-dha*.

བེ་སྣབས་ *be-snábs Cs.*, **thick slime** or **mucus,** e.g. the mucus flowing at childbirth from the vagina *Lt.*

བེ་བུམ་ *be-búm*, also *beu-búm*, **writing, scripture, book** *Glr.*, perh. the same word as the following.

བེ་འབུམ་ *be-˳bum*, are stated to be the sacred writings of the Bonpos, which — as our Lama candidly owned — 'are also perused by Buddhists for their edification'.

བེ་མོ་ *bé-mo* **cow-calf,** female calf *C.*

བེ་རྫི་ *be-rdzi* Nakshatra, v. *rgyu-skár* 3.

བེ་ཟ་ *bé-za W.*, from the *Hind.* ब्याज, **interest,** *ṫá-ka bé-za* a double paisa interest, of 1 rupee, = 4—6 pCt. pro month.

བེ་རག་ *be-rag* (spelling?), **fillet** of the women in *Ld.*, ornamented with coloured stones.

བེ་ལེ་ཀ་ *be-le-ka S.g.*, a kind of **surgical instrument.**

བེ་ལོག་ *be-log Sch.* **great-grandfather.**

བེ་ཤིང་ *be-šiṅ* **oak-tree,** = *ča-ra*; *be-ḱród* oak-forest *Wdṅ.*

བེག་གེ་ *beg-gé Lt.*, a disease; *Sch.*: measles.

བེག་ཙེ་ *bég-tse* a hidden **shirt of mail.**

བེང་ *beṅ Sch.*, **stick, cudgel, club.**

བེད་ *bed*, 1. = *ḱe, ḱe-béd*, **advantage, profit, gain, high price,** *ṫsá-la drúg-ču bed yód-pai skábs-su* at a time when salt was a sixty times dearer (than barley) *Glr.*; **bed ṫób-če** *W.* to gain, to make profit; *bed-čód Mil.* is stated to be the same as *loṅs-spyód*; *bed-čód ṫsod bčád-de* to be temperate, to keep moderation in the indulgence of the appetites. — 2. **interest,** *C.*, *W.*

བེན་ *ben* **a large pitcher; jug, beer-pot,** *Glr.*; **ču-bhén**, water-pot, *C.*

བེམ་པོ་ *bém-po* 1. **dead matter,** mostly applied to the body, as opp. to the soul, *rig-pa*, e.g. *bem rig ˳gye-dus* when body and soul are parting, *Mil., Thgr.*; *lus bem-rig ɣnyis-kyi so-mtsáms-su* on the boundary between the physical matter of the body and the soul *Mil.*; *Was.* (272) *bem-reg* is perh. a mistake in writing, although it also makes sense. — 2. *Sch.* **a pestilential disease**; in the *Mṅg. bem tol rgyáb-pa* seems to denote a surgical operation. — 3. some receptacle, **box, bag** etc., *bém-poi náṅ-nas ɣser bton* she took gold out of the . . .?

བེའུ་ *beu Cs.* **calf.**

བེའུ་བུམ་ *beu-búm* v. *be-búm, Mil.*

བེའུ་རས་ *beu-rás*, in *Stg.* mentioned as a material for clothing; *Schr.*: **'fine linen'**, which however is as yet unknown in Tibet.

བེར་ *ber* 1. **cloak,** *bér-gyi ťú-ba* tail of the cloak *Glr.*; *ber nág-po* a black cloak *Glr.* and elsewh.; *ˏǰol-bér* dress with a train *Wdk.*, *Pth.*; *ťsem-bér* a cloak patched up of many pieces *Pth.*; *ber-čen* gown of a priest, sacerdotal cloak, without sleeves, with *gos-čén* for a collar; *ber-ťúl* fur-cloak. — 2. **strength, sharpness, keenness, pungency,** of spices, spirits, snuff etc.; *ber-čan* sharp, pungent, piquant; **ȧ-rág-la ber máṅ-po yod** the gin is very strong *W.*; **bér-ra rag, lčeï bér-če máṅ-po rag** it bites, burns my tongue; *za-bér Cs.* the burning sensation caused by the stinging of nettles; cf. *gár-ba.*

བེར་ཀ་ *bér-ka W.*, *bér-ma, ber-lcág Mil.*, **stick, staff** (cf. *dbyúg-pa*); *spai bér-ma* cane, bamboo *Mil.*; *ber-ma lčag ɣčig* a simple staff *Mil.*; *lčags-bér* iron-bar, crow-bar; *smyug-bér* cane, walking-stick.

བེལ་ *bel Cs.* **leather bag.**

བཻ་ཌཱུ་རྱ་ *wai-dūr-ya, Ssk.*, **azure stone, lapis lazuli** *Dzl. wai-dūr-ya dkar-po* and *sṅon-po*, v. table of abbreviations.

བཻ་རོ་ཙ་ན་ *wai-ro-tsa-na Ssk., Tib.*: *rnam-par-snaṅ-mdzad*, 1. n. of the first Dhyani-Buddha. — 2. a Lotsawa v. *Köpp.* II., 69.

བོ་ *bo*, 1. num. figure: 135. — 2. **affix,** to designate some words as nouns.

བོ་ཏོག་པ་, བོ་ལོང་བ་ *bo-tóg-pa, bo-lóṅ-ba Ts.*, **ankle, ankle-bone.**

བོ་དེ་ *bo-de Cs.*: 'n. of a tree, the fruits of which are used as beads for rosaries'.

བོ་དྷི་ *bo-dhi Ssk.*, **wisdom;** also n. of **the Indian fig-tree,** ficus religiosa, *byaṅ-čub-śiṅ*; n. of the **white narcissus** (*Lh.*).

བོ་བ་ *bó-ba*, prob. pf. of *ˏbó-ba.*

བོ་མོ་ *bó-mo W.* for *bú-mo.*

བོ་ལོ་ *bó-lo*, **ball,** for playing *Ld.*

བོག་པ་ *bog-pa* v. *ˏbógs-pa.*

བོག་ར་ *bóg-ra Sch.* **roof.**

བོགས་ *bogs, Cs.*, **gain, profit, advantage;** *bogs ˏdón-pa Sch.* to yield profit; wherever I met with the word, it was used only in a religious sense: **gain for the mind,** benefit for the heart, furtherance of devotion of meditation, *Mil.*

བོང་ *boṅ* 1. also *boṅs*, **size, dimensions, volume, bulk,** *boṅ-čé, -čén* large, *boṅ če don čuṅ*, large of size, and small of significance are e. g. the lungs (in as far as roasted or boiled they yield little substantial food) *Mil.*; *lus-boṅ-čé, -čúṅ, ˏbriṅ* big, little, middling, as to size of body, *S.g.*; *boṅ-ťúṅ* little in stature; *boṅ-ťsád, boṅ-ťsód* = *rdzógs-pa* full size, a full-grown body *Thgy.* — 2. v. *boṅ-na.* — 3. also *bóṅ-ba, Cs.*: 'general name for small stones, pebbles etc.'; in medical works *ziṅ-gi bóṅ-ba* are mentioned as remedies; in *Pth.* the word occurs in an enumeration of temporal goods, precluding the above signification. — 4. v. *boṅ-bu.* — 5. provinc. for *baṅ Glr.*

བོང་ཁྲ་ *boṅ-kra Sch.* a species of **falcon.**

བོང་གུ་ *bóṅ-gu* v. *bóṅ-bu.*

བོང་ང་ *boṅ-ṅá*, various species of **wolf's bane,** aconite, *boṅ-dkár, -nág, -dmár, -sér*, used as medicines, or even as poisons.

བོང་ནག་ *boṅ-nág* v. the preceeding and the following article.

བོང་བུ་ *bóṅ-bu, Sch.* also *bóṅ-bo*, 1. **ass,** *bóṅ-po* or *po-bóṅ* he-ass, *bóṅ-mo* or *mo-bóṅ* she-ass, *boṅ-prúg* colt or foal of an ass; *boṅ-sgál* an ass's load; *boṅ-sbáṅ* dung of an ass; *boṅ-rdzi* keeper or driver of an ass; *dre-bóṅ Cs.* 'an ass generating a mule'. — 2. n. of insects, *rgyás-poi bóṅ-bu* sugar-mite, lepisma, *Ld.*; *boṅ-nág* (perh. *buṅ-nág*) dung-beetle *Lh.* — 3. *Cs.*: **blockhead, fool.**

བོད་ *bod* 1. *Ssk.* भोट, **Tibet,** *bód-(kyi) yul* id. 2. for *bód-pa, bod k̔a-čig* some **Tibetans** *Tar.*, *k̔yed bód-rnams* ye Tibetans. — 3. for *bód-skad* the **Tibetan language,** *bód-du bsgyur ˳jug* I will have it translated into Tibetan *Pth.*; *bód-skad*, in a more limited sense, also implies the common language of conversation, opp. to book-language *W.*; *bód-pa, bód-(kyi) mi* Tibetans, *bód-mo* fem.; *bód-kyi mi-rigs* or *mi-brgyúd* the people of Tibet, in contradistinction to other nations, *bod-˳báṅs* the Tibetan people, opp. to its ruler.

བོད་པ་ *bód-pa* 1. v. *bod.* — 2. = *˳bód-pa.*

བོན་ *bon* (acc. to *Schf.* = बीज) 1. n. of the early religion of Tibet, concerning which but very imperfect accounts are existing (v. Report of the Royal Bavarian Acad. of Sc., 13. Jan. 1866); so much is certain, that sorcery was the principal feature of it. When Buddhism became the religion of state, the former was considered heretical and condemnable, and *lha-čos* and *bon-čos*, or shorter *čos* and *bon*, were placed in opposition, as with us christianity and paganism; v. *Glr.* and *Mil.*; at the present time, both of them seem to exist peaceably side by side, and the primitive religion has not only numerous adherents and convents in *C.*, but manifold traces of it may be found still in the creed of the Tibetans of to-day. — 2. = *bón-po*, follower of this religion.

བོར་ *bor*, v. *˳bór-ba.*

བོར་ར་ *bór-ra*, **a sack of corn,** holding about 30 *k̔al W.*

བོལ་ *bol, bol-góṅ* 1. **the upper part of the foot** *Stg.* — 2. **the leg of a boot** *W.* — 3. **clod of earth** *C.* — 4. v. *˳bol.*

བོལ་གར་ *bol-gár* = *búl-ha-ri.*

བོལ་པོ་ *ból-po* v. *˳ból-po.*

བོས་ *bos*, v. *˳bód-pa.*

བྱ་ *bya* 1. sbst. **bird, fowl, hen,** cf. the following articles. (*Pur. biu* [v. *byiu*], *bi*). — 2. vb. fut. root of *byéd-pa*, v. this and the sbst. *byá-ba.* — 3. **ja čó-če* W.*, **to castrate, to geld.**

བྱཱ་ཀ་ར་ཎ་ *byā-ká-ra-ṇa*, व्याकरण, prop.: **explanation,** 1. = *luṅ-du-ston-pa* **prophecy,** cf. *Burn.* I, 54 sequ. — 2. in later times: **grammar.**

བྱ་ཀྲི་ *bya-kri Mṅg.*, *bya-tri Lt.*, n. of a medicine.

བྱ་རྐང་ *bya-rkáṅ*, 1. **a bird's foot.** — 2. n. of **a vein** *Med.* — 3. officinal plant, in *Lh.* a blue kind of orobanche.

བྱ་སྐད་ *bya-skád*, also *bya-sgrúṅs*, *bya-čós* title of a book of satirical fables, in which birds are introduced speaking.

བྱ་སྐོན་ *bya-skón* **fowler's net** *Lex.*

བྱ་སྐྱི་ *bya-skyi Stg.*; *Sch.*: **roof, shelter.**

བྱ་ཁང་ *bya-k̔áṅ Cs.* **bird-cage.**

བྱ་ཁྱུང་, ཁྲ་, ཁྲུང་ *bya-k̔yúṅ, -k̔rá, -k̔rúṅ* = *k̔yuṅ, k̔ra* and *k̔ruṅ-k̔rúṅ.*

བྱ་གག་ *bya-gág Dzl.* and elsewh., a species of ducks, *Sch.*: **the gray duck.**

བྱ་དགའ་ *bya-dgá* **gift, present,** esp. as a reward; *sbyin-pa* to bestow a gift, frq.; *bya-dgár* as a present, for a reward, *stér-ba* to give.

བྱ་རྒོད་ and རྒྱལ་ *bya-rgód* and *-rgyál* **bird of prey** *B.* and col.; *bya-rgod-spos Med.*, vulgo *la-da-ra* (v. *gla*) *bya-rgod-p̔úṅ-poi ri*, गृध्रकूट, vulture-hill, in Magadha, a preaching-place of Buddha.

བྱ་རྒྱ་ *bya-rgyá* **fowler's net.**

བྱ་སྒབ་ *bya-sgáb* n. of one of the smaller lobes of the lungs.

བྱ་སྙེན་ *bya-snyéṅ* v. *bya-rmyéṅ.*

བྱ་ཏྲི་ *bya-tri* v. *bya-kri.*

བྱ་ཐལ་ *bya-t̔ál Glr.* light-gray **bird's dung.**

བྱ་འདབ་ bya-ₒdáb 1. lit. **a bird's wing.** — 2. a part of the roof or vertical projection of the same, **a kind of façade**, admitting of pictorial decoration *Glr.*

བྱ་འདྲེ་ *bya-ₒdré Sch.*, a winged diabolical creature, **harpy.**

བྱ་ན་ *bya-na* (acc. to *Liš.* corrupted from व्यञ्जन) **seasoning, condiment, sauce,** in a legend; prob. also in **a** gen. sense: **meat, food,** *byá-nai yo-byád Lex.*, *byá-na-ma*, prob. id.; *ts̀á-ba byá-na-ma žig k̀yér-nas* bringing some warm food *Mil.*

བྱ་ནག་ *bya-nág* **raven,** or some similar bird *S.g.*; *bya-nag-rdó-rje Mil.* id., because the raven is said to reach an age of a thousand years.

བྱ་ནན་ *bya-nán Sch.* (sub. *byá-ra*) **earnest endeavour.**

བྱ་པ་ *byá-pa Cs.* **fowler, bird-catcher.**

བྱ་པོ་ *byá-po* 1. **cock,** the male of the domestic fowl, more definitely: *byá(-po) mts̀a-lu B.* and col.; *byá-po dáṅ-po, gnyis-pa* etc., the first, the second cock-crow *C.* — 2. **byá-po skyá-po** *W.* **sparrow.** — 3. *bya-po-tsi-tsi Med.*, a medicinal plant, stopping the monthly courses; in *Lh.* the great balsamine, Impatiens Roylei.

བྱ་སྤུ་ *byá-spu*, **down** (feather), *byai spu B.* and col.

བྱ་ཕོ་ *bya-p̀o*, **cock,** the male of any bird.

བྱ་ཕྲུག་ *bya-p̀rug* 1. **a young bird.** — 2. **a young fowl, chicken.**

བྱ་བ་ *byá-ba* 1. inf. and part. fut. of *byéd-pa*, q. v. — 2. sbst. **deed, action, work,** without any reference to time, *ₒjig-rtén-gyi byá-ba* and *čós-kyi byá-ba* secular and religious works, frq.; *mai byá-ba byéd-pa* to act as a mother, to perform a mother's part *Tar.*; *byá-ba zin-pa* an action completely past *Gram.*; *byá-ba maṅ yaṅ ₒbrás-bu čúṅ-ba* much labour and little fruit, much work and little profit *Tar.*; *der rgyál-po daṅ blón-po-rnams-kyi byá-ba byúṅ-ba yin* then the affairs of the kings and their officers, the concerns of the state and its functionaries, gained ground; also in an absolute sense *byá-ba* = **secularity, worldliness,** *byá-ba btáṅ-ba ǰig rgyún-du če* a resigning of worldly things is fraught with great blessing *Mil.*; *bya-byéd* the doing, doings: *bya-byed nyúṅ-ba ǰig rgyún-du če* the doing little brings great blessing, and so in a similar manner: *byá-rgyu byéd-rgyu ma maṅ ǰig* do not give way to a bustling disposition *Mil.*, i.e. do not permit your contemplative state to be interrupted by a distracting activity of your mind; *bstán-pa-la* (or *bstán-pai*) *byá-ba byás-pai lo-rgyús* an account of what has been done for the spread of the doctrine *Tar.*; *byá-ba daṅ ₒbrél-ba* seems to be a grammatical term relating to the verb.

བྱ་བང་ *bya-báṅ* v. *bya-wáṅ.*

བྱ་བལ་ *bya-bál Sch.* **down** (feathers); *Lt.* 121?

བྱ་བྲལ་བ་ *bya-brál-pa* one free from business, one that has renounced all worldly employment, **an ascetic,** *Ld.-Glr.*

བྱ་མ་ *byá-ma* **a female bird, hen, brood-hen.**

བྱ་མ་རྟ་ *byá-ma-rta* **courier, estafet.**

བྱ་མ་བུམ་ *bya-ma-búm* a tea-pot shaped vessel used in sacrificing.

བྱ་མ་བྱར་སྐྱག་ *bya-ma-byar-skyág* (?) **dandelion,** Taraxacum *Ld.*

བྱ་མ་བྱི་ *bya-ma-byi S.g.*; *Sch.* **flying squirrel.**

བྱ་མ་ལེབ་ *bya-ma-léb Sch.* **butterfly,** = *p̀yé-ma-léb.*

བྱ་མོ་ *byá-mo* 1. **the female** of any kind of birds. — 2. **hen, female fowl,** also in conjunction with *mts̀á-lu*, cf. *byá-po* (?).

བྱ་རྨྱང་བ་ *bya-rmyáṅ-ba Sch.*, *bya-rmyéṅ* (another reading *snyeṅ*) *byéd-pa*, **to yawn** *Mil.*

བྱ་དམར་ *bya-dmár* **flamingo** *Sch.*

བྱ་ཚང་ *bya-ts̀áṅ* **bird's nest.**

བྱ་ཚེ་རིང་ *bya-ts̀e-riṅ Sch.* **the white crane.**

བྱ་ཚོགས་ *bya-ts̀ógs* **a flight of birds.**

བྱ་རྫི་ *bya-rdzi* **one attending to poultry.**

བྱ་ཝང་ *bya-wáṅ S.g.; Sch.:* **night-hawk, goat-sucker,** caprimulgus; **bat.**

བྱ་བཞོན་ **bya-bžón** *Bal.* **egg.**

བྱ་ཟེ་ *bya-zé* **crest, tuft** (of feathers) of birds *Sch.*

བྱ་འུག་ *bya-ug* prob. **owl**; *Sch.* quail(?).

བྱ་ར་ *byá-ra Cs.*: 'heed, care, caution'. This word belonging to the language of the people and to later literature, is not so much an abstract, as a concrete noun, signifying **a watchman,** superintendent (chiefly by day, cf. *mél-ťse* night-watch); it denotes more particularly that individual of a community, who has to see to it, that the compulsory post-office duties be punctually performed, and that messages from the lord or magistrate of the place be duly dispatched and forwarded to their place of destination; in a more gen. sense *byá-ra byéd-pa Glr.*, *čó-če* *W.*, *ỵtoṅ-ba Mil.* c. *la*, **to give heed, to pay attention, to look sharp, not to lose sight of**; also, **to be on one's guard against, to take a thing seriously,** e.g. *nád-la* a disease *Lt.*; **ǰá-ra i-mig** (prop. *yid-mig*) **čo**, pay strict attention! *W.*

བྱ་རོག་ *bya-róg* **crow, raven,** mentioned in S.O. as an inveterate enemy of the *ug-pa* (owl).

བྱ་ལས་ *bya-lás,* **labour, work,** *zin-pa-méd-pai bya-lás* endless labours *Mil.*

བྱ་ལོ་པ་ *byá-lo-pa* 1. v. *lo.* — 2. *Sch.* 'keeping poultry'(?).

བྱ་སོ་མ་ *bya-so-ma Ts, Ld.* **bat.**

བྱག་(-པ་) *byág(-pa)* 1. *Cs.* **pliancy, nimbleness, agility of body**; *byag-mḱan* rope-dancer *Lex.* — 2. sometimes erron. for *ǰag* and *ǰág-pa.*

བྱང་ *byaṅ* 1. **north**; *byaṅ-p̓yógs* and prob. also *byáṅ-ḱa Mil.* id.; *byáṅ-gi, byaṅ-p̓yógs-kyi* northern; *byaṅ-ṅós* north side, northern brow or slope of a hill; also n. pr., *Glr.; byaṅ-ťáṅ* n. pr. the heaths or steppes in northern Tibet, more esp. those bordering in the west on *Ld.* — 2. **northern country,** coinciding with *byaṅ-ťáṅ: byáṅ-la bčúg-go* he was banished to the north country *Glr.; byáṅ-pa* a man from *Jaṅ-ťáṅ* — 3. the significations of *byaṅ-snyom-pa Sch.* **to tailor, to cut to a proper shape,** and of several other compounds, require a different etymology yet unknown. — 4. for *byáṅ-bu.*

བྱང་རྐྱང་ *byaṅ-rkyáṅ* **trowsers, small-clothes, breeches** *Mil.*

བྱང་ཁོག་ *byaṅ-ḱóg* 1. **the inside of the body,** *byaṅ-ḱog-stód* the upper part of the body, cavity of the chest, *byaṅ-ḱog-smád* lower part of the belly, abdomen, bowels *S.g.*; **ǰaṅ-ḱóg-la zug rag** I feel a pain in my bowels *W.* — 2. **rump**; opp. to *yan-lág* limbs *Lt.*

བྱང་ག་ *byáṅ-ga Lt.?*

བྱང་སྒྲ་མི་སྙན་ *byaṅ-sgra-mi-snyán* the northern continent of the ancient geography of India, v. *gliṅ.*

བྱང་ཆུབ་ *byaṅ-čúb,* **बोधि**, prop. wisdom; with the Buddhists **the highest perfection and holiness**, such as every Buddhist desires to obtain, which however to its full extent only the real Buddha himself possesses, v. *Köpp.* I, 425, 435; *byaṅ-čub-mčóg* id., frq.; *byaṅ-čub-mčóg-tu sems* (or resp. *ťugs*) *skyéd-pa* to create the thought of such holiness, to direct the mind to it *Dzl., Glr.*; *byaṅ-čub dód-pa* to aim at it, to be anxious to obtain it *Dzl.*; *lén-pa* to attain it; *byaṅ-čub-séms* the mind intent on and suited for it, universal charity; *snyiṅ-rǰe-byaṅ-čub-séms-kyis kun blaṅ-nas* submitting to every thing with a loving and charitable mind; *byaṅ-čub-séms-dpa,* **बोधिसत्त्व**, frq. with the addition of *sems-dpa-čen-po* the saint that has attained the highest station next to Buddha, merely for the welfare of men still tarrying in this world, designated Buddha, as it were; *Köp.* I, 422; *byaṅ-čub-séms-ma* fem. of it *Thgr.*; *byaṅ-čub-šiṅ,* **पिप्पल**, the bodhi-tree, holy fig-tree, ficus religiosa (not indica), emblem of mercy; *byaṅ-čub-snyiṅ-po* **बोधिमण्ड**, n. pr. = *rdo-rǰe-ydan.*

བྱང་རྡོ་ *byaṅ-rdo Cs.* **monument,** prop. inscription-stone.

བྱང་པ་ *byáṅ-pa* 1. v. *byaṅ.* — 2. *S.g.? byaṅ-pa-srin Sch.*: an insect.

བྱང་བ་ *byáṅ-ba*, pf. of *˳byáṅ-ba* q.v.; *byaṅ-séms* **a pure, holy mind** *Mil.*, prob. = *byaṅ-čub-séms.*

བྱང་བུ་ *byáṅ-bu*, བྱང་མ་ *byáṅ-ma* 1. **inscription, direction, label.** — 2. the **tablet** on which an inscription is written, *záṅs-kyi byáṅ-bu-la* (to write) on a copper plate or tablet *Glr.*; *yig-byáṅ*, *k'a-byáṅ*, resp. *žal-byaṅ*, = *byáṅ-bu* 1; *sgo-byáṅ* inscription over a door, *dur-byáṅ* on a sepulchre; *rtags-byáṅ* a mark on a thing *Cs.*; *brjed-byáṅ* list of marked luggage; *miṅ-byáṅ*, resp. *mtsan-byáṅ* list of names *Pth.*; *šog-byáṅ* cards *Sch.*; *byaṅ-rdó* a stone monument.

བྱད་ *byad* I. 1. *Cs.* **proportion, symmetry, beauty,** *dpe-byad Dzl.*, id.; *byád-čan* well-proportioned, fair, beautiful; *byad-méd* the contrary *Cs.* — 2. **face, countenance** *Lex.*; *byad spus k'éṅs-pa* a hairy face *Glr.*; *byád-kyi bkrags Thgy.*, *mdaṅs Lt.*, brightness, radiancy, beautiful complexion; *byad-bžin* face *Dzl.*, སྒྲ *Lex.*; *byad-yzúgs*, *Sch.*: stature, prob. more correctly: countenance and body *Dzl.* and elsewh. —

II. (*Cs.* also *byád-ma*) 1. **enemy.** — 2. **a wicked demon,** *byád-ma rmé-ša-čan Wdṅ.* — 3. also *byad-stem(s)*, *S.O.* and elsewh., **imprecation, malediction,** combined with sorcery, the name of an enemy being written on a slip of paper and hid in the ground, under various conjurations; *yžán-gyi byad*, *p'á-rol-poi byad-stéms* a malediction practised by another; *byád-du* or *stéms-su júg-pa*, prob. to curse a person with conjurations.

III. in compounds, *yo-byád*, *ča-byád* q.v. — IV. frq. for *byed.*

བྱན་ *byan* 1. *Ld.* frq. for *byá-na*, **jan čo-k'an, ján-ma** **cook.** — 2. v. the following.

བྱན་པོ་ *byán-po Cs.* **married man**; *Sch.*: a free man, one divorced from his wife; *byan-mo Cs.* **wife, spouse**; *Sch.*: 1. **a divorced woman.** — 2. **a whore.** Only this latter signification seems to be known among the common people, e.g. **ă-pe ján-mo**, as a vulgar abusive term; *byan-tsud-pa Sch.* 'to allure, entice, seduce'; these significations are, however, not sufficient to explain: *byán-moi byi-bor* (or *-por*) *raṅ byan tsud Lex.*, and: *séms-la raṅ byan tsud Mil.*

བྱབ་པ་ *byáb-pa* 1. **to clean, cleanse, wash, wipe,** *naṅ t'ams-čád-la* to clean the whole house *Domaṅ.* — 2. **to take up, to gather with both hands,** e.g. barley *C.*; *byab-zed Sch.* instrument for cleaning, brush; *byabs-k'rus Sch.* shower-bath.

བྱམས་པ་ *byáms-pa* 1. **kindness, love, affection,** *byáms-sems* id. — 2. **kind, loving, affectionate,** used of the love of parents to their children, of the beneficent to the needy, but not in the contrary order, nor of love to inanimate objects; *byáms-pái tiṅ-ṅe-˳dzin* the meditation of love, compassion, frq.; *mi kún-la byáms-šiṅ* being kind towards every body; *byáms-pai ynyen* kind, affectionate relations, frq.; *byáms-pa máṅ-na* when I have many well-wishers, patrons *Dom.*; *byáms-pa* as a n. pr., also *byáms-pa mgón-po* **Maitreya,** the Buddha of the future period of the world, who at present is enthroned in the Galdan heaven, and who is frequently represented in pictures, v. *Köpp.*; *byams-bžúgs* sitting like Maitreya, i.e. after European fashion on a chair, with his legs hanging down, opp. to *tub-bžúgs*, like Säkyathubpa; yet he is by no means uniformly represented in that posture.

བྱར་ *byar*, supine of *byéd-pa*; *byar-méd* 1. prop.: *non faciendum*, **not to be done.** — 2. sbst. **inactivity,** inaction in the specifically Buddhist sense, **apathy, indifference,** *byar-méd-kyi ṅáṅ-la ynás-par gyis Thgr.*

བྱས་པ་ *byás-pa*, pf. of *byéd-pa*; *byás-na* 'si feceris', 'sin feceris', after a preceding prohibitive *ma byed* also to be rendered by **else**; as sbst. 1. '*factor*'. 2. '*factus*': *byéd-pa byás-pa* a doer of deeds, as the first grade of holiness; *byás-pa šés-pa*, *yzó-ba Sch.* to keep in mind a thing done, to requite, to reward; *byas-čos Mil.*, also known in *C.*, seems to be a notion akin to our **conscience,** **jhe-čǘ záṅ-po, ṅém-pa** *C.*, **jhe-lé** id.

བྱི· *byi* 1. *Glr.*, *Pth.*, *byi byéd-pa* **to commit adultery** or **rape of females**, *byi-čád* punishment for it. — 2. v. *byi-ba*. — 3. *Pur.* **bi** **bird**, cf. *byiu*.

བྱི་དང་(ག་) *byi-táṅ(-ga)* **a medicine** *Med.*

བྱི་ཐུར· *byi-tur* or *dur*, 1. n. of an animal, inhabiting caves *S.g.*; *byi-dur-ma Sik.* **porcupine.** — 2. **spine** of a porcupine or a hedgehog *Sch.*

བྱི་དར· *byi-dár* a kind of silk stuff? *Wdk.*

བྱི་དུར· *byi-dúr* v. *byi-túr*.

བྱི་དོར· *byi-dór* **the wiping, cleaning;** *pyag-bdár žés-pa byi-dór-gyi las dei min* the word *pyag-bdár* denotes the act of cleaning *Lex.*; commonly *byi-dór byéd-pa* e.g. *gnás-su* to clean, to sweep a place *Dzl.*; spiritually; to cleanse one's thoughts *Mil.*; *byi-bdár byéd-pa Dzl.* **to dress, trim, decorate one's self, to make one's self smart.**

བྱི་པོ· *byi-po Sch.* **bosom.** — 2. *W.* **male-cat, tom-cat.**

བྱི་བ· *byi-ba* I. sbst. *B.* and *C.*; col. *C.* **ǰhi-tsi** *Ld.*, *Pur.* **bi-tse**, *Ld.*, *Lh.* **sa-bi-li(g)**, **rat, mouse,** and various other animals: *byi-ba-rkaṅ-riṅ Sch.* rabbit (?); *dṅúl-byi Sch.* white rabbit. — *byi-dkár Sch.* white hare. — *byi-kúṅ* mouse-hole. — *byi-rdo Sch.* rat's-bane, arsenic. — *byi-ldém* mouse-trap. — *byi-nág Sch.* fitchet, polecat. — *byi-prúg* young mouse. — *byi-brún Dzl.* mouse-dung. — *byi-blá* v. sub *byi-la*. — *byi-tsáṅ* mouse-nest, mouse-hole. — *byi-tsér* medicinal herb *Med.* — *byi-ₒdzín Cs.* mouse-trap; *byi-bzúṅ Lt.*, **bi-zúm** *W.*, etymol. id.; but applied to that troublesome plant, **the bur** (burdock), which is stuck into mouse-holes, to fasten in the skin of the mice. — *byi-loṅ* etym. blind-mouse *Sch.* mole. — II. vb.: *byi-ba byéd-pa Cs.*, = *byi byéd-pa* 1. **to mouse; to steal, to pilfer.** 2. **to commit adultery.** — III. pf. of *ₒbyi-ba* q. v.; *byi-ba spu*, *Sch.*, hair that has fallen off.

བྱི་བོ· *byi-bo Lex.*; *Sch.* **little child, infant,** = *byis-pa*.

བྱི་བཞིན· *byi-bžin* n. of one of the lunar mansions, v. *rgyu-skár*.

བྱི་ཟེ· *byi-zé Cs.* = *tabs*, **manner, way, method.**

བྱི་རུ· *byi-ru* **coral**, frq., also *byú-ru*; *byi-ru mdog* light red *Glr.*

བྱི་རུག· *byi-rúg* medicinal plant *Med.*

བྱི་ལ· *byi-la*, *B.*, *W.* **bi-la*, *bi-li** (*Hind.* **billā**), **cat;** *byi-lai brun*, cat's dung *Lt.*; *byi-bla Wdk.* id.? In the latter work it is mentioned as the name of a certain monster, whilst *byi-blai rgyal-mtsán* is an attribute of the gods, resembling a flag with a cat's head at the top.

བྱི་ལམ· *byi-lám Wdk.?*

བྱི་ཤང· *byi-šáṅ Wdk.?*

བྱིང་བ· *byiṅ-ba* v. *ₒbyiṅ-ba*.

བྱིང་བྱིང་ཐུ་ལུ· *byiṅ-byiṅ-tú-lu S.g.* n. of an animal (?).

བྱིངས་པ· *byiṅs-pa* 1. *Cs.* **general, common.** — 2. *Sch.* **hidden, concealed.** — 3. *Cs.* **root.** The word seems to be a secondary form of *spyi* and *dbyiṅs*, yet in various passages of medical works none of the above meanings is applicable.

བྱིན· *byin* 1. **pomp, splendour, magnificence,** e.g. of kings; *byin-čé-bar bžúgs-pa* to be enthroned in great splendour *Dzl.*; *gzi-brǰid daṅ byin če Dzl. mtu daṅ byin Dzl.*; *byin-čan* magnificent, splendid, brilliant, *byin-méd* the contrary. — 2. **blessing,** a bestowing of blessings, a power working for good, *byin-báb Lex.*, *-páb Sch.*: conferring blessings (?), *bčom-ldan-ₒdás-kyi byin-gyis* by the blessing, the miraculous power of Buddha; yet also applied to devils, v. below; most frq. *byin-gyis rlób-pa*, pf. *brlabs*, ft. *brlab*, imp. *rlobs*, **to bless,** *mi* a person, *sa-gzi* a place *Mil.*, also followed by the termin.: *séms-čan-gyi sdug-bsṅál ži-bar byiṅ-gyis rlobs* grant thy blessing, that the misery of beings may be assuaged *Mil.*; *bu mtun-rkyén ₒdzóm-bar byin-gyis rlobs* bless the son, that all happiness may be accumulated on him *Mil.*; *rgyud gnyén-po bzáṅ-bar* bless my soul, that it may be an efficient help (to these people) *Mil.*; relative to devils: *log-*

ₒdrén bdúd-kyis byin-gyis brlabs heretical teachers sent and fitted out by the devil; so also *Tar.* 46, 13; **to create, to change into** *Mil., Tar.*; hence *byiṅ-rlabs* blessing, *byin-rlabs byéd-pa*, resp. *mdzád-pa* frq., *ɣtóṅ-ba*, resp. *stsól-ba Cs.*, = *byiṅ-gyis rlób-pa*; *byin-rlabs-čan, byin-rlabs daṅ ldán-pa* blessed, sanctified, highly favoured, men or things *Pth.*; so also *byin-rlabs žúgs-pa Mil.*; *ₒdre-ₒdul byin-rlabs* blessing pronounced against demons, exorcism of devils *Mil.*; meton.: I am the *ₒṗágs-pai byin-rlabs* of all of you, he who will help you to go to heaven *Glr.*

བྱིན་རྟེན་ *byin-rtén Cs.*, the **relics** of a saint, or the place where they are kept ('depository of blessings'); also in the shape of pills, which liberal donors receive from their Lamas, and which they swallow, particularly in the hour of death.

བྱིན་པ་ *byin-pa* I. sbst. **calf of the leg,** *byin-pa ná-ba* pain in the calf; *byin-súl Cs.* 'hollow on the inward side of the thigh'(?). — II. pf. of *sbyin-pa*.

བྱིན་པོ་ *byin-po Sch.* **all, the whole; general;** *byin-gyis ṗrá-ba* by degrees, more and more fine etc.?

བྱིན་རླབས་ *byin-rlabs* v. *byin* 2.

བྱིབ་པ་ *byib-pa*, pf. *byibs* 1. **to cover, to wrap up,** *gós-kyis Lt.* — 2. *Cs.* **to hide, conceal, keep secret, hush up.**

བྱིའུ་ *byiu* 1. *Pur.* **biu**, **little bird, bird** *S.g.* — 2. *Sch.* **alpine hare.**

བྱིལ་བ་ *byil-ba* **to stroke,** *mgó-bo-la byil-byil byéd-pa* to stroke a person's head *Pth.*

བྱིལ་མོ་ *byil-mo* **naked** *Sch.*

བྱིས་པ་ *byis-pa* 1. **child,** esp. **little child;** *byis-(pai) nad* disease of children *Med.*; *byis-pa btsá-ṫabs* obstetric science *Med.*; *byis-stón* v. *ná-zla* sub *na* I, 2; *byis-pai blo Cs.* childishness, want of judgment; *byis-pai skyé-bo* **a plain, ignorant person,** a person not initiated *Thgy., S.O.*; *mo-byis* girl, lass *Mil.*; *byis-pa-zúṅ-žig Cs.*, twins. — 2. **boy, lad,** till about the age of 16 years, frq. (*W.* not in use).

བྱུ་རུ་ *byú-ru* = *byi-ru*.

བྱུག་པ་ *byúg-pa* 1. **unguent, ointment, salve,** whether as colouring-matter, medicine or sweet scent *Dzl., Med.*; *byúg-pa ska* thick ointment, thick plaster; *byúg-pa sla* thin unguent *Cs.* — 2. **foot-bath** *W.*, perh. better: *bčúg-pa*.

བྱུག་རིས་ *byug-ris*, *Lex.* = *gral*, **place,** in a certain succession or row; *byug-ris žog* make room, leave a place empty *Sch.*

བྱུགས་ *byugs* v. *ₒbyúg-pa*; *byugs-spos* **anointing-oil** *Sch.*

བྱུང་ *byuṅ* v. *ₒbyuṅ-ba*; *byúṅ-ṫsul* **history, story, particulars** of any event, *ṅai byúṅ-ṫsul dé-ltar ɣda* that is my story *Mil.*; *byuṅ-rábs Sch.* id.

བྱུར་ *byur B.*, esp. of later times and col., *Ld.* also *byus*, **misfortune, mishap, accident,** *byur čé-žiṅ bu mi ɣsós-na* if one has the great misfortune not to be able to keep a child alive *Dom.*; *mi-la byur ₒgél-ba* to draw down misfortune on a person *Dom.*; **ṅá-la ǰur čug soṅ** *W.*, **ǰhur** *C.*, I have had misfortune, I have been unfortunate; *byúr-gyi*, also *byúr-čan* unlucky, disastrous, perilous. — **ǰhur-nág** great calamity *C.* — *byur-sél* preservative against misfortune. — *raṅ-byur-rdó* was explained: a sling-stone with which one hits one's self.

བྱུར་པོ་ *byúr-po*, *Cs.* also *-bu*, vulg. *byur-byúr* **heaped,** a heaped measure of corn or meal; *byúr-por bkaṅ Thgy.*

བྱེ་ *bye* 1. = *byeu* **little bird,** *bye-gliṅ* bird's nest *Ma.*; *bye-ṗrúg* a young little bird *Dzl.*, also *bya-prúg*; *bye-brún* bird-dung *Wdṅ.*; *byeu ₒúr-pa Sch.* **partridge.** — 2. v. *byé-ma*.

བྱེ་མགོ་ *bye-mgó* 1. **bird's head.** — 2. **an officinal mineral** *S.g.*

བྱེ་བ་ *bye-ba* **ten million,** *byé-ba-ṗrag ɣsum daṅ sá-ya-ṗrag drug* thirty-six million; *byé-ba sa-ya*, eleven million; it seems to be among the larger numbers one of the most popular, as the word million is in English.

བྱེ་བྲག་ *bye-brág*, **विशेष**. 1. **difference, diversity,** *ḱó-bo daṅ saṅs-rgyás bye-brág či yod* what difference is there between me and Buddha? *Dzl.*; *bye-brág ₒbyéd-pa* to find, to show a difference, c. genit. in, of, between things; to analyze, to explain; variety, diversity *Was.* (266); *bye-brág bšád-pa* = *vibhāshā Was.* (147), also *bye-brag-bšad-mtsó* or *-ču-ytér*, title of books; *byé-brag-čan Cs.* different, *bye-brag-méd-pa Cs.*, *mi-pyéd-pa Dzl.* equal; *bye-brág-tu smrá-ba Thgy.*, *bye-brág-pa*, वैशेषिक, name of a school of philosophers, Atomists *Köpp.* I, 69. — 2. **division, section, class, species,** *dúd-*₀*groi*, *ról-moi bye-brag* a species of animals, a kind of musical instrument etc. *Lex.*; *yúl-gyi bye-brág* a part of the country, province, *Tar.* 33, 6; *bye-brág-tu* (to go through) according to the separate classes *Zam.*

བྱེ་མ་ *byé-ma* (*C.* **jhé-ma**, *W.* **bé-ma**) 1. **sand,** frq. — 2. **sandy plain, sands,** *ysér-gyi byé-mai dkyíl-na* in the middle of a plain of gold sand *Glr.* — 3. **gravel** (disease) *Schr.* — *byé-ma* ₀*bru yčig* a grain of sand *Cs.*; *gáṅ-pai klúṅ-gi byé-ma tsam* as much sand as there is on the Ganges; *bye-ma-ká-ra* brown sugar, ground sugar, *Hind.* चीनी, *C.* — *bye-dkár* white sand, *bye-nág* black sand. — *bye-čáb Lt.* sandy water, water standing on sandy ground. — *bye-ljóṅs* a sandy tract *Cs.* — *bye-táṅ* a plain of sand, a sandy desert *Glr.* — *bye-púṅ* heap of sand. — *bye-tsúb* sand raised by a whirlwind. — *bye-ríl* (*Schr. hril*), small sugar-balls, Indian sweet-meat, imported into Tibet, *C.*

བྱེད་པ་ *byéd-pa* I. vb., pf. *byas*, fut. *bya*, imp. *byos*, vulgo *byas* (*Sp.*, *Bal.* **béd-pa**; in *Ld.* and *Lh.* instead of it gen. **čó-če**), resp. *mdzád-pa*, eleg. *bgyíd-pa*, 1. **to make, to fabricate,** with the acc., e.g. a house, an armour etc.; with *las* or *la*, to make out of or of: *ysér-las* out of gold, *šín-la Tar.* 160, 11 of wood; with the acc. and termin. to form to, to work into, *págs-pa šog-šog-tu* to work or manufacture skin into parchment *Dzl.*; with the instrum.: to do with, to make of: ₀*dis či žig bya* what are you going to do with it, to make of it? *Dzl.* **to cause, to effect:** *lhúṅ-ba de ṅas byás-pa yin Mil.* it was I that caused this falling; with the supine, **to take care that:** *byéd-par* ₀*dod-par byéd-pa* to make him inclined to do it *Dzl.*, *ma šór-bar byos šig Pth.* take care, that he do not escape; *yód-par byéd-pa* **to produce, procure, provide,** *dei ynás-kaṅ-la sógs-pa byás-nas* he provided for him a dwelling with appurtenances *Dzl.*; to fit out, equip (a ship) *Glr.*; **to act:** *rgyál-po, draṅ-sróṅ* etc. *byéd-pa* to act a king, a saint, as much as: to rule as a king, to live as a saint *Dzl.*, *blá-ma byéd-pa* to be a priest *C.*; in a gen. sense: **to do:** *byá-ba daṅ bya-ba-ma-yin-pa stón-pa* to teach what men ought to do and what they ought not to do *Thgy.*; **to commit, perform, execute:** *nyés-pa byed-byéd-pa* one that has repeatedly committed himself, *las* or *byá-ba byéd-pa* to perform an action, *las či žig byed* what are you doing, what is your business? *tabs yód-de byéd-mkan med* there is an expedient, but no one that carries it into effect *Ma*; *mi byar mi rúṅ-bas* as it must be performed, lit. as it cannot remain undone *Dzl.*; *bsám-pa ltar myúr-du byás-na* if an intention is speedily executed, performed; *las byéd-pa* **to work, to be efficient** (of a medicine); **to act, proceed, pretend, affect:** *či ltar byás-na legs* how proceeding is good? i.e. which is the best way to proceed, how shall I manage best? *Glr.*; *bsám-ytan-la yód-pai lugs byas* he pretended, affected to meditate *Glr.*; *dei lúgs-su byao* I will act as he does, I will do like that man *Glr.*; *gá-le byéd-pa Mil.* to proceed slowly, to be slow; **to take, to assume, to count:** *žag bži-pa dáṅ-por byás-na* if the fourth day be taken for (counted as) the first *Wdn.*; *byéd-pa* with the termin. of the inf. is frequently used periphrastically or to give force to other verbs; such forms are: *ysód-par byéd-pa* to kill, *pa-más šés-par byos* (or *gyis*) *šig*, resp. *yab-yum-gyis mkyen-par mdzod čig* dear parents, you must know! *Dzl.*; on the other hand: *pá-la ríg-par gyis šig* let your father know about it *Tar.* 37, 7; in such cases the proper sense is merely to be gathered from the context. Besides the simple fut.: ₀*dúg-par byao* I shall remain *Tar.*, *kó-mo grogs byá-*

yis as I shall be with you *Glr.*; — the form *byao* frq. serves to express necessity: *btsál-bar bya* I must seek *Dzl.*; esp. with a negation: *brjód-par mi byao* they are by no means to be pronounced; the participles in the short forms of *ytoṅ-byéd* and *ytoṅ-byá* differ, in as much as the former is used in an active sense, e.g. one giving, a giver, the latter in a passive sense, one to be given; they may be formed of any verb. For specific combinations, in which *byéd-pa* is differently to be translated, as *dpe byéd-pa*, *yid-la byéd-pa* etc., refer to these words. — 2. **to say, to call**, yet chiefly only in the pf. tense: *žes byás-pa Dzl.* thus said, so called; *sṅar byás-pa bžin* according to what has been said before *Dzl.*; *byas-kyaṅ* though saying *Pth.* — and in the fut., which in that case, however, frq. stands for the present: (*žes*) *byá-bai sgra byúṅ-no* a voice thus speaking was heard *Glr.*; *dé-la dbyaṅs šes byao* these are called vowels *Gram.*; (*žes-*) *byás-pa*, or more frq. *byá-ba*, the so called, being often joined to a name, that is mentioned for the first time, e.g. Anu, the so called, whilst we should say, a man, called Anu, or of the name of A.; *byá-ba* also implies: of the purport, to the effect, just as *čés-pa* is also used: '*tsol-žig*' *byá-bai luṅ byúṅ-nas* an order being given to make a search *Glr.* — 3. **to go away, to disappear:** *byas soṅ* he disappeared *Glr.* —

II. sbst. 1. *byéd-pa* and *byéd-mḱan*, the person that does or has done a thing, **the doer, performer** etc.; **author**, *bstan-bčós byéd-mḱan* the author of the work *Tar.* — 2. *byéd-pa* **the instrumentative case** *Gram.* — 3. *byéd-pa* **the doing, dealings**, with noun in the instrum. case: *dé-ₒdra-ba mi-rigs-pa rgyál-pos byéd-pa* such wrong being done by the king, such unjust dealings of the king *Dzl.*; in the genit. case: *bló-yi byéd-pa dbyíṅs-su sbos* hide the working of your understanding in the heavens, i.e. let it disappear in nothingness; **effect**, also with the noun in the genit. case, *Wdṅ.* — 4. *byéd (-pa)-po*, **doer, accomplisher** etc., *mčód-sbyin byéd-pa-por bos* he invited him as sacrificing priest *Tar.*; *ₒdúl-bar byéd-pa-po* converter *Tar.*; *bkra-šis spél-bai byéd-po* augmenter of eternal happiness (from a hymn); *byéd-pa-po* **instrumentative case** *Gram.*; as the twelve *byéd-pa-poi skye-mčéd* I here cite the following from *Wdk.*, without being able to offer an explanation: *bdag*, *séms-čan*, *srog*, *ₒgró-ba*, *ysó-ba*, *skyés-bu*, *gaṅ-zág*, *šéd-čan*, *šed-bdág*, *byéd-pa-po*, *tsór-ba-po*, *šés-pa-po*, *mtóṅ-ba-po*, where, by the by, it is to be observed, that thirteen are here enumerated, *byed-pa-po* being mentioned again with the rest (a want of accuracy, which is not unfrequently to be met with in the scientific works of the Tibetans). — 5. *byá-ba* q. v.

བྱེའུ་ *byeu* (also *byiu* q.v.) **little bird**; *byeu-zúl byéd-pa* v. *zul*; *byeu-la-jug S.g.*, a medicinal herb *Cs.*

བྱེར་བ་ *byér-ba* v. *ₒbyér-ba*.

བྱེས་ *byes*, *Lexx.* and col.; **foreign country; abroad,** *byes tag-riṅ-ba* a far distant country *Cs.*; *byés-su ₒgró-ba* to go abroad, to travel; *byés-su ₒdég-pa* to remove, to emigrate *Lex.*; *byés-nas sléb-pa* to come from abroad *Lex.*; *byés-pa* traveller, foreigner, stranger; **lam-róg bés-pa yód-pa yin-te** *W.* proceeding together as fellow-travellers.

བྱོ་བ་ *byó-ba Cs.* *rná-ba byó-ba* **to hear, hearken, listen.**

བྱོན་པ་ *byón-pa* v. *ₒbyón-pa*.

བྱོལ་བ་ *byól-ba* v. *ₒbyól-ba*.

བྱོལ་སོང་ *byol-sóṅ* **animal**, esp. **quadruped;** *byol-sóṅ-bas glén-pa* more stupid than a brute *Mil.*; *byol-sóṅ rgyál-po* the lion *Mil.*

བྲ་ཀ་ *brá-ka* v. *ṭá-ka*.

བྲ་ཉེ་ *bra-nyé*, n. of a lunar mansion, v. *rgyu-skár* 2.

བྲ་བ་ *brá-ba*, 1. sbst., n. of a small **rodent,** living under ground (not mole *Cs.*, but rather **suslik, earless marmot** *Sch.*); *brá-pu-se Ld.* a similar animal (= *pra-li*?); *bra-mḱár*, *bra-tsáṅ Cs.*, burrow of it; *bra-brúṅ*

Lex., *bra-ríl Cs.*, dung of it; *bra-lpágs* skin of it. — 2. vb. **to have** or **to be in great plenty, to abound** (?), *ráṅ-gis za ma bra, btuṅ ma bra, gon ma bra* she allowed herself no abundance of food, drink, or clothing; **za-, tuṅ-, č̔in-, lab-, zér-ḍha-te** eating, drinking plentifully, walking, speaking, talking a great deal *C.*; **ts̔a-, ḍho-, ḍháṅ-ḍha-te** being very hot, warm, cold *C.*

བྲ་བོ *brá-bo* (prov. **brau**, *Pur.* **bro**) **buck-wheat**; *bra-p̔yé Lex.*, *rǰen Sch.* buck-wheat flour; *brá-sóg* buck-wheat straw, serving as a poor sort of fodder during winter.

བྲག *brag* **rock**, *brag rtse-γsúm-pa* a three-pointed rock; *brag-skéd* the middle height of a rock, opp. to *brag-mǰug* and *rtse* its foot and top *Cs.* — *brag-spós* prob. an aromatic herb, used for incense *Lt.* — *brag-skíbs* beetling rock. — *brag-rgyál* a prominent, high and precipitous rock, towering rock. — *brág-ča, -č̔a* echo; also fig. for something unsubstantial, shadowy, not existing *Mil.* — *brag-mǰúg* foot of a rock *Cs.* — *brag-p̔ug* rock-cavern. — *brag-p̔ye* dust produced by hewing stones *Glr.* — **ḍhag-bhóṅ** = *p̔a-bóṅ C.* — *brag-dmár* name of a rock in or near Lhasa, alledged not to be identic with *dmar-po-ri* (*Sch.*). — **ḍag-tsél-wa, ḍag-śig-pa** mite, tick *W.* — *brag-rtsáṅ* rock-lizard. — *brag-rtsé* top of a rock. — *brag-žún* mineral pitch, bitumen, is said to cure fevers and even fractures. — *brag-rí* rocky hill. — *brag-rúd* fall of a rock. — *brag-róṅ* chasm in a rock, ravine. — *brag-śig* v. *brag-rtsél-ba*.

བྲང *braṅ* 1. resp. *sku-bráṅ* **chest, breast,** (cf. *nú-ma*); *braṅ rdúṅ-ba* to beat one's breast *Glr.*; **ṭ̔ú-gu ḍáṅ-la čír-te k̔yér-če** *W.* to carry a child pressed against one's breast. — *braṅ-kyéd* (?) *Cs.* a high, prominent chest. — *braṅ-dkyil* middle of the breast, cardiac region. — *braṅ-lkóg Mil.* prob. = *lkóg-ma*. — *braṅ-skás Sch.* the dorsal vertebrae opposite to the chest. — **ḍaṅ-kúd** **string** of the *braṅ-k̔úṅ* (*-guṅ, -k̔oṅ, -goṅ*), **pellet-bow,** a bow furnished with two strings, to shoot pellets or small stones, *braṅ-rdi* or *-rdeu*, with it *W.* — **ḍhan-k̔óg** *C.* cardiac-region, pit of the stomach. — *braṅ-sgró* snake, serpent (like *lto-ₒgró*). — *braṅ-búr* the middle convex part of the *rdó-rǰe Ma.* — *braṅ-tsig Lh.*, prob. heart-burning. — *braṅ-(γ)žól Cs.* dew-lap. — *braṅ-ze Mil.* prob. breast-bone, sternum. — *braṅ-γyúṅ Sch.* tame, gentle. — *braṅ-rus Med.* breast-bone. — **ḍaṅ-lág** *W.* the hands crossed on the breast. — *braṅ-so Glr.* breast, brisket of a butchered animal. — 2. also *ₒbraṅ*, gen. *ₒbráṅ-sa*, eleg. *mč̔is-bráṅ* (q.v.), resp. *γzim-bráṅ, bžugs-bráṅ* **night-quarters, halting-place,** whether under a roof or in the open air; also as much as **stage** (of a journey); *bráṅ-sa ₒdébs-pa Tar.*, prob. also **bór-če** *W.*, to take up night-quarters; **dwelling,** particularly a temporary one, **lodgings;** but also a permanent **abode,** esp. in *W.*; **ḍáṅ-sa táṅ-če, yár-ce** to take in, to lodge a person over night *W.* (cf. *γnas* 2). — *bráṅ-k̔aṅ*, dwelling-house, dwelling-room *Pth.* — *braṅ-grógs* house-mate, bed-fellow. — *braṅ-dpón* master of the house, landlord. — *p̔o-bráṅ* v. *p̔o*; *bla-bráṅ* v. *bla*.

བྲང་ངེ *braṅ-ṅé Lex.* = *kraṅ-ṅé*.

བྲང་པ *bráṅ-pa* v. *ₒbráṅ-pa*.

བྲན *bran* 1. **slave, servant,** *mi-bráṅ* 'vir servus' *S.g.*; *bran byéd-pa* to be a servant, to serve *Cs.*; *brán-du ₒgyúr-ba* to become a servant *Cs.*; *brán-du ₒk̔ól-ba* to make another be a servant, to use him as a servant *B.*; *brán-du skúl-ba* to engage a person as a servant, to get him to work for one's self *Glr.*; *brán-du k̔as-bláṅs-so Pth.* they promised to serve him; *lus ṅag yid γsum brán-du p̔úl-te* devoting heart, mouth, and body to his service *Pth.*; *naṅ nub lto-gós-kyis brán-du k̔ol* morning and night I am a slave to food and clothing *Mil.*; **subject,** one owing allegiance, **la-dágs-si gyál-po-la ḍán-yul-ts̔o** a village subject to, belonging to, the king of Ladak *W.*; *brán-p̔o* servant, slave *Tar.*; *brán-mo* maid-servant, female slave; *bran-k̔ól, bran-γyóg* = *bran*; also collectively, servants, domestics, household. — 2. **texture,** in the compound *tags-brán byéd-pa* to weave *Mil.*; *nye-brán Mil.* seems to be some decoration of the shoes; *sño-brán Mil.* something similar. — *ču-brán Glr.*, and *mtso-brán??*

བྲན་པ་ *bran-pa* **to pour out** *Tar.*

བྲན་མོ་ *brán-mo* 1. v. *bran* 1. extr. — 2. also = **ḍan-tsós* W.* **finger, toe.**

བྲབ་པ་ *bráb-pa* v. *˳bráb-pa.*

བྲམ་ཟེ་ *brám-ze*, from ब्राह्मण् 1. **Brahmin,** Hindoo priest; *brám-ze-mo* female Brahmin; *brám-ze rig-byéd ˳dón-pai sgra* the voice of a Brahmin reciting the Vedas, being taken as a sign of good luck; *brámze-pa* an adherent of Brahma. — 2. **a priest** in general *S.O.* (Acc. to *Fouc.* transl. of *Gyatch.* 13 and 52 also = *brāhmaṇa*, the theological part of the Vedas; this is however against the tenor of the Tibetan text, which requires the word to be taken in the former sense.)

བྲལ་ *bral* v. *˳brál-ba.*

བྲི་ *bri* v. *˳brí-ba.*

བྲིད་པ་ *bríd-pa* 1. *Sch.* '**to continue, to reiterate, to repeat continually**; *bríd-la ytón-ba* to give again and again'. — 2. v. *˳bríd-pa.*

བྲིད་བྲིད་པ་ *brid-brid-pa Sch.* **to float,** to move confusedly, before one's eyes.

བྲིད་རྩ་ *brid-rtsa Lt.?*

བྲིམ(ས)་ *brim(s)* v. *˳brim-pa.*

བྲིས་ *bris* v. *˳brí-ba*; *bris-sku, sku-bris* **picture of a saint,** drawn or painted *Cs.* — *bris-˳búr* the art of painting and carving images. — *bris-ma* written book. — *nag-bris* a drawing *Cs.*; *tson-bris* a coloured picture.

བྲུ་བ་ *brú-ba* v. *˳brú-ba.*

བྲུ་བ་ཚ་ *bru-ba-tsá Lex.* **hunger.**

བྲུ་ཞ་ or བྲུ་ཤ་ *bru-žá* or *bru-šá Wdk.*, prob. = *gru-žá* and *gru-šá Pth.*, *˳bru-šál* or *˳bru-šál Ld.-Glr. Schl.* 19, b. 21, a. name of a country to the west of Tibet, bordering on Persia.

བྲུག་པ་ *brúg-pa* **to flow, to stream, to gush** *Cs.*; sbst. **current, flow, flux** *Cs.*; *ču brúg-pa* flowing-water *Lex.*

བྲུན་ *brun* **dirt, dung, excrements,** *mi-brún, bya-brún, sbrañ-brún* etc. feces of men, birds, flies etc. *Med.* and elsewh.

བྲུབ་པ་, བྲུབས་པ་ *brúb-pa, brúbs-pa* v. *˳brub-pa.*

བྲུལ་ *brul* **small particles, fritters, bits, crumbs,** *bag-brul C.* crumbs of bread; *brúl-ba Mil., C.* **to fall,** into an abyss *Thg.*; to fall off, fall out, fall down, of leaves, seeds etc.; *brúl-bu, brúl-lu* = *brul W.*

བྲུས་ *brus* v. *˳brú-ba.*

བྲེ་ *bre*, **ḍe**, *Sskr.* द्रोण, 1. a measure for dry things as well fluids, about 4 pints; acc. to *Cs:* $\frac{1}{20}$ of a *˳bo*; *bré-bo če, breu čún* large and small *bre, Cs.*; *ysér-pyę bre gañ Glr.* one (small) measure of gold-dust; *bre-do* two measures; *bré-la yšoñ* that will just fill a *bre Zam.*; *bres bšar-ba* to measure with a *bre Lex.*; *lha-kañ bre-tsad tsam žig* a miniature temple, not larger than a *bre Glr.*; vulgo also that part of the *Chod-rten*, which has the shape of a corn-measure; in a general sense, **measure,** *bre-sráñ ytán-la ˳bébs-pa Glr.* to regulate measures and weights. — 2. **bre* Ld. Lh.* **bre-sé* Kun.* Eremurus spectabilis, a plant of about a man's height, belonging to the asphodels. — 3. v. *bré-ba.*

བྲེ་ཀོ་ *bré-ko* **basin for washing** *C.*

བྲེ་ག་ *bré-ga* **medicinal herb**; *bré-gu*, id. (perh. the same plant) *Med.*

བྲེ་བ་ *bré-ba* v. *˳bre-ba*; *bla-bré, ka-bré Sch.* **capital, chapiter,** upper part of a column or pillar.

བྲེ་མོ་ *bré-mo Sch.* **unfit, useless, worthless;** *bré-moi ytam Thgy.*

བྲེགས་པ་ *brégs-pa* v. *˳brég-pa.*

བྲེང་བ་ *bréñ-ba* v. *˳bréñ-ba.*

བྲེད་པ་ *bréd-pa* **to be frightened, afraid, in fear** = *rtáb-pa*, *B.* and *C.*; *sbrúl-gyis dñañs-šiñ bréd-pa* to be frightened by a snake *Wdñ.*, or *bréd-čiñ dñáñs-pa Pth.*;

bdúd-kyis bréd-na if you are afraid of the devil *Glr.; bred-ˌtoms Lex.*; **ḍhé-po** fearful, frightful, terrible *C.*

བྲེལ་བ་ *brél-ba* I. vb. (not the same as *ˌbrél-ba*) 1. **to be employed, busy, engaged, to have business** or **work on hand**, *ṅed mkár-las-kyis brel-nas loṅ mi ˌdug* being engaged in building, we have no time to spare *Mil.; ˌdod kó-nas brél-na* if one is entirely taken up with lust and pleasure; **dhe-riṅ ṅá-la ḍhél-wa yọ', saṅ-nyin šog** to-day I have a great deal to do, come to-morrow *C.; brél-bas* on account of much business *Dzl.* — 2. synon. with *póṅs-pa* **to be poor, to be without, wanting, destitute of,** c. instrum.: *loṅs-spyod-kyis brél-ba Dzl.* ༢༣༠,7; more frq. with a negative: *čis kyaṅ mi brél-bar byás-so* they did not let him want anything *Dzl.* ༢༣༠,17, *Sch.; ˌtsó-bai yo-byád-kyis mi brél-bar* abounding in every necessary of life *Dzl.* ༢༦༦,3 (acc. to a better reading); combined with another word: *póṅs-brel-te; brel-poṅ-méd-čiṅ Dzl., mi brel-bar* not sparingly, scantily, niggardly, e.g. to bestow *Dzl.* frq. — II. sbst. 1. *C.* and *B.*, a being engaged in a **multiplicity of business** v. I, 1. — 2. *W.*: **business, affair, concern,** **ṅá-la ḍél-wa žig yod** I have some particular business, concern, suit; **ḍél-wa či yod** what do you want, what are you about, what are you doing there?

བྲེས་ *bres* 1., *W.* also *brés-kyu* **manger**; *rta-brés* manger for horses. — 2. v. *bre.* — 3. v. *ˌbré-ba.*

བྲོ་ *bro* 1. **oath,** *bro -tsál-ba* to take an oath (?) *Pth., bro ˌbór-ba* id., *dbu-bsnyuṅ daṅ bro bór-ro Glr.* they swore by their heads, nif. — 2. **dance,** *bro skráb-pa Lex., kráb-pa Mil., brdúṅ-ba Glr.*, resp. *žabs-bró mdzád-pa Mil.* to dance, leap, gambol, as a manifestation of gladness and mirth, whilst *gar byéd-pa* is a regular kind of dancing, with gentle and waving motions of the body; *ṙṅa-bró* drums and dancing *Glr.; bró-mkan Cs.* dancer. — 3. *Pur. bro* v. *brá-bo.* — 4. v. *bró-ba.* — 5. *bro-nád Lex., Mil.* and elsewh.; *Sch.* 'an epidemic disease'; *bro-ˌtsál Sch.* **'cold (in the head), cough, catarrh;'** *Tar.: págs-pa lo maṅ-por sku-bro ˌtsal-te; Mil.: šin-tu bro-ˌtsál-bar gyúr-nas.*

བྲོ་བ་ *bró-ba*, I. vb. 1. **to taste, to smell,** vb. a. & n.; *ynyid kyaṅ mi bró-bas,* not even enjoying (tasting) sleep *Dzl.; ká-ro skyá-ba bro* one has an astringent taste in the mouth *Med.; spos bro-o* it smells of incense *Dzl.; dri-ysúṅ žim-pa bro-o* it has a pleasant smell *Dzl.* — 2. *C.* **to desire, to wish,** = *ˌdód-pa, bló-bro-ba* id.; *ṅu bró-ste* being about to weep *Mil.* — II. sbst. **taste, savour, flavour,** col. *bro-blág* (**ḍob-lág**), *lán-tsa ka-zás kún-gyi bró-ba skyed* salt imparts flavour to any kind of food *S.g.; bro ltá-ba* or *myoṅ-ba,* col. **ḍob-lag nyaṅ-če* W.* to taste, to savour; to try the taste; *bró-ba-čan Cs., *ḍób-lag-čan* W.* savoury, pleasing to the organs of taste, exciting the appetite; *bro-(ba-)med* tasteless, insipid *Cs.*

བྲོ་མ་ *bró-ma* v. *gró-ma.*

བྲོག་ཞུ་ *bróg-žu* v. *próg-žu.*

བྲོད་ *brod*, = *bró-ba*, **taste** (*žim-po*) **ḍhọ'-čẹn* C., *ḍód-čan* W.,* well-tasted, savoury; **ḍhọ' čém-po* C.* of a strong, powerful taste.

བྲོད་པ་ *bród-pa* **joy, joyfulness,** *bród-pa skyéd-pa Mil.; dga-bród* id. *C.; či-bród* readiness to die *Mil.* — Here may be quoted also *drod* 2 and 3.

བྲོབ་, བྲོལ་ *brob, brol* v. *ˌbráb-pa, ˌbrál-ba.*

བྲོས་ *bros* 1. v. *bro* 5; *bros-tebs Sch.* — 2. v. *ˌbros-pa.*

བླ་ *bla* I. the space **over, above** a thing, chiefly occurring in compounds; *blá-na* above *Lex.; bla-na-méd-pa,* अनुत्तर, having nothing higher over it, the upper-most, the very highest, e.g. *byaṅ-čúb, šes-ráb* and the like frq ; *bla-na-méd-pai lam, bla-med-rdo-rjei tég-pa,* = *sṅágs-kyi lam,* the mystical method, v. *mdo* 3; *sá-bla,* above the earth, above ground, opp. to *sa-stéṅ, sa-ˌög* upon and under the earth. Generally fig.: **superior, better, preferable,** *baṅ-mdzód stoṅ yaṅ blao* then even an empty treasury is preferable *Dzl.*; commonly with the pf. root of a vb.:

tse *ₒjos kyaṅ blao Dzl.* then I will rather die; less frq. with *na*: *ši-na yaṅ blai* since even death is to be preferred *Dzl.*; frq. it may be rendered by 'may', *rgyál-bar gyur kyaṅ blao* then may rather . . . gain the victory (than that I should . . .) *Dzl.*; also pleon.: *kyod mig-gis mi mtoṅ yaṅ blai* be it that you do not see it (it is of no consequence whether you see or not) *Dzl.* ༢༧༩, 7. In the passage *Tar.* 123, 8 *bla* seems to stand as an adv. for 'very', *Schf.* —

Comp. *bla-gáb, bla-gós* (*W.* vulgo **tsá-dar, tsá-sar**) = *gzán-gos*, upper garment, cloth, serving Indians, and occasionally also Tibetans as a covering, = toga, ἱμάτιον; *bla-gáb ṗrúg-pa gčig-tu gzár-ba* to throw the toga over one shoulder, frq.; *bla-gab-méd-pa*, 1. without upper garment *Dzl.* 2. having no wish, no desire, free from passion(?) — *bla-bré*, also *bla-re*, canopy, dais *Dzl.* and elsewh. — *blá-ma* उत्तर 1. **the higher, upper, superior;** *blá-mar byéd-pa* to esteem highly, to honour, syn. to *bkúr-sti byéd-pa Domaṅ, Tar.*; the exact grammatical explanation of *mii blá-mai čós-kyi čo-ₒṗrúl Dzl.* ༥༦, or of the similar passage *mii čos blá-mai rdzu-ₒṗrúl Burn.* I, 164, offers some difficulties, although it is evident, that *Burn.* has hit the sense better than *Sch.* Of later date is the signification: 2. **the superior,** i.e. spiritual teacher, father confessor, गुरु, with the genit. of the person *Pth.*; in a more gen. sense: **ecclesiastic, priest, 'Lama'** *Thgr., Pth.*; in East. Tib. a title designing a high eccles. degree, something like 'D.D.' v. Desg. 247, 371; *bla-mčód* for *blá-ma daṅ mčod-gnás* ecclesiastic and sacrificing priest, whether it be one and the same person, or two different individuals *Pth., Mil.*; *bla-(ma-)čén(-po)* **chief Lama, Grand-Lama.** — *bla-bráṅ* resp. for dwelling-room or house of a Lama or Lamas, whilst *gzim-káṅ, ṗo-bráṅ* are the resp. expressions for secular dignitaries. — *bla-slób, blá-ma daṅ slób-ma*, the Lama and his disciple *Sch.* — *smán-gyi-bla* v. *sman.* —

II. *Sch.* **'soul, life'**; acc. to oral explanations: 1. **strength, power, vitality,** e.g. in food, scents etc., just like *bčud.* — 2. **blessing, power of blessings,** like *gyaṅ*, e.g. **ṭim-mé mi-la la čém-po mi dug = yaṅ mi čag* C.*, no blessing attends a contemner of the law. — 3. an object with which a person's life is ominously connected; thus very commonly *bla-šiṅ* a tree of fate (gen. a juniper or in *W.* a willow-tree, *ral-lcáṅ*), planted at a child's birth; *rgyál-poi bla-gyú* the king's turkois of life *Glr.*; *bla-dár* a little flag on the house-top, on which benedictions are written; *bla gnás* the omen is lasting, propitious, *nyams* it is vanishing, foreboding danger; so prob. also *Dzl.* ༢༠, 17, where it is not at once equivalent to 'soul' (*Sch.*). —

III. frq. incorr. for *sla.* — IV. in some combinations it has a signification not yet accounted for, e.g. *bla rdól-ba Sch.* to find fault with, to blame, abuse, without a reason; *bla-tse*(?) *Lex.*

བླ་གབ་, གོས་ *bla-gáb, gos* v. *bla* I.

བླ་ཆེན་, མཆོད་ *bla-čén, -mčód* v. *blá-ma* sub *bla* I.

བླ་གཉན་ *bla-gnyán Med.?*

བླ་ཐབས་ *bla-tábs Lex.*

བླ་དགས་ *bla-dágs Gram.; Sch.*: 'a primitive word, an abstract noun'.(?)

བླ་ན་ *blá-na* v. *bla* I.

བླ་བོར་ *blá-bor Sch.*: 'well! that may be! so much the better!'

བླ་བྲང་ *bla-bráṅ* v. *blá-ma* sub *bla* I.

བླ་འཚོ་, གླ་འཚོ་ *bla-tsó, gla-tso Sch.*: **hereditary portion, inheritance.**

བླ་གཡུ་ *bla-gyú*, བླ་ཤིང་ *bla-šiṅ* v. *bla* II.

བླ་རེ་ *bla-ré* v. *bla-bré* sub *bla* I.

བླག *blag* 1. sub *bde-blág* q.v. — 2. sub *btso-blag* q.v.

བླག་པ་ *blág-pa* 1. pf. *blags*, *rná-ba blág-pa* = *rná-ba gtád-pa Lex.*: **to incline one's ear to, to lend one's ear, to listen to** (*blág-pa* not by itself 'to hear' *Cs.*). —

2. *mčí-ma blág-pa* **to shed tears.** — 3. in *blág-pa méd-pa*, the free translation of **आभ्यवकाशिक**, *Burn.* 1, 309 takes it in the signification given by *Sch.* to *bde-blág*, and explains it by 'bare of every convenience or comfort'.

བླང་བ་ *bláṅ-ba* v. *lén-pa.*

བླད་པ་ *blád-pa* **to chew,** secondary form to *ldád-pa Lex.*

བླན་པ་ *blán-pa* = *glán-pa Cs.*

བླར་ *blar*, frq. incorr. for *slar.*

བླུ་བ་ *blú-ba,* pf. *blus,* **to buy off, to ransom, to redeem,** *mi de blú-ru γtóṅ-ba* to pay in order to redeem a man, to pay as a ransom for him *Glr.; p̀ug-ron-gyi srog blus* he redeemed the life of the dove *Dzl.*; *˳di-dag-gis rγyal-poi mgo blu-o* therewith I will redeem the king's head *Dzl.*; to recover, to redeem, *γté-ba,* a pawn, pledge, security *C.*; *blu-rín* the money or price paid for the redeeming of persons or goods, ransom.

བླུག་པ་ *blúg-pa* v. *ldúg-pa.*

བླུགས་སྐུ་ *blúgs-sku* **molten image**; *blúgs-pár* casting-mould; *blúgs-ma* **cast metal, statues, relievos** (cf. *˳búr-ba*); *blugs-γzár*, *dgáṅ-blugs* v. *γzar*; *ǰá-blugs* urn-shaped vessel for pouring out tea etc.; *spyi-blugs* v. *spyi-bo* sub *spyi*; *már-blugs* oil-pitcher.

བླུད་པ་ *blúd-pa* 1. vb. *ldud-pa.* — 2. sbst. to *blú-ba,* **release, ransom, redemption** *Sch.* — *blúd-bu* v. *rlúd-bu.*

བླུན་པ་ *blún-pa* **dull, stupid; stupidity, foolishness;** *blún-po* **stupid, foolish; fool, idiot;** *blún-po la-lá . . . ˳dzin* some fools consider it . . .; *blúṅ-poi lugs* foolery, fool's opinion, fool's wisdom, expressions frq. used in scientific works to defeat antagonistic views; *dgé-ba mi byéd-pai mi ni blún-po yin* the man without virtue is a fool; *˳dod-yón-la čags šin-tu blun* to be given to lust is folly *Pth.*; *byol-soṅ-p̀yúgs-pas blun* more stupid than a beast *Mil.; blún-γtam, blún-tsig* foolish talk, foolery; *blún-dad* superstition *Mil.* (cf. *dṅos-dad*).

བླུས་ *blus* v. *blú-ba; blús-ma* **ransom** *Cs.*

བློ་ *blo* I. rarely *bló-ba* **mind** (*Was.* 314 **बोधि**) 1. the intellectual power in man, **understanding,** *mk̀ás-pai blo daṅ ldán-pa Dzl.*, *blo rno-ba Glr.* talented, gifted; *blo čén-po* (*čúṅ-ṅu*) of great (small) mental abilities *C.*; *blo γsál-te* of a clear understanding, sharp-witted *Dzl.*; *šes-pai blo* sagacity, intelligence, judgment *Dzl.*; *blo-rgyá Sch.* comprehensive intellectual power; *blo myur-žiṅ* being of quick comprehension, sharp *Dzl.*; *blo-ráb*, -*˳briṅ*, -*dmán-pa* of sound, moderate, weak intellects or mental faculties *Mṅg.*, the last expression is frq. used in modestly speaking of one's self *Glr.* and elsewh.; *bló-yi mún-pa* intellectual darkness, a darkened mind *Glr.*; *blo-bág* narrow-minded, weak in intellect *Sch.; k̀yod ni blo nór-ro* you are mistaken; *blos-lčógs-pa* 'to be competent in mind or judgment' *Sch.*; *bló-na-˳bab* 'I understand' *Sch.* (?) — 2. **mind, thought, memory,** *čos daṅ yi-ge-la blo ǰúg-pa* to direct one's thoughts to religion and to learning to read *Glr.; bló-la sbyór-ba* to impresss on the mind, to inculcate *Glr.*; *bló-la bžúgs-pa* what is retained by, treasured up in the memory *Tar.*; *bló-la bzúṅ-ba* to learn by heart *Glr.*, *W.*: **loa* or *ló-na zúm-če**; *blo-t̀ag-čód* v. sub *t̀ág-pa* I. — 3. **mind, sentiment, disposition** (here in part = *yid*), *bló-la ˳dód-pa* to desire; *blo ˳dún-pa* interest, concern, v. *˳dún-pa; mčód-pa byéd-pai bló-čan de* he that has a mind, is disposed, to sacrifice *Dzl.; raṅ bdé-bar ˳dód-pai blo méd-par* without any regard to his own welfare *Thgy.; blo nyé-ba* friendly sentiment; also: kindly disposed *Glr.*; *sdáṅ-bai blo* a hating mind, malevolent disposition *Lt.*; *blo gró-ba Sch.*: 'to get soft, moved, touched, sad', acc. to a native authority: to be agreeably affected by; *blo mt̀ún-pa* to be of the same mind, like-minded, with supine also: to agree *Glr.*; perh. also: to be unanimous, peaceable, on friendly terms *Sch.*; *k̀yéd-kyi blo daṅ mt̀ún-pa* agreeably to your wish *Mil.*; *blor ma šoṅ Sch.* 'the mind could not take it in' *Tar.* 51, 7, *Schf.*: 'it did not please me, I could not reconcile myself to it'; **blo skyél-ba** *W.*, **k'el-ba** *C.*, *č'el-ba Cs.* (?), to rely, to depend upon, *blo gél-ba* to hope *Sch.* (the correct spelling as yet doubtful); *blos ɣtóṅ-ba* to give up, resign entirely, to risk, venture, e.g. *ráṅ-gi srog Glr.*, *Mil.*, *blo spáṅ-ba*, id. *Mil.*; **ts'e-ₒdi lŭ-táṅ** monk *C.*; *ₑó-čag blos ma t'óṅs-par* as she was so much attached to us *Mil.*; *raṅ-blos ma t'oṅs-pa* a man attached to himself, in love with himself; *blo ɣtód-pa Schr.* to trust, confide (cf. compounds); *dé-las blo zlóg-pa Thgy.*, to subtract, to draw off, divert, dissuade from; *blo brid-pa* to deceive, impose upon, cheat *Glr.* (*bló-yi bdag* 'conscience' *Sch.*, acc. to *Schr.* not an authenticated expression).

Comp. *blo-k'og-č'é* confident, courageous, intrepid, undaunted. — *blo-grós* **sense, intellect, understanding**; *blo-grós-kyi šés-bya* what is to be discerned by the understanding; *blo-grós daṅ ldán-pa*, *blo-grós-čan* sensible, judicious (of persons), *blo-grós č'én-po C.* of much sense, of an excellent understanding, *č'úṅ-nu C.*, *žán-pa Mil.* of little understanding; *blo-gros-méd* unintelligent, injudicious; *blo-gros-rgyal-po* n. of a medicinal plant, = *smug-č'úṅ Wdṅ.* — *bló-čan* having mind, sense; *byis-pai blo-čan* having the mind or sense of a child, thinking like a child *Cs.*; having a mind, v. above *mč'ód-pa byéd-pai bló-čan de.* — *blo-nyés* **ill-meaning, malicious** *Glr.* — *blo-ɣtád*, *blo-ɣdeṅ* **hope, confidence, assurance**, *bdág-gi blo-ɣdéṅ sú-la ₒč'a* in whom am I to place my confidence. — *blo-ɣdeṅ č'ós-la byéd-pa Glr.*; *W.*: **lor-tád* or *lo-dáṅ čó-če, kyél-če (s)**, c. *la.* — *blo-rtóg* prob. = *blo-grós*, *blo-rtóg t'a-dád-pa Pth.* people of different mental abilities. — *blo-stóbs* 1. *C.*, *W.* **courage.** 2. *W.*, **generosity, magnanimity,** or perh. also **equanimity, self-command,** e.g. if a person remains kind and forbearing towards disobedient servants. — *blo-t'ábs* counsel, expedient, *blo-t'ábs tsól-ba Ma.* — *blo-bde* **cheerful, happy.** — *blo-ₒdód* **covetous, greedy.** — *bló-sna* 1. *bló-sna maṅ-ba Glr.* was explained by our Lama: having manifold thoughts, being restless, flighty, giddy. 2. *W.* disposition, turn of mind, **ló-na rĭṅ-mo** slowness, irresolution, also longsuffering, **lo-na t'úṅ-se** resoluteness, determination, promptness, both also adj.: slow, irresolute, and: resolute, determined etc. — *blo-méd* injudicious, foolish *Cs.* (*Dzl.* ༢༤༤, 18 makes no sense, there being prob. an error in the text. The translation of *Sch.* seems to be a mere conjecture). — *blo-bzáṅ* 'sound sense', col. **'lob-zaṅ'**, a very common name of persons. — *blo-šéd Sch.* 'memory, intellectual power'. — *blo-séms* **mind, soul, heart,** *blo-sems-bdé* = *blo-bdé Mil.* — *blo-bsám* intellect; *W.*: **lo-sám méd-k'an** foolish, one not knowing what he is about.

II. frq. incorr. for *glo.*

བློ་བ་ *bló-ba* I. vb. **to be able** = *p'ód-pa*; *k'yod mi ló-na* if you cannot; **di mi lo** that you cannot (dare not) do, prob. only *W.* vulg. — II. sbst. = *blo*, frq. used by *Mil.* for the sake of the rhythm.

བློ་བུར་ *bló-bur* = *gló-bur* **sudden, suddenly;** *k'yed da-ltar-gyi dád-pa bló-bur yin* thy present faith is new, but just sprung up in thee *Mil.*; *mi-spyod bló-bur-du ₒgyur* the conduct of men suddenly changes *Ma.*

བློང་མོ་ *blóṅ-mo*, for *lóṅ-mo*, **bones** or **knuckles** used as dice *Mil.*

བློན་ *blon* 1. *Lex.* = *gros*, *blón ₒdébs-pa* **to give advice, to counsel;** *Cs.*: to make arrangements. — 2. v. the following.

བློན་པོ་ *blón-po* **officer** (prop. counsellor), any magisterial officer of higher rank; *blón-po daṅ ₒbaṅs* commanding and obeying, higher officers and subalterns *Glr.*; more particularly **minister** (of state); *blon(-po) č'en(-po) Glr.*, *blón-po bká-la ɣtógs-pa Glr.*, more commonly *bka-blón(-po)*, **high officer of state, minister, governor;** *k'rims-blón* minister of justice, officer of justice; *rgyal-blón* king and minister, also = council, privy-council, *Glr.*; *č'ós-blon* 1. (opp. to *bdúd-blon*) an orthodox, faithful minister etc. 2. *č'os-blon č'én-po* minister of public worship *Glr.*; *rje-blón* the same as *rgyal-blón Glr.* — *spyi-blon* chief officer *Cs.* — *p'yi naṅ bar ɣsúm-gyi blón-po Glr.*, lit. outer, inner, middle minister, a distinction not quite intelligible. — *dmág-blon* military, *yúl-blon* civil officer *Cs.* — *naṅ-blon* 1. v. above *p̔yi-naṅ* etc. 2. *Lh.* country-judge.

བྷ *bha*, sometimes written for བ, either from ignorance, or in order to appear learned, as is also དྷ for ད, and so forth.

བྷ་ག *bhá-ga Ssk.* **the female genitals,** *Pth.*

བྷ་ར་ཏ་ *bhá-ra-ta, bhá-ra-tai dúm-bu, bhár-ta, bár-dha, Ssk.* भरतखण्ड country between Lanka and the Sumeru, viz. Hindustan; also North-India, *Mil.* and elsewh.

བྷ་ལད *bha-lad, Urd.* ولايت, *Beng.* belati, 'a far distant country', = *p̔i-liṅ*, for **Europe.**

བྷང་གེ *bhaṅ-ge W., Ssk.* भङ्गा, **hemp.**

བྷེ་ད *bhe-da* v. *˳be-dha.*

དབའ *dba* 1. *Lex.* = *ẑe-sa* **reverence, respect,** obs. 2. (or *rba*) = the following.

དབའ་ཀློང *dba-klóṅ Glr., rba-kloṅ Mil., Dzl., dba-rlábs* **wave, billow;** *rba-skya* whitish waves *Mil.*; *dba-tsúb* surge, roar, turmoil of waves *Cs.*; *dba-byi* water-rat?

དབག་པ *dbág-pa*, pf. *dbags Sch.*, v. *dbog-pa* and *bag-pa.*

དབང *dbaṅ* (**waṅ*, vulg. *'aṅ**) 1. **might, power, potency,** *blón-po dbaṅ č̔és-pas* because the minister was very potent *Glr.*; *dbaṅ dge-˳dún-la ɣtad Glr.*, not only: 'he granted great privileges to the priesthood' *Sch.*, but: he invested it with magisterial power and jurisdiction; rarely used of physical power or strength *S.g.*; *bsdad-dbaṅ-med* it is not in my power to stay *Thgy.*; *búm-pa ǰó-moi yin-te dbaṅ ma mč̔is-so* as the pitcher belongs to my mistress, I have no power over it, I have not to dispose of it *Dzl.*; *sdod-dbaṅ-méd-par* having no strength, not being able to wait (from eagerness, avidity etc.) *Glr.*; *dbaṅ-méd*, prob. *sdod* to be supplied (if the text be correct), this won't do so any longer *Glr.*; *(raṅ-)dbaṅ-méd-du* or *par* involuntarily, not being able to help it, e.g. to weep, rejoice, believe, *Mil.*: *dbaṅ-méd-du mč̔i-ma ˳č̔ór-du ˳ǰúg-pa* to make one weep; *dbaṅ-méd-du ˳č̔ól-ba* to make a person powerless, to force by absolute power *Glr.*; *dbáṅ-du ˳gyúr-ba* to get into another's power, to be overpowered *Tar.*; *˳dód-pai* to get into the power of the passions, to be led away by them *Dzl.*; *dbáṅ-du gyúr-pa* seems also sometimes to mean: he who has brought every thing into his power (?), along with *nyon-moṅs-pa-méd-pa* and *sems-rnam-par-gról-ba*; *dbáṅ-du sdúd-pa* to reduce under one's power *Pth.*; *snyiṅ-rǰe* to make the principle of mercy one's own, to practise it freely *Glr.*, (where *˳dú-ba* stands); *˳gró-ba* to comprise all beings, *Glr.*; *dbáṅ-du byéd-pa* id.; *dbaṅ byéd-pa* c. la, 1. to rule over, to govern, frq. 2. to possess, *bdág-gis dbaṅ byar méd-pa* what one does not possess *Thgy.* — *dbaṅ-sgyúr-ba c. la*, to govern, to rule, frq.; *dbaṅ ˳grúb-pa* id. seldom. — *dbaṅ skúr-ba* v. *skur-ba* and *dbaṅ*, 2. **waṅ táṅ-če* W.* to make efforts, to exert one's self, also = the next. — *dbaṅ zá-ba* to offer violence *Dzl.* ༧༤༠, 3. — *dbáṅ-gis* like a postposition, by, by means of, in virtue of, in consequence of, e.g. *lás-kyi* of former actions *Glr.*; *ṅa-rgyál-gyi dbáṅ-gis* from or in consequence of pride *Tar.* — 2. more especially in mythology, *dbaṅ bču Dzl.* ༢༠༢, 14, also *stobs-bču Trigl.* 8, 6; *Gyatch.* II, 46, *Burn.* II, 781 seqq. 1. the ten powers of knowledge of Buddha, v. *Köpp.* I, 437 seqq. 2. in later times *ɣžan rǰés-su ˳dzin-pai dbaṅ bču* ten powers tending to the benefit of others are ascribed to the Bodhisattva, *Thgy.*: *ts̔é-la dbáṅ-ba* (respecting this form v. below) power over the length of one's own life; *séms-la dbáṅ-ba* power according to one's own pleasure to enter into any meditation; *yo-byád-la* to shower down provisions for the support of creatures; *lás-la* to mitigate the punishments for their sins; *skyé-ba-la* to effect one's own re-birth in the external world, without danger of being infected by its sin; *mós-pa-la* at pleasure to change one object into another; *smón-lam-la* to see every prayer for the welfare of others fulfilled; *rdzu-˳p̔rúl-la* to exhibit wonderful feats for bringing about the conversion of others; *ye-šés-la* to understand all writings on religion (ni f.); *čós-la* to convey the publication of religion to all creatures at the same time and in every language. 3. in practical mysticism: various supernatural powers (v. *skúr-ba*), e.g. *p̀yi naṅ ysáṅ-gi dbaṅ skúr-ba Pth.* is alledged to signify: to convey externally, i.e. into the mouth, the power of *snaṅ-ba-mťa-yás* (this and the two following are names of Buddhas and demons), internally, into the body, the power of *spyan-ras-yzigs* and lastly into the mind perfect purity, i.e. the *rta-mgrín*, and together with it power over the demons. — 3. **regard, consideration**(?). In later writings the composition of *dbáṅ-du byás-na* (*mdzád-na* etc.) c. genit. (instead of which in *C.* also *dbáṅ-du šór-na, šóṅ-na* are said to be in use), is frq. to be met with, signifying as much as: when... is concerned, when... is in question, for the purpose of, or merely: respecting, as regards: *légs-pai, j̀igs-pai, btsán-pai* when beauty, firmness, formidable appearance (of a royal castle) are concerned, are the points in question *Glr.*; *sṅágs-kyi dbáṅ-du rtsis-pai šló-ka* prob. the Slokas being numbered with a regard to the Mantras, i.e. including the latter *Tar.* 127, 16. — 4. symb. num.: 5 (*dbaṅ* being taken for *dbáṅ-po*).

Comp. and deriv. *dbaṅ-bskúr* consecration, inauguration, initiation *Was.* (189), = *dbaṅ-bskyúr* might, power, e.g. *saṅs-rgyás-kyi Glr.* — *dbaṅ-grál* the row of those that are to be ordained or consecrated. — *dbáṅ-čan* mighty, powerful *Cs.* — *dbaṅ-ťáṅ* 1. **might**, = *mṅa-ťaṅ*, *dbaṅ-ťaṅ-méd-pa* low, mean, of inferior rank *Dzl.* 2. **time, chronology** *Lexx.* 3. **destiny, fate, predestined fate**, or rather the destiny of any creature consequent to its former actions, *tse daṅ dbaṅ-ťáṅ*, frq.; *dbaṅ-ťaṅ-méd-pa* may therefore imply: having no destiny, i.e. no particular destiny. — *dbaṅ-ₒdus-p̀o-bráṅ* 'Angdophorung' of the Indian papers, n. of a fort in Tibet. — *dbaṅ-ldán* mighty, powerful; *dbaṅ-ldán-gyi p̀yogs Domaṅ, dbáṅ-poi p̀yogs Sbh.*, is said to be north-east. — *dbáṅ-po* v. the next article. — *dbaṅ-p̀yúg* 1. adj. mighty, also sbst.: *dbaṅ-p̀yúg yžán-las čé-ba Glr.* 2. symb. num.: 11. 3. **noun proper** a. Iswara, Siva *Glr.*, hence also the Lingam as his emblem *Glr.* b. Avalokitesvara *Glr.* — *dbáṅ-ba* 1. vb. c. *la* = *dbaṅ byéd-pa*, e.g. *rgyal-srid-la mi dbaṅ* he does not succeed to the throne; gen. with accus. *yèig ₒdi dbáṅ-ba yin* one... belongs to this one *Mil.*; *bdag dbáṅ-bai rgyal-p̀rán* the vassals under my sway *Dzl.* 2. sbst. = *dbaṅ*, e.g. *tsé-la dbáṅ-ba* (v. above). — *dbaṅ-ris* prob. domain, dominion. — *dbaṅ(-po)-lág(-pa)* a medicine, said to be prepared from a viscid, aromatic root, shaped like a hand. — *dbaṅ-šés* perception, by means of the organs of sense *Was.* (278).

དབང་པོ་ *dbáṅ-po* 1. **possessed of power, dominion**, *nór-gyi dbáṅ-por gyur Dzl.* (*Ms.*); **lord, ruler, sovereign**, esp. divine rulers: Indra, also *lhai dbáṅ-po*; further *rgyál-bai dbáṅ-po, ťúb-pai dbáṅ-po* the highest of the Buddhas *Glr.* — 2. **organ of sense**, *dbáṅ-po lṅa(-po)* a. the five organs of sense, eyes etc., also *dbáṅ-poi sgo lṅa Med.* b. *Trigl.* 17, 6, five immaterial, transcendent senses of Buddha, which are in unison with his five powers, *stobs lṅa*, as stated by *Burn.* II, 430, v. *Köpp.* I, 436. In natural philosophy six organs of sense frq. are mentioned, मनस् being added as the sixth; medical writings also treat of *dbáṅ-po dgu* or *dbáṅ-poi sgo dgu*, v. *bú-ga*. — 3. **sense, intellectual power**, *dbáṅ-po rnón-po* of acute intellect, *dbáṅ-po rdúl-po* of obtuse intellect, also as common expressions for sagacious or dull *Dzl.*; *dbáṅ-po nyams* the senses are weakened, become dull *Med.*; *lus sems dbáṅ-po* body, soul, and senses (are glad, are pure etc.) *Dom.*; *dbáṅ-po ysó-ba* to gladden, strengthen, revive, the senses *Mil.*; *ráṅ-gi séms-las dbáṅ-poi rnam-šés ₒbyuṅ* out of the spirit (of the personality which during the time between two periods of existence is in a disembodied state) the sense-endowed soul (of the new individual) is generated (in the process of conception)

S.g. — 4. **genitals,** *Wdṅ.* and elsewh.; *dbáṅ-po lúg-pa* v. *dbaṅ-lág* sub *dbaṅ.*

དབར་མི་ *dbár-mi Sch.* **a faint-hearted, timorous man.**

དབལ་ *dbal Lex.* = *tog* and *rtsé-mo* **top, summit, point** e.g. of a *mčod-rten Glr.*; the point, or acc. to some the grooves of the *p̓úr-pa* or exorcising dagger; *rtai dbal bzaṅ-ṅan Lex.?* — *dbál-ba* v. *˳bal-ba.*

དབུ་ *dbu* resp. for *mgo,* **head,** frq.; **beginning, commencement,** e.g. of holy doctrine *Glr.*; *'u lán-če* W.,* the mode of greeting between Lamas, by touching each other with their fore-heads; to bless (a layman by imposition of hands); *dbu mdzád-pa* to be the head, the principal person, e.g. in an assembly of believers *Mil.*; more definitely: *dbu mdzád-do* he was my instructor *Mil.* — *dbu-skrá* the hair of the head. — *dbu-rgyán* ornament of the head, diadem *Mil.* — *dbu-ṅás Sch.* pillow. — *dbu-čan* furnished with a head, i.e. with a thick stroke at the top (of a letter), hence the name of the Tibetan printing characters. — *dbu-čen* 1. **higher officer.** 2. *dbu-čuṅ* **subaltern officer** *Cs.* — *dbu-rje* **Reverence, Reverend,** title of Lamas. — *dbu-snyúṅ bžés-pa Sch., dbu-snyúṅ daṅ bro ˳bór-ba Glr.* resp. to swear by one's head. — *dbu-tód* royal cap, crown. — *dbu-mťún drúṅ-du* resp. the same as *žabs drúṅ-du* in directing letters: To ... — *dbu-˳p̓áṅ* **elevation, high rank, dignity,** *stód-pa* to praise, *smád-pa* to despise, to revile (dignities). — *dbú-ma* 1. n. of the goddess **Durga,** the wife of Siva. 2. **principal vein,** v. *rtsá-ba.* 3. **the middle** (-doctrine), **middle-road,** **मध्यम,** which endeavours to avoid the two extremes *Was.*, also *dbú-mai lam* or *ltá-ba*; *dbú-ma-pa* an adherent of this doctrine *Sch.*, cf. however *mdo* extr. — *dbu-méd* **the Tibetan current hand-writing,** cf. *dbú-čan.* — *dbu-rmóg Zam.* w.e.; in *W.* *gyál-po u'-móg čo žig* is said to signify: Long live the king! — *dbu-rtsé* the top, pinnacle, of a temple, monastery *Glr.* — *dbu-mdzád* (cf. *dbu mdzád-pa* above) **chairman, principal, warden,** in convents an official that takes the lead in performing the prayers. — *dbu-žwá* cap. — *dbu-šóg* title-page *Sch.*

དབུ་བ་ *dbú-ba* v. *lbú-ba.*

དབུགས་ *dbugs* 1. **breath, respiration,** *dbugs rṅúb-pa daṅ ˳byín-pa* or *˳byúṅ-ba* to respire, to inhale and exhale air *Med.*, *W.* *tón-če* for *˳byúṅ-ba; dbugs ˳byín-pa* to stop for rest, to recover one's breath *Sch.* (and perh. *Pth.*); *dbugs-dbyúṅ tób-pa* to be eased in one's mind, after despondency *Tar.*; *'ug gyaṅ bór-če* W.* to stop, to keep back one's breath; *'ug sub* or *kor táṅ-če* W.* to choke, suffocate, strangle, throttle; *skyé-˳gro ťams-čád-kyi dbugs lén-pa* to take away the breath of beings (which is ascribed to the demon *pe-dkár*) *Glr.*; *p̓yi-dbugs* seems to be the last breath of a dying man, but *náṅ-dbugs* is some fantastic physiological notion *Thgr.*; *dbugs mdé-ba* and *mi-bdé-ba* an easy and a hard breathing *Med.* frq.; *dbugs-ťúṅ* short breath; *dbugs rdzáṅ-ba* or *brdzáṅs-pa* shortness of breath, asthma, as a complaint of old age *Thgy.*; *dbugs lheb-lhéb byéd-pa* to pant, to be pursy *Med.* — *dbugs-rgód Lt.?* — *dbugs-ṅán Sch.* flatulence. — *dbugs ťebs-rél Sch.* 'in one breath'? — 2. **a breath, one respiration,** as smallest measure of time = $\frac{1}{1800}$ *kyim* = 4 seconds.

དབུང་ *dbuṅ Lex.* = *dbus.*

དབུབ་པ་ *dbúb-pa* v. *˳búbs-pa.*

དབུར་ *dbur* termin. of *dbu, Sch.* **first, at first.**

དབུར་བ་ *dbúr-ba,* also *˳úr-ba, 'úr-ba* **to smooth,** *šóg-bu* paper, *ras* woollen stuff, *γžál* a pavement *Cs.*; *'ur gyág-pa* C.*, *gyáb-če* W.* to iron, to smooth linen etc., *'ur-čag** smoothing-iron.

དབུལ་བ་ *dbúl-ba* I. vb. v. *˳búl-ba.* — II. adj. **poor, indigent** *Dzl.*; sbst. **poverty, want, penury,** *dbúl-ba sel-ba* to relieve want *Glr.*; *dbul-žiṅ ˳p̓óṅs-pai rigs* a poor and indigent generation *Dzl.*; hence frq. *dbúl-p̓oṅs* poor, a poor man, pauper *Mil.*; poverty *Glr.*; usually *dbúl-po,* fem. *dbúl-mo,* poor.

དབུས་ *dbus* (*Ld.* *'us*, *C.* *'ü*) 1. **middle, midst, centre,** *ťág-pai dbus tsám-du* *ǰyin-nas* having proceeded about to the middle of the rope *Dzl.*; *skyé-boi dbús-su* in the midst of the people *Tar.*; *ťaṅ γnyis-kyi dbus-ri* the hill (mountain) in the middle between the two plains *Glr.*; *dbús-kyi ri-rgyál* Sumeru standing in the centre (of the world) *Mil.*; seldom relative to time: *bžúgs-pai dbús-su* whilst he was sitting *Glr.*; in metaphysics: *dbus daṅ mťa* 'the medium and the extremes' *Cs.* Asiat. Researches XX, 577 — *dbús-ma* the middle one (of three or more persons) *Mil.*, (of inanimate things) *Glr.* — 2. in a specific sense: **the central province** of a country, a. of India, hence = Magadha, the holy land, land of Buddha *Thgy.* b. of Tibet, the province Ü; *dbús-pa* an inhabitant of it; *dbus-γtsán* Ü and *Tsaṅ*.

དབེན་པ་ *dbén-pa* **solitary, lonely,** e.g. a road *Dzl.*; **solitude, loneliness,** *dbén-pa* *ₒdi-na* in this solitude *Dzl.*; *dbén-par ₒgró-ba* or *γnás-pa* frq.; *dben*, id.: *dbén-la dga* *Ma.*; *dben-(pai) γnas, sa* solitary place, esp. hermitage; *dbén-γnas čén-po brgyád-kyi sa* earth from the eight great hermitages, sacred places of pilgrimage in India *Glr.*; like *bstoṅs-pa* the word is construed with the instrum. case: *mas dbén-pa*, solitary as to a mother, i.e. motherless; *snyiṅ-pos dbén-pa* = *snyiṅ-po méd-pa* *Tar.*

དབོ་ *dbo* 1. n. of a lunar mansion, v. *rgyu-skár*, no. 22. — 2. the belly-side of fur.

དབོ་བ་ *dbó-ba* v. *ₒbó-ba*.

དབོན་པོ་ *dbón-po* (*W.* *'ón-po*, *C.* *'ǫm-po*) 1. *B.* resp. for *ťsá-bo* **grandson; nephew**; *dbon-srás* id. *Glr.*; *dbón-mo* fem.; *mes-dbón* ancestor and grandchild *Glr.*; *dbon-žáṅ* *Glr.* 95 seems to denote son-in-law and brother-in-law, with which also *Sch.'s* Mongol transl. agrees, Geschichte d. Ost-Mong. p. 359 med. — 2. **Lama-servant** *C.* — 3. a certain sect of Lamas, clad in red, shorn, and married, = *sor-kyim-pa*, *C.*, *W.* — 4. a Lama skilled in astrology, who for instance, when a person has died, performs those ceremonies, that serve to avert harm from the survivors *W.*

དབོལ་བ་ *dból-ba* *Cs.* = *rtól-ba*, *Lex.* *rdziṅ dból-ba*.

དབྱངས་ *dbyaṅs*, *yaṅ(s)* 1. **singing, song, tune, melody,** *glu-dbyáṅs* id.; *luṅ-bstán-gyi dbyaṅs* prophetic song, psalm *Mil.*; *dbyaṅs(-su) lén-pa*, *dbyaṅs byéd-pa* to sing *Dzl.*; *stód(-pai) dbyaṅs* song of praise, hymn of thanksgiving, *ǰhé-pa* *C.*, *ǰúl-če* *W.*; *γduṅ-dbyáṅs* a song of aspiration *Mil.* — *dbyáṅs-čan* *Glr.* a deity, prob. = *ₒǰam-dbyáṅs-čan-ma* Saraswati, goddess of euphony. — *dbyaṅs-snyán* sweet singing. — *dbyáṅs-pa* singer *Cs.* — *yaṅ-žú* bow for a violin, fiddle-stick *W.* — 2. **vowel,** hence *dbyaṅs-yig* 1. the (four) **signs of the vowels,** *Gram.* 2. *Cs.*: **notes** (of music) or any contrivance for marking the modulation of sounds; so perh. also *Glr.*

དབྱར་ *dbyar* **summer,** in India: **rainy season** (cf. *dus*); also *dbyár-ka*, *dbyár-ka* *Mil.*, *W.*, *dbyár-dus*, *Cs.* *dbyár-mo*; *dbyar-dgun-méd-par* summer and winter *Mil.*; *dbyar B.*, *dbyár-ka-la* col. in summer; *dbyar-γnás* 1. summer-abode, *Sch.* 2. the solitary summer-fasting of the monks; *dbyar-skyés* 'summer-born'; *dbyar-ṅá* summer-drum, po. expression for thunder *Cs.* — *dbyar-čár* summer-rain *Cs.* — *dbyar-žwa* summer-hat.

དབྱར་པ་ *dbyár-pa* (*Pur.* *sbyár-pa*, elsewh. *yár-pa*) **poplar**, various kinds of which tree are found in the vicinity of villages, cultivated or growing wild. (*Wdṅ.* also *sbyár-pa.*)

དབྱི་ *dbyi* (*yi, com. 'i*) 1. **lynx,** *dbyi-mo* the female of this animal, *dbyi-ǰrúg* a young one; *dbyi-ťsáṅ* lair of it. — 2. in Ü: **beer,** = *čaṅ*.

དབྱི་གུ་ *dbyi-gu* = *dbyig-gu* **little stick,** cf. *dbyig-pa*.

དབྱི་བ་ *dbyi-ba*, prob. only fut. to *ₒǰyi-ba*, **to wipe off, to blot out, to efface,** *Lex.*: *ri-mo*, a drawing. *Sch.* however notices also a perf. *dbyis*.

དབྱི་མོ་ *dbyi-mo* **flax** (?).

དབྱི་མོང་ *dbyi-moṅ* medicinal herb, used against delirium *Med.*; *Cs.*: 'a plant of an acrid taste, used as tea'; in *Lh.* Potentilla Salesovii, of which neither the one nor the other fact is known to me.

དབྱིག(ས)་ *dbyig(s)* 1. = *nor* **wealth, riches, treasures**, *nor-dbyig* id. *Dzl.*; *dbyig-čan* rich, *dbyig-med* poor *Cs.*; *dbyig-mán Lex.* — 2. prob. = *dbyig-γnyén*, **precious stone** or a kind of such *Glr.* and elsewh.

དབྱིག་པ་ *dbyig-pa* **stick**, = *dbyúg-pa.*

དབྱིག་པུ་ *dbyig-pu Sch.*: 'implement for cleaning, scouring, polishing'.

དབྱིང་ཞ་ *dbyiṅ-ža Sch.*: **summer-hat** (?).

དབྱིངས་ *dbyiṅs* 1. syn. with *kloṅ*, com. *nám-mk'ai dbyiṅs* or *dbyiṅs* alone: **the heavens, celestial region**, *rgyáb-la brag dmar nám-mk'ai dbyiṅs* red rocks behind and the expanse of heaven *Mil.*; *k'yeu dbyiṅ-su yal* the youth disappearing was carried up to heaven *Pth.*; *dbyiṅs-na bžúgs-pai ḍá-ki-ma Mil.* — 2. **height** *Schr.*; the above passage was also rendered: red rocks behind, as high as heaven. — 3. in metaphysics an undefined idea of **extent, region, space**, धातु, (cf. *kloṅ*), *čós-kyi dbyiṅs*, धर्मधातु, not 'the wide diffusion of religion' *Sch.*, but a mere fanciful notion, or as it is expressed *Wts.* 143: le monde intellectuel de Bouddha; of highly learned Lamas the words are used: *tugs-dgóṅs čos-dbyiṅs-su tim C.*; and also *dbyiṅs* alone: *bló-yi byéd-pa dbyiṅs-su sbos Glr.* hide your mental activity in the heavens, i.e. let it be reduced to nothing; so prob. also *Tar.* 38, 10, *p'úṅ-po lhág-mo méd-pai dbyiṅs-su*, where nothing of the skandha is left remaining. *Sch.*: *dbyiṅs-su* in a body, in one mass, whole, entire (?).

དབྱིན་ *dbyin* or *γyin byéd-pa Sch.*, **to incite, instigate, set on.**

དབྱིབས་ *dbyibs* **shape, figure, form**, *byá-dbyibs-čan* having the shape of a bird *Lt.*; *šiṅ-rtai dbyibs daṅ ˳dra* shaped like a waggon or carriage *Glr.*; *skyés-pai dbyibs-la ṅós-bzuṅ-ba* to learn the nature (of plants) from the shape in which they grow; **á-mẹ yib dug** he quite resembles his mother in shape *W.*; *dbyibs légs-pa B.* a fine figure, **sóg-po** an ugly figure *W.*, or also: of a handsome (or ugly) form; *dbyibs zlúm-por yod* it has a round shape *Glr.*

དབྱུག་གུ་, དབྱུ་གུ་ *dbyúg-gu, dbyú-gu* 1. **small staff, wand, rod**, e.g. used as a magic wand, sun-dial etc. *Cs.* — 2. *Lex.*: = *ču-ťsod* q.v.; *Sch.*: *dbyúg-gu re-bži*, '64 equal parts of weight or measure; 64 quarters of an hour, or 16 hours'; but 64 *ču-ťsod* would make as much as 25$\frac{3}{5}$ hours.

དབྱུག་རྡོ་ *dbyúg-rdo W.* **sling-stone**; *B.*: *rdo-γyúg.*

དབྱུག་པ་ *dbyúg-pa* I. vb. pf. *dbyugs* 1. **to swing, brandish, flourish**, a stick, a sword; **to wag**, *rṅá-ma* the tail *Cs*; **yug yug ǰhe'-pa* W.*, to swing to and fro, to dangle; **yug toṅ* W.*, swing! dangle! — 2. **to throw, cast, fling**, **gyál-kar-nẹ do* C.*, to fling a stone through a window; to throw away, to throw down, **yúg-lẹ žog* C.* (= **p'áṅ-te bor* W.*), throw it away! — II. sbst, **stick**, *C.*; **yúg-pa gyáb-pa* C.* to strike, to beat with a stick. *dbyúg-to Glr.*, *dbyúg-to*, id. (*Sch.* club?) *Lex.*: = *bér-ka*, दण्ड; *dbyug-to-čan* wielding a stick; n.p.

དབྱུང་བ་ *dbyúṅ-ba*, fut., and in *C.* secondary form to the pres. *˳byin-pa.*

དབྱེ་བ་ *dbyé-ba*, (regular pronunciation **yé-wa*, com. *'é-wa**). I. vb. fut., and in *C.* secondary form of *˳byéd-pa.* — II. sbst. 1. **parting, partition, division, distinction, classification** *Thgy.* — 2. **section, part, class, species**, *dbyé-ba nyi-šu γsuṅs* twenty different species are named *Lt.*; *yi-ge ˳di dbyé-ba γnyis* these letters are divided into two classes; hence like *sna-ťsogs: sgyu-rtsál dbyé-ba* manifold arts, artifices *Smbh.* — *dbyé-brál Lex.*: **discord, dissension.**

དབྱེན་པ་ *dbyén-pa* (**yén-pa*, com. *'én-pa**, = *dbén-pa*), **difference, dissension, discord, schism**, *dge-˳dún-gyi dbyén-pa byéd-pa* to create discord, to cause a schism among the priesthood *Dzl.*; *dbyen ˳byéd pa* to make a difference, to discriminate *Sch.*

དབྱེར་མེད་, དབྱེ་རུ་མེད་པ་, དབྱེར་མི་ཕྱེད་པ་, *dbyer-méd, dbye-ru-méd-pa, dbyer-mi-p'yéd-pa* in-

separable, not to be distinguished, quite the same, identical *Gbr.* and elsewh.; *blá-mar dbyér-med* prob.: identical with a Lama; esp. in the higher philosophy in reference to the impossibility of distinguishing between good and evil (!).

དབྱེས་ *dbyes Schr.:* **magnitude, size, dimensions,** so perh. where *dprál-bai dbyes če* is mentioned as a characteristic of beauty.

དབྲག་ *dbrag*, v. *p̓rag*, **intermediate space, interstice;** ravine, glen, defile, *C.*; *Sch.* also: vise, handvise.

དབྲད་པ་ *dbrád-pa* v. *ₒbrád-pa.*

དབྲབ་པ་ *dbráb-pa* v. *ₒbráb-pa.*

དབྲལ་བ་ *dbrál-ba* v. *ₒbrál-ba.*

དབྲི་བ་ *dbri-ba* v. *ₒbri-ba.*

དབྲེ་བཙོང་ *dbre-btsóṅ* (?) *Sch.*; *Lex. dbre-btsog* dirt, filth.

དབྲོག་པ་ *dbróg-pa* v. *ₒp̓róg-pa.*

འབའ་ *ₒba Sch.:* 'seizure, distraint'; or rather the liability of paying higher interest, payment not having been made at the appointed time; *ₒba-gan*, *ₒba-gan-yig* warrant for thus proceeding against a debtor *C.*

འབའ་ཆ་ *ₒba-ča Wdṅ.*; *Sch.:* **lees from distilling brandy.**

འབའ་པོ་ *ₒbá-po* **magician, sorcerer, conjurer;** *ₒbá-mo* sorceress, witch *Cs.*, *W.*

འབའ་བ་ *ₒbá-ba* 1. **to bleat,** *W.* **ba tán-če**. — 2. **to bring, to carry,** *ₒbā-šog* bring it hither! *Sik.*, *ₒba-soṅ* take it there! — 3. **to commit adultery** *C.*

འབའ་བོ་ *ₒbá-bo*, *Cs.* = *p̓ug-pa*, **hole, cave, cavern,** *brág-gi* cleft in a rock, grotto; *ₒbá-bo-čan* **hollow, excavated.**

འབའ་བྱི་ *ₒbá-byi* a kind of cake, baked of parched rice or maize meal, frequently eaten with the tea *C.*

འབའ་ཞིག་ *ₒbá-žig B.* **only, solely, alone,** *bdag ₒbá-žig tár-ro* I alone escaped *Dzl.*; *rkáṅ-pa ₒbá-žig* the foot alone (appeared party-coloured) *Dzl.*; *blón-po de ₒbá-žig-gi čúṅ-ma* only this officer's wife *Dzl.*; **mere, nothing but,** *ysér daṅ dṅul ₒba-žig-gis gaṅ Sbh.*

འབག་ *ₒbag* 1. **mask, guise, disguise;** cf. also sub *sgo-lo.* — 2. **imitation, effigy, likeness, figure,** *ₒdra-ₒbág* resp. *sku-ₒbag*, *žal-ₒbág* id.; *ₒdra-ₒbag-gyon-mi* masked persons *Pth* — *ₒbag-ₒčam*, prop. **masquerade,** masked ball; *Cs.:* buffoonery, grimaces.

འབག་པ་ *ₒbág-pa* I. vb. pf. *ₒbags*, fut. *dbag?* cf. *sbág-pa*, **to defile, to pollute one's self,** *bud-méd daṅ* with women *Dzl.*; *ₒdod-čágs-la* through lust *Dzl.*; **to defile, to soil, to dirty,** *snód-la* a vessel *Dzl.* ༢༢༦, 7? — 2. *C.* **to take away, to steal, to rob; to covet, to wish to take,** c. *la Mil.* (acc. to oral information).

འབག་འབོག་ *ₒbag-ₒbóg* a slight elevation, **hillock** *W.*

འབག་རག་ *ₒbag-rág* **spider,** *ₒbag-rág-gi tsaṅ* cob-web *Sik.*

འབགས་ལྷག་ *ₒbags-lhag* **rest, remainder, remnant** (of food) *Mil.*

འབང་བ་ *ₒbáṅ-ba* **to be soaked, macerated,** softened by soaking *Cs.*, cf. *sbáṅ-ba.*

འབངས་ *ₒbaṅs* **subject,** *rgyál-po ₒbáṅs-su ₒoṅ* the king turns into a subject *Ma.*; *ₒbaṅs byéd-pa* to obey, *bkai ₒbaṅs bgyid-par* (or *bka-ₒbaṅs-su*) *k̓as-blaṅs-so* they promised to obey, to perform the commandment *Mil.* frq.; *báṅs-su byéd-pa Cs.* to reduce under one's dominion; gen. collectively: **the people, the subjects,** opp. to *blón-po* officers, magistrates, or *rje*, *rgyál-po* etc. — *lha-báṅs Tar.* 165, 22 *Schf.:* slaves belonging to a temple.

འབད་པ་ *ₒbád-pa* I. vb., imp. *ₒbod*, **to endeavour, to exert one's self, apply one's self,** c. *la* or the termin.; *dus-rgyún-du čós-la ₒbád-pa de* this (habit of) constantly applying one's self to religion *Mil.*; also c. acc.: *dká-ba brgya-p̓rág* to perform a hundred exercises of penance; col. **to cultivate, raise, rear, take care of,** *žiṅ* or *sa-yzi* to cultivate the ground, *rgun-ₒbrúm* to grow vines, *dúd-ₒgro* to breed cattle; *slób-par* to apply one's self to learning, *gléṅ-mo k̓ó-nar* to devote one's self exclusively to public speaking, preaching *C.* — II. sbst.

application, study, exertion, ˳*bád-pa drág-pos* with most persevering application; ˳*bád-pa daṅ rtsól-ba méd-par* without any exertion *Glr.;* hence ˳*bad-rtsól* id.; *skyés-bus srúb-pai* ˳*bad-rtsól* an assiduous rubbing with a human hand *Wdṅ.*; *dei* ˳*bad-rtsól-gyis* through his endeavours *Thgy.*; prob. also: **volition, energy of will** *S.g.*; the passage in *Thgy.: byaṅ-čúb či ťób-la* ˳*bad* ˳*tsál-lo,* is perh. not quite correct.

འབབ་ ˳*bab* 1. **a fall of snow** *Mil.* — 2. **tax, duty** *Sp.*

འབབ་པ་ ˳*báb-pa*, pf. *bab(s)*, imp. ˳*bob Cs.*, *bobs Glr.*, **to move downward** 1. **to descend,** *lá-nas* col., a defile, in *B.* gen. with *las*, e.g. *rtá-las Dzl.*, also *rtá-ḱa-nas Glr.* to alight from a horse, mostly with *la*, although *rí-la* ˳*báb-pa* may also mean: to alight (flying) on a mountain *Dzl.* ༢༥༣, 2. — 2. **to fall down,** *ɣnám-la ḱá-ba* ˳*bab* snow falls from heaven *Dzl.* — **to flow,** the usual word; to flow off; *mi-ɣtsáṅ* ˳*báb-pai ɣtór-ḱuṅ* sink-hole, for dirty water to run through *Lex.* — 4. **to alight on, to enter into,** of demons *Lt.* — 5. in a general sense, like **to get:** *nya skám-la* ˳*báb-pa* a fish that has got on dry ground; *ṅá-la ré-mos* ˳*bab Pth.*, or *res* ˳*bab Tar.* it is my turn; *sróg-la* ˳*báb-bo Dzl.* life is at stake; frq. in reference to time: *či-bai dús-la báb-bo* it has come to the time of dying, the hour of death has arrived; without a genit.: it is time; *skábs-la báb-bo* there is now an opportunity *Dzl.* — ˳*bab-ču* **river, rivulet, brook;** also **rain.** — ˳*bab-stégs* access or descent to the water, steps leading to a bathing-place *Hind.* *ghāṭ. — ˳*báb-mo** *W.* **condescending, affable.**

འབམ་ ˳*bam* 1. *rkaṅ-*˳*bám* a disease of the foot *Sch.*: **gout.** — 2. ˳*bám-yig* v. *yi-ge.*

འབམ་པ་ ˳*bám-pa Cs.* **putrefaction, rottenness; to be putrid, rotten,** cf. *bám-pa.*

འབར་བ་ ˳*bár-ba* (vb.n. to *sbár-ba*) 1. **to burn,** *me* ˳*bár-bai ḱáṅ-pa* a burning house *Thgy.*; **to catch fire, to be ignited; to blaze** *Dzl.*; also in reference to the passions frq.; **to beam, radiate,** ˳*ód-du* in light *Tar.*; ˳*bár-du rúṅ-ba Cs.* combustible. — 2. **to open, to begin to bloom, to blossom,** frq. — 3. **to talk, tattle, to be garrulous, babbling,** *˳*bar* ˳*ó-pa me'** it is not worth while to talk about it *C.*; *ḱo ṅá-la máṅ-po* ˳*bar* ˳*dug* he treats me to a long gossip *C*; esp. **to brawl, quarrel, chide,** *ḱa-*˳*bár* **quarrelsome, brawling** *Mil.*; *máṅ-du* ˳*bár-du byúṅ-ba-las* as she was going to brawl still longer *Mil.*; **bar-kád táṅ-če** to rail at a person *W.* — 4. *dpal* ˳*bar-ba Cs.* **to be celebrated,** famous.

འབར་འབར་ ˳*bar-*˳*bár* 1. sbst. **a high, pointed hill,** cf. ˳*bag-*˳*bóg.* — 2. adj. **uneven, rough; pock-marked.**

འབལ་བ་ ˳*bal-ba*, used only with *skra*, 1. **to part, dress, arrange,** the hair, as it is customary with the monks and nuns of certain sects; in Kham also national costume; *skra ɣyas* ˳*bal ɣyon* ˳*bal byéd-pa* (of a nun) *Pth.;* **bál-*˳*go-čen** a person wearing the hair thus dressed *C.; skrá-*˳*bal-čan,* prob. id.; *C.*: name of an old Indian sect. — 2. as a sign of mourning, **to have the hair disheveled,** hanging down in disorder *Pth.*; so also *Dzl.* ༧༦༥, 17, acc. to correct reading; ˳*bal-*˳*bál* **shaggy** *Sch.*

འབི་འབི་ ˳*bi-*˳*bi* **small lumps of clay** *Cs.*

འབིག(ས)་པ་ ˳*big(s)-pa*, pf. *ṕigs*, fut. *dbig*, imp. *ṕig(s)* and ˳*búg(s)-pa, ṕug, dbug, ṕug*, also *ṕig-pa, ṕúg-pa*, 1. **to sting,** of insects *Stg.*; **to pierce,** *rdó-rje-yis ni rin-čén ṕug* the diamond pierces the precious stone *Pth.;* **to bore,** *šiṅ-la búg-pa* ˳*búg-pa* to bore holes into wood *Glr.*; in a gen. sense, **to make a hole,** *rkáṅ-pa ḱyis ṕug* the dog bit my foot *Mil.; ḱáṅ-pa* ˳*big-pa Thgy.* and elsewh., **to break into, to break open;** *˳*big gyáb-pa**, id. *C.; ču-*˳*gágs* ˳*bigs* it removes strangury *Med.* — 2. *C.* **to deflower, to lie with,** obscene. — **búg-če** *W.* to make remarks on an absent person, **to criticize.** — *bigs-byéd*, n. p., n. of the Vindhya mountains (v. विन्ध्).

འབིང་ ˳*biṅ*, **jham-biṅ** *C.*, resp. **sol-*˳*biṅ** **tea-pot.**

འབིབ(ས)་པ་ ˳*bib(s)-pa* = ˳*búb(s)-pa Sch.*

འབུ་ ˳*bu* **worm, insect,** any small vermin, esp. euphem. for louse; ˳*bu-srin, srin-˳bu,* id.; ˳*bu-skyógs* **snail** *Med.*; ˳*bu-tags Cs.,* **cob-web**; **bu-yáṅ** (prob. a mere corruption of *búṅ-ba*) **humble-bee** *W.*; *˳*bu-riṅ** **snake** *W.*

འབུ་བ་ ˳*bú-ba,* pf. ˳*bus* 1. **to open, to unfold,** of flowers, esp. with *ḱa Pth.* — 2. *Cs.*: **to be lighted, kindled, set on fire.**

འབུམ་ ˳*bú-ma Sch.*: tool used in forging nails.

འབུ་རས་ ˳*bu-rás* a coarse silky material, stated to be imported into Tibet from Nepal, and to come from some other insect than the silk-worm.

འབུ་ལ་ ˳*bú-la* 1. *C., W.* shoe of plaited straw. — 2. *C.*: **kó-wa bú-la**, a kind of leather, resembling chagreen.

འབུ་སུ་ཧང་ ˳*bu-su-háṅ* medicinal herb *Med.*

འབུག་ ˳*bug Sch.* **awl, puncher; chisel.**

འབུགས་པ་ ˳*búgs-pa* v. ˳*bígs-pa.*

འབུངས་པ་ ˳*búṅs-pa,* prop.: **to fall upon in a body, to rush in upon,** = *rúb-pa*; *čós-la* ˳*buṅs* apply yourselves with might and main to religion! it is also used of one person: ˳*bad* ˳*buṅs* he summons all his strength, strains every nerve *Dzl.*

འབུད་པ་ ˳*búd-pa* I. pf. *bus, ṕu(s)* (the latter form prob. transit., the former intransit.) fut. *dbu,* imp. *ṕu(s)* 1. vb.n. **to blow,** *lás-kyi rluṅ* ˳*búd-čiṅ* whilst the wind of works is blowing; *čós-kyi duṅ bus* the trumpet of religion blew (was blown). — 2. vb. a. **to blow,** *duṅ* the trumpet; **to blow away,** *rluṅ-gis sbúr-ma bús-pa ltar* like chaff blown off by the wind *Dzl.*; to blow up, to fan, *me* the fire, frq.; **to blow into, to inject,** e.g. to apply a clyster *C.*; **to blow** or **breathe upon,** *bsér-bus* to be encountered by a cold wind *Med.*; **to inflate, to distend** by injecting air, *lus ḳuṇ bús-pa ltar skraṅs Mṅg.*; ˳*bud-˳duṅ Wdk.* = *duṅ* trumpet. Cf. *sbúd-pa* and *ṕu.* — *W.* **ṕú-če**. — II. pf. imp. *ṕud,* fut. *dbud W.* **ṕud-če**, trs.: 1. **to put off, pull off, take off** *C., W.,* the turban, hat, coat, ring etc. *Glr.* and elsewh.; **to throw down,** *ṕud bžág-go Glr.,* = **˳paṅ-sté** *bor W.,* v. sub ˳*ṕén-pa.* — 2. **to drive out, expel, cast out, chase away,** with the accus. of the person and place, *yul* out of the country *Tar.*; *yul-ṕud* an exile *Schr.*; *drag-pos* by force *Mil.*; **to let out** (out of a cage); **to set free, to set at liberty, to allow to pass** *W.*; **to lay out, to spend,** **ṅul tsam ṕud soṅ** how many rupees have been laid out, spent? — 3. **to pull out, tear out, extract, uproot,** *so* a tooth, *C., W.* — 4. **to take away, to subtract,** **gú-nẹ** (or *gu tóg-nẹ*) *ži ṕúd-pa* (or *ṕúd-na*) *ṅa lus** 4 taken from 9 leaves 5 *W.* — III. pf. ˳*bud,* vb.n. (limited perh. to *W.*) 1. **to fall from, escape from, drop, fall down,** **lág-pa-nẹ bud soṅ** it escaped, dropped out of my hand; **to fall off,** of leaves; **to fall through,** **sól-wa ḍa-mig-nẹ bud soṅ** the coals are fallen through the grate. — 2. **to go away, to leave,** e.g. to leave the service. — 3. **to go out of sight, to disappear,** **nyi-ma bud soṅ** the sun is gone down; **búd-ḱan** a departed (deceased) person; **the ancients, those of old,** *pristini*; **to pass away,** **dus-ťsód bud** time passes away (make haste!); **pid-ka šar-na gun bud soṅ** when spring begins, winter has passed away; **bud čug-če** **to cause to be lost,** or **to suffer to be lost, to lose.**

འབུན་པ་, བུན་པ་ ˳*bún-pa, bún-pa* **to itch;** **bun, zá-bun** **the itch, itching** *W.*; **bun rag** I feel an itching (*B. gyd-ba*).

འབུབ་པ་ ˳*búb-pa,* pf. *bub,* imp. *bub(s),* 1. **to be turned over, upside down,** frq. with *ḱa, ḱa-˳búb-tu nyal* he lies with his face undermost; *ḱa-˳bub-tu bžag* or *bor* it is placed with its top lowermost, inverted, tilted, turned over; *lag-˳búb* (or *-bubs*) *byéd-pa Sch.*: stumbling to fall on the hands. — 2. fig., **to be overthrown, destroyed, spoiled,** with regard to meditation *Mil.*

འབུབས་པ་ ˳*búbs-pa,* pf. imp. *ṕub(s),* fut. *dbub, W.* **ṕub-če**, **to put on a roof,** or something for a roof; *ťog* **to make, construct a roof;** *gur* to pitch a tent; *gru-ṕubs* corner-pavilion *S.g.*

འབུམ་ ˳*bum* **one hundred thousand,** ˳*búm-ťso* id.; *rgyai dmag* ˳*búm-ťso lṅa*

500 000 Chinese *Glr.*; ₒ*bum-ṗrág γčig* a hundred thousand; ₒ*búm-ťso drug* 600000; *mgur-ₒbúm* the 100 000 songs, v. *mgúr-ma*.

འབུམ་པ་ ₒ*búm-pa* **tomb, sepulchre** *Cs.*, *sku-ₒbúm*, *γduṅ-ₒbúm Cs.*, id.; *sku-ₒbúm* (**kum-búm**) n.p., a large monastery on the Chinese frontier, v. Huc, also *Köpp.*, who traces the name back to the preceding word.

འབུར་བ་ ₒ*búr-ba*, I. vb. 1. **to rise, to be prominent**, *sbáṅ-la brág-ri ₒbúr-ba čig* a rocky hill rising from the green-sward *Mil.*; ₒ*búr-du dód-pa* v. *dód-pa*; ₒ*búr-du rkó-ba* to emboss, to work out relievos *Glr.*; *ₒ*bur-kó gyáb-pa** *C*, **búr-la tón-če** *W.* id. — 2. **to spring up, come forth, bud, unfold,** **ño bur dug** it is getting green *W.* — 3. **to increase, augment,** **ño kyé-na ŏ-ma bur dug** when the fields are getting green, milk becomes more plentiful *W.* — *kyoṅ-ₒbur* gold and silver ornaments in relievo on some other metal. — *glo-ₒbúr*, *blo-ₒbur* seems to be a technical term for some part of a building *Glr.* — *bris-ₒbúr* paintings and sculptures. — ₒ*búr-rko-mḱan*, ₒ*búr-bzo-pa* engraver. — ₒ*búr-sku* relief-picture — ₒ*bur-rgód* (s.l.c.) *Ld.-Glr.*, *Schl.* 17, b., mentioned among various musical instruments(?). — ₒ*bur-ǰóms* with *byéd-pa* to reduce elevations, to smooth uneven ground; fig. *Mil.*, to prostrate an opponent in disputation. — ₒ*búr-po* 1. *Sch.*: **projecting, prominent; a protuberance, tumor,** *rús-pai ₒbúr-poi ldebs* near the protuberance of the bone *Med.* 2. **having protuberances, uneven, rough,** opp. to ₒ*ǰám-po*, of the skin *Med.* — ₒ*búr-ma* embossment, relievo — II. sbst. **protuberance,** e g. a boil, pustule etc.

འབུལ་བ་ ₒ*búl-ba* I. vb., pf. imp. *ṗul*, fut. *dbul* (**ul*, *ṳl**), *W.* **ṗúl-če** 1. **to give,** when the person receiving is considered to be of higher rank (cf. *γnáṅ-ba*), *či tsam žig dbúl-bar bgyi* how much shall we give you? *Feer Introd.* p. 70, 18; **to bring in,** e.g to place a criminal before the king *Dzl.*; *gar daṅ rtséd-mo rgyál-po-la ₒbúl-ba* to perform dances etc. before the king *Dzl.*; *γtsúg-lag-ḱaṅ rgyál-po-la γzígs-par ₒbúl-ba* to show the king the convent-temple *Glr.*; **to lay before, represent, report,** like *γsól-ba*, *ťsul rgyas ṗúl-bas* as they had given him a minute report of the manner in which ... *Mil.*; *ṗul žig* communicate it to me *Mil.*; ₒ*bul-bar ṗul-nas Mil.*, prob. proposing to give, offering; *lam* to put a person in the way of, to put in a condition, to enable *Mil.*; specifically in dating letters: *dkar-mdáṅs-nas ṗul* given at Kardang. — 2. **to add** (arith.) *Wdk.* II. sbst. **offering, gift, present,** ₒ*búl-ba maṅ-po ṗul Mil.*, also *byéd-pa Pth.*

འབུས་པ་ ₒ*bús-pa* 1. v. ₒ*bú-ba*. — 2. = ₒ*búr-bar*, **prominent.**

འབུས་ཤིང་ ₒ*bus-šiṅ Sch.* **a coppice of young trees.**

འབེ་དྷ་ ₒ*be-dha* (**bé-da**), a class of **itinerant musicians**, cf. *mon W.* (This seems not to be a Tibetan word, but to belong to one of the mountain dialects; its spelling also — acc. to *Ld.-Glr.*, *Schl.* 25, b. p. 15 — may be wrong).

འབེན་ ₒ*ben Pth.*, *ₒ*bem** *W.*, *C.*, 1. **aim, goal, target,** ₒ*ben ₒdzúgs-pa* to set up a target; ₒ*bén-la γtod-pa* to aim, to take aim; ₒ*bén-sa* the place where the target is to be set up; specifically: the central part of the target, the mark. — 2. **scope** *Cs.* — 3. **putrefaction** *Sch.*, = ₒ*bam*.

འབེན་དུག་ ₒ*ben-dúg Cs.* **rags, tatters.**

འབེབས་པ་ ₒ*bébs-pa*, pf. *ṗab*, fut. *dbab*, imp. *ṗob W.* **ṗáb-če**, causative to ₒ*báb-pa* 1. **to cast down, throw down,** *ltó-ba sa-la* to cast one's self on the ground *Dzl.*; *sa-rdúl ₒbebs bčug* he made (the pigeon) throw down dust *Glr.*; **to cause to rain** (e.g. jewels) frq.; *ḱyeu ču ₒbébs-kyi ri-mo* a picture representing two youths who, driven by piety, conveyed by means of an elephant skins filled with water to the fishes in a dried-up pool *Glr.*; *mig sna-rtsér* to keep one's eyes directed towards the tip of the nose. — 2. **to subject** *Dzl.* ༢༥༠, 12. — 3. **to put off, to lay aside,** e.g. *bug* I. — 4. used in a variety of phrases: *γnas ₒbébs-pa W.* **ži ṗáb-če** to take up one's residence in a place; *dpya ₒbébs-pa*, with *la*, to impose taxes *Tar.*, cf *˳bab; skyon ˳bébs-pa* to impute a crime to a person, to calumniate *Glr.*; **(s)kad ṕab-če* W.* to translate; *blo*, resp. *ṫugs*, e.g. *yul-ṕyogs ˳di-ru ˳bébs-pa* to direct one's thoughts to a certain place, to have a mind to settle there; *ytán-la ˳bébs-pa* v. *ytan*; **nā ṅúl-la ṕáb-ča** to turn the barley into money *Kun.*

འབེམ་ *˳bem* v. *ben.*

འབེར་ *˳ber Cs.*: 'a sort of plastic mass used by smiths'.

འབེལ་(མ་) *˳bel(-ma)* the hair on the forehead of a horse *Cs.*

འབེལ་པོ་ *˳bél-po Sch.*: **'temperate, saving, economical**; *˳bél-po ˳dug* a good deal has been saved (by economy), ample provision has been made; *˳bél-du ˳ǰúg-pa* to enjoin temperance, frugality' (?).

འབོ་ *˳bo* **a dry measure,** which seems to be very variable as to quantity, and little used; *ḱal-bó Cs.* **bushel.**

འབོ་བ་ *˳bó-ba*, pf. *˳bos, bo, ṕo*, fut. *dbo W.* **bo-če, ṕo-če**, **to pour out,** *ḱrag ˳bó-ba* to shed blood *Ma.*; *ma bó-ba byúṅ-nas* there being no spilling *Glr.*; *bdúd-rtsi ṕó-bas* pouring out nectar *Glr.*; **ṕos toṅ* Ld.* pour out! — 2. **to swell (up), to rise,** **bós-te rag** I see it has swelled *W.*; *˳bós-pai nas Sch.* swelled barley; *srán-ma ṕós-pa tsam* as big as a swelled pea *Lt.*; *srád-ma ṕos-ṕós* grain swelled, and afterwards parched. — 3. **to sprout, shoot forth,** of wild-growing plants, *sa ˳bo ˳dug* the ground is verdant *C.*

འབོག་ *˳bog*, a kind of **upper-garment,** *ṕo-˳bóg*, for men, *mo-˳bóg* for females *Cs.* — 2. *W.*: **a square cloth,** for wrapping up and carrying provisions, also **bog-ča**, hence **bog-ṭ̣es** a burden thus formed. — 3. *W.*, **a small hillock;** **sa-bóg, be-bóg** a sand-hill; **ri-bóg** a projecting hill, also a clod; **paṅ-bóg** a piece of turf.

འབོག་ཆོལ་ *˳bog-čol* v. *sbug-čol.*

འབོག་ཐོ་ *˳bog-ṫó, žwá-mo ˳bog-ṫo Cs.*, **hat** with a broad crown of yellow cloth, and trimmed with long-haired fur.

འབོག(ས་)པ་ *˳bog(s)-pa*, pf. *bog, ṕog*, fut. *dbog?* *W.* **bog-če**, **to be rooted out, uprooted, pulled out,** of teeth *W.*; **to be put out of joint,** *tsigs W.* — 2. **to be taken down** (opp. to *˳gél-ba*), *ḱál-rnams ṕog Glr.* the loads were taken off; **zaṅ mé-ne** the kettle from the fire *W.* — 3. **to grow loose, to come off, to drop off,** leaves from a tree *C.* — 4. **to sink down, to fall to the ground,** esp. in a fainting-fit, *˳bog-čiṅ brgyál-ba Thgy.*, *brgyál(-žiṅ) ˳bóg pa Pth*, id.; *˳bog yun-riṅ-na Lt.* prob.: when the fainting-fit has lasted a long time; *smyo-˳bóg* **madness, insanity,** *˳byuṅ* sets in, takes place *Glr.*; *˳bog-ši* being quickly carried off, by cholera etc. *W.* — 5. **to wade, to dip into, to submerge,** *čú-la Dzl.* also *ču Lex.* to wade through the water.

འབོགས་པ་ *˳bógs-pa*, pf. *ṕog*, fut *dbog, dbag*, imp. *ṕog*, 1. **to give, to impart,** *ydams-ṅág, luṅ* counsel, advice, directions *Tar.*; *ḱrid, bsláb-pa Mil.* instruction; *sdóm-pa* to impose religious duties, i.e. to receive into holy orders *Glr.*; to bequeath, to give (?), *nor Lex.* — 2. *yži-ma* **to fit up a dwelling,** = *˳bébs-pa Glr.*; *gro ˳bógs-pa* to take breakfast. — 3. **to blot, stain, pollute,** v. *˳bág-pa.*

འབོང་བ་ *˳bóṅ-ba Cs.*, **roundness, rotundity,** *˳boṅ-˳bóṅ*, **round**; acc. to my informants **boṅ-bóṅ** **loose, slack, incoherent** *W.* —

འབོད་ *˳bod* 1. v. *˳bód-pa.* — 2. v. *˳bád-pa.*

འབོད་པ་ *˳bód-pa, bód-pa*, pf. imp. *bos*, *W.* **bo-če, bos (boi, bo̤)**, 1. **to call, to exclaim,** *sdod čig čes bós-so* he exclaimed: wait! *Dzl.*; *mi žig B.*, *mi žig-la* col., to call a person; *rtsar Glr.*, *mdún-du Pth.* to call near; *náṅ-du* to call in; *˳bód-pai brda* or *tsig* **interjection** *Gram*; *čáṅ-la ˳bod-pa* to call, to invite, to a cup of beer *Dzl.*; *ma bós-par ˳óṅ-ba* to come uninvited *Dzl*; *ḱú-čos ˳bód-pa Wdṅ.*, *˳bod-grógs-pa Dzl.* to cry repeatedly; **bós-ra* Ld.*, **boi-ra, bo̤-ra* Lh.*, **ṫáṅ-če* or *gyáb-če** id. *W.*; *ṅu-˳bód* howling, v. *ṅú-ba.* — 2. **to call, to name, to denominate,** *yúl-skad... ˳bód-pa* commonly called, styled ... *Wdṅ.*

འབོབས་ ₒ*bobs*, not exactly 'stocking' (*Sch.*), but a soft, warm stuffing of the stockings; **bob-zóm** a shoe provided with such stuffing *C.*

འབོར་བ་ ₒ*bór-ba*, pf. imp. *bor*, 1. **to throw, cast, fling,** e.g. the mendicant's bowl up in the air, the sword to the ground *Dzl.*; *zám-pai ₒóg-tu* to precipitate a person from a bridge *Dzl.*; *p̀yir* to cast out *Thgy.*; **ma bhor-wa jhe'** *C.* don't throw it away! **bhor soṅ** I've lost it *C. bor-ytór, bor-stór, bor-dór, dór-ₒbor-ba Mil.* and elsewh. id.; to throw away, pour away, *č̀u* water *C.*; to waste, to squander *Dzl.* — 2. **to leave, forsake,** *k̀yim-t̀ab* husband or wife *Dzl.*; to leave behind, *mi žig bód-du* to leave a person behind in Tibet; *yáb-kyis bór-bai t̀se* when I was left by my father, when my father died *Pth.*; *de bór-la t̀oṅ* let that alone, give it up, keep away from it *Mil.*; **ṅa lé-ka bor taṅ yin** *W.* I shall now leave off working, I shall put aside my work. — 3. = ₒ*jóg-pa*, **to place, put, lay,** in *W.* the word commonly used, in *C.* and *B.* only in certain phrases: **'i-ru bor** put it here! **tán-ni k̀ar bór-če** to seat a person on the carpet, to invite to a seat on the carpet; **mii lág-tu t̀in bór-če** to place a charge into somebody's hands; **nyér-pa só-ma bór-če** to appoint a new manager; frq. with gerund: **k̀yi tág-te bór-če** to fasten a dog (to a chain). — 4. in particular combinations, e.g. *góm-pa.*

འབོལ་ ₒ*bol* (v. *bol*) **cushion, bolster, mattress;** *snye-ₒból* pillow, v. *snye-ba.*

འབོལ་པོ་ ₒ*ból-po B., C.,* **ₒból-mo** *W.* 1. **soft,** of the ground, beds, leather, fruit etc.; **soft, gentle, pliable,** also as to disposition of mind; ₒ*ból-le šig-ge sdód-pa* to sit still, to remain quiet, tranquil *Mil.* —. 2. *C.* = *mód-po.*

འབོས་ ₒ*bos* 1. v. ₒ*bo.* — 2. v. ₒ*bo-ba.* — 3. sbst. **boil, bump, tumour** *C.*

འབྱང་བ་ ₒ*byaṅ-ba* **to clean, cleanse, purify** *Cs.*, ₒ*byaṅ-k̀yád* custom *C., W.*

འབྱམས་པ་ ₒ*byám-pa,* pf. *byams Cs.*, **to flow over, to be diffused.** ₒ*byam-klás-pa Lex., Cs.*: unlimited, infinite; *rab-ₒbyáms Lex., Cs.*: widely diffused, far spread; *rab-ₒbyáms-pa Cs.*: a man of profound learning, a doctor of theology or philosophy; also *Schr.*; *Köpp.* II, 253.

འབྱར་བ་ ₒ*byár-ba* v. ₒ*byór-ba.*

འབྱི་བ་ ₒ*byi-ba,* pf. *byi,* also *p̀yi* and *p̀yis,* vb.n. of *p̀yi-ba* **to be wiped off, blotted out, effaced** *Cs.*; **to fall off,** of the hair *Dzl.* and elsewh.

འབྱིང་བ་ ₒ*byiṅ-ba,* pf. *byiṅ* 1. **to sink in, to sink down, to be swallowed up,** *šiṅ-rta byé-ma-la ₒbyiṅ Glr.* the carriage sticks fast in the sand; *gru č̀ú-la* the ship sinks in the water *Dzl.* and elsewh. — 2. **to grow faint, languid, remiss,** *rig-pa byiṅ-ba bsér-ba* to lift up again one's fainting soul *Mil.*; *byiṅ-rgod* seems to signify **languor, distraction,** *byiṅ-rmúgs Mil.*, id., *byiṅ-rmugs-méd-pai sgom*; so also *byiṅ-t̀ibs Lt.*; *sems-byiṅ-ba* **drowsiness, indolence, depression of spirits.** — 3. *C.* **jhiṅ soṅ, jhiṅ log soṅ**, they have dispersed, separated, are all gone home. — 4. v. ₒ*jiṅ*, 2.

འབྱིད་པ་ ₒ*byid-pa,* pf. *byid, p̀yid* 1. **to glide, to slip** *Lex.* = ₒ*dréd-pa.* — 2. **to disappear, to pass away,** e.g. *mi-t̀se ₒbyid* human life passes away *Lex.*; in *W.* **tse jid-če** vb.a., to earn a livelihood, **gár-ra čó-te** by smith's work (*C. lto zá-ba*).

འབྱིན་པ་ ₒ*byin-pa,* pf. imp. *p̀yuṅ,* fut. (in *C.* also pres.) *dbyuṅ Ld.* **p̀iṅ-če**, trs. of ₒ*byuṅ-ba,* **to cause to come forth: 1. to take out, to remove,** a pillar from its place *Dzl.*; **p̀iṅs(toṅ)** take it out (out of your pocket, out of the box etc.) *Ld.*; **to draw out, pull out,** a sword, a thorn etc., frq.; **to tear out, to put out,** one's eyes etc., *mig dbyúṅ-ba dé-dag* the men whose eyes are to be put out *Dzl.* p. ༢༩, 10, acc. to an emended reading; **to draw forth, produce, bring to light,** something that was hid *Dzl.* — 2. in a more gen. sense: **to let proceed from, to send out, to emit,** rays of light, frq.; *lus-la k̀rag* to draw blood by scratching one's self *Dzl.*; *mč̀i-ma Glr.* to shed tears; *skad* to make the voice to be heard, of a bird *Dzl.*; *sdug-bsṅál-gyi skad* to utter complaints, lamentations *Dzl.*; *skad čén-po* to cry aloud *Dzl.*; **to exhibit, to extol,** *bstán-pai čé-ba* the grandeur of the doctrine *Tar.* 48,9, *Schf.*; **to drive out, turn out, expel,** *ynas byin-pa Tar.*, **yúṅ-wa* Ts.*, to banish, so also *Ld.* **piṅ-če**; **to cast out, throw away** *Ts.*; **to save, rescue, liberate, release,** *nas* from, *Dom.*; absol. *Tar.* 121,19. — 3. particular phrases, such as *ḱól-du p̔yúṅ-ba, yid byin-pa* etc. v. in their own places.

འབྱུག་པ་ *byúg-pa*, pf. and imp. *byugs* 1. **to wet, moisten, smear, spread over, anoint,** with *la: ša skám-la ťsá-ču byúgs-pa* salt-meat *Glr.*; *ydóṅ-la sol-snúm byúg-pa* to daub one's face with coal-salve *Glr.*; also with accus. and instrum.: *lha-rtén spos daṅ byúg-pas* covering the little temple with spices and ointments *Dzl.*; *yser byúg-pa* prob. to gild *Pth.* — 2. **to stroke, to pat,** *mgó la* a person's head *Dzl.*

འབྱུང་བ་ *byúṅ-ba* I. vb., pf. imp. *byuṅ* (intrs of *byin-pa*) **to come out, to emerge,** often with a pleon. *p̔yir* etc., from the water, from an egg, a vessel etc. *Dzl.*; *ḱór-ba-las* = to be set free, to be liberated *Dom.*; to go out, *ḱyim-nas Dzl.*; *p̔yi-rol-tu byúṅ-ba* to go out into the open air *Dzl.*; **to make one's appearance, to become visible** *Dzl.*; **to show one's self, to appear** *rgyál-poi rmi-lam-du byúṅ-bai lha-yčig* the princess that appeared to the king in a dream *Glr.*; also: *ṅá-la rmi-lam bzáṅ-po byuṅ* I have had an auspicious dream *Mil.*: *sgrén-mor byúṅ-ba* to go abroad naked *Dzl.*; **to be heard, to resound,** *skad* frq.; **to be said, to be told** *Tar.*; **to turn out, to prove, to be found,** *ma bzi-ba su byúṅ-ba* he who is found not intoxicated *Glr.*; *ṅán-pa byuṅ* it proved to be ill founded *Mil.*; ...*pa su yaṅ ma byuṅ* none was to be found that ... *Pth.*; to step forward, from the crowd; to step forth, to appear *Glr.*; **to step up to,** with *rtsar* to *Glr.*; *brgyúgs-nas byuṅ* they came running up or near *Pth.*; **to go to, to proceed to, to come,** *rii rtsé-mor Dzl.*; **ka-náṅ-wa ma júṅ-na* W.* if no order (permission etc.) comes; *dbugs p̔yir byuṅ-nas* when breathing returned, when they recovered from fainting *Dzl.*; *mun-pai bskal-pa lṅa-brgya byuṅ-ṅo* then came, followed, 500 dark Kalpas *Pth.* — 2 **to rise,** as kings, frq.; **to arise, to originate, to become,** with *nas, las,* from, in consequence of, by, *dé-nas byuṅ* it derives its origin from that *Glr.*; *brás-bu byúṅ-bai šiṅ* trees on which fruit is growing *Stg.*; *mi byúṅ-bar gyúr ba* not to come to a fair beginning, to be suppressed in its first beginnings *Glr.*; *ḱyeu žig byuṅ dug* by that time a boy had become of it *Glr.*; *ynyis-su byuṅ* they became two, they split in two (systems of doctrine); *ráb-tu byúṅ-ba* to become a priest, v. *rab*; to come in (money); **to happen, to take place,** very frq., *ltas či byuṅ* what signs have taken place? *Dzl.*; *mi žig-la nyés-pa čén-po byuṅ* = a man has committed etc. *Dzl.* frq.; *ro di-rnams-la či byuṅ-ba yin* what has happened to these corpses, what is their history? *Glr.*; *sṅar byuṅ-ba* and *ma byuṅ-ba* things heard of and unheard of *Tar.*; *ḱá-p̔ye-nas yód-pa dé-aṅ de dús-su byúṅ-ṅo* 'at that time also the opened position (of the hands of the image) took place' *Glr.*; *blá-ma-la yaṅ byuṅ lágs-sam* did the same thing happen to your Reverence? *Mil.*; *ṅéd-kyis di-bžin byuṅ* it is I that brought this thing about *Glr.*; *p̔yis-byuṅ* or *byuṅ* the later time, time to come, also adv. afterwards, latterly, *Tar.* — 3. The word more and more assumes the character of an auxiliary in such phrases as the following: *gro-ťub-pa byuṅ* they were able to proceed (the possibility of proceeding was brought about) *Glr.*; *da bla-ma der bžúgs-pa byúṅ-na* in case your Reverence should stay there *Mil.*; with the supine: *búl-du, žér-du, stón-du byúṅ-ba-la(s)* as they gave, said, showed *Mil.*; *ťugs-dám p̔él-bar byuṅ* meditation increased; lastly, with the root only: *bod daṅ brel byuṅ* came into communication with Tibet *Glr.*; *sleb byúṅ-ba-la* when he appeared *Mil.*; *rdo dbyug byuṅ* he threw a stone; and so it is commonly used now, esp. in *C.*; it supplies the place of a copula in: *ysuṅ de kun séms-la šin-tu ťád-pa žig byuṅ* this song was truly heart-affecting *Mil.*

Comp. ˳byúṅ-k̔uṅs 1. = čʼu-mig **a well, spring** *Sambh.* 2. **origin** *Pth.* 3. **ablative case** *Gram.* — ˳byúṅ-k̔uṅs-kyi k̔ams *Cs.*, 'a mineral, *byuṅ-k̔uṅs-kyi k̔áms-kyi bčud* a mineral elixir' (?) — ˳*byuṅ-γnás* (सम्भव), **place of origin** (cf. *padma ˳byuṅ-γnás*); **primitive source,** *yón-tan t̔ams-čád-kyi ˳byuṅ-γnás* source of all accomplishments; *byuṅ-bai γži* id.; *p̔an-bdé t̔ams-čád ˳byúṅ-bai γži* primordial source of all happiness. — II. sbst. 1. **a coming forth, an originating, the state of being,** ˳*byuṅ-ba-nyid Tar.* 4, 4 *Schf.* the true state of a case. — 2. **element,** usually 4: ˳*byúṅ-ba bžii γnód-pa* damage done by fire, water, wind and sand *Glr.*; ˳*byuṅ-ba bžii lus* the physical body, very frq.; ˳*byúṅ ba γyo* the elements are in motion, are raging *Ma.*; higher philosophy numbers 5 elements, adding the ether, *mk̔a*, as the fifth; accordingly physiology teaches, that in the composition of the human body earth constitutes the mucus of the nose, water the saliva, fire produces the pictures formed in the eyes, air the sensations of the skin, ether the sensations of the ear; even 6 elements are spoken of, v. *Köpp.* I, 602. — 3. symb. num. for 5.

འབྱུང་པོ ˳*byúṅ-po* (भूत) 1. **being, creature,** ˳*byúṅ-po kun* all beings *Cs.*; ˳*byúṅ-po čʼén-po* the great being, Buddha *Cs.* — 2. **demon, evil spirit, foul sprite,** frq., ˳*byuṅ-po-srúṅ* a preservative, talisman, against such; ˳*byúṅ-mo* fem. *Cs.*

འབྱེ་བ ˳*byé-ba*, pf. and imp. *bye*, *W.* **be-če(s)**, intrs. of ˳*byéd-pa* 1. **to open,** *padma k̔á-bye-ba* a lotos-flower that has opened *Glr.*; *mṅal k̔á-bye-nas* when the mouth of the womb has opened itself *S.g.* — 2. **to divide, separate, resolve,** *ska sla γnyís-su bye* it resolves into thick and thin matter *Med.*; *dúm-bu stóṅ-du dbyé-bar ˳gyur* it separates into a thousand pieces *Glr.*; *bye-brág ma byé-bai bár-du* as long as the separation has not evidenced itself *Dzl.*

འབྱེད་པ ˳*byéd-pa*, pf. and imp. *p̔ye*, *p̔yed*, *p̔yes*, fut. *dbye*, *W.* **p̔é-če(s)**, pf. and imp. **p̔e(s)**, vb. a., 1. **to open,** **k̔a p̔e(s) toṅ** *W.* open your mouth; *sgo p̔yés-nas ˳ǰóg-pa Pth*, **p̔é-te bór-če** *W.* to open the door without shutting it again; fig. *čʼós-kyi sgo rnám-par ˳byéd-pa*; *mig* to open one's eyes, opp. to ˳*dzúm-pa*; *lóṅ-bai mig ˳byéd-pa* to open a blind man's eyes *Dzl.*; to open again what had been shut or stopped, to restore, *dáṅ-ga, yi-ga B.*, *k̔am W.* the appetite; *ba-p̔yéd* the open b, b pronounced like w, *Gram.*; to get out, work out, fetch out, stone-shivers by means of a chisel *Glr.* — 2. **to separate, to keep asunder, to disentangle,** threads *W.*; to disunite, to set at variance, *dé-dag dbyé-bai p̔yir* in order to set them at variance, to create enmity between them *Stg.*; to part, separate, *byaṅ-k̔óg-stod-smad mčʼin-dris dbyé-ba ste* the cavity of the chest and the abdomen being separated by the diaphragm *S.g.*; **to divide, classify,** *rígs-kyi sgó-nas dbyé-na* if they are classified according to the different species *Lt.*; **to pick, to sort,** pease; hence, **to pick out, choose, select,** **p̔é-te kyoṅ** make your choice, and bring it here! *W.*; *séms-čan-rnams lás kyis rnám-par p̔ye* the beings are severed by their deeds *Thgy.*; *k̔á-p̔ye-ba* to open, to separate, e.g. when hands, that were laid in each other, are separated again *Glr.*; *k̔á-p̔ye-ba* also **to open, to begin to bloom**; ˳*byéd-pa* **to dissect, to anatomize** *Thgy.*; esp. with *rnám-par*, **to analyze,** to explain grammatically and logically, *don*, the sense, import, *Stg.* frq.; as *sdúd-pa* is the opposite of it: ˳*byed-sdúd* **analysis and synthesis** *Cs.*; ˳*byed-sdúd-kyi sgra* term for the affix *am*, the disjunctive particle (ni f.) *Glr.*; *mi-p̔yéd-pa* **inseparable, indivisible, imperishable,** *sku Sch.*; **unshaken, immovable,** *dád-pa Mil.* frq.

འབྱེད་དཔྱད ˳*byed-dpyád Sch.* **tongs, pincers.**

འབྱེམ་པ ˳*byém-pa*, with *byéd-pa*, 'to act with promptness, determination and good success' *Sch.*

འབྱེར་བ ˳*byér-ba* pf. and imp. *byer*, **to disperse in flight,** to flee in different directions *Dzl.* *ts̔óṅ-˳dus byér-nas mi ˳dúg-ste* the market-people having fled, and no body remaining *Pth.*; **to give way, to be**

removed, of diseases *Lt.*, opp. to *rgyas* and *bsags*.

འབྱོ་བ་ ₒ*byó-ba*, pf. *ṗyo*, *ṗyos*, imp. *ṗyo*, *byo*, *byos*, **to pour out, to pour into another vessel, to transfuse** *Lex.* and *Cs.*

འབྱོག་པ་ ₒ*byóg-pa*, pf. *byogs* **to lick** *Lex.* and *Cs.*

འབྱོང་བ་ ₒ*byóṅ-ba* I. pf. *byáṅ-ba* 1. **to be cleansed,** purified, v. *byáṅ-ba*. — 2. **to be skilled, well versed,** *rig-byéd-la* in the Vedas *Tar.* — II. pf ₒ*byoṅs-pa* **to be finished, perfect, complete,** frq. with *snyiṅ-ṙje Mil* and elsewh., to exercise full compassion(?) cf. *sbyóṅ-ba*. (The above arrangement is nothing more than an attempt; in order to arrive at any certainty as to these roots, a far greater number of observations would be required.)

འབྱོན་པ་ ₒ*byón-pa*, pf. and imp. *byon*, resp. **to go, proceed, travel,** *dé-nas byón-pa-na* then in proceeding on the way *Glr.*; **to arrive, appear, become visible;** also for ₒ*byúṅ-ba*, e.g. *raṅ-byón*; with root of the verb: *ṗúr-byon-pas* preparing to fly *Mil.*; *ma-byón-pa* = *ma-ₒóṅs-pa* future (Buddhas) *S.O.*; to rise, to appear; with dat. inf. = ₒ*ǰúg-pa* **to begin, to set about** a certain work *Tar.* 125, 16.

འབྱོར་པ་ ₒ*byór-pa* **wealth, riches, goods, treasures,** ₒ*byor-pa zád-mi-šes-pa daṅ ldán-pa* one possessing inexhaustible wealth, *bdé-ba daṅ* ₒ*byór-pa* joy and treasures *S.O.*; ₒ*byór-pa drug Pth.*, prob. six kinds of temporal goods; *ráṅ-gi* ₒ*byór-pa lṅa* and *γžan-gyi* ₒ*byor-pa-lṅa* five subjective and five objective goods, of a similar nature as those mentioned sub *dal-*ₒ*byor*, yet without any evident reason for being thus divided *Thgy.*; ₒ*byor-ldán* rich, mostly used as a noun personal.

འབྱོར་བ་, འབྱར་བ་ ₒ*byór-ba*, ₒ*byár-ba* I. intrs. of *sbyór-ba* 1. **to stick to, adhere to** *Med.*; **ḱyág-la ǰar soṅ**, it is frozen fast *W.*; ₒ*byár-byed spyin* glue *Lex.*; ₒ*byor-sman* sticking-plaster *W.*; **to infect,** of diseases, ₒ*byor-nad* an infectious disease *Cs.* also mentally: **lo* or *sém-la ǰar** it sticks fast, is remembered, borne in mind.

2. **to be prepared,** ready, at hand, extant, *ša ma byór-nas* there being no meat prepared *Dzl.*; ₒ*ṗrál-du* ₒ*byór-ba ma yin* that is not at once in readiness *Dzl.*; *či* ₒ*byór-ba des mčód-pa byéd-pa* to offer sacrifice of such things as are at hand *Dzl.*; *či-ste* ₒ*byór-bar mi* ₒ*gyúr-na* but if he has not such a thing at his disposal *Sambh.* — 3. **to agree,** *mi-*ₒ*byór-ba ḱá-čig* some disagreements, contradictions *Tar.* — II. resp. **to come, arrive,** *W.*, *C.*; **ḱyé-kyi ku dǘn-du ǰár-gyu yin** I shall appear before your Honour *C.*; **nyár-du ǰar yoṅ** I shall immediately attend *C.*

འབྱོལ་བ་ ₒ*byól-ba*, pf. and imp. *byol*, fut. (and pres. in *C.*) *dbyol* **to give** or **make way, to turn out of the way, to step aside,** *γčig-gis γčig-la Dzl.*; ₒ*byól-te* ₒ*gro* in walking I make way (to people) *Dzl.*; *W.* with accus.: **rul, las, dig-pa ǰól-če** to step out of the way of, to shun, a serpent, toil, sin. Sometimes ₒ*ǰól-ba*.

འབྲ་གོ་ ₒ*brá-go* n. of a medicine *Med.*

འབྲང་ ₒ*braṅ* v. *braṅ* II.

འབྲང་རྒྱས་ ₒ*braṅ-rgyás Mil.* **sacrifice,** offering of eatables.

འབྲང་བ་ ₒ*bráṅ-ba* 1. pf. ₒ*braṅs*, imp. ₒ*broṅ*, **to bear, bring forth, give birth; to litter,** *bráṅ-mo* an animal going with young, bearing *Cs.* — 2. also ₒ*bréṅ-ba*, pf. ₒ*braṅs*, imp. ₒ*breṅs Mil.* (ₒ*broṅ Sch ?*) **to follow, to walk at another's heels,** with *ṗyir*, *ṗyi-bžin* (-*du*), *ṙjés-su*, *W.* **tíṅ-la** with genit., **to follow, pursue, hunt after,** *dbyúg-pas* with a stick *Pth.*; **to pursue,** in one's thoughts.

འབྲད་པ་, འདྲད་པ་ ₒ*brád-pa*, ₒ*drád-pa*, pf. *brad*, imp. *brod* **to scratch, to scrape,** with the nails, claws etc.; **to lacerate by scratching,** *γdoṅ Dzl.*; also **to gnaw, nibble at.**

འབྲབ་པ་ ₒ*bráb-pa*, pf. *brab*, imp. *brob* 1. **to catch suddenly, to snap away, snatch away,** a fly with one's hand, the prey with a bound. — 2. **to beat, to scourge,** *tser-lčág-gis* with thorns *Thgy.* — 3. **to throw out, to scatter,** magical objects, such as grains of barley etc.

འབྲལ་བ་ ˳*brál-ba*, pf. *bral*, imp. *brol*, intrs. of ˳*p̀rál-ba*, **to be separated, parted from, deprived of**, c. *daṅ*, e.g. from one's retinue, of the light of doctrine *Dzl.*; ˳*brál-bar mi p̀od bú-mo k̀yod* thou, my daughter, from whom I am not able to part *Glr.*; *č̀ún-ṅu-nas p̀a-má γnyis daṅ brál-te* from a child bereft of parents, an orphan from infancy *Pth.*; **to lose, to be bereft**, frq. used in reference to the death of near relations; *mdo-sdé daṅ lág-pa mi brál-žiṅ* as the sacred writings never came out of his hands; *skóm-pa daṅ brál-bar gyúr-to* he got rid of his thirst; *nad daṅ brál-bar gyúr-to* he recovered from his illness, frq. (in such cases often confounded by the illiterate with *nád-las bsgral* etc.); more particularly: *srog daṅ* etc. **to die, perish**, frq.; ˳*ǰig-č̀iṅ* ˳*brál-bar* ˳*gyúr-ba* to be dissolved, of the human body *Dzl.*; ˳*dú-ba yód-na* ˳*bral-bar oṅ* what was solid, is dissolved in dust *Dzl.*; ˳*bral(-bar) med (-pa)* **inseparable, indissoluble,** frq.

འབྲས་ ˳*bras*, *C.* also ˳*brás-mo*, resp. *bsaṅ-˳brás* (*Pur.* **bras**, *Ld.* **ḍas**, *Lh.* **ḍai**, *C.* **ḍe**) 1. **rice**; ˳*bras-dkár(-mo)* white rice, ˳*bras-dmár* red rice (the inferior and cheaper sort); of the former there seem to be distinguished: ˳*bo-tsa-li* (*Hd.* **basmati**), *rgyal-mo-γsáṅ*, *ham-dzém*, ˳*dzin-˳dzin* the second sort, acc. to *Cs.*; ˳*brás-kyi srus* peeled rice *Sch.*; ˳*bras-sá-lu* 'wild rice' *Sch.*; ˳*bras-so-ba Sch.* and *Schr.*, rice not husked ˳*brás-mo spos-šél* or *dkar-˳dzóm Ts.* maize.

Comp. ˳*bras-č̀áṅ* rice-wine, rice-beer. — ˳*bras-č̀án* boiled rice. — *ša-˳brás* rice mixed with small pieces of meat. — ˳*bras-t̀úg* rice-soup. — ˳*bras-žiṅ* rice-field. — ˳*bras-zán* dish of rice. — ˳*bras-yós* parched rice *Med.* — ˳*bras-síl C.* boiled rice, got up with butter, sugar, apricots etc., *W.* **p̀u-lá, p̀o-lá**, پلاو. — 2. **tumour,** esp. larger swellings in the groin etc.

འབྲས་ལྗོངས་ ˳*bras-ljóṅ* (**ḍe-ǰóṅ**) n. p., **Sikim.**

འབྲས་སྤུངས་ ˳*bras-spúṅs* n. p., monastery near Lhasa.

འབྲས་བུ་ ˳*brás-bu* 1. **fruit,** e.g. *šíṅ-gi Mil.*; ˳*brás-bu ye-méd-kyi sa* a country producing no fruit *Thgy.*; **corn, grain,** ˳*brás-bu zór-bas brṅá-ba Mil.*; ˳*bras-ṅan* a failure of fruit. — 2. **testicle** *Wdṅ.* cf. *rlig-pa*; *mig-˳brás* apple of the eye. — 3. fig. **effect, consequence,** esp. as opp. to *rgyu*, hence *rgyu-˳brás* cause and effect, more esp. in moral philosophy = **retribution, requital, recompense, reward,** three grades being distinguished: 1. *rnám-par smín-pai* ˳*brás-bu* full recompense, in the worst case by the punishments of hell; 2. *rgyu bt̀ún-pai* ˳*brás-bu* by adversity during life; 3. *dbáṅ-gi* ˳*brás-bu* by unpleasant local circumstances, — so *Thgy.*; *rgyu-˳brás* and ˳*brás-bu* also directly denote **the doctrine of final retribution,** ˳*brás-bu mi bden* the doctrine of requital is not true *Thgy.*; further: ˳*brás-bu* reward of ascetic exercises, the various grades of perfection, of which four are distinguished: a. *rgyún-du-žugs-pa* स्रोतापत्ति or as partic. ˳पन्न, he who enters the stream (that takes from the external world to Nirwana); b. *lan-γčig-p̀yir-˳oṅ-ba* सकृदागामिन्, he who returns once more (for the period of a human birth); c. *p̀yir-mi-˳oṅ-ba* अनागामिन् he who returns no more, being a candidate of Nirwana; d. *dgra-bčom-pa* अर्हन्त, the Arhat, the finished saint; v. *Köpp.* I, 398.

འབྲི་ཁུང་ or **གུང་** ˳*bri-kúṅ* or *-guṅ* sect of Lamas and monastery in Tibet, ˳*bri-kúṅ-pa* member of that sect.

འབྲི་ཏ་ ˳*bri-ta* a form of medicine, prob. a kind of extract *Med.*; ˳*bri-ta-sa-˳dzin* medicinal herb, an emetic, *Med.*; in *Lh.* Cuscuta, which however does not agree with the descriptions.

འབྲི་བ་ ˳*bri-ba*, I. pf. and imp. *bri*, intrs. of ˳*p̀ri-ba* **to lessen, decrease, diminish,** of water, frq. in conjunction with *k̀a*, at the surface, used with regard to size, number and intensity (synon. ˳*grib-pa*). — II. pf. and imp. *bris* (*Glr.* also *bri*) 1. **to draw, design, describe,** *dkyil-˳k̀or žig* to describe a circle or other figure; also to paint *Glr.* 2. **to write,** *yi-ge* letters, a letter (epistle); *yi-ger 'literis mandare'*, to record, to write down, something from hearing *Dzl.*: ˳*bri-smyúg* writing-reed, pen, pencil etc.

འབྲི་མོ་ ˳*bri-mo*, चमरी, **tame female yak**; *rgod-˳bri Pth.*, or *˳broṅ-˳bri Cs.*, wild female yak; *˳bri-zal* young female yak *Ld.-Glr.*, *˳bri-o* yak-milk; *˳bri-mar* yak-butter; *˳bri-mdzo* (*W.* **brim-dzo**) bastard of bull and yak.

འབྲི་མོག་ *˳bri-móg* medicinal herb *Med.*

འབྲིང་ *˳briṅ* **middle, midst, mean, middling, moderate**, *˳briṅ žig* something moderate, of middling quality, = *tsád-ma* or *tig-tsád W.*; *briṅ-po* the middle one, of three sons *Dzl.* and elsewh.; between *stobs-čé* and *čúṅ-ṅu Lt.*; *bzaṅ ṅan ˳briṅ γsum*; *rnal-˳byór ˳briṅ-po* one that is moderately advanced in contemplation *Thgr.*; *zlá-ba ˳briṅ-po* v. *zla-ba*; *˳briṅ-gis* **middling, moderately**, adv.

འབྲིང་བ་ *˳briṅ-ba*, in *žabs-˳briṅ byéd-pa* for *bráṅ-ba Mil.*

འབྲིད་པ་ *˳bríd-pa* 1. also *˳dríd-pa*, pf. *brid*, **to deceive, cheat, impose upon**, *blo ˳brid-pa* id. *Glr.*; *˳brid-de ṙṅód-pa-las Tar.*, as she wanted to seduce him deceitfully; *ka-mṅar-brid* deceitfully, insidiously sweet, being followed by a nauseous, acrid or burning taste *Med.* — 2. *Cs.* = *˳ṗri-ba.*

འབྲིམ་པ་ *˳brim-pa*, I. vb., pf. *brim(s)* 1. **to distribute, deal out, hand round**, sweet-meats, flowers, poems *Dzl.*, *Tar.*; ... *la*, to ... — 2. *Ld.* **to throw away**, what is worthless, = **ṗáṅ-čes**. — II. sbst. **distributer, dispenser, waiter at table** *Dzl.*; *˳brim (-pa) -po*, id. *Cs.*

འབྲུ་ *˳bru* **grain, corn, seed**, frq.; grain of sand, *byé-ma ˳bru rei stéṅ-na* on every grain of sand *Glr.*; *˳bru ˳tag-pa* to pound grains *Lex.* — 2. a single **grain, piece, letter**, *yi-ge ˳bru γčig* a single letter; also without *yi-ge*: *˳bru drúg* the six letters = *yi-ge-drúg-pa*, v. *drug*. — 3. collectively, **grain, corn**, in gen. *˳brui kal* a load of grain *Dzl.*; *˳brú-sna mi ˳kruṅs* no kind of grain is growing *Glr.*; *˳bru gáṅ-bu-čan* pulse, legume *S.g.*; *nor daṅ ˳bru-rnams ˳ṗel* money and corn multiply. — *˳bru-rdóg* grain of seed. — *˳brú-sna* v. above. — *˳bru-báṅ* granary. — *˳bru-˳bú* corn-worm, weevil *Cs.* *˳bru-már* oil extracted from seeds; lamp-oil *Dzl.* — *˳brú-tsoṅ-pa* oil-merchant.

འབྲུ་ཏང་ *˳bru-táṅ*, n. of a superior sort of tea.

འབྲུ་བ་, བྲུ་བ་ *˳brú-ba*, *bru-ba*, pf. and imp *brus*, *˳drú-ba*, *drus* 1. **to dig**, *kúṅ-bu*, *dur*, *doṅ* (cf. *rkó-ba*). — 2. **to chisel, carve, cut**. — 3. *Sch.* **to look through**, *yig* a writing; **to examine**, *˳bru* grain; hence *mtsaṅ ˳bru-ba* to spy out, smell out, faults, stirring up brawls and quarrels by it, *Stg.* **to irritate, vex, provoke**, *mtsaṅ ˳brú-bai tsig* provoking words *Lex.*; *snyad*, *snyon ˳brú-ba* **to accuse** *W.*

འབྲུ་མ་ *˳brú-ma* **tumour, swelling, weal** *Sch.*

འབྲུ་ཙ་ *˳bru-tsa* an angular kind of Tibetan current handwriting, v. *Csoma Gram.*

འབྲུ་ཤལ་, འབྲུ་ཤ་ *˳bru-šál*, *˳bru-šá* v. *bru-šá.*

འབྲུག་ *˳brug* (*Bal.* **blug**) 1. **thunder**, *˳brug-skád*, *˳brug-sgrá* id.; *skad-čen ˳brug* loud thunder; *˳brug ˳bód-pa Cs.*, *grág-pa Dzl.*, *ldír-ba Lex.* and elsewh., thundering. — 2. **dragon** (to which thunder is ascribed *Sch.*); *γyu-˳brúg sṅón-po* blue dragon *Glr*

འབྲུག་པ་ *˳brúg-pa* I. sbst. 1. **sect of Lamas**, clothed in red, *Schl.*73., established in the province of Bhotan, acc. to *Sch.* = *ža-dmár*, = *sá-skya*. — 2. **Bhotan**. —

II. vb. for *˳brúb-pa Mil.* frq.

འབྲུད་པ་ *˳brúd-pa*, = *˳brú-ba*, also *˳drúd-pa*.

འབྲུབ་པ་ *˳brúb-pa* 1. gen. with *ču*, **to cause to overflow, to gush, to spout forth to flow over**, *Mil.*, *Tar.* and elsewh.; *ču-˳brub Lex.*, *˳brubs Sch.* water that has flown over (?). *˳brub-po* **fluid, liquid; fluidity, a fluid**, *Cs.* (?). — 2. *Cs.* **to deal out**. — 3. *Sch.* **to shut up, wrap up.**

འབྲུམ་པ་ *˳brúm-pa* 1. *Cs.* **grain, minute particle**, *˳brum-rdog*, *˳bru-rdóg* a single grain, = *˳bru*; **fruit**, *rgun-˳brúm* grape; *se-˳brúm* hip (fruit of wild brier) *Sik.* — 2. **pustule, pock**, gen. *˳brúm-bu*; *˳brum-nad* small-pox; *˳brum-nág* black or deadly small-pox; *˳brum-dkár* white small-pox; *˳brum-krá* coloured small-pox *Med.*, *˳brum-*

pa and *ₒbrúm-pa nág-po* as name of a disease of the groin, prob. bubo *Med.* — *ₒbrum-rǰes* pock-mark. — *ₒbrúm-po* a large grain *Cs.; ₒbrúm-bu* a small grain; pock, pustule, v. above.

འབྲུམ་ལྷ་མོ་ *ₒbrum-lha-mo Sch.* a tutelar goddess of little children, worshipped by the Shamans.

འབྲེ་བ་ *ₒbré-ba*, pf. and imp. *bres* **to draw over** or **before, to spread, to stretch,** a net *Glr.*, a curtain *Glr.*, a canopy, awning *Lex.*; **to wrap a thing up in a cloth,** in order to carry it, as books, a corpse *Thgy.*

འབྲེག་པ་ *ₒbrég-pa*, pf. *breg(s)*, imp. *brog(s)*, also *ₒdrég-pa* **to cut off,** *śiṅ-ta-lai lo-ma bregs-pa* a plantain branch cut off, as representing a being irremediably cut off from its former state of existence *Mil.;* **to mow** *Sch.;* of parts of the body: *ske* to cut off a person's neck *Thgr.*, *ṗo-mtsán* the membrum virile *Schr.*, *rtai súg-pa* the foot of a horse, prob. only the tendon of it, as much as to lame, to disable *Glr.*; also to sever with a saw; most frq. in reference to the hair, to cut off, **to shave,** with the scissors or a razor, *skra daṅ ḱá-spu* frq.; *ₒbrég-mḱan* **barber, hair-cutter** *Dzl.; ₒbreg-spyád* a sharp small knife *Sch.*

འབྲེང་པ་ *ₒbréṅ-pa Cs.*, *bréṅ-ba* **strap, rope,** *ko-ₒbréṅ* leather strap; *śa-ₒbreṅ Mil.*; *ₒbreṅ-ťag Cs.* cane-ribbon, made of buck-leather; leading-rope, guide-line. — *ₒbréṅ-bu Cs.* cobbler's strap.

འབྲེང་བ་ *ₒbréṅ-ba* frq. for *ₒbráṅ-ba.*

འབྲེལ་ *ₒbrel* sbst. v. *ₒbrél-ba* II.

འབྲེལ་པ་ *ₒbrél-pa* **connection, conjunction,** yet only in certain applications: 1. **connection between cause and effect**, used also at once for **effect, consequence, efficacy,** *smón-lam-gyi ₒbrél-pa* the efficacy of prayer *Mil.* frq.; *ₒǰog-pa* to apply, make use of it *Mil.* — 2. **the vascular and nervous system conjunctively,** the two systems in their totality, ni f., *Med.* — 3. **genitive case**, the sixth case of Tibetan Grammarians, *ₒbrél-pai sgra*, the termination of it, *kyi.* — 4. **a small quantity, a little, a bit,** *zás-kyi ₒbrél-pa žig dgos* I ask for a little bit to eat *Mil.* frq.; *čos(-kyi) ₒbrél(-pa) ťób-pa* to snatch up a little bit of religion *Mil.*

འབྲེལ་བ་ *ₒbrél-ba* I. vb., intrs. of *sbrél-ba,* 1. **to hang together, to cohere, to be connected,** *rtsa daṅ rus-pa tsam ₒbrél-ba* connected only by veins and bones, nothing but skin and bone *Dzl.; ₒod-zér-gyi drá-bas ₒbrél-te* covered with a continuous net of rays *Glr.;* gen. with *daṅ, bod daṅ rgyai ₒbrél-ťsul* the connection with, or the intercourse between Tibet and China *Glr.; de dan ₒbrél-bai las* the functions connected with, and peculiar to (a certain organ) *Lt.; ₒbrel-mťsams* 1. **joint,** or **rivet** of pincers etc. *S.g.* 2. **boundary,** *W.* — 2. **to come together, to meet, to join,** *ₒbrél-γtam* gossipings in meeting on the road *Mil.* — 3. **to meet sexually, to cohabit,** *de daṅ lus ₒbrél-ba* to cohabit with (him or her) *Glr.; (lhán-du) ₒbrél-ba-la(s) bu skyes* they having cohabited, a child was born *Glr.* — II. sbst. *ₒbrél-ba* or *ₒbrel* **union, communication, connection,** *bod daṅ ₒbrel byuṅ* the union with Tibet took place *Glr.*; *rgya bod γnyis ₒbrel čád* the union ceases *Glr.; *nor-ḍél čò-če, nor-ḍél-la čá-če* W.*, to form a mercantile connection, to enter into commercial intercourse. — *las-ₒbrel = las-ₒṗro* q.v. — *γnyis-ₒbrél, γsum-ₒbrél* a double, triple consonant, e.g. *sk, skr.*

འབྲོག་ *ₒbrog* **solitude, wilderness, uncultivated land,** esp. **summer-pasture** for cattle in the mountains; thus *ₒbrog-skyoṅ-ba Ld.-Glr.*, *Schl.* 15, 6 might imply: to attend to a mountain dairy; *gám-ₒbrog* a near, *rgyáṅ-ₒbrog* a remote summer-pasture; *ₒbrog-ḱyi Cs.* a large shaggy shepherd's dog; *ₒbróg-dgon, ₒbróg-stoṅ, ₒbróg-sa = ₒbrog. ₒbróg-γnas* 1. **pasture-land** 2. **people occupying it.** — *ₒbróg-pa, ₒbróg-mi* id.; more particularly, **inhabitants of the steppe,** nomadic Tibetans *Sch.*, *ₒbróg-mo* wife, *ₒbrog-ṗrúg* child of such a nomad. — *ₒbrog-žád Sch.* rude, rough, boorish, *ₒbrog-žad stón-pa* to be rude etc.

འབྲོང་ *ₒbroṅ* 1. (चमर) = *γyag-rgod,* **wild yak** *Glr.*; *byáṅ-ḱai ₒbroṅ*, the yak of

Jang-thang; $_{o}$*broṅ-*$_{o}$*brí* cow, $_{o}$*broṅ-ṕrúg* calf, $_{o}$*broṅ-ko* skin, leather, $_{o}$*broṅ-ša* flesh, $_{o}$*broṅ-ru* or *-ra Glr.* horns of the wild yak. — 2. v. $_{o}$*bráṅ-ba.*

འབྲོམ་ $_{o}$*brom* noun personal; $_{o}$*brom-stón* a celebrated Lama and scholar in the 11th. century.

འབྲོས་པ་ $_{o}$*brós-pa*, pf. and imp. *bros*, **to flee, to run away** (*W.* **šor-će**), $_{o}$*brós-šiṅ gáb-pa* to flee and hide one's self *Dzl.*; *ṕyir* $_{o}$*brós-so* (the army) took to flight *Glr.*; $_{o}$*brós-pai ɣnas Dzl.*, $_{o}$*brós-sa Glr.* place of refuge; **fig.** *mig ḱuṅ-du bros* his eyes are sunk, hollow *S.g.* — $_{o}$*bros-ša* a large dorsal muscle *Med.* — *ɣnyid-*$_{o}$*brós-pa* = *ɣnyid-lóg-pa* (?) *Dzl.* ༢༧༤, 9.

རྦ་ *rba* v. *dba.*

རྦད་ *rbad* 1. *Sch.* a large species of **eagles.** — 2. *W.* **crutch,** = *paṅ - ka.* — 3. = *rbab.* — 4. **great** (?) v. *ka-rbad*; *rbad-sgra* a strong voice *Sch.*; cf. *rbod-rbód.* — 5. **quite, wholly, entirely** (?) *rbád-ɣćod-pa*, *rbad-tsér ɣćód-pa Mil.* to cut off entirely, to extirpate; **tag-ćú be'-ćó** **resolute** *C.*

རྦད་སྐྱོགས་ *rbad-skyógs Sch.* **residue, residuum, dregs, husks** etc.

རྦད་པ་ *rbád-pa* 1. vb., imp. *rbod*, **to set on, incite,** *Tar.*, *C.*, e.g. *ḱyi*; **to excite, instigate, animate,** *Cs.*; *rbad-ḱa S.g.* an inciting talk (?). — 2. adj. **undulating, undulatory** *Sch.*

རྦད་རྦོད་ *rbad-rbód*, **thick, dense, close, strong, great** *Cs.*, *skra rbad-rbód Lex.*

རྦབ་ *rbab*, 1. *Med.*, *Sch.*: a kind of **dropsy,** *skya-rbáb Sch.*, also *ša-rbab Lt.* id. (?) — 2. **the rolling down,** also *rbad*, e.g. *rdo-rbáb* loose stones rolling down, a frequent annoyance in high mountains *Pth.*, *rbab ži-bas* after the rolling of detritus had ceased *Mil.*; **bad ṕog soṅ** a piece of rock rolling down hit him *W.*; *rbab sgril-ba Lex.* to roll down, trs.; *rbáb-pa* id. intrs.; *már-la rbáb-tu šor* it rolled down and away *Mil.*

རྦེ་ *rbe Sch.* **'the fur of the stone-fox'.**

རྦོ་ *rbo Sch.* **milt of fish.**

རྦོད་ *rbod* v. *rbád-pa.*

ལྦ་བ་ *lbá-ba* 1. **wen, goitre.** — 2. **knots, excrescenses** on trees, on account of their speckled appearance often worked into drinking-bowls; *lbá - tsa Med.*, prob. a kind of salt, used as a curative of goitre.

ལྦག་ *lbag* **bubbles** (?), **ću bag gyáb-će** to strike the water, so as to make it splash and foam *W.*

ལྦུ་བ་, དབུ་བ་ *lbú-ba*, *dbú-ba* **bubble, foam, froth, slaver**; *ćú-lbu Lex.*; *lbú-bćas nyuṅ* producing little froth *Lt.*; *lbú-ba bsdú-ba* to scum or skim off *Cs.*; *grogs ćú-yi lbú-ba daṅ* $_{o}$*dra* a friend is like water-bubbles.

སྦ་ *sba* v. *spa.*

སྦ་ནག་ *sba-nág Sch.* **a mean house, hovel, hut.**

སྦ་བ་ *sbá-ba* 1. vb. fut. of *sbed-pa* q. v. — 2. sbst. **privy parts, pudenda** *Stg.*

སྦག་པ་ *sbúg-pa*, pf. *sbags*, imp. *sbogs* (cf. $_{o}$*bág-pa*), **to soil, stain, defile, pollute,** *dri-mas Lex.* — 2. **to mingle, intermix,** *Lex.*.

སྦང་བ་ *sbáṅ-ba* v. *sbóṅ-ba.*

སྦང་མ་ *sbáṅ-ma* malt from which beer has been brewed, v. *ćaṅ*; *sbaṅ-skóm* id. dried, *sbaṅ-ṕyé* id. reduced to flour (of an inferior quality) *Cs.*; *glum-sbáṅ Ts.* = *sbáṅ-ma*; *sbaṅ-ću* barm prepared from it *W.*

སྦངས་ *sbaṅs* dung of larger animals, *rtai sbaṅs Glr.* (**stal-báṅ(s)* Ld.*), *boṅ-sbaṅs*, *glaṅ-po-ćei sbaṅs Cs.*; *sbaṅs-lúd* id., used for manure; *sbaṅs-skám* id. dried for fuel.

སྦབ་ཅ་ *sbáb-ća C.*, **sbáb-ja* W.* a certain number or quantity of trading-articles, e.g. of paper, a quire of 10—100 sheets, a bundle of matches etc.

སྦམ་པ་ *sbám-pa*, pf. *sbams*, imp. *sboms*, **to put** or **place together, to collect, to gather,** *ṕyogs ɣćig-tu Lex.*; *smyúg-ma sbáms-pa* $_{o}$*dra* like reeds laid together *Wdṅ.*

སྦར་བ་ *sbár-ba*, v. *sbór-ba.*

སྦར་མོ་ *sbár-mo* v. *spár-mo.*

སྦལ་ *sbal* (perh. the same as the following *sbal-pa*), *lág-pai* the soft muscles of the inner hand, cf. also *ṗyag-sbál;* the soft part of the paw of animals.

སྦལ་པ་ and བ་ *sbál-pa* and *-ba* **frog** (rather scarce in Tibet), one *Lex.* **कर्कट, crab, crawfish** (?); *sbál-pa dkár-po Stg.* stated to be a large species of frog; *nágs-sbal Lt.* prob. tree-frog; *rús-sbal* **tortoise**; *sbal-čúṅ* or *-lčoṅ Pth.* 1. a young frog, **tadpole** *Cs.* 2. vulg. (from ignorance) **lizard**; *sbal-rgyáb S.g.* tortoise-shell.

སྦལ་མིག་ *sbal-mig* **bud, eye, gem, sprout, shoot,** *ˌton* comes forth, *ˌbye* opens *Stg.*

སྦིད་པ་ *sbíd-pa Ts.* for *sbúd-pa* **bellows,** instrument for blowing.

སྦུ་གུ་ *sbú-gu* **hollow, cavity,** in the stem of a plant or a grass-blade *Mil.*

སྦུ་བ་ *sbú-ba* v. *lbú-ba.*

སྦུ་ལ་ཁ་ *sbú-la-ḱa Ts.* = *bka-blon-śram* **sable,** *mustela zibellina.*

སྦུ་ལྷན་ *sbu-lhán Ts.* (**bu-hlén**) **plane,** tool used in joinery.

སྦུག་ཆོལ་, སྦུབ་ཆལ་, *sbug-čól, sbub-čál Cs.,* **ˌbog-ˌčol** (?) *Ld.-Glr.*; **sbug-žál, sbum-žól* W.* **large brass cymbal;** **dúṅ-ce, ṗáb-ce* W.* to play the cymbals..

སྦུག་པ་ *sbúg-pa* = *ˌbúgs-pa,* **to perforate, to pierce.**

སྦུག་(སྦུག་)པོ་ *sbug-(sbug-)po Cs.* **hollow.**

སྦུག་(ས་) *sbug(s),* more frq. *sbubs,* **hollow, cavity, excavation, interior space,** *ḱúṅ-bui Lex.* tubular cavity, in bones etc. *S.g.*; **subterraneous passage, conduit, sewer** *C.*; *sbúbs-su ˌǰúg-pa, sbúbs-nas ˌtón-pa* to put into an underground hole or recess, to come forth from it *Glr., Mil.*; *sbúg-tu nor sbá-ba* to hide money in such a place *Lex.;* **hiding-place, hidden recess,** = *saṅ-seṅ*; **hole** for inserting the handle of some instrument *Sch.; śáṅs kyi sbubs γnyis* hollow, expanded nostrils *Cs.; sbubs-ˌbyár Med.* disease of the penis, prob. stoppage of its orifice by gonorrhoea, cf. *m̌je.*

སྦུགས་ཧག་ *sbugs-hág* (**bu-hág**) 1. the **panting** of a dog *Sik.* — 2. **bassoon** with a large and nearly globular bell-mouth *W.* —

སྦུད་པ་ *sbúd-pa* 1. vb. **to light, kindle, set on fire,** seldom, *Lex.: mé-čas sbúd-pa* q. v. — sbst. **bellows,** usually consisting of two skin-bags, the orifices of which are opened and shut by the hands, and which are then squeezed together, so that the compressed air passing through a tube is driven into the fire; *sbúd-pa ˌbúd-pa Cs.* or *rgyáṅ-ba Sch.* to blow or work the bellows; *sbud-rgyál* = *sbúd-pa.*

སྦུན་པ་ *sbún-pa* v. *spún-pa.*

སྦུན་གཏེར་ *sbun-γtér Pth.* a small building in the style of a monument, in which sacred writings are deposited.

སྦུར་ *sbur* **ant** *Cs.*, prob. identical with the following (cf. *gróg-sbur*).

སྦུར་པ་ *sbúr-pa* **beetle,** *čú-sbur S.g.; sbur-čén, -čúṅ, -dmár, -mgyógs Cs.*, denoting various kinds of beetles.

སྦུར་མ་ *sbúr-ma,* = *sbún-pa,* **chaff, husks** etc.; *rlúṅ-gis sbúr-ma bús-pa ltar Dzl., sóg-sbur čus γyéṅ-ba ltar Pth.* like chaff scattered by the wind, carried along by the water; *sbu-lén* or *-lóṅ* **amber** *Wts.*

སྦེ་ག་ *sbé-ga Lex.* w. e.

སྦེ་བ་ *sbé-ba Sch.* **to scuffle, wrestle.**

སྦེག་པ་ *sbég-pa* **lean, lank, thin** *S.g.*

སྦེད་པ་ *sbéd-pa,* pf. *sbas,* fut. and common secondary form *sba,* imp. *sbos, W.* **sbá-ce**, pf. *sbas,* **to hide, conceal,** *γter* a treasure, *mdzód-du* in a store-house; *má-mo sbéd-pai ṗug* cavern in which a Mamo is concealed *Mil.*; *dpúṅ-gi ts̓ogs ts̓ál-du* to conceal troops in a wood *Dzl.*; *γtér-du* to deposit as a treasure *Glr.*; *sai ˌóg-tu* in the ground *Dzl.*; also as much as to inter, to bury *Dzl.;* **sbás-te* or *bé-te bor-ce* W.* = *sbéd-pa;* **sbás-te** **secretly, clandestinely, by stealth** *W.; mi sdíg-can-la lus sba ṗyir* in order to hide our form before sinful men, in order not to be recognized by them *Mil.*;

to hide from, to guard, secure, protect from, *srúṅ-źiṅ sbá-ba* id.; **to keep, preserve,** *sba-sri-med-par* (to bestow) freely, amply, without restriction.

སྦེད་མ་ *sbéd-ma* **a veiled woman;** name of a wife of Buddha *Cs.*

སྦོ་ *sbo Sch.* **the upper part of the belly;** *sbo-ṫsil* **bacon** *C.*; *sbo-rkún-pa* **pickpocket** *C.*

སྦོ་བ་ *sbó-ba* pf. *sbos* = *ₒbó-ba* 2, **to swell(up), to distend,** *ltó-ba sbos Lt.* the belly is swollen, turgid; *sbó-ₒḱrog-pa Sch.* 'to wheeze from inflation' (?).

སྦོག(ས)་པ་ *sbóg(s)-pa* v. *sbág-pa*; *ráṅ-gi bú-ṫsai ṫsig-sbóg Mil.*, seems to imply a man that is receiving abusive language from his own sons (?).

སྦོང་བ་ *sbóṅ-ba*, pf. *sbaṅs*, fut. *sbaṅ* **to steep** in water, **to soak, to drench;** **báṅ-te bor* W.* soak it in water!

སྦོད་པ་ *sbód-pa* **tassel, tuft.**

སྦོམ་པ་ *sbóm-pa*, more frq. *sbóm-po* **thick,** *ṗra-ba-las zlog sbóm-po Zam.* the contrary to *ṗrá-ba* is *sbóm-po*; *sbom-ṗrá daṅ riṅ-ṫúṅ mnyam* of equal length and thickness *Dzl.*; **stout; coarse, clumsy, heavy,** also applied to sins; *sbóm-ma* a stout woman *Cs.*; sbst. **thickness, stoutness, heaviness.**

སྦོར་བ་ *sbór-ba*, pf., fut. and secondary form *sbar*, trs. of *ₒbár-ba*, **to light, kindle, inflame.**

སྦོར་ལོ་ *sbór-lo* Anemone polyantha *Lh.*

སྦྱང་བ་ *sbyáṅ-ba* v. *sbyóṅ-ba.*

སྦྱར་བ་ *sbyár-ba* v. *sbyór-ba.*

སྦྱར་པ་ *sbyár-pa Wdṅ.*, n. of a tree, prob. = *dbyár-pa.*

སྦྱིག་པ་ *sbyig-pa*, *sbyig-mo Lex.* w. e.

སྦྱིན་པ་ *sbyin-pa*, I. vb., pf. and imp. *byin*, 1. **to give, to bestow** (in *B.* a common word, in *W.* almost unknown; yet v. *smin-pa* II.), without any ceremonial difference between high and low; **to hand, deliver; to give up, deliver over; to give back, give for a present; to offer, proffer, hold out,** *rín-la byin-no* he offered as an equivalent *Pth.*; *ma byin-par mi lén-pa* v. *dgé-ba.* — 2. **to add, to sum up** *Wdk.* —

II. sbst. **gift, present, alms;** the expression *sbyin-pa ysum* comprises: *zaṅ-ziṅ-gi* the bestowing of goods, *mi-ₒjigs-pai* the affording of protection, and *čós-kyi sbyin-pa*, the giving of moral instruction *Cs.*, *sbyin-ytóṅ* distribution of gifts, *sbyin-ytoṅ čen-po byed-pa Dzl.* — *sbyin-bdag* dispenser of gifts, more especially in the first beginnings of Buddhism a layman manifesting his piety by making presents to the priesthood, v. *Köpp.* I, 487, and in almost all legends; also the reverse, *len-pa* **the receiver of gifts,** Dulva v. Feer Introd. p. 71. — *sbyin-sreg*, होम, **burnt-offering,** v. *Was.* (194), *Schl.* 251 sqq.

སྦྱུ་ *sbyu*, sometimes for *sgyu Sch.*

སྦྱོང་བ་ *sbyóṅ-ba*, pf. *sbyaṅs*, fut. *sbyaṅ* शुध 1. **to clean, remove by cleaning,** clear away, as *ₒdág-pa*, esp. *sdig-pa Tar.*, *sgrib(-pa) Thgy.*; less frq. in a physical sense, e.g. removing phlegm by vomiting *Med.*, *ₒḱru-sbyóṅs* diarrhoea *Lex.*; **to cleanse,** *sbyóṅ-byed* 1. **cleansing, purifying,** *raṅ sbyoṅ-byed-kyi šes-rab Mil.* the knowledge how a man may be purified by his own doings. 2. *Med.*: **purging medicine.** — 2. **to remove, take away,** in a general sense *Cs.*; **to subtract,** *de-rnams ṫig-mtsams sbyaṅ-ste Wdk.*, 60 being subtracted, cf. *ₒṗri-ba*; **to cease,** of diseases *Med.* — 3. **to exercise, to train,** *blo* one's mind *Cs.*, *ḱa* one's mouth, hence *ḱa-sbyáṅ* eloquence *Mil.* (having reference also to *ḱa-yčáṅ* q. v.); *sṅon yón-tan sbyáṅs-pa sóṅ-bai mṫus* by dint of formerly cultivated abilities *Glr.*; *ṫugs yóṅs-su sbyáṅs-pai skyés-bu Mil.* a saint of a thoroughly cultivated (or purified) mind; **to exercise, to practise,** *da-rúṅ sbyaṅ dgos* that must be practised still better; **to study,** *sde-snód-la* the holy scriptures *Mil.*, and with accus. *yźuṅ-lugs Tar.* 14, 9 (where *byaṅ* stands); *rtsis-la sbyáṅ-ba* to learn mathematics *Pth.*; **to practise, to perform; to recite, to repeat,** formulas, *bšar-sbyáṅ byéd-pa Mil.*, **kor jaṅ čó-če* W.*; **to accustom, familiarize,** **mi daṅ* *ǰaṅ-ḱan** accustomed to man, tame, also without **mi daṅ** W.; **ǰaṅ-ḱyád** **custom, use, habit** W. — 4. **to accumulate** (?) *Cs.* — 5. **to conjure to the spot, to call by magic** (?) *Tar.* 76,15 *Schf.*

སྦྱོར་བ་ *sbyór-ba* I. vb., pf. and fut. *sbyar*, *W.* **žár-ċe**, trs. of *ₒbyór-ba*, 1. **to affix, attach, fasten, stick**, a writing, a plaster *W.*: **žar gyab-ċe**; **to apply** *lċé-rtse dḱán-la Gram.*; fig. *bló-la, séms-la* **to impress**; **ḱár-ya daṅ** **to solder** *W.*; **zer gyáb-la žor** nail it fast! *W.*; **me-sḱám žar ťsar** the trigger is drawn *W.*; **to put on**, a plaster, v. above, an arrow on the bow-string; **to subjoin, take up, resume**, a subject in a treatise *Thgy.*, *Tar.* 127,14; **to put together, to join, unite**, *rús-pa čág-pa Med.*, *dbáṅ-po ɣnyis* v. sub II.; **to compile, compose**, a book; *ḱa* 1. **to close, shut**, one's mouth, = *ₒťáms-pa Pth.* 2. **to kiss** *C.*; **to insert, to dispose** in proper classes or divisions *Gram.*, *byá-bai sgra ma sbyar yaṅ* also without the word *bya* being added; *bdé-ba-la, byaṅ-čúb-la Mil.*, like *ₒgód-pa* 3; **to join, connect, combine**, words, letters; *ťsig de don daṅ sbyár-tsa-na* if these sentences are joined with their significations, i.e. if their explanation is given *Mil.*; *rtsís-su* **to count together, to sum up** *Dzl.*; *sbyór-la*, gen. written *žor-la*, **joined, connected, combined**, **ťsig nyi sum žór-la yoṅ** two or three words are found joined to one another; this word is frq. used to express simultaneousness of action, where in English expressions as 'along with', 'together with', 'at the same time' etc. are used: *žór-la ₒgró-ba* to go along with (another person) *Mil.*; *žór-la ḱur-ḱyer* take this also along with it! **ḱo čá-te žor daṅ kal soṅ** *W.* as he was going, we sent it along with him; *žor-la gyel soṅ* it fell at the same time (by coming in contact with some other falling body); **žór-la ḱyér-wa** to take hold of and take away at the same time; *ḱó-la žor ṗóg-pa* he was also (simultaneously) affected by (the loss); **žór-la zér-ḱan žig** or even **ťsig-gi žor** a mere expletive, without any appreciable meaning *C.*; *bdag sdig-sgrib čés-pai žór-la* (the calamity has befallen the others too), owing to their connection with such a great sinner as I am *Mil.nt.* — 2. **to prepare, procure, to get ready**, *yo-byád* the appurtenances *Dzl.*, *ₒtsó-ba* victuals *Dzl.*; *rta daṅ sbyár-bai šíṅ-rta* a carriage ready to start *Stg.* (or acc. to no. 1, a carriage attached to the horses); **to mix**, *ču daṅ* with water *Dzl.* and elsewh.; *ɣžán-du* **to prepare, to turn one thing into another, to change, transform** *Thgy.*; frq. **to prepare one's own mind, to compose one's self**, *dád-pa-la sbyór-bar gyis* make up your mind to believe *Mil.* — **to join, fit together, adjust, make agree**, esp. one's course of action; **to conform one's self to**, with *daṅ*, *ḱó-moi yid daṅ sbyor čig* accommodate yourself to my wishes *Dzl.*; *ḱrims daṅ sbyár-ro Dzl.* then we must conform to the law; most frq.: ... *daṅ sbyár-nas* or *-te* **corresponding, agreeable to, according to**, *ḱrims* according to the law, to usage etc. *Dzl.*; *bú-moi yid* according to the wish of the daughter *Dzl.*; also **to compare** *Tar.* 89, 16, *Thgy.*; *ɣžan-rgyúd-la sbyór-ba* seems to imply: to gain knowledge by observing others, opp. to *raṅ-rgyúd-la brtág-pa*, to ascertain by one's own immediate judgment. — 4. **to compose poetry**, ... *kyis sbyár-bao* = *sdeb-pa* 5 — II. sbst. 1. **adjunction, conjunction, union**, *dbáṅ-po ɣnyís-kyi sbyór-ba byéd-pa*, '*membrorum amborum conjunctionem efficere*' *Wdṅ.*; hence **coition, cohabitation**, *bud-méd-la sbyór-ba byéd-pa* to effectuate it with a woman *Pth.*; *sgra-sbyor-ba* a joining or combination of sounds (letters), **orthography** (?) *Zam.* — 2. **a mingling, a mixture**, e.g. of medicines, also *sbyar-ťábs Med.*; *sbyor-sde-bži* the four departments of pharmacy *Glr.* (apparently the title of a book); **preparation** = *sṅón-ₒgro Schl.* 240, also mental preparation, esp. the preparation of the mind for prayer, and the arrangement of it, meditation preparatory to it (ni f.) cf. *mťsams sbyár-ba.* — 3. **syllogism** *Was.* (278). — 4. **comparison, agreement, harmony**, *ɣtám-gyi* the harmony of history *Schf.*

སྦྲ་ *sbra* 1. *W.* **(s)bra**, *C.* **ḍa** **felt-tent**, *sbra-gúr* id.; *sbra-ťág* ropes, *sbra-šíṅ* frame-work, *sbrá-pa* inmate, of such a tent. 2. v. sub *ytsan*.

སྦྲག་པ་ *sbrág-pa*, pf. *sbrags*, *C.* **ḍág-pa**, *W.* **rág-če** **to lay, to put**, a thing over or by the side of an other, *p̓yogs-yčig-tu Lex.*; gen. used only in the gerund: **ťsa dor rág-ne** together with salt and spices *W.*; **ńá-ža dan rág-te mi dug** he does not belong to us *W.*, or in compounds: *nyi-rág* **double-barreled gun** (one barrel beside the other), *W.*ran-bár ḍug-rág** six-barreled pistol, **revolver** *W.*, *bse-sgo bdun-sbrag Pth.*, sevenfold skin-door, used as a target for shooting at.

སྦྲག་མ་ *sbrág-ma* **hay-fork**, *Cs.*

སྦྲང་བུ་ *sbrán-bu C.* **ḍán-bu**, *W.* **rán-ńu, ra-un** **fly**, and similar insects without a sting; *sbrán-ma* 1. id. 2. *C.* **bee**, *sbrán-mai ťsogs* swarm of bees. — *sbrán-rtsi W.* **rán-si** **honey**; **rán-si rán-ńu** *W.* bee. — *sbrán-čan* **mead** or something similar. — *sbran-ťsán* and *sbran-dón Cs.* cells in a honey-comb, the honey-comb itself. — *sbran-búg* bee-hive *Sch.* — *sbran-byi* marten *Sch.* — *sbran-yáb* flap, fly-brush *Cs.*

སྦྲད་པ་ *sbrád-pa* = *ₒbrád-pa* **to scratch** *Sch.*

སྦྲན་པ་ *sbrán-pa* = *sbrón-pa*.

སྦྲམ་བུ་ *sbrám-bu* **unwrought gold** *Cs.*

སྦྲིད་པ་ *sbríd-pa* 1. **to sneeze** *Med.*; *sbríd-pa ₒbyun* I am seized with a sneezing *Med.* — 2. **to become numb, torpid**, **kán-pe nya ḍid son** my foot is asleep *W.* — 3. *Dzl.* ༢ཞ༠, 5 *Sch.* **to flutter** before one's eyes (?).

སྦྲུད་པ་ *sbrúd-pa*, pf. and imp. *sbrus*, fut. and sec. form *sbru*, *W.* **rú-če** **to stir** with one's hand, *zan Lex.*; **to knead** (*Cs.*) is *rdzi-ba* which is not identical with *sbrúd-pa*, at least not in *W.*

སྦྲུམ་པ་ *sbrúm-pa* **pregnant, big with young;** *mi dan srog-čags sbrum-ma-rnams Dzl.* women with child and beasts with young; *sbrúm-par ₒgyúr-ba* to conceive, to become pregnant, frq.; *sbrúm-par ťsór-nas* feeling pregnant *Pth.*; *p̓rú-gu sbrum byún-bas* having conceived, being with child *Pth.*

སྦྲུལ་ *sbrul*, *Pur. sbrul*, *Lh.* **rúl**, *C.* **ḍul** 1. **serpent, snake;** *sbrul* and *sbrúl-mo* also mythical demoniac beings; *sbrul ydúg-pa* or *dug-sbrul* venomous serpent; *sbrul ḱas sdígs-po Sch.* serpent-tamer; *sbrúl-gyi snyin-po* v. *tsán-dan*. — *sbrúl-mgo* 1. a serpent's head. 2. v. *ₒan-ke*. — *sbrul-sgón* a serpent's egg. — **ḍul-nyá** **eel** or some other esculent snake-like fish *C.* — *sbrul-dúg* venom of serpents. — *sbrul-míg* 1. a snake's eye. 2. n. of **a certain vein** *Med.* — *sbrul-ťsil* snake's grease *Med.* — *sbrul-žágs* v. *žags*. — *sbrul-ló* serpent-year, *sbrúl-lo-pa* one born in such a year v. *lo*. — *sbrul-šún* slough, skin of a snake. — 2. symb. num.: 8, = *klu*.

སྦྲེ(ད)་ *sbre(d) Lex.* n. of an animal; *Sch.*: **stone-fox.**

སྦྲེ་བོ, རེ་བོ, རེ་བ་ *sbré-bo, ré-bo, ré-ba* a coarse material manufactured of yak's hair for tent-coverings.

སྦྲེང་བ་ *sbrén-ba*, pf. *sbrens*, *Cs.*: **to play** an instrument; acc. to *Dzl.* ༦༤, 16, **to jerk**, a chord, a bow-string.

སྦྲེབས་པ་ *sbrébs-pa Cs.*: resp. for *ltógs-pa* **hungry.**

སྦྲེལ་བ་ *sbrél-ba*, *W.* **rél-če(s)** **to stitch together**, paper; **to stitch to, to sew on; to fasten on**, a package on a horse; *lčags-sgróg lág-pa sbrél-nas* having one's hands shackled together; *bar zám-gyis sbrel* the chasm is overarched by a bridge *Glr.*; (iron chains) *sén-ge dan* fastened to (stone) lions; in a gen. sense: **to connect, to join**, *ynyis-sbrél, ysum-sbrél* two or three consonants joined together, cf. *min-yži*.

སྦྲེས་པ་ *sbrés-pa Cs.* **frozen, stiff, hard.**

སྦྲོན་པ་ *sbrón-pa*, pf. and fut. *sbran* 1. **to call to the spot**, *rá-mda, grogs* for assistance *Lex.*; **to send for**, the minister *Glr.* — 2. **to call to** *Thgy.*; **to give information, notice, intelligence**, *rgyál-po-la rmí-lam-du* to warn the king by a dream *Dzl.*; *mi žig sbrán-du btán-nas Dzl.* to dispatch a man in order to convey intelligence. — 3. **to sprinkle, to stain, to pollute**, *ťig-les Sch.*

མ

མ *ma* 1. the letter **m.** — 2. numerical figure: 16.

མ་ *ma* I. sbst. 1. **mother,** col. *ă-ma*, resp. *yum; mai rum* womb, matrix; *rán-gi ma yčig-pai srín-mo* full sister by the same mother, whilst *mas dbén-pai srín-mo* denotes half-sister, step-sister, by another mother. — 2. frq. used metonymically, e.g. **capital,** v. below; **ma tsam yod* W.*, what is the amount of the sum advanced? **original text, copy to write after, pattern** v. below; **a letter** written **above** another. — **Comp.:** *ma-kál* amount in bushels of grain lent out. — *ma-kú* mother and uncle, v. *kú-bo*. — *ma-rgyúd Sch.* 1. **original, primary cause.** 2. **line of descent** by the mother's side, when however it should be spelt *brgyud.* — *má-ču* the first infusion of malt or stronger beer, v. *čan.* — *ma-čún Cs.:* 'a mother's younger sister', perh. more correctly: a father's second wife, as to rank; *ma-čen* 1. *Cs.:* 'a mother's elder sister', or a father's principal wife. 2. v. the respective article. — *ma-pár* capital and interest *W.* — *ma-bu* mother and son; capital and interest; original and copy; *ma-bú mtún-pa ˳bri-ba* to copy accurately *Schr.*; a letter written above and below another letter; principal and cross beam etc. — *má-mo* v. that article. — *ma-tsáb* foster-mother *Sch.* — *ma-yži* v. sub II. — *ma-yyár* step-mother *Cs.* — *ma-ró* a mother's corpse *Pth.*

II. a root signifying **below,** opp. to *ya: má-gi* the lower one, e.g. *čú-bo Mil.; ma-gi-na* below, at the bottom, *má-gi-nas* from below, out of the valley, in *Sik.:* from, out of, the Indian plain (v. *mta*); *má-mču* lower lip. — *má-tem* sill, threshold. — *má-tog* v. *tog* I, 2. — *má-rdo* = *rmán-rdo.* — *ma-rábs* mean descent, people of low extraction *Dzl.* — *ma-ri Sch.* downward (?) — *ma-ré* = *ma-tém*, v. *re.*

III. negative adv. **not,** however only in some cases: a. in the simplest form of prohibition, where in the Tibetan language inst. of the imperative the root of the present with *ma* is used: *ma ˳gro* do not go, *ma byed* do not do (it). With the form of the future *mi* is placed: *rjód-par mi byao* it shall not, should not be pronounced *Dom.*; *mi de dgrar mi bslan* they should not make the man their enemy *S.g.* — b. with the preterite: *ma son* he did not go, *ma byas* he did not do (it). — c. with the present tense also in conjunction with the words *yin, lags, mčis, red.* — d. without any evident reason, and perh. not always correctly, with many substantives and adjectives that are formed of infinitives or participles, and are conveying a negative sense: *ma-rig-pa* a not knowing, ignorance; *ma-rún-ba* v. *run-ba* (v. *mi*).

IV. In the col. language of *Lh. ma* is used as an **interrogative,** when a question is returned by a question: **kyód-di min či zer** what is your name? **min ma?** my name?

V. Affix, so-called article, frq. denoting the fem. of the masc. in *pa*, if *mo* is not used inst. of it; gen. put to the names of inanimate things, utensils etc., as also to compound adjectives: *zans ru-bži-ma* a four-handled kettle (cf. *bu lo-ynyis-pa* a boy two years old, sub *pa*).

VI. *mai nyin* **two days before yesterday** *C.,* = *snón-ma žag W.*

མ་འ *mā W.* always with a marked accent and long vowel, prob. abbrev. of *mans* **very,** before adjectives and adverbs, **mā mán-po** very much, **mā gyál-la** very good.

མ་ཀར་ *ma-kár* (Hind. مکار impostor) *W.* **deceit, imposition, intrigue,** **ma-kár čó-te zer** he speaks hypocritically, with some secret design; *ma-kar-čan,* **hypocritical, fawning.**

མ་ཀ་ར་ *ma-ka-ra Ssk.* **sea-monster.**

མ་ཁ་ *ma-ḱá* 1. *Lt.* = *mtsan-dbye.* — 2. **Mecca** *Stg.*

མ་ཁལ་ *ma-ḱál* v. *ma* I.

མ་མཁན་ *ma-mḱán* v. *ma-rgán.*

མ་གལ་ *ma-gál Wdṅ., W.* **poplar-tree.**

མ་གི་ *má-gi* v. *ma* II.

མ་རྒད་ *ma-rgád, *mar-gád* Glr.,* from मरकत, **emerald.**

མ་རྒན་ *ma-rgán W. *mar-gán** 1. **matron, grandam.** 2. *C.* also **ma-ḱẹ́n** **cook; quarter-master.**

མ་ཆེན་ *ma-čén* 1. v. *ma* I. — 2. **head-cook.**

མ་ཏྲི་མུ་ཏྲི་སཱ་ལ་འཛུ་ *ma-tri-mu-tri-sa-la-ₒdzu* is said to be a form of prayer of the Bonpos, as the Ommanipadmehūm is of the Buddhists; *Desg.* p. 242 has: *ma tchri mou me sa le gou.*

མ་དང་ (?) *ma-dáṅ Ld.* a place on the roof of a house cleared for spreading grain there.

མ་གདན་ *ma-γdán, W. *mag-dán*, C. *ma-dẹ́n** **ground, basis, foundation;** also for *ma-γdán-gyi ri-mo* **ground-plan.**

མ་རྡུ་, མ་དུ་ (?) *ma-rdú, *ma-dú W.* **thorn, prickle,** *má-rdu-čan* **thorny, prickly.**

མ་རྡོ་ *má-rdo, *mar-do* W.* prob. a careless pronunciation of *rmáṅ-rdo.*

མ་ནིང་ *ma-niṅ* 1. **without sexual distinction** *Med.* and *Gram.* — 2. **impotent, unable to beget** *S.g.* — 3. **barren, childless** *Wdṅ.* (explained by *bu-tsa-méd-pa*). — 4. *Cs.:* also **hermaphrodite,** *Wdṅ.* however denotes this explicitly by *mtsan-γnyis-pa.*

མ་ནུ་ *ma-nu Med.? Cs :* = मनु, मनस्, *yid;* as symb. num.: 14.

མ་ནུ་པ་ཏྲ་ *ma-nu-pa-tra* a medicine *Wdṅ.;* in *Lh.* Bryonia dioeca.

མ་ཎི་ *má-ṇi* (*Ssk.* precious stone) 1. abbrev. of Ommanipadmehūm; **má-ni táṅ-če* W.* 1. **to mutter prayers.** 2. **to purr like a cat.** Hence 2. **praying-cylinder,** prop. *ma-ni-ḱos-ₒḱór Schl.* 230. — 3. **consecrated stone-heaps** or **stone-walls** (Mongul *Obo*) *Schl.* 196; *ma-ni bka-ₒbúm* title of a book; as to its contents v. *Schl.* 84.

མ་ཕང་ *ma-p̀áṅ Mil., ma-p̀ám Cs.* = *ma-drós-pa,* v. *drós-pa.*

མ་མ་ *má-ma* **children's nurse** *Dzl., Glr., Cs.:* *nú-ma snún-pai* wet-nurse, *dri-ma ₒp̀yi-bai* nurse for cleaning, *p̀áṅ-du ₒḱúr-bai* for carrying, *rtséd-grogs-kyi* for playing.

མ་མུན་ *ma-mún Ld.* col. for *na-bún,* **fog.**

མ་མོ་ *má-mo* 1. *Sch.* **grandmother.** — 2. *Sch.* **ewe, sheep that has lambed.** — 3. *Mil.* and elsewh. frq., a kind of wicked demons.

མ་ཞི་ *ma-ží Lt.* medicinal plant (?).

མ་ཞུ་ *má-žú* v. *žú-ba.*

མ་གཞི་ *má-γži, W. *máb-ži** 1. **ground-work, basis, elementary principle, component part; prime colour; principal thing, main point.** — 2. *Sch.* **originally** (?).

མཱ་ཡཱ་ *mā-yā Ssk.* = *Tib. sgyu-ₒp̀rul-ma* **'delusion',** n. of the mother of Buddha Sākyamuni.

མ་གཡོག་ *ma-γyóg* = *t́ab-γyóg* **kitchen-boy, scullion** *W.*

མ་རི་, མ་རེ་ *ma-rí, ma-ré* v. *ma* II.

མ་རུ་ *má-ru* n. of a castle, perh. = *rmé-ru.*

མ་རུ་རྩེ་ *ma-ru-rtsé* 1. n. of a medicine *Med.* — 2. n. of a country *Pth.*

མ་ལ་ *ma-la Sch.* **excellent! capital!** — In *Feer Introd.* p. 69 it was explained by our Lama as = *'é-ma* **ah, well!** Also Feer has: *Eh bien!*

མ་ལ་ཁན་ *má-la-ḱan Ld.* **snake-charmer, conjurer.**

མ་ལ་ཡ་ *má-la-ya* **the western Ghauts** famous for sandal-wood; the tracts along their foot, **Malayalim, Malabar.**

མ་ལ་ལ་ཙེ་ *ma-la-la-tsé Ld.* **small lizard.**

མ་ལག་ *má-lag Ld.* **somerset;** **má-lag lóg-če** to perform a somerset, to play the tricks of a mountebank; to roll on the ground with legs turned up, of horses etc.

མ་ལམ་ *má-lam* **high-road, broad passage** *W.*

མ་ཤ་ *má-ša* 1. *Ssk.* माष, **pea**, Phaseolus radiatus, = *mon-srán* or *greu Wdň.* — 2. *W.* the contrary of *ya-ša*, **contempt, scorn, disregard.** — 3. *W.* **trigger of a musket.**

མ་ཤ་ཀ་ *ma-ša-ka Ssk.* माषक, *Cs.*: a small gold weight and coin in ancient India.

མ་ཤི་ཀ་ *ma-ši-ka* name formed from the Hebrew מָשִׁיחַ, for **Christ**, the Greek word not being adapted to the Tib. language *Chr. Prot.*

མ་ཧཱ་ *ma-hā Ssk.* **great**, used in names and titles: *ma-hā-kā-la* and *de-ba* = Siva *Glr.*; *ma-hā-tsi-na*, *ma-hā-tsin* the modern name of China, formerly *rgya-nág*; *ma-hā-tsi-nai skad* the Chinese language *Wdk.*; *ma-hā-rā-dzā* the great king, title of some princes, particularly that of Kashmere.

མ་ཧེ་ *ma-he*, *Ssk.* महिष, **buffalo** *Glr.*, *ma-he-mo* female of it.

མག་པ་ *mag-pa* 1. **son-in-law** *Dzl.*, *mag-skud* son-in-law and father-in-law *Dom.* 2. **bridegroom** col.

མག་མལ་ *mag-mal*, *Ar.* مخمل, **velvet** *W.*

མང་ *maṅ* 1. *C.* col. for *mi oṅ*, *mi ₒdug* (?); so also in some passages of the *Ma.* — 2. v. *máṅ-po.*

མང་ག་ལམ་ *maṅ-ga-lam Ssk.* = *bkra-šis.*

མང་པོ་ *máṅ-po* 1. **much, many**, *mi maṅ-po* (*rnams*) **many people**, also (like οἱ πολλοί) **most people, the gross** or **bulk of the people**, for which *W.* **máṅ-če**, e.g. **máṅ-če zer dug** most people say, or, mostly it is said etc.; *ₒkor máṅ-po* (*rnams*) the numerous retinue *Dzl.*; *máṅ-por* adverb **mostly** (not frq.) *Zam.*; *ču maṅ-nyúṅ ltos* look after the height of the water, whether there is much or little of it; *yčig bsgyúr-ba-la maṅ-nyuṅ med* if you multiply by 1, you will get neither more nor less *Wdk.* — 2. **very, very much**, with verbs, chiefly col., *maṅ-po ₒǰigs* I am very much afraid.

Comp. and deriv. *maṅ-bkúr* = *máṅ-pos bkúr-ba* v. *bkúr-ba* I. and II. — *maṅ-gé-mo* long ago, long since (?) *Cs.* — **maṅ-ṅa** *W.* col. for *máṅ-por*, *máṅ-ba*(*r*); **žag daṅ žag máṅ-ṅa máṅ-ṅa táṅ-če** to give a little more every day. — *máṅ-če* v. above. — *máṅ-ǰa* a liberal distribution of tea *Ld.-Glr. Schl.* fol. 27, a, and p. 72. *máṅ-du* is not only the termin. case, but also a compound of *maṅ* and the synon. *du*, being used exactly like *máṅ-po*, both in the nomin. and accus case, *ydams-ṅág máṅ-du bstán-pas ₒbrás-bu bži ťób-pa máṅ-du byuṅ* as he gave manifold instructions, many became obtainers of the four fruits *Tar.* 14, 3.

མང་བ་ *máṅ-ba* I. vb. pf. *maṅs*, **to be much**, *ₒdi máṅ-ṅam de maṅ* is this much or that? i.e. which is more, this or that? *Dzl.*; *dgra máṅs-pas* as the enemies had become very numerous *Dzl.*; *sman-dpyád máṅs-pas ṕán-rgyu med* by making much of medical treatment he will not grow well *Mil*; *ma máṅ čig* be it not much, let it not grow too much *Mil.* and elsewh.; *máṅs-kyis dógs-pa* fearing lest it should grow too much *Wdň.* — II. adj. 1. *máṅ-po.* — 2. **having much**, *bu maṅ-bar ₒgyúr-ba* to get many children, *bu-máṅs* rich in children *Pth.* — *máṅs-ťsig* a sign of the plural number, e.g. *dag Gram.* — III. also sbst. **plenty.**

མང་ཡུལ་ *máṅ-yul*, a province of Tibet bordering on Nepal, in which *skyid-gróṅ* is situated, v. *skyid.*

མན་ཛི་ར་ *man-dzi-ra S.g.* a mineral medicine; perh. *man-dza-ri Ssk.* **pearl.**

མཎྜལ་ *maṇḍal Ssk*, prop. *Tib. dkyil-ₒkor* jewels, viands etc. presented as offerings, and arranged in **a cirle** *Glr.* and elsewhere, cf. *ťsogs.*

མད་ *mad* 1. = *nad* (?) *lus mad-méd-čiṅ Sambh.* — 2. sometimes for *smad.*

མད་པ་ *mád-pa* **true**, *kyed mad ysúṅ-žiṅ* as you speak what is true *Mil.*; *ma nyés-pai bden-ťsig mád-po smras kyaṅ* although he solemnly declared not to have committed it *Pth.*

མན་ *man* I. sbst., also *mán-na*, *má-na Hind.* a **'man'** or Indian hundredweight, equal to about 80 pounds, anglicized **maund.** — II *W.* for *ma yin* (*B. min*) 1. it is not;

'i man this it is not; *mán-na* is it not so? isn't it? is it? In conjunction with a negative it is col. almost the only word for **only, but** etc.: *de mán-na mi yoṅ, de mán-na med* only this one is to be met with, besides this there are none; *la-dág-gi lug čún-se mán-na mi yoṅ* there are only small sheep in Ladak; *dún-la mán-na mi tóṅ-k'an* he who sees only what is close before him, a short-sighted person; *dé-bu lo gyad tiṅ-la mán-na mi yoṅ* fruit will appear only after a space of eight years; *di-riṅ mán-na ma toṅ* I have seen (him, it) only to-day, i.e. to-day for the first time cf. *min.* — 2. **no.** — III. = *ma* II., *man-yán* **below** and **above** *Cs.*; *man-čád, -c̀ád, -čód* 1. adv.and postp.c.accus., **below, downward, on the lower side of, as far as,** *lté-ba man-c̀ád ču náṅ-du nub Glr*, he was immerged in the water below his navel, i.e. up to his navel; inst. of *man-c̀ád* also merely *man: pús-mo goṅ man Mil.*, lit below the parts over the knee i.e. higher than the knee; *de man-čód*, below that *Glr.*; in reference to time, **from,** *do-núb man čad* from this evening *Mil.*; *de man-čád* **since, from that time forward** *Mil.*; *rmaṅ btiṅ-ba man rab-gnás mdzád-pa yán-la* from the foundation up to the consecration *Glr.*; **even to** (the last man), (all) **except** or **save** (one), also *mán-pa, mán-pe, mán-k'an, man-va* *W.* (*B. min-pa*). — 2. sbst. **lower part** of a country, **lowland,** thus in *Lh.* as a proper name.

མན་ངག་ *man-ṅag*, *Ssk.* उपदेश, **advice, direction, information,** *stón-pa* to give, *man-ṅag (-gi) rgyúd* v. *rgyud* 2; in later writings and in the mind of the common people, it coincides with *sṅags*, in as much as the esoteric doctrines of mysticism, i.e. magic art, are concerned, which are communicated in no other way than by word of mouth; cf. *k'a-rgyun.*

མན་ཅད་, ཆད་, ཆོད་, པ་, ཐག *man-c̀ad, čad, čod, pa, thag*, v. *man* II. and III.

མན་ད་ར་བ *man-da-ra-ba*, मन्दारव, a tree in paradise *Stg.*

མན་(ན་)མུན་(ནེ་) *man(-na)-mún(-ne) Ld.*, **turbid, muddy, dingy, dim, dull, dusky,** as to water, flames of light etc.

མན་ཙི་ *mán-tsi Sch.* a kind of silk-cloth.

མན་ཛི་ *man-dzi* 1. *Sch.* 'a small **square table**', acc. to others **a tripod** with long curved feet, for sacrificial purposes. — 2. *W.* **bed** *Hindi* मच.

མན་ཤེལ་ *man-šel* **crystal, glass** *Pth.*

མར་ *mar* I. sbst., resp. *gsol-már* 1. **butter** *Thgy*, *C.*, *W.* — 2. col. also **oil.** — **Comp.** *skya-már*, *Ld. k'ág-la mar* fresh, not melted butter; *ba-már* cow-butter; *ḥbri-már* yak-butter; *ḥbru-már* oil from oleaginous seeds, rape-seed oil etc. *Dzl.* and elsewhere; *rtsi-már* oil from the stones of apricots etc.; *mdzo-már* butter from the bastard-cow; *žun-már* melted butter, *ghi* (*Hind.*), the usual form of butter in India and frq. also in Tibet, highly esteemed both as food and as medicine; *žum-már-pa* *C.* **lamp;** *mar-dkár Med.* = *skya-már.* — *már-k'u* melted, liquid butter. — *mar-rnyiṅ* old, rancid butter, recommended by physicians for diseases of the mind, fainting-fits, wounds. — *mar-nág* *W.* oil, *nyuṅ-dkar-mar-nág* rape-seed oil. — *mar-blúg* *W.* a small urn-shaped vessel for butter or oil. — *mar-mé* **lamp,** at present only for holy uses, thus: *mar-mé ghyen-tsén* holy, heavenward burning lamp *C.* (formerly any lamp *Dzl.* VS, 11; *Glr.*); *mar me mdzád* Buddha Dipaṅkara, v. *Dzl.* XXXVII.; — *mar-žógs Mil.* a part cut off, one half of a *mar-ril*, i.e. a globular lump of fresh butter, about one pound in weight, not unfrequently offered to travellers as a gift of courtesy. — *mar-gsár* fresh butter *Lt.* — II. termin. of *ma* I., to or 'into' the mother; *mar-gyur ḥgró-ba* regarded as a mother, a creature loved like a mother, *Mil.*; v. *ma* II. down, downward, *már-la* id., *B.* and *C.*; v. *rbab* and *ḥgrib-pa*; *mar-ṅo* v. *ṅo* 5.

མར་ཀ་ལ་ག་ *mar-ka-la-ga* (?) a fine ochreous earth, found e. g. on the Baralasa pass between *Lh.* and *Ld.*, used as ground-colour in staining houses with *dkár-rtsi Ld.*

མར་རྒན་ *mar-rgán* v. *ma-rgán.*

མར་ངོ་ *mar-ṅó* v. *ṅo* 5.

མར་དོན་ *mar-dón* perh. *dmar-ˌdón.*

མར་པ་ *már-pa*, n. of a holy Lama, teacher of Milaraspa, by whom he was highly respected.

མར་བ་ *mar-ba* provinc. for *dmár-bu Sch.*

མར་ཡུལ་ *már-yul Ma.*, n.p. = *la-dwags* Ladak.

མལ་ *mal*, the place where a thing is, its **site, situation**, **mál-du ẑúg-pa** *C.* **bór-ĉe** *W.*, to put a thing in its own place; also where a thing has been, its **trace, vestige**, *śiṅ-rtai* rut, wheel-mark, track; *mal ycig-tu mi ˌdúg-pa* prob. to be unstable, changeable, fickle, restless; more esp. place of rest, **couch, bed**, *mál-gyi ˌog-tu* under the bed *Glr.*; *dgoṅs-mal* resp. for night-quarters *Dzl.* ༡༤༠, 3 (so acc. to the xylographic copy; *Sch.* having the less appropriate *dgons-lam*); **mal dúg-ĉe** *W.* to live in a strange place, ἐπιδημεῖν; *mal bdé-ba Sch.* a quiet sleep, *ṅai lus sems mál-du bde* I now may safely lie down, fig. for: the danger is now over *Glr.* — *mal-k'rí* bed-frame, bed-stead. — *mal-gós Cs.*, *mal-ć'á Lex.*, **mal-ć'é** *C.*, **-stán** *C.*, *W.*. *Dzl.* bedding, bed-clothes. — *mal-ldaṅ Sch.* 'cradle', rather improb., perh. hammock. — *mal-yól* bed-curtain. — *mál-sa*, resp. *yzims-mál* couch, bed.

མལ་ལ་མུལ་ལེ་ *mal-la-múl-le Ld.* **lukewarm,** tepid.

མལ་ལི་ཀ་ *mal-li-ka Ssk.*, properly name of a flower, Jasminum Champaca, used as an epithet in pompous titles of books.

མས་ *mas* 1. instrum. case of *ma* mother. — 2. v. *ma* II, **the lower part**, gen. however with terminative meaning, **downward, towards the lower parts**, *mas btáṅ-ba Med.* to move downward, to purge; **backward, last** *Sch.*; used also as a sbst.: *más-kyi* the last, e.g. *yi-ge* final letter *Cs.*; *más-la* downward, below *Sch.*, *más-nas* from below *Sch.*; cf. the contrary *yás.*

མི་ *mi*, I. num. figure: 46. — II. sbst. **man,** *mi ysod-pa* to kill men, to murder, *mi-méd ri-k'ród* uninhabited, desolate mountains *Mil.*; *mi-rnams ná-re* people said *Mil.*; *mí-la ma lab* tell no body else of it *Mil.*; *ráṅ-gis bsdágs-pa mi-yis spyod* what we gathered ourselves, is enjoyed by others *Mil.*; *mi-nor raṅ slóṅ-ba* to gather by begging what belongs to others *Mil.*; *mii bú-mo* 1. daughters of men, opp. to *lhai bú-mo* e.g. witches appear in the shape of daughters of men *Mil.* 2. daughters of others, opp. to *ráṅ-gi bú-mo Mil.*, cf. also *mi-bu* further on; pleon. before a pers. pron. of the first person: *mi-ṅá*, *mi-bdág* I, *Mil.* (cf. *p'o*), and with certain sbst.: *ytsó-bo mi drug* (we) six lords *Glr.*; plur. also *mi-ts'ó Sch.*

Comp. *mi-k'a*, (idle) talk of the people, common talk, *yúl-sdei náṅ-nas mi-k'a sdud* in the whole neighbourhood one is an object of gossip, nif.; defaming talk; imprecating speech, with or without *ṅán-pa*, *mi-k'á zug* or *p'og* (damnation) lights on (me, him) *Dom.* — *mi-kyim* 1. **human dwelling, house**, (the Chinese capital contained) *mi-kyim ˌbúm-ts'o* 100 000 houses *Glr.* 2. *Ld.-Glr. Schl.* 20. b. and *Glr.* 94, 7 it seems to imply **the people of a household, domestics,** the same as *k'yim-ghi mi.* — *mi-ˌgréṅ* v. *ˌgréṅ-ba.* — *mi-rgód* v. *rgód-pa* II. — *mi-brgyúd* v. *brgyud.* — *mi-rjé* sovereign, king, *mi-rjé mdzád-pa* to be king, to reign *Glr.* — *mi-nyid Cs.* 'humanity, honesty'; *mi-nyid-ĉan* 'humane, honest'(?) — *mi-brdág.* 1. = *mi-rjé.* 2. symb. num.: 16. — *mi-mda* (vulgo *mín-da*) *Mil.* and *C.*, *W.*: men, persons preceded by a numeral, e.g. six men, six women (prop. a line or row of people). — *mi-sdé* v. *sde. Sch.* has also: *lha-sdé mi-sdé* princes and nations. — *mi-sná* 1. **race of men, class of people** (seldom). 2. **messenger, delegate**, not frq met with in books, yet not unknown in *C.* and *W.*, and used esp. of messengers with an errand or charge given them in words; in our translations introduced for **apostle**, *ṗó-nya* having been adopted for 'angel'. — *mi-dpón* prefect *Glr.*, *C.* — *mi(i)-bu* 1. **a child of man, a mortal**, po., *Mil.*, cf. *mii bú-mo* above. 2. **son of man,** when Christ speaks of himself as such, otherwise *mii sras Chr. Prot.* — *mi-bo Cs.*, rarely for *mi.* — *mi-dbaṅ*, prince, potentate. — *mi-ma-yín(-pa)* **अमनुष**, one that is not a human being, *mi daṅ mi-ma-yin-pa ṫams-čád* all human and not human (adversaries) *Dom.*, esp. ghosts, demons, *dur-ḱród-kyi mi-ma-yin-pa-rnams* the ghosts of a grave-yard (not the souls of the dead); *mḱá-la rgyú-bai mi-ma-yín* the ghosts that walk in the air *Mil.*; *dkár-ṗyogs-kyi mi-ma yin-rnams* good genii *Mil.*; *mi-ma-yin-gyi čo-˳ṗrúl* apparitions of ghosts *Mil.* — *mi-mo* **woman,** yet only in contraposition to *lhá-mo* and other not human female beings *Mil.* and elsewh. — *mi(i)-yul* human world, lower world, earth, opp. to regions of the gods or of infernal beings *Glr.*, *Pth.* — *mi-rabs* mankind. — *mi-rigs* v. *rigs.* — *Mi-la-rás-pa*, often only *Mi-la*, name of a Buddhist ascetic, of the 11 century (*Wdk.*), who between the periods of his meditations itinerating in the southern part of Middle Tibet as a mendicant friar, instructed the people by his improvisations delivered in poetry and song, brought the indifferent to his faith, refuted and converted the heretics, wrought manifold miracles (*rdzu-˳ṗrúl*), and whose legends, written not without wit and poetical merit, are still at the present day the most popular and widely circulated book in Tibet. — *mi-lág* servant, **mi-lág-tu ˳dó-wa** to do servant's work, to perform drudgery *W.* — *mi-lús* 1. the human body. 2. v. *lús-pa.* — *mi-ser* 1. **subject, servant, menial, drudge.** 2. **robber, thief, sharper.** — 3. v. below.

III. negative adv.: **not,** in all such cases where *ma* (q.v.) is not used. With simple verbs the place of the negation is always immediately before them, in compound forms gen. before the last of the component parts, e.g. *˳byúṅ-bar mi ˳gyúr-ro*, unless logically it belongs to the first, in which case often *ma* inst. of *mi* is employed. This rule, however, is not always strictly observed, so *Glr.* 70: *de daṅ nám-du yaṅ mi ˳brál-bar gyis šig*, and immediately after: *skad ýčig kyaṅ ma brál-bar gyis šig* do never part with it

མི་ཉག་, **མེ་ཉག་** *mi-nyág*, *me-nyág*, and **ཏང་གུད་** Tanggud, names of two provinces closely connected with each other, situated in the north-eastern part of Tibet and forming in ancient times a separate kingdom *Glr.*

མི་མ་ *mi-ma Sch.* **tears.**

མི་སེར་ *mi-sér* 1. n.p., formed after مصر, *mi-sér yul* Egypt, *mi-sér-pa* Egyptian, *Chr. Prot.* — 2. v. *mi.*

མིའམ་ཅི་ *miam-či*, *Ssk.* **किंनर**, fabulous beings of Indian origin, nearly related to the *˳dri-za*, and belonging to the retinue of Kuvera; fem *miam-či-mo.*

མིའུ་ *miu* 1. **a little man, dwarf,** also *miu-ṫúṅ Wdn.*; *mig-gi miu* v. *mig.* — 2. perh. applicable also **to puppet, doll.**

མིག་ *mig*, resp. 1. **eye.** — 2. **eye of a needle; hole** in a hatchet or hammer, to insert the handle — 3. symb. num.: 2. — *mig-gi gaṅs Sch.*, the white of the eye; *mig-gi rgyál-mo* or *miu*, 'the queen or the little man in the eye': 1. **pupil.** 2. **iris** *Stg.*; *mig-gi snág-ṫsa* or *-mṫso Cs.*, vulgo *mig-gi nág-po* id.; *mig-gi mé-tog Sch.* the luminous point of the eye: *mig nyáms-pa Cs.* weak eyes; *mig ltá-ba* to see with the eyes, to look up, to look round *Glr.*; *mig ˳dzúm-pa* to shut the eyes, *˳byéd-pa* to open the eyes, v. *˳byéd-pa* 1; *˳dón-pa*, *˳byin-pa* to cut or tear out the eyes, to squeeze them out by a particular instrument, as a torture or punishment *C.*; *mig bčár-ba Lex.*, acc. to *Sch.* id.; *mdóṅs-pa*, *mdóṅs-par ˳gyúr-ba* to get blind or blinded, to be deprived of sight *Dzl.*; *mig ˳ḱyíd-pa Sch.*, to distort or roll the eyes; *mig skú-ba Dom.* (*bskú-ba?*) n. of a certain magic trick; *mig čid-pa* inflammation of the eyes through cold, snow-blindness *C.* (perh. *ṗyid-pa*); **mig zug soṅ**

it has struck my eyes, I should like to have it *C., W.*; **mig log ltá-ce** to eye one obliquely, with envy or jealousy *W.* —

Comp. *mig-kyóg* squinting *Sch.* — *mig-rkyén Mil.*, is said to be the same as *mig-ltós.* — **mig-skyór* W.* eye-ball. — *mig-skyág* the impurities in the eyes *Cs.* — *mig-ḱúṅ* eye-hole, socket *Sch.* — *mig-ₒḱrul Mil.* v. *mig-ₒṕrul.* — *mig-grogs* one's sweetheart *Cs.* — *mig-ₒgram* edge of the eye *Sch.* — *mig-rgyaṅ* 1. v. *rgyaṅ-ma.* 2. far-sightedness, *mig-rgyáṅ-ċan* one that is far-sighted, *mig rgyaṅ-ṫúṅ* short-sighted *Bhar.* *mig-sgyu* mirage, looming, Fata Morgana, *sós-kai ťáṅ-la mig-sgyu ₒgyú-ba bžin Thgr.* like the mirage on a plain in the hot season. — *mig-sgyur-ma* = *mḱá-ₒgro-ma Mil.* — *mig-ċaṅ* 1. having eyes. 2. having seeds or grains, fructified, of ears of corn *W.* — *mig-ċér* v. *ċe-re.* — *mig-lċibs* eye-lid *Med.* — *mig-ču* 1. tears *W.* 2. hydrophthalmia *Med.* 3. *mig-ču dzág-pa* blear-eyes *Schr.* — *mig-brnyás ₒḱyér-ba Mil.* c. dat., to slight, to treat contemptuously. — *mig-rtúl* dim, dull eyes *Sch.* — *mig-lta* (resp. *žál-lta, žál-ta*) *byéd-pa* to inspect, superintend (**mig-ta-ḱan** overseer of workmen); to keep, to guard; to care for, to minister, to serve. — *mig-ltág Sch.* = *mig-skyág*(?) — *mig-ltós* 1. eye-sight, look, mien *Cs.* 2. *C. W.* learning by observation and close ocular attention, **gár-ža-pe hín-dui mig-tós ḱur,* or *ḱyon,* or *lob dug* W.* the people of Lahoul copy the Hindoos; **mig-tós ṅán-pa ḱur,* or *lob soṅ* W.* he has imitated what is not good. — **mig-tọ́-la ṕém-pa,* or *nọ́'-pa* C.* to derive profit or harm from observing and imitating others(?) **mig-tọ́-la ṕém-pe 'ṭim** deterring punishment. — **mig-ťág tóṅ-wa** a kind of torture in *C.*, little hooks, connected by strings, being fastened in the lower eye-lids as well as in the chest, by which means the former are constantly drawn down and prevented from closing. — *mig-ṫúṅ* short-sightedness *Cs.*, *mig-ṫúṅ-ċan* short-sighted. — **mig-ḍa** snow-spectacles, shades formed of a texture of horse-hair. — **mig-dól* C.* = *ɣnyid-rdól.* — *mig-ldán* = *mig-ċan* po. needle. — *mig-nád*, disease of the eye. — *mig-po* = *mig Cs.*, *mig-po-čé* a large eye *Cs.* — **mig-ṕág* C., W.* eye-lid. — *mig-sprin* 'a white spot in the eye' *Sch.*; acc. to *Lt.* it seems to be the white of the eye, sclerotica, in *C.* the cataract is called so. — *mig-ṕór Cs.* = *mig-ḱúṅ.* — *mig-ₒḱrúl Mil.* optical deception, *mig-ₒḱrul-mḱan* a showman *Cs.* — *mig-bu* 'Augenklappe' *Sch.* (?) — *mig-ₒbúr* goggle-eyes. — *mig-ₒbras* apple of the eye, eye-ball, **mig-ḍás lóg-ċe,* or *mig-kór lóg-ċe* W.* to roll the eyes; *bdág-gi mig-gi ₒbras ltar ɣčés-na yaṅ* although she is as dear to me as the apple of my eye. — *mig-máṅ(s)* chess-board, game at tables, *mig-máṅ rtsé-ba Dzl.* to play at chess, *mig-maṅ-rís-su bris-pa Glr.* chequered, painted or in-laid work after the pattern of a chess-board. — *mig-méd* eyeless, blind. — *mig-dmár* 1. red eye, as a symptom of disease *Lt.* 2. the planet Mars. — *mig-smán* eye-medicine. — *mig-rtsa* 1. prob. Vena facialis externa *Med.* 2. the blood-vessels of the sclerotica, *mig-rtsa ₒḱrúgs-pa* the blood-vessels irritated, reddened *Med.* — **mig-sál* W.* sharp-sightedness, **mig-sál-ḱan** sharp-sighted, **mig-sal-nyám** the contrary. — *mig-rtség* the wrinkles of the eye-lid *Cs.* — *mig-ťsil*, 1. fat in the eye *Mil.* 2. the white in the eye *Cs.* — **mig-ťsig(-ċe)* W.* inflammation of the eye, **ḱá-mig-ťsig** caused by snow, **dúd-mig-ťsig** caused by smoke. — *mig-zi* mist before the eyes *Sch.* — *mig-zúr* corner of the eye *Sch.* — *mig-ɣzúgs S.g.* optical perception, a picture of objects being formed on the retina by reflected rays of light (merely guessed by Tibetan science, not ascertained by observation and research). **mig-yáṅ(s)* C., W.* liberal, bountiful. — *mig-yór*, 1. *Sch.* = *mig-rtúl.* 2. = *mig-sgyú Thgr.* — *mig-rig-rig Mil.* timidly, anxiously looking to and fro, hither and thither. — *mig-riṅ-ċan* = *mig-rgyáṅ-ċan Cs.* — *mig-ris* artificial eye-brows *Cs.* — *mig-rús* eye-bone *Cs.* — *mig-slobs* the act of accustoming the eyes to . . ., *mig-slóbs ṅán-pa skye Mil.* you habituate yourself to a faulty look, i. e.

downward, to what is earthly. — **mig-šóg** *W.* eye-lash. — *mig-sér* 1. jaundice, also **gya-nág mig-sér** *W.* 2. envy, jealousy, *mig-sér-čan* envious, jealous. — *mig-hu-ré* v. *hu-re.*

མིང་ *miṅ*, resp. *mtsan*, **name,** *k'yód-kyi miṅ či yin Mil.* or **či zer** *W.* what is your name? *dei miṅ yaṅ med Glr.* such a thing is or was not known at all, such a thing does not exist; *miṅ-tsam-gyi dge-slóṅ Dzl.* priest only by name; *W.*: **míṅ-gi náṅ-na** id.; *C.* also: **ṭál-gyi miṅ tsám-lẹ me** this tax exists only nominally; **appellation, designation, word,** *t'én-pai miṅ* a word for drawing (pulling) *Gram.*; *miṅ-gi mdzod* **dictionary;** **k'yod-sụ miṅ daṅ** or **sụ míṅ-ṅi náṅ-na** or **sụ miṅ nén-te** or **sụ míṅ-la tén-te ča dug** *W.* in whose name or business, upon whose order are you going? **čii miṅ daṅ** *W.* for what cause, in behalf of what affair? *míṅ-nas rjód-pa*, or *smó-ba Dzl.* and elsewh., to call by name, also to call upon the name of, hence . . . *kyi míṅ-nas brjód-de* in the name of; *miṅ ˳dógs-pa* to name v. *miṅ* 2; *dṅós-miṅ* v. *dṅos*; *btágs-miṅ* a name given (e.g. a Christian name) *Cs.*, *rjes-grúb-kyi miṅ* a surname *Cs.*, *rus-miṅ* a family name *Cs.*

Comp. *miṅ-rkyáṅ* a single syllable or name *Cs.*, cf. *miṅ-sbyár.* — *miṅ-grógs* one's name-sake *Cs.* — *miṅ-sgrá* a mere name, word, or sound (philosophical term.) *Was.* — *miṅ-ṅán* a bad name, infamy *Cs.* — *miṅ-čan* having a name, *dpal-˳byór miṅ-čan* one of the name of Paljor. — *miṅ-ťon* v. *˳ťón-pa.* — *miṅ-mťá* final letter *Cs.* — *miṅ-sbyár* compound name. — *miṅ-méd* 1. nameless. 2. the fourth finger. — *miṅ-tsig* word, appellation. — *miṅ-γži* the first letter of the root of a word, in contradistinction to the second, the third, and the prefix-letters, *miṅ-γži rkyáṅ-pa* a single initial, e. g. ཀ, including ཀྱ. ཀྲ, ཀླ, *Zam.*; *γnyis-sbrél*, *γsum-sbrél* a double, triple, letter, like རྐ. རྐྱ, *Cs.*(?) — *miṅ-bzáṅ* good reputation *Cs*

མིང་པོ་ *miṅ-po* **brother** in relation to his sister, *miṅ-sríṅ* brother and sister; *de ṅa daṅ miṅ-sriṅ-du byao Dzl.* her and myself I shall make to be sister and brother, i.e. I shall raise her to be my sister.

མིད་ *mid* **a large fish** *Cs.*; *mid-mid* id.

མིད་པ་ *mid-pa* 1. sbst. **gullet, oesophagus** *Mil.* and elsewh.; *mid-skráṅ* a tumour of it, incident to horses *Sch.* — 2. vb. **to swallow, to gulp down,** frq.

མིན་ *min*, *W.* **man**, 1. for *ma yin* (he, she, it) **is not,** *ša-min-ťsil-min Mil.* they are neither 'flesh nor fat'. — 2. abbrev. for *min-pa* and *min-par* v. below; *btaṅ-min* for **btaṅ yin-nam ma yin** *W.* will it be given or not? *min-pa* and *ma yin-pa* **to be not;** often as a participle supplying the place of a prep. or adv. (for *min-par*), **excepted, except, besides,** *de ma yin-pai šiṅ Stg.* the other trees except this one; *klu ma yin-pa γžan mi ťub Dzl.* except he that is a Lu cannot . . .; *saṅs-rgyás min-pa sus kyaṅ mi šes Mil.* besides Buddha no one knows of it, no one knows it except Buddha; *ṅas yug γčig min-pa mi bsdad Mil.* I have been sitting down only this moment; *ro zér-ba min-pa skyab-pai miṅ mi yoṅ-ba ˳dug Mil.* one can only say 'corpse', and the appellation '*skyab-pa*' is not admissible; *de min* **besides, otherwise, else, apart from, setting aside** *Mil.*; even: *de-min-rnams Glr.* those that are not doing so. Cf. *man.*

མིན་ད་ *min-da* v. *mi-mda*, sub *mi* compounds.

མིམ་ *mim*, the Hind. *mĕm*, **Madam,** *mim sá-heb* the mistress or lady of the house.

མིར་ *mir* termin., མིས་ *mis* instrum. case of *mi.*

མུ་ *mu* 1. num. fig.: 76. — 2. sbst. **border, boundary, limit, edge, end,** *žiṅ-mu-la γnás-pai lha* deity residing on the landmark; *mú-la skye* (the plant) grows on the edges of fields *Wdṅ.*; *mťa méd-čiṅ mu med Stg.* there is neither limit nor end; *mu bži = mťa bži Mil*, *S.g.* seems to be used in a philosophical sense for 'perfect limitedness'; *mu-k'yúd* **circumference, compass,** the **hoops** of a cask *Sch.*, the **rim** of a wheel *Stg.*; *mu-k'yud-˳dzin* n.p., the least of the seven mountains surrounding the Sumeru. *mú-stegs-pa*, also *mú-stegs-čan Ssk.* तीर्थिक (overlooking the word *stegs*) it is gen. explained in an intellectual sense, so by Cunningham: adherents of the doctrine of finite existence (Bhilsa Topes), *Cs.*: the doctrine of perpetual duration or of perpetual annihilation (?); but should not rather *mú-stegs* be the same as *ₒbáb-stegs* (v. *ₒbáb-pa*), being a literal translation of तीर्थ, and therefore prop. a Brahmanic ascetic (v. *Ssk.* dict.), in Buddhist literature always equivalent to Brahmanist, Non-Buddhist, heretic (infidel)? — 3. *Sch* has besides: *mú-la* in a circle, continuously; *mu-ltar* or *mú-nas* = *bžin-du C.*; in *W* they say: **mu čig-la bor** throw it together on a heap!

མུ་གེ་ *mú-ge* 1. *W.* **desire, appetite,** **zan za-če** or **čaṅ ťún-čči mú-ge rag** I have a longing for food, for beer; *mú-ge-čan* fond of dainties, lickerish, of men and animals. — 2. *B.* and col., **famine,** *mú-ge ₒbyuṅ Dzl.*, *Mil.* a famine is caused, breaks out.

མུ་ཅོར་ *mu-čór* **nonsense,** *smrá-ba Stg.* to talk nonsense.

མུ་ཏིག་ *mú-tig* **pearl** frq., *mú-tig-rgyan* a pearl ornament *Cs*; *mu-tig-čún-po*, *mu-tig-drá-ba Glr.* garland formed of pearls; *mu-tig-ṗreṅ* string of pearls.

མུ་ཐི་ལ་ *mu-ṫi-la* **mother of pearl** *Sch.* (?).

མུ་ནི་ *mu-ni Ssk.* **saint, ascetic, anchorite,** chiefly in names: *Sā-kya-mu-ni* the saint of the Sākyas, Buddha.

མུ་ནི་ཏི་ *mu-ni-ti Sch.* = *mu-tig* (?).

མུ་མེན་ *mu-mén Glr., Mil.* a precious stone, of a dark blue, yet inferior to the azure-stone, occasionally used for rosaries; mention is also made of *mu-mén dmár-po Wdṅ.*

མུ་རྩོད་ *mu-rtsód* (?) **colt's foot,** Tussilago farfara *Lh.*

མུ་ཟི་ *mú-zi* **brimstone, sulphur** *Med.*, *mú-zi-čan* containing sulphur, sulphurous; *mú-zii skyúr-rtsi* (*snum Schr.*) sulphuric acid *Cs.* (?).

མུ་རན་ *mu-rán* **hoop,** of casks etc. *Sch.*

མཱུ་ལ་ *mū-la Ssk.*, **root;** particular roots, such as those of Arum campanulatum, so perh. *Lt.*

མུག་གེ་ *múg-ge* sometimes for *mú-ge*.

མུག་པ་ *múg-pa*, 1. sbst. **moth, worm,** *múg-ma* id. *Glr.*, also *múṅ-ma*; *gós-mug* clothes-moth, *bál-mug* id., *lčágs-mug* a worm that eats iron away (?) *Cs.*; *múg-zan* moth-eaten, destroyed by worms *Cs.* — 2. vb. with *yid-*, *yi-*, resp. *ťugs-*, **to despair** *Pth.*; *blo múg-po* a gloomy, doleful way of thinking *Sch.*

མུན་པ་ *mun-pa* 1. sbst. **obscurity, darkness,** frq. — *mún-pai smag-rúm* id., frq.; *mún-pa-nas mún-par ₒgro Dzl.* they wander in eternal darkness; *mún-pa sél-ba* to lighten the darkness; frq. fig. with and without *bloi.* — 2. adj. **obscure, dark.** — 3. vb. in *W.*, *mun soṅ* he has become insensible. — **Comp.** *mún-ḱaṅ* dark room, e.g. the sanctuary containing the images of the gods *Glr.*; prison *Cs.* — *mún-ḱuṅ Dzl.* prison, dungeon. — **mun-ṭig* Lh.*, *mun-ḱród Dzl.*, **mun-nág* W., C.*, *mun-brág Sch.* and *Lh.* (?) close darkness. — **mun-ḍúl*, or *mun-nyúg táṅ-če* W.* to grope in the dark. — **mún-ču*, *núm-ču* W.* the dusk of evening, **mún (-ču) rub** sets in. — **mún-(s)pe-ra táṅ-če* W.* to talk confusedly, wildly. — *mun-sprúl Tar.* 56,17, to judge by the context: ignorance, stupidity; so *Schf.* — *mun-sribs Lex.* the darkness of night. — *mun-sró* furious passion, **mún-sro yoṅ dug* W.* he rages in his passion. — **mun-srós* = *mún-ču* W.*

མུམ་ *mum* (*Hind.*) *W.* **wax.**

མུར་ *mur* 1. termin. of *mu*, hence *mur-ťug* **to the extremity, till the end of** *Cs.*; perh. also *mur-dúm* (or *-zlum?*) *Ld.* **dull,** of knives, hatchets; *múr-ₒdug* = *mú-stegs-pa Sch.* — 2. **gills** of fish.

མུར་གོང་ *mur-goṅ* **the temples** *Sch.*; *mur-ₒgrám* id. *Cs*; **jaw, jaw-bone** *Sch.* — *mur-ťór* ulcers in the mouth *Sch.*

མུར་བ་ *múr-ba* 1. **to gnaw,** to destroy by gnawing, to bite asunder, e.g. bones *Thgr.* — 2. **to masticate, to chew** (?).

སྨུལ་ཐུག་ *mul-ťúg W.* **fist**, **mul-ťúg čó-če, gám-če** to threaten with the fist, **gyáb-če** to strike with the fist.

མེ་ *me* I. num. fig.: 106. — II. sbst. 1. resp. *žugs C.*, **náṅ-me* W.*, **fire**, *me ̥bar* the fire burns, *šor* breaks out, *mčed* spreads, *ši* is extinguished; **me són-na* W.* is the fire burning (again)? *K̔áṅ-pa mes* (vulgo **mé-la**) *bsregs, šor, k̔yer* the house is burnt down, **dugs soṅ* W.* ignited, burnt (partially); *me sbór-ba, ̥búd-pa, γtóṅ-ba B.*, **(s)bár-če, p̔ú-če, dúg-če* W.* to light a fire, *γsó-ba, *són-te čó-če* W.* to stir, poke, trim the fire, **nyál-če* W.* to cover the glowing embers with ashes, in order to preserve the heat; *rgyáb-pa* 1. **to set on fire,** *k̔yím-la* a house *Glr.* 2. **to strike fire** *W.*, *me ldé-ba B.* and col., to warm one's self at the fire. — 2. symb. num.: 3. —

Comp. *me-skám* cock (of a gun), **me-kám ǰar ťsar* W.* the gun is cocked. — *me-skyógs C.* a shovel for live coals. — *me-sgyógs, gyogs = sgyogs* 2. — *me-mgál* **firebrand,** *me-mgál-gyi k̔ór-lo* the circle made by a firebrand, when quickly swung round *Cs.* — **me-ḍọ́n** **torch** *C.* — *mé-čan* fiery, containing fire. — *me-lčágs* fire-steel, pocket-fire. — *mé-lče* flame of fire. — *me-čá* fire-steel (?) *Sch.*, **me-čẹ́* C.* every thing requisite for kindling a fire, as it is got in readiness for the following morning. — *me-mnyam-rlúṅ* v. *rluṅ.* — **me-tág* C.* 1. (*rtags*) a mark of burning. 2. (*ltag* or *stag*) **spark, sparklet,** a bit of live coal in the ashes. — *me-ťáb* fire-place, hearth; stove. — *me-dóṅ Dzl.* fire-pit, pool of fire. — *me-dród* v. *drod.* — **me-dá* C.*, musket, pistol; **me-da pag-čén** canon *Schr.*; **me-dá gyáb-pa** to discharge a gun; **me-da-šiṅ** resinous wood, the coal of which is particularly used for making gun-powder. — **me-dág** (*mdag*) *C.* coals glowing underneath the ashes. — *me-rdél* bullet, musket-ball *Sch.* — *me-rdó* flint *Cs.* — *me-núr Sch.* = *me-mdág.* — *me-snód*, or *-p̔ór* coal-pan, chafing-dish, perfuming-pan. — *me-p̔úṅ, me-búm* cupping-glass, cup *Lt.* — *mé-ba Dzl.* = *me.* — *mé-bo* = *me* a large fire, *mé-bo če Dzl.* — *me-dbál* a disease *Med.*; it is said to be a cutaneous eruption, hot and smarting, perh. erysipelas? — *me-múr* = *me-mdág Dzl.*; *me-ma-múr Thgy.* id.? — *me-btsá* v. *btsa.* — **me-ťsáǵ** spark *W.* — **me-dzẹ́** **gun-powder** *C.* — *me-γží* anvil *Sch.* — *me-γžób* mark of singeing, of having caught fire. — **me-zi* W.* = *me-ltág.* — *me-̥óbs* = *me-dóṅ Sch.* — *mé-ri* fire-mountain, introduced by us for **volcano.** — *me-ris* a figure resembling a flame *Sch.* — *me-ró* an extinguished fire, fig. *bstán-pai me-ró laṅ Glr.* the extinct doctrine revives again. — **me-liṅ* W.* flame. — *me-lén* fire-tongs. — *me-šél* burning-glass. — *me-lhá* the god of fire, v. *Schl.* 251 sqq. — III. v. also *mé-tog.*

མེ་ཉག་ *me-nyág* v. *mi-nyág.*

མེ་ཏོག་ *mé-tog, W. *mén-tog**, 1. **flower,** *mé-tog ̥bar, k̔a ̥bus* the flower opens, begins to bloom, *mé-tog-gi p̔réṅ-ba* chaplet, wreath of flowers. — 2. *W.* **tuft** or **crest** on the head of some birds. — 3. *W.* **snow-flake.**

མེ་ལོང་ *mé-loṅ* 1. **mirror, looking-glass,** frq.; *lás-kyi mé-loṅ* a magic mirror, revealing the future *Glr.*; also fig., esp. in titles of books, e.g. *rgyal-rábs-kyi γsál-bai mé-loṅ* A bright Mirror of the History of Kings. 2. **plain surface,** flat body extending in length and breadth, e.g. the flatness of the shoulder-blade, table-top, door-pannels etc., hence *sgo mé-loṅ-čan Glr.* an opening provided with a frame of boards to close it, not merely an 'ostium', of which description most of the inner doors in Tibetan houses are.

མེའོ་ *mea̤o* **the mewing of a cat.**

མེད་པ་ *méd-pa* for *mi yód-pa* **to be not, to exist not** (v. *yód-pa*), *med* he is not here, he is gone etc.; **k̔a-čúl-du soṅ-te med* W.* he is off, having gone to Kashmere; **čag-mag ǎ-pẹ k̔yér-te med* W.* the tinder-box is not here, father has taken it with him; **ši-te med* W.* he is dead and gone; *skabs med Dzl.* there is, or there was, no opportunity; *čos-kyi miṅ tsam yaṅ med Glr.* religious law does not, or did not, exist at all; *med kyaṅ* even if nothing is extant, though the thing does not exist in reality; **ni méd-na yaṅ yoṅ dug** the '*ni*' may be dispensed with, though '*ni*' be omitted, it will be all right; *rgyá-la méd-pai yi-ge drug Glr.* six letters not existing in Sanskrit; *méd-kyaṅ-ruṅ-bai yig-ₒbru γċig* a letter that may also be wanting, a dispensable letter, e.g. ཐྭ *Glr.*; *méd-kyaṅ dgós-pai k'ral-bsdúd Mil.* a taxation necessary, and even if one possesses nothing, yet as it were inexorable; *méd-pa* (*W.* **méd-k'an**) not being, not existing, not having; *blá-ma-la bżúgs-grogs méd-pa lágs-sam Mil.* has your Reverence no fellow-resident in your house? fem. *méd-ma Mil.*; *W.* **mā dud-pa-méd-k'an** very or quite smokeless; *mi brnáṅs-pa skyúg-tu méd-pa nád-du méd-pa Dzl.* a man about to be choked, being neither able to spit out, nor to swallow down; *bdag* (or *bdag-la*) *ċaṅ dbul-du med Dzl.* we are not able to give any thing; *med-mi-rúṅ-gi bu-ts'á Mil.* the sons and grandsons that are to get something (as a heritage); *k'yim der méd-du mi γtúb-pa*, or *mi rúṅ-ba* indispensable in the house *Thgy.*; so also *med-t'abs-méd-pai blón-po Glr.*; *méd-par ₒgyúr-ba* to be annihilated, to disappear, *stág-mo méd-par gyúr-to Pth.* the tigress disappeared; *γnam daṅ sa yaṅ med-gyur-na Dzl.* when heaven and earth shall pass away; **da ṅa ċiaṅ méd-k'an soṅ** *W.* now I am quite undone; *blón-po-rnams ₒgran-sems-méd-par gyur-to Glr.* the ministers lost their litigiousness, gave up quarreling; *zas brim-du méd-par gyúr-to Dzl.* the distribution of the dishes became impossible; **pé-ra zér-ċe méd-k'an soṅ** *W.* he became speechless; *med-par byéd-pa* to annihilate, an enemy *Dzl.*, to put an end to, a quarrel *Glr.*; frq. *méd-pa(r)* may be rendered by 'without': *rgyál-po żig méd-na mi ruṅ*, or *t'abs-méd Pth.* we cannot do without a king; *mt'a-rten-méd-pai mt'a* a termination without a final consonant *Gram.*; *rgyu méd-par S. g.* without cause; or by 'instead of': *rgyál-po méd-par Glr.* instead of the king, *sṅár-gyi lus méd-par Glr.* instead of the former shape; *nyin-mts'an-méd-par* making no difference between day and night, *p'o-mo-méd-par* between male and female, *rgan-byis-méd-par* old and young; vulgo also *nyin-med-mts'án-med* etc. — *méd-po*, *W.* **méd-k'an**, fem. *méd-mo*, a poor man, pauper.

མེན་ *men Mil.* **an ornament, piece of finery.**

མེནྡི་ *mendi*, *Ssk.* **मेन्धी**, Lawsonia alba, a plant used for staining the finger-nails red *Mil.*

མེན་ཙི་ *mén-tsi* **a coloured silk handkerchief** *W.*

མེན་ཧྲི་ *mén-hri* a kind of **fur**? *mén-hri dmár-poi slóg-pa* a fur-coat of red *men-hri* is mentioned as the vesture of a Lha.

མེར་ *mer* termin. of *me.*

མེར་བ་ *mér-ba Cs.*: 'a quaking; thinness; *mér-po*, *mer-mér* thin, as liquids'; *Sch.*: '*mér-gyis gaṅ* full to the brim'. I met with 1. *mer* in *żig-mér* q.v. — 2. *mér-ba* as adj. for *mts'o* the lake *Mil.* — 3. **mer-mér** *W.* adj. **like a thin pap,** and sbst. **a muddy substance,** e.g. street-mire; **mer-mér ċó-ċe** to make **a mire.** — 4. *mér-mer-ba* adj in connection with such sbst. as light, ray, beam, brightness *Thgr., Mil.* — 5. *mér-mer-po* used in medical writings in a similar manner as *núr-nur-po*, to define the shape of an embryo, **oblong, oval;** these descriptions, however, though partly founded on observation, are frequently very arbitrary, vague, and even contradictory. In *W.* the word has only the signification 3; a Lama from *C.* rendered it with **'full'**, which would agree with *Sch.* and no. 1, as well as with 'glittering, quivering', having some relation to no. 2 and no. 4.

མེལ་ཚེ་ or ཙེ་ *mél-ts'e* or *-tse* 1. **watch, watchman, sentinel; watcher, spy,** *mél-ts'e byéd-pa* to watch, to keep watch *Dzl.*; *ǰá-ra-mel-ts'e* = **mel-ts'e** *W.* — 2. **steatite** or **soap-stone,** of a greenish colour.

མེས་པོ་ *més-po*, vulgo **me-mé**, **grandfather;** also **forefather, ancestor, progenitor,** *saṅs-rgyás t'ams-ċád-kyi spyi-mes kun-tu-bzáṅ-po Thgr. Kuntuzaṅpo*, the common progenitor of all the Buddhas; *mes rgyál-po Glr.* merely equivalent to 'the old king';

pa-més the grandfather by the father's, *ma-més* by the mother's side *Cs*; *yaṅ-més* great-grandfather *Glr.*; *že-* or *yži-més Sch.* great-great-grandfather; *mes-dbón* grandfather and grandchildren, resp., e.g. *rgyál-po mes-dbón* the kings from one generation to another, the royal ancestors *Glr.*; *mes-rábs* id. *Sch.*; **me-mé**, reverential name given to men of a more advanced age *W.* also *C.*

མེ་ཏྲི་ *me-tri*, मैत्रेय, v. *byáms-pa Mil.*

མོ་ *mo*, I. num. figure: 136.

II. **woman, female,** opp. to *p̔o*, = *bud-méd*: *mo na-re* the woman said *Glr.*, *Mil.*; of animals: **female.** — **mo-kyáṅ* W.* virgin. — *mo-gós* woman's gown, petticoat. — *mo-brgyúd* female line of descent. — *mo-bí* female calf. — *mo-byis Mil.*, *mo-dbyis* (**mo-yi**) *C.* girl, female child. — *mo-btsún* nun *Glr.* — *mo-mt̔sán*, *moi dbáṅ-po* female genitals. — *mo-ráṅ-(mo)* **1. single, unmarried woman,** so perh. in the passage, *ydoṅ ṅán-gyi ḱyó-bas mo-ráṅ skyid* happier is a single woman than one with a husband of a bad face; more frq., the word implies 2. **a poor, destitute female,** one who did not get a husband *W.* 3. **she, herself** *C.*, *Lew.* — *mo-rí*, *mo-ré* a female kid. — *mo-rígs* female sex. *Cs.* — *mo-lús* the female body *Sch.* — *mo-yšám* a barren female, hence *mo-yšám-gyi bu* a nonsense, an incongruity.

III. **lot,** *mo ˳débs-pa* to cast the lot, always a religious ceremony performed by Lamas (cf. *rgyan* and *rtags-ríl*), which however does not preclude the possibility of an imposture; *mó-pa* one dealing with these practices, a soothsayer, *mó-pa ˳dre mt̔óṅ-ba* a soothsayer that pretends to have seen a ghost; *mó-mḱan Cs.*, *mó-rtsis-pa Glr.* id. (the latter expression in the respective passage = court-astrologer); *mo-ma* the feminine of it *Cs.*, which however is at variance with *Mil.*, who in several places has *bla-ma mḱas-pai mo-ma.*

IV. **affix**, so-called article, corresponding to the masc. terminations *po* and *pa*, and denoting the fem. gender of persons, *bú-mo* daughter, *bód-mo* a Tibetan woman.

མོ་ཁབ་ *mo-ḱáb* v. *ḱab.*

མོག་པ་ *móg-pa* **dark** (coloured) *Cs.*; *móg-ro* of horses, yellowish-brown *Glr.*

མོག་མོག་ *mog-móg* 1. *Cs.* = *móg-pa.* — 2. **meat-pie,** meat-balls in a cover of paste.

མོག་ཤ་ *móg-ša* **mushroom** *W.*

མོགས་ཙ་ར་ *mógs-tsa-ra Lt.* n. of a plant; in *Lh. mog-ša-ras* is a large species of Ferula or Dorema, of a yellow flower and a fetid smell.

མོང་གོལ་ *móṅ-gol* **a Mongul** *Tib. sóg-po.*

མོང་རྟུལ་ *moṅ-rtúl Lex.* = *blúṅ-po* **dull, stupid.**

མོང་ལོ་ *móṅ-lo*, *W.* for *lóṅ-mo* **knuckle, anklebone.**

མོད་ *mod* **moment,** occurring only in the following combinations: *láṅ-bai mod* (*de-nyid*)*-la* at the very moment of rising *Pth.*, *Mil.*, *dei mód-la* the moment after *Glr.*; gen. *mód-la* **instantly, immediately,** *mód-la dráṅs-so Glr.* he immediately pulled it out; *ḱra yaṅ mód-la p̔yin-te Dzl.* immediately after there came also the hawk; *dé-nas mód-la* id. *Dzl.*

མོད་པ་ *mód-pa* (cognate to *mád-pa?*) an emphatic word for **to be,** 1. as an augmentative of *yin*, sometimes superadded to this word; occasionally untranslatable, sometimes = **indeed, to be sure,** *žes smras mód-kyi Dzl.* though indeed you may say so; *dpag-tu-méd mód-kyi* though indeed it is immeasurable *Dzl.*; *ysa dé-ka ṅa yin mod Mil.* the snow-leopard indeed was I myself; *di ma yin mod ˳on-kyaṅ* ... to be sure, it is not this one, yet... *Tar.*; *˳gró-ba yin mod* (although not invited) yet after all you must go. — 2. as augmentative of *yod*, signifying abundance, plenty *B.*, *C.*, *W.*: *de mi byéd-na dgra mod* if you omit to do this, you will have plenty of enemies, *nad mod* plenty of diseases; *sti-bstáṅ-gi ḱrims šiṅ-tu mód-kyi* although they abounded in compliments; *mód-pa* having an abundance, *loṅs-spyód mód-par ˳gyur* he becomes the owner of great wealth *Dzl.*; *šiṅ-t̔og mód-*

pa Glr. abounding in tree-fruit; *mód-po* adj. plentiful, abounding, *kúl-lu-ru šiṅ mód-po* in Kullu wood is plentiful, or *šiṅ mód-poi yul* (Kullu is) a country abounding in wood, opp. to *dkón-po*, hence 'cheap' may occasionally stand for it.

མོན་ *mon* 1. n. p., general name for the different nations living between Tibet and the Indian plain *Mil : món-yul-gyi bán-dhe* a monk from Nepal; *Glr.: dpal-gro món-la* Paldo in Bhotan; *mon-ta-waṅ* is stated to be a commercial place in Assam, from whence much rice is brought to Tibet; the people of Lahoul are looked upon by the real Tibetans as Mon, though for the most part they speak the Tibetan language, and they in their turn consider the Hindoos in Kullu as Mon; that this appellation is often extended to the Hindoos in general, appears from such names as, *món-gre, món-sran* Indian pea, *Phaseolus radiatus*, माष; *món-č̣a-ra* the ever-green oak and its fruit, of the southern Himalaya ridges *Wdṅ.*; in *Ld.* the musicians (*Ld.-Glr. Schl.* 25, b), carpenters, and wood-cutters coming from the south, are likewise denominated Mon. — The form *mon-pa Cs.* is not known to me; *mon-mo* fem. *Pth.* — 2. sometimes for *mun*.

མོན་ཞ་ *mon-ža* (or perh. *γža*) *W.*, **popularity, respect, reputation**, *món-ža tob* he makes himself generally beloved, is highly respected; *món-ža-čan* **beloved, popular**.

མོར་ *mor* termin. of *mo*.

མོལ་བ་ *mól-ba* the usual resp. term, esp. in *W.*, for **to say, to speak**, as *bsgó-ba* and *bká-rtsal-ba* are used in earlier, and *γsúṅ-ba* in later literature and in *C.*, hence it is often to be rendered by 'to order'; **sá-heb-la sa-lám mol žu** have the goodness to present (say) my compliments to that gentleman; **mól-lče táṅ-če** to flatter, to caress; **mól-la táṅ-wa* C.* to make known(?).

མོས་པ་ *mós-pa* vb. and sbst. **to be pleased**, *la* **with, to wish, to have a mind**, *ₒgró-bar mós-so Glr.* I took a fancy to go there; *č̣u-la sógs-par mós-na Thgy.* if you wish for water or something of the kind; *mós-pa daṅ ₒdód-pa S.O.* desiring and coveting (are the origin of all the misery of sin); **to take pleasure in, to rejoice at**, *mós-pai glu Glr.* song of rejoicing; as sbst.: **pleasure, satisfaction, esteem**. — 2. **to respect, to esteem**, with *la*, to respect with devotion, **to revere, to adore** *č̣ós-la* frq.; *k̇yod gáṅ-la mos* to whom do you direct your devotions? *Mil.*; *mós-nas ₒbúl-ba yin* I give it merely from devout veneration, i.e. I shall take nothing for it *Pth.*; frq. joined with *gús-pa*: *yid-mos-gús drág-pos* with fervent veneration; *dad-mós* devotion; *mos spyód-pa* as participle, a pious man, a devotee *Tar.* 109, 7.

མྱ་ངན་ *mya-ṅán*, **trouble, misery, affliction**, *mya-ṅán-gyis γdúṅ-ste Dzl.*; *mya-ṅán či yaṅ med Dzl.* I have no trouble, no uneasiness, whatever; *mya-ṅán bsal Tar.* the time of mourning is at an end; *mya-ṅán byéd-pa* to lament, to wail; *mya-ṅan-méd*, अशोक, n. of a famous king of ancient India *Glr.*, *Tar.* ch. VI; *mya-ṅán-las ₒdás-pa*, abbr. *myaṅ-ₒdas* (and so also pronounced, as for instance in a verse of *Mil.*, where it occurs as a trochee) 'having been delivered from pain', the usual, illiteral, Tibetan version of निर्वाण, the absolute cessation of all motion and excitement both of body and mind, which is necessarily connected with personal existence; absolute rest, which by orientals is thought to be the highest degree of happiness, imagined by some as a perfect annihilation of existence, by others, more or less, only as a cessation of all that is unpleasant in human existence, — well set forth by *Köpp.* I. 304 sqq.

མྱ་ངམ་ *mya-ṅam* **a fearful desert** *Lex.*, *Thgy.*

མྱག་པ་ *myág-pa Sch.* **'to chew'**; acc. to medical writings, **the chemical decomposition** of the chyme in the stomach; **to cause putrefaction**; pf. *myags*; *myágs-par byéd-pa = myag-pa S.g.*; *rul-čiṅ myágs-pa Dzl.* decomposed, putrefied; *ro-myágs* the watery product of putrefaction, '*tabes*' *Thgy.*

མྱང་བ་ *myáṅ-ba* v. *myóṅ-ba*.

མྱད་པ་ *myád-pa Sch.* = *mid-pa* sbst.

སྨྱིང་ *myin Sch.* = *min.*

སྨྱུ་གུ་ *myú-gu*, སྨྱུག་ *myug*, 1. *Sch.* **reed, rush, flag**, also = *smyú-gu.* — 2. *Cs.* **sprout**, the first shoot of corn etc., *myú-gu snón-po Thgy.* the young green corn.

སྨྱུག་པ་ *myúg-pa, myúg-myug-pa* 1. **to run, roam, stroll idle about** *Sch.* — 2. **to show, exhibit ostentatiously, to boast with** *Cs.* v. *dmyúg-pa.*

སྨྱུར་བ་ *myúr-ba* **quick, swift, speedy,** *myúr-po* id. *Mil.*; mostly as adv., *myúr-du* **quickly, speedily; soon;** *ci-myúr* as speedily as possible; *myur-du-btsá-rtags* symptoms of immediate parturition *Med.*

སྨྱུལ་བ་ *myúl-ba* **to examine closely, to search into, to scrutinize,** c. accus. or termin. of place *Stg., Mil.*, prob. but a different spelling for *nyúl-ba.* — *lce-myúl Mng., Lt.* a symptom of disease, acc. to *Wise* p. 282: a quivering motion of the tongue.

སྨྱོ་བ་ *myó-ba* v. *smyó-ba.*

སྨྱོང་བ་ *myón-ba*, pf. *myans*, also *myon*, fut. *myan W. *nyán-ce**, 1. **to taste** *Dzl.*; **to try by tasting,** *myan-bas zim-po tsor-nas* perceiving the relish by tasting; *ro myón-ba *ḍob-lág nyán-ce* W.*, id.; **to enjoy,** *mto-ris-kyi lons-spyód* the bliss of paradise *Dzl.*; *myón-bar byéd-pa* to make, or to permit to, enjoy, *kyod cós-kyi zas myón-bar byao* I shall make thee enjoy the food of religious doctrine *Sch.*, yet it may be rendered also more simply: thou wilt enjoy ... *Dzl.* ༢༧༣, b. — 2. in philosophy: **to perceive,** in relation to the perceptions of sense, *Ssk.* वेदन. — 3. **to experience, to suffer,** both good and evil, *sdug-bsnal*, distress etc. frq.; **to get,** *mi-sdúg-pai lus* an ugly body; seldom with termin., *ynás-skabs yzán-du myón-bar ˳gyúr-bai lás-rnams* works which would bring upon their author another state of existence (after his death) *Thgy.*; *myón-bar mi ˳gyúr-ba* to be preserved from *Dom.*; *ran-gi byás-pa rán-gi myón-ba yin Pth.* your own doings are your own sufferings; as you have brewed, so you must drink. — 4. auxil. of the pf. like *byun*, but chiefly in negative sentences: *btsal ma myon Dzl.* I have never yet sought, *mton ma myon Mil.* I have never yet seen, *tos ma myon Mil.* I have never yet heard, — a construction, that has originated from the earlier one c. inf.: *rdzun smrá-ba ma myon, dgé-bai semsskyéd-pa ma myon* dealing with falsehood, producing virtuous thoughts, has never happened to me yet *Dzl.*

དམའ་བ་ *dmá-ba* **to be low,** *dbus dma mta ynyis mtó-na* if (in pregnancy) the middle parts of the body are low, and the sides high *Med.*; sbst. **lowness;** adj., also *dmá-mo*, **low**, low water, low voice, low rank, short measure or weight, frq.; *dmá-la kyád-du ysód-pa* to despise the low and humble *Lt.*; *dmá-na* if I live in humble circumstances *Dom.*; *ná-yis mto mto byás-pa dma dma byun* aspiring higher and higher, I fell deep *Pth.*; of religion: *cún-zad dmá-bai dús-su* as it had somewhat fallen into decay *Pth.*; *dma ˳bébs-pa* (frq. written *sma*) *W. *ma bab kál-ce**, and intrs. *dma ˳báb-pa* to lower, to degrade, by words: **to abuse, to vilify** *Do.* by deeds: **to deface, to deform, to mar** *Pth.*; **to disgrace, dishonour, profane** *Pth.*; **to humiliate** *Tar.*; **to oppress, to ruin** *Schr.*; **ma-bab-can* W.* humiliated, brought low. — *dmá-sa* 1. *Sch.* low land (?) 2. = *dmán-sa.* — Cf. *dmán-pa.*

དམག་ *dmag Lex.* सेना 1. **army, host,** *dmag-tsógs, dmag-dpún*, less frq. *dmag-yséb* id.; *dmag dan bcás-pa* with an army *Tar.*; *mi-la dmag skyúr-ba* to commit the command of an army to a person *Glr.*; *yúl-la dmag ˳dren-pa* to lead an army against, to invade a country, frq.; *dmag rgyág-pa Glr.*, **mag táb-pa* C.* to war, to make or wage war, *dmag-rgyág* (or *dmag-˳drén*) *res mán-du byéd-pa* to make war upon each other *Glr.*; *mú-stegs-pai dmág-gis bzun* he was made a prisoner by an army of Brahmanists *Glr.*; *dmag ston* 1000 men *Pth.*; *dmág-gi tsogs ston-prág súm-cu* an army of 30000 men *Dzl.* — 2. in a gen. sense, **multitude, number, host,** **mag-lin(s)* W.* a beating up of game, a battue; **mag-nór** property of the community, = **(s)pi-nor* W.* — 3. *Cs.* and *Sch.* **war.** —

Comp. *dmag-k̔rims* 'martial law' *Cs.* — **mag-ť́úg* W.* **war, contention, contest.** — *dmag-mgó Ma.* vanguard, front or first line of the army. — *dmag-sgár* encampment, *ₒdégs-pa* to pitch a camp. — *dmag-bsgrig* troops drawn up, battle-array *Sch* — *dmag-čás* requisites for war, military stores, ammunition *Pth.* — **mag-ťáb* C., W.* war. — *dmag-nór* v. above sub no. 2 *mag-nór.* — *dmag-sná* = *dmag-mgó Ma.* — *dmag-dpúṅ* army. — *dmag-dpón* commander, general. — *dmag-bráṅ* = *dmag-sgár.* — *dmag-mi* warrior, soldier. — *dmág-mo* = *dmag, dmág-mo če bskúr-ba Pth.* to send out a great army. — *dmag-ts̓ógs* = *dmag-dpúṅ.* — *dmag-líṅs* v. above.

དམག་པ་ *dmág-pa* v. མག་པ་ *mág-pa.*

དམངས་ *dmaṅs* **the common people, populace, multitude, vulgar;** *dmáṅs-kyi stón-mo* a banquet for all *Mil.*; *dmaṅs p̔ál-pa* the vulgar, the common people; one of the common people; *dmáṅs-rigs* id.; used also as an abusive word: **mean fellow;** when referred to Indian matters = शूद्र. the caste of craftsmen, not so low as *ydól-ba.*

དམད་པ་ *dmád-pa Sch.* invective, abuse, (does not suit to *S.g.* 21).

དམན་པ་ *dmán-pa* (cf. *dmá-ba*) 1. **low,** v. *mťó-ba*; gen. fig., in reference to quantity, **little,** *dman lhag log* either too little, or too much, or badly constituted, e.g. gall, and other humours of the human body *Med.*; *bsód-nams dmán-pa* having little merit, *blo dmán-pa* having little sense *Glr.*; with *skye-ba* v. *skye-ba* II.; in reference to quality: **indifferent, inferior** *Ssk.* हीन, *rim-pas dáṅ-po mčog yin p̔yi-ma dman* in the order (of enumeration) the first is always better, the next following inferior *S.g.*; **men-šár** maiden, girl, virgin *C.* (cf. *skye-dmán*); **depressed in spirits** *Wdṅ.*; **poor, pitiable,** *ri-dwágs dmán-ma* the poor deer *Mil.*; *dmán-sa* or *dman-ča, ₒdzín-pa* to choose the low, humble part, to be humble, to humble one's self, frq.; *dmán-sa, zuṅ daṅ mťó-sar sleb Mil.* choose what is low, and you will obtain what is high. — 2. *dman* for *skye-dmán* **woman,** opp. to *p̔o Mil.* — 3. in *Mil.* sometimes also for *má-mo, srin-mo.*

དམར་ *dmar* **profit, gain, good success,** *dmar čuṅ* a small profit *Mil*; *dmár-po* adj., *ťugs-dám dmár-po byúṅ-ṅam* did it go on well with your meditation? *Mil.*, *dmar-k̔rid Cs.* 'practical instruction', e.g. in the healing art; acc. to my authorities it signifies the last 'finishing' instruction, in religion *Mil.*, in medical science *Med.*

དམར་པོ་ *dmár-po,* fem. *dmár-mo* (seldom), *dmár-ba,* adj. 1. **red,** frq., *mdog-dmár-po* one red-coloured (lit. red as to colour) *Dom.*; *dmár-bai spyan* red eyes *Glr.*; *sna dmár-ba* having a red trunk or proboscis *Glr.*; *dmár-ba,* also **redness and to be red.** 2. v. *dmar.* — **Comp.** *dmar-skyá* pale red. — *dmar-k̔rá Lt.*, red-spotted. — *dmar-k̔rid* v. *dmar.* — **mar-žén** raw meat *W.* — *dmar-ljáṅ* greenish red *Mil.* — **már-ťag čod* W.* the red of evening has vanished from the mountains. — *dmar-ťáb?* — *dmar-ťór* v. *ťór-pa.* — *dmar-mdáṅs Sch.* 1. **bright red(?)** 2. **ruddy complexion.** — *dmar-ₒdon Lt.* medicinal herb; in *Lh.* = *bya-po-tsi-tsi.* — *dmar-nág, skud-pa dmar-nág ynyis* two threads, one black, the other red, used in magic. — *dmar-smyúg* blackish red. — *mar-zaṅ-záṅ* scarlet-red. — *dmar-yól* red chinaware (? opp. to *dkar-yól*) *Med.* — *dmar-bšál Sch.* dysentery, bloody flux. — *dmar-sér* (*-po*) reddish yellow, honey-coloured *Glr.*

དམས་པ་ *dmás-pa Cs.* **wounded.**

དམིག་པ་, དམིག་བུ་ *dmig-pa, dmig-bu Lex.* and *Cs.* **hole.**

དམིགས་ *dmigs* sbst. v. the following.

དམིགས་པ་ *dmigs-pa* 1. vb. (analogous to *sgom-pa*), **to fancy, to imagine** *Tar.* 73, 5. prob.; **to think, to construe in one's mind,** *dmigs-te Glr.* or vulgo *dmigs-la* in imagination, e.g. to do a thing in one's mind, which at the time one is not able to perform in reality; this according to a Buddhist's belief is permitted in various cases (e.g. **sém-mi mig-la p̔úl-če* W.*, to bring an offering in mind, in imagination); it is attended with the same beneficial effects, as if actually done, and in legends, especially, it is generally followed by a happy realisation of what had been desired. — *dmigs-so S.O.* prob.: it is imaginable, it may be done in mind; *don dmigs-pa* to intend a benefit or profit for another person *Mil.* — Generally 2. sbst., **thought, idea, fancy** **आलम्बन**. vulgo**mig(s)**; *dmigs-pai rten* prob.: a thing only supposed, an object imagined *Thgr.*; *dmigs-pa žig ston-pa, ˳bógs-pa* to give (to another person) an idea of, to make a suggestion *Mil.*; **mig-la ċo go* W.* means also: do it, execute it, according to your own mind, I cannot supply you an exact pattern of it; *dmigs-ċan* **ingenious, skilful** in contriving *W.*; *dmigs-pa-las ˳dás-pa = bsám-byai yúl-las ˳dás-pa?* — *yéns-med(-par) dmigs-pa (daṅ) brál-bas-na* indisturbable by fancies of the mind, free from every working of the imagination *Mil.*; *dmigs-pa-méd-pai snyiṅ-rje Mil.* seems to be, acc. to *Thgy.*. the pity which the accomplished saint, who has found every thing, even religion, to be vain and empty, feels towards all other beings, in as far as they are still subject to error and mistake, opp. to *séms-ċan-la dmigs-pai snyiṅ-rje,* and *čós-la dmigs-pai snyiṅ-rje* the tender sympathies called forth by the sight of beings that are really suffering and of those defective in morality — a play upon empty phrases, in as much as in the very narrative, from which the passage above is quoted, the natural softness of Milaraspa is evidently excited by a very positive case, and not by any reflexions of an abstract nature. — **mig-pa-ne zo-pa** (v. *bzó-ba*) *C.* done only in thought, supposed, fictitious; *dmigs ṫams-ċád brjéd-nas* forgetful of all the beautiful fancies, schemes, and airy notions; *dmigs-pa ɣtód-pa* prob.: to direct one's thoughts, fancies, *la* to *Tar.* 189, 2. (where, no doubt, *ɣtád-na* is to be read); *dmigs-ɣtád* **mental object,** *dmigs-ɣtád brál-bai rnál-˳byor-pa* a saint that is free from such objects; acc. to our Lama also = *ɣtád-so* q.v.; *dmigs-ɣsál Lex.*; (*Sch.*: 'a clear notion'), perh. misspelt for *dmigs-bsál* exception from a rule *Gram.*; a particular mention, marking out, exemption of a person, in magisterial orders or enactments *W.* — *dmigs-bu* a blind man's leader *Dzl.*, *Lex.* = *lóṅ-ḱrid-pa.* — *nyes-dmigs Mil.* and elsewh., punishment. In the last three examples the etymological relationship is not quite evident.

དམུ་, རྨུ་ *dmu, rmu* a kind of **evil demon,** rarely mentioned *Lex.*; *rmu-rgód* **wild, angry, passionate;** a violent fellow, not safe to deal with *Mil.*; *dmu-bló* a wild, irascible mind *Sch.*; hence *dmus-byúṅ* terrifying, frightful *Sch.*; perh. also *dmus-lóṅ* blind, bodily blind, whilst *loṅ-ba* may be applied also to spiritual blindness *Dzl.*, *Glr.* and elsewh., and *dmu-čú* **dropsy,** esp. in the chest and in the belly *Med.*; *dmu-skrán Sch.* an oedema, tumour filled with water.

དམུན་པ་ *dmún-pa* **darkened, obscured,** *blo*; *mún-pa.*

དམུལ་བ་ *dmúl-ba* v. *˳dzúm-pa.*

དམུར་བ་ *dmúr-ba* v. *múr-ba.*

དམུས་ལོང་ *dmús-loṅ* v. *dmu.*

དམེ་བ་ *dmé-ba* v. *rmé-ba.*

དམོད་པ་ *dmód-pa* I. vb. *Cs.* **to curse, accurse, execrate,** *dmód-pa byéd-pa* id. *Tar.* 14. 17. — II. sbst. *dmod-pa Dzl.*, *dmod, Glr.* and elsewh., **imprecation, execration, malediction;** *dmód-mo* id.; joined with *˳bór-ba, ˳dór-ba, ˳dzúg-pa, smó-ba:* 1. **to curse, to execrate,** *draṅ-sroṅ-gis dmod-pa bor-bai lo bċu-ɣnyis* the twelve years on which a curse had been pronounced by the saint *Dzl.* 2. **to swear,** to confirm a treaty by an oath *Glr.* 3. **to pronounce a prayer** or **conjuration,** *lha-la* to the deity *Glr.* 4. **to affirm,** e.g. to say' **kon-čóg še** or the like. The word seems to be nearly related both to *smód-pa,* and to *smón-pa,* but, as expressly stated by the *Lexx.*, is not synon. with these verbs.

དམྱལ་བ་ *dmyál-ba* I. vb. **to cut up,** to cut into little pieces, meat at dinner *Dzl.*, a punishment of hell *Dzl.* — II. sbst. **hell,** also *sems-ċan-dmyál-ba; dmyál-bar ˳gró-ba* to go to hell, *dmyál-ba bċo-brgyád* the 18 regions of hell; *tsa-dmyál* the hot hell, *gran-dmyál* the cold hell. — *dmyál-ba-pa, -po,* occupant of hell. — **nyál-wa-čan** W. **poor, miserable, wretched;** also like غریب *Urd.*, = my own little self, for 'I', in humble speech.

དམྱུག་པ་ *dmyúg-pa Cs.* **to show,** *dmyúg-dmyug-pa, dmyúg-pa byéd-pa* to show repeatedly, **to boast.** Yet cf. *myúg-pa.*

རྨ་ *rma* **wound** *B., C.*; *ná-la rma byuṅ* I was wounded; *rma ₒbyín-pa* to wound, *rma ɣsó-ba* to heal a wound; *rmai lhá-ba Sch.* 'a wound growing worse'; yet cf. *lhá-ba.* — *rmá-ka* 1. **the orifice** or **edges** of a wound. 2. *W.* inst. of *rma* **wound,** **rúl-li tám-te má-ka ton** he has been wounded by the bite of a serpent. — *rma-čás Sch.* **plaster, cataplasm, dressing, bandage.** — *rma-rjes Sch.* **scar,** cicatrix. — *rma-rnyiṅ* an old wound. — *rma-smán, rma-rtsis* medicine or salve for a wound. — *rma-mtsan* scar *Bhar.* — *rma-ró Sch.* scurf, scab. — *rma-šú* a festering, suppurating wound. — *rma-šúl* scar. — *rma-srol Sch.* the act of wounding, the wound received(?) — *rma-ɣsál* a fresh wound.

རྨ་ཆུ་ *rmá-ču* n.p., the river **Hoangho** *Glr.*

རྨ་ཆེན་ *rma-čén* v. *rmá-bya.*

རྨ་བ་ *rmá-ba*, pf. *rmas* 1. **to ask,** obs., *Lex.* 2. **to wound** *Dzl.*

རྨ་བྱ་ *rma-bya* (vulgo often **mab-ja**), मयूर, **peacock,** living wild in India, an object of superstition with Buddhists and Brahmanists. — *rma-bya-čén-po* n. of a deity *Dom.*; *rma-čén Wdk.*, महामायूरी *Will.*: 'one of the 5 tutelar deities of the Buddhists'; *Sch.*: *rma-čen ₒbom-ra* 'lord of the yellow stream' (?).

རྨང་ *rmaṅ*, provinc. *rmiṅ Glr.* **ground, foundation,** *rmaṅ ₒdiṅ-ba* to lay a foundation *Glr.*; *rtsig-rmáṅ* id.; *rmáṅ-rdo* foundation-stone.

རྨང་འཚེར་ *rmaṅ-ₒtsér, smaṅ-ₒtsér* or *-tsar Sch.* 1. **pincers** to pluck out hairs; *Cs.* instrument for cleaning the nostrils. — 2. *Sch.* **rake** (instrument).

རྨང་ལམ་ *rmáṅ-lam Sch.* = *rmi-lam*, of rare occurrence.

རྨད་པ་ *rmád-pa* or rather usually: *rmád-du byúṅ-ba, rmad-byúṅ* **wonderful, marvelous,** and *ṅo-mtsar-rmád-du ₒgyúr-ba* to wonder, to be surprised at, fq.

རྨན་པ་ *rmán-pa Sch.* **wounded;** *rmás-pa* v. *rmá-ba.*

རྨི་བ་ *rmi-ba*, pf. *rmis*, **to dream;** *rmi-lam* resp. *mnál-lam* **a dream,** *rmi-lam za-zi* a troubled dream *Lt.*; *mi-bzaṅ-ba* a portentous, ill-boding dream *S.g.*; *rmi-lam mtóṅ-ba, rmi-ba* to dream, *rmi-lam-du rál-bar rmis-so* he dreamt that he had been torn to pieces *Dzl.*; *rmi-lam-du ₒbyúṅ-ba* to appear in a dream *Dzl.*; *rmi-lam brtág-pa Cs.* to judge of dreams, *bšád-pa Cs.* to interpret dreams.

རྨིག་སྒ་ *rmig-sga Sch.* **a saddle** that may be folded together.

རྨིག་པ་ *rmig-pa* 1. **hoof,** *rmig-pa ka-brág, rmig-brág Cs.* a cloven hoof, *mig-pa-ka-brág-čan* cloven-footed; *rmig-zlúm* an undivided hoof; *rta-rmig* a horse's hoof, also name of a plant *Wdṅ.*; *ɣyág-rmig* a yak's hoof; *rmig-lčágs* **horse-shoe** *Cs.*; *rmig-(ɣ)zer* horse-shoe nail, hob-nail *Cs.* — 2. *W.* **horse-shoe,** *gyab-če* to put on a horse-shoe, to shoe.

རྨིག(སྨ)་པ་ *rmig(s)-pa* **lizard,** of a small kind *S.g.*

རྨིང་ *rmiṅ* v. *rmaṅ.*

རྨུ་ *rmu* v. *dmu.*

རྨུ་བ་ *rmú-ba Cs.* 1. **dullness, heaviness.** — 2. **fog.** — *rmus-pa* 1. *Cs.* **dull, heavy;** *Lex.* **peevish, loath, listless.** 2. **foggy, gloomy, dark,** *nam rmús-pa* a dark night *Dzl.*, cf. *rmúgs-pa*; covered with fog, *yul, Dzl.* — *rmu-tag* 1. a cord to which little flags are attached, on convents etc. 2. *Glr.* fol. 24, sqq., here the word seems to denote some supernatural means of communication between certain ancient kings and their ancestors dwelling among the gods.

རྨུག་པ་ *rmúg-pa*, pf. *rmugs*, 1. **to bite,** *B., C.,* — 2. **to hurt, to sting,** of bees etc. *W.*;

to gall, the feet by friction of the shoes *W.* — 3. **to bark** *W.*

རྨུགས་པ་ *rmúgs-pa* 1. **a dense fog,** *k'yim* fog is coming on, *ₒtib Cs.* id.; *sans* has cleared away *Cs.*; *rmúgs-pa-čan* **foggy;** *nam rmúgs-pa Dzl.* ༢༦༠, 12, a dark, foggy night (another reading: *rmús-pa*); *Dzl.* ༢༧༠, 15, *nyin-mtsán-du yul rmúgs-pa* (*rmús-pa*), covered with fog, wrapt in darkness. — 2. *Sch.* **eyes heavy with sleep.** — 3. **inertness, languor, laziness** *Mil.*; **inert, languid, sluggish,** *rmúgs-par byéd-pa Dom.*

རྨུན་པོ་ *rmún-po Cs.* **dull, heavy, stupid;** *žo rmún-po S.g.* sour milk (?).

རྨུར་བ་ *rmúr-ba* to gnarl and bite each other, of dogs *Lex.*

རྨུས་པ་ *rmús-pa* v. *rmú-ba.*

རྨེ་བ་ *rmé-ba* I. **to be economizing, parsimonious** *Lex.*; *bsris-* (*Sch. srid?*) and *sér-rme-ba Lex.* id. —

II. also *dmé-ba* and *smé-ba* 1. sbst. **spot, speck, mark,** a natural mark, on a cane *Mil.*; **mole, mother-spot;** **mé-žol* W.* mark of burning; **a detestable sin,** esp. murder; **uncleanness of food,** *rme-ytsan-méd* or *ytsan-rme-méd* making no difference as to clean or unclean food *Mil.*; *rme-grib* **moral defilement;** *rme-ša-čan Wdn.*, **me-ša za-kan* W.*, eating unclean flesh, as an animal that devours its own young. — 2. adj., also *rmé-ba-čan, rmé-čan Wdn.*, *rmé-po Lex.* **unclean, defiled, contaminated.**

རྨེ་རུ་ *rmé-ru,* n.p. 1. mountain on the Chinese frontier *Glr.* — 2. a castle in Lhasa *Glr.*

རྨེག་པ་ *rmeg-pa* = *ytan* **order, series, row** *Lex.*, *rmég-med-pa* disordered, not regulated.

རྨེད་ *rmed* **crupper,** attached to a saddle, *sgá-yi rméd Lexx.*; *gón-rmed Pth.*

རྨེད་པ་ *rméd-pa* I. also *sméd-pa,* pf. *rmes,* **to ask,** *dri-žin sméd-par mdzád-pa* id. resp. *Mil.*; *snyún-dri sméd-pa Mil.* = *snyún-dri žú-ba.* — II. **to plough and sow;** *rméd-du ǰúg-pa* to cause to be ploughed and sown, e.g. rice *Dzl.*

རྨེན་པ་ *rmen-pa Lex.* *rmén-bu Lt.*, *ša-rmén Mil.* and vulgo, **gland,** swelling of the glands, **wen.**

རྨེལ་བ་, སྨེལ་བ་ *rmél-ba, smél-ba* 1. **to pluck out,** *C.*, *W.*, *Lex.*, v. *bal.* — 2. **to become threadbare** *W.* — 3. *Sch.* **to appoint, to call, to invite.**

རྨོ་སྔགས་ *rmo-snags Sch.* = *snre-snágs.*

རྨོ་མོ་ *rmó-mo* 1. *Cs.* = *ma-čún.* — 2. *Sch.* **grandmother.**

རྨོ་བ་ *rmó-ba,* pf. and imp. *rmos* 1. **to plough** (**up**), *žin* frq.; **to sow and plough in** *ₒbras Dzl.*; *ma rmós-pai lo-tóg* 1. **a fabulous kind of grain** in the mythical age. 2. **maize,** *C.*, *W.* — *rmó-po, rmó-mk'an* ploughman. — 2. *ₒgyód-rmo-ba* v. *ₒgyód-pa.*

རྨོག་ *rmog* **helmet** *Glr.*; *rmog-tsáns Cs.* 'the padding in a helmet'; *k'rab-rmog* coat of mail and helmet.

རྨོང་བ་ *rmón-ba* vb. and sbst., pf. *rmons* **to be obscured; obscurity,** chiefly in a spiritual sense; also adj. **obscured, stultified** *Stg.*; more frq. *rmóns-pa,* e.g. *blo,* the mind darkened, by false doctrine *Thgy.*; by sorrow, despondency, = despairing, despondent, unnerved *Dzl.*, with *la* or termin., as to, with regard to . . .; *blo ma rmóns-pa,* or *rmons-méd Mil.* a mind lively, unimpaired, susceptible, *la* of; *kun-tu-rmón ša-čé-ba* an ample share of irrationality, the principal obstacle to the happiness (*ma-k'óm-pa*) of those beings which are born as beasts; *rmón-par ₒgyúr-ba* to be obscured, darkened, *byéd-pa* to obscure, to darken *Glr.*, also: to confound, perplex, deceive, = *mgo skór-ba Tar.*; *rmón-bu Lex.* without expl., *Cs.*: 'a kind of distemper'; *rmón-spu* hair of the abdomen and the pudenda, *ra-tug rmon-spus lhog-pa ǰom S.g.* the belly-hair of a he-goat tends to heal cancer.

རྨོད་པ་ *rmód-pa Cs.* **to plough,** *rmod-glán* a plough-ox; *rmod-lám Sch.* **furrow.**

རྨོན་པ་ *rmón-pa* 1. **the act of ploughing;** *rmón-pa rgyáb-pa* to plough *Cs.* — 2. **a plough-ox,** *rmon-dór* a yoke of plough-oxen.

རྨྱ་བ་ *rmyá-ba S.g.* **sickness, nausea,** *k'ams-rmyá Lex.* id.

རྨྱང་བ་, རྨྱེང་བ་ *rmyáṅ-ba, rmyéṅ-ba* = *snyéṅ-ba* **to stretch one's self**, to stretch forward the neck; *bya-rmyáṅ byéd-pa* id. *Cs.* also: to yawn.

སྨ་ *sma* v. *dma.*

སྨ་ར་ *smá-ra* **beard** *Mil.*, *smá-ra-čan* **bearded.**

སྨག་ *smag* 1. a sort of **medicine** of an astringent taste *Med.*; *smág-rgyu* **black pepper.** — 2. **dark; darkness**; *mún-pai smag-rúm* id. *Glr.*

སྨང་ཚེར་ *smaṅ-tsér* v. *rmaṅ-ₒtser.*

སྨད་ *smad*, अधर, 1. **the lower part**, opp. to *stod*; *smád-la* downward *Sch.*; *lús-kyi smad* the lower half of the human body, frq.; *smad ₒpyés-pa Sch.*: 'to move the posterior to and fro' (?). — *lus-smad-lṅa sá-la ytúg-pa* to bring the five lower parts of the body, the belly, the knees, and the points of the feet in close contact with the ground, i. e. to prostrate one's self; hence *čos-gos smad lṅa Dzl.* ༢༣°, 16, the five lower pieces of the priestly apparel, perh. breeches, stockings and boots; the meaning, however, of *sems-smád bčo-brgyád Pth.* I am not prepared to settle. — 2. **lowland** = *man-čád.* — 3. **low rank,** v. *smad-rigs* below. — 4. with regard to time, **the latter part, the second half,** उत्तर, of the night, *Dzl.*, of winter, of life etc. — 5. **children,** in relation to their mother, gen. preceded by *ma* or *bu*, thus: *ṅed ma-smád* I and my mother *Mil.*; *rgán-mo ma-smád ysum* the old woman with her (two) sons, those three *Dzl.*; also of animals: *rgód-ma ma-smád ynyis* the mare and her foal, the two *Dzl.*; *bu-smád* (*Cs.* also *mad*) wife and children, family; *nád-pa dei bu-smád Mil.* the sick man's family; *bu-smád-rnams* (my) wife and children *Mil.*

Comp. *smad-ₒčal* **lewdness, dissoluteness, prostitution,** *byéd-pa* to indulge in, to practise *Mil.* — *smad-ₒdógs* a subscribed letter *Gram.* — *smád-tsoṅ-ma* '*meretrix*', prostitute, harlot, frq. — *smad-yyógs* nether integuments, breeches, trowsers *Wdṅ.* — *smad-rigs* common people, lower caste *Dzl.*

སྨད་པ་ *smád-pa* I. vb. 1. **to bend down; to hand, to reach down,** the alms bowl to a little boy *Dzl.*; (*Sch.* 'to stoop'?); *ydoṅ smád-pa* to cast down one's eyes, to be abashed, dejected *Tar.*; *sems* to humble one's self, *la* before *Dzl.*, *tugs* id. resp.: **to be condescending, lowly, meek** *Dzl.* — 2. **to vilify,** c. *la* or accus.: **to blame, to chide,** *bú-mo* one's own daughter *Dzl.*, *bdág-gi séms-la* to blame one's self *Dzl*; **to abuse, defame, degrade, traduce,** *tsig ṅár-pas ₒpʼágs-pa-la* (to abuse) the venerable man with base words *Dzl.*, *dkon-mčóg-gi dbu-ₒpʼáṅ* (to degrade) the highness of the excellent, = to blaspheme; **to despise,** the doctrine *Glr.*; **to dishonour, violate, ravish,** *bu-moi lus* a girl *Pth.*; *má-ga-dha nyáms-smad-pai tse Tar.* 192 when (the country of) Magadha had been brought low, had decayed in its prosperity; *smád-pai tsig* or *ṅag* **abusive word, invective, libel;** *smád-ra* (prop. *sgra*) id., more in the language of the common people, but also *Mil.*; *smád-ra ytóṅ-ba Mil.*, **taṅ-če** *W.* to abuse, to revile; *smad-rigs* common people.

II. sbst. **blame, reproof, reproach, disgrace, contempt.**

སྨན་ *sman* 1. **medicine, physic, remedy,** both artificially prepared and crude: **medicinal herb, drug;** *rii sman ₒtú-ba* to gather officinal plants on the mountains *Dzl.*; *mén-la ₒdo* C.*, **man-la ča** *W*, (the plant) is used as a medicine; *sman sbyór-ba* to prepare a medicine, *ytóṅ-ba* to administer, *zá-ba* or *ₒtúṅ-ba* to take (physic); different forms of medicine are: *táṅ-gi sman* liquid medicine, infusion, decocture; *pʼyé-mai sman* powder; *ríl-bu* pill; *ldé-gu* electuary, sirup; *sman-már* oily medicine (*Tar.* 39, 8); *sman-čáṅ* prob. alcoholic tincture; *ₒbri-ta* extract(?). — Further: *kóṅ-sman* medicine taken internally, *byúg-sman* used externally, unguent; *ₒbyár-sman* plaster; *bzí-sman* soporiferous potion; *skyúg-sman* emetic; *bšál-sman* purgative. — *smán-gyi bla*, or *smán-bla Glr.* and *Med.*; *Sch.*: 'physician general', yet to my knowledge it is never used in that sense, but only as a god or Buddha of therapeutics; there are eight such gods, revered by students of medicine, and frequently invoked in medicinal writings, as well as in medical practice, v. *Schl.* p. 266 sqq. (*sman-gyi lha Glr.*, is prob. but a misprint). — Other compounds: *sman-rkyál* medicine-bag, smaller or larger leather-bags being the usual receptacles for the commodities of grocers and the drugs of physicians. — *smán-kan* apothecary's shop. — *sman-kúg* medicine-bag. — *sman-sgá* a kind of officinal ginger (?) *S.g.* — *sman-sgám* medicine-box. — *sman-mčód* the best, or a very superior medicine *Pth.* — *sman-ljóṅs* a country rich in medicinal plants. — *sman-rtá* the vehicle or substance in which medicine is taken *Med.* — *sman-snod* medicine glass or vessel. — *smán-pa* physician *Dzl.*, *Glr.*, *Med.* — *smán-dpe* medical book. — *sman-dpyád* v. *dpyád-pa*. — *sman-blá* v. above.

II. the same as, or something like *klu Glr.*, *Mil.*

III. *Lex.* = *pan*; *Sch.* also has: *sman-séms* 'a beneficent mind, a mind intent on working good'.

IV. incorr. for *dman.*

སྨར་བ་ *smár-ba* 1. sbst, **ready money,** gen. *smar-rkyáṅ*; *zoṅ min smar* money, and not goods *Lex.* — 2. vb. careless and incorr. pronunciation of *smrá-ba.*

སྨལ་པོ་ *smál-po* n. of a lunar mansion v. *rgyu-skár.*

སྨས་པ་ *smás-pa Sch.*, v. *rmás-pa.*

སྨིག་རྒྱུ་ *smig-rgyú* **mirage** *Lex.* = मरीचि; prob. also a reflection in water, *čur-ₒkrul-smig-rgyú.*

སྨིག་བུ་ *smig-bu* **lizard** *Sch.*, v. *rmig(s)-pa.*

སྨྱིག་མ་ *smig-ma*, provinc. for *smyúg-ma* **cane; reed** *Do.*

སྨིན་དྲུག་ *smin-drúg* 1. also *skár-ma-smin-drúg* कार्त्तिक **the Pleiades;** *smin-drug-zlá-ba* the month in which the moon standing near the Pleiades is full, Oct. or Nov., *Glr.*; *smin-drug-bú*, कार्त्तिकेय, the son of Siva, god of war *Lex.* — 2. *Pur.* Eremurus spectabilis, v. *bre.*

སྨིན་བདུན་, སྨེ་བདུན་ *smin-bdún*, *sme-bdún* **the Great Bear,** *Ursa major.*

སྨིན་པ་ *smín-pa*, I. (विपाक) **to ripen, ripeness, maturity;** most frq. **ripe,** *ₒbrás-bu smín-no B.*, *smin soṅ* vulgo, the fruit is ripe; *smin-par ₒgyúr-ba Glr.* *smin ₒdón-ba* to ripen; the growing on to maturity of an animal germ; also the 'stadium maturationis', or the full development of a disease *Med.*; applied to conversion *Pth.* and elsewh.; *rgyud smin-čiṅ gról-bar byín-gyis rlobs* give them the benediction for being saved (absorbed into Nirvana) after having attained to maturity of mind *Mil.*; *smin-gról-la* or *smin-gról-gyi lám-la ₒgód-pa* to lead to conversion and salvation *Glr.*; *rnám-par smín-pa* v. *rnám-pa.* — *smin-grol-gliṅ* n. of a monastery *Cs.*

II. *Bal.* to give (*sbyín-pa*).

སྨིན་མ་ *smín-ma* **eye-brow,** *smin(-mai) dbrág Med.*, *smin-prag Mil.*, *smin-mtsams Glr.* the space between the eye-brows.

སྨུག་ཆུང་ *smug-čuṅ Med.* a plant = *smug-rtsi* (?).

སྨུག་པ་ *smúg-pa Sch.* for *rmugs-pa* **fog.**

སྨུག་པོ་ *smúg-po* 1. sbst. a disease, acc. to *Cs.* = *ₒdus-nád*, v. *ₒdú-ba*, 1. — 2. adj. **dark bay, cherry-brown, purple-brown;** **gya-múg** *C.* violet coloured; *dmar-smug* brownish white *Wdn.*; *smug-smúg Sch.* dark red. — *smug-rtsi* 1. **red colour,** with which sacrificial utensils are painted *Lex.* — 2. Macrotomia, a plant with dark-red root, used for dyeing, *smug-tsós* paint or colour yielded by this plant *Cs.*

སྨེ་བདུན་ *sme-bdún* v. *smin-bdún.*

སྨེ་བ་ *smé-ba* 1. v. *rme-ba.* — 2. *rtsis-kyi smé-ba Lex.* a kind of arithmetical figure in geomancy, which is used together with the Chinese diagrams, *spar-ka Mil.*

སྨོ་བ་ *smó-ba*, pf. and imp. *smos*, not frq., yet in some cases of constant use, for *smrá-ba* **to say,** *miṅ-nas smó-ba* to call by name, to name *Do.*; . . . *čes smós-pa* the assertion that . . . *Wdn.*; *goṅ-du smós-pa* above-mentioned *Do.*; *lta či smos* v. *lta.*

སྨོད་པ་ *smód-pa*, pf. *smad, Lex.* निन्द v. *smád-pa*, **to blame,** *bdag stod γžan smod* to praise one's self, disparaging others; *γžogs-smód byéd-pa* to slander, calumniate *Thgy.*; **to depreciate, to make contemptible,** *smód-par ˳gyúr-bas Stg.* because it would be disreputable, would detract from his honour. For *smod-˳dzúg-pa* it would prob. be better to write *dmod-˳dzug-pa.*

སྨོན་པ་ *smón-pa* **to wish, to desire,** with *la*, *skyid-pa γžán-la ṅa mi smon* for another happiness I do not wish *Mil.*; more frq. with termin. of the infinitive, and then = to pray for, *rgyál-po skyé-bar* (to pray for) being re-born as a king *Dzl.*; *smón-pa bžin-du byéd-pa* to fulfil a prayer *Dzl.*; *smón-pai γnas* the object of a wish or prayer *Cs.*; *yid-smón* **wish, desire,** *de ťsúr-šog-gi yid-smon ṅá-la med* I do not wish that he should come *Mil.*; *rín-po-nas ˳di-lta-bur yid-smon byéd-par gyúr-te* having long ago entertained this wish *Stg.*; *yid-smon ˳os* worth wishing, desirable; *smon-˳ǰúg* a wish and its accomplishment, *smon-˳ǰúg γnyis*; *smón-lam,* प्रणिधि, prayer, whether it be in the general way of expressing a good wish or offering a petition to the deity, or in the specific Brahmanic-Buddhistic form, which is always united with some condition or asseveration, as: if such or such a thing be true, then may . . ., **wishing-prayer.** — *smon-(lam) lóg(-par) ˳débs-pa* to curse, to execrate.

སྨོན་མགྲིན་ or འདྲིན་ *smon-mgrin* or *˳drin* **comrade, companion, associate,** = *grógs-po Lex.*

སྨྱན་ *smyan? Sch.: smyan byéd-pa* to travel on business; *smyan-byed blo-žan* a traveling clerk not very shrewd *Bhar.* 108; this would seem preferable to the Ssk. equivalent, mentioned in *Schf.*'s edition.

སྨྱར་བ་ *smyár-ba Sch.* **to stretch one's self,** after sleep.

སྨྱི(ག)་གུ་, སྨྱུ(ག)་གུ་ *smyí(g)-gu, smyú(g)-gu* **thin cane, writing-cane, reed-pen;** **ḍoi nyi-gu* C.* goose-quill, **čág-gi nyi-gu* C.* steel-pen.

སྨྱིག་མ་, com. སྨྱུག་མ་ *smyig-ma, smyúg-ma* 1. **cane, bamboo,** *smyúg-mai sbubs* tube of bamboo *Cs.* — 2. **a pen of reed,** *˳ǰóg-pa, W. *žóg-če** to make a reed-pen; **ḍi-nyúg** id, improp. also lead-pencil.

Comp. *smyug-k'róg Cs.*, acc. to others, *smyug-sbróg* tube of bamboo; pen-case; small churn, = *gur-gúr Cs.* — **nyug-k'yim* C.* house constructed of bamboo. — *smyúg-mk'an* a worker in cane *Cs.* — *smyug-sgám* a chest made of reed *Cs.* — *smyug-gri* pen-knife. — *smyug-lčág* flag, flag-stick; long bamboo *Cs.* — **nyug-ťál* C.* a flat basket. — *smyug-ťógs* writer *Cs.* — *smyug-dóṅ Cs.* = *gur-gur.* — *smyug-γdán* mat of reed, cane-mat. — *smyug-γdúgs* an umbrella made of split reeds *Cs.* — *smyug-sdér* plate, dish or flat basket, coustructed of reed *C.* — **nyug-tsá-me-tog* C.*, Carthusian pink. — *smyug-ťsigs* knot, node, joint, of reeds. — **nyug-lóm* C.* flat basket. — *smyug-bšád* comb made of bamboo.

སྨྱུང་བ་ *smyúṅ-ba* **to fast, to observe a strict diet** *Med.*; often in a religious sense, *smyúṅ-bar byás-pa* and *ma byas-pa* he who has strictly observed fasting, and he who has not *Do.*; *smyuṅ-γnás* **the fast, the act of fasting;** **nyén-ne nyúṅ-ne zúm-če* W.* to fast, to practise abstinence. V. *Schl.* 240.

སྨྱུར་བ་ *smyúr-ba* **to be quick, expeditious, in a hurry, to hasten** *Cs.* Cf. *myúr-ba.*

སྨྱོ་བ་, མྱོ་བ་ *smyó-ba, myó-ba*, pf. *smyos, myos* **to be insane, mad,** *či-˳aṅ mi drán-par myós-so* they lost their senses and ran mad (with grief) *Dzl.*; *smyos-sam* is she mad? *Dzl.*; *snyiṅ myós-pas Do.*, being deranged; **nyo dug* W.* he is crazy; **to be mad,** as dogs *Schr.*; **to be intoxicated,** *smyó-bai k'ú-ba* intoxicating liquor *Dzl.*; *rťág-tu myós-pai γnas* pot-houses, fuddling-places *Stg.*; fig. *˳dod-čágs-kyis myos Dzl.* he is mad with lust; *smyó-bar byéd-pa* to make one mad or drunk. — *smyo-byéd* 1. **narcotic,** *smyo-byéd-kyi rdzas* narcotic medicine, soporiferous potion, maddening drink. 2. *smyo-byed(-kyi) γdon* a demon that causes a state of stupefaction or insanity. 3. **frenzy, madness.** 4. symb. num.: 13.

སྨྱོན་པ་ *smyón-pa* **insane, frantic, mad,** *la-dág-pa nyón-pa* a madman from Ladak; *glán-po-če Dzl.* a mad elephant, *ḱyi* a mad dog; **nyón-pa čo dug** *W.* he raves, he is stark mad; **čo-nyón žug** *W.* he has been seized with religious insanity, is deranged, which is stated to be occasionally the effect of severe and long continued meditation. Cf. *lhoṅ.*

སྨྲ་བ་ *smrá-ba*, sometimes སྨོ་བ་ *smó-ba*, also

སྨར་བ་ *smár-ba*, pf. *smras*, imp. *smros* 1. **to speak, to talk,** *smra ma nús-te Dzl.* growing dumb, speechless, not being able to speak (physically); *čaṅ mi smrá-bar gyúr-to* they grew speechless, did not know what to say *Dzl.*; *smra šés-nas mir gyúr-to* they received the faculty of speech and became men *Glr.*; *bslú-bai rnám-pas ḱyeu daṅ smrás-te Dzl.* speaking to the youth in a seductive manner; *ṫsig snyán-par smrá-ba Dzl.* to speak in a friendly way; *čos smrá-ba* **to preach,** *čos smrá-bai žál-la ltá-ba* to hang on the preacher's lips, to listen very attentively *Pth.*; *da ma smra žig Dzl.* do not lose another word; *smra-mḱas(-pa)* speaking shrewdly, well-spoken, eloquent *Dzl., Glr.*; *smra-˳dód* **talkative, loquacious** *Cs.*; *smra-nyúṅ* sparing of words, **taciturn,** *Lt.*; *smra-bčád* forbearing to speak; not being bound to speak *Mil.*; *smra-mčóg, smrá-bai dbaṅ-ṗyúg, smrá-bai rgyál-po* = *˳jam-dpál*; also **to treat of,** with reference to books *Was.* — 2. **to say,** *mi-la* to a person; when it precedes the words that are quoted as they were spoken, (the so-called 'oratio obliqua' being very seldom made use of, one instance v. further on): (*di-skad-čes*) *smrás-pa* or *smrás-so;* when placed after the words spoken, (*čes*) *smrás-so, smrás-te* etc.; *smrás-pa* also is equivalent to **he continued** *Dzl.*; sometimes it is used impersonally, **it is said,** e.g. it is said in that letter, where we should say, 'that letter says', *Stg.*; *smrá-rgyu ma byúṅ-ṅo* there remained nothing more for him to say (v. above); rarely with termin. inf.: *ytúg-par ni ṅa mi smrao* that they will reach it, I do not pretend to say *Thgy.*; *šés-par smrá-ba* to profess to know, to understand, like '*artem profiteri*' *Dzl.*; *dṅós-por smrá-ba* to acknowledge a thing in substance *Was.*, *méd-par smrá-ba* to deny it in sum and substance.

Note. The word which forms the subject of this article, though constantly to be met with in books, seems to be hardly ever used in conversational language.

སྨྲང་, སྨྲེང་ *smraṅ, smreṅ Cs.* **word, speech;** *smraṅ ysól-ba* to beg the word, to beg leave to speak

སྨྲེ་བ་ *smré-ba* 1. = *smrá-ba*(?) — 2. **to wail, to lament** *Pth.*; more com *smre-sṅágs ˳dón-pa* to utter lamentations; *smre-sṅágs-kyi sgó-nas* whining (with joy) *Mil.* — *smre-ytsáṅ?*

ཙ

ཙ *tsa*, 1. the letter sounding **ts**; tenuis, as in the words 'it got so cold', cf. however ཚ *tsa*; ཙ, ཚ and ཛ represent in *Ssk.* and Hindi-words the palatals **च, छ** and **ज** (ཛྷ = **झ**). — 2. num fig.: 17.

ཙྭ་ *tswa Ld.* **spunk,** German tinder.

ཙ་ཀོར་ *tsa-kór*, *Ssk.* **चकोर partridge,** = *srég-pa.*

ཙ་ཀྲ་བཱ་ཀ་ *tsa-kra-bā-ka* **red goose,** *Anas casarca.*

ཙ་དར་, ཙ་སར་ *tsa-dar, tsa-sar, Pers., Hind.* چدر **shawl, plaid, cloak, toga** *W.* —

ཙ་ན་, ཙ་ནས་, ཙ་ལ་ *tsá-na, tsá-nas, tsá-la* v. *tsam.*

ཙ་ན་ཀ་ *tsa-na-ka,* more corr. ཙ་ཎ་ཀ་ *Ssk.,* **chick-pea,** *Cicer arietinum.*

ཙ་བིག་ *tsá-big,* v. *ťsa-big.*

ཙ་རག་ *tsa-rág,* **tsa-rág zér-če** *Ld.* **to crackle,** of fire, breaking twigs etc.

ཙ་རུ་ *tsá-ru* 1. *W.* **curled, frizzled,** as hair and similar things. — 2. *Lex.*: *Ssk.* **meat-offering** to the manes.

ཙ་ཤ་(ཀ་) *tsa-ša(-ka),* चाष, *Coracias Indica,* **jay, roller.**

ཙག་གེ་ *tság-ge W.* **the black mark in a target,** *tság-ge-la gyob* hit the mark!

ཙན་དན་, ཙནྡན་ *tsán-dan, tsándan,* चन्दन, **sandal-tree,** *Sirium myrtifolium,* sandal-wood, used for elegant buildings, images of the gods, perfumes, medicines *Glr., Med.*; in different varieties: *dkár-po, dmár-po* etc., also of fabulous kinds: *tsán-dan sbrúl-gyi snyiṅ-po, gór-ši-ša, gláṅ-mgo Glr., Dzl.*; fig. **something superior in its kind,** *p̓a tsán-dan p̓ú-nu mi-lag-tu soṅ* the elder and younger sons of a distinguished father perform menial services.

ཙན་དོང་ *tsan-dóṅ* v. *btson-dóṅ.*

ཙབ་ཙུབ་, ཙབ་ཙོབ་, རྩབ་རྩུབ་ *tsab-tsúb, tsab-tsób, rtsab-rtsúb* **hurry, haste** *Cs., tsab-tsúb-čan* hasty *Cs.; tsab-tsúb mi bya Lex.* take your time, don't be in a hurry! *rtsab-rtsub-méd-par* not flitting, like a butterfly, from one object to another *Mil.; tsub-liṅ Sch.* hastily, in a hurry(?) — *rtsab-hrál Lex.*; *Sch.* a loose, dissolute course of life(?) — *rtsáb-pa Sch.* to hurry, to hasten(?).

ཙབས་རུ་ *tsabs-rú* 1. a kind of **salt,** *tsabs-ru-tsá S.g.* — 2. **a tube of horn** *Sch.*

ཙམ་ *tsam* mostly affixed as an enclitic, = *snyed* (sometimes carelessly for *tsám-pa* or *tsám-du*) I. in a relative sense; 1. **as much as** *ˌdi-tsam* as much as this, = so much, so many; *mi ˌdi tsam γsód-pa* to kill so many men *Glr.*; *dé-tsam* id.; also emphat.: *čos de tsam žig bšád-nas* after having given you so much religious instruction *Mil.*; by way of exclamation: *či-tsam* **how much!** *W.* and *B., či-tsam byas* how much have you not done! *Glr.; ǰi-tsam ... dé-tsam* how much... so much (as much as) *Cs.* — 2. denoting comparison, as to size, degree, intensity, **like, as-as, so-as, so that:** *ri-ráb tsam* like Sumeru (in height) *Cs; yúṅs-ˌbru tsam* as big as a grain of mustard-seed; **de ri ťón-po tsam dug dé-ťsogs di yaṅ yod** *W.* as high as yon mountain is also this one; *pús-mo núb-pa tsam* even to sinking in up to the knees (knee-deep); *nyi-ma ˌgrib-pa tsam* so much that the sun was darkened *Glr.; mťai rgyál-po yaṅ dbáṅ-du ˌdús-pa tsam byuṅ* he became so (powerful), that he could also subdue — or could have subdued — the neighbouring kings *Glr.* — 3. denoting contingency and restriction: **perhaps, if need be, almost, only, but, all but:** *ťsab ruṅ tsám-mo Wdṅ.* this may perhaps be used instead, this may, if need be, supply its place; *btaṅ-na nam-mkʻai bya yaṅ zin-(pa) tsam γda* if I let him loose, he might almost catch a bird in the air, = *zin-pa daṅ ˌdrao Mil.;* with a partic.: *rtags yód-pa tsám-la* = *rtags daṅ yód-pa-la* to every one that has the mark *Glr.; rtsa daṅ rús-pa tsam Dzl.* nothing but skin and bones; *ˌgro mi nús-pa ˌgóg-pa tsam Dzl.* one only creeping, not being able to walk; *ča tsam šes kyaṅ* if one knows but a particle, but a little bit; *sems tsám-mo* they exist only in our fancy *Was.*; *ťsigs-ma tsam yód-dam Dzl.* is not the sediment at least still left? *lhág-ma tsam žig Dzl.* but a remnant; *brgya tsam* may mean: about one hundred, or: only one hundred; in some cases *tsam* is untranslatable: *ṅa-brgyá tsam ťams-čád ťsei dus byas-so* the 500 merchants died all *Dzl.* (15,9 s.l.c.); *bdén-pa tsam yod Mil.* some grain of truth is in the matter; *ťsig daṅ rnám-par ˌdrá-ba tsam ˌdúg-na-ˌaṅ Mil.* though it is all but equal to the words, i.e. very much like the real tenor or wording; it may also be combined with the signs of the cases: *ṅa miṅ tsám-gyi dgé-sloṅ ma yin Dzl.* I am Bhikshu not only by name, I am not merely called so; *da tsám-gyi bár-du Dzl.* till about the present time (standing here rather pleon., as frq. is the case); *brám-ze ɣčig tsám-gyi slád-du Dzl.* for the sake of a single Brahmin; *spu nyág-ma tsám-gyi ₒgyód-pai sems Dzl.* but a whit (lit. a little hair) of repentance. — 4. *tsám-na* referring to time: **about a certain time, at the time when, when:** *nam-ṗyéd tsám-na* about midnight; *de tsám-na* then, at that time; esp. with verbs: *k̔yím-du ṗyin tsám-na Dzl.* when he came home; inst. of *tsám-na* it is very common to say *tsá-na; byéd-gin yod tsá-na* as he was just doing it *Glr.*; *ɣnyid sad tsá-na* when he awoke *Glr.; zlá-ba brgyad soṅ tsá-na* when eight months had passed *Glr.*; esp. col.: **yoṅ tsá-na* W.* as we came, on our journey hither, when incorr. **tsa-nẹ* (or *sá-nẹ*)* is said, which is justifiable only in such cases, as: **ă-ma kyé-sa-nẹ** from one's birth; *ǰi-tsam-na* or *-nas* **when,** yet mostly pleon., in as far as the sentence beginning with *ǰi-tsam-na* after all concludes with *nas, pa daṅ, dus-kyi t̔se* etc., v. *Feer Introd.* frq., also *Tar.* — 5. *tsám-du* denoting extent, degree, intensity: **as far as, about so far, nearly up to, even to, till, so that,** and *tsam* in various other applications: *lam ṗyed tsám-du* about half way; frq. with verbs: *bá-spu láṅs-pa tsám-du skrags Dzl.* he was so frightened, that his hair stood on end; *dúm-bur bčád-pa tsám-du sdug-bsṅál-gyis ɣdúṅs-te Dzl.* tormented by a pain, as if he were cut to pieces; *bus ma mtóṅ-ba tsám-du dgá-ste Dzl.* 'being glad even to a mother's being seen by her child', i.e. so glad as a child is, when beholding its mother again; sometimes *tsám-la* for *tsám-na* and *tsám-du Mil.* yet not frq. and more col.: *ḍib tsám-la* in the shade; **śíṅ-ni tsám-la* W.* under, before, near a tree; *tsám-gyis* instrum.: *ṅan-ṅon tsám-gyis čóg-śes-pa* content with every thing, as poor as it may be; com. added to the inf.: *smrás-pa tsám-du* as soon as it had been said *Dzl.* frq., or also: 'in the **mere** saying so' *Stg.*; inst. of it. col.: **zer tsam žig-la*; W.: *zér-ra tsám-žig-ga*.* — *tsam yaṅ* with a following negative: **not the least,** *mós-pa tsam yaṅ mi byéd-pa Mil.* to pay not the least respect; **not in the least, not at all:** *nyi-ma daṅ zlá-ba tsam yaṅ ltar med Dzl.* neither sun nor moon is to be seen at all. — *tsám-pa* adj., *mi-t̔sad-tsám-pa* man-sized, having the size of a man *Tar.* — *tsám-po Mil. mi tsám-po yóṅs-kyi sems-la ₒjug* prob: I shall enter into the soul of the very first man I meet with; also = *gaṅ* (cf. *rtags gaṅ yód-pa-la* above). — *Cs.* has besides: *tsám-po-ba* a comparing, estimating; *tsam-poi t̔sig* a comparative expression; *tsám-poi don* a comparative sense(?). II. used interrogatively: **how much? how many?** **rin tsam?* W.* how dear?

ཙམ་པ་ *tsám-pa* 1. v. *tsam* towards end of preced. article. — 2. sbst. **flour** from parched barley, v. *rtsám-pa.* — 3. n. of a country *Tar.* 10,14; 20,16; acc. to *Ssk. Lexx.* = Bhagalpore, v. *Köpp.* I, 96; in modern geography: the small Hindu mountain-province **Chamba** on the river Ravi, under British protection.

ཙམ་པ་ཀ་ *tsám-pa-ka Ssk.* **magnolia,** *Michelia Champaca.*

ཙམ་ཙོམ་ *tsam-tsóm* **tripping to and fro, fidgeting about** *W.* (cf. *tsab-tsób*).

ཙར་མ་ *tsár-ma* n. of a place, freq. resorted to by *Mil.*

ཙི་ *tsi* num. fig.: 47.

ཙི་ཏྲ་ཀ་ *tsi-tra-ka Ssk.* 1. a painted mark on the forehead, being the badge of various sects *Sch.* — 2. name of several plants, esp. *Ricinus communis,* so perh. *Lt.*; in *Lh.*: *Anemone rivularis,* common there.

ཙི་སྟག་ *tsi-stág* n. of a purgative *Med.*

ཙི་ན་ *tsi-na* चीन, *China Cs.*; now com. *ma-ha-tsin.*

ཙི་ཙི་ *tsi-tsi* **mouse** *C., tsi-ghi* id. *Ts.; tsi-čuṅ* **shrew** (mouse) *Sch.*; *t̔áṅ-gi tsi-tsi* **field-mouse** *Schr.; sai tsi-tsi* **mole** *Schr.*; *tsi-tsis-ₒdzin* n. of a plant *Wdṅ.*

ཙི་ཙི་རྫོ་ལ་ *tsi-tsi-dzó-la Cs.*, *tsi-tsi-dzó-ba Sch.* **cancer** (disease), said to be a Nepalese word.

ཙི་ཙེ་ *tsi-tsé* v. *tse-tsé.*

ཙིག་ཙིག་ *tsig-tsig byéd-pa* **to quarrel, to be at variance** *Sch.*

ཙིཏྟ་ *tsitta Ssk.* **the heart** as seat of the intellect, v. *Burn.* I, 637.

ཙིད་ *tsid* **anvil** *Sch.*

ཙུ་ *tsu* num. fig.: 77.

ཙུ་ད་ *tsú-da, tsú-dai śiṅ* n. of a tree *Sch.*

ཙུག་ *tsug* for *ċi-ltar* adv. interrog. and correlat., **how, as,** rarely occurring in books; *Pth.: de gar ₒgro, tsug byed* where she is going, and what she is doing. In *W.* com. in the form *zug*, in such combinations as: *gá-zug* for *ċi-tsug*, *ċi-ltar*; **ï-zug* or *ₒdí-zug*, and *á-zug** or **dé-zug**: **so**; **daṅ de-zug de-zug** and more of that kind; *de-tsug lags* in *Lexx.*

ཙུག་ཙུག་ *tsug-tsúg* the noise of **smacking** in eating, *tsug-tsúg mi bya* do not smack *Zam.*

ཙེ་ *tse* num. fig.: 107.

ཙེ་གུར་ *tse-gúr Sch.*: 1. a small **tube.** — 2. a **little.**

ཙེ་པོ་, ཙེལ་པོ་ *tsé-po, tsél-po* **a basket** carried on the back, dosser, esp. *W.*; **ċáṅ-tse* or *ċág-tse** a wicker basket, **nyúṅ-tse* or *nyúg-tse** a cane basket *Ts.*; **tsel-ċúg** the wands used for such a basket; **tsel-ċág** a broken dosser *W.*; **tsel-rá** the frame-work of a basket *Cs.*; **tsel-lúṅ** string or strap for carrying it.

ཙེ་ཙེ་, ཙི་ཙེ་ *tse-tsé, tsi-tsé* **millet** *Cs.*

ཙེ་རེ་ *tse-ré* 1. **song, tune** *Lex.* — 2. = *ťse-ré.*

ཙེག་ཙེག་ *tseg-tség, tseg-tség zér-ba* **to rustle,** 'to make a noise like dry hay' *Cs.*

ཙེབ་ཙེབ་ *tseb-tséb* **sharp-pointed,** of needles, thorns.

ཙེམ་ཙེ་ *tsém-tse* = *ċém-tse* **small scissors.**

ཙེའུ་རི་ *tseu-ri* a species of female demons *Thgr.*

ཙེར་ཙེར་ *tser-tsér, tser-tsér byéd-pa* **to tremble, shake, quake** *Sch.*

ཙེལ་པོ་ *tsél-po* v. *tsé-po.*

ཙོ་ *tso* num. fig.: 137.

ཙོ་ར་ *tsó-ra Wdṅ., Ssk.* n. for the medicinal herb *srúb-ka*; in *Ssk. Lexx.* no botanical explication is given, but only the notice, that it is a perfume; in Kullu a sweet-scented white lily is called so.

ཙོག་པུ་ *tsóg-pu* (acc. to one *Lex.* = उत्कटुक, which is not to be found; on the other hand *Burn.* I, 310 gives *tsóg-pu-pa* = नैषद्दिक. one sitting down) **the posture of cowering, squatting, crouching,** *tsog(-tsog)-pur sdód-pa*, *ₒdúg-pa* resp. *bžúgs-pa Pth.*, col. **tsoṅ-tsóṅ, tsom-tsóm**, **to cower, squat, crouch;** *tsóg-pu mi nus* he cannot even cower, of one sick unto death *Thgy.*; *tsog mi γzúg-pa* of a similar sense *Sch.* — (The version 'to sit on one leg drawn in' *Sch.*, which has also been adopted by *Burn.*, may possibly be founded on a mistake of *Sch.*, who in *Cs.*'s explanation: 'sitting in a crouching posture upon one's legs', prob. read 'upon one leg').

ཙོང་ཁ་ *tsóṅ-ka* n. of a place in Eastern Tibet *Ma.*; *tsóṅ-ka-pa* 1. inhabitant of that place. 2. n. of a celebrated teacher of religion and reformer, about the year 1400.

ཙོང་ཙོང་ *tsoṅ-tsóṅ* 1. = *tsog-tsóg* v. *tsóg-pu.* — 2. *tsoṅ-tsóṅ-la kur* carry it straight *W.*

ཙོན་དོང་ *tson-dóṅ* v. *btson-dóṅ.*

ཙོབ་ཙོབ་ *tsob-tsób*, **tsob-tsób-la dúg-ċe** *Ld.* to stand or sit in different groups, not in rows.

ཙོར་མོ་ *tsór-mo* **a five-finger pinch** *Cs.*

གཙག་པ་ *γtság-pa* v. *ₒtság-pa*; *γtság-bu* also *btságs-bu* **lancet** for bleeding.

གཙང་ *γtsaṅ* 1. **clean, pure** v. *γtsáṅ-ba.* — 2. n. of a province in *C.*, where Tasilhunpo is situated; *γtsáṅ-pa* inhabitant of it.

གཙང་བ་ *ytsaṅ-ba* 1. vb. **to be clean, pure** *Dom.* — 2. sbst. **cleanness, purity.** — 3. adj. **clean, pure.** Most frq. as sbst. with negation: *mi-ytsáṅ-ba* impurity, foulness, filth *Dzl.* and elsewh.; excrement *S.g.*; *mi-ytsáṅ-ba rnám-pa sna-tsógs-kyi p̔úṅ-po* heap of all kinds of filth, mass of corruption, sometimes applied to the human body *Dzl.*; *ytsáṅ-ma* adj., clean, as to the body, clothes etc.; *de ni rab-bkrús ytsáṅ-ma yin* that man is well washed and clean *S O.*; *ytsaṅ-btsog-méd(-pa)* one that knows no difference between clean and unclean (cf. *med*); **dirty, slovenly; rude, uncouth** *Glr.*; *ytsáṅ-mar byéd-pa* 1. **to clean.** 2. **to make one's self clean, smart, tidy**; **tsáṅ-ma ǰhé'-pa* C.*, **čó-če* W.* is said to be a euphemism for circumcision. — **šul-tsáṅ-po* C.* one that clears his plate, empties his cup; one that does a thing thoroughly. — *ytsáṅ-k̔aṅ Cs.*, com. *dri-ytsaṅ-k̔aṅ* v. *dri.* — *ytsaṅ-sbrá* religious purity, शुचि; *ytsaṅ-sbrá-čan* (or *daṅ ldán-pa*) morally pure, *ytsaṅ-sbra-méd-pa* impure *Do.* — *ytsaṅ-ris Sch.*: the pure country and its inhabitants, the pure, the saints.

གཙང་པོ་ *ytsáṅ-po*, *Ld.* **tsáṅs-po** **river, stream**; esp. the large stream flowing through Tibet from west to east, gen. called **Yarutsaṅpo**; *ytsaṅ-čú*, resp. *ytsaṅ-čáb*, id.

གཙང་བུ་ *ytsaṅ-bu* **screen, parasol** *Sch.*

གཙང་གཙོང་ *ytsaṅ-ytsoṅ* (or **ₒdzaṅ-ₒdzoṅ**?) *Ld.*, **steep, rugged, mountainous.**

གཙབ་པ་ *ytsáb-pa* **to detach with a crow-bar.**

གཙི་བ་ *ytsí-ba*, pf. *ytsis*, **to invite, summon, call, appoint** *Sch.*

གཙིགས་ *ytsigs* 1. **importance** *Cs.*, *ytsigs(su)-če* very important *Lex.*; *ytsigs čé-bar byéd-pa* to make much of *Cs.*; *Sch.* also *mi-ytsigs* **insignificant; unapt**, and *ma-ytsigs* **unimportant; without difficulty**, whereas in one *Lex.* *mi-ytsigs spyód-pa* is explained by *mi-rigs-pa.* — 2. *Pth.* 85: (but as a girl was born, the king and his ministers were quite in despair, and) *btsún-mo-la yaṅ t̔ugs ytsigs-čuṅ-bar gyur-to* also the queen's mind was much dejected(?). — 3. *Mil.*: *ytsigs-la ₒbébs-pa* frq.; by the context: **to subdue, to force, compel**, also with supine, *ₒbaṅs bgyid-par* to compel to obey. — 4. *Sch.*: *ytsigs-pai blo* quick comprehension, retentive memory.

གཙིགས་པ་ *ytsigs-pa*, with or without *mčé-ba*, **to show one's teeth, to grin** *Glr.*; *rnam-par ytsigs-pa* id. *Glr.*

གཙིར་བ་ *ytsir-ba* v. *ₒtsír-ba.*

གཙུག་ *ytsug* 1. **crown of the head, vertex** *Lt.*, *spyi-ytsug* id. *Glr.* frq.; *ytsúg-tu ₒčiṅ-ba* to fasten on the head; fig. *sá-yig ytsúg-tu bčiṅs-pai ga*, cf. *t̔od.* — 2. **tuft, crest**, of birds *Sch.* — 3. **whirlpool, eddy, vortex**; in the water *Sch.*; *ytsug-ₒk̔yil Wdṅ.*, also *rtsub-ₒkyil*, perh. id.(?); *ytsug-rgyán* head-ornament, *ytsug-(gi) nór(-bu)* jewel of the head; frq. fig.: most high, most glorious among ..., c.genit.; also *ytsúg-gi nór-bur gyúr-pa Glr.*, = *mčóg-tu gyúr-pa.* — *ytsug-tor* = *tor-čog*, उष्णीष, conical or flame-shaped hair-tuft on the crown of a Buddha, in later times represented as an excrescence of the skull itself, v. *Burn.* II., 558. *Schl.* 209.

གཙུག་ལག་ *ytsug-lág* 1. **sciences, '*literae*'**; *ytsug-lág rnám-pa bčo-brgyád* the eighteen sciences; *k̔yod ytsúg-lag čé-ziṅ ₒdzáṅs-pa* thou, who art rich in knowledge and wisdom. — 2. **scientific work** or **works**, frq.; *ytsug-lag-k̔áṅ* विहार, academy, convent-temple and school, cf. also *gándho-la*; *ytsúg-lag-mk̔an* or *-pa Cs.* a learned man.

གཙུགས་པ་ *ytsúgs-pa* **to bore out, scoop out, excavate** *Sch.*(?).

གཙུབ་པ་ *ytsúb-pa*, pf. *ytsubs*, **to rub**, *ytsub-šiṅ*, a piece of dry wood that is rubbed against another (*ytsub-stán* or *-ytán*) in order to make fire *Cs.*

གཙེ་བ་ *ytsé-ba*, pf. *ytses* v. *ₒtsé-ba.*

གཙེགས་པ་ *ytségs-pa* = *ₒdzigs-pa Sch.*

གཙེང་བ་ *ytséṅ-ba* = *ytsi-ba Sch.*

གཙེར་བ་ *ytsér-ba* = *ₒtsé-ba Lex.*

གཙོ་ *ytso* 1. v. *ytsó-bo.* — 2. v. *ytsod.*

གཙོ་བོ་ *ɣtsó-bo* (*Ssk.* **प्रधान**, consequently = *mčog*) 1. **the highest** in perfection, **the most excellent** in its kind, *ɣtsó-bor* or *ɣtsor byéd-pa, lén-pa* to place foremost, to consider the first or most excellent; *ɣtso byás-pai bú-mo lṅa* the five noblest of the girls *Mil.; ɣtso byéd-pa-rnams* the most respectable, the leaders, the heads *Mil.; des ɣtsó-byas dpon-ɣyóg-rnams* the higher and lower people subject to him *Pth.* (*ɣtsó-byed-pa* to be the first, belongs however rather under the head of no. 2); *sṅágs-kyi ɣtsó-bo, smón-lam-gyi ɣtsó-bo* (the same as *rgyál-po*) chief spell, principal prayer; *yi-ge ɣtsó-bo súm-ču* the 30 principal letters, (the letters of the alphabet) *Glr.; nad-rnams kún-gyi ɣtsó-bo* the principal disease, viz. fever *Lt.* (more correct from an Indian than from a Tibetan point of view); *ɣtso-čé-ba* **very important** *Thgr.;* **eminent** *Tar.; ɣtsó-bor* and *ɣtso-čér*, adv., **especially, chiefly, principally.** Hence: 2. **a chief, a principal, master, lord,** *rkaṅ-ɣnyis-kyi* (lord) of men, i.e. Buddha *Dzl.*; *rten-gyi ɣtso-bo* the 'lord' of the shrine, the deity to whom a shrine is consecrated, which in the lord's absence is guarded by some servant deity, e.g. *Dzl.* chap. VI.; *čós-kyi ɣtsó-bo čén-po* grand-master of the doctrine, a title of Sariibu *Dzl.*; **gentleman**, but chiefly as a title = Sir, Mr., *blón-po ɣtsó-bo drúg-po, ɣtsó-bo mi drug* the six (gentlemen) ministers *Glr.*; *ɣtsó-mo* the most distinguished lady, the noblest, first in rank, *bú-mo ɣtsó-mo* the most excellent among the girls; *ɣtsó-mor ˏós-pa žig* the one most deserving of preference, the one of the noblest appearance *Mil.*; *ɣtsó-mo mdzád-pa* to be mistress, resp.

གཙོམ་, བཙོམ་ *ɣtsó-ma, btsó-ma* **hemp** *Sch.*

གཙོད་, བཙོད་, གཙོ་ *ɣtsod, btsod, ɣtso* (*Ld.* vulgo **stsod**), **the so-called Tibetan antelope,** with straight horns standing close together and in the direction of the longitudinal axis of the head *S.g.*, *ɣtsód-mo* fem., *ɣtsod-p̀rúg* the young one, *ɣtsod-rús* the bones, *ɣtsod-k̀ul* the wool of it (used for shawls).

བཙའ་ *btsa* (*btsa-ba Sch.?*) 1. **rust,** *lčágs-kyi btsa* rust of iron; *btsas-zas Sch., k̀yer Lex.* destroyed by rust. — 2. **rust, blight, smut,** of corn *Sch.* — 3. = *btsag*, *Sch.* — *me-btsá* **moxa** *Lt.; mi-rus-btsa?*

བཙའ་བ་ *btsá-ba* 1. pf. *btsas,* **to bear, to bring forth,** *čuṅ-ma-la bu btsas* his wife bore, gave birth to, a son *Dzl.*; *bu btsá-bai t̀abs mi t̀ub* they could not bring forth *Dzl.; btsás-pa* what is begotten, new-born children or animals *Do.*; *btsá-zug laṅs* pains of labour ensued *Sch.* — 2. resp. **to watch, look on, spy,** *spyán-gyis Cs.*

བཙའ་མ་ *btsá-ma* **fruit** *Sch.* 2. = *btsa Sch.*

བཙག་ *btsag,* **गैरिक, red ochre** *Med.* and *Lex.*; used also of earths of a different colour; *btsag-t̀áṅ, btsag-ri, btsag-lúṅ* plain, hill, valley, of red earth; *btsag-yug* some other officinal mineral *Med.*

བཙག་པ་ *btság-pa* v. *ˬtság-pa.*

བཙག་མོ་ *btság-mo* a certain beverage, = *rtsáb-mo.*

བཙང་བ་ *btsáṅ-ba* prob. = *ˬtsáṅ-ba.*

བཙང་པོ་ *btsáṅ-po* title of sovereigns *Glr.*, alledged to be but Khams-dialect for *btsán-po.*

བཙན་ *btsan* 1. a species of demons, residing in the air, on high rocks etc., mischievous, *Glr., Dom.* — 2. v. the following article.

བཙན་(པོ་) *btsán(-po)* **strong, mighty, powerful,** of kings, ministers etc., esp. as title of honour: **high-potent,** *Dzl., Glr.*; hence of family, race, descent: **illustrious, noble,** *lhá-mo btsán-rnams* the queens of high descent, in opp. to a third of low extraction *Glr.*; *btsan-(žiṅ) p̀yug(-po)* noble and rich *Dzl., Mil.*; **strong, violent,** *btsan-dúg* a virulent poison *Dzl.;* **forcible, violent,** *btsan-ˬp̀rógs byéd-pa* to commit a robbery connected with violence *Pth.*; *btsan-tabs-su* by violent means *Pth.*; **coercive, strict, severe** *bka, k̀rims Glr.*, *btsán-par mdzád-pa* rigorously to enforce (a law); **firm, staunch, immovable, not wavering,** *ṅag-btsán* steadfastly abiding by one's word *Sch.*; **firm, safe,**

sure, *dben-ynás Mil.* a safe, inaccessible retreat; *rdzoṅ btsan* a firm stronghold *Lex.*; = concealed, hidden, hence *btsan-k'aṅ* the innermost dark room in a temple, in which the gods reside, or an apartment for the same purpose on the top of a house; **definite, decided, without uncertainty,** *saṅs-rgyás-kyi bstán-pa mi núb-ciṅ mt'a btsán-par byéd-pai p'yir* in order that the doctrine of Buddha by being accurately defined may be secured against subversion *Pth.*

བཙབ་པ་ *btsáb-pa* imp. *btsob,* **to cut small, to chop,** wood; **to hash, to mince,** meat *C.*; *bstab-stán* chopping-block *C.*

བཙམ(ས)་པ་ *btsám(s)-pa* for *ₒtsám-pa,* v. *to.*

བཙལ་བ་ *btsál-ba* v. *ₒtsól-ba.*

བཙས་པ་ *btsás-pa* v. *btsá-ba.*

བཙས་མ་ *btsás-ma* 1. also *rtsás-ma* **harvest,** *btsás-ma rṅa-ba* **to reap, to mow** *C.* and *Lex.*, *btsás-ma ran tsa-na* in harvest time *Mil.*— 2. **wages, pay,** *gru-btsás Lex.*, fare, passage-money; *la-btsás Lex.*, *la-čan-gyi btsas?*

བཙིར་བ་ *btsir-ba* v. *ₒtsir-ba.*

བཙུག(ས)་པ་ *btsúg(s)-pa* v. *ₒdzúgs-pa.*

བཙུད་པ་ *btsúd-pa* v. *ₒdzúd-pa, ₒtsúd-pa.*

བཙུན་པ་ *btsún-pa* 1. **respectable, noble,** of race, family, *rigs čé-žiṅ btsún-pa* id. *Dzl.*; *btsún-pai bud-méd Dzl.* a lady of rank. — 2. **reverend,** as title of ecclesiastics, *btsún-pa-rnams* the ecclesiastics, priests *Glr.*, = *ban-dhe* and *Ssk.* भदन्त (*Tar.* Transl. p. 4, note 7); even *btsún-pa k'rims-méd* wicked Reverends *Ma.* — 3. **creditable, honourable, faithful** in observing religious duties, so frq.: *mk'as btsun bzaṅ ysum* v. *mk'as-pa*; *tsig-btsún-pa* grave and virtuous discourse *Schr.*, *Sch.*: polite words (?), *tsig mi btsun-pa Thgy.* was explained to me: one whom nobody believes; applied to things: **good;** thus *Mil.* says of his cane: *spa čo-ris yé-nas btsún-pa de* this cane of quite an excellent quality. — *btsún-po* = *btsún-pa* 1., *rgya-rjé btsún-po* the noble emperor of China *Glr.*; as a title v. *snyuṅ*; *btsún-por byéd-pa Cs.* to reverence. — *btsún-ma* priestess *Cs.* — *btsún-mo* 1. woman of **rank, a lady;** also as a term of address: your ladyship, e.g. in a legend, when a merchant speaks to the wife of a judge *Dzl.*; **spouse, consort,** esp. **queen consort,** with and without *rgyál-poi,* frq.; *btsún-mo čé-ba* = *čen-ma* the principal wife; *btsun-mo-čan* having a wife, *btsun-mo-méd* not having a wife *Cs.* — 2. **nun,** *mo-btsún,* id. *Glr.*, *C.*

བཙུམ་པ་ *btsúm-pa* v. *ₒdzúm-pa.*

བཙེ་བ་ *btsé-ba* v. *ₒtsé-ba.*

བཙེམ་པ་ *btsém-pa* v. *tsem-pa.*

བཙོ་ *btso,* **purification, refining** (?) **ser-la tso taṅ-wa** *C.* to refine gold (which term eventually is the same as 'to boil') v. *ₒtsod-pa*; *btsó-ma, btsós-ma* a purified substance, *yser btsó-ma,* purified gold, very frq. with regard to a bright yellow colour *Glr.*

བཙོ་བ་ *btsó-ba* v. *ₒtsód-pa*; *btso-blag-pa* **to dye, to colour,** *btso-blág-mk'an* **a dyer,** *Lex.*

བཙོ་མ་ *btsó-ma* 1. = *ytsó-ma.* — 2. v. *btso.*

བཙོག་པ་ *btsóg-pa* I. vb. v. *ₒtsog-pa.*

II. adj., also *(b)rtsóg(s)-pa, W.* **sóg-po** 1. **unclean, dirty, nasty, vile,** *ₒdí-ni šin-tu rtsóg-pai sa yin* this is a very vile place, says the prince of hades to a saint visiting there; so also every Tibetan will say to a stranger entering his house; *ṅa btsog-čiṅ* when I am getting unclean, i.e. when I am confined *Dzl.*; *lus btsog-pa mnyam-pa ₒdi* this vile stinking body *Dzl.* — 2. in *W.* the common word for **bad** in every respect, **useless, spoiled, troublesome, perilous** (e.g. of a road); **injurious;** also in a more relative sense, **inferior, poor,** of goods; *btsog-nág* tobacco-juice, oil from the tobacco-pipe.

བཙོང་ *btsoṅ* **onion** *Med.* and vulgo, eschewed by pious Buddhists and ascetics, but a favourite food of the bulk of the people; *btsoṅ srég-pa* to roast onions.

བཙོང་བ་ *btsóṅ-ba* v. *˳tsóṅ-ba.*

བཙོད་ *btsod* n. of an animal, = *γtsod,* q v. — 2. n. of a plant, **madder** **मञ्जिष्ठा**, (*Rubia Manjit*); *btsod-˳bru* seeds of this plant, *btsod-žiṅ* field on which it is grown.

བཙོན་ *btson,* also *btsón-pa,* **a captive, prisoner,** *nyés-pa byás-pai btson žig* an imprisoned criminal *Dzl.*; *btsón-du ˳dzin-pa* to take prisoner *Dzl.*; *˳júg-pa* to put to prison; *btsón-nas ˳dón-pa* to set free, *ťár-ba* to be released; *bzáṅ-btson* undeserved imprisonment or detention (ni f.), e.g. of hostages, fig. of people that are snowed up *Mil* — *btsón-k̔aṅ, btson-rà* prison. — *btsón-doṅ* 1. **dungeon,** keep; *Mil.*: *γnás-skabs-kyi btsón-doṅ* the dungeon of life. — 2. *W.* **deep abyss, gulf,** **tsón-doṅ ťóṅ-na mi múṅ-poi go k̔or** many are getting dizzy, when looking into a deep abyss. — *btsón-rdzi, btsón-sruṅ* jailer, turnkey. — *btsón-rdzas* prison-fare.

བཙོལ་བ་ *btsól-ba* v. *˳tsól-ba.*

རྩ་ *rtsa* I. sbst., more col. *rtsá-ba* (*W.* **sá-wa**) or *rtsá-bo S.g.*5, 1. **vein,** *rtsa γčód-pa* to open a vein *Dzl.*, **sá-wa gyáb-če** *W.* id. Owing to the imperfect state of Indian and Tibetan anatomy, resulting from inveterate prejudices both of a religious and intellectual nature, great confusion prevails also in the department of angiology, many different vessels of the human body, and even part of the nerves being classed among the veins, so that it is impossible to find adequate terms for the Tibetan nomenclature. This applies e.g. to the division of the *rtsa* in *čágs-pai, srid-pai, ˳brél-pai,* and *ťséi* or *sróg-gi rtsa,* which last term does not correspond to what we understand by artery (*Cs.*); so it is also with respect to the three principal veins, which by a mystic theory are stated to proceed from the heart, *dbú-ma* the middle one, white, *rkyáṅ-ma* the left one, red, and *ró-ma* the right one, white, concerning which cf. the articles *γtúm-mo* and *tíg-le*; *rtsa-dkár,* also *rlúṅ-rtsa Med.,* are perh. in most cases the same as **artery,** acc. to the well-known supposition of the ancients, that the veins of dead men, appearing empty, contain air; *p̔ar-rtsa* id., as in the living body it pulsates; *rtsa-nág* or *k̔rág-rtsa,* vein, blood-vessel; *rtsa-sbúbs* is mentioned *Lt.* 147, 10, as a surgical instrument. Some names are more or less clear: *míg-rtsa* seems to be the Vena fac. ext., *rtsa-čúṅ* Vena jugul. ext., *rtsa-čén* or *rtsa-bo-čé* V. saphena magna, *p̔o-mtsan-ghi dbus-rtsa* V. dorsalis penis. *rgyú-grog-rtsa,* on the other hand, are the ureters, ni f., which are represented as proceeding from the small intestine. — *rtsa-rgyus Med.* 1. *Sch.*: 'veins and sinews' (?); *rtsa-rgyus-˳gag* an obstruction of the veins *S.g.* 2. title of a book: Directions how to feel the pulse. — *rtsa-čús, C. rtsa-˳dus* cramp. — *rtsa-mdúd* an inturgescence of the veins. — *rtsa-γnás Mil.* seems to be a net of veins, vascular plexus, any connection of things that may be compared to it, as e.g. the causal connection of the 12 Nidanas (v. *rten-˳brel* sub *rtén-pa* comp.) — *rtsa-spún* tissue of veins *Sch.* — 2. **pulse,** so in *rtsa ltá-ba,* or *rtog-pa Med.* to feel one's pulse, and *mťson-, kan-,* or *čag-rtsa* the feeling one's pulse with the second, third or fourth finger.

II. sbst, for *rtsá-ba.*

III. particle in conjunction with numerals: 1. gen. connecting the tens with the units, equivalent to **and**: *nyi-šu-rtsa-γčig* twenty and one; less frq. after *brgya* and *stoṅ,* where also *daṅ-rtsa* is not unusual, yet examples as the following: *S g.*, fol. 5, where the sum of 62, 33, 95 and 112 is stated to be = *sum-brgya-rtsa-γnyis,* and *Pth.* p. 34, twice *lṅa-brgyá-rtsa γčig* = *stoṅ-daṅ-rtsa-γnyis,* — exclude any doubt as to the proper use of the word. — 2. inst. of *nyi-šu-rtsa-γčig* to *nyi-šu-rtsa-dgu, rtsa-γčig* etc. is also used by itself, as an abbreviation, e.g. *S.g.* p. 3, in describing the growth of an embryo from week to week; this use of the word may account for the assumption, quite general in *W.* and *C.*, that *rtsa* in itself is equivalent to 20, for even Lamas of both districts could be convinced only by an arithmetical proof, that the numbers mentioned in the above passages were 302 and 1002, and not 322 and 1022. — 3. In *bċú-rtsa nyí-šu-rtsa, brgyá-rtsa*, without any units following, e.g *Tar.* 120, 10, the word evidently stands but pleonastically, like *ťam-pa.*

ར་ *rtswa* (*Bal., Pur. rtswa, stswa*) *C.* **tsa**, *Lh., Ld.,* **sa**, तृण, **grass, herb, plant,** *rtsa-ḱai* (or *rtsa-rtsei*) *zil-pa* the dew on the grass *Glr.*; *rtsa nyag γċig* a single blade of grass *Cs.*; *sṅó-yi rtsa, rtsa-sṅón* green grass; *rtsa-skám,* and often *rtsa* alone, **hay,** *rtsa rná-ba* to mow grass, *˳ťú-ba,* to gather (grass); *rtsá-ḱa C., W.* pasture, pasturage, **sá-ḱa gyál-la* W.* good pasturage. — *rtsá-ċan* covered with grass, grassy. — *rtsa-mċóg* Kusha-grass *Lex.*, v. *ku-ša*; *rtsa-mċog (-groṅ)* town in West Assam, where Buddha died *Glr.*; Kamarūpa. — *rtsa-ťág* grass-rope *Dzl.* — *rtsa-ťún* grass-gatherer *Sch.* — *rtsa-γdán* grass-mat *Sch.* — *rtsa-γyáb* manger *Sch.* — *rtsa-ras Sch.* 'linen', prop. the same as *la-ta* q. v. — 2. euphemism for *rkyag*; **tsa táṅ-wa* C.* to go to stool; *rtsa ču bsdams Mil.* he suffers from obstruction and strangury.

རྩ་བ་ *rtsá-ba*, 1. cf. *rtsaṅ* and *rtsad, Ssk.* मूल, 1. **root** (*W.* com. **bá-ťag** for it), **stalk of fruits;** *rtsá-ba lṅa* five (medicinal) roots, viz. *rá-mnye, lčá-ba, nyé-šiṅ, ắ-šo* (better *ắ-ša*)*-gandha, γzé-ma*; *rtsá-ba-nas ˳byin-pa* etc. to pull out with the root, to eradicate, extirpate, mostly fig., v. below. — 2. **the lower end** of a stick, **trunk** of a tree, pillar; *má-ťog rtsá-ba* id. *Mil.*; the **foot** of a hill, mountain-pass, the latter also *lá-rtsa W.* **lár-sa**; *rtsá-bai žal, lag* the lower faces or hands of those images, that represent deities with many faces and hands *Glr.*; *rtsá-bai ṅos* base of a triangle *Tar.* 204, 1; **fundament, foundation-pillar,** and the like; in later literature and vulgo *rtsá-bar* and *rtsar*, rarely (*Glr.*) *rtsá-ru* postp. with genit., **to, at,** e.g. to go to, to come to, to be at, both of persons and things, *bud-méd-kyi rtsar nyál-ba* or more euphem., *ṗyin-pa* to go to a woman *Glr.*, *šiṅ-gi rtsar*, even *čui rtsar Glr.*; **at, near,** **to,** a tree, river etc.; so also *rtsá-la* **to, at;** *rtsá(-ba)-na Glr.* and vulgo (incorr.) **tsá-ne* C.* **at, near;** without a case following: *rtsar byúṅ-nas* coming near, stepping up to *Glr.* — 3. **root** fig. · **origin, primary cause,** also *γži-rtsa*, e.g. *˳ḱor-bai γži-rtsa γċod-pa Mil.* to cut off the root of transmigration, to deliver a soul from tr.; *rtsá-ba-nas ˳byin-pa, ˳dón-pa, ˳góg-pa* etc., also *tsáṅ-nas, tsád-nas γċód-pa* etc., to exterminate (root and branch), to annihilate; on the other hand: *rtsa-brdár-γċod-pa Mil.*, *rtsád-γċod-pa* to examine closely, to investigate thoroughly. — *nyon-móṅs-kyi rtsá-ba γsum* are the three primary moral evils, viz. *˳dod-čágs, že-sdáṅ, γti-mug*; *rtsa-brál* therefore might signify: he who has freed himself from them; but it seems to mean also: without beginning or end, **unlimited,** e.g. *snyiṅ-rje Glr., sems nyid Mil.*; *dgé-bai rtsá-ba, dgé-rtsa* a virtuous deed, as a cause of future reward, *skyéd-pa, spyód-pa, byéd-pa* to perform such a deed; *rtsá-bai* . . . **the original, primary, principal** . . ., e.g. *don*, primitive or first meaning *Cs.*; *rtsá-bai nyon-móṅs-pa Cs.*: 'original sin', *Sch.*: 'sin inherited from former births'; at all events not identical with the original sin of Christian dogmatics, although the word grammatically might denote it; *rtsa (-bai) rgyud* an introductory treatise, giving a summary of the contents of a larger work, e.g. of the *rgyud-bži*, mentioned sub *brgyud*; also title of other works, *Ssk.* मूलतन्त्र, v. *Cs. Gram.*, chronol. table; whether *Sch.'s* translation 'cause and effect' is altogether correct, may admit of some doubt, yet v. below; *rtsá-ba daṅ ˳grél-ba Cs.* 'text and commentary'; in *rtsá-bai ma Thgy.* the genitive case stands prob. for the apposition: the mother that is the root of me, in a similar manner as *rtsá-bai raṅ-bžin* nature *Cs.*; *rtsá-bai blá-ma* seems to denote the teaching priest, the one by whom in any particular case the instruction is given, opp. to *brgyúd-pa*, he to whom it is imparted. A good deal of confusion however prevails here, owing to the ambiguity of the verbal form in *brgyúd-pa* and the variable spelling;

v. *rgyúd-pa* extr. — *rtsa-ṫór Sch.*: 'lower end and top' (?) (should perh. be *rtsa-ṫog*); *rtsa-mi Tar.* 191, 3 is rendered by *Schf.* with 'Haupt-Mann', principal man. — *rtsa-lág* (*Schr.*: root and branches) *Lex.* बन्धु relations, kindred; *rtsa-lag-čan* having relations, *rtsa-lag-med* without relations *Cs.* — *rtsa-šés Sch.*: primitive wisdom. — 4. symb. num.: 9. — II. v. *rtsa* **vein.**

Note. *rtsa*, vein, is traced by Tibetan scholars back to *rtsá-ba*, the veins being the 'roots of life'; in a dictionary the words are better treated separately.

ཙ་ལ་ *rtsá-la* v. *rtsá-ba* I, 2.

ཙང་ *rtsaṅ* = *rtsá-ba* seldom, v. *rtsá-ba* I, 3.

ཙངས་པ་ *rtsáṅs-pa* lizard, *brag-gi Lt.* (*W.* **gag-čig**).

ཙད་ *rtsad* = *rtsá-ba* **root,** *rtsád-nas γčód-pa Mil.* to root out, to eradicate; *rtsad γčód-pa,* = *rtsa-brdár γčód-pa,* = *ṫsar* and *γsar γčód-pa*, to search, investigate *Mil.*; *gar bžugs rtsad bčád-nas* to inquire, search for a person's place of abode *Pth.*

ཙབ་པ་, ཙབ་ཙབ་ *rtsab, rtsab-rtsab* v. *tsab-tsub.*

ཙབས་ *rtsabs* **ferment, barm, yeast,** prepared of barley-flour; *rtsabs-ḱur* a sweetish sort of bread, made up with it *Ld.*; *rtsábs-mo* a beverage brewed from roasted meal (*rtsám-pa*) and water, and made to ferment by adding butter-milk, esp. liked in winter; also called *btság-mo; žó-rtsabs Sch.* milk-brandy, not known to us.

ཙབས་རུ་ཚ་ *rtsabs-ru-ṫsa Lt.* n. of a medicine.

ཙམ་པ་ *rtsám-pa*, I. sbst. 1. **roast-flour,** flour from roasted grain, *ₒbras-rtsam* of rice, *gro-rtsam* of wheat, *nas-rtsam* of barley, this last the most common; stirred with water, beer, or tea into a pap, it is the usual food in *C.* — *rtsám-ₒbru* roast-flour and grain = victuals in gen. *Kun.* — *rtsám-rin* the price of flour *Sch.* — 2. **urine** *Lt.* *rtsam-mdóg* colour of urine.

II. vb. v. *rtsóm-pa.*

ཙར་ *rtsar* v. *rtsá-ba* I, 2.

ཙལ་ *rtsal* 1. **skill, dexterity, adroitness, accomplishment;** in the first place **physical skill,** *lag-rtsal-čan* of a skilful, practised hand *W.*; *sgyu-rtsál* id., *stobs daṅ sgyu-rtsál* strength and dexterity *Glr.*, skilfulness; *rtsal(daṅ) ldán(-pa)* skilful, expert, adroit, *rtsal-méd* the contrary; *rtsal ₒgran-pa* to vie in skill, *rtsal sbyóṅ-ba* to practise, or improve one's self in skill *Mil.*; *rtsal šor* all skill is gone, *rgud* id. *Sch.; stobs-(kyi) rtsal, Lex.* पराक्रम, strength, energy, *mṫu-rtsál* and *rtsal-mṫu* prob. id. *Dzl.*, *S.g.; rtsal-čé-ba* or *rtsal-po-čé* adroit as a gymnastic, wrestler etc.; also sbst. athlete, juggler etc. *Dzl.*; *rtsál-gyi mčoṅs* a gymnastic feat *Lex.*; *rtsal-sbyoṅ* bodily exercise, nimbleness, agility, *báṅ-rtsal-sbyoṅ* nimbleness in running, *γšóg-rtsal-sbyoṅ* agility in flying *Mil.*; *ču-rtsál* feats performed in the water; the art of swimming *Pth.*; vulgo *W.* also for natural, innate abilities: *mig-rtsal-mḱan* keen-sighted, *mig-rtsal nyams* of a weak sight; *rtsal-ṫón Sch* 'skilful, masterly' (?) — 2. in later times used in a special sense of **skill, expertness in contemplation,** cf. *sgóm-pa;* so frq. with *Mil.; byaṅ-čub-séms-kyi rtsal γsum*; *lam-ₒgag-méd-kyi rtsál-ḱa* such accomplishments 'as will clear the road', — ascetical terms familiar only to the initiated.

ཙས་མ་ *rtsás-ma* v. *btsás-ma.*

ཙི་ *rtsi* 1. all fluids of a somewhat greater consistency, such as the **juice** of some fruits, **paints, varnish** etc., *rtsi-čan* **viscid, sticky, clammy;** **tsi gyág-pa** *C.*, **si gyáb-če, kú-če, táṅ-če** *W.* to colour, to paint, **tsi táṅ-wa** *C.* also to solder; *ldab-pa*(?) *Sch.* to lacker, to varnish; *sbráṅ-rtsi* **honey;** *nád-kyi rkyen rtsi* a medical draught, potion *Dzl.* ༡༤, 7, (another reading: *sman*)*; bdúd-rtsi* nectar; *tsón-rtsi* painter's colour, *dkár-rtsi* white-wash, *nág-rtsi* black paint, *dmár-rtsi* red paint; **sér-tsi** *C.* gilding, **ṅúl-tsi** silvering *C.* — 2. applied to external appearance: **dóṅ-si** *W.* **complexion;** even *spa rtsi ₒjam ḱa-dóg légs-pa de* this cane, as to its outside smooth, as to colour beautiful *Mil.* (unless *rtsi* be = shell, bark, rind?)

— *rtsi-tóg* juicy fruit; *rtsi-śiṅ* 1. **fruit-tree** *Pth.* 2. **tree,** in gen. *Glr.* and elsewh., frq. — *rtsi-gu* fruit-kernel, the kernel in a fruit-stone (not the latter itself *Sch.*); *W.* for **tsi-gu**, q.v.; *rtsi-gu-mar-nag* oil extracted from the stones of apricots; *rtsi-már Lt.* id.

རྩི་བ་ *rtsi-ba*, pf. *(b)rtsis*, fut. *brtsi*, imp. *(b)rtsi(s)* 1. **to count,** **si-te bór-ċe* W.* to pay down, money; cf. also *rtsis.* — 2. **to count, reckon, calculate,** *mi ré-la pul re-rei ťád-du* reckoning a handful to each *Dzl.*; *žag súm-ċu-la zlá-ba γċig, zlá-ba bċu-γnyis-la lor rtsi-ba* to reckon a month at 30 days, a year at 12 months *Thgy.*; *mi-lo-ltar rtsi-ba* to count by the years of a man *Thgy.*; *gaṅ bzaṅ rtsi-ba* to calculate which (day) be a propitious one *Glr.*; *dus rtsi-ba* to reckon up, to compute the time *Mil.*; **če-miṅ ḍál-la si-ċe* W.* to reckon among the adults; *yón-tan-la skyón-du rtsi-ba* to consider good qualities as faults, = *ltá-ba* I, 2; *brduṅ rtsi* he may be reckoned to strike, i.e. he is very likely to strike, threatens to strike *C.*; *brtsis zin* 1. **the account is closed,** the bill is ready. 2. **product, sum total.**

རྩིའུ་ *rtsiu* n. of a plant, = *pri-yáṅ-ku Wdṅ.*

རྩིག་པ་ *rtsig-pa* I. vb., pf. *(b)rtsigs*, fut. *brtsig*, imp. *(b)rtsig(s)*, 1. **to build,** whether of stone or of wood, *ḱáṅ-pa.* — 2. **to wall up,** *sgo* a door *Glr.* — II. sbst. **wall, masonry.**

Comp. *rtsig-skyábs Stg.* is said to be = *rtsig-rmáṅ.* — *rtsig-ṅós* side of a wall. — *rtsig-rdó* stone for building. — *rtsig-dpón* master-mason, architect. — *rtsig-púr* a peg in a wall, wall-hook, to hang up things. — *rtsig-rmáṅ* fundament of a wall. — *rtsig-zúr* edge or ledge of a wall *Thgy.* — *rtsig-bzó-pa* brick-layer, mason. — *rtsig-γyóg* journeyman mason.

རྩིགས་ *rtsigs*, *Sch.*: '*rtsigs-čé* very gracious and well-affected' (?), prob. should be *rtsis-če* q. v. no. 3.

རྩིགས་མ་ *rtsigs-ma* **turbid matter, sediment, impurity,** = *tsigs-ma S.g.*

རྩིང་བ་ *rtsiṅ-ba* adj. and sbst., **coarse, clumsy, rough, rude; coarseness** etc., *B.*; *rtsiṅ-po B.* and *C.*, *rtsiṅ-ge C.*, *W.* id., but only adj.; *pye* coarse meal, grits (opp. to *žib-po*, *ˌȷám-po*); *spyód-pa rtsiṅ-ba* of rude manners *Glr.*

རྩིད་པ་ *rtsid-pa* **the long hair of the yak,** *rtsid-ťágs* = *re-ťágs* coarse cloth manufactured of it; *rtsid-stán* saddle-cloth *Mil.*; *rtsid-gúr* tent-covering made of it.

རྩིབ(ས)་མ་ *rtsib(s)-ma* 1. **rib,** *rtsib-mai bár-nas* from between the ribs *Glr.*; *rtsib-lógs γyas γyon* all the ribs of the right and left side *Dzl*; *rtsib-logs ná-ba* pain about the ribs *Do.*; *rtsib-riṅ* the upper ribs (?) — 2. **spoke** of a wheel, frq.; *rtsib-kyi mu-ḱyúd* fellies composing the rim of a wheel *Cs.*; in ornamental designs the *rtsib-ma* are often fanciful figures, supplying the radii of the circle; further: **the sticks** or **ribs** of a parasol, canopy etc. *Glr.*; **the spars** of a felt-tent, **the ribs** or **futtocks** of a boat *Schr.* — *rtsib-ri* n. of a mountain, = *śri-ri.*

རྩིས་ *rtsis* 1. **counting, numbering, numeration,** *rtsis-las ˳das-pa* innumerable *Mil.*; **bód si-la, món-si-la* W.* according to Tibetan, according to Indian counting or computation of time (is to-day the twentieth); **mí-si, ḍóṅ-si* W.* numbering of the people, of the domiciliated; **mág-si táṅ-ċe* W.* to hold a numbering of military forces. — 2. **account,** *rtsis byéd-pa Glr.*, *˳débs-pa Mil.*, *γyáb-pa C.*, *W.* **kor-ċe, (l)ta-ċe** **to calculate, to compute,** *rtsis-su sbyár-ba* to count together, to sum up *Dzl.*; **calculation, computation** (beforehand), **scheme;** **žag nyi-śu-la ˳gro- (or ča-rtsis yod)* W.* in about 20 days we calculate, i.e. we intend, to go; **śiṅ-ta gyúg-si yód-pe dus-tsód-la* Ld.* at the hour, when according to their calculation the carriage was to start; *rtsis-kyis* (or *rtsis byás-nas*) *ṅó-śes-pa* to find by computation *Glr.* — *skár-rtsis* **astrology, astronomy;** *dkár-rtsis, nág-rtsis*, acc. to *Cs.*: Indian and Chinese astronomy and chronology. — 3. **estimation, esteem,** *rtsis-po čén-po byéd-pa* to value, to make much of, *lús-kyi rtsis-po-če* one that makes much of his own body, by indulging and adorning it *Thgy.*; *rtsis-rtsis byéd-pa Sch.* id.; *dé-la bla-*

lhág-tu rtsis-su byed he respected her beyond measure *Tar.*, *Schf.* — **si-rúg** vulgo *W.* for *rtsis* in most of its significations.

རྩིས་པ་ *rtsis-pa* 1. also *rtsis-mk'an* **mathematician, astronomer, soothsayer; accountant** *Cs.* — 2. n. pr. *rtsis-pa á-mgrón* secular, *rtsis-pa mgron-ynyér* spiritual name of the late Resident of the Sikim government at Darjeeling, called by the English Cheboo Lama, † 1866, v. Hooker Journ. — *rtsis-dpon* a chief mathematician, chief accountant, receiver general *Cs.*

རྩུབ་པ་ *rtsúb-pa* I. vb. **to revile, abuse,** v. *ṅor rtsub-pa* sub *ṅo*.

II. adj., com. *rtsúb-po, rtsúb-mo* *Ssk.* **परुष, uneven, rough, rugged,** of the skin, cloth etc.; **coarse-grained,** powder; **rough, wild, dreary,** countries, *roṅ-rtsub* with wild ravines *Glr.*; **bristly,** hair; **harsh, tart, astringent,** of taste *Med.*; also applied to any thing of a highly **aromatic, pricking, pungent** or **acerb** taste, such as onions and similar vegetables, liable to cause both dietetic and religious scruples; *rtsub-zás* food of this description; in music: **strong, forte;** of sentiment and behaviour: **rude, unfeeling, regardless, callous** *S.g.*, *Glr.*

རྩེ་(མོ་) *rtse(-mo)* 1. **point, top, peak, summit,** *k'aṅ-, gri-, ri-, šiṅ-rtse*, or *k'aṅ-pai* etc., *rtsé-mo* **gable** of a house, point of a knife, top of a hill, head of a tree; of convents, royal palaces, resp.: *dbú-rtse Glr.*; *lá-rtse*, *W.* **lár-se** (cf. *rtsá-ba* I, 2.) **lá-se** **summit** of a mountain-pass; *rtse daṅ logs-su* terminal and lateral *Wdṅ.*; *rtsé-sgro Glr.* flag-feather, pinion; *ža rtse-riṅ* hat with a high crown *Tar.*; *rtse ycíl-ba Sch.*: to break off the point, to blunt; *rtse-reg-čé Mil.* very sensitive, touchy, not to be touched with the tip of the finger. — 2. **point, particular spot,** *rtse ycig-tu ltá-ba* to look at one point; also adv., to look **steadily, unremittingly,** as: *ráṅ-gi grib-ma-la rtse-ycig-tu ltá-ba Wdṅ.*, also *Tar.* frq.; *sems rtse ycig-tu byed-pa* to direct the mind to one point, frq.; *sems rtse-ycig-tu byás-pai tiṅ-ṅe-ₒdzin-la žúgs-te Dzl.*; aim, *ts'e ₒdii rtse ycig* as this life's only aim *Mil.*

རྩེ་བ་ *rtsé-ba*, pf. *rtses*, imp. *rtse(s)*, **क्रीड़,** (different from *brtsé-ba*) 1. **to play,** *mig-máṅ* at chess *Dzl.*; **to sport, to frolic,** used also of animals *Dzl.*; *rtse bro ytóṅ-ba* to run to and fro, playing and skipping, of deer *Mil.*; **to joke, to jest,** *rtsé-žiṅ dgá-ba, rtse-dgá spyád-pa* id.; **yáṅ(s)-pa sé-če** *W.* id.; **to enjoy, amuse, divert one's self, to take recreation,** *ts'al-gyi naṅ-du rtser soṅ* they went on a pleasure party into the woods *Dzl.*; euphem. of cohabitation, *ₒdi daṅ rtsé-bar byao Pth.* I mean to enjoy her.

Comp. *rtsé-mk'an* player, gambler, gamester. — *rtse-gróg*s, *rtsed-grógs* play-mate. — *rtse-dgá* v. above. — *rtse-rgód* sport and laughter. — *rtsé-sa* play-ground, place of amusement. — *rtse-sems* a mind fond of play; *k'yód-kyis rtsé-sems yin mod k'yaṅ* though you may still relish pleasures *Pth.*

2. **to touch,** *W.* **lág-pa ma se** do not touch it with your hand. — 3. **to shudder** (cf. *spu*).

རྩེ་ཆུང་ *rtse-čúṅ* = *rtsa-čúṅ*, Vena jugularis externa.

རྩེག་པ་ *rtség-pa*, pf. *(b)rtsegs*, fut. *brtseg*, imp. *rtsog*, *W.* **ság-če(s)** 1. **to lay one thing on or over another, to pile up, stack up, build up,** wood, boards; to put slices of meat on bread; fig.: *ná-ro ynyis brtseg* two 'naro' one above the other, ཻ, *Gram.*; gen. **double;** *k'aṅ-pa rtsegs-pa* 1. **'a house of two stories'** = a stately building, palace; by this word *Wdṅ.* explains *k'aṅ-bzáṅ*, v. *bzáṅ-po*. 2. acc. to other *Lexx.*, **an apartment built on another,** an upper chamber; balcony on the roof of a house, **कूटागार**; *rgya-grám brtségs-pai mč'ód-rten* a chod-ten with a cross (v. *rgya-grám*) on the top *Pth.* — 2. **to tuck up,** clothes *Cs.* — 3. *dbugs rtségs-pa, gyén-du dbugs(-kyis) rtség-pa Med.*, **short-breathed, asthmatic, panting, gasping,** from fright etc., or as a sign of approaching death. — *dkon(-mč'óg) brtségs(-pa)*; **रत्नकूट** title of a book.

རྩེང་བ་ *rtseṅ-ba*, pf. *brtseṅs*, fut. *brtseṅ*, imp. *(b)rtsoṅ(s)* **to tuck up, truss up.**

རྩེད་པ་ *rtséd-pa* I. also *rtsén-pa*, = *rtsé-ba* **to play;** *rtsed rtsé-ba* id.; *rtséd-mo*

play, game, *dgá-bai rtsèd-mo byed-pa Dzl.*; *glu gar rtsèd-mo byèd-pa* to sing, dance and play *Glr.*; *rtsèd-mo* **toy,** *byis-pai* children's toy *Mil.*; *rtsèd-mo-čan* **playful, sportive, merry** *Cs.*; *rkyál-, gár-, gri-, čól-, mčóṅ-, rtá-rtsed* the sport of swimming, dancing, fencing, dicing, leaping, riding *Cs.*; *γyeṅ-rtsèd* **play, amusement, diversion;** *rtsed-dgá* id. *Sch.*; *to-to-liṅ-liṅ rtsed* q.v.; *rtsèd-ˌǰo, rtsén-ˌǰo, W.* **sén-ǰo** **sport, public amusement, popular pleasure;** *γžón-nu rtsèd-ˌǰoi ṫsógs-kyis bskór-nas* surrounded by a number of youthful playmates; **sén-ǰo táṅ-če* W.* to arrange a sport.

II. **to varnish** (?).

རྩེད་མ་ *rtsèd-ma* the disagreeable feeling in the teeth produced by acids *Sch.*; *rsed-ám* a shivering, cold shudder *Sch.* v. *rtsé-ba* 3.

རྩེད་མོ་, རྩེན་པ་ *rtsèd-mo, rtsén-pa* v. *rtsèd-pa.*

རྩེན་གོག་ *rtsen-góg Mil*, acc. to *Sch.*: **calf of the leg.**

རྩེས་ *rtses* v. *rtsé-ba.*

རྩོག(ས་)པ་ *rtsóg(s)-pa* v. *brtsóg-pa.*

རྩོད་ལྡན་ *rtsod-ldán* n. of a certain era or period of the world v. *dus* 6.

རྩོད་པ་ *rtsód-pa*, I. vb., pf. *brtsad* **to contend, to fight with arms** *Dzl.*; with words: **to dispute, debate, wrangle,** frq., *daṅ* with, *la* about; *rtsód-čiṅ mi-snyán rǰód-pa* to speak evil words, to use bad language, in quarreling.

II. sbst. **dispute, contention, quarrel; disputation** *Glr.*; *rtsód-pa ˌgrán-pa* to compete in disputation *Glr.* — *ṫsád-mai rtsód-pa* a learned debate about words; *rtsód-pa-rnams* points of controversy *Tar.* 132,18, *Schf.* — *rtsod-γži* the subject of a disputation.

རྩོན(མ་) *rtsón(-ma) Pur.* **nausea, vomiting,** **rtson pog** he grows sick; **rtsón-čas** **to be sick, to vomit.**

རྩོམ་པ་ *rtsóm-pa* I. vb., pf. *(b)rtsams, rtsoms*, fut. *brtsam*, imp. *rtsom(s)* 1. **to begin, commence** a work, **to be about, to set about** an undertaking; *ˌbrós-par brtsáms-te* being about to run away *Dzl.*; *čós-las brtsáms-te rtsód-do* it was about religion that our dispute began *Tar.*; *ṅo-lóg brtsáms-pa-las* beginning, stirring up an insurrection *Glr.*; *dé-nas brtsáms-te* beginning at this place, **from here, from that time** (cf. *bzúṅs-te* sub *bzúṅ-ba*). — 2. **to make, to accomplish,** *γsó-bai las mi brtsám-mo* so he will not accomplish the business of healing; com. **to compose, to draw up,** in writing, *bstán-bčos rtsom-mi* author, writer, composer *Pth.*; *brtson-ˌgrús rtsóm-pa Dzl.* frq., to work diligently, carefully; **to take pains, to exert one's self,** *rtsóm-par*, or *rtsóm-pa-la mḱás-pa* a clever writer, an elegant composer, which title in Tibet is applied to any one, that exhibits in his style high-sounding bombast with a flourish of religious phrases; *čad rtsod rtsom γsum-gyi bšad-gra Glr.* prob. a school, in which religion is taught and explained, combined with disputations and written compositions. —

II. sbt. **beginning, commencement** (**आरंभ**), *rtsóm-pa daṅ-po* the first beginning *Ld.-Glr.*; **a doing, proceeding, undertaking, deed** *Tar.*

རྩོལ་བ་ *rtsól-ba* 1. vb. **to endeavour, to take pains, to give diligence;** *rtsól-bar* adv. **diligently, zealously;** *ḱyód-kyis rtsól-bai dús-la bab* now you must use dispatch *Pth.*; *rtsol-méd* **unsought,** *rtsol-méd ˌgró-bai don byéd-pa* to seek the welfare of beings without their caring for it *Glr.*; *srog rtsól-ba Lex.* and *Mil.*, acc. to *Sch.*: **to draw breath, to take fresh courage,** which seems to be implied by *dbugs rtsól-ba Ma.*; *nyal-po rtsol drag(-na)* if cohabitation is immoderately indulged in *Med.* — 2. sbst. **zeal, endeavour, exertion,** *rtsól-ba skyéd-pa* to use diligence *Zam.*

སྩོལ་བ་ *stsól-ba*, pf. and fut. *stsol* (**sól-wa, sál-wa**), 1. **to give, bestow, grant,** when the person that gives is respectfully spoken to, much the same as *γnaṅ-ba* q.v.; *stsál-du γsol* please to give, to grant etc. *Dzl.*; *bdág-gi lám-rgyags stsol čig* pray, give me provisions (provender) for the journey *Dzl.*; **to give back, to return** what had been lent *Dzl.*; **to grant, bestow, afford, give** (as a present); also for *ytón-ba* **to send, to send out,** so at least in *W.*; further: *W.* *ǰa sal, šu-gu sal, deb-sal** please to give me some tea, to lend me some paper, pray, give me change; or more pressingly: *ǰa sal gos** I earnestly request you for some tea etc., I entreat you to . . .; **sal mi gos** I thank you, I do not want it; *bká-stsal-ba* v. sub *bka*; *dṅos-grúb stsól-ba* to bestow spiritual gifts (?). — 3. sometimes incorr. for *bsál-ba* (*sél-ba*) **to clean, to clear, to remove** *Dzl.*

བརྩད་པ་, བརྩམ་པ་ *brtsád-pa*, *brtsám-pa* v. *rtsód-pa*, *rtsóm-pa*, sometimes incorr. for *btsád-pa*, *btsám-pa*.

བརྩེ་བ་ *brtsé-ba* vb. **to love,** sbst. **love, affection, kindness,** nearly the same as *byáms-pa*, frq. preceded by *snyiṅ*, resp. *tugs*, q. v.; *brtsé-bas* out of love, kindness, e. g. *ynáṅ-ba* to give something out of love; **with love, lovingly, kindly,** e. g. *skyóṅ-ba* to protect; *brtsé-bai tsig* words of love, kind exhortations *Glr.*; *brtsé-bai pyag-bris* your very kind letter; *snyiṅ-brtse-ba*, resp. *túgs-brtse-ba* = *brtsé-ba*; *brtsé-ba-čan*, *brtse-ldán* **loving, affectionate, kind;** *brtse(-ba)-méd(-pa)* **unkind, unmerciful, ungracious;** *brse-ydúṅ* **love, affection,** *pa-má brtse-ydúṅ če yaṅ či žig bya* what could even parental love do? *Glr.*; *lha-prúg yžón-nui brtse-ydúṅ de* this proof of love on the part of young goddesses towards me *Mil.*

བརྩོན་པ་ *brtsón-pa* 1. vb. with *la*, **to strive, to aim at, to exert one's self for,** *tsógs-pa-la* an accumulation of merits, frq.; *brtsón-par byéd-pa*, or *ₒgyúr-ba*, also with *mnón-par* preceding it; **to apply one's self,** *lás-la* to business, *tugs-dám-la* to meditation *Dzl.*, *Mil.* — 2. sbst. (*Ssk.* वीर्य *virtus*) **endeavour, effort, care, exertion,** *byá-ba-la brtsón-pa* alacrity, readiness to act *Wdṅ.*; more frq. *brtson-ₒgrús* v. below. — 3. adj. = *brtsón-pa-čan*, *brtson-ldán Mil.*, **diligent, assiduos, studious,** *sgrúb(-pa)-la* eager to obtain power over demons *Mil.*; *brtsón-par* **on purpose, with intention, wilfully;** as sbst. mostly *brtson-ₒgrús*, with *skyéd-pa*, *byéd-pa*, *rtsóm-pa* **to use diligence, to show energy, zeal** etc.; *brtson-ₒgrús drág-po* intense application; *brtson-ₒgrus-čan* **assiduous, studious,** *brtson-ₒgrus nyáms-te Stg.* having lost one's energy.

ཚ

ཚ 1. the letter *tsa*, the aspirate of ཙ (cf. ཙ), sounded *ts.* — 2. num. fig.: 18.

ཚ་ *tsa*, 1. **hot,** v. *tsa-ba.* — 2. **grandchild,** v. *tsá-bo.* — 3. v. *tsa-tsa.* — 4. resp. **illness, complaint** *C.*

ཚྭ་ *tswa* **salt,** *tswa ₒdébs-pa* **to salt,** with *la*; **tsa nyén-če** *W.* to taste, to try, food prepared with salt; *ka-ru-tswa* **alum** *Med.*; *rgya-tswa* **sal-ammoniac** *Med.*; *lče-myaṅ-tswa* **alum** *Lt.*; *rdo-tswa* **rock-salt** *Cs.*; *ba-tswa* **impure soda,** v. *bá-mo.* — *bód-tswa Lt.?* — *lán-tswa* = *tswa.* — *tswa-ka* salt mine *Cs.* — **tsa-(ku-)čan** *W.* **saline, salinous.** — *tswa-sgo* place where salt is found. — **tsa-tsé** **sal-ammoniac** *C.* — **tsa-ču** **salt-water, brine;** acc. to some, **vinegar** (?).

ཚ་སྐོར་ *tsa-skór* v. *tsá-bo.*

ཚ་ཁང་ *tsa-káṅ* v. *tsa-tsá.*

ཚ་འཁྲུ་ *tsa-ₒkrú* v. *tsa-ba.*

ཚ་ག་འབུ་ *tsá-ga-ₒbu*, also *čá-ga-ₒbu*, *tsag-tság* **grasshopper, locust** *C.*

ཚ་གཅིག་མ་ *tsa-yčig-ma* **thick blanket, quilt** *C.*

ཚ་ཆུ་ *tsa-ču* v. *tsa-ba.*

ཙྭ་ཚུ་ tswa-ču v. tswa.

ཚ་དྲག་ tsa-drág **haste, hurry,** *tsa-ḍág ǰhe šig* C., *tsa-rág toṅ* W. make haste! — adv. tsa-drág-tu Sch. but also *mā tsa-rág šog* W. come quickly, without delay!

ཚ་སྣ་ tsá-sna **anxiety** about, **tender care** for a thing, ni.f.; *tsa-na-čan* W. **solicitous, careful, attached,** *tsa-na-méd-k'an* W. **indifferent, unfeeling, callous;** k'án-pe *tsá-na k'ür-k'an* W. one that has to care for the welfare of a household or community, superintendent etc.

ཚ་སྣག་ tsa-snág Sch. = snág-tsa **ink.**

ཚ་པན་ཙེ་ tsa-pan-tsé C. **dresser, kitchen-table.**

ཚ་བིག་ tsá-big Ld. **a little.**

ཚ་བ་ tsá-ba I. vb. **to be hot,** só-ga-(la) nyi-mai ˏod-zér ráb-(tu-) tsá-bas as at the time of the Soga the rays of the sun are very hot.

II. sbst. 1. **heat,** tsá-bas ydúṅ-ba to be tormented by the heat S.g.; tsá-bai dus-su during the heat of the day, at noon, cf. dro Mil.; tsá-ba ni bsil-bar gyúr-to the heat changed into coolness Dzl.; tsa yzér-ba the burning of the heat, or of the sun Sch.; tsá-bai nad Lt. the fever-stage in diseases; tsa sél-ba to cure an acute disease Sch.; tsá-bas rmyá-ba to lose one's appetite in consequence of great heat Sch. — 2. **warm food,** stér-ba, ˳drén-pa Mil.; tsa-yčig-ma one that in twenty-four hours takes but one regular meal. — 3. **spice, condiment,** tsá-ba ysum त्रिकटुक, black pepper, long pepper, ginger.

III. adj. (vulgo *tsém-mo* C., *tsán-te* W.) 1. **hot, warm.** — 2. **sharp, biting, pungent,** of spices etc. — 3. **stinging, prickly, thorny** Pth. —

Comp. tsa-˳k'ru colic, gripes Lt. — tsa-góṅ forenoon Sch. — tsa-graṅ 1. hot and cold. 2. (relative) warmth. — *tsan-gyal* W. inflammatory fever. — tsa-lčib v. lčib. — *tsa-čú* 1. a hot spring C. 2. a warm bath C. — tsa-bra dinner Sch.(?) — tsa-mig red pepper Ld. — *tsém-mo C. hot, warm. — tsa-dmyál hot hell. — tsa-zér 'glowing ray', po. for sun. — *tsan-láṅ* W. hot, passionate, ardent; in the rut — tsa-lam Sch.: half a day's journey, a march before breakfast, = tsal-mai lam. — tsa-bsubs Lt.?

ཚ་བོ་ tsá-bo, resp. dbón-po B., sku-tsa C. 1. **grandchild, grandson,** Ld. *mé-mé-tsa-wo*. — 2. **nephew, brother's son** Dzl.; Ld.: *á-žáṅ-tsa-wo*. — bú-tsa v. bu; yáṅ-tsa **great-grandchild,** yúṅ-tsa **great-great-grandchild,** yži-tsa id. Sch. — tsa-skór grand-children Sch. — tsá-mo 1. **granddaughter.** 2. **niece.** 3. **wife** Lh. — tsa-žáṅ nephew and uncle Mil. — tsa-yzúg nephews and nieces Sch. — tsa-yúg **grandchildren,** tsa-yúg máṅ-poi čó-lo the many grandchildren's tattling Mil.; offspring, in gen., bu-tsa-yúg id. W., C.; *tsá-wo tsa-yúg yáṅ-tsa yúṅ-tsa* W. children and children's children.

ཚ་མིག་ tsa-mig v. tsá-ba comp.

ཚ་མོ་ tsá-mo 1. v. tsá-ba. — 2. v. tsá-bo.

ཚ་ཚ་ tsá-tsa 1. little images of Buddha, and conical figures, moulded of clay and used at sacrifices Schl. 194,206; tsá-k'aṅ place for keeping them Cs.; fig. k'á-nas mé-yi tsá-tsa ˳pro from his mouth proceeded cones of fire Pth. — 2. Bal. for tsa-drág **hastily, quickly;** tsa-tsa-méd **slow, slowly.**

ཚ་གཞུག་ tsa-yžúg v. tsá-bo.

ཚ་ཟར་ tsá-zar v. tsá-dar.

ཚ་རག་ tsa-rág v. tsa-drág.

ཚ་རུ་ tsa-rú **lamb-skin,** *tsar-lág* W. coat made of lamb-skins.

ཚ་ལ་ tsá-la a kind of medicine Med., acc. to Wdṅ. = dar-tsúr.

ཚ་ལུ་ tsa-lú 1. also mtsa-lú(?) **cock,** bya (-po)-tsá-lu Wdṅ., C.; in W. applied only to red-breasted cocks, from mtsal vermilion (Sch. hen?). — 2. v. tsál-ba.

ཚ་ལུམ་པ་ tsa-lúm-pa C. **sweet orange,** frq. in Sik.

ཚ་ལེ་ tsá-le 1. Ssk. सुभग, Hd. सुहागा, Pers. تنكار, Ar. بورق, **borax,** tsá-lei skyúr-

rtsi boracic acid *Cs.*; *tsa-le byéd-pa* to solder *Sch.*(?). — 2. *tsá-le zán-po Lh.*, n. of a flower, *Hemerocallis fulva.*

ཚག་ *tsag*, 1. v. *tsags.* — 2. *tság-sgra* **an appalling tone** *Sch.*(?); **tsag gyab* W.* a stinging pain is felt. — 3. **tsag-ṭúg, tsag-yá* W.* **twins**; **tsag-lúg** twin-sheep.

ཚག་པ་ *tság-pa* (cf. *ₒtság-pa*), *mar tság-pa* **oil-miller** *Sch.* — *tság-ma* **sieve, filter,** also *tsags*, q. v. — **tsag-ré** bolting-cloth, bolter *C.*, *W.* — *tsag-ró* residuum after sifting, as bran etc.

ཚག་ཚིག་ *tsag-tsig* **dark spots** or **speckles,** on wood etc. *Mil.*; **freckles** *C.*

ཚག་ཚེ་ *tsag-tse* **bruised barley** or **wheat** *Sch.*

ཚག་ཤ་ *tság-ša* **flesh of larger animals,** of cattle etc.

ཚགས་ *tsags* 1. **cap,** *gos-tságs* coat and cap *Dzl.* — 2. = *tság-ma, tsags-kyis, btsags Lex.*; *ko-tságs* a sieve made of leather, the one most in use; *ḱrol-tságs* = *tság-ma Lex.*; *nya-tságs* **weel,** for catching fish *C.* — 3. **thin-split bamboo,** for making baskets *Sik.* — 4. *Sch.*: **'the right sort, a choice article,** *tsags-bzáṅ byás-nas* making a good choice'. — 5. **density**(?) **tság-čan, tsag-ṭúg-mo* W.* standing close together, e. g. trees, books; *tsags-dám* dense and strong, as stuffs *Sch.*; *so tsags-dam-žiṅ* the teeth standing close and firm *Glr.*; **tsag čó-te dug** sit close together! *Ld.*; *tsags-lhód* not dense or compact *Sch.*; relative density. — 6. *tsags byéd-pa* (*W.* **čó-če**), *tságs-su ₒǰúg-pa* and *čúd-pa Mil.* **to save, spare, lay up** as provision for the future, *tse p̔yi-mai grabs či yaṅ tságs-su ma čud* I have not made any provision yet for the future life *Mil.*; **to economize, to be sparing,** *mé-la* of the fire; to be niggardly; *tságs-ₒdod-čan* **stingy, griping, avaricious.**

ཚང་ *tsaṅ* 1. **nest,** *byá-tsaṅ S.g.*; *tsaṅ bzó-ba* to build a nest *Sch.*; **den, hole, lair, kennel, burrow,** *stág-tsaṅ, wá-tsaṅ, p̔yi-tsaṅ* (cf. *p̔yi-ba*); **cell, honey-comb, hive,** *sbráṅ-tsaṅ Cs.* — 2. variously applied to human places of abode: *γnas-tsaṅ* **habitation, house;** *tsáṅ ₒčá-ba* to build a nest, to establish a household *Schr.*; *grwa-tsaṅ* v. *grwa*; **ṫab-tsáṅ** in *W.* the common word for **kitchen,** *γsól-ḱaṅ* being the resp. term for it; *tsáṅ-zla* perh. brothers and sisters, beside *p̔a-má Mil.* — 3. v. *ₒtsáṅ-ba.*

ཚང་ངུ་ *tsáṅ-ṅu* **cradle** *Sch.*

ཚང་བ་ *tsáṅ-ba* I. vb., pf. *tsaṅs,* **to be complete, full, entire,** *zlá-ba dgu tsáṅ-ba-na, tsáṅ-ba daṅ, tsáṅ(s)-nas* when the nine months were full, completed *Dzl.*, *zlá-ba tsáṅ-du nyé-bas* towards the end of the months of pregnancy *Dzl.*; **dá-wa tsaṅ soṅ = bud soṅ* W.* the month is completed, is expired; *rgyál-po γčig* (also *γčig-gis*) *ma tsáṅ-ba-la* as one king was still wanting, the number not being yet complete *Dzl.*; *tsaṅ-nas yod* they are complete (in number) *Pth.* —

II. sbst. (seldom) **completeness, entireness,** *yin-mín-gyi(s) ma-tsáṅ-ba byuṅ-na* when there is no completeness, no absolute certainty as to right and wrong. —

III. adj. 1. **complete, entire;** more frq.: 2. **having things complete,** *yón-tan dé-tso tsáṅ-bai bú-mo* a girl in full possession of all these qualities *Pth.*; *ḱa-dóg lṅa tsaṅ-ba* having all the five colours complete *Glr.*; *dbáṅ-po ma-tsáṅ-ba* one not in full possession of his five senses *Glr.* — *tsáṅ-ma* 1. **whole, entire, perfect** (the usual adjective form), *bya-p̔rúg tsáṅ-ma žig* a perfect young bird, i.e. perfectly developed *Dzl.* — 2. esp. *W.* **all,** for *tams-čád.* — **tsáṅ-ka* W.* **all together, in all,** with regard to smaller numbers. — *tsáṅ-po* forming a whole. — *tsaṅ-skám* **perfectly** dry, *tsaṅ-rlón* **perfectly** wet; *tsaṅ-ₒgrig* **all right,** frq., **tsaṅ-ḍig ǰhé-pa* or *čó-če* W.*

ཚང་ཚིང་ *tsaṅ-tsiṅ*, *Cs.*: **wood, grove, copse, thicket;** *Sch.*: a wild, dismal place; *tsaṅ-tsíṅ ₒḱrigs-pa Sch.*: 'dense thicket; horrible and awful'; *'tsaṅ-tsíṅ srid-pai γnas* the horrible existence in the external world *Mil.*

ཚང་ཡ་ *tsaṅ-yá* **double-barreled gun** *C.* and *W.*

ཚང་ར་ *tsaṅ-ra* v. *ₒtsaṅ-ra.*

ཚངས་ *tsaṅs*, *W.* **kú-lig-gi tsaṅs**, key-hole, col. for *mtsams* (?).

ཚངས་པ་ *tsáṅs-pa* (evid. preterite of *ₒtsáṅ-ba*) 1. **purified, clean, pure, holy**, *tsáṅs-par gyur čig* prob. be clean! be forgiven! *Dzl.* ༡༠༣, 13; *ₒgyod-tsáṅs, mtol-tsáṅs*, v. the two; *tsáṅs-par spyód-pa, tsáṅs-pai spyód-pa spyód-pa, tsáṅs-par mtsúṅs-par spyód-pa* 1. to be clean, chaste, holy, to do what is right, to lead an honest, upright life. 2. to be a priest, to belong to a holy order, and as sbst. priest, cleric; *mi-tsaṅs-par spyód-pa*, not to be clean, chaste etc., esp. with *bud-méd-la* to commit one's self with a woman *Mil.* — *tsaṅs-skúd*, *Sch.*: 'holy cord, the bond of spirits' (?) — *tsaṅs-tig* **equator**, prob. of *Cs.*'s construction, cf. *dguṅ* extr. — 2. ब्रह्म, **Brahma**, an Indian deity transplanted into Buddhism; he is occasionally called *lha čén-po* (*Glr.*) and proverbial for his melodious voice, yet otherwise not of any consequence. — *tsáṅs-pai bú-ga* = *mtsóg-ma Med., Pth.*

ཚད་ *tsad* (cf. *tsod*) 1. **measure**, a. in **a general** sense, **size**: *čc-čúṅ-gi tsád-la* according to the size, in size *Glr.*; *mi-tsad* size of a (full-grown) man *Tar.*; *sku-tsád* stature, size of body, resp. *Glr.*; *zlá-bai dkyil-ₒkór-gyi tsad* the size of the moon's disk *Stg.*; *stobs gyad stóbs-po-čei tsád-du p̔yin-te* his strength was equal to that of a powerful athlete *Dzl.*; **ṭu súm-čui tsad čo gos** *W.* make it thirty cubits in size; *k̔am-tsád-du yčód-pa* to cut into bits piecemeal *Dzl.*; *ču-rgyún k̔yab-tsád-du* as far as the waters covered it *Tar.*; *ṅóm-tsad(-du) ₒtúṅ-ba* to drink one's fill; *ynás-tsad* seems to express chronology *Wdk.*; *mnan-tsad* direction how the pulse is to be felt (or pressed) *Med.*; *k̔yéd-rnams-kyi čós-bslab-tsad* according to your view of religious studies *Mil.*; *dró-tsad* thermometer, *graṅ-droi tsad* id.; *yaṅ-ldii tsad* barometer; *mto-dman-gyi tsad* scale for the rising and falling (of the barometer); all these appear to be proposals of *Cs.* for the respective physical terms; *p̔a-tsád* distance (v. sub *p̔a* II); *tsad-méd(-pa)* **unmeasured, immeasurable, innumerable**, e.g. *yón-tan Dzl.*; *tsad-méd(-pa) bži* the four immeasurables (viz. merits): *byáms-pa, snyiṅ-rje, dká-ba* and *btaṅ-snyóm Dom.*, *spyod-pa* to practise them, *tob-pa* to attain to them *Dzl.*; *ṅa-bas mi tsad yžan yaṅ* an infinity of others besides me *Mil.*

b. **the full** measure, which is **not short** of the proper quantity, **standard**, *tsád-du p̔yin-pa, skyé-ba* (*Sch.* also *ₒk̔yól-ba*) to grow, so as to reach the proper measure; *tsád-du skyés-pa* grown up, full-sized, adj. *Dzl.*; **tsẹ' žág-pa** to set up a pattern, or as a pattern *C.* *tsad-ldán* right (as weight), about the same as 'gaged', just, fair, with regard to persons (ni f.) *C.*

c. **the right** measure, which does **not exceed** the proper quantity: *tsád-yčod-pa* to limit, *bed-čód* the enjoyment *Mil.*; *bza-btúṅ-la* to observe the proper measure in eating and drinking, **tsẹ' dzim-pa, or žág-pa** *C.* id.; *tsád-las ₒdá-ba, tál-ba* to exceed the proper measure frq.; *yid-p̔ám-pa-la tsád-las ₒdás-pa yoṅ* the dejection increases to an excess *Mil.* — To 1, a. may be referred d. those instances in which the word assuming the character of an affix serves to form abstract nouns, such as *ydeṅs-tsád*, or *rtogs-tsád*, *Mil.* in several passages (cf. also *tsod*) further to 1, b may be reckoned e. the signification **all**, *dgé-ba byed tsad* all the pious *Pth.*, to which also *Tar.* 54, 15 may be referred; *sna-tsád* **of every kind, of all sorts** *Glr.*; **žẹ tsẹ' čü'-du soṅ** *C.* all his eating agreed with him extremely well; *ₒdir ldóm-bu-ba byuṅ tsad* all the beggars that show themselves here *Mil.*; *mi yoṅs tsad* all the people that come; *snaṅ tsad čós-skur šar* all that happens appears as *čós-sku Glr.*; *ysuṅ tsad* all that is ordered, proclaimed *Sch.*; *tsogs tsád* all the people assembled *Sch.*; and f. **enough**, esp. with a negation: *ₒdra-ba mi tsad* not having enough of the comparisons, not resting satisfied with them; **ma tsád-de** *W.* = *ma zád-de B.* not only. — 2. a certain **definite measure**, in compounds: *dpag-tsád* a mile, *sor-tsád* an inch: also pleon. *k̔ru-tsad* an ell *Cs.* = *k̔ru*. — 3. **goal, mark**, the point to which racers run *C.*

— 4. *tsad rgyág-pa* **to guess, conjecture, suppose** *Sch.*, cf. *tsod.* — 5. sometimes for *tsád-pa* **heat**; for *tsad-ma* **logic**, *dbu-tsád* Madhyamika logic *Tar.* 179, 17, *Schf.*

ཚད་པ་ *tsád-pa* I. sbst. 1. **heat**, in gen.; *tsád-pa byuṅ-tse* when it grows hot *Glr.*; *tsád-pas γdúṅ-ba* to be tormented by the heat *Glr.*; *tsád-pas*, or vulg. *tsád-pa-nas*, *póg-pa* to be struck by the heat, to receive a sun-stroke; also to be taken ill with dysentery, to which the Tibetans, used to the dry atmosphere of the northern Himalaya, are very liable, when during summer they venture into the southern subtropical regions; *tsád-čan* hot, e.g. *yul*; *tsad-ldán* prob. id.; *me-búm tsád-čan, Lt.* a hot cupping-glass (?). 2. morbid heat of the body, **fever** (*W.* **tsan-žug**); *tsad-pai nad* id., but also **dysentery**, v. above *Glr.*, *C.*; *tsad-pa žag-γnyis-ma* tertian fever *Schr.*; *gya-tsẹ' Sik.* Indian or jungle-fever; **roṅ-tsẹ'** *Sik* common intermittent fever. — II. vb. *Cs.*: **to measure**, = *tsád-du byéd-pa*, *tsad ǰál-ba.*

ཚད་འབུ་ *tsád-ₒbu* **grasshopper, locust** *Sch.*

ཚད་མ་ *tsád-ma*, प्रमाण *Cs.*: **'measure, rule, model, proof, argument; logic'**; *tsád-ma-pa*, or *-mḱan*, *Cs.* logician, dialectitian; *tsád-mai bstan-bčós* a dialectical work *Pth.*; *tsad-ma γžuṅ* an original work on dialectics *Cs.*; *tsád-ma ₒgrél-ba* commentary to it *Cs.*; *saṅs-rgyás-kyi bka tsád-mar bžág-pa* the words of Buddha reduced to a dogmatical system (?) *Pth.* — *tsád-ma kun-ₒdús*, *tsád-ma sde bdun* titles of books mentioned by *Was.*

ཚན་ *tsan*, 1. a root = *tsa* in *tsá-ba* **hot, warm** *C.* and *B.*; *tsán-mo* (**tsẹ́m-mo**), *in W.* **tsán-te**, e.g. with *ču*, **ču tsẹ́m-mo** *C.*, **ču-tsán** *W.*, hot water *Dzl.*, warm water *Lt.*; *zan-drón tsán-mo* warm food *Lt.*; *ču-skól tsán-mo* boiling water *Mṅg.*; **ša tsọ́-pa tsẹ́m-mo** boiled meat, in Lhasa brought warm to the market; **tsẹn-ₒdí táṅ-wa** *C.* to proceed capitally against, ni. f.; *tsán-te* **sharp, biting, pungent**, *W.* also sbst.: **spice**, esp. **red pepper.** — *tsan-žug W.* **fever.** — *tsan-ró Sch.*: **'hot**, the sensation of heat'. — 2. = *tsá-bo*: **pa-tsẹ́n** cousin by the father's, **ma-tsẹ́n** by the mother's side *C.*; *pa-tsán* also = *pa-spún*; *ḱu-tsán* v. *ḱú-bo.* — 3. **series, order, class**, *sde-tsán* id.; *bži-tsán* a class or collection of four things, tetrad *Gram.*; *drug-tsán-du sdébs-pa* to put together in classes of six *Mil.*; *don-tsán Tar.* 96, 14, a certain class of ideas, range of thoughts *Schf.* — 4. as termination of some collective nouns: *γnyen-tsán*, *nye-tsan* **kindred, relations**, *nye-tsán bdúd-kyi bšol-ₒdébs yin Mil.*; *blón-po-tsan lṅá-po* the five embassies, ni f. *Glr.* — 5. *nán-tsan* **part**, of a country, **district**, *Tar.* 90, 20. — 6. *čos-tsan* any treatise under **a distinct head** or **title** in a volume *Cs.* — 7. **difference** *Sch.*; *le-tsan* different divisions, sections, chapters. — 8. **much, large, copious, great**, **ḱa tsan čin-te** *W.* much deep snow; *tsan-čé-ba*, *tsan-čen* **very much, a great deal**, *las ṅán ni tsan-čé* a great many bad actions *Thgr.*; *lo tsan-če-ba* a plentiful harvest, rich crop *Glr.*; hence *tsán-po* **a dignitary, grandee** *Pth.*; *ḱams-tsán*, 1. **prefect of a provincial association**, in large convents, such as Sera and others. 2. **association, club.**

ཚབ་ *tsab* (cf. *ₒtsáb-pa*), **representative**, com. *tsáb-po C.*, *W.*, **ḱó-la tsáb-po yod** he has got a representative, proxy; in reference to a thing: **equivalent, substitute**, *des tsab ruṅ* it may be replaced by this, *tsab ruṅ tsam-mo* this may perhaps be used as a substitute *Wdṅ.*; **táb-pii tsab čó-če** *W.* to use as a mop; *ṅas tsab byao* I shall supply his place *Tar.*; *tsáb-tu* **instead of, in the place of**, *már-mei* instead of a lamp, for a lamp *Glr.*; in *W.* **tsáb-la** very common. Chiefly in compounds: *sku-tsáb* resp. = *tsáb-po* **representative of a superior**, hence, as may be the case, **vice-roy, delegate, commissioner, agent.** — *rgyal-tsáb* v. *rgyál-ba.* — *do-tsab Schr.* prob. = *tsáb-po* = *sku-tsáb.* — *rta-tsáb* a thing given as an equivalent for a horse *Cs.* — *nor-tsáb* goods serving as a compensation for something else. — *pa-tsáb* **guardian, trustee.** — *bla-tsáb* representative of a Lama, **Vice-Lama.** — *bu-tsáb* **adopted child, foster-child.** — *mi-tsáb Schr.* **negociator, mediator; hostage** (?).

ཚབ་ཚབ་ *ťsab-ťsáb, mig ťsab-ťsáb byéd-pa* **to blink** or **twinkle** with the eyes *C.*, also *W.*

ཚབས་ *ťsabs* 1. mostly with *če, čén-po,* **very great, very much**, *sdig-pa ťsabs-čé-bar ₒdug* it proves a very great sin, *mgó-bo ₒk̔or ťsabs-čé-na* when much dizziness intervenes *Lt.*; **ţ im-dhan-gal ťsab čém-po* C.*, great, serious transgression; *ₒgál-ťsabs-čan* sinning heinously. — 2. *ťsábs-pa* and *-po Cs.*, who also designates it as resp., **peril, fear, sin** (rather questionable); **difficulty, trouble** (might perh. be more adequate); *búd-med ₒó-ťsabs-la p̔an Wdñ.* it is of use in milk-diseases of the women.

ཚམ་དམ་ *ťsam-dám* **noisy, blustering, alarming** *Sch.*

ཚམ་ཚུམ་, ཚམ་ཚོམ་ *ťsam-ťsúm, ťsam-ťsóm* (cf. *ťsóm-pa, tě-ťsom*) **doubt, hesitation, wavering,** *ťsam-ťsúm byéd-pa* **to doubt, hesitate, waver**; *ťsam-ťsúm-čan, ťsam-me-ťsom-mé* **doubtful, wavering, undecided,** *p̔an-ťsúñ p̔yág-la ťsam-me-ťsom-mér lús-pai ťse* whilst both of them were uncertain as to saluting (who should salute first) *Pth.*

ཚའི་ཏའུ་ *ťsai-tau* (Chinese) **chopping-knife** *C.*

ཚའི་སྐྱོགས་ *ťsai-skyógs* **scoop, basting-ladle** *C.*

ཚར་ *ťsar* 1. also *ťser* **time** *Pth.* vulgo; *ťsar-γčig* one time, once; *ťsar γčig-la* also = *srib-γčig-la* in one moment; *ťsar γsum* threefold, in three specimens, copies *Tar.*; *ťsar bži Dzl.* ༢༢༤, 8, in four divisions, sorts, qualities (?) — 2. also *ťsar-ťsar* **ends of threads, fringes,** in webs, *k̔a-ťsár Ld.* also *ru-ťsár* fringes at the beginning, *p̔on-ťsar* at the end of a web *Cs.* — 3. **thin strips of cane,** for wicker-work, *ťsar-zám* cane-bridge *C.* — 4. *ťsar-slág* v. *ťsa-ru.* — 5. v. *ₒťsar-ba.*

ཚར་བོང་ *ťsar-boñ* officinal plant in *Lh.*, *Carduus nutans*, but not agreeing with the description in *Wdñ.*

ཚར་མ་ *ťsár-ma*, fem. *ťsár-mo Bal.* **old.**

ཚར་ཚར་ *ťsar-ťsar* v. *ťsar* 2.

ཚལ་ *ťsal* 1. provinc. also *ťsol,* **wood, grove,** as a place for hunting and recreation, *ťsal stúg-po Dzl.*; *nags-ťsál* id.; **garden,** *mé-tog-gi* flower-garden *Ph.*; *ťsal yañ-tse (Chin.) C.* kitchen-garden. — 2. *smyu-gui-ťsal* one kind of the fabulous food of man in the primitive world *Glr.*; also the 'unploughed rice' is called *ₒbras sa-lu-ťsal.* — 3. v. *mťsal.*

ཚལ་པ་ *ťsál-pa* (*Sch. ťsal-ba?*) 1. also *šiñ-ťsal* **chip** (of wood), **splinter,** *nón-po* a sharp, piercing splinter *Dzl.*; **billet** *Glr.*; **thin board, veneer** etc.; **shiver, fragment,** *ťsál-pa bdún-du gas Dzl.*; *ťsál-bu* dimin., small chip or shiver *W.*: **ťsál-bu ťon soñ** a small piece is broken out. — 2. **bunch,** of flowers, of ears of corn etc., a lock of hair cut off *W.*

ཚལ་མ་ *ťsál-ma* vulgo for *dro,* **breakfast,** *ťsal-ma za-ba* **to breakfast,** *ťsál-ma zá-bu-rnams* 'companions at a great man's table' (?) *Cs.*; *ťsál-mai lam* = *ťsa-lám* v. *ťsá-ba* extr.; *ťsal bóg-pa* = *dro btáb-pa* to make a morning-halt on a journey; *ťsal-rtiñ* the time from breakfast till dinner, opp. to *sñá-dro*, q. v.

ཚས་ *ťsas* (*ťsás-po Cs.*) 1. *W.* for *ťsal* **garden,** *ťsas-skór, ťsás-k̔añ* garden-bed, *ťsás-mk̔an* gardener. — 2. of a woman in child-birth: *ťsas-kyis γso* (?) *Med.*

ཚི་ *ťsi* num. fig.: 48.

ཚི་ཀ་ *ťsi-ka* (or *ťsi-rka?*) *C.* **furrow** in a ploughed field.

ཚི་གུ་, ཚིག་གུ་ *ťsi-gu, ťsig-gu* 1. **kernel** or **nut** contained in the stone of a stone-fruit, *k̔ám-bui* of an apricot *Lt., C.* (*W.*: **rťsi-gu**). — 2. *Ld.* a large **muller** or **grinding-stone** = *ju-lúm*; **musket-ball, bullet.**

ཚི་བ་ *ťsi-ba C., W.* **ťsi** **tough, viscous, sticky matter,** esp. **clammy dirt,** e.g. in the wool of sheep; *ťsi dám-po* solid dirt, *bád-kan-gyi ťsi-ba Med.* **tenacious slime;** *ťsi(-ba)-čan* **sticky, clammy, dirty;** **ťsi-du* W.* **dirty, unclean, filthy,** esp. in a religious sense, = **kyug-ḍho* C.*; **ñe zúg-po ťsi-du soñ** says a girl euphemistically for: I have the menses.

ཚིག་ *ťsig* 1. **word,** in its strict sense, *'bdé-bar γšégs-pa ni' bde-ba dañ γšegs-pai ťsig γnyis-las med, bde-bar γšegs-pa* **are** only two words, viz. *bde-ba* and *γšegs-pa Lex.*; *˳dri-bai ťsig* interrogative (word), such as *či; ťsig sgrig-pa* to connect or arrange words; as a sbst.: **construction**, the order in which words are to be placed; **grammatical form**, *dá-ltar-gyi ťsig* form of the present tense; *ťsig-grógs, ťsig-grógs-kyi dbáṅ-gis Tar.; Schf.*: 'by the force of construction' (?) *ťsig-˳grél Tar.* **explanation of words**; *ťsig-˳grós Sch.*: '**course of speech**, connexion of words'; *ťsig-p̔rad, ťsig-rgyán* **particle**, a small word not inflected; *ťsig-˳brú Schr.*: **a separate word** or **syllable**, *ťsig-˳brú-γnyer-pa Sch.* 'linguist, philologist, purist'; *ťsig-˳bru-lčibs Lex.?* — 2. **word, saying, speech**, subject of a discourse, *ťsig-snyán(-pa)* kind word, friendly speech, *ťsig-˳ǰám* id., *brtse-bai ťsig* an affectionate word *Glr.*; **ťsig-súb* W.* hard, angry, bad words; **ťsig-ṅán, ťsig-zúr* W.* id.; *rtág-par ma mťóṅ-bai ťsig ťos-nas* always receiving the answer, that (she who was sought) had not been seen; *ťsig-med-par ˳gyúr-ba* not being able to utter a word (from pain) *Dzl.; but k̔a-ťsig-méd-par γsól-ba ˳débs-pa Mil.* prob. to pray without hypocrisy; *ťsig nyúṅ-la don čé-ba Mil.* saying much in few words; *ťsig-k̔yál-pa = kyal-ka Dzl.*; *γžán-gyi ťsig γčod-pa* to interrupt one in his speech; *ťsig-γsal* **a clear word, perspicuous style** *Cs.*; *ťsig-˳ból* **easy** or **fluent style** *Cs.*; *ťsig-la mk̔as-pa* skilful in selecting words *Cs.*; *bdén-ťsig* v. *bdén-pa* extr.; *brdzún-ťsig* **falsehood, lie** *Cs.*

ཚིག་གུ་ *ťsig-gu* v. *ťsi-gu.*

ཚིག་པ་ *ťsig-pa* 1. v. *˳ťsig-pa.* — 2. sbst., *W.* also *ťsig-po* **anger, indignation, vexation, provocation**, *ťsig-pa zá-ba* **to be angry** *Pth.*, frq.; **ťsig(-po) k̔ol* W.* his anger kindles.

ཚིག་པོ་ *ťsig-po* 1. = *ťsig Cs.* — 2. v. *ťsig-pa* 2.

ཚིགས་ *ťsigs*, less frq. *ťsigs-pa, ťsigs-ma* 1. **member** between two joints, hence *ťsigs-mtsáms* joint *S.g.*; **joint**, *sor-ťsigs* the joints of the fingers, **knuckles** *Cs.*; *ťsigs ˳búd-pa Cs.*, **ṭúl-če, bóg-če* W.* to put out of joint, **to dislocate, to sprain**; *ťsigs ˳ǰúg-pa* to reduce a dislocated joint *Cs.*; *ťsigs-nád, ťsigs-zúg* articular disease, pain in the joints, gout; joint of the back-bone, **vertebra**; **spine**, also *sgal-ťsigs*, vulgo *ťsigs-rús*, hence **ťsig-gúr* W.* hump, hunch; **joint, knee, knot,** *sog-ťsigs* knot of a stalk of corn or straw, *smyug-ťsigs* knot of cane *Cs.*; member of a generation *Glr.*; **metrical division, verse,** *ťsigs-su bčád-de smrá-ba* to speak in verse, *ťsigs (-su) bčad(-pa)* **strophe, stanza,** *ťsigs-bčád byéd-pa* to compose verses, to speak in verse *Dzl.; dus-ťsigs* **division of time,** e. g. season *Pth.* — 2. *ťsigs-ma* **sediment, residuum, residue,** *smán-gyi* of a medicine *Dzl.; már-gyi Dzl.* olive-husks, oil-cake; *ťsigs-ró = ťsigs-ma.*

ཚིབ(ས)་ *ťsib(s), ťsib-nad* **measles** *Sch.*

ཚིམ་པ་ *ťsim-pa* vb. **to be content**; gen. adj. **content, satisfied, satiated, consoled,** frq.: *yid ťsim-par gyur* he was satisfied, appeased, consoled; *ǰi ˳dód-pai yid ťsim-ste* all her (their) wishes being satisfied *Glr.*; *dga-bdés ťsim-par gyúr-čiṅ* being indeed over-happy *Pth.*; *ťsim-par byéd-pa* to satisfy, with the dat. or accus. of the person.

ཚིམ་ཚིམ་ *ťsim-ťsim, mig ťsim-ťsim ˳dug C.* the eye is **dazzled.**

ཚིར་ *ťsir* **order, course, succession, turn,** prob. only col., **ṅá-la ťsir yoṅ* or *bab** it is my turn; **ná-so ťsir-la** succession by seniority; **gán-ťsir žón-ťsir** id.; **ťsir-la, ťsir-du, ťsir daṅ** by turns, every one in his turn or course, one thing after the other.

ཚིར་བ་ *ťsir-ba* v. *˳ťsir-ba.*

ཚིལ་ *ťsil* **fat,** not melted, *ťsil-bu* id. *S.g.*; *lúg-ťsil* **mutton fat,** *p̔ág-ťsil* pork-fat, **bacon**; *k̔ál-ťsil, k̔óg-ťsil, gród-ťsil* **suet, lard**; *sbó-ťsil* **bacon**; *lóṅ-ťsil* **intestinal fat.** — *spra-ťsil* **wax** *B., C. (W. *mum*)*; *ťsil-ku* liquid fat, in the living body, or melted fat *Pth.* — *ťsil-čan, ťsil-ldán* **fat,** *ťsil-méd* **lean.** — *ťsil-ró* remains of lard after melting. — *ťsil-šúbs* 1. **straight-gut, rectum** *Med.* 2. **sausage** *Cs.* —

ཚིལ་དིང་ *ťsil-diṅ Ld.* **mortar and pestle.**

ཚིས་ *ťsis Mil., Thgy.* prob. secondary form of *rtsis.*

ཚུ་ *tsu* 1. num. fig.: 78. — 2. the contrary of *p'a* II., root of the words signifying **hitherward, on this side**; *tsú-k'a Cs.* (*tsúr-k'a* q v.), more frq. *tsú-rol* **this side** (opp. to *p'á-rol*), *tsú-rol-na* adv. **on this side**, postp. with genit. adj. **on this side**; *tsú-rol-tu*, this way, to this place; *tsú-rol-nas* from this side; *tsú-rol-pa* one on this side, one belonging to this (our) party *Stg.*; *tsu-bi* one of this side, *p'a-bi* one of the other side *Cs.*, provinc. (?). Cf. *tsun*, *tsur*.

ཚུ་འུ་ *tsu-u*(?) *C.*, prob. Chinese, for the Tibetan *skyúr-ru*, acc. to some: **vinegar**, acc. to others: **a pulpy product**, prepared of various kinds of fruit, mixed with vinegar, sugar, and spices, and having been left to ferment, used, like mustard, as a condiment, which in India is called 'chutney'.

ཚུག *tsug* 1. *Sch.*: **'group, object'**(?); *tsúg-so W.* all the households or villages placed under one Gopa. — 2. rarely for *tsug*; thus *ǰi-tsug Glr.* 49, inst. of *či-tsug*.

ཚུག་པ་(ལ་) *tsúg-pa(-la) W.* **to, up to, till**, *gaṅ tsúg-pa* **how far, how long?** **ṅa Nyúṅ-ti-ru čá-če tsúg-pa-la** until I go to Sultanpur; *gaṅ tsúg-pa ... de tsúg-pa* **so far as.**

ཚུགས་པ་ *tsugs-pa* 1. v. *ₒtsugs-pa.* — 2. **to do one harm, to hurt, to inflict**, mostly with a negative, *bar-čád ma tsúgs-par* without having hurt me *Mil.*; *ṅá-la mes, nad-kyis* etc. *mi tsugs* fire, disease etc. can do me no harm, *Glr.*, *Mil.*, frq. — 3. sbst., also *tsúgs-k'aṅ*, *W.* **tsug-sa**, **caravansary**, or merely a level, open place near a village, where traveller's may encamp, or where public business is transacted; also for **धर्मशाला, hall of judgment; hospital.**

ཚུད་པ་ *tsud-pa* v. *ₒtsud-pa.*

ཚུན་ *tsun* = *tsu* 2., gen. with *čad* or *čad* or *la*, signifying **within, by, not later than,** as postp. c. accus., *rabs bdun tsun-čád* within seven generations, (they will be happy) even to the seventh generation, *Dzl.*; *sáṅ-gi nyi-ma-p'yéd tsún-la* by to-morrow noon (it must be finished) *Glr.*; **dá-wa čé' tsun 'é leb** *C.* shall he come in less than half a month? *bu daṅ bú-mo tsun-čád* even to the children, not even the children being excluded *Tar.* 119, 3. —

Note. In the terms *p'an* and *tsun*, like *yan* and *man(-čad)*, the significations given by *Cs.*: **from, from a certain place or time forward, till, until,** are not properly inherent to the word, but are to be inferred in each separate instance from the figurative application of the original sense of the root.

ཚུབ་མ་ *tsúb-ma*, *ₒtsúb-ma* **storm**, *tsub-čéb*, *rluṅ-tsúb* **gale, hurricane**, *k'a-tsub* snow-storm; *bu-tsub* (*ǰu-tsub?*) gust of wind, (*lha*) *ₒdrei bu-tsub* whirlwind; fig. *p'rag-dóg-gi tsúb-ma Mil.* **a violent fit of envy**; *sems-tsúb* **trouble of mind** *Cs.*

ཚུར་ *tsur* **hither, to this place, hitherward** (cf. *p'ar*), *tsur šog* (resp. *ysegs*, in later lit. *byon*) come hither, come here! also in an objective sense: *tsur ₒóṅ-ba* **to return home** *Pth.*, *Tar.*; *ₒdi-nas tsur bšád-nas* speaking to me through this (tube) *Glr.*; almost pleon. in *tsúr-la nyon* listen to me! *Mil.* frq.; *tsúr-ka* **this side**, the this side river-bank, declivity, party etc., similarly: *tsúr-logs*, *tsúr-p'yogs*.

ཚུར་(མོ་), མཚུར་(མོ་) *tsúr(-mo)*, *mtsúr(-mo)* **colouring matter, pigment**, prob. = *sa-tsúr Stg.*, acc. to *Cs.* **mineral paint**, *nag-* black, *ser-* yellow, *dmar-tsúr* red-paint; for *nag tsúr Sch.* has: green vitriol; in *Zam.* also *rús-kyi tsur* is named.

ཚུལ་ *tsul* शील 1. **manner, way, form, character, nature**, *tsul ǰi-ltar ... de bžin-du* as — so *Wdṅ.*, *zér-tsul*, *ₒgrúl-tsul*, *bsám-tsul* the way in which a person speaks, walks, thinks; *ynás-tsul* v. *ynás-pa*; *ynás-tsul* and *snáṅ-tsul* **being** and **appearing**, philosoph. terms for **reality** and **appearance** *Was.* (297); *ytóṅ-tsul* the way of giving, i.e. a certain quantity given, dose *Stg.*; *mi sdug-pai sna-tsógs-kyis* (to damage) in various vicious ways *Mil.*; *tsul de k'ó-nas* by that same way of proceeding *Tar.*; hence *tsúl-gyis* in consequence of, by means of *Pth.* and elsewhere; *snan smrás-pai tsul* the character of his last speech *Dzl.*; *rgya-bód-kyi ₒbrél-tsul* the mode or kind of intercourse, the relations between Tibet and China *Glr.*; *p̔yág-gi tsúl-du* in a way as if he were saluting *Mil.*; *gus-gús-kyi tsúl(-du) byéd-pa* to make a semblance of veneration, to make gestures of reverence *Mil.*; *mi mḱyén-pai tsúl-du byás-te* pretending not to know *Mil.*; (cf. *tsúl-ₒčos-pa* v. *čos-pa*); *dge-slóṅ-gi tsúl-du* in the guise of a monk *Tar.*; *mai tsul ₒdzin-pa* to assume the mother's form, figure *Tar.*; *glaṅ-čén-gyi tsúl-du*, (Buddha came down) in the shape of, or as, an elephant *Glr.*; *dád-pai tsúl-gyis* in the way of faith, with a believing mind *Pth.*; *mi-rtág tsúl-du γda* it exists in the way of transientness, it is of a transitory nature *Mil.*; *mdzád-pa bču-γnyís-kyi tsúl-gyis* in the manner, in the order, of the twelve deeds *Glr.*; *šas čé-bai tsúl-gyis* for the most part, *Tar.* 50, 15; **way of acting, conduct, deportment, course of life,** *sṅá-mai tsul* your former conduct *Mil.*; *dé-lta-bui dgé-bai tsul de tós-nas* hearing such an example of virtue related. — 2. emphat.: **the right way,** good manners, order, rule; *tsul (daṅ) mṫún(-pa)* **orderly, regular, sensible, reasonable,** *brgyá-la tsul-mṫún re tsam ₒbyúṅ-na Mil.* if but once in a hundred cases something sensible is uttered; *tsul-ldán, tsúl-čan* regular, methodical *Cs.*; also **just,** conformable to duty, *tsúl-bžin-pa* adv. *tsul-bžin-du* id.; *tsul-méd, tsul-bžin-min* **irregular, unjust** *Cs.*; *srid-žui tsul spyód-čiṅ* fulfilling a child's duty; *tsúl-las nyams* **growing remiss in one's duty,** neglecting, breaking one's duty; esp. *tsúl-ḱrims* **religious or moral duty, moral law; monastic vows,** *tsúl-ḱrims-čan* 1. being bound by such *Sch.*; 2. observing such *Cs.*; *tsúl-ḱrims srúṅ-ba* to keep them, *ₒjig-pa, nyáms-pa* to break them; *tsúl-ḱrims,* as a personal name, is much in favour. — 3. **species, kind,** *nád-tsul* species or kind of disease, *zás-tsul* species of food *S.g.* (not frq.). — 4. joined to the root of a verb: *yóṅ tsul,* **when,** or **as,** he came, *W.*

ཚེ་ *tse* I. num. figure: 108.

II. sbst. 1. **time,** in a gen. sense, = *dus B.*; *yód(-pai) tse(-na),* **when** it is, **when** it was; *gáṅ(-gi) tse(-na), de(i) tse(-na)* **at which time, at that time, then,** frq. *tse-ré* all the time (?), *nyin-tse-ré* the whole day, *tsan-tse-ré* the whole night *W.* — 2. **time of life,** **tse-ghaṅ-tsọn-čug** imprisonment for life *C.*; *tse γčig-gi drós-pai gos* v. *drós-pa*; **life,** *tse ₒdi* this, the present, life, *tse-p̔yi(-ma)* a future period of life (also merely: *ₒdi p̔yi,* without *tse*); *tse sṅá-ma* an earlier period of existence, relative to the transmigration of souls, yet *tse ₒdi* and *p̔yi* may also be used in a Christian sense; *tse riṅ-ba* long life, *tse ṫúṅ-ba* short life; *tse-riṅ* is also a very common name both of men and women; *rgyál-ba daṅ tse-riṅ-bar šóg-čig* happiness and long life (to the king)! *Dzl.*; *tse(-daṅ) -ldán(-pa),* आयुष्मान्, title or epithet of Bodhisattwas; *tse-dpag-méd* name of Buddha; **tse p̔id-če** *W.* to earn a livelihood; *tse ₒḱyér-žiṅ šór-ba* to come off with one's life, to have a narrow escape; *tse ṫár-du ₒjúg-pa* v. *ṫár-ba*; *tse(-las) ₒdás(-pa)* having died *Dzl.* — 3. *Bal.* **sex,** **p̔ó-tse, mó-tse**, male, female sex.

Comp. *tse-skábs* v. *skabs.* — *tse-čú* water of life *Glr.* — *tse-γnyís-pa* of an amphibious nature *Cs.* — *tse-ltógs* a poor, starving vagrant, beggar *W.* — *tse-mdáṅs Lt.* = *byad-mdaṅs* healthy appearance, a fine, fresh complexion. — *tse-tsád* duration of life. — *tse-mdzad, Wdk.* 457, an attribute of the gods, resembling a small plate with fruit. — *tse-rábs* period of existence, duration of a re-birth, a great many of which acc. to Buddhist doctrine every man has to pass through *Dzl.*; *tse-rábs-kyi blá-ma Mil.* a man that is always re-born as a Lama.

ཚེ་དཔད་ *tse-pád Ephedra saxatilis,* a little alpine shrub with red berries, which are said to be roasted and pulverized, to give greater pungency to snuff.

ཚེ་རེ་ *tse-ré* 1. v. *tse.* — 2. v. *tsér-ka.*

ཚེག་ *tseg W.* **tsag** 1. **point, dot,** also *nag-tség.* — 2. more particularly **the point separating syllables,** *bar-tség,* id.; *p̔yi-tség* likewise, in as far as it follows a letter *Gram.*; *tseg-bar* that which stands between two points or tsegs, **a syllable.**

ཚེགས་ *ťsegs* **troublesome, difficult, hard,** *ťsegs-če* very troublesome, *rkaṅ ťsegs-čé Mil.* much (fruitless) running to and fro; *ťsegs-méd* it is not difficult; *ťsegs-méd(-par)* easily adv.; *ťségs-pa* trouble, toil, difficulty *Sch.*; *p̀ran-ťsegs* little troubles or difficulties *Cs.*

ཚེམ་(པོ་) *ťsém(-po)*, **seam,** cf. *ˌťsém-pa*; *ťsém-bzo-pa*, *ťsém-pa* **tailor** *W.*; *ťsém-po ˌgrol* the seam opens, comes loose; *ťsem-méd* without a seam; *ťsém-bu Lex., Sch.*: what has been stitched, darned, quilted.

ཚེམས་ *ťsems*, resp. **tooth,** *ťséms-šiṅ* tooth-pick *Dzl.*

ཚེམས་པ་ *ťsems-pa* to have the disadvantage, to come off a loser, not receiving a full share *Sch.*

ཚེར་ *ťser* 1. = *ťsar* **time** vulgo; *ťser-ťsér, Mil.*, prob. **many times, repeatedly.** — 2. v. the following.

ཚེར་ཀ་ *ťsér-ka W.* also *ťse-ré, ťse-ri* **sorrow, grief, pain, affliction,** **ťse-ré čo mi go** do not grieve! **ťser čúg-če** to afflict, to grieve (not in *B.*).

ཚེར་མ་ *ťsér-ma, W.***ťser-máṅ** 1. **thorn, prick, brier,** *Dzl. ťser zug soṅ* I have run a thorn into (my hand, foot); *ťser-mai mgo* a deer's head po. spoken of *Mil.*; *ťsér-ma ˌdón-pa* to pull out a thorn; *nya-ťsér* fish-bone *Sch.*; *ťsér-ma-čan* 1. thorny, prickly, briery. 2. like thorns, *Thgy.* — 2. **thorn-bush, bramble, brake** *ťser-dkár, ťser-stár*, buck-thorn, *Hippophaē rhamnoïdes*, **ťser-tar-lú-lu** *Ld.*, the berries of it (extremely sour). — *ťser-ťágs* thorn-hedge (in Tibet gen. dead hedges). — *ťser-lúm* yellow raspberry *Sik.* *ťser-lhág* n. of a disease *Lt.*

ཚེས་ *ťses* **अहन्,** 1. **day of the month,** *ťses-gráṅs* **date,** always expressed by the cardinal number, *ťses-γčig* etc., *ťses-bčú* the tenth, in certain months a festival day, *ťses-bču-mčód-pa* sacrifice and beer-drinking on that day; *ťses-bčúi ˌčám-yig* programme of the religious dances performed on that occasion; *zlá-ba ťsés-pa* and *ťses-γsum-zlá-ba.* — 2. symb. num.: 15.

ཚོ་ *ťso* 1. num. figure: 138. — 2. sbst. **troop, number, host,** yet hardly ever standing alone, or governing a genit. case, but like a termination affixed: *gróṅ-mi-ťso* the peasants (of the village), *k̀yéd rnál-ˌbyor-pa-ťso* ye saints! In some instances its substantive character is more apparent, thus in *ťsóṅ-pa-ťso, mk̀ás-pa-ťso, bá-ťso* it may be rendered by: a troop of merchants, a society of learned men (or the learned), a herd of cows (*Cs.*); but most frq. it stands (at least in later lit.) as plural termination of pronouns, so: *ṅéd-ťso* **we,** *k̀oṅ-ťso* **they,** *ˌdi-ťso* **these,** or it is affixed to numerals: *ˌbum-ťso* 100 000. — *yul-ťso* v. *yul.* — 3. adj. **hot** *Bal.*

ཚོ་བ་ *ťsó-ba* **fat, greasy,** *ťso-k̀ú* fat gravy, *ťso-ldír* unwieldy with fatness (*ťso ˌdug mi ˌdug*, or *bud ma bud*, is it fat or not? being with young or not? *Sch.*?)

ཚོ་ལོ་ *ťsó-lo W.* vulg. = *ˌp̀oṅs*, cf. *ˌp̀oṅ-ťsos.*

ཚོགས་ *ťsogs Ssk.* **गण,** (cf. *ˌťsógs-pa*) 1. **an assemblage** of men (implying, however, compared with *ťso*, a larger number of individuals, not at once to be surveyed), *Cs.*: *ťsogs sdú-ba* to call an assembly, *ˌgyéd-pa* to dismiss it; *ťsogs ˌdu* an assembly meets, *ˌgye* it dissolves; *W.*:**šol soṅ** it is adjourned, **ṭol soṅ** it is broken up; *dpuṅ(-gi), dmag (-gi)-ťsogs* army frq.; *yul-ťsogs* village community, country-parish, **yul-ťsog nyi laṅ-te yod** *W.* two parishes have set out; **human society,** *ťsógs-kyi náṅ-nas ˌbyúṅ-ba Stg.*, **ťsog ḍhaṅ gyé-wa** *C.* to retire from society; *ťsógs-naṅ mi ˌgró-ba* not mixing with society *Dó.*; *čós-ťsogs* has been introduced by us, with the concurrence of our native Christians, as the word for **'congregation, church,** ἐκκλησία'. — 2. **accumulation, multitude,** of things, **šiṅ-ťsog** *W.* wood, thicket, copse, bush, shrub; *mé-ťsogs* mass of fire, *Thgy.*; in a more special sense = *dgé-bai ťsogs*, or *bsód-nams-kyi ťsogs*, accumulation of merit acquired by virtue, *ťsogs γsóg-pa* to accumulate such frq.; *ťsogs ma bság-pai mi* almost the same as a wicked, godless person; *ťsogs(-kyi) ˌk̀or(-lo)*, **गणचक्र,** sacrificial offering, a quantity of victuals, trinkets, and other articles being disposed in a circle as an oblation, *Mil.* and elsewh.; *ťsogs-ₒk'ór skór-ba* prob., like *sóm-pa* to prepare such an offering; *ťsogs γnyis Glr.* was explained by *bsod-nams-kyi ťsogs daṅ ye-ses-kyi ťsogs*; *sna-ťsógs* of all kinds, merely signifies 'many'. — 3. *ťsogs drug Mil.* and elsewh., *Was.* 290, **'kinds' of perception** by the senses, which are supposed to be more or less in number, yet the etymology of the word rather suggests the groups of objects perceptible by means of the (6) senses. —

Comp. *ťsogs-k'áṅ* meeting-house *Cs.* — *ťsogs-ₒk'ór* v. above. — *ťsogs-grál Mil.* 1. row of people in an assembly 2. row of offerings, ni f. — *ťsógs-čan-ma Sch.* 'songstress, prostitute'. — *ťsogs-mčóg* a most splendid assemblage, *ťsogs-mčog-dge-ₒdún Thgy.* — *ťsogs-γtám* speech addressed to a meeting *Cs.* — *ťsogs-stón* a high sacrificial festival *Pth.* — *ťsogs(-kyi)-bdág(-po)* गणेश, son of Siwa, the god of wisdom, furnished with a thick belly and the head of an elephant; appears also in the Buddhism of later times. — *ťsogs-dpón* president or chairman of a meeting *Cs.* — *ťsogs-záṅs Sch.*: 'the meeting-kettle, the point of union or its symbol'. — *ťsogs-sa* place of meeting *Cs.* — *ťsogs-γsóg* accumulated merit, tantamount to offerings and gifts bestowed on priests, also any service or work done to or for a priest *Mil.*

ཚོང་ *ťsoṅ* (*Cs.* = *zoṅ* merchandize, but more corr.:) **trade, traffic, commerce,** **ṕag-ťsóṅ** *W.* smuggling-trade, **čó-če, tóṅ-če**; *ťsóṅ-gi k'e* profit, gain, *gun* loss in trading; *ťsoṅ byéd-pa Glr.*, **gyag-pa** *C.*, **gyab-če** *W.* (cf. above), to carry on trade; *ťsoṅ brgúd-pa* id. *Sch.*

Comp. *ťsoṅ-skad* commercial language, business-like style, terms of trade. — *ťsóṅ-k'aṅ* store-house, magazine. — *ťsoṅ-gru* trading-vessel, merchantman. — *ťsóṅ-grogs* commercial friend, correspondent. — *ťsoṅ-čaṅ* pledging in beer, after a bargain has been struck. — *ťsóṅ-čad* bill of purchase, deed of sale. — *ťsoṅ-mťun* commercial intercourse. — *ťsóṅ-ₒdus* market people *Pth.* — *ťsóṅ-ₒdus-sa* market-place. — *ťsóṅ-rdal* that quarter of a city which is chiefly inhabited by merchants. — *ťsoṅ-pa* **merchant, trader, seller**; *ₒbru-ťsoṅ-pa* corn-merchant, *čaṅ-ťsoṅ-pa* dealer in wine and other liquors. — *γser-daṅ-dnul-(gyi) ťsóṅ-pa* exchanger of gold and silver coins. — *ťsóṅ-dpon*, *Hind.* *čaudhari*, head of a commercial establishment, the principal merchant in a city, under whose control all the rest, and the market in general, are standing; the chief leader of a caravan, to whom all that have joined in it are subordinate *Glr.* — *ťsoṅ-spógs* proceeds of trade; *ťsoṅ-spógs byéd-pa*, *ťsoṅ-spógs-la ₒgró-ba* to engage in commercial speculations *Dzl.* — *ťsoṅ-ₒṕrúl* commerce, *ťsoṅ-ₒṕrúl-gyi γnas* market. — *ťsoṅ-zán* (cf. *ťsoṅ-čáṅ*) meal after settling a business. — *ťsoṅ-zóṅ* goods, merchandize. — *ťsóṅ-sa* commercial place, market.

ཚོང་ཚོང་ *ťsoṅ-ťsóṅ* 1. a kind of **ornament** *Cs.* 2. = *ťsoṅ-ťsóṅ*.

ཚོད་ *ťsod* (prop. the same as *ťsad*) 1. **measure, proportion,** in a general sense = **the right and just measure**; *ťsod ₒdzin-pa*, (*bzúṅ-ba*) *W.* **zúm-če** 1. to take measure, to measure, to measure out, to survey, *yul* land, **yul-ťsód-zum-k'an** land-surveyor *W.* 2. to estimate, to rate, to appraise, to tax, *raṅ-gi ťsod mi ₒdzin* he overrates himself (his own powers) *Dzl.* 3. to observe the right measure, to be temperate, *zas-čáṅ-la* in eating and drinking *Glr.*; *zás-ťsod ma zin čuṅs gyúr-na* when below the proper measure, i.e. when too little is eaten *Sg.* 4. to try, to tempt, to lead into temptation *W.*; *ťsod-ltá-ba*, *lén-pa B.* and vulg., *Cs.* also *ťsod bgám-pa* **to try, prove,** **ťsod ma ltos** I have not tried it yet *W.*, **tig-ťsód ma ltos** id., *ťsod ltá-ba*, *len-pa* also **to sound, to sift, examine, spy out,** *ťsód-len-pa* sbst., **spy**; *séms-kyi* or *nyáms-(kyi) ťsod lén-pa* to examine, find out or sift another's thoughts or sentiments, also **k'og-ťsǫ́' lém-pa** *C.*; *ťsod ₒjal-ba* to measure; *ťsod-ses-pa* **to keep measure,** and adj.: **observing due measure, temperate,** *ťsod-mi-sés-pa* not keeping measure, intemperate. — *ťsod-čan*, *ťsod-ldan* 1. **moderate.** 2. **punctilious, strict, grave** *W.* — *ťsod-méd* intemperate, immoderate, impudent. — 2. **measure, instrument for measuring,** *ču-tsód* water-clock. — 3. **division, portion, quantity,** *tsod-čig* part, **nor tsod čig** part of the money, of the estate *W.*; esp. of time, **point of time,** certain hour, cf. *ču-tsod* and *dus-tsod*; **duṅ pú-če tsód-la** *W.* at the time when the signal with the trumpet is given; **tsam tsod** *W.*, at which hour? — 4. **estimation, supposition, conjecture, guess;** *ṅai tsod-la* according to my estimation, *tsod ˳dzin-pa* v. above; **dha léb-pe tso' yo'** by this time he will have arrived, I guess *C.*; hence **tsod-če** *W.* to guess; *tsód-šes, tsód-bya* **riddle** *Cs.*, *tsód-šes smrá-ba* to propose a riddle, *mi-tsod* about men, *bem-tsód* about inanimate objects *Cs.*(?); **tsod-tsód'* *W.* at random *Sch.* — 5. *tsod* affixed to an adj. serves to form abstract nouns, thus: *rnyéd-par dká-tsód* the difficulty of obtaining, *˳jig-par slá-tsod* the facility of destroying, *ṗan-˳dógs čé-tsod* the greatness of the advantage *Thgy.*

ཚོད་མ་ *tsód-ma* 1. **vegetables, greens,** *tsód-ma rgod-skyés Cs.*: wild-growing greens, frequently gathered by the Tibetans in spring-time, such as dandelion, nettles, Eremurus etc.; *tsód-ma γyuṅ-skyés Cs.* cultivated vegetables. — 2. **boiled greens, vegetable-soup** *Mil.* and vulgo. — *sṅo-tsód* = *tsód-ma*; *nyuṅ-tsód* a dish of roots, turnips etc. *Cs.*; *ldum-tsód* a variety of roots *Cs.*(?) — *lo-tsód* all sorts of cabbage; *ša-tsód Cs.*, 'meat',(?) or more probably: prepared mushrooms. — *tsod-sdér* **plate, dish** *Sch.*

ཚོན་ *tson*, I. (cf. *tso-ba* and *tsos*) **colour,** 1. colouring matter, **paint,** = *tsón-rtsi*, or *rtsi-tsón*; *tsón-rtsi dkár-pos ˳brí-ba* to mark with white paint; *˳byúg-pa* **to paint;** *tson lén-pa* to take, imbibe colour *Cs.*; *tson sbyór-ba* to mix, to prepare colours *Cs.*; *tsón-gyis btso-ba* **to colour, to dye;** *tson-skúd* dyed thread *Do.*; *tson-spél* a coloured strip *W.* — 2. **colour** = *mdog W.* — II. v. *mtson.*

ཚོན་པོ་ *tson-po* 1. **fat, plump, well-fed** *W., C.* 2. **resinous.**

ཚོན་མོ་སྟེང་ *tson-mo-steṅ* a metal (not known) *Stg.*

ཚོབ་ *tsob* for *tsab Sch.*

ཚོམ་པ་ *tsóm-pa* I. also *tsóm-po Cs.* **bundle, bunch,** *tsóm-bu* id., *mé-tog-gi tsóm-bu* bunch of flowers *Pth.*; *rṅá-ma nág-poi tsóm-pa btágs-pa Mil.*, a kind of collar, made of black yak's tail; *pra-tsóm* a border or trimming set with jewels or pearls. Acc. to our authorities, however, the word properly signifies a mixture or variety of colours, something **variegated, gay-coloured,** e.g. **dii náṅ-du tsom máṅ-po** there is much colouring in this, it is manycoloured, **tsom-tsóm** id. — II. vb. **to doubt, hesitate;** to be timid, bashful, shy; to be ashamed *C.*; sbst. **doubt, timidity** etc.; *tsom-tsóm, tsam-tsóm, te-tsóm* id.

ཚོམས་ *tsoms C., W.* 1. = *ḱyams*, also *tsoms-skór* **court-yard,** *ḱan-pai tsoms Lex.* — 2. **set, division, part, chapter** *Sch.*, so perh. in the title of a book, *čéd-du brjód-pai tsoms Thgy.*; **kye-ču yu daṅ zii tsóm-čan** *W.* a neck-lace or string of pearls in sets, divided by turkois-drops and *γzi.*

ཚོམས་རྔམས་ *tsoms-rṅams* **noise, din, clatter** *Sch.*

ཚོར་བ་ *tsór-ba* 1. **to perceive,** sbst. **perception;** as one of the five skandhas = वेदना, a sensation, a feeling; **to perceive,** *γžán gyis ma tsór-bar* without any one perceiving it *Dzl.*; also without *γžán-gyis*: *ma tsór-bar rkú-ba* to steal unobserved, the contrary to robbing forcibly *Thgy.*; **žim-po tsor** he found it well-tasted; *sbrúm-pa tsór-nas* feeling herself to be with child *Pth.*; **yáṅ-mo tsor soṅ** *W.* it felt light to the touch. — 2. **to hear,** for *tós-pa*, common in *W.* —

ཚོར་ལོ་ *tsór-lo* a (flying) **report, rumour.**

ཚོལ་བ་ *tsól-ba* v. *˳tsól-ba.*

ཚོས་ *tsos* 1. **paint, dye, colouring matter;** *tsos rgyág-pa, rgyáb-pa* **to dye, to colour** *Sch.*; *tsos gyur* (or *log*) *soṅ* it has lost colour, it is faded; *tsós(-kyi) ḱu(-ba)* liquid paint, = *tsón-rtsi Glr.*; *tsós-mḱan* dyer, *tsos-lu Sch.*: a cosmetic, wash(?); *rgyá-tsos* a red pigment from India, perh. kermes *Med.* — 2. **a medicament** *Med.* — 3. v. *ḱur-tsos, ˳ṗoṅ-tsos.*

མཚའ་ལུ *mtsá-lu* 1. also *rtá-mtsa-lu Lex., Sch.:* a horse with white feet. — 2. v. *tsa-lu.*

མཚགས *mtsags Sch.* = *tsags* 4, *tsags-bzáṅ byéd-pa.*

མཚང *mtsaṅ* v. *ₒtsaṅ-ba.*

མཚན *mtsan* 1. resp. for *miṅ*, **name,** esp. the new name which every one receives that takes orders; *mtsan γsól-ba* 1. to give a name *Glr.* 2. to take, to assume, a name *Glr.*, title *W.* — 2. **mark, sign,** v. *mtsan-ma.* — 3. **night,** *mtsán-mo.*

མཚན(མ) *mtsán(-ma)* लक्षण, 1. **sign** (*rtags* and *ltas*), **mark, token, badge, symptom,** *dón-med-pai mtsán-ma yin* it is a sign that it would be fruitless *Wdṅ.; mtsán-ma ₒdébs-pa* to make a mark, to mark (e.g. with paint) *Glr.*; *btsún-mo-la ma ₒjígs-šig byás-pai mtsán-ma byin-nas* making a sign to the queen, signifying: do not fear! (that she had nothing to fear); *mtsán-mas mtsón-pa* to represent a thing by a sign or mark *Lex.; rgyal-poi mtsán-ma* (or *rtags*) *lṅá-po* (acc. to Indian notions) the five royal insignia, turban, parasol, sword, fly-flap and coloured sandals; **shape and peculiar characteristics of separate parts of the body,** *lus-kyi mtsan Dzl.* ༢༥༤, 5, esp. as marks of beauty, *skyés-bu čén-poi mtsan sum-ču-rtsa-γnyis* cf. *skyés-bu*; *mtsan daṅ dbyibs* as to limbs and stature *Dzl.*; *mtsan(-ma) bzáṅ(-po)* and *ṅán(-pa)* good and evil signs, tokens, symptoms, prognostics, frq.; *bkra-šís-pai dge-mtsan* propitious signs *Glr.*, emphat., good, favourable sign, some special (good) quality, *mtsan daṅ ldan-pa* possessing such quality, **superior, excellent,** frq.; *mtsán-ma rtóg-pa* to prove, to examine, signs; *mtsán-mar sgóm-pa* to take as an omen *Sch.*, *mtsán-mar ma bzuṅ* do not regard it as an (evil) omen, be not surprised or alarmed *Sch.* — *mtsan(daṅ) bčás(-pa)*, and *mtsan-méd* having characteristics and having none, (v. also *Was.* 297), terms with which Buddhist speculation loves to play, cf. *Köpp.* I, 597. — 2. **genitals** *Med., Pth.*, gen. preceded by *p̔o* or *mo*; *mtsan-dbye* prob. the genitals open themselves *Med.*; hence in Lhasa the word *tsan-zúg* (q. v.) might be misunderstood for painful affection of the genitals. — 3. *šín-tu mtsan čé-bar gyúr-te* is at one time applied to Buddha, at another to men, thus leaving the true meaning doubtful.

Comp. and deriv. *mtsán-mk̔an* soothsayer, astrologer, frq. — *mtsan-gráṅ* and *dgu-mtsan* prize, crown of victory *C.* — *mtsan-brjód* calling upon the name of a deity, enumerating its characteristics and attributes *Cs.*; *mtsan-dón* something similar(?). — *mtsan-nyid* prop.: **'the sign'**, the essential characteristic, sometimes even implying the true, innermost essence of a thing, whilst, on the other hand, it is also used merely for 'mark' in general; *čós-kyi mtsan-nyid stón-pa, k̔óṅ-du čúd-pa* prob. to show the true essence of doctrine, to receive it into one's own mind *Dzl.*; *mtsan-nyid-pa Mil.* n. of a philosophical school of the present day, stated to be the same as *bye-brág-pa;* it is much in favour with the Gelugpa-sect, and the principal object of their studies is, to ascertain the literal sense and original spirit of their doctrine; they love disputations on these subjects, and may be considered the representatives of speculative science among the Tibetan clergy. — *ₒdus-byás-kyi mtsan-nyid mi-rtág-pa yin* the essential property of all that is compounded is liability to decay *Glr.;* **property, quality** *Domaṅ*; **symptom, indication,** *nád-pa sós-pai mtsan-nyid* an indication that the patient will recover *S.g.*; *mtsan-nyid γsum* the three marks or characteristics in the doctrine of 'perception' of the Mahayanists, *kun-btágs, γžán-dbáṅ, yoṅs-grúb Was.* 291; *mtsan-nyid bšád-pa Schr.:* **definition;** so it seems to be used in *Thgy.* — *mtsan-rtágs* = *mtsán-ma Wdk.* — *mtsán-pa* **marked,** *ₒk̔ór-los* being marked with the figure of a wheel *Glr.* — *mtsán-dpe* for *mtsan daṅ dpe-byad Glr.* — *mtsan-γži Lex., Sch.:* 'the cause of a sign or symptom, an object' (?).

མཚན་མོ *mtsán-mo W.*, **tsan**, **night** **tsan ča dug**, *W.* night sets in; adv. **at**

night, by night, in the night time *Dzl., W.*: **tsan-la**; *dei mtsán-mo Dzl.* in that night; *tsan gáṅ, tsan tog-tág, W.* also **tsan-tse-ré**, the whole night; also adv., all night; *mtsan-dkyil, mtsan-gúṅ, mtsan-pyéd* **midnight;** *mtsan-stód, mtsan-smád* the first, the second half of the night; *mtsan-stód-kyi rmi-lam* a dream before midnight *Med.* — *mtsan-dús* **night time.** — *mtsan-byi* (*W. *tsan-bi**) **bat.** — *tsan-śiṅ W.* 1. **chip of pine-wood,** 2. **pine-wood.** 3. **pine-tree.** — *mtsan-só byéd-pa* to keep watch during the night *Sch.*

མཚམས་ *mtsams* 1. **intermediate space, interstice, border, boundary-line,** *rgya-gár daṅ bál-poi mtsáms-na, rgya-bál-gyi mtsáms-su* on the border between India and Nepal *Glr.*; *mtsáms-kyi nags-kród* boundary-forest *Glr.*; *sa-mtsáms* (vulgo *san-tsám*) frontier of the country *Glr.*; *dé-nas* ₒ*doms lṅa-brgyái mtsáms-nas* at a distance of 500 fathoms from that place; *bar-mtsams-na yod* it lies in the middle between; *ri taṅ mtsáms-su* where the mountains are contiguous to the plain; *byaṅ śar mtsáms-su* in the north-east (cf. no. 2 below); *ču* ₒ*gram mtsáms-su* (between the water and the river's bank) close to the edge *Wdṅ.*; *dei mtsáms-su* (with regard to a royal dynasty) **intervening, a usurper,** interrupting the regular succession *Glr.*; *čés-pai tsig mtsáms-nas* when these words were uttered, at these words *Tar.* 127, 11; *sgo(i)-mtsáms* a narrow opening of the door, *sgo-mtsáms-nas sleb* (he or it) enters through the cleft of a door, equivalent to our 'through the key-hole'; **tsám-la čug-če* W.* to preserve, to put (plants) between (paper), to pack up (glass in straw). — *mtsams sbyor-ba* 1. **to close interstices, to stitch up, to sew together** (the separate parts of a shoe) *Mil.* 2. *Sch.*: **to occupy a certain space, to enter a womb',** to embody one's self in human flesh, so it seems to be used in *Thgr.* and *Mil.* 3. **to take a resolution, to form a plan, to conceive an idea, to settle in one's mind,** like ₒ*gód-pa*, cf. *sbyór-ba* I, 2; II, 2 *C., W.* — *mtsams* ₒ*byé-ba* to split(?), *skra smin ysár-du mtsams-bye rtsub* ₒ*kyil S.g.* the hair of the head and the eye-brows splits, divides again, is growing thin, crisp, and interspersed with bald places, which is alledged to be a symptom of approaching death, yet hardly founded on correct observation, nor by any means clearly defined; *Schr.* has: *skra mtsams* ₒ*byéd-pa* to part the hair on the top of the head. — *mtsams-med-pa* 1. adj., *Ssk. ânantarya*, without interstices, continuous, = *go-mtsams-med-pa* v. *go* 1, *Dzl.* 2. sbst., *Ssk. ânantarya*, *Was.* (240), 'where nothing is to be interposed between a deed and its consequences, where the consequences are not to be averted', **a deadly, capital sin** *Dzl.* and elsewh.; *mtsáms-med-pa lṅa*, i e. inexpiable sins, are: parricide and matricide, murder of an Arhat (*dgrá-bčom-pa*), or of a Tathâgata, likewise causing divisions among the priesthood. — *dus-mtsáms* **intermediate time** *Cs.* — *mtsams-sbyór* the Sanskrit diphthongs ē, ō, ai, au; *mtsams-sbyór-pa* and *-ma*, a bawd, *Cs.* — *mtsams(-kyi)-žu(-ba)*, also ₒ*tsams-žu*, an expression gen. occurring in modern Tibetan letters, winding up the complimentary phrases of the introduction, and passing over to the proper business of the letter; for the immediate sense of the phrase I found no explanation. — 2. **the points of the compass,** *mtsams bži* the four cardinal points of the horizon; *mtsams brgyad* includes the intermediate points, south-east etc., *mtsams drug* denotes the four cardinal points together with the zenith and nadir. — 3. **demarcation, partition, break, pause, stop,** *mtsams γčod-pa* to make a stop or pause with the voice in reading *Gram.*; esp. to draw a line of demarcation about one's own person, whether it be by a magic circle (*Dom.*), or by retiring to a solitary house, either for the sake of private study (*Zam.*), or which is most frq. the case, for religious meditation, (**tsám-la dád-če* W.*) in the cell of a cloister, or in a hermitage or cave in the mountains, the seclusion lasting sometimes for several months, during which time the scanty food is silently received from without through a small aperture. Such seclusions are undergone by some in the sincere belief, that they will acquire thereby higher gifts and abilities, by others merely to increase their odour of sanctity. *mtsams sdóm-pa Mil.* has a similar signification. — *spyad-mtsáms* **rules, instructions,** defining the extent and limits of a person's duties. — 4. symb. num.: 6, v. *mtsams drug* above.

མཚར་བ་ *mtsár-ba* 1. **fair, fine, beautiful,** = *mdzés-pa Zam., Glr.* frq., *mtsar sdug daṅ ldán-pa* id, e.g. *bú-mo Glr.;* also of flowers; **bright, shining,** of metals *Stg.*; **nyám-tsar-wa, ló-tsar-wa** admirably fair, wonderfully fine. — 2. **wondrous, wonderful, marvelous,** gen. with *ṅo, ṅó-mtsar-čan žig* a wonderful, distinguished, eminent man *Mil.*; *rten ṅo-mtsar-čan* a wonderful image (of some deity) *Glr.*, in both instances equivalent to **wonder-working, miraculous;** *ṅo-mtsar-mčód-pa* a marvelous, extremely rich offering *Mil.*; more frq. *ṅo-mtsar-čé-ba* e.g. marvelous things, events, miracles *Dzl.; mi srid ṅo-mtsar-če* impossible! most wonderful! *Glr.*; *ṅo-mtsar-čé-ba ma yin* that is not so very wonderful *Dzl.*; **strange, ridiculous,** *ytam šin-tu ṅo-mtsar-čé Glr.* — 3. *ṅo-mtsár* **wonder, surprise, astonishment,** *ṅo-mtsár skyé-ba, ṅo-mtsár-du ˳gyur-ba* or *˳dzín-pa, ṅo-mtsar-rmád-du ˳gyúr-ba* to wonder, to be surprised. — 4. *ṅo-mtar-čé* an expression of thanks, = *bka-drin-če, dé-ltar yin-na k̔yed ŋnyis-ka ṅo-mtsar-čé* if that is so, then both of you receive my best thanks! *Mil.*; *yóṅs-pa ṅo-mtsar-čé* thanks to you for your coming! *Mil.*

མཚལ་ *mtsal Cs.* also *tsal* **vermilion,** used (among the rest) inst. of red ink for writing; *mtsal-pár* a printing with red ink *Cs.*; *mtsal-lčógs-pa(?) Sch.:* 'clear vermilion'(?); *sku-mtsál* resp. for *k̔rag* blood *Cs.*

མཚུངས་པ་ *mtsuṅs-pa* (*W.* **tsogs**) **similar, like, equal,** *k̔a-dog* as to colour *S.O.*, *sṅa-ma daṅ* like the former, *bdud-rtsir* like nectar *S.g.*; *bdud daṅ mtsuṅs* you are to me like a satan, you are a satan to me *Pth.; lhai sdug-bsṅál daṅ ča-mtsúṅs-pai stéṅ-du* besides their sharing all the imperfections of the gods *Thgy.*; *dús-mtsuṅs-pa* **a contemporary** *Mil.*; *mtsuṅs-méd, mtsuṅs-brál,* **without an equal, matchless, incomparable;** *sems daṅ mtsuṅs ldán-pa* explained by *Was.* (241) as: manifestations of mind, those outward signs by which the mind manifests itself as existing.

མཚུན་ *mtsun* (*Zam.* = *Ssk.* क्रव्य, raw flesh) 1. *Cs.:* **meat for the manes of the dead,** *ytóṅ-ba* to bring an offering to the dead, *skyel-ba* to send one; *mtsun-ytór* explained in *Wdṅ.* by *ši-bai dón-du ytór-ma ytóṅ-ba*; *mtsun-ytór stér-ba Wdṅ.* — 2. *Sch.:* **tutelar deities, household-gods,** or rather **the souls of ancestors;** so *Dzl.* ༢༠, 16 (another reading is *btsun*); also in *mtsun-ytor*, if *mtsun* be taken as a dat., it may have this signification; *mes-mtsún* household-gods of the Shamans *Sch.*

མཚུར་ *mtsur* v. *tsúr-mo.*

མཚུལ་པ་ *mtsúl-pa* **the lower part of the face,** nose and mouth, **the muzzle** of animals *Mil.; **bill, beak** Sch.; W.* **nám-tsul** **nose;** *mtsúl-pa ˳gag* the effect of the gall entering the nose(?) *Mṅg.*; *k̔a-mtsúl* (*W.* **k̔am-tsúl**) **face,** seldom in *B.*

མཚེ་སྐྱོང་ *mtse-skyóṅ Wdṅ.?*

མཚེ་ལྡུམ་ *mtse-ldúm* n. of a medicinal herb *S.g.*

མཚེ་མ་ *mtsé-ma* (*W.* **tsag-túg**) **twins,** *bu mtse-ma ŋnyis dus ŋčig-na ˳k̔ruṅs-so Pth.* two twin-sons were born simultaneously; *mtsé-ma ŋsúm-po* three-twin-child, trigemini *Wdṅ.*

མཚེད་ *mtsed, Sch.: dur-mtséd,* **place for burning the dead.**

མཚེའུ་ *mtseu* **a small lake,** *mtso daṅ mtseu* lakes and lakelets *Pth.*

མཚེར་བ་ *mtser-ba* = *˳tser-ba.*

མཚོ་ *mtso* 1. **lake,** frq. — 2. for *rgya-mtso* sea, rarely. — 3. symb. num.: 4. — **Comp.** *mtso-dkyil, mtso-dbús* the middle of a lake. — *mtso-˳k̔ór* an assemblage of many lakes *Cs.* — *mtso-˳k̔yóms* v. *˳k̔yoms.* — *mtso-˳grám, mtso-mtá* border of a lake. — *mtso-sṅón Glr.*, **sóg-po tso-ṅón** *C.* the blue lake, Kokonor, in Mongolia. — *mtso-čú* water, *mtso-rláṅs* vapours, *mtso-rlábs* waves of a lake. — **tso-lág** *C.* **inlet, creek, cove.** — **to-lag-ḍél** *C.* **strait, channel.**

མཚོག་པ་ *mtsóg-pa* v. *ₒtsóg-pa*.

མཚོག་མ་ *mtsóg-ma Lt.*, also *mtsog-yséṅ Cs.*, 'spot or tender part of the head', vacancy in the infant cranium, = *tsáṅs-pai bú-ga*.

མཚོགས་ *mtsogs* adv., **tsógs-se** adj., *W.* for *mtsuṅs* or *ₒdra*, **similar, like, equal;** **aṅ-ré-zi tsogs rgyál-la mi dug** they are not so good as the English; **ko daṅ ṅá-la dug-ṅál tsóg-se yod** with him and with me there is the like disaster, misfortune visits us equally.

མཚོན་ *mtson*, 1. also *mtsón-ča*, any **pointed or cutting instrument,** *mtsón-čas ytúb-pa* to cut to pieces with such an instrument *Dzl.*; **weapon, arms;** *mtson togs-pa* to seize a sword, to take up arms *Dzl.*; *mtsón-gyis ₒjig-pa* to destroy, to conquer, with the sword *Ma.*; *mtsón-ča rnám-pa bži Stg.*: sword, spear, dart, arrow; *go-mtsón* armory and arms; *ru-mtsón* v. *ru*; *mtson-krág* blood drawn by cuts or stabs (used for sorceries) *Lt.* — *mtsoṅ-gyi dru-bu* an attribute of the gods, resembling a coil or ball of thread *Wdṅ.*; *mtson-skúd sgríl-ma Thgr.* id. (?). — 2. also *tson* **fore-finger,** *mtsón-rtsa* the pulse to be felt with the fore-finger; *mtson gaṅ* a finger's breadth; *mtson gaṅ mar* a finger's breadth lower *Med.*; *mtsón-pa* a four-fingers' pinch(?); *šiṅ mtsón-pa žig* a handful of sticks *Mil.*

མཚོན་པ་ *mtson-pa* 1. v. *mtson*. — 2. vb. **to set forth, bring forward, adduce, state, quote, exhibit,** examples of grammatical forms etc. *Gram.*; *ₒdis mtsón-nas* illustrating it by this, setting this up as an example *Gram.*; *des kyaṅ sgyú-mai dpe čig mtson* also in this may be seen an instance of deception *Mil.*; *dpes mtsón-pa* to illustrate by parables *Mil.*; *mtsán-mas* by a sign *Gram.*; so prob. also: *ǎm-ban ɣnyis dei mtsón-pai dmág-mi* the soldiers brought forward by the two Chinese officials; it is also alledged to stand for **to make, to prepare** *C.* — *rnám-mka mtsón-pai rnál-ₒbyor-pa* prob.: the saint that represents the heavens, that resembles the heavenly space *Mil.*

འཚའ་ལུ་ *ₒtsa-lu* v. *mtsa-lu*.

འཚག་པ་ *ₒtsag-pa* 1. vb., pf. *tsags*, *btsags*, fut. *btsag*, imp. *tsog* (trans. to *ₒdzag-pa*), **to cause to trickle, to strain, filter, sift, squeeze, press out,** *ₒbru-már tság-pa* (partic.) oil-miller *Dzl.*; **to draw off,** *dmú-ču* to tap (a dropsical person) *S.g.* Cf. *tság-ma*, *tsags*. — 2. adj. **thick, fat, obese** *Lex.*

འཚང་, མཚང་ *ₒtsaṅ*, *mtsaṅ* **fault, error, offence, sin,** *de ₒtsáṅ-du če* that is very wicked, a great offence; *mii* or *mi-la ₒtsaṅ brú-ba* or *drú-ba* 1. **to spy out another's faults,** to upbraid him with them, to accuse him *Do.*, *C.*, *W.*; **tsaṅ ₒog ḍhú-wa** *C.* id. — 2. **to irritate, provoke, make angry** *C.*

འཚང་བ་ *ₒtsáṅ-ba*, vb. I. pf. *tsaṅs*, fut. *btsaṅ*(?) 1. **to press into, to stuff** *Sch.*, *ₒtsáṅ-ka byéd-pa* id. *Sch.*; *náṅ-du ₒtsáṅs-pa Lexx.* prob. pressed into, stuffed inside, so *Sch.*: *kri naṅ tsáṅs-čan* a stuffed seat; *dbugs kar ₒtsáṅs-pa* out of breath, panting (in the heat of pursuit) *Mil.*; *dbugs stod-du ₒtsaṅs-nas skad mi ton Mil.* I am pressed for breath, my breath stops, I cannot utter a word (for ardent longing); *stod-ₒtsáṅs*, *rluṅ-ₒtsáṅs*, *ₒtsáṅs-la pan*, all these expressions imply a want of breath, not sufficiently to be reconciled to the original meaning of the word. — 2. **sú-la tsáṅs-se yóṅ-če** *Ld.* to attack a person with open violence, opp. to a stealthy attack. — II. pf. *saṅs*, which verb, however, occurs only in *ₒtsaṅ-rgyá-bar ₒgyúr-ba* to become Buddha *Dzl.* frq., *ₒtsaṅ rgyá-bar ₒdód-pa* to aim at Buddhaship, and *saṅs-rgyás* (having become) Buddha. Besides this form, there exists also a verb *sáṅ-ba*, pf. (*b*)*saṅs*, to clean, as may easily be proved by examples. The whole will perh. become clear, if we presume, that the form *ₒtsaṅ-ba* for the present tense is now obsolete, occurring only in reference to Buddha, as quoted above, and that the root *saṅ* is now used as present tense in the following significations: 1. **to remove** (impurities) — like *ₒdág-pa* — **to make clean,** *daṅ sáṅ-te med* W. (the soot) having yesterday been removed, there is none just now; *saṅ dug, saṅ čos* W. it is cleansed, swept clean, *ₒbag saṅ, nyé-pa saṅ* the contamination, the sin, has been removed, done away with C.; *snyun saṅs* the disease is removed *Pth.*; *skyo-sáṅs byéd-pa* to remove melancholy, to recreate or amuse one's self; to comfort others; *skyo-sáṅs-la ₒgró-ba*, *skyo-sáṅs byéd-pa* to take a walk, to take a ride *Pth.*, *C.*; *mya-ṅáṅ sáṅ-ba* **to comfort** *Pth.*, **to console one's self;** esp. 2. **to recover, to come again to one's senses,** *ra-ro-ba-las* from intoxication *Dzl.*; *γzim-pa-las* from a deep sleep *Dzl.*; also construed as before: *bzi Glr.*, *ra* W. from a drunken fit, and this agrees with a sufficiently authenticated signification of the *Ssk.* root *budh*, so that *saṅs-rgyás* would after all be the literal translation of बुद्ध (contrary to *Burn.* I, 71 med.), taking the signification of the name, accord. to Tibetan notions, to be: 'the man that has entirely recovered from error and come to the knowledge of absolute truth'. That *saṅs-rgyás* be the same as **perfect, holy,** seems to be a mere etymological conjecture of *Cs.* — 3. **to take away, to take off,** *ḱeb sáṅ-wa* C. to uncover. — 4. **to be spoiled, to become unfit, useless,** *wó-ma saṅ soṅ* C. the milk is spoiled, *zom saṅ ₒdug* = *šaṅ ₒdug* the casks are leaky, are running out.

འཙང་ར་ *ₒtsaṅ-ra Sch.*: the neck of the thigh-bone; *tsáṅ-rai tsil* the fat attached to it *C.*

འཙབ་པ་ *ₒtsáb-pa*, pf. *tsabs*, *bsabs*, fut. *bsab*, imp. *tsob*, **to pay back, repay, refund,** *skyin-pa* a loan *Lex.*; cf. *tsab.*

འཙབ་འཚུབ་ *ₒtsab-ₒtsub* **hurry, confusion, perplexity, fear** *Sch.*; also: *ₒtsab-ₒtsáb-mor γnás-pa* to tarry in fear, to hesitate in apprehensions *Tar.*

འཙབས་པ་ *ₒtsábs-pa*, pf. *tsabs*, imp. *tsobs* *Sch.*: resp. **to be afraid;** *Lex. blo-ₒtsábs* id. (?).

འཙམ(ས)་པ་ *ₒtsám(s)-pa* 1. = *ₒčam-pa* (?) **fit, suitable, in accordance to, in conformity with,** *de daṅ ₒtsám-par S.g.*; *so-sói ₒbyór-pa daṅ ₒtsám-par Tar.* according to their ability, in proportion to their property. — 2. frq. and mostly erron. for *mtsáms-pa*.

འཙར་བ་ *ₒtsár-ba*, pf. *tsar* 1. **to be finished, completed, terminated,** *snón-la tsár-ro Glr.* it was the first that was finished; **to be at an end, consumed, spent,** *nor tsár-te soṅ* W. the money is all spent; esp. as an auxiliary, to denote an action that is perfectly past or completed (where in the earlier literature *zin* stands), in later books with the termin. inf., *yóṅs-su rdzógs-par tsár-te* when ... was completely finished *Glr.*; vulgo the mere root is used, esp. in *W.*, *tsog tsar-ra ma tsar* are they assembled, has the meeting begun already? *lam-la žug tsar, soṅ tsar, kal tsar* he is on the way, he is gone, it is dispatched; *tsár-ba byéd-pa*, *tsár-du ₒǰúg-pa Cs.*, *tsar čug-če* W. **to bring to a close, to finish, to terminate.** — *tsár-γčod-pa* 1. **to destroy, annihilate,** e. g. diabolic influences, infernal powers *Pth.*; **to defeat, overcome,** in disputation *Mil.*; **to excel, surpass,** *sgyu-rtsál-gyis Glr.*; **to punish** *Tar.* 2. for *γsár-γčod-pa Pth.* — 2. **to grow, grow up, thrive,** of little children *W.*; *ₒtsar-skyéd* growth *Mil.*

འཙལ་ *ₒtsal*, *sgro-bai-ₒtsal-gyi ḱa-brgyan Mil.?*

འཙལ་བ་ *ₒtsál-ba*, imp. *ₒtsol* eleg. 1. **to want, wish, desire, ask;** when followed by a verb, the latter stands in the termin. inf., or the mere root of it, and more esp. that of the perf. form, *yab daṅ mǰal ₒtsál-lo* I have a mind to go to see my father *Dzl.*; *bltás-par ₒtsál-te* wishing to see *Dzl.*; *túgs-la bžag ₒtsal* I wish it may be borne in mind *Glr.*; *γsuṅ ₒtsal* I beg you to speak *Mil.*, *bzuṅ ₒtsal* please take *Pth.*; pleon. *ₒḱrid-par žu ₒtsal Glr.*; esp. as an intimation of willingness, *dé-ltar ₒtsál-lo* yes, we will do that *Mil.*, or like our: very well! Further: *pʼá-la nor ma ₒtsál-tam* has he not asked the money from his father? *Dzl.*; *gum yaṅ či ₒtsál* why does (the king) want to kill me? *Dzl.*; *deï don mi ₒtsal* the profit of it I do not desire *Glr.* — 2. **to eat,** *btsan-dúg* poison *Dzl.*; *byi-bas ˳tsál-te* eaten by mice *Dzl.*; *ydon mi ˳tsál-bar* eleg. for *ydon mi zá-bar* without doubt *Dzl.* — 3. **to know** *Cs.*; so *ṅo-˳tsál-ba* appears to be used for *ṅo-šes-pa*, and in a passage of *S.O.* it seems to imply **to understand.** — 4. in certain phrases: *˳bad ˳tsál-ba* **to use diligence** *Thgy.*; *bro ˳tsál-ba* 1. **to swear** *Pth.*(?), 2. **to have a cold** *Mil.*; *p̀yag ˳tsál-ba* **to greet, salute,** v. *p̀yag*.

འཚལ་མ་ *˳tsál-ma Cs.* = *tsál-ma.*

འཚིག་པ་ *˳tsig-pa*, pf. *tsig*, **to burn, to destroy by fire,** *groṅ-k̀yer mi daṅ bčas-pa* (he burned) the town with its inhabitants *Pth.*; *mes*, *mer*, vulgo **mé-la** with fire; *rnám-par* entirely, completely *Dzl.*; more loosely: *tsig soṅ* he burnt himself, scalded himself etc.; also of food, burnt, injured by the heat; *˳tsig-gam* am I burning? (thinks one suffering of fever) *Med.*; of inflammation, v. *mig-˳tsig*; of any violent pain *Dom.*; **to be glowing,** of the evening-sky *W.*; **tsig ˳ǰug ˳dug** *C.* **to be in the rut,** the copulating of larger animals.

འཚིང་ and འཚིངས་པ་ *˳tsiṅ* and *˳tsiṅs-pa Mṅg.?*

འཚིར་བ་ *˳tsir-ba*, pf. *tsir*, *btsir*, fut. *ytsir*, *btsir*, imp. *tsir W.* **btsir-če* **to press,** *mig* with the finger on the eye *Med.*; *nán-gyis* to press hard *Stg.*; **to press out,** an ulcer; **to wring,** a wet cloth; **to crush out,** *til-már* sesame-oil *Lex.*; *˳o-ma ˳tsir-ba* **to milk**; **tsir tag ǰhé-pa*, or *tán-wa** *C.* **to press hard, to examine closely, to hold a rigorous inquest;** *btsún-mo-la yaṅ t̀ugs ytsir čúṅ-bar gyúr-to Pth.* also the queen's mind was much depressed.

འཚུགས་པ་ *˳tsúgs-pa*, pf. *tsugs* (intrs. of *˳dzúg-pa*), 1. **to go into** (more frq. *˳tsúd-pa*), **to enter upon, begin, commence,** *stód-pa ˳búl-ba-la tsugs* he began to praise, to flatter. — 2. **to penetrate by boring,** v. *p̀ur-pa*; **to take root, to establish one's self, to settle,** *rtsá-ba ma tsugs* it has not struck root; *˳brog ˳tsúgs-su ye ma-˳dod Mil.*, prob.: they had no longer any mind to establish themselves in this alpine solitude; *brtán-gyi skyíd-mgo dé-nas tsugs* this was the beginning of my lasting happiness *Mil.*; most frq. *tsúgs-pa* as partic. or adj.: **firm, steady,** *rk̀aṅ-lág ma tsúgs-te sá-la ˳gyél-to* his limbs not remaining firm (in consequence of a paralytic stroke), he fell to the ground *Dzl.*; **k̀áṅ-pa tsúg-kyin dug** sit quiet with your feet! *Ld.*; *˳dug mi tsúgs-pa Med.*, *sa yčig-tu mi tsugs-pa Pth.*, **dǒ-tsug mé-pa** *C.*, **dád-du mi tsúg-k̀an** *W.* not being able to sit still; not stationary, **unsettled, roving, restless, volatile, flighty, inattentive,** *spyód-pas skúd-čig kyaṅ mi tsúgs-pa Glr.* id.; **tsúg-la dod** *W.*, be attentive! **to be able** *C.*

འཚུད་པ་ *˳tsúd-pa*, pf. *tsud* (intrs. to *˳dzúd-pa*) **to be put into** (a hole), to prison *Glr.*; **to go into, to enter, to get into** (a good and wholesome way), **to go to** (hell); *k̀oṅ-du* v. *k̀oṅ ˳tsud-pa.*

འཚུབ་པ་ *˳tsub-pa*, pf. *tsubs*, 1. **to whirl,** of whirlwinds, snow-storms, smoke etc. *Mil.* and elsewh. — 2. **to be choked,** esp. **to be drowned,** *nya čab-la ˳p̀yo-ba ˳tsub mi srid* the fish swimming in the water cannot be drowned *Mil.*; *čus ˳tsúb-pa Mil.*; **tsub-te ši** *W.* he has been drowned. — 3. *spyód-pa ˳tsúb-pa* **pugnacity,** of fowl *Glr.*

འཚེ་བ་ *˳tse-ba* 1. vb. pf. *btses*, fut. *btse*, *ytse* (*Dzl.*) **to hurt, damage, injure, persecute, torment,** *mi-la ˳tsé-žiṅ ynód-pa byéd-pa*, or *ynód-čiṅ ˳tsé-bar byéd-pa* id.; also sbst., **enemy, persecutor** *Mil.*; *yčan-zán-la sógs-pai ˳tsé-ba daṅ bčás-pa* (a place) haunted by beasts of prey or any other noxious creatures *Thgy.*; the term is also applied to horses that bite each other. — 2. sbst. (spelling uncertain) **psalterium,** the third stomach of ruminating animals *W.*

འཚེག་པ་ *˳tség-pa*, pf. *tsegs*, imp. *tseg(s)*, **to repay** *Cs.*

འཚེང་བ་ *˳tséṅ-bá*, pf. prob. *˳tseṅs*, 1. **to increase, improve, thrive,** opp. to *˳ǰiṅ ba W.* — 2. **to be content, happy** *Mil.*

འཚེད་པ་ *˳tséd-pa* 1. v. *˳tsód-pa.* — 2. v. *bséd-pa.*

འཚེམ་པ་ *˳tsém-pa* pf. *tsems*, *btsems*, fut. *btsem*, imp. *tsems*, *W.* **tsém-če* **to sew,** **gos tsém-čeī ras** materials for a garment; ˳*ṫsem-skúd* **thread** for sewing; ˳*ṫsem-k'áb* **needle.** — ˳*ṫsem-drúb* **needle-work** *Cs.* — ˳*ṫsem-srúb W.* **seam.** — ˳*ṫsem-méd* without a seam; *Sch.* also: without interruption.

འཚེར་བ་ ˳*ṫsér-ba*, I. vb. **to neigh** *Pth.* and vulgo. — II. also *mṫsér-ba* 1. vb. **to grieve, to sorrow,** and sbst. **grief, sorrow,** resp. *ṫugs-˳ṫsér*, cf. *ṫsér-ka*; ˳*ṫsér-čan* **sorrowful, anxious,** ˳*ṫser-méd* **free from sorrow, easy.** — 2. **to be afraid, to fear** *C.*, *Mil.* — 3. **to shine, to glitter,** and sbst. **lustre, brightness, splendour, brilliancy,** of light *Lex.*, of jewels *Dzl.*; *dkár-žiṅ* (or *dkár-la*) ˳*ṫsér-ba* to be of a shining white *Mil.*

འཚེར་ས་, མཚེར་ས་ ˳*ṫsér-sa*, *mṫsér-sa* 1. *Sch.*: **cause of uneasiness, source of care.** — 2. an old deserted settlement or dwelling; ˳*ṫser-rnyiṅ* id. *Sch.*

འཚོ་བ་ ˳*ṫsó-ba*, I. vb. a. intrs., pf. and imp. *sos*, 1. **to live,** *riṅ-du* a long time, *lo brgya* a hundred years *Med.*; *nam* (or *ǰi-srid*) ˳*ṫsoï bár-du* **for life, life-long,** *čós-kyis*, *rig-pas*, *rṅón-pas* to gain a livelihood by religion, science, hunting *Cs.*, or: to lead the life of a cleric, scholar, hunter; *srid* ˳*ṫsó-ba* to pass life, **to continue** in a state, **to exist,** frq.; ˳*dú-˳dzii náṅ-du* ˳*ṫso mi ṗód-do* in the throng of the world I cannot exist *Dzl.* (*W.* **sóṅ-če* and *ṫse ṗíd-če**). — 2. **to remain alive,** to be maintained in life, ˳*di ma byás-na mi* ˳*ṫsoo* else we shall not remain alive, we shall not be able to live *Dzl.*; **to revive, to recover,** from sickness etc. *Dzl.*; *sós-par* ˳*gyúr-ba* id., frq.; *ṡi-ba-las* to be rescued from peril of death *Dzl.* — 3. **to last, to be durable,** of clothes etc., *W.*: **máṅ-po ṫsó-če** to last long, to be very durable; ˳*ṫsó-žiṅ sdód-pa* to remain valid, binding, to retain its virtue, efficacy, of laws, doctrine etc. — 4. **to feed, to graze.** — b. trs., pf. (*b*)*sos*, fut. *γso*, 1. **to nourish,** *lus* the body; to sustain, *srog* life; **to pasture, to feed,** *ṗyugs* ˳*ṫsó-ba-la kyér-ba* to lead the cattle to pasture *Pth.*, *ṗyugs* ˳*ṫsor ṗyin-pa* id. — 2. **to heal, to cure,** *nad Lt.*; in this sense the fut. form is used as a vb. for itself, q.v.; ˳*ṫso-byéd*, *ṫso-mdzád* **'life-giver'**, i.e. physician, medicine.

II. sbst., also ˳*ṫso*, 1. **life,** *mi žig-gi* ˳*ṫsó-ba bṡól-ba* to prolong life *Dzl.*; ˳*ó-čag* ˳*ṫsoï ǰe* the lord of our lives, viz. the king *Glr.*; ˳*ṫso skyóṅ-ba* to spare, preserve, protect another's life; **to rear, bring up, educate.** — 2. **livelihood, sustenance, nourishment, entertainment,** *zlá-ba γsúm-gyi bár-du* ˳*ṫsó-ba sbyór-ba* to board a person for three months *Dzl.*; ˳*ṫsó-ba-la ma bltá-ste* not caring for the entertainment *Dzl.*; ˳*ṫsó-bab záṅ-po* good eating and drinking *Mil.*

འཚོག་ཆས་ ˳*ṫsog-čas* **goods, effects, chattels, tools, necessaries,** = *yo-byad Lex.*; also **provisions, provender.**

འཚོག་པ་ ˳*ṫsóg-pa*, pf. *btsags*, fut. *btsog*, imp. *ṫsog*, *W.* **ṫsóg-če** 1. **to hew, chop, cut, pierce; to inoculate, vaccinate,** *brúm-pa* the small-pox. — 2. **to cudgel,** ˳*ṫsóg-čiṅ rdúṅ-ba Pth.*, *brdóg-˳ṫsog-pa* id. *Dzl.* — 3. also *mṫsóg-pa* **to find fault with, to blame, censure, carp at, teaze** *Sch.*

འཚོག་མ་, འཚོགས་མ་ ˳*ṫsóg-ma*, ˳*ṫsógs-ma* = *mṫsóg-ma*.

འཚོགས་པ་ ˳*ṫsogs-pa*, pf. and imp. *ṫsogs*, **to assemble, to gather, to meet,** frq.; *k'yed* ˳*dir ṫsogs*, ye, that are here assembled *Mil.*; *mi máṅ-po ṫsógs-pai mdún-du* before many assembled people *Dzl.*; ˳*byúṅ-ba lṅa ṫsógs-pa* the five elements meeting *S.g.*; ˳*ṫsogs rtén-gyi zas-čáṅ* food and drink to entertain the people assembled *Glr.*; **to unite, to join** in doing something, **to associate,** to make common cause; examples v. *lugs*.

འཚོང་བ་ ˳*ṫsóṅ-ba*, pf. *btsoṅs*, fut. *btsoṅ*, imp. *ṫsoṅ*, *W.* **ṫsóṅ-če**, **to sell,** *dri* ˳*ṫsóṅ-bai γnas* place where perfumes are sold *Stg.*; **daṅ gón-če ṫsóṅ-k'an-ni mi** *W.* the man that yesterday had a coat to sell.

འཚོད་པ་, འཚེད་པ་ ˳*ṫsód-pa*, ˳*ṫséd-pa*, (*Cs.* ˳*ṫsó-ba?*) pf. *btsos*, fut. *btso*, imp. *ṫsos*, *ṫsod*, *W.* **ṫsó-če**, 1. **to cook, to dress,** in boiling water, meat, vegetables; **ču-ṫsós** *W.* 'water-boiled', dumplings, = **čú-ta-gir**. — 2. **to bake** provinc. — 3. **to dye,** *gos* a garment. — 4. *ṫsós-pa*, **ṫsós-mk'an** *W.** **ripe,** **ṫsos soṅ** is ripe; **ldád-pa ma ṫsos** *Ld.*, he is a green-horn.

འཚོབ(ས)་པ་ ₒ*tsób(s)-pa* **to be a deputy, representative, substitute** *Cs.*; *rigs* ₒ*tsób-pa* to be the first-born male in a family, the support of a family *Dzl.*; ₒ*tsób-par byéd-pa* **to substitute,** to put in the place of another *Dzl.*; *ɣduṅ*-ₒ*tsób-po* resp. for **first-born** *Dzl.*

འཚོལ་བ་ ₒ*tsól-ba*, pf. and fut. *btsol*, imp. *tsol*, *W.* **tsál-ċe**, 1. **to seek, to search, to make research;** *tabs* **to think upon means.** — 2. **to try to obtain,** *zas*; **to procure, acquire** *Mil.*; **to fetch** *Thg.*

ཛ

ཛ *dza* 1. the letter sounding **dz**; cf. the observations to ཙ *tsa.* — 2. numerical figure: 19.

ཛ་ *dza* 1. v. *dza-ti.* — 2. *dzá-brduṅ-ba* **to break through** *Sch.*

ཛ་ཏི་ *dzá-ti*, prop. ཛཱ་ཏཱི་, *Ssk.* जाती, **nutmeg** *Lt.* and vulgo; sometimes *dza* for it, po. *Lt.*

ཛ་བོ་ཤིང་ *dza-bo-śiṅ Lex.* **a hollow tree** *Sch.*

ཛ་ཡ་ *dzá-ya* 1. *Sch.*: **'muddy deposit,** green slime in the water'. — 2. *C.* **the markings of wood,** speckled and variegated, in consequence of a disease of the tree, cf. *lbá-ba.* — 3. n. of an ancient king of China *Glr.*

ཛ་ལནྡྲ་ *dza-lantra*, more accur. ཛ་ལནྡྷ་ར་ *dza-lán-dha-ra*, n. of a province in the Punjâb, now 'Jellundur'.

ཛ་ལུ་ཀ་ *dzá-lu-ka, ċui dza-lu-ka Sch.* **'water-spider'**; in *Ssk.* however: **leech.**

ཛབ་ར་ *dzáb-ra*, prob. to be spelt *rdza-bra* q.v.

ཛམ་བུ་ *dzám-bu*, gen. ₒ*dzám-bu*, **जम्बु, the rose apple-tree**, *Eugenia*, which figures also in mythology; *dzám-bui gliṅ, dzam-bu-gliṅ, dzam-gliṅ*, **जम्बुद्वीप**, acc. to the ancient geography of India and Tibet, that part of the world which comprizes these countries, the triangular peninsula of Hindostan, occasionally including the immediate border-lands; but as in Brahman and Buddhist literature all that does not belong to these two religions is considered as not existing, or at least as hardly human, ₒ*dzam-bu-gliṅ* is simply used for **earth, world,** and ₒ*dzam-bu-gliṅ-pa*, for inhabitant of the world, **man.**

ཛམ་བྷ་ལ་ *dzám-bha-la*, also *dzám-bha*, *Glr.* the Tibetan **Plutos, god of riches,** = *rnam-tos-srás*, also *rmugs*-ₒ*dzin Lex.*, *ɣnod*-ₒ*dzin*, and acc. to *Schf.*'s conjecture (*Tar.* 6, 1) also *ɣnód-pa-ċan*; *dzam-sér* this god painted yellow, *dzam-nág* painted black *Cs.*

ཛི་ *dzi*, num. figure: 49.

ཛི་ན་མི་ཏྲ་ *dzi-na-mi-tra Ssk.* n. of a Buddhist scholar.

ཛུ་ *dzu*, num. figure: 79.

ཛུ་ཏ་ *dzu-ta Hindi*: **shoe** *C.*, *W.*

ཛུབ་ཛུབ་ *dzub-dzúb C.* **dhsub-dhsúb ǰhé-pa** **to wag, to whisk** the tail, of horses and cattle.

ཛེ་ *dze*, num. figure: 109.

ཛེ་ཙེ་ *dze-tse C.* **dhse-tse**, vent-hole for the smoke, **chimney.**

ཛོ་ *dzo* num. figure: 139.

ཛོ་ཀི་, ཛྭོ་ཀི་ *dzó-ki, dzwo-ki Mil.*, *Wdṅ.*, vulg. for *yó-gi*, v. *rnál*-ₒ*byor-pa.*

མཛའ་བ་ *mdzá-ba* (*Lex.* = *mtún-pa*) **to love,** as friends or kinsmen do, *Kyo-sùg* *mdzá-ba-rnams* a loving married couple *Dzl.*; *mdza-žiń sdúg-par* ₒ*gyúr-ba* loving each other, e.g. like brothers or sisters, *Dzl.*; *mi-mdzá-ba tams-čád* any hostile, malignant (creatures or powers) *Dom.*; *mi-mdzá-ba-rnams sdúm-pa* to reconcile those that are at variance *Thgy.*; *brám-ze mdzá-žiń šés-pa žig yód-de* he had a Brahmin for his intimate friend *Dzl.*; *mdza-bšés* **friend**, frq. in conjunction with *nyé-du* or *k'yim-mtses Glr.*; *mdzá-bo* id. *Dzl.* etc. and vulgo, rarely *mdzao Thgy.*; still more vulg. *Ts.*: **dzán-te, dzá-mo** fem.; **dzá-wo ǰhé-pa**, *C.*, = *mdzá-ba*; *mdza-grógs* intimate friend *Sch.*; *C.*: husband, wife.

མཛངས་པ་ *mdzańs-pa* (*Ssk.* पण्डित) 1. **wise, learned**, frq.; *mk'ás-šiń mdzáńs-pa, ytsug-lag-če-žiń mdzáńs-pa*; *mdzańs-blun* the wise man and the fool, a relig. composition, publ. by Schmidt, together with a German translation, containing an endless variety of examples relative to the Buddhist doctrine of future rewards and punishments; *mdzáńs-ma* a wise woman *Glr.* — 2. **gentle, noble**, distinguished as to rank, *ya-rábs mdzáńs-kyi bu Glr.* po. — (The spelling ₒ*dzáńs-pa* is not of unfrequent occurrence, but seems to be objectionable.)

མཛད་པ་ *mdzád-pa*, imp. *mdzod* (*W.* also **dzad**), **to do, to act**, resp. for *byéd-pa* in all its significations, whenever the person acting is the object of respect, hence almost without exception with regard to Buddha; but also in common life: **či dzad dug** *W.* what is your honour doing? also together with *byed-pa*, *grogs byéd-par mdzód čig* pray, help me! further as a sbst.: **the act of doing, the thing done, the deed**, *mdzád-pa bču-gnyís* the twelve deeds (or prop. incidents) of an incarnated Buddha, viz. the descending from the gods, conception, birth, exhibition of skill (i.e. going through certain chivalrous exercises), conjugal diversion, relinquishing family-ties, engaging in penitential exercises, conquering the devil, becoming Buddha, preaching, dying, being deposited in the shape of relics; sometimes even hundred (or rather 125) such deeds are enumerated *Cs.* —

Comp. and deriv. *mdzád(-pa)-po* a maker, composer etc.; also to be used for creator. — *mdzad-spyód* resp. deed, action *Mil.*; deportment, conduct, like *spyód-lam Mil.*; course of life, way of acting, e.g. of a heretical king *Pth.*

མཛར་ར་མཛེར་རེ་ *mdzár-ra-mdzer-ré Ld.* pitted with the small-pox, **pock-marked; warty, blotchy**, v. *mdzér-pa*.

མཛུབ་མོ་, vulgo མཛུག་གུ་ *mdzúb-mo, mdzúg-gu*, 1. **finger**, esp. **fore-finger**; *tams-čád k'ar mdzúb-mo čúg-la sdod Glr.* now sit down and put your finger into your mouth (for our: put your finger upon your mouth), i.e. be silent, as becomes the vanquished; **dzúg-gu tŭ'-pa** *C.* a kind of covenanting, the two parties wetting their fingers with saliva and then striking them against one another, which ceremony is considered more stringent than that of **do čóg-pa**, v. *rdo*. The different fingers are: *(m)t'é-bo, (m)t'éb-mo* **thumb**; *mdzúb-mo B.*, **dzúg-gu** vulgo, *ston-byéd Cs.*, *mtsod Med.* **fore-finger**; *srin-lád, bar-mdzúb Cs.*, **gúń-dzug** *C.*, *kán-ma Med.* **middle-finger**; *srin-mdzub Cs.*, **srín-dzug** vulgo, *miń-méd* (*Cs.*, acc. to *Ssk.*) *čad Med.* **the fourth finger**; *(m)t'e(-ba)* or *t'eu-čúń*, **dzug-čúń** *C.* **the little finger.** — 2. **toe.** — 3. **claw.**

Comp. *mdzub-kér, -kyér* or *-kyáń Cs.* a stiff finger. — *mdzub-brkyáńs Cs.* an extended finger. — *mdzub-skyis* finger-ring (= *ser-ydub*) *Lew.* — *mdzub-k'rid* a pointing with the finger, hint, intimation, direction, *blo-t'é-tsom sél-bai mdzub-k'rid byas* he made an intimation that removed every scruple of the mind *Glr.* — **dzug-gáń** *W.* a span, measured with thumb and fore-finger. — *mdzub-gúg* a crooked finger *Cs.* — **mdzub-rtén** vulgo, thimble — *mdzub-mt'ó* 'a span measured with the thumb and middle-finger' *Sch.* prob. = *mdzug-gań*. — *mdzub-rdúb* a mutilated finger *Cs.* — *mdzub-brdá* a hint or sign given with a finger *Cs.* — *mdzub-rtsé* tip of a finger *Cs.* — *mdzub-tsigs* joint of a finger *Cs.* — *mdzub-žá* thimble *Cs.* — *dzug-ri* *W.* = *mdzub-brdá*, *dzug-ri-táṅ-če* to beckon. — *mdzub-šúbs* a fingered glove *Sch.*

མཛེ་ *mdze*, *Ssk.* कुष्ठ, **leprosy** (not cancer, yet infectious, the skin growing white and chapped) *Glr.*, *Med.*; *mdzé-čan* **leprous.**

མཛེར་པ་, འཛེར་པ་ *mdzer-pa*, *ₒdzér-pa* **knot, excrescence** of the skin, **wart** etc. *Med.*; *rus-mdzér S.g.* bony excrescence, exostosis (?); **knag, knot,** in wood *Dzl.*; *mdzer-mál* knot-hole, in boards.

མཛེས་པ་ *mdzés-pa* **fair, handsome, beautiful,** *mdzés-pai* or *-mai bú-mo Glr.*; *bú-mo mdzés-pa* as a tender address to a daughter *Glr.*; *ri-bo nags-ťsál dú-mas mdzés-pa* a mountain beautified by numerous woods; *mdzés-par byá-bai pyir* for show, serving as finery, ornament *Stg.*; fig.: *spyód-lam mdzés-pa* a deportment outwardly unblamable *Dzl.*; *lus-mdzés* a well-made body, *ydoṅ-mdzés* a handsome face, *mig-mdzes* a beautiful eye *Cs.*; *mdzes-mdzés* **pomp, extravagance, profusion, debauchery** *Sch.* — *ynod-mdzés* name of the *rig-sṅágs-kyi rgyál-po*(?) *Dom.*, *Lex.*

མཛོ་ *mdzo* mongrel-breed of the yak-bull and common cow *Lt.*, whilst *ₒbri-mdzo* (*W.* *brim-dzo*) is the hybrid of a common bull and a yak-cow, *mdzó-po* a male, *mdzó-mo* a female animal of the kind, both valued as domestic cattle; *mdzó-mo-kyu* a herd of such animals; *mdzo-rgód* wild cattle; *mdzo-prúg* calf of such cattle; *mdzo-kó* leather, *mdzo-már* butter from a bastard cow, *mdzo-sgál* load for the same *Cs.*; *mdzo-ťsá Wdṅ.* n. of a medicine (cf. *ba-ťsá?*).

མཛོ་མོ་ *mdzó-mo*, 1. v. *mdzo.* — 2. **oats** *Sch.*

མཛོད་ *mdzod*, *Ssk.* कोष, 1. sbst. **store-house, magazine, depository, strong-box,** *mdzód-du ₒjúg-pa, sbéd-pa* to secure, to hide a thing in a depository, *mdzód-nas ₒdón-pa* to fetch forth from it; *dkor-mdzód, yter-mdzód Glr.* treasury; *baṅ-mdzód* corn-magazine, granary; *dbyig-mdzód* a safe for valuables, *yser-mdzód* for gold; *pyag-mdzód* (*Cs.* also *mdzód-pa*) **treasurer,** with kings, in large monasteries; *miṅ-gi mdzod* a treasury of words, **dictionary.** — *mdzod-kaṅ* store-room, larder. — *mdzod-sruṅ* treasurer *Dzl.* — 2. vb. v. *mdzád-pa.*

མཛོད་སྤུ་ *mdzód-spu*, *Ssk.* ऊर्णा, *smin-mtsams-kyi mdzód-spu Glr.*, acc. to *Cs.* **a single hair,** acc. to the majority, **a circle of hair,** between the eye-brows, in the middle of the forehead, one of the particular marks of a Buddha, from which, e.g., he is able to send forth magic or divine rays of light.

མཛོལ་བུ་ *mdzól-bu Lex.*; *Sch.*: **'grief, dejection; a snare, a trap'**(?).

འཛའ་ *ₒdza* 1. **exchange, agio** *C.* — 2. **interest** or **premium** paid for the use of money borrowed *Lh.*

འཛའ་བ་ *ₒdzá-ba*, prob. only in the word *čúd-ₒdza-ba* **to be expended in vain** *Cs.* (?).

འཛག་པ་ *ₒdzág-pa*, pf. (*y*)*zags*, fut. *yzag*, (intrs. to *ₒtsag-pa*), **to drop, drip, trickle,** *sna-krág, sna-ču dzag* blood, water, dripping from the nose *Med.*; *ṅal-ťag zág-če* the menstrual flow of females (plain expression for it) *W.*; *mči-ma Dzl.*; *ₒó-ma ₒdzág-pa dé-las ₒbyuṅ* milk is trickling from it *Wdṅ.*; *ₒdzag-ₒdzág-pa* to trickle constantly *Sch.*; in a more gen. sense: **to flow out** spouting; *krag yzágs-pa* the blood that has been shed *Dzl.*; *mtso žábs-nas zágs-te méd-par soṅ* flowing off at the bottom, the lake dwindled away *Mil.*; *ká-ču zag dug* *W.* he foams (with rage); *bžin zags-te* the face dripping (with perspiration); *šú-gu zags soṅ* *W.* the paper runs, blots; sometimes used transitively: *kún-la snyiṅ-btse mči-ma yzag* he is shedding tears of universal pity *Dzl.* 22, 16; *sor bar-nas ₒdzág-nas* letting (the ashes) fall through between his fingers *Mil.*

འཛག་འཛོག་ *ₒdzag-ₒdzóg* **mixed, mingled, promiscuously, pell-mell** *Lexx.* = *ₒkrúgs-pa.*

འཛང་འཛོང་ *ₒdzaṅ-ₒdzóṅ* = *ytsaṅ-ytsóṅ.*

འཛངས་པ་ *ₒdzaṅs-pa*, *Lex.* = *zád-pa* **spent, consumed, exhausted,** construed with *nor*, of rare occurrence.

འཛད་པ་ *°dzád-pa*, pf. *zad* **1. to be on the decline, pf. to be consumed, spent,** frq., *bságs-pai nor °dzad* the gathered wealth goes to an end *Pth.*; *snúm-zad-kyi már-me* a lamp the oil of which is exhausted *Glr.*; *k̒yód-kyi bsód-nams zád-pai ts̒óṅ-p̒rug-rnams* ye (poor) partners in trade, whose stored-up merits are now at an end (whilst the speaker by the strength of his virtue is saved from the danger in which the others perish) *Glr.*; *rgyágs-la zad* that has been spent for provisions *Mil.*; *brlai ša zad kyaṅ yaṅ-ṅo* the flesh of the upper part of the thigh, even after it had been used (after all had been laid on the scales), was nevertheless lighter than .... *Dzl.*; *t̒abs-zád* helpless *Glr.*; *ts̒e-yóṅs-su zád-pa-las* whilst life is consuming itself *Do.*; *ts̒e-zád-kar Do.*, prob. the same as *°č̒i-k̒ar*, at the hour of death; frq. referred to sin: *°dod-č̒ágs-kyi sems, dri-ma kun, nyés-pai skyon t̒ams-čád, °dód-pa kun yóṅs-su zád-de* sensuality and all sin, desire and defilement being done away with, having ceased *Dzl.*; *dug lṅai lás-la zád-pa med* the effects of the five poisons (q.v.) never cease; *°dré-la zad-pa med* of devils there is an infinite number *Mil.*; *zad (-pa) méd(-pa), zad-mi-šes-pa* incessant, endless, everlasting — 2. *°dis zad* **with this it is done,** i.e. a. this is **the only thing,** besides which no second is existing; *°dis don-ɣnyer-žiṅ °ts̒ó-bar zád-na* as this is our **only means** of making a living *Dzl.*; *bu ni k̒yod ɣčig-pur zád-de* as thou art **our only son** *Dzl.*; *mt̒óṅ-ba k̒ó-mo k̒ó-nar zád-de* as I am **the only person** that has seen .... *Tar.*; *mts̒óṅ-bar zád-de* this is limited to seeing, this refers **only** to sight *Dzl.* ༢༠, 12; *ɣnyis ni miṅ ɣčig-pa tsám-du zád-pas* as the two have **only one name** *Tar.*; hence the frequent *ma zád-de* with the termin. case, **not only,** *srog °dór-ba °di °bá-žig-tu ma zád-de* having lost his life not only this time (but often so before) *Dzl.* ༢༣, 13; *der ma zad(-kyi)* not enough with that, still more, further, yea even *Thgy.* — b. **it is decided, settled, unquestionable,** *nor rgyál-pos bžés-par zád-na* as the fortune unquestionably falls to the king.

འཛུབ་ *°dzub* **magic sentence,** *bzlá-ba* to pronounce one *Lex.*

འཛབ(ས)་པ་ *°dzáb(s)-pa* **to strive, endeavour; to be studious, to give diligence** *Sch.*

འཛམ་བུ་ *°dzám-bu* v. *dzám-bu.*

འཛམ་བུར་ *°dzam-búr*, **gun, cannon,** **gyáb-pa** *C.* to discharge.

འཛར་ *°dzar* **bob, tassel, tuft** *Lex.*

འཛར་བ་ *°dzár-ba Cs.*: **'to hang down'**; yet it is evidently the prop. present-form to the pf. *bzar* and the fut. *ɣzar*, which frq. are used without regard to tense: **to hang up,** clothes on a line *Dzl.*; **to hang** or **throw over,** the toga over one's shoulder *Dzl.* and elsewh.

འཛི་བ་ *°dzí-ba* **to abstain from, to be abstinent, temperate** *Sch.*

འཛིང་བ་ *°dziṅ-ba* **to quarrel, contend, fight,** *mč̒e-, sder-, rwa-°dziṅ byéd-pa* to fight with tusks, claws, horns *Cs.*; *°dzíṅ-mo* **quarrel, contention, dispute.**

འཛིངས་པ་, གཟིང་བ་ *°dzíṅs-pa, ɣziṅ-ba*, gen. with *skra*, rarely with *mgo Glr.*, **bristly, rugged, shaggy,** of beggars *Dzl*, infernal monsters *Dzl.* — *sprin-sna °dziṅs-mt̒iṅ-nág Mil.?*

འཛིན་ *°dzin* I. **the act of seizing, seizure, grasp, gripe,** v. *°dzin-pa*, e.g. *nyi-°dzin* eclipse of the sun, *zla-°dzin* lunar eclipse, (the heavenly bodies being seized by the dragon Rāhula, v. *sgra-ɣčan*), *ril-°dzin* total, *č̒a-°dzin* partial eclipse *Wdk.* — 2. **he that seizes, holds fast, a holder, keeper; receptacle;** *rdo-rje-°dzin* v. *rdó-rje*; *č̒u-°dzin* po. cloud, *ro-°dzin* po. tongue *Lex.*; **adherent,** e.g. in *srol-°dzin.* — 3. **bond, obligation, certificate,** e.g. *p̒rod-°dzin* **receipt, acquittance.** — 4. **contract, agreement, treaty,** **žág-pa** *C.*, **táṅ-če** *W.*, to conclude, make, a bargain, a treaty; *yig-°dzin* **a written agreement.**

འཛིན་ཅན་ *°dzin-čan W.* **sticky, glutinous** (?).

འཛིན་པ་ *°dzin-pa* I. vb. pf. *(b)zuṅ*, fut. *ɣzuṅ*, imp. *zuṅ(s)*, also *ɣzúṅ-ba, bzúṅ-ba* and *zin-pa* in all tenses, *W.* **zúm-če**, *Bal.* **zúṅ-čas**, 1. **to take hold of, to seize, grasp,** *lág-pa-nas* to grasp a person's hand *Mil.*; *mgó-nas* taking hold of a skull *Dzl.* ༢༡, 6; *gós-kyi mťá-ma* to seize the coat-tail *Dzl.*; *mi* a man, = to catch, frq.; *čúṅ-mar* ˳*dzin-pa* to take wives *Glr.*; **to hold,** *lág-na rál-gri* to hold a sword in one's hand *Glr.*; **ḱyi zum toṅ* W.*, **ḱyi dzin* (or *zin*) *rog ǰhę* C.*, hold the dog fast! **to catch,** a ball, rain-water etc.; *bzuṅ-bas mi zin capiendo non capitur*, it (the soul) cannot be taken hold of *Mil.*; *bdág-gi ẏduṅ-brgyúd* ˳*dzin-pai rgyál-bu* a prince upholding my race *Glr.*; **to hold, support,** a certain doctrine; **to embrace,** another religion *Glr.*, v. below; to take upon one's self, some religious duty. — 2. **to get, receive, obtain.** — 3. **to occupy, to take possession of,** hold in possession, a country *Ma.*, *rgyál-sa* the throne; **to be seized,** *nád-kyis zin-pa* seized with a malady *Mil.*, — 4. intellectually: **to take in, comprehend, grasp, conceive,** by the faculty of perception or imagination: *dbáṅ-po-rnams-kyi nús-pa zad-pas yul mi* ˳*dzin-pa-am ẏžán-du* ˳*dzin-pa* to perceive things not as they are, or not at all, in consequence of weakened senses *Thgy.*; with reference to mind or memory: *séms-la, yid-la, bló-la B.* and *col.*; **to be taken in, affected, seized, captivated,** *sdíg-pas zin-pa* to be affected, taken, by sin *Mil.*; *ťúgs-rǰes zin-pa* to be kindly, graciously, affected towards a person; *ťugs-ma zin-pa* to be not graciously inclined *Mil. nt.*; *bú-mos zin-pa* taken in love with a girl *Pth.*; ˳*dzin-pa ťams-čád* all that captivates me; **to choose, to follow,** *ri-ḱród* to choose the solitude of mountains *Mil.*, *dmán-sa* to follow humility, to choose lowliness *Mil.* and elsewh.; **to embrace,** another religion, v. above; **to take for, to consider, esteem,** *ṅa-la dgrar* taking me for an enemy *Dzl.*; *mi* or *mí-la ẏčés-par* or *sdúg-par* to value, esteem, love, a person, v. *ẏčés-pa*; *ṗar, mar* to esteem, respect one, as a father, as a mother *Stg.*; *méd-pa-la yód-par* to consider the not existing as existing *Thgr.*; *ẏnyis-su* to consider as different, to find a difference between two things, which according to Buddhist philosophy are one and the same, cf. *ẏnyis-*˳*dzin*; also absolutely, without an object being mentioned: *dṅós-por* ˳*dzin-pa* to believe in the reality (of a thing) *Mil.* — 5. *rǰés-su* ˳*dzin-pa* v. *rǰes*.

II. sbst. 1. **he that seizes, holds, occupies,** *rigs-sṅags* ˳*dzin-pa* the holder of a magic sentence; **adherent, keeper** etc. — 2. **that which affects, captivates,** in an intellectual sense, v. above ˳*dzin-pa ťams-čád*; the being seized or affected with, or as we should say, **taking an interest in,** v. sub *spóṅ-ba*; also cf. *ẏzuṅ-*˳*dzin*. — ˳*dzin-skyóṅ*, *ṗo-bráṅ* ˳*dii* ˳*dzin-skyóṅ gyis* occupy this palace and take care of it *Glr.* — ˳*dzin-pa* **the earth,** as a receptacle of beings *Sch.*

འཛིམ་པ་ ˳*dzim-pa Lt.?* acc. to one *Lex.* = ˳*dzin-pa*.

འཛིར་བ་ ˳*dzir-ba*, = འཛག་པ *dzág-pa* **to drop, to drip** *Lex.*

འཛུ་བ་ ˳*dzu-ba*, pf. ˳*dzus*, **to enter** *Sch.*

འཛུགས་པ་ and ཟུག་པ་ ˳*dzugs-pa* and *zug-pa*, pf. *btsugs, zugs*, fut. *ẏzugs*, imp. *zug(s)*, (trs. to ˳*ťsugs-pa*) 1. **to prick** or **stick into, to set,** to prick a stick, to set a plant, into the ground, **to plant,** frq.; **to run, thrust, pierce,** to run one's self a splinter into the flesh etc. *W.*; **to erect,** a pillar, **to raise,** a standard. — 2. **to put down, to place,** a kettle *Dzl.*; to place before, *mi-la ṗór-pa* to place a drinking-bowl before a person (more genteel than *bžag-pa*) *Glr.*; **to put or place on, to touch with,** *mdzúb-mo* the finger; esp. *pús-mo(-i lha-ṅá) sá-la* to place the knee on the ground, to kneel down, v. *pús-mo*; *žábs-*˳*dzugs-kyi dga-ston* feast given, when a little child begins to walk *Glr.* — 3. **to lay out,** a garden, **to found,** a town, a convent; **to institute,** a sacrificial festival *Glr.*; **to introduce,** *srol* a custom *Lex.*, hence in a general sense, **to begin, commence,** any business, with or without *mgo*; **ku-rím tsúg-sa ma tsugs* W.* has the ceremony already begun? is it a going? *rgól-ba* ˳*dzúgs-pa* to offer resistance *Pth.* — 4. **to prick, sting, pierce,** *mdas* with arrows *Dzl.*, fig. *mi-ḱa zúg-pa* hurting by malicious words *Do.*;

tsig kún-tu zúg-pa a sarcastic, offensive speech *Stg.* — 5. intrs., **to bore or force itself into, to penetrate, to take hold, to stick to,** mostly fig., e.g. *sman ma zug* the medicine has not taken hold yet, does not work *Thgy.*; *zlá-la Kyéd-kyis mi zug* you do not cling or stick to a companion *Mil.*; **dé-la sem zúg-pa* C.* to be attached to, to be pleased with a thing; **zúg-pa* C.*, attached. — 6. **to sting,** like nettles, **to prick,** *tser ltar* like a thorn *Mil.*; *ló-ma zúg-par byed* the leaves sting *Wdñ.*; *zug-rgyu-méd-pa* not smarting *Wdñ.*

འཛུད་པ་ *ₒdzúd-pa*, pf. *btsud*, *Sch.* also *zud*, imp. *tsud* (trs. to *ₒtsúd-pa*, synon. to *ₒjúg-pa*), **to put, to lay,** into a box, into the grave; **to lead, to guide,** into the right way, to virtue, to religion = to convert; to reduce, to despair, *sdig-pa-la* to seduce to sin *Pth.*; **to prompt** one to do a thing *Gyatch.*; *ₒdzúd-ₒdzud-pa* to put into *Sch.*

འཛུབ་མོ་ *ₒdzub-mo*, sometimes erron. for *mdzúb-mo.*

འཛུམ་ *ₒdzum* **smile,** *bydms-pai ₒdzúm-γyis* with a friendly smile; *ₒdzum byéd-pa* **to smile;** *ₒdzum dañ ldan* **smiling** *Pth.*; *ₒdzum skyóñ-ba* to preserve a friendly countenance, to be always mild and gentle; *ₒdzum-skyoñ* in a special sense, the exhortation given to every daughter on her marriage, to treat visitors with a friendly smile; also fig., **an engaging appearance,** *rí-mo ₒdzúm-gyis ma bslús-par* not to be deceived by an enticing appearance of colour *Mil.*; *ño-ₒdzúm*, **smile,** in a relative sense, *ǎ-nei ño-ₒdzúm dkar nag bltas* I watched whether the smile, the mien, of my aunt was friendly or unfriendly *Mil.*; *ño-ₒdzúm nág-ste* looking sad *Dzl.*

འཛུམ་པ་ *ₒdzum-pa*, pf. *btsum*, *zum*, fut. *γzum*, imp. *tsum* 1. **to close, to shut,** yet only in certain applications, more esp. **to close one's eyes, to shut one's mouth,** *mig mi-ₒdzúm-par ltá-žiñ* to have one's eyes immovably fixed upon *Dzl.*; also *pád-mai Ka zum bžin S.g.* just as the lotus-flower closes; *má-Ka mi zúm-žiñ Wdñ.* if the wound will not close; *Ka zum* the orifice (of the urethra) is closed *Mñg.* — 2. **to wink,** prob. only **dzum-dzúm ǰhé'-pa* and *čó-če*.* — 3. **to smile,** *rdb-tu* to look very friendly *Glr.*; sbst. **the smile,** *bčom-ldan-ₒdás-kyi žal ₒdzúm-pa dañ bčás-pai sgó-nas* from the portals of Buddha's countenance graced with a smile *Glr.*; *žal-ₒdzúm mdzád-pa* resp. to smile *Glr.*; *bžin-gyi ₒdzum* the smile of the countenance; adj. **smiling; sweet, beautiful** *Mil.*

Comp. *ₒdzúm-Ka* a smiling mouth; *lha-mo ₒdzúm-Ka-mo* a smiling goddess *Mil.* — *ₒdzúm-bag-čan* (of a child) sweetly smiling *Mil.* — *ₒdzum-ltag-dgyé Cs.:* 'a smile between the teeth, a sardonic smile, a grin'; *ₒdzum-mdáñs* a smiling air *Cs.* — *ₒdzum-múl* or *-dmúl* a smile; *dzum-múl-gyis šor* a smile escaped him *Glr.*; *ₒdzum-(d)múl-ba* to smile. — *ₒdzum-méd* frowning, austere *Cs.* — *ₒdzum-ₒdzúm* 1. the winking. 2. the smiling; *ₒdzum-wañ-wáñ Cs.:* smiling look.

འཛུར་ *ₒdzur*, 1. sup. of *ₒdzu-ba.* 2. v. the following.

འཛུར་བ་ *ₒdzur-ba*, pf. *bzur*, fut. *γzur*, imp. *zur*, *Cs.* **zúr-wa** **to give** or **make way,** *lam(-nas)* to step aside; **to keep aloof** *Mil.*; *lás-la ₒdzúr-ba* to shun work, to evade labour *Lex.*

འཛུལ་བ་ *ₒdzúl-ba* 1. vb. **to slip in,** *rtsa-γséb-tu* between the grass *Thgy.*, *sgor* through the door *Lex.*; *čú-la*, *čur* into the water, i.e. to dive. — 2. sbst. *Sch.:* **'a tippler'.**

འཛུས་ *ₒdzus* v. *ₒdzú-ba.*

འཛེག་པ་ *ₒdzég-pa*, pf. *ₒdzegs*, imp. *ₒdzog*, **to ascend,** *rí-la* frq.; *šiñ-sdoñ-po-la Glr.*

འཛེང་ *ₒdzeñ*, *ₒdzeñ-rdo* **whsettone, hone** *Lex.*

འཛེང་བ་ *ₒdzéñ-ba* **to stick** or **jut out, to project, to be prominent** *Sch.*

འཛེད་པ་ *ₒdzéd-pa*, pf. *bzed*, fut. *γzed*, vulgo *bzéd-pa*, **zé'-pa* C.*, **zéd-če* W.*, **to hold out** or **forth,** *Kud* the coat-tail, *snod* a vessel *Dzl.* (The significations given by *Cs.*: **to receive,** and by *Sch.:* **to meet with,** seem not to be sufficiently warranted.)

འཛེམ་པ་ *ₒdzém-pa* **to shrink,** *la*, from, **to shun, avoid,** *mi-dgé-ba-la Glr.*, *sdig-*

pa-la frq.; ṅó-tsa-la mi ₒdzém-pa Cs. **insensible to shame, shameless**; nád-rigs-la-mi ₒdzém-na unless one is on his guard against the several diseases; also **to feel ashamed**, *ṅe'-nam-la mi ₒdzem-mam* C. do you not feel abashed in our presence? ₒdzém-pa-čan ₒdzém-bag-čan **bashful, modest, temperate** Cs.; ₒdzém(-pa)-med(-pa) the contrary; k'rel-ₒdzém **modesty** Cs.

འཛེར་པ་ ₒdzér-pa v. mdzér-pa.

འཛེར་བ་ ₒdzér-ba 1. **to say**, to speak, Stg. ཁ་ 57, 6, obs., v. zér-ba. — 2. **to be hoarse**, ₒdzér-po hoarse, skad Dzl., Med.; skad ₒdzer-ₒdzér-du ṅú-ba to weep with a very hoarse voice Pth. — 3. **to solder** Sch.

འཛོ་སྒྲེལ་ ₒdzo-sgrél Mil.?

འཛོག་པ་ ₒdzóg-pa, pf. btsogs, fut. btsog **to heap together, to jumble, to throw disorderly together** Cs.

འཛོང་འཛོང་ ₒdzoṅ-ₒdzóṅ Ts. *ₒdzog-ₒdzóg* 1. **jagged, pointed, conical**. — 2. **oblong, cylindrical** C.

འཛོམ(ས)་པ་ ₒdzóm(s)-pa **to come together, to meet**, *dzom tsár-ra ma tsar* are they already assembled? dúg-pa mṅón-dgai žiṅ-k'ams der ₒó-skol ₒdzóm-par ɣdon mi za that we shall meet again in the realms of pure bliss, that is certain Mil.; tses bčo-lṅá daṅ ₒdzóms-pas as it just fell upon the 15th. Glr.; *dzom mi dzom* W. they do not agree with each other; dé-rnams rnyéd-par dká-ste mi ₒdzom as it is difficult to obtain these things, we shall not be able to get all of them together Glr.; *dzóm-pa mé'-pa čig kyaṅ me'* C. there is nothing that does not find its way there, that is not to be had there; **to be plentiful** Mil.; as partic. with termin. case: **rich in, abounding** Mil. — dál-ₒbyor ₒdzóm-pai lus Mil. v. dál-ba. — k'un-ₒdzóm 'where all meet', name of mountain-passes, e. g. between Lh. and Sp., and of females; in a similar manner yaṅ-ₒdzóm and ₒbyor-ₒdzóm ('conflux of goods'). — ₒdzóm-po rich in C., rtsa-ču ₒdzóm-po abounding in grass and water, fertile C.; mt'un-rkyén ₒdzóm-po fortunate, successful, through a favourable concurrence of circumstances; tsos-sna-ₒdzóm-po variegated, many-coloured.

འཛོལ་པ་ ₒdzól-pa **fault, error, mistake**, dé-la ₒdzól-pa ɣsum byuṅ he fell into three mistakes, committed three errors Glr.

འཛོལ་བ་ ₒdzól-ba **to shake about, to stir** or **shake up**, e.g. a feather-bed; **to confound, to confuse**, p'rin goṅ-ₒog ₒdzol-ba to deliver a message confusedly, making a mess of it Glr.; W.: *zol-zól čo-če*. — *ₒdzól-tso* C., *zol-zól* W. **difference**.

ཛ་ rdza, W. *za*, 1. **clay**, gen. rdzá-sa. — 2. in comp. for rdzá-ma, e.g. čáṅ-rdza **beer-jug**, čú-rdza **water-pitcher** Cs. —

Comp. and deriv. rdza-kór earthen bowl, little dish. — rdza-k'áṅ pottery Schr. — rdza-k'úṅ clay-pit. — rdza-mk'án potter, rdza-mk'án-gyi ₒkór-lo skór-ba to turn the potter's wheel Dom. — rdza-rṅá kettle-drum of burnt clay. — rdza-čág potsherd. — rdza-čú, or more refined rdza-čáb, water issuing from clay-slate rocks Mil. and elsewh. — rdza-čén a large, rdza-čúṅ a little pot, v. rdzá-ma. — rdza-snód, rdza-spyád earthen vessel. — rdza-pág tile, (Dutch) tile for stoves. — rdza-p'ór C. = rdza-kór. — rdza-búm 1. **pitcher, jar, bottle**, formed of clay. 2. **jar**, in gen., lčágs-kyi rdza-búm iron jar Stg. — rdzá-bo an earthen vessel Cs. — rdzá-ma **pot** (unglazed, urn-shaped, bellied vessels of various size, not for cooking, but only for holding water, butter and the like). — rdza-ɣžóṅ earthen basin. — rdza-ri mountain consisting of clay-slate. — rdza-sá argillaceous earth, clay. — dza-brá, C. *dzab-ra*, W. *zab-ra* a mole-like animal.

ཛ་ཀི་ rdzá-ki Mil., for dzó-gi, yó-gi.

ཛང་ rdzaṅ **chest, box**, for various store = báṅ-ba Thgy.

ཛང་བ་ rdzáṅ-ba v. rdzóṅ-ba.

ཛབ་ rdzab, ₒdam-rdzáb, **mud, mire** (Cs. **clay**); rdzab-dóṅ **sink, slough**.

ཛབ་ཛུབ་ rdzab-rdzúb **sham, emptiness, falsehood**, rmi-lam rdzab-rdzúb-čan an empty dream Cs.

རྫས་ *rdzas* 1. **thing, matter, object** (= *dṅós-po Lex.*), *rdzas dkar sér-por mtoṅ* white objects appear yellow *Lt.*; *rdzas ḱa-sáṅ yód-pa dé-riṅ med* the thing of yesterday is to-day no more *Mil.*; *mi-ɣtsáṅ-bai rdzas* something impure *Pth.*; natural bodies, **substances,** from which e.g. medicines are prepared *S.g.*; **materials, requisites,** *dei rdzas* requisites for this purpose; especially for sacrifices, sorceries etc., hence also used as identical with **magic agency** *Wdṅ.*; **remedy,** *smyo-byéd-kyi* narcotic, soporific *Glr.*; **ointment,** v. *rkáṅ-pa* and *bábs*; *rdzás-las ˳byúṅ-bai bsód-nams Tar.* 20, 9, not: merits arising 'from works or any material causes', but: the good, the blessing accruing from a right application of *rdzas*, wonder-working medicines, and consisting in long life etc., with which also *Trigl.* fol. 20, b is in unison, if the Sanskrit word is read *dzaiwatrikam*; *srog-rdzás* **provisions, victuals** *Pth.*; in the context *rdzas* is also found standing alone in the same sense, where it perh. would be more correct to read *zas*; *mé-mdai rdzas*, *me-rdzás*, also *rdzas* alone, **gun-powder,** **dzę-ḱúg* C.* cartridge-box, **dzę-mé'** (a gun) not loaded *C.*; **goods, property,** *rdzas gaṅ yód-pa-rnams* all his property *Mil.*; *nor (daṅ) rdzas* money and money's worth *Mil.* and elsewh.; **treasures, jewels, valuable productions,** *rgya-gár-gyi Glr.* — 2. in philosophy: **matter** *Was.*; **real substance, realities** *Was.*

རྫི་ *rdzi*, *W.* **zi**, 1. **wind,** *rdzi-rlúṅ* id., also *bsér-bui*, *rlúṅ-gi rdzi Do.*; *ṗu-rdzi*, or *stod-rdzi* a wind blowing down the valley, *luṅ-* or *mdo-rdzi* blowing up the valley; *dri-rdzi ldaṅ* a fragrant breeze, a wind fraught with the odours of flowers is blowing *Stg.*; **šár-zi yóṅ-ṅa rag* W.* I perceive an east-wind is setting in; *rdzi-čár* heavy rain with wind, *rdzi-čár drág-po* rain-storm *Tar.* and elsewh.; **zi núm-če** or *tsór-če* W.* **to smell, sniff, snuffle,** of dogs. — 2. in comp. for *rdzi-bo*, *rdzi-ma*. — 3. v. *zi*.

རྫི་བ་ *rdzi-ba*, pf. *(b)rdzis*, fut. *brdzi*, imp. *(b)rdzi(s)*, *W.*, **zi-če**, *Pur.* **dzi-čas** **to press, to knead,** dough; **to tread, to beat** (clay, *gyaṅ* q. v.); *gál-te tsér-ma brdzis-na* if I should tread into a thorn *Dzl.*; **to crush,** a worm; **to oppress, to distress;** *rdzi-méd Lex., Sch.*: 'powerless', but *stóbs-rnams-la rdzi-ba-med-pa Stg.* evidently signifies: of invincible strength.

རྫི་བོ་ *rdzi-bo* **herdsman, shepherd, keeper,** frq.; also *rdziu Dzl.*; *rdzi-ṗo* a male, *rdzi-mo* a female keeper; *ṗyúgs-rdzi* herdsman, *ɣnág-rdzi* neat-herd, *gláṅ-rdzi* cow-keeper; *rá-rdzi* (**rár-zi* W.*) goat-herd; *ḱyi-rdzi* dog-feeder, *byá-rdzi* person attending to the poultry; *mi-rdzi* 'guarder of man, a god' *Cs.* yet a king might also be thus designated; *rdzi-skór* shepherd's hut = *pu-lu*. *Sch.* has besides: *dpe-rdzi* **index, register.**

རྫི་མ་ *rdzi-ma* (vulgo **zi-ma**) **eye-lashes** (the eye-lashes of Buddha are sometimes compared to those of a cow).

རྫིག་རྫིག་ *rdzig-rdzig*, with **taṅ-wa* C.*, **to address harshly, to fly at.**

རྫིང་ *rdziṅ* **pond,** gen. *rdziṅ-bu* e. g. for bathing *Dzl.*; v. also *skyil-ba*; *rdziṅ-po* or *-čén* a large pond *Cs.*

རྫིངས་ *rdziṅs*, *gru-rdziṅs Lt.*, gen. *ɣziṅs* **ship, ferry.**

རྫིའུ་ *rdziu* 1. for *rdzi-bo*. — 2. **fin of a fish** *Sch.*

རྫུ་བ་ *rdzú-ba*, pf. *(b)rdzus*, fut. *brdzu*, imp. *(b)rdzu(s)* **to give a deceptive representation,** to make a thing appear different from what it is (cf. *sprúl-ba*), with termin. case **to change into,** also **to change** (one's self), **to be changed,** *srin-por* to change into a Rakshasa *Zam.*; **to disguise** one's self, *rnál-byor-par* as a mendicant friar; *rdzús-te skyé-ba* v. *skyé-ba*; *yig-rdzu* a letter filled with falsehoods, a lying epistle *Mil. nt.*; *šá-ru rdzú-bai rgyú-ma* entrails feigning to be flesh, looking like flesh *Mil.*; *rdzu-˳ṗrúl* (*Ssk.* ऋद्धि) **delusion, miraculous appearances, transformations,** *stón-pa* to produce such, *˳ǰig-pa* to destroy the illusion, e.g. by seeing through it *Mil.*; *rdzu-˳ṗrúl-gyi mtu*, or *stobs* **witchcraft, magic;** *rdzu-˳ṗrul-čan* gifted with magic power *Thgy.* *rdzu-˳ṗrul* is the highest manifestation of the acquired moral perfection, that is known to Buddhism; there is, however, an essential difference between it and the miracles of holy writ, the former bearing the stamp of non-reality and mere appearance, as is not only implied by the name, but also universally acknowledged; and it differs again from *čo-ₒṗrul*, in as much as the latter requires the help of natural magic (jugglery), or of demoniacal influences, and never can be produced, like *rdzu-ₒṗrúl*, at the pleasure of the saint by his own immanent power. Yet there is no doubt that the term *čo-ₒṗrul* is also often used in connection with *rdzu-ₒṗrúl*, and as identical with it; v. *Dzl.* ༣༦ and ༡༠༩.

རྫུན་ *rdzun, C.* **dzun**, *W.* **zun**, *Pur.* **rdzun**, also *brdzun* **untruthful speech, falsehood, lie, fiction, fable**; *rdzun-ťsig*, id.; *mi-bden rdzún* that is falsehood and not truth *Glr.*; *rdzun-smrá-ba*, resp. *ysúṅ-ba B.*, *byéd-pa B., C.*, **zér-če** *W.* **to lie**, *rgyál-ba-rnams-kyis rdzun ysúṅ-ba mi srid* it is impossible that Buddhas should lie; **to tell tales, to make believe, to impose upon**; **zun yin** *W.* you are not in earnest, you only want to quiz me; **zun gyáb-če** *W.* to lie, to act the hypocrite; **mi še zun gyab** *W.* to feign, to pretend ignorance, to disown a person or thing, **mi ťsor zun gyab** *W.* he pretends not to hear it. — *rdzun-ₒḱrúb Sch.*: 'an adroit liar and deceiver'. — *rdzún-ma* 1. = *rdzun Dzl.* 2. **liar** *Mil.* — **zún-yag-čan** *W.* **clown, buffoon, merry Andrew.**

རྫུབ་ *rdzub* **deceit, imposture** *Lex.*, *byéd-pa* **to make a false assertion** *Tar.*; cf. *rdzab-rdzub.*

རྫུས་མ་ *rdzús-ma* something **counterfeit, feigned, dissembled,** *rdzús-mai spráṅ-po* a disguised beggar *Glr.*

རྫེ་བ་ *rdzé-ba* pf. *(b)rdzes*, fut. *brdze*, imp. *(b)rdze(s) W.* **zé-če**, 1. **to tuck up, truss up,** clothes; **to cock,** a hat; **to turn up,** the upper-lip *Wdṅ.*; *skra gyén-du brdzés-pa* the hair bristling *Do.*; **so* or *čé-wa zé-če** *W.* to show one's teeth, to grin. — 2. **to threaten** *Cs.*

རྫེའུ་ *rdzéu* dimin. of *rdzá-ma*, **a small pot, pipkin.**

རྫོག(ས)་ *rdzog(s)?* **fist,** also **dzog-ril** *C.*

རྫོགས་པ་ *rdzogs-pa* 1. vb. **to be finished, to be at an end, to terminate** (*Lex.* = *zín-pa*), *lam rdzógs-pai mťsáms-su* just where the road terminates *Mil.*; **dá-wa zóg-nę** *W.* as the month has expired; **ťi-ru pí-ti yúl-ťso zog soṅ** *W.* here the villages of Spiti have an end; *mdzád-pa yóṅs-su rdzógs-nas* having accomplished all his deeds *Glr.*; *ji-ltar smón-pa bžin-du yoṅs rdzógs-pas* all prayers and wishes being fully realized *Dzl.*; *yóṅs-su rdzógs-par ťsár-te* when the whole (of the building) was completed *Glr.* — 2. adj. **perfect, complete, blameless,** **gó-lo zog dug** *W.* the body (of this horse) is without fault; *stón-pa dág-par rdzógs-pai saṅs-rgyás* the most perfect teacher, Buddha *Glr.*; so in a similar manner *rdzogs (-pa)-čén(-po)*; also *yé-šes yóṅs-su rdzógs-pa* is an appellation of Buddha. — *rdzógs-par* adv. **perfectly, completely, fully** (cf. *lhúg-par*), *bsnyád-pa* to report circumstantially *Dzl.*, *ydams-ṅág ynáṅ-ba* to counsel well *Mil.*; *rdzógs-par šés-pa žig* one thoroughly conversant *Mil.*; *rdzógs-par bsláb-pa* to learn thoroughly *Mil.* — *bsnyén-par rdzógs-pa* or *bsnyen-rdzógs mdzád-pa* to ordain, v. *bsnyén-pa.* —

Comp. *rdzogs-ldán* v. *dus* 6. — *rdzogs-ťsig* v. *slár-sdu-ba.* — **dzog-yél** *C.* obeisance to Chinese officers, in a kneeling posture. — *rdzogs-rim* v. sub *skyéd-pa.*

རྫོང(ས)་ *rdzoṅ(s)*, 1. (*C.* vulgo **dzum**) **castle, fortress**; *rdzóṅ-dpon* lord or governor of a castle, commander of a fortress; **dzoṅ-kyél** *C.*, **zoṅ-lén** *W.* letter-post from one nobleman's seat to another. — 2. **the act of accompanying, escorting,** *ₒdebs-pa* **to accompany, to escort** *Dzl.*, **fee for safe-conduct,** travelling-present; **dowry,** *byéd-pa* to bestow.

རྫོང་བ་ *rdzóṅ-ba* pf. *(b)rdzaṅ(s)*, fut. *(b)rdzaṅ* **to send, to dispatch,** presents, ambassadors; **to expedite, send off, dismiss; to give to take along with.** — *dbugs rdzóṅ-ba* **shortness of breath, asthma** *Thgy.* and elsewh.

རྫོབ་པོ་, -མོ་ *rdzób-po, -mo*, 1. **vain, empty, spurious, void**; *kun-rdzób* v. *kun.* — 2. **vain, fond of dress** *W.*

ཝ

ཝ wa 1. the letter **w**, which occurs but rarely, and only as an initial, yet it is a true Tibetan letter, the *Ssk.* व being gen. represented by བ, and as second constituent of a double consonant denoted by ྭ (called *wa-zúr* angular or small *wa*); the pronunciation in general is the same as that of the English w. — 2. num. fig.: 20.

ཝ་ *wa* 1. **water-channel, gutter,** gen. of wood (*Cs.* also: trough); *wa-ḱa Lex.* id., *Cs.*; *wa-mču* **spout, lip,** or **beak** of vessels. — 2. **fox** (the name corresponding to the sound of barking) *Dzl.*, vulgo *wa-tsé; wa brgyal* the fox yelps *Sch.* The fox is the riding-beast of the goblins; whenever his barking is heard, it is in consequence of his receiving lashes from his rider. — *wa-skyés* fox-born *Cs.* — *wa-gró* a bluish fox, *gro-gró* a gray fox *Sch.* — *wa-rgán* **an old fox, a knave** *Cs.* — *wa-ldéb* fox-trap *W.* — *wa-nág* a blackish fox *Sch.* — *wa-lpágs* fox's skin. — *wa-spyaṅ Mil*, *wá-ma-spyaṅ Cs.* **jackall.** — *wa-ṕrúg* young fox, cub. — *wá-mo* she-fox. — *wa-ťsaṅ* fox-hole. — *wa-róg* black fox *Sch.* — *wa-ťswá* a kind of salt *S.g.* — 3. n. of **a lunar mansion,** v. *rgyu-skár*. — 4. *wa-lóg-pa* **to perform somersets** *Sch.* — 5. *W.* **ho!** calling for one.

ཝ་ར་ཎ་སཱི་, or སེ་, བ་ར་ན་སི་ *wa-ra-ṇa-sí* or *sé*, *ba-ra-na-si* **Banaras,** a city in the valley of the Ganges, frq. mentioned in legends, as a residence of Buddha, at the present time a principal seat of Brahmanism.

ཝ་ལེ་, ཝལ་ལེ་, ཝལ་ལེ་བ་ *wa-lé*, *wal-lé*, *wal-lé-ba* **clear, distinct, plain,** *wa-lér drán-pa* to recollect distinctly *Cs.*; *yid-la* floating distinctly before one's mind *Lex.*; *don wa-lé gyis* try to gain a clear understanding of the sense of it *Mil.*; also *skad-wál* = क्षाशब्द(?).

ཝ་སི་ *wa-si* a kind of apples *Sch.*

ཝི་ *wi* num fig.: 50.

ཝུ་ *wu* num fig.: 80.

ཝུ་རྡོ་ *wu-rdo* **pumice stone** *Sch.*

ཝེ་ *we* num. fig.: 110.

ཝོ་ *wo* num. fig.: 140.

ཞ

ཞ *ža*, 1. a letter of the alphabet, represented by *ž*, originally, and in the frontier-provinces to the present day, the soft sibilant, which is pronounced like *j* in French, or like the English s in leisure, (*zh*), (still more accurately like the Polish *z* in *zima*); in *C.* it differs now from ཤ only by the following vowel being deep-toned. — 2. numerical figure: 21.

ཞྭ་, ཞྭ་མོ་ *žwa*, *žwa-mo*, resp. *dbu-žwa*, a covering of the head, **hat, cap;** fig. *ṅa yig sá-yi žwá-čan* the letter ང having ས for a cap: སྔ *Zam.*; *žwa gón-pa*, *gyón-pa* to put the cap on, *ḅúd-pa* to take it off (in *Ts.* by way of salutation); *rgya-*, *bod-*, *sog-žwa* Chinese, Tibetan, Mongolian cap; *dgun-žwa* winter-cap, *dbyar-žwa* summer-hat (light felt-hats adapted to the warmer season); *p̀yiṅ-žwa* hat or cap made of felt; *wa-žwa* cap made of the fur of a fox. — *žwa-dkár*, *-nág*, *-dmár*, *-sér* white, black, red, yellow cap, denoting occasionally also **the wearers** of such caps, esp. **red-caps** and **yellow-caps**, as belonging to different Lama-sects. — *žwa-k̀ébs* the covering of a hat *Cs.* — *žwa-tog* top ornament of a hat *Cs.*, prob. a button, v. *tog*. — *žwa-γžól* brim, *žwa-ri* crown of a hat *Cs.*, in *Ld.* however *ri* denotes the brim or flap. — *Schl.* p. 171 calls a low conical cap of the Chief Lama *ná-t̀on-ža*.

ཞ་ཉེ་ or ཞ་ནེ་ *žá-nye* or *žá-ne*, also *rá-nye Cs.*, **lead**, *žá-nyei γtiṅ-rdo* **sounding-lead, plummet** *Pth.*; *ža-nye-rdó* **lead-ore** *Cs.*; *žá-nyei čus sbyár-ba* to fill up (a groove or juncture) with molten lead *Glr.*; *žá-nye dkár-po C.*, **tin**, also *ža-dkár*, *γša-* or *bša-dkár*; *žá-nye nág-po* lead, (*Cs.*'s 'white lead and black lead' seem to be a mere conjecture); *ža-šóg* (**tin-foil** *Sch.* (?)), thin plates of lead.

ཞ་བ་ *žá-ba* **lame**; **lameness**; gen. *žá-bo* **lame, halting**; a lame person, **cripple**, *B.* and col.; *žá-mo* fem.; **žá-wo čo dug** *W.* he is lame, he limps; *rkáṅ-* or *lág-ža-čan* having a lame foot or hand.

ཞ་འབྲིང་ *ža-˳briṅ* v. *žabs* extr.

ཞ་ལ་ *žá-la Glr.* and vulgo, v. *žál-ba*.

ཞ་ལུ་ *žá-lu* **cup, bowl**, = *p̀or-pa*, *ko-re Cs.*

ཞ་ལུ་པ་ *žá-lu-pa*, *žá-lu lóts-tsa-ba* or *lo-čén* n. of the author of a little glossary, called **Zamatog**.

ཞག *žag* 1. *žág-pa* (only *Schr.*, *Cs.*), **žág-po** *W*, **žág-ma** *Lt.*, *W.*, resp. *dguṅ-žág* **a day**, the time from one sun-rise to another (cf. on the other hand *nyí-ma* 2); *žag čig* **a day**, and adv : **once day, once**; **žag čig-gi žág-la** *W.* is also used of a future day: **žag čig de dus leb yin** *W.* once the time will come; *žag ˳ga-nas* after a few days *Mil.*; *žag dú-ma lón-par* after many days *Dzl.*; **ṅa di-riṅ ná-niṅ léb-žag** *W.* this is the day of our arrival a year ago; **dé-žag** *W.* **lately**, the other day, a short time ago; **dáṅ-žag** *W.* **yesterday; recently**, **dáṅ-zag za-nyi-ma** *W.* last sunday; **nán-žag** *W.* some time ago, **nán-žag stón-ka** *W.* last autumn; **k̀ár-saṅ-žag** *W.* **the day before yesterday**; *žág-nas žág-tu* **from day to day**; **žág-daṅ(-žag)** *W.* **every day, always**; *žag bdun* seven days, *žag-bdun-p̀rág* **a week**, *žag-bdun-p̀rág že-brgyád* forty-eight weeks *Thgy.* — *žag-gráṅs* **the date**, **žag-dáṅ gyáb-če** *W.* **to date**. — *žag-mál* **a station, day's journey, quarters** *Cs.*, *žág-sa* id. *Cs.* — **žag-záṅ** *W.* **holiday**. — 2. **fat, grease**, in a liquid state, = *tsíl-k̀u S.g.*; also melted and congealed again *W.*; fig. **the fat of the country, fertility**, *yúl-la žag med* the country is barren *Ma.*; *žág-čan* greasy, oily, *žag-méd* lean; *žag-p̀ór* a cup, vessel, for grease *Cs.* — 3. **fog, smoke, dry vapour**, filling the atmosphere in autumn.

ཞགས་པ་ *žágs-pa* **leash**, rope with a noose, e.g. for catching wild horses, *žags-tág Cs*, *žags-dbyúg Sch.* id., *rgyáb-pa Cs.*, *p̀en pa Sch.* to throw the noose; *žags-pas*, *žags-tag-gis ˳dzín-pa* frq. fig., as *Schl.* 213; *sbrul-žágs* noose consisting of a serpent, for catching any hurtful creature *Glr.*; frq. as an attribute of the gods.

ཞང་(པོ) *žáṅ(-po)*, vulgo *á-žaṅ*, **uncle** by the mother's side, **mother's brother**; *žaṅ-brgyúd* his offspring *Cs.*; *žaṅ-nyén* in a gen. sense, relations by the mother's side *Dom.*; *žaṅ-tsá* sister's son. — *tsa-žáṅ*, resp. *dbon-žáṅ* 1. nephew and uncle, by the mother's side, also applied to spiritual brotherhood *Mil.* — 2. **son-in-law** and **brother-in-law** *Glr.*

ཞང་བློན་ *žaṅ-blón Glr.* seems to be a kind of **title** given to a minister (or magistrate).

ཞང་ཞུང་ *žaṅ-žúṅ* ancient n. of the province of **Guge** *Glr.*

ཞན་པ་ *žán-pa* **weak, feeble**, frq., the opp. to *drág-po*; *ṅa ji-ltar žan yaṅ* as weak, as miserable as I am (says a cripple) *Pth.*;

K̔ams žán-pa Mil. of a weak body, of delicate health; also applied **to sounds, accent** and the like; cf. *ṅá-ro*; **ugly** opp. to *légs-pa*, v. *skye-sgo.*

ཞབས་ *žabs* 1. **bottom** of a lake, of a vessel *Dzl., Mil.*; lower end of a staff *Mil.*; for **under** in compounds, as *mṅa-žábs* q. v. — 2. resp. for *rkáṅ-pa* **foot,** *mi žíg-gi žábs-la* *ₒdúd-pa Cs., mgó-bos btúg-pa S.b., ₒo byéd-pa Cs.* to bow down at another person's feet, to touch them with one's head, to kiss them; *žabs drúṅ-du* c. genit **to the feet of . . .,** for **to . . .,** in directions of letters; *žabs rjén-par* **barefooted,** e. g. *γségs-pa Mil.*; *žabs ₒdegs-pa Sch.* to help, prob. = *žabs-tóg byéd-pa* v. below; *žabs ₒčág-pa* = *ₒčág-pa* II. —

Comp. For the most part they are the same as those of *rkáṅ-pa;* there are to be mentioned more especially: *žábs-kyu* **1. spur** *Cs.* (?). 2. n. of the vowel-sign ͜ for u *Gram.* — *žábs-mgo Tar.* point of the foot *Schf.* — *žabs-sgróg* garter *Cs.* — *žabs-bčágs Sch.*, 1. partic. of *žabs-ₒčag-pa.* 2. = *žábs-čágs.* 3. **grounds, territory.** — *žabs-čág(s), -p̔yágs,* resp. shoe, boot. — *žabs-tóg* 1. **service** rendered to superiors, esp. to priests, convents etc., by the erection of buildings, or keeping them in repair, or by any aid or work done in their behalf; *ₒtsó-bai žabs-tóg* or *žabs-tog* alone: distribution of victuals, *žabs-tóg bzáṅ-po p̔ul* he placed dainty food before him *Mil.*; *žabs-tóg ₒo mi brgyál-ba ₒbul* we shall provide you with every thing, so that you shall not suffer want *Mil.*; *žabs-tóg byéd-pa* a. **to render such services** b. **to feed, treat, provide,** offer, *Glr.* and elsewh. 2. = *žabs-tóg-pa* 1. **servant,** regularly employed in monasteries, by Lamas etc., **an official,** *rgyál-poi sku-γsuṅ-túgs-kyi žabs-tóg* royal page, *Glr.* 2. **dispenser, benefactor** *žabs-tóg-ma* fem. — *žabs-rtíṅ* **heel.** — *žabs-rtén* 1. **footstool** *Cs.* 2. **boot** *Sch.* — *žabs-ₒdrén* **shame, disgrace,** from *mii žabs ₒdrén-pa* to bring shame upon another, to be a disgrace to him, e.g. a child proving a disgrace to his parents, by a dissolute life, disrespectful deportment etc. *Thgy. žabs-rdul* dust on one's feet *Cs.* — *žabs-pád* lit.: 'a padma below the foot', seems to be an attribute of divine persons, but sometimes nothing more than a high-sounding complimental expression for 'foot'; *byin-pa 'e-na-ya ₒdra žabs-pad ₒbur* his leg displays a calf like that of Enaya *Pth.*; *žabs-pad-la, Zam.* init., seems to stand like *žabs druṅ-du,* so also *žabs-pád k̔ri drúṅ-du,* in letters; *mii žabs-pad stén-pa Tar.,* fig. for *žabs-tóg byéd-pa* **to serve; to be a scholar, pupil** *Schf.* — *žábs-p̔yi* **servant** (male or female), in the widest sense of the word, servant to an individual, as well as a minister of the state or the church, only that the latter service is always referred by an Asiatic to the 'person' of the king or priest; collectively: **retinue;** occasionally also to be understood as **an attending, a waiting on,** thus: *rjé-yi žábs-p̔yi ₒgran,* we will vie with one another in our attending the lord *Glr.*; *žábs-p̔yir ₒbráṅ-ba, žábs-ₒbraṅ-ba* or *ₒbriṅ-ba* to follow as a servant, *žam-ₒbriṅ(-pa) Do., žam-riṅ Cs., ža-ₒbriṅ Sch.* servant. — *žabs-bró, žabs-bró mdzád-pa* **to dance** *Sch.* — *žabs-ma* drawers, under-petticoat. — *žabs-sén* nail of the toe *Sch.* — *žabs-bsíl* water for washing an honoured person's feet. — *žabs-lhám* = *žabs-čág.*

ཞམ་ཅུ་ *žám-ču Sch.:* 'the scum left by the evaporation of water' (?); **žám-če** *W.* to take off, *lbú-ba* the froth, scum; yet cf. *γžám-pa.*

ཞམ་མེ་བ་ *žám-me-ba* **being plentiful, abounding in** *Mil.*

ཞར་བ་ *žár-ba,* fem. *ma,* 1. = *yan lag ma tsaṅ* being not in full possession of one's members, *mig-žár* **one-eyed, half or totally blind;** *lag-žár* having only one hand, being lame in one or both hands; so in a similar manner *rkaṅ-žár.* — 2. (= *mig-žár*) *C., W.* **blind,** rarely in *B.* — **žar-tḙ** (*žar-ltas*) the winking with one eye *C.*

ཞར་ལ་ *žar-la, Schr.* **'following, succeeding',** prob. = *žór-la,* q.v.

ཞལ་ *žal* resp. for *k̔a* 1. **mouth** 2. **face, countenance** *žál-du γsól-ba, W. *žál-la rág-če**, to eat, to drink; **tsá-big žál-la rag** or **žal-rág dzod** please to take some . . .!

rgyal-poi žál-nas ysuṅs the king spoke *Glr.* frq.; *žál-gyi sgo* the door of the face, the mouth (cf. also *ˌdzúm-pa*); *žál-la mi nyán-pa Glr.* to be disobedient; *žál-gyis bžés-pa Glr.* or *ˌčé-ba Sch.* to promise, and other significations of *ḱas lén-pa*, e.g. to accept *Tar.* 126, 10; *žal bgrád-pa* and *ydáṅ-ba* **to gape** *Sch.*, *ˌbyéd-pa* to open the mouth, *žal ˌdzúm-pa* to smile; with *ltá-ba* 1. *žál-la ltá-ba*, e.g. *čos smrá-bai* to watch the mouth of the preacher, to hang on his lips *Pth.*; in a similar manner: *gús-pai séms-kyis ṅá-yi žál-la lta Pth.* 2. *žal ltá-ba, žál-lta byéd-pa* **to serve** (v. *žál-ta*), *žal yaṅ ḱyéd-la lta mčód-pa yaṅ ḱyéd-la ˌbul* they serve you and honour you *Glr.*; *žál-lta-ru byuṅ* he came to serve him *Mil.*; *žal ydáms-pa* **to bid, order, exhort** *Glr.*; *žal dón-pa* **to pronounce, to deliver, state, report**; *žal mjál-ba Mil.* **to visit, to come to see**; *žal mtóṅ-ba* to see a person's face *Tar.*; 'in order to attain the highest *dṅos-grúb*, one must *séms-kyi raṅ-žál mtóṅ-ba*, and in order to be able to do this, one must penetrate into the Buddhist doctrine' — thus *Mil.* teaches a Bonpa; *ṕyis žal mtóṅ-bao* afterwards his face was seen, he made his appearance *Tar.*; *žal-yzigs-pa* v. sbst. *žal-yzig.*

Comp. For the most part expressions of civility: *žal-kár*, resp. for *kar-yól* plates and drinking-vessels. — *žal-dkyil* face *Cs.* — *žal-bkód* order, ordinance *Sch.*(?). — *žal-skóm, žal-skyéms* drink. — *žal-skyin Glr.* countenance. — *žal-skyógs* cup, goblet *Mil.* — *žal-ḱébs* cover of an image of Buddha *Sch.* — *žal-ḱrid* oral or personal instruction *Mil.* — *žal-ˌḱaṅ* biting words of a superior (*Sch.* prob. not quite correct). — **žal-gyá*' (*rgya? brgya*) **ǰhé'-pa* or *žé-pa** to promise *C.* — *žal-rgyán* mustaches *C.* — *žal-ṅó* 1. = *ṅo*, *žal-ṅó nág-par bžugs* he was sitting there with a mournful face *Glr.* 2. *ṫsogs-čen-žal-ṅó* title of the chief-justices of the great monasteries of Sera, Gadan and Depung. 3. *Sch.*: '*žal-ṅo* or *ṅor*(?), noble sons, princes'(?) — *žal-dṅós* **bodily**, in one's own body or person, *saṅs-rgyás žal-dṅós-kyi ˌḱrúṅs-yul Pth.*, the place where Buddha was born bodily; *žal-dṅós-su mjál-bar yod Glr.* he is bodily to be seen. — *žal-sṅa Cs.* = *spyan-sṅa.* — *žal-čol* resp. for *'ar-čól* handkerchief, napkin *C.* — *žal-čád* v. *ḱa-čád.* — *žal-ču, žal-čáb Schr.*, *Cs.* spittle, saliva. — *žal-mčú* lip, v. *ḱa-mčú.* — *žal-čé* **judgment, decision**; *des ˌú-bu-čag-yi žal-čé ycád-do* he shall pass sentence on us *Dzl.* ༢༦༢, 15, and elsewh. (the text of *Sch.* is not quite correct); *žal-čé bču-drúg-pa* and *bču-ysúm-pa* '(the code) with the 16 and that with the 13 judgments'; these are two distinct bodies of law, both of them in *C.* of standard authority; *žal-čé-pa* judge *Dzl.* — *žal-čéms* v. *čems* 2. — *žal-nyód* favourite dish *Sch.* — *žál-ta* 1. also *žál-lta* a. **service, turn.** b. **inspection, visitation, revision**; *žál-ta byéd-pa* a. **to serve,** b. **to inspect, review, superintend; to visit,** the poor, the sick and to take care of them; **to guard,** *žiṅ-la* the field. 2. resp. for *ḱá-ta, ḱa-ydáms* **direction, instruction, counsel, advice,** *žál-ta žib-rgyás žú-ba* to ask for accurate and detailed instructions *Mil.*; *žál-ta-pa* = *sku-mdún-pa, žábs-ṕyi* waiting-man, valet-de-chambre *C.*, *Tar.* 56,2: servant in a convent; more frq. fem., *žál-ta-ma* waiting-woman, lady's maid, chamber-maid. — *žal-ydáms* **instruction, advice,** *ǰig-rtén-la dgós-pai žal-ydáms ysúṅs-so* he imparted to her useful maxims *Glr.*; **order, command** *Glr.* (v. above); also, *žal-ydáms bris-mḱan* **author,** in as much as all printed books are considered to be sacred, and the authors generally are Lamas, whose words are looked upon as divine. — *žal-ydóṅ* **countenance.** — *žal-bdág* in large religious meetings a Lama, who walks about with a wand in order to preserve good order, a verger. — *žal-ˌdébs* **a free-will offering** or **present** *Cs.* — *žal-ṗágs* **lip.** — *žal-ṕyis* resp. **napkin.** — *žal-bád* (or *pad?*) *C.* **chief overseer, superintendent.** — *žal-byáṅ* **title, superscription, inscription.** — *žal-ṫsóm* (for *ág-ṫsóm*) *Pth.* **beard.** — *žal-tsós Sch.* (*Cs.* *žal-ṫsus*) = *žal-zás Dzl.* **food.** — *žal-zág* **tobacco-pipe,** v. *gaṅ-zag.* — *žal-yzigs* 1. **looking with the face,** *lhor*, southward *Glr.* 2. **apparition,** *žal-yzigs ṫób-pa* to see an apparition, *bžúgs-par žal-yzigs-šiṅ* appearing in a sitting posture *Mil. nt.* (cf. *spyan-rás*). — *žal-bsró Tar.* 76, 12, *Schf.*: **the act of consecrating**, e.g. a temple.

ཞལ་བ་ *žál-ba* I. sbst., also *žal, žá-la, žál-rtsa* or *-rdza Sch.* **clay, lime-floor,** *Lex.: žál-ba = skyáṅ-núl*; *mfíl-gyi žá-la Glr.* **clay, cement of a floor,** cf. *ăr-ga*; **plastering, rough-cast,** *sgó-la žal bgyis-te* plastering the door with clay *Glr.*, also applied to the anointing of sacrificial objects with butter *Mil.* — II. vb. **to serve up food, to spread a repast** *Sch.*

ཞི་ *ži* num. fig.: 51.

ཞི་གིལ་ *ži-gil* **chaff** and other impurities removed from the grain by washing.

ཞི་བ་ *ži-ba*, *Ssk.* शम, **to become quiet, calm, to abate, to subside; to settle,** of a swelling *W.*; **to be allayed,** of passion, malice etc. *Glr.*; **to be appeased, relieved, to cease,** of pain, quarrels, intoxication, maladies etc. *Glr.* and elsewh.; **to be atoned, blotted out,** of sins *Tar.*; *ži-bar ₒgyúr-ba B.*, **ži čá-če* W.*, id.; **ra, šro ži soṅ* W.* the drunken fit, the paroxysm of passion has passed over; *ži-la soṅ* (the hobgoblins) became quiet, held their peace *Mil.*; *ži-bar byéd-pa* **to still, sooth, appease, mitigate,** **ži čúg-če* W.*; *ži-byed* a composing draught, संशमन *Wise* 130; more particularly with reference to the affections: **to be dispassionate**, not subject to any mental emotion, *ži-ba čén-por ₒgyur* he is getting very free from passion *Do.*, v. below *ži-ynás;* also sbst. **tranquillity, calmness,** and adj. **tranquil, calm,** *ži-ba daṅ bde-légs-su ₒgyúr-bar mdzád-du ysol* permit us to attain to peace and happiness *Dom.*; *ži-bai fábs-kyis* **amicably, in a fair way** *Glr.*; so also *ži-bai ytam smrá-ba Glr.; ži-bas mi ful drág-pos ₒdul dgos ₒdug Pth.* if he will not submit by fair means, he must be converted or subdued by force; *ži-bai žal Pth.* the expression of calmness about his mouth, his peaceful countenance; *ži-bar yšégs-pa* to go to rest, to die *Cs.*; *ži-bai* or *lóṅs-skui lha-tsogs žé-ynyis Thgr.* the good, the peaceable deities, opp. to those called *kró-bo;* differently again the word is used in: *ži-ba daṅ kró-ba daṅ ži-ma-kro Pth.*, which has been explained by *Sch.* as: the medium between calmness and passion, 'calm indignation'. *Cs.* moreover mentions *ži-ba* or *rtag-ži-ba*, as 'a name or epithet of Iswara and certain Buddhas', so that *ži-ba* would be equal in sound as well as in meaning to शिव, *ži-ba-pa* and *-ma* being his male and female disciples. A good deal of obscurity attaches, further, to the frequent mention of the *ži-rgyas-dbaṅ-drag*, as the characteristic properties of the four parts of the world (v. *glin*), and likewise as qualities and functions of the Buddhas, gods and saints, viz. allaying diseases, conferring happiness and wealth, ruling over all creatures and subduing all that is unruly and hostile; to which are to be added four kinds of burnt-offerings, in the same fourfold sense, v. *Schl.* 250. Finally, in mysticism the term *ži-ba* acts a prominent part: *ži(-bar) ynás(-pa)* and *lhag(-par) mfoṅ(-ba)*, शमथ and विपश्यन, shortened *ži-lhág*, implies an absolute inexcitability of mind, and a deadening of it against any impressions from without, combined with an absorption in the idea of Buddha, or which in the end amounts to the same thing, in the idea of emptiness and nothingness. This is the aim to which the contemplating Buddhist aspires, when, placing an image of Buddha, as *rten*, (v. *rten* 1) before him, he looks at it immovably, until every other thought is lost, and no sensual impressions from the outer world any longer reach or affect his mind. By continued practice he acquires the ability of putting himself, also without *rten*, merely by his own effort, into this state of perfect apathy, and of attaining afterwards even to *dṅos-grub*, the supernatural powers of a saint. The stories that are related of such achievements, and with which the work of Taranâtha abounds, are, notwithstanding their absurdity, readily believed by every faithful Buddhist. That there are also cases of failures, cf. *smyón-pa*.

ཞི་མ་ *ži-ma* **sieve,** of cane or wood *Ts.*

ཞི་མི་ *ži-mi Schr.* and *Wts.* (where *ši-mi* stands), gen. *žim-bu Glr.*, or *žúm-bu* **cat**, *C.*

ཞིག *žig* 1. = *čig*. — 2. v. *˳jig-pa* I., 2, *žig-rál-ba* **demolished, ruined** *Mil.*

ཞིག་མེར་ *žig-mér* (sbst. or adj.?) **dense throng, or crowded together** in a mass *W.*

ཞིང་ *žiṅ*, I. sbst. **ཞིང** (*Cs.*: *žiṅ-ma, žiṅ-po, žiṅ-bu*, perh. provincialisms), 1. **field, ground, soil, arable land**; *táṅ-žiṅ* fields in a plain, level land, *rí-žiṅ* fields on a mountain, hill-land; *túl-žiṅ W.* (ni f.) cultivated land; *žiṅ-ḱa* = *žiṅ*, *žíṅ-ḱai bú-mo* the girls in the field *Mil.*; *žiṅ rmó-ba* frq., to plough a field; to carry on agriculture; *˳débs-pa* to till, to sow a field, *mi yčig-gis btáb-pai* a field that has been sowed by one man *Glr.*; *žiṅ ˳ćú-ba* to irrigate a field (?) *Cs.*; *rná-ba* to mow, to reap, a field, *žíṅ-mḱan* **reaper**; **žiṅ bád-če* W.* to pursue husbandry; *žiṅ bgód-pa* to divide or distribute land *Cs.* — 2. fig., cf. *žíṅ-ḱams, bsód-nams-kyi žiṅ daṅ ˳ṕrád-pa* to enter the field of merit, to turn into the path of virtue *Dzl.*; *ydúl-byai žíṅ-du yzigs-te Pth.* seeing him in the land of conversion (yet v. also 3, a.); **region**, *žiṅ bču* (*Sch.*: 'the ten regions') is said to signify something like: the reign of Evil.— 3. equivalent to *saṅs-rgyás-kyi žiṅ* the kingdom of Buddha, a. in an earthly sense: **a holy land, a land of salvation**, where Buddha resides, or at least where Buddhism prevails; so also *˳dúl-bai žiṅ* land of conversion *Glr.*; acc. to *Wts.* it is a name of the earthly seat of Buddha, the residence of the Dalai Lama at Lhasa; b. supernaturally: **heaven, paradise, Elysium** i.e. one of the heavens inhabited by the Buddhist gods, or also the state of non-existence, Nirwāna; *žiṅ-la ṕéb-pa* = *bdé-bar yšégs-pa* **to die**. — 4. **body**, v. *žiṅ-čén, žiṅ-lpágs*. —

Comp. and deriv. *žiṅ-bkód* map *C.*, *W.*, *žiṅ-gi bkód-pa* v. *Asiat. Res.* XX., 425. — *žiṅ-ḱaṅ* 1. summer-house, pleasure-house, pavilion *W.* 2. field and house, the whole estate or property *W.* (= *yul-yžis*) — *žiṅ-ḱáms* = *žiṅ* 2 and 3, frq. — *žiṅ-˳ḱrúṅs, žiṅ-gi ḱrúṅs-pa* or *-ma* the produce of the field *Cs.* — *žiṅ-ḱród* many fields together *Cs.* — *žiṅ-rgód* rough, uncultivated ground *Sch.* — *žiṅ-čén* and *-čúṅ* **a large and a small field**; also: a large and a small body or corpse *Thgr.* — *žiṅ-mčóg* paradise, a most delightful country, an Eden, an Eldorado *Pth.* — *žiṅ-bdág* proprietor of a field, land-owner. — *žiṅ-pa* husbandman, farmer *Dzl.* — *žiṅ-lpags* a skin (pulled off), hide. — *žiṅ-mu* boundary of a field, landmark. — *žiṅ-bzáṅ* good land, productive soil *Cs.* — *žiṅ-yšin* dead, arid, burnt soil *Cs.* —*žiṅ-sa* 1. ground, soil, arable land *Cs.* 2. province *Sch.*

II. gerundial termin. = *čiṅ*, q.v.

ཞིབ་ *žib*, resp. **fine flour**, also **flour in general**, *žib-ḱúg* bag, *žib-ṕór* box, for flour *Cs.*

ཞིབ་པ་ *žib-pa, B.*, *žib-po Cs.*, *žib-mo C.*, *W.* 1. **fine**, of powder and similar things, *žib-rtsiṅ* fine and coarse *Zam.*; *žib-par byéd-pa, B.** *žib-mo čó-če* W.*, to make fine, to pound, to reduce to powder. — 2. **accurate, exact, strict, precise**, *ltá-ba yáṅs-šiṅ spyód-lam žib-par mdzod* be wide in your views, but strict in your actions *Glr.*; so *Sch.* understands also *žib-žib yod, žib-po med, žib-rgyu med*, which ought however to be translated: 'I have accurate information, I have no precise information, I have no particulars to communicate'; *žib-mo šés-pa* to know accurately; more frq. adv. *žib-par, žib-tu B.*, **žib-ča* *vulg., **exactly, precisely, thoroughly** *žib-tu ysól-ba, ytam žib-tu byéd-pa* to report accurately *Dzl.* (the former resp.); *žib-par bšád-pa Glr.* id.; *žib-par* (*šes-*) *˳dód-na* if you wish to know it accurately *Glr.*; *bka žib-tu bgros-pa* resp., to consult carefully *Pth.*; *bka-mčid ysuṅ-gléṅ žib-tu bgyid* gentlemen, discourse as freely as you please! *Mil.*; *las-rgyu-˳bras žib-tu mi rtsí-na* if one does not strictly regard the doctrine of retaliation *Mil.*; **žib-ča ltos* (or *to**) *W.* look at it well, carefully; **žib-ča zer* W.* pronounce it accurately; **žib-ča čo'-pa* C.* to examine closely; **žib-sál* W.* accurately and distinctly.

ཞིམ་ཐོག་ལེ་ *žim-tog-le* n. of a medicinal herb *Med.*

ཞིམ་པ་ *žim-pa*, gen. *žim-po*, **well-tasted, sweet-scented**, **žim-po rag* W.* I find the taste or smell of it agreeable; *ša ₒdi lhág-par žim-na* this meat being of a better taste *Dzl.*; *žim-rgyui zas* food prepared of savoury things *Zam.*; *dri-žim, dri-ysúṅ žim-po* pleasant odour *Dzl.*; *dri mi žim-pa* disagreeable smell *Glr.*; **žim-ze** also **žim-žim** *C.*, **žim-zag** *W.* sweet-meats, confectionery; **žim-zag-tsóṅ-k'aṅ** *W.* confectioner; **žim-lto-čan** *W.* dainty-mouthed, a sweet-tooth.

ཞིམ་བུ་ *žim-bu* v. *ží-mi.*

ཞུ་ *žu*, 1. num. figure: 81. — 2. v. *žú-ba.*

ཞུ་དག་ *žu-dág*, ཞུས་དག་ *žus-dág* **amendment, improvement, correction**; the word is also added at the end of written books, e.g. of Taranātha, as an attestation of a careful revision; *žu-dág byéd-pa* **to mend, improve, correct**; *raṅ-rgyúd žu-dág byéd-pa* to examine and reform one's self *Cs.* *žu-dag-mk'an* **reviser, corrector, censor** *Cs.*, *žu-čén-gyi lóts-tsa-ba* a great corrector or commentator (of *Ssk.* writings), seems to have become a current title.

ཞུ་བ་ *žú-ba* I. vb., pf. *žus* (esp. in later writings and vulgo, in ancient literature gen. *ysól-bar* for it) signifies 1. every kind of speaking to a person of higher rank, therefore **to request, to prefer a suit or petition, to make a report, to put a question** etc., *žú-žiṅ ysól-ba-la ₒgró-bai tse* when I have to bring in a petition *Dzl.*; '*mnál-lam de yžán-la mi ysúṅ-bar žu*' *žús-so* 'pray, do not relate the dream to others', he begged *Glr.*; *ynáṅ-bar žu byás-pas* **saying**, 'I beg you will permit', *Glr.*; *sṅar mtóṅ-bai dṅós-po dé-dag žuo* I will ask him about the things lately seen, I shall request an explanation of him *Dzl.*; *ṅá-la gáṅ-dag žú-ba de légs-so* it is very right of you, thus to ask me about every thing *Do.*; *rgyál-poi drúṅ-du rmi-lam žús-pa* he related the dream before the king *Pth.*; *ston-pa žu* (*pa* col. for *par*) I request (you) to explain *Mil.*; *der ₒbyón-pa žu* 'thither to come I request' *Mil.*; *dé-la mk'án-po žus* they besought him to be their abbot *Glr.*; *ynáṅ-ba žú-ba* to ask permission *Cs.* — 2. In *W.* this *žu* has become a word of civility to the widest extent, as it is not only added to almost every sentence of a speech or a letter, something like our 'with your permission' or 'if you please', e.g. **žan či méd-na ṅa ḍo yin žu** if you have nothing further (to say), I shall go, with your permission; **k'o leb soṅ žu** he is arrived, if you please; but it also supplies every kind of salutation in coming or going, hence **žu zér-če**, resp. **žu žú-če**, to make or give one's compliments, **ǎ-pa-ne žu máṅ-po žu dug** my father's best respects (cf. *p̔yag*). Inst. of *žu*, *ǰu* is also frq. heard (vulgo), e.g. **ǰu sab ǰu!** good day, Sir, good day! which prob. is only an intensation of sound, and not to be referred to the Indian जी. — **či-la žu** *W.* **why, well then, mind!** **či-la žu, nyi-ráṅ ṅe tsar ma kyód-pa yun-riṅ kyod** well, I have not seen you this age! — The word is also used as a sbst., for **request, wish, question**, **žú-wa ₒbúl-ba** *C.*, **p̔úl-če** *W.*, *ytóṅ-ba Glr.* to make a request, to put a question; *ydan-ₒdrén-pai žú-ba nán-čan p̔úl-bas Mil.* assailing him with pressing invitations.

II. (prop. fut. of *ₒǰú-ba*) pf. (*b*)*žu*(*s*), fut. (*b*)*žu*, (imp.?) 1. **to melt**, trs. and intrs., *bžu-btúl* v. sub *lugs*; *bžu-byai yser* gold to be melted *Cs.*; *žú-bai k'ams* whatever is melting or fusible, **metals** *Sch.*; *žuo* it melted (from the heat) *Dzl.*; *ₒód-du žu-nas* dissolving in light *Glr.* frq. — 2. **to digest**, *žú-byed-kyi sman* digestive medicine *Cs.* (cf. *ₒǰu-byéd*); *ma-žú(-ba)* undigested, *zas ma žú-ba* undigested food, also **indigestion**, sufferings arising from it; *ma-žúi nad* id.; *ma-žú ₒǰú-ba* to decompose what is undigested *Med.*; opp. to *žu-rǰés* it seems to denote more particularly **the chyme** before it is mixed with bile, and perh. also **the duodenum** where this takes place; so the region of *žu daṅ ma-žúi bár-na* is stated to be the place, where the bile is principally operating *S.g.* Cf. *ₒǰú-ba.*

Comp. *žu-skyogs W.* crucible, melting-spoon. — *žú-mk'an* 1. **petitioner.** 2. **digester**; n. of an officinal plant, = *spaṅ-žún Wdṅ.*

— *žu-glén, žu-gléṅ byéd-pa* to address, accost, resp. *C.* — *žu-rgyá* (v. *rgya-ma*) 1. petitionary letter, petition, suit. 2. any writing addressed to superiors. — *žu-rgyú* the subject of a petition or suit. — **žu-ṅó-pa**, *C.*, intercessor, advocate, mediator, **žu-ṅó ǰhé-pa** to intercede, to advocate. — *žu-rǰés* 1. **the chyme mixed with bile** (cf. *ma-žu* above). 2. **the place of it**, *žu-rǰés na* I feel a pain there *Med.* 3. **eructation, rising,** *ḱá-la zu-rǰés skyur S.g.* caused by beer; *ro daṅ žu-rǰés mṅár-mo Med.* a sweetish taste and rising (from the stomach). — *žu-rtén* **the present** which, according to oriental notions, has necessarily to attend or introduce a petition. — *žu-dón* prop. drift, subject of a petition; in a general sense = *žú-ba* request, suit, address, communication etc. — *žu-sná* (pronounced **žu-ná**) *W.* = *žu-ṅó.* — *žú-po, žú-ba-po* = *žú-mḱan* 1. — *žu-byéd* v. above — *žu-ₒbúl*, pronounced **žum-búl**, petitioning, making a suit in an humble posture with folded hands *Cs.* — *žú-yig, žú-šog, žú-bai ṗrin-yig* a petition, *žú-yig-gi rten* = *žu-rten.* — *žu-lán* answer to a petition. — *žu-lóg* a feigned, false, designing suit, **gyáb-pa** to address such a one *C.*

ཞུགས་ *žugs*, resp. **fire**, e.g. the fire lighted for cremation *Tar.* 7, 4.

ཞུགས་པ་ *žúgs-pa* v. *ₒjúg-pa.*

ཞུང་ཞུང་ *žuṅ-žúṅ* with *byéd-pa* **to nod or bow repeatedly,** of a pigeon *Mil.*

ཞུད་པ་ *žúd-pa* 1. **to twine, to twist** *W.* **žúd-če, žú-če**. — 2. **to spin** *Cs.*, *žu-ḱór* spindle, distaff. — 3. **to rub** *Cs.* — 4. **to hang up, to suspend** *Ts.* — *žud-ťúg* = *dpyaṅ-ťúg.*

ཞུན་པ་ *žún-pa* **melted** *Cs.*; **žun ťáṅ-če** *W.* **to melt,** trs ; *žun-ťár byéd-pa* to melt and beat to pieces *Mil.*; *žun-ťigs* spark flying from red-hot iron *W.*; *žún-ma* that which is melted, *ysei sogs žún-mai ṗúṅ-po* heaps of melted gold and other metals *Glr.* — *žun-mar* v. *mar.* — *žún-mo* melted, whatever melts easily *Cs.* (who spells it *bžun-mo*).

ཞུམ་པ་ *žúm-pa* 1. sbst. **fear, dismay, despondency, faint-heartedness,** *sems žúm-na* if I continue undismayed *Dzl.*; *dkon-mčóg ysúm-la žúm-pa-med-par bkúr-bsti byéd-pa* to honour the three most Precious undauntedly, with a cheerful heart; *sems ráb-tu žúm-par gyúr-to* they became greatly dejected in mind, their spirits were much cast down *Pth.* — 2. vb. **lbú-wa žúm-če** *W.* **to scum, to skim** (off).

ཞུམ་བུ་ *žúm-bu* = *ži-mi.*

ཞུར་ *žur*, 1. **snout, muzzle, trunk.** — 2. sup. of *žú-ba.*

ཞུལ་ཞུལ་ *žul-žúl, Ts.*: **žü-žü ǰhé-pa** **to stroke, to caress.**

ཞུས་དག་ *žus-dág* v. *žu-dág*, ཞུས་པ་ *žús-pa* v. *zú-ba.*

ཞེ་ *že* (cf. *žen*) 1. **inclination, affection, heart, mind; volition;** there is a proverb in *C.*: **mi ḱá-ṗo-čé-la že me', ču nyóg-po-čé-la tiṅ me'** a braggart has no mind, as muddy water has no bottom, i.e. as in muddy water you cannot see the bottom, so you cannot rely on the solid principles of a braggart; *ḱa-žé* v. *ḱa*, comp.; *že bkon-pa* or *ₒḱon-pa* a hating mind, *rkám-pa Sch.* a covetous, *ťág-pa Mil.* a sincere, *nág-po C.* a wicked, *ytsáṅ-ba Sch.* a pure heart or mind, or also hating, covetous etc. as to mind (several other combinations of this kind, given by *Sch.*, are too doubtful to be copied); *že-yčód-pa Sch.*: 'to lose courage, to have no longer any inclination for', perh. better, **to resign,** and *že-bčád* **resignation,** as a Buddhist virtue *Mil.*; on the other hand, *že yčod-pai ťsig Sch.*: 'slanderous words' which, e.g. *Dzl.* ༢༠, 11, well agrees with the context, but is not clear in point of etymology. — *že-dúg* damage, destruction *Sch.*, *byéd-pa* to cause, to inflict. — *že-lóg* v. *žen-lóg* sub *žén-pa.* — *že-sún* angry, cross, ill-humoured, vexed. — 2. numerical word for *bži-bču* in the abridged numbers *že-yčig* etc., 41 to 49. — 3. numerical figure: 111.

ཞེ་ན་ *žé-na*, rarely *žés-na*, v. *čé-na.*

ཞེ་ས་ *žé-sa* **reverence, respect, civility, politeness,** *žé-sa daṅ bčás-pa* **reverential, respectful** *Pth.*; *dei dús-su mis ṗyag daṅ* *žé-sa mi šés-pas* because at that time people knew little of compliments and politeness *Pth.*; *žé-sa byéd-pa* to show honour, respect, *rnám-gyur mdzés-pai žé-sa ˳bul-ba* to arrange mimic performances in honour of some persons, (which also at the present time is frequently done in these countries); complimentary word (for *žé-sai tsig*), *rná-bai žé-sa snyan* the complimentary word for *rna-ba* is *snyan Zam.*

ཞེང་, གཞེང་ *žeṅ, yžeṅ Cs.* (*W.* **žaṅ**) 1. **breadth, width,** *žéṅ-čan* **broad** (road, valley), **wide, spacious,** **žéṅ ka-čém-po** *C.* id.; *žeṅ-méd, žeṅ-p̓rá-mo,* **žeṅ-čúṅ-se** *W.* **narrow;** *žéṅ-du* in breadth *Sambh.*; *žeṅ-šiṅ* writing-tablet = *snum-glegs.* — 2. **plain, surface, side,** *žeṅ-čé-ba ɣnyis* the two broad sides (of a pillar) *Glr.*

ཞེད་པ་ *žéd-pa* **to fear, to be afraid,** synon. to *˳jigs-pa Thgr.* frq.; *žéd-nas* full of apprehensions *Pth.*

ཞེན་པ་ *žén-pa* (cf. *že*), vb. c. *la*, 1. **to desire, to long for, to be attached to, to be partial to, to be taken with,** *kyéd-la žén-čiṅ čags* I love you ardently (ἐρῶ) *Glr.*; *bod-˳báṅs ṅá-la žen-čé-žiṅ dgá-ba-rnams* the people of Tibet, that are affectionately attached to me *Glr.*; sbst.: **desire, longing,** e.g. to hear more of a thing *Mil.*; also **greediness, covetousness;** *ráṅ-˳dod-žen-pa* **self-love, selfishness, egotism** *Glr.*; *p̓yógs-žen Tar.* 184, 22, **party-spirit, party-agitation;** *čágs-med žén-med* free from passion or interest *Mil.*; *žén-pa zlog* suppress your passion *Mil.*; *tse ˳dí-la žen ldóg-pa* to be disgusted with this life *Thgy.*; **žém-pa ma lóg-na dhé'-pa mi yoṅ** *C.* before one has renounced every desire, one cannot believe. —

Comp. *žén-ka, žé-ka = žén-pa* sbst., *Sch.* — *žen-kris Mil.*, *žen-čágs* frq., also vulgo, *žen-˳dzin Glr.* inclination, desire, passion, attachment, **žen-dzin čó-če** *W.* to love, to be attached. — *žen-dón*, resp. *bžed-dón*, object of desire *Cs.* — *žen-lóg(-pa*, cf. above), disinclination, antipathy, disgust; in an ascetic sense: resignation *Mil.*; *˳jig-rtén žen-lóg-gi gaṅ-zdg* a man tired of this world *Mil.*; *žen-lóg-pa*, or *-mkan* fastidious, squeamish, easily disgusted; **že-mi-lóg-ken** *C.* one that is not easily disgusted, not squeamish. — 2. = *ljén-pa* **to penetrate, to be fixed,** of colours etc., *ras dkar-po tson žen-pa ltar* as a colour is fixed in white cloth, is **lasting** *Dzl.*

ཞེམ་ཞེམ་ *žem-žém Ld.* an inferior kind of silk, of which the handkerchiefs consist, that are presented to foreign visitors etc. as a welcome or mark of respect, cf. *ka-btágs.*

ཞེར་ *žer, žer ˳débs-par byéd-pa Cs.*: **to chide, rebuke,** which, however, in the only passage, where I met with the word, does not suit the sense very well.

ཞེར་པོ་ *žer-po* **'mean, pitiful, coarse'** *Cs.*

ཞེས་ *žes* v. *čes.*

ཞོ་ *žo*, 1. **dram,** a small weight = $\frac{1}{10}$ ounce, of *skar-lṅa*, v. *skár-ma*; *ɣser-žo-gaṅ Pth.* a dram of gold; *ɣser žo ɣsum-brgyá* between 1 and 2 pounds of gold; as a coin it is stated to be = $^2/_3$ rupee. — 2. resp. *ɣsol-žo* **thick milk, curds,** *žo bsnyál-ba* to place milk to curdle; **milk** in gen., esp. *mai nú-žo Dzl.*, *má-žo* col., mother's milk; *žo-˳t̓úṅ dús-na* during the time of suckling, *žo-spáṅs zas zai dús-na* after the child has been weaned *Med.*; *žo dkróg-pa, skróg-pa, bsrúb-pa* **to churn, to butter** *Lex.* — 3. **a small white spot,** *sen-žo* on a finger nail, *so-žo* on a tooth *Glr.* — 4. num. figure: 141.

Comp. *žó-ka* prob. = *žo, Thgy.* — *žo-skyá Med.?* — *žo-čágs Med.?* - *žo-p̓rúm Sch.*: 'a vessel for thick milk' (?), perh. *p̓ru.* — *žo-rás Med., Sch.*: spoiled milk. — **žo-ri** *W.*, (like *rú-ma C.*) **sour milk,** used to acidify new milk; in a gen. sense: **ferment, leaven,** **žo-dzi** *Ts.* — *žo-ši Sch.* = *žo-rás.* — *žo-sri, žoi spris-ma Wdṅ.* **cream.**

ཞོ་ཤ་ *žo-šá* 1. **force, efficiency** *Cs.* — 2. n. of a medicinal fruit, *žo-šá ɣsum*, viz. *mkál-žo-ša* kidney-shaped, healing diseases of the kidneys (in *W.* the chesnut bears this name), *snyiṅ-žo-ša* heart-shaped, healing diseases of the heart; *gla-gor-žo-ša* is said to be given to horses; besides *mčín-pa-*

and mčér-pa-žo-ša are mentioned. — 3. **toll** (?), **pay** (?), žo-šás ₒtsó-ba *Tar.*, *Stg.* a publican *Cs.*, a soldier *Schr.*, prob. any officer that receives salary or pay.

ཞོག་ *žog*, imp. of ₒjóg-pa.

ཞོགས་ *žogs* v. *mar-žógs*.

ཞོགས་པ་ *žógs-pa Med.*, *žóg-ka Sch.*, = *sňá-dro* **morning, fore-noon**; *žógs-ja* **tea at breakfast** *Cs.*

ཞོང་ *žoṅ* **lower, nether,** *žóṅ-k'aṅ-pa* the lower part of the house, *žoṅ-rtsé* the lower and the upper part; *žoṅ-žóṅ* **deepened, excavated, hollow, uneven** *C.*

ཞོད་ *žod* 1. the original meaning of the word is yet uncertain; at present used in *C.*: **žo' dé-wa, žo-jág**, **peace, quietness, tranquillity,** **k'o žo'-dé-la mi žag** he gives him no rest, causes him much trouble; **sém-kyi zo' dé-mo** peace of mind, evenness of temper; **žo'* or *zo' dé-mo* or ₒ*jám-pa* gentleness, meekness. — 2. *Sch.*: **high-water, floods, inundations** *Wts.*, *C.*; *sňa t'an p'yi žod* first drought, then inundation *Wdk.* — 3. **udder** *W.*, *C.*

ཞོན་པ་ *žón-pa*, resp. ₒ*čib-pa* **to mount,** c. *la*; *rtá-la žón-pa* to ride, on horseback, *šiṅ-rta-la* to ride, in a carriage, frq.; *rtá-la žón-nas lhó-p'yogs-su* ₒ*gró-ba* to ride southward, to travel on horseback towards the south *S.g.*; also c. accus.: *bžón-pa žón-pa* to mount a horse or a carriage *Lex.*; *žón-du* ₒ*júg-pa* (= *skyón-pa*) to let mount.

ཞོམ་པ་ *žóm-pa*, = ₒ*jóms-pa?* *rgas žóm-ste* **weighed down by old age** *Sch.*; cf. *γžóm-pa.*

ཞོར་ *žór*, ཞོར་ལ་ *žór-la* etc. v. *sbyór-la.*

ཞོལ་ *žol* 1. *žol-γyág*, **yak-bull,** *Bos grunniens Sch.*; *rá-ma žól-mo* a long-haired goat *Mil. nt.* — 2. **village belonging to a convent** *Mil.*, so Shikatse is the *sde-žól* of Tashi-lhunpo. — 3. postp., **under,** *Sch.* (cf *γžol-ba* II).

གཞའ་བ་ *γža-ba Sch.*: 1. **to sport, joke, play, sing,** (cf. *ga-γža*). — 2. **to believe, trust, confide.**

གཞའ་ཚོན་ *γža-tson* earlier form for ₒ*ja-tsón* **rain-bow.**

གཞའ་གསང་ *γža-γsaṅ* = *γyuṅ-druṅ Lex.*

གཞག་པ་ *γžag-pa* v. ₒ*jóg-pa.*

གཞང་ *γžaṅ* 1. **anus** *Med.*, *γžáṅ-k'a* id.; *γžaṅ-nád*, *γžaṅ*-ₒ*brúm* **piles, hemorrhoids** *Med.*; *γžaṅ-srín* a kind of intestinal worms *Lt.* — 2. **privy parts,** **žaṅ*-ₒ*ť ág** *W.* catamenial blood; **žáṅ-tsoṅ-ma** *W.* = *smád-tsoṅ-ma*; **žaṅ-sťoṅ** *W.*, without breeches, with a bare posterior.

གཞད་གད་, གཞད་མོ་ *γžad-gád*, *γžád-mo* v. *bžád-pa.*

གཞན་ *γžan*, *γžán-pa*, *γžán-ma* (the last esp. in *W.*), 1. adj. and sbst., **other, the other, another,** *žan mi* the other men *Dzl.*, *γžán-pas lhág-par* more than others *Dzl.*; *slób-ma γžán-dag* the other scholars *Dzl.*; *mtsan γžán-pa* the other signs *Dzl.*; *blón-po γžán-ma-rnams* the other ministers *Glr.*; *bú-mo γžán-pas čé-rgyu med* she is not taller than the other girls (*pas* = *las*, not from *pa*) *Glr.*; *γžan rgol ma nus* others were not able to resist them (= nobody could do them any harm) *Glr.*; *γžán-du* to some other place, ₒ*gró-ba* to go (to some other place) = **to go away, to start; elsewhere; in another way,** v. example ₒ*dzín-pa* 1, 4; also: *γžán-du ma sems šig Dzl.*, suppose or believe nothing else, do not think that the matter can be otherwise, frq. used like our 'of course'; *γžán-na* **elsewhere;** *γžán-nas* **from some other place;** *γžán-nas* ₒ*grúb-tu med* it cannot be accomplished from any other quarter, by any body else *Mil.* — 2. adv. **otherwise, else, on the other hand** *W.*; *γžán-yaṅ* **further, furthermore, or else,** (just) to mention some other circumstance, frq. — *γžan-bsgrúb Lex.* seems to be some logical term *Gram.* — *γžan*-ₒ*p'rúl* n. of a heaven inhabited by certain gods *Glr.*, *Mil.* — *γžan-dbáṅ* **dependent on others** *Was*, cf. *raṅ-dbáṅ.*

གཞབ་པ་ *γžáb-pa* **to lick** *Sch.*

གཞམས་པ་ *γžáms-pa* v. *bžáms-pa.*

གཞར་ཡང་ γžár-yaṅ *Lex.* = *nám-yaṅ*; *Pth.*: *γžar-yaṅ mi* **never** (*Sch.* and *Schr.* prob. incorr.).

གཞལ་བ་ γžál-ba, fut. of *ˏǰál-ba*, **to weigh**, *sráṅ-la γžál-bar nús-kyi* if one could weigh with a pair of scales *Glr.*; *γžál-dgos-kyi rdzas Sch.*; 'goods for which duties are to be paid', liable to duty, to custom; *γžal-du-méd-pa* **imponderable** *Stg.*; **immensely much** *Pth.*; **immeasurable, incomparable, infinite, vast**; *γžal méd*, *γžal-γás* id.; *γžal-med-ḱáṅ*, more frq. *γžal-yas-ḱaṅ*, also *γžal-med-kaṅ-bžaṅ* palace, rarely used of human palaces (so *Glr.* in one passage, when speaking of the house of a Brahmin), mostly of the abode of gods *Pth.* and elsewh.; also Tibet, in po. language, is called a *lha-γnás γžal-yas-ḱáṅ*, the heavens with the sun a *ṅo-mtsár lhai γžal-yas-ḱáṅ*. — *γžal-ṫsád* **measure, scale, standard** *Sch.*

གཞས་ γžas **play, sport, jest, joke** *Sch*, *Lex.*: *glu-γžas.*

གཞི་(མ་) γži(-ma) 1. that from which and on which a thing arises, exists, depends; **ground, foundation, original cause, exciting cause** (**मूल** *Was.* 234); *dge-légs ṫams-ċád ˏbyúṅ-bai γži(-ma)* the primitive source of all happiness (is the doctrine of Buddha) *Glr.*; *γži-skye-méd* without origin and birth *Mil.*; *γžir bžág-pa* prob.: to use as a foundation *Mil.*, *Tar.*; **gór-ži* W.* cause of delay; *ma-γži* v. as an article of its own sub *ma*; *rtsig-γži* foundation of a wall *Cs.*; *nyúṅ-γži*, *lá-γži* turnips, radishes, left for seed (being the foundations, as it were, of new plants); in *γži-sems-nyid*, *γži-č̓os-nyid* it prob. stands as an apposition, in the sense of *kun-γži*: the spirit, the primeval cause; in a special sense: the innermost essence, inherent nature; *γži-nas* **actually**, opp. to 'apparently' *Mil.*; **fundamental law, statute**, *γži čén-po* title of a book *Was.* 264; in certain cases it may be translated by **action**, v. *ruṅ-ba* 2, c. — 2. **ground, floor**, *γži-ma gru-bží* a square floor *Glr.*; *stéṅ-gi γži* the upper base, top-surface *Stg.* — 3. **residence, abode, home**, *γži ˏdzin-pa* to take up one's residence in a place *Mil.* and elsewh.; *γži ˏbébs-pa W.* **ṗab-ċe** id.; *γži-ma rab ċig ṗóg-nas bžág-go* he assigned to him a nice dwelling-place and established him there *Glr.*; **seat, place**, *č̓os-γži* seat of religion, monastery *Tar.* and elsewh.; school of religion *Tar.* **44**, 17; *γži γċig-tu skád-ċig kyaṅ mi sdód-de* in no place resting for a moment (the arrow flies towards its goal) *Thgy.*; **ži ċig-tu* C.* the same as *rtse γċig-tu*. — 4. in philosophy: **axiom, proposition** *Was.* (58); **contents, tenor** (299); **basis, support** (273). — 5. *Sch.*: **enmity**?? — 6. also *že* (cf. *γžes*) a definition of time or of relationship: *γži-niṅ*, *že-niṅ* two years ago, *γži-més* great-great-grandfather, *γži-més-mo* great-great-grandmother, *γži-ṫsá* great-great-grandchild *Sch.* —

Comp. *γži-dgón* monastery of the place, in or near a village, usually very small and harbouring but a few monks. — *γži-ǰi-bžin-pa* a recluse, 'who stays where he is' *Burn.* I, 310. — *γži-bdág* lord of the manor, lord of the soil, may denote a king or nobleman, but gen. it is **a local deity**, presiding over a certain district, to whom travellers are bound to offer sacrifice, and whom to offend they must carefully avoid.

གཞིག་པ་ γžig-pa 1. **to examine, search, try**, *rtog-* (or *brtag-*) *γžig légs-par γtóṅ-ba* to select and arrange carefully, e.g. books *Pth.*; *lo daṅ zlá-bar rtog-γžig žib-tu γtóṅ-ba* to search minutely as to the day and year *Pth.*; *bsam-γžig γtóṅ-ba* = *bsam-bló γtóṅ-ba* to weigh, consider *Pth.* — 2. fut. of *ˏǰig-pa*.

གཞིབ་པ་ γžib-pa fut. of *ˏǰib-pa*.

གཞིབས་པ་ γžibs-pa **to put** or **lay in order** *Lex.*, **žib-žib ċó-ċe(s)* W.*, **toṅ-wa* C.* id.

གཞིལ་བ་ γžil-ba fut. of *ˏǰil-ba*, = *ˏǰóms-pa*.

གཞིས་ཀ་ γžis-ka **native place, native country** *Lex.*; *yul-γžis* house, estate, property *Mil.* = *žiṅ-ḱáṅ* paternal estate; *ṗa-γžis* the father's domicile as inheritance; *γžis sgríl-ba* to change one's abode, to remove to another place *Sch.*; *γžis-pa* **a native** *Sch.*; *γžis-mad* **family, household, wife, children** and

domestics; *γẑi-byés Sch.*: native and foreign, at home and abroad.

གཞུ་ *γẑu*, also *γẑu-mo Mil.*, resp. *γnam-rú B.* and col., 1. **bow**, for shooting, *γẑu bčos* he constructed a bow *Glr.*; *γẑu ˳géṅ-ba*, *W.* **káṅ-če**, to bend the bow and have it ready, frq.; *˳tén-pa Pth.*, and *˳gúgs-pa Cs.*, id.; *˳búd-pa* to unbend (the bow) *Cs.*; *rdúṅ-ba* (*Dzl.* ཌོ, 15, ༢ཤ༢, 11. *Gyatch.* ༢༣, 10), acc. to explanations given by Lamas: to make the bow-string sound by a sudden pull or jerk, = *γẑú-rgyúd sbréṅ-ba Dzl.*, which both as to matter and language seems preferable to other explanations that have been given. — 2. **arch**, in architecture *Cs.*, *γẑú-lugs-su ˳búb-pa* 'to arch in the form of a bow' *Cs.*; **capital, chapiter**, v. *ka-ba*. — 3. resp. for **ẑum-már-pa** **lamp**, **zim-ẑu** id., **góṅ-ẑu** lantern *C.* (spelling uncertain).

Comp. *γẑú-mk'an* bow-maker. — *γẑu-rgyúd* bow-string *Dzl.* — *γẑú-čan*, *γẑu-ldán* furnished with a bow. — *γẑu-mčog Lex.*, *Sch.*: 'the two ends of a bow'; *γẑu-mčóg ˳dzúgs-pa* to rest one end of the bow on some object(?) *Mil.* — *γẑu-tóg* an arched roof *Cs.* — *γẑu-tógs* holding a bow, archer *Ld.-Glr.* — *γẑu-brtán* n. of an ancient Indian king *Gl.* — *γẑu-dóms* a cord, fathom, as a standard measure, opp. to any abitrary measure (so explained by a Lama). — *γẑú-pa* bow-man, archer. — *γẑur-šúbs*, bow-case *Wdṅ.*

གཞུ་བ་ *γẑú-ba* **to strike, to lash**, *lčág-gis* with a whip.

གཞུག་ *γẑug* 1. = *mjug*, q. v., **end, extremity**; *γẑug-gu*, *γẑug-čuṅ Med.* **coccyx; rump** or **ventlet** of birds *Sch.*; *γẑug-rmén* the glands of it *Sch.*; *gral-γẑúg* the end of a row *Glr.*; *mgo-γẑúg* upper and lower end, e.g. of a stick *Glr.*; *lo-γẑúg-la* at the end of the year *Mil.*; *mṅag-γẑúg* household-servants, suite *Sch.* — 2. v. *˳júg-pa*.

གཞུང་ *γẑuṅ* 1. **the middle, midst.** — 2. **spinal marrow** *S.g.*, also *klad-γẑuṅ Sch.*, *γẑuṅ-riṅs Mil.* — **gyab-ẑúṅ-la zug rag** *W.* I feel a pain in the middle of my back; *lče-γẑuṅ* the middle of the tongue; *γẑuṅ-nas* in a direct way, opp. to *zúr-nas*.

Comp. **ẑúṅ-go** *C.* middle door, principal door or gate. **ẑuṅ-čág** *W.* partition-wall, **ṭád-če** to construct one. — *γẑúṅ-pa* a man from the middle part of the country, neither *stód-pa* nor *šám-pa W.* — *γẑúṅ-ma* 1. **the middle of a thing** *Cs.*; as a proper name: the middle part of Lhasa, containing the royal palace, also *γẑuṅ-sa-dga-ldán*. 2. the back-part of fur *Sch.* 3. **kernel, pith, main substance** *Sch.* 4. **the original, the source, text**; *γẑuṅ-lúgs* id. *Tar.*

གཞུང་བ་ *γẑúṅ-ba* pf. *γẑuṅs Cs.*: '**to attend, to be heedful; attention**, *γẑúṅs-pa* heedful'; *Sch.* has: 'sincere, orderly', and for the current phrase *yid γẑúṅs-pa* he gives: 'a quiet and prudent mind or behaviour'. But the way in which the word is used in books, where it frequently occurs in conjunction with *mk'ás-pa*, as well as in the popular expressions *ẑúṅ-k'an* and *ẑuṅ-méd-k'an* = *blo-rnó* and *blo-dmán*, would rather suggest the version: **acuteness of perception**, a good and quick comprehension.

གཞུད་པ་ *γẑud-pa Sch.*: '**to go, to walk, to put into**'.

གཞུན་པོ་ *γẑún-po* **excellent in its kind**, *γser γẑún-po* the purest gold, *ston-tóg γẑún-po* a capital crop *C.*

གཞུར་བ་ *γẑúr-ba* **to shear, shave, cut off**, **ṭa** the hair *C.*, leaves, branches *Cs.* (cf. *bẑár-ba*?).

གཞེ་ར་ *γẑé-ra* **parsley** *C.*

གཞེང་ *γẑeṅ* v. *ẑeṅ*.

གཞེན་ *γẑen* the act of **remembering** or **reminding**, **nyiṅ-la ẑen yóṅ-če ṗi-la ḍi** *W.* in order not to forget it, I have written it down; *γẑen skúl-ba Lex.* to remind a person; *γẑen btád-pa* or acc. to another reading *btáb-pa*, i.e. *˳débs-pa* to admonish, exhort *Dzl.* ༢༧༢, 9.

གཞེན་པ་ *γẑén-pa* **to light, kindle, inflame** *Sch.*; *ráṅ-byuṅ-gi mes ẑúgs-la*, prob. to be set in flames by spontaneous fire (?) *Tar.* 7, 4.

གཞེས་ *γẑes* **the second day after to-morrow** *Lex.*; **to-re naṅ-la ẑe-la** *W.* to-morrow, the day after to-morrow, on the fourth day; yžes-rnyiṅ Cs. = yži-niṅ.

གཞེས་པ་ yžés-pa (= bžugs-pa yet less used), resp. for **to sit, stay, wait,** čuṅ tsam yžes šig wait a little! Dzl. 222, 12 (another reading: bžugs šig).

གཞོ་བ་ yžó-ba for bžó-ba, v. ˎjó-ba.

གཞོག་པ་ yžóg-pa v. ˎjóg-pa.

གཞོགས་ yžogs **the side of the body,** = glo; yžogs yyas yyon the right and left side Sch.; yžógs-su sideways Sch.; yžogs slóṅ-ba Lex., yžogs-sloṅ byéd-pa Cs. to speak allusively; yžogs-smód byéd-pa to prejudice a person against another insidiously, to create enmity Thgy.; it is also used like a verb: yžógs-te rtsáb-pa to be insolent with a fair appearance, opp. to ṅor downright Thgy. — yžogs-p̔yéd ná-ba Do. prob. an inaccurate expression for pain in one side.

གཞོང་པ་ yžóṅ-pa **wooden basin, trough, tub, washing-tub;** k̔yi-yžóṅ (col. *k̔yib-žóṅ*) trough for feeding dogs and other animals, also manger W.; *ṭ̔ud-žoṅ* W. prob. id.; *čag-žóṅ* W. trough for dry horse-meat; *ṭab-žóṅ* winnowing-tray, inst. of a shovel; in books the word is used in a wider sense, in such expressions as yser-, dṅul-, ˎk̔ar-, rdo-yzoṅ.

གཞོངས་ yžoṅs Lex. = ljoṅs.

གཞོན་པ་ yžón-pa 1. sbst. v. bžón-pa. — 2. adj. **young,** yžón-pa de na-ré the younger one said Mil.; rgyál-po sku-ná yžón-pa the young king; bdag yžón-pas as I am still young, I as the younger one, the youngest Dzl.; yžón-pa ˎgá-žig some young people Mil.; yžón-dus bu-méd who in their younger years had no children; yžón-nu **a youth,** frq., yžón-nu-tso plur. Mil.; yžón-nu-ma or bú-mo yžón-nu Dzl. **virgin, maiden, girl;** sé-ba yžón-nu a young rose Wdṅ.; yžón-nu daṅ brál-bar byéd-pa to deprive a girl of her virginity Cs., yžon-nu-brál a girl that has lost her virginity Cs.; yžón-nu-nas from a child, from infancy Mil.; yžon-grógs youthful companion Mil.; yžón-ša-čan with youthful flesh, yžón-ša-čan-du ˎgyúr-ba Glr. to grow young again.

གཞོབ་ yžob 1. me-yžób **singeing,** or what has been **singed,** wool, hair, feathers etc.; **a mark** from burning; yžób-dri Sch. also yžob-ró smell of singeing; yžób-tu ˎgyúr-ba to be singed, seared Pth.; *žob gyáb-pa* C. to singe off; fig. ṅai lus-séms yžób-tu ṭal Glr. my body and soul were seared, deeply afflicted. — 2. W. **a crash,** e.g. of a tree breaking down.

གཞོམ་པ་ yžóm-pa 1. v. ˎjoms-pa. — 2. **to break in two, to tear** Sch.; in W. used of metal vessels **bent** or **bruised.**

གཞོར་ yžor v. ˎjor.

གཞོལ་བ་ yžól-ba 1. **to apply one's self diligently** Cs., čós-la ṭ̔ugs yžól-ba Pth. id. resp. — 2. **to comprehend, to fathom**(?) Sch. — 3. resp. for ˎbáb-pa **to alight, light from, dismount,** v. čibs; cf. also žol.

གཞོས་ yžos for bžos, v. ˎjó-ba.

བཞའ་ bža, in Lexx. mentioned as the same with brlán-pa.

བཞག་ bžag 1. **large intestine,** = ynyé-ma; bžag-sgór-mo the windings of the intestines Glr., Mil. — 2. certain muscles under the arms Mṅg. — 3. Sch.: 'flesh of animals that died of disease'.

བཞག་པ་ bžág-pa 1. v. ˎjóg-pa. — 2. **to tear, wear,** intrs., of cloth etc.; **to burst, crack, split** C., W.

བཞད་ bžad, also bžád-pa Pth. **swan;** bžad-dkár Lex.; bžad-ldán Schr.: 'a pond with swans on it'.

བཞད་པ་, གཞད་པ་ bžád-pa, yžád-pa **to laugh, smile** Glr.; bžád-k̔a-ma a girl with a smiling face Mil.; bžad-gád **laughter,** ṭég-pa to raise (a laughter) Mil., bžad-gád-mk̔an Tar. buffoon, jester; bžád-mo **smile, laughing, laughter,** bžád-mo bžád-pa to laugh; bžád-pa-mo, bžad-ldán-ma n. of a goddess, Ssk. Hūsawati Cs.

བཞབ་པ་ bžáb-pa v. ˎjáb-pa.

བཞམས་པ་ bžáms-pa 1. also yžáms-pa Schr.? **to stroke,** p̔yág-gis resp. with the hand, **to coax, caress;** hence bžáms-te Dzl.

༢༢,5, might perh. be rendered: **to appease, to pacify.** — 2. *bžams-bsgó byéd-pa Lex.* **to remind of, to call to mind.**

བཞར་བ་ *bžár-ba* **to scrape,** with a knife, **to shave** or **shear,** with a razor *Med.*; *skra bžár-ba* the hair.

བཞི་ *bži* 1. **four**; *bži-pa, bži-po* cf. *dgu*; *bži-bču* (col. **žib-ču**) 40, *bži-bču-rtsa-γčig* (*W.*žib-ču-že-čig*), *že-γčig* etc. the numbers 41—49; *bži-brgyá* 400, *bži-stoṅ* 4000 etc.; *bži-ča* one fourth, a quarter; *bži-ṫsan-gyi-sdé-pa pyed-daṅ-brgyád* the 7½ tetrads (of letters) *Gram.* — 2. often incorr. for *ži* or *γži.*

བཞིན་ *bžin* 1. sbst. **face, countenance,** *ráb-tu mi-sdúg-pa* (of) a very ugly face *Dzl.*, *légs-pa, mdzés-pa Glr.* (of) a handsome, a pretty face; *bžin-mdzés-ma* a woman or girl with a pretty face; *bžin zúgs-te* the face dripping (from perspiration); *bžin ₒdzúm-pa daṅ bčas-pa* with a friendly smiling countenance *Mil.*; *bžin-pags sér-po* the skin of the face being yellow (as in bilious complaints) *Mṅg.*; *bžin-rás* the appearance, *ṅán-pa Med.*; *bžin-bzáṅ*, fem. *bzin-bzaṅ-ma*, a polite address: my dear Sir; *kye bžin-bzaṅ-dag* much respected gentlemen! also in other instances as a word of politeness: *bžin-bzáṅ-ma dé-dag laṅs-te* the ladies rose and ...; it seems to be particularly in favour, when apparitions are addressed *Mil.* — 2. particle, the meaning of which corresponds in part to that of the Greek prep. *κατά* c. acc., gen. used as an adv. *bžin-du* or *bžin*, but also as an adj. with *pa:* a. joined to verbal roots, *bžin* serves to form with them a partic. pres., and *bžin-du* a gerund, *ṫugs-mnyés-bžin-pai ṅáṅ-la* in a rejoicing frame of mind, in a joyful mood *Mil.*; *ḱri-la bžúgs-bžin-du* sitting on the chair *Dzl.*; *skrág-bžin-du* from fear *Dzl.* (cf. *καϑ' ὕπνον*); *mdaṅs ₒgyur bžin-du* whilst his colour changes *Dzl.*; *mi šes bžin-du šes-so žes zer* not knowing it he pretends to know it *Stg.*; *dád-bžin-du log soṅ* 'credentes discesserunt', believing they went away *Mil.* b. *bžin(-du)* as postp. c. acc., **agreeably, in conformity, according to,** very frq.; *čos bžin-du* according to the precepts of religion *Dzl.* (cf. *κατὰ νόμον*), *rgyál-pos bsgó-ba bžin-du sgrúb-pa* to execute a thing according to the king's command, to perform his order frq.; *ḱyod ǰi-skad smrás-pa bžin-du γžán-dag-la bsnyád-de* relating to the others according to what has been said by you, = relating what you have said *Dzl.*; *yid-bžin-du* to heart's content frq.; **like, as,** *ri ₒgyél-ba* like the breaking down of a mountain *Dzl.*; also with a pleonastic *ltar: mḱán-po ǰi-ltar γsúṅ-ba bžin Glr.*, or, which would be the same, *ǰi-bžin γsúṅ-ba ltar*, as the very learned gentleman has said, foretold; *de bžin-du* **so** = *dé-ltar; de-de-bžin-no* yes, that is so; *de-bžin-nyid* (तथता), **truth, reality, substance, essentiality** *Was.* (272), **identity** (297), in mysticism = *čos-nyid Thgy.*, v. *čos*, comp.

c. *pyi-bžin(-du), pyir-bžin(-du)* **afterwards, subsequently** (cf. *κατόπισϑε*). — d. distrib. *nyin-ré-bžin(-du)*, **daily, per day** (*καϑ' ἡμέραν*), *nyin-γčig-bžin-du* id.; *re-re-bžin-gyi mdzad-pa Glr.* his daily doings.

བཞུ་བ་ *bžú-ba*, v. *žú-ba* II. and *ₒju-ba*, **to melt.**

བཞུགས་པ་ *bžúgs-pa*, resp. for *sdód-pa* and *ₒdúg-pa*, 1. **to sit,** *bžúgs-su γsol B*, *bžugs (-žu)* col., please sit down! — *bžúgs-ḱri* chair; throne. — 2. **to dwell, reside,** *bžúgs-pai po-bráṅ* castle of residence *Dzl.*; *bžúgs-pai rten* a small temple in which a deity resides *Dzl.*; *bžugs-grógs* fellow-lodger: — 3. **to remain, stay, exist, live,** *ₒjig-rtén-du bžúgs-pa* to be in the world, to live on earth, of Buddha and saints; also, still to remain in the world; *stón-pa bžúgs-pai dús-su* during the life-time of the Teacher (Buddha) *Tar.*; *ḱyed ₒdir bžugs čos-mdzád* ye devout here present = my devout friends! *Mil.*; **žug yǫ́-dham* C.* are you at home? **ku žug naṅ yǫ́-dham* C.* are you coming? = welcome! well-met!; transferred to writings, texts etc., **to be contained,** so in titles of books: *mdzaṅs-blún žes-byá-ba bžúgs-so* the so-styled 'Sage and Fool' is contained (in the present volume); *bló-la bžúgs-pa daṅ glegs-bám-du bžúgs-pa ṫams-čád yi-ger spel* all that was found in the memories (of individual persons) and in books, was recorded *Tar.*

བཞུད་པ་ *bžúd-pa*, resp. **to go away, to depart,** *B.* frq.; *p̓ar bžud* pray, go away! (opp. to *t̓sur-byon*).

བཞུན་ *bžun* v. *žun*.

བཞུར་བ་ *bžúr-ba* 1. = *γzúr-ba, bžár-ba Cs.* — 2. **to strain, filter,** *Sch.*

བཞུས་པ་ *bžús-pa* v. *žú-ba*.

བཞེང་བ་ *bžéṅ-ba*, pf. and imp. *bžeṅs Glr.*, resp. for *slóṅ-ba*, **to raise, erect, set up,** an image, temple; **to manufacture, compose,** sacred things, e.g. pictures, books; **to draw up, frame, write, print,** or cause it to be done; **to found, endow, give,** books to monasteries etc.

བཞེངས་པ་ *bžéṅs-pa* 1. pf. of *bžéṅ-ba*. — 2. resp. for *láṅ-ba* **to rise, get up,** intrs. to *bžéṅ-ba*; also with *yár(-la) Glr.*; **nyi-ráṅ žáṅs(-sa*) W.* are you risen? **žaṅ(s)** please to get up!

བཞེད་པ་ *bžéd-pa* I. vb., resp. for *ₒdód-pa*, **to wish, desire,** *rgyál-po γzigs bžéd-dam* does your Reverence wish to see the king? *Dzl.*; *rgyál-po náṅ-du ₒbyón-par bžéd-pa-la* as the king wished to enter *Glr.*; *rta mi bžéd-na* if your Reverence does not wish to have the horse *Mil.*; in science: **to accept,** *mk̓án-pa p̓yi-ma-dag mi bžéd--pa legs* it is well that learned men of later times do not accept it, approve of it *Gram.*; **to assert, maintain,** *so-sói bžéd-t̓sul máṅ-na yaṅ* although many different propositions are to be met with *Wdk.*; *sṅá-mas bžed* earlier writers are of opinion, insist on *Gram.*; of letters: *ga-ₒp̓ul bžed* certain letters require ག for a prefix *Zam.* — II. **supposition, view, opinion** *Tar.* 113, 21. — *bžed-don* resp. **wish, desire** *Cs.*, *bžed-don ₒgrub* it happens according to one's wish, as one could wish *Cs.*

བཞེས་པ་ *bžés-pa* I. vb., resp. for *lén-pa* **to take, receive, accept; to seize, confiscate,** *B.*, *C.* (*W. *nám-če** synon.); *k̓áb-tu bžés-pa* and *žál-gyis bžés-pa* v. *k̓ab* and *žal*; esp. at meals, **to take, to eat,** *ǰi bžéd-pa bžes šig Dzl.* please take whatever you like, *bžés-na* if he would take it, if it should be to his liking *Mil.*; instead of *lón-pa* in: *dgúṅ-lo bču-γnyís bžés-pa* he got twelve years old. — II. sbst. **food, meat,** *bžés-pa ₒdrén-pa* to offer, to serve up meat *Mil.*, *Pth.* — **Comp.** **žē-ḍho* C.* food, sweet-meats (cf. *gro*) *bžes-t̓áṅ* food (?) *Sch.* — **žē-ḍhúṅ** (?) *Ts.* beer. —**žē-bhág*C.* bread. —**žē-rág* W.* brandy. —**žē-hór* C.*, hookah, oriental tobacco-pipe, the smoke of which passes through water.

བཞོ་བ་, བཞོས་པ་ *bžó-ba, bžós-pa* **to milk.**

བཞོག་པ་ *bžog-pa* v. *ₒǰog-pa*.

བཞོགས་ *bžogs = γžogs*.

བཞོང་ *bžoṅ = γžoṇ*.

བཞོན་པ་ *bžón-pa* (sometimes incorr. *γžón-pa*) vehiculum, **riding-beast, carriage, vehicle;** *bžón-pa šóm-pa* to order the horses to be put to *Dzl.*; *bžon-pas ₒbrós-pa* to take to flight in a vehicle or on horseback *Dzl.*; *mi-srun bžón-pa* a not gentle riding-beast *S.g.*

བཞོན་མ་ *bžón-ma* **milking cow** *Cs*, *bžon-p̓yugs* milking cattle *Glr.*

ཟ

ཟ *za* 1. the letter **z,** originally, and in the frontier-provinces to the present-day, sounding like the English z, in *C.* differing from ས, s, only by the following vowel being deep-toned. — 2. numer. figure: 22.

ཟ་, ཟས་ *za, zas, Ld.* any thing **small, neat, elegant, of a miniature size,** **pé-ča za žig** a little book, pocket-edition, **nod-čád za zig** a little pot or can, **čaṅ za žig** a drop of beer.

ཟྭ་ *zwa*, **nettle**, stinging nettle, gen. *zwa-tsód*, being, when young, eaten as greens (v. *tsód-ma*); *zwa(i)-pyi(mo)*, *'a-ya-zwa-tsód*, *Wdn.*, blind or dead nettle; *zwa-lčág* scourge made of stinging nettles, *zwa-lčág brgyáb-pa* to flog with it *Cs.*; *zwa-ber*, the smart produced by the stinging of nettles *Cs.*; *zwa-ₒbrúm Wdn.* (?).

ཟ་ཁུ་ *za-ḱu Med.*, e.g. *bad-kan za-ḱur ₒgyur Mng.* prob. the same word which *Sch.* spells *za-gu*, explaining it by gonorrhoea, morbid discharge of seminal fluid, semen pruriens.

ཟ་བ་ *za-ba, bza-ba* I. vb., perf. *zos, bzas*, fut. *bza*, imp. *zo, zos* (*C.* *zę*) 1. **to eat**, both of men and animals, *zá-bya*, *zá-rgyu* what may or must be eaten, *za-čig-pa Dzl.* (perh. better *bza-γčig-pa*) one that takes only one meal a day, or perh.: one that takes a solitary meal; *zós-pas* having eaten *Dzl.*; *zós-pai ₒóg-tu* after he had eaten *Dzl.*; *zos-ₒgrogs* 'immediately after dinner' (??) *Sch.*; *ma-lús-par zá-ba Dzl.*, **dág-mo za-če** *W.*, to eat up, consume, to clear the plate, the manger; *bzá-ru rún-ba* or *mi-rúṅ-ba* what may or may not be eaten; *Dzl.* ༢༦, 16 has also a supine *zós-su*: *bu zos-su ₒoṅ* she will even be constrained to eat her own young (s. l. c.); *žim-du zo Zam.* may you enjoy your dinner! ni f.; *zá-ḱar* at dinner-time *Sch.*; *za-zá-ba* 'to eat often, to be a glutton' *Cs.* — 2. **to live upon, to live by**, *gla zá-ba* to gain one's subsistence as a day-labourer *Dzl.* — 3. **to itch**, *za ₒṕrúg-pa* v. *ₒṕrug-pa*. — 4. fig. for **to steal**, **ḱún-ma, gṓn-mo zos soṅ** *Ld.*, a thief, a witch, has made away with it. — 5. fig. of affections of the mind: **to entertain, to give way to**, *ḱóṅ-ḱro, tsig-pa, té-tsom zá-ba* to give way to resentment, anger, doubts. — II. sbst. **food, meat, victuals**, *za ču žim* good eating and drinking *Mil.*; **zá-če zá-če, čó-če** *W.* to eat food, to prepare food. — *za-rkóṅ* v. *rkoṅ*. — *za-ḱaṅ* dining-room; eating-house, cook's shop *C.* — *za-ḱu* v. the preceding article. — *zá-mḱan* one that is eating, an eater. — **za-čóg** *W.* what may be eaten, **za-mi-čóg** what may not be eaten. — **za-túr** *C.* chop-sticks. — *zá-ma* **food, victuals**, *zá-ma mi ster ruṅ* though you do not give me any food *Mil.* — *za-yón* meat-offering to saints etc. *Mil.* — For more refer to *bza*.

ཟ་མ་ *zá-ma* 1. v. above. — 2. also *zá-ma-tog Ssk.* करण्ड, **basket**, in Tibetan only fig., mostly as a title of books, but also used in connection with mysticism.

ཟ་ཟི་ *za-zi* **trouble, noise** *Cs.*, **troublesome chatting** *Sch.*; **troubled, bewildered, perplexed** *Schr.*; in the passage *rmi-lam za-zi maṅ Med.* it seems to signify troubled dreams.

ཟ་ཟོམ་ *za-zóm* a fine cotton fabric *Sch.*

ཟ་ར་ *zá-ra?* **zá-ra ṕi-mo** *W.* the later part of the afternoon, v. *rdzá-ra*.

ཟ་རུ་ *zá-ru* v. *γzár-bu*.

ཟ་འོག་ *za-ₒóg* **heavy silk cloth**, *za-ₒóg-gi gos* a garment made of it *Glr.*; *za-ₒóg dgu brtsegs ḱri* a seat formed of nine silk quilts. — *za-báb* id.

ཟ་ཧོར་ *za-hor* n. of a town or district, acc. to *Cs.* in Bengal, acc. to *Pth.* in the north-west of India, by the statements of Lamas the present **Mandi**, a small principality under British protection, in the Punjâb, between the rivers Byās and Ravi, where there is a sacred lake, celebrated as a place of pilgrimage, from which the Brahmins residing there derive a considerable income.

ཟག་པ་ *zág-pa* 1. sometimes for *γzág-pa*, from *ₒdzágs-pa*. — 2. sbst., *Ssk.* आस्रव **misery, affliction, sorrow**, esp. as a consequence of sin, hence frq. = sin, *zág-pa zad* the woe of this world is over, frq.; *zág-pa-med-pai las* works spotless or without sin *Thgy.*; *zag-méd-kyi bde-ba* untroubled happiness *Glr.*; *zag-bčás* burdened with misery and sin, *zag-bčás-kyi las γsum* the three sinful works *Thgy.*; *zag-bčas-kyi mṅon(-par)-šes(-pa) Glr.* and *Thgr.?*

ཟང་ *zaṅ? Sch.*: *zaṅ-tál-du* **penetrating.**

ཟང་ཟང་ *zaṅ-záṅ* 1. v. *dmár-po* extr. — 2. also *zaṅ-ziṅ, ziṅ-ziṅ, γziṅ-ba*, v. *ₒdziṅs-pa*; *W.* also: **muddled, rather tipsy.**

ཟང་ཟིང་ *zaṅ-zíṅ* 1. sbst. **matter, object, goods,** = *rdzas*, *zaṅ-zin čúṅ-zad tsám-gyi* *p'yir* even for the most trifling matter *Stg.*; *p'yi-rol-gyi zaṅ-ziṅ* external goods, earthly possessions, (opp. to internal, spiritual gifts) *Dzl.*; also *zaṅ-ziṅ* by itself: what is earthly, pertaining to this world *Mil.* — 2. adj., **confused in mind, stupefied** *Sch.*, v. the preceding article.

ཟངས་ *zaṅs* 1. **copper**, *ysér-zaṅs* gilt copper, *záṅs-kyi btsa* prob. verdigris. — 2. **kettle** *B.*, *C.*, v. *p'an-dil*; *záṅs-su skól-ba* to boil in a kettle *Dzl.*; *zaṅs k'ól-pa* a boiling kettle *Dzl.*; *ₒk'ár-zaṅs* bronze or brass kettle, *lċags-zaṅs* iron kettle. — *zaṅs-rkyán* copper can or jug. — *zaṅs-skyógs* copper ladle. — *zaṅs-čén* a large, *zaṅs-čúṅ* a small kettle. — *zaṅs-tig* a small species of gentian. — *zaṅs-tib* copper tea-pot. — **záṅ-ton-sa** *W.* copper-mine. — *zaṅs-t'ál* copper slacks *Glr.* — *zaṅs-mdóg* copper colour. — *zaṅs-sdér* copper plate or dish *Sch.* — *zaṅs-snód* copper vessel. — **záṅ-bu** *C.*, *W.*, = *zaṅs* 2; **záṅ-bu če čuṅ nyi** two copper kettles, a large one and a little one. — *záṅs-ma* = *záṅs-bu?* *Mṅg.* — *záṅs-yya* *Cs.*: 'copper-green', prob. verdigris. — *záṅs-sa* copper-ore *Cs.*

ཟངས་དཀར་ *záṅs-dkar* south-western province of Ladak, *záṅs-dkar-pa*, *-ma* man or woman of that province.

ཟད་པ་ *zád-pa* v. *ₒdzád-pa.*

ཟན་ *zan*, *C.* **zęn**, I. resp. *bsáṅ-ma*, also *k'am-zán* *Mil.* 1. **pap, porridge,** of flour and water, thick, boiled or not boiled, warm or cold, also called *bág-zan*, esp. as dough for baking; in *C.* porridge is gen. made of *rtsám-pa*, and if possible of tea; *ₒbrás-zan* rice-p., *ₒó-zan*, milk-p.; porridge being the daily food, as bread is with us, the word is used also 2. for **food** in gen : *zan zá-ba* to take food, to eat, *bdag daṅ zan mi zá-na* if you will not eat with me *Dzl.*; *zan-gráṅ* cold, *zan-drón* warm food, *zan-čaṅ* meat and drink, *S.g.*; *zan btsos-pa* boiled food; **zan-kón** dearth *W.*; *zan zos* 1. he was eating porridge. 2. as one word: *Bal.* wife, cf. *bza*; fig. *lkog-zán zá-ba* to take unlawful interest *Sch.* — 3. **fodder, provender,** v. *bzan.* —

II. inst. of *za* **eater,** as second part of a compound: *ša-zán* meat-eater; carnivorous animal *Glr.*; *nya-zán* fish-eater, ichthyophagist; *p'ag-zén* pork-eater.

ཟན་པོ་ *zán-po* v. *yzán-po.*

ཟབ་ *zab* **silk,** fine or heavy silk, v. *dar-záb*; *zab-čén* costly silk cloth *Sch.*; *zab-skúd* *Lt.*, *Mil.* silk-cord; *zab-ₒból* silk covering for a seat, bolster *Pth.*

ཟབ་པ་ *záb-pa*, vb., adj. and sbst., **to be deep, deep, depth,** *záb-po*, gen. *záb-mo*, adj., deep, frq.; often fig., *blo-záb* *Cs.*: a profound mind or understanding; *zab-záb byas kyaṅ záb-mo raṅ mi ₒdug* although people call it deep, it is not deep *Sch.*; *zab-lám*, *záb-moi sgom-k'rid* a term of Buddhist mysticism, doctrine of witchcraft, = *dbú-mai lam*, or *p'yág-rgya čén-po.* — *zab-k'yád* depth, = *zabs*, *Dzl.*, *Mil.*

ཟབས་ *zabs* **depth,** *zábs-su ₒdom bčui doṅ* a pit ten fathoms in depth.

ཟམ་པ་ *zám-pa* **bridge,** *grú-zam* bridge of boats *Cs.*; *lcágs-zam* iron bridge, wire-bridge; *lčúg-zam* suspension-bridge, by means of cables of twisted birch-tree branches; *ₒdrén-zam* draw-bridge *Cs.*; *rdó-zam* 1. stone-bridge. 2. natural rock-bridge; *rtswá-zam* common expression for *lčúg-zam* and *ťsár-zam*; the latter: suspension-bridge by cables formed of thin split cane; *šiṅ-zam* wooden bridge; *zám-pa ₒdzúgs-pa* to throw a bridge *Cs.*; *zám-pai ká-ba* or *rkáṅ-pa* the piers or foundations, *spaṅ-léb*, *spaṅ-sgó* the boards or planks, *mda-yáb* or *lag-rtén* parapet, *yžu-ťóg* arch, *zam-ydúṅ* beam of a bridge, *Cs.*; *zam-čén* a large bridge, *zam-čúṅ* a little one *Cs.*, *zám-bu* id.

ཟར་ *zar* 1. supine of *zá-ba*; *zar ₒjúg-pa* **to give to eat.** — 2. **pitch-fork,** for shaking up the corn, hay-fork, dung-fork; forks at dinner are not yet used in Tibet, spoons and knives, and in Lhasa chop-sticks, answering their end sufficiently.

ཟར་བབས་ *zar-bábs* *Sch.*: **tassel**; acc. to our authorities: **gold-brocade.**

ཟར་བུ་ *zár-bu* *Glr.*, *Mil.* seems to be **tassel.**

ཟར་མ་ *zar-ma Dzl., Med.* **sesame-seed**; *zar-mai me-tog* flower of sesame, *Sch.*; *zar-ma-ču* is mentioned in *Pth.* as Aphrodisiacum; yet *zar-mai ras* is stated to be a fabric, manufactured from *zwa-tsód*, muslin?

ཟལ་ *zal Ld.* a small and uninhabited river-island.

ཟལ་མོ་ *zál-mo* 1. **young cow, heifer,** *ˏbri-zál* yak-heifer. — 2. a fabulous bird *Sch.*

ཟས་ *zas* **food, nourishment,** for men and animals, also in a wider fig. sense; *zas-bčád smyúṅ-γnas* fasting, abstaining from or withholding food *Lex.*; *zas-bzáṅ(-po)* 1. dainty food *Dzl.* 2. nourishing fare, *Wdṅ.*, *zas-ṅán(-pa)* the contrary; *zas-ni* as to diet . : . *Med.*; *zás-su či za* what does it feed on? *Dzl.*; *zás-sukrag ˏtúṅ-ba* to drink blood for nourishment *Do.*; *zas ˏtsól-ba* to seek to obtain a livelihood *Ma.*; *ˏtsó-ba zas, Mil.* a pleon. expression = *zas*; *k̔a-zás* (resp. *žal-zas B., sól-wa* col.) **food, meat,** for human beings; *dkár-zas* v. *dkár-ba*; *dmár-zas Sch.*: 'festival dishes', perh. more corr. flesh-meat, animal food? *gró-zas Sch.*: 'dry traveller's fare'; *ǰán-zas*, wholesome nutritive food *Med.* —

Comp. **zẹ-kọ́n* C.* dearth, scarcity. — *zas-skom* meat and drink, solid and liquid food *Med.*; *zas-čáṅ*, id., as travelling-provisions *Glr.* — *zas-spyód* food and exercise, diet, in a wider sense *Med.* — *zas-tsód* the due measure of food, *zas-tsód ma zin* the portion or share was not full, it was not the full allowance, *S.g.* — *zas-γtsáṅ-ma* (clean food), n.p. शुद्धोदन, the father of Buddha; *bdúd-rtsi-zas*, *bré-bo-zas*, *zas-dkár* the names of his three brothers, *zas-γtsaṅ-srás* appellation of Buddha himself.

ཟི་ *zi*, I. num. figure: 52. — II. *W.* 1. something of a very **small size** or **quantity**, **zi yaṅ mi dug** not an atom is left, **zi-med-k̔an čo** eat it up to the last crumb! **mé-zi** a spark in the ashes ever so small. — 2. **the black mark** in a target. (cf. *ža*).

ཟི་ཉིལ་ *zi-ñíl* v. *zi-liṅ*.

ཟི་བ་ *zi-ba* v. *γzi-ba*.

ཟི་མ་ *zi-ma, Sch.*: **green slime** on standing water, *zi-ma-čan* what is covered with such a slime.

ཟི་ར་ *zi-ra, Ssk.* and *Hindi* जीर, **the Asiatic caraway,** *Cuminum Cyminum*, exported from Tibet to India, of a powerful aroma, which to the taste of Europeans is often disagreeable; two kinds are distinguished, *zi-ra dkár-po*, and *nág-po*.

ཟི་རི་རི་ *zi-ri-ri* **the humming of bees,** the singing of a kettle *W.*

ཟི་རུ་ *zi-ru* col. for *γzér-bu*.

ཟི་ལིང་ *zi-liṅ* I. also **zi-ñil, zi-lóṅ* W.* **noise, bustle, tumult.** —

II. from the Chinese 1. also *zi-lím, zi-láṅ* **a composition metal,** similar to German silver, *zi-liṅ-pan-tse* or *baṅ-tse C.* a basin of that metal. — 2. n. p., province, adjoining the Kokonor, *zi-liṅ-ǰa* tea from thence.

ཟིང་ཟིང་ *ziṅ-ziṅ* v. *zaṅ-ziṅ*.

ཟིང་རེལ་ *ziṅ-rél W.*, prob. for *ˏdziṅ-sbrél*, with **čó-če**, to prepare for battle, or to begin fighting.

ཟིན་པ་ *zin-pa* 1. v. *ˏdzin-pa*. — 2. = *ˏdzád-pa*, esp. in the pf. tense, **to draw near to an end, to be at an end, to be finished, exhausted, consumed**; *zin-pai p̔úṅ-po* the perishable, mortal body *Thgy.*; **to be finished, terminated,** *nam yaṅ mi zin-to Dzl.* it will never be finished; **to finish, to get done with,** building a wall *Glr.*, **zin čúg-če* W.* id.; *ˏtuṅ ma zin dógs-pas* fearing not to be able to drink it all *Glr.*; *rtsé-ba zin-pas* as the playing has ceased, or, as he has done playing *Dzl.*; *zin(-pa) méd(-pai) las* endless working, unceasing labour *Mil.*; hence = *tsár-ba*, to denote an action that is **perfectly past**, esp. in *B.*, *p̔rú-gu skyés-su zin kyaṅ* although the child is already born *Do.*; *γsón-poi tsé-na ˏṅ-čag-gis de spyad zin* we had enjoyed it during our life-time; *zin-bris Cs.*: 1. **abridgment, general view, synopsis.** 2. **lecture,** so *Schf. Tar.* 210, 22. 3. **receipt, quittance; bond** (of obligation), **bill of debt.**

ཟིམ་བུ་ *zim-bu* **fine, thin, slender,** *čar zim-bu mi drág-po žig bab* a fine, drizzling rain was falling *Dzl.*, *Mil.*; *čar zim-zim dál-gyis báb-pa Mil.*, id.; *zim-zim* or *ziṅ-ziṅ* **fine, hair-shaped, capillary**, e.g. the leaves of some plants.

ཟིར་བ་ *zir-ba*, (*γzir-ba?*), gen. **zir táṅ-če* W.*, **to aim**, *zir-po*, *zir-čan* a good aimer, marksman *W.*; *zir-sa* **aim, dispart**, **nẹ-zir** sight (of a gun) *W.*

ཟིར་མོ་ *zir-mo*, **zir-mo gyún-če* W.* to slide down a snow-hill on the coat spread under, a winter-diversion of children.

ཟིལ་ *zil* 1. (*Cs. zil-ma*), **brightness, splendour, brilliancy, glory**, *rje-btsún-gyi túgs-rjei zil ma bzód-par* not being able to bear the brightness of his Reverence's grace, (the adversary fell down the mountain) *Mil.*; *zíl-čan* **brilliant, resplendent**; *zil-gyis nón-pa* to overcome, vanquish, *koi zil-gyis nón-te* overpowered by him *Pth.*; *zil-bar ₒgró-ba* to increase, multiply, spread *Sch.* — 2. in botany: *stoṅ-zil, Corydalis meïfolia*; *γser-zil, dṅul-zil? S.g.*

ཟིལ་དངར་ *zil-dṅár* v. *dṅar.*

ཟིལ་པ་ *zil pa* **dew**, *zil-pa krom-mé* a sparkling dew-drop *Pth.*; *zil-dkár* **hoar-frost** *Sch.*; *zil-mṅar Cs.* = *mdúd-rtsi* **nectar.**

ཟིལ་བུན་པ་ *zil-bún-pa* a slight **shuddering** from fear.

ཟུ་ *zu*, num. figure: 82.

ཟུག་ *zug* 1. also *γzug*, **pain, torment**, physical and mental; **distemper, illness, complaint**, esp. *W.* **zúg rag** I feel a pain, I am ill, **gó-la zug rág-ga** have you the head-ache? **zug čo dug** he is ill, he is suffering from pain; **só-zug** toothache; *zúg-rṅu, zug-γzér*, resp. *snyún* or *snyúṅ-zug*, *B.* and col. = *zug*, *mya-ṅán-gyi zúg-rṅus sdúg-bsṅal-žiṅ* weighed down by the grief of misery, *nyon-móṅs-kyi zúg-rṅu Mil.*, of the like import. — 2. also *γzug*, the principal or main pieces in cutting up an animal, **quarters**, *zúg-tu ₒprál-ba* to cut into such pieces *Mil.*; 1 *zug* = 3 *lhu*, = 6 *dum* = 12 *rgya-ri*. — 3. v. *tsug.*

ཟུག་རྔུ་ *zúg-rṅu* v. *zug* 1.

ཟུག་པ་ *zúg-pa* I. vb. 1. v. *ₒdzúgs-pa.* — 2. **to bark** *Dzl.*

II. sbst. **building, erection**, **zúg-pa gyáb-pa* Ts.* to build (cf. *ₒdzúgs-pa* 3).

ཟུང་ *zuṅ* 1. earlier literat. and *W.* **a pair, couple**, *zúṅ-du ma mčis* not occurring in pairs *Wdṅ.*; **čá-bu zuṅ čig*, Ld.* a pair of pendants (for the ears); *nyi-zlá zuṅ γčig btsón-du bzuṅ* sun and moon are both shut up (covered by clouds) *Mil.*; *zuṅ-mčóg* the model-pair, the two principal disciples of Buddha, Sariibu and Maudgalgyibu, *Köpp.* I, 101; *zuṅ-ldán* **agreeing** in sound, **rhyming** *Cs.*; *zuṅ-ₒbrél* **connection, junction, union**, *zuṅ-ₒbrel ₒdód-na* if one wishes both things to be united *Glr.*; *zuṅ-brél-du* one after the other, or one with the other *Pth.*; *zuṅ sdéb-pa* **to join, connect, unite** *Mil.*; *zuṅ-yá* one half of a pair, a single one, e.g. shoe etc. *Cs.* — 2. **a single, separate piece** *C.* and sometimes in later literat.; *ka-dród zuṅ čig* a bit or mouthful of food *Thgy.*; *tsar re zuṅ re bltás-pas* when he had seen a single piece but once, (he knew it immediately) *Tar.* — 3. symb. num.: 2; *zuṅ-pyógs* id. — *zuṅ-ₒjúg* a technical term of practical mysticism, the forcing the mind (*sems*) into the principal artery, in order to prevent distraction (of mind) (!) *Mil.* (v. *γtúm-mo*).

ཟུང་མཁར་ *zuṅ-mkár* n. of a royal castle *Glr.*

ཟུང་བ་ *zúṅ-ba* v. *ₒdzin-pa.*

ཟུངས་ *zuṅs* v. *γzuṅs.*

ཟུབ་པ་ *zúb-pa* inst. of *bsúbs-pa*, pf. of *sub-pa Glr.*

ཟུམ་པ་ *zúm-pa* 1. v. *ₒdzúm-pa.* — 2. *W.* for *bzúṅ-ba*, v. *ₒdzin-pa*; hence *zum-káb* **pin, brooch.**

ཟུར་ *zur* 1. **edge**, *gad-zúr* edge of a steep river-bank or precipice consisting of conglomerate *Cs.*; *ču-zúr* edge of the water, border, brink, bank, *ču-zúr-pa* one that lives on the bank of a river; *zúr-na* at the border (of the place where one happens to be) *Mil.* **žiṅ-zúr-nẹ lum yod* W.* the road leads along the field; **board**, of a ship. — 2. **edge, corner**, *ká-ba zur-brgyád-pa* octangular pillar *Stg.*, (v. *zúr-čan* and *zúl-ma* below); *zur bži* the four corners *Sch.* — 3. **side**, **zúr-du* (or *lóg-su*) *žag-pa** *C.* to lay aside; *zúr(-du) bkól-ba Lex.*, *Sch.*: to lay up, put by, spare, save; *zúr-du ˳krid-pa* to take aside, apart, for a private conversation; so also *zur ṗyin-pa Stg.*; *zúr-du*, *zúr-gyis B*, **zúr-na* W.*, **indirectly, by the way, by the by, incidentally,** *zúr-du smrá-ba* to speak indirectly, by hints *Cs.*; *zúr-gyis mtśón-pa Tar.* to note, point out only by hints or insinuations *Schf.*; hence perh. *ṫsig zúr* **invective speech,** **ṫsig-zúr ma zer* W.* no invectives! don't be personal! *zur zá-ba* is prob. the same, where *Sch.* has: to address harshly; **zúr-ne láb-če* W.* to learn or study privately (out of school-time, or, not with the appointed master); *zur bžugs-pa Cs.* (prob. for *zúr-du*) **to lead a private life** (cf. *zúr-pa*); *zur mig ltá-ba* **to look sideways, askance, to leer, squint** *Sch.* — 4. **outline,** *ḱyod daṅ zur ˳dra tsam yaṅ sa steṅ med* none on earth is like you, or can be compared to you, even in a general outline *Pth.*; *˳di - dag zur tsam bsdú - ba yin-gyis* this is merely a brief outline, extract, sketch *Glr.* and elsewh., frq., also *zur tsam yin-gyis Glr.* —

Comp. *zur-bkód*, *zúr-˳débs*, *Sch.*: 'founded for a special purpose'. — *zúr-čan* cornered, angular, *yi-ge Glr.* p. 31, a sort of type or printing-letter, = *klui yi-ge*, v. also no. 2 above. — *zur-čág Sch.*: prop., having a broken edge, damaged by being knocked about; gen. fig., of words and grammatical forms: faulty, corrupted, misapplied; *Lis.* and elsewh., *Ssk.* **अपभ्रंश**. the most vitiated Prakrit-dialect *Was.* (267). — *zur-˳débs* = *zur-bkód-zur-nór* private goods *Cs.* — *zur-pa* one out of office, a private individual *Cs.* — *zúr-ma* = *zur* prov. — *zur-γsós* educated by strangers *Sch.*

ཟུར་མོ་ *zúr-mo* **pain,** = *zug*, vulg.

ཟུར་ཕུད་ *zur-ṗúd Glr.* **hair-knot, dressed hair** *Sch.*

ཟུལ་མ་ *zúl-ma W.* **cornered, angular,** = *zúr-čan*; **ṗé-zúl** lotus-edged, of bowls, dishes, plates, that are of a polygonal or radiated shape.

ཟེ་ *ze* I. num. figure: 112.

II., also *zé-ba B.*, *W.*, *zeu Cs.* 1. **hump** of a camel, zebu etc. *Cs.* — 2. **crest**, of birds, dragons etc. *Glr.*, *S.g.*; also *ze-próg Lex.* — *zé-ḱa Cs.*: 1. 'hump. 2. decorated pad or cushion'. — *ze-rṅóg Cs.* = *zé-ba*. — *ze-˳brú*, *zeu-˳brú Glr.*, *Mṅg.* the anthers of a flower.

ཟེ་འབུག་ *ze-búg W.* **the maw or fourth stomach** of ruminating animals.

ཟེ་མ་ *zé-ma W.* **elastic spring.**

ཟེ་ཚྭ་ *zé-ṫswa* **saltpetre** *S.g.*; *zé-ṫswa-čan* containing saltpetre, nitrous; *zé-ṫsai skyúr-rtsi* nitric acid *Cs.*

ཟེགས་མ་ *zégs-ma* **impurity, smut, dirt** *Sch.*

ཟེང་ *zeṅ*, *ṫú-ba γyás-zeṅ γyón-zeṅ byás-pa* the skirts of the coat on the right and left side folded back, tucked up *Mil.*

ཟེད་ *zed* I. sbst. 1. **brush,** *ṗag-zéd* brush of hog's bristles; *byab-zéd* clothes-brush, dust-brush *Cs.*; *so-zéd* tooth-brush *Cs.* — 2. **edge** *C.* — II. adj *Sch.*: **'broken off, damaged, injured;** *zéd-laṅs* **chink, crack, rent;** *zéd-˳dug-pa* to crumble at the top' (?).

ཟེམ་ *zem* 1. **cask, barrel, tun,** often sonsisting merely of an excavated piece of a willow-tree, the Tibetans knowing but little of coopery *C.*, *W.* — 2. **box, chest** *W.* — *zem-śiṅ* the body or wood of a vessel, *zem-mṫil* the bottom of a vessel *Cs.*

ཟེར་ *zer* 1. v. *γzer*. — 2. **talk,** cf. *brjod*. — 3. n of a small animal *Med.*

ཟེར་བ་ *zér-ba* 1. (seldom *˳dzér-ba*) **to say,** esp. later literat. and vulg.; *ḱyod zér-ba bdén-no* you say rightly *Dzl.* (where at other times always *smra-ba* is used inst. of it); *he he zer bgád-pas* they laughed he, he! *Glr.*; *čos dar zer rgyai yig-ṫsaṅ-na ˳dug* then the doctrine was diffused, say the Chinese records *Glr.*; after words quoted: ... *zér-bar ˳dúg-pas* thus having been spoken, read, heard *Glr.*; *'yin' zer bsnyon byás-so* saying 'it is he', she told a lie *Glr.*, and so frq. *zer*, where in earlier literat. *žes* is used; *zér-na* 1. **if one says,** esp. for the older *že-*

na, frq. 2. **if I may say so, so to speak, as it were**; **dí-la ċi zer** what is this called? frq., also without *la*; to make a noise, e.g. **sag sag zér-wa* C.* to foam with a hissing noise, to sparkle, of wine, beer; *zér-mkan* 1. he that is saying. 2. *W.*, said, called, mentioned, esp. for the older *žes byá-ba*. — **zér-ke'* C.* rumour, report. — **zér-pog-ċan* W.* speaking in an uncivil or offensive manner. — *zer-ri C.* rumour. — 2 **to drive in**, nails, v. *γzér-ba*.

ཟེལ་མ་ *zél-ma* **small chip**, *šiṅ-zél* **wood-shavings** *W.*

ཟོ་ *zo* I. num. figure: 142.

II. imp. of *zá-ba*.

III. sbst. resp. *sku-zó*, = *lus-kyi k'ams* **physical constitution**, *sku-zo mdog légs-la* as the appearance of your majesty's bodily constitution is so excellent *Glr.*; *zo bzáṅ-ba* a good complexion *Cs.* — 2. **figure, delineation, representation**, perh. better to be spelt *bzo* (?) — 3. **mould**, *zo-ċágs* showing mouldy spots *Sch.* (?); *zo-már* old, mouldy butter, so prob. *S.g.*; *zo-ša Lt.* mouldy meat

ཟོ་བ་ *zo-ba* 1. sbst., **pail, bucket**, *šiṅ-zo* wooden pail, *ču-zo* water-pail. — 2. vb. v. *bzó-ba*.

ཟོག་ *zog* 1. **deceit, fraud, falsehood** (*Lex.* = *rdzub*), *zóg-ċan* 1. **lying, deceitful; liar** *W.* 2. **adulterate, counterfeit** *W.*; *zog-ldán*, *zóg-po Cs.* id., *zog-méd* the opp.; *sgyu-zóg* (religious) **hypocrisy** *Pth.*; *čos-zóg* **priestcraft** *Mil.*; **zol-zóg** = *zog W.* — 2. vulg. pronunciation in *C.* and *W.*, inst. of the following.

ཟོང་ *zoṅ* (vulgo *zog*) 1. **ware, merchandise, goods**, *zoṅ-min-smár* not goods but ready money *Lex.*; *rgyágs-zoṅ* goods taken by travellers along with them to be bartered for provisions; *smán-zoṅ* drugs; *ts'óṅ-zoṅ* **merchandise** *Cs.*; *zóṅ-rnams rnám-pa sna-tsógs* goods of all kinds; **zóg-gi dág-po* Ts.* owner of the goods, master of the estate, heir, = *nór-bdag*. — 2. *Sch.* **worth, price**(?). — 3. *Sch.* **doubt**(?). — 4. *Sch.* **lie**(?).

ཟོན་ *zon* **attention, heed, care**, gen. *zon byéd-pa*, to pay attention, to take heed, to beware, *dgrá-la* of an enemy *Pth.*; also c. accus. *Mil.*; *zon sdig-pa spoṅ mi šes* seems to mean: not knowing the attention needful for renouncing sin *Thgy.*; *zon-méd* **heedless**; *zon-grábs* **provision, precaution, preventive measure** *Sch.*

ཟོན་པ་ *zón-pa Ts.*, **stuff- or woolen shoes**; **bob-zọn** id., covered with leather.

ཟོབ་ *zob Ts.*, **zob-zób ǰhé'-pa** **to shake thoroughly**, = *ₒdzól-ba*.

ཟོམ་ *zom* 1. **point, top**, *rdo-rǰei* of the *dor-ǰe Dom*; **summit**, of the Rirab and some other mountains *S.O.* and elsewh.; *zom-k'óg* **dull, simple, stupid**, *Sch.* — 2. **cave** *Sch.*, *brag-zóm* rock-cavern.

ཟོར་ *zor*, 1. sup. of *zó-ba*, *bzó-ba Sch.* — 2. sbst. the weapons employed in combating the evil spirits in the *γtór-ma*, such as knife, sword, sling, bow and arrows etc.; *zor-k'a* the fore- or front-part, the edge, of the weapons directed against the demons, *zór-k'a ₒp'én-pa Cs.*: to fling those weapons a gainst the spirits.

ཟོར་བ་ *zór-ba* **sickle**, *zór-bas rṅá-ba Mil.*, *γċód-pa Cs.* to cut with a sickle, *zór-lče* sickle-blade; *zor-čúṅ* small, *zor-čén* large sickle, scythe, though in Tibet as yet hardly known; *zor-rtúl* blunt, dull, *zor-rnón* sharp sickle; *zór-bu* = *zor-čúṅ*.

ཟོར་ཡང་ *zor-yáṅ Sch.*: **small, short** (?).

ཟོལ་ཚོ་ *zól-tso* v. *ₒdzól-ba*.

ཟོལ་ཟོག་ *zol-zóg* **deceit, fraud, imposture, falsehood**, *zol-zóg byéd-pa*, *W.* **ċo-ċe**, **to deceive, impose on**, e.g in traffic *Thgy.*, *zól-zog-ċan* **deceitful, fraudulent**, *zol(-zog)-méd* without deceit, free from guile, artless *Mil.*

ཟོས་ *zos* v. *zá-ba*.

ཟླ་ *zla* 1. for *zlá-ba*. — 2. for *zlá-bo*.

ཟླ་བ་ *zlá-ba* I. sbst. 1. prov. *zla*, **moon**, frq.; *mk'ai zlá-ba* **celestial moon** *Lex.*, to distinguish it from 2. *dús-kyi zlá-ba* **temporal moon or month**, *zlá-ba γċig*, *B*, *W.*, **da ċig* C.*, one month; **zlá-ba ma ₒk'or šog** come before the end of the month *Sch.*; *zlá-ba ts'áṅ-du nyé-bas* towards the expiration of the months (of pregnancy) *Dzl.*; *zla-dús ťém-pa daṅ* at the expiration of those months *Glr*; cf. also *ṅo* 5. — 3. symb. num: 1. — **Combinations and comp.** *zlá-bai dkyil-ₒk'or, zla-dkyil,* **da kyír-mo** *W.* disk of the moon; **da gaṅ soṅ** *W.* the moon is full; **da gaṅ-po* or *soṅ-te** *W. zlá-ba rgyás-pa Pth., nya-rgyás zlá-ba Pth.* full moon; *nya* day of full moon; *zla(-ba) k'ám(-pa), zla-gám, W.* **da-p'éd** half moon, i.e. the first and last quarter; **semicircle,** *zlá-ba k'ám-pa ltá-bur bżág-go* they are placed round in a semicircle *Do.*; *dbyibs zla-gám ltá-bur yod* it is semicircular in shape *Glr.*; *zlá-bai ṅo* v. *ṅo*; *zla-ťéb = zla-šól*; *zla-nág* new moon *Sch.* (?); *zla-p'ógs* monthly wages; *zla-tsés* 1. = *zlá-ba ťsés-pa, ťses-ysum-zlá-ba Mil.* the moon on the first two or three evenings of her being visible; **crescent,** *zla-ťsés ltá-bu* in the shape of a crescent, *S.g.*; it is also used as an image of speedy decay. — 2. **date** *Schr.* (?) — *zla-mťsán* the monthly courses; also the discharges of them, *zla-mťsán ₒdzag* the catamenial discharges flow *Cs*; *zla-mťsán-čan Stg., zla-mťsán daṅ ldán-pa S.g.* having the monthly courses; *zla(-ba)-šól, -żól, -ťéb, zla-lhág, W.* **da-ṭ'úl** **intercalary month**; the separate months of the year are usually counted from *zlá-ba dáṅ-po* to *bču-ynyis-pa*, yet there are also particular names for them, viz. acc. to *Cs.*:

1. *ₒbrúg-zla, ťui zlá-ba, rtá-pa zlá-ba,* माघ
2. *sbrúl-zla, k'rá-zla, dbó-zla,* उत्तरफल्गुनी
3. *rta(i) zla(-ba), nág-zla,* चैत्र
4. *lúg-zla, sá-ga-zla-ba,* वैशाख
5. *spré-zla, snrón-zla,* ज्येष्टा
6. *byá-zla, ču-snód-zla-ba,* पूर्वाषाढा
7. *k'yi-zla, gró-bżin-zla-ba,* उत्तरषाढा
8. *p'ág-zla, k'rúm-zla,* भद्रपदा
9. *byi-zla, ťa-skár-zlá-ba,* अश्विनी
10. *glaṅ-zla, smin-drúg-zla-ba,* कात्तिका
11. *stág-zla, mgó-zla,* मृगशिर
12. *yós-zla, rgyál-zla,* पौष्या

II. vb., also *zló-ba, zlós-pa,* pf. *bzlas, bzlos,* fut. *bzlo,* imp. *zlos,* 1. **to say, tell, express,** *zloam mi zlo* shall you tell it or not? *Pth.*; *yżán-la zló-ba Lex.* to tell others; *yid-ma-raṅs-pa-nyid p'yir zlós-par byéd-pa* to express one's dissatisfaction *Stg.* (?). — 2. **to murmur** or **mutter over,** to recite softly or quite silently, prayers, spells etc., also *żúb-bus zlá-ba Zam.*; *yi-ge-drúg-pa lan-čig bzlás-pai bsód-nams Glr.* the merit of saying once the six-syllable prayer, and as such saying generally is done repeatedly, it is synon. with **to repeat.** — 3. **to answer, reply** *Cs.*; *Mil.* ni f. — 4. undoubtedly a less correct spelling for *ₒda-ba* (for which reason the secondary forms with o are wanting), **to pass, to get beyond,** *la zlá-ba* to cross a mountain-pass, *nád-kyi la zlá-ba* to be past hope of recovery *Cs.*; also trs., *mya-ṅán-las zlá-ba* to deliver from pain, to help to eternal happiness.

ཟླ་བོ་ *zlá-bo* 1. = *grogs, W.* **yá-do**, **companion, associate,** *zlá-bo byéd-pa* **to accompany, attend, assist,** *rkún-zla* a thief's accomplice *Dzl.*; *ₒgrán-zla* **rival, competitor** (v. *ₒgrán-pa* extr.); *ynyén-zla,* v. *ynyen*; *bzá-zla* **spouse, consort** (male or female) *Lex.* — *srid-zla Mil.* partner for life; *zla-yzán* a woman whose husband is dead ('who has eaten him'). — 2. **friend, acquaintance** *B.* and col. — 3. **lover, bridegroom; spouse** in *C.* To *zla* standing for *zlá-bo*, may be referred *zlas-dbyé Zam.*, expl. by द्वन्द्व, **pair, couple, combination,** viz. of a thing and its reverse, hence *zlas-p'yé-ba* **reverse, contrary,** e.g. *yód-pai zlas-p'yé-ba méd-pa Sch.*

ཟླུག(ས)་པ་ *zlúg(s)-pa,* pf. *bzlugs,* fut. *bzlug,* **to give notice, send word, inform** *Sch.*, *p'rín-yig-gis bzlúgs-pa* he informed him by a letter *Stg.*, not frq.; in *Lexx.* explained by *yżán-la snyád-pa,* and *gó-bar byed ₒjúg-pa.* —

ཟླུམ་པ་ *zlúm-pa* 1. adj., more frq. *zlúm-po,* (= **kor-kór** *C.*, **kyir-kyír** *W.*) **round, circular,** *dbyibs* in shape *Glr.*; **roundish, rounded, obtuse,** *zlúm-por rtsíg-pa* to erect a round, cylindrical wall, e.g. for a monument; **clubby, clumsy,** e.g. of a short and thick tobacco-pipe; *rkáṅ-pa zlúm-pa* club-footed *Stg.*; **globular, spherical,** e.g. cavities in the human body *S.g.*; *dku-zlúm Zam.*

(acc. to the *Ssk.*) the interior rounding of the abdomen. — 2. vb. 1. **to mix together** *Sch.*; **to put together, collect,** *ts'ogs* merit *Lexx.* 2. for *btúm-pa Pth.*: *dgé-ₒdún dbu-zlúm żabs-rjén* clerics with their heads wrapt up and barefooted. 3. for *ₒdúm-pa.* — *zlum-ril* **globular** *Cs.* — **zlúm-bu** *W.* **host, swarm, troop, crowd.**

ཟླུམ་ཕུ་སེ་ *zlúm-p'u-se* (or *rtse?*) a mole-like animal *Ld.* (whether the same as *rdza-bra?*).

ཟློ་བ་ *zló-ba* v. *zlá-ba,* II.

ཟློག་པ་ *zlóg-pa,* pf. *zlogs,* fut. *bzlog,* trs. to *ldóg-pa,* **to cause to return:** 1. **to drive back, repulse,** an army *Dzl.;* **to dispel, expel,** evil spirits *Dom.*; **to send back.** — 2. in a gen. sense: **to send, dispatch,** people to fetch something *Dzl.* frq. — 3. **to turn off, divert,** *bsám-pa-las* from an intention *Dzl.;* with *blo* to divert the mind from, to dismiss a thought, to give up, to banish from one's thoughts *Thgy.*, *γnyén-gyi γduṅ-séms zlog dka* it is hard to give up the love of kindred altogether *Mil.; dei t'ugs slar zlóg-tu γsol* we beg you to dismiss the thought of it *Dzl.*; **to dissuade from** *Tar.* 40, 5; **to avert,** injury, evil consequences, frq.; **to prevent,** *nad-sél* the healing of a disease *S.g.* — *zlog-t'ábs* antidote *Ma.* — 4 **to subvert, overthrow** (?). 5. *mii ṅo* **to resist, to be unyielding, uncompliant** *Dzl.*

ཟློས་གར་, ཟློད་གར་ *zlós-gar*, *zlód-gar Stg.* **a dance,** *zlós-gar byéd-pa* **to dance,** *slób-pa* to teach or learn dancing; *zlós-gar-mk'an* a dancer.

ཟློས་པ་ *zlós-pa* v. *zlá-ba.*

གཟའ་ *γza* I. ग्रह 1. **planet,** *γza bdun* the well-known seven heavenly bodies called in ancient times planets, viz. Sun, Moon, Mercury, Venus, Mars, Jupiter and Saturn; sometimes the ascending knot (राहु) is added to the number, sometimes also the descending knot (केतु), and then there are *γza brgyad* or *γza dgu,* eight or nine planets. The former seven denote also the days of the week: *γza-nyí-ma* Sunday, *γza-zlá-ba* Monday, *γza-mig-dmár* Tuesday, *γza-lhág-ma* Wednesday, *γza-p'úr-bu* Thursday, *γza-pa* (or *-wa*)*-sáṅs* Friday, *γza-spén-pa* Saturday, and the signs for them in the calendar are ༡, ༢, ༣, ☾, ♈, ♋, ○; *γzai γnód-pa* hurtful influence of the planets. — 2. *γza-čén-po,* and often *γza* alone, = *rá-hu,* hence *nyí-zla-γzas-ₒdzin* or *γzas-bzuṅ* **eclipse** of the sun or moon, v. *sgra-γčan*; acc. to *Pth.* every uncommon or alarming sidereal phenomenon seems to be personified as *γza.* — 3. symb. num.: 9. — 4. vulgo: **rainbow.** — *γza-skár,* 1. **planets and fixed stars,** *nyi-zla-γza-skár* the sun, moon, planets, and stars. — 2. **constellation,** *γza-skar-ṅán* an adverse configuration *S.g.* — *γza-k'yim Cs.* 'the place', more corr. 'the house' of a planet, the constellation in which the planet stands. — *γza-nád Cs.* and *Schr.*: **apoplexy;** in *W.* it seems to be used only for **epilepsy;** *γza p'óg-pa* id.; *γzá-p'og-mkan*, *γzá-brgyab-pa* epileptic. — *blá-γza, sróg-γza, γšéd-γza, má-γza grógs-γza, bú-γza, dgrá-γza, klúṅ-si-dar-γza Wdk.* and several more, are astrological terms, not to be clearly defined. — II. sometimes for *bza,* q.v. — III. *W.* **rubble-stones, bowlders, detritus,** *γza-róṅ* ravine filled with detritus; a better spelling seems to be *rdza.*

གཟག་པ་ *γzág pa* v. *ₒtság-pa, ₒdzág-pa.*

གཟགས་པ་ *γzágs-pa* 1. v. *γzábs-pa.* — 2. **to magnify, multiply** *Sch.*

གཟན་ *γzan* 1. v. *bzan* and *γzan-pa; γčan-γzan,* q.v. — 2. esp. *W.*, commonly *γzan-gós* **plaid,** = *bla-gós* v. *bla.* *γzan-stán Zam.* id.? *rṅul-γzán* **napkin,** nif. *Lex.*

གཟན་པ་ *γzán-pa* 1. **to eat, devour** *Cs.* — 2. **to gnaw,** mostly fig.: *tsér-ma żábs-la γzan* the thorn hurts, annoys, the foot *Mil.;* of clothes: **to wear out** *C.*; adj. *γzán-pa* and *γzán-po* **worn-out, threadbare;** *séms-la γzan* it gnaws at the heart *Mil.*, *sróg-la* it preys upon life *Mil.*, **ná-wa-la** *C.* it deafens the ears, = *sún-ₒbyin-pa; γzán-du skyúr-ba* (lit. to give to devour, e.g. a body to demons), **to scorn, slight, despise** *Mil.*; **to throw away, squander, waste, lavish,** gen. in the forms (*čud*)*-γzón-pa,* ; *són-pa,* v. *čud.*

གཟབ་པ་ γzáb-pa I. *Cs.* **'clean'**, *Sch.* also **'clear, careful'**; *bzáb-pa Cs.* **'fine, elegant'**. In books I met with neither form; in col. language, however, are used: **záb-mo** 1. **dressed up, smart,** = *mčór-po.* 2. **fond of dress, vain.** — **zab-če* W.* to dress one's self up. — **záb-gos* W.* festival raiment, holiday-clothes (opp. to *rgyún-gos*). — **zab-ṭód* W.*, **zab-ṭö* C.* (lit.: *sprod*) **taṅ soṅ** he is dressed up, very smart. — *Sch.*: *γzáb-yig*, 'elegant writing', the Tibetan printed letters, *dbú-čan.* —

II. v. *γzábs-pa.*

གཟབ་མ་ *γzáb-ma* **bundle, bunch,** of grapes *C.*

གཟབས་པ་ *γzábs-pa*, also *γzáb-pa*, *γzágs-pa Lex.*, imp. *γzobs*, **to use care, diligence,** *lo γčig zas-spyód γzábs-pas* by a careful diet continued for a year *Mṅg.*; **to take care, to beware,** *dé-las γzobs* beware of it, be on your guard against it *Sch.*

གཟར་ *γzar Lex.*, **peg, hook, wooden nail,** for hanging up things; *γzar-sláṅ* a pan that may be hung up.

གཟར་བུ་ *γzár-bu* (col. *zá-ru*) **ladle,** gen. of wood, *γzár-bu ˳pyar* she wields the ladle, she swings it for a blow *Mil.*; *dgáṅ-γzar* and *blúgs-γzar* two spoons or ladles, with long handles, used at burnt-offerings *Schl.* 249.

གཟར་བ་ *γzár-ba* 1. adj. *γzár-po*, **steep, rugged, precipitous,** *brag mtó-la γzár-ba-la* near a high, precipitous rock *Mil.*; *ri γzár-po, brag γzár-po* slope, declivity, of a hill or rock; *brag-γyaṅ-γzár Mṅg.* id.; *ri γzár-gyi ṅos* steep declivity, cliff *Thgy.*; *ri-γzar-ču* waterfall, cataract *Glr.*; *γzar-kyóm-pa* to get dizzy on a steep height *Sch.* — 2. vb. v. *˳dzár-ba.*

གཟས་པ་ *γzás-pa* **to be about, to be on the point, to prepare,** *mčóṅs-par, bsád-par γzás-pa-las* when he was on the point of leaping, of killing *Dzl.*; *rkó-bar γzás-so* he prepared, began, to dig out.

གཟི་ *γzi* 1. **shine, brightness, clearness, splendour;** **táṅ-zi* W.* **looming, mirage.** — 2. n. of a half-precious stone, variously coloured, brown, gray, streaked *Glr*, *Pth.* — 3. v. sub *γzir-ba.* — 4. v. *bzi.* —

Comp. *γzi-čan* shining, bright, e. g. a star *W.* — *γzi-brjid* 1. **brightness, beauty,** a fair, healthy complexion, = *mdaṅs*, or joined with it, frq; **majesty,** e. g. of deities etc. *Dzl.* 2. **honour, esteem, celebrity;** *γzi-brjid-čan* 1. bright, beautiful, majestic. 2. celebrated, famous, distinguished. — *γzi-mdáṅs* 1. **healthy appearance** *S.g.* 2. vulgo also **evening-red, evening-sky,** ni f. — *γzi-byin* = *γzi-brjid* 1; *γzi-byin nyáms-pa* looking poor, emaciated, worn out, from hunger, sufferings *Stg.*; *γzi-byin-čan* bright, shining; *γzi-˳ód* bright gloss or lustre *Lex.*

གཟི་རུ་ *γzi-ru* col. for *γzér-bu* **a little nail** *W.*

གཟིག་ *γzig* **leopard;** *γzig-ris* its colour.

གཟིག་མོ་ *γzig-mo* **porcupine** *Ssk.*, *γzig-móṅ* id.?

གཟིགས་པ་ *γzigs-pa*, resp. for *mtóṅ-ba* and *ltá-ba* 1. **to see,** *˳óṅs-par* seeing that he had come *Dzl.*; in indirect questions, to see whether? — what sort of? — etc.; **to see through, to get an insight** *Tar.* 94, 6; *Schf.*; **to look,** *šár-la* towards the east *Glr.*; **to look (for),** *γzigs-pas mi ˳dug* when he looked (for it), there was nothing to be seen; **to look at, to regard, mind, esteem,** *sku-tsé-la mi γzigs-pa* not regarding your Honour's life *Dzl.* — 2. equivalent to: **to give, grant,** *sá-bon žig tugs-rje γzigs dgos* have the goodness to give me some seed, prob. only breviloquence for *sá-bon žig γnáṅ-bar tugs-brtsé-bar γzigs šig.* — *γzigs-rtén* resp. **present, gift,** *γzigs-rtén-du skúr-ba* to charge a person with the delivery of a present *Pth.* — **zig-dod-čan* W.* vain. — **zig-po* W.* neat, well dressed, resp. for *mčór-po.* — — *γzigs-mo* resp. for *ltád-mo*, *mé-tog dé-la γzigs-mor byón-pa-las* as he came in order to look at the flower *Pth.*

གཟིང་བ་ *γziṅ-ba* for *˳dziṅs-pa Glr.*

གཟིངས་ *γziṅs* **vessel, ship, float, ferry,** also fig.; *gru-γziṅs* id., frq.; *γziṅs čén-po žig byás-te* equipping a large vessel *Glr.*;

γziṅs-čuṅ a small vessel *Cs.*; γziṅs-pa ship-master, captain.

གཟིམ་པ་ *γzim-pa*, also with *mnal*, resp. for *γnyid-log-pa*, 1. **to fall asleep** *Dzl.* — 2. **to sleep,** *rgyál-po γzim-pa-las* whilst the king was sleeping *Glr.* — 3. **to expire, to die** *Tar.* 4, 20. —

Comp. **zim-kyoṅ** W., resp. for *rkyóṅ-rtse*, candle, lamp. — *γzim-k̔aṅ* 1. sleeping-room. 2. dwelling, habitation. — *γzim-k̔ebs* quilt. — *γzim-k̔om* cloak-bag, portmanteau. — *γzim-k̔ri* bedstead. — *γzim-gur* sleeping-tent. — **zim-gág** C. porter, door-keeper. — *γzim-ča* bedding, bed-clothes *Gyatch.* — **zim-tiṅ, zim-ter** W. lamp. — **zim-tiṅ** (lit. *-btiṅ*) *Sik.* bedstead? — *γzim-t̔úl* sheep-skins for night-quarters. — *γzim-dpon* body-servant, valet-de-chambre, = *sku-mdún-pa*; *γzim-p̔rúg* his subordinate servants or pages. — *γzim-mál* bed-linen. — *γzim-yól* bed-curtain.

གཟིམ་གཟིམ་ *γzim-γzim W., C., *mig zim-zim ča dug* W.* the eyes are dazzled, by a glaring light.

གཟིར་བ་ *γzir-ba* (acc. to *Cs.* fut. of *ₒtsir-ba*, certainly related to it, but chiefly used in an intellectual sense), **to be pressed, harassed, troubled, to suffer,** to be pressed by necessity, to suffer from hunger, disease etc. *B., C.* — *Sch.* also *γzi γzir-ba* a stinging pain in the chest.

གཟིལ་ *γzil, γzil-bun-pa C.* = *spu-ziṅ byed-pa.*

གཟུ་བ་ *γzú-ba* **a lever, bar;** = *γsó-mo Cs.*; *γzu-rṅás* a prop *Cs.*

གཟུ་བོ་ *γzú-bo Cs.*: 1. **straight, right.** — 2. **upright, honest.** *Lexx.*: *t̔ugs γzú-bo*, from which it appears to be a word of civility, but little known. *Sch.* has besides: *γzu-dpáṅ*, which he renders by 'witness, mediator'.

གཟུ་ལུམ་(ས)་ *γzu-lúm(s) Lexx.* = *bab-čol* and **सहसा**, hence signifying **rashness, impetuosity,** so *Cs.*, and therefore *γzu-lúm-čan* **inconsiderate;** *γzu-lúm byéd-pa* **to act rashly;** *Sch.* also: **disobedience, pride, haughtiness.**

གཟུག་ *γzug* 1. v. *zug.* — 2. **top,** *lai* of a mountain-pass *Mil.*

གཟུག་གེ་བ་ *γzúg-ge-ba* **hurting, giving pain,** *žes γzúg-ge-ba žús-nas* as she spoke words that gave so much pain *Mil.nt.*

གཟུག་པ་ *γzúg-pa* **to be able to bear, to sustain,** v. sub *tsog.*

གཟུགས་ *γzugs, Ssk.* **रूप**, 1. **figure, form, shape,** *p̔yi-rol-gyi γzúgs-rnams* the forms of the sensible world, the impressions that are made on the eye *Wdṅ.*; *mig-gis γzúgs-rnams mt̔oṅ* the forms (of things) are seen with the eyes; *ráb-tu-byuṅ-bai γzugs* the (painted) figure of a priest *Glr.*; sim. *klui γzugs γsér-las byás-pa Tar.*; *lus-γzúgs* shape of body, stature, frq.; *srin-moi γzúgs-su byéd-pa* to transform one's self into a Rakshasi *Glr.*; *rnál-ₒbyor-pai γzugs byéd-pa* to assume the outward appearance of a hermit *Mil.*; in metaphysics: form, body, as one of the five Skandhas, v. *p̔úṅ-po.* — 2. resp. *sku-γzúgs, W *zúg-po** = *lus,* **body,** **zúg-po ṭú-če* W.* to wash the body, to bathe; **zúg-po zâṅ-wa mi dug, mi-dé-wa dug* C., *dé-mo mi dug* W.* euphem. for: she has just her courses. — *γzugs-ṅán* ill-formed, too short in stature *S.g.*; *γzugs ₒk̔úm-pa* to bend, twist one's body, and *γzúgs-kyis ₒtsó-ba, quaestum corpore facere*, are given by *Sch.*; *γzugs riṅ-mo* long-stalked *Glr.* — 3. in physics: **body, matter, substance,** *γzúgs-čan, γzúgs-su snáṅ-ba* composed of matter, material, substantial; *γzúgs-čan ma yin-pa, γzúgs-su mi snáṅ-ba, γzugs-méd* immaterial, unsubstantial; *γzúgs-med-pai* (or *-kyi*) *skad* a ghostlike voice *Mil.*; *γzugs-k̔áms* the range of the material world. — *γzugs-brnyán* v. *brnyan.*

གཟུགས་པ་ *γzúgs-pa* v. *ₒdzúg-pa.*

གཟུང་བ་ *γzúṅ-ba* v. *ₒdzin-pa*; *γzuṅ-ₒdzin Mil.* frq., **interest, inclination, bias,** *γzuṅ-ₒdzin-brál* being free from interest, unbiased, apathetic, which always is praised as an indispensable quality and the true happiness of an ascetic, and the literal equivalent to which in *Ssk.* may be regarded to be **ग्राह्यग्राह**; yet *Was.* p. 304 renders it by 'idea and reason'. — *γzuṅ-γzér* peg on a wall, = *rtsig-púr*; a hold, support, rail, balustrade (?) *Stg.*

གཟུངས་ *γzuṅs*, frq. spelt *zuṅs*, yet properly only in compounds, lit. **a hold,** i.e. 1. **power, strength** *Schr.*; *γzuṅs-žán Sch.*: **loose, weak, without a hold, untenable;** *γzuṅs-zád* **weakened, debilitated,** esp. of women by loss of blood *Cs.*; *γzuṅs-rtén* **prop, support.** — 2. *lus-zúṅs* the seven constituents necessary for **healthy life,** धातु, chyle, blood, fat, muscle, bone, marrow, semen *Med.* — 3. धारणी, also *γzuṅs-sṅágs*, **spells, magic sentences,** first used in the doctrine of Mahâyâna, from which the mysticism of later times originated, v. *Was.* (142, 177); they are for the most part but short, and always end in a string of Sanskrit syllables, that are devoid of any meaning. Whole volumes are filled with them.

གཟུད་པ་ *γzúd-pa*, fut. of *ₒdzúd-pa*.

གཟུམ་པ་, གཟུར་བ་, གཟུལ་བ་ *γzúm-pa, γzúr-ba, γzúl-ba* v. *ₒdzúm-pa* etc.

གཟེ་བ་ *γzé-ba Sch.* 1. **pannier, dosser** *Dzl.* ༢༥༢, 14. — 2. **home, habitation, nest.** — 3. **swift,** in running *Thgy.*, **quick,** in comprehending *Sch.*

གཟེ་མ་ *γzé-ma Med.*; *Cs.*: 'a horned aquatic plant'; *γzé-mai čaṅ Med.* beer made of it.

གཟེ་རུ་ *γzé-ru*, for *γzér-bu* **a little nail.**

གཟེ་རེ་ *γze-ré* **looking poorly** *Sch.*; *γze-ré byéd-pa* **to be poorly, ailing, ill** *Sch.*

གཟེག་(ས)་ *γzeg(s)*, कण. **a little grain, atom;** *γzeg ča čuṅ* a small particle *Lex.*; *γzég-ma* prob. id. (*Cs.* also: filth?) *γzeg-zán* कणाद. 'atom-eater', n. of the founder of the Vaiseshika-philosophy, also called Kâsyapa; *γzeg-zán-pa* its professors *Wdṅ.*

གཟེག་མོ་བྱི་ *γzég-mo-byi* **hedgehog** *Sch.*

གཟེངས་ *γzeṅs* **height, loftiness, sublimity, gloriousness,** esp. in *γzeṅs stód-pa*, also *yar γzeṅs stód-pa Pth.*; to praise, extol, glorify *Mil.* (cf. *seṅ*).

གཟེད་པ་ *γzéd-pa* I. vb. 1. v. *ₒdzéd-pa*. — 2. **to hit** *Sch.* — II. sbst. *Sch.*: 'a long spike'.

གཟེད་མ་ *γzéd-ma Cs*, gen. *γzéb-ma*, also *γzebs Sch.* 1. **pannier,** with lid *Kun.*; a box-shaped **basket** with lid *C.* — 2. **cage, aviary** *Lex.*; **prison** *Sch.* — 3. **net, snare** *Sch.*

གཟེམ་པ་ *γzém-pa*, 1. *Cs.* = *ₒdzém-pa*. — 2. **to do a thing gently,** **zém-te dul-wa* C.* to walk softly, **žág-pa* C.* to put down softly.

གཟེར་ *γzer*, also *zer*, 1. **nail, tack,** *šiṅ-γzer* wooden nail, *lčágs-γzer* iron nail; *γnám-γzer* 'plug or bolt for fastening a door (at the top)' *Cs.*; **gyáb-če* W.*, **gyág-pa* C.*, *γzér-ba Glr.*, *ₒdzúg-pa Lex.*, *ₒdébs-pa* and more frq. *γzér-gyis ₒdébs-pa B.* to knock in, drive in, nails; *lag-zér gyág-pa* driving red-hot tacks into the finger-ends, a kind of torture in *C.*; *γzér-bu*, vulgo **zé-ru, zí-ru** a little nail. — 2. **a help to memory,** for retaining a lesson or doctrine, **mnemonic verse** *Mil.* — 3. **ray, beam,** *nyi-γzér* sun-beam, *ₒod-γzér* ray of light; *ts̓a-γzér* 'a hot beam', *bsil-γzér* 'a cool beam' (?) *Cs.* — 4. **pain, ache, illness,** (*γ*)*zug-γzér* id., *mgo-γzér* headache, *rgyu-γzér* gripes, colic, *p̓o-γzér* stomach-ache, *rtsib-γzér* pleurisy, *so-γzér* toothache *Cs.*; **zer-kyáṅ ṅá-la gyáb-ba rag*, or *táṅ-ṅa rág* W.* I feel the pains of labour; **zer-láṅ* W.* spasms in the stomach or something similar; *γzer-ₒp̓rig-pa* to writhe with pain; *γzer ₒp̓o* the pain passes from one part of the body to another *S.g.*

གཟེར་བ་ *γzer-ba* 1. **to bore into, drive** or **knock into,** *zer C.* nails, **ná-da* C.* an arrow through the ear, Chinese punishment. — 2. **to feel pain, to be suffering** (= *γzír-ba?*); *čaṅ-ₒt̓úṅ γzer* beer-tippling produces pain *Med.*

གཟེར་བུ་ *γzér-bu*, v. *γzer* 1, extr.

གཟོ་བ་ *γzó-ba* 1. v. *bzó-ba*. — 2. **to remember, keep in mind, own, acknowledge,** esp. *drin* a favour, also *byás-pa*, **as much as to be grateful;** *dé-dag-gi byas-pa γzó-bai p̓yir* from gratefulness for their kindness *Dzl.*; *byas mi γzo* they are ungrateful; *drin γzó-*

ba, drin γzó-bai sems gratitude, *drin mi γzó-ba* ingratitude; *drin-γzo-čan* **grateful.**

གཟོང་, གཟོང་བུ་ *γzoṅ, γzóṅ-bu* **chisel, graving-tool, puncheon.**

གཟོད་ *γsod* 1. **now, this moment,** (opp. to *dá či*, before, a little time ago) *Mil.*; at least just now, *Mil.; da-γzod (-čig)*, id.; *da-γzód bu yin-par ča yod* now I know that it is my son; **not until now, then for the first time** (in narratives with preterite tenses) *Pth.*; **then at length** *Pth.* — *γzód-tsor-ba, tos-pa, -rdog-pa Dzl.* **to hear, to receive information, to be informed, to be told,** *γšégs-pa* that he was gone *Dzl.* — 3. *γzód-ma* **beginning, commencement** v. *γdód-ma.*

གཟོན་པ་ *γzon-pa, γsón-pa* with *čud*, v. *čud* and *γzán-pa* extr.; *bsgó-ba rnar γzón-pa* the precept was wastled in the ear, it entered at one ear and left at the other; one *Lex.* gives the explanation: *bsláb-bya-la mi nyán-pai don.*

གཟོབ་པ་ *γzób-pa* 1. *Sch.* **quick, sharp, clever; caution, circumspection.** — 2. v. *γzáb-pa.*

བཟང་ *bzaṅ* 1. n. of a medicinal plant in Tibet *Wdṅ.* — 2. whatever is **good**, v. *bzáṅ-ba.* — 3. **agreement, treaty,** v. *sgrig-pa.*

བཟང་བ་ *bzáṅ-ba* adj. and sbst., *bzáṅ-po* adj 1. **good,** (**भद्र**), in every respect, answering its purpose, excellent, suited, morally good; *bsam-pa bzaṅ-po* a good resolution *Mil.; bdag bzaṅ-na* if I behave well, keep myself free from blame, *Do.* (cf. *légs-pa*). — 2. **fair, beautiful,** as to the body, frq.; *nags-tsal bzáṅ-po* a beautiful wood *Mil.; γzugs-bzáṅ* of a fine, tall stature. — sbst.: *bzaṅ* the good, that which is good in the abstract; *bzáṅ-nas byuṅ* 'it came from good' i.e. from a good heart; *dei γzáṅ-lan-du* as an acknowledgment of his goodness *Glr.* —

Comp. *bzáṅ-kyi* a species of large dogs *Cs.* — *bzaṅ-sgrig* treaty of peace, **ǰhé-pa** *C.*, **čó-če** *W.* to make peace, to come to an agreement, to conclude a treaty, frq.; *bzaṅ-sgrig-pa* id. — *bzaṅ-ṅán* good and bad, good and ill, *bzaṅ-ṅan-ₒbriṅ γsum* good, bad, and indifferent; *bzaṅ-ṅán ₒbyéd-pa* to discern between good and evil, to choose one or the other *Schr.; bzaṅ-ṅán rtógs-pai sems* is an attempt to find an adequate expression for the word 'conscience' *Chr. P.* — *bzaṅ-tál* a good exit out of the *ₒkór-ba* (the cycle of transmigrations), a happy departure *Thgr.* — *bzaṅ-drúg* 'the six good things' (nutmeg, cloves, saffron, cardamom, camphor, sandal-wood) *C.*; used by *Mil.* also in a fig. sense; in *W.* simply: cloves. — *bzaṅ-ₒdód* self-complacency. — *bzaṅ-spyód* 1. *Cs.* good action. 2. n. of a prayer of particular efficacy *Glr.*, also called *smón-lam-gyi rgyál-po.* — *bzaṅ-btsón* v. *btson.* — **zaṅ-lúg** *W.* good behaviour, good treatment, **mi žig-nẹ tób-če** to experience such from a person, **mi-la čó-če** to show it to a person.

བཟངས་ *bzaṅs*, only in *kaṅ-bzáṅs*, which *Wdṅ.* explains by *káṅ-pa brtségs-pa* a large house of several stories, applied only to the abodes of gods; in *W.* also the cubical part of the Chodten is called so.

བཟད་པ་ *bzád-pa* rarely for *bzod-pa*; *mi-bzád-pa* 1. **intolerable** *Dzl., Do.* — 2. **irresistible** *Do.*

བཟན་ *bzan*, sometimes for *zan*, esp. **food of animals,** *bzan ₒtsól-ba* to seek food *Mil*; **pasture, pasturage,** *bzán-la skyél-ba* to place in pasture, to let feed *Glr.*; *bzán-pa Ts.* id.

བཟབ་པ་ *bzáb-pa* v. *γzáb-pa.*

བཟའ་ *bza*, I. vb., fut. of *zá-ba*, **to eat,** *bza* this is to be eaten, in dietetic prescriptions; v. also *zá-ba.* — II. sbst. 1. (rarely *γza*) seems to denote the members of a family, they being conceived as **eaters** or **fellow-boarders;** *bzá-tso máṅ-poi pa-má* parents that have a large family *Mil.; bza maṅs náṅ-na* among a numerous household *Mil.*; *bza-drúg* a family, a company at table, of six persons, ni f. *C.*; in certain combinations: **wife, spouse,** *rgyá-mo bza* the Chinese spouse, *bál-mo bza* the Nepalese spouse (of the king), *Glr.* frq. — 2. **meat, food,** *bzá-ba daṅ btúṅ-ba* meat and drink, specially the quality and quantity of food, *zá-*

ma bčud če-la bza če-ba nutritive and substantial food *Mil. nt.*

Comp. *bza-ytád, bzá-bai ytád-so* store of provisions, *bzá-ytad-méd-pa* not having such a store *Mil.* — *bza-mi* 1. = *k'yo-šug* **husband and wife,** *byéd-pa* to become husband and wife, to marry each other, *k'yod dan ṅa ynyis bza-mi byao* we will marry each other *Glr.*; *bza-mir byin-gyis rlób-pa* to give the nuptial benediction, to unite in wedlock, to marry *Glr.*; *dbúl-po bza-mi ynyis* a poor married couple *Glr.* 2. in a wider sense: **household,** *bza-mi nyi-šu-rtsa-ynyis* a household of twenty two persons *Mil.* — *bza-med* **ill-fed, lean** *Mil.* — *bzá-tso* plur. of *bza.* — **za-dá** (lit. *za-zlá*) *W., C.* partner, wife. — *bza-šiṅ* **fruit-tree,** *bza-šiṅ-rá-ba* orchard, *bza-šiṅ-ra-ba-srúṅ-pa* watchman or keeper of it *Dzl.* — *bza-šúg* (vulg. **-šúb**) = *bza-mi C.*

བཟར་ *bzar* sometimes for *zar*; *bzár-ba* v. *ₒdzár-ba.*

བཟས་པ་ *bzás-pa* v. *zá-ba* and *yzás-pa.*

བཟི་ *bzi* (sometimes *yzi, zi*), **drunken fit, intoxication, stupefaction**; *bzi sáṅs-te* having become sober again after intoxication *Glr.*; **zi-čan** *W.* intoxicated, muddled, *bzi-ba* 1. vb. **to become intoxicated, to get drunk,** *bzi-bar ₒgyúr-ba* id.; *bzi-bar byéd-pa* to intoxicate, to make drunk *Cs.* 2. sbst. **state of intoxication.** 3. adj. **drunk, intoxicated** *C.*

བཟུང་བ་ *bzúṅ-ba* v. *ₒdzin-pa*; it is used as an adv. in the form of *bzúṅs-te*, e.g. *dei núb-mo-nas bzúṅs-te* from that evening (prop. beginning with that evening), ever since that evening *Mil.*; *tses brgyad-nas bzuṅs-te nyai bar-du* during the time from the 8 th. to the 15 th. (day of the month).

བཟུར་ *bzur* v. *dzúr-ba.*

བཟེ་རེ་ *bze-ré*, also *bze Sch.*: **pain,** *bze-re-čan* suffering pain, *bze-ré byéd-pa* to inflict pain, to torment. (*Cs.*: 'indignation; angry; to be angry with.')

བཟེད་ *bzed* 1. in comp.: *p'yag-bzéd* **(hand-) basin** *Cs.*; *lhuṅ-bzéd* **beggar's bowl, alms-pot,** frq.; *bzed-snód* **salver** *Sch.*; *bzed-žál Lex.*, also *žal-bzéd Cs.*: 'spitting-box; acc. to oral expl. a cup into which the higher class of people skim off the superabundant grease swimming on the tea (v. *ja*); *bzéd-pa* v. *ₒdzéd-pa.* — 2. *bzed-snyóms-pa* **wire-drawing** *Sch.*

བཟོ་ *bzo* 1. **work, labour,** *bzoi rnam-ₒgyur* the beauty of a work or workmanship *Glr.*; *bzo rgya-nág-gi lugs* as to the workmanship it is in Chinese style *Glr.* (by some the word is taken in these passages in the signification 3). — *bzó-la sréd-pa* liking labour, laborious, = *las Stg.*; **zo te-rél, mi-la ma (s)tan** *W.* the work is not yet finished, do not let people see it yet! *snai bzo byed-gin ₒdug-pas* being just occupied with working out the noses *Glr.* — 2. **manufacture, art, trade, handicraft,** *rin-po-čei* art of a jeweler, *gos-* trade of a tailor, *dṅul-* art of a silversmith, *lčags-* trade of a blacksmith, *tag-* of a rope-maker, *rdo-* of a stone-cutter, *rtsig-* of a mason, *bzaṅ-* of a copper-smith, *šiṅ-* of a joiner or carpenter, *yser-* art of a goldsmith, *lha-* of an image-maker, *lham-bzo* trade of a shoemaker. — 3. also *zo,* **figure, image, picture, resemblance,** = *dbyibs,* **ǎ-mẹ zo dug** *W.* he is the exact likeness of his mother; **appearance, physical constitution,** v. *zo.* — 4. sometimes for *bzó-pa, bzó-bo,* so that all the words enumerated sub 2 may also denote the artist or workman. —

Comp. and deriv. *bzó-k'aṅ* **workshop.** — *bzo-k'yád, bzoi kyad Glr.* **work of art,** masterpiece, elegant piece of workmanship. — *bzo-k'yúd, bzo-k'yun Cs.*: 1. potter's wheel. 2. a hydraulic machine(?). — *bzo-grá* academy of arts, mechanics' institution *Cs.* — *bzo-rgyú* working-materials *Glr.* — **zó-bsta(?), zób-sta, zó-sta** *W.* **form, fashion,** e.g. **style** of a house, its architecture; form, of a bottle, a lamp or candle stick, of any production of art; **zor-dó** anvil-stone *W.* (*bzo-rdo*). — *bzó-pa* **artist,** mechanic, *dṅúl-bzo-pa,* silversmith, and so forth. — *bzo-dpón* **master,** over journey-men or the students of an art. — *bzó-ba,* pf. *bzos,* **to make, to manufacture** *C.* (for the *byéd-pa* of *B.*, and **čo-če** of *W.*), **par zó-wa** to print; **sém-kyi zó-wa** *C.* to frame in one's mind, contrive, invent; **zo-**

*pę tsa** manufactured salt, **zǫ́-pę ser** artificial gold *Wdṅ.* — *bzó-bo* = *bzó-pa, bzó-bo mḱás-pa* a skilful artist *Mil.; bzo-byéd* 1. id. 2. **imaginative faculty, imagination,** ni f. — *bzo-lás* work *Sch.*

བཟོད་པ་ *bzód-pa* (rarely *bżád-pa*) I. vb., क्षम, 1. **to suffer, bear, endure,** c. acc., *mig ná-ba ma bzód-nas* not being able to bear the pain in his eyes *Dzl.*; *lus ₒdis na mi bzod* with this body pain, disease, cannot be endured *Thgy.*; *saṅs-rgyás-kyi túgs-rje čé-bas ma bzód-nas* seems to imply: Buddha in his mercy not suffering this, but checking the mischief; — also c. dat.: *ₒjám-po-la mi bzod* he cannot bear what is soft or smooth *Dzl.*; *ma-bdé-ba búg-tsam-la bzód-pa mi byéd-de* getting so fretful through a slight indisposition *Mil.*; *ltá-bas mi bzód-de* finding it unbearable for his eyes *Pth.*; *dráṅ-pas mi bzód-de* as much as: so that he almost lost his senses over it *Pth.*; *bzód-tabs* (or *bzod-glags*)*-méd-par ₒbyúṅ-ba* or *ₒgyúr-ba* not to be able to bear . . . any longer, frq.; *mi-bzód-pa* or *-bzád-pa* adj., **unbearable, intolerable,** also **irresistible**; *ma bzód-nas* not being able to resist any longer *Dzl.* — 2. **to forgive, pardon,** *sṅan-čad to-ₒtsám-pa bzód-par ɣsol* to pardon our former tricks is what we beg *Mil.*; *rtá-la ma skyón-pa bzód-par bżes ₒtsal* that I did not request you to mount, this I beg you to forgive me *Mil.*; *bzód-par ɣsól-lo byas kyaṅ* although she begged pardon *Pth.*; *skyón-rnams yé-šes-spyan-ldan-rnams-la bzód-par ɣsol* with respect to the deficiencies I pray for the indulgence of the very wise (readers); *bzod-ɣsól byéd-pa* to ask pardon, forbearance *Pth.* —

II. sbst. 1. **patience** (*Ssk.* क्षान्ति), *bzód-pa sgóm-pa* to exercise one's self in patience *Dzl.* ༥, 12; but also, to have patience, to show forbearance; *bzód-pa bżés-pa,* id. resp. (v. also above I, 2); *bzód-pa-čan* **patient**; *bzod-sráṅ* unwearied patience; *bzod-pa-čuṅ* impatient *Mil.*, *bzod-med Cs.* id. — 2. in asceticism: **perseverance, stedfast adherence to the four truths,** constancy in pursuing the path that has been entered upon, *mi skye-bui čos-la bzod-pa* acc. to *Was.* id., being at the same time no longer subject to rebirths, p. (140). —

Observ. So far as 'to forgive' implies patience, forbearance, it may be rendered by *bzód-pa*; but as the Scriptural view of 'forgiveness of sin' involves more than that, other expressions, such as *bú-lon sél-ba,* must be resorted to with reference to the latter.

བཟོབ་པ་ *bzób-pa Sch.* = *ɣsób-pa.*

བཟོམ་ *bzom* **tub,** carried on the back, to convey water, v. *ču-bzóm* sub *ču.*

བཟླ་བ་ *bzlá-ba* v. *zlá-ba.*

བཟླས་བརྗོད་ *bzlas-brjód* (cf. *zlá-ba* II, 2); *zlá-ba* in a strict sense, is stated to be **the silent,** *brjód-pa* **the soft, yet audible pronouncing of spells** etc., *bzlas-brjod* signifying both together; *bzlas-brjód byéd-pa* to mutter over *Glr.*; *mú-stegs-pai bzlas-brjód* Brahmanical spell-murmuring *Thgy.*

བཟླུམ་པ་ *bzlúm-pa* v. *zlúm-pa.*

བཟློ་བ་ *bzló-ba* v. *zló-ba.*

བཟློག་ *bzlog* **the contrary, the reverse,** *prá-ba-las bzlog sbóm-po* the contrary of thin is thick *Lex.*

བཟློས་ *bzlos,* v. *zló-ba.*

འ

འ *a,* 1. a letter peculiar to the Tibetan language, which, contrary to ཨ (q.v.) denotes the pure vowel, without any admixture of a consonant sound. The difficulty which attaches to the articulation of this vowel, requiring an opening of the glottis before it is sounded, has occasioned a great variety of pronunciation in the different provincial dialects. Vide Phonetic Table with its explications. — 2. numerical figure: 23.

འ་ཅག་ ˏá-čag, *Cs.* **we**, v. ˏú-čag.

འ་ཅི་ ˏa-či n. of a country *Glr.*

འ་ཏི་ཝ་ ˏa-ti-wa, with *lóg-pa*, *Sch.*: **to perform somersets, to tumble over, to roll.**

འ་ན་ཡང་ ˏa-na-yaṅ **although**, *Sch.*; ˏa-na-ma-na *Sch.*; **perfectly alike, having a striking resemblance** (?).

འ་མ་ ˏá-ma **but**, e.g. ˏá-ma ma rjed čig but do not forget! *Cs.*

འ་འུར་ ˏa-úr *Sch.*: **'shaking or rattling sounds'** cf. ˏur-ˏúr.

འང་ ˏaṅ 1. like *yaṅ*, attached to conjunctions, and corresponding to the English **ever, soever**, after vowels, col. also after consonants, e.g. nam-ˏaṅ. — 2 ˏáṅ-sgra, bóṅ-bui *Cs.* the braying of an ass.

འང་ཀི་ ˏáṅ-ke (not ident. with *ǎṅ-gi* number), a mystical character, frq. occurring in certain finical ornaments or flourishes called *sbrúl-mgo*, occasionally also in written words.

འབ་པ་ ˏáb-pa *Ts.* **to bark.**

འར་པོ་, འར་ཅན་ ˏár-po, ˏár-čan *Ts.* **angry** = *γtúm-po.*

འར་བ་ ˏár-ba *C.* **lot**, *rgyáb-pa* to cast, = *rgyan rgyáb-pa.*

འར་འུར་ ˏar-ˏúr v. ˏur-ˏúr.

འར་ཡང་ ˏár-yaṅ **also, too, likewise** *Sch.*

འི་ ˏi 1. num. figure: 53. — 2. *W.* demonstr. pron. inst. of ˏdi, **this**, also *'i-po.*

འུ་ ˏu 1. num. figure: 83. — 2. sbst. **kiss**, v. ˏo. — 3. also ˏo, *Cs.*: demonstr. pron., **this**, ˏú-ni-ru, ˏú-nir, ˏó-nir, **hither**; *Ts.* *wú-ahi* **this.**

འུ་སྒྲ་ ˏú-sgra *Glr.* **noise of many foot-steps**, prob. = ˏúr-sgra.

འུ་ཅག་ ˏú-čag 1. also ˏó-čag *Glr.*, ˏó-čog *Thgy.*, ˏú-bu-čag *Dzl.* pers. pron. **we.** — 2. **chimney** *W.* (?).

འུ་ཐུག་ ˏu-ťúg *Sch.*: 'Lüderlichkeit, auch འུ་ཚུགས་ *'u-tsúgs'*; but in *W.* *'un-ťug čó-če* means **to break out into a violent passion**, and *'ún-ťug-ḱan* or *-čan* **angry**; in *C.* *mú-ťug-pa* and *dúg-ťug-pa* **to be at a loss**; so also in *Mil.*

འུ་བུ་ ˏú-bu v. ˏú-čag.

འུ་རུ་རུ་ ˏu-ru-rú *Sch.* = *ur.*

འུ་ལག་ ˏu-lág **compulsory post-service**, the gratuitous forwarding of letters, luggage and persons, the supply of the requisite porters and beasts of burden (also more immediately these themselves), — originally a socage-service rendered to lords and proprietors, government officers and priests; in more recent times remunerated and legally regulated in those parts that are visited by European travellers; *mi-la* ˏu-lág *skúl-ba* to impose such services, by exacting porters etc. *Pth.*, ˏgél-ba id.; *skyél-ba* prob. to forward by Ulag; (*Cs.* limits the signification too much).

འུ་སུ་ ˏú-su *Lt.* **coriander seed.**

འུག་པ་ ˏúg-pa, **owl**, *Lt.*; ˏug-rgán *Sch.* the great horn-owl, ˏug(-gu)-čúṅ the little owl; ˏug-míg owl's eyes (*Cs.* 'large languishing eyes', *Sch.*: 'large protruding eyes'); ˏúg-mig-čan having such eyes, ˏúg mig-pa or -ma a goggle-eyed man or woman *Cs.* — 2. *Ld.* also for *yug-po* **oats.**

འུག་སིངས་ ˏug-siṅs v. *siṅs-po.*

འུད་ ˏud 1. *Cs.* **swaggering, bragging, bombast, fustian**; ˏud čer smra-ba to swagger, brag, gen. *wur śe-pa*, *C.* — 2. = *yud Thgy.*, ˏud-kyis, **in a moment, instantly, suddenly.** — 3. **command, order** (?), *Sch.*: ˏud-sgrog-pa to make known an order.

འུབ་པ་ ˏub-pa **to sweep** or **rake together** with one's hands, *paṅ-pas* ˏub-kyis *bsdus-te Pth.* with the arms gathering all into one heap.

འུམ་བུ་གླང་མཁར་ ˏum-bu-glaṅ-mḱar n. of the palace of the ancient Tibetan king **Thothori**, *Glr.*

འུར་ ˏur 1. **noise, din, clashing, cracking, roar** of a tempest etc., but also and not less,

a low, humming noise, *rná-bai bú-ga bkág-pai ťse ‚ur-‚úr žés-pai sgra* the humming in the ears produced by stopping them *Wdṅ.*, *‚ur-‚úr-po-yi sgra* id. *Wdṅ.; rná-ba ‚úr-la ₒkrog* there is a buzzing in my ear *S.g.; ‚ur ldaṅ* or *ₒbyuṅ* a noise is heard; *Cs.* more particularly: **talk, babbling, chit-chat,** *‚ur-ɣtoṅ-ba* to talk, to chat; **toṅ-‚ur** *C.* (lit. *stoṅ*) bragging, humbug; *‚ur-sgra* = *‚ur* noise caused by many voices, many footsteps, cf. *‚u-sgra*; of the howling of a tempest, *‚úr-sgra če* although it (the thunder) makes a great noise *Mil.*; *‚ur-tiṅ* a brass basin, used to make a noise by striking it *Sch.*; *‚úr-ba* sbst. **a humming insect, beetle** *Sch.*; vb., **to be noisy, chattering,** *Cs.; dga-grágs ‚úr-te* shouting, rejoicing *Mil.*; **‚ur čó-če** to set a dog on a person *W.*; **‚ur bšád-pa, ‚ur-brdáb btáṅ-ba** *C., W.* to exaggerate, brag, boast. — 2. *bag-dró ‚ur-‚úr Pth.* seems to describe the feeling of a genial warmth pervading the body. — 3. **wur gyág-pa** *C.*, *'*ur gyáb-če, táṅ-če** *W.* to smooth, v. *dbur-ba.* — 4. *‚úr-rdo* a sling *Sch.*, *‚úr-rdo ₒṗén-pa* to throw with a sling.

འེ་ *‚e* num. figure: 113.

འོ་ *‚o* I. num. figure: 143. —

II. sbst. 1. provinc. *‚u* **kiss** (**चुम्ब**), *‚o byéd-pa* **to kiss** *Lt.*, *ḱá-la* on the mouth *Pth.; ṗyag, žabs* resp. on the hand, the foot *Cs.*; *‚o ɣtóṅ-ba Cs.*, *'*u lán-če** *W.*, = *‚o byed-pa.* — 2. v. *‚o-ma.* —

III. pron. 1. pers. pron. **we**, v. *‚u-čag.* — 2. dem. pron. **this** *Cs.* v. *‚u* III. — IV. interj. (*o ‚ŏ*) 1. like **oh, yes!** as a reply: *‚o lágs-so* oh very well! *Mil*; *'*o yóṅ-ṅog, 'o ḍig-gog, 'o gyál-log W.*, **‚o yóṅ-ṅe** *C.* well! it's all right to me! well, do so! — *‚o‚o, ‚ŏ‚ŏ,* so! well! very well! in *W.* it is a common reply, indicating nothing more, than that attention has been paid to the words spoken, like the English well! indeed! — 2. as a positive affirmative, **yes!** *W.*, cf. *‚o-ná.*

འོ་སྐོལ་ *‚ó-skol*, also with *rnams* and *čag*, (*Cs.* also *‚ú-skol*), *Ld.* '*á-χŏ*, **we,** *Mil., Tar., Thgy.*, e.g. (if all men must die), *‚o-skol lta či smos* of course also we *Thgy.*; it is very often used as a reciprocal pronoun: *‚ó-skol ma ši ṗrád-pa* the fact, that we have seen each other once more before we die *Mil.*

འོ་བརྒྱལ་ *‚o-brgyál*, resp. **fatigue, weariness, want,** any kind of hardship, **ṗéb-lam-la ob-gyál ma kyód-da** *W.* has not your walk hither fatigued you? *‚o-brgyál yóṅ-lugs* the getting into difficulties *Mil.*; more frq. as vb.: *‚o-brgyál-ba, ḱyéd-čag-rnams ‚o ma brgyál-lam* are you perhaps fatigued? *Glr.; žabs-tóg ‚o mi brgyal-ba ₒbul* a short expression for: everything shall be at your service, so that you shall not want anything *Mil.; ‚o-re-brgyál* = *‚o-brgyál* 1. **trouble, drudgery, annoyance** *Mil.* 2. **decay, decline, ruin,** of religion, usages etc.

འོ་སྙིག་ *‚o-snyig* **sour cream** *Sch.*

འོ་སྙིགས་ *‚o-snyigs* **birch-tree** *Sch.*

འོ་དོད་ *‚o-dod* **lamentation, wailing, cry for help,** gen. as vb. *‚o-dód ₒbód-pa* to lament, to call for help *Glr., Pth., Wdṅ.*; *‚o-dód-pa* one that seeks help, support, redress, a client, a plaintiff, more in pop. language.

འོ་ན་ *‚o-ná* (cf. *‚o, ‚on, ‚ón-kyaṅ*), comes nearest to the Greek ἀλλά, used esp. to introduce a new thought or proposition in speech: **now,** what shall you do in that case? *Dzl.;* **well,** what did he say? *Dzl.;* **well,** I hope you have at least ... *Dzl.;* **why, ay,** *Mil.;* **but now** *Thgy.;* **but,** the Latin *autem*, when a new clause is added *Mil., Thgy.;* **yea,** in a climax, e.g.: I met with a naked man, yea, an insane ascetic *Mil.* — 2. as an answer in the affirmative, **yes** *W.* —

འོ་མ་ *‚ó-ma* **milk,** *‚ó-ma ₒjó-ba* **to milk** *Glr.*; *snyól-ba* to let it curdle *Cs.*, *srúb-pa* to churn it *Cs.*; *‚ó-ma čags* the milk thickens, coagulates *Cs.* —

Comp. *‚o-ťáṅ* 'milk-meadow', the plain in which Lhasa now stands; of the former lake, *‚o-ťáṅ-gi mťso Glr.*, a sedgy moor is said to be still remaining. — *‚o-ťúg* milk-soup *Tar.* — *‚o-ťúd* cheese, v. *ťud.* — *‚o-ₒťúṅ* suckling-child, baby, = *žo-ₒťuṅ.* — *‚o-*

snól milk-vessel. — *o-spri, o-sri,* cream. — *o-már* 1. milk and butter *Sch.* 2. termin. of *ó-ma* into the milk. — *o-zó* milk-pail.

འོ་མ་ཟི་ཟི་ *o-ma-zi-zi W.* **pater-noster pea,** the seed of Abrus precatorius, used as beads for rosaries.

འོ་ཡོ་, འོ་ཡོག་ *o-yó, o-yóg* **terrier** *Sch.*

འོ་རེ་བརྒྱལ་ *o-re-brgyál* v. *o-brgyál.*

འོ་ཤོ་ *ó-šo W.*, only in **'ó-šo táṅ-ce* or *gyáb-ce** **to laugh at,** deride, to feel a pleasure at the misfortune of others.

འོ་སེ་ *o-se* **mulberry,** *ó-se-šiṅ* mulberry-tree; *ba-ós Med.*, perh. strawberry spinach, Blitum, which in *W.* is called *ba-o-se,* cow-mulberry.

འོག་ *og, W. *yog*, Ts. *wág**, 1. root signifying **below,** or with reference to time, **after,** opp. to *goṅ; óg-tu, W. *yóg-la** 1. adv. **down, below, underneath; afterwards, later;** in paging books it denotes the second page of a leaf, v. *goṅ;* it is used as an expedient to correct errors in numbering, or to make additions, as with us e.g. 'page 24, b'. 2. postp. **under,** with accus., less frq. with dat., **down from; after** (as to time, rank, succession). — *óg-na, W. *yóg-na**, 1. adv. **underneath, below.** 2. postp. c. gen. **under, after.** — *óg-nas, W. *yóg-nas** 1. adv. **from under, from below.** 2. postp. c. genit. **forth from below** *óg-tu júg-pa* to put underneath, to subject, subdue *Glr.*; *ka-óg Ts.* = *óg-tu,* e g. **šiṅ-gi ka-wág** under the tree; sometimes (less corr.) with accus. inst. of genit., also *og* alone, inst. of *óg-tu, óg-na: *Rutog Gu-lab-siṅ 'og mi dug* W.* Rutog does not stand under, is not subordinate to, Gulab Singh; *ldiṅ-og* the division of soldiers under the Dingpon, or a century (division of hundred); *bcu-og* a body of ten men under a *bcú-dpon* or corporal. — 2. testicles, of animals, *og-can* not castrated; **wog cé-pa** (*spyad-pa*) to cover, copulate *C.*

Comp. and deriv. *óg-sgo* the lower orifices of the body for the discharge of the excretions, *óg-sgo γnyis S.g.*; more partic. the anus *Pth.* — *og-rdo* anvil *Sch.* — *og-pag* v. *pag.* — *óg-ma* adj. the lower, later, following one, *dei óg-ma* the one following after that, the second in turn; **lá-me san ge-nyén yóg-ma žig duy* W.* a Genyen is inferior to a Lama. *og-min,* **अकनिष्ठ,** 'the not inferiors' i.e. the highest, the inmates of a certain heaven inhabited by gods, or also that heaven itself. — *óg-rol-tu* = *óg-tu Tar.* — *og-rlúṅ Lt.* vapour, flatulence. — *og-šál* crop, craw of birds.

འོང་བ་ *óṅ-ba,* pf. *oṅs,* imp. *šog, B.* and *Bal.* (**'óṅ-cas**), for which in common life almost always, and in more recent literature not seldom, *yóṅ-ba, W. *yóṅ-ce**, is used, 1. **to come,** *ma óṅ-ba mtóṅ-nas Dzl.* when he saw his mother coming; *náṅ-du oṅs, Dzl.* he came in; *pyir oṅ-ba Glr.* to come back; *mi γnyis ṅai drúṅ-du óṅ-rgyu yin-pa Glr.* two men that were about to come to me; *óṅ-bai lám-du Pth.* when being on their way; *ti-se-la sgóm-du yóṅs-pa yin Mil.* we come to the Tise in order to meditate; *óṅs-pa légs-so* you are welcome *Cs.*; *ṅas o-dód byas kyaṅ óṅ-mkan med Pth.* although I was crying for help, nobody came; *kyer óṅs-so Glr.* they came to bring, they brought with them; *krid-šog* bring hither! *krid óṅs-so Glr.* they brought thither; with reference to time: *ma-óṅs-pa* not yet come, i.e. future, *dus* etc. very frq.; also poet.: *ma-óṅs dón-du* for the benefit of those that are to come, i.e. of posterity; *čaṅ yóṅ-bai rigs, Wdṅ.*, the kinds (of cerealia) from which beer comes (is made). — 2. **to happen,** *yód-pa yóṅ-gin dúg-pas Mil.* as it sometimes happens that there are . . .; more frq. **to occur, to be met with,** *gréṅ-bu oṅ gyúr-na* whenever an e occurs, wherever an e stands *Gram.*; *mii yul-na mi oṅ* such a thing does not occur on earth *Glr.*; **di-ru mi yóṅ(-ce)* W.* that is not to be met with here. — 3. **to fall to the lot of, to be given, to come upon,** c. dat., *sras óṅ-bai γsól-ba btáb-bo Pth.* she prayed that a son might be given to her; **ko-la nad yoṅs* W.* a disease came upon him; **sód-nyom yoṅ** I receive alms, **sod-nam yoṅ** I acquire merit *W.;* to come in, *yoṅ-sgo* income, revenue *Schr.*, cf. *yoṅ-*

taṅ sub *taṅ* 2. — 4. **to be suitable, practicable, to do,** *bstán-pa γčig-la stón-pa γnyis mi ˏóṅs-pas Glr.* as two preceptors for one doctrine will not do; *yúl-du lóg-pa mi ˏóṅ-bas Glr.* as a journey home is not practicable; *ˏo-yóṅ-ṅog* v. *ˏo*; *lús-la óṅ-bai bár-du* as long as he was fit for work; **to go on well, to do well** *C.*, **da yóṅ-ṅa** *W.* will it do now? — 5. when connected with verbs, it serves to indicate futurity, like the English auxiliaries **shall** and **will**, as becomes evident from such expressions as the following: *˳či-ba nam yoṅ ča med Mil.* when dying comes, i.e. when we shall die, is uncertain; *mdog ˳gyúr-ba ˏoṅ Glr.* a change of colour is coming, i.e. the colour will, or is going to, change; *˳gró-ba mi yoṅ-bar ˳dug Mil.* I am not likely (*dúg-pa*, 4) to go there any more; **ṭel-če mi yoṅ** *W.* he will not be put to shame, not be disappointed; also with the supine: *srog daṅ brál-bar ˳gyúr-du ˏoṅ Dzl.* it will even come to his dying, it will be his death; *zós-su ˏoṅ Dzl.* he will even get so far as to eat . . .; *ši-bar ˏoṅ* he will die; still more free and popular are those turns, in which the gerund or the mere root is used: *γnaṅ-ste ˏoṅ Pth.* he will assent to it, allow it; *γčig min kyaṅ γčig yin-te ˏoṅ Glr.* if it is not the one, it will be the other; *sleb yoṅ* he will come *Mil.* and in *C.* very common; *yid-čés mi ˏoṅ* they will not believe it; it is also used to express the passive voice, and the English **to become, to grow, to get:** *šés-na ṅa γsod ˏóṅ-bas Glr.* as I should be killed, if she heard of it; **zer yoṅ** *C.* so it is said, expressed, i.e. this is the usual way of expressing it; **pél-te yoṅ** *W.* it is getting larger, increases; or with a noun: *smin ˏoṅ Glr.* it is growing ripe; *rgyál-po ˳baṅs-su ˏoṅ Ma.* the king becomes a subject.

འོང་མོལ་ *ˏoṅ-mól Ld.* for *ˏól-mo.*

འོད་ *ˏod*, **light, shine, brightness,** *šar* flames up, shines, *˳pro* spreads, proceeds from; *ˏod spró-ba* to emit light, *bkyé-ba* to spread *Sch.*; *ˏod lham-mér mdzád-pa* resp., to shine with a bright light *Sch.*; *ˏod kéṅs-pa* filled with light *Sch.*; *lús-la ˏod yód-pa* self-luminous, a property of primeval man *Glr.*; *nyi-ˏód* sun-light, *zla-ˏód* moon-light, *skar-ˏód* star-light *Cs.*; *γnam-ˏod* brightness of the night-heavens, zodiacal-light *Cs.*; *me-ˏod* fire-shine *Cs.*; lustre, brightness, of polished metal, *ˏod byin-pa* to elicit a gloss or lustre, to give a bright polish *Sch.*; metaphor. fair complexion, external beauty, **káṅ-pe 'od pélte yoṅ** the splendour of the house increases, **bud ča dug** declines, decays *W.*; *ˏod daṅ ldán-pa B.*, *ˏód-čan* 1. **luminous, emitting light;** 2. **bright, polished.** 3. **light,** **da 'od-čan ča yin** *W.* now it will grow light. 4. **of a fine colour, of a blooming appearance** *Glr.* 5. **beautiful, splendid, stately;** *ˏod-med*, vulgo *ˏod-med-kan*, the contrary.

Comp. *ˏod-kór* or *skor* a luminous circle *Lex.* — *ˏod-dkar* 1. white light. 2. symb. num.: 1. — *ˏód-čan*, v. above. — *ˏod-dpag-méd*, अमिताभ, also *snaṅ-ba-mta-yás* the fourth Dhyani-Buddha, v. *saṅs-rgyás.* — *ˏód-spro* (or *˳pro?*) light? — **ŏd-ṭo** *W.*, **ód-ṭo tog** hold up the light! **ód-ṭo bu** glow-worm, fire-fly; *ˏod-˳pro* sometimes occurring in the names of gods. — *ˏod-γzér* ray of light *Dzl.* and elsewh. frq.; *ˏod-γzér-čan* n. of a god, *ˏod-γzér-čan-ma* of a goddess *Do.* — *ˏod-srúṅ* n. p. 1. the human Buddha of the preceding period of the world. 2. a king of Tibet, son of Langdarma. — *ˏod-γsál* 1. a bright light or gloss, *ˏod-γsál mdaṅs daṅ ldán-pa* very glossy, of leaves. 2. com. of the supernatural enlightening of the saints, *ˏod-γsál-gyi ṅáṅ-nas γzigs-te Mil.* knowing, beholding, by means of prophetic light.

འོད་མ་ *ˏód-ma* **cane, bamboo,** *ˏód-ma tsal*, वेणुवन, cane-grove; such a grove near Rājagriha was a favourite retreat of Buddha.

འོན་ *ˏon W.* **but** (*sed, autem*); (not so often used as in English).

འོན་ཀྱང་ *ˏon-kyaṅ* **but, yet, notwithstanding** *Dzl.* and elsewh., frq. in *B.*; rarely *ˏon-yaṅ* for it *Mil.*; it stands at the beginning of sentences, but is also preceded by a gerund with *-kyi*, in which case it is almost pleonastic; *Lexx.* give उताहो as the

Ssk. word for it, which however seems not to agree with its use.

འོན་དང་ *ˏón-taṅ* = *ˏón-kyaṅ Lex.*

འོན་ཏེ་ *ˏón-te B.* and *C.* **or if not, or else, or also,** in double-questions after the termination *am* of the first question.

འོན་པ་ *ˏón-pa* 1. **deaf,** also **to be deaf;** *ˏón-pa-pa, ˏón-pa-po, ˏón-po* a deaf man, *ˏón-pa-mo, ˏon-mo* a deaf woman *Cs.*; *ˏon-loṅ* deaf and blind. — 2. **to give, to bring,** chiefly as imp. *ˏón-čig Dzl.*

འོན་སེང་ *ˏon-seṅ,* with *byéd-pa,* **to pay attention, to watch, to spy** *Sch.*

འོབ་ *ˏob* 1. also *ˏobs* **ditch, trench, pit** *Dzl.*; *me-ˏób* fiery pit; also fig.: the fire-pool of passions. — 2. v. *yob.*

འོམ་བུ་ *ˏóm-bu* 1. **tamarisk,** Myricaria *Med.* not unfrequent near the rivers of Tibet. — 2. *Sch.*: 'a town, settlement' (?).

འོར་ *ˏor* 1. **dropsy,** viz. the species **anasarca,** nif., = *págs-ču*; *dbu-ˏor* prob. id. *Med.* — 2. **eddy, whirlpool** *Sch.*

འོར་བ་ *ˏór-ba* 1. **to put** or **lay down** *Cs.* — 2. **to feed,** e. g. a little child *W.*

འོལ་ *ˏol* **clover, trefoil,** viz. snail-clover, medic, (Medicago); *ˏol-táṅ* a plain covered with such clover; **'ol-kyog* W.* snail.

འོལ་མདུད་ *ˏol-mdúd* v. *'ol-mdúd.*

འོལ་པ་ *ˏól-pa* **vulture** *Sch.* (?)

འོལ་སྤྱི་ *ˏól-spyi* **in a general way, generally speaking, about,** *ˏól-spyir* id. *Sch.*; *ˏól-spyi tsám-du dus mnyám-mo* they are about contemporaries *Tar.*

འོལ་བ་ *ˏól-ba* **black horse** *Mil., Ld.-Glr.* (*Ts.* **wál-ba**).

འོལ་མོ་ *ˏól-mo Ld.* **oṅ-mol** **besom, broom, brush,** *stag-ˏól* birch-broom, *zed-ˏól* hair-broom *Cs.*

འོལ་མོ་སེ་ *ˏol-mo-sé Wdṅ.* an officinal plant; *Cs.*: '*ˏol-ma-sa* 1. a certain small berry. — 2. a small weight'.

འོས་ *ˏos* 1. v. the following. — 2. v. *ˏo-se.*

འོས་པ་ *ˏós-pa* 1. vb. and adj. **to be worthy, suitable; becoming, appropriate,** with termin. inf., in later times and vulgo, with the root, *sbyín-par ˏos* it is becoming, it is meet to give; *ₒdi γzigs-par mi ˏos* it is not decent to see this; **ku-lón čá-če 'os* W.* he is worthy to be a vizier; **ĭ-sam la taṅ mi 'os* W.* he is not worth such high wages; **la nán-te taṅ 'os* W.* he deserves extra-pay; *yid-smón ˏos* to be wished, desirable; *ṗyag bya-bar ˏos-par ₒgyur* he becomes adorable; *stód-ˏos* to be praised, laudable; *bkúr-ˏos* deserving honour *Cs.*; *ṫams-čád-la ṗóg-ˏos-pai čád-pa* the punishment condign to all; rarely with genit.: *kún-gyis bkúr-žiṅ mčód-pai ˏos Mil.* he is deserving of universal honour and respect, and even: *rjei ˏos min* he was not worth to be a king, for which more frq. the termin. is used: *γtsó-mor ˏós-pa žig Glr.* the one that is the most deserving of being mistress, i.e. she that has the genteelest appearance, that is most of a gentlewoman; *grógs-su ˏós-pa* he is worthy to be his colleague, nif. *Mil.* — 2. more particularly in colloquial language: **right,** *W.* **ós-čan, ŏ-šan**; with a negative **mi-ós-pa, os-méd, os-mín* W.*, **mi-ŏ-pa** etc. *C.* wrong (for the *rigs-pa* and *mi-rigs-pa* of earlier lit.); *mi ˏós-pai spyod-pa byed-pa Glr.* to entertain illicit intercourse; *rdzas ˏós-pa* a lawful, *mi ˏós-pa* an unlawful matter *Schr.*; **ŏ-min-ghi ṭim-gál* C.* a wrong, immoral act, sinful transgression; **'os mi-ós ṗé-če* W.* to discern between right and wrong; with regard to a man's words, **credible, trustworthy,** or the contrary. — *Sch.* has besides: *ˏos či yod,* 'what other means or way is there?' and: *ˏos spyi-ba* 'to finish (a thing) for the most part; to be good or tolerably good' (??).

ཡ

ཡ *ya* 1. the consonant y, pronounced like the English initial y, in yard, yoke etc., in *C.* deep-toned; *yá-btags, yá-ta Glr.* the subscribed y or ྱ. — 2. num. fig.: 24.

ཡ་ *ya* I. often with *γčig*, one of two things that belong together as being of one kind, or forming a pair, also one of two opponents; *mig ya-γčig lóṅ-ba Pth.* blind of one eye; *lham ya-γčig Glr.* one of a pair of boots, an odd boot; *lag-pa ya-γčig-tu γser ťogs, lág-pa ya-γčig-tu bú-mo ḱrid-de Dzl.* in one hand holding the gold, with the other leading his daughter; *stóṅ-pa daṅ γsál-ba γnyis ya ma brál-bar Thgr.* the empty and the clear (emptiness and clearness) being inseparable from each other; *ya-gyál* one of several, e.g. of three things *Gram.*; of six *Lex.*; **yá-do** in *W.* the common word for *grogs* or *zlá-bo* **associate, companion, assistant**, **yá-do čó-če** to assist; **nyī-ka ya yǫ'* C.* they are equal to each other, a match, one as good as the other, **ḱó-la ya mé'*, or *ḱǫ ya ǰhe'-ḱen mi dug* C.* he finds none that is a match to him, **di lé-kę ya ṅę mi ťub* C.* I am not equal to the task; *ḱai ya* v. *ḱá-ya*; *ya-méd = do-méd*; *˳ťáb-ya* adversary, antagonist; *ya-žár* one-eyed; *ya-ma-zúṅ* and *ya-má-brla, ya-ya* v. below. —

II. root signifying **above, up** etc. (opp. to *ma*), cf. *goṅ*; adj. *yá-gi* (also *yá-ki Mil.*), *p̔u yá-gi* the upper or highest part of a valley *Glr.*, *rí-bo yá-gi* the hill up yonder *Mil.*; *yá-gi* upper = heavenly *Mil.*, opp. to *má-gi*; *yar* and *yas* v. the respective articles; the word, otherwise, occurs only in compounds: *yá-rkan* palate; *ya-gád* (for *skad*) ladder *Sch.*; *ya-góṅ* above, over *Sch.*; *ya-mgál, ya-mčú, ya-ťém, ya-ťóg, ya-rábs, ya-ré, ya-só* v. *mgal* etc.; *ya-mťá* the upper end, i. e. the beginning e.g. of a word, opp. to *ma-mťa* the end *Cs.*; *yá-ša* **esteem, honour, love,** shown to a person *W.* (= *že-sa B., C.*), **yá-šę spé-ra** expressions of respect; **yá-šę p̔í-la zér-na** if one speaks respectfully; *ya-ša-méd-ḱan* uncivil, regardless, reckless, unfeeling; **yá-ša čó-če** to show love, regard, to treat with tenderness, to fondle, a child, animal etc., opp. to *má-ša*, which however is less in use.

ཡ་ཁ་ *yá-ḱa* **mutual revilings** *Ma.*: *ma smád-la yaṅ yá-ḱa sgrags* mother and children abuse one another. *Cs.*: *yá-ga* bad reputation (?).

ཡ་རྒྱལ་ *ya-gyál* v. *ya* I.

ཡ་ང་(བ་) *yá-ṅa(-ba) C.* also **yá-ṅa-bo** (prob. for *γya ṅán-pa*) **shuddering, fright, anguish,** with genit. or accus. of that which is the cause of it *Do.*; *yá-ṅa-bai dmag-ťsógs Mil.* a formidable host; *yá-ṅai gegs* terrible danger *Pth.*

ཡ་ཏ་ *yá-ta* v. letter *ya*.

ཡ་ཏྲ་ prop. ཡཱ་ཏྲཱ་ *ya-tra* (procession and feast, in honour of some idol) *W.*: **festivity, reveling,** in beer with dumplings and pastry, held in autumn or winter, in memory and for the benefit of the souls of those that died during the last year.

ཡ་དོ་ *yá-do* v. *ya* I.

ཡ་པོ་ *yá-po* **butcher; executioner** *Schr.*

ཡ་བ་ *yá-ba* prob. = *γya-ba*. — *Mil.?*

ཡ་བ་ཀྵཱ་ར་ *ya-ba-kšā-ra Ssk.* **saltpetre** *Med.*

ཡ་མ་ *yá-ma* 1. **the temples.** — 2. **a severe cold, catarrh.** *Med.*; **yá-ma rag* W.* I have a bad cold. — 3. n. of a goddess, = *brtán-ma*.

ཡ་མ་ཟུང་ *ya-ma-zúṅ* **unsymmetrical, incongruous, not fitting together,** e. g. two unequal shoes; of religions, languages, customs, that have sprung from heterogeneous elements; of behaviour: **inconsistent; unheard of, prodigious,** *ǒo-ₒprúl* magic feats *Tar.*

ཡ་མ་བརླ་ *ya-ma-brla*, **ya-má-la**, *Ü: ya-ma-la-po*, *Ts.: *ya-ma-lẹn-te**, *Lis.:* — *snyiṅ-po-med-pa*, *mi-bdén-pa* **vain, unstable, fickle, not to be trusted** or **depended upon.**

ཡ་མཚན་ *yá-mtsan* 1. **wonder, miracle, supernatural occurrence,** adopted also as the term for the miracles of Scripture *Chr. Prot.*; *ltás-sam yá-mtsan ci byuṅ Dzl.* what signs and wonders have happened? *yá-mtsan-du ₒgyúr-ba Dzl.* to happen, to come to pass in a marvelous manner; *yá-mtsan-ste Pth.* being a wonderful man; *kyód-la ₒdi-tsam rig-pa-méd-pa ni yá-mtsan-čeo* that you are so ignorant is very strange (wonderful); **yá-tsẹm-po* C.* marvelous, miraculous; *yá-tsam-čan* id. *Schr.* — 2. **wonder, astonishment, amazement,** *rgyál-po yá-mtsan čén-po skyés-te Tar.* the king greatly wondering; **yám-tsan tsór-če, čó-če* W.* to wonder; *yá-mtsan-gyi ɣnás-so Tar.* it is a thing to be wondered at; *dé-tsam yá-mtsan-rgyu med Mil.* that is not so very astonishing.

ཡ་ཡ་ *yá-ya* 1. *Cs.:* **differing, diverse,** *yá-ya-ba* **diversity;** *yá-ya-bor gyúr-ba Sch.:* a subject of dispute, contrariety of opinion. — 2. *ɣyá-ya.*

ཡ་ཡོ་ *ya-yó* **crooked, wry,** col. *Cs.*

ཡ་ལད་ *ya-lád* **corselet and helmet, mail, armour,** *ɣsér-gyi* of gold; also fig. *B.*

ཡ་ཤ་ *yá-ša* v. *ya* II.

ཡ་ཧུ་དཱ་ *ya-hu-dá* **Judah,** *ya-hu-dá-pa* **jew** *Chr. Prot.*

ཡ་ཧོ་ཝཱ་ *ya-ho-wá* **Jehovah** *Chr. Prot.*

ཡག་པ་ *yág-pa* **a small mattock, hoe,** *čág-yag* iron hoe, *šiṅ-yag* wooden hoe *Ts.*

ཡག་པོ་ *yág-po*, prov. also *ɖág-po*, seldom in B., but otherwise common in *C.* and *W.* **good,** in all its significations, both as to men and things, = *bzáṅ-po*; **dei pi-la di yág-po* W.* for that purpose this is good, fit, serviceable; **yág-po ɟhé-pa* C.*, **čó-če* W.*, c. c. *la*, **to caress, to flirt,** also in an obscene sense; *yág-po yág-po* well, well!

ཡང་ *yaṅ* 1. (accented), **again, once more; likewise, also, further,** frq., *yaṅ yaṅ Mil.*, *yaṅ daṅ yáṅ-du Tar.*, *yáṅ-nas yáṅ-du Dzl.* **again and again**; joined to adj. and adv. denoting a higher degree, **still:** *yaṅ čuṅ Mil.* still smaller, *ₒdi či-yaṅ-las yaṅ dgá-ba žig byuṅ Mil.* that was still more pleasing than any thing before; *yáṅ sgos Mil.* still more in detail; **yáṅ-ṅon-žag* W.* the third day before yesterday. — 2. (unaccented, throwing the accent back on the preceding word), after the final letters g, d, b, s, gen. *kyaṅ*, after vowels often *ₒaṅ*, **also, too,** the Latin *quoque*, *ṅa yaṅ*, *bdag kyaṅ* I too; *bu čé-ba yaṅ Dzl.* my eldest boy too; *bsód-nams daṅ yaṅ ldán-pa Dzl.* having also merit; *yaṅ — yaṅ —*, both — and —; *ₒdi yaṅ — de yaṅ* both this and that, *ṗyi-rol yaṅ naṅ yaṅ* both outside and inside; followed by a negative, **neither — nor;** *yaṅ* singly, with a negative: **not even,** *kar-šá-pa-ni ɣčig kyaṅ mi sbyin-no Dzl.* I shall not even give a cowry for it; *yaṅ* with a comparative (as above) **still,** *sṅár-bas kyaṅ lhág-par* still more than formerly; as effect of a preceding cause, **so then,** *kyeu de yaṅ tse ₒdas-so Dzl.* so then the boy died, *bsád-pa yaṅ graṅs-méd-do Dzl.* so then there were people killed without number; emphat., **even,** *ríṅ-por ma lón-par smra yaṅ šés-so Dzl.* within a short time he was even able to speak; *sṅa-čád kyaṅ Dzl.* even before this; *kar-šá-pa-ni ₒbum yaṅ* even so much as a hundred thousand cowries (I would give); also joined to a verbal root: *tams-čad ₒdus kyaṅ* even if all without exception be gathered; **although,** *btsal kyaṅ ma rnyed* although they were seeking, they did not find, or, they were seeking indeed, **but** did not find; this latter turn is frequently used, where we use **but, yet, nevertheless** etc.

ཡང་སྐྱར་ *yaṅ-skyár* 1. sbst. **postscript.** *Cs.* — 2. adv. **again, afresh, anew** *C.*

ཡང་གེ་ *yáṅ-ge* v. *yáṅ-po.*

ཡང་སྒོས་ *yáṅ-sgos* v. *yaṅ* 1.

ཡང་ཅར་ *yáṅ-čar Bhot.* and *Schr.*

ཡང་ལྕི་ *yaṅ-lči* v. *yáṅ-po.*

ཡང་འཇུག་ *yáṅ-ǰug* the second of two final letters, viz. *s* after *g, ṅ, b, m.*

ཡང་ཏྲི, ཡང་གི་ཁ་ *yáṅ-tri, yáṅ-gi-ka* (spelling uncertain), is said to be the n. of a green stone, which is worked into handles of knives etc. *W.*

ཡང་དག་པ་ *yáṅ-dag-pa* v. *dág-pa.*

ཡང་ན་ *yáṅ-na* **or**, in *B.*, com. pleon. after the affixed *am* (*gam, nam* etc.), which in itself already expresses the **or**; it is also preceded by *daṅ*; **further**, *Thgy.*; **either — or —**, *yaṅ-na (ni) — yaṅ-na (ni) —.*

ཡང་སྤྲུལ་ *yáṅ-sprul* v. *sprúl-pa.*

ཡང་པོ་ *yáṅ-po Cs.*, **yáṅ-mo** *C.* and *W.* **yáṅ-ghe** *Ts.* adj., *yáṅ-ba* adj. and sbst., **light, lightness,** opp. to *lči-ba,* q. cf.; — fig. *ǰam-žiṅ yáṅ-ba* what is soft and light, commodious and easy *Dzl.;* of food cf. *lči-ba* II.; **weak,** **de saṅ yáṅ-mo yin** *W.* this is a weaker, less emphatic, word than that; **ṅo yáṅ-mo** *C., W.* cheerful, happy.

ཡང་མ་ *yáṅ-ma* **early barley,** v. *nas* I.

ཡང་མེས་པོ་ *yáṅ-mes-po* **great-grandfather,** *yáṅ-mes-mo* **great-grandmother** *Sch.*

ཡང་རྩལ་ *yáṅ-rtsal* **very high skill, consummate art** *Mil.*

ཡང་རྩེ་ *yáṅ-rtse* **the highest point, summit,** fig. **the height of perfection.**

ཡང་ཚ་ *yáṅ-tsa* **great-grandson** *Sch.*

ཡང་ར་ *yáṅ-ra W.* **buck, ram, he-goat,** = *pá-ra.*

ཡང་ལ་ *yáṅ-la* prob. = *yáṅ-na S.g.*

ཡང་སོས་ *yáṅ-sos* n. of a hell *Thgy.*

ཡངས་པ་ *yáṅs-pa* 1. also *-po*, **wide, broad, large,** *taṅ, sa-γži* a large or wide field, plain *Glr.*; *yaṅs-šiṅ rgya-če-ba* large and spacious, of a house *S.O.*; **gá-sa* (or *né-sa*) *yaṅ-pa dug** *W.* here is much room; fig. **mig-yáṅ** *C., W.* liberal, generous, bounteous; **yaṅ-méd-la, yaṅ-yáṅ-pa-la** *W.* sudden, unexpected, unawares; **yaṅ-lúg čó-če** *W.* to hang or throw a coat over, without getting into the sleeves; *yaṅ-šam byéd-pa* id., *Sch.;* **yaṅ-hlúb** *C., W.* wide, of clothes. — 2. v. *γyéṅ-ba.*

ཡངས་པ་ཅན་ *yáṅs-pa-čan*, *Ssk.* **वैशाली**, *Dzl.* and elsewh., city in ancient India, now **Allahabad.**

ཡན་ *yan* (= *ya* II, opp. to *man* III q. v.) **what is uppermost,** *man-yan* **below** and **above** *Cs.*; *yán-na Cs.:* **above, in the beginning, in the first part;** gen. *yan* stands as adv. or postp. with accus., = *yán-la, yan-čád(-la), yan-čód(-la),* **above, in the upper part,** *lté-ba yan stéṅ-la yód-de Glr.* lit. above the navel standing out of (the water), i.e. standing in (the water) up to the navel; *sta-zúr yan-čád Dzl.* above the hips; *lo-brgyád yan-čád Pth.* above eight years old; otherwise when referring to time, always **till, to**; often preceded by *nas*, **from . . . forth,** *Glr.*

ཡན་གླིང་ *yan-ljiṅ* **dulcimer,** musical instrument in *Ts.*

ཡན་པ་ *yán-pa* adj., **free, vacant, unoccupied, having no owner,** of places and things that are common property, like the air, rocks and stones etc.; *kyi yán-pa* a dog without a master, vagrant dog; *gral yán-la yod* there are yet places unoccupied; of fields: **untilled, fallow-ground;** *yan kyár-la ma ča,* v. *kyár-ba*; *yán-gar-ba* **separate, apart, by itself** *Lis.*, *rgyal-rigs yán-gar-ba žig* a separate dynasty, a dynasty of its own; *yán-gar-du* id., adv. *Was.* (281); *rgya-yán* the external world, *rgya-yán(-gyi) γnyén-pa Glr.* a helper from the external world; *sems rgya-yán-du ma šór-bar byos* take care that the mind be not distracted by outward things; **yan ča-če** *W.* to disperse, **lug, nor tsaṅ-ma, sam-pa yan soṅ** *W.*, the sheep have dispersed (or a sheep has strayed), the fortune is gone, the thoughts are lost, wandering; *yán-du ǰúg-pa* to suffer (the sheep) to disperse on the pasture; *nad yán-*

pa wandering (contagious) disease, = *yams* *Sch.* (*yán-pa* to run about, to wander *Sch.*, is rather doubtful).

ཡན་ལག་ *yán-lag* 1. **member, limb,** *yán-lag lňa* arms, legs, and head *Mṅg.*; *yán-lag skyón-čan* an injured or defective limb *Lex.*; *yán-lag nyams-pa* weak in the limbs, decrepit, crazy, = *žá-ba Lex.* — 2. fig. **branch of a river, branch of a tree;** *dge-bsnyén-gyi yán-lag γzúṅ-bar bgyio Do.* was explained: I wish to be counted a branch, i.e. a member, of the community of novices; **appendage,** something subordinate to a greater thing, like **branch-establishment** *Tar.* 175, 3; also with reference to books: **appendix, supplement** *Tar.* — 3. **branch, section, separate part** of a doctrine or science, frq., a **particular head, point, thought,** in a treatise.

ཡབ་ *yab*, resp. for *ṗa*, **father,** *rgyál-po yab yum γsum Glr.* the king and his two consorts; *rgyál-po yab yum* denotes also king and queen as father and mother to the country *Glr.*; *yab rgyál-po-la γsól-to Dzl.* he said to his royal father; *yab-srás* **father and son,** in a spiritual sense: **master and disciple;** *yab-mes* 1. **father and grandfather.** 2. **progenitor, ancestors** *Glr.*

ཡབ་པ་, གཡབ་པ་ *yáb-pa, γyáb-pa* 1. **to lock, lock up, secure, cover over** *Sch.*, *yab-ča* things well secured, under safe keeping; *yáb-yob-pa* to hide, conceal *Sch.*; *γyab* or *γyab-sa* **covered place, covert, shelter** *Sch.*; *yab riṅ-po* **portico, veranda,** e.g. of the monastery at Tashilhunpo; *yab-ras* **awning, tent** *Sch.* — 2. *C.* **to skim, to scoop off,** from the surface of a fluid. — 3. *W.* **to move to and fro, hither and thither,** v. *γyób-pa.* —

ཡབ་མོ་, གཡབ་མོ་ *yáb-mo, γyáb-mo* 1. **the act of fanning, waving,** *lág-pa yáb-mo byéd-čiṅ ₒčí-ba* dying whilst waving the hand to and fro, considered as a sign of peace *Do.*; *gós-kyi yáb-mo byéd-pa Glr.* to beckon by waving with one's clothes; hence fig. — 2. **the bringing on, provoking,** *dgrá-boi* of an enemy *Mil.*, *ₒṗuṅ-γžii* a calamity *Mil.*; *yáb-mo ǰhe'-pa* or *γyág-pa* to beckon to come, to bring (something adverse) upon one's self. — 3. **fan,** *rňa-yáb* a. a yak-tail fan *Cs.* b. kettle-drum stick *Sch.*; *sbraṅ-yáb* fly-brush *Cs.*; *rluṅ-yáb* ventilating- or cooling-fan *Cs.*; *bsil-yáb* **pankah** (*Hind.*), a large fan suspended from the ceiling and set in motion by means of a string. — 4. **sail** *Cs.?*

ཡམ་བུ་ *yám-bu* = *rdo-tsád* v. *rdo* comp.

ཡམ་མེ་བ་ *yám-me-ba* 1. *Sch.*: **coarsely, roughly, of a coarse make, rough-hewn.** — 2. *Mil.*: *čui ká-na ṗár-la yám-me γšegs* he walked softly gliding across the water to the other bank.

ཡམ་ཡོམ་ *yam-yóm Cs.* also *yam-yám Thgr.* **tottering, not steady** *Cs. yam-yóm byéd-pa* **to totter.**

ཡམས་ *yams, yams-nád Cs.*, *nad-yáms Glr.* **epidemic** or **contagious disease, plague,** *má-yams* a plague caused by evil spirits, v. *má-mo.*

ཡར་ *yar*, from *ya*, **up, upward,** also *yár-la*, e.g. *γzigs-pa* to look up *Glr.*, *yár-ₒgro már-ₒgro byéd-pa Glr.* to travel up and down; *yar mar ₒčág-pa B.*, **kyód-če** *W.* resp., to walk up and down; *yár-la ḱyer šog* bring or fetch up *Pth.*; *yar ma sgyugs mar ma ₒtón-par Pth.* as it would go off neither upward by vomiting, nor downward; *yár-nas már-la* from top to bottom; *yar ₒtón-pa Thgy.* to come up again, from a depth; **yar mar tsaṅ-ma-ru** *W.* in every direction, all over; in such expressions as *yar laṅ-ba* **to rise, get up,** *yar ₒṗél-ba* **to increase,** it stands pleon.; *yár-la* also denotes a relation to that which is higher, the intercourse with, the deportment towards, superiors (*már-la* the contrary) *Glr.*; esp. with reference to the transmigration of souls and their final deliverance: *yar γčód-pa* to cut off the way to the three upper classes of beings, the so-called 'good natures', *yar skyé-ba* to be reborn in the upper classes, the reverse of which is *mar ₒgríb-pa* to sink down to the lower; *yar ₒdrén-pa* to draw or lift up to heaven.

ཡར་ལྟོས་ *yár-ltos* **imitation** *Sch.*

ཡར་བ་ *yár-ba* **to disperse, ramble, stray** *C.* (= **yan čá-če* W.*); **to spring** or **leap off** *Cs.*; **to be scattered** *Sch.*

ཡར་ལུང་ *yar-lun Glr.* a large tributary of the Yangtsekyang coming from the north, in western China, east of the town of Bathang; nevertheless Tibetan historians, from a partiality to old legends, describe it as flowing near the mountain of Yarlha-sampo. V. *Köpp.* II, 50.

ཡར་ལྷ་ཤམ་པོ་ *Yarlhašampo*, a snowy mountain, between Lhasa and the frontier of Bhotan, near which according to tradition the first king of Tibet, *γnya-k̔ri-γtsáṅ-po, Nyaṭ̔ itsángpo*, coming from India, first entered the country.

ཡལ་ག་ *yál-ga* **branch, bough,** frq., *yál-gai ts̔úl-du* ramified *S. g.*, *yál-ga-čan* branchy, full of boughs; *yal-p̔rán Cs.*, *yál-ga p̔reu Sch.* small branch, twig; *yal-ₒdáb* a branch full of leaves *Cs.*

ཡལ་བ་ *yál-ba* **to dwindle, fail; disappear, vanish,** *drod yal* animal heat (in a living being) diminishes, (an inanimate object) cools down, grows cold; *ṅad yal* it evaporates *Lt.*; of beer: to get stale, dead (*W.: *yal čá-če**); **(s)kug(s) gyál-k̔an-la yal ča dug* W.* the stake is lost in going to the winner; *ₒǰa yál-ba bžín-du Glr.* like the vanishing of the rainbow; *yal-šúl Wdn.* in a fruit the remnants of the withered blossom; **to be obliged to yield, to be dislodged** *Glr.* fol. 25, but perh. the signification: **to disappear** is also here admissible; *lus daṅ srog yal Dzl.* body and soul are trifled away, are lost; **go-yál** (v. *sgó-po*) one who has lost himself by gambling and has thus become the slave of another; *yál-bar ₒdór-ba, ₒbór-ba*, 1. *Sch.* **to annihilate, annul.** 2. *Cs.* **to despise,** *γžan* other people. Cf. *yól-ba.*

ཡལ་ཡལ་ *yal-yál Cs.* 100 000 octillions, *yal-yál čén-po* a nonillion; yet cf. *dkrigs-pa.*

ཡལ་ཡོལ་, -ཡུལ་ *yal-yól, -yúl* **inconstancy, inattention, carelessness** *Cs.*, *Sch.*

ཡས་ *yas*, from *ya*, 1. **from above,** *ₒbáb-pa* to come down from above *Cs.*; **above,** *yás-kyi* the one above, the upper one *Do.*; *yás-nas* from above *C.*, *yas mas*, a. from above and from below *Cs.* b. upward and downward *Cs.*; *yas-byón* coming from above *Mil.* — 2. **off, away,** *yas γtóṅ-ba, ₒp̔aṅ-yás γtóṅ-ba, γtor-yas byéd-pa Glr.* and elsewh., to throw away. — 3. in comp. **without,** *mt̔a-yás* without an end, endless, frq.; *bgraṅ-yás* numberless *Gram.*

ཡི་ *yi*, 1. num. fig.: 54. — 2. in some combinations inst. of *yid*, *so yi γčód-pa yi(d) čád-pa* 1. **to forget,** e.g. a benefactor *Glr.* 2. more frq. **to give up, to despair** *Dzl.*; **despondency, despair** *Mil.*; *yi-p̔ri-ba* a disliking, hatred *Cs.*; *yi(d)-múg-pa, yi-múg-par ₒgyúr-ba* to despair, frq.; *yi-ráṅ-ba* to be glad, to rejoice, v. *ráṅ-ba*; *yi-γsúd-pa Cs.* = *yi-múg-pa.*

ཡི་ག་ *yi-ga* **appetite,** *yi-ga ₒgag, ldog* the appetite is lost, aversion, disgust is felt, *yi-ga sdaṅ* id. *Sch.*; *ₒčus* id. *Med.*; *yi-gar ₒoṅ* it is grateful to the taste, it tastes well *Med.*

ཡི་གེ་ *yi-ge* in comp. *yig*, 1. **letter,** *yi-ge dbú-čan* (*W. *róm-yig**) the Tibetan printed letters, *dbu-méd* (*W. *ṭ̔a-yig**) current handwriting, of which there are again different kinds: *dpé-yig* the more distinct and careful, used in copying books, *ₒk̔yúg-yig* the cursory and often rather illegible writing in letters, and *ₒbam-yig*, the very large and regular style invented for the use of elementary writing-schools (v. specimens of all of them in the lithogr. supplement to *Cs.*'s grammar). — *yi-ge-drúg-pa* the six-syllable (prayer), **the Ommanipadmehum** *Glr.* and elsewh.; *yi-ge-bdún-pa* and *brgyá-pa Mil.?* *yi-ge bsláb-pa* to learn reading and writing, *yig-rtsís* reading, writing, and cyphering; *ká-yig* the letter k. — 2. anything that is written, **note, card, bill, document; inscription, title** (more accurately *k̔á-yig*), esp. **letter, epistle;** *yi-ge bžág-pa* a deposited document, bond *C.*; *dge-sdig-gi yi-ge* register of virtues and iniquities; *yi-gei lan* a written answer *Glr.*; *yi-gei šubs* a. **envelope,** b. **letter-case, pocket-book;** *yi-ge ₒbri-ba* to write a letter, *spriṅ-ba W. *kál-če** to send off, *t̔ob-*

pa to receive a letter; *yi-ge sleb* a letter arrives; *yi-ger* ˳*bri-ba Dzl.*, ˳*gód-pa* to compose, to pen down; *yi-ger* ˳*brir* ˳*jûg-pa* to get copied; *yi-ger bris* ˳*jóg pa literis mandatum deponere*; *skú-yig* letter, circular epistle; *k'á-yig* v. above; *čád-yig* contract, bargain; ˳*čáms-yig* dancing-book, rules relating to religious dances; ˳*čól-yig* letter of recommendation *Cs.*; *rtágs-yig* 1. **stamp, signature** *Cs.* 2. **certificate, credentials** *W.*; *γnás-yig* description of a place; *sprińs-* or ˳*p'riń-yig* = *skúr-yig*; *bú-yig* 1. copy. 2. commentary, opp. to *má-yig* 1. original, first copy; 2. text *Cs.*; ˳*dzin-yig* = *rtágs-yig* 2 *W.*; *žú-yig* memorial, petition; *lán-yig* letter in answer, reply; *lám-yig* 1. **hand-book, road-book, guide,** *šám-bha-lai lam-yig* description of the road to Sambhala (a fantastical book). 2. **itinerary, travelling-journal** (?). 3. **pass-port** *Cs.*

ཡི་དྭགས་ *yi-dwags* (from etymol. subtility written also *yid-tags* or *yid-btags*), प्रेत, the fifth class of beings of Buddhist cosmography, condemned in a fore-hell to suffer perpetual hunger and thirst, a grade of punishment preceding the final and full torments of hell; they are represented as giants with huge bellies, and very narrow throats, inhabiting the air *Köpp.* I, 245.

ཡི་དམ་ *yi-dam*, less frq. *yid-dam* (= *dam-bča*) resp. *túgs-dam* 1. **oath, vow, asseveration, promise,** *yi-dam-la brtén-pas* because he firmly adhered to his word *Dzl.* — 2. a 'wishing prayer' (v. *smon-lam*), *yi-dam bčá-ba* to make a vow *Dzl.*, to pronounce a wishing prayer *Dzl.* — 3. **meditation** (this signification rests only on the analogy with *tugs-dam*, and has yet to be confirmed by quotations from literature). — 4. also *yi-dam-lhá* **tutelar god,** a deity whom a person chooses to be his patron, whether for his whole life, or only for some particular undertaking, and with whom he enters into an intimate union by meditation; frequently also it is a defunct saint or teacher (so e.g. the *yi-dam* of Milaraspa was *rdo-rje-*˳*čań*); sometimes such a connection subsists from infancy through life, or the deity makes advances to the respective person by special revelations, so in the case of king *Sroń-btsan-sgam-po Glr.* — 5. acc. to *Cs.*'s proposition: **sacrament**; yet our Christian converts preferred the more popular *dam-bča.*

ཡིག་ *yig* = *yi-ge* as an affix, v. *yi-ge.*

ཡིག་བསྐུར་ *yig-bskúr*, also *yig-mgó*, **epistolary guide**, containing the different addresses and customary phrases used in writing letters *W.* — *yig-k'áń* **library** *C.*, **chancery** *Schr.* — *yig-mk'an* **secretary, book-keeper, clerk** *Glr.* and elsewh. — *yig-ča Glr.*, *Tar.* **written accounts, records, books of history.** — *yig-dpon* a 'master-writer' *Cs.* — *yig-p'réń* line, written or printed. — *yig-*˳*bru* a single letter. — *yig-tsáń* 1. **archives, records, documents** *Glr.* 2. **book-case** *Glr.* — *yig-*˳*dzin* **written contract,** *bžág-pa* to indent (articles of agreement).

ཡིད་ *yid*, resp. *tugs*, I. 1. **soul, mind,** esp. the powers of perception, volition and imagination, cf. *blo*; *yid bžin-du* as one would wish, to heart's content, frq.; *yid-bžin-gyi nór-bu* a jewel or talisman that grants every wish; *yid-du* ˳*oń-ba* adj., rarely *yid-*˳*oń-po Mil.* **engaging, winning, pleasing,** *skyé-bo máń-poi yid-du* ˳*óń-ba Do.* beloved with many; **nice, pretty,** of girls, houses etc., frq.; also *yid-kyi* inst. of it, e.g. *yid-kyi mto* a pretty lake *Sbh.*; *ńai-yid* ˳*oń* my dearest! my darling! *Pth.*; *yid-du-mi-*˳*oń-bai tsig smrá-ba Wdń.* to say some unpleasant word; whereas *W.*: **da yid-la yoń* or *juń** now it comes into my mind; *ńa yid-du mi rag* I do not recollect; *C.*: **yi'-la ma soń** it would not go down with him, he had no mind for it; *ńai yid-la mi* ˳*bab Tar.* it does not please me, I do not like it; *yid-la šar kyań ro mi myoń Mil.* though you may fancy it in your mind, yet you do not perceive the taste; *yid-la byéd-pa*, ˳*dzin-pa W.*: **čo-če, bór-če**, **to comprehend, perceive, remember, mind, take to heart,** frq.; *yid-kyis byéd-pa* to do a thing in one's mind, fancy, e.g. sacrificing, like *dmigs-la Thgr.*; *yid-kyis byás-pa* fancied, imaginary, ideal *Cs.*; **yi'-*

kyi lóg-pa* C. to read mentally, softly, inaudibly; before many verbs *yid* stands almost pleon.: **yid kul-ce* W.* **to exhort**; *yid ˳kul-ba Sch.* 'mental suffering', perh. better: **to be uneasy, troubled, harassed**; *yid ˳krúl-ba* **to be mistaken**; *yid-čad-pa* v. *yi-ɣčod-pa*; *yid-čes-pa* **to believe,** with the accus. or dat. of the thing which one believes, with the dat. of the person whom one believes, ... *par*, that ... (cf. *dád-pa*); *kyód-la čuṅ žig yid ma čés-pas Mil.* having become a little distrustful towards you; **yid (or dén)-čé-čeï spé-ra* W.* credible words; *yid-brtan-dká-ba Tar.* not to be depended upon, hardly to be believed; *yid-ɣnyis* **doubt**; *té-tsom daṅ yid-ɣnyis ma byed čig Mil.*; *yid ˳pám-pa Mil.* **to be cast down, dejected, depressed**; *yid ˳próg-pa Mil.* **to prepossess, to infatuate**; *yid bloṅ-ba* **to be afraid, full of anxiety** (?) *Sch.*; *yid ˳byuṅ-ba*, resp. *tugs-˳byuṅ-ba Mil.* **to be sad, unhappy, discontented,** *la*, on account of; *ṅa kor-bai čos-la yid-byuṅ-nas Mil.* I was wearied of the way of (constantly moving in) the orb of transmigration; *yid-˳byin-pa* to make discontented or weary; *yid-múg-pa* v. *yi-mug-pa*; *yid ˳tsim-par ˳gyúr-ba Dzl.* to become satisfied, contented; **yid tsim čo-ce* W.* to satisfy; *yid-log-pa* **to be tired** or **weary of** *Sch.*; *yid-túṅ Dzl.* **forward, rash, overhasty**; *yid-dúṅs* v. *duṅs*; *yid-myós* fuddled, tipsy; *yid-smón* v. *smón-pa*; *yid-ɣžúṅs* v. *ɣzúṅs*; *yid-srúbs Lexx., Sch.*: 'a refractory, stubborn mind', which however does not suit the connection. — 2. symb. num.: 14. — II. = *yud*, *yid-tsam* for *yud-tsam*, *Wdṅ* frq.

ཡིད་དྭགས་ *yid-tags* v. *yi-dags*.

ཡིན་པ་ *yin-pa*, resp. and eleg. *lágs-pa* I. **to be,** with neg. *ma yin* or *min*, *W.* **man**; *kyod su yin* who are you? *bsa de-ka ṅa yin Mil.* I was the leopard (you saw); with genit., *ṅai yin* that is mine, belongs to me; **di-riṅ za-nyi-ma yin* W.* to-day is Sunday; *gáṅ-nas yin Mil.* whence are you? *˳di med-pas yin Pth.* it is because this is not here ...; *ṅa bú-moi dús-na yin-te Glr.* when I was still a girl; **yin kyaṅ* C.*, **yin-na yaṅ* W.*, *C.* for *˳on kyaṅ* **yet, nevertheless, notwithstanding**; *yin-graṅ(-na)* v. *gráṅ-ba* extr.; *yin* for optat or imp.: *de yin* 1. **so it is, yes.** 2. **that may be,** *mi ˳dod ruṅ de yin Mil.* if you feel no inclination, never mind, let it be so! *dgrá-bo yin-na-˳aṅ yin Mil.* if he is an enemy, let him be so! *yin-na* stands also pleon. with adverbs etc.: *sṅar yin-na* = *sṅar Mil.*; *yin*, so it is! yes! *min*, *W.* **man**, no! *yin-min* truth in a relative sense, *yin-min-gyi té-tsom bsal Glr.* it removes all doubts as to the truth, e.g. the historical truth; *ma yin-pa*, *min-pa* 1. vb. not to be a thing. 2. adj. not being a certain thing, *ma yin-par*, adv.; *čos ma yin-par* 'not being law', i.e. contrary to the law of religion, **wrong, unjust,** = *mi rigs-par*; *yul, dus, tsod, rigs-pa ma yin-par spyód-pa Thgy.* to do a thing at a wrong time or place, without observing due measure, in an improper or unnatural manner; hence also *ma-yin-pa* alone: **wrong, unjust**; **ma-yim-pe čö-pa jhé-ken-la ten-šig zer* C.* whoever commits an improper action is called **ten-šig**; hence also *yin-min* right and wrong. — 3. v. *min.* Cf. moreover *yód-pa* and *˳dúg-pa*, which may be used for *yin-pa*, but not inversely. Sometimes it implies **to mean, to signify**: *ṅa de či yin Glr.* what does this drumming mean? *rgyál-po koṅ-ráṅ yin dgoṅs* the king thought (the prophecy) meant him, referred to himself; *tóg-ma ṅéd-kyi pyir ma yin-pas Dzl.* as from the very beginning it was not aimed at me, had no reference to me; also in other instances, where we have to use words of a more precise character: *kyód-kyi lo gaṅ yin-pa-la kó-wo dgú-gis Tar.* whilst the sensibility that was with you, i.e. the discretion shown by you, gives me much pleasure. — II. *yin* is joined to a partic. pres., quite analogous to our English construction: *˳gró-ba yin* **I am going** *Mil., C.*; *kyód-la lám-mkan yód-pa é yin? Mil.* (are you having) have you a guide? *dei náṅ-na su yód-pa yin? Glr.* who is within? it is also joined to a partic. pf., when referring to the past: *ṅa-ráṅ-la skyés-pa yin Glr.* I have born him; *čád-pa yin-pas Glr.*

because he is descended from . . .; *ci byúṅ-ba yiṅ, Glr.* what has become of him? *de-dus ci byas-pa yin Mil.* what were you doing just then? so esp. *W.: *zér-pa yin, zér-pen** he has said it, **kál-pen** it has been sent off; joined to the partic. fut., (or to the partic. pres. or pf., in as far as these are sometimes used also for the fut.) it expresses futurity: *ŝi-ba yin Pth.* I shall die; *ṅo su ŝés-pa-la bskúr-ba yin Glr.* she shall be given to him, that will know her, find her out from amongst the rest; *ₒgró-ba yin mod Glr.* indeed you will have to go now. When joined to a root, it is only in *W.* that it denotes the future: **léb yin, léb-bin** he will come, **táṅ yin** he will give.

Comp. **yin-tog-čan* W.* thinking one's self to be something (great), proud, conceited. — *yin-tsul Mil.* **property, attribute,** ni f. — *yin-lugs* 1. circumstances, **condition** (= *ynás-lugs?*); *k'óṅ-rnams-kyi yin-lugs brjod Mil.* she related to him her circumstances. 2. nature or essence of things *Mil.*

ཡིབ་ *yib*, v. *čar-yib* **eaves, shed** *Mil. nt.*, yet cf. the following.

ཡིབ་པ་ *yib-pa* **to hide one's self** *C., W.*; *čar yib byéd-pa Pth.* to take shelter from the rain; **yib-te bór-če* W.* to hide, conceal; *yib-ma* **something hidden** *Sch.*; *yib-sa* **place of concealment, hiding-corner.**

ཡིས *yis*, termination of the instrum. case after vowels, po.

ཡུ་ *yu* 1. sbst.? *yu byéd-pa* **to calumniate** *Sch.* (?); *yu-na* if it is true *Sch.* (??) — 2. num. figure: 84.

ཡུ་གུ, -ཁུ་ *yu-gu, -k'u* **oats,** or a similar kind of grain, which, in case of need, may serve for food *C.*

ཡུ་གུ་ཤིང་ *yú-gu-ŝiṅ* officinal tree, yielding a remedy for wounds and sores *S.g.*; also fig. *Wdṅ.*

ཡུ་གུར, ཡུ་གེ་ར་ *yu-gúr, yu-gé-ra*, n. of a country and people, *Cs.*, which *Sch.* gratuitously identifies with *Taṅ-gúd*; however *Glr.* p. 32 is stated, that Tibet derived mathematical science and works of art from the east, viz. China and Minyag (i.e. *Taṅ-gúd*), laws and specimens of workmanship from the north, viz. Hor and Yugera (which are frequently mentioned together *Ma.*) — a passage which *Sch.* (History of the Eastern Monguls, 328) translated, but owing to an obscurity in the Mongul text, he failed to recognize Yugera, instead of which he has the word 'Gugi', questionable even to himself. (*Sch.* on the 'Phantom of the Turkish Uigures', v. Preface to *Dzl.* IX.).

ཡུ་བ་ *yú-ba* **handle, hilt, shaft,** *gri-yu* haft of a knife; *stár-yu* helve of an axe; *débs-yu* handle of an awl; *lhám-yu* leg of a boot *Cs.*; *yú(-ba)-čan* provided with a handle, *yu-méd* without a handle *Cs.*; *yu-bčád* 'shoes, slippers' *Sch.* (?).

ཡུ་བུ་ཅག་ *yú-bu-čag Cs.* = *ₒú-bu-čag.*

ཡུ་བོ, ཡུ་མོ་ *yú-bo, yú-mo* ox, cow, having no horns *Cs.*; for *yú-mo Sch.* has 'hind, female of a stag'; it seems to be little known. *yú-mo srol-góṅ* and *yú-mo mdeu-ₒbyín* names of plants *Wdṅ.*

ཡུག་ *yug* (= *bubs*) 1. **piece of cloth** or **stuff;** *gós-su ras-yúg ycig-las mi bdóg-ste Dzl.* as they had but one cotton cloth for their clothing. Cotton cloth is generally of very small width, but the silk fabric, designated by *dár-yúg*, seems not to exceed much the breadth of ribbons *Glr.* — 2. for *yud Mil.*

ཡུག་པོ་ *yúg-po, Ld. ₒúg-pa* **oats,** prob. the same as *yú-ku.*

ཡུག(ས)་ས, ཡུག(ས)་ཟ་ *yúg(s)-sa, yúg(s)-za* **mourning** for a deceased husband or wife, and the state of uncleanness consequent to it, the duration of which varies according to circumstances, whether the first or second spouse has died, and also with respect to the different countries; *yúg(s)-sa-pa*, also *yúg(s)-sa* **widower,** *yúg(s)-sa-mo* **widow;** *yúg(s)-sa p'óg-pa* being unclean in consequence of mourning; *sáṅs-pa* cleansed, viz. by the expiration of the time of mourning *Cs.*

ཡུང་བ་ *yúṅ-ba Med., *yúṅ-pe* W.,* **turmeric.**

ཡུང་མ་ *yúṅ-ma*, for *nyúṅ-ma*, **turnip** *Glr.*

ཡུངས་(ད)ཀར་ *yuṅs-(d)kár* **white mustard,** *yuṅs-nág* **black mustard;** *yuṅs-ₒbrú* **grain of mustard-seed,** *yuṅs-ₒbru tsam* as small as a grain of mustard-seed *S.g.*; *yuṅs-már* oil of mustard.

ཡུད་ *yud* 1. rarely *yug*, a very small portion of time, **moment,** acc. to *S.g.* = **कला,** stated to be a space of time varying from 8 seconds to 2½ minutes; *yúd tsam (žig)*, *yud ré* but one moment, *yúd-tsam-pa Do.* of a moment's duration; *tse ₒdi yud tsam yin ṗyí-ma-la mta-méd* this life is but like a moment, the future without end; *yúd-kyis*, *yúd-du* in a moment, e.g. *γnás-su ṗyin-pa* to get to a place *S.g.*; for a moment, *nám-mḱa-la ltá-ba* looking up to heaven *Wdṅ.* — 2. acc. to *Stg. ḱu*, fol. 53, *yud* is a space of time of longer duration, 48 minutes; acc. to *Schr.* in *Bhot.* = *č̒u-ts̒ód* 24 minutes. — **3. a black** or coloured stripe on woven fabrics, *yud-čan* striped, black or white *W.*

ཡུད་བུ་ *yúd-bu* = *yú-bu*, *ₔú-bu Cs.* (?).

ཡུད་ཡུད་ *yud-yúd Sch.*: *yud-yúd bríd-pa* **a dim and indistinct glimmering** before one's eyes.

ཡུན་ *yun* **time,** when denoting a certain space or length of time, *klog ₒkyúg-pai yun tsam ma lón-par der ṗyin-nas Mil.* in no longer time than a flash of lightning takes he arrived there; *yun riṅ-po*, *W.* **-mo**, a long time, *yun riṅ-por*, *yun riṅ-du* during a long time, *yun riṅ-po-nas* a long time since or past; **yun máṅ-po bud č̒a dug** *W.* a long time passes; **yun riṅ-ṅi ḱá-na** *W.* by degrees, gradually; *yún-du Glr.* for a long time to come; *yun či srid-du* how long? *yun ťúṅ-ba* a short time.

ཡུམ་ *yum*, resp. for *ma*, 1. **mother,** *btsún-mo yum*, *yum btsún-mo* the queen mother. — 2. *Ssk.* **मातृका**, title of the third and latest part of the sacred writings, which contains the **Abhidharma**, or metaphysical portion (*Köpp.* I, 595. *Burn.* I, 48); *Sch.* mentions also an extract of it, *yum-č̒úṅ*.

ཡུམ་པ་ *yúm-pa*, only *W.* **to strew,** salt on food, ashes on the snow.

ཡུར་བ་ *yúr-ba* I. vb. 1. **to slumber,** *W.* also **ťom yur-čé**. — 2. v. *yúr-ma*.

II. sbst. **aqueduct, conduit, water-course, ditch** *Glr.*; *yúr-po če* a large trench, channel, canal, *yur-ṗrán* a small one; *sbubs-yur* a covered, subterraneous canal *Cs.*; *yur(-bai) č̒u* water conveyed by a canal.

ཡུར་མ་ *yúr-ma* **the act of weeding** *C., W.*; **yur-ma yur-wa**, *C., W.* also **čo-če** to pull out weeds; metaph. to purify the mind, cleanse the heart, e.g. by disburdening one's conscience.

ཡུལ་ *yul* 1. **place,** a. **an inhabited place,** as opp. to desolation, *ťaṅ stoṅ-pa mi daṅ yul med-čiṅ Pth.* a desert in which there are neither men nor dwelling-places; b. **place,** with reference to a sacred community (college, monastery etc.) near it, e.g. some of the students live in the college, others in the place: so *yul-dgón* village and monastery, *yul-dgón-rnams Mil.* for *yúl-mi daṅ dgón-pa-pa-rnams* laymen and clerics. c. **place, province, country,** in a gen. sense, *yúl-(gyi) skad* provincial dialect, provincialism; *yul-(gyi) mťil*, *mč̒og* chief place, capital; *yul č̒en-po brgyad* chief places; as such are enumerated in *Pth.*, without any regard to geography, Singhala, Thogar, Li, Balpo, Kashmir, Zahor, Urgyan, Magata; *rgya-gar(-gyi) yul* India; *rgyá-yul*, *bód-yul*, *sóg-yul* India (or China), Tibet, Mongolia; whenever *yul* precedes a word, as in **yul wa-ra-ṇa-sér**, it is to be understood in this way: as to the place (situation), in Banāras; *skyid-yul* a lucky place, *sdug-yul* an unlucky one; *ṗá-yul* fatherland, native country, home; *raṅ-yul* one's own country, *γžán-yul* a foreign country; *ₒbróg-yul* country consisting of steppes, *róṅ-yul* country full of ravines; *lha(i)-yul* **land of gods,** abode of the *lha*, also fig., a particularly pleasant country or scenery; *mí(i)-yul* **abode of men,** (*ἡ οἰκουμένη*) **the inhabited world, earth,** yet in the Tibetan sense always as opp. to the abodes of good or evil deities; *mii yúl-na mi ₔoṅ Glr.* in the world such a thing is not to be found; *rnám-šes dbáṅ-poi yúl-las ₒdás-pa Wdṅ.* the soul that has left the external world, (yet cf. no. 2); *spyód-yul*, q.v. — 2. **the object or objects of perception by means of the senses**; *p'yii yul drug* the provinces of the six senses, viz. forms (the external appearances of bodies), sounds etc. *Mil.*; so prob. also: *yúl-rnams-la lóṅs-spyod-par rmóṅs-te Wdṅ.* dead to sensual pleasures; *yul mi ₒdzín-pa*, or *γžán-du ₒdzín-pa Thgy.* to perceive things either not at all, or not correctly; *brjód-pai yúl-las ₒdás-pa* is stated to imply: exceeding the limits of speech, unspeakable, unutterable; *bsám-byai yúl-las ₒdás-pa = bsám-gyis mi k'yáb-pa* frq. unimaginable, inconceivable, which term, however, does not seem to be fully adequate; also *Was.* (311) translates *yul* with **object**; cf. *γnas*, 5. — 3. **weather**, or rather in a more gen. sense, **climatic state** of a country, and condition of the beings in it, v. below *yul-ṅán, yul-bzáṅ*.

Comp. and deriv. *yul-k'áms* kingdom, e.g. of Nepal, China, *Glr.* — *yul-ₒk'ór* country, province *Glr.* — *yul-gru* id. *Glr.* — *yul-dgón* v. above. — *yul-ṅán C.* tempest, *yul-ṅán-gyi ts'úb-ma* the turmoil of the tempest *Glr.*; also public calamities, such as famine, murrain etc, *Glr.* — *yúl-čan* 1. **suited, proper, being in its place, fulfilling its purpose,** *Cs.* (?) 2. **that which is treated 'objectively'** *Was* 311, cf. no. 2 above. — *yúl-čos* characteristic properties, manners etc. of a country. — *yul-ljóṅs* district, tract of country. — **yul tum-túm* Ld.* the separate villages of a whole cluster bearing one common name. — *yul-sdé* 1. **district** *C.*, *W.* 2. **village magistrate.** — *yúl-pa* **inhabitant, native,** *gaṅ yúl-pa yin* whence are you? what is your country? — **citizen, burgher** *Mil.*; *yúl-pa-rnams* the people, the public *Mil.* — *yúl-po* gen. with *če*, a large country, *Mil.* — *yúl-dpon* village magistrate, district judge. — *yul-p'yógs* region, neighbourhood *Mil.* — *yúl-ma* a native woman. — *yúl-mi* 1. = *yúl-pa*. 2. **countryman, compatriot** *Do.* — *yul-méd* 1. **improper, not in its place** *Cs.* 2. *ráṅ-snaṅ yul-méd bstán-du γsol Glr.* was explained: what has no place in my mind, what I do not know or understand, I beg you to teach me. — *yúl-ts'o* **village, borough,** = *gróṅ-ts'o*. — **yul-ts'ód-zum-k'an* W.* landsurveyor, engineer. — *yul-γžis* v. *γžis*. — *yul-bzáṅ* fair weather *Cs.*, yet cf. *yul-ṅán*. — *yúl-yod-pa* = *yúl-čan Cs.* — *yúl-len* the mode of forwarding letters from village to village, instead of expediting them in longer and regular stages. — *yul-bšád* geography or topography. — *yul-sá* dwelling-place, habitation *W.* — *yul-srid* government of a country *Schr.* — *yul-sréd* = *yul-la ₒdód-pa* attachment to one's native place, the love of country and of home, *Mil.*

ཡུལ་བ་ *yúl-ba*, less corr. spelling for *nyúl-ba Tar.*

ཡུས་ *yus* 1. **boasting, bragging, puff,** *yus če don čuṅ Mil.* much bragging, and nothing in it, *yus če šes čuṅ Mil.* one that boasts much, and knows very little; *yus brjod-pa, byed-pa* to boast *Cs.* — 2. **pride,** *k'oṅ yus ma če žig* do not take too much pride in your heart *Mil.*; *lás-la byas yus čé-na ṅó-so čuṅ* the more a man is pleased with himself after his deed, the less (real) happiness. — 3. **blame, charge, accusation** *Schr.* (?), false accusation *Sch.* (?), *yus byéd-pa* to charge, accuse *Schr.* — 4. **ardour, fervour, transport,** *dád-pai yús-kyis* in the fervour of devotion, e.g. to shed tears, to fall down on the ground *Pth.* — 5. *yus ₒtúd-pa* to fasten one cord to another, **to knit or join things together** *Sch.*

ཡེ་ *ye*, 1. *Cs.*: '*yé-ma* **beginning and eternity,** *ye-ldán* **eternal'.** This word is known to me only as an adv., **completely, perfectly, highly, quite**; *yé-nas* id.; *ye-dág* quite clean, *ye-rdzógs* quite perfect, *yé-nas bzáṅ-po* altogether good; with a negative following, **not at all,** *ye ma ₒdod* I felt no inclination at all, *ye ma žig-par ₒdug Mil.* he was not hurt at all, *yé-nas mi byed dgos* that is not to be done by any means; *ye-šés* (vulgo *Ld.* **'i-šes**) ज्ञान, the perfect, absolute, heavenly, divine **wisdom**; less frq. resp. *ye-mkyén*; *ye-šés lṅa* the five kinds of divine wisdom, of which, acc. to some, every Buddha is possessed, acc. to others, only Adibuddha; *ye-šés*, in a great measure at least, is inherent to all great saints and divine beings; it will suddenly break forth from the bodies of the terrifying gods in the shape of fire, which puts the demons to flight *Glr.*; *rań-byúń ye-šés* the self-originated wisdom occasionally is personified in a similar manner, as Wisdom is in the Proverbs of Solomon; in later times this conception coincides in the popular mind also with *stoń-pa-nyid.* — 2. provinc. for *yin Glr.* 75. — 3. provinc. for ... *am*, *K̒yed blá-ma-čan ₒgró-ye Mil.* are you going to the Lama? — 4. in comp. for *ye-šés*, v. *ye-ťig.* — 5. num. figure: 114.

ཡེ་ཏིག་ *ye-ťig Sch.*: **'the trace, line, or manifestation of divine wisdom'.**

ཡེ་དངས་ *ye-dáńs Bal.* for *nyid-rán*, **you,** the pronoun of polite address.

ཡེ་འབྲོག་ *ye-ₒbróg* a contagious disease *Cs.*; acc. to oral explanation: **injury inflicted on the soul, harm done to the mind,** which may take place in 360 different ways *Mil.* —

ཡེ་རང་ *ye-ráń* n. of a city, next to Khobom (Katmandu), the first in Nepal *Mil.*

ཡེ་རེ་ *ye-ré* v. *yér-re-ba.*

ཡེ་ཤུ་ *yé-šu* **Jesus** *Chr. Prot.*

ཡེགས་པ་ *yégs-pa* **rough, shaggy, hairy** *Cs.*

ཡེང་བ་ *yéń-ba* v. *γyéń-ba.*

ཡེད་པོ་ *yéd-po* provinc. for *yág-po.*

ཡེན་ *yen*, prob. only in *yén-la* joined to *γtóń-ba* and synonyms, **to bestow liberally, amply, plentifully;** *zas dań spyód-lam yen-la γtad-par bya* food and exercise should be amply provided for *Lt.*

ཡེར་ *yer Lt.* = *γnyid-yer* q.v.

ཡེར་པ་ *yér-pa? p̒yág-tu yér-pa žig mdzád-nas* to raise one's hand with the palm turned upward, as a gesture of (willingly or respectfully) **offering,** *Mil.nt.* (This term might perh. be applied to the 'waving' of the wave-offerings, ordained by the Mosaic law.)

ཡེར་བ་ *yér-ba* **sprinkled, sputtered, spouted**(?) *Sch.*

ཡེར་རེ་བ་ *yér-re-ba* **pure, clear, genuine, unadulterated** *Mil.*; *sńo ye-ré* a pure blue, *dkar ye-ré* a pure white *C.*

ཡེལ་ཡེལ་ *yel-yél, Pth.* frq., e.g. *mdańs yel-yél, sems-dgá yel-yél* **clear, light, bright** or something like it(?).

ཡེས་མེས་ *yes-més* **ancestor** *Sch.*

ཡོ་ *yo* numerical figure: 144.

ཡོ་ག་ *yó-ga Ssk.* = *rnal-ₒbyór*, *yó-gi* = *yo-ga-pa*, *yó-gi-ni* = *yó-ga-ma*; more about this word v. *Williams Ssk. Dict.*

ཡོ་བ་ *yó-ba* 1. adj. and sbst., **oblique, sloping, slanting, awry, crooked; obliquity, slope, slant;** *čuń-yó-ba* a little slanting, crooked *Glr.*; *k̒a yo* the mouth awry *S.g.*; *yón-po*, col. **yón-te**, adj., id.; *yo sróń-ba, yón-po bsrań-ba, Lexx.*, to make the crooked straight; **zám-pa yon-yón čo dug* W.* the bridge is unsteady, swings to and fro; fig. **twisted, distorted, perverted, erroneous;** *yon-dpyad* wrong interpretation, false judgment; going crooked ways, **deceitful, crafty,** and sbst. **crookedness,** deceitful dealings *Cs.*; more frq. *γyo.* — 2. **everything, altogether, whole** (?) *Sch.*

ཡོ་བྱད་ *yo-byád*, **tools, implements, chattels, household furniture, necessaries,** *ₒtsó-bai* necessaries of life; *mčod-pai* requisites for sacrificing; *yo-byád sbyór-ba* to procure the needful, to make preparations *Dzl.*; *yo-byád ťams-čád-kyis* (or *bzáń-pos*) *stób-pa Tar.* to provide a person with everything necessary, to fit out well; *yo-byád srél-ba* id. (?) *Sch.*; *yo-byád-kyis ₒbrál-ba* to be in want of the needful; *nor p̒yugs yo-byád* money, cattle, and furniture, as a specification of property.

ཡོ་འབོག་ *yo-ₒbóg Wdń.* n. of a tree, which by the Lamas of Sikim is stated to grow in Tibet; *Sch.*: **elm,** and in another place: *rii yo-ₒbóg* **linden-tree,** less prob.

ཡོག་ *yog* 1. col. but also sometimes in *B.*, for *ₒog* **below, down stairs,** *yog-k̒áń* **ground-floor; cellar.** — 2. v. *γyóg-pa.*

ཡོག་པོ་ *yóg-po* 1. *Sch. yóg-mo, W. yóg-šiṅ,* **pole** or **stick for stirring the fire, poker** *Mil. nt.* — 2. v. *γyóg-po.*

ཡོག་གཅིན་ *yóg-γčin* one that is wetting his bed *Sch.*

ཡོང་བ་ *yóṅ-ba*, pf. *yoṅs*, used throughout Tibet (except in Balti, where they say *'óṅ-čas*); not unfrq. also in later literature, for *ˌóṅ-ba* **to come**; *Sch.* has also *yoṅ-čad (-tsad?)* time and place of coming, and *yoṅ-yé* ever before, at all times (?).

ཡོངས་ *yoṅs*, **all, whole,** *mgo-nág yóṅs-kyi rje Glr.* lord of all the black-haired (i.e. of all men); *yoṅs-ₒdu-ₒtsal-gyi p̓o-bráṅ Mil.* the palace in which all wish to meet, ni f.; *yóṅs-su* adv. **wholly, completely, altogether,** *yóṅs-su dág-pa* quite clean, *yóṅs-su spáṅ-ba* to give up entirely; *yóṅs-su bslád-de* quite lost in perverseness; **generally, universally,** *žes yóṅs-su grágs-so Glr.* so he was universally called; *yóṅs-grágs-kyi bu čen bži Mil.nt.*, four disciples, followers, of universal fame; *sdug-bsṅál-las yóṅs-su ma gról-la Stg.*, seems to mean: he is not yet quite delivered; cf. however *yé-nas* with a negative. — *yoṅs-grúb* **the absolute**, what is independent and complete in itself *Was.* (202). —

ཡོད་པ་ *yód-pa*, resp. and eleg. *mčís-pa* 1. **to be,** = *yin-pa, sgyu yod Dzl.* it is deceit, humbug; often with the termin., like *ₒdúg-pa, dúd-pa ltá-bur yod Glr.* it is smoke-coloured; *šin-tu mtún-par yod ₒdúg-pas Glr.* as they are very intimate with each other; with a participle joined to it (or a gerund, vulgo, esp. in *W.*), *gró-ba yod* **it is becoming, growing, getting** *Pth.*; *šár-p̓yogs-su bstán-pa yod* it is pointing towards the east, *stsál-nas yod* he gives, has given; *brtsig-nas yod* he is building, he was building; *léb(s)-te yod* *W.* he is (has) come; with a root often pleon.: *ṅas bšags yod k̓yod-kyis k̓ol čig Mil.* I have been splitting (the tree), do you carry it away now; *ṅan čén-po byas yod Glr.* he has been committing a great evil; *soṅ yód-pas Pth.* as he was gone. — 2. **to be in a certain place,** *der rdziṅ-bu žig yód-pai ndṅ-na Dzl.* ina pond which is in that place; *ṅai yúl-mi-las bú-mo yód-pa-rnam Dzl.* the girls that are among my subjects; *de náṅ-na yód-k̓an tsáṅ-ma* *W.* all that is in it; *yód-sa*, pop. for *gáṅ-na-ba*, place of abode. — 3. **to exist, to be on hand,** *bdé-ba yod ma yin Pth.* no happiness exists; *čúṅ-zad yod kyaṅ srid-kyis Dzl.* as possibly a little might still be on hand; *'é yod* is, or are there (even now)? *Glr.*; *snáṅ-ba yód-pai dús-su Thgy.* whilst there is day-light. — 4. with genit. or dat. for **to have** (like the Latin *est mihi* I have): *sú-la-ˌaṅ yod ma yin Pth.* nobody has . . .; *rgyál-po-la ₒdód-pa čén-po yód-par ₒdug* the king seems to have yet a great wish; *rgyál-moi γyóg-mo žig yód-pa de Pth.* a maid-servant whom the queen had; so in a like manner without a case: *gri žig yód-pa de Mil.* the knife which he had about (him); *yód-pa Thgy.* the things which one has, τὰ ὑπάρχοντα; *k̓rón-pa ₒdom bču-dgu yód-pa Glr.* a well having a depth of 19 fathoms. — 5. *yód-par ₒgyur* a. fut. of *yód-pa* **shall or will be.** b. **to originate, appear,** *bsáṅs-pai šúl-du da-rúṅ yaṅ yód-par gyúr-nas Dzl.* as in the place of (the gold-pieces) that were taken away, always new ones appeared. c. **to get, receive,** *k̓ri γdugs kyaṅ yód-par gyur čig Dzl.* the throne should also receive a canopy! *yód-par byéd-pa* **to beget, produce, effect,** frq., *bu yód-par gyis šig Dzl.* get her a child!

Comp. *Cs.: yod-pa-nyid* existence, *yod-min-nyid* non-existence; *Sch.: yod-táṅ* 'thoroughly clear'; *yod-tsód yin* 'it has the semblance of being' (?); *yod-med* a. being and not being, *yod-méd go-bzlóg snaṅ* optical illusions, when one imagines to see what is not existing, or the reverse. b. in *W. yod* is also used merely to give force to *med*, as *yod med* there is not at all . . .

ཡོན་ *yon* 1. **gift, offering**, of free will, to priests and mendicant friars, frq., *zás-yon* a gift consisting in food, *yon ₒbúl-ba* to bestow a gift, to bring an offering; *yón-du ₒbúl-ba* to present as a gift; **fee,** *smán-yon* physician's fee *Cs.*; *yon sṅó-ba* to bless the gift received, to return a blessing for it. — 2. = *yon-tan.*

Comp. *yon-mčód* 1. = *yón-bdag Glr.* 2. for *yón-bdag daṅ mčód-γnas Mil.* dispenser (of gifts) and priest. — *yón-bdag* vulgo and in more recent literature for the *sbyín-bdag* of earlier writings, **dispenser of gifts, entertainer, host**, in point of fact identic with **house-owner, citizen, farmer**, and also at the present time used in that sense without any religious bearing; it is also the title generally used by mendicant friars in their addresses, something like 'your honour'. — *yón-γnas* the receiver of a gift *Cs.*

ཡོན་ཏན་ *yón-tan* गुण (opp. to *skyon*) 1. **good quality, excellence, valuable properties**, e.g. the medicinal virtues of plants; also **acquirements, accomplishments, attainments**, *yón-tan slób-pa* to learn something useful *Pth.* and vulgo; *ₒdi bui yón-tan yin Dzl.* for that you are indebted to the boy, this is the boy's merit; **property, quality**, in gen., e.g. the different tastes and effects of medicines *Méd.*; also mystic or fantastic properties *Glr.* — *bdag blus kyaṅ yón-tan med Glr.*, even if one would ransom me, it would be to no purpose, not worth while; *ₒdód(-pai) yón(-tan)* v. *ₒdód-pa*; *p̔an-yon* v. *p̔án-pa*. — 2. num.: 3.

ཡོན་པོ་ *yón-po* v. *yó-ba*.

ཡོབ་, འོབ་ *yob, ₒob*, **stirrup** *Cs.*; *yob-góṅ* instep of the foot *Cs.*; *yob-lčágs* 'the iron of the stirrup' *Cs.*; *yob-čén* = *yob Cs.*; *yob-t̔ág* stirrup-leather *Cs.*, *yob-mt̔il* the footing, *yob-lúṅ* (*Sch. yob-lóṅ*) the hoop of the stirrup.

ཡོབ་པ་ *yób-pa* v. *γyób-pa*.

ཡོམ་པ་ *yóm-pa Cs.* vb., adj. sbst., **to swing, totter, tremble, to be unsteady; swinging etc., the swinging etc.**; *yóm-po*, adj., *yom-yóm Pth.*, *yóm-me-ba Mil.* id.

ཡོར་པོ་ *yór-po* 1. **dull, heavy, blunt** *Cs.*; *Tar.*: *yór-yor-ba*; but the expressions *t̔om-yór* shaking, tottering, trembling, like an old man *Mil.*, and *mig-yór* mirage, seem to indicate that the proper signification is **trembling**. — 2. **oblique, slanting**, *C.*

ཡོལ་གོ་, ཡོལ་མ་ *yól-go, yól-ma* **earthenware, crockery** *Schr.*, *Cs.*, *dkar-yól* **china-ware, porcelain**, frq.; *yol-gór* **cup, bowl**, *Sch.*

ཡོལ་བ་ *yól-ba* I. sbst. **curtain**, *yól-bas ₒbré-ba Glr.* to stretch a curtain over; *yól-ba ten-pa Glr.* to draw a curtain; *yól-ba γčod-pa* to close the curtain (of a door), *yól-ba ₒbyéd-pa* to open it *Cs.*; *dar-yól* silk-curtain, *ras-yól* calico-curtain; *sgo-yól* curtain before a door. — II. vb. 1. **to be past**, *nyi-ma-p̔yed yol* mid-day is past, it is afternoon (about 2 o'cl.) *Wdk.* (v. *nyin-žág*); *srod yol soṅ* the evening-twilight is gone, it is complete night (about 11 o'cl.) *C.*; *nyi-ma yól-la k̔ad* day is almost over, evening is drawing on, *Dzl.* ༢༥, 6; *dús-las yól-ba* **to be past**, both impers., it is past, it is over, and pers., he is past his prime, old, decrepit *Dzl.*; *rluṅ daṅ čar dús-las mi yól-bas* wind and rain setting in and ceasing at the proper time *Dzl.* — 2. also *γyól-ba C.*, *dbyól-ba*, *ₒbyól-ba* **to evade, shun, to go not to a place**, *mig yól-ba* to look away; **lé-yol čém-po yin** he is very shy of work, averse to labour *C.*

ཡོས་ *yos*, 1. **slightly roasted corn**, mostly barley or wheat, which on account of its transportability is generally taken by travellers along with them, as their fare on the road; fresh prepared it is much relished by the people; *ₒbrás-yos* rice, thus prepared *S.g.* — 2. **hare**, but only as an astronomical term, *yós-lo* the hare-year.

གཡག་ *γyag*, चमर, **the yak**, Bos grunniens (reckoned by the Hindu among the antilopes), fem. v. *ₒbri-mo*; *p̔o-γyág* male yak; *p̔a-γyág* uncastrated yak-bull; *γyag-rú* horn of a yak, also n. of a plant, Morina *Ld.*; *γyag-rog-žol-čén* a very long-haired, shaggy yak *Sch.*

གཡང་ *γyaṅ* 1. *Ssk.* श्री, synon. *dpal*, **happiness, blessing, prosperity**, *γyaṅ čágs* blessing comes (from), grows (out of), nif. *Mil.*; *šor* it departs, it is gone; *γyaṅ-skyób*, *γyaṅ-ₒgúgs Schl.* 263, **yaṅ-k̔úg* W.* a calling forth of blessing, sacrifices and other ceremonies performed, in order to secure happiness and prosperity. — *γyaṅ-skár* **propitious stars** or **aspects**; the lunar mansions no. ༢

to ??? v. rgyu-skár. — γyaṅ-k̔úg beggar's bag of the Lamas. — γyáṅ-čan happy, blessed, prosperous, γyaṅ-méd the contrary. — γyaṅ-yig a written benediction Glr. — γyaṅ-lhá a deity of the Shamans, dispensing happiness Sch. — 2. gulf, abyss, gen. γyáṅ-sa also γyaṅ-γzáṅ; ǰi-tsam mto bžin γyáṅ-sa če so high as you stand, so deep is the gulf; lus γyáṅ-du γtóṅ-ba to plunge, to precipitate one's self Dzl.; γyáṅ-du or γyáṅ-la ltúṅ-ba to fall down Dzl.; mčóṅ-ba to leap Glr.; ṅán-soṅ-gi γyáṅ-la ˳k̔or Pth. he totters on the brink of the abyss of hell; γyáṅ-sa-las ˳dzin-pa to snatch from the abyss, to save Thgy.; brag-γyaṅ-γzár rocky precipice Mṅg.

གཡང་ཏི་ γyaṅ-ti Sch.: 'the precious stone chas'.

གཡང་ཚེ་ γyaṅ-tsé Mil. nt., C. a bowl or cup of clay or wood.

གཡང་ལྤགས་ γyaṅ-lúgs C. also yaṅ-lús, = γzán-gos skin of an animal, used for clothing; Mil. also fig.: bzód-pai γyaṅ-lúgs gyon he wrapped himself in the mantle of patience; γyaṅ-γži Lex. अजिन, skin of an antilope, the customary couch of the members of religious orders; also skin, couch, covering, in general Pth.

གཡན་པ་ γyán-pa Lexx. w.e. Sch.: a cutaneous eruption, akin to the itch, which is said to invade any part of the body, and to be combined with a copious discharge of matter; hereditary, and not contagious.

གཡབ་ γyab, γyáb-pa, γyáb-mo v. yab etc.

གཡམ་ γyam Sch.: 'the following a good or bad example, with the respective consequences(?)'.

གཡམ་པ་ γyám-pa Sch.: 'a certain stone'; *yam-p̔áṅ* W. a slab of slate, roof-slate, for γya-spáṅ.

གཡའ་ γya 1. rust, incorr. verdigris; lčags-γyá id.; lčags gya čags Lt. iron rusts; *ya k̔or, or ǰuṅ, or yoṅ* W. id.: *ya čád-če* W. to scrape the rust off (from metals), to clean, polish; γya-dág-pa freed from rust, clear, polished, e.g. a mirror; γyá-pa rusty Sch.; fig. for infection, contamination Mil.; γya ˳drúl-ba to be mouldy Sch. or more corr. to get rusty, to get covered with foul extraneous matter; lčé-la γya-˳drúl byed Lt. the tongue gets furred. — 2. also γyá-ma, vulgo *yá-máṅ*, slate, slab of slate; γya-spáṅ 1. id. 2. Cs. also oil of vitriol, sulphuric-acid(?) 3. in C. verdigris; γya-tig 1. a line drawn with a slate- or lead-pencil. 2. slate-pencil, lead-pencil, also γya-smyúg. 3. bolt, bar, γya rgáb-pa to bolt, to bar, γya p̔yé-ba to unbolt, to unbar; γyá-šir = γya; *˳dzin-ya* C. pin. — 4. v. γyá-ba.

གཡའ་ཀྱི་མ་ γyá-kyi-ma Lt. n. of a plant, in Lh. a small high-alpine Saussurea.

གཡའ་བ་ γyá-ba 1. to shrink, to start up, in consequence of a sudden irritation, tickling etc., to shudder, skyi-γya-ba id. Mil.; W.: *ya čúg-če* to cause to shrink or start, to tickle, Cs. also: γyá-ba to feel a horror. — 2. to itch, dei lus γyá-bas Dzl. because he felt an itching.

གཡའ་ཡ་ γyá-ya C. *yá-ya* yes! in speaking to inferiors.

གཡའ་ལི་ γyá-li maple Sik.; the dried leaves of it are said to be boiled by the poor instead of tea.

གཡར་དམ་ γar-dám Lex., oath(?) Sch.

གཡར་བ་ γyár-ba to borrow, to lend; to hire; with reference to money, only provinc. (Lh., Ts.); p̔o-braṅ-nas már-me γyár-te Glr. having borrowed a lamp in the castle; γnas-tsáṅ γyár-ba Tar., C., *dáṅ-sa yár-če* W. with la, to ask for reception, night-quarters; k̔áṅ-pa γyár-mk̔an lessee, tenant, lodger; γyar byed-pa = γyár-ba Sch.; *p̔an-yár čo-če* W. to succour a person by an advance of money; p̔a-γyár step-father, ma-γyár step-mother, bu-γyár adopted child; γyár-po credit for what has been lent, advanced; *yár-po táṅ-če* W. to lend, a thing, Schr. to let, lodgings.

གཡར་ཚུས་ γyar-tsus food, nourishment, victuals Sch.

གཡས་པ་ γyás-pa right, γyás-ma the right hand, γyás-na on the right (hand), γyás-su to the right, γyás-nas from the right;

mig-γyás the right eye, *lag-γyás* the right hand, *rkaṅ-γyás* the right foot; *γyas-ṅos*, *-p̔yógs*, *-lógs* the right (hand) side: *γyas-γyón* right and left; *γyas-γyón-la ltá-ba* to look all round; *γyas-rú* 1. the right wing. 2. p.n., district in *Ts.*; **Yé-ru tsáṅ-po** n. of the principal river in Tibet v. *tsáṅ-po*.

གཡི་, དབྱི་ *γyi, dbyi* **lynx** (*Cs.* erron. ermine).

གཡིག(ས)་པ་ *γyig(s)-pa* **to be hindered** *Cs.*; *Lex.*: *γyér-mas γyigs-pa?*

གཡུ་ *γyu* **turkois,** *mdún-γyu* the front-turkois in the head-dress of females; *p̔rá-γyu* little turkois-stones; *γyui* frq. for turkois-blue; **yu-dán** *W.* the ribbon on which the turkois-stones of the head-dress are fastened; *γyu-mtsó* a blue-glittering lake, po. *Mil.*; **yu-žún-men-tog** forget-me-not *Sp*; *γyu-rál* a mane of turkois-colour *Glr.* — *γyu-rúṅ* for *γyuṅ-druṅ Glr.*

གཡུག་པ་ *γyúg-pa*, incorr. spelling for *dbyúg-pa.* —

གཡུང་དྲུང་ *γyuṅ-drúṅ*, **स्वस्तिका** (also *γža-γsaṅ*), **the cross cramponee** ⊹, the principal symbol of the Bonpos, but also much in favour in Buddhist mysticism and popular superstition; *γyuṅ-drúṅ-pa* = *bón-po*; *γyuṅ-drúṅ dgón-pa* the Buddhist monastery Lama Yurru in Ladak, v. Cunningham.

གཡུང་བ་ *γyúṅ-ba* **tame,** opp. to *rgod.*

གཡུང་མོ་ *γyúṅ-mo* (*Lex.* **छिम्बिका**, **a libidinous woman**), *Cs.*: 'a woman having always the menses'.

གཡུར་ *γyur* 1. **sleep** *Sch.* — 2. v. *γyul-k̔a.*

གཡུར་བ་ *γyúr-ba Lex.*, *C.* also **yór-ba** **to droop, to hang or sink down,** of fading flowers etc.; *γyur zá-ba Lex.* w.e.; *Sch.*: what has become ripe and eatable.

གཡུལ་ *γyul Schr.*: **army;** *Cs.*: **battle;** neither of the two meanings appears to be quite exact (cf. *dmag*); prob. both *γyul* and *γyul-ṅó* denote an army facing the enemy and ready for battle; *γyúl-las rgyál-ba* and *p̔ám-pa* to conquer and to be conquered frq.; *γyul ˳gyéd-pa Do.*, *spród-pa Do.*, *Pth.*, *˳t̔áb-pa* to fight, strive, struggle, *daṅ* with; *γyúl-du* or *γyul-ṅor žúgs-pa* to go to battle *Do.*; *γyul šóm-pa* to prepare for battle *Lex.*; *dug lṅai γyúl-ṅo zlóg-pa* to repulse the warlike host of the five poisons *Mil.*

གཡུལ་ཁ་, གཡུལ་འཐག་ *γyul-k̔a*, *γyul-˳t̔ag* **thrashing-floor;** both these words appear to be not everywhere current, but provinc., cf. *k̔o-γyu*; *γyul-k̔a γčóg-pa Sch.*, **yur ǰhé-pa** *C.* **to thrash.**

གཡེང་བ་ *γyéṅ-ba*, less frq. *yéṅ-ba*, pf. *(γ)yeṅs*, **to move a thing softly to and fro,** e.g. an infant on one's arms, to lull it to sleep *Thgy.*; esp. with reference to the water: *čus γyeṅs-te* moved by the waves to and fro *Dzl.*; fig. to run to and fro, like a hunted hare *Ma.*; **to stream into, to overflow,** *yul-k̔áms-su* a country, to inundate it, of floods, hostile armies etc *Ma.*; **to rummage, turn over,** *dpé-rnams* books *Mil* — 2. **to turn off the attention, to disturb the mind,** *rgyál-po spyan γyéṅs-pa daṅ Glr.* the king looking away, directing his attention to something else; *sems bdud-kyis γyeṅs Mil.* the soul is disturbed by the devil; *čos ˳dód-pa-rnams γyéṅs-par byéd-pa Thgy.* to put out or confound those that are seeking religion; *ma-γyéṅs-par nyón čig* now be all attention! *γyéṅ-ba*, *γyéṅs-pa* sbst., **inattention, wandering, absence of mind,** *γyéṅs-su ˳ǰúg-pa Thgr.* to give one's self to inattention; adj. *rnám-par γyéṅs-pa* very absent, wandering; *rnám-par mi-γyéṅ-ba* or *-γyéṅs-pa* quite attentive, not to be disturbed by anything, inexcitable, a character in which Buddha excels, and which every one of his followers must strive to attain. — 3. sbst. *γyéṅs-pa* **diversion, pleasure, recreation,** **yáṅ(s)-pa-la čá-če**, resp. **t̔ug-yáṅ(s)-la (s)kyód-če** *W.* to take a walk, **yáṅ(s)-pa sé-če** *W.* to be playful, like children, kittens etc.; **jest, joke,** **yáṅ-pa man, don-dám yin** *W.* I am not joking, I am serious; **yáṅ(s)-pa-čan** *W.* jester, buffoon; *yéṅs-˳dod-kyi k̔a-krám ma yin Mil.*, these are no falsehoods spoken in jest. — *γyéṅs-ma*, a wanton female, prostitute *Sch.*

གཡེན་ *γyen?* *γyen-sbyór-ba S.g.* **to calumniate** ni f.

གཡེམ་པ་ *γyém-pa, Lex.* **मिथ्याचर्या, being untrue** in one's dealings, acting **wrongfully,** which also my referees confirmed to be the general import of the word; in books, however, it is usually joined to *ₒdód-pas,* or *ₒdód-pa-la,* adding *lóg-par,* as: *ₒdód-pa-la lóg-par γyém-pa,* or it stands alone as in *γyém byéd-pa,* signifying **'to commit adultery, fornication'** *Dzl* and elsewh.; *log-γyém* sbst. —

གཡེར་ཁ་ *γyér-ka* (vulg. **'er-ka*), **bell, set of bells,** or **peal** *Glr.*

གཡེར་པོ་ *γyér-po* **wise, prudent, circumspect, thorough-going** *Sch.*

གཡེར་བག་ *γyer-bág Lex., Sch.:* **a light, luminous place.**

གཡེར་མ་ *γyér-ma Med.* frq., **Guinea pepper,** *Capsicum W. *nyér-ma*; γyer-šiṅ-pa* medicinal herb *S.g.*

གཡེལ་བ་ *γyél-ba* 1. **to be idle, lazy, slothful; idleness, laziness;** *γyel-ba-méd-par* incessantly, continually, e.g. to pray, to guard *Mil., S.O.* — 2. *ṭugs γyél-ba* resp. to forget *W.*

གཡོ་ *γyo* (rarely *yo*) **craft, cunning, deceit,** more frq. *γyo-sgyú, γyo-zól; γyó-čan* crafty, deceitful, *γyo-méd* honest, *γyo byéd-pa* to deceive.

གཡོ་བ་ *γyó-ba* I. vb., pf. and imp. *γyos,* 1. **to move,** to cause to change place; **to be moved,** agitated, shaken, *γnam sa γyós-so* heaven and earth were shaken *Dzl.; des ni sa ₒdi γyo-bar ₒgyur* thereby the earth may be shaken *Do.;* **to bend, incline, tilt,** e.g. a vessel; **zúg-po yos toṅ* W.* make a bow! *sku γyós-par ₒgyúr-to* the image began to move *Glr.; sa-γyós* earthquake; **to begin to move** or to march *Ma.; ṭugs-rje ytiṅ-nas γyós-pai rtags* it is a sign that his heart is moved by grace *Mil. nt.; dgé-bai p̔yógs-la ₒdu-šés čuṅ-zad kyaṅ ma γyos* he did not allow the least virtuous impulses to rise (in his heart), he kept down every sense of virtue; *γyó-ba* partic., continually moving, restless, uneasy, of the mind *Mil., mi-γyó-ba* **unmoved,** immovable, n. of Siva and of other terrifying deities *Glr.* (cf. **अचल** *Will.*) — 2. **to prepare,** victuals for the table *γyós-subyéd-pa* id.; *γyós-kaṅ* kitchen, bake-house, *γyós-mkan* baker, cook.

II. sbst. **moveableness, mobility,** *yáṅ-žiṅ γyo-ba-nyíd* an easy mobility *Wdṅ.*

གཡོག་ *γyog* (v. *yog, ₒog*) *Tar.* and elsewh., usually occurring in the more definite form *γyóg-po,* **servant, man-servant,** *γyóg-mo* **maid-servant, female servant,** waiting-maid; when distinguished from *kól-po, kól-mo* and *bran,* it denotes a higher degree, e.g. *γyóg-mo γnyis* two waiting-maids and besides 500 *kól-mo* maid-servants *Pth.; γyóg-po daṅ yáṅ-γyog daṅ nyíṅ-γyog* servant, servant's servant, and the servant again of these *Pth.; mii γyog byéd-pa* to be in a person's service, to obey a person; *dpon-γyóg* master (mistress) and domestics, master and attendants, frq.; *nad-γyóg,* a nurse, one that tends sick persons *Dzl.; γyog-ₒkór* attendants, e.g. *γyog-ₒkór bču-drúg* attendants and retinue of 16 persons, *ₒkor daṅ γyog* id.

གཡོག་ནང་ཟན་ *γyog-naṅ-zán* a house-servant *C.* —

གཡོག་པ་ *γyóg-pa,* pf. and imp. *γyogs,* rarely *yóg-pa* 1. **to cover,** *bu gós-kyis γyóg-pa* to cover a child with a garment *Dzl., mgó-la rdzá-ma γyóg-pa* to cover one's head with a pot *Glr.;* also: *rdzá-mai mgó-la drá-bas γyóg-pa* to cover the opening of a pot with a wire grate *Glr.; p̔yii págs-pa γyogs* the external cutaneous covering appears (in the embryo) *S.g.; ri-mgo ka-bas γyogs* the hill-tops were covered with snow *Mil.;* **to pour over** or **upon,** to cover in pouring, *krág-gis* with blood *Dzl.;* **to overlay,** with gold *Dzl.;* **to sprinkle over, besprinkle,** **sig-pa-la ṭág* W.* the wall with blood; **to strew over,** **ká-la gog-ṭál* W.* ashes over the snow. — 2. **to pour away,** to throw away; so *W.;* the people in *W.* understand the words *Dzl.* ༩༩, 6: **ma yógs-pai lhág-ma** the rest which has not been thrown away, whereas others, e.g. the people of Sikkim explain it: the rest that has not been taken possession or care of.

གཡོགས་ *γyogs* 1. **cover, covering,** *mgo-γyógs Lex.* covering for the head, cap; also fig. and po. for self-delusion, self-deception (prop.: a veiling of the head) *Mil.*; *steṅ-γyógs, stod-γyógs* upper-garment, mantle, toga, *smad-γyógs* trowsers, breeches *Tar.* — 2. **cover, envelope,** *γyógs-čan* having a cover.

གཡོད་ *γyod C.* the large intestine, colon.

གཡོན་ཅན་ *γyón-čan Pth*; *Cs.* = *γyó-čan* crafty; perh. also **fornicator**, as *γyón-ma*, acc. to *Lex.* and *Sch.*: harlot.

གཡོན་པ་ *γyón-pa* **left**, *γyón-ma* the left hand, *γyón-na* on the left, to the left, *γyón-du* towards the left, *γyón-nas* from the left; *γyón-lógs* the left side or hand, *γyon-lág-byed-pa Pth.* left-handed, *γyon-rú Sch.* the left wing, of an army.

གཡོབ་པ་ *γyób-pa*, pf. *γyobs* **to move about, to swing, brandish,** *γšóg-pa* the wings; *rkaṅ-lág γyób-pa* to kick, to strike, with the arms and legs.

གཡོར་མོ་ *γyór-mo* 1. **sail**, *γyor-yól* id *Cs.*, *γyor-šiṅ* sail-yard *Cs.*, also mast, in a rather obscure description of a ship in *Zam.*, where the sail is called *dar*, cloth. — 2. **wave, billow,** *rgyá-mtsoi Glr.*

Note. Tibetan writers knowing of ships and navigation about as much as a blind man of colours, the obscurity of passages relating to such matters may easily be accounted for.

གཡོར་བ་ *γyór-ba* 1. v. *γyúr-ba*. — 2. v. *γyár-ba*. — 3. v. *yor*.

གཡོལ་བ་ *γyól-ba* v. *yól-ba*.

གཡོས་ *γyos* 1. prov. for *γyas*, in *γyos-skór* circumambulation from left to right (so that the right side is towards the person or object that is reverentially to be saluted) *Wdṅ.* — 2. v. *γyo-ba*.

ར

ར *ra* 1. the consonant r, always pronounced with the tongue. — 2. num. fig.: 25.

ར་ *ra* stands for: 1 *rá-ba*, 2. *rá-ma*, 3. *rá-mda*, 4. *rá-ro*.

རྭ་ *rwa* (cf. *ru*) 1. **horn** *W.* **rá-čó** id. — 2. **sting** e.g. of the scorpion. — 3. *Sch.*: 'the inward side, the horn-side, of a bow'. — *rwa-čan* horned. — *rwa-snyiṅ* the pith of a horn *Cs.* — *rwa-myúg* 'the first germ of seed that appears after sowing' *Cs.*; *rwá-rtsa* 'the root or bottom of a horn' *Cs.*, *rwá-rtse* 'the top or point of a horn' *Cs.*, *rwá-tsa S.g.* (?).

ར་གན་ *rá-gan*, in comp. *rag*, **brass**, *rá-gan-gyi búm-pa*, *rag-búm* brass cup, can, vessel, *rag-dúṅ* a brass trumpet; *rag-skyá Sch.*: white-copper, packfong, German silver.

ར་སྒོ་ *rá-sgo* hoof, claw *C.*, *W.*

ར་ཉེ་ *rá-nye*, provinc. for *žá-nye* **lead.**

ར་མཉེ་ *rá-mnye* an officinal root *Med.*, *Sch.*: **carrot.**

ར་ཏི་ *rá-ti Cs.*: 'a small weight, a drachm (60 grains)'; but रती (not to be found in *Will.*) is prob. the Hindi word for रत्तिका, the seed or grain of *Abrus precatorius*, as a weight about = 2 grains.

ར་མདའ་ *rá-mda* **help, assistance** (*Cs.* also: companion, **assistant**), *rá-mda ˳bód-pa* to cry out for help *Glr.*, *rá-mdar sbrón-pa Cs.* to call (upon a person) for assistance, *ra ˳dégs-pa W.* **ram tág-če** (cf. *žabs ˳dégs-pa*) **to help,** to assist *Sch.*, *ra ˳drén-pa* id. *Mil. nt.*; *rá-mda-pa* **helper, assistant** *Glr.*; *rá-mdai dpuṅ-tsóg* **auxiliary forces** or army *Cs.*

ར་སྡོང་ *ra-sdóṅ Sch.* **weeping willow.**

ར་སྣ་ *ra-sná* n. of a medicinal herb *Wdṅ.* 166, = *sgrón-šiṅ* fir-tree.

ར་བ་ *rá-ba* 1. **enclosure, fence, wall,** frq., esp. in *W.*, also the space inclosed by a fence, wall etc., **yard, court-yard, pen, fold** etc.; *rá-bas skór-ba* to inclose with a fence *Stg.*, *rá-čan*(?), *ra-ldán* having an enclosure, fence, wall etc. *Cs.*; *smyúg-mai rá-ba* bamboo-hedge, bamboo-fence, *ts̔ér-mai rá-ba* thorn-hedge, thorn-fence, *šiṅ-gi rá-ba* wooden fence, fence of boards, pickets or rails *C.*; *rá-mo* id., *ra-mo-čé* a large pen or fold *Mil.* and *C.*; *kun-dga-rá-ba*, *k̔ún-ra*, v. *kun*; *k̔ríms-ra* place of execution; *lčáṅ-ra* garden with willow-trees; *nyág-ra*(?) wall of stones put loosely together *Ld.*; *rtá-ra* stable or pen for horses; *rdó-ra* 1. stone-wall. 2. circle of dancers; *p̔ág-ra* v. *rags*. — *bá-ra* cow-house, pen for cows; *rtsig-ra Sch.*: wall round a court-yard; *brtsón-ra* v. *brtson*; *lúg-ra* sheepcot, sheepfold; *šiṅ-ra* v. above. — *ra-šúl* the remnants or traces of an old pen. — 2. the first of the three (or two) months of a season, *zla ra-ba*.

ར་མ་ *rá-ma* (rarely *ra Glr.*) **goat, she-goat,** frq. — *ra-kyál* bag made of a goat's skin. — *ra-skyés Tar.*; *Sch.*: a gelded he-goat. — *rá-gu*, col. *rí-gu*, young goat, **kid.** — *ra-rgód* wild goat, = *ra-po-čé Cunningh. Ld.* p. 199. — *ra-t̔úg S.g.* and *p̔á-ra* he-goat. — *ra-t̔óṅ* 1. a he-goat of two years *C.* 2. a gelded he-goat *W.* — *ra-dó*(?) thread made of goat's hair *W.* — *ra-lpágs* goat's skin. — *ra-p̔ó* a gelded he-goat. — *ra-lúg* goats and sheep; *ra-ma-lúg* id., when a particular stress is laid on the impropriety of both species of animals being mixed together; also fig. of improper intermixtures. — *ra-šá* goat's flesh. — *ra-slóg* a coat made of goat's skins.

ར་མེད་ *ra-méd* **infallible,** certain, sure *Sch.*

ར་མོ་ཆེ་ *ra-mo-čé* n. of a plain near Lhasa where the Chinese wife of *Sroṅbtsansgampo* ordered a large Buddhist temple to be built *Glr.*; as a com noun v. sub *rá-ba*.

ར་རི་ *ra-ri Sch.*: *ra-ri-méd-pa* neither high nor low.

ར་རིལ་ *ra-ril* **treddles, dung** of goats.

ར་རེས་ *ra-rés* = *rés-mos*, **skyid dug ra-rés yoṅ dug** *Ld.* good fortune and misfortune come by turns.

ར་རོ་ *rá-ro* 1. **intoxication, drunkenness.** — 2. **intoxicated** *B.* and col.; *Sch.*: *rá-ro dáṅ-po bag-méd-pa*, v. sub *bag* I. *rá-ro γnyis-pa glaṅ-po-če smyon-pa daṅ ₒdra* drunkenness while continued resembles a furious elephant, *rá-ro γsúm-pa ši-ro ₒdra* the end (of it) resembles a corpse; *ra ži* or *saṅs*, also *γdaṅs* (?) *W.* the drunken fit is over; *rá-ro-ba B.*, *C.*, *rá-ro(-čan) W.* intoxicated, drunk, *rá-ro-bar byéd-pa* to make drunk *Dzl.*, *rá-ro-ba-las sáṅs-te* having come to one's self again after a drunken fit, being sober again *Dzl.*

ར་ས་འཕྲུལ་སྣང་ *ra-sa-ₒp̔rul-snáṅ* n. of a Buddhist temple erected in Lhasa by the Nepalese wife of *Sroṅbtsansgampo Glr.*

ར་སི་ *rá-si Hind.* **rope,** in *Lh.* **hempen rope,** and as such distinguished from *t̔ág-pa*, rope made of goat's hair, which is the one most in use in Tibet.

ར་སིད་ *ra-sid* (Pers. رسيد), **receipt,** **ra-sid ṭi-ked** money-stamp.

རཱ་ཧུ་ and རཱ་ཧུ་ལ་ *rā-hu* and *rā-hu-la* v. *sgra-γčán*.

རཀྟ་ *rakta Ssk.* **blood, saffron, minium, cinnabar** *Mil.*

རག་ *rag* 1. sbst. v. *ra-gán*. — 2. adj. (*Ssk.*: *adhīna*) subject, subservient, dependent, *rag lás-pa* or *lús-pa B.*, *C.*, *W.*, **rag-ldom-pa** *W.*, with *la*, **to depend on,** *de k̔yód-kyi nús-pa-la rag-lús* that depends on your strength *Mil.*; *dbugs rṅúb-pa sems-la rag-lás-pa yin* breathing depends on the soul *Stg.*; *ₒtsó-ba γžán-la rag-lás-šiṅ* as they depend on others for their lives *Tar.*; *Bhar.* 22 *k̔yod rgyal-srid byed-la rag-go Schf.*: 'regno operam nava!' — 3. *W.* for *reg*, *grags*, *dregs*, *sbrag*, v. *rag-pa*; *rag-čan W.* for *drégs-pa-čan* **proud,** haughty; for *grágs-čan* **famous; glorious, splendid; angry** (?).

རག་པ་ *rág-pa* 1. vb. *W.* for *rég-pa* **to touch, feel,** and in a more generalized sense

= ˳ts̓ór-ba **to perceive,** to scent, taste, hear, see, e.g. **dáṅ-mo rag** I feel cold, **dáṅ-mo rag-ga** do you feel cold? (but **dáṅ-mo dug** it is cold); **gó-la zug rag** (*C. *rig**) my head aches; **tóg-ri rag** I feel hungry, **tóg-ri rág-ga** are you hungry? **ṅai miṅ žód-du rag** I hear my name called; **go k̓ád-da rag** I perceive the door sticks; **'i lúṅ-po k̓yér-ra rag** I see, the wind will carry that away; **go p̓é-te mi rag** the door seems to be locked. — 2. adj. **dark-russet, brownish,** of rocks, horses *W.*

རག་མ་ *rág-ma* 1. *W.* adj. to the gerund **rág-te** (*sbrág-ste*): **be-rág yu-dán** (lit. *ydan*) **rág-te** a fillet together with a strip set with turkoises. — 2. prop. n. of a village *Mil.*

རག་ཙེ་ *rág-tse* **stone** in fruits *W.*

རག་ཤ་ *rág-ša* **a bead of a rosary,** acc. to *Lis̓.* from रुद्राक्ष Elaeocarpus Janitrus, the berries of which are used for such beads.

རག་ཤི་ *rag-ší* n. of a country.

རགས་ *rags* 1. **dam, mole, dike, embankment,** also *č̓u-rágs, č̓u-lón* — 2. any construction of a similar shape: *p̓ág-rags* (also *p̓ág-ra*) **intrenchment, breast-work;** *p̓úb-rags* stack, rick; *šiṅ-rágs* stack of wood.

རགས་པ་ *rágs-pa* **coarse, thick, gross,** *lús-kyi rnám-pa p̓ra-rágs-rnams Wdṅ.* the more delicate and the coarser component parts of the body; *rags-pai dbáṅ-du byás-na Wdṅ.*, reckoning one with another, on an average; **rough,** as in: *rágs-rtsis-su* by a rough estimate *Tar.*; *rágs-pai mi-rtág-pa daṅ p̓rá-bai mi-rtág-pa* the perishableness of the whole mass and of the single parts *Thgy.*; *yán-lag rágs-pa* prob.: strong, firm limbs *Pth.*; of Buddhas is said that they appear *rágs-pai ts̓úl-gyis* i.e. **bodily,** or **substantially;** *rags-ris byed-pa Sch.:* to work, mould, form, sketch etc. roughly.

རང་ *raṅ* 1. **self** *B.* and col. (*nyid*, with few exceptions, is, in *W.* at least, colloquially not in use) *ṅa-ráṅ k̓yod-ráṅ* **I myself, thou thyself** etc., in col. language also = **I, thou** etc.; sometimes the person is only indicated by the context, the pronoun I etc. being omitted; *raṅ-čag, ráṅ-rnams* plur.; *ráṅ-gi* my, thy etc.; *č̓úṅ-ma de ráṅ-gi lús-la č̓ágs-pas* this wife fond of herself, in love with herself *Dzl.* (yet cf. *de-ráṅ*, below); *des ráṅ-gi ma yin-par rig-nas* he perceiving that it was his own mother *Pth.*; *ráṅ-la ráṅ-gis skra bčád-de* shaving one's own head *Dzl.*; also in a gen. sense: *ráṅ-bas ṅán-pa* an inferior person than one's self *Thgy.*, in like manner: *ráṅ-las č̓é-ba Thgr.*; *ráṅ-la bu méd-na* if a man has no son of his own *Mil.*; *ráṅ-gi srúṅ-ba* to keep, to guard one's own property *Thgy.*; **raṅ mi-˳dód-pe kyen ts̓áṅ-ma* C.* all the disagreeable things that fall to one's lot; in compounds: *raṅ-séms* one's own soul (opp. to *yžan-lús*) *Mil.*; v. also *˳dré-ba* extr.; *raṅ-rig raṅ-ysal raṅ-bde ysum* self-created knowledge, clearness, and happiness (the three fruits of the spirit) *Mil.*; *raṅ-sróg ráṅ-gis yčod* you will take your own life *Glr.* — 2. **spontaneously, of one's own accord,** *žal-zás raṅ-˳óṅ-ṅo Dzl.*; *ráṅ-byon-pa, ráṅ-byuṅ-ba* originated of itself, v. below; *raṅ ˳gról-ba* 1. to get loose, come loose of itself. 2. to become clear or intelligible spontaneously, by intuition. 3. to save one's self; *ráṅ-šar-ba* = *ráṅ-˳grol-ba* 2. — 3. **just, exactly, precisely, the very,** *de ráṅ* the very same; *de raṅ yin* so it is! exactly so! just so! **dhá-ta raṅ* C.*, **dá-či raṅ, dág-sa raṅ* W.* just-now, **dí-riṅ raṅ* just to-day *W.*; **already,** *sṅá-mo raṅ* already early in the morning *Mil.*; **barely, merely, the mere, the very,** *ṅa daṅ p̓rád-pa ráṅ-gis* by the mere meeting with me *Mil.*; *mi raṅ* a person travelling all alone, i.e. without baggage, horse or companion *Kun.*; *mo-ráṅ* v. *mo.* — **really, indeed, actually, truly** (the verb being repeated): *mi-la-rás-pa de yin raṅ yin-nam?* art thou really that same Milaraspa? **yoṅ raṅ yoṅ-gyu yin* C.* he will truly or certainly come; **even,** *sdáṅ-po raṅ byas* now they even hated him *Mil.*

Comp. *raṅ-skal* a person's own share. — *raṅ skyu* (?) *t̓úb-pa Sch.:* to act after one's own mind. — *raṅ-skyur* vinegar *Cs.*(?)

— raṅ-ḱa Sch. = ráṅ-bu? — raṅ-ḱóṅs = raṅ-ḱúl territory, district C. (?) — raṅ-°ḱós one's own worth, affairs, necessities Sch. — raṅ-grub not made or produced by men, **self-produced.** — ráṅ-dga-ba **free, independent,** ráṅ-dga-pa an unmarried man Sch. — raṅ-rgyál 1. Stg.: = raṅ-saṅs-rgyás. 2. raṅ-rgyál-gyis °gró-ba Sch.: to live after one's own option or pleasure (?) — raṅ-rgyú Sch.: 'die eigene Ursache, Selbstfolge' (?!) — raṅ-ṅó one's own nature, śes-pa to know Mil. — raṅ-nyid himself, herself etc., one's self Mil., raṅ-nyid °gról-ba to deliver one's self Thgy., bdud raṅ-nyíd the devil himself in his own person Tar. — raṅ-°ťág **mill, water-mill.** — raṅ-mťóṅ **pride,** self-complacency, self-sufficiency Mil., Glr. — raṅ-dón one's own affairs, one's own profit, raṅ-dón byéd-pa to look to one's own advantage Do., raṅ-°dód **selfishness,** v. raṅ-rtsis. — raṅ-snáṅ v. sub snáṅ-ba; Sch. also: self-born. — raṅ-po Cs. = po-raṅ an unmarried man. — raṅ-bábs v. babs. — ráṅ-bu 1. Cs. single, alone, ráṅ-bur adv. singly, alone, without a consort. 2. Cs.: a single life (?). 3. Schr.: one's own child. — raṅ-byúṅ, raṅ-byón self-born, having originated of itself, = raṅ-grúb frq. raṅ-dbaṅ **independence, liberty,** raṅ-dbáṅ ťób-pa to become free Glr.; ɣnás-la raṅ-dbaṅ-méd they are not master of the place i.e. they are not free to choose the place Thgy., in the same sense, gar skye raṅ-dbaṅ-med Mil.; *raṅ-wáṅ °júg-pa* to set free C.; raṅ-dbáṅ-čan **free** W. — raṅ-°bar Cs.: **'musket',** in W. it is only used for **pistol;** *raṅ-bár ḍug-rág* W. **a revolver.** — ráṅ-mo Cs. = mo-ráṅ an unmarried woman. — raṅ-rtsis the opinion which one has of one's self, raṅ-rtsis daṅ raṅ-°dód ma če žig think little of your own self! Mil. — raṅ-bžín, स्वभाव, natural **disposition,** state or **constitution, nature, temper,** raṅ-bžin-las ɣžán-du °gyúr-ba to change one's natural constitution Wdṅ., °bab dé-ltar čé-bai raṅ-bžín-gyis as a natural consequence of so heavy a snow-fall Mil.; raṅ-bžín-gyis **of itself, by itself,** from its very nature, **naturally, spontaneously** Dzl., in col. language, raṅ-bžin-nas id., also for **self** in the sense: I, he etc. without the aid and independently of others; °byúṅ-ba lṅai raṅ-bžin-čan-gyi lus °di this body participating of the nature of the five elements Wdṅ.; draṅ-poi raṅ-bžin-čan-gyi p'yir for raṅ-bžin-čan yin-pai p'yir Sbh. — *raṅ-žin ǰö'-pa* C. needless words, where it is a matter of course; also: talk without any serious intent; *de da raṅ-žin-la zér-če žig yod* W. that is nothing but talk. — raṅ-bzó. 1. Lex.: the right, proper form (of a word)? 2. self-determination, opp. to a punctilious adhering to tradition Mil. — raṅ-raṅ **each ... himself, each ... his,** her, its etc. (not reciprocally, as Sch. has it), raṅ-ráṅ-gi ḱrii °óg-tu sbas he buried each (idol) under its own seat Glr., raṅ-ráṅ-gi leur ɣsal each (subject) will be explained in its own chapter Lt. — raṅ-raṅ-lao each (final consonant) has itself (joined), i.e. is doubled Gram. — raṅ-ré 1. = raṅ-ráṅ: raṅ-réi sna-ťág raṅ-rés zuṅ each may lead himself, may be his own guide. 2. **we,** raṅ-réi sgo drúṅ-na at our own door Mil., raṅ-ré-rnams we (the Lamas, opp. to the laymen) Mil. 3. polite way of addressing, for our **you** or the German 'Sie' Thgr.? — raṅ-šúgs-la **of itself,** spontaneously W. — ráṅ-sa, ráṅ-so one's own place, ráṅ-sa °dzín-pa to maintain one's place, one's station Mil., prob. like ráṅ-mgo °ťón-pa; ráṅ-sar, ráṅ-sor 1. bžág-pa to put (a thing) in its place, fig. for: to leave undecided, to let the matter alone, ni f. Mil. 2. of itself, e.g. ráṅ-sor ži (a storm) abates of itself. — raṅ-saṅs-rgyas Pratyekabuddha, i.e. a Buddha who has obtained his Buddhaship alone by his own exercises of penance, but who does not promote the welfare of other beings.

རང་ག་བ་ ráṅ-ga-ba Cs. **coarseness, meanness.**

རང་བ་ ráṅ-ba, pf. raṅs, **to rejoice,** sems mi-ráṅs-par **discontented,** yid-ráṅ-ba or yi-ráṅ-ba id., frq.; *dhé-la ga-ráṅ-ḍhug-te* highly pleased with it C.; yid ma ráṅs-šiṅ mi myú-bar gyúr-te being very much dissatisfied Stg.; ma-ráṅ-bžin-du unwillingly, reluctantly.

རང་རོང་ཅན་ *rań-roń-čan Cs.* **rough, craggy,** uneven.

རངས་པ་ *rańs-pa* 1. v. *rań-ba.* — 2. *nyin-ráńs-par* for *ťo-ráńs-kyi dús-su* early in the morning *Tar.* 111, 17. — 3. in *W.* for *réńs-pa.*

རངས་པོ་ *ráńs-po Sch.* **rough, rude, unpolished.**

རད་པ་ *rád-pa W.* for *bgrád-pa.*

རད་རོད་ *rad-ród* v. *ród-po.*

རན་ད་ *rán-da* (*Pers.* رندا, رنده) **a plane** *Ld.*

རན་པ་ *rán-pa* 1. vb. and adj. to keep, or keeping, the proper mean, **to be proportionate, just right,** adv. *rán-par* **moderately,** *rán-par sro* warm yourself moderately (tolerably) *Lt., zas-ťsód rán-par zá-ba* to eat moderately *S.g.; ₒdí-tsam ni rán-no* this is about the proper measure *Dzl.*; with the root of the vb.: *žiń rńá-ran-nas* as it was (the proper) time for harvest *Dzl., ₒgro-ran* it is time to go *Pth., ši ma rán-par ší-ba* to die an untimely death; *bág-mar γtań-rán-pa dań* when it was time to give her in marriage *Dzl.;* not so often with a sbst.: *rtsás-ma rán-tsa-na* when harvest-time had come *Mil.* — 2. *rtsa rán-pa C.* **shave-grass,** *Equisetum arvense.* — 3. col. for *ₒdrén-pa* **to lead** (water); for *bran-pa* v. *ťags.*

རབ་ *rab* I. **superior, excellent;** the eldest, of three sons, opp. to *bríń-po* and *ťa-čúń,* frq.; *gań-zág dbań-po-ráb-rnams* very able or clever persons (opp. to *ₒbríń-po* or *ťá-ma* having moderate or very little capacity) *Mil., Thgr.,* inst. of which *rab ₒbriń γsum* is often used *Thgy.; ťébs-na rab* if rightly understood, that will be the best *Thgr.,* frq. for: so it is right, that will do; **much, plentiful,** *rab-skrái ₔóg-nas* also with a full head of hair (you may be a holy man) *Mil.; ráb-tu* adv. **very,** with adjectives and verbs, *ráb-tu sdoms* lock (the door) well *Dzl.; ráb-tu ḱrós-par gyúr-te Tar.;* it occurs also in the following phrases: *ráb-tu ₒbyin-pa* to receive or admit into a religious order, *ráb-tu ₒbyúń-ba* to enter into a religious community, to take orders, *slób-dpon čos-ₒbańs-las* being with, or being ordained by the teacher Chosbangs; *rgyál-poi rígs-las* (to take orders) as a descendant of the royal family, of the caste of noblemen *Tar.; ráb-(tu) byúń(-ba)* he that has taken orders, a novice, or in gen.: **a clerical person;** *rab-byúń* is also the name of the first year of the cycle of sixty years; *rab-(tu) γnás(-par) byéd-pa, mdzád-pa* c. acc. or *la,* prop. 'to make firm or permanent', **to consecrate, to hallow,** a new house, esp. a temple, an idol; by this act a house is secured against accidents, and an idol is supposed to acquire life and to become the abode of the respective deity, which occasionally manifests itself by sundry miracles *Glr.*; *ráb-tu ₒbyéd-pa* (also erron. *byéd-pa*) *Cs.* to analyze, but *Tar.* 96 it is equivalent to प्रकरण treatise, dissertation. *rab-ₒbyáms-pa* v. *ₒbyáms-pa; rab-ₔóg* the second in rank, next in value, excellence etc., thus *Dzl.* ༢༦༤, 5 (as a better reading for *ₒbriń-mo*); *rab-yáńs* very wide, very extensive *Sch.; rab-γsál* 1. very clear, quite evident. 2. sbst. a small **balcony** or **gallery,** frequently seen in Tibetan houses. 3. *Sch.* history (?).

II. also *rabs,* **ford,** *rab-méd* without a ford, *rab-só* = *rabs Sch.*

རབ་རིབ་ *rab-rib,* col. also *hrab-hrib,* **mist, dimness,** e. g. before the eyes, in consequence of impaired vision; **ḱo šrab-šrib mán-na mi ťoń** he sees only a mist before his eyes, *W.*; *skár-ma rab-rib* the faint glimmering of a star.

རབས་ *rabs* 1. **lineage, succession of families, race, family,** *rgyal-rábs* royal family or lineage, nobility; succession of kings; *mi-rábs* human race; *rabs-čád* a person whose lineage is broken off, i.e. **childless,** issueless, *rabs-čád bza-mi γnyis* a married couple without children *Mil.*; *yá-rabs* the higher class of people, noblemen; *má-rabs* the lower class, also: one belonging to the higher or lower class; collectively: *rgán-rabs* old men, aged people, *γžón-rabs* youth, young persons; *sńón-rabs* **the ancients** (*veteres*), *p̓yi-rabs* men of modern times, descendants, posterity *Glr., sńon-ₒrabs-sgrúń* an old legend, ancient history *Zam.*, *sṅón-ɣyi rabs bċo-brgyad* the 18 Puranas *Tar.* 4, 11. — 2. **generation** *Dzl.*, resp. *ɣdun-rábs Glr.*, *ṅá-nas ɣdun-rábs lṅá-pa-na* in the fifth generation after me; with respect to individuals, period of life, viz. one of the many periods, which every person is supposed to pass through, or sometimes pleon. denoting a person as being the representative of his generation: *saṅs-rgyás rabs bdun* the seven Buddhas. — 3. in gen.; **succession, series, development**, e. g. the propagation of the Buddhist doctrine *Tar.* 205, 21; *bskal-rábs* successions of Kalpas, *bskal-rábs-nas bskal-rábs-su.*

རམ་པ་ *rám-pa* 1. *W.* **quick**-(quitch-)grass. — 2. = *rán-pa? Lt., Glr.*

རམ་བུ་ *rám-bu* 1. prob. only in: *rám-bu ˳degs-pa* to join in singing, to take part in a song, to fall in with, *Dzl.* ༢*V*, 13 (not: to set up a dismal cry *Sch.*), v. also *˳ċol-ba.* 2. = *na-rám Polygonum viviparum.*

རམས་ *rams* 1. **indigo** *B.*, col. — 2. *Cs.*: 'degree of doctorship, *sṅags-* or *go-* or *druṅ-ráms-pa* one having such a degree'.

རལ་ *ral* 1. **goat's hair.** — 2. **rent, cleft,** *p̓u ral ɣnyis* a sloping valley dividing into two parts at its upper end; *ral-ɣsum* n. of Lahoul on account of its consisting of three valleys; cf. *rál-ba.* — 3. v. *rál-pa.*

རལ་ཀ་ *rál-ka* v. *rál-gu.*

རལ་ཁ་ *rál-k̓a* v. *rál-gri.*

རལ་ག་ *rál-ga Sch.* = *yál-ga.*

རལ་གུ་ *rál-gu* 1. *Sch.*: **cleft, chink, fissure.** — 2. *dar-dkár-gyi rál-gu* and *rál-ka Pth.?*

རལ་གྲི་ *ral-gri*, col. **ral-gyi, ra-gyi** **sword,** also for rapier and other thrust-blades *Dzl.*; *ral-grii ˳dáb-ma* or *lċe* **blade,** *so* edge, *šubs* scabbard of a sword *Cs.*; *rál-gri-pa Cs.* a sword-man; a fighting man; *rál-k̓a* = *rál so*; *rál-k̓a spród-pa* 'to bring the blades together', to fight hand to hand, (*ral-k̓a sbrad-pa Sch.* is prob. a misprint).

རལ་པ་ *rál-pa* **long hair, lock, curl; mane** (of the lion, not of the horse etc.); *rál-pa-ċan* having or wearing long hair, n. of a Tibetan king that distinguished himself by his bigotry and by his servility to the priests; *ral-lċaṅ* a willow planted at the birth of a child, under which a lock of the child's hair is buried, when it is seven years old *Ld.*

རལ་བ་ *rál-ba* = *drál-ba* and *hrál-ba*, pf. of *˳drál-ba*, **torn,** of clothes etc., *mtsóṅ-gyis* lacerated, slashed, cut to pieces by the sword *Dzl.*; *žig-rál-ba* id.; *žig-rál* breach, **destruction,** *k̓áṅ-pa-la žig-rál byúṅ-na* when the house gives way *Glr.*; *k̓a-rál, rna-rál, sna-rál* a lip, ear or nose, that has been lacerated by wearing rings etc.

རས་ *ras* 1. sbst. **cotton cloth,** cottons, also a piece of cotton cloth, handkerchief etc., *ras sbóm-pa* thick, strong cotton cloth; *lág-ras, p̓yis-ras Cs.* handkerchief, napkin; *t̓ód-ras* **turban** *Cs.*; *p̓rá-ras* a fine sort of cotton stuff, = *k̓á-ši-kai ras.*

Comp. *ras-rkyáṅ* cotton cloth. — *ras-skúd Cs.* cotton thread. — *ras-k̓úg* a small bag made of cotton. — *ras-k̓ra* **calico, chintz** *Cs. ras-gós* **cotton dress, gown.** — *rẹ-˳gá* a strong cotton fabric brought from *Sik.*, *C. ras bċós-bu Cs.* calico, chintz. — *ras-t̓ág* **fillet, bandage.** — *rás-pa* a person wearing cotton clothes *Mil.*, frq. — *ras-bál* raw cotton. — *ras-búbs* a whole piece of cotton cloth. — *rás-ma* a small piece, a rag *Lex.* **rẹ-zẹ́n** *C.* a long, loose cotton garment, shawl. — *ras-yúg* = *ras-búbs.* — *ras-rú* v. *re-rú.* — *ras-slág* a furred garment covered with cotton cloth *W.* — 2. adj. *k̓a-rás* (**rē**, for *reṅs?*) hard snow that will bear a man.

རས་པ་ *rás-pa* 1. vb., *Ld.* **ras-ċe** **to get or grow hoarse,** **skad ras soṅ** the voice has grown hoarse, **skad ras-sa rag** I feel a hoarseness in my throat. — 2. sbst. v. sub *ras.*

རི་ *ri*, also *ri-bo B.*, **rí-ga** *W.* 1. **mountain, hill,** *ri pó-ta-la* the mountain (called) Potala *Lis.*; *ri-bo dpal-˳bár Mil.*, *rgyal-gyi-śri ri Mil.* the mountain *Pal-bár, Gyal-gyisri*; *rir* on the mountain *Mil.*, *ri-la* id.

frq.; *ri-ťaṅ-mťsams-su* at the foot of the mountains or hills *Med.*; *rir-gán-pa* one living in close vicinity to a mountain, *W.*; *gáṅs-ri* an ice-mountain, snowy mountain, glacier, *nágs-ri* or *šiṅ-ri* a hill covered with wood, *brág-ri* a rocky mountain, *γyá-ri* a mountain or hill consisting of slate-stone or schist; *spaṅ-ri* a hill covered with grass. — 2. **brim** of a hat or cap; **side-leather**, side-piece of a shoe. — 3. symb. num.: 7. — 4. num. figure: 55. — 5. v. *ri-mo.*

Comp. and deriv. *ri-skéd* v. *rkéd-pa.* — *ri-skyégs Stg.*, v. *skyegs.* — *ri-ḱród* chain of mountains, assemblage of hills or mountains, esp. as abode of hermits who, on that account, are called *ri-ḱród-pa*; also directly = *dgón-pa* hermitage. — *ri-mgó* mountain top. — *ri-rgyál*, *rii rgyál-po* a very high mountain, e.g. Tise *Mil.*, Gandharā *Sbh.*, esp. = *ri-ráb*, q.v. — *ri-rgyúd* chain of mountains, ridge of hills. — *ri-čan* mountainous, hilly. — *ri-čén*, *ri-bo-čé* a great mountain. — *ri-nyín* the sunny side, the southern slope of a mountain. — *ri-rnyíl* fall of a mountain, land-slip *Sch.* — *ri-stóṅ* v. *stóṅ-pa.* — *ri-deu* (or *rdeu*) *čúṅ Sch.*, **ri-bóg, ri-de-bóg* W.*, a mountain spur abounding in stones. — **ri-dód* W.* (perh. to be spelled *ri-ḱród*) a hermit (living) in the mountains. — *ri-sná* mountain spur. — *ri-pa* an inhabitant of the mountains, mountaineer, from a Tibetan point of view equivalent to the Latin *paganus* and *agrestis* as opp. to *urbanus*, therefore = peasant, poor uncivilized person. — *ri-ṕrán* a little hill or mountain. — *rí-bo* = *ri*, v. above. — *ri-bór-pa Tar.*, *Cs.*: *ri-ₒór-pa*; = *ri-ḱród-pa*, *ri-bór-gyi groṅ* mountain village *Tar.* — *ri-brág, brág-ri* rocky mountain. — *ri-ₒbóg* spur. — *ri-sbúg* mountain cavern. — *ri-rtsá* foot, *ri-rtsé* top of a mountain, *nyi-ma ri-rtsé-la ṕóg-na* when the rising sun illumines the mountain tops. — *ri-rtsé-kan Cs.* n. of a mischievous spirit. — *ri-rdzóṅ* mountain fortress, fort. — *ri-ráb* the centre of the world and king of the mountains, the fabulous Sumeru or Meru, also *ri-rab-lhún-po, ri-rgyál, ri-bo-mčog-ráb Mil.* — *ri-lúṅ* mountain and valley. — *ri-γséb Sch.* = *ri-ḱród.* — *ri-sribs* the side not exposed to the sun, shady side, north-side of the mountains.

རི་གུ་ *ri-gu* young goat, **kid** *W.*

རི་རྒྱ་ *ri-rgyá Sch.*: foxes or fox-skins(?).

རི་དྭགས་ *ri-dwags* animals of chase, **game.**

རི་བ་ *ri-ba W.* **ri-če** to be worth, gen. as adj. **worth,** **lug di ṅul čig ri-če yin** this sheep is worth one rupee *W.*; *dṅul brgya ri-bai rta* a horse worth one hundred rupees *Cs.*. cf. *riṅ* and *rib*; *ri-bai rin-ťáṅ* the full price *Sch.*

རི་བོང་ *ri-bóṅ* **hare,** *ri-bóṅ-mo Cs.* female hare; it lives in *Ld.*, but not in the smaller valleys, e.g. not in Lahoul; *ri-bóṅ-gi rwa* the horn of a hare, a nonentity, a thing not existing, cf. *mo-šám-gyi bu.*

རི་མོ་ *ri-mo* 1. **figure, picture, painting, drawing,** *lha-ḱáṅ-gi Glr.*; *ri-mo-mḱan* **painter;** *ri-mo-čan, ri-mo-ldan* marked with figures; *ri-mor byéd-pa* to represent by means of figures and colours, to paint *Do.*; **markings** (streaks, speckles etc.) *šai* markings of a (tiger's) skin *Tar.*; *ri-ḱrá* having stripes of various colours, spotted, speckled; *ri-mo* also draught, plan, design, and fig. **pattern,** rule of conduct, law written into the heart. — 2. = *rím-gro* reverence, **veneration,** *ri-mor byéd-pa* to honour, to venerate *Stg.*

རི་ལུ་ *ri-lu* col., but also *Tar.* 63, for *ríl-bu.*

རི་ཤི་ *ri-ši*, ऋषि, = *draṅ-sróṅ* q. v.

རི་ཤོ་ *ri-šó* n. of a medicinal herb *Med.*

རིག་ *rig* in *Ld.* col. and provinc. for *žig:* **maṅ-ṅa rig** or **nyuṅ-ṅu rig toṅ** give much! give little!

རིག་པ་ *rig-pa* I. vb., 1. **to know, to understand,** = *šés-pa* with the termin. of a sbst.: to know (a person etc.) as, with the termin. of the inf.: to know that, **to perceive,** observe, *ḱrós-par rig-nas* perceiving that he became angry *Dzl.*; *ṕá-la rig-par gyis* let your father know it, inform your father of it *Tar.*; *zlóg-tu-rig-par byed* (it or he) teaches how to avert, prevent etc. — 2. v. *sgrig-pa.*

II. sbst. 1. **knowing, knowledge; prudence, talents, natural gifts** *Glr.*; *rig-pa dan ldán-pa* **talented, rich in knowledge, learned** *Dzl.*; *rig-pa ysar-ba* new informations, disclosures, knowledge; **news,** *lóg-gi rig-pa bsgrés-na* if one compares the absurd news *Tar.* 174, *Schf.*; *ma-rig-pa* 1. sbst. **अविद्या ignorance,** mostly used in the specific Buddhist sense, viz. for the innate principal and **fundamental error** of considering perishable things as permanent and of looking upon the external world as one really existing, with Buddhists in a certain manner the original sin, from which every evil is proceeding, v. *Köpp.* I, 163 (but cf. *yti-mug*). 2. adj. void of reason, **unreasonable,** irrational, *dúd-ₒgro ma-rig-pa Mil.* — 2. **science, learning, literature,** *nán-gi rig-pa* the orthodox or sacred literature, *p̔yii rig-pa* the heterodox or profane literature *Cs.*, *tun-mon-gi rig-pa* literature or science common to both religions (Buddhists and Brahmans) *Cs.*; *rig-pai ynas* and *rig-pa* any single science (philosophy, medicine etc.) v. *rig-ynás*; *rig-pai ról-ts̔o* or *rig-pai ynas t̔ams-čád Cs.* circle of science, **encyclopedia.** — 3. **soul** (prob. only in later literature), *rig-pa lus dan brál-ba* the soul separated from the body, *rten dan brál-ba* the soul separated from her hold or from her abode *Thgr.*; often opp. to *bem Mil.*

Comp. *rig-mk̔an*, *rig(-pa)-po Cs.*, *Sch.* a knowing person, a learned man. — *rig-rgyud* **character** *Mil.* — *rig-snágs* **a spell, charm, magic formula,** *rig-snags-mk̔an* a person skilled in charms. — *rig-ynás* a science, one of the sciences; *rig-ynás ĉé-ba lna* the five great sciences or classes of science, frq.; these are: *sgrá-rig-pa* science of language, *ytan-ts̔igs-rig-pa* dialectics, *ysó-ba-rig-pa* medicine, *bzó-rig-pa* science of mechanical arts, *nan-dón-rig-pa* religious philosophy; of less consequence are: *rig-ynás čún-ba lna* the five minor sciences; and the *rig-ynás* or *rig-pa bčo-brgyad* (also; *tsug-lag* ?L), which need not be particularly enumerated, though they are often mentioned in the *Dzl.*; they are named by *Cs.* and *Sch.* — *rig(-pa)-po* v. *rig-mk̔an.* — *rig-byéd* 1. conveying knowledge, **instructive,** prob. also learned, *na rig-byéd glú-mk̔an ma yin-te* I am no schooled, accomplished, singer *Mil.* 2. **instruction,** a book conveying knowledge, a scientific work, *bzoi rig-byéd* a technological work *Glr.* 3. **वेद** Veda, the (four) sacred writings of ancient Brahmanism, hence 4. as symb. num.: 4. — *rig-ma*, **वेदमातृ**, Veda-mother, *Gāyatrī*, a certain metre, verse and hymn of the Rigveda, personified as a deity *Mil.* — *rig-ₒdzin*, from *rig-pa ₒdzín-pa* to comprehend a science with ease, to be of quick parts *Dzl.*, as partic.: **a man of parts, a clever fellow;** but usually *rig-ₒdzin* (like *rig-ₒčan*, of rarer occurrence), *Ssk.* **विद्याधर,** denotes a kind of spirits to whom a high degree of wisdom is attributed, like the Dākinis. — *rig-šés* the faculty of **reason** *Tar.* 90, 2, *Schf.*

རིག་རིག་ *rig-rig, mig rig-rig byéd-pa* or *dúg-pa* to look about, esp. in an anxious manner, shyly *Tar.*, *Mil.*

རིགས་ *rigs* 1. **family, lineage, extraction, birth, descent,** *rigs-rús* lineage and family *Glr.*, *mai rigs-su nyé-ba* or *ytógs-pa* a relation by the mother's side *Dzl.*; emph.: **noble birth** or extraction: *rigs-kyi bu* or *bú-mo* noble or honoured sir! honoured madam! a respectful address, which is also more generally applied; thus in *Thgr.* it is the regular way of addressing the soul of a deceased person; *mi-rigs* 1. the human race, mankind *Cs.* 2. **nation, tribe** *Glr.*; *sdé-rigs* **tribe** *Cs.* 3. rarely = sex, *mó-rigs* female sex *Wdn.* — 2. in a special sense: **caste, class** in society, **rank.** In Tibet five ranks are usually distinguished. viz.: *rgyál-rigs* royal state, royalty, *brám-ze-rigs* caste of priests (Brahman caste), *rjé-rigs* nobility, aristocracy, *dmáns-rigs* the citizens, *ydól-pai rigs* the common people. When speaking of India, the appellations of these classes are applied to the castes of Brahmanism, although they do not correspond to each other in every respect. — 3. **kind, sort, species,** *groi rigs ysum yod* there are three sorts of wheat, *skád-*

rigs gós-rigs mi-ₒdrá-ba different languages and costumes; *ċi-rigs* of every sort, *ċi-rigs-su* in every possible manner, e g. *čos stón-pa* to teach religion; *nyin-moi rigs-kyis* or *rigs-la* by the day, **by days, daily** *Glr.*; *rigs* is also used for **some, certain,** *nád-rigs-la mi ₒdzém-na* if one is not on his guard against certain diseases; sometimes pleon.: *ɣán-lag rigs bži* the four limbs, viz. hands and feet *Glr.; rgyal-čén rigs bži* the four great spirit-kings *Thgy.*, *rigs ɣsum mgón-po* the three tutelar saints (*spyan-ras-ɣzigs, p̓yag-rdór, ₒǰam-dbyáṅs) Glr.; saṅs-rgyás rigs lṅai žiṅ-k̓ams Thgr.* — *rigs-pa* vb. **to have the way, manner, custom, quality of,** *mgo p̓yir ₒbyúṅ-bai rigs-so* the upper end (of a stick, part of which is in the water) has the way of sticking out, i.e. sticks out; often to be translated: **must** necessarily (according to the laws of nature or to circumstances); as partic. or adj.: **necessary,** also **proper, suitable, right, suited to its purpose,** in the earlier literature gen. with the genit. of the infin., sometimes with the termin. of the infin., in later times with the root of the verb; thus: *t̓ós-nas ldáṅ-bai rigs-so* you must get up as soon as you hear . . . *Dzl.; da ri žig snáṅ-bai rigs* now a mountain must appear *Dzl.; bžág-pai rigs-sam* would it not be expedient to appoint...? *Dzl.*; *rigs-kyi dús-la báb-bo* it is just the right time *Dzl.*; *mi smrá-bai mi rigs-so* it is not right to be silent *Dzl.*; *smád-par mi rigs-so* it is not right to abuse *Glr.*; *ₒóṅ-rigs ₒdúg-pas* because (he) might possibly come *Mil. nt.*; *drán-pa mi zin rigs-la* if he should perhaps not retain the recollection of, if there should be any danger of his not remembering *Thgr.*; *ṅan-sóṅ-du ₒgró-bai rigs-la* as there is a possibility of going to hell *Thgr.*; *ɣdúl-bai rigs-pa* those fit for conversion *Dzl.; lhar skyé-ba ni rigs-pa ma lags* his being re-born as a deity is not befitting, or also: not possible, not probable *Dzl.*; *mi-rigs-pa* wrong, not right, unbecoming, improper etc., mostly as adv.: *mi-rigs-par byéd-pa* to act wrong, to do badly, frq. — *rigs-kyi rǰes-ₒbráṅ Was.* (274) v. sub *luṅ.*

Comp. *rigs-brgyúd* race, **lineage,** extraction, **family** *Cs.*, *rigs-brgyud-ₒdzin* **male issue,** *rigs-brgyúd ₒp̓él-bar ₒgyúr-ba* the rising of a numerous progeny *Dom.* — *rigs-ṅán* 1. low birth or extraction, **k̓yod mi rig-ṅán-pa daṅ nyám-po ḍé-ċe man** you must not mingle with people of low extraction, with common people *W.*; *rigs-ṅán dpón-du skyó-ba* to raise a child of low extraction to the royal dignity *Glr.* 2. **hangman** *Dzl.* (cf. *ɣdól-pa*). — *rigs-ċan, rigs-ldán* of noble birth. — *rigs-mnyám-pa, mt̓ún-pa, ₒdrá-ba* of the same rank etc., of the same species. — *rigs-nyáms* **degenerated,** *rigs-nyáms dge-slóṅ* a monk disgracing his profession *Pth.* — *rigs-méd* = *rigs-ṅán* no. 1.

རིགས་པ་ *rigs-pa* 1. v. *rigs.* — 2. often erron. for *rig-pa.* — 3. adj. of *rigs*: *rgyál-rigs-pa* belonging to the reigning family or caste; *ċi-rigs-pai sgó-nas* in every possible manner *Mil.*; *ċi-rigs-par snyán-pai ts̓ig-gis* with ever so many kind words *Dzl.*; also: in any way, any how, to a certain degree or extent, in part, partly *Tar.* 4, 3 etc. — 4. sbst., translation of न्याय **logic, dialectics** *Trigl.* 15; an infallible, not deceptive idea *Was.* (297).

རིང་ངེ་བ་ *riṅ-ṅe-ba* **continual** (?), **daily** (?) *k̓a-tsá riṅ-ṅe-ba Mil. nt.* every day warm meals.

རིང་བ་ *riṅ-ba* I. adj , also *riṅ-po C., B.*, **riṅ-mo** *W.* 1. **long, high, tall,** relating to space; *riṅ-mo* **k̓ur** *W.* carry it lengthwise; it also implies distance, in which case *t̓ag-riṅ* (q. v.) is the more precise form; *da-dúṅ yúl-las riṅ-ste* as he is still at a great distance from the place *Dzl.*; more frq. with *daṅ*: *ɣnas ₒdi groṅ-k̓yér daṅ riṅ-bas* because this place is far from the town *Dzl.*; *mi riṅ-ba-na* at no great distance. — 2. **long,** with respect to **time,** *ts̓e riṅ-ba* sbst. a long life, adj. long-lived, *rgyál-ba daṅ ts̓e riṅ-bar šog ċig* may he be victorious and live long! *Dzl.*; *yun riṅ-po* (or *mo*) a long time; *yun riṅ-po-nas* from a long time, a long time since, *riṅ-por ma lón-par*, less accurately: *riṅ-po ma lón-par* soon afterwards, relating to things past, *riṅ-por mi t̓ogs-par* id. with respect to the future, = after a little while, in a short time, frq.; *mi-riṅ-bar* id. *Tar.*; *dé-nas mi riṅ-bar* not long after that *Tar.*; *riṅ žig* a long time, *riṅ žig lón-pa daṅ* after a long time *Dzl.*; *riṅ žig-tu* adv. **long, a long while, for a long time,** *riṅ žig-tu ma ˳oṅs-pas* as he did not come for a long time *Dzl.*; *riṅ žig-na* after or during a long time *Glr.*; *riṅ-la*, resp. *sku-riṅ-la* c. genit. **during, at,** *nyín-gyi riṅ-la* in the day-time, during the day *Pth.*, *˳dir bžugs rin* (provinc. for *riṅ*?) *˳tso-čas* or *rgyags* provisions for the time of his stay *Mil.*; esp. of kings etc.: **under** a king; during the reign or life of a king, frq.; *dé-riṅ B., C.*, **di-riṅ** (more correct form, but only in *W.*) **to-day.** — 3. **old,** *riṅ žig-na Sch.* long ago, long since, v. also *riṅ-lugs.* —

II. **length, distance** etc., more definite form, but of rare occurrence: *riṅ-ba-nyid*, *dé-nas mi-riṅ-ba-nyid-na* a very short time afterwards *Tar.*

Comp. *riṅ-kyád* **length.** — **riṅ-táb** *W.* length, copiousness (of account). — *riṅ-túṅ* 1. long and short. 2. length, relatively. — *riṅ-gág*, also *stod-gág* jacket or waistcoat of a Lama, without sleeves.

རིང་ལུགས་ *riṅ-lúgs Cs.*: 'the sect or followers of a person', *Sch.*: 'old customs'; *Glr.* 92, 2 (?).

རིང་བསྲེལ་ *riṅ-bsrél* ('things which are to be preserved for a long time'), धातु, relics of a Buddha or a saint, viz. small, hard particles, acc. to Burnouf the remnants of burnt bones.

རིངས་ *riṅs* sometimes for *riṅ.*

རིངས་པ་ *riṅs-pa* **swift, speedy,** *riṅs-par rgyúg-pa* to run fast, to hasten, hurry; *riṅs-par yod* I am in a hurry *Mil.*; **riṅ-pa toṅ** *W.* be quick! make haste! *riṅs ruṅ* though you be in a hurry *Mil.*; *riṅs-pai bsód-snyoms* alms, gifts of charity (requiring haste), urgently requested, and out of the common course, *Burn.* I, 269. 628 **za-riṅs, ˳tuṅ-riṅs**, waiting impatiently for one's meal, **˳grul-riṅs** for setting out *W.*; *riṅs-stábs-su* most speedily *Mil.*

རིད་པ་ *rid-pa* 1. **meager, emaciated** *Dzl.* and elsewh. — 2. *Sch.* also: **rare.**

རིད་པང་ *rid-páṅ* the Neosa pine-tree *Kun.*

རིན་ *rin* 1. **price, value,** *rin γčód-pa* to fix, to determine the price *Cs.* (cf. *taṅ*), *rin rtóg-pa* to ascertain the price, to estimate the value *Cs.*; *rin ˳bébs-pa* to abate, to lessen the price *Cs.*; *rin ˳báb-pa, rin ˳bri-ba* to go down, to sink or fall in value *Cs.*; **rin tsam** *W.*, **rin gha-tsö** *C.* how dear (is it)? what does it cost? *rin-la mi čog Sch.* to sell under cost-price; *rin-čan* dear, costly; *rin-méd* worthless, also: **for nothing, gratis;** *rin-góṅ, rin-táṅ, rin-tsád Tar.* ༢༠༢, 17 = *rin*; *rin-čén-po, rin-po-čé* v. the next article. — 2. for *riṅ*, v. *riṅ-ba* I, 2.

རིན་ཆེན་(པོ་) *rin-čen(-po)*, also *rin-po-če*, 1. **very dear, precious, valuable;** usually: 2. sbst, रत्न, **a precious thing, treasure, jewel, precious stone, precious metal; metal** in general; *Glr.* 7, five jewels of the gods are enumerated, sapphire, indragopa and other three, prob. fabulous, stones, and five jewels as the property of man: gold,. silver, pearls, corals, lapis lazuli; in other books other jewels are specified as such. In the Buddha-legends frq. mention is made of the *rin-po-če sna bdun,* i.e. the extraordinary treasures of a Tshakravartin king, viz. the precious wheel (v. *˳kor-lo*), the precious elephant, the precious horse, the precious jewel, the precious wife, the precious minister and the precious general (or inst. of him, the precious citizen) v. Gyatch. chap. III. Sometimes *rin-po-čei* may be understood literally: consisting of jewels, of precious stones, at other times it is merely equivalent to: valuable, precious; *rin-po-čei gliṅ Glr.* seems frq. to signify a holy, happy land inhabited by gods. — 3. **a title,** used not only in *rgya-mtso rin-po-če* and *paṇ-čen rin-po-če* (the honorary titles of the high-priests of Lhasa and of Tashilunpo), but also a title of every Lama of a higher class.

རིན་དི་ *rin-di W.* (*riṅ-dri Bun.*) 1. **lead.** — 2. **musket-ball.**

རིབ་ *rib* = *ri-ba Sch.* (*Dzl.* ༢༢༧, 8. 15, and in *Sch.'s* dictionary): **worth,** costing, standing at; to the Tibetans asked by us the word seemed to be unknown, and the MS. of Kyelang has *ri-ba* in the above cited passage.

རིབ་མ་ **rib-ma* W.*, **ḍib-ma* C.*, **fence, hedge, enclosure** to protect the fields from cold winds, intruders etc.

རིམ་གྲི་ *rim-gri* resp. for **ltógs-ri** **hunger** *W.*

རིམ་(འ)གྲོ་ *rim-gro* or *rim-ₒgro*, resp. *sku-rim* **honour, homage,** shown more esp. to gods, saints, and priests, **offerings** and other ceremonies (v. sub *sku*), *rim-gros ťar-bar ₒgyur* he will yet be cured by religious ceremonies (if medical advise should prove insufficient) *S.g.*; *dei rim-gro-la* as a ceremony for him (the sick person) *Mil.*; *zaṅ-ziṅ-gi rim-gros* by offerings in goods, cattle etc.) *Mil.*; *rim-ₒgro čén-po byas* he arranged a great sacrificial festival *Pth.*; *rim-gro-pa* servant, waiting-man, valet de chambre.

རིམ་པ་ *rim-pa*, *Ssk.* क्रम, 1. **series, succession,** *rim-(pa) bžin(-du) Dzl.*, *rim-par Glr.*, in a row or line, in rows, by turns, successively, one after another, also = by degrees, gradually; *rim-gyis, rim-pas Dzl.* id.; *rim-pas dáṅ-po mčog yin ṗyi-ma dman* v. sub *dmán-pa*; *byá-ba ťob-rim bžin byéd-pa* to do a business by turns, each taking a certain share of the work *Glr.* — 2. **the place** in a row or file, constituent part or member of a series, *dei mi-brgyúd rim-pa lṅas rgyál-sa bzuṅ* five members of his lineage occupied the throne *Glr.*, and in a still more general sense: *sgo rim-pa bdun* a sevenfold door *Dzl.*; *rim-ldábs Sch.* and *nyis-rim S.g.* double; *rim-γčig = lan-γčig* one time, once. — 3. **order, method,** *ₒcád-par ₒgyúr-bai rim-pa ₒdis* by this method which will be explained immediately, *Sbh.*; *rim-bral* disorderly, irregular *Cs.* — *rim γnyis* v. *skyed-rim.*

རིམས་(ནད་) *rims(-nad)* contagious disease, **epidemy, plague,** *ṅan-rims* id. *Glr.*; *rims γtoṅ-ba* to send, to cause a plague, as demons do *Dzl.*; *dus γdon γnyis-kyis ma skyed rims mi ₒbyuṅ* plagues, epidemies, are caused by nothing but the season or by demons; **ťu-rim* W.* **dysentery, diarrhoea,** bloody flux; *rims-só* the 'tooth' of an epidemy, i.e. its contagium, virulency.

རིལ་ཏིང་ *ril-tiṅ Ld.* = *ša-rág.*

རིལ་བ་ *ril-ba* I. more frq. *ril-po, ril-mo B., C.*; **ril-ril* W.* 1. **round, globular,** in *C.* also **cylindrical;** *srán-ma ril-mo* peas are round *Wdṅ.*; **ril-ril* W.* also sbst.: a round, globular object, such as a cabbage-head, a round lump of butter etc.; *ril-bai spyi-blugs Glr., Sch.:* 'a bottle, narrow in the middle, a gourd-bottle'. — 2. **whole, entire; wholly, quite** **ǩoṅ-ril** quite crippled, lamed *C.*; **nag-ril-ril* W.* very black, quite black; *rtág-pa daṅ ril-por ₒdzin-pa* to consider a thing lasting and entire (not compounded) *Thgy.*; *ril-por ṅa dbáṅ-na* if it belongs to me entirely *Mil.*; *ril-po* the whole, the entire thing (opp. to a part), also in arithmetic *Wdk.*; *ril-poi lhág-ma* the remainder of the whole *Wdk.*; *bubs-ril lus* the whole body *S.g.*; *ril-gyis γyógs-pa* entirely, completely, enveloped, or wrapped up *Sch.*; *ril-mid-pa Sch.:* 'to swallow a thing entire'; *dé-dag daṅ ril-gyis mči-am ṗyed daṅ mči-ba bka-stsól čig* tell me whether I am to come with all, or only with one half (of them) *Dzl.* ༡༥༢, 5 (acc. to the manuscript of Kyelang); *ril-bu*, col. **ril-lu**, **small ball, globule, pill,** *ril-bur bsgril-ba srán-ma tsam* formed into a pill of the size of a pea *Lt.*; *ril-ma* globular dung of some animals, *byi-bai ril* mouse-dung *Mṅg.* (where Piper longum is compared with it), *glá-bai ril* dung of the musk-deer; *lúg-ril* tirdles, sheep-pellets, *ša-ril* 1. dung of the argali *Ld.* 2. small meat-balls *C.* — II. 1. *W.*: **ril-če** (for *gril-ba*) **to fall.** — 2. *Bal.* **ril-čas** (for *sgril-ba*) **to wrap up.**

རིས་ *ris* 1. cognate to *ri-mo* and perh. to *ₒbri-ba*: **figure, form, design,** *pádma-ris* the figure of a lotus-flower *Glr.*, *mig-maṅ-ris-su bris-pa Glr.* painted like a chess-board; *skya-ris* the blank parts of a picture, *tson-ris* the painted parts of a picture *Cs.* — 2. *Cs.*: **part, region, quarter,** hence *mťo-ris* **heaven,** v. *mťo*; *dbaṅ-ris* share of power or of territory; *mṅa-ris* id. and n. of a part of

Tibet; *pyogs-ris* **party**; *Cs.* has also: *ráṅ-ris* one's own party, *ɣžán-ris* another's party, *ris-čan* **partial, prejudiced,** *ris-méd* **impartial, indifferent,** hence also **hermit,** because he ought to feel indifferent to every thing. — 3. *Sch.: 'ris-su* difference, *ris-su čád-pa* equality'(??). — 4. *ris-ɣza* symb. num.: 7, derived from the number of the great planets together with sun and moon.

རུ་ *ru* 1. **horn,** = *rwa; rá-ru* goat's horn, *lúg-ru* ram's horn. — 2. parts of vessels etc. resembling a horn, e.g. the handle of a stew-pan *Mil. nt.*; **gó-ru* C.* door-post. — 3. **part, division,** *dmág-gi* of an army *Stg.*, wing *Cs.*; of a country, *dbu-ɣtsáṅ-ru-bži Mil.*; *ɣyás-ru* the right side or wing, *ɣyón-ru* the left side or wing, *ɣžuṅ-ru* the middle part or centre *Cs.* — 4. as num. figure: 85.

Comp. *ru-dár Wdk, Mil., ru-mtsón Sch.* military ensign, **banner, colours,** *ₒpyár-ba* to display, to hoist (a flag). — *ru-sná* division of an army *Sch.* — *rú-pa* 'troops, advanced posts of the enemy' *Sch.* — *ru-dpón* commander of a regiment, colonel.

རུ་ང་ *ru-ṅá* **hatred, grudge, malice,** (of rare occurrence); *ru-ṅa-čan* spiteful, malicious.

རུ་རྟ་ *ru-rtá Cs.*: 'a kind of spicy root'; in *Lh. Inula Helenium.*

རུ་ཐོག་ or རྡོག་ *ru-tóg* or *ru-rdóg Cs.* n. of a district in Tibet contiguous to Ladak; an extensive plain, east of lake *Paṅkoṅ.*

རུ་པ་ *rú-pa* v. *ru.*

རུ་པོ་ *rú-po* **ram** *W.*

རུ་བ་ or རེ་གུར་ *rú-ba* or *re-gur* a tent-covering made of yak's hair; *rú-ba-pa* a person living in such a tent; *rú-bai tsogs* a number of such tents, a tent-village.

རུ་མ་ *rú-ma* **curdled milk,** used as a ferment *C.*, *ₒó-mar rú-ma blug-ₒdra* as when sweet and curdled milk are put together *S.g.*; as to its effect, it may also stand for **leaven.**

རུ་ཚར་ *ru-tsár* **fringes** *Ld.* = *ka-tsár.*

རུ་རཀྵ་ *ru-rakša Med.*; *Cs.*: a sort of berry.

རུ་རུ་ *ru-ru Stg.*; *Sch.*: a kind of deer; a species of fruit-trees.

རུ་ལེབ་ *ru-léb* 'flat-horn', acc. to *Sch.* the reindeer (*šá-ba ru-léb* the domesticated, and *ₒbróg-gi ru-léb* the wild r.), more prob. **the elk,** v. *ka-ša.*

རུག་གེ་ *rug-gé* appearing (?), *žiṅ snum rug-gé* the field had a luxuriant appearance *Mil. nt.*

རུག་པ་ *rúg-pa* 1. *Cs.* a kind of potato. — 2. *W.* **to collect, gather, pluck,** v. *sgrúg-pa.*

རུང་ཁང་ *rúṅ-kaṅ Cs.*: **bake-house, kitchen.**

རུང་བ་ *rúṅ-ba* 1. vb. **to be fit, calculated, suitable, right,** and adj.: **fit** etc., gen. with termin., rarely with the root of the verb, *tsig ₒdi ₒjigs-su ruṅ* this word is calculated to terrify, is terrible *Dzl.*; *btsoṅ-du ruṅ* it is salable, vendible *Dzl.*; *slob-dpón-du mi ruṅ* he is not fit to be a teacher *Dzl.*; *ɣžán-du mi ruṅ* he is good for nothing else, but also in the sense: he is too good for anything else, nothing inferior can be offered to him *Glr.*; *grub rúṅ-du yód-pa* one that is able to perform it *Tar.*; *mi rnyed mi ruṅ* it must be procured by all means *Dzl.*, *mi byar mi ruṅ* it must be done *Dzl.*; *nyál-du mi ruṅ* it would not do to sleep *Dzl.*; *med kyaṅ ruṅ* I (you etc.) can also do without (him) *Glr.*; *dei tse ɣtáṅ-du rúṅ-ṅam mi ruṅ* would it not be as well to let him go once more? *Dzl.*; *či-ltar yid-čes-su ruṅ* how can one believe you? *Dzl.*; **kon-čóg zun zer mi ruṅ* W.* God cannot tell a lie; *ₒdi yaṅ ruṅ* this, too, is correct, will do *Gram.*; *tsab ruṅ tsam* it may perhaps be used instead *Wdṅ.*; *ṅá-la mós-pa ma byas kyaṅ rúṅ-ste* that they do not show me any honour is not so great a loss; but ... *Mil.*; *ₒdis ruṅ-ṅam* is that the right thing? will that do? *de-ltar ruṅ* (*W.* **čog**) well, let it be so! for aught I care! — 2. several other phrases with *ruṅ*: a. *lus ₒdi či ruṅ* why should we care so much for this our body? *Dzl.*; esp. *či ma ruṅ,* preceded by *na* or (rarely) by *yaṅ*: **why should** not...? i.e. **o that! would that!** *ˌdi bdág-gi yin-na či ma ruṅ* would that this were mine! *Thgy.*; *ṅai bú-mo mín-na či ma ruṅ* I only wish, she were not my daughter! would it were not my daughter! *Pth.* b. *ruṅ* = *yaṅ* after a verbal root: *de tsam žig bsdad ruṅ* though I have been sitting so long *Mil.*; *mi dgos ruṅ* though it is not necessary *Mil.*; *ŝes ruṅ mi ŝes-pa ltar byéd-pa* to plead ignorance although one knows the thing *Mil.*; *či-la ťug ruṅ* whatever may happen to me, = at all events, at any rate; *či yin ruṅ* whatever it may be *Mil.*; *log yin ruṅ min ruṅ* whether it be an erroneous (opinion) or not *Mil.*; *ŝi ruṅ γson ruṅ* whether I live or die, living or dead *Pth.*; *gaṅ yaṅ ruṅ, či yan ruṅ* whosoever he may be, whatsoever it may be, frq.; *sa ču gaṅ yaṅ rúṅ-ba-la* on earth, water or whatever it be *Do.* c. *mi-rúṅ-ba* **illicit, improper, unfit,** v. above; *mi-rúṅ-bai γži bču* ten illicit actions, differently specified *Tar.* 33, 9, *Köpp.* I, 147, partly moral offences, partly only infractions of discipline; but *ma-rúṅ-ba, ma-rúṅs-pa* 1. **pernicious, dangerous, atrocious,** as enemies, beasts of prey, malignant gods and spirits, reckless destroyers etc. 2. **spoiled, destroyed, ruined,** *ma-rúṅ-bar byéd-pa* to destroy etc., *ma-rúṅ-bar ˌgyúr-ba* to be destroyed etc. *Dzl.*

རུད་ *rud* **a falling** or **fallen mass,** as: *ǩa-rúd* snow-slip, avalanche, *ču-rúd* deluge, inundation, flood (by the rupture of an embankment and the like), *sa-rúd* land-slide, descent of a great mass of earth; *rúd-zam* a snow-bridge, formed by avalanches.

རུབ་ཆུ་ *rub-čú* prop. n., a district in the south of *Ld.*

རུབ་པ་ *rúb-pa* **to rush in upon, to attack, assault,** *p̌yag žabs kún-nas rub-rúb ˌjús-te* rushing in upon him from every side in order to touch his hands and feet *Mil.*; *bzán-la rúb-pa* **to pounce on** the prey, to fall upon the food *Glr.*; **do-rub táṅ-te sád-če* W.* to kill with stones, to stone; **čog-čig-la rúb-pa* W.* to press or crowd together towards one side; *ǩa-rúb byéd-pa* to outcry, to bear down by a louder crying *Mil.*; **ˌgo-rub-rúb ˌdug* C.*, **go-rúb taṅ dug* W.* they put their heads together; **ŝrod rub soṅ,* or *mún-ču rub soṅ* W.* darkness draws on, night is setting in, for which in *C.* **sa rub soṅ** is said to be used, so that it might also be translated by **to darken, to obscure.**

རུབ་ཤོ་ *rub-ŝó* **currant** *W.*

རུམ་ *rum* 1. **womb, uterus,** = *mṅal*, but less frq.: *rum mi bde-ba* sensations of pain during pregnancy *Dzl.*, *rúm-du ˌjúg-pa* to enter into the womb. — 2. **darkness, obscurity,** *mún-pai rum Glr.*, gen. *smag-rúm.* — 3. prop. n., **Turkey, the Ottoman empire,** the site of which is but vaguely known to the Tibetans, though some commodities from thence find their way to Lhasa; *rúm-pa* a man from Turkey, a Turk; *rum-ŝam* (شام) Syria *Cs.*

རུལ་བ་ *rúl-ba* **to rot, to get rotten, to become putrid, to turn rancid** etc., *rúl-bar ˌgyúr-ba B.*, **rul čá-če* W.* id.; *ˌo-ma rul soṅ* the milk is spoiled, *ǩa rul* the snow does no longer bear, **be rul* W.* **drift-sand, quicksand;** *rul-skyúr* 'sour by putrefaction' *Sch*; *rúl-dri* a putrid smell; *rúl-po* for *hrúl-po Cs.* — Cf. *ˌdrul-ba.*

རུས་ *rus* 1., *W. rus-pa*, **lineage, family,** *miṅ daṅ rus ni ˌdi-ltar-ro* their name and lineage are such and such *Glr.*; **ṅa-raṅ-ghi* (or *ṅa-raṅ dhaṅ*) *ru-čig-pa* or *-ḍá-wa* C. B.*, **rús-pa čig-čig* W.* we are of the same family; *rus-γčig-pa γsód-pa* a murderer of persons related to him by blood *Lex.*; *ťu-mi rus Lex.*: *Thu-mi*, a family-name; *rus mťó-ba* high extraction, *rus dmá-ba* low extraction *Cs.* — 2. v. the next article.

རུས་པ་ *rús-pa* (resp. *γduṅ*) 1. **bone,** *rus-čág* fracture of a bone *Med.*; *rús-pai dúm-bu* prob. small bones of which the Tibetan anatomy enumerates 360. — *mi-rus* human bone; *rkáṅ-rus* bone of the foot; *mgó-rus* bone of the skull; *rús-pai rgyan Mil.* a decoration of terrifying deities and magicians, consisting of human bones suspended from the girdle; *rús-pai rgyan drug Pth.*, the like ornament, but fastened to six different parts of the body, the top of the head, the ears, the neck, the upper arm, the wrists, and the feet; *rus ₒbol-ba* mentioned as a morbid symptom *Lt.?* — 2. **the stone** of apricots and other stone-fruits *C.*, *W.*; grape-stone *Wdṅ.* — 3. **energy**, *snyiṅ-gi Mil.*, gen. *snyiṅ-rus* q.v. — 4. v. *rus*.

Comp, *rus-kráṅ* skeleton, **rus-ṭáṅ tsóg-se** *W.* he is nothing but skin and bones. — *rús-ḱu Lt.* bone-broth(?). — *rus-gróg Sch.*: a dry bone (?). — *rus-bčúd Lt.?* — *rus-nád W.* caries. — *rús-bu* 1. small bone. 2. bones in general *Dzl.* — *rus-tsád, rus-tsód Med.?* — *rus-šiṅ* 1. *Sch.* firmness, perseverance, repentance. 2. n. of a part of the body (?) *Lt.*

རེ *re* 1. indefinite num. or pron., **single, a single one, some** (persons), **something; one to each, one at a time,** *re-ré* or *re* **every, every one, every body, each,** *ráṅ-la bu re méd-na yid-ₒṗam-pa re yóṅ-gi ₒdug, dés-na ḱyéd-la-aṅ bu re dgos* despair comes from having no son, therefore you, too, should have a son *Mil.*; *yud re* for a moment, = *yud tsam Thgr.*; *lan re lan ɣnyis* once or twice *Mil.*; *mi brgya re tsam žon čóg-pa* (a horse) sufficiently (large) for being mounted by about a hundred men *Glr.*; *lo re tsam ma-ɣtógs* with the exception of one year about *Glr.*; *ras-gos-rkyáṅ re* a single cotton garment *Mil.*; *čos-ₒbrél re* a small amount of spiritual instruction *Mil.*; *W.*: **bal re** some wool, **šú-gu re** some paper (= *žig*), **ḱú-šu re** some apples; *bčú-la ṗúr-pa re ɣtád-nas* handing to each of the ten a *ṗur-pa Pth.*; *lág-na dóṅ-tse re-ré yod* in each of his hands there was a gold-coin *Dzl.*; *nyin ré-la séms-čan ḱri re bsad Glr.* he slaughtered every day 10 000 living beings, *ra lṅa lṅa bsad* five goats (every day); *mi res lug re bsad* each man killed one sheep *Glr.*; in a somewhat different sense: **lo ré-ne lo re čúṅ-se yod** *W.* they grow smaller from year to year; *nyuṅ re* little at a time *Glr.*; *re-re ɣnyis-ɣnyis* one and all, one with another, indiscriminately *Mil.*, *re-re-bžin-gyi mgo* every single person's head *Tar.*; *re žig* **somebody, something; some** (persons), **a little;** (with or without *dus*) **a little while,** *re žig sdod* wait a little! *Dzl.*; *re žig čig-na* after a little while, *Bhar.* 37; **once, one day, one time, at a future time,** also *dus re žig-gi tse Pth* — 2. **mutual, reciprocal** (in this sense it is perh. to be spelled *res*, though it is certainly cognate to *re*), *dpon slob re ₒḱaṅ ₒbyuṅ Mil.* there arises mutual discord between teachers and disciples *Mil.*; **different, differing?** *ré-lta-bu* 'of a different kind or nature' *Sch.* — 3. sbst. a. the wooden parts of a door, *re bži* the four parts of a door-frame, *yá-re* the head-piece, the lintel, *má-re* the sill or threshold (= *yá-tem* and *má-tem*), **yá-re má-re ḍal toṅ** *W.* pull it down entirely! *logs-ré* the side posts (*C. sgo-ru*). b. v. *re-mos* and *reu*. — 4. In such forms as *mór-ra-re, mčís-sa-re, gyúr-ta-re* (*Dzl.* ༥༤, 1. ༢༦, 9. ༢༦༢, 2) it may be rendered by an adverb, as: certainly, undoubtedly. — 5. vb., v. *réd-pa* and *ré-ba*. — 6. particle, mostly put between two closely connected words: *nyams-re-dgá, blo-re-bdé Glr.*, *ₒo-re brgyál, skyug-re-lóg, že-re-ₒjigs, yi-re-múg, don-re-čúṅ, snyiṅ-re-rjé* (this last very frq.), without essentially modifying the signification, yet only used in emphatic speech. — 7. num. for *drug-ču* in the abbreviated forms of the numbers 61 to 69. — 8. num. figure: 115.

རེ་སྐན *re-skán* (etymology?), acc. to the passages which came to my knowledge a strong negative (like *οὐ μή*), **by no means, never,** *yoṅ re-skan Mil.* frq., that can never happen, that is absolutely impossible (parallel to *yoṅ mi srid*); *tsím-par ₒgyur re-skán* they never can be satisfied with it *Tar.*

རེ་སྐོན *re-skón* n. of a bitter medicinal herb.

རེ་ཁ *re-ḱá Sch.* **a picture, painting.**

རེ་འཁན *re-ₒḱán* v. *re-ba*.

རེ་འཁང *re-ₒḱáṅ Sch.*: *re-ₒḱáṅ ₒbyúṅ-ba* to be not too much (?).

རེ་གུར *re-gur* v. *ré-ba* sbst.

རེ་གྲོན *re-grón* **addition, increase.**

རེ་ལྕགས་པ་ or རེའུ་ལྕགས་པ་ *re-lčágs-pa* or *reu-lčágs-pa*, *Med.*, a mezereon with white blossoms in the South-Himalaya, of which paper is made.

རེ་ཏོ་ *ré-to* pumpkin *Kun.*

རེ་དོགས་ *re-dógs* v. *ré-ba.* vb.

རེ་ལྡེ་ *re-ldé* v. *ré-ba* sbst

རེ་སྣམ་ *ré-snám* v. *ré-ba* sbst.

རེ་འཕགས་ *re-ₒp̓ágs* prop. n., **Triloknath**, a much frequented place of pilgrimage in Chamba, with a famous image and sanctuary of *Avalokitešvara.*

རེ་བ་ *ré-ba Cs.* sbst., also *ré-bo,* acc. to some *sbré-bo*, *W.* **re-snam**, *Cs.* sack-cloth, a kind of cloth of yak's-hair, a tent-cloth (also *re-ldé* and *re-yól Cs.*); *re-gúr* a tent of such cloth.

རེ་བ་ *ré-ba* I. vb., 1. **to hope,** *t̓ams-čád mt̓óṅ-du reo* all hoped to see *Dzl.*; *dé-la p̓án-du ré-nas* hoping it might be good for it *Mil.*; *sú-la re* in whom should they place their hope, in whom should they trust? *loṅ yód-du ré-la* whilst you are hoping still to have time (enough) *Mil.*; *ré-žiṅ ltós-pa* to look up full of hope *Glr.* — 2. **to wish,** v. II. — 3. to beg, to ask alms, **to go a begging,** for victuals, **k̓o ré-a-la yoṅ* W.* he comes to beg.

II. आशा sbst. **hope; wish,** frq., *ré-ba skóṅ-ba*, *ré-ba sgrúb-pa* to fulfil a hope; *rnyéd-pa, t̓ób-pa* to get it fulfilled, to obtain what one has hoped for, *ré-ba ltar ₒgyur* it goes to one's wish, as well as one could wish; *ré-ba daṅ ldán-pa* hoping, full of hope, *ré-ba méd-pa* hopeless, despairing.

Comp. *re-t̓ág* v. *t̓ág-pa.* — *re-dógs* hope and fear, *re-dógs med* being without hope and without fear (the principal aim and prerogative of ascetics) *Mil.* — *ré-(bai) ɣnas Cs.:* room for hope; prob. also = *ré-sa* the person or thing whereon one's hopes are placed *C.*, *W.*

རེ་མོས་, རེས་མོས་ *ré-mos, rés-mos* **turn, series,** or more accurately: the order or change of the series, *ṅéd-la sdúg-pai ré-mos bab* then misfortune came to be our turn *Mil.*; *re-mos-su Pth.*, **ré-mos čós-la* Ld.* by turns, alternately, e.g. to strike one's breast with the hands; **ré-mos ré-mos* W.* by degrees, gradually; *re-móṅs* id. *Ma.*

རེ་ཞིག་ *ré-žig* v. *re* 1.

རེ་རལ་ *re-rál* n. of a medicine *Med.*

རེ་རུ་ (རས་རུ་?) *re-rú* (*ras-ru?*) *W.* the spread- or warp-beam of a loom.

རེ་ས་ *ré-sa* v. *ré-ba.*

རེག་ *reg* 1. *Sch.*: *reg-ɣzig-pa* 'notes taken down, and extracts made, during a course of study'.—2. v. the following article.

རེག་པ་ *rég-pa* I. vb., 1. (*W.*rág-če = nyúg-če**, the latter being more in use) **to touch,** to come in contact with, *lág-pa sá-la gar rég-par* where his hands touched the ground *Dzl.*; *rluṅ yál-ga-la rég-na* when the wind touches the branches *Dzl.*; *k̓á-reg-pa* c.dat.: to eat, to taste, to take, *dúg-la-k̓á-reg ré-ba yod* in taking poison there is hope, (viz. so bad are the times) *Ma.*; **ts̓á-big žal rag dzod* or *žál-la rag* W.* please, taste a little of it! *sá-la k̓ru gaṅ tsam-gyis ma rég-par ₒbyón-pa* to walk not touching the ground by an ell, i.e. to move in the air, about a cubit distant from the ground *Pth.*; *rég-pa-med-pa* intangible, unapproachable, out of reach, *Glr.* — 2. to feel, to perceive *Cs.?* — II. sbst. *reg* (prob. only abbreviation of *reg-bya*) feeling, touch, sense of feeling *S.g.* 10, 5?

Comp. *reg-dúg* ('poison that has entered the body by contact') *S.g.* 29, is said to signify now in *C.* venereal disease, syphilis. — *rég-bya* 1. what is felt or may be felt, anything palpable or tangible, *reg-bya mi ts̓or* what may be felt is felt no longer *Wdṅ.* 2. **feeling, sense of feeling,** *p̓ágs-pa-reg-bya* the feeling of the skin, *lús-po p̓yii rég-bya gráṅ-la* whilst the outside of the body appears cold to the touch, *rég-bya-rtsúb* rough to the touch *Med.* — *rég-ma Cs.* n. of a goddess.

རེང་བ་ *reṅ-ba*, pf. *reṅs* **to be stiff, hard, rigid,** *rmai reṅ sbyaṅs* to remove the hard parts, of a wound (to clear, to cleanse) *Wdṅ.*; **raṅs soṅ* W.* (the blood) has coagulated, congealed, also of a dead body: it has grown stiff; **ráṅs-te dad dug* W.* he makes himself stiff, he struggles against; *réṅs-pa* **solid** (opp. to liquid), **coagulated, stiff, hard;** *reṅs-par byed-pa* to make hard or stiff; fig.: **stiffnecked, obstinate, unwilling,** *Do.*

རེང་བུ་ *réṅ-bu* 1. **pastil for fumigating** *Lt.*, v. *spos.* — 2. *Sch.:* separate, not belonging to anything else.

རེངས་ *reṅs* sometimes for *raṅs*, v. *ñyin-reṅs, to-reṅs.*

རེངས་པོ་ *reṅs-po Sch.* **alone, single.**

རེད་པ་ *réd-pa* 1. **to be,** = *yín-pa*, in *Sp.* and *C.*, rarely in *B.*; also *ré-pa (ré-ba)* is met with; *ḱyed pʹyugs-rdzi ma red rdo-rje-semsdpar snaṅ* you are not a herdsman, no, you are *Vajrasattva* (viz. a deity)! *Pth.*; **čaṅ yǒ-pa re' mè-pa re'*?* is there any beer here or not? *C.* — 2. *Cs.:* **to be ready,** *red mda* a ready arrow *Cs.*; *red daṅ ma red rma* a healed wound and one not yet healed (?) *Sch.* — 3. **to be withered** *Ts.*

རེབ་རེབ་པ་ *reb-réb-pa Sch.*: **to be in a great haste or hurry, to be very zealous,** *W.*: **reb log čó-če** to do something wicked again and again.

རེམ་པ་ *rém-pa* vb. and adj. (to be) strong, vigorous, durable, sound, hearty, of men and animals, **rem-pa soṅ* W.* now I feel strong again; **gyóg-pa ḍúl-če-la rém-pa čo!* W.* exert yourself to walk fast! *čos spyod rem* show your ability, in performing ceremonies or incantations *Mil.*; *rém-čig rém-čig ₒdré-ťsogs-rnams* be strong, ye hobgoblins, show your power; do your best! (ironically) *Mil.*

རེའུ་ *reu Mil.* prob. **panel** or **square,** of a wainscoted wall, of a chessboard etc.; *re(u)-mig* id.

རེར་ *rer* termin. of *re*, to each individually; . . . a piece.

རེས་ *res* 1. inst. of *re.* — 2. **change, turn, time, times,** *da ṅed byéd-pai rés-la bábste* it being now our turn of acting *Dzl.*; **di-riṅ ču-ré ḱoi yod* W.* to-day it is his turn to irrigate (the field); *res byéd-pa* with verbal root, to do a thing by turns with another person, *čáṅ-la ₒťuṅ-rés byéd-pa*, resp.: *skéms-la ysol-rés mdzád-pa* to vie with one another in drinking beer *Glr.*; *skyes ₒbul-rés byéd-pa* to send mutual presents to one another *Glr.*; *res ₒjóg-pa* to change *Sch.*; *rés-kyis* relieving one another (in service), doing (a thing) alternately or by turns, e g. *nyál-la mél-ťse byéd-pa* to sleep and to keep watch *Dzl.*; *res* is also used as an adv.: 1. *res če res čuṅ* now great, now small, or partly great, partly small; *res yod res med* at one time it is there, at another not *Cs.* 2. at a time, every time, distributively: *res pʹye ťúr-mgo re tsam ₒgams* I always take the tip of a spoon full of meal at a time *Mil.*; *res yčig* once, once upon a time *Tar.*, *res ₒga* sometimes, *res . . . res* now — now, at one time — at another, frq.; **lu-ré* W.* a change of singing, an alternative song; *rés-mos* v. *re-mos; res-yzá* a changing (wandering) star, **a planet** *Cs.*; *res-ₒgrogs-zla-skár* the stars with which the moon is successively in conjunction *Sch.*

རེས་པོ་ *rés-po* **old,** v. *bgre-ba.*

རོ་ *ro* I. sbst. **taste, flavour, savour,** *ḱa-ro* id.; *ro-myóṅ-ba* to taste; six different kinds of taste are distinguished: *mṅár-ba* sweet, *skyúr-ba* sour, *lán-ťswa-ba* salt, *ḱá-ba* bitter, *ťsá-ba* acrid, *bská-ba* astringent, and the medicines accordingly are also divided into six classes; *ro brgya daṅ ldan-pa* of a hundredfold taste, i.e. of the most exquisite and manifold flavour, frq. — II. sbst. 1. also *ró-ma?* resp.: *spur*, **dead body, corpse, carcass,** *mi-ro* a dead man, *rtá-ro* dead horse, *srín-bui ro* dead insects *Dzl*; *ro srég-pa* to burn a corpse. — 2. **body,** v. comp. — 3. **residue, remains, sediment,** *ťság-ro* (or *ₒťság-ro*) that which remains in a sieve or filter, impurities, husks etc., *já-ro* tea-leaves in a teapot, *ťsíl-ro* the remains of bacon after having been fried, greaves; *gál-ro*, *rdó-ro*, *sá-ro* rubbish; *skúd-ro* the ends of threads in a seam; v. also *ro-tó*.

Comp. *ro-ḱáń*, col. **rom-ḱan** place for burning or burying the dead, a favourite spot for conjurations and sorceries. — *ro-grib* defilement by contact with dead bodies. — *ro-rgyáb* **back, back part** *Lt.* — *ro-sgám* **coffin.** — *ro-tó Ld.* (= *ro* II, 3) **residue**; **rań-sii ro-to** **wax**; **sig-pę ro-tó** ruins of walls. — *ro-stód* the upper part of the human body, chest and back *Stg.*; esp. back *Mil.* — *ro-dóm* fees given to the Lamas for performing the burial or cremation ceremonies *Mil.* — *ro-búg Sch.* **grave, tomb.** — *ro-myágs* v. *myags* — *ro-smád* the lower part of the body *Med.*, *ro-smád sbrúl-du ̥ḱyil-ba* the lower part of the body like a winding serpent *Wdk.* — *ro-rás* cloth of cotton for wrapping up a dead body before cremation; upon it incantations are frequently written against demons and malignant spirits *Pth.* — *ro-lańs* = **वेताल** (evil) spirit, or goblin that occupies a dead body (*Will.*) *Tar.* 158. — *ro-śiń* wood for burning a dead body.

རོ་ཉེ་ *ro-nyé Stg.* = *ra-nyé*, *ża-nyé* **lead.**

རོ་མ་ *ró-ma* 1. sometimes for *ro Cs.*, *Schr.* — 2. v. *rtsa* I.

རོ་ཙ་, རོ་གཙའ་ *ró-tsa*, *ró-ytsa* **sexual instinct, carnal desire,** lust *Med.*, *ró-tsa skyéd-pa* to excite, to increase the carnal appetite by medicine *Cs.*; also: to feel it; *ró-tsa-ba* 1. voluptuous, sensual, lustful *Mil.* 2. exciting or animating the sexual instinct *Wdń.*

རོག་པོ་ *róg-po* 1. *C.* **black,** cf. *bya-* and *ṕo-róg.* — 2. *W.*=*rág-pa* **reddish, yellowish-brown,** of rocks. — *róg-ge-ba* shining dimly; *żal ̥dzum-nág róg-ge-ba* with a face glowing gloomily as it were *Mil.nt.* — *rog-róg* 1. *C.* jet-black. 2. 'dark-grey' *Sch.*, prob. = *róg-po* 2. — 3. **rogue, villain** *Cs.* (a man of dark deeds?).

རོགས་ *rogs*, vulgar pronunciation of *grogs*, **friend, companion, associate, assistant** v. *grogs*; *rogs-méd yċig-pa* quite alone *Pth.*; **rog-rám ċó-ċe** *W.* = *ra-mda byéd-pa*; **rógs-po** *Ld.* adulterer, **róg-po ċó-ċe** (of a husband) and **róg-mo ċó-ċe** (of a wife) to commit adultery.

རོང་ *roń* **narrow passage, defile, cleft** in a hill, also **valley;** *brag-róń* dell or chasm between rocks, **ravine,** *roń-rtsúb* a rough country full of ravines, so Tibet is called *Glr.*; *róń-yul* id.; *róń-mi*, *róń-rta*, *róń-lċań* a man coming from, a horse bred in, a willow growing in such a country.

རོད་ *rod* **pride, haughtiness** *Ts.*

རོད་པ་, རོད་པོ་ *ród-pa*, *ród-po* **stiff,** unable to help one's self, *ród-lċi-ba Sch.* id.; *Ld.*: **rod-da-rod-dé** of decrepit or sick people.

རོམ་ཁང་ *róm-ḱań W.* for *ro-ḱań.*

རོམ་པོ་ *róm-po W.* (for *sbóm-po C., B.*) **thick, big, stout,** of men, trees, sticks; **massive, massy, plump; deep,** of sounds, opp. to *ṕrá-mo.* — *róm-yig* type, types, letters used in printing, opp. to *ṕra-yig*, v. *yi-ge.*

རོལ་ *rol* 1. **side,** only in the comp.: *náń-rol* inside, *ṕyi-rol* outside, *ṕá-rol*, *tsú-rol* etc.; *mál-gyi ṕyi-rol* the outside of the bed (e.g. has been soiled) *Glr.*; mostly as postposition: *ydáńs-pa-ċan-gyi náń-rol-na* within the town of *Yań-pa-ċan*; *náń-rol-nas ̥búl-ba* to reach, to hand from within *Dzl.*; *ċui ṕá-rol-na*, *tsú-rol-na* (or *tsú-rol-tu*) on the other side or on this side of the water; *yyás-rol*, *yyón-rol* the right side, the left side; also in a looser sense: *ṕyi-rol-tu bzuń-ba* to look upon a thing as externally or really existing *Mil.*; often pleon.: *sńón-rol-nas* **before, previously** *Thgy.*; *̥óg-rol-tu* for *̥óg-tu* **after** *Pth.*, *Tur.*; *̥di-nas nyi-ma-núb-kyi ṕyógs-rol-na* to the west from here. — 2. *Sch.*: *rol(-tu) bsád-pa* to destroy completely, to kill on the spot (?). — 3. (*Cs.* also *rol-mo*) **furrow;** *rol rmód-pa* to make furrows, to plough.

རོལ་རྟ་ *ról-rta Sch.*: **the near horse** in a team, the right-hand horse.

རོལ་པ་ *ról-pa* = *sprúl-pa*, v. *ról-ba* 3.

རོལ་བ་ *ról-ba* 1. **to amuse** or **divert one's self** (synon. with *rtsé-ba*), thus one of the twelve actions of a Buddha is *btsun-moi ̥ḱor-*

du ról-ba diverting himself with his wives; *bdag-yód daṅ ról-ba* to divert one's self with a married woman (sensu obsc.) *Schr.*; in *rgya-čer-ról-pa* (v. sub *rgya*), and in *ról-pa bkód-pa* (the n. of a certain kind of contemplation *Gyatch.*), it is used for **ललित**, playing. — 2. **to take, taste, eat, drink,** *srín-mo ḱrág-la ról-ba* witches or ogresses reveling in blood *Mil.*; *ról-pai stábs-su bžugs* there he sits with greedy mien. — 3. = *sprúl-ba* **to practice sorcery, to cause to appear** by magic power, *rnám-par ról-pa* = *rnám-par sprúl-pa*; *yé-šes ról-pai ḱyeu lṅa Pth.* for: *yé-šes-kyi sprúl-pa* incarnations of the divine Wisdom; *rol-pai mtso* prob. **enchanted lake,** occurs in the description of the Sumeru, but no Lama seemed to know its exact meaning. — 4. vulg.: **to thrash,** to cudgel.

རོལ་མ་ *ról-ma* 1. v. *rol* 3. — 2. col. for *sgról-ma*.

རོལ་མོ་ *ról-mo* (cf. *ról-ba* 1). 1. **music,** *ról-mo byéd-pa*, *W.* **čò-če**, to make music, *ról-mo spyád-pa Sch.* id. — 2. **musical instrument,** = *ról-moi ča-byád Dzl.*, *ról-ča Cs.*, in *W.* esp. cymbal.

རླ་ and རླག *rla* and *rlag* sometimes for *bla* and *glags*.

རླག་པ་ *rlág-pa* v. *rlóg-pa*.

རླངས་པ་ *rláṅs-pa* **vapour, steam,** *ḱa-rláṅs* **breath, exhalation,** **ḱa-láṅ táṅ-če** to breathe, to exhale *W.*; **gaṅ-láṅ** cloud-like snow-drifts on high hills, *ču-rláṅs* steam, watery vapour; *rláṅs-ču ˳dón-pa Schr.* **to distil.**

རླན་ *rlan* 1. **moisture, humidity,** *rlan spáṅ-ba* to avoid the wet *Med.*, *rlan steṅ nyál-ba* to sleep in the wet *Lt.* — 2. **a liquid,** *rlan-rlón* id., *rlan-rlón čaṅ* the liquid (called) beer *Lex.*; *rlán-čan* moist, wet, humid, e.g. a country, *rlan-méd* dry. Cf. *rlón-pa*, *brlan*.

རླབ(ས)་པ་ *rláb(s)-pa Sch.*: 'to remove, to clear away'.

རླབས་ *rlabs* **wave, billow, flood,** *rgyá-mtsoi rlabs Med.*; *ču-rlábs* and *dba-rlábs* or *rba-rlábs* = *rlabs*; *dus-rlabs* ebb and flood, tides *Stg.*; *rlabs γyó-ba* or *˳ḱrúg-pa* the tumult of the waves *Cs.*; *rlabs-po-čé* or *rlabs-čén*, *Lex.*: **महोर्मि**, a large wave or billow, a rolling swell of the sea, surf, surge; also fig.: a high degree, e.g. of diligence *Thgy.*

རླམ་པ་ *rlám-pa* v. *rlóm-pa*; *rlam-ḱyér Sch.* pride (?).

རླིག་པ་ *rlig-pa*, resp. *γsaṅ-rlig*, **testicle, stone,** *˳byín-pa*, *˳ṗyid-pa*, *W.* **tón-če** **to castrate,** emasculate (a man), to cut or geld (an animal), *rlig-ṗyúṅ*, *rlig-méd* castrated, emasculated, *rlig-čan* having testicles, *rlig-γčig-pa* having only one testicle; *rlig-bu*, *rlig-šúbs* scrotum; *rlig-skráṅs* swollen testicles; *rlig-rlúgs Lt.*, *rlig-blúgs S.g.*, id. (acc. to *Cs.*).

རླིངས་ *rliṅs Sch.* **good, quick,** cf. *brliṅ-ba*.

རླིད་ *rlid Sch.* a closed leather-bag.

རླིད་བུ་ *rlid-bu Sch.*: 'a whole, a lump or mass'; but this seems not applicable in the phrase *dúd-˳groi rlid-bu Lex.*, and otherwise it is not known to me.

རླུག(ས)་པ་ *rlúg(s)-pa* 1. *Cs.*: '**to purge,** *mṅal rlúgs-par byéd-pa* to cause an abortion, *rlugs-byéd* purging, procuring abortion; *rlúgs-ma Sch.*: 'the casting out, effusion'; acc. to one *Lex.* excretion of indigested food. — 2. *Ts.*: to overthrow, to pull down, v. *lug-pa*.

རླུང་ *rluṅ* **वायु** 1. *W.* *rluṅ-po* **breeze, wind,** *rluṅ ló-ma-la reg* the wind touches the leaves *Dzl.*, *rluṅ-gis skyod* (a thing) is moved by the wind *Dzl.*, blown away by the wind *Glr.*; **luṅ laṅ* C.*, **lúṅ-po ṗu dug* W.*, the wind blows, also for: there is a draught (here); **lúṅ-rag máṅ-po yoṅ dug* W.* one feels the wind (here) very much; *rluṅ čén-po Mil.*, *drág-po* a high wind, a gale; *šár-rluṅ* east-wind etc., *čar-rlúṅ* rain and wind; *skám-rluṅ* a dry wind *Cs.*; **lúṅ-po yób-če* W.* to fan; *˳og-luṅ* wind (from the stomach), **flatulence** *Lt.*; fig.: *lás-kyi rlúṅ-gis déd-de* impelled or pushed on by the wind of actions, i.e. involved in the consequences of one's actions; and in a similar manner in other instances, frq. — 2. **air,** atmospheric air, *rlúṅ-gyi dkyil-˳ḱor* **atmosphere**; *rlúṅ-gi ˳ṗrúl-ḱor* air-pump *Cs.*, *rlúṅ-gi gru* air-balloon *Cs.* — 3. in physiology: one of the three humours of the body (v. *nyés-pa*) supposed to exist in nearly all the parts and organs of the body, circulating in veins of its own, producing the arbitrary and the involuntary motions, and causing various other physiological phenomena. When deranged, it is the cause of many diseases, esp. of such complaints the origin and seat of which is not known, as rheumatism, nervous affections etc. This *rluṅ* or humour is divided into five species, viz.: *srog-ₒdzín* cause of breathing, *gyén-rgyu* faculty of speaking, *ḱyab-byéd* cause of muscular motion, *me-mnyám* of digestion and assimilation, *ťur-sél* of excretion; *rlúṅ-las gyúr-pa yin* (the disease) arises from *rluṅ Glr.*; *rlúṅ-gis bzúṅ-ste*=*rluṅ-nád-kyis btáb-ste*. — These notions concerning *rluṅ* are one of the weakest points of Tibetan physiology and pathology. — 4. **in mysticism** *rluṅ ₒdzín-pa* seems to be = *dbugs bsgyáṅ-ba*, and to denote the drawing in and holding one's breath during the procedure called *ɣtum-mo* (q.v.), which is as much as to prepare one's self for contemplation, or enter into a state of ecstasy *Mil.*; *rluṅ séms-la dbaṅ ťób-pa Mil.*, frq., is said to imply that high degree of mystical ecstasy, when *rluṅ* and *sems* have been joined into one; he who has attained to the *mgyogs-rlúṅ* is able to perform extraordinary things, e.g. with a heavy burden on his back he is able to run with the greatest speed, and the like. —

Comp. *rlúṅ-rta* **the airy horse**, n. of little flags, frequently to be seen waving in the wind on Tibetan houses, on heaps of stones, bridges etc. The figure of a horse which together with various prayers is printed on these flags signifies (acc. to *Schl.* 253) the deity *rta-mčog*. Huc also mentions superstitious practices that may be called *rluṅ-rta*. — *rluṅ-mdá Sch.* air-gun. — *rluṅ-nád* disease caused by *rluṅ*, v. above. — *rluṅ-dmár*, *rluṅ nág-po* prop. dust-storm, a storm whirling up clouds of dust; further: **storm, tempest** in general, also a gale at sea *Glr.* and elsewh. — *rluṅ-ťsúb* whirlwind, **snow-storm** *Mil.* — *rluṅ-séms* v. above, *rluṅ* 4. — *rluṅ-sér*, *rluṅ-bsér-bu*, *rluṅ bsír-ba*, a violent wind *Cs.*

རླུབས་ *rlubs* 1. in *C.*: **corner, hole, place for hiding** a thing; *Lex.*: *ḱuṅ-bui rlubs*. — 2. *Sch.*: **ditch, pit, pool, abyss,** *mei rlubs* fire-pool.

རློག་པ་ *rlóg-pa*, pf. *brlags*, fut. *brlag*, imp. *rlog(s)*, *brlag*, vb. a. to *ldóg-pa*, 1. **to overthrow, to destroy**; *ťál-bar* or *rdál-du rlóg-pa* to reduce to powder, to destroy entirely *Thgy.* and elsewh.; *rtsa-ba-nas*, or *rnám-par*, to annihilate, e.g. all the infidels *Pth.*, **to break, to smash** e.g. a vessel *C.*; **to lose** *C.*, *'á-ma lag-soṅ* I have lost my mother *C.*, *lug čig lag soṅ* one sheep has perished *C.* — 2. fig. **to pervert, to infatuate,** *nyés-pai dri-mas yóṅs-su brlágs-te* quite corrupted by the filth of sin *Dzl.*; *čúṅ-mar ₒdzín-pai bsám-rlags-ťso* those infatuated by thoughts of marriage *Glr.*; *brlág-po* **foolish, stupid,** of a little child *Thgy.*

རློང་ *rloṅ* sometimes erron. for *kloṅ* or *loṅ*.

རློན་པ་ *rlón-pa* I. 1. adj. (*Cs.* 'moist') *W.* **wet,** *ťsaṅ-rlón* quite wet, wet through; hence of meat, vegetables and the like, **fresh, green, raw** *B.* and col. — 2. vb., pf. and fut. *brlan*, **to make wet, to moisten,** *čus*, *čar-pas Dzl.*

II. *Sch.*: **to answer,** with *lan*, also *glón-pa*, *ldón-pa*, *blán-pa*, *zlón-pa*.

རློབ་པ་ *rlób-pa*, pf. *brlabs*, fut. *brlab*, imp. *rlobs*, v. *byin*.

རློམ་པ་ *rlóm-pa* I. vb., pf. *brlams*, fut. *brlam* 1. **to be proud of, to glory in, to boast of,** with termin., *bder rlóm-pa* to boast of one's good fortune, *ɣčíg-par* or *ɣčíg-tu rlóm-pa* to be proud of the identity with ... *Tar.* — 2. **to love, to adhere to, to be attached to** *W.*, **to strive after,** *ɣžán-gyi nór-la*. — 3. **to be possessed,** of demons, *ydón-gyis brláms-pa Lt.* — II. sbst. **pride,** *bsags kyaṅ rlóm-pas ₒḱyer* if perhaps (any merit) has been gathered, it is taken away again by pride *Mil.* — Deriv. *rlóm-po* **a boaster,** an arrogant person *Cs.*; *rlóm-sems* **pride, arrogance.**

བརླ་(བོ་? *Cs.*) *brla* (*-bo?*) **the thigh,** *brla ná-ba* a pain in the thigh *Do.*, *brla ɣyas* the right thigh *Glr.*, *brla-rkáṅ* femoral bone (*Sch.*: hip-bone?). **brla-ḱuṅ** groin *W.*; *brla-bar Sch.*: junction of the legs, genitals; *brla-rús* femoral bone; *brla-šá* muscular part of the thigh; *brla-súl Cs.*: 'side of the thigh'.

བརླག་པ་ *brlág-pa* v. *rlóg-pa.*

བརླང་པོ་ *brláṅ-po Lex.* and *Sch.* **abusive word, invective, abusive language** (*Sch.* also: 'rude fellow, brute'?), *rtsub-brláṅ-ba ma yin-pa* refraining from abusive language *Thgy.*; *brláṅ-po-rnams byéd-pa* to make use of such language *Stg.*; *brlaṅ-spyód byéd-pa* to be coarse, churlish *Sch.*

བརླན་པ་ *brlán-pa* v. *rlón-pa.*

བརླབ་པ་ *brláb-pa* v. *rlób-pa.*

བརླམ་པ་ *brlám-pa* v. *rlóm-pa.*

བརླིང་བ་ *brliṅ-ba C.* **firm, secure, safe** (*Sch.*: quick?), *brliṅ-po* id., both of men and things, **liṅ-ghyi ǰhe-la ḱur** *C.* carry it safely, carefully! *brliṅ-lóg Sch.*: confused, disorderly, not to be trusted.

བརླུག་པ་ *brlúg-pa Sch.*: = *mdzá-bo* friend, assistant, helper; one *Lex.* explains *bló-brlug* by *grogs.*

བརླུབས་ *brlubs* v. *rlubs.*

ལ

ལ *la* 1. the letter l. — 2. numeral: 26.

ལ་ *la* I. sbst. **mountain pass,** road or passage over a mountain, *lai gyen* the up-hill road or ascent of a mountain, *lai ṫur* the down-hill road or descent *Cs.*; *la rgál-ba B., C.* (*W.*: **gyáb-če**) to cross a mountain pass; *lá-la ˳gró-ba Cs.* id.

Comp. *la-rkéd* or *skéd* the declivity or slope of a mountain pass. — *la-ḱá* the highest point of the pass, *la-mgó* the head, or top, of a mountain pass. — *la-sgó, Sch.*: 'turnpike of a pass'. — *la-γčán-pa* a collector of duties on a ghat or pass *Cs.* — *la-čúṅ* a small pass *Glr.* — *la-mǰúg* = *la-rtsa.* *la-stóṅ* v. *stóṅ-pa.* — *la-ṫóg* = *la-rtsé.* — *la-rtsá* (*W.* **lar-sa**) foot of a mountain pass *la-rtsé* (*W.* **lar-sé**) top of it. — *la-šán Sch.*: = *la-rkéd.*

II. sbst., also *lá-ba,* **wax-light, wax-candle, taper,** from the Chinese *láh* **wax,** *C.*

III. In compounds for *la-ṗug* and *la-ča.*

IV. postpos. c. acc. 1. denoting local relations in quite a general sense, in answer to the questions **where** and **whither:** *sá-la ˳gré-ba* to roll (one's body) on the ground, *sá-la ˳gril-ba* to fall down on the ground, *nám-mka-la ˳ṗág-pa* to rise to heaven, *nám-mka-la ˳ṗúr-ba* to fly in the air, *mé-la* at, on, in, to, the fire, *rí-la* on, to, the mountain, *čú-la* in, into, to, on, the water, *šár-la* to, towards the east, eastward (e.g. to look), *bód-la* in, to, Tibet; also where we should say: from, as: *γnám-la ḱá-ba ˳bab* snow falls from heaven, *rtá-la ˳bab* he alights from his horse, *brág-la mčoṅs* he leaps down from the rock *Dzl.*, *lús-la ḱrag ˳byin-pa* to draw blood from the body by scratching. This latter use of *la* occurs so frequently, that it cannot always be looked upon as a misspelling for *las,* though this would be the more exact word. — 2. with reference to time: *žag γsúm-pa-la* on the third day, *lo nyi-šú-pa-la* in the twentieth or during the twentieth year, *zlá-ba γsúm-la* (finish it) within three months *Glr.*, *ṗyag dáṅ-po-la* at, during, the first obeisance *Glr.* — 3. in other bearings: *dé-la rtén-nas* (prop. relying on, keeping to) relative to, with respect to, in consequence of; also *dé-la*, without *rtén-nas* id.; with verbs expressing feelings of the mind: **at, off, concerning** etc., *dé-la dgá-ste* glad of, rejoicing at it; *sdíg-pa-la ₒdzém-pa* to be afraid of sin; *ma byúṅ-ba ₒdi-la ɣdams-ṅág ɣsól-to* he asked advice with respect to this not having been done *Mil.*; in introducing a new subject: *rgyál-sa me-nyág-la šór-bai lo-rgyús-la* now, as to the fact of the supremacy having been transferred to *Taṅ-gud*, it ... *Glr.*; in headings of chapters etc., e.g. *gliṅ bži'i miṅ-la* names of the four parts of the globe *Trig.*; *če-čuṅ-gi tsad-la* with respect to size *Glr.*; *bre-sráṅ-la ɣyo mi byéd-pa* not to cheat by measure and weight *Glr.*; for the Latin *erga* and *contra*, as: *dgra-la rgol-ba* to struggle against or with an enemy; *bu-la snyiṅ-brtse-nas* from love to her son; *nad-stóbs-kyi če-čúṅ-la dpág-pa* to proportion (the medicines) to the degree of the illness *Lt.; sṅár-gyi rgyún-la* in comparison with the former time *Tar.*; *rgyál-poi túgs-rje-la* by, or according to the king's favour; *ṅai lúgs-la* by my way of proceeding, according to my system *Mil.; žábs-pyi-la* (to go with a person) as a companion. — 4. most frq. *la* is used as sign of the dat. case, col. also of the accus. following a vb. a. — 5. in all the relations mentioned above, *la* is added to the inf., partic. and root of a vb., wherever the verb will at all admit of it, and besides it is used as gerundial particle in a similar sense as *te:* a. after the inf. (only in *B.*): *lha-rtén žig yód-pa-la* as there was in that place an idol-shrine *Dzl.;* often also to be translated by **although.** b. added to the root (*B.* and col.): *mtóṅ-la ma btags* (though) having seen it, yet he did not fasten it *Dzl.*; col. esp. when the root is doubled, for **while, whilst:** **ṅe ša tub-túb-la kyod šiṅ kur** fetch thou wood, whilst I am cutting the meat into pieces *W.*; in *C.* and *B.* = *čiṅ*, also added to adjectives, *lus mi-sdúg-čiṅ túṅ-la dbyaṅs snyán-pa* ugly as to his body (and) of small stature, (but) having a fine voice *Dzl.*; in sentences containing an imp. it is added to the root of it: *šóg-la ltos šig* come and look!

ལ་ཁྱི་མོ་ *la-kyi-mo W.* **the mountain-weasel**; = *sre-moṅ?*

ལ་རྒྱ་ *la-rgyá Sch.*: government, administration (?).

ལ་ཚ་ *la-cá* **sealing-wax**, *Wdṅ.*; **la-kyir* W.* balls of sealing-wax, with a hole for stringing them, used like our sticks of sealing-wax; *la-tig* drops of sealing-wax; *la-tig rgyág-pa* to drop melted sealing-wax upon (a person), as a torture.

ལ་ཉུང་ *la-nyúṅ Glr.*, either a sort of turnip, or (more prob.) for *lá-pug daṅ nyúṅ-ma* radish and turnip.

ལ་ཉེ་ *la-nyé Sch.*: 'a mark' (?).

ལ་ཏ་ *la-tá Hind.* لتّه? an imported material like flax or a sort of linen-cloth, not in general use; hence in many parts of the country unknown.

ལ་ཏུ་, ལ་ཐུ་, ལ་དུ་ *la-tu, la-tu, la-du*, prop. लड्डू, a sort of pastry of India, composed of suet, coarse meal, sugar and spices; the word may also be used for our gingerbread.

ལ་ཐིག་ *la-tig* v. *la-ča.*

ལ་ཐོད་ *la-tód* **turban** *Glr.*

ལ་དྭགས་ *la-dwágs*, also *már-yul*, **Ladág, Ladák,** province in the valley of the Indus between *mṅa-ris* and Bálti, inhabited by Tibetans and formerly belonging to Tibet, afterwards an independent kingdom, but recently conquered by Gulab Singh of Kashmere and hindooized as much as possible by his son and successor; capital **Le.**

ལ་པ་ཤ་, ལ་པ་ཤག་ *lá-pa-ša* or *lá-pa-šag Cs.* a kind of upper garment without a girdle.

ལ་པོ་ *lá-po* **buttermilk**, boiled, but not yet dried into vermicelli (*čúr-ba*).

ལ་ཕུག་ *lá-pug* **radish**, *bod lá-pug* the common black radish, ni f.; *rgya lá-pug* a red species, of an acidulous taste. The carrot (*Daucus carota*) is in *C.* also col. called *la-pug sér-po.* — *la-bdár*, gen. **lab-*

*dár**, a contrivance for grating radishes, either made of wood, or consisting of a quartz-stone with a crystallized, rough surface.

ལ་བ་ *lá-ba* v. *la* II.

ལྭ་བ་, ལྭ་ཝ་ *lwá-ba, lwá-wa, Ssk.* कम्बल, *Will.:* 'a woolen blanket or cloth; a sort of deer'; *skrai lwá-ba Stg.* frq. a kind of woolen cloth. The seat of Buddha is often a slab resembling a *lwá-ba Do.*

ལ་མ་ *la-ma Sch.:* a certain herb.

ལ་མ་སྲོ་ *la-ma-sró* **raspberry** *Kun.*

ལ་འུར་ *la-ʼúr Cs.*, also *la-gór Sch.*, **quick, swift, speedy,** *k'yod ma ʼdug ma ʼdug la-ʼúr ʼden Mil.* make haste, go without stopping (on the road).

ལ་ཡོགས་ *la-yógs* **retribution,** punishments overtaking a sinner during this life (cf. *lan-čags*) *C., W.*; **la-yóg tob yin** that will come home to you! *Sch.* has *la-yogs-pa* to return, to come back (?).

ལ་རེ་ *la-ré W.* a sort of long-legged and swift-moving centiped, frequent in houses.

ལ་ལ་ *la-la C., B.* (is said to be pronounced *la-lá* in *Sp.*, but *Thgy.* sometimes accentuates *lá-la*, according to the metre) **some, a few**; when put twice: **partly — partly, what — what;** *la-la žig* also as a singular: some body, some one *Dzl. VV*, 1.

ལ་ལ་ཕུད་ *lá-la-p̀ud* a medicinal herb; in *Lh.* a Bupleurum.

ལ་སོ་ *la-so Sch.* **list** (of cloth), **selvage.**

ལ་སོགས་ *la-sógs* v. *sogs.*

ལག་ *lag*, also *dbón-lag, dgón-lag, Sch.*: little, not much.

ལག(པ་) *lág(-pa)* 1. resp. *p̀yag*, **hand, arm,** **lág-pa tán-ċe** *W.* to shake hands, also to offer one's hand, as a pledge of faith (for *C.* v. *mdzúg-gu*); *lág-pa-nas ʼjú-ba* to take, to seize by the hand *Dzl.*; *lag-pai rgyab* or *bol* the back of the hand; *lág-pai mdun* the palm of the hand *Cs.*; *lág-tu lén-pa* **to take in hand, to exercise, to practise,** *sgóm-pa* meditation *Mil.*, *ts'ig-dón* to study and practise the import of a word, to live accordingly *Mil.*, metaph.: *mtso-lág* **arm of the sea,** gulf, **bay,** *mtso-lag-ʼbrél* narrow sea, **straits;** *glin-lág, yul-lág* tongue of land, *glin-lag-ʼbrél* isthmus, neck of land *C.*; fig. for **power,** authority, *mii lág-tu ʼgró-ba* to get into a person's power, to be at his mercy *Thgy.*, *lág-nas ʼp̀róg-pa* to snatch out of a person's hand, to deliver from another's power *Glr.* — 2. **fore-paw;** also **paw** or **foot** in gen., e.g. foot of a cock *Glr.* — 3. symb. num.: 2.

Comp. *lag-kod* **bundle, bunch, armful,** sheaf of corn *Ld.* (?). — *lag-skór Ld.*: **hand-mill.** — *lag-k'úg* **pouch, hand-bag** *Schr.* — *lag-mgó* 1. *lag-mgo tsam* like a fist *Glr.*, or acc. to others: both hands put together in the shape of a globe or ball. 2. a glove with only a thumb, a mitten *C.* — *lag-grám* leaning one's head on the hand *W.* — *lag-rgyúgs* **railing.** — *lag-rgyún* accustomed manner, **use, habit** *Cs* — *lag-ṅár* **the fore-arm** *Wdn.* — *lág-ča* **utensils, tools, implements;** object carried in the hands, e.g. royal insignia at a festival procession *Glr.*; also in a more gen. sense, like *ċá-lag, ʼk'or-γyóg lág-ča dan bċás-pa ton žig* supply servants and things (wanted for the journey)! *Glr.* — *lag-čág* a broken hand, a lame hand *Cs., Schr.* — **lag-čad** *W.* solemn promise by shaking or joining hands. — *lag-rjés* 1. impression, mark, of the hand, of the fingers. 2. a work which immortalizes a person's name, *lag-rjes ʼjóg-pa* to leave such a work behind *Glr.* — *lag-nyá*, one *Lex.* has: *lag-nyás* = *stér-mk'an-med-par lén-pa* to take what is not given, hence *lag-nya* prob. a sbst.: a grasp, a snatch. — **lag-nyár** *W.* for *lag-ṅar.* — *lag-tig* (or *dig?*) travelling-bag, pouch *Ld.* — *lag-rtags* 1. resp. *p̀yag-rtágs* q.v., sign or mark made with the hand, as a seal of verification, impressed on a legal document, but often only with the finger dipped in ink. 2. any small object, e.g. a needle, which the deliverer of a letter has to hand over together with the letter; present in general? — *lag-stábs Sch.* = *lag-*

len. — *lag-mtil* **the palm** of the hand. — *lag-dám Mil.*, *lag-dám-po C.* **close-fisted,** stingy, niggardly. — *lag-dar Lex.*, prob. the same as *láb-dár* (*W.*col.) **grater.** — *lag-γdúb* **bracelet.** — *lag-bdé Mil., C.*, the person that pours out the tea at a tea-carousal. — *lag-ˌdón Cs.* a vassal or subject paying his landlord in money or kind, opp. to *rkaṅ-ˌgró* who performs his services as an errand-goer or a porter. — *lag-rdúm Mil.* having a mutilated or crippled hand. — *lag-ldán* having a hand or a trunk, hence = **elephant,** *Cs.* — *lag-brdá* **sign** or signal made by the hand, **beckoning.** — *lag-na-rdó-rje*, *lag-rdór* v. *rdó-rje.* — *lag-na-γżoṅ-ṫogs Cs.* 'holding a basin in his hand', n. of a deity. — *lag-snód* = *lag-ṫig.* — *lag-dpón* workmaster, overseer, esp. builder *Dzl., Glr.* — *lag-ṗyís* a piece of cloth for wiping the hands, **towel, napkin.** — *lag-búbs* v. *ˌbúb-pa. lag-bér* **walking-staff.** — *lag-mi* **bail,** surety. — *lag-dmár C.* **hangman.** — *lag-btsúg* **shoot, scion.** — *lag-ṫsigs* joint of the hand, **wrist; elbow-joint.** — *lag-γzúṅs*, *W.* **lag-zúm**, **balustrade,** banister, railing. — *lág-γyog-pa* **companion, assistant, associate.** — *lag-ris* the lines in the palm of the hand *Sch.* — *lag-lén*, resp. *ṗyag-lén*, *Sch.* also *lag-stabs*, **practice, practical knowledge, dexterity,** *Cs.*: *čós-kyi lag-lén* the practice of religion, *ḱríms-kyi* of the law, *rtsis-kyi* of mathematics. — *lag-šúbs* **glove.**

ལགས་པ་ *lágs-pa*, resp. and eleg. for *yin-pa* and *ˌgyúr-ba*, **to be;** *lágs-so* like *yin*, as answer to a question: so it is! yes to be sure! very well! at your service! When a Lama asks a shepherd: *ḱyéd-kyi miṅ či yin* what is your name? the latter answers: *N.N. byá-ba lags* my name, if you please, is N.N., and asks on his part: *blá-ma ḱyed či skad byá-ba lags* what may be the name of your Reverence? *Mil.* — *de ḱyed lágs-sam* is it you, Sir? *Pth.*; *dge-sloṅ de su lags* who is this reverend gentleman? *Dzl.*; *či ltar lags-pa* (for *gyur-pa*) *γsol-pa* he reported (to Buddha) what had happened, *Dzl.*; *blá-ma-la bžugs-grogs med-pa lags-sam Mil.* has your Reverence no attendant? *ltá-ba ma lágs-kyi* that does not mean: to behold, but ... *Dzl.*; *ˏoṅ-ba či lags* 'what is it that this comes here?' i.e. how does this happen to come here? *Glr.*; *rje či lags* what is that, Sir? (when one is surprised at any thing strange or unaccountable, at an unreasonable demand etc., also when we should say: God forbid!) *Glr.*; *yin lags*, *γda lags*, *yod lags* there is, it is *Glr.*; *žal-zás γsol lágs-nas* when we shall have done dining *Dzl.*; a Lama asks: *btsal-le* (= *btsal-lam*) have you looked for it? and the disciple answers: *btsal lags* yes, I have! *Mil.*; in addressing a person: *blá-ma lags* (prop: you that are a Lama) for the mere vocative case, ὦ ἱερεῦ, *Mil.*, frq. — In *W. lags* is not in use now (cf. however *le* 3), but in *C.* it is of frq. occurrence, e.g. in Lhasa: **lā*, *lā-so*, *lā yọ'*, *lā yin** for: yes, Sir! very well, Sir! **lā? lā-am? lā-sam?** please? what did you say?

ལགས་མོ་ *lágs-mo* W. **clean,** for *légs-pa.*

ལང་ཀ་ *laṅ-ka* **Ceylon,** *laṅ-ka-pu-ri* city of the Rakshasa in Ceylon, which island is the abode of these beings, according to the belief of many people in Tibet and northern India even at the present day; *laṅ-kar γšegs-pai mdo* the *Sutra Laṅkāvatāra* in the *Kangyur.*

ལང་(ང་)ལོང་(ངེ་) *laṅ(-ṅa)-loṅ(-ṅe)* **weak,** e.g. from hunger, disease *Ld.*

ལང་ཐང་ *laṅ-ṫaṅ Scopolia praealta Don.*, a common weed with pale yellowish flowers *Med.*; in *Lh.* a species of Hyoscyamus, of frq. occurrence, seems to be understood by the same name.

ལང་བ་ *láṅ-ba* (provinc. *lóṅ-ba*), pf. *laṅs*, imp. *loṅ(s)*, = *ldaṅ-ba*, I. **to rise, to get up,** *da loṅs* get up now! also with *yar* (pleon.); *laṅs-te sdod-pa* **to stand,** *Lt.* and col.; **to arise,** e.g. of a contest *W., C.*; to go away, to depart, esp. fig.,–of the night: *nam láṅs-te* at daybreak; **to come forward, to step forth,** from among the crowd *Do.*; *ṗyir láṅ-ba* **to recover,** to be restored, to grow well, **to come to one's self,** after a fainting fit *Dzl.*; *bstán-pai mé-ro láṅs-pa yin* the dying embers of religion were blown into a flame again *Glr.*; **to appear, to break out,** of a disease, *nad-laṅs-dus* when a disease is in its first beginnings *Lt.* — II. *laṅ-ba* and *loṅ-ba*, pf. *loṅs* to come up to, to arrive at, **to be equal, to reach,** *ₒdi loṅ soṅ* with this it is made up, that will do *C.*; *ₒdrén-gyis ma laṅ* lit.: the serving up (of many dishes) would not do, i.e. there would be no end of serving up *Mil.*; *gráṅs-kyis láṅ-ba* to be numerable *Mil.*, cf. also *ča* (init.) and *rǰód-pa* (extr.).

ལང་ཚོ་ *láṅ-tso* **youth,** youthful age, *dei láṅ-tso-la ma čágs-pas* not falling in love with, not being enticed or led away by their youthful appearance *Glr.*, *láṅ-tso rgyás-pas* grown up to adolescence; *laṅ-tsoi dpal* the charms of youth *Pth.*; *láṅ-tso srin-moi ydoṅ* the face of the youthful Srinmo *Glr.*; *laṅ-tso-čan Cs.* adolescent, young; *laṅ-tso-ma* **girl,** maiden *Sb.*

ལང་ལིང་བ་ *láṅ-liṅ-ba Sch.* to be in a confused whirling motion (v. *loṅ-loṅ*); *laṅ-ma-liṅ Mil.* seems to be a word descriptive of the rising of a cloud, of the soaring of a bird of prey, *sprin-dkár laṅ-ma-liṅ.*

ལང་ལོང་ *laṅ-lóṅ* v. *laṅ-ṅa-loṅ-ṅe.*

ལང་ཤོར་ *laṅ-šór Cs.* **stubbornness, obstinacy,** adj. *laṅ-šór-čan*; sometimes *laṅ-šór* (without *čan*) seems to be also used adjectively, e.g.: *ₒdre k'yéd-pas láṅ-šor búg-čags yin Mil.* evil passion is more obstinate (i.e. more difficult to be got rid of) than ye hobgoblins.

ལད་པ་ *lád-pa Cs.* **weak, faint, exhausted,** of men and animals; **blunt, dull,** of knives; *Sch.* also **rotten, decayed.**

ལད་མོ་ *lád-mo* **imitation,** *lád-mo byéd-pa B.*, *C.*, **čo-če**, *gyab-če* W.*, **to imitate, to mimic, to say after,** *smón-lam ₒdi-skad bdág-gi lád-mo gyis* say after me the following prayer *Thgr.*; *ṅéd-kyi lád-mo k'yéd-kyis mi ₒoṅ Mil.* you cannot imitate me.

ལན་ *lan* (orig. perh.: 'turn', hence): 1. **time, times,** *lan-yčig* 1. once, one time. 2. also *dus-lan-yčig Glr.* once, one day, both as to the past and the future. 3. once for all, decidedly *Glr.* 4. for this time, first, first of all, before all, **lan čig lé-ka ₒdi čo** this work must be done first of all; *da-lán* id.; *lan ynyis* **twice,** *lan-bču* ten times etc.; *lan bdun (nam) ysum* seven times or three times, frq. in rules about ceremonies; *bsgór-ba lan máṅ-du byás-te* circumambulating round it many times *Mil.*; *lan graṅs dpag-tu-méd-pa* innumerable times *Thgy.*; *W.*: **ži lan nyi la tsam p'el** how many are 2 times 4? *bži lan ynyís-la brgyad soṅ* 2 times 4 are 8. — 2. **return, retribution, retaliation,** *lan byéd-pa* (*W.* **čó-če**), *lan ₒǰál-ba* **to return, retaliate, repay;** *p'án-lan ynód-pas* or *légs-pai lan nyés-pas ₒǰál-ba B.*, **p'ém-pe lén-la nǒ-pa ǰhé-pa* C.*, **p'án-pe lán-la nód-pa čo-če* W.* to return evil for good; **lan-zó čó-če W.* to show gratefulness, to be grateful; **punishment,** ... *bčúg-pas lan dug* that is the punishment for having allowed... *Glr.*; *lan lén-pa*, *W.*: **lan k'ór-če, táṅ-če, dug-lan ldón-če**, to take vengeance, to revenge one's self; *mig-la mig-lan só-la só-lan šróg-la šróg-lan* eye for eye, tooth for tooth, life for life; *dei lán-la* in return for that; *lan-gráṅs* a number of retributions *Thgy.*; *drín-lan* recompense for benefits received, requital of a good action, *bzaṅ-lán* id., *dei bzáṅ-lan-du* as an acknowledgment for it *Glr.*; hence *ṅan-lan* signifies: taking revenge for an injury received, returning evil for evil, not as *Cs.* gives: *bzaṅ-lan* gratefulness, *ṅan-lan* ungratefulness (?) — 3. **answer, reply,** *k'yód-kyi ysúṅ-ba dei lán-du* as answer to your majesty's question *Glr.*; *lan ₒdébs-pa* frq., also *ₒtébs-pa, klón-pa, ldón-pa Dzl.*, *W.* **zér-če** **to answer;** *lan ysól-ba, žú-ba* id. in answering to the questions of a person superior by rank, age or office,— *lan mdzád-pa* if he, the superior, answers; *ytám-lan glú-yis ₒǰal* I answer to the speech by a song *Mil.*; *dris-lan* an answer to a question, *p'rin-lan* a reply to a dispatch received, *rtsód-lan Cs.* a defendant's reply (in law), *yig-lan* answer to a letter.

ལན་ཀན, ལན་གན་ *lán-kan*, *lán-gan* **railing, fence, enclosure** *Stg.*; *Lex.*: = *pu-šu.*

ལན་སྐྱར་ *lan-skyár W.* prob. = *lan*, **retribution, return**, **de lan-kyár yin** that is all he has gained by it!

ལན་གྱོག་ *lan-gyóg Thgy.*, prob. = *lan-čags;* or perh. the original form of *la-yógs?*

ལན་ཆགས་ *lan-čágs* **misfortune, adversity, calamity,** as a supposed punishment for what has been done in a former life; every unlucky accident, that happens to a person without his own fault, being looked upon as a retribution for former crimes. Thus *lan-čags* denotes about what Non-Buddhists would call **destiny, fate, disaster.**

ལན་བུ་ *lán-bu* **braid, plait, tress of hair** (*Cs.* curl, lock of hair? *Sch.* pigtail?) *lán-bu slé-ba* or *lhé-ba* to make plaits, to plait the hair; *lan-tsár* ornaments, worn in the hair *Mil.*

ལན་ཚ་ *lán-tsa*, more accurately *lańtsa* (acc. to Hodgson corrupted from रञ्जा) n. of a style of writing in use among Nepalese Buddhists. It is a kind of ornamental writing, used by caligraphists for inscriptions and titles of books.

ལན་ཚྭ་ *lán-tswa* **salt,** prob. = *tswa*, *lán-tswa čú-la tim-pa* salt which dissolves in water *Thgy.*; *lán-tswa k'a-zás kún-gyi bró-ba skyed* salt gives a relish to every dish *S.g.*; *lán-tswai ču* salt-water *Lex.*; *lán-tswa-ba* saline, briny *Med.*

ལབ་བདར་ *lab-bdár* v. *la-bdár* in *la-púg.*

ལབ་པ་ *láb-pa* **to speak, talk, tell,** *mi-la ma lab* do not tell anybody *Mil.*; *rdzún-ytam láb-pa Bhot.* **to lie,** to utter a falsehood; *lab tsól-ba Sch.:* 'to speak unseemly, to brawl(?)'. — *lab tsám-pa Sch.:* to speak while dreaming, to be delirious. *lab ytóń-ba Cs.*, **lab gyáb-če* W.* **to talk, to chat;** **k'á-lab-čen** **eloquent,** fluent of words *C., W.*; *rgya-láb* a great deal of talk, *rgya-láb-čan* **talkative** *C., W.*

Comp. *láb-ga Cs.*, **láb-ča* C., W.* **talk.** — *lab-grógs Mil.* companion, intimate friend *Mil.* — *lab-rdól* talking unbecomingly *Sch.* — **láb-ra** (prop. *láb-sgra*) 'noise of tattling', **tattle, talk,** **láb-ra tán-če* W.* **to chat, babble.** — **lab-lób* or *lab-lo**, with **gyáb-če** to speak indistinctly, to mumble; to speak in one's sleep; **lab-lób-te dul** he walks speaking in his sleep, he is a somnambulist *W.*

ལབ་ཙེ་ *láb-tse* a heap of stones in which a pole with little flags is fastened, esp. on mountain passes *Schl.* 198.

ལམ་ *lam* 1. **way, road,** *lam-čén*, *rgyá-lam*, *stóń-lam Cs.*, **má-lam* W.* **highway, main road, high-road;** *gyén-lam* an up-hill road, an ascent, *túr-lam* a down-hill road, *préd-lam*, *rtsíbs-lam* a horizontal or a sloping road, that leads alongside a hill, *lam-prán* a narrow footpath, *lam dóg-mo* a strait path, *lam yáńspa* a broad one; **lam dé-mo** a good, easy road, **lam sóg-po** a difficult, dangerous, road *W.*; *lam tár* the road is open, may be passed, is not obstructed by snow etc. *Glr.*; *lam byéd-pa Sch.*, **lam čó-če, sál-če* W.* to clear a path, to construct a road; *rgya-gár-gyi lam* or *rgya-gar-du ₒgró-bai lam* the way to India *Pth.*; *gri-lam* the way of the knife, i.e. **a cut, slit, slash;** **'i-ne dúd-pe lam** here is the way for the smoke, here the smoke escapes *W.* — 2. way, space or distance travelled over, **journey,** *lám-du* on the road, on the journey; *bal-bód-kyi lam* the journey from Nepal to Tibet *Glr.*, *lám-du ₒjúg-pa* to set out, to travel, also: to continue one's journey, *lam-pyéd tsám-du pyin-pa dań* as we had done about half the way *Dzl.*, *lám-nas ldóg-pa* to return home from a journey, *k'rús-la ₒgró-bai lám-du* when he went to bathe *Dzl.* — 3. गति, fig. **way** or **manner** of acting, in order to obtain a certain end; *tár(-pai) lam* the way of deliverance, viz. for Buddhists: from the cycle of transmigrations, for Christians: from sin and its consequences; hence the way to happiness, to eternal bliss. The six (sometimes only five) classes of beings (v. *ₒgró-ba*) are sometimes called the six ways of re-birth within the orb of transmigration. In mystical writings *lam lńa* are spoken of as the ways leading to the *sa bču* (q. v.) *Thgy.*; *lam(-gyi) rim(-pa) Cs.*: 'a degree of advance; the several steps towards perfection'; also the title of sundry mystical writings; *záb-lam* the profound method or way, *tábs-lam* method of the (proper) means (ni f.) *Mil.*; *bla-med-rdó-rjei lam*, col. *snágs-kyi lam* denotes the Uma-doctrine or mysticism, v. *dbú-ma; skyés-bu čún-bai, ˳brín-poi*, and *čén-poi lam* three ways: that of a natural (sinful) man, that of the more advanced believer (but not: 'the happy mean' *Cs.*) and that of the saint, or the walk and conversation of the righteous, so also in *draṅ-sroṅ-gi lam* the saint's or hermit's course of life; *dgé-ba bčui lás-kyi lam spyód-pa* to walk the way of practising the ten virtues *Dzl.*

Comp. and deriv. *lám-ka* prob. = *lam*, *lám-ka-na* (another reading *lám-k'ar*), by the road-side *Dzl.* — *lam-mk'an* one well acquainted with the road, **a guide** *Pth.*, also fig. — *lam-gól* by-way, secret path *Sch.* — — *lam-grógs* **fellow-traveller**, travelling companion. — *lam-rgyúd* = *lam* 3? *lam-rgyúd lṅa Dzl.* ༢༥༤, 18, the five classes of beings, cf. *˳gró-ba* II. — *lam-rgyús-pa* = *lám-mk'an*. — *lam-čén Schr.* = *rgya-lám*. — *lam-rtágs* the signs of the way being nearly accomplished i.e. the acquirements and perfections of a saint *Mil.* — *lam-ltar-snaṅ* something looking like a road, but a spurious, wrong way *Sch.* — *lam-stégs* seat, resting-place by the way-side; also fig. *Glr.* — *lam-mdó* v. *mdo.* — *lam-˳drén-pa*, *lam-sná-pa* **guide.** — *lám-pa* 1. **police-officer** stationed on high-roads for seizing thieves or fugitives; **toll-gatherer.** 2. **traveller,** wayfarer *Cs.* 3. **bell-wether** *W.* — *lám-po* = *lam*, *lam-po-čé.* 1. **highway** *Sb.*; also as a place for practising magic, ni f. 2. **way to heaven,** = **t'ar-lam** *W.*(?) — *lám-yig* v. *yi-ge* extr. — *lam-lóg* erroneous *Mil.* — *lam-sraṅ* **lane, street.**

ལར་ *lar* 1. **but, yet, still, however** *Mil.*, *Thgy.*, *Glr.*; *lár-ni* and *lár-na* id.; occurs scarcely any more in col. language. — 2. **lar** (or **la-re**) *me'* *C.* none at all(?).

ལས་ *las* I. sbst., col. *lás-ka*, resp. *p'yag-lás* *W.* **ṭ in-lẹ**. 1. **action, act, deed, work,** *byi-dór-gyi las* the act of sweeping *Lex.*; *las-bzáṅ*, *las-dkár* a good work, virtuous action, *las-ṅán*, *las-nág* a bad, a wicked action, frq.; *lus daṅ ṅag daṅ yid-kyi las* actions, words, thoughts *Dzl.*; *lás-kyi rnam-smin* retribution, reward or punishment for human actions, frq. (cf. *las-rgyu-˳bras* below); *lás-kyi mé-loṅ* mirror of fate, mirror foreshadowing future events *Glr.*; *lás-kyi búm-pa* a certain vessel used in religious ceremonies *Schl.* 248; *las ma zád-pas* because the measure of his deeds was not yet full, his destiny was not yet fulfilled *Dzl.*; also **destination** in a general sense *Was.* (282); *lás-kyi lhág-ma lús-pa des* in consequence of the yet remaining rest of (unrequited) works *Stg.*; *sṅón-las* former action; *las dbaṅ-bčós-su-méd-pa Pth.* an accident which cannot be prevented; **performance, transaction, business,** *las t'ams-čad nus-pa* one who can do or perform every thing *Do.*; also the **functions** of some organ of the body *Lt.*; **work; labour, manual labour,** **lé-ka tób-pa** to get work; *las byéd-pa B.*, *C.*, **lẹ-ka čó-če, táṅ-če** *W.* to do or perform a work, **to work,** also of things: **to operate, to produce effects** *Wdṅ*; *mk'ar-las-byed-mi* workmen employed in building *Mil.*; *dúr-las byéd-pa* to attend to the graves, i.e. to perform the sepulchral rites and ceremonies; *zaṅ-ziṅ-las byéd-pa* to carry on business, to trade, to traffic *Mil.*; *lás-su* as a task, according to one's occupation, trade, or business, by virtue of one's office, **ex officio** (ni f.) *Mil.*; *lás-su rúṅ-bar* duly, rightly, perfectly, *comme il faut Mil.*; *lás-su byá-ba* v. below (extr.). — 2. sometimes: **secular business,** **lé-kẹ náṅ-na** in business-affairs, in practical life. — 3. **effect** of actions, and in a special sense: **merit,** *las zád-pa* the merits being over, having an end *Thgy.* (cf. 1, above). — 4. the doctrine of works and their consequences, of retribution, *las mi bden* that doctrine is not true *Thgy.*

Comp. and deriv. *lás-ka* 1. col. work, labour, v. above. 2. *Sch.* and *Wts.*: **dignity, rank, title.** — *las-skál* retributive fate, = *las-p'ró.* — *lás-mk'an* **workman** *Cs.* — *las-rgyu-˳brás* either for: *las daṅ rgyu-˳bras* works and their fruits (which in *Thgy.* are divided into *bsód-nams-ma-yin-pai las-rgyu-˳brás* sinful deeds, *bsód-nams-kyi las-rgyu-˳bras* virtuous actions, *mi-yyo-bai las-rgyu-ₒbrás* ascetic or mystical works *W.*), or for *lás-kyi rgyu-ₒbrás*: **fruits** of works, retribution and the doctrine of it. — *lás-sgo* **trading-place, emporium** *Glr.* — *lás-čan* 1. laborious, industrious *Cs.* 2. (v. above *las* 3) having acquired merit, **worthy** *Mil.* — *las-čé* in *C.* used for expressing probability, as in *W.* *ₒgro* with the gerund is used, v. *ₒgro-ba* I, 5; *mtoṅ las-čé* he will probably have seen it *Mil. nt.*; *ṅas ₒdi ₒbor las-čé* as possibly I may put this yet aside; *ḱyod mi-la-ni min las-čé* you are not Mila, are you? *Mil.* — *las ťog-pa Sch.*: **a person employed, an official, a functionary.** — *las-rtágs Sch.* **dignity, rank, title** incident to the office held. — *las-dáṅ-po-pa* v. *daṅ-po.* — *las-dár Sch.*: 'parade, ceremonial'(?) — *lás-pa* 1. **workman, labourer** *Cs.* 2. *Sp.*: vice-magistrate of a village. — *lás-dpon* overseer of workmen. — *las-spyód* works, actions, way of life, *byaṅ-čúb-kyi las-spyód skyéd-pa* to lead a holy life *Pth.* — *las-ₒṗró* 'continuation, prosecution of works', blessings following meritorious deeds, *ḱyed daṅ ṅa yaṅ sṅón-gyi las-ₒṗró-yód-pa yin* a bond of connection is formed between you and me by the merits we acquired in former periods of life *Pth.*; — **happiness,** prosperity in consequence of good works, good luck, fortunate event, opp. to *lan-čags.* — *las-ₒbrél Glr.* prob. id. — *lás-mi* **work-man.** — *las-méd* **idle, lazy, inactive.** — *las-ťsán* 1. **office, post, service,** *las-ťsán-du ₒǰúg-pa* to put into office, to appoint, *las-ťsán-nas ₒdón-pa* to put out of office, to dismiss *Cs.* 2. **official, functionary** **yúl-gyi lę-ťsęn** elders of a village-community *C.*, *las-ťsán-pa* id. — **lę-lam-ḱan** **diligent, industrious,** **lę-mi-lám-ḱan** **idle, lazy** *W.* — *las-su byá-ba* the second case of Tibetan grammar, the **dative** case.

II. only in *B.* and *C.*: postp. c. accus. mostly corresponding in its application to the English prepos. **from,** used also for expressing the ablative case (having nearly the same sense as *nas*): 1. **from,** e.g. delivering from, coming from, often = **through,** e.g. shining into a room through the window *Dzl.*; to hear, get, borrow a thing from a person etc.; to call, to denominate a thing **from** or **after,** according to; *ťsád-las dpág-pa* to define **by** or **according to** measure *S.g.*; in quotations: *ₒdúl-ba-las* **out of** the, **from** the Dulva, sometimes also for: **in** the Dulva; for denoting the material **of** which a thing is made: of earth, of clay etc.; partitively: *ₒbras dé-las šas γčig* a part of this rice, *slób-ma-las γčig* one of the disciples *Dzl.*; *ṅai yúl-mi-las bú-mo yód-pa-rnams* the girls that are found **among** my subjects *Dzl.*, *kún-las ₒṗágs-pa* distinguished **amongst** all, more excellent than all the others *Dzl.*; hence 2. **than** after the comparative degree: *ná-niṅ-las bzaṅ* more beautiful than last year *Mil.*; with a negative: *lo bču-drúg-las ma lón-te* not older than sixteen years *Dzl.*; *zlá-ba lṅá-las mi sdod* I shall not stay **longer than** five months *Glr.*; *ras-yúg γčig-las mi bdóg-ste* possessing **nothing but** one sheet of cotton cloth *Dzl.*; *ṅá-las med* there is none besides myself *Glr.*; *brnyas ₒḱyér-ba-las mi yoṅ* in the end you will probably do nothing else but despise me *Mil.*; in a brief mode of speaking: *γsa-γčig-las rǰe-btsun ma mtoṅ* we saw nothing but the leopard, your Reverence we did not see *Mil.*; *mi ṗán-žiṅ γnód-pa-las med* it is good for nothing, it only does harm *Mil.* — 3. added to the inf. of verbs it signifies not so much **from** as **after,** from doing, i.e. after doing, *nyál-ba-las láṅ-ba* to rise from lying, to rise after having been lying down; **during,** frq., the verbal root being repeated, *soṅ-sóṅ-ba-las* during my going or travelling on *Dzl.*; *náṅ-du ₒgró-bar bsám-pa-las* when (I) intended to walk in, when (I) was on the point of walking in *Dzl.*

ལས་པ་ *lás-pa Cs.* for *lús-pa*; in *rág-las-pa* and a few other expressions occurring also in *B.*

ལི་ *li* I. **bell-metal,** *li-sku, li-ťál, li-ťúr, li-snód* an idol, a plate, spoon, vessel made of that metal; *li-ma* in gen.: utensil, instrument that is cast of *li Glr.*

II. **apple,** = *sli C.*

III. *li-yul Glr.*, acc. to *Was.* (74) Buddhist countries in northern Tibet, esp. Khoten; acc. to others in northern India or Nepal.

ལི་ཀ་ར་ *li-ka-ra* or *li-ka-ra Cs.* a sort of **sugar.**

ལི་ཁྲི་ *li-kri Glr.* and elsewh., an orange-coloured powder, acc. to *Lis.* सिन्दूर red lead, **minium.**

ལི་ཐང་ *li-tán Cs.*: 'n. of a province of Tibet near the Chinese frontier', *li-tán-pa* inhabitant of that province.

ལི་བ་ *li-ba* **squinting, squint-eyed** *Sch.*, *li-ba mig* squinting eyes *Sch.*

ལི་ཙ་བྱི་ *li-tsa-byi* n. of a noble family of ancient India, often mentioned in the history of Buddha *Dzl.*, *Gyatch.*

ལི་ཡུལ་ *li-yul* v. *li* III.

ལི་ལམ་ *li-lam, Hind.* नीलाम, acc. to Shakspeare from the Portuguese *leilam*, **auction, public sale.**

ལི་ཤི་ *li-ši* 1. *Ssk.* लवङ्ग **cloves** *Med.*, *C.* — 2. *Hind.* इलाएची cardamom *W.*

ལིག་བུ་མིག་ *lig-bu-mig S g.*, *Sch.*: 'malachite'.

ལིང་ག་ *lin-ga Ssk.* 1. **sign, mark.** — 2. the image of an enemy which is burnt in the *sbyin-srég* in order thus to kill him by witchcraft *Lt.* — 3. membrum virile *Pth.*

ལིང་གོལ་མ་ *lin-gol-ma* **a large hornet** *Sik.*

ལིང་ངེ་ *lin-né* **dangling, waving, floating,** in the wind *Mil.*; *sprin žig lin byun-bas* a floating cloud? *Mil.*; **lin-lin čó-če* W.* **to dangle,** to hang dangling, e.g. on the gallows, **lin-lin sé-če* W.* **to swing, to see-saw**; *rkan-lág pra lin-né ˳dug-pa* an infant struggling with hands and feet *Pth.*

ལིང་ཏོག་ *lin-tóg* or *lin-tóg* **a film or pellicle** on the eye *Med.*

ལིང་བ་ *lin-ba C.*, also *lin-po* or *lin* alone, **a whole piece,** *lin γčig* of one piece, *lin bži* four pieces or parts, = *rnám-pa*; *γsér-gyi lin-ba Cs.*: a piece of unwrought gold; *dar-lin Cs.* a piece of silk; *lin-gis ˳dril-ba* to pack up into a parcel, to roll up into one packet *Sch.*

ལིང་ཚེ་ *lin-tse* gratings, **lattice** *Cs.*

ལིང་ལིང་ *lin-lin* v. *lin-né.*

ལིངས་ *lins* **a hunting** or **chase** in which a number of people are engaged; *dmág-lins* id. (cf. *kyi-ra*); *byá-lins Cs.* falconry, hawking; *lins-la ˳gró-ba* to go a shooting, a hunting; *lins ˳débs-pa Sch.* to hunt, to arrange a hunting party; *lins γtón-ba* to get by hunting, to hunt down, *lins btán-ba* what has been got by hunting, game shot or caught; *lins-pa* hunter, huntsman, *lins-pa-mo* huntress *Cs.*; *lins-kyi* hound, *lins-kra* hunting falcon or hawk.

ལིངས་སྐོར་ *lins-skór* hand-mill *W.* (?)

ལིངས་པ་ *lins-pa Sch.*: quite round or globular; *dkár-por lins-te Pth.*: prob.: being quite white, cf. **ldins-se* Ld.* quite.

ལིབ་ *lib*, **all,** *Ld.*: **lib du-če** to sweep all together with the hands; *C.*: **ká-wę lib kab son** all being covered with snow.

ལུ་ *lu* 1. **knag, knot, snag,** = *˳dzér-pa*; **lu-big** knot-hole *Ts.* — 2 num. for 86.

ལུ་ཀང་ *lu-kan* (perh. a misspelling for *lugs-kon?*) **crucible** for gold and silver *Sch.*

ལུ་གུ་, ལུག་གུ་ *lú-gu*, *lúg-gu*, diminutive of *lug*, **lamb,** frq.; *lu-gu-rgyúd* 1. rope to which the lambs are fastened, or strung; hence 2. small chain, e.g. watch-chain, chain or row of stitches on knitting-needles; lace-trimming and the like.

ལུ་བ་ *lú-ba* 1. vb. **to cough,** to throw up phlegm, to clear the throat. — 2. sbst. **the cough** *Cs.*

ལུ་མ་ *lú-ma Sb.* pool containing a spring, ground full of springs, *lú-ma-čan* rich in springs.

ལུ་ལུ་ *lú-lu* the fruit of some thorny shrubs, *šib-ši-lu-lu* hip, fruit of the wild rose-tree, *tser-stár-lu-lu* berry of *Hippophaë.*

ལུག་ *lug* **sheep,** **ḍó-lug, ši-lug, bšád-lug* W.* sheep for slaughter. — *lúg-kyu* flock of sheep. — *lúg-gu* v. *lú-gu.* — *lug-sgál* sheep's load — *lug-ňál-ba* and *lug-čún-ba* names of medicinal herbs *Cs.*, *Wdn.* — *lug-snyíd Sch.* **wether.** — *lug-túg* **ram** *B.*, *C.*; *lug-túg-gi rwa dbyibs* like a ram's horn *Wdn.*; *rgya-ru-lug-túg* a Saiga ram *S.g.* —

lug-ťóṅ Sch. wether. — lúg-pa 1. sbst. shepherd, keeper of sheep Ma. 2. to stick the heads together like timid sheep, to be sheepish in behaviour Ma. — lug-míg n. of a flower Med. — lug-múr and lug-rtsí medicinal herbs. — lug-tsúgs a sheep-skin with little wool on it Ld. — lug-rá sheep-fold, pen, sheep-cot. — lug-rú ram's horn; n. of several species of Pedicularis. — *lug-lóg* sheep-skin Ld.

ལུག་པ་ lúg-pa I. sbst. and vb., v. sub lug. — II. vb., **to give way, to fall down,** cf. rlúg-pa Ts.

ལུགས་ lugs 1. **the casting, founding,** of metal, lúgs-su blúg-pa Glr., *lúg-la lúg-pa* col. C., to found, to cast; lúgs-ma **a cast,** rgya-gár lúgs-ma an image (statue, idol) cast in India Glr. — 2. **way, manner, fashion, mode, method,** bód-kyi lúgs su gyis šig Glr. make it according to the fashion of Tibet; ṅai lúgs-kyis bon byed dgos you must live according to our, i.e. the Bon-fashion Mil.; bsam-γtán-la yód-pai lúgs-su byas he feigned meditation Glr.; di yin-pai lúgs-su byed they speak, act, make it appear, as if it really were so Tar. 184, 21; ṅa-ráṅ-gi lúgs-kyi mḱár-las my way of building, what I call my style of building Mil.; **opinion, view, judgment, way of proceeding,** ḱyed-ráṅ-gi lúgs-la according to you, if we followed your advice Mil.; čós-lugs **religion,** i.e. a certain system of faith and worship, p̓yi naṅ γnyis čós-lugs gaṅ bzaṅ which of the two religions, the Brahman or the Buddhist be the better one Glr.; **established manner, custom, usage, rite,** čá-lugs mode of dress, fashion, čós-lugs religious rites, rgyá-lugs Chinese (or Indian) manners, bód-lugs Tibetan manners etc.; ráṅ-lugs one's own way, γžán-lugs other people's way or manners; ráṅ-lugs-la γnás-pa (= raṅ-sa ₒdzin-pa) Glr.; seems to be only another expression for that Buddhist virtue of absolute indifference to all objects of the outer world; lugs is also used concretely, meaning the adherents of a custom or religion, hence = **sect, school, religious party, denomination,** mdo-lugs follower of the Sutras, the Sutra sect, sṅags-lugs a follower of the Tantras, the Tantra sect; in a special sense: lugs γnyis the two principal classes with regard to religious life, ₒjig-rtén-gyi lugs the laical or profane class, laymen, čós-kyi lugs the clerical or sacred class, priests Cs.; lúgs-kyi that which relates to manners or morals, **ethical** Cs. (v. As. Res. XX, 583). — 3. in conjunction with a verbal root or with the genit. of the inf. it often corresponds to the English termination **ing** as: ldáṅ-lugs the rising, getting up, ₒgró-lugs the going, sdód-lugs the sitting Mil., ₒo-rgyál yóṅ-lugs sogs šól-ₒdebs-kyi žú-ba the (possibility of) getting into difficulties and other reasons for inducing him to postpone (his setting out) Mil.; bsam-yás bžéṅs-lugs bris he described the building of Sam-yé Glr.; méd-lugs the (circumstance of) not having Mil.; yin-lugs **the condition, state** Mil.; dá-ltu ná-lugs či-ltar na as to your present illness, in what does it consist? Mil.; ťsógs-nas skyóṅ-bai lúgs-su yód-pa they joined in educating them, they educated them together Mil.; it is also added to adjectives: čé-lugs **greatness** Mil.

ལུགས་མ་ lúgs-ma v. lugs 1.

ལུང་ luṅ I. 1. **a strap,** slung over the shoulder or round the waist, for carrying things; **handle, ear** (curved), of vessels, baskets etc., different from yú-ba a straight handle, hilt. — 2. 'foot-stalk of fruits' Cs.; lúṅ-ťag Cs.: a rosary, string of beads, suspended by the girdle.

II. Ssk. **आगम,** = bka, used of words spoken by secular persons commanding respect: p̓as γnáṅ-bai luṅ ťób-nas obtaining (his) father's word of permission Dzl, luṅ ₒbyuṅ an **order** is issued (by the king) Glr., tú-ru-ška-la luṅ len dgós-pa being obliged to accept orders from the Turuskas Tar.; more frq.: **spiritual exhortation,** admonition, **instruction,** luṅ γnáṅ-ba to give it (sometimes only: to pronounce forms of prayer etc. before devotees); luṅ γtóṅ-ba id., *luṅ taṅ-ḱen* instructor, teacher, admonisher C.; luṅ stón-pa, also lúṅ-du stón-pa to instruct, to give spiritual precepts, also with regard to supernatural voices etc. *Mil.*; esp. **to prophesy,** predict, **to reveal secrets,** with termin.: *dā-na-šī-la yín-par luṅ bstan* it is prophesied that it is Dānasīla, the prediction relates to D., *saṅs-rgyás-su lúṅ-bstan-to* he has received a prediction concerning (his obtaining) the Buddhaship *Dzl.*; *mdaṅ mkā-ʼgros lúṅ-bstan-pai skyés-bu de* the man foreshown yesterday by the Dākini *Mil.*, hence *lúṅ-ma-bstan-pa* unheard of, unprecedented *Mil. nt.* (*Cs.* also: to demonstrate, *lúṅ-du brtán-du yód-pa* demonstrable?); *luṅ ʼgód-pa Cs.* to make, to establish, precepts; *luṅ ʼdrén-pa Cs.* to cite, to quote, an authority *Tar.* 210, 2; *lúṅ-gi rjes-ʼbráṅ Was.* (274) those who stick to the letter (opp. to *rigs-kyi rjes-bráṅ* to the real quality, viz. the spirit); *luṅ-bstán* exhortation, precept, commandment, *lhai luṅ-bstán bšád-pa* to communicate the precept of the god *Tar.*, . . . *žes byá-bai luṅ-bstán byuṅ* there came a divine order or prophecy of this purport, to this effect; hence *luṅ-ston-pa* **prophet** *Chr. Prot.*

ལུང་ཏག་ *luṅ-ťág* v. above *luṅ* I.

ལུང་པ་ *lúṅ-pa* 1. **valley,** *ri-lúṅ* mountain and valley; *luṅ-čén* a large valley, *luṅ-čúṅ* or *luṅ-ʼprán* a little valley; *luṅ-kóg Sch.*: 'the cavity of the valley'; *luṅ-stóṅ* a desolate, a solitary valley, as a fit abode for hermits, frq. — 2. **furrow, hollow, groove,** e.g. on the surface of a stick *Mil.*, of the liver *Med.*

ལུད་ *lud* **manure, dung,** *lug-lúd* sheep's dung; *lud ʼgrém-pa* to spread manure (on fields) *Cs.*, *lud ʼdrén-pa* to carry manure (to the fields) *Cs.*, **gyáb-če, táb-če, táṅ-če** *W.* to manure the ground; *lud-ku* dung-water; *lud-dóṅ* dung-hole; *lud-púṅ* dung-hill; *lúd-ʼbu* grubs etc. in a dung-hill.

ལུད་པ་ *lud-pa* 1. sbst. **phlegm, mucus,** *rnag-krág-gi lúd-pas bkaṅ-ste* full of phlegm, matter and blood *Glr.*; esp. in the organs of respiration: *lúd-pa čig bskyúr-bas* throwing up some phlegm *Glr.*; *lúd-pa lú-ba* to throw up by coughing *Dzl.*, *sbríd-pa* by sneezing *S.g.*; *lúd-por* spittoon, spitting-box *C.* — 2. vb., **to boil over** *ču lúd-pas* the water boiling over *Dzl.*; *mtso lúd-pa* the running over of lakes, **inundation** *Ma.*; *ču lúd-nas lúd-nas bkáṅ-ba yin* it filled, by the water rising higher and higher.

ལུམས་ *lums* **a bath** used as a medical cure; **fomentation.**

ལུམ་བི་, ལུམ་བི་ནི་ *lúm-bi, lúm-bi-ni*, n. of a queen, and of a grove called after her, situated in the north of India, where Buddha is said to have been born.

ལུས་ *lus*, also *lús-po*, **body,** *lus sá-la brdáb-pa* to prostrate one's self, frq., *lus stón-pa* to show one's self, to appear, to make one's self visible, as gods *Dzl.*, and in a similar manner *lus* is often used for expressing our reflective verbs, when relating to physical processes, cf. *sems*; *lús-kyi dbáṅ-po* the sense of feeling, in as far as it resides in the skin and the whole body of man *Med.*; *rgyál-poi ydúṅ-brgyúd* (or *rgyal-bu*) *lús-la yod* I bear a prince under my bosom *Glr.*; *lus smád-pa* **to violate, to ravish** *Pth.*; *lus ʼgrúb-pai ťóg-ma* the beginning of the development of a body as embryo *Wdṅ.*; *grúb-pa lus* v. *grúb-pa*; *lús-la čágs-šiṅ* from love of life *Dzl.*; *lus daṅ sróg-la sdó-ba* to risk or stake one's life *Dzl.*; *mi-lus ťób-pa* or *bláṅ-ba* to be born as a human being, *lus-ṅán* (to be born) as an animal, or also as a woman *Mil.*; — often for the whole person of a man: *brán-gyi lus kyaṅ dpón-du ʼgyur* even a servant may become a master *S.g.*; *lús-kyis mi bzód-par nya-ṅán-gyis ydúṅs-te* is used (*Dzl.* ༡༥༡, ༢) of an exclusively mental suffering or infirmity. — In mysticism and speculative science several expressions are employed which, however, do not differ much in their import: *sgyú-lus, ʼjá-lus, bde-ʼgro mto-ris-kyi lus*; *rig-pa ʼdzin-pai lus* (*Tar.* 56, 20), *yid-kyi lus* (frq.), लिङ्गशरीर, the immaterial body which is enclosed in the grosser material frame, accompanying the soul in all its transmigrations and not destroyed by death (*Köpp.* I., 66), *yid-kyi lus* might be rendered by 'spiritual body'; another explanation given by Lamas is: the body which exists only in our imagination (*yid*); in that case it would be identical with *sgyu-lús*.

Comp. *lus-rgyágs* a fat body *Cs.*, *lus-ríd* a mean, thin, lean body, *lus-sbóm* a thick stout figure, *lus-rín* a long tall body, *lus-tún* a short body *Cs.* — *lús-čan* having a body, hence as sbst. = *séms-čan* creature, being, *lús-čan kún-gyi yid-du ₒoṅ* a favourite of every creature *Stg.* — *lus-stód* upper part of the body, *lus-smád* lower part of the body. — *lus-bóṅs* the bulk of a body. — *lus-byád* form of the body. — *lus-med* having no body, incorporeal, ghostlike, ghostly, *lus-méd-pai skad* a ghostly voice *Mil.* — *lus-smád* v. *lus-stód*. — *lus-zúṅs* v. sub *γzuṅs*.

ལུས་པ་ *lús-pa*, *C.* also *lás-pa*, to remain behind or at home, *bód-du zlá-ba γnyis* to remain in Tibet for two months *Glr.*; **to be remaining or left** *Dzl.*; **to be forgotten,** omitted, left behind; *γyén-du lús-pa* to remain uppermost, floating to remain standing, sitting, lying, e.g. **k'a lús-sa mi dug** *W.* the snow does not remain, will soon melt away; *lús-par byéd-pa Pth.*, *lús-su ₒjúg-pa*, **lus čúg-če** *Ld.* to leave behind, to leave a remainder; *ma-lús-par* entirely, wholly, without remainder, without exception, *ₒgró-ba ma-lús* or *mi-lús Mṅg.*, all creatures without exception; *má-lus-par* prob. also: surely, undoubtedly, at any rate, in any case, ni f. — *lús-ma*, *rjés-lus*, *p'yír-lus*, *lhág-lus Cs.* **remainder, balance, residue.**

ལེ་ *le* 1. a small not cultivated **river-island** *C.*, = *gliṅ-ka* and *zal.* — 2. v. *leu.* — 3. *W.* a word expressive of civility and respect, and added to other words or sentences, like Sir! and Madam! in English, **zu-lé** good day, Sir! it is also added to the word *sa-heb* gentleman, and then *sa-heb-le* is about equivalent to: honoured Sir, dear Sir. — 4. num.: 16.

ལེ་བརྒན་, ལེབ་རྒན་ *le-brgan*, *leb-rgán* 1. *Med.* frq., *Lex.* = वरं saffron, whereas *Cs.* has: 'poppy, *le-brgan-rtsi* the juice of poppies, opium, *le-brgán-ghi mé-tog* the poppy flower, *le-brgán-ghi ₒbrás-bu* poppy-seed', and *Sch.* adds: *le-brgan-mdóg* poppy-coloured, light-red, and he translates also *le-brgán Dzl.* ༣༤, 1, by 'poppy-coloured', although it is mentioned there amongst various species of Lotus. But in *W.* poppy and opium are usually called by the Hindi name افيم, *p'im*; neither in *W.* nor in *Sik.* did I meet with any body, who knew the significations given by *Cs.* and *Sch.*, but only: 2. **diapered design** of woven fabrics; thus also *Mil.*: *le-brgán dmár-poi γdan* a flowered carpet, *le-brgán ₒjol-bér Pth.* a flowered dress with a train.

ལེ་ན་ *lé-na* the soft downy wool of goats (esp. those of Jangtháng) below the long hair, **the shawl wool**; fine woolen-cloth.

ལེ་མ་ *lé-ma* v. *leu.*

ལེ་ལག་ *le-lág* **appendix, supplement, addition** *Cs.*

ལེ་ལན་ *le-lán Cs.*: consequence; *Sch.*: rebuke, reprimand, reproof, and *le-lán-pa*, *le-lán bdá-ba* to blame, rebuke, reprove; *le-lán-čan Cs.* consequential, important (?).

ལེ་ལམ་མཁན་ *le-lám-mk'an* v. *las-lám-mk'an.*

ལེ་ལོ་ *lé-lo*, *lé-lo-nyid* **indolence, laziness, tardiness,** *lé-lo ma byed čig* don't be lazy! *Glr.*; *γčig lé-lo byás-nas* as one (of them) had been lazy *Dzl.*; *lé-los ₒk'yer* he is overcome by laziness *Mil.*; *lé-loi rjés-su ₒgró-ba* to be given to laziness *Ld.-Glr.*; *lé-lo-čaṅ* **lazy, indolent, slothful.** — **le-šól** *W.* = *le-lo.*

ལེགས་པ་ *légs-pa B.*, *légs-po* and *-mo C.* (cf. also no. 3) 1. **good,** serving the purpose, with regard to things; adv. *légs-par* well, duly, properly, *légs-par ₒtsól-ba* to search, to investigate accurately *Glr.*; *bsú-ba légs-po gyis* do care for a proper reception! *Glr.*; *légs-par gyur čig* (*Schr.* adds *k'yéd-la*) may you prosper! *Sch.*, *légs-par ₒóṅs-so* you are welcome *Sch.*; **happy, comfortable,** *bdag légs-na* when I am well off (opp. to *nyés-na*) *Do.*; *legs nyes stón-pai mé-loṅ* mirror of fate, of the future *Glr.*; *lo(-tog) légs(-pa) B.*, **lo lag-mo** *W.*, a rich, healthy, happy year; *či ltar byás-na legs* which is the best way of doing it? *Glr.*,

Tar.; *sems-čan mis byás-na légs-pa gaṅ yin* which of the actions of human beings are good (in this connection it is nearly the same as *bzáṅ-po*, morally good); *legs* is also used in politely hinting or requesting, like the English 'you had better': *k'yod p'yin-pa légs(-so) Glr.*, and still more polite: *yšégs-par legs* your Highness had perhaps better go etc. *Pth*; *nús-na šin-tu légs-so* if you can do it, very well! *Dzl.*; also *légs-so* alone, very well! well done! *légs-so légs-so* excellent! capital! — 2. **neat, elegant, graceful, beautiful** *C.* — 3. **lág-mo* W.* **good, due,** and adv. **well, duly, properly,** like *légs-par* (v. above), e.g. **me lág-mo ˳bar ˳dug** the fire burns well, **lé-ka lág-mo čos** you have worked well; but most frq.: **clean, pure, clear,** **ču lag-mo** pure or clear water (opp. to *rtsóg-pa*); **fine,** of powder, = *žib-mo*; **lág-mo čó-če** to clean, clear, wash, wipe, sweep etc.; to reduce to fine powder, to pulverize.

Comp. *légs-čan Sch.*, *legs-ldán Cs.* virtuous (?). — *legs-byás*, resp. *legs-mdzád* good deed, good work *Cs.* — *legs-sbyár*, संस्कृत, well constructed, skilfully arranged, highwrought, hence: the Sanskrit language. — *legs-smón* **patron, protector, well-wisher,** congratulator *Cs.* — *legs-bšad* a remarkable saying, a sententious remark *Mil.*, two works, called after their authors *goṅ-dkár* and *sa-skya-legs-bšád*, are recommended to students of the language. — *legs-ysol* resp. **thanks, acknowledgment,** gratitude *C.*

ལེན་པ་ *lén-pa* (rarely *lóṅ-ba, lón-pa*), pf. *bloṅs* (rarely *loṅs*), fut. *blaṅ*, imp. *lon Cs.*, *loṅ(s) Dzl., Mil., blaṅs Cs., W.*: **lén-če, nén-če, bláṅ-če** to take, i.e. 1. **to receive, get, obtain,** *ynas-ṅán* an inferior place viz. for being re-born *Thgy.* — 2. **to accept,** what is offered or given, opp. to *˳dór-ba*; also **to bear, to suffer patiently, to put up with.** — 3. **to seize, catch,** lay hold of, **grasp,** e.g. one that is about to leap into the water *Dzl.*; **to catch up; to catch, to take prisoner,** a culprit *Dzl.*; **to carry off,** e.g. the arms of killed enemies; *ma byin-par* to take what is not given, **to steal, to rob**; *lén-pa-˳dra* it is as if it had been stolen from me *Glr.*; *čúṅ-ma lén-pa* to get or take a wife, frq., also to procure one for another person; *srog lén-pa* = *˳p'róg-pa* to deprive of life, **to kill** *Mṅg.*; **to fetch,** *lén-du* (*W. *lén-na-la**) *soṅ* go and fetch it! to take possession of, **to occupy** (by force of arms) *Glr.*

ལེབ་མོ་ *léb-mo* (*Cs.* also *léb-po*) **flat,** *mon-sráṅ léb-mo* Indian pease are flat, lenticular; *léb-čan, leb-léb* id. col., **leb-léb-la bor** lay it down flat! *léb-ma, leb-tágs* **lace, bandage, ribbon** *Cs.*, *dar-skúd-kyi leb-tágs* lace of silk thread; *bhag-leb* a flat loaf of bread *C.*; *šiṅ-léb, leb-šiṅ* board, plank, *rdo-léb* a slab, cf. *gléb-pa*.

ལེའུ་ *leu* **division, section** of a speech, of a treatise, of a book, **chapter,** of very different length; *léu-čan Cs.*, *leur byás-pa Zam.* having sections or chapters, being divided into chapters; abbreviated *le*, *bšags-le daṅ šer-le čad-pa yin* the chapters (treating) of the confession of sins and of wisdom are wanting *Tar.*; *lé-ma Cs.*, *le-tsán Sch.* id.

ལོ་ *lo* 1. **year** (resp. *dgúṅ-lo*, v. *dguṅ*), *lo lṅa-bču-pa Ma.* usually *lo lṅa-bču lon-pa* (*W. *lon-k'an**) fifty years old, of fifty years; *bú-mo lo-ynyis-ma* a girl two years old *Ma.*; *lo daṅs lo, lo-ré (-re)-bžin, ló-ltar* (*Sch.* also *bstár!*) **annually, yearly;** *ló-nas ló-ru* from year to year; *sṅá-lo, ˳dás-lo* last year; *˳di-lo*, usually **dá-lo**, this year; *p'yi-lo, C. sáṅ-lo* next year; *lo ˳k'ór-te* after one year had passed, *srás-kyis lo k'or-te* when the prince was one year old *Glr.*; the names of the twelve years of the small cycle (v. below) are those of the following twelve animals: *byi* mouse, *glaṅ* ox, *stag* tiger, *yos* hare, *˳brug* dragon, *sbrul* serpent, *rta* horse, *lug* sheep, *spre* ape, *bya* hen, *kyi* dog, *p'ag* hog; thus the first year is called *byi-lo* the mouse-year, and *byí-lo-pa* is a person born in that year etc. — 2. for *lo-tóg*, v. the compounds; for *ló-ma* leaf, for *ló-tsa-ba*. — 3. prob.: **talk, report, rumour, saying,** added (like *skad*) to the word or sentence to which it belongs, *če-gé-mo ši lo zér-ba t'os tsá-na* when a rumour is heard, that N.N. has died

Thgy.; *W.*: **da lam far lo** they say the road is open now; also with a definitive subject: **'a-čé'kú-lig toṅ' lo** the mistress asks for the key; **ko kóm-se rag lo** he says he is thirsty (yet also in these cases a speaking on hearsay may be meant: somebody tells me that Mrs. N.N. asks for etc.); **ṫsór-lo** **report, rumour** *W.*, also **ṫóṅ-lo** and **lób* (?)-*lo** are said to have a similar signification; **šé-lo** and **rig-lo** *W.* are expressions of which I cannot give a satisfactory explanation; *bšád-lo byas kyaṅ krám-pa yin Mil.*, prob.: though he may get a name (in the world) by his learned discussions, he is after all a liar. — *lo* 3 prob. occurs only in col. language and more recent pop. literature; *Dzl.* ༢༧༢, 17 *lo* is a corrupt reading for *ysol*. — 4. num.: 146.

Comp. *lo-skor* (*Cs.* also *lo-kor*) **cycle of years**, a period of twelve years; it is the usual manner of determining the exact time of an event, which also tolerably well suffices for the short space of a man's life. If for instance a person in a dog-year (e.g. 1874) says that he is a *byi-lo-pa*, it may be guessed by his appearance, whether he is 10 or 22, 34, 46 etc. years old, and thus also in other cases accidental circumstances must help to determine the precise date of an event. Occasionally, however, the cycles are counted, e.g. *lo-skór brgyad* 96 years *Glr.* Besides this cycle of 12 years there exists another of 60 years which is formed (in imitation of Chinese chronology) by combining those 12 names of animals with the names of the (so called) five elements, *šiṅ* wood, *me* fire, *sa* earth, *lčags* iron, *ču* water. Each of these elements is named twice, followed, the first time by *po*, and the second by *mo*; which signs of gender may also be omitted without altering any thing in the matter. Thus *šiṅ(-po)-kyi-lo*, *šiṅ(-mo)-pag-lo*, *me(-po)-byi-lo*, *me(-mo)-glaṅ-lo* are our years 1834, 35, 36, 37, and 1894, 95, 96, 97 etc. — *lo-krims* (v. *lo-tóg-gi krims*) ceremonies, at the beginning of harvest. — *lo-gráṅs* prop. date (of the year), *Sch.* also: *lo-gráṅs ṫsáṅ-ma* **being of** (full) **age.** — *lo-mgó Cs.* the beginning of a year, new-year's day. — *lo-rgyús* v. *rgyus*. — *lo-ṅán* a bad year, a poor harvest. — *lo-čág Cs.* 'every second year'. — *lo-čúṅ* or *nyúṅ C.* young, *lo-nyuṅ-nyúṅ* very young. — *lo-nyés* = *lo-ṅán*. — *lo-snyiṅ Sch.* 'year, period or stage of life' (?). — *lo-tóg* or *-tóg* the produce of the year, **harvest, crop,** *lo-tóg rṅá-ba* to reap it, to gather it in. — *lo-ṫó* **almanac.** — *lo-ₒdod Mil.* earthly-minded, sinner? — *lo-dpyá* annual tribute. — **lo-pü** = *srus-púd*, *C.* — *lo-pyág* (*Ld.* **lob-čag**) embassy sent every year to the king to renew the oath of allegiance. — *lo-pyéd* half a year. — *lo-ṫsán* annual produce, harvest, *lo-ṫsan čé-ba* a rich, abundant harvest *Glr.* — *lo-légs* v. *légs-pa*. — *lo-bšád* = *lo-ṫó Cs.* — *lo-yséb Sch.* a stack, a heap of corn (?).

ལོ་ཀ་ *ló-ka Ssk.* **world,** *lo-ke-šwa-ra* = **अवलोकितेश्वर.**

ལོ་ཐོག་ *lo-tóg*, or *lo-tóg*, v. *lo*, compounds.

ལོ་འདབ་ *lo-ₒdáb* v. *ló-ma*.

ལོ་མ་ *ló-ma*, *W.* **lób-ma**, **leaf,** *ló-ma lhuṅ*, *brul B., C.*, **lób-ma ḍil* or *ḍul soṅ** *W.* the leaves have fallen; **lób-ma ṭá-mo** an acerose or pine-leaf; *lo-ₒdáb* = *ló-ma*.

ལོ་ཙ་, ལོ་ཙཱ་ *lo-tsa*, *lo-tsā* (v. *Ssk.* लोच् to speak?) the (art of) **translating,** *sgra daṅ ló-tsa slób-pa* to learn the language and the (art of) translating *Glr.*; also *ló-tsa sgyúr-ba* to translate *Pth.*; *ló-tsa-ba* translator (of Buddhist works) *lo-čén* great translator, seems to be a certain title; *lo-páṇ* for *ló-tsa-ba daṅ páṇḍi-ta*.

ལོ་ལི་མ་ *ló-li-ma Ld.* (*Urd.* لولی) **prostitute, harlot.**

ལོག་གེ་བ་ *lóg-ge-ba* seems to be nearly the same as *lóg-pa* adj., *te-ṫsom lóg-ge-bai ṅáṅ-la* prob.: entertaining irrational doubts or scruples; *baṅ-rim lóg-ge-ba* an inverted *baṅ-rim* q.v.; *lóg-ge-ba-la kyer* he took it back again *Mil.*

ལོག་པ་ *lóg-pa* I. vb., pf. and secondary form of *ldóg-pa*, q.v., **1. to return, to go back,** *yúl-du Glr.*; **nam lóg-te ča dug** *W.*, **nam lóg-ne ḍó-gyu yin** *C.* when will you return? *lóg-pa ₒtad Glr.*, *lóg-la ₒdól-do Glr.* let us turn back, *ṗyir lóg-pai lam* **the way back.** — 2. **to come back, to come again.** — 3. **to turn round, to be turned upside down, to tumble down** *W.*, e.g. of a pile of wood etc.; *ṅo lóg-pa* or *ldóg-pa* to turn away one's face, always used fig. for to turn one's back on, to apostatize *ₒḱór-bai yul ṅó-ldóg-na* if you mean to turn your back to the land of the cycle of existences, more frq.: *lóg-pa byéd-pa* **to revolt, to rebel,** *lóg-pa rtsóm-pa* to plot, to stir up, an insurrection *Glr.*, *lóg-pa-mḱan* a rebel *Glr.*; **lóg-pa-ċan** rebellious, seditious *W.*

II. adj. **reversed, inverted; irrational, wrong,** *lóg-pai lam*, *lam lóg-pa Mil.* a wrong way; *lóg-pa-la žúgs-pa* ('to rush into error, to turn to what is wrong?'), also euphemism for **to fornicate** *Stg.*; *lta-(ba)- log(-pa)* v. *ltá-ba*; *ċ̌os-lóg* a wrong faith, false doctrine, **heresy;** *grwa-lóg*, *jo-lóg* col. an apostate monk or nun; *lóg-par* and (col.) *log* adv. wrong, amiss, erroneously, *lóg-par sém-pa* to think evil, to have suspicions (about a thing), often = *lta-lóg skyéd-pa* **to sin;** frq.: **log ₒdrén-pa** to mislead, seduce *B.*; **log yóṅ-ċe** *W.* to come back, to return, **ši-lóg yóṅ-ċe** to recover life, to revive (after having been nearly lifeless), to rise from the dead, prob. also: to appear as a ghost *W.*; **nad log-gyáb taṅ** *W.* the disease has become worse again, there has been a relapse; **la-lóg (bla-lóg) ṗó-ċe** *W.* to turn, e.g. the roast; **ċud log taṅ-ċe** v. *γċud.*

Comp. *log-ċ̌os Ma.* = *ċ̌os-lóg.* — *log-rtógs* wrong judgment, false knowledge. — *lóg-lta* = *lta-lóg*, v. *ltá-ba.* — *log-spyod*, *Lt.*: *lóg-spyod ṅán-pa* perverse conduct, a sinful life. — *lóg-ₒtso* with *sgrúb-pa* to live in a sinful manner, as much as: to live by crime, by vice *Mil.*

ལོགས་ *logs* 1. **side,** *rtsig-logs* the side of a wall, *mdún-logs* fore-side, front-side, *rgyáb-logs* back, back part of a thing; *lógs-re* 1. **side-post of a door** (opp. to *yá-* and *má-re*). 2. each side (v. *re* 3); *logs-bzáṅ* the right or upper side, *logs-ṅán* the left or lower side (of a cloth) *Cs.*; **surface,** *sai* of the earth; **side, direction, region,** *rkáṅ-pai-lógs-nas* from the part of the feet, up from the feet (e.g. a pain in the body proceeding up from the feet) *Sch.*; *γyas-logs* the right side, *γyón-logs* the left side, frq.; *tsú(r)-logs* this side, on this side, *ṗá(r)-logs* the other side, on the other side; *lógs-su*, *lógs-la* **aside,** apart, **žág-pa** *C.* to lay by, to put aside, to put out of the way, to clear away, *lógs-su dgár-ba*, *bkár-ba* means about the same; *lógs-su bkál-ba* to hang aside, to hang up in another place; *lógs-na yód-pa* to be distinct, separate, to live by one's self, solitarily *Schf.*, *Tar.* 45, 18; *lógs-pa* other, additional, by-, co-, spare-, *rgyags logs-pa* spare-provision, so also *logs γċig*: *ṫág-pai snė́-mo logs γċig* the other end of a rope. — 2. **wall,** **log-žál** *W.* id.; *logs-bris* mural or fresco painting *Tar.*

ལོང་ *loṅ* 1. **leisure,** spare-time, vacant time, **time,** *loṅ yód-du ré-la nám-zla ₒdas* whilst you are always hoping to have (still) time (enough), you allow the favourable moment to pass away *Mil.*; similarly: *loṅ yod snyam-la mi-tse zad Mil.*; *sdód-pai loṅ méd-par* without delay, immediately, directly *Glr.*; **ṅa yóṅ-loṅ med** *C.*, *W.* I have not time to come; **ṗéb-loṅ yód-na** if your honour have time to come *C.*, *W.*; *rdég-loṅ yóṅ-bas* as there will be yet plenty of time to beat (me, you had better hear me now) *Mil.*; *loṅ-γtam Sch.*: 'cheerful talk, animated conversation'. — 2. imp. of *laṅ-ba* and *len-pa.*

ལོང་ཀ་, ལོང་ཁ་, ལོང་ག་ *loṅ-ka*, *loṅ-ḱa*, *loṅ-ga Med.* **intestines, entrails, guts;** strictly taken it is said to denote only the blind gut(?); *yár-'oṅ*, *már-loṅ Cs.*: the upper gut, the lower gut or thin guts, thick guts; *loṅ-nád* a disease of the guts.

ལོང་བ་ *lóṅ-ba* 1. pf. and secondary form of *ldoṅ-ba*, as vb.: **to be blind,** and fig.: **to be infatuated;** as adj.: blind, blinded etc., as sbst.: blind man *Dzl.* — *loṅ-ḱrid* (or *ₒḱrid-pa*) the guide of a blind man *Lex.*; *lóṅ-po*, *lóṅ-ba-po* a blind man *Cs.*; **nye-lóṅ** *W.* an empty ear of corn, a tare. — 2. also *loṅs-pa*, = *lén-pa Glr.* or *laṅ-ba* 1, 2 *Glr.*

ལོང་བུ་ *lóṅ-bu Stg*, *lóṅ-mo Mil.* **ankle-bone, astragal.**

ལོང་ལོང་ *loṅ-loṅ* being in pieces, in fragments *C.*, cf. *bun-loṅ.*

ལོངས་ *loṅs*, 1. pf. and imp. of *lóṅ-ba.* — 2. in conjunction with *spyód-pa:* **to use,** to make use of, to have the use or benefit of, **to enjoy,** e.g. *bdé-ba daṅ skyid-pa-la* happiness and prosperity; *lóṅ-spyod-par byá-bai rgyu* the object of enjoyment, the thing enjoyed *Stg.*; *loṅs-spyód* (*Ssk.* भोग) 1. **enjoyment, fruition,** use, esp. with regard to eating and drinking, *loṅs-spyód šá-la byed* they fed on meat, *loṅs-spyód šiṅ dé-las byed* they lived on (the fruits of) this tree *Pth.* 2. **plenty, abundance,** *bza-btúṅ-gi lóṅs-spyod dpag-tu-méd-pa bsag Glr.* they produced or procured an enormous quantity of food and drink; esp.: **riches,** *loṅs-spyod čé-ba* great riches; **wealth, property,** *lóṅs-spyod-kyi bdág-por gyur* he became owner of the property *Dzl.*; *mčód-pa byá-bai lóṅs-spyod med* he was not rich enough to bring an offering (to Buddha) *Dzl.*

ལོད་པ་, ལོད་པོ་ *lód-pa, lód-po,* v. *lhód-pa.*

ལོད་པོ་ *lód-po Sch.*: 'half through, through the middle, one half(?)'.

ལོན་ *lon* **notice, tidings, message,** *lon-bzáṅ* good news, *spriṅ-ba* to give notice, send word, send a message; *lon kyur* or *lon zer* has also the special sense: send in my name! *C.*; *lon žig k'yér-la šog* let me know, send me word *Pth.*

ལོན་པ་ *lón-pa = lén-pa* 1. **to take, to receive** etc. *Glr., Pth., ču lón-nam* have you fetched the water? i. e. are you bringing the water? *Pth.*; *nór-bu mi lon* I shall not receive the jewel! *Pth.* — 2. more frq. the word is used with reference to time: **to elapse, to pass,** a. in a general sense, *lo máṅ-po žig lón-pa daṅ* after many years had elapsed *Dzl.*, *riṅ-žig lón-te* after a long time, *riṅ-por ma lón-par* after a short time. b. with regard to the age of a person: *lo či tsam lon* how old are you? *bču-drúg-lon* I am sixteen *Mil.*

ལོབ་ *lob W.* sometimes for *lo* year, and *lób-ma* for *ló-ma* leaf.

ལོབ་པ་ *lób-pa,* pf., imp. *lobs,* **to learn,** rarely for *slób-pa*; *lóbs-pa* the act of learning *Dzl.*

ལོས་ *los,* **in truth, indeed,** *mgón-skyabs raṅ los yin* he is indeed the helper (from a hymn in praise of Buddha).

ཤ

ཤ 1. the letter *ša*, the English **sh**, but palatal; in *C.* it is distinguished from ཞ (*ža*) only by the following vowel being sounded in the high tone. — 2. num.: 27.

ཤ་ *ša* I. 1. **flesh, meat,** *γyág-ša* yak's flesh, *lúg-ša* mutton; *ša ₒtsód-pa* (*W.* *tsó-če*) to boil meat; *ša rṅod-pa* (*W.* *ṅó-če, šrág-če* or *lám-če*) to roast meat; '*p'yi-ša* outward flesh, *náṅ-ša* or *náṅ-ča* inward flesh, or the entrails' *Cs.*(?); *šá-nas čád-pai bu Glr.* the child of my own flesh and blood; *ša ₒk'rig-pa* sexual instinct; *'á-pę ša, 'á-mę ša* in *W.* a vulgar form of attestation; **surface of the body,** *šai ri-mo* spots, stripes etc. on the skin (of an animal) *Tar.* — 2. **muscle,** *nú-ša* thoracic muscle *Mṅg.* — 2. for *ša-k'óg* v. compounds.

II. v. *šá-ba* and *ša-mo.*

Comp. *ša-bkra* n. of a cutaneous disease *Med.* — *ša-skám* meat dried in the sun. — *ša-k'áṅ* **larder**; butcher's stall. — *ša-k'ú* broth. — *ša-k'óg* the body of a slaughtered animal, without the skin, head, and entrails, *če-ša* of a large — *čuṅ-ša* of a small animal. — *ša-ḱrág* flesh and blood, meton. 1. for body, *ša-ḱrág γsál-ba* a sound body *Mil.* 2. for: children born of the same parents *Cs.* — *ša-rgyágs* fat meat. — **ša-čúg** (*ša bčug*) meat cut into strips and hung up to dry in the sun *W.*, *C.* (*Hook.* II, 183). — *ša-rǰén* raw meat. — *ša-nyóg Sch.*: 'soup with greens in it'. — *ša-rnyiṅ* old meat. — *ša-mdóg* colour of the skin, complexion *Dzl.* and elsewh. — *ša-mdog-lóg-pa Cs.*: *erysipelas*, St. Anthony's fire? — *ša-nág* the lean of meat *Cs.* — *ša-nád* a certain disease *Lt.* — **šá-na** (lit.-*sna*) *W.* ardour, zeal? — *šá-spu* feathers, downs. — **ša-spin** meat boiled down to jelly *W.* — *ša-°ṕróg Mil.?* — **šá-bhag-leb** a sort of pie baked in oil *C.* — *ša-bo* sheep, cattle or other animals destined for slaughter *Mil. nt.* — *šá-°bu* **a maggot.** — **ša-búr** *W.* **boil, abscess, ulcer**; *Sch.*: mark left by a lash, weal. — **ša-dé** rice boiled with small pieces of meat *C.* — *ša-sbráṅ* **flesh-fly,** blue-bottle-fly. — *ša-rmén* fleshy excrescence, a little lump in the muscular flesh. — *ša-btsós* boiled meat. — *ša-ťsá* 1. hot meat. 2. friend *Pth.*, *S.g.*, *ša-ťsa-čan* amicable, attached *W.* — *ša-ťsán dmár-po Sch.*: 'a tumour resembling a weal or a wart'. — *ša-tsil* the fat of flesh. — *šá-ťsoṅ-pa* butcher, dealer in meat. — *ša-°dzin* 1. a hook for taking meat out of a kettle *C.*, *W.* 2. the **fork** of Europeans. — *ša-°dzér* wart. — *ša-zá*, *ša-zán* 1. prop.: flesh-eater, carnivorous animal. 2. gen.: a class of demons, described as fierce and malignant, *Ssk.* पिशाच. — *ša-zúg*, *ša-γzúg* = *zug* 2. — *ša-rág* dried apricots, with little pulp, and almost as hard as stone. — *ša-ríd* lean flesh. — *ša-ril* 1. little meat-pies. 2. v. *ša-ba*. — *ša-rúg* sauce, gravy *C.* — *ša-rúl* putrid meat. — *ša-ró* a disease *Wdṅ.*, is said to be an induration of the skin, callus, or perh. scirrhus. — *ša-rlón* fresh meat, raw meat, *ša-γsár* flesh of an animal that has just been killed.

ཤྭ་ *šwa* 1. *Dzl.* ?ཀ་?, 1. *Sch.*: high water, flood, inundation. — 2. *Lt.*: a certain hereditary disease or infirmity?

ཤ་ཀ་ *ša-ka* some kind of game (?) *Wdṅ.*

ཤ་ཀ་མ་ *ša-ka-ma*, *ḱa-če ša-ka-ma* **saffron** *C.*

ཤ་ཀར་ *ša-kar Cs.* a kind of sugar.

ཤ་ཀོན་ *ša-kón*, or *ša-°ḱón*, *Wdṅ.*; *Sch.*: grudge, resentment, **hatred.**

ཤཱཀྱ་ *šá-kya Ssk.*, *ṕód-pa Tib.*, **the mighty, the powerful, the bold,** n. of the family of Buddha, the founder of the Buddhist religion, and hence often n. of Buddha himself, also *šā-kya-ťúb-pa* (*Mil.* rather boldly abbreviates it into *šāk-ťub*), *šā-kya-mú-ni*, *šā-kya-seṅ-ge*.

ཤ་དཀར་ *ša-dkár* v. *γša-dkar*.

ཤ་སྐད་ *ša-skád* the cawing or croaking of ravens *W.*

ཤ་སྐྱོ་ *ša-skyó Mṅg.?* perh. dough mixed with meat.

ཤ་ཁ་མ་, ཤ་ཁ་ར་ *šá-ḱa-ma*, *šá-ḱa-ra* = *ša-ka-ma* and *ša-ka-ra*.

ཤ་ཁུག་ *ša-ḱúg Sch.* a small bag or purse.

ཤ་ཁྱི་ *ša-ḱyi Sch.* a shaggy dog, a poodle.

ཤ་འཁོན་ *ša-°ḱón* v. *ša-kón*.

ཤ་གོས་ *ša-gós*, col. for *šam-gós*.

ཤ་ཆེན་ *ša-čén Lt.?*

ཤ་ཉམ(ས)་ *ša-nyám(s) Lex.*, as explanation of *dbal?*

ཤ་སྟ་ *ša-sta*, = *klu Wdṅ.*

ཤ་སྟག་ *šá-stag* 1. also *ša-dag* **mere, merely, only,** *ḱyeu šá-dag btsás-te* only sons being born *Dzl.*; *mi dbúl-°ṕoṅs-pa šá-stag-ste* as they are all of them poor people *Dzl.*; *bdén-pa-mťoṅ-ba šá-stag-tu gyúr-to* they all come to the knowledge of the truth *Tar.* — 2. *Ld.* for (*rtai*) *šám*(-*la*)-*btags*(-*pa*) a pack, a bundle, fastened to the saddle behind the rider, **šá-stag-la ḱol* or *rel toṅ** tie it up, fasten it behind!

ཤ་དི་ *šá-di Ld.*, *Pur.* **ape, monkey.**

ཤ་ན་ *ša-na* 1. *Ssk.* शण **hemp,** *Cs.*: **flax,** *šá-nai ras Stg.*, *Sch.*: **'fine linen'**, *šá-nai* *gos* a garment made of fine linen. — 2. v. *śá-sna*, sub *śa*.

ཤ་པོས་ *śá-pos* a thick blanket *Ld.*

ཤ་བ་, ཤྭ་བ་ *śá-ba, śwa-ba Cs. W., C., B.* **a hart, a stag,** col. usually **śa-wa-ra-ćú* or *ru-ću**; *śá-p̀o* the male animal, *śá-mo* the hind, roe, *śa-p̀rúg* a young deer, fawn; cf. *Ḱa-śwa.*

ཤ་མ་ *śa-ma* 1. **after-birth,** placenta. — 2. an ordinary coat made of cloth which has not been napped *W.*

ཤ་མི་ལིག་ *śa-mi-lig* **parsley** *Ld.*

ཤ་མོ་ *śá-mo C., B.* (*W.* **móg-śa**) **mushroom;** the various species of fungus receive their appellations from their colour (*dkar-śá, nag-śa, smug-śa, ser-śa*) or from the place where they grow (*kluṅs-śa, ću-śa, lud-śa, śiṅ-śa*); the damp climate of Sikkim produces moreover **sọ-kẹ, Ḱá-wa* and *dẹ́-mo* (*sgre-mo*) *-śa-mo**, etc. *Cs.* has also *śa-maṅ*, a thick kind of mushroom.

ཤ་ར་ཤོ་རེ་ *śa-ra śo-ré* (cf. *γśér-pa*) *W.* **moist.**

ཤཱ་རི་ཀ་ *śā-ri-ka Ssk.* n. of a bird, *Gracula religiosa;* a species of jay.

ཤཱ་རིའི་བུ་ *śā-rii-bu*, शारिपुत्र, n. of one of the two principal disciples of Buddha.

ཤ་རུ་ *śá-ru* 1. **hartshorn** *Med.* — 2. n. of a vein *Med.*

ཤ་ལོག་ *śa-lóg* **warped, oblique, aslant** *W.*

ཤཀ་ཏི་ *śák-ti Ssk.*: spear, lance, pike, sword, *Cs.* also trident; *Dzl.*

ཤག་ *śag*, in *śag-ter-gás* it broke, it burst asunder *Sch.*

ཤག་མ་ *śág-ma* 1. *C.* small stones or pebbles, **gravel,** *śág-ma-ćan* gravelly, *śag-ṫáṅ* a plain abounding with gravel. — 2. *W.* **pebble,** *śag-rád* rocky ground, covered with a thin layer of mould which only by dint of much irrigation will yield a scanty produce; *śag-rúg* gravel, *śág-sa* earth mixed up with pebbles, stony, sterile ground.

ཤགས་ *śags* 1. **joke, jest, fun,** *śags ćé-ba byéd-pa* to rally maliciously, to turn into ridicule with sarcasms *Glr.; ṅan-śágs Mil.* a bad joke; *Ḱa-śágs* v. *Ḱa.* — 2. cause of a contention, object of a dispute or a quarrel, **matter in dispute** *Mil.;* quarrel, dispute, contention, in gen., **śag gyág-pa* C.* to fight, to quarrel, to dispute.

ཤང་ *śaṅ* v. *γśaṅ.*

ཤང་པོ་, ཤང་སྐུལ་ཅེས་, ཤང་རིག་ *śáṅ-po, *śaṅ kúl-će*, śaṅ-rig* v. *γćaṅ-po; *śaṅ-lág** a kind of fur, perh. for *sbyaṅ-slág* fur-coat of wolf's skin *Lh.*

ཤང་ལང་ *śaṅ-láṅ* **sabre, sword** *Pth.*

ཤང་ཤང་ *śaṅ-śáṅ* a fabulous creature with wings and bird's feet, but otherwise like a human being; *śaṅ-śaṅ-ṫéu Cs*: pheasant or partridge (**जीवजीव**).

ཤངས་ *śaṅs*, resp. for *sna*, **the nose,** *śaṅs-rgyúd Pth., śaṅs-sna* id.; *śaṅs-Ḱúṅ* nostril, *śaṅs-rtsé* tip of the nose.

ཤད་ *śad* 1. the mark of punctuation: །, also *rḱyaṅ-śád* or *ćig-śád;* it is a diacritical sign of about the value of our comma or semicolon; *nyis-śád* the double shad, ༎, dividing sentences, or, in metrical compositions, verses; *bži-śád* the fourfold shad, ༎༎, at the end of sections and chapters; *ṭseg-śád* the dotted shad (༏), an ornamental form of the ordinary shad, always made use of, when a shad is to be put after the first syllable of a line; *śad byéd-pa Lex.*, *ₒṫén-pa Sch.*, to make a shad. — 2. v. the following article.

ཤད་པ་, གཤད་པ་, གཤོད་པ་ *śád-pa, γśád-pa, γśód-pa Cs.* 1. **to comb, to curry,** (a horse), also *śad rgyág-pa.* — 2. **to brush, to stroke,** to rub gently with the hand *W.*; *śád-ma Sch.* **curry-comb,** horse-comb; **śiṅ-śẹ** a wooden rake, **ćág-śẹ** an iron rake *C.*

ཤན་ *śan* 1. **iron hoop** of a barrel *Cs.* — 2. **small boat,** **śẹ́m-pa** ferry-man *C.* — 3. snow-leopard *W.* (cf. *γsa*). — 4. **difference, distinction,** *śan ₒbyéd-pa* to distinguish, decide, determine *Mil.* and elsewh., *γžan-gyis śan mi byéd-pas* as nobody else is able to decide it *Glr.*; *skad-γnyis-śan-sbyór* is said to be the title of a certain dictionary.

ཤན་ཁ་ *śán-Ḱa* 1. **oblique** *W.*, **śán-Ḱa-la dẹ́-će** to cut off obliquely; *śan-ṫér* id.,

lam šan-tér-la ča dug the road has an oblique direction. — 2. *C.*: place of passing over a river.

ཤན་པ་ *šán-pa* 1. also *bšan-pa*, slaughterer, **butcher** *Glr.*, sometimes also **hangman;** *šán-kań* slaughter-house, butcher's shop, *šán-gri* butcher's knife, *šan-grib* pollution by the sin of slaughtering an animal. — 2. master or rower of a boat, **boatman.**

ཤབ་ཤུབ་ *šab-šúb* 1. *W.* **whispering,** **šab-šúb táń-če, zér-če** to whisper. — 2. also *šab-šób* **lie, falsehood,** *šab-šób byéd-pa* to lie, to cheat; *šab-šúb-čan* deceitful, fraudulent, crafty.

ཤམ་, གཤམ་ *šam, yšam* the lower part of a thing, e.g. of a country, *šám-pa* a lowlander (opp. to *yžúń-pa* and *stód-pa*); *yšám-du* adv. and postp. **below,** at foot, *ráń-leui šám-du ₒčad* they will be treated of in their respective chapters *Lt.*; *dei šám-du* under it, underneath (e g. to write); *šam-gós, šam-tábs*, resp. *sku-šám* a garment like **a petticoat,** worn by Tibetan priests and monks.

ཤམ་བུ་ *šám-bu* **flounces, fringes, trimmings.**

ཤམ་བྷ་ལ་ *šám-bha-la Ssk.*. in pure Tibetan *bde-ₒbyúń*, n. of a fabulous country in the north west of Tibet, fancied to be a kind of paradise; *šám-bha-lai lám-yig* (not passport, but:) 'guide for the journey to Shambhala'.

ཤར་ *šar* (from *šár-ba*) 1. **east,** *šar-p̀yógs* id.; *šár-pa* inhabitant of an eastern country; *šar-lhó* south-east. — 2. termin. of *ša*, into the flesh.

ཤར་པ་ *šár-pa* 1. young men, grown-up youth (collective noun) *W.;* perh. also: a young man. — 2. v. the preceding article.

ཤར་པོ་ *šár-po* 1. *W.* **adulterer,** **šár-po čó-če** or *ḱúr-če** to commit adultery, (on the part of the husband.) — 2. = *šar-pa* 1.

ཤར་ཕོ་ *šár-p̀o* a young man, *šár-p̀o yžón-nu ysum* three young men *Mil.*

ཤར་བ་ *šár-ba* pf. and secondary form of *ₒčár-ba*.

ཤར་མ་ *šár-ma* 1. *Sch.*: **a strip** *Schr. šar rgyáb-pa* to sew in long stitches, to baste (*Sch.: zuńs ydáb-pa*). — 2. *W., C.* **grown-up girls** (collective noun); **a female** (?)

ཤར་མོ་ *šár-mo* **adulteress,** cf. *šár-po*.

ཤར་ཤར་ *šar-šár* **straightway, directly,** *šar-šár ₒgró-ba Cs.*

ཤར་ཤུར་ *šar-šur Ld.* furrowed, having small elevations and hollows.

ཤལ་ *šal*, in *rna-šál* **ear-lap,** tip of the ear.

ཤལ་བ་ *šál-ba* 1. *Sch.* **stone-pavement.** — 2. **a harrow,** *šál-šal-ba Sch.*, **šál-la ḍúd-če** *Ld.* to harrow.

ཤལ་མ་ *šál-ma Cs.*: **a flint, sharp-edged stone;** *W.*: stony ground; mountain side consisting of detritus; *šál-ma-čan* full of sharp stones *Cs.*

ཤལ་མ་ལི་ *šál-ma-li Ssk.* the seven-leaved silk-cotton tree, *Bombax heptaphyllum Stg.*

ཤས་ *šas* 1. **part,** *ča-šas* id.; *ₒbras de-las šas yčig* part of this rice *Dzl.*; *šas-šás-su bgó-ba* to distribute, . . . *la* among *Dzl.*; *šas-čé-ba* a good deal, much, the greater part of, *zla-mtsán šas-čé-bai ḱu-ḱrág* generative fluid in which uterine blood predominates (cf. *ḱu-ḱrág* in *ḱú-ba*) *Wdń.*; *yti-mug šas-čé-bar ₒgyúr-ba* excess of dullness or stupidity *Thgr.;* *šas-čér, šas-čés, šas-čén* in an eminent degree, in an exceeding measure. — 2. **some, a few,** *žag-šás* some days *Mil.;* *ₒga-šas* some, a few *Mil.* — 3. instr. of *ša*.

ཤི་ *ši* num.: 57.

ཤི་བ་ *ši-ba* pf. and secondary form of *ₒči-ba*. 1. vb. **to die, to expire, to go out** (as light, fire); *ši-bar gyur-pa-las* when she was in a dying state *Pth.*, *ši-zin-pai ₒóg-tu* after her death; **ši-te lóg(-yoń)-če** *W.* to rise again from the dead, **láń-če** (lit. *slań-čes*) to raise from the dead. — 2. sbst. the state of dying, expiring, *ši-ba-las sos* awakened from a dying state frq.; cf. also comp. — 3. partic. and adj. *ši-ba sós-par byéd-par gyur* one already dying still recovers *Do.*; *ši-bai lus* the body of the deceased *Do.*

Comp. *śi-ki-ma, ˳či-k'a-ma* 1. sbst. **dying, death,** *śi-ki-ma-ru* in dying. — 2. adj. **dying,** *śi-ki-ma yod* (or *˳či-k'a-ma yod*) he is at the point of death, he is at death's door. — **śi-k'an** col. the deceased, the dead. — *śi-sño Sch.*: 'blessing for one deceased'. — *śi-čos* religious ceremonies for the dead *Sch.* — *śi-śa* flesh of animals that have died of themselves, the only flesh which a strict Buddhist is allowed to eat, and which accordingly in Buddhist countries is frequently consumed.

ཤི་རིག་ *śi-rig W.* clinking, jingling.

ཤི་རོག་ *śi-róg W.* a sort of early barley.

ཤཱི་ལ་ *śī-la Ssk.* for *k'rims, tsúl-k'rims* custom, manner, moral law.

ཤིག་ *śig* 1. for *čig* (q. v.) after a final s. — 2. **louse,** *mi-śig* common louse, *lúg-śig* sheep-louse, tick, *k'yi-śig* flea, *(lha)-˳dre-śig* bug; **ḍag* (lit. *brag*)*-śig-pa* W.* mite, wood-louse, tick; *śig ˳tú-ba B., *ltá-če, rúg-če* W.* to look for lice, to louse, *śig bsál-ba* to clean from lice; *śig-čan Sch.* also *śig-po* or *śig-śig-po* infested with lice, lousy; *śig-nád* pedicular disease; *śig-sró* lice and nits *S.g.*

ཤིག་གེ་བ་, ཤིག་ཤིག་ *śig-ge-ba, śig-śig* 1. standing or lying close together, **close-banded** *Mil. nt., C.* cf. *γśig-pa, γśib-pa.* — 2. **trembling, tottering, wavering;** with *mig:* looking this way and that, looking about, perh. also: rolling (the eyes).

ཤིགས་(སེ་)ཤིགས་ *śigs(-se)-śigs* **rocking,** as trees moved by the wind *Mil.; śigs-śigs yom-yóm* waving, moving to and fro, shaken etc., also fig. *Pth.*

ཤིང་ *śiṅ* I. gerundial particle for *čiṅ* after a final s.

II. sbst. 1. **tree,** *bzá-śiṅ* fruit-tree, *rtsí-śiṅ* v. *rtsi; ljón-śiṅ* a beautiful green leafy tree, *skám-śiṅ* a dry withered tree. — 2. **wood,** *śiṅ žig* some wood; *k'áṅ-śiṅ* timber, timber-wood, *búd-śiṅ* firewood, fuel, *skám-śiṅ* dry wood; *yám-śiṅ Cs.*: 'a small quantity of wood thrown into the fire for sacrifice'. — 3. **a piece of wood, log, billet,** **śiṅ nyi sum tob* W.* put two or three pieces (to the fire); **stump, stub** of a tree *Glr.; *tú-pag-gi śiṅ* W.* gun-stock; *sróg-śiṅ* axle, axle-tree.

Comp. *śiṅ-kir-ti* **a carrying-frame** *Lh.* — *śiṅ-kyu* a wooden hook. — *śiṅ-rkaṅ Schr.* **a wooden leg, a crutch.** — *śiṅ-rkéd* the upper part of the trunk of a tree. — *śiṅ-k'aṅ* 1. a wooden house, log-house. 2. shed or out-house for wood. — *śiṅ-k'u* sap, juice of trees. — *śiṅ-k'ur* a load of wood. — *śiṅ-k'ri* wooden chair. — *śiṅ-mk'an* worker in wood, **carpenter, joiner.** — *śiṅ-rgón Sch.* **wood pecker,** *śiṅ-rgon k'rá-bo* the spotted woodpecker, *śiṅ-rgon mgo-nág* black woodpecker. — *śiṅ-rgyál* a tree of extraordinary height or circumference, **a giant-tree.** — *śiṅ-ṅár* **licorice** *Sch., Wts.;* a sort of cinnamon *W.* — *śiṅ-čás* 1. wooden utensils, implements. 2. tools for working wood *Sch.* — *śiṅ-tog, śiṅ-t'og* fruits of trees, **fruit.** — *śiṅ-rta* v. that article. — *śiṅ-stan* **chopping-block** *Ld.* — *śiṅ-t'ags* wooden enclosure. — *śiṅ-t'ún* wood-picker, gatherer of wind-fallen wood. — *śiṅ-dúm* log, billet, block. — *śiṅ-dra* wooden lattice-work; wooden paling *C., W.* — *śiṅ-druṅ-pa* one sitting under a tree, i. e. an ascetic, *Burn.* I, 309. — *śiṅ-γdúgs* the leafy crown of a tree *Sch.* — *śiṅ-sdóṅ* trunk, **stem of a tree; a tree; block.** — *śiṅ-p'rán* **a small tree, a shrub, bush** *Sch.* — *śiṅ-bál* cotton from the cotton-tree *Cs.*, cf. *śal-ma-li-śiṅ.* — *śiṅ-bu* a small piece of wood, *śiṅ-bu sor-bži-pa* a piece of wood four inches broad or long *Tar.* — *śiṅ-˳brás* fruit. — *śiṅ-smán* medicine prepared from wood *Sch.* — *śiṅ-rtsá* root of a tree. — *śiṅ-rtsi* **resin** *Cs.* — *śiṅ-rtsé* **top of a tree.** — *śiṅ-ts'a* **cinnamon** (having a 'saltish' taste, as is expressly stated *S.g.*); **śiṅ-ts'ẹ lób-ma* W.* **bay-leaf, laurel-leaf.** — *śiṅ-tsál* **chip, shaving, splinter.** **śiṅ-ts'óqs* W.* **forest.** — *śiṅ-γžoṅ* a wooden basin, trough, tub. — **śiṅ-žóg** (lit. *bžogs*) **chip, splint** *W.*; shavings brought off by the plane *C.* — *śiṅ-zán* **wood-rasp** *Sch.* — **śiṅ-žél** **a small chip,** a very small and thin piece of wood, a splinter, **śiṅ-žél zug soṅ* W.* I have run a splinter into (my hand or foot).

— *śiṅ-zóg W.* **a rasp.** — *śiṅ-ysér* **a peg.** — *śiṅ-léb* board, plank. — *śiṅ-śún* the bark of trees. — *śiṅ-sél* a rasp.

ཤིང་ཀུན་ *śiṅ-kun* **asa foetida,** used as medicine, and (like garlic) as a spice; also n. of a mountain pass between Lahoul and Zaṅkar.

ཤིང་རྟ་ *śiṅ-rta* ('wooden horse') **waggon, cart,** carriage, also fig. = *ṫég-pa*, e.g. *śiṅ-rta čén-po* frq. in the writings of *Tsoṅḱapa*; *śiṅ-rta-ₒḱór-lo* id.; *śiṅ-rtai ḱaṅ-bzáṅ* the body of a carriage, *śiṅ-rtai mda* the pole, beam, shaft of a cart, *ₒṗáṅ-lo* the wheel, *rǰes, lam, śul, srol* the track, rut (of a cart) *Cs.*; *śiṅ-rta rkaṅ-yčig Sch.* wheelbarrow; *śiṅ-rta-mḱan Cs.* maker of carts, cartwright; *śiṅ-rta-pa* 1. carter, driver, coachman. 2. charioteer.

ཤིད་ *śid* 1. *Sch.* **hazel-nut.** — 2. also *yśid-yśid-ma, yśid-stón, yśid-zán* **funeral repast,** of which every body may partake; *śid-čós* religious funeral ceremony; *śid-sa Sch.* 1. burying ground, cemetery. 2. a fruitful field = *yśin-sa*. Cf. *yśin*.

ཤིན་ཏུ་ *śin-tu* **very, greatly,** esp. before adj. and adv., in *B.* frq.

ཤིབ་ *śib* v. *śib*.

ཤིབ་པ་ *śib-pa* v. *śúb-pa* **to whisper.**

ཤིབ་ཤི་ལུ་ལུ་ *śib-śi-lú-lu* or *rú-ru Ld.* **hip,** the fruit of the dog-rose.

ཤིམ་ཤ་པ་ *śim-śa-pa Cs.* a kind of tree or wood.

ཤིར་, ཤིར་ཤིར་ *śir, śir-śir*, with *ₒtón-pa Cs.* to gush out, to stream forth with a noise.

ཤིལ་བ་ *śil-ba W.* to drip through.

ཤིལ་ལི་ *śil-li* a gauze-like texture *W.*; *śil-śil* 1. id. 2. *Cs.*: 'a cant word denoting the noise of any thing'.

ཤིས་ *śis* **good luck, fortune, bliss;** *de ₒbyúṅ-na śis* if that happens, it will be an auspicious sign, *śis-pai miṅ* a name foreboding good *Lt.*, *mi śis-pai ltas* an omen foreboding ill *Wdṅ.*; *bstán-pai śis* acc. to *Schl.* 232 denotes the religious plays performed in the convents. *Cs.*: *śis(-pa)-po* one blessed, *śis-pa yin-pa* to be blessed, *śis-par ₒgyúr-ba* to become blessed, *śis-par byéd-pa* to make blessed, to bless; *bkra-śis* v. *bkrá-ba*.

ཤུ་ *śu* 1. acc. to Cunningham and other English authorities the Tibetan word for **stag;** yet as none of the many Tibetans, from different parts of the country, that were consulted by us, seemed to know this word, it is not unlikely, that in consequence of indistinct hearing it is but a corruption of *śa-ba* (q. v.). — 2. **śu-śú ǰhé-pa** *C.* **to whistle.** — 3. num.: 87.

ཤུ་དག་ *śu-dág* n. of a plant *Med.*; *Sch.*: **the rush.**

ཤུ་བ་ *śú-ba* I. sbst. 1. **an abscess, ulcer, sore** *Cs.*: *śú-ba ₒton* an abscess rises, *na* gives pain, *ṗan* heals; **śu-ₒbúr** *W.*, and prob. also *śu-ṫór Med.*, id.; **śu-nág* and *bá-śu** *W.* a sore that has become inflamed and rankling. — 2. **scab, scurf, scald** *W.*

II. vb., pf. *(b)śus*, fut. *bśu*, imp. *(b)śu(s)*, 1. **to take off,** pull off, draw off, *yżán-gyi gos* to take off a person's clothes, *gó-ča* armour, *mtśón-ča* arms, weapons *Pth.*; **to strip, strip off,** e.g. leaves, twigs, *ṗágs-pa* the skin, the peel, hence (also without *ṗágs-pa*) **to skin, to pare, to peel** *W.*, e.g. **'á-lu śú-če** to peel potatoes; *gyab-śús* coat of wool shorn from a sheep, fleece *Ld.* — 2. **to copy,** *dpe* a book, resp. *żal-śús byéd-pa* *Cs.*; *dpe-bśús* a copied book *C.*

ཤུ་བྷཾ་ *śu-bham Ssk.*, sometimes at the end of books, hail! all hail!

ཤུ་ར་སེ་(ན་) *śu-ra-se(-na)* n. of a tract of land in the neighbourhood of Mathura, not far from Agra *Wdk.*

ཤུ་ཨི་ཀ་ *śú-'i-ka Tar.* 63, 8, prob. also *śu-lig Sch.*, n. of a fabulous country in the north-west.

ཤུག་ *śug* 1. **a thrust, push, knock,** **śug čém-po ǰhé-pa** **to push off,** to give a knock, to elbow, differing from *ₒṗúl-ba* to shove (by a more gentle motion) *C.* — 2. in comp.: *ḱyo-śúg*, v. *ḱyo*; *śúg-bza* **wife,** consort, spouse *Schr.* — 3. *W.*: **old,** but still fit for use. — 4. *śug-śúg-la* col. for *śúb-bur* **softly, gently,** e.g. *ₒgró-ba* to walk, to tread etc.

ཤུག་གུ *śúg-gu W.* for *śóg-bu.*

ཤུག་པ *śúg-pa* 1. the high, cypress-like **juniper-tree** of the Himalaya mountains, **the pencil cedar** (*Juniperus excelsa*). It covers large mountain tracts, is considered sacred, and much used in religious ceremonies; its berries (*śug-ˌbrás*) are burnt as incense. — *śug-dúd* the smoke or perfume of juniper.—*śug-ṫsér Med.* the young pointed sprouts of this tree. — *sug-ṫsód* a sort of mistletoe, *Viscum Oxycedri*, growing on it and gradually killing it. The leaves have a slightly sour taste and are used for culinary purposes *W.* — *rgya-śug* acc. to *Cs.* = *spá-ma Juniperus squamosa*, a low shrub and similar to our *Juniperus communis*. But a passage of the *Stg.* shows that its fruits are eaten like pease or rice, which cannot be imagined of juniper-berries or cypress cones; cf. *spá-ma.* — 2. in *śúg-pa ˌpúd-pa Sch.*, v. sub *ˌpúd-pa.*

ཤུགས *śugs* 1. **inherent strength, power, energy,** c. genit.: *dád-pai, byáms-pai, dgá-bai śúgs-kyis* by the power or ardour of faith, love, joy, e.g. to shed tears, = to weep with joy etc. *Glr.* and elsewh.; *ɣċin-gyi śugs dgag mi bya* the impulse to make water must not be suppressed *Med.*; *ˌdi-dag sṅón-gyi sbyin-śugs yin* this is the power of former alms or presents *Glr.*; *ṫúgs-rǰei śúgs-kyis* by the power of grace *Do.*; *der sléb-pai śugs* the power or ability of attaining to that place *Thgr.*; without a genit.: *śúgs-kyis* = *ráṅ-śugs-kyis* spontaneously, of one's own accord, *śúgs-kyis yoṅ* they will, no doubt, come of their own accord *Mil.*; *śugs byéd-pa* to exert one's self(?); *śugs-stóbs* = *śugs*; *sṅá-śugs ˌdrén-pa Cs.*: 'the accenting the first syllable'. — 2. col. also *śubs* and *śud*, mostly in compounds: *śúgs-skad Mil.*, *śúgs-sgra*, col. **śúg-ra** **a whistling,** a whistle or whiff; *śúgs-glu* 1. a whistling. 2. a whistled tune, **śúg-ḍa ǰhé'-pa** to whistle a tune *C.*; *śúgs-pa* a small whistle which, in sounding it, is put quite into the mouth.

ཤུགས་ནར *śugs-nár* (*W.* **k̔óg-śúg**), *śugs-riṅ* **sigh, groan,** *śugs nar byéd-pa* or *ˌbyin-pa* to sigh, to groan, *śugs-riṅ nar nár ˌdug* **he heaves a deep sigh** *Mil. nt.*

ཤུང་བ *śúṅ-ba*, pf. *śuṅs*, 1. **to snore.** — 2. **to hum, to buzz,** e.g. of a large beetle.

ཤུད *śud* v. *śugs* 2.

ཤུད་པ *śúd-pa* pf. fut. *bśud*, 1. **to rub,** e.g. one thing against another *C.* — 2. **to get scratched, excoriated, galled** (cf. *śún-pa*). — 3. *śud byéd-pa* (*W.* **ċó-ċe**) **to steal silently away, to sneak off** unperceived.

ཤུན་པ *śún-pa* **bark, rind, peel, skin,** *śun-kóg*, *śun-págs* id., the last expression is also used of the skin of animals *Lex.* — *p̔yi-śun* the outer rind or skin, *náṅ-śun* the inner rind; *bár-śun* the middle rind, the bast, esp. of willows *Sch.*: *śun-kóg láṅs-pa* the spontaneous chapping or peeling off of the skin; *śun-máṅ* **box-wood.**

ཤུབ་པ *śúb-pa*, also *śíb-pa*, pf. imp. *śubs*, to speak in a low voice, **to whisper,** *śub byéd-pa* id.; **k̔og-śúb-la sil-ċe** *W.* to read in a low voice, to read whispering; *śúb-bu* a whispering, *śúb-bus zlá-ba* to recite in a low voice *Lex.*, *śúb-bur smrá-ba B.*, **śúb-la zér-ċe** *W.* to speak softly; *śúb-bus smód-pa* to reprehend in a whisper *B.*

ཤུབས *śubs* **case, covering, sheath, paper bag** etc. frq.; *rkaṅ-śúbs*, resp. *ža͏bs-śúbs* stocking, sock, *gri-śúbs* knife-case or sheath, *mǰe-śúbs* v. *mǰe*; *lag-śúbs*, resp. *p̔yag-śúbs* **glove.**

ཤུམ་པ *śúm-pa*, pf. (*b*)*śums*, ft. *bśum*, imp. (*b*)*śum*(*s*), 1. **to weep,** *ma śum mdzod* do not weep! *ṅu-śúm Mil.* **weeping, lamentation.** — 2. to tremble(?) *graṅ-śúm Lt.*, *Schr. graṅ-śúm byéd-pa* to tremble or shiver with cold, to shudder.

ཤུར་བ *śúr-ba*, pf. fut. *bśur*, imp. (*b*)*śur*, 1. to burn slightly, **to singe.** — 2. **to cut off.**

ཤུར་བུ *śúr-bu* 1. **girdle, belt** *Lex.*; *śur-bu-p̔réu Zam.* id. (acc. to *Sch.*). — 2. *Cs.*: **sore, ulcer.** — 3. *Ts.*: **dumpling of flour,** = *k̔o-lag.*

ཤུལ *śul* 1. **an empty place,** a place that has been left, that is no longer occupied, *ráṅ-śul stóṅs-nas* your own place becoming empty, by your quitting it *Mil.* *šúl-du lús-pai nor* all the things left behind in the camp *Glr.*; *dón-tse lúis-pai šúl-du* instead of the coin which had been taken away (there appeared . . .) *Dzl.*; *k̀yód-kyi šúl-du* in the place which you occupied during your life *Thgr.*; hence in a looser sense: *btsún-mo méd-pai šúl-du* on the occasion of the queen's absence *Glr.*; in the same manner *Tar.* 103, 16, 19, and also thus: *dei šúl-du Glr.* 51 during her absence. — 2. **track, rut,** of a carriage, **furrow,** of a plough *Dzl.*, **way, road;** also in a gen. sense: *šul t̀ag-riṅ* a long way *Glr.*; *šul-lám* = *šul*; acc. to *Cs.* also **manner, method.** — 3. any thing left behind by a person departed, or by a thing removed, as *ču-šul, mar-šul, p̀ye-šul* that little water, butter or flour which adheres to the vessel emptied, but not washed; *me-šul* the extinguished cinders left by a fire; **property left** by a deceased person *šul ťsáṅ-ma yóg-po-la ťob* his servant gets all the property left (by his master) *W.*, *C.*, *p̀a-šul* paternal inheritance, patrimony; *p̀a-šul-ₒdzin-pa* the heir *C.*; *šul yaṅ mi ₒdug* nothing at all is left; **šúl-med-k̀an čo** *W.* finish it at once! eat it all up! *šu-tsaṅ-po* one that eats all up, clears his trencher (a good trencher-man) *Ts.*

ཤུལ་པ་ *šúl-pa, bšúl-pa Cs.*: **backbone, back, posteriors;** *šul-šá* the flesh, the muscles of the back, *šul-rgyús* the fibres, the nerves of the back; *Sch.*: *bšul-drí* smell of excrements, *šul-byí* **polecat, fitchet.**

ཤུས་ *šus* 1. v. *šú-ba.* — 2. *šus ₒdébs-pa* to whistle *S.g.*

ཤུས་མ་ *šús-ma* any thing copied, **a copy** *Cs.*

ཤེ་ *še* 1. *Cs.* *še-stag, še-dag* = *ša-stág* **mere, only,** nothing but. — 2. num.: 117.

ཤེ་ན་ *šé-na* v. *čé-na.*

ཤེ་པ་ *šé-pa* v. *šés-pa.*

ཤེ་བམ་ *še-bám Cs.*: = *ťo-yig* a kind of contract or bargain.

ཤེ་མ་ *šé-ma* (for *rjé-ma* or *yčés-ma?*) *W.* **noblewoman,** lady of rank or quality, **lady,** **šé-ma čuṅ-ṅu, šem-čúṅ** nobleman's daughter, **young lady, Miss.**

ཤེ་མོང་ *še-móṅ Sch.*: 'divine predestination, divine protection; nature, fate, destiny; power; origin of power or authority; strength', force, the latter signification also in *Wts.*(?).

ཤེ་རུལ་ *še-rul Sch.*: **fetid, putrid.**

ཤེག་ *šeg* 1. imp. of *yšégs-pa*, resp. for *šog.* — 2. the Arabian شيخ, chieftain, elder, senior. — 3. *C.* col. for *šed* I.

ཤེད་ *šed* I. **strength, force,** = *stóbs, mťu, C.* also *šeg*; *dpá-žiṅ šed-čé* a mighty hero *Thgy.*; *šéd-čan* **strong, vigorous, powerful;** *šéd-mo* 1. sbst. = *šed?* 2. adj. = *šed-čan Ts.*, **šė-mo gyág-pa yin** he is strong and stout, *šed-méd* **powerless, weak,** *šed-méd-kyi rtá-bas rkaṅ-ťáṅ mgyogs* one travels quicker on foot than on a weak horse; *šed-čúṅ* **weak, feeble, frail,** e.g. *lus Lt.*; *šed ₒbri* strength decreases, begins to fail, *ysos* is restored, *nyams* is impaired; *šed skyéd-pa* to grow fat *Sch.*: 'to protect; to make haste'; **mi žig-la šed čúg-če** *W.* **to strengthen a** person; **šed daṅ nyé-če** *W.* to rub well, forcibly; **šed žár-te (sbyar-te) čoṅ** run and jump! **šed žár-te gyob** swing your arm and throw! *W.*; **šed-kyer-nág-po** by force, with violence, e.g. **taṅ** he forced it on (me) *W.* (cf. *nan*); *šed-po-čé* a strong, powerful man *Thgy.*; *šéd-bu Lex.* id.; *šed-bdág Sch.* one having power or authority, a lord, ruler. — **šed-wáṅ** *W.* **force, violence,** **šed-wáṅ daṅ** by force, e.g. to take, **šed-wáṅ táṅ-če** *W.* to violate, to force (a girl).

II. the approximate **direction, region, quarter,** *nyi-mai ₒog šéd-na* below the sun, i.e. between the sun and the horizon *Mil.*; *W.*: **gaṅ šéd-la** in what direction? whereto? **de šéd-la** about in that direction; **gaṅ šed ne** (lit. *ynas*) *šig-tu** to some place or other.

ཤེན་ *šen*(?) **floor** of a house or room *W.*

ཤེར་ཕྱིན་ *šer-p̀yin* abbreviation for *šes-ráb-kyi p̀á-rol-tu p̀yin-pa*, the title of a division of the *Kan-gyur.*

ཤེར་བ་ **šér-ba**, pf. *bšer*, **to compare, to confront** *Cs.*

ཤེལ་ **šel crystal, glass** *Dzl.* and elsewh.; acc. to *Stg.* the moon also consists of such crystal *Cs.*: *rán-šel* native crystal, *bžú-šel* artificial crystal, glass; *mán-šel Pth.* prob. = *šel; spos-šél* amber; *me-šél* burning-glass, *ču-šél* चन्द्रकान्त a fabulous magic stone supposed to have the power of producing water or even rain.

Comp. *šel-kór* or *-por* a tumbler. — *šel-dkár* = *šel Glr.* — *šel-kán* glass-works, glass-manufactory *Schr.* — *šel-sgóṅ* globe of glass *Mil.* — *šel-sgó* glass-door. — *šel-rdó* crystal. — *šel-snód, šel-spyád* a crystal or glass vessel. — *šel-préṅ* a string of glass-beads. — *šel-búm* glass-bottle. — *šel-mig* spectacles, spy-glass, telescope.

ཤེས་ *šes* v. *čes.*

ཤེས་པ་ *šés-pa* (synon. *rig-pa*, resp. *mkyén-pa*) I. vb., 1. **to know, perceive, apprehend,** *bzáṅ-bar šés-pa* to find, to know a thing to be good *Glr.*; *brtágs-na mi šes* when (the soul) is searched for, it is not to be perceived or apprehended *Mil.*; *šés-pai blo ingenium sapiens Dzl.*; *mi-šes-pa-dag* those who do not care for knowing (a thing) *Dzl.*; *su šés B., C.,* **či šē** *W.* (like the Hindi क्या जाने) who can tell? may be; *čiaṅ mi šē-kan* a know-nothing, ignoramus, dunce; **ko-ráṅ mā šé-kan čén-mo žig tsor dug** *W.* he is said to be an extremely clever (learned etc.) man; *mi-šés dgu šés-pa* knowing (even) the unknown things, knowing every thing *Thgy.*; *čaṅ-šés* id.; **ṅa-ráṅ toṅ šē** *W.* I know it from having seen it; *šés-par gyur* 1. he will know. 2. he comes to know, he learns; *šes-par gyis šig* 1. know! 2. let it be known! *šes-bžin-du* **knowing, knowingly,** with (my) knowledge; *ṅó-šes-pa* = *šés-pa*, yet cf. sub *ṅo.* — 2. **to understand,** = *gó-ba, don* the sense *Glr.*; *ṅas rtsis šes* I understand mathematics; **to be able,** in a general sense, also physically: **ghaṅ šē-pa** *C.* to one's best ability, to the utmost of one's power (= *ji nus-kyis B.,* **či túb-kan** *W.*); *krág-gi goṅ ₒgul šés-pa* a clot of blood that could only quiver (though, in fact, a human being) *Glr.*; esp. with a negative: *smra mi šés-pa* not being able to speak, *dgye dgu mi šes* they cannot be bent or curved *Med.* — 3. **to be convinced, to be of opinion, to think,** *sú-la yaṅ mdzá-bor ma šes* do not think anybody to be your friend!

II. sbst. (= *rig-pa*) 1. **the knowing** (about a thing), **knowledge.** — 2. **science, learning,** *šés-pa-la zóg-tu ltá-ba* to look upon science as a (sort of) cheating. — 3. **intellectual power, intelligence,** *šés-pa tibs* the intellect (of infants) is still very weak *Lt.*, *ysal* is clear *Pth.* — 4. **the soul** or spirit, separate from the body *Thgy., Mil.*

Comp. **šē-gyá** talent(?) *C., W.* — **šē-gyü** **character** *C., W.,* **šē-gyü ṅém-pa** a bad character. — *šes-ₒdód* **desire of knowledge, curiosity** of mind *Mil.* *šes-ldan, šes-blo-ldán-pa* 1. knowing, rich in wisdom. 2. very learned Sir! — *šés-po, šés-pa-po* one that knows or understands, a knower *Cs.* — *šés-bya* 1. what may be known or ought to be known, *šés-bya kun* every thing worth knowing, all the sciences. 2. knowing, conscious, wilful? *šés-byai sgrib-pa* contamination by wilful sins *Do.?* — *šes-byed* that which knows, the understanding. — *šés-bžin* **consciousness** (v. above *šes-bžin-du*), *dran-pa daṅ šes-bžin-čan yin-te Gyatch.* ༢༢༤, 14 (cf. *Burn.* II, 806, 5); *šés-bžin* may, accordingly, be used for **'conscience'** in a christian sense. — *šés-yoṅ Ts.* = *šes-rgya.* — *šes-ráb* (प्रज्ञा) 1. 'great knowledge', **wisdom, intelligence, understanding, talent,** *šes-rab če-ba* very talented, gifted (e.g. a boy) *Mil.*; *šes-ráb daṅ ldán-pa* id.; *šes-rab-spyan* the (mystic) eye of wisdom *Schl.* p. 210. — *šes-rab-rtswa Taraxacum*, dandelion, also used as food. — *šes-ráb-kyi pá-rol-tu pyin-pa*, प्रज्ञापारमिता, the having arrived at the other side of wisdom, n. of that section of the *Kangyur* which treats of philosophical matters.

ཤོ་ *šo* (*Cs.*: *šó-mo*) I. **die, dice,** *šo rgyáb-pa* **to dice,** *šo rtsé-ba* to play at dice, *šo-ₒgyéd-pa* (*Sch. kyé-žig* as imp.) id.? — *šo rgyál-ba* or *pám-pa* to win or lose at playing;

šo-rgyán *Cs.* the money or stake deposited at dice-playing; *rtsis-šoi rdeu Mil.*, *šo-rdél Wdk.*, an attribute of certain deities; *šo-míg* the points of dice, *šo-mig γsúm-par* (or *-pa-la*) *ₒbáb-na* when three points are thrown. Tibetans play with three dice marked with 6 and 1, 5 and 4, 3 and 2 on opposite sides, hence from 3 to 18 points may be thrown.

II. 1. the white willow of *Spiti*, *Ld.* and other Himalayan districts. — 2. other plants *rgya-šo*, *lug-šo? Wdṅ.*

III. = *btsa-ma* blast, blight, smut, mildew *Cs.*

IV. for *šo-gam*, q. v.

V. num.: 147.

ཤོ་གམ་ *šo-gám* **custom, duty, tax,** *šo-gám lči-ba W.* **lčin-te** high duty, *šo-gam len-pa* to take toll, to levy a duty; *šo-gám bzlá-ba Sch.*: 'to smuggle, to circumvent or defraud the customs'(?); *šo-gám-gyi γnas* custom-house; *šo-gám-pa* receiver of the customs, toll-gatherer; **šo-ṭ ál, šo-dúṅ* Ts.* tax, duty.

ཤོ་ཆ་ *šó-ča* a kind of steel-yard *C.*

ཤོ་མ་ *šó-ma*, v. *šá-mo*, **mushroom** *Mil.*

ཤོ་མང་ *šo-máṅ* a medicinal herb *Med.*

ཤོ་ར་ *šó-ra* **saltpetre,** nitre, *šó-ra-čan* nitrous.

ཤོ་རེ་ *šo-ré*, adj., **damaged, spoiled,** by being partially broken, torn etc., sbst.: **a defect, flaw, notch, gap,** also **hare-lip**; **šo-ré soṅ** it is damaged, **šo-ré ťon soṅ** a notch, chink, crack has been caused; **ka-šór, na-šór**, with a slit lip, a slit nose.

ཤོ་ལོ་ཀ་ *šó-lo-ka* v. *šlo-ka.*

ཤོག་ *šog* I. *šóg-čig*, prop. from *γšégs-pa*, imp. of *ₒóṅ-ba*, 1. come! let him come! *ₒbrás-bu ťsúr-šog-gi yid-smón ṅá-la med* I do not wish that fruit should come to me from without *Mil.*; *kur šog, kyer šog bskyal šog* bring hither, (with *soṅ* inst. of *šog*: take away!) *šog zér-ba* **to invite,** *ṅed-la šog kyaṅ mi zer Glr.* we are not so much as invited, you know. — 2. with the imp. = *gyur-čig*, *bsad-par-šog* may (he, I etc.) be killed! *Dzl.* — II. v. *šos.*

ཤོག་པ་ *šóg-pa* I. sbst., also frq. *γšóg-pa*, 1. **wing,** *γšog-rkyaṅ-ba* to spread the wings, also to spread like wings; **šóg-pa dé-če, čád-če, ḍúm-če* W.* to clip the wings; *γšóg-pa-čan*, *γšog-ldán* provided with wings, winged, a bird. — 2. **wing-feather, pinion,** *ₒdab-γšóg*, *γšóg-sgro* id.; *mǰug-γšog* tail-feather. — 3. **fin,** of fishes. — 4. other things resembling a wing or a feather, *mig-γšog*, resp. *spyán-γšog* eye-lash; *raṅ-tág-gi γšóg-pa* prob.: wing or float-board of a water-mill; of course it might also be used for: wing, sail, of a windmill, though these are not yet known in Tibet.

II. vb., v. sub *γšog-pa.*

ཤོག་བུ་ *šóg-bu*, *W.* **šúg-gu**, 1. **sheet of paper,** and **paper** collectively, *rgya-šóg* China paper, *bod-šóg* Tibet paper, *dar-šóg* silk-paper, *ras-šóg* cotton-paper (also paper of linen-rags), *šiṅ-šóg* bast-paper, *pags-šóg* leather-paper, skin-paper, parchment; *mťiṅ-šóg*, *nag-šóg* dark-blue or black paper, for writing on in gold or silver; *mgo-šóg*, resp. *dbu-šóg*, upper leaf, i. e. cover, covering, wrapper. — 2. *Bal.*: **book.**

Comp. *šog-káṅ* **paper-maker's form.** — *šog-gáṅ* a sheet of paper. — *šog-gráṅs* number of leaves in a book. — *šog-sgril*, *šog-dril*, *W.* **šog-ril** **paper-roll, codex.** — *šog-ldéb Sch.*: 'leaf, sheet'? — *šog-ťsár* scrap of paper. — *šog-šiṅ Sch.* palm-tree? — *šog-hril γčig* = *šog-gáṅ*, *Sch.*

ཤོང་(ས)་, གཤོང་(ས)་ *šoṅ(s)*, *γšoṅ(s)* (*Lex.*: खात 'elevated plain, ridge of a mountain') 1. **mountain-ridge** *Wts.* Usual meaning: 2. **pit, hole, cavity, excavation, valley,** *ču-šóṅs* cavity filled with water *Dzl.*; *spaṅ-šoṅs* valley with meadows, low ground overgrown with grass; *snai bya-γšóg-gi γšoṅs* the cavities near the wings of the nose *Mil. nt.*; *šóṅ-du* valley-ward, down hill *Dzl.*; *šóṅs-čan*, (*γ*)*šoṅ-*(*γ*)*šóṅ* full of cavities, **uneven,** *Sch.* also: **rough, rugged, steep;** *šóṅs-bu* **furrow,** *šóṅs-bu ₒtén-pa* to make furrows, to furrow.

ཤོང་བ་ *šóṅ-ba* I. to go in, **to have room** in or on, with term., *mi šoṅ*, *W.* also: **šóṅ-če mi dug** that is not to be got in, there is no room for it; *bre lṅa šóṅ-bai búm-pa* a can holding five quarts *Dzl.*

II. pf. *bšaṅs*, fut. *bšaṅ*, imp. *šoṅ(s)*, **to empty, remove, carry or take away,** *W.* stones, earth etc., but gen. (with or without *rkyág-pa*) to go to stool, to ease nature, *B.* and col.

ཤོད་ *šod* 1. the lower, the inferior part of a thing, *rtse-šod* upper and lower part, top and bottom *C.*; *rgya-šod Wdṅ.* a low tract of land, with a milder climate, where e.g. apricots are thriving, opp. to *ṗu-lhágs* elevated cold region, scarcely fit for the cultivation of corn and barley; *šód-du* to or towards the bottom, **down, downwards,** *C.*, **šǫ'-du báb-pa** to descend, come down, **šǫ'-nẹ ˳dzég-pa** to ascend *C.* — 2. imp. of *˳čád-pa, bšád-pa*; yet cf. also:

ཤོད་པ་ *šod-pa*, pf. *bšád-pa*, 1. **to say, to declare** *C.* — 2. **to comb** *Cs.*

ཤོབ་, གཤོབ་ *šob, γšob* **a fib, falsehood, lie,** *smrá-ba, W. *gyáb-če**, to tell a lie.

ཤོབ་ཤོབ་ *šob-šób* **loose, soft,** as leaves etc. *W.*

ཤོམ་པ་ *šom-pa*, pf. *(b)šoms, bšams*, fut. *bšam*, imp. *(b)šom(s)*, **to prepare, make ready, arrange, put in order, fit out,** *γnas* lodgings, *γdan* a seat, *stón-mo* a festive entertainment, *bžón-pa* a carriage, i.e. to have the horses put to *Dzl.*; *dpúṅ-gi ṫsogs* an army *Dzl.* — *šóm-ra* 1. **preparation, arrangement, fitting out,** *šóm-ra byéd-pa* = *šóm-pa C.*, so also *Cs.*; but *Sch.*: 2. *šóm-ra* **state, pomp, splendour,** with *byéd-pa* to show off, to dress smartly, *šóm-čan* stately, grand (?).

ཤོར་ *šor* v. *šo-ré.*

ཤོར་བ་ *šór-ba* 1. v. *˳čór-ba.* — 2. to measure *Mil.*, v. *γšór-ba.*

ཤོལ་བ་ *šól-ba* 1. **intercalation, insertion** *Cs.*, *zla-šól* intercalary month. — 2. *Cs*: pres. tense of *bšól-ba* q.v.

ཤོལ་པོ་ *šól-po Sch.*: 'a species of willow', v. *γšól-po.*

ཤོས་ *šos* 1. almost always in conjunction with *γčig*, **the other,** of two, e.g. *bud-méd γčig-šós* the other woman *Dzl.* — 2. *Zam.* तर, col. *šog*, a termination indicating the comparative or superlative degree: *čuṅ-šós, γžon-šós* the younger, the youngest, of two or of several, *btsún-mo lṅa-brgyái čuṅ-šós Pth.*; **riṅ-šóg* W.* the tallest; *yun-riṅ-šós Thgy.* the most long-lived; *drin-če-šós* the principal benefactress, cf. *drin*; *nad če-šós rgás-nad ˳ṫébs-pas* because one is suffering under the chief disease, viz. old age, *Thgy.*

ཤྲཱི་ *šrī Ssk.*, = *dpal* **glory, magnificence; magnificent, splendid, grand;** *šrī-ri Mil.*, pr. n., a naked mountain in a sandy plain, about a ten day's journey to the west of Tashi-lhunpo, covered with monasteries, and perh. on that account considered as *nyams-mṫsár-ba. šrī-ḱaṇḍa* v. *dpál-gyi dum-bu.*

ཤློ་ཀ་ *šló-ka Ssk.*, also *šo-lo-ka*, **strophe, stanza,** esp. one consisting of four catalectic trochaical dimeters.

གཤའ་ *γša* I. 1. also *γšá-ma, bšá-ma*, **worthy, becoming, fitting, suitable,** *˳ṫsé-ba mi γšai* as it is unworthy, unbecoming, improper, to persecute (others) *Dzl.*; **de ḱyód-la ša yod** or **šá-če yod* Ld.* that serves you right. — 2. **righteous, upright, honest, good,** = *skyón-med-pa, C.*; *blo γšá-ma* an upright, true heart, *Thgy.*; **lẹ šá-ma ǰhé'-pa* C.* to perform a work faithfully, in good earnest.

II. **only, merely; mere, nothing but,** (= *šá-stag*) *C.*

གཤའ་དཀར་, བཤའ་དཀར་ *γša-dkár, bša-dkár S.g., Wdṅ., C.* **tin,** *W. kar-ya*; yet cf. *ža-nye.*

གཤའ་རིང་ *γša-riṅ* a long skirt or coat-tail *Sch.*

གཤག་པ་ *γšág-pa* v. *γšóg-pa.*

གཤགས་ *γšags* **right, justice,** *Lex.* and esp. *W.*; *γšags ˳byed-pa Lex.* to investigate the rightfulness (of an action), = **ye dig ṗé-če* W.*; **ṭim-šág táṅ-če** to administer justice, to sit in judgment **ṭim-šág-taṅ-ḱan** judge, **šag (go-) lóg táṅ-če** to warp justice, to judge contrary to justice and right; **ṭim-šág žú-če** to go to law, to bring an action, **šág-pon** superior judge, chief-justice, *W.* — *bka-γšágs* v. *bka* extr.

གཤང་ γšaṅ a musical instrument, esp. used by the Bonpo, *Glr.*, *γšaṅ ˳ḱról-ba* to play on that instrument *Mil.*

གཤང་བ་ *γšáṅ-pa Sch.* = *bšáṅ-ba.*

གཤང་གཤོང་ *γšaṅ-γšóṅ* rough, rugged places or tracts *Cs:*

གཤད་པ་ *γšád-pa* 1. = *šód-pa* **to comb.** — 2. = *˳čád-pa* II., **to explain, to relate.**

གཤམ་ *γšam* 1. **the lower part** of a thing, *γšám-du* a. adv. **down.** b. postp. **under, below, beneath**; also adv. **farther down,** more towards the end, in the course of; examples v. sub *leu*; postp. *dei γšám-du* under it. — 2. **barren,** *B.* and col., *mo-γšám, rgod-γšám, ba-γšám* a barren woman, mare, cow.

གཤར་ *γšar Sch.*: a certain style of writing.

གཤས་མ་ *γšás-ma Sch.* = *γšá-ma.*

གཤིག་པ་ *γšig-pa* v. *γšib-pa.*

གཤིན་པ་ *γšín-pa* 1. also *γšín-po* **good, fine,** *žiṅ šín-pa B., C.* a fertile field, *sa-ǰyógs γšín-pa* a rich country *Stg.*; *γšín-par rmó-ba* to plough well; *γšín-sa* 1. fertile field or land. 2. v. *γšín-po.* — 2. = *γšim-pa.*

གཤིན་པོ་ *γšín-po* **one deceased, a dead man,** *γšín-mo* a dead woman, e.g. **šin-mó ǰor-zóm** the deceased, the late Jorzóm; it may have reference to the body, as well as to the soul, or to both together. — *γšin-rje* the god of the dead, of the lower regions, of hades, also regarded as the judge of the dead, *Ssk.* **यम**; *γšin-rjei γšed* a. id., Yama the destroyer. b. the destroyer of Yama, Siwa; *Ssk.* **यमान्तक**, cf. also *Schl.* 93. **čin-dúd** **knot,** opp. to **ṭol-dúd** a bow, a slip-knot *W.* — *γšin-˳dré* the soul as a ghost or spectre *Sch.* — *γšin-˳prás* the convulsive motions, the writhings of a dying creature. — *γšin-zas* food presented to the Lamas when a person has died (*Cs.*: food prepared, or exposed for the dead?). *šín-sa* 1. **burying ground, cemetery,** 2. fertile field.

གཤིབ(ས)་པ་, བཤིབ(ས)་པ་ *γšib(s)-pa, bšib(s)-pa,* also *γšig-pa,* 1. *Sch.*: to range, **to compare;** *Ld.* to be ranged, to draw up in files; **gral γšig rgyáb-pa** *C.* to induce assembled people by means of a stick to stand or sit closer; cf. *žal-bdág.* — 2. *ral-gri γšib-pa Wdṅ.?*

གཤིམ་པ་, གཤིན་པ་ *γšim-pa, γšin-pa Sch.*: 'ground, crushed'.

གཤིམས་བཟང་བ་ *γšims-bzáṅ-ba Sch.* to be irresolute, unsettled in opinion; to be distrustful, suspicious.

གཤིས་ *γšis,* often also *bšis,* 1. **nature, temper, natural disposition,** *γšis-ka* col. id., *raṅ-γšis yin* it is their nature, their natural disposition *Mil.* — *γšis-kyis* by the very nature of the case, without secondary causes, naturally, quite of itself *Mil.*; *γšis-ñán Mil., Do.* was also explained by *rgyú-med-par,* prob. implying merely: not having been one's self the efficient cause. — 2. **person, body,** *γšis ťams-čád-du ˳byúg-go* they anointed the whole body *Do.*

གཤུང་བ་ *γšuṅ-ba Cs.* to rebuke, reproach; the *Lexx.* explain it by: *šúb-bur smád-pa* to blame in a whisper, i.e. behind a person's back.

གཤུམ་པ་ *γšúm-pa* v. *šúm-pa.*

གཤེ་བ་ *γšé-ba,* pf. *γšes,* **to abuse, revile,** with *la, Dzl.* and elsewh.; *γše yaṅ slar mi γšé-ba* even when reviled, (one should) not revile again (rule for monks) *Cs.*

གཤེག་པ་ *γšég-pa* v. *γšóg-pa.*

གཤེགས་པ་ *γšégs-pa* (imp. *γšegs, Dulva* in *Feer Introd.* etc. p. 68; but *šog* is prob. the original and older form), *Bal.* **šags-čas**, resp. **to go, to go away,** opp. to *˳byón-pa* to come *Glr.*; in other passages **to come** *Dzl.*; *γšegs-grábs mdzad* he made preparations for setting out *Mil.*; *nám-mḱa-la ˳ṗúr-žiṅ γšegs* he ascended to heaven *Tar.*; *slar γšégs-pa* **to return, to come back.** *γšégs-pa* is col. seldom used, but often in books, and mostly of Buddha and great saints; *bdé-bar γšégs-pa* **to die,** of saints and kings; *sku γšegs-pa Glr.*; *dgúṅ-du* or *dgúṅ-la γšégs-pa Mil., mḱar γšégs-pa Glr.,* id.; *bdé(-bar)-γšegs(-pa)* as partic. = **सुगत** **Buddha;** *de-bžin-γšegs-pa* **तथागत** acc. to the explanation now generally accepted: he that walks in the same ways (as his predecessors), a very frq. epithet of the Buddhas. — *γšégs-bskyés* parting-(beer-) cup, parting-feast or treat *Mil.* — *γšegs-zón Cs.* a banquet or dinner, after the death of a great person.

གཤེད་མ་ *γšed-ma*, rarely *γšed*, 1. **executioner, hangman** *Stg.*; *γšéd-ma skó-ba* to engage a hangman, i.e. to pay a murderer *Glr*; fig.: *p'an tsun γčig-gi γšed γčig-gis byá-ste Wdṅ.* prob. means: one destroying the other. — 2. in a special sense: gods of vengeance, tormenting the condemned in hell, or fighting against evil spirits, *drag-γšéd Schl.*

གཤེན་རབ(ས)་ *γšen-rab(s) Glr.*, the founder of the Bon-religion, his full name being *bon γšen-rabs-γyuṅ-drúṅ C.* prob. identic with the Chinese philosopher *Lao-tse* — *ye-γšen Mil.* id. — *sgrub-γšén* the Bon-doctrine (opp. to *dam-čós Mil.*)

གཤེར(བ་) *γšér(-ba) B., C.*: **wet, wetness;** *γšér-ba, γšér-pa, γšér-po* adj, *γšér-bar ₒgyúr-ba* to get thoroughly wet, to be drenched *Dzl.*, to get moist, to be moistened; *γšér-bar byéd-pa C., B.*, *šér-pa čó-če* *W.* to wet, to moisten. In *C.* and in *B.* *γšer-ba* seems to be mainly used for **wet**, in *W.* for **moist.**

གཤེར་བ་ *γšér-ba* I. sbst. and adj. v. the preceding article.

II. vb.. 1. **to ask for, beg for,** *šér-te t'ob soṅ* I got it by asking for it (I did not buy it) *W.* — 2. **to ask** *šér-len-pa* (lit. *γšér-len-pa*) **to interrogate, to question, to try** (judicially); as partic. and sbst.; the examining or criminal judge *C.* — 3. = *γšór-ba* **to measure** *C.*

གཤོ་བ་ *γšó-ba*, pf. *γšos*, 1. **to pour out, to pour away** *C.*, prob. the same as *bšo-ba.* — 2 (?) *k'a šós-te k'yer* he has **alienated** him, enticed him to join his own party *Ld.*

གཤོ་མོ་ *γšó-mo* **lever** *šó-mo gyáb-pa* *C., W*, *taṅ-če* *W..* *šó-mo kán-pa* *W.*, *kémpa* *C.* to put a lever to (a thing).

གཤོག་པ་ *γšóg-pa* I. sbst. v. *šóg-pa.*

II. vb., also *bšóg-pa, γšág-pa, γšég-pa, ₒčégs-pa*, pf. *γšags, bšags*, fut. *γšag, bšag*, imp. *γšog, Pth.*, 1. **to cleave, to split,** *šiṅ* wood, *rnám-par* entirely, *tsál-pa bžir* into four pieces *Glr*, *dúm-bur* into pieces; *sgo γšág-pa* **to break open** a door (with a hatchet) *Pth.*; **to break or pierce through,** *dkyil* through the middle *Mil.*, *gaṅs bšóg-pa Mil.* to break through the snow, by means of yaks sent in advance to beat a path (v. *Huc.*), *lam bšog-pa* in a gen. sense: to beat a path; *lam mi šog* or *ma šog-par ₒdug Glr.* the road is not practicable; *sóg-les γšég-pa Thg.* to saw lengthwise; — *γšeg-pa* is also used for: **to rend, to tear,** to make a rent or slit into a dress etc. *C., W.* — 2. **to confess,** *sdig-pa, nyés-pa, ltúṅ-ba* to confess a sin, and thus **to expiate it,** which two, according to the views of a Buddhist, are always united, at least as it regards lighter transgressions. Hence *sdig-pa bšags* frq. means: the sin is atoned for, is blotted out, and *γšeg-pa* is the usual word for **'to forgive'.** *sdig-bšágs* **atonement, expiation,** *sbrul bsád-pai-sdig-bšágs-su* as an atonement for having killed a serpent *Glr*; *mtol-bšágs* = *sdig-bšágs, mtol-bšágs-la ša-k'óg ₒbúl-ba* to offer a killed animal (a sheep) as an atonement *Mil.*; *sdig-bšags-smón-lam Glr.* **penitential prayer.**

གཤོང(ས)་ *γšoṅ(s)* v. *šoṅ.*

གཤོད་པ་ *γšód-pa* to comb *Cs.*

གཤོན་པ་ *γšón-pa Cs.*: = *skyón-pa* to put on (?).

གཤོབ་ *γšob* = *šob.*

གཤོམ་པ་ *γšóm-pa Thgy.* = *šóm-pa.*

གཤོར་ *γšor Sch.* a basin or **reservoir** of water, seems to be not much known; but in *Zam.* *yúr-bai γšor* is to be found.

གཤོར་བ་ *γšór-ba* I. vb., *C.* also *γšér-ba*, pf. fut. *bšar, bšor*, 1. **to count,** e.g. sheep, by letting them pass one by one through one's hands, the beads of a rosary (through one's fingers), hence *čos-brjod-bšar-sbyaṅ maṅ-po byed* to read prayers etc. (cf. *sbyaṅ-ba*, 3). — 2. **to measure,** *bres* by the peck *Lex.*; **to weigh;** *γsér-la rá-gan γšár-ba* to weigh out (to exchange) brass for gold. — 3. **to hunt, to chase,** = °čór-ba, *ri-dwags* game *Lex.*; *nya-γšór-ba* **to fish** *Dzl.* — 4. *Sch.* to cut through (?).

II. adj., also *γšér-ba*, **rough, bristly, shaggy,** *skra*, *spu Stg.*, opp. to °*ǰam-po* (*Sch.* rough, gruff, rude?)

གཤོལ་ *γšol* **plough** *Glr.*, *toṅ*, *tóṅ-γšol* id. The plough in India and Tibet consists only of a crooked beam, *γšol-mda*, (without wheels) with the share (*γšol-lčágs*, *toṅ-lčágs*) at the lower end; *γšol-mdá °dzin-pa* **to plough,** lit. to take hold of the plough-beam.

གཤོལ་པོ་ *γšól-po* **poplar-tree** *C.*

གཤོས་པ་ *γšos-pa* 1. *γšo-ba* and *bšo-ba*.

བཤའ་ *bša* 1. in *bgo-bša* **portion, share, allowance, ration** *Lex.*, evidently a secondary form of *šas.* — 2. *Dzl.* ༢༧༠, 1 **inundation,** flood; *šwa*, the reading of the manuscript of Kyelang, seems to be preferable.

བཤའ་བ་ *bšá-ba*, pf. *bšas*, **to slaughter, to kill** (animals for food); in a story of *Glr.* it follows the slaughtering and must be understood to denote the cutting to pieces of the killed animal; but our Lama preferred to read *bšús-pa* to skin.

བཤའ་མ་ *bšá-ma* v. *γšá-ma*.

བཤག་པ་ *bšág-pa* v. *γšóg-pa*.

བཤང་བ་ *bšáṅ-ba*, *Sch.* also *γšaṅ-ba*, alvine discharges, *bšáṅ-ba °byin-pa* to make open bowels, of food, medicines *Med.*; *bšaṅ-dgág* **constipation** *Med.*; *bšaṅ-γči* excrements and urine, *bšaṅ-γčis skú-ba* to dirty therewith *Dzl.*; *bšaṅ-γči bsri-ba* to retain stool and urine *Sch.*; *bšaṅ-lám* the anus *Med.*

བཤངས་པ་ *bšáṅs-pa* **leaky, leaking, full of crevices,** **ču-zóm nyi-ma-la bór-na šaṅ dug** *W.* the water-pail will become leaky, if it is left standing in the sun.

བཤད་པ་ *bšád-pa* (prob. pf. of °*čád-pa* q.v.) 1. **to explain,** expound; **to declare,** pronounce, *čos-bšád-pa* to explain religion, to lecture on religious subjects, **to preach;** °*či-ba daṅ °drar bšad* he must be set down for dead *Wdṅ.*; *bú-mo skyé-bar bšad* this **indicates** that a girl will be born *Lt.*; *bšád-kyis mi láṅ-ṅo* it is **ineffable, unspeakable; to say,** °*báb-par bšad* they say it flows down *Wdṅ.*, *tá-mar bšad* he is said to be on the lowest stage *Thgy.*, *ṅán-par bšad* it is said or declared to be bad, *smán-du bšad* it is **mentioned** as a medicine *Wdṅ.*; **to tell, to relate,** col. the usual word. — 2. **to comb,** v. *šód-pa.* — *bšad-grwa* **school-room, lecture-room.** — **šad-dón** *W.* the subject of a talk. *bšad-γdám* a public lecture *Sch.* (?). *bšad-ló byéd-pa* to make many words *Mil.*

བཤན་པ་ *bšán-pa* v *šán-pa.*

བཤར་ *bšar*, supine of *bšá-ba.*

བཤར་བ་ *bšár-ba* v *γšór-ba.*

བཤལ་བ་ *bšál-ba* 1. **to wash, to wash out or off, to clean by washing, to rinse,** plates, dishes, etc. — 2. *ltó-ba bšál-ba* **to purge** the body, hence in gen. *bšál-ba* to suffer from diarrhoea, and *W.* col. **šal* **diarrhoea, looseness, flux,** **šal rag** I have d., **šal dug** he suffers from d., **šal yoṅ** d. begins; *bšal-ǰám* a mild d., *bšal-°pyés*(?) a violent flux *Sch.*; *bšal-nád* indisposition from d.; *bšal-byéd B.*, *bšal-smán B.* and col. **laxative,** aperient medicine.

བཤས་པ་ *bšás-pa* v. *bšá-ba.*

བཤིག་པ་ *bšig-pa* v. °*dzig-pa* I.

བཤིབ་པ་ *bšib-pa* v. *γšib-pa.*

བཤུ་བ་ *bšú-ba* v. *šú-ba.*

བཤུག་པ་ *bšúg-pa* to sell *Cs.*

བཤུད་པ་ *bšúd-pa* 1. v. *šud-pa.* — 2. *Sch.*: to purify by fire, *bšúd-me* purifying fire (?).

བཤུབ་པ་ *bšúb-pa* to put into the scabbard, **to sheathe** *Sch.*

བཤུམ་པ་ *bšúm-pa* — བཤེར་བ་ *bšér-ba* v. ཤུམ་པ་ *šúm-pa* etc.

བཤེའུ་ *bšeu* (cf. *bša*, *šwa*) **inundation, flood** *Mil.*

བཤེས་པ་ *bšés-pa*, prop. pf. of *šés-pa*, **to know** (a person or thing), **to be acquainted,** *dan* with *Dzl.; ɣnyen-bšés* **a relation, relative,** *ɣnyen-bšes-la p̓án-ɣtogs-par sems-so* they are intent on being of use to their relatives *Dzl.; ɣnyen* and *bšes* may also be separated: *k̓yód-la ɣnyen med bšes kyan med, Mil.; bšes-ɣnyén* on the other hand means: **friend,** *dgé-bai bšes-, nyén* (*Ssk.* कल्याणमित्र) friend to virtue, **spiritual adviser,** opp. to *mi-dgéi bšes- nyén* **seducer,** *Glr.* (cf. *sdig-pai grógs-po*); *dge-bšés* 1. = *dgé-bai bšes-ɣnyén.* 2. = *dge-bsnyén* **lay-brother.** — *no-bšés* v. *no-šés.* — *mdza-bšés* **friend.**

བཤོ་བ་ *bšó-ba*, pf. *bšos*, 1. also *ɣšó-ba*, **to pour out** *Lex.* — 2. **to lie with,** to have sexual intercourse with, = *ₒk̓rig-pa byéd-pa*, e.g.: *de dan bšós-pas bu skyes* after having slept with him, she bore him a son *Pth.*; **to engender, to generate, to beget** (v.a.), *p̓ág-rdzis bšós-pai bu* the son begotten by the swine-herd *Pth.*, (*bšo-ba* seems not to be considered obscene).

བཤོག་པ་ *bšóg-pa* v. *ɣšóg-pa.*

བཤོད་པ་ *bšód-pa* = *bšád-pa*, **šo'-ri** *C.* **rumour, report,** **šo-ri-la dhé-ḍa zer dúg-te yi' mi če** though it is rumoured I cannot believe it *C.*

བཤོར་བ་ *bšór-ba* v. *ɣšór-ba.*

བཤོར་པོ་ *bšór-po C., W.* **liberal, munificent,** *Schr.*: squanderer, spendthrift(?).

བཤོལ་བ་ *bšól-ba* 1. **to put off, postpone, defer, delay,** *bód-la ₒgró-ba* the going to Tibet *Glr.*; absolutely: *bšól-ba bzan* it is good to wait; — **to prolong,** e.g. *mi žig-gi ₒtsó-ba* the life of a person (by a reprieve) *Dzl.*, also **to grant, to allow** viz. a respite, a reprieve, *bdág-la žag bdun žig bšól-te* granting me a respite of seven days *Dzl.*; **to stop, detain,** e.g. the sun in his course *Thgy.*, a traveller wishing to set out *Pth.*; **to omit,** to neglect doing *Mil.* (ni f.); *p̓yi bšól-ba* **to put off, postpone,** *p̓yi-bšól byéd-pai gán-zag* a person that is always postponing his religious duties *Mil.*; *čós-la p̓yi-bšól byar mi run Mil.* there should be no putting off, whenever religion is concerned; *bšol ₒdebs-pa* and *ₒtebs-pa* = *bšol-ba* frq.; *bšol ma tebs* he could not be detained, kept back, diverted from his purpose *Pth.;* relatives are called *bdúd-kyi bšol-ₒdébs* a hinderance on the way of the believer, caused by the devil.

བཤོས་ *bšos* resp. for *zan* or *spags*, **food, victuals, provisions of the table;** *bšos-la ɣšegs-pa* to go to dine, to go to dinner *Dzl.*; *dge-ₒdún-la bšos ɣsol-ba* to treat the priests to a meal *Dzl.*; now almost exclusively applied to food **offered to the gods,** = *lha-bšos*; *bšos-bu Mil.* offering-morsels, e.g. small pieces of butter offered to the gods or the ghosts.

བཤོས་པ་ *bšos-pa* **begotten, generated,** v. *bšo-ba.*

ས

ས *sa* 1. the letter **s,** the sharp English *s*, in *C.* distinguished from **z,** (which is sounded there also as sharp s) only by the following vowel being high-toned. — 2. num.: 28.

ས་ *sa* 1. **earth,** as elementary substance, *sa ču me rlun* earth, water, fire, air, the four elements, *sa nyún-zad čig* a small quantity of earth, opp. to: *sa čén-poi sa* the mass of the whole earth *Dzl.*; *rdzá-sa* clay, argillaceous earth, **bé-sa** *W.* sand and earth, *šág-sa* flint and earth; also for **ore, metal** (like *rdo*), *ɣsér-sa* gold-ore, *dnúl-sa* silver-ore *Cs.*; *k̓yim-sa* sweepings, offscourings;

the ground, *sá-la* (*W.* also **sa̤ K'á-na**) *₀dúg-pa* to sit on the ground, *sá-la ltúṅ-ba, ɣyél-ba* to fall to the ground; *sa-₄óg, sa-stéṅ, sa-blá*, under, on, above the ground; *sa-₄og-spyód* the Nagas (*klu*); **the earth,** the globe which we inhabit, usually more accurately *sa čén-po* v. above. — 2. **place, spot, space,** = *ɣnas*, and col. more in use than this, *rwai sa ₀búr-ba Stg.* 'swollen in the places of the horns', i.e. men that had been oxen in a former life, and in consequence of it are distinguished by little knobs corresponding to their former horns; **ṗóg-sa ghá-la dug* C.* where have you been hit or hurt? *₀dá-sa* and *₀bém-sa* sharp-shooters' stand and place of the target *C.*; *yod-sa* the place where a person lives, (in the old classical style usually expressed by *gaṅ-na-ba*);**čin-taṅ-sa** vulg. 1. orifice of the urethra. 2. privy, water-closet; *ṅá-la grós-₀dri-sa čig yod* I have a place where to ask advice, I have an oracle *Glr.*; in a wider sense: **occasion, opportunity, possibility,** *lús-la rég-sa med* one cannot get near him *Glr.*, *rje K'yód-kyi ɣšégs-sa dé-na med* you cannot go to that place, Sir! *Mil.*; *nor-gyis blú-sa med* you cannot ransom yourself by money *Mil.*; also with respect to men: *ṅa ɣžán-lu zér-sa* (*žú-sa, ré-sa*) *med* I cannot address myself to any body else with my words (requests, hopes); **place, step, degree, grade,** *čun-ma čé-sar bzuṅ* he took and treated his second wife in the place of the first, i.e. he showed the second the honour due to the first; *sa-bču* v. compounds. — 3. it is also said to be the name of a quadruped of the size and appearance of a badger, but not identic with *ɣsa Sik.*

Comp. *sa-dkár* =*dkar-rtsi Cs.* – *sa-skám Sch.* arid soil, dry ground, **steppe.** — *sa-skyóṅ, sa-skyór Lex.* protector of the earth i.e. king. — *sa-K'u* made dirty by earth, dust etc., **soiled, turbid.**— **sa-K'yád* W.* (for *ɣnas B.*, *sá-ča C.*) **place,** **sa-K'yád kám-po** a dry place, also: the dry land; **a piece of ground,****sa-K'yád čig taṅ** he gave him landed property, **sa-K'yád-di dág-po** landlord; **dwelling-place, place of residence,** **K'yód-di sa-K'yád gá-ru yod** where is your home? — *sa-K'yáb Cs.* = *sa-bdag.* — *sa-K'yon Cs.*: 'the earth's extension or compass'. — **sa-ṭa** (*sa-Kra*) **map** *C.* — *sá-mK'an* one who is well acquainted with a particular place or country, a guide *Dzl.* — *sa-mK'ar Glr.* a castle the walls of which consist for the most part of earth. — *sa-gyóṅ Sch.* hard ground. — *sa-dgá* and *sa-dgyés Lex.* = *ku-mu-da.* — *sa-dgra Glr.* the enemy of a country, i.e. in many cases nothing but a demon. — **saṅ-gúl* W.* earthquake. — *sa-ṅós* surface of the earth. — *sa-sṅón Cs.* blue earth. — *sa-bču*, दशभूमि, acc. to one explanation the ten steps or degrees of perfection which must be attained by those striving after the prize of Buddhaship; *sa ťób-pa* to reach one step (viz. the first) *Do.*; *sa čén-po* a high degree, e.g. the eighth *Thgy.*; *Foucaux* enumerates them all *Gyatch. Transl.* p. 3. According to another supposition *sa-bču* signifies the ten worlds or dominions of the Bodhisattvas *Was.* (124). — *sa-čá Glr., Mil., C.* **place, country** (*W.* **sa-K'yád**). — *sa-čen* 1. v. above *sa* 1.; 2. v. *sa-bču*; 3. v. *sa-skya.* — *sa-stéṅ* v. above *sa* 1. — *sa-dúg* evaporation, damp, injurious to those sleeping on the bare ground. — *sa-dó* (v. *do-po*) half a load of earth, a sackful of earth, being half the load of a donkey *Mil.* — **sa-dóṅ* W.* **pit,** hole. — *sa-bdág* 1. **landlord,** master or lord of the ground, sovereign *Stg.*, *sá-yi bdág-po sá-yi rje* are words used in addressing a king *Mil.* 2. more frq.: **god of the ground** of the country, supposed to be a jealous and angry being, of terrific appearance, to whom on many occasions sacrifices are brought, and who prob. was worshipped already before the spread of Buddhism cf. *Schl.* 271. — *sa-mda* 1. mouse-trap, also a large trap for catching leopards and other animals. 2. a fabulous plant (?). — *sa-rdó* a stone of earthy fracture; earth and stones; **sa-dó ḍa tsi-wa** to slight, to disregard, to neglect *C.* — *sa-ɣnás* (= *ɣnás-sa*) **place, region, country, landscape,** *nyams-dgá-bai sa-ɣnás* a lovely landscape *Glr.* — *sa-sna-lṅá* soil of five different places. — *sá-*

pa inhabitant of the earth, of our globe *Sch.* — *sa-spyód* possessing the earth, man *Cs.* — *sa-p̓ág Glr.*, prob. = *so-p̓ág* brick, dried in the sun. — *sa-p̓úg* cavern, cave. — *sa-p̓yógs* **place, region, tract,** *ˏǰigs-pai sa-p̓yogs* an unsafe place or region *Thgy.* — **sá-bi-lig* W.* 1. **mouse, rat** 2. *Ld.* also **bar, bolt,** door-bar? — *sa-blá* v. above *sa* 1. — *sa-dbáṅ Cs.* = *sa-bdág*, v. above *sa* no. 1. — *sa-ˏbol Cs.* soft earth. — *sa-ma-rdó* or *sa-min-rdó-min Sch.:* 'neither earth nor stone', i.e. a kind of conglomerate. — *sa-min Sch.*: 'white sand' (??). — *sa-mós Sch.* = *kú-mu-da* or *úd-pa-la.* — *sa-dmár* red earth; *sa-dmar-ˏbóṅ* n. of a monastery in the neighbourhood of Darjeeling, situated on a mountain-slope, which consists of a red-coloured soil (*Hook.*I, 171 calls it Simonbong). — **sa-tse* W.* sand or gravel found in roasted barley etc. — *sa-ŕtsig, sa-rtsis, sa-ts̓ig* **stage, post-station.** — *sa-mtsams, W. *san-tsam*,* **border, frontier, boundary** *Glr.*; *sa-mtsáms ˏgéys-pa* to fix the borders or limits, to mark out the boundaries. — *sa-žag* dust floating on water *Pth.* — *sa-γži* **ground, soil, footing, floor; estate** *Tar.* 99. — *sa-ˎóg* v. above *sa* 1; *sa-ˎog-spyód* the Nagas (*klu*). — *sa-yáṅs* a wide place or space, an extensive tract of land. — *sa-yúl* = *sa-č̓á Glr.* — *sa-γyos, sa γyó-ba* earthquake. — *sa-rigs* species of earth. — *sa-ris Pth.?* — *sa-rúl Cs.* rotten or decayed earth (?) — **sa-ró* W.* **rubbish,** (*Sch.* fallow-ground, fallow field?) — *sa-lám Mil.*, perh. for *sa-bčui lam.* — *sa-šún Sch.* crust of the earth (?) — *sa-bšin* fertile land, rich soil. — *sa-srán* hard ground. — *sa-sráṅ Cs.* = *sa-bdag* v. above *sa* no. 1. — *sa-srós* evening twilight, dusk *Cs.*

ས་སྐྱ་ *sa-skyá* a large monastery, S.W. of Lhasa, also the Lamas belonging to it, clothed in red, *Wts.* 132. *Schl.* 73. *sa (-skya)-č̓én(-po)* honorary title of the Lama *Kun-dga-snyiṅ-po*, born in the year 1090 after Christ; *sa-skyá páṇḍi-ta* a famous Lama of this monastery, born 1180.

ས་ག་ *sá-ga* n. of one of the lunar mansions, v. *rgyu-skár* no. ༡༦, and hence also n. of a month, part of March and April, ni f.

སཱ་ག་ར་ *sā-ga-ra Skr.* **the sea.**

ས་གུ་ཙེ་ *sa-gu-tsé* **worm** *C.*

ས་ཏྲ་ *sa-tra Tar.* 184 and 187, *Schf.*: **diploma, patent,** not to be found in *Ssk.* dictionaries.

ས་ཐེལ་ནག་པོ་ *sa-t̓el-nág-po* deity of the *Hór-pa.*

ས་བོན་ *sá-bon* 1. **seed,** *sá-bon ˏdébs-pa* to sow, *sá-bon btáb-mk̓an* sower, *sá-bon-du byéd-pa* to use as seed-corn *Dzl.*; **seed-corn, corn, grain,** also green corn, *sá-bon tsám-la ṙṅá-ba* to mow off as if it were green corn *Ma.* — 2. = *k̓u-k̓rág*, v. *k̓ú-ba Med.*; also = *k̓ú-ba*, e.g. *sá-bon ˏdzin-pa* **conception** *S.g.*, *sa-bon zág-pa emissio seminis Glr.*; fig.: **propagation, progeny, issue,** *sá-bon byed mi nus* then no propagation can take place; *sa-bon čig žog* 'propagate thyself!' — 3. fig.: *dgé-bai sá-bon* the seeds or germs of virtue, *sdig-pai sá-bon* the germs of vice, *da sá-bon ma bskyéd-na* if I do not now produce seeds viz. of virtue (else more frq.: 'a root of virtue') *Dzl.*; *byaṅ-č̓úb-kyi sá-bon Tar.* — 4. *W.* **soap,** acc. to the Hind. سَابُن, more accurately صَابُن

ས་འཚོ་མ་ *sa-ˏtsó-ma* Gopa, the wife of Buddha.

ས་ཡ་ *sá-ya* **a million;** this number, however, is not much in use with Indians and Tibetans, whereas the lāk, *ˏbum*, 100,000, frq. serves to represent a very large sum.

ས་ཡབ་ *sa-yáb* (sovereign, 'father to a country') a not unfrequent perversion of the title *sa-heb W.*

ས་ར་སོ་རེ་ *sa-ra-so-ré* also *sar-sór*, coarse-grained and fine-grained (corn, seeds etc.) mixed together *W.*

ས་རི་ *sa-ri* n. of a lunar mansion, v. *rgyu-skár* ༢༥.

སཱ་ལ་ *sā-la Ssk.* n. of an Indian tree, *Shorea robusta*, with which also some superstitious fables are connected.

ས་ལང་གི་ *sa-láṅ-gi, Hind.* सारङ्गी, a kind of violin,

ས་ལུ་ *sa-lu Ssk.* शाली, *Oryza sativa,* **rice,** as a plant; acc. to *Sch.* also Indian corn (?).

སཱ་ལེ་སྦྲམ་ *sa-le-sbrám* (cf. *sbram-bu*) *Wdṅ.* **fine gold.**

སཱ་ཧེབ་ *sá-heb*, col. *sāb*, *sab*, *Arab.* صَاحِب, formerly in India title of Moslems of high rank, now title of every European, = **gentleman, sir.**

སག་ *sag*, also *nya-sag Cs*, 1. brawn, callosity; *Sch.* also: hair-side (of a skin); *sag-čan* brawny, *sag-₀túg* a thick brawn. — 2. *W.* **scale,** (of a fish) *nya-sag-čan* scaly.

སག་གདར་ *sag-γdár C.*, **sab-dár** *W.*, *γsag-brdár Sch.* **a rasp,** *sag-γdár rgyag-pa* **to rasp.**

སག་པ་ *ság-pa C.* a little bubble, **sag sag zér-wa** to sparkle, to effervesce.

སག་རམ་རྩི་ *sag-ram-rtsí* **sulphuric acid** *Cs.*

སག(ས)་རི་ *sag(s)-ri* **shagreen.**

སག་ལད་ *sag-lád*, *Pers.* سَقلاط, 1. fine **cloth,** made of *lé-na*, *C.* **go-nam** (v. *snam-bu*). European broadcloth *W.* — 2. round or twisted lace, round tape, strips of cloth set with spangles? *W.*

སང་ *saṅ* 1. *B.*, *C.* **to-morrow,** *saṅ-nyín* id. *Glr.*; *sáṅ-gi γdúgs-la* for to-morrow noon *Dzl.*; *saṅ náṅ-par Cs.*, *saṅ sñá-bar Glr.* to-morrow morning; also absolutely: on the following day *Pth.*, *dei-saṅ* id.; *saṅ-p̓ód*, more frq. *saṅ-lo* next year; *saṅ-p̓ód da tsám-du* a year hence, this time a year. — 2. *W.* particle denoting the comparative degree, inst. of *las* or *pas* of *B.*, **de saṅ i' gyál-la** this is better than that. — 3. *Ld.*, *Balt.* sometimes for *yaṅ*.

སཾ་སྐྲྀ་ཏའི་སྐད་ *saṅ-kritai skad* **the Sanskrit language** *Glr.*

སང་གི་ཀ་ *sáṅ-gi-ka*(?) a greenish stone of which knife-handles and similar articles are said to be made *W.*

སང་ངང་ *saṅ-ṅá*, *saṅ-ṅé*, *saṅ-sún Ld.* **secretly, privately, whisperingly, by report,** = *sám-súm.*

སང་སེང་ *saṅ-séṅ* **hiding-place, chink, crevice,** *Kyim-gyi* of the house *Stg.*, for hiding money and treasures, = *sbugs*; *gós-kyi* folds of the dress, that are a haunt of vermin.

སང་བ་ *sáṅ-ba*, pf. (*b*)*saṅs*, fut. (*b*)*saṅ*, 1. **to do away with,** to remove (dirt etc.), **to cleanse,** cf. *₀tsáṅ-ba*, where also examples are given. — 2. in a more gen. sense: **to take away** or **off,** *Kebs sáṅ-ba* to uncover; **Ko-la nyi' saṅ soṅ** *C.* his sleep is gone, he cannot sleep. — 3. **to spoil,** to render unfit or useless, **wó-ma saṅ soṅ** *C.* the milk is spoiled, **zem saṅ soṅ** the cask or tub leaks *C.* Cf. *seṅ.*

སངས་རྒྱས་ *saṅs-rgyás* the Tibetan equivalent for बुद्ध; as to the etymology of the word v. sub *₀tsáṅ-ba.* The first historical Buddha is *Saṅs-rgyas śā-kya túb-pa*, whose family name is *Gaú-ta-ma* and his personal name *Don-grúb*, सिद्धार्थ, which, however, is not much used. In course of time several imaginary predecessors were given to him: *₍Od-srúṅ*, *Gser-túb* and *₀Kor-ba-₀jíg*, as having existed and reigned in former periods of the world. A successor also, *Byáms-pa*, was assigned to him, of whom it is supposed that he will reign at the period following this present one. According to others, however, *Sākyatubpa* was already the seventh Buddha that appeared on earth, the four above-named having been preceded by *Tams-čad-skyób*, *Gtsug-tor-čan* and *Rnam-par-γzigs*, this last one being the first of them all. These seven Buddhas then are comprised under the name of *Saṅs-rgyas-rabs-bdún.* — But the fertile imagination of devote Buddhists has further increased the number of future Buddhas to not less than one thousand (?), appropriate names for each of them have been invented, and Prof. Schmidt has thought it worth his while, to have these thousand names reprinted in a special pamphlet. Mysticism, however, generally knows only of the five first-named Buddhas (*Gautama*, his three predecessors and his first successor) and to each of these five 'human' Buddhas a celestial Buddha corresponds, called 'Dhyani Buddha' or the Buddha of contemplation, whilst to every Dhyani Buddha again his Dhyani Bodhisattwa is associated. In later times there is even mentioned a supreme or highest god, Adi-Buddha, *tóg-mai Saṅs-rgyás*, which doctrine, however, seems not to have been generally accepted. — Cf. *Köpp.* II, 15—29.

སད་ *sad* **frost, cold air, cold, coldness,** *sád-kyis* *ˌkyér-ba* to be destroyed by frost *Glr.*; often in conjunction with *sér-ba*, hail.

སད་པ་ *sád-pa* I. **to examine, see, try, test,** *kyod bzód-dam mi bzod sád-par byao* I shall see, whether you are patient *Dzl.*; *ɣser ltar sád-nas mṅón-par ˌgyur* like gold, it is approved by testing *Dzl.*; *nyáms-sad-pa* v. *nyams*; *sád-mi mi bdun* 'the seven men of trial', i.e. the seven most distinguished and talented among the young Tibetans sent by king *Kri-sroṅ-lde-btsan* to *'Kanpo* Bodhisattwa, for being thoroughly instructed in religion and sciences *Glr.* 86, also *Tar.* 162, 22; *las sád-pai gáṅ-zag Mil.* a tried, a tested man?

II. frq. in conjunction with *ɣnyid*, resp. *mnal* 1. to cease to sleep, **to awake,** *rmis ma-tóg-tu* directly from that dream *Dzl.*, *ɣzim-pa-las* from sleep *Dzl.* — 2. **to rouse,** from sleep, **to waken,** more precisely *sád-par byéd-pa*; also fig.: *dgé-bai rtsá-ba* good, virtuous, emotions *Tar.*

སན་གིན་ *san-gin*, *Pers.* سنگین, **bayonet** *W.*

སབ་ *sab*, col. for *sa-heb.*

སམ་ཏ་ *sam-ta Schr.*, *brtsam-grwa Cs.*, others: *bsám-kra*, *sáb-dra*, pocket-book, note-book, memorandum-book, tablets *C.*, *W.* (*Cs.* a small writing-desk?).

སམ་དལ་ *sam-dál Ld.*, *yar-sam Lh.* **mustaches.**

སམ་(མ་)སུམ་(མེ་) *sam(-ma)-sum(-me)* with a low voice, **lowly, softly,** e.g. **zér-ce**, from politeness etc.; **sam-súm zer** speak in a low voice! *W.*

སར་ *sar* 1. termin. of *sa*, *ćé-sar ˌdón-pa Cs.* to promote to high rank or dignity, *sar-ɣnas-dpá-bo* (in a hymn) was explained by: *sa bcú-la ɣnás-pai dpá-bo* i.e. Buddha. — 2. *sár-ɣcod-pa* v. *ɣsar.* — 3. sbst. **wick** *W.*

ས་རྫི་ཀ་ *sa-rdzi-ka Ssk.* **soda,** in *Wdṅ.* it is mentioned as a plant, yielding soda.

སར་སོར་ *sar-sor* v. *sa-ra-so-re.*

སལ་བབ་ *sal-báb W.*, and prob. also *sal-síl Mil.*, gold ornament, **gold lace,** and the like, ni. f.

སལ་ལེ་བ་ *sál-le-ba* **clear, bright, brilliant** *Mil.*, *sal-lér snáṅ-ba* lighted up brilliantly, well lighted *Pth.*, *mdaṅs sal-sál* id. *Pth.*

སས་ *sas* instr. of *sa.*

སི་ *si* 1. in some parts of *Ld.* the termination of the instrum. after vowels, like *su* in *Kun.* — 2. also *si-si*, the sound of whistling through the teeth, *si-skad*, *si-sgra* whistling, whistle; *si-brda* whistling, whistle, as a call or sign; *si-glu* a whistled tune. — 3. num.: 58.

སཱི་ཏཱ *sī-tā* n. of one of the four fabulous streams of the world.

སི་རི་ *si-ri* 1. **pack-thread, twine** *C.*, *W.* — 2. **bar, bolt, door-bar,** **si-ri cúg-ce** or *gyáb-ce** to bolt, to bolt up, **si-ri tón-ce** to unbolt, unbar *W.*

སི་རི་འབུ་ *si-ri-ˌbu* **centiped** *W.*

སི་རིལ་ *si-ril* a kind of inkhorn, case for carrying an inkstand in one's pocket *Ld.*

སི་ལ་ *si-la Ssk.* सिह्लकी a sort of incense.

སི་ལི་མ་ *si-li-ma* the breaking up of the ice *Sch.*

སིག་པ་ *sig-pa* **to hitch up,** to give a hitch, as porters do with a load on their back *Cs.*

སིག་བུ་ *sig-bu Sch.*, *sig-ra Schr.*, a sort of basket.

སིང་ *siṅ* v. *siṅ-siṅ.*

སིང་སྐྱུར་ *siṅ-skyúr Sch.* curdled milk, sour milk.

སིང་ག་གླིང་ *siṅ-ga-gliṅ Cs.*, *siṅ-ga-lai gliṅ Glr.*, सिंहल, **Ceylon.**

སིང་གེ་ *siṅ-ge* 1. frq. for *seṅ-ge.* — 2. v. *rtsiṅ-ge.*

སིང་བ་ *siṅ-ba* 1. vb., **bal siṅ-ce** **to pick out, sort out,** wool for the third time, by which the finest is obtained. — 2. adj. in compounds: *nág-siṅ-ba* jet-black, very black *Thgy.*; *spró-siṅ-ba* v. *spro.*

སིང་བུ་ *siṅ-bu* liquor made of mare's milk, Tartar arrack *Sch.*

སིང་ཚལ་ *siṅ-tsál Ts.* **tea-pot, tea-kettle.**

སིང་ཡོལ་ *siṅ-yól* v. *seṅ-rás* in *seṅ-po.*

སིང་རི་ *siṅ-rí* 1. n. of a mountain *Glr.* — 2. = *siṅs-po.*

སིང་སིང་ *siṅ-siṅ* **thin, limpid,** of fluids *W.* (yet cf. *séṅ-po*), **siṅ čug-če** to clarify, to purify.

སིངས་པོ་ *siṅs-po* 1. adj. **thin, clear** *W.* — 2. sbst. *Cs.*, also *čaṅ(-ba)-siṅs Pth.*, *Lt.*, **ug-siṅ* Ld.* **small-beer,** the fourth infusion of 'chang', a weak beverage, without any intoxicating qualities, yet not disrelished on that account.

སིད་པ་ *síd-pa* **to whistle** *Sch.*, *sid-sgra* = *si-sgra.*

སིནྡྷུ་ར་ *sindhu-ra*, for सिन्दूर **minium,** red lead, = *li-ḱri Glr.*

སིབ་པ་ *síb-pa* **to evaporate, to soak in, to be imbibed,** of fluids, *sib-sib* or *sib-kyis*, also *sib-kyis ťim-pa* to evaporate quickly.

སིབ་བུ་ *sib-bu Lt.*; *Cs.*: a sort of **small-pox;** *Schr.*: **the measles.**

སིམ་པ་ *sim-pa Lex.* = *bdé-ba*, सुख, sbst. **good health, prosperity,** vb. **to be well, to be well off.**

སིམ་བིད་(ལ་) *sim-bid(-la)* adv. **sliding, gliding, slipping,** with **čá-če** to move along in this way *Ld.*

སིལ་བུ, གསིལ་བུ་ *sil-bu*, *ɣsil-bu* a little piece, **a fragment,** *ro sil-bur ˳gyur* the corpse falls to pieces *Mil.*; *sil-sil* col. id.; **sil čó-če** to reduce to small pieces, by breaking, crumbling, plucking etc. *W.*

སིལ་སྙན་ *sil-snyán* (also *sil* and *sil-sil Lex.*) **cymbal,** *lčágs-kyi sil ˳ḱról-ba Lex.*, *sil snyán ról-mo ˳ḱról-ba Glr.*, *Dzl.* to strike the cymbals; *sil-snyán-ma* a female cymbal-player *Tar.*

སིལ་མ་ *sil-ma* 1. the tinkling sound of a cymbal, *rdza-čáb sil-mas snyán-pa brjod* tunefully flows the brook over its clay-slate bed *Mil.*; *sil-čáb* gurgling water, rippling brook *Mil.*— 2. also *sil-dṅúl* the rupee of Ladak, = 4 *jau*, = ⅘ of an Indian rupee, **sil-ṅul gyad-di nas** a patch of barley worth 8 Silma *Ld.*

སུ་ *su* I. pron., also *su žig*, 1. interrog. pron. **who?** *˳di-na su yod* who is here? *ḱyod su yin* who are you? *su čí-skad byá-ba yod* who is it and what is his name? *Mil.*; **which?** = *gaṅ*, *rgyál-poi bu su žig* which son of the king? *Tar.*, *sú-rnams*, *sú-dag*, col. **sú-su** plural form; in certain popular phrases: **su-gyóg** race, running-match *W.*, **su tob gyáb-pa** to pounce upon, to snatch away, to plunder *C.*, *W.*—2. correlative and indefinite pron.: *su mi di ɣsód-pa dé-la ... sbyin-no* to him that kills this man, I shall give ... *Stg.*; *ḱyod sṅar sú-la yaṅ ɣsól-ba ma btáb-bam* have not you already asked somebody before? *Dzl.* ᒪᘓ, 14 (acc. to a better reading); *su de čáṅ-bai gán-du mčio* I shall go to him who has it *Do.*; *su ťod-ťód* whom it concerns *Sch.* (?); *su yaṅ (ruṅ)* **whosoever,** whoever, any body who, also absolutely: **every, every one, all,** *sú-bas kyaṅ p̔yis* later than all (the others) *Dzl.*, when followed by a negative: **nobody,** frq.; *su byuṅ Mil.* = *su yaṅ*; *su med kyaṅ* though nobody be present. *Pth.*; *su*, *su žig*, *su gaṅ* is also used for **somebody, some one, a certain** (but not frq. and more in col. or vulg. language): *su gaṅ mdzá-bo žig* a certain friend; *su sér-sna-čan žig* a (certain) miser; also in the following manner: **su čad dug su tsem dug** one cuts out, the other sews *W.*; **bóṅ-bu su lo-ču-nyi-pa, su lo-čú-pa yin** some of the donkeys are twelve, others ten years old. — II. termination: 1. of the term. after a final s, cf. *tu*, *du*, *ru*. — 2. of the instr. in *Kun.*: **'á-pa-su** from or by the father, inst. of the *p̔as* of *B.* (cf. सु in the Brūj-dialect of the Hindi). — 3. expletive after *nas Mil.* and elsewh. — III. num.: 88.

སུ་གི་ *sú-gi* vulgar corruption of *dzo-ki* q.v.

སུ་མི་ *su-mi* a medicinal root serving as an antidote *Cs.*

སུ་རུ་པན་ཚ་, སུར་པན་ *su-ru-pan-tsá, sur-pán* Guinea pepper, *Capsicum annuum C., W.*

སུ་ལུ་ *sú-lu? sú-lui ťsúl-du bžúgs-pa* denotes perh. the usual sitting posture of Milaraspa who, while reciting his songs, used to stretch out his left leg, drawing up the other, and supporting his right arm on it, on which his head was leaning.

སུ་སུ་ *su-su* 1. v. *su.* — 2. *su-sú zer-wa* denotes **the drawing in the breath** in blowing up a fire, the lips being nearly closed, to prevent ashes or smoke from entering the mouth.

སུག་ *sug* **reward, recompense,** *sug-rnán* id., *sug-rjéd* mark of honour as a reward *Cs.*; *pag-súg* a bribe, frq.

སུག་པ་ *súg-pa* I. sbst. 1. **the hand** *Med.*; *sug-bris* handwriting *Sch.* — 2. the lower part of the leg of animals, *rtai súg-bži*; **súg-gu* W.* id. — 3. a medicinal herb *Wdn.*

II. vb. **to push, jog, nudge** a person, in order to waken him, or to make him attentive; **to push open,** a door with a stick *Mil.*; *súg-pa žig byéd-pa Mil.*, **sug gyáb-pa* C.* **to push, to shove, to displace,** **sug ča yin** it will get out of its place *W.*

སུག་སྨེལ་ *sug-rmél Cs.*: 'a kind of spice, betel, betel-nut' (?); *sug-smél Lt.* and *C.* **cardamom.**

སུད་པ་ *súd-pa* **to cough, to breathe with difficulty** *Cs.*, *súd-de ši-ba* to be choked or suffocated *Sch.*

སུན་པ་ *sun-pa* vb. and adj. 1. **to be tired of, weary of, sick of; tired, weary, out of humour** *rná-ba mi sún-te* not tired of hearing *Mil.*; *yid sún-par gyúr-ba* to become tired, to get weary of; the more precise form of the adj. is *sún-po*: **žág-dan ḍe zá-na sún-po rag* or *sún-na rag* W.* if one eats rice every day, one gets tired of it; **sems sún-po** id.; **'ám-čog sun son* C.* one gets tired of hearing *C.*; **sú-heb nyen sun run** though it may be disagreeable to you, Sir, to hear it *C.*; *ťugs-sún dgóns-pa yin-pa dug* I suppose your Reverence will be tired of it *Mil.*; **sun** (*C. *sun**) **čug-če** **to make** (a person) **tired of** (a thing), **to vex, annoy, to stun** or **drown with noise,** to deafen. — 2. *sún-par byéd-pa Dzl.*, and more frq. *sún-par byin-pa* 1. to drown with, to overpower by noise, to silence (thus prob. *Mil.* ch. 34 init.); hence 2. **to refute, confute, disprove** *Tar.* 3. c. acc. **to insult, defame, disgrace, dishonour** *Schr., Dzl.* ༢༢༢, 1, 3, ༢༠༥, 2; *Bhar.* 67, *Schf.*; so perh. also *sun-pa* in the following passage of *Mil.*: *ťúgs-rje drág-po sun ma byin* we will not put to shame the great favour (of the Lama). 4. **to renounce,** to resign, *sun byin-pai stobs* strength to renounce (the world).

སུབ་པ་ *súb-pa*, pf. *(b)subs*, fut. *bsub*, 1. **to stop up, plug up, close, cork; to keep shut,** closed, locked up, **to stop,** *ka sna lág-pas* to stop one's mouth and nose with one's hand *Lt.*; *dbugs súb-pa* to strangle, suffocate, choke (a person); **to fill up,** choke up (with earth, rubbish etc.) a lake *Glr.*; *sna-sub* a disease of the nose? *Lt.* — 2. **to cover, close, shut up** *Sch.*, more frq., fig. *rkan-rjés súb-pa* to cover the trace or track, to efface every vestige; **ti-pi ťúr-la súb-če** to turn down the brim of the hat; **to blot out, erase,** *ri-mo* a drawing, *bú-lon-pai min* the name of a debtor; **to hush up, conceal, cover,** e.g. other people's offences; **to suppress, to avoid,** e.g. obscene words; to allow to settle, the mash, in brewing; in all these instances in *W.* also **súb-te bór-če** is used.

སུམ་ *sum*, for *gsum*, **three,** in compounds before consonants: *súm-ču* 30, *sum-brgya* 300, *sum-stón* 3000; *súm-ča, Sch.* also *sum-yar*, **a third,** the third part, *dzam-bu-glin súm-ča gnyis* (or only *sum-gnyis*) two thirds of Dzambuling (i.e. of the world) *Dz.*, *bod sum gnyis* two thirds of (all) the Tibetans *Ma.*; *sum-skyá Sch.* a cord of three twisted threads; *sum-ču-rtsa-gsum* the 33 ancient gods (of the Vedas); *súm-ču-pa* the thirty, i.e. 30 letters, the Tibetan alphabet, *súm-ču-pa dan rtags-jug Zam.* the alphabet and the punctuation, abbreviated: *sum-rtágs Lexx.*

སུམ་(ཅུ་)ཏིག་ *sum(-ču)-tig* a medicinal herb *Med.*

སུམ་པ་, སུམས་པ་ *súm-pa, súms-pa* I. adj. **putrid, rancid, rotten.**

II. vb., pf. *bsums*? fut. *bsum*, *Sch.* **to bind** or **tie together**, to draw together; **to condense.**

སུར་ན་ *súr-na*, *Pers.* سُرْنا, **hautboy**, larger than the *gliṅ-bu* and sounding sharper; for profane use.

སུར་པན་ *súr-pán* v. *su-ru-pan-tsá.*

སུར་ཡ་ or སཱུརྱ་ *sur-ya* or *surya Med.*, सूर्य, **colocynth.**

སུར་སུར་ *sur-sur* **coarse-grained**, e.g. grits *W.*

སུལ་ *sul* an artificial **plait** or **gather** made in a dress *W.*; **furrow, channel, groove, trench, ditch** (*Cs.*); *ri-súl* lateral valley, ravine, hollow, *ri-súl-gyi groṅ-kyér* ravine as a haunt of evil spirits; *brag-sul* narrow ravine between rocks; *ku-súl* the fluting in a column; *súl-čan* furrowed, having plaits or folds; *súl-ma* an angular, not round, vessel; *sul-mál* the third stomach of ruminating animals, the psalterium or book-tripe *Sch.*, *sul-máṅs Lt.*

སུས་ *sus* 1. instr. of *su.* — 2. *kyeu-sús Gyatch.* ༢༥, 13, also *Stg.?*

སེ་ *se* 1. *Ld.* inst. of *te* after *s*, e.g. **zós-se** — 2. num.: 118.

སེ་གོལ་ *se-gól* 1. **snapping** one's fingers. — 2. the time it takes to do this, i.e. **a very short time, a moment, a twinkling** *Cs.*, *se-gól-gyi sgra* the sound produced by snapping the fingers, *se-gól-gyi brda* a signal given by it *Cs.*; *se-gól γtóg-pa Mil.*, *byéd-pa Mil.*, *brdáb-pa Glr.* to snap one's fingers as a sign of contempt or indignation.

སེ་ཏྲང་ *se-tráṅ* yellow beads of a rosary, coming from the central part of Tibet, accounted more valuable than **rág-ša* W.*

སེ་དུག་ *se-dúg* v. *se-šiṅ.*

སེ་དྲི་, བསེ་དྲི་ *se-dri, bse-dri* the disagreeable smell of the sweat of the arm-pits *Lt.*, *se-dri bsnám-pa* having that smell *Pth.*

སེ་ནམ་ *se-nam* vulgar for *bsód-snyoms*, **alms.**

སེ་སྤུར་ *se-spur Sch.* **dung-beetle.**

སེ་བ་, གསེ་བ་, བསེ་བ་ *sé-ba, γsé-ba, bsé-ba* 1. **rose-bush, rose-tree; rose;** *γser-mdog-sé-ba-me* (for *mé-tog*) *Lt.*, prob. the yellow rose; wild roses with beautiful and rich blossoms frequently adorn the slopes of the lower hills in the Himalaya mountains; whether the *se-rgód Med.* and the 'wild rose' of *Cs.* are identical, seems to be questionable; **se-ḍúm* C.* **hip, haw.** — *šiṅ-sé-ba* is mentioned as the food of the silk-worm *Glr.*, hence = *ₒó-se-šiṅ.* — 3. thorn?

སེ་བོ་ *se-bo* **gray,** *skra se-bo* gray hair; *mgo se-bo* (resp. *dbu se-bo*) a gray-headed person. — In col. language many things which we call gray, are styled white.

སེ་འབྲུ་, སེའུ་ *se-ₒbru, seu* (*C.* **sen-ḍú**, *W.* **sem-rú**) **pomegranate.**

སེ་མོ་དོ་ *sé-mo-do* or *sé-mo-to Mil.* a kind of **ornament,** e.g. made of pearls.

སེ་མོག་ *se-móg C.* **the venereal disease;** *se-rmá* syphilitic ulcers *Sch.*

སེ་ཡབ་, བསེ་ཡབ་ *se-yáb, bse-yáb* **fig** *Med.*

སེ་ར་ *sé-ra*, n. of a large monastery near Lhasa.

སེ་རག་དུར་སྨན་ *se-rag-dur-smán* **carrot** *W.*

སེ་རེལ་ *se-rél* half open, **se-rél čúg-če** to open half (doors, lids, covers etc.) *W.*

སེ་ཤིང་, བསེ་ཤིང་ *sé-šiṅ, bsé-šiṅ Cs.*: 'a tree or shrub, good for hedges', *se-dúg* 1. poison contained in that shrub. 2. = *se-móg Cs.*

སེག་, སེག་སེག་ *seg, seg-ség* **obliquely, awry, sideways,** *ség-γčod-pa Cs.*, **ség-ḍhe-la ḍhá-wa* C.*, **ség-ḍe-la ḍé-če* W.* to cut off obliquely (opp. to **ṭe'-kaṅ-la** straight *C.*).

སེག་མ་ *seg-ma* **small stones, gravel** *W.*

སེང་ *señ* v. *γseṅ.*

སེང་གེ་ *séṅ-ge*, *W.* **siṅ-ge**, **lion,** *séṅ-ge-mo* lioness, *séṅ-gei rál-pa* the mane of a lion; *seṅ-gei ḱri* **सिंहासन a throne** ('said to be so called from its being supported by golden lions' *Will.*); *seṅ-mgó* lion's head *Glr.*; *seṅ-ydoṅ-ma Sch.*, = *sī-ha-mu-ka* lion's face, **a goddess,** *Glr.; seṅ-prúg* a lion's whelp, *seṅ-tsáṅ* a lion's den.

སེང་ལྡང་ *seṅ-ldáṅ S.g*, *seṅ-ṫsér Wdṅ.*, a tree growing on the southern, lower ranges of the Himalayas, having red wood, and a bark which by poor people is used for tea (*sdoṅ-ja*); its sap serves as an official drug, *Lt.*; acc. to *Schf.* **खदिर** *Acacia Catechu.*

སེང་པོ་, བསེང་པོ་ *séṅ-po, bséṅ-po* 1. **clean, white,** cf. *skya-séṅ.* — 2. *Sch.:* **thin, airy, transparent, not dense or tight,** *seṅ-séṅ* id. (*Sch.:* **open, free, roomy, spacious**); *skyé-bo seṅ-séṅ-por gyur* they became very thin, lean, pale people, **siṅ-siṅ-po, síngs-po* W.* id.; *seṅ-rás Sch.*, **siṅ-yol* W.* a thin curtain, thin cotton cloth.

སེང་བ་ *séṅ-ba*, pf. *bsaṅs*, fut. *bsaṅ, bseṅ,* **to lift up, to raise** what was hanging down or drooping *W.* **saṅ ċo-ċe* or *taṅ-ċe** to lift up (the eyes, the hands, the dress etc.); *sku-ḱáms bséṅ-ba-la ₒbyon* (his Reverence) goes to take some recreation *Mil.; ḱams dúb-pa séṅ-ba* to refresh the wearied body *Mil.*; *ḱams rmúgs-pa bséṅ-bai rluṅ-ñád* bracing air; *skyo-bsáṅ-ba* to unbend the mind, to divert one's self; *skyo-séṅ-la ₒgró-ba* (resp. *ₒbyón-pa*) to take a walk, *séṅ-la mdzád-pa* to drive out, to take the air in a carriage *Pth.; mya-ṅán bsáṅs-te* consolatory, giving comfort *Pth.*

སེང་ཤིང་, སེང་ཤང་ *seṅ-śiṅ, seṅ-śáṅ* v. *yseg-śáṅ.*

སེད་ *sed* **a file,** **ċag-sé** id., **śiṅ-sé** **a rasp.**

སེན་ཐབས་ *sen-ṫábs Mil.?*

སེན་མོ་ *sén-mo*, **resp.** *ṗyag-sen* or *żabs-sén*, **nail** of a **finger or toe;** *sen-ṫóg* **a gripe, pinch, nip, twitch;** a pinch (of snuff) *sén-mo ₒdébs-pa, W.* **ṫáb-ċe* or *gyáb-ċe** **to pinch, squeeze,** **sen-ċus gyáb-ċe** to bore with the knuckles *W.; sen-tsám Sch.* as much as may be put on a finger-nail, a small quantity; *sen-żó* a white spot, such as will sometimes appear on the nails of the fingers.

སེབ་ *seb* v. *yseb.*

སེམ་, སེམས་ *sem*, usually *sems*, *Ssk.* **सत्त्व**, resp. ཐུགས་, **soul;** esp. as power of perception and volition, **mind,** cf. *yid* and *blo; sems na* the mind is disturbed, disordered *Mṅg.; sem ₒḱrúgs-pa* a mind agitated and troubled by sorrow, affliction, vexation etc., *sem ḱóṅ-du* (or *ḱóṅs-su*) *ċúd-pa* one very much grieved, deeply concerned; *sem ċúṅ-ba* a timid mind, **sem ṫsér-ċan* W.* a compassionate disposition, **sem nyé-mo* W.* a friendly disposition; *sem ysó-ba B.*, **sem so táṅ-ċe* or *ċúg-ċe* W.* **to console,** comfort, appease; the mind as imaginative faculty, intellectual power, *sem stór-ba* to lose one's senses *Do.;* **spirit,** *kun-yżii sem* the (eternal) spirit (opp. to *ₒbyúṅ-ba bżii lus* the material, perishable body) *Mil.*; *sém-kyi spyód-pa* intellectual power, mental faculties *Wdṅ.*; *dṅós-po ṫams-ċád ráṅ-gi sems yin-te* 'as things with me are only mind', i.e. as they exist only in my mind, in my imagination *Thgr.*, cf. *Was.* (136); *sém-la ma soṅ* 'it did not enter his mind', he had no mind, did not like *W.*; *sems ₒgyur* (his) mind is changed, *sems sgyur-ba* to change one's mind, *μετανοεῖν*; *bzód-pai sems* patient indurance, fortitude, **constancy;** *ynod-sems* **malice;** *śes-ráb daṅ ldán-pai sems* **wisdom,** knowledge; *sems skyéd-pa*, c. genit., to suffer thoughts or inclinations to rise in one's mind, as e.g. *ₒdod-ċágs-kyi* libidinous (thoughts), frq.; also: to nourish, indulge (desires, passions), to give way to them; often used for our reflective verbs: *sems smád-pa* to humble one's self (*mi żig-la* before a person); also: *bdág-gi séms-la smad* he blamed, scolded, himself *Dzl.* ༧༥, 3, cf. *lus.*

Comp. *séms-mḱan* **intelligent, sensible,** *séms-mḱan mi yċig kyaṅ ma byuṅ* not one sensible person was present *Glr.*— *sems-ₒḱrál* a mind afflicted, painfully agitated *Sch.* — *sems-ċan* animated being, **man, animal,** very frq.; *séms-ċan daṅ ldán-pa* being with child, pregnant; *sems-ċan-dmyál-ba* = *dmyál-ba*·

— *sems-nyid Glr.*, *Thgy.*, 'the very soul', but this is often nearly the same as 'spirit', and in the language of the N. T. it may fitly be used for *πνεῦμα*, and *tugs-nyid* for *πνεῦμα ἅγιον*, Holy Spirit. — *sems-rtén* **keepsake, token** *Pth.* and col. — *sems-dón* an intellectual or spiritual good, gift, or possession *Mil.* — *sems-bdé* **cheerful, merry** *Mil.* — *sems-nád* **heart-grief, affliction**, *séms-kyi nád-du če* he has much heart-grief *Glr.* — *sems-dpá* a brave mind; *byaṅ-čub-sems-dpá* v. *byaṅ-čúb*; *sems-dpa-čén-po*, महासत्त्व, a frq. apposition to it. — *séms-tsam* a mere thought, idea *Was.* (134), *séms-tsam-pa* (*Cs.*: योगाचार्य) a mystic *Köpp.* II, 25. — *sems-ťsér* **fatigue, weariness, disgust** *Sch.*

སེམ(ས)་པ་ *sém(s)-pa*, pf. *sems*, *bsams*, fut. *bsam*, imp. *som*, *W.* **sám-če**, **to think**, *ₒdi snyám-du séms-so* or *bsáms-so* he thought as follows, he had the following thoughts; *lóg-par sém-pa* to think ill (of a person) *Dzl.*; **to meditate, muse, ponder**, *sém-bžin-du* absorbed in meditation, lost in thought *Dzl.*, *mi-dgá-bar sém-šiṅ* immersed in melancholy thoughts *Dzl.*; in *C.* **sém-žin-du** signifies at the present time: knowingly, wilfully, purposely, = *šes bžin-du*; *šin-tu soms šig* think over it seriously! *Dzl.*; **to think of**, c. accus., *gráṅ-bai ɣnas* (to think) of a cool place, i. e. to long for coolness *Dzl.*, and c. dat.: *ráṅ-gi yúl-la ma bsám-par* forgetful of home, forgetting one's native soil *Glr.*, *yi-ge ₒdi-la ma bsám-par* disregarding this contract *Glr.*; also with termin.: *ɣžán-du ma sems šig* do not think of anybody else; **to intend, purpose, have in view**, e.g. *ɣnód-par byá-bar* to do harm *Dzl.*; construed in the same manner, it also signifies: **to fancy, imagine** *Do.*; with *daṅ ₒdrá-bar* and similar expressions: **to hold, think, consider, to take for, to look upon as**; *da ₒk'ór-bai nyes-dmigs bsám-šes-na* (for *bsám-žiṅ*) now that you know with full consciousness the punishment of (going through) the cycle (of animal existences) *Mil.* (yet cf. *bsám-šes* in *bsám-pa*). Sometimes it denotes only an act of memory, a remembering: *lhá-čos ťos-bsam-byéd-pa-rnams* those who have heard and kept in their memory the religion of Buddha, (who remember the words even without understanding them) *Mil.* Cf. *bsám-pa*.

སེའུ་ *seu* 1. **a little tooth** *Lt.* — 2. **pomegranate.**

སེར་, སེར་རུ་ *ser*, *sér-ru* corruption, putrefaction? **már-la sér-ru gyab** *C.* the butter turns yellow and rancid, *sér-čan* **rancid** *S.g.*

སེར་ཀ་ *sér-ka*, *sér-k'a*, *sér-ga* 1. **a cleft, slit, fissure, crevice, gap**, *brag-sér* chasm or cleft in a rock; *rgya-sér* a large gap, cleft, chasm; *sér-ka súb-pa* to close, stop up a hole *Pth.* — 2. v. *sér-po.*

སེར་སྐྱ་ *ser-skyá* **Lamas and laymen**, **ser-kyá kun ₒdúm-ma ǰhé-pa** a promiscuous convention, parish council *C.* — 2. v. *skyá-bo.*

སེར་ཁྱིམ་པ་ *sér-k'yim-pa* a sect of Lamas = *dbón-po.*

སེར་ག་མ་ *sér-ga-ma Sch.* turmeric, *Curcuma.*

སེར་ཆེ་ *ser-čé Lt.* a yellow aquatic flower; **ser-čen** *W. Saxifraga flagellaris.*

སེར་སྣ་ *sér-sna* **avarice**, frq.; *sér-sna byéd-pa* to be avaricious *Dzl.*

སེར་པོ་ *sér-po* **yellow**; *ser-ₒpréṅ* clerical procession, parade *Mil.nt.*

སེར་བ་ *sér-ba* **hail**; *ser-k'rál* a kind of insurance against damage done by hail, i.e. money paid to the Lama for his preventive ceremonies.

སེར་བུ་ *sér-bu* v. *bsér-bu.*

སེར་མོ་ *sér-mo* 1. *C.* col. **finger.** — 2. *W.* six-rowed barley, **late barley.** — *sér-mo-ba* the Lamas *Sch.*

སེལ་ *sel* 1. **discord, dissension**, *naṅ-sél* domestic dispute. — 2. a kind of **incantation**, like *brtad*, *sel ₒǰúg-pa* to exorcise, to make use of conjurations or incantations *Mil.*

སེལ་བ་ *sel-ba*, pf., fut. *bsal*, imp. *sol*, **to remove**, esp. impurities, hence **to cleanse; to pick, pick off; to blot out, cross out**, *bú-lon* a debt; **to clear**, **lam sál-če** *W.* to make a path or road; very frq. fig.: **to remove**, to remedy (an evil), to cure (a disease), to repair (a damage), to redress grievances), to dispel (darkness) etc.

སོ་ *so*, I. sbst. 1. resp. *ťsems*, **tooth**, *stén-so*, *yá-so* upper tooth; *ˏóg-so*, *má-so* lower tooth; *mdún-so Sch.* *ɣčád-so*, *Stg.* *so-drúṅ* fore-tooth, front-tooth; *sbúbs-so*, *grám-so*, *ráṅ-ťag-so Sch.* *ldán-so* cheek-tooth, molar-tooth, grinder, *mčé-so Cs*, **čód-ten-so** *W.* eye-tooth, corner-tooth, canine-tooth. — 2. **tooth** of a saw, wheel, comb. — 3. **edge** of a knife.

II. sbst. for *sa*, in conjunction with certain words, e.g. *ṅan-sor skye-ba* to be born in an inferior place *Mil.*; v. also *ráṅ-so*, *sór-bžag-pa*, *ˏkrúl-so*.

III. sbst. **joy** (?), *so bsod-pa* id. *Cs.* and *Lex.*; cf. *ṅó-so*.

IV. sbst., also *bso*, **look-out, guard, spying,** *so byéd-pa* to spy, to look out; *só-kʻuṅ* peep-hole; *só-pa* keeper, guard, watchman, spy, emissary, *zas nor bdúd-kyi só-pa yin* money and dainties are the devil's emissaries *Mil.*; *mé-bso* a guard or watch kept by several persons round a fire; *só-sgra* 1. watchword, = *sgar-miṅ*. 2. v. comp.

V. grammatical termination: **tén-so** provinc. for *rtén-no C.*, also *Glr.*

VI. num. for *súm-ču* in the abbreviated numbers 31—39.

VII. num.: 148.

Comp. *so-grí* a saw. — *só-sgra* the whistling through the teeth, in the magic performances of the Bonpo, *só-sgra ˏdébs-pa Glr.* — *so-čág* a broken tooth. — *so-drég* tartar? *Med.* — *so-búd* a tooth that has come out. — *so-máṅ* comb. — *so-žó* a small white spot on a tooth, cf. *sén-žo.* — *so-zéd* **tooth-brush.** — *so-šíṅ* **toothpick.** — *so-srúb* gap in the teeth *Sch.*

སོ་ག་ *só-ga* = *sós-ka.*

སོ་ཅ་ *só-ča* n. of an emetic *Med.*

སོ་ནམ(ས་) *so-nám(s)* **agriculture, husbandry,** *so-náms byéd-pa* to till the ground, to practise agriculture, farming, *sgrúb-pa*, *ˏbád-pa* id., *so-nám-pa Cs.* husbandman, farmer.

སོ་པ་ *só-pa* v. *so* IV.

སོ་པ་རི་ *só-pa-ri Cs.* a kind of berry, beneficial to the teeth.

སོ་ཕག་ *so-pʻág* **brick, tile;** also collective noun, brickwork, tiling.

སོ་བ་ *só-ba* course, thick-shelled **barley,** used for fodder.

སོ་བྱ་ *só-bya* an aquatic bird *S.g.*

སོ་མ་ *só-ma* 1. sbst. *Ssk.* (prop. a climbing plant the juice of which was offered in libations to the gods and was also worshipped itself, on account of its intoxicating qualities, hence): **hemp,** also *ɣtsó-ma*, *btsó-ma*; *so-ma-rá-dza* id., *so-ma-rá-dzai ras* **hemp-linen** *Schr.*, *so-ma-rá-dzai ťág-pa* **hempen rope** *Pth.* — 2. adj. **new, fresh,** esp. *W.* **só-mo náṅ-na zer gos** this ought to have been mentioned directly (when it was still fresh in every body's memory).

སོ་ཚིས་, སོ་ཚིགས་ *so-ťsís*, *so-ťsigs* **house-keeping,** management of domestic concerns, **husbandry,** cf. *so-nam* agriculture.

སོ་ལུག་ *so-lug* **lees** of liquors, yeast of beer *Sch.*

སོ་ལོག་ *so-log* **high-road, causeway** *W.*

སོ་སོ་ *so-só* distinct, separate, singly, individually, *zas so-sói lág-tu ˏóṅs-so* the victuals came into the hands of the individual persons *Dzl.*; *so-só-nas* adv. frq.: *so-só-nas snod bzéd-de* 'singulatim', each for himself, holding forth his vessel *Dzl.*; **various** e.g. **na so-só** *W.* for *sna-ťsogs* of *B.*; **diverse, different** *sám-pa so-só* different opinions, a dissension; **separate, distinct,** *so-só byéd-pa*, *W.* **so-só čó-če** to separate, disjoin, divide, *so-sór bžág-pa*, *W.* **so-só bór-če** to set, put, lay apart. — *so-soi skye-bo*, **पृथग्जन**, prop. one separated (from the saints), one outside the pale, a man of the lower classes, of low caste; with Buddhists: **a layman,** and as to his spiritual condition: a man in his natural state, one not yet enlightened (like ψυχικός I Cor. 2, 14, though on account of its derivation, the above term cannot well be used for the Greek word); also the lower classes of clerical persons, monks. — *so-só(s)-ťar-pa*, *so-ťár*, **प्रतिमोक्ष**,

liberation, **deliverance,** *so-só-ťar-pai mdo* the book of deliverance, code of the moral law, containing about 250 precepts for the priesthood, the monastic rules of the Buddhists.

སོ་སོ་ཚ་ *so-so-ča* a medicinal herb, an emetic *Wdn.*

སོག་ *sog* 1. v. *sob*. — 2. for **srog** *Ü.*

སོག་པ་ *sóg-pa* 1. sbst, also *sógs-pa*, **shoulder-blade,** scapula, *sóg-pai mé-lon* the flat part of it, *sog-yu* the narrow extremity of it; *sog-mó ͦdébs-pa* (v. *mo* III.) to divine from the shoulder-blade; *sog-lhú* shoulder as a piece of meat for boiling (I Sam. 9, 24). — 2. vb. (also: *ysóg-pa, bsóg-pa, sógs-pa*) pf. *(b)ags*, fut. *bsag*, imp. *sogs, bsag*, *W.* **ság-če**, **to gather, heap up, hoard up,** *ṕral sog-ͦjog-méd-pa* without having collected and deposited the daily requisites, the things wanted every day *Mil.*, *bsód-nams sóg-pa Mil.*, *ťsogs sóg-pa* frq. to collect, to hoard up merits of virtue, *las-ṅán sóg-pa* to heap up sins; *ysog-ldáṅ* morbid matter consisting in too great an accumulation of humours, ni f., *Med.; dmág-gi dpuṅ sóg-pa* to collect an army *Dzl.;* **to assemble,** children *Glr.;* hence **sag(s)* W.* **all** (of them), **lug sag tsam** how many sheep are there in all?

སོག་པོ་ *sóg-po* **a Mongol** *Glr.*, *sóg-mo* a Mongol woman, *sog-ṕrúg* Mongol child, Mongol boy, *sog-čás* Mongol dress or fashion of dress, *sog-rta* Mongol horse.

སོག་མ་ *sóg-ma* **blade, stalk; straw;** *sog-ͦbru* *Sch.* green corn that begins to sprout; *sog-ťsigs* a knot on a stalk *Cs.*; *sog-sbúr* a small blade of straw, chaff *Pth.*; *sóg-mai ͦbú-la* a shoe of straw; *sog-rú, sog-rúm, sog-ldúm* stubbles.

སོག་ལེ་ *sóg-le B., C.,* **čad-sóg, gya-sóg** *W.* **a saw,** *sóg-les ycód-pa B.* to saw to pieces, **gya-sóg šrúl-ce** *W.* to saw; *sog-le-ka* the toothed edge of a saw, also botanical term.: serrate, serrated (of leaves) *Wdn.*

སོགས་ *sogs* **and so forth, and the like,** mostly preceded by *la: mi-la sógs-pai srog-čágs homo et cetera animantia*, prop. the beings in addition to man; *ba-dán-la sógs-pas brgyán-te* decorated with little flags and the like; less frq.: *la sógs-te*, inst. of which always *la-sógs-pa* or *pai* may be used; often *sogs* alone, also in prose; after *(la) sógs(-pa)* usually a comma is to be supplied, and the words following are to be considered as an apposition: *yi-ge rtsis-la sógs-pa rig-pai ynas lṅa* writing, arithmetic and so on, the five sciences; hence often applicable, when a comprehensive noun appellative does not exist: *yser sogs* gold and the other, viz. metals, *Glr.; tsa sogs ysum* the three *tsa*-sounds, *tsa, ťsa* and *dza Gram.*

Note. In course of time the original grammatical sense seems to have been forgotten, in as much as *la* is now read together with *sógs-pa*, and often also the dot separating the syllables is omitted.

སོང་ *soṅ* perf. and imp. of *ͦgró-ba* to go, 1. **I went, I have** (thou hast etc.) **gone,** v. *ͦgro-ba* 1 and 2, e.g. *der soṅ yód-pas* when he had gone thither *Pth.*, *soṅ-sóṅ-ba-las* going on continually, *Dzl.*, continuing to do a thing *Dzl.*; *sóṅ-ba yin* it is gone, it is no longer extant *Mil.; dbáṅ-du soṅ* (he or it) came into the power of... *S.g.*; *da sdig-pa-la sóṅ-na Thgy.* if we now go on to (the topic of sins) *W.:* **da-rúṅ ṅa ma soṅ** it is not yet past five o'clock; **'i-nẹ sóṅ-pa 'a tsúg-pa** from here (adverbially, like *bzúṅs-te*) to that place *Ld.*; imp.: **dí-ru ma dug! soṅ!** do not stand here! walk on! — 2. **became, turned** etc. *Kyi-mo žig-tu soṅ* she became a bitch, was changed into a bitch *Mil.*, *dkár-por soṅ* it turned white *Glr.*, **doṅ nág-po soṅ** *W.* his face grew dark; **bi-gáṅ soṅ** *W.* a hole has been made, it got a hole; **gyál-sẹ ka-čúd sóṅ-nẹ** as she got a taste for the town *W.; *nod ču gaṅ soṅ** the vessel was already full of water (when I came) *W.* — **soṅ-ťó** *W.* account of expenses.

སོད་པ་ *sód-pa* 1. *C.* **to wake, rouse.** — 2. sometimes for *ysód-pa*.

སོན་ *son* rarely for *soṅ*; frq. only in *nár-son-pa*, v. *na*.

སོན་པ་ *són-pa* 1. v. *son*. — 2. v. *ysón-pa, ysón-po*.

སོབ་ *sob* 1. also *sog, γsob, γsog*, **null, void, vain, empty, bad in its quality, not durable.** — 2. also *γsob* something **stuffed** (as a chair), *nán-sob, ḱóṅ-sob, ḱóg-sob Wdṅ.* prob. id.; *sob-stán* **cushion, bolster, mattress,** *pags-sób* the stuffed skin of an animal, *seṅ(-gei) sób* the stuffed skin of a lion *Pth.*

སོམ་ *som* 1. also *γsom, sóm-śiṅ* **fir-tree, pine-tree.** — 2. also *soms*, imp. of *sém-pa.*

སོར་ *sor* 1. also *γsor*, **gimlet,** *rús-pa ˳búgs-pai sor S.g.* prob. a sort of **trephine.** — 2. v. *sór-mo.* — 3. v. *sar, sor bžag-pa* to put in its place (*Sch.* also: 'quite the same'?); *ráṅ-sor* v. *raṅ* compounds. — 4. (cognate to *só-ma?*) *sor čúd-pa* (*Sch.* ˳*jud-pa*) **to restore, renew,** e.g. exhausted strength *Dzl.*, the doctrine of Buddha *Pth.* — 5. term. of *so.*

སོར་མོ་ *sór-mo*, resp. *p̔yag-sór Mil., žabs-sór*, 1. **finger, toe;** *sor-γdúb* finger-ring, *sor-ṫsígs* the joint of a finger. — 2. **inch,** *sor-bži-pa* four-inched.

སོལ་བ་ *sól-ba* **coal,** esp. charcoal, = *sol-nág; sól-bai me* coal-fire *Lt.*; **sol-mé** *W.* live coal, burning coal.

སོལ་པོ་ *sól-po* resp. **friendly, kind, affable** *C., W.*

སོས་ *sos* 1. inst. of *so, sos btáb-pa* **to bite,** *Sch.* also **to backbite,** to calumniate. — 2. v. *γsó-ba* and ˳*ṫsó-ba.*

སོས་ཀ་, སོ་ག་ *sós-ka, só-ga,* 1. in Tibet: **spring,** = *dpyid, Mil.* — 2. in India: **the hot season,** from about the middle of April till the middle of June.

སོས་དལ་ *sos-dál or sos-bsdal Sch.*: **slow.**

སོས་ཟིན་ *sos-zín* disease of the membrum virile, in five forms (prob. different stages of gonorrhea) *Mṅg.*

སྲ་བ་ *srá-ba* 1. adj., also *srá-bo* and *srá-mo Cs.*, col. **srán-te** (cf. *srán-pa*), **hard, solid, compact, firm,** and abstract noun: **solidity, hardness, compactness,** of wood, meat etc., and often fig.: *γžu-srán* a bow difficult to be bent *S.g.*, *rgas-srá* hearty vigorous old age *S.g.*; *mṫson ḱar sra* proof against cut and thrust, also: proof against malicious words *Mil.* — *sra-brkyaṅ*, कठिनास्तर, the coarse blanket of a monk. — *sa-rtsí* **varnish.** — 2. vb. *W.*, **to empty.**

སྲང་ *sraṅ* I. (cf. *sróṅ-ba*) 1. **pair of scales, balance** *B., sráṅ-la ˳dégs-pa Cs., γžál-ba, ṫsád-pa Sch., sráṅ-ba Sp.* to weigh, to balance. — 2. **steel-yard,** **sraṅ tág-če** to hold the steel-yard, in weighing. — 3. **weight,** in a general sense, *bre-sráṅ* weight and measure, *rgya-sráṅ* Chinese weights *Cs.* — 4. **an ounce,** *sraṅ gáṅ* one ounce, *sraṅ do* two ounces, *sman sráṅ* ༢༢, two pounds of medicine, the daily quantity taken by Buddha when he had caught cold *Dzl.* ༤༢, 3. — *sráṅ-ča Sch.* balance and what belongs to it. — *sraṅ-mdá* scale-beam or lever of a pair of scales *Sch.* — *sraṅ-p̔ór* scale. — *sraṅ-ṫsád Cs.* weight. — *sráṅ-ba* vb. v. above.

II. **street,** *lam-sráṅ* id.; *sraṅ-yár Sch.*: tortuous path, labyrinth (?). — *rgya-sráṅ* street, lane *Glr.*; *rgyu-sráṅ* the road which a person habitually walks.

སྲན་བུ་ *srán-bu* **thread, yarn,** ˳*ḱál-ba, sgríl-ba.*

སྲད་མ་ *srád-ma* v. *srán-ma.*

སྲན་པ་ *srán-pa* (cf. *srá-ba*) *Cs.*: pf. fut. *bsran*, imp. *sron*, W. **śrán-če** **to suffer, bear** (with patience), **endure, to be hardened** *W.* frq., **śrán-ṫub-ḱan* or *śrán-ṫeg-ḱan** one that can endure much; **ḱyod śran gos** *Ld.* you must hold out, you must stand it; in *B. sran ˳dzugs-pa* is used in the same sense; **ḱyág-śran-čan** hardened, accustomed to frost, **dúg-śran-čan** inured to hardships *W.* — **śrán-te** col. frq. adj.: 1. = *srá-ba* (opp. to *lhód-po* and ˳*ból-mo*) **hard, firm, durable, rigid, strict.** 2. fig. **hard, severe, bitter.** — *sdug-srán* hardiness *Mil.*; *sran-čé-ba* = *srán-ṫub-mḱan. Cs.*: *srán-pa* sbst. hardship, severe distress or toil, *srán-par* toilsomely, rigorously, *srán-pa-po* one that hardens himself (?).

སྲན་མ་, སྲད་མ་ *srán-ma, srád-ma* 1. **pease, beans, lentils,** *Cs.* mentions also *srad-dkár, srad-nág* and *srad-sṅón*, also *mḱal-srán*, in *W.*, however, we only met with the common field pea and some dry imported Indian sorts of it (*mon-srán*); *rgya-srán* (*Cs. mon-srán*) was the name the natives were inclined to give to our European bean. — *sran-ṗúṅ* a heap of pease, *sran-ṗúb* pease-straw, *sran-ṗyé* flour of pease, *sran-mé* blossom of pease. — 2. **grain,** like *rdóg-po*, e.g. of Indian corn; even *lčágs-kyi sran-čuṅ Wdṅ.* grains of shot(?).

སྲབ་ *srab* **bridle,** *rtai; srab sga stan ťsáṅ-po* a complete riding-gear; **šrab čúg-če** *W.* **to bridle, to bit** (a horse), **šrab gyúr-če** **to govern, to rein** (a horse) *srab-skyógs Cs.* **the reins,** — *srab-lčags Cs.* **the bit.** — *srab-mťúr Sch.* **the halter.** — *srab-mdá Stg., Ld.:* **šram-dá** **reins.**

སྲབ་པ་ *sráb-pa B.,* **sráb-mo** *W.* **thin, tender, fine,** e.g. skin *Dzl.*, cloth, leather, paper, clouds; **shallow, loose,** not close; *srab-mťil Sch.* inner sole, welt; *srab-mťúg* thickness, dimension.

སྲབ་སྲིབ་ *srab-srib Cs.* **dark, obscure.**

སྲམ་ *sram,* उद्र 1. **otter,** the flesh of which is considered very nourishing, the liver is used as a remedy for strangury *S g.*, but encountering this animal is regarded as an evil omen *S.g.*; *ču-sram* id.? (*Cs.* beaver?) *nyá-sram Mil.*, either the same, or: fishes and otters; *brag-srám* rock-otter? sable? **ka-lon-šram** *W.* prob. **sable;** it is nearly black and stated to live near Yarkand, in the mountains as well as in the flat country. The ear-coverings worn by the ladies of Ladak are made of the fur of this animal. — 2. **otter-skin, sable-skin.**

སྲར་ *srar* adv. *Sch.*: **severely, rigorously.**

སྲས་(པོ་) *sras(-po)* resp. for *bu*, **son, child,** *dpon-srás, rgyal-srás* son of the sovereign, a prince; *rgyal-srás* also: son of Buddha, a Buddha; *lha(i) sras(-po)* 1. son of a god *Dzl.* 2. a prince; *ťugs-srás* spiritual son or daughter *Mil.*; in this sense *sras* may be applied to females: *saṅs-rgyás-kyi sras dág-pao* she has become a spotless child of Buddha *Dzl.* — *srás-bu* = *sras.* — *srás-mo* **daughter, young lady, princess.** — *sras-ťsáb Cs.* adopted child.

སྲི་ *sri* 1. a species of **devil** or **demon,** devouring esp. children, **a vampire,** also *sri-ṅán Schl., čúṅ-sri Glr., ṗúṅ-sri Mil.* a devil bringing misfortune; they are supposed to live in underground places, and are therefore also called *ṅás-kyi sri*; *sri laṅ* a devil rises from below; *sri nón-pa B.,* **nán-če** *W.* to lay, suppress a devil.

སྲི་བ་ *sri-ba* I. pf. *bsris*, fut. *bsri*, 1. **to retain,** e g. *bšáṅ-ba, gčin* constipation, strangury. — 2. **to be parsimonious, niggardly,** esp. with *nor*; *sba-sri-méd-par gnáṅ-ba Mil.* to give unsparingly, to bestow very liberally; **šri-šes-k̒an** *W.* parsimonious.

II. *W.* **to wind, to wrap round,** for *dkri-ba.*

སྲི་ཞུ་ *sri-žu*, less frq. *srid-žu*, **respect, reverence, deference,** *sri-žu-pa, sri-žu-mk̒an* one paying his regards, his respects, showing deference.

སྲིང་བ་ *sriṅ-ba* pf. *bsriṅs*, fus. *bsriṅ* 1. (cognate to *riṅ-ba*) **to extend, stretch, stretch out,** the arm, **to hand, reach,** **de dul soṅ, ṅá-la šriṅ toṅ** it has fallen down, hand it to me *W.*; **to fling far away** *C.* — 2. **to postpone, put off,** *ₒči-bai ťse Glr.* the term of death; **to prolong,** *ťse* life *S.g.*; **to wait, to tarry,** *'*á-ťsig šriṅ** *Lh.* wait a little, **dag-sa yoṅ-ṅa ťsa-big šriṅ-te yoṅ?** shall (I, you, he etc.) come directly or after a while? *Ld.*; **nam dir šriṅ-če ča dug?** how long shall you stay here? *W.* — 3. **to send** (*skúr-ba Lex.*) *ṗrin, yo-byád Sch.* — 4. *skyéd-sriṅ-ba* **to bring up, train up, to rear** *Glr.*

སྲིང་མོ་ *sriṅ-mo* **sister** (of a male person, cf. *miṅ-po*) *bu-sriṅ, miṅ-sriṅ*, resp. *lčam-sriṅ* brother and sister, cousins.

སྲིད་ *srid* 1. **length, extension,** *ṗug srid-du k̒ru-bčo-brgyád-pa* a cavern 18 cubits long *Tar.*; more frq. with regard to time: *ₒdi* or *de-srid(-kyi bar)-du* (for) so long (a time), *či-srid-du*, also *či-srid-de*, how long (a time)? also: as long as; when followed by *yaṅ*: be it ever so long (in this case *ji* would be more correct); also *srid-par*, or *srid* alone, for *srid-du.* — 2. **dominion, government,** *srid-la ma ₒčám-pas* falling out with one another about the government *Glr.*, esp. *rgyal-srid, dbaṅ-srid* id.; *srid byéd-pa* to reign, to govern, *srid ₒťsó-ba* id. *Dzl.*; *ₒdi gnyis-kyi srid gaṅ yód-rnams ṗrog* he seized upon their territorial shares *Glr.*; *bla-srid Cs.* a Lama's dominion. — *sde-srid* **province**; *čos-srid* clerical government, ecclesiastical dominion. — 3. **ruler, commander, regent, reigning prince**; so also in the compounds just mentioned.

སྲིད་པ་ *srid-pa* I. vb., 1. to be, to exist (?). — 2. **to be possible,** often preceded by *yaṅ*; *skyé-ba daṅ ˳jig-pa kún-la srid-na* since springing up and passing away is the lot of all men *Dzl.*; *p̔án-pa žig srid* healing is possible *Pth.*; *˳di-las sla yaṅ srid* it might be easier (for me) then than now *Dzl.*; *de-bžin-du bden srid snyám-nas* thinking this might possibly be true; the verb is usually put in the infinitive mood terminating in *pa*: *de yin-pa-aṅ srid* after all it might be this man, it might be he *Mil.*; *˳dir ˳óṅ-ba mi srid-do, bód-du brós-pa srid* he will scarcely come back, he will have escaped to Tibet *Glr.*; sometimes with the root of the verb: *yoṅ mi srid Mil.*; *bdag t̔ar kyaṅ srid-kyis* as it is a possible case, that we might be released *Dzl.*; *ma srid čig* about the same as: God forbid! by no means! In *W.* nearly = **to be obliged:** **k̔yer-wa-la šrid** now it will be my lot, now I shall be obliged, to carry (twice as much), **sád-če-la šrid** (*B.*: *bab* or *t̔ug*) he deserves death, he must die.

II. sbst. भुवनं 1. **existence,** state of being, **life,** *srid-pa γžan nyáms-su myóṅ-ba* to experience, to pass through, other periods of existence *Wdṅ.*, *srid p̔yi-ma Sch.*: the future period of life, of existence. — 2. things existing, **the world,** *srid(-pa) γsum* the three worlds, *srid-pai ˳k̔ór-lo Cs.*: the revolving system (the world's cycle); *srid-pai mtso* the ocean of existence, *srid-pai ču-klúṅ čén-po* the stream of existence *Mil.*; also a single **being,** commonly however *srid-pa-pa*; *bár-doi srid-pa, bár-srid-pa Thgy.*, *bár-ma-doi srid-pa-pa Stg.* the beings in the Bardo, v. *bár-do*. — The meaning of *srid* in *srid-pai bar-do*, and in some other expressions, have yet to be determined. — 3. symb. num.: 14.

སྲིན་ཀླད་ *srin-klád Sch.*: a sort of **flint-stone.**

སྲིན་གླང་ *srin-gláṅ Lt.? W.* **srin-gláṅ-čan** having the staggers (of horses); being mad.

སྲིན་པོ་ *srin-po*, *Ssk.* राक्षस, fem. *srin-mo*, **demons,** figuring in Indian and Tibetan mythology. They are supposed to be, for the most part, of an enormous size, generally hostile to mankind, going about at night, to ensnare and even to devour human beings. Their chief abode was Ceylon, and also Tibet was originally inhabited by them. The Tibetans are even said to be the descendants of an ape (sent by, or emanated from, Avalokitēshvara) and of a Tibetan Srinmo. *brág-srin* rock-Srinpo or Srinmo; *˳dre-srin* goblins and Srinpos; *čú-srin* v. the following article.

སྲིན་བུ་ *srin-bu*, = *˳bu*, **insect, worm, vermin;** *srin-bu pád-ma* (*srin-pa Sik.*) **leech,** *srin-bu me-˳k̔yér* **glow-worm;** *rgyu-srin*, *k̔oṅ-srin* **intestinal worm;** *p̔yi-srin* vermin living on the skin *Lt.*; *dár-srin* **silk-worm;** *srin-bál* acc. to *Wdṅ.* = *rás-bál* **cotton,** *Sch.*, *Schr.*: **flock-silk;** raw silk; *srin-byá* nocturnal bird, **owl** etc. *Lt.*; *srin-t̔ór* **small ulcer** or tumour; *srin-šiṅ Med.*, *Sch.*: **mulberry-tree;** *ču-srin* a monster living in the water.

སྲིན་ལག་ *srin-lág* **the ring-finger.**

སྲིབ(ས)་ *srib*(*s*) 1. **darkness, gloom, night.** — 2. **shady side, north side** of a mountain. — *sríb-pa* vb., to grow dark or dusky, *C.*: **sa šrib soṅ** night has begun.

སྲིའུ་ནག་ *sriu-nág* **mulberry-tree.**

སྲིལ་ *sril Sch.* **silk-worm.**

སྲུ་ *sru Glr.*, *srú-mo Lex.* and *C.* mother's sister, **aunt.**

སྲུག་པ་ *srúg-pa*, *W.* for *sprúg-pa*, *srúb-pa* and *dkrúg-pa*: 1. **to shake, to shake out.** — 2. **to stir, stir up, twirl.** — 3. **to shake,** to make to totter.

སྲུང་བ་ *srúṅ-ba* I. vb., pf. (*b*)*sruṅs*, fut. *bsruṅ*, imp. (*b*)*sruṅ*(*s*), *Ssk.* रक्ष, 1. **to watch, to keep guard** intrs.; but gen. trans., i.e. **to watch, to keep, to guard, to keep in custody,** *k̔yim* the house *Dzl.*; **to save from, to pro-**

tect, to shelter, e.g. *lus*, the body, but also: **to keep** unpolluted, pure, chaste; *bdag srúṅ-ba* to guard one's self, in a special sense: to live as a *bdag-srúṅ*, as a hermit *Dzl.*; **to preserve,** *bdag ɣnód-pa ṫams-ċád-las sruṅs śig* may I be preserved from every harm! *Do.*; with *la: bdág-la srúṅ-du ɣsol* I pray to preserve, to protect me *Do.* — 2. **to beware of, to guard against,** *lus daṅ ṅág-gi nyés-pa Dzl.*, = *lus daṅ ṅag srúṅ-ba* (v. above no. 1) *Dzl.* — 3. **to keep, to observe faithfully,** a promise, laws; *bká-sruṅ-mḱan* **obedient, faithful, trustworthy.** — 4. **to hinder,** forbid, prohibit, *rígs-kyis, bdág-pos, ċós-kyis sruṅ* it is forbidden, it is prohibited, by the degree of kindred, by the husband, by religion in general *Thgy.*; **to prevent, to be a preservative** or **preventive** *S.g.* — 5. **to wait,** = *srúṅ-ba*, e.g. **žag nyi** for two days *W.*

II. sbst. 1. **the keeping, guarding, the heed, guard.** — 2. the person or the thing keeping, guarding, esp. **amulet, preventive, preservative,** *btágs-pa* to suspend (an amulet, to the neck or other part of the body).

Comp. and deriv. *sruṅ-skúd*, -*ₒḱór* or -*mdúd* an amulet consisting of threads. — *srúṅ-mḱan* **keeper, guardian, watchman,** **tsáṅ-la śrúṅ-ḱan** *W.* (night-) watchman; *srúṅ-pa B.* = *srúṅ-mḱan*, *bzá-śiṅ-ra-ba srúṅ-pa* keeper of a fruit-garden *Dzl.*; *srúṅ-po Cs.* = *srúṅ-mḱan*; *srúṅ-ma B.* id., *dmyal-bai sruṅ-ma* guardian of the infernal regions frq. *Dzl.*; *ċós-skyoṅ-bai srúṅ-ma ṫams-ċád* all the tutelar gods of religion *Mil.*; collectively: body of watchmen, *lhá-rnams-kyi srúṅ-ma dáṅ-po* the first corps of watchmen of the gods, the Nūga; *rgyál-poi srúṅ-mai mi* the men of the king's body-guard *Stg.* —*srúṅ-sems* the taking heed, being cautious.

སྲུན་པ་, བསྲུན་པ་ *srún-pa, bsrún-pa,* **calm, soft, mild,** and: **mildness, gentleness, meekness;** *srún-po* adj. = *srún-pa*, esp. of horses: **quiet, tame;** *śín-tu mi-bsrún-žiṅ* very **malicious, malignant,** of demons *Mil.*

སྲུབ་ *srub* v. *srus.*

སྲུབ་པ་ *srúb-pa*, pf. imp. (*b*)*srubs*, fut. *bsrub*, 1. **to stir, stir up, stir about,** *žo srúb-pa* to churn, to make butter. — 2. **to rummage, to rake up, to stir, to turn over.** — 3. **to rub,** two pieces of wood against each other *Wdṅ.* — **śrub-śiṅ** *C.* 1. twirling-stick. 2. mischiefmaker, disturber of the peace.

སྲུབས་ *srubs* 1. **a cleft, slit, gap, fissure,** *brag-srúbs* chasm or cleft in a rock, smaller than *sér-ka Mil.*; **intermediate space,** interval, interstice; **rent** in a dress; **disunion, separation; wound** *Lt.*; *srubs ₒbye Lt.*, *srubs ₒṫor Sch.* a severing, a wound has been made; *srubs ɣtór-ba* to rend asunder, to tear *Sch.* **tsem-śrúb ḍól-ċe** *W.* to rip, to cut open a seam. — 2. seam? — 3. *W.* col. for *srus.*

སྲུམ་ *srum* resp. for **meat,** flesh of animals used as food, *srum-ḱóg* an animal slaughtered and cut up, for a person of quality.

སྲུལ་པོ་ *srúl-po* 1. **evil demon, malignant spirit** *Mil.*; *lús-srul-po Lex.* **sorcerer.** — 2. **putrid, rotten** *Cs.*

སྲུལ་བ་ *srúl-ba*, pf. and fut. *bsrul*, I. **to be corrupted, decomposed,** of the humours of the body *Wdṅ.*

II. *W.* **śrúl-ċe*, = *śrúg-ċe** 1. **to stir,** **ṫúg-pa** the soup, **to mix** and stir, **ċú-la p̀e** flour with water. — 2. **to shove, to move,** to and fro, **p̀ág-te śrúl-ċe** to plane, **ċad-sóg śrul-ċe** to saw. — 3. **ṫa śrul-ċe** to put a horse to a gallop?

སྲུས་ *srus*, *W.* also **śrub**, **unripe ears** of wheat etc. **śrub nyé-ċe** *W.* to rub them between the hands; the grains, thus being shelled, are considered a rural dainty; *ₒbrás-kyi srus* a shelled grain of rice.

སྲུས་པ་ *srús-pa Sch.* **to thicken, to become more consistent,** by evaporation, by boiling.

སྲེ་ད་ *sré-da Wdṅ.*, *sred S.g.*, a species of corn (?).

སྲེ་ནག་ *sre-nág Lex.* **soot;** *W.* **śre-móg**.

སྲེ་བ་ *sré-ba* I. sbst. a certain shrub *Cs.*

II. vb., pf. *bsres*, fut. *bsre*, imp. (*b*)*sres*, trans. to *ₒdré-ba* 1. **to mix with, to mingle, to admix,** *már-la sré-ba* to mix with butter *Lt.*, *čaṅ ču sre-ba* to mix beer with water *Med.*; *dreu sré-ba* to breed mules; *bsrés-pa* mixed up, **confused,** of a narration *Tar.*; fig. *k'a* or *lus sré-ba* to communicate with another, i.e. to live, to eat, drink, smoke with a person *Do.*; *skyid sdug sré-ba* to share pleasure and pain, joy and sorrow *Glr.*; *W.*, like **żé-če**, **to exchange for**: **zan daṅ śrog** to risk one's life for a subsistence. — 2. **to add; to add up,** cast up, sum up *Wdk.*, **nyī daṅ nyī śre żi** 2 and 2 make 4 *W.*

སྲེ་མོག་ *sre-móg* v. *sre-nág.*

སྲེ་མོང་ *sre-móṅ* **weasel,** prob. = **la-k'yi-mo** *W.*; *sré-mo Lex.*

སྲེ་ལོང་ *sre-lóṅ* 1. *Sch.*: the sinew above the heel. — 2 n. of a medicine?

སྲེག་པ་ *srég-pa* I. sbst. (*W.* **śrag-pa**) **partridge.**

II. vb., pf. (*b*)*sregs*, fut. *bsreg*, imp. (*b*)*sreg*(*s*), *W.* **śrág-če** **to burn,** i.e. 1. **to consume, to destroy by or with fire** (*mes, mé-la*) e.g. a corpse, *dág-mo*, or *W.* **nán-tan**, altogether, entirely, *dgra* an enemy (sc. in effigy); *sbyin-sreg* **burnt-offering; to make red-hot,** *lčags-bsrégs* red-hot iron *Thgy.* — 2. **to roast, fry, bake,** on a spit *C.*, or in a pan, **már-la** in butter *W.*; **tá-gir śrág-če** to bake bread *W.*; **to tan,** to make swarthy, *nyi-mas* (to be tanned) by the sun *Dzl.*; *bsrég-k'aṅ Sch.* shed for storing up fire-wood.

སྲེང་ *sreṅ*, *mi-sréṅ C.* = *mi-rkyáṅ*, v. *rkyaṅ-pa.*

སྲེད་ *sred* v. *sré-da.*

སྲེད་རྒྱལ་མ་ *sréd-rgyal-ma* a deity of the Bonpo *Mil.*

སྲེད་པ་ *sréd-pa* 1. vb., sbst., adj. **to desire, the desire, desirous,** *zás-la* of food *Lt.*, *k'a-tsai ró-la* of acid or hot substances *Med.*, *ról-mo-la* (liking) music *Stg.*; *yúl-sred-pa čúṅ-ba* not much attached to his native country; *ₒjig-rtén(-la) sréd-pa* **avarice, covetousness** *Mil.*, *ₒdod-sred-čan* covetous, greedy *Pth.*, *čágs-sred-čan* lecherous, libidinous *Pth.*; *sréd-pa-las yóṅs-su gról-ba* quite free of any desire, (so is Buddha); *sréd-po Cs.* lover, *sréd-ma Cs.* sweet-heart. — 2. symb. num.: 8.

སྲེན་ *sren* (?) **floor** *W.*

སྲེལ་བ་ *srél-ba*, pf. and fut. *bsrel Cs.*, *W.* **śrál če** **to bring up, to rear, to nurse up, to train,** infants, young animals, **śrál-k'an** nourisher, fosterer, nurse etc.

སྲེས་ *sres Ts.* = *ži-gil* q.v.

སྲོ་ *sro*, resp. *t'ugs-sro. W.*, **heat, ardour, passion, wrath, anger,** **śro yoṅ** anger rises (in a person), he (etc.) grows angry, **śro bab, śro bud** the anger abates; **śro-riṅ-mo** slow to wrath, **śró-čan** furious, raging, **śro-t'úṅ** hot, ardent, passionate.

སྲོ་བ་ *sró-ba*, pf. (*b*)*sros*, fut. *bsro*, imp. (*b*)*sro*(*s*), **to warm,** to make warm or hot at the fire, or in the sun *Glr.*, *Lt.*; *ₒjám-pai dród-kyis bu bsro* (a mother) foments her child with a gentle warmth *Thgy.*

སྲོ་མ་ *sró-ma* 1. **egg** of a louse, **a nit** *C.*, *W.*, *šig-sro ₒdu* nits are increasing fast *S.g.* — 2. small **bubble** *W.*, **čáṅ-la śró-ma k'ol** the beer foams, froths in fermentation. — 3. *sró-ma nág-po*, *sró-ma séṅ-ge* n. of a medicinal herb *Med.*

སྲོ་ལོ་ *sró-lo Med.*, Sedum and similar plants.

སྲོག་ *srog* **life,** *srog γčód-pa* to kill, frq.; *srog lén-pa*, *ₒp'róg-pa* id., esp. when done by demons; *srog daṅ ₒprál-ba* id., esp. to execute, to put to death *Glr.*, *srog daṅ ₒbrál-ba* to die; *srog ₒbúl-ba Dzl.* ༢༥་༢, 12 *Sch.*: to sacrifice, to yield up one's life, but the manuscript of Kyelang has: *srog daṅ ₒbrál-lo*, and *šá-bai srog k'yéd-la ₒbúl-lo* (*Mil.*) means: I make you a present of the stag's life, i.e. I spare its life for your sake; *srog ₒdór-ba* to sacrifice, one's life, prop. to cast it away *Dzl.*; *srog-la mi ltá-ba* to make light of one's life frq.; *srog daṅ bsdó-ba* to risk, to hazard one's life, frq.; *srog skyób-pa* to save life *Dzl.*, *srog ₒbyin-pa*, *ₒdon-pa* id., *Thgy.*: to save, to preserve (a child's) life (by well caring for it); *srog ₒtsó-ba* id. *Dzl.*, *S.g.* (*Sch.* also: to recover, to grow well again); *sróg-gi ká-ba* n. of a vein; *sróg-gi snyiṅ-po Mil.?*

Comp. **sróg-skyób** *W.* **deliverer, redeemer, saviour.** — *sróg-k'uṅ Mil.* the deep cut or stab, by which Tibetan butchers kill animals (*Huc* I, 443), *sróg-k'uṅ* ˳*byéd-pa* to stab in this manner. — *sróg-čan, srog-ldán* having life, living, alive. — *srog-čágs* animated being, *mi-la sógs-pai srog-čágs ťams-čád* all men and other living beings *Dzl.*, *srog-ťág = dpyaṅ-ťág.* — *srog-bdág čén-po = pe-dkár Glr.* — *srog-méd* lifeless, inanimate. — *srog-rtsá* 'root of life, vein of life', aorta *S.g.*, chiefly used rhetor. and fig. — *srog-lén* **deadly, fatal** *Lt.* — *srog-šíṅ* **axle, axle-tree;** *mčod-rtén-gyi srog-šíṅ* the pole in a Chodten; fig. **prop,** *séms-kyi srog-šíṅ Mil.*

སྲོང་བ་ *sróṅ-ba*, pf. *bsraṅs*, fut. *bsraṅ*, imp. *sroṅ(s)*, *bsraṅ*, *W.* **šráṅ-če**, **to make straight, to straighten,** *yón-po* what is awry, crooked *Lex.*, *yzer sróṅ-ba* to beat out nails; **to equal** *Sch.*; *sku dráṅ-por bsráṅs-te* (he sat) straight and erect, cf. also *sraṅ* and *bsráṅ-po.* — *W.*: **sráṅ-te ča dúg-ga 'i-ru dad** will he pass straight through or does he stay here?

སྲོང་བཙན་སྒམ་པོ་ *sroṅ-btsan-sgám-po* Srong-tsangampo, n. of the most famous king of Tibet, a contemporary of Mohammed; he introduced the Tibetan letters, and was the chief promoter of Buddhism and its literature.

སྲོད་, སྲོད་འཇིང་ *srod, srod-*˳*ǰiṅ* **dusk of the evening, twilight,** **šrod rub** *W.* the dusk of evening draws near, it is getting dusky, *srod daṅ ťo-raṅs* in the evening and morning *Lt.*; *srod byiṅ soṅ* night has set in; *srod yol soṅ* id., viz. the time about 11 o'clock at night *C.*; *srod-la* in the dusk of evening *Mil.* — *srod-*˳*k'or-p̀ag Cs.* (?) the *k'yim* of evening-twilight, v. *nyin-žag.* — *srod-loṅ* dayblind, nyctalops, seeing better in a mild than in a bright light.

སྲོལ་ *srol* **usage, custom, common use, habitual practice, habit,** *der yi-gei srol méd-pas* as the art of writing is not yet in use there *Glr.*; *sňár-srol bzáṅ-po-la dgoṅs šig* keep in mind the good old customs *Glr.*; *srol čágs-pa, sról-du* ˳*gyúr-ba Cs.*, *sról-du* ˳*ťsúd-pa* to grow into a habit, to become the custom (of a person, a country); *srol* ˳*dzúgs-pa* to introduce a practice *Glr.*; *srol ytód-pa Lex.* prob. the same; *bka-sról = srol,* but at the same time expressive of reverence for the originator of the custom *Zam.*; *p̀yag-sról Mil.* is said to be a respectful expression for *lag-lén-gyi srol* (?); *legs-pai dpe-srol btsug-ste Glr.* having introduced good customs for imitation; *ťob-sról* **claim, title, right,** founded on old custom.

སྲོས་ *sros* 1. v. *sro-ba.* — 2. *Cs.* sbst. = *srod* twilight, dusk of evening, *mún-sros-pa* dusky, dark; *Glr.*: *sa srós-nas* when it grew dark.

སླ(ང)་ང་ *sla(ṅ)-ṅá* a large iron **pan** for parching grain, *slaṅ-dreg*s soot adhering to a pan.

སླ་བ་ *slá-ba* I. adj., also *slá-mo* 1. **thin,** of fluids (opp. to *ská-ba, ťúg-po, réṅs-pa*) *W.* **lan-te**. — 2. **easy,** opp. to *dká-bo* difficult, *šés-pa slá-ba ma yin* knowledge is not easily obtained *Dzl.*; usually with the supine: *ríg-par slao* it may easily be found out *Dzl.*, or with the root of the verb: *go-slá* easy to be comprehended.

II. vb., v. *slé-ba.*

སླག་པ་, སློག་པ་ *slág-pa, slóg-pa* **fur-coat,** *sgo-slóg Mil.*, more corr. *dgo-slog,* hunting-coat, made of the skin of an antelope; *spyaṅ-slág, W.* **šaṅ-lag** fur-coat of a wolf's skin; *ťsar-slág* coat of lamb's skins; *ras-slág* prob.: a fur-coat covered with calico *Glr.*

སླང་ *slaṅ* 1. v. sub *sla-ṅa.* — 2. v. *slóṅ-ba.*

སླང་ཁ་ *sláṅ-k'a* **shelf, shelves, stand.**

སླང་བ་ *sláṅ-ba* v. *slóṅ-ba.*

སླད་ *slad,* eleg. = *p̀yi* I, II, IV, 1. *slad-ról* **hind part, back part** *Lex.*, *slád-bžin-du* or *slád-bžin-par* behind, e.g. ˳*bráṅ-ba* to walk behind one, *slád-sa = p̀yí-sa* (गूथ) dung *Bhar.* — 2. **after,** *slád-na* c. genit. = ˳*óg-tu Dzl.*; *slád-nas* adv. afterwards, hereafter, subsequently *Lex.* and *C.*; *slád-kyi* subsequent, later, posterior; *slád-ma Cs.*:

the hind part, that which comes after, the later or latter part; *slád-mar*, *slád-kyis* afterwards, hereafter, *slád-mar yaṅ* also for the future. — 3. *slád-du* **on account of, for the sake of.**

སླད་པ་ *slád-pa*, pf. *bslad*, (cf. *lhád-pa*) **to mix**, esp. with something of an inferior quality, hence **to adulterate, vitiate, to spoil, to corrupt**, *skyón-gyis* or *lhád-kyis ma slád-pa* not marred by any defects *Lex.*, *p̔yin-ci-lóg-gis yoṅs-su slád-de* quite unfitted by perversity *Dzl.*; *gáṅ-gis kyaṅ ma slád-pa* without any thing detrimental operating, not subject to any noxious influence *Wdṅ.*; *de myós-šiṅ slád-par byás-te* making him drunk and thus disabling him *Dzl.*

སླན་ *slan* 1. (?) **na-slán* W.* the furred car-coverings of Tibetan ladies. — 2. = *slad*; *slan-čád* = *p̔yin-čád.*

སླན་ཏེ་ *slán-te* v. *slá-ba.*

སླན་པ་ *slán-pa* 1. **to mend, patch** *Sch.* — 2. v. *bslan.*

སླམ་པ་ *slám-pa*, 1. to roast slightly, **to parch**, to make brown by exposing to heat, e.g. meal *C.*, *W.* — 2. **to roast, to fry**, **már-la* W.*

སླར་ *slar*, eleg. = *p̔yir*, 1. **again, over again, once more.** — 2. **afterwards, hereafter**, *slár-nas* id. *C.* — *slar yaṅ ˳jug-pa* to be affixed or added again (of letters, to the end of a word) *Gram.*; *slar ˛óṅ-ba* to come back, to return *Dzl.*; *slar-γšegs* he went away again *Dzl.*; *slar stobs skyed* he regains strength *S.g.*; *slár-bsdu-ba* the final o of a verb, indicating the end of a sentence *Gram.*

སླས་ *slas* 1. v. *lhas.* — 2. **retinue, train, attendants**, wives and servants, *p̔o-bráṅ-gi slas* a king's or prince's retinue, **the court**, people at court *Dzl.*

སླི་ *sli C.* acc. to some authorities: a yellowish red **apple**, or Indian apple (opp. to *kú-šu* Tibetan apple); acc. to *Cs.* **cherry**; cherries, however, are scarcely known in Tibet. — *sli-tsí* small, wild-growing, cherry-like dwarf-apples, *Pyrus baccata*; **bi-li-tsi* W.* gooseberry; **wám-p̔u-li-tsi** the white berries of a species of mountain-ash, *Pyrus ursina* (**wamp̔u** in the Bunan language: 'bear').

སླུ་བ་ *slú-ba*, pf. *bslus*, fut. *bslu*, imp. (*b*)*slu*(*s*), **to entice, allure, ensnare, beguile, seduce**, e.g. to be ensnared by wordly sorrows; less frq. in a direct sense: **to impose on, to deceive**, *rdzun byás-te* by a falsehood *Dzl.*; *slu-k̔ríd* enticement, seduction, means of seduction, bait; *bzáṅ-poi slu-k̔ríd* enticement to a good purpose; *bslú-ba-mk̔an* deceiver, deluder, impostor *Glr.*; *mi-slú*(*-ba*) infallible, sure *Mil.*

སླེ་ *sle* 1. a coarse blanket *Ts.*, = *čá-ra*, *čá-ri.* — 2. n. of the capital of Ladak.

སླེ་ཏྲེས་ *sle-trés Med.* n. of a creeper or climbing plant.

སླེ་པོ་ *slé-po* Ü, *slé-ba*, *slé-bo Cs.* a flat **basket.**

སླེ་བ་ *slé-ba* I. vb., *bsle-ba*, *lhé-ba.* pf. *lhas B.*, **lá-če* W.* **to twist, plait, braid,** the hair, (to make) a basket etc.; **to knit.**

II. sbst. 1. v. no. I. — 2. **distortion, dislocation** (of a limb) *Cs.*; *slé-bo* one that has a distorted limb *Cs.*; *sle-míg* a distorted eye *Cs.*

སླེ་ཡོན་ *sle-yón* **craft, deceit, trickery,** *sle-yón byéd-pa* **to cheat, deceive, impose upon** *Cs.*

སླེད་ *sled* knitting-needle(?) *Ld.*

སླེབ་པ་ *sléb-pa*, pf. (*b*)*slebs*, fut. *bsleb*, resp. *˳byón-pa*, *p̔éb-pa* (cf. *˛óṅ-ba*), 1. **to arrive**, with termin.; *bslebs-zin* I have arrived, he has arrived; in *Ld.* however the future **slebs yin** is also pronounced **leb zin**. — 2. **to reach, to extend**, to a certain place or point *Pth.* and col. — 3. **to come in** (of interest, rent, duties), hence *sleb* income, revenue, public revenue, receipt of customs etc.; *sléb-t̔o* account of receipts.

སློ་དྲོན་ *slo-drón* warm fresh **dung** *Sch.*

སློག་པ་ *slog-pa* I. sbst. v. *slóg-pa.*

II. vb., pf. *bslogs*, fut. *bslog*, *Cs.* (trs. to *ldog-pa*) **to turn**, to turn round or about, to turn upside down, inside out, *rkyál-pa p̔yi-náṅ slóg-pa* to turn out the inside of a bag; *mig slóg-pa* to roll one's eyes; **boṅ-bu má-lag slog ˳dug** the donkey is rolling on his back; *sa slóg-pa* to plough up, turn up, to dig the soil; in arithmetic: **sum nyi lóg-pa ḍug** W. two times three are six.

སློང་བ, སླང་བ *slóṅ-ba, sláṅ-ba*, pf. *(b)slaṅs*, fut. *(b)slaṅ*, imp. *sloṅ(s)*, W. **láṅ-ċe**, I. causat. and transit. form to *ldáṅ-ba*. 1. **to cause to rise, to help to rise**, one lying on the ground; *dgrá-ru slóṅ-ba* to cause a person to rise as an enemy (cf. *dgrar ldáṅ-ba*), i.e. to make a person one's enemy *S.g.*; *bsád-pai mi-ró slóṅ-ba* to resuscitate the slain; **to excite, cause, inspire,** compassion, fear, terror etc.; *p̒rag-dog-gis, skyo-ṡas-kyis kun-nas bslaṅs-te Glr., Mil.* quite excited by envy and hatred, ni f.; esp. in pathology of the procatarctic or exciting causes of diseases: **to kindle** (a disease) **into action,** hence *sloṅ-rkyén* the exciting cause (of a disease); — **to raise, to erect,** a pile, post, wall *Mil.; sláṅ-ṡiṅ* a pile, stay, prop, erected or set up. — *kun-slóṅ Lex., Mil.: nyon-móṅs-kyi sloṅ-kun-sloṅ* excitement (??).

II. (perh. originally quite a different word), 1. **to ask, require,** ccdp. *klu ẓig ṅá-la dpe sloṅ* a Lu asks me for the book *Dzl.; bú-mo čúṅ-mar slóṅ-ba* to ask a man's daughter in marriage *Dzl.;* esp. **to beg,** to try to get by begging: *ċúṅ-zad bsláṅ-ṅo* we beg for a little of it! *Dzl., p̒á-la sláṅs-nas k̒yer* he obtained it from his father by begging *Mil.; bsód-snyoms slóṅ-ba* to collect alms by begging (*slóṅ-ba* partic. and sbst. beggar, mendicant *Dzl*, *slóṅ-mk̒an, slóṅ-ba-po* id.); hence. — 2. **to collect, to gather,** *nor Cs.* riches. — 3. **to examine, to probe** (a wound), *rma-ysar mdzúb-mos* a fresh wound with the finger *Thgy.;* also: **to search** a man's **house.** — 4. **to give,** *k̒a-lhág ċig sdús-la sloṅ ċig* gather some of the remnants of the meal, and give them to me! *Mil.*, so in *Sp.* and *C.* frq.

སློང་མོ *slóṅ-mo* **alms,** *slóṅ-mo slóṅ-ba Lex., byéd-pa Cs.* to ask alms, to beg; *slóṅ-mos ₒtsó-ba* to live on alms; *slóṅ-mo-pa* beggar *Pth.*

སློན་པ *slón-pa* 1. *Sch.* **to patch, to mend.** — 2. *Sch.*: *dpáṅ-po p̒yir slón-par byéd-pa* to dissemble, to feign (?) — 3. *Cs.*: to thrust out.

སློབ *slob* the act of learning, study, *slob ma myóṅ-ba* to have had no instruction or education; *slob ₒk̒rid-pa* to teach.

སློབ་པ *slób-pa*, I. vb., pf. *bslabs*, fut. *bslab*, imp. *slob(s)*, W. **láb-ċe**, **to learn, to teach,** *ṅa* or *ṅá-la slob* I learn, *ṅas slob* I teach, *dé-la mk̒an slob ynyis-kyis lo-tsts̒a bslabs* both the abbot and the instructor taught him the art of translating *Pth.*; *ṅa rtsis ṡig slob ₒdód-pas slobs* as I should like to learn something of mathematics, teach me! *Pth.*; *bslábs-pas ṡés-te* when he had learned it *Pth.; bslάb-ċiṅ lóbs-pa yaṅ dka* as learning is difficult, even if one is taught *Dzl.*; *slób-tu ₒjúg-pa* to let one take lessons, to have or get one instructed *Dzl.; *ṭ ú-gu-la gom-ṫáṅ láb-ċe** to teach a little child to walk *W.; mi-la yi-ge bslabs* schools were established *Glr.; yón-tan slób-pa* to teach (to learn) good, useful, things *Pth.* and frq.

II. sbst. 1. the act of **learning** *Dzl.* — 2. **teacher, instructor,** *brám-ze slób-pa* a Brahman as instructor *Dzl.*; *ₒp̒ágs-pa slób-pa-rnams* the venerable preceptors (more than *dge-slóṅ*, less than *dgrá-bċom-pa*) *Tar.* 5, 1. 31, 9.

Comp. **lob-k̒yád** W. **use, practice, exercise.** — *slob-grwá* **school, school-room, school-house;** **lob-ḍa-k̒áṅ** W. id. — *slob-grógs* school-fellow, co-disciple. — *slob-ynyér* student, scholar, *slob-ynyér gáṅ-du bgyis* where have you studied? at what college have you been a student? *Mil.* — *slób-dpon* **teacher, instructor, master,** frq.; also a college-title like our bachelor etc.; **'the teacher'** by way of eminence, is either Buddha or *Pad-ma-byuṅ-ynás.* — *slob-ₒbáṅs* **scholar, pupil, disciple,** = *bu-slób Mil.* — *slób-ma* id., frq. **lob-ló** **report, rumour, fame** W. — Cf. *bslabs.*

སློབས *slobs* **exercise, practice, experience;** *mig-slobs ṅan-pa skye Mil.* a bad custom of seeing begins to prevail (viz. that of looking downward, and minding only earthly things).

གསའ, བསའ *ysa, bsa Mil., C.* (W. **ṡan**) **the snow-leopard,** nearly white, with small clusters of black spots; living on the higher mountains.

གསག་པ་ *ɣsúg-pa Sch.* **to sew together.**

གསང་ what is **secret, hidden,** *ɣsaṅ šor* the secret comes out, is made known *Dzl.*

གསང་བ་ *ɣsáṅ-ba* I. vb. **to do a thing secretly, to conceal,** *ṅa-la ɣsaṅ-du mi ruṅ* it is not right of you to be so close to me *Mil.*; *ɣsáṅ-ste brkús-nas* stealing secretly, *ɣsáṅ-ste bskyál-nas* sending underhand, furtively *Dzl.*; **to hide one's self, to be concealed** *dbén-pai ɣnas šig-tu ɣsáṅ-ste* betaking one's self secretly to a solitary place *Dzl.*, *yid-mṫún-par ɣsáṅ-ste* keeping it secret with one consent *Dzl.*; **saṅ-nę dad-če* W.* to sit concealed.

II. sbst. 1. **secret things, a secret;** *ɣsaṅ-bai bdag-po* = *ɣsaṅ-dbaṅ* v. below. — 2. **secret parts** *Med.*, also *ɣsaṅ-ɣnás Med.*, *ɣsáṅ-bai pád-ma Med.*, sometimes the anus included; *ɣsáṅ-bai nad* diseases of the sexual organs *Med.*

III. adj. 1. **secret, hidden, concealed,** *ɣsáṅ-bai čos* esoteric doctrine *Dzl.*; *p̔yi-naṅ-ɣsáṅ* v. *p̔yi* III. — 2. *K̔yi-mo nyan-gyi rna ɣsaṅ-ba* a female dog of very sharp hearing (v. *ɣseṅ-ba*).

Comp. *ɣsáṅ-kaṅ* a secret room *Cs.* — *ɣsáṅ-sgo* a secret door *Pth.* — *ɣsaṅ-sgro S.g.?* — *ɣsaṅ-sṅágs* secret charms, mysterious incantations, frq.; even in medical works they are praised as the 'best medicine'. — *ɣsaṅ-mǰe* v. *mǰe.* — *ɣsaṅ-ɣnás* 1. a secret place. 2. **mystery,** nif.: *ɣsáṅ-bai ɣnas dú-ma ɣsuṅs* he taught many mysteries, many secret doctrines. 3. **privities, pudenda.** — *ɣsaṅ-spyód* **privy, necessary,** water-closet. — *ɣsaṅ-dbáṅ*, *ɣsaṅ-rdór Mil.*, *ɣsaṅ-bai-bdág-po Do.* = *rdo-rǰe-ˌčaṅ*, v. *rdo-rǰe*, comp.

གསན་པ་ *ɣsán-pa* resp. **to hear, to listen** *Dzl.*; *k̔yod ɣsan daṅ* listen (to me)! *Mil.*; *bdag-gi ṫsig-la ɣson* id. *Glr.*; with *las* or *la:* to hear a person teaching, expounding etc. *Tar.* Cf. *ɣsón-pa.*

གསབ་པ་ *ɣsáb-pa* v. *ɣsób-pa.*

གསར་བ་ *ɣsár-ba, ɣsár-pa,* usually *ɣsár-po* **new, fresh,** *lúg-ša ɣsár-ba* fresh mutton *Lt.*; *rma ɣsár-pa* a raw wound *Thgy.*; *búg-ma ɣsár-pa* the young, (recently married) wife *Dzl.*; **bhú-mo sár-pa** a girl that is still a virgin *C.*; *ɣsár-du* adv., *ɣsár-du bsád-pai ša* flesh of animals that have just been slaughtered, lit.: fresh-slaughtered flesh *Dzl.*; *k̔a-ɣsár* a new edge; *k̔aṅ-ɣsár* new house, also a name of villages, castles etc.; *gos-ɣsár*, *mar-ɣsár Lt.*; *rta-ɣsár Schr.* a horse not yet broken in. — *ɣsar ˌgrógs-pa Sch.*: 'to tell each other news; to make a new acquaintance'. **sar-zúg čó-če* W.* to plant (a piece of land) for the first time, to cultivate, to people, to stock with inhabitants. — *ɣsar-rñiṅ* old and new, stale and fresh; age, duration, existence. — *ɣsar ɣčód-pa* frq., also *ṫsar ɣčód-pa Pth.*, **to search, inquire into, investigate thoroughly, to examine, to study,** *skad* a language. — *ɣsár-bu* **new beginner, tyro, novice** *Mil.*

གསལ་བ་ *ɣsál-ba* vb., **to be clear, distinct, bright,** *slar šár-žiṅ ɣsál-na* when (the sun) shines bright again; *már-me ˌči-k̔ar ɣsál-ba bžin* flaming up once more, like an extinguishing lamp *Glr.*; *lhaṅ-ṅé lham-mér ɣsál-te* appearing bright, clear and distinct *Dzl.*; *ɣsál-lo* it is clear, it is evident; it stands written, it may be read, *ˌdúl-ba-na ɣsál-lo* it may be read in the Dulva *Glr.*. *Tar.*; *ɣsál-po* (प्रकाश) **visible** to a great distance, **conspicuous, distinct,** obvious, intelligible; *kun-ɣsál* id.; **mig sál-po ṫoṅ mi ṫub, ṅag sál-po zer mi še* W.* his eye, — his speech, is not clear, he is not able to see, to speak distinctly; *ɣsal-dag-snyan-ɣsúm B.* = the popular *sgra-dag-ɣsal-ɣsúm*, v. *sgra*; *yi-ge ɣsál-po* a plain, legible handwriting; **clear, bright,** *ɣsál-bai mé-loṅ* a bright mirror (a frq. title of books); **bright, light, pure,** of colours, *dkar-ɣsál* pure white *Glr.*; **pure,** free from faults and deficiencies, **sál-po gyúb-če* W.* **to correct;** *sa-p̔yógs kyaṅ ɣsál-bar gyúr-ro* also his whole neighbourhood will be freed from defects, will become **happy** *Do.*; *ɣsál-le-ba* = *ɣsal-ba*; *ɣsál-k̔a Tar.* prob. = *ɣsál-ča, Mil.*: *ɣsál-ča žig ɣnáṅ-ba žu* I request (you) to give me a detailed account, inst. of which also only *sal čig* may be said.

གསལ་ཤིང་ ysál-šiṅ (like σταυρὸς in its original meaning) **a pointed stake,** for empaling malefactors, *ysál-šiṅ-du* or *ysál-šiṅ-gi ṫsé-la skyón-pa* to empale. — Cf. *rkyaṅ-šiṅ.*

གསས་མོ་ *ysás-mo Lexx.*; in *Lt.* prob.: **mother's milk.**

གསིག་པ་ *ysig-pa Cs.*, also *bsig-pa*, to throw up in a backward direction; in *Thgr.* is said of a lion: *rál-pa ysig* he shakes his mane; *dpuṅ-bsig Cs.*: 'the shaking of one's shoulder' (prob. for: **shrugging**); **to winnow, to fan, to sift** *Stg.*; *W.*

གསིང་མ་ *ysiṅ-ma* 1. **pasture-ground, meadow** *Dzl.* — 2. moor, fen *Sch.?*

གསིར་བ་ *ysir-ba Sch.*, *bsir-ba Cs.* 1. **to whirl about** or round, to twirl, *ṗaṅ* a spindle, *mda ysir-ba Cs.*: 'to whirl an arrow'. — 2. *W.* **to move** by a repeated pushing, *ṗág-ste* a plane; **to smooth, to even,** with a plane, a knife etc.; **to slide, glide, slip,** down a slope.

གསིལ་བ་ *ysil-ba* 1. **to cut to pieces, to divide, split,** *lhú-ru Mil.*, *dúm-bur Lex.*, *ysor-gyis ysil-ba* to saw to pieces, to saw up. — 2. **to toll, sound, ring,** *dril-bu ysil-ba* to ring a bell *Cs.*, hence *mḱar-ysil* v. *mḱar-ba.* — 3. **sil-če* W.* **to read.** — *ysil-bu* and *ysil-ma* v. *síl-bu.*

གསུང་ *ysuṅ*, resp. for *skad* and *ytam*, 1. **voice,** *ysuṅ byuṅ* a voice sounded, was heard *Glr.*, *ysuṅ dág-pa* a clear voice, like that of Buddha *Dzl.* — 2. **the act of speaking, talking,** *ysuṅ gléṅ-ba* to converse, discourse, *ysuṅ ͺdré-ba*, *ysuṅ-ͺdré mdzád-pa* id.; that which is spoken, the words uttered, **the speech,** *ḱyéd-kyi ysuṅ dei lán-du* in answer to your words *Glr.*; *ysuṅ klóg-pa* to read the sayings, the apothegms (of Buddha) *Ma.*

གསུང་བ་ *ysúṅ-ba* I. vb., pf. *ysuṅs*, resp. for *smrá-ba B.* and *C.* (in *W.* **mól-če** is used inst. of it) **to speak, talk, say,** the latter also with the termin. of the infin., inst. of direct speech, but rarely; *dé-skad ma ysuṅ* your Reverence should not say so! *Mil.*; *ysuṅ ma ynaṅ* it did not please him to speak *Mil.*; *rdzun ysúṅ-ba* to tell a falsehood, to lie; **to explain,** *don Mil.*; **to ask;** *mi ͺdod mi ysuṅ bžés-par žu Mil.* please accept it without ceremonies (without a refusal); *žal-ydáms ysúṅ-ba* to give advice etc. *Glr.*; *čos ysúṅ-ba* to preach *Glr.*; *mgúr-ma ysúṅ-ba* to recite or to sing a song (but also: *mgúr-ma smrá-ba*, *zér-ba* is said).

Comp. *ysuṅ-bgrós* **report, statement, opinion.** — *ysuṅ-mčog* **principal word, main dogma** e.g. the Ommanipadmehum *Glr.* — *ysuṅ-snyán* a harmonious voice, an agreeable, pleasant speech; *Mil.* uses it also of the singing of birds (and the screaming of peacocks!) — *ysuṅ-sprós*, *ysuṅ-ͺṗró* **conversation** between persons of rank, or between such and inferior people. *ysuṅ-ráb* = *ysuṅ-mčóg*, also sacred writing, **Holy Scripture** *Chr. Pr.* — *ysuṅ-šóg* = *bka-šóg.*

གསུད་པ་, བསུད་པ་ *ysúd-pa*, *bsúd-pa* 1. *Sch.* **to be lost, to be dispersed.** — 2. *W.* to fill with food beyond satiety, **to stuff, to cram.** *Bhar.* 124 *smán-pa ysud* stands for *Ssk.* **विसूचिका** (*Will.*: spasmodic cholera), which elsewh. is rendered *zas ma žu-ba*; the meaning is prob. to overeat one's self.

གསུམ་ *ysum* three (cf. *sum*), *ysúm-ḱa*, *ysúm-ga* the three, all the three; *ysúm-pa* the third; containing three; *ysúm-po* the three; *ysum* also elliptically for *dkon-mčog-ysúm*: *ysúm-la skyábs-su ͺdóṅ-ba* to seek the protection of the Three Precious *Do.*; *bskál-pa gráṅs-med(-pa) ysum* three times innumerable Kalpas (appeared) *Dzl.*, *Glr.*; *rgán-mo ma smad ysum-po ͺdi* the old (woman) with her (two) sons, the three *Dzl.*; *rgyál-po yab yum ysum* the king and his (two) queens, the three *Glr.*; *rab ͺbriṅ ysum* the big, the middle (and the little one), the three. — *ysúm-sprul* emanation of the third degree, = *nyiṅ-sprul.*

གསུར་མ་ *ysúr-ma* a thing slightly burnt, **singed** *Cs.*, *ysur-drí* the smell of it.

གསུས་པ་ *ysús-pa* **belly, stomach,** *ysús-pa sbos* the belly is swollen or distended *Lex.*; *ysus-nád* dropsy of the belly; *ysus-rked* the middle part of the body, the waist *Sch.*; *ysus-ͺṗyaṅ-po* a deity.

གསེ་བ་ ysé-ba 1. v. sé-ba. — 2. v. ysèd-pa.

གསེག་བརྡར་ yseg-brdár *Sch.* **a file** (instrument), v. *sag-ydar*.

གསེག་མ་ ysèg-ma **small stones**; *yseg-seb-čan* full of small stones.

གསེག་གཤང་ *yseg-yśàṅ* = *mk̔ar-ysil Lex.*

གསེང་, སེང་ ysеṅ, seṅ 1. **cleft, chink, crevice, fissure, leak**, v. *k̔oṅ-sèṅ* sub *k̔oṅ* extr.; *sgo-ysèṅ* chink of a door *Tar.*; *yseṅ bsrúb-pa Sch.* to stop up, plug up, crevices etc.; *ysèṅs-pa* leaky, cracked, full of fissures *Sch.* — 2. **harmonious**, well-sounding. — 3. *rná-ba yseṅ Sch.*: a sharp, acute, quick ear, cf. *ysáṅ-ba* II, 2.

གསེད་ *ysed* several larger species of Lonicera.

གསེད་པ་ *ysèd-pa*, also *bsèd-pa* (pf. *yses?*) **to pick, sort, assort**, hair, wool; **to pull or pluck in pieces.**

གསེབ་ *yseb* I. **stallion**, a male horse or camel.

II. also *seb*, 1. the narrow **interstices** between persons or things thronged together, hence with *na*, *tu* and *la*, **between, among**, with *nas* **from between**, *k̔yi mii ysèb-la mčoṅ* the dog leaps into the midst of the people, *lò-mai ysèb-tu ₒjòg-pa* to put between leaves, *sprín-gyi ysèb-nas lus p̔yed ₒton* half of his body protrudes from between the clouds, = rises above etc.; *groṅ-ysèb-tu bžúgs-pa* to sit among the villagers; *k̔yèd-čag-gi ysèb-na Meu-dgál byá-bai bud-méd yód-dam?* is there a woman among you named *Meu-dgal?* *ysèb-lam* a secret path, by-way, between rocks or underwood. — 2. **multitude, crowd**, *dmág-yseb* army, *nágs-yseb* forest.

གསེར་ *yser* (*Pers.* زر) **gold**; *ysèr-gyi* of gold, golden, *ysèr-gyi mé-tog* n. of a medicinal herb.

Comp. *yser-skúd S.g.* n. of an officinal herb. — *yser-skyèms* v. *skyems*. — *ysèr-k̔a* a gold mine. — *yser-mk̔ár* an imperial castle *Wts.* — *yser-gliṅ* Malacca *Cs.* — *yser-ₒgyur-rtsí* prob. much the same as: 'philosopher's stone' *Pth.* — *yser-t̔úb* n. of the second Buddha, Kanakamuni. — *yser-mdóg* gold-colour, *ysèr-mdog-čan* n. of a monastery. — *ysèr-pa* gold-searcher, gold-washer *Gram.*; *yser-p̔ud* n. of a medicinal herb, an emetic *Med.* — *yser-ₒp̔réṅ* a gold chain. — *yser-byé* gold-sand. — *yser-mé* = *ysèr-gyi-mé-tog Med.* — *yser-ytsó-ma*, *yser-btsó-ma* refined gold *Glr.*, *Pth.* — **ser-zàṅ** *W.* gilt copper. — *yser-bzó-pa*, *yser-mgár Cs.* goldsmith. — *yser-yíg-pa* 'bearer of a gold-letter', ambassador, envoy *Glr.* — *yser-śóg* leaf-gold, gold-foil, foliated gold *Sch.* — *yser-sraṅ* one ounce of gold; a coin = 16 rupees, gold-mohur.

གསེས་ *yses? raṅ-ysés* **reciprocal, mutual** *Wdṅ.*

གསོ་བ་ *ysó-ba* pf. *ysos*, (*b*)*sos* (= *ₒtsó-ba*) 1. **to feed, nourish** *Dzl.*; **to bring up, nurse up, rear, train,** *bu* a child, *dúd-ₒgro* an animal; also *ysó-skyoṅ-ba*, *yso-skyóṅ byéd-pa*. — 2. **to cure,** *nad, rma*; **to stop, remove,** to put an end to, *ṅal* fatigue, i.e. to recruit one's self, to rest; **to mend, to repair,** *k̔yim* a house *Cs.*; **to restore, rebuild, re-establish,** what had been destroyed, **to kindle again, stir up again,** a fire; *žig-* or *śig-yso-ba* id.; **to refresh, recreate,** *sems*, resp. *t̔ugs*, the soul, i.e. to comfort, console.

Comp. *yso-mk̔an* **restorer** *Glr.* *yso-t̔ábs* **way of curing,** manner of healing *Med.* — *ysó-ba-po* **physician** *Med.* — *ysó-bya* the thing to be cured, the disease *Med.*; *yso-byéd* the healing substance, **the remedy**; the healing person, **the physician.** — *yso-sbyóṅ-ba* v. the following article. — *yso-ts̔úl* = *yso-t̔ábs*. — *yso-rig* **pharmacology.**

གསོ་སྦྱོང་བ་ *yso-sbyóṅ-ba*, for *ṅyés-pa ysó-ba daṅ sdig-pa sbyoṅ-ba* to get quit of sin, by making confession to a priest and thus restoring the former state of virtuousness, **to confess**; also *yso-sbyoṅ len-pa*, *yso-sbyoṅ-la ynas-pa*; such confession does not entail any penalties, but only a renewal of obligations, cf. *Fouc. Gyatch.* II, 16.

གསོ་རས་ *yso-rás Lex.*; *Sch.*: **rag, tatter.**

གསོག་པ་ *ysóg-pa* 1. v. *sóg-pa* II. — 2. v. *sob.*

གསོང་པོ་ *ysóṅ-po* **sincere,** *ysóṅ-por smrá-ba* to speak the truth.

གསོང་བ་ *ysóṅ-ba Cs.* and *Lex.*; usually *ysáṅ-ba.*

གསོད་པ་ γsód-pa, pf. *bsad*, fut. (*Lex.* γ*sad*, usually:) *bsad*, imp. *sod*, *W.* **sád-če**, 1. **to kill, slay, murder, slaughter.** γ*sód-pa-la dgá-ba* to delight in killing *Dzl.*; *bsad ma-ťág-pai ša*, γ*sár-du bsád-pai ša* v. γ*sár-ba*; *rgyál-pos* γ*sód-pa* to be executed by the authority *Dzl.*; (*ťse*) *bsád-pa-la ťúg-nas* when he was just on the point of being executed *Dzl.*; **p̀ag ǰáb-te sád-tan-če* W.* to assassinate; *bsád-do! bčóm-mo!* I am lost! it is all over with me! *Wdṅ.* — 2. **to put out, extinguish** frq. — 3. *k̀yád-*γ*sod-pa* to despise, v. *k̀yad* extr.

Comp. γ*sod-*γ*čód* **the act of murdering, murder,** slaughter, γ*sod-*γ*čód-kyi* *jigs-pa* fear of murder *Mil.*; γ*sod-*γ*čód máṅ-po byed* he is murdering, slaughtering, a great deal. — γ*sod-byéd* killer, murderer, γ*sod-byéd rṅón-pa* the murderous huntsman *Lex.*; γ*sod-byéd-kyi* γ*nas* slaughter-house *Stg.* — γ*sód-sa* place of execution *Thgy.* — γ*sód-lugs* way of killing, *sṅar ma byas* a new (way of killing) *Tar.*

གསོན་པ་ γsón-pa I. A. vb., 1. intrs. **to live, to be alive,** γ*són-no* he (she etc.) is alive, **de méd-na mi són-če mi ťub** without that a man cannot live *W.*; **to remain alive, to save or preserve one's own life,** *rdzún-du smrás-na* γ*son kyaṅ* though I could save my life by (telling) a falsehood *Dzl.*; γ*són-par mi dod* I do not wish to live (any longer) *Dzl.*; of the fire: **to burn,** **da són-na* W.* does it burn now? — 2. trs. **to wake, to rouse** from sleep **by shaking, to urge on, to hurry on** (lazy people), by force, whereas *skúl-ba* is only done by words. — B. sbst. **life,** γ*són-pai ťsé-na* or γ*són-pai dús-su* **during** (my, your etc.) **life, in lifetime,** frq.; hence: γ*son-pa-nyid* for ζωή John 1, 4 etc. *Chr. P.* — C. adj. **living, alive,** frq. γ*són-po*, col. **γsón-te**, *kyé-ma bu* γ*són-po mťóṅ-ṅo* ah, there I see my son again alive! *Stg.*; γ*són-por byéd-pa* to call into life, to animate, γ*són-por dúr-du* *júg-pa* to bury alive *Dzl.*, γ*són-pai rgyú-ma* *drén-pa* to tear out the bowels of a living man; **son-te* W.* also: **healthy, whole, restored to health again,** **kaṅ-pa, mig, me són-te čó-če** to cure a foot, an eye, to blow a fire into flame again; **entire, whole, undivided,** **són-te k̀yóṅ-ṅa** am I to bring it entire (or cut into pieces etc.)? of the moon: **full.** — γ*són-ma* rarely for γ*són-po*, *p̀úg-ron* γ*són-ma* a live pigeon *Pth.*; γ*son-*γ*šin* both the living and the dead *Cs.*; γ*son bsrégs* a creature burnt alive, *mi žig(-la)* γ*son-bsrégs byéd-pa* to burn a person alive *Pth.*

II. vb., pf. *bsan*, fut. γ*san*, imp. γ*son Cs.*, prob. the original form of γ*sán-pa* **to hear.**

III. *čúd-*γ*son-pa* v. *čud.*

གསོབ་ γsob v. *sob.*

གསོབ་པ་ γsób-pa, pf. *bsab*, fut. γ*sab*, 1. **to fill out or up, to supply, complete, make up,** *hór-k̀oṅs* a gap (?) *Sch.*, **to cure,** wounds *W.*, **sob-mán** balm, ointment for wounds. — 2. **to pay, repay, return,** *skyin-pa* a loan *Sch.*, *drin* γ*sób-pa* to return a kindness *Glr.*

གསོར་ γsor 1. v. *sór* I. — 2. supine of γ*só-ba.*

གསོར་བ་ γsórba **to brandish, flourish,** a staff *Cs.*

གསོལ་བ་ γsól-ba I. vb., 1. = *žú-ba* 1, q.v.; *rgyál-po-la sróg-gi skyabs* γ*sól-to* he besought the king to save his life *Dzl.*; *stón-pa-la smón-lam btáb-par* γ*sol čig* ask the teacher to say the prayers *Dzl.*; *bstán-du* γ*sol* I beg to explain, frq.; *lha* γ*sól-ba* to worship a god, by offerings, libations etc. *Glr.* and elsewh. Tibetans when arriving on the top of a mountain-pass generally mutter the words: γ*sól-lo* γ*sól-lo*, prob. to express their thankfulness for having been preserved from harm so far, and to implore further protection. — 2. resp. for *gón-pa* and *skón-pa* **to put on:** (*skú-la*) *ná-bza*, *čos-gos*, *dbú-la ťod*, *žábs-la čag* (to put on) a garment, clerical robes, cap, shoes *Dzl.*, *Glr.*; *slób-dpon-la ber-čén skú-la* γ*sól-te* putting the cloak on the teacher *Ma.*; for *zá-ba*, *ťúṅ-ba*, also for *drén-pa*, **to eat, to drink, to offer a meal** *Dzl.*; *rgyál-po* *bras-čáṅ* γ*sól-nas* as the king had drunk rice-wine *Glr.*; **to take, to give, administer** (medicine) *Dzl.*; **to place** (food etc.) **before, to**

serve up for (clerical persons) *Dzl.*, *γsól-lo mčód-čig* I place it before you, help yourself! moreover: *rgyál-pos čáb-la sku-ḱrús γsol* the king took a bath *Glr.*; *srás-la sku-ḱrús γsól-lo* they administered a bath to the prince *Glr.*; *mtsan γsól-ba* to assume, to receive, a name *Glr.*, to give a name *Glr.*; even thus: *dei ťúgs-la γdon γsol* a demon enters his (the king's) body (clothes himself with it) *Glr.*

Comp. **sol-kár** *W.*, resp. for *kar-yol* earthen ware, crockery. — *γsol-skrúm* meat prepared for the table of a man of rank. *γsol-ḱá* 1. request, prayer *Sch.* 2. meat and drink *Sch.* — **sól-ḱań** resp. for **yó-ḱań** *C.*, **ťab-tsáń** *W.* **kitchen.** — *γsol-ńán* poisoned food *Glr.* — *γsol-lčóg* **table.** — *γsol-mčód* **prayer** and **offerings.** — *γsol-ǰá* **tea.** — *γsol-nyá* fish destined or dressed for the table of a respected person, *rgyál-poi Pth.* — *γsol-tág*, *γsol-stégs* **table.** — *γsol-tib* **tea-pot.** — *γsol-ťáb* **fire-place, kitchen.** — *γsol-ldóń* = *gur-gúr.* — *γsól-dpon* prop. head-cook, master-cook, gen. **cup-bearer, butler, waiter.** — *γsol-ṕógs* **salary** *Sch.* — **γsol-ₒbiń** *C.* = *γsol-tib.* — *γsol-már* **butter.** — *γsol-tsígs* **dinner.** — *γsol-žib* fine parched **barley-flour.** *γsol-γyóg* under-waiter, under-butler. — *γsol-rás* **distribution of victuals**, by a person of rank to common people, hence *Chr. P.* for **Lord's supper**, holy communion; **donation, gift, present** in gen.

II. sbst. 1. **request, demand, entreaty,** *γsol-ba ₒdebs-pa* to make a request, to entreat frq. — 2. **food** **sól-wa žé-pa** to eat, dine, sup *C.*

གསོས་པ་ *γsós-pa* v. *γsó ba*, *γsos byéd-pa* **to cure** *Sch.*; *bu mi γsos-pa* not keeping, retaining a child alive *Do.*; *γsós-bu* foster-son, **adoptive son**; *γsós-ma* cure? medicine? *γsós-ma ₒdébs-pa Thgy.*

བསའ་ *bsa* v. *γsa.*

བསག་པ་ *bság-pa* v. *γsóg-pa.*

བསང་བུ་ *bsáń-bu* resp. for *zan* **food, fare** *Glr.*; **bsáń-ma** id. *W.*; *bsań-ₒbrás* resp. a dish of rice.

བསད་པ་ *bsád-pa* v. *γsód-pa.*

བསབ་པ་ *bsáb-pa* v. *γsób-pa.*

བསམ་ *bsam*, **thought, thinking,** *bsám-gyis mi ḱyáb-pa* beyond the reach of human intellect, **incomprehensible** etc. frq.; *čos bzáń-las bsam bzań lhág-pa yin* a good way of thinking is worth more than good (external) religion *Mil.*; *W.*: **sam-ńan-čan** **malicious, wicked.**

བསམ་པ་ *bsám-pa* I. fut. tense and secondary form of *sém-pa.*

II. sbst. सङ्कल्प, 1. **thought**, imagination, fancy, *bsám-pa ńán-pa sém-pa* to foster bad thoughts *Do.*; *bsám-pa tsám-gyis* quick as thought; *rtág-tu ₒdi snyám-du bsám-pa skyes* he was constantly haunted by these thoughts *Dzl.* — 2. **will,** *mi žig-gi bsám-pa ltar* (or *bžin-du*) *sgrúb-pa* to execute, to carry out a person's will frq.; *bsám-pa ltar ma gyúr-pas* as it did not go according to their **wish**; *bsam-pa ₒdi-las ma zlog čig* do not try to divert me from my **purpose** *Dzl.*; *bsám-pa bzáń-po* good **intention** or **design** *Mil.*; **desire, mind, inclination, liking,** *γnód-pai* or *γdúg-pai* thirst for blood, murderous disposition *Glr.* — 3. **soul, heart** (of rare occurrence), *bsám-pai dón mi ₒgrub* then (by doing so) you injure your own soul *Mil*

Comp. *bsam-γtán*, ध्यान, 1. **state of complete abstraction,** acc. to *Burn.* '*contemplation*' (cf. *tiń-ńe-ₒdzín*, समाधि, समापत्ति, *Burn.* '*méditation*'), *bsam-γtán byéd-pa* to transpose one's self into the state of contemplation or meditation (the difference between the two is not easily defined), v. *Köpp.* I, 586. With this extraordinary state of mind a strange conception is associated, viz. 2. of **certain regions,** where besides gods and other beings also such men have their abode, that are growing more and more perfect and are stripping off every personal quality, whether good or bad, v. *Köpp.* I, 255. — *bsam-mnó* or *-bló*, also *blo-bsám* **thinking,** wishing etc., *bsam-mnó byéd-pa* or *γtóń-ba*, resp. *ťugs-bsám γtóń-ba Pth.*, **to think, to meditate, consider, think upon** frq.; *bzáń-byed-kyi bsam-*

bló a mind, directed towards what is good, **honesty, probity** *Glr.* — *bsam-sbyór* **design, device, project** *Mil., bzáṅ-po, ṅán-pa; bsam-byór byéd-pa* to plan, to scheme, to project a plan *C.* — *bsam-šés* **consciousness,** **sam-šé ṅém-pa** *C.* bad conscience (?).

བསམ་བསེའུ་ *bsam-bséu* 1. **seminal vesicle.** — 2. ovary?

བསལ་བ་ *bsál-ba* v. *sél-ba.*

བསིག་པ་ *bsig-pa* v. *γsig-pa.*

བསིད་པ་ *bsid-pa* **to mend, repair, put in order** *Sch.*

བསིར་བ་ *bsir-ba* 1. = *γsir-ba.* — 2. *W.* **to sip,** **sir-te tuṅ** he drinks sipping.

བསིལ་བ་ *bsil-ba* I. adj. and sbst. **cool, the cool** (of the day), **coolness,** *ḱáṅ-pa bsil-ba žig* a cool house *Dzl.*, *bsil-ba ṕan* coolness is wholesome *Lt.*, *ṫsá-ba bsil-bar ₒgyur* the heat changes to coolness *Dzl.*; *bsil* id., **sil-la dod** sit down in the shade *W.*, *lčaṅ-bsil* 'willow-shade', shady place under willow-trees; *bsil-žiṅ gráṅ-ba* **cold** *Dzl., Glr.*; *bsil-mo* id., **sil-mo ṕi-la** *W.* for the sake of coolness.

II. vb., **to cool,** resp. for *ₒḱrúd-pa* **to wash,** *žal* mouth and face, *žabs* the feet, *žábs-bsil* water for washing the feet *Cs.*; even: *ču drón-mos sku bsil-bar mdzád-pa* to wash the body with warm water *Cs.*; **to shed,** *spyan-čáb máṅ-po* many tears *Mil.*

Comp. *bsil-ḱaṅ* a cool room, a summer-house, summer-residence *Stg.* — *bsil-grib* cool shade *Cs.* — *bsil-ₒṫúṅ* a cooling drink or beverage *Sch.* — *bsil-γdúgs* parasol *Do.* — *bsil-bu* coolness (?); *bsil-bui rluṅ* a cool breeze *Cs.* — *bsil-smán* a cooling medicine. — *bsil-zás* cooling food. — *bsil-ₒyáb* a fan.

བསུ་བ་ *bsú-ba*, pf. and imp. *bsus,* **to go to meet,** *ma bu bsur ₒoṅ* the mother goes to meet her son *Dzl.* (usually with accus. as in the preceding case, col. also with dat.); *bsus šig* let him come to meet me *Thgr.*; **to join,** of two armies, generals, kings *Dzl.*; **to make advances, to interest one's self for;** most frq.: **to go to meet** (solemnly), **to welcome** a respected person, *ṕo-bráṅ-gi náṅ-du* into the castle *Dzl.*; *páṇḍi-ta ₒbyón-pa-la bsú-ba byéd-do* I will go to meet the arriving Pandit *Glr.*; *bsú-ba rgya-čén-po* very great festivities of reception *Pth.*; *bág-mar bsú-ba yin* we will lead her home as your bride *Mil.*; *γdóṅ-bsu-ba* = *bsú-ba Mil.*; **dan sú-če** *W.* for *ₒdan-* or *spyan-ₒdren-pa* of *B.* — **su-kyel* or *kyal** *W.* reception and conduct of honour.

བསུ་སྨན་ *bsu-smán Sch.* **clyster,** *W.* **sur-nyig**.

བསུང་ *bsuṅ* **smell,** esp. **sweet scent** *Dzl.*; *dri-bsúṅ* id.; *dri-bsúṅ žim-pa broo* it is sweet, scented, fragrant *Dzl.*: *bsuṅ-ṅád Sch.* fragrance; *ro bsúṅ-ba* filled with a cadaverous smell *Dzl.*; **mar suṅ soṅ dog** *W.* the butter smells (rancid).

བསུན་བསྐྱུར་ *bsun-bskyúr Sch.*: irregularity of life, **dissoluteness**; *bsún-par byed-pa Sch.*: to be dissolute; to be dirty; *bsún-tsam* disgusting, obscene *Sch.*

བསུམ་པ་ *bsum-pa* 1. = *ₒdzúm-pa.* — 2. = *súm-pa Cs.*

བསུར་སྙིག་ *bsur-snyig W.* **clyster,** cf. *bsu-smán.*

བསེ་ *bse* 1. v. *se, se-ba, se-dri, se-šin.* — 2. also: *bse-ḱó,* **tanned leather,** *bse-ḱráb Lex.* a coat of mail made of leather; *bse-sgám, bsei sgróm-bu Pth.* leather-box, or a box covered with leather; *bse-sgó* leather-door, or a door-like target made of hides *Pth.* — 3. *bse* or *bse-ru* (*Lex.* [Sanskrit] 'a certain animal') **unicorn,** *Hook.* II., 157 'tchiru', **an antelope,** prob. = *γtsod*; **rhinoceros** *Tar.* 185, 20.

བསེགས་པ་ *bségs-pa Sch.* to come from one side, to come across one's way.

བསེད་པ་ *bséd-pa* v. *γséd-pa.*

བསེད་དཔྱད་ *bsed-dpyád Sch.* the bow for setting a drill in motion.

བསེན་མོ་ *bsen-mo Sch*: a female devil.

བསེར་, སེར་, གསེར་བུ་ *bser, ser, γsér-bu* 1. **a fresh, cold breeze,** *bsér-gyis ṕog* he is exposed to a cold wind *Sch.* — 2. of persons, resp. **the feeling cold, catching cold,** *bsér-du yoṅ* you will feel cold *Mil*; also *bsér-mo* adj. or sbst.: **sér-mo* *sér-mo máṅ-po ma kyód-da* W. did you not feel very cold on your way? bser-mai nad resp. a catarrh, a cold Dzl.

བསེལ་(བ་) bsél(-ba), gen. lam-bsél **convoy, safe-conduct, escort**; Lex.: ˳jag-skyób-kyi kyél-ma (escort) against robbers; bsél-pa safeguard, guide, (lam-) bsél byéd-pa to accompany and protect on the way, to escort.

བསོག་པ་ bsóg-pa v. ság-pa.

བསོད་སྙོམས་ bsod-snyóms, **पिण्ड, alms, gifts** presented to clerical persons, bsod-snyóms-gyis ˳tso-ba to live on alms, on charity, bsod-snyóms byéd-pa, sóg-pa, ˳júg-pa Cs., bsod-snyóms-la rgyú-ba, resp. ;ségs-pa to beg, ask, collect alms; bsod-snyóms sbyór-ba to prepare an entertainment for the priesthood.

བསོད་པ་ bsód-pa 1. vb., **to be pleased with, to take a delight in, to like**, W.: *de-la kon-čog sod-če man* God is not pleased with that. — 2. adj., **pleasing, agreeable.** *nyiṅ sod tsor dug* W. I feel well, I am quite happy; bsód-pa daṅ ṅán-pa good and bad; bsód-pai zas is explained by one Lex.: zas bzáṅ-poi miṅ good food, good provisions, by another: = **प्रणीत** prepared, dressed, boiled.— bsód-bde, bsód-nams, resp. sku-bsód 1. **good fortune, happiness, felicity**, bsód-bde-čan happy, bsód-bde-med unhappy Cs. 2. **destiny, fate,** = dbaṅ-táṅ, *tam-čád sód-de-nẹ juṅ* every thing happens according to a decree of fate W.; prob. also sku-bsód šín-tu če Ld.-Glr. 11, b. Schl., his destiny is a very high one; kyód-kyi bsód-bde-la brdúṅ-ba yód-pa yin it belongs to your destiny that you get a drubbing. — 3. **merit, virtue, good action,** byéd-pa to perform (a good action) Dzl., bsód-bde sóg-pa to gather merit, bsód-nams ma yin-pai las sinful deed Thgy.

བསོས་ bsos **indemnification, damages** paid for bodily injury.

བསོས་པ་ bsós-pa v. ɣsos-pa.

བསྲང་བ་ bsráṅ-ba v. sróṅ-ba; bsráṅ-po **straight, upright,** *yór-po dug šráṅ-po-la žog* C. it stands aslant, put it straight!

བསྲད་པ་ bsrád-pa v. bsród-pa.

བསྲན་པ་ bsrán-pa v. srán-pa.

བསྲབ་པ་ bsráb-pa, v. srab, **to bridle, keep under, restrain, check, curb, refrain,** bag-čágs the passions, mún-pa or sgríb-pa bsráb-pa Cs. to dispel darkness (prob. only in a spiritual sense).

བསྲལ་བ་ bsrál-ba v. srél-ba.

བསྲི་བ་ bsri-ba etc. v. sri-ba etc.

བསྲུང་ bsrun Cs. **a tutelar genius.**

བསྲུན་པ་, བསྲུབ་པ་, བསྲུལ་བ་, བསྲེ་བ་, བསྲེག་པ་, བསྲེལ་བ་, བསྲོ་བ་ bsrún-pa, bsrúb-pa, bsrúl-ba, bsré-ba, bsrég-pa, bsrél-ba, bsró-ba v. srún-pa, srúb-pa etc.

བསྲོད་པ་, བསྲད་པ་ bsród-pa, bsrád-pa, = sró-ba, **to dry,** by exposing to the rays of the sun Sch.

བསླ་བ་, བསླང་བ་, བསླད་པ་ etc. bslá-ba, bsláṅ-ba, bslád-pa etc. v. slá-ba, sláṅ-ba etc.

བསླབ་པ་ bsláb-pa 1. vb., v. slob-pa. — 2. sbst. **doctrine,** bsláb-pa ɣsum Glr., acc. to an explanation in the Triglot: lhág-pai tsul-krims, lhág-pai sems, lhág-pai šes-ráb (expressions which I am not able to interpret satisfactorily); our Lama explained bsláb-pa ɣsúm-gyi sdóm-pa Mil. by: so-tár, byaṅ-séms and ɣsaṅ-sṅágs-kyi sdóm-pa; bsláb-pai ɣnas **dogma, tenet** Tar. — *lab-kan* W. **teacher.** — *lab-(s)tán táṅ-če* W. to teach, to keep school. — bslab-bya what is to be learned, **doctrine, precept, admonition,** ˳jig-rtén mi-čos-la dgos-pai bsláb-bya mdzád-do he imparted to her some practical doctrines or rules of life and social intercourse Glr., bsláb-bya stón-pa B., *táṅ-če* W. to give admonitions, to exhort, reprimand.

བསླུ་བ་, བསླེ་བ་, བསླེབ་པ་, བསློག་པ་ bslú-ba, bslé-ba, bsléb-pa, bslóg-pa v. slu-ba, sle-ba etc.

ཧ

ཧ *ha* 1. the letter *h*. — 2. numeral: 29.

ཧ་ *ha* 1. *W.* **a yawn**, **ha yoṅ dug** I cannot help yawning. 2. **breath**, *ha ˳débs-pa* to breathe. — 3. **the sound of laughter**, **hab-gód čó-če* W.* to laugh out or aloud, cf. *ha-há*.

ཧྭ་ *hwa* 1. *gós-kyi hwa* **collar** of a coat. — 2. **shin, shin-bone** *Sch.* — 3. **hă, hŏ* W.* very well! — 4. col. nearly = *pa* II., **yonder,** farther off, **há-la gyug* C.* get you gone! be off! begone!; **há-čog* = *pá-rol** the other side, yonder side, **há-gi** that (man) there, **há-gi-ru** there, there above, up there, there behind, thither, that way *C., W.*

ཧ་གོ་བ་ *há-go-ba W.* **to understand,** **ha mi go-a** don't you understand it?

ཧ་ཅང་ *há-čaṅ* **very,** sometimes **too much, too,** *mya-ṅán-las ˳da-ba há-čaṅ yaṅ myur-čés-so* his removal (prop. disappearing) from misery happens really too soon! *Dzl.*; *há-čaṅ-nas* id., **há-čaṅ-ne k'é-pa* C.* very learned, possessed of extensive information.

ཧ་ན་ཧོ་ནེ་, ཧན་ཧོན་ *ha-na-ho-né, han-hón* **very angry,** much enraged *Ld.*

ཧ་ནི་ *há-ni* **all** of them, **all together, in a body** *Sch.*

ཧ་བ་ཧ་བ་ *há-ba-há-ba* **to breathe out steam** or vapour.

ཧ་བོ་ *há-bo* n. of a medicinal herb *Lt.*

ཧ་ཡེགས་ *ha-yégs* **woe** (to you etc.)! *W.*

ཧ་ར་ *há-ra*, with **gyáb-če**, *W.* **to play at dice.**

ཧ་ར་ཧུ་རེ་ *ha-ra-hu-ré W.* **impetuous, violent, rude, impudent.**

ཧ་རམ་ *ha-rám* with **čó-če* W.* **to deny, disown, disavow.**

ཧ་རི་ *há-ri Ssk.* **parrot.**

ཧ་རི་ཏ་ཀ་ *ha-ri-ta-ka Ssk.* **vegetables, greens, pot-herbs** *Wdṅ.*

ཧ་རི་དྲ་ *ha-ri-dra Ssk.* the turmeric plant, **Curcuma** *S.g.*

ཧ་རི་ཙནྡན་ *ha-ri-tsan-dan Ssk.* **sandal-wood.**

ཧ་རི་ཙམ་ *ha-ri-tsam Pur.* **centipede.**

ཧ་རིབ་ *ha-rib Ld.* music (?).

ཧ་རེ་ཎུ་ཀ་ *ha-re-ṇu-ka Ssk.* a medicine *Med.*

ཧ་ལ་, ཧ་ལ་ཧ་ལ་ *ha-la, ha-la-ha-la Wdṅ.*, a certain poison, also **poison** in general, *Ssk.*

ཧ་ལ་ཧ་ལ་ *ha-la-há-la Cs.*: a name of *spyan-ras-γzigs*, v. *spyan.*

ཧ་ལམ་ *há-lam* **about, near, nearly, pretty, tolerably, rather,** *de daṅ há-lam ˳drá-ba* about or nearly like that *Wdṅ.*

ཧ་ལལ་ *ha-lál Ar.*, **ha-lál čó-če**, *Urd.* حلال کرنا, to kill (an animal) in the manner prescribed by the Mahometan law *W.*

ཧ་ལས་ *ha-lás* col., **astonished, frightened,** **ha-la-śi** or **ha-la-śe** id., **ha-lé čá-če* W.*, *ha-lás-pa B.* **to be astonished, frightened** *Mil., Pth.*

ཧ་ལོ་ *ha-ló* **flower,** esp. a large beautiful **garden-flower** *Glr., ha-ló rkyáṅ-pa* a simple flower, *ha-ló stoṅ-˳dáb* a double flower; **ha-ló-ka** mallow *W.* (?)

ཧ་ཤང་ *ha-śáṅ* 1. *Cs.*: (Chinese word) **a Buddhist priest, doctor, scholar** *Glr.* — 2. id., represented by **a mask** in religious plays, *ha-p'rúg* an old doctor with boys, his pupils.

ཧ་ཤིག *ha-śig* a mineral medicine, used as a remedy for the stone; acc. to *Wdṅ.* = *tód-le-kór*, alabaster.

ཧ་ཧ་, ཧཧ *ha-há, hā-hā* the natural sound of laughter *Mil., ha-há rgód-pa* to laugh out, to set up a loud laugh;

to *Sch.* also an interjection expressive of pain (?).

ཧའི་ *hai* a Chinese word, **shoe** *C.*

ཧའུ་སྤ་བ་ *hau-spa-ba* n. of a medicinal herb *Med.*

ཧགས་ *hags Lex.* **sugar, treacle** *Cs.*, *hágs-kyi lá-tu.*

ཧང་ *hañ? hañ-ₒdzom-pa* **to squander, to dissipate** *Sch.*, *hañ-ča-byed* **a squanderer** *Sch.*

ཧང་བ་ *háñ-ba, W.* **háñ-če** **to pant, to gasp.**

ཧད་ཀྱིས་ *hád-kyis* **suddenly** *Sch.* — *had-po? Mil.*

ཧད་ཧད་ *had-hád* or *hur-húr*, with **čó-če** **to exert one's self,** to strive *W.*

ཧན་ལྡང་ *han-ldáñ W.* 1. **dumb, mute,** **han-dáñ-ńi* (s)*pé ra** **a stammering,** also: a confused, unmeaning speech. — 2. **imbecile, weak of mind.**

ཧན་ཧོན་ *han-hón* v. *ha-na-ho-né.*

ཧབ་ *hab* 1. **a mouthful,** *háb-za byéd-pa*, *hab-háb zá-ba* to devour greedily, e.g. of dogs, pigs etc., *hab-bčád* a needy wretch, a starveling, famishing person.— 2. **a stitch,** in sewing, also **háb-ka** *C.* **háb-so** *W.*, *hab-ₒtsem-pa* to make here a stitch and there a stitch, as in quilting *Mil. nt.* — 3. *hab-gód* v. *ha* 3. — 4. v. the following article.

ཧབ་ཤ་ *háb-ša* **a dispute, a quarrel,** *háb-ša byéd-pa Mil.*, *Thgr.*, to dispute, to quarrel; *ḥab-tób byéd pa* to scramble for, to strive or contend for *Pth.*

ཧམ་པ་ *hám-pa* 1. **avarice, covetousness, greediness;** *W.* also vb.: to covet, **žán-ni nór-la** after a person's wealth; **to long for,** to yearn after, **k̔oi 'á-ne hám-te dad dug** his wife sits yearning (after him); *hám-pa byéd-pa Sch.*: to be covetous. — 2. **strength** *Cs.;* **courage, bravery** *W.*, of men and animals. — 3. white film on liquids etc., **mould** *C.*, **hám-ḍi* or *-ri** a musty, fusty smell *C.*, *W.*; **hám-por čág-k̔an** *W.* **mouldy, musty,** **ham-če** *W.* to get mouldy. — 4. **lie,** falsehood, *C.* — *hám-pa-čan* 1. **covetous, avaricious; greedy, voracious.** 2. **courageous;** one *Lex.* explains *rlam-k̔yér* by *hám-pas k̔yér-ba*(?); **hám-pa čúñ-se** *W.* cowardly.

ཧམ་བུར་ *hám-bur W.* rime, hoar-frost?

ཧར་ *har* **suddenly,** *har láñ-ba* to rise suddenly *Mil.*; **har sę' ǰhé'-pa** to rouse suddenly from sleep *C.*; *har-gyis* (*Sch. had-kyis*) more precise form of the adv. *Tar.*

ཧར་རེ་ *hár-re* **empty, open,** *Tar.* 115,16 *Schf.*

ཧལ་པ་ *hál-pa* a porridge, made of milk, butter and honey.

ཧལ་བ་ *hál-ba* **to pant, to wheeze, to snort,** *hal-kyi* a panting dog *Sch.*; **hal-méd** *W.* **weak.**

ཧས་ *has* **exaggeration, hyperbole,** *has-čer smrá-ba Cs*, **hę gyab-če** *W.* **to exaggerate, to talk big, to brag.**

ཧས་པོ་རི་ *hás-po-ri* n. of a mountain in *C.*, *Glr.*

ཧི་ *hi* numeral: 59.

ཧི་དིག་ *hi-dig*, or *hig-dig*, *W.* **zér-če** **to blow one's nose.**

ཧི་མཱ་ལ་ཡ་ *hi-mā-la-ya Ssk.*, = *gañs-čan* the snowy mountains, **Him:laya.**

ཧི་ར་ *hi-ra Ssk.* **diamond.**

ཧི་རི་ *hi-ri* **corn-stack,** **hi-ri gyáb-če** *W.* to pile up a stack of corn.

ཧི་ལིང་ *hi-liñ* **noise,****hi-liñ táñ-k̔an** *W.*, **bully, brawler.**

ཧི་ཧི་ *hi-hi* = *ha-há.*

ཧིའི་ཀ་ *hii ka Sch.* **breast-bone.**

ཧིག, ཧིག་ཀ་ *hig, hig-ka* **the act of sobbing,** **hig táñ-te dug* or *gyáb-te dug** he is sobbing *W.*; **hig ǰáñ* (lit. *sbyañ*) *dug** is said to be an expression used of a Lama, when he is watching the gradual departing of the soul of a dying man.

ཧིང་ *hiñ*, **हिङ्गु**, = *šiñ-kun*, *Asa foetida.*

ཧིན་དུ་སྟཱ་ནི་ *hin-du-stá-ni*, *C.*: **hin-du-tá-ni kę'**, Hindoostanee, the language of the Hindoos.

ཧིས་ *his Pur.*: **hiz yoñ** **he is panting.**

ཧུ་ *hu* 1. *W.* **breath,** **hu gyáb-če** to breathe. — 2. num.: 89.

ཧུ་ཀ་ *hú-ka*, *Ar.* حقه **the hookah**, with an inflexible tube.

ཧུ་ཀམ་ *hu-kám W.*, حکم *Urdu*, **order, command.**

ཧུ་ཁྱུ་ *hu-kyú* the sound of sighing *Pth.*

ཧུ་ན་ *hú-na Cs : Ssk.* (*hū-na*) n. of an ancient people, the Huns (?).

ཧུ་འང་དྷི་ *hu-.aṅ-dhi* (?) *Sch.*: title of the Chinese emperor.

ཧུ་རེ་ *hu-ré*, *mig hu-ré ˳dug* **he stares, he goggles,** with wonder, horror, confusion *Mil.*, *Glr.*; *mig-húr Mṅg.*

ཧུ་ཤར་ *hu-šār* (from the *Hind. hōšyār?*) (grown) **well again,** being again lively, active; **diligent, sedulous** *W.*

ཧུ་ཧུ་ *hu-hú* 1. interj. expressive of pain from cold *Cs.* — 2. 'the sound of one's mouth in eating' *Cs.* — 3. **hu-hú táṅ-če** *W.* **to whistle.**

ཧཱུྃ་ *hūm*, हुम्, हूम्, mystical interjection, e.g. in the prayer of six syllables, v. ཨོཾ་

ཧུན་ *hun W.* (= *ča, lon, ṗrin*) **news,** tidings, intelligence, information, **hun taṅ-če* to give account or notice, to inform, acquaint, let know, **tsar-na hun toṅ** tell me (let me know) as soon as it is finished! **hun tsór-če** to get intelligence, to receive news; **hun ma yoṅ* or *mi duġ** we have no news yet; **disclosure, explanation, opinion, idea,** **či yód-pę hun kyód-la ǰuṅ yin** you shall get an idea of what kind of ... are to be found, **sém-čan tún-čan ži̇g yin-pę hun ṅá-la ǰuṅ** I have got the notion that this is a very quiet animal; **re-reï hun čil-tar šè** whence have you such accurate information of every one of them? **ser-dub ḍil-te hun ma juṅ** he did not perceive it when the ring fell off; **hun-méd-la** **unexpectedly, unawares.**

ཧུབ་ *hub* as much as is swallowed at once, **a gulp, a draught.** *tóg-mar húb re ˳tuṅ ži̇g* at first take only one mouthful, one draught at a time *Glr.*; *hub ṗčig* one mouthful, *hub do* two mouthfuls *Cs.*; *húb-kyis* by draughts *Sch.*; *hub-húb byéd-pa* to drink in large draughts, to gulp.

ཧུར་ *hur* 1. v. *hu-ré*. — 2. *hur-húr* v. *had-had.*

ཧུར་བ་ *húr-ba* **dexterity, cleverness, skilfulness** *C.*, *hur-ṫáġ* id., also **zeal, diligence** *Sch.*; *húr-po* 1. **quick, alert, dexterous, clever.** 2. **hot, hasty, passionate** *Ld.*; *rta húr-po* a fleet, spirited, fine horse *Cs.*

ཧུས་ *hus Cs.* **moisture, humidity,** *hús-čan* wet.

ཧེ་ *he* 1. num.: 119. — 2. interj.: **o! holla!** *Cs.*; *he-he* 1. id. *Cs.* 2. = *ha-há*, *he-hé zer bgád-pas* she laughed: he, he! *Glr.*

ཧེ་ཏུ་ *hé-tu Ssk.* **cause, reason, argument, logic.**

ཧེ་བག་ *he-baġ* **provocation, taunts, sarcasms.**

ཧེ་བཛྲ་ *Ssk. he-wajra*, ཀྱེ་རྡོ་རྗེ་ *Tibet. kye-rdo-rje Cs.*: n. of a god; n. of a series of treatises.

ཧེ་རུ་ཀ་ *hé-ru-ka* **terrifying deities,** also *krag-˳ṫuṅ*, *Thgr.* frq., *hé-ru-kai rgyud* legends of wrathful deities.

ཧེག་པོ་ *hég-po* having become **putrid, rancid.**

ཧེལ་གེ་ *hél-ge Sch.*: **soft leather, wash-leather.**

ཧེལ་པོ་ *hél-po*, *hél-čan*, **hel-hél** *W.* **wide, extended**; of garments: **wide, easy**; *hél-ba* id. and sbst.: **width** *Sch.*

ཧོ་ *ho* num.: 149.

ཧོ་མ་ *hó-ma Ssk.* prop.: **burnt-offering** of butter; = *sbyin-srég* v. *Was.* (194); *Schl.* 251; *hó-ma byéd-pa* **to sacrifice;** *hom-kuṅ* a small pit or a triangular box used as an altar for such an offering.

ཧོ་ཧོ་ *ho-hó* interj. of admiration *Cs.*

ཧོང་ལེན་ *hoṅ-lén* a medicinal herb, *Picrorrhiza*, frequently to be found on the mountains, *Hook.* I., 272.

ཧོན་ཧོན་ *hon-hón* **stupid, foolish** *Cs.*

ཧོབ་པ་ *hób-pa*, *W.*: **hób-te duġ** it has got **bent in** or **battered,** of tin ware.

ཧོམ་ *hom* (Mongol word?) a pad, placed under a camel's load.

ཧོམ་པ་ *hóm-pa W.* **to fall away,** to lose flesh, e.g. of hollow cheeks, **to shrink, to shrivel,** of withered fruit.

ཧོར་ *hor* 1. formerly: **a Mongol** *ḥor ǰiṅ-gin-ḱan* the Mongol Djingiskhan; *hor-sér Shara Sharaighol* n. of a Mongol tribe *Glr.*; *hór-yul Mongolia.* — 2. at present: in *C.* the people living near the *Tengri-nor* (*ɣnam-mtso*); in *W.* the Turks; *hór-zla* a Turkish month.

Note. *Cs.* has only the second of these significations, *Sch.* only the first (the latter using *Cs.*'s examples and changing all the Turks into Mongols!) The suppositions of Latham seem still less consistent with the real state of the case.

ཧོར་ཁོངས་ *hor-ḱoṅs Sch.:* deficiencies, gaps; separation' (?).

ཧོར་འདྲ་ *hór-ḥdra Sch.:* 'confiscation, *hór-ḥdra bábs-pa* to confiscate' (?).

ཧོར་པ་ *hór-pa* **wood-grouse** or cock of the wood *Sch.*, *hór-pa dkár-po* a species of hawk *Sch.* (?).

ཧོལ་ཧོལ་ *hol-hól W.* **soft, loose, light,** as the soil in spring, **hol táṅ-ce, hól-te bór-ce** to break up, to loosen (the soil).

ཧྲག་པ་ *hrág-pa* 1. vb., **to require more and more,** to covet incessantly *Ma., W.* — 2. sbst., adj. **hardness, hard** *Cs.*

ཧྲང་བ་ *hráṅ-ba* 1. **alone,** cf. *raṅ*, **šraṅ-šráṅ-la yoṅ soṅ** I came alone *C.*, *p̓o-hráṅ, mo-hráṅ* single man and woman, = *p̓o-ráṅ* etc. *C.* — 2. with *dmar* preceding, **naked** *C.*

ཧྲད་པ་ *hrád-pa* 1. **to thrust, to push violently, to stem** firmly, **káṅ-pa sig-pa-la* W.* to stem the foot against the wall. — 2. **to scratch,** *sgó-la p̓yag-hrád-pa ḥga mdzád-pa* (his Reverence) made several scratchings with his hand, scratched several times, at the door *Mil.* — 3. **to exert one's self,** to make every effort *W.*, **šrád-čan zúm-ce** or *táṅ-ce** id. *W.*

ཧྲབ་ཧྲིབ་ *hrab-hrib C.* **šrab-ba-šrib-be* Ld.*, v. *rab-rib.*

ཧྲལ་བ་ *hrál-ba* **to rend, tear up, tear to pieces** e.g. of a beast of prey: to tear up a person's body; **šral soṅ** he has torn it to pieces *C., W*, *hral-hrál Lex.*

ཧྲི་ *hri Cs.:* '*Ssk.* essence, substance; a mystical word'.

ཧྲིག་ *hrig W.* **šrig-la táṅ-ce, šríg-ga táṅ-ce** **to hang** (a thief), **šrig-la ši-ce** to hang one's self.

ཧྲིག་པ་ *hrig-pa Cs.*, *mig* (or resp. *spyaṅ*) *hrig-hrig byéd-pa* or *ḥdúg-pa*, (= *rig-rig*), to look this way and that, hither and thither *Mil. nt.*; *hrig-ge-ba* looking in that manner *Thgr.*

ཧྲིད་ *hrid; S.g.*; *rná-ba hrid ḥbyar* is explained by *Wdṅ.*: *rná-ba lhág-pa p̓yógs-su byar* the ear leans feebly on the neck, as a sign of death.

ཧྲིལ་པོ་ *hril-po* 1. **round, globular,** *hril-hril byéd-pa* to writhe with pain, *hril-hril kar-kár byéd-pa* to be writhing, and then again stretching one's self or starting up *Pth.* — 2. **whole,** *ṫse hril-por* for the whole life *Glr.*, *mgo hril-gyis ɣtúm-nas* wrapping up his whole head *Glr.* — 3. **close, dense,** *hril ḥdús-te ḥdúg-pa* to sit or stand close together in rows *Mil., C., W.* Cf. *ril-ba.*

ཧྲུད་པ་ *hrúd-pa* adj. and abstract noun, **rough, rugged; severe, austere; roughness** etc.; *hrúd-po* adj. id. *Cs.*

ཧྲུམ་པ་ *hrúm-pa* **to break, to smash** *Sch.*

ཧྲུལ་བ་ *hrúl-ba* adj. and abstr. sbst. **ragged, tattered; raggedness,** *hrul-bai dug-po* a ragged coat *Mil.*; *hrúl-po* id., *gos hrúl-po Dzl.* and elsewh. frq. — 2. sbst.: **rags, tatters,** *gós-su hrúl-po gyón-pa* to put on rags for a garment *Pth.*; *hrúl-ḱaṅ* a ruin, **ruins** *Sch.*

ཧྲེམ་པ་ *hrém-pa* **swollen** *Sch.*, *hrem-mé* id. *Mṅg.*

ལྷ་ *lha*, *Ssk.* देव, 1. the first class of beings subject to metempsychosis, **the gods,** both those of Brahminical mythology, and the various national and local gods, with whom Buddhism came in contact. These local gods were incorporated into the system of Buddhism, when they were found to be too numerous and too much endeared to the people, to be entirely discarded and given up; so, most of them are worshipped even nowadays and presented with various offerings. They are also supposed to enjoy a blissful existence (hence: *dé-riṅ lhá-yi nyi-ma šar* 'this day was a day of happiness to me' *Glr.*, and similar expressions are of frq. occurrence; v. also *lha-yul*) and to be possessed of qualities and capacities superior to those of ordinary human beings. Nevertheless, when compared with any Buddhist saint, they are considered to be of inferior rank and power; and a local '*lha*' can never attain to Buddhaship, without having previously assumed the nature of man; v. *Köpp.* I, 122. 248. II, 296. *lhai bu* or *sras, bú-mo* or *srás-mo* descendant from the gods, son or daughter of the gods *Dzl.* and elsewh.; *lha mi ťób-pa* to obtain the birth as a god or as man *Thgy.*; *lhai yi-ge* the Lantsa-letters, v. *lan-tsa*; *lha ˳báb-pa* the (mystical) entering of a deity into a human being, **inspiration**, so that the person inspired pronounces the oracles of the god, *lha žúgs-pa* id. pop.; also: the person thus inspired; *lha ni ǩyab-˳ǰúg-la mos* as for gods, they worshipped Vishnu *Pth.*, *lha má-mo-la byed* they worshipped the Mamo as a '*lha*' *Pth.*; *lhai dbáṅ-po, lha-bdág,* = *brgya-byin* Indra; in another sense: *lhai rgyál-po byéd-pa* to make the gods subject to one's self, (said to be the blessed consequence of a certain charm) *Do.*; the following gods are occasionally mentioned: *nám-mkai lha* the deity of heaven *Tar.*; that of the sea *Dzl.*; the gods of trees, of houses etc.; *dgrá-lha* and *ṗó-lha* are two personal gods of every human individual, the one being the god of the right side, the other of the left side of his body *Glr.*, *Mil.*; *yi-dam-lha* v. *yi-dam*. — 2. **the image of a god**, in as much as it is really thought to be inhabited by a deity, after having been duly inaugurated (*ráb-tu gnás-pa*) *Glr.*; the local '*lha*' are not always represented by figures resembling human beings, but even by sticks, stones and similar fetishes; gods also of non-Buddhist nations are called '*lha*' and are acknowledged as such. — 3. fig.: *mii lha* **a king** *Mil.*, and hence '*lha*' is often used in addressing a king, like the French *Sire! lha-rgyal-yab-yúm* the royal father and mother *Pth.*; *lhá-yi lha* the lord of lords, the supreme being, **Buddha** *Cs.*

Comp. *lha-ǩáṅ* **an idol-shrine.** — *lha-gčig* 1. dear Sir! dear Lord and King! *Pth.* 2. **princess** *Glr.* — *lha-lčám* **a princess** *Pth.* — *lha-čén* a great and mighty deity. — *lhá-čos* v. *čos* no. 2. — *lhá-rje* **physician** *Wdṅ.* — *lha-rtén* **image** or temple of a god or of the gods. — *lha-ťó* (prob. for *lhai ťo-yór*) **heaps of stones,** erected on mountain passes or on the tops of mountains. — *lha-˳dre* gods and goblins, *lha klu ˳dre srin gdúg-pa maṅ Glr.* 2. **goblin, hobgoblin;** **lhá-˳dre-ber-ka** mullein (Verbascum) *Lh.*; **lán-de non soṅ** *W.* I have had the night-mare. — *lhá-sde, mi-sde* the class of the gods, the class of men. — *lha-nád Sch.*: **hysterics; madness.** — *lha-ṗyág* honours shown to the '*lha*', worship paid to them, *ṗyogs bžir lha-ṗyág mán-po btsál-te* bowing towards the four points of the compass in token of reverence to the '*lha*' *Pth.*, often only: **compliments, kind regards,** offered to respected persons, in letters. — *lha-ṗyi* n. of a mountain in the south of Tibet *Mil.* — *lha-ṗrúg* a descendant from the gods, child of the gods; as a mask *Schl.* 235. — *lha-ṗrán* inferior deities. — *lha-bris-mǩan* or *-pa* a painter of gods. — *lha-˳báṅs Tar.*; *Schf.*: **slaves** (doing service) **in temples.** — *lha-ma-yin, lha-min,* असुर, one of the six classes of beings, living on the slopes of the Sumeru below the '*lha*' against whom, like Titans, they are continually fighting; also *lha-ma-yin-mo* are mentioned. — *lha-ma-srin* gods, Asuras and Rakshasas, or perh. also: *lha-ma-srin sde brgyad* the eight classes of the gods, Asuras, Rākshasas etc., i.e. the whole world of spirits. — *lhá-mo* **goddess.** — *lha-ma-rtá Sch.*: a certain insect. — *lhá-bzo* 1. the art of making images of gods *Pth.* 2. also *lha-bzó-bo* a framer of gods *Glr.* — *lhá-yul* 1. the region of the world where the gods reside, the heaven, seat or abode of the gods. 2. fig.: a blessed country, a paradise. — *lhá-sa* (in early times *lha-ldán*) *Sch.*, *Köpp.* II, 332, n. of the capital of Tibet. — *lha-srin* gods and Rakshasas; *steṅ lha-*

srin. ˛og klu-γnyán, bar γži-bdág, are often mentioned in connexion. — lha-sríṅ **tutelar god**, bód-kyi Glr.

ལྷ་ང་ lha-ṅá **knee-pan**, pús-mo γyás-pai lha-ṅá sá-la ˳dzúg-pa to kneel down on the right knee frq.; lha-k̔úṅ the bend of the knee W.

ལྷ་བ་ lhá-ba Med. and Pth., acc. to Wdṅ. also klad-rgyás, Sch.: 'the bloody marrow in the bones; whilst he translates rmai lhá-ba by: 'the growing worse of a wound'.

ལྷ་རུ་ lha-rú Med.; Sch. **cartilage** (cf. lha-gór sub lkóg-ma).

ལྷག་ lhag 1. **more, beyond,** *dá-wa čig lag soṅ* more than a month has passed W., *nyi-ma-p̔yèd lag soṅ* W. it is already past noon, rgyá-mtso-bas kyaṅ lhág-ste as this alone would be more than the whole sea Dzl.; nyi-šus lhag more by twenty S.g. — 2. = lhág-ma. — lhág-pa 1. adj. **surpassing, excelling, superior,** ˳di-las lhág-pai γžan čos med Dzl.; nyam-t̔ág-pa ṅá-las lhág-pa yód-dam is there any one that is thinner than I? Dzl.; dé-rnams-kyi náṅ-nas lhág-pa the best amongst these Glr.; rgya hor γnyís-las lhág-pa ṅed bod yin we Tibetans surpass the Chinese and Mongols (in sagacity) Glr. 2. rarely = lhág-ma: dé-las lhág-pa the others, the remaining S.g. 6, 1. de-lhag **besides, moreover.** — lhág-par adv. **more** (magis) frq., mostly with adj., but also with verbs, šin-tu lhág-par **far more; very, exceedingly, uncommonly,** lhág-par légs-pa uncommonly beautiful Dzl.; čes lhág-par **extremely**, excessively Stg.; **further**, furthermore, moreover. — lhág-ge-ba = lhag-pa, lhág-ge mdzád-nas making it project. — lhág-ma 1. **remains, scrapings,** sṅar bšad-pai lhág-ma (the letters) which at the last discussion remained, were left, (unexplained) Gram.; lha lhág-ma-rnams the other, the remaining gods Stg.; **the remainder,** in subtracting Wdk. — 2. **razor-stone, razor-strap** Sch. — 3. being above, being at the upper part of, groṅ the place lying higher up (the valley), opp. to ˛óg-ma Dzl.

Comp. lhag-bčas 1. having **more than** so and so much, bhā-ra-ta šlo-ka ˳bum lhag-bčas the Bharata of more than 100,000 verses Tar. 2. the gerund in te (ste etc.) Gram. — lhag-mt̔óṅ 'seeing more' (than other mortals), in certain states of contemplation v. ži-γnas sub ži.

ལྷག་གིས་ lhág-gis = lhaṅ-ṅer, lhag-gis ˳čar Thgr., ˳byuṅ Mil. he shines bright, lhág-ge-ba = lhaṅ-ṅe-ba Mil.

ལྷག་པ་ lhág-pa I. sbst., also γza lhág-pa 1. **Mercury.** 2. **Wednesday.** — II. adj. **more excellent**, v. lhag.

ལྷག(ས)་པ་ lhag(s)-pa I. sbst. **cold wind,** lág-pa p̔og the cold wind has withered them (the flowers) W.; lo-γsár lhágs-pa the cold new year's wind Mil. — II. vb., **to come together**, to meet, to assemble, with other persons; perh. also: to join, to be adjacent or contiguous, of houses, beams etc.

ལྷང་ངེ་ lhaṅ-ṅe, lhan-ne, lham-me, also lhag-ge, lam-me, lham-pa **clear, distinct,** to the sight as well as to the ear; lhaṅ-ṅe lham-mer γsal-te (Buddha) appearing clearly and distinctly Dzl., in a similar sense: lham-me lhaṅ-ṅe lhan-ner bžúgs-so Pth.; clear, sonorous; k̔yi-skad lhaṅ-lhaṅ-pa Mil. the clear (loud) barking of dogs; k̔yod lhaṅ-lhaṅ glú-len-pa Mil thou clear-voiced songster; lhaṅ-lháṅ brǰód-la speaking with a clear, sonorous voice. — Cs. has: **majestic, glorious, sublime, august.**

ལྷད་ lhad a baser substance mixed with a finer one, an **alloy,** lhad ˳ǰúg-pa or sré-ba with la, lhád-kyis slád-pa with accus. Mil., **to alloy, adulterate,** lhád-čan **adulterated,** e.g. milk C., lhad-méd **unadulterated, pure, genuine, real**; *tsig hlę̀ šor* C. or *žug soṅ* W. spurious words are admixed, falsehoods have been artfully introduced; p̔yis lhád-du bčúg-pai tsig Tar. a later interpolation. — 2. Bal., *γlad*, **fatigued, exhausted.**

ལྷན་ lhan **together,** lhán-gyis (when referring to the subject of the action), lhán-nas (as ablative case), lhán-du (the most frq. form) **with one another, together,** lhan-γčig (-tu), and often lhan-čig(-tu) id.:-bdag dan lhan-γčig zan mi zá-na if you will not eat together with me Dzl., rta bčus lhán-du rgyúgs-pa ltá-bui sgra a noise as if ten horses were trotting together *Glr.*; *rtá-pa brgya dan lhán-du* accompanied by a hundred men on horseback *Glr.*; *lhan(-čig)-skyes(-pa)* **born together with**, e.g. the '*lha*' or '*ₒdre*' born together with every human being *Mil.*; *lhan-skyes nad, rma* a hereditary disease or defect *Med.* *lhan-rgyás* 1. 'partner of the seal', i.e. a colleague using the same seal in official business (*lhan-rgyás-kyi té-tse*, or *spyi-dám*). 2. = *lhan-γčig*, **hlen-gyé-la tsog* or *žug** they have come together.

ལྷན་པ་ *lhán-pa* I. vb., **to join, to unite**, **ka lán-če** *W.* **to kiss**, **'u lán-če** id. resp.

II. sbst. 1. **a patch**, *lhán-pas klán-pa B.*, **hlém-pa gyág-pa** *C.*, **gyáb-če** *W.*, *ₒdébs-pa, rdáb-pa Mil.* **to patch, mend.** — 2. **spot, speck, blot**, place differently coloured, *ₒod-zér šár-čin lhán-pa bžin-du* a sunbeam forming by reflection a bright spot *Dzl.*; *lhan-tábs* **appendix, supplement**, title of a medical book.

ལྷབ་ལྷབ་པ་ *lhab-lháb-pa, lhabs-se lhabs Sch.*: 'to flutter to and fro, to glimmer, glisten' (?).

ལྷབ་ལྷུབ་ *lhab-lhúb* **wide, flowing**, *dar-bér lhab-lhúb* a wide silk cloak; prob. also sbst.: the moving to and fro, waving, *mé-tog-gi* of flowers *Do.*, **hlab-hlúb-tu sol** *C.* loosen your dress! make yourself comfortable!

ལྷམ་ *lham* **boot**, also **shoe**; *mčil-lham* id.; *rgyá-lham* a Chinese boot, *sóg-lham* a Mongol boot.

Comp. *lham-skúd* twine, used by shoemakers *Schr.* — *lham-kan-čén* (prob. a Chinese word) strong Chinese boots *C.* — *lhám-mkan* shoemaker *Schr.* — *lham-sgróg* shoe-strap, latchet; string for lacing felt-leggings. — *lham-mtil* boot-sole. — *lham-yú* leg of a boot *Cs.*, *lham yu-rin* boots with long legs *Sch.* — *Sch.*: *lham-krád* or *-skrád* pieces of leather, used for the patching of soles; *lham-góg* worn-out boots; *lham-ₒgrám* the upper-leather, the vamp; *lham sgró-gu-čan* buskins; *lham yu-čád* a sort of slippers to which cotton leggings are sewed (?); *rtín-lham* quarter-piece (of a shoe).

ལྷམས་ཀྱིས་ *lháms-kyis* at once, all, every thing *Sch.* Cf. *lhem.*

ལྷས་(མ་) *lhas(-ma)* 1. **pen, fold**, inclosure for sheep *C.*, *W.*; also **hlé-ra**. 2. also *lhés(-ma)* **braid**; **wicker-work**; **texture**; also of pastry, **twisted cake** or **bun, cracknel** (*W.* **žim-zag**), also *lhas-dóg.*

ལྷས་བསྟན་ *lhas-bstán* n. of the birth-place of the mother of Buddha, *Ssk.* देवदर्शित.

ལྷས་པ་ *lhás-pa* v. under *slé-ba.*

ལྷས་བྱིན་ *lhas-byín*, देवदत्त, n. of a cousin of Buddha who, as the legends have it, was continually annoying Buddha by malicious artifices, whereby, however, the blameless character of the latter showed itself but the more conspicuously; hence proverbially used for any malicious character *Cs.*

ལྷིང་ *lhin*, cf. *lins-pa*; *lhin-skrán Sch.*: a tumor filled with matter, **an abscess**, *lhín-rtsa* a full vein; *lhin čád-pa Lt.*, acc. to *Sch.*: completely separated.

ལྷུ་ *lhu* **part, portion** of the body of an animal, = ⅓ *zug*, *lhu-tsigs bču-γnyís Sch.*: the 12 chief parts (of an animal) resulting from this way of dividing it, — but elsewhere 18 such parts are mentioned; *lhú-ru γsíl-ba* to divide, to parcel out *Mil.*; **share** in plough-land, v. sub *spyod-pa* I, 2.

ལྷུག་ *lhug* v. *ldúg-pa* to pour *Cs.*

ལྷུག་པ་ *lhúg-pa, Cs.*: '*lhug-pa* and *lhug-ma* **prose**; *lhug-po* **wide, diffuse, luxurious**, *gos lhug-lhug-po* a very ample robe; *lhug-par* **amply, copiously, plentifully**; *lhug-par smra-ba* to speak diffusely, copiously, to speak in prose'. *Sch.* adds: '*lhugs* successive, continuous; *lhugs-tsig* and *lhug-pa* continuous prose'. The principal meaning, however, seems to be: **uninterrupted, having no gaps**; unreserved; *lhúg-par bšád-pa* = *spas-γsán-med-par bšád-pa* to explain completely, without omitting any thing, **lug tán-če** *Ld.* to give unreservedly, without limitation; hence also: liberally, plentifully; *mči-ma* *lhúg-par śor* or *byuṅ Mil.*, tears were flowing abundantly. — In some other passages the meaning of *lhúg-pa* is not quite clear.

ལྷུང་བ་ *lhúṅ-ba*, pf. of *ltúṅ-ba; lhuṅ lhuṅ snyán-pai sgra sgróg-ċiṅ ₒbáb-bo* sweetly murmuring (the gentle stream) descends *Mil.*

ལྷུང་བཟེད་ *lhuṅ-bzéd*, *Ssk.* पिण्डपात्र, **the alms-bowl** of Buddha and of the mendicant friars.

ལྷུན་ *lhun* **mass, bulk,** *lhún-ċan* **massy, bulky; well-fed,** **lun-ťúg-po* W.*, *lhun-čé-ba* very large; *lhun-(gyis) grub(-pa)* acc. to *Cs.*: 'formed in mass, or all at once', self-created, not contrived by human labour; *bgó-ba daṅ bzá-ba lhún-gyis grúb-pas* clothes and food coming forth of themselves *Dzl.*; also used of palaces, sacred buildings, images, though in such instances often only by way of compliment; *lhun-grúb* is also noun personal. — *lhún-po, ri-rab-lhún-po* the mountain of the universe, **Meru, Sumeru,** frq. *lhun-stúg Sch., lhun-ťúg Thgy.* very great, in reference to the mental darkness produced by sin; prob. also: considerable, sublime, grand.

ལྷུབ་པ་ *lhúb-pa* 1. sbst. **width,** *lhúb-pa-ċan Cs., yan(s)-hlúb, hlub-hlúb W., C.* **wide,** of clothes. — 2. vb.: **to bind, tie, fasten,** e.g. ornaments to the ear *Ts.*, = *klúb-pa.*

ལྷུམས་ *lhums*, resp. for *mṅal* **the womb** frq., *lhúms-su žúgs-pai dus-mčód* sacrificial festival of the conception (of Buddha) *Sch.*

ལྷུར་ *lhur*, with *lén-pa* or *byéd-pa* c. acc. **to apply one's self to, bestow pains upon,** = *don-γnyér byéd-pa Dzl.* and elsewh.

ལྷེ་བ་ *lhé-ba* v. *slé-ba.*

ལྷེན་ *lhen Cs.* 'filth or dross in the bowels, causing obstruction'; acc. to others: internal excrescences, v. *skran*; *Sch.: lhen* or *lhen-snά* pit of the heart.

ལྷེབ་ *lheb*, *dbugs lheb-lheb-tu ₒdug-pa Pth.* **'ug leb leb ǰhed-de* C.* gasping for breath.

ལྷེམ་ *lhem* **now, at present, directly, instantly** *C.*; **all** (of them) cf. *lhams.*

ལྷེས་མ་ *lhés-ma* = *lhás-ma* 2; also: the act of twisting, plaiting, **hlé-ma gyáb-pa* C.* to twist, **to plait.**

ལྷོ་ *lho* **south,** *lho-núb* south-west, *śar-lhó* south-east; *lhor, lho-p̓yógs-su* to the south, towards the south; *lhó-k̓a* prob. = *lho*; *lhó-k̓a món-nas ₒoṅs Mil.* they came from the Mon in the south; *lhó-pa, lho-ₒbrúg-pa* an inhabitant of Bhotan; *lhó-yul* acc. to *Cunn.* the original form of the name of that province which is now called Lāhul or Lāhōl by the Hindoos, and Lahoul by the English; *lho-búr Sch.* (also *lho-ₒú-ma*), = *k̓ug-rna.*

ལྷོག་པ་ *lhóg-pa, glóg-pa Cs.* **a large ulcer** or **sore,** *Sch.*: **carbuncle, anthrax,** *sbyóṅ-ba* to cure it; in *Med.* also *nya-lhóg* and *gag-lhóg* are mentioned. According to the description, however, which Tibetan physicians gave us of the *lhóg-pa*, it seems to denote a cancerous ulcer, against which they employ the *Aconitum ferox* of Nepal, or in default of it some other species of aconite.

ལྷོང་ *lhoṅ Sch.* vexation, anger, wrath(?); but: '*lhoṅ śor* he has lost the *lhoṅ*', is said of one who was not equal to the exertions of incessant meditation, and who in consequence has lost his senses, v. sub *smyón-pa.*

ལྷོད་པ་ *lhód-pa, glod-pa, lod-pa* or *-po, lhod, lhód-po* 1. **loose, relaxed, unstrung, slackened,** *yan-lág* of the limbs, e.g. when death approaches *S.g.*, **zúg-po lód-po čá-na* W.* when one gets tired (one cannot help yawning). *lhód-pa sgrím-pa* to tighten what is loose, *lhod lhod γtóṅ-ba* to slacken; fig. **'ó-ma lód-po* W.* the milk begins to fail, milk is scarce. — 2. of the mind: **easy, careless, unconcerned,** *lhód-de nyol ċig* sleep well! sleep soundly! *Glr.*; *blo lhod gyis-la śod* relate the matter calmly, coolly *Mil.*; *śes-pa lhod-ċiṅ* in good spirits, of a cheerful temper *Pth.*; *ťabs śig yod-kyi rgyal-po ťugs lhod mdzod* there is yet a help; therefore, o king, be of good cheer! *Pth.*

ལྷོན་པ་ *lhón-pa, glón-pa* **to return, to give** or **pay back** *Cs.*

ཨ

ཨ *a*, 1. the consonant which is formed in the lowest and hindmost part of the organs of speech, being produced by the opening of the glottis, like the Greek spiritus lenis, the Hebrew Aleph and the Arabian Elif. (In our modern languages the opening of the glottis is not regarded as a consonant, nor expressed by a particular letter or sign.). Combined with the Tibetan vowel-signs, ཨ, ཨི, ཨུ, ཨེ, ཨོ, it is pronounced *'a*, *'i*, *'u*, *'e*, *'o* (cf. འ). It is also called *skye-ba-méd-pai yi-ge*, probably because all speaking depends on and is rendered possible only by a previous opening of the glottis; hence this letter is a symbol of the deity, of the *č'ós-sku* that was before every thing else. *Spyan-ras-zig*, therefore, addresses a celestial Buddha with *'a: 'a skye-méd rnam-dág č'ós-kyi dbyiṅs*. — 2. num.: 30.

ཨ་(འ་?) *'a* (*ₒa?*) 1. in *Ld.* and *Kh.* the col. demonstr. pron, for *de* that (q.v.); *'*á-ng** from thence, there, *'á-ru* there, thither, that way. — 2. *Lh.*, pronounced very short and sharp, **well? what is the matter? yes! here!**

ཨཿ *'a Cs.: 'Ssk.:* अः, a mystical exclamation'.

ཨ་ཀ་(ཨ་ཁ་?) *'á-ka* (*'á-k'a?*) acc.to *Huc* II, 160 = *'á-jo Kh.*

ཨ་ཀ་རུ་ *'á-ka-ru Cs.*, v. *'á-ga-ru*.

ཨ་ཀཱ་ལ་ *'a-kā-la Lt., Ssk.:* **untimely.**

ཨ་ཀྲོང་ *'a-kroṅ* an alpine plant, in *Lh. Arenaria Roylea.*

ཨ་ཁ་ཁ་, ཨ་ཁག *'á-k'a-k'a*, *'a-k'ág* an exclamation expressive of contempt and detestation, opp. to *'á-la-la;* acc. to *Cs. 'a-k'ag* is also adj. = *mi-sdug-pa.*

ཨ་ཁུ་ *'a-k'ú*, *W.* also *'a-kú*, col. for *k'ú-bo* 1. **father's brother, uncle** *Mil., C., W.* — 2. **husband, consort** *W.*

ཨ་ག་རུ་ *'á-ga-ru*, **अगरु**, **aloe-wood**, agallochum, calambac.

ཨ་གྱིས་ *'a-gyis* caressing word used by mothers soothing their babies, prob. without any particular signification *Thgy.*

ཨ་ཅུག *'a-čúg* **ankle-bone** *Lt.*

ཨ་ཆུ་, ཨ་ཆུ་ཆུ་ *'a-č'ú*, *'á-č'u-č'u* interj. expressive of pain from cold, hence *'a-č'ú-zer-ba* n. of one of the cold hells.

ཨ་ཆེ་ *'a-č'é*, *'a-čé*, *Bal. 'a-šé*, col. for *čé-že* 1. **an elder sister** of a female person. — 2. *W.* **wife, mistress, madam,** used as address and otherwise.

ཨ་ཇོ་ *'a-jó C., W., jo-jó C.* (v. *jó-bo*) 1. **an elder brother** of a male person. — 2. **Sir, Mr., gentleman, lord,** used in addressing and otherwise; also like our: **friend!** ho there! hollo! I say! *'a-jho lág C.* **the old Squire,** = *ga-gá Ld.*

ཨ་ཏི་ཤ་ *'a-ti-ša Ssk.*, *p'ul-du-byuṅ-ba Tib.*, n. of a celebrated Pandit of Bengal, who lived for many years in Tibet, and died there in the eleventh century of our era.

ཨ་ཐོ་བ་ *'a-t'ó-ba* beautiful, good *Sch* (?).

ཨ་འཐས་ *'a-ₒt'as Pth.?*

ཨ་དོགས་ *'a-dogs Sch.* table(?)

ཨ་དོན་ *'a-dón Sch.:* 'without sexual distinction; sense of the letter *'a*'.

ཨ་དྲུང་ *'a-drúṅ C.* **horse-boy,** one tending horses.

ཨ་ན་(ན་) *'á-na(-na)* an interjection expressive of grief *Sch.*

ཨ་ན་མ་ན་ *'a-na-ma-na Sch.:* having a striking likeness(?).

ཨ་ནུ་ *'á-nu* Hindi man's name, also used in Tibet *Glr.*

ཨ་ནེ་ *'á-ne* 1. = *né-ne-mo* **father's sister, aunt; grand-aunt** *Glr.* — 2. *Cs.:* **nun.**

3. *W.* **wife, partner, spouse,** *'*á-ne kúr-ce*' to take a wife, to marry, *(s)kyá-wo 'á-ne kur čog* a layman is at liberty to marry; *'á-ne-la čó-ce* to treat, to use as a wife, sensu obsc. = to sleep with. — 4. **a woman, a female.** — 5. *Sch.* an old woman (?).

ཨ་པ་ *'á-pa = 'á-p̔a.*

ཨ་པོ་ *'a-po Ü:* **building** (= *k̔ar-lén* *W.*), *'á-po gyáb-pa* to construct a house, to build.

ཨ་པྲ་ *'á-pra Sch.* **zizel**, earless marmot, souslik (*Spermophilus citillus*).

ཨ་ཕ་ *'á-p̔a, 'á-pa* col. for *p̔a*, in *B.* of rare occurrence; *'á-pa čén-po* the elder, *čún-nu* the younger, of the husbands of a person's mother, hence occasionally = **uncle;** *'á-pe̥ ša* *W.* a vulgar oath; also (like *p̔a*) uncastrated male animal, cf. *p̔a.*

ཨ་ཕོ་ང་ *'a-p̔o-ná C.* col.: **I**, cf. *k̔o-bo-ná.*

ཨ་ཕྱི་ *'a-p̔yi Mil.*, *'a-p̔i, 'a-pi*, for *p̔yi-mo* **grandmother.**

ཨ་ཕྱིམ་ *'a-p̔yim* **old woman, goody, dame** *Sch.*

ཨ་ཕྲག་ *'a-p̔rág Sch.:* the bosom of a garment, *'a-p̔rág-tu sdú-ba* to put into the bosom, = *'am-bág.*

ཨ་ཝ་དྷུ་ཏི་ *'a-wa-dhu-ti* v. *dhu-ti.*

ཨ་བང་ *'a-bań,* for *bań-po,* the husband of the father's or the mother's sister *Cs.*

ཨ་བི་ཥ་ *'a-bi-ṣa Ssk.:* 'antivenomous', n. of a medicinal herb *Wdň.*

ཨ་བོ་ *'a-bo* 1. *Sch.* = *'a-j̔o.* — 2. a medicine *S.g.*

ཨ་བོ་ཙེ་ *'a-bo-tse Sch.:* **'good, tolerable, middling'**, cf. *Bun.: eb-bo* good.

ཨ་བྱག་ *'a-byag* and *'a-̥bras* names of medicines *Med.*

ཨ་མ་ *'á-ma* col. and sometimes in *B.* = *ma* **mother;** *'á-me̥ ša* a vulgar oath; *'á-ma drin-čén* so a king addresses a wonder-working nun *Pth.*

ཨ་མ་གྱིས་ *'a-ma-gyis Cs.* interj., prob. similar to *a-gyis.*

ཨ་མི་དེ་བ་ *'a-mi-de-ba* the usual Tibetan corruption of **अमिताभ**, v. *̥od-dpag-méd.*

ཨ་མྲ་ *'á-mra Ssk.* **the mango tree** and **-fruit** *Dzl.*

ཨ་མྲི་ཏ་ *'a-mri-ta* (*Ssk.* **अमृत ambrosia;** also various fruits etc.), in the *Lt.* perh. the **guava** fruit, which in Hindoostani is now called *amrūt.*

ཨ་ཙ་(མ་) *'a-tsa(-ma)* interj. expressive of pain by touching hot objects *Sch.*; also used in various other instances, when disagreeably surprised, startled etc. *bdag ma gról-ba ̥di 'á-tsa-ma* alas! I am not yet released! *Thgr.*; *'á-tsa-ma yi-dwags snyiṅ re-r̔jé* alas! ye poor Yidags folk! *Mil.*

ཨ་ཙ་ར་ *'a-tsa-ra Mil.* a species of hobgoblins, or spectres; in *C.* a Bengalee, acc. to *Lew.* The observations of *Huc* (II, 271) concerning this word seem to be mixed with some errors.

ཨ་ཙརྱ་ *'a-tsarya, Ssk.* **आचार्य, spiritual guide** or **father, instructor, professor, doctor.**

ཨ་ཚ་(ཚ་) *'a-ts̔a(-ts̔a)* an interj. expressing discomfort occasioned by heat.

ཨ་མཚར་ *'a-mts̔ar Sch.:* oh dear, what a wonder!

ཨ་ཛ་ན་ *'á-dza-na Wdň., 'á-dzi-na Stg.,* **अजिन** *Will.:* the hairy skin of a black antelope, which serves the religious student for a couch, seat, covering etc.; Tibetan writers use it for the animal itself: *ri-dwags 'á-dzi-nai págs-pa Stg.*

ཨ་ཞང་ *'a-žáń* 1. col. for *žáń-po* **mother's brother,** *'a-žań-ts̔á-wo* **nephew.** — 2. *Cs.:* 'an address' (?).

ཨ་ཝ་ *'á-wa* a medicinal herb *S.g.?*

ཨ་བརྟ་ *'ā-warta, 'ā-barta(-na) Ssk.* ('whirl, whirlpool, eddy') a disease of the *rluṅ,* q.v.; perh. **dizziness?** *Med.*

ཨའུ་ཙི་ *'au-tsi* 1. *Sch.:* it is of no consequence, it does not matter. — 2. n. of a plant = *bya-po-tsi-tsi.*

ཨ་ཡ་ཟྭ་ཚོད་ *'a-ya-zwa-ts̔ód* dead-nettle *Med.*

ཨ་ཡུ་ *'a-yu C.* (= *k̔u-yu*) **hornless,** of cattle.

ཨ་ར་ *'á-ra* **beard** *Ts.*

ཨ་ར་ 'ā-rā *Hind.* **a saw.**

ཨ་ར་པ་ཙ་ན་ *'a-ra-pa-tsa-na* a mystical and symbolical word, *Was.* (183)

ཨ་རག་ *'a-rág*, resp. *bšes-rág C.*, *ₒdon-rág W.*, **arrack, brandy,** the usual barley-brandy, which is distilled in the convents and in nearly every manor-house.

ཨ་རུ་ *'á-ru* 1. prob. *Ssk.* a medicinal plant, *Med.* — 2. v. *'a.*

ཨ་རུ་ར་ *'á-ru-ra* **myrobalan,** an astringent medicinal fruit *Med.* frq.

ཨ་རུམ་ *'a-rum* a species of garlic, with a pale-red blossom, *Allium strictum.*

ཨ་རེ་ *'a-re* an interj. the meaning of which is stated differently, *Mil.*; *'a-re pans* well then! throw it away!

ཨ་རོག་ *'a-róg Sch.*: = *rogs-po, grogs,* **companion, mate, fellow, comrade, friend;** *'a-rog-kya* or *gya Sch.*: 'a complimentary phrase or form of salutation'.

ཨ་ལ་(ལ་) *'á-la (-la) Mil.*, also *'ál-la* id. interj. expressive of joyful surprise: aye, ah, that is capital! *dés-na 'á-la-la* well, that is excellent or splendid indeed! *Mil.*; also adjectively: **de san di 'á-la-la* W.* this is much better than that!

ཨ་ལི་ *'á-li* the Tibetan vowels, *'ā-li-ká-li* the series of the vowels together with the consonants; *'a-pren* id.

ཨ་ལི་ *'a-li* a little *C.*

ཨ་ལི་ཁུག་ཏ་ *'a-li-kug-ta* **a swallow** *Cs.*

ཨ་ལུང་ *'a-lún Sch.* **buckle, clasp** (?).

ཨ་ལོང་ *'a-lón* **a ring.**

ཨ་ཤད་ *'a-šád* v. sub *γtúm-mo.*

ཨ་ཤུ་ *'a-šú* **apricot.**

ཨ་ཤོ་ཀ་ *'a-šo-ka* n. of a tree and of a king.

ཨ་སམ་ *'a-sám Sch.*: a thick sauce or broth, soup; *'a-sbyár* a thin broth.

ཨ་སྲུ་ *'a-srú* for *srú-mo* **aunt** *Sch.*

ཨ་གསལ་ལ་ *'a-γsál-la* adv. **openly, manifestly, publicly,** = *mnon-súm-du.*

ཨ་ཧ་ཧ་ *'a-ha-há* interj. expressing joy, pleasure, satisfaction.

ཨ་ཧོ་ཡེ་ *'a-ho-yé* yea, nay even (?).

ཨག་པོ་ *'ág-po* **bad** *C.*

ཨག་ཙེ་ *'ag-tsé Melia Azedarachta,* **the 'neem'** of Anglo-Indians, an important remedy for cutaneous diseases.

ཨག་ཚོམ་ *'ag-tsóm Glr., 'og-tsóm Sch.,* resp *žal-tsóm Pth.,* **beard of the chin, chin-tuft.**

ཨང་ *'an* 1. sbst. = *ₒdoms? 'án-rta, 'án-ras* loin-cloth *C., W.*; *'an-tún* **under-garment,** χιτών, (hence also to be used for shirt and shift); *'an-rág* **trowsers,** breeches *Pth.* — 2. interj.: **well then! now then! well!** in French: *eh bien!* at the beginning of a speech also *'án-ge, 'án-ke, 'án-ki, Mil.,* without any regard to rank.

ཨང་གི་ *'án-gi* or *'án-ki, Ssk.* अङ्क, **figure, number, cipher,** also *'an-grans, 'an-yig Cs.*; the last word, acc. to others, means **secret characters,** cryptography.

ཨང་གུ་ལི་ *'an-gu-li Ssk.* **finger** *Do.*

ཨང་གར་འཇིག་ *'an-rgar-ₒjig* acc. to *Lew.* **English,** *Hd. angrezi.*

ཨང་མ་ཙི་ *'an-ma-tsi Sch.* **flies,** winged insects.

ཨན་ *'an W.* **white chalk.**

ཨན་སྟོང་ *'an-ston Med., Sch.*: cervical vertebra.

ཨན་གདོས་ *'an-γdos C.*: **stocks,** **'an-dó-la ₒjúg-pa** to put (a person) into the stocks.

ཨན་འདར་ *'an-ₒdár C.* 1. **board, plank, deal.** — 2. *lčags-kyi 'an-ₒdár Cs.* an iron instrument of torture; acc. to *Thgy.* a kind of press.

ཨནྡྲ་རྙི་ལ་ *'andra-rnyi-la Lex.,* corrupted form for *'indra-ni-la.*

ཨམ་ཅོག, ཨམ་བག་ **'am-čog, 'am-bag** col. *C.* for *rna-mčog, snam-brag* **ear; bosom.**

ཨམ་བན་ *'am-ban* a Chinese resident, Chinese superior civil officer, in the chief cities and provincial towns of the tributary countries of China.

ཨར་ཀ་ *'ár-ka, 'ár-ga, 'ár-ka, 'ér-ka* 1. *Cs.* **marble.** — 2. **plaster-floor** made of pulverized marble and oil, also *'a-žál.*

ཨར་གོན་ *'ar-gon* an offspring of parents not having the same rank, nor the same religion, and not belonging to the same nation *Ld.*

ཨ་རྒྷཾ་ *'a-rgam Sch.:* 'the offering of sacrifices'; *Will.:* **अर्घ** respectful offering to a god or Brāhman.

ཨརྫ་ཀ་ *'ar-dza-ka Ssk., Sch.:* **cotton,** *'ár-dza-kai dóg-pa Glr.* cotton-capsule. (This signification is not to be found in our *Ssk.*-dictionaries.)

ཨར་ལ་གཏད་པ་ *'ár-la ytád-pa Sch.:* 'to be reduced to extremities, to extreme misery' (?).

ཨལ་གཅིག་ *'al-γčig Sch.:* 'the one half of a pair, e.g. **one** eye', = *ya-γčig.*

ཨལ་ད་ *'ál-ta* (for *da-lta*) *Bal.* 1. **now, at present.** — 2. **to-day.**

ཨལ་ཏིང་ *'al-tin, *al-tin-la kur-če* W.* to carry something bulky tied up in the girdle.

ཨལ་ཏོ་, ཨལ་ཚེ་ *'al-tó, 'al-tsé* earthen kitchen-pot *Ld.*

ཨལ་ལ་ *'al-la* v. *'a-la-la.*

ཨསྨ་གརྦྷ་ *'asma-gar-bha, Tar.: nór-bu asma-gar-bha Schf.:* **emerald.**

ཨི་ *'i* 1. **beer,** = *čan, C.* — 2. vulgar pronunciation of *dbyi, *yi*,* **the lynx.** — 3. num.: 60.

ཨི་ཁུག་ *'i-k'ug, 'ig, W.* **hiccough, sob,** *'i-k'ug yóṅ-ṅa rag** I have got the hiccough, *'i-k'ug gyab dug** he hiccoughs.

ཨིནྡྲ་གོ་པ་ *'indra-go-pa,* **इन्द्रगोप, cochineal;** yet among the substances devoted to a costly Chodten it is mentioned as one of the five divine jewels *Glr.* 7.

ཨིནྡྲ་ནཱི་ལ་ *'indra-nī-la* **sapphire** (*Sch.:* emerald?).

ཨུ་ *'u* num.: 90.

ཨུ་ཆུག་ *'u-čúg,* with *čó-če* W.* **to persuade,** e.g. to buy something.

ཨུ་དུམ་བ་ར་ *'u-dum-ba-ra* (*Ssk. Ficus glomerata*) in Tibetan literature a fabulous lotos of immense size.

ཨུ་མ་ *'u-ma Ssk.,* prob. also spelled *dbú-ma,* n. of the wife of Siwa (Durga, Kāli etc.).

ཨུ་ཙུགས་ *'u-tsúgs Sch.* = *'u-túg.*

ཨུ་རྒྱན་ *'u-rgyán* 1. also *'oḍiyana Cs.,* (not mentioned in *Ssk.* dictionaries), often written in the abbreviated form ཨུརྒྱན, a fabulous country in the north-west of India (though *Cs.* supposes it to be Ujain), frequently represented as a kind of paradise. — 2. now a noun personal of frq. occurrence; *'u-rgyan-padma* v. *padma-₀byuṅ-γnás.*

ཨུག་ཆོས་ *'ug-čós* n. of a remedy *Med.*

ཨུང་གུ་ *'úṅ-gu* **oil-lamp** *C.*

ཨུཏྤ་ལ་, ཨུད་པ་ལ་ *'ut-pa-la, 'ud-pa-la* a blue lotos which is also used for medicinal purposes. In *Lh.* this name seems to be transferred to *Polemonium caeruleum.*

ཨུན་ཐུག་ *'un-túg* v. *₀u-túg.*

ཨུམ་ *'um* **a kiss,** *'um ǰór-wa* or *gyág-pa** **to kiss** *C.*

ཨུར་རྒྱ་ *'ur-rgyá* a warm meal-porridge; fermenting **dough** *C.*

ཨུར་རྡོ་ *'ur-rdó* v. *ur-rdó.*

ཨུར་བ་ *'úr-ba* v. *dbúr-ba.*

ཨུལ་འཐག་ *'ul-₀tág* col. for *γyul-₀tág.*

ཨེ་ *'e* 1. in *C.* and later literature, an interrogative, pronounced short, accented, and usually put immediately before the vb. or the pron. which stands in the place of the vb.: *dé-mo ě yǒ'*? do you feel well? are you well? are you getting on well? *k'yed daṅ 'e ₀prad mi šes* I do not know whether I shall see you again *Mil.*; *'e nus mi nus* whether we shall be able or not *Mil.*; rarely for **even if, though, although,** *'e sus kyaṅ mi túb-na* though nobody is really able to do it. — 2. num.: 120.

ཨེ་ཉ་ཡ་ *'e-nya-ya, 'e-na-ya, Ssk.* **एण**, a fabulous black antelope with short legs and black eyes.

ཨེ་མ་ *'é-ma, 'e-ma‿ó, 'e-ma-hó* interj. expressing joy, surprise, astonishment, **hey! hey day! indeed! you don't say so!** in asking, beseeching, requesting a person's attention: **please, pray, I say**; or expressive of lamentation, compassion: **alas! oh! would to God! O dear!** e.g.: *'é-ma séms-čan snyiṅ-re-rjé* alas, the poor people! *Glr.*

ཨེ་ཝྃ་ *'e-wam, Ssk.* **एवम्, yes, certainly, to be sure** *Wdk.* and elsewh.

ཨེ་ར་ཀ་ *'e-ra-ka Cs.*: 'n. of a country, Irak? Chaldaea?' (In *Ssk.* it denotes a sort of grass, or a woollen carpet.)

ཨེ་ལ་ *'e-la, Ssk.* **एला**, *'é-la p̀rá-mo Wdṅ.* small **cardamoms**, seed of *Electeria Cardamomum.*

ཨེན་ཙམ་ *'én-tsam* **a little, some, a small bit,** *Ü* and *B.*

ཨེན་རེ་ *'en-ré* **quick, fast, speedy** *Sch.*

ཨེན་འདར་ *'en-ₒdár* v. *'an-ₒdar.*

ཨེམ་ཆི་ *'ém-či, 'ám-či* (Turkish word) **physician** *W.*

ཨེར་ཀ་ *'ér-ka C.* v. *'ár-ka.*

ཨོ་ *'o* 1. for འོ *'o* **a kiss,** *Pth.* — 2. num.: 150.

ཨོ་དཀར་ *'o-dkár W.* = *lkog-dkór*, v. *lkóg-ma.*

ཨོ་ཌི་ཡན་ *'o-ḍi-yán* v. *'u-rgyán.*

ཨོཌྲ་ *'óndra,* **ओड्र** *Oḍra,* the northern part of Orissa, *Wdk.*

ཨོ་མོ་སུ་ *'ó-mo-su* (Mongol word) **stocking** *C.*

ཨོ་ལྡོང་ *'o-ldóṅ, 'o-dóṅ,* col. **'ó-šo* Cs.*, **windpipe**; **'o-lé* W.* **throat**; **'o-lé dám-te ši soṅ** he is suffocated.

ཨོ་ལོ་ *'ó-lo* (Mongol word?) *Sch.*: the place where two rivers flow together, **the confluence** of two rivers.

ཨོ་རྒྱན་ *'o-rgyán* = *'u-rgyán Pth.*

ཨོཾ་ *ŏm, Ssk.* **ओम्**, mystical interjection, in later Hindooism the symbol of the Hindoo triad, in as much as it consists of the three sounds, a (Vishnu), u (Shiva), and m (Brahma). This interjection frequently occurs in the prayers of the northern Buddhists of Tibet, and especially in the famous 'six-syllable prayer', ཨོཾ་མ་ཎི་པདྨེ་ཧཱུྃ་, *ŏm maṇi pad-me hūm,* the literal version of which is: 'O thou jewel in the lotus, *hūm*!' The person addressed in these words is not Buddha, but *Spyan-ras-yzigs* (v. *spyan*); by some he is thought to be the author of them. Concerning the import of this short apostrophy the best information is to be found *Köpp.* II, 59—61. — The Tibetans themselves are ignorant of the proper sense of these six syllables, if sense at all there be in them, and it is not unlikely that some shrewd priest invented this form of prayer, in order to furnish the common people with a formula or symbol, easily to be retained by the memory, and the frequent recital of which might satisfy their religious wants. And though there may be no obvious meaning in such exclamations or prayers, yet their efficacy is sure to be firmly believed in by a people, whose practical religion chiefly consists in the performance of certain rites and ceremonies, in a devout veneration of their Lamas, combined with frequent oblations to them, in abstaining from gross sins (regarding even the killing of live animals as such), and in the Pradakshina (v. *skor-ba* 2). — The numerous attempts that have been made to explain the Ommanipadmehūm satisfactorily, and to discover a deeper sense or even a hidden wisdom in it, have proved more or less unsuccessful. The most simple and popular, but also the flattest of these explanations is derived from the purely extrinsic circumstance, that the Sanskrit words of the prayer consist of six syllables, and accordingly it is suggested, that each of these syllables, when pronounced by a pious Buddhist, conveys a blessing upon one of the 'six classes of beings'. — The conjecture with which *Köpp.* closes his disquisition, is certainly nothing but a smart thought of that learned author.

ཨོཾ་ཨཿཧཱུྃ་ *'ŏ-'a-hūm*, another mystical formula, used e. g. for transforming the *mi-ɣtsáṅ-ba bću* into *bdud-rtsi*, v. the explanation given under *naṅ-mčód*.

ཨོཾ་ཙུགས་ *'ŏ-tsugs Sch.*: propping one's chin on both fists, *'ŏ-tsúgs mdzad Mil.*

ཨོག་རྒྱ་ *'og-rgyá* **beard**; *'og-tsúm* = *'ag-tsóm*.

ཨོག་མ་ *'óg-ma* **throat, neck,** = *lkóg-ma*; *'og-żó* a beautiful white neck, a 'milk-neck' *Glr.*; *'og-skó* prob. = *'os-sko Med.*

ཨོང་གུ་ *'oṅ-gu* **a lamp,** *'oṅ-rás* **the wick** of a lamp *C.*

ཨོང་ལེ་ *'oṅ-lé W.* resp. for *'a*, at your service! at your commands!

ཨོང་ལོག་ *'oṅ-log* **ptarmigan** *Sch.*

ཨོམ་མོག་ *'om-móg* **throat and chest** *Sch.*

ཨོལ་མ་ *'ol-ma C.* **throat, windpipe,** = *'ol-ldoṅ*; **'ól-ma dám-te sé-pa** to strangle, throttle; *'ol-rko, 'ol-goṅ, 'ol-kroṅ* id., or acc. to others = *'ol-mdud* the fore-part of the larynx.

ཨོས་སྐོ་ *'os-sko*, also **ŏ-ku* C.* **the chin,** resp. *żal-ko*.

ཨོས་ཚོས་ *'os-čos Ts.* **ö̱-čö̱** *Pedicularis Hookeriana.*

ENGLISH-TIBETAN VOCABULARY.

English-Tibetan Vocabulary.

The figures, here and there attached to Tibetan words, refer to the page where the respective article is to be found. — The accent is marked only when, exceptionally, it rests on the last syllable of a word.

A

A, An, article *čig* 140.
Abandon *skyur-ba*; *spon-ba*; *ₒbor-ba*.
Abate *ži-ba*.
Abbot *mḱan-po*.
Abdomen *čal*, esp. *sku-čál*.
Ability *nus-pa*; *rtsal*.
Ablative case *ₒbyuṅ-ḱuṅs*.
Able *mḱas-pa*; to be — *ₒkyud-pa*; *lčogs-pa*; *nyan-pa*; *ťub-pa*; *nus-pa*; *p̀od-pa*; *ₒťsugs-pa*; *šes-pa*.
Ablution *ḱrus*.
Abode *mčis-bráṅ*; *ₒdug-γnas*; *ₒdug-sa*; *γnas* (*-tsaṅ*); *γži-ma*.
Abolish *ₒjig-pa*; *snub-pa*.
Abortion *skyur-ma*; *mṅal rlugs-pa*.
Abounding *rgyas-pa* 109, *mod-po*, *ₒdzom-po*.
About *tsam-na*, *tsa-na*; round — v. *p̀yogs* 352; to be — *ča-ba* 152; *ťas-pa*.
Above adv. *steṅ-na*; *bla*; *yan*, *yan-la* 506; prep. *ḱa-na*, *ḱa-ru*, *ḱa-la*, *ḱar* 34; *goṅ-du*; *ltag-nas*, *ltag*; *ťog-tu*.
Abridge *sdud-pa*.
Abridgment *zin-bris*.
Abroad v. *byes*; to go — *byes-su ₒgro-ba*.
Abscess *ču-búr*; *p̀ol*.
Absolutely *čis-kyaṅ*; *ga-na-méd*.
Abstinence *dge-ba*; *ťsod-šes-pa* 452.
Abundant *ḱrigs*.
Abuse s. (reviling words) *skur-pa* 23; vb. a. (to revile) *skur ₒdebs-pa* (*byed-pa*; *smra-ba*); *dma ₒbab-pa*; *smad-pa*.
Abyss *btson-doṅ*; *γyaṅ-sa*.
Academy *γtsug-lag-ḱáṅ*.
Accept *bžed-pa*, *bžes-pa*; *len-pa*.
Acceptable, to be — *ₒťad-pa*.
Access *ₒgro-sa*; v. also *γtoṅ-ba* 208 and *mjal-ba* 173.
Accident *rkyen*; unfortunate — *ₒgal-rkyén*; fatal — *bar-čád*; *byur*, *byus*.
Accompany *skyel-ba*; *zla-bo byed-pa*.
Accomplish v. *grub-pa*; *čom-pa*; *spyod-pa*; *rtsom-pa*.
Accomplished *pul-tu byuṅ-ba* 344.
Accomplishment *rtsal*; *yon-tan* 516.
Accord, Accordance *ₒčam-pa*.
According to **naṅ-tar** *W. C.*; *daṅ sbyar-nas*; *bžin-du*.
Account s. *rtsis*, *lo-rgyús* 113; *γnas-ťsúl*; on — of v. *rkyen*; *čed-du*; *p̀yir*; *slad-du*.
Account vb. a. *rtsis byed-pa* (*ₒdebs-pa*, *gyab-pa*).
Accountant *rtsis-pa*.
Accumulate *spuṅ-ba*.
Accurate *žib-pa*.
Accusation, false — *snyad*.
Accuse *ₒgel-ba*; *rgol-ba*.
Accustomed *goms-pa*; *ₒdris-pa*; to be — *ₒdris-pa*.
Ache vb. n. *na-ba*.
Acid, Acidity *skyur-ba*.
Acknowledge *ḱas len-pa*; frq. only *smra-ba*, *zer-ba* etc.
Aconite *boṅ-ṅa*.
Acquaintance (friend) *ṅo-šés*.
Acquainted, to be — *bšés-pa*.
Acquiesce *ḱo-ťag γčod-pa*; *mi rgol-ba*; *daṅ-du len-pa*.
Acquitted, to be — *rgyal-ba*.
Across *p̀red*, *ₒp̀red*.
Act vb. *byed-pa*; *spyod-pa*; *bgyid-pa*; to — the part of *byed-pa*.
Action *spyod-pa*; *bya-ba*; *las*; former actions *sṅon-lás*.
Action (law-suit) *ḱrims*, *šags* *W.* 51.
Activity *spyod-pa*.

Actual ṅes-pa-čan; ṅo-rtóg; γdán-dag-pa.
Actually γži-nas.
Acute rno-ba.
Adage ḱa-dpe.
Add snon-pa; sre-ba; rǰes-su °ǰug-pa; v. °god-pa.
Addict, to — one's self sten-pa.
Adduce v. mťson-pa and dpe.
Adequate °grig-pa; mťun-pa.
Adhere °byor-ba, °byar-ba; γnas-pa.
Adherent ṕyogs-pa; °dzin-pa.
Adieu v. ṕyi-ṕyag 347.
Adibuddha kun-γži 4.
Adjust sbyor-ba; sgrig-pa; °god-pa.
Admit γtoṅ-ba; ḱas len-pa.
Admonish skul-ba.
Admonition bskul-ba, bskul-ma; bslab-bya.
Adolescent s. ḱyeu.
Adore mos-pa.
Adorn v. °god-pa; sgron-pa; brgyan-pa; spra-ba.
Adult s. če-mi, nar son-pa 298.
Adulterate slad-pa.
Adulterer šar-po, adulteress šar-mo.
Adultery, to commit — v. °ǰug-pa 177, byi byed-pa; γyem byed-pa.
Advantage don; bogs; °ḱyer-so; rgyal-ḱa, ḱa-rgyál.
Adversary ṕa-rol-po.
Advice bka-γdáms; ḱa-bsgos; ḱa-ta, ḱa-γdáms; gros; γdams-pa; °dun-ma; man-ṅág; to ask — bgro-ba.
Advise γdam-pa, °dom-pa.
Adviser bka-γdams-pa.
Affair don.
Affect bčos-pa 147.
Affection čags-pa; byams-pa, byams-sems; brtse-ba.
Affectionate brtse-ba-čan.
Affix sbyor-ba.
Affliction sdug-pa; mya-ṅán; ťser-ka W.
Afore-said sṅa-ma.
Afraid, to be — skrág-pa, dṅaṅ-ba; °ǰigs-pa; bag ťsa-ba; bred-pa.
After adv. rgyab-tu; ṕyi 349; °og; slad-na.
After prep. rǰes, °og; slad; rtiṅ; mťar; nas.
After-birth ša-ma.
Afterwards rǰes-la, rǰes-su; rtiṅ-du; de-nas; ṕyin-čád; ṕyis; ṕyi-bžin; slad-nas; slar.
Again čed-du; ṕyir; slar; yaṅ; — and — yaṅ-nas yaṅ-du.
Age na-ťsód, na-so; dus.
Aged rgad-pa; to be — rga-ba.
Agent byed(-pa)-po, byed-mḱan; ťsab-po, resp. sku-ťsab.
Agressor sṅa-rgol.
Agility byag-pa.
Agio non-ka; ṕar; °dza.
Agitate dkrug-pa; skyod-pa; skyom-pa; sgul-ba; to be agitated °gul-ba; °ḱrug-pa.
Agitation ḱrag-°ḱrúgs.
Ago sṅun-la; long — sṅa-mo-nas.
Agony γšin-°ṕras; koṅ-°ḱrúgs; sems ḱoṅ-du °ťsud-pa.
Agree °grig-pa; °čam-pa; stun-pa; mťun-pa.
Agreeable dga-ba; yid-du °oṅ-ba.
Agreement ḱa-čád, resp. žal-čád; gan-rgyá; čad, čad-so; °čam-pa; bzaṅ.
Agriculture so-nám(s).
Ague ťsad-pai nád; ťsan-zug W.
Aim s. °gro-sa 102; °ben.
Aim vb. zir-ba; v. γtod-pa no. 3.
Air (atmospheric air) ṅá-ra; ṅad; rluṅ; cold — ṅad.
Air (tune) mgur, glu, dbyaṅs.
Air (mien) ṅo, γdoṅ.
Alabaster ḱa-ma-ru; ťod-le-kór.
Alas kye-ma.
Alienism °gron.
Alight °bab-pa, resp. γšol-ba.
Alive γson-po.
All kun; v. gaṅ; ťams-čád; mťá-dag, ťsad; yoṅs; — right! ťsaṅ-°grig; — seeing kun-γzigs; — uniting kun-°dus; not at — ťsam yaṅ mi (ma); ye mi (ma).
Allegory °dra-dpe.
Allow γnaṅ-ba; to be —ed čog-pa, ruṅ-ba.
Almanac lo-ťó.
Almighty kun-dbaṅ.
Almond ba-dám.
Alms ldom-bu; sloṅ-mo; bsod-snyóms.
Alone γčig, γčig-γčig, γčig-pu, γčig-po.
Along with žor-la.
Alphabet ka-ṕreṅ, ka-ḱá; kā-li 2.
Alpine pastures neu-γsíṅ; ne-ťaṅ C.
Also yaṅ 505.
Altar mčod-stégs, mčod-ḱri.
Alter sgyur-ba; spo-ba.
Alteration °gyur-ba.
Although yaṅ 505.
Altogether kun, yoṅs-su.
Alum ḱa-ru-ťsa; lče-myaṅ-ťsá.
Always rgyun-du; rtag-tu; nam-yaṅ.
Amalgam gyim-bág.
Ambassador ṕo-nya.
Amber spos-šél.
Ambitious grags-pa-la čags-pa; mťon-dod-čan.
Ambush v. (lkog-)°ǰab.
Amendment žu-dág, žus-dág.
Among naṅ, naṅ-na 301; las 546.
Amusement γyeṅ-rtséd.
Analogy v. dpe.
Anasarca pags-ču.
Anatomy lus-kyi γnas-lugs.
Ancestor ṕa-mes, mes-po; brgyud.

Ancient *sṅa-ba*; — ly *sṅa-sor*; *sṅon-dús*.
And *daṅ* 248; v. also *čiṅ* 140.
Angel *p̓o-nya* 345.
Anger *k̓ro-ba*; *k̓oṅ-k̓ro*; *k̓on-pa*; *sro*, resp. *t̓ugs-sro W.*; *že-sdaṅ*.
Angle *grwa* 75; *gru*.
Angry *k̓ro-ba*, *k̓ro-bo*, *k̓ro-mo*; to be — °*k̓ro-ba*; *sdaṅ-ba*.
Angular *zul-ma*.
Animal s. *dud-°gro*; *srog-čágs*.
Animated being *srog-čágs*; *sems-čan*.
Animosity °*k̓aṅ*.
Annals *lo-rgyús*; — of the kings *rgyal-rábs*.
Annihilate *med-par byed-pa*; to be annihilated *med-par °gyur-ba*.
Annotation *mčan-bu*.
Announce *lon sgyur-ba*; *sbrón-pa*; *p̓rin smra-ba*; *ṡes-par byed-pa*.
Annoy °*k̓aṅ-ba*; *sṅog-pa*; *sun °ǰug-pa*.
Annually *lo-ltar*, *lo daṅ lo*.
Anoint *skud-pa*; *bsgo-ba*; °*byug-pa*.
Another *bdag-méd*; *yžan-ma*.
Answer vb. *lan °debs-pa*.
Ant *gre-mog-°bu*; *grog-ma*.
Antagonist °*t̓ab-ya*; *p̓a-rol-pa* (or *po*).
Antelope *dgo-ba*; the Tibetan — *ytsod*, *btsod*, *ytso*.
Antidote *ynyen-po*.
Antipathy *žen-lóg*.
Antiquity *sṅa-dús*, *sṅa-ba*; *sṅon-tsé*, *sṅon-dus*, *sṅon-rabs*.
Anus *rkub*; *yžaṅ*, *yžaṅ-k̓a*; *bṡaṅ-lám*.
Anxiety **k̓og-ṭúg**; col. *nyams-ṅa*.
Anxious (*sems*) *k̓oṅ-du čud-pa*; v. also *bag-tsa*.
Any v. *gaṅ* 65; — one *gaṅ žig*; — thing *či žig*, *či-yaṅ*; — whatever *čaṅ*.
Apathy *btaṅ-snyoms*; *byar-méd*.
Aperture *sgo*; *bu-ga*.
Apostle *mi-sná*.
Apothecary's shop *sman-k̓aṅ*.
Apparition *snaṅ-ba*; *žal-yzigs*.
Appear °*čar-ba*; *ston-pa*; *snaṅ-ba*; °*byuṅ-ba*; *yod-par °gyur-ba*.
Appearance °*k̓yer-so*; *ča-byád*, *ča-lugs*; *čas*; *snaṅ-tsúl*.
Appease *ži-bar byed-pa*.
Appendix *k̓a-skoṅ*.
Appertain *ytogs-pa*.
Appetite *k̓am*; *daṅ-ga*.
Apple *ku-ṡu*; *sli*; — of the eye *spyan-°bras*.
Application °*bad-pa*; *brtson-°grus*.
Apply *bkan-pa*; to — one's self *brtson-pa*.
Appoint *skul-ba*; *sko-ba*; °*gel-ba*; °*čol-ba*; °*ǰug-pa*.
Apprehend *yčags-pa*; *dogs-pa*.
Apprentice *mčan-bu*.
Approach vb. *k̓ad-pa*; *nye-ba*; *bsnyen-pa*.
Approach s. °*gro-sa*.
Approve *bžed-pa*.

Appurtenance *rgyu-čá*; —s *skor*.
Apricot *k̓am-bu*; *ču-li*, *čo-li*; dried — *ču-li C.*, *p̓a-tiṅ W.*; *mṅa-ris k̓am-bu C.*
Apron *dun-k̓ebs*, *paṅ-k̓ébs*.
Aqueduct *yur-ba*.
Arch *yžu*, *yžu-mo*.
Archer °*p̓oṅ-mk̓an*; —y °*p̓oṅ*.
Architect *rtsig-dpón*.
Archives *yig-tsáṅ*.
Area v. *dkyil-°k̓or*; *k̓yon*, *rgya-k̓yón*; *ču-žéṅ*.
Argali *ynyan*.
Argue *bgro-ba*, *rtsod-pa*.
Argument *mṅon-rtágs*; *rtags*.
Arise *skye-ba*; °*k̓or-ba*; °*k̓ruṅ-ba*; *čags-pa*; *ldaṅ-ba*.
Arm *lag*(*-pa*), resp. *p̓yag*.
Armful *lag-kód*; v. also *paṅ*.
Armour *go-k̓ráb*; *go-ča*.
Armpit *mčan-k̓uṅ*.
Arms *mt̓son*, *mt̓son-ča*, °*t̓ab-grabs*.
Army *dpuṅ*; *dmag*; *dmag-dpúṅ*.
Aroma *ṅad*.
Aromatic *ṅad-čan*.
Arrange *sgrig-pa*; °*ǰog-pa*; *ytan-la °bebs-pa* 205.
Arrangement *grabs*; *rgyu*; *ynas-lugs*.
Arrive *sleb-pa*; °*byon-pa*; °*byor-ba*.
Arrogance *ṅa-rgyal*; *p̓o-so*.
Arrow *mda*.
Arsenal *go-k̓áṅ*.
Arsenic *ba-bla*.
Art *sgyu-rtsál*; *bzo*.
Artery *rtsa-dkár*; *rluṅ-rtsa*.
Artifice *sgyu*.
Artificial *bčos-pa*.
Artist *bzo-pa*.
As (like) *ltar*; *bžin-du*; (when) v. *čiṅ* 140; *na* 299; *pas* 323; as — as *tsam* 430; — far — *tsam-du*, *bar-du*, *tug*, *t̓sug-pa*; — much — *ga-tsám*; — soon — *ma-k̓ád*, *ma-t̓ag-tu*.
Ascend °*dzeg-pa*.
Ascending node *sgra-yčán*.
Ascetic s. *sgom-po*, *sgom-mk̓an*; *sdom-sruṅ*.
Ashamed, to feel — *skyeṅ-ba*; *k̓rel-ba*; °*dzem-pa*.
Ash-coloured *gro-mo*.
Ashes *gog-t̓ál*; *t̓al-ba*.
Aside *zur-du*; *logs-su*, *logs-la*.
Ask °*dri-ba*, *ysol-ba*, *žu-ba*; *ṡer-ba*; *sloṅ-ba*; 'if one asks so' v. *če-na* 142.
Asleep, to fall — *ynyid-du °gro-ba*.
Aspire *snyeg-pa*.
Ass *boṅ-bu*, *boṅ-bo*; wild — *rkyaṅ*.
Assailant *sṅa-rgol*.
Assassinate v. °*ǰab-pa* 174.
Assemblage *k̓rod-pa*; *tsogs*.
Assemble vb. n. °*du-ba*; °*tsogs-pa*; *lhags-pa*; vb. a. *sdud-pa*; *sog-pa*.
Assert *dam °ča-ba*; *bžed-pa*.
Assiduous *brtson-pa-čan*.

Assist *zla-bo* or *grogs byed-pa.*
Assistance *skyabs*; *skyobs*; *ra-mda.*
Assistant *grogs*; *ya-do W.*; *ra-mda-pa.*
Associate s. *grogs*; *zla-bo*; *ya-do W.*; *rogs.*
Associate vb. *ₒtsogs-pa*; to be –d *ₒgrogs-pa.*
Assume *ₒčaṅ-ba.*
Assurance *γdeṅ*; *blo-γtád*, *blo-γdéṅ.*
Asterism *skar-ma.*
Asthma *dbugs rdzaṅ-ba.*
Astonished, to be – *ha-las-pa.*
Astonishment *ṅo-mtsár*; *ya-mtsan.*
Astray, to go – *ₒkyar-ba*; v. also sub *yan-pa* 506.
Astride, to put – *skyon-pa.*
Astringent *bska-ba.*
Astrology *skar-dpyád*, *skar-rtsís.*
Astronomy *skar-rtsis* 439.
Asunder *so-sor* 578; to tear – *ₒdral-ba.*
At *kar*; *mdun-du*; *na* 298; *rtsar* 437.
Athlete *gyad.*
Atmosphere *rluṅ-gyi dkyil-ₒkor* 11.
Atom *rdul.*
Atonement *sdig-bšágs.*
Attach *ₒdogs-pa*; *sdom-pa*, *rtod-pa.*
Attached *zug-pa C.* 466; to be – *čags-pa*; *žen-pa.*
Attachment *ₒkri-ba*; *čags-pa*; *žen-ₒdzin.*
Attack *rub-pa.*
Attain *sgrub-pa*; *tob-pa*; *rnyed-pa*; v also *pyin-pa.*
Attend vb. n. *skyoṅ-ba*; vb. a. *zla-bo byed-pa*; *nya-ra byed-pa.*
Attendant *ₒkor*, *ₒkor-mkan*; *ₒkor-γyog*, *γyog-ₒkor.*
Attention *γnyer-ka*; *zon.*
Attentive *γčaṅ-po.*
Attitude *staṅs*; *spyod-lam*; *rnam-ₒgyur*, *tsul*, *sdod-tsul.*
Attribute s. *brjod-pa* gramm.; *rtags*; *mtsan*, *mtsan-nyid.*
Auction *ni-lam.*
Auditory (in a monastery) *kun-dga-ra-ba* 4.
Augment vb. n. *rgyas-pa*; *ₒpel-ba*; vb. a. *spel-ba.*
Aunt *ne-ne-mo*; *'a-ne*; *sru.*
Auspice *ča*; *rten-ₒbrél.*
Authentic *ṅes-pa*
Author *byed-mkan*; *žal-γdams bris-mkan* 473.
Authority *čab*; *mtu.*
Authorize *dbaṅ skur-ba.*
Autumn *ston*, *ston-ka.*
Avalanche *ka-rúd.*
Avarice *ser-sna*; *ham-pa.*
Aversion *skyo-šas*; *krel*; to feel an – *skyo-ba.*
Avert *zlog-pa*; *γčod-pa.*
Avoid *γčod-pa*; *spoṅ-ba*; *ₒdzem-pa.*
Await *sgug-pa.*
Away *par* 341; *yas* 508.
Awkward *rtsal-méd*; *mi šes-pa.*
Awn *gra-ma.*
Awry *kyom-kyóm*; *ča-čús*; *yo-ba.*
Axe *sta-ré*; *ste-po.*
Axiom *γži-ma.*
Axle-tree *srog-šiṅ.*
Ay *ₒo-ná.*

B

Babbling s. *čol-čúṅ.*
Baby *pru-gu čuṅ-ṅu.*
Back s. *rgyab*; *ltag-pa*; the small of the – *sgal-pa.*
Back adv. *rgyab-tu*; *pyir.*
Background *mtil.*
Bacon *sbo-tsil.*
Bad *ṅan-pa*; *tu-ba*; *gyi-na*; *btsog-po W.*
Badger *grum-pa.*
Bag *sgyiu*, *sgyig-gu*; *sgye-mo*; *pad*; leather – *rkyal-pa*; small – *rkyal-bu.*
Bail (person) *dge-rgán*; *lag-mi.*
Bakehouse *bkad-sa.*
Baker *γyos-mkan.*
Balance (pair of scales) *tu-lā*; *bat-ti*; *sraṅ.*
Balcony *rab-γsál.*
Bald *ter.*
Ball *go-la*; *bo-lo*; musket *rdeu C.*, *rin-di W.*; cannon – *tu-lúm.*
Ballista *sgyogs.*
Balustrade *lag-γžúṅs.*
Banana *skyes-sdóṅ.*
Band (gang) *kyu*, *kyu-bo.*
Bandage *ras-tág*; *leb-ma*, *leb-tágs.*
Bandeleer *ga-ša.*
Bandy-legged *rkaṅ-kyóg.*
Banish *spyug-pa.*
Bank (shore) *ₒkris*; *ₒgram*; *ṅogs*; *dṅo*; – of a river *ču-ka*, *ču-ₒgram*, *ču-mtu.*
Banker *bun-bdág.*
Banquet s. *mgron.*
Baptism *krus* 51.
Baptize *krus γsol-ba.*
Barbarian *kla-klo.*
Barbarous *ₒkob.*
Barber *ₒbreg-mkan.*
Barberry *skyer-pa W.*
Bare *rjen-pa*; – footed *rkaṅ-rjén.*
Bark s. *pags-pa*; *šun-pa*; – of a species of willow *sgro-ba*; – of the birch-tree *gro-ga.*

Bark vb. n. *zug-pa.*
Barley *nas*; *so-ba*; boiled — *glum*; — corn *nas.*
Barm *ṕabs*; *sbaṅ-ču.*
Barter vb. *rje-ba*; *sdeb-pa.*
Base s. *γži*; *rmaṅ.*
Bashful *ṅo-bab-pa*; *dzem-bag-čan.*
Bashfulness *ḱrel.*
Basin *ka-to-ra*; *zi-liṅ-pan-tse.*
Basis *₀gram-γži*; *ma-γži.*
Basket *pe-ra*; *tse-po*; *γzed-ma*; a small — of reed *bag-tse.*
Bat (animal) *ṕa-wáṅ.*
Bath *ḱrus.*
Bathe *₀ḱru-ba*, *₀ḱrud-pa.*
Battle *γyul*, *₀ṫab-mo.*
Bawling adj. *ča-čo-čan.*
Bay (gulf) *ḱug*; *ču-ḱúg*; *mṫso-lág.*
Bay-coloured *smug-po.*
Bayonet *san-gin W.*
Bazar *ḱrom.*
Be *yin-pa*, resp. *lags-pa*; *yod-pa*; *₀dug-pa*; *mčis-pa*; *mṅa-ba*; *γnas-pa*; there is, there are *₀dug*; *mčis.*
Beadle (in a monastery) *dge-bskós*; *dge-γyóg.*
Beam (timber) *γduṅ-ma*; — of light *γzer*; *₀od-γzér.*
Bear vb. a. (to bring forth) *btsa-ba*; *skyed-pa*; (to carry) *₀ḱur-ba*, *₀ḱyer-ba*; *ṫeg-pa*, *₀ṫogs-pa*; (to suffer) *γzod-pa*, *ṫub-pa.*
Bear s, brown — *dom*; yellow — *dred* 261; the Great Bear *smin-bdún.*
Beard *rgya-bo*; *sma-ra*; *'ag-ṫsóm*; — of corn *gra-ma.*
Beast *dud-₀gro*; — of burden *ḱal-ma*; — of prey *γčan-zán.*
Beat *rgyab-pa*; *rduṅ-ba*; *rdegs-pa*; *₀ṕam-par byed-pa*; to — the drum *skrog-pa*; to — the gong, the cymbal v. *₀ḱrol-ba*; to be beaten *₀ṕam-pa.*
Beautiful *mdzes-pa*; *bzaṅ-ba*; *legs-pa*; *sdug-pa*; *dga-ba*; *bde-ba*; — appearance or colour *bkrag*; *mdaṅs*; — form *rnam-₀gyúr.*
Because v. *kyi* 6; *pas* 323.
Beckon *lag-brdá byed-pa.*
Become *skye-ba*; *₀gyur-ba*; *ča-ba W.*
Becoming (comely), to be — *₀os-pa.*
Bed *mčis-mál*; *nyal-ḱri.*
Bed (garden) *ṫsas-ḱaṅ.*
Bedding *mal-gós*, *mal-čá*; *γzim-čá.*
Bedfellow *mal-grogs*, resp. *γzim-grogs.*
Bedstead *mal-ḱri*; *mčis-mál.*
Bee *buṅ-ba*; *sbraṅ-ma.*
Beer *čaṅ*; — carousal *čaṅ-sa*; — house *čaṅ-ḱaṅ.*
Beetle *sbur-pa.*
Befool *mgo skor-ba.*
Before adv. *sṅa-ma*, *sṅa-góṅ* 135; *sṅan*, *sṅar*, *sṅun* 136; *sṅon*, *sṅon-du* 137; prep. *druṅ-du* 263; *mdun-du* 273.
Beforehand v. *sṅa*; *sṅan*, *sṅar*; to be — *sṅa-ba.*
Beg *žu-ba*; *γsol-ba.*
Beget *bšo-ba*; *skyed-pa.*
Beggar *spraṅ-po*; *ldom-bu-ba*; — boy *spraṅ-ṕrúg.*
Begin vb. n. *čas-pa*; *ǰug-pa*; *mgo ₀dzug-pa*; to — to exist *skye-ba*; vb. a. *rtsom-pa*; *₀dzugs-pa.*
Beginner *las-daṅ-po-pa.*
Beginning s. *mgo*, *mgo-ma*; *₀go-ma*; *sgo-mo*; *sṅon-ma*; *ṫog-ma*; — and end (head and tail) *mgo-mǰug.*
Begotten *čad-pa*; to be — *čags-pa.*
Behalf v. *don* no. 3, 259.
Behave *₀grul-ba.*
Behaviour *rnam-₀gyur*; *spyod-pa.*
Behead *ske γčod-pa.*
Behind adv. *rtiṅ*; *ṕa-rol-na* 338; *ṕyi*, *ṕyis*; prep. *₀gab*; v. *rgyab* 107.
Behold interj. *kye-hó* 7.
Being s. *₀gro-ba*; *lus-čan*, *sems-čan.*
Belch s. *sgreg-pa*; vb. n. *sgreg-pa ₀don-pa.*
Believe vb. n. *dad-pa* 249; vb. a. *yid* (*ṫugs* or *blen*) *čes-pa.*
Bell *dril*; — metal *mḱar-ba*, *₀ḱar-ba*; — wether *ḱyu-mčóg.*
Bellows *sbud-pa.*
Belly *grod-pa*; *lto-ba*, *γsus-pa.*
Belong *γtogs-pa*; *mṅa-ba*; belonging together *ṫe-mḱan W.*
Beloved *γčes-pa*; *mon-ža-čan.*
Below adv. *ma* 408; *man-čád*, *man-čód*; prep. *₀og* 501.
Bench *gral.*
Bend vb. a. *kug-kúg byed-pa*; *skyil-ba*; *dgu-ba*; *gugs-pa*; *gum-pa*; *₀dud-pa*; vb. n. *mgo dgur-ba*; *dgye-ba.*
Benefit v. *skyed* 29; *don* no. 3, 259; *ṕan-pa*, *ṕan-yón*; for the — of *ṕyogs-su*; *don-du*
Benevolence *ṕan-pai sems.*
Bent (crooked) *ḱoṅs*; *₀ḱyog-po*; *gug-ge-ba*; *dgu-ba.*
Benumbed v. *sbrid-pa.*
Bereave *₀ṕral-ba*; to be bereft *₀bral-ba.*
Besides *ḱa-ru*, *ḱar*; *steṅ-du*; *min*, *min-pa.*
Besiege *skor-ba.*
Besprinkle *čag-čág byed-pa* or *₀debs-pa.*
Best s. *mčog* 166; *don* no. 3, 259.
Bestow *sbyin-pa*; *ster-ba.*
Better, to get the — of *ṫub-pa*; *rgyal-ba.*
Between *bar-la*, *de-bár*; *γseb-na*, *γseb-la*; from — *bar-nas.*
Beverage *skyems*; *btuṅ-ba* 244.
Beyond *ṕa-rol-na*; *ṕan-čád.*
Bhotan *₀brug-pa.*
Bice, blue — *sṅo-skyá.*

Bid *sgo-ba*; *ǰug-pa*; *ₒdom-pa*.
Bier *ḱyogs*; *dgu-ḱri*.
Big *čen-po*; — with child *sems-čan daṅ ldan-pa*; — with young *sbrum-pa*.
Bigness *ḱo-lág*.
Bile *mḱris-pa*.
Billet of wood *mgal-pa*; *šiṅ-dum*.
Billow *ču-ri*, *ču-rlabs*; *dba-klóṅ*.
Bind *ₒčiṅ-ba*; *ₒdogs-pa*; *sdom-pa*; *ₒḱyig-pa*.
Biped *rkaṅ-γnyis-pa*.
Birch-tree *stag-pa*.
Bird *bya*; *dab-čágs*; little — *mčil-pa*.
Birdcage *bya-ḱáṅ*.
Birdsnest *bya-ťsáṅ*.
Birth v. *skye-ba* 28; high — *skye-ba mťo-ba*; low — *skye-ba dma-ba*.
Birthplace *skye-γnás*.
Bishop *do-dam-pa* 257.
Bison (Indian) *glaṅ-to*.
Bit (small piece) *ḱam*, *ḱam-ťsád*; *čag-dúm*; *brul*.
Bit (of a bridle) *srab-lčágs*.
Bitch *ḱyi-mo*.
Bite vb. *rmug-pa*; *ₒča-ba*.
Bitter *ḱa*, *ḱa-po*, *ḱa-ba* 36.
Bittern *ču-skyar*.
Bitumen *brag-žún*.
Black adj. *nag-po*.
Black s. (centre of a target) *rtags*.
Blacksmith *lčags-mgár*.
Bladder (urinary) *lgaṅ-pa*.
Blade (of grass) *ǰag-ma*; *sog-ma*.
Blade (of a sword) *lče*.
Blame vb. a. *spyó-ba*; *smad-pa*, *smod-pa*.
Blame s. *klan-ka*.
Blank adj. *stoṅ-pa*.
Blanket *grum-tse*; *tsa-dar*; *ča-ra* 152; *ša-pos Ld.*
Blasphemy *skur-pa*.
Blast vb. *γčog-pa*.
Blaze s. *mdoṅs*.
Bleat *ₒba-ba*.
Bleed *γtar-ba*, *rtsa γčod-pa*.
Bless *sṅo-ba*.
Blessed *skal-ldán*; *bde-ₒgro*; *γyaṅ-čan*.
Blessing s. *byin*, *byin-rlábs*; *bkra-šis*; *bsṅo-ba*; *ṕan-yón*; *γyaṅ*; *rgyan* 107.
Blind *mdoṅs-pa*; *žar-ba*, *mig-žár*; *loṅ-ba*.
Blister s. (pustule) *ču-sgaṅ*; *ču-bur*; (plaster) *ǰibs-sman*.
Blister vb. *ǰibs-pa*; *ǰibs-sman ǰug-pa*.
Blood *ḱrag*; —y *ḱrag-čan*.
Blooming *bkra-ba*.
Blossom vb. *ₒbar-ba*.
Blot out *ₒṕyid-pa*; *sel-ba*.
Blow vb. *ₒbud-pa*.
Blow s. *lčag*.
Blue *sṅon-po*, *sṅo-bo*; deep — *sṅo-nag*; pale — *sṅo-skyá*; *sṅo-saṅs*; sky — *mťiṅ*.
Bluff s. *gad-pa*.
Blunt *rtul-po*; vb. also *ḱa* IV. no. 5.
Blushing (the act of) *ṅo-ťsa*.
Board s. *spaṅ-léb*; *šiṅ-léb*; *glegs*; *sgo-rnám*; — of a door *sgo-glégs*; — of a ship *zur*.
Boast vb. *rlom-pa*.
Boasting s. *ḱa-ťso*, *ḱa-ṕo*; *yus*.
Boat *gru*.
Boatman *gru-pa*; *ko-mḱan*; *mnyan-pa*.
Bodily *dṅos-su*; *mṅon-sum-du*; *žal-dṅós*.
Body *lus*; *γzugs*; *sku*; — linen *gos-lág*.
Boil s. (ulcer) *ču-búr*; *ša-búr W.*
Boil vb. a. *skol-ba*; to — down *sgor-ba*; vb. n. *ₒḱol-ba*; to — over *lud-pa*.
Boiling adj. *ḱol-pa*, *ḱol-ma*.
Boldness *ṅo-mig*; *rtul-ṕod-pa*.
Bolster *sṅas*; *γdan*.
Bolt s. *bur*; v. also *γya* and *si-ri*.
Bolt vb. a. *γya rgyab-pa*; *si-ri čug-če W.*
Bond *ₒdzin*; *zin-brís*.
Bonds *bčiṅ-ba*, *bčiṅs-pa*; *ₒčiṅ-ba*.
Bone *γduṅ*; *rus-pa*; —s of fish *gra-ma*.
Book *dpe*; *glegs-bám*; *po-ti*.
Books (literature) *čos*; book-language *čos-skad*.
Bookstand *dpe-ḱri*.
Boot *lham*; leather half-boot *krad-pa* 8.
Border s. *gru*; *mťa-ma*; *sna*; *mu*; *mťsams*.
Bore vb. *rtol-ba*; *ₒbigs-pa*.
Born *čad-pa*; to be — *skye-ba*; *btsa-ba*; *ₒḱruṅ-ba*, *kruṅs-pa*; *ltams-pa*.
Borough *groṅ-ťso*.
Borrow *skyi-ba*; *brnyan-pa*; *γyar-ba*.
Bosom *snam-brág*; *paṅ-ḱébs*.
Botch vb. *glan-pa*.
Both *γnyis*.
Bottle *bum-pa*.
Bottom *γtiṅ*; *mťil*; *žabs*.
Bough *yal-ga*.
Bound vb. n. *ₒṕar-ba*.
Boundary *mťsams*, *sa-mťsams*.
Bow vb. *ₒdud-pa*; **skyed kug taṅ-če** 16 *W.*
Bow s. (compliment) *ṕyag*.
Bow s. (for shooting) *γžu*.
Bowels *rgyu-ma*; *naṅ-ḱról*.
Bowl s. *ko-re W.*; *koṅ-po*; *pa-tra*; *ṕor-pa*; *γžoṅ-pa*; beggar's — *lhuṅ-bzéd*; — of a tobacco-pipe *gaṅ-mgó*.
Box s. (chest) *sgam*; *sgrom*; *gau*; *pa-ri*; — on the ear *ₒgram-lčag*.
Boy *byis-pa*; infant — *ḱyeu*.
Bracelet *γdu-bu*; *lag-γdúb*.
Brag *sgeg-pa*.
Brahma *ťsaṅs-pa*.
Brahmin *bram-ze*.
Braid vb. *γčud-pa*.
Brain *klad-pa*; *glad*; *mgo-klád*.
Bramble *ťser-ma*.
Bran *ťsag-ro*.
Branch (bough) *yal-ga*; *gel-pa*; v. also *lčug-pa* 149.

Brandish *dbyug-pa.*
Brandy *'a-rág.*
Brass *ra-gan*; — can *čab-rkyan.*
Brave adj. *des-pa*; *dpa(-ba)*; *spa-ba.*
Brawls v. *klan-ka* 8.
Bread *bag-leb C.*; *ta-gir W.*
Breadth *ka-żeṅ*; *żeṅ*, *γżeṅ.*
Break vb. a. *γčog-pa*; to — one's promise *ₒgal-ba*; v. *ₒčal-ba*; v. *ₒjig-pa*; vb.n. *ₒgas-pa*; *ₒčag-pa*; to — forth *rdol-ba*; to - out *ₒčor-ba*; *laṅ-ba.*
Breakfast s. *gro*; *dro C.*; *tsal-ma W.*
Breakfast vb. *tsal-ma za-ba.*
Breast *nu-ma*; *braṅ*, resp. *sku-bráṅ.*
Breath *rṅam-pa*; *dbugs*; *rlaṅs-pa*; to be out of — *dṅaṅ-ba.*
Breathe *rṅam-pa.*
Breeze *rluṅ.*
Bribe s. *pag-súg.*
Brick *pag*, *pag-bu*; *so-pag.*
Bricklayer *rtsig-bzo-pa*
Bride *bag-ma*; —'s maid *bag-grogs-mo.*
Bridegroom *bag-po*, *mag-pa* col.
Bridge *zam-pa.*
Bridle s. *srab.*
Brier *tser-ma.*
Bright *bkrag-čan*; *krol-król*; *γżi-brjid-čan*; *ₒod-čan*; *γsal-ba.*
Brightness *bkrag*; *dṅom-pa*; *mdaṅs*; *ₒtser-ba*; *zil*; *γzi*; *γzi-brjid*; *ₒod.*
Brilliant *zil-čan.*
Brim *gru.*
Bring *skyel-ba*; *ₒkyer-ba*; *ₒkyog-pa*; *ₒkyoṅ-ba*; *ₒkyol-ba*; to — along with *ₒkrid-pa*; to — on *skyed-pa*; to — round *skul-ba*; to — together *sprod-pa*; to — up *γsos skyed-pa.*
Brisk *kram-pa.*
Bristle s. *kab-spú.*
Bristly *rtsub-po.*
Brittle *krol-mo.*
Broad *pal-čan*; *żeṅ-čan.*
Broken *dkrum-pa*; *čag-pa*, *čag-po*; - country *lčaṅ-lčóṅ.*
Bronze v. *kro* 52; *mkar-ba*, *ₒkar-ba.*
Brook s. *grog-ču*; *ču*; *bab-ču*; *ču-pran.*
Broom *pyag-ma*; *ₒol-mo.*
Broth *śa-kú.*
Brother *spun*, resp. *mčed*; father's — *ku-bo*; mother's — *żaṅ-po*, *'a-żaṅ W.*; a sister's — *miṅ-po*; elder — *jo-bo*, col. *'a-jó*; resp. *γčen*; younger — *nu-bo*; *γčuṅ-po*; *no W.*; religious — *čoś-spun*; brother — in law *skud-po.*

Bruise vb. *grug-pa.*
Brush s. *pir*; *zed.*
Brute *byol-sóṅ.*
Bubble s. *ču-búr*; *lbu-ba*, *dbu-ba.*
Bubbling *kol-pa.*
Bucket *ču-bzóm.*
Buckle s. *čab-ma.*
Buckler *pa-li*; *pub.*
Buckwheat *bra-bo.*
Bud s *sbal-mig*; leaf — *kyi-gu.*
Bud vb. *skye-ba.*
Buddha *saṅs-rgyas*; *rgyal-ba*; *rgyal-ba goṅ-ma.*
Buddhist *naṅ-pa.*
Buffalo *ma-he.*
Bug *ča-ré*; (*lha*) *ₒdre-śig.*
Build *rtsig-pa*; *ₒčos-pa*; *ₒgod-pa.*
Building s. *bkod-pa.*
Bulk *boṅ*; *lhun.*
Bull *glaṅ-túg*; *ba-glaṅ.*
Bullet *go-la*; *tsi-gu*; — mould *ka-lib.*
Bullock *glaṅ*; *spo-to C.*
Bun *lhas(-ma)*; *lhas-dóg*; *żim-zag W.*
Bunch *čam-pód*; *čag-pa*; *čag-bu*, *čag-mo*; *čun-po*; *tsom-pa*; *γzab-ma.*
Bundle *čun-po*; *pon-po*; *lag-kód.*
Bung *ka-ₒdig.*
Burden s. *kal*; *kur*, *kur-po*; *kres-po*; *ₒgaṅ (-po).*
Burn vb. a. *ₒtsig-pa*; *sreg-pa*; vb. n. *ₒbar-ba.*
Burning-glass *me-śél.*
Burst vb. a. *γčog-pa*; vb. n. *ₒgas-pa*; *ₒtor-ba*; *rdol-ba.*
Bury *skuṅ-ba.*
Bushel *kal-bó.*
Business *las*; *don*; *kag*; *gaṅ-po*; *spros-pa*; **ḍel-wa** 382 *W.*
Busy, to be — *brel-ba.*
But adv. (only) *tsam*; v. *man* 411; conj. v. *kyi*; *ₒon-kyaṅ*; *ₒo-ná.*
Butcher *śan-pa*; *śa-tsoṅ-pa.*
Butler *γsol-dpon.*
Butter *mar*; fresh — *skya-már.*
Butterfly *pye-ma-léb.*
Buttermilk *da-ra*; *dar-ba.*
Buttock *rkub*; *ₒpoṅ-tsos.*
Button s. *sgrog-gu*, *sgrog-ril*; *tob-či*, *tob-ču.*
Buy *nyo-ba.*
Buzz vb. *ₒkrog-pa.*
Buzzing s. *ₒur.*
By *kyi*; v. sub *rkyen*; *sgo-nas*; *pas*; *pyir*; close — *druṅ-du.*

C

Cabbage *kram*; Chinese white — *pe-tsé, pi-tsi.*
Cairn *to-yór*; *dur-puṅ.*
Calamity *bkra-mi-šis*; *rkyen*; *ₒgal-rkyen.*
Calamus *ču-tág.*
Calculate *rtsi-ba*; *rtsis byed-pa*; *bgraṅ-ba.*
Calculation *rtsis.*
Calendar *lo-to.*
Calf *be-to, be-do*; *beu*; — of the leg *sgyid-pa*; *byin-pa.*
Call vb. a. *skad-pa*; *skul-ba*; *kug-pa*; *ₒgugs-pa*; *sgrog-pa*; *ₒbod-pa*; v. also *byed-pa* I, 2 and *miṅ ₒdogs-pa* 280; so-called *žes byas-pa*; vb. n. to — to a person *ke' taṅ-wa C.*; *skad gyab-če W.*; *sgrog-pa*; *brgyaṅ-ba.*
Calm adj. *gya-ma-gyú*; v. *dal-ba.*
Calm vb. a. *ži-bar byed-pa.*
Calumny *pra-ma.*
Camel *rṅa-bóṅ*; male — *rṅa-γséb*, female — *rṅa-mo.*
Camp *sgar.*
Camphor *ga-pur.*
Can s. *rkyan, čab-rkyán* 155.
Cancer (disease) *lhog-pa*; (constellation) *kar-ka-ta.*
Candle *rkyoṅ-tse.*
Candy *kaṇ-ḍa.*
Cane *spa, sba*; *smyi-gu, smyug-ma*; *ₒod-ma.*
Canine tooth *mče-ba, mče-só.*
Cannon *gyogs, sgyogs*; *ₒdzam-búr*; — ball *tu-lúm.*
Canopy *γdugs.*
Caoutchouc *gyig.*
Cap *tod-kebs.*
Caper vb. n. *dkyu-ba.*
Capital adj. *kyad-par-čan.*
Capital s. (stock in trade) v. *ma* I, 2; *tog* III.; (chief city) *mtil*; *rgyal-sa W.*
Captain *ₒgo-pa*; *brgya-dpon.*
Captivate *ₒdzin-pa.*
Captive s. *btson.*
Caravansary *tsugs-kaṅ.*
Caraway 1. Carum *go-snyod.* 2. Cumin *zi-ra.*
Carcass *ro, teṅ-ro*; *γzugs.*
Card *yi-ge.*
Cardamom *sug-rmél*; *li-ši W.*
Cardinal points *pyogs* 352.
Care s. *nya-ra*; *γnyer-ka*; to take — **ka-dar čo-če**; to take — of *skyoṅ-ba*; **čag-pa ǰhé-pa* C.*; *γnyer-ba*; to use — *γzabs-pa.*
Careless *bag-méd.*
Caress vb. a. *mtun-par byed-pa*; *yag-po*; *ₒǰag-po byed-pa.*
Carpenter *šiṅ-mkan.*
Carpet *stan.*
Carriage (conveyance) *bčibs-pa*; *bžon-pa*; *teg-pa.*
Carrion *ₒkrums.*
Carrot *guṅ-dmar-la-pug*; *lča-ba*; *se-rag-dur-sman W.*
Carry *ₒkur-ba*; *ₒkyer-ba, ₒkyog-pa*; *ₒkyol-ba*; *skya-ba*; *skyed-pa*; to — away *skyel-ba*; *bda-ba*; to be able to — *teg-pa* 235.
Cart *šiṅ-rta.*
Carter *šiṅ-rta-pa.*
Cartilage *čag-krúm.*
Carve *ₒǰog-pa*; *ₒbru-ba, bru-ba.*
Case (incident) *rkyen*; *skabs*; in — *gal-te* 68; *na* 299; (sheath) *šubs*; (grammar) *rnam-dbyé* 314.
Cash *rnags* 313.
Cashmere *ka-čúl, ka-čé.*
Cask *zem.*
Cast vb. a. *skyur-ba*; *rgyag-pa*; *ₒdebs-pa*; *ₒpen-pa*; to — away *ₒdor-ba*; to — down *ₒbebs-pa*; *ₒbor-ba*; to (metals) *ldugs-pa.*
Casting-mould *lug-koṅ.*
Castle *mkar*; *po-braṅ*; *rdzoṅs.*
Castrate *rlig-pa ₒbyin-pa.*
Cat *byi-la*; *bi-la, bi-li, pi-ši W. žim-bu, žum-bu C.*
Catapult *sgyogs* 119.
Cataract *ri-γzar-čú.*
Catarrh *čam-pa*; *bro-ₒtsúl.*
Catch *ₒdzin-pa.*
Catgut *rgyus-skúd.*
Cattle *pyugs*; breeding — *rkaṅ-ₒgrós*; hornless — *mgo-ril W.*
Caul (anatomy) *rgyu-sgróg.*
Cause s. *rkyen*; *rgyu*; *rgyu-mtsan*; original = *γži-ma.*
Cause vb. a. v. *gugs-pa*; *ₒǰug-pa*; *γtoṅ-ba*; *byed-pa.*
Causeway *so-log.*
Caution s. *γnyer-ka.*
Cautious v. *ka-dár*; *gya-ma-gyú*; to be — **ka-dar čo-če**; *ₒgab-pa.*
Cave, Cavern *pug-pa.*
Cavity *kuṅ*; *sbugs.*
Cease *ₒgag-pa*; *ₒčad-pa*; *ži-ba.*
Ceiling *tog, ya-tog.*
Celebrated *gzi-brǰid-čan.*
Cell *grwa*; **da-šág** 75.
Cellar *ša-káṅ.*
Cemetery *dur-krod.*
Censer *pog-pór, spos-pór.*
Censor (of a monastery) *dge-bskos* 85.
Censure s. *klan-ka.*
Centiped *la-ré W.*; *si-ri-ₒbu W.*
Centre *lte-ba*; *mtil*; *dbus.*
Cerebellum *klad-čuṅ.*
Ceremony *čo-ga*; *sku-rím.*

Certain *ńes-pa*; *gor-ma-čág*; *ńo-rtóg*; a — one *ɣčig-čig*.
Certainly *ɣdon-mi-za-bar*.
Certainty *ńes-pa*; *tag-čód*.
Ceylon *laṅ-ka*.
Chaff *spun-pa*, *sbun-pa*; *sbur-ma*.
Chain s. *lčags-tág*; *nyag-tág*.
Chair *ḱri*; *rgya-ḱrí C.*
Chairman *ḱri-pa*.
Chalk *to-lé dkar-po*.
Chamber *naṅ*; *ḱaṅ-mig*.
Champion *gyad*.
Chance s. *rgyu* 110.
Change s. *ₒgyur-ba*; *res*.
Change vb. a *sgyur-ba*; *ɹje-ba*; *spo-ba*; *rdzu-ba*; to — place *ₒṕo-ba*; vb. n. *ₒgyur-ba*; *ₒṕo-ba*.
Chant vb. *dgyer-ba*.
Chap vb. *ₒgas-pa*.
Chapter *leu*.
Character (disposition) *rgyud*; *ńaṅ*; *ńo-bo-nyid*; *tsul*; *rig-rgyud*; **šē-gyú* C.* 562.
Characteristic s. *rgyu-mtsán* 111.
Charge vb. *sko-ba*; *rgol-ba*; *mńag-pa*; to — with (to commission) *ₒgel-ba*.
Charge s. (commission) *ḱag*.
Charity *snyiṅ-rje*.
Charming *dga-ba*; *yid-du ˬoṅ-ba*.
Chase vb. *ₒčor-ba*.
Chase s. *ḱyi-ra*.
Chasm s. *rgya-sér*.
Chastisement *čad-pa*; *tul*.
Chastity *ḱrel-yod*; *tsaṅs-par spyod-pa*.
Chat vb. *ˬur ɣtoṅ-ba*; *lab ɣtoṅ-ba*.
Chattering s. *čo-lo*.
Cheap *ḱye-mo W.*; *rin čuṅ-ba*.
Cheat vb. *blo brid-pa*; *slu-ba*; *ɣyo-zól byed-pa*; *mgo skor-ba*.
Cheek *ₒgram-pa*; — bone *ₒgram-rús*; — tooth *ₒgram-so*.
Cheer vb. *glod-pa*; *spro-ba skyed-pa*; *dga-bar byed-pa*.
Cheerful *ḱrul-po*; *dga-mo*; *sems-bdé*, *blo-bdé*.
Cheese *tud*; *ˬo-túd*.
Chess-board *mig-máṅ*; to play at chess *mig-maṅ rtse-ba*.
Chest (box) *gau*; *sgam*; *sgrom*; (thorax) *braṅ*, resp. *sku-bráṅ*.
Chew *ldad-pa*.
Chicken *bya-ṕrug*.
Chief adj. *dpon*; *ɣtso*; — justice *ḱrims-dpon*.
Chief s. *ₒgo-pa*; *dpon-po*; *ɣtso-bo*; *ḱyu-mčóg*.
Chiefly *ɣtso-bor*, *ɣtso-čér*.
Child *ṕru-gu*; *byis-pa*; *bu*; v. *ḱyeu*.
Children *bu-ṕrug*; — of the same parents (brothers, sisters) *spun*.
Chill s. *kyi-bún*.
Chin *ko-kó*; *ma-lé*.
China *rgya-nág*; *rgya-yúl*; modern name: *ma-hā-či-na*, *ma-hā-čin*; — clay *ḱam-pa*; — ware *kar-yól*; *dkar-yól*; resp. *žal-kar C.*; *sol-kar W.*
Chinese s. *rgya-nag-pa*, *rgya-bo*; fem. *rgya-nag-ma*, *rgya-mo*; *rgya-mí*; plur. *rgya-rnams*.
Chinese adj. *rgyai*, *rgya-nag-gi*, — language *rgya-skád*; — paper *rgya-šóg*.
Chink *sgo-bár*.
Chip *tsal-pa*; *šiṅ-tsal*.
Chirping s. *ča-čó*.
Chisel vb. *ₒbru-ba*.
Chit-chat s. *ˬur*.
Choice adj. *mčog-tu bkrab*; *ḱyad-par ṕags-pa*; *ḱyad-par-čan*.
Choke *dbugs sub-pa*; **skye tsir taṅ-če* W.*; *ske bsdam-ste ɣsod-pa*; to be choked *rnaṅ-ba*; *ske bsdam-ste ₒči-ba*; *ₒtsub-pa*.
Cholera *ḱoṅ-lóg W.*; *nya-lóg Sik.*
Choose vb. a. *bkrab-pa*; *ₒbyed-pa*; *ₒdzin-pa*; vb. n. (to like) *dgyes-pa*.
Chop vb. *btsab-pa*; to — off *ɣčod-pa*.
Chopping-block *šiṅ-stan*.
Chopsticks *tur-ma*.
Chord *rgyud* 111
Christ *skyabs-mgón* 26; *ma-ši-ka* 410.
Chronic adj. *yun riṅ-bai*; — disease *ɣčoṅ-nád*.
Chronicle *lo-rgyús*.
Churn vb. *dkrog-pa*; *žo dkrog-pa*.
Churn s. v. *gur-gúr* 70.
Chutney (Indian condiment) *tsu-u* 449.
Chyle *dwaṅs-ma* 249.
Cimeter *gri-gúg*.
Cinamon *šiṅ-tsa*.
Cipher s. *mḱa*; *tig-le*.
Circle s. *skor*, *ₒḱor*, *ₒḱor-lo*; *dkyil-ₒḱor*; *sgor-mo*, *sgor-tig*.
Circular adj. *kyir-kyir*; *gor-mo*.
Circumference *dkyil-ₒḱor*; *ₒḱor*; *ḱo-ra*; *ḱyon*; *mu-ḱyúd*.
Circumstance *rkyen*; *skabs*.
Citadel *mḱar*; *rdzoṅ*.
Citizen *ḱyim-bdág*; *yul-pa*; *yon-bdag*.
Citron *yam-bu-ra W.*; *spyod-pad C.*
City *groṅ-ḱyér*.
Civilize *ₒdul-ba*.
Claim s. *tob-tsir*, *tob-sról*.
Clairvoyance *mńon-šés* 133.
Clammy *rtsi-čan*.
Clamour s. *ku*, *ku-sgra*, *ku-čo*; *skad-lóg*; *ča-čó*.
Clandestinely *sbas-te W.*; v. also *lkog-tu*, *ɣsaṅ-ba*.
Clap vb., to — the hands *čag-čág byed-pa*.
Clap s. (crash) *sguṅ W.*; *ldim W.*; *ldir-sgra*.
Clasp vb. a. *ₒḱyud-pa*; *ₒḱril-ba*.
Clasp s. *čab-ma*; — knife *ltab-gri*.

Class s. *gral*; *ča-tsán*; *bye-brág*; *dbye-ba*; *tsan*, *sde-tsán*.
Classify *rnam-par bžag-pa*; *ₒbyed-pa*.
Claw *kron*; *sder(-mo)*; *spar-ba*.
Clay *ₒǰim-pa*; *rdza*; *žal-ba*; — floor *skyań-nul*.
Clean adj. *dag-pa*, *γtsań-ba*; *lag-mo W.*; — food *dkar-zás*.
Clean, Cleanse vb. a. *pyi-bdar byed-pa*; *sań-ba*; *sel-ba*; to be cleansed *ₒbyoń-ba*.
Clear adj. *mńon-pa*; *tur-re*; *wa-lè*; *wa-le-ba*; *lag-mo W.*; *sińs-po W.*; *lhań-ńe*.
Clear vb. a. *ₒdag-pa*; *sel-ba*.
Cleave *ₒges-pa*; *ₒčeg-pa*; to be cleft *ₒgas-pa*.
Cleft s. *rgya-sér*; *ral*; *srubs*.
Clerk *yig-mkan*.
Clever *γčań-po*; *sgrin-po*; *tabs-čan*; *spyań-po*; a — writer *rtsom-par mkas-pa*.
Clew s. *gru-gu*.
Climb *ₒdzeg-pa*; *rgal-ba*.
Cling *čags-pa*; *ča-bžag-pa*.
Clip *ₒgrum-pa*.
Cloak s. *ber*.
Clock *ču-tsod*; *ču-tsod-ₒkor-lo*.
Close vb. a. *ₒgegs-pa*; v. also *ₒdzum-pa*.
Close adj. *gya-ma-gyu* 73; — fisted *kroń-po*; *lag-dam-po*; adv. *ₒǰam-pa* 174; — over *glad-la*.
Clot s. *goń-po*; — of blood *krag-góń*.
Cloth *sag-lád*; *prug*; *ter-ma*; *dar*; a piece of — *yug*, *bubs*.
Clothes *gos*, *gos-lág*; *bgo-ba*; to change — *gos brǰe-ba*; to put on — *gos gon-pa*; to take off — *gos ₒbud-pa*; suit of — *go-lus-ča-tsań W.*
Clothes-brush *byab-zéd*.
Clothes-stand *γdań*, *rdań*.
Clothing s. *bgo-ba*; *ča-byád*, *ča-lúgs*.
Cloud s. *sprin*; — of dust *bud*.
Clouded, to be — *ₒkrig-pa*.
Cloudy, it has become — *kor-soń*.
Clove *li-ši C.*; *bzań-drúg W.*; *zer-bu W.*
Club (mace) *ga-da*.
Clumsy *sbom-pa*; *zlum-pa*.
Cluster s. *čag-mo*.
Clyster s. *ₒkos*; *bsur-smyig*; — pipe *čeu*.
Coachman *šiń-rta-pa*.
Coagulate *ₒkyags-pa*.
Coal *sol-ba*.
Coarse *rtsiń-ba*; *rags-pa*; — grained *rtsub-po*.
Coast *ₒkris*.
Coat s. *gos*; *dug-po Ü*; *ču-pa Ts.*; — lap *kud*; — of mail *krab*.
Coat vb. a. *ₒtum-pa*.
Cock s. *bya-po*, *bya-po*; *kyim-bya*; of a gun *to-čúń*; *me-skám*.
Cock vb. a. *rdze-ba*.
Coetaneous *na-mnyám*, *na-ₒdrá*.
Coffee *ka-bu* 37, III.
Coffer *sgrom*.
Coffin *dur-sgám*, *ro-sgám*.
Cohabit *ₒbrel-ba*; *ₒkrig-pa spyod-pa*.
Cohabitation *sbyor-ba*.
Cohere *ₒbrel-ba*.
Coil vb. (of snakes) *ₒkri-ba*.
Coin s. *doń-tse*.
Coition, Coitus *ₒkrig-pa*; *čags-spyód*; *nyal-po*.
Colander *tsag-ma*.
Cold adj. *grań-ba*; — air *ńa-ra*; *ńad*; — wind *ńar-ba*; *lhags-pa*; to feel — *ₒkyags-pa*; v. *kyi-bún*; to get, to grow — *grań-ba*, *grańs-pa*.
Cold s. *kyags-pa*; *grań-ba*; *ńad*; *ńar-ba*; to have a — *bro-ₒtsal-ba*; a — in the head *čam-pa*; *bro-ₒtsál*; *ya-ma*.
Colic *glań*, *glań-tábs*; *rgyu-γzér*; *tsa-ₒkru*.
Collar s. *goń-ba*, *gos-kyi goń-ba*; to seize by the — *goń-ba-nas ₒdzin-pa*.
Collect vb. a. *sgrug-pa*, *sloń-pa*; *sdud-pa*; *sog-pa*.
Colonel *ru-dpón*.
Colour s. *ka*; *ka-dog*; *mdog*; *tson*; beautiful — *bkrag*; prime — *ma-γži*; to lose — *dkyug-pa*.
Colt *tur-bu*; — of an ass *ku-rúg*, *gu-rúg*.
Comb s. *so-mań*.
Comb vb. a. *šad-pa*, *γšad-pa*, *γšod-pa*.
Combat s. *ₒtab-mo*; *ₒkrug-pa*.
Combat vb. *ₒtab-mo ₒgyed-pa*, *ₒtab-pa*; *ₒkrab-pa*; *rgol-ba*.
Come *ₒoń-ba*, resp *ₒbyor-ba*, *ₒbyon-pa*; *pebpa*; eleg. *mči-ba*; come! *šog*; to — again *ldog-pa*, *log-pa*; to — back *pyir-ₒgro-ba*; to — forth *čags-pa*; to — out *ₒbyuń-ba*, *ₒton-pa*; to — to *ₒkyol-ba*; *γnas-su ₒgyur-ba*; to — together *ₒdzom-pa*; to — up (of seeds) *ₒkruń-ba*, *rdol-ba*.
Comfort vb. a. *glod-pa*; *mya-ńan sań-ba*; *spro-ba skyed-pa*.
Comforter *skyo-grógs*.
Command vb. a. *bka γnań-ba*, *γnań-ba*; (an army) *ₒkrid-pa*.
Command s. *žal-γdáms*.
Commander *dmag-ₒgo*; *dmag-dpón*.
Commandment *bka*, *bka-krims*, *bka-bsgos*; *krims*.
Commence *rtsom-pa*; *ₒdzugs-pa*.
Commend *sńag-pa*; *ₒčol-ba*.
Comment vb. a. *ₒgrel-ba*, *ₒgrol-ba*.
Commerce *tsoń*.
Commissary *sku-tsáb*.
Commission vb. a. *sko-ba*; *ₒgel-ba*; *mńag-pa*.
Commit *skur-ba*; *ₒčol-ba*; (sin etc.) *byed-pa*.
Common *dkyus-ma*; *tun*; *pal-pa*; *pral*; the — people *pal* 341.
Communication *bka-rgya*; *ₒbrel*, *ₒbrel-ba*.

Communion *˳brel-ba*; *˳grogs-lugs*; holy — *ɣsol-rás* 592.
Compact adj *mk'raṅ*; *˳čag-čan*.
Companion *grogs*; *rogs*; *skyo-grógs*; *zla-bo*; *ya-do* W.
Company *kyu*; in — *tun-moṅ-du*; *˳grogs-te*.
Comparative degree v. *ǰe* 172; *las* II, *pas*, *saṅ*.
Compare *sdur-ba*; *sgrun-pa*; *sgre-ba*.
Comparison *dpe* 327.
Compass (circumference) *mu-kyúd*; points of the — *mtsams* 455.
Compasses, pair of, *skor-tig*.
Compassion *snyiṅ-rǰe*; *snyiṅ-brtse-ba*.
Compel v. *nan-gyis* 302; *šed-kyer-nag-pos* W.; to be compelled *dgos-pa*.
Competitor *˳gran-zla*.
Compile *sgrig-pa*.
Complaint *zug*, *ɣzug* 488, *nad*.
Complete adj. *grub-pa*; *rgyas-pa*; *tam-pa*; *p̓un-tsógs*; *rdzogs-pa*; *tsaṅ-ba*; to be — *tsaṅ-ba*.
Complete vb. a. *sgrub-pa*; *tog ˳gel-ba*; to be completed *˳kor-ba*; *˳tsar-ba*.
Completely *ɣtan-du*; *ye-nas*.
Complex of fields *kluṅs*.
Complicate adj. *krag-krúg*.
Compliment s. *p̓yag*; compliments v. *stod-pa* 223.
Compose *˳god-pa*; *rtsom-pa*; to — verses *sdeb-pa*; *sbyor-ba*.
Comprehend *go-ba*; *˳dzin-pa*; *yid-la byed-pa*.
Comprehension *go-ba*.
Comprehensive *kyab-če-ba*.
Comprise *kyab-pa*; *sdud-pa*.
Compulsion *gal* 68; *nan* 302.
Computation *rtsis*.
Compute *rtsi-ba*.
Comrade *grogs*.
Concave *koṅ*.
Conceal *sbed-pa*; *ɣsaṅ-ba*; *sgoṅ-ba*; *˳čab-pa*.
Concealment *p̓ag*.
Conceited *mčor-po*.
Conception *dmigs-pa*.
Concerning (as regards) *rten-nas*; *dbaṅ-du byas-na* 387.
Concession *ɣnaṅ-ba*.
Concord *mtun-pa*.
Condemn *žal-če ɣčod-pa*; *krims ɣčod-pa* or *ɣtoṅ-ba*.
Condescending *če-tabs-med-pa*; to be — *mtun-pa byed-pa*.
Condiment *skyu-rúm*; *sdor*.
Condition (state) *ɣnas-skabs*; *ɣnas-tsúl* 311; *yin-lugs* 518.
Conduct vb. a. *skyel-ba*; *˳krid-pa*; *˳dren-pa*.
Conduct s. *spyod-pa*.
Cone *tsa-tsa*.
Confess *˳čey-pa*; *mtol-ba*; *ɣšog-pa*; *ɣso-sbyoṅ-ba* 590.
Confession (creed) *čos-rgyud* 164.
Confide (*yid*) *rton-pa* 215; v. *blo-ɣdéṅ* 385.
Confidence *blo-ɣtád*, *blo-ɣdéṅ*.
Confidential speaking *snyiṅ-ɣtam*.
Confine vb. *dgar-ba*.
Conform vb. *sbyor-ba*.
Confound *dkrug-pa*; *˳dzol-ba*.
Confused, to be — *rtab-pa*.
Confusion *˳kral-˳krúl*.
Congeal *˳kyags-pa*.
Conglomerate s. *gad-pa*.
Congratulate *bkra-šis mṅa ɣsol-ba*.
Conjuncture *bsgaṅ*; *dus*.
Conjure (implore) *nan-gyis žu-ba*.
Conjure up *˳gugs-pa*.
Conjurer *˳ba-po*.
Connect *sbyor-ba*; *sbrel-ba*; *zuṅ sdebs-pa*.
Connected with *bčas-pa*; to be — *˳brel-ba*.
Connection *˳brel-pa*, *zuṅ-˳brél*; v. also *rgyu-rkyén* 110.
Conquer *bčom-pa*; *˳joms-pa*; *rgyal-ba*; *˳p̓am-par byed-pa* 356; to be conquered *˳p̓am-pa*.
Conqueror *rgyal-ba*.
Conscience *gal-mtun šes-pa*; *šes-bžin*; v. also *byas-čos* and *ɣnoṅ-ba*.
Conscientious *krel-čan*.
Consciousness *šes-pa*; *dran-pa*; — of guilt *ɣnoṅ-ba*.
Consecrate *skur-ba*; *rab(-tu) ɣnas(-par) byed-pa* 524.
Consequence *mǰug*; *˳bras-bu*; in — of *dbaṅ-gis*.
Consider vb. a. *graṅ-ba*; *˳dzin-pa*; *bsam-mnó byed-pa*; vb. n. *sgom-pa*; *mno-ba*.
Consideration *dran-pa* 262.
Consign *skur-ba*.
Consist *˳dus-pa*, *bsdus-pa*.
Consistence *ska-slád*.
Consistency *srab-˳túg*.
Console *sems ɣso-ba*; *mya-ṅan-bsaṅ-ba*.
Consort s. *čuṅ-ma*; royal — *lčam-mo*; *btsun-mo*.
Conspicuous *mṅon-pa*; *ɣsal-po*.
Constable *dge-ɣyóg* 86.
Constellation *skar-ma*; *ɣza-skár*.
Constipation *bšaṅ-dgág*.
Constitute *gel-ba*; *sko-ba*; *˳jug-pa* II, 2.
Constraint *gal*.
Construct *bčo-ba*; v. *˳ča-ba*; *˳čos-pa*; *ɣtoṅ-ba*; *˳god-pa*; *rtsig-pa*.
Construction (grammatical) *tsig sgrig-pa*.
Consult *bka-bgro-ba*.
Consultation *gros-gléṅ*; *˳dun-ma*.
Consume *čud ɣzon-pa*; *zin ˳jug-pa*; to be

consumed *ča-ba*; *čad-pa*; *ₒtsar-ba*; *ₒdzad-pa*; *zin-pa*.
Consumption *γčon*.
Contain v. *šoṅ-ba*; to be contained *ₒgro-ba*; v. *ₒdug-pa* no. 2.
Contamination *grib*.
Contemplate *sgom-pa*.
Contemplation *sgom*; *tiṅ-ṅe-ₒdzin*.
Contempt *ṅnan-čen*; *brnyas-pa*; *smad-pa*.
Contend (fight) *ₒkrug-pa*; *rtsod-pa*; (to strive) *ₒgran-pa*.
Content adj. *čog šes-pa*; *tsim-pa*; to be — *mgu-ba*; to heart's — *yid bžin-du*.
Contention *ₒgran-sems*; *ₒdziṅ-mo*.
Contentment *snyiṅ-tsim*.
Contest s. *tob-šá*.
Continent *gliṅ*.
Continually *rgyun-du*; *čar*, *ča-ré*; *γtan-du*.
Continuation *ₒpro*.
Continue *ₒpro-ba*.
Contract vb. a. *skum-pa*; vb. n. *ₒkor-ba*.
Contract s. *gan-rgyá*; *čad-yig*; *ₒdzin*, *yig-ₒdzin*.
Contradiction, to be in — *ₒgal-ba*.
Contrary s. *bzlog*, *go-bzlóg*; *go-ldóg*, *go-lóg*.
Contrivance *grabs*.
Convent s. *čos-sde*; *sde*; *dgon-pa*.
Convention *ka-čád*.
Conversation *gleṅ-brjód*.
Converse vb. *gleṅ-ba*; *gleṅ-mo byed-pa*; *gros-byéd bgro-ba*.
Convert vb. *čos-su ₒjug-pa*.
Convey *skya-ba*; *skyed-pa*; *skyel-ba*; *ₒkur-ba*.
Convoy s. *skyel-ma*.
Cook vb. *ₒtsod-pa*.
Cook s. *gyos-mkan*; head — *γsol-dpon*, *ma-čen*.
Cool *graṅ-ba*; *bsil-ba*.
Cooly (carrier) *kur-pa*; (workman) *gla-pa*.
Coot *skyegs*.
Copious *rgyas-pa*.
Copper *zaṅs*.
Copulation *ₒkrig-pa*; *čags-spyod*.
Copy vb. *šu-ba*.
Copy s. (transcript) *bkod-pa*; *bu-dpe*; (pattern) *ma*, *ma-dpe*.
Coral *byi-ru*.
Cord s. *rgyud*; *sgrogs*; *ta-gu*; *ₒpreṅ-ba*.
Cordial s. *bčud*.
Core *kog-šiṅ*.
Coriander seed *ₒu-su*.
Cork *ka-γčod*, *ka-ₒdig*.
Corn (grain) *ₒbru*; boiled — *čan*; slightly roasted *yos*; stack of — *rags*, *pub-rags*; *hi-ri*; corn on a toe *rkaṅ-mdzub-dzer-pa*.
Corner *kug*; *gru*; *grwa*; *zur*.
Corporal *bču-dpon*.
Corpse *ro*, resp. *spur*.
Correct adj. *skyon-méd*; *nor-méd*; to be — *ₒgrig-pa*.
Correct vb. *sgyur-ba*; *žu-dag byed-pa*.
Correction *žu-dág*, *žus-dág*.
Correspond (to be adequate) *ₒgrig-pa*.
Correspondent (in business) *tsoṅ-grogs*.
Corrupt vb. a. *slad-pa*.
Corruptness *kun-dkris*.
Costly *gus-po*, *rin-čan*.
Cottage *kan-bu*; *ku-tu*.
Cotton *ras-bal*, *srin-bal*, *šiṅ-bal*; — cloth (*ka-ši-kai*) *ras*.
Couch s. *kri*; *nyal-kri*; *mal*.
Cough s. *glo*; *kogs*; *bro-ₒtsál*; vb. *kogs-pa*.
Council *gros*, *gros-gleṅ*; *ₒdun-ma*.
Counsel s. *gros*; *bka-γdáms*; *ₒdun-ma*.
Counselor *bka-γšags*.
Count vb. *bgraṅ-ba*; *ₒdren-pa*; *rtsi-ba*; *γšor-ba*; *si kor-če W.*
Countenance *γdoṅ*; *bžin*; *ṅo*; *skye-sgo*; *sgo-lo*.
Counteract *ₒgal-ba*.
Counterfeit adj. *rdzus-ma*.
Counterparty *pa-rol*
Counting s. *rtsis*.
Country *yul*, *yul-ₒkór*, *yul-grú*; *sa-čá*; *rgyal-kág*; love of — *yul-sréd*; *yul-la ₒdod-pa*.
Couple s. *zuṅ*; married — *bza-mí*.
Courage *snyiṅ-stobs*, *snyiṅ-rús*; *spobs-pa*.
Courageous *ham-pa-čan*; *dpa-ba*, *dpa-čan*.
Courier *rta-zam-pa*.
Course s. *tsir*.
Court s. (residence of a prince) *kab*; — of justice *bka-γšags*; *krims-kaṅ*.
Courtyard *kyams*; *tsoms*, *tsoms-skór*.
Cove *kug*.
Covenant s. *ka-čád*.
Cover vb. *ₒkeb-pa*; *ₒgebs-pa*; *klub-pa*; *ₒtum-pa*.
Cover, Covering s. *ka-kebs*, *ka-gab*, *ka-γčod*, *ka-leb*; *kebs*, *kyebs*, *kebs-ma*; *go-šog*; *tums*; *γyogs*; *šubs*; covering for the head *mgo-γyógs*.
Cowry *ₒgron-bu*.
Crab *sdig-srin*.
Crack vb. a. *γčog-pa*; vb. n. *ₒgas-pa*.
Crack s. *sguṅ*.
Craft (cunning) *dku-lto*.
Crafty *yó-ba*.
Cram *sgrim-pa*.
Crane (bird) *kruṅ-kruṅ*.
Crash s. *sguṅ*.
Crave *ṅnab-pa*.
Craw *lkog-šóg*.
Crawfish *sdig-srin*.
Crawl *gog-pa*; *ₒpye-ba*.
Cream *spri-ma*, *spris-ma*, *sris-ma*; *ₒo-sri*; *žo-sri*.

Create ˳yod-pa.
Creator ˳yod-pa-po; mdzad-po.
Creature bkod-pa; ˳gro-ba, lus-c̀an.
Credible ˳os-pa.
Creditor bun-bdág.
Creed čos-rgyud, čos-lugs.
Creek ḱug, ḱugs.
Creep ˳ṕye-ba, gog-pa.
Crescent s. zla-ts̀es lta-bui ri-mo or dbyibs.
Crest (of fowl) c̀od-ṕán.
Crevice γseṅ, seṅ.
Cricket (insect) c̀og-c̀og-pa W.
Crime nyes-pa; noṅs-pa.
Cripple ża-bo.
Crippled ḱoṅs-ḱan W.; ḱoṅ-ril C.; grum-pa.
Criticise ˳bigs-pa.
Crocodile kum-bi-ra.
Crooked kug; kum-pa, koṅ; kyog-po; ḱoṅs; ˳ḱyog-po; dgur; to be — dgye-ba.
Crop vb. γtog-pa.
Crop s. lo-tóg.
Cross s. brkyaṅ-s̀iṅ; sku-ru-ka.
Cross vb. γc̀od-pa; rgal-ba.
Crouch čum-pa.
Croup, he has the — ḱoi lkog-ma skraṅs soṅ (his throat is swollen).
Crow s. ḱa-ta; ṕo-róg.
Crow-bar gal-ta; lc̀ags-bér.
Crowd s. ḱrod-pa; ḱrom; γseb.
Crowd vb. a. bčar-ba C., bc̀er-ba W.
Crown s. c̀od-ṕán; — of the head spyi-bo; γtsug.
Crown vb. a. c̀od-pan-gyis brgyan-pa; v. also tog ˳gel-ba.
Crucible koṅ-po W.; żu-skyógs C.
Cruel γnyan-pa; drag-s̀ul-c̀an.
Crumb čag-dúm; brul; bir-bir W.
Crumble vb. a. grug-pa; vb. n. gog-pa.
Crupper sgal-pa; rmed.
Crush glem-pa; rdzi-ba.
Cry vb. n. ˳grags-pa, ˳grogs-pa.
Cry s. ṅa-ro; skad, skad-ṅan; c̀a-c̀ó; — for help ˳o-dód.
Crystal man-s̀el, s̀el.
Cubit ḱru 61.
Cuckoo ḱu-byúg; kug-se W.
Cucumber ka ku-ráṅ Kun.
Cultivate ˳bad-pa; cultivated land kluṅs.
Cunning s. dku-lto.
Cup ko-ré, kor; koṅ-po; tiṅ; ṕor-pa; — bearer γsol-dpon.
Cupboard ˳ča.
Cupping-glass me-búm, me-ṕúṅ.
Curd żo, resp. γsol-żó.
Cure vb. γc̀od-pa; bc̀os-pa; ˳ts̀o-ba; γso-ba.
Curious (inquisitive) snob-zog-c̀an.
Curl s. (of hair) ral-pa.
Curled tsa-ru W.
Currant nyaṅ-ka Sp.; rub-s̀o W.; (raisins) ba-s̀o Ld., ba-s̀o-ka C.
Current s. rgyun; ču-rgyún.
Current adj., to be — (of coins) ˳grul-ba, rgyug-pa.
Curse s. ṅan; dmod-pa.
Curse vb. a. ṅan ˳debs-pa; dmod-pa ˳bor-ba.
Curtain yol-ba.
Curve s. gye-gu.
Curve vb. a. kug-kug byed-pa; ˳gum-pa; curved ḱyog-po; kyag-kyóg W.; to be curving dgye-ba.
Cushion sṅas; stan; ˳bol, snye-˳ból; sob-stán.
Custom (use) ḱrims; čos; srol; (toll) s̀o-gám.
Cut vb. a. γc̀od-pa; ˳ǰog-pa; dra-ba; (to mow) rṅa-ba; to — into pieces sgral-ba; ˳tub-pa; v. ˳čad-pa; to — off grum-pa; ˳breg-pa, ˳dreg-pa; v. čod-pa; v. čad-pa; to — open ˳ges-pa; to — out v. γc̀ar-ba 143; to — up γtubs-pa; dmyal-ba.
Cut s. ḱram-ka; (blow) lc̀ag; a short — *gyog-lám*.
Cylinder ˳ḱor-lo 58; praying — čos-kyi ˳ḱor-lo.
Cylindrical ril-ba; to be — ˳gril-ba.
Cymbal sbug-żál; sbum-żól W.; sil-snyán.
Cypress spa-ma Sik.

D

Daily adv. nyin-re-bżin(-du); żag-daṅ żag.
Dalai Lama ta-lai bla-ma.
Dam s. ču-rags; ču-lon.
Dam up vb. skyil-ba.
Damage s. skyon; gud, gun; god; nyes-pa; γnod-pa; vb. a. γnod-pa.
Damp adj. rlan-c̀an.
Dance vb. ˳čam-pa; bro-brduṅ-ba or ḱrab-pa; s. gar; bro.
Dancer gar-mḱan.
Dandelion ḱur-ma, ḱur-ts̀od.
Dandy ˳ṕyor-dga.
Danger nyen.
Dangerous ma-ruṅ-ba, ma-ruṅs-pa; γdug-pa-c̀an; btsog-pa W.
Daring adj. rtul-ṕod-pa; spobs-pa-c̀an; dpa-c̀an, dpa-bo.
Dark adj. sgrib-pa; mun-pa; smag; to grow — ˳tibs-pa; ˳grib-pa.
Darken vb. a. sgrib-pa; vb. n. ˳grib-pa.

Darkness *mun-pa*; *smag-rum*.
Darling, my —! *ṅai yid˳oṅ*; cf. also *sdug-pa*.
Darn *tur-ba*; *snol-ba*.
Dart s. *mda*; vb. n. *˳ḱyug-pa* 60.
Date s. (time) *zag-gráṅs*; (fruit) *ḱa-zúr*.
Daub vb. *skud-pa*.
Daughter *bu-mo*, *bo-mo*; *sras-mo*; — in-law *mna-ma*.
Dawn s. *skya-ód*, *skya-réṅs*; *ťo-ráṅs*; vb. it dawns *skya-reṅs šar*.
Day *nyi-ma*; *nyin-mo*; *žag*; — and night *nyin-mťsán*; — by — *žag daṅ žag*; all the — long *nyin-ťse-ré*; every — *žag-daṅ W.*; from — to — *žag-nas žag-tu*; one —, some — *deu-re*; the other — *de-žag* 471 *W.*; this — five days *dgus*.
Day-break *nam-laṅs*; at — *nam-laṅs-te* or *nas*.
Dazzle vb. n. *ťom-par ˳gyur-ba*.
Dazzling *ḱrol-po*; *lčam-me-ba*.
Dead adj. v. *ši-ba*; a — man *γšin-po*; *ro*.
Deaf *˳on-pa*.
Deal with vb. *spyod-pa*.
Deal s., a good — *ga-čén*.
Dear *γčig*; *γčes-pa*; *dkon-pa*; *gus-po*; *rin-ťaṅ-čan*, *rin-čan*; to hold — *γče-ba*.
Dearth *zas-dkon C.*
Death *˳či-ba*; forebodings of — *˳či-ltas*; hour of — *˳da-ga*; to seek — *lčeb-pa*.
Debate s. *rtsod-pa*; vb. *bgro gleṅ byed-pa*.
Debt *bu-lon*; the — is cleared *bu-lon ḱor*.
Debtor *bu-lon-pa*.
Decapitate *ske γčod-pa*.
Decay s. *˳ǰig-pa*.
Decay vb. *nyil-ba*; *˳tor-ba*; *nub-pa*.
Decayed *˳ḱogs-pa*.
Deceased *γšin-po*.
Deceit *mgo-skór*; *ṅo-lkog*; *rdzub*; *zog*, *zol-zóg*.
Deceitful *lče-γnyis-pa*.
Deceive *mgo skor-ba*; *rṅod-pa*; *blo ˳brid-pa*, *˳brid-pa*; *slu-ba*.
Deceived *˳ḱrul-pa*.
Decency *ḱrel-yod*.
Decent *˳gab-pa*.
Deception *sgyu-zóg*.
Decide *γčod-pa*; *ťag-γčod-pa*.
Decided *zad*; v. *˳dzad-pa*; to be — *čad-pa*.
Declare *bšad-pa*.
Declination (of the sun) v. *bgrod-pa*; north — *byaṅ-bgrod*, south — *lho-bgrod*.
Decline (decay) vb. n. *rgud-pa*.
Declivity *gud*; *ri γzar-po*, *brag γzar-po*.
Decoction *ťaṅ-gi sman*.
Decorate *sgron-pa*; *brgyan-pa*; *spra-ba*.
Decoration *rgyan*.
Decrease vb. *˳gyur-ba*; *˳grib-pa*; *˳bri-ba*.
Decree s. *bka-šog*, *bka-ḱrims*; *ḱra-ma*.
Decrepit *˳ḱogs-pa*.

Dedicate *sṅo-ba*.
Deed *las*; *bya-ba*.
Deep adj. *γtiṅ-riṅ-ba*; *zab-pa*; — (of sounds) *rom-po W.*
Deer *ka-ša Sik.*
Deface *dma ˳bebs-pa*.
Defeat vb. *˳pam-par byed-pa*.
Defect s. *skyon*.
Defective *skyon-čan*.
Defence *skyabs*.
Defend *skyoṅ-ba*; *skyob-pa*.
Defender (of religion) *čos-skyóṅ*.
Defer v. *˳gyaṅ-ba*.
Deficient *sgob-sgób*.
Defile s. *roṅ*.
Defile vb. *bsgo-ba*; *˳bag-pa*.
Defilement *grib*.
Deform vb. *mi sdug-par byed-pa*.
Degenerate adj. *brgyud-méd*; *rigs-nyáms*.
Degree (rank) *ťem-pa*, *ťem-rim*; *sa* no. 2; *go*, *go-ṗaṅ*; a high — v. *rlabs*; by degrees *ḱad-kyis*; *mťar-gyis*; *rim-gyis*, *rim-pa bžin du*
Dejected *žum-pa*; *mi dga-ba*, v. *dga-ba* III; *dman-pa*.
Delay s. *bšol-ba*.
Delay vb., to be delayed *˳gyaṅ-ba*.
Delegate vb. a. *mṅag-pa*.
Delegate s. *ťsab-po*, resp. *sku-ťsáb*.
Deliberate vb. *bka-bgro-ba*, *bgro-ba*.
Deliberation *grabs*, *˳dun-ma*, *˳dun-gros*.
Delight s. *dga-ba*; *dga-spró*, *dga-ťsór*, *dga-ráṅs*, *dga-mgú*; to take — in *dga-ba*, resp. *dgyes-pa* or *mnyes-pa*; *spro-ba*.
Delighted *dga-mo*, *dga-ba*, *dga-raṅs*; to be *dga-ba*.
Delightful *dga-mo*, *dga-ťsor če-ba*.
Delineation *bkod-pa*; *ris*, *ri-mo*.
Deliver (rescue) *sgrol-ba*; (transfer) *sprod-pa*; *γtod-pa*; *skur-ba*.
Deliverance (liberation) *grol-ba*.
Deliverer *skyabs-mgón*; *srog-skyób W.*
Dell *grog-po*.
Delude *mgo skor-ba*.
Deluge s. *ču-rúd*.
Delusion *snaṅ-˳ḱrúl*.
Delusive *kun-rdzób*; *˳ḱrul-snaṅ-čan*.
Demand vb. *˳dod-pa*.
Demeanour *spyod-lam*.
Demon *bgegs*; *˳goṅ-po*.
Den *ťsaṅ*.
Denomination *čos-lugs*.
Dense *stugs-po*; *˳ťug-po*.
Density *ska-sláď*.
Depart *čas-pa*; *bžud-pa*; (deviate) *˳gyur-ba*.
Depend upon *rten-pa*; *blo skyel-ba W.*, *ḱel-ba C.*
Deportment *spyod-pa*.
Depository *mdzod*.

Depression (incision) *lton-ga.*
Deprive *°p̓rog-pa; °p̓ral-ba;* to be deprived *°bral-ba.*
Depth *zab-k̓yád; ytiṅ; zab-pa; zabs.*
Deranged *°k̓rul-ba* no. 3.
Derangement *skyon.*
Descend *°bab-pa.*
Descendants *brgyud.*
Describe *ston-pa; °bri-ba.*
Description *bśad-pa; bstan-pa; ynas-t̓sul, ynas-lugs; rnam-t̓ar; byed-t̓sul, yod-t̓sul.*
Desert s. *dgon-pa; °brog(-stoṅ).*
Deserted *stoṅ-pa.*
Deserve v. *°os-pa.*
Design vb.a. (delineate) *°bri-ba; °god-pa;* (intend for) *sṅo-ba*
Design s. *ri-mo.*
Desirable *mk̓o-ba.*
Desire s. *t̓ob-bló; °dod-pa.*
Desire vb. *°dod-pa; smon-pa; żen-pa; sred-pa; rṅam-pa; rṅub-pa; rkam-pa.*
Desolate adj. *ṅo bab-pa; żum-pa.*
Despair s. *yi(d) yčod-pa; yi(d) mug-pa.*
Despair vb. *k̓o-tag yčod-pa; yi(d)-mug-pa.*
Despise *brnyas-pa; rṅan-čen byed-pa; k̓yad-du ysod-pa; °gyiṅ-ba; smad-pa.*
Despond *spa-sgoṅ-ba.*
Despondency *żum-pa; yi(d) mug.*
Destine *sko-ba; sṅo-ba.*
Destiny *skal-ba; sko-ba; bsod-bdé; dbaṅ-t̓áṅ.*
Destitute *kun-gyis btaṅ-ba; mgon-méd; rten-méd.*
Destroy *°gem-pa; rṅam-pa; °jig-pa; °joms-pa; t̓sar-yčod-pa* 458; *ma-ruṅ-bar byed-pa; med-par byed-pa.*
Destruction *żig-ral,* v. *ral-ba.*
Detail s., in — *rgyas-par* 109.
Detain *skyil-ba; bśol-ba.*
Detect *rnyed-pa; t̓ob-pa.*
Determine vb. a. (induce) *skul-ba;* vb. n. (resolve) *t̓ag yčod-pa.*
Detest *spoṅ-ba.*
Develop vb. n. *rgyas-pa* 109.
Deviate *°k̓yar-ba; °gol-ba.*
Devil *bdud; bgegs.*
Devise *dmigs-pa-nas* (or *sems-kyis*) *yzo-ba; dgoṅs-pa.*
Devote vb. *sṅo-ba.*
Devotion *gus-pa, daṅ-ba.*
Devour *čur mid-pa; hab-háb za-ba.*
Devout *skal-ldán; gus-pa; čos-čan; daṅ-ba.*
Dew s. *zil-pa.*
Dexterity *sgyu-rtsál.*
Dexterous *skyen-pa; rtsal-čan.*
Diadem *čod-p̓án.*
Diagram *dkyil-°k̓or.*
Dialect *skad-lúgs.*
Diamond *rdo-rje, dor-je-p̓a-lám.*
Diaphragm *mčin-ri.*
Diarrhoea *°k̓ru-ba; śal W.* 567.

Dictionary *miṅ-gi mdzod.*
Die, dice s. *čo-lo, čol; śo;* to play at — *śo rtse-ba; śo gyed-pa.*
Die vb. n. *°či-ba, śi-ba;* resp. *dgoṅs-pa,* and *°groṅ-ba;* eleg. *°gum-pa;* v. *°da-ba;* to — out *°čad-pa.*
Diet *spyod-lam;* lenten — *dkar-zás.*
Difference *k̓yad, k̓yad-par; bye-brag;* to find a — *ynyis-su °dzin-pa.*
Different *mi-yčig; t̓a-dad-pa; so-só; mi-°dra-ba;* not — *yčig-pa.*
Difficult *dka-ba, dka-bo; k̓ag-po, k̓ab-le.*
Diffuse vb. *°gyed-pa.*
Dig *rko-ba; bru-ba.*
Digest *°ju-ba; żu-ba.*
Digestion *°ju-ba.*
Dignitary *t̓san-po.*
Dignity *go-grál, go-p̓áṅ; go-sá; gras; dbu-°p̓áṅ.*
Dike *ču-rags, ču-lon; rags.*
Dilapidated *gog-po.*
Diligence *brtson-°grus; snyiṅ-rús;* to use — *rtsol-ba skyed-pa.*
Diligent *brtson-pa-čan.*
Diligently *rtsol-bar.*
Dim adj. *dkrigs-pa; bkrag-čór; man-mún Ld.;* to grow — *°grib-pa.*
Diminish vb. a. *°p̓ri-ba;* vb. n. *°grib-pa.*
Dimness *rab-rib, hrab-hrib.*
Din *°du-°dzi.*
Dip vb. *spag-pa.*
Diploma *bka-rgya, bka-śog;* — of nobility *dpal-gyi ynaṅ-śóg.*
Direct vb. a. *ytod-pa;* to be —ed *ston-pa, lta-ba.*
Direction *ṅo, ṅos; p̓yogs; man-ṅág; żal-ta; śed.*
Directly *de-ma-t̓ag-tu.*
Director **°go-pón* C.*
Dirt *dri-ma; dreg-pa; rkyag-pa; lčags-dregs.*
Dirty adj. *dri-ma-čan; btsog-pa; gos-pa; mi-ytsaṅ-ba; t̓si-du W.*
Dirty vb. a. *°go-ba.*
Disadvantage *skyon.*
Disagreeable *mi-sdug-pa; yid-du-mi-°oṅ-ba.*
Disappear *mi-snaṅ-bar °gyur-ba; yal-ba; med-par °gyur-ba; °jig-pa; °bul-pa.*
Disapprove *°dor-ba; mi ynaṅ-ba.*
Disciple *grwa-pa; nye-ynas; slob-°báṅs.*
Discontented *skyo-mo; mi dga-ba.*
Discontinue *yčod-pa.*
Discord *dbyen-pa; sel.*
Discouraged *ṅo °bab-pa.*
Discourse s. *gleṅ-brjód, gleṅ-mo; lda-gu.*
Discuss *bgro-ba.*
Disdain s. *rṅan-čén.*
Disease s. *nad; na-ba; snyuṅ;* chronic — *yčoṅ;* fatal — *°či-nád.*
Disfigured *gya-ba.*

Disgrace s. *rkaṅ-˳drén, žabs-˳drén.*
Disgrace vb. a. *dma-˳bebs-pa.*
Disguise s. *˳bag; rdzu-ba.*
Disguise vb. a. *˳gebs-pa*; v. *čas* 156.
Disgust s. *skyo-śás; ḱrel; rnam-rtóg.*
Dish *ka-to-ra; sder-ma; spags; skyu-rúm W.*
Disheartened *skyo-mo.*
Dishonour vb. *smad-pa; dma ˳bebs-pa.*
Disk *kyir-kyir; dkyil-˳ḱór; ˳ḱor-lo; sgor-mo.*
Dislocated, to be — *˳ḱrul-ba.*
Dismay s. *žum-pa.*
Dismiss *bka ˳grol-ba; ˳gyed-pa; γtoṅ-ba; ˳don-pa.*
Disorder s. *˳ḱrug-pa; skyon; ˳ḱrul-˳ḱrúl.*
Dispatch vb. *rdzoṅ-ba; zlog-pa; γtoṅ-ba, mṅag-pa.*
Dispel *zlog-pa.*
Dispense vb. (deal out) *˳brim-pa.*
Disperse vb. a. *˳gye-ba, ˳gyed-pa; γċor-ba*; vb. n. *˳byer-ba: yan ča-ċe W.*
Display vb. *˳grems-pa; γċal-ba.*
Disposition s. (character) *rgyud; ṅaṅ; ṅaṅ-rgyúd; raṅ-bžin; γšis.*
Disputation *rtsod-pa.*
Dispute vb. n. *rgol-ba; rtsod-pa.*
Dispute s. *ḱa-mču, rtsod-pa, ˳dziṅ-mo.*
Dissatisfaction *mi-dga-bai sems.*
Dissatisfied *mi-dga-ba*; also *˳ḱon-pa.*
Dissect *˳byed-pa.*
Dissension *˳ḱon-po; naṅ-sel, sel; dbyen-pa.*
Dissertation *rgyud, mdo.*
Dissimilarity *ḱyad-par; mi-˳dra-ba.*
Dissolute *˳čol-pa*; to be — *mi ṫsaṅs-par spyod-pa.*
Dissolve vb. a. *˳ǰig-pa*; to be dissolved *ťim-pa.*
Dissuade *sgyur-ba; zlog-pa.*
Distance *rgyaṅ-ma; nye-riṅ; ťag; ṗa-ṫsad, ṗa-zád.*
Distant *ťag-riṅ(-mo).*
Distend *rkyoṅ-ba.*
Distinct *ḱrol-po; čod-po; wa-lé, wal-le-ba.*
Distinction *ḱyad; dbye-ba.*
Distinguish *rnam(-par) bžag(-pa).*
Distinguished *˳ṗags-pa; ḱyad-par-ċan.*
Distorted *ċa-ċús*; to be — *˳ḱrul-ba.*
Distress s. *sdug-bsṅal, mya-ṅan, dka-las.*
Distribute *bgod-pa; ˳brim-pa*; v. *˳gyed-pa.*
District *yul-ḱág; yul-lǰóṅs; yul-sde; ḱul; sde.*
Disturb *dkrug-pa; γyeṅs-par byed-pa; bar-du γċod-pa*; to be disturbed *˳ḱrug-pa.*
Disturber *bstan-śig.*
Ditch *ču-˳óbs; ˳obs.*
Diverse *sna-ṫsogs; sna-so-só.*
Diversity *bye-ba; mi ˳dra-ba.*
Divert *sgyur-ba; rtse-ba; zlog-pa.*
Divide *bgod-pa; ˳gyed-pa; ˳byed-pa; ˳ges-pa*; to be divided *˳gye-ba*
Dividend *bgo-byá.*
Divine s. *čos-pa.*
Division *dbye-ba; bye-brág; ḱyad, ḱyad-par; ču-ṫsán; rnam-pa; ḱag.*
Divisor *bgod-byéd.*
Dizzy, I am — *mgo ˳ḱor.*
Do *byed-pa; spyod-pa*; eleg. *bgyid-pa*; resp. *mdzad-pa*; that will — **ǰig-pa yin* C.*; *des čog.*
Doctrine *čos; bstan-pa.*
Dog *ḱyi*, male — *ḱyi-ṗo*, fem. *ḱyi-mo*; mad — *ḱyi smyon-pa*; — kennel *ḱyi-ḱáṅ, ḱyi-pul.*
Doll *miu.*
Domain *ḱams; ḱul; dbaṅ-ris.*
Domicile *mčis-bráṅ.*
Dominion *ḱams* 39; v. *rgyal-ḱams* 108; *ṅaṅ; mṅa; čab-˳óg; dbaṅ-ris; srid.*
Door *sgo; čab-sgo*; large — *sgo-mo*; little — *sgeu*; principal — *rgyal-sgo*; — bar *γtan-pa*; — frame *sgo-˳drig*; — hinge *sgo-ḱor, go-ṗiṅ W.*; — keeper *sgo-pa*, resp. *čabs-sgo-pa, sgo-sruṅ.*
Dose s. *ťun.*
Dosser *ṫse-po, ṫsel-po.*
Dot s. *ṫseg.*
Double adj. *γnyis-ldáb*; — tongued *lċe-γnyis-pa*; — barreled gun *nyi-rag W.*; (v. *sbrag-pa*); *ṫsaṅ-yá.*
Double vb. a. *skum-pa.*
Doubt s. *ṫe-ṫsóm; ṫsom-pa; ṫsom-ṫsóm; yid-γnyis.*
Doubtful *γtol-méd.*
Dough *skyo-ma; bag-zan.*
Down adv. *ťur; ťeṅ-la C.; γšam-du*; to go — *nub-pa, ˳bab-pa.*
Downward *mar, mas; ˳og-tu, šod-du.*
Dowry *rdzoṅs.*
Doze vb. *nyid ťom-pa.*
Drag vb. *˳drud-pa.*
Dragon *˳brug.*
Dram s. (weight) *žo* 478.
Draught s. (drawing) *bkod-pa; ri-mo*; (drink) *hub.*
Draw (pull) *˳ťen-pa; ˳dren-pa*; to — in *rṅub-pa; skum-pa*; to — out *˳ťen-pa; ˳byin-pa*; to — up (to compose) *˳god-pa.*
Dreadful *˳ǰigs-pa.*
Dream s. *rmi-lam*, resp. *mnal-lam*; vb. *rmi-ba.*
Dress s. *gos, čas*; resp. *na-bza.*
Dress vb. a. (to clothe) *skon-pa*; (to cook) *˳ṫsod-pa, ˳ṫsed-pa*; to — wounds *sdom-pa.*
Dressed up *zab-mo.*
Dried *skam-po*; — up *kum-pa.*
Drink vb. *˳ťuṅ-ba.*
Drink s. *skyems; žal-skóm*; meat and *bza-btúṅ.*

Drinkable water *skems-ču*
Drinking-cup *skyogs*; *čaṅ-čan*, *ṗor-pa*, *ko-re W.*
Drip vb. *˳dzag-pa*.
Drive vb. *˳ded-pa*; to — back *˳gogs-pa*; *zlog-pa*; to — out *skrod-pa*; *bda-ba*.
Driver *˳ded-mi*.
Drop s. *ṫigs-pa*.
Drop vb. a. *ḱrul ytoṅ-ba*; vb. n. *˳dzag-pa*; *˳čor-ba*.
Dropsy *pags-ču*; *snyiṅ-ču*; *dmu-ču*.
Dross *lčags-drėgs*.
Drowned, to be — *˳ṫsub-pa*; *čus ˳ḱyer-ba*.
Drum s. *ṙṅa*; — skin *ṙṅa-lpágs*; — stick *ṙṅa-lčág*.
Drummer *ṙṅa-pa*.
Drunk *ra-ro-ba*; *bzi-čan W.*; to get — *bzi-ba*.
Drunkard *čaṅ-dad-čan W.*
Drunkenness *ra-ro*.
Dry adj. *skam-pa*, *skam-po*; *skem-pa*; — weather, drought *ṫan-pa*.
Dry vb. a. *skem-pa*.
Dryness *skam-pa*.
Duck s. (water-fowl) *ṅur-ba*.
Due adj. *dgos-pa*.
Duel s. *˳ḱrug-pa*.
Dulcimer *yaṅ-ljin Ts.*
Dull adj. *ḱugs-pa*; *glen-pa*; *rtul-po*; *blun-pa*.
Dullness *rmu-ba*.
Dumb *lkugs-pa*; *smra-mi-nus-pa*.
Dumpling *ču-ṫa-gir W.*
Dung s. *lča Ld.*; *lči-ba W.*; *brun*.
Dungeon *ḱri-mán*; *btson-doṅ*.
Dupe vb. a. *mgo skor byed-pa* 25.
During prep. *ḱons-su*; *na* 298; *riṅ-la*.
Dusky *nan-mún*.
Dust s. *ḱyim-sa*; *ṫal-ba*; *rdul*; *ṗye-ma*; cloud of — *bud*.
Duty *ḱag*; *ḱrims*; *sdom-pa*; moral — *ṫsul-ḱrims*; (tax) *dpya*; *šo-gám*.
Dwarf *miu*.
Dwell *ynas-pa*, *˳dug-pa*; *sdod-pa*; resp. *bžugs-pa*; *˳ḱod-pa*.
Dwelling s. *ynas-ḱaṅ*, *ynas-ṫsaṅ*; eleg. *mčis-braṅ*; temporary — *˳braṅ-sa*.
Dwindle *yal-ba*.
Dye s. *ṫsos*; vb. a. *ṫsos rgyag-pa*.
Dynasty *rgyal-brgyúd*; *rgyal-rábs*.

E

Each *kun*; *re*, *re-ré*
Eager *˳dod-čan*, *˳dod-ldan*; to be — *˳dod-pa*; *sred-pa*.
Eagle *go-bo*; *glag*.
Ear *rna-ba*; resp *snyan*; — ache *rna-ba na-ba*; — hole *rna-ḱúṅ*; — shot *rgyaṅ-grágs*; — wax *klog-pa*; *rna-ḱyág*; — of corn *snye-ma*.
Early adj. and adv. v. *sṅa* 135; earlier *sṅa-ma*, *sṅa-mo*; earlier or later *sṅa-rtiṅ-du*.
Earn *ḱug-pa*.
Earnest s., in good — *don-dám*.
Earnestly *snyiṅ-nas*; v. also *yaṅ-dag-pa*, sub. *dag-pa* 248.
Earth *sa*; *sa čen-po*; — quake *sa-yyós*; *saṅ-gúl W.*
East *šar*.
Easy *sla-ba*; *lhod-pa*.
Eat *za-ba*, *bza-ba*; resp. *ysol-ba*; *mčod-pa*; v. also *˳ṫuṅ-ba*; to — up *ma-lus-par za-ba*.
Echo s. *brag-ča*; *sgra-brnyán*.
Eclipse of the moon *zla-˳dzin*, of the sun *nyi-˳dzin*.
Edge *ḱa*; *ča-ga*; *mṫa*; *zur*; — of a knife *dṅo*.
Edict *bka-šog*, *ysuṅ-šog*; *bkar-btags-pa*.
Edifice *bkod-pa* 96.
Educate *˳ṫso-ba*; *yso-ba*, *yso-skyoṅ byed-pa*.
Effect vb. a. *byed-pa*.
Effect s. *˳bras-bu*; effects (goods) *ča-lag W.*, *lag-ča*, *yo-byad*.
Effervesce *˳ḱol-ba*.
Efficacy *nus-pa*.
Egg *sgo-ṅá*, *ṫul W.*
Egotism *bdag-˳dzin* 268.
Egypt *mi-sér yul*.
Eight num. *brgyad*; eighth *brgyad-pa*; eighteen *ču-brgyad*; eighteenth *ču-brgyad-pa*; eighty *brgyad-ču*; eightieth *brgyad-ču-pa*.
Either — or *yaṅ-na* — *yaṅ-na*.
Eject *skrod-pa*; *˳dor-ba*.
Elapse *˳da-ba*.
Elbow *gru-mo*, *gre-mo*; *dre-bo*.
Elder adj. *če-ba*, *čen-po*; — brother *jo-bo*; *ṫu-bo*.
Elder s. *rgad-po*.
Election *ydam-ka*.
Electuary *lde-gu*.
Element *˳byuṅ-ba*; *ḱams*.
Elephant *glaṅ*, *glaṅ-po-čé*, *glaṅ-čén*.
Elevate *sgro-˳dogs-pa*; *˳degs-pa*; *spar-ba*; *seṅ-ba*.
Eleven *bču-yčig*; eleventh *bču-yčig-pa*.
Elk *ḱa-šá ša-ba*.
Eloquence *ḱa-sbyaṅ*.
Eloquent *ṅag-dbáṅ*; *ḱa-sbyaṅ-po*; *ḱa-šugs-čan W.*
Elsewhere *yžan-du*.

Emanate *˳ṕro-ba.*
Emanation *sprul-ba* 336.
Emboss *ṕur-ba.*
Embrace vb. *˳ḱyud-pa*; *˳ḱril-ba*; *˳dzin-pa*; *ḱyab-pa.*
Emerald *ma-rgád,*
Emerge *˳byuṅ-ba.*
Emetic *skyug-smán.*
Eminent *kyad-par-ċan*; *ṕun-sum-t́sogs-pa*; *rgyal-ba*; *ṕul-tu byúṅ-ba.*
Emit *˳byin-pa.*
Emmet *gre-mog-bu W.*; *grog-ma.*
Empale *γsal-ṡiṅ-la skyon-pa.*
Emperor *rgyal-po čen-po.*
Empire *ḱams*; *yul-ḱáms*; *rgyal-ḱág.*
Employ *skyel-ba*; *spyod-pa*; to be –ed or busy *brel-ba.*
Empty *stoṅ-pa*; to make – *stoṅs-pa.*
Emulate *˳gran-pa.*
Emulation *˳gran-sems.*
Enabled, to be – *ḱom-pa* 44.
Encampment *sgar*; *dmag-sgár.*
Enchanter *˳goṅ-po*; enchantress *˳goṅ-ba-mo.*
Encircle *skor-ba.*
Enclose *skor-ba.*
Enclosure *skor-ba*; *ra-ba.*
Encompass *˳ḱyigs-pa*; *˳ḱyud-pa*; *skor-ba.*
End s. *mǰug*; *mt́a*, *mt́a-ma*; *ṕug*; *γžug*; towards or at the – *mt́a-ru*, *mt́ar*; to be at an – *rdzogs-pa*, *zin-pa.*
Endeavour vb. *rtsol-ba*; *lhur len-pa*; *don-du γnyer-ba*; s. *˳grus-pa.*
Endless *mt́a-yás*; *mt́a-méd.*
Enemy *dgra*, *dgra-bo*; *ṕa-rol-po*; *˳t́se-ba.*
Energy *ṡugs.*
Engagement (promise) *čad*; *sdom-pa*; v. also *las*, *brel-ba.*
Engrave *rko-ba.*
Enjoin *skul-ba.*
Enjoy *loṅs spyod-pa*; – one's self *rtse-ba.*
Enjoyment *loṅs-spyód*; *nyams-myoṅ.*
Enlarge *rgyas-pa*; *˳ṕel-ba*; *dar-ba*; – upon *spro-ba.*
Enough *t́sad*; *čog-pa*; to be – *˳ḱyed-pa*; *˳grig-pa.*
Ensnare *dkri-ba.*
Enter vb. a. *˳ǰug-pa*; *˳t́sugs-pa*; *˳t́sud-pa*; vb. n. *čud-pa.*
Entertainment *mgron*; v. also *mčod-stón.*
Entire *tsaṅ-ma*; *ril-ba*; *son-te W.*
Entity *ṅo-bo-nyid* 129; *čos-nyid* 164.
Entrails *rgyu-ma*, *naṅ-ḱrol.*
Entrance (vestibule) *sgo-ḱáṅ.*
Entrust *˳čol-ba*; *γtod-pa*, *γnyer-ḱa γtad-pa.*
Enumerate *sgraṅ-ba*, *bsgraṅ-ba*; *˳dren-pa.*
Enumeration *rnam-gráṅs.*
Envelope *yi-gei ṡubs.*
Envious *ṕrag-dog-ċan*; v. also *ċe-ré.*

Envoy *ṕo-nya.*
Envy s. *ṕrag-dóg*; *mig-sér.*
Envy vb. *ṕrag-pa.*
Epidemy *rims(-nad)*; *ṅan-rims.*
Epilepsy *ḱyab-˳ǰug*; *γza-nád*; *γza-ṕog-pa.*
Epistle *yi-ge.*
Epitaph *dur-byaṅ.*
Equal *mnyam-pa*; *snyoms-po* 201; *˳dra-ba*; *mt́suṅs-pa.*
Equality *mnyam-pa-nyid*; *˳dra-mi-˳dra.*
Equanimity *snyoms-pa*; *btaṅ-snyóms.*
Equivalent s. *dod*; *t́sab.*
Eradicate *rtsad-nas γċod-pa.*
Erect adj. *kye-ré*; *ḱroṅ-ṅe.*
Erect vb. a. *sgreṅ-ba*; *˳dzugs-pa*; *bžeṅ-ba.*
Err *˳ḱyar-ba*; *˳ḱrul-ba*; *˳gol-ba*; *nor-ba.*
Error *˳gal-sa*; *˳ḱrul-so*, *˳ḱrul-γží.*
Eructation *skyug-ldád*; *sgreg-pa.*
Escape vb. *˳čor-ba*; *˳bud-pa.*
Escort s. *skyel-ma*; *bsel(-ba)*, *lam-bsél.*
Escort vb. *rdzoṅ* *˳debs-pa.*
Especially *ḱyad-par-du.*
Essence *ṅo-bo-nyid* 129; *bċud* (quintessence) 147.
Establish *˳god-pa.*
Estafet *rta-zam-pa.*
Esteem s. *ṕu-dúd*; *rtsis*; *ya-ṡa.*
Esteem vb. a. *bkur-ba*; *γċes-par byed-pa* or *˳dzin-pa.*
Estimation *rtsis*; *t́sod* 453.
Eternal *rtag-pa*; *skye-˳či-med-pa.*
Eternity *rtag-tu-ba* (?).
Ether *mḱa.*
Etymology *t́a-snyád.*
Eunuch *nyug-rúm.*
Euphony *sgra-dbyaṅs.*
Europe *rgya-pi-liṅ*; *ṕyi-gliṅ*, vulgo *ṕi-liṅ.*
European s. *ṕa-ráṅ*, *ṕe-ráṅ*; *ṕi-liṅ-pa.*
Evade *˳ǰur-ba*, *˳dzur-ba*; *˳ǰol-ba*; *˳čor-ba.*
Evangelist *ṕrin-bzaṅ sgrog-pa(-po).*
Evaporate *t́im-pa.*
Even adj. *mnyam-pa.*
Even vb. a (to level) *snyom-pa.*
Even adv. *t́a-na*; *yaṅ*; not – v. *yaṅ* 505.
Evening *nub*; *nub-mo*; *dgoṅs.*
Evenness *nyam-pa-nyid.*
Event *rkyen*; *dṅos-po*; at all events *ċis kyaṅ*, *gaṅ yin kyaṅ* 65; *ga-na-méd W.*, *gar-méd W.*
Ever *rtag-tu*; *γtan-du*; *dus-rgyun-du.*
Every *kun*; *re*, *re-ré*; v. *gaṅ* 65; – day *dkyus-ma*; *žag daṅ žag* 248; – thing *ċaṅ*; *ċi*; *kun.*
Everywhere *kun-tu*; v. *ċir* 141.
Evidence *rgyu-mt́san* 111.
Evident *mṅon-pa.*
Evidently v. *ṅes-pa* 128.
Evil s. *ṅan*; *nyes-pa.*
Evil adj. *ṅan-pa*; *t́u-ba*; – spirit *˳goṅ-po.*
Exact adj. *žib-pa.*

Exactly *ḱo-na*; *raṅ*; — that *de-dé* 256.
Exaggerate *sgro-˳dogs-pa*.
Exalt *sgro-˳dogs-pa*.
Exalted *˳ṕags-pa*.
Examination *brtags-dpyad*.
Examine *rtog-pa*; *dpyod-pa*; *yžig-pa*; *sad-pa*.
Example *dpe*; *dpe-brǰód*.
Excavate *yčoṅ-ba*; *sbug-pa*.
Excavation *sbugs*; *šoṅ*.
Excellence *dṅos-grub*; *če-ba*.
Excellent *rgyal ba*; *ḱyad-par-čan*; *yčes-pa*; *ṕun-tsógs*; *˳ṕags-pa*.
Except prep. *ma ytogs-par*; *min, min-par*.
Exchange s. (agio) *ṕar*.
Excite *sloṅ-ba, dkrog-pa*.
Exclaim *˳bod-pa*.
Exclusively *ḱo-na*.
Excrement *rkyag-pa*; *rtug-pa*; *dri-ma*.
Excrescence *lba-ba*; *mdzer-pa*; *˳dzer-pa*.
Execrate *ṅan ˳debs-pa*; *mnan-pa*; *dmod-pa ˳bor-ba*.
Exercise s. (bodily) *spyod-lam* 335; — of religion *čos-spyod*.
Exercise vb. a. *sbyoṅ-ba*; *lag-tu len-pa*.
Exert one's self *˳bad-pa*.
Exertion *˳bad-pa*; *brtson-pa*; *don-ynyér*; *dka-ba*.
Exhausted *nyams-ťag-pa*; to be — (consumed) *˳dzad-pa*; *zin-pa*; (tired) *˳čad-pa*; *ṅal-˳čad-pa, ťaṅ-˳čad-pa*.
Exhort *skul-ba*; *skul-čag byed-pa*; *bslab-bya byed-pa*, or *ston-pa*, or *btaṅ-ba*.
Exhortation *bskul-ba, bskul-ma*; *snyiṅ-ytam*; *luṅ, luṅ-bstán*; *bslab-bya*; farewell — *ḱa-čéms*.
Exile vb. a. *ynas-nas dgar-ba*.
Exist cf. *˳dug-pa*; *yod-pa*; *skye-ba*.
Existence *skye-ba*; *srid-pa*.
Exorcise *dam-la ˳dogs-pa*.
Expanse *kloṅ*; *ḱa-žéṅ*.
Expect *sgug-pa*.
Expedient adj. *ṕan-˳dogs-pa, ṕan-ťogs-čan*; *rigs-pa* 528; *don-byed-nus-pa*
Expel *skrod-pa*; *˳ǰil-ba*; *˳don-pa*; *spyug-pa*; *˳bud-pa*; *zlog-pa*.
Expend *skyag-pa*.
Expenditure, Expense *˳gro-sgo*; *skyag-pa, skyag-sgo*.
Expensive *gus-po*.
Experience vb. a. *myoṅ-ba, nyams-su myoṅ-ba*; v. also *sbyoṅ-ba*.
Experience s. *slobs*.
Experienced (skilled) *mḱas-pa*.
Expiation *sdig-bšágs*.
Expire *˳da-ba*.
Explain *˳grel-ba, ˳grol-ba*; *ṅo sprod-pa*; *˳čad-pa*; *bšad-pa*.
Explanation *brda-spród*.
Exploit *ḱyo ga*.
Expressly *čed-du*.
Exquisite *mčog-tu bkrab*; *kyad-par ˳ṕags-pa*.
Extend *rkyoṅ-ba*; *bsnar-ba*.
Extension *ḱyon*; *gu*.
Extensive *rgyas-pa*; *yaṅs-pa*.
Extent *ḱyon*; *rgya, rgya-ḱyon, rgya-ba*; *ču-žeṅ* 158.
Exterior s. *rnam-pa*; *ča-byad* 152.
External *ṕyii*, v. *ṕyi* III 319; — appearance *ča-byad, ṕyi-rol*.
Extinct, to become — *˳čad-pa*; *ši-ba*.
Extinguish *ysod-pa*.
Extra *˳ťeb*.
Extract vb. a. *bku-ba*; *˳byin-pa*; *˳don-pa*.
Extraction (descent) *rigs*.
Extremity (end) *mťa-ma, zur*.
Eye s. *mig*, resp. *spyan*; — brow *smin-ma*; — lash *rdzi-ma*; *mig-yšog*, resp. *spyan-yšog*; — lid *mig-pág C. W.*

F

Fable s. *sgruṅs*.
Fabricate vb. a. *˳čos-pa*; *bčo-ba*; *byed-pa*; *bzo-ba*; to be fabricated *grub-pa*.
Face s. *ydoṅ*; *ṅo*; *ḱa*; *skye-sgó*; *sgo-lo*; *bžin*; in the — of *ḱa-ru, ḱar*.
Face vb. (to be directed towards) *ston-pa*.
Fail vb. (to miss) *mi ḱes-pa C.*; *mi-˳ťebs-pa W.*; (to err) *˳gol-ba*; (to dwindle) *yal-ba*.
Faint adj. *nyams-čuṅ*; to get — *yčoṅ-ba*.
Faint vb. n. *brgyal-ba*; *˳ḱam-pa*.
Fair adj. *mdzes-pa*; *mťsar-ba*; *bzaṅ-ba*.
Faith *dad-pa*.
Faithful *dad-pa*; *ydeṅs-pa*; *slu-méd*; *gyo-sgyu-méd*.
Falchion *gri-gug*.
Falcon *ḱra*.
Fall vb. *˳gril-ba*; *˳gyel-ba*; *ltuṅ-ba*; *˳bab-pa*; to — in drops *˳ťig-pa*; to — off *˳byi-ba*; to — to pieces *˳ǰig-pa*; *˳gril-ba W.*; to — upon *˳buṅs-pa*.
Fall s. *ltuṅ-ba*.
Fallow *yan-pa*.
False *mi bden-pa*; *rdzus-ma*; *yyo-čan*; charge *ḱa-yog*; *snyad*; conception *bčos-pa*; — sentiment *lta-lóg, log-lta*.
Falsehood *dkyus*; *ḱa-šób*; *rdzun*.
Fame *grags-pa*.
Family *brgyud*; *ydun*; *bu-smád*; *yžis-mad*; *rabs*; *rigs-brgyúd*; *rus*.

Famine *mu-ge.*
Famous *grags-ċan.*
Fan s. *ṙṅa-yáb.*
Fan vb. a. *°ḱrab-pa*; v. *yab-mo.*
Fancy vb. a. *sgom-pa*; *dmigs-pa*; *sems-pa*; vb. n. *mno-ba.*
Fancy s. *dmigs-pa*; *sems-kyi snaṅ-ba.*
Fang *ḱron*; *mče-ba, mče-so.*
Far *rgyaṅ-riṅ-po, rgyaṅs* 107; (*ṫag-*)*riṅ-ba*; *mi nye-ba*; as — as *bar-du, ḱad-du*; — famed *sgra-čé*; — from *ltu či smos* 215.
Farewell v. *ga-le* 64; to say — v. *ṗyi-ṗyag*, sub *ṗyag.*
Farm s *groṅ-bžis*; — steward *γnyer-pa* 194.
Farmer *ḱyim-pa-pa*; *žiṅ-pa* 475.
Farsightedness *mig-rgyáṅ* 414.
Farther *ṗar.*
Fashion s. *ċos*; *lugs.*
Fast adj. *mgyogs-pa*; *mgyur-ba.*
Fast vb. n. *smyuṅ-ba*; *dge-ba sruṅ-ba.*
Fasten *sdom-pa*; *°grogs-pa*; *°dogs-pa*; *sgril-ba*; *sbyor-ba*; *sbrel-ba.*
Fasting s. *bsnyen-γnas, smyuṅ-γnas.*
Fat adj. *rgyas-pa*; *ṫso-ba*; *ṫson-po.*
Fat s. *ṫsil*; melted — *ṫsil-ḱu*; *žag.*
Fatal *byur-gyi*; *nyen-čan*; *ma-ruṅ-ba*; *šrog-len, šrog-°ṗrog.*
Fate *skal-ba, las-bskos* v. *sko-ba* 24; *bsod-pa*; *dbaṅ-ṫáṅ*; cf. also *lan-čags* and *las-°ṗro.*
Father *ṗa*, resp *yab*; — in law *gyos-po*; *skud-po.*
Fathom s. *°doms-pa.*
Fatigue s. *ṅal*, resp. *°o-brgyál.*
Fatigue vb. a. *ṅal °ǰug-pa*; to be fatigued *ṅal-ba*, resp. *sku-ṅal-ba, ṫugs ṅal-ba.*
Fault *skyon*; *noṅs-pa*; *°ṫsaṅ.*
Faulty *skyon-čan.*
Favour s. *bka-drin*; v. *γnaṅ-ba* II 309.
Favourable *mṫun-pa*; — circumstance *mṫun-rkyén.*
Favourite s. *snyiṅ-sdúg*; *sdug-pa.*
Fear s. *°ǰigs-pa, °ǰigs-skrag, °ǰigs-ri*; *bag-ṫsa* (*-ba*).
Fear vb. *°ǰigs-pa*; *dṅaṅ-ba*; *dogs pa.*
Fearless *°ǰigs-méd*; *bag-méd.*
Feast s. *dga-ston*; *mgron*; *ston-mo.*
Feather *spu*; quill — *sgro.*
Fee s. *gla*; *ṙṅan-pa*; *baq-šis.*
Feeble *kyar-kyór*; *kyór*; *nya-ra-nyo-ré.*
Feed *stob-pa*; *snyod-pa*; *°or-ba W.*; *°ṫso-ba, γso-ba.*
Feel *reg-pa, ṫsor-ba*; to — cold *°ḱyags-pa.*
Feeling s. *reg-bya.*
Feign vb. n. *bčos-pa* 148; v. *lugs byed-pa* (*lugs* no. 2, 548); *ṫsul-du byed-pa* (*ṫsul* no. 1, 450).
Fellow *grogs*; *ya-do W.*; — labourer *las-grogs*; — lodger *°dug-grogs, braṅ-grogs*, resp. *bžugs-grogs*; traveller *lam-grogs.*
Felt s. *ṗyiṅ-pa.*
Female *mo.*
Fen *°dam*; *gram-pa.*
Fence s. *ḱo-ra*; *skyor-ba*; *ta-bèr W.*; *pu-šu*; *ra-ba.*
Ferment vb. *°ḱol-ba*; s. *žo-ri W.* 478; *ru-ma.*
Fern *skyes-ma.*
Ferocious *ṅar-po.*
Ferry s. *gru*; *rdziṅs, γziṅs.*
Ferry-man *gru-pa*; *ču-ṗyag-pa*; *mnyan-pa.*
Festival *dus-čén.*
Fetter vb. a. *sbrel-ba*; *°ḱyig-pa*; *°čiṅ-ba.*
Fetters s. *sgrogs*; *lčags, lčags-sgrog*; *bčiṅs-pa.*
Fever *ṫsad-pai nád C.*; *ṫsan-zug W.*
Few *nyuṅ-ṅu*; a few *°ga, °ga tsam*; *nyuṅ-ṅu žig*; *čig* 140; *la-lá C.*
Fib s. *šob, γšob.*
Fibre *rgyus-pa.*
Fickle *gyi-na*; *ya-ma-brla*; *°gyur-ldog*; *skad γčig kyaṅ mi ṫsugs-pa.*
Fickleness *°gyur-ldog, ldog-°gyur.*
Fictitious *bčos-pa*; *dmigs-pa-nas bzos-pa.*
Fidget vb. *°ṗar-ba.*
Field *žiṅ*; *kluṅs*; — terrace *daṅ-tse W.*
Fife *gliṅ-bu.*
Fifth *lṅa-pa*; fifteen *bčo-lṅa*; fifteenth *bčo-lṅa-pa*; fifty *lṅa-bču*; fiftieth *lṅa-bču-pa.*
Fight s. *°ṫab-mo.*
Fight vb. a. *gyed-pa*; *rgol-ba*; *°ṫab-pa*; *°ṫab-mo byed-pa*; vb. n. *°ḱrug-pa*; *°gran-pa*; *rgol-ba*; *rtsod-pa*; *°dziṅ-ba.*
Figure s. *dkyil-ḱor*; *skye-γzúgs*; *blod-pa*; *rnam-°gyúr*; *dbyibs*; *γzugs*; *bzo, zo*; *ri-mo*; *ris.*
Figured (variegated) *či-tra W.*
File s. (tool) *lčags-bdar*; *sed.*
File vb. (to string) *rgyud-pa*; *star-ba.*
Fill vb. *ḱyab-pa*; *°geṅs-pa.*
Filter s. *ṫsag-ma*; vb. a *°ṫsag-pa.*
Filth *dri-ma*; *mi-γtsaṅ-ba* 433; *grib.*
Find *ṫob-pa*; *rnyed-pa*; *ḱug-pa.*
Fine adj. (beautiful) *mdzes-pa*; *sdug-pa*; *mṫsar-ba*; (not coarse) *žib-pa*; *lag-mo W.*; (thin) *srab-pa.*
Fine s. (penalty) *rgyal, stoṅ.*
Finger *ser-mo, sor-mo*, resp. *ṗyag-sór*; *mdzub-mo, mdzug-gu*; — ring *ser-γdúb, sor-γdúb.*
Finish vb. *sgrub-pa*; to be finished *°grub-pa*; *ṫsar-ba*; *rdzogs-pa*; *°dzad-pa*; *zin-pa.*
Fir *ṫaṅ-šiṅ*; *som, γsom, som-šiṅ.*
Fire s. *me*; — brand *gal-mé*; — fly *°od-ṗro-°bu W.*; — place *ṫab, me-ṫab*; — tongs *me-lèn.*
Firm (solid) *mḱraṅ*; *mḱregs-pa*; *sra-ba*; (trodden) *čag-čan* 167; (tight) *ṫaṅ-po, dam-po*; (sure) *btsan*; *ṅes-pa*; (steady) v. *ṫsugs-pa.*

Firmness (of mind) *snyiṅ-rús.*
First *daṅ-po*; *sṅa-ma*; *mgo-ma*; born *mgo-bu*; *sṅon-skyes*; — part *stod* 223; adv. (at first) *mgo-ma* W.; *sṅa-sór*, *sṅa-góṅ*; *sṅar*; *γčig-tu*; *ťog-mar.*
Firstfruits *p̓ud*
Firstly *daṅ-por.*
Fish s. *nya*; — bone *nya-grá.*
Fish vb. *nya rṅon-pa*; *nya γšor ba.*
Fishing-hook *mčil-pa.*
Fishing-net *nya-rgya*, *nya·dól.*
Fissure *rgya-sér*; *ser-ka.*
Fist *k̓u-ťsúr.*
Fit vb. a. v. *sgrig-pa* 120; to — out *šom-pa*; to be — *°ťad-pa*; *ruṅ-ba.*
Five *lṅa.*
Fix vb. a. *°god-pa*; *sbyor-ba*; — a time *dus byed-pa.*
Flabby *kyom.*
Flag s. *dar*; — staff *dar-po-čé.*
Flageolet *gliṅ-bu*
Flame s. *lče*, *me-lče.*
Flannel *ťer-ma.*
Flap s. *gos sgáb.*
Flash vb. *°k̓yug-pa.*
Flat adj. *leb-mo*; *mnyam-pa.*
Flatten vb. a. *gleb-pa.*
Flatter *stod-pa*; *mol-lče btaṅ-ba* W.
Flatterer *ṅo stod-k̓an.*
Flattery *γčam-bu.*
Flatulence *p̓yen*; *°og-rluṅ.*
Flavour s. *bro-ba*; *ro.*
Flaw s. *šo-ré* W.
Flea *k̓yi-šig*; *°ji-ba.*
Flee *°bros-pa.*
Fleece s. *bal-rgyáb.*
Flesh *ša*; — fly *ša-sbráṅ.*
Flexible *kyom*; *mnyen-pa.*
Fling vb. *rgyab-pa*; *rgyag-pa* C.; *dbyug-pa* C.; *°p̓en-pa*; *skyur-ba*; *°bor-ba.*
Flint *lčag-rdo*; *lčags-mag.*
Float vb. n. *ldiṅ-ba.*
Flock s. *k̓yu*, *k̓yu-bo.*
Flog *lčag-gis γžu-ba*, v. also *skar-ba.*
Flood s. *ču-log.*
Floor s. *γži-ma*; (bottom) *mťil* 240; *šen* W.; *'an-°dar* C.; ground — *°og-k̓aṅ.*
Flour s. *p̓ye*; *žib.*
Flourish vb. *ble-ba*; *°ťseṅ-ba.*
Flourish s. (in writing) *ri-mo kyag-kyog.*
Flow vb. *°bab-pa*; s. *rgyun* 112.
Flower s. *me-tog*; — bed *rka*; — garden *sdum-ra.*
Fluid s. *k̓u-ba.*
Flute *p̓red-gliṅ.*
Flutter s. *k̓rag-k̓rug* 49.
Fly vb. *°p̓ur-ba*; to — up *°p̓ar-ba* 356.
Fly s. *sbraṅ-ma.*
Foal *rteu*; — of an ass *gu-rug.*
Foam s. *lbu-ba*, *dbu-ba.*

Fodder s. *čag.*
Foe *dgra*, *dgra-bo*; *p̓a-rol-pa* and *po.*
Fog *kug-rna*; *na-bún*; *rmugs-pa.*
Fold s. (plait) *ltab-ma*; (pen) *lhas-ma.*
Fold vb. a. (to plait) *ltab-pa*; (to pen) *dgar-ba.*
Follow *°braṅ-ba*, *r̀jes-su °gro-ba*; *γčod-pa.*
Follower *bstan-°dzin.*
Following *p̓yi(s)*, *p̓yir* 1, 2; *°di.*
Fond, to be — of . . . *la čags-pa*, *žen-pa.*
Fondness *k̓ri ba*; *žen-k̓ris*, *žen-čags-pa.*
Fontanel *klad-sgo*; *mťsogs-ma*; *°ťsaṅs-pai bu-ga.*
Food *zas*, resp. *žal-zás*, *bžes-pa*; *bšos*; *ka-zás*; *za-ba*, *za-ma*; *lto*; — of animals *bzan.*
Fool s. *glen-pa*; *blun-pa*, *blun-po.*
Foolish *glen-pa*; *blun-pa*; *blo-méd.*
Foot *rkaṅ pa*, resp. *žabs*; — bridge *dem-tsi* Lh; — path *rkaṅ-lam*; *°p̓raṅ*, *lam-°p̓raṅ*; — race *baṅ*; — ring *rkaṅ-γdub*; — soldier *rkaṅ-ťaṅ-pa*; — stool *rkaṅ-stegs*; — of a hill *rtsa-ba*; on foot *rkaṅ-ťaṅ-du* or *la.*
Footprint, Footstep *rkaṅ-r̀jés.*
For *don-du*; v. *p̓yogs* 352; — forty days *žag bži-bčui bar-du*, *žag bži-bču ťug* W.
Forbear vb. a. *°gyod-mi rmo-ba* 98.
Forbid *°gegs-pa*; *mi γnaṅ-ba.*
Force s. *mťu*; *dbaṅ*; *ṅar-ba*; *šed-dbáṅ* W.
Force vb. *dbaṅ-med-du °čol-ba*; v. also *nan-gyis*; *šed-k̓yer-nag-pos* W.
Ford vb *rgal-ba.*
Fore, — arm *lag-ṅár*; — finger *mdzub-mo*; — part, — side *ṅar*, *k̓a*, *mdun ṅos.*
Foregoing *sṅon-gro*; *sṅa-ma.*
Forehead *ťod-pa*; *dpral-ba.*
Foreign *yan-pa*; *γžan-ma*; *p̓yii*; — country *byes.*
Forenoon *sṅa-ťóg*; *sṅa-dro.*
Foreskin *sgo-pur*; *mdun-lpags*, *°dom-lpags.*
Forest *nags(-ma)*, *nags-γseb*; *nags-ťsal*, *nags-k̓rod*; *ťsal.*
Forget *r̀jed-pa*; *yi-γčod-pa*, resp. *ťugs γyel-ba* W.
Forgive vb. a. (not resenting) *bzod-pa* 498; (to leave unpunished) *°gyod-mi rmo-ba*; (to efface) *sel-ba*; (to wash away) *dag-pa.*
Fork *k̓a-brág*; *ša-°dzin.*
Form s. (mould) *par*; (figure) *dbyibs*; *γzugs*; *čas*; grammatical — *ťsig.*
Form vb a. *skyed-pa.*
Former adj. *goṅ*, *goṅ-ma*; *sṅon-°gro*; *daṅ-po*; — part *stod*; — time *sṅon-rol.*
Formerly *sṅa-čád*, *sṅa-goṅ*, *sṅa-bar*; *sṅan*, *sṅar*; *sṅon.*
Fornicate *°čal-ba*; v. *γyem-pa.*
Fornicator *°čál-pa.*
Forsake *skyur-ba*; *°bor-ba*; *γtoṅ-ba.*
Fort *mk̓ar.*

Forte (in music) *rtsub-po.*
Forth *sogs; p̓ar; yas.*
Fortress *rdzoṅ(s).*
Fortune (lot) *p̓ya*; (wealth) *k̓a-rje C.*; good - *bkra-šis*; —teller *p̓ya-mk̓an*; *ṅan-sṅags-mk̓an.*
Forward vb. *₀k̓al-ba.*
Found vb. *₀god-pa*; *rgyag-pa*; *₀debs-pa*; *₀dzugs-pa.*
Foundation *rmaṅ*; — of a house *mt̓il*; *k̓aṅ-rtsá.*
Fountain *ču-mig.*
Four *bži*; fourth *bži-pa*; fourteen *ču-bži*; fourteenth *ču-bži-pa*; forty *bži-bču*; fortieth *bži-bču-pa.*
Fourfooted *rkaṅ-bži-pa.*
Fowl *bya*; domestic — *k̓yim-bya.*
Fowler *bya-pa.*
Fox *wa*; — coloured *k̓am-pa.*
Fragile *k̓rol-mo W.*
Fragment *čag-k̓rúm, čag-dúm*; (*γ*)*sil-bu.*
Fragrance *ṅad.*
Frail, to get — *rgud-pa.*
Frame s. *k̓ri*; vb. a. *₀god-pa* 95.
Frankincense *bdug-pa, gu-gul.*
Fraud *ṅo-lkog*; *zog, zol-zóg.*
Free adj. *yan-pa*; *t̓ar-pa*; to become — *₀grol-ba*; *t̓ar-ba*; to set — *t̓ar-du ₀jug-pa*; *₀bud-pa.*
Freeze *₀k̓yags-pa*; *p̓yid-pa.*
Freight s. *k̓al.*
Frenzy *₀k̓rul-pa.*
Fresh *γsar-ba, γsar-po*; *so-ma W.*; — butter *skya-már W.*
Friday *γza-pa(-wa)-saṅs.*
Friend *grogs, rog*; *ṅo-šés, mdza-bšés, bšes-γnyén*; *mdza-bo*; *zla-bo.*
Friendly *sṅyiṅ-nyé*; resp. *sol-po.*
Fright s. *₀jigs-pa.*
Frighten *skrag-pa.*
Frightened *skrag-pa*; to be — *rtab-pa.*
Fringes *k̓a-t̓sar.*
Frog *sbal-pa.*
From *nas* 304; *man-čad* 411; *las* 546; — within *k̓oṅ-nas* 43.
Frontier *sa-mt̓sáms.*
Front-side *k̓a*; *ṅar.*
Frost *k̓yags-pa*; *sad.*
Froth *lbu-ba, dbu-ba.*
Frozen *k̓yags-pa.*
Fruit *šiṅ-tóg*; *₀bras-bu*; — tree *bza-šiṅ*; *rtsi-šiṅ.*
Fry vb. *sreg-pa, slam-pa, rṅód-pa.*
Fuel *bud-šiṅ.*
Fulfil *skoṅ-ba*; *sgrub-pa*; *₀geṅs-pa.*
Full *gaṅ-ba*; *ltem-pa*; *mt̓on-po*; to be — *ltams-pa*; *₀k̓eṅs-pa*; to make — *k̓yab-pa.*
Fully *rgyas-par.*
Fumigate *bdug-pa.*
Fun *pra-čál*; *šags.*
Functionary *blon-po*
Fundament *rtsa-ba*; *rkub.*
Fur-coat *slag-pa, slog-pa*; *t̓ul-pa.*
Furious *γtum-pa.*
Furnish (supply) *sgrub-pa.*
Furniture *yo-byád.*
Furrow s. *rka.*
Further *γžan-yaṅ, yaṅ.*
Furtherance *mt̓un-rkyen.*
Futurity *ma ₀ons-pai dus*; *p̓ugs.*

G

Gain vb. a. *rgyal-ba, rnyed-pa, sgrub-pa.*
Gain s. *skyed*; *k̓e, k̓ye*; *k̓a-rgyál, rgyál-k̓a*; *rnyed-pa*; *spogs, bogs.*
Gait *bgrod.*
Galaxy *dgu-t̓sigs.*
Gale *rluṅ-dmár, rluṅ nag-po.*
Gall s. *mk̓ris-pa.*
Gallop vb. n. *rta rgyug-pa.*
Gallows *čar-šiṅ.*
Game s. (animals of chase) *ri-dwags.*
Gander *ṅaṅ-pa.*
Ganges *gaṅ-gā.*
Gap *rgya-sér*; *ser-ka, ser-ga.*
Gape vb. *sgyiṅ-ba*; *γdaṅ-ba.*
Garden *t̓sal*; *t̓sas W.*; *ldum-ra*; *sdum-ra*; — flower *ha-ló.*
Garlic *sgog-pa.*
Garment *gos*; *čas*, resp. *na-bza*; under — *'aṅ-t̓úṅ*; upper — *bla-gáb, bla-gós, γzan-gos.*
Garret *steṅ-k̓aṅ.*
Gate *rgyal-sgo*; *sgo-mo.*
Gather vb. a. *sgrug-pa*; *₀t̓u-ba*; *sog-pa*; vb. n. *₀k̓or-ba*; *₀gugs-pa*; *₀t̓ibs-pa.*
Gatherer *t̓un, ₀t̓un.*
Gear s. *go-ča.*
Gelding s. *p̓o-rtá.*
General adj. *spyi* 333; *t̓un-moṅ.*
General s. *dmag-dpón.*
Generate *skyed-pa.*
Generation *rgyal-brgyúd*; *γduṅ-rabs, rabs.*
Genesis *čags-rábs.*
Genitals *mt̓san(-ma).*
Genitive case *₀brel-pa.*
Gentian *tig-ta*; *kyi-lčé.*

Gentle *˳jam-po, ˳bol-po; mťun-ċan; sgye-mo.*

Gentleman *ytso-bo; sa-heb;* old —, old squire, *ga-gá Ld., 'a-jo-lag C.*

Gently *ṅaṅ-gis; ga-le C., gu-le W.*

Gentry *drag-rigs.*

Genuine *dṅos; ṅo-rtóg; lhad-méd.*

Geography *ynas-bšád, yul-bšád.*

Germinate vb. n. *skye-ba;* to cause to — *skyed-pa.*

Gesture s. *brda; rnam-gyúr;* v. also *ťsul.*

Get vb. a. *ḱug-pa; rnyed-pa; ťob-pa; ˳dzin-pa; yod-par ˳gyur-ba;* vb. n. *˳gro-ba; ča-ba W.;* to — into *ċud-pa; ˳bab-pa;* to — through *ťar-ba, bgrod-pa;* to — up *ldaṅ-ba, laṅ-ba,* resp. *bžeṅs-pa.*

Ghost *mi-ma-yin(-pa); sems-nyid.*

Ghostlike *yzugs-méd* 494; *lus-méd.*

Gift s. *˳ḱyos-pa; ynaṅ-ba; bya-dgá; ˳bul-ba; sbyin-pa; yon.*

Gild *čus ytoṅ-ba, yser-čus ˳byug-pa.*

Gills *nya-skyogs.*

Gimlet *sor.*

Ginger *sga, sgeu; lċa-sga.*

Girdle s. *ska-rágs.*

Girl *bu-mo; yžon-nu-ma; na-čuṅ.*

Give *skur-ba; ster-ba; ynaṅ-ba; ˳bul-ba* 394; *˳bogs-pa; sbyin-pa; stsol-ba;* to — an entertainment *˳gyed-pa;* to — up *sgyur-ba; yċod-pa; spoṅ-ba; blos ytoṅ-ba;* to be given to *skyoṅ-ba; rten-pa.*

Glacier *gaṅs, gaṅs-ċan.*

Glad adj. *dga-ba;* — tidings *ytam-snyán;* to be — *dga-ba; mgu-ba;* to make — **sem ťad ċug-ċe* W.*

Glass *šel, man-šel;* — beads *ga-šél;* — bottle *šel-búm.*

Gleaner *snye-ťun.*

Glide *˳dred-pa; ˳byid-pa.*

Glistening *ḱrom-mé, ḱrol-po; ċam.*

Glitter vb. *˳ťser-ba.*

Globe *ril W.*

Globular *zlum-pa, ril-ba;* a — stone *rdo-ril.*

Glorious *grags-ċan; ˳ṕags-pa.*

Glory s. *grags-pa; dpal, dpal-byór.*

Glory vb. *rlom-pa, ṕo-ťsod ˳ċud-pa;* v. *ṕo-so.*

Gloss *bḱrag; ˳od-ysál.*

Glossy *bḱra-ba.*

Glove *lag-šúbs.*

Glue s. *spyin.*

Gnash *so ḱrig-ḱrig byed-pa, so bdar-ba; so sdom-pa.*

Gnaw *yzan-pa; ˳ča-ba, mur-ba.*

Go *˳gro-ba; ˳doṅ-ba; ča-ba W.; rgyu-ba; bgrod-pa; ṕyin-pa,* eleg. *mči-ba,* resp. *ṕeb-pa;* to — about *˳grim-pa;* to — abroad *˳gron-du ˳gro-ba, byes-su ˳gro-ba;* to — astray *˳ḱyar-ba;* to — away *˳gye-ba,* resp. *bžud-pa, yšegs-pa;* to — in or into *čud-pa, ˳jug-pa;* to — out *˳ton-pa; spro-ba;* to — round *˳ḱor-ba, skor-ba.*

Goal *ťsad.*

Goat *ra-ma;* wild — *ra-rgód, ra-po-čé; skyin.*

Goat's hair *ral.*

Goblet *skyogs.*

Goblin *˳dre, lha-˳dre.*

God *dkon-mčog;* a god *lha,* a goddess *lha-mo;* a tutelar god *yi-dam-lhá, lha-sruṅ; mgon-po.*

Going s. (the act of) *gros.*

Goitre *lba-ba.*

Gold *yser.*

Gong *˳ḱar-rṅá.*

Good adj. *bzaṅ-ba; legs-pa; dga-bdé C.; rgyal-ba W.;* col. *yag-po;* to be — (of coins) *˳grul-ba.*

Good s. (advantage) *don.*

Good-bye *da ča yin W.*152; **ṭa-ši-šig* W.;* v. *ga-le C.* 64.

Goods *dṅos-po; ka-ċa; ḱa-rjé C.; spus; zoṅ.*

Goose *ṅaṅ-pa, ṅaṅ-ma.*

Gorge s. (ravine) *roṅ.*

Gossip s. (idle talk) *ḱa-bšád; rgya-láb.*

Gourd *ka-béd, ku-ba, gon W., ċuṅ C.*

Gout *draṅ-nád W.; grum-bu, grum-nád, drag-grúm; dreg-nad, ťsigs-nad, ťsigs-zúg.*

Govern *sgyur-ba; rgyal-srid skyoṅ-ba; dbaṅ sgyur-ba.*

Government *rgyal-po, rgyal-srid.*

Governor *sde-pa; bka-blón.*

Grace s. *bka-drin, ťugs-rje.*

Gracious *ťugs-rje-ċan.*

Gradually *ṅaṅ-gis; gu-le gu-le W.*

Graft s. *pe-bán.*

Grain s. *čag-tse, rdog-po, ˳bru.*

Grammar *byā-ka-ra-ṇa* 372.

Grandchild *ťsa-bo;* — daughter *ťsa-mo;* — father *mes-po;* — mother *ma-mo, ṕyi-mo;* — son *ťsa-bo,* resp. *dbon-po.*

Grant vb. (*bka*) *ynaṅ-ba; ˳grub-pa; stsol-ba; yzigs-pa.*

Granulous *čag-tse-ċan W.*

Grape *rgun, rgun-˳brúm; čag-mo.*

Grasp vb. *˳ju-ba, ˳dzin-pa;* cf. *yċags-pa.*

Grass *rtswa.*

Grasshopper *ċog-ċog-pa, ča-ga-˳bu.*

Grate s. *dra-pa, lċags-dra.*

Grateful *drin-yzo-ċan;* to be — *drin yzo-ba.*

Grater *lag-dár, lab-dár.*

Gratitude *drin dran-pa.*

Grave s. *dur-ḱuṅ.*

Gravel s. *gyo-mo; šag-ma.*

Gravy *spags; ša-rúg,* resp. *skyu-rúm.*

Gray *se-bo;* light — *skya-bo.*

Grease s. *snum-pa;* vb. *snum-gyis skud-pa.*

Greasy *snum-ċan; ťso-ba.*

Great *čé-ba, čen-po, rgyas-pa.*

Greatness *če-ba, če-kyád.*
Greedy *₀dod-sred-čan; blo-₀dód; ham-pa-čan.*
Green *ño-ba, ñon-po; ljan-ku.*
Greens s. *ño-tsód, ldum, tsod-ma.*
Greensward *na-ka; ne-táñ.*
Grieve vb. n. *skyo-ba, ₀gyod-pa.*
Grind *₀tag-pa; bdar-ba*; to — the teeth so *bdar-ba.*
Gripes *glañ, glañ-tabs.*
Gristle *čag-krúm.*
Grit (gravel) *gyo-mo.*
Groan s. *₀kog-šúgs W., šugs-nár, šugs-riñ.*
Groan vb. *₀kun-pa.*
Groom *rta-rdzi.*
Grope *snom-pa.*
Grotto *gyam, pug-pa.*
Ground s. *žiñ; γži(-ma)* 480; *sa-γži* 570.
Grouse *ri-skyégs; goñ-mo.*
Grove *skyed-mos-tsal.*
Grow vb. n. *čer skye-ba; ₀kruñ-ba; ₀gyur-ba; rgyas-pa; ča-ba*; to — dark *₀tibs-pa*; to — old *bgre-ba*; to cause to grow *skyed-pa.*
Growth *skyed, skye.*
Grudge s. *kon-pa*; to bear a — *₀kon-pa.*
Grumbling s. **to-tá* W.*
Grunt vb. *ñug-pa, ñur-ba, kun-pa.*
Guard vb. *skyoñ-ba, skyob-pa, sruñ-ba.*
Guardian *pa-tsáb*; — of the world *jig-rten-skyoñ.*
Guess s. v. *tsod* 453.
Guide s. *lam-mkan, lam-₀dren-pa, lam-yig.*
Guitar *sgra-snyan; ko-poñs W.*
Gulf *kug, ču-kug*; (abyss) *btson-doñ.*
Gullet *lkog-ma.*
Gulp s. *hub; skyu-gáñ, čor-gáñ.*
Gum s. *tañ-ču.*
Gun *sgyogs; tu-pag W.; me-mda C.*
Gunpowder *tu-pag-man W.; me-rdzás C.*
Gunstock *₀gu-mdá; sgum-da.*
Gut, great — or colon *γnye-ma.*
Gutter *wa.*
Guttural s. *lče-rtsa-čan* 150.

H

Habitation *groñ; γnas-tsañ, γnas-kañ, γži-ma.*
Haft *yu-ba.*
Hail s. (frozen rain) *ser-ba*; (salutation) v. *rgyal-ba* I 108.
Hair *skra; spu*, a little — *ba-spu.*
Hairy *ba-spu-čan; skra-čan.*
Half (one half) s. *ča* 151.
Half adj. *pyed*; — boot *krad-pa.*
Hall *bkad-sa*; — of judgment *tsugs-kañ.*
Halo *kyim.*
Halter *tur-mgo; srab-mtúr.*
Halting-place *sti-bai γnas*; (night quarters) *₀brañ-sa*, resp. *γzim-bráñ.*
Hammer s. *to-čúñ*; large — *to-ba.*
Hand s. *lag(-pa)*, resp. *pyag.*
Hand vb. a. *sriñ-ba*; to — over *skur-ba.*
Handicraft *bzo.*
Handful *kyá-le; kyor; ₀čañs-pa; spar-ba; pul.*
Handkerchief *sna-pyis*; — of salutation *ka-btágs* 37.
Handle s. *kab-za, lčibs, yu-ba.*
Handsome *mčor-po, mdzes-pa.*
Handspike *gal-ta.*
Hang vb. a. (a man) **čar-la tañ-če* W.*; to — up *skar-ba, dgar-ba, ₀gel-ba; ₀pyar-ba*; vb. n. to — down *₀jol-ba, ₀pyañ-ba.*
Hangman *γšed-ma.*
Hank *gru-gu.*
Happen *₀gyur-ba, ₀byuñ-ba, ₀oñ-ba.*
Happiness *dge-ba, skyid-pa, γyañ; bkra-šis.*
Happy *bkra-šis-pa; skal-ldán, skyid-po; legs-pa*; to be — *bde-ba, skyid-pa*; may you be — *bkra-šis-šig W.*
Hard *kyoñ, mkrañ, mkregs-pa; sra-ba*; — to bear *kag-po*; — water *ču kyoñ-po.*
Hardened *šran-čan.*
Hardness *ñar-ba.*
Hardship *dka-ba, nyon-moñs-pa* 191.
Hardware *lčags-čas.*
Hare *ri-bóñ.*
Harm s. *skyon*; to do — *tsugs-pa, γnod-pa byed-pa* or *skyel-ba*; vb. to — *snad-pa.*
Harmony (musical concord) *sgra-dbyañs*; (agreement) *mtun-pa*; concord amongst kinsmen *γnyen-₀dún.*
Harness s. *čibs-čas.*
Harrow s. *šal-ba*; vb. to — *šal-ba ₀drud-pa.*
Harsh *gyoñ-po; rtsub-po.*
Hartshorn *ša-ru.*
Harvest s. *btsas-ma; lo-tóg* 552.
Haste s. *tsa-drag*; to make — *rgyug-pa*; make haste! **tsa-rag toñ* W.; *riñ-pa toñ* W.*
Hasten vb. n. *snyegs-pa; riñs-pa.*
Hasty *spro tuñ-ba; yid tuñ-ba.*
Hate vb. *₀kon-pa, ₀gras-pa, sdañ-ba.*
Hatred *sdañ-sems, že-sdáñ.*
Haughtiness *če-tábs, po-so.*
Haughty *ka-drág, keñs-pa; če-tabs-čan, po-so-čan*
Hautboy *dge-gliñ; sur-na.*
Have (possess) *bdog-pa*; having v. *čan* 138,

v. *bčas-pa* 146; I have *ṅa-la yod* 515; I have to v. *rgyu* no. 3, 110.
Hawk s. *ḱra*.
Hay *rtsa-skám*; — fork *sbrag-ma*.
Haze *ḱug-rná*.
He *ḱo, ḱoṅ, de* 255; — who *gaṅ* no. 2 65.
Head s. *mgo*, resp. *dbu*; (chief) *ḱyu-mčog* 47; *γtso-bo* 434; (of an argument) *yan-lag*; — master *˳go-dpón*.
Head vb. a. *˳ḱrid-pa, sna ˳dren-pa*.
Headache *mgo-nád*; *klad-γzér*.
Headman *˳go-pa, rgad-po*.
Heal vb. a. *˳tso-ba* 460, *γso-ba*; *bčos-pa*.
Health *ḱams*; *nad-med-pa*.
Healthy *nad-méd*.
Heap s. *ṗuṅ-po*.
Heap vb. a *sgril-ba, bčer-ba, spuṅ-ba*; to — up *sog-pa*.
Heaped *byur-po, byur-byúr* 377; *gaṅ-ba W.* 66.
Hear vb. a. *ťos-pa, ťsor-ba W., nyan-pa*; hear! *ka-yé*.
Hearer *nyan-pa* or *-po*.
Heart *snyiṅ*, resp. *ťugs*; *naṅ*; *rgyud* 112; *že* 477; to know by — *ḱa-ťon-du šes-pa* 35.
Heart-grief *sems-nád*.
Hearth *me-ťáb*; *sgyid-bu* 118; — stone *sgyed-po*.
Heartily *snyiṅ ťag-pa-nas*.
Hearty *že-ťag-pa*; a — request *že-ťag-pai žu-ba*.
Heat *tsa-ba, tsad-pa*; *ťan-pa*.
Heated *dros-pa* 264.
Heaven *mḱa, nam-mḱa*; *γnam, mťo-ris* 242.
Heavens *mḱa, dbyiṅs* 390.
Heavy *lči-ba*.
Hedgehog *rgaṅ, ˳gaṅ-γzer-ma*.
Heed s., to give — *bya-ra byed-pa*.
Heedless *zon-méd*.
Heel s. *rtiṅ-pa*.
Heifer *zal-mo*.
Height *mťo-ḱyad*; *ḱyon*; *rṅams*; *dpaṅs*; *˳ṗaṅ* 355.
Heir s. *nor-bdag*; joint — *go-ḱan W.*
Hellebore *spru-ma*.
Helm s. *ḱa-lo*.
Helmet *rmog*.
Help s. *skyabs, skyobs, ra-mda*.
Help vb. a. *skyabs byed-pa, grogs byed-pa*.
Helper *skyabs-mgon, skyabs-γnas*; *γnyen-po, dpuṅ-γnyén, dpuṅ-grogs*.
Hem s. *sne-mo, ča-ga*.
Hemorrhoids *γžaṅ-nád, γžaṅ-brúm*.
Hemp *so-ma, γtso-ma, btso-ma*; *bhaṅ-ge W.*
Hen *bya-mo*; *ḱyim-bya*.
Henceforth *da-ste, da ṗyis* 247, *da ṗyin-čád* 350.
Herb *sṅo, sṅo-ťsód, rtswa*.
Herd *ḱyu, ḱyu-bo*.
Herdsman *rdzi-bo, ṗyugs-rdzi*.
Here *˳di-ru* 275.
Hereafter *ṗugs-na, da-ste, da-ṗyis, da ṗyin-čad*.
Heresy *čos-lóg*.
Heritage *nor-skal*.
Hermit *dgon-pa-pa*; *bdag-bsrúṅ*.
Hermitage *dgon-pa, γnas*.
Hero *ḱyo-ga*.
Heron *kaṅ-ka*; *skyar-mo*.
Hesitation *ťsam-ťsúm*.
Hew *˳ǰog-pa, ˳ťsog-pa*; v. also cleave.
Hiccough s. *skyig-bu*; *'i-ḱug, 'ig W.*; vb. to — *skyig-pa*.
Hide s. *ko-ba, ko-lpags, pags-pa* or *-po*.
Hide vb. a. *skuṅ-ba, sbed-pa*; to — one's self *˳gab-pa, yib-pa, γsaṅ-ba*.
Hiding-place *bskuṅs-sa*.
High *mťo-ba, mťon-po*; — and low *drag-žán* 261; — road, — way *rgya-lám*; *ma-lam W.*
Hill *ri*; v. *sgaṅ*.
Hilt *kab-za, lčibs, yu-ba*.
Hinder vb. a. *˳gegs-pa, ˳ḱegs-pa*; to be -ed *ťogs-pa*.
Hind-foot *rkaṅ-pa*.
Hind-part *mǰug*.
Hindrance *gegs, bgegs, bar-čód*.
Hinge s. *sgo-˳ḱór*.
Hip s. (joint) *sta-zúr, dpyi*; (fruit) *šib-ši-lu-lu Ld.*
Hire s. *rṅan-pa*, vb. to — *γyar-ba*.
History *lo-rgyús, byuṅ-ťsul*.
Hit vb. a. *ḱes-pa, rgyab-pa, ťug-pa, ˳ṗog-pa, ˳ťebs-pa W.*
Hit s. *lčag* 148.
Hither *ťsur*; — to *sṅa-čad*.
Hive s. *ťsaṅ*.
Hoangho *rma-ču*.
Hoarfrost *ba-mo*.
Hoarse *ṅar-ṅar-po, ˳dzer-po*; to be — *˳dzer-ba*; *ras-pa Ld.*
Hoarseness *skad-gágs*.
Hoe vb. a. *rko-ba*.
Hog s. *ṗag*.
Hoist vb. a. *˳ṗyar-ba*.
Hold vb. a. *čaṅ-ba, snom-pa, ˳dzin-pa*; to — forth *˳dzed-pa*; to — out (suffice) *˳ḱyed-pa*; vb. n. *rten-pa* 213.
Hold s. *rten*; to take — of *˳ǰu-ba*. [413.
Hole s. *ḱuṅ, bi-gán, bi-yán W., bu-ga*; *mig*
Hollo interj. *ka-yé*; *kye, kye-hó*; *W. wa!*
Hollow adj. *ḱoṅ-stóṅ*.
Hollow s. *ḱuṅ, sbug(s)*; the — of the hand *skyor*.
Holly *sgom-˳bróg*.
Holy *skal-ldán, dam-pa*; a — man, saint, *skyes-bu dam-pa*.
Homage s. *bkur-ba, bkur-sti*; *rim-gro*, resp. *sku-rim*.
Home s. *ḱyim*; to be at — *ḱyim-du sdod-pa*.

Homeless *nes-méd.*
Hone s. *₀dzeṅ.*
Honest *draṅ-po, ćos draṅ-po.*
Honey *sbraṅ-rtsi, raṅ-si W.*
Honour s. *bkur-ba, bkur-sti; sti-staṅ; ya-ša; rim-gro,* resp. *sku-rim; grags pa, ṗu-dúd.*
Honour vb. a. *bkur-ba, mćod-pa, rje-ba.*
Honourable *btsun-pa.*
Hood s. *ṫod-k̔ebs.*
Hoof *rmig-pa.*
Hook s. *kug.*
Hookah (Turkish pipe) *ći-lim;* resp. *žē-k̔ór C.*
Hoop s. *šan.*
Hoopoe *ṗu-šúd.*
Hope s. *re-ba; blo-ydéṅ, blo-ytád;* vb. to — *re-ba.*
Horizon *mṫoṅ-₀k̔or.*
Horn *rwa, ru.*
Hornet *liṅ-gol-ma.*
Hornless *k̔u-yú.*
Horse s. *rta,* resp. *ćibs;* black — *₄ol-ba;* — dung *rta-sbaṅs;* — tail *rta-ṙna;* — whip *rta-lćag.*
Horseman *rta-pa.*
Horseshoe *rmig-lćágs.*
Hospital *nad-k̔aṅ, ṫsugs-k̔aṅ.*
Host (number of men) *dpuṅ, ṗal-po-će;* (army) *dmag.*
Hot *ṫsa-ba, ṫsan;* to be — *ṫsa-ba;* the — time of the day *dro* 264.
Hour *ću-ṫsod* 158; double — *k̔yim* 47.
House s. *k̔aṅ-pa; k̔yim; groṅ; mk̔ar; sdum-pa C.; naṅ;* — owner *k̔yim-bdag, k̔yim-pa-pa;* — rent *k̔aṅ-glá.*
Household *yžis-mad; bza-mi* 497.
Housekeeping *so-tsis, so-tsigs.*
Housewife *k̔yim-ṫab-mo, k̔yim-bdag-mo.*
How *ći* 139, *ći-ltar, ći-tsug, ga-zug, ći-ne Bal.;* — much *ga-ṫsód;* (*ći-*)*tsam.*
However *₄on-kyaṅ.*
Howl vb. *ṅu-ba;* (of animals) *ṅur-ba.*
Howling s. (of a tempest) *₄ur-sgra* 500.
Hug vb. a. *₀k̔yud-pa.*
Hum s. *di-ri-ri* 252; *₄ur-sgra* 500.
Hum vb. *₀k̔rog-pa.*
Human *mii;* — being *skye-bo.*
Humble adj. *gus-pa.*
Humbleness *yćam-bu.*
Humidity *bad.*
Humours (of the body) v. *nyes-pa* 191.
Humming (noise) *₄ur-₄ur;* — of bees *di-ri-ri, zi-ri-ri.*
Hump, Hunch s. *ṙnog; gye-gu.*
Hundred *brgya.*
Hunger s. *ltogs-pa; bkres-pa.*
Hungry *ltogs-pa, bkren-pa, bkres-pa.*
Hunt, Hunting s. *kyi-ra.*
Hunt vb. a. *ṙṅon-pa, ₀ćor-ba, yšor-ba.*
Hunter *ṙṅon-pa, kyi-ra-ba, liṅs-pa.*
Hurricane *rluṅ-ṫsúb.*
Hurry vb. *grim-pa; rgyug-pa.*
Hurry s. *tsab-tsúb.*
Hurt vb. a. *ynod-pa skyel-ba; ynod-pa, ₀k̔aṅ-ba, ṫsugs-pa, ₀tse-ba.*
Husband s. *k̔yo, k̔yim-ṫabs, k̔yim-bdag; skyes-pa; dga-grogs; bdag-po;* — and wife (couple) *k̔yo-šúg.*
Husbandry *so-ṫsis, so-ṫsigs.*
Husk s. *lgaṅ-bu, spun-pa, sbur-ma.*
Hut s. *k̔u-tu, pu-lu, spyil-po.*
Hydrophobia *k̔yi-smyón.*
Hypocrisy *k̔a-ćos; sgyu-zóg; ṫsul-₀ćos.*
Hypocrite *k̔a-že mi mṫsuṅs-pa.*

I

I pron. *ṅa, ṅed, ṅed-raṅ* 128, *ṅos* 130, *bdag-nyid* 268; I myself *ṅa-raṅ, ṅed-raṅ.*
Ice *dar, ćab-brom, gaṅs, k̔yags-pa.*
Icicle *k̔yags-sdóṅ.*
Idea *₀du-šes; dmigs-pa.*
Identic *mi-ynyis-pa* 192.
Idiocrasy *ṅaṅ* 125.
Idle adj. *le-lo-ćan; kyaṅ-kyóṅ W.*
If *na* 299, *gal-te* 68; but if *ći-ste* 140.
Ignoble *skye-ba dma-ba.*
Ignorance *yti-mug, ma-rig-pa.*
Ill adj. and adv. (sick) *nad-pa;* — fed *dṅos-ṅán; bza-méd;* — humoured *skyo-ba;* — looking *spus-méd;* — luck *rkyen;* to be — *na-ba.*
Illness *nad, na-ba, zug W.*
Illusion *₀k̔rul-snáṅ, sgyu-ma.*
Illustrate *₀grel-bá;* to — by parables *dpes mṫson-pa.*
Image *sku;* molten — *blugs-sku.*
Imagine vb. a. *go-ba, sgom-pa, dmigs-pa, sems-pa;* vb. n. *snyam-pa.*
Imbecile *glen-pa, han-ldáṅ W.*
Imbibe *₀jibs-pa;* to be imbibed *ṫim-pa.*
Imitate *lad-mo byed-pa.*
Imitation *lad-mo; ₀bag.*
Immaterial (not existing) *dṅos-med, yzugs-méd.*
Immeasurable *ṫsad-méd, yžal-du-med-pa.*
Immediate *₀ṗral, ṗral.*
Immediately *mod-la, de ma-ṫag-tu* 227.
Immoderate *ṫsod méd.*
Immoral *₀ćol-pa, mi tsaṅs-pa* 445.
Impaired *nyams-pa.*

Impart *ˌbogs-pa.*
Impartial *p̓yogs-méd.*
Impartiality *mnyam-pa-nyid.*
Impeded, to be — *k̓ad-pa.*
Impediment *gegs, ˌgal-rkyén, bar-č̓ód.*
Imperative mood *ɣdams-ṅag ˌdoms-pai t̓sig* 265.
Imperishable *mi-ˌǰig-pa, rtag-pa.*
Impetuous *ṅar-ma.*
Impious *skal-méd; sdig-byéd.*
Implements *č̓a-byad, č̓a-lag, go-č̓a, yo-byád.*
Impolite *gyoṅ-po*; very — *k̓a-gyoṅ-č̓é.*
Imponderable *ɣžal-du-med-pa.*
Importance *k̓ag, ˌk̓os, gal, do-gál, ɣtsigs.*
Important *ċ̓i-ba, k̓ag-ċan, ˌk̓os-ċan.*
Impose vb. a. (lay on) *ˌgel-ba, skul-ba*; (to deceive) *ˌbrid-pa, mgo skor-ba.*
Imposture *mgo-skór; sgyu, ṅo lkog; rdzub.*
Imprecation *ṅan; byad, byad-stems.*
Impress vb. (on the mind) *k̓oṅ-du č̓ud-pa*; *ɣċags-pa.*
Improper *mi-ruṅ-ba.*
Improve vb. n. *ˌp̓el-ba, t̓seṅ-ba.*
Improvement *skyed.*
Impure *skyug-bro, ma-dag-pa.*
In prep. *na, naṅ-na.*
Inattention *ɣyeṅ-ba, ɣyeṅs-pa.*
Inattentive *mi ˌtsugs-pa.*
Incantation *sṅags, ɣsaṅ-sṅags, ɣzuṅs.*
Incense s. *kun-du-ru, gu-gul, bdug-pa.*
Incessantly *k̓or-yug-tu. rgyun-č̓ad-med-par, rgyun-du.*
Inch *sor-mo.*
Inclination *ɣzuṅ-ba, bag-č̓ags.*
Incline vb. n. (to lean) *ˌk̓ra-ba.*
Inclined, to be — (disposed) *ˌdod-pa*
Income *sleb.*
Incongruous *ya-ma-zúṅ.*
Inconsiderate *ɣzu-lum-ċan, blo-gros-med.*
Inconstant *č̓ol, mi ˌtsugs-pa, ˌgyur-ldóg.*
Incorporeal *lus-méd.*
Incorrect *skyon-ċan.*
Increase vb. a. *sgro-ˌdogs-pa, snon-pa, spel-ba*; vb. n. *rgyas-pa, ˌp̓el-ba.*
Increase s. *skyed, non-ka.*
Incredible *mi srid-pa, ˌos-méd W.*; *yid-* [*č̓es-su mi ruṅ-ba.*
Indecorous *ṅo-tsa.*
Indeed *de-ka yod* 255, *mod-pa.*
Indefatigably *skyo mi-ṡes-par.*
Indented *ċoṅ-ċóṅ.*
Independence *raṅ-dbáṅ.*
Index *dkar-č̓ag, gleṅ-ɣži; t̓o.*
India *rgya-gár*, British — *rgya-p̓i-liṅ.*
Indian s. *rgya-gar-pa.*
India rubber *gyig.*
Indicate *ston-pa.*
Indication *mtsan-nyid*
Indifferent *stoṅ-pa*; to be — to ... *la mi lta-ba.*
Indigence *gyoṅ, dbul-ba, ˌp̓oṅs-pa.*
Indigent *dbul-po, dbul-ˌp̓oṅs.*
Indigestion *zas ma žu-ba.*
Indigo *rams*: — colour *mt̓iṅ.*
Indirectly *zur-du, zur-na W.*
Indivisible *mi-p̓yed-pa.*
Indolent *kyaṅ-kyóṅ W., rgod-bag-ċan.*
Indubitable *gor-ma-č̓ag-pa, ɣdon-mi-za-* [*ba.*
Induce *skul-ba.*
Indulge in vb. n. *č̓ags-pa*; v. also *bag-med-pa* 363
Industrious *le-lam-k̓an W.*; *brtson-pa-ċan.*
Inexplicable *ɣya-nyés*; it is — to me *rgyu-mtsan mi ṡes* or *bṡad mi nus.*
Infallible *mi-nor-ba.*
Infant *č̓u-ma-lóṅ Ld.*; *p̓ru-gu č̓uṅ-ba*; — boy *k̓yeu.*
Infect *ˌgo-ba, bsgo-ba.*
Inflammation *ˌt̓sig-pa*; — of the eyes *mig-t̓sig (ċe) W.*
Inflate *ˌbud-pa*; *p̓u ˌdebs-pa.*
Inflection *dgu-ba.*
Inflict *skyel-ba.*
Influence s. *dbaṅ*; vb. a. *skul-ba.*
Inform vb. a. *spriṅ-ba, lon zer-ba C., hun taṅ-č̓e W.*
Information *man-ṅág*; *hun W.*
Infringe *ˌgal-ba.*
Infuse *ˌǰug-pa.*
Infusion *t̓aṅ-gi sman.*
Ingenious *dmigs-ċan.*
Inheritance *skal-nór, nor-skal.*
Inject *ˌǰug-pa.*
Injure *ˌtse-ba, ɣnod-pa.*
Injured *nyams-pa.*
Injury *ɣnod-pa.*
Ink *snag-t̓sa*; — powder *snag-p̓yé.*
Inkstand *snag-k̓oṅ*; **nag-bhum* C.*
Inlet *t̓so-lág C.*
Inmate *naṅ-gi mi.*
Inn *ˌgron-k̓áṅ.*
Inner *naṅ-gi* 301.
Innumerable *graṅs-méd-pa*; *tsad-méd.*
Inquire *ˌdri-ba*; to — closely *žib-tu ˌdri-ba*; to — rigorously **skar-t̓ag taṅ-č̓e* W.*
Inquiry *brtags-pa.*
Inquisitive *rtogs-ˌdod-ċan.*
Insane *smyon-pa*; to be — *ˌk̓rul-ba, smyó-* [*ba.*
Insanity *smyo-ˌbóg.*
Inscription *byaṅ-bu, byaṅ-ma*; *žal-byáṅ.*
Insect *rkaṅ-drug-ldan-pa*; *ˌbu.*
Insensible *k̓al-k̓ól*; to get — *ˌk̓ol-ba.*
Inseparable *mi-p̓yed-pa, ˌbral-méd.*
Insert *ˌdzud-pa.*
Inside s. *k̓oṅ-pa, naṅ-rol.*
Inspect *lta-ba, mgo byed-pa* 91, *žal-ta byed-pa* 473.
Inspection *žal-ta.*
Instance *dpe*; for — *ˌdi-lta-ste, dper-na.*
Instant s. *dar, skad, yud.*

Instantly *mod-la.*
Instantaneous *dar ỳcig-gi; ˳p̓ral-gyi; yud-tsam-pa.*
Instantaneously *glo-bur.*
Instead *dod-du; t̓sab-tu, šul-du.*
Instigate *ṅar ˳don-pa.*
Instinct v. *raṅ-bžin,* v. *šugs;* sexual — *ro-tsa.*
Institute vb. a. *˳dzugs-pa.*
Instruction *bka-ỳdams, bka-naṅ; k̓rid; žal-ta;* instructions *spyad-mt̓sáms* 456.
Instructive *k̓rid-˳debs-su ruṅ-ba.*
Instructor *mk̓an-po;* instructress *mk̓an-mo.*
Instrument *č̓a-byád, č̓a-lag.*
Insult vb. *˳k̓u-ba; ˳k̓aṅ-ba; t̓sig rtsub* (or *ṅan*) *zer-ba.*
Insurrection *sde-k̓rugs, ˳k̓rug-pa.*
Intellect *blo-grós.*
Intelligence (knowledge) *rgyus;* (news) *č̓a.*
Intelligent *sems-mk̓an, blo-rno-ba.*
Intelligible *k̓rol-po; go-sla-ba.*
Intemperate *t̓sod-méd.*
Intend *dgoṅs-pa, dga-ba, č̓a-ba W., ˳dod-pa; sems-pa; sṅo-ba* 137.
Intent s. *don, bsam-pa.*
Inter vb. a. *skuṅ-ba.*
Intercalary month *zla(-ba)-šol, *da-t̓ul* W.* 491.
Intercessor *ṅo-č̓en* 129.
Intercourse *˳brel-ba* 402; to have — *˳dre-ba, k̓a-bsre-ba, sdeb-pa.*
Interest s. (money) *skyed, p̓ar, bed;* (concern) *ỳzuṅ-ba.*
Interfere *k̓a ˳jug-pa.*
Interior s. *k̓og, k̓oṅ-pa, naṅ* I 301.
Intermediate *bar* 366.
Interpret *˳grol-ba.*
Interpreter *skad-pa.*
Interstice *bar, dbrag.*
Interval *bar-skabs, bar-˳t̓sáms.*
Intestines *rgyu-ma, loṅ-k̓a, loṅ-ga.*
Into *naṅ-du.*
Intolerable *mi-bzad-pa.*
Intoxicated *č̓aṅ-č̓em-č̓an* 154, *ra-ro-ba* 521, *zi-č̓an W.*
Intoxication *bzi, ra-ro.*
Intrenchment *rags, p̓ag-rags.*
Intrigue s. *gya-gyú.*
Introduce *˳dzugs-pa.*
Introduction (preface) *sṅon-˳gro.*
Inundate *ỳyeṅ-ba, lud-pa.*
Inundation *č̓u ˳k̓yam-pa, č̓u-nag, č̓u-rúd.*
Inured v. *sran-pa* 580.
Invective *smad-pai t̓sig.*
Inveigh *ỳše-ba, k̓a kye-č̓e W.*
Invent *dmigs-pa-nas bzo-ba; bsam-blo* or *-mno byas-te sgrub-pa; blo-t̓abs ˳t̓sol-ba.*
Investigate *lta-ba, lta-rtog byed-pa.*
Invincible *ỳžan-gyis mi t̓ub-pa* 234.
Invisible *mi-snaṅ-ba.*
Invite *˳dren-pa, ỳdan-˳dren-pa, spyan-˳dren-pa; šog zer-ba.*
Involuntarily *ga-č̓ád,* (*raṅ*) *dbaṅ-med-du.*
Inward *naṅ-gi* II 301.
Iron s. *lč̓ags;* — ore *lč̓ags-sa;* — slag *lč̓ags-drégs.*
Iron adj. *lč̓ags-kyi.*
Irreligious *skal-méd, č̓os-méd.*
Irresistible *rgol mi nus-pa.*
Irritable *rtse-reg-č̓e* 440.
Irritate **gob-non-č̓o-č̓e* W., t̓saṅ ˳bru-ba.*
Isabel (horse) *ṅaṅ-pa.*
Ischury *č̓u-gags* 157.
Isinglass *nya-spyin.*
Island *gliṅ-p̓rán.*
Issue vb. n. *˳gye-ba, ˳p̓ro-ba.*
Issue s. *bu-rgyúd.*
Isthmus *č̓u-bar, gliṅ-lag-˳brél* 541.
It pron. *k̓o* 42, *de* 255.
Itch s. (disease) *rkoṅ-pa.*
Itching s. *˳bun-pa.*
Itself pron. v. *ṅo* 129; *dṅos-ỳži* 131.
Ivory *ba-so.*

J

Jackal *č̓e-spyaṅ, dur-spyaṅ, wa-spyáṅ.*
Jackdaw *skyuṅ-ka, lč̓uṅ-ka.*
Jacket *k̓eu-rtse, ke-rtse.*
Jagged *č̓oṅ-č̓óṅ.*
Jar s. *rdza-búm.*
Jaundice *mig-sér;* black — *k̓sa-ya nag-po.*
Jawbone *mgal, ˳gram-rús.*
Jealous *č̓e-ré, mig-ser-č̓an.*
Jealousy *gran-sems, č̓ags-sdaṅ, mig-sér.*
Jehovah *ya-ho-wá.*
Jejune *lto-stoṅ.*
Jelly (gelatine) *˳grig-˳grig C.*
Jessamine *kun-da.*
Jesus *ye-šu.*
Jest s. *ku-ré, kyal-ka, k̓a-šágs, ga-ža.*
Jest vb. *ku-re byed-pa; rtse-ba.*
Jet of water *č̓u-mda.*
Jewel *rdo-rje; nor-bu; p̓ra, ˳p̓ra; rin-po-č̓e.*
Join vb. a. *sgrig-pa, ˳dogs-pa, sdud-pa, sbyor-ba, sbrel-ba, zuṅ sdebs-pa;* vb. n. *sdeb-pa;* to — (in singing) *ram-bu ˳degs-pa.*
Joined *sbyor-la, žor-la.*
Joint s. *˳brel-mt̓sams* 402; *t̓sigs* 448.
Jointly *skyus* 28.

Joke s. *ku-re, kyal-ka, ḱa-śágs, ga-ża.*
Joke vb. *rtse-ba.*
Journey s. *lam* 514; a day's — *dgoṅs, dgoṅs-żág.*
Journeyman *las-grogs.*
Joy s. *dga-ba* II 83, *dga-bdé, dga-ťsór; ṅo-só, spro-ba* II 337, *brod-pa.*
Joyful, to be — *mgu-ba.*
Joyous *dga-mo.*
Judah *ya-hu-dá.*
Judge s. *ḱrims-dpon*; district — *yul-dpon.*
Judgment-hall *bka-ẏśágs.*
Jug *ču-snod, ben.*
Juggler *sgyu-ma-mḱan.*
Jugglery *ₒṗrul, čo-ₒṗrul.*
Juice *bčud, rtsi.*
Jump vb. *ₒḱrab-pa.*
Juniper *śpa-ma.*
Jupiter (*ẏza*) *ṗur-bu.*
Just adj. *draṅ-po, ťsul-čan* 450.
Just adv. v. *raṅ* no. 3 522; — before *ḱa-draṅ* 35; — by *ₒgram-du* 98; — he, the very, *ḱo-na* 43; — now *ma-ťág* 227; — so *de-ḱa-ltar* 255.
Justice v. *ḱrims* 50; *ẏśags* 564; chief — *śag-dpon W.*
Justification *rnam-dag rtsi-ba* 314.

K

Kalpa s. v. *bskal-pa* 33.
Keep vb. a. *ₒčaṅ-ba, sruṅ-ba, skyoṅ-ba* 31; to — back *ₒgegs-pa, skyil-ba*; to — in mind *ₒčaṅ-ba*; vb. n. *rten-pa* 213.
Keeper *rdzi-bo* 468; *sruṅ-mḱan* 583.
Kernel *rkaṅ; rtsi-gu, ťsi-gu.*
Kettle *zaṅs, zaṅs-bu*; — drum *rṅa.*
Key *lde-mig*; (*ṗe-*) *ku-lig W.*
Khams v. *ḱams* 39.
Khatmandu v. *ḱo-bóm* 43.
Kick s. *rdog-pa, ₒṗra-śags.*
Kick vb. a. *ₒṗra-ba*, v. also *rdog-pa.*
Kid *ra-gu, ri-gu W.*
Kidney *mḱal-ma.*
Kill *ẏsod-pa, srog ẏčod-pa*, resp. *ₒgum-pa, ₒgem-pa.*
Kind s. *ḱyad-par, rigs, sna* 316; *rnam-pa* 313; *bye-brag*; of every — *sna-ťsad.*
Kind adj. *driṅ-čan, byams-pa*; to be — *mťun-po byed-pa.*
Kindle *dugs-pa, sbor-ba.*
Kindness *drin, bka-drin, bdag-rkyén, brtse-ba.*
King *rgyal-po, rje-bo.*
Kingdom *rgyal-ḱáms, rgyal-ḱág.*
Kiss s. *ₒo, ₒu.*
Kiss vb. *ₒo byed-pa, ḱa ẏtugs-pa, *ḱa lan-če* W.*
Kitchen *bkud-sa, ẏyos-ḱaṅ; ťab-ťsaṅ W., sol-ḱaṅ C.*; — garden *ldum-ra W.*
Knag *mdzer-pa.*
Knapsack *ḱab-ta-ka, ḱom; ṫi-ka W.*
Knead *rdzi-ba.*
Knee *pus-mo*; — joint *sgyid-pa*; — pan *lha-ṅá.*
Knife *gri.*
Knit *slé-ba.*
Knock s. (the sound of knocking) *tag-tág*; there is a — *tag-tág zer W.*
Knocker *ẏtun.*
Knot s. *mdud-pa* 273; *mdzer-pa* 463.
Know *śes-pa, ṅo-śes-pa, rig-pa*, resp. *mḱyen-pa, ṅes-pa C.*; to — by heart *ḱa-ton-du śes-pa.*
Knowledge *rgyus, rig-pa, śes-pa.*
Known adj. *rgyus-yod-pa, ča-yod-pa*; not *ẏtol-méd, rgyus-med-pa, ča-med-pa.*
Knuckle s. *sor-ťsigs*; knuckles used as dice *bloṅ-mo.*
Kunawar v. *ḱu-nu* 40.

L

Label s. *byaṅ-bu, byaṅ-ma.*
Labour s. *las*, resp. *ṗrin-las, bzo.*
Labour vb. a. *las byed-pa.*
Labourer *las-pa.*
Laconic *ḱa-nyúṅ, ťsig-nyúṅ.*
Lad *byis-pa.*
Ladder *skad, skas-ka.*
Lade (water) *ₒču-ba.*
Ladle s. *ťum-bu, ẏzar-bu, ču-ẏzar, skyogs.*
Lady *jo-mo, btsun-mo*; — of rank *rje-ma*, col. *śe-ma*; young — *śem-čúṅ W.*
Lahul *gar-źa* 67.
Lair *ťsaṅ.*
Lake *mťso.*
Lama *bla-ma*; Grand — *bla(-ma) čen-po.*
Lamb *lu-gu, lug-gu.*
Lame adj. *ża-ba, ża-bo, rkaṅ-rdúm.*
Lamed *grum-pa.*
Lament vb. n. *smre-ba, mya-ṅan byed-pa, čo-ṅe debs-pa.*
Lamentation *čo-ṅe, ₒo-dód.*
Lamp *mar-mé, sgron-ma, 'oṅ-gu, *żum-mar-pa* C., rkyoṅ-tse W.*
Lampblack *sgron-dregs.*

Lampoon s. *sgo-yig.*
Land s. (cultivated) *kluṅs*; (dry land) *skam-sa*; — owner *ẑiṅ-bdág.*
Landlord (of a house) *bran-dpon*; — (of the ground) *sa-bdág.*
Landscape *sa-ynás.*
Landslip *sa-rúd.*
Lane *lam-sraṅ.*
Language *skad, sgra*; — master *skad-pa.*
Languid *nyams-čuṅ, nyams-ťag-pa, yčoṅ-ba C., šed-méd W.*; to get — *rgod-pa.*
Lantern *sgron-ma*, paper — *goṅ-ẑu.*
Lap s. (coat-tail) *grwa*; (bosom) *paṅ*, resp. *sku-páṅ.*
Lard s. *grod-ťsil.*
Large *rgyas-pa, čen-po, rgya-čen-po, yaṅs-pa.*
Lark *čò-ga, lčo-ga*; *ča-čir Ld.*
Larynx *lkol-mdúd, 'ol-mdúd.*
Last adj. *rjes* 181, *ťa-ma* 226, *p̓yi-ma, rtiṅ-ma W.*; — night *mdaṅ*; — will *k̓a-čḗms, bka-čḗms*; — year *k̓a-niṅ, sṅa-lo, na-níṅ.*
Last vb. n. *ₒťso-ba.*
Lasting adj. *rtag-po.*
Lastly *mťar* 240.
Latch s. *ₒk̓or-gyág, ₒk̓or-yya.*
Late *p̓yi-mo*; later (subsequent) *p̓yi-ma*; to be late *ₒp̓yi-ba.*
Lately *da-či, *de-zag-la** 275.
Lath *lčam, p̓yam.*
Lathe *skor-spyád.*
Latter *p̓yi-ma.*
Lattice *dra-ba.*
Laudable *stod-ₒos.*
Laugh vb. n. *dgod-pa, rgod-pa, bẑad-pa.*
Laughter *gad-mo, rgod.*
Laurel, — leaf **šiṅ-tse lo-ma* W.*
Law *k̓rims, bka-k̓rims*; to go to — **ťim ẑu-če* W.*
Lawsuit *k̓rims, k̓rim-šágs.*
Lawyer *k̓rims-pa.*
Lax adj. *kyom.*
Laxative s. *bšal-smán.*
Lay vb. a. *snyol-ba, sgyel-ba, bsnyal-te bẑag-pa*; *ₒgrems-pa*; to — aside *skyuṅ-ba, ₒp̓ud-pa*; to — on *ₒgel-ba, stad-pa*; to — out (to expend) *skyag-pa, ₒdzugs-pa*; (to plan) *ₒgod-pa*; (to display) *yčal-ba*; to — over (to spread over) *sgron-pa*; to — up *bkri-ba, bdog-pa.*
Layman *k̓yim-pa, gaṅ-zág*; *mi-nag skye-bo* 29.
Laziness *le-lo, le-lo-nyid.*
Lazy *le-lo-čan, kyaṅ-k̓yóṅ W.*
Lead s. *ẑa-nye, ẑa-ne, ra-nye*; *rin-di W.*; — pencil *yya-ťig, ₒbri-smyúg.*
Lead vb. a. *ₒk̓rid-pa, ťog ₒdren-pa, sna ₒdren-pa.*
Leaf *lo-ma.*
Leak vb. n. *rdol-ba.*

Lean adj. *skam-ši, skem-po, ẑag-méd.*
Lean vb. (against) *snye-ba.*
Leap vb. *mčoṅ-ba, ₒp̓ar-ba.*
Learn *slob-pa.*
Learned adj. *mk̓as-pa.*
Learning s. *rig-pa, šes-pa.*
Lease s., to take a — *nyo-ba.*
Leather s. *ko-ba, ko-lpags, bse*; — shoe *ko-k̓rád*; — sieve *ko-ťsag.*
Leave s. *ynaṅ-ba*; — of absence *bka-bkrol, dgoṅs-pa*; to take — v. *p̓yag* 347.
Leave vb. *ₒǰog-pa, ytoṅ-ba, ₒbor-ba.*
Leaven s *ẑo-ri W.*; v. *ru-ma* 531.
Lecture s. *gleṅ-brǰod, gleṅ-mo.*
Lecturer *sgrog-pa-po*; — 's chair *čos-k̓ri.*
Leech s. *k̓rag-ₒťuṅ-ₒbu W.*; *srin-bu pad-ma.*
Leek *sgog-pa.*
Left adj. *yyon-pa*; — hand *yyon-ma*; — handed *yyon-lag-byed-pa*; *gyog-po.*
Leg *rkaṅ-pa.*
Legalize *bkar-ₒdogs-pa.*
Legend *sgruṅs.*
Legendary tales *rnam-ťár.*
Leisure *loṅ, čog-ka*; to have — *čog-pa.*
Lemon *gam-bu-ra, spyod-pád.*
Lend *yyar-ba.*
Length *dkyus, riṅ-k̓yád, srid.*
Leopard *yzig*; snow — *ysa.*
Leprosy *rṅo, mdze.*
Lessen vb. n. *ₒgrib-pa*; *ǰe-nyuṅ ǰe-nyuṅ-bar ₒgyur-ba.*
Lesson s. *k̓a-ta*, resp. *ẑal-ta*; *rgyugs W.*
Lest conj. v. *dogs-pa* 258.
Let vb. (to — in, to — loose etc.) *ytoṅ-ba*; *ₒǰug-pa* II, no. 2 178
Letter (of the alphabet) *yi-ge*; (epistle) *yi-ge*, resp. *bka-šóg*; — case *yi-gei šubs.*
Lettuce *ldum.*
Level vb. a. *snyoms-pa.*
Lever *yšo-mo.*
Liar *k̓ram-pa, zog-čan.*
Libation *mčod-pa, mčod-ston* 166.
Libel s. *sgo-yig.*
Liberal *mig-yáṅs.*
Liberate *ₒgrol-ba.*
Liberty *ťar-pa, raṅ-dbáṅ*; to be at — *čog-pa.*
Libidinous *čags-sred-čan, ₒčol-pa.*
Librarian *deb-ťer-pa.*
Library *kun-dga-ra-ba*; *yig-k̓aṅ.*
Lick vb. *ldag-pa.*
Lid *k̓a-k̓ébs, k̓a-gáb, k̓a-yčód, k̓a-leb*; *čab-ma.*
Lie s. *rdzun, šob, šab-šób W.*
Lie vb. (to tell a lie) *rdzun smra-bā* or *byed-pa.*
Lie vb. (down) *nyal-ba*; to — with **ťig-pa čo-če* W., bšo-ba.*
Life *srog, ₒťso-ba, yson-pa, ťse* 450; — long *nam ₒťsoi bar-du.*

Lift vb. *ker-ba, ͦk'yog-pa, ͦdegs-pa, spor-ba, ͦp'yar-ba, seṅ-ba.*
Light s. *ͺod, snaṅ-ba.*
Light adj. (not heavy) *yaṅ-po*; (not dark) *skya-bo*; — blue *sṅo-skya*; — gray *dkar-skya*; — green *ljaṅ-skya*; — red *dkar-dmar*; — yellow *ser-skya.*
Light vb. a. *sgron-pa, sbor-ba.*
Lightning s. *glog, glog-ka, tog*
Like adj. (similar) *mnyam-pa, mtsuṅs-pa, tsogs-se W.*; adv. (in the same manner) *lta, ltar. naṅ-tar W. C.*
Like vb. a. . . . *la dga-ba.*
Likelihood *ṅo.*
Likeness *bzo, zo.*
Likewise *yaṅ.*
Limb *yan-lag.*
Lime *rdo-żó.*
Limit s. *mta, mu.*
Line s. *tig; yig-p'rén.*
Lineage *brgyud, rigs, rigs-brgyúd, rus, rus-pa.*
Linger *ͦgor-ba.*
Lining s. *naṅ-ša.*
Lion *seṅ-ge*; lioness *seṅ-ge-mo.*
Lip *k'a-lpágs, mču, k'a-mču.*
Liquid s. *k'u-ba, rlan-rlón.*
List s. *to*; — of goods *rjed-byáṅ.*
Listen *nyan-pa.*
Literature *čos, rig-pa.*
Litter s. (palanquin) *k'ad, k'yogs, ͦk'yogs*; (bier) *dgu-k'ri C.*
Little adj. *čuṅ-ba, nyuṅ-ba, p'ra-ba, p'ran, p'ran-bu, dman-pa.*
Little s. (a little) *čig, čuṅ, čuṅ-żig, tig-tsám, tsa-big, 'a-tsig W., a-li C.*; adj. *čuṅ-ba.*
Live vb. n. (to be alive) *ysoṅ-pa* 591; (to dwell) *ynas-pa* 310, *ͦdug-pa* 277, *ͦk'od-pa* 56; (to behave) *ͦgrul-ba* 100; to — by or on *za-ba* 485, *ͦtso-ba* 460.
Lively *yčaṅ-po, k'ram-pa.*
Liver *mčin-pa* 165.
Lizard *skyin-gór, da-byid, rgag-čig Ld.* 103, *ma-la-la-tsé Ld.* 409.
Load s. *k'al, k'ur, rgyab, rgyab-k'al* 107, *sgal* 114, *dos* 260.
Load vb. a. *ͦgel-ba, ͦk'el-ba*
Loadstone *k'ab-lén.*
Loaf *kor-kór, dog W.* 257.
Loan s. *skyin-pa*, resp. *kar-skyin.*
Locality *ynas, skye-ynás* 28.
Lock s. (of hair) *ral-pa.*
Lock s. (of a door) *lčags, *go-čag* C., ku-lig W.*
Lock vb. a. *yčod-pa*; to — up *ͦgegs-pa*; *gar-te* or *gyaṅ-du bor-če W.*, v. *sgyoṅ-ba* 119.
Locust *tsa-ga-ͦbu, ča-ga-ͦbu.*
Lodgings *ynas-tsaṅ, ͦbraṅ-sa.*
Log *dog W.*
Logic *tsad-ma, rigs-pa.*
Loins *rked-pa.*
Loiter *ͦgor-ba.*
Lonely *dben-pa.*
Long adj. *riṅ-ba, dkyus-riṅ*; as — as v. *bar* 366.
Long vb. n. *rkam-pa, skam-pa, ydun-ba, żen-pa.*
Look vb. (to view) *lta-ba*, resp. *yzigs-pa*; (to appear) *snaṅ-ba*; to — at or on *ltos-pa*; to — down upon *ͦgyiṅ-ba*; to — upon as *sgom-pa.*
Look s. *lta-staṅs, ṅo*; — out *so, bso.*
Loose adj. *kyom, lhod-pa.*
Loose, Loosen vb. a. *glod-pa, ͦgrol-ba.*
Looseness *ͦk'ru-ba.*
Lop vb. a. *ͦgrum-pa.*
Lord s. *mgon-po, jo-bo, rje-bo, dpon-po, dbaṅ-po, ytso-bo*; — of the manor *yżi-bdág.*
Lose *rlog-pa, ͦbud-pa W.*; to — colour *dkyug-pa*; to be lost *stor-ba.*
Loss *gud, gun, god, god-pa, god-ma.*
Lot s. (fortune) *skal-ba*, resp. *sku-skál*; *las-bskos* (v. *sko-ba*); *p'ya*; to cast lots *mo ͦdebs-pa, rgyan rgyab-pa* 107, *rtags-ril btaṅ-ba W.* 212.
Lotus *ku-mu-da, pad-ma* 322.
Loud *mton-po, skad čen-po.*
Louse s. *šig.*
Love vb. a. *čags-pa, *čags-żen čo-če* W., ydun-ba, ͦp'reṅ-ba, brtse-ba, mdza-ba* 461, **żen-ͦdzin čo-če* W., yčes-par byed-pa* or *ͦdzin-pa.*
Love s. *čags-pa, snyiṅ-brtse-ba*, resp. *tugs-brtse-ba, duṅs-pa, dran-séms, byams-pa, byams-sems.*
Lover *ͦdod-grogs, mdza-grogs, bzaṅ-grogs*; *ͦdod-mk'an.*
Low *dma-mo, dman-pa*; *snyan-pa.*
Lower adj., — part of a thing *smad, šam, yšam, šod*; — — of the body *ro-smád.*
Lowland *smad, man-čád.*
Luck s., good — *šis*, bad — *rkyen.*
Lucky *bkra-šis-pa.*
Luggage *ča-lág.*
Lukewarm *mal-la-mul-le.*
Luminous *ͺod-čan.*
Lump *goṅ-po, goṅ-bu, gog, dog.*
Lunar *zla-bai*; — mansions *rgyu-skar* 111.
Lunch, Luncheon s. *dro* 264.
Lungs *glo-ba.*
Lurk *sgug-pa, ͦjab-ste sdod-pa, lkog-ͦjab byas-te lta-ba.*
Lurking-place *bskuṅs-sa.*
Lust s *ͦdod-pa, ͦdod-čags, čags-pa, ro-tsa.*
Lustful *čags-sred-čan, ͦčol-pa.*
Lustre *bkrag, ͦtser-ba.*
Lynx *dbyi, yyi.*

M

Mace (club) *ga-da.*

Machine *˳ṕrul-˳ḱor.*

Mad *smyon-pa*; to be — *smyo-ba.*

Madam, dear — *bžin-bzaṅ-ma.*

Madder, *btsod.*

Madness *˳ḱrul-pa, smyo-˳bóg.*

Magazine *tsoṅ-ḱaṅ, mdzod.*

Maggot *ša-˳bu.*

Magic s. *˳ṕrul*; adj. *˳ṕrul-gyi*; — sentence *γzuṅs*; — tricks *čo-˳ṕrul*; — wheel *˳ṕrul-˳ḱor.*

Magician *˳ba-po.*

Magistrate *˳go-pa, ˳go-γod Ld.*; village — *yul-dpon.*

Magnificence *rṅam-pa, dpal, dpal-byór, byin.*

Magnolia *tsam-pa-ka.*

Magpie *skya-ga, ka-ta ḱra-bo.*

Maid, Maiden *bu-mo*; lady's — *žal-ta-ma*; — servant *ḱol-mo, γyog-mo.*

Mail (armour) *ḱrab, ya-lád.*

Maim vb.a. *ṕran γčod-pa, sug-pa ˳dreg-pa.*

Main adj. *mčog*, v. also *γžuṅ*; — dogma *γsuṅ-mčog*; — point *don* 259, *γnad*; — substance *ṅo-bo-nyid.*

Maintain *smra-ba, ˳dod-pa*, resp. *bžed-pa*; *smras-pa-la brtan-par γnas-pa.* [*tsáb* 375.

Maitreya *byams-pa mgon-po* 109; *rgyal-*

Majestic *rṅom-bag-čan, γzi-brǰid-čan.*

Majesty *rṅam-pa, rṅom-brǰid.*

Make vb. a. *byed-pa*, eleg. *bgyid-pa*, resp. *mdzad-pa, sgrub-pa, ˳ča-ba, bzo-ba, ˳ǰug-pa, bčo-ba*; to be made *˳grub-pa.*

Maker *mdzad-po.*

Malabar *ma-la-ya.*

Male adj. *ṕo*; — child *ḱyeu*; *bu*; — person *skyes-pa.*

Malediction *byad, byad-stem(s).*

Malice *γnod-sems.*

Malicious *blo-nyés.*

Mallow *čam-pa ta-lo.*

Man s. (human being) *mi, rkaṅ-γnyis-pa*; *laṅs-gro, skye-bo, skyes-bu, gaṅ-zag*; (male) *ṕo, skyes-pa*; — servant *ḱol-po, bran-ḱól*; waiting — *žal-ta-pa.*

Mane *rṅog, ltag-spu.*

Manger *ḱyi-γžóṅ*; *bres.*

Manifest adj. *mṅon-pa.*

Manifestly *ṅos-su.*

Manifold *sna-tsogs, sna-maṅ-ba*; *ṕal-čér.*

Mankind *skye-bo, skye-dgú, skye-rgú*; *mi-rabs, mi-rigs.*

Manly *ḱyo-gai*; — age *dar-ma.*

Manner *tsul, lugs, rnam-pa* no. 4,313; *stabs, staṅs, sgros, čos* no. 5, 168.

Mansion, lunar — *rgyu-skar* 111.

Manufacture s. *bzo.*

Manufacture vb.a. *˳god-pa, sgrub-pa, bčo-ba, bzo-ba.*

Manure s. *lud*; vb. a. *lud γtoṅ-ba.*

Many *maṅ-po, du-ma, dgu*, a good — *ga-čén*; how —? *du*; so — *de-snyéd.*

Map s. *bkod-pa, žiṅ-bkod W.*; **sa-ṭa* C.*

Maple *γya-li Sik.*

March vb.n. *˳grod-pa, ˳grul-ba*; to — about *˳grim-pa.*

March s. *rkaṅ-grós.*

Mare *rgod-ma, mo-rta.*

Margin *ṅos, zur, mta.*

Marigold *gur-kúm.* [*bkur-sti.*

Mark s. *rtags, mtsan(-ma)*; — of honour

Market *tsoṅ-˳dus*; — place *ḱrom.*

Marmot *ṕyi-ba, ˳ṕyi-ba.*

Married adj., a — man or woman *ḱyim-tab*; a — woman *bdag-tu byas-pai bud-med*; to get — (both of man and woman) *ḱyo-šug-tu ˳du-ba* 276; (of a woman) *mi žig-gi čuṅ-mar byed-pa* 159.

Marrow *rkaṅ*; *ṅo-bo-nyid*; spinal — *klad-γžuṅ.*

Marry vb. a. (to take a wife) *čuṅ-ma len-pa*; (to unite in matrimony) *ḱyo-šug-tu sdud-pa.*

Mars *mig-dmár.*

Marsh *gram-pa*; *˳dam.*

Marvelous (*ṅo*) *mtsar-ba* 456; v. also *ya-mtsan-po* 505.

Mask s. *˳bag.*

Mason *rtsig-bzo-pa.*

Masquerade *˳bag-˳čam.*

Mass (lump) *goṅ-po*, (heap) *ṕuṅ-po*, (bulk) *lhun*, (multitude) *ḱrod-pa.*

Mast (flag-staff) *dar-po-čé.*

Master *mgon-po, mṅa-bdág, bdag-po, dpon-*

Mat s. *stan.* [*po.*

Match s. (equal) *ḱa-ya, do*; v. *čar* 156; v. *ya* 504; (lunt) *ṕa-til, pa-til.*

Matchless *˳gran-zla-med-pa, ˳gran-ya-méd, do-méd, mtsuṅs-méd.*

Mate s. (companion) *do-zla*; *ya-do W.*

Material s. *rgyu.*

Material adj. *dṅos-čan, γzugs-čan.*

Mathematician *rtsis-pa.*

Matter s (substance) *rgyu, dṅos-po, rdzas, zaṅ-ziṅ*; (in physics) *bem-po, γzugs*; (pus) *ču-ser, ču-rnag, rnag.*

Matter vb. n.; it does not — *čaṅ mi sto*; what does it —? *či sto.*

Mattock *˳ǰor, tog-tse.*

Mattress *sob-stán.*

Maw *lkog-sóg, ze-búg.*

Maxim *bka-rtags.*

Meadow *spaṅ, spaṅ-po, ne-ṫán, ne-ma.*

Meagre *skem-pa, rid-pa.*

Meal (flour) *ṗye.*
Mean adj. *gyi-na, ṅan-pa, btsog-pa.*
Mean vb. *go-ba, snyam-pa, ˳du-šes-pa; yin-pa* 510.
Meaning s. *bsam-pa,* resp. *dgoṅs-pa; don.*
Means s. *grabs, ṫabs;* by all — *ṅes-par, gaṅ-gis kyaṅ, či kyaṅ;* by no — *re-skán;* by what —? *čis;* by — of *sgo-nas* 115
Measure s. *skar-ṫsád, bre, ṫsad, ṫsod;* to take — *skad-če, ṫsod ˳dzin-pa;* measures (arrangements) *grabs;* to take — *grabs byed-pa.*
Measure vb.a. *˳jal-ba, dpog-pa, ṫsod ˳dzin-pa, nyams-len-pa, ẏšor-ba.*
Meat s. *ša,* resp. *skrum; za-ba,* resp. *bžes-pa;* dried — *skam-saṅ;* — and drink *bza-btúṅ;* — jelly *ša-spyin;* — pie *mog-móg W.*
Mecca *ma-ḱá.*
Mechanic s. *bzo-pa;* mechanics' institution *bzo-grá.*
Meddle *ḱa ˳jug-pa, ṫe-ba.*
Mediator *bar-mi.*
Medicine *sman.*
Meditate *sems-pa,* resp. *dgoṅs-pa, lta-ba, sgom-pa, bsam-mno byed-pa,* resp. *ṫugs-bsam ẏtoṅ-ba.*
Meditation *sgom, sgom-pa, rnal-˳byór.*
Medley *čug-ga-čog-gé.*
Meet vb. a. *ṫug-pa, ˳prad-pa, m̀jal-ba;* vb. n. *˳dzom-pa;* to go to — *ẏdan-˳dren-pa.*
Meeting s. *˳du-ba, ˳dus-pa;* — house *˳dun-ḱaṅ, ṫsogs-ḱaṅ;* — place *˳dus-sa.*
Melody *mgur, dbyaṅs.*
Melon *ga-gón.*
Melt vb. a. *˳ju-ba, žu-ba;* melted, molten *žuṇ-pa, žun-mo;* melting-spoon *žu-kyóg.*
Member *yan-lag, ṫsigs* 448.
Memorandum-book *r̀jed-ṫo.*
Memorial stone *r̀jed-rdó.*
Memory *dran-pa.*
Menace vb. *˳gam-pa.*
Mend vb. a. *glan-pa.*
Mendacious *ḱram-sems-čan.*
Mendicant adj. *spraṅ-po;* — friar *spraṅ-bán.*
Menses, Menstruation *ḱrag ˳dzag-pa, zla-mṫsán.*
Mention vb. a. *˳god-pa;* to be mentioned (in a book etc.) *˳byuṅ-ba.*
Merciful *snyiṅ-r̀je-čan,* resp. *ṫugs-r̀je-čan.*
Mercury (planet) *lhag-pa;* (metal) *dṅul-ču.*
Mercy *snyiṅ-r̀je, ṫugs-r̀je.*
Mere *˳ba-žig.*
Merely *ša-stag, ša-dag.*
Merit s. *bsod-pa.*
Merry *ḱrul-po, sems-spro-ba, spro-sems-čan; dga-ba, dga-mo.*
Mesh *˳gug(s) W.*
Mess (dish) *skyu-rúm, spags.*
Message *ṗrin, ˳ṗrin, lon,* resp. *bka-ṗrin.*
Messenger *ṗo-nya, mi-sná.*
Metal *žu-bai ḱams;* cast — *blugs-ma.*
Metaphor *ṅag-snyán, ˳dra-dpe.*
Meteor *ke-tu.*
Method *čo-ga, ṫabs, ṫsul, lugs.*
Metropolis *rgyal-sa, mṫil.*
Mewing s. (of a cat) *mea˳o.*
Mid-day *nyin-guṅ, dguṅ, ẏdugs.*
Middle s. *dkyil, rked-pa, koṅs, guṅ, dguṅ, dbus, ẏžuṅ.*
Middle adj. *bar-pa, bar-ma, briṅ;* — finger *kan-ma, guṅ-mo, bar-mdzub.*
Midnight *nam-ṗyéd, mṫsan-dkyil, mṫsan-guṅ, mṫsan-ṗyed, dguṅ,* v. *guṅ* 69.
Midriff *mčin-dri*
Midst s. *koṅs, dbus.*
Might *mṅa, mṅa-ṫáṅ, dbaṅ, dbaṅ-ṫáṅ.*
Mighty *ḱa-drág, rgyas-pa, dbaṅ-čan, btsan-po.*
Migrate *˳ṗo-ba.*
Milch cow *bžon-ma.*
Mild *dul-ba, srun-pa, bsrun-pa.*
Mile *dpag-ṫsád.*
Milk s. *žo, ˳o-ma;* sour — *žo-ri W, ru-ma C.;* — pail *˳o-zó.*
Milk vb. a. *˳jo-ba, ˳o-ma ˳jo-ba, ˳o-ma ˳ṫsir-ba.*
Milky-way *dgu-ṫsigs.*
Mill s. *raṅ-˳ṫag.*
Millet *ḱre, či-tse.*
Million *sa-ya;* ten — *bye-ba.*
Millstone *ḱod.*
Milt *mčer-pa.*
Mind s. *sems, blo, yid, nyams, snyiṅ, snyam-pa, že,* resp. *ṫugs;* to have a — *dga-ba, ˳dod-pa;* to keep in — *dran-pa, ẏzo-ba.*
Mind vb. a. *lta-ba, ẏnyer-ḱa byed-pa* 194; never —! v. *čis kyaṅ* 141.
Mine s. *ḱuṅs, ẏter-ḱa.*
Mine pron. *ṅai* 124.
Minister s. *blon-po;* prime — *bka-blón.*
Mint (plant) *dag-či Lh.*
Minute s. *ču-sraṅ.*
Minute adj. *ṗra-ba, žib-pa.*
Miracle *ltas, ya-mṫsan.*
Mirage *dri-zai groṅ, mig-sgyu.*
Mischief *skag, ṅan;* — maker *bstan-šig.*
Miserable *gyi-na, ṅan-pa, ṫu-ba, sdug-bsṅal-čan.*
Miserly *bkren-pa.*
Misery *nyon-moṅs-pa, zag-pa.*
Misfortune *bkra-mi-šis, rkyen, skyon, ṅan, byur, byus.*
Mishap *gal-rkyén.*
Miss s. (young lady) *šem-čúṅ W.*
Miss vb. *ṫal-ba, mi ḱes-pa.*
Missive s. *bka-rgya, če-dón* 160

Mist *na-bún, rmugs-pa.*
Mistake s. *ˌḱrul-pa, ˌḱrul-yži, ˌgol-sa, nor-ba, ˌdzol-pa.*
Mistake vb. *nor-ba, ˌḱrul-ba.*
Mistaken adj. *ˌḱrul-ba, ˌḱrul-pa.*
Mistress (instructress) *mḱan-mo*; (head of a household) *jo-mo, dpon-mo*; (lady) *btsun-mo* 435.
Mix *sdeb-pa, spel-ba* 331, *sre-ba*; to be mixed with *ˌdre-ba.*
Mixture *spel-ma, sbyor-ba* II no. 2, 406.
Mock vb. *ťo-ˌtsam-pa.*
Mode (manner) *skabs, stabs, lugs.*
Model s. *dpe* 327.
Moderate adj. *ˌbriṅ, ťsod-čan.*
Moderately *ˌbriṅ-gis*; *ran-par.*
Modest *ḱan-man, ḱram-pa, ˌdzem-bag čan.*
Modesty *ḱrel, ḱrel-yod, ḱrel-ˌdzém.*
Mohammedan, Mohammedanism *kla-klo.*
Moisture *bčud, bad.*
Moment *skad, bsgaṅ, yud.*
Monastery *dgon-pa, čos-sdé, grwa-sa.*
Monday *γza-zla-ba.*
Money *dṅul, nor*; ready — *rnags*; *smar-ba, smar-rkyáṅ*; — changer *nor-bdag.*
Mongol *sog-po.*
Monk *grwa-pa, mgo-reg, čos-pa.*
Monkey *spra* 335, *spre, spreu* 337.
Month *zla-ba*; intercalary — *da-ťúl W.* 51.
Moon *zla-ba, zla*; full — *nya-rgyas zla-ba*; half — i. e. first und last quarter *da-p̓éd W.*; new — *zla-nág* 491; waxing and waning — *ṅo, ṅos* v. *ṅo* no. 5, 129.
Moral adj. *ťsul-čan, ťsul daṅ mťun-pa*; *mťsul-krims-kyi*; *dge-bai*; *čos-kyi*; also *sems-kyi, yid-kyi*; — doctrine *čos* no. 2, 163.
More *lhag* 600.
Moreover *deï steṅ-du* 222.
Morning *sṅa-dro, sṅa-mo W., naṅ-mo*; the next — *ťo-ráṅs, naṅ-par*; this — *da-náṅ*; yesterday — *ḱa-náṅ*; — twilight *skya-réṅs, skya-'ód W.*
Morrow, to — *saṅ, ťo-re W.*
Mortal s. *mi(i)-bu*; adj. (perishable) *zin-pai*; *mi rtag-pa*; (deadly) *srog-len.*
Mortar (for pounding) *mčig*; (short cannon) *sgyogs*; (cement) *ˌjim-pa, ka-lag W.*
Most *kun-las lhag* or *maṅ-po*; v. also *p̓al-čér* 342.
Moth *mug-pa.*
Mother *ma*, resp. *yum*; *'a-ma*; — in law *sgyug-mo*; *gyos-mo.*
Motherless *mas dben-pa.*
Mother-of-pearl *nya-p̓yis.*
Motion *ˌgul-ba, γyo-ba.*
Motionless adv. *ma γyo-bar, ma ˌgul-bar, ma γyens-par.*
Motive *rgyu.*
Mould s. (form) *par* 323; (fungus) *ham-pa.*
Mould vb. a. *ˌgod-pa, ˌčos-pa, ˌdag-pa* 274.
Mouldy *ham-por čags-mḱan W.*
Mound *dur-p̓uṅ* 254.
Mount vb. *žon-pa*, resp. *ˌčib-pa.*
Mountain *ri*; — pass *la*; — pasture *ˌbrog.*
Mourn *mya-ṅan byed-pa.*
Mournful *mya-ṅan-gyi*; — song *skyo-glu.*
Mouse s. *byi-ba, tsi-tsi*; *sa-bi-lig W.*
Mouth *ḱa*, resp. *žal.*
Mouthful s. *čor-gáṅ, čor-čig.*
Move vb. a. *skyod-pa, sgul-ba, γyo-ba*; to — to and fro *γyeṅ-ba* 518; **šrul-če** *W.* (v. *srul-ba* 583); vb. n. *rgyu-ba, ˌgul-ba*, resp. *ˌčags-pa* 167; to — a little *nur-ba* 305; to — on *ˌgro-ba*; to — quickly to and fro *ˌgyu-ba* 96; to — round *skor-ba.*
Mow *rṅa-ba, rṅab-pa.*
Much *drags, maṅ-po, rab*; as — as *ga-tsám W., tsam* 430; so — *ˌdi-snyéd, de-snyéd*; very — *maṅ-drags, šin-tu maṅ-po.*
Mucus *snabs, lud-pa.*
Mud *ka-lag, ˌjim-pa, ˌdam, mer-ba, rdzab, ˌdam-rdzáb*; — floor *skyaṅ-núl.*
Muddy *man-mún.*
Mulberry *ˌo-se.*
Mule *dre, dre-po, dre-mo.*
Multiply vb. a. *sgyur-ba, sgril-ba, sgre-ba, spel-ba, ˌp̓el-ba.*
Multitude *ḱrod-pa, ḱrom, dmag, γseb.*
Murder vb. a. *γsod-pa*; s. *γsod-γčód.*
Murderer *γsod-byéd.*
Muscle (anatomy) *ša, nya.*
Muse vb. n. *rtog-pa.*
Mushroom *ša-mo, mog-ša W.*
Music *rol-mo.*
Musk *gla-rtsi*; — bag *gla-bai lte-ba*; — deer *gla-ba.*
Musket *me-dá C.*; — ball *rdeu, rde.*
Mustard *ske-ťsé, skye-ťsé, yuṅs* 512.
Mute adj. *lkugs-pa, han-ldáṅ W.*
Mutter vb. a. *sam(-ma) sum(-me) zer-ba W.*; to — prayers *ma-ṇi taṅ-če W., zla-ba, zlo-ba* 491.
Muzzle s. *ḱa-mťsúl, mťsúl-pa.*
My pron. *nai*, eleg. *bdag-gi, ṅed-kyi.*
Myriad (*čig-*)*ḱri.*
Mystic s. *rgyud-pa.*

—

N

Nail s. *yzer, zer, ṗur-pa*; a little — *yzi-ru, yzer-bu*; — of a finger or toe *sen-mo*, resp. *ṗyag-sén, žabs-sén.*
Naked *sgren-mo, ỳèer-bu, rjen-pa.*
Name s. *miṅ*, resp. *mtsan.*
Name vb. *miṅ ytogs-pa, skad-pa, ₒgrag-pa, zer-ba.*
Namely *de-yaṅ, de ˌaṅ; ₒdi-lta-ste.*
Nape *ltag-pa.*
Napkin *ka-ṗyis, lag-ṗyis, paṅ-keb.*
Narcotic adj. *smyo-byéd.*
Narrative s. *lo-rgyús.*
Narrow adj. *ṗal-méd, žeṅ-méd, dog-pa.*
Nasty *btsog-pa. (b)rtsog(s)-pa.*
Nation *mi-brgyúd* 124, *sde* 295, *rigs* 527.
Native s. *yul-pa*
Native-place *yžis-ka.*
Natural *dṅos-ma, ma bčos-pa.*
Naturally *raṅ-bžin-gyis, yžis-kyis* 565.
Nature *ṅaṅ, čos-nyid, ṅo-bo-nyid* 129.
Naught (cipher) *mka.*
Naughty *ṅa-rgyal-čan.*
Nausea *skyug-bro-ba, kam-lóg, kams-rmyá.*
Navel *lte-ba.*
Near adj. *nye-ba*; adv *nye-bar, rtsar* 437, *gram-du; rgyaṅ ťuṅ-ba; ldan-la, ldan-du* 289; to be — *nye-ba, rten-pa* 214.
Neat adj. *sdug-pa, sdug-gu.*
Necessaries s. *yo-byád.*
Necessary adj. *dgos-pa, rigs-pa* 528; to be — *dgos-pa.*
Necessity *dgos-pa.*
Neck *ske, mgur, mgul, mgrin-pa, ₒjiṅ-pa; ynya-ba*; — cloth *ka-dkri, ka-ras.*
Neckerchief *dkri-ma, mgul-čiṅs.*
Necklace *ske-čá.*
Need s. *gyoṅ.*
Needful *dgos-pa.*
Needle *kab, ₒtsem-káb.*
Negative s. *dgag-pa* 94, *ₒgag-pai sgra.*
Neglect vb. *ₒgyiṅ-ba, . . . la mi lta-ba.*
Neigh *ₒtser-ba.*
Neighbour *kyim-mtsés, ṗa-rol-po.*
Neighbourhood *sa-ṗyógs, yul-ṗyógs.*
Nepal *bal-po, bal-yúl.*
Nephew *tsa-bo*, resp. *dbon-po, dbon-srás.*
Nerve *ču-rtsá.*
Nest *tsaṅ.*
Net *rgya, rgya-mo, dol*; — work *dra-ba.*
Nettle *zwa.*
Neutralize *ₒriṅ-ba.*
Never v. *nam-yaṅ* 303.
Nevertheless *yin-kyaṅ, yin-na yaṅ W.*
New *so-ma, ysar-ba, ysar-po.*
News *ťa, skad, ṗrin, ₒṗrin, lon, lnun W.*; good — *lon-bzáṅ.*

Nice *sdug-pa.*
Night *nam, mtsan-mo*; — quarters *ₒbraṅ-sa*, eleg. *mčis-bráṅ*, resp. *yzim-bráṅ*; — watch *ťun.*
Nimble *skyen-pa*; — footed *rkaṅ-mgyogs-pa.*
Nine num. *dgu*; ninth *dgu-pa*; nineteen *bču-dgu*; nineteenth *bču-dgu-pa*; ninety *dgu-bču*; ninetieth *dgu-bču-pa.*
Nip vb. a. *grum-pa.*
Nipple *nu-ma* 305, *pi-pi.*
Nitre *šo-ra.*
No, none v. *gaṅ* 65.
Nobility *dpal* no. 4, 326.
Noble adj. *drag-pa, btsun-pa, skye-mtó.*
Nobleman *rje-bo, mi-drag-pa, no-nó* 306.
Noblewoman *btsun-mo, še-ma W.*
Nod vb. a. (beckon) *lag-brda byed-pa*; **go kug taṅ-če* W.*
Node, ascending — *sgra-yčan*; descending — *ke-tu.*
Noise *klag-čór, grag-pa, sgra, ˌur, ku, ku-sgra*; — made by thunder etc. *čems-čéms* 161; to make a — *ₒkrol-ba.*
Noisome *ṅam-pa.*
Nominate *sko-ba, ₒčol-ba.*
Nonsense *čab-čob, čal-čól*; to talk — *čal-čól smra-ba.*
Nook *kug, kugs.*
Noon *dguṅ.*
North *byaṅ.*
Nose *sna, *nam-tsul* W.*
Nostril *sna-kúṅ.*
Not *ma* 408, *mi* 413, *med* v. *med-pa* 417.
Notch s. *kram-ka, nya-ga, ltoṅ-ga.*
Note s. *mčan-bu, yi-ge* no. 2, 508.
Nothing *čaṅ mi* 138, *či mi* 140; — but *ša-stag*, col. *ka-rkyaṅ* (v. *rkyaṅ-pa*); *ₒba-žig* 391.
Notice s. *rgyus, ťa, lon*; to give — *lon spriṅ-ba.*
Notion *du-šes.*
Notwithstanding *ˌon-kyaṅ* 502.
Noun substantive *dṅos-miṅ* 131
Nourish *ₒtso-ba, yso-ba.*
Nourishing adj. *nyams-brtas byed-pa.*
Nourishment *zas.*
Novice *dge-bsnyén* 85.
Now *da, da-lta, yzod, ˌo-na* 500; — and then *bar-bar-du* or *la*; just — *ma-ťag* 227; not until — *da-yzód* 247.
Nowhere v. *čir* 141.
Noxious *mi-dgos-pa, nyes-pa, ydug-pa.*
Null adj. *sob, sog, ysob, ysog.*
Number s. *graṅs.*
Number vb. a. *bgraṅ-ba, rtsi-ba.*

Numberless *bgran-yás.*
Numerous *rgyas-pa.*
Nun *čos-ma, btsun-mo, mo-btsún* 435; *jo-mo* 173.
Nurse s. (children's) *má-ma.*
Nurse up vb. a. *ysos skyed-pa, skyed srin-ba* 30.
Nutriment *bčud.*
Nutritious *bčud-čan, lči-ba.*

O

Oak *ča-ra, be-šiṅ*; — forest *be-ḱród.*
Oar *skya, gru-ḱyém.*
Oath *yi-dám,* resp. *ťugs-dám, mna, bro.*
Oats *ka-rtsam, yug-po.*
Obedient *bka nyan-pa.*
Obey *ḱa-la* (or resp. *žal-la*) *nyan-pa.*
Object s. *ynas, rdzas, zaṅ-ziṅ, dṅos-po* 131; — of perception *yul* 513; mental — *dmigs-ytád.*
Oblation *mčod-pa, sbyin-pa* 405.
Oblige (compel) v. *nan-gyis* 303.
Obliged, to feel — *drin-dran-pa.*
Oblique *ḱyom-ḱyóm, yo-ba, šan-ḱa.*
Oblong *nar-mo, kyoṅ.*
Obscuration *sgrib-pa* 120.
Obscure adj. *mun-pa, go-dka-ba* 71.
Obscure vb. a. *sgrib-pa*; obscured *dkrigs-pa, rmoṅ-ba, rmoṅs-pa.*
Obscurity *mun-pa.*
Observe *sruṅ-ba,* . . . *la lta-ba* I no. 3, 216.
Obstinate *kyoṅ-po, go-ťag-čan W.* (lit. *mgo-mḱregs-čan*).
Obstruct *ₒgegs-pa, bčur-ba.*
Obstruction *bgegs, ₒgag.*
Obtain *sgrub-pa, rnyed-pa, ťob-pa, len-pa.*
Obviate *yčod-pa, zlog-pa.*
Occasion s. *rkyen, glags, skabs*; on — of *skabs-su.*
Occupy *ₒdzin-pa* no. 3, 465.
Occur *ₒgyur-ba, ₒťon-pa, ₒoṅ-ba.*
Occurrence *rkyen, dṅos-po.*
Ocean *rgya-mťso.*
Odour *dri, dri-ma.*
Oesophagus *lkog-ma.*
Of prep. *kyi* 6, *nas* 304, *las* 546.
Off adv. *ṕar* 341, *yas* 508.
Offence *sdig-pa*; to commit an — *nyes-pa, sdig-pa byed-pa.*
Offend *ₒḱaṅ-ba, ₒḱu-ba.*
Offensive *šin-tu ťu-ba, mi žim-pa*; *yid-du mi ₒoṅ-ba.*
Offer *sbyin-pa.*
Offering s. *mčod-pa, ₒbul-ba, yon*; — lamp *mčod-sdoṅ*; — table *mčod-ḱri, mčod-stégs*; house or place of — *mčod-ḱaṅ.*
Office *ₒgaṅ-po.*
Officer *ₒgo-pa, blon-po.*
Official s. *bka-blon, bka-yšags.*
Official adj. *blon-poi, bka-blon-gyi*; — paper *bka-šog.*
Offspring *brgyud, ba-rgyúd.*
Oh interj. *ka, ka-ye, kye, kye-ma* 7; oh very well! *ₒo lags-so.*
Oil *mar, mar-nág W.*; — cake *mar-gyi ťsigs-ma*; — lamp *'uṅ-gu.*
Ointment *skud*; *byug-pa.*
Old *rgad-pa, čen-mo W., rnyiṅ-pa, bčad-po*; — age *rgas-ka*; — man *rgad-po*, — woman *rgad-mo*; — squire *ga-ga* 63; to be — *rga-ba*; to grow — *bgre-ba.*
Oleander *ka-ra-bi-ra.*
Olive *skyu-ru, ḱa-skyur-po Sik.*; — tree *skyu-ru šiṅ, ḱa-skyur-poi šiṅ Sik.*
Omen *sṅa-ltás, ltas, rtags.*
Omit *bšol-ba.*
Omniscient *kun-mkyén.*
On prep. *ḱa-ru, ḱar* 34, *ḱa-ťog-la, ka-tod-la* 35, *dgaṅ-la, dgeṅ-la, sgeṅ-la* 114, *ťog-tu* 237, *na* 298.
Once (one time) *lan-yčig*; — more *čed-du, du-ruṅ, ṕyir, yaṅ, slar*; at — v. *čar* 139; (at the same time) *ṕyogs yčig-la* 352.
One num. *yčig*, — at a time *yčig-čig* 144; — eyed *mig-žár*; — footed *rkaṅ-yčig-pa*; the one — the other *yčig* . . . *yčig, yčig-po.*
One pron. (French 'on') *skyes-bu* 31; — another *yčig-gis yčig* 143; by one's self *yčig-* [*yčig* 141.
Onion *btsoṅ.*
Only adj. *yčig-ka, yčig-pu* 144; *zad* (v. *ₒdzad-pa* 464).
Only adv. *ka-rkyaṅ* (v. *rkyaṅ-pa* 17), *ša-stag* 555; *ḱo-na* 43, *yčig-tu* 144; *ₒba-žig* 391, *man-na mi* 411, *tsam* 430; not — *ma zad-de* 445.
Open adj. *ṕyes-pa, ṕyes-te,* vulgo *ṕe-te*; *bkag-pa ma yin-pa.*
Open vb. a. *ḱa ₒbyed-pa, bgrad-pa*; vb. n. *ₒbye-ba, ḱa ₒbye-ba.*
Opening s. *ḱa, bu-ga.*
Openly *ṅos-su* 130, *mṅon-sum-du* 133; *'a-ysal-la W.* 605.
Opinion *grub-mtá, lta-ba, sṅaṅ-ba*; in my — *ṅas bltas-pas* 216.
Opportunity *skabs, glags, rgyu, stabs, ťabs, sa.*
Opposite *ḱa-draṅ, go-ldog*; — side *ṕar-ḱa, ṕa-rol, ṕar-ṅos.*
Opposition, to be or act in — *ₒgal-ba* c. *las* or *daṅ.*
Oppress *nón-pa.*

Optical deception *mig-°ḱrúl*.
Or *yaṅ-na* 506.
Oracle *gros-°dri-sa*.
Orally *ḱa-nas*, col. *ḱa-na*.
Orange *ťsa-lum-pa*.
Orb *°ḱor-lo*; — of transmigration *°ḱor-ba* 58.
Orchard *bza-ṡiṅ-ra-ba*, *ldum-ra*.
Ordain *bsnyen-par rdzogs-pa*, *bsnyen-rdzogs mdzad-pa* 469.
Order s. (succession) *go-rim* 71; to put in — *ṡom-pa*, *γtan-la °bebs-pa*; (command) *bka*, *bka btags-pa*, *bka-ťaṅ*, *bka-γnaṅ-ba*; *żal-γdáms*; *hu-kúm* W.; (purpose) in — to *don-du* 259, *ṕyir-du* 351
Order vb. a. (command) *bka γnaṅ-ba* 13, *sgo-ba* 116.
Orderly adj. *ťsul-mťún*.
Ordinarily *rgyun*, *ṕal-čér*.
Organ (of sense) *dbaṅ-po*.
Orifice *ḱa*, *bu-ga*.
Origin *ḱuṅs*, *byuṅ-ḱuṅs*, *°go-ma*, *ťog-ma*, *čags-ťsúl*, *rtsa-ba*.
Originate vb. n. *ḱruṅ-ba*, *čags-pa*
Ornament s. *rgyan*, *čun-po*.
Orphan *da-ṕrúg*.
Orthography *dag-yig*, *yi-gei sdeb-sbyór*, *brda-spród*.
Other *γżan*, *γżan-pa*, *γżan-ma*, *ṡos*, *γċig-ṡós*.
Otter *sram*.
Ought v. *rgyu* 110.
Ounce *sraṅ*.
Our, ours *ṅai* 124, *ṅed-kyi* 127.
Out adv. *ṕyir* 351, *ṕyi-rol-tu* 349; to be — (mistaken) *°ḱrul-ba*; out of prep. *nas*, *ḱoṅ-nas*.
Outcast s. *γdol-pa*.
Outcry *grags-pa*.
Outlet *sgo*.
Outside s. *ḱa*, *ṕyi-rol*.
Outside adv. *ṕyi* III 349.
Outward adj. *pyii*; — appearance *ča-byád*.
Over prep. *goṅ-du*, *bar-snaṅ* or *la*; *bla*; — against *ḱa-draṅ*, *ťad(-ka)*; adv. to be — (past) *ťal-ba* II no. 5, 231.
Overcome vb. a. *ťub-pa*, *non-pa*; vb. n. *sran-pa*.
Overflow vb. a. *γyeṅ-ba*; vb. n. *lud-pa*.
Overhasty *ha-ċaṅ riṅs-pa*, *ha-ċaṅ myur-čes-pa*.
Overseer *skul-ḱan*, *do-dam-pa*, *mgo byed-pai mi*.
Overshadow *°ḱeb-pa*.
Overtake *snyegs-pa*, *γtug-pa*.
Overthrow vb. *sgyel-ba*, *rlog-pa*.
Overturn vb. *sgyel-ba*, *rtib-pa*.
Owl *°ug-pa*.
Own adj. *raṅ-gi*, *nyid-kyi*.
Own vb. (possess) *bdog-pa*, *dbaṅ-ba*; owning *mṅa-ba*.
Owner *mṅa-bdág*.
Ox *glaṅ*, *ba-glaṅ*.

P

Pace s. *gom-pa*; *°čag-pa*, *gom-°čag-pa*.
Pace vb. *gom-pa °bor-ba*.
Pack vb. a., to — on *°ḱel-ba*; to — up *teg-pa*.
Paddle-wheel *sku-ru*.
Padlock *doṅ-pa*.
Page s. (waiting-boy) *go-re-lóṅ*; *sku-druṅ-pa*, *sku-mdun-pa*; — of a book *ṡog-logs*.
Pail *zo-ba*.
Pain s. (bodily) *zug*, *γzug*; *γzer*; (mental) *mya-ṅán* 420, *sdug-bsṅal* 294; to take pains *°gru-ba*, *°bad-pa*; *brtson-°grus byed-pa*.
Pain vb. a. *°ťse-ba*; to be pained *γduṅ-ba*.
Paint s. *ťson*; vb. a. *skud-pa*.
Painter *ri-mo-mḱan*.
Painting s. *ri-mo*, *ťaṅ-ka*.
Pair s. *zuṅ*, *dor*.
Pairing s. (copulation) *°ḱrig-pa*.
Palace *ṕo-braṅ*.
Palanquin *°ḱyogs*; **ḱyog-ċáṅ** W., **ṕeb-ċáṅ** C. (v. *dpyaṅ-ba* 328).
Palate *dkan*, *rkan*
Pale adj. **kya-ko-ré*, *kya-te-ré** 25.
Palm s. (of the hand) *lag-mťil*, *ťal-mo*.
Pan (large) *sla(ṅ)-ṅa*; (small) *dra-zu*; (flat) *ta-ba*.
Pancake **ťul-ta-gir** W. 231.
Pankah (fan) *bsil-γáb*.
Pannier *γzed-ma*.
Pant vb. n. *rṅam-pa*, *dṅaṅ-ba*.
Pap (porridge) *skyo-ma*, *ḱo-lág*.
Paper s. *ṡog-bu* 563; a sheet of — *gre-ga*; official — *bka-ṡog*.
Parable *dpe* 327, *°dra-dpe*.
Paradigm *dpe-brjód*.
Paradise *mťo-ris*
Paragraph *rnam-bċad-pa*.
Paralyze *°čiṅ-ba*; *nyams-par byed-pa*.
Parasol *γdugs*.
Parcel s. (package) *ťums* 231.
Parch *rṅod-pa*, *slam-pa*.
Pardon vb. a. (to use forbearance) *bzod-pa* 498; (to leave unpunished) *°gyod mi rmo-ba*, *čad-pas mi γċod-pa*.
Pare *kog-pa ṡu-ba*.
Parenthesis *yi-geī mčan-bu*.
Parents *ṕa-má*.
Park *skyed-mos-ťsál*.

Parrot *ne-tso.*
Parsimonious *šri-šes-ḱan W.*
Parsley *ẏže-ra C., ša-mi-lig W.*
Part s. *ča, ča-šds, šas, rnam-pa, ḱa, ḱag, ga-šas, lhu*; in — (partly) *ča* ˳*dra tsam*; at equal parts *ča-snyoms.*
Part vb. a. ˳*ṕral-ba*; vb. n. ˳*gye-ba,* ˳*bral-ba.*
Partake *ča ṫob-pa, ṫob-ča* ˳*dzin-pa, bgo-skal ṫob-pa.*
Partaker **go-ḱan* W.*
Partial (biased) *nye-riṅ.*
Particle (grammatical) *tsig-ṕrad.*
Particularly *ḱyad-par-du, mčog-tu.*
Partition *dbye-ba*; — wall *čod, bar-skya.*
Partizan *ṕyogs-pa.*
Partly *ča tsam, ga-šas*; v. also *la-lá* 541; *ḱa-čig* 34.
Partner *ḱa-ya, ya, ya-do W., grogs, zla-bo.*
Partridge *sreg-pa.*
Party (part) *ṕyogs* 352.
Pas (in dancing) *gom-pa.*
Pass vb. n. *skyod-pa,* ˳*grul-ba, rgyug-pa, rgyud-pa,* ˳*čor-ba, ṫal-ba*; to — away ˳*ḱor-ba,* ˳*da-ba,* ˳*bud-pa W.*; vb. a. (to cross) *rgal-ba, zla-ba*; to — over a certain space ˳*da-ba.*
Passage (entrance or exit) *sgo, lam.*
Passion *čags-pa,* ˳*dod-čágs, bag-čágs.*
Passport *bka-šog, lam-yig.*
Past adj. ˳*das-pa*; — ages *sṅa-rol*; to be — *yol-ba.*
Paste s. *skyo-ma*; vb. a. *sbyor-ba.*
Pastry ˳*ḱur-ba.*
Pasturage *bzan.*
Pasture s. *neu-ẏsiṅ*; — land ˳*ol-ṫáṅ,* ˳*brog-ẏnas.*
Pat vb. a. ˳*byug-pa.*
Patch s. *lhan-pa*; vb. a. *lhan-pas* ˳*debs-pa, glan-pa.*
Patience *bzod-pa.*
Patient adj. *bzod-pa-čan.*
Patron *mgo-skyóṅ, mgo-*˳*drén, mgon-po.*
Pattern *dpe, ma, ri-mo.*
Pauper *dbul-ṕoṅs*; *med-po, med-mo.*
Pavement *skyaṅ-núl.*
Paw s. *spar-ba.*
Pay vb. a. *sprod-pa,* ˳*jal-ba.*
Pay s. *gla, ṕogs.*
Pea, pease *sran-ma, srad-ma.*
Peace *žod, dus-bde, ži-bde.*
Peach *ka-ṫa ra, ḱam-bu, bun-ču li.*
Peacock *rma-bya.*
Peak *rtse(-mo).*
Pear *nyu-ti, nyo-ti.*
Pearl *mu-tig.*
Peasant *groṅ-pa, groṅ-mi*; *kyim-pa-pa, žiṅ-pa.*
Pebble *rdeu, rde*; *ču-rdó*; *šag-ma.*
Pedestrian *rkaṅ-ṫaṅ-pa.*
Peel s. *ḱog-pa, šun-pa.*
Peel vb. a. *ḱog-pa šu-ba, šu-ba.*
Peep-hole *so-ḱuṅ* 578.
Peg *rtod-pa, ẏdaṅ-bu, ṕur-pa.*
Pen s. *smyug-gu*; — knife *smyug-gri.*
Pen vb. a. (sheep etc.) *skyil-ba,* ˳*gegs-pa.*
Penalty *rgyal, stoṅ.*
Penance *dka-ṫúb, dka-spyód*; *brtul-žúgs.*
Pencil *ẏya-ṫig,* ˳*bri-smyúg*; *pir.*
Pencil-cedar *šug-pa.*
Penetrate *ḱyub-pa,* ˳*dzugs-pa.*
Penis *mje, sgro-ba C.*
Penitent adj. *dka-ṫúb, brtul-žúgs.*
Pent-roof *čar-skyibs.*
People s. *skyes-bu*; common — *dmaṅs, smad-rigs.*
Pepper s. *ṕo-ba-ri*; Guinea — *ẏyer-ma C.*, **nyer-ma** or **ṫsan-te** or *su-ru-ṕan-ṫsá W.*
Peppermint *ṕo-lo-liṅ W.*
Perambulate ˳*grim-pa.*
Perceive *rtogs-pa, ṫsor-ba, yid-la byed-pa, rag-pa W., rig-pa.*
Perception *go-ba, rtogs-pa*; object of *yul* 513.
Perfect adj. *grub-pa, ṕun-ṫsógs, ṕul-byúṅ, tsaṅ-ma, rdzogs-pa.*
Perfection *dṅos-grúb*; state of — *grub-pa.*
Perfectly *ṫsaṅ, rdzogs-par.*
Perform *byed-pa, sgrub-pa, bčo-ba W., spyod-pa.*
Perfume s. *spos.*
Perhaps *gal-te-na, graṅ*; *su šes, či šes W.*
Peril s. *nyen, bar-čód,* ˳*ḱrul-so.*
Perimeter *mṫa-skór.*
Period *dus-ṫsigs, dus-mṫsams*; *ẏnas-skabs*; former — *sṅon-rol.*
Perish ˳*jig-pa, med-par* ˳*gyur-ba.*
Permission *dgoṅs-pa, bka ẏnaṅ-ba*; with your — *žu W.* 476.
Permit *bka ẏnaṅ-ba*; to be permitted *čog-pa, ruṅ-ba.*
Pernicious *ṅan-pa*; *ma-ruṅ-ba.*
Perpendicular *gyeṅ-la draṅ-po W.*
Perpetual *rtag-pa.*
Perpetually *rgyun-du.*
Persecute *snyeg-pa,* ˳*ded-pa,* ˳*ṫse-ba.*
Persevbrance *yid yoṅs-su mi-skyo-ba* or *mi* ˳*gyur-ba.*
Persia *ta-zig.*
Person *gaṅ-zág.*
Personal *dṅos.*
Personally *mṅon-sum-du, dṅos-su.*
Perspiration *rṅul.*
Pertinacious *mgo-mḱregs-čan.*
Peruke *skra-ṫsab.*
Perverse *go-ldog.*
Perversity *ṕyin-či-lóg.*
Pervert *rlog-pa.*
Pestle *ẏtun, dgog-tiṅ C.*
Petting adj. *mnyo-mnyo-čan-W.*

Petroleum *rdo-snúm*.
Petticoat *mo-gós*, *śam-gós*.
Pewter *dkar-γyá*.
Philology *sgra-rig-pa*.
Philosophy *naṅ-don-rig-pa* 527.
Phlegm *bad-kan*, *lud-pa*.
Phlegmatic *ṅaṅ-brgyud riṅ-ba*; — disposition **śe-gyu'-dhal-wa* C.* (lit. *śes-rgyud dal-ba*).
Physician *sman-pa*; *'em-či*, *'am-či*; *γso-ba-po* 590.
Piccolo-flute *p̓red-gliṅ*.
Pick vb. a. *˳byed-pa*; to — up *sgrug-pa*.
Pickle s. *skyu-rúm*.
Picture s. *bzo*, *zo*, *ri-mo*; *t̓aṅ-ka*, resp. *żal-t̓aṅ*; — of a saint *bris-sku*, *sku-bris*.
Piebald *k̓ra-bo*.
Piece s. *čag-krum*, *čag-dum*, *dum*, *rnam-pa*; a single — *zuṅ* 488; a small — *k̓ol-bu*; to fall to pieces *rdib-pa*.
Pierce *˳big(s)-pa*.
Piety *k̓rel*; *čos-la dga-bai sems*.
Pig *p̓ag*.
Pigeon *p̓u-rón*, *p̓ug-rón*.
Pigtail *ču-ti W.*, *lčaṅ-lo C.*
Pilaw *p̓u-la*, *p̓o-la*.
Pile vb. a. *sgril-ba*, *bčer-ba*, *rtseg-pa*.
Pilfer *byi byed-pa*.
Pilgrimage, to go on a — *mjal-ba*.
Pill s. *ril-bu*.
Pillar *ka-ba*.
Pillow *sṅas*, *snye-stán*, *snye-˳ból*.
Pin s. *t̓ur-pa*, *˳dzin-γya C.*, *zum-k̓áb W.*
Pincers *skam-čuṅ*.
Pinch vb., the shoe pinches **k̓ab-ša dam dug* W.* 297.
Pious *skal-ldan*; *k̓rel-čan*, *čos-čan*, *čos-sem-čan W.*; *čos-la dga-ba*.
Pisé *gyaṅ*, *gyeṅ* 74.
Pistol **me-dá* C.*, **raṅ-˳bár* W.*
Pit s. *k̓uṅ*, *k̓uṅs*, *doṅ*.
Pitcher *ču-snód*, *ču-rdzá*, *ben*, *rdza-búm*.
Pitchfork *zar*.
Pith *γnad*.
Pitiable *dman-pa*.
Pity s. *snyiṅ-brtse-ba*.
Place s. *k̓ag*, *sa*, *sa-k̓yad*, *go*, *yul-gru*, *yul*, *γnas*, *sa-ča*, *groṅ*; to take — *˳gyur-ba*, *˳byuṅ-ba*.
Place vb. a. *˳ǰog-pa*, *˳bor-ba*, *˳dzugs-pa*; to be placed *k̓od-pa*.
Plague s. *γnyan*, *˳go-bai nad*, *˳go-bai rims*; *ṅan-rims*, *rims-nád*.
Plaid *γzan-gós*.
Plain s. *t̓aṅ*; *ṅos*.
Plain adj. (without ornament) *˳ǰam-saṅ*, *rgyan-méd*.
Plaintiff **t̓im żu-k̓an* W.*
Plait s. *lan-bu*; vb. a. *lan-bu sle-ba*; *γčud-pa*.
Plan s. *bkob-lta*, *bkod-pa*; vb. a. *˳god-pa*.
Plane s. *p̓ag-ste W.*; vb. a. **p̓ag-sté šrul-če* W.*
Planet *γza* 492.
Plank *spaṅ*, *spaṅ-léb*.
Plant s. *sṅo*, *rtswa*; vb. a. *˳dzugs-pa*.
Plantain *skyes-sdóṅ*; *ta-la*
Plaster s. (in surgery) *˳byor-sman*.
Plaster vb. a. (to pave) *skyaṅ-nul byed-pa*.
Plastering s. *żal-ba* 474.
Plate s. *glegs*, *gra-ti Ld.*, *ta-bag W.*; tin — *t̓a-li W.*; iron — *lčags-t̓ál*.
Plate vb. a. *čus γtoṅ-ba* 160.
Play vb. (to sport) *rtse-ba*, *rtsed-pa*; to — on an instrument *˳k̓rol-ba*, *skrog-pa*; to — a trick *γnod-pa skyel-ba*.
Play-fellow *rtse-gróγs*, *grogs-k̓yeu*.
Play-ground *rtse-sa*
Pleasant *sdug-pa*, *yid-du ˳oṅ-ba*; to be — *˳t̓ad-pa*.
Pleasantness *˳k̓yer-so*.
Please vb. a. *dga-bar byed-pa*; vb. n. v. *mk̓yen-pa* 55; if you please *żu* 476; to be pleased *dgyes-pa*, *bsod-pa*.
Pleasing adj. *dga-mo*, *bsod-pa*.
Pleasure *dga-ba*, *rtsed-mo*, *γyeṅ-rtsed*, *rtsed-˳ǰo*; *snyiṅ dga-ba* or *bde-ba*; at — *raṅ-dgár*, *yid bżin-du*.
Plebeian *ma-rabs*, *p̓al-pa*.
Pledge s. *rgyan*, *γta-ma*, *γte-pa*.
Pleiades *smin-drúg*.
Plentiful *k̓rigs*, *rgyas-pa*, *mod-po*; to be — *˳dzom-pa*.
Plenty s. *loṅs-spyód*.
Pliable, Pliant *mnyen-pa*, *mnyen-lčug*, *lčug-pa*.
Plough s. *γšol*; vb. a. *γšol-mda ˳dzin-pa*; *rmo-ba*.
Pluck s. (of an animal) *snyiṅ-luṅ*.
Pluck vb. *sgrug-pa*.
Plummet *ża-nyei γtiṅ-rdo*.
Plump *lkob*; *rom-po W.*
Plunder vb. *˳gog-pa*, **kog-te k̓yer-če W.* 95.
Pock s. *˳brum-pa*; — marked *mdzar-ra-mdzer-ré Ld.*
Pocket s. *čan-da*, *dku-mda*, *k̓ud-pa*; — book *yi-gei šubs*; *sam-ta*, *sab-dra*; — fire *me-lčags*; — handkerchief *na-či C.*, *na-p̓i W.*
Pocket vb. a. *˳k̓ur-ba*.
Pod *gaṅ-bu*, *lgaṅ-bu*.
Poem *ṅag-snyán*; *snyan-ṅags*.
Poetry *sdeb-sbyór*.
Point s. *t̓seg*, *nag-t̓seg*; main — *don*, *ma-γži*; to be on the — *ča-ba*; v. also *las* II extr. 546.
Poison *dug*.
Poker *yog-po*.
Polecat *šul-byi*.
Polish vb. *bdar-ba*.

Polished adj. *₄od-čan.*
Politeness *že-sa.*
Pollute *₀bag-pa.*
Pollution *grib.*
Pomatum *šra-skúd.*
Pomegranate *se-₀bru, seu.*
Pond *rdziṅ.*
Ponder *sems-pa,* resp. *dgoṅs-pa; bsam-blo γtoṅ-ba.*
Pool *ču-kyil, lteṅ-ka.*
Poor *dbul-ba, ṗoṅs-pa, ṅan-pa, gyi-na, ḱas-dmán, ḱas-žán*; the poor people! *snyiṅ-re-rǰe.*
Poplar *dbyar-pa; ma-gál W.; γšol-po.*
Popular *mon-ža-čan W.*
Popularity *mon-ža W.*
Porcelain *kar-yól, dkar-yól*; — clay *ḱam-pa.*
Porch *sgo-ḱáṅ.*
Porcupine *rgaṅ, byi-ṫur, γzig-mo.*
Pore *spui ḱuṅ-bu, ba-spui bu-ga.*
Porridge *zan* 486.
Portal *sgo-ḱáṅ.*
Portion s. *skal-ba, ča* 150, *ča-šás; ṫsod, lhu* 601; — of meat *rgya-ri, sder-gáṅ.*
Position *go* 70.
Positive adj. *dṅos.*
Possess, to be possessed of *bdog-pa.*
Possessing adj. *bčas-pa* 146.
Possession, to hold in — *₀dzin-pa* 465.
Possibility *glags, go-skábs, rgyu, sa.*
Possible, to be — *srid-pa.*
Post s. (pillar) *ka-ba.*
Posteriors *rkub, mǰug, ṗum-ṗúm, šul-pa.*
Postillion *rta-zam-pa.*
Postpone *bšol-ba, sriṅ-ba.*
Postscript *yaṅ-skyár.*
Post-service *₄u-lág* 499.
Post-station *rta-zám.*
Pot s. *ḱog-ma, rdza-ma, ṗan-dil W.*; — cloth *ṫsa-lčibs*; — house *čaṅ-ḱaṅ.*
Potato *skyi-ba, *kyi-u* C., *ḍho-ma, gya-ḍho* C.* 78; *'a-lu W.*
Potency *dbaṅ.*
Potsherd *gyo-mo, čag-po.*
Pouch s. *rkyal-bu, ḱug-ma, ḱab-ta-ka Ld.*
Poultry *ḱyim-bya.*
Pound vb.a. *rduṅ-ba, ḱrum-ḱrum byed-pa.*
Pour *ldugs-pa, ₀byo-ba, ₀bo-ba.*
Poverty *ṗoṅs-pa, dbul-ba.*
Powder s. *ṗye-ma.*
Power *mṅa, mṅa-tdṅ, mṫu, nus-pa.*
Powerful *rgyags-pa, ṅar-ma, btsan-po.*
Powerless *dbaṅ-méd*; to render — *dbaṅ-med-du ₀čol-ba.*
Practice s. *lag-lén,* resp. *ṗyag-lén; lob-ḱyád W.*
Practise vb. a. *sbyoṅ-ba.*
Praise s. *sṅag-γsól*; vb.a. *sṅag-pa, stod-pa.*
Prattle s. *čol-čúṅ.*
Pray vb. n. *γsol-ba, žu-ba.*
Prayer *γsol-ba*; — mill *čos-ḱor, ma-ni-čos-ḱor.*
Preach *čos sgrog-pa,* resp. *čos-kyi sgrog-gleṅ mdzad-pa.*
Precede *sṅon-du ₀gro-ba.*
Preceding *sṅa-ma, sṅon-₀gro.*
Precept *bka-bsgos, bka-rtags, ḱrims, čos, γdams-pa, bslab-bya.*
Precious *dkon-pa, γčes-pa, rin-čen, rin-po-čé*; the most — thing *dkon-mčog* 10.
Precipitous *γzar-ba.*
Precisely *raṅ, ḱo-na.*
Preface s. *sṅon-₀gro.*
Prefect *yul-dpon, mi-dpón.*
Preferable *bla.*
Prefix s. *sṅon-ǰúg, ₀ṗul(-yig).*
Pregnant *sbrum-pa; sems-čan daṅ ldan-pa* 290.
Preparation *grabs, rgyu, sta-gón.*
Prepare *šom-pa, sbyor-ba* I, no. 2,406; *bčo-ba W., dger-ba C., ₀ča-ba* 168; to — victuals for the table *γyo-ba, γyos-su byed-pa.*
Prepuce *mdun-pags, ₀dom-pags.*
Prerogative *don.*
Presage s. *sṅa-ltás.*
Presence, in — of *mdun-du,* resp. *spyan-sṅar.*
Present s. (gift) *skyes, rten, žu-rtén,* resp. *γzigs-rtén, ₀ḱyos-pa, bya-dgá, sbyin-pa.*
Preserve vb. *skyoṅ-ba, skyob-pa, sruṅ-ba.*
Press vb. *bkan-pa, bčar-ba, glem-pa C., non-pa, ₀ṫsir-ba,* to — hard (in an inquest) *tsir tag ǰhé-pa C.*
Pressingly *nan-gyis* 303.
Presume (arrogate) *ḱas-len-pa* 34.
Pretty adj. *mčor-po, sdug-pa, dga-mo.*
Prevail on *₀ǰug-pa.*
Prevent *₀gogs-pa, γčod-pa, zlog-pa.*
Preventive s. *sruṅ-ba.*
Previous adj. *sṅon-₀gro.*
Previously *sṅa-na, sṅa-goṅ, sṅan, sṅar, sṅon.*
Price *goṅ, ṫaṅ, rin.*
Prick vb. a. *snun-pa, ₀dzugs-pa* 465.
Pricking (pungent) *rtsub-po.*
Pricks fastened to the feet for climbing mountains *rkaṅ-mdzer.*
Pride s. *ṅa-rgyal, dregs-pa, ṗo-so, rlom-pa, rlom-sems.*
Priest *bla-ma.*
Priestcraft *čos-zog.*
Priesthood *dge-₀dun.*
Primary adj. v. *rtsa-ba.*
Prime minister *bka-blón.*
Prince *rgyal-bu, rgyal-srás.*
Principal adj. *mčog, γtso-bo*; — part *mgo.*
Principal s. *mgon-po, ₀go-dpon.*
Principally *γtso-bor.*
Print vb. *par-du ₀debs-pa, par rgyab-pa W.*

Printer *par-pa.*
Printing-office *par-Kan.*
Prison *btson-Kan, Kri-mun.*
Prisoner *btson.*
Private, Privately *sgos.*
Privilege s. *γnan-ba.*
Privities *ₒdoms, sba-ba.*
Privy s. *čab-Kun, γsan-spyód.*
Prize s. (reward) *dgu-mtsán.*
Probationer *dge-bsnyén.*
Proboscis *glan-sná.*
Proceed *ₒgye-ba, spro-ba*; to let — *ₒgyed-pa* 97.
Proclaim *bka bkod-pa, bka ₒdogs-pa, sgrog-pa, sgyur-ba W.*
Proclamation *bka bkod-pa, bka btags-pa, bka-ₒdogs-pa.*
Procreate *skyed-pa, bšo-ba.*
Procure *sgrub-pa, γnyer-ba, sbyor-ba, ₒtsol-ba.*
Produce s. *tog.*
Produce vb. *skyed-pa*; to be produced *čags-pa.*
Product s. (sum total) *brtsis-zin.*
Professor *mKan-po.*
Profit s. *skyed, Ke, Kye, don, spogs*; *pan-pa, pan-togs, bed.*
Profitable *drug, pan-ₒdogs-pa.*
Profound *zab-pa.*
Prognostic s. *sna-ltas.*
Progress s. *skyed.*
Prohibit *ₒKegs-pa, ₒgegs-pa.*
Project vb. a. *ₒgod-pa*; vb. n. *tal-ba.*
Prolong *bšol-ba, srin-ba.*
Prolongation *stud-ma.*
Prominent, to be — *tal-ba.*
Promise s. *čad*; vb. *čad-pa, ₒče-ba, Kas-len-pa, dam ₒča-ba.*
Promulgate *sgrog-pa, rjod-pa.*
Pronounce *ₒdon-pa, rjod-pa.*
Pronunciation *lčogs, zer-lčogs, zer-tsul W., klog-tsul, rjod-dbyans C.*
Proof s. *mnon-rtágs, rtags, rgyu-mtsan.*
Prop s. *rgyab-rtén*; vb. a. *skyor-ba.*
Propagation *sa-bon*; *dar-ba.*
Propensity *bag-čágs.*
Proper *dnos* 131; — place *go*; — time *bsgan.*
Property *yon-tan, lons-spyód*; — left *šul* 561.
Prophesy vb. *lun ston-pa.*
Prophet *lun-ston-pa.*
Prophetic sight *mnon-šes, ₒod-γsal*, resp. *tugs-mKyén.*
Propitious *bkra-šis-pa, dge-ba.*
Proportion *tig-tsád, byad.*
Propound *rjod-pa, ston-pa, ₒčad-pa.*
Proprietor *bdag-po.*
Prospect (likelihood) *no* 129, *ča* 151.
Prosperity *bkra-šis.*
Prosperous *γyan-čan.*

Prostitute s. *ₒpyon-ma, smad-tson-ma.*
Protect *skyob-pa, ₒgebs-pa, srun-ba, skyabs byed-pa.*
Protection *skyabs.*
Protector *skyabs-mgón*; *mgo-skyon, mgo-ₒdren, mgon-po*; — of religion *čos-skyon* 31.
Proud *Kens-pa, grags-čan, rgyags-pa, dregs-pa*; to be — *snyems-pa.*
Proverb *Ka-dpe.*
Provide *sbyor-ba, yod-par byed-pa.*
Provided with (having, possessing) *čan* 138, *ldan-pa* 290.
Province *Kag, Kul, sde, sde-srid*;* *yul-gyi kyad-par.*
Provincialism *gron-tsig.*
Provisions *rgyags*; *srog-rdzás*, resp. *bšos*; store of — *γtad-so.*
Provoke *nyams ₒbru-ba, ₒtsan ₒbru-ba.*
Provost *dge-bskos.*
Prudent *mKas-pa, grun-ba, rgod-pa, sgrin-po.*
Prune vb. *ₒgrum-pa.*
Ptarmigan *gon-mo.*
Public s. *yul-pa-rnams* 513.
Publication *bkar-btags-pa, bka bkod-pa, gram-yig.*
Publicly *mnon-sum-du.*
Publish *bkar-ₒdogs-pa, sgyur-ba, sgrog-pa.*
Puddle s. *ču-ₒKyil.*
Puff s. (ostentation) *γus* 513.
Puff-ball *lgo, pa-ba-dgo-dgó.*
Pull vb. a. *ₒdren-pa, ₒten-pa*; to — along *ₒdrud-pa*; to — down *snyil-ba, rtib-pa, ₒdral-ba*; to — off *šu-ba*; to — out *ₒbyin-pa, ₒgog-pa.*
Pulpit *čos-Kri.*
Pumpkin *gon, čun.*
Pungency *ber.*
Pungent *ber-čan, rtsub-po, tsa-ba, tsan-te.*
Punish *ₒjun-pa, čad-pas γčod-pa* 155.
Punishment *čad-pa, Kral, ga-sir Ld., god, dgra, lan* 548.
Pupil (scholar) *mKan-bu*; *slob-ma, slob-prug, slob-bans, bu-slob.*
Puppy *Kyi-gu.*
Purchase vb. *nyo-ba.*
Pure *dan-ba, γtsan-ba, tsans-pa*; *lag-mo W.*; *γsal-ba, dga-mo, lhad-méd.*
Purgative s. *bšal-sman.*
Purge vb. *bšal-ba.*
Purity *γtsan-ba.*
Purpose s. *dgos-pa, don*; on — *brtson-par.*
Purpose vb. *dgons-pa, sems-pa.*
Purposely *čed-du.*
Purr vb. n. *nug-pa*, v. *ma-ni.*
Purse s. *sgyiu, sgyig-gu, sgye-mo.*
Pursue *rnon-pa, snyegs-pa, ₒded-pa.*
Pus (matter) *ču-rnag, rnag, ču-ser.*
Push vb. a. *rdegs-pa, ₒpul-ba, sug-pa.*
Pustule *ₒbrum-pa.*

Put vb. a. *bkan-pa, ₒgod-pa, ₒǰug-pa, ₒǰog-pa, ₒbor-ba W.*; to — astride (e.g. in empaling) *skyon-pa*; to — down *grems-pa, ₒgrol-ba, sgyel-ba, ₒǰog-pa*; to — in or into *sgyoṅ-ba, ċud-pa, ₒǰug-pa, teg-pa, ₒdzud-pa*; to — in order *sgrig-pa*; to — off *bud-pa, bšol-ba*; to — on *ₒgebs-pa, gon-pa*, resp. *ɣsol-ba*; to — together *snol-ba*.
Putrid *rul-ba*.
Putty s. *bag-sbyin* 364.

Q

Quadrangle *dkyil-ₒk̔or gru-bži-pa.*
Quadrate s. *k̔a-gáṅ*; adj. *k̔a-gaṅ-ba.*
Quadruped *rkaṅ-bži-pa.*
Quail s. *big-bi-lig W.*
Quality *č̔os-nyid*; good — *yon-tan* 516.
Quarrel s. *k̔a-mč̔u, ₒdziṅ-mo, hab-ša, rtsod-pa.*
Quarrel vb. *ₒk̔rug-pa, rgol-ba, ₒgran-pa*; quarreling words *ₒgran-ts̔ig.*
Quarrelsome, — temper *ₒgran-sems.*
Quarter of the heavens *p̔yogs* 352.
Quarters *ɣnas, ɣnas-ts̔aṅ C., braṅ-sa W.*
Quartz *ċag-dkár.*
Queen *rgyal-mo*; — consort *btsun-mo* (*rgyal-poi*).
Question s. *dri-ba, žu-ba.*
Queue (pigtail) *lċaṅ-lo C., ċu-ti Ld.*
Quick adj. *mgyogs-pa, myur-ba, skyen-pa, k̔ram-pa*; be —! **riṅ-pa toṅ* W.*
Quickly *mgyogs-par*; *myur-du.*
Quicksand **be-rul* W.*
Quicksilver *dṅul-č̔u.*
Quiet adj. *dal-ba, gya-ma-gyú, srun-po*; to become — *ži-ba.*
Quill *rkaṅ.*
Quilt s. *ts̔a-ɣċig-ma C.*
Quintessence *ṅo-bo-nyid, bċud, snyiṅ-po.*
Quit vb. a. *ₒbor-ba* 396, *ₒǰog-pa* 179, *skyur-ba* 28; *ₒgye-ba, ɣtoṅ-ba.*
Quite *ye, ye-nas, yons-su*; *ldiṅ-se Ld.*
Quittance *ₒp̔rod-ₒdzín.*
Quiver s. *mda-dóṅ.*
Quiver vb. n. *ₒdar-ba.*
Quotient *t̔ob-nór.*

R

Race s. (generation) *mi-snú, rabs.*
Race s. (contest in running) *baṅ* 364; to run a — *dkyu-ba.*
Radish *la-p̔ug, guṅ-la-p̔ug.*
Rafter *lċam, gral-ma.*
Rag *hrul-ba.*
Rage vb. n. *rṅam-pa.*
Ragged adj. *č̔ad-po, hrul-po.*
Rail s. *lag-rgyúgs* 541.
Rain s. *č̔ar, č̔ar-pa*; — cloak *č̔ar-k̔ebs*; — water *č̔ar-č̔u.*
Rain vb.n. *č̔ar ₒbab-pa*, it rains *č̔ar ₒbab W.*
Rainbow *ₒǰa, ₒǰa-ts̔on.*
Rainy *č̔ar-ċan*; — season *č̔ar-dus.*
Raise *sgreṅ-ba, ₒdon-pa, ker-ba, ₒp̔yar-ba, ₒdzugs-pa, bžeṅ-ba, seṅ-ba, sloṅ-ba.*
Raisin *rgun-rgód, rgun-ₒbrúm.*
Rake s. (gardening) *k̔a-ɣzé W., rgya-ɣzéb C.*
Ram s. *lug-t̔úg.*
Ramble vb. *ₒk̔yam-pa, ₒk̔or-ba W.*
Rampart *ₒk̔or-yúg.*
Range s. (row) *gral, rim-pa*; — of vision *mt̔oṅ-ₒk̔or, mt̔oṅ-mt̔a.*
Range vb. n. *rgyu-ba, ₒgrim-pa.*
Rank s. *go, go-p̔aṅ, go-sá, go-grál, go-grás, rigs.*
Ransom s. *glud, blud, glud-ts̔ab*; *blud-pa*; vb. a. *blu-ba.*
Rare *dkon-pa.*
Rash adj. *yid-t̔úṅ* 570.
Rashness *bab-ċol, ɣzu-lúm.*
Rasp s. *sa-bdar, sag-ɣdár C.*; *šiṅ-zóg W., šiṅ-séd W.*
Rasp vb. a. *bdar-ba, sag-ɣdar rgyag-pa C.*
Raspberry *ts̔er-lum Sik., la-ma-sró Kun.*
Rat s. *byi-ba, sa-bi-lig W.*
Rather *č̔a-lam*; v. *bla* 382.
Ration *zas-skál.*
Raven *k̔a-ta, bya-róg, p̔o-róg, bya-nág.*
Ravine *grog-po, roṅ, sul.*
Raw *rǰen-pa.*
Ray s. *ɣzer, ₒod-ɣzér.*
Razor *spu-gri.*
Reach vb. a. *ɣtug-pa, t̔ug-pa, sriṅ-ba*; to — down *smad-pa.*
Reach of hearing *rgyaṅ-grágs.*
Read vb. *klog-pa, sgrog-pa, *sil-ċe* W.*
Reading-desk *č̔os-k̔ri.*
Ready *p̔ral-grig* 359; to be made — *grub-pa, ₒgrub-pa*; — money *rnags, smar-ba, smar-rkyáṅ.*
Real *ṅes-pa-ċan, dṅos, dṅos-ċan*; *ṅo-rtóg W.*
Reality *dṅos*; *yaṅ-dag-pa-nyíd* 248; *ɣnas-ts̔ul* 449.
Really *ṅes-pa-ċan-du*; (bodily) *dṅos-su* 131.
Realm *k̔ams*; *rgyal-k̔ams* 108.

Reap *rña-ba.*
Reaper *žiṅ-mk'an.*
Reaping-hook *zor-ba, rgya-zór.*
Rear vb. (bring up) *srel-ba, ɣso-ba.*
Reason s. (intellect) *blo, blo-grós*; (cause) *rgyu.*
Reasonable *tsul-mtun* 450.
Rebel vb. *ño-log byed-pa* 553, **gyab-log ǰhe'-pa* C.*
Rebel s. *ño-log-mk'an.*
Re-born, to be — *skye-ba* 28.
Rebound vb. n. *ꜥp'ar-ba.*
Rebuke s. *bka-bkyón, brgyad-kág*; vb. a. *brgyad-kag byed-pa.*
Receipt *ꜥp'rod-ꜥdzín, zin-brís.*
Receive *len-pa*, resp. *bžes-pa*; *tob-pa*; *rǰes-su ꜥdzin-pa.*
Receptacle *rten* no. 2, 213.
Recite *skyor-ba, sgrog-pa.*
Reckon (count) *rtsi-ba.*
Recline *bkyed-pa, snye-ba.*
Recommend *sñag-pa*; *stod-pa.*
Recommendation, letter of — *mtun-ꜥgyur-gyi yi-ge.*
Recompense s. *rñan-pa, ɣnaṅ-sbyin, bya-dga.*
Recompense vb. a. *brñan-pa.*
Reconcile vb. a. *sdum-pa*; to — one's self *ko-tág yčod-pa.*
Record vb. *ꜥgod-pa* no. 5, 95.
Records s. *deb-tér, yig-ča.*
Recover vb n. *tso-ba, p'yir laṅ-ba.*
Recreation *skyo-sáṅs*; *ɣyeṅs-pa W.*; to take — *rtse-ba*; *skyo-saṅs-la ꜥgro-ba*, resp. *byon-pa.*
Rector *ꜥgo-dpón C.*
Red *dmar-po, dmar-ba*; light — *dkar-dmar.*
Redeem *ꜥgrol-ba, blu-ba.*
Redeemer *skyabs-mgón.*
Redemption *blud-pa.*
Reduce (the wages) *yčod-pa.*
Reed *ꜥdam-bu*; — pen *snyug-gu, smyi-gu, *di-nyúg* W.*
Reel vb. n. *ꜥk'yom-pa, ꜥk'yor-ba.*
Reflection (consideration) *sgom, rtog-pa.*
Refuge *skyabs-ɣnas.*
Refuse s. *gal-ró.*
Refuse vb. *ꜥdor-ba, mi ɣnaṅ-ba.*
Regard vb. a. *ɣzigs-pa*; to — as *dgoṅs-pa*; as regards *dbaṅ-du byas-na, -la* 540.
Regard s., to have — to *lta-ba* I, no. 3, 216.
Regardful *yčaṅ-po.*
Regent *rgyal-tsáb* 109; *sde-srid, srid.*
Region *k'ams, gliṅ, ljoṅs, sa-p'yógs, yul-p'yógs.*
Register s. *dkar-čág*; *to.*
Regular *tsul-čan.*
Reign s. *rgyal-srid.*
Reinforcements *dmag-tsógs snon-ma.*

Reins (of a bridle) *srab-skyógs, srab-mdá.*
Reins (kidneys) *mk'al-ma.*
Reject *spoṅ-ba.*
Rejoice vb. n *dga-ba*, resp. *dgyes-pa*; *mgu-ba, rǰes-su yi-raṅ-ba* 182.
Relate vb. a. *skad-pa, ꜥčad-pa, snyad-pa.*
Relation (kindred) *brgyud*; *nye-du, nye-brél*; (reference) *rgyud.*
Relative s. (kinsman) *nyen, ɣnyen, ɣnyen-bšés.*
Relax vb. a. *glod-pa.*
Release vb. a. *ꜥgrol-ba*; to be released *ꜥgrol-ba.*
Release s. *blud-pa, tar-du ꜥǰug-pa.*
Relic *riṅ-bsrél* 529.
Religion *čos, čos-lugs.*
Religious *čos-kyi*; *čos-la dga-ba*; *k'rel-čan W.*
Religiously, to live — *čos byed-pa.*
Reluctantly *ṅam-šúgs Sch.*
Rely *rten-pa.*
Remain *ꜥdug-pa, bžugs-pa, lus-pa.*
Remainder *lus-ma, lhag-ma.*
Remains (dead body) *ro.*
Remedy s. *ɣnyen, rdzas, ɣso-byéd.*
Remember *dgoṅs-pa, dran-pa, rǰes-su dran-pa*; *yid-la byed-pa*; *ṅes-pa* 128.
Remind *yid skul-ba.*
Remove vb. *ꜥgrol-ba, sgrol-ba*; *ꜥbyin-pa, sbyoṅ-ba.*
Rend *yčod-pa, ꜥdral-ba, ɣšeg-pa, hral-ba.*
Renounce *spoṅ-ba.*
Renown *grags-pa, snyan-pa.*
Renowned *grags-pa-čan, grags-čan, sgra-čé.*
Rent adj. *čad-po*; to be — *ꜥgas-pa.*
Rent s. (fissure) *ral*; (house-rent) *k'aṅ-gla.*
Repair vb. a. *ɣso-ba.*
Repay *ꜥǰal-ba, ɣsob-pa.*
Repeat *skyor-ba, sgre-ba, stud-pa, ldab-pa.*
Repent *ꜥgyod-pa.*
Repentance *ꜥgyod-pa.*
Repertory *tob-yig.*
Reply s. *k'a-lán, lan*; vb. *lan ꜥdebs-pa, glon-pa.*
Report s. (of a gun) *sguṅ*; (rumour) **(s)lob-lo* W.*
Representative s *tsab-po.*
Reprimand s. *bka-bkyón.*
Reproach vb. a. *čo ꜥdri-ba, smad-pa, smad-ra ɣtoṅ-ba.*
Reproach s. *brgyad-k'ág*; *smad-pa.*
Reproduce *skyed-pa.*
Reproof *smad-pa.*
Repulse vb. *zlog-pa.*
Reputation *grags-pa.*
Request s. *žu-ba, ɣsol-ba*; vb. *žu-ba.*
Require *bžed-pa* 484.
Requisite s. *čas* 156; requisites *rdzas* 468.

Requital *ḱa-lán*; *ₒbras-bu*.
Rescue vb. a. *sgrol-ba*, *skyob-pa*, *skyabs byed-pa*, *ťar-bar byed-pa*.
Resentment *ḱon-pa*.
Reserved adj. *gya-ma-gyu* 73.
Reside *bžugs-pa*.
Residence *ḱab*, *rgyal-sa*; *γži-ma*.
Residue *ro*.
Residuum *ťsigs-ma*.
Resign *ḱo-ťág γčod-pa*.
Resin *ťaṅ-ču*.
Resist *rgol-ba*.
Resolute *lo-na ťuṅ-se W*.
Resolve vb. n. (decide) *bgro-ba*, *ťag-γčod-pa*.
Resound *ₒḱrol-ba*.
Respect s. *bkur-ba*, *bkur-sti*; *sku-rim*, *gus-pa*; *ṕu-dúd*, *sri-žu*; to pay one's respects *rje-sa* or *že-sa byed-pa*; best respects! *žu W*. 476; in every — *rnam-pa kun-tu*; with — to *la* 540.
Respect vb. a. *rtsis byed-pa*.
Respectable *btsun-pa*.
Respectful *gus-pa*.
Respiration *dbugs*.
Respire *dbugs rṅub-pa daṅ ₒbyin-pa*.
Responsibility *ḱag*.
Rest s. (remainder) *mťa*, *lus-ma*, *lhag-ma*.
Rest s. (repose) *sti-ba*; vb. *sti-ba*; *ṅal γso-ba* 127.
Resting-place *lam-stégs*.
Restless *ₒdug mi ťsugs-pa* 459.
Restore *γso-ba*.
Restrain *ₒdul-ba*; *ₒjun-pa*; to be restrained *dog-par ₒgyur-ba*.
Restrict vb. **skar-tág taṅ-če* W*.
Retain *skyil-ba*, *ₒgegs-pa* 94, *sgyoṅ-ba* 110.
Retaliation *rnam(-par) smin(-pa)*; *lan* 543.
Retinue *ₒḱor*, *ₒḱor-γyog*, *ₒḱor-ₒdab*; *žabs-ṕyi*, *slas*.
Retribution *ₒbras-bu* 400, *la-γógs* 541; *lan*; doctrine of — *bgo-skdl* 89.
Return vb. a. *lan byed-pa*, *lan ₒjal-ba*; to — an answer *glon-pa*; vb. n. *ₒḱor-ba*, *log-pa*, *ṕyir ₒgro-ba*.
Revenge s. *dugs*, *lan*; to take — **dug** or **lan ḱor-če* W*.
Revere *mos-pa*.
Reverence *sku-rim*, *gus-pa*, *bsnyen-bkúr*, *bag-yod(-pa)*, *že-sa*.
Reverend (title) *rje-btsún*, *btsun-pa*, *dbu-rjé*.
Reverse s. (side opposite) *rgyab-lógs*; (contrary) *zlas-ṕye-ba*; *bzlog*, *go-ldóg*, *go-lóg*.
Revile vb. a. *smad-pa*, *γše-ba*.
Revise vb. a. *sgyur-ba*, *lta-ba*.
Revision *žal-ta* 473.
Revolt vb. *gyab-lóg byed-pa*, *ṅo-lóg byed-pa*.

Revolver **raṅ-bar ḍug-rág* W*. 523.
Reward s. *rṅan-pa*, *sug*; vb. *rṅan-pa*.
Rheumatism *grum-bu*, *grum-nád*; *grum-pa W*., **zer-ne* C*.
Rhododendron *ba-lu*, *da-lí*.
Rhubarb *ču-čú*, *la-čú*.
Rhyming adj. *zuṅ-ldán*.
Rib *rtsib(s)-ma*.
Ribbon *ₒčiṅ-ba*, *leb-ma*.
Rice *ₒbras*; boiled — *ₒbras-čán*; parched — *ₒbras-yos*.
Rich adj. *ṕyug-po*; — in *rgyas-pa*, *ₒdzom-po*.
Riches s. *dkor*, *nor*, *dbyig(s)*, *ₒbyor-pa*.
Rick *ṕub-rags*.
Riddle s. (enigma) *ldem-po*.
Ride vb. (on horseback) *rta-la žon-te ₒgro-ba*; (in a carriage) *šiṅ-ta-la žon-te ₒgro-ba*.
Riding-beast *bžon-pa*.
Right adj. (right-hand) *γyas-pa*; (not wrong) *draṅ-po*, *ₒos-pa*; all right! *ťsaṅ-grig*; — measure *čag-ťsad*; to be — *ₒgrig-pa*, *ran-pa*.
Right s. *ḱrims* 50.
Righteous *čos-draṅ-po*.
Rim *ḱyud-mo*.
Rind *ḱog-pa*.
Ring s. *'a-lóṅ*; — dove *ku-hu*; — worm *ḱe*.
Ring vb. a. (a bell etc.) *ₒḱrol-ba*.
Rinse *bšal-ba*.
Ripe adj. *smin-pa*.
Rise vb. n. (to get up) *ldaṅ-ba*, *laṅ-ba*, *ḱar* or *ḱer-laṅ-ba*, resp. *bžeṅs-pa*; (as the sun) *ₒčar-ba*; (in the air) *ₒṕag-pa*; (to come forth) *ₒbur-ba*, *ₒbyuṅ-ba*.
Risk s. *nyen*, *bar-čod*.
Risk vb. a. *skyel-ba*, *sdo-ba*, *blos-γtoṅ-ba* 385.
Rival s. *ₒgran-zla*.
River *ču*, *ₒbab-ču*, *ču-kluṅ*, *ču-bo*, *γtsaṅ-po* 433.
Rivet s. *ₒbrel-mťsams*.
Rivulet *ču-ṕran*.
Road *lam*, *šul*, *šul-lám*, *ₒgro-sa*; — book *lam-yig*.
Roam *ₒḱor-ba*, *ₒṕyo-ba*, *ₒgrim-pa*, *yar-ba*.
Roar vb. n. *ₒḱrog-pa*, *ṅu-ba*, *ldir-ba*, *ṅa-ro sgrog-pa*.
Roar, Roaring s. *ṅa-ro*, *ṅar-skad*, *ₒur* 409.
Roast vb. a. *rṅod-pa*, *sreg-pa*.
Roast-flour *rtsam-pa*.
Rob *rku-ba*, *ₒṕrog-pa*, **kog-te ḱyer-če* W*.
Robber *mi-śér*.
Robbery *čoms*, *bčom-pa*.
Rock s. *brag*; — salt *rdo-ťswa*.
Rock vb. n. *ₒḱyom-pa*, *dpyaṅ-ba*; vb. a. *dpyaṅ-la γtoṅ-ba* 328.
Rod *lčag*, *lčug-ma*, *dbyug-gu*.
Roll s. *gril*, *ₒḱor-lo*; paper — *šog-sgril*, *šog-ril W*.

Roll vb. a. *sgril-ba, sgre-ba*; to — one's self *₀k'ri-ba, ₀gre-ba*; vb. n. *ldir-ba*; the rolling of thunder *ldi-ri-ri.*
Roof s. *tog.*
Room s. (apartment) *k'aṅ-pa, k'aṅ-bu, k'aṅ-mig, naṅ-mig C. W.*; (space) *gu, go*; to find — v. *₀gro-ba, šoṅ-ba.*
Root s. *ba-tag W.*; *rtsa-ba, rtsad.*
Root up vb. a. *rtsad-nas γčod-pa.*
Rope *sgrogs, tag-pa.*
Rosary *₀p'reṅ-ba.*
Rose *se-ba, γse-ba, bse-ba.*
Rose-coloured *dkar-rgyá.*
Rot vb. n. *₀drul-ba, rul-ba.*
Rouge *skeg-tsós.*
Rough *gyoṅ-po, rtsub-po, rags-pa, rtsiṅ-ba.*
Roughness *ṅad* 126.
Round adj. *kor-kór*; *kyir-kyir W.*; *gor-mo, sgor-mo*; *zlum-pa*; *ril-ba*; to make — *sgoṅ-ba*; to be made — *₀gril-ba.*
Round about adv. *kun-nas, p'yogs bžir.*
Round s., the — of transmigration *₀k'or-ba* 58.
Rouse *dkrog-pa*; **šaṅ skul-če* W.* 23.
Rove *₀grim-pa, rgyu-ba.*
Row vb. *skya rgyab-pa.*
Row s. (series) *gral, rim-pa.*
Row s. (fray) *₀tab-mo, ₀dziṅ-mo.*
Royal *rgyal-poi*; — family *rgyal-rigs*; — residence *rgyal-sa.*
Rub vb. *bdar-ba, ₀drud-pa.*
Rubbish *gal-ró, rdo-ro, sa-ró W.*
Ruby *pad-ma-ra-ga.*
Rudder *skya-mǰug.*
Rude *₀k'ob*; *rtsiṅ-ba*; *gyoṅ-po*, very — *k'a-gyoṅ-če.*
Rugged *γtsaṅ-γtsoṅ, rtsub-po.*
Ruin vb. a. *₀gud-pa*; to be ruined *₀ǰig-pa.*
Ruinous *gog-po.*
Ruins s., a house in — *k'aṅ-rul, k'aṅ-gog.*
Rule s. (regulation) *k'rims* 51; (special direction) *spyad-mtsáms* 456.
Rule vb. a. *₀god-pa, dbaṅ sgyur-ba* or *byed-pa.*
Ruler (governor) *mṅa-bdag*; *dbaṅ-po*; *srid*; (instrument) *tig-šiṅ.*
Rumination (chewing the cud) *skyug-ldád.*
Rumour s. *grag-pa, γtam, bšod-pa*; **zer-ke'* C.*; *tsor-lo W.*
Rump *byaṅ-k'óg.*
Run vb. *rgyug-pa, ₀čor-ba*; to — about *₀k'yam-pa*; to — (flow) off *rdol-ba*; to — a race *dkyu-ba.*
Rupee *dṅul*; *kyir-mo Ld., gir-mo* 68, *gor-mo W.*; Tibetan — **čo̤'-táṅ* C.* 145.
Rupture *čag-čád.*
Rush s. (reed) *snyug-ma.*
Rush vb. *₀k'rog-pa, rgyug-pa.*
Russia *rgya-sér.*
Russian s. *rgya-ser-pa.*
Rust s. *btsa, γya, lčags-γya.*
Rut (track) *mal, šul.*

S

Sable s. *bka-blon sram W., brag-sram W.*
Sack s. *p'ad.*
Sacrament *dam-bča* 250.
Sacred *dag-pa.*
Sacrifice vb. a. *mčod-pa* 166.
Sacrificial, — ceremony *sku-rím* 22; — feast *mčod-ston.*
Saddle s. *sga, rta-sga*; — cloth *ka-lé, sga-k'ébs*; — girth *glo W.*
Saddle vb. a. *sga bstad-pa*, resp. *čibs-sga bstad-pa.*
Safe adj. *brtan-pa, btsan-po.*
Saffron *gur-kúm*; *k'a-če-skyes* 36.
Saiga-antelope *rgya-ra.*
Sail s. *dar, γyor-mo.*
Sail vb. *gru-la žon-te lam-du ₀gro-ba*; v. also *rgal-ba* 103.
Saint *grub-tób* 78; *skyes-bu dam-pa* 31; *rnal-₀byor-pa* 315.
Sake, for the — of *p'yir* 351.
Sal ammoniac *rgya-tsá*; *tsa-tsé C.*
Salary *p'ogs.*
Salt s. *tswa, lan-tswa*; vb. a. *tswa ₀debs-pa.*
Saltpetre *ze-tswa, šo-ra.*
Salutation *p'yag.*
Salute vb. a. *p'yag ₀tsal-ba, ₀bul-ba* or *byed-pa.*
Same adj. *nyid*; at the — time *γčig-čar*; of the — kind *γčig-pa, γčig-γčig W.*; one and the — *γčig*; the very — *de-k'o-na, de-ka*; *de raṅ, de-ka raṅ.*
Sample *bkod-pa.*
Sanctuary *mčod-γnas.*
Sand *bye-ma.*
Sandal-tree *tsan-dan.*
Sanskrit *nā-ga-ri.*
Sap s. *bčud, k'u-ba.*
Satiate *₀graṅ-ba.*
Satisfaction *skaṅ-γso.*
Satisfied *tsim-pa.*
Satisfy vb. a. v. *graṅ-ba* 98; v. *ṅom-pa* 130.
Saturday. Saturn *γza-spen-pa.*
Sauce *skyu-rum, spags.*
Sausage *sgyu-ma.*
Save vb. a. (deliver) *skyabs byed-pa, skyoṅ-ba, sgrol-ba, skyob-pa, ₀p'aṅs-pa, sruṅ-ba*; (lay up) *sri-ba* 581, *p'aṅ-ba* 340; to be —d *tar-ba* 230.

Saviour *skyabs-mgon* 26; *srog-skyób W.*
Savour s. *bro-ba.*
Saw s. *sog-le C.*, *čad-* or *rgya-sóg W.*; vb. a. **čad-sog šrul-če* W.*
Say *sgo-ba*, resp. *mol-ba W.*; *smra-ba*, *zer-ba*, *bšad-pa*, resp. *γsuṅ-ba*; *bka-rtsol-ba*; he says, he said *na-re* 300; to — nothing of (let alone) *lta či smos.*
Scale s. (of a fish) *k̔rab*; (of a balance) *k̔u-le*; (for measuring) *skar-tsád*; pair of scales *sraṅ.*
Scale off vb. n. *gog-pa.*
Scar s. *rmai r̀jes*, or *šul*, or *mal.*
Scarce adj. *dkon-pa.*
Scarf *ska-rags*; — of salutation *k̔a-btágs* 37.
Scatter vb. a. *̥grems-pa*, *γtor-ba*; to be scattered *̥t̔or-ba.*
Scene *groṅ-k̔yér*, *ltad-mo*; v. *gleṅ-γži.*
Scenery *snaṅ-tsúl.*
Scent s. (odour) *ṅad*, *dri-bsuṅ.*
Scholar (pupil) *grwa-pa*, *slob-ma*, *slob-baṅs*, *slob-p̔rug*, *k̔rid-p̔rúg*, *mk̔an-bu*, *rgyud-pa*; (man of letters) *mk̔as-po.*
School s. *grwa*, *slob-grwá*, *čos-gra*; — boy *grwa-p̔rug*; — house *grwa-kaṅ*; — master *grwa-dpón*; — room *bšad-grwá*; — table *čos-k̔ri.*
Science *rig-pa*; sciences *γtsug-lág.*
Scientific, — work *bstan-bčos.*
Scissors *čan-pa* 155, *čem-tse C.*, *grim-tse Sik.*
Sclerotic of the eye *gaṅs.*
Scold vb. *bka-bkyon-pa*, *spyo-ba.*
Scoop s. *skyogs*; vb. a. *̥ču-ba.*
Scope *̥gro-sa*, *spyod-yul.*
Scorn vb. *t̔o-̥tsam-pa.*
Scrap *čag-dúm.*
Scrape vb. *̥brad-pa*, *̥drad-pa.*
Scratch vb. *spar-mos ̥brad-pa.*
Scream vb. *sgrog-pa.*
Screaming s. *skad-ṅán*, *skad-lóg.*
Screw s. *γču-ba.*
Scripture, Holy scripture, *γsuṅ-ráb*, *γsuṅ-mčóg.*
Scrotum *rlig-bu*, *rlig-šúbs.*
Scruple s. *rtog-pa*, *rnam-rtóg.*
Scullion *ma-γyóg*, *t̔ab-γyóg.*
Sculpture *brkos-ma.*
Sea *rgya-mtso*; — captain *ded-dpon*; — monster *ču-srin.*
Seal s. (stamp) *rgya*, resp. *p̔yag-rgyá*; *t̔e-mo*, col. *t̔e-tse*; *dam-k̔a*, resp. *p̔yag-dám*; vb. a. *dam-k̔a brgyab-pa.*
Sealing-wax *la-ča.*
Seam s. *mt̔a-ma*, *sne-mo*, *tsem (-po).*
Search vb. *̥tsol-ba*, *γžig-pa*; to — into *sar-* or *tsar-γčod-pa.*
Season *dus* 255, **nam-da, nam-la** 304.
Seat s. *k̔ri*, *rten*, *γži-ma* 480.
Seclusion *dben-pa*, *dben-γnas* 389.

Secrecy *lkog.*
Secret s. and adj. *γsaṅ-ba.*
Secretary *yig-mk̔an*; *bka-druṅ C.*
Sect *čos-lugs*, *lugs.*
Section *k̔ag*, *skabs*, *skor*, *rnam-pa*, *bam-po*, *dbye-ba*; *yan-lag.*
Sedan-chair *̥k̔yogs*, *k̔yogs-dpyaṅ*, *p̔eb-dpyaṅ C.*
Sediment *snyigs-pa*, *tsigs-ma*, *ro.*
Seduce *rṅod-pa*, *slu-ba.*
Seducer *mi-dgei bšes-nyén.*
See vb. *mt̔oṅ-ba*, resp. *γzigs-pa*; to be seen *snaṅ-ba.*
Seed s. *sa-bon.*
Seek *̥tsol-ba.*
Seize *̥jug-pa*, *̥t̔am-pa*, *̥t̔ogs-pa*, *̥dzin-pa*, *len-pa*, resp. *bžes-pa.*
Seizure *̥dzin.*
Select vb. *̥dam-pa*, *̥byed-pa.*
Self *ṅo* 129, *ṅos*, *nyid*, *bdag*, *raṅ*, I myself *ṅed-raṅ* 128, *ṅa-raṅ* 522; — dependant *raṅ-dbaṅ.*
Selfish *dṅos-̥dzin-čan*; to be — *ṅos ̥dzin-pa.*
Selfishness *dṅos-̥dzin*, *raṅ-̥dód.*
Sell *̥tsoṅ-ba*; to be sold *̥gyag-pa*, *̥grim-pa W.*
Send *skur-ba*, *̥k̔al-ba*, *mṅag-pa*, *γtoṅ-ba*, *rdzoṅ-ba*, *zlog-pa*; to — for *̥gugs-pa*; to — forth *̥byin-pa*; to — word *spriṅ-ba.*
Senior (elder) *rgad-po.*
Sense s. (intellectual power) *blo-grós* 385, *dbaṅ-po* 387; (meaning) *dgoṅs-pa* 87, *don* 258.
Sensible *tsul-mt̔ún.*
Sentence *žal-čé*; to pass — *žal-če γčod-pa*; *t̔ag-čod-pa byed-pa.*
Sentiment *blo* 384; false — *lta-lóg* 217.
Sentinel *mel-tse*, *bya-ra.*
Separate vb. a. *dgar-ba*; vb. n. *̥gol-ba*, *̥gye-ba*, *̥p̔ral-ba*; *so-só byed-pa*; to be separated *̥bral-ba.*
Separate adj. *sgos*; *so-so.*
Separation *gud* 69.
Sepulchre *baṅ-so.*
Series *gral*, *gras*, *rim-pa.*
Serpent *sbrul*; — demon *klu* 8.
Serrated *čoṅ-čóṅ.*
Serum *ču-sér.*
Servant *γyog-po*, *γyog-mo*; *k̔ol-po*, *k̔ol-mo*; *bran-po*, *bran-mo*; *bran-k̔ól*; *mi-lág*; *žabs-p̔yi*, *mṅag-γžug*; your servant! *da čen žu W.* 152.
Serve vb. *žal-ta byed-pa*; to — up *̥dren-pa.*
Service *žabs-t̔óg* 472; at your — *-oṅ-le*, *'a W.*
Sesame *til*; — oil *til-már.*
Set vb. a. to — about *rtsom-pa*, *čas-pa*; to - at *p̔yo-p̔yó*; to — forth *r̀jod-pa*; to — in order *̥god-pa*, *γtan-la ̥bebs-pa*; vb. n.

to — (of the sun) *nub-pa, skyod-pa W.*; to — out (depart) *čas-pa.*
Settle vb. a., to — a business *go čod-pa*; vb. n. *ₒtsugs-pa* 459.
Settled adj. (decided) *zad-pa*; (at an end) *zin-pa, rdzogs-pa.*
Settlement (colony) *babs-sa.*
Seven num. *bdun*; seventh *bdun-pa*; seventeen *bču-bdun*; seventeenth *bču-bdun-pa*; seventy *bdun-ču*; seventieth *bdun-ču-pa.*
Several *ka-čig, ₒga, mi-ₒdra-ba.*
Severe *ynyan-pa, drag-pa.*
Severity *ṅad W.*
Sew *ₒtsem-pa.*
Sex *rten* no. 4, 213.
Sexual *rten-gyi.*
Shackle s. *lčags, lčags-sgrog.*
Shade s. *grib.*
Shadow s. *grib-ma.*
Shake vb. a. *skyod-pa, skyom-pa, sgul-ba, sprug-pa*; vb. n. *ₒgul-ba, lčogs-pa.*
Sham, to perform a — work *bčos-su byed-pa.*
Shame s. *krel, ṅo-tsa, bag-yod(-pa)* 364, *žabs-ₒdrén* 472; it is a —! *krel-ba yod W.* (**fel-wa yod**).
Shamefaced *ṅo-tsa-čan.*
Shameless *krel-méd; ṅo-tsa-med-pa.*
Shape s. *dbyibs, yzugs, čas, bkod-pa.*
Share vb. *bgod-pa*; s. *bgo-skal, skal-ba; ča, ča-šás.*
Sharer *go-kan W.*
Sharp adj. (not blunt) *rno-ba*; (to the taste) *tsa-ba; ber-čan.*
Sharpness (of an edge) *ka* IV, no. 5, 35.
Sharpsightedness *mig-sál W.*
Shave *ₒbreg-pa, bžar-ba.*
Shawl *do-šā-lā.*
She pron. *ko, koṅ* 41, *de* 255.
Sheaf *lag-kód.*
Shears v. *čan-pa* 155.
Sheath s. *šubs.*
Shed s. (slight building) *bkad-sa* 12.
Shed vb. a. *ldug-pa, blug-pa*; (tears) *bsil-ba.*
Sheep *lug*; flock of — *lug-kyu*; — fold *lug-rá.*
Sheet of paper *gre-ga C., šog-bu; šog-gáṅ W.*
Shelf *slaṅ-ka.*
Shell s. (husk) *kog-pa, gaṅ-bu, lgaṅ-bu*; (mollusk) *duṅ* 253, *ₒgron-bu* 102; vb. a. *bgrud-pa.*
Shell-lac *rgya-skyégs.*
Shelter s. *skyibs; skyabs-ynás; yyam; čar-skyibs.*
Shepherd *lug-pa.*
Shield s. *pa-li, pub.*
Shift vb. n. *ₒpo-ba.*
Shine vb. n. *čar-ba, ₒtser-ba, snaṅ-ba*; s. *ₒod.*
Shining (bright) *čem-me-ba, lčam-me-ba; krol-krol W.*
Ship s. *gru, gru-bo, yziṅs*; — master *gru-dpon.*
Shirt s. *myo-kár Ld.*
Shiver vb. *ₒgul-ba.*
Shoe s. *lham*; soft — *ba-bu*; — of plaited straw *bu-la*; — strap *lham-sgróg.*
Shoot s. *lčug-ma*; vb. n. *ₒkruṅ-ba*; vb. a. *ₒpen-pa.*
Shooting-star *ke-tu, skar-mdá.*
Shore *ₒgram, skam-sa.*
Short *tuṅ-ba*; in — *sgril-bas* 120, *mdor-na* 273; cf. also *zur-tsam* 489.
Shortsighted *mig-rgyaṅ-túṅ.*
Shoulder s. *dpuṅ-pa, prag-pa*; — blade *sog-pa.*
Shout vb. *ₒgrags-pa, sgrog-pa.*
Shovel s. *kyem*; coal — *me-skyogs.*
Show vb. a. *ston-pa, ṅom-pa, sdigs-pa.*
Showman *ltad-mo-mkan.*
Shrewd *mkas-pa.*
Shrine *rten.*
Shrink vb. n. (to be contracted) *ₒkum-pa*, (to recoil) *ₒdzem-pa, čum-pa.*
Shriveled, Shrunk, *kums-pa.*
Shudder vb *yya-ba.*
Shun *spoṅ-ba, ₒdzem-pa.*
Shut vb. a. (a door) *ₒgegs-pa*; (the eyes) *ₒdzum-pa*; to — off or out *ₒkegs-pa*; to — up *skyil-ba, sgyoṅ-ba.*
Shuttle *doṅ-po.*
Shy vb. n. (of horses) *ₒdrog-pa.*
Shy adj. *ₒdrog-čan.*
Sick *nad-pa*; v. also *yi-ga čus* 508.
Sickle *zor-ba, rgya-zór.*
Sickly *nad-bu-čan.*
Side s. *logs, ṅo, ṅos, ṅogs, ₒdabs, rol* 536, *kud-ma*; (of the body) *dku, yžogs, glo, ₒgram*, (direction) *pyogs* 352.
Sieve *lčags-tsags.*
Sigh s. *kog-šúgs W., šugs-nár, sugs-riṅ.*
Sight *ltad-mo, snaṅ-ba, mtoṅ-snáṅ.*
Sign s. *rgya*, resp. *pyag-rgya; mtsan-ma, mtsan-nyid, rgyu-mtsan; rtags; brda* 297.
Signature *rgya-rtags.*
Signification *don.*
Signify v. *yin-pa* 510.
Sikim *ₒbras-ljóṅs.*
Silence *čem-me-ba.*
Silent, to be — *ka-rog-pa; čaṅ mi smra-ba.*
Silk *dar, gos*; — cloth *za-ₒóg*; — thread *gos-skúd*; silks *gos-čén*, col. *go-šén.*
Silk-worm *dar-srin.*
Silver s. *dṅul*; — in bars *gag.*
Similar *ₒdra-ba*; **tsogs-se* W.*
Similitude *dpe.*
Simple *rkyaṅ-pa.*
Simultaneously *yčig-čar.*

Sin s. *sdig-pa, nyes-pa, nyon-moṅs-pa skyon, sgrib-pa*; heinous — *rme-ba* 425; deadly — *mtsams-med-pa* 455.
Since adv. (ever since) *bzuṅs-te*; conj. *pas.*
Sincere *draṅ-po.*
Sinew *ču-ba.*
Sinful *sdig-čan, skyon-čan.*
Sing *glu len-pa.*
Singed, Singeing *me-γžób.*
Single adj. (separate) *γčig-ka, γčig-pu* 144; *nyag-ma, rkyaṅ-pa*; (unmarried) *k̔yo-méd*; *čuṅ-ma-méd*; — combat *k̔rug-pa, ₒdziṅ-mo.*
Sink vb. n. *rgud-pa, nub-pa. ₒbyiṅ-ba.*
Sinner *sdig-po, sgrib-pa.*
Sir *γtso-bo* 434; *sa-heb*, col. *sāb* 571; *'a-ǰó* 603; dear Sir *bžin-bzáṅ* 483.
Sister *sriṅ-mo, mčed*, resp. *lčam-mo*; elder — *'a-če* 603; younger — *nu-mo* 305.
Sit *sdod-pa*, resp. *bžugs-pa*; *ₒdug-pa, ₒk̔od-pa*; sitting cross-legged *skyil-krúṅ* 27.
Site *mal.*
Situated, to be — towards *lta-ba.*
Situation *γnas-skabs.*
Six num. *drug*, sixth *drug-pa*; sixteen *bču-drug*, sixteenth *bču-drug-pa*; sixty *drug-ču*, sixtieth *drug-ču-pa.*
Size *če-kyad, če-čuṅ, tsad, boṅ, k̔yon, rgya.*
Skeleton *keṅ-rus.*
Sketch s. *bkod-pa*; *zur tsam bsdu-ba* 489.
Skilful *mk̔as-pa, sgrin-po, t̔abs-šes-pa*; *t̔abs-čan W.*; *skyen-pa, spyaṅ-po.*
Skill *sgyu-rtsál.*
Skin s. *pags-pa, ko-ba.*
Skirt s. *gos-sgab, gos-mt̔a, t̔u-ba.*
Skull *t̔od-pa.*
Sky *nam-mk̔a, γnam.*
Slab *spaṅ, γya-ma.*
Slacken vb. a. *glod-pa.*
Slackened adj. *lhod-pa, lhod-po.*
Slander s. *p̔ra-ma, smad-sgra.*
Slander vb. *p̔ra-ma byed-pa*, or *smra-ba*, or *ₒǰug-pa*, resp. *γsol-ba, žu-ba.*
Slanderer *p̔ra-ma-mk̔an.*
Slanting *yo-ba, yon-po.*
Slate *γya-ma.*
Slaughter s. *γsod-γčod*; vb. a. *γsod-pa, ske γčod-pa*, resp. *ₒgom-pa.*
Slave s. *bran, mṅag-γžúg.*
Sleep s. *γnyid*, resp. *mnal.*
Sleep vb. *nyal-ba, γnyid-log-pa*, resp. *γzim-pa.*
Sleeping-room *γzim-k̔aṅ.*
Sleet s. *k̔a-ma-čár.*
Sleeve *p̔u-dúṅ.*
Slender *kyaṅ-po*; *kyaṅ-kyaṅ riṅ-mo W.*
Slide vb. n. *ₒdred-pa.*
Slight adj. *p̔ra-ba.*
Slight vb. a. *ₒgyiṅ-ba, ₒgyiṅ-bag byed-pa*; *čo-ₒdri-ba.*
Sling s. *sgu-rdo*; — stone *rdo-γyúg.*

Slip in vb. n. *ₒkril-ba, ₒk̔yud-pa, ₒdzul-ba.*
Slope s. *gud, ṅogs.*
Sloping *gyiṅ-mo W.*
Slow *bul-po, dal-ba*; (irresolute) **lo-sna maṅ-ba*; *lo-sna riṅ-mo* W.*
Slowly *ṅaṅ-gis, gul-gúl*; *gu-le W., ga-le C.*
Slowness *dal-ba, dal-bu.*
Smack vb. *k̔a brdab-pa*; *dkan-sgra ₒdebs-pa W.*
Small *čuṅ-ba, čuṅ-tse W.*; *p̔ra-ba.*
Small-pox *ₒbrum-nad.*
Smart adj. (gaily dressed) *rnam-ₒgyur-čan*; *γzab-mo, γzab-sprod*; *mčor-po.*
Smash *γčog-pa, rduṅ-ba.*
Smear *skud-pa, ₒbyug-pa.*
Smell s. *bsuṅ*; vb. a. *snom-pa*; vb. n. *mnam-pa.*
Smile s. *ₒdzum*, vb. n. *ₒdzum-pa.*
Smith *mgar-ba.*
Smoke s. *dud-pa*; vb. a. (tobacco) *ₒt̔uṅ-ba.*
Smooth adj. *ₒǰam-pa.*
Smooth vb. a. *dbur-ba, ₒur-ba, 'ur-ba.*
Smoothing-iron *lčags-bsró.*
Smuggle *p̔ag-tsoṅ byed-pa.*
Smut s. *sre-nag*; *sre-mog W.*
Snail *skyogs-lto-bu*; — clover *ₒol.*
Snake *sbrul, ₒbu-ríṅ, lto-ₒgro.*
Snap s. (with the fingers) *skad-čig* 19.
Snare s. *rnyi, snyi.*
Snatch vb. *ₒgog-pa.*
Sneak vb. *ₒǰab-pa.*
Sneeze vb. *sbrid-pa.*
Snipe *skyar-po, ču-skyar*; *tiṅ-ti-liṅ Ld.*
Snivel s. *snabs.*
Snore vb. *ṅug-pa, sṅur-ba.*
Snow s. *k̔a-ba, gaṅs*; — ball *k̔a-goṅ*; — bridge *rud-zam*; — fall *ₒbab*; — leopard *γsa. bsa*; — shoe *dkyar*; — slip *k̔a-rúd*; — storm *k̔a-tsúb, rluṅ-tsúb, bu-yug.*
Snuff s. *sna-ₒdág W.*
So *čes* 142, *de-ltar* 256, *ₒdi-ltar* 275, *de-bžin-du* 256, *de-ₒdras* 282; just — *de-ka-ltar* 255; so as *tsam* 430; so that *tsam-du*; so then *yaṅ* 505.
Soak *sboṅ-ba.*
Soap s. *glaṅ-glád C., sa-bon W.*
Soar *ldiṅ-ba, ₒp̔yo-ba.*
Sob s. *ṅud-mo.*
Socage *ₒu-lag* 499.
Society, human — *tsogs* 451.
Socket of the eye *mig-k̔úṅ.*
Sod *skaṅ-ša.*
Soda *bul.*
Soft *ₒǰam-pa, mnyen-pa, snyi-ba, ₒbol-po.*
Softly *ga-le C., gu-le W.*
Soil s. *sa-γži.*
Soil vb. *bsgo-ba.*
Solder *k̔ro-čus sdom-pa*; **kar-ya daṅ žar-če* W.*
Soldier *dmag-mi.*

Sole of the foot *rkaṅ-mtil.*
Sole adj. *γčig, γčig-pu* 144.
Solely *K̔o-na, ₒba-žig.*
Solid adj. (not hollow) *K̔oṅ-gaṅ, gar-bu, pu-ri med-K̔an W.*; (not liquid) *reṅs-pa*; (firm) *mK̔raṅ, ₒčag-čan W., sra-ba.*
Solitary adj. *dben-pa*; — place *dgon-pa.*
Solitude *dben-pa, ₒbrog, gud.*
Some *K̔a-čig, ga-čen, ga-šas, gaṅ-žig, ₒga, res-ₒga*; *či γtoṅ W., čig, čuṅ-žig*; *č̔a-lam*; *re-žig*; *la-lá.*
Somebody, some one, *γčig, γčig-čig.*
Somerset *ma-lág.*
Something *či žig*; *či-γtoṅ W.*
Somnambulism *γnyid-rdól.*
Son *bu, bu-p̔o, bu-tsa W.*, resp. *sras*; — in-law *mag-pa*; — of man *mi bu, mii-sras.*
Song *glu, mgur, dbyaṅs.*
Sonorous *sgra-čan, sgra-ldaṅ.*
Soon *sṅa, mgyogs-pa*; *myur-du*; as — as *ma-K̔ad, ma t̔ag-tu* 227, *tsam-gyis* 431; sooner or later *sṅa-p̔yi.*
Soot *dreg-pa, sre-nág.*
Soothe *ži-bar byed-pa.*
Soothsayer *č̔a-mK̔an, rtsis-pa, mtsan-mK̔an.*
Sorcerer *ₒgoṅ-po, ₒba-po*; sorceress *ₒba-mo.*
Sorcery *rnam-p̔rul, p̔ra-mén*; to practise — *sprul-ba, rol-ba.*
Sorrel adj. *K̔am-pa.*
Sorrow s. *K̔oṅ-ₒK̔rugs*, col. **K̔og-t̔úg*.*
Sorrowful *mi dga-ba.*
Sorry *koṅ-du č̔ud-pa, mi dga-ba, blo mi bde-ba, sems skyo-mo.*
Sort s. *K̔yad-par, sna, rigs*; of what — *či lta-bu.*
Soul *nyams*, resp. *t̔ugs-nyáms, dgoṅs-pa*; *rgyud*; *rnam-šes, sems.*
Sound s *skad, K̔rol*; *sgra, sgra-skád.*
Sound vb.n. *K̔rol-ba, ₒgrags-pa*; vb.a. *sgra* [*sgrog-pa.*
Sound adj. *rem-pa, bde-ba.*
Soup *t̔ug-pa.*
Sour adj. *skyur-ba, skyur-po C., skyur-mo W.*
Source *č̔u-mig, č̔u-mgo*; *K̔uṅs, ₒgo-ma.*
South *lho.*
Sovereign s. *dbaṅ-po.*
Sow s. *p̔ag-mo*; — thistle *K̔al-pa.*
Sow vb. a. *sa-bon ₒdebs-pa.*
Space *gu, go.*
Spade *lčags-K̔yém.*
Span s. *mt̔o.*
Spare vb. *p̔aṅ-ba.*
Spark *me-ltág, me-tság.*
Sparkle *ₒK̔ol-ba W., sag-ság zer-ba C.*
Sparrow *bya-po skya-bo W.*; — hawk *K̔ra, mč̔il-K̔ra.*
Spasm *rtsa-č̔us* or *-ₒdus*; *ₒč̔iṅ-ba C.*
Spawn s. *sgo-ṅa, sgoṅ.*
Speak *smra-ba*, resp. *bka-stsol-ba*; *mol-ba W.*; *lab-pa*, resp. *γsuṅ-ba, zer-ba.*
Spear s. *mduṅ.*
Specimen v. *p̔ud* 344.
Speck *rme-ba, sme-ba.*
Spectacles *šel-mig*; snow — **mig-ḍa*.*
Spectator *ltad-mo-pa.*
Speech *skad, ṅag, γtam, t̔sig, brjod*, resp. *bka*, resp. *γsuṅ*; *dpe-sgra W.*
Speed, good —! **t̔am-pa č̔o* W.*
Speedily *myur-du, nye-bar.*
Speedy *mgyogs-pa, mgyogs-riṅs W.*; *myúr-ba, riṅs-pa.*
Spell s. *γzuṅs, γzuṅs-sṅags.*
Spend *skyag-pa, č̔ud γzon-pa*; to be spent *č̔a-ba, ₒgro-ba, ₒgyag-pa, ₒtsar-ba, ₒdzad-pa.*
Sphere *dkyil-ₒK̔or* 11; *groṅ* 79, *ṅaṅ* 126; — of activity *spyod-yul.*
Spice *sdor, spod*; *t̔san-te W.*
Spider *t̔ags-gru-ₒbu, ₒbag-rág.*
Spin *ₒK̔al-ba, ₒK̔el-ba.*
Spindle *p̔aṅ.*
Spirit *sems, sems-nyid*; *kun-γži* 4; evil — *γdon* 267, *ₒgoṅ-po* 95.
Spirited *hur-po.*
Spit vb. *t̔u gyab-če W., t̔o-le ₒdebs-pa W.*
Spittle *mč̔il-ma*, resp. *žal-č̔ab.*
Spleen (milt) *mč̔er-pa.*
Splendid *ₒod-čan, grags-čan.*
Splendour *rṅam-pa, dṅom-pa, rṅom-brjid, brjid, dpal, byin, zil, γzi, γzi-brjid.*
Splint (for a broken limb) *č̔ag-šiṅ.*
Splinter s. *t̔sal-pa, šiṅ-t̔sal*; *šiṅ-zél W.*
Split vb. a. *ₒges-pa, γčog-pa, γšog-pa, č̔eg-pa*; vb. n. *ₒgas-pa.*
Spoil vb. a. (plunder) *ₒjoms-pa*; *γčil-ba.*
Spoiled (corrupted) *K̔ag-po*; to be — *saṅ-ba.*
Spoke *rtsib-ma.*
Sponge s. *č̔u-ₒK̔úr.*
Spontaneously *raṅ, raṅ-bžin-gyis, šugs-kyis, rgyu med-du* 110.
Spoon *t̔ur-ma*; tip of a — *t̔ur-mgo.*
Spoon-bill *skyar-léb.*
Sport vb. n. (frolic) *rtse-ba.*
Sportsman *K̔yi-ra-ba.*
Spot s. (locality) *go*; (stain) *grib*; (mark) *t̔ig-le.*
Spouse (wife) *č̔uṅ-ma, btsun-mo, K̔ab.*
Spout s. *wa-mč̔ú.*
Sprain vb. a. *t̔sigs ₒbud-pa* or *ₒbog-pa*; to be sprained *ₒK̔rul-ba.*
Spread vb. a. *rkyoṅ-ba, ₒgebs-pa, ₒK̔eb-pa, γčal-ba, rdal-ba, spel-ba, ₒdiṅ-ba, ₒbre-ba, ₒgrems-pa*; vb.n. *mč̔ed-pa, ₒgye-ba, rgyas-pa, dar-ba, ldaṅ-ba.*
Sprightly *γčaṅ-po.*
Spring up vb. n. *č̔ags-pa* 153.

Spring s. (fountain) *ču-mig*, *k'ron-pa*; (season) *dpyid*.
Sprinkle *ₒgrems-pa*, *čag-čag byed-pa*.
Sprout s. *sbál-mig*, *myu-gu*, *myug*.
Sprout vb. n. *skye-ba*, *ₒk'ruṅ-ba*, *rdol-ba*.
Spunk *spra-ba*; *tsa Ld*.
Spur s. (of horsemen) *rtiṅ-lčags*; mountain — *sgaṅ*.
Spy s. *lta-nyul-pa*, *mel-tse*; — glass *dur-bín*, *šel-mig*.
Spy vb. *so-byed-pa*; to — out (another's faults) *ₒtsaṅ bru-ba*.
Squander *γzan-pa*.
Square s. *k'a-gáṅ*; adj. *k'a-gaṅ-ba*, *k'a-gaṅ-ma*.
Squash vb. *glem-pa*.
Squat vb. *tsog-pur sdod-pa* 432.
Squeeze vb. *glem-pa*, *bčer-ba*.
Squire v. *ga-gá*.
Stack s. *p'ub-rags*.
Staff *mk'ar-ba*, *ₒk'ar-ba*, *ber-ka*.
Stag *ša-ba* 556.
Stage (of a journey) *ₒbraṅ-sa*.
Stain vb. (sully) *bsgo-ba*; stained *nyams-pa*.
Staircase *t'em-pa*, *rgya-skás*; *gya-šrás W*.
Stairs *t'em-pa*; up — *ya-t'og*, down — *ma-t'og*.
Stake s. (in the ground) *rtod-pa*; (in a wager) *rgyal-rgyan*.
Stalk s. *rkaṅ*, *sdoṅ-po*, *ba-t'ag*, *rtsa-ba*, *sog-ma*.
Stallion *γseb*.
Stammerer *k'a-ldig-mk'an W*.
Stamp s. *rgya*, resp. *p'yag-rgyá*.
Stamp vb. *ₒk'rab-pa* 61.
Stanch vb. (the flowing blood) *sdom-pa*.
Stand vb. a. (bear) *bzod pa* 498; to be able to — *t'ub-pa*, *t'eg-pa*; vb. n. *greṅ-ba*, *laṅs-te sdod-pa*.
Stand s. *stegs* 221.
Star *skar-ma*; shooting — *skar-mdá*.
Start vb. (set out) *rgyug-pa*; (from alarm) *ₒdrog-pa*.
State s. (condition) *γnas-skabs*, *γnas-tsúl*.
Stately *ₒod-čan*.
Statue *sku*, *rdo-sku*.
Stature *sgo-po*, *sgo-bo*.
Stay vb. n. *ₒdug-pa*, *sdod-pa*, *γnas-pa*, *bžugs-pa*.
Steadfast *brtan-po*.
Steady *ₒtsugs-pa*.
Steal vb. a. *rku-ba*, *ma-sbyin-par leṅ-pa*; vb. n. (slip) *ₒdab-pa*, *nyul-ba*, *ₒdzul-ba*.
Stealth, by — *sbas-te W*.
Steam *rlaṅs-pa*.
Steel **čag-záṅ**, *p'o-ldd*.
Steelyard *rgya-ma*, *nya-ga*; *pur*, *spor*, *spo-ré*, *sraṅ*.
Steep adj. *γtsaṅ-γtsoṅ*, *γzar-ba*.
Steer vb. a. *k'a-lo sgyur-ba*.
Stench *dri ṅan-pa*, *dri ṅa-ba*, *dri-mnam*.
Step s. *gom-pa*, *rdog-pa*; — of a ladder *šral-daṅ* 21; vb. n. *bgom-pa*, *gom-pa ₒbor-ba*, *ₒgrul-ba*, *ₒčag-pa*.
Stepfather *p'a-γyár*; stepmother *ma-gyár*.
Stick s. *ber-ka*, *dbyug-pa*.
Stick vb. n. *k'ad-pa*, *ₒbyor-ba*; vb. a. *sbyor-ba*, *ₒdzugs-pa*.
Sticky *rtsi-čan*.
Stiff *reṅs-pa*; to be — *reṅ-ba*.
Still adj. (quiet) *dal-ba*, *mi γyo-bar*; (silent) v. *k'a rog-pa*.
Still adv. *da-rúṅ*, *yaṅ*.
Sting s. *mduṅ*; vb. a. *ₒbig(s)-pa*, *ₒdzug-pa* 466.
Stingy *lag-dam-po*, *t'sags-ₒdod-čan*.
Stink vb. *mnam-pa*.
Stir vb. a. *dkrug-pa*, *srub-pa*; to — up *rnyog-pa*, *sprug-pa*.
Stirrup *yob*, *ₒob*.
Stitch vb. *sbrel-ba*.
Stocking *rkaṅ-šúbs*, resp. *žabs-šúbs*.
Stomach *grod-pa*, *p'o-ba*.
Stone s. *rdo*; — of fruits *rus-pa*; vb. a. *rdo-rub-la btaṅ-če W*.
Stool *stegs* 221.
Stoop vb. *mgo dgu-ba*, *mgo dgur-ba* or *ₒgug-pa*.
Stop vb. a. *sub-pa*, *ₒgegs-pa*; vb. n. *ₒgag-pa*, *sdod-pa*.
Stopple, stopper *k'a-ₒdig*.
Store s. *mdzod*; — room *mdzod-k'aṅ*, *baṅ-ba*, *baṅ-k'aṅ*, *t'soṅ-k'aṅ*.
Storm s. *t'sub-ma*, *rluṅ čen-po*, *drag-po*.
Story s. (floor) *t'og*; (tale) *γnas-t'súl*, *lo-rgyus*.
Stout adj. *sbom-pa*, *rom-po*; (of cloth) *t'sags-dam*; to grow — *brta-ba*.
Stove *t'ab*, *me-t'áb*.
Straight adj. *draṅ-po*, *groṅs-po*, *bsraṅs-pa*.
Straighten *sroṅ-ba*.
Strain vb. a. (filter) *ₒt'sag-pa*.
Strainer *ču-t'sags*.
Straits *sa-bár*, *mt'so-lag-ₒbrél*.
Stranger *p'yi-mi*, *byes-pa*.
Strangle *ske bsdam-ste γsod-pa*.
Strangury *γčin-ₒgág*.
Strap s. *ko-t'ág*, *sgrog-gu*, *rog-bu W.*, *luṅ*.
Stratagem *dku-lto*.
Straw *sog-ma*, *p'ub-ma*.
Strawberry *dpal-byór W*.
Stray v. *yan-pa* 506.
Street *rgya-sráṅ*, *lam-sráṅ*.
Strength *nyams-stóbs*, *stobs-po*; *šed*; — of spirits etc. *ber*.
Strengthen *šed čug-če W*.
Stretch vb. *rkyoṅ-ba*, *sriṅ-ba*.
Strew *γtor-ba*, *ₒdiṅ-ba*.
Strewing-oblation *γtor-ma* 210.

Strict *dam-po.*
Stride vb. *bgom-pa.*
Strike vb. *ₒp'og-pa, rgyab-pa, rduṅ-ba, rdeg-pa.*
String s. *rgyud, sgrog, ₒčiṅ-ba, ₒpreṅ-ba, ta-gu.*
Strip vb. *šu-ba, gos ₒbud-pa.*
Strive for vb. *snyegs-pa, ₒgraṅ-pa, brtson-pa.*
Stroke s. *lčag, ₒp'ras-pa.*
Stroke vb. *byil-ba, ₒbyug-pa.*
Strong *gar-ba, drags-po, btsan-po, rem-pa* 535, *šed-čan.*
Structure *bkod-pa.*
Stubborn *mgo-k'regs-pa.*
Student *slob-ynyér.*
Studious *brtson-ₒgrus-čan.*
Study s. *ₒbad-pa.*
Stuff s. (cloth) *ras.*
Stuff vb. a *ₒtsaṅ-ba.*
Stunned *k'al-k'ól.*
Stupid *glen-pa, blun-pa, blo-gros-méd.*
Style s. *bzo, zo-sta W.* 497.
Subdue *ₒjoms-pa.*
Subject s. *skor, gleṅ-yži, mṅa-žábs, bran, ₒbaṅs.*
Subject vb.a. *ₒjoms-pa, ₒog-tu ₒjug-pa* 501.
Subsequent *p'yi-ma.*
Subside *ži-ba.*
Subsidy *ₒtud-ma.*
Subsistence *ₒtso-t'abs.*
Substance *dṅos-po, rdzas* 468.
Substantive *dṅos-miṅ.*
Substitute s. *t'sab.*
Subtract *ₒdor-ba, sbyoṅ-ba, ₒbud-pa.*
Succession *t'sir, rabs* 525, *rim-pa* 530.
Such *ₒdi-ₒdra-ba* 282, *de-lta-bu* 256.
Suck *ₒjibs-pa, ₒtuṅ-ba.*
Suckling baby *žo-ₒt'úṅs.*
Suddenly *glo-bur, glo-bur-du, har(-gyis); yaṅ-med-la W.*
Suet *grod-t'sil, k'oṅ-t'sil.*
Suffer vb. a. *myoṅ-ba, bzod-pa*; vb. n. *mṅar-ba, yzir-ba.*
Suffice *ₒk'yed-pa, ldaṅ-ba*; *čog-pa.*
Sugar *ka-ra, k'a-ra*; raw — *bu-rám*; — cane *ₒdam-búr W.*
Suit s., a complete — of clothes *mgo-lus ča tsáṅ.*
Suitable, to be — *ₒoṅ-ba* 502, *ₒos-pa, ruṅ-ba.*
Suitor *ₒdod-mk'an.*
Sully *bsgo-ba.*
Sulphur *mu-zi.*
Sum s. *brtsis-zin*; vb. to — up *sgril-ba, sdom-pa, sre-ba.*
Summary s. *sdom.*
Summer *dbyar.*
Summit *mgo, spo, rtse(-mo).*
Summon vb. a. *ₒgugs-pa.*

Sun *nyi-ma*; — beam *nyi-yžér*; — dial *nyi-tsód.*
Sunday *yza-nyi-ma.*
Superficies *ṅos, k'a, ydoṅ.*
Superintend *žal-ta byed-pa.*
Superintendence *do-dám.*
Superior adj. *k'yad, goṅ-ma, rgyal-ba, bla, rab*; s. *goṅ-ma, bla-ma.*
Supernumerary adj. *ₒt'eb.*
Supine adj. *gan-kyál.*
Supper *dgoṅs-zas*; Lord's — *ysol-ras* 592.
Supple *mnyen-pa.*
Supplement *k'a-skóṅ, yan-lag, lhan-t'ábs.*
Supply vb. *sgrub-pa.*
Support vb. *skyoṅ-ba, ₒdegs-pa, ₒdzin-pa*; s. *rten-pa, rgyab-rtén.*
Supposition resp. *bsam-pa, snaṅ-ba, bžed-pa, bžed-t'sul.*
Suppress *non-pa, ₒjoms-pa, snub-pa, sub-pa, ₒgegs-pa*
Sure *gor-ma-čág,* eleg. *gor-ma-bkúm* 73; *btsan-po* 431; to be sure! **tig, dig, de-ka yod** 255.
Surely *ṅes-par, nan-čágs* 303.
Surety *brtan-pa, ydeṅ-t'sad.*
Surface *k'a, ṅos, logs, ₒk'od, ydoṅ-pa.*
Surpass *ₒda-ba.*
Surround *skor-ba.*
Suspend *dpyaṅ-ba, spyaṅ-ba* 328.
Swaddling-cloth *ču-stán W.*
Swallow s. *k'ug-ta.*
Swallow vb. *mid-pa, k'yur-mid-pa.*
Swamp s. *gram-pa.*
Swan *bžad, bžad-pa; ṅaṅ-pai rgyal-po.*
Swear *bro ₒtsal-ba, dmod-mo ₒbor-ba* 423.
Sweat s. *rṅul.*
Sweep vb. *p'yag bdar-ba*; to — together *sdud-pa.*
Sweepings *pyag-dár.*
Sweet *dṅar-ba*; — scented *žim-po.*
Sweet-heart *ₒdod-grogs, mig-grogs, mdza-grogs, bzaṅ-grogs.*
Sweet-meats *žim-zé, žim-žim C., žim-zág W.*
Swell vb. n. *skraṅ-ba, ₒbo-ba.*
Swift adj. *skyen-pa, myur-ba, riṅs-pa.*
Swim *rkyal-ba, ₒp'yo-ba.*
Swine *p'ag.*
Swing vb. a. *dbyug-pa, yyob-pa.*
Switch s. *lčag.*
Swoon vb. n. *brgyal-ba.*
Sword *ral-gri.*
Syllable *sgra* 119, *t'seg-bar* 450.
Symbol *rten* 213.
Symmetry *dpe-byad, byad.*
Symptom *mt'san(-ma), rtags.*
Synonym *skad-dód* 258.
Syphilis *p'a-ráṅ, reg-dug.*
Syria *rum-šam.*
Syringe *yčiu.*

T

Tabernacle *gur-mčóg* 69.
Table *lčog-tse* 150, resp. *ysol-lčóg* 592; *ysol-stegs*; European — *rgya-lčóg*.
Tablet, bearing an inscription *byaṅ-bu*, *byaṅ-ma*.
Taciturn *smra-nyúṅ*.
Tail *rṅa-ma*, *mǰug-ma*.
Tailor *tsem-pa*.
Take vb. a. *len-pa*, *ₒtogs-pa*, *ₒdzin-pa*, resp. *bžes-pa*; **nam-če** W; to — for *ₒdzin-pa* 465, *sems-pa*; to — off *ₒbud-pa*, *šu-ba*; to — out *ₒgog-pa*, *ₒdon-pa*, *ₒbyin-pa*; take away! *k'ur soṅ* C., *k'ur k'yer* W.
Tale *lo-rgyús*, *sgruṅ(s)*.
Talent *blo*, *rig-pa*, *yon-tan*, *šes-rab*.
Talk s. *ytam*, *ₒur*; vb. *smra-ba*, *lab-pa*, *gleṅ-ba*, *ₒbar-ba*, *ₒur ytoṅ-ba*.
Talkative *smra-ₒdód*, *rgya-lab-čan*.
Tall col. *sgo-po riṅ-mo*, *kyaṅ-kyaṅ riṅ-mo*, *ₒǰoṅ-ₒǰóṅ*.
Tallow-candle *tsil-sdóṅ*.
Tamarisk *ₒom-bu*.
Tame adj. *dul-ba*, *ₒdris-pa*, *yyuṅ-ba*; vb. a. *ₒdul-ba*, *t'ul-ba*.
Tan vb a. *mnyed-pa*.
Tanner *ko-ba mnyed-mk'an* C.
Tardy *bul-po*.
Target *ₒben*.
Tarry vb. *ₒgor-ba*.
Tartar (incrusting the teeth) *so-dreg*.
Task s. *k'ag*; *rgyugs* W.
Taste s. (savour) *bro-ba*, *ro*; vb. a. *myoṅ-ba*; vb. n. *bro-ba*.
Tattered *čad-po*.
Tavern *čaṅ-k'aṅ*
Tax s. *k'ral*, *dpya*; *ₒbab* Sp; vb. a. (appraise) *ₒǰal-ba*.
Tea *ǰa*, resp. *ysol-ǰá*; — pot *tib-ril*, resp. *ysol-tib*; — party *ǰa-mgrón*.
Teach vb. *ston-pa*, *slob-pa*.
Teacher *ston-pa*, *slob-pa*, *slob-dpon*; *rgyud-pa*.
Team of bullocks *glaṅ-dór*.
Tear s. *mči-ma*; to shed tears *mči-ma blag-pa*.
Tear vb. a. *yšeg-pa*; to — out *ₒp'yid-pa*, *ₒbyin-pa*; to — to pieces *ₒdral-ba*, *hral-ba*.
Tease *gob-nón čo-če* W.
Tedder vb. *btod-pa*; s. *btod-t'ág*.
Tell *ₒčad-pa*, *snyod-pa*, *smra-ba*, *zer-ba*, *zlo-ba*, *zlos-pa*.
Temperate *t'sod šes-pa*.
Temperature *graṅ-dro*.
Tempest *rluṅ čen-po* or *drag-po*, *rluṅ-dmár*, *yul-ṅán*.
Temple *mčod-k'aṅ*.
Temporal *t'se ₒdii*; — life *ynas-skabs*.
Tempt *nyams sad-pa*, *t'sod ₒdzin-pa*.
Ten num. *bču*, *čig bču*; — thousand *k'ri*; tenth *bču-pa*.
Tenant *k'aṅ-pa yyar-mk'an*.
Tend vb. a. *skyoṅ-ba*.
Tender adj. *snyi-ba*, *ₒǰam-pa*; *byams-pa*.
Tendon *nya-ču*.
Tenet *č'os*.
Tent *gur*, resp. *bžugs-gur*.
Term s. (limited time) *čad-so*.
Terminate vb. n. *zin-pa*; vb. a. *ₒt'sar-bar byed-pa*.
Termination *mt'a* 239.
Terrace *steṅ-ka*, *steṅ-tse*.
Terrify *ₒǰigs-pa*, *ₒǰigs-skrag ₒdon-pa* C.; **ǰig-ri skul-če** W.; to be terrified *skrag-pa*.
Test vb. a. *nyams sad-pa*; *t'sod lta-ba* 216.
Testament *bka-čéms*, *k'a-čéms*.
Testicle *rlig-pa*, resp. *ysaṅ-rlig*, euphem. *ₒbras-bu*.
Testimony *če-bži*; v. *dpaṅ(-po)* 326.
Texture *t'ags*.
Than *las* 546, *pas*, *saṅ* W. 571.
Thank vb. *ytaṅ-rág byed-pa* or *ₒbul-ba*.
Thanks s. *ytaṅ-rág*, *legs-ysól*; many —! *bka-drin-čé*, *ṅo-mt'sar-čé* 456; *žu* W.
That pron. *de* 255; *so-či-ltar* 218.
The def. art. v. *de* 255.
Theatre *ltad-mo lta-bai sa*, *ltad-mo-k'aṅ*.
Theft *rkun-ma*.
Theme *skor*.
Then *de-tsa-na*, *der* 256.
Theory *lta-ba* II, no. 3, 217.
There *de-na*, *de-ru* 256, *p'a-gir* 338.
Therefore *de-bas-na*, *des-na*, *des* 256.
Therein *naṅ-na*.
They *k'o-pa*; *k'o-wa* W.; *k'o-t'so*, *k'o-čag* C.; *de-dag*, *de-rnams*.
Thick *ₒt'ug-pa*, *stugs-po*, *sbom-pa*, *rom-po*; (of fluids) *ska-ba*, *rnyog-pa*.
Thicket *t'saṅ-t'siṅ* 444.
Thickness *srab-ₒt'úg* 244.
Thief *rkun-ma*.
Thimble *lčuṅ-mo*, *mdzub-rtén*.
Thin adj. *p'ra-ba*, *zim-bu*, *siṅs-po* W.; *srab-pa*, *sla-ba*, *sla-mo*.
Thing *dṅos-po*, *ča*, *ča-byád*, *čas*, *rdzas*; things (goods) *ča*, *ča-lag*.
Think (suppose) *snyam-pa*; (meditate) *sem(s)-pa*; *bsam-mno byed-pa* or *ytoṅ-ba*, resp. *dgoṅs-pa*; to — of *dran-pa* 261, *dgoṅs-pa*.
Third num. *sum-pa*; thirteen *bču-sum*; thirteenth *bču-sum-pa*; thirty *sum-ču*; thirtieth *sum-ču-pa*; a third, third part *sum-ča*, *sum-yar*.
Thirst s. *skom*, *skom-pa*, *skom-dád*; vb. *skom-pa*.

This *ₒdi* 275.
Thither *de-ru, der* 256; *p̓yogs der* 352.
Thong *ko-ťág.*
Thorn *ťser-ma.*
Thoroughly *k̓yon-nas.*
Thou *k̓yed, k̓yod*, resp. *nyid.*
Though v. *kyi* 6.
Thought *bsam-pa*, resp. *dgoṅs-pa, snyam-pa, snaṅ-ba, dmigs-pa, ₒčar-sgo, nyams.*
Thousand num. *stoṅ*; ten — *k̓ri, k̓ri-k̓rag, k̓ri-ťso*; hundred — *ₒbum, ₒbum-ťso.*
Thrash vb. *γyul-k̓a γčog-pa, γyur byed-pa C.,*k̓o-yu skor-če* W.*
Thread s. *skud-pa, ₒťsem-skúd; snal-ma* 319, *nyag-ťág* 185.
Threaten *gam-pa W.*
Three num. *γsum, sum.*
Threshold *ťem-pa, sgo-ťém.*
Thrifty *paṅ-sems-čan.*
Throat *mgul*, resp. *mgur, lkog-ma, ske, gre-ba, mgrin-pa, 'o-lé W.*; sore — *mgul-nad.*
Throb vb. *ₒp̓ar-ba.*
Throne s. *rgyal-sa, k̓ri, sen-ge-k̓ri.*
Through *ltaṅ, lteṅ* 217; *p̓yir* 351.
Throughout *ťog-ťág* 237.
Throw vb. a. *rgyab-pa, rgyag-pa, skyur-ba, γtor-ba, ₒp̓en-pa, dbyug-pa; ₒbor-ba C.*; to — down *ₒbud-pa, ₒbebs-pa*; to — off *spoṅ-ba.*
Thumb s. *ťe-bo, mťe-bo.*
Thunder s. *ₒbrug, ₒbrug-skád, ₒbrug-sgrá.*
Thunderbolt *ťog, lče, rdo-rje, γnam-lčags.*
Thursday *γza-p̓ur-bu.*
Thus *de-ltar, ₒdi-ltar, de-bžin-du, de-ₒdras C., de-tsug W.*
Thwart (frustrate) *sgyel-ba.*
Tiara *čod-pán.*
Tibet *bod.*
Tibetan m. *bod-pa*, f. *bod-mo*; — language *bod-skad*; — printing-characters *dbu-čan* 388; — current handwriting *dbu-méd.*
Tick s. *lug-šig.*
Tickle vb. **ki-tsi kug-če* W.*; *gug-pa W.*
Tide s. *dus-rlábs.*
Tidings *p̓rin*; glad — *γtam-snyán*; (gospel) *p̓rin bzaṅ-po.*
Tie s. *ₒčiṅ-ba*, vb. a. *ₒčiṅ-ba, ₒk̓yig-pa.*
Tiger *stag.*
Tight *dam-po, ťaṅ-po.*
Till, until *bar-du* 366, *ťug C.*; *ťsug-pa W.*
Till vb. a. *ₒdul-ba.*
Time s. *dus, ťse, skabs*; (while) *yun*; time, times *lan*; one —, once *lan-γčig*; ten — *lan-bču*; point of —, proper — for *bsgaṅ* 124.
Timid *ₒjigs-pa, ₒjigs-mk̓an, ₒjigs-pa-čan; sems-čuṅ-ba.*
Tin s. *ža-nye dkar-po, ža-dkár, dkar-ya*; — plate *ta-lí W.*
Tinder-box *lčags-mag.*
Tire vb. a. *ṅal ₒjug-pa.*
Tired *dub-pa*; to be — *dub-pa, skyo-ba.*
Tithe s. *ču-k̓ág W.*
Title s. *mťsan*; (claim) *ťob-srol.*
To prep. *mdun* 273, *druṅ-du*, resp. *žabs-druṅ-du* 263, *rtsar* 437, *gan-du* 66.
Tobacco *ťa-ma-k̓a*; — pipe *gaṅ-zág, žal-zág.*
To-day *de-riṅ C., ₒdi-riṅ W.*
Toe *rkaṅ-sór, sor-mo*; the big — *rkaṅ-pai mťe-bo.*
Together *γčig-tu, lhan-čig-tu*; — with *bčas-pa, mnyam-du.*
Token *mťsan-ma*
Tola (Indian half ounce) *dṅul*, col. *mul.*
Toll s. *šo-gam.*
Tomb *dur, baṅ-so.*
Tongs *rkam-pa.*
Tongue *lče*, resp. *ljags.*
Too adv. (too much) *ha-čaṅ*; conj. (also) *yaṅ.*
Tool *čas*; tools *yo-byád, lag-ča.*
Tooth *so*, resp. *ťsems*; — ache *so-zug*; — brush *so-zéd*; — pick *ťsems-šiṅ, so-šiṅ.*
Top s. *rtse(-mo).*
Topography *γnas-bšád, yul-bšád.*
Torch *gal-mé, sgron-ma.*
Torment vb.a. *ₒťse-ba; sdug-bsṅal* or *γnag ston-pa W.*
Torn adj. *ral-ba, čad-po.*
Tortoise *rus-sbal.*
Torture vb. a. *mi-la γnag ston-pa W.*
Totter *yam-yóm byed-pa.*
Touch vb. *nyug-pa, γtug-pa, ťug-pa, reg-pa.*
Toupet *ťor-čóg, ťor-ťsúgs.*
Towards *ťog-tu* 237, *ťad-du, p̓yogs-su.*
Towel *lag-ₒp̓yis.*
Tower *mk̓ar dgu-ťog.*
Town *groṅ, groṅ-kyer*; *yul-gru*; *rgyal-sa W.*
Toy s. *rtsed-mo.*
Trace s. *rkaṅ-rjés, mal.*
Track s. *rjes, šul.*
Trackless *rjes-méd.*
Tractable *srab-k̓a dul-mo.*
Trade s. *ťsoṅ, bzo.*
Tradesman *k̓e-pa.*
Trading-place *las-sgo.*
Traffic s. *ťsoṅ.*
Train vb. a. *sbyoṅ-ba*; to — up *skyed-sriṅ-ba.*
Trample vb.a. *rdzi-ba, rdog-pas rduṅ-ba.*
Tranquil *ži-ba.*
Tranquillity *žod.*
Transaction *las.*
Transfer vb. *spo-ba, ₒgod-pa.*
Transform *sgyur-ba*; to — one's self *sprul-ba* 336; to be transformed into *ₒgyur-ba* 96, *ₒgro-ba* 101.

Transformation *rdzu-ₒṗrul.*
Transgress *ₒgal-ba*; *ₒda-ba.*
Transgression *ₒgal-ḱrúl.*
Translate *sgyur-ba.*
Transmigration, the round of — *ₒḱor-ba* 58.
Transplant *spo-ba.*
Transport vb. *skyel-ba*, *ₒḱyer-ba.*
Trap s. *rnyi*, *snyi*; *ldem-pa W.*; — door *ɣnam-sgo*; mouse — *bi-ldém W.*, fox *wa-ldém W.*
Travel vb. *ₒgro-ba*, *ₒgrod-pa*, *bgrod-pa*; *č̌a-ba W.*
Tread vb. a. *rdzi-ba*; **čag-čag ċo-ċe* W.*; vb. n. *ₒčag-pa*, *ₒčags-pa.*
Treadle *rkaṅ-śiṅ.*
Treasure s. *ɣter.*
Treasurer *dkor-pa*, *ṗyag-mdzód.*
Treasury *dkor-mdzód.*
Treat s (feast) *mgron.*
Treat vb. n. (to use) *spyod-pa* 334; (to regale) *mgron-du ɣnyer-ba*; to — medically *bċos-pa*; *sman-dpyad byed-pa* 329; vb. n. to — of *ṙjod-pa* 182.
Treatise *rgyud*, *rgyud-sdé.*
Treatment, good — *bzaṅ-lúgs W.*
Treaty *bzaṅ-sgrig.*
Tree *śiṅ*, *sdoṅ-po*, *śiṅ-sdóṅ.*
Tremble *ₒgul-ba*, *ₒdar-ba.*
Trespass vb. n. *bar-du ɣċod-pa* 367.
Trevet *lċags-sgyid.*
Trial (before a tribunal) *ɣtam-sdúr W.*
Tribe *sde.*
Tribunal *ḱrims-ḱaṅ.*
Tribute *dpya*
Trick s. *bar-čad*; to play tricks *ṫo-ₒṫsam-pa.*
Trickle vb. n. *ₒdzag-pa.*
Trifling adj. *ṗra-ba.*
Tripod *sgyid-bu*, *lċags-sgyid.*
Troop s. *ḱyu*, *pal-po-č̌e*, *ṫso*; troops *dpuṅ.*
Trophy *rgyal-mṫsán.*
Trot vb. *ₒdur-ba*; s. *ₒdur-ₒgro.*
Trouble s. *nyon-moṅs-pa*, *dka-sdúg*, *mya-ṅán*; vb. a. *dkrug-pa.*
Troublesome *ṫsegs.*
Trowsers *rkaṅ-snam*, *gos-ṫúṅ*, *dor-ma*, *byaṅ-rkyaṅ*, *smad-ɣyógs.*
True *bden-pa*, *ṅo-rtóg.*
Trumpet *duṅ.*
Trunk (of a tree) *sdoṅ-po*; (of an elephant) *glaṅ-sna*; (box) *sgam*, *sgrom.*
Truss s. *ṗon-po*; vb. to — up *rdze-ba.*
Trustee *ṗa-ṫsáb.*
Trustworthy *ₒos-pa.*
Truth *ṅes-pa*, *bden-pa*, *yin-min* 510.
Try *nyams sad-pa* 186, *dpyod-pa*, col. *ṫsod-lta-ba.*
Tub *ɣżoṅ-pa*, *bzom.*
Tube *doṅ-po*, *pu-ri.*
Tuck up *rdze-ba.*
Tuesday *ɣza-mig-dmár.*
Tuft *ṗon*; — of wool *bal-ₒdab W.*
Tumble vb. *ₒgyel-ba.*
Tumbler (drinking-glass) *śel-kór*, *śel-ṗór.*
Tumult *ₒḱrug-pa.*
Tun *zem.*
Tune s. *glu.*
Turban *ṫod*, *la-ṫód.*
Turbid *ska-ba*, *nyog-pa.*
Turf *spaṅ*, *spaṅ-po*
Turkey *rum.*
Turkois *ɣyu.*
Turmeric *yuṅ-ba.*
Turn vb. a *sgyur-ba*; to — off *zlog-pa*; to — out *ₒbyin-pa*; to — round *ₒḱor-ba*; to — up *rdze-ba*; to — upside down *spub-pa*, *slog-pa*; vb. n. *ṗyogs-pa*, *ₒgro-ba*, *č̌a-ba W.*; to — away *ldog-pa.*
Turn s. *ṫsir* 448, *res* 535; by turns *ṫsir-la*, *ṫsir-du*, *ṫsir daṅ*, *res-la.*
Turnip *nyuṅ-ma.*
Turret *speu*, *spiu.*
Tusk *mč̌e-ba*, *mč̌e-so.*
Tutelar god *yi-dam-lha*, *ṫugs-dám.*
Twelve *bċu-ɣnyis*; twelfth *bċu-ɣnyis-pa.*
Twenty *nyi-śu*; twentieth *nyi-śu-pa.*
Twice *lan-ɣnyis.*
Twilight *srod*, *srod-ₒjiṅ.*
Twine s. *skud-pa*, *si-ri W.*
Twins **ṫsag-ṫúg**, *mṫse-ma.*
Twirling-stick *ja-bkrúg.*
Twist vb. a. *sgrim-pa*, *ɣċud-pa*, *sle-ba.*
Two *ɣnyis*; v. also *do* 256.
Two-legged *rkaṅ-ɣnyis-pa.*
Tyrant *dpon-po drag-po* or *drag-śul-ċan.*

U

Ugly *mi-sdug-pa.*
Ulcer *śu-ba*; *ba-śu W.*; *ṗol*, *lhog-pa.*
Ultimately *ṗugs-na.*
Umbrella *nyi-rib*, *ɣdugs.*
Unable *mi śes-pa*, *ċaṅ mi śes-pa.*
Unaccustomed *mi gom-pa.*
Unadulterated *ma-ₒdres-pa*, *lhad-méd.*
Unaware *yaṅ-med-la W.*
Unbearable *mi-bzod-pa.*
Unbecoming *mi-rigs-pa.*
Unbelieving *ma-dad-pa*, *dad-méd.*
Unbutton vb. a. *ₒgrol-ba.*
Unchangeable *ₒgyur-méd*
Unchastity *ₒdod-lóg.*

Uncle *ḱu-bo*; *žaṅ(-po)*, *'a-žaṅ*, *'a-ḱú W.*
Unclean *mi-ytsaṅ-ba*, *dri-ma-čan*; *ťsi-du W.*, *skyug-bro C.*
Uncommon *ťun-mín*, *ťun-moṅs ma yin-pa* 231; *srol-méd*, *ťa-mal-pa ma yin-pa* 227.
Undefined *ṅes-med*.
Under *˳og*, *˳og-na* 501; v. also *šam* 557.
Under-garment *'aṅ-ťúṅ*.
Undergo *mtoṅ-ba*, *bzod-pa*, *snyoṅ-ba*.
Understand *mḱyen-pa*, *go-ba*, *ṅos-˳ṕrod-pa*, *rig-pa*, *šes-pa*; *ha-go-ba W.*
Understanding s. *blo*, *blo-grós*; good — (agreement) *mťun* 241.
Undertaking s. *rtsom-pa* 441.
Undoubtedly *ydon-mi-za-bar*.
Uneasy *koṅ-du čud-pa*, *mi ťsim-pa*, *mi dga-ba*, *mi dga-ste*.
Unequal *mi-˳dra-ba*.
Unequalled *˳gran-ya-med*.
Uneven *rtsub-po*.
Unexpectedly *hun-med-la W.*, *yaṅ-med-la W.*; *glo-bur-du*, *har(-gyis) C.*
Unfasten *˳grol-ba*.
Unfinished *ťe-rél W.*
Unfit adj. *mi-ruṅ-ba*.
Unfold *˳bu-ba*, *ḱa ˳bu-ba*.
Ungracious *brtse-méd*.
Unguent *byug-sman*.
Unhappy *bkra-mi-šis-pa*, *sdug-bsṅal-čan*, *yyaṅ-med-pa*.
Unimpaired *ma-nyams-pa*.
Universally *ṕal-čér*.
Universe *˳jig-rtén*.
Unjust *ťsul-méd*; *čos ma yin-pa*.
Unkind *brtse-méd*.
Unmarried (male or female) *ḱyim-ťabs-méd*; (female) *ḱyo-méd*.
Unobserved adv. *ma-ťsor-bar*.
Unoccupied *yan-pa*.
Unquestionable *ťag-bčad-pa* 227.
Unquestionably *ydon mi za-bar*.
Unreasonable *mi-rig-pa* 528.
Unripe *rjen-pa*.
Unsought *rtsol-méd*.
Unsteady *˳dug mi ťsugs-pa* 459.
Unsubstantial *yzugs-méd* 494.
Unsymmetrical *ya-ma-zúṅ*.
Untie *˳grol-ba*.
Until *bar-du*, *ťug C.*, *ťsug-pa W.*; *ṕan-la* 340, *yan-la* 506.
Untoward *mi-˳dod-pa*.
Untruth *šab-šób*.
Up to prep. *gan*, *druṅ-du*, *mdun-du*, *ldan-du W.* 289; *rtsar* 437; adv. *yar*, *gyen*.
Upbraid *bka-bkyon byed-pa*.
Up-hill *gyen-du*.
Upon *ḱa-ru*, *ḱar* 35, *ťog-tu* 237, *steṅ-du* 222.
Upper adj. *ya-gi*; — end *ťog-ma*; — part *stod*.
Upright (erect) *kye-ré*; *kroṅ-króṅ W.*; (honest) *čos-draṅ-po*.
Up-stairs *ya-ťog*.
Urge vb. a. v. *nan* 302.
Urgently *nye-bar*.
Urinary organs *ču-só*.
Urine *yčin*, *ču*, *dri-ču*.
Usage (custom) *srol*.
Use vb. a. *spyod-pa*.
Use s. *krims*; *ṕan-pa*; *lob-ḱyád W.*
Useful *dgos-pa*, *ṕan-ťogs-pa*; to be — *ṕan-pa*.
Useless *mi-dgos-pa*, *ṕan-méd*, *don-méd*; *čon W.* 162.
Usual *ťun*, *tun-móṅ*, *ṕal-pa*.
Usurp *˳ṕrog-pa*.
Utensils *lag-ča*.
Uterus *bu-snód*, *ṕru-ma*.
Utmost v. *bla-ma* 382, *ṕi* 172.
Utter *rjod-pa*, *˳don-pa*.
Uvula *lče-čúṅ*.

V

Vacuity *stoṅ-pa-ñyid* 223.
Vagina *mṅal-sgo* 132.
Vagrant adj. *yan-pa*.
Vain (fond of dress) *mčor-po*, *rdzob-po*, col. *zab-mo*.
Valid *stobs-čan*.
Valley *luṅ-pa*; lower part of a — *mdo*, upper part *ṕu*.
Valuable *dkon-pa*, *rin-po-če*.
Value s. (price) *goṅ*, *ťaṅ*, *rin*; (importance) *˳ḱos*.
Vanish *yal-ba*, *mi-snaṅ-bar ˳gyur-ba* 317.
Vapour s. *ṅad*, *rlaṅs-pa*.
Variegated *bkra-ba*.
Various *sna-ťsogs*, *sna-so-só*, *so-só*, *rigs mi-yčig-pa*.
Varnish s. *rtsí*.
Vegetables *sṅo-ťsód*, *ťsod-ma*, *ldum*.
Vehicle *ťeg-pa*, *bžon-pa*.
Veil s. *ydoṅ-ḱebs*.
Vein (of the body) *rtsa*; (of minerals) *yter-ḱa* 208, *rdo-ḱá* 287.
Venerable *btsun-pa*.
Vengeance *dugs W.*; to take — **dug kor-če*, *lan kor-če* W.*
Venture vb. *spobs-pa*.
Venus *pa(-wa)-saṅs*.
Verdant, the ground becomes — *sa ˳bo C.* 395; or *sṅo skyé* 136.

Vermicelli *γčur-ṗe, čur-ba.*
Vermilion s. *mts̀al, ts̀al.*
Vermin *sriṅ-bu, ˳bu.*
Verse s. *rkaṅ-pa* 15, *ts̀igs* 448.
Vertex *mgo-dkyil, γtsug.*
Vertical *gyen-la draṅ-po W.*
Very *rab-tu, śin-tu*; *ha-čaṅ* 595; *mā W.* 408; the very *k̀o-na* 43.
Vessel (receptacle) *snod*; (anatom.) *bu-ga*; (ship) *γziṅs, gru.*
Vestibule *sgo-k̀aṅ.*
Vestige *mal.*
Vice s. *sdig-pa, mi-dge-ba.*
Vice-roy *rgyal-ts̀ab.*
Vicissitude *˳gyur-ba* II 97.
Victorious, to be — *rgyal-ba.*
Victory *rgyal.*
Victuals *k̀a-zás, za-ba, za-ma.*
Vie with *˳gran-pa.*
View s. *snaṅ-ba* 317; point of — (mode of viewing things) *mt̀oṅ-snáṅ* 318, *γzigs-snáṅ*; vb. a. *lta-ba.*
Vigorous *rem-pa.*
Vile *btsog-pa.*
Vilify *smad-pa, dma-˳bebs-pa, ma-bab kal-ba W.* 421.
Village *yul-gru, groṅ, groṅ-tso, groṅ-yul, yul-ts̀o.*
Villager *groṅ-pa.*
Vine *rgun, rgun-śiṅ.*

Vinegar *skyur-k̀u, skyur-ru Sik., skyur-mo Lh.*
Vineyard *rgun-ts̀ás.*
Violate (infringe) *γčog-pa, ˳čal-ba*; (deflower) *lus smad-pa.*
Violent *drags-po, btsan.*
Virgin *bu-mo, bu-mo γsar-ma.*
Virtue *dge-ba, bsod-pa*; by — of *stobs-kyis* 224.
Virtuous *dge-ba, dge-ldán.*
Viscid *rtsi-čan.*
Vishnu *k̀yab-ǰúg* 46.
Visible *mṅon-pa, γsal-po, mt̀oṅ-du ruṅ-ba.*
Vision (act of seeing) *snaṅ-ba, mt̀oṅ-snaṅ*; range of — *mt̀oṅ-˳k̀or*; (phantom) *żal-γzigs.*
Visit vb. a. *żal-lta byed-pa*; … *daṅ t̀ug-pa-la ˳gro-ba*, … *daṅ mǰal-ba* or *ṗrad-pa.*
Visitation (inspection) *żal-ta, żal-lta.*
Voice *skad, sgra, sgra-skad*, resp. *γsuṅ*; loud — *skad-čé.*
Volcano *me-ri.*
Voluptuousness *˳dod-pa, ˳dod-čags.*
Vomit vb. *skyug-pa*; s. *skyugs-pa.*
Vortex *γtsug.*
Vow s. *t̀ugs-dám, dam, dam-ts̀ig, yi-dam*; to make a — *t̀ugs-dam bča-ba.*
Vowel *dbyaṅs.*
Vulgar s. *dmaṅs* 422; adj. *t̀a-mal-pa* 227.
Vulture *go-bo, glag, bya-glág.*

W

Wag vb. a. *sgril-ba.*
Wages *gla, ṗogs.*
Waggon *śiṅ-rta*; — wheel *śiṅ-rtai ṗaṅ-ló.*
Wailings s. *smre-sṅágs.*
Waist *rked-pa.*
Wait vb. n. *sgug-pa, sdod-pa, sriṅ-ba*; to — on *mǰal-ba*; to lie in — *sgug-pa*; to keep one waiting *sgug-tu ˳ǰug-pa.*
Waiting-man *sku-mdun-pa, żabs-ṗyi*; *druṅ-k̀ór.*
Wake vb. a. *sod-pa, γnyid sad-pa.*
Walk vb. n. *bgrod-pa, ˳grul-ba, ˳gro-ba, ˳čag-pa*; resp. *skyod-pa, γśegs-pa, ˳byon-pa*; to take a — *skyo-saṅs-la ˳gro-ba* 458; v. also *γyeṅs-pa* 518; the act of walking *˳gros*; manner of — *spyod-˳grós.*
Wall s. *rtsig-pa, lčags-ri, skya.*
Walnut *star-ka, dar-sga.*
Wand s. *dbyug-gu, dbyu-gu.*
Wander *˳k̀yam-pa, rgyu-ba.*
Want vb. a. *dgos-pa, ˳ts̀al-ba, ˳k̀o-ba*; I — *ṅa-la dgos* 87; I do not want it *˳k̀o-če med W.* 56.
War s. *˳k̀rug-pa*; *mag-t̀áb C., mag-t̀úg W.*
Wardrobe *gos-sgám.*

Warm adj. *dro-ba, dron-mo, ts̀a-ba.*
Warm vb. a. *sro-ba*; *dugs-pa W.*; to — one's self *lde-ba.*
Warmth *ts̀a-graṅ, drod.*
Warp s. *rgyu.*
Warrior *dmag-mí.*
Wart *mdzer-pa.*
Wash vb. a. *˳k̀rud-pa*, resp. *bsil-ba.*
Washing s. *k̀rus*; water for — *k̀rus-k̀u.*
Waste adj. *gog-po, stoṅ-pa.*
Watch vb. a. *sruṅ-ba.*
Watchman *sruṅ-mk̀an.*
Water *ču*, eleg. *čab*; — carrier *ču-pa*; — channel *wa*; — closet *ṗyag-ra*; *γsaṅ-spyód*; — jar *ču-rdzá*; — snake *ču-sbrul*; — spout *˳dre-ṗu-ts̀ub W.*; — tub *ču-zém.*
Wave s. *rlabs, dba-klóṅ.*
Wavering s. *ts̀am-ts̀úm.*
Wax s. *spra-ts̀il C., mum W.*
Way (road) *˳gro-sa, lam*, (manner) *rnam-pa, ts̀abs, lugs, ts̀ul*; by or in the — of *sgo-nas* 115; to have the — of *rigs-pa* 528; to give — *˳byer-ba*; to make — *˳byol-ba, ˳dzur-ba.* [*˳o, ˳u-čag.*
We pron. *ṅa* 124, *ṅa-čag, ṅed, ṅed-raṅ, ṅos,*

Weak adj. žan-pa, šed-med, šed-čuṅ, hal-med W.; nyams-čuṅ, ˳ǰam-po W.
Weal (mark) col. nya.
Wealth nor, dkor, ṗyug-ḱyád, dbyig(s), byor-pa, loṅs-spyód 551.
Weapon mṫson.
Wear vb. a. gyon-pa, bgo-ba.
Weariness ṅal-ba, ˏo-brgyál.
Weary adj., to be — skyo-ba, sun-pa.
Weary vb. n. ṅal ˳ǰug-pa; to be wearied ṅal-ba.
Weather, clear — ẏnam daṅ-ba, ẏnam dwaṅs, ẏnam ṫaṅ; dry — ṫan-pa 229.
Weave vb. a. ˳ṫag-pa.
Weaver ṫa-ga-pa.
Wedge s. ka-ru.
Wednesday ẏza-lhag-ma.
Weed s. rtsa-ṅan.
Weeding (the act of) ẏur-ma.
Week bdun-ṗrág.
Weep ṅu-ba, šum-pa.
Weft spun.
Weigh vb. a. ˳ǰal-ba, ˳degs-pa, ẏžal-ba, ẏšor-ba.
Weight rdo 286, sraṅ 580.
Welcome, you are — ˏoṅs-pa legs-so 501.
Welfare bde-ba, bde-˳ǰágs.
Well s. ḱron-pa, ču-doṅ, ˳byuṅ-ḱuṅs, ču-míg.
Well adj., are you —? de-mo 'e yo C.; adv. ˏo-ná 500; very — de-ltar ˳ṫsal-lo; well, well! yag-po yag-po; — sounding snyan-pa; — tasted žim-po.
Wen lba-ba.
Went, I went soṅ 579.
West nub.
Wet adj. rlon-pa, ẏšer-ba; s. rlan.
Wether ṫoṅ-pa.
What interr. ċi 139, gaṅ 65, ċi-ltar 140, ǰi 172.
Whatever ċi-yaṅ; — it may be ċi yaṅ ruṅ 532.
Wheat gro; — flour bag-ṗyé.
Wheel s. ˳ḱor-lo; paddle — sku-ru.
When ḱa-ru, ḱar; ċiṅ; interr. nam, dus-nam-žig 303.
Where ga-na, ga-ru, gar; — is? ga-ré.
Whetstone ˳dzeṅ.
Which interr. gaṅ 65.
While s. yun; a little — ṫen, dar-ẏċig, re žig (dus); a long — riṅ žig-tu.
Whilst la 540, las 546.
Whip s. lċag, rta-lċag.
Whirl vb. n. ˳ṫsub-pa.
Whirlpool ẏtsug, ẏtsug-˳ḱyil.
Whirlwind ˳dre-pu-ṫsúb W.
Whisper s. šab-šúb; vb. šub-pa, šib-pa.
Whistle vb. šugs-sgra ẏtoṅ-ba; v. also hu-hú 597.
White adj. dkar-ba; — wash dkar-rtsi.
Whither ga-ru, ga-la 64, gar 67.
Who interr. gaṅ 65, su 573.
Whole adj. ṫams-ċád 230; ṫsaṅ-ma, ril-ba, hril-po; s. ril-po.
Wholly yoṅs-su.
Why interr. ċi, ċi-la 140, ċii ṗyir 351; ga-la rten-nas 214; interj. ˏo-ná 500.
Wick s. snyiṅ-po, sdoṅ-ras C., sar W.
Wicked adj. čos-méd, sdig-pa-la dga-ba.
Wide žeṅ-ċan, yaṅs-pa, hel-po, hel-ċan.
Widow yugs(s)-sa-mo.
Widower yug(s)-sa-pa, yug-sa; skyes-nág
Width ḱyon, ẏžeṅ. [C.
Wife čuṅ-ma, čuṅ-grogs; 'a-ne W.; ḱab 38, ḱyo-mo 48; (housewife) ḱyim-ṫab-mo, ḱyim-pa-ma 47.
Wild adj. rgod-pa, ẏnyan-pa.
Wilderness dgon pa, ˳brog.
Will s. bsam-pa, ṫugs, resp. ṫugs-dgoṅs.
Willing, to be — ˳dod-pa.
Willow lċaṅ-ma.
Wind s. rdzi, rluṅ; cold — lhag(s)-pa.
Wind vb. a. dkri-ba, ˳ḱri-ba, ˳ḱyil-ba, sgril-ba; vb. n. ˳ḱril-ba.
Window rgyal-dkar C.; — hole dkar-ḱuṅ.
Windpipe ḱru-ḱrú W., lkog-ma.
Wine rgun-čaṅ, resp. rgun-skyéms; čaṅ.
Wing s. šog-pa, ˏdab-ma.
Wink vb. n. mig ḱrab-ḱráb or ṫsab-ṫsáb or ˳dzum-˳dzúm byed-pa.
Winter s. dgun, dgun-ka.
Wipe vb. a. ˳ṗyi-ba; to be wiped off ˳byi-ba.
Wire lċags-skúd.
Wisdom ye-šes, šes-ráb.
Wise adj. mḱas-pa, gruṅ-ba, mdzaṅs-pa.
Wish s. ˳dod-pa, yid-smon; resp. dgoṅs-pa, bžed-don; vb. a. ˳dod-pa, smon-pa, ˳ṫsal-ba, bžed-pa.
Witchcraft mṫu, ṗra-mén.
With daṅ 248, mnyam-du 195, bċas-su.
Withdraw vb. a. ẏċod-pa, mi sder-ba; vb. n. ˳gye-ba.
Wither vb. n. rnyid-pa.
Within ṫsun-čád.
Without prep. med-pa(r) 418.
Witness s. dpaṅ(-po).
Wolf spyaṅ-ki.
Woman bud-méd, mo, 'a-ne W.
Womb mṅal 132, bu-snod 319, rum.
Wonder s. ya-mṫsan.
Wonderful nyams-mṫsar-ba, ṅo-mṫsar-ba; ya-mṫsan-po C., ya-mṫsan-ċan W.
Wont, Wonted adj. goms-pa.
Wood (forest) nags(-ma), ṫsal; (timber) šiṅ; — shavings šiṅ-zél.
Woodpecker šiṅ-rgón.
Woof spun.
Wool bal.
Word ṫsig, miṅ, sgra, ṅág 125; resp. bka.

Work s. *bya-ba, bzo, las*, resp. *ṕrin-las*; vb. a. *las byed-pa*.
Workman *las-pa, las-mi*.
Workmanship *bzo* 497.
Workmaster *lag-dpón*.
Workshop *bzo-ḱaṅ*.
World *°ǰig-rtén, srid-pa* 582.
Worldliness *°ǰig-rtén °di-la čags-pai sems*; v. *bya-ba*.
Worm *°bu, srin-bu, nyal-°gro*.
Worn out *čad-po*.
Worst, to get the — of *°ṕam-pa*.
Worth s. *°ḱos, goṅ, rin, ťaṅ*.
Worth adj. *ri-ba*.
Worthless *rin-méd*.
Worthy *γša, γša-ma*; to be — *ʼos-pa*.
Wound s. *rma, rma-ḱa W.*
Wrap vb. a. *dkri-ba*; to — round *sgril-ba*; to — up *°dril-ba*.
Wrath *ḱro-ba, že-sdaṅ*.
Wrest vb. a. *snol-ba*.
Wrestle vb. n. *snol-ba*.
Wretched *sdug-po*; *nyal-ba-čan W.*
Wring *°ťsir-ba*.
Wrinkle s. *γnyer-ma*.
Wrist *lag-ťsigs*.
Write *°bri-ba*.
Wrong adj. *mi-rigs-pa, log-pa, mi-ʼos-pa*; *ʼos-med W.*
Wry adj. *°ču-ba, °čus-pa* 170.

Y

Yak *γyag*; male — *ṕo-γyág*; female — *°bri-mo*; wild — *°broṅ*.
Yard (court-yard) *ḱyams*.
Yarn *snal-ma, sran-bu*.
Yawn vb. *glal-ba, sgyiṅ-ba* 118.
Yea *ʼo-ná* 500.
Year *lo*; this — *da-lo*.
Yeast *ṕabs, rtsabs*.
Yellow *ser-po*.
Yes *ʼo, de yin*; *ʼa W.*; yes, yes! *de-ka yod* 255; —, so it is *de-de-bžin-no*.
Yesterday *ḱa-rtsáṅ, mdaṅ*.
Yet *ʼon kyaṅ, yin kyaṅ, yin na yaṅ W.*; *gal-te*.
Yield vb. a. *γtoṅ-ba*; vb. n. *daṅ-du len-pa*.
Yoke of oxen *glaṅ-dór*.
Yonder *ṕa-gi*.
You pron. *ḱyed, ḱyod* 48, *nyid* 188.
Young adj. *γžon-pa, čuṅ-ba*; the youngest (son) *ťa-čúṅ*; s. *ṕrug*.
Youth s. (youthful age) *laṅ-ťso*; (boy or young man) *ḱyeu, γžon-nu*.

Z

Zeal *rtsol-ba, brtson-°grus, °bad-pa, bag-čags*.
Zealous *brtson-°grus daṅ ldan-pa*; to be — *brtson-°grus skyed-pa, brtson-par byed-pa*.
Zealously *rtsol-bar*.
Zero *ťig-le*.
Zinc *ti-ťsa*.
Zodiac *ḱyim-gyi °ḱor-lo*.

Final remark. The Tibetan words, given in the Vocabulary, are not in every instance to be regarded as exact equivalents for whatever word happens to be sought, but rather as hints, how to attain to the wished for expression. It will, therefore, be frequently indispensable to refer to the Tib. Engl. Dictionary for further explanation, and to examine the different bearings and relations of the word in question, so far as they may have been traced there. — Although this Vocabulary is by no means complete in itself, yet it is to be hoped that it will not prove quite unuseful, but answer the purpose for which it was intended.

CORRECTIONS.

A revision of the Dictionary has brought such a number of misprints to light that, on second thoughts, it seems absolutely necessary not to leave them unnoticed, but to register all that are of any consequence. The unfortunate fact, that such corrections should be required, has to be ascribed to two circumstances, in regard to which the reader's indulgence has already been appealed to in the Preface, namely, the author's weak state of health, and the difficulties with which the printing of a book of this character is necessarily attended. —

---

p. page; a b the respective column, left or right; l. line; when the lines are counted from foot of page, the numerals are provided with an asterisk.

p.	col.	l.		
2	a	8	read	*ka-ma-la-ṥí-la*
2	b	17	„	*ka-sa ǰu*
3	b	3*	„	to beckon
8	a	18	„	*ṭud-kyi*
9	b	21	„	*dka-ťub-la*
15	a	9	„	*ṭa-ṥi-lhüm-po*
16	a	19*	„	*rkaṅ-˳bám*
16	b	7*	„	dig out
17	a	9*	„	affix denoting
17	a	19*	„	*rkyaṅ-pa*
20	b	10*	„	frequently
21	a	6	„	*skal-nór*
21	b	2	„	*ṭé*
26	a	5	„	*skyaṅ*
27	a	11*	„	*skyil-ldir*
27	b	13*	„	*skyur-mo*
28	a	6	„	*γyaṅ-skyúr*
28	a	15*	„	re-born
28	b	19	„	*kyer-mén*
31	b	16*	„	*lag-lén*
32	b	16	dele	2. to paste. —
32	b	5*	read	*skra-séṅ*
33	a	5*	„	*ḱ*
33	b	7	„	*ḍá-ru skróg-pa*
33	b	12	„	caste
34	a	5	„	soft mouth
34	a	15*	„	to lie on the face
35	b	2*	„	*ḱa-γdáms*
38	a	1	„	*lás-ka*
38	a	10	„	*Ld.*
39	a	6	„	*zas ḱam γčig* id. — 2.
41	a	20	„	*ḱúg-tu*
41	a	4*	„	*rna-ḱúṅ*
44	a	18	„	*kóg-pa ṅan-pa*
51	a	14*	read	*ḱrims-ḱáṅ*
52	b	24	„	**ťó-pa**
54	b	13	„	requisites
56	b	5	„	འཁྲིལ་བ་
56	b	15	„	*˳ḱo-byéd*
59	a	20*	„	འཁྲུག(ས)་པ་
59	a	10*	„	*˳ḱyam-pa*
59	b	20*	„	*˳ód-˳ḱyims*
63	a	6*	„	= *gaṅ.* — 3. bald, *W. ga-pi* (v. *spyi* 333).
65	a	24*	„	*˳óṅ-ba de-ni*
66	a	16*	„	*gaṅ-zúg-*
66	a	14*	„	*lóg-lta-čan-gyi*
66	b	15	„	*mdzod-lṅá*
67	a	20	„	གཉ་རྡོ་ལ་
69	b	17*	„	*gun-dúm*
74	a	18	„	*gyád-kyi*
74	a	13*	„	*gyi* for *kyi*
75	a	11	„	*gyón-rgyu*
76	b	6	„	*ťáb-grabs*
77	b	18	„	གྲུ་གུ་
78	b	22*	„	*gróg-ču*
79	a	18	„	*mčód-rten*
81	a	11	„	*-rtséd-mo*
84	b	5	„	stoop
85	b	18	„	उपासिका
86	b	11	„	*mdo*; *dge-slóṅ-ma* a nun; *dge-slob-ma* etc.
87	a	19	„	*bstán-pa-la*

p.	col.	l.		
89	b	2*	read	*ċes bgrós-nas*
92	a	4	„	*'u-ṡóg*
95	a	11*	„	*ṅan-*
95	b	3	„	འགྲོགས་པ་
95	b	21	„	establish
96	a	10*	„	*ₒgor*
96	b	1	„	*ₒgyág-pa*
96	b	3	„	*ₒgyaṅ-ba*
96	b	15	„	*ṡél-gyí*
98	a	14	„	*ₒgyód-par*
111	b	22	„	རྒྱུག་པ་
112	a	20*	„	*tiṅ-ṅe-ₒdzin*
113	b	7	„	*na-ťsa*
121	a	20	„	*bsgrub-*
122	a	4	vide	emendation p. XXII.
122	a	8*	read	སྒྲོག(ས)་
122	b	24*	„	*sgrón-pa*
128	a	4	„	*ṅéd-ċag*
128	b	4	„	*dé-ₒdra-ba*
128	b	6	„	*ₒčí-ba*
128	b	2*	„	*ṅo dkár-po*
131	a	16*seqq.	„	*ₒdzin*
132	b	5*	„	*ċis*
132	b	3*	„	*mṅón-no*
135	a	4	„	*Lex.*
139	b	6	„	*ċii* of what?
140	b	1	„	ཅི་ཅེ་
141	b	17	„	*ċuṅ*
143	a	20*	„	gallinaceous
146	b	10*, 8*	„	**vċu**
147	b	23	„	**vċom-ldan-ₒdé**
158	a	17	„	*ču-búr*
158	b	14*	„	the water; also =
161	b	10*	„	*dris-pas* (instead of
163	b	10*	„	*čós-skad*
164	a	3*	„	irreligious
165	b	18*	„	*mčé-ba*
166	b	15	„	पूज
168	b	20*	„	*zá-ba*
170	a	13	„	*ₒču-ba* to draw etc.
170	a	22	„	vb. n. to *ₒǰún-pa*
170	b	2*	„	*ǩro-bo-ₒčól-pa*
171	a	12	„	*Lex.*
176	b	24	„	*ₒǰig-ṭág*
177	a	5	„	*ₒǰiṅ-ǩúṅ*
184	b	10*	„	*nyá-ra byéd-pa*
185	a	13*	„	*dpon-gyi*
186	b	4*	„	*nyal-ǩrí*
195	a	21	„	**mnyé-ċe**
195	b	6	„	རྐྱང་བ་
195	b	7*	„	*ɣnyid*
200	a	13*	read	སྙིན་པ་
205	a	4	„	*Cs.*
219	b	7	„	*ma byed*
226	a	11*	„	178. 3. — *Was.* (296): 2.
231	b	7	„	*ťig-skúd*
232	a	3*	„	*żib-ċu*
233	b	18	„	*Ld.-Glr.*,
233	b	23*	„	translates it
233	b	19*	„	**ťun ċad** *W.*
235	b	24	„	*mi-ťeg ǩúr-ba*
237	a	9*	„	*ṅá-ťog*
237	b	15	„	*spyi-ťóg*
238	a	14*	„	*ťod*
256	a	9	„	from thence
256	b	12	„	རིབ་(མ)་
259	b	14	„	*don* 1. — *don-dám*
264	b	7*	„	དྲོན་མོ་
265	a	10	„	like an arctic sea
267	a	14	dele	(Pinus abies)
270	b	14	read	*bdé-mo*
273	b	2*	„	डोली
274	a	4*	dele	the words: marked or
275	a	9 seqq.	read	*ₒdas-pa*
275	b	6*	„	*p̀yi*
287	b	16	„	precious stone
287	b	22	„	*Pth.* having obtained im mortality
291	a	5	„	*ₒbrug*
292	b	23	„	*sdáṅ-ba*
293	a	3*	„	*sdíg-to-ċan*
293	b	1	„	སྡི(ག)ས་པ་ *sdi(g)s-pa*
301	b	22	„	*lo tóṅ-ṅi*
303	b	23	„	*zín-to*
304	b	22	„	prep.
305	b	21*	„	ནུར་ནུར་པོ་
312	a	3*	„	མཚོལ་གྲིབ་
316	b	8	„	*smin-pa*
317	b	12*	„	apparition
318	b	14	„	brightly
322	b	8*	„	*dkár(-po)*
325	a	10	„	*gru-ₒdzin*
326	b	4	„	Durga, Uma
327	a	17	„	*żág-pe̥ pe*
328	a	18*	„	*koṅ-ǰo*
338	a	14*	„	the defunct ancestors
338	b	2*	„	postp. c. gen.
340	a	21	„	abstrusely
340	b	17	„	*Gram.*;
353	b	15	„	*ₒǰúg-pa*
354	a	9*	„	*ₒp̀rál-ba*

p.	col.	l.	
357	b	12*	read ₒpʻóṅ-mkʻan
374	a	12*	„ བྱུག་(པ་)
383	b	10*	„ གླ་འཚོ་ gla-ₒtsó
389	a	12*	„ dbón-mo
407	a	17*	„ སྦྲིད་པ་
410	b	13*	„ circle
412	b	21*, 19*	„ mi-kʻyim
415	a	24*	„ to name v. ₒdogs-pa 2;
427	a	12	„ sman-mčóg
431	a	1*	„ tsám-gyis
433	a	2*	„ yaṅ
439	a	19	„ mii
439	b	14*	„ ₒgro- (or ča-) rtsis yod
442	a	7*	„ nyáṅ-če
442	b	17	„ assiduous
446	a	3*	„ tsan-zug
449	a	12*	„ travellers
460	b	10	„ ₒtsó-ba
466	b	11*	read whetstone
474	a	20*	„ soothe
480	a	13	„ γžal-med-kʻaṅ-bzaṅ
493	b	18	„ Sik.
496	a	5	„ γzod
496	a	18	„ wasted
508	b	12	„ so yi γčód-pa, yi čád-pa
522	a	2 3	„ ḍáṅ-mo
530	b	5	„ རིལ་བ་
540	a	4	„ of
567	a	5*	„ prop.
576	a	14*	skyo-séṅ mdzád-pa
578	b	3	„ སོ་ཕག་ so-pʻág
587	a	20, 21	„ nyon-móṅs-kyi kun-slóṅ
589	a	1	„ གསལ་ཤིང་
591	b	23*	„ vb. 1. to beg, to pray = žú-ba
592	a	9	„ (the king's) soul

In several of the longer articles some confusion in the use of the figures in large and small type has occurred. In order to restrict this catalogue within the smallest possible limits, these and other slight inaccuracies have not been entered.

www.ingramcontent.com/pod-product-compliance
Lightning Source LLC
Chambersburg PA
CBHW021928110726
47901CB00003B/750
* 9 7 8 3 7 4 2 8 4 5 5 0 4 *